Anne of Green Gables

Word Cloud Classics

A Christmas Carol and Other Holiday Treasures

Adventures of Huckleberry Finn

The Adventures of Sherlock Holmes

Aesop's Fables

The Age of Innocence

Anna Karenina

The Art of War

The Brothers Grimm: 101 Fairy Tales

The Brothers Grimm Volume II: 110 Grimmer Fairy Tales

Common Sense and Selected Works of Thomas Paine

The Count of Monte Cristo

Don Quixote

Dracula

Emma

Frankenstein

Great Expectations

Inferno

Jane Eyre

Lady Chatterley's Lover

Les Misérables

Little Women

Madame Bovary

Moby-Dick

Narrative of the Life of Frederick Douglass and Other Works

Persuasion

The Picture of Dorian Gray

Pride and Prejudice

The Prince and Other Writings

The Red Badge of Courage and Other Stories

The Scarlet Letter

The Secret Garden

Sense and Sensibility

The Three Musketeers

Twenty Thousand Leagues Under the Sea

Uncle Tom's Cabin

Walden and Civil Disobedience

The Wizard of Oz

Anne of Green Gables

By Lucy Maud Montgomery

CANTERBURY CLASSICS
San Diego

All correspondence concerning the content of this
book should be addressed to:
Canterbury Classics
10350 Barnes Canyon Road, Suite 100
San Diego, CA 92121

Publisher: Peter Norton
Publishing Team: Lori Asbury, Ana Parker
Director Editorial and Production: JoAnn Padgett
Editor: Melinda Allman

Library of Congress Cataloging-in-Publication Data

Montgomery, L. M. (Lucy Maud), 1874-1942.
Anne of Green Gables / Lucy Maud Montgomery.
p. cm.
Summary: Anne, an eleven-year-old orphan, is sent by mistake to live with a lonely, middle-aged brother and sister on a Prince Edward Island farm and proceeds to make an indelible impression on everyone around her.
ISBN 978-1-60710-728-6 (pbk.)
[1. Orphans--Fiction. 2. Friendship--Fiction. 3. Islands--Fiction. 4. Country life--Prince Edward Island--Fiction. 5. Prince Edward Island--History--20th century--Fiction. 6. Canada--History--1867-1914--Fiction.] I. Title.
PZ7.M768An 2013
[Fic]--dc23

2012029996

PRINTED IN CHINA

4 5 6 7 8 19 18 17 16 15

CONTENTS

CHAPTER I

MRS. RACHEL LYNDE IS SURPRISED

Mrs. Rachel Lynde lived just where the Avonlea main road dipped down into a little hollow, fringed with alders and ladies' eardrops and traversed by a brook that had its source away back in the woods of the old Cuthbert place; it was reputed to be an intricate, headlong brook in its earlier course through those woods, with dark secrets of pool and cascade; but by the time it reached Lynde's Hollow it was a quiet, well-conducted little stream, for not even a brook could run past Mrs. Rachel Lynde's door without due regard for decency and decorum; it probably was conscious that Mrs. Rachel was sitting at her window, keeping a sharp eye on everything that passed, from brooks and children up, and that if she noticed anything odd or out of place she would never rest until she had ferreted out the whys and wherefores thereof.

There are plenty of people in Avonlea and out of it, who can attend closely to their neighbor's business by dint of neglecting their own; but Mrs. Rachel Lynde was one of those capable creatures who can manage their own concerns and those of other folks into the bargain. She was a notable housewife; her work was always done and well done; she "ran" the Sewing Circle, helped run the Sunday school, and was the strongest prop of the Church Aid Society and Foreign Missions Auxiliary. Yet with all this Mrs. Rachel found abundant time to sit for hours at her kitchen window, knitting "cotton warp" quilts—she had knitted sixteen of them, as Avonlea housekeepers were wont to tell in awed voices—and keeping a sharp eye on the main road that crossed the hollow and wound up the steep red hill beyond. Since Avonlea occupied a little triangular peninsula jutting out into the Gulf of St. Lawrence with water on two sides of it, anybody who went out of it or into it had to pass over that hill road and so run the unseen gauntlet of Mrs. Rachel's all-seeing eye.

She was sitting there one afternoon in early June. The sun was coming in at the window warm and bright; the orchard on the slope below the house was in a bridal flush of pinky-white bloom, hummed over by a myriad of bees. Thomas Lynde—a meek little man whom Avonlea people called "Rachel Lynde's husband"—was sowing his late turnip seed on the hill field beyond the barn; and Matthew Cuthbert ought to have been sowing his on the big red brook field away over by Green Gables. Mrs. Rachel knew that he ought because she had heard him tell Peter Morrison the evening before in William J. Blair's store over at Carmody that he meant to sow his turnip seed the next afternoon. Peter had asked him, of course, for Matthew Cuthbert had never been known to volunteer information about anything in his whole life.

And yet here was Matthew Cuthbert, at half-past three on the afternoon of a busy day, placidly driving over the hollow and up the hill; moreover, he wore a white collar and his best suit of clothes, which was plain proof that he was going out of Avonlea; and he had the buggy and the sorrel mare, which betokened that he was going a considerable distance. Now, where was Matthew Cuthbert going and why was he going there?

Had it been any other man in Avonlea, Mrs. Rachel, deftly putting this and that together, might have given a pretty good guess as to both questions. But Matthew so rarely went from home that it must be something pressing and unusual which was taking him; he was the shyest man alive and hated to have to go among strangers or to any place where he might have to talk. Matthew, dressed up with a white collar and driving in a buggy, was something that didn't happen often. Mrs. Rachel, ponder as she might, could make nothing of it and her afternoon's enjoyment was spoiled.

"I'll just step over to Green Gables after tea and find out from Marilla where he's gone and why," the worthy woman finally concluded. "He doesn't generally go to town this time of year and he never visits; if he'd run out of turnip seed he wouldn't dress up and take the buggy to go for more; he wasn't driving fast enough to be going for a doctor. Yet something must have happened since last night to start him off. I'm clean puzzled, that's what, and I won't know a minute's peace of mind or conscience until I know what has taken Matthew Cuthbert out of Avonlea today."

Accordingly after tea Mrs. Rachel set out; she had not far to go; the big, rambling, orchard-embowered house where the Cuthberts lived was a scant quarter of a mile up the road from Lynde's Hollow. To be sure, the long lane made it a good deal further. Matthew Cuthbert's father, as shy and silent as his son after him, had got as far away as he possibly could from his fellow men without actually retreating into the woods when he founded his homestead. Green Gables was built at the furthest edge of his cleared land and there it was to this day, barely visible from the main road along which all the other Avonlea houses were so sociably situated. Mrs. Rachel Lynde did not call *living* in such a place living at all.

"It's just *staying*, that's what," she said as she stepped along the deep-rutted, grassy lane bordered with wild rose bushes. "It's no wonder Matthew and Marilla are both a little odd, living away back here by themselves. Trees aren't much company, though dear knows if they were there'd be enough of them. I'd ruther look at people. To be sure, they seem contented enough; but then, I suppose, they're used to it. A body can get used to anything, even to being hanged, as the Irishman said."

With this Mrs. Rachel stepped out of the lane into the backyard of Green Gables. Very green and neat and precise was that yard, set about on one side with great patriarchal willows and the other with prim Lombardies. Not a stray stick nor stone was to be seen, for Mrs. Rachel would have seen it if there had been. Privately she was of the opinion that Marilla Cuthbert swept that yard over as often as she swept her house. One could have eaten a meal off the ground without overbrimming the proverbial peck of dirt.

Mrs. Rachel rapped smartly at the kitchen door and stepped in when bidden to do so. The kitchen at Green Gables was a cheerful apartment—or would have been cheerful if it had not been so painfully clean as to give it something of the appearance of an unused parlor. Its windows looked east and west; through the west one, looking out on the back yard, came a flood of mellow June sunlight; but the east one, whence you got a glimpse of the bloom white cherry trees in the left orchard and nodding, slender birches down in the hollow by the brook, was greened over by a tangle of vines. Here sat Marilla Cuthbert, when she sat at all, always slightly distrustful of sunshine, which seemed to her too dancing and irresponsible a thing for a world which was meant to be taken seriously; and here she sat now, knitting, and the table behind her was laid for supper.

Mrs. Rachel, before she had fairly closed the door, had taken a mental note of everything that was on that table. There were three plates laid, so that Marilla must be expecting some one home with Matthew to tea; but the dishes were everyday dishes and there was only crab-apple preserves and one kind of cake, so that the expected company could not be any particular company. Yet what of Matthew's white collar and the sorrel mare? Mrs. Rachel was getting fairly dizzy with this unusual mystery about quiet, unmysterious Green Gables. "Good evening, Rachel," Marilla said briskly. "This is a real fine evening, isn't it? Won't you sit down? How are all your folks?"

Something that for lack of any other name might be called friendship existed and always had existed between Marilla Cuthbert and Mrs. Rachel, in spite of—or perhaps because of—their dissimilarity.

Marilla was a tall, thin woman, with angles and without curves; her dark hair showed some gray streaks and was always twisted up in a hard little knot behind with two wire hairpins stuck aggressively through it. She looked like a woman of narrow experience and rigid conscience, which she was; but there was a saving something about her mouth which, if it had been ever so slightly developed, might have been considered indicative of a sense of humor.

"We're all pretty well," said Mrs. Rachel. "I was kind of afraid YOU weren't, though, when I saw Matthew starting off today. I thought maybe he was going to the doctor's."

Marilla's lips twitched understandingly. She had expected Mrs. Rachel up; she had known that the sight of Matthew jaunting off so unaccountably would be too much for her neighbor's curiosity.

"Oh, no, I'm quite well although I had a bad headache yesterday," she said. "Matthew went to Bright River. We're getting a little boy from an orphan asylum in Nova Scotia and he's coming on the train tonight."

If Marilla had said that Matthew had gone to Bright River to meet a kangaroo from Australia Mrs. Rachel could not have been more astonished. She was actually stricken dumb for five seconds. It was unsupposable that Marilla was making fun of her, but Mrs. Rachel was almost forced to suppose it.

"Are you in earnest, Marilla?" she demanded when voice returned to her.

"Yes, of course," said Marilla, as if getting boys from orphan asylums in Nova Scotia were part of the usual spring work on any well-regulated Avonlea farm instead of being an unheard of innovation.

Mrs. Rachel felt that she had received a severe mental jolt. She thought in exclamation points. A boy! Marilla and Matthew Cuthbert of all people adopting a boy! From an orphan asylum! Well, the world was certainly turning upside down! She would be surprised at nothing after this! Nothing!

"What on earth put such a notion into your head?" she demanded disapprovingly.

This had been done without her advice being asked, and must perforce be disapproved.

"Well, we've been thinking about it for some time—all winter in fact," returned Marilla. "Mrs. Alexander Spencer was up here one day before Christmas and she said she was going to get a little girl from the asylum over in Hopeton in the spring. Her cousin lives there and Mrs. Spencer has visited here and knows all about it. So Matthew and I have talked it over off and on ever since. We thought we'd get a boy. Matthew is getting up in years, you know—he's sixty—and he isn't so spry as he once was. His heart troubles him a good deal. And you know how desperate hard it's got to be to get hired help. There's never anybody to be had but those stupid, half-grown little French boys; and as soon as you do get one broke into your ways and taught something he's up and off to the lobster canneries or the States. At first Matthew suggested getting a Home boy. But I said 'no' flat to that. 'They may be all right—I'm not saying they're not—but no London street Arabs for me,' I said. 'Give me a native born at least. There'll be a risk, no matter who we get. But I'll feel easier in my mind and sleep sounder at nights if we get a born Canadian.' So in the end we decided to ask Mrs. Spencer to pick us out one when she went over to get her little girl. We heard last week she was going, so we sent her word by Richard Spencer's folks at Carmody to bring us a smart, likely boy of about ten or eleven. We decided that would be the best age—old enough to be of some use in doing chores right off and young enough to be trained up proper. We mean to give him a good home and schooling. We had a telegram from Mrs. Alexander Spencer today—the mail-man brought it from the station—saying they were coming on the five-thirty train tonight. So Matthew went to Bright River to meet him. Mrs. Spencer will drop him off there. Of course she goes on to White Sands station herself."

Mrs. Rachel prided herself on always speaking her mind; she

proceeded to speak it now, having adjusted her mental attitude to this amazing piece of news.

"Well, Marilla, I'll just tell you plain that I think you're doing a mighty foolish thing—a risky thing, that's what. You don't know what you're getting. You're bringing a strange child into your house and home and you don't know a single thing about him nor what his disposition is like nor what sort of parents he had nor how he's likely to turn out. Why, it was only last week I read in the paper how a man and his wife up west of the Island took a boy out of an orphan asylum and he set fire to the house at night—set it *on purpose*, Marilla—and nearly burnt them to a crisp in their beds. And I know another case where an adopted boy used to suck the eggs—they couldn't break him of it. If you had asked my advice in the matter—which you didn't do, Marilla—I'd have said for mercy's sake not to think of such a thing, that's what."

This Job's comforting seemed neither to offend nor to alarm Marilla. She knitted steadily on.

"I don't deny there's something in what you say, Rachel. I've had some qualms myself. But Matthew was terrible set on it. I could see that, so I gave in. It's so seldom Matthew sets his mind on anything that when he does I always feel it's my duty to give in. And as for the risk, there's risks in pretty near everything a body does in this world. There's risks in people's having children of their own if it comes to that—they don't always turn out well. And then Nova Scotia is right close to the Island. It isn't as if we were getting him from England or the States. He can't be much different from ourselves."

"Well, I hope it will turn out all right," said Mrs. Rachel in a tone that plainly indicated her painful doubts. "Only don't say I didn't warn you if he burns Green Gables down or puts strychnine in the well—I heard of a case over in New Brunswick where an orphan asylum child did that and the whole family died in fearful agonies. Only, it was a girl in that instance."

"Well, we're not getting a girl," said Marilla, as if poisoning wells were a purely feminine accomplishment and not to be dreaded in the case of a boy. "I'd never dream of taking a girl to bring up. I wonder at Mrs. Alexander Spencer for doing it. But there, *she* wouldn't shrink from adopting a whole orphan asylum if she took it into her head."

Mrs. Rachel would have liked to stay until Matthew came home with his imported orphan. But reflecting that it would be a good two hours at least before his arrival she concluded to go up the road to Robert Bell's and tell the news. It would certainly make a sensation second to none, and Mrs. Rachel dearly loved to make a sensation. So she took herself away, somewhat to Marilla's relief, for the latter felt her doubts and fears reviving under the influence of Mrs. Rachel's pessimism.

"Well, of all things that ever were or will be!" ejaculated Mrs. Rachel when she was safely out in the lane. "It does really seem as if I must be dreaming. Well, I'm sorry for that poor young one and no mistake. Matthew and Marilla don't know anything about children and they'll expect him to be wiser and steadier that his own grandfather, if so be's he ever had a grandfather, which is doubtful. It seems uncanny to think of a child at Green Gables somehow; there's never been one there, for Matthew and Marilla were grown up when the new house was built—if they ever *were* children, which is hard to believe when one looks at them. I wouldn't be in that orphan's shoes for anything. My, but I pity him, that's what."

So said Mrs. Rachel to the wild rose bushes out of the fulness of her heart; but if she could have seen the child who was waiting patiently at the Bright River station at that very moment her pity would have been still deeper and more profound.

CHAPTER II

MATTHEW CUTHBERT IS SURPRISED

Matthew Cuthbert and the sorrel mare jogged comfortably over the eight miles to Bright River. It was a pretty road, running along between snug farmsteads, with now and again a bit of balsamy fir wood to drive through or a hollow where wild plums hung out their filmy bloom. The air was sweet with the breath of many apple orchards and the meadows sloped away in the distance to horizon mists of pearl and purple; while

"The little birds sang as if it were
The one day of summer in all the year."

Matthew enjoyed the drive after his own fashion, except during the moments when he met women and had to nod to them—for in Prince Edward Island you are supposed to nod to all and sundry you meet on the road whether you know them or not.

Matthew dreaded all women except Marilla and Mrs. Rachel; he had an uncomfortable feeling that the mysterious creatures were secretly laughing at him. He may have been quite right in thinking so, for he was an odd-looking personage, with an ungainly figure and long iron-gray hair that touched his stooping shoulders, and a full, soft brown beard which he had worn ever since he was twenty. In fact, he had looked at twenty very much as he looked at sixty, lacking a little of the grayness.

When he reached Bright River there was no sign of any train; he thought he was too early, so he tied his horse in the yard of the small Bright River hotel and went over to the station house. The long platform was almost deserted; the only living creature in sight being a girl who was sitting on a pile of shingles at the extreme end. Matthew, barely noting that it *was* a girl, sidled past her as quickly as possible without looking at her. Had he looked he could hardly have failed to notice the tense rigidity and expectation of her attitude and expression. She was sitting there waiting for something or somebody and, since sitting and waiting was the only thing to do just then, she sat and waited with all her might and main.

Matthew encountered the stationmaster locking up the ticket office preparatory to going home for supper, and asked him if the five-thirty train would soon be along.

"The five-thirty train has been in and gone half an hour ago," answered that brisk official. "But there was a passenger dropped off for you—a little girl. She's sitting out there on the shingles. I asked her to go into the ladies' waiting room, but she informed me gravely that she preferred to stay outside. 'There was more scope for imagination,' she said. She's a case, I should say."

"I'm not expecting a girl," said Matthew blankly. "It's a boy I've come for. He should be here. Mrs. Alexander Spencer was to bring him over from Nova Scotia for me."

The stationmaster whistled.

"Guess there's some mistake," he said. "Mrs. Spencer came off the train with that girl and gave her into my charge. Said you and your sister were adopting her from an orphan asylum and that you would be along for her presently. That's all I know about it—and I haven't got any more orphans concealed hereabouts."

"I don't understand," said Matthew helplessly, wishing that Marilla was at hand to cope with the situation.

"Well, you'd better question the girl," said the station master carelessly. "I dare say she'll be able to explain—she's got a tongue of her own, that's certain. Maybe they were out of boys of the brand you wanted."

He walked jauntily away, being hungry, and the unfortunate Matthew was left to do that which was harder for him than bearding a lion in its den—walk up to a girl—a strange girl—an orphan girl—and demand of her why she wasn't a boy. Matthew groaned in spirit as he turned about and shuffled gently down the platform towards her.

She had been watching him ever since he had passed her and she had her eyes on him now. Matthew was not looking at her and would not have seen what she was really like if he had been, but an ordinary observer would have seen this: A child of about eleven, garbed in a very short, very tight, very ugly dress of yellowish-gray wincey. She wore a faded brown sailor hat and beneath the hat, extending down her back, were two braids of very thick, decidedly red hair. Her face was small, white and thin, also much freckled; her mouth was large and so were her eyes, which looked green in some lights and moods and gray in others.

So far, the ordinary observer; an extraordinary observer might have seen that the chin was very pointed and pronounced; that the big eyes were full of spirit and vivacity; that the mouth was sweet-lipped and expressive; that the forehead was broad and full; in short, our discerning extraordinary observer might have concluded that no commonplace soul inhabited the body of this stray woman-child of whom shy Matthew Cuthbert was so ludicrously afraid.

Matthew, however, was spared the ordeal of speaking first, for as soon as she concluded that he was coming to her she stood up, grasping with one thin brown hand the handle of a shabby, old-fashioned carpet-bag; the other she held out to him.

"I suppose you are Mr. Matthew Cuthbert of Green Gables?" she said in a peculiarly clear, sweet voice. "I'm very glad to see you. I was beginning to be afraid you weren't coming for me and I was imagining all the things that might have happened to prevent you. I had made up my mind that if you didn't come for me tonight I'd go down the track to that big wild cherry tree at the bend, and climb up into it to stay all night. I wouldn't be a bit afraid, and it would be lovely to sleep in a wild cherry tree all white with bloom in the moonshine, don't you think? You could imagine you were dwelling in marble halls, couldn't you? And I was quite sure you would come for me in the morning, if you didn't tonight."

Matthew had taken the scrawny little hand awkwardly in his; then and there he decided what to do. He could not tell this child with the glowing eyes that there had been a mistake; he would take her home and let Marilla do that. She couldn't be left at Bright River anyhow, no matter what mistake had been made, so all questions and explanations might as well be deferred until he was safely back at Green Gables.

"I'm sorry I was late," he said shyly. "Come along. The horse is over in the yard. Give me your bag."

"Oh, I can carry it," the child responded cheerfully. "It isn't heavy. I've got all my worldly goods in it, but it isn't heavy. And if it isn't carried in just a certain way the handle pulls out—so I'd better keep it because I know the exact knack of it. It's an extremely old carpet-bag. Oh, I'm very glad you've come, even if it would have been nice to sleep in a wild cherry tree. We've got to drive a long piece, haven't we? Mrs. Spencer said it was eight miles. I'm glad because I love driving. Oh, it seems so wonderful that I'm going to live with you and belong to you. I've never belonged to anybody—not really. But the asylum was the worst. I've only been in it four months, but that was enough. I don't suppose you ever were an orphan in an asylum, so you can't possibly understand what it is like. It's worse than anything you could imagine. Mrs. Spencer said it was wicked of me to talk like that, but I didn't mean to be wicked. It's so easy to be wicked without knowing it, isn't it? They were good, you know—the asylum people. But there is so little scope for the imagination in an asylum—only just in the other orphans. It was pretty interesting to imagine things about them—to imagine that perhaps the girl who sat next to you was really the daughter of a belted earl, who had been stolen away from her parents in her infancy by a cruel nurse who died before she could confess. I used to lie awake at nights and imagine things like that, because I didn't have time in the day. I guess that's why I'm so thin—I *am* dreadful thin, ain't I? There isn't a pick on my bones. I do love to imagine I'm nice and plump, with dimples in my elbows."

With this Matthew's companion stopped talking, partly because she was out of breath and partly because they had reached the buggy. Not another word did she say until they had left the village and were driving down a steep little hill, the road part of which had been cut so deeply into the soft soil that the banks, fringed with blooming wild cherry trees and slim white birches, were several feet above their heads.

The child put out her hand and broke off a branch of wild plum that brushed against the side of the buggy.

"Isn't that beautiful? What did that tree, leaning out from the bank, all white and lacy, make you think of?" she asked.

"Well now, I dunno," said Matthew.

"Why, a bride, of course—a bride all in white with a lovely misty veil. I've never seen one, but I can imagine what she would look like. I don't ever expect to be a bride myself. I'm so homely nobody will ever want to marry me—unless it might be a foreign missionary. I suppose a foreign missionary mightn't be very particular. But I do hope that some day I shall have a white dress. That is my highest ideal of earthly bliss. I just love pretty clothes. And I've never had a pretty dress in my life that I can remember—but of course it's all the more to look forward to, isn't it? And then I can imagine that I'm dressed gorgeously. This morning when I left the asylum I felt so ashamed because I had to wear this horrid old wincey dress. All the orphans had to wear them, you know. A merchant in Hopeton last winter donated three hundred yards of wincey to the asylum. Some people said it was because he couldn't sell it, but I'd rather believe that it was out of the kindness of his heart, wouldn't you? When we got on the train I felt as if everybody must be looking at me and pitying me. But I just went to work and imagined that I had on the most beautiful pale blue silk dress—because when you *are* imagining you might as well imagine something worth while—and a big hat all flowers and nodding plumes, and a gold watch, and kid gloves and boots. I felt cheered up right away and I enjoyed my trip to the Island with all my might. I wasn't a bit sick coming over in the boat. Neither was Mrs. Spencer although she generally is. She said she hadn't time to get sick, watching to see that I didn't fall overboard. She said she never saw the beat of me for prowling about. But if it kept her from being seasick it's a mercy I did prowl, isn't it? And I wanted to see everything that was to be seen on that boat, because I didn't know whether I'd ever have another opportunity. Oh, there are a lot more cherry trees all in bloom! This Island is the bloomiest place. I just love it already, and I'm so glad I'm going to live here. I've always heard that Prince Edward Island was the prettiest place in the world, and I used to imagine I was living here, but I never really expected I would. It's delightful when your imaginations come true, isn't it? But those red roads are so funny. When we got into the train at Charlottetown and the red roads began to flash past I asked Mrs. Spencer what made them red and she said she didn't know and for pity's sake not to ask her any more questions. She said I must have asked her a thousand already. I suppose I had, too, but how are you going to find out about things if you don't ask questions? And what *does* make the roads red?"

"Well now, I dunno," said Matthew.

"Well, that is one of the things to find out sometime. Isn't it splendid to think of all the things there are to find out about? It just makes me feel glad to be alive—it's such an interesting world. It wouldn't be half so interesting if we knew all about everything, would it? There'd be no scope for imagination then, would there? But am I talking too much? People are always telling me I do. Would you rather I didn't talk? If you say so I'll stop. I *can* stop when I make up my mind to it, although it's difficult."

Matthew, much to his own surprise, was enjoying himself. Like most quiet folks he liked talkative people when they were willing to do the talking themselves and did not expect him to keep up his end of it. But he had never expected to enjoy the society of a little girl. Women were bad enough in all conscience, but little girls were worse. He detested the way they had of sidling past him timidly, with sidewise glances, as if they expected him to gobble them up at a mouthful if they ventured to say a word. That was the Avonlea type of well-bred little girl. But this freckled witch was very different, and although he found it rather difficult for his slower intelligence to keep up with her brisk mental processes he thought that he "kind of liked her chatter." So he said as shyly as usual:

"Oh, you can talk as much as you like. I don't mind."

"Oh, I'm so glad. I know you and I are going to get along together fine. It's such a relief to talk when one wants to and not be told that children should be seen and not heard. I've had that said to me a million times if I have once. And people laugh at me because I use big words. But if you have big ideas you have to use big words to express them, haven't you?"

"Well now, that seems reasonable," said Matthew.

"Mrs. Spencer said that my tongue must be hung in the middle. But it isn't—it's firmly fastened at one end. Mrs. Spencer said your place was named Green Gables. I asked her all about it. And she said there were trees all around it. I was gladder than ever. I just love trees. And there weren't any at all about the asylum, only a few poor weeny-teeny things out in front with little whitewashed cagey things about them. They just looked like orphans themselves, those trees did. It used to make me want to cry to look at them. I used to say to them, 'Oh, you *poor* little things! If you were out in a great big woods with other trees all around you and little mosses and Junebells growing over your roots and a brook not far away and birds singing in you branches, you could grow, couldn't you? But you can't where you are. I know just exactly how you feel, little trees.' I felt sorry to leave them behind this morning. You do get so attached to things like that, don't you? Is there a brook anywhere near Green Gables? I forgot to ask Mrs. Spencer that."

"Well now, yes, there's one right below the house."

"Fancy. It's always been one of my dreams to live near a brook. I never expected I would, though. Dreams don't often come true, do they? Wouldn't it be nice if they did? But just now I feel pretty nearly perfectly happy. I can't feel exactly perfectly happy because—well, what color would you call this?"

She twitched one of her long glossy braids over her thin shoulder and held it up before Matthew's eyes. Matthew was not used to deciding on the tints of ladies' tresses, but in this case there couldn't be much doubt.

"It's red, ain't it?" he said.

The girl let the braid drop back with a sigh that seemed to come from her very toes and to exhale forth all the sorrows of the ages.

"Yes, it's red," she said resignedly. "Now you see why I can't be perfectly happy. Nobody could who has red hair. I don't mind the other things so much—the freckles and the green eyes and my skinniness. I can imagine them away. I can imagine that I have a beautiful rose-leaf complexion and lovely starry violet eyes. But I *cannot* imagine that red hair away. I do my best. I think to myself, 'Now my hair is a glorious black, black as the raven's wing.' But all the time I *know* it is just plain red and it breaks my heart. It will be my lifelong sorrow. I read of a girl once in a novel who had a lifelong sorrow but it wasn't red hair. Her hair was pure gold rippling back from her alabaster brow. What is an alabaster brow? I never could find out. Can you tell me?"

"Well now, I'm afraid I can't," said Matthew, who was getting a little dizzy. He felt as he had once felt in his rash youth when another boy had enticed him on the merry-go-round at a picnic.

"Well, whatever it was it must have been something nice because she was divinely beautiful. Have you ever imagined what it must feel like to be divinely beautiful?"

"Well now, no, I haven't," confessed Matthew ingenuously.

"I have, often. Which would you rather be if you had the choice—divinely beautiful or dazzlingly clever or angelically good?"

"Well now, I—I don't know exactly."

"Neither do I. I can never decide. But it doesn't make much real difference for it isn't likely I'll ever be either. It's certain I'll never be angelically good. Mrs. Spencer says—oh, Mr. Cuthbert! Oh, Mr. Cuthbert!! Oh, Mr. Cuthbert!!!"

That was not what Mrs. Spencer had said; neither had the child tumbled out of the buggy nor had Matthew done anything astonishing. They had simply rounded a curve in the road and found themselves in the "Avenue."

The "Avenue," so called by the Newbridge people, was a stretch of road four or five hundred yards long, completely arched over with huge, wide-spreading apple trees, planted years ago by an eccentric old farmer. Overhead was one long canopy of snowy fragrant bloom. Below the boughs the air was full of a purple twilight and far ahead a glimpse of painted sunset sky shone like a great rose window at the end of a cathedral aisle.

Its beauty seemed to strike the child dumb. She leaned back in the buggy, her thin hands clasped before her, her face lifted rapturously to the white splendor above. Even when they had passed out and were driving down the long slope to Newbridge she never moved or spoke. Still with rapt face she gazed afar into the sunset west, with eyes that saw visions trooping splendidly across that glowing background. Through Newbridge, a bustling little village where dogs barked at them and small boys hooted and curious faces peered from the windows, they drove, still in silence. When three more miles had dropped away behind them the child had not spoken. She could keep silence, it was evident, as energetically as she could talk.

"I guess you're feeling pretty tired and hungry," Matthew ventured to say at last, accounting for her long visitation of dumbness with the only reason he could think of. "But we haven't very far to go now—only another mile."

She came out of her reverie with a deep sigh and looked at him with the dreamy gaze of a soul that had been wondering afar, star-led.

"Oh, Mr. Cuthbert," she whispered, "that place we came through—that white place—what was it?"

"Well now, you must mean the Avenue," said Matthew after a few moments' profound reflection. "It is a kind of pretty place."

"Pretty? Oh, *pretty* doesn't seem the right word to use. Nor beautiful, either. They don't go far enough. Oh, it was wonderful—wonderful. It's the first thing I ever saw that couldn't be improved upon by imagination. It just satisfies me here"—she put one hand on her breast—"it made a queer funny ache and yet it was a pleasant ache. Did you ever have an ache like that, Mr. Cuthbert?"

"Well now, I just can't recollect that I ever had."

"I have it lots of times—whenever I see anything royally beautiful. But they shouldn't call that lovely place the Avenue. There is no meaning in a name like that. They should call it—let me see—the White Way of Delight. Isn't that a nice imaginative name? When I don't like the name of a place or a person I always imagine a new one and always think of them so. There was a girl at the asylum whose name was Hepzibah Jenkins, but I always imagined her as Rosalia DeVere. Other people may call that place the Avenue, but I shall always call it the White Way of Delight. Have we really only another mile to go before we get home? I'm glad and I'm sorry. I'm sorry because this drive has been so pleasant and I'm always sorry when pleasant things end. Something still pleasanter may come after, but you can never be sure. And it's so often the case that it isn't pleasanter. That has been my experience anyhow. But I'm glad to think of getting home. You see, I've never had a real home since I can remember. It gives me that pleasant ache again just to think of coming to a really truly home. Oh, isn't that pretty!"

They had driven over the crest of a hill. Below them was a pond, looking almost like a river so long and winding was it. A bridge spanned it midway and from there to its lower end, where an amber-hued belt of sand-hills shut it in from the dark blue gulf beyond, the water was a glory of many shifting hues—the most spiritual shadings of crocus and rose and ethereal green, with other elusive tintings for which no name has ever been found. Above the bridge the pond ran up into fringing groves of fir and maple and lay all darkly translucent in their wavering shadows. Here and there a wild plum leaned out from the bank like a white-clad girl tip toeing to her own reflection. From the marsh at the head of the pond came the clear, mournfully-sweet chorus of the frogs. There was a little gray house peering around a white apple orchard on a slope beyond and, although it was not yet quite dark, a light was shining from one of its windows.

"That's Barry's pond," said Matthew.

"Oh, I don't like that name, either. I shall call it—let me see—the Lake of Shining Waters. Yes, that is the right name for it. I know because of the thrill. When I hit on a name that suits exactly it gives me a thrill. Do things ever give you a thrill?"

Matthew ruminated.

"Well now, yes. It always kind of gives me a thrill to see them ugly white grubs that spade up in the cucumber beds. I hate the look of them."

"Oh, I don't think that can be exactly the same kind of a thrill. Do you think it can? There doesn't seem to be much connection between grubs and lakes of shining waters, does there? But why do other people call it Barry's pond?"

"I reckon because Mr. Barry lives up there in that house. Orchard Slope's the name of his place. If it wasn't for that big bush behind it you could see Green Gables from here. But we have to go over the bridge and round by the road, so it's near half a mile further."

"Has Mr. Barry any little girls? Well, not so very little either—about my size."

"He's got one about eleven. Her name is Diana."

"Oh!" with a long indrawing of breath. "What a perfectly lovely name!"

"Well now, I dunno. There's something dreadful heathenish about it, seems to me. I'd ruther Jane or Mary or some sensible name like that. But when Diana was born there was a schoolmaster boarding there and they gave him the naming of her and he called her Diana."

"I wish there had been a schoolmaster like that around when I was born, then. Oh, here we are at the bridge. I'm going to shut my eyes tight. I'm always afraid going over bridges. I can't help imagining that perhaps just as we get to the middle, they'll crumple up like a jack-knife and nip us. So I shut my eyes. But I always have to open them for all when I think we're getting near the middle. Because, you see, if the bridge *did* crumple up I'd want to *see* it crumple. What a jolly rumble it makes! I always like the rumble part of it. Isn't it splendid there are so many things to like in this world? There, we're over. Now I'll look back. Good night, dear Lake of Shining Waters. I always say good night to the things I love, just as I would to people. I think they like it. That water looks as if it was smiling at me."

When they had driven up the further hill and around a corner Matthew said:

"We're pretty near home now. That's Green Gables over—"

"Oh, don't tell me," she interrupted breathlessly, catching at his partially raised arm and shutting her eyes that she might not see his gesture. "Let me guess. I'm sure I'll guess right."

She opened her eyes and looked about her. They were on the crest of a hill. The sun had set some time since, but the landscape was still clear in the mellow afterlight. To the west a dark church spire rose up against a marigold sky. Below was a little valley and beyond a long, gently-rising slope with snug farmsteads scattered along it. From one to another the child's eyes darted, eager and wistful. At last they lingered on one away to the left, far back from the road, dimly white with blossoming trees in the twilight of the surrounding woods. Over it, in the stainless southwest sky, a great crystal-white star was shining like a lamp of guidance and promise.

"That's it, isn't it?" she said, pointing.

Matthew slapped the reins on the sorrel's back delightedly.

"Well now, you've guessed it! But I reckon Mrs. Spencer described it so's you could tell."

"No, she didn't—really she didn't. All she said might just as well have been about most of those other places. I hadn't any real idea what it looked like. But just as soon as I saw it I felt it was home. Oh, it seems as if I must be in a dream. Do you know, my arm must be black and blue from the elbow up, for I've pinched myself so many times today. Every little while a horrible sickening feeling would come over me and I'd be so afraid it was all a dream. Then I'd pinch myself to see if it was real—until suddenly I remembered that even supposing it was only a dream I'd better go on dreaming as long as I could; so I stopped pinching. But it *is* real and we're nearly home."

With a sigh of rapture she relapsed into silence. Matthew stirred uneasily. He felt glad that it would be Marilla and not he who would have to tell this waif of the world that the home she longed for was not to be hers after all. They drove over Lynde's Hollow, where it was already quite dark, but not so dark that Mrs. Rachel could not see them from her window vantage, and up the hill and into the long lane of Green Gables. By the time they arrived at the house Matthew was shrinking from the approaching revelation with an energy he did not understand. It was not of Marilla or himself he was thinking of or the trouble this mistake was probably going to make for them, but of the child's disappointment. When he thought of that rapt light being quenched in her eyes he had an uncomfortable feeling that he was going to assist at murdering something—much the same feeling that came over him when he had to kill a lamb or calf or any other innocent little creature.

The yard was quite dark as they turned into it and the poplar leaves were rustling silkily all round it.

"Listen to the trees talking in their sleep," she whispered, as he lifted her to the ground. "What nice dreams they must have!"

Then, holding tightly to the carpet-bag which contained "all her worldly goods," she followed him into the house.

CHAPTER III

MARILLA CUTHBERT IS SURPRISED

Marilla came briskly forward as Matthew opened the door. But when her eyes fell on the odd little figure in the stiff, ugly dress, with the long braids of red hair and the eager, luminous eyes, she stopped short in amazement.

"Matthew Cuthbert, who's that?" she ejaculated. "Where is the boy?"

"There wasn't any boy," said Matthew wretchedly. "There was only *her*."

He nodded at the child, remembering that he had never even asked her name.

"No boy! But there *must* have been a boy," insisted Marilla. "We sent word to Mrs. Spencer to bring a boy."

"Well, she didn't. She brought *her*. I asked the stationmaster. And I had to bring her home. She couldn't be left there, no matter where the mistake had come in."

"Well, this is a pretty piece of business!" ejaculated Marilla.

During this dialogue the child had remained silent, her eyes roving from one to the other, all the animation fading out of her face. Suddenly she seemed to grasp the full meaning of what had been said. Dropping her precious carpet-bag she sprang forward a step and clasped her hands.

"You don't want me!" she cried. "You don't want me because I'm not a boy! I might have expected it. Nobody ever did want me. I might have known it was all too beautiful to last. I might have known nobody really did want me. Oh, what shall I do? I'm going to burst into tears!"

Burst into tears she did. Sitting down on a chair by the table, flinging her arms out upon it, and burying her face in them, she proceeded to cry stormily. Marilla and Matthew looked at each other deprecatingly across the stove. Neither of them knew what to say or do. Finally Marilla stepped lamely into the breach.

"Well, well, there's no need to cry so about it."

"Yes, there *is* need!" The child raised her head quickly, revealing a tear-stained face and trembling lips. "*You* would cry, too, if you were an orphan and had come to a place you thought was going to be home and found that they didn't want you because you weren't a boy. Oh, this is the most *tragical* thing that ever happened to me!"

Something like a reluctant smile, rather rusty from long disuse, mellowed Marilla's grim expression.

"Well, don't cry any more. We're not going to turn you out-of-doors tonight. You'll have to stay here until we investigate this affair. What's your name?"

The child hesitated for a moment.

"Will you please call me Cordelia?" she said eagerly.

"*Call* you Cordelia? Is that your name?"

"No-o-o, it's not exactly my name, but I would love to be called Cordelia. It's such a perfectly elegant name."

"I don't know what on earth you mean. If Cordelia isn't your name, what is?"

"Anne Shirley," reluctantly faltered forth the owner of that name, "but, oh, please do call me Cordelia. It can't matter much to you what you call me if I'm only going to be here a little while, can it? And Anne is such an unromantic name."

"Unromantic fiddlesticks!" said the unsympathetic Marilla. "Anne is a real good plain sensible name. You've no need to be ashamed of it."

"Oh, I'm not ashamed of it," explained Anne, "only I like Cordelia better. I've always imagined that my name was Cordelia—at least, I always have of late years. When I was young I used to imagine it was Geraldine, but I like Cordelia better now. But if you call me Anne please call me Anne spelled with an *e*."

"What difference does it make how it's spelled?" asked Marilla with another rusty smile as she picked up the teapot.

"Oh, it makes *such* a difference. It *looks* so much nicer. When you hear a name pronounced can't you always see it in your mind, just as if it was printed out? I can; and A-n-n looks dreadful, but A-n-n-e looks so much more distinguished. If you'll only call me Anne spelled with an *e* I shall try to reconcile myself to not being called Cordelia."

"Very well, then, Anne spelled with an *e*, can you tell us how this mistake came to be made? We sent word to Mrs. Spencer to bring us a boy. Were there no boys at the asylum?"

"Oh, yes, there was an abundance of them. But Mrs. Spencer said *distinctly* that you wanted a girl about eleven years old. And the matron said she thought I would do. You don't know how delighted I was. I couldn't sleep all last night for joy. Oh," she added reproachfully, turning to Matthew, "why didn't you tell me at the station that you didn't want me and leave me there? If I hadn't seen the White Way of Delight and the Lake of Shining Waters it wouldn't be so hard."

"What on earth does she mean?" demanded Marilla, staring at Matthew.

"She—she's just referring to some conversation we had on the road," said Matthew hastily. "I'm going out to put the mare in, Marilla. Have tea ready when I come back."

"Did Mrs. Spencer bring anybody over besides you?" continued Marilla when Matthew had gone out.

"She brought Lily Jones for herself. Lily is only five years old and she is very beautiful and has nut-brown hair. If I was very beautiful and had nut-brown hair would you keep me?"

"No. We want a boy to help Matthew on the farm. A girl would be of no use to us. Take off your hat. I'll lay it and your bag on the hall table."

Anne took off her hat meekly. Matthew came back presently and they sat down to supper. But Anne could not eat. In vain she nibbled at the bread and butter and pecked at the crab-apple preserve out of the little scalloped glass dish by her plate. She did not really make any headway at all.

"You're not eating anything," said Marilla sharply, eyeing her as if it were a serious shortcoming.

Anne sighed.

"I can't. I'm in the depths of despair. Can you eat when you are in the depths of despair?"

"I've never been in the depths of despair, so I can't say," responded Marilla.

"Weren't you? Well, did you ever try to *imagine* you were in the depths of despair?"

"No, I didn't."

"Then I don't think you can understand what it's like. It's a very uncomfortable feeling indeed. When you try to eat a lump comes right up in your throat and you can't swallow anything, not even if it was a chocolate caramel. I had one chocolate caramel once two years ago and it was simply delicious. I've often dreamed since then that I had a lot of chocolate caramels, but I always wake up just when I'm going to eat them. I do hope you won't be offended because I can't eat. Everything is extremely nice, but still I cannot eat."

"I guess she's tired," said Matthew, who hadn't spoken since his return from the barn. "Best put her to bed, Marilla."

Marilla had been wondering where Anne should be put to bed. She had prepared a couch in the kitchen chamber for the desired and expected boy. But, although it was neat and clean, it did not seem quite the thing to put a girl there somehow. But the spare room was out of the question for such a stray waif, so there remained only the east gable room. Marilla lighted a candle and told Anne to follow her, which Anne spiritlessly did, taking her hat and carpet-bag from the hall table as she passed. The hall was fearsomely clean; the little gable chamber in which she presently found herself seemed still cleaner.

Marilla set the candle on a three-legged, three-cornered table and turned down the bedclothes.

"I suppose you have a nightgown?" she questioned.

Anne nodded.

"Yes, I have two. The matron of the asylum made them for me. They're fearfully skimpy. There is never enough to go around in an asylum, so things are always skimpy—at least in a poor asylum like ours. I hate skimpy night-dresses. But one can dream just as well in them as in lovely trailing ones, with frills around the neck, that's one consolation."

"Well, undress as quick as you can and go to bed. I'll come back in a few minutes for the candle. I daren't trust you to put it out yourself. You'd likely set the place on fire."

When Marilla had gone Anne looked around her wistfully. The whitewashed walls were so painfully bare and staring that she thought they must ache over their own bareness. The floor was bare, too, except for a round braided mat in the middle such as Anne had never seen before. In one corner was the bed, a high, old-fashioned one, with four dark, low-turned posts. In the other corner was the aforesaid three-corner table adorned with a fat, red velvet pin-cushion hard enough to turn the point of the most adventurous pin. Above it hung a little six-by-eight mirror. Midway between table and bed was the window, with an icy white muslin frill over it, and opposite it was the wash-stand.

The whole apartment was of a rigidity not to be described in words, but which sent a shiver to the very marrow of Anne's bones. With a sob she hastily discarded her garments, put on the skimpy nightgown and sprang into bed where she burrowed face downward into the pillow and pulled the clothes over her head. When Marilla came up for the light various skimpy articles of raiment scattered most untidily over the floor and a certain tempestuous appearance of the bed were the only indications of any presence save her own.

She deliberately picked up Anne's clothes, placed them neatly on a prim yellow chair, and then, taking up the candle, went over to the bed.

"Good night," she said, a little awkwardly, but not unkindly.

Anne's white face and big eyes appeared over the bedclothes with a startling suddenness.

"How can you call it a *good* night when you know it must be the very worst night I've ever had?" she said reproachfully.

Then she dived down into invisibility again.

Marilla went slowly down to the kitchen and proceeded to wash the supper dishes. Matthew was smoking—a sure sign of perturbation of mind. He seldom smoked, for Marilla set her face against it as a filthy habit; but at certain times and seasons he felt driven to it and then Marilla winked at the practice, realizing that a mere man must have some vent for his emotions.

"Well, this is a pretty kettle of fish," she said wrathfully. "This is what comes of sending word instead of going ourselves. Richard Spencer's folks have twisted that message somehow. One of us will have to drive over and see Mrs. Spencer tomorrow, that's certain. This girl will have to be sent back to the asylum."

"Yes, I suppose so," said Matthew reluctantly.

"You *suppose* so! Don't you know it?"

"Well now, she's a real nice little thing, Marilla. It's kind of a pity to send her back when she's so set on staying here."

"Matthew Cuthbert, you don't mean to say you think we ought to keep her!"

Marilla's astonishment could not have been greater if Matthew had expressed a predilection for standing on his head.

"Well, now, no, I suppose not—not exactly," stammered Matthew, uncomfortably driven into a corner for his precise meaning. "I suppose—we could hardly be expected to keep her."

"I should say not. What good would she be to us?"

"We might be some good to her," said Matthew suddenly and unexpectedly.

"Matthew Cuthbert, I believe that child has bewitched you! I can see as plain as plain that you want to keep her."

"Well now, she's a real interesting little thing," persisted Matthew. "You should have heard her talk coming from the station."

"Oh, she can talk fast enough. I saw that at once. It's nothing in her favour, either. I don't like children who have so much to say. I don't want an orphan girl and if I did she isn't the style I'd pick out. There's something I don't understand about her. No, she's got to be dispatched straightway back to where she came from."

"I could hire a French boy to help me," said Matthew, "and she'd be company for you."

"I'm not suffering for company," said Marilla shortly. "And I'm not going to keep her."

"Well now, it's just as you say, of course, Marilla," said Matthew rising and putting his pipe away. "I'm going to bed."

To bed went Matthew. And to bed, when she had put her dishes away, went Marilla, frowning most resolutely. And upstairs, in the east gable, a lonely, heart-hungry, friendless child cried herself to sleep.

CHAPTER IV

MORNING AT GREEN GABLES

It was broad daylight when Anne awoke and sat up in bed, staring confusedly at the window through which a flood of cheery sunshine was pouring and outside of which something white and feathery waved across glimpses of blue sky.

For a moment she could not remember where she was. First came a delightful thrill, as something very pleasant; then a horrible remembrance. This was Green Gables and they didn't want her because she wasn't a boy!

But it was morning and, yes, it was a cherry tree in full bloom outside of her window. With a bound she was out of bed and across the floor. She pushed up the sash—it went up stiffly and creakily, as if it hadn't been opened for a long time, which was the case; and it stuck so tight that nothing was needed to hold it up.

Anne dropped on her knees and gazed out into the June morning, her eyes glistening with delight. Oh, wasn't it beautiful? Wasn't it a lovely place? Suppose she wasn't really going to stay here! She would imagine she was. There was scope for imagination here.

A huge cherry tree grew outside, so close that its boughs tapped against the house, and it was so thick-set with blossoms that hardly a leaf was to be seen. On both sides of the house was a big orchard, one of apple trees and one of cherry trees, also showered over with blossoms; and their grass was all sprinkled with dandelions. In the garden below were lilac trees purple with flowers, and their dizzily sweet fragrance drifted up to the window on the morning wind.

Below the garden a green field lush with clover sloped down to the hollow where the brook ran and where scores of white birches grew, upspringing airily out of an undergrowth suggestive of delightful possibilities in ferns and mosses and woodsy things generally. Beyond it was a hill, green and feathery with spruce and fir; there was a gap in it where the gray gable end of the little house she had seen from the other side of the Lake of Shining Waters was visible.

Off to the left were the big barns and beyond them, away down over green, low-sloping fields, was a sparkling blue glimpse of sea.

Anne's beauty-loving eyes lingered on it all, taking everything greedily in. She had looked on so many unlovely places in her life, poor child; but this was as lovely as anything she had ever dreamed.

She knelt there, lost to everything but the loveliness around her, until she was startled by a hand on her shoulder. Marilla had come in unheard by the small dreamer.

"It's time you were dressed," she said curtly.

Marilla really did not know how to talk to the child, and her uncomfortable ignorance made her crisp and curt when she did not mean to be.

Anne stood up and drew a long breath.

"Oh, isn't it wonderful?" she said, waving her hand comprehensively at the good world outside.

"It's a big tree," said Marilla, "and it blooms great, but the fruit don't amount to much never—small and wormy."

"Oh, I don't mean just the tree; of course it's lovely—yes, it's *radiantly* lovely—it blooms as if it meant it—but I meant everything, the garden and the orchard and the brook and the woods, the whole big dear world. Don't you feel as if you just loved the world on a morning like this? And I can hear the brook laughing all the way up here. Have you ever noticed what cheerful things brooks are? They're always laughing. Even in wintertime I've heard them under the ice. I'm so glad there's a brook near Green Gables. Perhaps you think it doesn't make any difference to me when you're not going to keep me, but it does. I shall always like to remember that there is a brook at Green Gables even if I never see it again. If there wasn't a brook I'd be *haunted* by the uncomfortable feeling that there ought to be one. I'm not in the depths of despair this morning. I never can be in the morning. Isn't it a splendid thing that there are mornings? But I feel very sad. I've just been imagining that it was really me you wanted after all and that I was to stay here forever and ever. It was a great comfort while it lasted. But the worst of imagining things is that the time comes when you have to stop and that hurts."

"You'd better get dressed and come downstairs and never mind your imaginings," said Marilla as soon as she could get a word in edgewise. "Breakfast is waiting. Wash your face and comb your hair. Leave the window up and turn your bedclothes back over the foot of the bed. Be as smart as you can."

Anne could evidently be smart to some purpose for she was downstairs in ten minutes' time, with her clothes neatly on, her hair brushed and braided, her face washed, and a comfortable consciousness pervading her soul that she had fulfilled all Marilla's requirements. As a matter of fact, however, she had forgotten to turn back the bedclothes.

"I'm pretty hungry this morning," she announced as she slipped into the chair Marilla placed for her. "The world doesn't seem such a howling wilderness as it did last night. I'm so glad it's a sunshiny morning. But I like rainy mornings real well, too. All sorts of mornings are interesting, don't you think? You don't know what's going to happen through the day, and there's so much scope for imagination. But I'm glad it's not rainy today because it's easier to be cheerful and bear up under affliction on a sunshiny day. I feel that I have a good deal to bear up under. It's all very well to read about sorrows and imagine yourself living through them heroically, but it's not so nice when you really come to have them, is it?"

"For pity's sake hold your tongue," said Marilla. "You talk entirely too much for a little girl."

Thereupon Anne held her tongue so obediently and thoroughly that her continued silence made Marilla rather nervous, as if in the presence of something not exactly natural. Matthew also held his tongue—but this was natural,—so that the meal was a very silent one.

As it progressed Anne became more and more abstracted, eating mechanically, with her big eyes fixed unswervingly and unseeingly on the sky outside the window. This made Marilla more nervous than ever; she had an uncomfortable feeling that while this odd child's body might be there at the table her spirit was far away in some remote airy cloudland, borne aloft on the wings of imagination. Who would want such a child about the place?

Yet Matthew wished to keep her, of all unaccountable things! Marilla felt that he wanted it just as much this morning as he had the night before, and that he would go on wanting it. That was Matthew's way—take a whim into his head and cling to it with the most amazing silent persistency—a persistency ten times more potent and effectual in its very silence than if he had talked it out.

When the meal was ended Anne came out of her reverie and offered to wash the dishes.

"Can you wash dishes right?" asked Marilla distrustfully.

"Pretty well. I'm better at looking after children, though. I've had so much experience at that. It's such a pity you haven't any here for me to look after."

"I don't feel as if I wanted any more children to look after than I've got at present. *You're* problem enough in all conscience. What's to be done with you I don't know. Matthew is a most ridiculous man."

"I think he's lovely," said Anne reproachfully. "He is so very sympathetic. He didn't mind how much I talked—he seemed to like it. I felt that he was a kindred spirit as soon as ever I saw him."

"You're both queer enough, if that's what you mean by kindred spirits," said Marilla with a sniff. "Yes, you may wash the dishes. Take plenty of hot water, and be sure you dry them well. I've got enough to attend to this morning for I'll have to drive over to White Sands in the afternoon and see Mrs. Spencer. You'll come with me and we'll settle what's to be done with you. After you've finished the dishes go upstairs and make your bed."

Anne washed the dishes deftly enough, as Marilla, who kept a sharp eye on the process, discerned. Later on she made her bed less successfully, for she had never learned the art of wrestling with a feather tick. But it was done somehow and smoothed down; and then Marilla, to get rid of her, told her she might go out-of-doors and amuse herself until dinner time.

Anne flew to the door, face alight, eyes glowing. On the very threshold she stopped short, wheeled about, came back and sat down by the table, light and glow as effectually blotted out as if some one had clapped an extinguisher on her.

"What's the matter now?" demanded Marilla.

"I don't dare go out," said Anne, in the tone of a martyr relinquishing all earthly joys. "If I can't stay here there is no use in my loving Green Gables. And if I go out there and get acquainted with all those trees and flowers and the orchard and the brook I'll not be able to help loving it. It's hard enough now, so I won't make it any harder. I want to go out so much—everything seems to be calling to me, 'Anne, Anne, come out to us. Anne, Anne, we want a playmate'—but it's better not. There is no use in loving things if you have to be torn from them, is there? And it's so hard to keep from loving things, isn't it? That was why I was so glad when I thought I was going to live here. I thought I'd have so many things to love and nothing to hinder me. But that brief dream is over. I am resigned to my fate now, so I don't think I'll go out for fear I'll get unresigned again. What is the name of that geranium on the window sill, please?"

"That's the apple-scented geranium."

"Oh, I don't mean that sort of a name. I mean just a name you gave it yourself. Didn't you give it a name? May I give it one then? May I call it—let me see—Bonny would do—may I call it Bonny while I'm here? Oh, do let me!"

"Goodness, I don't care. But where on earth is the sense of naming a geranium?"

"Oh, I like things to have handles even if they are only geraniums. It makes them seem more like people. How do you know but that it hurts a geranium's feelings just to be called a geranium and nothing else? You wouldn't like to be called nothing but a woman all the time. Yes, I shall call it Bonny. I named that cherry tree outside my bedroom window this morning. I called it Snow Queen because it was so white. Of course, it won't always be in blossom, but one can imagine that it is, can't one?"

"I never in all my life saw or heard anything to equal her," muttered Marilla, beating a retreat down to the cellar after potatoes. "She is kind of interesting as Matthew says. I can feel already that I'm wondering what on earth she'll say next. She'll be casting a spell over me, too. She's cast it over Matthew. That look he gave me when he went out said everything he said or hinted last night over again. I wish he was like other men and would talk things out. A body could answer back then and argue him into reason. But what's to be done with a man who just *looks*?"

Anne had relapsed into reverie, with her chin in her hands and her eyes on the sky, when Marilla returned from her cellar pilgrimage. There Marilla left her until the early dinner was on the table.

"I suppose I can have the mare and buggy this afternoon, Matthew?" said Marilla.

Matthew nodded and looked wistfully at Anne. Marilla intercepted the look and said grimly:

"I'm going to drive over to White Sands and settle this thing. I'll take Anne with me and Mrs. Spencer will probably make arrangements to send her back to Nova Scotia at once. I'll set your tea out for you and I'll be home in time to milk the cows."

Still Matthew said nothing and Marilla had a sense of having wasted words and breath. There is nothing more aggravating than a man who won't talk back—unless it is a woman who won't.

Matthew hitched the sorrel into the buggy in due time and Marilla and Anne set off. Matthew opened the yard gate for them and as they drove slowly through, he said, to nobody in particular as it seemed:

"Little Jerry Buote from the Creek was here this morning, and I told him I guessed I'd hire him for the summer."

Marilla made no reply, but she hit the unlucky sorrel such a vicious clip with the whip that the fat mare, unused to such treatment, whizzed indignantly down the lane at an alarming pace. Marilla looked back once as the buggy bounced along and saw that aggravating Matthew leaning over the gate, looking wistfully after them.

CHAPTER V

ANNE'S HISTORY

Do you know," said Anne confidentially, "I've made up my mind to enjoy this drive. It's been my experience that you can nearly always enjoy things if you make up your mind firmly that you will. Of course, you must make it up *firmly*. I am not going to think about going back to the asylum while we're having our drive. I'm just going to think about the drive. Oh, look, there's one little early wild rose out! Isn't it lovely? Don't you think it must be glad to be a rose? Wouldn't it be nice if roses could talk? I'm sure they could tell us such lovely things. And isn't pink the most bewitching color in the world? I love it, but I can't wear it. Redheaded people can't wear pink, not even in imagination. Did you ever know of anybody whose hair was red when she was young, but got to be another color when she grew up?"

"No, I don't know as I ever did," said Marilla mercilessly, "and I shouldn't think it likely to happen in your case either."

Anne sighed.

"Well, that is another hope gone. 'My life is a perfect graveyard of buried hopes.' That's a sentence I read in a book once, and I say it over to comfort myself whenever I'm disappointed in anything."

"I don't see where the comforting comes in myself," said Marilla.

"Why, because it sounds so nice and romantic, just as if I were a heroine in a book, you know. I am so fond of romantic things, and a graveyard full of buried hopes is about as romantic a thing as one can imagine isn't it? I'm rather glad I have one. Are we going across the Lake of Shining Waters today?"

"We're not going over Barry's pond, if that's what you mean by your Lake of Shining Waters. We're going by the shore road."

"Shore road sounds nice," said Anne dreamily. "Is it as nice as it sounds? Just when you said 'shore road' I saw it in a picture in my mind, as quick as that! And White Sands is a pretty name, too; but I don't like it as well as Avonlea. Avonlea is a lovely name. It just sounds like music. How far is it to White Sands?"

"It's five miles; and as you're evidently bent on talking you might as well talk to some purpose by telling me what you know about yourself."

"Oh, what I *know* about myself isn't really worth telling," said Anne eagerly. "If you'll only let me tell you what I *imagine* about myself you'll think it ever so much more interesting."

"No, I don't want any of your imaginings. Just you stick to bald facts. Begin at the beginning. Where were you born and how old are you?"

"I was eleven last March," said Anne, resigning herself to bald facts with a little sigh. "And I was born in Bolingbroke, Nova Scotia. My father's name was Walter Shirley, and he was a teacher in the Bolingbroke High School. My mother's name was Bertha Shirley. Aren't Walter and Bertha lovely names? I'm so glad my parents had nice names. It would be a real disgrace to have a father named—well, say Jedediah, wouldn't it?"

"I guess it doesn't matter what a person's name is as long as he behaves himself," said Marilla, feeling herself called upon to inculcate a good and useful moral.

"Well, I don't know." Anne looked thoughtful. "I read in a book once that a rose by any other name would smell as sweet, but I've never been able to believe it. I don't believe a rose *would* be as nice if it was called a thistle or a skunk cabbage. I suppose my father could have been a good man even if he had been called Jedediah; but I'm sure it would have been a cross. Well, my mother was a teacher in the High School, too, but when she married father she gave up teaching, of course. A husband was enough responsibility. Mrs. Thomas said that they were a pair of babies and as poor as church mice. They went to live in a weeny-teeny little yellow house in Bolingbroke. I've never seen that house, but I've imagined it thousands of times. I think it must have had honeysuckle over the parlor window and lilacs in the front yard and lilies of the valley just inside the gate. Yes, and muslin curtains in all the windows. Muslin curtains give a house such an air. I was born in that house. Mrs. Thomas said I was the homeliest baby she ever saw, I was so scrawny and tiny and nothing but eyes, but that mother thought I was perfectly beautiful. I should think a mother would be a better judge than a poor woman who came in to scrub, wouldn't you? I'm glad she was satisfied with me anyhow, I would feel so sad if I thought I was a disappointment to her—because she didn't live very long after that, you see. She died of fever when I was just three months old. I do wish she'd lived long enough for me to remember calling her mother. I think it would be so sweet to say 'mother,' don't you? And father died four days afterwards from fever too. That left me an orphan and folks were at their wits' end, so Mrs. Thomas said, what to do with me. You see, nobody wanted me even then. It seems to be my fate. Father and mother had both come from places far away and it was well known they hadn't any relatives living. Finally Mrs. Thomas said she'd take me, though she was poor and had a drunken husband. She brought me up by hand. Do you know if there is anything in being brought up by hand that ought to make people who are brought up that way better than other people? Because whenever I was naughty Mrs. Thomas would ask me how I could be such a bad girl when she had brought me up by hand—reproachful-like.

"Mr. and Mrs. Thomas moved away from Bolingbroke to Marysville, and I lived with them until I was eight years old. I helped look after the Thomas children—there were four of them younger than me—and I can tell you they took a lot of looking after. Then Mr. Thomas was killed falling under a train and his mother offered to take Mrs. Thomas and the children, but she didn't want me. Mrs. Thomas was at *her* wits' end, so she said, what to do with me. Then Mrs. Hammond from up the river came down and said she'd take me, seeing I was handy with children, and I went up the river to live with her in a little clearing among the stumps. It was a very lonesome place. I'm sure I could never have lived there if I hadn't had an imagination. Mr. Hammond worked a little sawmill up there, and Mrs. Hammond had eight children. She had twins three times. I like babies in moderation, but twins three times in succession is *too much*. I told Mrs. Hammond so firmly, when the last pair came. I used to get so dreadfully tired carrying them about.

"I lived up river with Mrs. Hammond over two years, and then Mr. Hammond died and Mrs. Hammond broke up housekeeping. She divided her children among her relatives and went to the States. I had to go to the asylum at Hopeton, because nobody would take me. They didn't want me at the asylum, either; they said they were overcrowded as it was. But they had to take me and I was there four months until Mrs. Spencer came."

Anne finished up with another sigh, of relief this time. Evidently she did not like talking about her experiences in a world that had not wanted her.

"Did you ever go to school?" demanded Marilla, turning the sorrel mare down the shore road.

"Not a great deal. I went a little the last year I stayed with Mrs. Thomas. When I went up river we were so far from a school that I couldn't walk it in winter and there was a vacation in summer, so I could only go in the spring and fall. But of course I went while I was at the asylum. I can read pretty well and I know ever so many pieces of poetry off by heart—'The Battle of Hohenlinden' and 'Edinburgh after Flodden,' and 'Bingen of the Rhine,' and most of the 'Lady of the Lake' and most of 'The Seasons' by James Thompson. Don't you just love poetry that gives you a crinkly feeling up and down your back? There is a piece in the Fifth Reader—'The Downfall of Poland'—that is just full of thrills. Of course, I wasn't in the Fifth Reader—I was only in the Fourth—but the big girls used to lend me theirs to read."

"Were those women—Mrs. Thomas and Mrs. Hammond—good to you?" asked Marilla, looking at Anne out of the corner of her eye.

"O-o-o-h," faltered Anne. Her sensitive little face suddenly flushed scarlet and embarrassment sat on her brow. "Oh, they *meant* to be—I know they meant to be just as good and kind as possible. And when people mean to be good to you, you don't mind very much when they're not quite—always. They had a good deal to worry them, you know. It's very trying to have a drunken husband, you see; and it must be very trying to have twins three times in succession, don't you think? But I feel sure they meant to be good to me."

Marilla asked no more questions. Anne gave herself up to a silent rapture over the shore road and Marilla guided the sorrel abstractedly while she pondered deeply. Pity was suddenly stirring in her heart for the child. What a starved, unloved life she had had—a life of drudgery and poverty and neglect; for Marilla was shrewd enough to read between the lines of Anne's history and divine the truth. No wonder she had been so delighted at the prospect of a real home. It was a pity she had to be sent back. What if she, Marilla, should indulge Matthew's unaccountable whim and let her stay? He was set on it; and the child seemed a nice, teachable little thing.

"She's got too much to say," thought Marilla, "but she might be trained out of that. And there's nothing rude or slangy in what she does say. She's ladylike. It's likely her people were nice folks."

The shore road was "woodsy and wild and lonesome." On the right hand, scrub firs, their spirits quite unbroken by long years of tussle with the gulf winds, grew thickly. On the left were the steep red sandstone cliffs, so near the track in places that a mare of less steadiness than the sorrel might have tried the nerves of the people behind her. Down at the base of the cliffs were heaps of surf-worn rocks or little sandy coves inlaid with pebbles as with ocean jewels; beyond lay the sea, shimmering and blue, and over it soared the gulls, their pinions flashing silvery in the sunlight.

"Isn't the sea wonderful?" said Anne, rousing from a long, wide-eyed silence. "Once, when I lived in Marysville, Mr. Thomas hired an express wagon and took us all to spend the day at the shore ten miles away. I enjoyed every moment of that day, even if I had to look after the children all the time. I lived it over in happy dreams for years. But this shore is nicer than the Marysville shore. Aren't those gulls splendid? Would you like to be a gull? I think I would—that is, if I couldn't be a human girl. Don't you think it would be nice to wake up at sunrise and swoop down over the water and away out over that lovely blue all day; and then at night to fly back to one's nest? Oh, I can just imagine myself doing it. What big house is that just ahead, please?"

"That's the White Sands Hotel. Mr. Kirke runs it, but the season hasn't begun yet. There are heaps of Americans come there for the summer. They think this shore is just about right."

"I was afraid it might be Mrs. Spencer's place," said Anne mournfully. "I don't want to get there. Somehow, it will seem like the end of everything."

CHAPTER VI

MARILLA MAKES UP HER MIND

Get there they did, however, in due season. Mrs. Spencer lived in a big yellow house at White Sands Cove, and she came to the door with surprise and welcome mingled on her benevolent face.

"Dear, dear," she exclaimed, "you're the last folks I was looking for today, but I'm real glad to see you. You'll put your horse in? And how are you, Anne?"

"I'm as well as can be expected, thank you," said Anne smilelessly. A blight seemed to have descended on her.

"I suppose we'll stay a little while to rest the mare," said Marilla, "but I promised Matthew I'd be home early. The fact is, Mrs. Spencer, there's been a queer mistake somewhere, and I've come over to see where it is. We sent word, Matthew and I, for you to bring us a boy from the asylum. We told your brother Robert to tell you we wanted a boy ten or eleven years old."

"Marilla Cuthbert, you don't say so!" said Mrs. Spencer in distress. "Why, Robert sent word down by his daughter Nancy and she said you wanted a girl—didn't she Flora Jane?" appealing to her daughter who had come out to the steps.

"She certainly did, Miss Cuthbert," corroborated Flora Jane earnestly.

"I'm dreadful sorry," said Mrs. Spencer. "It's too bad; but it certainly wasn't my fault, you see, Miss Cuthbert. I did the best I could and I thought I was following your instructions. Nancy is a terrible flighty thing. I've often had to scold her well for her heedlessness."

"It was our own fault," said Marilla resignedly. "We should have come to you ourselves and not left an important message to be passed along by word of mouth in that fashion. Anyhow, the mistake has been made and the only thing to do is to set it right. Can we send the child back to the asylum? I suppose they'll take her back, won't they?"

"I suppose so," said Mrs. Spencer thoughtfully, "but I don't think it will be necessary to send her back. Mrs. Peter Blewett was up here yesterday, and she was saying to me how much she wished she'd sent by me for a little girl to help her. Mrs. Peter has a large family, you know, and she finds it hard to get help. Anne will be the very girl for her. I call it positively providential."

Marilla did not look as if she thought Providence had much to do with the matter. Here was an unexpectedly good chance to get this unwelcome orphan off her hands, and she did not even feel grateful for it.

She knew Mrs. Peter Blewett only by sight as a small, shrewish-faced woman without an ounce of superfluous flesh on her bones. But she had heard of her. "A terrible worker and driver," Mrs. Peter was said to be; and discharged servant girls told fearsome tales of her temper and stinginess, and her family of pert, quarrelsome children. Marilla felt a qualm of conscience at the thought of handing Anne over to her tender mercies.

"Well, I'll go in and we'll talk the matter over," she said.

"And if there isn't Mrs. Peter coming up the lane this blessed minute!" exclaimed Mrs. Spencer, bustling her guests through the hall into the parlor, where a deadly chill struck on them as if the air had been strained so long through dark green, closely drawn blinds that it had lost every particle of warmth it had ever possessed. "That is real lucky, for we can settle the matter right away. Take the armchair, Miss Cuthbert. Anne, you sit here on the ottoman and don't wiggle. Let me take your hats. Flora Jane, go out and put the kettle on. Good afternoon, Mrs. Blewett. We were just saying how fortunate it was you happened along. Let me introduce you two ladies. Mrs. Blewett, Miss Cuthbert. Please excuse me for just a moment. I forgot to tell Flora Jane to take the buns out of the oven."

Mrs. Spencer whisked away, after pulling up the blinds. Anne sitting mutely on the ottoman, with her hands clasped tightly in her lap, stared at Mrs Blewett as one fascinated. Was she to be given into the keeping of this sharp-faced, sharp-eyed woman? She felt a lump coming up in her throat and her eyes smarted painfully. She was beginning to be afraid she couldn't keep the tears back when Mrs. Spencer returned, flushed and beaming, quite capable of taking any and every difficulty, physical, mental or spiritual, into consideration and settling it out of hand.

"It seems there's been a mistake about this little girl, Mrs. Blewett," she said. "I was under the impression that Mr. and Miss Cuthbert wanted a little girl to adopt. I was certainly told so. But it seems it was a boy they wanted. So if you're still of the same mind you were yesterday, I think she'll be just the thing for you."

Mrs. Blewett darted her eyes over Anne from head to foot.

"How old are you and what's your name?" she demanded.

"Anne Shirley," faltered the shrinking child, not daring to make any stipulations regarding the spelling thereof, "and I'm eleven years old."

"Humph! You don't look as if there was much to you. But you're wiry. I don't know but the wiry ones are the best after all. Well, if I take you you'll have to be a good girl, you know—good and smart and respectful. I'll expect you to earn your keep, and no mistake about that. Yes, I suppose I might as well take her off your hands, Miss Cuthbert. The baby's awful fractious, and I'm clean worn out attending to him. If you like I can take her right home now."

Marilla looked at Anne and softened at sight of the child's pale face with its look of mute misery—the misery of a helpless little creature who finds itself once more caught in the trap from which it had escaped. Marilla felt an uncomfortable conviction that, if she denied the appeal of that look, it would haunt her to her dying day. Moreover, she did not fancy Mrs. Blewett. To hand a sensitive, "highstrung" child over to such a woman! No, she could not take the responsibility of doing that!

"Well, I don't know," she said slowly. "I didn't say that Matthew and I had absolutely decided that we wouldn't keep her. In fact I may say that Matthew is disposed to keep her. I just came over to find out how the mistake had occurred. I think I'd better take her home again and talk it over with Matthew. I feel that I oughtn't to decide on anything without consulting him. If we make up our mind not to keep her we'll bring or send her over to you tomorrow night. If we don't you may know that she is going to stay with us. Will that suit you, Mrs. Blewett?"

"I suppose it'll have to," said Mrs. Blewett ungraciously.

During Marilla's speech a sunrise had been dawning on Anne's face. First the look of despair faded out; then came a faint flush of hope; her eyes grew deep and bright as morning stars. The child was quite transfigured; and, a moment later, when Mrs. Spencer and Mrs. Blewett went out in quest of a recipe the latter had come to borrow she sprang up and flew across the room to Marilla.

"Oh, Miss Cuthbert, did you really say that perhaps you would let me stay at Green Gables?" she said, in a breathless whisper, as if speaking aloud might shatter the glorious possibility. "Did you really say it? Or did I only imagine that you did?"

"I think you'd better learn to control that imagination of yours, Anne, if you can't distinguish between what is real and what isn't," said Marilla crossly. "Yes, you did hear me say just that and no more. It isn't decided yet and perhaps we will conclude to let Mrs. Blewett take you after all. She certainly needs you much more than I do."

"I'd rather go back to the asylum than go to live with her," said Anne passionately. "She looks exactly like a—like a gimlet."

Marilla smothered a smile under the conviction that Anne must be reproved for such a speech.

"A little girl like you should be ashamed of talking so about a lady and a stranger," she said severely. "Go back and sit down quietly and hold your tongue and behave as a good girl should."

"I'll try to do and be anything you want me, if you'll only keep me," said Anne, returning meekly to her ottoman.

When they arrived back at Green Gables that evening Matthew met them in the lane. Marilla from afar had noted him prowling along it and guessed his motive. She was prepared for the relief she read in his face when he saw that she had at least brought Anne back with her. But she said nothing to him, relative to the affair, until they were both out in the yard behind the barn milking the cows. Then she briefly told him Anne's history and the result of the interview with Mrs. Spencer.

"I wouldn't give a dog I liked to that Blewett woman," said Matthew with unusual vim.

"I don't fancy her style myself," admitted Marilla, "but it's that or keeping her ourselves, Matthew. And since you seem to want her, I suppose I'm willing—or have to be. I've been thinking over the idea until I've got kind of used to it. It seems a sort of duty. I've never brought up a child, especially a girl, and I dare say I'll make a terrible mess of it. But I'll do my best. So far as I'm concerned, Matthew, she may stay."

Matthew's shy face was a glow of delight.

"Well now, I reckoned you'd come to see it in that light, Marilla," he said. "She's such an interesting little thing."

"It'd be more to the point if you could say she was a useful little thing," retorted Marilla, "but I'll make it my business to see she's trained to be that. And mind, Matthew, you're not to go interfering with my methods. Perhaps an old maid doesn't know much about bringing up a child, but I guess she knows more than an old bachelor. So you just leave me to manage her. When I fail it'll be time enough to put your oar in."

"There, there, Marilla, you can have your own way," said Matthew reassuringly. "Only be as good and kind to her as you can without spoiling her. I kind of think she's one of the sort you can do anything with if you only get her to love you."

Marilla sniffed, to express her contempt for Matthew's opinions concerning anything feminine, and walked off to the dairy with the pails.

"I won't tell her tonight that she can stay," she reflected, as she strained the milk into the creamers. "She'd be so excited that she wouldn't sleep a wink. Marilla Cuthbert, you're fairly in for it. Did you ever suppose you'd see the day when you'd be adopting an orphan girl? It's surprising enough; but not so surprising as that Matthew should be at the bottom of it, him that always seemed to have such a mortal dread of little girls. Anyhow, we've decided on the experiment and goodness only knows what will come of it."

CHAPTER VII

ANNE SAYS HER PRAYERS

When Marilla took Anne up to bed that night she said stiffly:

"Now, Anne, I noticed last night that you threw your clothes all about the floor when you took them off. That is a very untidy habit, and I can't allow it at all. As soon as you take off any article of clothing fold it neatly and place it on the chair. I haven't any use at all for little girls who aren't neat."

"I was so harrowed up in my mind last night that I didn't think about my clothes at all," said Anne. "I'll fold them nicely tonight. They always made us do that at the asylum. Half the time, though, I'd forget, I'd be in such a hurry to get into bed nice and quiet and imagine things."

"You'll have to remember a little better if you stay here," admonished Marilla. "There, that looks something like. Say your prayers now and get into bed."

"I never say any prayers," announced Anne.

Marilla looked horrified astonishment.

"Why, Anne, what do you mean? Were you never taught to say your prayers? God always wants little girls to say their prayers. Don't you know who God is, Anne?"

"'God is a spirit, infinite, eternal and unchangeable, in His being, wisdom, power, holiness, justice, goodness, and truth,'" responded Anne promptly and glibly.

Marilla looked rather relieved.

"So you do know something then, thank goodness! You're not quite a heathen. Where did you learn that?"

"Oh, at the asylum Sunday school. They made us learn the whole catechism. I liked it pretty well. There's something splendid about some of the words. 'Infinite, eternal and unchangeable.' Isn't that grand? It has such a roll to it—just like a big organ playing. You couldn't quite call it poetry, I suppose, but it sounds a lot like it, doesn't it?"

"We're not talking about poetry, Anne—we are talking about

saying your prayers. Don't you know it's a terrible wicked thing not to say your prayers every night? I'm afraid you are a very bad little girl."

"You'd find it easier to be bad than good if you had red hair," said Anne reproachfully. "People who haven't red hair don't know what trouble is. Mrs. Thomas told me that God made my hair red *on purpose*, and I've never cared about Him since. And anyhow I'd always be too tired at night to bother saying prayers. People who have to look after twins can't be expected to say their prayers. Now, do you honestly think they can?"

Marilla decided that Anne's religious training must be begun at once. Plainly there was no time to be lost.

"You must say your prayers while you are under my roof, Anne."

"Why, of course, if you want me to," assented Anne cheerfully. "I'd do anything to oblige you. But you'll have to tell me what to say for this once. After I get into bed I'll imagine out a real nice prayer to say always. I believe that it will be quite interesting, now that I come to think of it."

"You must kneel down," said Marilla in embarrassment.

Anne knelt at Marilla's knee and looked up gravely.

"Why must people kneel down to pray? If I really wanted to pray I'll tell you what I'd do. I'd go out into a great big field all alone or into the deep, deep, woods, and I'd look up into the sky—up—up—up—into that lovely blue sky that looks as if there was no end to its blueness. And then I'd just *feel* a prayer. Well, I'm ready. What am I to say?"

Marilla felt more embarrassed than ever. She had intended to teach Anne the childish classic, "Now I lay me down to sleep." But she had, as I have told you, the glimmerings of a sense of humor—which is simply another name for a sense of fitness of things; and it suddenly occurred to her that that simple little prayer, sacred to white-robed childhood lisping at motherly knees, was entirely unsuited to this freckled witch of a girl who knew and cared nothing about God's love, since she had never had it translated to her through the medium of human love.

"You're old enough to pray for yourself, Anne," she said finally. "Just thank God for your blessings and ask Him humbly for the things you want."

"Well, I'll do my best," promised Anne, burying her face in Marilla's lap. "Gracious heavenly Father—that's the way the ministers say it in church, so I suppose it's all right in private prayer, isn't it?" she interjected, lifting her head for a moment.

"Gracious heavenly Father, I thank Thee for the White Way of Delight and the Lake of Shining Waters and Bonny and the Snow Queen. I'm really extremely grateful for them. And that's all the blessings I can think of just now to thank Thee for. As for the things I want, they're so numerous that it would take a great deal of time to name them all so I will only mention the two most important. Please let me stay at Green Gables; and please let me be good-looking when I grow up. I remain,

"Yours respectfully,
Anne Shirley."

"There, did I do all right?" she asked eagerly, getting up. "I could have made it much more flowery if I'd had a little more time to think it over."

Poor Marilla was only preserved from complete collapse by remembering that it was not irreverence, but simply spiritual ignorance on the part of Anne that was responsible for this extraordinary petition. She tucked the child up in bed, mentally vowing that she should be taught a prayer the very next day, and was leaving the room with the light when Anne called her back.

"I've just thought of it now. I should have said, 'Amen' in place of 'yours respectfully,' shouldn't I?—the way the ministers do. I'd forgotten it, but I felt a prayer should be finished off in some way, so I put in the other. Do you suppose it will make any difference?"

"I—I don't suppose it will," said Marilla. "Go to sleep now like a good child. Good night."

"I can only say good night tonight with a clear conscience," said Anne, cuddling luxuriously down among her pillows.

Marilla retreated to the kitchen, set the candle firmly on the table, and glared at Matthew.

"Matthew Cuthbert, it's about time somebody adopted that child and taught her something. She's next door to a perfect heathen. Will you believe that she never said a prayer in her life till tonight? I'll send her to the manse tomorrow and borrow the Peep of the Day series, that's what I'll do. And she shall go to Sunday school just as soon as I can get some suitable clothes made for her. I foresee that I shall have my hands full. Well, well, we can't get through this world without our share of trouble. I've had a pretty easy life of it so far, but my time has come at last and I suppose I'll just have to make the best of it."

CHAPTER VIII

ANNE'S BRINGING-UP IS BEGUN

For reasons best known to herself, Marilla did not tell Anne that she was to stay at Green Gables until the next afternoon. During the forenoon she kept the child busy with various tasks and watched over her with a keen eye while she did them. By noon she had concluded that Anne was smart and obedient, willing to work and quick to learn; her most serious shortcoming seemed to be a tendency to fall into daydreams in the middle of a task and forget all about it until such time as she was sharply recalled to earth by a reprimand or a catastrophe.

When Anne had finished washing the dinner dishes she suddenly confronted Marilla with the air and expression of one desperately determined to learn the worst. Her thin little body trembled from head to foot; her face flushed and her eyes dilated until they were almost black; she clasped her hands tightly and said in an imploring voice:

"Oh, please, Miss Cuthbert, won't you tell me if you are going to send me away or not? I've tried to be patient all the morning, but I really feel that I cannot bear not knowing any longer. It's a dreadful feeling. Please tell me."

"You haven't scalded the dishcloth in clean hot water as I told you to do," said Marilla immovably. "Just go and do it before you ask any more questions, Anne."

Anne went and attended to the dishcloth. Then she returned to Marilla and fastened imploring eyes on the latter's face.

"Well," said Marilla, unable to find any excuse for deferring her explanation longer, "I suppose I might as well tell you. Matthew and I have decided to keep you—that is, if you will try to be a good little girl and show yourself grateful. Why, child, whatever is the matter?"

"I'm crying," said Anne in a tone of bewilderment. "I can't think why. I'm glad as glad can be. Oh, *glad* doesn't seem the right word at all. I was glad about the White Way and the cherry blossoms—but this! Oh, it's something more than glad. I'm so happy. I'll try to be so good. It will be uphill work, I expect, for Mrs. Thomas often told me I was desperately wicked. However, I'll do my very best. But can you tell me why I'm crying?"

"I suppose it's because you're all excited and worked up," said Marilla disapprovingly. "Sit down on that chair and try to calm yourself. I'm afraid you both cry and laugh far too easily. Yes, you can stay here and we will try to do right by you. You must go to school; but it's only a fortnight till vacation so it isn't worth while for you to start before it opens again in September."

"What am I to call you?" asked Anne. "Shall I always say Miss Cuthbert? Can I call you Aunt Marilla?"

"No; you'll call me just plain Marilla. I'm not used to being called Miss Cuthbert and it would make me nervous."

"It sounds awfully disrespectful to just say Marilla," protested Anne.

"I guess there'll be nothing disrespectful in it if you're careful to speak respectfully. Everybody, young and old, in Avonlea calls me Marilla except the minister. He says Miss Cuthbert—when he thinks of it."

"I'd love to call you Aunt Marilla," said Anne wistfully. "I've never had an aunt or any relation at all—not even a grandmother. It would make me feel as if I really belonged to you. Can't I call you Aunt Marilla?"

"No. I'm not your aunt and I don't believe in calling people names that don't belong to them."

"But we could imagine you were my aunt."

"I couldn't," said Marilla grimly.

"Do you never imagine things different from what they really are?" asked Anne wide-eyed.

"No."

"Oh!" Anne drew a long breath. "Oh, Miss—Marilla, how much you miss!"

"I don't believe in imagining things different from what they really are," retorted Marilla. "When the Lord puts us in certain circumstances He doesn't mean for us to imagine them away. And that reminds me. Go into the sitting room, Anne—be sure your feet are clean and don't let any flies in—and bring me out the illustrated card that's on the mantelpiece. The Lord's Prayer is on it and you'll devote your spare time this afternoon to learning it off by heart. There's to be no more of such praying as I heard last night."

"I suppose I was very awkward," said Anne apologetically, "but then, you see, I'd never had any practice. You couldn't really expect a person to pray very well the first time she tried, could you? I thought out a splendid prayer after I went to bed, just as I promised you I would. It was nearly as long as a minister's and so poetical. But would you believe it? I couldn't remember one word when I woke up this morning. And I'm afraid I'll never be able to think out another one as good. Somehow, things never are so good when they're thought out a second time. Have you ever noticed that?"

"Here is something for you to notice, Anne. When I tell you to do a thing I want you to obey me at once and not stand stock-still and discourse about it. Just you go and do as I bid you."

Anne promptly departed for the sitting-room across the hall; she failed to return; after waiting ten minutes Marilla laid down her knitting and marched after her with a grim expression. She found Anne standing motionless before a picture hanging on the wall between the two windows, with her eyes astar with dreams. The white and green light strained through apple trees and clustering vines outside fell over the rapt little figure with a half-unearthly radiance.

"Anne, whatever are you thinking of?" demanded Marilla sharply.

Anne came back to earth with a start.

"That," she said, pointing to the picture—a rather vivid chromo entitled, "Christ Blessing Little Children"—"and I was just imagining I was one of them—that I was the little girl in the blue dress, standing off by herself in the corner as if she didn't belong to anybody, like me. She looks lonely and sad, don't you think? I guess she hadn't any father or mother of her own. But she wanted to be blessed, too, so she just crept shyly up on the outside of the crowd, hoping nobody would notice her—except Him. I'm sure I know just how she felt. Her heart must have beat and her hands must have got cold, like mine did when I asked you if I could stay. She was afraid He mightn't notice her. But it's likely He did, don't you think? I've been trying to imagine it all out—her edging a little nearer all the time until she was quite close to Him; and then He would look at her and put His hand on her hair and oh, such a thrill of joy as would run over her! But I wish the artist hadn't painted Him so sorrowful looking. All His pictures are like that, if you've noticed. But I don't believe He could really have looked so sad or the children would have been afraid of Him."

"Anne," said Marilla, wondering why she had not broken into this speech long before, "you shouldn't talk that way. It's irreverent—positively irreverent."

Anne's eyes marveled.

"Why, I felt just as reverent as could be. I'm sure I didn't mean to be irreverent."

"Well I don't suppose you did—but it doesn't sound right to talk so familiarly about such things. And another thing, Anne, when I send you after something you're to bring it at once and not fall into mooning and imagining before pictures. Remember that. Take that card and come right to the kitchen. Now, sit down in the corner and learn that prayer off by heart."

Anne set the card up against the jugful of apple blossoms she had brought in to decorate the dinner-table—Marilla had eyed that decoration askance, but had said nothing—propped her chin on her hands, and fell to studying it intently for several silent minutes.

"I like this," she announced at length. "It's beautiful. I've heard it before—I heard the superintendent of the asylum Sunday school say it over once. But I didn't like it then. He had such a cracked voice and he prayed it so mournfully. I really felt sure he thought praying was a disagreeable duty. This isn't poetry, but it makes me feel just the same way poetry does. 'Our Father who art in heaven hallowed be Thy name.' That is just like a line of music. Oh, I'm so glad you thought of making me learn this, Miss—Marilla."

"Well, learn it and hold your tongue," said Marilla shortly.

Anne tipped the vase of apple blossoms near enough to bestow a soft kiss on a pink-cupped bud, and then studied diligently for some moments longer.

"Marilla," she demanded presently, "do you think that I shall ever have a bosom friend in Avonlea?"

"A—a what kind of friend?"

"A bosom friend—an intimate friend, you know—a really kindred spirit to whom I can confide my inmost soul. I've dreamed of meeting her all my life. I never really supposed I would, but so many of my loveliest dreams have come true all at once that perhaps this one will, too. Do you think it's possible?"

"Diana Barry lives over at Orchard Slope and she's about your age. She's a very nice little girl, and perhaps she will be a playmate for you when she comes home. She's visiting her aunt over at Carmody just now. You'll have to be careful how you behave yourself, though. Mrs. Barry is a very particular woman. She won't let Diana play with any little girl who isn't nice and good."

Anne looked at Marilla through the apple blossoms, her eyes aglow with interest.

"What is Diana like? Her hair isn't red, is it? Oh, I hope not. It's bad enough to have red hair myself, but I positively couldn't endure it in a bosom friend."

"Diana is a very pretty little girl. She has black eyes and hair and rosy cheeks. And she is good and smart, which is better than being pretty."

Marilla was as fond of morals as the Duchess in Wonderland, and was firmly convinced that one should be tacked on to every remark made to a child who was being brought up.

But Anne waved the moral inconsequently aside and seized only on the delightful possibilities before it.

"Oh, I'm so glad she's pretty. Next to being beautiful oneself—and that's impossible in my case—it would be best to have a beautiful bosom friend. When I lived with Mrs. Thomas she had a bookcase in her sitting room with glass doors. There weren't any books in it; Mrs. Thomas kept her best china and her preserves there—when she had any preserves to keep. One of the doors was broken. Mr. Thomas smashed it one night when he was slightly intoxicated. But the other was whole and I used to pretend that my reflection in it was another little girl who lived in it. I called her Katie Maurice, and we were very intimate. I used to talk to her by the hour, especially on Sunday, and tell her everything. Katie was the comfort and consolation of my life. We used to pretend that the bookcase was enchanted and that if I only knew the spell I could open the door and step right into the room where Katie Maurice lived, instead of into Mrs. Thomas's shelves of preserves and china. And then Katie Maurice would have taken me by the hand and led me out into a wonderful place, all flowers and sunshine and fairies, and we would have lived there happy forever after. When I went to live with Mrs. Hammond it just broke my heart to leave Katie Maurice. She felt it dreadfully, too, I know she did, for she was crying when she kissed me good-bye through the bookcase door. There was no bookcase at Mrs. Hammond's. But just up the river a little way from the house there was a long green little valley, and the loveliest echo lived there. It echoed back every word you said, even if you didn't talk a bit loud. So I imagined that it was a little girl called Violetta and we were great friends and I loved her almost as well as I loved Katie Maurice—not quite, but almost, you know. The night before I went to the asylum I said good-bye to Violetta, and oh, her good-bye came back to me in such sad, sad tones. I had become so attached to her that I hadn't the heart to imagine a bosom friend at the asylum, even if there had been any scope for imagination there."

"I think it's just as well there wasn't," said Marilla dryly. "I don't approve of such goings-on. You seem to half believe your own imaginations. It will be well for you to have a real live friend to put such nonsense out of your head. But don't let Mrs. Barry hear you talking about your Katie Maurices and your Violettas or she'll think you tell stories."

"Oh, I won't. I couldn't talk of them to everybody—their memories are too sacred for that. But I thought I'd like to have you know about them. Oh, look, here's a big bee just tumbled out of an apple blossom. Just think what a lovely place to live—in an apple blossom! Fancy going to sleep in it when the wind was rocking it. If I wasn't a human girl I think I'd like to be a bee and live among the flowers."

"Yesterday you wanted to be a sea gull," sniffed Marilla. "I think you are very fickle minded. I told you to learn that prayer and not talk. But it seems impossible for you to stop talking if you've got anybody that will listen to you. So go up to your room and learn it."

"Oh, I know it pretty nearly all now—all but just the last line."

"Well, never mind, do as I tell you. Go to your room and finish learning it well, and stay there until I call you down to help me get tea."

"Can I take the apple blossoms with me for company?" pleaded Anne.

"No; you don't want your room cluttered up with flowers. You should have left them on the tree in the first place."

"I did feel a little that way, too," said Anne. "I kind of felt I shouldn't shorten their lovely lives by picking them—I wouldn't want to be picked if I were an apple blossom. But the temptation was *irresistible*. What do you do when you meet with an irresistible temptation?"

"Anne, did you hear me tell you to go to your room?"

Anne sighed, retreated to the east gable, and sat down in a chair by the window.

"There—I know this prayer. I learned that last sentence coming upstairs. Now I'm going to imagine things into this room so that they'll always stay imagined. The floor is covered with a white velvet carpet with pink roses all over it and there are pink silk curtains at the windows. The walls are hung with gold and silver brocade tapestry. The furniture is mahogany. I never saw any mahogany, but it does sound *so* luxurious. This is a couch all heaped with gorgeous silken cushions, pink and blue and crimson and gold, and I am reclining gracefully on it. I can see my reflection in that splendid big mirror hanging on the wall. I am tall and regal, clad in a gown of trailing white lace, with a pearl cross on my breast and pearls in my hair. My hair is of midnight darkness and my skin is a clear ivory pallor. My name is the Lady Cordelia Fitzgerald. No, it isn't—I can't make *that* seem real."

She danced up to the little looking-glass and peered into it. Her pointed freckled face and solemn gray eyes peered back at her.

"You're only Anne of Green Gables," she said earnestly, "and I see you, just as you are looking now, whenever I try to imagine I'm the Lady Cordelia. But it's a million times nicer to be Anne of Green Gables than Anne of nowhere in particular, isn't it?"

She bent forward, kissed her reflection affectionately, and betook herself to the open window.

"Dear Snow Queen, good afternoon. And good afternoon dear birches down in the hollow. And good afternoon, dear gray house up on the hill. I wonder if Diana is to be my bosom friend. I hope she will, and I shall love her very much. But I must never quite forget Katie Maurice and Violetta. They would feel so hurt if I did and I'd hate to hurt anybody's feelings, even a little bookcase girl's or a little echo girl's. I must be careful to remember them and send them a kiss every day."

Anne blew a couple of airy kisses from her fingertips past the cherry blossoms and then, with her chin in her hands, drifted luxuriously out on a sea of daydreams.

CHAPTER IX

MRS. RACHEL LYNDE IS PROPERLY HORRIFIED

Anne had been a fortnight at Green Gables before Mrs. Lynde arrived to inspect her. Mrs. Rachel, to do her justice, was not to blame for this. A severe and unseasonable attack of grippe had confined that good lady to her house ever since the occasion of her last visit to Green Gables. Mrs. Rachel was not often sick and had a well-defined contempt for people who were; but grippe, she asserted, was like no other illness on earth and could only be interpreted as one of the special visitations of Providence. As soon as her doctor allowed her to put her foot out-of-doors she hurried up to Green Gables, bursting with curiosity to see Matthew and Marilla's orphan, concerning whom all sorts of stories and suppositions had gone abroad in Avonlea.

Anne had made good use of every waking moment of that fortnight. Already she was acquainted with every tree and shrub about the place. She had discovered that a lane opened out below the apple orchard and ran up through a belt of woodland; and she had explored it to its furthest end in all its delicious vagaries of brook and bridge, fir coppice and wild cherry arch, corners thick with fern, and branching byways of maple and mountain ash.

She had made friends with the spring down in the hollow—that wonderful deep, clear icy-cold spring; it was set about with smooth red sandstones and rimmed in by great palm-like clumps of water fern; and beyond it was a log bridge over the brook.

That bridge led Anne's dancing feet up over a wooded hill beyond, where perpetual twilight reigned under the straight, thick-growing firs and spruces; the only flowers there were myriads of delicate "June bells," those shyest and sweetest of woodland blooms, and a few pale, aerial starflowers, like the spirits of last year's blossoms. Gossamers glimmered like threads of silver among the trees and the fir boughs and tassels seemed to utter friendly speech.

All these raptured voyages of exploration were made in the odd half hours which she was allowed for play, and Anne talked Matthew and Marilla half-deaf over her discoveries. Not that Matthew complained, to be sure; he listened to it all with a wordless smile of enjoyment on his face; Marilla permitted the "chatter" until she found herself becoming too interested in it, whereupon she always promptly quenched Anne by a curt command to hold her tongue.

Anne was out in the orchard when Mrs. Rachel came, wandering at her own sweet will through the lush, tremulous grasses splashed with ruddy evening sunshine; so that good lady had an excellent chance to talk her illness fully over, describing every ache and pulse beat with such evident enjoyment that Marilla thought even grippe must bring its compensations. When details were exhausted Mrs. Rachel introduced the real reason of her call.

"I've been hearing some surprising things about you and Matthew."

"I don't suppose you are any more surprised than I am myself," said Marilla. "I'm getting over my surprise now."

"It was too bad there was such a mistake," said Mrs. Rachel sympathetically. "Couldn't you have sent her back?"

"I suppose we could, but we decided not to. Matthew took a fancy to her. And I must say I like her myself—although I admit she has her faults. The house seems a different place already. She's a real bright little thing."

Marilla said more than she had intended to say when she began, for she read disapproval in Mrs. Rachel's expression.

"It's a great responsibility you've taken on yourself," said that lady gloomily, "especially when you've never had any experience with children. You don't know much about her or her real disposition, I suppose, and there's no guessing how a child like that will turn out. But I don't want to discourage you I'm sure, Marilla."

"I'm not feeling discouraged," was Marilla's dry response. "When I make up my mind to do a thing it stays made up. I suppose you'd like to see Anne. I'll call her in."

Anne came running in presently, her face sparkling with the delight of her orchard rovings; but, abashed at finding herself in the unexpected presence of a stranger, she halted confusedly inside the door. She certainly was an odd-looking little creature in the short tight wincey dress she had worn from the asylum, below which her thin legs seemed ungracefully long. Her freckles were more numerous and obtrusive than ever; the wind had ruffled her hatless hair into over-brilliant disorder; it had never looked redder than at that moment.

"Well, they didn't pick you for your looks, that's sure and certain," was Mrs. Rachel Lynde's emphatic comment. Mrs. Rachel was one of those delightful and popular people who pride themselves on speaking their mind without fear or favor. "She's terrible skinny and homely, Marilla. Come here, child, and let me have a look at you. Lawful heart, did any one ever see such freckles? And hair as red as carrots! Come here, child, I say."

Anne "came there," but not exactly as Mrs. Rachel expected. With one bound she crossed the kitchen floor and stood before Mrs. Rachel, her face scarlet with anger, her lips quivering, and her whole slender form trembling from head to foot.

"I hate you," she cried in a choked voice, stamping her foot on the floor. "I hate you—I hate you—I hate you—" a louder stamp with each assertion of hatred. "How dare you call me skinny and ugly? How dare you say I'm freckled and redheaded? You are a rude, impolite, unfeeling woman!"

"Anne!" exclaimed Marilla in consternation.

But Anne continued to face Mrs. Rachel undauntedly, head up, eyes blazing, hands clenched, passionate indignation exhaling from her like an atmosphere.

"How dare you say such things about me?" she repeated vehemently. "How would you like to have such things said about you? How would you like to be told that you are fat and clumsy and probably hadn't a spark of imagination in you? I don't care if I do hurt your feelings by saying so! I hope I hurt them. You have hurt mine worse than they were ever hurt before even by Mrs. Thomas's intoxicated husband. And I'll *never* forgive you for it, never, never!"

Stamp! Stamp!

"Did anybody ever see such a temper!" exclaimed the horrified Mrs. Rachel.

"Anne go to your room and stay there until I come up," said Marilla, recovering her powers of speech with difficulty.

Anne, bursting into tears, rushed to the hall door, slammed it until the tins on the porch wall outside rattled in sympathy, and fled through the hall and up the stairs like a whirlwind. A subdued slam above told that the door of the east gable had been shut with equal vehemence.

"Well, I don't envy you your job bringing *that* up, Marilla," said Mrs. Rachel with unspeakable solemnity.

Marilla opened her lips to say she knew not what of apology or deprecation. What she did say was a surprise to herself then and ever afterwards.

"You shouldn't have twitted her about her looks, Rachel."

"Marilla Cuthbert, you don't mean to say that you are upholding her in such a terrible display of temper as we've just seen?" demanded Mrs. Rachel indignantly.

"No," said Marilla slowly, "I'm not trying to excuse her. She's been very naughty and I'll have to give her a talking to about it. But we must make allowances for her. She's never been taught what is right. And you *were* too hard on her, Rachel."

Marilla could not help tacking on that last sentence, although she was again surprised at herself for doing it. Mrs. Rachel got up with an air of offended dignity.

"Well, I see that I'll have to be very careful what I say after this, Marilla, since the fine feelings of orphans, brought from goodness knows where, have to be considered before anything else. Oh, no, I'm not vexed—don't worry yourself. I'm too sorry for you to leave any room for anger in my mind. You'll have your own troubles with that child. But if you'll take my advice—which I suppose you won't do, although I've brought up ten children and buried two—you'll do that 'talking to' you mention with a fair-sized birch switch. I should think *that* would be the most effective language for that kind of a child. Her temper matches her hair I guess. Well, good evening, Marilla. I hope you'll come down to see me often as usual. But you can't expect me to visit here again in a hurry, if I'm liable to be flown at and insulted in such a fashion. It's something new in *my* experience."

Whereat Mrs. Rachel swept out and away—if a fat woman who always waddled *could* be said to sweep away—and Marilla with a very solemn face betook herself to the east gable.

On the way upstairs she pondered uneasily as to what she ought to do. She felt no little dismay over the scene that had just been enacted. How unfortunate that Anne should have displayed such temper before Mrs. Rachel Lynde, of all people! Then Marilla suddenly became aware of an uncomfortable and rebuking consciousness that she felt more humiliation over this than sorrow over the discovery of such a serious defect in Anne's disposition. And how was she to punish her? The amiable suggestion of the birch switch—to the efficiency of which all of Mrs. Rachel's own children could have borne smarting testimony—did not appeal to Marilla. She did not believe she could whip a child. No, some other method of punishment must be found to bring Anne to a proper realization of the enormity of her offense.

Marilla found Anne face downward on her bed, crying bitterly, quite oblivious of muddy boots on a clean counterpane.

"Anne," she said not ungently.

No answer.

"Anne," with greater severity, "get off that bed this minute and listen to what I have to say to you."

Anne squirmed off the bed and sat rigidly on a chair beside it, her face swollen and tear-stained and her eyes fixed stubbornly on the floor.

"This is a nice way for you to behave, Anne! Aren't you ashamed of yourself?"

"She hadn't any right to call me ugly and redheaded," retorted Anne, evasive and defiant.

"You hadn't any right to fly into such a fury and talk the way you did to her, Anne. I was ashamed of you—thoroughly ashamed of you. I wanted you to behave nicely to Mrs. Lynde, and instead of that you have disgraced me. I'm sure I don't know why you should lose your temper like that just because Mrs. Lynde said you were red-haired and homely. You say it yourself often enough."

"Oh, but there's such a difference between saying a thing yourself and hearing other people say it," wailed Anne. "You may know a thing is so, but you can't help hoping other people don't quite think it is. I suppose you think I have an awful temper, but I couldn't help it. When she said those things something just rose right up in me and choked me. I *had* to fly out at her."

"Well, you made a fine exhibition of yourself I must say. Mrs. Lynde will have a nice story to tell about you everywhere—and she'll tell it, too. It was a dreadful thing for you to lose your temper like that, Anne."

"Just imagine how you would feel if somebody told you to your face that you were skinny and ugly," pleaded Anne tearfully.

An old remembrance suddenly rose up before Marilla. She had been a very small child when she had heard one aunt say of her to another,

"What a pity she is such a dark, homely little thing." Marilla was every day of fifty before the sting had gone out of that memory.

"I don't say that I think Mrs. Lynde was exactly right in saying what she did to you, Anne," she admitted in a softer tone. "Rachel is too outspoken. But that is no excuse for such behavior on your part. She was a stranger and an elderly person and my visitor—all three very good reasons why you should have been respectful to her. You were rude and saucy and"—Marilla had a saving inspiration of punishment—"you must go to her and tell her you are very sorry for your bad temper and ask her to forgive you."

"I can never do that," said Anne determinedly and darkly. "You can punish me in any way you like, Marilla. You can shut me up in a dark, damp dungeon inhabited by snakes and toads and feed me only on bread and water and I shall not complain. But I cannot ask Mrs. Lynde to forgive me."

"We're not in the habit of shutting people up in dark damp dungeons," said Marilla dryly, "especially as they're rather scarce in Avonlea. But apologize to Mrs. Lynde you must and shall and you'll stay here in your room until you can tell me you're willing to do it."

"I shall have to stay here forever then," said Anne mournfully, "because I can't tell Mrs. Lynde I'm sorry I said those things to her. How can I? I'm *not* sorry. I'm sorry I've vexed you; but I'm *glad* I told her just what I did. It was a great satisfaction. I can't say I'm sorry when I'm not, can I? I can't even *imagine* I'm sorry."

"Perhaps your imagination will be in better working order by the morning," said Marilla, rising to depart. "You'll have the night to think over your conduct in and come to a better frame of mind. You said you would try to be a very good girl if we kept you at Green Gables, but I must say it hasn't seemed very much like it this evening."

Leaving this Parthian shaft to rankle in Anne's stormy bosom, Marilla descended to the kitchen, grievously troubled in mind and vexed in soul. She was as angry with herself as with Anne, because, whenever she recalled Mrs. Rachel's dumbfounded countenance, her lips twitched with amusement and she felt a most reprehensible desire to laugh.

CHAPTER X

ANNE'S APOLOGY

Marilla said nothing to Matthew about the affair that evening; but when Anne proved still refractory the next morning an explanation had to be made to account for her absence from the breakfast table. Marilla told Matthew the whole story, taking pains to impress him with a due sense of the enormity of Anne's behavior.

"It's a good thing Rachel Lynde got a calling down; she's a meddlesome old gossip," was Matthew's consolatory rejoinder.

"Matthew Cuthbert, I'm astonished at you. You know that Anne's behavior was dreadful, and yet you take her part! I suppose you'll be saying next thing that she oughtn't to be punished at all!"

"Well now—no—not exactly," said Matthew uneasily. "I reckon she ought to be punished a little. But don't be too hard on her, Marilla. Recollect she hasn't ever had anyone to teach her right. You're—you're going to give her something to eat, aren't you?"

"When did you ever hear of me starving people into good behavior?" demanded Marilla indignantly. "She'll have her meals regular, and I'll carry them up to her myself. But she'll stay up there until she's willing to apologize to Mrs. Lynde, and that's final, Matthew."

Breakfast, dinner, and supper were very silent meals—for Anne still remained obdurate. After each meal Marilla carried a well-filled tray to the east gable and brought it down later on not noticeably depleted. Matthew eyed its last descent with a troubled eye. Had Anne eaten anything at all?

When Marilla went out that evening to bring the cows from the back pasture, Matthew, who had been hanging about the barns and watching, slipped into the house with the air of a burglar and crept upstairs. As a general thing Matthew gravitated between the kitchen and the little bedroom off the hall where he slept; once in a while he ventured uncomfortably into the parlor or sitting room when the minister came to tea. But he had never been upstairs in his own house since the spring he helped Marilla paper the spare bedroom, and that was four years ago.

He tiptoed along the hall and stood for several minutes outside the door of the east gable before he summoned courage to tap on it with his fingers and then open the door to peep in.

Anne was sitting on the yellow chair by the window gazing mournfully out into the garden. Very small and unhappy she looked, and Matthew's heart smote him. He softly closed the door and tiptoed over to her.

"Anne," he whispered, as if afraid of being overheard, "how are you making it, Anne?"

Anne smiled wanly.

"Pretty well. I imagine a good deal, and that helps to pass the time. Of course, it's rather lonesome. But then, I may as well get used to that."

Anne smiled again, bravely facing the long years of solitary imprisonment before her.

Matthew recollected that he must say what he had come to say without loss of time, lest Marilla return prematurely.

"Well now, Anne, don't you think you'd better do it and have it over with?" he whispered. "It'll have to be done sooner or later, you know, for Marilla's a dreadful determined woman—dreadful determined, Anne. Do it right off, I say, and have it over."

"Do you mean apologize to Mrs. Lynde?"

"Yes—apologize—that's the very word," said Matthew eagerly. "Just smooth it over so to speak. That's what I was trying to get at."

"I suppose I could do it to oblige you," said Anne thoughtfully. "It would be true enough to say I am sorry, because I *am* sorry now. I wasn't a bit sorry last night. I was mad clear through, and I stayed mad all night. I know I did because I woke up three times and I was just furious every time. But this morning it was over. I wasn't in a temper anymore—and it left a dreadful sort of goneness, too. I felt so ashamed of myself. But I just couldn't think of going and telling Mrs. Lynde so. It would be so humiliating. I made up my mind I'd stay shut up here forever rather than do that. But still—I'd do anything for you—if you really want me to—"

"Well now, of course I do. It's terrible lonesome downstairs without you. Just go and smooth things over—that's a good girl."

"Very well," said Anne resignedly. "I'll tell Marilla as soon as she comes in I've repented."

"That's right—that's right, Anne. But don't tell Marilla I said anything about it. She might think I was putting my oar in and I promised not to do that."

"Wild horses won't drag the secret from me," promised Anne solemnly. "How would wild horses drag a secret from a person anyhow?"

But Matthew was gone, scared at his own success. He fled hastily to the remotest corner of the horse pasture lest Marilla should suspect what he had been up to. Marilla herself, upon her return to the house, was agreeably surprised to hear a plaintive voice calling, "Marilla" over the banisters.

"Well?" she said, going into the hall.

"I'm sorry I lost my temper and said rude things, and I'm willing to go and tell Mrs. Lynde so."

"Very well." Marilla's crispness gave no sign of her relief. She had been wondering what under the canopy she should do if Anne did not give in. "I'll take you down after milking."

Accordingly, after milking, behold Marilla and Anne walking down the lane, the former erect and triumphant, the latter drooping and dejected. But halfway down Anne's dejection vanished as if by enchantment. She lifted her head and stepped lightly along, her eyes fixed on the sunset sky and an air of subdued exhilaration about her. Marilla beheld the change disapprovingly. This was no meek penitent such as it behooved her to take into the presence of the offended Mrs. Lynde.

"What are you thinking of, Anne?" she asked sharply.

"I'm imagining out what I must say to Mrs. Lynde," answered Anne dreamily.

This was satisfactory—or should have been so. But Marilla could not rid herself of the notion that something in her scheme of punishment was going askew. Anne had no business to look so rapt and radiant.

Rapt and radiant Anne continued until they were in the very presence of Mrs. Lynde, who was sitting knitting by her kitchen window. Then the radiance vanished. Mournful penitence appeared on every feature. Before a word was spoken Anne suddenly went down on her knees before the astonished Mrs. Rachel and held out her hands beseechingly.

"Oh, Mrs. Lynde, I am so extremely sorry," she said with a quiver in her voice. "I could never express all my sorrow, no, not if I used up a whole dictionary. You must just imagine it. I behaved terribly to you—and I've disgraced the dear friends, Matthew and Marilla, who have let me stay at Green Gables although I'm not a boy. I'm a dreadfully wicked and ungrateful girl, and I deserve to be punished and cast out by respectable people forever. It was very wicked of me to fly into a temper because you told me the truth. It *was* the truth; every word you said was true. My hair is red and I'm freckled and skinny and ugly. What I said to you was true, too, but I shouldn't have said it. Oh, Mrs. Lynde, please, please, forgive me. If you refuse it will be a lifelong sorrow on a poor little orphan girl. You wouldn't like to inflict lifelong sorrow on a poor little orphan girl, would you, even if she had a dreadful temper? Oh, I am sure you wouldn't. Please say you forgive me, Mrs. Lynde."

Anne clasped her hands together, bowed her head, and waited for the word of judgment.

There was no mistaking her sincerity—it breathed in every tone of her voice. Both Marilla and Mrs. Lynde recognized its unmistakable ring. But the former understood in dismay that Anne was actually enjoying her valley of humiliation—was reveling in the thoroughness of her abasement. Where was the wholesome punishment upon which she, Marilla, had plumed herself? Anne had turned it into a species of positive pleasure.

Good Mrs. Lynde, not being overburdened with perception, did not see this. She only perceived that Anne had made a very thorough apology and all resentment vanished from her kindly, if somewhat officious, heart.

"There, there, get up, child," she said heartily. "Of course I forgive you. I guess I was a little too hard on you, anyway. But I'm such an outspoken person. You just mustn't mind me, that's what. It can't be denied your hair is terrible red; but I knew a girl once—went to school with her, in fact—whose hair was every mite as red as yours when she was young, but when she grew up it darkened to a real handsome auburn. I wouldn't be a mite surprised if yours did, too—not a mite."

"Oh, Mrs. Lynde!" Anne drew a long breath as she rose to her feet. "You have given me a hope. I shall always feel that you are a benefactor. Oh, I could endure anything if I only thought my hair would be a handsome auburn when I grew up. It would be so much easier to be good if one's hair was a handsome auburn, don't you think? And now may I go out into your garden and sit on that bench under the apple trees while you and Marilla are talking? There is so much more scope for imagination out there."

"Laws, yes, run along, child. And you can pick a bouquet of them white June lilies over in the corner if you like."

As the door closed behind Anne Mrs. Lynde got briskly up to light a lamp. "She's a real odd little thing. Take this chair, Marilla; it's easier than the one you've got; I just keep that for the hired boy to sit on. Yes, she certainly is an odd child, but there is something kind of taking about her after all. I don't feel so surprised at you and Matthew keeping her as I did—nor so sorry for you, either. She may turn out all right. Of course, she has a queer way of expressing herself—a little too—well, too kind of forcible, you know; but she'll likely get over that now that she's come to live among civilized folks. And then, her temper's pretty quick, I guess; but there's one comfort, a child that has a quick temper, just blaze up and cool down, ain't never likely to be sly or deceitful. Preserve me from a sly child, that's what. On the whole, Marilla, I kind of like her."

When Marilla went home Anne came out of the fragrant twilight of the orchard with a sheaf of white narcissi in her hands.

"I apologized pretty well, didn't I?" she said proudly as they went down the lane. "I thought since I had to do it I might as well do it thoroughly."

"You did it thoroughly, all right enough," was Marilla's comment. Marilla was dismayed at finding herself inclined to laugh over the recollection. She had also an uneasy feeling that she ought to scold Anne for apologizing so well; but then, that was ridiculous! She compromised with her conscience by saying severely:

"I hope you won't have occasion to make many more such apologies. I hope you'll try to control your temper now, Anne."

"That wouldn't be so hard if people wouldn't twit me about my looks," said Anne with a sigh. "I don't get cross about other things; but I'm *so* tired of being twitted about my hair and it just makes me boil right over. Do you suppose my hair will really be a handsome auburn when I grow up?"

"You shouldn't think so much about your looks, Anne. I'm afraid you are a very vain little girl."

"How can I be vain when I know I'm homely?" protested Anne. "I love pretty things; and I hate to look in the glass and see something that isn't pretty. It makes me feel so sorrowful—just as I feel when I look at any ugly thing. I pity it because it isn't beautiful."

"Handsome is as handsome does," quoted Marilla.

"I've had that said to me before, but I have my doubts about it," remarked skeptical Anne, sniffing at her narcissi. "Oh, aren't these flowers sweet! It was lovely of Mrs. Lynde to give them to me. I have no hard feelings against Mrs. Lynde now. It gives you a lovely, comfortable feeling to apologize and be forgiven, doesn't it? Aren't the stars bright tonight? If you could live in a star, which one would you pick? I'd like that lovely clear big one away over there above that dark hill."

"Anne, do hold your tongue," said Marilla, thoroughly worn out trying to follow the gyrations of Anne's thoughts.

Anne said no more until they turned into their own lane. A little gypsy wind came down it to meet them, laden with the spicy perfume of young dew-wet ferns. Far up in the shadows a cheerful light gleamed out through the trees from the kitchen at Green Gables. Anne suddenly came close to Marilla and slipped her hand into the older woman's hard palm.

"It's lovely to be going home and know it's home," she said. "I love Green Gables already, and I never loved any place before. No place ever seemed like home. Oh, Marilla, I'm so happy. I could pray right now and not find it a bit hard."

Something warm and pleasant welled up in Marilla's heart at touch of that thin little hand in her own—a throb of the maternity she had missed, perhaps. Its very unaccustomedness and sweetness disturbed her. She hastened to restore her sensations to their normal calm by inculcating a moral.

"If you'll be a good girl you'll always be happy, Anne. And you should never find it hard to say your prayers."

"Saying one's prayers isn't exactly the same thing as praying," said Anne meditatively. "But I'm going to imagine that I'm the wind that is blowing up there in those tree tops. When I get tired of the trees I'll imagine I'm gently waving down here in the ferns—and then I'll fly over to Mrs. Lynde's garden and set the flowers dancing—and then I'll go with one great swoop over the clover field—and then I'll blow over the Lake of Shining Waters and ripple it all up into little sparkling waves. Oh, there's so much scope for imagination in a wind! So I'll not talk any more just now, Marilla."

"Thanks be to goodness for that," breathed Marilla in devout relief.

CHAPTER XI

ANNE'S IMPRESSIONS OF SUNDAY SCHOOL

"Well, how do you like them?" said Marilla.

Anne was standing in the gable room, looking solemnly at three new dresses spread out on the bed. One was of snuffy colored gingham which Marilla had been tempted to buy from a peddler the preceding summer because it looked so serviceable; one was of black-and-white checkered sateen which she had picked up at a bargain counter in the winter; and one was a stiff print of an ugly blue shade which she had purchased that week at a Carmody store.

She had made them up herself, and they were all made alike—plain skirts fulled tightly to plain waists, with sleeves as plain as waist and skirt and tight as sleeves could be.

"I'll imagine that I like them," said Anne soberly.

"I don't want you to imagine it," said Marilla, offended. "Oh, I can see you don't like the dresses! What is the matter with them? Aren't they neat and clean and new?"

"Yes."

"Then why don't you like them?"

"They're—they're not—pretty," said Anne reluctantly.

"Pretty!" Marilla sniffed. "I didn't trouble my head about getting pretty dresses for you. I don't believe in pampering vanity, Anne, I'll tell you that right off. Those dresses are good, sensible, serviceable dresses, without any frills or furbelows about them, and they're all you'll get this summer. The brown gingham and the blue print will do you for school when you begin to go. The sateen is for church and Sunday school. I'll expect you to keep them neat and clean and not to tear them. I should think you'd be grateful to get most anything after those skimpy wincey things you've been wearing."

"Oh, I *am* grateful," protested Anne. "But I'd be ever so much gratefuller if—if you'd made just one of them with puffed sleeves. Puffed sleeves are so fashionable now. It would give me such a thrill,

Marilla, just to wear a dress with puffed sleeves."

"Well, you'll have to do without your thrill. I hadn't any material to waste on puffed sleeves. I think they are ridiculous-looking things anyhow. I prefer the plain, sensible ones."

"But I'd rather look ridiculous when everybody else does than plain and sensible all by myself," persisted Anne mournfully.

"Trust you for that! Well, hang those dresses carefully up in your closet, and then sit down and learn the Sunday school lesson. I got a quarterly from Mr. Bell for you and you'll go to Sunday school tomorrow," said Marilla, disappearing downstairs in high dudgeon.

Anne clasped her hands and looked at the dresses.

"I did hope there would be a white one with puffed sleeves," she whispered disconsolately. "I prayed for one, but I didn't much expect it on that account. I didn't suppose God would have time to bother about a little orphan girl's dress. I knew I'd just have to depend on Marilla for it. Well, fortunately I can imagine that one of them is of snow-white muslin with lovely lace frills and three-puffed sleeves."

The next morning warnings of a sick headache prevented Marilla from going to Sunday school with Anne.

"You'll have to go down and call for Mrs. Lynde, Anne," she said. "She'll see that you get into the right class. Now, mind you behave yourself properly. Stay to preaching afterwards and ask Mrs. Lynde to show you our pew. Here's a cent for collection. Don't stare at people and don't fidget. I shall expect you to tell me the text when you come home."

Anne started off irreproachable, arrayed in the stiff black-and-white sateen, which, while decent as regards length and certainly not open to the charge of skimpiness, contrived to emphasize every corner and angle of her thin figure. Her hat was a little, flat, glossy, new sailor, the extreme plainness of which had likewise much disappointed Anne, who had permitted herself secret visions of ribbon and flowers. The latter, however, were supplied before Anne reached the main road, for being confronted halfway down the lane with a golden frenzy of wind-stirred buttercups and a glory of wild roses, Anne promptly and liberally garlanded her hat with a heavy wreath of them. Whatever other people might have thought of the result it satisfied Anne, and she tripped gaily down the road, holding her ruddy head with its decoration of pink and yellow very proudly.

When she had reached Mrs. Lynde's house she found that lady gone. Nothing daunted, Anne proceeded onward to the church alone. In the porch she found a crowd of little girls, all more or less gaily attired in whites and blues and pinks, and all staring with curious eyes at this stranger in their midst, with her extraordinary head adornment. Avonlea little girls had already heard queer stories about Anne. Mrs. Lynde said she had an awful temper; Jerry Buote, the hired boy at Green Gables, said she talked all the time to herself or to the trees and flowers like a crazy girl. They looked at her and whispered to each other behind their quarterlies. Nobody made any friendly advances, then or later on when the opening exercises were over and Anne found herself in Miss Rogerson's class.

Miss Rogerson was a middle-aged lady who had taught a Sunday school class for twenty years. Her method of teaching was to ask the printed questions from the quarterly and look sternly over its edge at the particular little girl she thought ought to answer the question. She looked very often at Anne, and Anne, thanks to Marilla's drilling, answered promptly; but it may be questioned if she understood very much about either question or answer.

She did not think she liked Miss Rogerson, and she felt very miserable; every other little girl in the class had puffed sleeves. Anne felt that life was really not worth living without puffed sleeves.

"Well, how did you like Sunday school?" Marilla wanted to know when Anne came home. Her wreath having faded, Anne had discarded it in the lane, so Marilla was spared the knowledge of that for a time.

"I didn't like it a bit. It was horrid."

"Anne Shirley!" said Marilla rebukingly.

Anne sat down on the rocker with a long sigh, kissed one of Bonny's leaves, and waved her hand to a blossoming fuchsia.

"They might have been lonesome while I was away," she explained. "And now about the Sunday school. I behaved well, just as you told me. Mrs. Lynde was gone, but I went right on myself. I went into the church, with a lot of other little girls, and I sat in the corner of a pew by the window while the opening exercises went on. Mr. Bell made an awfully long prayer. I would have been dreadfully tired before he got through if I hadn't been sitting by that window. But it looked right out on the Lake of Shining Waters, so I just gazed at that and imagined all sorts of splendid things."

"You shouldn't have done anything of the sort. You should have listened to Mr. Bell."

"But he wasn't talking to me," protested Anne. "He was talking to God and he didn't seem to be very much interested in it, either. I think he thought God was too far off to make it worthwhile. There was a long row of white birches hanging over the lake and the sunshine fell down through them, 'way, 'way down, deep into the water. Oh, Marilla, it was like a beautiful dream! It gave me a thrill and I just said, 'Thank you for it, God,' two or three times."

"Not out loud, I hope," said Marilla anxiously.

"Oh, no, just under my breath. Well, Mr. Bell did get through at last and they told me to go into the classroom with Miss Rogerson's class. There were nine other girls in it. They all had puffed sleeves. I tried to imagine mine were puffed, too, but I couldn't. Why couldn't I? It was as easy as could be to imagine they were puffed when I was alone in the east gable, but it was awfully hard there among the others who had really truly puffs."

"You shouldn't have been thinking about your sleeves in Sunday school. You should have been attending to the lesson. I hope you knew it."

"Oh, yes; and I answered a lot of questions. Miss Rogerson asked ever so many. I don't think it was fair for her to do all the asking. There were lots I wanted to ask her, but I didn't like to because I didn't think she was a kindred spirit. Then all the other little girls recited a paraphrase. She asked me if I knew any. I told her I didn't, but I could recite, 'The Dog at His Master's Grave' if she liked. That's in the *Third Royal Reader*. It isn't a really truly religious piece of poetry, but it's so sad and melancholy that it might as well be. She said it wouldn't do and she told me to learn the nineteenth paraphrase for next Sunday. I read it over in church afterwards and it's splendid. There are two lines in particular that just thrill me.

> *"Quick as the slaughtered squadrons fell*
> *In Midian's evil day."*

"I don't know what 'squadrons' means nor 'Midian,' either, but it sounds *so* tragical. I can hardly wait until next Sunday to recite it. I'll practice it all the week. After Sunday school I asked Miss Rogerson—

because Mrs. Lynde was too far away—to show me your pew. I sat just as still as I could and the text was Revelations, third chapter, second and third verses. It was a very long text. If I was a minister I'd pick the short, snappy ones. The sermon was awfully long, too. I suppose the minister had to match it to the text. I didn't think he was a bit interesting. The trouble with him seems to be that he hasn't enough imagination. I didn't listen to him very much. I just let my thoughts run and I thought of the most surprising things."

Marilla felt helplessly that all this should be sternly reproved, but she was hampered by the undeniable fact that some of the things Anne had said, especially about the minister's sermons and Mr. Bell's prayers, were what she herself had really thought deep down in her heart for years, but had never given expression to. It almost seemed to her that those secret, unuttered, critical thoughts had suddenly taken visible and accusing shape and form in the person of this outspoken morsel of neglected humanity.

CHAPTER XII

A SOLEMN VOW AND PROMISE

It was not until the next Friday that Marilla heard the story of the flower-wreathed hat. She came home from Mrs. Lynde's and called Anne to account.

"Anne, Mrs. Rachel says you went to church last Sunday with your hat rigged out ridiculous with roses and buttercups. What on earth put you up to such a caper? A pretty-looking object you must have been!"

"Oh. I know pink and yellow aren't becoming to me," began Anne.

"Becoming fiddlesticks! It was putting flowers on your hat at all, no matter what color they were, that was ridiculous. You are the most aggravating child!"

"I don't see why it's any more ridiculous to wear flowers on your hat than on your dress," protested Anne. "Lots of little girls there had bouquets pinned on their dresses. What's the difference?"

Marilla was not to be drawn from the safe concrete into dubious paths of the abstract.

"Don't answer me back like that, Anne. It was very silly of you to do such a thing. Never let me catch you at such a trick again. Mrs. Rachel says she thought she would sink through the floor when she saw you come in all rigged out like that. She couldn't get near enough to tell you to take them off till it was too late. She says people talked about it something dreadful. Of course they would think I had no better sense than to let you go decked out like that."

"Oh, I'm so sorry," said Anne, tears welling into her eyes. "I never thought you'd mind. The roses and buttercups were so sweet and pretty I thought they'd look lovely on my hat. Lots of the little girls had artificial flowers on their hats. I'm afraid I'm going to be a dreadful trial to you. Maybe you'd better send me back to the asylum. That would be terrible; I don't think I could endure it; most likely I would go into consumption; I'm so thin as it is, you see. But that would be better than being a trial to you."

"Nonsense," said Marilla, vexed at herself for having made the child cry. "I don't want to send you back to the asylum, I'm sure. All I want is that you should behave like other little girls and not make yourself ridiculous. Don't cry any more. I've got some news for you. Diana Barry came home this afternoon. I'm going up to see if I can borrow a skirt pattern from Mrs. Barry, and if you like you can come with me and get acquainted with Diana."

Anne rose to her feet, with clasped hands, the tears still glistening on her cheeks; the dish towel she had been hemming slipped unheeded to the floor.

"Oh, Marilla, I'm frightened—now that it has come I'm actually frightened. What if she shouldn't like me! It would be the most tragical disappointment of my life."

"Now, don't get into a fluster. And I do wish you wouldn't use such long words. It sounds so funny in a little girl. I guess Diana'll like you well enough. It's her mother you've got to reckon with. If she doesn't like you it won't matter how much Diana does. If she has heard about your outburst to Mrs. Lynde and going to church with buttercups round your hat I don't know what she'll think of you. You must be polite and well behaved, and don't make any of your startling speeches. For pity's sake, if the child isn't actually trembling!"

Anne *was* trembling. Her face was pale and tense.

"Oh, Marilla, you'd be excited, too, if you were going to meet a little girl you hoped to be your bosom friend and whose mother mightn't like you," she said as she hastened to get her hat. They went over to Orchard Slope by the short cut across the brook and up the firry hill grove. Mrs. Barry came to the kitchen door in answer to Marilla's knock. She was a tall black-eyed, black-haired woman, with a very resolute mouth. She had the reputation of being very strict with her children.

"How do you do, Marilla?" she said cordially. "Come in. And this is the little girl you have adopted, I suppose?"

"Yes, this is Anne Shirley," said Marilla.

"Spelled with an *e*," gasped Anne, who, tremulous and excited as she was, was determined there should be no misunderstanding on that important point.

Mrs. Barry, not hearing or not comprehending, merely shook hands and said kindly:

"How are you?"

"I am well in body although considerable rumpled up in spirit, thank you, ma'am," said Anne gravely. Then aside to Marilla in an audible whisper, "There wasn't anything startling in that, was there, Marilla?"

Diana was sitting on the sofa, reading a book which she dropped when the callers entered. She was a very pretty little girl, with her mother's black eyes and hair, and rosy cheeks, and the merry expression which was her inheritance from her father.

"This is my little girl Diana," said Mrs. Barry. "Diana, you might take Anne out into the garden and show her your flowers. It will be better for you than straining your eyes over that book. She reads entirely too much—" this to Marilla as the little girls went out—"and I can't prevent her, for her father aids and abets her. She's always poring over a book. I'm glad she has the prospect of a playmate—perhaps it will take her more out-of-doors."

Outside in the garden, which was full of mellow sunset light streaming through the dark old firs to the west of it, stood Anne and Diana, gazing bashfully at each other over a clump of gorgeous tiger lilies.

The Barry garden was a bowery wilderness of flowers which would have delighted Anne's heart at any time less fraught with destiny. It was encircled by huge old willows and tall firs, beneath which flourished flowers that loved the shade. Prim, right-angled paths, neatly bordered with clamshells, intersected it like moist red ribbons and in the beds between old-fashioned flowers ran riot. There were rosy bleeding-hearts and great splendid crimson peonies; white, fragrant narcissi and thorny, sweet Scotch roses; pink and blue and white columbines and lilac-tinted Bouncing Bets; clumps of southernwood and ribbon grass and mint; purple Adam-and-Eve, daffodils, and masses of sweet clover white with its delicate, fragrant, feathery sprays; scarlet lightning that shot its fiery lances over prim white musk-flowers; a garden it was where sunshine lingered and bees hummed, and winds, beguiled into loitering, purred and rustled.

"Oh, Diana," said Anne at last, clasping her hands and speaking almost in a whisper, "oh, do you think you can like me a little—enough to be my bosom friend?"

Diana laughed. Diana always laughed before she spoke.

"Why, I guess so," she said frankly. "I'm awfully glad you've come to live at Green Gables. It will be jolly to have somebody to play with. There isn't any other girl who lives near enough to play with, and I've no sisters big enough."

"Will you swear to be my friend forever and ever?" demanded Anne eagerly.

Diana looked shocked.

"Why, it's dreadfully wicked to swear," she said rebukingly.

"Oh no, not my kind of swearing. There are two kinds, you know."

"I never heard of but one kind," said Diana doubtfully.

"There really is another. Oh, it isn't wicked at all. It just means vowing and promising solemnly."

"Well, I don't mind doing that," agreed Diana, relieved. "How do you do it?"

"We must join hands—so," said Anne gravely. "It ought to be over running water. We'll just imagine this path is running water. I'll repeat the oath first. I solemnly swear to be faithful to my bosom friend, Diana Barry, as long as the sun and moon shall endure. Now you say it and put my name in."

Diana repeated the "oath" with a laugh fore and aft. Then she said:

"You're a queer girl, Anne. I heard before that you were queer. But I believe I'm going to like you real well."

When Marilla and Anne went home Diana went with them as far as the log bridge. The two little girls walked with their arms about each other. At the brook they parted with many promises to spend the next afternoon together.

"Well, did you find Diana a kindred spirit?" asked Marilla as they went up through the garden of Green Gables.

"Oh yes," sighed Anne, blissfully unconscious of any sarcasm on Marilla's part. "Oh Marilla, I'm the happiest girl on Prince Edward Island this very moment. I assure you I'll say my prayers with a right good-will tonight. Diana and I are going to build a playhouse in Mr. William Bell's birch grove tomorrow. Can I have those broken pieces of china that are out in the woodshed? Diana's birthday is in February and mine is in March. Don't you think that is a very strange coincidence? Diana is going to lend me a book to read. She says it's perfectly splendid and tremendously exciting. She's going to show me a place back in the woods where rice lilies grow. Don't you think Diana has got very soulful eyes? I wish I had soulful eyes. Diana is going to teach me to sing a song called 'Nelly in the Hazel Dell.' She's going to give me a picture to put up in my room; it's a perfectly beautiful picture, she says—a lovely lady in a pale blue silk dress. A sewing-machine agent gave it to her. I wish I had something to give Diana. I'm an inch taller than Diana, but she is ever so much fatter; she says she'd like to be thin because it's so much more graceful, but I'm afraid she only said it to soothe my feelings. We're going to the shore some day to gather shells. We have agreed to call the spring down by the log bridge the Dryad's Bubble. Isn't that a perfectly elegant name? I read a story once about a spring called that. A dryad is sort of a grown-up fairy, I think."

"Well, all I hope is you won't talk Diana to death," said Marilla. "But remember this in all your planning, Anne. You're not going to play all the time nor most of it. You'll have your work to do and it'll have to be done first."

Anne's cup of happiness was full, and Matthew caused it to overflow. He had just got home from a trip to the store at Carmody, and he sheepishly produced a small parcel from his pocket and handed it to Anne, with a deprecatory look at Marilla.

"I heard you say you liked chocolate sweeties, so I got you some," he said.

"Humph," sniffed Marilla. "It'll ruin her teeth and stomach. There, there, child, don't look so dismal. You can eat those, since Matthew has gone and got them. He'd better have brought you peppermints. They're wholesomer. Don't sicken yourself eating all them at once now."

"Oh, no, indeed, I won't," said Anne eagerly. "I'll just eat one tonight, Marilla. And I can give Diana half of them, can't I? The other half will taste twice as sweet to me if I give some to her. It's delightful to think I have something to give her."

"I will say it for the child," said Marilla when Anne had gone to her gable, "she isn't stingy. I'm glad, for of all faults I detest stinginess in a child. Dear me, it's only three weeks since she came, and it seems as if she'd been here always. I can't imagine the place without her. Now, don't be looking I told-you-so, Matthew. That's bad enough in a woman, but it isn't to be endured in a man. I'm perfectly willing to own up that I'm glad I consented to keep the child and that I'm getting fond of her, but don't you rub it in, Matthew Cuthbert."

CHAPTER XIII

THE DELIGHTS OF ANTICIPATION

It's time Anne was in to do her sewing," said Marilla, glancing at the clock and then out into the yellow August afternoon where everything drowsed in the heat. "She stayed playing with Diana more than half an hour more'n I gave her leave to; and now she's perched out there on the woodpile talking to Matthew, nineteen to the dozen, when she knows perfectly well she ought to be at her work. And of course he's listening to her like a perfect ninny. I never saw such an infatuated man. The more she talks and the odder the things she says, the more he's delighted evidently. Anne Shirley, you come right in here this minute, do you hear me!"

A series of staccato taps on the west window brought Anne flying in from the yard, eyes shining, cheeks faintly flushed with pink, unbraided hair streaming behind her in a torrent of brightness.

"Oh, Marilla," she exclaimed breathlessly, "there's going to be a Sunday school picnic next week—in Mr. Harmon Andrews's field, right near the lake of Shining Waters. And Mrs. Superintendent Bell and Mrs. Rachel Lynde are going to make ice cream—think of it, Marilla—*ice cream*! And, oh, Marilla, can I go to it?"

"Just look at the clock, if you please, Anne. What time did I tell you to come in?"

"Two o'clock—but isn't it splendid about the picnic, Marilla? Please can I go? Oh, I've never been to a picnic—I've dreamed of picnics, but I've never—"

"Yes, I told you to come at two o'clock. And it's a quarter to three. I'd like to know why you didn't obey me, Anne."

"Why, I meant to, Marilla, as much as could be. But you have no idea how fascinating Idlewild is. And then, of course, I had to tell Matthew about the picnic. Matthew is such a sympathetic listener. Please can I go?"

"You'll have to learn to resist the fascination of Idle-whatever-you-call-it. When I tell you to come in at a certain time I mean that time and not half an hour later. And you needn't stop to discourse with sympathetic listeners on your way, either. As for the picnic, of course you can go. You're a Sunday school scholar, and it's not likely I'd refuse to let you go when all the other little girls are going."

"But—but," faltered Anne, "Diana says that everybody must take a basket of things to eat. I can't cook, as you know, Marilla, and—and—I don't mind going to a picnic without puffed sleeves so much, but I'd feel terribly humiliated if I had to go without a basket. It's been preying on my mind ever since Diana told me."

"Well, it needn't prey any longer. I'll bake you a basket."

"Oh, you dear good Marilla. Oh, you are so kind to me. Oh, I'm so much obliged to you."

Getting through with her "ohs" Anne cast herself into Marilla's arms and rapturously kissed her sallow cheek. It was the first time in her whole life that childish lips had voluntarily touched Marilla's face. Again that sudden sensation of startling sweetness thrilled her. She was secretly vastly pleased at Anne's impulsive caress, which was probably the reason why she said brusquely:

"There, there, never mind your kissing nonsense. I'd sooner see you doing strictly as you're told. As for cooking, I mean to begin giving you lessons in that some of these days. But you're so featherbrained, Anne, I've been waiting to see if you'd sober down a little and learn to be steady before I begin. You've got to keep your wits about you in cooking and not stop in the middle of things to let your thoughts rove all over creation. Now, get out your patchwork and have your square done before teatime."

"I do *not* like patchwork," said Anne dolefully, hunting out her workbasket and sitting down before a little heap of red and white diamonds with a sigh. "I think some kinds of sewing would be nice; but there's no scope for imagination in patchwork. It's just one little seam after another and you never seem to be getting anywhere. But of course I'd rather be Anne of Green Gables sewing patchwork than Anne of any other place with nothing to do but play. I wish time went as quick sewing patches as it does when I'm playing with Diana, though. Oh, we do have such elegant times, Marilla. I have to furnish most of the imagination, but I'm well able to do that. Diana is simply perfect in every other way. You know that little piece of land across the brook that runs up between our farm and Mr. Barry's. It belongs to Mr. William Bell, and right in the corner there is a little ring of white birch trees—the most romantic spot, Marilla. Diana and I have our playhouse there. We call it Idlewild. Isn't that a poetical name? I assure you it took me some time to think it out. I stayed awake nearly a whole night before I invented it. Then, just as I was dropping off to sleep, it came like an inspiration. Diana was *enraptured* when she heard it. We have got our house fixed up elegantly. You must come and see it, Marilla—won't you? We have great big stones, all covered with moss, for seats, and boards from tree to tree for shelves. And we have all our dishes on them. Of course, they're all broken but it's the easiest thing in the world to imagine that they are whole. There's a piece of a plate with a spray of red and yellow ivy on it that is especially beautiful. We keep it in the parlor and we have the fairy glass there, too. The fairy glass is as lovely as a dream. Diana found it out in the woods behind their chicken house. It's all full of rainbows—just little young rainbows that haven't grown big yet—and Diana's mother told her it was broken off a hanging lamp they once had. But it's nice to imagine the fairies lost it one night when they had a ball, so we call it the fairy glass. Matthew is going to make us a table. Oh, we have named that little round pool over in Mr. Barry's field Willowmere. I got that name out of the book Diana lent me. That was a thrilling book, Marilla. The heroine had five lovers. I'd be satisfied with one, wouldn't you? She was very handsome and she went through great tribulations. She could faint as easy as anything. I'd love to be able to faint, wouldn't you, Marilla? It's so romantic. But I'm really very healthy for all I'm so thin. I believe I'm getting fatter, though. Don't you think I am? I look at my elbows every morning when I get up to see if any dimples are coming. Diana is having a new dress made with elbow sleeves. She is going to wear it to the picnic. Oh, I do hope it will be fine next Wednesday. I don't feel that I could endure the disappointment if anything happened to prevent me from getting to the picnic. I suppose I'd live through it, but I'm certain it would be a lifelong sorrow. It wouldn't matter if I got to a hundred picnics in after years; they wouldn't make up for missing this one. They're going to have boats on the Lake of Shining Waters—and ice cream, as I told you. I have never tasted ice cream. Diana tried to explain what it was like, but I guess ice cream is one of those things that are beyond imagination."

"Anne, you have talked even on for ten minutes by the clock," said

Marilla. "Now, just for curiosity's sake, see if you can hold your tongue for the same length of time."

Anne held her tongue as desired. But for the rest of the week she talked picnic and thought picnic and dreamed picnic. On Saturday it rained and she worked herself up into such a frantic state lest it should keep on raining until and over Wednesday that Marilla made her sew an extra patchwork square by way of steadying her nerves.

On Sunday Anne confided to Marilla on the way home from church that she grew actually cold all over with excitement when the minister announced the picnic from the pulpit.

"Such a thrill as went up and down my back, Marilla! I don't think I'd ever really believed until then that there was honestly going to be a picnic. I couldn't help fearing I'd only imagined it. But when a minister says a thing in the pulpit you just have to believe it."

"You set your heart too much on things, Anne," said Marilla, with a sigh. "I'm afraid there'll be a great many disappointments in store for you through life."

"Oh, Marilla, looking forward to things is half the pleasure of them," exclaimed Anne. "You mayn't get the things themselves; but nothing can prevent you from having the fun of looking forward to them. Mrs. Lynde says, 'Blessed are they who expect nothing for they shall not be disappointed.' But I think it would be worse to expect nothing than to be disappointed."

Marilla wore her amethyst brooch to church that day as usual. Marilla always wore her amethyst brooch to church. She would have thought it rather sacrilegious to leave it off—as bad as forgetting her Bible or her collection dime. That amethyst brooch was Marilla's most treasured possession. A seafaring uncle had given it to her mother who in turn had bequeathed it to Marilla. It was an old-fashioned oval, containing a braid of her mother's hair, surrounded by a border of very fine amethysts. Marilla knew too little about precious stones to realize how fine the amethysts actually were; but she thought them very beautiful and was always pleasantly conscious of their violet shimmer at her throat, above her good brown satin dress, even although she could not see it.

Anne had been smitten with delighted admiration when she first saw that brooch.

"Oh, Marilla, it's a perfectly elegant brooch. I don't know how you can pay attention to the sermon or the prayers when you have it on. I couldn't, I know. I think amethysts are just sweet. They are what I used to think diamonds were like. Long ago, before I had ever seen a diamond, I read about them and I tried to imagine what they would be like. I thought they would be lovely glimmering purple stones. When I saw a real diamond in a lady's ring one day I was so disappointed I cried. Of course, it was very lovely but it wasn't my idea of a diamond. Will you let me hold the brooch for one minute, Marilla? Do you think amethysts can be the souls of good violets?"

CHAPTER XIV

ANNE'S CONFESSION

On the Monday evening before the picnic Marilla came down from her room with a troubled face.

"Anne," she said to that small personage, who was shelling peas by the spotless table and singing, "Nelly of the Hazel Dell" with a vigor and expression that did credit to Diana's teaching, "did you see anything of my amethyst brooch? I thought I stuck it in my pincushion when I came home from church yesterday evening, but I can't find it anywhere."

"I—I saw it this afternoon when you were away at the Aid Society," said Anne, a little slowly. "I was passing your door when I saw it on the cushion, so I went in to look at it."

"Did you touch it?" said Marilla sternly.

"Y-e-e-s," admitted Anne, "I took it up and I pinned it on my breast just to see how it would look."

"You had no business to do anything of the sort. It's very wrong in a little girl to meddle. You shouldn't have gone into my room in the first place and you shouldn't have touched a brooch that didn't belong to you in the second. Where did you put it?"

"Oh, I put it back on the bureau. I hadn't it on a minute. Truly, I didn't mean to meddle, Marilla. I didn't think about its being wrong to go in and try on the brooch; but I see now that it was and I'll never do it again. That's one good thing about me. I never do the same naughty thing twice."

"You didn't put it back," said Marilla. "That brooch isn't anywhere on the bureau. You've taken it out or something, Anne."

"I did put it back," said Anne quickly—pertly, Marilla thought. "I don't just remember whether I stuck it on the pincushion or laid it in the china tray. But I'm perfectly certain I put it back."

"I'll go and have another look," said Marilla, determining to be just. "If you put that brooch back it's there still. If it isn't I'll know you didn't, that's all!"

Marilla went to her room and made a thorough search, not only over the bureau but in every other place she thought the brooch might possibly be. It was not to be found and she returned to the kitchen.

"Anne, the brooch is gone. By your own admission you were the last person to handle it. Now, what have you done with it? Tell me the truth at once. Did you take it out and lose it?"

"No, I didn't," said Anne solemnly, meeting Marilla's angry gaze squarely. "I never took the brooch out of your room and that is the truth, if I was to be led to the block for it—although I'm not very certain what a block is. So there, Marilla."

Anne's "so there" was only intended to emphasize her assertion, but Marilla took it as a display of defiance.

"I believe you are telling me a falsehood, Anne," she said sharply. "I know you are. There now, don't say anything more unless you are prepared to tell the whole truth. Go to your room and stay there until you are ready to confess."

"Will I take the peas with me?" said Anne meekly.

"No, I'll finish shelling them myself. Do as I bid you."

When Anne had gone Marilla went about her evening tasks in a very disturbed state of mind. She was worried about her valuable brooch. What if Anne had lost it? And how wicked of the child to deny having taken it, when anybody could see she must have! With such an innocent face, too!

"I don't know what I wouldn't sooner have had happen," thought Marilla, as she nervously shelled the peas. "Of course, I don't suppose she meant to steal it or anything like that. She's just taken it to play with or help along that imagination of hers. She must have taken it, that's clear, for there hasn't been a soul in that room since she was in it, by her own story, until I went up tonight. And the brooch is gone, there's nothing surer. I suppose she has lost it and is afraid to own up for fear she'll be punished. It's a dreadful thing to think she tells falsehoods. It's a far worse thing than her fit of temper. It's a fearful responsibility to have a child in your house you can't trust. Slyness and untruthfulness—that's what she has displayed. I declare I feel worse about that than about the brooch. If she'd only have told the truth about it I wouldn't mind so much."

Marilla went to her room at intervals all through the evening and searched for the brooch, without finding it. A bedtime visit to the east gable produced no result. Anne persisted in denying that she knew anything about the brooch but Marilla was only the more firmly convinced that she did.

She told Matthew the story the next morning. Matthew was confounded and puzzled; he could not so quickly lose faith in Anne but he had to admit that circumstances were against her.

"You're sure it hasn't fell down behind the bureau?" was the only suggestion he could offer.

"I've moved the bureau and I've taken out the drawers and I've looked in every crack and cranny" was Marilla's positive answer. "The brooch is gone and that child has taken it and lied about it. That's the plain, ugly truth, Matthew Cuthbert, and we might as well look it in the face."

"Well now, what are you going to do about it?" Matthew asked forlornly, feeling secretly thankful that Marilla and not he had to deal with the situation. He felt no desire to put his oar in this time.

"She'll stay in her room until she confesses," said Marilla grimly, remembering the success of this method in the former case. "Then we'll see. Perhaps we'll be able to find the brooch if she'll only tell where she took it; but in any case she'll have to be severely punished, Matthew."

"Well now, you'll have to punish her," said Matthew, reaching for his hat. "I've nothing to do with it, remember. You warned me off yourself."

Marilla felt deserted by everyone. She could not even go to Mrs. Lynde for advice. She went up to the east gable with a very serious face and left it with a face more serious still. Anne steadfastly refused to confess. She persisted in asserting that she had not taken the brooch. The child had evidently been crying and Marilla felt a pang of pity which she sternly repressed. By night she was, as she expressed it, "beat out."

"You'll stay in this room until you confess, Anne. You can make up your mind to that," she said firmly.

"But the picnic is tomorrow, Marilla," cried Anne. "You won't keep me from going to that, will you? You'll just let me out for the afternoon, won't you? Then I'll stay here as long as you like *afterwards* cheerfully. But I *must* go to the picnic."

"You'll not go to picnics nor anywhere else until you've confessed, Anne."

"Oh, Marilla," gasped Anne.

But Marilla had gone out and shut the door.

Wednesday morning dawned as bright and fair as if expressly made to order for the picnic. Birds sang around Green Gables; the Madonna lilies in the garden sent out whiffs of perfume that entered in on viewless winds at every door and window, and wandered through halls and rooms like spirits of benediction. The birches in the hollow waved joyful hands as if watching for Anne's usual morning greeting from the east gable. But Anne was not at her window. When Marilla took her breakfast up to her she found the child sitting primly on her bed, pale and resolute, with tight-shut lips and gleaming eyes.

"Marilla, I'm ready to confess."

"Ah!" Marilla laid down her tray. Once again her method had succeeded; but her success was very bitter to her. "Let me hear what you have to say then, Anne."

"I took the amethyst brooch," said Anne, as if repeating a lesson she had learned. "I took it just as you said. I didn't mean to take it when I went in. But it did look so beautiful, Marilla, when I pinned it on my breast that I was overcome by an irresistible temptation. I imagined how perfectly thrilling it would be to take it to Idlewild and play I was the Lady Cordelia Fitzgerald. It would be so much easier to imagine I was the Lady Cordelia if I had a real amethyst brooch on. Diana and I make necklaces of roseberries but what are roseberries compared to amethysts? So I took the brooch. I thought I could put it back before you came home. I went all the way around by the road to lengthen out the time. When I was going over the bridge across the Lake of Shining Waters I took the brooch off to have another look at it. Oh, how it did shine in the sunlight! And then, when I was leaning over the bridge, it just slipped through my fingers—so—and went down—down—down, all purply-sparkling, and sank forevermore beneath the Lake of Shining Waters. And that's the best I can do at confessing, Marilla."

Marilla felt hot anger surge up into her heart again. This child had taken and lost her treasured amethyst brooch and now sat there calmly reciting the details thereof without the least apparent compunction or repentance.

"Anne, this is terrible," she said, trying to speak calmly. "You are the very wickedest girl I ever heard of."

"Yes, I suppose I am," agreed Anne tranquilly. "And I know I'll have to be punished. It'll be your duty to punish me, Marilla. Won't you please get it over right off because I'd like to go to the picnic with nothing on my mind."

"Picnic, indeed! You'll go to no picnic today, Anne Shirley. That shall be your punishment. And it isn't half severe enough either for what you've done!"

"Not go to the picnic!" Anne sprang to her feet and clutched Marilla's hand.

"But you *promised* me I might! Oh, Marilla, I must go to the picnic. That was why I confessed. Punish me any way you like but that. Oh, Marilla, please, please, let me go to the picnic. Think of the ice cream! For anything you know I may never have a chance to taste ice cream again."

Marilla disengaged Anne's clinging hands stonily.

"You needn't plead, Anne. You are not going to the picnic and that's final. No, not a word."

Anne realized that Marilla was not to be moved. She clasped her hands together, gave a piercing shriek, and then flung herself face downward on the bed, crying and writhing in an utter abandonment of disappointment and despair.

"For the land's sake!" gasped Marilla, hastening from the room. "I believe the child is crazy. No child in her senses would behave as she does. If she isn't she's utterly bad. Oh dear, I'm afraid Rachel was right from the first. But I've put my hand to the plow and I won't look back."

That was a dismal morning. Marilla worked fiercely and scrubbed the porch floor and the dairy shelves when she could find nothing else to do. Neither the shelves nor the porch needed it—but Marilla did. Then she went out and raked the yard.

When dinner was ready she went to the stairs and called Anne. A tear-stained face appeared, looking tragically over the banisters.

"Come down to your dinner, Anne."

"I don't want any dinner, Marilla," said Anne, sobbingly. "I couldn't eat anything. My heart is broken. You'll feel remorse of conscience someday, I expect, for breaking it, Marilla, but I forgive you. Remember when the time comes that I forgive you. But please don't ask me to eat anything, especially boiled pork and greens. Boiled pork and greens are so unromantic when one is in affliction."

Exasperated, Marilla returned to the kitchen and poured out her tale of woe to Matthew, who, between his sense of justice and his unlawful sympathy with Anne, was a miserable man.

"Well now, she shouldn't have taken the brooch, Marilla, or told stories about it," he admitted, mournfully surveying his plateful of unromantic pork and greens as if he, like Anne, thought it a food unsuited to crises of feeling, "but she's such a little thing—such an interesting little thing. Don't you think it's pretty rough not to let her go to the picnic when she's so set on it?"

"Matthew Cuthbert, I'm amazed at you. I think I've let her off entirely too easy. And she doesn't appear to realize how wicked she's been at all—that's what worries me most. If she'd really felt sorry it wouldn't be so bad. And you don't seem to realize it, neither; you're making excuses for her all the time to yourself—I can see that."

"Well now, she's such a little thing," feebly reiterated Matthew. "And there should be allowances made, Marilla. You know she's never had any bringing up."

"Well, she's having it now," retorted Marilla.

The retort silenced Matthew if it did not convince him. That dinner was a very dismal meal. The only cheerful thing about it was Jerry Buote, the hired boy, and Marilla resented his cheerfulness as a personal insult.

When her dishes were washed and her bread sponge set and her hens fed Marilla remembered that she had noticed a small rent in her best black lace shawl when she had taken it off on Monday afternoon on returning from the Ladies' Aid. She would go and mend it.

The shawl was in a box in her trunk. As Marilla lifted it out, the sunlight, falling through the vines that clustered thickly about the window, struck upon something caught in the shawl—something that glittered and sparkled in facets of violet light. Marilla snatched at it with a gasp. It was the amethyst brooch, hanging to a thread of the lace by its catch!

"Dear life and heart," said Marilla blankly, "what does this mean? Here's my brooch safe and sound that I thought was at the bottom of Barry's pond. Whatever did that girl mean by saying she took it and lost it? I declare I believe Green Gables is bewitched. I remember now that when I took off my shawl Monday afternoon I laid it on the bureau for a minute. I suppose the brooch got caught in it somehow. Well!"

Marilla betook herself to the east gable, brooch in hand. Anne had cried herself out and was sitting dejectedly by the window.

"Anne Shirley," said Marilla solemnly, "I've just found my brooch hanging to my black lace shawl. Now I want to know what that rigmarole you told me this morning meant."

"Why, you said you'd keep me here until I confessed," returned Anne wearily, "and so I decided to confess because I was bound to get to the picnic. I thought out a confession last night after I went to bed and made it as interesting as I could. And I said it over and over so that I wouldn't forget it. But you wouldn't let me go to the picnic after all, so all my trouble was wasted."

Marilla had to laugh in spite of herself. But her conscience pricked her.

"Anne, you do beat all! But I was wrong—I see that now. I shouldn't have doubted your word when I'd never known you to tell a story. Of course, it wasn't right for you to confess to a thing you hadn't done—it was very wrong to do so. But I drove you to it. So if you'll forgive me, Anne, I'll forgive you and we'll start square again. And now get yourself ready for the picnic."

Anne flew up like a rocket.

"Oh, Marilla, isn't it too late?"

"No, it's only two o'clock. They won't be more than well gathered yet and it'll be an hour before they have tea. Wash your face and comb your hair and put on your gingham. I'll fill a basket for you. There's plenty of stuff baked in the house. And I'll get Jerry to hitch up the sorrel and drive you down to the picnic ground."

"Oh, Marilla," exclaimed Anne, flying to the washstand. "Five minutes ago I was so miserable I was wishing I'd never been born and now I wouldn't change places with an angel!"

That night a thoroughly happy, completely tired-out Anne returned to Green Gables in a state of beatification impossible to describe.

"Oh, Marilla, I've had a perfectly scrumptious time. Scrumptious is a new word I learned today. I heard Mary Alice Bell use it. Isn't it very expressive? Everything was lovely. We had a splendid tea and then Mr. Harmon Andrews took us all for a row on the Lake of Shining Waters—six of us at a time. And Jane Andrews nearly fell overboard. She was leaning out to pick water lilies and if Mr. Andrews hadn't caught her by her sash just in the nick of time she'd have fallen in and prob'ly been drowned. I wish it had been me. It would have been such a romantic experience to have been nearly drowned. It would be such a thrilling tale to tell. And we had the ice cream. Words fail me to describe that ice cream. Marilla, I assure you it was sublime."

That evening Marilla told the whole story to Matthew over her stocking basket.

"I'm willing to own up that I made a mistake," she concluded candidly, "but I've learned a lesson. I have to laugh when I think of Anne's 'confession,' although I suppose I shouldn't for it really was a falsehood. But it doesn't seem as bad as the other would have been, somehow, and anyhow I'm responsible for it. That child is hard to understand in some respects. But I believe she'll turn out all right yet. And there's one thing certain, no house will ever be dull that she's in."

CHAPTER XV

A TEMPEST IN THE SCHOOL TEAPOT

What a splendid day!" said Anne, drawing a long breath. "Isn't it good just to be alive on a day like this? I pity the people who aren't born yet for missing it. They may have good days, of course, but they can never have this one. And it's splendider still to have such a lovely way to go to school by, isn't it?"

"It's a lot nicer than going round by the road; that is so dusty and hot," said Diana practically, peeping into her dinner basket and mentally calculating if the three juicy, toothsome, raspberry tarts reposing there were divided among ten girls how many bites each girl would have.

The little girls of Avonlea school always pooled their lunches, and to eat three raspberry tarts all alone or even to share them only with one's best chum would have forever and ever branded as "awful mean" the girl who did it. And yet, when the tarts were divided among ten girls you just got enough to tantalize you.

The way Anne and Diana went to school *was* a pretty one. Anne thought those walks to and from school with Diana couldn't be improved upon even by imagination. Going around by the main road would have been so unromantic; but to go by Lover's Lane and Willowmere and Violet Vale and the Birch Path was romantic, if ever anything was.

Lover's Lane opened out below the orchard at Green Gables and stretched far up into the woods to the end of the Cuthbert farm. It was the way by which the cows were taken to the back pasture and the wood hauled home in winter. Anne had named it Lover's Lane before she had been a month at Green Gables.

"Not that lovers ever really walk there," she explained to Marilla, "but Diana and I are reading a perfectly magnificent book and there's a Lover's Lane in it. So we want to have one, too. And it's a very pretty name, don't you think? So romantic! We can't imagine the lovers into it, you know. I like that lane because you can think out loud there without people calling you crazy."

Anne, starting out alone in the morning, went down Lover's Lane as far as the brook. Here Diana met her, and the two little girls went on up the lane under the leafy arch of maples—"maples are such sociable trees," said Anne; "they're always rustling and whispering to you"—until they came to a rustic bridge. Then they left the lane and walked through Mr. Barry's back field and past Willowmere. Beyond Willowmere came Violet Vale—a little green dimple in the shadow of Mr. Andrew Bell's big woods. "Of course there are no violets there now," Anne told Marilla, "but Diana says there are millions of them in spring. Oh, Marilla, can't you just imagine you see them? It actually takes away my breath. I named it Violet Vale. Diana says she never saw the beat of me for hitting on fancy names for places. It's nice to be clever at something, isn't it? But Diana named the Birch Path. She wanted to, so I let her; but I'm sure I could have found something more poetical than plain Birch Path. Anybody can think of a name like that. But the Birch Path is one of the prettiest places in the world, Marilla."

It was. Other people besides Anne thought so when they stumbled on it. It was a little narrow, twisting path, winding down over a long hill straight through Mr. Bell's woods, where the light came down sifted through so many emerald screens that it was as flawless as the heart of a diamond. It was fringed in all its length with slim young birches, white stemmed and lissom boughed; ferns and starflowers and wild lilies-of-the-valley and scarlet tufts of pigeonberries grew thickly along it; and always there was a delightful spiciness in the air and music of bird calls and the murmur and laugh of wood winds in the trees overhead. Now and then you might see a rabbit skipping across the road if you were quiet—which, with Anne and Diana, happened about once in a blue moon. Down in the valley the path came out to the main road and then it was just up the spruce hill to the school.

The Avonlea school was a whitewashed building, low in the eaves and wide in the windows, furnished inside with comfortable substantial old-fashioned desks that opened and shut, and were carved all over their lids with the initials and hieroglyphics of three generations of school children. The schoolhouse was set back from the road and behind it was a dusky fir wood and a brook where all the children put their bottles of milk in the morning to keep cool and sweet until dinner hour.

Marilla had seen Anne start off to school on the first day of September with many secret misgivings. Anne was such an odd girl. How would she get on with the other children? And how on earth would she ever manage to hold her tongue during school hours?

Things went better than Marilla feared, however. Anne came home that evening in high spirits.

"I think I'm going to like school here," she announced. "I don't think much of the master, through. He's all the time curling his mustache and making eyes at Prissy Andrews. Prissy is grown up, you know. She's sixteen and she's studying for the entrance examination into Queen's Academy at Charlottetown next year. Tillie Boulter says the master is *dead gone* on her. She's got a beautiful complexion and curly brown hair and she does it up so elegantly. She sits in the long seat at the back and he sits there, too, most of the time—to explain her lessons, he says. But Ruby Gillis says she saw him writing something on her slate and when Prissy read it she blushed as red as a beet and giggled; and Ruby Gillis says she doesn't believe it had anything to do with the lesson."

"Anne Shirley, don't let me hear you talking about your teacher in that way again," said Marilla sharply. "You don't go to school to criticize the master. I guess he can teach *you* something, and it's your business to learn. And I want you to understand right off that you are not to come home telling tales about him. That is something I won't encourage. I hope you were a good girl."

"Indeed I was," said Anne comfortably. "It wasn't so hard as you might imagine, either. I sit with Diana. Our seat is right by the window and we can look down to the Lake of Shining Waters. There are a lot of nice girls in school and we had scrumptious fun playing at dinnertime. It's so nice to have a lot of little girls to play with. But of course I like Diana best and always will. I *adore* Diana. I'm dreadfully far behind the others. They're all in the fifth book and I'm only in the fourth. I feel that it's kind of a disgrace. But there's not one of them has such an imagination as I have and I soon found that out. We had reading and geography and Canadian history and dictation today. Mr. Phillips said my spelling was disgraceful and he held up my slate so that everybody could see it, all marked over. I felt so mortified, Marilla; he might have been politer to a stranger, I think. Ruby Gillis gave me an apple and Sophia Sloane lent me a lovely pink card with 'May I see you home?' on it. I'm to give it back to her tomorrow. And Tillie Boulter let me wear her bead ring all the afternoon. Can I have some of those pearl beads off the old pincushion in the garret to make myself a ring? And oh,

Marilla, Jane Andrews told me that Minnie MacPherson told her that she heard Prissy Andrews tell Sara Gillis that I had a very pretty nose. Marilla, that is the first compliment I have ever had in my life and you can't imagine what a strange feeling it gave me. Marilla, have I really a pretty nose? I know you'll tell me the truth."

"Your nose is well enough," said Marilla shortly. Secretly she thought Anne's nose was a remarkable pretty one; but she had no intention of telling her so.

That was three weeks ago and all had gone smoothly so far. And now, this crisp September morning, Anne and Diana were tripping blithely down the Birch Path, two of the happiest little girls in Avonlea.

"I guess Gilbert Blythe will be in school today," said Diana. "He's been visiting his cousins over in New Brunswick all summer and he only came home Saturday night. He's *aw'fly* handsome, Anne. And he teases the girls something terrible. He just torments our lives out."

Diana's voice indicated that she rather liked having her life tormented out than not.

"Gilbert Blythe?" said Anne. "Isn't it his name that's written up on the porch wall with Julia Bell's and a big 'Take Notice' over them?"

"Yes," said Diana, tossing her head, "but I'm sure he doesn't like Julia Bell so very much. I've heard him say he studied the multiplication table by her freckles."

"Oh, don't speak about freckles to me," implored Anne. "It isn't delicate when I've got so many. But I do think that writing take-notices up on the wall about the boys and girls is the silliest ever. I should just like to see anybody dare to write my name up with a boy's. Not, of course," she hastened to add, "that anybody would."

Anne sighed. She didn't want her name written up. But it was a little humiliating to know that there was no danger of it.

"Nonsense," said Diana, whose black eyes and glossy tresses had played such havoc with the hearts of Avonlea schoolboys that her name figured on the porch walls in half a dozen take-notices. "It's only meant as a joke. And don't you be too sure your name won't ever be written up. Charlie Sloane is *dead gone* on you. He told his mother—his *mother*, mind you—that you were the smartest girl in school. That's better than being good looking."

"No, it isn't," said Anne, feminine to the core. "I'd rather be pretty than clever. And I hate Charlie Sloane, I can't bear a boy with goggle eyes. If anyone wrote my name up with his I'd *never* get over it, Diana Barry. But it *is* nice to keep head of your class."

"You'll have Gilbert in your class after this," said Diana, "and he's used to being head of his class, I can tell you. He's only in the fourth book although he's nearly fourteen. Four years ago his father was sick and had to go out to Alberta for his health and Gilbert went with him. They were there three years and Gil didn't go to school hardly any until they came back. You won't find it so easy to keep head after this, Anne."

"I'm glad," said Anne quickly. "I couldn't really feel proud of keeping head of little boys and girls of just nine or ten. I got up yesterday spelling 'ebullition.' Josie Pye was head and, mind you, she peeped in her book. Mr. Phillips didn't see her—he was looking at Prissy Andrews—but I did. I just swept her a look of freezing scorn and she got as red as a beet and spelled it wrong after all."

"Those Pye girls are cheats all round," said Diana indignantly, as they climbed the fence of the main road. "Gertie Pye actually went and put her milk bottle in my place in the brook yesterday. Did you ever? I don't speak to her now."

When Mr. Phillips was in the back of the room hearing Prissy Andrews's Latin, Diana whispered to Anne, "That's Gilbert Blythe sitting right across the aisle from you, Anne. Just look at him and see if you don't think he's handsome."

Anne looked accordingly. She had a good chance to do so, for the said Gilbert Blythe was absorbed in stealthily pinning the long yellow braid of Ruby Gillis, who sat in front of him, to the back of her seat. He was a tall boy, with curly brown hair, roguish hazel eyes, and a mouth twisted into a teasing smile. Presently Ruby Gillis started up to take a sum to the master; she fell back into her seat with a little shriek, believing that her hair was pulled out by the roots. Everybody looked at her and Mr. Phillips glared so sternly that Ruby began to cry. Gilbert had whisked the pin out of sight and was studying his history with the soberest face in the world; but when the commotion subsided he looked at Anne and winked with inexpressible drollery.

"I think your Gilbert Blythe *is* handsome," confided Anne to Diana, "but I think he's very bold. It isn't good manners to wink at a strange girl."

But it was not until the afternoon that things really began to happen.

Mr. Phillips was back in the corner explaining a problem in algebra to Prissy Andrews and the rest of the scholars were doing pretty much as they pleased eating green apples, whispering, drawing pictures on their slates, and driving crickets, harnessed to strings, up and down aisle. Gilbert Blythe was trying to make Anne Shirley look at him and failing utterly, because Anne was at that moment totally oblivious not only to the very existence of Gilbert Blythe, but of every other scholar in Avonlea school itself. With her chin propped on her hands and her eyes fixed on the blue glimpse of the Lake of Shining Waters that the west window afforded, she was far away in a gorgeous dreamland hearing and seeing nothing save her own wonderful visions.

Gilbert Blythe wasn't used to putting himself out to make a girl look at him and meeting with failure. She *should* look at him, that red-haired Shirley girl with the little pointed chin and the big eyes that weren't like the eyes of any other girl in Avonlea school.

Gilbert reached across the aisle, picked up the end of Anne's long red braid, held it out at arm's length and said in a piercing whisper:

"Carrots! Carrots!"

Then Anne looked at him with a vengeance!

She did more than look. She sprang to her feet, her bright fancies fallen into cureless ruin. She flashed one indignant glance at Gilbert from eyes whose angry sparkle was swiftly quenched in equally angry tears.

"You mean, hateful boy!" she exclaimed passionately. "How dare you!"

And then—thwack! Anne had brought her slate down on Gilbert's head and cracked it—slate not head—clear across.

Avonlea school always enjoyed a scene. This was an especially enjoyable one. Everybody said "Oh" in horrified delight. Diana gasped. Ruby Gillis, who was inclined to be hysterical, began to cry. Tommy Sloane let his team of crickets escape him altogether while he stared open-mouthed at the tableau.

Mr. Phillips stalked down the aisle and laid his hand heavily on Anne's shoulder.

"Anne Shirley, what does this mean?" he said angrily.

Anne returned no answer. It was asking too much of flesh and blood to expect her to tell before the whole school that she had been called "carrots." Gilbert it was who spoke up stoutly.

"It was my fault, Mr. Phillips. I teased her."

Mr. Phillips paid no heed to Gilbert.

"I am sorry to see a pupil of mine displaying such a temper and such a vindictive spirit," he said in a solemn tone, as if the mere fact of being a pupil of his ought to root out all evil passions from the hearts of small imperfect mortals. "Anne, go and stand on the platform in front of the blackboard for the rest of the afternoon."

Anne would have infinitely preferred a whipping to this punishment under which her sensitive spirit quivered as from a whiplash. With a white, set face she obeyed. Mr. Phillips took a chalk crayon and wrote on the blackboard above her head.

"Ann Shirley has a very bad temper. Ann Shirley must learn to control her temper," and then read it out loud so that even the primer class, who couldn't read writing, should understand it. Anne stood there the rest of the afternoon with that legend above her. She did not cry or hang her head. Anger was still too hot in her heart for that and it sustained her amid all her agony of humiliation. With resentful eyes and passion-red cheeks she confronted alike Diana's sympathetic gaze and Charlie Sloane's indignant nods and Josie Pye's malicious smiles. As for Gilbert Blythe, she would not even look at him. She would *never* look at him again! She would never speak to him!!

When school was dismissed Anne marched out with her red head held high. Gilbert Blythe tried to intercept her at the porch door.

"I'm awfully sorry I made fun of your hair, Anne," he whispered contritely. "Honest I am. Don't be mad for keeps, now."

Anne swept by disdainfully, without look or sign of hearing. "Oh how could you, Anne?" breathed Diana as they went down the road half reproachfully, half admiringly. Diana felt that *she* could never have resisted Gilbert's plea.

"I shall never forgive Gilbert Blythe," said Anne firmly. "And Mr. Phillips spelled my name without an *e*, too. The iron has entered into my soul, Diana."

Diana hadn't the least idea what Anne meant but she understood it was something terrible.

"You mustn't mind Gilbert making fun of your hair," she said soothingly. "Why, he makes fun of all the girls. He laughs at mine because it's so black. He's called me a crow a dozen times; and I never heard him apologize for anything before, either."

"There's a great deal of difference between being called a crow and being called carrots," said Anne with dignity. "Gilbert Blythe has hurt my feelings *excruciatingly*, Diana."

It is possible the matter might have blown over without more excruciation if nothing else had happened. But when things begin to happen they are apt to keep on.

Avonlea scholars often spent noon hour picking gum in Mr. Bell's spruce grove over the hill and across his big pasture field. From there they could keep an eye on Eben Wright's house, where the master boarded. When they saw Mr. Phillips emerging therefrom they ran for the schoolhouse; but the distance being about three times longer than Mr. Wright's lane they were very apt to arrive there, breathless and gasping, some three minutes too late.

On the following day Mr. Phillips was seized with one of his spasmodic fits of reform and announced, before going home to dinner, that he should expect to find all the scholars in their seats when he returned. Anyone who came in late would be punished.

All the boys and some of the girls went to Mr. Bell's spruce grove as usual, fully intending to stay only long enough to "pick a chew." But spruce groves are seductive and yellow nuts of gum beguiling; they picked and loitered and strayed; and as usual the first thing that recalled them to a sense of the flight of time was Jimmy Glover shouting from the top of a patriarchal old spruce, "Master's coming."

The girls, who were on the ground, started first and managed to reach the schoolhouse in time but without a second to spare. The boys, who had to wriggle hastily down from the trees, were later; and Anne, who had not been picking gum at all but was wandering happily in the far end of the grove, waist deep among the bracken, singing softly to herself, with a wreath of rice lilies on her hair as if she were some wild divinity of the shadowy places, was latest of all. Anne could run like a deer, however; run she did with the impish result that she overtook the boys at the door and was swept into the schoolhouse among them just as Mr. Phillips was in the act of hanging up his hat.

Mr. Phillips's brief reforming energy was over; he didn't want the bother of punishing a dozen pupils; but it was necessary to do something to save his word, so he looked about for a scapegoat and found it in Anne, who had dropped into her seat, gasping for breath, with her forgotten lily wreath hanging askew over one ear and giving her a particularly rakish and disheveled appearance.

"Anne Shirley, since you seem to be so fond of the boys' company we shall indulge your taste for it this afternoon," he said sarcastically. "Take those flowers out of your hair and sit with Gilbert Blythe."

The other boys snickered. Diana, turning pale with pity, plucked the wreath from Anne's hair and squeezed her hand. Anne stared at the master as if turned to stone.

"Did you hear what I said, Anne?" queried Mr. Phillips sternly.

"Yes, sir," said Anne slowly, "but I didn't suppose you really meant it."

"I assure you I did"—still with the sarcastic inflection which all the children, and Anne especially, hated. It flicked on the raw. "Obey me at once."

For a moment Anne looked as if she meant to disobey. Then, realizing that there was no help for it, she rose haughtily, stepped across the aisle, sat down beside Gilbert Blythe, and buried her face in her arms on the desk. Ruby Gillis, who got a glimpse of it as it went down, told the others going home from school that she'd "acksually never seen anything like it—it was so white, with awful little red spots in it."

To Anne, this was as the end of all things. It was bad enough to be singled out for punishment from among a dozen equally guilty ones; it was worse still to be sent to sit with a boy, but that that boy should be Gilbert Blythe was heaping insult on injury to a degree utterly unbearable. Anne felt that she could *not* bear it and it would be of no use to try. Her whole being seethed with shame and anger and humiliation.

At first the other scholars looked and whispered and giggled and nudged. But as Anne never lifted her head and as Gilbert worked fractions as if his whole soul was absorbed in them and them only, they soon returned to their own tasks and Anne was forgotten. When Mr. Phillips called the history class out Anne should have gone, but Anne did not move, and Mr. Phillips, who had been writing some verses "To Priscilla" before he called the class, was thinking about an obstinate rhyme still and never missed her. Once, when nobody was looking, Gilbert took from his desk a little pink candy heart with a gold motto on it, "You are sweet," and slipped it under the curve of Anne's arm. Whereupon Anne arose, took the pink heart gingerly between the tips of her fingers, dropped it on the floor, ground it to powder beneath her heel, and resumed her position without deigning to bestow a glance on Gilbert.

When school went out Anne marched to her desk, ostentatiously took out everything therein, books and writing tablet, pen and ink, testament and arithmetic, and piled them neatly on her cracked slate.

"What are you taking all those things home for, Anne?" Diana wanted to know, as soon as they were out on the road. She had not dared to ask the question before.

"I am not coming back to school any more," said Anne. Diana gasped and stared at Anne to see if she meant it.

"Will Marilla let you stay home?" she asked.

"She'll have to," said Anne. "I'll *never* go to school to that man again."

"Oh, Anne!" Diana looked as if she were ready to cry. "I do think you're mean. What shall I do? Mr. Phillips will make me sit with that horrid Gertie Pye—I know he will because she is sitting alone. Do come back, Anne."

"I'd do almost anything in the world for you, Diana," said Anne sadly. "I'd let myself be torn limb from limb if it would do you any good. But I can't do this, so please don't ask it. You harrow up my very soul."

"Just think of all the fun you will miss," mourned Diana. "We are going to build the loveliest new house down by the brook; and we'll be playing ball next week and you've never played ball, Anne. It's tremendously exciting. And we're going to learn a new song—Jane Andrews is practicing it up now; and Alice Andrews is going to bring a new Pansy book next week and we're all going to read it out loud, chapter about, down by the brook. And you know you are so fond of reading out loud, Anne."

Nothing moved Anne in the least. Her mind was made up. She would not go to school to Mr. Phillips again; she told Marilla so when she got home.

"Nonsense," said Marilla.

"It isn't nonsense at all," said Anne, gazing at Marilla with solemn, reproachful eyes. "Don't you understand, Marilla? I've been insulted."

"Insulted fiddlesticks! You'll go to school tomorrow as usual."

"Oh, no." Anne shook her head gently. "I'm not going back, Marilla. I'll learn my lessons at home and I'll be as good as I can be and hold my tongue all the time if it's possible at all. But I will not go back to school, I assure you."

Marilla saw something remarkably like unyielding stubbornness looking out of Anne's small face. She understood that she would have trouble in overcoming it; but she resolved wisely to say nothing more just then.

"I'll run down and see Rachel about it this evening," she thought. "There's no use reasoning with Anne now. She's too worked up and I've an idea she can be awful stubborn if she takes the notion. Far as I can make out from her story, Mr. Phillips has been carrying matters with a rather high hand. But it would never do to say so to her. I'll just talk it over with Rachel. She's sent ten children to school and she ought to know something about it. She'll have heard the whole story, too, by this time."

Marilla found Mrs. Lynde knitting quilts as industriously and cheerfully as usual.

"I suppose you know what I've come about," she said, a little shamefacedly.

Mrs. Rachel nodded.

"About Anne's fuss in school, I reckon," she said. "Tillie Boulter was in on her way home from school and told me about it."

"I don't know what to do with her," said Marilla. "She declares she won't go back to school. I never saw a child so worked up. I've been expecting trouble ever since she started to school. I knew things were going too smooth to last. She's so high strung. What would you advise, Rachel?"

"Well, since you've asked my advice, Marilla," said Mrs. Lynde amiably—Mrs. Lynde dearly loved to be asked for advice—"I'd just humor her a little at first, that's what I'd do. It's my belief that Mr. Phillips was in the wrong. Of course, it doesn't do to say so to the children, you know. And of course he did right to punish her yesterday for giving way to temper. But today it was different. The others who were late should have been punished as well as Anne, that's what. And I don't believe in making the girls sit with the boys for punishment. It isn't modest. Tillie Boulter was real indignant. She took Anne's part right through and said all the scholars did, too. Anne seems real popular among them, somehow. I never thought she'd take with them so well."

"Then you really think I'd better let her stay home," said Marilla in amazement.

"Yes. That is, I wouldn't say school to her again until she said it herself. Depend upon it, Marilla, she'll cool off in a week or so and be ready enough to go back of her own accord, that's what, while, if you were to make her go back right off, dear knows what freak or tantrum she'd take next and make more trouble than ever. The less fuss made the better, in my opinion. She won't miss much by not going to school, as far as *that* goes. Mr. Phillips isn't any good at all as a teacher. The order he keeps is scandalous, that's what, and he neglects the young fry and puts all his time on those big scholars he's getting ready for Queen's. He'd never have got the school for another year if his uncle hadn't been a trustee—*the* trustee, for he just leads the other two around by the nose, that's what. I declare, I don't know what education in this Island is coming to."

Mrs. Rachel shook her head, as much as to say if she were only at the head of the educational system of the Province things would be much better managed.

Marilla took Mrs. Rachel's advice and not another word was said to Anne about going back to school. She learned her lessons at home, did her chores, and played with Diana in the chilly purple autumn twilights; but when she met Gilbert Blythe on the road or encountered him in Sunday school she passed him by with an icy contempt that was no whit thawed by his evident desire to appease her. Even Diana's efforts as a peacemaker were of no avail. Anne had evidently made up her mind to hate Gilbert Blythe to the end of life.

As much as she hated Gilbert, however, did she love Diana, with all the love of her passionate little heart, equally intense in its likes and dislikes. One evening Marilla, coming in from the orchard with a basket of apples, found Anne sitting along by the east window in the twilight, crying bitterly.

"Whatever's the matter now, Anne?" she asked.

"It's about Diana," sobbed Anne luxuriously. "I love Diana so, Marilla. I cannot ever live without her. But I know very well when we grow up that Diana will get married and go away and leave me. And oh, what shall I do? I hate her husband—I just hate him furiously. I've been imagining it all out—the wedding and everything—Diana dressed in snowy garments, with a veil, and looking as beautiful and regal as a queen; and me the bridesmaid, with a lovely dress too, and puffed sleeves, but with a breaking heart hid beneath my smiling face. And then bidding Diana goodbye-e-e—" Here Anne broke down entirely and wept with increasing bitterness.

Marilla turned quickly away to hide her twitching face, but it was no use; she collapsed on the nearest chair and burst into such a hearty and unusual peal of laughter that Matthew, crossing the yard outside, halted in amazement. When had he heard Marilla laugh like that before?

"Well, Anne Shirley," said Marilla as soon as she could speak, "if you must borrow trouble, for pity's sake borrow it handier home. I should think you had an imagination, sure enough."

CHAPTER XVI

DIANA IS INVITED TO TEA WITH TRAGIC RESULTS

October was a beautiful month at Green Gables, when the birches in the hollow turned as golden as sunshine and the maples behind the orchard were royal crimson and the wild cherry trees along the lane put on the loveliest shades of dark red and bronzy green, while the fields sunned themselves in aftermaths.

Anne reveled in the world of color about her.

"Oh, Marilla," she exclaimed one Saturday morning, coming dancing in with her arms full of gorgeous boughs, "I'm so glad I live in a world where there are Octobers. It would be terrible if we just skipped from September to November, wouldn't it? Look at these maple branches. Don't they give you a thrill—several thrills? I'm going to decorate my room with them."

"Messy things," said Marilla, whose aesthetic sense was not noticeably developed. "You clutter up your room entirely too much with out-of-doors stuff, Anne. Bedrooms were made to sleep in."

"Oh, and dream in too, Marilla. And you know one can dream so much better in a room where there are pretty things. I'm going to put these boughs in the old blue jug and set them on my table."

"Mind you don't drop leaves all over the stairs then. I'm going to a meeting of the Aid Society at Carmody this afternoon, Anne, and I won't likely be home before dark. You'll have to get Matthew and Jerry their supper, so mind you don't forget to put the tea to draw until you sit down at the table as you did last time."

"It was dreadful of me to forget," said Anne apologetically, "but that was the afternoon I was trying to think of a name for Violet Vale and it crowded other things out. Matthew was so good. He never scolded a bit. He put the tea down himself and said we could wait awhile as well as not. And I told him a lovely fairy story while we were waiting, so he didn't find the time long at all. It was a beautiful fairy story, Marilla. I forgot the end of it, so I made up an end for it myself and Matthew said he couldn't tell where the join came in."

"Matthew would think it all right, Anne, if you took a notion to get up and have dinner in the middle of the night. But you keep your wits about you this time. And—I don't really know if I'm doing right—it may make you more addlepated than ever—but you can ask Diana to come over and spend the afternoon with you and have tea here."

"Oh, Marilla!" Anne clasped her hands. "How perfectly lovely! You *are* able to imagine things after all or else you'd never have understood how I've longed for that very thing. It will seem so nice and grown-uppish. No fear of my forgetting to put the tea to draw when I have company. Oh, Marilla, can I use the rosebud spray tea set?"

"No, indeed! The rosebud tea set! Well, what next? You know I never use that except for the minister or the Aids. You'll put down the old brown tea set. But you can open the little yellow crock of cherry preserves. It's time it was being used anyhow—I believe it's beginning to work. And you can cut some fruit cake and have some of the cookies and snaps."

"I can just imagine myself sitting down at the head of the table and pouring out the tea," said Anne, shutting her eyes ecstatically. "And asking Diana if she takes sugar! I know she doesn't but of course I'll ask her just as if I didn't know. And then pressing her to take another piece of fruit cake and another helping of preserves. Oh, Marilla, it's a wonderful sensation just to think of it. Can I take her into the spare room to lay off her hat when she comes? And then into the parlor to sit?"

"No. The sitting room will do for you and your company. But there's a bottle half full of raspberry cordial that was left over from the church social the other night. It's on the second shelf of the sitting-room closet and you and Diana can have it if you like, and a cooky to eat with it along in the afternoon, for I daresay Matthew'll be late coming in to tea since he's hauling potatoes to the vessel."

Anne flew down to the hollow, past the Dryad's Bubble and up the spruce path to Orchard Slope, to ask Diana to tea. As a result just after Marilla had driven off to Carmody, Diana came over, dressed in *her* second-best dress and looking exactly as it is proper to look when asked out to tea. At other times she was wont to run into the kitchen without knocking; but now she knocked primly at the front door. And when Anne, dressed in her second best, as primly opened it, both little girls shook hands as gravely as if they had never met before. This unnatural solemnity lasted until after Diana had been taken to the east gable to lay off her hat and then had sat for ten minutes in the sitting room, toes in position.

"How is your mother?" inquired Anne politely, just as if she had not seen Mrs. Barry picking apples that morning in excellent health and spirits.

"She is very well, thank you. I suppose Mr. Cuthbert is hauling potatoes to the *Lily Sands* this afternoon, is he?" said Diana, who had ridden down to Mr. Harmon Andrews's that morning in Matthew's cart.

"Yes. Our potato crop is very good this year. I hope your father's crop is good too."

"It is fairly good, thank you. Have you picked many of your apples yet?"

"Oh, ever so many," said Anne, forgetting to be dignified and jumping up quickly. "Let's go out to the orchard and get some of the Red Sweetings, Diana. Marilla says we can have all that are left on the tree. Marilla is a very generous woman. She said we could have fruit cake and cherry preserves for tea. But it isn't good manners to tell your company what you are going to give them to eat, so I won't tell you what she said we could have to drink. Only it begins with an *r* and a *c* and it's a bright red color. I love bright red drinks, don't you? They taste twice as good as any other color."

The orchard, with its great sweeping boughs that bent to the ground with fruit, proved so delightful that the little girls spent most of the afternoon in it, sitting in a grassy corner where the frost had spared the green and the mellow autumn sunshine lingered warmly, eating apples and talking as hard as they could. Diana had much to tell Anne of what went on in school. She had to sit with Gertie Pye and she hated it; Gertie squeaked her pencil all the time and it just made her—Diana's—blood run cold; Ruby Gillis had charmed all her warts away, true's you live, with a magic pebble that old Mary Joe from the Creek gave her. You had to rub the warts with the pebble and then throw it away over your left shoulder at the time of the new moon and the warts would all go. Charlie Sloane's name was written up with Em White's on the porch wall and Em White was *awful mad* about it; Sam Boulter had "sassed" Mr. Phillips in class and Mr. Phillips whipped him and Sam's father came down to the school and dared Mr. Phillips to lay a hand on one of his children again; and Mattie Andrews had a new red hood and a blue crossover with tassels on it and the airs she put on about it were perfectly sickening; and Lizzie Wright didn't speak to Mamie Wilson because Mamie Wilson's grown-up sister had cut out Lizzie Wright's grown-up sister with her beau; and everybody missed Anne so and wished she'd come to school again; and Gilbert Blythe—

But Anne didn't want to hear about Gilbert Blythe. She jumped up hurriedly and said suppose they go in and have some raspberry cordial.

Anne looked on the second shelf of the room pantry but there was no bottle of raspberry cordial there. Search revealed it away back on the top shelf. Anne put it on a tray and set it on the table with a tumbler.

"Now, please help yourself, Diana," she said politely. "I don't believe I'll have any just now. I don't feel as if I wanted any after all those apples."

Diana poured herself out a tumblerful, looked at its bright-red hue admiringly, and then sipped it daintily.

"That's awfully nice raspberry cordial, Anne," she said. "I didn't know raspberry cordial was so nice."

"I'm real glad you like it. Take as much as you want. I'm going to run out and stir the fire up. There are so many responsibilities on a person's mind when they're keeping house, isn't there?"

When Anne came back from the kitchen Diana was drinking her second glassful of cordial; and, being entreated thereto by Anne, she offered no particular objection to the drinking of a third. The tumblerfuls were generous ones and the raspberry cordial was certainly very nice.

"The nicest I ever drank," said Diana. "It's ever so much nicer than Mrs. Lynde's, although she brags of hers so much. It doesn't taste a bit like hers."

"I should think Marilla's raspberry cordial would prob'ly be much nicer than Mrs. Lynde's," said Anne loyally. "Marilla is a famous cook. She is trying to teach me to cook but I assure you, Diana, it is uphill work. There's so little scope for imagination in cookery. You just have to go by rules. The last time I made a cake I forgot to put the flour in. I was thinking the loveliest story about you and me, Diana. I thought you were desperately ill with smallpox and everybody deserted you, but I went boldly to your bedside and nursed you back to life; and then I took the smallpox and died and I was buried under those poplar trees in the graveyard and you planted a rosebush by my grave and watered it with your tears; and you never, never forgot the friend of your youth who sacrificed her life for you. Oh, it was such a pathetic tale, Diana. The tears just rained down over my cheeks while I mixed the cake. But I forgot the flour and the cake was a dismal failure. Flour is so essential to cakes, you know. Marilla was very cross and I don't wonder. I'm a great trial to her. She was terribly mortified about the pudding sauce last week. We had a plum pudding for dinner on Tuesday and there was half the pudding and a pitcherful of sauce left over. Marilla said there was enough for another dinner and told me to set it on the pantry shelf and cover it. I meant to cover it just as much as could be, Diana, but when I carried it in I was imagining I was a nun—of course I'm a Protestant but I imagined I was a Catholic—taking the veil to bury a broken heart in cloistered seclusion; and I forgot all about covering the pudding sauce. I thought of it next morning and ran to the pantry. Diana, fancy if you can my extreme horror at finding a mouse drowned in that pudding sauce! I lifted the mouse out with a spoon and threw it out in the yard and then I washed the spoon in three waters. Marilla was out milking and I fully intended to ask her when she came in if I'd give the sauce to the pigs; but when she did come in I was imagining that I was a frost fairy going through the woods turning the trees red and yellow, whichever they wanted to be, so I never thought about the pudding sauce again and Marilla sent me out to pick apples. Well, Mr. and Mrs. Chester Ross from Spencervale came here that morning. You know they are very stylish people, especially Mrs. Chester Ross. When Marilla called me in dinner was all ready and everybody was at the table. I tried to be as polite and dignified as I could be, for I wanted Mrs. Chester Ross to think I was a ladylike little girl even if I wasn't pretty. Everything went right until I saw Marilla coming with the plum pudding in one hand and the pitcher of pudding sauce, *warmed up*, in the other. Diana, that was a terrible moment. I remembered everything and I just stood up in my place and shrieked out, 'Marilla, you mustn't use that pudding sauce. There was a mouse drowned in it. I forgot to tell you before.' Oh, Diana, I shall never forget that awful moment if I live to be a hundred. Mrs. Chester Ross just *looked* at me and I thought I would sink through the floor with mortification. She is such a perfect housekeeper and fancy what she must have thought of us. Marilla turned red as fire but she never said a word—then. She just carried that sauce and pudding out and brought in some strawberry preserves. She even offered me some, but I couldn't swallow a mouthful. It was like heaping coals of fire on my head. After Mrs. Chester Ross went away, Marilla gave me a dreadful scolding. Why, Diana, what is the matter?"

Diana had stood up very unsteadily; then she sat down again, putting her hands to her head.

"I'm—I'm awful sick," she said, a little thickly. "I—I—must go right home."

"Oh, you mustn't dream of going home without your tea," cried Anne in distress. "I'll get it right off—I'll go and put the tea down this very minute."

"I must go home," repeated Diana, stupidly but determinedly.

"Let me get you a lunch anyhow," implored Anne. "Let me give you a bit of fruit cake and some of the cherry preserves. Lie down on the sofa for a little while and you'll be better. Where do you feel bad?"

"I must go home," said Diana, and that was all she would say. In vain Anne pleaded.

"I never heard of company going home without tea," she mourned. "Oh, Diana, do you suppose that it's possible you're really taking the smallpox? If you are I'll go and nurse you, you can depend on that. I'll never forsake you. But I do wish you'd stay till after tea. Where do you feel bad?"

"I'm awful dizzy," said Diana.

And indeed, she walked very dizzily. Anne, with tears of disappointment in her eyes, got Diana's hat and went with her as far as the Barry yard fence. Then she wept all the way back to Green Gables, where she sorrowfully put the remainder of the raspberry cordial back into the pantry and got tea ready for Matthew and Jerry, with all the zest gone out of the performance.

The next day was Sunday and as the rain poured down in torrents from dawn till dusk Anne did not stir abroad from Green Gables. Monday afternoon Marilla sent her down to Mrs. Lynde's on an errand. In a very short space of time Anne came flying back up the lane with tears rolling down her cheeks. Into the kitchen she dashed and flung herself face downward on the sofa in an agony.

"Whatever has gone wrong now, Anne?" queried Marilla in doubt and dismay. "I do hope you haven't gone and been saucy to Mrs. Lynde again."

No answer from Anne save more tears and stormier sobs!

"Anne Shirley, when I ask you a question I want to be answered. Sit right up this very minute and tell me what you are crying about."

Anne sat up, tragedy personified.

"Mrs. Lynde was up to see Mrs. Barry today and Mrs. Barry was in an awful state," she wailed. "She says that I set Diana *drunk* Saturday and sent her home in a disgraceful condition. And she says I must be a thoroughly bad, wicked little girl and she's never, never going to let Diana play with me again. Oh, Marilla, I'm just overcome with woe."

Marilla stared in blank amazement.

"Set Diana drunk!" she said when she found her voice. "Anne, are you or Mrs. Barry crazy? What on earth did you give her?"

"Not a thing but raspberry cordial," sobbed Anne. "I never thought raspberry cordial would set people drunk, Marilla—not even if they drank three big tumblerfuls as Diana did. Oh, it sounds so—so—like Mrs. Thomas's husband! But I didn't mean to set her drunk."

"Drunk fiddlesticks!" said Marilla, marching to the sitting room pantry. There on the shelf was a bottle which she at once recognized as one containing some of her three-year-old homemade currant wine for which she was celebrated in Avonlea, although certain of the stricter sort, Mrs. Barry among them, disapproved strongly of it. And at the same time Marilla recollected that she had put the bottle of raspberry cordial down in the cellar instead of in the pantry as she had told Anne.

She went back to the kitchen with the wine bottle in her hand. Her face was twitching in spite of herself.

"Anne, you certainly have a genius for getting into trouble. You went and gave Diana currant wine instead of raspberry cordial. Didn't you know the difference yourself?"

"I never tasted it," said Anne. "I thought it was the cordial. I meant to be so—so—hospitable. Diana got awfully sick and had to go home. Mrs. Barry told Mrs. Lynde she was simply dead drunk. She just laughed silly-like when her mother asked her what was the matter and went to sleep and slept for hours. Her mother smelled her breath and knew she was drunk. She had a fearful headache all day yesterday. Mrs. Barry is so indignant. She will never believe but what I did it on purpose."

"I should think she would better punish Diana for being so greedy as to drink three glassfuls of anything," said Marilla shortly. "Why, three of those big glasses would have made her sick even if it had only been cordial. Well, this story will be a nice handle for those folks who are so down on me for making currant wine, although I haven't made any for three years ever since I found out that the minister didn't approve. I just kept that bottle for sickness. There, there, child, don't cry. I can't see as you were to blame although I'm sorry it happened so."

"I must cry," said Anne. "My heart is broken. The stars in their courses fight against me, Marilla. Diana and I are parted forever. Oh, Marilla, I little dreamed of this when first we swore our vows of friendship."

"Don't be foolish, Anne. Mrs. Barry will think better of it when she finds you're not to blame. I suppose she thinks you've done it for a silly joke or something of that sort. You'd best go up this evening and tell her how it was."

"My courage fails me at the thought of facing Diana's injured mother," sighed Anne. "I wish you'd go, Marilla. You're so much more dignified than I am. Likely she'd listen to you quicker than to me."

"Well, I will," said Marilla, reflecting that it would probably be the wiser course. "Don't cry any more, Anne. It will be all right."

Marilla had changed her mind about it being all right by the time she got back from Orchard Slope. Anne was watching for her coming and flew to the porch door to meet her.

"Oh, Marilla, I know by your face that it's been no use," she said sorrowfully. "Mrs. Barry won't forgive me?"

"Mrs. Barry indeed!" snapped Marilla. "Of all the unreasonable women I ever saw she's the worst. I told her it was all a mistake and you weren't to blame, but she just simply didn't believe me. And she rubbed it well in about my currant wine and how I'd always said it couldn't have the least effect on anybody. I just told her plainly that currant wine wasn't meant to be drunk three tumblerfuls at a time and that if a child I had to do with was so greedy I'd sober her up with a right good spanking."

Marilla whisked into the kitchen, grievously disturbed, leaving a very much distracted little soul in the porch behind her. Presently Anne stepped out bareheaded into the chill autumn dusk; very determinedly and steadily she took her way down through the sere clover field over the log bridge and up through the spruce grove, lighted by a pale little moon hanging low over the western woods. Mrs. Barry, coming to the door in answer to a timid knock, found a white-lipped eager-eyed supplicant on the doorstep.

Her face hardened. Mrs. Barry was a woman of strong prejudices and dislikes, and her anger was of the cold, sullen sort which is always hardest to overcome. To do her justice, she really believed Anne had made Diana drunk out of sheer malice prepense, and she was honestly anxious to preserve her little daughter from the contamination of further intimacy with such a child.

"What do you want?" she said stiffly.

Anne clasped her hands.

"Oh, Mrs. Barry, please forgive me. I did not mean to—to—intoxicate Diana. How could I? Just imagine if you were a poor little orphan girl that kind people had adopted and you had just one bosom friend in all the world. Do you think you would intoxicate her on purpose? I thought it was only raspberry cordial. I was firmly convinced it was raspberry cordial. Oh, please don't say that you won't let Diana play with me any more. If you do you will cover my life with a dark cloud of woe."

This speech, which would have softened good Mrs. Lynde's heart in a twinkling, had no effect on Mrs. Barry except to irritate her still more. She was suspicious of Anne's big words and dramatic gestures and imagined that the child was making fun of her. So she said, coldly and cruelly:

"I don't think you are a fit little girl for Diana to associate with. You'd better go home and behave yourself."

Anne's lips quivered.

"Won't you let me see Diana just once to say farewell?" she implored.

"Diana has gone over to Carmody with her father," said Mrs. Barry, going in and shutting the door.

Anne went back to Green Gables calm with despair.

"My last hope is gone," she told Marilla. "I went up and saw Mrs. Barry myself and she treated me very insultingly. Marilla, I do *not* think she is a well-bred woman. There is nothing more to do except to pray and I haven't much hope that that'll do much good because, Marilla, I do not believe that God Himself can do very much with such an obstinate person as Mrs. Barry."

"Anne, you shouldn't say such things," rebuked Marilla, striving to overcome that unholy tendency to laughter which she was dismayed to find growing upon her. And indeed, when she told the whole story to Matthew that night, she did laugh heartily over Anne's tribulations.

But when she slipped into the east gable before going to bed and found that Anne had cried herself to sleep an unaccustomed softness crept into her face.

"Poor little soul," she murmured, lifting a loose curl of hair from the child's tear-stained face. Then she bent down and kissed the flushed cheek on the pillow.

CHAPTER XVII

A NEW INTEREST IN LIFE

The next afternoon Anne, bending over her patchwork at the kitchen window, happened to glance out and beheld Diana down by the Dryad's Bubble beckoning mysteriously. In a trice Anne was out of the house and flying down to the hollow, astonishment and hope struggling in her expressive eyes. But the hope faded when she saw Diana's dejected countenance.

"Your mother hasn't relented?" she gasped.

Diana shook her head mournfully.

"No; and oh, Anne, she says I'm never to play with you again. I've cried and cried and I told her it wasn't your fault, but it wasn't any use. I had ever such a time coaxing her to let me come down and say good-bye to you. She said I was only to stay ten minutes and she's timing me by the clock."

"Ten minutes isn't very long to say an eternal farewell in," said Anne tearfully. "Oh, Diana, will you promise faithfully never to forget me, the friend of your youth, no matter what dearer friends may caress thee?"

"Indeed I will," sobbed Diana, "and I'll never have another bosom friend—I don't want to have. I couldn't love anybody as I love you."

"Oh, Diana," cried Anne, clasping her hands, "do you *love* me?"

"Why, of course I do. Didn't you know that?"

"No." Anne drew a long breath. "I thought you *liked* me of course but I never hoped you *loved* me. Why, Diana, I didn't think anybody could love me. Nobody ever has loved me since I can remember. Oh, this is wonderful! It's a ray of light which will forever shine on the darkness of a path severed from thee, Diana. Oh, just say it once again."

"I love you devotedly, Anne," said Diana stanchly, "and I always will, you may be sure of that."

"And I will always love thee, Diana," said Anne, solemnly extending her hand. "In the years to come thy memory will shine like a star over my lonely life, as that last story we read together says. Diana, wilt thou give me a lock of thy jet-black tresses in parting to treasure forevermore?"

"Have you got anything to cut it with?" queried Diana, wiping away the tears which Anne's affecting accents had caused to flow afresh, and returning to practicalities.

"Yes. I've got my patchwork scissors in my apron pocket fortunately," said Anne. She solemnly clipped one of Diana's curls. "Fare thee well, my beloved friend. Henceforth we must be as strangers though living side by side. But my heart will ever be faithful to thee."

Anne stood and watched Diana out of sight, mournfully waving her hand to the latter whenever she turned to look back. Then she returned to the house, not a little consoled for the time being by this romantic parting.

"It is all over," she informed Marilla. "I shall never have another friend. I'm really worse off than ever before, for I haven't Katie Maurice and Violetta now. And even if I had it wouldn't be the same. Somehow, little dream girls are not satisfying after a real friend. Diana and I had such an affecting farewell down by the spring. It will be sacred in my memory forever. I used the most pathetic language I could think of and said 'thou' and 'thee.' 'Thou' and 'thee' seem so much more romantic than 'you.' Diana gave me a lock of her hair and I'm going to sew it up in a little bag and wear it around my neck all my life. Please see that it is buried with me, for I don't believe I'll live very long. Perhaps when she sees me lying cold and dead before her Mrs. Barry may feel remorse for what she has done and will let Diana come to my funeral."

"I don't think there is much fear of your dying of grief as long as you can talk, Anne," said Marilla unsympathetically.

The following Monday Anne surprised Marilla by coming down from her room with her basket of books on her arm and hip and her lips primmed up into a line of determination.

"I'm going back to school," she announced. "That is all there is left in life for me, now that my friend has been ruthlessly torn from me. In school I can look at her and muse over days departed."

"You'd better muse over your lessons and sums," said Marilla, concealing her delight at this development of the situation. "If you're going back to school I hope we'll hear no more of breaking slates over people's heads and such carryings on. Behave yourself and do just what your teacher tells you."

"I'll try to be a model pupil," agreed Anne dolefully. "There won't be much fun in it, I expect. Mr. Phillips said Minnie Andrews was a model pupil and there isn't a spark of imagination or life in her. She is just dull and poky and never seems to have a good time. But I feel so depressed that perhaps it will come easy to me now. I'm going round by the road. I couldn't bear to go by the Birch Path all alone. I should weep bitter tears if I did."

Anne was welcomed back to school with open arms. Her imagination had been sorely missed in games, her voice in the singing and her dramatic ability in the perusal aloud of books at dinner hour. Ruby Gillis smuggled three blue plums over to her during testament reading; Ella May MacPherson gave her an enormous yellow pansy cut from the covers of a floral catalogue—a species of desk decoration much prized in Avonlea school. Sophia Sloane offered to teach her a perfectly elegant new pattern of knit lace, so nice for trimming aprons. Katie Boulter gave her a perfume bottle to keep slate water in, and Julia Bell copied carefully on a piece of pale pink paper scalloped on the edges the following effusion:

To Anne

When twilight drops her curtain down
And pins it with a star
Remember that you have a friend
Though she may wander far.

"It's so nice to be appreciated," sighed Anne rapturously to Marilla that night.

The girls were not the only scholars who "appreciated" her. When Anne went to her seat after dinner hour—she had been told by Mr. Phillips to sit with the model Minnie Andrews—she found on her desk a big luscious "strawberry apple." Anne caught it up all ready to take a bite when she remembered that the only place in Avonlea where strawberry apples grew was in the old Blythe orchard on the other side of the Lake of Shining Waters. Anne dropped the apple as if it were a red-hot coal and ostentatiously wiped her fingers on her handkerchief. The apple lay untouched on her desk until the next morning, when little Timothy Andrews, who swept the school and kindled the fire, annexed it as one of his perquisites. Charlie Sloane's slate pencil, gorgeously bedizened with striped red and yellow paper, costing two cents where ordinary pencils cost only one, which he sent up to her after dinner hour, met with a more favorable reception. Anne was graciously pleased to accept it and rewarded the donor with a smile which exalted that infatuated youth straightway into the seventh heaven of delight and caused him to make such fearful errors in his dictation that Mr. Phillips kept him in after school to rewrite it.

But as,

> *"The Caesar's pageant shorn of Brutus' bust*
> *Did but of Rome's best son remind her more,"*

so the marked absence of any tribute or recognition from Diana Barry who was sitting with Gertie Pye embittered Anne's little triumph.

"Diana might just have smiled at me once, I think," she mourned to Marilla that night. But the next morning a note, most fearfully and wonderfully twisted and folded, and a small parcel were passed across to Anne.

> "Dear Anne," ran the former, "Mother says I'm not to play with you or talk to you even in school. It isn't my fault and don't be cross at me, because I love you as much as ever. I miss you awfully to tell all my secrets to and I don't like Gertie Pye one bit. I made you one of the new bookmarkers out of red tissue paper. They are awfully fashionable now and only three girls in school know how to make them. When you look at it remember
>
> Your true friend ,
> Diana Barry."

Anne read the note, kissed the bookmark, and dispatched a prompt reply back to the other side of the school.

> My own darling Diana:—
>
> Of course I am not cross at you because you have to obey your mother. Our spirits can commune. I shall keep your lovely present forever. Minnie Andrews is a very nice little girl—although she has no imagination—but after having been Diana's busum friend I cannot be Minnie's. Please excuse mistakes because my spelling isn't very good yet, although much improoved.
>
> Yours until death us do part
> Anne or Cordelia Shirley.

P.S. I shall sleep with your letter under my pillow tonight.
A. or C.S.

Marilla pessimistically expected more trouble since Anne had again begun to go to school. But none developed. Perhaps Anne caught something of the "model" spirit from Minnie Andrews; at least she got on very well with Mr. Phillips thenceforth. She flung herself into her studies heart and soul, determined not to be outdone in any class by Gilbert Blythe. The rivalry between them was soon apparent; it was entirely good-natured on Gilbert's side; but it is much to be feared that the same thing cannot be said of Anne, who had certainly an unpraiseworthy tenacity for holding grudges. She was as intense in her hatreds as in her loves. She would not stoop to admit that she meant to rival Gilbert in schoolwork, because that would have been to acknowledge his existence which Anne persistently ignored; but the rivalry was there and honors fluctuated between them. Now Gilbert was head of the spelling class; now Anne, with a toss of her long red braids, spelled him down. One morning Gilbert had all his sums done correctly and had his name written on the blackboard on the roll of honor; the next morning Anne, having wrestled wildly with decimals the entire evening before, would be first. One awful day they were ties and their names were written up together. It was almost as bad as a take-notice and Anne's mortification was as evident as Gilbert's satisfaction. When the written examinations at the end of each month were held the suspense was terrible. The first month Gilbert came out three marks ahead. The second Anne beat him by five. But her triumph was marred by the fact that Gilbert congratulated her heartily before the whole school. It would have been ever so much sweeter to her if he had felt the sting of his defeat.

Mr. Phillips might not be a very good teacher; but a pupil so inflexibly determined on learning as Anne was could hardly escape making progress under any kind of teacher. By the end of the term Anne and Gilbert were both promoted into the fifth class and allowed to begin studying the elements of "the branches"—by which Latin, geometry, French, and algebra were meant. In geometry Anne met her Waterloo.

"It's perfectly awful stuff, Marilla," she groaned. "I'm sure I'll never be able to make head or tail of it. There is no scope for imagination in it at all. Mr. Phillips says I'm the worst dunce he ever saw at it. And Gil—I mean some of the others are so smart at it. It is extremely mortifying, Marilla. Even Diana gets along better than I do. But I don't mind being beaten by Diana. Even although we meet as strangers now I still love her with an *inextinguishable* love. It makes me very sad at times to think about her. But really, Marilla, one can't stay sad very long in such an interesting world, can one?"

CHAPTER XVIII

ANNE TO THE RESCUE

All things great are wound up with all things little. At first glance it might not seem that the decision of a certain Canadian Premier to include Prince Edward Island in a political tour could have much or anything to do with the fortunes of little Anne Shirley at Green Gables. But it had.

It was in January the Premier came, to address his loyal supporters and such of his nonsupporters as chose to be present at the monster mass meeting held in Charlottetown. Most of the Avonlea people were on Premier's side of politics; hence on the night of the meeting nearly all the men and a goodly proportion of the women had gone to town thirty miles away. Mrs. Rachel Lynde had gone too. Mrs. Rachel Lynde was a red-hot politician and couldn't have believed that the political rally could be carried through without her, although she was on the opposite side of politics. So she went to town and took her husband—Thomas would be useful in looking after the horse—and Marilla Cuthbert with her. Marilla had a sneaking interest in politics herself, and as she thought it might be her only chance to see a real live Premier, she promptly took it, leaving Anne and Matthew to keep house until her return the following day.

Hence, while Marilla and Mrs. Rachel were enjoying themselves hugely at the mass meeting, Anne and Matthew had the cheerful kitchen at Green Gables all to themselves. A bright fire was glowing in the old-fashioned Waterloo stove and blue-white frost crystals were shining on the windowpanes. Matthew nodded over a *Farmer's Advocate* on the sofa and Anne at the table studied her lessons with grim determination, despite sundry wistful glances at the clock shelf, where lay a new book that Jane Andrews had lent her that day. Jane had assured her that it was warranted to produce any number of thrills, or words to that effect, and Anne's fingers tingled to reach out for it. But that would mean Gilbert Blythe's triumph on the morrow. Anne turned her back on the clock shelf and tried to imagine it wasn't there.

"Matthew, did you ever study geometry when you went to school?"

"Well now, no, I didn't," said Matthew, coming out of his doze with a start.

"I wish you had," sighed Anne, "because then you'd be able to sympathize with me. You can't sympathize properly if you've never studied it. It is casting a cloud over my whole life. I'm such a dunce at it, Matthew."

"Well now, I dunno," said Matthew soothingly. "I guess you're all right at anything. Mr. Phillips told me last week in Blair's store at Carmody that you was the smartest scholar in school and was making rapid progress. 'Rapid progress' was his very words. There's them as runs down Teddy Phillips and says he ain't much of a teacher, but I guess he's all right."

Matthew would have thought anyone who praised Anne was "all right."

"I'm sure I'd get on better with geometry if only he wouldn't change the letters," complained Anne. "I learn the proposition off by heart and then he draws it on the blackboard and puts different letters from what are in the book and I get all mixed up. I don't think a teacher should take such a mean advantage, do you? We're studying agriculture now and I've found out at last what makes the roads red. It's a great comfort. I wonder how Marilla and Mrs. Lynde are enjoying themselves. Mrs. Lynde says Canada is going to the dogs the way things are being run at Ottawa and that it's an awful warning to the electors. She says if women were allowed to vote we would soon see a blessed change. What way do you vote, Matthew?"

"Conservative," said Matthew promptly. To vote Conservative was part of Matthew's religion.

"Then I'm Conservative too," said Anne decidedly. "I'm glad because Gil—because some of the boys in school are Grits. I guess Mr. Phillips is a Grit too because Prissy Andrews's father is one, and Ruby Gillis says that when a man is courting he always has to agree with the girl's mother in religion and her father in politics. Is that true, Matthew?"

"Well now, I dunno," said Matthew.

"Did you ever go courting, Matthew?"

"Well now, no, I dunno's I ever did," said Matthew, who had certainly never thought of such a thing in his whole existence.

Anne reflected with her chin in her hands.

"It must be rather interesting, don't you think, Matthew? Ruby Gillis says when she grows up she's going to have ever so many beaus on the string and have them all crazy about her; but I think that would be too exciting. I'd rather have just one in his right mind. But Ruby Gillis knows a great deal about such matters because she has so many big sisters, and Mrs. Lynde says the Gillis girls have gone off like hot cakes. Mr. Phillips goes up to see Prissy Andrews nearly every evening. He says it is to help her with her lessons but Miranda Sloane is studying for Queen's too, and I should think she needed help a lot more than Prissy because she's ever so much stupider, but he never goes to help her in the evenings at all. There are a great many things in this world that I can't understand very well, Matthew."

"Well now, I dunno as I comprehend them all myself," acknowledged Matthew.

"Well, I suppose I must finish up my lessons. I won't allow myself to open that new book Jane lent me until I'm through. But it's a terrible temptation, Matthew. Even when I turn my back on it I can see it there just as plain. Jane said she cried herself sick over it. I love a book that makes me cry. But I think I'll carry that book into the sitting room and lock it in the jam closet and give you the key. And you must *not* give it to me, Matthew, until my lessons are done, not even if I implore you on my bended knees. It's all very well to say resist temptation, but it's ever so much easier to resist it if you can't get the key. And then shall I run down the cellar and get some russets, Matthew? Wouldn't you like some russets?"

"Well now, I dunno but what I would," said Matthew, who never ate russets but knew Anne's weakness for them.

Just as Anne emerged triumphantly from the cellar with her plateful of russets came the sound of flying footsteps on the icy board walk outside and the next moment the kitchen door was flung open and in rushed Diana Barry, white faced and breathless, with a shawl wrapped hastily around her head. Anne promptly let go of her candle and plate in her surprise, and plate, candle, and apples crashed together down the cellar ladder and were found at the bottom embedded in melted grease, the next day, by Marilla, who gathered them up and thanked mercy the house hadn't been set on fire.

"Whatever is the matter, Diana?" cried Anne. "Has your mother relented at last?"

"Oh, Anne, do come quick," implored Diana nervously. "Minnie May is awful sick—she's got croup, Young Mary Joe says—and Father and Mother are away to town and there's nobody to go for the doctor. Minnie May is awful bad and Young Mary Joe doesn't know what to do—and oh, Anne, I'm so scared!"

Matthew, without a word, reached out for cap and coat, slipped past Diana and away into the darkness of the yard.

"He's gone to harness the sorrel mare to go to Carmody for the doctor," said Anne, who was hurrying on hood and jacket. "I know it as well as if he'd said so. Matthew and I are such kindred spirits I can read his thoughts without words at all."

"I don't believe he'll find the doctor at Carmody," sobbed Diana. "I know that Dr. Blair went to town and I guess Dr. Spencer would go too. Young Mary Joe never saw anybody with croup and Mrs. Lynde is away. Oh, Anne!"

"Don't cry, Di," said Anne cheerily. "I know exactly what to do for croup. You forget that Mrs. Hammond had twins three times. When you look after three pairs of twins you naturally get a lot of experience. They all had croup regularly. Just wait till I get the ipecac bottle—you mayn't have any at your house. Come on now."

The two little girls hastened out hand in hand and hurried through Lover's Lane and across the crusted field beyond, for the snow was too deep to go by the shorter wood way. Anne, although sincerely sorry for Minnie May, was far from being insensible to the romance of the situation and to the sweetness of once more sharing that romance with a kindred spirit.

The night was clear and frosty, all ebony of shadow and silver of snowy slope; big stars were shining over the silent fields; here and there the dark pointed firs stood up with snow powdering their branches and the wind whistling through them. Anne thought it was truly delightful to go skimming through all this mystery and loveliness with your bosom friend who had been so long estranged.

Minnie May, aged three, was really very sick. She lay on the kitchen sofa feverish and restless, while her hoarse breathing could be heard all over the house. Young Mary Joe, a buxom, broad-faced French girl from the creek, whom Mrs. Barry had engaged to stay with the children during her absence, was helpless and bewildered, quite incapable of thinking what to do, or doing it if she thought of it.

Anne went to work with skill and promptness.

"Minnie May has croup all right; she's pretty bad, but I've seen them worse. First we must have lots of hot water. I declare, Diana, there isn't more than a cupful in the kettle! There, I've filled it up, and, Mary Joe, you may put some wood in the stove. I don't want to hurt your feelings but it seems to me you might have thought of this before if you'd any imagination. Now, I'll undress Minnie May and put her to bed and you try to find some soft flannel cloths, Diana. I'm going to give her a dose of ipecac first of all."

Minnie May did not take kindly to the ipecac but Anne had not brought up three pairs of twins for nothing. Down that ipecac went, not only once, but many times during the long, anxious night when the two little girls worked patiently over the suffering Minnie May, and Young Mary Joe, honestly anxious to do all she could, kept up a roaring fire and heated more water than would have been needed for a hospital of croupy babies.

It was three o'clock when Matthew came with a doctor, for he had been obliged to go all the way to Spencervale for one. But the pressing need for assistance was past. Minnie May was much better and was sleeping soundly.

"I was awfully near giving up in despair," explained Anne. "She got worse and worse until she was sicker than ever the Hammond twins were, even the last pair. I actually thought she was going to choke to death. I gave her every drop of ipecac in that bottle and when the last dose went down I said to myself—not to Diana or Young Mary Joe, because I didn't want to worry them any more than they were worried, but I had to say it to myself just to relieve my feelings—'This is the last lingering hope and I fear 'tis a vain one.' But in about three minutes she coughed up the phlegm and began to get better right away. You must just imagine my relief, doctor, because I can't express it in words. You know there are some things that cannot be expressed in words."

"Yes, I know," nodded the doctor. He looked at Anne as if he were thinking some things about her that couldn't be expressed in words. Later on, however, he expressed them to Mr. and Mrs. Barry.

"That little redheaded girl they have over at Cuthbert's is as smart as they make 'em. I tell you she saved that baby's life, for it would have been too late by the time I got there. She seems to have a skill and presence of mind perfectly wonderful in a child of her age. I never saw anything like the eyes of her when she was explaining the case to me."

Anne had gone home in the wonderful, white-frosted winter morning, heavy-eyed from loss of sleep, but still talking unweariedly to Matthew as they crossed the long white field and walked under the glittering fairy arch of the Lover's Lane maples.

"Oh, Matthew, isn't it a wonderful morning? The world looks like something God had just imagined for His own pleasure, doesn't it? Those trees look as if I could blow them away with a breath—pouf! I'm so glad I live in a world where there are white frosts, aren't you? And I'm so glad Mrs. Hammond had three pairs of twins after all. If she hadn't I mightn't have known what to do for Minnie May. I'm real sorry I was ever cross with Mrs. Hammond for having twins. But, oh, Matthew, I'm so sleepy. I can't go to school. I just know I couldn't keep my eyes open and I'd be so stupid. But I hate to stay home, for Gil—some of the others will get head of the class, and it's so hard to get up again—although of course the harder it is the more satisfaction you have when you do get up, haven't you?"

"Well now, I guess you'll manage all right," said Matthew, looking at Anne's white little face and the dark shadows under her eyes. "You just go right to bed and have a good sleep. I'll do all the chores."

Anne accordingly went to bed and slept so long and soundly that it was well on in the white and rosy winter afternoon when she awoke and descended to the kitchen where Marilla, who had arrived home in the meantime, was sitting knitting.

"Oh, did you see the Premier?" exclaimed Anne at once. "What did he look like Marilla?"

"Well, he never got to be Premier on account of his looks," said Marilla. "Such a nose as that man had! But he can speak. I was proud of being a Conservative. Rachel Lynde, of course, being a Liberal, had no use for him. Your dinner is in the oven, Anne, and you can get yourself some blue plum preserve out of the pantry. I guess you're hungry. Matthew has been telling me about last night. I must say it was fortunate you knew what to do. I wouldn't have had any idea myself, for I never saw a case of croup. There now, never mind talking till you've had your dinner. I can tell by the look of you that you're just full up with speeches, but they'll keep."

Marilla had something to tell Anne, but she did not tell it just then for she knew if she did Anne's consequent excitement would lift her clear out of the region of such material matters as appetite or dinner. Not until Anne had finished her saucer of blue plums did Marilla say:

"Mrs. Barry was here this afternoon, Anne. She wanted to see you, but I wouldn't wake you up. She says you saved Minnie May's life, and she is very sorry she acted as she did in that affair of the currant wine. She says she knows now you didn't mean to set Diana drunk, and she hopes you'll forgive her and be good friends with Diana again. You're to go over this evening if you like for Diana can't stir outside the door on account of a bad cold she caught last night. Now, Anne Shirley, for pity's sake don't fly up into the air."

The warning seemed not unnecessary, so uplifted and aerial was Anne's expression and attitude as she sprang to her feet, her face irradiated with the flame of her spirit.

"Oh, Marilla, can I go right now—without washing my dishes? I'll wash them when I come back, but I cannot tie myself down to anything so unromantic as dishwashing at this thrilling moment."

"Yes, yes, run along," said Marilla indulgently. "Anne Shirley—are you crazy? Come back this instant and put something on you. I might as well call to the wind. She's gone without a cap or wrap. Look at her tearing through the orchard with her hair streaming. It'll be a mercy if she doesn't catch her death of cold."

Anne came dancing home in the purple winter twilight across the snowy places. Afar in the southwest was the great shimmering, pearl-like sparkle of an evening star in a sky that was pale golden and ethereal rose over gleaming white spaces and dark glens of spruce. The tinkles of sleigh bells among the snowy hills came like elfin chimes through the frosty air, but their music was not sweeter than the song in Anne's heart and on her lips.

"You see before you a perfectly happy person, Marilla," she announced. "I'm perfectly happy—yes, in spite of my red hair. Just at present I have a soul above red hair. Mrs. Barry kissed me and cried and said she was so sorry and she could never repay me. I felt fearfully embarrassed, Marilla, but I just said as politely as I could, 'I have no hard feelings for you, Mrs. Barry. I assure you once for all that I did not mean to intoxicate Diana and henceforth I shall cover the past with the mantle of oblivion.' That was a pretty dignified way of speaking wasn't it, Marilla? I felt that I was heaping coals of fire on Mrs. Barry's head. And Diana and I had a lovely afternoon. Diana showed me a new fancy crochet stitch her aunt over at Carmody taught her. Not a soul in Avonlea knows it but us, and we pledged a solemn vow never to reveal it to anyone else. Diana gave me a beautiful card with a wreath of roses on it and a verse of poetry:

"If you love me as I love you
Nothing but death can part us two.

"And that is true, Marilla. We're going to ask Mr. Phillips to let us sit together in school again, and Gertie Pye can go with Minnie Andrews. We had an elegant tea. Mrs. Barry had the very best china set out, Marilla, just as if I was real company. I can't tell you what a thrill it gave me. Nobody ever used their very best china on my account before. And we had fruit cake and pound cake and doughnuts and two kinds of preserves, Marilla. And Mrs. Barry asked me if I took tea and said 'Pa, why don't you pass the biscuits to Anne?' It must be lovely to be grown up, Marilla, when just being treated as if you were is so nice."

"I don't know about that," said Marilla, with a brief sigh.

"Well, anyway, when I am grown up," said Anne decidedly, "I'm always going to talk to little girls as if they were too, and I'll never laugh when they use big words. I know from sorrowful experience how that hurts one's feelings. After tea Diana and I made taffy. The taffy wasn't very good, I suppose because neither Diana nor I had ever made any before. Diana left me to stir it while she buttered the plates and I forgot and let it burn; and then when we set it out on the platform to cool the cat walked over one plate and that had to be thrown away. But the making of it was splendid fun. Then when I came home Mrs. Barry asked me to come over as often as I could and Diana stood at the window and threw kisses to me all the way down to Lover's Lane. I assure you, Marilla, that I feel like praying tonight and I'm going to think out a special brand-new prayer in honor of the occasion."

CHAPTER XIX

A CONCERT, A CATASTROPHE, AND A CONFESSION

Marilla, can I go over to see Diana just for a minute?" asked Anne, running breathlessly down from the east gable one February evening.

"I don't see what you want to be traipsing about after dark for," said Marilla shortly. "You and Diana walked home from school together and then stood down there in the snow for half an hour more, your tongues going the whole blessed time, clickety-clack. So I don't think you're very badly off to see her again."

"But she wants to see me," pleaded Anne. "She has something very important to tell me."

"How do you know she has?"

"Because she just signaled to me from her window. We have arranged a way to signal with our candles and cardboard. We set the candle on the window sill and make flashes by passing the cardboard back and forth. So many flashes mean a certain thing. It was my idea, Marilla."

"I'll warrant you it was," said Marilla emphatically. "And the next thing you'll be setting fire to the curtains with your signaling nonsense."

"Oh, we're very careful, Marilla. And it's so interesting. Two flashes mean, 'Are you there?' Three mean 'yes' and four 'no.' Five mean, 'Come over as soon as possible, because I have something important to reveal.' Diana has just signaled five flashes, and I'm really suffering to know what it is."

"Well, you needn't suffer any longer," said Marilla sarcastically. "You can go, but you're to be back here in just ten minutes, remember that."

Anne did remember it and was back in the stipulated time, although probably no mortal will ever know just what it cost her to confine the discussion of Diana's important communication within the limits of ten minutes. But at least she had made good use of them.

"Oh, Marilla, what do you think? You know tomorrow is Diana's birthday. Well, her mother told her she could ask me to go home with her from school and stay all night with her. And her cousins are coming over from Newbridge in a big pung sleigh to go to the Debating Club concert at the hall tomorrow night. And they are going to take Diana and me to the concert—if you'll let me go, that is. You will, won't you, Marilla? Oh, I feel so excited."

"You can calm down then, because you're not going. You're better at home in your own bed, and as for that club concert, it's all nonsense, and little girls should not be allowed to go out to such places at all."

"I'm sure the Debating Club is a most respectable affair," pleaded Anne.

"I'm not saying it isn't. But you're not going to begin gadding about to concerts and staying out all hours of the night. Pretty doings for children. I'm surprised at Mrs. Barry's letting Diana go."

"But it's such a very special occasion," mourned Anne, on the verge of tears. "Diana has only one birthday in a year. It isn't as if birthdays were common things, Marilla. Prissy Andrews is going to recite 'Curfew Must Not Ring Tonight.' That is such a good moral piece, Marilla, I'm sure it would do me lots of good to hear it. And the choir are going to sing four lovely pathetic songs that are pretty near as good as hymns. And oh, Marilla, the minister is going to take part; yes, indeed, he is; he's going to give an address. That will be just about the same thing as a sermon. Please, mayn't I go, Marilla?"

"You heard what I said, Anne, didn't you? Take off your boots now and go to bed. It's past eight."

"There's just one more thing, Marilla," said Anne, with the air of producing the last shot in her locker. "Mrs. Barry told Diana that we might sleep in the spare room bed. Think of the honor of your little Anne being put in the spare room bed."

"It's an honor you'll have to get along without. Go to bed, Anne, and don't let me hear another word out of you."

When Anne, with tears rolling over her cheeks, had gone sorrowfully upstairs, Matthew, who had been apparently sound asleep on the lounge during the whole dialogue, opened his eyes and said decidedly:

"Well now, Marilla, I think you ought to let Anne go."

"I don't then," retorted Marilla. "Who's bringing this child up, Matthew, you or me?"

"Well now, you," admitted Matthew.

"Don't interfere then."

"Well now, I ain't interfering. It ain't interfering to have your own opinion. And my opinion is that you ought to let Anne go."

"You'd think I ought to let Anne go to the moon if she took the notion, I've no doubt," was Marilla's amiable rejoinder. "I might have let her spend the night with Diana, if that was all. But I don't approve of this concert plan. She'd go there and catch cold like as not, and have her head filled up with nonsense and excitement. It would unsettle her for a week. I understand that child's disposition and what's good for it better than you, Matthew."

"I think you ought to let Anne go," repeated Matthew firmly. Argument was not his strong point, but holding fast to his opinion certainly was. Marilla gave a gasp of helplessness and took refuge in silence. The next morning, when Anne was washing the breakfast dishes in the pantry, Matthew paused on his way out to the barn to say to Marilla again:

"I think you ought to let Anne go, Marilla."

For a moment Marilla looked things not lawful to be uttered. Then she yielded to the inevitable and said tartly:

"Very well, she can go, since nothing else'll please you."

Anne flew out of the pantry, dripping dishcloth in hand.

"Oh, Marilla, Marilla, say those blessed words again."

"I guess once is enough to say them. This is Matthew's doings and I wash my hands of it. If you catch pneumonia sleeping in a strange bed or coming out of that hot hall in the middle of the night, don't blame me, blame Matthew. Anne Shirley, you're dripping greasy water all over the floor. I never saw such a careless child."

"Oh, I know I'm a great trial to you, Marilla," said Anne repentantly. "I make so many mistakes. But then just think of all the mistakes I don't make, although I might. I'll get some sand and scrub up the spots before I go to school. Oh, Marilla, my heart was just set on going to that concert. I never was to a concert in my life, and when the other girls talk about them in school I feel so out of it. You didn't know just how I felt about it, but you see Matthew did. Matthew understands me, and it's so nice to be understood, Marilla."

Anne was too excited to do herself justice as to lessons that morning in school. Gilbert Blythe spelled her down in class and left her clear out of sight in mental arithmetic. Anne's consequent humiliation was less than it might have been, however, in view of the concert and the spare room bed. She and Diana talked so constantly about it all day that with a stricter teacher than Mr. Phillips dire disgrace must inevitably have been their portion.

Anne felt that she could not have borne it if she had not been going to the concert, for nothing else was discussed that day in school. The Avonlea Debating Club, which met fortnightly all winter, had had several smaller free entertainments; but this was to be a big affair, admission ten cents, in aid of the library. The Avonlea young people had been practicing for weeks, and all the scholars were especially interested in it by reason of older brothers and sisters who were going to take part. Everybody in school over nine years of age expected to go, except Carrie Sloane, whose father shared Marilla's opinions about small girls going out to night concerts. Carrie Sloane cried into her grammar all the afternoon and felt that life was not worth living.

For Anne the real excitement began with the dismissal of school and increased therefrom in crescendo until it reached to a crash of positive ecstasy in the concert itself. They had a "perfectly elegant tea;" and then came the delicious occupation of dressing in Diana's little room upstairs. Diana did Anne's front hair in the new pompadour style and Anne tied Diana's bows with the especial knack she possessed; and they experimented with at least half a dozen different ways of arranging their back hair. At last they were ready, cheeks scarlet and eyes glowing with excitement.

True, Anne could not help a little pang when she contrasted her plain black tam and shapeless, tight-sleeved, homemade gray-cloth coat with Diana's jaunty fur cap and smart little jacket. But she remembered in time that she had an imagination and could use it.

Then Diana's cousins, the Murrays from Newbridge, came; they all crowded into the big pung sleigh, among straw and furry robes. Anne reveled in the drive to the hall, slipping along over the satin-smooth roads with the snow crisping under the runners. There was a magnificent sunset, and the snowy hills and deep-blue water of the St. Lawrence Gulf seemed to rim in the splendor like a huge bowl of pearl and sapphire brimmed with wine and fire. Tinkles of sleigh bells and distant laughter, that seemed like the mirth of wood elves, came from every quarter.

"Oh, Diana," breathed Anne, squeezing Diana's mittened hand

under the fur robe, "isn't it all like a beautiful dream? Do I really look the same as usual? I feel so different that it seems to me it must show in my looks."

"You look awfully nice," said Diana, who having just received a compliment from one of her cousins, felt that she ought to pass it on. "You've got the loveliest color."

The program that night was a series of "thrills" for at least one listener in the audience, and, as Anne assured Diana, every succeeding thrill was thrillier than the last. When Prissy Andrews, attired in a new pink-silk waist with a string of pearls about her smooth white throat and real carnations in her hair—rumor whispered that the master had sent all the way to town for them for her—"climbed the slimy ladder, dark without one ray of light," Anne shivered in luxurious sympathy; when the choir sang "Far Above the Gentle Daisies" Anne gazed at the ceiling as if it were frescoed with angels; when Sam Sloane proceeded to explain and illustrate "How Sockery Set a Hen" Anne laughed until people sitting near her laughed too, more out of sympathy with her than with amusement at a selection that was rather threadbare even in Avonlea; and when Mr. Phillips gave Mark Antony's oration over the dead body of Caesar in the most heart-stirring tones—looking at Prissy Andrews at the end of every sentence—Anne felt that she could rise and mutiny on the spot if but one Roman citizen led the way.

Only one number on the program failed to interest her. When Gilbert Blythe recited "Bingen on the Rhine" Anne picked up Rhoda Murray's library book and read it until he had finished, when she sat rigidly stiff and motionless while Diana clapped her hands until they tingled.

It was eleven when they got home, sated with dissipation, but with the exceeding sweet pleasure of talking it all over still to come. Everybody seemed asleep and the house was dark and silent. Anne and Diana tiptoed into the parlor, a long narrow room out of which the spare room opened. It was pleasantly warm and dimly lighted by the embers of a fire in the grate.

"Let's undress here," said Diana. "It's so nice and warm."

"Hasn't it been a delightful time?" sighed Anne rapturously. "It must be splendid to get up and recite there. Do you suppose we will ever be asked to do it, Diana?"

"Yes, of course, someday. They're always wanting the big scholars to recite. Gilbert Blythe does often and he's only two years older than us. Oh, Anne, how could you pretend not to listen to him? When he came to the line,

> *'There's another,* not *a sister,'*

he looked right down at you."

"Diana," said Anne with dignity, "you are my bosom friend, but I cannot allow even you to speak to me of that person. Are you ready for bed? Let's run a race and see who'll get to the bed first."

The suggestion appealed to Diana. The two little white-clad figures flew down the long room, through the spare-room door, and bounded on the bed at the same moment. And then—something—moved beneath them, there was a gasp and a cry—and somebody said in muffled accents:

"Merciful goodness!"

Anne and Diana were never able to tell just how they got off that bed and out of the room. They only knew that after one frantic rush they found themselves tiptoeing shiveringly upstairs.

"Oh, who was it—*what* was it?" whispered Anne, her teeth chattering with cold and fright.

"It was Aunt Josephine," said Diana, gasping with laughter. "Oh, Anne, it was Aunt Josephine, however she came to be there. Oh, and I know she will be furious. It's dreadful—it's really dreadful—but did you ever know anything so funny, Anne?"

"Who is your Aunt Josephine?"

"She's father's aunt and she lives in Charlottetown. She's awfully old—seventy anyhow—and I don't believe she was *ever* a little girl. We were expecting her out for a visit, but not so soon. She's awfully prim and proper and she'll scold dreadfully about this, I know. Well, we'll have to sleep with Minnie May—and you can't think how she kicks."

Miss Josephine Barry did not appear at the early breakfast the next morning. Mrs. Barry smiled kindly at the two little girls.

"Did you have a good time last night? I tried to stay awake until you came home, for I wanted to tell you Aunt Josephine had come and that you would have to go upstairs after all, but I was so tired I fell asleep. I hope you didn't disturb your aunt, Diana."

Diana preserved a discreet silence, but she and Anne exchanged furtive smiles of guilty amusement across the table. Anne hurried home after breakfast and so remained in blissful ignorance of the disturbance which presently resulted in the Barry household until the late afternoon, when she went down to Mrs. Lynde's on an errand for Marilla.

"So you and Diana nearly frightened poor old Miss Barry to death last night?" said Mrs. Lynde severely, but with a twinkle in her eye. "Mrs. Barry was here a few minutes ago on her way to Carmody. She's feeling real worried over it. Old Miss Barry was in a terrible temper when she got up this morning—and Josephine Barry's temper is no joke, I can tell you that. She wouldn't speak to Diana at all."

"It wasn't Diana's fault," said Anne contritely. "It was mine. I suggested racing to see who would get into bed first."

"I knew it!" said Mrs. Lynde, with the exultation of a correct guesser. "I knew that idea came out of your head. Well, it's made a nice lot of trouble, that's what. Old Miss Barry came out to stay for a month, but she declares she won't stay another day and is going right back to town tomorrow, Sunday and all as it is. She'd have gone today if they could have taken her. She had promised to pay for a quarter's music lessons for Diana, but now she is determined to do nothing at all for such a tomboy. Oh, I guess they had a lively time of it there this morning. The Barrys must feel cut up. Old Miss Barry is rich and they'd like to keep on the good side of her. Of course, Mrs. Barry didn't say just that to me, but I'm a pretty good judge of human nature, that's what."

"I'm such an unlucky girl," mourned Anne. "I'm always getting into scrapes myself and getting my best friends—people I'd shed my heart's blood for—into them too. Can you tell me why it is so, Mrs. Lynde?"

"It's because you're too heedless and impulsive, child, that's what. You never stop to think—whatever comes into your head to say or do you say or do it without a moment's reflection."

"Oh, but that's the best of it," protested Anne. "Something just flashes into your mind, so exciting, and you must out with it. If you stop to think it over you spoil it all. Haven't you never felt that yourself, Mrs. Lynde?"

No, Mrs. Lynde had not. She shook her head sagely.

"You must learn to think a little, Anne, that's what. The proverb you need to go by is 'Look before you leap'—especially into spare room beds."

Mrs. Lynde laughed comfortably over her mild joke, but Anne

remained pensive. She saw nothing to laugh at in the situation, which to her eyes appeared very serious. When she left Mrs. Lynde's she took her way across the crusted fields to Orchard Slope. Diana met her at the kitchen door.

"Your Aunt Josephine was very cross about it, wasn't she?" whispered Anne.

"Yes," answered Diana, stifling a giggle with an apprehensive glance over her shoulder at the closed sitting-room door. "She was fairly dancing with rage, Anne. Oh, how she scolded. She said I was the worst-behaved girl she ever saw and that my parents ought to be ashamed of the way they had brought me up. She says she won't stay and I'm sure I don't care. But Father and Mother do."

"Why didn't you tell them it was my fault?" demanded Anne.

"It's likely I'd do such a thing, isn't it?" said Diana with just scorn. "I'm no telltale, Anne Shirley, and anyhow I was just as much to blame as you."

"Well, I'm going in to tell her myself," said Anne resolutely.

Diana stared.

"Anne Shirley, you'd never! Why—she'll eat you alive!"

"Don't frighten me any more than I am frightened," implored Anne. "I'd rather walk up to a cannon's mouth. But I've got to do it, Diana. It was my fault and I've got to confess. I've had practice in confessing, fortunately."

"Well, she's in the room," said Diana. "You can go in if you want to. I wouldn't dare. And I don't believe you'll do a bit of good."

With this encouragement Anne bearded the lion in its den—that is to say, walked resolutely up to the sitting-room door and knocked faintly. A sharp "Come in" followed.

Miss Josephine Barry, thin, prim, and rigid, was knitting fiercely by the fire, her wrath quite unappeased and her eyes snapping through her gold-rimmed glasses. She wheeled around in her chair, expecting to see Diana, and beheld a white-faced girl whose great eyes were brimmed up with a mixture of desperate courage and shrinking terror.

"Who are you?" demanded Miss Josephine Barry, without ceremony.

"I'm Anne of Green Gables," said the small visitor tremulously, clasping her hands with her characteristic gesture, "and I've come to confess, if you please."

"Confess what?"

"That it was all my fault about jumping into bed on you last night. I suggested it. Diana would never have thought of such a thing, I am sure. Diana is a very ladylike girl, Miss Barry. So you must see how unjust it is to blame her."

"Oh, I must, hey? I rather think Diana did her share of the jumping at least. Such carryings on in a respectable house!"

"But we were only in fun," persisted Anne. "I think you ought to forgive us, Miss Barry, now that we've apologized. And anyhow, please forgive Diana and let her have her music lessons. Diana's heart is set on her music lessons, Miss Barry, and I know too well what it is to set your heart on a thing and not get it. If you must be cross with anyone, be cross with me. I've been so used in my early days to having people cross at me that I can endure it much better than Diana can."

Much of the snap had gone out of the old lady's eyes by this time and was replaced by a twinkle of amused interest. But she still said severely:

"I don't think it is any excuse for you that you were only in fun. Little girls never indulged in that kind of fun when I was young. You don't know what it is to be awakened out of a sound sleep, after a long and arduous journey, by two great girls coming bounce down on you."

"I don't *know*, but I can *imagine*," said Anne eagerly. "I'm sure it must have been very disturbing. But then, there is our side of it too. Have you any imagination, Miss Barry? If you have, just put yourself in our place. We didn't know there was anybody in that bed and you nearly scared us to death. It was simply awful the way we felt. And then we couldn't sleep in the spare room after being promised. I suppose you are used to sleeping in spare rooms. But just imagine what you would feel like if you were a little orphan girl who had never had such an honor."

All the snap had gone by this time. Miss Barry actually laughed—a sound which caused Diana, waiting in speechless anxiety in the kitchen outside, to give a great gasp of relief.

"I'm afraid my imagination is a little rusty—it's so long since I used it," she said. "I dare say your claim to sympathy is just as strong as mine. It all depends on the way we look at it. Sit down here and tell me about yourself."

"I am very sorry I can't," said Anne firmly. "I would like to, because you seem like an interesting lady, and you might even be a kindred spirit although you don't look very much like it. But it is my duty to go home to Miss Marilla Cuthbert. Miss Marilla Cuthbert is a very kind lady who has taken me to bring up properly. She is doing her best, but it is very discouraging work. You must not blame her because I jumped on the bed. But before I go I do wish you would tell me if you will forgive Diana and stay just as long as you meant to in Avonlea."

"I think perhaps I will if you will come over and talk to me occasionally," said Miss Barry.

That evening Miss Barry gave Diana a silver bangle bracelet and told the senior members of the household that she had unpacked her valise.

"I've made up my mind to stay simply for the sake of getting better acquainted with that Anne-girl," she said frankly. "She amuses me, and at my time of life an amusing person is a rarity."

Marilla's only comment when she heard the story was, "I told you so." This was for Matthew's benefit.

Miss Barry stayed her month out and over. She was a more agreeable guest than usual, for Anne kept her in good humor. They became firm friends.

When Miss Barry went away she said:

"Remember, you Anne-girl, when you come to town you're to visit me and I'll put you in my very sparest spare-room bed to sleep."

"Miss Barry was a kindred spirit, after all," Anne confided to Marilla. "You wouldn't think so to look at her, but she is. You don't find it right out at first, as in Matthew's case, but after a while you come to see it. Kindred spirits are not so scarce as I used to think. It's splendid to find out there are so many of them in the world."

CHAPTER XX

A GOOD IMAGINATION GONE WRONG

Spring had come once more to Green Gables—the beautiful capricious, reluctant Canadian spring, lingering along through April and May in a succession of sweet, fresh, chilly days, with pink sunsets and miracles of resurrection and growth. The maples in Lover's Lane were red budded and little curly ferns pushed up around the Dryad's Bubble. Away up in the barrens, behind Mr. Silas Sloane's place, the Mayflowers blossomed out, pink and white stars of sweetness under their brown leaves. All the school girls and boys had one golden afternoon gathering them, coming home in the clear, echoing twilight with arms and baskets full of flowery spoil.

"I'm so sorry for people who live in lands where there are no Mayflowers," said Anne. "Diana says perhaps they have something better, but there couldn't be anything better than Mayflowers, could there, Marilla? And Diana says if they don't know what they are like they don't miss them. But I think that is the saddest thing of all. I think it would be *tragic*, Marilla, not to know what Mayflowers are like and *not* to miss them. Do you know what I think Mayflowers are, Marilla? I think they must be the souls of the flowers that died last summer and this is their heaven. But we had a splendid time today, Marilla. We had our lunch down in a big mossy hollow by an old well—such a *romantic* spot. Charlie Sloane dared Arty Gillis to jump over it, and Arty did because he wouldn't take a dare. Nobody would in school. It is very *fashionable* to dare. Mr. Phillips gave all the Mayflowers he found to Prissy Andrews and I heard him say 'sweets to the sweet.' He got that out of a book, I know; but it shows he has some imagination. I was offered some Mayflowers too, but I rejected them with scorn. I can't tell you the person's name because I have vowed never to let it cross my lips. We made wreaths of the Mayflowers and put them on our hats; and when the time came to go home we marched in procession down the road, two by two, with our bouquets and wreaths, singing 'My Home on the Hill.' Oh, it was so thrilling, Marilla. All Mr. Silas Sloane's folks rushed out to see us and everybody we met on the road stopped and stared after us. We made a real sensation."

"Not much wonder! Such silly doings!" was Marilla's response.

After the Mayflowers came the violets, and Violet Vale was empurpled with them. Anne walked through it on her way to school with reverent steps and worshipping eyes, as if she trod on holy ground.

"Somehow," she told Diana, "when I'm going through here I don't really care whether Gil—whether anybody gets ahead of me in class or not. But when I'm up in school it's all different and I care as much as ever. There's such a lot of different Annes in me. I sometimes think that is why I'm such a troublesome person. If I was just the one Anne it would be ever so much more comfortable, but then it wouldn't be half so interesting."

One June evening, when the orchards were pink blossomed again, when the frogs were singing silverly sweet in the marshes about the head of the Lake of Shining Waters, and the air was full of the savor of clover fields and balsamic fir woods, Anne was sitting by her gable window. She had been studying her lessons, but it had grown too dark to see the book, so she had fallen into wide-eyed reverie, looking out past the boughs of the Snow Queen, once more bestarred with its tufts of blossom.

In all essential respects the little gable chamber was unchanged. The walls were as white, the pincushion as hard, the chairs as stiffly and yellowly upright as ever. Yet the whole character of the room was altered. It was full of a new vital, pulsing personality that seemed to pervade it and to be quite independent of schoolgirl books and dresses and ribbons, and even of the cracked blue jug full of apple blossoms on the table. It was as if all the dreams, sleeping and waking, of its vivid occupant had taken a visible although unmaterial form and had tapestried the bare room with splendid filmy tissues of rainbow and moonshine. Presently Marilla came briskly in with some of Anne's freshly ironed school aprons. She hung them over a chair and sat down with a short sigh. She had had one of her headaches that afternoon, and although the pain had gone she felt weak and "tuckered out," as she expressed it. Anne looked at her with eyes limpid with sympathy.

"I do truly wish I could have had the headache in your place, Marilla. I would have endured it joyfully for your sake."

"I guess you did your part in attending to the work and letting me rest," said Marilla. "You seem to have got on fairly well and made fewer mistakes than usual. Of course it wasn't exactly necessary to starch Matthew's handkerchiefs! And most people when they put a pie in the oven to warm up for dinner take it out and eat it when it gets hot instead of leaving it to be burned to a crisp. But that doesn't seem to be your way evidently."

Headaches always left Marilla somewhat sarcastic.

"Oh, I'm so sorry," said Anne penitently. "I never thought about that pie from the moment I put it in the oven till now, although I felt instinctively that there was something missing on the dinner table. I was firmly resolved, when you left me in charge this morning, not to imagine anything, but keep my thoughts on facts. I did pretty well until I put the pie in, and then an irresistible temptation came to me to imagine I was an enchanted princess shut up in a lonely tower with a handsome knight riding to my rescue on a coal-black steed. So that is how I came to forget the pie. I didn't know I starched the handkerchiefs. All the time I was ironing I was trying to think of a name for a new island Diana and I have discovered up the brook. It's the most ravishing spot, Marilla. There are two maple trees on it and the brook flows right around it. At last it struck me that it would be splendid to call it Victoria Island because we found it on the Queen's birthday. Both Diana and I are very loyal. But I'm sorry about that pie and the handkerchiefs. I wanted to be extra good today because it's an anniversary. Do you remember what happened this day last year, Marilla?"

"No, I can't think of anything special."

"Oh, Marilla, it was the day I came to Green Gables. I shall never forget it. It was the turning point in my life. Of course it wouldn't seem so important to you. I've been here for a year and I've been so happy. Of course, I've had my troubles, but one can live down troubles. Are you sorry you kept me, Marilla?"

"No, I can't say I'm sorry," said Marilla, who sometimes wondered how she could have lived before Anne came to Green Gables, "no, not exactly sorry. If you've finished your lessons, Anne, I want you to run over and ask Mrs. Barry if she'll lend me Diana's apron pattern."

"Oh—it's—it's too dark," cried Anne.

"Too dark? Why, it's only twilight. And goodness knows you've gone over often enough after dark."

"I'll go over early in the morning," said Anne eagerly. "I'll get up at sunrise and go over, Marilla."

"What has got into your head now, Anne Shirley? I want that pattern to cut out your new apron this evening. Go at once and be smart too."

"I'll have to go around by the road, then," said Anne, taking up her hat reluctantly.

"Go by the road and waste half an hour! I'd like to catch you!"

"I can't go through the Haunted Wood, Marilla," cried Anne desperately.

Marilla stared.

"The Haunted Wood! Are you crazy? What under the canopy is the Haunted Wood?"

"The spruce wood over the brook," said Anne in a whisper.

"Fiddlesticks! There is no such thing as a haunted wood anywhere. Who has been telling you such stuff?"

"Nobody," confessed Anne. "Diana and I just imagined the wood was haunted. All the places around here are so—so—*commonplace*. We just got this up for our own amusement. We began it in April. A haunted wood is so very romantic, Marilla. We chose the spruce grove because it's so gloomy. Oh, we have imagined the most harrowing things. There's a white lady walks along the brook just about this time of the night and wrings her hands and utters wailing cries. She appears when there is to be a death in the family. And the ghost of a little murdered child haunts the corner up by Idlewild; it creeps up behind you and lays its cold fingers on your hand—so. Oh, Marilla, it gives me a shudder to think of it. And there's a headless man stalks up and down the path and skeletons glower at you between the boughs. Oh, Marilla, I wouldn't go through the Haunted Wood after dark now for anything. I'd be sure that white things would reach out from behind the trees and grab me."

"Did ever anyone hear the like!" ejaculated Marilla, who had listened in dumb amazement. "Anne Shirley, do you mean to tell me you believe all that wicked nonsense of your own imagination?"

"Not believe *exactly*," faltered Anne. "At least, I don't believe it in daylight. But after dark, Marilla, it's different. That is when ghosts walk."

"There are no such things as ghosts, Anne."

"Oh, but there are, Marilla," cried Anne eagerly. "I know people who have seen them. And they are respectable people. Charlie Sloane says that his grandmother saw his grandfather driving home the cows one night after he'd been buried for a year. You know Charlie Sloane's grandmother wouldn't tell a story for anything. She's a very religious woman. And Mrs. Thomas's father was pursued home one night by a lamb of fire with its head cut off hanging by a strip of skin. He said he knew it was the spirit of his brother and that it was a warning he would die within nine days. He didn't, but he died two years after, so you see it was really true. And Ruby Gillis says—"

"Anne Shirley," interrupted Marilla firmly, "I never want to hear you talking in this fashion again. I've had my doubts about that imagination of yours right along, and if this is going to be the outcome of it, I won't countenance any such doings. You'll go right over to Barry's, and you'll go through that spruce grove, just for a lesson and a warning to you. And never let me hear a word out of your head about haunted woods again."

Anne might plead and cry as she liked—and did, for her terror was very real. Her imagination had run away with her and she held the spruce grove in mortal dread after nightfall. But Marilla was inexorable. She marched the shrinking ghost-seer down to the spring and ordered her to proceed straightaway over the bridge and into the dusky retreats of wailing ladies and headless specters beyond.

"Oh, Marilla, how can you be so cruel?" sobbed Anne. "What would you feel like if a white thing did snatch me up and carry me off?"

"I'll risk it," said Marilla unfeelingly. "You know I always mean what I say. I'll cure you of imagining ghosts into places. March, now."

Anne marched. That is, she stumbled over the bridge and went shuddering up the horrible dim path beyond. Anne never forgot that walk. Bitterly did she repent the license she had given to her imagination. The goblins of her fancy lurked in every shadow about her, reaching out their cold, fleshless hands to grasp the terrified small girl who had called them into being. A white strip of birch bark blowing up from the hollow over the brown floor of the grove made her heart stand still. The long-drawn wail of two old boughs rubbing against each other brought out the perspiration in beads on her forehead. The swoop of bats in the darkness over her was as the wings of unearthly creatures. When she reached Mr. William Bell's field she fled across it as if pursued by an army of white things, and arrived at the Barry kitchen door so out of breath that she could hardly gasp out her request for the apron pattern. Diana was away so that she had no excuse to linger. The dreadful return journey had to be faced. Anne went back over it with shut eyes, preferring to take the risk of dashing her brains out among the boughs to that of seeing a white thing. When she finally stumbled over the log bridge she drew one long shivering breath of relief.

"Well, so nothing caught you?" said Marilla unsympathetically.

"Oh, Mar—Marilla," chattered Anne, "I'll b-b-be contt-tented with c-c-commonplace places after this."

CHAPTER XXI

A NEW DEPARTURE IN FLAVORINGS

"Dear me, there is nothing but meetings and partings in this world, as Mrs. Lynde says," remarked Anne plaintively, putting her slate and books down on the kitchen table on the last day of June and wiping her red eyes with a very damp handkerchief. "Wasn't it fortunate, Marilla, that I took an extra handkerchief to school today? I had a presentiment that it would be needed."

"I never thought you were so fond of Mr. Phillips that you'd require two handkerchiefs to dry your tears just because he was going away," said Marilla.

"I don't think I was crying because I was really so very fond of him," reflected Anne. "I just cried because all the others did. It was Ruby Gillis started it. Ruby Gillis has always declared she hated Mr. Phillips, but just as soon as he got up to make his farewell speech she burst into tears. Then all the girls began to cry, one after the other. I tried to hold out, Marilla. I tried to remember the time Mr. Phillips made me sit with Gil—with a boy; and the time he spelled my name without an *e* on the blackboard; and how he said I was the worst dunce he ever saw at geometry and laughed at my spelling; and all the times he had been so horrid and sarcastic; but somehow I couldn't, Marilla, and I just had to cry too. Jane Andrews has been talking for a month about how glad she'd be when Mr. Phillips went away and she declared she'd never shed a tear. Well, she was worse than any of us and had to borrow a handkerchief from her brother—of course the boys didn't cry—because she hadn't brought one of her own, not expecting to need it. Oh, Marilla, it was heartrending. Mr. Phillips made such a beautiful farewell speech beginning, 'The time has come for us to part.' It was very affecting. And he had tears in his eyes too, Marilla. Oh, I felt dreadfully sorry and remorseful for all the times I'd talked in school and drawn pictures of him on my slate and made fun of him and Prissy. I can tell you I wished I'd been a model pupil like Minnie Andrews. She hadn't anything on her conscience. The girls cried all the way home from school. Carrie Sloane kept saying every few minutes, 'The time has come for us to part,' and that would start us off again whenever we were in any danger of cheering up. I do feel dreadfully sad, Marilla. But one can't feel quite in the depths of despair with two months' vacation before them, can they, Marilla? And besides, we met the new minister and his wife coming from the station. For all I was feeling so bad about Mr. Phillips going away I couldn't help taking a little interest in a new minister, could I? His wife is very pretty. Not exactly regally lovely, of course—it wouldn't do, I suppose, for a minister to have a regally lovely wife, because it might set a bad example. Mrs. Lynde says the minister's wife over at Newbridge sets a very bad example because she dresses so fashionably. Our new minister's wife was dressed in blue muslin with lovely puffed sleeves and a hat trimmed with roses. Jane Andrews said she thought puffed sleeves were too worldly for a minister's wife, but I didn't make any such uncharitable remark, Marilla, because I know what it is to long for puffed sleeves. Besides, she's only been a minister's wife for a little while, so one should make allowances, shouldn't they? They are going to board with Mrs. Lynde until the manse is ready."

If Marilla, in going down to Mrs. Lynde's that evening, was actuated by any motive save her avowed one of returning the quilting frames she had borrowed the preceding winter, it was an amiable weakness shared by most of the Avonlea people. Many a thing Mrs. Lynde had lent, sometimes never expecting to see it again, came home that night in charge of the borrowers thereof. A new minister, and moreover a minister with a wife, was a lawful object of curiosity in a quiet little country settlement where sensations were few and far between.

Old Mr. Bentley, the minister whom Anne had found lacking in imagination, had been pastor of Avonlea for eighteen years. He was a widower when he came, and a widower he remained, despite the fact that gossip regularly married him to this, that, or the other one, every year of his sojourn. In the preceding February he had resigned his charge and departed amid the regrets of his people, most of whom had the affection born of long intercourse for their good old minister in spite of his shortcomings as an orator. Since then the Avonlea church had enjoyed a variety of religious dissipation in listening to the many and various candidates and "supplies" who came Sunday after Sunday to preach on trial. These stood or fell by the judgment of the fathers and mothers in Israel; but a certain small, red-haired girl who sat meekly in the corner of the old Cuthbert pew also had her opinions about them and discussed the same in full with Matthew, Marilla always declining from principle to criticize ministers in any shape or form.

"I don't think Mr. Smith would have done, Matthew," was Anne's final summing up. "Mrs. Lynde says his delivery was so poor, but I think his worst fault was just like Mr. Bentley's—he had no imagination. And Mr. Terry had too much; he let it run away with him just as I did mine in the matter of the Haunted Wood. Besides, Mrs. Lynde says his theology wasn't sound. Mr. Gresham was a very good man and a very religious man, but he told too many funny stories and made the people laugh in church; he was undignified, and you must have some dignity about a minister, mustn't you, Matthew? I thought Mr. Marshall was decidedly attractive; but Mrs. Lynde says he isn't married, or even engaged, because she made special inquiries about him, and she says it would never do to have a young unmarried minister in Avonlea, because he might marry in the congregation and that would make trouble. Mrs. Lynde is a very farseeing woman, isn't she, Matthew? I'm very glad they've called Mr. Allan. I liked him because his sermon was interesting and he prayed as if he meant it and not just as if he did it because he was in the habit of it. Mrs. Lynde says he isn't perfect, but she says she supposes we couldn't expect a perfect minister for seven hundred and fifty dollars a year, and anyhow his theology is sound because she questioned him thoroughly on all the points of doctrine. And she knows his wife's people and they are most respectable and the women are all good housekeepers. Mrs. Lynde says that sound doctrine in the man and good housekeeping in the woman make an ideal combination for a minister's family."

The new minister and his wife were a young, pleasant-faced couple, still on their honeymoon, and full of all good and beautiful enthusiasms for their chosen lifework. Avonlea opened its heart to them from the start. Old and young liked the frank, cheerful young man with his high ideals, and the bright, gentle little lady who assumed the mistress-ship of the manse. With Mrs. Allan Anne fell promptly and wholeheartedly in love. She had discovered another kindred spirit.

"Mrs. Allan is perfectly lovely," she announced one Sunday afternoon. "She's taken our class and she's a splendid teacher. She said right away she didn't think it was fair for the teacher to ask all the questions, and you know, Marilla, that is exactly what I've always thought. She said we could ask her any question we liked and I asked ever so many. I'm good at asking questions, Marilla."

"I believe you" was Marilla's emphatic comment.

"Nobody else asked any except Ruby Gillis, and she asked if there was to be a Sunday school picnic this summer. I didn't think that was a very proper question to ask because it hadn't any connection with the lesson—the lesson was about Daniel in the lions' den—but Mrs. Allan just smiled and said she thought there would be. Mrs. Allan has a lovely smile; she has such *exquisite* dimples in her cheeks. I wish I had dimples in my cheeks, Marilla. I'm not half so skinny as I was when I came here, but I have no dimples yet. If I had perhaps I could influence people for good. Mrs. Allan said we ought always to try to influence other people for good. She talked so nice about everything. I never knew before that religion was such a cheerful thing. I always thought it was kind of melancholy, but Mrs. Allan's isn't, and I'd like to be a Christian if I could be one like her. I wouldn't want to be one like Mr. Superintendent Bell."

"It's very naughty of you to speak so about Mr. Bell," said Marilla severely. "Mr. Bell is a real good man."

"Oh, of course he's good," agreed Anne, "but he doesn't seem to get any comfort out of it. If I could be good I'd dance and sing all day because I was glad of it. I suppose Mrs. Allan is too old to dance and sing and of course it wouldn't be dignified in a minister's wife. But I can just feel she's glad she's a Christian and that she'd be one even if she could get to heaven without it."

"I suppose we must have Mr. and Mrs. Allan up to tea someday soon," said Marilla reflectively. "They've been most everywhere but here. Let me see. Next Wednesday would be a good time to have them. But don't say a word to Matthew about it, for if he knew they were coming he'd find some excuse to be away that day. He'd got so used to Mr. Bentley he didn't mind him, but he's going to find it hard to get acquainted with a new minister, and a new minister's wife will frighten him to death."

"I'll be as secret as the dead," assured Anne. "But oh, Marilla, will you let me make a cake for the occasion? I'd love to do something for Mrs. Allan, and you know I can make a pretty good cake by this time."

"You can make a layer cake," promised Marilla.

Monday and Tuesday great preparations went on at Green Gables.

Having the minister and his wife to tea was a serious and important undertaking, and Marilla was determined not to be eclipsed by any of the Avonlea housekeepers. Anne was wild with excitement and delight. She talked it all over with Diana Tuesday night in the twilight, as they sat on the big red stones by the Dryad's Bubble and made rainbows in the water with little twigs dipped in fir balsam.

"Everything is ready, Diana, except my cake which I'm to make in the morning, and the baking-powder biscuits which Marilla will make just before teatime. I assure you, Diana, that Marilla and I have had a busy two days of it. It's such a responsibility having a minister's family to tea. I never went through such an experience before. You should just see our pantry. It's a sight to behold. We're going to have jellied chicken and cold tongue. We're to have two kinds of jelly, red and yellow, and whipped cream and lemon pie, and cherry pie, and three kinds of cookies, and fruit cake, and Marilla's famous yellow plum preserves that she keeps especially for ministers, and pound cake and layer cake, and biscuits as aforesaid; and new bread and old both, in case the minister is dyspeptic and can't eat new. Mrs. Lynde says ministers are dyspeptic, but I don't think Mr. Allan has been a minister long enough for it to have had a bad effect on him. I just grow cold when I think of my layer cake. Oh, Diana, what if it shouldn't be good! I dreamed last night that I was chased all around by a fearful goblin with a big layer cake for a head."

"It'll be good, all right," assured Diana, who was a very comfortable sort of friend. "I'm sure that piece of the one you made that we had for lunch in Idlewild two weeks ago was perfectly elegant."

"Yes; but cakes have such a terrible habit of turning out bad just when you especially want them to be good," sighed Anne, setting a particularly well-balsamed twig afloat. "However, I suppose I shall just have to trust to Providence and be careful to put in the flour. Oh, look, Diana, what a lovely rainbow! Do you suppose the dryad will come out after we go away and take it for a scarf?"

"You know there is no such thing as a dryad," said Diana. Diana's mother had found out about the Haunted Wood and had been decidedly angry over it. As a result Diana had abstained from any further imitative flights of imagination and did not think it prudent to cultivate a spirit of belief even in harmless dryads.

"But it's so easy to imagine there is," said Anne. "Every night before

I go to bed, I look out of my window and wonder if the dryad is really sitting here, combing her locks with the spring for a mirror. Sometimes I look for her footprints in the dew in the morning. Oh, Diana, don't give up your faith in the dryad!"

Wednesday morning came. Anne got up at sunrise because she was too excited to sleep. She had caught a severe cold in the head by reason of her dabbling in the spring on the preceding evening; but nothing short of absolute pneumonia could have quenched her interest in culinary matters that morning. After breakfast she proceeded to make her cake. When she finally shut the oven door upon it she drew a long breath.

"I'm sure I haven't forgotten anything this time, Marilla. But do you think it will rise? Just suppose perhaps the baking powder isn't good? I used it out of the new can. And Mrs. Lynde says you can never be sure of getting good baking powder nowadays when everything is so adulterated. Mrs. Lynde says the Government ought to take the matter up, but she says we'll never see the day when a Tory Government will do it. Marilla, what if that cake doesn't rise?"

"We'll have plenty without it" was Marilla's unimpassioned way of looking at the subject.

The cake did rise, however, and came out of the oven as light and feathery as golden foam. Anne, flushed with delight, clapped it together with layers of ruby jelly and, in imagination, saw Mrs. Allan eating it and possibly asking for another piece!

"You'll be using the best tea-set, of course, Marilla," she said. "Can I fix the table with ferns and wild roses?"

"I think that's all nonsense," sniffed Marilla. "In my opinion it's the eatables that matter and not flummery decorations."

"Mrs. Barry had *her* table decorated," said Anne, who was not entirely guiltless of the wisdom of the serpent, "and the minister paid her an elegant compliment. He said it was a feast for the eye as well as the palate."

"Well, do as you like," said Marilla, who was quite determined not to be surpassed by Mrs. Barry or anybody else. "Only mind you leave enough room for the dishes and the food."

Anne laid herself out to decorate in a manner and after a fashion that should leave Mrs. Barry's nowhere. Having abundance of roses and ferns and a very artistic taste of her own, she made that tea table such a thing of beauty that when the minister and his wife sat down to it they exclaimed in chorus over it loveliness.

"It's Anne's doings," said Marilla, grimly just; and Anne felt that Mrs. Allan's approving smile was almost too much happiness for this world. Matthew was there, having been inveigled into the party only goodness and Anne knew how. He had been in such a state of shyness and nervousness that Marilla had given him up in despair, but Anne took him in hand so successfully that he now sat at the table in his best clothes and white collar and talked to the minister not uninterestingly. He never said a word to Mrs. Allan, but that perhaps was not to be expected.

All went merry as a marriage bell until Anne's layer cake was passed. Mrs. Allan, having already been helped to a bewildering variety, declined it. But Marilla, seeing the disappointment on Anne's face, said smilingly:

"Oh, you must take a piece of this, Mrs. Allan. Anne made it on purpose for you."

"In that case I must sample it," laughed Mrs. Allan, helping herself to a plump triangle, as did also the minister and Marilla.

Mrs. Allan took a mouthful of hers and a most peculiar expression crossed her face; not a word did she say, however, but steadily ate away at it. Marilla saw the expression and hastened to taste the cake.

"Anne Shirley!" she exclaimed, "what on earth did you put into that cake?"

"Nothing but what the recipe said, Marilla," cried Anne with a look of anguish. "Oh, isn't it all right?"

"All right! It's simply horrible. Mr. Allan, don't try to eat it. Anne, taste it yourself. What flavoring did you use?"

"Vanilla," said Anne, her face scarlet with mortification after tasting the cake. "Only vanilla. Oh, Marilla, it must have been the baking powder. I had my suspicions of that bak—"

"Baking powder fiddlesticks! Go and bring me the bottle of vanilla you used."

Anne fled to the pantry and returned with a small bottle partially filled with a brown liquid and labeled yellowly, "Best Vanilla."

Marilla took it, uncorked it, smelled it.

"Mercy on us, Anne, you've flavored that cake with *anodyne liniment*. I broke the liniment bottle last week and poured what was left into an old empty vanilla bottle. I suppose it's partly my fault—I should have warned you—but for pity's sake why couldn't you have smelled it?"

Anne dissolved into tears under this double disgrace.

"I couldn't—I had such a cold!" and with this she fairly fled to the gable chamber, where she cast herself on the bed and wept as one who refuses to be comforted.

Presently a light step sounded on the stairs and somebody entered the room.

"Oh, Marilla," sobbed Anne, without looking up, "I'm disgraced forever. I shall never be able to live this down. It will get out—things always do get out in Avonlea. Diana will ask me how my cake turned out and I shall have to tell her the truth. I shall always be pointed at as the girl who flavored a cake with anodyne liniment. Gil—the boys in school will never get over laughing at it. Oh, Marilla, if you have a spark of Christian pity don't tell me that I must go down and wash the dishes after this. I'll wash them when the minister and his wife are gone, but I cannot ever look Mrs. Allan in the face again. Perhaps she'll think I tried to poison her. Mrs. Lynde says she knows an orphan girl who tried to poison her benefactor. But the liniment isn't poisonous. It's meant to be taken internally—although not in cakes. Won't you tell Mrs. Allan so, Marilla?"

"Suppose you jump up and tell her so yourself," said a merry voice.

Anne flew up, to find Mrs. Allan standing by her bed, surveying her with laughing eyes.

"My dear little girl, you mustn't cry like this," she said, genuinely disturbed by Anne's tragic face. "Why, it's all just a funny mistake that anybody might make."

"Oh, no, it takes me to make such a mistake," said Anne forlornly. "And I wanted to have that cake so nice for you, Mrs. Allan."

"Yes, I know, dear. And I assure you I appreciate your kindness and thoughtfulness just as much as if it had turned out all right. Now, you mustn't cry any more, but come down with me and show me your flower garden. Miss Cuthbert tells me you have a little plot all your own. I want to see it, for I'm very much interested in flowers."

Anne permitted herself to be led down and comforted, reflecting that it was really providential that Mrs. Allan was a kindred spirit. Nothing more was said about the liniment cake, and when the guests went away Anne found that she had enjoyed the evening more than could have been expected, considering that terrible incident. Nevertheless, she sighed deeply.

"Marilla, isn't it nice to think that tomorrow is a new day with no mistakes in it yet?"

"I'll warrant you'll make plenty in it," said Marilla. "I never saw your beat for making mistakes, Anne."

"Yes, and well I know it," admitted Anne mournfully. "But have you ever noticed one encouraging thing about me, Marilla? I never make the same mistake twice."

"I don't know as that's much benefit when you're always making new ones."

"Oh, don't you see, Marilla? There must be a limit to the mistakes one person can make, and when I get to the end of them, then I'll be through with them. That's a very comforting thought."

"Well, you'd better go and give that cake to the pigs," said Marilla. "It isn't fit for any human to eat, not even Jerry Boute."

CHAPTER XXII

ANNE IS INVITED OUT TO TEA

"And what are your eyes popping out of your head about, now?" asked Marilla, when Anne had just come in from a run to the post office. "Have you discovered another kindred spirit?"

Excitement hung around Anne like a garment, shone in her eyes, kindled in every feature. She had come dancing up the lane, like a wind-blown sprite, through the mellow sunshine and lazy shadows of the August evening.

"No, Marilla, but oh, what do you think? I am invited to tea at the manse tomorrow afternoon! Mrs. Allan left the letter for me at the post office. Just look at it, Marilla. 'Miss Anne Shirley, Green Gables.' That is the first time I was ever called 'Miss.' Such a thrill as it gave me! I shall cherish it forever among my choicest treasures."

"Mrs. Allan told me she meant to have all the members of her Sunday school class to tea in turn," said Marilla, regarding the wonderful event very coolly. "You needn't get in such a fever over it. Do learn to take things calmly, child."

For Anne to take things calmly would have been to change her nature. All "spirit and fire and dew," as she was, the pleasures and pains of life came to her with trebled intensity. Marilla felt this and was vaguely troubled over it, realizing that the ups and downs of existence would probably bear hardly on this impulsive soul and not sufficiently understanding that the equally great capacity for delight might more than compensate. Therefore Marilla conceived it to be her duty to drill Anne into a tranquil uniformity of disposition as impossible and alien to her as to a dancing sunbeam in one of the brook shallows. She did not make much headway, as she sorrowfully admitted to herself. The downfall of some dear hope or plan plunged Anne into "deeps of affliction." The fulfillment thereof exalted her to dizzy realms of delight. Marilla had almost begun to despair of ever fashioning this waif of the world into her model little girl of demure manners and prim deportment. Neither would she have believed that she really liked

Anne much better as she was.

Anne went to bed that night speechless with misery because Matthew had said the wind was round northeast and he feared it would be a rainy day tomorrow. The rustle of the poplar leaves about the house worried her, it sounded so like pattering raindrops, and the full, faraway roar of the gulf, to which she listened delightedly at other times, loving its strange, sonorous, haunting rhythm, now seemed like a prophecy of storm and disaster to a small maiden who particularly wanted a fine day. Anne thought that the morning would never come.

But all things have an end, even nights before the day on which you are invited to take tea at the manse. The morning, in spite of Matthew's predictions, was fine and Anne's spirits soared to their highest.

"Oh, Marilla, there is something in me today that makes me just love everybody I see," she exclaimed as she washed the breakfast dishes. "You don't know how good I feel! Wouldn't it be nice if it could last? I believe I could be a model child if I were just invited out to tea every day. But oh, Marilla, it's a solemn occasion too. I feel so anxious. What if I shouldn't behave properly? You know I never had tea at a manse before, and I'm not sure that I know all the rules of etiquette, although I've been studying the rules given in the Etiquette Department of the *Family Herald* ever since I came here. I'm so afraid I'll do something silly or forget to do something I should do. Would it be good manners to take a second helping of anything if you wanted to *very* much?"

"The trouble with you, Anne, is that you're thinking too much about yourself. You should just think of Mrs. Allan and what would be nicest and most agreeable to her," said Marilla, hitting for once in her life on a very sound and pithy piece of advice. Anne instantly realized this.

"You are right, Marilla. I'll try not to think about myself at all."

Anne evidently got through her visit without any serious breach of "etiquette," for she came home through the twilight, under a great, high-sprung sky gloried over with trails of saffron and rosy cloud, in a beatified state of mind and told Marilla all about it happily, sitting on the big red-sandstone slab at the kitchen door with her tired curly head in Marilla's gingham lap.

A cool wind was blowing down over the long harvest fields from the rims of firry western hills and whistling through the poplars. One clear star hung over the orchard and the fireflies were flitting over in Lover's Lane, in and out among the ferns and rustling boughs. Anne watched them as she talked and somehow felt that wind and stars and fireflies were all tangled up together into something unutterably sweet and enchanting.

"Oh, Marilla, I've had a most *fascinating* time. I feel that I have not lived in vain and I shall always feel like that even if I should never be invited to tea at a manse again. When I got there Mrs. Allan met me at the door. She was dressed in the sweetest dress of pale-pink organdy, with dozens of frills and elbow sleeves, and she looked just like a seraph. I really think I'd like to be a minister's wife when I grow up, Marilla. A minister mightn't mind my red hair because he wouldn't be thinking of such worldly things. But then of course one would have to be naturally good and I'll never be that, so I suppose there's no use in thinking about it. Some people are naturally good, you know, and others are not. I'm one of the others. Mrs. Lynde says I'm full of original sin. No matter how hard I try to be good I can never make such a success of it as those who are naturally good. It's a good deal like geometry, I expect. But don't you think the trying so hard ought to count for something? Mrs. Allan is one of the naturally good people. I love her passionately. You know there are some people, like Matthew and Mrs. Allan that you can love right off without any trouble. And there are others, like Mrs. Lynde, that you have to try very hard to love. You know you *ought* to love them because they know so much and are such active workers in the church, but you have to keep reminding yourself of it all the time or else you forget. There was another little girl at the manse to tea, from the White Sands Sunday school. Her name was Laurette Bradley, and she was a very nice little girl. Not exactly a kindred spirit, you know, but still very nice. We had an elegant tea, and I think I kept all the rules of etiquette pretty well. After tea Mrs. Allan played and sang and she got Lauretta and me to sing too. Mrs. Allan says I have a good voice and she says I must sing in the Sunday school choir after this. You can't think how I was thrilled at the mere thought. I've longed so to sing in the Sunday school choir, as Diana does, but I feared it was an honor I could never aspire to. Lauretta had to go home early because there is a big concert in the White Sands Hotel tonight and her sister is to recite at it. Lauretta says that the Americans at the hotel give a concert every fortnight in aid of the Charlottetown hospital, and they ask lots of the White Sands people to recite. Lauretta said she expected to be asked herself someday. I just gazed at her in awe. After she had gone Mrs.

Allan and I had a heart-to-heart talk. I told her everything—about Mrs. Thomas and the twins and Katie Maurice and Violetta and coming to Green Gables and my troubles over geometry. And would you believe it, Marilla? Mrs. Allan told me she was a dunce at geometry too. You don't know how that encouraged me. Mrs. Lynde came to the manse just before I left, and what do you think, Marilla? The trustees have hired a new teacher and it's a lady. Her name is Miss Muriel Stacy. Isn't that a romantic name? Mrs. Lynde says they've never had a female teacher in Avonlea before and she thinks it is a dangerous innovation. But I think it will be splendid to have a lady teacher, and I really don't see how I'm going to live through the two weeks before school begins, I'm so impatient to see her."

CHAPTER XXIII

ANNE COMES TO GRIEF IN AN AFFAIR OF HONOR

Anne had to live through more than two weeks, as it happened. Almost a month having elapsed since the liniment cake episode, it was high time for her to get into fresh trouble of some sort, little mistakes, such as absentmindedly emptying a pan of skim milk into a basket of yarn balls in the pantry instead of into the pigs' bucket, and walking clean over the edge of the log bridge into the brook while wrapped in imaginative reverie, not really being worth counting.

A week after the tea at the manse Diana Barry gave a party.

"Small and select," Anne assured Marilla. "Just the girls in our class."

They had a very good time and nothing untoward happened until after tea, when they found themselves in the Barry garden, a little tired of all their games and ripe for any enticing form of mischief which might present itself. This presently took the form of "daring."

Daring was the fashionable amusement among the Avonlea small fry just then. It had begun among the boys, but soon spread to the girls, and all the silly things that were done in Avonlea that summer because the doers thereof were "dared" to do them would fill a book by themselves.

First of all Carrie Sloane dared Ruby Gillis to climb to a certain point in the huge old willow tree before the front door; which Ruby Gillis, albeit in mortal dread of the fat green caterpillars with which said tree was infested and with the fear of her mother before her eyes if she should tear her new muslin dress, nimbly did, to the discomfiture of the aforesaid Carrie Sloane.

Then Josie Pye dared Jane Andrews to hop on her left leg around the garden without stopping once or putting her right foot to the ground; which Jane Andrews gamely tried to do, but gave out at the third corner and had to confess herself defeated.

Josie's triumph being rather more pronounced than good taste permitted, Anne Shirley dared her to walk along the top of the board fence which bounded the garden to the east. Now, to "walk" board fences requires more skill and steadiness of head and heel than one might suppose who has never tried it. But Josie Pye, if deficient in some qualities that make for popularity, had at least a natural and inborn gift, duly cultivated, for walking board fences. Josie walked the Barry fence with an airy unconcern which seemed to imply that a little thing like that wasn't worth a "dare." Reluctant admiration greeted her exploit, for most of the other girls could appreciate it, having suffered many things themselves in their efforts to walk fences. Josie descended from her perch, flushed with victory, and darted a defiant glance at Anne.

Anne tossed her red braids.

"I don't think it's such a very wonderful thing to walk a little, low, board fence," she said. "I knew a girl in Marysville who could walk the ridgepole of a roof."

"I don't believe it," said Josie flatly. "I don't believe anybody could walk a ridgepole. *You* couldn't, anyhow."

"Couldn't I?" cried Anne rashly.

"Then I dare you to do it," said Josie defiantly. "I dare you to climb up there and walk the ridgepole of Mr. Barry's kitchen roof."

Anne turned pale, but there was clearly only one thing to be done. She walked toward the house, where a ladder was leaning against the kitchen roof. All the fifth-class girls said, "Oh!" partly in excitement, partly in dismay.

"Don't you do it, Anne," entreated Diana. "You'll fall off and be killed. Never mind Josie Pye. It isn't fair to dare anybody to do anything so dangerous."

"I must do it. My honor is at stake," said Anne solemnly. "I shall walk that ridgepole, Diana, or perish in the attempt. If I am killed you are to have my pearl bead ring."

Anne climbed the ladder amid breathless silence, gained the ridgepole, balanced herself uprightly on that precarious footing, and started to walk along it, dizzily conscious that she was uncomfortably high up in the world and that walking ridgepoles was not a thing in which your imagination helped you out much. Nevertheless, she managed to take several steps before the catastrophe came. Then she swayed, lost her balance, stumbled, staggered, and fell, sliding down over the sun-baked roof and crashing off it through the tangle of

Virginia creeper beneath—all before the dismayed circle below could give a simultaneous, terrified shriek.

If Anne had tumbled off the roof on the side up which she had ascended Diana would probably have fallen heir to the pearl bead ring then and there. Fortunately she fell on the other side, where the roof extended down over the porch so nearly to the ground that a fall therefrom was a much less serious thing. Nevertheless, when Diana and the other girls had rushed frantically around the house—except Ruby Gillis, who remained as if rooted to the ground and went into hysterics—they found Anne lying all white and limp among the wreck and ruin of the Virginia creeper.

"Anne, are you killed?" shrieked Diana, throwing herself on her knees beside her friend. "Oh, Anne, dear Anne, speak just one word to me and tell me if you're killed."

To the immense relief of all the girls, and especially of Josie Pye, who, in spite of lack of imagination, had been seized with horrible visions of a future branded as the girl who was the cause of Anne Shirley's early and tragic death, Anne sat dizzily up and answered uncertainly:

"No, Diana, I am not killed, but I think I am rendered unconscious."

"Where?" sobbed Carrie Sloane. "Oh, where, Anne?" Before Anne could answer Mrs. Barry appeared on the scene. At sight of her Anne tried to scramble to her feet, but sank back again with a sharp little cry of pain.

"What's the matter? Where have you hurt yourself?" demanded Mrs. Barry.

"My ankle," gasped Anne. "Oh, Diana, please find your father and ask him to take me home. I know I can never walk there. And I'm sure I couldn't hop so far on one foot when Jane couldn't even hop around the garden."

Marilla was out in the orchard picking a panful of summer apples when she saw Mr. Barry coming over the log bridge and up the slope, with Mrs. Barry beside him and a whole procession of little girls trailing after him. In his arms he carried Anne, whose head lay limply against his shoulder.

At that moment Marilla had a revelation. In the sudden stab of fear that pierced her very heart she realized what Anne had come to mean to her. She would have admitted that she liked Anne—nay, that she was very fond of Anne. But now she knew as she hurried wildly down the slope that Anne was dearer to her than anything else on earth.

"Mr. Barry, what has happened to her?" she gasped, more white and shaken than the self-contained, sensible Marilla had been for many years.

Anne herself answered, lifting her head.

"Don't be very frightened, Marilla. I was walking the ridgepole and I fell off. I expect I have sprained my ankle. But, Marilla, I might have broken my neck. Let us look on the bright side of things."

"I might have known you'd go and do something of the sort when I let you go to that party," said Marilla, sharp and shrewish in her very relief. "Bring her in here, Mr. Barry, and lay her on the sofa. Mercy me, the child has gone and fainted!"

It was quite true. Overcome by the pain of her injury, Anne had one more of her wishes granted to her. She had fainted dead away.

Matthew, hastily summoned from the harvest field, was straightway dispatched for the doctor, who in due time came, to discover that the injury was more serious than they had supposed. Anne's ankle was broken.

That night, when Marilla went up to the east gable, where a white-faced girl was lying, a plaintive voice greeted her from the bed.

"Aren't you very sorry for me, Marilla?"

"It was your own fault," said Marilla, twitching down the blind and lighting a lamp.

"And that is just why you should be sorry for me," said Anne, "because the thought that it is all my own fault is what makes it so hard. If I could blame it on anybody I would feel so much better. But what would you have done, Marilla, if you had been dared to walk a ridgepole?"

"I'd have stayed on good firm ground and let them dare away. Such absurdity!" said Marilla.

Anne sighed.

"But you have such strength of mind, Marilla. I haven't. I just felt that I couldn't bear Josie Pye's scorn. She would have crowed over me all my life. And I think I have been punished so much that you needn't be very cross with me, Marilla. It's not a bit nice to faint, after all. And the doctor hurt me dreadfully when he was setting my ankle. I won't be able to go around for six or seven weeks and I'll miss the new lady teacher. She won't be new any more by the time I'm able to go to school. And Gil—everybody will get ahead of me in class. Oh, I am an afflicted mortal. But I'll try to bear it all bravely if only you won't be cross with me, Marilla."

"There, there, I'm not cross," said Marilla. "You're an unlucky child, there's no doubt about that; but as you say, you'll have the suffering of it. Here now, try and eat some supper."

"Isn't it fortunate I've got such an imagination?" said Anne. "It will help me through splendidly, I expect. What do people who haven't any imagination do when they break their bones, do you suppose, Marilla?"

Anne had good reason to bless her imagination many a time and oft during the tedious seven weeks that followed. But she was not solely dependent on it. She had many visitors and not a day passed without one or more of the schoolgirls dropping in to bring her flowers and books and tell her all the happenings in the juvenile world of Avonlea.

"Everybody has been so good and kind, Marilla," sighed Anne happily, on the day when she could first limp across the floor. "It isn't very pleasant to be laid up; but there is a bright side to it, Marilla. You find out how many friends you have. Why, even Superintendent Bell came to see me, and he's really a very fine man. Not a kindred spirit, of course; but still I like him and I'm awfully sorry I ever criticized his prayers. I believe now he really does mean them, only he has got into the habit of saying them as if he didn't. He could get over that if he'd take a little trouble. I gave him a good broad hint. I told him how hard I tried to make my own little private prayers interesting. He told me all about the time he broke his ankle when he was a boy. It does seem so strange to think of Superintendent Bell ever being a boy. Even my imagination has its limits, for I can't imagine *that*. When I try to imagine him as a boy I see him with gray whiskers and spectacles, just as he looks in Sunday school, only small. Now, it's so easy to imagine Mrs. Allan as a little girl. Mrs. Allan has been to see me fourteen times. Isn't that something to be proud of, Marilla? When a minister's wife has so many claims on her time! She is such a cheerful person to have visit you, too. She never tells you it's your own fault and she hopes you'll be a better girl on account of it. Mrs. Lynde always told me that when she came to see me; and she said it in a kind of way that made me feel she might hope I'd be a better girl but didn't really believe I would. Even Josie Pye came to see me. I received her as politely as I could, because

I think she was sorry she dared me to walk a ridgepole. If I had been killed she would have to carry a dark burden of remorse all her life. Diana has been a faithful friend. She's been over every day to cheer my lonely pillow. But oh, I shall be so glad when I can go to school for I've heard such exciting things about the new teacher. The girls all think she is perfectly sweet. Diana says she has the loveliest fair curly hair and such fascinating eyes. She dresses beautifully, and her sleeve puffs are bigger than anybody else's in Avonlea. Every other Friday afternoon she has recitations and everybody has to say a piece or take part in a dialogue. Oh, it's just glorious to think of it. Josie Pye says she hates it but that is just because Josie has so little imagination. Diana and Ruby Gillis and Jane Andrews are preparing a dialogue, called 'A Morning Visit,' for next Friday. And the Friday afternoons they don't have recitations Miss Stacy takes them all to the woods for a 'field' day and they study ferns and flowers and birds. And they have physical culture exercises every morning and evening. Mrs. Lynde says she never heard of such goings on and it all comes of having a lady teacher. But I think it must be splendid and I believe I shall find that Miss Stacy is a kindred spirit."

"There's one thing plain to be seen, Anne," said Marilla, "and that is that your fall off the Barry roof hasn't injured your tongue at all."

CHAPTER XXIV

MISS STACY AND HER PUPILS GET UP A CONCERT

It was October again when Anne was ready to go back to school—a glorious October, all red and gold, with mellow mornings when the valleys were filled with delicate mists as if the spirit of autumn had poured them in for the sun to drain—amethyst, pearl, silver, rose, and smoke-blue. The dews were so heavy that the fields glistened like cloth of silver and there were such heaps of rustling leaves in the hollows of many-stemmed woods to run crisply through. The Birch Path was a canopy of yellow and the ferns were sear and brown all along it. There was a tang in the very air that inspired the hearts of small maidens tripping, unlike snails, swiftly and willingly to school; and it *was* jolly to be back again at the little brown desk beside Diana, with Ruby Gillis nodding across the aisle and Carrie Sloane sending up notes and Julia Bell passing a "chew" of gum down from the back seat. Anne drew a long breath of happiness as she sharpened her pencil and arranged her picture cards in her desk. Life was certainly very interesting.

In the new teacher she found another true and helpful friend. Miss Stacy was a bright, sympathetic young woman with the happy gift of winning and holding the affections of her pupils and bringing out the best that was in them mentally and morally. Anne expanded like a flower under this wholesome influence and carried home to the admiring Matthew and the critical Marilla glowing accounts of schoolwork and aims.

"I love Miss Stacy with my whole heart, Marilla. She is so ladylike and she has such a sweet voice. When she pronounces my name I feel *instinctively* that she's spelling it with an *e*. We had recitations this afternoon. I just wish you could have been there to hear me recite 'Mary, Queen of Scots.' I just put my whole soul into it. Ruby Gillis told me coming home that the way I said the line, 'Now for my father's arm, she said, my woman's heart farewell,' just made her blood run cold."

"Well now, you might recite it for me some of these days, out in the barn," suggested Matthew.

"Of course I will," said Anne meditatively, "but I won't be able to do it so well, I know. It won't be so exciting as it is when you have a whole schoolful before you hanging breathlessly on your words. I know I won't be able to make your blood run cold."

"Mrs. Lynde says it made *her* blood run cold to see the boys climbing to the very tops of those big trees on Bell's hill after crows' nests last Friday," said Marilla. "I wonder at Miss Stacy for encouraging it."

"But we wanted a crow's nest for nature study," explained Anne. "That was on our field afternoon. Field afternoons are splendid, Marilla. And Miss Stacy explains everything so beautifully. We have to write compositions on our field afternoons and I write the best ones."

"It's very vain of you to say so then. You'd better let your teacher say it."

"But she *did* say it, Marilla. And indeed I'm not vain about it. How can I be, when I'm such a dunce at geometry? Although I'm really beginning to see through it a little, too. Miss Stacy makes it so clear. Still, I'll never be good at it and I assure you it is a humbling reflection. But I love writing compositions. Mostly Miss Stacy lets us choose our own subjects; but next week we are to write a composition on some remarkable person. It's hard to choose among so many remarkable people who have lived. Mustn't it be splendid to be remarkable and have compositions written about you after you're dead? Oh, I would dearly love to be remarkable. I think when I grow up I'll be a trained nurse and go with the Red Crosses to the field of battle as a messenger of mercy. That is, if I don't go out as a foreign missionary. That would be very romantic, but one would have to be very good to be a missionary, and that would be a stumbling block. We have physical culture exercises every day, too. They make you graceful and promote digestion."

"Promote fiddlesticks!" said Marilla, who honestly thought it was all nonsense.

But all the field afternoons and recitation Fridays and physical culture contortions paled before a project which Miss Stacy brought forward in November. This was that the scholars of Avonlea school should get up a concert and hold it in the hall on Christmas night, for the laudable purpose of helping to pay for a schoolhouse flag. The pupils one and all taking graciously to this plan, the preparations for a program were begun at once. And of all the excited performers-elect none was so excited as Anne Shirley, who threw herself into the undertaking heart and soul, hampered as she was by Marilla's disapproval. Marilla thought it all rank foolishness.

"It's just filling your heads up with nonsense and taking time that ought to be put on your lessons," she grumbled. "I don't approve of children's getting up concerts and racing about to practices. It makes them vain and forward and fond of gadding."

"But think of the worthy object," pleaded Anne. "A flag will cultivate a spirit of patriotism, Marilla."

"Fudge! There's precious little patriotism in the thoughts of any of you. All you want is a good time."

"Well, when you can combine patriotism and fun, isn't it all right? Of course it's real nice to be getting up a concert. We're going to have six choruses and Diana is to sing a solo. I'm in two dialogues—'The Society for the Suppression of Gossip' and 'The Fairy Queen.' The boys are going to have a dialogue too. And I'm to have two recitations, Marilla. I just tremble when I think of it, but it's a nice thrilly kind of tremble. And we're to have a tableau at the last—'Faith, Hope and Charity.' Diana and Ruby and I are to be in it, all draped in white with flowing hair. I'm to be Hope, with my hands clasped—so—and my eyes uplifted. I'm going to practice my recitations in the garret. Don't be alarmed if you hear me groaning. I have to groan heartrendingly in one of them, and it's really hard to get up a good artistic groan, Marilla. Josie Pye is sulky because she didn't get the part she wanted in the dialogue. She wanted to be the fairy queen. That would have been ridiculous, for who ever heard of a fairy queen as fat as Josie? Fairy queens must be slender. Jane Andrews is to be the queen and I am to be one of her maids of honor. Josie says she thinks a red-haired fairy is just as ridiculous as a fat one, but I do not let myself mind what Josie says. I'm to have a wreath of white roses on my hair and Ruby Gillis is going to lend me her slippers because I haven't any of my own. It's necessary for fairies to have slippers, you know. You couldn't imagine a fairy wearing boots, could you? Especially with copper toes? We are going to decorate the hall with creeping spruce and fir mottoes with pink tissue-paper roses in them. And we are all to march in two by two after the audience is seated, while Emma White plays a march on the organ. Oh, Marilla, I know you are not so enthusiastic about it as I am, but don't you hope your little Anne will distinguish herself?"

"All I hope is that you'll behave yourself. I'll be heartily glad when all this fuss is over and you'll be able to settle down. You are simply good for nothing just now with your head stuffed full of dialogues and groans and tableaus. As for your tongue, it's a marvel it's not clean worn out."

Anne sighed and betook herself to the back yard, over which a young new moon was shining through the leafless poplar boughs from an apple-green western sky, and where Matthew was splitting wood. Anne perched herself on a block and talked the concert over with him, sure of an appreciative and sympathetic listener in this instance at least.

"Well now, I reckon it's going to be a pretty good concert. And I expect you'll do your part fine," he said, smiling down into her eager, vivacious little face. Anne smiled back at him. Those two were the best of friends and Matthew thanked his stars many a time and oft that he had nothing to do with bringing her up. That was Marilla's exclusive duty; if it had been his he would have been worried over frequent conflicts between inclination and said duty. As it was, he was free to "spoil Anne"—Marilla's phrasing—as much as he liked. But it was not such a bad arrangement after all; a little "appreciation" sometimes does quite as much good as all the conscientious "bringing up" in the world.

CHAPTER XXV

MATTHEW INSISTS ON PUFFED SLEEVES

Matthew was having a bad ten minutes of it. He had come into the kitchen, in the twilight of a cold, gray December evening, and had sat down in the woodbox corner to take off his heavy boots, unconscious of the fact that Anne and a bevy of her schoolmates were having a practice of "The Fairy Queen" in the sitting room. Presently they came trooping through the hall and out into the kitchen, laughing and chattering gaily. They did not see Matthew, who shrank bashfully back into the shadows beyond the woodbox with a boot in one hand and a bootjack in the other, and he watched them shyly for the aforesaid ten minutes as they put on caps and jackets and talked about the dialogue and the concert. Anne stood among them, bright eyed and animated as they; but Matthew suddenly became conscious that there was something about her different from her mates. And what worried Matthew was that the difference impressed him as being something that should not exist. Anne had a brighter face, and bigger, starrier eyes, and more delicate features than the other's; even shy, unobservant Matthew had learned to take note of these things; but the difference that disturbed him did not consist in any of these respects. Then in what did it consist?

Matthew was haunted by this question long after the girls had gone, arm in arm, down the long, hard-frozen lane and Anne had betaken herself to her books. He could not refer it to Marilla, who, he felt, would be quite sure to sniff scornfully and remark that the only difference she saw between Anne and the other girls was that they sometimes kept their tongues quiet while Anne never did. This, Matthew felt, would be no great help.

He had recourse to his pipe that evening to help him study it out, much to Marilla's disgust. After two hours of smoking and hard reflection Matthew arrived at a solution of his problem. Anne was not dressed like the other girls!

The more Matthew thought about the matter the more he was convinced that Anne never had been dressed like the other girls—never since she had come to Green Gables. Marilla kept her clothed in plain, dark dresses, all made after the same unvarying pattern. If Matthew knew there was such a thing as fashion in dress it was as much as he did; but he was quite sure that Anne's sleeves did not look at all like the sleeves the other girls wore. He recalled the cluster of little girls he had seen around her that evening—all gay in waists of red and blue and pink and white—and he wondered why Marilla always kept her so plainly and soberly gowned.

Of course, it must be all right. Marilla knew best and Marilla was bringing her up. Probably some wise, inscrutable motive was to be served thereby. But surely it would do no harm to let the child have one pretty dress—something like Diana Barry always wore. Matthew decided that he would give her one; that surely could not be objected to as an unwarranted putting in of his oar. Christmas was only a fortnight off. A nice new dress would be the very thing for a present. Matthew, with a sigh of satisfaction, put away his pipe and went to bed, while Marilla opened all the doors and aired the house.

The very next evening Matthew betook himself to Carmody to buy the dress, determined to get the worst over and have done with it. It would be, he felt assured, no trifling ordeal. There were some things Matthew could buy and prove himself no mean bargainer; but he knew he would be at the mercy of shopkeepers when it came to buying a girl's dress.

After much cogitation Matthew resolved to go to Samuel Lawson's store instead of William Blair's. To be sure, the Cuthberts always had gone to William Blair's; it was almost as much a matter of conscience with them as to attend the Presbyterian church and vote Conservative. But William Blair's two daughters frequently waited on customers there and Matthew held them in absolute dread. He could contrive to deal with them when he knew exactly what he wanted and could point it out; but in such a matter as this, requiring explanation and consultation, Matthew felt that he must be sure of a man behind the counter. So he would go to Lawson's, where Samuel or his son would wait on him.

Alas! Matthew did not know that Samuel, in the recent expansion of his business, had set up a lady clerk also; she was a niece of his wife's and a very dashing young person indeed, with a huge, drooping pompadour, big, rolling brown eyes, and a most extensive and bewildering smile. She was dressed with exceeding smartness and wore several bangle bracelets that glittered and rattled and tinkled with every movement of her hands. Matthew was covered with confusion at finding her there at all; and those bangles completely wrecked his wits at one fell swoop.

"What can I do for you this evening, Mr. Cuthbert?" Miss Lucilla Harris inquired, briskly and ingratiatingly, tapping the counter with both hands.

"Have you any—any—any—well now, say any garden rakes?" stammered Matthew.

Miss Harris looked somewhat surprised, as well she might, to hear a man inquiring for garden rakes in the middle of December.

"I believe we have one or two left over," she said, "but they're upstairs in the lumber room. I'll go and see."

During her absence Matthew collected his scattered senses for another effort.

When Miss Harris returned with the rake and cheerfully inquired: "Anything else tonight, Mr. Cuthbert?" Matthew took his courage in both hands and replied: "Well now, since you suggest it, I might as well—take—that is—look at—buy some—some hayseed."

Miss Harris had heard Matthew Cuthbert called odd. She now concluded that he was entirely crazy.

"We only keep hayseed in the spring," she explained loftily. "We've none on hand just now."

"Oh, certainly—certainly—just as you say," stammered unhappy Matthew, seizing the rake and making for the door. At the threshold he recollected that he had not paid for it and he turned miserably back. While Miss Harris was counting out his change he rallied his powers for a final desperate attempt.

"Well now—if it isn't too much trouble—I might as well—that is—I'd like to look at—at—some sugar."

"White or brown?" queried Miss Harris patiently.

"Oh—well now—brown," said Matthew feebly.

"There's a barrel of it over there," said Miss Harris, shaking her bangles at it. "It's the only kind we have."

"I'll—I'll take twenty pounds of it," said Matthew, with beads of perspiration standing on his forehead.

Matthew had driven halfway home before he was his own man again. It had been a gruesome experience, but it served him right, he thought, for committing the heresy of going to a strange store. When he reached home he hid the rake in the tool house, but the sugar he carried in to Marilla.

"Brown sugar!" exclaimed Marilla. "Whatever possessed you to get so much? You know I never use it except for the hired man's porridge or black fruit cake. Jerry's gone and I've made my cake long ago. It's not good sugar, either—it's coarse and dark—William Blair doesn't usually keep sugar like that."

"I—I thought it might come in handy sometime," said Matthew, making good his escape.

When Matthew came to think the matter over he decided that a woman was required to cope with the situation. Marilla was out of the question. Matthew felt sure she would throw cold water on his project at once. Remained only Mrs. Lynde; for of no other woman in Avonlea would Matthew have dared to ask advice. To Mrs. Lynde he went accordingly, and that good lady promptly took the matter out of the harassed man's hands.

"Pick out a dress for you to give Anne? To be sure I will. I'm going to Carmody tomorrow and I'll attend to it. Have you something particular in mind? No? Well, I'll just go by my own judgment then. I believe a nice rich brown would just suit Anne, and William Blair has some new gloria in that's real pretty. Perhaps you'd like me to make it up for her, too, seeing that if Marilla was to make it Anne would probably get wind of it before the time and spoil the surprise? Well, I'll do it. No, it isn't a mite of trouble. I like sewing. I'll make it to fit my niece, Jenny Gillis, for she and Anne are as like as two peas as far as figure goes."

"Well now, I'm much obliged," said Matthew, "and—and—I dunno—but I'd like—I think they make the sleeves different nowadays to what they used to be. If it wouldn't be asking too much I—I'd like them made in the new way."

"Puffs? Of course. You needn't worry a speck more about it, Matthew. I'll make it up in the very latest fashion," said Mrs. Lynde. To herself she added when Matthew had gone:

"It'll be a real satisfaction to see that poor child wearing something decent for once. The way Marilla dresses her is positively ridiculous, that's what, and I've ached to tell her so plainly a dozen times. I've held my tongue though, for I can see Marilla doesn't want advice and she thinks she knows more about bringing children up than I do for all she's an old maid. But that's always the way. Folks that has brought up children know that there's no hard and fast method in the world that'll suit every child. But them as never have think it's all as plain and easy as Rule of Three—just set your three terms down so fashion, and the sum'll work out correct. But flesh and blood don't come under the head of arithmetic and that's where Marilla Cuthbert makes her mistake. I suppose she's trying to cultivate a spirit of humility in Anne by dressing her as she does; but it's more likely to cultivate envy and discontent. I'm sure the child must feel the difference between her clothes and the other girls'. But to think of Matthew taking notice of it! That man is waking up after being asleep for over sixty years."

Marilla knew all the following fortnight that Matthew had something on his mind, but what it was she could not guess, until Christmas Eve, when Mrs. Lynde brought up the new dress. Marilla behaved pretty well on the whole, although it is very likely she distrusted Mrs. Lynde's diplomatic explanation that she had made the dress because Matthew was afraid Anne would find out about it too soon if Marilla made it.

"So this is what Matthew has been looking so mysterious over and grinning about to himself for two weeks, is it?" she said a little stiffly but tolerantly. "I knew he was up to some foolishness. Well, I must say I don't think Anne needed any more dresses. I made her three good, warm, serviceable ones this fall, and anything more is sheer extravagance. There's enough material in those sleeves alone to make a waist, I declare there is. You'll just pamper Anne's vanity, Matthew, and she's as vain as a peacock now. Well, I hope she'll be satisfied at last, for I know she's been hankering after those silly sleeves ever since they came in, although she never said a word after the first. The puffs have been getting bigger and more ridiculous right along; they're as big as balloons now. Next year anybody who wears them will have to go through a door sideways."

Christmas morning broke on a beautiful white world. It had been a very mild December and people had looked forward to a green Christmas; but just enough snow fell softly in the night to transfigure Avonlea. Anne peeped out from her frosted gable window with delighted eyes. The firs in the Haunted Wood were all feathery and wonderful; the birches and wild cherry trees were outlined in pearl; the plowed fields were stretches of snowy dimples; and there was a crisp tang in the air that was glorious. Anne ran downstairs singing until her voice reechoed through Green Gables.

"Merry Christmas, Marilla! Merry Christmas, Matthew! Isn't it a lovely Christmas? I'm so glad it's white. Any other kind of Christmas doesn't seem real, does it? I don't like green Christmases. They're not green—they're just nasty faded browns and grays. What makes people call them green? Why—why—Matthew, is that for me? Oh, Matthew!"

Matthew had sheepishly unfolded the dress from its paper swathings and held it out with a deprecatory glance at Marilla, who feigned to be contemptuously filling the teapot, but nevertheless watched the scene out of the corner of her eye with a rather interested air.

Anne took the dress and looked at it in reverent silence. Oh, how pretty it was—a lovely soft brown gloria with all the gloss of silk; a skirt with dainty frills and shirrings; a waist elaborately pintucked in the most fashionable way, with a little ruffle of filmy lace at the neck. But the sleeves—they were the crowning glory! Long elbow cuffs, and above them two beautiful puffs divided by rows of shirring and bows of brown-silk ribbon.

"That's a Christmas present for you, Anne," said Matthew shyly. "Why—why—Anne, don't you like it? Well now—well now."

For Anne's eyes had suddenly filled with tears.

"*Like* it! Oh, Matthew!" Anne laid the dress over a chair and clasped her hands. "Matthew, it's perfectly exquisite. Oh, I can never thank you enough. Look at those sleeves! Oh, it seems to me this must be a happy dream."

"Well, well, let us have breakfast," interrupted Marilla. "I must say, Anne, I don't think you needed the dress; but since Matthew has got it for you, see that you take good care of it. There's a hair ribbon Mrs. Lynde left for you. It's brown, to match the dress. Come now, sit in."

"I don't see how I'm going to eat breakfast," said Anne rapturously. "Breakfast seems so commonplace at such an exciting moment. I'd rather feast my eyes on that dress. I'm so glad that puffed sleeves are still fashionable. It did seem to me that I'd never get over it if they went out before I had a dress with them. I'd never have felt quite satisfied, you see. It was lovely of Mrs. Lynde to give me the ribbon too. I feel that I ought to be a very good girl indeed. It's at times like this I'm sorry I'm not a model little girl; and I always resolve that I will be in future. But somehow it's hard to carry out your resolutions when irresistible temptations come. Still, I really will make an extra effort after this."

When the commonplace breakfast was over Diana appeared, crossing the white log bridge in the hollow, a gay little figure in her crimson ulster. Anne flew down the slope to meet her.

"Merry Christmas, Diana! And oh, it's a wonderful Christmas. I've something splendid to show you. Matthew has given me the loveliest dress, with *such* sleeves. I couldn't even imagine any nicer."

"I've got something more for you," said Diana breathlessly. "Here—this box. Aunt Josephine sent us out a big box with ever so many things in it—and this is for you. I'd have brought it over last night, but it didn't come until after dark, and I never feel very comfortable coming through the Haunted Wood in the dark now."

Anne opened the box and peeped in. First a card with "For the Anne-girl and Merry Christmas," written on it; and then, a pair of the daintiest little kid slippers, with beaded toes and satin bows and glistening buckles.

"Oh," said Anne, "Diana, this is too much. I must be dreaming."

"*I* call it providential," said Diana. "You won't have to borrow Ruby's slippers now, and that's a blessing, for they're two sizes too big for you, and it would be awful to hear a fairy shuffling. Josie Pye would be delighted. Mind you, Rob Wright went home with Gertie Pye from the practice night before last. Did you ever hear anything equal to that?"

All the Avonlea scholars were in a fever of excitement that day, for the hall had to be decorated and a last grand rehearsal held.

The concert came off in the evening and was a pronounced success. The little hall was crowded; all the performers did excellently well, but Anne was the bright particular star of the occasion, as even envy, in the shape of Josie Pye, dared not deny.

"Oh, hasn't it been a brilliant evening?" sighed Anne, when it was all over and she and Diana were walking home together under a dark, starry sky.

"Everything went off very well," said Diana practically. "I guess we must have made as much as ten dollars. Mind you, Mr. Allan is going to send an account of it to the Charlottetown papers."

"Oh, Diana, will we really see our names in print? It makes me thrill to think of it. Your solo was perfectly elegant, Diana. I felt prouder than you did when it was encored. I just said to myself, 'It is my dear bosom friend who is so honored.'"

"Well, your recitations just brought down the house, Anne. That sad one was simply splendid."

"Oh, I was so nervous, Diana. When Mr. Allan called out my name I really cannot tell how I ever got up on that platform. I felt as if a million eyes were looking at me and through me, and for one dreadful moment I was sure I couldn't begin at all. Then I thought of my lovely puffed sleeves and took courage. I knew that I must live up to those sleeves, Diana. So I started in, and my voice seemed to be coming from ever so far away. I just felt like a parrot. It's providential that I practiced those recitations so often up in the garret, or I'd never have been able to get through. Did I groan all right?"

"Yes, indeed, you groaned lovely," assured Diana.

"I saw old Mrs. Sloane wiping away tears when I sat down. It was splendid to think I had touched somebody's heart. It's so romantic to take part in a concert, isn't it? Oh, it's been a very memorable occasion indeed."

"Wasn't the boys' dialogue fine?" said Diana. "Gilbert Blythe was just splendid. Anne, I do think it's awful mean the way you treat Gil. Wait till I tell you. When you ran off the platform after the fairy dialogue one of your roses fell out of your hair. I saw Gil pick it up and put it in his breast pocket. There now. You're so romantic that I'm sure you ought to be pleased at that."

"It's nothing to me what that person does," said Anne loftily. "I simply never waste a thought on him, Diana."

That night Marilla and Matthew, who had been out to a concert for the first time in twenty years, sat for a while by the kitchen fire after Anne had gone to bed.

"Well now, I guess our Anne did as well as any of them," said Matthew proudly.

"Yes, she did," admitted Marilla. "She's a bright child, Matthew. And she looked real nice too. I've been kind of opposed to this concert scheme, but I suppose there's no real harm in it after all. Anyhow, I was proud of Anne tonight, although I'm not going to tell her so."

"Well now, I was proud of her and I did tell her so 'fore she went upstairs," said Matthew. "We must see what we can do for her some of these days, Marilla. I guess she'll need something more than Avonlea school by and by."

"There's time enough to think of that," said Marilla. "She's only thirteen in March. Though tonight it struck me she was growing quite a big girl. Mrs. Lynde made that dress a mite too long, and it makes Anne look so tall. She's quick to learn and I guess the best thing we can do for her will be to send her to Queen's after a spell. But nothing need be said about that for a year or two yet."

"Well now, it'll do no harm to be thinking it over off and on," said Matthew. "Things like that are all the better for lots of thinking over."

CHAPTER XXVI

THE STORY CLUB IS FORMED

Junior Avonlea found it hard to settle down to humdrum existence again. To Anne in particular things seemed fearfully flat, stale, and unprofitable after the goblet of excitement she had been sipping for weeks. Could she go back to the former quiet pleasures of those faraway days before the concert? At first, as she told Diana, she did not really think she could.

"I'm positively certain, Diana, that life can never be quite the same again as it was in those olden days," she said mournfully, as if referring to a period of at least fifty years back. "Perhaps after a while I'll get used to it, but I'm afraid concerts spoil people for everyday life. I suppose that is why Marilla disapproves of them. Marilla is such a sensible woman. It must be a great deal better to be sensible; but still, I don't believe I'd really want to be a sensible person, because they are so unromantic. Mrs. Lynde says there is no danger of my ever being one, but you can never tell. I feel just now that I may grow up to be sensible yet. But perhaps that is only because I'm tired. I simply couldn't sleep last night for ever so long. I just lay awake and imagined the concert over and over again. That's one splendid thing about such affairs—it's so lovely to look back to them."

Eventually, however, Avonlea school slipped back into its old groove and took up its old interests. To be sure, the concert left traces. Ruby Gillis and Emma White, who had quarreled over a point of precedence in their platform seats, no longer sat at the same desk, and a promising friendship of three years was broken up. Josie Pye and Julia Bell did not "speak" for three months, because Josie Pye had told Bessie Wright that Julia Bell's bow when she got up to recite made her think of a chicken jerking its head, and Bessie told Julia. None of the Sloanes would have any dealings with the Bells, because the Bells had declared that the Sloanes had too much to do in the program, and the Sloanes had retorted that the Bells were not capable of doing the little they had to do properly. Finally, Charlie Sloane fought Moody

Spurgeon MacPherson, because Moody Spurgeon had said that Anne Shirley put on airs about her recitations, and Moody Spurgeon was "licked"; consequently Moody Spurgeon's sister, Ella May, would not "speak" to Anne Shirley all the rest of the winter. With the exception of these trifling frictions, work in Miss Stacy's little kingdom went on with regularity and smoothness.

The winter weeks slipped by. It was an unusually mild winter, with so little snow that Anne and Diana could go to school nearly every day by way of the Birch Path. On Anne's birthday they were tripping lightly down it, keeping eyes and ears alert amid all their chatter, for Miss Stacy had told them that they must soon write a composition on "A Winter's Walk in the Woods," and it behooved them to be observant.

"Just think, Diana, I'm thirteen years old today," remarked Anne in an awed voice. "I can scarcely realize that I'm in my teens. When I woke this morning it seemed to me that everything must be different. You've been thirteen for a month, so I suppose it doesn't seem such a novelty to you as it does to me. It makes life seem so much more interesting. In two more years I'll be really grown up. It's a great comfort to think that I'll be able to use big words then without being laughed at."

"Ruby Gillis says she means to have a beau as soon as she's fifteen," said Diana.

"Ruby Gillis thinks of nothing but beaus," said Anne disdainfully. "She's actually delighted when anyone writes her name up in a take-notice for all she pretends to be so mad. But I'm afraid that is an uncharitable speech. Mrs. Allan says we should never make uncharitable speeches; but they do slip out so often before you think, don't they? I simply can't talk about Josie Pye without making an uncharitable speech, so I never mention her at all. You may have noticed that. I'm trying to be as much like Mrs. Allan as I possibly can, for I think she's perfect. Mr. Allan thinks so too. Mrs. Lynde says he just worships the ground she treads on and she doesn't really think it right for a minister to set his affections so much on a mortal being. But then, Diana, even ministers are human and have their besetting sins just like everybody else. I had such an interesting talk with Mrs. Allan about besetting sins last Sunday afternoon. There are just a few things it's proper to talk about on Sundays and that is one of them. My besetting sin is imagining too much and forgetting my duties. I'm striving very hard to overcome it and now that I'm really thirteen perhaps I'll get on better."

"In four more years we'll be able to put our hair up," said Diana. "Alice Bell is only sixteen and she is wearing hers up, but I think that's ridiculous. I shall wait until I'm seventeen."

"If I had Alice Bell's crooked nose," said Anne decidedly, "I wouldn't—but there! I won't say what I was going to because it was extremely uncharitable. Besides, I was comparing it with my own nose and that's vanity. I'm afraid I think too much about my nose ever since I heard that compliment about it long ago. It really is a great comfort to me. Oh, Diana, look, there's a rabbit. That's something to remember for our woods composition. I really think the woods are just as lovely in winter as in summer. They're so white and still, as if they were asleep and dreaming pretty dreams."

"I won't mind writing that composition when its time comes," sighed Diana. "I can manage to write about the woods, but the one we're to hand in Monday is terrible. The idea of Miss Stacy telling us to write a story out of our own heads!"

"Why, it's as easy as wink," said Anne.

"It's easy for you because you have an imagination," retorted Diana, "but what would you do if you had been born without one? I suppose you have your composition all done?"

Anne nodded, trying hard not to look virtuously complacent and failing miserably.

"I wrote it last Monday evening. It's called 'The Jealous Rival; or In Death Not Divided.' I read it to Marilla and she said it was stuff and nonsense. Then I read it to Matthew and he said it was fine. That is the kind of critic I like. It's a sad, sweet story. I just cried like a child while I was writing it. It's about two beautiful maidens called Cordelia Montmorency and Geraldine Seymour who lived in the same village and were devotedly attached to each other. Cordelia was a regal brunette with a coronet of midnight hair and duskly flashing eyes. Geraldine was a queenly blonde with hair like spun gold and velvety purple eyes."

"I never saw anybody with purple eyes," said Diana dubiously.

"Neither did I. I just imagined them. I wanted something out of the common. Geraldine had an alabaster brow, too. I've found out what an alabaster brow is. That is one of the advantages of being thirteen. You know so much more than you did when you were only twelve."

"Well, what became of Cordelia and Geraldine?" asked Diana, who was beginning to feel rather interested in their fate.

"They grew in beauty side by side until they were sixteen. Then Bertram DeVere came to their native village and fell in love with the fair Geraldine. He saved her life when her horse ran away with her in a carriage, and she fainted in his arms and he carried her home three miles; because, you understand, the carriage was all smashed up. I found it rather hard to imagine the proposal because I had no experience to go by. I asked Ruby Gillis if she knew anything about how men proposed because I thought she'd likely be an authority on the subject, having so many sisters married. Ruby told me she was hid in the hall pantry when Malcolm Andres proposed to her sister Susan. She said Malcolm told Susan that his dad had given him the farm in his own name and then said, 'What do you say, darling pet, if we get hitched this fall?' And Susan said, 'Yes—no—I don't know—let me see'—and there they were, engaged as quick as that. But I didn't think that sort of a proposal was a very romantic one, so in the end I had to imagine it out as well as I could. I made it very flowery and poetical and Bertram went on his knees, although Ruby Gillis says it isn't done nowadays. Geraldine accepted him in a speech a page long. I can tell you I took a lot of trouble with that speech. I rewrote it five times and I look upon it as my masterpiece. Bertram gave her a diamond ring and a ruby necklace and told her they would go to Europe for a wedding tour, for he was immensely wealthy. But then, alas, shadows began to darken over their path. Cordelia was secretly in love with Bertram herself and when Geraldine told her about the engagement she was simply furious, especially when she saw the necklace and the diamond ring. All her affection for Geraldine turned to bitter hate and she vowed that she should never marry Bertram. But she pretended to be Geraldine's friend the same as ever. One evening they were standing on the bridge over a rushing turbulent stream and Cordelia, thinking they were alone, pushed Geraldine over the brink with a wild, mocking, 'Ha, ha, ha.' But Bertram saw it all and he at once plunged into the current, exclaiming, 'I will save thee, my peerless Geraldine.' But alas, he had forgotten he couldn't swim, and they were both drowned, clasped in each other's arms. Their bodies were washed ashore soon afterwards. They were buried in the one grave and their funeral was most imposing, Diana. It's so much more romantic to end a story up with a funeral than a wedding. As for Cordelia, she went insane with remorse and was shut up in a lunatic asylum. I thought that was a poetical retribution for her crime."

"How perfectly lovely!" sighed Diana, who belonged to Matthew's school of critics. "I don't see how you can make up such thrilling things out of your own head, Anne. I wish my imagination was as good as yours."

"It would be if you'd only cultivate it," said Anne cheeringly. "I've just thought of a plan, Diana. Let you and me have a story club all our own and write stories for practice. I'll help you along until you can do them by yourself. You ought to cultivate your imagination, you know. Miss Stacy says so. Only we must take the right way. I told her about the Haunted Wood, but she said we went the wrong way about it in that."

This was how the story club came into existence. It was limited to Diana and Anne at first, but soon it was extended to include Jane Andrews and Ruby Gillis and one or two others who felt that their imaginations needed cultivating. No boys were allowed in it—although Ruby Gillis opined that their admission would make it more exciting—and each member had to produce one story a week.

"It's extremely interesting," Anne told Marilla. "Each girl has to read her story out loud and then we talk it over. We are going to keep them all sacredly and have them to read to our descendants. We each write under a nom-de-plume. Mine is Rosamond Montmorency. All the girls do pretty well. Ruby Gillis is rather sentimental. She puts too much lovemaking into her stories and you know too much is worse than too little. Jane never puts any because she says it makes her feel so silly when she has to read it out loud. Jane's stories are extremely sensible. Then Diana puts too many murders into hers. She says most of the time she doesn't know what to do with the people so she kills them off to get rid of them. I mostly always have to tell them what to write about, but that isn't hard for I've millions of ideas."

"I think this story-writing business is the foolishest yet," scoffed Marilla. "You'll get a pack of nonsense into your heads and waste time that should be put on your lessons. Reading stories is bad enough but writing them is worse."

"But we're so careful to put a moral into them all, Marilla," explained Anne. "I insist upon that. All the good people are rewarded and all the bad ones are suitably punished. I'm sure that must have a wholesome effect. The moral is the great thing. Mr. Allan says so. I read one of my stories to him and Mrs. Allan and they both agreed that the moral was excellent. Only they laughed in the wrong places. I like it better when people cry. Jane and Ruby almost always cry when I come to the pathetic parts. Diana wrote her Aunt Josephine about our club and her Aunt Josephine wrote back that we were to send her some of our stories. So we copied out four of our very best and sent them. Miss Josephine Barry wrote back that she had never read anything so amusing in her life. That kind of puzzled us because the stories were all very pathetic and almost everybody died. But I'm glad Miss Barry liked them. It shows our club is doing some good in the world. Mrs. Allan says that ought to be our object in everything. I do really try to make it my object but I forget so often when I'm having fun. I hope I shall be a little like Mrs. Allan when I grow up. Do you think there is any prospect of it, Marilla?"

"I shouldn't say there was a great deal" was Marilla's encouraging answer. "I'm sure Mrs. Allan was never such a silly, forgetful little girl as you are."

"No; but she wasn't always so good as she is now either," said Anne seriously. "She told me so herself—that is, she said she was a dreadful mischief when she was a girl and was always getting into scrapes. I felt so encouraged when I heard that. Is it very wicked of me, Marilla, to feel encouraged when I hear that other people have been bad and mischievous? Mrs. Lynde says it is. Mrs. Lynde says she always feels shocked when she hears of anyone ever having been naughty, no matter how small they were. Mrs. Lynde says she once heard a minister confess that when he was a boy he stole a strawberry tart out of his aunt's pantry and she never had any respect for that minister again. Now, I wouldn't have felt that way. I'd have thought that it was real noble of him to confess it, and I'd have thought what an encouraging thing it would be for small boys nowadays who do naughty things and are sorry for them to know that perhaps they may grow up to be ministers in spite of it. That's how I'd feel, Marilla."

"The way I feel at present, Anne," said Marilla, "is that it's high time you had those dishes washed. You've taken half an hour longer than you should with all your chattering. Learn to work first and talk afterwards."

CHAPTER XXVII

VANITY AND VEXATION OF SPIRIT

Marilla, walking home one late April evening from an Aid meeting, realized that the winter was over and gone with the thrill of delight that spring never fails to bring to the oldest and saddest as well as to the youngest and merriest. Marilla was not given to subjective analysis of her thoughts and feelings. She probably imagined that she was thinking about the Aids and their missionary box and the new carpet for the vestry room, but under these reflections was a harmonious consciousness of red fields smoking into pale purply mists in the declining sun, of long, sharp-pointed fir shadows falling over the meadow beyond the brook, of still, crimson-budded maples around a mirrorlike wood pool, of a wakening in the world and a stir of hidden pulses under the gray sod. The spring was abroad in the land and Marilla's sober, middle-aged step was lighter and swifter because of its deep, primal gladness.

Her eyes dwelt affectionately on Green Gables, peering through its network of trees and reflecting the sunlight back from its windows in several little coruscations of glory. Marilla, as she picked her steps along the damp lane, thought that it was really a satisfaction to know that she was going home to a briskly snapping wood fire and a table nicely spread for tea, instead of to the cold comfort of old Aid meeting evenings before Anne had come to Green Gables.

Consequently, when Marilla entered her kitchen and found the fire black out, with no sign of Anne anywhere, she felt justly disappointed and irritated. She had told Anne to be sure and have tea ready at five o'clock, but now she must hurry to take off her second-best dress and prepare the meal herself against Matthew's return from plowing.

"I'll settle Miss Anne when she comes home," said Marilla grimly, as she shaved up kindlings with a carving knife and with more vim than was strictly necessary. Matthew had come in and was waiting patiently for his tea in his corner. "She's gadding off somewhere with Diana, writing stories or practicing dialogues or some such tomfoolery, and never thinking once about the time or her duties. She's just got to be pulled up short and sudden on this sort of thing. I don't care if Mrs. Allan does say she's the brightest and sweetest child she ever knew. She may be bright and sweet enough, but her head is full of nonsense and there's never any knowing what shape it'll break out in next. Just as soon as she grows out of one freak she takes up with another. But there! Here I am saying the very thing I was so riled with Rachel Lynde for saying at the Aid today. I was real glad when Mrs. Allan spoke up for Anne, for if she hadn't I know I'd have said something too sharp to Rachel before everybody. Anne's got plenty of faults, goodness knows, and far be it from me to deny it. But I'm bringing her up and not Rachel Lynde, who'd pick faults in the Angel Gabriel himself if he lived in Avonlea. Just the same, Anne has no business to leave the house like this when I told her she was to stay home this afternoon and look after things. I must say, with all her faults, I never found her disobedient or untrustworthy before and I'm real sorry to find her so now."

"Well now, I dunno," said Matthew, who, being patient and wise and, above all, hungry, had deemed it best to let Marilla talk her wrath out unhindered, having learned by experience that she got through with whatever work was on hand much quicker if not delayed by untimely argument. "Perhaps you're judging her too hasty, Marilla. Don't call her untrustworthy until you're sure she has disobeyed you. Mebbe it can all be explained—Anne's a great hand at explaining."

"She's not here when I told her to stay," retorted Marilla. "I reckon she'll find it hard to explain *that* to my satisfaction. Of course I knew you'd take her part, Matthew. But I'm bringing her up, not you."

It was dark when supper was ready, and still no sign of Anne, coming hurriedly over the log bridge or up Lover's Lane, breathless and repentant with a sense of neglected duties. Marilla washed and put away the dishes grimly. Then, wanting a candle to light her way down the cellar, she went up to the east gable for the one that generally stood on Anne's table. Lighting it, she turned around to see Anne herself lying on the bed, face downward among the pillows.

"Mercy on us," said astonished Marilla, "have you been asleep, Anne?"

"No," was the muffled reply.

"Are you sick then?" demanded Marilla anxiously, going over to the bed.

Anne cowered deeper into her pillows as if desirous of hiding herself forever from mortal eyes.

"No. But please, Marilla, go away and don't look at me. I'm in the depths of despair and I don't care who gets head in class or writes the best composition or sings in the Sunday school choir any more. Little things like that are of no importance now because I don't suppose I'll ever be able to go anywhere again. My career is closed. Please, Marilla, go away and don't look at me."

"Did anyone ever hear the like?" the mystified Marilla wanted to know. "Anne Shirley, whatever is the matter with you? What have you done? Get right up this minute and tell me. This minute, I say. There now, what is it?"

Anne had slid to the floor in despairing obedience.

"Look at my hair, Marilla," she whispered.

Accordingly, Marilla lifted her candle and looked scrutinizingly at Anne's hair, flowing in heavy masses down her back. It certainly had a very strange appearance.

"Anne Shirley, what have you done to your hair? Why, it's *green*!"

Green it might be called, if it were any earthly color—a queer, dull, bronzy green, with streaks here and there of the original red to heighten the ghastly effect. Never in all her life had Marilla seen anything so grotesque as Anne's hair at that moment.

"Yes, it's green," moaned Anne. "I thought nothing could be as bad as red hair. But now I know it's ten times worse to have green hair. Oh, Marilla, you little know how utterly wretched I am."

"I little know how you got into this fix, but I mean to find out," said Marilla. "Come right down to the kitchen—it's too cold up here—and tell me just what you've done. I've been expecting something queer for some time. You haven't got into any scrape for over two months, and I was sure another one was due. Now, then, what did you do to your hair?"

"I dyed it."

"Dyed it! Dyed your hair! Anne Shirley, didn't you know it was a wicked thing to do?"

"Yes, I knew it was a little wicked," admitted Anne. "But I thought it was worth while to be a little wicked to get rid of red hair. I counted the cost, Marilla. Besides, I meant to be extra good in other ways to make up for it."

"Well," said Marilla sarcastically, "if I'd decided it was worth while to dye my hair I'd have dyed it a decent color at least. I wouldn't have dyed it green."

"But I didn't mean to dye it green, Marilla," protested Anne dejectedly. "If I was wicked I meant to be wicked to some purpose. He said it would turn my hair a beautiful raven black—he positively assured me that it would. How could I doubt his word, Marilla? I know what it feels like to have your word doubted. And Mrs. Allan says we should never suspect anyone of not telling us the truth unless we have proof that they're not. I have proof now—green hair is proof enough for anybody. But I hadn't then and I believed every word he said *implicitly*."

"Who said? Who are you talking about?"

"The peddler that was here this afternoon. I bought the dye from him."

"Anne Shirley, how often have I told you never to let one of those Italians in the house! I don't believe in encouraging them to come around at all."

"Oh, I didn't let him in the house. I remembered what you told me, and I went out, carefully shut the door, and looked at his things on the step. Besides, he wasn't an Italian—he was a German Jew. He had a big box full of very interesting things and he told me he was working hard to make enough money to bring his wife and children out from Germany. He spoke so feelingly about them that it touched my heart. I wanted to buy something from him to help him in such a worthy object. Then all at once I saw the bottle of hair dye. The peddler said it was warranted to dye any hair a beautiful raven black and wouldn't wash off. In a trice I saw myself with beautiful raven-black hair and the temptation was irresistible. But the price of the bottle was seventy-five cents and I had only fifty cents left out of my chicken money. I think the peddler had a very kind heart, for he said that, seeing it was me, he'd sell it for fifty cents and that was just giving it away. So I bought it, and as soon as he had gone I came up here and applied it with an old hairbrush as the directions said. I used up the whole bottle, and oh, Marilla, when I saw the dreadful color it turned my hair I repented of being wicked, I can tell you. And I've been repenting ever since."

"Well, I hope you'll repent to good purpose," said Marilla severely, "and that you've got your eyes opened to where your vanity has led you, Anne. Goodness knows what's to be done. I suppose the first thing is to give your hair a good washing and see if that will do any good."

Accordingly, Anne washed her hair, scrubbing it vigorously with soap and water, but for all the difference it made she might as well have been scouring its original red. The peddler had certainly spoken the truth when he declared that the dye wouldn't wash off, however his veracity might be impeached in other respects.

"Oh, Marilla, what shall I do?" questioned Anne in tears. "I can never live this down. People have pretty well forgotten my other mistakes—the liniment cake and setting Diana drunk and flying into a temper with Mrs. Lynde. But they'll never forget this. They will think I am not respectable. Oh, Marilla, 'what a tangled web we weave when first we practice to deceive.' That is poetry, but it is true. And oh, how Josie Pye will laugh! Marilla, I *cannot* face Josie Pye. I am the unhappiest girl in Prince Edward Island."

Anne's unhappiness continued for a week. During that time she went nowhere and shampooed her hair every day. Diana alone of outsiders knew the fatal secret, but she promised solemnly never to tell, and it may be stated here and now that she kept her word. At the end of the week Marilla said decidedly:

"It's no use, Anne. That is fast dye if ever there was any. Your hair must be cut off; there is no other way. You can't go out with it looking like that."

Anne's lips quivered, but she realized the bitter truth of Marilla's remarks. With a dismal sigh she went for the scissors.

"Please cut it off at once, Marilla, and have it over. Oh, I feel that my heart is broken. This is such an unromantic affliction. The girls in books lose their hair in fevers or sell it to get money for some good deed, and I'm sure I wouldn't mind losing my hair in some such fashion half so much. But there is nothing comforting in having your hair cut off because you've dyed it a dreadful color, is there? I'm going to weep all the time you're cutting it off, if it won't interfere. It seems such a tragic thing."

Anne wept then, but later on, when she went upstairs and looked in the glass, she was calm with despair. Marilla had done her work thoroughly and it had been necessary to shingle the hair as closely as possible. The result was not becoming, to state the case as mildly as may be. Anne promptly turned her glass to the wall.

"I'll never, never look at myself again until my hair grows," she exclaimed passionately.

Then she suddenly righted the glass.

"Yes, I will, too. I'd do penance for being wicked that way. I'll look at myself every time I come to my room and see how ugly I am. And I won't try to imagine it away, either. I never thought I was vain about my hair, of all things, but now I know I was, in spite of its being red, because it was so long and thick and curly. I expect something will happen to my nose next."

Anne's clipped head made a sensation in school on the following Monday, but to her relief nobody guessed the real reason for it, not even Josie Pye, who, however, did not fail to inform Anne that she looked like a perfect scarecrow.

"I didn't say anything when Josie said that to me," Anne confided that evening to Marilla, who was lying on the sofa after one of her headaches, "because I thought it was part of my punishment and I ought to bear it patiently. It's hard to be told you look like a scarecrow and I wanted to say something back. But I didn't. I just swept her one scornful look and then I forgave her. It makes you feel very virtuous when you forgive people, doesn't it? I mean to devote all my energies to being good after this and I shall never try to be beautiful again. Of course it's better to be good. I know it is, but it's sometimes so hard to believe a thing even when you know it. I do really want to be good, Marilla, like you and Mrs. Allan and Miss Stacy, and grow up to be a credit to you. Diana says when my hair begins to grow to tie a black velvet ribbon around my head with a bow at one side. She says she thinks it will be very becoming. I will call it a snood—that sounds so romantic. But am I talking too much, Marilla? Does it hurt your head?"

"My head is better now. It was terrible bad this afternoon, though. These headaches of mine are getting worse and worse. I'll have to see a doctor about them. As for your chatter, I don't know that I mind it—I've got so used to it."

Which was Marilla's way of saying that she liked to hear it.

CHAPTER XXVIII

AN UNFORTUNATE LILY MAID

"Of course you must be Elaine, Anne," said Diana. "I could never have the courage to float down there."

"Nor I," said Ruby Gillis, with a shiver. "I don't mind floating down when there's two or three of us in the flat and we can sit up. It's fun then. But to lie down and pretend I was dead—I just couldn't. I'd die really of fright."

"Of course it would be romantic," conceded Jane Andrews, "but I know I couldn't keep still. I'd be popping up every minute or so to see where I was and if I wasn't drifting too far out. And you know, Anne, that would spoil the effect."

"But it's so ridiculous to have a redheaded Elaine," mourned Anne. "I'm not afraid to float down and I'd love to be Elaine. But it's ridiculous just the same. Ruby ought to be Elaine because she is so fair and has such lovely long golden hair—Elaine had 'all her bright hair streaming down,' you know. And Elaine was the lily maid. Now, a red-haired person cannot be a lily maid."

"Your complexion is just as fair as Ruby's," said Diana earnestly, "and your hair is ever so much darker than it used to be before you cut it."

"Oh, do you really think so?" exclaimed Anne, flushing sensitively with delight. "I've sometimes thought it was myself—but I never dared to ask anyone for fear she would tell me it wasn't. Do you think it could be called auburn now, Diana?"

"Yes, and I think it is real pretty," said Diana, looking admiringly at the short, silky curls that clustered over Anne's head and were held in place by a very jaunty black velvet ribbon and bow.

They were standing on the bank of the pond, below Orchard Slope, where a little headland fringed with birches ran out from the bank; at its tip was a small wooden platform built out into the water for the convenience of fishermen and duck hunters. Ruby and Jane were spending the midsummer afternoon with Diana, and Anne had come over to play with them.

Anne and Diana had spent most of their playtime that summer on and about the pond. Idlewild was a thing of the past, Mr. Bell having ruthlessly cut down the little circle of trees in his back pasture in the spring. Anne had sat among the stumps and wept, not without an eye to the romance of it; but she was speedily consoled, for, after all, as she and Diana said, big girls of thirteen, going on fourteen, were too old for such childish amusements as playhouses, and there were more fascinating sports to be found about the pond. It was splendid to fish for trout over the bridge and the two girls learned to row themselves about in the little flat-bottomed dory Mr. Barry kept for duck shooting.

It was Anne's idea that they dramatize Elaine. They had studied Tennyson's poem in school the preceding winter, the Superintendent of Education having prescribed it in the English course for the Prince Edward Island schools. They had analyzed and parsed it and torn it to pieces in general until it was a wonder there was any meaning at all left in it for them, but at least the fair lily maid and Lancelot and Guinevere and King Arthur had become very real people to them, and Anne was devoured by secret regret that she had not been born in Camelot. Those days, she said, were so much more romantic than the present.

Anne's plan was hailed with enthusiasm. The girls had discovered that if the flat were pushed off from the landing place it would drift down with the current under the bridge and finally strand itself on another headland lower down which ran out at a curve in the pond. They had often gone down like this and nothing could be more convenient for playing Elaine.

"Well, I'll be Elaine," said Anne, yielding reluctantly, for, although she would have been delighted to play the principal character, yet her artistic sense demanded fitness for it and this, she felt, her limitations made impossible. "Ruby, you must be King Arthur and Jane will be Guinevere and Diana must be Lancelot. But first you must be the brothers and the father. We can't have the old dumb servitor because there isn't room for two in the flat when one is lying down. We must pall the barge all its length in blackest samite. That old black shawl of your mother's will be just the thing, Diana."

The black shawl having been procured, Anne spread it over the flat and then lay down on the bottom, with closed eyes and hands folded over her breast.

"Oh, she does look really dead," whispered Ruby Gillis nervously, watching the still, white little face under the flickering shadows of the birches. "It makes me feel frightened, girls. Do you suppose it's really right to act like this? Mrs. Lynde says that all play-acting is abominably wicked."

"Ruby, you shouldn't talk about Mrs. Lynde," said Anne severely. "It spoils the effect because this is hundreds of years before Mrs. Lynde was born. Jane, you arrange this. It's silly for Elaine to be talking when she's dead."

Jane rose to the occasion. Cloth of gold for coverlet there was none, but an old piano scarf of yellow Japanese crepe was an excellent substitute. A white lily was not obtainable just then, but the effect of a tall blue iris placed in one of Anne's folded hands was all that could be desired.

"Now, she's all ready," said Jane. "We must kiss her quiet brows and, Diana, you say, 'Sister, farewell forever,' and Ruby, you say, 'Farewell, sweet sister,' both of you as sorrowfully as you possibly can. Anne, for goodness sake smile a little. You know Elaine 'lay as though she smiled.' That's better. Now push the flat off."

The flat was accordingly pushed off, scraping roughly over an old embedded stake in the process. Diana and Jane and Ruby only waited long enough to see it caught in the current and headed for the bridge before scampering up through the woods, across the road, and down to the lower headland where, as Lancelot and Guinevere and the King, they were to be in readiness to receive the lily maid.

For a few minutes Anne, drifting slowly down, enjoyed the romance of her situation to the full. Then something happened not at all romantic. The flat began to leak. In a very few moments it was necessary for Elaine to scramble to her feet, pick up her cloth of gold coverlet and pall of blackest samite and gaze blankly at a big crack in the bottom of her barge through which the water was literally pouring. That sharp stake at the landing had torn off the strip of batting nailed on the flat. Anne did not know this, but it did not take her long to realize that she was in a dangerous plight. At this rate the flat would fill and sink long before it could drift to the lower headland. Where were the oars? Left behind at the landing!

Anne gave one gasping little scream which nobody ever heard; she was white to the lips, but she did not lose her self-possession. There was one chance—just one.

"I was horribly frightened," she told Mrs. Allan the next day, "and it seemed like years while the flat was drifting down to the bridge and the water rising in it every moment. I prayed, Mrs. Allan, most earnestly, but I didn't shut my eyes to pray, for I knew the only way God could save me was to let the flat float close enough to one of the bridge piles for me to climb up on it. You know the piles are just old tree trunks and there are lots of knots and old branch stubs on them. It was proper to pray, but I had to do my part by watching out and right well I knew it. I just said, 'Dear God, please take the flat close to a pile and I'll do the rest,' over and over again. Under such circumstances you don't think much about making a flowery prayer. But mine was answered, for the flat bumped right into a pile for a minute and I flung the scarf and the shawl over my shoulder and scrambled up on a big providential stub. And there I was, Mrs. Allan, clinging to that slippery old pile with no way of getting up or down. It was a very unromantic position, but I didn't think about that at the time. You don't think much about romance when you have just escaped from a watery grave. I said a grateful prayer at once and then I gave all my attention to holding on tight, for I knew I should probably have to depend on human aid to get back to dry land."

The flat drifted under the bridge and then promptly sank in midstream. Ruby, Jane, and Diana, already awaiting it on the lower headland, saw it disappear before their very eyes and had not a doubt but that Anne had gone down with it. For a moment they stood still, white as sheets, frozen with horror at the tragedy; then, shrieking at the tops of their voices, they started on a frantic run up through the woods, never pausing as they crossed the main road to glance the way of the bridge. Anne, clinging desperately to her precarious foothold, saw their flying forms and heard their shrieks. Help would soon come, but meanwhile her position was a very uncomfortable one.

The minutes passed by, each seeming an hour to the unfortunate lily maid. Why didn't somebody come? Where had the girls gone? Suppose they had fainted, one and all! Suppose nobody ever came! Suppose she grew so tired and cramped that she could hold on no longer! Anne looked at the wicked green depths below her, wavering with long, oily shadows, and shivered. Her imagination began to suggest all manner of gruesome possibilities to her.

Then, just as she thought she really could not endure the ache in her arms and wrists another moment, Gilbert Blythe came rowing under the bridge in Harmon Andrews's dory!

Gilbert glanced up and, much to his amazement, beheld a little white scornful face looking down upon him with big, frightened but also scornful gray eyes.

"Anne Shirley! How on earth did you get there?" he exclaimed.

Without waiting for an answer he pulled close to the pile and extended his hand. There was no help for it; Anne, clinging to Gilbert Blythe's hand, scrambled down into the dory, where she sat, drabbled and furious, in the stern with her arms full of dripping shawl and wet crepe. It was certainly extremely difficult to be dignified under the circumstances!

"What has happened, Anne?" asked Gilbert, taking up his oars.

"We were playing Elaine," explained Anne frigidly, without even looking at her rescuer, "and I had to drift down to Camelot in the barge—I mean the flat. The flat began to leak and I climbed out on the pile. The girls went for help. Will you be kind enough to row me to the landing?"

Gilbert obligingly rowed to the landing and Anne, disdaining assistance, sprang nimbly on shore.

"I'm very much obliged to you," she said haughtily as she turned away. But Gilbert had also sprung from the boat and now laid a detaining hand on her arm.

"Anne," he said hurriedly, "look here. Can't we be good friends? I'm awfully sorry I made fun of your hair that time. I didn't mean to vex you and I only meant it for a joke. Besides, it's so long ago. I think your hair is awfully pretty now—honest I do. Let's be friends."

For a moment Anne hesitated. She had an odd, newly awakened consciousness under all her outraged dignity that the half-shy, half-eager expression in Gilbert's hazel eyes was something that was very good to see. Her heart gave a quick, queer little beat. But the bitterness of her old grievance promptly stiffened up her wavering determination. That scene of two years before flashed back into her recollection as vividly as if it had taken place yesterday. Gilbert had called her "carrots" and had brought about her disgrace before the whole school. Her resentment, which to other and older people might be as laughable as its cause, was in no whit allayed and softened by time seemingly.

She hated Gilbert Blythe! She would never forgive him!

"No," she said coldly, "I shall never be friends with you, Gilbert Blythe; and I don't want to be!"

"All right!" Gilbert sprang into his skiff with an angry color in his cheeks. "I'll never ask you to be friends again, Anne Shirley. And I don't care either!"

He pulled away with swift defiant strokes, and Anne went up the steep, ferny little path under the maples. She held her head very high, but she was conscious of an odd feeling of regret. She almost wished she had answered Gilbert differently. Of course, he had insulted her terribly, but still—! Altogether, Anne rather thought it would be a relief to sit down and have a good cry. She was really quite unstrung, for the reaction from her fright and cramped clinging was making itself felt.

Halfway up the path she met Jane and Diana rushing back to the pond in a state narrowly removed from positive frenzy. They had found nobody at Orchard Slope, both Mr. and Mrs. Barry being away. Here Ruby Gillis had succumbed to hysterics, and was left to recover from them as best she might, while Jane and Diana flew through the Haunted Wood and across the brook to Green Gables. There they had found nobody either, for Marilla had gone to Carmody and Matthew was making hay in the back field.

"Oh, Anne," gasped Diana, fairly falling on the former's neck and weeping with relief and delight, "oh, Anne—we thought—you were—drowned—and we felt like murderers—because we had made—you be—Elaine. And Ruby is in hysterics—oh, Anne, how did you escape?"

"I climbed up on one of the piles," explained Anne wearily, "and Gilbert Blythe came along in Mr. Andrews's dory and brought me to land."

"Oh, Anne, how splendid of him! Why, it's so romantic!" said Jane, finding breath enough for utterance at last. "Of course you'll speak to him after this."

"Of course I won't," flashed Anne, with a momentary return of her old spirit. "And I don't want ever to hear the word 'romantic' again, Jane Andrews. I'm awfully sorry you were so frightened, girls. It is all my fault. I feel sure I was born under an unlucky star. Everything I do gets me or my dearest friends into a scrape. We've gone and lost your father's flat, Diana, and I have a presentiment that we'll not be allowed to row on the pond any more."

Anne's presentiment proved more trustworthy than presentiments are apt to do. Great was the consternation in the Barry and Cuthbert households when the events of the afternoon became known.

"Will you *ever* have any sense, Anne?" groaned Marilla.

"Oh, yes, I think I will, Marilla," returned Anne optimistically. A good cry, indulged in the grateful solitude of the east gable, had soothed her nerves and restored her to her wonted cheerfulness. "I think my prospects of becoming sensible are brighter now than ever."

"I don't see how," said Marilla.

"Well," explained Anne, "I've learned a new and valuable lesson today. Ever since I came to Green Gables I've been making mistakes, and each mistake has helped to cure me of some great shortcoming. The affair of the amethyst brooch cured me of meddling with things that didn't belong to me. The Haunted Wood mistake cured me of letting my imagination run away with me. The liniment cake mistake cured me of carelessness in cooking. Dyeing my hair cured me of vanity. I never think about my hair and nose now—at least, very seldom. And today's mistake is going to cure me of being too romantic. I have come to the conclusion that it is no use trying to be romantic in Avonlea. It was probably easy enough in towered Camelot hundreds of years ago, but romance is not appreciated now. I feel quite sure that you will soon see a great improvement in me in this respect, Marilla."

"I'm sure I hope so," said Marilla skeptically.

But Matthew, who had been sitting mutely in his corner, laid a hand on Anne's shoulder when Marilla had gone out.

"Don't give up all your romance, Anne," he whispered shyly, "a little of it is a good thing—not too much, of course—but keep a little of it, Anne, keep a little of it."

CHAPTER XXIX

AN EPOCH IN ANNE'S LIFE

Anne was bringing the cows home from the back pasture by way of Lover's Lane. It was a September evening and all the gaps and clearings in the woods were brimmed up with ruby sunset light. Here and there the lane was splashed with it, but for the most part it was already quite shadowy beneath the maples, and the spaces under the firs were filled with a clear violet dusk like airy wine. The winds were out in their tops, and there is no sweeter music on earth than that which the wind makes in the fir trees at evening.

The cows swung placidly down the lane, and Anne followed them dreamily, repeating aloud the battle canto from "Marmion"—which had also been part of their English course the preceding winter and which Miss Stacy had made them learn off by heart—and exulting in its rushing lines and the clash of spears in its imagery. When she came to the lines:

The stubborn spearsmen still made good
Their dark impenetrable wood,

she stopped in ecstasy to shut her eyes that she might the better fancy herself one of that heroic ring. When she opened them again it was to behold Diana coming through the gate that led into the Barry field and looking so important that Anne instantly divined there was news to be told. But betray too eager curiosity she would not.

"Isn't this evening just like a purple dream, Diana? It makes me so glad to be alive. In the mornings I always think the mornings are best; but when evening comes I think it's lovelier still."

"It's a very fine evening," said Diana, "but oh, I have such news, Anne. Guess. You can have three guesses."

"Charlotte Gillis is going to be married in the church after all and Mrs. Allan wants us to decorate it," cried Anne.

"No. Charlotte's beau won't agree to that, because nobody ever has been married in the church yet, and he thinks it would seem too much like a funeral. It's too mean, because it would be such fun. Guess again."

"Jane's mother is going to let her have a birthday party?"

Diana shook her head, her black eyes dancing with merriment.

"I can't think what it can be," said Anne in despair, "unless it's that Moody Spurgeon MacPherson saw you home from prayer meeting last night. Did he?"

"I should think not," exclaimed Diana indignantly. "I wouldn't be likely to boast of it if he did, the horrid creature! I knew you couldn't guess it. Mother had a letter from Aunt Josephine today, and Aunt Josephine wants you and me to go to town next Tuesday and stop with her for the Exhibition. There!"

"Oh, Diana," whispered Anne, finding it necessary to lean up against a maple tree for support, "do you really mean it? But I'm afraid Marilla won't let me go. She will say that she can't encourage gadding about. That was what she said last week when Jane invited me to go with them in their double-seated buggy to the American concert at the White Sands Hotel. I wanted to go, but Marilla said I'd be better at home learning my lessons and so would Jane. I was bitterly disappointed, Diana. I felt so heartbroken that I wouldn't say my prayers when I went to bed. But I repented of that and got up in the middle of the night and said them."

"I'll tell you," said Diana, "we'll get Mother to ask Marilla. She'll be more likely to let you go then; and if she does we'll have the time of our lives, Anne. I've never been to an Exhibition, and it's so aggravating to hear the other girls talking about their trips. Jane and Ruby have been twice, and they're going this year again."

"I'm not going to think about it at all until I know whether I can go or not," said Anne resolutely. "If I did and then was disappointed, it would be more than I could bear. But in case I do go I'm very glad my new coat will be ready by that time. Marilla didn't think I needed a new coat. She said my old one would do very well for another winter and that I ought to be satisfied with having a new dress. The dress is very pretty, Diana—navy blue and made so fashionably. Marilla always makes my dresses fashionably now, because she says she doesn't intend to have Matthew going to Mrs. Lynde to make them. I'm so glad. It is ever so much easier to be good if your clothes are fashionable. At least, it is easier for me. I suppose it doesn't make such a difference to naturally good people. But Matthew said I must have a new coat, so Marilla bought a lovely piece of blue broadcloth, and it's being made by a real dressmaker over at Carmody. It's to be done Saturday night, and I'm trying not to imagine myself walking up the church aisle on Sunday in my new suit and cap, because I'm afraid it isn't right to imagine such things. But it just slips into my mind in spite of me. My cap is so pretty. Matthew bought it for me the day we were over at Carmody. It is one of those little blue velvet ones that are all the rage, with gold cord and tassels. Your new hat is elegant, Diana, and so becoming. When I saw you come into church last Sunday my heart swelled with pride to think you were my dearest friend. Do you suppose it's wrong for us to think so much about our clothes? Marilla says it is very sinful. But it is such an interesting subject, isn't it?"

Marilla agreed to let Anne go to town, and it was arranged that Mr. Barry should take the girls in on the following Tuesday. As Charlottetown was thirty miles away and Mr. Barry wished to go and return the same day, it was necessary to make a very early start. But Anne counted it all joy, and was up before sunrise on Tuesday morning. A glance from her window assured her that the day would be fine, for the eastern sky behind the firs of the Haunted Wood was all silvery and cloudless. Through the gap in the trees a light was shining in the western gable of Orchard Slope, a token that Diana was also up.

Anne was dressed by the time Matthew had the fire on and had the breakfast ready when Marilla came down, but for her own part was much too excited to eat. After breakfast the jaunty new cap and jacket were donned, and Anne hastened over the brook and up through the firs to Orchard Slope. Mr. Barry and Diana were waiting for her, and they were soon on the road.

It was a long drive, but Anne and Diana enjoyed every minute of it. It was delightful to rattle along over the moist roads in the early red sunlight that was creeping across the shorn harvest fields. The air was fresh and crisp, and little smoke-blue mists curled through the valleys and floated off from the hills. Sometimes the road went through woods where maples were beginning to hang out scarlet banners; sometimes it crossed rivers on bridges that made Anne's flesh cringe with the old, half-delightful fear; sometimes it wound along a harbor shore and passed by a little cluster of weather-gray fishing huts; again it mounted to hills whence a far sweep of curving upland or misty-blue sky could be seen; but wherever it went there was much of interest to discuss. It was almost noon when they reached town and found their way to "Beechwood." It was quite a fine old mansion, set back from the street in a seclusion of green elms and branching beeches. Miss Barry met them at the door with a twinkle in her sharp black eyes.

"So you've come to see me at last, you Anne-girl," she said. "Mercy, child, how you have grown! You're taller than I am, I declare. And you're ever so much better looking than you used to be, too. But I dare say you know that without being told."

"Indeed I didn't," said Anne radiantly. "I know I'm not so freckled as I used to be, so I've much to be thankful for, but I really hadn't dared to hope there was any other improvement. I'm so glad you think there is, Miss Barry."

Miss Barry's house was furnished with "great magnificence," as Anne told Marilla afterward. The two little country girls were rather abashed by the splendor of the parlor where Miss Barry left them when she went to see about dinner.

"Isn't it just like a palace?" whispered Diana. "I never was in Aunt Josephine's house before, and I'd no idea it was so grand. I just wish Julia Bell could see this—she puts on such airs about her mother's parlor."

"Velvet carpet," sighed Anne luxuriously, "and silk curtains! I've dreamed of such things, Diana. But do you know I don't believe I feel very comfortable with them after all. There are so many things in this room and all so splendid that there is no scope for imagination. That is one consolation when you are poor—there are so many more things you can imagine about."

Their sojourn in town was something that Anne and Diana dated from for years. From first to last it was crowded with delights.

On Wednesday Miss Barry took them to the Exhibition grounds and kept them there all day.

"It was splendid," Anne related to Marilla later on. "I never imagined anything so interesting. I don't really know which department was the most interesting. I think I liked the horses and the flowers and the fancywork best. Josie Pye took first prize for knitted lace. I was real glad she did. And I was glad that I felt glad, for it shows I'm improving, don't you think, Marilla, when I can rejoice in Josie's success? Mr.

Harmon Andrews took second prize for Gravenstein apples and Mr. Bell took first prize for a pig. Diana said she thought it was ridiculous for a Sunday school superintendent to take a prize in pigs, but I don't see why. Do you? She said she would always think of it after this when he was praying so solemnly. Clara Louise MacPherson took a prize for painting, and Mrs. Lynde got first prize for homemade butter and cheese. So Avonlea was pretty well represented, wasn't it? Mrs. Lynde was there that day, and I never knew how much I really liked her until I saw her familiar face among all those strangers. There were thousands of people there, Marilla. It made me feel dreadfully insignificant. And Miss Barry took us up to the grandstand to see the horse races. Mrs. Lynde wouldn't go; she said horse racing was an abomination and, she being a church member, thought it her bounden duty to set a good example by staying away. But there were so many there I don't believe Mrs. Lynde's absence would ever be noticed. I don't think, though, that I ought to go very often to horse races, because they *are* awfully fascinating. Diana got so excited that she offered to bet me ten cents that the red horse would win. I didn't believe he would, but I refused to bet, because I wanted to tell Mrs. Allan all about everything, and I felt sure it wouldn't do to tell her that. It's always wrong to do anything you can't tell the minister's wife. It's as good as an extra conscience to have a minister's wife for your friend. And I was very glad I didn't bet, because the red horse *did* win, and I would have lost ten cents. So you see that virtue was its own reward. We saw a man go up in a balloon. I'd love to go up in a balloon, Marilla; it would be simply thrilling; and we saw a man selling fortunes. You paid him ten cents and a little bird picked out your fortune for you. Miss Barry gave Diana and me ten cents each to have our fortunes told. Mine was that I would marry a dark-complected man who was very wealthy, and I would go across water to live. I looked carefully at all the dark men I saw after that, but I didn't care much for any of them, and anyhow I suppose it's too early to be looking out for him yet. Oh, it was a never-to-be-forgotten day, Marilla. I was so tired I couldn't sleep at night. Miss Barry put us in the spare room, according to promise. It was an elegant room, Marilla, but somehow sleeping in a spare room isn't what I used to think it was. That's the worst of growing up, and I'm beginning to realize it. The things you wanted so much when you were a child don't seem half so wonderful to you when you get them."

Thursday the girls had a drive in the park, and in the evening Miss Barry took them to a concert in the Academy of Music, where a noted prima donna was to sing. To Anne the evening was a glittering vision of delight.

"Oh, Marilla, it was beyond description. I was so excited I couldn't even talk, so you may know what it was like. I just sat in enraptured silence. Madame Selitsky was perfectly beautiful, and wore white satin and diamonds. But when she began to sing I never thought about anything else. Oh, I can't tell you how I felt. But it seemed to me that it could never be hard to be good any more. I felt like I do when I look up to the stars. Tears came into my eyes, but, oh, they were such happy tears. I was so sorry when it was all over, and I told Miss Barry I didn't see how I was ever to return to common life again. She said she thought if we went over to the restaurant across the street and had an ice cream it might help me. That sounded so prosaic; but to my surprise I found it true. The ice cream was delicious, Marilla, and it was so lovely and dissipated to be sitting there eating it at eleven o'clock at night. Diana said she believed she was born for city life. Miss Barry asked me what my opinion was, but I said I would have to think it over very seriously before I could tell her what I really thought. So I thought it over after I went to bed. That is the best time to think things out. And I came to the conclusion, Marilla, that I wasn't born for city life and that I was glad of it. It's nice to be eating ice cream at brilliant restaurants at eleven o'clock at night once in a while; but as a regular thing I'd rather be in the east gable at eleven, sound asleep, but kind of knowing even in my sleep that the stars were shining outside and that the wind was blowing in the firs across the brook. I told Miss Barry so at breakfast the next morning and she laughed. Miss Barry generally laughed at anything I said, even when I said the most solemn things. I don't think I liked it, Marilla, because I wasn't trying to be funny. But she is a most hospitable lady and treated us royally."

Friday brought going-home time, and Mr. Barry drove in for the girls.

"Well, I hope you've enjoyed yourselves," said Miss Barry, as she bade them good-bye.

"Indeed we have," said Diana.

"And you, Anne-girl?"

"I've enjoyed every minute of the time," said Anne, throwing her arms impulsively about the old woman's neck and kissing her wrinkled cheek. Diana would never have dared to do such a thing and felt rather aghast at Anne's freedom. But Miss Barry was pleased, and she stood on her veranda and watched the buggy out of sight. Then she went back into her big house with a sigh. It seemed very lonely, lacking those fresh young lives. Miss Barry was a rather selfish old lady, if the truth must be told, and had never cared much for anybody but herself. She valued people only as they were of service to her or amused her. Anne had amused her, and consequently stood high in the old lady's good graces. But Miss Barry found herself thinking less about Anne's quaint speeches than of her fresh enthusiasms, her transparent emotions, her little winning ways, and the sweetness of her eyes and lips.

"I thought Marilla Cuthbert was an old fool when I heard she'd adopted a girl out of an orphan asylum," she said to herself, "but I guess she didn't make much of a mistake after all. If I'd a child like Anne in the house all the time I'd be a better and happier woman."

Anne and Diana found the drive home as pleasant as the drive in—pleasanter, indeed, since there was the delightful consciousness of home waiting at the end of it. It was sunset when they passed through White Sands and turned into the shore road. Beyond, the Avonlea hills came out darkly against the saffron sky. Behind them the moon was rising out of the sea that grew all radiant and transfigured in her light. Every little cove along the curving road was a marvel of dancing ripples. The waves broke with a soft swish on the rocks below them, and the tang of the sea was in the strong, fresh air.

"Oh, but it's good to be alive and to be going home," breathed Anne. When she crossed the log bridge over the brook the kitchen light of Green Gables winked her a friendly welcome back, and through the open door shone the hearth fire, sending out its warm red glow athwart the chilly autumn night. Anne ran blithely up the hill and into the kitchen, where a hot supper was waiting on the table.

"So you've got back?" said Marilla, folding up her knitting.

"Yes, and oh, it's so good to be back," said Anne joyously. "I could kiss everything, even to the clock. Marilla, a broiled chicken! You don't mean to say you cooked that for me!"

"Yes, I did," said Marilla. "I thought you'd be hungry after such a drive and need something real appetizing. Hurry and take off your things, and we'll have supper as soon as Matthew comes in. I'm glad you've got back, I must say. It's been fearful lonesome here without you, and I never put in four longer days."

After supper Anne sat before the fire between Matthew and Marilla, and gave them a full account of her visit.

"I've had a splendid time," she concluded happily, "and I feel that it marks an epoch in my life. But the best of it all was the coming home."

CHAPTER XXX

THE QUEEN'S CLASS IS ORGANIZED

Marilla laid her knitting on her lap and leaned back in her chair. Her eyes were tired, and she thought vaguely that she must see about having her glasses changed the next time she went to town, for her eyes had grown tired very often of late.

It was nearly dark, for the full November twilight had fallen around Green Gables, and the only light in the kitchen came from the dancing red flames in the stove.

Anne was curled up Turk-fashion on the hearthrug, gazing into that joyous glow where the sunshine of a hundred summers was being distilled from the maple cordwood. She had been reading, but her book had slipped to the floor, and now she was dreaming, with a smile on her parted lips. Glittering castles in Spain were shaping themselves out of the mists and rainbows of her lively fancy; adventures wonderful and enthralling were happening to her in cloudland—adventures that always turned out triumphantly and never involved her in scrapes like those of actual life.

Marilla looked at her with a tenderness that would never have been suffered to reveal itself in any clearer light than that soft mingling of fireshine and shadow. The lesson of a love that should display itself easily in spoken word and open look was one Marilla could never learn. But she had learned to love this slim, gray-eyed girl with an affection all the deeper and stronger from its very undemonstrativeness. Her love made her afraid of being unduly indulgent, indeed. She had an uneasy feeling that it was rather sinful to set one's heart so intensely on any human creature as she had set hers on Anne, and perhaps she performed a sort of unconscious penance for this by being stricter and more critical than if the girl had been less dear to her. Certainly Anne herself had no idea how Marilla loved her. She sometimes thought wistfully that Marilla was very hard to please and distinctly lacking in sympathy and understanding. But she always checked the thought reproachfully, remembering what she owed to Marilla.

"Anne," said Marilla abruptly, "Miss Stacy was here this afternoon when you were out with Diana."

Anne came back from her other world with a start and a sigh.

"Was she? Oh, I'm so sorry I wasn't in. Why didn't you call me, Marilla? Diana and I were only over in the Haunted Wood. It's lovely in the woods now. All the little wood things—the ferns and the satin leaves and the crackerberries—have gone to sleep, just as if somebody had tucked them away until spring under a blanket of leaves. I think it was a little gray fairy with a rainbow scarf that came tiptoeing along the last moonlight night and did it. Diana wouldn't say much about that, though. Diana has never forgotten the scolding her mother gave her about imagining ghosts into the Haunted Wood. It had a very bad effect on Diana's imagination. It blighted it. Mrs. Lynde says Myrtle Bell is a blighted being. I asked Ruby Gillis why Myrtle was blighted, and Ruby said she guessed it was because her young man had gone back on her. Ruby Gillis thinks of nothing but young men, and the older she gets the worse she is. Young men are all very well in their place, but it doesn't do to drag them into everything, does it? Diana and I are thinking seriously of promising each other that we will never marry but be nice old maids and live together forever. Diana hasn't quite made up her mind though, because she thinks perhaps it would be nobler to marry some wild, dashing, wicked young man and reform him. Diana and I talk a great deal about serious subjects now, you know. We feel that we are so much older than we used to be that it isn't becoming to talk of childish matters. It's such a solemn thing to be almost fourteen, Marilla. Miss Stacy took all us girls who are in our teens down to the brook last Wednesday, and talked to us about it. She said we couldn't be too careful what habits we formed and what ideals we acquired in our teens, because by the time we were twenty our characters would be developed and the foundation laid for our whole future life. And she said if the foundation was shaky we could never build anything really worth while on it. Diana and I talked the matter over coming home from school. We felt extremely solemn, Marilla. And we decided that we would try to be very careful indeed and form respectable habits and learn all we could and be as sensible as possible, so that by the time we were twenty our characters would be properly developed. It's perfectly appalling to think of being twenty, Marilla. It sounds so fearfully old and grown up. But why was Miss Stacy here this afternoon?"

"That is what I want to tell you, Anne, if you'll ever give me a chance to get a word in edgewise. She was talking about you."

"About me?" Anne looked rather scared. Then she flushed and exclaimed:

"Oh, I know what she was saying. I meant to tell you, Marilla, honestly I did, but I forgot. Miss Stacy caught me reading *Ben Hur* in school yesterday afternoon when I should have been studying my Canadian history. Jane Andrews lent it to me. I was reading it at dinner hour, and I had just got to the chariot race when school went in. I was simply wild to know how it turned out—although I felt sure *Ben Hur* must win, because it wouldn't be poetical justice if he didn't—so I spread the history open on my desk lid and then tucked *Ben Hur* between the desk and my knee. I just looked as if I were studying Canadian history, you know, while all the while I was reveling in Ben Hur. I was so interested in it that I never noticed Miss Stacy coming down the aisle until all at once I just looked up and there she was looking down at me, so reproachful-like. I can't tell you how ashamed I felt, Marilla, especially when I heard Josie Pye giggling. Miss Stacy took *Ben Hur* away, but she never said a word then. She kept me in at recess and talked to me. She said I had done very wrong in two respects. First, I was wasting the time I ought to have put on my studies; and secondly, I was deceiving my teacher in trying to make it appear I was reading a history when it was a storybook instead. I had never realized until that moment, Marilla, that what I was doing was deceitful. I was shocked. I cried bitterly, and asked Miss Stacy to forgive me and I'd never do such a thing again; and I offered to do penance by never so much as looking at *Ben Hur* for a whole week, not even to see how the chariot race turned out. But Miss Stacy said she wouldn't require that, and she forgave me freely. So I think it wasn't very kind of her to come up here to you about it after all."

"Miss Stacy never mentioned such a thing to me, Anne, and its only your guilty conscience that's the matter with you. You have no business to be taking storybooks to school. You read too many novels anyhow. When I was a girl I wasn't so much as allowed to look at a novel."

"Oh, how can you call *Ben Hur* a novel when it's really such a religious book?" protested Anne. "Of course it's a little too exciting to be proper reading for Sunday, and I only read it on weekdays. And I never read *any* book now unless either Miss Stacy or Mrs. Allan thinks it is a proper book for a girl thirteen and three-quarters to read. Miss Stacy made me promise that. She found me reading a book one day called, *The Lurid Mystery of the Haunted Hall.* It was one Ruby Gillis had lent me, and, oh, Marilla, it was so fascinating and creepy. It just curdled the blood in my veins. But Miss Stacy said it was a very silly, unwholesome book, and she asked me not to read any more of it or any like it. I didn't mind promising not to read any more like it, but it was *agonizing* to give back that book without knowing how it turned out. But my love for Miss Stacy stood the test and I did. It's really wonderful, Marilla, what you can do when you're truly anxious to please a certain person."

"Well, I guess I'll light the lamp and get to work," said Marilla. "I see plainly that you don't want to hear what Miss Stacy had to say. You're more interested in the sound of your own tongue than in anything else."

"Oh, indeed, Marilla, I do want to hear it," cried Anne contritely. "I won't say another word—not one. I know I talk too much, but I am really trying to overcome it, and although I say far too much, yet if you only knew how many things I want to say and don't, you'd give me some credit for it. Please tell me, Marilla."

"Well, Miss Stacy wants to organize a class among her advanced students who mean to study for the entrance examination into Queen's. She intends to give them extra lessons for an hour after school. And she came to ask Matthew and me if we would like to have you join it. What do you think about it yourself, Anne? Would you like to go to Queen's and pass for a teacher?"

"Oh, Marilla!" Anne straightened to her knees and clasped her hands. "It's been the dream of my life—that is, for the last six months, ever since Ruby and Jane began to talk of studying for the Entrance. But I didn't say anything about it, because I supposed it would be perfectly useless. I'd love to be a teacher. But won't it be dreadfully expensive? Mr. Andrews says it cost him one hundred and fifty dollars to put Prissy through, and Prissy wasn't a dunce in geometry."

"I guess you needn't worry about that part of it. When Matthew and I took you to bring up we resolved we would do the best we could for you and give you a good education. I believe in a girl being fitted to earn her own living whether she ever has to or not. You'll always have a home at Green Gables as long as Matthew and I are here, but nobody knows what is going to happen in this uncertain world, and it's just as well to be prepared. So you can join the Queen's class if you like, Anne."

"Oh, Marilla, thank you." Anne flung her arms about Marilla's waist and looked up earnestly into her face. "I'm extremely grateful to you and Matthew. And I'll study as hard as I can and do my very best to be a credit to you. I warn you not to expect much in geometry, but I think I can hold my own in anything else if I work hard."

"I dare say you'll get along well enough. Miss Stacy says you are bright and diligent." Not for worlds would Marilla have told Anne just what Miss Stacy had said about her; that would have been to pamper vanity. "You needn't rush to any extreme of killing yourself over your books. There is no hurry. You won't be ready to try the Entrance for a year and a half yet. But it's well to begin in time and be thoroughly grounded, Miss Stacy says."

"I shall take more interest than ever in my studies now," said Anne blissfully, "because I have a purpose in life. Mr. Allan says everybody should have a purpose in life and pursue it faithfully. Only he says we must first make sure that it is a worthy purpose. I would call it a worthy purpose to want to be a teacher like Miss Stacy, wouldn't you, Marilla? I think it's a very noble profession."

The Queen's class was organized in due time. Gilbert Blythe, Anne Shirley, Ruby Gillis, Jane Andrews, Josie Pye, Charlie Sloane, and Moody Spurgeon MacPherson joined it. Diana Barry did not, as her parents did not intend to send her to Queen's. This seemed nothing short of a calamity to Anne. Never, since the night on which Minnie May had had the croup, had she and Diana been separated in anything. On the evening when the Queen's class first remained in school for the extra lessons and Anne saw Diana go slowly out with the others, to walk home alone through the Birch Path and Violet Vale, it was all the former could do to keep her seat and refrain from rushing impulsively after her chum. A lump came into her throat, and she hastily retired behind the pages of her uplifted Latin grammar to hide the tears in her eyes. Not for worlds would Anne have had Gilbert Blythe or Josie Pye see those tears.

"But, oh, Marilla, I really felt that I had tasted the bitterness of death, as Mr. Allan said in his sermon last Sunday, when I saw Diana go out alone," she said mournfully that night. "I thought how splendid it would have been if Diana had only been going to study for the Entrance, too.

But we can't have things perfect in this imperfect world, as Mrs. Lynde says. Mrs. Lynde isn't exactly a comforting person sometimes, but there's no doubt she says a great many very true things. And I think the Queen's class is going to be extremely interesting. Jane and Ruby are just going to study to be teachers. That is the height of their ambition. Ruby says she will only teach for two years after she gets through, and then she intends to be married. Jane says she will devote her whole life to teaching, and never, never marry, because you are paid a salary for teaching, but a husband won't pay you anything, and growls if you ask for a share in the egg and butter money. I expect Jane speaks from mournful experience, for Mrs. Lynde says that her father is a perfect old crank, and meaner than second skimmings. Josie Pye says she is just going to college for education's sake, because she won't have to earn her own living; she says of course it is different with orphans who are living on charity—*they* have to hustle. Moody Spurgeon is going to be a minister. Mrs. Lynde says he couldn't be anything else with a name like that to live up to. I hope it isn't wicked of me, Marilla, but really the thought of Moody Spurgeon being a minister makes me laugh. He's such a funny-looking boy with that big fat face, and his little blue eyes, and his ears sticking out like flaps. But perhaps he will be more intellectual-looking when he grows up. Charlie Sloane says he's going to go into politics and be a member of Parliament, but Mrs. Lynde says he'll never succeed at that, because the Sloanes are all honest people, and it's only rascals that get on in politics nowadays."

"What is Gilbert Blythe going to be?" queried Marilla, seeing that Anne was opening her Caesar.

"I don't happen to know what Gilbert Blythe's ambition in life is—if he has any," said Anne scornfully.

There was open rivalry between Gilbert and Anne now. Previously the rivalry had been rather one-sided, but there was no longer any doubt that Gilbert was as determined to be first in class as Anne was. He was a foeman worthy of her steel. The other members of the class tacitly acknowledged their superiority, and never dreamed of trying to compete with them.

Since the day by the pond when she had refused to listen to his plea for forgiveness, Gilbert, save for the aforesaid determined rivalry, had evinced no recognition whatever of the existence of Anne Shirley. He talked and jested with the other girls, exchanged books and puzzles with them, discussed lessons and plans, sometimes walked home with one or the other of them from prayer meeting or Debating Club. But Anne Shirley he simply ignored, and Anne found out that it is not pleasant to be ignored. It was in vain that she told herself with a toss of her head that she did not care. Deep down in her wayward, feminine little heart she knew that she did care, and that if she had that chance of the Lake of Shining Waters again she would answer very differently. All at once, as it seemed, and to her secret dismay, she found that the old resentment she had cherished against him was gone—gone just when she most needed its sustaining power. It was in vain that she recalled every incident and emotion of that memorable occasion and tried to feel the old satisfying anger. That day by the pond had witnessed its last spasmodic flicker. Anne realized that she had forgiven and forgotten without knowing it. But it was too late.

And at least neither Gilbert nor anybody else, not even Diana, should ever suspect how sorry she was and how much she wished she hadn't been so proud and horrid! She determined to "shroud her feelings in deepest oblivion," and it may be stated here and now that she did it, so successfully that Gilbert, who possibly was not quite so indifferent as he seemed, could not console himself with any belief that Anne felt his retaliatory scorn. The only poor comfort he had was that she snubbed Charlie Sloane, unmercifully, continually, and undeservedly.

Otherwise the winter passed away in a round of pleasant duties and studies. For Anne the days slipped by like golden beads on the necklace of the year. She was happy, eager, interested; there were lessons to be learned and honors to be won; delightful books to read; new pieces to be practiced for the Sunday school choir; pleasant Saturday afternoons at the manse with Mrs. Allan; and then, almost before Anne realized it, spring had come again to Green Gables and all the world was abloom once more.

Studies palled just a wee bit then; the Queen's class, left behind in school while the others scattered to green lanes and leafy wood cuts and meadow byways, looked wistfully out of the windows and discovered that Latin verbs and French exercises had somehow lost the tang and zest they had possessed in the crisp winter months. Even Anne and Gilbert lagged and grew indifferent. Teacher and taught were alike glad when the term was ended and the glad vacation days stretched rosily before them.

"But you've done good work this past year," Miss Stacy told them on the last evening, "and you deserve a good, jolly vacation. Have the best time you can in the out-of-door world and lay in a good stock of health and vitality and ambition to carry you through next year. It will be the tug of war, you know—the last year before the Entrance."

"Are you going to be back next year, Miss Stacy?" asked Josie Pye.

Josie Pye never scrupled to ask questions; in this instance the rest of the class felt grateful to her; none of them would have dared to ask it of Miss Stacy, but all wanted to, for there had been alarming rumors running at large through the school for some time that Miss Stacy was not coming back the next year—that she had been offered a position in the grade school of her own home district and meant to accept. The Queen's class listened in breathless suspense for her answer.

"Yes, I think I will," said Miss Stacy. "I thought of taking another school, but I have decided to come back to Avonlea. To tell the truth, I've grown so interested in my pupils here that I found I couldn't leave them. So I'll stay and see you through."

"Hurrah!" said Moody Spurgeon. Moody Spurgeon had never been so carried away by his feelings before, and he blushed uncomfortably every time he thought about it for a week.

"Oh, I'm so glad," said Anne, with shining eyes. "Dear Miss Stacy, it would be perfectly dreadful if you didn't come back. I don't believe I could have the heart to go on with my studies at all if another teacher came here." When Anne got home that night she stacked all her textbooks away in an old trunk in the attic, locked it, and threw the key into the blanket box.

"I'm not even going to look at a schoolbook in vacation," she told Marilla. "I've studied as hard all the term as I possibly could and I've pored over that geometry until I know every proposition in the first book off by heart, even when the letters *are* changed. I just feel tired of everything sensible and I'm going to let my imagination run riot for the summer. Oh, you needn't be alarmed, Marilla. I'll only let it run riot within reasonable limits. But I want to have a real good jolly time this summer, for maybe it's the last summer I'll be a little girl. Mrs. Lynde says that if I keep stretching out next year as I've done this I'll have to put on longer skirts. She says I'm all running to legs and eyes. And when I put on longer skirts I shall feel that I have to live up to them and be very dignified. It won't even do to believe in fairies then, I'm afraid;

so I'm going to believe in them with all my whole heart this summer. I think we're going to have a very gay vacation. Ruby Gillis is going to have a birthday party soon and there's the Sunday school picnic and the missionary concert next month. And Mr. Barry says that some evening he'll take Diana and me over to the White Sands Hotel and have dinner there. They have dinner there in the evening, you know. Jane Andrews was over once last summer and she says it was a dazzling sight to see the electric lights and the flowers and all the lady guests in such beautiful dresses. Jane says it was her first glimpse into high life and she'll never forget it to her dying day."

Mrs. Lynde came up the next afternoon to find out why Marilla had not been at the Aid meeting on Thursday. When Marilla was not at Aid meeting people knew there was something wrong at Green Gables.

"Matthew had a bad spell with his heart Thursday," Marilla explained, "and I didn't feel like leaving him. Oh, yes, he's all right again now, but he takes them spells oftener than he used to and I'm anxious about him. The doctor says he must be careful to avoid excitement. That's easy enough, for Matthew doesn't go about looking for excitement by any means and never did, but he's not to do any very heavy work either and you might as well tell Matthew not to breathe as not to work. Come and lay off your things, Rachel. You'll stay to tea?"

"Well, seeing you're so pressing, perhaps I might as well stay," said Mrs. Rachel, who had not the slightest intention of doing anything else.

Mrs. Rachel and Marilla sat comfortably in the parlor while Anne got the tea and made hot biscuits that were light and white enough to defy even Mrs. Rachel's criticism.

"I must say Anne has turned out a real smart girl," admitted Mrs. Rachel, as Marilla accompanied her to the end of the lane at sunset. "She must be a great help to you."

"She is," said Marilla, "and she's real steady and reliable now. I used to be afraid she'd never get over her featherbrained ways, but she has and I wouldn't be afraid to trust her in anything now."

"I never would have thought she'd have turned out so well that first day I was here three years ago," said Mrs. Rachel. "Lawful heart, shall I ever forget that tantrum of hers! When I went home that night I says to Thomas, says I, 'Mark my words, Thomas, Marilla Cuthbert'll live to rue the step she's took.' But I was mistaken and I'm real glad of it. I ain't one of those kind of people, Marilla, as can never be brought to own up that they've made a mistake. No, that never was my way, thank goodness. I did make a mistake in judging Anne, but it weren't no wonder, for an odder, unexpecteder witch of a child there never was in this world, that's what. There was no ciphering her out by the rules that worked with other children. It's nothing short of wonderful how she's improved these three years, but especially in looks. She's a real pretty girl got to be, though I can't say I'm overly partial to that pale, big-eyed style myself. I like more snap and color, like Diana Barry has or Ruby Gillis. Ruby Gillis's looks are real showy. But somehow—I don't know how it is but when Anne and them are together, though she ain't half as handsome, she makes them look kind of common and overdone—something like them white June lilies she calls narcissus alongside of the big, red peonies, that's what."

CHAPTER XXXI

WHERE THE BROOK AND RIVER MEET

Anne had her "good" summer and enjoyed it wholeheartedly. She and Diana fairly lived outdoors, reveling in all the delights that Lover's Lane and the Dryad's Bubble and Willowmere and Victoria Island afforded. Marilla offered no objections to Anne's gypsyings. The Spencervale doctor who had come the night Minnie May had the croup met Anne at the house of a patient one afternoon early in vacation, looked her over sharply, screwed up his mouth, shook his head, and sent a message to Marilla Cuthbert by another person. It was:

"Keep that redheaded girl of yours in the open air all summer and don't let her read books until she gets more spring into her step."

This message frightened Marilla wholesomely. She read Anne's death warrant by consumption in it unless it was scrupulously obeyed. As a result, Anne had the golden summer of her life as far as freedom and frolic went. She walked, rowed, berried, and dreamed to her heart's content; and when September came she was bright-eyed and alert, with a step that would have satisfied the Spencervale doctor and a heart full of ambition and zest once more.

"I feel just like studying with might and main," she declared as she brought her books down from the attic. "Oh, you good old friends, I'm glad to see your honest faces once more—yes, even you, geometry. I've had a perfectly beautiful summer, Marilla, and now I'm rejoicing as a strong man to run a race, as Mr. Allan said last Sunday. Doesn't Mr. Allan preach magnificent sermons? Mrs. Lynde says he is improving every day and the first thing we know some city church will gobble him up and then we'll be left and have to turn to and break in another green preacher. But I don't see the use of meeting trouble halfway, do you, Marilla? I think it would be better just to enjoy Mr. Allan while we have him. If I were a man I think I'd be a minister. They can have such an influence for good, if their theology is sound; and it must be thrilling to preach splendid sermons and stir your hearers' hearts. Why can't women be ministers, Marilla? I asked Mrs. Lynde that and she was shocked and said it would be a scandalous thing. She said there might be female ministers in the States and she believed there was, but thank goodness we hadn't got to that stage in Canada yet and she hoped we never would. But I don't see why. I think women would make splendid ministers. When there is a social to be got up or a church tea or anything else to raise money the women have to turn to and do the work. I'm sure Mrs. Lynde can pray every bit as well as Superintendent Bell and I've no doubt she could preach too with a little practice."

"Yes, I believe she could," said Marilla dryly. "She does plenty of unofficial preaching as it is. Nobody has much of a chance to go wrong in Avonlea with Rachel to oversee them."

"Marilla," said Anne in a burst of confidence, "I want to tell you something and ask you what you think about it. It has worried me terribly—on Sunday afternoons, that is, when I think specially about such matters. I do really want to be good; and when I'm with you or Mrs. Allan or Miss Stacy I want it more than ever and I want to do just what would please you and what you would approve of. But mostly when I'm with Mrs. Lynde I feel desperately wicked and as if I wanted to go and do the very thing she tells me I oughtn't to do. I feel irresistibly tempted to do it. Now, what do you think is the reason I feel like that? Do you think it's because I'm really bad and unregenerate?"

Marilla looked dubious for a moment. Then she laughed.

"If you are I guess I am too, Anne, for Rachel often has that very effect on me. I sometimes think she'd have more of an influence for good, as you say yourself, if she didn't keep nagging people to do right. There should have been a special commandment against nagging. But there, I shouldn't talk so. Rachel is a good Christian woman and she means well. There isn't a kinder soul in Avonlea and she never shirks her share of work."

"I'm very glad you feel the same," said Anne decidedly. "It's so encouraging. I shan't worry so much over that after this. But I dare say there'll be other things to worry me. They keep coming up new all the time—things to perplex you, you know. You settle one question and there's another right after. There are so many things to be thought over and decided when you're beginning to grow up. It keeps me busy all the time thinking them over and deciding what is right. It's a serious thing to grow up, isn't it, Marilla? But when I have such good friends as you and Matthew and Mrs. Allan and Miss Stacy I ought to grow up successfully, and I'm sure it will be my own fault if I don't. I feel it's a great responsibility because I have only the one chance. If I don't grow up right I can't go back and begin over again. I've grown two inches this summer, Marilla. Mr. Gillis measured me at Ruby's party. I'm so glad you made my new dresses longer. That dark-green one is so pretty and it was sweet of you to put on the flounce. Of course I know it wasn't really necessary, but flounces are so stylish this fall and Josie Pye has flounces on all her dresses. I know I'll be able to study better because of mine. I shall have such a comfortable feeling deep down in my mind about that flounce."

"It's worth something to have that," admitted Marilla.

Miss Stacy came back to Avonlea school and found all her pupils eager for work once more. Especially did the Queen's class gird up their loins for the fray, for at the end of the coming year, dimly shadowing their pathway already, loomed up that fateful thing known as "the Entrance," at the thought of which one and all felt their hearts sink into their very shoes. Suppose they did not pass! That thought was doomed to haunt Anne through the waking hours of that winter, Sunday afternoons inclusive, to the almost entire exclusion of moral and theological problems. When Anne had bad dreams she found herself staring miserably at pass lists of the Entrance exams, where Gilbert Blythe's name was blazoned at the top and in which hers did not appear at all.

But it was a jolly, busy, happy swift-flying winter. Schoolwork was as interesting, class rivalry as absorbing, as of yore. New worlds of thought, feeling, and ambition, fresh, fascinating fields of unexplored knowledge seemed to be opening out before Anne's eager eyes.

"Hills peeped o'er hill and Alps on Alps arose."

Much of all this was due to Miss Stacy's tactful, careful, broadminded guidance. She led her class to think and explore and discover for themselves and encouraged straying from the old beaten paths to a degree that quite shocked Mrs. Lynde and the school trustees, who viewed all innovations on established methods rather dubiously.

Apart from her studies Anne expanded socially, for Marilla, mindful of the Spencervale doctor's dictum, no longer vetoed occasional outings. The Debating Club flourished and gave several concerts; there were one or two parties almost verging on grown-up affairs; there were sleigh drives and skating frolics galore.

Betweentimes Anne grew, shooting up so rapidly that Marilla was astonished one day, when they were standing side by side, to find the girl was taller than herself.

"Why, Anne, how you've grown!" she said, almost unbelievingly. A sigh followed on the words. Marilla felt a queer regret over Anne's inches. The child she had learned to love had vanished somehow and here was this tall, serious-eyed girl of fifteen, with the thoughtful brow and the proudly poised little head, in her place. Marilla loved the girl as much as she had loved the child, but she was conscious of a queer sorrowful sense of loss. And that night, when Anne had gone to prayer meeting with Diana, Marilla sat alone in the wintry twilight and indulged in the weakness of a cry. Matthew, coming in with a lantern, caught her at it and gazed at her in such consternation that Marilla had to laugh through her tears.

"I was thinking about Anne," she explained. "She's got to be such a big girl—and she'll probably be away from us next winter. I'll miss her terrible."

"She'll be able to come home often," comforted Matthew, to whom Anne was as yet and always would be the little, eager girl he had brought home from Bright River on that June evening four years before. "The branch railroad will be built to Carmody by that time."

"It won't be the same thing as having her here all the time," sighed Marilla gloomily, determined to enjoy her luxury of grief uncomforted. "But there—men can't understand these things!"

There were other changes in Anne no less real than the physical change. For one thing, she became much quieter. Perhaps she thought all the more and dreamed as much as ever, but she certainly talked less. Marilla noticed and commented on this also.

"You don't chatter half as much as you used to, Anne, nor use half as many big words. What has come over you?"

Anne colored and laughed a little, as she dropped her book and looked dreamily out of the window, where big fat red buds were bursting out on the creeper in response to the lure of the spring sunshine.

"I don't know—I don't want to talk as much," she said, denting her chin thoughtfully with her forefinger. "It's nicer to think dear, pretty thoughts and keep them in one's heart, like treasures. I don't like to have them laughed at or wondered over. And somehow I don't want to use big words any more. It's almost a pity, isn't it, now that I'm really growing big enough to say them if I did want to. It's fun to be almost grown up in some ways, but it's not the kind of fun I expected, Marilla. There's so much to learn and do and think that there isn't time for big words. Besides, Miss Stacy says the short ones are much stronger and better. She makes us write all our essays as simply as possible. It was hard at first. I was so used to crowding in all the fine big words I could think of—and I thought of any number of them. But I've got used to it now and I see it's so much better."

"What has become of your story club? I haven't heard you speak of it for a long time."

"The story club isn't in existence any longer. We hadn't time for it—and anyhow I think we had got tired of it. It was silly to be writing about love and murder and elopements and mysteries. Miss Stacy sometimes has us write a story for training in composition, but she won't let us write anything but what might happen in Avonlea in our own lives, and she criticizes it very sharply and makes us criticize our own too. I never thought my compositions had so many faults until I began to look for them myself. I felt so ashamed I wanted to give up altogether, but Miss Stacy said I could learn to write well if I only trained myself to be my own severest critic. And so I am trying to."

"You've only two more months before the Entrance," said Marilla. "Do you think you'll be able to get through?"

Anne shivered.

"I don't know. Sometimes I think I'll be all right—and then I get horribly afraid. We've studied hard and Miss Stacy has drilled us thoroughly, but we mayn't get through for all that. We've each got a stumbling block. Mine is geometry of course, and Jane's is Latin, and Ruby and Charlie's is algebra, and Josie's is arithmetic. Moody Spurgeon says he feels it in his bones that he is going to fail in English history. Miss Stacy is going to give us examinations in June just as hard as we'll have at the Entrance and mark us just as strictly, so we'll have some idea. I wish it was all over, Marilla. It haunts me. Sometimes I wake up in the night and wonder what I'll do if I don't pass."

"Why, go to school next year and try again," said Marilla unconcernedly.

"Oh, I don't believe I'd have the heart for it. It would be such a disgrace to fail, especially if Gil—if the others passed. And I get so nervous in an examination that I'm likely to make a mess of it. I wish I had nerves like Jane Andrews. Nothing rattles her."

Anne sighed and, dragging her eyes from the witcheries of the spring world, the beckoning day of breeze and blue, and the green things upspringing in the garden, buried herself resolutely in her book. There would be other springs, but if she did not succeed in passing the Entrance, Anne felt convinced that she would never recover sufficiently to enjoy them.

CHAPTER XXXII

THE PASS LIST IS OUT

With the end of June came the close of the term and the close of Miss Stacy's rule in Avonlea school. Anne and Diana walked home that evening feeling very sober indeed. Red eyes and damp handkerchiefs bore convincing testimony to the fact that Miss Stacy's farewell words must have been quite as touching as Mr. Phillips's had been under similar circumstances three years before. Diana looked back at the schoolhouse from the foot of the spruce hill and sighed deeply.

"It does seem as if it was the end of everything, doesn't it?" she said dismally.

"You oughtn't to feel half as badly as I do," said Anne, hunting vainly for a dry spot on her handkerchief. "You'll be back again next winter, but I suppose I've left the dear old school forever—if I have good luck, that is."

"It won't be a bit the same. Miss Stacy won't be there, nor you nor Jane nor Ruby probably. I shall have to sit all alone, for I couldn't bear to have another deskmate after you. Oh, we have had jolly times, haven't we, Anne? It's dreadful to think they're all over."

Two big tears rolled down by Diana's nose.

"If you would stop crying I could," said Anne imploringly. "Just as soon as I put away my hanky I see you brimming up and that starts me off again. As Mrs. Lynde says, 'If you can't be cheerful, be as cheerful as you can.' After all, I dare say I'll be back next year. This is one of the times I *know* I'm not going to pass. They're getting alarmingly frequent."

"Why, you came out splendidly in the exams Miss Stacy gave."

"Yes, but those exams didn't make me nervous. When I think of the real thing you can't imagine what a horrid cold fluttery feeling comes round my heart. And then my number is thirteen and Josie Pye says it's so unlucky. I am *not* superstitious and I know it can make no difference. But still I wish it wasn't thirteen."

"I do wish I was going in with you," said Diana. "Wouldn't we have a perfectly elegant time? But I suppose you'll have to cram in the evenings."

"No; Miss Stacy has made us promise not to open a book at all. She says it would only tire and confuse us and we are to go out walking and not think about the exams at all and go to bed early. It's good advice, but I expect it will be hard to follow; good advice is apt to be, I think. Prissy Andrews told me that she sat up half the night every night of her Entrance week and crammed for dear life; and I had determined to sit up *at least* as long as she did. It was so kind of your Aunt Josephine to ask me to stay at Beechwood while I'm in town."

"You'll write to me while you're in, won't you?"

"I'll write Tuesday night and tell you how the first day goes," promised Anne.

"I'll be haunting the post office Wednesday," vowed Diana.

Anne went to town the following Monday and on Wednesday Diana haunted the post office, as agreed, and got her letter.

"Dearest Diana," wrote Anne, "here it is Tuesday night and I'm writing this in the library at Beechwood. Last night I was horribly lonesome all alone in my room and wished so much you were with me. I couldn't 'cram' because I'd promised Miss Stacy not to, but it was as hard to keep from opening my history as it used to be to keep from reading a story before my lessons were learned.

"This morning Miss Stacy came for me and we went to the Academy, calling for Jane and Ruby and Josie on our way. Ruby asked me to feel her hands and they were as cold as ice. Josie said I looked as if I hadn't slept a wink and she didn't believe I was strong enough to stand the grind of the teacher's course even if I did get through. There are times and seasons even yet when I don't feel that I've made any great headway in learning to like Josie Pye!

"When we reached the Academy there were scores of students there from all over the Island. The first person we saw was Moody Spurgeon sitting on the steps and muttering away to himself. Jane asked him what on earth he was doing and he said he was repeating the multiplication table over and over to steady his nerves and for pity's sake not to interrupt him, because if he stopped for a moment he got frightened and forgot everything he ever knew, but the multiplication table kept all his facts firmly in their proper place!

"When we were assigned to our rooms Miss Stacy had to leave us. Jane and I sat together and Jane was so composed that I envied her. No need of the multiplication table for good, steady, sensible Jane! I wondered if I looked as I felt and if they could hear my heart thumping clear across the room. Then a man came in and began distributing the English examination sheets. My hands grew cold then and my head fairly whirled around as I picked it up. Just one awful moment—Diana, I felt exactly as I did four years ago when I asked Marilla if I might stay at Green Gables—and then everything cleared up in my mind and my heart began beating again—I forgot to say that it had stopped altogether!—for I knew I could do something with that paper anyhow.

"At noon we went home for dinner and then back again for history in the afternoon. The history was a pretty hard paper and I got dreadfully mixed up in the dates. Still, I think I did fairly well today. But oh, Diana, tomorrow the geometry exam comes off and when I think of it it takes every bit of determination I possess to keep from opening my Euclid. If I thought the multiplication table would help me any I would recite it from now till tomorrow morning.

"I went down to see the other girls this evening. On my way I met Moody Spurgeon wandering distractedly around. He said he knew he had failed in history and he was born to be a disappointment to his parents and he was going home on the morning train; and it would be easier to be a carpenter than a minister, anyhow. I cheered him up and persuaded him to stay to the end because it would be unfair to Miss Stacy if he didn't. Sometimes I have wished I was born a boy, but when I see Moody Spurgeon I'm always glad I'm a girl and not his sister.

"Ruby was in hysterics when I reached their boardinghouse; she had just discovered a fearful mistake she had made in her English paper. When she recovered we went uptown and had an ice cream. How we wished you had been with us.

"Oh, Diana, if only the geometry examination were over! But there, as Mrs. Lynde would say, the sun will go on rising and setting whether I fail in geometry or not. That is true but not especially comforting. I think I'd rather it didn't go on if I failed!

Yours devotedly,
Anne"

The geometry examination and all the others were over in due time and Anne arrived home on Friday evening, rather tired but with an air of chastened triumph about her. Diana was over at Green Gables when she arrived and they met as if they had been parted for years.

"You old darling, it's perfectly splendid to see you back again. It seems like an age since you went to town and oh, Anne, how did you get along?"

"Pretty well, I think, in everything but the geometry. I don't know whether I passed in it or not and I have a creepy, crawly presentiment that I didn't. Oh, how good it is to be back! Green Gables is the dearest, loveliest spot in the world."

"How did the others do?"

"The girls say they know they didn't pass, but I think they did pretty well. Josie says the geometry was so easy a child of ten could do it! Moody Spurgeon still thinks he failed in history and Charlie says he failed in algebra. But we don't really know anything about it and won't until the pass list is out. That won't be for a fortnight. Fancy living a fortnight in such suspense! I wish I could go to sleep and never wake up until it is over."

Diana knew it would be useless to ask how Gilbert Blythe had fared, so she merely said:

"Oh, you'll pass all right. Don't worry."

"I'd rather not pass at all than not come out pretty well up on the list," flashed Anne, by which she meant—and Diana knew she meant—that success would be incomplete and bitter if she did not come out ahead of Gilbert Blythe.

With this end in view Anne had strained every nerve during the examinations. So had Gilbert. They had met and passed each other on the street a dozen times without any sign of recognition and every time Anne had held her head a little higher and wished a little more earnestly that she had made friends with Gilbert when he asked her, and vowed a little more determinedly to surpass him in the examination. She knew that all Avonlea junior was wondering which would come out first; she even knew that Jimmy Glover and Ned Wright had a bet on the question and that Josie Pye had said there was no doubt in the world that Gilbert would be first; and she felt that her humiliation would be unbearable if she failed.

But she had another and nobler motive for wishing to do well. She wanted to "pass high" for the sake of Matthew and Marilla—especially Matthew. Matthew had declared to her his conviction that she "would beat the whole Island." That, Anne felt, was something it would be foolish to hope for even in the wildest dreams. But she did hope fervently that she would be among the first ten at least, so that she might see Matthew's kindly brown eyes gleam with pride in her achievement. That, she felt, would be a sweet reward indeed for all her hard work and patient grubbing among unimaginative equations and conjugations.

At the end of the fortnight Anne took to "haunting" the post office also, in the distracted company of Jane, Ruby, and Josie, opening the Charlottetown dailies with shaking hands and cold, sinkaway feelings as bad as any experienced during the Entrance week. Charlie and Gilbert were not above doing this too, but Moody Spurgeon stayed resolutely away.

"I haven't got the grit to go there and look at a paper in cold blood," he told Anne. "I'm just going to wait until somebody comes and tells me suddenly whether I've passed or not."

When three weeks had gone by without the pass list appearing Anne began to feel that she really couldn't stand the strain much longer. Her appetite failed and her interest in Avonlea doings languished. Mrs. Lynde wanted to know what else you could expect with a Tory superintendent of education at the head of affairs, and Matthew, noting Anne's paleness and indifference and the lagging steps that bore her home from the post office every afternoon, began seriously to wonder if he hadn't better vote Grit at the next election.

But one evening the news came. Anne was sitting at her open window, for the time forgetful of the woes of examinations and the cares of the world, as she drank in the beauty of the summer dusk, sweet-scented with flower breaths from the garden below and sibilant and rustling from the stir of poplars. The eastern sky above the firs was flushed faintly pink from the reflection of the west, and Anne was wondering dreamily if the spirit of color looked like that, when she saw Diana come flying down through the firs, over the log bridge, and up the slope, with a fluttering newspaper in her hand.

Anne sprang to her feet, knowing at once what that paper contained. The pass list was out! Her head whirled and her heart beat until it hurt her. She could not move a step. It seemed an hour to her before Diana came rushing along the hall and burst into the room without even knocking, so great was her excitement.

"Anne, you've passed," she cried, "passed the *very first*—you and Gilbert both—you're ties—but your name is first. Oh, I'm so proud!"

Diana flung the paper on the table and herself on Anne's bed, utterly breathless and incapable of further speech. Anne lighted the lamp, oversetting the match safe and using up half a dozen matches before her shaking hands could accomplish the task. Then she snatched up the paper. Yes, she had passed—there was her name at the very top of a list of two hundred! That moment was worth living for.

"You did just splendidly, Anne," puffed Diana, recovering sufficiently to sit up and speak, for Anne, starry-eyed and rapt, had not uttered a word. "Father brought the paper home from Bright River not ten minutes ago—it came out on the afternoon train, you know, and won't be here till tomorrow by mail—and when I saw the pass list I just rushed over like a wild thing. You've all passed, every one of you, Moody Spurgeon and all, although he's conditioned in history. Jane and Ruby did pretty well—they're halfway up—and so did Charlie. Josie just scraped through with three marks to spare, but you'll see she'll put on as many airs as if she'd led. Won't Miss Stacy be delighted? Oh, Anne, what does it feel like to see your name at the head of a pass list like that? If it were me I know I'd go crazy with joy. I am pretty near crazy as it is, but you're as calm and cool as a spring evening."

"I'm just dazzled inside," said Anne. "I want to say a hundred things, and I can't find words to say them in. I never dreamed of this—yes, I did too, just once! I let myself think *once*, 'What if I should come out first?' quakingly, you know, for it seemed so vain and presumptuous to think I could lead the Island. Excuse me a minute, Diana. I must run right out to the field to tell Matthew. Then we'll go up the road and tell the good news to the others."

They hurried to the hayfield below the barn where Matthew was coiling hay, and, as luck would have it, Mrs. Lynde was talking to Marilla at the lane fence.

"Oh, Matthew," exclaimed Anne, "I've passed and I'm first—or one of the first! I'm not vain, but I'm thankful."

"Well now, I always said it," said Matthew, gazing at the pass list delightedly. "I knew you could beat them all easy."

"You've done pretty well, I must say, Anne," said Marilla, trying to hide her extreme pride in Anne from Mrs. Rachel's critical eye. But that good soul said heartily:

"I just guess she has done well, and far be it from me to be backward in saying it. You're a credit to your friends, Anne, that's what, and we're all proud of you."

That night Anne, who had wound up the delightful evening with a serious little talk with Mrs. Allan at the manse, knelt sweetly by her open window in a great sheen of moonshine and murmured a prayer of gratitude and aspiration that came straight from her heart. There was in it thankfulness for the past and reverent petition for the future; and when she slept on her white pillow her dreams were as fair and bright and beautiful as maidenhood might desire.

CHAPTER XXXIII

THE HOTEL CONCERT

"Put on your white organdy, by all means, Anne," advised Diana decidedly.

They were together in the east gable chamber; outside it was only twilight—a lovely yellowish-green twilight with a clear-blue cloudless sky. A big round moon, slowly deepening from her pallid luster into burnished silver, hung over the Haunted Wood; the air was full of sweet summer sounds—sleepy birds twittering, freakish breezes, faraway voices and laughter. But in Anne's room the blind was drawn and the lamp lighted, for an important toilet was being made.

The east gable was a very different place from what it had been on that night four years before, when Anne had felt its bareness penetrate to the marrow of her spirit with its inhospitable chill. Changes had crept in, Marilla conniving at them resignedly, until it was as sweet and dainty a nest as a young girl could desire.

The velvet carpet with the pink roses and the pink silk curtains of Anne's early visions had certainly never materialized; but her dreams had kept pace with her growth, and it is not probable she lamented them. The floor was covered with a pretty matting, and the curtains that softened the high window and fluttered in the vagrant breezes were of pale-green art muslin. The walls, hung not with gold and silver brocade tapestry, but with a dainty apple-blossom paper, were adorned with a few good pictures given Anne by Mrs. Allan. Miss Stacy's photograph occupied the place of honor, and Anne made a sentimental point of keeping fresh flowers on the bracket under it. Tonight a spike of white lilies faintly perfumed the room like the dream of a fragrance. There was no "mahogany furniture," but there was a white-painted bookcase filled with books, a cushioned wicker rocker, a toilet table befrilled with white muslin, a quaint, gilt-framed mirror with chubby pink Cupids and purple grapes painted over its arched top, that used to hang in the spare room, and a low white bed.

Anne was dressing for a concert at the White Sands Hotel. The guests had got it up in aid of the Charlottetown hospital, and had hunted out all the available amateur talent in the surrounding districts to help it along. Bertha Sampson and Pearl Clay of the White Sands Baptist choir had been asked to sing a duet; Milton Clark of Newbridge was to give a violin solo; Winnie Adella Blair of Carmody was to sing a Scotch ballad; and Laura Spencer of Spencervale and Anne Shirley of Avonlea were to recite. As Anne would have said at one time, it was "an epoch in her life," and she was deliciously athrill with the excitement of it. Matthew was in the seventh heaven of gratified pride over the honor conferred on his Anne and Marilla was not far behind, although she would have died rather than admit it, and said she didn't think it was very proper for a lot of young folks to be gadding over to the hotel without any responsible person with them.

Anne and Diana were to drive over with Jane Andrews and her brother Billy in their double-seated buggy; and several other Avonlea girls and boys were going too. There was a party of visitors expected out from town, and after the concert a supper was to be given to the performers.

"Do you really think the organdy will be best?" queried Anne anxiously. "I don't think it's as pretty as my blue-flowered muslin—and it certainly isn't so fashionable."

"But it suits you ever so much better," said Diana. "It's so soft and frilly and clinging. The muslin is stiff, and makes you look too dressed up. But the organdy seems as if it grew on you."

Anne sighed and yielded. Diana was beginning to have a reputation for notable taste in dressing, and her advice on such subjects was much sought after. She was looking very pretty herself on this particular night in a dress of the lovely wild-rose pink, from which Anne was forever debarred; but she was not to take any part in the concert, so her appearance was of minor importance. All her pains were bestowed upon Anne, who, she vowed, must, for the credit of Avonlea, be dressed and combed and adorned to the Queen's taste.

"Pull out that frill a little more—so; here, let me tie your sash; now for your slippers. I'm going to braid your hair in two thick braids, and tie them halfway up with big white bows—no, don't pull out a single curl over your forehead—just have the soft part. There is no way you do your hair suits you so well, Anne, and Mrs. Allan says you look like a Madonna when you part it so. I shall fasten this little white house rose just behind your ear. There was just one on my bush, and I saved it for you."

"Shall I put my pearl beads on?" asked Anne. "Matthew brought me a string from town last week, and I know he'd like to see them on me."

Diana pursed up her lips, put her black head on one side critically, and finally pronounced in favor of the beads, which were thereupon tied around Anne's slim milk-white throat.

"There's something so stylish about you, Anne," said Diana, with unenvious admiration. "You hold your head with such an air. I suppose it's your figure. I am just a dumpling. I've always been afraid of it, and now I know it is so. Well, I suppose I shall just have to resign myself to it."

"But you have such dimples," said Anne, smiling affectionately into the pretty, vivacious face so near her own. "Lovely dimples, like little dents in cream. I have given up all hope of dimples. My dimple-dream will never come true; but so many of my dreams have that I mustn't complain. Am I all ready now?"

"All ready," assured Diana, as Marilla appeared in the doorway, a gaunt figure with grayer hair than of yore and no fewer angles, but with a much softer face. "Come right in and look at our elocutionist, Marilla. Doesn't she look lovely?"

Marilla emitted a sound between a sniff and a grunt.

"She looks neat and proper. I like that way of fixing her hair. But I expect she'll ruin that dress driving over there in the dust and dew with it, and it looks most too thin for these damp nights. Organdy's the most unserviceable stuff in the world anyhow, and I told Matthew so when he got it. But there is no use in saying anything to Matthew nowadays. Time was when he would take my advice, but now he just buys things for Anne regardless, and the clerks at Carmody know they can palm anything off on him. Just let them tell him a thing is pretty and fashionable, and Matthew plunks his money down for it. Mind you keep your skirt clear of the wheel, Anne, and put your warm jacket on."

Then Marilla stalked downstairs, thinking proudly how sweet Anne looked, with that

"One moonbeam from the forehead to the crown"

and regretting that she could not go to the concert herself to hear her girl recite.

"I wonder if it *is* too damp for my dress," said Anne anxiously.

"Not a bit of it," said Diana, pulling up the window blind. "It's a perfect night, and there won't be any dew. Look at the moonlight."

"I'm so glad my window looks east into the sun-rising," said Anne, going over to Diana. "It's so splendid to see the morning coming up over those long hills and glowing through those sharp fir tops. It's new every morning, and I feel as if I washed my very soul in that bath of earliest sunshine. Oh, Diana, I love this little room so dearly. I don't know how I'll get along without it when I go to town next month."

"Don't speak of your going away tonight," begged Diana. "I don't want to think of it, it makes me so miserable, and I do want to have a good time this evening. What are you going to recite, Anne? And are you nervous?"

"Not a bit. I've recited so often in public I don't mind at all now. I've decided to give 'The Maiden's Vow.' It's so pathetic. Laura Spencer is going to give a comic recitation, but I'd rather make people cry than laugh."

"What will you recite if they encore you?"

"They won't dream of encoring me," scoffed Anne, who was not without her own secret hopes that they would, and already visioned herself telling Matthew all about it at the next morning's breakfast table. "There are Billy and Jane now—I hear the wheels. Come on."

Billy Andrews insisted that Anne should ride on the front seat with him, so she unwillingly climbed up. She would have much preferred to sit back with the girls, where she could have laughed and chattered to her heart's content. There was not much of either laughter or chatter in Billy. He was a big, fat, stolid youth of twenty, with a round, expressionless face, and a painful lack of conversational gifts. But he admired Anne immensely, and was puffed up with pride over the prospect of driving to White Sands with that slim, upright figure beside him.

Anne, by dint of talking over her shoulder to the girls and occasionally passing a sop of civility to Billy—who grinned and chuckled and never could think of any reply until it was too late—contrived to enjoy the drive in spite of all. It was a night for enjoyment. The road was full of buggies, all bound for the hotel, and laughter, silver-clear, echoed and re-echoed along it. When they reached the hotel it was a blaze of light from top to bottom. They were met by the ladies of the concert committee, one of whom took Anne off to the performers' dressing room which was filled with the members of a Charlottetown Symphony Club, among whom Anne felt suddenly shy and frightened and countrified. Her dress, which, in the east gable, had seemed so dainty and pretty, now seemed simple and plain—too simple and plain, she thought, among all the silks and laces that glistened and rustled around her. What were her pearl beads compared to the diamonds of the big, handsome lady near her? And how poor her one wee white rose must look beside all the hothouse flowers the others wore! Anne laid her hat and jacket away, and shrank miserably into a corner. She wished herself back in the white room at Green Gables.

It was still worse on the platform of the big concert hall of the hotel, where she presently found herself. The electric lights dazzled her eyes, the perfume and hum bewildered her. She wished she were sitting down in the audience with Diana and Jane, who seemed to be having a splendid time away at the back. She was wedged in between a stout lady in pink silk and a tall, scornful-looking girl in a white-lace dress. The stout lady occasionally turned her head squarely around and surveyed Anne through her eyeglasses until Anne, acutely sensitive of being so scrutinized, felt that she must scream aloud; and the white-lace girl kept talking audibly to her next neighbor about the "country bumpkins" and "rustic belles" in the audience, languidly anticipating "such fun" from the displays of local talent on the program. Anne believed that she would hate that white-lace girl to the end of life.

Unfortunately for Anne, a professional elocutionist was staying at the hotel and had consented to recite. She was a lithe, dark-eyed woman in a wonderful gown of shimmering gray stuff like woven moonbeams, with gems on her neck and in her dark hair. She had a marvelously flexible voice and wonderful power of expression; the audience went wild over her selection. Anne, forgetting all about herself and her troubles for the time, listened with rapt and shining eyes; but when the recitation ended she suddenly put her hands over her face. She could never get up and recite after that—never. Had she ever thought she could recite? Oh, if she were only back at Green Gables!

At this unpropitious moment her name was called. Somehow Anne—who did not notice the rather guilty little start of surprise the white-lace girl gave, and would not have understood the subtle compliment implied therein if she had—got on her feet, and moved dizzily out to the front. She was so pale that Diana and Jane, down in the audience, clasped each other's hands in nervous sympathy. Anne was the victim of an overwhelming attack of stage fright. Often as she had recited in public, she had never before faced such an audience as this, and the sight of it paralyzed her energies completely. Everything was so strange, so brilliant, so bewildering—the rows of ladies in evening dress, the critical faces, the whole atmosphere of wealth and culture about her. Very different this from the plain benches at the Debating Club, filled with the homely, sympathetic faces of friends and neighbors. These people, she thought, would be merciless critics. Perhaps, like the white-lace girl, they anticipated amusement from her "rustic" efforts. She felt hopelessly, helplessly ashamed and miserable. Her knees trembled, her heart fluttered, a horrible faintness came over her; not a word could she utter, and the next moment she would have fled from the platform despite the humiliation which, she felt, must ever after be her portion if she did so.

But suddenly, as her dilated, frightened eyes gazed out over the audience, she saw Gilbert Blythe away at the back of the room, bending forward with a smile on his face—a smile which seemed to Anne at once triumphant and taunting. In reality it was nothing of the kind. Gilbert was merely smiling with appreciation of the whole affair in general and of the effect produced by Anne's slender white form and spiritual face against a background of palms in particular. Josie Pye, whom he had driven over, sat beside him, and her face certainly was both triumphant and taunting. But Anne did not see Josie, and would not have cared if she had. She drew a long breath and flung her head up proudly, courage and determination tingling over her like an electric shock. She *would not* fail before Gilbert Blythe—he should never be able to laugh at her, never, never! Her fright and nervousness vanished; and she began her recitation, her clear, sweet voice reaching to the farthest corner of the room without a tremor or a break. Self-possession was fully restored to her, and in the reaction from that horrible moment of powerlessness she recited as she had never done before. When she finished there were bursts of honest applause. Anne, stepping back to her seat, blushing with shyness and delight, found her hand vigorously clasped and shaken by the stout lady in pink silk.

"My dear, you did splendidly," she puffed. "I've been crying like a baby, actually I have. There, they're encoring you—they're bound to have you back!"

"Oh, I can't go," said Anne confusedly. "But yet—I must, or Matthew will be disappointed. He said they would encore me."

"Then don't disappoint Matthew," said the pink lady, laughing.

Smiling, blushing, limpid-eyed, Anne tripped back and gave a quaint, funny little selection that captivated her audience still further. The rest of the evening was quite a little triumph for her.

When the concert was over, the stout, pink lady—who was the wife of an American millionaire—took her under her wing, and introduced her to everybody; and everybody was very nice to her. The professional elocutionist, Mrs. Evans, came and chatted with her, telling her that she had a charming voice and "interpreted" her selections beautifully. Even the white-lace girl paid her a languid little compliment. They had supper in the big, beautifully decorated dining room; Diana and Jane were invited to partake of this, also, since they had come with Anne, but Billy was nowhere to be found, having decamped in mortal fear of some such invitation. He was in waiting for them, with the team, however, when it was all over, and the three girls came merrily out into the calm, white moonshine radiance. Anne breathed deeply, and looked into the clear sky beyond the dark boughs of the firs.

Oh, it was good to be out again in the purity and silence of the night! How great and still and wonderful everything was, with the murmur of the sea sounding through it and the darkling cliffs beyond like grim giants guarding enchanted coasts.

"Hasn't it been a perfectly splendid time?" sighed Jane, as they drove away. "I just wish I was a rich American and could spend my summer at a hotel and wear jewels and low-necked dresses and have ice cream and chicken salad every blessed day. I'm sure it would be ever so much more fun than teaching school. Anne, your recitation was simply great, although I thought at first you were never going to begin. I think it was better than Mrs. Evans's."

"Oh, no, don't say things like that, Jane," said Anne quickly, "because it sounds silly. It couldn't be better than Mrs. Evans's, you know, for she is a professional, and I'm only a schoolgirl, with a little knack of reciting. I'm quite satisfied if the people just liked mine pretty well."

"I've a compliment for you, Anne," said Diana. "At least I think it must be a compliment because of the tone he said it in. Part of it was anyhow. There was an American sitting behind Jane and me—such a romantic-looking man, with coal-black hair and eyes. Josie Pye says he is a distinguished artist, and that her mother's cousin in Boston is married to a man that used to go to school with him. Well, we heard him say—didn't we, Jane?—'Who is that girl on the platform with the splendid Titian hair? She has a face I should like to paint.' There now, Anne. But what does Titian hair mean?"

"Being interpreted it means plain red, I guess," laughed Anne. "Titian was a very famous artist who liked to paint red-haired women."

"*Did* you see all the diamonds those ladies wore?" sighed Jane. "They were simply dazzling. Wouldn't you just love to be rich, girls?"

"We *are* rich," said Anne staunchly. "Why, we have sixteen years to our credit, and we're happy as queens, and we've all got imaginations, more or less. Look at that sea, girls—all silver and shadow and vision of things not seen. We couldn't enjoy its loveliness any more if we had millions of dollars and ropes of diamonds. You wouldn't change into any of those women if you could. Would you want to be that white-lace girl and wear a sour look all your life, as if you'd been born turning up your nose at the world? Or the pink lady, kind and nice as she is, so stout and short that you'd really no figure at all? Or even Mrs. Evans, with that sad, sad look in her eyes? She must have been dreadfully unhappy sometime to have such a look. You *know* you wouldn't, Jane Andrews!"

"I *don't* know—exactly," said Jane unconvinced. "I think diamonds would comfort a person for a good deal."

"Well, I don't want to be anyone but myself, even if I go uncomforted by diamonds all my life," declared Anne. "I'm quite content to be Anne of Green Gables, with my string of pearl beads. I know Matthew gave me as much love with them as ever went with Madame the Pink Lady's jewels."

CHAPTER XXXIV

A QUEEN'S GIRL

The next three weeks were busy ones at Green Gables, for Anne was getting ready to go to Queen's, and there was much sewing to be done, and many things to be talked over and arranged. Anne's outfit was ample and pretty, for Matthew saw to that, and Marilla for once made no objections whatever to anything he purchased or suggested. More—one evening she went up to the east gable with her arms full of a delicate pale green material.

"Anne, here's something for a nice light dress for you. I don't suppose you really need it; you've plenty of pretty waists; but I thought maybe you'd like something real dressy to wear if you were asked out anywhere of an evening in town, to a party or anything like that. I hear that Jane and Ruby and Josie have got 'evening dresses,' as they call them, and I don't mean you shall be behind them. I got Mrs. Allan to help me pick it in town last week, and we'll get Emily Gillis to make it for you. Emily has got taste, and her fits aren't to be equaled."

"Oh, Marilla, it's just lovely," said Anne. "Thank you so much. I don't believe you ought to be so kind to me—it's making it harder every day for me to go away."

The green dress was made up with as many tucks and frills and shirrings as Emily's taste permitted. Anne put it on one evening for Matthew's and Marilla's benefit, and recited "The Maiden's Vow" for them in the kitchen. As Marilla watched the bright, animated face and graceful motions her thoughts went back to the evening Anne had arrived at Green Gables, and memory recalled a vivid picture of the odd, frightened child in her preposterous yellowish-brown wincey dress, the heartbreak looking out of her tearful eyes. Something in the memory brought tears to Marilla's own eyes.

"I declare, my recitation has made you cry, Marilla," said Anne gaily stooping over Marilla's chair to drop a butterfly kiss on that lady's cheek. "Now, I call that a positive triumph."

"No, I wasn't crying over your piece," said Marilla, who would have scorned to be betrayed into such weakness by any poetry stuff. "I just couldn't help thinking of the little girl you used to be, Anne. And I was wishing you could have stayed a little girl, even with all your queer ways. You've grown up now and you're going away; and you look so tall and stylish and so—so—different altogether in that dress—as if you didn't belong in Avonlea at all—and I just got lonesome thinking it all over."

"Marilla!" Anne sat down on Marilla's gingham lap, took Marilla's lined face between her hands, and looked gravely and tenderly into Marilla's eyes. "I'm not a bit changed—not really. I'm only just pruned down and branched out. The real *me*—back here—is just the same. It won't make a bit of difference where I go or how much I change outwardly; at heart I shall always be your little Anne, who will love you and Matthew and dear Green Gables more and better every day of her life."

Anne laid her fresh young cheek against Marilla's faded one, and reached out a hand to pat Matthew's shoulder. Marilla would have given much just then to have possessed Anne's power of putting her feelings into words; but nature and habit had willed it otherwise, and she could only put her arms close about her girl and hold her tenderly to her heart, wishing that she need never let her go.

Matthew, with a suspicious moisture in his eyes, got up and went out-of-doors. Under the stars of the blue summer night he walked agitatedly across the yard to the gate under the poplars.

"Well now, I guess she ain't been much spoiled," he muttered, proudly. "I guess my putting in my oar occasional never did much harm after all. She's smart and pretty, and loving, too, which is better than all the rest. She's been a blessing to us, and there never was a luckier mistake than what Mrs. Spencer made—if it *was* luck. I don't believe it was any such thing. It was Providence, because the Almighty saw we needed her, I reckon."

The day finally came when Anne must go to town. She and Matthew drove in one fine September morning, after a tearful parting with Diana and an untearful practical one—on Marilla's side at least—with Marilla. But when Anne had gone Diana dried her tears and went to a beach picnic at White Sands with some of her Carmody cousins, where she contrived to enjoy herself tolerably well; while Marilla plunged fiercely into unnecessary work and kept at it all day long with the bitterest kind of heartache—the ache that burns and gnaws and cannot wash itself away in ready tears. But that night, when Marilla went to bed, acutely and miserably conscious that the little gable room at the end of the hall was untenanted by any vivid young life and unstirred by any soft breathing, she buried her face in her pillow, and wept for her girl in a passion of sobs that appalled her when she grew calm enough to reflect how very wicked it must be to take on so about a sinful fellow creature.

Anne and the rest of the Avonlea scholars reached town just in time to hurry off to the Academy. That first day passed pleasantly enough in a whirl of excitement, meeting all the new students, learning to know the professors by sight and being assorted and organized into classes. Anne intended taking up the Second Year work being advised to do so by Miss Stacy; Gilbert Blythe elected to do the same. This meant getting a First Class teacher's license in one year instead of two, if they were successful; but it also meant much more and harder work. Jane, Ruby, Josie, Charlie, and Moody Spurgeon, not being troubled with the stirrings of ambition, were content to take up the Second Class work. Anne was conscious of a pang of loneliness when she found herself in a room with fifty other students, not one of whom she knew, except the tall, brown-haired boy across the room; and knowing him in the fashion she did, did not help her much, as she reflected pessimistically. Yet she was undeniably glad that they were in the same class; the old rivalry could still be carried on, and Anne would hardly have known what to do if it had been lacking.

"I wouldn't feel comfortable without it," she thought. "Gilbert looks awfully determined. I suppose he's making up his mind, here and now, to win the medal. What a splendid chin he has! I never noticed it before. I do wish Jane and Ruby had gone in for First Class, too. I suppose I won't feel so much like a cat in a strange garret when I get acquainted, though. I wonder which of the girls here are going to be my friends. It's really an interesting speculation. Of course I promised Diana that no Queen's girl, no matter how much I liked her, should ever be as dear to me as she is; but I've lots of second-best affections to bestow. I like the look of that girl with the brown eyes and the crimson waist. She looks vivid and red-rosy; there's that pale, fair one gazing out of the window. She has lovely hair, and looks as if she knew a thing or two about dreams. I'd like to know them both—know them well—well enough to walk with my arm about their waists, and call them nicknames. But just now I don't know them and they don't know me, and probably don't want to know me particularly. Oh, it's lonesome!"

It was lonesomer still when Anne found herself alone in her hall bedroom that night at twilight. She was not to board with the other girls, who all had relatives in town to take pity on them. Miss Josephine Barry would have liked to board her, but Beechwood was so far from the Academy that it was out of the question; so Miss Barry hunted up a boarding-house, assuring Matthew and Marilla that it was the very place for Anne.

"The lady who keeps it is a reduced gentlewoman," explained Miss Barry. "Her husband was a British officer, and she is very careful what sort of boarders she takes. Anne will not meet with any objectionable persons under her roof. The table is good, and the house is near the Academy, in a quiet neighborhood."

All this might be quite true, and indeed, proved to be so, but it did not materially help Anne in the first agony of homesickness that seized upon her. She looked dismally about her narrow little room, with its dull-papered, pictureless walls, its small iron bedstead and empty book-case; and a horrible choke came into her throat as she thought of her own white room at Green Gables, where she would have the pleasant consciousness of a great green still outdoors, of sweet peas growing in the garden, and moonlight falling on the orchard, of the brook below the slope and the spruce boughs tossing in the night wind beyond it, of a vast starry sky, and the light from Diana's window shining out through the gap in the trees. Here there was nothing of this; Anne knew that outside of her window was a hard street, with a network of telephone wires shutting out the sky, the tramp of alien feet, and a thousand lights gleaming on stranger faces. She knew that she was going to cry, and fought against it.

"I *won't* cry. It's silly—and weak—there's the third tear splashing down by my nose. There are more coming! I must think of something funny to stop them. But there's nothing funny except what is connected with Avonlea, and that only makes things worse—four—five—I'm going home next Friday, but that seems a hundred years away. Oh, Matthew is nearly home by now—and Marilla is at the gate, looking down the lane for him—six—seven—eight—oh, there's no use in counting them! They're coming in a flood presently. I can't cheer up—I don't *want* to cheer up. It's nicer to be miserable!"

The flood of tears would have come, no doubt, had not Josie Pye appeared at that moment. In the joy of seeing a familiar face Anne forgot that there had never been much love lost between her and Josie. As a part of Avonlea life even a Pye was welcome.

"I'm so glad you came up," Anne said sincerely.

"You've been crying," remarked Josie, with aggravating pity. "I suppose you're homesick—some people have so little self-control in that respect. I've no intention of being homesick, I can tell you. Town's too jolly after that poky old Avonlea. I wonder how I ever existed there so long. You shouldn't cry, Anne; it isn't becoming, for your nose and eyes get red, and then you seem *all* red. I'd a perfectly scrumptious time in the Academy today. Our French professor is simply a duck. His moustache would give you kerwollops of the heart. Have you anything eatable around, Anne? I'm literally starving. Ah, I guessed likely Marilla'd load you up with cake. That's why I called round. Otherwise I'd have gone to the park to hear the band play with Frank Stockley. He boards same place as I do, and he's a sport. He noticed you in class today, and asked me who the redheaded girl was. I told him you were an orphan that the Cuthberts had adopted, and nobody knew very much about what you'd been before that."

Anne was wondering if, after all, solitude and tears were not more satisfactory than Josie Pye's companionship when Jane and Ruby appeared, each with an inch of Queen's color ribbon—purple and scarlet—pinned proudly to her coat. As Josie was not "speaking" to Jane just then she had to subside into comparative harmlessness.

"Well," said Jane with a sigh, "I feel as if I'd lived many moons since the morning. I ought to be home studying my Virgil—that horrid old professor gave us twenty lines to start in on tomorrow. But I simply couldn't settle down to study tonight. Anne, methinks I see the traces of tears. If you've been crying *do* own up. It will restore my self-respect, for I was shedding tears freely before Ruby came along. I don't mind being a goose so much if somebody else is goosey, too. Cake? You'll give me a teeny piece, won't you? Thank you. It has the real Avonlea flavor."

Ruby, perceiving the Queen's calendar lying on the table, wanted to know if Anne meant to try for the gold medal.

Anne blushed and admitted she was thinking of it.

"Oh, that reminds me," said Josie, "Queen's is to get one of the

Avery scholarships after all. The word came today. Frank Stockley told me—his uncle is one of the board of governors, you know. It will be announced in the Academy tomorrow."

An Avery scholarship! Anne felt her heart beat more quickly, and the horizons of her ambition shifted and broadened as if by magic. Before Josie had told the news Anne's highest pinnacle of aspiration had been a teacher's provincial license, First Class, at the end of the year, and perhaps the medal! But now in one moment Anne saw herself winning the Avery scholarship, taking an Arts course at Redmond College, and graduating in a gown and mortar board, before the echo of Josie's words had died away. For the Avery scholarship was in English, and Anne felt that here her foot was on native heath.

A wealthy manufacturer of New Brunswick had died and left part of his fortune to endow a large number of scholarships to be distributed among the various high schools and academies of the Maritime Provinces, according to their respective standings. There had been much doubt whether one would be allotted to Queen's, but the matter was settled at last, and at the end of the year the graduate who made the highest mark in English and English Literature would win the scholarship—two hundred and fifty dollars a year for four years at Redmond College. No wonder that Anne went to bed that night with tingling cheeks!

"I'll win that scholarship if hard work can do it," she resolved. "Wouldn't Matthew be proud if I got to be a B.A.? Oh, it's delightful to have ambitions. I'm so glad I have such a lot. And there never seems to be any end to them—that's the best of it. Just as soon as you attain to one ambition you see another one glittering higher up still. It does make life so interesting."

CHAPTER XXXV

THE WINTER AT QUEEN'S

Anne's homesickness wore off, greatly helped in the wearing by her weekend visits home. As long as the open weather lasted the Avonlea students went out to Carmody on the new branch railway every Friday night. Diana and several other Avonlea young folks were generally on hand to meet them and they all walked over to Avonlea in a merry party. Anne thought those Friday evening gypsyings over the autumnal hills in the crisp golden air, with the home lights of Avonlea twinkling beyond, were the best and dearest hours in the whole week.

Gilbert Blythe nearly always walked with Ruby Gillis and carried her satchel for her. Ruby was a very handsome young lady, now thinking herself quite as grown up as she really was; she wore her skirts as long as her mother would let her and did her hair up in town, though she had to take it down when she went home. She had large, bright-blue eyes, a brilliant complexion, and a plump showy figure. She laughed a great deal, was cheerful and good-tempered, and enjoyed the pleasant things of life frankly.

"But I shouldn't think she was the sort of girl Gilbert would like," whispered Jane to Anne. Anne did not think so either, but she would not have said so for the Avery scholarship. She could not help thinking, too, that it would be very pleasant to have such a friend as Gilbert to jest and chatter with and exchange ideas about books and studies and ambitions. Gilbert had ambitions, she knew, and Ruby Gillis did not seem the sort of person with whom such could be profitably discussed.

There was no silly sentiment in Anne's ideas concerning Gilbert. Boys were to her, when she thought about them at all, merely possible good comrades. If she and Gilbert had been friends she would not have cared how many other friends he had nor with whom he walked. She had a genius for friendship; girl friends she had in plenty; but she had a vague consciousness that masculine friendship might also be a good thing to round out one's conceptions of companionship and furnish broader standpoints of judgment and comparison. Not that Anne could have put her feelings on the matter into just such clear definition. But she thought that if Gilbert had ever walked home with her from the train, over the crisp fields and along the ferny byways, they might have had many and merry and interesting conversations about the new world that was opening around them and their hopes and ambitions therein. Gilbert was a clever young fellow, with his own thoughts about things and a determination to get the best out of life and put the best into it. Ruby Gillis told Jane Andrews that she didn't understand half the things Gilbert Blythe said; he talked just like Anne Shirley did when she had a thoughtful fit on and for her part she didn't think it any fun to be bothering about books and that sort of thing when you didn't have to. Frank Stockley had lots more dash and go, but then he wasn't half as good-looking as Gilbert and she really couldn't decide which she liked best!

In the Academy Anne gradually drew a little circle of friends about her, thoughtful, imaginative, ambitious students like herself. With the "rose-red" girl, Stella Maynard, and the "dream girl," Priscilla Grant, she soon became intimate, finding the latter pale spiritual-looking maiden to be full to the brim of mischief and pranks and fun, while the vivid, black-eyed Stella had a heartful of wistful dreams and fancies, as aerial and rainbow-like as Anne's own.

After the Christmas holidays the Avonlea students gave up going home on Fridays and settled down to hard work. By this time all the Queen's scholars had gravitated into their own places in the ranks and the various classes had assumed distinct and settled shadings of individuality. Certain facts had become generally accepted. It was admitted that the medal contestants had practically narrowed down to three—Gilbert Blythe, Anne Shirley, and Lewis Wilson; the Avery scholarship was more doubtful, any one of a certain six being a possible winner. The bronze medal for mathematics was considered as good as won by a fat, funny little up-country boy with a bumpy forehead and a patched coat.

Ruby Gillis was the handsomest girl of the year at the Academy; in the Second Year classes Stella Maynard carried off the palm for beauty, with small but critical minority in favor of Anne Shirley. Ethel Marr was admitted by all competent judges to have the most stylish modes of hair-dressing, and Jane Andrews—plain, plodding, conscientious Jane—carried off the honors in the domestic science course. Even Josie

Pye attained a certain preeminence as the sharpest-tongued young lady in attendance at Queen's. So it may be fairly stated that Miss Stacy's old pupils held their own in the wider arena of the academical course.

Anne worked hard and steadily. Her rivalry with Gilbert was as intense as it had ever been in Avonlea school, although it was not known in the class at large, but somehow the bitterness had gone out of it. Anne no longer wished to win for the sake of defeating Gilbert; rather, for the proud consciousness of a well-won victory over a worthy foeman. It would be worth while to win, but she no longer thought life would be insupportable if she did not.

In spite of lessons the students found opportunities for pleasant times. Anne spent many of her spare hours at Beechwood and generally ate her Sunday dinners there and went to church with Miss Barry. The latter was, as she admitted, growing old, but her black eyes were not dim nor the vigor of her tongue in the least abated. But she never sharpened the latter on Anne, who continued to be a prime favorite with the critical old lady.

"That Anne-girl improves all the time," she said. "I get tired of other girls—there is such a provoking and eternal sameness about them. Anne has as many shades as a rainbow and every shade is the prettiest while it lasts. I don't know that she is as amusing as she was when she was a child, but she makes me love her and I like people who make me love them. It saves me so much trouble in making myself love them."

Then, almost before anybody realized it, spring had come; out in Avonlea the Mayflowers were peeping pinkly out on the sere barrens where snow-wreaths lingered; and the "mist of green" was on the woods and in the valleys. But in Charlottetown harassed Queen's students thought and talked only of examinations.

"It doesn't seem possible that the term is nearly over," said Anne. "Why, last fall it seemed so long to look forward to—a whole winter of studies and classes. And here we are, with the exams looming up next week. Girls, sometimes I feel as if those exams meant everything, but when I look at the big buds swelling on those chestnut trees and the misty blue air at the end of the streets they don't seem half so important."

Jane and Ruby and Josie, who had dropped in, did not take this view of it. To them the coming examinations were constantly very important indeed—far more important than chestnut buds or Maytime hazes. It was all very well for Anne, who was sure of passing at least, to have her moments of belittling them, but when your whole future depended on them—as the girls truly thought theirs did—you could not regard them philosophically.

"I've lost seven pounds in the last two weeks," sighed Jane. "It's no use to say don't worry. I *will* worry. Worrying helps you some—it seems as if you were doing something when you're worrying. It would be dreadful if I failed to get my license after going to Queen's all winter and spending so much money."

"*I* don't care," said Josie Pye. "If I don't pass this year I'm coming back next. My father can afford to send me. Anne, Frank Stockley says that Professor Tremaine said Gilbert Blythe was sure to get the medal and that Emily Clay would likely win the Avery scholarship."

"That may make me feel badly tomorrow, Josie," laughed Anne, "but just now I honestly feel that as long as I know the violets are coming out all purple down in the hollow below Green Gables and that little ferns are poking their heads up in Lovers' Lane, it's not a great deal of difference whether I win the Avery or not. I've done my best and I begin to understand what is meant by the 'joy of the strife.' Next to trying and winning, the best thing is trying and failing. Girls, don't talk about exams! Look at that arch of pale green sky over those houses and picture to yourself what it must look like over the purply-dark beechwoods back of Avonlea."

"What are you going to wear for commencement, Jane?" asked Ruby practically.

Jane and Josie both answered at once and the chatter drifted into a side eddy of fashions. But Anne, with her elbows on the window sill, her soft cheek laid against her clasped hands, and her eyes filled with visions, looked out unheedingly across city roof and spire to that glorious dome of sunset sky and wove her dreams of a possible future from the golden tissue of youth's own optimism. All the Beyond was hers with its possibilities lurking rosily in the oncoming years—each year a rose of promise to be woven into an immortal chaplet.

CHAPTER XXXVI

THE GLORY AND THE DREAM

On the morning when the final results of all the examinations were to be posted on the bulletin board at Queen's, Anne and Jane walked down the street together. Jane was smiling and happy; examinations were over and she was comfortably sure she had made a pass at least; further considerations troubled Jane not at all; she had no soaring ambitions and consequently was not affected with the unrest attendant thereon. For we pay a price for everything we get or take in this world; and although ambitions are well worth having, they are not to be cheaply won, but exact their dues of work and self-denial, anxiety and discouragement. Anne was pale and quiet; in ten more minutes she would know who had won the medal and who the Avery. Beyond those ten minutes there did not seem, just then, to be anything worth being called Time.

"Of course you'll win one of them anyhow," said Jane, who couldn't understand how the faculty could be so unfair as to order it otherwise.

"I have not hope of the Avery," said Anne. "Everybody says Emily Clay will win it. And I'm not going to march up to that bulletin board and look at it before everybody. I haven't the moral courage. I'm going straight to the girls' dressing room. You must read the announcements and then come and tell me, Jane. And I implore you in the name of our old friendship to do it as quickly as possible. If I have failed just say so, without trying to break it gently; and whatever you do *don't* sympathize with me. Promise me this, Jane."

Jane promised solemnly; but, as it happened, there was no necessity for such a promise. When they went up the entrance steps of Queen's they found the hall full of boys who were carrying Gilbert Blythe around on their shoulders and yelling at the tops of their voices, "Hurrah for Blythe, Medalist!"

For a moment Anne felt one sickening pang of defeat and disappointment. So she had failed and Gilbert had won! Well, Matthew would be sorry—he had been so sure she would win.

And then!

Somebody called out:

"Three cheers for Miss Shirley, winner of the Avery!"

"Oh, Anne," gasped Jane, as they fled to the girls' dressing room amid hearty cheers. "Oh, Anne I'm so proud! Isn't it splendid?"

And then the girls were around them and Anne was the center of a laughing, congratulating group. Her shoulders were thumped and her hands shaken vigorously. She was pushed and pulled and hugged and among it all she managed to whisper to Jane:

"Oh, won't Matthew and Marilla be pleased! I must write the news home right away."

Commencement was the next important happening. The exercises were held in the big assembly hall of the Academy. Addresses were given, essays read, songs sung, the public award of diplomas, prizes and medals made.

Matthew and Marilla were there, with eyes and ears for only one student on the platform—a tall girl in pale green, with faintly flushed cheeks and starry eyes, who read the best essay and was pointed out and whispered about as the Avery winner.

"Reckon you're glad we kept her, Marilla?" whispered Matthew, speaking for the first time since he had entered the hall, when Anne had finished her essay.

"It's not the first time I've been glad," retorted Marilla. "You do like to rub things in, Matthew Cuthbert."

Miss Barry, who was sitting behind them, leaned forward and poked Marilla in the back with her parasol.

"Aren't you proud of that Anne-girl? I am," she said.

Anne went home to Avonlea with Matthew and Marilla that evening. She had not been home since April and she felt that she could not wait another day. The apple blossoms were out and the world was fresh and young. Diana was at Green Gables to meet her. In her own white room, where Marilla had set a flowering house rose on the window sill, Anne looked about her and drew a long breath of happiness.

"Oh, Diana, it's so good to be back again. It's so good to see those pointed firs coming out against the pink sky—and that white orchard and the old Snow Queen. Isn't the breath of the mint delicious? And that tea rose—why, it's a song and a hope and a prayer all in one. And it's *good* to see you again, Diana!"

"I thought you liked that Stella Maynard better than me," said Diana reproachfully. "Josie Pye told me you did. Josie said you were *infatuated* with her."

Anne laughed and pelted Diana with the faded "June lilies" of her bouquet.

"Stella Maynard is the dearest girl in the world except one and you are that one, Diana," she said. "I love you more than ever—and I've so many things to tell you. But just now I feel as if it were joy enough to sit here and look at you. I'm tired, I think—tired of being studious and ambitious. I mean to spend at least two hours tomorrow lying out in the orchard grass, thinking of absolutely nothing."

"You've done splendidly, Anne. I suppose you won't be teaching now that you've won the Avery?"

"No. I'm going to Redmond in September. Doesn't it seem wonderful? I'll have a brand new stock of ambition laid in by that time after three glorious, golden months of vacation. Jane and Ruby are going to teach. Isn't it splendid to think we all got through even to Moody Spurgeon and Josie Pye?"

"The Newbridge trustees have offered Jane their school already," said Diana. "Gilbert Blythe is going to teach, too. He has to. His father can't afford to send him to college next year, after all, so he means to earn his own way through. I expect he'll get the school here if Miss Ames decides to leave."

Anne felt a queer little sensation of dismayed surprise. She had not known this; she had expected that Gilbert would be going to Redmond also. What would she do without their inspiring rivalry? Would not work, even at a coeducational college with a real degree in prospect, be rather flat without her friend the enemy?

The next morning at breakfast it suddenly struck Anne that Matthew was not looking well. Surely he was much grayer than he had been a year before.

"Marilla," she said hesitatingly when he had gone out, "is Matthew quite well?"

"No, he isn't," said Marilla in a troubled tone. "He's had some real bad spells with his heart this spring and he won't spare himself a mite. I've been real worried about him, but he's some better this while back and we've got a good hired man, so I'm hoping he'll kind of rest and pick up. Maybe he will now you're home. You always cheer him up."

Anne leaned across the table and took Marilla's face in her hands.

"You are not looking as well yourself as I'd like to see you, Marilla. You look tired. I'm afraid you've been working too hard. You must take a rest, now that I'm home. I'm just going to take this one day off to visit all the dear old spots and hunt up my old dreams, and then it will be your turn to be lazy while I do the work."

Marilla smiled affectionately at her girl.

"It's not the work—it's my head. I've got a pain so often now—behind my eyes. Doctor Spencer's been fussing with glasses, but they don't do me any good. There is a distinguished oculist coming to the Island the last of June and the doctor says I must see him. I guess I'll have to. I can't read or sew with any comfort now. Well, Anne, you've done real well at Queen's I must say. To take First Class License in one year and win the Avery scholarship—well, well, Mrs. Lynde says pride goes before a fall and she doesn't believe in the higher education of women at all; she says it unfits them for woman's true sphere. I don't believe a word of it. Speaking of Rachel reminds me—did you hear anything about the Abbey Bank lately, Anne?"

"I heard it was shaky," answered Anne. "Why?"

"That is what Rachel said. She was up here one day last week and said there was some talk about it. Matthew felt real worried. All we have saved is in that bank—every penny. I wanted Matthew to put it in the Savings Bank in the first place, but old Mr. Abbey was a great friend of Father's and he'd always banked with him. Matthew said any bank with him at the head of it was good enough for anybody."

"I think he has only been its nominal head for many years," said Anne. "He is a very old man; his nephews are really at the head of the institution."

"Well, when Rachel told us that, I wanted Matthew to draw our money right out and he said he'd think of it. But Mr. Russell told him yesterday that the bank was all right."

Anne had her good day in the companionship of the outdoor world. She never forgot that day; it was so bright and golden and fair, so free from shadow and so lavish of blossom. Anne spent some of its rich hours in the orchard; she went to the Dryad's Bubble and Willowmere and Violet Vale; she called at the manse and had a satisfying talk with Mrs. Allan; and finally in the evening she went with Matthew for the cows, through Lovers' Lane to the back pasture. The woods were all gloried through with sunset and the warm splendor of it streamed down through the hill gaps in the west. Matthew walked slowly with bent head; Anne, tall and erect, suited her springing step to his.

"You've been working too hard today, Matthew," she said reproachfully. "Why won't you take things easier?"

"Well now, I can't seem to," said Matthew, as he opened the yard gate to let the cows through. "It's only that I'm getting old, Anne, and keep forgetting it. Well, well, I've always worked pretty hard and I'd rather drop in harness."

"If I had been the boy you sent for," said Anne wistfully, "I'd be able to help you so much now and spare you in a hundred ways. I could find it in my heart to wish I had been, just for that."

"Well now, I'd rather have you than a dozen boys, Anne," said Matthew patting her hand. "Just mind you that—rather than a dozen boys. Well now, I guess it wasn't a boy that took the Avery scholarship, was it? It was a girl—my girl—my girl that I'm proud of."

He smiled his shy smile at her as he went into the yard. Anne took the memory of it with her when she went to her room that night and sat for a long while at her open window, thinking of the past and dreaming of the future. Outside the Snow Queen was mistily white in the moonshine; the frogs were singing in the marsh beyond Orchard Slope. Anne always remembered the silvery, peaceful beauty and fragrant calm of that night. It was the last night before sorrow touched her life; and no life is ever quite the same again when once that cold, sanctifying touch has been laid upon it.

CHAPTER XXXVII

THE REAPER WHOSE NAME IS DEATH

"Matthew—Matthew—what is the matter? Matthew, are you sick?"

It was Marilla who spoke, alarm in every jerky word. Anne came through the hall, her hands full of white narcissus—it was long before Anne could love the sight or odor of white narcissus again—in time to hear her and to see Matthew standing in the porch doorway, a folded paper in his hand, and his face strangely drawn and gray. Anne dropped her flowers and sprang across the kitchen to him at the same moment as Marilla. They were both too late; before they could reach him Matthew had fallen across the threshold.

"He's fainted," gasped Marilla. "Anne, run for Martin—quick, quick! He's at the barn."

Martin, the hired man, who had just driven home from the post office, started at once for the doctor, calling at Orchard Slope on his way to send Mr. and Mrs. Barry over. Mrs. Lynde, who was there on an errand, came too. They found Anne and Marilla distractedly trying to restore Matthew to consciousness.

Mrs. Lynde pushed them gently aside, tried his pulse, and then laid her ear over his heart. She looked at their anxious faces sorrowfully and the tears came into her eyes.

"Oh, Marilla," she said gravely. "I don't think—we can do anything for him."

"Mrs. Lynde, you don't think—you can't think Matthew is—is—" Anne could not say the dreadful word; she turned sick and pallid.

"Child, yes, I'm afraid of it. Look at his face. When you've seen that look as often as I have you'll know what it means."

Anne looked at the still face and there beheld the seal of the Great Presence.

When the doctor came he said that death had been instantaneous and probably painless, caused in all likelihood by some sudden shock. The secret of the shock was discovered to be in the paper Matthew had held and which Martin had brought from the office that morning. It contained an account of the failure of the Abbey Bank.

The news spread quickly through Avonlea, and all day friends and neighbors thronged Green Gables and came and went on errands of kindness for the dead and living. For the first time shy, quiet Matthew Cuthbert was a person of central importance; the white majesty of death had fallen on him and set him apart as one crowned.

When the calm night came softly down over Green Gables the old house was hushed and tranquil. In the parlor lay Matthew Cuthbert in his coffin, his long gray hair framing his placid face on which there was a little kindly smile as if he but slept, dreaming pleasant dreams. There were flowers about him—sweet old-fashioned flowers which his mother had planted in the homestead garden in her bridal days and for which Matthew had always had a secret, wordless love. Anne had gathered them and brought them to him, her anguished, tearless eyes burning in her white face. It was the last thing she could do for him.

The Barrys and Mrs. Lynde stayed with them that night. Diana, going to the east gable, where Anne was standing at her window, said gently:

"Anne dear, would you like to have me sleep with you tonight?"

"Thank you, Diana." Anne looked earnestly into her friend's face. "I think you won't misunderstand me when I say I want to be alone. I'm not afraid. I haven't been alone one minute since it happened—and I want to be. I want to be quite silent and quiet and try to realize it. I can't realize it. Half the time it seems to me that Matthew can't be dead; and the other half it seems as if he must have been dead for a long time and I've had this horrible dull ache ever since."

Diana did not quite understand. Marilla's impassioned grief, breaking all the bounds of natural reserve and lifelong habit in its stormy rush, she could comprehend better than Anne's tearless agony. But she went away kindly, leaving Anne alone to keep her first vigil with sorrow.

Anne hoped that the tears would come in solitude. It seemed to her a terrible thing that she could not shed a tear for Matthew, whom she had loved so much and who had been so kind to her, Matthew who had walked with her last evening at sunset and was now lying in the dim room below with that awful peace on his brow. But no tears came at first, even when she knelt by her window in the darkness and prayed, looking up to the stars beyond the hills—no tears, only the same horrible dull ache of misery that kept on aching until she fell asleep, worn out with the day's pain and excitement.

In the night she awakened, with the stillness and the darkness about her, and the recollection of the day came over her like a wave of sorrow. She could see Matthew's face smiling at her as he had smiled when they parted at the gate that last evening—she could hear his voice saying, "My girl—my girl that I'm proud of." Then the tears came and Anne wept her heart out. Marilla heard her and crept in to comfort her.

"There—there—don't cry so, dearie. It can't bring him back. It—it—isn't right to cry so. I knew that today, but I couldn't help it then. He'd always been such a good, kind brother to me—but God knows best."

"Oh, just let me cry, Marilla," sobbed Anne. "The tears don't hurt me like that ache did. Stay here for a little while with me and keep your arm round me—so. I couldn't have Diana stay, she's good and kind and sweet—but it's not her sorrow—she's outside of it and she couldn't come close enough to my heart to help me. It's our sorrow—yours and mine. Oh, Marilla, what will we do without him?"

"We've got each other, Anne. I don't know what I'd do if you weren't here—if you'd never come. Oh, Anne, I know I've been kind of strict and harsh with you maybe—but you mustn't think I didn't love you as well as Matthew did, for all that. I want to tell you now when I can. It's never been easy for me to say things out of my heart, but at times like this it's easier. I love you as dear as if you were my own flesh and blood and you've been my joy and comfort ever since you came to Green Gables."

Two days afterwards they carried Matthew Cuthbert over his homestead threshold and away from the fields he had tilled and the orchards he had loved and the trees he had planted; and then Avonlea settled back to its usual placidity and even at Green Gables affairs slipped into their old groove and work was done and duties fulfilled with regularity as before, although always with the aching sense of "loss in all familiar things." Anne, new to grief, thought it almost sad that it could be so—that they *could* go on in the old way without Matthew. She felt something like shame and remorse when she discovered that the sunrises behind the firs and the pale pink buds opening in the garden gave her the old inrush of gladness when she saw them—that Diana's visits were pleasant to her and that Diana's merry words and ways moved her to laughter and smiles—that, in brief, the beautiful world of blossom and love and friendship had lost none of its power to please her fancy and thrill her heart, that life still called to her with many insistent voices.

"It seems like disloyalty to Matthew, somehow, to find pleasure in these things now that he has gone," she said wistfully to Mrs. Allan one evening when they were together in the manse garden. "I miss him so much—all the time—and yet, Mrs. Allan, the world and life seem very beautiful and interesting to me for all. Today Diana said something funny and I found myself laughing. I thought when it happened I could never laugh again. And it somehow seems as if I oughtn't to."

"When Matthew was here he liked to hear you laugh and he liked to know that you found pleasure in the pleasant things around you," said Mrs. Allan gently. "He is just away now; and he likes to know it just the same. I am sure we should not shut our hearts against the healing influences that nature offers us. But I can understand your feeling. I think we all experience the same thing. We resent the thought that anything can please us when someone we love is no longer here to share the pleasure with us, and we almost feel as if we were unfaithful to our sorrow when we find our interest in life returning to us."

"I was down to the graveyard to plant a rosebush on Matthew's grave this afternoon," said Anne dreamily. "I took a slip of the little white Scotch rosebush his mother brought out from Scotland long ago; Matthew always liked those roses the best—they were so small and sweet on their thorny stems. It made me feel glad that I could plant it by his grave—as if I were doing something that must please him in taking it there to be near him. I hope he has roses like them in heaven. Perhaps the souls of all those little white roses that he has loved so many summers were all there to meet him. I must go home now. Marilla is all alone and she gets lonely at twilight."

"She will be lonelier still, I fear, when you go away again to college," said Mrs. Allan.

Anne did not reply; she said good night and went slowly back to Green Gables. Marilla was sitting on the front door-steps and Anne sat down beside her. The door was open behind them, held back by a big pink conch shell with hints of sea sunsets in its smooth inner convolutions.

Anne gathered some sprays of pale-yellow honeysuckle and put them in her hair. She liked the delicious hint of fragrance, as some aerial benediction, above her every time she moved.

"Doctor Spencer was here while you were away," Marilla said. "He says that the specialist will be in town tomorrow and he insists that I must go in and have my eyes examined. I suppose I'd better go and have it over. I'll be more than thankful if the man can give me the right kind of glasses to suit my eyes. You won't mind staying here alone while I'm away, will you? Martin will have to drive me in and there's ironing and baking to do."

"I shall be all right. Diana will come over for company for me. I shall attend to the ironing and baking beautifully—you needn't fear that I'll starch the handkerchiefs or flavor the cake with liniment."

Marilla laughed.

"What a girl you were for making mistakes in them days, Anne. You were always getting into scrapes. I did use to think you were possessed. Do you mind the time you dyed your hair?"

"Yes, indeed. I shall never forget it," smiled Anne, touching the heavy braid of hair that was wound about her shapely head. "I laugh a little now sometimes when I think what a worry my hair used to be to me—but I don't laugh *much*, because it was a very real trouble then. I did suffer terribly over my hair and my freckles. My freckles are really gone; and people are nice enough to tell me my hair is auburn now—all but Josie Pye. She informed me yesterday that she really thought it was redder than ever, or at least my black dress made it look redder, and she asked me if people who had red hair ever got used to having it. Marilla, I've almost decided to give up trying to like Josie Pye. I've made what I would once have called a heroic effort to like her, but Josie Pye won't *be* liked."

"Josie is a Pye," said Marilla sharply, "so she can't help being disagreeable. I suppose people of that kind serve some useful purpose in society, but I must say I don't know what it is any more than I know the use of thistles. Is Josie going to teach?"

"No, she is going back to Queen's next year. So are Moody Spurgeon and Charlie Sloane. Jane and Ruby are going to teach and they have both got schools—Jane at Newbridge and Ruby at some place up west."

"Gilbert Blythe is going to teach too, isn't he?"

"Yes"—briefly.

"What a nice-looking fellow he is," said Marilla absently. "I saw him in church last Sunday and he seemed so tall and manly. He looks a lot like his father did at the same age. John Blythe was a nice boy. We used to be real good friends, he and I. People called him my beau."

Anne looked up with swift interest.

"Oh, Marilla—and what happened?—why didn't you—"

"We had a quarrel. I wouldn't forgive him when he asked me to. I meant to, after awhile—but I was sulky and angry and I wanted to punish him first. He never came back—the Blythes were all mighty independent. But I always felt—rather sorry. I've always kind of wished I'd forgiven him when I had the chance."

"So you've had a bit of romance in your life, too," said Anne softly.

"Yes, I suppose you might call it that. You wouldn't think so to look at me, would you? But you never can tell about people from their outsides. Everybody has forgot about me and John. I'd forgotten myself. But it all came back to me when I saw Gilbert last Sunday."

CHAPTER XXXVIII

THE BEND IN THE ROAD

Marilla went to town the next day and returned in the evening. Anne had gone over to Orchard Slope with Diana and came back to find Marilla in the kitchen, sitting by the table with her head leaning on her hand. Something in her dejected attitude struck a chill to Anne's heart. She had never seen Marilla sit limply inert like that.

"Are you very tired, Marilla?"

"Yes—no—I don't know," said Marilla wearily, looking up. "I suppose I am tired but I haven't thought about it. It's not that."

"Did you see the oculist? What did he say?" asked Anne anxiously.

"Yes, I saw him. He examined my eyes. He says that if I give up all reading and sewing entirely and any kind of work that strains the eyes, and if I'm careful not to cry, and if I wear the glasses he's given me he thinks my eyes may not get any worse and my headaches will be cured. But if I don't he says I'll certainly be stone-blind in six months. Blind! Anne, just think of it!"

For a minute Anne, after her first quick exclamation of dismay, was silent. It seemed to her that she could *not* speak. Then she said bravely, but with a catch in her voice:

"Marilla, *don't* think of it. You know he has given you hope. If you are careful you won't lose your sight altogether; and if his glasses cure your headaches it will be a great thing."

"I don't call it much hope," said Marilla bitterly. "What am I to live for if I can't read or sew or do anything like that? I might as well be blind—or dead. And as for crying, I can't help that when I get lonesome. But there, it's no good talking about it. If you'll get me a cup of tea I'll be thankful. I'm about done out. Don't say anything about this to any one for a spell yet, anyway. I can't bear that folks should come here to question and sympathize and talk about it."

When Marilla had eaten her lunch Anne persuaded her to go to bed. Then Anne went herself to the east gable and sat down by her window in the darkness alone with her tears and her heaviness of heart. How sadly things had changed since she had sat there the night after coming home! Then she had been full of hope and joy and the future had looked rosy with promise. Anne felt as if she had lived years since then, but before she went to bed there was a smile on her lips and peace in her heart. She had looked her duty courageously in the face and found it a friend—as duty ever is when we meet it frankly.

One afternoon a few days later Marilla came slowly in from the front yard where she had been talking to a caller—a man whom Anne knew by sight as Sadler from Carmody. Anne wondered what he could have been saying to bring that look to Marilla's face.

"What did Mr. Sadler want, Marilla?"

Marilla sat down by the window and looked at Anne. There were tears in her eyes in defiance of the oculist's prohibition and her voice broke as she said:

"He heard that I was going to sell Green Gables and he wants to buy it."

"Buy it! Buy Green Gables?" Anne wondered if she had heard aright. "Oh, Marilla, you don't mean to sell Green Gables!"

"Anne, I don't know what else is to be done. I've thought it all over. If my eyes were strong I could stay here and make out to look after things and manage, with a good hired man. But as it is I can't. I may lose my sight altogether; and anyway I'll not be fit to run things. Oh, I never thought I'd live to see the day when I'd have to sell my home. But things would only go behind worse and worse all the time, till nobody would want to buy it. Every cent of our money went in that bank; and there's some notes Matthew gave last fall to pay. Mrs. Lynde advises me to sell the farm and board somewhere—with her I suppose. It won't bring much—it's small and the buildings are old. But it'll be enough for me to live on I reckon. I'm thankful you're provided for with that scholarship, Anne. I'm sorry you won't have a home to come to in your vacations, that's all, but I suppose you'll manage somehow."

Marilla broke down and wept bitterly.

"You mustn't sell Green Gables," said Anne resolutely.

"Oh, Anne, I wish I didn't have to. But you can see for yourself. I can't stay here alone. I'd go crazy with trouble and loneliness. And my sight would go—I know it would."

"You won't have to stay here alone, Marilla. I'll be with you. I'm not going to Redmond."

"Not going to Redmond!" Marilla lifted her worn face from her hands and looked at Anne. "Why, what do you mean?"

"Just what I say. I'm not going to take the scholarship. I decided so the night after you came home from town. You surely don't think I could leave you alone in your trouble, Marilla, after all you've done for me. I've been thinking and planning. Let me tell you my plans. Mr. Barry wants to rent the farm for next year. So you won't have any bother over that. And I'm going to teach. I've applied for the school here—but I don't expect to get it for I understand the trustees have promised it to Gilbert Blythe. But I can have the Carmody school—Mr. Blair told me so last night at the store. Of course that won't be quite as nice or convenient as if I had the Avonlea school. But I can board home and drive myself over to Carmody and back, in the warm weather at least. And even in winter I can come home Fridays. We'll keep a horse for that. Oh, I have it all planned out, Marilla. And I'll read to you and keep you cheered up. You shan't be dull or lonesome. And we'll be real cozy and happy here together, you and I."

Marilla had listened like a woman in a dream.

"Oh, Anne, I could get on real well if you were here, I know. But I can't let you sacrifice yourself so for me. It would be terrible."

"Nonsense!" Anne laughed merrily. "There is no sacrifice. Nothing could be worse than giving up Green Gables—nothing could hurt me more. We must keep the dear old place. My mind is quite made up, Marilla. I'm *not* going to Redmond; and I *am* going to stay here and teach. Don't you worry about me a bit."

"But your ambitions—and—"

"I'm just as ambitious as ever. Only, I've changed the object of my ambitions. I'm going to be a good teacher—and I'm going to save your eyesight. Besides, I mean to study at home here and take a little college course all by myself. Oh, I've dozens of plans, Marilla. I've been thinking them out for a week. I shall give life here my best, and I believe it will give its best to me in return. When I left Queen's my future seemed to stretch out before me like a straight road. I thought I could see along it for many a milestone. Now there is a bend in it. I don't know what lies around the bend, but I'm going to believe that the best does. It has a fascination of its own, that bend, Marilla. I wonder how the road beyond it goes—what there is of green glory and soft, checkered light and shadows—what new landscapes—what new beauties—what curves and hills and valleys further on."

"I don't feel as if I ought to let you give it up," said Marilla, referring to the scholarship.

"But you can't prevent me. I'm sixteen and a half, 'obstinate as a mule,' as Mrs. Lynde once told me," laughed Anne. "Oh, Marilla, don't you go pitying me. I don't like to be pitied, and there is no need for it. I'm heart glad over the very thought of staying at dear Green Gables. Nobody could love it as you and I do—so we must keep it."

"You blessed girl!" said Marilla, yielding. "I feel as if you'd given me new life. I guess I ought to stick out and make you go to college—but I know I can't, so I ain't going to try. I'll make it up to you though, Anne."

When it became noised abroad in Avonlea that Anne Shirley had given up the idea of going to college and intended to stay home and teach there was a good deal of discussion over it. Most of the good folks, not knowing about Marilla's eyes, thought she was foolish. Mrs. Allan did not. She told Anne so in approving words that brought tears of pleasure to the girl's eyes. Neither did good Mrs. Lynde. She came up one evening and found Anne and Marilla sitting at the front door in the warm, scented summer dusk. They liked to sit there when the twilight came down and the white moths flew about in the garden and the odor of mint filled the dewy air.

Mrs. Rachel deposited her substantial person upon the stone bench by the door, behind which grew a row of tall pink and yellow hollyhocks, with a long breath of mingled weariness and relief.

"I declare I'm getting glad to sit down. I've been on my feet all day, and two hundred pounds is a good bit for two feet to carry round. It's a great blessing not to be fat, Marilla. I hope you appreciate it. Well, Anne, I hear you've given up your notion of going to college. I was real glad to hear it. You've got as much education now as a woman can be comfortable with. I don't believe in girls going to college with the men and cramming their heads full of Latin and Greek and all that nonsense."

"But I'm going to study Latin and Greek just the same, Mrs. Lynde," said Anne laughing. "I'm going to take my Arts course right here at Green Gables, and study everything that I would at college."

Mrs. Lynde lifted her hands in holy horror.

"Anne Shirley, you'll kill yourself."

"Not a bit of it. I shall thrive on it. Oh, I'm not going to overdo things. As 'Josiah Allen's wife,' says, I shall be 'mejum'. But I'll have lots of spare time in the long winter evenings, and I've no vocation for fancy work. I'm going to teach over at Carmody, you know."

"I don't know it. I guess you're going to teach right here in Avonlea. The trustees have decided to give you the school."

"Mrs. Lynde!" cried Anne, springing to her feet in her surprise. "Why, I thought they had promised it to Gilbert Blythe!"

"So they did. But as soon as Gilbert heard that you had applied for it he went to them—they had a business meeting at the school last night, you know—and told them that he withdrew his application, and suggested that they accept yours. He said he was going to teach at White Sands. Of course he knew how much you wanted to stay with Marilla, and I must say I think it was real kind and thoughtful in him, that's what. Real self-sacrificing, too, for he'll have his board to pay at White Sands, and everybody knows he's got to earn his own way through college. So the trustees decided to take you. I was tickled to death when Thomas came home and told me."

"I don't feel that I ought to take it," murmured Anne. "I mean—I don't think I ought to let Gilbert make such a sacrifice for—for me."

"I guess you can't prevent him now. He's signed papers with the White Sands trustees. So it wouldn't do him any good now if you were to refuse. Of course you'll take the school. You'll get along all right, now that there are no Pyes going. Josie was the last of them, and a good thing she was, that's what. There's been some Pye or other going to Avonlea school for the last twenty years, and I guess their mission in life was to keep school teachers reminded that earth isn't their home. Bless my heart! What does all that winking and blinking at the Barry gable mean?"

"Diana is signaling for me to go over," laughed Anne. "You know we keep up the old custom. Excuse me while I run over and see what she wants."

Anne ran down the clover slope like a deer, and disappeared in the firry shadows of the Haunted Wood. Mrs. Lynde looked after her indulgently.

"There's a good deal of the child about her yet in some ways."

"There's a good deal more of the woman about her in others," retorted Marilla, with a momentary return of her old crispness. But crispness was no longer Marilla's distinguishing characteristic. As Mrs.

Lynde told her Thomas that night. "Marilla Cuthbert has got *mellow*. That's what."

Anne went to the little Avonlea graveyard the next evening to put fresh flowers on Matthew's grave and water the Scotch rosebush. She lingered there until dusk, liking the peace and calm of the little place, with its poplars whose rustle was like low, friendly speech, and its whispering grasses growing at will among the graves. When she finally left it and walked down the long hill that sloped to the Lake of Shining Waters it was past sunset and all Avonlea lay before her in a dreamlike afterlight—"a haunt of ancient peace." There was a freshness in the air as of a wind that had blown over honey-sweet fields of clover. Home lights twinkled out here and there among the homestead trees. Beyond lay the sea, misty and purple, with its haunting, unceasing murmur. The west was a glory of soft mingled hues, and the pond reflected them all in still softer shadings. The beauty of it all thrilled Anne's heart, and she gratefully opened the gates of her soul to it.

"Dear old world," she murmured, "you are very lovely, and I am glad to be alive in you."

Halfway down the hill a tall lad came whistling out of a gate before the Blythe homestead. It was Gilbert, and the whistle died on his lips as he recognized Anne. He lifted his cap courteously, but he would have passed on in silence, if Anne had not stopped and held out her hand.

"Gilbert," she said, with scarlet cheeks, "I want to thank you for giving up the school for me. It was very good of you—and I want you to know that I appreciate it."

Gilbert took the offered hand eagerly.

"It wasn't particularly good of me at all, Anne. I was pleased to be able to do you some small service. Are we going to be friends after this? Have you really forgiven me my old fault?"

Anne laughed and tried unsuccessfully to withdraw her hand.

"I forgave you that day by the pond landing, although I didn't know it. What a stubborn little goose I was. I've been—I may as well make a complete confession—I've been sorry ever since."

"We are going to be the best of friends," said Gilbert, jubilantly. "We were born to be good friends, Anne. You've thwarted destiny enough. I know we can help each other in many ways. You are going to keep up your studies, aren't you? So am I. Come, I'm going to walk home with you."

Marilla looked curiously at Anne when the latter entered the kitchen.

"Who was that came up the lane with you, Anne?"

"Gilbert Blythe," answered Anne, vexed to find herself blushing. "I met him on Barry's hill."

"I didn't think you and Gilbert Blythe were such good friends that you'd stand for half an hour at the gate talking to him," said Marilla with a dry smile.

"We haven't been—we've been good enemies. But we have decided that it will be much more sensible to be good friends in the future. Were we really there half an hour? It seemed just a few minutes. But, you see, we have five years' lost conversations to catch up with, Marilla."

Anne sat long at her window that night companioned by a glad content. The wind purred softly in the cherry boughs, and the mint breaths came up to her. The stars twinkled over the pointed firs in the hollow and Diana's light gleamed through the old gap.

Anne's horizons had closed in since the night she had sat there after coming home from Queen's; but if the path set before her feet was to be narrow she knew that flowers of quiet happiness would bloom along it. The joy of sincere work and worthy aspiration and congenial friendship were to be hers; nothing could rob her of her birthright of fancy or her ideal world of dreams. And there was always the bend in the road!

"'God's in his heaven, all's right with the world,'" whispered Anne softly.

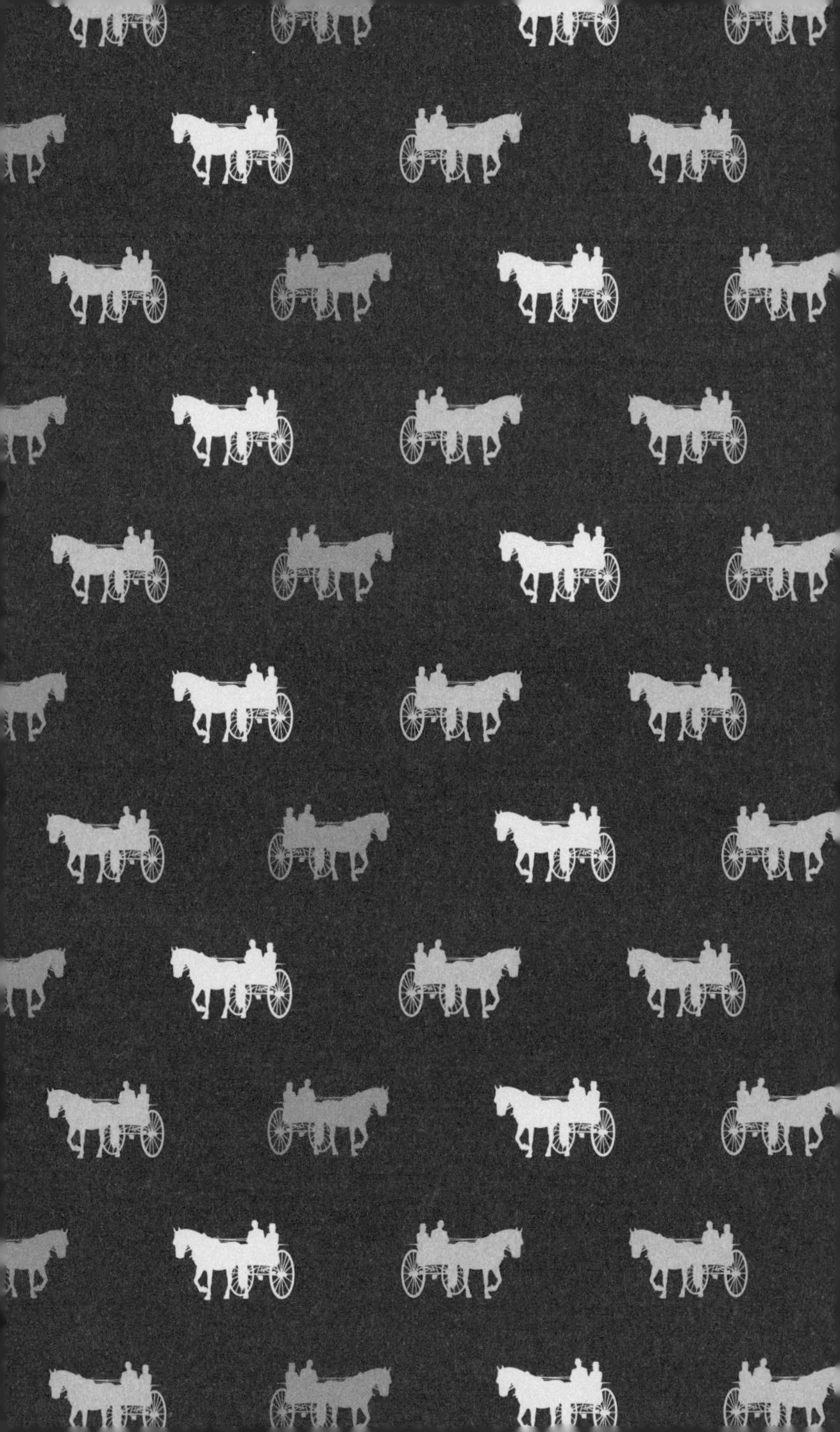

Emma

Word Cloud Classics

A Christmas Carol and Other Holiday Treasures

Adventures of Huckleberry Finn

The Adventures of Sherlock Holmes

Aesop's Fables

The Age of Innocence

Anna Karenina

Anne of Green Gables

The Art of War

The Brothers Grimm: 101 Fairy Tales

The Brothers Grimm Volume II: 110 Grimmer Fairy Tales

Common Sense and Selected Works of Thomas Paine

The Count of Monte Cristo

Don Quixote

Dracula

Frankenstein

Great Expectations

Inferno

Jane Eyre

Lady Chatterley's Lover

Les Misérables

Little Women

Madame Bovary

Moby-Dick

Persuasion

The Picture of Dorian Gray

Pride and Prejudice

The Prince and Other Writings

The Red Badge of Courage and Other Stories

The Scarlet Letter

The Secret Garden

Narrative of the Life of Frederick Douglass and Other Works

Sense and Sensibility

The Three Musketeers

Twenty Thousand Leagues Under the Sea

Uncle Tom's Cabin

Walden and Civil Disobedience

The Wizard of Oz

Emma

JANE AUSTEN

CANTERBURY CLASSICS
San Diego

All correspondence concerning the content of this book should be addressed to: Canterbury Classics
10350 Barnes Canyon Road, Suite 100
San Diego, CA 92121

Publisher: Peter Norton
Publishing Team: Lori Asbury, Ana Parker
Director Editorial and Production: JoAnn Padgett
Editor: Melinda Allman

Library of Congress Cataloging-in-Publication Data

Austen, Jane, 1775-1817.
Emma / Jane Austen.
pages ; cm.
ISBN-13: 978-1-60710-946-4 (alk. paper)
ISBN-10: 1-60710-946-8 (alk. paper)
1. Young women--Fiction. 2. Mate selection--Fiction. 3. Female friendship--Fiction. 4. Fathers and daughters--Fiction. 5. England--Social life and customs--19th century--Fiction. I. Title.

PR4034.E5 2013
823'.7--dc23

2013005727

PRINTED IN CHINA

3 4 5 6 7 19 18 17 16 15

CONTENTS

VOLUME I

CHAPTER I

Emma Woodhouse, handsome, clever, and rich, with a comfortable home and happy disposition, seemed to unite some of the best blessings of existence; and had lived nearly twenty-one years in the world with very little to distress or vex her.

She was the youngest of the two daughters of a most affectionate, indulgent father; and had, in consequence of her sister's marriage, been mistress of his house from a very early period. Her mother had died too long ago for her to have more than an indistinct remembrance of her caresses; and her place had been supplied by an excellent woman as governess, who had fallen little short of a mother in affection.

Sixteen years had Miss Taylor been in Mr. Woodhouse's family, less as a governess than a friend, very fond of both daughters, but particularly of Emma. Between *them* it was more the intimacy of sisters. Even before Miss Taylor had ceased to hold the nominal office of governess, the mildness of her temper had hardly allowed her to impose any restraint; and the shadow of authority being now long passed away, they had been living together as friend and friend very mutually attached, and Emma doing just what she liked; highly esteeming Miss Taylor's judgment, but directed chiefly by her own.

The real evils, indeed, of Emma's situation were the power of having rather too much her own way, and a disposition to think a little too well of herself; these were the disadvantages which threatened alloy to her many enjoyments. The danger, however, was at present so unperceived, that they did not by any means rank as misfortunes with her.

Sorrow came—a gentle sorrow—but not at all in the shape of any disagreeable consciousness.—Miss Taylor married. It was Miss Taylor's loss which first brought grief. It was on the wedding-day of this beloved friend that Emma first sat in mournful thought of any continuance. The wedding over, and the bride-people gone, her father and herself were left to dine together, with no prospect of a third to cheer a long evening. Her father composed himself to sleep after dinner, as usual, and she had then only to sit and think of what she had lost.

The event had every promise of happiness for her friend. Mr. Weston was a man of unexceptionable character, easy fortune, suitable age, and pleasant manners; and there was some satisfaction in considering with what self-denying, generous friendship she had always wished and promoted the match; but it was a black morning's work for her. The want of Miss Taylor would be felt every hour of every day. She recalled her past kindness—the kindness, the affection of sixteen years—how she had taught and how she had played with her from five years old—how she had devoted all her powers to attach and amuse her in health—and how nursed her through the various illnesses of childhood. A large debt of gratitude was owing here; but the intercourse of the last seven years, the equal footing and perfect unreserve which had soon followed Isabella's marriage, on their being left to each other, was yet a dearer, tenderer recollection. She had been a friend and companion such as few possessed: intelligent, well-informed, useful, gentle, knowing all the ways of the family, interested in all its concerns, and peculiarly interested in herself, in every pleasure, every scheme of hers—one to whom she could speak every thought as it arose, and who had such an affection for her as could never find fault.

How was she to bear the change?—It was true that her friend was going only half a mile from them; but Emma was aware that great must be the difference between a Mrs. Weston, only half a mile from them, and a Miss Taylor in the house; and with all her advantages, natural and domestic, she was now in great danger of suffering from intellectual solitude. She dearly loved her father, but he was no companion for her. He could not meet her in conversation, rational or playful.

The evil of the actual disparity in their ages (and Mr. Woodhouse had not married early) was much increased by his constitution and habits; for having been a valetudinarian all his life, without activity of mind or body, he was a much older man in ways than in years; and though everywhere beloved for the friendliness of his heart and his amiable temper, his talents could not have recommended him at any time.

Her sister, though comparatively but little removed by matrimony, being settled in London, only sixteen miles off, was much beyond her daily reach; and many a long October and November evening must be struggled through at Hartfield, before Christmas brought the next visit from Isabella and her husband, and their little children, to fill the house, and give her pleasant society again.

Highbury, the large and populous village, almost amounting to a town, to which Hartfield, in spite of its separate lawn, and shrubberies, and name, did really belong, afforded her no equals. The Woodhouses were first in consequence there. All looked up to them. She had many acquaintance in the place, for her father was universally civil, but not one among them who could be accepted in lieu of Miss Taylor for even half a day. It was a melancholy change; and Emma could not but sigh over it, and wish for impossible things, till her father awoke, and made it necessary to be cheerful. His spirits required support. He was a nervous man, easily depressed; fond of every body that he was used to, and hating to part with them; hating change of every kind. Matrimony, as the origin of change, was always disagreeable; and he was by no means yet reconciled to his own daughter's marrying, nor could ever speak of her but with compassion, though it had been entirely a match of affection, when he was now obliged to part with Miss Taylor too; and from his habits of gentle selfishness, and of being never able to suppose that other people could feel differently from himself, he was very much disposed to think Miss Taylor had done as sad a thing for herself as for them, and would have been a great deal happier if she had spent all the rest of her life at Hartfield. Emma smiled and chatted as cheerfully as she could, to keep him from such thoughts; but when tea came, it was impossible for him not to say exactly as he had said at dinner,

"Poor Miss Taylor!—I wish she were here again. What a pity it is that Mr. Weston ever thought of her!"

"I cannot agree with you, papa; you know I cannot. Mr. Weston is such a good-humoured, pleasant, excellent man, that he thoroughly deserves a good wife;—and you would not have had Miss Taylor live with us for ever, and bear all my odd humours, when she might have a house of her own?"

"A house of her own!—But where is the advantage of a house of her own? This is three times as large.—And you have never any odd humours, my dear."

"How often we shall be going to see them, and they coming to see us!—We shall be always meeting! *We* must begin; we must go and pay wedding visit very soon."

"My dear, how am I to get so far? Randalls is such a distance. I could not walk half so far."

"No, papa, nobody thought of your walking. We must go in the carriage, to be sure."

"The carriage! But James will not like to put the horses to for such a little way;—and where are the poor horses to be while we are paying our visit?"

"They are to be put into Mr. Weston's stable, papa. You know we have settled all that already. We talked it all over with Mr. Weston last night. And as for James, you may be very sure he will always like going to Randalls, because of his daughter's being housemaid there. I only doubt whether he will ever take us anywhere else. That was your doing, papa. You got Hannah that good place. Nobody thought of Hannah till you mentioned her—James is so obliged to you!"

"I am very glad I did think of her. It was very lucky, for I would not have had poor James think himself slighted upon any account; and I am sure she will make a very good servant: she is a civil, pretty-spoken girl; I have a great opinion of her. Whenever I see her, she always curtseys and asks me how I do, in a very pretty manner; and when you have had her here to do needlework, I observe she always turns the lock of the door the right way and never bangs it. I am sure she will be an excellent servant; and it will be a great comfort to poor Miss Taylor to have somebody about her that she is used to see. Whenever James goes over to see his daughter, you know, she will be hearing of us. He will be able to tell her how we all are."

Emma spared no exertions to maintain this happier flow of ideas, and hoped, by the help of backgammon, to get her father tolerably through the evening, and be attacked by no regrets but her own. The backgammon-table was placed; but a visitor immediately afterwards walked in and made it unnecessary.

Mr. Knightley, a sensible man about seven or eight-and-thirty, was not only a very old and intimate friend of the family, but particularly connected with it, as the elder brother of Isabella's husband. He lived about a mile from Highbury, was a frequent visitor, and always welcome, and at this time more welcome than usual, as coming directly from their mutual connexions in London. He had returned to a late dinner, after some days' absence, and now walked up to Hartfield to say that all were well in Brunswick Square. It was a happy circumstance, and animated Mr. Woodhouse for some time. Mr. Knightley had a cheerful manner, which always did him good; and his many inquiries after "poor Isabella" and her children were answered most satisfactorily. When this was over, Mr. Woodhouse gratefully observed, "It is very kind of you,

Mr. Knightley, to come out at this late hour to call upon us. I am afraid you must have had a shocking walk."

"Not at all, sir. It is a beautiful moonlight night; and so mild that I must draw back from your great fire."

"But you must have found it very damp and dirty. I wish you may not catch cold."

"Dirty, sir! Look at my shoes. Not a speck on them."

"Well! that is quite surprising, for we have had a vast deal of rain here. It rained dreadfully hard for half an hour while we were at breakfast. I wanted them to put off the wedding."

"By the bye—I have not wished you joy. Being pretty well aware of what sort of joy you must both be feeling, I have been in no hurry with my congratulations; but I hope it all went off tolerably well. How did you all behave? Who cried most?"

"Ah! poor Miss Taylor! 'Tis a sad business."

"Poor Mr. and Miss Woodhouse, if you please; but I cannot possibly say 'poor Miss Taylor.' I have a great regard for you and Emma; but when it comes to the question of dependence or independence!—At any rate, it must be better to have only one to please than two."

"Especially when *one* of those two is such a fanciful, troublesome creature!" said Emma playfully. "That is what you have in your head, I know—and what you would certainly say if my father were not by."

"I believe it is very true, my dear, indeed," said Mr. Woodhouse, with a sigh. "I am afraid I am sometimes very fanciful and troublesome."

"My dearest papa! You do not think I could mean *you*, or suppose Mr. Knightley to mean *you*. What a horrible idea! Oh no! I meant only myself. Mr. Knightley loves to find fault with me, you know—in a joke—it is all a joke. We always say what we like to one another."

Mr. Knightley, in fact, was one of the few people who could see faults in Emma Woodhouse, and the only one who ever told her of them: and though this was not particularly agreeable to Emma herself, she knew it would be so much less so to her father, that she would not have him really suspect such a circumstance as her not being thought perfect by every body.

"Emma knows I never flatter her," said Mr. Knightley, "but I meant no reflection on any body. Miss Taylor has been used to have two persons to please; she will now have but one. The chances are that she must be a gainer."

"Well," said Emma, willing to let it pass—"you want to hear about the wedding; and I shall be happy to tell you, for we all behaved charmingly. Every body was punctual, every body in their best looks: not a tear, and hardly a long face to be seen. Oh no; we all felt that we were going to be only half a mile apart, and were sure of meeting every day."

"Dear Emma bears every thing so well," said her father. "But, Mr. Knightley, she is really very sorry to lose poor Miss Taylor, and I am sure she *will* miss her more than she thinks for."

Emma turned away her head, divided between tears and smiles. "It is impossible that Emma should not miss such a companion," said Mr. Knightley. "We should not like her so well as we do, sir, if we could suppose it; but she knows how much the marriage is to Miss Taylor's advantage; she knows how very acceptable it must be, at Miss Taylor's time of life, to be settled in a home of her own, and how important to her to be secure of a comfortable provision, and therefore cannot allow herself to feel so much pain as pleasure. Every friend of Miss Taylor must be glad to have her so happily married."

"And you have forgotten one matter of joy to me," said Emma, "and a very considerable one—that I made the match myself. I made the match, you know, four years ago; and to have it take place, and be proved in the right, when so many people said Mr. Weston would never marry again, may comfort me for any thing."

Mr. Knightley shook his head at her. Her father fondly replied, "Ah! my dear, I wish you would not make matches and foretell things, for whatever you say always comes to pass. Pray do not make any more matches."

"I promise you to make none for myself, papa; but I must, indeed, for other people. It is the greatest amusement in the world! And after such success, you know!—Every body said that Mr. Weston would never marry again. Oh dear, no! Mr. Weston, who had been a widower so long, and who seemed so perfectly comfortable without a wife, so constantly occupied either in his business in town or among his friends here, always acceptable wherever he went, always cheerful—Mr. Weston need not spend a single evening in the year alone if he did not like it. Oh no! Mr. Weston certainly would never marry again. Some people even talked of a promise to his wife on her deathbed, and others of the son and the uncle not letting him. All manner of solemn nonsense was talked on the subject, but I believed none of it.

"Ever since the day—about four years ago—that Miss Taylor and I met with him in Broadway Lane, when, because it began to drizzle, he darted away with so much gallantry, and borrowed two umbrellas for us from Farmer Mitchell's, I made up my mind on the subject. I planned the match from that hour; and when such success has blessed me in this instance, dear papa, you cannot think that I shall leave off match-making."

"I do not understand what you mean by 'success,'" said Mr. Knightley. "Success supposes endeavour. Your time has been properly and delicately spent, if you have been endeavouring for the last four years to bring about this marriage. A worthy employment for a young lady's mind! But if, which I rather imagine, your making the match, as you call it, means only your planning it, your saying to yourself one idle day, 'I think it would be a very good thing for Miss Taylor if Mr. Weston were to marry her,' and saying it again to yourself every now and then afterwards, why do you talk of success? Where is your merit? What are you proud of? You made a lucky guess; and *that* is all that can be said."

"And have you never known the pleasure and triumph of a lucky guess?—I pity you.—I thought you cleverer—for, depend upon it a lucky guess is never merely luck. There is always some talent in it. And as to my poor word 'success,' which you quarrel with, I do not know that I am so entirely without any claim to it. You have drawn two pretty pictures; but I think there may be a third—a something between the do-nothing and the do-all. If I had not promoted Mr. Weston's visits here, and given many little encouragements, and smoothed many little matters, it might not have come to any thing after all. I think you must know Hartfield enough to comprehend that."

"A straightforward, open-hearted man like Weston, and a rational, unaffected woman like Miss Taylor, may be safely left to manage their own concerns. You are more likely to have done harm to yourself, than good to them, by interference."

"Emma never thinks of herself, if she can do good to others," rejoined Mr. Woodhouse, understanding but in part. "But, my dear, pray do not make any more matches; they are silly things, and break up one's family circle grievously."

"Only one more, papa; only for Mr. Elton. Poor Mr. Elton! You like Mr. Elton, papa,—I must look about for a wife for him. There is nobody in Highbury who deserves him—and he has been here a whole year, and has fitted up his house so comfortably, that it would be a shame to have him single any longer—and I thought when he was joining their hands to-day, he looked so very much as if he would like to have the same kind office done for him! I think very well of Mr. Elton, and this is the only way I have of doing him a service."

"Mr. Elton is a very pretty young man, to be sure, and a very good young man, and I have a great regard for him. But if you want to shew him any attention, my dear, ask him to come and dine with us some day. That will be a much better thing. I dare say Mr. Knightley will be so kind as to meet him."

"With a great deal of pleasure, sir, at any time," said Mr. Knightley, laughing, "and I agree with you entirely, that it will be a much better thing. Invite him to dinner, Emma, and help him to the best of the fish and the chicken, but leave him to chuse his own wife. Depend upon it, a man of six or seven-and-twenty can take care of himself."

CHAPTER II

Mr. Weston was a native of Highbury, and born of a respectable family, which for the last two or three generations had been rising into gentility and property. He had received a good education, but, on succeeding early in life to a small independence, had become indisposed for any of the more homely pursuits in which his brothers were engaged, and had satisfied an active, cheerful mind and social temper by entering into the militia of his county, then embodied.

Captain Weston was a general favourite; and when the chances of his military life had introduced him to Miss Churchill, of a great Yorkshire family, and Miss Churchill fell in love with him, nobody was surprized, except her brother and his wife, who had never seen him, and who were full of pride and importance, which the connexion would offend.

Miss Churchill, however, being of age, and with the full command of her fortune—though her fortune bore no proportion to the family-estate—was not to be dissuaded from the marriage, and it took place, to the infinite mortification of Mr. and Mrs. Churchill, who threw her off with due decorum. It was an unsuitable connexion, and did not produce much happiness. Mrs. Weston ought to have found more in it, for she had a husband whose warm heart and sweet temper made him think every thing due to her in return for the great goodness of being in love with him; but though she had one sort of spirit, she had not the best. She had resolution enough to pursue her own will in spite of her brother, but not enough to refrain from unreasonable regrets at that brother's unreasonable anger, nor from missing the luxuries of her former home. They lived beyond their income, but still it was nothing in comparison of Enscombe: she did not cease to love her husband, but she wanted at once to be the wife of Captain Weston, and Miss Churchill of Enscombe.

Captain Weston, who had been considered, especially by the Churchills, as making such an amazing match, was proved to have much the worst of the bargain; for when his wife died, after a three years' marriage, he was rather a poorer man than at first, and with a child to maintain. From the expense of the child, however, he was soon relieved. The boy had, with the additional softening claim of a lingering illness of his mother's, been the means of a sort of reconciliation; and Mr. and Mrs. Churchill, having no children of their own, nor any other young creature of equal kindred to care for, offered to take the whole charge of the little Frank soon after her decease. Some scruples and some reluctance the widower-father may be supposed to have felt; but as they were overcome by other considerations, the child was given up to the care and the wealth of the Churchills, and he had only his own comfort to seek, and his own situation to improve as he could.

A complete change of life became desirable. He quitted the militia and engaged in trade, having brothers already established in a good way in London, which afforded him a favourable opening. It was a concern which brought just employment enough. He had still a small house in Highbury, where most of his leisure days were spent; and between useful occupation and the pleasures of society, the next eighteen or twenty years of his life passed cheerfully away. He had, by that time, realised an easy competence—enough to secure the purchase of a little estate adjoining Highbury, which he had always longed for—enough to marry a woman as portionless even as Miss Taylor, and to live according to the wishes of his own friendly and social disposition.

It was now some time since Miss Taylor had begun to influence his schemes; but as it was not the tyrannic influence of youth on youth, it had not shaken his determination of never settling till he could purchase Randalls, and the sale of Randalls was long looked forward to; but he had gone steadily on, with these objects in view, till they were accomplished. He had made his fortune, bought his house, and obtained his wife; and was beginning a new period of existence, with every probability of greater happiness than in any yet passed through. He had never been an unhappy man; his own temper had secured him from that, even in his first marriage; but his second must shew him how delightful a well-judging and truly amiable woman could be, and must give him the pleasantest proof of its being a great deal better to choose than to be chosen, to excite gratitude than to feel it.

He had only himself to please in his choice: his fortune was his own; for as to Frank, it was more than being tacitly brought up as his uncle's heir, it had become so avowed an adoption as to have him assume the name of Churchill on coming of age. It was most unlikely, therefore, that he should ever want his father's assistance. His father had no apprehension of it. The aunt was a capricious woman, and governed her husband entirely; but it was not in Mr. Weston's nature to imagine that any caprice could be strong enough to affect one so dear, and, as he believed, so deservedly dear. He saw his son every year in London, and was proud of him; and his fond report of him as a very fine young man had made Highbury feel a sort of pride in him too. He was looked on as sufficiently belonging to the place to make his merits and prospects a kind of common concern.

Mr. Frank Churchill was one of the boasts of Highbury, and a lively curiosity to see him prevailed, though the compliment was so little returned that he had never been there in his life. His coming to visit his father had been often talked of but never achieved.

Now, upon his father's marriage, it was very generally proposed, as a most proper attention, that the visit should take place. There was not a dissentient voice on the subject, either when Mrs. Perry drank tea with Mrs. and Miss Bates, or when Mrs. and Miss Bates returned the visit. Now was the time for Mr. Frank Churchill to come among them; and the hope strengthened when it was understood that he had written to his new mother on the occasion. For a few days, every morning visit in Highbury included some mention of the handsome letter Mrs. Weston had received. "I suppose you have heard of the handsome letter Mr. Frank Churchill has written to Mrs. Weston? I understand it was a very handsome letter, indeed. Mr. Woodhouse told me of it. Mr. Woodhouse saw the letter, and he says he never saw such a handsome letter in his life."

It was, indeed, a highly prized letter. Mrs. Weston had, of course, formed a very favourable idea of the young man; and such a pleasing attention was an irresistible proof of his great good sense, and a most welcome addition to every source and every expression of congratulation which her marriage had already secured. She felt herself a most fortunate woman; and she had lived long enough to know how fortunate she might well be thought, where the only regret was for a partial separation from friends whose friendship for her had never cooled, and who could ill bear to part with her.

She knew that at times she must be missed; and could not think, without pain, of Emma's losing a single pleasure, or suffering an hour's ennui, from the want of her companionableness: but dear Emma was of no feeble character; she was more equal to her situation than most girls would have been, and had sense, and energy, and spirits that might be hoped would bear her well and happily through its little difficulties and privations. And then there was such comfort in the very easy distance of Randalls from Hartfield, so convenient for even solitary female walking, and in Mr. Weston's disposition and circumstances, which would make the approaching season no hindrance to their spending half the evenings in the week together.

Her situation was altogether the subject of hours of gratitude to Mrs. Weston, and of moments only of regret; and her satisfaction—her more than satisfaction—her cheerful enjoyment, was so just and so apparent, that Emma, well as she knew her father, was sometimes taken by surprize at his being still able to pity 'poor Miss Taylor,' when they left her at Randalls in the centre of every domestic comfort, or saw her go away in the evening attended by her pleasant husband to a carriage of her own. But never did she go without Mr. Woodhouse's giving a gentle sigh, and saying, "Ah, poor Miss Taylor! She would be very glad to stay."

There was no recovering Miss Taylor—nor much likelihood of ceasing to pity her; but a few weeks brought some alleviation to Mr. Woodhouse. The compliments of his neighbours were over; he was no longer teased by being wished joy of so sorrowful an event; and the wedding-cake, which had been a great distress to him, was all ate up. His own stomach could bear nothing rich, and he could never believe other people to be different from himself. What was unwholesome to him he regarded as unfit for any body; and he had, therefore, earnestly tried to dissuade them from having any wedding-cake at all, and when that proved vain, as earnestly tried to prevent any body's eating it. He had been at the pains of consulting Mr. Perry, the apothecary, on the subject. Mr. Perry was an intelligent, gentlemanlike man, whose frequent visits were one of the comforts of Mr. Woodhouse's life; and upon being applied to, he could not but acknowledge (though it seemed rather against the bias of inclination) that wedding-cake might certainly disagree with many—perhaps with most people, unless taken moderately. With such an opinion, in confirmation of his own, Mr. Woodhouse hoped to influence every visitor of the newly married pair; but still the cake was eaten; and there was no rest for his benevolent nerves till it was all gone.

There was a strange rumour in Highbury of all the little Perrys being seen with a slice of Mrs. Weston's wedding-cake in their hands: but Mr. Woodhouse would never believe it.

CHAPTER III

Mr. Woodhouse was fond of society in his own way. He liked very much to have his friends come and see him; and from various united causes, from his long residence at Hartfield, and his good nature, from his fortune, his house, and his daughter, he could command the visits of his own little circle, in a great measure, as he liked. He had not much intercourse with any families beyond that circle; his horror of late hours, and large dinner-parties, made him unfit for any acquaintance but such as would visit him on his own terms. Fortunately for him, Highbury, including Randalls in the same parish, and Donwell Abbey in the parish adjoining, the seat of Mr. Knightley, comprehended many such. Not unfrequently, through Emma's persuasion, he had some of the chosen and the best to dine with him: but evening parties were what he preferred; and, unless he fancied himself at any time unequal to company, there was scarcely an evening in the week in which Emma could not make up a card-table for him.

Real, long-standing regard brought the Westons and Mr. Knightley; and by Mr. Elton, a young man living alone without liking it, the privilege of exchanging any vacant evening of his own blank solitude for the elegancies and society of Mr. Woodhouse's drawing-room, and the smiles of his lovely daughter, was in no danger of being thrown away.

After these came a second set; among the most come-at-able of whom were Mrs. and Miss Bates, and Mrs. Goddard, three ladies almost always at the service of an invitation from Hartfield, and who were fetched and carried home so often, that Mr. Woodhouse thought it no hardship for either James or the horses. Had it taken place only once a year, it would have been a grievance.

Mrs. Bates, the widow of a former vicar of Highbury, was a very old lady, almost past every thing but tea and quadrille. She lived with her single daughter in a very small way, and was considered with all the regard and respect which a harmless old lady, under such untoward circumstances, can excite. Her daughter enjoyed a most uncommon degree of popularity for a woman neither young, handsome, rich, nor married. Miss Bates stood in the very worst predicament in the world for having much of the public favour; and she had no intellectual superiority to make atonement to herself, or frighten those who might hate her into outward respect. She had never boasted either beauty or cleverness. Her youth had passed without distinction, and her middle of life was devoted to the care of a failing mother, and the endeavour to make a small income go as far as possible. And yet she was a happy woman, and a woman whom no one named without good-will. It was her own universal good-will and contented temper which worked such wonders. She loved every body, was interested in every body's happiness, quicksighted to every body's merits; thought herself a most fortunate creature, and surrounded with blessings in such an excellent mother, and so many good neighbours and friends, and a home that wanted for nothing. The simplicity and cheerfulness of her nature, her contented and grateful spirit, were a recommendation to every body, and a mine of felicity to herself. She was a great talker upon little matters, which exactly suited Mr. Woodhouse, full of trivial communications and harmless gossip.

Mrs. Goddard was the mistress of a school—not of a seminary, or an establishment, or any thing which professed, in long sentences of refined nonsense, to combine liberal acquirements with elegant morality, upon new principles and new systems—and where young ladies for enormous pay might be screwed out of health and into vanity—but a real, honest, old-fashioned boarding-school, where a reasonable quantity of accomplishments were sold at a reasonable price, and where girls might be sent to be out of the way, and scramble themselves into a little education, without any danger of coming back prodigies. Mrs. Goddard's school was in high repute—and very deservedly; for Highbury was reckoned a particularly healthy spot: she had an ample house and garden, gave the children plenty of wholesome food, let them run about a great deal in the summer, and in winter dressed their chilblains with her own hands. It was no wonder that a train of twenty young couple now walked after her to church. She was a plain, motherly kind of woman, who had worked hard in her youth, and now thought herself entitled to the occasional holiday of a tea-visit; and having formerly owed much to Mr. Woodhouse's kindness, felt his particular claim on her to leave her neat parlour, hung round with fancy-work, whenever she could, and win or lose a few sixpences by his fireside.

These were the ladies whom Emma found herself very frequently able to collect; and happy was she, for her father's sake, in the power; though, as far as she was herself concerned, it was no remedy for the absence of Mrs. Weston. She was delighted to see her father look comfortable, and very much pleased with herself for contriving things so well; but the quiet prosings of three such women made her feel that every evening so spent was indeed one of the long evenings she had fearfully anticipated.

As she sat one morning, looking forward to exactly such a close of the present day, a note was brought from Mrs. Goddard, requesting, in most respectful terms, to be allowed to bring Miss Smith with her; a most welcome request: for Miss Smith was a girl of seventeen, whom Emma knew very well by sight, and had long felt an interest in, on account of her beauty. A very gracious invitation was returned, and the evening no longer dreaded by the fair mistress of the mansion.

Harriet Smith was the natural daughter of somebody. Somebody had placed her, several years back, at Mrs. Goddard's school, and somebody had lately raised her from the condition of scholar to that of parlour-boarder. This was all that was generally known of her history. She had no visible friends but what had been acquired at Highbury, and was now just returned from a long visit in the country to some young ladies who had been at school there with her.

She was a very pretty girl, and her beauty happened to be of a sort which Emma particularly admired. She was short, plump, and fair, with a fine bloom, blue eyes, light hair, regular features, and a look of great sweetness, and, before the end of the evening, Emma was as much pleased with her manners as her person, and quite determined to continue the acquaintance.

She was not struck by any thing remarkably clever in Miss Smith's conversation, but she found her altogether very engaging—not inconveniently shy, not unwilling to talk—and yet so far from pushing, shewing so proper and becoming a deference, seeming so pleasantly grateful for being admitted to Hartfield, and so artlessly impressed by the appearance of every thing in so superior a style to what she had been used to, that she must have good sense, and deserve encouragement. Encouragement should be given. Those soft blue eyes, and all those natural graces, should not be wasted on the inferior society of Highbury and its connexions. The acquaintance she had already formed were unworthy of her. The friends from whom she had just parted, though very good sort of people, must be doing her harm. They were a family of the name of Martin, whom Emma well knew by character, as renting a large farm of Mr. Knightley, and residing in the parish of Donwell—very creditably, she believed—she knew Mr. Knightley thought highly of them—but they must be coarse and unpolished, and very unfit to be the intimates of a girl who wanted only a little more knowledge and elegance to be quite perfect. *She* would notice her; she would improve her; she would detach her from her bad acquaintance, and introduce her into good society; she would form her opinions and her manners. It would be an interesting, and certainly a very kind undertaking; highly becoming her own situation in life, her leisure, and powers.

She was so busy in admiring those soft blue eyes, in talking and listening, and forming all these schemes in the in-betweens, that the evening flew away at a very unusual rate; and the supper-table, which always closed such parties, and for which she had been used to sit and watch the due time, was all set out and ready, and moved forwards to the fire, before she was aware. With an alacrity beyond the common impulse of a spirit which yet was never indifferent to the credit of doing every thing well and attentively, with the real good-will of a mind delighted with its own ideas, did she then do all the honours of the meal, and help and recommend the minced chicken and scalloped oysters, with an urgency which she knew would be acceptable to the early hours and civil scruples of their guests.

Upon such occasions poor Mr. Woodhouse's feelings were in sad warfare. He loved to have the cloth laid, because it had been the fashion of his youth, but his conviction of suppers being very unwholesome made him rather sorry to see any thing put on it; and while his hospitality would have welcomed his visitors to every thing, his care for their health made him grieve that they would eat.

Such another small basin of thin gruel as his own was all that he could, with thorough self-approbation, recommend; though he might constrain himself, while the ladies were comfortably clearing the nicer things, to say:

"Mrs. Bates, let me propose your venturing on one of these eggs. An egg boiled very soft is not unwholesome. Serle understands boiling an egg better than any body. I would not recommend an egg boiled by any body else; but you need not be afraid, they are very small, you see—

one of our small eggs will not hurt you. Miss Bates, let Emma help you to a *little* bit of tart—a *very* little bit. Ours are all apple-tarts. You need not be afraid of unwholesome preserves here. I do not advise the custard. Mrs. Goddard, what say you to *half* a glass of wine? A *small* half-glass, put into a tumbler of water? I do not think it could disagree with you."

Emma allowed her father to talk—but supplied her visitors in a much more satisfactory style, and on the present evening had particular pleasure in sending them away happy. The happiness of Miss Smith was quite equal to her intentions. Miss Woodhouse was so great a personage in Highbury, that the prospect of the introduction had given as much panic as pleasure; but the humble, grateful little girl went off with highly gratified feelings, delighted with the affability with which Miss Woodhouse had treated her all the evening, and actually shaken hands with her at last!

CHAPTER IV

Harriet Smith's intimacy at Hartfield was soon a settled thing. Quick and decided in her ways, Emma lost no time in inviting, encouraging, and telling her to come very often; and as their acquaintance increased, so did their satisfaction in each other. As a walking companion, Emma had very early foreseen how useful she might find her. In that respect Mrs. Weston's loss had been important. Her father never went beyond the shrubbery, where two divisions of the ground sufficed him for his long walk, or his short, as the year varied; and since Mrs. Weston's marriage her exercise had been too much confined. She had ventured once alone to Randalls, but it was not pleasant; and a Harriet Smith, therefore, one whom she could summon at any time to a walk, would be a valuable addition to her privileges. But in every respect, as she saw more of her, she approved her, and was confirmed in all her kind designs.

Harriet certainly was not clever, but she had a sweet, docile, grateful disposition, was totally free from conceit, and only desiring to be guided by any one she looked up to. Her early attachment to herself was very amiable; and her inclination for good company, and power of appreciating what was elegant and clever, shewed that there was no want of taste, though strength of understanding must not be expected. Altogether she was quite convinced of Harriet Smith's being exactly the young friend she wanted—exactly the something which her home required. Such a friend as Mrs. Weston was out of the question. Two such could never be granted. Two such she did not want. It was quite a different sort of thing, a sentiment distinct and independent. Mrs. Weston was the object of a regard which had its basis in gratitude and esteem. Harriet would be loved as one to whom she could be useful. For Mrs. Weston there was nothing to be done; for Harriet every thing.

Her first attempts at usefulness were in an endeavour to find out who were the parents, but Harriet could not tell. She was ready to tell every thing in her power, but on this subject questions were vain. Emma was obliged to fancy what she liked—but she could never believe that in the same situation *she* should not have discovered the truth. Harriet had no penetration. She had been satisfied to hear and believe just what Mrs. Goddard chose to tell her; and looked no farther.

Mrs. Goddard, and the teachers, and the girls and the affairs of the school in general, formed naturally a great part of the conversation—and but for her acquaintance with the Martins of Abbey-Mill Farm, it must have been the whole. But the Martins occupied her thoughts a good deal; she had spent two very happy months with them, and now loved to talk of the pleasures of her visit, and describe the many comforts and wonders of the place. Emma encouraged her talkativeness—amused by such a picture of another set of beings, and enjoying the youthful simplicity which could speak with so much exultation of Mrs. Martin's having "*two* parlours, two very good parlours, indeed; one of them quite as large as Mrs. Goddard's drawing-room; and of her having an upper maid who had lived five-and-twenty years with her; and of their having eight cows, two of them Alderneys, and one a little Welch cow, a very pretty little Welch cow indeed; and of Mrs. Martin's saying as she was so fond of it, it should be called *her* cow; and of their having a very handsome summer-house in their garden, where some day next year they were all to drink tea:—a very handsome summer-house, large enough to hold a dozen people."

For some time she was amused, without thinking beyond the immediate cause; but as she came to understand the family better, other feelings arose. She had taken up a wrong idea, fancying it was a mother and daughter, a son and son's wife, who all lived together; but when it appeared that the Mr. Martin, who bore a part in the narrative, and was always mentioned with approbation for his great good-nature in doing something or other, was a single man; that there was no young Mrs. Martin, no wife in the case; she did suspect danger to her poor little friend from all this hospitality and kindness, and that, if she were not taken care of, she might be required to sink herself for-ever.

With this inspiriting notion, her questions increased in number and meaning; and she particularly led Harriet to talk more of Mr. Martin, and there was evidently no dislike to it. Harriet was very ready to speak of the share he had had in their moonlight walks and merry evening games; and dwelt a good deal upon his being so very good-humoured and obliging. He had gone three miles round one day in order to bring her some walnuts, because she had said how fond she was of them, and in every thing else he was so very obliging. He had his shepherd's son into the parlour one night on purpose to sing to her. She was very fond of singing. He could sing a little himself. She believed he was very clever, and understood every thing. He had a very fine flock, and, while she was with them, he had been bid more for his wool than any body in the country. She believed every body spoke well of him. His mother and sisters were very fond of him. Mrs. Martin had told her one day (and there was a blush as she said it) that it was impossible for any body to be a better son, and therefore she was sure, whenever he married, he would make a good husband. Not that she *wanted* him to marry. She was in no hurry at all.

"Well done, Mrs. Martin!" thought Emma. "You know what you are about."

"And when she had come away, Mrs. Martin was so very kind as to send Mrs. Goddard a beautiful goose—the finest goose Mrs. Goddard had ever seen. Mrs. Goddard had dressed it on a Sunday, and asked all the three teachers, Miss Nash, and Miss Prince, and Miss Richardson, to sup with her."

"Mr. Martin, I suppose, is not a man of information beyond the line of his own business? He does not read?"

"Oh yes!—that is, no—I do not know—but I believe he has read a good deal—but not what you would think any thing of. He reads the Agricultural Reports, and some other books that lay in one of the window seats—but he reads all *them* to himself. But sometimes of an evening, before we went to cards, he would read something aloud out of the *Elegant Extracts*, very entertaining. And I know he has read the *Vicar of Wakefield*. He never read the *Romance of the Forest*, nor *The Children of the Abbey*. He had never heard of such books before I mentioned them, but he is determined to get them now as soon as ever he can."

The next question was—

"What sort of looking man is Mr. Martin?"

"Oh! not handsome—not at all handsome. I thought him very plain at first, but I do not think him so plain now. One does not, you know, after a time. But did you never see him? He is in Highbury every now and then, and he is sure to ride through every week in his way to Kingston. He has passed you very often."

"That may be, and I may have seen him fifty times, but without having any idea of his name. A young farmer, whether on horseback or on foot, is the very last sort of person to raise my curiosity. The yeomanry are precisely the order of people with whom I feel I can have nothing to do. A degree or two lower, and a creditable appearance might interest me; I might hope to be useful to their families in some way or other. But a farmer can need none of my help, and is, therefore, in one sense, as much above my notice as in every other he is below it."

"To be sure. Oh yes! It is not likely you should ever have observed him; but he knows you very well indeed—I mean by sight."

"I have no doubt of his being a very respectable young man. I know, indeed, that he is so, and, as such, wish him well. What do you imagine his age to be?"

"He was four-and-twenty the 8th of last June, and my birthday is the 23rd, just a fortnight and a day's difference—which is very odd."

"Only four-and-twenty. That is too young to settle. His mother is perfectly right not to be in a hurry. They seem very comfortable as they are, and if she were to take any pains to marry him, she would probably repent it. Six years hence, if he could meet with a good sort of young woman in the same rank as his own, with a little money, it might be very desirable."

"Six years hence! Dear Miss Woodhouse, he would be thirty years old!"

"Well, and that is as early as most men can afford to marry, who are not born to an independence. Mr. Martin, I imagine, has his fortune entirely to make—cannot be at all beforehand with the world. Whatever money he might come into when his father died, whatever his share of the family property, it is, I dare say, all afloat, all employed in his stock, and so forth; and though, with diligence and good luck, he may be rich in time, it is next to impossible that he should have realised any thing yet."

"To be sure, so it is. But they live very comfortably. They have no indoors man, else they do not want for any thing; and Mrs. Martin talks of taking a boy another year."

"I wish you may not get into a scrape, Harriet, whenever he does marry;—I mean, as to being acquainted with his wife—for though his sisters, from a superior education, are not to be altogether objected to, it does not follow that he might marry any body at all fit for you to notice. The misfortune of your birth ought to make you particularly careful as to your associates. There can be no doubt of your being a gentleman's daughter, and you must support your claim to that station by every thing within your own power, or there will be plenty of people who would take pleasure in degrading you."

"Yes, to be sure, I suppose there are. But while I visit at Hartfield, and you are so kind to me, Miss Woodhouse, I am not afraid of what any body can do."

"You understand the force of influence pretty well, Harriet; but I would have you so firmly established in good society, as to be independent even of Hartfield and Miss Woodhouse. I want to see you permanently well connected, and to that end it will be advisable to have as few odd acquaintance as may be; and, therefore, I say that if you should still be in this country when Mr. Martin marries, I wish you may not be drawn in by your intimacy with the sisters, to be acquainted with the wife, who will probably be some mere farmer's daughter, without education."

"To be sure. Yes. Not that I think Mr. Martin would ever marry any body but what had had some education—and been very well brought up. However, I do not mean to set up my opinion against yours—and I am sure I shall not wish for the acquaintance of his wife. I shall always have a great regard for the Miss Martins, especially Elizabeth, and should be very sorry to give them up, for they are quite as well educated as me. But if he marries a very ignorant, vulgar woman, certainly I had better not visit her, if I can help it."

Emma watched her through the fluctuations of this speech, and saw no alarming symptoms of love. The young man had been the first admirer, but she trusted there was no other hold, and that there would be no serious difficulty, on Harriet's side, to oppose any friendly arrangement of her own.

They met Mr. Martin the very next day, as they were walking on the Donwell road. He was on foot, and after looking very respectfully at her, looked with most unfeigned satisfaction at her companion. Emma was not sorry to have such an opportunity of survey; and walking a few yards forward, while they talked together, soon made her quick eye sufficiently acquainted with Mr. Robert Martin. His appearance was very neat, and he looked like a sensible young man, but his person had no other advantage; and when he came to be contrasted with gentlemen, she thought he must lose all the ground he had gained in Harriet's inclination. Harriet was not insensible of manner; she had voluntarily noticed her father's gentleness with admiration as well as wonder. Mr. Martin looked as if he did not know what manner was.

They remained but a few minutes together, as Miss Woodhouse must not be kept waiting; and Harriet then came running to her with a smiling face, and in a flutter of spirits, which Miss Woodhouse hoped very soon to compose.

"Only think of our happening to meet him!—How very odd! It was quite a chance, he said, that he had not gone round by Randalls. He did not think we ever walked this road. He thought we walked towards Randalls most days. He has not been able to get the *Romance of the Forest* yet. He was so busy the last time he was at Kingston that he quite forgot it, but he goes again to-morrow. So very odd we should happen to meet! Well, Miss Woodhouse, is he like what you expected? What do you think of him? Do you think him so very plain?"

"He is very plain, undoubtedly—remarkably plain:—but that is nothing compared with his entire want of gentility. I had no right to expect much, and I did not expect much; but I had no idea that he could be so very clownish, so totally without air. I had imagined him, I confess, a degree or two nearer gentility."

"To be sure," said Harriet, in a mortified voice, "he is not so genteel as real gentlemen."

"I think, Harriet, since your acquaintance with us, you have been repeatedly in the company of some such very real gentlemen, that you must yourself be struck with the difference in Mr. Martin. At Hartfield, you have had very good specimens of well-educated, well-bred men. I should be surprized if, after seeing them, you could be in company with Mr. Martin again without perceiving him to be a very inferior creature—and rather wondering at yourself for having ever thought him at all agreeable before. Do not you begin to feel that now? Were not you struck? I am sure you must have been struck by his awkward look and abrupt manner, and the uncouthness of a voice which I heard to be wholly unmodulated as I stood here."

"Certainly, he is not like Mr. Knightley. He has not such a fine air and way of walking as Mr. Knightley. I see the difference plain enough. But Mr. Knightley is so very fine a man!"

"Mr. Knightley's air is so remarkably good that it is not fair to compare Mr. Martin with *him*. You might not see one in a hundred with *gentleman* so plainly written as in Mr. Knightley. But he is not the only gentleman you have been lately used to. What say you to Mr. Weston and Mr. Elton? Compare Mr. Martin with either of *them*. Compare their manner of carrying themselves; of walking; of speaking; of being silent. You must see the difference."

"Oh yes!—there is a great difference. But Mr. Weston is almost an old man. Mr. Weston must be between forty and fifty."

"Which makes his good manners the more valuable. The older a person grows, Harriet, the more important it is that their manners should not be bad; the more glaring and disgusting any loudness, or coarseness, or awkwardness becomes. What is passable in youth is detestable in later age. Mr. Martin is now awkward and abrupt; what will he be at Mr. Weston's time of life?"

"There is no saying, indeed," replied Harriet rather solemnly.

"But there may be pretty good guessing. He will be a completely gross, vulgar farmer, totally inattentive to appearances, and thinking of nothing but profit and loss."

"Will he, indeed? That will be very bad."

"How much his business engrosses him already is very plain from the circumstance of his forgetting to inquire for the book you recommended. He was a great deal too full of the market to think of any thing else—which is just as it should be, for a thriving man. What has he to do with books? And I have no doubt that he *will* thrive, and be a very rich man in time—and his being illiterate and coarse need not disturb *us*."

"I wonder he did not remember the book"—was all Harriet's answer, and spoken with a degree of grave displeasure which Emma thought might be safely left to itself. She, therefore, said no more for some time. Her next beginning was,

"In one respect, perhaps, Mr. Elton's manners are superior to Mr. Knightley's or Mr. Weston's. They have more gentleness. They might be more safely held up as a pattern. There is an openness, a quickness, almost a bluntness in Mr. Weston, which every body likes in *him*, because there is so much good-humour with it—but that would not do to be copied. Neither would Mr. Knightley's downright, decided, commanding sort of manner, though it suits *him* very well; his figure, and look, and situation in life seem to allow it; but if any young man were to set about copying him, he would not be sufferable. On the contrary, I think a young man might be very safely recommended to take Mr. Elton as a model. Mr. Elton is good-humoured, cheerful, obliging, and gentle. He seems to me to be grown particularly gentle of late. I do not know whether he has any design of ingratiating himself with either of us, Harriet, by additional softness, but it strikes me that his manners are softer than they used to be. If he means any thing, it must be to please you. Did not I tell you what he said of you the other day?"

She then repeated some warm personal praise which she had drawn from Mr. Elton, and now did full justice to; and Harriet blushed and smiled, and said she had always thought Mr. Elton very agreeable.

Mr. Elton was the very person fixed on by Emma for driving the young farmer out of Harriet's head. She thought it would be an excellent match; and only too palpably desirable, natural, and probable, for her to have much merit in planning it. She feared it was what every body else must think of and predict. It was not likely, however, that any body should have equalled her in the date of the plan, as it had entered her brain during the very first evening of Harriet's coming to Hartfield. The longer she considered it, the greater was her sense of its expediency. Mr. Elton's situation was most suitable, quite the gentleman himself, and without low connexions; at the same time, not of any family that could fairly object to the doubtful birth of Harriet. He had a comfortable home for her, and Emma imagined a very sufficient income; for though the vicarage of Highbury was not large, he was known to have some independent property; and she thought very highly of him as a good-humoured, well-meaning, respectable young man, without any deficiency of useful understanding or knowledge of the world.

She had already satisfied herself that he thought Harriet a beautiful girl, which she trusted, with such frequent meetings at Hartfield, was foundation enough on his side; and on Harriet's there could be little doubt that the idea of being preferred by him would have all the usual weight and efficacy. And he was really a very pleasing young man, a young man whom any woman not fastidious might like. He was reckoned very handsome; his person much admired in general, though not by her, there being a want of elegance of feature which she could not dispense with:—but the girl who could be gratified by a Robert Martin's riding about the country to get walnuts for her might very well be conquered by Mr. Elton's admiration.

CHAPTER V

"I do not know what your opinion may be, Mrs. Weston," said Mr. Knightley, "of this great intimacy between Emma and Harriet Smith, but I think it a bad thing."

"A bad thing! Do you really think it a bad thing?—why so?"

"I think they will neither of them do the other any good."

"You surprize me! Emma must do Harriet good: and by supplying her with a new object of interest, Harriet may be said to do Emma good. I have been seeing their intimacy with the greatest pleasure. How very differently we feel!—Not think they will do each other any good! This will certainly be the beginning of one of our quarrels about Emma, Mr. Knightley."

"Perhaps you think I am come on purpose to quarrel with you, knowing Weston to be out, and that you must still fight your own battle."

"Mr. Weston would undoubtedly support me, if he were here, for he thinks exactly as I do on the subject. We were speaking of it only yesterday, and agreeing how fortunate it was for Emma, that there should be such a girl in Highbury for her to associate with. Mr. Knightley, I shall not allow you to be a fair judge in this case. You are so much used to live alone, that you do not know the value of a companion; and, perhaps no man can be a good judge of the comfort a woman feels in the society of one of her own sex, after being used to it all her life. I can imagine your objection to Harriet Smith. She is not the superior young woman which Emma's friend ought to be. But on the other hand, as Emma wants to see her better informed, it will be an inducement to her to read more herself. They will read together. She means it, I know."

"Emma has been meaning to read more ever since she was twelve years old. I have seen a great many lists of her drawing-up at various times of books that she meant to read regularly through—and very good lists they were—very well chosen, and very neatly arranged—sometimes alphabetically, and sometimes by some other rule. The list she drew up when only fourteen—I remember thinking it did her judgment so much credit, that I preserved it some time; and I dare say she may have made out a very good list now. But I have done with expecting any course of steady reading from Emma. She will never submit to any thing requiring industry and patience, and a subjection of the fancy to the understanding. Where Miss Taylor failed to stimulate, I may safely affirm that Harriet Smith will do nothing.—You never could persuade her to read half so much as you wished.—You know you could not."

"I dare say," replied Mrs. Weston, smiling, "that I thought so *then*;—but since we have parted, I can never remember Emma's omitting to do any thing I wished."

"There is hardly any desiring to refresh such a memory as *that*,"—said Mr. Knightley, feelingly; and for a moment or two he had done. "But I," he soon added, "who have had no such charm thrown over my senses, must still see, hear, and remember. Emma is spoiled by being the cleverest of her family. At ten years old, she had the misfortune of being able to answer questions which puzzled her sister at seventeen. She was always quick and assured: Isabella slow and diffident. And ever since she was twelve, Emma has been mistress of the house and of you all. In her mother she lost the only person able to cope with her. She inherits her mother's talents, and must have been under subjection to her."

"I should have been sorry, Mr. Knightley, to be dependent on *your* recommendation, had I quitted Mr. Woodhouse's family and wanted another situation; I do not think you would have spoken a good word for me to any body. I am sure you always thought me unfit for the office I held."

"Yes," said he, smiling. "You are better placed *here*; very fit for a wife, but not at all for a governess. But you were preparing yourself to be an excellent wife all the time you were at Hartfield. You might not give Emma such a complete education as your powers would seem to promise; but you were receiving a very good education from *her*, on the very material matrimonial point of submitting your own will, and doing as you were bid; and if Weston had asked me to recommend him a wife, I should certainly have named Miss Taylor."

"Thank you. There will be very little merit in making a good wife to such a man as Mr. Weston."

"Why, to own the truth, I am afraid you are rather thrown away, and that with every disposition to bear, there will be nothing to be borne. We will not despair, however. Weston may grow cross from the wantonness of comfort, or his son may plague him."

"I hope not *that.*—It is not likely. No, Mr. Knightley, do not foretell vexation from that quarter."

"Not I, indeed. I only name possibilities. I do not pretend to Emma's genius for foretelling and guessing. I hope, with all my heart, the young man may be a Weston in merit, and a Churchill in fortune.—But Harriet Smith—I have not half done about Harriet Smith. I think her the very worst sort of companion that Emma could possibly have. She knows nothing herself, and looks upon Emma as knowing every thing. She is a flatterer in all her ways; and so much the worse, because undesigned. Her ignorance is hourly flattery. How can Emma imagine she has any thing to learn herself, while Harriet is presenting such a delightful inferiority? And as for Harriet, I will venture to say that *she* cannot gain by the acquaintance. Hartfield will only put her out of conceit with all the other places she belongs to. She will grow just refined enough to be uncomfortable with those among whom birth and circumstances have placed her home. I am much mistaken if Emma's doctrines give any strength of mind, or tend at all to make a girl adapt herself rationally to the varieties of her situation in life.—They only give a little polish."

"I either depend more upon Emma's good sense than you do, or am more anxious for her present comfort; for I cannot lament the acquaintance. How well she looked last night!"

"Oh! you would rather talk of her person than her mind, would you? Very well; I shall not attempt to deny Emma's being pretty."

"Pretty! say beautiful rather. Can you imagine any thing nearer perfect beauty than Emma altogether—face and figure?"

"I do not know what I could imagine, but I confess that I have seldom seen a face or figure more pleasing to me than hers. But I am a partial old friend."

"Such an eye!—the true hazle eye—and so brilliant! regular features, open countenance, with a complexion! oh! what a bloom of full health, and such a pretty height and size; such a firm and upright figure! There is health, not merely in her bloom, but in her air, her head, her glance. One hears sometimes of a child being 'the picture of health;' now, Emma always gives me the idea of being the complete picture of grown-up health. She is loveliness itself. Mr. Knightley, is not she?"

"I have not a fault to find with her person," he replied. "I think her all you describe. I love to look at her; and I will add this praise, that I do not think her personally vain. Considering how very handsome she is, she appears to be little occupied with it; her vanity lies another way. Mrs. Weston, I am not to be talked out of my dislike of Harriet Smith, or my dread of its doing them both harm."

"And I, Mr. Knightley, am equally stout in my confidence of its not doing them any harm. With all dear Emma's little faults, she is an excellent creature. Where shall we see a better daughter, or a kinder sister, or a truer friend? No, no; she has qualities which may be trusted; she will never lead any one really wrong; she will make no lasting blunder; where Emma errs once, she is in the right a hundred times."

"Very well; I will not plague you any more. Emma shall be an angel, and I will keep my spleen to myself till Christmas brings John and Isabella. John loves Emma with a reasonable and therefore not a blind affection, and Isabella always thinks as he does; except when he is not quite frightened enough about the children. I am sure of having their opinions with me."

"I know that you all love her really too well to be unjust or unkind; but excuse me, Mr. Knightley, if I take the liberty (I consider myself, you know, as having somewhat of the privilege of speech that Emma's mother might have had) the liberty of hinting that I do not think any possible good can arise from Harriet Smith's intimacy being made a matter of much discussion among you. Pray excuse me; but supposing any little inconvenience may be apprehended from the intimacy, it cannot be expected that Emma, accountable to nobody but her father, who perfectly approves the acquaintance, should put an end to it, so long as it is a source of pleasure to herself. It has been so many years my province to give advice, that you cannot be surprized, Mr. Knightley, at this little remains of office."

"Not at all," cried he; "I am much obliged to you for it. It is very good advice, and it shall have a better fate than your advice has often found; for it shall be attended to."

"Mrs. John Knightley is easily alarmed, and might be made unhappy about her sister."

"Be satisfied," said he, "I will not raise any outcry. I will keep my ill-humour to myself. I have a very sincere interest in Emma. Isabella does not seem more my sister; has never excited a greater interest; perhaps hardly so great. There is an anxiety, a curiosity in what one feels for Emma. I wonder what will become of her!"

"So do I," said Mrs. Weston gently, "very much."

"She always declares she will never marry, which, of course, means just nothing at all. But I have no idea that she has yet ever seen a man she cared for. It would not be a bad thing for her to be very much in love with a proper object. I should like to see Emma in love, and in some doubt of a return; it would do her good. But there is nobody hereabouts to attach her; and she goes so seldom from home."

"There does, indeed, seem as little to tempt her to break her resolution at present," said Mrs. Weston, "as can well be; and while she is so happy at Hartfield, I cannot wish her to be forming any attachment which would be creating such difficulties on poor Mr. Woodhouse's account. I do not recommend matrimony at present to Emma, though I mean no slight to the state, I assure you."

Part of her meaning was to conceal some favourite thoughts of her own and Mr. Weston's on the subject, as much as possible. There were wishes at Randalls respecting Emma's destiny, but it was not desirable to have them suspected; and the quiet transition which Mr. Knightley soon afterwards made to "What does Weston think of the weather; shall we have rain?" convinced her that he had nothing more to say or surmise about Hartfield.

CHAPTER VI

Emma could not feel a doubt of having given Harriet's fancy a proper direction and raised the gratitude of her young vanity to a very good purpose, for she found her decidedly more sensible than before of Mr. Elton's being a remarkably handsome man, with most agreeable manners; and as she had no hesitation in following up the assurance of his admiration by agreeable hints, she was soon pretty confident of creating as much liking on Harriet's side, as there could be any occasion for. She was quite convinced of Mr. Elton's being in the fairest way of falling in love, if not in love already. She had no scruple with regard to him. He talked of Harriet, and praised her so warmly, that she could not suppose any thing wanting which a little time would not add. His perception of the striking improvement of Harriet's manner, since her introduction at Hartfield, was not one of the least agreeable proofs of his growing attachment.

"You have given Miss Smith all that she required," said he; "you have made her graceful and easy. She was a beautiful creature when she came to you, but, in my opinion, the attractions you have added are infinitely superior to what she received from nature."

"I am glad you think I have been useful to her; but Harriet only wanted drawing out, and receiving a few, very few hints. She had all the natural grace of sweetness of temper and artlessness in herself. I have done very little."

"If it were admissible to contradict a lady," said the gallant Mr. Elton.

"I have perhaps given her a little more decision of character, have taught her to think on points which had not fallen in her way before."

"Exactly so; that is what principally strikes me. So much superadded decision of character! Skilful has been the hand!"

"Great has been the pleasure, I am sure. I never met with a disposition more truly amiable."

"I have no doubt of it." And it was spoken with a sort of sighing animation, which had a vast deal of the lover. She was not less pleased another day with the manner in which he seconded a sudden wish of hers, to have Harriet's picture.

"Did you ever have your likeness taken, Harriet?" said she: "did you ever sit for your picture?"

Harriet was on the point of leaving the room, and only stopt to say, with a very interesting naivete,

"Oh! dear, no, never."

No sooner was she out of sight, than Emma exclaimed,

"What an exquisite possession a good picture of her would be! I would give any money for it. I almost long to attempt her likeness myself. You do not know it I dare say, but two or three years ago I had a great passion for taking likenesses, and attempted several of my friends, and was thought to have a tolerable eye in general. But from one cause or another, I gave it up in disgust. But really, I could almost venture, if Harriet would sit to me. It would be such a delight to have her picture!"

"Let me entreat you," cried Mr. Elton; "it would indeed be a delight! Let me entreat you, Miss Woodhouse, to exercise so charming a talent in favour of your friend. I know what your drawings are. How could you suppose me ignorant? Is not this room rich in specimens of your landscapes and flowers; and has not Mrs. Weston some inimitable figure-pieces in her drawing-room, at Randalls?"

Yes, good man!—thought Emma—but what has all that to do with taking likenesses? You know nothing of drawing. Don't pretend to be in raptures about mine. Keep your raptures for Harriet's face. "Well, if you give me such kind encouragement, Mr. Elton, I believe I shall try what I can do. Harriet's features are very delicate, which makes a likeness difficult; and yet there is a peculiarity in the shape of the eye and the lines about the mouth which one ought to catch."

"Exactly so—The shape of the eye and the lines about the mouth—I have not a doubt of your success. Pray, pray attempt it. As you will do it, it will indeed, to use your own words, be an exquisite possession."

"But I am afraid, Mr. Elton, Harriet will not like to sit. She thinks so little of her own beauty. Did not you observe her manner of answering me? How completely it meant, 'why should my picture be drawn?'"

"Oh! yes, I observed it, I assure you. It was not lost on me. But still I cannot imagine she would not be persuaded."

Harriet was soon back again, and the proposal almost immediately made; and she had no scruples which could stand many minutes against the earnest pressing of both the others. Emma wished to go to work directly, and therefore produced the portfolio containing her various attempts at portraits, for not one of them had ever been finished, that they might decide together on the best size for Harriet. Her many beginnings were displayed. Miniatures, half-lengths, whole-lengths, pencil, crayon, and water-colours had been all tried in turn. She had always wanted to do every thing, and had made more progress both in drawing and music than many might have done with so little labour as she would ever submit to. She played and sang;—and drew in almost every style; but steadiness had always been wanting; and in nothing had she approached the degree of excellence which she would have been glad to command, and ought not to have failed of. She was not much deceived as to her own skill either as an artist or a musician, but she was not unwilling to have others deceived, or sorry to know her reputation for accomplishment often higher than it deserved.

There was merit in every drawing—in the least finished, perhaps the most; her style was spirited; but had there been much less, or had there been ten times more, the delight and admiration of her two companions would have been the same. They were both in ecstasies. A likeness pleases every body; and Miss Woodhouse's performances must be capital.

"No great variety of faces for you," said Emma. "I had only my own family to study from. There is my father—another of my father—but the idea of sitting for his picture made him so nervous, that I could only take him by stealth; neither of them very like therefore. Mrs. Weston again, and again, and again, you see. Dear Mrs. Weston! always my kindest friend on every occasion. She would sit whenever I asked her. There is my sister; and really quite her own little elegant figure!—and the face not unlike. I should have made a good likeness of her, if she would have sat longer, but she was in such a hurry to have me draw her four children that she would not be quiet. Then, here come all my attempts at three of those four children;—there they are, Henry and John and Bella, from one end of the sheet to the other, and any one of them might do for any one of the rest. She was so eager to have them drawn that I could not refuse; but there is no making children of three or four years old stand still you know; nor can it be very easy to take any likeness of them, beyond the air and complexion, unless they are coarser featured than any of mama's children ever were. Here is my sketch of the fourth, who was a baby. I took him as he was sleeping on the sofa, and it is as strong a likeness of his cockade as you would wish to see. He had nestled down his head most conveniently. That's very like. I am rather proud of little George. The corner of the sofa is very good. Then here is my last,"—unclosing a pretty sketch of a gentleman in small size, whole-length—"my last and my best—my brother, Mr. John Knightley.—This did not want much of being finished, when I put it away in a pet, and vowed I would never take another likeness. I could not help being provoked; for after all my pains, and when I had really made a very good likeness of it—(Mrs. Weston and I were quite agreed in thinking it *very* like)—only too handsome—too flattering—but that was a fault on the right side—after all this, came poor dear Isabella's cold approbation of—'Yes, it was a little like—but to be sure it did not do him justice.' We had had a great deal of trouble in persuading him to sit at all. It was made a great favour of; and altogether it was more than I could bear; and so I never would finish it, to have it apologised over as an unfavourable likeness, to every morning visitor in Brunswick Square;—and, as I said, I did then forswear ever drawing any body again. But for Harriet's sake, or rather for my own, and as there are no husbands and wives in the case *at present*, I will break my resolution now."

Mr. Elton seemed very properly struck and delighted by the idea, and was repeating, "No husbands and wives in the case at present indeed, as you observe. Exactly so. No husbands and wives," with so interesting a consciousness, that Emma began to consider whether she had not better leave them together at once. But as she wanted to be drawing, the declaration must wait a little longer.

She had soon fixed on the size and sort of portrait. It was to be a whole-length in water-colours, like Mr. John Knightley's, and was destined, if she could please herself, to hold a very honourable station over the mantelpiece.

The sitting began; and Harriet, smiling and blushing, and afraid of not keeping her attitude and countenance, presented a very sweet mixture of youthful expression to the steady eyes of the artist. But there was no doing any thing, with Mr. Elton fidgeting behind her and watching every touch. She gave him credit for stationing himself where he might gaze and gaze again without offence; but was really obliged to put an end to it, and request him to place himself elsewhere. It then occurred to her to employ him in reading.

"If he would be so good as to read to them, it would be a kindness indeed! It would amuse away the difficulties of her part, and lessen the irksomeness of Miss Smith's."

Mr. Elton was only too happy. Harriet listened, and Emma drew in peace. She must allow him to be still frequently coming to look; any thing less would certainly have been too little in a lover; and he was ready at the smallest intermission of the pencil, to jump up and see the progress, and be charmed.—There was no being displeased with such an encourager, for his admiration made him discern a likeness almost before it was possible. She could not respect his eye, but his love and his complaisance were unexceptionable.

The sitting was altogether very satisfactory; she was quite enough pleased with the first day's sketch to wish to go on. There was no want of likeness, she had been fortunate in the attitude, and as she meant to throw in a little improvement to the figure, to give a little more height, and considerably more elegance, she had great confidence of its being in every way a pretty drawing at last, and of its filling its destined place with credit to them both—a standing memorial of the beauty of one, the skill of the other, and the friendship of both; with as many other agreeable associations as Mr. Elton's very promising attachment was likely to add.

Harriet was to sit again the next day; and Mr. Elton, just as he ought, entreated for the permission of attending and reading to them again.

"By all means. We shall be most happy to consider you as one of the party."

The same civilities and courtesies, the same success and satisfaction, took place on the morrow, and accompanied the whole progress of the picture, which was rapid and happy. Every body who saw it was pleased, but Mr. Elton was in continual raptures, and defended it through every criticism.

"Miss Woodhouse has given her friend the only beauty she wanted,"—observed Mrs. Weston to him—not in the least suspecting that she was addressing a lover.—"The expression of the eye is most correct, but Miss Smith has not those eyebrows and eyelashes. It is the fault of her face that she has them not."

"Do you think so?" replied he. "I cannot agree with you. It appears to me a most perfect resemblance in every feature. I never saw such a likeness in my life. We must allow for the effect of shade, you know."

"You have made her too tall, Emma," said Mr. Knightley.

Emma knew that she had, but would not own it; and Mr. Elton warmly added,

"Oh no! certainly not too tall; not in the least too tall. Consider, she is sitting down—which naturally presents a different—which in short gives exactly the idea—and the proportions must be preserved, you know. Proportions, fore-shortening.—Oh no! it gives one exactly the idea of such a height as Miss Smith's. Exactly so indeed!"

"It is very pretty," said Mr. Woodhouse. "So prettily done! Just as your drawings always are, my dear. I do not know any body who draws so well as you do. The only thing I do not thoroughly like is, that she seems to be sitting out of doors, with only a little shawl over her shoulders—and it makes one think she must catch cold."

"But, my dear papa, it is supposed to be summer; a warm day in summer. Look at the tree."

"But it is never safe to sit out of doors, my dear."

"You, sir, may say any thing," cried Mr. Elton, "but I must confess that I regard it as a most happy thought, the placing of Miss Smith out of doors; and the tree is touched with such inimitable spirit! Any other situation would have been much less in character. The naivete of Miss Smith's manners—and altogether—Oh, it is most admirable! I cannot keep my eyes from it. I never saw such a likeness."

The next thing wanted was to get the picture framed; and here were a few difficulties. It must be done directly; it must be done in London; the order must go through the hands of some intelligent person whose taste could be depended on; and Isabella, the usual doer of all commissions, must not be applied to, because it was December, and Mr. Woodhouse could not bear the idea of her stirring out of her house in the fogs of December. But no sooner was the distress known to Mr. Elton, than it was removed. His gallantry was always on the alert. "Might he be trusted with the commission, what infinite pleasure should he have in executing it! he could ride to London at any time. It was impossible to say how much he should be gratified by being employed on such an errand."

"He was too good!—she could not endure the thought!—she would not give him such a troublesome office for the world,"—brought on the desired repetition of entreaties and assurances,—and a very few minutes settled the business.

Mr. Elton was to take the drawing to London, chuse the frame, and give the directions; and Emma thought she could so pack it as to ensure its safety without much incommoding him, while he seemed mostly fearful of not being incommoded enough.

"What a precious deposit!" said he with a tender sigh, as he received it.

"This man is almost too gallant to be in love," thought Emma. "I should say so, but that I suppose there may be a hundred different ways of being in love. He is an excellent young man, and will suit Harriet exactly; it will be an 'Exactly so,' as he says himself; but he does sigh and languish, and study for compliments rather more than I could endure as a principal. I come in for a pretty good share as a second. But it is his gratitude on Harriet's account."

CHAPTER VII

The very day of Mr. Elton's going to London produced a fresh occasion for Emma's services towards her friend. Harriet had been at Hartfield, as usual, soon after breakfast; and, after a time, had gone home to return again to dinner: she returned, and sooner than had been talked of, and with an agitated, hurried look, announcing something extraordinary to have happened which she was longing to tell. Half a minute brought it all out. She had heard, as soon as she got back to Mrs. Goddard's, that Mr. Martin had been there an hour before, and finding she was not at home, nor particularly expected, had left a little parcel for her from one of his sisters, and gone away; and on opening this parcel, she had actually found, besides the two songs which she had lent Elizabeth to copy, a letter to herself; and this letter was from him, from Mr. Martin, and contained a direct proposal of marriage. "Who could have thought it? She was so surprized she did not know what to do. Yes, quite a proposal of marriage; and a very good letter, at least she thought so. And he wrote as if he really loved her very much—but she did not know—and so, she was come as fast as she could to ask Miss Woodhouse what she should do." Emma was half-ashamed of her friend for seeming so pleased and so doubtful.

"Upon my word," she cried, "the young man is determined not to lose any thing for want of asking. He will connect himself well if he can."

"Will you read the letter?" cried Harriet. "Pray do. I'd rather you would."

Emma was not sorry to be pressed. She read, and was surprized. The style of the letter was much above her expectation. There were not merely no grammatical errors, but as a composition it would not have disgraced a gentleman; the language, though plain, was strong and unaffected, and the sentiments it conveyed very much to the credit of the writer. It was short, but expressed good sense, warm attachment, liberality, propriety, even delicacy of feeling. She paused over it, while Harriet stood anxiously watching for her opinion, with a "Well, well," and was at last forced to add, "Is it a good letter? or is it too short?"

"Yes, indeed, a very good letter," replied Emma rather slowly—

"so good a letter, Harriet, that every thing considered, I think one of his sisters must have helped him. I can hardly imagine the young man whom I saw talking with you the other day could express himself so well, if left quite to his own powers, and yet it is not the style of a woman; no, certainly, it is too strong and concise; not diffuse enough for a woman. No doubt he is a sensible man, and I suppose may have a natural talent for—thinks strongly and clearly—and when he takes a pen in hand, his thoughts naturally find proper words. It is so with some men. Yes, I understand the sort of mind. Vigorous, decided, with sentiments to a certain point, not coarse. A better written letter, Harriet (returning it,) than I had expected."

"Well," said the still waiting Harriet;—"well—and—and what shall I do?"

"What shall you do! In what respect? Do you mean with regard to this letter?"

"Yes."

"But what are you in doubt of? You must answer it of course—and speedily."

"Yes. But what shall I say? Dear Miss Woodhouse, do advise me."

"Oh no, no! the letter had much better be all your own. You will express yourself very properly, I am sure. There is no danger of your not being intelligible, which is the first thing. Your meaning must be unequivocal; no doubts or demurs: and such expressions of gratitude and concern for the pain you are inflicting as propriety requires, will present themselves unbidden to *your* mind, I am persuaded. You need not be prompted to write with the appearance of sorrow for his disappointment."

"You think I ought to refuse him then," said Harriet, looking down.

"Ought to refuse him! My dear Harriet, what do you mean? Are you in any doubt as to that? I thought—but I beg your pardon, perhaps I have been under a mistake. I certainly have been misunderstanding you, if you feel in doubt as to the *purport* of your answer. I had imagined you were consulting me only as to the wording of it."

Harriet was silent. With a little reserve of manner, Emma continued:

"You mean to return a favourable answer, I collect."

"No, I do not; that is, I do not mean—What shall I do? What would you advise me to do? Pray, dear Miss Woodhouse, tell me what I ought to do."

"I shall not give you any advice, Harriet. I will have nothing to do with it. This is a point which you must settle with your feelings."

"I had no notion that he liked me so very much," said Harriet, contemplating the letter. For a little while Emma persevered in her silence; but beginning to apprehend the bewitching flattery of that letter might be too powerful, she thought it best to say,

"I lay it down as a general rule, Harriet, that if a woman *doubts* as to whether she should accept a man or not, she certainly ought to refuse him. If she can hesitate as to 'Yes,' she ought to say 'No' directly. It is not a state to be safely entered into with doubtful feelings, with half a heart. I thought it my duty as a friend, and older than yourself, to say thus much to you. But do not imagine that I want to influence you."

"Oh! no, I am sure you are a great deal too kind to—but if you would just advise me what I had best do—No, no, I do not mean that—As you say, one's mind ought to be quite made up—One should not be hesitating—It is a very serious thing.—It will be safer to say 'No,' perhaps.—Do you think I had better say 'No?'"

"Not for the world," said Emma, smiling graciously, "would I advise you either way. You must be the best judge of your own happiness. If you prefer Mr. Martin to every other person; if you think him the most agreeable man you have ever been in company with, why should you hesitate? You blush, Harriet.—Does any body else occur to you at this moment under such a definition? Harriet, Harriet, do not deceive yourself; do not be run away with by gratitude and compassion. At this moment whom are you thinking of?"

The symptoms were favourable.—Instead of answering, Harriet turned away confused, and stood thoughtfully by the fire; and though the letter was still in her hand, it was now mechanically twisted about without regard. Emma waited the result with impatience, but not without strong hopes. At last, with some hesitation, Harriet said—

"Miss Woodhouse, as you will not give me your opinion, I must do as well as I can by myself; and I have now quite determined, and really almost made up my mind—to refuse Mr. Martin. Do you think I am right?"

"Perfectly, perfectly right, my dearest Harriet; you are doing just what you ought. While you were at all in suspense I kept my feelings to myself, but now that you are so completely decided I have no hesitation in approving. Dear Harriet, I give myself joy of this. It would have grieved me to lose your acquaintance, which must have been the consequence of your marrying Mr. Martin. While you were in the smallest degree wavering, I said nothing about it, because I would not influence; but it would have been the loss of a friend to me. I could not have visited Mrs. Robert Martin, of Abbey-Mill Farm. Now I am secure of you for ever."

Harriet had not surmised her own danger, but the idea of it struck her forcibly.

"You could not have visited me!" she cried, looking aghast. "No, to be sure you could not; but I never thought of that before. That would have been too dreadful!—What an escape!—Dear Miss Woodhouse, I would not give up the pleasure and honour of being intimate with you for any thing in the world."

"Indeed, Harriet, it would have been a severe pang to lose you; but it must have been. You would have thrown yourself out of all good society. I must have given you up."

"Dear me!—How should I ever have borne it! It would have killed me never to come to Hartfield any more!"

"Dear affectionate creature!—*You* banished to Abbey-Mill Farm!—*You* confined to the society of the illiterate and vulgar all your life! I wonder how the young man could have the assurance to ask it. He must have a pretty good opinion of himself."

"I do not think he is conceited either, in general," said Harriet, her conscience opposing such censure; "at least, he is very good-natured, and I shall always feel much obliged to him, and have a great regard for—but that is quite a different thing from—and you know, though he may like me, it does not follow that I should—and certainly I must confess that since my visiting here I have seen people—and if one comes to compare them, person and manners, there is no comparison at all, *one* is so very handsome and agreeable. However, I do really think Mr. Martin a very amiable young man, and have a great opinion of him; and his being so much attached to me—and his writing such a letter—but as to leaving you, it is what I would not do upon any consideration."

"Thank you, thank you, my own sweet little friend. We will not be parted. A woman is not to marry a man merely because she is asked, or because he is attached to her, and can write a tolerable letter."

"Oh no;—and it is but a short letter too."

Emma felt the bad taste of her friend, but let it pass with a "very true; and it would be a small consolation to her, for the clownish manner which might be offending her every hour of the day, to know that her husband could write a good letter."

"Oh! yes, very. Nobody cares for a letter; the thing is, to be always happy with pleasant companions. I am quite determined to refuse him. But how shall I do? What shall I say?"

Emma assured her there would be no difficulty in the answer, and advised its being written directly, which was agreed to, in the hope of her assistance; and though Emma continued to protest against any assistance being wanted, it was in fact given in the formation of every sentence. The looking over his letter again, in replying to it, had such a softening tendency, that it was particularly necessary to brace her up with a few decisive expressions; and she was so very much concerned at the idea of making him unhappy, and thought so much of what his mother and sisters would think and say, and was so anxious that they should not fancy her ungrateful, that Emma believed if the young man had come in her way at that moment, he would have been accepted after all.

This letter, however, was written, and sealed, and sent. The business was finished, and Harriet safe. She was rather low all the evening, but Emma could allow for her amiable regrets, and sometimes relieved them by speaking of her own affection, sometimes by bringing forward the idea of Mr. Elton.

"I shall never be invited to Abbey-Mill again," was said in rather a sorrowful tone.

"Nor, if you were, could I ever bear to part with you, my Harriet. You are a great deal too necessary at Hartfield to be spared to Abbey-Mill."

"And I am sure I should never want to go there; for I am never happy but at Hartfield."

Some time afterwards it was, "I think Mrs. Goddard would be very much surprized if she knew what had happened. I am sure Miss Nash would—for Miss Nash thinks her own sister very well married, and it is only a linen-draper."

"One should be sorry to see greater pride or refinement in the teacher of a school, Harriet. I dare say Miss Nash would envy you such an opportunity as this of being married. Even this conquest would appear valuable in her eyes. As to any thing superior for you, I suppose she is quite in the dark. The attentions of a certain person can hardly be among the tittle-tattle of Highbury yet. Hitherto I fancy you and I are the only people to whom his looks and manners have explained themselves."

Harriet blushed and smiled, and said something about wondering that people should like her so much. The idea of Mr. Elton was certainly cheering; but still, after a time, she was tender-hearted again towards the rejected Mr. Martin.

"Now he has got my letter," said she softly. "I wonder what they are all doing—whether his sisters know—if he is unhappy, they will be unhappy too. I hope he will not mind it so very much."

"Let us think of those among our absent friends who are more cheerfully employed," cried Emma. "At this moment, perhaps, Mr. Elton is shewing your picture to his mother and sisters, telling how much more beautiful is the original, and after being asked for it five or six times, allowing them to hear your name, your own dear name."

"My picture!—But he has left my picture in Bond-street."

"Has he so!—Then I know nothing of Mr. Elton. No, my dear little modest Harriet, depend upon it the picture will not be in Bond-street till just before he mounts his horse to-morrow. It is his companion all this evening, his solace, his delight. It opens his designs to his family, it introduces you among them, it diffuses through the party those pleasantest feelings of our nature, eager curiosity and warm prepossession. How cheerful, how animated, how suspicious, how busy their imaginations all are!"

Harriet smiled again, and her smiles grew stronger.

CHAPTER VIII

Harriet slept at Hartfield that night. For some weeks past she had been spending more than half her time there, and gradually getting to have a bed-room appropriated to herself; and Emma judged it best in every respect, safest and kindest, to keep her with them as much as possible just at present. She was obliged to go the next morning for an hour or two to Mrs. Goddard's, but it was then to be settled that she should return to Hartfield, to make a regular visit of some days.

While she was gone, Mr. Knightley called, and sat some time with Mr. Woodhouse and Emma, till Mr. Woodhouse, who had previously made up his mind to walk out, was persuaded by his daughter not to defer it, and was induced by the entreaties of both, though against the scruples of his own civility, to leave Mr. Knightley for that purpose. Mr. Knightley, who had nothing of ceremony about him, was offering by his short, decided answers, an amusing contrast to the protracted apologies and civil hesitations of the other.

"Well, I believe, if you will excuse me, Mr. Knightley, if you will not consider me as doing a very rude thing, I shall take Emma's advice and go out for a quarter of an hour. As the sun is out, I believe I had better take my three turns while I can. I treat you without ceremony, Mr. Knightley. We invalids think we are privileged people."

"My dear sir, do not make a stranger of me."

"I leave an excellent substitute in my daughter. Emma will be happy to entertain you. And therefore I think I will beg your excuse and take my three turns—my winter walk."

"You cannot do better, sir."

"I would ask for the pleasure of your company, Mr. Knightley, but I am a very slow walker, and my pace would be tedious to you; and, besides, you have another long walk before you, to Donwell Abbey."

"Thank you, sir, thank you; I am going this moment myself; and I think the sooner *you* go the better. I will fetch your greatcoat and open the garden door for you."

Mr. Woodhouse at last was off; but Mr. Knightley, instead of being immediately off likewise, sat down again, seemingly inclined for more chat. He began speaking of Harriet, and speaking of her with more voluntary praise than Emma had ever heard before.

"I cannot rate her beauty as you do," said he; "but she is a pretty little creature, and I am inclined to think very well of her disposition. Her character depends upon those she is with; but in good hands she will turn out a valuable woman."

"I am glad you think so; and the good hands, I hope, may not be wanting."

"Come," said he, "you are anxious for a compliment, so I will tell you that you have improved her. You have cured her of her school-girl's giggle; she really does you credit."

"Thank you. I should be mortified indeed if I did not believe I had been of some use; but it is not every body who will bestow praise where they may. *You* do not often overpower me with it."

"You are expecting her again, you say, this morning?"

"Almost every moment. She has been gone longer already than she intended."

"Something has happened to delay her; some visitors perhaps."

"Highbury gossips!—Tiresome wretches!"

"Harriet may not consider every body tiresome that you would."

Emma knew this was too true for contradiction, and therefore said nothing. He presently added, with a smile,

"I do not pretend to fix on times or places, but I must tell you that I have good reason to believe your little friend will soon hear of something to her advantage."

"Indeed! how so? of what sort?"

"A very serious sort, I assure you;" still smiling.

"Very serious! I can think of but one thing—Who is in love with her? Who makes you their confidant?"

Emma was more than half in hopes of Mr. Elton's having dropt a hint. Mr. Knightley was a sort of general friend and adviser, and she knew Mr. Elton looked up to him.

"I have reason to think," he replied, "that Harriet Smith will soon have an offer of marriage, and from a most unexceptionable quarter:—Robert Martin is the man. Her visit to Abbey-Mill, this summer, seems to have done his business. He is desperately in love and means to marry her."

"He is very obliging," said Emma; "but is he sure that Harriet means to marry him?"

"Well, well, means to make her an offer then. Will that do? He came to the Abbey two evenings ago, on purpose to consult me about it. He knows I have a thorough regard for him and all his family, and, I believe, considers me as one of his best friends. He came to ask me whether I thought it would be imprudent in him to settle so early; whether I thought her too young: in short, whether I approved his choice altogether; having some apprehension perhaps of her being considered (especially since *your* making so much of her) as in a line of society above him. I was very much pleased with all that he said. I never hear better sense from any one than Robert Martin. He always speaks to the purpose; open, straightforward, and very well judging. He told me every thing; his circumstances and plans, and what they all proposed doing in the event of his marriage. He is an excellent young man, both as son and brother. I had no hesitation in advising him to marry. He proved to me that he could afford it; and that being the case, I was convinced he could not do better. I praised the fair lady too, and altogether sent him away very happy. If he had never esteemed my opinion before, he would have thought highly of me then; and, I dare say, left the house thinking me the best friend and counsellor man ever had. This happened the night before last. Now, as we may fairly suppose, he would not allow much time to pass before he spoke to the lady, and as he does not appear to have spoken yesterday, it is not unlikely that he should be at Mrs. Goddard's to-day; and she may be detained by a visitor, without thinking him at all a tiresome wretch."

"Pray, Mr. Knightley," said Emma, who had been smiling to herself through a great part of this speech, "how do you know that Mr. Martin did not speak yesterday?"

"Certainly," replied he, surprized, "I do not absolutely know it; but it may be inferred. Was not she the whole day with you?"

"Come," said she, "I will tell you something, in return for what you have told me. He did speak yesterday—that is, he wrote, and was refused."

This was obliged to be repeated before it could be believed; and Mr. Knightley actually looked red with surprize and displeasure, as he stood up, in tall indignation, and said,

"Then she is a greater simpleton than I ever believed her. What is the foolish girl about?"

"Oh! to be sure," cried Emma, "it is always incomprehensible to a man that a woman should ever refuse an offer of marriage. A man always imagines a woman to be ready for any body who asks her."

"Nonsense! a man does not imagine any such thing. But what is the meaning of this? Harriet Smith refuse Robert Martin? madness, if it is so; but I hope you are mistaken."

"I saw her answer!—nothing could be clearer."

"You saw her answer!—you wrote her answer too. Emma, this is your doing. You persuaded her to refuse him."

"And if I did, (which, however, I am far from allowing) I should not feel that I had done wrong. Mr. Martin is a very respectable young man, but I cannot admit him to be Harriet's equal; and am rather surprized indeed that he should have ventured to address her. By your account, he does seem to have had some scruples. It is a pity that they were ever got over."

"Not Harriet's equal!" exclaimed Mr. Knightley loudly and warmly; and with calmer asperity, added, a few moments afterwards, "No, he is not her equal indeed, for he is as much her superior in sense as in situation. Emma, your infatuation about that girl blinds you. What are Harriet Smith's claims, either of birth, nature or education, to any connexion higher than Robert Martin? She is the natural daughter of nobody knows whom, with probably no settled provision at all, and certainly no respectable relations. She is known only as parlour-boarder at a common school. She is not a sensible girl, nor a girl of any information. She has been taught nothing useful, and is too young and too simple to have acquired any thing herself. At her age she can have no experience, and with her little wit, is not very likely ever to have any that can avail her. She is pretty, and she is good tempered, and that is all. My only scruple in advising the match was on his account, as being beneath his deserts, and a bad connexion for him. I felt that, as to fortune, in all probability he might do much better; and that as to a rational companion or useful helpmate, he could not do worse. But I could not reason so to a man in love, and was willing to trust to there being no harm in her, to her having that sort of disposition, which, in good hands, like his, might be easily led aright and turn out very well. The advantage of the match I felt to be all on her side; and had not the smallest doubt (nor have I now) that there would be a general cry-out upon her extreme good luck. Even *your* satisfaction I made sure of. It crossed my mind immediately that you would not regret your friend's leaving Highbury, for the sake of her being settled so well. I remember saying to myself, 'Even Emma, with all her partiality for Harriet, will think this a good match.'"

"I cannot help wondering at your knowing so little of Emma as to say any such thing. What! think a farmer, (and with all his sense and all his merit Mr. Martin is nothing more,) a good match for my intimate friend! Not regret her leaving Highbury for the sake of marrying a man whom I could never admit as an acquaintance of my own! I wonder you should think it possible for me to have such feelings. I assure you mine are very different. I must think your statement by no means fair. You are not just to Harriet's claims. They would be estimated very differently by others as well as myself; Mr. Martin may be the richest of the two, but he is undoubtedly her inferior as to rank in society.—The sphere in which she moves is much above his.—It would be a degradation."

"A degradation to illegitimacy and ignorance, to be married to a respectable, intelligent gentleman-farmer!"

"As to the circumstances of her birth, though in a legal sense she may be called Nobody, it will not hold in common sense. She is not to pay for the offence of others, by being held below the level of those with whom she is brought up.—There can scarcely be a doubt that her father is a gentleman—and a gentleman of fortune.—Her allowance is very liberal; nothing has ever been grudged for her improvement or comfort.—That she is a gentleman's daughter, is indubitable to me; that she associates with gentlemen's daughters, no one, I apprehend, will deny.—She is superior to Mr. Robert Martin."

"Whoever might be her parents," said Mr. Knightley, "whoever may have had the charge of her, it does not appear to have been any part of their plan to introduce her into what you would call good society. After receiving a very indifferent education she is left in Mrs. Goddard's hands to shift as she can;—to move, in short, in Mrs. Goddard's line, to have Mrs. Goddard's acquaintance. Her friends evidently thought this good enough for her; and it *was* good enough. She desired nothing better herself. Till you chose to turn her into a friend, her mind had no distaste for her own set, nor any ambition beyond it. She was as happy as possible with the Martins in the summer. She had no sense of superiority then. If she has it now, you have given it. You have been no friend to Harriet Smith, Emma. Robert Martin would never have proceeded so far, if he had not felt persuaded of her not being disinclined to him. I know him well. He has too much real feeling to address any woman on the haphazard of selfish passion. And as to conceit, he is the farthest from it of any man I know. Depend upon it he had encouragement."

It was most convenient to Emma not to make a direct reply to this assertion; she chose rather to take up her own line of the subject again.

"You are a very warm friend to Mr. Martin; but, as I said before, are unjust to Harriet. Harriet's claims to marry well are not so contemptible as you represent them. She is not a clever girl, but she has better sense than you are aware of, and does not deserve to have her understanding spoken of so slightingly. Waiving that point, however, and supposing her to be, as you describe her, only pretty and good-natured, let me tell you, that in the degree she possesses them, they are not trivial recommendations to the world in general, for she is, in fact, a beautiful girl, and must be thought so by ninety-nine people out of an hundred; and till it appears that men are much more philosophic on the subject of beauty than they are generally supposed; till they do fall in love with well-informed minds instead of handsome faces, a girl, with such loveliness as Harriet, has a certainty of being admired and sought after, of having the power of chusing from among many, consequently a claim to be nice. Her good-nature, too, is not so very slight a claim, comprehending, as it does, real, thorough sweetness of temper and manner, a very humble opinion of herself, and a great readiness to be pleased with other people. I am very much mistaken if your sex in general would not think such beauty, and such temper, the highest claims a woman could possess."

"Upon my word, Emma, to hear you abusing the reason you have, is almost enough to make me think so too. Better be without sense, than misapply it as you do."

"To be sure!" cried she playfully. "I know *that* is the feeling of you all. I know that such a girl as Harriet is exactly what every man delights in—what at once bewitches his senses and satisfies his judgment. Oh! Harriet may pick and chuse. Were you, yourself, ever to marry, she is the very woman for you. And is she, at seventeen, just entering into life, just beginning to be known, to be wondered at because she does not accept the first offer she receives? No—pray let her have time to look about her."

"I have always thought it a very foolish intimacy," said Mr.

Knightley presently, "though I have kept my thoughts to myself; but I now perceive that it will be a very unfortunate one for Harriet. You will puff her up with such ideas of her own beauty, and of what she has a claim to, that, in a little while, nobody within her reach will be good enough for her. Vanity working on a weak head, produces every sort of mischief. Nothing so easy as for a young lady to raise her expectations too high. Miss Harriet Smith may not find offers of marriage flow in so fast, though she is a very pretty girl. Men of sense, whatever you may chuse to say, do not want silly wives. Men of family would not be very fond of connecting themselves with a girl of such obscurity—and most prudent men would be afraid of the inconvenience and disgrace they might be involved in, when the mystery of her parentage came to be revealed. Let her marry Robert Martin, and she is safe, respectable, and happy for ever; but if you encourage her to expect to marry greatly, and teach her to be satisfied with nothing less than a man of consequence and large fortune, she may be a parlour-boarder at Mrs. Goddard's all the rest of her life—or, at least, (for Harriet Smith is a girl who will marry somebody or other), till she grow desperate, and is glad to catch at the old writing-master's son."

"We think so very differently on this point, Mr. Knightley, that there can be no use in canvassing it. We shall only be making each other more angry. But as to my *letting* her marry Robert Martin, it is impossible; she has refused him, and so decidedly, I think, as must prevent any second application. She must abide by the evil of having refused him, whatever it may be; and as to the refusal itself, I will not pretend to say that I might not influence her a little; but I assure you there was very little for me or for any body to do. His appearance is so much against him, and his manner so bad, that if she ever were disposed to favour him, she is not now. I can imagine, that before she had seen any body superior, she might tolerate him. He was the brother of her friends, and he took pains to please her; and altogether, having seen nobody better (that must have been his great assistant) she might not, while she was at Abbey-Mill, find him disagreeable. But the case is altered now. She knows now what gentlemen are; and nothing but a gentleman in education and manner has any chance with Harriet."

"Nonsense, errant nonsense, as ever was talked!" cried Mr. Knightley.—"Robert Martin's manners have sense, sincerity, and good-humour to recommend them; and his mind has more true gentility than Harriet Smith could understand."

Emma made no answer, and tried to look cheerfully unconcerned, but was really feeling uncomfortable and wanting him very much to be gone. She did not repent what she had done; she still thought herself a better judge of such a point of female right and refinement than he could be; but yet she had a sort of habitual respect for his judgment in general, which made her dislike having it so loudly against her; and to have him sitting just opposite to her in angry state, was very disagreeable. Some minutes passed in this unpleasant silence, with only one attempt on Emma's side to talk of the weather, but he made no answer. He was thinking. The result of his thoughts appeared at last in these words.

"Robert Martin has no great loss—if he can but think so; and I hope it will not be long before he does. Your views for Harriet are best known to yourself; but as you make no secret of your love of match-making, it is fair to suppose that views, and plans, and projects you have;—and as a friend I shall just hint to you that if Elton is the man, I think it will be all labour in vain."

Emma laughed and disclaimed. He continued,

"Depend upon it, Elton will not do. Elton is a very good sort of man, and a very respectable vicar of Highbury, but not at all likely to make an imprudent match. He knows the value of a good income as well as any body. Elton may talk sentimentally, but he will act rationally. He is as well acquainted with his own claims, as you can be with Harriet's. He knows that he is a very handsome young man, and a great favourite wherever he goes; and from his general way of talking in unreserved moments, when there are only men present, I am convinced that he does not mean to throw himself away. I have heard him speak with great animation of a large family of young ladies that his sisters are intimate with, who have all twenty thousand pounds apiece."

"I am very much obliged to you," said Emma, laughing again. "If I had set my heart on Mr. Elton's marrying Harriet, it would have been very kind to open my eyes; but at present I only want to keep Harriet to myself. I have done with match-making indeed. I could never hope to equal my own doings at Randalls. I shall leave off while I am well."

"Good morning to you,"—said he, rising and walking off abruptly. He was very much vexed. He felt the disappointment of the young man, and was mortified to have been the means of promoting it, by the sanction he had given; and the part which he was persuaded Emma had taken in the affair, was provoking him exceedingly.

Emma remained in a state of vexation too; but there was more indistinctness in the causes of hers, than in his. She did not always feel so absolutely satisfied with herself, so entirely convinced that her opinions were right and her adversary's wrong, as Mr. Knightley. He walked off in more complete self-approbation than he left for her. She was not so materially cast down, however, but that a little time and the return of Harriet were very adequate restoratives. Harriet's staying away so long was beginning to make her uneasy. The possibility of the young man's coming to Mrs. Goddard's that morning, and meeting with Harriet and pleading his own cause, gave alarming ideas. The dread of such a failure after all became the prominent uneasiness; and when Harriet appeared, and in very good spirits, and without having any such reason to give for her long absence, she felt a satisfaction which settled her with her own mind, and convinced her, that let Mr. Knightley think or say what he would, she had done nothing which woman's friendship and woman's feelings would not justify.

He had frightened her a little about Mr. Elton; but when she considered that Mr. Knightley could not have observed him as she had done, neither with the interest, nor (she must be allowed to tell herself, in spite of Mr. Knightley's pretensions) with the skill of such an observer on such a question as herself, that he had spoken it hastily and in anger, she was able to believe, that he had rather said what he wished resentfully to be true, than what he knew any thing about. He certainly might have heard Mr. Elton speak with more unreserve than she had ever done, and Mr. Elton might not be of an imprudent, inconsiderate disposition as to money matters; he might naturally be rather attentive than otherwise to them; but then, Mr. Knightley did not make due allowance for the influence of a strong passion at war with all interested motives. Mr. Knightley saw no such passion, and of course thought nothing of its effects; but she saw too much of it to feel a doubt of its overcoming any hesitations that a reasonable prudence might originally suggest; and more than a reasonable, becoming degree of prudence, she was very sure did not belong to Mr. Elton.

Harriet's cheerful look and manner established hers: she came back, not to think of Mr. Martin, but to talk of Mr. Elton. Miss Nash had been telling her something, which she repeated immediately with great delight. Mr. Perry had been to Mrs. Goddard's to attend a sick child, and Miss Nash had seen him, and he had told Miss Nash, that as he was coming back yesterday from Clayton Park, he had met Mr. Elton, and found to his great surprize, that Mr. Elton was actually on his road to London, and not meaning to return till the morrow, though it was the whist-club night, which he had been never known to miss before; and Mr. Perry had remonstrated with him about it, and told him how shabby it was in him, their best player, to absent himself, and tried very much to persuade him to put off his journey only one day; but it would not do; Mr. Elton had been determined to go on, and had said in a *very particular* way indeed, that he was going on business which he would not put off for any inducement in the world; and something about a very enviable commission, and being the bearer of something exceedingly precious. Mr. Perry could not quite understand him, but he was very sure there must be a *lady* in the case, and he told him so; and Mr. Elton only looked very conscious and smiling, and rode off in great spirits. Miss Nash had told her all this, and had talked a great deal more about Mr. Elton; and said, looking so very significantly at her, "that she did not pretend to understand what his business might be, but she only knew that any woman whom Mr. Elton could prefer, she should think the luckiest woman in the world; for, beyond a doubt, Mr. Elton had not his equal for beauty or agreeableness."

CHAPTER IX

Mr. Knightley might quarrel with her, but Emma could not quarrel with herself. He was so much displeased, that it was longer than usual before he came to Hartfield again; and when they did meet, his grave looks shewed that she was not forgiven. She was sorry, but could not repent. On the contrary, her plans and proceedings were more and more justified and endeared to her by the general appearances of the next few days.

The Picture, elegantly framed, came safely to hand soon after Mr. Elton's return, and being hung over the mantelpiece of the common sitting-room, he got up to look at it, and sighed out his half sentences of admiration just as he ought; and as for Harriet's feelings, they were visibly forming themselves into as strong and steady an attachment as her youth and sort of mind admitted. Emma was soon perfectly satisfied of Mr. Martin's being no otherwise remembered, than as he furnished a contrast with Mr. Elton, of the utmost advantage to the latter.

Her views of improving her little friend's mind, by a great deal of useful reading and conversation, had never yet led to more than a few first chapters, and the intention of going on to-morrow. It was much easier to chat than to study; much pleasanter to let her imagination range and work at Harriet's fortune, than to be labouring to enlarge her comprehension or exercise it on sober facts; and the only literary pursuit which engaged Harriet at present, the only mental provision she was making for the evening of life, was the collecting and transcribing all the riddles of every sort that she could meet with, into a thin quarto of hot-pressed paper, made up by her friend, and ornamented with ciphers and trophies.

In this age of literature, such collections on a very grand scale are not uncommon. Miss Nash, head-teacher at Mrs. Goddard's, had written out at least three hundred; and Harriet, who had taken the first hint of it from her, hoped, with Miss Woodhouse's help, to get a great many more. Emma assisted with her invention, memory and taste; and as Harriet wrote a very pretty hand, it was likely to be an arrangement of the first order, in form as well as quantity.

Mr. Woodhouse was almost as much interested in the business as the girls, and tried very often to recollect something worth their putting in. "So many clever riddles as there used to be when he was young—he wondered he could not remember them! but he hoped he should in time." And it always ended in "Kitty, a fair but frozen maid."

His good friend Perry, too, whom he had spoken to on the subject, did not at present recollect any thing of the riddle kind; but he had desired Perry to be upon the watch, and as he went about so much, something, he thought, might come from that quarter.

It was by no means his daughter's wish that the intellects of Highbury in general should be put under requisition. Mr. Elton was the only one whose assistance she asked. He was invited to contribute any really good enigmas, charades, or conundrums that he might recollect; and she had the pleasure of seeing him most intently at work with his recollections; and at the same time, as she could perceive, most earnestly careful that nothing ungallant, nothing that did not breathe a compliment to the sex should pass his lips. They owed to him their two or three politest puzzles; and the joy and exultation with which at last he recalled, and rather sentimentally recited, that well-known charade,

> My first doth affliction denote,
> Which my second is destin'd to feel
> And my whole is the best antidote
> That affliction to soften and heal.—

made her quite sorry to acknowledge that they had transcribed it some pages ago already.

"Why will not you write one yourself for us, Mr. Elton?" said she; "that is the only security for its freshness; and nothing could be easier to you."

"Oh no! he had never written, hardly ever, any thing of the kind in his life. The stupidest fellow! He was afraid not even Miss Woodhouse"—he stopt a moment—"or Miss Smith could inspire him."

The very next day however produced some proof of inspiration. He called for a few moments, just to leave a piece of paper on the table containing, as he said, a charade, which a friend of his had addressed to a young lady, the object of his admiration, but which, from his manner, Emma was immediately convinced must be his own.

"I do not offer it for Miss Smith's collection," said he. "Being my friend's, I have no right to expose it in any degree to the public eye, but perhaps you may not dislike looking at it."

The speech was more to Emma than to Harriet, which Emma could understand. There was deep consciousness about him, and he found it easier to meet her eye than her friend's. He was gone the next moment:—after another moment's pause,

"Take it," said Emma, smiling, and pushing the paper towards Harriet—"it is for you. Take your own."

But Harriet was in a tremor, and could not touch it; and Emma, never loth to be first, was obliged to examine it herself.

To Miss———

CHARADE.
My first displays the wealth and pomp of kings,
Lords of the earth! their luxury and ease.
Another view of man, my second brings,
Behold him there, the monarch of the seas!
But ah! united, what reverse we have!
Man's boasted power and freedom, all are flown;
Lord of the earth and sea, he bends a slave,
And woman, lovely woman, reigns alone.
Thy ready wit the word will soon supply,
May its approval beam in that soft eye!

She cast her eye over it, pondered, caught the meaning, read it through again to be quite certain, and quite mistress of the lines, and then passing it to Harriet, sat happily smiling, and saying to herself, while Harriet was puzzling over the paper in all the confusion of hope and dulness, "Very well, Mr. Elton, very well indeed. I have read worse charades. *Courtship*—a very good hint. I give you credit for it. This is feeling your way. This is saying very plainly—'Pray, Miss Smith, give me leave to pay my addresses to you. Approve my charade and my intentions in the same glance.'

May its approval beam in that soft eye!

Harriet exactly. Soft is the very word for her eye—of all epithets, the justest that could be given.

Thy ready wit the word will soon supply.

Humph—Harriet's ready wit! All the better. A man must be very much in love, indeed, to describe her so. Ah! Mr. Knightley, I wish you had the benefit of this; I think this would convince you. For once in your life you would be obliged to own yourself mistaken. An excellent charade indeed! and very much to the purpose. Things must come to a crisis soon now."

She was obliged to break off from these very pleasant observations, which were otherwise of a sort to run into great length, by the eagerness of Harriet's wondering questions.

"What can it be, Miss Woodhouse?—what can it be? I have not an idea—I cannot guess it in the least. What can it possibly be? Do try to find it out, Miss Woodhouse. Do help me. I never saw any thing so hard. Is it kingdom? I wonder who the friend was—and who could be the young lady. Do you think it is a good one? Can it be woman?

> And woman, lovely woman, reigns alone.

Can it be Neptune?

> Behold him there, the monarch of the seas!

Or a trident? or a mermaid? or a shark? Oh, no! shark is only one syllable. It must be very clever, or he would not have brought it. Oh! Miss Woodhouse, do you think we shall ever find it out?"

"Mermaids and sharks! Nonsense! My dear Harriet, what are you thinking of? Where would be the use of his bringing us a charade made by a friend upon a mermaid or a shark? Give me the paper and listen.

For Miss ———, read Miss Smith.

> My first displays the wealth and pomp of kings,
> Lords of the earth! their luxury and ease.

That is *court*.

> Another view of man, my second brings;
> Behold him there, the monarch of the seas!

That is *ship*;—plain as it can be.—Now for the cream.

> But ah! united (*courtship*, you know), what reverse we have!

Man's boasted power and freedom, all are flown.
Lord of the earth and sea, he bends a slave,
And woman, lovely woman, reigns alone.

A very proper compliment!—and then follows the application, which I think, my dear Harriet, you cannot find much difficulty in comprehending. Read it in comfort to yourself. There can be no doubt of its being written for you and to you."

Harriet could not long resist so delightful a persuasion. She read the concluding lines, and was all flutter and happiness. She could not speak. But she was not wanted to speak. It was enough for her to feel. Emma spoke for her.

"There is so pointed, and so particular a meaning in this compliment," said she, "that I cannot have a doubt as to Mr. Elton's intentions. You are his object—and you will soon receive the completest proof of it. I thought it must be so. I thought I could not be so deceived; but now, it is clear; the state of his mind is as clear and decided, as my wishes on the subject have been ever since I knew you. Yes, Harriet, just so long have I been wanting the very circumstance to happen what has happened. I could never tell whether an attachment between you and Mr. Elton were most desirable or most natural. Its probability and its eligibility have really so equalled each other! I am very happy. I congratulate you, my dear Harriet, with all my heart. This is an attachment which a woman may well feel pride in creating. This is a connexion which offers nothing but good. It will give you every thing that you want—consideration, independence, a proper home—it will fix you in the centre of all your real friends, close to Hartfield and to me, and confirm our intimacy for ever. This, Harriet, is an alliance which can never raise a blush in either of us."

"Dear Miss Woodhouse!"—and "Dear Miss Woodhouse," was all that Harriet, with many tender embraces could articulate at first; but when they did arrive at something more like conversation, it was sufficiently clear to her friend that she saw, felt, anticipated, and remembered just as she ought. Mr. Elton's superiority had very ample acknowledgment.

"Whatever you say is always right," cried Harriet, "and therefore I suppose, and believe, and hope it must be so; but otherwise I could not have imagined it. It is so much beyond any thing I deserve. Mr. Elton, who might marry any body! There cannot be two opinions about *him*.

He is so very superior. Only think of those sweet verses—'To Miss ———.' Dear me, how clever!—Could it really be meant for me?"

"I cannot make a question, or listen to a question about that. It is a certainty. Receive it on my judgment. It is a sort of prologue to the play, a motto to the chapter; and will be soon followed by matter-of-fact prose."

"It is a sort of thing which nobody could have expected. I am sure, a month ago, I had no more idea myself!—The strangest things do take place!"

"When Miss Smiths and Mr. Eltons get acquainted—they do indeed—and really it is strange; it is out of the common course that what is so evidently, so palpably desirable—what courts the pre-arrangement of other people, should so immediately shape itself into the proper form. You and Mr. Elton are by situation called together; you belong to one another by every circumstance of your respective homes. Your marrying will be equal to the match at Randalls. There does seem to be a something in the air of Hartfield which gives love exactly the right direction, and sends it into the very channel where it ought to flow.

The course of true love never did run smooth—

A Hartfield edition of Shakespeare would have a long note on that passage."

"That Mr. Elton should really be in love with me—me, of all people, who did not know him, to speak to him, at Michaelmas! And he, the very handsomest man that ever was, and a man that every body looks up to, quite like Mr. Knightley! His company so sought after, that every body says he need not eat a single meal by himself if he does not chuse it; that he has more invitations than there are days in the week. And so excellent in the Church! Miss Nash has put down all the texts he has ever preached from since he came to Highbury. Dear me! When I look back to the first time I saw him! How little did I think!—The two Abbots and I ran into the front room and peeped through the blind when we heard he was going by, and Miss Nash came and scolded us away, and staid to look through herself; however, she called me back presently, and let me look too, which was very good-natured. And how beautiful we thought he looked! He was arm-in-arm with Mr. Cole."

"This is an alliance which, whoever—whatever your friends may be, must be agreeable to them, provided at least they have common sense; and we are not to be addressing our conduct to fools. If they are anxious to see you *happily* married, here is a man whose amiable character gives every assurance of it;—if they wish to have you settled in the same country and circle which they have chosen to place you in, here it will be accomplished; and if their only object is that you should, in the common phrase, be *well* married, here is the comfortable fortune, the respectable establishment, the rise in the world which must satisfy them."

"Yes, very true. How nicely you talk; I love to hear you. You understand every thing. You and Mr. Elton are one as clever as the other. This charade!—If I had studied a twelvemonth, I could never have made any thing like it."

"I thought he meant to try his skill, by his manner of declining it yesterday."

"I do think it is, without exception, the best charade I ever read."

"I never read one more to the purpose, certainly."

"It is as long again as almost all we have had before."

"I do not consider its length as particularly in its favour. Such things in general cannot be too short."

Harriet was too intent on the lines to hear. The most satisfactory comparisons were rising in her mind.

"It is one thing," said she, presently—her cheeks in a glow—"to have very good sense in a common way, like every body else, and if there is any thing to say, to sit down and write a letter, and say just what you must, in a short way; and another, to write verses and charades like this."

Emma could not have desired a more spirited rejection of Mr. Martin's prose.

"Such sweet lines!" continued Harriet—"these two last!—But how shall I ever be able to return the paper, or say I have found it out?—Oh! Miss Woodhouse, what can we do about that?"

"Leave it to me. You do nothing. He will be here this evening, I dare say, and then I will give it him back, and some nonsense or other will pass between us, and you shall not be committed.—Your soft eyes shall chuse their own time for beaming. Trust to me."

"Oh! Miss Woodhouse, what a pity that I must not write this beautiful charade into my book! I am sure I have not got one half so good."

"Leave out the two last lines, and there is no reason why you should not write it into your book."

"Oh! but those two lines are"—

"The best of all. Granted;—for private enjoyment; and for private enjoyment keep them. They are not at all the less written you know, because you divide them. The couplet does not cease to be, nor does its meaning change. But take it away, and all *appropriation* ceases, and a very pretty gallant charade remains, fit for any collection. Depend upon it, he would not like to have his charade slighted, much better than his passion. A poet in love must be encouraged in both capacities, or neither. Give me the book, I will write it down, and then there can be no possible reflection on you."

Harriet submitted, though her mind could hardly separate the parts, so as to feel quite sure that her friend were not writing down a declaration of love. It seemed too precious an offering for any degree of publicity.

"I shall never let that book go out of my own hands," said she.

"Very well," replied Emma; "a most natural feeling; and the longer it lasts, the better I shall be pleased. But here is my father coming: you will not object to my reading the charade to him. It will be giving him so much pleasure! He loves any thing of the sort, and especially any thing that pays woman a compliment. He has the tenderest spirit of gallantry towards us all!—You must let me read it to him."

Harriet looked grave.

"My dear Harriet, you must not refine too much upon this charade.—You will betray your feelings improperly, if you are too conscious and too quick, and appear to affix more meaning, or even quite all the meaning which may be affixed to it. Do not be overpowered by such a little tribute of admiration. If he had been anxious for secrecy, he would not have left the paper while I was by; but he rather pushed it towards me than towards you. Do not let us be too solemn on the business. He has encouragement enough to proceed, without our sighing out our souls over this charade."

"Oh! no—I hope I shall not be ridiculous about it. Do as you please."

Mr. Woodhouse came in, and very soon led to the subject again, by the recurrence of his very frequent inquiry of "Well, my dears, how does your book go on?—Have you got any thing fresh?"

"Yes, papa; we have something to read you, something quite fresh. A piece of paper was found on the table this morning—(dropt, we suppose, by a fairy)—containing a very pretty charade, and we have just copied it in."

She read it to him, just as he liked to have any thing read, slowly and distinctly, and two or three times over, with explanations of every part as she proceeded—and he was very much pleased, and, as she had foreseen, especially struck with the complimentary conclusion.

"Aye, that's very just, indeed, that's very properly said. Very true. 'Woman, lovely woman.' It is such a pretty charade, my dear, that I can easily guess what fairy brought it.—Nobody could have written so prettily, but you, Emma."

Emma only nodded, and smiled.—After a little thinking, and a very tender sigh, he added,

"Ah! it is no difficulty to see who you take after! Your dear mother was so clever at all those things! If I had but her memory! But I can remember nothing;—not even that particular riddle which you have heard me mention; I can only recollect the first stanza; and there are several.

> Kitty, a fair but frozen maid,
> Kindled a flame I yet deplore,
> The hood-wink'd boy I called to aid,
> Though of his near approach afraid,
> So fatal to my suit before.

And that is all that I can recollect of it—but it is very clever all the way through. But I think, my dear, you said you had got it."

"Yes, papa, it is written out in our second page. We copied it from the *Elegant Extracts*. It was Garrick's, you know."

"Aye, very true.—I wish I could recollect more of it.

> Kitty, a fair but frozen maid.

The name makes me think of poor Isabella; for she was very near being christened Catherine after her grandmama. I hope we shall have her here next week. Have you thought, my dear, where you shall put her—and what room there will be for the children?"

"Oh! yes—she will have her own room, of course; the room she always has;—and there is the nursery for the children,—just as usual, you know. Why should there be any change?"

"I do not know, my dear—but it is so long since she was here!—not since last Easter, and then only for a few days.—Mr. John Knightley's being a lawyer is very inconvenient.—Poor Isabella!—she is sadly taken away from us all!—and how sorry she will be when she comes, not to see Miss Taylor here!"

"She will not be surprized, papa, at least."

"I do not know, my dear. I am sure I was very much surprized when I first heard she was going to be married."

"We must ask Mr. and Mrs. Weston to dine with us, while Isabella is here."

"Yes, my dear, if there is time.—But—(in a very depressed tone)—she is coming for only one week. There will not be time for any thing."

"It is unfortunate that they cannot stay longer—but it seems a case of necessity. Mr. John Knightley must be in town again on the 28th, and we ought to be thankful, papa, that we are to have the whole of the time they can give to the country, that two or three days are not to be taken out for the Abbey. Mr. Knightley promises to give up his claim this Christmas—though you know it is longer since they were with him, than with us."

"It would be very hard, indeed, my dear, if poor Isabella were to be anywhere but at Hartfield."

Mr. Woodhouse could never allow for Mr. Knightley's claims on his brother, or any body's claims on Isabella, except his own. He sat musing a little while, and then said,

"But I do not see why poor Isabella should be obliged to go back so soon, though he does. I think, Emma, I shall try and persuade her to stay longer with us. She and the children might stay very well."

"Ah! papa—that is what you never have been able to accomplish, and I do not think you ever will. Isabella cannot bear to stay behind her husband."

This was too true for contradiction. Unwelcome as it was, Mr. Woodhouse could only give a submissive sigh; and as Emma saw his spirits affected by the idea of his daughter's attachment to her husband, she immediately led to such a branch of the subject as must raise them.

"Harriet must give us as much of her company as she can while my brother and sister are here. I am sure she will be pleased with the children. We are very proud of the children, are not we, papa? I wonder which she will think the handsomest, Henry or John?"

"Aye, I wonder which she will. Poor little dears, how glad they will be to come. They are very fond of being at Hartfield, Harriet."

"I dare say they are, sir. I am sure I do not know who is not."

"Henry is a fine boy, but John is very like his mama. Henry is the eldest, he was named after me, not after his father. John, the second, is named after his father. Some people are surprized, I believe, that the eldest was not, but Isabella would have him called Henry, which I thought very pretty of her. And he is a very clever boy, indeed. They are all remarkably clever; and they have so many pretty ways. They will come and stand by my chair, and say, 'Grandpapa, can you give me a bit of string?' and once Henry asked me for a knife, but I told him knives were only made for grandpapas. I think their father is too rough with them very often."

"He appears rough to you," said Emma, "because you are so very gentle yourself; but if you could compare him with other papas, you would not think him rough. He wishes his boys to be active and hardy; and if they misbehave, can give them a sharp word now and then; but he is an affectionate father—certainly Mr. John Knightley is an affectionate father. The children are all fond of him."

"And then their uncle comes in, and tosses them up to the ceiling in a very frightful way!"

"But they like it, papa; there is nothing they like so much. It is such enjoyment to them, that if their uncle did not lay down the rule of their taking turns, whichever began would never give way to the other."

"Well, I cannot understand it."

"That is the case with us all, papa. One half of the world cannot understand the pleasures of the other."

Later in the morning, and just as the girls were going to separate in preparation for the regular four o'clock dinner, the hero of this inimitable charade walked in again. Harriet turned away; but Emma could receive him with the usual smile, and her quick eye soon discerned in his the consciousness of having made a push—of having thrown a die; and she imagined he was come to see how it might turn up. His ostensible reason, however, was to ask whether Mr. Woodhouse's party could be made up in the evening without him, or whether he should be in the smallest degree necessary at Hartfield. If he were, every thing else must give way; but otherwise his friend Cole had been saying so much about his dining with him—had made such a point of it, that he had promised him conditionally to come.

Emma thanked him, but could not allow of his disappointing his friend on their account; her father was sure of his rubber. He re-urged—she re-declined; and he seemed then about to make his bow, when taking the paper from the table, she returned it—

"Oh! here is the charade you were so obliging as to leave with us; thank you for the sight of it. We admired it so much, that I have ventured to write it into Miss Smith's collection. Your friend will not take it amiss I hope. Of course I have not transcribed beyond the first eight lines."

Mr. Elton certainly did not very well know what to say. He looked rather doubtingly—rather confused; said something about "honour,"—glanced at Emma and at Harriet, and then seeing the book open on the table, took it up, and examined it very attentively. With the view of passing off an awkward moment, Emma smilingly said,

"You must make my apologies to your friend; but so good a charade must not be confined to one or two. He may be sure of every woman's approbation while he writes with such gallantry."

"I have no hesitation in saying," replied Mr. Elton, though hesitating a good deal while he spoke; "I have no hesitation in saying—at least if my friend feels at all as *I* do—I have not the smallest doubt that, could he see his little effusion honoured as *I* see it, (looking at the book again, and replacing it on the table), he would consider it as the proudest moment of his life."

After this speech he was gone as soon as possible. Emma could not think it too soon; for with all his good and agreeable qualities, there was a sort of parade in his speeches which was very apt to incline her to laugh. She ran away to indulge the inclination, leaving the tender and the sublime of pleasure to Harriet's share.

CHAPTER X

Though now the middle of December, there had yet been no weather to prevent the young ladies from tolerably regular exercise; and on the morrow, Emma had a charitable visit to pay to a poor sick family, who lived a little way out of Highbury.

Their road to this detached cottage was down Vicarage Lane, a lane leading at right angles from the broad, though irregular, main street of the place; and, as may be inferred, containing the blessed abode of Mr. Elton. A few inferior dwellings were first to be passed, and then, about a quarter of a mile down the lane rose the Vicarage, an old and not very good house, almost as close to the road as it could be. It had no advantage of situation; but had been very much smartened up by the present proprietor; and, such as it was, there could be no possibility of the two friends passing it without a slackened pace and observing eyes.—Emma's remark was—

"There it is. There go you and your riddle-book one of these days."—Harriet's was:

"Oh, what a sweet house!—How very beautiful!—There are the yellow curtains that Miss Nash admires so much."

"I do not often walk this way *now*," said Emma, as they proceeded, "but *then* there will be an inducement, and I shall gradually get intimately acquainted with all the hedges, gates, pools and pollards of this part of Highbury."

Harriet, she found, had never in her life been within side the Vicarage, and her curiosity to see it was so extreme, that, considering exteriors and probabilities, Emma could only class it, as a proof of love, with Mr. Elton's seeing ready wit in her.

"I wish we could contrive it," said she; "but I cannot think of any tolerable pretence for going in;—no servant that I want to inquire about of his housekeeper—no message from my father."

She pondered, but could think of nothing. After a mutual silence of some minutes, Harriet thus began again—

"I do so wonder, Miss Woodhouse, that you should not be married, or going to be married! so charming as you are!"—

Emma laughed, and replied,

"My being charming, Harriet, is not quite enough to induce me to marry; I must find other people charming—one other person at least. And I am not only not going to be married, at present, but have very little intention of ever marrying at all."

"Ah!—so you say; but I cannot believe it."

"I must see somebody very superior to any one I have seen yet, to be tempted; Mr. Elton, you know, (recollecting herself,) is out of the question: and I do *not* wish to see any such person. I would rather not be tempted. I cannot really change for the better. If I were to marry, I must expect to repent it."

"Dear me!—it is so odd to hear a woman talk so!"—

"I have none of the usual inducements of women to marry. Were I to fall in love, indeed, it would be a different thing! but I never have been in love; it is not my way, or my nature; and I do not think I ever shall. And, without love, I am sure I should be a fool to change such a situation as mine. Fortune I do not want; employment I do not want; consequence I do not want: I believe few married women are half as much mistress of their husband's house as I am of Hartfield; and never, never could I expect to be so truly beloved and important; so always first and always right in any man's eyes as I am in my father's."

"But then, to be an old maid at last, like Miss Bates!"

"That is as formidable an image as you could present, Harriet; and if I thought I should ever be like Miss Bates! so silly—so satisfied—so smiling—so prosing—so undistinguishing and unfastidious—and so apt to tell every thing relative to every body about me, I would marry to-morrow. But between *us*, I am convinced there never can be any likeness, except in being unmarried."

"But still, you will be an old maid! and that's so dreadful!"

"Never mind, Harriet, I shall not be a poor old maid; and it is poverty only which makes celibacy contemptible to a generous public! A single woman, with a very narrow income, must be a ridiculous, disagreeable old maid! the proper sport of boys and girls, but a single woman, of good fortune, is always respectable, and may be as sensible and pleasant as any body else. And the distinction is not quite so much against the candour and common sense of the world as appears at first; for a very narrow income has a tendency to contract the mind, and sour the temper. Those who can barely live, and who live perforce in a very small, and generally very inferior, society, may well be illiberal and cross. This does not apply, however, to Miss Bates; she is only too good-natured and too silly to suit me; but, in general, she is very much to the taste of every body, though single and though poor. Poverty certainly has not contracted her mind: I really believe, if she had only a shilling in the world, she would be very likely to give away sixpence of it; and nobody is afraid of her: that is a great charm."

"Dear me! but what shall you do? how shall you employ yourself when you grow old?"

"If I know myself, Harriet, mine is an active, busy mind, with a great many independent resources; and I do not perceive why I should be more in want of employment at forty or fifty than one-and-twenty. Woman's usual occupations of hand and mind will be as open to me then as they are now; or with no important variation. If I draw less, I shall read more; if I give up music, I shall take to carpet-work. And as for objects of interest, objects for the affections, which is in truth the great point of inferiority, the want of which is really the great evil to be avoided in *not* marrying, I shall be very well off, with all the children of a sister I love so much, to care about. There will be enough of them, in all probability, to supply every sort of sensation that declining life can need. There will be enough for every hope and every fear; and though my attachment to none can equal that of a parent, it suits my ideas of comfort better than what is warmer and blinder. My nephews and nieces!—I shall often have a niece with me."

"Do you know Miss Bates's niece? That is, I know you must have seen her a hundred times—but are you acquainted?"

"Oh! yes; we are always forced to be acquainted whenever she comes to Highbury. By the bye, *that* is almost enough to put one out of conceit with a niece. Heaven forbid! at least, that I should ever bore people half so much about all the Knightleys together, as she does about Jane Fairfax. One is sick of the very name of Jane Fairfax. Every letter from her is read forty times over; her compliments to all friends go round and round again; and if she does but send her aunt the pattern of a stomacher, or knit a pair of garters for her grandmother, one hears of nothing else for a month. I wish Jane Fairfax very well; but she tires me to death."

They were now approaching the cottage, and all idle topics were superseded. Emma was very compassionate; and the distresses of the poor were as sure of relief from her personal attention and kindness, her counsel and her patience, as from her purse. She understood their ways, could allow for their ignorance and their temptations, had no romantic expectations of extraordinary virtue from those for whom education had done so little; entered into their troubles with ready sympathy, and always gave her assistance with as much intelligence as good-will. In the present instance, it was sickness and poverty together which she came to visit; and after remaining there as long as she could give comfort or advice, she quitted the cottage with such an impression of the scene as made her say to Harriet, as they walked away,

"These are the sights, Harriet, to do one good. How trifling they make every thing else appear!—I feel now as if I could think of nothing but these poor creatures all the rest of the day; and yet, who can say how soon it may all vanish from my mind?"

"Very true," said Harriet. "Poor creatures! one can think of nothing else."

"And really, I do not think the impression will soon be over," said Emma, as she crossed the low hedge, and tottering footstep which ended the narrow, slippery path through the cottage garden, and brought them into the lane again. "I do not think it will," stopping to look once more at all the outward wretchedness of the place, and recall the still greater within.

"Oh! dear, no," said her companion.

They walked on. The lane made a slight bend; and when that bend was passed, Mr. Elton was immediately in sight; and so near as to give Emma time only to say farther,

"Ah! Harriet, here comes a very sudden trial of our stability in good thoughts. Well, (smiling,) I hope it may be allowed that if compassion has produced exertion and relief to the sufferers, it has done all that is truly important. If we feel for the wretched, enough to do all we can for them, the rest is empty sympathy, only distressing to ourselves."

Harriet could just answer, "Oh! dear, yes," before the gentleman joined them. The wants and sufferings of the poor family, however, were the first subject on meeting. He had been going to call on them. His visit he would now defer; but they had a very interesting parley about what could be done and should be done. Mr. Elton then turned back to accompany them.

"To fall in with each other on such an errand as this," thought Emma; "to meet in a charitable scheme; this will bring a great increase of love on each side. I should not wonder if it were to bring on the declaration. It must, if I were not here. I wish I were anywhere else."

Anxious to separate herself from them as far as she could, she soon afterwards took possession of a narrow footpath, a little raised on one side of the lane, leaving them together in the main road. But she had not been there two minutes when she found that Harriet's habits of dependence and imitation were bringing her up too, and that, in short, they would both be soon after her. This would not do; she immediately stopped, under pretence of having some alteration to make in the lacing of her half-boot, and stooping down in complete occupation of the footpath, begged them to have the goodness to walk on, and she would follow in half a minute. They did as they were desired; and by the time she judged it reasonable to have done with her boot, she had the comfort of farther delay in her power, being overtaken by a child from the cottage, setting out, according to orders, with her pitcher, to fetch broth from Hartfield. To walk by the side of this child, and talk to and question her, was the most natural thing in the world, or would have been the most natural, had she been acting just then without design; and by this means the others were still able to keep ahead, without any obligation of waiting for her. She gained on them, however, involuntarily: the child's pace was quick, and theirs rather slow; and she was the more concerned at it, from their being evidently in a conversation which interested them. Mr. Elton was speaking with animation, Harriet listening with a very pleased attention; and Emma, having sent the child on, was beginning to think how she might draw back a little more, when they both looked around, and she was obliged to join them.

Mr. Elton was still talking, still engaged in some interesting detail; and Emma experienced some disappointment when she found that he was only giving his fair companion an account of the yesterday's party at his friend Cole's, and that she was come in herself for the Stilton cheese, the north Wiltshire, the butter, the cellery, the beet-root, and all the dessert.

"This would soon have led to something better, of course," was her consoling reflection; "any thing interests between those who love; and any thing will serve as introduction to what is near the heart. If I could but have kept longer away!"

They now walked on together quietly, till within view of the vicarage pales, when a sudden resolution, of at least getting Harriet into the house, made her again find something very much amiss about her boot, and fall behind to arrange it once more. She then broke the lace off short, and dexterously throwing it into a ditch, was presently obliged to entreat them to stop, and acknowledged her inability to put herself to rights so as to be able to walk home in tolerable comfort.

"Part of my lace is gone," said she, "and I do not know how I am to contrive. I really am a most troublesome companion to you both, but I hope I am not often so ill-equipped. Mr. Elton, I must beg leave to stop at your house, and ask your housekeeper for a bit of ribband or string, or any thing just to keep my boot on."

Mr. Elton looked all happiness at this proposition; and nothing could exceed his alertness and attention in conducting them into his house and endeavouring to make every thing appear to advantage. The room they were taken into was the one he chiefly occupied, and looking forwards; behind it was another with which it immediately communicated; the door between them was open, and Emma passed into it with the housekeeper to receive her assistance in the most comfortable manner. She was obliged to leave the door ajar as she found it; but she fully intended that Mr. Elton should close it. It was not closed, however, it still remained ajar; but by engaging the housekeeper in incessant conversation, she hoped to make it practicable for him to chuse his own subject in the adjoining room. For ten minutes she could hear nothing but herself. It could be protracted no longer. She was then obliged to be finished, and make her appearance.

The lovers were standing together at one of the windows. It had a most favourable aspect; and, for half a minute, Emma felt the glory of having schemed successfully. But it would not do; he had not come to the point. He had been most agreeable, most delightful; he had told Harriet that he had seen them go by, and had purposely followed them; other little gallantries and allusions had been dropt, but nothing serious.

"Cautious, very cautious," thought Emma; "he advances inch by inch, and will hazard nothing till he believes himself secure."

Still, however, though every thing had not been accomplished by her ingenious device, she could not but flatter herself that it had been the occasion of much present enjoyment to both, and must be leading them forward to the great event.

CHAPTER XI

Mr. Elton must now be left to himself. It was no longer in Emma's power to superintend his happiness or quicken his measures. The coming of her sister's family was so very near at hand, that first in anticipation, and then in reality, it became henceforth her prime object of interest; and during the ten days of their stay at Hartfield it was not to be expected—she did not herself expect—that any thing beyond occasional, fortuitous assistance could be afforded by her to the lovers. They might advance rapidly if they would, however; they must advance somehow or other whether they would or no. She hardly wished to have more leisure for them. There are people, who the more you do for them, the less they will do for themselves.

Mr. and Mrs. John Knightley, from having been longer than usual absent from Surry, were exciting of course rather more than the usual interest. Till this year, every long vacation since their marriage had been divided between Hartfield and Donwell Abbey; but all the holidays of this autumn had been given to sea-bathing for the children, and it was therefore many months since they had been seen in a regular way by their Surry connexions, or seen at all by Mr. Woodhouse, who could not be induced to get so far as London, even for poor Isabella's sake; and who consequently was now most nervously and apprehensively happy in forestalling this too short visit.

He thought much of the evils of the journey for her, and not a little of the fatigues of his own horses and coachman who were to bring some of the party the last half of the way; but his alarms were needless; the sixteen miles being happily accomplished, and Mr. and Mrs. John Knightley, their five children, and a competent number of nursery-maids, all reaching Hartfield in safety. The bustle and joy of such an arrival, the many to be talked to, welcomed, encouraged, and variously dispersed and disposed of, produced a noise and confusion which his nerves could not have borne under any other cause, nor have endured much longer even for this; but the ways of Hartfield and the feelings of her father were so respected by Mrs. John Knightley, that in spite of maternal solicitude for the immediate enjoyment of her little ones, and for their having instantly all the liberty and attendance, all the eating and drinking, and sleeping and playing, which they could possibly wish for, without the smallest delay, the children were never allowed to be long a disturbance to him, either in themselves or in any restless attendance on them.

Mrs. John Knightley was a pretty, elegant little woman, of gentle, quiet manners, and a disposition remarkably amiable and affectionate; wrapt up in her family; a devoted wife, a doating mother, and so tenderly attached to her father and sister that, but for these higher ties, a warmer love might have seemed impossible. She could never see a fault in any of them. She was not a woman of strong understanding or any quickness; and with this resemblance of her father, she inherited also much of his constitution; was delicate in her own health, over-careful of that of her children, had many fears and many nerves, and was as fond of her own Mr. Wingfield in town as her father could be of Mr. Perry. They were alike too, in a general benevolence of temper, and a strong habit of regard for every old acquaintance.

Mr. John Knightley was a tall, gentleman-like, and very clever man; rising in his profession, domestic, and respectable in his private character; but with reserved manners which prevented his being generally pleasing; and capable of being sometimes out of humour. He was not an ill-tempered man, not so often unreasonably cross as to deserve such a reproach; but his temper was not his great perfection; and, indeed, with such a worshipping wife, it was hardly possible that any natural defects in it should not be increased. The extreme sweetness of her temper must hurt his. He had all the clearness and quickness of mind which she wanted, and he could sometimes act an ungracious, or say a severe thing.

He was not a great favourite with his fair sister-in-law. Nothing wrong in him escaped her. She was quick in feeling the little injuries to Isabella, which Isabella never felt herself. Perhaps she might have passed over more had his manners been flattering to Isabella's sister, but they were only those of a calmly kind brother and friend, without praise and without blindness; but hardly any degree of personal compliment could have made her regardless of that greatest fault of all in her eyes which he sometimes fell into, the want of respectful forbearance towards her father. There he had not always the patience that could have been wished. Mr. Woodhouse's peculiarities and fidgetiness were sometimes provoking him to a rational remonstrance or sharp retort equally ill-bestowed. It did not often happen; for Mr. John Knightley had really a great regard for his father-in-law, and generally a strong sense of what was due to him; but it was too often for Emma's charity, especially as there was all the pain of apprehension frequently to be endured, though the offence came not. The beginning, however, of every visit displayed none but the properest feelings, and this being of necessity so short might be hoped to pass away in unsullied cordiality. They had not been long seated and composed when Mr. Woodhouse, with a melancholy shake of the head and a sigh, called his daughter's attention to the sad change at Hartfield since she had been there last.

"Ah, my dear," said he, "poor Miss Taylor—It is a grievous business."

"Oh yes, sir," cried she with ready sympathy, "how you must miss her! And dear Emma, too!—What a dreadful loss to you both!—I have been so grieved for you.—I could not imagine how you could possibly do without her.—It is a sad change indeed.—But I hope she is pretty well, sir."

"Pretty well, my dear—I hope—pretty well.—I do not know but that the place agrees with her tolerably."

Mr. John Knightley here asked Emma quietly whether there were any doubts of the air of Randalls.

"Oh! no—none in the least. I never saw Mrs. Weston better in my life—never looking so well. Papa is only speaking his own regret."

"Very much to the honour of both," was the handsome reply.

"And do you see her, sir, tolerably often?" asked Isabella in the plaintive tone which just suited her father.

Mr. Woodhouse hesitated.—"Not near so often, my dear, as I could wish."

"Oh! papa, we have missed seeing them but one entire day since they married. Either in the morning or evening of every day, excepting one, have we seen either Mr. Weston or Mrs. Weston, and generally both, either at Randalls or here—and as you may suppose, Isabella, most frequently here. They are very, very kind in their visits. Mr. Weston is really as kind as herself. Papa, if you speak in that melancholy way, you will be giving Isabella a false idea of us all. Every body must be aware that Miss Taylor must be missed, but every body ought also to be assured that Mr. and Mrs. Weston do really prevent our missing her by any means to the extent we ourselves anticipated—which is the exact truth."

"Just as it should be," said Mr. John Knightley, "and just as I hoped it was from your letters. Her wish of shewing you attention could not be doubted, and his being a disengaged and social man makes it all easy. I have been always telling you, my love, that I had no idea of the change being so very material to Hartfield as you apprehended; and now you have Emma's account, I hope you will be satisfied."

"Why, to be sure," said Mr. Woodhouse—"yes, certainly—I cannot deny that Mrs. Weston, poor Mrs. Weston, does come and see us pretty often—but then—she is always obliged to go away again."

"It would be very hard upon Mr. Weston if she did not, papa.—You quite forget poor Mr. Weston."

"I think, indeed," said John Knightley pleasantly, "that Mr. Weston has some little claim. You and I, Emma, will venture to take the part of the poor husband. I, being a husband, and you not being a wife, the claims of the man may very likely strike us with equal force. As for Isabella, she has been married long enough to see the convenience of putting all the Mr. Westons aside as much as she can."

"Me, my love," cried his wife, hearing and understanding only in part.—"Are you talking about me?—I am sure nobody ought to be, or can be, a greater advocate for matrimony than I am; and if it had not been for the misery of her leaving Hartfield, I should never have thought of Miss Taylor but as the most fortunate woman in the world; and as to slighting Mr. Weston, that excellent Mr. Weston, I think there is nothing he does not deserve. I believe he is one of the very best-tempered men that ever existed. Excepting yourself and your brother, I do not know his equal for temper. I shall never forget his flying Henry's kite for him that very windy day last Easter—and ever since his particular kindness last September twelvemonth in writing that note, at twelve o'clock at night, on purpose to assure me that there was no scarlet fever at Cobham, I have been convinced there could not be a more feeling heart nor a better man in existence.—If any body can deserve him, it must be Miss Taylor."

"Where is the young man?" said John Knightley. "Has he been here on this occasion—or has he not?"

"He has not been here yet," replied Emma. "There was a strong expectation of his coming soon after the marriage, but it ended in nothing; and I have not heard him mentioned lately."

"But you should tell them of the letter, my dear," said her father.

"He wrote a letter to poor Mrs. Weston, to congratulate her, and a very proper, handsome letter it was. She shewed it to me. I thought it very well done of him indeed. Whether it was his own idea you know, one cannot tell. He is but young, and his uncle, perhaps—"

"My dear papa, he is three-and-twenty. You forget how time passes."

"Three-and-twenty!—is he indeed?—Well, I could not have thought it—and he was but two years old when he lost his poor mother! Well, time does fly indeed!—and my memory is very bad. However, it was an exceeding good, pretty letter, and gave Mr. and Mrs. Weston a great deal of pleasure. I remember it was written from Weymouth, and dated Sept. 28th—and began, 'My dear Madam,' but I forget how it went on; and it was signed 'F. C. Weston Churchill.'—I remember that perfectly."

"How very pleasing and proper of him!" cried the good-hearted Mrs. John Knightley. "I have no doubt of his being a most amiable young man. But how sad it is that he should not live at home with his father! There is something so shocking in a child's being taken away from his parents and natural home! I never could comprehend how Mr. Weston could part with him. To give up one's child! I really never could think well of any body who proposed such a thing to any body else."

"Nobody ever did think well of the Churchills, I fancy," observed Mr. John Knightley coolly. "But you need not imagine Mr. Weston to have felt what you would feel in giving up Henry or John. Mr. Weston is rather an easy, cheerful-tempered man, than a man of strong feelings; he takes things as he finds them, and makes enjoyment of them somehow or other, depending, I suspect, much more upon what is called society for his comforts, that is, upon the power of eating and drinking, and playing whist with his neighbours five times a week, than upon family affection, or any thing that home affords."

Emma could not like what bordered on a reflection on Mr. Weston, and had half a mind to take it up; but she struggled, and let it pass. She would keep the peace if possible; and there was something honourable and valuable in the strong domestic habits, the all-sufficiency of home to himself, whence resulted her brother's disposition to look down on the common rate of social intercourse, and those to whom it was important.—It had a high claim to forbearance.

CHAPTER XII

Mr. Knightley was to dine with them—rather against the inclination of Mr. Woodhouse, who did not like that any one should share with him in Isabella's first day. Emma's sense of right however had decided it; and besides the consideration of what was due to each brother, she had particular pleasure, from the circumstance of the late disagreement between Mr. Knightley and herself, in procuring him the proper invitation.

She hoped they might now become friends again. She thought it was time to make up. Making-up indeed would not do. *She* certainly had not been in the wrong, and *he* would never own that he had. Concession must be out of the question; but it was time to appear to forget that they had ever quarrelled; and she hoped it might rather assist the restoration of friendship, that when he came into the room she had one of the children with her—the youngest, a nice little girl about eight months old, who was now making her first visit to Hartfield, and very happy to be danced about in her aunt's arms. It did assist; for though he began with grave looks and short questions, he was soon led on to talk of them all in the usual way, and to take the child out of her arms with all the unceremoniousness of perfect amity. Emma felt they were friends again; and the conviction giving her at first great satisfaction, and then a little sauciness, she could not help saying, as he was admiring the baby,

"What a comfort it is, that we think alike about our nephews and nieces. As to men and women, our opinions are sometimes very different; but with regard to these children, I observe we never disagree."

"If you were as much guided by nature in your estimate of men and women, and as little under the power of fancy and whim in your dealings with them, as you are where these children are concerned, we might always think alike."

"To be sure—our discordancies must always arise from my being in the wrong."

"Yes," said he, smiling—"and reason good. I was sixteen years old when you were born."

"A material difference then," she replied—"and no doubt you were much my superior in judgment at that period of our lives; but does not the lapse of one-and-twenty years bring our understandings a good deal nearer?"

"Yes—a good deal *nearer.*"

"But still, not near enough to give me a chance of being right, if we think differently."

"I have still the advantage of you by sixteen years' experience, and by not being a pretty young woman and a spoiled child. Come, my dear Emma, let us be friends, and say no more about it. Tell your aunt, little Emma, that she ought to set you a better example than to be renewing old grievances, and that if she were not wrong before, she is now."

"That's true," she cried—"very true. Little Emma, grow up a better woman than your aunt. Be infinitely cleverer and not half so conceited. Now, Mr. Knightley, a word or two more, and I have done. As far as good intentions went, we were *both* right, and I must say that no effects on my side of the argument have yet proved wrong. I only want to know that Mr. Martin is not very, very bitterly disappointed."

"A man cannot be more so," was his short, full answer.

"Ah!—Indeed I am very sorry.—Come, shake hands with me."

This had just taken place and with great cordiality, when John Knightley made his appearance, and "How d'ye do, George?" and "John, how are you?" succeeded in the true English style, burying under a calmness that seemed all but indifference, the real attachment which would have led either of them, if requisite, to do every thing for the good of the other.

The evening was quiet and conversable, as Mr. Woodhouse declined cards entirely for the sake of comfortable talk with his dear Isabella, and the little party made two natural divisions; on one side he and his daughter; on the other the two Mr. Knightleys; their subjects totally distinct, or very rarely mixing—and Emma only occasionally joining in one or the other.

The brothers talked of their own concerns and pursuits, but principally of those of the elder, whose temper was by much the most communicative, and who was always the greater talker. As a magistrate, he had generally some point of law to consult John about, or, at least, some curious anecdote to give; and as a farmer, as keeping in hand the home-farm at Donwell, he had to tell what every field was to bear next year, and to give all such local information as could not fail of being interesting to a brother whose home it had equally been the longest part of his life, and whose attachments were strong. The plan of a drain, the change of a fence, the felling of a tree, and the destination of every acre for wheat, turnips, or spring corn, was entered into with as much equality of interest by John, as his cooler manners rendered possible; and if his willing brother ever left him any thing to inquire about, his inquiries even approached a tone of eagerness.

While they were thus comfortably occupied, Mr. Woodhouse was enjoying a full flow of happy regrets and fearful affection with his daughter.

"My poor dear Isabella," said he, fondly taking her hand, and interrupting, for a few moments, her busy labours for some one of her five children—"How long it is, how terribly long since you were here! And how tired you must be after your journey! You must go to bed early, my dear—and I recommend a little gruel to you before you go.—You and I will have a nice basin of gruel together. My dear Emma, suppose we all have a little gruel."

Emma could not suppose any such thing, knowing as she did, that both the Mr. Knightleys were as unpersuadable on that article as herself;—and two basins only were ordered. After a little more discourse in praise of gruel, with some wondering at its not being taken every evening by every body, he proceeded to say, with an air of grave reflection,

"It was an awkward business, my dear, your spending the autumn at South End instead of coming here. I never had much opinion of the sea air."

"Mr. Wingfield most strenuously recommended it, sir—or we should not have gone. He recommended it for all the children, but particularly for the weakness in little Bella's throat,—both sea air and bathing."

"Ah! my dear, but Perry had many doubts about the sea doing her any good; and as to myself, I have been long perfectly convinced, though perhaps I never told you so before, that the sea is very rarely of use to any body. I am sure it almost killed me once."

"Come, come," cried Emma, feeling this to be an unsafe subject, "I must beg you not to talk of the sea. It makes me envious and miserable;—I who have never seen it! South End is prohibited, if you please. My dear Isabella, I have not heard you make one inquiry about Mr. Perry yet; and he never forgets you."

"Oh! good Mr. Perry—how is he, sir?"

"Why, pretty well; but not quite well. Poor Perry is bilious, and he has not time to take care of himself—he tells me he has not time to take care of himself—which is very sad—but he is always wanted all round the country. I suppose there is not a man in such practice anywhere. But then there is not so clever a man any where."

"And Mrs. Perry and the children, how are they? Do the children grow? I have a great regard for Mr. Perry. I hope he will be calling soon. He will be so pleased to see my little ones."

"I hope he will be here to-morrow, for I have a question or two to ask him about myself of some consequence. And, my dear, whenever he comes, you had better let him look at little Bella's throat."

"Oh! my dear sir, her throat is so much better that I have hardly any uneasiness about it. Either bathing has been of the greatest service to her, or else it is to be attributed to an excellent embrocation of Mr. Wingfield's, which we have been applying at times ever since August."

"It is not very likely, my dear, that bathing should have been of use to her—and if I had known you were wanting an embrocation, I would have spoken to—"

"You seem to me to have forgotten Mrs. and Miss Bates," said Emma. "I have not heard one inquiry after them."

"Oh! the good Bateses—I am quite ashamed of myself—but you mention them in most of your letters. I hope they are quite well. Good old Mrs. Bates—I will call upon her to-morrow, and take my children.—They are always so pleased to see my children.—And that excellent Miss Bates!—such thorough worthy people!—How are they, sir?"

"Why, pretty well, my dear, upon the whole. But poor Mrs. Bates had a bad cold about a month ago."

"How sorry I am! But colds were never so prevalent as they have been this autumn. Mr. Wingfield told me that he has never known them more general or heavy—except when it has been quite an influenza."

"That has been a good deal the case, my dear; but not to the degree you mention. Perry says that colds have been very general, but not so heavy as he has very often known them in November. Perry does not call it altogether a sickly season."

"No, I do not know that Mr. Wingfield considers it *very* sickly except—"

"Ah! my poor dear child, the truth is, that in London it is always a sickly season. Nobody is healthy in London, nobody can be. It is a dreadful thing to have you forced to live there! so far off!—and the air so bad!"

"No, indeed—*we* are not at all in a bad air. Our part of London is very superior to most others!—You must not confound us with London in general, my dear sir. The neighbourhood of Brunswick Square is very different from almost all the rest. We are so very airy! I should be unwilling, I own, to live in any other part of the town;—there is hardly any other that I could be satisfied to have my children in: but *we* are so remarkably airy!—Mr. Wingfield thinks the vicinity of Brunswick Square decidedly the most favourable as to air."

"Ah! my dear, it is not like Hartfield. You make the best of it—but after you have been a week at Hartfield, you are all of you different creatures; you do not look like the same. Now I cannot say, that I think you are any of you looking well at present."

"I am sorry to hear you say so, sir; but I assure you, excepting those little nervous head-aches and palpitations which I am never entirely free from anywhere, I am quite well myself; and if the children were rather pale before they went to bed, it was only because they were a little more tired than usual, from their journey and the happiness of coming. I hope you will think better of their looks to-morrow; for I assure you Mr. Wingfield told me, that he did not believe he had ever sent us off altogether, in such good case. I trust, at least, that you do not think Mr. Knightley looking ill," turning her eyes with affectionate anxiety towards her husband.

"Middling, my dear; I cannot compliment you. I think Mr. John Knightley very far from looking well."

"What is the matter, sir?—Did you speak to me?" cried Mr. John Knightley, hearing his own name.

"I am sorry to find, my love, that my father does not think you looking well—but I hope it is only from being a little fatigued. I could have wished, however, as you know, that you had seen Mr. Wingfield before you left home."

"My dear Isabella,"—exclaimed he hastily—"pray do not concern yourself about my looks. Be satisfied with doctoring and coddling yourself and the children, and let me look as I chuse."

"I did not thoroughly understand what you were telling your

brother," cried Emma, "about your friend Mr. Graham's intending to have a bailiff from Scotland, to look after his new estate. What will it answer? Will not the old prejudice be too strong?"

And she talked in this way so long and successfully that, when forced to give her attention again to her father and sister, she had nothing worse to hear than Isabella's kind inquiry after Jane Fairfax; and Jane Fairfax, though no great favourite with her in general, she was at that moment very happy to assist in praising.

"That sweet, amiable Jane Fairfax!" said Mrs. John Knightley.—"It is so long since I have seen her, except now and then for a moment accidentally in town! What happiness it must be to her good old grandmother and excellent aunt, when she comes to visit them! I always regret excessively on dear Emma's account that she cannot be more at Highbury; but now their daughter is married, I suppose Colonel and Mrs. Campbell will not be able to part with her at all. She would be such a delightful companion for Emma."

Mr. Woodhouse agreed to it all, but added,

"Our little friend Harriet Smith, however, is just such another pretty kind of young person. You will like Harriet. Emma could not have a better companion than Harriet."

"I am most happy to hear it—but only Jane Fairfax one knows to be so very accomplished and superior!—and exactly Emma's age."

This topic was discussed very happily, and others succeeded of similar moment, and passed away with similar harmony; but the evening did not close without a little return of agitation. The gruel came and supplied a great deal to be said—much praise and many comments—undoubting decision of its wholesomeness for every constitution, and pretty severe Philippics upon the many houses where it was never met with tolerable;—but, unfortunately, among the failures which the daughter had to instance, the most recent, and therefore most prominent, was in her own cook at South End, a young woman hired for the time, who never had been able to understand what she meant by a basin of nice smooth gruel, thin, but not too thin. Often as she had wished for and ordered it, she had never been able to get any thing tolerable. Here was a dangerous opening.

"Ah!" said Mr. Woodhouse, shaking his head and fixing his eyes on her with tender concern.—The ejaculation in Emma's ear expressed, "Ah! there is no end of the sad consequences of your going to South

End. It does not bear talking of." And for a little while she hoped he would not talk of it, and that a silent rumination might suffice to restore him to the relish of his own smooth gruel. After an interval of some minutes, however, he began with,

"I shall always be very sorry that you went to the sea this autumn, instead of coming here."

"But why should you be sorry, sir?—I assure you, it did the children a great deal of good."

"And, moreover, if you must go to the sea, it had better not have been to South End. South End is an unhealthy place. Perry was surprized to hear you had fixed upon South End."

"I know there is such an idea with many people, but indeed it is quite a mistake, sir.—We all had our health perfectly well there, never found the least inconvenience from the mud; and Mr. Wingfield says it is entirely a mistake to suppose the place unhealthy; and I am sure he may be depended on, for he thoroughly understands the nature of the air, and his own brother and family have been there repeatedly."

"You should have gone to Cromer, my dear, if you went anywhere.—Perry was a week at Cromer once, and he holds it to be the best of all the sea-bathing places. A fine open sea, he says, and very pure air. And, by what I understand, you might have had lodgings there quite away from the sea—a quarter of a mile off—very comfortable. You should have consulted Perry."

"But, my dear sir, the difference of the journey;—only consider how great it would have been.—An hundred miles, perhaps, instead of forty."

"Ah! my dear, as Perry says, where health is at stake, nothing else should be considered; and if one is to travel, there is not much to chuse between forty miles and an hundred.—Better not move at all, better stay in London altogether than travel forty miles to get into a worse air. This is just what Perry said. It seemed to him a very ill-judged measure."

Emma's attempts to stop her father had been vain; and when he had reached such a point as this, she could not wonder at her brother-in-law's breaking out.

"Mr. Perry," said he, in a voice of very strong displeasure, "would do as well to keep his opinion till it is asked for. Why does he make it any business of his, to wonder at what I do?—at my taking my family to one part of the coast or another?—I may be allowed, I hope, the use of my judgment as well as Mr. Perry.—I want his directions no more than his drugs." He paused—and growing cooler in a moment, added, with only sarcastic dryness, "If Mr. Perry can tell me how to convey a wife and five children a distance of an hundred and thirty miles with no greater expense or inconvenience than a distance of forty, I should be as willing to prefer Cromer to South End as he could himself."

"True, true," cried Mr. Knightley, with most ready interposition—"very true. That's a consideration indeed.—But John, as to what I was telling you of my idea of moving the path to Langham, of turning it more to the right that it may not cut through the home meadows, I cannot conceive any difficulty. I should not attempt it, if it were to be the means of inconvenience to the Highbury people, but if you call to mind exactly the present line of the path—the only way of proving it, however, will be to turn to our maps. I shall see you at the Abbey to-morrow morning I hope, and then we will look them over, and you shall give me your opinion."

Mr. Woodhouse was rather agitated by such harsh reflections on his friend Perry, to whom he had, in fact, though unconsciously, been attributing many of his own feelings and expressions;—but the soothing attentions of his daughters gradually removed the present evil, and the immediate alertness of one brother, and better recollections of the other, prevented any renewal of it.

CHAPTER XIII

There could hardly be a happier creature in the world than Mrs. John Knightley, in this short visit to Hartfield, going about every morning among her old acquaintance with her five children, and talking over what she had done every evening with her father and sister. She had nothing to wish otherwise, but that the days did not pass so swiftly. It was a delightful visit;—perfect, in being much too short.

In general their evenings were less engaged with friends than their mornings; but one complete dinner engagement, and out of the house too, there was no avoiding, though at Christmas. Mr. Weston would take no denial; they must all dine at Randalls one day;—even Mr. Woodhouse was persuaded to think it a possible thing in preference to a division of the party.

How they were all to be conveyed, he would have made a difficulty if he could, but as his son and daughter's carriage and horses were actually at Hartfield, he was not able to make more than a simple question on that head; it hardly amounted to a doubt; nor did it occupy Emma long to convince him that they might in one of the carriages find room for Harriet also.

Harriet, Mr. Elton, and Mr. Knightley, their own especial set, were the only persons invited to meet them;—the hours were to be early, as well as the numbers few; Mr. Woodhouse's habits and inclination being consulted in every thing.

The evening before this great event (for it was a very great event that Mr. Woodhouse should dine out, on the 24th of December) had been spent by Harriet at Hartfield, and she had gone home so much indisposed with a cold, that, but for her own earnest wish of being nursed by Mrs. Goddard, Emma could not have allowed her to leave the house. Emma called on her the next day, and found her doom already signed with regard to Randalls. She was very feverish and had a bad sore throat: Mrs. Goddard was full of care and affection, Mr. Perry was talked of, and Harriet herself was too ill and low to resist the authority which excluded her from this delightful engagement, though she could not speak of her loss without many tears.

Emma sat with her as long as she could, to attend her in Mrs.

Goddard's unavoidable absences, and raise her spirits by representing how much Mr. Elton's would be depressed when he knew her state; and left her at last tolerably comfortable, in the sweet dependence of his having a most comfortless visit, and of their all missing her very much. She had not advanced many yards from Mrs. Goddard's door, when she was met by Mr. Elton himself, evidently coming towards it, and as they walked on slowly together in conversation about the invalid—of whom he, on the rumour of considerable illness, had been going to inquire, that he might carry some report of her to Hartfield—they were overtaken by Mr. John Knightley returning from the daily visit to Donwell, with his two eldest boys, whose healthy, glowing faces shewed all the benefit of a country run, and seemed to ensure a quick despatch of the roast mutton and rice pudding they were hastening home for. They joined company and proceeded together. Emma was just describing the nature of her friend's complaint;—"a throat very much inflamed, with a great deal of heat about her, a quick, low pulse, etc. and she was sorry to find from Mrs. Goddard that Harriet was liable to very bad sore-throats, and had often alarmed her with them." Mr. Elton looked all alarm on the occasion, as he exclaimed,

"A sore-throat!—I hope not infectious. I hope not of a putrid infectious sort. Has Perry seen her? Indeed you should take care of yourself as well as of your friend. Let me entreat you to run no risks. Why does not Perry see her?"

Emma, who was not really at all frightened herself, tranquillised this excess of apprehension by assurances of Mrs. Goddard's experience and care; but as there must still remain a degree of uneasiness which she could not wish to reason away, which she would rather feed and assist than not, she added soon afterwards—as if quite another subject,

"It is so cold, so very cold—and looks and feels so very much like snow, that if it were to any other place or with any other party, I should really try not to go out to-day—and dissuade my father from venturing; but as he has made up his mind, and does not seem to feel the cold himself, I do not like to interfere, as I know it would be so great a disappointment to Mr. and Mrs. Weston. But, upon my word, Mr. Elton, in your case, I should certainly excuse myself. You appear to me a little hoarse already, and when you consider what demand of voice and what fatigues to-morrow will bring, I think it would be no more than common prudence to stay at home and take care of yourself to-night."

Mr. Elton looked as if he did not very well know what answer to make; which was exactly the case; for though very much gratified by the kind care of such a fair lady, and not liking to resist any advice of her's, he had not really the least inclination to give up the visit;—but Emma, too eager and busy in her own previous conceptions and views to hear him impartially, or see him with clear vision, was very well satisfied with his muttering acknowledgment of its being "very cold, certainly very cold," and walked on, rejoicing in having extricated him from Randalls, and secured him the power of sending to inquire after Harriet every hour of the evening.

"You do quite right," said she;—"we will make your apologies to Mr. and Mrs. Weston."

But hardly had she so spoken, when she found her brother was civilly offering a seat in his carriage, if the weather were Mr. Elton's only objection, and Mr. Elton actually accepting the offer with much prompt satisfaction. It was a done thing; Mr. Elton was to go, and never had his broad handsome face expressed more pleasure than at this moment; never had his smile been stronger, nor his eyes more exulting than when he next looked at her.

"Well," said she to herself, "this is most strange!—After I had got him off so well, to chuse to go into company, and leave Harriet ill behind!—Most strange indeed!—But there is, I believe, in many men, especially single men, such an inclination—such a passion for dining out—a dinner engagement is so high in the class of their pleasures, their employments, their dignities, almost their duties, that any thing gives way to it—and this must be the case with Mr. Elton; a most valuable, amiable, pleasing young man undoubtedly, and very much in love with Harriet; but still, he cannot refuse an invitation, he must dine out wherever he is asked. What a strange thing love is! he can see ready wit in Harriet, but will not dine alone for her."

Soon afterwards Mr. Elton quitted them, and she could not but do him the justice of feeling that there was a great deal of sentiment in his manner of naming Harriet at parting; in the tone of his voice while assuring her that he should call at Mrs. Goddard's for news of her fair friend, the last thing before he prepared for the happiness of meeting her again, when he hoped to be able to give a better report; and he sighed and smiled himself off in a way that left the balance of approbation much in his favour.

After a few minutes of entire silence between them, John Knightley began with—

"I never in my life saw a man more intent on being agreeable than Mr. Elton. It is downright labour to him where ladies are concerned. With men he can be rational and unaffected, but when he has ladies to please, every feature works."

"Mr. Elton's manners are not perfect," replied Emma; "but where there is a wish to please, one ought to overlook, and one does overlook a great deal. Where a man does his best with only moderate powers, he will have the advantage over negligent superiority. There is such perfect good-temper and good-will in Mr. Elton as one cannot but value."

"Yes," said Mr. John Knightley presently, with some slyness, "he seems to have a great deal of good-will towards you."

"Me!" she replied with a smile of astonishment, "are you imagining me to be Mr. Elton's object?"

"Such an imagination has crossed me, I own, Emma; and if it never occurred to you before, you may as well take it into consideration now."

"Mr. Elton in love with me!—What an idea!"

"I do not say it is so; but you will do well to consider whether it is so or not, and to regulate your behaviour accordingly. I think your manners to him encouraging. I speak as a friend, Emma. You had better look about you, and ascertain what you do, and what you mean to do."

"I thank you; but I assure you you are quite mistaken. Mr. Elton and I are very good friends, and nothing more;" and she walked on, amusing herself in the consideration of the blunders which often arise from a partial knowledge of circumstances, of the mistakes which people of high pretensions to judgment are for ever falling into; and not very well pleased with her brother for imagining her blind and ignorant, and in want of counsel. He said no more.

Mr. Woodhouse had so completely made up his mind to the visit, that in spite of the increasing coldness, he seemed to have no idea of shrinking from it, and set forward at last most punctually with his eldest daughter in his own carriage, with less apparent consciousness of the weather than either of the others; too full of the wonder of his own going, and the pleasure it was to afford at Randalls to see that it was cold, and too well wrapt up to feel it. The cold, however, was severe; and by the time the second carriage was in motion, a few flakes of snow were finding their way down, and the sky had the appearance of being so overcharged as to want only a milder air to produce a very white world in a very short time.

Emma soon saw that her companion was not in the happiest humour. The preparing and the going abroad in such weather, with the sacrifice of his children after dinner, were evils, were disagreeables at least, which Mr. John Knightley did not by any means like; he anticipated nothing in the visit that could be at all worth the purchase; and the whole of their drive to the vicarage was spent by him in expressing his discontent.

"A man," said he, "must have a very good opinion of himself when he asks people to leave their own fireside, and encounter such a day as this, for the sake of coming to see him. He must think himself a most agreeable fellow; I could not do such a thing. It is the greatest absurdity—Actually snowing at this moment!—The folly of not allowing people to be comfortable at home—and the folly of people's not staying comfortably at home when they can! If we were obliged to go out such an evening as this, by any call of duty or business, what a hardship we should deem it;—and here are we, probably with rather thinner clothing than usual, setting forward voluntarily, without excuse, in defiance of the voice of nature, which tells man, in every thing given to his view or his feelings, to stay at home himself, and keep all under shelter that he can;—here are we setting forward to spend five dull hours in another man's house, with nothing to say or to hear that was not said and heard yesterday, and may not be said and heard again to-morrow. Going in dismal weather, to return probably in worse;—four horses and four servants taken out for nothing but to convey five idle, shivering creatures into colder rooms and worse company than they might have had at home."

Emma did not find herself equal to give the pleased assent, which no doubt he was in the habit of receiving, to emulate the "Very true, my love," which must have been usually administered by his travelling companion; but she had resolution enough to refrain from making any answer at all. She could not be complying, she dreaded being quarrelsome; her heroism reached only to silence. She allowed him to talk, and arranged the glasses, and wrapped herself up, without opening her lips.

They arrived, the carriage turned, the step was let down, and Mr. Elton, spruce, black, and smiling, was with them instantly. Emma thought with pleasure of some change of subject. Mr. Elton was all obligation and cheerfulness; he was so very cheerful in his civilities indeed, that she began to think he must have received a different account of Harriet from what had reached her. She had sent while dressing, and the answer had been, "Much the same—not better."

"*My* report from Mrs. Goddard's," said she presently, "was not so pleasant as I had hoped—'Not better' was *my* answer."

His face lengthened immediately; and his voice was the voice of sentiment as he answered.

"Oh! no—I am grieved to find—I was on the point of telling you that when I called at Mrs. Goddard's door, which I did the very last thing before I returned to dress, I was told that Miss Smith was not better, by no means better, rather worse. Very much grieved and concerned—I had flattered myself that she must be better after such a cordial as I knew had been given her in the morning."

Emma smiled and answered—"My visit was of use to the nervous part of her complaint, I hope; but not even I can charm away a sore throat; it is a most severe cold indeed. Mr. Perry has been with her, as you probably heard."

"Yes—I imagined—that is—I did not—"

"He has been used to her in these complaints, and I hope to-morrow morning will bring us both a more comfortable report. But it is impossible not to feel uneasiness. Such a sad loss to our party to-day!"

"Dreadful!—Exactly so, indeed.—She will be missed every moment."

This was very proper; the sigh which accompanied it was really estimable; but it should have lasted longer. Emma was rather in dismay when only half a minute afterwards he began to speak of other things, and in a voice of the greatest alacrity and enjoyment.

"What an excellent device," said he, "the use of a sheepskin for carriages. How very comfortable they make it;—impossible to feel cold with such precautions. The contrivances of modern days indeed have rendered a gentleman's carriage perfectly complete. One is so fenced and guarded from the weather, that not a breath of air can find its way unpermitted. Weather becomes absolutely of no consequence. It is a very cold afternoon—but in this carriage we know nothing of the matter.—Ha! snows a little I see."

"Yes," said John Knightley, "and I think we shall have a good deal of it."

"Christmas weather," observed Mr. Elton. "Quite seasonable; and extremely fortunate we may think ourselves that it did not begin yesterday, and prevent this day's party, which it might very possibly have done, for Mr. Woodhouse would hardly have ventured had there been much snow on the ground; but now it is of no consequence. This is quite the season indeed for friendly meetings. At Christmas every body invites their friends about them, and people think little of even the worst weather. I was snowed up at a friend's house once for a week. Nothing could be pleasanter. I went for only one night, and could not get away till that very day se'nnight."

Mr. John Knightley looked as if he did not comprehend the pleasure, but said only, coolly,

"I cannot wish to be snowed up a week at Randalls."

At another time Emma might have been amused, but she was too much astonished now at Mr. Elton's spirits for other feelings. Harriet seemed quite forgotten in the expectation of a pleasant party.

"We are sure of excellent fires," continued he, "and every thing in the greatest comfort. Charming people, Mr. and Mrs. Weston;—Mrs. Weston indeed is much beyond praise, and he is exactly what one values, so hospitable, and so fond of society;—it will be a small party, but where small parties are select, they are perhaps the most agreeable of any. Mr. Weston's dining-room does not accommodate more than ten comfortably; and for my part, I would rather, under such circumstances, fall short by two than exceed by two. I think you will agree with me, (turning with a soft air to Emma), I think I shall certainly have your approbation, though Mr. Knightley perhaps, from being used to the large parties of London, may not quite enter into our feelings."

"I know nothing of the large parties of London, sir—I never dine with any body."

"Indeed! (in a tone of wonder and pity,) I had no idea that the law had been so great a slavery. Well, sir, the time must come when you will be paid for all this, when you will have little labour and great enjoyment."

"My first enjoyment," replied John Knightley, as they passed through the sweep-gate, "will be to find myself safe at Hartfield again."

CHAPTER XIV

Some change of countenance was necessary for each gentleman as they walked into Mrs. Weston's drawing-room;—Mr. Elton must compose his joyous looks, and Mr. John Knightley disperse his ill-humour. Mr. Elton must smile less, and Mr. John Knightley more, to fit them for the place.—Emma only might be as nature prompted, and shew herself just as happy as she was. To her it was real enjoyment to be with the Westons. Mr. Weston was a great favourite, and there was not a creature in the world to whom she spoke with such unreserve, as to his wife; not any one, to whom she related with such conviction of being listened to and understood, of being always interesting and always intelligible, the little affairs, arrangements, perplexities, and pleasures of her father and herself. She could tell nothing of Hartfield, in which Mrs. Weston had not a lively concern; and half an hour's uninterrupted communication of all those little matters on which the daily happiness of private life depends, was one of the first gratifications of each.

This was a pleasure which perhaps the whole day's visit might not afford, which certainly did not belong to the present half-hour; but the very sight of Mrs. Weston, her smile, her touch, her voice was grateful to Emma, and she determined to think as little as possible of Mr. Elton's oddities, or of any thing else unpleasant, and enjoy all that was enjoyable to the utmost.

The misfortune of Harriet's cold had been pretty well gone through before her arrival. Mr. Woodhouse had been safely seated long enough to give the history of it, besides all the history of his own and Isabella's coming, and of Emma's being to follow, and had indeed just got to the end of his satisfaction that James should come and see his daughter, when the others appeared, and Mrs. Weston, who had been almost wholly engrossed by her attentions to him, was able to turn away and welcome her dear Emma.

Emma's project of forgetting Mr. Elton for a while made her rather sorry to find, when they had all taken their places, that he was close to her. The difficulty was great of driving his strange insensibility towards Harriet from her mind, while he not only sat at her elbow, but was continually obtruding his happy countenance on her notice, and solicitously addressing her upon every occasion. Instead of forgetting him, his behaviour was such that she could not avoid the internal suggestion of "Can it really be as my brother imagined? Can it be possible for this man to be beginning to transfer his affections from Harriet to me?—Absurd and insufferable!"—Yet he would be so anxious for her being perfectly warm, would be so interested about her father, and so delighted with Mrs. Weston; and at last would begin admiring her drawings with so much zeal and so little knowledge as seemed terribly like a would-be lover, and made it some effort with her to preserve her good manners. For her own sake she could not be rude; and for Harriet's, in the hope that all would yet turn out right, she was even positively civil; but it was an effort; especially as something was going on amongst the others, in the most overpowering period of Mr. Elton's nonsense, which she particularly wished to listen to. She heard enough to know that Mr. Weston was giving some information about his son; she heard the words "my son," and "Frank," and "my son," repeated several times over; and, from a few other half-syllables very much suspected that he was announcing an early visit from his son; but before she could quiet Mr. Elton, the subject was so completely past that any reviving question from her would have been awkward.

Now, it so happened that in spite of Emma's resolution of never marrying, there was something in the name, in the idea of Mr. Frank Churchill, which always interested her. She had frequently thought—especially since his father's marriage with Miss Taylor—that if she *were* to marry, he was the very person to suit her in age, character and condition. He seemed by this connexion between the families, quite to belong to her. She could not but suppose it to be a match that every body who knew them must think of. That Mr. and Mrs. Weston did think of it, she was very strongly persuaded; and though not meaning to be induced by him, or by any body else, to give up a situation which she believed more replete with good than any she could change it for, she had a great curiosity to see him, a decided intention of finding him pleasant, of being liked by him to a certain degree, and a sort of pleasure in the idea of their being coupled in their friends' imaginations.

With such sensations, Mr. Elton's civilities were dreadfully ill-timed; but she had the comfort of appearing very polite, while feeling very cross—and of thinking that the rest of the visit could not possibly pass without bringing forward the same information again, or the substance of it, from the open-hearted Mr. Weston.—So it proved;—for when happily released from Mr. Elton, and seated by Mr. Weston, at dinner, he made use of the very first interval in the cares of hospitality, the very first leisure from the saddle of mutton, to say to her,

"We want only two more to be just the right number. I should like to see two more here,—your pretty little friend, Miss Smith, and my son—and then I should say we were quite complete. I believe you did not hear me telling the others in the drawing-room that we are expecting Frank. I had a letter from him this morning, and he will be with us within a fortnight."

Emma spoke with a very proper degree of pleasure; and fully assented to his proposition of Mr. Frank Churchill and Miss Smith making their party quite complete.

"He has been wanting to come to us," continued Mr. Weston, "ever since September: every letter has been full of it; but he cannot command his own time. He has those to please who must be pleased, and who (between ourselves) are sometimes to be pleased only by a good many sacrifices. But now I have no doubt of seeing him here about the second week in January."

"What a very great pleasure it will be to you! and Mrs. Weston is so anxious to be acquainted with him, that she must be almost as happy as yourself."

"Yes, she would be, but that she thinks there will be another put-off. She does not depend upon his coming so much as I do: but she does not know the parties so well as I do. The case, you see, is—(but this is quite between ourselves: I did not mention a syllable of it in the other room. There are secrets in all families, you know)—The case is, that a party of friends are invited to pay a visit at Enscombe in January; and that Frank's coming depends upon their being put off. If they are not put off, he cannot stir. But I know they will, because it is a family that a certain lady, of some consequence, at Enscombe, has a particular dislike to: and though it is thought necessary to invite them once in two or three years, they always are put off when it comes to the point. I have not the smallest doubt of the issue. I am as confident of seeing Frank here before the middle of January, as I am of being here myself: but your good friend there (nodding towards the upper end of the table) has so few vagaries herself, and has been so little used to them at Hartfield, that she cannot calculate on their effects, as I have been long in the practice of doing."

"I am sorry there should be any thing like doubt in the case," replied Emma; "but am disposed to side with you, Mr. Weston. If you think he will come, I shall think so too; for you know Enscombe."

"Yes—I have some right to that knowledge; though I have never been at the place in my life.—She is an odd woman!—But I never allow myself to speak ill of her, on Frank's account; for I do believe her to be very fond of him. I used to think she was not capable of being fond of any body, except herself: but she has always been kind to him (in her way—allowing for little whims and caprices, and expecting every thing to be as she likes). And it is no small credit, in my opinion, to him, that he should excite such an affection; for, though I would not say it to any body else, she has no more heart than a stone to people in general; and the devil of a temper."

Emma liked the subject so well, that she began upon it, to Mrs. Weston, very soon after their moving into the drawing-room: wishing her joy—yet observing, that she knew the first meeting must be rather alarming.—Mrs. Weston agreed to it; but added, that she should be very glad to be secure of undergoing the anxiety of a first meeting at the time talked of: "for I cannot depend upon his coming. I cannot be so sanguine as Mr. Weston. I am very much afraid that it will all end in nothing. Mr. Weston, I dare say, has been telling you exactly how the matter stands?"

"Yes—it seems to depend upon nothing but the ill-humour of Mrs. Churchill, which I imagine to be the most certain thing in the world."

"My Emma!" replied Mrs. Weston, smiling, "what is the certainty of caprice?" Then turning to Isabella, who had not been attending before—"You must know, my dear Mrs. Knightley, that we are by no means so sure of seeing Mr. Frank Churchill, in my opinion, as his father thinks. It depends entirely upon his aunt's spirits and pleasure; in short, upon her temper. To you—to my two daughters—I may venture on the truth. Mrs. Churchill rules at Enscombe, and is a very odd-tempered woman; and his coming now, depends upon her being willing to spare him."

"Oh, Mrs. Churchill; every body knows Mrs. Churchill," replied Isabella: "and I am sure I never think of that poor young man without the greatest compassion. To be constantly living with an ill-tempered person, must be dreadful. It is what we happily have never known any thing of; but it must be a life of misery. What a blessing, that she never had any children! Poor little creatures, how unhappy she would have made them!"

Emma wished she had been alone with Mrs. Weston. She should then have heard more: Mrs. Weston would speak to her, with a degree of unreserve which she would not hazard with Isabella; and, she really believed, would scarcely try to conceal any thing relative to the Churchills from her, excepting those views on the young man, of which her own imagination had already given her such instinctive knowledge. But at present there was nothing more to be said. Mr. Woodhouse very soon followed them into the drawing-room. To be sitting long after dinner, was a confinement that he could not endure. Neither wine nor conversation was any thing to him; and gladly did he move to those with whom he was always comfortable.

While he talked to Isabella, however, Emma found an opportunity of saying,

"And so you do not consider this visit from your son as by any means certain. I am sorry for it. The introduction must be unpleasant, whenever it takes place; and the sooner it could be over, the better."

"Yes; and every delay makes one more apprehensive of other delays. Even if this family, the Braithwaites, are put off, I am still afraid that some excuse may be found for disappointing us. I cannot bear to imagine any reluctance on his side; but I am sure there is a great wish on the Churchills' to keep him to themselves. There is jealousy. They are jealous even of his regard for his father. In short, I can feel no dependence on his coming, and I wish Mr. Weston were less sanguine."

"He ought to come," said Emma. "If he could stay only a couple of days, he ought to come; and one can hardly conceive a young man's not having it in his power to do as much as that. A young *woman*, if she fall into bad hands, may be teazed, and kept at a distance from those she wants to be with; but one cannot comprehend a young *man*'s being under such restraint, as not to be able to spend a week with his father, if he likes it."

"One ought to be at Enscombe, and know the ways of the family, before one decides upon what he can do," replied Mrs. Weston. "One ought to use the same caution, perhaps, in judging of the conduct of any one individual of any one family; but Enscombe, I believe, certainly must not be judged by general rules: *she* is so very unreasonable; and every thing gives way to her."

"But she is so fond of the nephew: he is so very great a favourite. Now, according to my idea of Mrs. Churchill, it would be most natural, that while she makes no sacrifice for the comfort of the husband, to whom she owes every thing, while she exercises incessant caprice towards *him*, she should frequently be governed by the nephew, to whom she owes nothing at all."

"My dearest Emma, do not pretend, with your sweet temper, to understand a bad one, or to lay down rules for it: you must let it go its own way. I have no doubt of his having, at times, considerable influence; but it may be perfectly impossible for him to know beforehand *when* it will be."

Emma listened, and then coolly said, "I shall not be satisfied, unless he comes."

"He may have a great deal of influence on some points," continued Mrs. Weston, "and on others, very little: and among those, on which she is beyond his reach, it is but too likely, may be this very circumstance of his coming away from them to visit us."

CHAPTER XV

Mr. Woodhouse was soon ready for his tea; and when he had drank his tea he was quite ready to go home; and it was as much as his three companions could do, to entertain away his notice of the lateness of the hour, before the other gentlemen appeared. Mr. Weston was chatty and convivial, and no friend to early separations of any sort; but at last the drawing-room party did receive an augmentation. Mr. Elton, in very good spirits, was one of the first to walk in. Mrs. Weston and Emma were sitting together on a sofa. He joined them immediately, and, with scarcely an invitation, seated himself between them.

Emma, in good spirits too, from the amusement afforded her mind by the expectation of Mr. Frank Churchill, was willing to forget his late improprieties, and be as well satisfied with him as before, and on his making Harriet his very first subject, was ready to listen with most friendly smiles.

He professed himself extremely anxious about her fair friend—her fair, lovely, amiable friend. "Did she know?—had she heard any thing about her, since their being at Randalls?—he felt much anxiety—he must confess that the nature of her complaint alarmed him considerably." And in this style he talked on for some time very properly, not much attending to any answer, but altogether sufficiently awake to the terror of a bad sore throat; and Emma was quite in charity with him.

But at last there seemed a perverse turn; it seemed all at once as if he were more afraid of its being a bad sore throat on her account, than on Harriet's—more anxious that she should escape the infection, than that there should be no infection in the complaint. He began with great earnestness to entreat her to refrain from visiting the sick-chamber again, for the present—to entreat her to *promise him* not to venture into such hazard till he had seen Mr. Perry and learnt his opinion; and though she tried to laugh it off and bring the subject back into its proper course, there was no putting an end to his extreme solicitude about her. She was vexed. It did appear—there was no concealing it—exactly like the pretence of being in love with her, instead of Harriet; an inconstancy, if real, the most contemptible and abominable! and she had difficulty in behaving with temper. He turned to Mrs. Weston to implore her assistance, "Would not she give him her support?—would not she add her persuasions to his, to induce Miss Woodhouse not to go to Mrs. Goddard's till it were certain that Miss Smith's disorder had no infection? He could not be satisfied without a promise—would not she give him her influence in procuring it?"

"So scrupulous for others," he continued, "and yet so careless for herself! She wanted me to nurse my cold by staying at home to-day, and yet will not promise to avoid the danger of catching an ulcerated sore throat herself. Is this fair, Mrs. Weston?—Judge between us. Have not I some right to complain? I am sure of your kind support and aid."

Emma saw Mrs. Weston's surprize, and felt that it must be great, at an address which, in words and manner, was assuming to himself the right of first interest in her; and as for herself, she was too much provoked and offended to have the power of directly saying any thing to the purpose. She could only give him a look; but it was such a look as she thought must restore him to his senses, and then left the sofa, removing to a seat by her sister, and giving her all her attention.

She had not time to know how Mr. Elton took the reproof, so rapidly did another subject succeed; for Mr. John Knightley now came into the room from examining the weather, and opened on them all with the information of the ground being covered with snow, and of its still snowing fast, with a strong drifting wind; concluding with these words to Mr. Woodhouse:

"This will prove a spirited beginning of your winter engagements, sir. Something new for your coachman and horses to be making their way through a storm of snow."

Poor Mr. Woodhouse was silent from consternation; but every body else had something to say; every body was either surprized or not surprized, and had some question to ask, or some comfort to offer. Mrs. Weston and Emma tried earnestly to cheer him and turn his attention from his son-in-law, who was pursuing his triumph rather unfeelingly.

"I admired your resolution very much, sir," said he, "in venturing out in such weather, for of course you saw there would be snow very soon. Every body must have seen the snow coming on. I admired your spirit; and I dare say we shall get home very well. Another hour or two's snow can hardly make the road impassable; and we are two carriages; if one is blown over in the bleak part of the common field there will be the other at hand. I dare say we shall be all safe at Hartfield before midnight."

Mr. Weston, with triumph of a different sort, was confessing that he had known it to be snowing some time, but had not said a word, lest it should make Mr. Woodhouse uncomfortable, and be an excuse for his hurrying away. As to there being any quantity of snow fallen or likely to fall to impede their return, that was a mere joke; he was afraid they would find no difficulty. He wished the road might be impassable, that he might be able to keep them all at Randalls; and with the utmost good-will was sure that accommodation might be found for every body, calling on his wife to agree with him, that with a little contrivance, every body might be lodged, which she hardly knew how to do, from the consciousness of there being but two spare rooms in the house.

"What is to be done, my dear Emma?—what is to be done?" was Mr. Woodhouse's first exclamation, and all that he could say for some time. To her he looked for comfort; and her assurances of safety, her representation of the excellence of the horses, and of James, and of their having so many friends about them, revived him a little.

His eldest daughter's alarm was equal to his own. The horror of being blocked up at Randalls, while her children were at Hartfield, was full in her imagination; and fancying the road to be now just passable for adventurous people, but in a state that admitted no delay, she was eager to have it settled, that her father and Emma should remain at Randalls, while she and her husband set forward instantly through all the possible accumulations of drifted snow that might impede them.

"You had better order the carriage directly, my love," said she; "I dare say we shall be able to get along, if we set off directly; and if we do come to any thing very bad, I can get out and walk. I am not at all afraid. I should not mind walking half the way. I could change my shoes, you know, the moment I got home; and it is not the sort of thing that gives me cold."

"Indeed!" replied he. "Then, my dear Isabella, it is the most extraordinary sort of thing in the world, for in general every thing does give you cold. Walk home!—you are prettily shod for walking home, I dare say. It will be bad enough for the horses."

Isabella turned to Mrs. Weston for her approbation of the plan. Mrs. Weston could only approve. Isabella then went to Emma; but Emma could not so entirely give up the hope of their being all able to get away; and they were still discussing the point, when Mr. Knightley, who had left the room immediately after his brother's first report of the snow, came back again, and told them that he had been out of doors to examine, and could answer for there not being the smallest difficulty in their getting home, whenever they liked it, either now or an hour hence. He had gone beyond the sweep—some way along the Highbury road—the snow was nowhere above half an inch deep—in many places hardly enough to whiten the ground; a very few flakes were falling at present, but the clouds were parting, and there was every appearance of its being soon over. He had seen the coachmen, and they both agreed with him in there being nothing to apprehend.

To Isabella, the relief of such tidings was very great, and they were scarcely less acceptable to Emma on her father's account, who was immediately set as much at ease on the subject as his nervous constitution allowed; but the alarm that had been raised could not be appeased so as to admit of any comfort for him while he continued at Randalls. He was satisfied of there being no present danger in returning home, but no assurances could convince him that it was safe to stay; and while the others were variously urging and recommending, Mr. Knightley and Emma settled it in a few brief sentences—thus:

"Your father will not be easy; why do not you go?"

"I am ready, if the others are."

"Shall I ring the bell?"

"Yes, do."

And the bell was rung, and the carriages spoken for. A few minutes more, and Emma hoped to see one troublesome companion deposited in his own house, to get sober and cool, and the other recover his temper and happiness when this visit of hardship were over.

The carriage came: and Mr. Woodhouse, always the first object on such occasions, was carefully attended to his own by Mr. Knightley and Mr. Weston; but not all that either could say could prevent some renewal of alarm at the sight of the snow which had actually fallen, and the discovery of a much darker night than he had been prepared for. "He was afraid they should have a very bad drive. He was afraid poor Isabella would not like it. And there would be poor Emma in the carriage behind. He did not know what they had best do. They must keep as much together as they could;" and James was talked to, and given a charge to go very slow and wait for the other carriage.

Isabella stept in after her father; John Knightley, forgetting that he did not belong to their party, stept in after his wife very naturally; so that Emma found, on being escorted and followed into the second carriage by Mr. Elton, that the door was to be lawfully shut on them, and that they were to have a tête-à-tête drive. It would not have been the awkwardness of a moment, it would have been rather a pleasure, previous to the suspicions of this very day; she could have talked to him of Harriet, and the three-quarters of a mile would have seemed but one. But now, she would rather it had not happened. She believed he had been drinking too much of Mr. Weston's good wine, and felt sure that he would want to be talking nonsense.

To restrain him as much as might be, by her own manners, she was immediately preparing to speak with exquisite calmness and gravity of the weather and the night; but scarcely had she begun, scarcely had they passed the sweep-gate and joined the other carriage, than she found her subject cut up—her hand seized—her attention demanded, and Mr. Elton actually making violent love to her: availing himself of the precious opportunity, declaring sentiments which must be already well known, hoping—fearing—adoring—ready to die if she refused him; but flattering himself that his ardent attachment and unequalled love and unexampled passion could not fail of having some effect, and in short, very much resolved on being seriously accepted as soon as possible. It really was so. Without scruple—without apology—without much apparent diffidence, Mr. Elton, the lover of Harriet, was professing himself *her* lover. She tried to stop him; but vainly; he would go on, and say it all. Angry as she was, the thought of the moment made her resolve to restrain herself when she did speak. She felt that half this folly must be drunkenness, and therefore could hope that it might belong only to the passing hour. Accordingly, with a mixture of the serious and the playful, which she hoped would best suit his half and half state, she replied,

"I am very much astonished, Mr. Elton. This to *me*! you forget yourself—you take me for my friend—any message to Miss Smith I shall be happy to deliver; but no more of this to *me*, if you please."

"Miss Smith!—message to Miss Smith!—What could she possibly mean!"—And he repeated her words with such assurance of accent, such boastful pretence of amazement, that she could not help replying with quickness,

"Mr. Elton, this is the most extraordinary conduct! and I can account for it only in one way; you are not yourself, or you could not speak either to me, or of Harriet, in such a manner. Command yourself enough to say no more, and I will endeavour to forget it."

But Mr. Elton had only drunk wine enough to elevate his spirits, not at all to confuse his intellects. He perfectly knew his own meaning; and having warmly protested against her suspicion as most injurious, and slightly touched upon his respect for Miss Smith as her friend,—but acknowledging his wonder that Miss Smith should be mentioned at all,—he resumed the subject of his own passion, and was very urgent for a favourable answer.

As she thought less of his inebriety, she thought more of his inconstancy and presumption; and with fewer struggles for politeness, replied,

"It is impossible for me to doubt any longer. You have made yourself too clear. Mr. Elton, my astonishment is much beyond any thing I can express. After such behaviour, as I have witnessed during the last month, to Miss Smith—such attentions as I have been in the daily habit of observing—to be addressing me in this manner—this is an unsteadiness of character, indeed, which I had not supposed possible! Believe me, sir, I am far, very far, from gratified in being the object of such professions."

"Good Heaven!" cried Mr. Elton, "what can be the meaning of this?—Miss Smith!—I never thought of Miss Smith in the whole course of my existence—never paid her any attentions, but as your friend: never cared whether she were dead or alive, but as your friend. If she has fancied otherwise, her own wishes have misled her, and I am very sorry—extremely sorry—But, Miss Smith, indeed!—Oh! Miss Woodhouse! who can think of Miss Smith, when Miss Woodhouse is near! No, upon my honour, there is no unsteadiness of character. I have thought only of you. I protest against having paid the smallest attention to any one else. Every thing that I have said or done, for many weeks past, has been with the sole view of marking my adoration of yourself. You cannot really, seriously, doubt it. No!—(in an accent meant to be insinuating)—I am sure you have seen and understood me."

It would be impossible to say what Emma felt, on hearing this—which of all her unpleasant sensations was uppermost. She was too completely overpowered to be immediately able to reply: and two moments of silence being ample encouragement for Mr. Elton's sanguine state of mind, he tried to take her hand again, as he joyously exclaimed—

"Charming Miss Woodhouse! allow me to interpret this interesting silence. It confesses that you have long understood me."

"No, sir," cried Emma, "it confesses no such thing. So far from having long understood you, I have been in a most complete error with respect to your views, till this moment. As to myself, I am very sorry that you should have been giving way to any feelings—Nothing could be farther from my wishes—your attachment to my friend Harriet—your pursuit of her, (pursuit, it appeared), gave me great pleasure, and I have been very earnestly wishing you success: but had I supposed that she were not your attraction to Hartfield, I should certainly have thought you judged ill in making your visits so frequent. Am I to believe that you have never sought to recommend yourself particularly to Miss Smith?—that you have never thought seriously of her?"

"Never, madam," cried he, affronted in his turn: "never, I assure you. *I* think seriously of Miss Smith!—Miss Smith is a very good sort of girl; and I should be happy to see her respectably settled. I wish her extremely well: and, no doubt, there are men who might not object to—Every body has their level: but as for myself, I am not, I think, quite so much at a loss. I need not so totally despair of an equal alliance, as to be addressing myself to Miss Smith!—No, madam, my visits to Hartfield have been for yourself only; and the encouragement I received—"

"Encouragement!—I give you encouragement!—Sir, you have been entirely mistaken in supposing it. I have seen you only as the admirer of my friend. In no other light could you have been more to me than a common acquaintance. I am exceedingly sorry: but it is well that the mistake ends where it does. Had the same behaviour continued, Miss Smith might have been led into a misconception of your views; not being aware, probably, any more than myself, of the very great inequality which you are so sensible of. But, as it is, the disappointment is single, and, I trust, will not be lasting. I have no thoughts of matrimony at present."

He was too angry to say another word; her manner too decided to invite supplication; and in this state of swelling resentment, and mutually deep mortification, they had to continue together a few minutes longer, for the fears of Mr. Woodhouse had confined them to a foot-pace. If there had not been so much anger, there would have been desperate awkwardness; but their straightforward emotions left no room for the little zigzags of embarrassment. Without knowing when the carriage turned into Vicarage Lane, or when it stopped, they found themselves, all at once, at the door of his house; and he was out before another syllable passed.—Emma then felt it indispensable to wish him a good night. The compliment was just returned, coldly and proudly; and, under indescribable irritation of spirits, she was then conveyed to Hartfield.

There she was welcomed, with the utmost delight, by her father, who had been trembling for the dangers of a solitary drive from Vicarage Lane—turning a corner which he could never bear to think of—and in strange hands—a mere common coachman—no James; and there it seemed as if her return only were wanted to make every thing go well: for Mr. John Knightley, ashamed of his ill-humour, was now all kindness and attention; and so particularly solicitous for the comfort of her father, as to seem—if not quite ready to join him in a basin of gruel—perfectly sensible of its being exceedingly wholesome; and the day was concluding in peace and comfort to all their little party, except herself.—But her mind had never been in such perturbation; and it needed a very strong effort to appear attentive and cheerful till the usual hour of separating allowed her the relief of quiet reflection.

CHAPTER XVI

The hair was curled, and the maid sent away, and Emma sat down to think and be miserable.—It was a wretched business indeed!—Such an overthrow of every thing she had been wishing for!—Such a development of every thing most unwelcome!—Such a blow for Harriet!—that was the worst of all. Every part of it brought pain and humiliation, of some sort or other; but, compared with the evil to Harriet, all was light; and she would gladly have submitted to feel yet more mistaken—more in error—more disgraced by mis-judgment, than she actually was, could the effects of her blunders have been confined to herself.

"If I had not persuaded Harriet into liking the man, I could have borne any thing. He might have doubled his presumption to me—but poor Harriet!"

How she could have been so deceived!—He protested that he had never thought seriously of Harriet—never! She looked back as well as she could; but it was all confusion. She had taken up the idea, she supposed, and made every thing bend to it. His manners, however, must have been unmarked, wavering, dubious, or she could not have been so misled.

The picture!—How eager he had been about the picture!—and the charade!—and an hundred other circumstances;—how clearly they had seemed to point at Harriet. To be sure, the charade, with its "ready wit"—but then the "soft eyes"—in fact it suited neither; it was a jumble without taste or truth. Who could have seen through such thick-headed nonsense?

Certainly she had often, especially of late, thought his manners to herself unnecessarily gallant; but it had passed as his way, as a mere error of judgment, of knowledge, of taste, as one proof among others that he had not always lived in the best society, that with all the gentleness of his address, true elegance was sometimes wanting; but, till this very day, she had never, for an instant, suspected it to mean any thing but grateful respect to her as Harriet's friend.

To Mr. John Knightley was she indebted for her first idea on the subject, for the first start of its possibility. There was no denying that those brothers had penetration. She remembered what Mr. Knightley had once said to her about Mr. Elton, the caution he had given, the conviction he had professed that Mr. Elton would never marry indiscreetly; and blushed to think how much truer a knowledge of his character had been there shewn than any she had reached herself. It was dreadfully mortifying; but Mr. Elton was proving himself, in many respects, the very reverse of what she had meant and believed him; proud, assuming, conceited; very full of his own claims, and little concerned about the feelings of others.

Contrary to the usual course of things, Mr. Elton's wanting to pay his addresses to her had sunk him in her opinion. His professions and his proposals did him no service. She thought nothing of his attachment, and was insulted by his hopes. He wanted to marry well, and having the arrogance to raise his eyes to her, pretended to be in love; but she was perfectly easy as to his not suffering any disappointment that need be cared for. There had been no real affection either in his language or manners. Sighs and fine words had been given in abundance; but she could hardly devise any set of expressions, or fancy any tone of voice, less allied with real love. She need not trouble herself to pity him. He only wanted to aggrandise and enrich himself; and if Miss Woodhouse of Hartfield, the heiress of thirty thousand pounds, were not quite so easily obtained as he had fancied, he would soon try for Miss Somebody else with twenty, or with ten.

But—that he should talk of encouragement, should consider her as aware of his views, accepting his attentions, meaning (in short), to marry him!—should suppose himself her equal in connexion or mind!—look down upon her friend, so well understanding the gradations of rank below him, and be so blind to what rose above, as to fancy himself shewing no presumption in addressing her!—It was most provoking.

Perhaps it was not fair to expect him to feel how very much he was her inferior in talent, and all the elegancies of mind. The very want of such equality might prevent his perception of it; but he must know that in fortune and consequence she was greatly his superior. He must know that the Woodhouses had been settled for several generations at Hartfield, the younger branch of a very ancient family—and that the Eltons were nobody. The landed property of Hartfield certainly was inconsiderable, being but a sort of notch in the Donwell Abbey estate, to which all the rest of Highbury belonged; but their fortune, from other sources, was such as to make them scarcely secondary to Donwell Abbey itself, in every other kind of consequence; and the Woodhouses had long held a high place in the consideration of the neighbourhood which Mr. Elton had first entered not two years ago, to make his way as he could, without any alliances but in trade, or any thing to recommend him to notice but his situation and his civility.—But he had fancied her in love with him; that evidently must have been his dependence; and after raving a little about the seeming incongruity of gentle manners and a conceited head, Emma was obliged in common honesty to stop and admit that her own behaviour to him had been so complaisant and obliging, so full of courtesy and attention, as (supposing her real motive unperceived) might warrant a man of ordinary observation and delicacy, like Mr. Elton, in fancying himself a very decided favourite. If *she* had so misinterpreted his feelings, she had little right to wonder that *he*, with self-interest to blind him, should have mistaken hers.

The first error and the worst lay at her door. It was foolish, it was wrong, to take so active a part in bringing any two people together. It was adventuring too far, assuming too much, making light of what ought to be serious, a trick of what ought to be simple. She was quite concerned and ashamed, and resolved to do such things no more.

"Here have I," said she, "actually talked poor Harriet into being very much attached to this man. She might never have thought of him but for me; and certainly never would have thought of him with hope, if I had not assured her of his attachment, for she is as modest and humble as I used to think him. Oh! that I had been satisfied with persuading her not to accept young Martin. There I was quite right. That was well done of me; but there I should have stopped, and left the rest to time and chance. I was introducing her into good company, and giving her the opportunity of pleasing some one worth having; I ought not to have attempted more. But now, poor girl, her peace is cut up for some time. I have been but half a friend to her; and if she were *not* to feel this disappointment so very much, I am sure I have not an idea of any body else who would be at all desirable for her;—William Coxe—Oh! no, I could not endure William Coxe—a pert young lawyer."

She stopt to blush and laugh at her own relapse, and then resumed a more serious, more dispiriting cogitation upon what had been, and might be, and must be. The distressing explanation she had to make to Harriet, and all that poor Harriet would be suffering, with the awkwardness of future meetings, the difficulties of continuing or discontinuing the acquaintance, of subduing feelings, concealing resentment, and avoiding eclat, were enough to occupy her in most unmirthful reflections some time longer, and she went to bed at last with nothing settled but the conviction of her having blundered most dreadfully.

To youth and natural cheerfulness like Emma's, though under temporary gloom at night, the return of day will hardly fail to bring return of spirits. The youth and cheerfulness of morning are in happy analogy, and of powerful operation; and if the distress be not poignant enough to keep the eyes unclosed, they will be sure to open to sensations of softened pain and brighter hope.

Emma got up on the morrow more disposed for comfort than she had gone to bed, more ready to see alleviations of the evil before her, and to depend on getting tolerably out of it.

It was a great consolation that Mr. Elton should not be really in love with her, or so particularly amiable as to make it shocking to disappoint him—that Harriet's nature should not be of that superior sort in which the feelings are most acute and retentive—and that there could be no necessity for any body's knowing what had passed except the three principals, and especially for her father's being given a moment's uneasiness about it.

These were very cheering thoughts; and the sight of a great deal of snow on the ground did her further service, for any thing was welcome that might justify their all three being quite asunder at present.

The weather was most favourable for her; though Christmas Day, she could not go to church. Mr. Woodhouse would have been miserable had his daughter attempted it, and she was therefore safe from either exciting or receiving unpleasant and most unsuitable ideas. The ground covered with snow, and the atmosphere in that unsettled state between frost and thaw, which is of all others the most unfriendly for exercise, every morning beginning in rain or snow, and every evening setting in to freeze, she was for many days a most honourable prisoner. No intercourse with Harriet possible but by note; no church for her on Sunday any more than on Christmas Day; and no need to find excuses for Mr. Elton's absenting himself.

It was weather which might fairly confine every body at home; and though she hoped and believed him to be really taking comfort in some society or other, it was very pleasant to have her father so well satisfied with his being all alone in his own house, too wise to stir out; and to hear him say to Mr. Knightley, whom no weather could keep entirely from them,—

"Ah! Mr. Knightley, why do not you stay at home like poor Mr. Elton?"

These days of confinement would have been, but for her private perplexities, remarkably comfortable, as such seclusion exactly suited her brother, whose feelings must always be of great importance to his companions; and he had, besides, so thoroughly cleared off his ill-humour at Randalls, that his amiableness never failed him during the rest of his stay at Hartfield. He was always agreeable and obliging, and speaking pleasantly of every body. But with all the hopes of cheerfulness, and all the present comfort of delay, there was still such an evil hanging over her in the hour of explanation with Harriet, as made it impossible for Emma to be ever perfectly at ease.

CHAPTER XVII

Mr. and Mrs. John Knightley were not detained long at Hartfield. The weather soon improved enough for those to move who must move; and Mr. Woodhouse having, as usual, tried to persuade his daughter to stay behind with all her children, was obliged to see the whole party set off, and return to his lamentations over the destiny of poor Isabella;—which poor Isabella, passing her life with those she doated on, full of their merits, blind to their faults, and always innocently busy, might have been a model of right feminine happiness.

The evening of the very day on which they went brought a note from Mr. Elton to Mr. Woodhouse, a long, civil, ceremonious note, to say, with Mr. Elton's best compliments, "that he was proposing to leave Highbury the following morning in his way to Bath; where, in compliance with the pressing entreaties of some friends, he had engaged to spend a few weeks, and very much regretted the impossibility he was under, from various circumstances of weather and business, of taking a personal leave of Mr. Woodhouse, of whose friendly civilities he should ever retain a grateful sense—and had Mr. Woodhouse any commands, should be happy to attend to them."

Emma was most agreeably surprized.—Mr. Elton's absence just at this time was the very thing to be desired. She admired him for contriving it, though not able to give him much credit for the manner in which it was announced. Resentment could not have been more plainly spoken than in a civility to her father, from which she was so pointedly excluded. She had not even a share in his opening compliments.—Her name was not mentioned;—and there was so striking a change in all this, and such an ill-judged solemnity of leave-taking in his graceful acknowledgments, as she thought, at first, could not escape her father's suspicion.

It did, however.—Her father was quite taken up with the surprize of so sudden a journey, and his fears that Mr. Elton might never get safely to the end of it, and saw nothing extraordinary in his language. It was a very useful note, for it supplied them with fresh matter for thought and conversation during the rest of their lonely evening. Mr. Woodhouse talked over his alarms, and Emma was in spirits to persuade them away with all her usual promptitude.

She now resolved to keep Harriet no longer in the dark. She had reason to believe her nearly recovered from her cold, and it was desirable that she should have as much time as possible for getting the better of her other complaint before the gentleman's return. She went to Mrs. Goddard's accordingly the very next day, to undergo the necessary penance of communication; and a severe one it was.—She had to destroy all the hopes which she had been so industriously feeding—to appear in the ungracious character of the one preferred—and acknowledge herself grossly mistaken and mis-judging in all her ideas on one subject, all her observations, all her convictions, all her prophecies for the last six weeks.

The confession completely renewed her first shame—and the sight of Harriet's tears made her think that she should never be in charity with herself again.

Harriet bore the intelligence very well—blaming nobody—and in every thing testifying such an ingenuousness of disposition and lowly opinion of herself, as must appear with particular advantage at that moment to her friend.

Emma was in the humour to value simplicity and modesty to the utmost; and all that was amiable, all that ought to be attaching, seemed on Harriet's side, not her own. Harriet did not consider herself as having any thing to complain of. The affection of such a man as Mr. Elton would have been too great a distinction.—She never could have deserved him—and nobody but so partial and kind a friend as Miss Woodhouse would have thought it possible.

Her tears fell abundantly—but her grief was so truly artless, that no dignity could have made it more respectable in Emma's eyes—and she listened to her and tried to console her with all her heart and understanding—really for the time convinced that Harriet was the superior creature of the two—and that to resemble her would be more for her own welfare and happiness than all that genius or intelligence could do.

It was rather too late in the day to set about being simple-minded and ignorant; but she left her with every previous resolution confirmed of being humble and discreet, and repressing imagination all the rest of her life. Her second duty now, inferior only to her father's claims, was to promote Harriet's comfort, and endeavour to prove her own affection in some better method than by match-making. She got her to Hartfield, and shewed her the most unvarying kindness, striving to occupy and amuse her, and by books and conversation, to drive Mr. Elton from her thoughts.

Time, she knew, must be allowed for this being thoroughly done; and she could suppose herself but an indifferent judge of such matters in general, and very inadequate to sympathise in an attachment to Mr. Elton in particular; but it seemed to her reasonable that at Harriet's age, and with the entire extinction of all hope, such a progress might be made towards a state of composure by the time of Mr. Elton's return, as to allow them all to meet again in the common routine of acquaintance, without any danger of betraying sentiments or increasing them.

Harriet did think him all perfection, and maintained the non-existence of any body equal to him in person or goodness—and did, in truth, prove herself more resolutely in love than Emma had foreseen; but yet it appeared to her so natural, so inevitable to strive against an inclination of that sort *unrequited*, that she could not comprehend its continuing very long in equal force.

If Mr. Elton, on his return, made his own indifference as evident and indubitable as she could not doubt he would anxiously do, she could not imagine Harriet's persisting to place her happiness in the sight or the recollection of him.

Their being fixed, so absolutely fixed, in the same place, was bad for each, for all three. Not one of them had the power of removal, or of effecting any material change of society. They must encounter each other, and make the best of it.

Harriet was farther unfortunate in the tone of her companions at Mrs. Goddard's; Mr. Elton being the adoration of all the teachers and great girls in the school; and it must be at Hartfield only that she could have any chance of hearing him spoken of with cooling moderation or repellent truth. Where the wound had been given, there must the cure be found if anywhere; and Emma felt that, till she saw her in the way of cure, there could be no true peace for herself.

CHAPTER XVIII

Mr. Frank Churchill did not come. When the time proposed drew near, Mrs. Weston's fears were justified in the arrival of a letter of excuse. For the present, he could not be spared, to his "very great mortification and regret; but still he looked forward with the hope of coming to Randalls at no distant period."

Mrs. Weston was exceedingly disappointed—much more disappointed, in fact, than her husband, though her dependence on seeing the young man had been so much more sober: but a sanguine temper, though for ever expecting more good than occurs, does not always pay for its hopes by any proportionate depression. It soon flies over the present failure, and begins to hope again. For half an hour Mr. Weston was surprized and sorry; but then he began to perceive that Frank's coming two or three months later would be a much better plan; better time of year; better weather; and that he would be able, without any doubt, to stay considerably longer with them than if he had come sooner.

These feelings rapidly restored his comfort, while Mrs. Weston, of a more apprehensive disposition, foresaw nothing but a repetition of excuses and delays; and after all her concern for what her husband was to suffer, suffered a great deal more herself.

Emma was not at this time in a state of spirits to care really about Mr. Frank Churchill's not coming, except as a disappointment at Randalls. The acquaintance at present had no charm for her. She wanted, rather, to be quiet, and out of temptation; but still, as it was desirable that she should appear, in general, like her usual self, she took care to express as much interest in the circumstance, and enter as warmly into Mr. and Mrs. Weston's disappointment, as might naturally belong to their friendship.

She was the first to announce it to Mr. Knightley; and exclaimed quite as much as was necessary, (or, being acting a part, perhaps rather more) at the conduct of the Churchills, in keeping him away. She then proceeded to say a good deal more than she felt, of the advantage of such an addition to their confined society in Surry; the pleasure of looking at somebody new; the gala-day to Highbury entire, which the sight of him would have made; and ending with reflections on the Churchills again, found herself directly involved in a disagreement with Mr. Knightley; and, to her great amusement, perceived that she was taking the other side of the question from her real opinion, and making use of Mrs. Weston's arguments against herself.

"The Churchills are very likely in fault," said Mr. Knightley, coolly; "but I dare say he might come if he would."

"I do not know why you should say so. He wishes exceedingly to come; but his uncle and aunt will not spare him."

"I cannot believe that he has not the power of coming, if he made a point of it. It is too unlikely, for me to believe it without proof."

"How odd you are! What has Mr. Frank Churchill done, to make you suppose him such an unnatural creature?"

"I am not supposing him at all an unnatural creature, in suspecting that he may have learnt to be above his connexions, and to care very little for any thing but his own pleasure, from living with those who have always set him the example of it. It is a great deal more natural than one could wish, that a young man, brought up by those who are proud, luxurious, and selfish, should be proud, luxurious, and selfish too. If Frank Churchill had wanted to see his father, he would have contrived it between September and January. A man at his age—what is he?—three or four-and-twenty—cannot be without the means of doing as much as that. It is impossible."

"That's easily said, and easily felt by you, who have always been your own master. You are the worst judge in the world, Mr. Knightley, of the difficulties of dependence. You do not know what it is to have tempers to manage."

"It is not to be conceived that a man of three or four-and-twenty should not have liberty of mind or limb to that amount. He cannot want money—he cannot want leisure. We know, on the contrary, that he has so much of both, that he is glad to get rid of them at the idlest haunts in the kingdom. We hear of him for ever at some watering-place or other. A little while ago, he was at Weymouth. This proves that he can leave the Churchills."

"Yes, sometimes he can."

"And those times are whenever he thinks it worth his while; whenever there is any temptation of pleasure."

"It is very unfair to judge of any body's conduct, without an intimate knowledge of their situation. Nobody, who has not been in the interior of a family, can say what the difficulties of any individual of that family may be. We ought to be acquainted with Enscombe, and with Mrs. Churchill's temper, before we pretend to decide upon what her nephew can do. He may, at times, be able to do a great deal more than he can at others."

"There is one thing, Emma, which a man can always do, if he chuses, and that is, his duty; not by manoeuvring and finessing, but by vigour and resolution. It is Frank Churchill's duty to pay this attention to his father. He knows it to be so, by his promises and messages; but if he wished to do it, it might be done. A man who felt rightly would say at once, simply and resolutely, to Mrs. Churchill—'Every sacrifice of mere pleasure you will always find me ready to make to your convenience; but I must go and see my father immediately. I know he would be hurt by my failing in such a mark of respect to him on the present occasion. I shall, therefore, set off to-morrow.'—If he would say so to her at once, in the tone of decision becoming a man, there would be no opposition made to his going."

"No," said Emma, laughing; "but perhaps there might be some made to his coming back again. Such language for a young man entirely dependent, to use!—Nobody but you, Mr. Knightley, would imagine it possible. But you have not an idea of what is requisite in situations directly opposite to your own. Mr. Frank Churchill to be making such a speech as that to the uncle and aunt, who have brought him up, and are to provide for him!—Standing up in the middle of the room, I suppose, and speaking as loud as he could!—How can you imagine such conduct practicable?"

"Depend upon it, Emma, a sensible man would find no difficulty in it. He would feel himself in the right; and the declaration—made, of course, as a man of sense would make it, in a proper manner—would do him more good, raise him higher, fix his interest stronger with the people he depended on, than all that a line of shifts and expedients can ever do. Respect would be added to affection. They would feel that they could trust him; that the nephew who had done rightly by his father, would do rightly by them; for they know, as well as he does, as well as all the world must know, that he ought to pay this visit to his father; and while meanly exerting their power to delay it, are in their hearts not thinking the better of him for submitting to their whims. Respect for right conduct is felt by every body. If he would act in this sort of manner, on principle, consistently, regularly, their little minds would bend to his."

"I rather doubt that. You are very fond of bending little minds; but where little minds belong to rich people in authority, I think they have a knack of swelling out, till they are quite as unmanageable as great ones. I can imagine, that if you, as you are, Mr. Knightley, were to be transported and placed all at once in Mr. Frank Churchill's situation, you would be able to say and do just what you have been recommending for him; and it might have a very good effect. The Churchills might not have a word to say in return; but then, you would have no habits of early obedience and long observance to break through. To him who has, it might not be so easy to burst forth at once into perfect independence, and set all their claims on his gratitude and regard at nought. He may have as strong a sense of what would be right, as you can have, without being so equal, under particular circumstances, to act up to it."

"Then it would not be so strong a sense. If it failed to produce equal exertion, it could not be an equal conviction."

"Oh, the difference of situation and habit! I wish you would try to understand what an amiable young man may be likely to feel in directly opposing those, whom as child and boy he has been looking up to all his life."

"Our amiable young man is a very weak young man, if this be the first occasion of his carrying through a resolution to do right against the will of others. It ought to have been a habit with him by this time, of following his duty, instead of consulting expediency. I can allow for the fears of the child, but not of the man. As he became rational, he ought to have roused himself and shaken off all that was unworthy in their authority. He ought to have opposed the first attempt on their side to make him slight his father. Had he begun as he ought, there would have been no difficulty now."

"We shall never agree about him," cried Emma; "but that is nothing extraordinary. I have not the least idea of his being a weak young man: I feel sure that he is not. Mr. Weston would not be blind to folly, though in his own son; but he is very likely to have a more yielding, complying, mild disposition than would suit your notions of man's perfection. I dare say he has; and though it may cut him off from some advantages, it will secure him many others."

"Yes; all the advantages of sitting still when he ought to move, and of leading a life of mere idle pleasure, and fancying himself extremely expert in finding excuses for it. He can sit down and write a fine flourishing letter, full of professions and falsehoods, and persuade himself that he has hit upon the very best method in the world of preserving peace at home and preventing his father's having any right to complain. His letters disgust me."

"Your feelings are singular. They seem to satisfy every body else."

"I suspect they do not satisfy Mrs. Weston. They hardly can satisfy a woman of her good sense and quick feelings: standing in a mother's place, but without a mother's affection to blind her. It is on her account that attention to Randalls is doubly due, and she must doubly feel the omission. Had she been a person of consequence herself, he would have come I dare say; and it would not have signified whether he did or no. Can you think your friend behindhand in these sort of considerations? Do you suppose she does not often say all this to herself? No, Emma, your amiable young man can be amiable only in French, not in English. He may be very 'aimable,' have very good manners, and be very agreeable; but he can have no English delicacy towards the feelings of other people: nothing really amiable about him."

"You seem determined to think ill of him."

"Me!—not at all," replied Mr. Knightley, rather displeased; "I do not want to think ill of him. I should be as ready to acknowledge his merits as any other man; but I hear of none, except what are merely personal; that he is well-grown and good-looking, with smooth, plausible manners."

"Well, if he have nothing else to recommend him, he will be a treasure at Highbury. We do not often look upon fine young men, well-bred and agreeable. We must not be nice and ask for all the virtues into the bargain. Cannot you imagine, Mr. Knightley, what a *sensation* his coming will produce? There will be but one subject throughout the parishes of Donwell and Highbury; but one interest—one object of curiosity; it will be all Mr. Frank Churchill; we shall think and speak of nobody else."

"You will excuse my being so much over-powered. If I find him conversable, I shall be glad of his acquaintance; but if he is only a chattering coxcomb, he will not occupy much of my time or thoughts."

"My idea of him is, that he can adapt his conversation to the taste of every body, and has the power as well as the wish of being universally agreeable. To you, he will talk of farming; to me, of drawing or music; and so on to every body, having that general information on all subjects which will enable him to follow the lead, or take the lead, just as propriety may require, and to speak extremely well on each; that is my idea of him."

"And mine," said Mr. Knightley warmly, "is, that if he turn out any thing like it, he will be the most insufferable fellow breathing! What! at three-and-twenty to be the king of his company—the great man—the practised politician, who is to read every body's character, and make every body's talents conduce to the display of his own superiority; to be dispensing his flatteries around, that he may make all appear like fools compared with himself! My dear Emma, your own good sense could not endure such a puppy when it came to the point."

"I will say no more about him," cried Emma, "you turn every thing to evil. We are both prejudiced; you against, I for him; and we have no chance of agreeing till he is really here."

"Prejudiced! I am not prejudiced."

"But I am very much, and without being at all ashamed of it. My love for Mr. and Mrs. Weston gives me a decided prejudice in his favour."

"He is a person I never think of from one month's end to another," said Mr. Knightley, with a degree of vexation, which made Emma immediately talk of something else, though she could not comprehend why he should be angry.

To take a dislike to a young man, only because he appeared to be of a different disposition from himself, was unworthy the real liberality of mind which she was always used to acknowledge in him; for with all the high opinion of himself, which she had often laid to his charge, she had never before for a moment supposed it could make him unjust to the merit of another.

VOLUME II

CHAPTER I

Emma and Harriet had been walking together one morning, and, in Emma's opinion, had been talking enough of Mr. Elton for that day. She could not think that Harriet's solace or her own sins required more; and she was therefore industriously getting rid of the subject as they returned;—but it burst out again when she thought she had succeeded, and after speaking some time of what the poor must suffer in winter, and receiving no other answer than a very plaintive—"Mr. Elton is so good to the poor!" she found something else must be done.

They were just approaching the house where lived Mrs. and Miss Bates. She determined to call upon them and seek safety in numbers. There was always sufficient reason for such an attention; Mrs. and Miss Bates loved to be called on, and she knew she was considered by the very few who presumed ever to see imperfection in her, as rather negligent in that respect, and as not contributing what she ought to the stock of their scanty comforts.

She had had many a hint from Mr. Knightley and some from her own heart, as to her deficiency—but none were equal to counteract the persuasion of its being very disagreeable,—a waste of time—tiresome women—and all the horror of being in danger of falling in with the second-rate and third-rate of Highbury, who were calling on them for ever, and therefore she seldom went near them. But now she made the sudden resolution of not passing their door without going in—observing, as she proposed it to Harriet, that, as well as she could calculate, they were just now quite safe from any letter from Jane Fairfax.

The house belonged to people in business. Mrs. and Miss Bates occupied the drawing-room floor; and there, in the very moderate-sized apartment, which was every thing to them, the visitors were most cordially and even gratefully welcomed; the quiet neat old lady, who with her knitting was seated in the warmest corner, wanting even to give up her place to Miss Woodhouse, and her more active, talking daughter, almost ready to overpower them with care and kindness, thanks for their visit, solicitude for their shoes, anxious inquiries after Mr. Woodhouse's health, cheerful communications about her mother's, and sweet-cake from the beaufet—"Mrs. Cole had just been there, just called in for ten minutes, and had been so good as to sit an hour with them, and *she* had taken a piece of cake and been so kind as to say she liked it very much; and, therefore, she hoped Miss Woodhouse and Miss Smith would do them the favour to eat a piece too."

The mention of the Coles was sure to be followed by that of Mr. Elton. There was intimacy between them, and Mr. Cole had heard from Mr. Elton since his going away. Emma knew what was coming; they must have the letter over again, and settle how long he had been gone, and how much he was engaged in company, and what a favourite he was wherever he went, and how full the Master of the Ceremonies' ball had been; and she went through it very well, with all the interest and all the commendation that could be requisite, and always putting forward to prevent Harriet's being obliged to say a word.

This she had been prepared for when she entered the house; but meant, having once talked him handsomely over, to be no farther incommoded by any troublesome topic, and to wander at large amongst all the Mistresses and Misses of Highbury, and their card-parties. She had not been prepared to have Jane Fairfax succeed Mr. Elton, but he was actually hurried off by Miss Bates; she jumped away from him at last abruptly to the Coles, to usher in a letter from her niece.

"Oh! yes—Mr. Elton, I understand—certainly as to dancing—Mrs. Cole was telling me that dancing at the rooms at Bath was—Mrs. Cole was so kind as to sit some time with us, talking of Jane; for as soon as she came in, she began inquiring after her, Jane is so very great a favourite there. Whenever she is with us, Mrs. Cole does not know how to shew her kindness enough; and I must say that Jane deserves it as much as any body can. And so she began inquiring after her directly, saying, 'I know you cannot have heard from Jane lately, because it is not her time for writing;' and when I immediately said, 'But indeed we have, we had a letter this very morning,' I do not know that I ever saw any body more surprized. 'Have you, upon your honour?' said she; 'well, that is quite unexpected. Do let me hear what she says.'"

Emma's politeness was at hand directly, to say, with smiling interest—

"Have you heard from Miss Fairfax so lately? I am extremely happy. I hope she is well?"

"Thank you. You are so kind!" replied the happily deceived aunt, while eagerly hunting for the letter.—"Oh! here it is. I was sure it could not be far off; but I had put my huswife upon it, you see, without being aware, and so it was quite hid, but I had it in my hand so very lately that I was almost sure it must be on the table. I was reading it to Mrs. Cole, and since she went away, I was reading it again to my mother, for it is such a pleasure to her—a letter from Jane—that she can never hear it often enough; so I knew it could not be far off, and here it is, only just under my huswife—and since you are so kind as to wish to hear what she says;—but, first of all, I really must, in justice to Jane, apologise for her writing so short a letter—only two pages you see—hardly two—and in general she fills the whole paper and crosses half. My mother often wonders that I can make it out so well. She often says, when the letter is first opened, 'Well, Hetty, now I think you will be put to it to make out all that checker-work'—don't you, ma'am?—And then I tell her, I am sure she would contrive to make it out herself, if she had nobody to do it for her—every word of it—I am sure she would pore over it till she had made out every word. And, indeed, though my mother's eyes are not so good as they were, she can see amazingly well still, thank God! with the help of spectacles. It is such a blessing! My mother's are really very good indeed. Jane often says, when she is here, 'I am sure, grandmama, you must have had very strong eyes to see as you do—and so much fine work as you have done too!—I only wish my eyes may last me as well.'"

All this spoken extremely fast obliged Miss Bates to stop for breath; and Emma said something very civil about the excellence of Miss Fairfax's handwriting.

"You are extremely kind," replied Miss Bates, highly gratified; "you who are such a judge, and write so beautifully yourself. I am sure there is nobody's praise that could give us so much pleasure as Miss Woodhouse's. My mother does not hear; she is a little deaf you know. Ma'am," addressing her, "do you hear what Miss Woodhouse is so obliging to say about Jane's handwriting?"

And Emma had the advantage of hearing her own silly compliment repeated twice over before the good old lady could comprehend it. She was pondering, in the meanwhile, upon the possibility, without seeming very rude, of making her escape from Jane Fairfax's letter, and had almost resolved on hurrying away directly under some slight excuse, when Miss Bates turned to her again and seized her attention.

"My mother's deafness is very trifling you see—just nothing at all. By only raising my voice, and saying any thing two or three times over, she is sure to hear; but then she is used to my voice. But it is very remarkable that she should always hear Jane better than she does me. Jane speaks so distinct! However, she will not find her grandmama at all deafer than she was two years ago; which is saying a great deal at my mother's time of life—and it really is full two years, you know, since she was here. We never were so long without seeing her before, and as I was telling Mrs. Cole, we shall hardly know how to make enough of her now."

"Are you expecting Miss Fairfax here soon?"

"Oh yes; next week."

"Indeed!—that must be a very great pleasure."

"Thank you. You are very kind. Yes, next week. Every body is so surprized; and every body says the same obliging things. I am sure she will be as happy to see her friends at Highbury, as they can be to see her. Yes, Friday or Saturday; she cannot say which, because Colonel Campbell will be wanting the carriage himself one of those days. So very good of them to send her the whole way! But they always do, you know. Oh yes, Friday or Saturday next. That is what she writes about. That is the reason of her writing out of rule, as we call it; for, in the common course, we should not have heard from her before next Tuesday or Wednesday."

"Yes, so I imagined. I was afraid there could be little chance of my hearing any thing of Miss Fairfax to-day."

"So obliging of you! No, we should not have heard, if it had not been for this particular circumstance, of her being to come here so soon. My mother is so delighted!—for she is to be three months with us at least. Three months, she says so, positively, as I am going to have the pleasure of reading to you. The case is, you see, that the Campbells are going to Ireland. Mrs. Dixon has persuaded her father and mother to come over and see her directly. They had not intended to go over till the summer, but she is so impatient to see them again—for till she married, last October, she was never away from them so much as a week, which must make it very strange to be in different kingdoms, I was going to say, but however different countries, and so she wrote a very urgent letter to her mother—or her father, I declare I do not know which it was, but we shall see presently in Jane's letter—wrote in Mr.

Dixon's name as well as her own, to press their coming over directly, and they would give them the meeting in Dublin, and take them back to their country seat, Baly-craig, a beautiful place, I fancy. Jane has heard a great deal of its beauty; from Mr. Dixon, I mean—I do not know that she ever heard about it from any body else; but it was very natural, you know, that he should like to speak of his own place while he was paying his addresses—and as Jane used to be very often walking out with them—for Colonel and Mrs. Campbell were very particular about their daughter's not walking out often with only Mr. Dixon, for which I do not at all blame them; of course she heard every thing he might be telling Miss Campbell about his own home in Ireland; and I think she wrote us word that he had shewn them some drawings of the place, views that he had taken himself. He is a most amiable, charming young man, I believe. Jane was quite longing to go to Ireland, from his account of things."

At this moment, an ingenious and animating suspicion entering Emma's brain with regard to Jane Fairfax, this charming Mr. Dixon, and the not going to Ireland, she said, with the insidious design of farther discovery,

"You must feel it very fortunate that Miss Fairfax should be allowed to come to you at such a time. Considering the very particular friendship between her and Mrs. Dixon, you could hardly have expected her to be excused from accompanying Colonel and Mrs. Campbell."

"Very true, very true, indeed. The very thing that we have always been rather afraid of; for we should not have liked to have her at such a distance from us, for months together—not able to come if any thing was to happen. But you see, every thing turns out for the best. They want her (Mr. and Mrs. Dixon) excessively to come over with Colonel and Mrs. Campbell; quite depend upon it; nothing can be more kind or pressing than their *joint* invitation, Jane says, as you will hear presently; Mr. Dixon does not seem in the least backward in any attention. He is a most charming young man. Ever since the service he rendered Jane at Weymouth, when they were out in that party on the water, and she, by the sudden whirling round of something or other among the sails, would have been dashed into the sea at once, and actually was all but gone, if he had not, with the greatest presence of mind, caught hold of her habit—(I can never think of it without trembling!)—But ever since we had the history of that day, I have been so fond of Mr. Dixon!"

"But, in spite of all her friends' urgency, and her own wish of seeing Ireland, Miss Fairfax prefers devoting the time to you and Mrs. Bates?"

"Yes—entirely her own doing, entirely her own choice; and Colonel and Mrs. Campbell think she does quite right, just what they should recommend; and indeed they particularly *wish* her to try her native air, as she has not been quite so well as usual lately."

"I am concerned to hear of it. I think they judge wisely. But Mrs. Dixon must be very much disappointed. Mrs. Dixon, I understand, has no remarkable degree of personal beauty; is not, by any means, to be compared with Miss Fairfax."

"Oh! no. You are very obliging to say such things—but certainly not. There is no comparison between them. Miss Campbell always was absolutely plain—but extremely elegant and amiable."

"Yes, that of course."

"Jane caught a bad cold, poor thing! so long ago as the 7th of November, (as I am going to read to you) and has never been well since. A long time, is not it, for a cold to hang upon her? She never mentioned it before, because she would not alarm us. Just like her! so considerate!—But however, she is so far from well, that her kind friends the Campbells think she had better come home, and try an air that always agrees with her; and they have no doubt that three or four months at Highbury will entirely cure her—and it is certainly a great deal better that she should come here, than go to Ireland, if she is unwell. Nobody could nurse her, as we should do."

"It appears to me the most desirable arrangement in the world."

"And so she is to come to us next Friday or Saturday, and the Campbells leave town in their way to Holyhead the Monday following—as you will find from Jane's letter. So sudden!—You may guess, dear Miss Woodhouse, what a flurry it has thrown me in! If it was not for the drawback of her illness—but I am afraid we must expect to see her grown thin, and looking very poorly. I must tell you what an unlucky thing happened to me, as to that. I always make a point of reading Jane's letters through to myself first, before I read them aloud to my mother, you know, for fear of there being any thing in them to distress her. Jane desired me to do it, so I always do: and so I began to-day with my usual caution; but no sooner did I come to the mention of her being unwell, than I burst out, quite frightened, with 'Bless me! poor Jane is ill!'—which my mother, being on the watch, heard distinctly, and was sadly alarmed at. However, when I read on, I found it was not near so bad as I had fancied at first; and I make so light of it now to her, that she does not think much about it. But I cannot imagine how I could be so off my guard. If Jane does not get well soon, we will call in Mr. Perry. The expense shall not be thought of; and though he is so liberal, and so fond of Jane that I dare say he would not mean to charge any thing for attendance, we could not suffer it to be so, you know. He has a wife and family to maintain, and is not to be giving away his time. Well, now I have just given you a hint of what Jane writes about, we will turn to her letter, and I am sure she tells her own story a great deal better than I can tell it for her."

"I am afraid we must be running away," said Emma, glancing at Harriet, and beginning to rise—"My father will be expecting us. I had no intention, I thought I had no power of staying more than five minutes, when I first entered the house. I merely called, because I would not pass the door without inquiring after Mrs. Bates; but I have been so pleasantly detained! Now, however, we must wish you and Mrs. Bates good morning."

And not all that could be urged to detain her succeeded. She regained the street—happy in this, that though much had been forced on her against her will, though she had in fact heard the whole substance of Jane Fairfax's letter, she had been able to escape the letter itself.

CHAPTER II

Jane Fairfax was an orphan, the only child of Mrs. Bates's youngest daughter.

The marriage of Lieut. Fairfax of the _______ regiment of infantry, and Miss Jane Bates, had had its day of fame and pleasure, hope and interest; but nothing now remained of it, save the melancholy remembrance of him dying in action abroad—of his widow sinking under consumption and grief soon afterwards—and this girl.

By birth she belonged to Highbury: and when at three years old, on losing her mother, she became the property, the charge, the consolation, the fondling of her grandmother and aunt, there had seemed every probability of her being permanently fixed there; of her being taught only what very limited means could command, and growing up with no advantages of connexion or improvement, to be engrafted on what nature had given her in a pleasing person, good understanding, and warm-hearted, well-meaning relations.

But the compassionate feelings of a friend of her father gave a change to her destiny. This was Colonel Campbell, who had very highly regarded Fairfax, as an excellent officer and most deserving young man; and farther, had been indebted to him for such attentions, during a severe camp-fever, as he believed had saved his life. These were claims which he did not learn to overlook, though some years passed away from the death of poor Fairfax, before his own return to England put any thing in his power. When he did return, he sought out the child and took notice of her. He was a married man, with only one living child, a girl, about Jane's age: and Jane became their guest, paying them long visits and growing a favourite with all; and before she was nine years old, his daughter's great fondness for her, and his own wish of being a real friend, united to produce an offer from Colonel Campbell of undertaking the whole charge of her education. It was accepted; and from that period Jane had belonged to Colonel Campbell's family, and had lived with them entirely, only visiting her grandmother from time to time.

The plan was that she should be brought up for educating others; the very few hundred pounds which she inherited from her father making independence impossible. To provide for her otherwise was out of Colonel Campbell's power; for though his income, by pay and appointments, was handsome, his fortune was moderate and must be all his daughter's; but, by giving her an education, he hoped to be supplying the means of respectable subsistence hereafter.

Such was Jane Fairfax's history. She had fallen into good hands, known nothing but kindness from the Campbells, and been given an excellent education. Living constantly with right-minded and well-informed people, her heart and understanding had received every advantage of discipline and culture; and Colonel Campbell's residence being in London, every lighter talent had been done full justice to, by the attendance of first-rate masters. Her disposition and abilities were equally worthy of all that friendship could do; and at eighteen or nineteen she was, as far as such an early age can be qualified for the care of children, fully competent to the office of instruction herself; but she was too much beloved to be parted with. Neither father nor mother could promote, and the daughter could not endure it. The evil day was put off. It was easy to decide that she was still too young; and Jane remained with them, sharing, as another daughter, in all the rational pleasures of an elegant society, and a judicious mixture of home and amusement, with only the drawback of the future, the sobering suggestions of her own good understanding to remind her that all this might soon be over.

The affection of the whole family, the warm attachment of Miss Campbell in particular, was the more honourable to each party from the circumstance of Jane's decided superiority both in beauty and acquirements. That nature had given it in feature could not be unseen by the young woman, nor could her higher powers of mind be unfelt by the parents. They continued together with unabated regard however, till the marriage of Miss Campbell, who by that chance, that luck which so often defies anticipation in matrimonial affairs, giving attraction to what is moderate rather than to what is superior, engaged the affections of Mr. Dixon, a young man, rich and agreeable, almost as soon as they were acquainted; and was eligibly and happily settled, while Jane Fairfax had yet her bread to earn.

This event had very lately taken place; too lately for any thing to be yet attempted by her less fortunate friend towards entering on her path of duty; though she had now reached the age which her own judgment had fixed on for beginning. She had long resolved that one-and-twenty should be the period. With the fortitude of a devoted novitiate, she had resolved at one-and-twenty to complete the sacrifice, and retire from all the pleasures of life, of rational intercourse, equal society, peace and hope, to penance and mortification for ever.

The good sense of Colonel and Mrs. Campbell could not oppose such a resolution, though their feelings did. As long as they lived, no exertions would be necessary, their home might be hers for ever; and for their own comfort they would have retained her wholly; but this would be selfishness:—what must be at last, had better be soon. Perhaps they began to feel it might have been kinder and wiser to have resisted the temptation of any delay, and spared her from a taste of such enjoyments of ease and leisure as must now be relinquished. Still, however, affection was glad to catch at any reasonable excuse for not hurrying on the wretched moment. She had never been quite well since the time of their daughter's marriage; and till she should have completely recovered her usual strength, they must forbid her engaging in duties, which, so far from being compatible with a weakened frame and varying spirits, seemed, under the most favourable circumstances, to require something more than human perfection of body and mind to be discharged with tolerable comfort.

With regard to her not accompanying them to Ireland, her account to her aunt contained nothing but truth, though there might be some truths not told. It was her own choice to give the time of their absence to Highbury; to spend, perhaps, her last months of perfect liberty with those kind relations to whom she was so very dear: and the Campbells, whatever might be their motive or motives, whether single, or double, or treble, gave the arrangement their ready sanction, and said, that they depended more on a few months spent in her native air, for the recovery of her health, than on any thing else. Certain it was that she was to come; and that Highbury, instead of welcoming that perfect novelty which had been so long promised it—Mr. Frank Churchill—must put up for the present with Jane Fairfax, who could bring only the freshness of a two years' absence.

Emma was sorry;—to have to pay civilities to a person she did not like through three long months!—to be always doing more than she wished, and less than she ought! Why she did not like Jane Fairfax might be a difficult question to answer; Mr. Knightley had once told her it was because she saw in her the really accomplished young woman, which she wanted to be thought herself; and though the accusation had been eagerly refuted at the time, there were moments of self-examination in which her conscience could not quite acquit her. But "she could never get acquainted with her: she did not know how it was, but there was such coldness and reserve—such apparent indifference whether she pleased or not—and then, her aunt was such an eternal talker!—and she was made such a fuss with by every body!—and it had been always imagined that they were to be so intimate—because their ages were the same, every body had supposed they must be so fond of each other." These were her reasons—she had no better.

It was a dislike so little just—every imputed fault was so magnified by fancy, that she never saw Jane Fairfax the first time after any considerable absence, without feeling that she had injured her; and now, when the due visit was paid, on her arrival, after a two years' interval, she was particularly struck with the very appearance and manners, which for those two whole years she had been depreciating. Jane Fairfax was very elegant, remarkably elegant; and she had herself the highest value for elegance. Her height was pretty, just such as almost every body would think tall, and nobody could think very tall; her figure particularly graceful; her size a most becoming medium, between fat and thin, though a slight appearance of ill-health seemed to point out the likeliest evil of the two. Emma could not but feel all this; and then, her face—her features—there was more beauty in them altogether than she had remembered; it was not regular, but it was very pleasing beauty. Her eyes, a deep grey, with dark eye-lashes and eyebrows, had never been denied their praise; but the skin, which she had been used to cavil at, as wanting colour, had a clearness and delicacy which really needed no fuller bloom. It was a style of beauty, of which elegance was the reigning character, and as such, she must, in honour, by all her principles, admire it:—elegance, which, whether of person or of mind, she saw so little in Highbury. There, not to be vulgar, was distinction, and merit.

In short, she sat, during the first visit, looking at Jane Fairfax with twofold complacency; the sense of pleasure and the sense of rendering justice, and was determining that she would dislike her no longer. When she took in her history, indeed, her situation, as well as her beauty; when she considered what all this elegance was destined to, what she was going to sink from, how she was going to live, it seemed impossible to feel any thing but compassion and respect; especially, if to every well-known particular entitling her to interest, were added the highly probable circumstance of an attachment to Mr. Dixon, which she had so naturally started to herself. In that case, nothing could be more pitiable or more honourable than the sacrifices she had resolved on. Emma was very willing now to acquit her of having seduced Mr. Dixon's actions from his wife, or of any thing mischievous which her imagination had suggested at first. If it were love, it might be simple, single, successless love on her side alone. She might have been unconsciously sucking in the sad poison, while a sharer of his conversation with her friend; and from the best, the purest of motives, might now be denying herself this visit to Ireland, and resolving to divide herself effectually from him and his connexions by soon beginning her career of laborious duty.

Upon the whole, Emma left her with such softened, charitable feelings, as made her look around in walking home, and lament that Highbury afforded no young man worthy of giving her independence; nobody that she could wish to scheme about for her.

These were charming feelings—but not lasting. Before she had committed herself by any public profession of eternal friendship for Jane Fairfax, or done more towards a recantation of past prejudices and errors, than saying to Mr. Knightley, "She certainly is handsome; she is better than handsome!" Jane had spent an evening at Hartfield with her grandmother and aunt, and every thing was relapsing much into its usual state. Former provocations reappeared. The aunt was as tiresome as ever; more tiresome, because anxiety for her health was now added to admiration of her powers; and they had to listen to the description of exactly how little bread and butter she ate for breakfast, and how small a slice of mutton for dinner, as well as to see exhibitions of new caps and new workbags for her mother and herself; and Jane's offences rose again. They had music; Emma was obliged to play; and the thanks and praise which necessarily followed appeared to her an affectation of candour, an air of greatness, meaning only to shew off in higher style her own very superior performance. She was, besides, which was the worst of all, so cold, so cautious! There was no getting at her real opinion. Wrapt up in a cloak of politeness, she seemed determined to hazard nothing. She was disgustingly, was suspiciously reserved.

If any thing could be more, where all was most, she was more reserved on the subject of Weymouth and the Dixons than any thing. She seemed bent on giving no real insight into Mr. Dixon's character, or her own value for his company, or opinion of the suitableness of the match. It was all general approbation and smoothness; nothing delineated or distinguished. It did her no service however. Her caution was thrown away. Emma saw its artifice, and returned to her first surmises. There probably *was* something more to conceal than her own preference; Mr. Dixon, perhaps, had been very near changing one friend for the other, or been fixed only to Miss Campbell, for the sake of the future twelve thousand pounds.

The like reserve prevailed on other topics. She and Mr. Frank Churchill had been at Weymouth at the same time. It was known that they were a little acquainted; but not a syllable of real information could Emma procure as to what he truly was. "Was he handsome?"—"She believed he was reckoned a very fine young man." "Was he agreeable?"—"He was generally thought so." "Did he appear a sensible young man; a young man of information?"—"At a watering-place, or in a common London acquaintance, it was difficult to decide on such points. Manners were all that could be safely judged of, under a much longer knowledge than they had yet had of Mr. Churchill. She believed every body found his manners pleasing." Emma could not forgive her.

CHAPTER III

Emma could not forgive her;—but as neither provocation nor resentment were discerned by Mr. Knightley, who had been of the party, and had seen only proper attention and pleasing behaviour on each side, he was expressing the next morning, being at Hartfield again on business with Mr. Woodhouse, his approbation of the whole; not so openly as he might have done had her father been out of the room, but speaking plain enough to be very intelligible to Emma. He had been used to think her unjust to Jane, and had now great pleasure in marking an improvement.

"A very pleasant evening," he began, as soon as Mr. Woodhouse had been talked into what was necessary, told that he understood, and the papers swept away;—"particularly pleasant. You and Miss Fairfax gave us some very good music. I do not know a more luxurious state, sir, than sitting at one's ease to be entertained a whole evening by two such young women; sometimes with music and sometimes with conversation. I am sure Miss Fairfax must have found the evening pleasant, Emma. You left nothing undone. I was glad you made her play so much, for having no instrument at her grandmother's, it must have been a real indulgence."

"I am happy you approved," said Emma, smiling; "but I hope I am not often deficient in what is due to guests at Hartfield."

"No, my dear," said her father instantly; "*that* I am sure you are not. There is nobody half so attentive and civil as you are. If any thing, you are too attentive. The muffin last night—if it had been handed round once, I think it would have been enough."

"No," said Mr. Knightley, nearly at the same time; "you are not often deficient; not often deficient either in manner or comprehension. I think you understand me, therefore."

An arch look expressed—"I understand you well enough;" but she said only, "Miss Fairfax is reserved."

"I always told you she was—a little; but you will soon overcome all that part of her reserve which ought to be overcome, all that has its foundation in diffidence. What arises from discretion must be honoured."

"You think her diffident. I do not see it."

"My dear Emma," said he, moving from his chair into one close by her, "you are not going to tell me, I hope, that you had not a pleasant evening."

"Oh! no; I was pleased with my own perseverance in asking questions; and amused to think how little information I obtained."

"I am disappointed," was his only answer.

"I hope every body had a pleasant evening," said Mr. Woodhouse, in his quiet way. "I had. Once, I felt the fire rather too much; but then I moved back my chair a little, a very little, and it did not disturb me. Miss Bates was very chatty and good-humoured, as she always is, though she speaks rather too quick. However, she is very agreeable, and Mrs. Bates too, in a different way. I like old friends; and Miss Jane Fairfax is a very pretty sort of young lady, a very pretty and a very well-behaved young lady indeed. She must have found the evening agreeable, Mr. Knightley, because she had Emma."

"True, sir; and Emma, because she had Miss Fairfax."

Emma saw his anxiety, and wishing to appease it, at least for the present, said, and with a sincerity which no one could question—

"She is a sort of elegant creature that one cannot keep one's eyes from. I am always watching her to admire; and I do pity her from my heart."

Mr. Knightley looked as if he were more gratified than he cared to express; and before he could make any reply, Mr. Woodhouse, whose thoughts were on the Bateses, said—

"It is a great pity that their circumstances should be so confined! a great pity indeed! and I have often wished—but it is so little one can venture to do—small, trifling presents, of any thing uncommon—Now we have killed a porker, and Emma thinks of sending them a loin or a leg; it is very small and delicate—Hartfield pork is not like any other pork—but still it is pork—and, my dear Emma, unless one could be sure of their making it into steaks, nicely fried, as ours are fried, without the smallest grease, and not roast it, for no stomach can bear roast pork—I think we had better send the leg—do not you think so, my dear?"

"My dear papa, I sent the whole hind-quarter. I knew you would wish it. There will be the leg to be salted, you know, which is so very nice, and the loin to be dressed directly in any manner they like."

"That's right, my dear, very right. I had not thought of it before, but that is the best way. They must not over-salt the leg; and then, if it is not over-salted, and if it is very thoroughly boiled, just as Serle boils ours, and eaten very moderately of, with a boiled turnip, and a little carrot or parsnip, I do not consider it unwholesome."

"Emma," said Mr. Knightley presently, "I have a piece of news for you. You like news—and I heard an article in my way hither that I think will interest you."

"News! Oh! yes, I always like news. What is it?—why do you smile so?—where did you hear it?—at Randalls?"

He had time only to say,

"No, not at Randalls; I have not been near Randalls," when the door was thrown open, and Miss Bates and Miss Fairfax walked into the room. Full of thanks, and full of news, Miss Bates knew not which to give quickest. Mr. Knightley soon saw that he had lost his moment, and that not another syllable of communication could rest with him.

"Oh! my dear sir, how are you this morning? My dear Miss Woodhouse—I come quite over-powered. Such a beautiful hind-quarter of pork! You are too bountiful! Have you heard the news? Mr. Elton is going to be married."

Emma had not had time even to think of Mr. Elton, and she was so completely surprized that she could not avoid a little start, and a little blush, at the sound.

"There is my news:—I thought it would interest you," said Mr. Knightley, with a smile which implied a conviction of some part of what had passed between them.

"But where could *you* hear it?" cried Miss Bates. "Where could you possibly hear it, Mr. Knightley? For it is not five minutes since I received Mrs. Cole's note—no, it cannot be more than five—or at least ten—for I had got my bonnet and spencer on, just ready to come out—I was only gone down to speak to Patty again about the pork—Jane was standing in the passage—were not you, Jane?—for my mother was so afraid that we had not any salting-pan large enough. So I said I would go down and see, and Jane said, 'Shall I go down instead? for I think you have a little cold, and Patty has been washing the kitchen.'—'Oh! my dear,' said I—well, and just then came the note. A Miss Hawkins—that's all I know. A Miss Hawkins of Bath. But, Mr. Knightley, how could you possibly have heard it? for the very moment Mr. Cole told Mrs. Cole of it, she sat down and wrote to me. A Miss Hawkins—"

"I was with Mr. Cole on business an hour and a half ago. He had just read Elton's letter as I was shewn in, and handed it to me directly."

"Well! that is quite—I suppose there never was a piece of news more generally interesting. My dear sir, you really are too bountiful. My mother desires her very best compliments and regards, and a thousand thanks, and says you really quite oppress her."

"We consider our Hartfield pork," replied Mr. Woodhouse—"indeed it certainly is, so very superior to all other pork, that Emma and I cannot have a greater pleasure than—"

"Oh! my dear sir, as my mother says, our friends are only too good to us. If ever there were people who, without having great wealth themselves, had every thing they could wish for, I am sure it is us. We may well say that 'our lot is cast in a goodly heritage.' Well, Mr. Knightley, and so you actually saw the letter; well—"

"It was short—merely to announce—but cheerful, exulting, of course."—Here was a sly glance at Emma. "He had been so fortunate as to—I forget the precise words—one has no business to remember them. The information was, as you state, that he was going to be married to a Miss Hawkins. By his style, I should imagine it just settled."

"Mr. Elton going to be married!" said Emma, as soon as she could speak. "He will have every body's wishes for his happiness."

"He is very young to settle," was Mr. Woodhouse's observation. "He had better not be in a hurry. He seemed to me very well off as he was. We were always glad to see him at Hartfield."

"A new neighbour for us all, Miss Woodhouse!" said Miss Bates, joyfully; "my mother is so pleased!—she says she cannot bear to have the poor old Vicarage without a mistress. This is great news, indeed. Jane, you have never seen Mr. Elton!—no wonder that you have such a curiosity to see him."

Jane's curiosity did not appear of that absorbing nature as wholly to occupy her.

"No—I have never seen Mr. Elton," she replied, starting on this appeal; "is he—is he a tall man?"

"Who shall answer that question?" cried Emma. "My father would say 'yes,' Mr. Knightley 'no;' and Miss Bates and I that he is just the happy medium. When you have been here a little longer, Miss Fairfax, you will understand that Mr. Elton is the standard of perfection in Highbury, both in person and mind."

"Very true, Miss Woodhouse, so she will. He is the very best young man—But, my dear Jane, if you remember, I told you yesterday he was precisely the height of Mr. Perry. Miss Hawkins,—I dare say, an excellent young woman. His extreme attention to my mother—wanting her to sit in the vicarage pew, that she might hear the better, for my mother is a little deaf, you know—it is not much, but she does not hear quite quick. Jane says that Colonel Campbell is a little deaf. He fancied bathing might be good for it—the warm bath—but she says it did him no lasting benefit. Colonel Campbell, you know, is quite our angel. And Mr. Dixon seems a very charming young man, quite worthy of him. It is such a happiness when good people get together—and they always do. Now, here will be Mr. Elton and Miss Hawkins; and there are the Coles, such very good people; and the Perrys—I suppose there never was a happier or a better couple than Mr. and Mrs. Perry. I say, sir," turning to Mr. Woodhouse, "I think there are few places with such society as Highbury. I always say, we are quite blessed in our neighbours.—My dear sir, if there is one thing my mother loves better than another, it is pork—a roast loin of pork—"

"As to who, or what Miss Hawkins is, or how long he has been acquainted with her," said Emma, "nothing I suppose can be known. One feels that it cannot be a very long acquaintance. He has been gone only four weeks."

Nobody had any information to give; and, after a few more wonderings, Emma said,

"You are silent, Miss Fairfax—but I hope you mean to take an interest in this news. You, who have been hearing and seeing so much of late on these subjects, who must have been so deep in the business on Miss Campbell's account—we shall not excuse your being indifferent about Mr. Elton and Miss Hawkins."

"When I have seen Mr. Elton," replied Jane, "I dare say I shall be interested—but I believe it requires *that* with me. And as it is some months since Miss Campbell married, the impression may be a little worn off."

"Yes, he has been gone just four weeks, as you observe, Miss Woodhouse," said Miss Bates, "four weeks yesterday.—A Miss Hawkins!—Well, I had always rather fancied it would be some young lady hereabouts; not that I ever—Mrs. Cole once whispered to me—but I immediately said, 'No, Mr. Elton is a most worthy young man—but'—In short, I do not think I am particularly quick at those sort of discoveries. I do not pretend to it. What is before me, I see. At the same time, nobody could wonder if Mr. Elton should have aspired—Miss Woodhouse lets me chatter on, so good-humouredly. She knows I would not offend for the world. How does Miss Smith do? She seems quite recovered now. Have you heard from Mrs. John Knightley lately? Oh! those dear little children. Jane, do you know I always fancy Mr. Dixon like Mr. John Knightley. I mean in person—tall, and with that sort of look—and not very talkative."

"Quite wrong, my dear aunt; there is no likeness at all."

"Very odd! but one never does form a just idea of any body beforehand. One takes up a notion, and runs away with it. Mr. Dixon, you say, is not, strictly speaking, handsome?"

"Handsome! Oh! no—far from it—certainly plain. I told you he was plain."

"My dear, you said that Miss Campbell would not allow him to be plain, and that you yourself—"

"Oh! as for me, my judgment is worth nothing. Where I have a regard, I always think a person well-looking. But I gave what I believed the general opinion, when I called him plain."

"Well, my dear Jane, I believe we must be running away. The weather does not look well, and grandmama will be uneasy. You are too obliging, my dear Miss Woodhouse; but we really must take leave. This has been a most agreeable piece of news indeed. I shall just go round by Mrs. Cole's; but I shall not stop three minutes: and, Jane, you had better go home directly—I would not have you out in a shower!—We think she is the better for Highbury already. Thank you, we do indeed. I shall not attempt calling on Mrs. Goddard, for I really do not think she cares for any thing but *boiled* pork: when we dress the leg it will be another thing. Good morning to you, my dear sir. Oh! Mr. Knightley is coming too. Well, that is so very!—I am sure if Jane is tired, you will be so kind as to give her your arm.—Mr. Elton, and Miss Hawkins!—Good morning to you."

Emma, alone with her father, had half her attention wanted by him while he lamented that young people would be in such a hurry to marry—and to marry strangers too—and the other half she could give to her own view of the subject. It was to herself an amusing and a very welcome piece of news, as proving that Mr. Elton could not have suffered long; but she was sorry for Harriet: Harriet must feel it—and all that she could hope was, by giving the first information herself, to save her from hearing it abruptly from others. It was now about the time that she was likely to call. If she were to meet Miss Bates in her way!—and upon its beginning to rain, Emma was obliged to expect that the weather would be detaining her at Mrs. Goddard's, and that the intelligence would undoubtedly rush upon her without preparation.

The shower was heavy, but short; and it had not been over five minutes, when in came Harriet, with just the heated, agitated look which hurrying thither with a full heart was likely to give; and the "Oh! Miss Woodhouse, what do you think has happened!" which instantly burst forth, had all the evidence of corresponding perturbation. As the blow was given, Emma felt that she could not now shew greater kindness than in listening; and Harriet, unchecked, ran eagerly through what she had to tell. "She had set out from Mrs. Goddard's half an hour ago—she had been afraid it would rain—she had been afraid it would pour down every moment—but she thought she might get to Hartfield first—she had hurried on as fast as possible; but then, as she was passing by the house where a young woman was making up a gown for her, she thought she would just step in and see how it went on; and though she did not seem to stay half a moment there, soon after she came out it began to rain, and she did not know what to do; so she ran on directly, as fast as she could, and took shelter at Ford's."—Ford's was the principal woollen-draper, linen-draper, and haberdasher's shop united; the shop first in size and fashion in the place.—"And so, there she had set, without an idea of any thing in the world, full ten minutes, perhaps—when, all of a sudden, who should come in—to be sure it was so very odd!—but they always dealt at Ford's—who should come in, but Elizabeth Martin and her brother!—Dear Miss Woodhouse! only think. I thought I should have fainted. I did not know what to do. I was sitting near the door—Elizabeth saw me directly; but he did not; he was busy with the umbrella. I am sure she saw me, but she looked away directly, and took no notice; and they both went to quite the farther end of the shop; and I kept sitting near the door!—Oh! dear; I was so miserable! I am sure I must have been as white as my gown. I could not go away you know, because of the rain; but I did so wish myself anywhere in the world but there.—Oh! dear, Miss Woodhouse—well, at last, I fancy, he looked round and saw me; for instead of going on with her buyings, they began whispering to one another. I am sure they were talking of me; and I could not help thinking that he was persuading her to speak to me—(do you think he was, Miss Woodhouse?)—for presently she came forward—came quite up to me, and asked me how I did, and seemed ready to shake hands, if I would. She did not do any of it in the same way that she used; I could see she was altered; but, however, she seemed to *try* to be very friendly, and we shook hands, and stood talking some time; but I know no more what I said—I was in such a tremble!—I remember she said she was sorry we never met now; which I thought almost too kind! Dear, Miss Woodhouse, I was absolutely miserable! By that time, it was beginning to hold up, and I was determined that nothing should stop me from getting away—and then—only think!—I found he was coming up towards me too—slowly you know, and as if he did not quite know what to do; and so he came and spoke, and I answered—and I stood for a minute, feeling dreadfully, you know, one can't tell how; and then I took courage, and said it did not rain, and I must go; and so off I set; and I had not got three yards from the door, when he came after me, only to say, if I was going to Hartfield, he thought I had much better go round by Mr. Cole's stables, for I should find the near way quite floated by this rain. Oh! dear, I thought it would have been the death of me! So I said, I was very much obliged to him: you know I could not do less; and then he went back to Elizabeth, and I came round by the stables—I believe I did—but I hardly knew where I was, or any thing about it. Oh! Miss Woodhouse, I would rather done any thing than have it happen: and yet, you know, there was a sort of satisfaction in seeing him behave so pleasantly and so kindly. And Elizabeth, too. Oh! Miss Woodhouse, do talk to me and make me comfortable again."

Very sincerely did Emma wish to do so; but it was not immediately in her power. She was obliged to stop and think. She was not thoroughly comfortable herself. The young man's conduct, and his sister's, seemed the result of real feeling, and she could not but pity them. As Harriet described it, there had been an interesting mixture of wounded affection and genuine delicacy in their behaviour. But she had believed them to be well-meaning, worthy people before; and what difference did this make in the evils of the connexion? It was folly to be disturbed by it. Of course, he must be sorry to lose her—they must be all sorry. Ambition, as well as love, had probably been mortified. They might all have hoped to rise by Harriet's acquaintance: and besides, what was the value of Harriet's description?—So easily pleased—so little discerning;—what signified her praise?

She exerted herself, and did try to make her comfortable, by considering all that had passed as a mere trifle, and quite unworthy of being dwelt on,

"It might be distressing, for the moment," said she; "but you seem to have behaved extremely well; and it is over—and may never—can never, as a first meeting, occur again, and therefore you need not think about it."

Harriet said, "very true," and she "would not think about it;" but still she talked of it—still she could talk of nothing else; and Emma, at last, in order to put the Martins out of her head, was obliged to hurry on the news, which she had meant to give with so much tender caution; hardly knowing herself whether to rejoice or be angry, ashamed or only amused, at such a state of mind in poor Harriet—such a conclusion of Mr. Elton's importance with her!

Mr. Elton's rights, however, gradually revived. Though she did not feel the first intelligence as she might have done the day before, or an hour before, its interest soon increased; and before their first conversation was over, she had talked herself into all the sensations of curiosity, wonder and regret, pain and pleasure, as to this fortunate Miss Hawkins, which could conduce to place the Martins under proper subordination in her fancy.

Emma learned to be rather glad that there had been such a meeting. It had been serviceable in deadening the first shock, without retaining any influence to alarm. As Harriet now lived, the Martins could not get at her, without seeking her, where hitherto they had wanted either the courage or the condescension to seek her; for since her refusal of the brother, the sisters never had been at Mrs. Goddard's; and a twelvemonth might pass without their being thrown together again, with any necessity, or even any power of speech.

CHAPTER IV

Human nature is so well disposed towards those who are in interesting situations, that a young person, who either marries or dies, is sure of being kindly spoken of.

A week had not passed since Miss Hawkins's name was first mentioned in Highbury, before she was, by some means or other, discovered to have every recommendation of person and mind; to be handsome, elegant, highly accomplished, and perfectly amiable: and when Mr. Elton himself arrived to triumph in his happy prospects, and circulate the fame of her merits, there was very little more for him to do, than to tell her Christian name, and say whose music she principally played.

Mr. Elton returned, a very happy man. He had gone away rejected and mortified—disappointed in a very sanguine hope, after a series of what appeared to him strong encouragement; and not only losing the right lady, but finding himself debased to the level of a very wrong one. He had gone away deeply offended—he came back engaged to another—and to another as superior, of course, to the first, as under such circumstances what is gained always is to what is lost. He came back gay and self-satisfied, eager and busy, caring nothing for Miss Woodhouse, and defying Miss Smith.

The charming Augusta Hawkins, in addition to all the usual advantages of perfect beauty and merit, was in possession of an independent fortune, of so many thousands as would always be called ten; a point of some dignity, as well as some convenience: the story told well; he had not thrown himself away—he had gained a woman of 10,000£ or thereabouts; and he had gained her with such delightful rapidity—the first hour of introduction had been so very soon followed by distinguishing notice; the history which he had to give Mrs. Cole of the rise and progress of the affair was so glorious—the steps so quick, from the accidental rencontre, to the dinner at Mr. Green's, and the party at Mrs. Brown's—smiles and blushes rising in importance—with consciousness and agitation richly scattered—the lady had been so easily impressed—so sweetly disposed—had in short, to use a most intelligible phrase, been so very ready to have him, that vanity and prudence were equally contented.

He had caught both substance and shadow—both fortune and affection, and was just the happy man he ought to be; talking only of himself and his own concerns—expecting to be congratulated—ready to be laughed at—and, with cordial, fearless smiles, now addressing all the young ladies of the place, to whom, a few weeks ago, he would have been more cautiously gallant.

The wedding was no distant event, as the parties had only themselves to please, and nothing but the necessary preparations to wait for; and when he set out for Bath again, there was a general expectation, which a certain glance of Mrs. Cole's did not seem to contradict, that when he next entered Highbury he would bring his bride.

During his present short stay, Emma had barely seen him; but just enough to feel that the first meeting was over, and to give her the impression of his not being improved by the mixture of pique and pretension, now spread over his air. She was, in fact, beginning very much to wonder that she had ever thought him pleasing at all; and his sight was so inseparably connected with some very disagreeable feelings, that, except in a moral light, as a penance, a lesson, a source of profitable humiliation to her own mind, she would have been thankful to be assured of never seeing him again. She wished him very well; but he gave her pain, and his welfare twenty miles off would administer most satisfaction.

The pain of his continued residence in Highbury, however, must certainly be lessened by his marriage. Many vain solicitudes would be prevented—many awkwardnesses smoothed by it. A *Mrs. Elton* would be an excuse for any change of intercourse; former intimacy might sink without remark. It would be almost beginning their life of civility again.

Of the lady, individually, Emma thought very little. She was good enough for Mr. Elton, no doubt; accomplished enough for Highbury—handsome enough—to look plain, probably, by Harriet's side. As to connexion, there Emma was perfectly easy; persuaded, that after all his own vaunted claims and disdain of Harriet, he had done nothing. On that article, truth seemed attainable. *What* she was, must be uncertain; but *who* she was, might be found out; and setting aside the 10,000£, it did not appear that she was at all Harriet's superior. She brought no name, no blood, no alliance. Miss Hawkins was the youngest of the two daughters of a Bristol—merchant, of course, he must be called;

but, as the whole of the profits of his mercantile life appeared so very moderate, it was not unfair to guess the dignity of his line of trade had been very moderate also. Part of every winter she had been used to spend in Bath; but Bristol was her home, the very heart of Bristol; for though the father and mother had died some years ago, an uncle remained—in the law line—nothing more distinctly honourable was hazarded of him, than that he was in the law line; and with him the daughter had lived. Emma guessed him to be the drudge of some attorney, and too stupid to rise. And all the grandeur of the connexion seemed dependent on the elder sister, who was *very well married*, to a gentleman in a *great way*, near Bristol, who kept two carriages! That was the wind-up of the history; that was the glory of Miss Hawkins.

Could she but have given Harriet her feelings about it all! She had talked her into love; but, alas! she was not so easily to be talked out of it. The charm of an object to occupy the many vacancies of Harriet's mind was not to be talked away. He might be superseded by another; he certainly would indeed; nothing could be clearer; even a Robert Martin would have been sufficient; but nothing else, she feared, would cure her. Harriet was one of those, who, having once begun, would be always in love. And now, poor girl! she was considerably worse from this reappearance of Mr. Elton. She was always having a glimpse of him somewhere or other. Emma saw him only once; but two or three times every day Harriet was sure *just* to meet with him, or *just* to miss him, *just* to hear his voice, or see his shoulder, *just* to have something occur to preserve him in her fancy, in all the favouring warmth of surprize and conjecture. She was, moreover, perpetually hearing about him; for, excepting when at Hartfield, she was always among those who saw no fault in Mr. Elton, and found nothing so interesting as the discussion of his concerns; and every report, therefore, every guess—all that had already occurred, all that might occur in the arrangement of his affairs, comprehending income, servants, and furniture, was continually in agitation around her. Her regard was receiving strength by invariable praise of him, and her regrets kept alive, and feelings irritated by ceaseless repetitions of Miss Hawkins's happiness, and continual observation of, how much he seemed attached!—his air as he walked by the house—the very sitting of his hat, being all in proof of how much he was in love!

Had it been allowable entertainment, had there been no pain to her friend, or reproach to herself, in the waverings of Harriet's mind, Emma would have been amused by its variations. Sometimes Mr. Elton predominated, sometimes the Martins; and each was occasionally useful as a check to the other. Mr. Elton's engagement had been the cure of the agitation of meeting Mr. Martin. The unhappiness produced by the knowledge of that engagement had been a little put aside by Elizabeth Martin's calling at Mrs. Goddard's a few days afterwards. Harriet had not been at home; but a note had been prepared and left for her, written in the very style to touch; a small mixture of reproach, with a great deal of kindness; and till Mr. Elton himself appeared, she had been much occupied by it, continually pondering over what could be done in return, and wishing to do more than she dared to confess. But Mr. Elton, in person, had driven away all such cares. While he staid, the Martins were forgotten; and on the very morning of his setting off for Bath again, Emma, to dissipate some of the distress it occasioned, judged it best for her to return Elizabeth Martin's visit.

How that visit was to be acknowledged—what would be necessary—and what might be safest, had been a point of some doubtful consideration. Absolute neglect of the mother and sisters, when invited to come, would be ingratitude. It must not be: and yet the danger of a renewal of the acquaintance!—

After much thinking, she could determine on nothing better, than Harriet's returning the visit; but in a way that, if they had understanding, should convince them that it was to be only a formal acquaintance. She meant to take her in the carriage, leave her at the Abbey Mill, while she drove a little farther, and call for her again so soon, as to allow no time for insidious applications or dangerous recurrences to the past, and give the most decided proof of what degree of intimacy was chosen for the future.

She could think of nothing better: and though there was something in it which her own heart could not approve—something of ingratitude, merely glossed over—it must be done, or what would become of Harriet?

CHAPTER V

Small heart had Harriet for visiting. Only half an hour before her friend called for her at Mrs. Goddard's, her evil stars had led her to the very spot where, at that moment, a trunk, directed to *The Rev. Philip Elton, White-Hart, Bath*, was to be seen under the operation of being lifted into the butcher's cart, which was to convey it to where the coaches passed; and every thing in this world, excepting that trunk and the direction, was consequently a blank.

She went, however; and when they reached the farm, and she was to be put down, at the end of the broad, neat gravel walk, which led between espalier apple-trees to the front door, the sight of every thing which had given her so much pleasure the autumn before, was beginning to revive a little local agitation; and when they parted, Emma observed her to be looking around with a sort of fearful curiosity, which determined her not to allow the visit to exceed the proposed quarter of an hour. She went on herself, to give that portion of time to an old servant who was married, and settled in Donwell.

The quarter of an hour brought her punctually to the white gate again; and Miss Smith receiving her summons, was with her without delay, and unattended by any alarming young man. She came solitarily down the gravel walk—a Miss Martin just appearing at the door, and parting with her seemingly with ceremonious civility.

Harriet could not very soon give an intelligible account. She was feeling too much; but at last Emma collected from her enough to understand the sort of meeting, and the sort of pain it was creating. She had seen only Mrs. Martin and the two girls. They had received her doubtingly, if not coolly; and nothing beyond the merest commonplace had been talked almost all the time—till just at last, when Mrs. Martin's saying, all of a sudden, that she thought Miss Smith was grown, had brought on a more interesting subject, and a warmer manner. In that very room she had been measured last September, with her two friends. There were the pencilled marks and memorandums on the wainscot by the window. *He* had done it. They all seemed to remember the day, the hour, the party, the occasion—to feel the same consciousness, the same regrets—to be ready to return to the same good understanding; and they were just growing again like themselves, (Harriet, as Emma must suspect, as ready as the best of them to be cordial and happy) when the carriage reappeared, and all was over. The style of the visit, and the shortness of it, were then felt to be decisive. Fourteen minutes to be given to those with whom she had thankfully passed six weeks not six months ago!—Emma could not but picture it all, and feel how justly they might resent, how naturally Harriet must suffer. It was a bad business. She would have given a great deal, or endured a great deal, to have had the Martins in a higher rank of life. They were so deserving, that a *little* higher should have been enough: but as it was, how could she have done otherwise?—Impossible!—She could not repent. They must be separated; but there was a great deal of pain in the process—so much to herself at this time, that she soon felt the necessity of a little consolation, and resolved on going home by way of Randalls to procure it. Her mind was quite sick of Mr. Elton and the Martins. The refreshment of Randalls was absolutely necessary.

It was a good scheme; but on driving to the door they heard that neither "master nor mistress was at home;" they had both been out some time; the man believed they were gone to Hartfield.

"This is too bad," cried Emma, as they turned away. "And now we shall just miss them; too provoking!—I do not know when I have been so disappointed." And she leaned back in the corner, to indulge her murmurs, or to reason them away; probably a little of both—such being the commonest process of a not ill-disposed mind. Presently the carriage stopt; she looked up; it was stopt by Mr. and Mrs. Weston, who were standing to speak to her. There was instant pleasure in the sight of them, and still greater pleasure was conveyed in sound—for Mr. Weston immediately accosted her with,

"How d'ye do?—how d'ye do?—We have been sitting with your father—glad to see him so well. Frank comes to-morrow—I had a letter this morning—we see him to-morrow by dinner-time to a certainty—he is at Oxford to-day, and he comes for a whole fortnight; I knew it would be so. If he had come at Christmas he could not have staid three days; I was always glad he did not come at Christmas; now we are going to have just the right weather for him, fine, dry, settled weather. We shall enjoy him completely; every thing has turned out exactly as we could wish."

There was no resisting such news, no possibility of avoiding the influence of such a happy face as Mr. Weston's, confirmed as it all was by the words and the countenance of his wife, fewer and quieter, but not less to the purpose. To know that *she* thought his coming certain was enough to make Emma consider it so, and sincerely did she rejoice in their joy. It was a most delightful reanimation of exhausted spirits. The worn-out past was sunk in the freshness of what was coming; and in the rapidity of half a moment's thought, she hoped Mr. Elton would now be talked of no more.

Mr. Weston gave her the history of the engagements at Enscombe, which allowed his son to answer for having an entire fortnight at his command, as well as the route and the method of his journey; and she listened, and smiled, and congratulated.

"I shall soon bring him over to Hartfield," said he, at the conclusion.

Emma could imagine she saw a touch of the arm at this speech, from his wife.

"We had better move on, Mr. Weston," said she, "we are detaining the girls."

"Well, well, I am ready;"—and turning again to Emma, "but you must not be expecting such a *very* fine young man; you have only had *my* account you know; I dare say he is really nothing extraordinary:"—though his own sparkling eyes at the moment were speaking a very different conviction.

Emma could look perfectly unconscious and innocent, and answer in a manner that appropriated nothing.

"Think of me to-morrow, my dear Emma, about four o'clock," was Mrs. Weston's parting injunction; spoken with some anxiety, and meant only for her.

"Four o'clock!—depend upon it he will be here by three," was Mr. Weston's quick amendment; and so ended a most satisfactory meeting. Emma's spirits were mounted quite up to happiness; every thing wore a different air; James and his horses seemed not half so sluggish as before. When she looked at the hedges, she thought the elder at least must soon be coming out; and when she turned round to Harriet, she saw something like a look of spring, a tender smile even there.

"Will Mr. Frank Churchill pass through Bath as well as Oxford?"—was a question, however, which did not augur much.

But neither geography nor tranquillity could come all at once, and

Emma was now in a humour to resolve that they should both come in time.

The morning of the interesting day arrived, and Mrs. Weston's faithful pupil did not forget either at ten, or eleven, or twelve o'clock, that she was to think of her at four.

"My dear, dear anxious friend,"—said she, in mental soliloquy, while walking downstairs from her own room, "always overcareful for every body's comfort but your own; I see you now in all your little fidgets, going again and again into his room, to be sure that all is right." The clock struck twelve as she passed through the hall. "'Tis twelve; I shall not forget to think of you four hours hence; and by this time to-morrow, perhaps, or a little later, I may be thinking of the possibility of their all calling here. I am sure they will bring him soon."

She opened the parlour door, and saw two gentlemen sitting with her father—Mr. Weston and his son. They had been arrived only a few minutes, and Mr. Weston had scarcely finished his explanation of Frank's being a day before his time, and her father was yet in the midst of his very civil welcome and congratulations, when she appeared, to have her share of surprize, introduction, and pleasure.

The Frank Churchill so long talked of, so high in interest, was actually before her—he was presented to her, and she did not think too much had been said in his praise; he was a *very* good looking young man; height, air, address, all were unexceptionable, and his countenance had a great deal of the spirit and liveliness of his father's; he looked quick and sensible. She felt immediately that she should like him; and there was a well-bred ease of manner, and a readiness to talk, which convinced her that he came intending to be acquainted with her, and that acquainted they soon must be.

He had reached Randalls the evening before. She was pleased with the eagerness to arrive which had made him alter his plan, and travel earlier, later, and quicker, that he might gain half a day.

"I told you yesterday," cried Mr. Weston with exultation, "I told you all that he would be here before the time named. I remembered what I used to do myself. One cannot creep upon a journey; one cannot help getting on faster than one has planned; and the pleasure of coming in upon one's friends before the look-out begins, is worth a great deal more than any little exertion it needs."

"It is a great pleasure where one can indulge in it," said the young man, "though there are not many houses that I should presume on so far; but in coming *home* I felt I might do any thing."

The word *home* made his father look on him with fresh complacency. Emma was directly sure that he knew how to make himself agreeable; the conviction was strengthened by what followed. He was very much pleased with Randalls, thought it a most admirably arranged house, would hardly allow it even to be very small, admired the situation, the walk to Highbury, Highbury itself, Hartfield still more, and professed himself to have always felt the sort of interest in the country which none but one's *own* country gives, and the greatest curiosity to visit it. That he should never have been able to indulge so amiable a feeling before, passed suspiciously through Emma's brain; but still, if it were a falsehood, it was a pleasant one, and pleasantly handled. His manner had no air of study or exaggeration. He did really look and speak as if in a state of no common enjoyment.

Their subjects in general were such as belong to an opening acquaintance. On his side were the inquiries,—"Was she a horsewoman?—Pleasant rides?—Pleasant walks?—Had they a large neighbourhood?—Highbury, perhaps, afforded society enough?—There were several very pretty houses in and about it.—Balls—had they balls?—Was it a musical society?"

But when satisfied on all these points, and their acquaintance proportionably advanced, he contrived to find an opportunity, while their two fathers were engaged with each other, of introducing his stepmother, and speaking of her with so much handsome praise, so much warm admiration, so much gratitude for the happiness she secured to his father, and her very kind reception of himself, as was an additional proof of his knowing how to please—and of his certainly thinking it worth while to try to please her. He did not advance a word of praise beyond what she knew to be thoroughly deserved by Mrs. Weston; but, undoubtedly he could know very little of the matter. He understood what would be welcome; he could be sure of little else. "His father's marriage," he said, "had been the wisest measure, every friend must rejoice in it; and the family from whom he had received such a blessing must be ever considered as having conferred the highest obligation on him."

He got as near as he could to thanking her for Miss Taylor's merits, without seeming quite to forget that in the common course of things it was to be rather supposed that Miss Taylor had formed Miss

Woodhouse's character, than Miss Woodhouse Miss Taylor's. And at last, as if resolved to qualify his opinion completely for travelling round to its object, he wound it all up with astonishment at the youth and beauty of her person.

"Elegant, agreeable manners, I was prepared for," said he; "but I confess that, considering every thing, I had not expected more than a very tolerably well-looking woman of a certain age; I did not know that I was to find a pretty young woman in Mrs. Weston."

"You cannot see too much perfection in Mrs. Weston for my feelings," said Emma; "were you to guess her to be *eighteen*, I should listen with pleasure; but *she* would be ready to quarrel with you for using such words. Don't let her imagine that you have spoken of her as a pretty young woman."

"I hope I should know better," he replied; "no, depend upon it, (with a gallant bow,) that in addressing Mrs. Weston I should understand whom I might praise without any danger of being thought extravagant in my terms."

Emma wondered whether the same suspicion of what might be expected from their knowing each other, which had taken strong possession of her mind, had ever crossed his; and whether his compliments were to be considered as marks of acquiescence, or proofs of defiance. She must see more of him to understand his ways; at present she only felt they were agreeable.

She had no doubt of what Mr. Weston was often thinking about. His quick eye she detected again and again glancing towards them with a happy expression; and even, when he might have determined not to look, she was confident that he was often listening.

Her own father's perfect exemption from any thought of the kind, the entire deficiency in him of all such sort of penetration or suspicion, was a most comfortable circumstance. Happily he was not farther from approving matrimony than from foreseeing it.—Though always objecting to every marriage that was arranged, he never suffered beforehand from the apprehension of any; it seemed as if he could not think so ill of any two persons' understanding as to suppose they meant to marry till it were proved against them. She blessed the favouring blindness. He could now, without the drawback of a single unpleasant surmise, without a glance forward at any possible treachery in his guest, give way to all his natural kind-hearted civility in solicitous inquiries after Mr. Frank Churchill's accommodation on his journey, through the sad evils of sleeping two nights on the road, and express very genuine unmixed anxiety to know that he had certainly escaped catching cold—which, however, he could not allow him to feel quite assured of himself till after another night.

A reasonable visit paid, Mr. Weston began to move.—"He must be going. He had business at the Crown about his hay, and a great many errands for Mrs. Weston at Ford's, but he need not hurry any body else." His son, too well-bred to hear the hint, rose immediately also, saying,

"As you are going farther on business, sir, I will take the opportunity of paying a visit, which must be paid some day or other, and therefore may as well be paid now. I have the honour of being acquainted with a neighbour of yours, (turning to Emma,) a lady residing in or near Highbury; a family of the name of Fairfax. I shall have no difficulty, I suppose, in finding the house; though Fairfax, I believe, is not the proper name—I should rather say Barnes, or Bates. Do you know any family of that name?"

"To be sure we do," cried his father; "Mrs. Bates—we passed her house—I saw Miss Bates at the window. True, true, you are acquainted with Miss Fairfax; I remember you knew her at Weymouth, and a fine girl she is. Call upon her, by all means."

"There is no necessity for my calling this morning," said the young man; "another day would do as well; but there was that degree of acquaintance at Weymouth which—"

"Oh! go to-day, go to-day. Do not defer it. What is right to be done cannot be done too soon. And, besides, I must give you a hint, Frank; any want of attention to her *here* should be carefully avoided. You saw her with the Campbells, when she was the equal of every body she mixed with, but here she is with a poor old grandmother, who has barely enough to live on. If you do not call early it will be a slight."

The son looked convinced.

"I have heard her speak of the acquaintance," said Emma; "she is a very elegant young woman."

He agreed to it, but with so quiet a "Yes," as inclined her almost to doubt his real concurrence; and yet there must be a very distinct sort of elegance for the fashionable world, if Jane Fairfax could be thought only ordinarily gifted with it.

"If you were never particularly struck by her manners before," said she, "I think you will to-day. You will see her to advantage; see her and hear her—no, I am afraid you will not hear her at all, for she has an aunt who never holds her tongue."

"You are acquainted with Miss Jane Fairfax, sir, are you?" said Mr. Woodhouse, always the last to make his way in conversation; "then give me leave to assure you that you will find her a very agreeable young lady. She is staying here on a visit to her grandmama and aunt, very worthy people; I have known them all my life. They will be extremely glad to see you, I am sure; and one of my servants shall go with you to shew you the way."

"My dear sir, upon no account in the world; my father can direct me."

"But your father is not going so far; he is only going to the Crown, quite on the other side of the street, and there are a great many houses; you might be very much at a loss, and it is a very dirty walk, unless you keep on the footpath; but my coachman can tell you where you had best cross the street."

Mr. Frank Churchill still declined it, looking as serious as he could, and his father gave his hearty support by calling out, "My good friend, this is quite unnecessary; Frank knows a puddle of water when he sees it, and as to Mrs. Bates's, he may get there from the Crown in a hop, step, and jump."

They were permitted to go alone; and with a cordial nod from one, and a graceful bow from the other, the two gentlemen took leave. Emma remained very well pleased with this beginning of the acquaintance, and could now engage to think of them all at Randalls any hour of the day, with full confidence in their comfort.

CHAPTER VI

The next morning brought Mr. Frank Churchill again. He came with Mrs. Weston, to whom and to Highbury he seemed to take very cordially. He had been sitting with her, it appeared, most companionably at home, till her usual hour of exercise; and on being desired to chuse their walk, immediately fixed on Highbury.—"He did not doubt there being very pleasant walks in every direction, but if left to him, he should always chuse the same. Highbury, that airy, cheerful, happy-looking Highbury, would be his constant attraction."—Highbury, with Mrs. Weston, stood for Hartfield; and she trusted to its bearing the same construction with him. They walked thither directly.

Emma had hardly expected them: for Mr. Weston, who had called in for half a minute, in order to hear that his son was very handsome, knew nothing of their plans; and it was an agreeable surprize to her, therefore, to perceive them walking up to the house together, arm in arm. She was wanting to see him again, and especially to see him in company with Mrs. Weston, upon his behaviour to whom her opinion of him was to depend. If he were deficient there, nothing should make amends for it. But on seeing them together, she became perfectly satisfied. It was not merely in fine words or hyperbolical compliment that he paid his duty; nothing could be more proper or pleasing than his whole manner to her—nothing could more agreeably denote his wish of considering her as a friend and securing her affection. And there was time enough for Emma to form a reasonable judgment, as their visit included all the rest of the morning. They were all three walking about together for an hour or two—first round the shrubberies of Hartfield, and afterwards in Highbury. He was delighted with every thing; admired Hartfield sufficiently for Mr. Woodhouse's ear; and when their going farther was resolved on, confessed his wish to be made acquainted with the whole village, and found matter of commendation and interest much oftener than Emma could have supposed.

Some of the objects of his curiosity spoke very amiable feelings. He begged to be shewn the house which his father had lived in so long, and which had been the home of his father's father; and on recollecting that an old woman who had nursed him was still living, walked in quest of her cottage from one end of the street to the other; and though in some points of pursuit or observation there was no positive merit, they shewed, altogether, a good-will towards Highbury in general, which must be very like a merit to those he was with.

Emma watched and decided, that with such feelings as were now shewn, it could not be fairly supposed that he had been ever voluntarily absenting himself; that he had not been acting a part, or making a parade of insincere professions; and that Mr. Knightley certainly had not done him justice.

Their first pause was at the Crown Inn, an inconsiderable house, though the principal one of the sort, where a couple of pair of post-horses were kept, more for the convenience of the neighbourhood than from any run on the road; and his companions had not expected to be detained by any interest excited there; but in passing it they gave the history of the large room visibly added; it had been built many years ago for a ball-room, and while the neighbourhood had been in a particularly populous, dancing state, had been occasionally used as such;—but such brilliant days had long passed away, and now the highest purpose for which it was ever wanted was to accommodate a whist club established among the gentlemen and half-gentlemen of the place. He was immediately interested. Its character as a ball-room caught him; and instead of passing on, he stopt for several minutes at the two superior sashed windows which were open, to look in and contemplate its capabilities, and lament that its original purpose should have ceased. He saw no fault in the room, he would acknowledge none which they suggested. No, it was long enough, broad enough, handsome enough. It would hold the very number for comfort. They ought to have balls there at least every fortnight through the winter. Why had not Miss Woodhouse revived the former good old days of the room?—She who could do any thing in Highbury! The want of proper families in the place, and the conviction that none beyond the place and its immediate environs could be tempted to attend, were mentioned; but he was not satisfied. He could not be persuaded that so many good-looking houses as he saw around him, could not furnish numbers enough for such a meeting; and even when particulars were given and families described, he was still unwilling to admit that the inconvenience of such a mixture would be any thing, or that there would be the smallest difficulty in every body's returning into their proper place the next morning. He argued like a young man very much bent on dancing; and Emma was rather surprized to see the constitution of the Weston prevail so decidedly against the habits of the Churchills. He seemed to have all the life and spirit, cheerful feelings, and social inclinations of his father, and nothing of the pride or reserve of Enscombe. Of pride, indeed, there was, perhaps, scarcely enough; his indifference to a confusion of rank, bordered too much on inelegance of mind. He could be no judge, however, of the evil he was holding cheap. It was but an effusion of lively spirits.

At last he was persuaded to move on from the front of the Crown; and being now almost facing the house where the Bateses lodged, Emma recollected his intended visit the day before, and asked him if he had paid it.

"Yes, oh! yes"—he replied; "I was just going to mention it. A very successful visit:—I saw all the three ladies; and felt very much obliged to you for your preparatory hint. If the talking aunt had taken me quite by surprize, it must have been the death of me. As it was, I was only betrayed into paying a most unreasonable visit. Ten minutes would have been all that was necessary, perhaps all that was proper; and I had told my father I should certainly be at home before him—but there was no getting away, no pause; and, to my utter astonishment, I found, when he (finding me nowhere else) joined me there at last, that I had been actually sitting with them very nearly three-quarters of an hour. The good lady had not given me the possibility of escape before."

"And how did you think Miss Fairfax looking?"

"Ill, very ill—that is, if a young lady can ever be allowed to look ill. But the expression is hardly admissible, Mrs. Weston, is it? Ladies can never look ill. And, seriously, Miss Fairfax is naturally so pale, as almost always to give the appearance of ill health.—A most deplorable want of complexion."

Emma would not agree to this, and began a warm defence of Miss Fairfax's complexion. "It was certainly never brilliant, but she would not allow it to have a sickly hue in general; and there was a softness and delicacy in her skin which gave peculiar elegance to the character of her face." He listened with all due deference; acknowledged that he had heard many people say the same—but yet he must confess, that to him nothing could make amends for the want of the fine glow of health. Where features were indifferent, a fine complexion gave beauty to them all; and where they were good, the effect was—fortunately he need not attempt to describe what the effect was.

"Well," said Emma, "there is no disputing about taste.—At least you admire her except her complexion."

He shook his head and laughed.—"I cannot separate Miss Fairfax and her complexion."

"Did you see her often at Weymouth? Were you often in the same society?"

At this moment they were approaching Ford's, and he hastily exclaimed, "Ha! this must be the very shop that every body attends every day of their lives, as my father informs me. He comes to Highbury himself, he says, six days out of the seven, and has always business at Ford's. If it be not inconvenient to you, pray let us go in, that I may prove myself to belong to the place, to be a true citizen of Highbury. I must buy something at Ford's. It will be taking out my freedom.—I dare say they sell gloves."

"Oh! yes, gloves and every thing. I do admire your patriotism. You will be adored in Highbury. You were very popular before you came, because you were Mr. Weston's son—but lay out half a guinea at Ford's, and your popularity will stand upon your own virtues."

They went in; and while the sleek, well-tied parcels of "Men's Beavers" and "York Tan" were bringing down and displaying on the counter, he said—"But I beg your pardon, Miss Woodhouse, you were speaking to me, you were saying something at the very moment of this burst of my *amor patriae*. Do not let me lose it. I assure you the utmost stretch of public fame would not make me amends for the loss of any happiness in private life."

"I merely asked, whether you had known much of Miss Fairfax and her party at Weymouth."

"And now that I understand your question, I must pronounce it to be a very unfair one. It is always the lady's right to decide on the degree of acquaintance. Miss Fairfax must already have given her account.—I shall not commit myself by claiming more than she may chuse to allow."

"Upon my word! you answer as discreetly as she could do herself. But her account of every thing leaves so much to be guessed, she is so very reserved, so very unwilling to give the least information about any body, that I really think you may say what you like of your acquaintance with her."

"May I, indeed?—Then I will speak the truth, and nothing suits me so well. I met her frequently at Weymouth. I had known the Campbells a little in town; and at Weymouth we were very much in the same set. Colonel Campbell is a very agreeable man, and Mrs. Campbell a friendly, warm-hearted woman. I like them all."

"You know Miss Fairfax's situation in life, I conclude; what she is destined to be?"

"Yes—(rather hesitatingly)—I believe I do."

"You get upon delicate subjects, Emma," said Mrs. Weston smiling; "remember that I am here.—Mr. Frank Churchill hardly knows what to say when you speak of Miss Fairfax's situation in life. I will move a little farther off."

"I certainly do forget to think of *her*," said Emma, "as having ever been any thing but my friend and my dearest friend."

He looked as if he fully understood and honoured such a sentiment.

When the gloves were bought, and they had quitted the shop again, "Did you ever hear the young lady we were speaking of, play?" said Frank Churchill.

"Ever hear her!" repeated Emma. "You forget how much she belongs to Highbury. I have heard her every year of our lives since we both began. She plays charmingly."

"You think so, do you?—I wanted the opinion of some one who could really judge. She appeared to me to play well, that is, with considerable taste, but I know nothing of the matter myself.—I am excessively fond of music, but without the smallest skill or right of judging of any body's performance.—I have been used to hear hers admired; and I remember one proof of her being thought to play well:—a man, a very musical man, and in love with another woman—engaged to her—on the point of marriage—would yet never ask that other woman to sit down to the instrument, if the lady in question could sit down instead—never seemed to like to hear one if he could hear the other. That, I thought, in a man of known musical talent, was some proof."

"Proof indeed!" said Emma, highly amused.—"Mr. Dixon is very musical, is he? We shall know more about them all, in half an hour, from you, than Miss Fairfax would have vouchsafed in half a year."

"Yes, Mr. Dixon and Miss Campbell were the persons; and I thought it a very strong proof."

"Certainly—very strong it was; to own the truth, a great deal stronger than, if *I* had been Miss Campbell, would have been at all agreeable to me. I could not excuse a man's having more music than love—more ear than eye—a more acute sensibility to fine sounds than to my feelings. How did Miss Campbell appear to like it?"

"It was her very particular friend, you know."

"Poor comfort!" said Emma, laughing. "One would rather have a stranger preferred than one's very particular friend—with a stranger it might not recur again—but the misery of having a very particular friend always at hand, to do every thing better than one does oneself!—Poor Mrs. Dixon! Well, I am glad she is gone to settle in Ireland."

"You are right. It was not very flattering to Miss Campbell; but she really did not seem to feel it."

"So much the better—or so much the worse:—I do not know which. But be it sweetness or be it stupidity in her—quickness of friendship, or dulness of feeling—there was one person, I think, who must have felt it: Miss Fairfax herself. She must have felt the improper and dangerous distinction."

"As to that—I do not—"

"Oh! do not imagine that I expect an account of Miss Fairfax's sensations from you, or from any body else. They are known to no human being, I guess, but herself. But if she continued to play whenever she was asked by Mr. Dixon, one may guess what one chuses."

"There appeared such a perfectly good understanding among them all—" he began rather quickly, but checking himself, added, "however, it is impossible for me to say on what terms they really were—how it might all be behind the scenes. I can only say that there was smoothness outwardly. But you, who have known Miss Fairfax from a child, must be a better judge of her character, and of how she is likely to conduct herself in critical situations, than I can be."

"I have known her from a child, undoubtedly; we have been children and women together; and it is natural to suppose that we should be intimate,—that we should have taken to each other whenever she visited her friends. But we never did. I hardly know how it has happened; a little, perhaps, from that wickedness on my side which was prone to take disgust towards a girl so idolized and so cried up as she always was, by her aunt and grandmother, and all their set. And then, her reserve—I never could attach myself to any one so completely reserved."

"It is a most repulsive quality, indeed," said he. "Oftentimes very convenient, no doubt, but never pleasing. There is safety in reserve, but no attraction. One cannot love a reserved person."

"Not till the reserve ceases towards oneself; and then the attraction may be the greater. But I must be more in want of a friend, or an agreeable companion, than I have yet been, to take the trouble of conquering any body's reserve to procure one. Intimacy between Miss Fairfax and me is quite out of the question. I have no reason to think ill of her—not the least—except that such extreme and perpetual cautiousness of word and manner, such a dread of giving a distinct idea about any body, is apt to suggest suspicions of there being something to conceal."

He perfectly agreed with her: and after walking together so long, and thinking so much alike, Emma felt herself so well acquainted with him, that she could hardly believe it to be only their second meeting. He was not exactly what she had expected; less of the man of the world in some of his notions, less of the spoiled child of fortune, therefore better than she had expected. His ideas seemed more moderate—his feelings warmer. She was particularly struck by his manner of considering Mr. Elton's house, which, as well as the church, he would go and look at, and would not join them in finding much fault with. No, he could not believe it a bad house; not such a house as a man was to be pitied for having. If it were to be shared with the woman he loved, he could not think any man to be pitied for having that house. There must be ample room in it for every real comfort. The man must be a blockhead who wanted more.

Mrs. Weston laughed, and said he did not know what he was talking about. Used only to a large house himself, and without ever thinking how many advantages and accommodations were attached to its size, he could be no judge of the privations inevitably belonging to a small one. But Emma, in her own mind, determined that he *did* know what he was talking about, and that he shewed a very amiable inclination to settle early in life, and to marry, from worthy motives. He might not be aware of the inroads on domestic peace to be occasioned by no housekeeper's room, or a bad butler's pantry, but no doubt he did perfectly feel that Enscombe could not make him happy, and that whenever he were attached, he would willingly give up much of wealth to be allowed an early establishment.

CHAPTER VII

Emma's very good opinion of Frank Churchill was a little shaken the following day, by hearing that he was gone off to London, merely to have his hair cut. A sudden freak seemed to have seized him at breakfast, and he had sent for a chaise and set off, intending to return to dinner, but with no more important view that appeared than having his hair cut. There was certainly no harm in his travelling sixteen miles twice over on such an errand; but there was an air of foppery and nonsense in it which she could not approve. It did not accord with the rationality of plan, the moderation in expense, or even the unselfish warmth of heart, which she had believed herself to discern in him yesterday. Vanity, extravagance, love of change, restlessness of temper, which must be doing something, good or bad; heedlessness as to the pleasure of his father and Mrs. Weston, indifferent as to how his conduct might appear in general; he became liable to all these charges. His father only called him a coxcomb, and thought it a very good story; but that Mrs. Weston did not like it, was clear enough, by her passing it over as quickly as possible, and making no other comment than that "all young people would have their little whims."

With the exception of this little blot, Emma found that his visit hitherto had given her friend only good ideas of him. Mrs. Weston was very ready to say how attentive and pleasant a companion he made himself—how much she saw to like in his disposition altogether. He appeared to have a very open temper—certainly a very cheerful and lively one; she could observe nothing wrong in his notions, a great deal decidedly right; he spoke of his uncle with warm regard, was fond of talking of him—said he would be the best man in the world if he were left to himself; and though there was no being attached to the aunt, he acknowledged her kindness with gratitude, and seemed to mean always to speak of her with respect. This was all very promising; and, but for such an unfortunate fancy for having his hair cut, there was nothing to denote him unworthy of the distinguished honour which her imagination had given him; the honour, if not of being really in love with her, of being at least very near it, and saved only by her own indifference—(for still her resolution held of never marrying)—

the honour, in short, of being marked out for her by all their joint acquaintance.

Mr. Weston, on his side, added a virtue to the account which must have some weight. He gave her to understand that Frank admired her extremely—thought her very beautiful and very charming; and with so much to be said for him altogether, she found she must not judge him harshly. As Mrs. Weston observed, "all young people would have their little whims."

There was one person among his new acquaintance in Surry, not so leniently disposed. In general he was judged, throughout the parishes of Donwell and Highbury, with great candour; liberal allowances were made for the little excesses of such a handsome young man—one who smiled so often and bowed so well; but there was one spirit among them not to be softened, from its power of censure, by bows or smiles—Mr. Knightley. The circumstance was told him at Hartfield; for the moment, he was silent; but Emma heard him almost immediately afterwards say to himself, over a newspaper he held in his hand, "Hum! just the trifling, silly fellow I took him for." She had half a mind to resent; but an instant's observation convinced her that it was really said only to relieve his own feelings, and not meant to provoke; and therefore she let it pass.

Although in one instance the bearers of not good tidings, Mr. and Mrs. Weston's visit this morning was in another respect particularly opportune. Something occurred while they were at Hartfield, to make Emma want their advice; and, which was still more lucky, she wanted exactly the advice they gave.

This was the occurrence:—The Coles had been settled some years in Highbury, and were very good sort of people—friendly, liberal, and unpretending; but, on the other hand, they were of low origin, in trade, and only moderately genteel. On their first coming into the country, they had lived in proportion to their income, quietly, keeping little company, and that little unexpensively; but the last year or two had brought them a considerable increase of means—the house in town had yielded greater profits, and fortune in general had smiled on them. With their wealth, their views increased; their want of a larger house, their inclination for more company. They added to their house, to their number of servants, to their expenses of every sort; and by this time were, in fortune and style of living, second only to the family at

Hartfield. Their love of society, and their new dining-room, prepared every body for their keeping dinner-company; and a few parties, chiefly among the single men, had already taken place. The regular and best families Emma could hardly suppose they would presume to invite—neither Donwell, nor Hartfield, nor Randalls. Nothing should tempt *her* to go, if they did; and she regretted that her father's known habits would be giving her refusal less meaning than she could wish. The Coles were very respectable in their way, but they ought to be taught that it was not for them to arrange the terms on which the superior families would visit them. This lesson, she very much feared, they would receive only from herself; she had little hope of Mr. Knightley, none of Mr. Weston.

But she had made up her mind how to meet this presumption so many weeks before it appeared, that when the insult came at last, it found her very differently affected. Donwell and Randalls had received their invitation, and none had come for her father and herself; and Mrs. Weston's accounting for it with "I suppose they will not take the liberty with you; they know you do not dine out," was not quite sufficient. She felt that she should like to have had the power of refusal; and afterwards, as the idea of the party to be assembled there, consisting precisely of those whose society was dearest to her, occurred again and again, she did not know that she might not have been tempted to accept. Harriet was to be there in the evening, and the Bateses. They had been speaking of it as they walked about Highbury the day before, and Frank Churchill had most earnestly lamented her absence. Might not the evening end in a dance? had been a question of his. The bare possibility of it acted as a farther irritation on her spirits; and her being left in solitary grandeur, even supposing the omission to be intended as a compliment, was but poor comfort.

It was the arrival of this very invitation while the Westons were at Hartfield, which made their presence so acceptable; for though her first remark, on reading it, was that "of course it must be declined," she so very soon proceeded to ask them what they advised her to do, that their advice for her going was most prompt and successful.

She owned that, considering every thing, she was not absolutely without inclination for the party. The Coles expressed themselves so properly—there was so much real attention in the manner of it—so much consideration for her father. "They would have solicited the honour earlier, but had been waiting the arrival of a folding-screen from London, which they hoped might keep Mr. Woodhouse from any draught of air, and therefore induce him the more readily to give them the honour of his company." Upon the whole, she was very persuadable; and it being briefly settled among themselves how it might be done without neglecting his comfort—how certainly Mrs. Goddard, if not Mrs. Bates, might be depended on for bearing him company—Mr. Woodhouse was to be talked into an acquiescence of his daughter's going out to dinner on a day now near at hand, and spending the whole evening away from him. As for *his* going, Emma did not wish him to think it possible, the hours would be too late, and the party too numerous. He was soon pretty well resigned.

"I am not fond of dinner-visiting," said he—"I never was. No more is Emma. Late hours do not agree with us. I am sorry Mr. and Mrs. Cole should have done it. I think it would be much better if they would come in one afternoon next summer, and take their tea with us—take us in their afternoon walk; which they might do, as our hours are so reasonable, and yet get home without being out in the damp of the evening. The dews of a summer evening are what I would not expose any body to. However, as they are so very desirous to have dear Emma dine with them, and as you will both be there, and Mr. Knightley too, to take care of her, I cannot wish to prevent it, provided the weather be what it ought, neither damp, nor cold, nor windy." Then turning to Mrs. Weston, with a look of gentle reproach—"Ah! Miss Taylor, if you had not married, you would have staid at home with me."

"Well, sir," cried Mr. Weston, "as I took Miss Taylor away, it is incumbent on me to supply her place, if I can; and I will step to Mrs. Goddard in a moment, if you wish it."

But the idea of any thing to be done in a *moment*, was increasing, not lessening, Mr. Woodhouse's agitation. The ladies knew better how to allay it. Mr. Weston must be quiet, and every thing deliberately arranged.

With this treatment, Mr. Woodhouse was soon composed enough for talking as usual. "He should be happy to see Mrs. Goddard. He had a great regard for Mrs. Goddard; and Emma should write a line, and invite her. James could take the note. But first of all, there must be an answer written to Mrs. Cole."

"You will make my excuses, my dear, as civilly as possible. You will say that I am quite an invalid, and go no where, and therefore must decline their obliging invitation; beginning with my *compliments*, of course. But you will do every thing right. I need not tell you what is to be done. We must remember to let James know that the carriage will be wanted on Tuesday. I shall have no fears for you with him. We have never been there above once since the new approach was made; but still I have no doubt that James will take you very safely. And when you get there, you must tell him at what time you would have him come for you again; and you had better name an early hour. You will not like staying late. You will get very tired when tea is over."

"But you would not wish me to come away before I am tired, papa?"

"Oh! no, my love; but you will soon be tired. There will be a great many people talking at once. You will not like the noise."

"But, my dear sir," cried Mr. Weston, "if Emma comes away early, it will be breaking up the party."

"And no great harm if it does," said Mr. Woodhouse. "The sooner every party breaks up, the better."

"But you do not consider how it may appear to the Coles. Emma's going away directly after tea might be giving offence. They are good-natured people, and think little of their own claims; but still they must feel that any body's hurrying away is no great compliment; and Miss Woodhouse's doing it would be more thought of than any other person's in the room. You would not wish to disappoint and mortify the Coles, I am sure, sir; friendly, good sort of people as ever lived, and who have been your neighbours these *ten* years."

"No, upon no account in the world, Mr. Weston; I am much obliged to you for reminding me. I should be extremely sorry to be giving them any pain. I know what worthy people they are. Perry tells me that Mr. Cole never touches malt liquor. You would not think it to look at him, but he is bilious—Mr. Cole is very bilious. No, I would not be the means of giving them any pain. My dear Emma, we must consider this. I am sure, rather than run the risk of hurting Mr. and Mrs. Cole, you would stay a little longer than you might wish. You will not regard being tired. You will be perfectly safe, you know, among your friends."

"Oh yes, papa. I have no fears at all for myself; and I should have no scruples of staying as late as Mrs. Weston, but on your account. I am only afraid of your sitting up for me. I am not afraid of your not being exceedingly comfortable with Mrs. Goddard. She loves piquet, you know; but when she is gone home, I am afraid you will be sitting up by yourself, instead of going to bed at your usual time—and the idea of that would entirely destroy my comfort. You must promise me not to sit up."

He did, on the condition of some promises on her side: such as that, if she came home cold, she would be sure to warm herself thoroughly; if hungry, that she would take something to eat; that her own maid should sit up for her; and that Serle and the butler should see that every thing were safe in the house, as usual.

CHAPTER VIII

Frank Churchill came back again; and if he kept his father's dinner waiting, it was not known at Hartfield; for Mrs. Weston was too anxious for his being a favourite with Mr. Woodhouse, to betray any imperfection which could be concealed.

He came back, had had his hair cut, and laughed at himself with a very good grace, but without seeming really at all ashamed of what he had done. He had no reason to wish his hair longer, to conceal any confusion of face; no reason to wish the money unspent, to improve his spirits. He was quite as undaunted and as lively as ever; and, after seeing him, Emma thus moralised to herself:—

"I do not know whether it ought to be so, but certainly silly things do cease to be silly if they are done by sensible people in an impudent way. Wickedness is always wickedness, but folly is not always folly.—It depends upon the character of those who handle it. Mr. Knightley, he is *not* a trifling, silly young man. If he were, he would have done this differently. He would either have gloried in the achievement, or been ashamed of it. There would have been either the ostentation of a coxcomb, or the evasions of a mind too weak to defend its own vanities.—No, I am perfectly sure that he is not trifling or silly."

With Tuesday came the agreeable prospect of seeing him again, and for a longer time than hitherto; of judging of his general manners, and by inference, of the meaning of his manners towards herself; of guessing how soon it might be necessary for her to throw coldness into her air; and of fancying what the observations of all those might be, who were now seeing them together for the first time.

She meant to be very happy, in spite of the scene being laid at Mr. Cole's; and without being able to forget that among the failings of Mr. Elton, even in the days of his favour, none had disturbed her more than his propensity to dine with Mr. Cole.

Her father's comfort was amply secured, Mrs. Bates as well as Mrs. Goddard being able to come; and her last pleasing duty, before she left the house, was to pay her respects to them as they sat together after dinner; and while her father was fondly noticing the beauty of her dress, to make the two ladies all the amends in her power, by helping them to large slices of cake and full glasses of wine, for whatever unwilling self-denial his care of their constitution might have obliged them to practise during the meal.—She had provided a plentiful dinner for them; she wished she could know that they had been allowed to eat it.

She followed another carriage to Mr. Cole's door; and was pleased to see that it was Mr. Knightley's; for Mr. Knightley keeping no horses, having little spare money and a great deal of health, activity, and independence, was too apt, in Emma's opinion, to get about as he could, and not use his carriage so often as became the owner of Donwell Abbey. She had an opportunity now of speaking her approbation while warm from her heart, for he stopped to hand her out.

"This is coming as you should do," said she; "like a gentleman.—I am quite glad to see you."

He thanked her, observing, "How lucky that we should arrive at the same moment! for, if we had met first in the drawing-room, I doubt whether you would have discerned me to be more of a gentleman than usual.—You might not have distinguished how I came, by my look or manner."

"Yes I should, I am sure I should. There is always a look of consciousness or bustle when people come in a way which they know to be beneath them. You think you carry it off very well, I dare say, but with you it is a sort of bravado, an air of affected unconcern; I always observe it whenever I meet you under those circumstances. *Now* you have nothing to try for. You are not afraid of being supposed ashamed. You are not striving to look taller than any body else. *Now* I shall really be very happy to walk into the same room with you."

"Nonsensical girl!" was his reply, but not at all in anger.

Emma had as much reason to be satisfied with the rest of the party as with Mr. Knightley. She was received with a cordial respect which could not but please, and given all the consequence she could wish for. When the Westons arrived, the kindest looks of love, the strongest of admiration were for her, from both husband and wife; the son approached her with a cheerful eagerness which marked her as his peculiar object, and at dinner she found him seated by her—and, as she firmly believed, not without some dexterity on his side.

The party was rather large, as it included one other family, a proper unobjectionable country family, whom the Coles had the advantage of naming among their acquaintance, and the male part of Mr. Cox's family, the lawyer of Highbury. The less worthy females were to come in the evening, with Miss Bates, Miss Fairfax, and Miss Smith; but already, at dinner, they were too numerous for any subject of conversation to be general; and, while politics and Mr. Elton were talked over, Emma could fairly surrender all her attention to the pleasantness of her neighbour. The first remote sound to which she felt herself obliged to attend, was the name of Jane Fairfax. Mrs. Cole seemed to be relating something of her that was expected to be very interesting. She listened, and found it well worth listening to. That very dear part of Emma, her fancy, received an amusing supply. Mrs. Cole was telling that she had been calling on Miss Bates, and as soon as she entered the room had been struck by the sight of a pianoforte—a very elegant looking instrument—not a grand, but a large-sized square pianoforte; and the substance of the story, the end of all the dialogue which ensued of surprize, and inquiry, and congratulations on her side, and explanations on Miss Bates's, was, that this pianoforte had arrived from Broadwood's the day before, to the great astonishment of both aunt and niece—entirely unexpected; that at first, by Miss Bates's account, Jane herself was quite at a loss, quite bewildered to think who could possibly have ordered it—but now, they were both perfectly satisfied that it could be from only one quarter;—of course it must be from Colonel Campbell.

"One can suppose nothing else," added Mrs. Cole, "and I was only surprized that there could ever have been a doubt. But Jane, it seems, had a letter from them very lately, and not a word was said about it. She knows their ways best; but I should not consider their silence as any reason for their not meaning to make the present. They might chuse to surprize her."

Mrs. Cole had many to agree with her; every body who spoke on the subject was equally convinced that it must come from Colonel Campbell, and equally rejoiced that such a present had been made; and there were enough ready to speak to allow Emma to think her own way, and still listen to Mrs. Cole.

"I declare, I do not know when I have heard any thing that has given me more satisfaction!—It always has quite hurt me that Jane Fairfax, who plays so delightfully, should not have an instrument. It seemed quite a shame, especially considering how many houses there are where fine instruments are absolutely thrown away. This is like giving ourselves a slap, to be sure! and it was but yesterday I was telling Mr. Cole, I really was ashamed to look at our new grand pianoforte in the drawing-room, while I do not know one note from another, and our little girls, who are but just beginning, perhaps may never make any thing of it; and there is poor Jane Fairfax, who is mistress of music, has not any thing of the nature of an instrument, not even the pitifullest old spinet in the world, to amuse herself with.—I was saying this to Mr. Cole but yesterday, and he quite agreed with me; only he is so particularly fond of music that he could not help indulging himself in the purchase, hoping that some of our good neighbours might be so obliging occasionally to put it to a better use than we can; and that really is the reason why the instrument was bought—or else I am sure we ought to be ashamed of it.—We are in great hopes that Miss Woodhouse may be prevailed with to try it this evening."

Miss Woodhouse made the proper acquiescence; and finding that nothing more was to be entrapped from any communication of Mrs. Cole's, turned to Frank Churchill.

"Why do you smile?" said she.

"Nay, why do you?"

"Me!—I suppose I smile for pleasure at Colonel Campbell's being so rich and so liberal.—It is a handsome present."

"Very."

"I rather wonder that it was never made before."

"Perhaps Miss Fairfax has never been staying here so long before."

"Or that he did not give her the use of their own instrument—which must now be shut up in London, untouched by any body."

"That is a grand pianoforte, and he might think it too large for Mrs. Bates's house."

"You may *say* what you chuse—but your countenance testifies that your *thoughts* on this subject are very much like mine."

"I do not know. I rather believe you are giving me more credit for acuteness than I deserve. I smile because you smile, and shall probably suspect whatever I find you suspect; but at present I do not see what there is to question. If Colonel Campbell is not the person, who can be?"

"What do you say to Mrs. Dixon?"

"Mrs. Dixon! very true indeed. I had not thought of Mrs. Dixon. She must know as well as her father, how acceptable an instrument would be; and perhaps the mode of it, the mystery, the surprize, is more like a young woman's scheme than an elderly man's. It is Mrs. Dixon, I dare say. I told you that your suspicions would guide mine."

"If so, you must extend your suspicions and comprehend *Mr.* Dixon in them."

"Mr. Dixon.—Very well. Yes, I immediately perceive that it must be the joint present of Mr. and Mrs. Dixon. We were speaking the other day, you know, of his being so warm an admirer of her performance."

"Yes, and what you told me on that head, confirmed an idea which I had entertained before.—I do not mean to reflect upon the good intentions of either Mr. Dixon or Miss Fairfax, but I cannot help suspecting either that, after making his proposals to her friend, he had the misfortune to fall in love with *her*, or that he became conscious of a little attachment on her side. One might guess twenty things without guessing exactly the right; but I am sure there must be a particular cause for her chusing to come to Highbury instead of going with the Campbells to Ireland. Here, she must be leading a life of privation and penance; there it would have been all enjoyment. As to the pretence of trying her native air, I look upon that as a mere excuse.—In the summer it might have passed; but what can any body's native air do for them in the months of January, February, and March? Good fires and carriages would be much more to the purpose in most cases of delicate health, and I dare say in hers. I do not require you to adopt all my suspicions, though you make so noble a profession of doing it, but I honestly tell you what they are."

"And, upon my word, they have an air of great probability. Mr. Dixon's preference of her music to her friend's, I can answer for being very decided."

"And then, he saved her life. Did you ever hear of that?—A water party; and by some accident she was falling overboard. He caught her."

"He did. I was there—one of the party."

"Were you really?—Well!—But you observed nothing of course, for it seems to be a new idea to you.—If I had been there, I think I should have made some discoveries."

"I dare say you would; but I, simple I, saw nothing but the fact, that Miss Fairfax was nearly dashed from the vessel and that Mr. Dixon caught her.—It was the work of a moment. And though the consequent shock and alarm was very great and much more durable—indeed I believe it was half an hour before any of us were comfortable again—yet that was too general a sensation for any thing of peculiar anxiety to be observable. I do not mean to say, however, that you might not have made discoveries."

The conversation was here interrupted. They were called on to share in the awkwardness of a rather long interval between the courses, and obliged to be as formal and as orderly as the others; but when the table was again safely covered, when every corner dish was placed exactly right, and occupation and ease were generally restored, Emma said,

"The arrival of this pianoforte is decisive with me. I wanted to know a little more, and this tells me quite enough. Depend upon it, we shall soon hear that it is a present from Mr. and Mrs. Dixon."

"And if the Dixons should absolutely deny all knowledge of it we must conclude it to come from the Campbells."

"No, I am sure it is not from the Campbells. Miss Fairfax knows it is not from the Campbells, or they would have been guessed at first. She would not have been puzzled, had she dared fix on them. I may not have convinced you perhaps, but I am perfectly convinced myself that Mr. Dixon is a principal in the business."

"Indeed you injure me if you suppose me unconvinced. Your reasonings carry my judgment along with them entirely. At first, while I supposed you satisfied that Colonel Campbell was the giver, I saw it only as paternal kindness, and thought it the most natural thing in the world. But when you mentioned Mrs. Dixon, I felt how much more probable that it should be the tribute of warm female friendship. And now I can see it in no other light than as an offering of love."

There was no occasion to press the matter farther. The conviction seemed real; he looked as if he felt it. She said no more, other subjects took their turn; and the rest of the dinner passed away; the dessert succeeded, the children came in, and were talked to and admired amid the usual rate of conversation; a few clever things said, a few downright silly, but by much the larger proportion neither the one nor the other—nothing worse than everyday remarks, dull repetitions, old news, and heavy jokes.

The ladies had not been long in the drawing-room, before the other ladies, in their different divisions, arrived. Emma watched the entree of her own particular little friend; and if she could not exult in her dignity and grace, she could not only love the blooming sweetness and the artless manner, but could most heartily rejoice in that light, cheerful, unsentimental disposition which allowed her so many alleviations of pleasure, in the midst of the pangs of disappointed affection. There she sat—and who would have guessed how many tears she had been lately shedding? To be in company, nicely dressed herself and seeing others nicely dressed, to sit and smile and look pretty, and say nothing, was enough for the happiness of the present hour. Jane Fairfax did look and move superior; but Emma suspected she might have been glad to change feelings with Harriet, very glad to have purchased the mortification of having loved—yes, of having loved even Mr. Elton in vain—by the surrender of all the dangerous pleasure of knowing herself beloved by the husband of her friend.

In so large a party it was not necessary that Emma should approach her. She did not wish to speak of the pianoforte, she felt too much in the secret herself, to think the appearance of curiosity or interest fair, and therefore purposely kept at a distance; but by the others, the subject was almost immediately introduced, and she saw the blush of consciousness with which congratulations were received, the blush of guilt which accompanied the name of "my excellent friend Colonel Campbell."

Mrs. Weston, kind-hearted and musical, was particularly interested by the circumstance, and Emma could not help being amused at her perseverance in dwelling on the subject; and having so much to ask and to say as to tone, touch, and pedal, totally unsuspicious of that wish of saying as little about it as possible, which she plainly read in the fair heroine's countenance.

They were soon joined by some of the gentlemen; and the very first of the early was Frank Churchill. In he walked, the first and the handsomest; and after paying his compliments en passant to Miss Bates and her niece, made his way directly to the opposite side of the circle, where sat Miss Woodhouse; and till he could find a seat by her, would not sit at all. Emma divined what every body present must be thinking. She was his object, and every body must perceive it. She introduced him to her friend, Miss Smith, and, at convenient moments afterwards, heard what each thought of the other. "He had never seen so lovely a face, and was delighted with her naivete." And she, "Only to be sure it was paying him too great a compliment, but she did think there were some looks a little like Mr. Elton." Emma restrained her indignation, and only turned from her in silence.

Smiles of intelligence passed between her and the gentleman on first glancing towards Miss Fairfax; but it was most prudent to avoid speech. He told her that he had been impatient to leave the dining-room—hated sitting long—was always the first to move when he could—that his father, Mr. Knightley, Mr. Cox, and Mr. Cole, were left very busy over parish business—that as long as he had staid, however, it had been pleasant enough, as he had found them in general a set of gentlemanlike, sensible men; and spoke so handsomely of Highbury altogether—thought it so abundant in agreeable families—that Emma began to feel she had been used to despise the place rather too much. She questioned him as to the society in Yorkshire—the extent of the neighbourhood about Enscombe, and the sort; and could make out from his answers that, as far as Enscombe was concerned, there was very little going on, that their visitings were among a range of great families, none very near; and that even when days were fixed, and invitations accepted, it was an even chance that Mrs. Churchill were not in health and spirits for going; that they made a point of visiting no fresh person; and that, though he had his separate engagements, it was not without difficulty, without considerable address *at times*, that he could get away, or introduce an acquaintance for a night.

She saw that Enscombe could not satisfy, and that Highbury, taken at its best, might reasonably please a young man who had more retirement at home than he liked. His importance at Enscombe was very evident. He did not boast, but it naturally betrayed itself, that he had persuaded his aunt where his uncle could do nothing, and on her laughing and noticing it, he owned that he believed (excepting one or two points) he could *with time* persuade her to any thing. One of those points on which his influence failed, he then mentioned. He had wanted very much to go abroad—had been very eager indeed to be allowed to travel—but she would not hear of it. This had happened the year before. *Now*, he said, he was beginning to have no longer the same wish.

The unpersuadable point, which he did not mention, Emma guessed to be good behaviour to his father.

"I have made a most wretched discovery," said he, after a short pause.—"I have been here a week to-morrow—half my time. I never knew days fly so fast. A week to-morrow!—And I have hardly begun to enjoy myself. But just got acquainted with Mrs. Weston, and others!—I hate the recollection."

"Perhaps you may now begin to regret that you spent one whole day, out of so few, in having your hair cut."

"No," said he, smiling, "that is no subject of regret at all. I have no pleasure in seeing my friends, unless I can believe myself fit to be seen."

The rest of the gentlemen being now in the room, Emma found herself obliged to turn from him for a few minutes, and listen to Mr. Cole. When Mr. Cole had moved away, and her attention could be restored as before, she saw Frank Churchill looking intently across the room at Miss Fairfax, who was sitting exactly opposite.

"What is the matter?" said she.

He started. "Thank you for rousing me," he replied. "I believe I have been very rude; but really Miss Fairfax has done her hair in so odd a way—so very odd a way—that I cannot keep my eyes from her. I never saw any thing so outré!—Those curls!—This must be a fancy of her own. I see nobody else looking like her!—I must go and ask her whether it is an Irish fashion. Shall I?—Yes, I will—I declare I will—and you shall see how she takes it;—whether she colours."

He was gone immediately; and Emma soon saw him standing before Miss Fairfax, and talking to her; but as to its effect on the young lady, as he had improvidently placed himself exactly between them, exactly in front of Miss Fairfax, she could absolutely distinguish nothing.

Before he could return to his chair, it was taken by Mrs. Weston.

"This is the luxury of a large party," said she:—"one can get near every body, and say every thing. My dear Emma, I am longing to talk to you. I have been making discoveries and forming plans, just like yourself, and I must tell them while the idea is fresh. Do you know how Miss Bates and her niece came here?"

"How?—They were invited, were not they?"

"Oh! yes—but how they were conveyed hither?—the manner of their coming?"

"They walked, I conclude. How else could they come?"

"Very true.—Well, a little while ago it occurred to me how very sad it would be to have Jane Fairfax walking home again, late at night, and cold as the nights are now. And as I looked at her, though I never saw her appear to more advantage, it struck me that she was heated, and would therefore be particularly liable to take cold. Poor girl! I could not bear the idea of it; so, as soon as Mr. Weston came into the room, and I could get at him, I spoke to him about the carriage. You may guess how readily he came into my wishes; and having his approbation, I made my way directly to Miss Bates, to assure her that the carriage would be at her service before it took us home; for I thought it would be making her comfortable at once. Good soul! she was as grateful as possible, you may be sure. 'Nobody was ever so fortunate as herself!'—but with many, many thanks—'there was no occasion to trouble us, for Mr. Knightley's carriage had brought, and was to take them home again.' I was quite surprized;—very glad, I am sure; but really quite surprized. Such a very kind attention—and so thoughtful an attention!—the sort of thing that so few men would think of. And, in short, from knowing his usual ways, I am very much inclined to think that it was for their accommodation the carriage was used at all. I do suspect he would not have had a pair of horses for himself, and that it was only as an excuse for assisting them."

"Very likely," said Emma—"nothing more likely. I know no man more likely than Mr. Knightley to do the sort of thing—to do any thing really good-natured, useful, considerate, or benevolent. He is not a gallant man, but he is a very humane one; and this, considering Jane Fairfax's ill-health, would appear a case of humanity to him;—and for an act of unostentatious kindness, there is nobody whom I would fix on more than on Mr. Knightley. I know he had horses to-day—for we arrived together; and I laughed at him about it, but he said not a word that could betray."

"Well," said Mrs. Weston, smiling, "you give him credit for more simple, disinterested benevolence in this instance than I do; for while Miss Bates was speaking, a suspicion darted into my head, and I have never been able to get it out again. The more I think of it, the more probable it appears. In short, I have made a match between Mr. Knightley and Jane Fairfax. See the consequence of keeping you company!—What do you say to it?"

"Mr. Knightley and Jane Fairfax!" exclaimed Emma. "Dear Mrs. Weston, how could you think of such a thing?—Mr. Knightley!—Mr. Knightley must not marry!—You would not have little Henry cut out from Donwell?—Oh! no, no, Henry must have Donwell. I cannot at all consent to Mr. Knightley's marrying; and I am sure it is not at all likely. I am amazed that you should think of such a thing."

"My dear Emma, I have told you what led me to think of it. I do not want the match—I do not want to injure dear little Henry—but the idea has been given me by circumstances; and if Mr. Knightley really wished to marry, you would not have him refrain on Henry's account, a boy of six years old, who knows nothing of the matter?"

"Yes, I would. I could not bear to have Henry supplanted.—Mr. Knightley marry!—No, I have never had such an idea, and I cannot adopt it now. And Jane Fairfax, too, of all women!"

"Nay, she has always been a first favourite with him, as you very well know."

"But the imprudence of such a match!"

"I am not speaking of its prudence; merely its probability."

"I see no probability in it, unless you have any better foundation than what you mention. His good-nature, his humanity, as I tell you, would be quite enough to account for the horses. He has a great regard for the Bateses, you know, independent of Jane Fairfax—and is always glad to shew them attention. My dear Mrs. Weston, do not take to match-making. You do it very ill. Jane Fairfax mistress of the Abbey!—Oh! no, no;—every feeling revolts. For his own sake, I would not have him do so mad a thing."

"Imprudent, if you please—but not mad. Excepting inequality of fortune, and perhaps a little disparity of age, I can see nothing unsuitable."

"But Mr. Knightley does not want to marry. I am sure he has not the least idea of it. Do not put it into his head. Why should he marry?—He is as happy as possible by himself; with his farm, and his sheep, and his library, and all the parish to manage; and he is extremely fond of his brother's children. He has no occasion to marry, either to fill up his time or his heart."

"My dear Emma, as long as he thinks so, it is so; but if he really loves Jane Fairfax—"

"Nonsense! He does not care about Jane Fairfax. In the way of love, I am sure he does not. He would do any good to her, or her family; but—"

"Well," said Mrs. Weston, laughing, "perhaps the greatest good he could do them, would be to give Jane such a respectable home."

"If it would be good to her, I am sure it would be evil to himself; a very shameful and degrading connexion. How would he bear to have Miss Bates belonging to him?—To have her haunting the Abbey, and thanking him all day long for his great kindness in marrying Jane?—

'So very kind and obliging!—But he always had been such a very kind neighbour!' And then fly off, through half a sentence, to her mother's old petticoat. 'Not that it was such a very old petticoat either—for still it would last a great while—and, indeed, she must thankfully say that their petticoats were all very strong.'"

"For shame, Emma! Do not mimic her. You divert me against my conscience. And, upon my word, I do not think Mr. Knightley would be much disturbed by Miss Bates. Little things do not irritate him. She might talk on; and if he wanted to say any thing himself, he would only talk louder, and drown her voice. But the question is not, whether it would be a bad connexion for him, but whether he wishes it; and I think he does. I have heard him speak, and so must you, so very highly of Jane Fairfax! The interest he takes in her—his anxiety about her health—his concern that she should have no happier prospect! I have heard him express himself so warmly on those points!—Such an admirer of her performance on the pianoforte, and of her voice! I have heard him say that he could listen to her for ever. Oh! and I had almost forgotten one idea that occurred to me—this pianoforte that has been sent here by somebody—though we have all been so well satisfied to consider it a present from the Campbells, may it not be from Mr. Knightley? I cannot help suspecting him. I think he is just the person to do it, even without being in love."

"Then it can be no argument to prove that he is in love. But I do not think it is at all a likely thing for him to do. Mr. Knightley does nothing mysteriously."

"I have heard him lamenting her having no instrument repeatedly; oftener than I should suppose such a circumstance would, in the common course of things, occur to him."

"Very well; and if he had intended to give her one, he would have told her so."

"There might be scruples of delicacy, my dear Emma. I have a very strong notion that it comes from him. I am sure he was particularly silent when Mrs. Cole told us of it at dinner."

"You take up an idea, Mrs. Weston, and run away with it; as you have many a time reproached me with doing. I see no sign of attachment—I believe nothing of the pianoforte—and proof only shall convince me that Mr. Knightley has any thought of marrying Jane Fairfax."

They combated the point some time longer in the same way; Emma rather gaining ground over the mind of her friend; for Mrs. Weston was the most used of the two to yield; till a little bustle in the room shewed them that tea was over, and the instrument in preparation;—and at the same moment Mr. Cole approaching to entreat Miss Woodhouse would do them the honour of trying it. Frank Churchill, of whom, in the eagerness of her conversation with Mrs. Weston, she had been seeing nothing, except that he had found a seat by Miss Fairfax, followed Mr. Cole, to add his very pressing entreaties; and as, in every respect, it suited Emma best to lead, she gave a very proper compliance.

She knew the limitations of her own powers too well to attempt more than she could perform with credit; she wanted neither taste nor spirit in the little things which are generally acceptable, and could accompany her own voice well. One accompaniment to her song took her agreeably by surprize—a second, slightly but correctly taken by Frank Churchill. Her pardon was duly begged at the close of the song, and every thing usual followed. He was accused of having a delightful voice, and a perfect knowledge of music; which was properly denied; and that he knew nothing of the matter, and had no voice at all, roundly asserted. They sang together once more; and Emma would then resign her place to Miss Fairfax, whose performance, both vocal and instrumental, she never could attempt to conceal from herself, was infinitely superior to her own.

With mixed feelings, she seated herself at a little distance from the numbers round the instrument, to listen. Frank Churchill sang again. They had sung together once or twice, it appeared, at Weymouth. But the sight of Mr. Knightley among the most attentive, soon drew away half Emma's mind; and she fell into a train of thinking on the subject of Mrs. Weston's suspicions, to which the sweet sounds of the united voices gave only momentary interruptions. Her objections to Mr. Knightley's marrying did not in the least subside. She could see nothing but evil in it. It would be a great disappointment to Mr. John Knightley; consequently to Isabella. A real injury to the children—a most mortifying change, and material loss to them all;—a very great deduction from her father's daily comfort—and, as to herself, she could not at all endure the idea of Jane Fairfax at Donwell Abbey. A Mrs. Knightley for them all to give way to!—No—Mr. Knightley must never marry. Little Henry must remain the heir of Donwell.

Presently Mr. Knightley looked back, and came and sat down by her. They talked at first only of the performance. His admiration was certainly very warm; yet she thought, but for Mrs. Weston, it would not have struck her. As a sort of touchstone, however, she began to speak of his kindness in conveying the aunt and niece; and though his answer was in the spirit of cutting the matter short, she believed it to indicate only his disinclination to dwell on any kindness of his own.

"I often feel concern," said she, "that I dare not make our carriage more useful on such occasions. It is not that I am without the wish; but you know how impossible my father would deem it that James should put-to for such a purpose."

"Quite out of the question, quite out of the question," he replied;—"but you must often wish it, I am sure." And he smiled with such seeming pleasure at the conviction, that she must proceed another step.

"This present from the Campbells," said she—"this pianoforte is very kindly given."

"Yes," he replied, and without the smallest apparent embarrassment.—"But they would have done better had they given her notice of it. Surprizes are foolish things. The pleasure is not enhanced, and the inconvenience is often considerable. I should have expected better judgment in Colonel Campbell."

From that moment, Emma could have taken her oath that Mr. Knightley had had no concern in giving the instrument. But whether he were entirely free from peculiar attachment—whether there were no actual preference—remained a little longer doubtful. Towards the end of Jane's second song, her voice grew thick.

"That will do," said he, when it was finished, thinking aloud—"you have sung quite enough for one evening—now be quiet."

Another song, however, was soon begged for. "One more;—they would not fatigue Miss Fairfax on any account, and would only ask for one more." And Frank Churchill was heard to say, "I think you could manage this without effort; the first part is so very trifling. The strength of the song falls on the second."

Mr. Knightley grew angry.

"That fellow," said he, indignantly, "thinks of nothing but shewing off his own voice. This must not be." And touching Miss Bates, who at that moment passed near—"Miss Bates, are you mad, to let your niece sing herself hoarse in this manner? Go, and interfere. They have no mercy on her."

Miss Bates, in her real anxiety for Jane, could hardly stay even to be grateful, before she stept forward and put an end to all farther singing. Here ceased the concert part of the evening, for Miss Woodhouse and Miss Fairfax were the only young lady performers; but soon (within five minutes) the proposal of dancing—originating nobody exactly knew where—was so effectually promoted by Mr. and Mrs. Cole, that every thing was rapidly clearing away, to give proper space. Mrs. Weston, capital in her country-dances, was seated, and beginning an irresistible waltz; and Frank Churchill, coming up with most becoming gallantry to Emma, had secured her hand, and led her up to the top.

While waiting till the other young people could pair themselves off, Emma found time, in spite of the compliments she was receiving on her voice and her taste, to look about, and see what became of Mr. Knightley. This would be a trial. He was no dancer in general. If he were to be very alert in engaging Jane Fairfax now, it might augur something. There was no immediate appearance. No; he was talking to Mrs. Cole—he was looking on unconcerned; Jane was asked by somebody else, and he was still talking to Mrs. Cole.

Emma had no longer an alarm for Henry; his interest was yet safe; and she led off the dance with genuine spirit and enjoyment. Not more than five couple could be mustered; but the rarity and the suddenness of it made it very delightful, and she found herself well matched in a partner. They were a couple worth looking at.

Two dances, unfortunately, were all that could be allowed. It was growing late, and Miss Bates became anxious to get home, on her mother's account. After some attempts, therefore, to be permitted to begin again, they were obliged to thank Mrs. Weston, look sorrowful, and have done.

"Perhaps it is as well," said Frank Churchill, as he attended Emma to her carriage. "I must have asked Miss Fairfax, and her languid dancing would not have agreed with me, after yours."

CHAPTER IX

Emma did not repent her condescension in going to the Coles. The visit afforded her many pleasant recollections the next day; and all that she might be supposed to have lost on the side of dignified seclusion, must be amply repaid in the splendour of popularity. She must have delighted the Coles—worthy people, who deserved to be made happy!—And left a name behind her that would not soon die away.

Perfect happiness, even in memory, is not common; and there were two points on which she was not quite easy. She doubted whether she had not transgressed the duty of woman by woman, in betraying her suspicions of Jane Fairfax's feelings to Frank Churchill. It was hardly right; but it had been so strong an idea, that it would escape her, and his submission to all that she told, was a compliment to her penetration, which made it difficult for her to be quite certain that she ought to have held her tongue.

The other circumstance of regret related also to Jane Fairfax; and there she had no doubt. She did unfeignedly and unequivocally regret the inferiority of her own playing and singing. She did most heartily grieve over the idleness of her childhood—and sat down and practised vigorously an hour and a half.

She was then interrupted by Harriet's coming in; and if Harriet's praise could have satisfied her, she might soon have been comforted.

"Oh! if I could but play as well as you and Miss Fairfax!"

"Don't class us together, Harriet. My playing is no more like hers, than a lamp is like sunshine."

"Oh! dear—I think you play the best of the two. I think you play quite as well as she does. I am sure I had much rather hear you. Every body last night said how well you played."

"Those who knew any thing about it, must have felt the difference. The truth is, Harriet, that my playing is just good enough to be praised, but Jane Fairfax's is much beyond it."

"Well, I always shall think that you play quite as well as she does, or that if there is any difference nobody would ever find it out. Mr. Cole said how much taste you had; and Mr. Frank Churchill talked a great deal about your taste, and that he valued taste much more than execution."

"Ah! but Jane Fairfax has them both, Harriet."

"Are you sure? I saw she had execution, but I did not know she had any taste. Nobody talked about it. And I hate Italian singing.—There is no understanding a word of it. Besides, if she does play so very well, you know, it is no more than she is obliged to do, because she will have to teach. The Coxes were wondering last night whether she would get into any great family. How did you think the Coxes looked?"

"Just as they always do—very vulgar."

"They told me something," said Harriet rather hesitatingly; "but it is nothing of any consequence."

Emma was obliged to ask what they had told her, though fearful of its producing Mr. Elton.

"They told me—that Mr. Martin dined with them last Saturday."

"Oh!"

"He came to their father upon some business, and he asked him to stay to dinner."

"Oh!"

"They talked a great deal about him, especially Anne Cox. I do not know what she meant, but she asked me if I thought I should go and stay there again next summer."

"She meant to be impertinently curious, just as such an Anne Cox should be."

"She said he was very agreeable the day he dined there. He sat by her at dinner. Miss Nash thinks either of the Coxes would be very glad to marry him."

"Very likely.—I think they are, without exception, the most vulgar girls in Highbury."

Harriet had business at Ford's.—Emma thought it most prudent to go with her. Another accidental meeting with the Martins was possible, and in her present state, would be dangerous.

Harriet, tempted by every thing and swayed by half a word, was always very long at a purchase; and while she was still hanging over muslins and changing her mind, Emma went to the door for amusement.—Much could not be hoped from the traffic of even the busiest part of Highbury;—Mr. Perry walking hastily by, Mr. William Cox letting himself in at the office-door, Mr. Cole's carriage-horses returning from exercise, or a stray letter-boy on an obstinate mule, were the liveliest objects she could presume to expect; and when her eyes fell only on the butcher with his tray, a tidy old woman travelling homewards from shop with her full basket, two curs quarrelling over a dirty bone, and a string of dawdling children round the baker's little bow-window eyeing the gingerbread, she knew she had no reason to complain, and was amused enough; quite enough still to stand at the door. A mind lively and at ease, can do with seeing nothing, and can see nothing that does not answer.

She looked down the Randalls road. The scene enlarged; two persons appeared; Mrs. Weston and her stepson; they were walking into Highbury;—to Hartfield of course. They were stopping, however, in the first place at Mrs. Bates's; whose house was a little nearer Randalls than Ford's; and had all but knocked, when Emma caught their eye.—Immediately they crossed the road and came forward to her; and the agreeableness of yesterday's engagement seemed to give fresh pleasure to the present meeting. Mrs. Weston informed her that she was going to call on the Bateses, in order to hear the new instrument.

"For my companion tells me," said she, "that I absolutely promised Miss Bates last night, that I would come this morning. I was not aware of it myself. I did not know that I had fixed a day, but as he says I did, I am going now."

"And while Mrs. Weston pays her visit, I may be allowed, I hope," said Frank Churchill, "to join your party and wait for her at Hartfield—if you are going home."

Mrs. Weston was disappointed.

"I thought you meant to go with me. They would be very much pleased."

"Me! I should be quite in the way. But, perhaps—I may be equally in the way here. Miss Woodhouse looks as if she did not want me. My aunt always sends me off when she is shopping. She says I fidget her to death; and Miss Woodhouse looks as if she could almost say the same. What am I to do?"

"I am here on no business of my own," said Emma; "I am only waiting for my friend. She will probably have soon done, and then we shall go home. But you had better go with Mrs. Weston and hear the instrument."

"Well—if you advise it.—But (with a smile) if Colonel Campbell should have employed a careless friend, and if it should prove to have an indifferent tone—what shall I say? I shall be no support to Mrs. Weston. She might do very well by herself. A disagreeable truth would be palatable through her lips, but I am the wretchedest being in the world at a civil falsehood."

"I do not believe any such thing," replied Emma.—"I am persuaded that you can be as insincere as your neighbours, when it is necessary; but there is no reason to suppose the instrument is indifferent. Quite otherwise indeed, if I understood Miss Fairfax's opinion last night."

"Do come with me," said Mrs. Weston, "if it be not very disagreeable to you. It need not detain us long. We will go to Hartfield afterwards. We will follow them to Hartfield. I really wish you to call with me. It will be felt so great an attention! and I always thought you meant it."

He could say no more; and with the hope of Hartfield to reward him, returned with Mrs. Weston to Mrs. Bates's door. Emma watched them in, and then joined Harriet at the interesting counter,—trying, with all the force of her own mind, to convince her that if she wanted plain muslin it was of no use to look at figured; and that a blue ribbon, be it ever so beautiful, would still never match her yellow pattern. At last it was all settled, even to the destination of the parcel.

"Should I send it to Mrs. Goddard's, ma'am?" asked Mrs. Ford.—"Yes—no—yes, to Mrs. Goddard's. Only my pattern gown is at Hartfield. No, you shall send it to Hartfield, if you please. But then, Mrs. Goddard will want to see it.—And I could take the pattern gown home any day. But I shall want the ribbon directly—so it had better go to Hartfield—at least the ribbon. You could make it into two parcels, Mrs. Ford, could not you?"

"It is not worth while, Harriet, to give Mrs. Ford the trouble of two parcels."

"No more it is."

"No trouble in the world, ma'am," said the obliging Mrs. Ford.

"Oh! but indeed I would much rather have it only in one. Then, if you please, you shall send it all to Mrs. Goddard's—I do not know—No, I think, Miss Woodhouse, I may just as well have it sent to Hartfield, and take it home with me at night. What do you advise?"

"That you do not give another half-second to the subject. To Hartfield, if you please, Mrs. Ford."

"Aye, that will be much best," said Harriet, quite satisfied, "I should not at all like to have it sent to Mrs. Goddard's."

Voices approached the shop—or rather one voice and two ladies: Mrs. Weston and Miss Bates met them at the door.

"My dear Miss Woodhouse," said the latter, "I am just run across to entreat the favour of you to come and sit down with us a little while, and give us your opinion of our new instrument; you and Miss Smith. How do you do, Miss Smith?—Very well I thank you.—And I begged Mrs. Weston to come with me, that I might be sure of succeeding."

"I hope Mrs. Bates and Miss Fairfax are—"

"Very well, I am much obliged to you. My mother is delightfully well; and Jane caught no cold last night. How is Mr. Woodhouse?—I am so glad to hear such a good account. Mrs. Weston told me you were here.—Oh! then, said I, I must run across, I am sure Miss Woodhouse will allow me just to run across and entreat her to come in; my mother will be so very happy to see her—and now we are such a nice party, she cannot refuse.—'Aye, pray do,' said Mr. Frank Churchill, 'Miss Woodhouse's opinion of the instrument will be worth having.'—But, said I, I shall be more sure of succeeding if one of you will go with me.—'Oh,' said he, 'wait half a minute, till I have finished my job;'—For, would you believe it, Miss Woodhouse, there he is, in the most obliging manner in the world, fastening in the rivet of my mother's spectacles.—The rivet came out, you know, this morning.—So very obliging!—For my mother had no use of her spectacles—could not put them on. And, by the bye, every body ought to have two pair of spectacles; they should indeed. Jane said so. I meant to take them over to John Saunders the first thing I did, but something or other hindered me all the morning; first one thing, then another, there is no saying what, you know. At one time Patty came to say she thought the kitchen chimney wanted sweeping. Oh, said I, Patty do not come with your bad news to me. Here is the rivet of your mistress's spectacles out. Then the baked apples came home, Mrs. Wallis sent them by her boy; they are extremely civil and obliging to us, the Wallises, always—I have heard some people say that Mrs. Wallis can be uncivil and give a very rude answer, but we have never known any thing but the greatest attention from them. And it cannot be for the value of our custom now, for what is our consumption of bread, you know? Only three of us.—besides dear Jane at present—and she really eats nothing—makes such a shocking breakfast, you would be quite frightened if you saw it. I dare not let my mother know how little she eats—so I say one thing and then I say another, and it passes off. But about the middle of the day she gets hungry, and there is nothing she likes so well as these baked apples, and they are extremely wholesome, for I took the opportunity the other day of asking Mr. Perry; I happened to meet him in the street. Not that I had any doubt before—I have so often heard Mr. Woodhouse recommend a baked apple. I believe it is the only way that Mr. Woodhouse thinks the fruit thoroughly wholesome. We have apple-dumplings, however, very often. Patty makes an excellent apple-dumpling. Well, Mrs. Weston, you have prevailed, I hope, and these ladies will oblige us."

Emma would be "very happy to wait on Mrs. Bates, etc.," and they did at last move out of the shop, with no farther delay from Miss Bates than,

"How do you do, Mrs. Ford? I beg your pardon. I did not see you before. I hear you have a charming collection of new ribbons from town. Jane came back delighted yesterday. Thank ye, the gloves do very well—only a little too large about the wrist; but Jane is taking them in."

"What was I talking of?" said she, beginning again when they were all in the street.

Emma wondered on what, of all the medley, she would fix.

"I declare I cannot recollect what I was talking of.—Oh! my mother's spectacles. So very obliging of Mr. Frank Churchill! 'Oh!' said he, 'I do think I can fasten the rivet; I like a job of this kind excessively.'—Which you know shewed him to be so very. . . . Indeed I must say that, much as I had heard of him before and much as I had expected, he very far exceeds any thing. . . . I do congratulate you, Mrs. Weston, most warmly. He seems every thing the fondest parent could. . . . 'Oh!' said he, 'I can fasten the rivet. I like a job of that sort excessively.' I never shall forget his manner. And when I brought out the baked apples from the closet, and hoped our friends would be so very obliging as to take some, 'Oh!' said he directly, 'there is nothing in the way of fruit half so good, and these are the finest-looking home-baked apples I ever saw in my life.' That, you know, was so very. . . . And I am sure, by his manner, it was no compliment. Indeed they are very delightful apples, and Mrs. Wallis does them full justice—only we do not have them baked more than twice, and Mr. Woodhouse made us promise to have them done three times—but Miss Woodhouse will be so good as not to mention it. The apples themselves are the very finest sort for baking, beyond a doubt; all from Donwell—some of Mr. Knightley's most liberal supply. He sends us a sack every year; and certainly there never was such a keeping apple anywhere as one of his trees—I believe there is two of them. My mother says the orchard was always famous in her younger days. But I was really quite shocked the other day—for Mr. Knightley called one morning, and Jane was eating these apples, and we talked about them and said how much she enjoyed them, and he asked whether we were not got to the end of our stock. 'I am sure you must be,' said he, 'and I will send you another supply; for I have a great many more than I can ever use. William Larkins let me keep a larger quantity than usual this year. I will send you some more, before they get good for nothing.' So I begged he would not—for really as to ours being gone, I could not absolutely say that we had a great many left—it was but half a dozen indeed; but they should be all kept for Jane; and I could not at all bear that he should be sending us more, so liberal as he had been already; and Jane said the same. And when he was gone, she almost quarrelled with me—No, I should not say quarrelled, for we never had a quarrel in our lives; but she was quite distressed that I had owned the apples were so nearly gone; she wished I had made him believe we had a great many left. Oh, said I, my dear, I did say as much as I could. However, the very same evening William Larkins came over with a large basket of apples, the same sort of apples, a bushel at least, and I was very much obliged, and went down and spoke to William Larkins and said every thing, as you may suppose. William Larkins is such an old acquaintance! I am always glad to see him. But, however, I found afterwards from Patty, that William said it was all the apples of *that* sort his master had; he had brought them all—and now his master had not one left to bake or boil. William did not seem to mind it himself, he was so pleased to think his master had sold so many; for William, you know, thinks more of his master's profit than any thing; but Mrs. Hodges, he said, was quite displeased at their being all sent away. She could not bear that her master should not be able to have another apple-tart this spring. He told Patty this, but bid her not mind it, and be sure not to say any thing to us about it, for Mrs. Hodges *would* be cross sometimes, and as long as so many sacks were sold, it did not signify who ate the remainder. And so Patty told me, and I was excessively shocked indeed! I would not have Mr. Knightley know any thing about it for the world! He would be so very. . . . I wanted to keep it from Jane's knowledge; but, unluckily, I had mentioned it before I was aware."

Miss Bates had just done as Patty opened the door; and her visitors walked upstairs without having any regular narration to attend to, pursued only by the sounds of her desultory good-will.

"Pray take care, Mrs. Weston, there is a step at the turning. Pray take care, Miss Woodhouse, ours is rather a dark staircase—rather darker and narrower than one could wish. Miss Smith, pray take care. Miss Woodhouse, I am quite concerned, I am sure you hit your foot. Miss Smith, the step at the turning."

CHAPTER X

The appearance of the little sitting-room as they entered, was tranquillity itself; Mrs. Bates, deprived of her usual employment, slumbering on one side of the fire, Frank Churchill, at a table near her, most deedily occupied about her spectacles, and Jane Fairfax, standing with her back to them, intent on her pianoforte.

Busy as he was, however, the young man was yet able to shew a most happy countenance on seeing Emma again.

"This is a pleasure," said he, in rather a low voice, "coming at least ten minutes earlier than I had calculated. You find me trying to be useful; tell me if you think I shall succeed."

"What!" said Mrs. Weston, "have not you finished it yet? You would not earn a very good livelihood as a working silversmith at this rate."

"I have not been working uninterruptedly," he replied, "I have been assisting Miss Fairfax in trying to make her instrument stand steadily, it was not quite firm; an unevenness in the floor, I believe. You see we have been wedging one leg with paper. This was very kind of you to be persuaded to come. I was almost afraid you would be hurrying home."

He contrived that she should be seated by him; and was sufficiently employed in looking out the best baked apple for her, and trying to make her help or advise him in his work, till Jane Fairfax was quite ready to sit down to the pianoforte again. That she was not immediately ready, Emma did suspect to arise from the state of her nerves; she had not yet possessed the instrument long enough to touch it without emotion; she must reason herself into the power of performance; and Emma could not but pity such feelings, whatever their origin, and could not but resolve never to expose them to her neighbour again.

At last Jane began, and though the first bars were feebly given, the powers of the instrument were gradually done full justice to. Mrs. Weston had been delighted before, and was delighted again; Emma joined her in all her praise; and the pianoforte, with every proper discrimination, was pronounced to be altogether of the highest promise.

"Whoever Colonel Campbell might employ," said Frank Churchill, with a smile at Emma, "the person has not chosen ill. I heard a good deal of Colonel Campbell's taste at Weymouth; and the softness of the upper notes I am sure is exactly what he and *all that party* would particularly prize. I dare say, Miss Fairfax, that he either gave his friend very minute directions, or wrote to Broadwood himself. Do not you think so?"

Jane did not look round. She was not obliged to hear. Mrs. Weston had been speaking to her at the same moment.

"It is not fair," said Emma, in a whisper; "mine was a random guess. Do not distress her."

He shook his head with a smile, and looked as if he had very little doubt and very little mercy. Soon afterwards he began again,

"How much your friends in Ireland must be enjoying your pleasure on this occasion, Miss Fairfax. I dare say they often think of you, and wonder which will be the day, the precise day of the instrument's coming to hand. Do you imagine Colonel Campbell knows the business to be going forward just at this time?—Do you imagine it to be the consequence of an immediate commission from him, or that he may have sent only a general direction, an order indefinite as to time, to depend upon contingencies and conveniences?"

He paused. She could not but hear; she could not avoid answering,

"Till I have a letter from Colonel Campbell," said she, in a voice of forced calmness, "I can imagine nothing with any confidence. It must be all conjecture."

"Conjecture—aye, sometimes one conjectures right, and sometimes one conjectures wrong. I wish I could conjecture how soon I shall make this rivet quite firm. What nonsense one talks, Miss Woodhouse, when hard at work, if one talks at all;—your real workmen, I suppose, hold their tongues; but we gentlemen labourers if we get hold of a word—Miss Fairfax said something about conjecturing. There, it is done. I have the pleasure, madam, (to Mrs. Bates,) of restoring your spectacles, healed for the present."

He was very warmly thanked both by mother and daughter; to escape a little from the latter, he went to the pianoforte, and begged Miss Fairfax, who was still sitting at it, to play something more.

"If you are very kind," said he, "it will be one of the waltzes we danced last night;—let me live them over again. You did not enjoy them as I did; you appeared tired the whole time. I believe you were glad we danced no longer; but I would have given worlds—all the worlds one ever has to give—for another half-hour."

She played.

"What felicity it is to hear a tune again which *has* made one happy!—If I mistake not that was danced at Weymouth."

She looked up at him for a moment, coloured deeply, and played something else. He took some music from a chair near the pianoforte, and turning to Emma, said,

"Here is something quite new to me. Do you know it?—Cramer.—And here are a new set of Irish melodies. That, from such a quarter, one might expect. This was all sent with the instrument. Very thoughtful of Colonel Campbell, was not it?—He knew Miss Fairfax could have no music here. I honour that part of the attention particularly; it shews it to have been so thoroughly from the heart. Nothing hastily done; nothing incomplete. True affection only could have prompted it."

Emma wished he would be less pointed, yet could not help being amused; and when on glancing her eye towards Jane Fairfax she caught the remains of a smile, when she saw that with all the deep blush of consciousness, there had been a smile of secret delight, she had less scruple in the amusement, and much less compunction with respect to her.—This amiable, upright, perfect Jane Fairfax was apparently cherishing very reprehensible feelings.

He brought all the music to her, and they looked it over together.—Emma took the opportunity of whispering,

"You speak too plain. She must understand you."

"I hope she does. I would have her understand me. I am not in the least ashamed of my meaning."

"But really, I am half ashamed, and wish I had never taken up the idea."

"I am very glad you did, and that you communicated it to me. I have now a key to all her odd looks and ways. Leave shame to her. If she does wrong, she ought to feel it."

"She is not entirely without it, I think."

"I do not see much sign of it. She is playing *Robin Adair* at this moment—*his* favourite."

Shortly afterwards Miss Bates, passing near the window, descried Mr. Knightley on horse-back not far off.

"Mr. Knightley I declare!—I must speak to him if possible, just to thank him. I will not open the window here; it would give you all cold; but I can go into my mother's room you know. I dare say he will come in when he knows who is here. Quite delightful to have you all meet so!—Our little room so honoured!"

She was in the adjoining chamber while she still spoke, and opening the casement there, immediately called Mr. Knightley's attention, and every syllable of their conversation was as distinctly heard by the others, as if it had passed within the same apartment.

"How d'ye do?—how d'ye do?—Very well, I thank you. So obliged to you for the carriage last night. We were just in time; my mother just ready for us. Pray come in; do come in. You will find some friends here."

So began Miss Bates; and Mr. Knightley seemed determined to be heard in his turn, for most resolutely and commandingly did he say,

"How is your niece, Miss Bates?—I want to inquire after you all, but particularly your niece. How is Miss Fairfax?—I hope she caught no cold last night. How is she to-day? Tell me how Miss Fairfax is."

And Miss Bates was obliged to give a direct answer before he would hear her in any thing else. The listeners were amused; and Mrs. Weston gave Emma a look of particular meaning. But Emma still shook her head in steady scepticism.

"So obliged to you!—so very much obliged to you for the carriage," resumed Miss Bates.

He cut her short with,

"I am going to Kingston. Can I do any thing for you?"

"Oh! dear, Kingston—are you?—Mrs. Cole was saying the other day she wanted something from Kingston."

"Mrs. Cole has servants to send. Can I do any thing for *you*?"

"No, I thank you. But do come in. Who do you think is here?—Miss Woodhouse and Miss Smith; so kind as to call to hear the new pianoforte. Do put up your horse at the Crown, and come in."

"Well," said he, in a deliberating manner, "for five minutes, perhaps."

"And here is Mrs. Weston and Mr. Frank Churchill too!—Quite delightful; so many friends!"

"No, not now, I thank you. I could not stay two minutes. I must get on to Kingston as fast as I can."

"Oh! do come in. They will be so very happy to see you."

"No, no; your room is full enough. I will call another day, and hear the pianoforte."

"Well, I am so sorry!—Oh! Mr. Knightley, what a delightful party last night; how extremely pleasant.—Did you ever see such dancing?—Was not it delightful?—Miss Woodhouse and Mr. Frank Churchill; I never saw any thing equal to it."

"Oh! very delightful indeed; I can say nothing less, for I suppose Miss Woodhouse and Mr. Frank Churchill are hearing every thing that passes. And (raising his voice still more) I do not see why Miss Fairfax should not be mentioned too. I think Miss Fairfax dances very well; and Mrs. Weston is the very best country-dance player, without exception, in England. Now, if your friends have any gratitude, they will say something pretty loud about you and me in return; but I cannot stay to hear it."

"Oh! Mr. Knightley, one moment more; something of consequence—so shocked!—Jane and I are both so shocked about the apples!"

"What is the matter now?"

"To think of your sending us all your store apples. You said you had a great many, and now you have not one left. We really are so shocked! Mrs. Hodges may well be angry. William Larkins mentioned it here. You should not have done it, indeed you should not. Ah! he is off. He never can bear to be thanked. But I thought he would have staid now, and it would have been a pity not to have mentioned. . . . Well, (returning to the room,) I have not been able to succeed. Mr. Knightley cannot stop. He is going to Kingston. He asked me if he could do any thing. . . ."

"Yes," said Jane, "we heard his kind offers, we heard every thing."

"Oh! yes, my dear, I dare say you might, because you know, the door was open, and the window was open, and Mr. Knightley spoke loud. You must have heard every thing to be sure. 'Can I do any thing for you at Kingston?' said he; so I just mentioned. . . . Oh! Miss Woodhouse, must you be going?—You seem but just come—so very obliging of you."

Emma found it really time to be at home; the visit had already lasted long; and on examining watches, so much of the morning was perceived to be gone, that Mrs. Weston and her companion taking leave also, could allow themselves only to walk with the two young ladies to Hartfield gates, before they set off for Randalls.

CHAPTER XI

It may be possible to do without dancing entirely. Instances have been known of young people passing many, many months successively, without being at any ball of any description, and no material injury accrue either to body or mind;—but when a beginning is made—when the felicities of rapid motion have once been, though slightly, felt—it must be a very heavy set that does not ask for more.

Frank Churchill had danced once at Highbury, and longed to dance again; and the last half-hour of an evening which Mr. Woodhouse was persuaded to spend with his daughter at Randalls, was passed by the two young people in schemes on the subject. Frank's was the first idea; and his the greatest zeal in pursuing it; for the lady was the best judge of the difficulties, and the most solicitous for accommodation and appearance. But still she had inclination enough for shewing people again how delightfully Mr. Frank Churchill and Miss Woodhouse danced—for doing that in which she need not blush to compare herself with Jane Fairfax—and even for simple dancing itself, without any of the wicked aids of vanity—to assist him first in pacing out the room they were in to see what it could be made to hold—and then in taking the dimensions of the other parlour, in the hope of discovering, in spite of all that Mr. Weston could say of their exactly equal size, that it was a little the largest.

His first proposition and request, that the dance begun at Mr. Cole's should be finished there—that the same party should be collected, and the same musician engaged, met with the readiest acquiescence. Mr. Weston entered into the idea with thorough enjoyment, and Mrs. Weston most willingly undertook to play as long as they could wish to dance; and the interesting employment had followed, of reckoning up exactly who there would be, and portioning out the indispensable division of space to every couple.

"You and Miss Smith, and Miss Fairfax, will be three, and the two Miss Coxes five," had been repeated many times over. "And there will be the two Gilberts, young Cox, my father, and myself, besides Mr. Knightley. Yes, that will be quite enough for pleasure. You and Miss Smith, and Miss Fairfax, will be three, and the two Miss Coxes five; and for five couple there will be plenty of room."

But soon it came to be on one side,

"But will there be good room for five couple?—I really do not think there will."

On another,

"And after all, five couple are not enough to make it worth while to stand up. Five couple are nothing, when one thinks seriously about it. It will not do to *invite* five couple. It can be allowable only as the thought of the moment."

Somebody said that *Miss* Gilbert was expected at her brother's, and must be invited with the rest. Somebody else believed *Mrs.* Gilbert would have danced the other evening, if she had been asked. A word was put in for a second young Cox; and at last, Mr. Weston naming one family of cousins who must be included, and another of very old acquaintance who could not be left out, it became a certainty that the five couple would be at least ten, and a very interesting speculation in what possible manner they could be disposed of.

The doors of the two rooms were just opposite each other. "Might not they use both rooms, and dance across the passage?" It seemed the best scheme; and yet it was not so good but that many of them wanted a better. Emma said it would be awkward; Mrs. Weston was in distress about the supper; and Mr. Woodhouse opposed it earnestly, on the score of health. It made him so very unhappy, indeed, that it could not be persevered in.

"Oh! no," said he; "it would be the extreme of imprudence. I could not bear it for Emma!—Emma is not strong. She would catch a dreadful cold. So would poor little Harriet. So you would all. Mrs. Weston, you would be quite laid up; do not let them talk of such a wild thing. Pray do not let them talk of it. That young man (speaking lower) is very thoughtless. Do not tell his father, but that young man is not quite the thing. He has been opening the doors very often this evening, and keeping them open very inconsiderately. He does not think of the draught. I do not mean to set you against him, but indeed he is not quite the thing!"

Mrs. Weston was sorry for such a charge. She knew the importance of it, and said every thing in her power to do it away. Every door was now closed, the passage plan given up, and the first scheme of dancing only in the room they were in resorted to again; and with such good-will on Frank Churchill's part, that the space which a quarter of an hour before had been deemed barely sufficient for five couple, was now endeavoured to be made out quite enough for ten.

"We were too magnificent," said he. "We allowed unnecessary room. Ten couple may stand here very well."

Emma demurred. "It would be a crowd—a sad crowd; and what could be worse than dancing without space to turn in?"

"Very true," he gravely replied; "it was very bad." But still he went on measuring, and still he ended with,

"I think there will be very tolerable room for ten couple."

"No, no," said she, "you are quite unreasonable. It would be dreadful to be standing so close! Nothing can be farther from pleasure than to be dancing in a crowd—and a crowd in a little room!"

"There is no denying it," he replied. "I agree with you exactly. A crowd in a little room—Miss Woodhouse, you have the art of giving pictures in a few words. Exquisite, quite exquisite!—Still, however, having proceeded so far, one is unwilling to give the matter up. It would be a disappointment to my father—and altogether—I do not know that—I am rather of opinion that ten couple might stand here very well."

Emma perceived that the nature of his gallantry was a little self-willed, and that he would rather oppose than lose the pleasure of dancing with her; but she took the compliment, and forgave the rest. Had she intended ever to *marry* him, it might have been worth while to pause and consider, and try to understand the value of his preference, and the character of his temper; but for all the purposes of their acquaintance, he was quite amiable enough.

Before the middle of the next day, he was at Hartfield; and he entered the room with such an agreeable smile as certified the continuance of the scheme. It soon appeared that he came to announce an improvement.

"Well, Miss Woodhouse," he almost immediately began, "your inclination for dancing has not been quite frightened away, I hope, by the terrors of my father's little rooms. I bring a new proposal on the subject:—a thought of my father's, which waits only your approbation to be acted upon. May I hope for the honour of your hand for the two first dances of this little projected ball, to be given, not at Randalls, but at the Crown Inn?"

"The Crown!"

"Yes; if you and Mr. Woodhouse see no objection, and I trust you cannot, my father hopes his friends will be so kind as to visit him there. Better accommodations, he can promise them, and not a less grateful welcome than at Randalls. It is his own idea. Mrs. Weston sees no objection to it, provided you are satisfied. This is what we all feel. Oh! you were perfectly right! Ten couple, in either of the Randalls rooms, would have been insufferable!—Dreadful!—I felt how right you were the whole time, but was too anxious for securing *any thing* to like to yield. Is not it a good exchange?—You consent—I hope you consent?"

"It appears to me a plan that nobody can object to, if Mr. and Mrs. Weston do not. I think it admirable; and, as far as I can answer for myself, shall be most happy—It seems the only improvement that could be. Papa, do you not think it an excellent improvement?"

She was obliged to repeat and explain it, before it was fully comprehended; and then, being quite new, farther representations were necessary to make it acceptable.

"No; he thought it very far from an improvement—a very bad plan—much worse than the other. A room at an inn was always damp and dangerous; never properly aired, or fit to be inhabited. If they must dance, they had better dance at Randalls. He had never been in the room at the Crown in his life—did not know the people who kept it by sight.—Oh! no—a very bad plan. They would catch worse colds at the Crown than anywhere."

"I was going to observe, sir," said Frank Churchill, "that one of the great recommendations of this change would be the very little danger of any body's catching cold—so much less danger at the Crown than at Randalls! Mr. Perry might have reason to regret the alteration, but nobody else could."

"Sir," said Mr. Woodhouse, rather warmly, "you are very much mistaken if you suppose Mr. Perry to be that sort of character. Mr. Perry is extremely concerned when any of us are ill. But I do not understand how the room at the Crown can be safer for you than your father's house."

"From the very circumstance of its being larger, sir. We shall have no occasion to open the windows at all—not once the whole evening; and it is that dreadful habit of opening the windows, letting in cold air upon heated bodies, which (as you well know, sir) does the mischief."

"Open the windows!—but surely, Mr. Churchill, nobody would think of opening the windows at Randalls. Nobody could be so imprudent! I never heard of such a thing. Dancing with open windows!—I am sure, neither your father nor Mrs. Weston (poor Miss Taylor that was) would suffer it."

"Ah! sir—but a thoughtless young person will sometimes step behind a window-curtain, and throw up a sash, without its being suspected. I have often known it done myself."

"Have you indeed, sir?—Bless me! I never could have supposed it. But I live out of the world, and am often astonished at what I hear. However, this does make a difference; and, perhaps, when we come to talk it over—but these sort of things require a good deal of consideration. One cannot resolve upon them in a hurry. If Mr. and Mrs. Weston will be so obliging as to call here one morning, we may talk it over, and see what can be done."

"But, unfortunately, sir, my time is so limited—"

"Oh!" interrupted Emma, "there will be plenty of time for talking every thing over. There is no hurry at all. If it can be contrived to be at the Crown, papa, it will be very convenient for the horses. They will be so near their own stable."

"So they will, my dear. That is a great thing. Not that James ever complains; but it is right to spare our horses when we can. If I could be sure of the rooms being thoroughly aired—but is Mrs. Stokes to be trusted? I doubt it. I do not know her, even by sight."

"I can answer for every thing of that nature, sir, because it will be under Mrs. Weston's care. Mrs. Weston undertakes to direct the whole."

"There, papa!—Now you must be satisfied—Our own dear Mrs. Weston, who is carefulness itself. Do not you remember what Mr. Perry said, so many years ago, when I had the measles? 'If *Miss Taylor* undertakes to wrap Miss Emma up, you need not have any fears, sir.' How often have I heard you speak of it as such a compliment to her!"

"Aye, very true. Mr. Perry did say so. I shall never forget it. Poor little Emma! You were very bad with the measles; that is, you would have been very bad, but for Perry's great attention. He came four times a day for a week. He said, from the first, it was a very good sort—which was our great comfort; but the measles are a dreadful complaint. I hope whenever poor Isabella's little ones have the measles, she will send for Perry."

"My father and Mrs. Weston are at the Crown at this moment," said Frank Churchill, "examining the capabilities of the house. I left them there and came on to Hartfield, impatient for your opinion, and hoping you might be persuaded to join them and give your advice on the spot. I was desired to say so from both. It would be the greatest pleasure to them, if you could allow me to attend you there. They can do nothing satisfactorily without you."

Emma was most happy to be called to such a council; and, her father engaging to think it all over while she was gone, the two young people set off together without delay for the Crown. There were Mr. and Mrs. Weston; delighted to see her and receive her approbation, very busy and very happy in their different way; she, in some little distress; and he, finding every thing perfect.

"Emma," said she, "this paper is worse than I expected. Look! in places you see it is dreadfully dirty; and the wainscot is more yellow and forlorn than any thing I could have imagined."

"My dear, you are too particular," said her husband. "What does all that signify? You will see nothing of it by candlelight. It will be as clean as Randalls by candlelight. We never see any thing of it on our club-nights."

The ladies here probably exchanged looks which meant, "Men never know when things are dirty or not;" and the gentlemen perhaps thought each to himself, "Women will have their little nonsenses and needless cares."

One perplexity, however, arose, which the gentlemen did not disdain. It regarded a supper-room. At the time of the ballroom's being built, suppers had not been in question; and a small card-room adjoining, was the only addition. What was to be done? This card-room would be wanted as a card-room now; or, if cards were conveniently voted unnecessary by their four selves, still was it not too small for any comfortable supper? Another room of much better size might be secured for the purpose; but it was at the other end of the house, and a long awkward passage must be gone through to get at it. This made a difficulty. Mrs. Weston was afraid of draughts for the young people in that passage; and neither Emma nor the gentlemen could tolerate the prospect of being miserably crowded at supper.

Mrs. Weston proposed having no regular supper; merely sandwiches, etc., set out in the little room; but that was scouted as a wretched suggestion. A private dance, without sitting down to supper, was pronounced an infamous fraud upon the rights of men and women;

and Mrs. Weston must not speak of it again. She then took another line of expediency, and looking into the doubtful room, observed,

"I do not think it *is* so very small. We shall not be many, you know."

And Mr. Weston at the same time, walking briskly with long steps through the passage, was calling out,

"You talk a great deal of the length of this passage, my dear. It is a mere nothing after all; and not the least draught from the stairs."

"I wish," said Mrs. Weston, "one could know which arrangement our guests in general would like best. To do what would be most generally pleasing must be our object—if one could but tell what that would be."

"Yes, very true," cried Frank, "very true. You want your neighbours' opinions. I do not wonder at you. If one could ascertain what the chief of them—the Coles, for instance. They are not far off. Shall I call upon them? Or Miss Bates? She is still nearer.—And I do not know whether Miss Bates is not as likely to understand the inclinations of the rest of the people as any body. I think we do want a larger council. Suppose I go and invite Miss Bates to join us?"

"Well—if you please," said Mrs. Weston rather hesitating, "if you think she will be of any use."

"You will get nothing to the purpose from Miss Bates," said Emma. "She will be all delight and gratitude, but she will tell you nothing. She will not even listen to your questions. I see no advantage in consulting Miss Bates."

"But she is so amusing, so extremely amusing! I am very fond of hearing Miss Bates talk. And I need not bring the whole family, you know."

Here Mr. Weston joined them, and on hearing what was proposed, gave it his decided approbation.

"Aye, do, Frank.—Go and fetch Miss Bates, and let us end the matter at once. She will enjoy the scheme, I am sure; and I do not know a properer person for shewing us how to do away difficulties. Fetch Miss Bates. We are growing a little too nice. She is a standing lesson of how to be happy. But fetch them both. Invite them both."

"Both sir! Can the old lady?" . . .

"The old lady! No, the young lady, to be sure. I shall think you a great blockhead, Frank, if you bring the aunt without the niece."

"Oh! I beg your pardon, sir. I did not immediately recollect.

Undoubtedly if you wish it, I will endeavour to persuade them both." And away he ran.

Long before he reappeared, attending the short, neat, brisk-moving aunt, and her elegant niece,—Mrs. Weston, like a sweet-tempered woman and a good wife, had examined the passage again, and found the evils of it much less than she had supposed before—indeed very trifling; and here ended the difficulties of decision. All the rest, in speculation at least, was perfectly smooth. All the minor arrangements of table and chair, lights and music, tea and supper, made themselves; or were left as mere trifles to be settled at any time between Mrs. Weston and Mrs. Stokes.—Every body invited, was certainly to come; Frank had already written to Enscombe to propose staying a few days beyond his fortnight, which could not possibly be refused. And a delightful dance it was to be.

Most cordially, when Miss Bates arrived, did she agree that it must. As a counsellor she was not wanted; but as an approver, (a much safer character) she was truly welcome. Her approbation, at once general and minute, warm and incessant, could not but please; and for another half-hour they were all walking to and fro, between the different rooms, some suggesting, some attending, and all in happy enjoyment of the future. The party did not break up without Emma's being positively secured for the two first dances by the hero of the evening, nor without her overhearing Mr. Weston whisper to his wife, "He has asked her, my dear. That's right. I knew he would!"

CHAPTER XII

One thing only was wanting to make the prospect of the ball completely satisfactory to Emma—its being fixed for a day within the granted term of Frank Churchill's stay in Surry; for, in spite of Mr. Weston's confidence, she could not think it so very impossible that the Churchills might not allow their nephew to remain a day beyond his fortnight. But this was not judged feasible. The preparations must take their time, nothing could be properly ready till the third week were entered on, and for a few days they must be planning, proceeding and hoping in uncertainty—at the risk—in her opinion, the great risk, of its being all in vain.

Enscombe however was gracious, gracious in fact, if not in word. His wish of staying longer evidently did not please; but it was not opposed. All was safe and prosperous; and as the removal of one solicitude generally makes way for another, Emma, being now certain of her ball, began to adopt as the next vexation Mr. Knightley's provoking indifference about it. Either because he did not dance himself, or because the plan had been formed without his being consulted, he seemed resolved that it should not interest him, determined against its exciting any present curiosity, or affording him any future amusement. To her voluntary communications Emma could get no more approving reply, than,

"Very well. If the Westons think it worth while to be at all this trouble for a few hours of noisy entertainment, I have nothing to say against it, but that they shall not chuse pleasures for me.—Oh! yes, I must be there; I could not refuse; and I will keep as much awake as I can; but I would rather be at home, looking over William Larkins's week's account; much rather, I confess.—Pleasure in seeing dancing!—not I, indeed—I never look at it—I do not know who does.—Fine dancing, I believe, like virtue, must be its own reward. Those who are standing by are usually thinking of something very different."

This Emma felt was aimed at her; and it made her quite angry. It was not in compliment to Jane Fairfax however that he was so indifferent, or so indignant; he was not guided by *her* feelings in reprobating the ball, for *she* enjoyed the thought of it to an extraordinary degree. It made her animated—open hearted—she voluntarily said;—

"Oh! Miss Woodhouse, I hope nothing may happen to prevent the ball. What a disappointment it would be! I do look forward to it, I own, with *very* great pleasure."

It was not to oblige Jane Fairfax therefore that he would have preferred the society of William Larkins. No!—she was more and more convinced that Mrs. Weston was quite mistaken in that surmise. There was a great deal of friendly and of compassionate attachment on his side—but no love.

Alas! there was soon no leisure for quarrelling with Mr. Knightley. Two days of joyful security were immediately followed by the overthrow of every thing. A letter arrived from Mr. Churchill to urge his nephew's instant return. Mrs. Churchill was unwell—far too unwell to do without him; she had been in a very suffering state (so said her husband) when writing to her nephew two days before, though from her usual unwillingness to give pain, and constant habit of never thinking of herself, she had not mentioned it; but now she was too ill to trifle, and must entreat him to set off for Enscombe without delay.

The substance of this letter was forwarded to Emma, in a note from Mrs. Weston, instantly. As to his going, it was inevitable. He must be gone within a few hours, though without feeling any real alarm for his aunt, to lessen his repugnance. He knew her illnesses; they never occurred but for her own convenience.

Mrs. Weston added, "that he could only allow himself time to hurry to Highbury, after breakfast, and take leave of the few friends there whom he could suppose to feel any interest in him; and that he might be expected at Hartfield very soon."

This wretched note was the finale of Emma's breakfast. When once it had been read, there was no doing any thing, but lament and exclaim. The loss of the ball—the loss of the young man—and all that the young man might be feeling!—It was too wretched!—Such a delightful evening as it would have been!—Every body so happy! and she and her partner the happiest!—"I said it would be so," was the only consolation.

Her father's feelings were quite distinct. He thought principally of Mrs. Churchill's illness, and wanted to know how she was treated; and as for the ball, it was shocking to have dear Emma disappointed; but they would all be safer at home.

Emma was ready for her visitor some time before he appeared; but if this reflected at all upon his impatience, his sorrowful look and total want of spirits when he did come might redeem him. He felt the going away almost too much to speak of it. His dejection was most evident. He sat really lost in thought for the first few minutes; and when rousing himself, it was only to say,

"Of all horrid things, leave-taking is the worst."

"But you will come again," said Emma. "This will not be your only visit to Randalls."

"Ah!—(shaking his head)—the uncertainty of when I may be able to return!—I shall try for it with a zeal!—It will be the object of all my thoughts and cares!—and if my uncle and aunt go to town this spring—but I am afraid—they did not stir last spring—I am afraid it is a custom gone for ever."

"Our poor ball must be quite given up."

"Ah! that ball!—why did we wait for any thing?—why not seize the pleasure at once?—How often is happiness destroyed by preparation, foolish preparation!—You told us it would be so.—Oh! Miss Woodhouse, why are you always so right?"

"Indeed, I am very sorry to be right in this instance. I would much rather have been merry than wise."

"If I can come again, we are still to have our ball. My father depends on it. Do not forget your engagement."

Emma looked graciously.

"Such a fortnight as it has been!" he continued; "every day more precious and more delightful than the day before!—every day making me less fit to bear any other place. Happy those, who can remain at Highbury!"

"As you do us such ample justice now," said Emma, laughing, "I will venture to ask, whether you did not come a little doubtfully at first? Do not we rather surpass your expectations? I am sure we do. I am sure you did not much expect to like us. You would not have been so long in coming, if you had had a pleasant idea of Highbury."

He laughed rather consciously; and though denying the sentiment, Emma was convinced that it had been so.

"And you must be off this very morning?"

"Yes; my father is to join me here: we shall walk back together, and I must be off immediately. I am almost afraid that every moment will bring him."

"Not five minutes to spare even for your friends Miss Fairfax and Miss Bates? How unlucky! Miss Bates's powerful, argumentative mind might have strengthened yours."

"Yes—I *have* called there; passing the door, I thought it better. It was a right thing to do. I went in for three minutes, and was detained by Miss Bates's being absent. She was out; and I felt it impossible not to wait till she came in. She is a woman that one may, that one *must* laugh at; but that one would not wish to slight. It was better to pay my visit, then"—

He hesitated, got up, walked to a window.

"In short," said he, "perhaps, Miss Woodhouse—I think you can hardly be quite without suspicion"—

He looked at her, as if wanting to read her thoughts. She hardly knew what to say. It seemed like the forerunner of something absolutely serious, which she did not wish. Forcing herself to speak, therefore, in the hope of putting it by, she calmly said,

"You are quite in the right; it was most natural to pay your visit, then"—

He was silent. She believed he was looking at her; probably reflecting on what she had said, and trying to understand the manner. She heard him sigh. It was natural for him to feel that he had *cause* to sigh. He could not believe her to be encouraging him. A few awkward moments passed, and he sat down again; and in a more determined manner said,

"It was something to feel that all the rest of my time might be given to Hartfield. My regard for Hartfield is most warm"—

He stopt again, rose again, and seemed quite embarrassed.—He was more in love with her than Emma had supposed; and who can say how it might have ended, if his father had not made his appearance? Mr. Woodhouse soon followed; and the necessity of exertion made him composed.

A very few minutes more, however, completed the present trial. Mr. Weston, always alert when business was to be done, and as incapable of procrastinating any evil that was inevitable, as of foreseeing any that was doubtful, said, "It was time to go;" and the young man, though he might and did sigh, could not but agree, to take leave.

"I shall hear about you all," said he; "that is my chief consolation. I shall hear of every thing that is going on among you. I have engaged Mrs. Weston to correspond with me. She has been so kind as to promise it. Oh! the blessing of a female correspondent, when one is really interested in the absent!—she will tell me every thing. In her letters I shall be at dear Highbury again."

A very friendly shake of the hand, a very earnest "Good-bye," closed the speech, and the door had soon shut out Frank Churchill. Short had been the notice—short their meeting; he was gone; and Emma felt so sorry to part, and foresaw so great a loss to their little society from his absence as to begin to be afraid of being too sorry, and feeling it too much.

It was a sad change. They had been meeting almost every day since his arrival. Certainly his being at Randalls had given great spirit to the last two weeks—indescribable spirit; the idea, the expectation of seeing him which every morning had brought, the assurance of his attentions, his liveliness, his manners! It had been a very happy fortnight, and forlorn must be the sinking from it into the common course of Hartfield days. To complete every other recommendation, he had *almost* told her that he loved her. What strength, or what constancy of affection he might be subject to, was another point; but at present she could not doubt his having a decidedly warm admiration, a conscious preference of herself; and this persuasion, joined to all the rest, made her think that she *must* be a little in love with him, in spite of every previous determination against it.

"I certainly must," said she. "This sensation of listlessness, weariness, stupidity, this disinclination to sit down and employ myself, this feeling of every thing's being dull and insipid about the house!—I must be in love; I should be the oddest creature in the world if I were not—for a few weeks at least. Well! evil to some is always good to others. I shall have many fellow-mourners for the ball, if not for Frank Churchill; but Mr. Knightley will be happy. He may spend the evening with his dear William Larkins now if he likes."

Mr. Knightley, however, shewed no triumphant happiness. He could not say that he was sorry on his own account; his very cheerful look would have contradicted him if he had; but he said, and very steadily, that he was sorry for the disappointment of the others, and with considerable kindness added,

"You, Emma, who have so few opportunities of dancing, you are really out of luck; you are very much out of luck!"

It was some days before she saw Jane Fairfax, to judge of her honest regret in this woeful change; but when they did meet, her composure was odious. She had been particularly unwell, however, suffering from headache to a degree, which made her aunt declare, that had the ball taken place, she did not think Jane could have attended it; and it was charity to impute some of her unbecoming indifference to the languor of ill-health.

CHAPTER XIII

Emma continued to entertain no doubt of her being in love. Her ideas only varied as to the how much. At first, she thought it was a good deal; and afterwards, but little. She had great pleasure in hearing Frank Churchill talked of; and, for his sake, greater pleasure than ever in seeing Mr. and Mrs. Weston; she was very often thinking of him, and quite impatient for a letter, that she might know how he was, how were his spirits, how was his aunt, and what was the chance of his coming to Randalls again this spring. But, on the other hand, she could not admit herself to be unhappy, nor, after the first morning, to be less disposed for employment than usual; she was still busy and cheerful; and, pleasing as he was, she could yet imagine him to have faults; and farther, though thinking of him so much, and, as she sat drawing or working, forming a thousand amusing schemes for the progress and close of their attachment, fancying interesting dialogues, and inventing elegant letters; the conclusion of every imaginary declaration on his side was that she *refused him*. Their affection was always to subside into friendship. Every thing tender and charming was to mark their parting; but still they were to part. When she became sensible of this, it struck her that she could not be very much in love; for in spite of her previous and fixed determination never to quit her father, never to marry, a strong attachment certainly must produce more of a struggle than she could foresee in her own feelings.

"I do not find myself making any use of the word *sacrifice*," said she.—"In not one of all my clever replies, my delicate negatives, is there any allusion to making a sacrifice. I do suspect that he is not really necessary to my happiness. So much the better. I certainly will not persuade myself to feel more than I do. I am quite enough in love. I should be sorry to be more."

Upon the whole, she was equally contented with her view of his feelings.

"*He* is undoubtedly very much in love—every thing denotes it—very much in love indeed!—and when he comes again, if his affection continue, I must be on my guard not to encourage it.—It would be most inexcusable to do otherwise, as my own mind is quite made up. Not that

I imagine he can think I have been encouraging him hitherto. No, if he had believed me at all to share his feelings, he would not have been so wretched. Could he have thought himself encouraged, his looks and language at parting would have been different.—Still, however, I must be on my guard. This is in the supposition of his attachment continuing what it now is; but I do not know that I expect it will; I do not look upon him to be quite the sort of man—I do not altogether build upon his steadiness or constancy.—His feelings are warm, but I can imagine them rather changeable.—Every consideration of the subject, in short, makes me thankful that my happiness is not more deeply involved.—I shall do very well again after a little while—and then, it will be a good thing over; for they say every body is in love once in their lives, and I shall have been let off easily."

When his letter to Mrs. Weston arrived, Emma had the perusal of it; and she read it with a degree of pleasure and admiration which made her at first shake her head over her own sensations, and think she had undervalued their strength. It was a long, well-written letter, giving the particulars of his journey and of his feelings, expressing all the affection, gratitude, and respect which was natural and honourable, and describing every thing exterior and local that could be supposed attractive, with spirit and precision. No suspicious flourishes now of apology or concern; it was the language of real feeling towards Mrs. Weston; and the transition from Highbury to Enscombe, the contrast between the places in some of the first blessings of social life was just enough touched on to shew how keenly it was felt, and how much more might have been said but for the restraints of propriety.—The charm of her own name was not wanting. *Miss Woodhouse* appeared more than once, and never without a something of pleasing connexion, either a compliment to her taste, or a remembrance of what she had said; and in the very last time of its meeting her eye, unadorned as it was by any such broad wreath of gallantry, she yet could discern the effect of her influence and acknowledge the greatest compliment perhaps of all conveyed. Compressed into the very lowest vacant corner were these words—"I had not a spare moment on Tuesday, as you know, for Miss Woodhouse's beautiful little friend. Pray make my excuses and adieus to her." This, Emma could not doubt, was all for herself. Harriet was remembered only from being *her* friend. His information and prospects as to Enscombe were neither worse nor better than had been anticipated; Mrs. Churchill was recovering, and he dared not yet, even in his own imagination, fix a time for coming to Randalls again.

Gratifying, however, and stimulative as was the letter in the material part, its sentiments, she yet found, when it was folded up and returned to Mrs. Weston, that it had not added any lasting warmth, that she could still do without the writer, and that he must learn to do without her. Her intentions were unchanged. Her resolution of refusal only grew more interesting by the addition of a scheme for his subsequent consolation and happiness. His recollection of Harriet, and the words which clothed it, the "beautiful little friend," suggested to her the idea of Harriet's succeeding her in his affections. Was it impossible?—No.—Harriet undoubtedly was greatly his inferior in understanding; but he had been very much struck with the loveliness of her face and the warm simplicity of her manner; and all the probabilities of circumstance and connexion were in her favour.—For Harriet, it would be advantageous and delightful indeed.

"I must not dwell upon it," said she.—"I must not think of it. I know the danger of indulging such speculations. But stranger things have happened; and when we cease to care for each other as we do now, it will be the means of confirming us in that sort of true disinterested friendship which I can already look forward to with pleasure."

It was well to have a comfort in store on Harriet's behalf, though it might be wise to let the fancy touch it seldom; for evil in that quarter was at hand. As Frank Churchill's arrival had succeeded Mr. Elton's engagement in the conversation of Highbury, as the latest interest had entirely borne down the first, so now upon Frank Churchill's disappearance, Mr. Elton's concerns were assuming the most irresistible form.—His wedding-day was named. He would soon be among them again; Mr. Elton and his bride. There was hardly time to talk over the first letter from Enscombe before "Mr. Elton and his bride" was in every body's mouth, and Frank Churchill was forgotten. Emma grew sick at the sound. She had had three weeks of happy exemption from Mr. Elton; and Harriet's mind, she had been willing to hope, had been lately gaining strength. With Mr. Weston's ball in view at least, there had been a great deal of insensibility to other things; but it was now too evident that she had not attained such a state of composure as could stand against the actual approach—new carriage, bell-ringing, and all.

Poor Harriet was in a flutter of spirits which required all the reasonings and soothings and attentions of every kind that Emma could give. Emma felt that she could not do too much for her, that Harriet had a right to all her ingenuity and all her patience; but it was heavy work to be for ever convincing without producing any effect, for ever agreed to, without being able to make their opinions the same. Harriet listened submissively, and said "it was very true—it was just as Miss Woodhouse described—it was not worth while to think about them—and she would not think about them any longer," but no change of subject could avail, and the next half-hour saw her as anxious and restless about the Eltons as before. At last Emma attacked her on another ground.

"Your allowing yourself to be so occupied and so unhappy about Mr. Elton's marrying, Harriet, is the strongest reproach you can make *me*. You could not give me a greater reproof for the mistake I fell into. It was all my doing, I know. I have not forgotten it, I assure you.—Deceived myself, I did very miserably deceive you—and it will be a painful reflection to me for ever. Do not imagine me in danger of forgetting it."

Harriet felt this too much to utter more than a few words of eager exclamation. Emma continued,

"I have not said, exert yourself Harriet for my sake; think less, talk less of Mr. Elton for my sake; because for your own sake rather, I would wish it to be done, for the sake of what is more important than my comfort, a habit of self-command in you, a consideration of what is your duty, an attention to propriety, an endeavour to avoid the suspicions of others, to save your health and credit, and restore your tranquillity. These are the motives which I have been pressing on you. They are very important—and sorry I am that you cannot feel them sufficiently to act upon them. My being saved from pain is a very secondary consideration. I want you to save yourself from greater pain. Perhaps I may sometimes have felt that Harriet would not forget what was due—or rather what would be kind by me."

This appeal to her affections did more than all the rest. The idea of wanting gratitude and consideration for Miss Woodhouse, whom she really loved extremely, made her wretched for a while, and when the violence of grief was comforted away, still remained powerful enough to prompt to what was right and support her in it very tolerably.

"You, who have been the best friend I ever had in my life—Want gratitude to you!—Nobody is equal to you!—I care for nobody as I do for you!—Oh! Miss Woodhouse, how ungrateful I have been!"

Such expressions, assisted as they were by every thing that look and manner could do, made Emma feel that she had never loved Harriet so well, nor valued her affection so highly before.

"There is no charm equal to tenderness of heart," said she afterwards to herself. "There is nothing to be compared to it. Warmth and tenderness of heart, with an affectionate, open manner, will beat all the clearness of head in the world, for attraction, I am sure it will. It is tenderness of heart which makes my dear father so generally beloved—which gives Isabella all her popularity.—I have it not—but I know how to prize and respect it.—Harriet is my superior in all the charm and all the felicity it gives. Dear Harriet!—I would not change you for the clearest-headed, longest-sighted, best-judging female breathing. Oh! the coldness of a Jane Fairfax!—Harriet is worth a hundred such—And for a wife—a sensible man's wife—it is invaluable. I mention no names; but happy the man who changes Emma for Harriet!"

CHAPTER XIV

Mrs. Elton was first seen at church: but though devotion might be interrupted, curiosity could not be satisfied by a bride in a pew, and it must be left for the visits in form which were then to be paid, to settle whether she were very pretty indeed, or only rather pretty, or not pretty at all.

Emma had feelings, less of curiosity than of pride or propriety, to make her resolve on not being the last to pay her respects; and she made a point of Harriet's going with her, that the worst of the business might be gone through as soon as possible.

She could not enter the house again, could not be in the same room to which she had with such vain artifice retreated three months ago, to lace up her boot, without *recollecting*. A thousand vexatious thoughts would recur. Compliments, charades, and horrible blunders; and it was not to be supposed that poor Harriet should not be recollecting too; but she behaved very well, and was only rather pale and silent. The visit was of course short; and there was so much embarrassment and occupation of mind to shorten it, that Emma would not allow herself entirely to form an opinion of the lady, and on no account to give one, beyond the nothing-meaning terms of being "elegantly dressed, and very pleasing."

She did not really like her. She would not be in a hurry to find fault, but she suspected that there was no elegance;—ease, but not elegance.—She was almost sure that for a young woman, a stranger, a bride, there was too much ease. Her person was rather good; her face not unpretty; but neither feature, nor air, nor voice, nor manner, were elegant. Emma thought at least it would turn out so.

As for Mr. Elton, his manners did not appear—but no, she would not permit a hasty or a witty word from herself about his manners. It was an awkward ceremony at any time to be receiving wedding visits, and a man had need be all grace to acquit himself well through it. The woman was better off; she might have the assistance of fine clothes, and the privilege of bashfulness, but the man had only his own good sense to depend on; and when she considered how peculiarly unlucky poor Mr. Elton was in being in the same room at once with the woman he had just married, the woman he had wanted to marry, and the woman whom he had been expected to marry, she must allow him to have the right to look as little wise, and to be as much affectedly, and as little really easy as could be.

"Well, Miss Woodhouse," said Harriet, when they had quitted the house, and after waiting in vain for her friend to begin; "Well, Miss Woodhouse, (with a gentle sigh) what do you think of her?—Is not she very charming?"

There was a little hesitation in Emma's answer.

"Oh! yes—very—a very pleasing young woman."

"I think her beautiful, quite beautiful."

"Very nicely dressed, indeed; a remarkably elegant gown."

"I am not at all surprized that he should have fallen in love."

"Oh! no—there is nothing to surprize one at all.—A pretty fortune; and she came in his way."

"I dare say," returned Harriet, sighing again, "I dare say she was very much attached to him."

"Perhaps she might; but it is not every man's fate to marry the woman who loves him best. Miss Hawkins perhaps wanted a home, and thought this the best offer she was likely to have."

"Yes," said Harriet earnestly, "and well she might, nobody could ever have a better. Well, I wish them happy with all my heart. And now, Miss Woodhouse, I do not think I shall mind seeing them again. He is just as superior as ever;—but being married, you know, it is quite a different thing. No, indeed, Miss Woodhouse, you need not be afraid; I can sit and admire him now without any great misery. To know that he has not thrown himself away, is such a comfort!—She does seem a charming young woman, just what he deserves. Happy creature! He called her 'Augusta.' How delightful!"

When the visit was returned, Emma made up her mind. She could then see more and judge better. From Harriet's happening not to be at Hartfield, and her father's being present to engage Mr. Elton, she had a quarter of an hour of the lady's conversation to herself, and could composedly attend to her; and the quarter of an hour quite convinced her that Mrs. Elton was a vain woman, extremely well satisfied with herself, and thinking much of her own importance; that she meant to shine and be very superior, but with manners which had been formed in a bad school, pert and familiar; that all her notions were drawn from one set of people, and one style of living; that if not foolish she was ignorant, and that her society would certainly do Mr. Elton no good.

Harriet would have been a better match. If not wise or refined herself, she would have connected him with those who were; but Miss Hawkins, it might be fairly supposed from her easy conceit, had been the best of her own set. The rich brother-in-law near Bristol was the pride of the alliance, and his place and his carriages were the pride of him.

The very first subject after being seated was Maple Grove, "My brother Mr. Suckling's seat;"—a comparison of Hartfield to Maple Grove. The grounds of Hartfield were small, but neat and pretty; and the house was modern and well-built. Mrs. Elton seemed most favourably impressed by the size of the room, the entrance, and all that she could see or imagine. "Very like Maple Grove indeed!—She was quite struck by the likeness!—That room was the very shape and size of the morning-room at Maple Grove; her sister's favourite room."—Mr. Elton was appealed to.—"Was not it astonishingly like?—She could really almost fancy herself at Maple Grove."

"And the staircase—You know, as I came in, I observed how very like the staircase was; placed exactly in the same part of the house. I really could not help exclaiming! I assure you, Miss Woodhouse, it is very delightful to me, to be reminded of a place I am so extremely partial to as Maple Grove. I have spent so many happy months there! (with a little sigh of sentiment). A charming place, undoubtedly. Every body who sees it is struck by its beauty; but to me, it has been quite a home. Whenever you are transplanted, like me, Miss Woodhouse, you will understand how very delightful it is to meet with any thing at all like what one has left behind. I always say this is quite one of the evils of matrimony."

Emma made as slight a reply as she could; but it was fully sufficient for Mrs. Elton, who only wanted to be talking herself.

"So extremely like Maple Grove! And it is not merely the house—the grounds, I assure you, as far as I could observe, are strikingly like. The laurels at Maple Grove are in the same profusion as here, and stand very much in the same way—just across the lawn; and I had a glimpse of a fine large tree, with a bench round it, which put me so exactly in mind! My brother and sister will be enchanted with this place. People who have extensive grounds themselves are always pleased with any thing in the same style."

Emma doubted the truth of this sentiment. She had a great idea that people who had extensive grounds themselves cared very little for the extensive grounds of any body else; but it was not worth while to attack an error so double-dyed, and therefore only said in reply,

"When you have seen more of this country, I am afraid you will think you have overrated Hartfield. Surry is full of beauties."

"Oh! yes, I am quite aware of that. It is the garden of England, you know. Surry is the garden of England."

"Yes; but we must not rest our claims on that distinction. Many counties, I believe, are called the garden of England, as well as Surry."

"No, I fancy not," replied Mrs. Elton, with a most satisfied smile. "I never heard any county but Surry called so."

Emma was silenced.

"My brother and sister have promised us a visit in the spring, or summer at farthest," continued Mrs. Elton; "and that will be our time for exploring. While they are with us, we shall explore a great deal, I dare say. They will have their barouche-landau, of course, which holds four perfectly; and therefore, without saying any thing of *our* carriage, we should be able to explore the different beauties extremely well. They would hardly come in their chaise, I think, at that season of the year. Indeed, when the time draws on, I shall decidedly recommend their bringing the barouche-landau; it will be so very much preferable. When people come into a beautiful country of this sort, you know, Miss Woodhouse, one naturally wishes them to see as much as possible; and Mr. Suckling is extremely fond of exploring. We explored to King's-Weston twice last summer, in that way, most delightfully, just after their first having the barouche-landau. You have many parties of that kind here, I suppose, Miss Woodhouse, every summer?"

"No; not immediately here. We are rather out of distance of the very striking beauties which attract the sort of parties you speak of; and we are a very quiet set of people, I believe; more disposed to stay at home than engage in schemes of pleasure."

"Ah! there is nothing like staying at home for real comfort. Nobody can be more devoted to home than I am. I was quite a proverb for it at Maple Grove. Many a time has Selina said, when she has been going to Bristol, 'I really cannot get this girl to move from the house. I absolutely must go in by myself, though I hate being stuck up in the barouche-landau without a companion; but Augusta, I believe, with her own good-will, would never stir beyond the park paling.' Many a time has she said so; and yet I am no advocate for entire seclusion. I think, on the contrary, when people shut themselves up entirely from society, it is a very bad thing; and that it is much more advisable to mix in the world in a proper degree, without living in it either too much or too little. I perfectly understand your situation, however, Miss Woodhouse (looking towards Mr. Woodhouse)—Your father's state of health must be a great drawback. Why does not he try Bath?—Indeed he should. Let me recommend Bath to you. I assure you I have no doubt of its doing Mr. Woodhouse good."

"My father tried it more than once, formerly; but without receiving any benefit; and Mr. Perry, whose name, I dare say, is not unknown to you, does not conceive it would be at all more likely to be useful now."

"Ah! that's a great pity; for I assure you, Miss Woodhouse, where the waters do agree, it is quite wonderful the relief they give. In my Bath life, I have seen such instances of it! And it is so cheerful a place, that it could not fail of being of use to Mr. Woodhouse's spirits, which, I understand, are sometimes much depressed. And as to its recommendations to *you*, I fancy I need not take much pains to dwell on them. The advantages of Bath to the young are pretty generally understood. It would be a charming introduction for you, who have lived so secluded a life; and I could immediately secure you some of the best society in the place. A line from me would bring you a little host of acquaintance; and my particular friend, Mrs. Partridge, the lady I have always resided with when in Bath, would be most happy to shew you any attentions, and would be the very person for you to go into public with."

It was as much as Emma could bear, without being impolite. The idea of her being indebted to Mrs. Elton for what was called an *introduction*—of her going into public under the auspices of a friend of Mrs. Elton's—probably some vulgar, dashing widow, who, with the help of a boarder, just made a shift to live!—The dignity of Miss Woodhouse, of Hartfield, was sunk indeed!

She restrained herself, however, from any of the reproofs she could have given, and only thanked Mrs. Elton coolly; "but their going to Bath was quite out of the question; and she was not perfectly convinced that the place might suit her better than her father." And then, to prevent farther outrage and indignation, changed the subject directly.

"I do not ask whether you are musical, Mrs. Elton. Upon these occasions, a lady's character generally precedes her; and Highbury has long known that you are a superior performer."

"Oh! no, indeed; I must protest against any such idea. A superior performer!—very far from it, I assure you. Consider from how partial a quarter your information came. I am doatingly fond of music—passionately fond;—and my friends say I am not entirely devoid of taste; but as to any thing else, upon my honour my performance is *mediocre* to the last degree. You, Miss Woodhouse, I well know, play delightfully. I assure you it has been the greatest satisfaction, comfort, and delight to me, to hear what a musical society I am got into. I absolutely cannot do without music. It is a necessary of life to me; and having always been used to a very musical society, both at Maple Grove and in Bath, it would have been a most serious sacrifice. I honestly said as much to Mr. E. when he was speaking of my future home, and expressing his fears lest the retirement of it should be disagreeable; and the inferiority of the house too—knowing what I had been accustomed to—of course he was not wholly without apprehension. When he was speaking of it in that way, I honestly said that *the world* I could give up—parties, balls, plays—for I had no fear of retirement. Blessed with so many resources within myself, the world was not necessary to *me*. I could do very well without it. To those who had no resources it was a different thing; but my resources made me quite independent. And as to smaller-sized rooms than I had been used to, I really could not give it a thought. I hoped I was perfectly equal to any sacrifice of that description. Certainly I had been accustomed to every luxury at Maple Grove; but I did assure him that two carriages were not necessary to my happiness, nor were spacious apartments. 'But,' said I, 'to be quite honest, I do not think I can live without something of a musical society. I condition for nothing else; but without music, life would be a blank to me.'"

"We cannot suppose," said Emma, smiling, "that Mr. Elton would hesitate to assure you of there being a *very* musical society in Highbury; and I hope you will not find he has outstepped the truth more than may be pardoned, in consideration of the motive."

"No, indeed, I have no doubts at all on that head. I am delighted to find myself in such a circle. I hope we shall have many sweet little concerts together. I think, Miss Woodhouse, you and I must establish a musical club, and have regular weekly meetings at your house, or ours.

Will not it be a good plan? If *we* exert ourselves, I think we shall not be long in want of allies. Something of that nature would be particularly desirable for *me*, as an inducement to keep me in practice; for married women, you know—there is a sad story against them, in general. They are but too apt to give up music."

"But you, who are so extremely fond of it—there can be no danger, surely?"

"I should hope not; but really when I look around among my acquaintance, I tremble. Selina has entirely given up music—never touches the instrument—though she played sweetly. And the same may be said of Mrs. Jeffereys—Clara Partridge, that was—and of the two Milmans, now Mrs. Bird and Mrs. James Cooper; and of more than I can enumerate. Upon my word it is enough to put one in a fright. I used to be quite angry with Selina; but really I begin now to comprehend that a married woman has many things to call her attention. I believe I was half an hour this morning shut up with my housekeeper."

"But every thing of that kind," said Emma, "will soon be in so regular a train—"

"Well," said Mrs. Elton, laughing, "we shall see."

Emma, finding her so determined upon neglecting her music, had nothing more to say; and, after a moment's pause, Mrs. Elton chose another subject.

"We have been calling at Randalls," said she, "and found them both at home; and very pleasant people they seem to be. I like them extremely. Mr. Weston seems an excellent creature—quite a first-rate favourite with me already, I assure you. And *she* appears so truly good—there is something so motherly and kind-hearted about her, that it wins upon one directly. She was your governess, I think?"

Emma was almost too much astonished to answer; but Mrs. Elton hardly waited for the affirmative before she went on.

"Having understood as much, I was rather astonished to find her so very lady-like! But she is really quite the gentlewoman."

"Mrs. Weston's manners," said Emma, "were always particularly good. Their propriety, simplicity, and elegance, would make them the safest model for any young woman."

"And who do you think came in while we were there?"

Emma was quite at a loss. The tone implied some old acquaintance—and how could she possibly guess?

"Knightley!" continued Mrs. Elton; "Knightley himself!—Was not it lucky?—for, not being within when he called the other day, I had never seen him before; and of course, as so particular a friend of Mr. E.'s, I had a great curiosity. 'My friend Knightley' had been so often mentioned, that I was really impatient to see him; and I must do my *caro sposo* the justice to say that he need not be ashamed of his friend. Knightley is quite the gentleman. I like him very much. Decidedly, I think, a very gentleman-like man."

Happily, it was now time to be gone. They were off; and Emma could breathe.

"Insufferable woman!" was her immediate exclamation. "Worse than I had supposed. Absolutely insufferable! Knightley!—I could not have believed it. Knightley!—never seen him in her life before, and call him Knightley!—and discover that he is a gentleman! A little upstart, vulgar being, with her Mr. E., and her *caro sposo*, and her resources, and all her airs of pert pretension and underbred finery. Actually to discover that Mr. Knightley is a gentleman! I doubt whether he will return the compliment, and discover her to be a lady. I could not have believed it! And to propose that she and I should unite to form a musical club! One would fancy we were bosom friends! And Mrs. Weston!—Astonished that the person who had brought me up should be a gentlewoman! Worse and worse. I never met with her equal. Much beyond my hopes. Harriet is disgraced by any comparison. Oh! what would Frank Churchill say to her, if he were here? How angry and how diverted he would be! Ah! there I am—thinking of him directly. Always the first person to be thought of! How I catch myself out! Frank Churchill comes as regularly into my mind!"—

All this ran so glibly through her thoughts, that by the time her father had arranged himself, after the bustle of the Eltons' departure, and was ready to speak, she was very tolerably capable of attending.

"Well, my dear," he deliberately began, "considering we never saw her before, she seems a very pretty sort of young lady; and I dare say she was very much pleased with you. She speaks a little too quick. A little quickness of voice there is which rather hurts the ear. But I believe I am nice; I do not like strange voices; and nobody speaks like you and poor Miss Taylor. However, she seems a very obliging, pretty-behaved young lady, and no doubt will make him a very good wife. Though I think he had better not have married. I made the best excuses I could for not having been able to wait on him and Mrs. Elton on this happy occasion; I said that I hoped I *should* in the course of the summer. But I ought to have gone before. Not to wait upon a bride is very remiss. Ah! it shews what a sad invalid I am! But I do not like the corner into Vicarage Lane."

"I dare say your apologies were accepted, sir. Mr. Elton knows you."

"Yes: but a young lady—a bride—I ought to have paid my respects to her if possible. It was being very deficient."

"But, my dear papa, you are no friend to matrimony; and therefore why should you be so anxious to pay your respects to a *bride*? It ought to be no recommendation to *you*. It is encouraging people to marry if you make so much of them."

"No, my dear, I never encouraged any body to marry, but I would always wish to pay every proper attention to a lady—and a bride, especially, is never to be neglected. More is avowedly due to *her*. A bride, you know, my dear, is always the first in company, let the others be who they may."

"Well, papa, if this is not encouragement to marry, I do not know what is. And I should never have expected you to be lending your sanction to such vanity-baits for poor young ladies."

"My dear, you do not understand me. This is a matter of mere common politeness and good-breeding, and has nothing to do with any encouragement to people to marry."

Emma had done. Her father was growing nervous, and could not understand *her*. Her mind returned to Mrs. Elton's offences, and long, very long, did they occupy her.

CHAPTER XV

Emma was not required, by any subsequent discovery, to retract her ill opinion of Mrs. Elton. Her observation had been pretty correct. Such as Mrs. Elton appeared to her on this second interview, such she appeared whenever they met again,—self-important, presuming, familiar, ignorant, and ill-bred. She had a little beauty and a little accomplishment, but so little judgment that she thought herself coming with superior knowledge of the world, to enliven and improve a country neighbourhood; and conceived Miss Hawkins to have held such a place in society as Mrs. Elton's consequence only could surpass.

There was no reason to suppose Mr. Elton thought at all differently from his wife. He seemed not merely happy with her, but proud. He had the air of congratulating himself on having brought such a woman to Highbury, as not even Miss Woodhouse could equal; and the greater part of her new acquaintance, disposed to commend, or not in the habit of judging, following the lead of Miss Bates's good-will, or taking it for granted that the bride must be as clever and as agreeable as she professed herself, were very well satisfied; so that Mrs. Elton's praise passed from one mouth to another as it ought to do, unimpeded by Miss Woodhouse, who readily continued her first contribution and talked with a good grace of her being "very pleasant and very elegantly dressed."

In one respect Mrs. Elton grew even worse than she had appeared at first. Her feelings altered towards Emma.—Offended, probably, by the little encouragement which her proposals of intimacy met with, she drew back in her turn and gradually became much more cold and distant; and though the effect was agreeable, the ill-will which produced it was necessarily increasing Emma's dislike. Her manners, too—and Mr. Elton's, were unpleasant towards Harriet. They were sneering and negligent. Emma hoped it must rapidly work Harriet's cure; but the sensations which could prompt such behaviour sunk them both very much.—It was not to be doubted that poor Harriet's attachment had been an offering to conjugal unreserve, and her own share in the story, under a colouring the least favourable to her and the most soothing to him, had in all likelihood been given also. She was, of course, the object of their joint dislike.—When they had nothing else to say, it must be always easy to begin abusing Miss Woodhouse; and the enmity which they dared not shew in open disrespect to her, found a broader vent in contemptuous treatment of Harriet.

Mrs. Elton took a great fancy to Jane Fairfax; and from the first. Not merely when a state of warfare with one young lady might be supposed to recommend the other, but from the very first; and she was not satisfied with expressing a natural and reasonable admiration—but without solicitation, or plea, or privilege, she must be wanting to assist and befriend her.—Before Emma had forfeited her confidence, and about the third time of their meeting, she heard all Mrs. Elton's knight-errantry on the subject.—

"Jane Fairfax is absolutely charming, Miss Woodhouse.—I quite rave about Jane Fairfax.—A sweet, interesting creature. So mild and ladylike—and with such talents!—I assure you I think she has very extraordinary talents. I do not scruple to say that she plays extremely well. I know enough of music to speak decidedly on that point. Oh! she is absolutely charming! You will laugh at my warmth—but, upon my word, I talk of nothing but Jane Fairfax.—And her situation is so calculated to affect one!—Miss Woodhouse, we must exert ourselves and endeavour to do something for her. We must bring her forward. Such talent as hers must not be suffered to remain unknown.—I dare say you have heard those charming lines of the poet,

Full many a flower is born to blush unseen,
And waste its fragrance on the desert air.

We must not allow them to be verified in sweet Jane Fairfax."

"I cannot think there is any danger of it," was Emma's calm answer—"and when you are better acquainted with Miss Fairfax's situation and understand what her home has been, with Colonel and Mrs. Campbell, I have no idea that you will suppose her talents can be unknown."

"Oh! but dear Miss Woodhouse, she is now in such retirement, such obscurity, so thrown away.—Whatever advantages she may have enjoyed with the Campbells are so palpably at an end! And I think she feels it. I am sure she does. She is very timid and silent. One can see that she feels the want of encouragement. I like her the better for it. I must confess it is a recommendation to me. I am a great advocate for timidity—and I am sure one does not often meet with it.—But in those who are at all inferior, it is extremely prepossessing. Oh! I assure you,

Jane Fairfax is a very delightful character, and interests me more than I can express."

"You appear to feel a great deal—but I am not aware how you or any of Miss Fairfax's acquaintance here, any of those who have known her longer than yourself, can shew her any other attention than"—

"My dear Miss Woodhouse, a vast deal may be done by those who dare to act. You and I need not be afraid. If *we* set the example, many will follow it as far as they can; though all have not our situations. *We* have carriages to fetch and convey her home, and *we* live in a style which could not make the addition of Jane Fairfax, at any time, the least inconvenient.—I should be extremely displeased if Wright were to send us up such a dinner, as could make me regret having asked *more* than Jane Fairfax to partake of it. I have no idea of that sort of thing. It is not likely that I *should*, considering what I have been used to. My greatest danger, perhaps, in housekeeping, may be quite the other way, in doing too much, and being too careless of expense. Maple Grove will probably be my model more than it ought to be—for we do not at all affect to equal my brother, Mr. Suckling, in income.—However, my resolution is taken as to noticing Jane Fairfax.—I shall certainly have her very often at my house, shall introduce her wherever I can, shall have musical parties to draw out her talents, and shall be constantly on the watch for an eligible situation. My acquaintance is so very extensive, that I have little doubt of hearing of something to suit her shortly.—I shall introduce her, of course, very particularly to my brother and sister when they come to us. I am sure they will like her extremely; and when she gets a little acquainted with them, her fears will completely wear off, for there really is nothing in the manners of either but what is highly conciliating.—I shall have her very often indeed while they are with me, and I dare say we shall sometimes find a seat for her in the barouche-landau in some of our exploring parties."

"Poor Jane Fairfax!"—thought Emma.—"You have not deserved this. You may have done wrong with regard to Mr. Dixon, but this is a punishment beyond what you can have merited!—The kindness and protection of Mrs. Elton!—'Jane Fairfax and Jane Fairfax.' Heavens! Let me not suppose that she dares go about, Emma Woodhouse-ing me!—But upon my honour, there seems no limits to the licentiousness of that woman's tongue!"

Emma had not to listen to such paradings again—to any so

exclusively addressed to herself—so disgustingly decorated with a "dear Miss Woodhouse." The change on Mrs. Elton's side soon afterwards appeared, and she was left in peace—neither forced to be the very particular friend of Mrs. Elton, nor, under Mrs. Elton's guidance, the very active patroness of Jane Fairfax, and only sharing with others in a general way, in knowing what was felt, what was meditated, what was done.

She looked on with some amusement.—Miss Bates's gratitude for Mrs. Elton's attentions to Jane was in the first style of guileless simplicity and warmth. She was quite one of her worthies—the most amiable, affable, delightful woman—just as accomplished and condescending as Mrs. Elton meant to be considered. Emma's only surprize was that Jane Fairfax should accept those attentions and tolerate Mrs. Elton as she seemed to do. She heard of her walking with the Eltons, sitting with the Eltons, spending a day with the Eltons! This was astonishing!—She could not have believed it possible that the taste or the pride of Miss Fairfax could endure such society and friendship as the Vicarage had to offer.

"She is a riddle, quite a riddle!" said she.—"To chuse to remain here month after month, under privations of every sort! And now to chuse the mortification of Mrs. Elton's notice and the penury of her conversation, rather than return to the superior companions who have always loved her with such real, generous affection."

Jane had come to Highbury professedly for three months; the Campbells were gone to Ireland for three months; but now the Campbells had promised their daughter to stay at least till Midsummer, and fresh invitations had arrived for her to join them there. According to Miss Bates—it all came from her—Mrs. Dixon had written most pressingly. Would Jane but go, means were to be found, servants sent, friends contrived—no travelling difficulty allowed to exist; but still she had declined it!

"She must have some motive, more powerful than appears, for refusing this invitation," was Emma's conclusion. "She must be under some sort of penance, inflicted either by the Campbells or herself. There is great fear, great caution, great resolution somewhere.—She is *not* to be with the *Dixons*. The decree is issued by somebody. But why must she consent to be with the Eltons?—Here is quite a separate puzzle."

Upon her speaking her wonder aloud on that part of the subject, before the few who knew her opinion of Mrs. Elton, Mrs. Weston ventured this apology for Jane.

"We cannot suppose that she has any great enjoyment at the Vicarage, my dear Emma—but it is better than being always at home. Her aunt is a good creature, but, as a constant companion, must be very tiresome. We must consider what Miss Fairfax quits, before we condemn her taste for what she goes to."

"You are right, Mrs. Weston," said Mr. Knightley warmly, "Miss Fairfax is as capable as any of us of forming a just opinion of Mrs. Elton. Could she have chosen with whom to associate, she would not have chosen her. But (with a reproachful smile at Emma) she receives attentions from Mrs. Elton, which nobody else pays her."

Emma felt that Mrs. Weston was giving her a momentary glance; and she was herself struck by his warmth. With a faint blush, she presently replied,

"Such attentions as Mrs. Elton's, I should have imagined, would rather disgust than gratify Miss Fairfax. Mrs. Elton's invitations I should have imagined any thing but inviting."

"I should not wonder," said Mrs. Weston, "if Miss Fairfax were to have been drawn on beyond her own inclination, by her aunt's eagerness in accepting Mrs. Elton's civilities for her. Poor Miss Bates may very likely have committed her niece and hurried her into a greater appearance of intimacy than her own good sense would have dictated, in spite of the very natural wish of a little change."

Both felt rather anxious to hear him speak again; and after a few minutes silence, he said,

"Another thing must be taken into consideration too—Mrs. Elton does not talk *to* Miss Fairfax as she speaks *of* her. We all know the difference between the pronouns he or she and thou, the plainest spoken amongst us; we all feel the influence of a something beyond common civility in our personal intercourse with each other—a something more early implanted. We cannot give any body the disagreeable hints that we may have been very full of the hour before. We feel things differently. And besides the operation of this, as a general principle, you may be sure that Miss Fairfax awes Mrs. Elton by her superiority both of mind and manner; and that, face to face, Mrs. Elton treats her with all the respect which she has a claim to. Such a woman as Jane Fairfax probably never fell in Mrs. Elton's way before—and no degree of vanity can prevent her acknowledging her own comparative littleness in action, if not in consciousness."

"I know how highly you think of Jane Fairfax," said Emma. Little Henry was in her thoughts, and a mixture of alarm and delicacy made her irresolute what else to say.

"Yes," he replied, "any body may know how highly I think of her."

"And yet," said Emma, beginning hastily and with an arch look, but soon stopping—it was better, however, to know the worst at once—she hurried on—"And yet, perhaps, you may hardly be aware yourself how highly it is. The extent of your admiration may take you by surprize some day or other."

Mr. Knightley was hard at work upon the lower buttons of his thick leather gaiters, and either the exertion of getting them together, or some other cause, brought the colour into his face, as he answered,

"Oh! are you there?—But you are miserably behindhand. Mr. Cole gave me a hint of it six weeks ago."

He stopped.—Emma felt her foot pressed by Mrs. Weston, and did not herself know what to think. In a moment he went on—

"That will never be, however, I can assure you. Miss Fairfax, I dare say, would not have me if I were to ask her—and I am very sure I shall never ask her."

Emma returned her friend's pressure with interest; and was pleased enough to exclaim,

"You are not vain, Mr. Knightley. I will say that for you."

He seemed hardly to hear her; he was thoughtful—and in a manner which shewed him not pleased, soon afterwards said,

"So you have been settling that I should marry Jane Fairfax?"

"No indeed I have not. You have scolded me too much for match-making, for me to presume to take such a liberty with you. What I said just now, meant nothing. One says those sort of things, of course, without any idea of a serious meaning. Oh! no, upon my word I have not the smallest wish for your marrying Jane Fairfax or Jane any body. You would not come in and sit with us in this comfortable way, if you were married."

Mr. Knightley was thoughtful again. The result of his reverie was, "No, Emma, I do not think the extent of my admiration for her will ever take me by surprize.—I never had a thought of her in that way, I assure you." And soon afterwards, "Jane Fairfax is a very charming young woman—but not even Jane Fairfax is perfect. She has a fault. She has not the open temper which a man would wish for in a wife."

Emma could not but rejoice to hear that she had a fault. "Well," said she, "and you soon silenced Mr. Cole, I suppose?"

"Yes, very soon. He gave me a quiet hint; I told him he was mistaken; he asked my pardon and said no more. Cole does not want to be wiser or wittier than his neighbours."

"In that respect how unlike dear Mrs. Elton, who wants to be wiser and wittier than all the world! I wonder how she speaks of the Coles—what she calls them! How can she find any appellation for them, deep enough in familiar vulgarity? She calls you, Knightley—what can she do for Mr. Cole? And so I am not to be surprized that Jane Fairfax accepts her civilities and consents to be with her. Mrs. Weston, your argument weighs most with me. I can much more readily enter into the temptation of getting away from Miss Bates, than I can believe in the triumph of Miss Fairfax's mind over Mrs. Elton. I have no faith in Mrs. Elton's acknowledging herself the inferior in thought, word, or deed; or in her being under any restraint beyond her own scanty rule of good-breeding. I cannot imagine that she will not be continually insulting her visitor with praise, encouragement, and offers of service; that she will not be continually detailing her magnificent intentions, from the procuring her a permanent situation to the including her in those delightful exploring parties which are to take place in the barouche-landau."

"Jane Fairfax has feeling," said Mr. Knightley—"I do not accuse her of want of feeling. Her sensibilities, I suspect, are strong—and her temper excellent in its power of forbearance, patience, self-control; but it wants openness. She is reserved, more reserved, I think, than she used to be—And I love an open temper. No—till Cole alluded to my supposed attachment, it had never entered my head. I saw Jane Fairfax and conversed with her, with admiration and pleasure always—but with no thought beyond."

"Well, Mrs. Weston," said Emma triumphantly when he left them, "what do you say now to Mr. Knightley's marrying Jane Fairfax?"

"Why, really, dear Emma, I say that he is so very much occupied by the idea of *not* being in love with her, that I should not wonder if it were to end in his being so at last. Do not beat me."

CHAPTER XVI

Every body in and about Highbury who had ever visited Mr. Elton, was disposed to pay him attention on his marriage. Dinner-parties and evening-parties were made for him and his lady; and invitations flowed in so fast that she had soon the pleasure of apprehending they were never to have a disengaged day.

"I see how it is," said she. "I see what a life I am to lead among you. Upon my word we shall be absolutely dissipated. We really seem quite the fashion. If this is living in the country, it is nothing very formidable. From Monday next to Saturday, I assure you we have not a disengaged day!—A woman with fewer resources than I have, need not have been at a loss."

No invitation came amiss to her. Her Bath habits made evening-parties perfectly natural to her, and Maple Grove had given her a taste for dinners. She was a little shocked at the want of two drawing rooms, at the poor attempt at rout-cakes, and there being no ice in the Highbury card-parties. Mrs. Bates, Mrs. Perry, Mrs. Goddard and others, were a good deal behind-hand in knowledge of the world, but she would soon shew them how every thing ought to be arranged. In the course of the spring she must return their civilities by one very superior party—in which her card-tables should be set out with their separate candles and unbroken packs in the true style—and more waiters engaged for the evening than their own establishment could furnish, to carry round the refreshments at exactly the proper hour, and in the proper order.

Emma, in the meanwhile, could not be satisfied without a dinner at Hartfield for the Eltons. They must not do less than others, or she should be exposed to odious suspicions, and imagined capable of pitiful resentment. A dinner there must be. After Emma had talked about it for ten minutes, Mr. Woodhouse felt no unwillingness, and only made the usual stipulation of not sitting at the bottom of the table himself, with the usual regular difficulty of deciding who should do it for him.

The persons to be invited, required little thought. Besides the Eltons, it must be the Westons and Mr. Knightley; so far it was all of course—and it was hardly less inevitable that poor little Harriet must be asked to make the eighth:—but this invitation was not given with equal satisfaction, and on many accounts Emma was particularly pleased by Harriet's begging to be allowed to decline it. "She would rather not be in his company more than she could help. She was not yet quite able to see him and his charming happy wife together, without feeling uncomfortable. If Miss Woodhouse would not be displeased, she would rather stay at home." It was precisely what Emma would have wished, had she deemed it possible enough for wishing. She was delighted with the fortitude of her little friend—for fortitude she knew it was in her to give up being in company and stay at home; and she could now invite the very person whom she really wanted to make the eighth, Jane Fairfax.—Since her last conversation with Mrs. Weston and Mr. Knightley, she was more conscience-stricken about Jane Fairfax than she had often been.—Mr. Knightley's words dwelt with her. He had said that Jane Fairfax received attentions from Mrs. Elton which nobody else paid her.

"This is very true," said she, "at least as far as relates to me, which was all that was meant—and it is very shameful.—Of the same age—and always knowing her—I ought to have been more her friend.—She will never like me now. I have neglected her too long. But I will shew her greater attention than I have done."

Every invitation was successful. They were all disengaged and all happy.—The preparatory interest of this dinner, however, was not yet over. A circumstance rather unlucky occurred. The two eldest little Knightleys were engaged to pay their grandpapa and aunt a visit of some weeks in the spring, and their papa now proposed bringing them, and staying one whole day at Hartfield—which one day would be the very day of this party.—His professional engagements did not allow of his being put off, but both father and daughter were disturbed by its happening so. Mr. Woodhouse considered eight persons at dinner together as the utmost that his nerves could bear—and here would be a ninth—and Emma apprehended that it would be a ninth very much out of humour at not being able to come even to Hartfield for forty-eight hours without falling in with a dinner-party.

She comforted her father better than she could comfort herself, by representing that though he certainly would make them nine, yet he always said so little, that the increase of noise would be very immaterial. She thought it in reality a sad exchange for herself, to have him with his grave looks and reluctant conversation opposed to her instead of his brother.

The event was more favourable to Mr. Woodhouse than to Emma. John Knightley came; but Mr. Weston was unexpectedly summoned to town and must be absent on the very day. He might be able to join them in the evening, but certainly not to dinner. Mr. Woodhouse was quite at ease; and the seeing him so, with the arrival of the little boys and the philosophic composure of her brother on hearing his fate, removed the chief of even Emma's vexation.

The day came, the party were punctually assembled, and Mr. John Knightley seemed early to devote himself to the business of being agreeable. Instead of drawing his brother off to a window while they waited for dinner, he was talking to Miss Fairfax. Mrs. Elton, as elegant as lace and pearls could make her, he looked at in silence—wanting only to observe enough for Isabella's information—but Miss Fairfax was an old acquaintance and a quiet girl, and he could talk to her. He had met her before breakfast as he was returning from a walk with his little boys, when it had been just beginning to rain. It was natural to have some civil hopes on the subject, and he said,

"I hope you did not venture far, Miss Fairfax, this morning, or I am sure you must have been wet.—We scarcely got home in time. I hope you turned directly."

"I went only to the post-office," said she, "and reached home before the rain was much. It is my daily errand. I always fetch the letters when I am here. It saves trouble, and is a something to get me out. A walk before breakfast does me good."

"Not a walk in the rain, I should imagine."

"No, but it did not absolutely rain when I set out."

Mr. John Knightley smiled, and replied,

"That is to say, you chose to have your walk, for you were not six yards from your own door when I had the pleasure of meeting you; and Henry and John had seen more drops than they could count long before. The post-office has a great charm at one period of our lives. When you have lived to my age, you will begin to think letters are never worth going through the rain for."

There was a little blush, and then this answer,

"I must not hope to be ever situated as you are, in the midst of every dearest connexion, and therefore I cannot expect that simply growing older should make me indifferent about letters."

"Indifferent! Oh! no—I never conceived you could become

indifferent. Letters are no matter of indifference; they are generally a very positive curse."

"You are speaking of letters of business; mine are letters of friendship."

"I have often thought them the worst of the two," replied he coolly. "Business, you know, may bring money, but friendship hardly ever does."

"Ah! you are not serious now. I know Mr. John Knightley too well—I am very sure he understands the value of friendship as well as any body. I can easily believe that letters are very little to you, much less than to me, but it is not your being ten years older than myself which makes the difference, it is not age, but situation. You have every body dearest to you always at hand, I, probably, never shall again; and therefore till I have outlived all my affections, a post-office, I think, must always have power to draw me out, in worse weather than to-day."

"When I talked of your being altered by time, by the progress of years," said John Knightley, "I meant to imply the change of situation which time usually brings. I consider one as including the other. Time will generally lessen the interest of every attachment not within the daily circle—but that is not the change I had in view for you. As an old friend, you will allow me to hope, Miss Fairfax, that ten years hence you may have as many concentrated objects as I have."

It was kindly said, and very far from giving offence. A pleasant "thank you" seemed meant to laugh it off, but a blush, a quivering lip, a tear in the eye, shewed that it was felt beyond a laugh. Her attention was now claimed by Mr. Woodhouse, who being, according to his custom on such occasions, making the circle of his guests, and paying his particular compliments to the ladies, was ending with her—and with all his mildest urbanity, said,

"I am very sorry to hear, Miss Fairfax, of your being out this morning in the rain. Young ladies should take care of themselves.—Young ladies are delicate plants. They should take care of their health and their complexion. My dear, did you change your stockings?"

"Yes, sir, I did indeed; and I am very much obliged by your kind solicitude about me."

"My dear Miss Fairfax, young ladies are very sure to be cared for.—I hope your good grand-mama and aunt are well. They are some of my very old friends. I wish my health allowed me to be a better neighbour. You do us a great deal of honour to-day, I am sure. My daughter and I are both highly sensible of your goodness, and have the greatest satisfaction in seeing you at Hartfield."

The kind-hearted, polite old man might then sit down and feel that he had done his duty, and made every fair lady welcome and easy.

By this time, the walk in the rain had reached Mrs. Elton, and her remonstrances now opened upon Jane.

"My dear Jane, what is this I hear?—Going to the post-office in the rain!—This must not be, I assure you.—You sad girl, how could you do such a thing?—It is a sign I was not there to take care of you."

Jane very patiently assured her that she had not caught any cold.

"Oh! do not tell *me*. You really are a very sad girl, and do not know how to take care of yourself.—To the post-office indeed! Mrs. Weston, did you ever hear the like? You and I must positively exert our authority."

"My advice," said Mrs. Weston kindly and persuasively, "I certainly do feel tempted to give. Miss Fairfax, you must not run such risks.—Liable as you have been to severe colds, indeed you ought to be particularly careful, especially at this time of year. The spring I always think requires more than common care. Better wait an hour or two, or even half a day for your letters, than run the risk of bringing on your cough again. Now do not you feel that you had? Yes, I am sure you are much too reasonable. You look as if you would not do such a thing again."

"Oh! she *shall not* do such a thing again," eagerly rejoined Mrs. Elton. "We will not allow her to do such a thing again:"—and nodding significantly—"there must be some arrangement made, there must indeed. I shall speak to Mr. E. The man who fetches our letters every morning (one of our men, I forget his name) shall inquire for yours too and bring them to you. That will obviate all difficulties you know; and from *us* I really think, my dear Jane, you can have no scruple to accept such an accommodation."

"You are extremely kind," said Jane; "but I cannot give up my early walk. I am advised to be out of doors as much as I can, I must walk somewhere, and the post-office is an object; and upon my word, I have scarcely ever had a bad morning before."

"My dear Jane, say no more about it. The thing is determined, that is (laughing affectedly) as far as I can presume to determine any thing without the concurrence of my lord and master. You know, Mrs. Weston, you and I must be cautious how we express ourselves. But I do flatter myself, my dear Jane, that my influence is not entirely worn out. If I meet with no insuperable difficulties therefore, consider that point as settled."

"Excuse me," said Jane earnestly, "I cannot by any means consent to such an arrangement, so needlessly troublesome to your servant. If the errand were not a pleasure to me, it could be done, as it always is when I am not here, by my grandmama's."

"Oh! my dear; but so much as Patty has to do!—And it is a kindness to employ our men."

Jane looked as if she did not mean to be conquered; but instead of answering, she began speaking again to Mr. John Knightley.

"The post-office is a wonderful establishment!" said she.—"The regularity and despatch of it! If one thinks of all that it has to do, and all that it does so well, it is really astonishing!"

"It is certainly very well regulated."

"So seldom that any negligence or blunder appears! So seldom that a letter, among the thousands that are constantly passing about the kingdom, is even carried wrong—and not one in a million, I suppose, actually lost! And when one considers the variety of hands, and of bad hands too, that are to be deciphered, it increases the wonder."

"The clerks grow expert from habit.—They must begin with some quickness of sight and hand, and exercise improves them. If you want any farther explanation," continued he, smiling, "they are paid for it. That is the key to a great deal of capacity. The public pays and must be served well."

The varieties of handwriting were farther talked of, and the usual observations made.

"I have heard it asserted," said John Knightley, "that the same sort of handwriting often prevails in a family; and where the same master teaches, it is natural enough. But for that reason, I should imagine the likeness must be chiefly confined to the females, for boys have very little teaching after an early age, and scramble into any hand they can get. Isabella and Emma, I think, do write very much alike. I have not always known their writing apart."

"Yes," said his brother hesitatingly, "there is a likeness. I know what you mean—but Emma's hand is the strongest."

"Isabella and Emma both write beautifully," said Mr. Woodhouse;

"and always did. And so does poor Mrs. Weston"—with half a sigh and half a smile at her.

"I never saw any gentleman's handwriting"—Emma began, looking also at Mrs. Weston; but stopped, on perceiving that Mrs. Weston was attending to some one else—and the pause gave her time to reflect, "Now, how am I going to introduce him?—Am I unequal to speaking his name at once before all these people? Is it necessary for me to use any roundabout phrase?—Your Yorkshire friend—your correspondent in Yorkshire;—that would be the way, I suppose, if I were very bad.—No, I can pronounce his name without the smallest distress. I certainly get better and better.—Now for it."

Mrs. Weston was disengaged and Emma began again—"Mr. Frank Churchill writes one of the best gentleman's hands I ever saw."

"I do not admire it," said Mr. Knightley. "It is too small—wants strength. It is like a woman's writing."

This was not submitted to by either lady. They vindicated him against the base aspersion. "No, it by no means wanted strength—it was not a large hand, but very clear and certainly strong. Had not Mrs. Weston any letter about her to produce?" No, she had heard from him very lately, but having answered the letter, had put it away.

"If we were in the other room," said Emma, "if I had my writing-desk, I am sure I could produce a specimen. I have a note of his.—Do not you remember, Mrs. Weston, employing him to write for you one day?"

"He chose to say he was employed"—

"Well, well, I have that note; and can shew it after dinner to convince Mr. Knightley."

"Oh! when a gallant young man, like Mr. Frank Churchill," said Mr. Knightley dryly, "writes to a fair lady like Miss Woodhouse, he will, of course, put forth his best."

Dinner was on table.—Mrs. Elton, before she could be spoken to, was ready; and before Mr. Woodhouse had reached her with his request to be allowed to hand her into the dining-parlour, was saying—

"Must I go first? I really am ashamed of always leading the way."

Jane's solicitude about fetching her own letters had not escaped Emma. She had heard and seen it all; and felt some curiosity to know whether the wet walk of this morning had produced any. She suspected that it *had*; that it would not have been so resolutely encountered but in full expectation of hearing from some one very dear, and that it had not been in vain. She thought there was an air of greater happiness than usual—a glow both of complexion and spirits.

She could have made an inquiry or two, as to the expedition and the expense of the Irish mails;—it was at her tongue's end—but she abstained. She was quite determined not to utter a word that should hurt Jane Fairfax's feelings; and they followed the other ladies out of the room, arm in arm, with an appearance of good-will highly becoming to the beauty and grace of each.

CHAPTER XVII

When the ladies returned to the drawing-room after dinner, Emma found it hardly possible to prevent their making two distinct parties;—with so much perseverance in judging and behaving ill did Mrs. Elton engross Jane Fairfax and slight herself. She and Mrs. Weston were obliged to be almost always either talking together or silent together. Mrs. Elton left them no choice. If Jane repressed her for a little time, she soon began again; and though much that passed between them was in a half-whisper, especially on Mrs. Elton's side, there was no avoiding a knowledge of their principal subjects: The post-office—catching cold—fetching letters—and friendship, were long under discussion; and to them succeeded one, which must be at least equally unpleasant to Jane—inquiries whether she had yet heard of any situation likely to suit her, and professions of Mrs. Elton's meditated activity.

"Here is April come!" said she, "I get quite anxious about you. June will soon be here."

"But I have never fixed on June or any other month—merely looked forward to the summer in general."

"But have you really heard of nothing?"

"I have not even made any inquiry; I do not wish to make any yet."

"Oh! my dear, we cannot begin too early; you are not aware of the difficulty of procuring exactly the desirable thing."

"I not aware!" said Jane, shaking her head; "dear Mrs. Elton, who can have thought of it as I have done?"

"But you have not seen so much of the world as I have. You do not know how many candidates there always are for the *first* situations. I saw a vast deal of that in the neighbourhood round Maple Grove. A cousin of Mr. Suckling, Mrs. Bragge, had such an infinity of applications; every body was anxious to be in her family, for she moves in the first circle. Wax-candles in the schoolroom! You may imagine how desirable! Of all houses in the kingdom Mrs. Bragge's is the one I would most wish to see you in."

"Colonel and Mrs. Campbell are to be in town again by Midsummer," said Jane. "I must spend some time with them; I am sure they will want it;—afterwards I may probably be glad to dispose of myself. But I would not wish you to take the trouble of making any inquiries at present."

"Trouble! aye, I know your scruples. You are afraid of giving me trouble; but I assure you, my dear Jane, the Campbells can hardly be more interested about you than I am. I shall write to Mrs. Partridge in a day or two, and shall give her a strict charge to be on the look-out for any thing eligible."

"Thank you, but I would rather you did not mention the subject to her; till the time draws nearer, I do not wish to be giving any body trouble."

"But, my dear child, the time is drawing near; here is April, and June, or say even July, is very near, with such business to accomplish before us. Your inexperience really amuses me! A situation such as you deserve, and your friends would require for you, is no everyday occurrence, is not obtained at a moment's notice; indeed, indeed, we must begin inquiring directly."

"Excuse me, ma'am, but this is by no means my intention; I make no inquiry myself, and should be sorry to have any made by my friends. When I am quite determined as to the time, I am not at all afraid of being long unemployed. There are places in town, offices, where inquiry would soon produce something—Offices for the sale—not quite of human flesh—but of human intellect."

"Oh! my dear, human flesh! You quite shock me; if you mean a fling at the slave-trade, I assure you Mr. Suckling was always rather a friend to the abolition."

"I did not mean, I was not thinking of the slave-trade," replied Jane; "governess-trade, I assure you, was all that I had in view; widely different certainly as to the guilt of those who carry it on; but as to the greater misery of the victims, I do not know where it lies. But I only mean to say that there are advertising offices, and that by applying to them I should have no doubt of very soon meeting with something that would do."

"Something that would do!" repeated Mrs. Elton. "Aye, *that* may suit your humble ideas of yourself;—I know what a modest creature you are; but it will not satisfy your friends to have you taking up with any thing that may offer, any inferior, commonplace situation, in a family not moving in a certain circle, or able to command the elegancies of life."

"You are very obliging; but as to all that, I am very indifferent; it would be no object to me to be with the rich; my mortifications, I think, would only be the greater; I should suffer more from comparison. A gentleman's family is all that I should condition for."

"I know you, I know you; you would take up with any thing; but I shall be a little more nice, and I am sure the good Campbells will be quite on my side; with your superior talents, you have a right to move in the first circle. Your musical knowledge alone would entitle you to name your own terms, have as many rooms as you like, and mix in the family as much as you chose;—that is—I do not know—if you knew the harp, you might do all that, I am very sure; but you sing as well as play;—yes, I really believe you might, even without the harp, stipulate for what you chose;—and you must and shall be delightfully, honourably and comfortably settled before the Campbells or I have any rest."

"You may well class the delight, the honour, and the comfort of such a situation together," said Jane, "they are pretty sure to be equal; however, I am very serious in not wishing any thing to be attempted at present for me. I am exceedingly obliged to you, Mrs. Elton, I am obliged to any body who feels for me, but I am quite serious in wishing nothing to be done till the summer. For two or three months longer I shall remain where I am, and as I am."

"And I am quite serious too, I assure you," replied Mrs. Elton gaily, "in resolving to be always on the watch, and employing my friends to watch also, that nothing really unexceptionable may pass us."

In this style she ran on; never thoroughly stopped by any thing till Mr. Woodhouse came into the room; her vanity had then a change of object, and Emma heard her saying in the same half-whisper to Jane,

"Here comes this dear old beau of mine, I protest!—Only think of his gallantry in coming away before the other men!—what a dear creature he is;—I assure you I like him excessively. I admire all that quaint, old-fashioned politeness; it is much more to my taste than modern ease; modern ease often disgusts me. But this good old Mr. Woodhouse, I wish you had heard his gallant speeches to me at dinner. Oh! I assure you I began to think my *caro sposo* would be absolutely jealous. I fancy I am rather a favourite; he took notice of my gown. How do you like it?—Selina's choice—handsome, I think, but I do not know whether it is not over-trimmed; I have the greatest dislike to the idea of being over-trimmed—quite a horror of finery. I must put on a few ornaments now, because it is expected of me. A bride, you know, must appear like a bride, but my natural taste is all for simplicity; a simple style of dress is so infinitely preferable to finery. But I am quite in the minority, I believe; few people seem to value simplicity of dress,—show and finery are every thing. I have some notion of putting such a trimming as this to my white and silver poplin. Do you think it will look well?"

The whole party were but just reassembled in the drawing-room when Mr. Weston made his appearance among them. He had returned to a late dinner, and walked to Hartfield as soon as it was over. He had been too much expected by the best judges, for surprize—but there was great joy. Mr. Woodhouse was almost as glad to see him now, as he would have been sorry to see him before. John Knightley only was in mute astonishment.—That a man who might have spent his evening quietly at home after a day of business in London, should set off again, and walk half a mile to another man's house, for the sake of being in mixed company till bed-time, of finishing his day in the efforts of civility and the noise of numbers, was a circumstance to strike him deeply. A man who had been in motion since eight o'clock in the morning, and might now have been still, who had been long talking, and might have been silent, who had been in more than one crowd, and might have been alone!—Such a man, to quit the tranquillity and independence of his own fireside, and on the evening of a cold sleety April day rush out again into the world!—Could he by a touch of his finger have instantly taken back his wife, there would have been a motive; but his coming would probably prolong rather than break up the party. John Knightley looked at him with amazement, then shrugged his shoulders, and said, "I could not have believed it even of *him*."

Mr. Weston meanwhile, perfectly unsuspicious of the indignation he was exciting, happy and cheerful as usual, and with all the right of being principal talker, which a day spent anywhere from home confers, was making himself agreeable among the rest; and having satisfied the inquiries of his wife as to his dinner, convincing her that none of all her careful directions to the servants had been forgotten, and spread abroad what public news he had heard, was proceeding to a family communication, which, though principally addressed to Mrs. Weston, he had not the smallest doubt of being highly interesting to every body in the room. He gave her a letter; it was from Frank, and to herself; he had met with it in his way, and had taken the liberty of opening it.

"Read it, read it," said he, "it will give you pleasure; only a few lines—will not take you long; read it to Emma."

The two ladies looked over it together; and he sat smiling and talking to them the whole time, in a voice a little subdued, but very audible to every body.

"Well, he is coming, you see; good news, I think. Well, what do you say to it?—I always told you he would be here again soon, did not I?—Anne, my dear, did not I always tell you so, and you would not believe me?—In town next week, you see—at the latest, I dare say; for *she* is as impatient as the black gentleman when any thing is to be done; most likely they will be there to-morrow or Saturday. As to her illness, all nothing of course. But it is an excellent thing to have Frank among us again, so near as town. They will stay a good while when they do come, and he will be half his time with us. This is precisely what I wanted. Well, pretty good news, is not it? Have you finished it? Has Emma read it all? Put it up, put it up; we will have a good talk about it some other time, but it will not do now. I shall only just mention the circumstance to the others in a common way."

Mrs. Weston was most comfortably pleased on the occasion. Her looks and words had nothing to restrain them. She was happy, she knew she was happy, and knew she ought to be happy. Her congratulations were warm and open; but Emma could not speak so fluently. *She* was a little occupied in weighing her own feelings, and trying to understand the degree of her agitation, which she rather thought was considerable.

Mr. Weston, however, too eager to be very observant, too communicative to want others to talk, was very well satisfied with what she did say, and soon moved away to make the rest of his friends happy by a partial communication of what the whole room must have overheard already.

It was well that he took every body's joy for granted, or he might not have thought either Mr. Woodhouse or Mr. Knightley particularly delighted. They were the first entitled, after Mrs. Weston and Emma, to be made happy;—from them he would have proceeded to Miss Fairfax, but she was so deep in conversation with John Knightley, that it would have been too positive an interruption; and finding himself close to Mrs. Elton, and her attention disengaged, he necessarily began on the subject with her.

CHAPTER XVIII

"I hope I shall soon have the pleasure of introducing my son to you," said Mr. Weston.

Mrs. Elton, very willing to suppose a particular compliment intended her by such a hope, smiled most graciously.

"You have heard of a certain Frank Churchill, I presume," he continued—"and know him to be my son, though he does not bear my name."

"Oh! yes, and I shall be very happy in his acquaintance. I am sure Mr. Elton will lose no time in calling on him; and we shall both have great pleasure in seeing him at the Vicarage."

"You are very obliging.—Frank will be extremely happy, I am sure.—He is to be in town next week, if not sooner. We have notice of it in a letter to-day. I met the letters in my way this morning, and seeing my son's hand, presumed to open it—though it was not directed to me—it was to Mrs. Weston. She is his principal correspondent, I assure you. I hardly ever get a letter."

"And so you absolutely opened what was directed to her! Oh! Mr. Weston—(laughing affectedly) I must protest against that.—A most dangerous precedent indeed!—I beg you will not let your neighbours follow your example.—Upon my word, if this is what I am to expect, we married women must begin to exert ourselves!—Oh! Mr. Weston, I could not have believed it of you!"

"Aye, we men are sad fellows. You must take care of yourself, Mrs. Elton.—This letter tells us—it is a short letter—written in a hurry, merely to give us notice—it tells us that they are all coming up to town directly, on Mrs. Churchill's account—she has not been well the whole winter, and thinks Enscombe too cold for her—so they are all to move southward without loss of time."

"Indeed!—from Yorkshire, I think. Enscombe is in Yorkshire?"

"Yes, they are about one hundred and ninety miles from London. A considerable journey."

"Yes, upon my word, very considerable. Sixty-five miles farther than from Maple Grove to London. But what is distance, Mr. Weston, to people of large fortune?—You would be amazed to hear how my brother, Mr. Suckling, sometimes flies about. You will hardly believe me—but twice in one week he and Mr. Bragge went to London and back again with four horses."

"The evil of the distance from Enscombe," said Mr. Weston, "is, that Mrs. Churchill, *as we understand*, has not been able to leave the sofa for a week together. In Frank's last letter she complained, he said, of being too weak to get into her conservatory without having both his arm and his uncle's! This, you know, speaks a great degree of weakness—but now she is so impatient to be in town, that she means to sleep only two nights on the road.—So Frank writes word. Certainly, delicate ladies have very extraordinary constitutions, Mrs. Elton. You must grant me that."

"No, indeed, I shall grant you nothing. I always take the part of my own sex. I do indeed. I give you notice—You will find me a formidable antagonist on that point. I always stand up for women—and I assure you, if you knew how Selina feels with respect to sleeping at an inn, you would not wonder at Mrs. Churchill's making incredible exertions to avoid it. Selina says it is quite horror to her—and I believe I have caught a little of her nicety. She always travels with her own sheets; an excellent precaution. Does Mrs. Churchill do the same?"

"Depend upon it, Mrs. Churchill does every thing that any other fine lady ever did. Mrs. Churchill will not be second to any lady in the land for"—

Mrs. Elton eagerly interposed with,

"Oh! Mr. Weston, do not mistake me. Selina is no fine lady, I assure you. Do not run away with such an idea."

"Is not she? Then she is no rule for Mrs. Churchill, who is as thorough a fine lady as any body ever beheld."

Mrs. Elton began to think she had been wrong in disclaiming so warmly. It was by no means her object to have it believed that her sister was *not* a fine lady; perhaps there was want of spirit in the pretence of it;—and she was considering in what way she had best retract, when Mr. Weston went on.

"Mrs. Churchill is not much in my good graces, as you may suspect—but this is quite between ourselves. She is very fond of Frank, and therefore I would not speak ill of her. Besides, she is out of health now; but *that* indeed, by her own account, she has always been. I would not say so to every body, Mrs. Elton, but I have not much faith in Mrs. Churchill's illness."

"If she is really ill, why not go to Bath, Mr. Weston?—To Bath, or to Clifton?"

"She has taken it into her head that Enscombe is too cold for her. The fact is, I suppose, that she is tired of Enscombe. She has now been a longer time stationary there, than she ever was before, and she begins to want change. It is a retired place. A fine place, but very retired."

"Aye—like Maple Grove, I dare say. Nothing can stand more retired from the road than Maple Grove. Such an immense plantation all round it! You seem shut out from every thing—in the most complete retirement.—And Mrs. Churchill probably has not health or spirits like Selina to enjoy that sort of seclusion. Or, perhaps she may not have resources enough in herself to be qualified for a country life. I always say a woman cannot have too many resources—and I feel very thankful that I have so many myself as to be quite independent of society."

"Frank was here in February for a fortnight."

"So I remember to have heard. He will find an *addition* to the society of Highbury when he comes again; that is, if I may presume to call myself an addition. But perhaps he may never have heard of there being such a creature in the world."

This was too loud a call for a compliment to be passed by, and Mr. Weston, with a very good grace, immediately exclaimed,

"My dear madam! Nobody but yourself could imagine such a thing possible. Not heard of you!—I believe Mrs. Weston's letters lately have been full of very little else than Mrs. Elton."

He had done his duty and could return to his son.

"When Frank left us," continued he, "it was quite uncertain when we might see him again, which makes this day's news doubly welcome. It has been completely unexpected. That is, *I* always had a strong persuasion he would be here again soon, I was sure something favourable would turn up—but nobody believed me. He and Mrs. Weston were both dreadfully desponding. 'How could he contrive to come? And how could it be supposed that his uncle and aunt would spare him again?' and so forth—I always felt that something would happen in our favour; and so it has, you see. I have observed, Mrs. Elton, in the course of my life, that if things are going untowardly one month, they are sure to mend the next."

"Very true, Mr. Weston, perfectly true. It is just what I used to say to a certain gentleman in company in the days of courtship, when, because things did not go quite right, did not proceed with all the rapidity which suited his feelings, he was apt to be in despair, and exclaim that he was sure at this rate it would be *May* before Hymen's saffron robe would be put on for us. Oh! the pains I have been at to dispel those gloomy ideas and give him cheerfuller views! The carriage—we had disappointments about the carriage;—one morning, I remember, he came to me quite in despair."

She was stopped by a slight fit of coughing, and Mr. Weston instantly seized the opportunity of going on.

"You were mentioning May. May is the very month which Mrs. Churchill is ordered, or has ordered herself, to spend in some warmer place than Enscombe—in short, to spend in London; so that we have the agreeable prospect of frequent visits from Frank the whole spring—precisely the season of the year which one should have chosen for it: days almost at the longest; weather genial and pleasant, always inviting one out, and never too hot for exercise. When he was here before, we made the best of it; but there was a good deal of wet, damp, cheerless weather; there always is in February, you know, and we could not do half that we intended. Now will be the time. This will be complete enjoyment; and I do not know, Mrs. Elton, whether the uncertainty of our meetings, the sort of constant expectation there will be of his coming in to-day or to-morrow, and at any hour, may not be more friendly to happiness than having him actually in the house. I think it is so. I think it is the state of mind which gives most spirit and delight. I hope you will be pleased with my son; but you must not expect a prodigy. He is generally thought a fine young man, but do not expect a prodigy. Mrs. Weston's partiality for him is very great, and, as you may suppose, most gratifying to me. She thinks nobody equal to him."

"And I assure you, Mr. Weston, I have very little doubt that my opinion will be decidedly in his favour. I have heard so much in praise of Mr. Frank Churchill.—At the same time it is fair to observe, that I am one of those who always judge for themselves, and are by no means implicitly guided by others. I give you notice that as I find your son, so I shall judge of him.—I am no flatterer."

Mr. Weston was musing.

"I hope," said he presently, "I have not been severe upon poor Mrs. Churchill. If she is ill I should be sorry to do her injustice; but there are some traits in her character which make it difficult for me to speak of her with the forbearance I could wish. You cannot be ignorant, Mrs. Elton, of my connexion with the family, nor of the treatment I have met with; and, between ourselves, the whole blame of it is to be laid to her. She was the instigator. Frank's mother would never have been slighted as she was but for her. Mr. Churchill has pride; but his pride is nothing to his wife's: his is a quiet, indolent, gentlemanlike sort of pride that would harm nobody, and only make himself a little helpless and tiresome; but her pride is arrogance and insolence! And what inclines one less to bear, she has no fair pretence of family or blood. She was nobody when he married her, barely the daughter of a gentleman; but ever since her being turned into a Churchill she has out-Churchill'd them all in high and mighty claims: but in herself, I assure you, she is an upstart."

"Only think! well, that must be infinitely provoking! I have quite a horror of upstarts. Maple Grove has given me a thorough disgust to people of that sort; for there is a family in that neighbourhood who are such an annoyance to my brother and sister from the airs they give themselves! Your description of Mrs. Churchill made me think of them directly. People of the name of Tupman, very lately settled there, and encumbered with many low connexions, but giving themselves immense airs, and expecting to be on a footing with the old established families. A year and a half is the very utmost that they can have lived at West Hall; and how they got their fortune nobody knows. They came from Birmingham, which is not a place to promise much, you know, Mr. Weston. One has not great hopes from Birmingham. I always say there is something direful in the sound: but nothing more is positively known of the Tupmans, though a good many things I assure you are suspected; and yet by their manners they evidently think themselves equal even to my brother, Mr. Suckling, who happens to be one of their nearest neighbours. It is infinitely too bad. Mr. Suckling, who has been eleven years a resident at Maple Grove, and whose father had it before him—I believe, at least—I am almost sure that old Mr. Suckling had completed the purchase before his death."

They were interrupted. Tea was carrying round, and Mr. Weston, having said all that he wanted, soon took the opportunity of walking away.

After tea, Mr. and Mrs. Weston, and Mr. Elton sat down with Mr. Woodhouse to cards. The remaining five were left to their own powers, and Emma doubted their getting on very well; for Mr. Knightley seemed little disposed for conversation; Mrs. Elton was wanting notice, which nobody had inclination to pay, and she was herself in a worry of spirits which would have made her prefer being silent.

Mr. John Knightley proved more talkative than his brother. He was to leave them early the next day; and he soon began with—

"Well, Emma, I do not believe I have any thing more to say about the boys; but you have your sister's letter, and every thing is down at full length there we may be sure. My charge would be much more concise than hers, and probably not much in the same spirit; all that I have to recommend being comprised in, do not spoil them, and do not physic them."

"I rather hope to satisfy you both," said Emma, "for I shall do all in my power to make them happy, which will be enough for Isabella; and happiness must preclude false indulgence and physic."

"And if you find them troublesome, you must send them home again."

"That is very likely. You think so, do not you?"

"I hope I am aware that they may be too noisy for your father—or even may be some encumbrance to you, if your visiting engagements continue to increase as much as they have done lately."

"Increase!"

"Certainly; you must be sensible that the last half-year has made a great difference in your way of life."

"Difference! No indeed I am not."

"There can be no doubt of your being much more engaged with company than you used to be. Witness this very time. Here am I come down for only one day, and you are engaged with a dinner-party!—When did it happen before, or any thing like it? Your neighbourhood is increasing, and you mix more with it. A little while ago, every letter to Isabella brought an account of fresh gaieties; dinners at Mr. Cole's, or balls at the Crown. The difference which Randalls, Randalls alone makes in your goings-on, is very great."

"Yes," said his brother quickly, "it is Randalls that does it all."

"Very well—and as Randalls, I suppose, is not likely to have less influence than heretofore, it strikes me as a possible thing, Emma, that Henry and John may be sometimes in the way. And if they are, I only beg you to send them home."

"No," cried Mr. Knightley, "that need not be the consequence. Let them be sent to Donwell. I shall certainly be at leisure."

"Upon my word," exclaimed Emma, "you amuse me! I should like to know how many of all my numerous engagements take place without your being of the party; and why I am to be supposed in danger of wanting leisure to attend to the little boys. These amazing engagements of mine—what have they been? Dining once with the Coles—and having a ball talked of, which never took place. I can understand you—(nodding at Mr. John Knightley)—your good fortune in meeting with so many of your friends at once here, delights you too much to pass unnoticed. But you, (turning to Mr. Knightley,) who know how very, very seldom I am ever two hours from Hartfield, why you should foresee such a series of dissipation for me, I cannot imagine. And as to my dear little boys, I must say, that if Aunt Emma has not time for them, I do not think they would fare much better with Uncle Knightley, who is absent from home about five hours where she is absent one—and who, when he is at home, is either reading to himself or settling his accounts."

Mr. Knightley seemed to be trying not to smile; and succeeded without difficulty, upon Mrs. Elton's beginning to talk to him.

VOLUME III

CHAPTER I

A very little quiet reflection was enough to satisfy Emma as to the nature of her agitation on hearing this news of Frank Churchill. She was soon convinced that it was not for herself she was feeling at all apprehensive or embarrassed; it was for him. Her own attachment had really subsided into a mere nothing; it was not worth thinking of;—but if he, who had undoubtedly been always so much the most in love of the two, were to be returning with the same warmth of sentiment which he had taken away, it would be very distressing. If a separation of two months should not have cooled him, there were dangers and evils before her:—caution for him and for herself would be necessary. She did not mean to have her own affections entangled again, and it would be incumbent on her to avoid any encouragement of his.

She wished she might be able to keep him from an absolute declaration. That would be so very painful a conclusion of their present acquaintance! and yet, she could not help rather anticipating something decisive. She felt as if the spring would not pass without bringing a crisis, an event, a something to alter her present composed and tranquil state.

It was not very long, though rather longer than Mr. Weston had foreseen, before she had the power of forming some opinion of Frank Churchill's feelings. The Enscombe family were not in town quite so soon as had been imagined, but he was at Highbury very soon afterwards. He rode down for a couple of hours; he could not yet do more; but as he came from Randalls immediately to Hartfield, she could then exercise all her quick observation, and speedily determine how he was influenced, and how she must act. They met with the utmost friendliness. There could be no doubt of his great pleasure in seeing her. But she had an almost instant doubt of his caring for her as he had done, of his feeling the same tenderness in the same degree. She watched him well. It was a clear thing he was less in love than he had been. Absence, with the conviction probably of her indifference, had produced this very natural and very desirable effect.

He was in high spirits; as ready to talk and laugh as ever, and seemed delighted to speak of his former visit, and recur to old stories: and he was not without agitation. It was not in his calmness that she read his comparative difference. He was not calm; his spirits were evidently fluttered; there was restlessness about him. Lively as he was, it seemed a liveliness that did not satisfy himself; but what decided her belief on the subject, was his staying only a quarter of an hour, and hurrying away to make other calls in Highbury. "He had seen a group of old acquaintance in the street as he passed—he had not stopped, he would not stop for more than a word—but he had the vanity to think they would be disappointed if he did not call, and much as he wished to stay longer at Hartfield, he must hurry off." She had no doubt as to his being less in love—but neither his agitated spirits, nor his hurrying away, seemed like a perfect cure; and she was rather inclined to think it implied a dread of her returning power, and a discreet resolution of not trusting himself with her long.

This was the only visit from Frank Churchill in the course of ten days. He was often hoping, intending to come—but was always prevented. His aunt could not bear to have him leave her. Such was his own account at Randalls. If he were quite sincere, if he really tried to come, it was to be inferred that Mrs. Churchill's removal to London had been of no service to the wilful or nervous part of her disorder. That she was really ill was very certain; he had declared himself convinced of it, at Randalls. Though much might be fancy, he could not doubt, when he looked back, that she was in a weaker state of health than she had been half a year ago. He did not believe it to proceed from any thing that care and medicine might not remove, or at least that she might not have many years of existence before her; but he could not be prevailed on, by all his father's doubts, to say that her complaints were merely imaginary, or that she was as strong as ever.

It soon appeared that London was not the place for her. She could not endure its noise. Her nerves were under continual irritation and suffering; and by the ten days' end, her nephew's letter to Randalls communicated a change of plan. They were going to remove immediately to Richmond. Mrs. Churchill had been recommended to the medical skill of an eminent person there, and had otherwise a fancy for the place. A ready-furnished house in a favourite spot was engaged, and much benefit expected from the change.

Emma heard that Frank wrote in the highest spirits of this arrangement, and seemed most fully to appreciate the blessing of having two months before him of such near neighbourhood to many dear friends—for the house was taken for May and June. She was told that now he wrote with the greatest confidence of being often with them, almost as often as he could even wish.

Emma saw how Mr. Weston understood these joyous prospects. He was considering her as the source of all the happiness they offered. She hoped it was not so. Two months must bring it to the proof.

Mr. Weston's own happiness was indisputable. He was quite delighted. It was the very circumstance he could have wished for. Now, it would be really having Frank in their neighbourhood. What were nine miles to a young man?—An hour's ride. He would be always coming over. The difference in that respect of Richmond and London was enough to make the whole difference of seeing him always and seeing him never. Sixteen miles—nay, eighteen—it must be full eighteen to Manchester-street—was a serious obstacle. Were he ever able to get away, the day would be spent in coming and returning. There was no comfort in having him in London; he might as well be at Enscombe; but Richmond was the very distance for easy intercourse. Better than nearer!

One good thing was immediately brought to a certainty by this removal,—the ball at the Crown. It had not been forgotten before, but it had been soon acknowledged vain to attempt to fix a day. Now, however, it was absolutely to be; every preparation was resumed, and very soon after the Churchills had removed to Richmond, a few lines from Frank, to say that his aunt felt already much better for the change, and that he had no doubt of being able to join them for twenty-four hours at any given time, induced them to name as early a day as possible.

Mr. Weston's ball was to be a real thing. A very few to-morrows stood between the young people of Highbury and happiness.

Mr. Woodhouse was resigned. The time of year lightened the evil to him. May was better for every thing than February. Mrs. Bates was engaged to spend the evening at Hartfield, James had due notice, and he sanguinely hoped that neither dear little Henry nor dear little John would have any thing the matter with them, while dear Emma were gone.

CHAPTER II

No misfortune occurred, again to prevent the ball. The day approached, the day arrived; and after a morning of some anxious watching, Frank Churchill, in all the certainty of his own self, reached Randalls before dinner, and every thing was safe.

No second meeting had there yet been between him and Emma. The room at the Crown was to witness it;—but it would be better than a common meeting in a crowd. Mr. Weston had been so very earnest in his entreaties for her arriving there as soon as possible after themselves, for the purpose of taking her opinion as to the propriety and comfort of the rooms before any other persons came, that she could not refuse him, and must therefore spend some quiet interval in the young man's company. She was to convey Harriet, and they drove to the Crown in good time, the Randalls party just sufficiently before them.

Frank Churchill seemed to have been on the watch; and though he did not say much, his eyes declared that he meant to have a delightful evening. They all walked about together, to see that every thing was as it should be; and within a few minutes were joined by the contents of another carriage, which Emma could not hear the sound of at first, without great surprize. "So unreasonably early!" she was going to exclaim; but she presently found that it was a family of old friends, who were coming, like herself, by particular desire, to help Mr. Weston's judgment; and they were so very closely followed by another carriage of cousins, who had been entreated to come early with the same distinguishing earnestness, on the same errand, that it seemed as if half the company might soon be collected together for the purpose of preparatory inspection.

Emma perceived that her taste was not the only taste on which Mr. Weston depended, and felt, that to be the favourite and intimate of a man who had so many intimates and confidantes, was not the very first distinction in the scale of vanity. She liked his open manners, but a little less of open-heartedness would have made him a higher character.—General benevolence, but not general friendship, made a man what he ought to be.—She could fancy such a man. The whole party walked about, and looked, and praised again; and then, having nothing else to do, formed a sort of half-circle round the fire, to observe in their various modes, till other subjects were started, that, though *May*, a fire in the evening was still very pleasant.

Emma found that it was not Mr. Weston's fault that the number of privy councillors was not yet larger. They had stopped at Mrs. Bates's door to offer the use of their carriage, but the aunt and niece were to be brought by the Eltons.

Frank was standing by her, but not steadily; there was a restlessness, which shewed a mind not at ease. He was looking about, he was going to the door, he was watching for the sound of other carriages,—impatient to begin, or afraid of being always near her.

Mrs. Elton was spoken of. "I think she must be here soon," said he. "I have a great curiosity to see Mrs. Elton, I have heard so much of her. It cannot be long, I think, before she comes."

A carriage was heard. He was on the move immediately; but coming back, said,

"I am forgetting that I am not acquainted with her. I have never seen either Mr. or Mrs. Elton. I have no business to put myself forward."

Mr. and Mrs. Elton appeared; and all the smiles and the proprieties passed.

"But Miss Bates and Miss Fairfax!" said Mr. Weston, looking about. "We thought you were to bring them."

The mistake had been slight. The carriage was sent for them now. Emma longed to know what Frank's first opinion of Mrs. Elton might be; how he was affected by the studied elegance of her dress, and her smiles of graciousness. He was immediately qualifying himself to form an opinion, by giving her very proper attention, after the introduction had passed.

In a few minutes the carriage returned.—Somebody talked of rain.—"I will see that there are umbrellas, sir," said Frank to his father: "Miss Bates must not be forgotten:" and away he went. Mr. Weston was following; but Mrs. Elton detained him, to gratify him by her opinion of his son; and so briskly did she begin, that the young man himself, though by no means moving slowly, could hardly be out of hearing.

"A very fine young man indeed, Mr. Weston. You know I candidly told you I should form my own opinion; and I am happy to say that I am extremely pleased with him.—You may believe me. I never compliment. I think him a very handsome young man, and his manners are precisely what I like and approve—so truly the gentleman, without the least conceit or puppyism. You must know I have a vast dislike to puppies—quite a horror of them. They were never tolerated at Maple Grove. Neither Mr. Suckling nor me had ever any patience with them; and we used sometimes to say very cutting things! Selina, who is mild almost to a fault, bore with them much better."

While she talked of his son, Mr. Weston's attention was chained; but when she got to Maple Grove, he could recollect that there were ladies just arriving to be attended to, and with happy smiles must hurry away.

Mrs. Elton turned to Mrs. Weston. "I have no doubt of its being our carriage with Miss Bates and Jane. Our coachman and horses are so extremely expeditious!—I believe we drive faster than any body.—What a pleasure it is to send one's carriage for a friend!—I understand you were so kind as to offer, but another time it will be quite unnecessary. You may be very sure I shall always take care of *them*."

Miss Bates and Miss Fairfax, escorted by the two gentlemen, walked into the room; and Mrs. Elton seemed to think it as much her duty as Mrs. Weston's to receive them. Her gestures and movements might be understood by any one who looked on like Emma; but her words, every body's words, were soon lost under the incessant flow of Miss Bates, who came in talking, and had not finished her speech under many minutes after her being admitted into the circle at the fire. As the door opened she was heard,

"So very obliging of you!—No rain at all. Nothing to signify. I do not care for myself. Quite thick shoes. And Jane declares—Well!—(as soon as she was within the door) Well! This is brilliant indeed!—This is admirable!—Excellently contrived, upon my word. Nothing wanting. Could not have imagined it.—So well lighted up!—Jane, Jane, look!—did you ever see any thing? Oh! Mr. Weston, you must really have had Aladdin's lamp. Good Mrs. Stokes would not know her own room again. I saw her as I came in; she was standing in the entrance. 'Oh! Mrs. Stokes,' said I—but I had not time for more." She was now met by Mrs. Weston.—"Very well, I thank you, ma'am. I hope you are quite well. Very happy to hear it. So afraid you might have a headache!—seeing you pass by so often, and knowing how much trouble you must have. Delighted to hear it indeed. Ah! dear Mrs. Elton, so obliged to you for the carriage!—excellent time. Jane and I quite ready. Did not keep the horses a moment. Most comfortable carriage.—Oh! and I am sure our thanks are due to you, Mrs. Weston, on that score. Mrs. Elton had most kindly sent Jane a note, or we should have been.—But two such offers in one day!—Never were such neighbours. I said to my mother, 'Upon my word, ma'am—.' Thank you, my mother is remarkably well. Gone to Mr. Woodhouse's. I made her take her shawl—for the evenings are not warm—her large new shawl—Mrs. Dixon's wedding-present.—So kind of her to think of my mother! Bought at Weymouth, you know—Mr. Dixon's choice. There were three others, Jane says, which they hesitated about some time. Colonel Campbell rather preferred an olive. My dear Jane, are you sure you did not wet your feet?—It was but a drop or two, but I am so afraid:—but Mr. Frank Churchill was so extremely—and there was a mat to step upon—I shall never forget his extreme politeness.—Oh! Mr. Frank Churchill, I must tell you my mother's spectacles have never been in fault since; the rivet never came out again. My mother often talks of your good-nature. Does not she, Jane?—Do not we often talk of Mr. Frank Churchill?—Ah! here's Miss Woodhouse.—Dear Miss Woodhouse, how do you do?—Very well I thank you, quite well. This is meeting quite in fairy-land!—Such a transformation!—Must not compliment, I know (eyeing Emma most complacently)—that would be rude—but upon my word, Miss Woodhouse, you do look—how do you like Jane's hair?—You are a judge.—She did it all herself. Quite wonderful how she does her hair!—No hairdresser from London I think could.—Ah! Dr. Hughes I declare—and Mrs. Hughes. Must go and speak to Dr. and Mrs. Hughes for a moment.—How do you do? How do you do?—Very well, I thank you. This is delightful, is not it?—Where's dear Mr. Richard?—Oh! there he is. Don't disturb him. Much better employed talking to the young ladies. How do you do, Mr. Richard?—I saw you the other day as you rode through the town—Mrs. Otway, I protest!—and good Mr. Otway, and Miss Otway and Miss Caroline.—Such a host of friends!—and Mr. George and Mr. Arthur!—How do you do? How do you all do?—Quite well, I am much obliged to you. Never better.—Don't I hear another carriage?—Who can this be?—very likely the worthy Coles.—Upon my word, this is charming to be standing about among such friends! And such a noble fire!—I am quite roasted. No coffee, I thank you, for me—never take coffee.—A little tea if you please, sir, by and bye,—no hurry—Oh! here it comes. Every thing so good!"

Frank Churchill returned to his station by Emma; and as soon as

Miss Bates was quiet, she found herself necessarily overhearing the discourse of Mrs. Elton and Miss Fairfax, who were standing a little way behind her.—He was thoughtful. Whether he were overhearing too, she could not determine. After a good many compliments to Jane on her dress and look, compliments very quietly and properly taken, Mrs. Elton was evidently wanting to be complimented herself—and it was, "How do you like my gown?—How do you like my trimming?—How has Wright done my hair?"—with many other relative questions, all answered with patient politeness. Mrs. Elton then said, "Nobody can think less of dress in general than I do—but upon such an occasion as this, when every body's eyes are so much upon me, and in compliment to the Westons—who I have no doubt are giving this ball chiefly to do me honour—I would not wish to be inferior to others. And I see very few pearls in the room except mine.—So Frank Churchill is a capital dancer, I understand.—We shall see if our styles suit.—A fine young man certainly is Frank Churchill. I like him very well."

At this moment Frank began talking so vigorously, that Emma could not but imagine he had overheard his own praises, and did not want to hear more;—and the voices of the ladies were drowned for a while, till another suspension brought Mrs. Elton's tones again distinctly forward.—Mr. Elton had just joined them, and his wife was exclaiming,

"Oh! you have found us out at last, have you, in our seclusion?—I was this moment telling Jane, I thought you would begin to be impatient for tidings of us."

"Jane!"—repeated Frank Churchill, with a look of surprize and displeasure.—"That is easy—but Miss Fairfax does not disapprove it, I suppose."

"How do you like Mrs. Elton?" said Emma in a whisper.

"Not at all."

"You are ungrateful."

"Ungrateful!—What do you mean?" Then changing from a frown to a smile—"No, do not tell me—I do not want to know what you mean.—Where is my father?—When are we to begin dancing?"

Emma could hardly understand him; he seemed in an odd humour. He walked off to find his father, but was quickly back again with both Mr. and Mrs. Weston. He had met with them in a little perplexity, which must be laid before Emma. It had just occurred to Mrs. Weston that Mrs. Elton must be asked to begin the ball; that she would expect it; which interfered with all their wishes of giving Emma that distinction.—Emma heard the sad truth with fortitude.

"And what are we to do for a proper partner for her?" said Mr. Weston. "She will think Frank ought to ask her."

Frank turned instantly to Emma, to claim her former promise; and boasted himself an engaged man, which his father looked his most perfect approbation of—and it then appeared that Mrs. Weston was wanting *him* to dance with Mrs. Elton himself, and that their business was to help to persuade him into it, which was done pretty soon.—Mr. Weston and Mrs. Elton led the way, Mr. Frank Churchill and Miss Woodhouse followed. Emma must submit to stand second to Mrs. Elton, though she had always considered the ball as peculiarly for her. It was almost enough to make her think of marrying. Mrs. Elton had undoubtedly the advantage, at this time, in vanity completely gratified; for though she had intended to begin with Frank Churchill, she could not lose by the change. Mr. Weston might be his son's superior.—In spite of this little rub, however, Emma was smiling with enjoyment, delighted to see the respectable length of the set as it was forming, and to feel that she had so many hours of unusual festivity before her.—She was more disturbed by Mr. Knightley's not dancing than by any thing else.—There he was, among the standers-by, where he ought not to be; he ought to be dancing,—not classing himself with the husbands, and fathers, and whist-players, who were pretending to feel an interest in the dance till their rubbers were made up,—so young as he looked!—He could not have appeared to greater advantage perhaps anywhere, than where he had placed himself. His tall, firm, upright figure, among the bulky forms and stooping shoulders of the elderly men, was such as Emma felt must draw every body's eyes; and, excepting her own partner, there was not one among the whole row of young men who could be compared with him.—He moved a few steps nearer, and those few steps were enough to prove in how gentlemanlike a manner, with what natural grace, he must have danced, would he but take the trouble.—Whenever she caught his eye, she forced him to smile; but in general he was looking grave. She wished he could love a ballroom better, and could like Frank Churchill better.—He seemed often observing her. She must not flatter herself that he thought of her dancing, but if he were criticising her behaviour, she did not feel afraid. There was nothing like flirtation between her and her partner.

They seemed more like cheerful, easy friends, than lovers. That Frank Churchill thought less of her than he had done, was indubitable.

The ball proceeded pleasantly. The anxious cares, the incessant attentions of Mrs. Weston, were not thrown away. Every body seemed happy; and the praise of being a delightful ball, which is seldom bestowed till after a ball has ceased to be, was repeatedly given in the very beginning of the existence of this. Of very important, very recordable events, it was not more productive than such meetings usually are. There was one, however, which Emma thought something of.—The two last dances before supper were begun, and Harriet had no partner;—the only young lady sitting down;—and so equal had been hitherto the number of dancers, that how there could be any one disengaged was the wonder!—But Emma's wonder lessened soon afterwards, on seeing Mr. Elton sauntering about. He would not ask Harriet to dance if it were possible to be avoided: she was sure he would not—and she was expecting him every moment to escape into the card-room.

Escape, however, was not his plan. He came to the part of the room where the sitters-by were collected, spoke to some, and walked about in front of them, as if to shew his liberty, and his resolution of maintaining it. He did not omit being sometimes directly before Miss Smith, or speaking to those who were close to her.—Emma saw it. She was not yet dancing; she was working her way up from the bottom, and had therefore leisure to look around, and by only turning her head a little she saw it all. When she was half-way up the set, the whole group were exactly behind her, and she would no longer allow her eyes to watch; but Mr. Elton was so near, that she heard every syllable of a dialogue which just then took place between him and Mrs. Weston; and she perceived that his wife, who was standing immediately above her, was not only listening also, but even encouraging him by significant glances.—The kind-hearted, gentle Mrs. Weston had left her seat to join him and say, "Do not you dance, Mr. Elton?" to which his prompt reply was, "Most readily, Mrs. Weston, if you will dance with me."

"Me!—oh! no—I would get you a better partner than myself. I am no dancer."

"If Mrs. Gilbert wishes to dance," said he, "I shall have great pleasure, I am sure—for, though beginning to feel myself rather an old married man, and that my dancing days are over, it would give me very great pleasure at any time to stand up with an old friend like Mrs. Gilbert."

"Mrs. Gilbert does not mean to dance, but there is a young lady disengaged whom I should be very glad to see dancing—Miss Smith."

"Miss Smith!—oh!—I had not observed.—You are extremely obliging—and if I were not an old married man.—But my dancing days are over, Mrs. Weston. You will excuse me. Any thing else I should be most happy to do, at your command—but my dancing days are over."

Mrs. Weston said no more; and Emma could imagine with what surprize and mortification she must be returning to her seat. This was Mr. Elton! the amiable, obliging, gentle Mr. Elton.—She looked round for a moment; he had joined Mr. Knightley at a little distance, and was arranging himself for settled conversation, while smiles of high glee passed between him and his wife.

She would not look again. Her heart was in a glow, and she feared her face might be as hot.

In another moment a happier sight caught her;—Mr. Knightley leading Harriet to the set!—Never had she been more surprized, seldom more delighted, than at that instant. She was all pleasure and gratitude, both for Harriet and herself, and longed to be thanking him; and though too distant for speech, her countenance said much, as soon as she could catch his eye again.

His dancing proved to be just what she had believed it, extremely good; and Harriet would have seemed almost too lucky, if it had not been for the cruel state of things before, and for the very complete enjoyment and very high sense of the distinction which her happy features announced. It was not thrown away on her, she bounded higher than ever, flew farther down the middle, and was in a continual course of smiles.

Mr. Elton had retreated into the card-room, looking (Emma trusted) very foolish. She did not think he was quite so hardened as his wife, though growing very like her;—*she* spoke some of her feelings, by observing audibly to her partner,

"Knightley has taken pity on poor little Miss Smith!—Very good-natured, I declare."

Supper was announced. The move began; and Miss Bates might be heard from that moment, without interruption, till her being seated at table and taking up her spoon.

"Jane, Jane, my dear Jane, where are you?—Here is your tippet.

Mrs. Weston begs you to put on your tippet. She says she is afraid there will be draughts in the passage, though every thing has been done—One door nailed up—Quantities of matting—My dear Jane, indeed you must. Mr. Churchill, oh! you are too obliging! How well you put it on!—so gratified! Excellent dancing indeed!—Yes, my dear, I ran home, as I said I should, to help grandmama to bed, and got back again, and nobody missed me.—I set off without saying a word, just as I told you. Grandmama was quite well, had a charming evening with Mr. Woodhouse, a vast deal of chat, and backgammon.—Tea was made downstairs, biscuits and baked apples and wine before she came away: amazing luck in some of her throws: and she inquired a great deal about you, how you were amused, and who were your partners. 'Oh!' said I, 'I shall not forestall Jane; I left her dancing with Mr. George Otway; she will love to tell you all about it herself to-morrow: her first partner was Mr. Elton, I do not know who will ask her next, perhaps Mr. William Cox.' My dear sir, you are too obliging.—Is there nobody you would not rather?—I am not helpless. Sir, you are most kind. Upon my word, Jane on one arm, and me on the other!—Stop, stop, let us stand a little back, Mrs. Elton is going; dear Mrs. Elton, how elegant she looks!—Beautiful lace!—Now we all follow in her train. Quite the queen of the evening!—Well, here we are at the passage. Two steps, Jane, take care of the two steps. Oh! no, there is but one. Well, I was persuaded there were two. How very odd! I was convinced there were two, and there is but one. I never saw any thing equal to the comfort and style—Candles everywhere.—I was telling you of your grandmama, Jane,—There was a little disappointment.—The baked apples and biscuits, excellent in their way, you know; but there was a delicate fricassee of sweetbread and some asparagus brought in at first, and good Mr. Woodhouse, not thinking the asparagus quite boiled enough, sent it all out again. Now there is nothing grandmama loves better than sweetbread and asparagus—so she was rather disappointed, but we agreed we would not speak of it to any body, for fear of its getting round to dear Miss Woodhouse, who would be so very much concerned!—Well, this is brilliant! I am all amazement! could not have supposed any thing!—Such elegance and profusion!—I have seen nothing like it since—Well, where shall we sit? where shall we sit? Anywhere, so that Jane is not in a draught. Where *I* sit is of no consequence. Oh! do you recommend this side?—Well, I am sure,

Mr. Churchill—only it seems too good—but just as you please. What you direct in this house cannot be wrong. Dear Jane, how shall we ever recollect half the dishes for grandmama? Soup too! Bless me! I should not be helped so soon, but it smells most excellent, and I cannot help beginning."

Emma had no opportunity of speaking to Mr. Knightley till after supper; but, when they were all in the ballroom again, her eyes invited him irresistibly to come to her and be thanked. He was warm in his reprobation of Mr. Elton's conduct; it had been unpardonable rudeness; and Mrs. Elton's looks also received the due share of censure.

"They aimed at wounding more than Harriet," said he. "Emma, why is it that they are your enemies?"

He looked with smiling penetration; and, on receiving no answer, added, "*She* ought not to be angry with you, I suspect, whatever he may be.—To that surmise, you say nothing, of course; but confess, Emma, that you did want him to marry Harriet."

"I did," replied Emma, "and they cannot forgive me."

He shook his head; but there was a smile of indulgence with it, and he only said,

"I shall not scold you. I leave you to your own reflections."

"Can you trust me with such flatterers?—Does my vain spirit ever tell me I am wrong?"

"Not your vain spirit, but your serious spirit.—If one leads you wrong, I am sure the other tells you of it."

"I do own myself to have been completely mistaken in Mr. Elton. There is a littleness about him which you discovered, and which I did not: and I was fully convinced of his being in love with Harriet. It was through a series of strange blunders!"

"And, in return for your acknowledging so much, I will do you the justice to say, that you would have chosen for him better than he has chosen for himself.—Harriet Smith has some first-rate qualities, which Mrs. Elton is totally without. An unpretending, single-minded, artless girl—infinitely to be preferred by any man of sense and taste to such a woman as Mrs. Elton. I found Harriet more conversable than I expected."

Emma was extremely gratified.—They were interrupted by the bustle of Mr. Weston calling on every body to begin dancing again.

"Come Miss Woodhouse, Miss Otway, Miss Fairfax, what are you all doing?—Come Emma, set your companions the example. Every body is lazy! Every body is asleep!"

"I am ready," said Emma, "whenever I am wanted."

"Whom are you going to dance with?" asked Mr. Knightley.

She hesitated a moment, and then replied, "With you, if you will ask me."

"Will you?" said he, offering his hand.

"Indeed I will. You have shewn that you can dance, and you know we are not really so much brother and sister as to make it at all improper."

"Brother and sister! no, indeed."

CHAPTER III

This little explanation with Mr. Knightley gave Emma considerable pleasure. It was one of the agreeable recollections of the ball, which she walked about the lawn the next morning to enjoy.—She was extremely glad that they had come to so good an understanding respecting the Eltons, and that their opinions of both husband and wife were so much alike; and his praise of Harriet, his concession in her favour, was peculiarly gratifying. The impertinence of the Eltons, which for a few minutes had threatened to ruin the rest of her evening, had been the occasion of some of its highest satisfactions; and she looked forward to another happy result—the cure of Harriet's infatuation.—From Harriet's manner of speaking of the circumstance before they quitted the ballroom, she had strong hopes. It seemed as if her eyes were suddenly opened, and she were enabled to see that Mr. Elton was not the superior creature she had believed him. The fever was over, and Emma could harbour little fear of the pulse being quickened again by injurious courtesy. She depended on the evil feelings of the Eltons for supplying all the discipline of pointed neglect that could be farther requisite.—Harriet rational, Frank Churchill not too much in love, and Mr. Knightley not wanting to quarrel with her, how very happy a summer must be before her!

She was not to see Frank Churchill this morning. He had told her that he could not allow himself the pleasure of stopping at Hartfield, as he was to be at home by the middle of the day. She did not regret it.

Having arranged all these matters, looked them through, and put them all to rights, she was just turning to the house with spirits freshened up for the demands of the two little boys, as well as of their grandpapa, when the great iron sweep-gate opened, and two persons entered whom she had never less expected to see together—Frank Churchill, with Harriet leaning on his arm—actually Harriet!—A moment sufficed to convince her that something extraordinary had happened. Harriet looked white and frightened, and he was trying to cheer her.—The iron gates and the front-door were not twenty yards asunder;—they were all three soon in the hall, and Harriet immediately sinking into a chair fainted away.

A young lady who faints, must be recovered; questions must be answered, and surprizes be explained. Such events are very interesting, but the suspense of them cannot last long. A few minutes made Emma acquainted with the whole.

Miss Smith, and Miss Bickerton, another parlour boarder at Mrs. Goddard's, who had been also at the ball, had walked out together, and taken a road, the Richmond road, which, though apparently public enough for safety, had led them into alarm.—About half a mile beyond Highbury, making a sudden turn, and deeply shaded by elms on each side, it became for a considerable stretch very retired; and when the young ladies had advanced some way into it, they had suddenly perceived at a small distance before them, on a broader patch of greensward by the side, a party of gipsies. A child on the watch, came towards them to beg; and Miss Bickerton, excessively frightened, gave a great scream, and calling on Harriet to follow her, ran up a steep bank, cleared a slight hedge at the top, and made the best of her way by a short cut back to Highbury. But poor Harriet could not follow. She had suffered very much from cramp after dancing, and her first attempt to mount the bank brought on such a return of it as made her absolutely powerless—and in this state, and exceedingly terrified, she had been obliged to remain.

How the trampers might have behaved, had the young ladies been more courageous, must be doubtful; but such an invitation for attack could not be resisted; and Harriet was soon assailed by half a dozen children, headed by a stout woman and a great boy, all clamorous, and impertinent in look, though not absolutely in word.—More and more frightened, she immediately promised them money, and taking out her purse, gave them a shilling, and begged them not to want more, or to use her ill.—She was then able to walk, though but slowly, and was moving away—but her terror and her purse were too tempting, and she was followed, or rather surrounded, by the whole gang, demanding more.

In this state Frank Churchill had found her, she trembling and conditioning, they loud and insolent. By a most fortunate chance his leaving Highbury had been delayed so as to bring him to her assistance at this critical moment. The pleasantness of the morning had induced him to walk forward, and leave his horses to meet him by another road, a mile or two beyond Highbury—and happening to have borrowed a pair of scissors the night before of Miss Bates, and to have forgotten to restore them, he had been obliged to stop at her door, and go in for a few minutes: he was therefore later than he had intended; and being on foot, was unseen by the whole party till almost close to them. The terror which the woman and boy had been creating in Harriet was then their own portion. He had left them completely frightened; and Harriet eagerly clinging to him, and hardly able to speak, had just strength enough to reach Hartfield, before her spirits were quite overcome. It was his idea to bring her to Hartfield: he had thought of no other place.

This was the amount of the whole story,—of his communication and of Harriet's as soon as she had recovered her senses and speech.—He dared not stay longer than to see her well; these several delays left him not another minute to lose; and Emma engaging to give assurance of her safety to Mrs. Goddard, and notice of there being such a set of people in the neighbourhood to Mr. Knightley, he set off, with all the grateful blessings that she could utter for her friend and herself.

Such an adventure as this,—a fine young man and a lovely young woman thrown together in such a way, could hardly fail of suggesting certain ideas to the coldest heart and the steadiest brain. So Emma thought, at least. Could a linguist, could a grammarian, could even a mathematician have seen what she did, have witnessed their appearance together, and heard their history of it, without feeling that circumstances had been at work to make them peculiarly interesting to each other?—How much more must an imaginist, like herself, be on fire with speculation and foresight!—especially with such a groundwork of anticipation as her mind had already made.

It was a very extraordinary thing! Nothing of the sort had ever occurred before to any young ladies in the place, within her memory; no rencontre, no alarm of the kind;—and now it had happened to the very person, and at the very hour, when the other very person was chancing to pass by to rescue her!—It certainly was very extraordinary!—And knowing, as she did, the favourable state of mind of each at this period, it struck her the more. He was wishing to get the better of his attachment to herself, she just recovering from her mania for Mr. Elton. It seemed as if every thing united to promise the most interesting consequences. It was not possible that the occurrence should not be strongly recommending each to the other.

In the few minutes' conversation which she had yet had with him, while Harriet had been partially insensible, he had spoken of her terror, her naivete, her fervour as she seized and clung to his arm, with a sensibility amused and delighted; and just at last, after Harriet's own account had been given, he had expressed his indignation at the abominable folly of Miss Bickerton in the warmest terms. Every thing was to take its natural course, however, neither impelled nor assisted. She would not stir a step, nor drop a hint. No, she had had enough of interference. There could be no harm in a scheme, a mere passive scheme. It was no more than a wish. Beyond it she would on no account proceed.

Emma's first resolution was to keep her father from the knowledge of what had passed,—aware of the anxiety and alarm it would occasion: but she soon felt that concealment must be impossible. Within half an hour it was known all over Highbury. It was the very event to engage those who talk most, the young and the low; and all the youth and servants in the place were soon in the happiness of frightful news. The last night's ball seemed lost in the gipsies. Poor Mr. Woodhouse trembled as he sat, and, as Emma had foreseen, would scarcely be satisfied without their promising never to go beyond the shrubbery again. It was some comfort to him that many inquiries after himself and Miss Woodhouse (for his neighbours knew that he loved to be inquired after), as well as Miss Smith, were coming in during the rest of the day; and he had the pleasure of returning for answer, that they were all very indifferent—which, though not exactly true, for she was perfectly well, and Harriet not much otherwise, Emma would not interfere with. She had an unhappy state of health in general for the child of such a man, for she hardly knew what indisposition was; and if he did not invent illnesses for her, she could make no figure in a message.

The gipsies did not wait for the operations of justice; they took themselves off in a hurry. The young ladies of Highbury might have walked again in safety before their panic began, and the whole history dwindled soon into a matter of little importance but to Emma and her nephews:—in her imagination it maintained its ground, and Henry and John were still asking every day for the story of Harriet and the gipsies, and still tenaciously setting her right if she varied in the slightest particular from the original recital.

CHAPTER IV

A very few days had passed after this adventure, when Harriet came one morning to Emma with a small parcel in her hand, and after sitting down and hesitating, thus began:

"Miss Woodhouse—if you are at leisure—I have something that I should like to tell you—a sort of confession to make—and then, you know, it will be over."

Emma was a good deal surprized; but begged her to speak. There was a seriousness in Harriet's manner which prepared her, quite as much as her words, for something more than ordinary.

"It is my duty, and I am sure it is my wish," she continued, "to have no reserves with you on this subject. As I am happily quite an altered creature in *one respect*, it is very fit that you should have the satisfaction of knowing it. I do not want to say more than is necessary—I am too much ashamed of having given way as I have done, and I dare say you understand me."

"Yes," said Emma, "I hope I do."

"How I could so long a time be fancying myself! . . ." cried Harriet, warmly. "It seems like madness! I can see nothing at all extraordinary in him now.—I do not care whether I meet him or not—except that of the two I had rather not see him—and indeed I would go any distance round to avoid him—but I do not envy his wife in the least; I neither admire her nor envy her, as I have done: she is very charming, I dare say, and all that, but I think her very ill-tempered and disagreeable—I shall never forget her look the other night!—However, I assure you, Miss Woodhouse, I wish her no evil.—No, let them be ever so happy together, it will not give me another moment's pang: and to convince you that I have been speaking truth, I am now going to destroy—what I ought to have destroyed long ago—what I ought never to have kept—I know that very well (blushing as she spoke).—However, now I will destroy it all—and it is my particular wish to do it in your presence, that you may see how rational I am grown. Cannot you guess what this parcel holds?" said she, with a conscious look.

"Not the least in the world.—Did he ever give you any thing?"

"No—I cannot call them gifts; but they are things that I have valued very much."

She held the parcel towards her, and Emma read the words *Most precious treasures* on the top. Her curiosity was greatly excited. Harriet unfolded the parcel, and she looked on with impatience. Within abundance of silver paper was a pretty little Tunbridge-ware box, which Harriet opened: it was well lined with the softest cotton; but, excepting the cotton, Emma saw only a small piece of court-plaister.

"Now," said Harriet, "you *must* recollect."

"No, indeed I do not."

"Dear me! I should not have thought it possible you could forget what passed in this very room about court-plaister, one of the very last times we ever met in it!—It was but a very few days before I had my sore throat—just before Mr. and Mrs. John Knightley came—I think the very evening.—Do not you remember his cutting his finger with your new penknife, and your recommending court-plaister?—But, as you had none about you, and knew I had, you desired me to supply him; and so I took mine out and cut him a piece; but it was a great deal too large, and he cut it smaller, and kept playing some time with what was left, before he gave it back to me. And so then, in my nonsense, I could not help making a treasure of it—so I put it by never to be used, and looked at it now and then as a great treat."

"My dearest Harriet!" cried Emma, putting her hand before her face, and jumping up, "you make me more ashamed of myself than I can bear. Remember it? Aye, I remember it all now; all, except your saving this relic—I knew nothing of that till this moment—but the cutting the finger, and my recommending court-plaister, and saying I had none about me!—Oh! my sins, my sins!—And I had plenty all the while in my pocket!—One of my senseless tricks!—I deserve to be under a continual blush all the rest of my life.—Well—(sitting down again)—go on—what else?"

"And had you really some at hand yourself? I am sure I never suspected it, you did it so naturally."

"And so you actually put this piece of court-plaister by for his sake!" said Emma, recovering from her state of shame and feeling divided between wonder and amusement. And secretly she added to herself, "Lord bless me! when should I ever have thought of putting by in cotton a piece of court-plaister that Frank Churchill had been pulling about! I never was equal to this."

"Here," resumed Harriet, turning to her box again, "here is something still more valuable, I mean that *has been* more valuable, because this is what did really once belong to him, which the court-plaister never did."

Emma was quite eager to see this superior treasure. It was the end of an old pencil,—the part without any lead.

"This was really his," said Harriet.—"Do not you remember one morning?—no, I dare say you do not. But one morning—I forget exactly the day—but perhaps it was the Tuesday or Wednesday before *that evening*, he wanted to make a memorandum in his pocket-book; it was about spruce-beer. Mr. Knightley had been telling him something about brewing spruce-beer, and he wanted to put it down; but when he took out his pencil, there was so little lead that he soon cut it all away, and it would not do, so you lent him another, and this was left upon the table as good for nothing. But I kept my eye on it; and, as soon as I dared, caught it up, and never parted with it again from that moment."

"I do remember it," cried Emma; "I perfectly remember it.—Talking about spruce-beer.—Oh! yes—Mr. Knightley and I both saying we liked it, and Mr. Elton's seeming resolved to learn to like it too. I perfectly remember it.—Stop; Mr. Knightley was standing just here, was not he? I have an idea he was standing just here."

"Ah! I do not know. I cannot recollect.—It is very odd, but I cannot recollect.—Mr. Elton was sitting here, I remember, much about where I am now."—

"Well, go on."

"Oh! that's all. I have nothing more to shew you, or to say—except that I am now going to throw them both behind the fire, and I wish you to see me do it."

"My poor dear Harriet! and have you actually found happiness in treasuring up these things?"

"Yes, simpleton as I was!—but I am quite ashamed of it now, and wish I could forget as easily as I can burn them. It was very wrong of me, you know, to keep any remembrances, after he was married. I knew it was—but had not resolution enough to part with them."

"But, Harriet, is it necessary to burn the court-plaister?—I have not a word to say for the bit of old pencil, but the court-plaister might be useful."

"I shall be happier to burn it," replied Harriet. "It has a disagreeable look to me. I must get rid of every thing.—There it goes, and there is an end, thank Heaven! of Mr. Elton."

"And when," thought Emma, "will there be a beginning of Mr. Churchill?"

She had soon afterwards reason to believe that the beginning was already made, and could not but hope that the gipsy, though she had *told* no fortune, might be proved to have made Harriet's.—About a fortnight after the alarm, they came to a sufficient explanation, and quite undesignedly. Emma was not thinking of it at the moment, which made the information she received more valuable. She merely said, in the course of some trivial chat, "Well, Harriet, whenever you marry I would advise you to do so and so"—and thought no more of it, till after a minute's silence she heard Harriet say in a very serious tone, "I shall never marry."

Emma then looked up, and immediately saw how it was; and after a moment's debate, as to whether it should pass unnoticed or not, replied,

"Never marry!—This is a new resolution."

"It is one that I shall never change, however."

After another short hesitation, "I hope it does not proceed from—I hope it is not in compliment to Mr. Elton?"

"Mr. Elton indeed!" cried Harriet indignantly.—"Oh! no"—and Emma could just catch the words, "so superior to Mr. Elton!"

She then took a longer time for consideration. Should she proceed no farther?—should she let it pass, and seem to suspect nothing?—Perhaps Harriet might think her cold or angry if she did; or perhaps if she were totally silent, it might only drive Harriet into asking her to hear too much; and against any thing like such an unreserve as had been, such an open and frequent discussion of hopes and chances, she was perfectly resolved.—She believed it would be wiser for her to say and know at once, all that she meant to say and know. Plain dealing was always best. She had previously determined how far she would proceed, on any application of the sort; and it would be safer for both, to have the judicious law of her own brain laid down with speed.—She was decided, and thus spoke—

"Harriet, I will not affect to be in doubt of your meaning. Your resolution, or rather your expectation of never marrying, results from an idea that the person whom you might prefer, would be too greatly your superior in situation to think of you. Is not it so?"

"Oh! Miss Woodhouse, believe me I have not the presumption to suppose—Indeed I am not so mad.—But it is a pleasure to me to admire him at a distance—and to think of his infinite superiority to all the rest of the world, with the gratitude, wonder, and veneration, which are so proper, in me especially."

"I am not at all surprized at you, Harriet. The service he rendered you was enough to warm your heart."

"Service! oh! it was such an inexpressible obligation!—The very recollection of it, and all that I felt at the time—when I saw him coming—his noble look—and my wretchedness before. Such a change! In one moment such a change! From perfect misery to perfect happiness!"

"It is very natural. It is natural, and it is honourable.—Yes, honourable, I think, to chuse so well and so gratefully.—But that it will be a fortunate preference is more that I can promise. I do not advise you to give way to it, Harriet. I do not by any means engage for its being returned. Consider what you are about. Perhaps it will be wisest in you to check your feelings while you can: at any rate do not let them carry you far, unless you are persuaded of his liking you. Be observant of him. Let his behaviour be the guide of your sensations. I give you this caution now, because I shall never speak to you again on the subject. I am determined against all interference. Henceforward I know nothing of the matter. Let no name ever pass our lips. We were very wrong before; we will be cautious now.—He is your superior, no doubt, and there do seem objections and obstacles of a very serious nature; but yet, Harriet, more wonderful things have taken place, there have been matches of greater disparity. But take care of yourself. I would not have you too sanguine; though, however it may end, be assured your raising your thoughts to *him*, is a mark of good taste which I shall always know how to value."

Harriet kissed her hand in silent and submissive gratitude. Emma was very decided in thinking such an attachment no bad thing for her friend. Its tendency would be to raise and refine her mind—and it must be saving her from the danger of degradation.

CHAPTER V

In this state of schemes, and hopes, and connivance, June opened upon Hartfield. To Highbury in general it brought no material change. The Eltons were still talking of a visit from the Sucklings, and of the use to be made of their barouche-landau; and Jane Fairfax was still at her grandmother's; and as the return of the Campbells from Ireland was again delayed, and August, instead of Midsummer, fixed for it, she was likely to remain there full two months longer, provided at least she were able to defeat Mrs. Elton's activity in her service, and save herself from being hurried into a delightful situation against her will.

Mr. Knightley, who, for some reason best known to himself, had certainly taken an early dislike to Frank Churchill, was only growing to dislike him more. He began to suspect him of some double-dealing in his pursuit of Emma. That Emma was his object appeared indisputable. Every thing declared it; his own attentions, his father's hints, his stepmother's guarded silence; it was all in unison; words, conduct, discretion, and indiscretion, told the same story. But while so many were devoting him to Emma, and Emma herself making him over to Harriet, Mr. Knightley began to suspect him of some inclination to trifle with Jane Fairfax. He could not understand it; but there were symptoms of intelligence between them—he thought so at least—symptoms of admiration on his side, which, having once observed, he could not persuade himself to think entirely void of meaning, however he might wish to escape any of Emma's errors of imagination. *She* was not present when the suspicion first arose. He was dining with the Randalls family, and Jane, at the Eltons'; and he had seen a look, more than a single look, at Miss Fairfax, which, from the admirer of Miss Woodhouse, seemed somewhat out of place. When he was again in their company, he could not help remembering what he had seen; nor could he avoid observations which, unless it were like Cowper and his fire at twilight,

"Myself creating what I saw," brought him yet stronger suspicion of there being a something of private liking, of private understanding even, between Frank Churchill and Jane.

He had walked up one day after dinner, as he very often did, to spend his evening at Hartfield. Emma and Harriet were going to walk; he joined them; and, on returning, they fell in with a larger party, who, like themselves, judged it wisest to take their exercise early, as the weather threatened rain; Mr. and Mrs. Weston and their son, Miss Bates and her niece, who had accidentally met. They all united; and, on reaching Hartfield gates, Emma, who knew it was exactly the sort of visiting that would be welcome to her father, pressed them all to go in and drink tea with him. The Randalls party agreed to it immediately; and after a pretty long speech from Miss Bates, which few persons listened to, she also found it possible to accept dear Miss Woodhouse's most obliging invitation.

As they were turning into the grounds, Mr. Perry passed by on horseback. The gentlemen spoke of his horse.

"By the bye," said Frank Churchill to Mrs. Weston presently, "what became of Mr. Perry's plan of setting up his carriage?"

Mrs. Weston looked surprized, and said, "I did not know that he ever had any such plan."

"Nay, I had it from you. You wrote me word of it three months ago."

"Me! impossible!"

"Indeed you did. I remember it perfectly. You mentioned it as what was certainly to be very soon. Mrs. Perry had told somebody, and was extremely happy about it. It was owing to *her* persuasion, as she thought his being out in bad weather did him a great deal of harm. You must remember it now?"

"Upon my word I never heard of it till this moment."

"Never! really, never!—Bless me! how could it be?—Then I must have dreamt it—but I was completely persuaded—Miss Smith, you walk as if you were tired. You will not be sorry to find yourself at home."

"What is this?—What is this?" cried Mr. Weston, "about Perry and a carriage? Is Perry going to set up his carriage, Frank? I am glad he can afford it. You had it from himself, had you?"

"No, sir," replied his son, laughing, "I seem to have had it from nobody.—Very odd!—I really was persuaded of Mrs. Weston's having mentioned it in one of her letters to Enscombe, many weeks ago, with all these particulars—but as she declares she never heard a syllable of it before, of course it must have been a dream. I am a great dreamer. I dream of every body at Highbury when I am away—and when I have gone through my particular friends, then I begin dreaming of Mr. and Mrs. Perry."

"It is odd though," observed his father, "that you should have had such a regular connected dream about people whom it was not very likely you should be thinking of at Enscombe. Perry's setting up his carriage! and his wife's persuading him to it, out of care for his health—just what will happen, I have no doubt, some time or other; only a little premature. What an air of probability sometimes runs through a dream! And at others, what a heap of absurdities it is! Well, Frank, your dream certainly shews that Highbury is in your thoughts when you are absent. Emma, you are a great dreamer, I think?"

Emma was out of hearing. She had hurried on before her guests to prepare her father for their appearance, and was beyond the reach of Mr. Weston's hint.

"Why, to own the truth," cried Miss Bates, who had been trying in vain to be heard the last two minutes, "if I must speak on this subject, there is no denying that Mr. Frank Churchill might have—I do not mean to say that he did not dream it—I am sure I have sometimes the oddest dreams in the world—but if I am questioned about it, I must acknowledge that there was such an idea last spring; for Mrs. Perry herself mentioned it to my mother, and the Coles knew of it as well as ourselves—but it was quite a secret, known to nobody else, and only thought of about three days. Mrs. Perry was very anxious that he should have a carriage, and came to my mother in great spirits one morning because she thought she had prevailed. Jane, don't you remember grandmama's telling us of it when we got home? I forget where we had been walking to—very likely to Randalls; yes, I think it was to Randalls. Mrs. Perry was always particularly fond of my mother—indeed I do not know who is not—and she had mentioned it to her in confidence; she had no objection to her telling us, of course, but it was not to go beyond: and, from that day to this, I never mentioned it to a soul that I know of. At the same time, I will not positively answer for my having never dropt a hint, because I know I do sometimes pop out a thing before I am aware. I am a talker, you know; I am rather a talker; and now and then I have let a thing escape me which I should not. I am not like Jane; I wish I were. I will answer for it *she* never betrayed the least thing in the world. Where is she?—Oh! just behind. Perfectly remember Mrs. Perry's coming.—Extraordinary dream, indeed!"

They were entering the hall. Mr. Knightley's eyes had preceded Miss Bates's in a glance at Jane. From Frank Churchill's face, where he thought he saw confusion suppressed or laughed away, he had involuntarily turned to hers; but she was indeed behind, and too busy with her shawl. Mr. Weston had walked in. The two other gentlemen waited at the door to let her pass. Mr. Knightley suspected in Frank Churchill the determination of catching her eye—he seemed watching her intently—in vain, however, if it were so—Jane passed between them into the hall, and looked at neither.

There was no time for farther remark or explanation. The dream must be borne with, and Mr. Knightley must take his seat with the rest round the large modern circular table which Emma had introduced at Hartfield, and which none but Emma could have had power to place there and persuade her father to use, instead of the small-sized Pembroke, on which two of his daily meals had, for forty years been crowded. Tea passed pleasantly, and nobody seemed in a hurry to move.

"Miss Woodhouse," said Frank Churchill, after examining a table behind him, which he could reach as he sat, "have your nephews taken away their alphabets—their box of letters? It used to stand here. Where is it? This is a sort of dull-looking evening, that ought to be treated rather as winter than summer. We had great amusement with those letters one morning. I want to puzzle you again."

Emma was pleased with the thought; and producing the box, the table was quickly scattered over with alphabets, which no one seemed so much disposed to employ as their two selves. They were rapidly forming words for each other, or for any body else who would be puzzled. The quietness of the game made it particularly eligible for Mr. Woodhouse, who had often been distressed by the more animated sort, which Mr. Weston had occasionally introduced, and who now sat happily occupied in lamenting, with tender melancholy, over the departure of the "poor little boys," or in fondly pointing out, as he took up any stray letter near him, how beautifully Emma had written it.

Frank Churchill placed a word before Miss Fairfax. She gave a slight glance round the table, and applied herself to it. Frank was next to Emma, Jane opposite to them—and Mr. Knightley so placed as to see them all; and it was his object to see as much as he could, with as little apparent observation. The word was discovered, and with a faint smile pushed away. If meant to be immediately mixed with the others, and buried from sight, she should have looked on the table instead of looking just across, for it was not mixed; and Harriet, eager after every fresh word, and finding out none, directly took it up, and fell to work. She was sitting by Mr. Knightley, and turned to him for help. The word was *blunder*; and as Harriet exultingly proclaimed it, there was a blush on Jane's cheek which gave it a meaning not otherwise ostensible. Mr. Knightley connected it with the dream; but how it could all be, was beyond his comprehension. How the delicacy, the discretion of his favourite could have been so lain asleep! He feared there must be some decided involvement. Disingenuousness and double-dealing seemed to meet him at every turn. These letters were but the vehicle for gallantry and trick. It was a child's play, chosen to conceal a deeper game on Frank Churchill's part.

With great indignation did he continue to observe him; with great alarm and distrust, to observe also his two blinded companions. He saw a short word prepared for Emma, and given to her with a look sly and demure. He saw that Emma had soon made it out, and found it highly entertaining, though it was something which she judged it proper to appear to censure; for she said, "Nonsense! for shame!" He heard Frank Churchill next say, with a glance towards Jane, "I will give it to her—shall I?"—and as clearly heard Emma opposing it with eager laughing warmth. "No, no, you must not; you shall not, indeed."

It was done however. This gallant young man, who seemed to love without feeling, and to recommend himself without complaisance, directly handed over the word to Miss Fairfax, and with a particular degree of sedate civility entreated her to study it. Mr. Knightley's excessive curiosity to know what this word might be, made him seize every possible moment for darting his eye towards it, and it was not long before he saw it to be *Dixon*. Jane Fairfax's perception seemed to accompany his; her comprehension was certainly more equal to the covert meaning, the superior intelligence, of those five letters so arranged. She was evidently displeased; looked up, and seeing herself watched, blushed more deeply than he had ever perceived her, and saying only, "I did not know that proper names were allowed," pushed away the letters with even an angry spirit, and looked resolved to be engaged by no other word that could be offered. Her face was averted from those who had made the attack, and turned towards her aunt.

"Aye, very true, my dear," cried the latter, though Jane had not spoken a word—"I was just going to say the same thing. It is time for us to be going indeed. The evening is closing in, and grandmama will be looking for us. My dear sir, you are too obliging. We really must wish you good night."

Jane's alertness in moving, proved her as ready as her aunt had preconceived. She was immediately up, and wanting to quit the table; but so many were also moving, that she could not get away; and Mr. Knightley thought he saw another collection of letters anxiously pushed towards her, and resolutely swept away by her unexamined. She was afterwards looking for her shawl—Frank Churchill was looking also—it was growing dusk, and the room was in confusion; and how they parted, Mr. Knightley could not tell.

He remained at Hartfield after all the rest, his thoughts full of what he had seen; so full, that when the candles came to assist his observations, he must—yes, he certainly must, as a friend—an anxious friend—give Emma some hint, ask her some question. He could not see her in a situation of such danger, without trying to preserve her. It was his duty.

"Pray, Emma," said he, "may I ask in what lay the great amusement, the poignant sting of the last word given to you and Miss Fairfax? I saw the word, and am curious to know how it could be so very entertaining to the one, and so very distressing to the other."

Emma was extremely confused. She could not endure to give him the true explanation; for though her suspicions were by no means removed, she was really ashamed of having ever imparted them.

"Oh!" she cried in evident embarrassment, "it all meant nothing; a mere joke among ourselves."

"The joke," he replied gravely, "seemed confined to you and Mr. Churchill."

He had hoped she would speak again, but she did not. She would rather busy herself about any thing than speak. He sat a little while in doubt. A variety of evils crossed his mind. Interference—fruitless interference. Emma's confusion, and the acknowledged intimacy, seemed to declare her affection engaged. Yet he would speak. He owed it to her, to risk any thing that might be involved in an unwelcome interference, rather than her welfare; to encounter any thing, rather than the remembrance of neglect in such a cause.

"My dear Emma," said he at last, with earnest kindness, "do you think you perfectly understand the degree of acquaintance between the gentleman and lady we have been speaking of?"

"Between Mr. Frank Churchill and Miss Fairfax? Oh! yes, perfectly.—Why do you make a doubt of it?"

"Have you never at any time had reason to think that he admired her, or that she admired him?"

"Never, never!" she cried with a most open eagerness—"Never, for the twentieth part of a moment, did such an idea occur to me. And how could it possibly come into your head?"

"I have lately imagined that I saw symptoms of attachment between them—certain expressive looks, which I did not believe meant to be public."

"Oh! you amuse me excessively. I am delighted to find that you can vouchsafe to let your imagination wander—but it will not do—very sorry to check you in your first essay—but indeed it will not do. There is no admiration between them, I do assure you; and the appearances which have caught you, have arisen from some peculiar circumstances—feelings rather of a totally different nature—it is impossible exactly to explain:—there is a good deal of nonsense in it—but the part which is capable of being communicated, which is sense, is, that they are as far from any attachment or admiration for one another, as any two beings in the world can be. That is, I *presume* it to be so on her side, and I can *answer* for its being so on his. I will answer for the gentleman's indifference."

She spoke with a confidence which staggered, with a satisfaction which silenced, Mr. Knightley. She was in gay spirits, and would have prolonged the conversation, wanting to hear the particulars of his suspicions, every look described, and all the wheres and hows of a circumstance which highly entertained her: but his gaiety did not meet hers. He found he could not be useful, and his feelings were too much irritated for talking. That he might not be irritated into an absolute fever, by the fire which Mr. Woodhouse's tender habits required almost every evening throughout the year, he soon afterwards took a hasty leave, and walked home to the coolness and solitude of Donwell Abbey.

CHAPTER VI

After being long fed with hopes of a speedy visit from Mr. and Mrs. Suckling, the Highbury world were obliged to endure the mortification of hearing that they could not possibly come till the autumn. No such importation of novelties could enrich their intellectual stores at present. In the daily interchange of news, they must be again restricted to the other topics with which for a while the Sucklings' coming had been united, such as the last accounts of Mrs. Churchill, whose health seemed every day to supply a different report, and the situation of Mrs. Weston, whose happiness it was to be hoped might eventually be as much increased by the arrival of a child, as that of all her neighbours was by the approach of it.

Mrs. Elton was very much disappointed. It was the delay of a great deal of pleasure and parade. Her introductions and recommendations must all wait, and every projected party be still only talked of. So she thought at first;—but a little consideration convinced her that every thing need not be put off. Why should not they explore to Box Hill though the Sucklings did not come? They could go there again with them in the autumn. It was settled that they should go to Box Hill. That there was to be such a party had been long generally known: it had even given the idea of another. Emma had never been to Box Hill; she wished to see what every body found so well worth seeing, and she and Mr. Weston had agreed to chuse some fine morning and drive thither. Two or three more of the chosen only were to be admitted to join them, and it was to be done in a quiet, unpretending, elegant way, infinitely superior to the bustle and preparation, the regular eating and drinking, and picnic parade of the Eltons and the Sucklings.

This was so very well understood between them, that Emma could not but feel some surprise, and a little displeasure, on hearing from Mr. Weston that he had been proposing to Mrs. Elton, as her brother and sister had failed her, that the two parties should unite, and go together; and that as Mrs. Elton had very readily acceded to it, so it was to be, if she had no objection. Now, as her objection was nothing but her very great dislike of Mrs. Elton, of which Mr. Weston must already be perfectly aware, it was not worth bringing forward again:—it could not be done without a reproof to him, which would be giving pain to his wife; and she found herself therefore obliged to consent to an arrangement which she would have done a great deal to avoid; an arrangement which would probably expose her even to the degradation of being said to be of Mrs. Elton's party! Every feeling was offended; and the forbearance of her outward submission left a heavy arrear due of secret severity in her reflections on the unmanageable good-will of Mr. Weston's temper.

"I am glad you approve of what I have done," said he very comfortably. "But I thought you would. Such schemes as these are nothing without numbers. One cannot have too large a party. A large party secures its own amusement. And she is a good-natured woman after all. One could not leave her out."

Emma denied none of it aloud, and agreed to none of it in private.

It was now the middle of June, and the weather fine; and Mrs. Elton was growing impatient to name the day, and settle with Mr. Weston as to pigeon-pies and cold lamb, when a lame carriage-horse threw every thing into sad uncertainty. It might be weeks, it might be only a few days, before the horse were useable; but no preparations could be ventured on, and it was all melancholy stagnation. Mrs. Elton's resources were inadequate to such an attack.

"Is not this most vexatious, Knightley?" she cried.—"And such weather for exploring!—These delays and disappointments are quite odious. What are we to do?—The year will wear away at this rate, and nothing done. Before this time last year I assure you we had had a delightful exploring party from Maple Grove to Kings Weston."

"You had better explore to Donwell," replied Mr. Knightley. "That may be done without horses. Come, and eat my strawberries. They are ripening fast."

If Mr. Knightley did not begin seriously, he was obliged to proceed so, for his proposal was caught at with delight; and the "Oh! I should like it of all things," was not plainer in words than manner. Donwell was famous for its strawberry-beds, which seemed a plea for the invitation: but no plea was necessary; cabbage-beds would have been enough to tempt the lady, who only wanted to be going somewhere. She promised him again and again to come—much oftener than he doubted—and was extremely gratified by such a proof of intimacy, such a distinguishing compliment as she chose to consider it.

"You may depend upon me," said she. "I certainly will come. Name your day, and I will come. You will allow me to bring Jane Fairfax?"

"I cannot name a day," said he, "till I have spoken to some others whom I would wish to meet you."

"Oh! leave all that to me. Only give me a carte-blanche.—I am Lady Patroness, you know. It is my party. I will bring friends with me."

"I hope you will bring Elton," said he: "but I will not trouble you to give any other invitations."

"Oh! now you are looking very sly. But consider—you need not be afraid of delegating power to *me*. I am no young lady on her preferment. Married women, you know, may be safely authorised. It is my party. Leave it all to me. I will invite your guests."

"No,"—he calmly replied,—"there is but one married woman in the world whom I can ever allow to invite what guests she pleases to Donwell, and that one is—"

"—Mrs. Weston, I suppose," interrupted Mrs. Elton, rather mortified.

"No—Mrs. Knightley;—and till she is in being, I will manage such matters myself."

"Ah! you are an odd creature!" she cried, satisfied to have no one preferred to herself.—"You are a humourist, and may say what you like. Quite a humourist. Well, I shall bring Jane with me—Jane and her aunt.—The rest I leave to you. I have no objections at all to meeting the Hartfield family. Don't scruple. I know you are attached to them."

"You certainly will meet them if I can prevail; and I shall call on Miss Bates in my way home."

"That's quite unnecessary; I see Jane every day:—but as you like. It is to be a morning scheme, you know, Knightley; quite a simple thing. I shall wear a large bonnet, and bring one of my little baskets hanging on my arm. Here,—probably this basket with pink ribbon. Nothing can be more simple, you see. And Jane will have such another. There is to be no form or parade—a sort of gipsy party. We are to walk about your gardens, and gather the strawberries ourselves, and sit under trees;—and whatever else you may like to provide, it is to be all out of doors—a table spread in the shade, you know. Every thing as natural and simple as possible. Is not that your idea?"

"Not quite. My idea of the simple and the natural will be to have the table spread in the dining-room. The nature and the simplicity of gentlemen and ladies, with their servants and furniture, I think is best observed by meals within doors. When you are tired of eating strawberries in the garden, there shall be cold meat in the house."

"Well—as you please; only don't have a great set out. And, by the bye, can I or my housekeeper be of any use to you with our opinion?—Pray be sincere, Knightley. If you wish me to talk to Mrs. Hodges, or to inspect any-thing—"

"I have not the least wish for it, I thank you."

"Well—but if any difficulties should arise, my housekeeper is extremely clever."

"I will answer for it, that mine thinks herself full as clever, and would spurn any body's assistance."

"I wish we had a donkey. The thing would be for us all to come on donkeys, Jane, Miss Bates, and me—and my *caro sposo* walking by. I really must talk to him about purchasing a donkey. In a country life I conceive it to be a sort of necessary; for, let a woman have ever so many resources, it is not possible for her to be always shut up at home;—and very long walks, you know—in summer there is dust, and in winter there is dirt."

"You will not find either, between Donwell and Highbury. Donwell Lane is never dusty, and now it is perfectly dry. Come on a donkey, however, if you prefer it. You can borrow Mrs. Cole's. I would wish every thing to be as much to your taste as possible."

"That I am sure you would. Indeed I do you justice, my good friend. Under that peculiar sort of dry, blunt manner, I know you have the warmest heart. As I tell Mr. E., you are a thorough humourist.—Yes, believe me, Knightley, I am fully sensible of your attention to me in the whole of this scheme. You have hit upon the very thing to please me."

Mr. Knightley had another reason for avoiding a table in the shade. He wished to persuade Mr. Woodhouse, as well as Emma, to join the party; and he knew that to have any of them sitting down out of doors to eat would inevitably make him ill. Mr. Woodhouse must not, under the specious pretence of a morning drive, and an hour or two spent at Donwell, be tempted away to his misery.

He was invited on good faith. No lurking horrors were to upbraid him for his easy credulity. He did consent. He had not been at Donwell for two years. "Some very fine morning, he, and Emma, and Harriet, could go very well; and he could sit still with Mrs. Weston, while the dear girls walked about the gardens. He did not suppose they could be damp now, in the middle of the day. He should like to see the old house again exceedingly, and should be very happy to meet Mr. and Mrs. Elton, and any other of his neighbours.—He could not see any objection at all to his, and Emma's, and Harriet's going there some very fine morning. He thought it very well done of Mr. Knightley to invite them—very kind and sensible—much cleverer than dining out.—He was not fond of dining out."

Mr. Knightley was fortunate in every body's most ready concurrence. The invitation was everywhere so well received, that it seemed as if, like Mrs. Elton, they were all taking the scheme as a particular compliment to themselves.—Emma and Harriet professed very high expectations of pleasure from it; and Mr. Weston, unasked, promised to get Frank over to join them, if possible; a proof of approbation and gratitude which could have been dispensed with.—Mr. Knightley was then obliged to say that he should be glad to see him; and Mr. Weston engaged to lose no time in writing, and spare no arguments to induce him to come.

In the meanwhile the lame horse recovered so fast, that the party to Box Hill was again under happy consideration; and at last Donwell was settled for one day, and Box Hill for the next,—the weather appearing exactly right.

Under a bright mid-day sun, at almost Midsummer, Mr. Woodhouse was safely conveyed in his carriage, with one window down, to partake of this al-fresco party; and in one of the most comfortable rooms in the Abbey, especially prepared for him by a fire all the morning, he was happily placed, quite at his ease, ready to talk with pleasure of what had been achieved, and advise every body to come and sit down, and not to heat themselves.—Mrs. Weston, who seemed to have walked there on purpose to be tired, and sit all the time with him, remained, when all the others were invited or persuaded out, his patient listener and sympathiser.

It was so long since Emma had been at the Abbey, that as soon as she was satisfied of her father's comfort, she was glad to leave him, and look around her; eager to refresh and correct her memory with more particular observation, more exact understanding of a house and grounds which must ever be so interesting to her and all her family.

She felt all the honest pride and complacency which her alliance with the present and future proprietor could fairly warrant, as she viewed the respectable size and style of the building, its suitable, becoming, characteristic situation, low and sheltered—its ample gardens stretching down to meadows washed by a stream, of which the Abbey, with all the old neglect of prospect, had scarcely a sight—and its abundance of timber in rows and avenues, which neither fashion nor extravagance had rooted up.—The house was larger than Hartfield, and totally unlike it, covering a good deal of ground, rambling and irregular, with many comfortable, and one or two handsome rooms.—It was just what it ought to be, and it looked what it was—and Emma felt an increasing respect for it, as the residence of a family of such true gentility, untainted in blood and understanding.—Some faults of temper John Knightley had; but Isabella had connected herself unexceptionably. She had given them neither men, nor names, nor places, that could raise a blush. These were pleasant feelings, and she walked about and indulged them till it was necessary to do as the others did, and collect round the strawberry-beds.—The whole party were assembled, excepting Frank Churchill, who was expected every moment from Richmond; and Mrs. Elton, in all her apparatus of happiness, her large bonnet and her basket, was very ready to lead the way in gathering, accepting, or talking—strawberries, and only strawberries, could now be thought or spoken of.—"The best fruit in England—every body's favourite—always wholesome.—These the finest beds and finest sorts.—Delightful to gather for one's self—the only way of really enjoying them.—Morning decidedly the best time—never tired—every sort good—hautboy infinitely superior—no comparison—the others hardly eatable—hautboys very scarce—Chili preferred—white wood finest flavour of all—price of strawberries in London—abundance about Bristol—Maple Grove—cultivation—beds when to be renewed—gardeners thinking exactly different—no general rule—gardeners never to be put out of their way—delicious fruit—only too rich to be eaten much of—inferior to cherries—currants more refreshing—only objection to gathering strawberries the stooping—glaring sun—tired to death—could bear it no longer—must go and sit in the shade."

Such, for half an hour, was the conversation—interrupted only once by Mrs. Weston, who came out, in her solicitude after her stepson, to inquire if he were come—and she was a little uneasy.—She had some fears of his horse.

Seats tolerably in the shade were found; and now Emma was obliged to overhear what Mrs. Elton and Jane Fairfax were talking of.—A situation, a most desirable situation, was in question. Mrs. Elton had received notice of it that morning, and was in raptures. It was not with Mrs. Suckling, it was not with Mrs. Bragge, but in felicity and splendour it fell short only of them: it was with a cousin of Mrs. Bragge, an acquaintance of Mrs. Suckling, a lady known at Maple Grove. Delightful, charming, superior, first circles, spheres, lines, ranks, every thing—and Mrs. Elton was wild to have the offer closed with immediately.—On her side, all was warmth, energy, and triumph—and she positively refused to take her friend's negative, though Miss Fairfax continued to assure her that she would not at present engage in any thing, repeating the same motives which she had been heard to urge before.—Still Mrs. Elton insisted on being authorised to write an acquiescence by the morrow's post.—How Jane could bear it at all, was astonishing to Emma.—She did look vexed, she did speak pointedly—and at last, with a decision of action unusual to her, proposed a removal.—"Should not they walk? Would not Mr. Knightley shew them the gardens—all the gardens?—She wished to see the whole extent."—The pertinacity of her friend seemed more than she could bear.

It was hot; and after walking some time over the gardens in a scattered, dispersed way, scarcely any three together, they insensibly followed one another to the delicious shade of a broad short avenue of limes, which stretching beyond the garden at an equal distance from the river, seemed the finish of the pleasure grounds.—It led to nothing; nothing but a view at the end over a low stone wall with high pillars, which seemed intended, in their erection, to give the appearance of an approach to the house, which never had been there. Disputable, however, as might be the taste of such a termination, it was in itself a charming walk, and the view which closed it extremely pretty.—The considerable slope, at nearly the foot of which the Abbey stood, gradually acquired a steeper form beyond its grounds; and at half a mile distant was a bank of considerable abruptness and grandeur, well clothed with wood;—and at the bottom of this bank, favourably placed and sheltered, rose the Abbey-Mill Farm, with meadows in front, and the river making a close and handsome curve around it.

It was a sweet view—sweet to the eye and the mind. English

verdure, English culture, English comfort, seen under a sun bright, without being oppressive.

In this walk Emma and Mr. Weston found all the others assembled; and towards this view she immediately perceived Mr. Knightley and Harriet distinct from the rest, quietly leading the way. Mr. Knightley and Harriet!—It was an odd tête-à-tête; but she was glad to see it.—There had been a time when he would have scorned her as a companion, and turned from her with little ceremony. Now they seemed in pleasant conversation. There had been a time also when Emma would have been sorry to see Harriet in a spot so favourable for the Abbey-Mill Farm; but now she feared it not. It might be safely viewed with all its appendages of prosperity and beauty, its rich pastures, spreading flocks, orchard in blossom, and light column of smoke ascending.—She joined them at the wall, and found them more engaged in talking than in looking around. He was giving Harriet information as to modes of agriculture, etc. and Emma received a smile which seemed to say, "These are my own concerns. I have a right to talk on such subjects, without being suspected of introducing Robert Martin."—She did not suspect him. It was too old a story.—Robert Martin had probably ceased to think of Harriet.—They took a few turns together along the walk.—The shade was most refreshing, and Emma found it the pleasantest part of the day.

The next remove was to the house; they must all go in and eat;—and they were all seated and busy, and still Frank Churchill did not come. Mrs. Weston looked, and looked in vain. His father would not own himself uneasy, and laughed at her fears; but she could not be cured of wishing that he would part with his black mare. He had expressed himself as to coming, with more than common certainty. "His aunt was so much better, that he had not a doubt of getting over to them."—Mrs. Churchill's state, however, as many were ready to remind her, was liable to such sudden variation as might disappoint her nephew in the most reasonable dependence—and Mrs. Weston was at last persuaded to believe, or to say, that it must be by some attack of Mrs. Churchill that he was prevented coming.—Emma looked at Harriet while the point was under consideration; she behaved very well, and betrayed no emotion.

The cold repast was over, and the party were to go out once more to see what had not yet been seen, the old Abbey fish-ponds; perhaps get as far as the clover, which was to be begun cutting on the morrow, or, at any rate, have the pleasure of being hot, and growing cool again.—

Mr. Woodhouse, who had already taken his little round in the highest part of the gardens, where no damps from the river were imagined even by him, stirred no more; and his daughter resolved to remain with him, that Mrs. Weston might be persuaded away by her husband to the exercise and variety which her spirits seemed to need.

Mr. Knightley had done all in his power for Mr. Woodhouse's entertainment. Books of engravings, drawers of medals, cameos, corals, shells, and every other family collection within his cabinets, had been prepared for his old friend, to while away the morning; and the kindness had perfectly answered. Mr. Woodhouse had been exceedingly well amused. Mrs. Weston had been shewing them all to him, and now he would shew them all to Emma;—fortunate in having no other resemblance to a child, than in a total want of taste for what he saw, for he was slow, constant, and methodical.—Before this second looking-over was begun, however, Emma walked into the hall for the sake of a few moments' free observation of the entrance and ground-plot of the house—and was hardly there, when Jane Fairfax appeared, coming quickly in from the garden, and with a look of escape.—Little expecting to meet Miss Woodhouse so soon, there was a start at first; but Miss Woodhouse was the very person she was in quest of.

"Will you be so kind," said she, "when I am missed, as to say that I am gone home?—I am going this moment.—My aunt is not aware how late it is, nor how long we have been absent—but I am sure we shall be wanted, and I am determined to go directly.—I have said nothing about it to any body. It would only be giving trouble and distress. Some are gone to the ponds, and some to the lime walk. Till they all come in I shall not be missed; and when they do, will you have the goodness to say that I am gone?"

"Certainly, if you wish it;—but you are not going to walk to Highbury alone?"

"Yes—what should hurt me?—I walk fast. I shall be at home in twenty minutes."

"But it is too far, indeed it is, to be walking quite alone. Let my father's servant go with you.—Let me order the carriage. It can be round in five minutes."

"Thank you, thank you—but on no account.—I would rather walk.—And for *me* to be afraid of walking alone!—I, who may so soon have to guard others!"

She spoke with great agitation; and Emma very feelingly replied, "That can be no reason for your being exposed to danger now. I must order the carriage. The heat even would be danger.—You are fatigued already."

"I am,"—she answered—"I am fatigued; but it is not the sort of fatigue—quick walking will refresh me.—Miss Woodhouse, we all know at times what it is to be wearied in spirits. Mine, I confess, are exhausted. The greatest kindness you can shew me, will be to let me have my own way, and only say that I am gone when it is necessary."

Emma had not another word to oppose. She saw it all; and entering into her feelings, promoted her quitting the house immediately, and watched her safely off with the zeal of a friend. Her parting look was grateful—and her parting words, "Oh! Miss Woodhouse, the comfort of being sometimes alone!"—seemed to burst from an overcharged heart, and to describe somewhat of the continual endurance to be practised by her, even towards some of those who loved her best.

"Such a home, indeed! such an aunt!" said Emma, as she turned back into the hall again. "I do pity you. And the more sensibility you betray of their just horrors, the more I shall like you."

Jane had not been gone a quarter of an hour, and they had only accomplished some views of St. Mark's Place, Venice, when Frank Churchill entered the room. Emma had not been thinking of him, she had forgotten to think of him—but she was very glad to see him. Mrs. Weston would be at ease. The black mare was blameless; *they* were right who had named Mrs. Churchill as the cause. He had been detained by a temporary increase of illness in her; a nervous seizure, which had lasted some hours—and he had quite given up every thought of coming, till very late;—and had he known how hot a ride he should have, and how late, with all his hurry, he must be, he believed he should not have come at all. The heat was excessive; he had never suffered any thing like it—almost wished he had staid at home—nothing killed him like heat—he could bear any degree of cold, etc., but heat was intolerable—and he sat down, at the greatest possible distance from the slight remains of Mr. Woodhouse's fire, looking very deplorable.

"You will soon be cooler, if you sit still," said Emma.

"As soon as I am cooler I shall go back again. I could very ill be spared—but such a point had been made of my coming! You will all be going soon I suppose; the whole party breaking up. I met *one* as I came—Madness in such weather!—absolute madness!"

Emma listened, and looked, and soon perceived that Frank Churchill's state might be best defined by the expressive phrase of being out of humour. Some people were always cross when they were hot. Such might be his constitution; and as she knew that eating and drinking were often the cure of such incidental complaints, she recommended his taking some refreshment; he would find abundance of every thing in the dining-room—and she humanely pointed out the door.

"No—he should not eat. He was not hungry; it would only make him hotter." In two minutes, however, he relented in his own favour; and muttering something about spruce-beer, walked off. Emma returned all her attention to her father, saying in secret—

"I am glad I have done being in love with him. I should not like a man who is so soon discomposed by a hot morning. Harriet's sweet easy temper will not mind it."

He was gone long enough to have had a very comfortable meal, and came back all the better—grown quite cool—and, with good manners, like himself—able to draw a chair close to them, take an interest in their employment; and regret, in a reasonable way, that he should be so late. He was not in his best spirits, but seemed trying to improve them; and, at last, made himself talk nonsense very agreeably. They were looking over views in Swisserland.

"As soon as my aunt gets well, I shall go abroad," said he. "I shall never be easy till I have seen some of these places. You will have my sketches, some time or other, to look at—or my tour to read—or my poem. I shall do something to expose myself."

"That may be—but not by sketches in Swisserland. You will never go to Swisserland. Your uncle and aunt will never allow you to leave England."

"They may be induced to go too. A warm climate may be prescribed for her. I have more than half an expectation of our all going abroad. I assure you I have. I feel a strong persuasion, this morning, that I shall soon be abroad. I ought to travel. I am tired of doing nothing. I want a change. I am serious, Miss Woodhouse, whatever your penetrating eyes may fancy—I am sick of England—and would leave it to-morrow, if I could."

"You are sick of prosperity and indulgence. Cannot you invent a few hardships for yourself, and be contented to stay?"

"*I* sick of prosperity and indulgence! You are quite mistaken. I do not look upon myself as either prosperous or indulged. I am thwarted in every thing material. I do not consider myself at all a fortunate person."

"You are not quite so miserable, though, as when you first came. Go and eat and drink a little more, and you will do very well. Another slice of cold meat, another draught of Madeira and water, will make you nearly on a par with the rest of us."

"No—I shall not stir. I shall sit by you. You are my best cure."

"We are going to Box Hill to-morrow;—you will join us. It is not Swisserland, but it will be something for a young man so much in want of a change. You will stay, and go with us?"

"No, certainly not; I shall go home in the cool of the evening."

"But you may come again in the cool of to-morrow morning."

"No—It will not be worth while. If I come, I shall be cross."

"Then pray stay at Richmond."

"But if I do, I shall be crosser still. I can never bear to think of you all there without me."

"These are difficulties which you must settle for yourself. Chuse your own degree of crossness. I shall press you no more."

The rest of the party were now returning, and all were soon collected. With some there was great joy at the sight of Frank Churchill; others took it very composedly; but there was a very general distress and disturbance on Miss Fairfax's disappearance being explained. That it was time for every body to go, concluded the subject; and with a short final arrangement for the next day's scheme, they parted. Frank Churchill's little inclination to exclude himself increased so much, that his last words to Emma were,

"Well;—if *you* wish me to stay and join the party, I will."

She smiled her acceptance; and nothing less than a summons from Richmond was to take him back before the following evening.

CHAPTER VII

They had a very fine day for Box Hill; and all the other outward circumstances of arrangement, accommodation, and punctuality, were in favour of a pleasant party. Mr. Weston directed the whole, officiating safely between Hartfield and the Vicarage, and every body was in good time. Emma and Harriet went together; Miss Bates and her niece, with the Eltons; the gentlemen on horseback. Mrs. Weston remained with Mr. Woodhouse. Nothing was wanting but to be happy when they got there. Seven miles were travelled in expectation of enjoyment, and every body had a burst of admiration on first arriving; but in the general amount of the day there was deficiency. There was a languor, a want of spirits, a want of union, which could not be got over. They separated too much into parties. The Eltons walked together; Mr. Knightley took charge of Miss Bates and Jane; and Emma and Harriet belonged to Frank Churchill. And Mr. Weston tried, in vain, to make them harmonise better. It seemed at first an accidental division, but it never materially varied. Mr. and Mrs. Elton, indeed, shewed no unwillingness to mix, and be as agreeable as they could; but during the two whole hours that were spent on the hill, there seemed a principle of separation, between the other parties, too strong for any fine prospects, or any cold collation, or any cheerful Mr. Weston, to remove.

At first it was downright dulness to Emma. She had never seen Frank Churchill so silent and stupid. He said nothing worth hearing—looked without seeing—admired without intelligence—listened without knowing what she said. While he was so dull, it was no wonder that Harriet should be dull likewise; and they were both insufferable.

When they all sat down it was better; to her taste a great deal better, for Frank Churchill grew talkative and gay, making her his first object. Every distinguishing attention that could be paid, was paid to her. To amuse her, and be agreeable in her eyes, seemed all that he cared for—and Emma, glad to be enlivened, not sorry to be flattered, was gay and easy too, and gave him all the friendly encouragement, the admission to be gallant, which she had ever given in the first and most animating period of their acquaintance; but which now, in her own estimation, meant nothing, though in the judgment of most people looking on it must have had such an appearance as no English word but flirtation could very well describe. "Mr. Frank Churchill and Miss Woodhouse flirted together excessively." They were laying themselves open to that very phrase—and to having it sent off in a letter to Maple Grove by one lady, to Ireland by another. Not that Emma was gay and thoughtless from any real felicity; it was rather because she felt less happy than she had expected. She laughed because she was disappointed; and though she liked him for his attentions, and thought them all, whether in friendship, admiration, or playfulness, extremely judicious, they were not winning back her heart. She still intended him for her friend.

"How much I am obliged to you," said he, "for telling me to come to-day!—If it had not been for you, I should certainly have lost all the happiness of this party. I had quite determined to go away again."

"Yes, you were very cross; and I do not know what about, except that you were too late for the best strawberries. I was a kinder friend than you deserved. But you were humble. You begged hard to be commanded to come."

"Don't say I was cross. I was fatigued. The heat overcame me."

"It is hotter to-day."

"Not to my feelings. I am perfectly comfortable to-day."

"You are comfortable because you are under command."

"Your command?—Yes."

"Perhaps I intended you to say so, but I meant self-command. You had, somehow or other, broken bounds yesterday, and run away from your own management; but to-day you are got back again—and as I cannot be always with you, it is best to believe your temper under your own command rather than mine."

"It comes to the same thing. I can have no self-command without a motive. You order me, whether you speak or not. And you can be always with me. You are always with me."

"Dating from three o'clock yesterday. My perpetual influence could not begin earlier, or you would not have been so much out of humour before."

"Three o'clock yesterday! That is your date. I thought I had seen you first in February."

"Your gallantry is really unanswerable. But (lowering her voice)—nobody speaks except ourselves, and it is rather too much to be talking nonsense for the entertainment of seven silent people."

"I say nothing of which I am ashamed," replied he, with lively impudence. "I saw you first in February. Let every body on the Hill hear me if they can. Let my accents swell to Mickleham on one side, and Dorking on the other. I saw you first in February." And then whispering—"Our companions are excessively stupid. What shall we do to rouse them? Any nonsense will serve. They *shall* talk. Ladies and gentlemen, I am ordered by Miss Woodhouse (who, wherever she is, presides) to say, that she desires to know what you are all thinking of?"

Some laughed, and answered good-humouredly. Miss Bates said a great deal; Mrs. Elton swelled at the idea of Miss Woodhouse's presiding; Mr. Knightley's answer was the most distinct.

"Is Miss Woodhouse sure that she would like to hear what we are all thinking of?"

"Oh! no, no"—cried Emma, laughing as carelessly as she could—"Upon no account in the world. It is the very last thing I would stand the brunt of just now. Let me hear any thing rather than what you are all thinking of. I will not say quite all. There are one or two, perhaps, (glancing at Mr. Weston and Harriet,) whose thoughts I might not be afraid of knowing."

"It is a sort of thing," cried Mrs. Elton emphatically, "which *I* should not have thought myself privileged to inquire into. Though, perhaps, as the *Chaperon* of the party—*I* never was in any circle—exploring parties—young ladies—married women—"

Her mutterings were chiefly to her husband; and he murmured, in reply,

"Very true, my love, very true. Exactly so, indeed—quite unheard of—but some ladies say any thing. Better pass it off as a joke. Every body knows what is due to *you*."

"It will not do," whispered Frank to Emma; "they are most of them affronted. I will attack them with more address. Ladies and gentlemen—I am ordered by Miss Woodhouse to say, that she waives her right of knowing exactly what you may all be thinking of, and only requires something very entertaining from each of you, in a general way. Here are seven of you, besides myself, (who, she is pleased to say, am very entertaining already) and she only demands from each of you either one thing very clever, be it prose or verse, original or repeated—or two things moderately clever—or three things very dull indeed, and she engages to laugh heartily at them all."

"Oh! very well," exclaimed Miss Bates, "then I need not be uneasy. 'Three things very dull indeed.' That will just do for me, you know. I shall be sure to say three dull things as soon as ever I open my mouth, shan't I? (looking round with the most good-humoured dependence on every body's assent)—Do not you all think I shall?"

Emma could not resist.

"Ah! ma'am, but there may be a difficulty. Pardon me—but you will be limited as to number—only three at once."

Miss Bates, deceived by the mock ceremony of her manner, did not immediately catch her meaning; but, when it burst on her, it could not anger, though a slight blush shewed that it could pain her.

"Ah!—well—to be sure. Yes, I see what she means, (turning to Mr. Knightley,) and I will try to hold my tongue. I must make myself very disagreeable, or she would not have said such a thing to an old friend."

"I like your plan," cried Mr. Weston. "Agreed, agreed. I will do my best. I am making a conundrum. How will a conundrum reckon?"

"Low, I am afraid, sir, very low," answered his son;—"but we shall be indulgent—especially to any one who leads the way."

"No, no," said Emma, "it will not reckon low. A conundrum of Mr. Weston's shall clear him and his next neighbour. Come, sir, pray let me hear it."

"I doubt its being very clever myself," said Mr. Weston. "It is too much a matter of fact, but here it is.—What two letters of the alphabet are there, that express perfection?"

"What two letters!—express perfection! I am sure I do not know."

"Ah! you will never guess. You, (to Emma), I am certain, will never guess.—I will tell you.—M. and A.—Em-ma.—Do you understand?"

Understanding and gratification came together. It might be a very indifferent piece of wit, but Emma found a great deal to laugh at and enjoy in it—and so did Frank and Harriet.—It did not seem to touch the rest of the party equally; some looked very stupid about it, and Mr. Knightley gravely said,

"This explains the sort of clever thing that is wanted, and Mr. Weston has done very well for himself; but he must have knocked up every body else. *Perfection* should not have come quite so soon."

"Oh! for myself, I protest I must be excused," said Mrs. Elton; "*I* really cannot attempt—I am not at all fond of the sort of thing. I had an acrostic once sent to me upon my own name, which I was not at all pleased with. I knew who it came from. An abominable puppy!—You know who I mean (nodding to her husband). These kind of things are very well at Christmas, when one is sitting round the fire; but quite out of place, in my opinion, when one is exploring about the country in summer. Miss Woodhouse must excuse me. I am not one of those who have witty things at every body's service. I do not pretend to be a wit. I have a great deal of vivacity in my own way, but I really must be allowed to judge when to speak and when to hold my tongue. Pass us, if you please, Mr. Churchill. Pass Mr. E., Knightley, Jane, and myself. We have nothing clever to say—not one of us.

"Yes, yes, pray pass *me*," added her husband, with a sort of sneering consciousness; "*I* have nothing to say that can entertain Miss Woodhouse, or any other young lady. An old married man—quite good for nothing. Shall we walk, Augusta?"

"With all my heart. I am really tired of exploring so long on one spot. Come, Jane, take my other arm."

Jane declined it, however, and the husband and wife walked off. "Happy couple!" said Frank Churchill, as soon as they were out of hearing:—"How well they suit one another!—Very lucky—marrying as they did, upon an acquaintance formed only in a public place!—They only knew each other, I think, a few weeks in Bath! Peculiarly lucky!—for as to any real knowledge of a person's disposition that Bath, or any public place, can give—it is all nothing; there can be no knowledge. It is only by seeing women in their own homes, among their own set, just as they always are, that you can form any just judgment. Short of that, it is all guess and luck—and will generally be ill-luck. How many a man has committed himself on a short acquaintance, and rued it all the rest of his life!"

Miss Fairfax, who had seldom spoken before, except among her own confederates, spoke now.

"Such things do occur, undoubtedly."—She was stopped by a cough. Frank Churchill turned towards her to listen.

"You were speaking," said he, gravely. She recovered her voice.

"I was only going to observe, that though such unfortunate circumstances do sometimes occur both to men and women, I cannot imagine them to be very frequent. A hasty and imprudent attachment may arise—but there is generally time to recover from it afterwards. I would be understood to mean, that it can be only weak, irresolute characters, (whose happiness must be always at the mercy of chance) who will suffer an unfortunate acquaintance to be an inconvenience, an oppression for ever."

He made no answer; merely looked, and bowed in submission; and soon afterwards said, in a lively tone,

"Well, I have so little confidence in my own judgment, that whenever I marry, I hope some body will chuse my wife for me. Will you? (turning to Emma.) Will you chuse a wife for me?—I am sure I should like any body fixed on by you. You provide for the family, you know, (with a smile at his father). Find some body for me. I am in no hurry. Adopt her, educate her."

"And make her like myself."

"By all means, if you can."

"Very well. I undertake the commission. You shall have a charming wife."

"She must be very lively, and have hazle eyes. I care for nothing else. I shall go abroad for a couple of years—and when I return, I shall come to you for my wife. Remember."

Emma was in no danger of forgetting. It was a commission to touch every favourite feeling. Would not Harriet be the very creature described? Hazle eyes excepted, two years more might make her all that he wished. He might even have Harriet in his thoughts at the moment; who could say? Referring the education to her seemed to imply it.

"Now, ma'am," said Jane to her aunt, "shall we join Mrs. Elton?"

"If you please, my dear. With all my heart. I am quite ready. I was ready to have gone with her, but this will do just as well. We shall soon overtake her. There she is—no, that's somebody else. That's one of the ladies in the Irish car party, not at all like her.—Well, I declare—"

They walked off, followed in half a minute by Mr. Knightley. Mr. Weston, his son, Emma, and Harriet, only remained; and the young man's spirits now rose to a pitch almost unpleasant. Even Emma grew tired at last of flattery and merriment, and wished herself rather walking quietly about with any of the others, or sitting almost alone, and quite unattended to, in tranquil observation of the beautiful views beneath her. The appearance of the servants looking out for them to give notice of the carriages was a joyful sight; and even the bustle of collecting and preparing to depart, and the solicitude of Mrs. Elton to have *her* carriage first, were gladly endured, in the prospect of the quiet drive home which was to close the very questionable enjoyments of this day of pleasure. Such another scheme, composed of so many ill-assorted people, she hoped never to be betrayed into again.

While waiting for the carriage, she found Mr. Knightley by her side. He looked around, as if to see that no one were near, and then said,

"Emma, I must once more speak to you as I have been used to do: a privilege rather endured than allowed, perhaps, but I must still use it. I cannot see you acting wrong, without a remonstrance. How could you be so unfeeling to Miss Bates? How could you be so insolent in your wit to a woman of her character, age, and situation?—Emma, I had not thought it possible."

Emma recollected, blushed, was sorry, but tried to laugh it off.

"Nay, how could I help saying what I did?—Nobody could have helped it. It was not so very bad. I dare say she did not understand me."

"I assure you she did. She felt your full meaning. She has talked of it since. I wish you could have heard how she talked of it—with what candour and generosity. I wish you could have heard her honouring your forbearance, in being able to pay her such attentions, as she was for ever receiving from yourself and your father, when her society must be so irksome."

"Oh!" cried Emma, "I know there is not a better creature in the world: but you must allow, that what is good and what is ridiculous are most unfortunately blended in her."

"They are blended," said he, "I acknowledge; and, were she prosperous, I could allow much for the occasional prevalence of the ridiculous over the good. Were she a woman of fortune, I would leave every harmless absurdity to take its chance, I would not quarrel with you for any liberties of manner. Were she your equal in situation—but, Emma, consider how far this is from being the case. She is poor; she has sunk from the comforts she was born to; and, if she live to old age, must probably sink more. Her situation should secure your compassion. It was badly done, indeed! You, whom she had known from an infant, whom she had seen grow up from a period when her notice was an honour, to have you now, in thoughtless spirits, and the pride of the moment, laugh at her, humble her—and before her niece, too—and before others, many of whom (certainly *some*) would be entirely guided by *your* treatment of her.—This is not pleasant to you, Emma—and it is very far from pleasant to me; but I must, I will,—I will tell you truths while I can; satisfied with proving myself your friend by very faithful counsel, and trusting that you will some time or other do me greater justice than you can do now."

While they talked, they were advancing towards the carriage; it was ready; and, before she could speak again, he had handed her in. He had misinterpreted the feelings which had kept her face averted, and her tongue motionless. They were combined only of anger against herself, mortification, and deep concern. She had not been able to speak; and, on entering the carriage, sunk back for a moment overcome—then reproaching herself for having taken no leave, making no acknowledgment, parting in apparent sullenness, she looked out with voice and hand eager to shew a difference; but it was just too late. He had turned away, and the horses were in motion. She continued to look back, but in vain; and soon, with what appeared unusual speed, they were half way down the hill, and every thing left far behind. She was vexed beyond what could have been expressed—almost beyond what she could conceal. Never had she felt so agitated, mortified, grieved, at any circumstance in her life. She was most forcibly struck. The truth of this representation there was no denying. She felt it at her heart. How could she have been so brutal, so cruel to Miss Bates! How could she have exposed herself to such ill opinion in any one she valued! And how suffer him to leave her without saying one word of gratitude, of concurrence, of common kindness!

Time did not compose her. As she reflected more, she seemed but to feel it more. She never had been so depressed. Happily it was not necessary to speak. There was only Harriet, who seemed not in spirits herself, fagged, and very willing to be silent; and Emma felt the tears running down her cheeks almost all the way home, without being at any trouble to check them, extraordinary as they were.

CHAPTER VIII

The wretchedness of a scheme to Box Hill was in Emma's thoughts all the evening. How it might be considered by the rest of the party, she could not tell. They, in their different homes, and their different ways, might be looking back on it with pleasure; but in her view it was a morning more completely misspent, more totally bare of rational satisfaction at the time, and more to be abhorred in recollection, than any she had ever passed. A whole evening of back-gammon with her father, was felicity to it. *There*, indeed, lay real pleasure, for there she was giving up the sweetest hours of the twenty-four to his comfort; and feeling that, unmerited as might be the degree of his fond affection and confiding esteem, she could not, in her general conduct, be open to any severe reproach. As a daughter, she hoped she was not without a heart. She hoped no one could have said to her, "How could you be so unfeeling to your father?—I must, I will tell you truths while I can." Miss Bates should never again—no, never! If attention, in future, could do away the past, she might hope to be forgiven. She had been often remiss, her conscience told her so; remiss, perhaps, more in thought than fact; scornful, ungracious. But it should be so no more. In the warmth of true contrition, she would call upon her the very next morning, and it should be the beginning, on her side, of a regular, equal, kindly intercourse.

She was just as determined when the morrow came, and went early, that nothing might prevent her. It was not unlikely, she thought, that she might see Mr. Knightley in her way; or, perhaps, he might come in while she were paying her visit. She had no objection. She would not be ashamed of the appearance of the penitence, so justly and truly hers. Her eyes were towards Donwell as she walked, but she saw him not.

"The ladies were all at home." She had never rejoiced at the sound before, nor ever before entered the passage, nor walked up the stairs, with any wish of giving pleasure, but in conferring obligation, or of deriving it, except in subsequent ridicule.

There was a bustle on her approach; a good deal of moving and talking. She heard Miss Bates's voice, something was to be done in a hurry; the maid looked frightened and awkward; hoped she would be pleased to wait a moment, and then ushered her in too soon. The aunt and niece seemed both escaping into the adjoining room. Jane she had a distinct glimpse of, looking extremely ill; and, before the door had shut them out, she heard Miss Bates saying, "Well, my dear, I shall *say* you are laid down upon the bed, and I am sure you are ill enough."

Poor old Mrs. Bates, civil and humble as usual, looked as if she did not quite understand what was going on.

"I am afraid Jane is not very well," said she, "but I do not know; they *tell* me she is well. I dare say my daughter will be here presently, Miss Woodhouse. I hope you find a chair. I wish Hetty had not gone. I am very little able—Have you a chair, ma'am? Do you sit where you like? I am sure she will be here presently."

Emma seriously hoped she would. She had a moment's fear of Miss Bates keeping away from her. But Miss Bates soon came—"Very happy and obliged"—but Emma's conscience told her that there was not the same cheerful volubility as before—less ease of look and manner. A very friendly inquiry after Miss Fairfax, she hoped, might lead the way to a return of old feelings. The touch seemed immediate.

"Ah! Miss Woodhouse, how kind you are!—I suppose you have heard—and are come to give us joy. This does not seem much like joy, indeed, in me—(twinkling away a tear or two)—but it will be very trying for us to part with her, after having had her so long, and she has a dreadful headache just now, writing all the morning:—such long letters, you know, to be written to Colonel Campbell, and Mrs. Dixon. 'My dear,' said I, 'you will blind yourself'—for tears were in her eyes perpetually. One cannot wonder, one cannot wonder. It is a great change; and though she is amazingly fortunate—such a situation, I suppose, as no young woman before ever met with on first going out—do not think us ungrateful, Miss Woodhouse, for such surprising good fortune—(again dispersing her tears)—but, poor dear soul! if you were to see what a headache she has. When one is in great pain, you know one cannot feel any blessing quite as it may deserve. She is as low as possible. To look at her, nobody would think how delighted and happy she is to have secured such a situation. You will excuse her not coming to you—she is not able—she is gone into her own room—I want her to lie down upon the bed. 'My dear,' said I, 'I shall say you are laid down upon the bed:' but, however, she is not; she is walking about the room. But, now that she has written her letters, she says she shall soon be well. She will be extremely sorry to miss seeing you, Miss Woodhouse, but your kindness will excuse her. You were kept waiting at the door—I was quite ashamed—but somehow there was a little bustle—for it so happened that we had not heard the knock, and till you were on the stairs, we did not know any body was coming. 'It is only Mrs. Cole,' said I, 'depend upon it. Nobody else would come so early.' 'Well,' said she, 'it must be borne some time or other, and it may as well be now.' But then Patty came in, and said it was you. 'Oh!' said I, 'it is Miss Woodhouse: I am sure you will like to see her.'—'I can see nobody,' said she; and up she got, and would go away; and that was what made us keep you waiting—and extremely sorry and ashamed we were. 'If you must go, my dear,' said I, 'you must, and I will say you are laid down upon the bed.'"

Emma was most sincerely interested. Her heart had been long growing kinder towards Jane; and this picture of her present sufferings acted as a cure of every former ungenerous suspicion, and left her nothing but pity; and the remembrance of the less just and less gentle sensations of the past, obliged her to admit that Jane might very naturally resolve on seeing Mrs. Cole or any other steady friend, when she might not bear to see herself. She spoke as she felt, with earnest regret and solicitude—sincerely wishing that the circumstances which she collected from Miss Bates to be now actually determined on, might be as much for Miss Fairfax's advantage and comfort as possible. "It must be a severe trial to them all. She had understood it was to be delayed till Colonel Campbell's return."

"So very kind!" replied Miss Bates. "But you are always kind."

There was no bearing such an "always;" and to break through her dreadful gratitude, Emma made the direct inquiry of—

"Where—may I ask?—is Miss Fairfax going?"

"To a Mrs. Smallridge—charming woman—most superior—to have the charge of her three little girls—delightful children. Impossible that any situation could be more replete with comfort; if we except, perhaps, Mrs. Suckling's own family, and Mrs. Bragge's; but Mrs. Smallridge is intimate with both, and in the very same neighbourhood:—lives only four miles from Maple Grove. Jane will be only four miles from Maple Grove."

"Mrs. Elton, I suppose, has been the person to whom Miss Fairfax owes—"

"Yes, our good Mrs. Elton. The most indefatigable, true friend. She would not take a denial. She would not let Jane say, 'No;' for when Jane first heard of it, (it was the day before yesterday, the very morning we were at Donwell) when Jane first heard of it, she was quite decided against accepting the offer, and for the reasons you mention; exactly as you say, she had made up her mind to close with nothing till Colonel Campbell's return, and nothing should induce her to enter into any engagement at present—and so she told Mrs. Elton over and over again—and I am sure I had no more idea that she would change her mind!—but that good Mrs. Elton, whose judgment never fails her, saw farther than I did. It is not every body that would have stood out in such a kind way as she did, and refuse to take Jane's answer; but she positively declared she would *not* write any such denial yesterday, as Jane wished her; she would wait—and, sure enough, yesterday evening it was all settled that Jane should go. Quite a surprize to me! I had not the least idea!—Jane took Mrs. Elton aside, and told her at once, that upon thinking over the advantages of Mrs. Smallridge's situation, she had come to the resolution of accepting it.—I did not know a word of it till it was all settled."

"You spent the evening with Mrs. Elton?"

"Yes, all of us; Mrs. Elton would have us come. It was settled so, upon the hill, while we were walking about with Mr. Knightley. 'You *must all* spend your evening with us,' said she—'I positively must have you *all* come.'"

"Mr. Knightley was there too, was he?"

"No, not Mr. Knightley; he declined it from the first; and though I thought he would come, because Mrs. Elton declared she would not let him off, he did not;—but my mother, and Jane, and I, were all there, and a very agreeable evening we had. Such kind friends, you know, Miss Woodhouse, one must always find agreeable, though every body seemed rather fagged after the morning's party. Even pleasure, you know, is fatiguing—and I cannot say that any of them seemed very much to have enjoyed it. However, *I* shall always think it a very pleasant party, and feel extremely obliged to the kind friends who included me in it."

"Miss Fairfax, I suppose, though you were not aware of it, had been making up her mind the whole day?"

"I dare say she had."

"Whenever the time may come, it must be unwelcome to her and all her friends—but I hope her engagement will have every alleviation that is possible—I mean, as to the character and manners of the family."

"Thank you, dear Miss Woodhouse. Yes, indeed, there is every thing in the world that can make her happy in it. Except the Sucklings and Bragges, there is not such another nursery establishment, so liberal and elegant, in all Mrs. Elton's acquaintance. Mrs. Smallridge, a most delightful woman!—A style of living almost equal to Maple Grove—and as to the children, except the little Sucklings and little Bragges, there are not such elegant sweet children anywhere. Jane will be treated with such regard and kindness!—It will be nothing but pleasure, a life of pleasure.—And her salary!—I really cannot venture to name her salary to you, Miss Woodhouse. Even you, used as you are to great sums, would hardly believe that so much could be given to a young person like Jane."

"Ah! madam," cried Emma, "if other children are at all like what I remember to have been myself, I should think five times the amount of what I have ever yet heard named as a salary on such occasions, dearly earned."

"You are so noble in your ideas!"

"And when is Miss Fairfax to leave you?"

"Very soon, very soon, indeed; that's the worst of it. Within a fortnight. Mrs. Smallridge is in a great hurry. My poor mother does not know how to bear it. So then, I try to put it out of her thoughts, and say, Come ma'am, do not let us think about it any more."

"Her friends must all be sorry to lose her; and will not Colonel and Mrs. Campbell be sorry to find that she has engaged herself before their return?"

"Yes; Jane says she is sure they will; but yet, this is such a situation as she cannot feel herself justified in declining. I was so astonished when she first told me what she had been saying to Mrs. Elton, and when Mrs. Elton at the same moment came congratulating me upon it! It was before tea—stay—no, it could not be before tea, because we were just going to cards—and yet it was before tea, because I remember thinking—Oh! no, now I recollect, now I have it; something happened before tea, but not that. Mr. Elton was called out of the room before tea, old John Abdy's son wanted to speak with him. Poor old John, I have a great regard for him; he was clerk to my poor father twenty-seven years; and now, poor old man, he is bed-ridden, and very poorly with the rheumatic gout in his joints—I must go and see him to-day; and so will Jane, I am sure, if she gets out at all. And poor John's son came to talk to Mr. Elton about relief from the parish; he is very well-to-do himself, you know, being head man at the Crown, ostler, and every thing of that sort, but still he cannot keep his father without some help; and so, when Mr. Elton came back, he told us what John ostler had been telling him, and then it came out about the chaise having been sent to Randalls to take Mr. Frank Churchill to Richmond. That was what happened before tea. It was after tea that Jane spoke to Mrs. Elton."

Miss Bates would hardly give Emma time to say how perfectly new this circumstance was to her; but as without supposing it possible that she could be ignorant of any of the particulars of Mr. Frank Churchill's going, she proceeded to give them all, it was of no consequence.

What Mr. Elton had learned from the ostler on the subject, being the accumulation of the ostler's own knowledge, and the knowledge of the servants at Randalls, was, that a messenger had come over from Richmond soon after the return of the party from Box Hill—which messenger, however, had been no more than was expected; and that Mr. Churchill had sent his nephew a few lines, containing, upon the whole, a tolerable account of Mrs. Churchill, and only wishing him not to delay coming back beyond the next morning early; but that Mr. Frank Churchill having resolved to go home directly, without waiting at all, and his horse seeming to have got a cold, Tom had been sent off immediately for the Crown chaise, and the ostler had stood out and seen it pass by, the boy going a good pace, and driving very steady.

There was nothing in all this either to astonish or interest, and it caught Emma's attention only as it united with the subject which already engaged her mind. The contrast between Mrs. Churchill's importance in the world, and Jane Fairfax's, struck her; one was every thing, the other nothing—and she sat musing on the difference of woman's destiny, and quite unconscious on what her eyes were fixed, till roused by Miss Bates's saying,

"Aye, I see what you are thinking of, the pianoforte. What is to become of that?—Very true. Poor dear Jane was talking of it just now.—'You must go,' said she. 'You and I must part. You will have no business here.—Let it stay, however,' said she; 'give it houseroom till Colonel Campbell comes back. I shall talk about it to him; he will settle for me; he will help me out of all my difficulties.'—And to this day, I do believe, she knows not whether it was his present or his daughter's."

Now Emma was obliged to think of the pianoforte; and the remembrance of all her former fanciful and unfair conjectures was so little pleasing, that she soon allowed herself to believe her visit had been long enough; and, with a repetition of every thing that she could venture to say of the good wishes which she really felt, took leave.

CHAPTER IX

Emma's pensive meditations, as she walked home, were not interrupted; but on entering the parlour, she found those who must rouse her. Mr. Knightley and Harriet had arrived during her absence, and were sitting with her father.—Mr. Knightley immediately got up, and in a manner decidedly graver than usual, said,

"I would not go away without seeing you, but I have no time to spare, and therefore must now be gone directly. I am going to London, to spend a few days with John and Isabella. Have you any thing to send or say, besides the 'love,' which nobody carries?"

"Nothing at all. But is not this a sudden scheme?"

"Yes—rather—I have been thinking of it some little time."

Emma was sure he had not forgiven her; he looked unlike himself. Time, however, she thought, would tell him that they ought to be friends again. While he stood, as if meaning to go, but not going—her father began his inquiries.

"Well, my dear, and did you get there safely?—And how did you find my worthy old friend and her daughter?—I dare say they must have been very much obliged to you for coming. Dear Emma has been to call on Mrs. and Miss Bates, Mr. Knightley, as I told you before. She is always so attentive to them!"

Emma's colour was heightened by this unjust praise; and with a smile, and shake of the head, which spoke much, she looked at Mr. Knightley.—It seemed as if there were an instantaneous impression in her favour, as if his eyes received the truth from hers, and all that had passed of good in her feelings were at once caught and honoured.—He looked at her with a glow of regard. She was warmly gratified—and in another moment still more so, by a little movement of more than common friendliness on his part.—He took her hand;—whether she had not herself made the first motion, she could not say—she might, perhaps, have rather offered it—but he took her hand, pressed it, and certainly was on the point of carrying it to his lips—when, from some fancy or other, he suddenly let it go.—Why he should feel such a scruple, why he should change his mind when it was all but done, she could not perceive.—He would have judged better, she thought, if he had not stopped.—The intention, however, was indubitable; and whether it was that his manners had in general so little gallantry, or however else it happened, but she thought nothing became him more.—It was with him, of so simple, yet so dignified a nature.—She could not but recall the attempt with great satisfaction. It spoke such perfect amity.—He left them immediately afterwards—gone in a moment. He always moved with the alertness of a mind which could neither be undecided nor dilatory, but now he seemed more sudden than usual in his disappearance.

Emma could not regret her having gone to Miss Bates, but she wished she had left her ten minutes earlier;—it would have been a great pleasure to talk over Jane Fairfax's situation with Mr. Knightley.—Neither would she regret that he should be going to Brunswick Square, for she knew how much his visit would be enjoyed—but it might have happened at a better time—and to have had longer notice of it, would have been pleasanter.—They parted thorough friends, however; she could not be deceived as to the meaning of his countenance, and his unfinished gallantry;—it was all done to assure her that she had fully recovered his good opinion.—He had been sitting with them half an hour, she found. It was a pity that she had not come back earlier!

In the hope of diverting her father's thoughts from the disagreeableness of Mr. Knightley's going to London; and going so suddenly; and going on horseback, which she knew would be all very bad; Emma communicated her news of Jane Fairfax, and her dependence on the effect was justified; it supplied a very useful check,—interested, without disturbing him. He had long made up his mind to Jane Fairfax's going out as governess, and could talk of it cheerfully, but Mr. Knightley's going to London had been an unexpected blow.

"I am very glad, indeed, my dear, to hear she is to be so comfortably settled. Mrs. Elton is very good-natured and agreeable, and I dare say her acquaintance are just what they ought to be. I hope it is a dry situation, and that her health will be taken good care of. It ought to be a first object, as I am sure poor Miss Taylor's always was with me. You know, my dear, she is going to be to this new lady what Miss Taylor was to us. And I hope she will be better off in one respect, and not be induced to go away after it has been her home so long."

The following day brought news from Richmond to throw every thing else into the background. An express arrived at Randalls to announce the death of Mrs. Churchill! Though her nephew had had no particular reason to hasten back on her account, she had not lived above six-and-thirty hours after his return. A sudden seizure of a different nature from any thing foreboded by her general state, had carried her off after a short struggle. The great Mrs. Churchill was no more.

It was felt as such things must be felt. Every body had a degree of gravity and sorrow; tenderness towards the departed, solicitude for the surviving friends; and, in a reasonable time, curiosity to know where she would be buried. Goldsmith tells us, that when lovely woman stoops to folly, she has nothing to do but to die; and when she stoops to be disagreeable, it is equally to be recommended as a clearer of ill-fame. Mrs. Churchill, after being disliked at least twenty-five years, was now spoken of with compassionate allowances. In one point she was fully justified. She had never been admitted before to be seriously ill. The event acquitted her of all the fancifulness, and all the selfishness of imaginary complaints.

"Poor Mrs. Churchill! no doubt she had been suffering a great deal: more than any body had ever supposed—and continual pain would try the temper. It was a sad event—a great shock—with all her faults, what would Mr. Churchill do without her? Mr. Churchill's loss would be dreadful indeed. Mr. Churchill would never get over it."—Even Mr. Weston shook his head, and looked solemn, and said, "Ah! poor woman, who would have thought it!" and resolved, that his mourning should be as handsome as possible; and his wife sat sighing and moralising over her broad hems with a commiseration and good sense, true and steady. How it would affect Frank was among the earliest thoughts of both. It was also a very early speculation with Emma. The character of Mrs. Churchill, the grief of her husband—her mind glanced over them both with awe and compassion—and then rested with lightened feelings on how Frank might be affected by the event, how benefited, how freed. She saw in a moment all the possible good. Now, an attachment to Harriet Smith would have nothing to encounter. Mr. Churchill, independent of his wife, was feared by nobody; an easy, guidable man, to be persuaded into any thing by his nephew. All that remained to be wished was, that the nephew should form the attachment, as, with all her good-will in the cause, Emma could feel no certainty of its being already formed.

Harriet behaved extremely well on the occasion, with great self-command. What ever she might feel of brighter hope, she betrayed nothing. Emma was gratified, to observe such a proof in her of strengthened character, and refrained from any allusion that might endanger its maintenance. They spoke, therefore, of Mrs. Churchill's death with mutual forbearance.

Short letters from Frank were received at Randalls, communicating all that was immediately important of their state and plans. Mr. Churchill was better than could be expected; and their first removal, on the departure of the funeral for Yorkshire, was to be to the house of a very old friend in Windsor, to whom Mr. Churchill had been promising a visit the last ten years. At present, there was nothing to be done for Harriet; good wishes for the future were all that could yet be possible on Emma's side.

It was a more pressing concern to shew attention to Jane Fairfax, whose prospects were closing, while Harriet's opened, and whose engagements now allowed of no delay in any one at Highbury, who wished to shew her kindness—and with Emma it was grown into a first wish. She had scarcely a stronger regret than for her past coldness; and the person, whom she had been so many months neglecting, was now the very one on whom she would have lavished every distinction of regard or sympathy. She wanted to be of use to her; wanted to shew a value for her society, and testify respect and consideration. She resolved to prevail on her to spend a day at Hartfield. A note was written to urge it. The invitation was refused, and by a verbal message. "Miss Fairfax was not well enough to write;" and when Mr. Perry called at Hartfield, the same morning, it appeared that she was so much indisposed as to have been visited, though against her own consent, by himself, and that she was suffering under severe headaches, and a nervous fever to a degree, which made him doubt the possibility of her going to Mrs. Smallridge's at the time proposed. Her health seemed for the moment completely deranged—appetite quite gone—and though there were no absolutely alarming symptoms, nothing touching the pulmonary complaint, which was the standing apprehension of the family, Mr. Perry was uneasy about her. He thought she had undertaken more than she was equal to, and that she felt it so herself, though she would not own it. Her spirits seemed overcome. Her present home, he could not but observe, was unfavourable to a nervous disorder:—confined always to one room;—he could have wished it otherwise—and her good aunt, though his very old friend, he must acknowledge to be not the best companion for an invalid of that description. Her care and attention could not be questioned; they were, in fact, only too great. He very much feared that Miss Fairfax derived more evil than good from them. Emma listened with the warmest concern; grieved for her more and more, and looked around eager to discover some way of being useful. To take her—be it only an hour or two—from her aunt, to give her change of air and scene, and quiet rational conversation, even for an hour or two, might do her good; and the following morning she wrote again to say, in the most feeling language she could command, that she would call for her in the carriage at any hour that Jane would name—mentioning that she had Mr. Perry's decided opinion, in favour of such exercise for his patient. The answer was only in this short note:

"Miss Fairfax's compliments and thanks, but is quite unequal to any exercise."

Emma felt that her own note had deserved something better; but it was impossible to quarrel with words, whose tremulous inequality shewed indisposition so plainly, and she thought only of how she might best counteract this unwillingness to be seen or assisted. In spite of the answer, therefore, she ordered the carriage, and drove to Mrs. Bates's, in the hope that Jane would be induced to join her—but it would not do;—Miss Bates came to the carriage door, all gratitude, and agreeing with her most earnestly in thinking an airing might be of the greatest service—and every thing that message could do was tried—but all in vain. Miss Bates was obliged to return without success; Jane was quite unpersuadable; the mere proposal of going out seemed to make her worse.—Emma wished she could have seen her, and tried her own powers; but, almost before she could hint the wish, Miss Bates made it appear that she had promised her niece on no account to let Miss Woodhouse in. "Indeed, the truth was, that poor dear Jane could not bear to see any body—any body at all—Mrs. Elton, indeed, could not be denied—and Mrs. Cole had made such a point—and Mrs. Perry had said so much—but, except them, Jane would really see nobody."

Emma did not want to be classed with the Mrs. Eltons, the Mrs. Perrys, and the Mrs. Coles, who would force themselves anywhere; neither could she feel any right of preference herself—she submitted, therefore, and only questioned Miss Bates farther as to her niece's appetite and diet, which she longed to be able to assist. On that subject poor Miss Bates was very unhappy, and very communicative; Jane would hardly eat any thing:—Mr. Perry recommended nourishing food; but every thing they could command (and never had any body such good neighbours) was distasteful.

Emma, on reaching home, called the housekeeper directly, to an examination of her stores; and some arrowroot of very superior quality was speedily despatched to Miss Bates with a most friendly note. In half an hour the arrowroot was returned, with a thousand thanks from Miss Bates, but "dear Jane would not be satisfied without its being sent back; it was a thing she could not take—and, moreover, she insisted on her saying, that she was not at all in want of any thing."

When Emma afterwards heard that Jane Fairfax had been seen wandering about the meadows, at some distance from Highbury, on the afternoon of the very day on which she had, under the plea of being unequal to any exercise, so peremptorily refused to go out with her in the carriage, she could have no doubt—putting every thing together—that Jane was resolved to receive no kindness from *her*. She was sorry, very sorry. Her heart was grieved for a state which seemed but the more pitiable from this sort of irritation of spirits, inconsistency of action, and inequality of powers; and it mortified her that she was given so little credit for proper feeling, or esteemed so little worthy as a friend: but she had the consolation of knowing that her intentions were good, and of being able to say to herself, that could Mr. Knightley have been privy to all her attempts of assisting Jane Fairfax, could he even have seen into her heart, he would not, on this occasion, have found any thing to reprove.

CHAPTER X

One morning, about ten days after Mrs. Churchill's decease, Emma was called downstairs to Mr. Weston, who "could not stay five minutes, and wanted particularly to speak with her."—He met her at the parlour-door, and hardly asking her how she did, in the natural key of his voice, sunk it immediately, to say, unheard by her father,

"Can you come to Randalls at any time this morning?—Do, if it be possible. Mrs. Weston wants to see you. She must see you."

"Is she unwell?"

"No, no, not at all—only a little agitated. She would have ordered the carriage, and come to you, but she must see you *alone*, and that you know—(nodding towards her father)—Humph!—Can you come?"

"Certainly. This moment, if you please. It is impossible to refuse what you ask in such a way. But what can be the matter?—Is she really not ill?"

"Depend upon me—but ask no more questions. You will know it all in time. The most unaccountable business! But hush, hush!"

To guess what all this meant, was impossible even for Emma. Something really important seemed announced by his looks; but, as her friend was well, she endeavoured not to be uneasy, and settling it with her father, that she would take her walk now, she and Mr. Weston were soon out of the house together and on their way at a quick pace for Randalls.

"Now,"—said Emma, when they were fairly beyond the sweep gates,—"now Mr. Weston, do let me know what has happened."

"No, no,"—he gravely replied.—"Don't ask me. I promised my wife to leave it all to her. She will break it to you better than I can. Do not be impatient, Emma; it will all come out too soon."

"Break it to me," cried Emma, standing still with terror.—"Good God!—Mr. Weston, tell me at once.—Something has happened in Brunswick Square. I know it has. Tell me, I charge you tell me this moment what it is."

"No, indeed you are mistaken."—

"Mr. Weston do not trifle with me.—Consider how many of my dearest friends are now in Brunswick Square. Which of them is it?—I charge you by all that is sacred, not to attempt concealment."

"Upon my word, Emma."—

"Your word!—why not your honour!—why not say upon your honour, that it has nothing to do with any of them? Good Heavens!—What can be to be *broke* to me, that does not relate to one of that family?"

"Upon my honour," said he very seriously, "it does not. It is not in the smallest degree connected with any human being of the name of Knightley."

Emma's courage returned, and she walked on.

"I was wrong," he continued, "in talking of its being *broke* to you. I should not have used the expression. In fact, it does not concern you—it concerns only myself,—that is, we hope.—Humph!—In short, my dear Emma, there is no occasion to be so uneasy about it. I don't say that it is not a disagreeable business—but things might be much worse.—If we walk fast, we shall soon be at Randalls."

Emma found that she must wait; and now it required little effort. She asked no more questions therefore, merely employed her own fancy, and that soon pointed out to her the probability of its being some money concern—something just come to light, of a disagreeable nature in the circumstances of the family,—something which the late event at Richmond had brought forward. Her fancy was very active. Half a dozen natural children, perhaps—and poor Frank cut off!—This, though very undesirable, would be no matter of agony to her. It inspired little more than an animating curiosity.

"Who is that gentleman on horseback?" said she, as they proceeded—speaking more to assist Mr. Weston in keeping his secret, than with any other view.

"I do not know.—One of the Otways.—Not Frank;—it is not Frank, I assure you. You will not see him. He is half way to Windsor by this time."

"Has your son been with you, then?"

"Oh! yes—did not you know?—Well, well, never mind."

For a moment he was silent; and then added, in a tone much more guarded and demure,

"Yes, Frank came over this morning, just to ask us how we did."

They hurried on, and were speedily at Randalls.—"Well, my dear," said he, as they entered the room—"I have brought her, and now I hope you will soon be better. I shall leave you together. There is no use in delay. I shall not be far off, if you want me."—And Emma distinctly heard him add, in a lower tone, before he quitted the room,—"I have been as good as my word. She has not the least idea."

Mrs. Weston was looking so ill, and had an air of so much perturbation, that Emma's uneasiness increased; and the moment they were alone, she eagerly said,

"What is it my dear friend? Something of a very unpleasant nature, I find, has occurred;—do let me know directly what it is. I have been walking all this way in complete suspense. We both abhor suspense. Do not let mine continue longer. It will do you good to speak of your distress, whatever it may be."

"Have you indeed no idea?" said Mrs. Weston in a trembling voice. "Cannot you, my dear Emma—cannot you form a guess as to what you are to hear?"

"So far as that it relates to Mr. Frank Churchill, I do guess."

"You are right. It does relate to him, and I will tell you directly;" (resuming her work, and seeming resolved against looking up.) "He has been here this very morning, on a most extraordinary errand. It is impossible to express our surprize. He came to speak to his father on a subject,—to announce an attachment—"

She stopped to breathe. Emma thought first of herself, and then of Harriet.

"More than an attachment, indeed," resumed Mrs. Weston; "an engagement—a positive engagement.—What will you say, Emma—what will any body say, when it is known that Frank Churchill and Miss Fairfax are engaged;—nay, that they have been long engaged!"

Emma even jumped with surprize;—and, horror-struck, exclaimed,

"Jane Fairfax!—Good God! You are not serious? You do not mean it?"

"You may well be amazed," returned Mrs. Weston, still averting her eyes, and talking on with eagerness, that Emma might have time to recover—"You may well be amazed. But it is even so. There has been a solemn engagement between them ever since October—formed at Weymouth, and kept a secret from every body. Not a creature knowing it but themselves—neither the Campbells, nor her family, nor his.—It is so wonderful, that though perfectly convinced of the fact, it is yet almost incredible to myself. I can hardly believe it.—I thought I knew him."

Emma scarcely heard what was said.—Her mind was divided

between two ideas—her own former conversations with him about Miss Fairfax; and poor Harriet;—and for some time she could only exclaim, and require confirmation, repeated confirmation.

"Well," said she at last, trying to recover herself; "this is a circumstance which I must think of at least half a day, before I can at all comprehend it. What!—engaged to her all the winter—before either of them came to Highbury?"

"Engaged since October,—secretly engaged.—It has hurt me, Emma, very much. It has hurt his father equally. *Some part* of his conduct we cannot excuse."

Emma pondered a moment, and then replied, "I will not pretend *not* to understand you; and to give you all the relief in my power, be assured that no such effect has followed his attentions to me, as you are apprehensive of."

Mrs. Weston looked up, afraid to believe; but Emma's countenance was as steady as her words.

"That you may have less difficulty in believing this boast, of my present perfect indifference," she continued, "I will farther tell you, that there was a period in the early part of our acquaintance, when I did like him, when I was very much disposed to be attached to him—nay, was attached—and how it came to cease, is perhaps the wonder. Fortunately, however, it did cease. I have really for some time past, for at least these three months, cared nothing about him. You may believe me, Mrs. Weston. This is the simple truth."

Mrs. Weston kissed her with tears of joy; and when she could find utterance, assured her, that this protestation had done her more good than any thing else in the world could do.

"Mr. Weston will be almost as much relieved as myself," said she. "On this point we have been wretched. It was our darling wish that you might be attached to each other—and we were persuaded that it was so.—Imagine what we have been feeling on your account."

"I have escaped; and that I should escape, may be a matter of grateful wonder to you and myself. But this does not acquit *him*, Mrs. Weston; and I must say, that I think him greatly to blame. What right had he to come among us with affection and faith engaged, and with manners so *very* disengaged? What right had he to endeavour to please, as he certainly did—to distinguish any one young woman with persevering attention, as he certainly did—while he really belonged to another?—

How could he tell what mischief he might be doing?—How could he tell that he might not be making me in love with him?—very wrong, very wrong indeed."

"From something that he said, my dear Emma, I rather imagine—"

"And how could *she* bear such behaviour! Composure with a witness! to look on, while repeated attentions were offering to another woman, before her face, and not resent it.—That is a degree of placidity, which I can neither comprehend nor respect."

"There were misunderstandings between them, Emma; he said so expressly. He had not time to enter into much explanation. He was here only a quarter of an hour, and in a state of agitation which did not allow the full use even of the time he could stay—but that there had been misunderstandings he decidedly said. The present crisis, indeed, seemed to be brought on by them; and those misunderstandings might very possibly arise from the impropriety of his conduct."

"Impropriety! Oh! Mrs. Weston—it is too calm a censure. Much, much beyond impropriety!—It has sunk him, I cannot say how it has sunk him in my opinion. So unlike what a man should be!—None of that upright integrity, that strict adherence to truth and principle, that disdain of trick and littleness, which a man should display in every transaction of his life."

"Nay, dear Emma, now I must take his part; for though he has been wrong in this instance, I have known him long enough to answer for his having many, very many, good qualities; and—"

"Good God!" cried Emma, not attending to her.—"Mrs. Smallridge, too! Jane actually on the point of going as governess! What could he mean by such horrible indelicacy? To suffer her to engage herself—to suffer her even to think of such a measure!"

"He knew nothing about it, Emma. On this article I can fully acquit him. It was a private resolution of hers, not communicated to him—or at least not communicated in a way to carry conviction.—Till yesterday, I know he said he was in the dark as to her plans. They burst on him, I do not know how, but by some letter or message—and it was the discovery of what she was doing, of this very project of hers, which determined him to come forward at once, own it all to his uncle, throw himself on his kindness, and, in short, put an end to the miserable state of concealment that had been carrying on so long."

Emma began to listen better.

"I am to hear from him soon," continued Mrs. Weston. "He told me at parting, that he should soon write; and he spoke in a manner which seemed to promise me many particulars that could not be given now. Let us wait, therefore, for this letter. It may bring many extenuations. It may make many things intelligible and excusable which now are not to be understood. Don't let us be severe, don't let us be in a hurry to condemn him. Let us have patience. I must love him; and now that I am satisfied on one point, the one material point, I am sincerely anxious for its all turning out well, and ready to hope that it may. They must both have suffered a great deal under such a system of secrecy and concealment."

"*His* sufferings," replied Emma dryly, "do not appear to have done him much harm. Well, and how did Mr. Churchill take it?"

"Most favourably for his nephew—gave his consent with scarcely a difficulty. Conceive what the events of a week have done in that family! While poor Mrs. Churchill lived, I suppose there could not have been a hope, a chance, a possibility;—but scarcely are her remains at rest in the family vault, than her husband is persuaded to act exactly opposite to what she would have required. What a blessing it is, when undue influence does not survive the grave!—He gave his consent with very little persuasion."

"Ah!" thought Emma, "he would have done as much for Harriet."

"This was settled last night, and Frank was off with the light this morning. He stopped at Highbury, at the Bates's, I fancy, some time—and then came on hither; but was in such a hurry to get back to his uncle, to whom he is just now more necessary than ever, that, as I tell you, he could stay with us but a quarter of an hour.—He was very much agitated—very much, indeed—to a degree that made him appear quite a different creature from any thing I had ever seen him before.—In addition to all the rest, there had been the shock of finding her so very unwell, which he had had no previous suspicion of—and there was every appearance of his having been feeling a great deal."

"And do you really believe the affair to have been carrying on with such perfect secrecy?—The Campbells, the Dixons, did none of them know of the engagement?"

Emma could not speak the name of Dixon without a little blush.

"None; not one. He positively said that it had been known to no being in the world but their two selves."

"Well," said Emma, "I suppose we shall gradually grow reconciled to the idea, and I wish them very happy. But I shall always think it a very abominable sort of proceeding. What has it been but a system of hypocrisy and deceit,—espionage, and treachery?—To come among us with professions of openness and simplicity; and such a league in secret to judge us all!—Here have we been, the whole winter and spring, completely duped, fancying ourselves all on an equal footing of truth and honour, with two people in the midst of us who may have been carrying round, comparing and sitting in judgment on sentiments and words that were never meant for both to hear.—They must take the consequence, if they have heard each other spoken of in a way not perfectly agreeable!"

"I am quite easy on that head," replied Mrs. Weston. "I am very sure that I never said any thing of either to the other, which both might not have heard."

"You are in luck.—Your only blunder was confined to my ear, when you imagined a certain friend of ours in love with the lady."

"True. But as I have always had a thoroughly good opinion of Miss Fairfax, I never could, under any blunder, have spoken ill of her; and as to speaking ill of him, there I must have been safe."

At this moment Mr. Weston appeared at a little distance from the window, evidently on the watch. His wife gave him a look which invited him in; and, while he was coming round, added, "Now, dearest Emma, let me intreat you to say and look every thing that may set his heart at ease, and incline him to be satisfied with the match. Let us make the best of it—and, indeed, almost every thing may be fairly said in her favour. It is not a connexion to gratify; but if Mr. Churchill does not feel that, why should we? and it may be a very fortunate circumstance for him, for Frank, I mean, that he should have attached himself to a girl of such steadiness of character and good judgment as I have always given her credit for—and still am disposed to give her credit for, in spite of this one great deviation from the strict rule of right. And how much may be said in her situation for even that error!"

"Much, indeed!" cried Emma feelingly. "If a woman can ever be excused for thinking only of herself, it is in a situation like Jane Fairfax's.—Of such, one may almost say, that 'the world is not their's, nor the world's law.'"

She met Mr. Weston on his entrance, with a smiling countenance, exclaiming,

"A very pretty trick you have been playing me, upon my word! This was a device, I suppose, to sport with my curiosity, and exercise my talent of guessing. But you really frightened me. I thought you had lost half your property, at least. And here, instead of its being a matter of condolence, it turns out to be one of congratulation.—I congratulate you, Mr. Weston, with all my heart, on the prospect of having one of the most lovely and accomplished young women in England for your daughter."

A glance or two between him and his wife, convinced him that all was as right as this speech proclaimed; and its happy effect on his spirits was immediate. His air and voice recovered their usual briskness: he shook her heartily and gratefully by the hand, and entered on the subject in a manner to prove, that he now only wanted time and persuasion to think the engagement no very bad thing. His companions suggested only what could palliate imprudence, or smooth objections; and by the time they had talked it all over together, and he had talked it all over again with Emma, in their walk back to Hartfield, he was become perfectly reconciled, and not far from thinking it the very best thing that Frank could possibly have done.

CHAPTER XI

"Harriet, poor Harriet!"—Those were the words; in them lay the tormenting ideas which Emma could not get rid of, and which constituted the real misery of the business to her. Frank Churchill had behaved very ill by herself—very ill in many ways,—but it was not so much *his* behaviour as her *own*, which made her so angry with him. It was the scrape which he had drawn her into on Harriet's account, that gave the deepest hue to his offence.—Poor Harriet! to be a second time the dupe of her misconceptions and flattery. Mr. Knightley had spoken prophetically, when he once said, "Emma, you have been no friend to Harriet Smith."—She was afraid she had done her nothing but disservice.—It was true that she had not to charge herself, in this instance as in the former, with being the sole and original author of the mischief; with having suggested such feelings as might otherwise never have entered Harriet's imagination; for Harriet had acknowledged her admiration and preference of Frank Churchill before she had ever given her a hint on the subject; but she felt completely guilty of having encouraged what she might have repressed. She might have prevented the indulgence and increase of such sentiments. Her influence would have been enough. And now she was very conscious that she ought to have prevented them.—She felt that she had been risking her friend's happiness on most insufficient grounds. Common sense would have directed her to tell Harriet, that she must not allow herself to think of him, and that there were five hundred chances to one against his ever caring for her.—"But, with common sense," she added, "I am afraid I have had little to do."

She was extremely angry with herself. If she could not have been angry with Frank Churchill too, it would have been dreadful.—As for Jane Fairfax, she might at least relieve her feelings from any present solicitude on her account. Harriet would be anxiety enough; she need no longer be unhappy about Jane, whose troubles and whose ill-health having, of course, the same origin, must be equally under cure.—Her days of insignificance and evil were over.—She would soon be well, and happy, and prosperous.—Emma could now imagine why her own attentions had been slighted. This discovery laid many smaller matters open. No doubt it had been from jealousy.—In Jane's eyes she had been a rival; and well might any thing she could offer of assistance or regard be repulsed. An airing in the Hartfield carriage would have been the rack, and arrowroot from the Hartfield storeroom must have been poison. She understood it all; and as far as her mind could disengage itself from the injustice and selfishness of angry feelings, she acknowledged that Jane Fairfax would have neither elevation nor happiness beyond her desert. But poor Harriet was such an engrossing charge! There was little sympathy to be spared for any body else. Emma was sadly fearful that this second disappointment would be more severe than the first. Considering the very superior claims of the object, it ought; and judging by its apparently stronger effect on Harriet's mind, producing reserve and self-command, it would.—She must communicate the painful truth, however, and as soon as possible. An injunction of secrecy had been among Mr. Weston's parting words. "For the present, the whole affair was to be completely a secret. Mr. Churchill had made a point of it, as a token of respect to the wife he had so very recently lost; and every body admitted it to be no more than due decorum."—Emma had promised; but still Harriet must be excepted. It was her superior duty.

In spite of her vexation, she could not help feeling it almost ridiculous, that she should have the very same distressing and delicate office to perform by Harriet, which Mrs. Weston had just gone through by herself. The intelligence, which had been so anxiously announced to her, she was now to be anxiously announcing to another. Her heart beat quick on hearing Harriet's footstep and voice; so, she supposed, had poor Mrs. Weston felt when *she* was approaching Randalls. Could the event of the disclosure bear an equal resemblance!—But of that, unfortunately, there could be no chance.

"Well, Miss Woodhouse!" cried Harriet, coming eagerly into the room—"is not this the oddest news that ever was?"

"What news do you mean?" replied Emma, unable to guess, by look or voice, whether Harriet could indeed have received any hint.

"About Jane Fairfax. Did you ever hear any thing so strange? Oh!—you need not be afraid of owning it to me, for Mr. Weston has told me himself. I met him just now. He told me it was to be a great secret; and, therefore, I should not think of mentioning it to any body but you, but he said you knew it."

"What did Mr. Weston tell you?"—said Emma, still perplexed.

"Oh! he told me all about it; that Jane Fairfax and Mr. Frank Churchill are to be married, and that they have been privately engaged to one another this long while. How very odd!"

It was, indeed, so odd; Harriet's behaviour was so extremely odd, that Emma did not know how to understand it. Her character appeared absolutely changed. She seemed to propose shewing no agitation, or disappointment, or peculiar concern in the discovery. Emma looked at her, quite unable to speak.

"Had you any idea," cried Harriet, "of his being in love with her?—You, perhaps, might.—You (blushing as she spoke) who can see into every body's heart; but nobody else—"

"Upon my word," said Emma, "I begin to doubt my having any such talent. Can you seriously ask me, Harriet, whether I imagined him attached to another woman at the very time that I was—tacitly, if not openly—encouraging you to give way to your own feelings?—I never had the slightest suspicion, till within the last hour, of Mr. Frank Churchill's having the least regard for Jane Fairfax. You may be very sure that if I had, I should have cautioned you accordingly."

"Me!" cried Harriet, colouring, and astonished. "Why should you caution me?—You do not think I care about Mr. Frank Churchill."

"I am delighted to hear you speak so stoutly on the subject," replied Emma, smiling; "but you do not mean to deny that there was a time—and not very distant either—when you gave me reason to understand that you did care about him?"

"Him!—never, never. Dear Miss Woodhouse, how could you so mistake me?" turning away distressed.

"Harriet!" cried Emma, after a moment's pause—"What do you mean?—Good Heaven! what do you mean?—Mistake you!—Am I to suppose then?—"

She could not speak another word.—Her voice was lost; and she sat down, waiting in great terror till Harriet should answer.

Harriet, who was standing at some distance, and with face turned from her, did not immediately say any thing; and when she did speak, it was in a voice nearly as agitated as Emma's.

"I should not have thought it possible," she began, "that you could have misunderstood me! I know we agreed never to name him—but considering how infinitely superior he is to every body else, I should not have thought it possible that I could be supposed to mean any other person. Mr. Frank Churchill, indeed! I do not know who would ever look at him in the company of the other. I hope I have a better taste than to think of Mr. Frank Churchill, who is like nobody by his side. And that you should have been so mistaken, is amazing!—I am sure, but for believing that you entirely approved and meant to encourage me in my attachment, I should have considered it at first too great a presumption almost, to dare to think of him. At first, if you had not told me that more wonderful things had happened; that there had been matches of greater disparity (those were your very words);—I should not have dared to give way to—I should not have thought it possible—But if *you*, who had been always acquainted with him—"

"Harriet!" cried Emma, collecting herself resolutely—"Let us understand each other now, without the possibility of farther mistake. Are you speaking of—Mr. Knightley?"

"To be sure I am. I never could have an idea of any body else—and so I thought you knew. When we talked about him, it was as clear as possible."

"Not quite," returned Emma, with forced calmness, "for all that you then said, appeared to me to relate to a different person. I could almost assert that you had *named* Mr. Frank Churchill. I am sure the service Mr. Frank Churchill had rendered you, in protecting you from the gipsies, was spoken of."

"Oh! Miss Woodhouse, how you do forget!"

"My dear Harriet, I perfectly remember the substance of what I said on the occasion. I told you that I did not wonder at your attachment; that considering the service he had rendered you, it was extremely natural:—and you agreed to it, expressing yourself very warmly as to your sense of that service, and mentioning even what your sensations had been in seeing him come forward to your rescue.—The impression of it is strong on my memory."

"Oh, dear," cried Harriet, "now I recollect what you mean; but I was thinking of something very different at the time. It was not the gipsies—it was not Mr. Frank Churchill that I meant. No! (with some elevation) I was thinking of a much more precious circumstance—of Mr. Knightley's coming and asking me to dance, when Mr. Elton would not stand up with me; and when there was no other partner in the room. That was the kind action; that was the noble benevolence and generosity; that was the service which made me begin to feel how superior he was to every other being upon earth."

"Good God!" cried Emma, "this has been a most unfortunate—most deplorable mistake!—What is to be done?"

"You would not have encouraged me, then, if you had understood me? At least, however, I cannot be worse off than I should have been, if the other had been the person; and now—it *is* possible—"

She paused a few moments. Emma could not speak.

"I do not wonder, Miss Woodhouse," she resumed, "that you should feel a great difference between the two, as to me or as to any body. You must think one five hundred million times more above me than the other. But I hope, Miss Woodhouse, that supposing—that if—strange as it may appear—. But you know they were your own words, that *more* wonderful things had happened, matches of *greater* disparity had taken place than between Mr. Frank Churchill and me; and, therefore, it seems as if such a thing even as this, may have occurred before—and if I should be so fortunate, beyond expression, as to—if Mr. Knightley should really—if *he* does not mind the disparity, I hope, dear Miss Woodhouse, you will not set yourself against it, and try to put difficulties in the way. But you are too good for that, I am sure."

Harriet was standing at one of the windows. Emma turned round to look at her in consternation, and hastily said,

"Have you any idea of Mr. Knightley's returning your affection?"

"Yes," replied Harriet modestly, but not fearfully—"I must say that I have."

Emma's eyes were instantly withdrawn; and she sat silently meditating, in a fixed attitude, for a few minutes. A few minutes were sufficient for making her acquainted with her own heart. A mind like hers, once opening to suspicion, made rapid progress. She touched—she admitted—she acknowledged the whole truth. Why was it so much worse that Harriet should be in love with Mr. Knightley, than with Frank Churchill? Why was the evil so dreadfully increased by Harriet's having some hope of a return? It darted through her, with the speed of an arrow, that Mr. Knightley must marry no one but herself!

Her own conduct, as well as her own heart, was before her in the same few minutes. She saw it all with a clearness which had never blessed her before. How improperly had she been acting by Harriet! How inconsiderate, how indelicate, how irrational, how unfeeling had been her conduct! What blindness, what madness, had led her on! It struck her with dreadful force, and she was ready to give it every bad name in the world. Some portion of respect for herself, however, in spite of all these demerits—some concern for her own appearance, and a strong sense of justice by Harriet—(there would be no need of *compassion* to the girl who believed herself loved by Mr. Knightley—but justice required that she should not be made unhappy by any coldness now) gave Emma the resolution to sit and endure farther with calmness, with even apparent kindness.—For her own advantage indeed, it was fit that the utmost extent of Harriet's hopes should be enquired into; and Harriet had done nothing to forfeit the regard and interest which had been so voluntarily formed and maintained—or to deserve to be slighted by the person, whose counsels had never led her right.—Rousing from reflection, therefore, and subduing her emotion, she turned to Harriet again, and, in a more inviting accent, renewed the conversation; for as to the subject which had first introduced it, the wonderful story of Jane Fairfax, that was quite sunk and lost.—Neither of them thought but of Mr. Knightley and themselves.

Harriet, who had been standing in no unhappy reverie, was yet very glad to be called from it, by the now encouraging manner of such a judge, and such a friend as Miss Woodhouse, and only wanted invitation, to give the history of her hopes with great, though trembling delight.—Emma's tremblings as she asked, and as she listened, were better concealed than Harriet's, but they were not less. Her voice was not unsteady; but her mind was in all the perturbation that such a development of self, such a burst of threatening evil, such a confusion of sudden and perplexing emotions, must create.—She listened with much inward suffering, but with great outward patience, to Harriet's detail.—Methodical, or well arranged, or very well delivered, it could not be expected to be; but it contained, when separated from all the feebleness and tautology of the narration, a substance to sink her spirit—especially with the corroborating circumstances, which her own memory brought in favour of Mr. Knightley's most improved opinion of Harriet.

Harriet had been conscious of a difference in his behaviour ever since those two decisive dances.—Emma knew that he had, on that occasion, found her much superior to his expectation. From that evening, or at least from the time of Miss Woodhouse's encouraging her to think of him, Harriet had begun to be sensible of his talking to her much more than he had been used to do, and of his having indeed quite a different manner towards her; a manner of kindness and sweetness!—Latterly she had been more and more aware of it. When they had been all walking together, he had so often come and walked by her, and talked so very delightfully!—He seemed to want to be acquainted with her. Emma knew it to have been very much the case. She had often observed the change, to almost the same extent.—Harriet repeated expressions of approbation and praise from him—and Emma felt them to be in the closest agreement with what she had known of his opinion of Harriet. He praised her for being without art or affectation, for having simple, honest, generous, feelings.—She knew that he saw such recommendations in Harriet; he had dwelt on them to her more than once.—Much that lived in Harriet's memory, many little particulars of the notice she had received from him, a look, a speech, a removal from one chair to another, a compliment implied, a preference inferred, had been unnoticed, because unsuspected, by Emma. Circumstances that might swell to half an hour's relation, and contained multiplied proofs to her who had seen them, had passed undiscerned by her who now heard them; but the two latest occurrences to be mentioned, the two of strongest promise to Harriet, were not without some degree of witness from Emma herself.—The first, was his walking with her apart from the others, in the lime-walk at Donwell, where they had been walking some time before Emma came, and he had taken pains (as she was convinced) to draw her from the rest to himself—and at first, he had talked to her in a more particular way than he had ever done before, in a very particular way indeed!—(Harriet could not recall it without a blush.) He seemed to be almost asking her, whether her affections were engaged.—But as soon as she (Miss Woodhouse) appeared likely to join them, he changed the subject, and began talking about farming:—The second, was his having sat talking with her nearly half an hour before Emma came back from her visit, the very last morning of his being at Hartfield—though, when he first came in, he had said that he could not stay five minutes—and his having told her, during their conversation, that though he must go to London, it was very much against his inclination that he left home at all, which was much more (as Emma felt) than he had acknowledged to *her*. The superior degree of confidence towards Harriet, which this one article marked, gave her severe pain.

On the subject of the first of the two circumstances, she did, after a little reflection, venture the following question. "Might he not?—Is not it possible, that when enquiring, as you thought, into the state of your affections, he might be alluding to Mr. Martin—he might have Mr. Martin's interest in view? But Harriet rejected the suspicion with spirit.

"Mr. Martin! No indeed!—There was not a hint of Mr. Martin. I hope I know better now, than to care for Mr. Martin, or to be suspected of it."

When Harriet had closed her evidence, she appealed to her dear Miss Woodhouse, to say whether she had not good ground for hope.

"I never should have presumed to think of it at first," said she, "but for you. You told me to observe him carefully, and let his behaviour be the rule of mine—and so I have. But now I seem to feel that I may deserve him; and that if he does chuse me, it will not be any thing so very wonderful."

The bitter feelings occasioned by this speech, the many bitter feelings, made the utmost exertion necessary on Emma's side, to enable her to say on reply,

"Harriet, I will only venture to declare, that Mr. Knightley is the last man in the world, who would intentionally give any woman the idea of his feeling for her more than he really does."

Harriet seemed ready to worship her friend for a sentence so satisfactory; and Emma was only saved from raptures and fondness, which at that moment would have been dreadful penance, by the sound of her father's footsteps. He was coming through the hall. Harriet was too much agitated to encounter him. "She could not compose herself—Mr. Woodhouse would be alarmed—she had better go;"—with most ready encouragement from her friend, therefore, she passed off through another door—and the moment she was gone, this was the spontaneous burst of Emma's feelings: "Oh God! that I had never seen her!"

The rest of the day, the following night, were hardly enough for her thoughts.—She was bewildered amidst the confusion of all that had rushed on her within the last few hours. Every moment had brought a fresh surprize; and every surprize must be matter of humiliation to her.—How to understand it all! How to understand the deceptions she had been thus practising on herself, and living under!—The blunders, the blindness of her own head and heart!—she sat still, she walked about, she tried her own room, she tried the shrubbery—in every place, every posture, she perceived that she had acted most weakly; that she had been imposed on by others in a most mortifying degree; that she had been imposing on herself in a degree yet more mortifying; that she was wretched, and should probably find this day but the beginning of wretchedness.

To understand, thoroughly understand her own heart, was the first endeavour. To that point went every leisure moment which her father's claims on her allowed, and every moment of involuntary absence of mind.

How long had Mr. Knightley been so dear to her, as every feeling declared him now to be? When had his influence, such influence begun?—When had he succeeded to that place in her affection, which Frank Churchill had once, for a short period, occupied?—She looked back; she compared the two—compared them, as they had always stood in her estimation, from the time of the latter's becoming known to her—and as they must at any time have been compared by her, had it—oh! had it, by any blessed felicity, occurred to her, to institute the comparison.—She saw that there never had been a time when she did not consider Mr. Knightley as infinitely the superior, or when his regard for her had not been infinitely the most dear. She saw, that in persuading herself, in fancying, in acting to the contrary, she had been entirely under a delusion, totally ignorant of her own heart—and, in short, that she had never really cared for Frank Churchill at all!

This was the conclusion of the first series of reflection. This was the knowledge of herself, on the first question of inquiry, which she reached; and without being long in reaching it.—She was most sorrowfully indignant; ashamed of every sensation but the one revealed to her—her affection for Mr. Knightley.—Every other part of her mind was disgusting.

With insufferable vanity had she believed herself in the secret of every body's feelings; with unpardonable arrogance proposed to arrange every body's destiny. She was proved to have been universally mistaken; and she had not quite done nothing—for she had done mischief. She had brought evil on Harriet, on herself, and she too much feared, on Mr. Knightley.—Were this most unequal of all connexions to take place, on her must rest all the reproach of having given it a beginning; for his attachment, she must believe to be produced only by a consciousness of Harriet's;—and even were this not the case, he would never have known Harriet at all but for her folly.

Mr. Knightley and Harriet Smith!—It was a union to distance every wonder of the kind.—The attachment of Frank Churchill and Jane Fairfax became commonplace, threadbare, stale in the comparison, exciting no surprize, presenting no disparity, affording nothing to be said or thought.—Mr. Knightley and Harriet Smith!—Such an elevation on her side! Such a debasement on his! It was horrible to Emma to think how it must sink him in the general opinion, to foresee the smiles, the sneers, the merriment it would prompt at his expense; the mortification and disdain of his brother, the thousand inconveniences to himself.—Could it be?—No; it was impossible. And yet it was far, very far, from impossible.—Was it a new circumstance for a man of first-rate abilities to be captivated by very inferior powers? Was it new for one, perhaps too busy to seek, to be the prize of a girl who would seek him?—Was it new for any thing in this world to be unequal, inconsistent, incongruous—or for chance and circumstance (as second causes) to direct the human fate?

Oh! had she never brought Harriet forward! Had she left her where she ought, and where he had told her she ought!—Had she not, with a folly which no tongue could express, prevented her marrying the unexceptionable young man who would have made her happy and respectable in the line of life to which she ought to belong—all would have been safe; none of this dreadful sequel would have been.

How Harriet could ever have had the presumption to raise her thoughts to Mr. Knightley!—How she could dare to fancy herself the chosen of such a man till actually assured of it!—But Harriet was less humble, had fewer scruples than formerly.—Her inferiority, whether of mind or situation, seemed little felt.—She had seemed more sensible of Mr. Elton's being to stoop in marrying her, than she now seemed of Mr. Knightley's.—Alas! was not that her own doing too? Who had been at pains to give Harriet notions of self-consequence but herself?—Who but herself had taught her, that she was to elevate herself if possible, and that her claims were great to a high worldly establishment?—If Harriet, from being humble, were grown vain, it was her doing too.

CHAPTER XII

Till now that she was threatened with its loss, Emma had never known how much of her happiness depended on being *first* with Mr. Knightley, first in interest and affection.—Satisfied that it was so, and feeling it her due, she had enjoyed it without reflection; and only in the dread of being supplanted, found how inexpressibly important it had been.—Long, very long, she felt she had been first; for, having no female connexions of his own, there had been only Isabella whose claims could be compared with hers, and she had always known exactly how far he loved and esteemed Isabella. She had herself been first with him for many years past. She had not deserved it; she had often been negligent or perverse, slighting his advice, or even wilfully opposing him, insensible of half his merits, and quarrelling with him because he would not acknowledge her false and insolent estimate of her own—but still, from family attachment and habit, and thorough excellence of mind, he had loved her, and watched over her from a girl, with an endeavour to improve her, and an anxiety for her doing right, which no other creature had at all shared. In spite of all her faults, she knew she was dear to him; might she not say, very dear?—When the suggestions of hope, however, which must follow here, presented themselves, she could not presume to indulge them. Harriet Smith might think herself not unworthy of being peculiarly, exclusively, passionately loved by Mr. Knightley. *She* could not. She could not flatter herself with any idea of blindness in his attachment to *her*. She had received a very recent proof of its impartiality.—How shocked had he been by her behaviour to Miss Bates! How directly, how strongly had he expressed himself to her on the subject!—Not too strongly for the offence—but far, far too strongly to issue from any feeling softer than upright justice and clear-sighted good-will.—She had no hope, nothing to deserve the name of hope, that he could have that sort of affection for herself which was now in question; but there was a hope (at times a slight one, at times much stronger) that Harriet might have deceived herself, and be overrating his regard for *her*.—Wish it she must, for his sake—be the consequence nothing to herself, but his remaining single all his life. Could she be secure of that, indeed, of his never marrying at all, she believed she should be perfectly satisfied.—Let him but continue the same Mr. Knightley to her and her father, the same Mr. Knightley to all the world; let Donwell and Hartfield lose none of their precious intercourse of friendship and confidence, and her peace would be fully secured.—Marriage, in fact, would not do for her. It would be incompatible with what she owed to her father, and with what she felt for him. Nothing should separate her from her father. She would not marry, even if she were asked by Mr. Knightley.

It must be her ardent wish that Harriet might be disappointed; and she hoped, that when able to see them together again, she might at least be able to ascertain what the chances for it were.—She should see them henceforward with the closest observance; and wretchedly as she had hitherto misunderstood even those she was watching, she did not know how to admit that she could be blinded here.—He was expected back every day. The power of observation would be soon given—frightfully soon it appeared when her thoughts were in one course. In the meanwhile, she resolved against seeing Harriet.—It would do neither of them good, it would do the subject no good, to be talking of it farther.—She was resolved not to be convinced, as long as she could doubt, and yet had no authority for opposing Harriet's confidence. To talk would be only to irritate.—She wrote to her, therefore, kindly, but decisively, to beg that she would not, at present, come to Hartfield; acknowledging it to be her conviction, that all farther confidential discussion of *one* topic had better be avoided; and hoping, that if a few days were allowed to pass before they met again, except in the company of others—she objected only to a tête-à-tête—they might be able to act as if they had forgotten the conversation of yesterday.—Harriet submitted, and approved, and was grateful.

This point was just arranged, when a visitor arrived to tear Emma's thoughts a little from the one subject which had engrossed them, sleeping or waking, the last twenty-four hours—Mrs. Weston, who had been calling on her daughter-in-law elect, and took Hartfield in her way home, almost as much in duty to Emma as in pleasure to herself, to relate all the particulars of so interesting an interview.

Mr. Weston had accompanied her to Mrs. Bates's, and gone through his share of this essential attention most handsomely; but she having then induced Miss Fairfax to join her in an airing, was now returned with much more to say, and much more to say with satisfaction, than a quarter of an hour spent in Mrs. Bates's parlour, with all the encumbrance of awkward feelings, could have afforded.

A little curiosity Emma had; and she made the most of it while her friend related. Mrs. Weston had set off to pay the visit in a good deal of agitation herself; and in the first place had wished not to go at all at present, to be allowed merely to write to Miss Fairfax instead, and to defer this ceremonious call till a little time had passed, and Mr. Churchill could be reconciled to the engagement's becoming known; as, considering every thing, she thought such a visit could not be paid without leading to reports:—but Mr. Weston had thought differently; he was extremely anxious to shew his approbation to Miss Fairfax and her family, and did not conceive that any suspicion could be excited by it; or if it were, that it would be of any consequence; for "such things," he observed, "always got about." Emma smiled, and felt that Mr. Weston had very good reason for saying so. They had gone, in short—and very great had been the evident distress and confusion of the lady. She had hardly been able to speak a word, and every look and action had shewn how deeply she was suffering from consciousness. The quiet, heart-felt satisfaction of the old lady, and the rapturous delight of her daughter—who proved even too joyous to talk as usual, had been a gratifying, yet almost an affecting, scene. They were both so truly respectable in their happiness, so disinterested in every sensation; thought so much of Jane; so much of every body, and so little of themselves, that every kindly feeling was at work for them. Miss Fairfax's recent illness had offered a fair plea for Mrs. Weston to invite her to an airing; she had drawn back and declined at first, but, on being pressed had yielded; and, in the course of their drive, Mrs. Weston had, by gentle encouragement, overcome so much of her embarrassment, as to bring her to converse on the important subject. Apologies for her seemingly ungracious silence in their first reception, and the warmest expressions of the gratitude she was always feeling towards herself and Mr. Weston, must necessarily open the cause; but when these effusions were put by, they had talked a good deal of the present and of the future state of the engagement. Mrs. Weston was convinced that such conversation must be the greatest relief to her companion, pent up within her own mind as every thing had so long been, and was very much pleased with all that she had said on the subject.

"On the misery of what she had suffered, during the concealment of so many months," continued Mrs. Weston, "she was energetic. This was one of her expressions. 'I will not say, that since I entered into the engagement I have not had some happy moments; but I can say, that I have never known the blessing of one tranquil hour:'—and the quivering lip, Emma, which uttered it, was an attestation that I felt at my heart."

"Poor girl!" said Emma. "She thinks herself wrong, then, for having consented to a private engagement?"

"Wrong! No one, I believe, can blame her more than she is disposed to blame herself. 'The consequence,' said she, 'has been a state of perpetual suffering to me; and so it ought. But after all the punishment that misconduct can bring, it is still not less misconduct. Pain is no expiation. I never can be blameless. I have been acting contrary to all my sense of right; and the fortunate turn that every thing has taken, and the kindness I am now receiving, is what my conscience tells me ought not to be. Do not imagine, madam,' she continued, 'that I was taught wrong. Do not let any reflection fall on the principles or the care of the friends who brought me up. The error has been all my own; and I do assure you that, with all the excuse that present circumstances may appear to give, I shall yet dread making the story known to Colonel Campbell.'"

"Poor girl!" said Emma again. "She loves him then excessively, I suppose. It must have been from attachment only, that she could be led to form the engagement. Her affection must have overpowered her judgment."

"Yes, I have no doubt of her being extremely attached to him."

"I am afraid," returned Emma, sighing, "that I must often have contributed to make her unhappy."

"On your side, my love, it was very innocently done. But she probably had something of that in her thoughts, when alluding to the misunderstandings which he had given us hints of before. One natural consequence of the evil she had involved herself in," she said, "was that of making her *unreasonable*. The consciousness of having done amiss, had exposed her to a thousand inquietudes, and made her captious and irritable to a degree that must have been—that had been—hard for him to bear. 'I did not make the allowances,' said she, 'which I ought to have done, for his temper and spirits—his delightful spirits, and that gaiety, that playfulness of disposition, which, under any other circumstances, would, I am sure, have been as constantly bewitching to me, as they were at first.' She then began to speak of you, and of the great kindness you had shewn her during her illness; and with a blush which shewed me how it was all connected, desired me, whenever I had an opportunity, to thank you—I could not thank you too much—for every wish and every endeavour to do her good. She was sensible that you had never received any proper acknowledgment from herself."

"If I did not know her to be happy now," said Emma, seriously, "which, in spite of every little drawback from her scrupulous conscience, she must be, I could not bear these thanks;—for, oh! Mrs. Weston, if there were an account drawn up of the evil and the good I have done Miss Fairfax!—Well (checking herself, and trying to be more lively), this is all to be forgotten. You are very kind to bring me these interesting particulars. They shew her to the greatest advantage. I am sure she is very good—I hope she will be very happy. It is fit that the fortune should be on his side, for I think the merit will be all on hers."

Such a conclusion could not pass unanswered by Mrs. Weston. She thought well of Frank in almost every respect; and, what was more, she loved him very much, and her defence was, therefore, earnest. She talked with a great deal of reason, and at least equal affection—but she had too much to urge for Emma's attention; it was soon gone to Brunswick Square or to Donwell; she forgot to attempt to listen; and when Mrs. Weston ended with, "We have not yet had the letter we are so anxious for, you know, but I hope it will soon come," she was obliged to pause before she answered, and at last obliged to answer at random, before she could at all recollect what letter it was which they were so anxious for.

"Are you well, my Emma?" was Mrs. Weston's parting question.

"Oh! perfectly. I am always well, you know. Be sure to give me intelligence of the letter as soon as possible."

Mrs. Weston's communications furnished Emma with more food for unpleasant reflection, by increasing her esteem and compassion, and her sense of past injustice towards Miss Fairfax. She bitterly regretted not having sought a closer acquaintance with her, and blushed for the envious feelings which had certainly been, in some measure, the cause. Had she followed Mr. Knightley's known wishes, in paying that attention to Miss Fairfax, which was every way her due; had she tried to know her better; had she done her part towards intimacy; had she endeavoured to find a friend there instead of in Harriet Smith; she must, in all probability, have been spared from every pain which pressed on her now.—Birth, abilities, and education, had been equally marking one as an associate for her, to be received with gratitude; and the other—what was she?—Supposing even that they had never become intimate friends; that she had never been admitted into Miss Fairfax's confidence on this important matter—which was most probable—still, in knowing her as she ought, and as she might, she must have been preserved from the abominable suspicions of an improper attachment to Mr. Dixon, which she had not only so foolishly fashioned and harboured herself, but had so unpardonably imparted; an idea which she greatly feared had been made a subject of material distress to the delicacy of Jane's feelings, by the levity or carelessness of Frank Churchill's. Of all the sources of evil surrounding the former, since her coming to Highbury, she was persuaded that she must herself have been the worst. She must have been a perpetual enemy. They never could have been all three together, without her having stabbed Jane Fairfax's peace in a thousand instances; and on Box Hill, perhaps, it had been the agony of a mind that would bear no more.

The evening of this day was very long, and melancholy, at Hartfield. The weather added what it could of gloom. A cold stormy rain set in, and nothing of July appeared but in the trees and shrubs, which the wind was despoiling, and the length of the day, which only made such cruel sights the longer visible.

The weather affected Mr. Woodhouse, and he could only be kept tolerably comfortable by almost ceaseless attention on his daughter's side, and by exertions which had never cost her half so much before. It reminded her of their first forlorn tete-a-tete, on the evening of Mrs. Weston's wedding-day; but Mr. Knightley had walked in then, soon after tea, and dissipated every melancholy fancy. Alas! such delightful proofs of Hartfield's attraction, as those sort of visits conveyed, might shortly be over. The picture which she had then drawn of the privations of the approaching winter, had proved erroneous; no friends had deserted them, no pleasures had been lost.—But her present forebodings she feared would experience no similar contradiction. The prospect before her now, was threatening to a degree that could not be entirely dispelled—that might not be even partially brightened. If all took place that might take place among the circle of her friends,

Hartfield must be comparatively deserted; and she left to cheer her father with the spirits only of ruined happiness.

The child to be born at Randalls must be a tie there even dearer than herself; and Mrs. Weston's heart and time would be occupied by it. They should lose her; and, probably, in great measure, her husband also.—Frank Churchill would return among them no more; and Miss Fairfax, it was reasonable to suppose, would soon cease to belong to Highbury. They would be married, and settled either at or near Enscombe. All that were good would be withdrawn; and if to these losses, the loss of Donwell were to be added, what would remain of cheerful or of rational society within their reach? Mr. Knightley to be no longer coming there for his evening comfort!—No longer walking in at all hours, as if ever willing to change his own home for their's!—How was it to be endured? And if he were to be lost to them for Harriet's sake; if he were to be thought of hereafter, as finding in Harriet's society all that he wanted; if Harriet were to be the chosen, the first, the dearest, the friend, the wife to whom he looked for all the best blessings of existence; what could be increasing Emma's wretchedness but the reflection never far distant from her mind, that it had been all her own work?

When it came to such a pitch as this, she was not able to refrain from a start, or a heavy sigh, or even from walking about the room for a few seconds—and the only source whence any thing like consolation or composure could be drawn, was in the resolution of her own better conduct, and the hope that, however inferior in spirit and gaiety might be the following and every future winter of her life to the past, it would yet find her more rational, more acquainted with herself, and leave her less to regret when it were gone.

CHAPTER XIII

The weather continued much the same all the following morning; and the same loneliness, and the same melancholy, seemed to reign at Hartfield—but in the afternoon it cleared; the wind changed into a softer quarter; the clouds were carried off; the sun appeared; it was summer again. With all the eagerness which such a transition gives, Emma resolved to be out of doors as soon as possible. Never had the exquisite sight, smell, sensation of nature, tranquil, warm, and brilliant after a storm, been more attractive to her. She longed for the serenity they might gradually introduce; and on Mr. Perry's coming in soon after dinner, with a disengaged hour to give her father, she lost no time in hurrying into the shrubbery.—There, with spirits freshened, and thoughts a little relieved, she had taken a few turns, when she saw Mr. Knightley passing through the garden door, and coming towards her.—It was the first intimation of his being returned from London. She had been thinking of him the moment before, as unquestionably sixteen miles distant.—There was time only for the quickest arrangement of mind. She must be collected and calm. In half a minute they were together. The "How d'ye do's" were quiet and constrained on each side. She asked after their mutual friends; they were all well.—When had he left them?—Only that morning. He must have had a wet ride.—Yes.—He meant to walk with her, she found. "He had just looked into the dining-room, and as he was not wanted there, preferred being out of doors."—She thought he neither looked nor spoke cheerfully; and the first possible cause for it, suggested by her fears, was, that he had perhaps been communicating his plans to his brother, and was pained by the manner in which they had been received.

They walked together. He was silent. She thought he was often looking at her, and trying for a fuller view of her face than it suited her to give. And this belief produced another dread. Perhaps he wanted to speak to her, of his attachment to Harriet; he might be watching for encouragement to begin.—She did not, could not, feel equal to lead the way to any such subject. He must do it all himself. Yet she could not bear this silence. With him it was most unnatural. She considered—resolved—and, trying to smile, began—

"You have some news to hear, now you are come back, that will rather surprize you."

"Have I?" said he quietly, and looking at her; "of what nature?"

"Oh! the best nature in the world—a wedding."

After waiting a moment, as if to be sure she intended to say no more, he replied,

"If you mean Miss Fairfax and Frank Churchill, I have heard that already."

"How is it possible?" cried Emma, turning her glowing cheeks towards him; for, while she spoke, it occurred to her that he might have called at Mrs. Goddard's in his way.

"I had a few lines on parish business from Mr. Weston this morning, and at the end of them he gave me a brief account of what had happened."

Emma was quite relieved, and could presently say, with a little more composure,

"*You* probably have been less surprized than any of us, for you have had your suspicions.—I have not forgotten that you once tried to give me a caution.—I wish I had attended to it—but—(with a sinking voice and a heavy sigh) I seem to have been doomed to blindness."

For a moment or two nothing was said, and she was unsuspicious of having excited any particular interest, till she found her arm drawn within his, and pressed against his heart, and heard him thus saying, in a tone of great sensibility, speaking low,

"Time, my dearest Emma, time will heal the wound.—Your own excellent sense—your exertions for your father's sake—I know you will not allow yourself—." Her arm was pressed again, as he added, in a more broken and subdued accent, "The feelings of the warmest friendship—Indignation—Abominable scoundrel!"—And in a louder, steadier tone, he concluded with, "He will soon be gone. They will soon be in Yorkshire. I am sorry for *her*. She deserves a better fate."

Emma understood him; and as soon as she could recover from the flutter of pleasure, excited by such tender consideration, replied,

"You are very kind—but you are mistaken—and I must set you right.—I am not in want of that sort of compassion. My blindness to what was going on, led me to act by them in a way that I must always be ashamed of, and I was very foolishly tempted to say and do many things which may well lay me open to unpleasant conjectures, but I have no other reason to regret that I was not in the secret earlier."

"Emma!" cried he, looking eagerly at her, "are you, indeed?"—but checking himself—"No, no, I understand you—forgive me—I am pleased that you can say even so much.—He is no object of regret, indeed! and it will not be very long, I hope, before that becomes the acknowledgment of more than your reason.—Fortunate that your affections were not farther entangled!—I could never, I confess, from your manners, assure myself as to the degree of what you felt—I could only be certain that there was a preference—and a preference which I never believed him to deserve.—He is a disgrace to the name of man.—And is he to be rewarded with that sweet young woman?—Jane, Jane, you will be a miserable creature."

"Mr. Knightley," said Emma, trying to be lively, but really confused—"I am in a very extraordinary situation. I cannot let you continue in your error; and yet, perhaps, since my manners gave such an impression, I have as much reason to be ashamed of confessing that I never have been at all attached to the person we are speaking of, as it might be natural for a woman to feel in confessing exactly the reverse.—But I never have."

He listened in perfect silence. She wished him to speak, but he would not. She supposed she must say more before she were entitled to his clemency; but it was a hard case to be obliged still to lower herself in his opinion. She went on, however.

"I have very little to say for my own conduct.—I was tempted by his attentions, and allowed myself to appear pleased.—An old story, probably—a common case—and no more than has happened to hundreds of my sex before; and yet it may not be the more excusable in one who sets up as I do for understanding. Many circumstances assisted the temptation. He was the son of Mr. Weston—he was continually here—I always found him very pleasant—and, in short, for (with a sigh) let me swell out the causes ever so ingeniously, they all centre in this at last—my vanity was flattered, and I allowed his attentions. Latterly, however—for some time, indeed—I have had no idea of their meaning any thing.—I thought them a habit, a trick, nothing that called for seriousness on my side. He has imposed on me, but he has not injured me. I have never been attached to him. And now I can tolerably comprehend his behaviour. He never wished to attach me. It was merely a blind to conceal his real situation with another.—It was his object to blind all about him; and no one, I am sure, could be more effectually blinded than myself—except that I was *not* blinded—that it was my good fortune—that, in short, I was somehow or other safe from him."

She had hoped for an answer here—for a few words to say that her conduct was at least intelligible; but he was silent; and, as far as she could judge, deep in thought. At last, and tolerably in his usual tone, he said,

"I have never had a high opinion of Frank Churchill.—I can suppose, however, that I may have underrated him. My acquaintance with him has been but trifling.—And even if I have not underrated him hitherto, he may yet turn out well.—With such a woman he has a chance.—I have no motive for wishing him ill—and for her sake, whose happiness will be involved in his good character and conduct, I shall certainly wish him well."

"I have no doubt of their being happy together," said Emma; "I believe them to be very mutually and very sincerely attached."

"He is a most fortunate man!" returned Mr. Knightley, with energy. "So early in life—at three-and-twenty—a period when, if a man chuses a wife, he generally chuses ill. At three-and-twenty to have drawn such a prize! What years of felicity that man, in all human calculation, has before him!—Assured of the love of such a woman—the disinterested love, for Jane Fairfax's character vouches for her disinterestedness; every thing in his favour,—equality of situation—I mean, as far as regards society, and all the habits and manners that are important; equality in every point but one—and that one, since the purity of her heart is not to be doubted, such as must increase his felicity, for it will be his to bestow the only advantages she wants.—A man would always wish to give a woman a better home than the one he takes her from; and he who can do it, where there is no doubt of *her* regard, must, I think, be the happiest of mortals.—Frank Churchill is, indeed, the favourite of fortune. Every thing turns out for his good.—He meets with a young woman at a watering-place, gains her affection, cannot even weary her by negligent treatment—and had he and all his family sought round the world for a perfect wife for him, they could not have found her superior.—His aunt is in the way.—His aunt dies.—He has only to speak.—His friends are eager to promote his happiness.—He had used every body ill—and they are all delighted to forgive him.—He is a fortunate man indeed!"

"You speak as if you envied him."

"And I do envy him, Emma. In one respect he is the object of my envy."

Emma could say no more. They seemed to be within half a sentence of Harriet, and her immediate feeling was to avert the subject, if possible. She made her plan; she would speak of something totally different—the children in Brunswick Square; and she only waited for breath to begin, when Mr. Knightley startled her, by saying,

"You will not ask me what is the point of envy.—You are determined, I see, to have no curiosity.—You are wise—but *I* cannot be wise. Emma, I must tell you what you will not ask, though I may wish it unsaid the next moment."

"Oh! then, don't speak it, don't speak it," she eagerly cried. "Take a little time, consider, do not commit yourself."

"Thank you," said he, in an accent of deep mortification, and not another syllable followed.

Emma could not bear to give him pain. He was wishing to confide in her—perhaps to consult her;—cost her what it would, she would listen. She might assist his resolution, or reconcile him to it; she might give just praise to Harriet, or, by representing to him his own independence, relieve him from that state of indecision, which must be more intolerable than any alternative to such a mind as his.—They had reached the house.

"You are going in, I suppose?" said he.

"No,"—replied Emma—quite confirmed by the depressed manner in which he still spoke—"I should like to take another turn. Mr. Perry is not gone." And, after proceeding a few steps, she added—"I stopped you ungraciously, just now, Mr. Knightley, and, I am afraid, gave you pain.—But if you have any wish to speak openly to me as a friend, or to ask my opinion of any thing that you may have in contemplation—as a friend, indeed, you may command me.—I will hear whatever you like. I will tell you exactly what I think."

"As a friend!"—repeated Mr. Knightley.—"Emma, that I fear is a word—No, I have no wish—Stay, yes, why should I hesitate?—I have gone too far already for concealment.—Emma, I accept your offer—Extraordinary as it may seem, I accept it, and refer myself to you as a friend.—Tell me, then, have I no chance of ever succeeding?"

He stopped in his earnestness to look the question, and the expression of his eyes overpowered her.

"My dearest Emma," said he, "for dearest you will always be, whatever the event of this hour's conversation, my dearest, most beloved Emma—tell me at once. Say 'No,' if it is to be said."—She could really say nothing.—"You are silent," he cried, with great animation; "absolutely silent! at present I ask no more."

Emma was almost ready to sink under the agitation of this moment. The dread of being awakened from the happiest dream, was perhaps the most prominent feeling.

"I cannot make speeches, Emma:" he soon resumed; and in a tone of such sincere, decided, intelligible tenderness as was tolerably convincing.—"If I loved you less, I might be able to talk about it more. But you know what I am.—You hear nothing but truth from me.—I have blamed you, and lectured you, and you have borne it as no other woman in England would have borne it.—Bear with the truths I would tell you now, dearest Emma, as well as you have borne with them. The manner, perhaps, may have as little to recommend them. God knows, I have been a very indifferent lover.—But you understand me.—Yes, you see, you understand my feelings—and will return them if you can. At present, I ask only to hear, once to hear your voice."

While he spoke, Emma's mind was most busy, and, with all the wonderful velocity of thought, had been able—and yet without losing a word—to catch and comprehend the exact truth of the whole; to see that Harriet's hopes had been entirely groundless, a mistake, a delusion, as complete a delusion as any of her own—that Harriet was nothing; that she was every thing herself; that what she had been saying relative to Harriet had been all taken as the language of her own feelings; and that her agitation, her doubts, her reluctance, her discouragement, had been all received as discouragement from herself.—And not only was there time for these convictions, with all their glow of attendant happiness; there was time also to rejoice that Harriet's secret had not escaped her, and to resolve that it need not, and should not.—It was all the service she could now render her poor friend; for as to any of that heroism of sentiment which might have prompted her to entreat him to transfer his affection from herself to Harriet, as infinitely the most worthy of the two—or even the more simple sublimity of resolving to refuse him at once and for ever, without vouchsafing any motive, because he could not marry them both, Emma had it not. She felt for Harriet, with pain and with contrition; but no flight of generosity run mad, opposing all that could be probable or reasonable, entered her brain. She had led her friend astray, and it would be a reproach to her for ever; but her judgment was as strong as her feelings, and as strong as it had ever been before, in reprobating any such alliance for him, as most unequal and degrading. Her way was clear, though not quite smooth.—She spoke then, on being so entreated.—What did she say?—Just what she ought, of course. A lady always does.—She said enough to shew there need not be despair—and to invite him to say more himself. He *had* despaired at one period; he had received such an injunction to caution and silence, as for the time crushed every hope;—she had begun by refusing to hear him.—The change had perhaps been somewhat sudden;—her proposal of taking another turn, her renewing the conversation which she had just put an end to, might be a little extraordinary!—She felt its inconsistency; but Mr. Knightley was so obliging as to put up with it, and seek no farther explanation.

Seldom, very seldom, does complete truth belong to any human disclosure; seldom can it happen that something is not a little disguised, or a little mistaken; but where, as in this case, though the conduct is mistaken, the feelings are not, it may not be very material.—Mr. Knightley could not impute to Emma a more relenting heart than she possessed, or a heart more disposed to accept of his.

He had, in fact, been wholly unsuspicious of his own influence. He had followed her into the shrubbery with no idea of trying it. He had come, in his anxiety to see how she bore Frank Churchill's engagement, with no selfish view, no view at all, but of endeavouring, if she allowed him an opening, to soothe or to counsel her.—The rest had been the work of the moment, the immediate effect of what he heard, on his feelings. The delightful assurance of her total indifference towards Frank Churchill, of her having a heart completely disengaged from him, had given birth to the hope, that, in time, he might gain her affection himself;—but it had been no present hope—he had only, in the momentary conquest of eagerness over judgment, aspired to be told that she did not forbid his attempt to attach her.—The superior hopes which gradually opened were so much the more enchanting.—The affection, which he had been asking to be allowed to create, if he could, was already his!—Within half an hour, he had passed from a thoroughly distressed state of mind, to something so like perfect happiness, that it could bear no other name.

Her change was equal.—This one half-hour had given to each the same precious certainty of being beloved, had cleared from each the same degree of ignorance, jealousy, or distrust.—On his side, there had been a long-standing jealousy, old as the arrival, or even the expectation, of Frank Churchill.—He had been in love with Emma, and jealous of Frank Churchill, from about the same period, one sentiment having probably enlightened him as to the other. It was his jealousy of Frank Churchill that had taken him from the country.—The Box Hill party had decided him on going away. He would save himself from witnessing again such permitted, encouraged attentions.—He had gone to learn to be indifferent.—But he had gone to a wrong place. There was too much domestic happiness in his brother's house; woman wore too amiable a form in it; Isabella was too much like Emma—differing only in those striking inferiorities, which always brought the other in brilliancy before him, for much to have been done, even had his time been longer.—He had stayed on, however, vigorously, day after day—till this very morning's post had conveyed the history of Jane Fairfax.—Then, with the gladness which must be felt, nay, which he did not scruple to feel, having never believed Frank Churchill to be at all deserving Emma, was there so much fond solicitude, so much keen anxiety for her, that he could stay no longer. He had ridden home through the rain; and had walked up directly after dinner, to see how this sweetest and best of all creatures, faultless in spite of all her faults, bore the discovery.

He had found her agitated and low.—Frank Churchill was a villain.—He heard her declare that she had never loved him. Frank Churchill's character was not desperate.—She was his own Emma, by hand and word, when they returned into the house; and if he could have thought of Frank Churchill then, he might have deemed him a very good sort of fellow.

CHAPTER XIV

What totally different feelings did Emma take back into the house from what she had brought out!—she had then been only daring to hope for a little respite of suffering;—she was now in an exquisite flutter of happiness, and such happiness moreover as she believed must still be greater when the flutter should have passed away.

They sat down to tea—the same party round the same table—how often it had been collected!—and how often had her eyes fallen on the same shrubs in the lawn, and observed the same beautiful effect of the western sun!—But never in such a state of spirits, never in any thing like it; and it was with difficulty that she could summon enough of her usual self to be the attentive lady of the house, or even the attentive daughter.

Poor Mr. Woodhouse little suspected what was plotting against him in the breast of that man whom he was so cordially welcoming, and so anxiously hoping might not have taken cold from his ride.—Could he have seen the heart, he would have cared very little for the lungs; but without the most distant imagination of the impending evil, without the slightest perception of any thing extraordinary in the looks or ways of either, he repeated to them very comfortably all the articles of news he had received from Mr. Perry, and talked on with much self-contentment, totally unsuspicious of what they could have told him in return.

As long as Mr. Knightley remained with them, Emma's fever continued; but when he was gone, she began to be a little tranquillised and subdued—and in the course of the sleepless night, which was the tax for such an evening, she found one or two such very serious points to consider, as made her feel, that even her happiness must have some alloy. Her father—and Harriet. She could not be alone without feeling the full weight of their separate claims; and how to guard the comfort of both to the utmost, was the question. With respect to her father, it was a question soon answered. She hardly knew yet what Mr. Knightley would ask; but a very short parley with her own heart produced the most solemn resolution of never quitting her father.—She even wept over the idea of it, as a sin of thought. While he lived, it must be only an engagement; but she flattered herself, that if divested of the danger of drawing her away, it might become an increase of comfort to him.—How to do her best by Harriet, was of more difficult decision;—how to spare her from any unnecessary pain; how to make her any possible atonement; how to appear least her enemy?—On these subjects, her perplexity and distress were very great—and her mind had to pass again and again through every bitter reproach and sorrowful regret that had ever surrounded it.—She could only resolve at last, that she would still avoid a meeting with her, and communicate all that need be told by letter; that it would be inexpressibly desirable to have her removed just now for a time from Highbury, and—indulging in one scheme more—nearly resolve, that it might be practicable to get an invitation for her to Brunswick Square.—Isabella had been pleased with Harriet; and a few weeks spent in London must give her some amusement.—She did not think it in Harriet's nature to escape being benefited by novelty and variety, by the streets, the shops, and the children.—At any rate, it would be a proof of attention and kindness in herself, from whom every thing was due; a separation for the present; an averting of the evil day, when they must all be together again.

She rose early, and wrote her letter to Harriet; an employment which left her so very serious, so nearly sad, that Mr. Knightley, in walking up to Hartfield to breakfast, did not arrive at all too soon; and half an hour stolen afterwards to go over the same ground again with him, literally and figuratively, was quite necessary to reinstate her in a proper share of the happiness of the evening before.

He had not left her long, by no means long enough for her to have the slightest inclination for thinking of any body else, when a letter was brought her from Randalls—a very thick letter;—she guessed what it must contain, and deprecated the necessity of reading it.—She was now in perfect charity with Frank Churchill; she wanted no explanations, she wanted only to have her thoughts to herself—and as for understanding any thing he wrote, she was sure she was incapable of it.—It must be waded through, however. She opened the packet; it was too surely so;—a note from Mrs. Weston to herself, ushered in the letter from Frank to Mrs. Weston.

"I have the greatest pleasure, my dear Emma, in forwarding to you the enclosed. I know what thorough justice you will do it, and have scarcely a doubt of its happy effect.—I think we shall never materially disagree about the writer again; but I will not delay you by a long preface.—We are quite well.—This letter has been the cure of all the little nervousness I have been feeling lately.—I did not quite like your looks on Tuesday, but it was an ungenial morning; and though you will never own being affected by weather, I think every body feels a north-east wind.—I felt for your dear father very much in the storm of Tuesday afternoon and yesterday morning, but had the comfort of hearing last night, by Mr. Perry, that it had not made him ill.

—Yours ever,
"A. W."

[To Mrs. Weston.]
Windsor—July

My Dear Madam,

If I made myself intelligible yesterday, this letter will be expected; but expected or not, I know it will be read with candour and indulgence.—You are all goodness, and I believe there will be need of even all your goodness to allow for some parts of my past conduct.—But I have been forgiven by one who had still more to resent. My courage rises while I write. It is very difficult for the prosperous to be humble. I have already met with such success in two applications for pardon, that I may be in danger of thinking myself too sure of yours, and of those among your friends who have had any ground of offence.—You must all endeavour to comprehend the exact nature of my situation when I first arrived at Randalls; you must consider me as having a secret which was to be kept at all hazards. This was the fact. My right to place myself in a situation requiring such concealment, is another question. I shall not discuss it here. For my temptation to *think* it a right, I refer every caviller to a brick house, sashed windows below, and casements above, in Highbury. I dared not address her openly; my difficulties in the then state of Enscombe must be too well known to require definition; and I was fortunate enough to prevail, before we parted at Weymouth, and to induce the most upright female mind in the creation to stoop in charity to a secret engagement.—Had she refused, I should have gone mad.—But you will be ready to say, what was your hope in doing this?—What did you look forward to?—To any thing, every thing—to time, chance, circumstance, slow effects, sudden bursts, perseverance and weariness, health and sickness. Every possibility of good was before me, and the first of blessings secured, in obtaining her promises of faith and correspondence. If you need farther explanation, I have the honour, my dear madam, of being your husband's son, and the advantage of inheriting a disposition to hope for good, which no inheritance of houses or lands can ever equal the value of.—See me, then, under these circumstances, arriving on my first visit to Randalls;—and here I am conscious of wrong, for that visit might have been sooner paid. You will look back and see that I did not come till Miss Fairfax was in Highbury; and as *you* were the person slighted, you will forgive me instantly; but I must work on my father's compassion, by reminding him, that so long as I absented myself from his house, so long I lost the blessing of knowing you. My behaviour, during the very happy fortnight which I spent with you, did not, I hope, lay me open to reprehension, excepting on one point. And now I come to the principal, the only important part of my conduct while belonging to you, which excites my own anxiety, or requires very solicitous explanation. With the greatest respect, and the warmest friendship, do I mention Miss Woodhouse; my father perhaps will think I ought to add, with the deepest humiliation.—A few words which dropped from him yesterday spoke his opinion, and some censure I acknowledge myself liable to.—My behaviour to Miss Woodhouse indicated, I believe, more than it ought.—In order to assist a concealment so essential to me, I was led on to make more than an allowable use of the sort of intimacy into which we were immediately thrown.—I cannot deny that Miss Woodhouse was my ostensible object—but I am sure you will believe the declaration, that had I not been convinced of her indifference, I would not have been induced by any selfish views to go on.—Amiable and delightful as Miss Woodhouse is, she never gave me the idea of a young woman likely to be attached; and that she was perfectly free from any tendency to being attached to me, was as much my conviction as my wish.—She received my attentions with an easy, friendly, good-humoured playfulness, which exactly suited me. We seemed to understand each other. From our relative situation, those attentions were her due, and were felt to be so.—Whether Miss Woodhouse began really to understand me before the expiration of that fortnight, I cannot say;—when I called to take leave of her, I remember that I was within a moment of confessing the truth, and I then fancied she was not without suspicion; but I have no doubt of her having since detected me, at least in some degree.—She may not have surmised the whole, but her quickness must have penetrated a part. I cannot doubt it. You will find, whenever the subject becomes freed from its present restraints, that it did not take her wholly by surprize. She frequently gave me hints of it. I remember her telling me at the ball, that I owed Mrs. Elton gratitude for her attentions to Miss Fairfax.—I hope this history of my conduct towards her will be admitted by you and my father as great extenuation of what you saw amiss. While you considered me as having sinned against Emma Woodhouse, I could deserve nothing from either. Acquit me here, and procure for me, when it is allowable, the acquittal and good wishes of that said Emma Woodhouse, whom I regard with so much brotherly affection, as to long to have her as deeply and as happily in love as myself.—Whatever strange things I said or did during that fortnight, you have now a key to. My heart was in Highbury, and my business was to get my body thither as often as might be, and with the least suspicion. If you remember any queernesses, set them all to the right account.—Of the pianoforte so much talked of, I feel it only necessary to say, that its being ordered was absolutely unknown to Miss F———, who would never have allowed me to send it, had any choice been given her.—The delicacy of her mind throughout the whole engagement, my dear madam, is much beyond my power of doing justice to. You will soon, I earnestly hope, know her thoroughly yourself.—No description can describe her. She must tell you herself what she is—yet not by word, for never was there a human creature who would so designedly suppress her own merit.—Since I began this letter, which will be longer than I foresaw, I have heard from her.—She gives a good account of her own health; but as she never complains, I dare not depend. I want to have your opinion of her looks. I know you will soon call on her; she is living in dread of the visit. Perhaps it is paid already. Let me hear from you without delay; I am impatient for a thousand particulars. Remember how few minutes I was at Randalls, and in how bewildered, how mad a state: and I am not much better yet; still insane either from happiness or misery. When I think of the kindness and favour I have met with, of her excellence and patience, and my uncle's generosity, I am mad with joy: but when I recollect all the uneasiness I occasioned her, and how little I deserve to be forgiven, I am mad with anger. If I could but see her again!—But I must not propose it yet. My uncle has been too good for me to encroach.—I must still add to this long letter. You have not heard all that you ought to hear. I could not give any connected detail yesterday; but the suddenness, and, in one light, the unseasonableness with which the affair burst out, needs explanation; for though the event of the 26th ult., as you will conclude, immediately opened to me the happiest prospects, I should not have presumed on such early measures, but from the very particular circumstances, which left me not an hour to lose. I should myself have shrunk from any thing so hasty, and she would have felt every scruple of mine with multiplied strength and refinement.—But I had no choice. The hasty engagement she had entered into with that woman—Here, my dear madam, I was obliged to leave off abruptly, to recollect and compose myself.—I have been walking over the country, and am now, I hope, rational enough to make the rest of my letter what it ought to be.—It is, in fact, a most mortifying retrospect for me. I behaved shamefully. And here I can admit, that my manners to Miss W., in being unpleasant to Miss F., were highly blameable. *She* disapproved them, which ought to have been enough.—My plea of concealing the truth she did not think sufficient.—She was displeased; I thought unreasonably so: I thought her, on a thousand occasions, unnecessarily scrupulous and cautious: I thought her even cold. But she was always right. If I had followed her judgment, and subdued my spirits to the level of what she deemed proper, I should have escaped the greatest unhappiness I have ever known.—We quarrelled.—Do you remember the morning spent at Donwell?—*There* every little dissatisfaction that had occurred before came to a crisis. I was late; I met her walking home by herself, and wanted to walk with her, but she would not suffer it. She absolutely refused to allow me, which I then thought most unreasonable. Now, however, I see nothing in it but a very natural and consistent degree of discretion. While I, to blind the world to our engagement, was behaving one hour with objectionable particularity to another woman, was she to be consenting the next to a proposal which might have made every previous caution useless?—Had we been met walking together between Donwell and Highbury, the truth must have been suspected.—I was mad enough, however, to resent.—I doubted her affection. I doubted it more the next day on Box Hill; when, provoked by such conduct on my side, such shameful, insolent neglect of her, and such apparent devotion to Miss W., as it would have been impossible for any woman of sense to endure, she spoke her resentment in a form of words perfectly intelligible to me.—In short, my dear madam, it was a quarrel blameless on her side, abominable on mine; and I returned the same evening to Richmond, though I might have staid with you till the next morning, merely because I would be as angry with her as possible. Even then, I was not such a fool as not to mean to be reconciled in time; but I was the injured person, injured by her coldness, and I went away determined that she should make the first advances.—I shall always congratulate myself that you were not of the Box Hill party. Had you witnessed my behaviour there, I can hardly suppose you would ever have thought well of me again. Its effect upon her appears in the immediate resolution it produced: as soon as she found I was really gone from Randalls, she closed with the offer of that officious Mrs. Elton; the whole system of whose treatment of her, by the bye, has ever filled me with indignation and hatred. I must not quarrel with a spirit of forbearance which has been so richly extended towards myself; but, otherwise, I should loudly protest against the share of it which that woman has known.—'Jane,' indeed!—You will observe that I have not yet indulged myself in calling her by that name, even to you. Think, then, what I must have endured in hearing it bandied between the Eltons with all the vulgarity of needless repetition, and all the insolence of imaginary superiority. Have patience with me, I shall soon have done.—She closed with this offer, resolving to break with me entirely, and wrote the next day to tell me that we never were to meet again.—*She felt the engagement to be a source of repentance and misery to each: she dissolved it.*—This letter reached me on the very morning of my poor aunt's death. I answered it within an hour; but from the confusion of my mind, and the multiplicity of business falling on me at once, my answer, instead of being sent with all the many other letters of that day, was locked up in my writing-desk; and I, trusting that I had written enough, though but a few lines, to satisfy her, remained without any uneasiness.—I was rather disappointed that I did not hear from her again speedily; but I made excuses for her, and was too busy, and—may I add?—too cheerful in my views to be captious.—We removed to Windsor; and two days afterwards I received a parcel from her, my own letters all returned!—and a few lines at the same time by the post, stating her extreme surprize at not having had the smallest reply to her last; and adding, that as silence on such a point could not be misconstrued, and as it must be equally desirable to both to have every subordinate arrangement concluded as soon as possible, she now sent me, by a safe conveyance, all my letters, and requested, that if I could not directly command hers, so as to send them to Highbury within a week, I would forward them after that period to her at———: in short, the full direction to Mr. Smallridge's, near Bristol, stared me in the face. I knew the name, the place, I knew all about it, and instantly saw what she had been doing. It was perfectly accordant with that resolution of character which I knew her to possess; and the secrecy she had maintained, as to any such design in her former letter, was equally descriptive of its anxious delicacy. For the world would not she have seemed to threaten me.—Imagine the shock; imagine how, till I had actually detected my own blunder, I raved at the blunders of the post.—What was to be done?—One thing only.—I must speak to my uncle. Without his sanction I could not hope to be listened to again.—I spoke; circumstances were in my favour; the late event had softened away his pride, and he was, earlier than I could have anticipated, wholly reconciled and complying; and could say at last, poor man! with a deep sigh, that he wished I might find as much happiness in the marriage state as he had done.—I felt that it would be of a different sort.—Are you disposed to pity me for what I must have suffered in opening the cause to him, for my suspense while all was at stake?—No; do not pity me till I reached

Highbury, and saw how ill I had made her. Do not pity me till I saw her wan, sick looks.—I reached Highbury at the time of day when, from my knowledge of their late breakfast hour, I was certain of a good chance of finding her alone.—I was not disappointed; and at last I was not disappointed either in the object of my journey. A great deal of very reasonable, very just displeasure I had to persuade away. But it is done; we are reconciled, dearer, much dearer, than ever, and no moment's uneasiness can ever occur between us again. Now, my dear madam, I will release you; but I could not conclude before. A thousand and a thousand thanks for all the kindness you have ever shewn me, and ten thousand for the attentions your heart will dictate towards her.—If you think me in a way to be happier than I deserve, I am quite of your opinion.—Miss W. calls me the child of good fortune. I hope she is right.—In one respect, my good fortune is undoubted, that of being able to subscribe myself,

Your obliged and affectionate Son,

F. C. Weston Churchill.

CHAPTER XV

This letter must make its way to Emma's feelings. She was obliged, in spite of her previous determination to the contrary, to do it all the justice that Mrs. Weston foretold. As soon as she came to her own name, it was irresistible; every line relating to herself was interesting, and almost every line agreeable; and when this charm ceased, the subject could still maintain itself, by the natural return of her former regard for the writer, and the very strong attraction which any picture of love must have for her at that moment. She never stopt till she had gone through the whole; and though it was impossible not to feel that he had been wrong, yet he had been less wrong than she had supposed—and he had suffered, and was very sorry—and he was so grateful to Mrs. Weston, and so much in love with Miss Fairfax, and she was so happy herself, that there was no being severe; and could he have entered the room, she must have shaken hands with him as heartily as ever.

She thought so well of the letter, that when Mr. Knightley came again, she desired him to read it. She was sure of Mrs. Weston's wishing it to be communicated; especially to one, who, like Mr. Knightley, had seen so much to blame in his conduct.

"I shall be very glad to look it over," said he; "but it seems long. I will take it home with me at night."

But that would not do. Mr. Weston was to call in the evening, and she must return it by him.

"I would rather be talking to you," he replied; "but as it seems a matter of justice, it shall be done."

He began—stopping, however, almost directly to say, "Had I been offered the sight of one of this gentleman's letters to his stepmother a few months ago, Emma, it would not have been taken with such indifference."

He proceeded a little farther, reading to himself; and then, with a smile, observed, "Humph! a fine complimentary opening: But it is his way. One man's style must not be the rule of another's. We will not be severe."

"It will be natural for me," he added shortly afterwards, "to speak my opinion aloud as I read. By doing it, I shall feel that I am near you. It will not be so great a loss of time: but if you dislike it—"

"Not at all. I should wish it."

Mr. Knightley returned to his reading with greater alacrity.

"He trifles here," said he, "as to the temptation. He knows he is wrong, and has nothing rational to urge.—Bad.—He ought not to have formed the engagement.—'His father's disposition:'—he is unjust, however, to his father. Mr. Weston's sanguine temper was a blessing on all his upright and honourable exertions; but Mr. Weston earned every present comfort before he endeavoured to gain it.—Very true; he did not come till Miss Fairfax was here."

"And I have not forgotten," said Emma, "how sure you were that he might have come sooner if he would. You pass it over very handsomely—but you were perfectly right."

"I was not quite impartial in my judgment, Emma:—but yet, I think—had *you* not been in the case—I should still have distrusted him."

When he came to Miss Woodhouse, he was obliged to read the whole of it aloud—all that related to her, with a smile; a look; a shake of the head; a word or two of assent, or disapprobation; or merely of love, as the subject required; concluding, however, seriously, and, after steady reflection, thus—

"Very bad—though it might have been worse.—Playing a most dangerous game. Too much indebted to the event for his acquittal.—No judge of his own manners by you.—Always deceived in fact by his own wishes, and regardless of little besides his own convenience.—Fancying you to have fathomed his secret. Natural enough!—his own mind full of intrigue, that he should suspect it in others.—Mystery; Finesse—how they pervert the understanding! My Emma, does not every thing serve to prove more and more the beauty of truth and sincerity in all our dealings with each other?"

Emma agreed to it, and with a blush of sensibility on Harriet's account, which she could not give any sincere explanation of.

"You had better go on," said she.

He did so, but very soon stopt again to say, "the pianoforte! Ah! That was the act of a very, very young man, one too young to consider whether the inconvenience of it might not very much exceed the pleasure. A boyish scheme, indeed!—I cannot comprehend a man's wishing to give a woman any proof of affection which he knows she would rather dispense with; and he did know that she would have prevented the instrument's coming if she could."

After this, he made some progress without any pause. Frank Churchill's confession of having behaved shamefully was the first thing to call for more than a word in passing.

"I perfectly agree with you, sir,"—was then his remark. "You did behave very shamefully. You never wrote a truer line." And having gone through what immediately followed of the basis of their disagreement, and his persisting to act in direct opposition to Jane Fairfax's sense of right, he made a fuller pause to say, "This is very bad.—He had induced her to place herself, for his sake, in a situation of extreme difficulty and uneasiness, and it should have been his first object to prevent her from suffering unnecessarily.—She must have had much more to contend with, in carrying on the correspondence, than he could. He should have respected even unreasonable scruples, had there been such; but hers were all reasonable. We must look to her one fault, and remember that she had done a wrong thing in consenting to the engagement, to bear that she should have been in such a state of punishment."

Emma knew that he was now getting to the Box Hill party, and grew uncomfortable. Her own behaviour had been so very improper! She was deeply ashamed, and a little afraid of his next look. It was all read, however, steadily, attentively, and without the smallest remark; and, excepting one momentary glance at her, instantly withdrawn, in the fear of giving pain—no remembrance of Box Hill seemed to exist.

"There is no saying much for the delicacy of our good friends, the Eltons," was his next observation.—"His feelings are natural.—What! actually resolve to break with him entirely!—She felt the engagement to be a source of repentance and misery to each—she dissolved it.—What a view this gives of her sense of his behaviour!—Well, he must be a most extraordinary—"

"Nay, nay, read on.—You will find how very much he suffers."

"I hope he does," replied Mr. Knightley coolly, and resuming the letter. "'Smallridge!'—What does this mean? What is all this?"

"She had engaged to go as governess to Mrs. Smallridge's children—a dear friend of Mrs. Elton's—a neighbour of Maple Grove; and, by the bye, I wonder how Mrs. Elton bears the disappointment?"

"Say nothing, my dear Emma, while you oblige me to read—not

even of Mrs. Elton. Only one page more. I shall soon have done. What a letter the man writes!"

"I wish you would read it with a kinder spirit towards him."

"Well, there *is* feeling here.—He does seem to have suffered in finding her ill.—Certainly, I can have no doubt of his being fond of her. 'Dearer, much dearer than ever.' I hope he may long continue to feel all the value of such a reconciliation.—He is a very liberal thanker, with his thousands and tens of thousands.—'Happier than I deserve.' Come, he knows himself there. 'Miss Woodhouse calls me the child of good fortune.'—Those were Miss Woodhouse's words, were they?—And a fine ending—and there is the letter. The child of good fortune! That was your name for him, was it?"

"You do not appear so well satisfied with his letter as I am; but still you must, at least I hope you must, think the better of him for it. I hope it does him some service with you."

"Yes, certainly it does. He has had great faults, faults of inconsideration and thoughtlessness; and I am very much of his opinion in thinking him likely to be happier than he deserves: but still as he is, beyond a doubt, really attached to Miss Fairfax, and will soon, it may be hoped, have the advantage of being constantly with her, I am very ready to believe his character will improve, and acquire from hers the steadiness and delicacy of principle that it wants. And now, let me talk to you of something else. I have another person's interest at present so much at heart, that I cannot think any longer about Frank Churchill. Ever since I left you this morning, Emma, my mind has been hard at work on one subject."

The subject followed; it was in plain, unaffected, gentlemanlike English, such as Mr. Knightley used even to the woman he was in love with, how to be able to ask her to marry him, without attacking the happiness of her father. Emma's answer was ready at the first word. "While her dear father lived, any change of condition must be impossible for her. She could never quit him." Part only of this answer, however, was admitted. The impossibility of her quitting her father, Mr. Knightley felt as strongly as herself; but the inadmissibility of any other change, he could not agree to. He had been thinking it over most deeply, most intently; he had at first hoped to induce Mr. Woodhouse to remove with her to Donwell; he had wanted to believe it feasible, but his knowledge of Mr. Woodhouse would not suffer him to deceive himself long; and now he confessed his persuasion, that such a transplantation would be a risk of her father's comfort, perhaps even of his life, which must not be hazarded. Mr. Woodhouse taken from Hartfield!—No, he felt that it ought not to be attempted. But the plan which had arisen on the sacrifice of this, he trusted his dearest Emma would not find in any respect objectionable; it was, that he should be received at Hartfield; that so long as her father's happiness—in other words his life—required Hartfield to continue her home, it should be his likewise.

Of their all removing to Donwell, Emma had already had her own passing thoughts. Like him, she had tried the scheme and rejected it; but such an alternative as this had not occurred to her. She was sensible of all the affection it evinced. She felt that, in quitting Donwell, he must be sacrificing a great deal of independence of hours and habits; that in living constantly with her father, and in no house of his own, there would be much, very much, to be borne with. She promised to think of it, and advised him to think of it more; but he was fully convinced, that no reflection could alter his wishes or his opinion on the subject. He had given it, he could assure her, very long and calm consideration; he had been walking away from William Larkins the whole morning, to have his thoughts to himself.

"Ah! there is one difficulty unprovided for," cried Emma. "I am sure William Larkins will not like it. You must get his consent before you ask mine."

She promised, however, to think of it; and pretty nearly promised, moreover, to think of it, with the intention of finding it a very good scheme.

It is remarkable, that Emma, in the many, very many, points of view in which she was now beginning to consider Donwell Abbey, was never struck with any sense of injury to her nephew Henry, whose rights as heir-expectant had formerly been so tenaciously regarded. Think she must of the possible difference to the poor little boy; and yet she only gave herself a saucy conscious smile about it, and found amusement in detecting the real cause of that violent dislike of Mr. Knightley's marrying Jane Fairfax, or any body else, which at the time she had wholly imputed to the amiable solicitude of the sister and the aunt.

This proposal of his, this plan of marrying and continuing at Hartfield—the more she contemplated it, the more pleasing it became.

His evils seemed to lessen, her own advantages to increase, their mutual good to outweigh every drawback. Such a companion for herself in the periods of anxiety and cheerlessness before her!—Such a partner in all those duties and cares to which time must be giving increase of melancholy!

She would have been too happy but for poor Harriet; but every blessing of her own seemed to involve and advance the sufferings of her friend, who must now be even excluded from Hartfield. The delightful family party which Emma was securing for herself, poor Harriet must, in mere charitable caution, be kept at a distance from. She would be a loser in every way. Emma could not deplore her future absence as any deduction from her own enjoyment. In such a party, Harriet would be rather a dead weight than otherwise; but for the poor girl herself, it seemed a peculiarly cruel necessity that was to be placing her in such a state of unmerited punishment.

In time, of course, Mr. Knightley would be forgotten, that is, supplanted; but this could not be expected to happen very early. Mr. Knightley himself would be doing nothing to assist the cure;—not like Mr. Elton. Mr. Knightley, always so kind, so feeling, so truly considerate for every body, would never deserve to be less worshipped than now; and it really was too much to hope even of Harriet, that she could be in love with more than *three* men in one year.

CHAPTER XVI

It was a very great relief to Emma to find Harriet as desirous as herself to avoid a meeting. Their intercourse was painful enough by letter. How much worse, had they been obliged to meet!

Harriet expressed herself very much as might be supposed, without reproaches, or apparent sense of ill-usage; and yet Emma fancied there was a something of resentment, a something bordering on it in her style, which increased the desirableness of their being separate.—It might be only her own consciousness; but it seemed as if an angel only could have been quite without resentment under such a stroke.

She had no difficulty in procuring Isabella's invitation; and she was fortunate in having a sufficient reason for asking it, without resorting to invention.—There was a tooth amiss. Harriet really wished, and had wished some time, to consult a dentist. Mrs. John Knightley was delighted to be of use; any thing of ill health was a recommendation to her—and though not so fond of a dentist as of a Mr. Wingfield, she was quite eager to have Harriet under her care.—When it was thus settled on her sister's side, Emma proposed it to her friend, and found her very persuadable.—Harriet was to go; she was invited for at least a fortnight; she was to be conveyed in Mr. Woodhouse's carriage.—It was all arranged, it was all completed, and Harriet was safe in Brunswick Square.

Now Emma could, indeed, enjoy Mr. Knightley's visits; now she could talk, and she could listen with true happiness, unchecked by that sense of injustice, of guilt, of something most painful, which had haunted her when remembering how disappointed a heart was near her, how much might at that moment, and at a little distance, be enduring by the feelings which she had led astray herself.

The difference of Harriet at Mrs. Goddard's, or in London, made perhaps an unreasonable difference in Emma's sensations; but she could not think of her in London without objects of curiosity and employment, which must be averting the past, and carrying her out of herself.

She would not allow any other anxiety to succeed directly to the place in her mind which Harriet had occupied. There was a communication before her, one which *she* only could be competent to make—the confession of her engagement to her father; but she would have nothing to do with it at present.—She had resolved to defer the disclosure till Mrs. Weston were safe and well. No additional agitation should be thrown at this period among those she loved—and the evil should not act on herself by anticipation before the appointed time.—A fortnight, at least, of leisure and peace of mind, to crown every warmer, but more agitating, delight, should be hers.

She soon resolved, equally as a duty and a pleasure, to employ half an hour of this holiday of spirits in calling on Miss Fairfax.—She ought to go—and she was longing to see her; the resemblance of their present situations increasing every other motive of good-will. It would be a *secret* satisfaction; but the consciousness of a similarity of prospect would certainly add to the interest with which she should attend to any thing Jane might communicate.

She went—she had driven once unsuccessfully to the door, but had not been into the house since the morning after Box Hill, when poor Jane had been in such distress as had filled her with compassion, though all the worst of her sufferings had been unsuspected.—The fear of being still unwelcome, determined her, though assured of their being at home, to wait in the passage, and send up her name.—She heard Patty announcing it; but no such bustle succeeded as poor Miss Bates had before made so happily intelligible.—No; she heard nothing but the instant reply of, "Beg her to walk up;"—and a moment afterwards she was met on the stairs by Jane herself, coming eagerly forward, as if no other reception of her were felt sufficient.—Emma had never seen her look so well, so lovely, so engaging. There was consciousness, animation, and warmth; there was every thing which her countenance or manner could ever have wanted.—She came forward with an offered hand; and said, in a low, but very feeling tone,

"This is most kind, indeed!—Miss Woodhouse, it is impossible for me to express—I hope you will believe—Excuse me for being so entirely without words."

Emma was gratified, and would soon have shewn no want of words, if the sound of Mrs. Elton's voice from the sitting-room had not checked her, and made it expedient to compress all her friendly and all her congratulatory sensations into a very, very earnest shake of the hand.

Mrs. Bates and Mrs. Elton were together. Miss Bates was out, which accounted for the previous tranquillity. Emma could have wished Mrs. Elton elsewhere; but she was in a humour to have patience with every body; and as Mrs. Elton met her with unusual graciousness, she hoped the rencontre would do them no harm.

She soon believed herself to penetrate Mrs. Elton's thoughts, and understand why she was, like herself, in happy spirits; it was being in Miss Fairfax's confidence, and fancying herself acquainted with what was still a secret to other people. Emma saw symptoms of it immediately in the expression of her face; and while paying her own compliments to Mrs. Bates, and appearing to attend to the good old lady's replies, she saw her with a sort of anxious parade of mystery fold up a letter which she had apparently been reading aloud to Miss Fairfax, and return it into the purple and gold reticule by her side, saying, with significant nods,

"We can finish this some other time, you know. You and I shall not want opportunities. And, in fact, you have heard all the essential already. I only wanted to prove to you that Mrs. S. admits our apology, and is not offended. You see how delightfully she writes. Oh! she is a sweet creature! You would have doated on her, had you gone.—But not a word more. Let us be discreet—quite on our good behaviour.—Hush!—You remember those lines—I forget the poem at this moment:

For when a lady's in the case,
You know all other things give place.

Now I say, my dear, in *our* case, for *lady*, read——mum! a word to the wise.—I am in a fine flow of spirits, an't I? But I want to set your heart at ease as to Mrs. S.—*My* representation, you see, has quite appeased her."

And again, on Emma's merely turning her head to look at Mrs. Bates's knitting, she added, in a half whisper,

"I mentioned no *names*, you will observe.—Oh! no; cautious as a minister of state. I managed it extremely well."

Emma could not doubt. It was a palpable display, repeated on every possible occasion. When they had all talked a little while in harmony of the weather and Mrs. Weston, she found herself abruptly addressed with,

"Do not you think, Miss Woodhouse, our saucy little friend here is charmingly recovered?—Do not you think her cure does Perry the highest credit?—(here was a side-glance of great meaning at Jane.) Upon my word, Perry has restored her in a wonderful short time!—Oh! if you had seen her, as I did, when she was at the worst!"—And when Mrs. Bates was saying something to Emma, whispered farther, "We do not say a word of any *assistance* that Perry might have; not a word of a certain young physician from Windsor.—Oh! no; Perry shall have all the credit."

"I have scarce had the pleasure of seeing you, Miss Woodhouse," she shortly afterwards began, "since the party to Box Hill. Very pleasant party. But yet I think there was something wanting. Things did not seem—that is, there seemed a little cloud upon the spirits of some.—So it appeared to me at least, but I might be mistaken. However, I think it answered so far as to tempt one to go again. What say you both to our collecting the same party, and exploring to Box Hill again, while the fine weather lasts?—It must be the same party, you know, quite the same party, not *one* exception."

Soon after this Miss Bates came in, and Emma could not help being diverted by the perplexity of her first answer to herself, resulting, she supposed, from doubt of what might be said, and impatience to say every thing.

"Thank you, dear Miss Woodhouse, you are all kindness.—It is impossible to say—Yes, indeed, I quite understand—dearest Jane's prospects—that is, I do not mean.—But she is charmingly recovered.—How is Mr. Woodhouse?—I am so glad.—Quite out of my power.—Such a happy little circle as you find us here.—Yes, indeed.—Charming young man!—that is—so very friendly; I mean good Mr. Perry!—such attention to Jane!"—And from her great, her more than commonly thankful delight towards Mrs. Elton for being there, Emma guessed that there had been a little show of resentment towards Jane, from the vicarage quarter, which was now graciously overcome.—After a few whispers, indeed, which placed it beyond a guess, Mrs. Elton, speaking louder, said,

"Yes, here I am, my good friend; and here I have been so long, that anywhere else I should think it necessary to apologise; but, the truth is, that I am waiting for my lord and master. He promised to join me here, and pay his respects to you."

"What! are we to have the pleasure of a call from Mr. Elton?—That will be a favour indeed! for I know gentlemen do not like morning visits, and Mr. Elton's time is so engaged."

"Upon my word it is, Miss Bates.—He really is engaged from morning to night.—There is no end of people's coming to him, on some pretence or other.—The magistrates, and overseers, and churchwardens, are always wanting his opinion. They seem not able to do any thing without him.—'Upon my word, Mr. E.,' I often say, 'rather you than I.—I do not know what would become of my crayons and my instrument, if I had half so many applicants.'—Bad enough as it is, for I absolutely neglect them both to an unpardonable degree.—I believe I have not played a bar this fortnight.—However, he is coming, I assure you: yes, indeed, on purpose to wait on you all." And putting up her hand to screen her words from Emma—"A congratulatory visit, you know.—Oh! yes, quite indispensable."

Miss Bates looked about her, so happily!—

"He promised to come to me as soon as he could disengage himself from Knightley; but he and Knightley are shut up together in deep consultation.—Mr. E. is Knightley's right hand."

Emma would not have smiled for the world, and only said, "Is Mr. Elton gone on foot to Donwell?—He will have a hot walk."

"Oh! no, it is a meeting at the Crown, a regular meeting. Weston and Cole will be there too; but one is apt to speak only of those who lead.—I fancy Mr. E. and Knightley have every thing their own way."

"Have not you mistaken the day?" said Emma. "I am almost certain that the meeting at the Crown is not till to-morrow.—Mr. Knightley was at Hartfield yesterday, and spoke of it as for Saturday."

"Oh! no, the meeting is certainly to-day," was the abrupt answer, which denoted the impossibility of any blunder on Mrs. Elton's side.—"I do believe," she continued, "this is the most troublesome parish that ever was. We never heard of such things at Maple Grove."

"Your parish there was small," said Jane.

"Upon my word, my dear, I do not know, for I never heard the subject talked of."

"But it is proved by the smallness of the school, which I have heard you speak of, as under the patronage of your sister and Mrs. Bragge; the only school, and not more than five-and-twenty children."

"Ah! you clever creature, that's very true. What a thinking brain you have! I say, Jane, what a perfect character you and I should make, if we could be shaken together. My liveliness and your solidity would produce perfection.—Not that I presume to insinuate, however, that *some* people may not think *you* perfection already.—But hush!—not a word, if you please."

It seemed an unnecessary caution; Jane was wanting to give her words, not to Mrs. Elton, but to Miss Woodhouse, as the latter plainly saw. The wish of distinguishing her, as far as civility permitted, was very evident, though it could not often proceed beyond a look.

Mr. Elton made his appearance. His lady greeted him with some of her sparkling vivacity.

"Very pretty, sir, upon my word; to send me on here, to be an encumbrance to my friends, so long before you vouchsafe to come!—But you knew what a dutiful creature you had to deal with. You knew I should not stir till my lord and master appeared.—Here have I been sitting this hour, giving these young ladies a sample of true conjugal obedience—for who can say, you know, how soon it may be wanted?"

Mr. Elton was so hot and tired, that all this wit seemed thrown away. His civilities to the other ladies must be paid; but his subsequent object was to lament over himself for the heat he was suffering, and the walk he had had for nothing.

"When I got to Donwell," said he, "Knightley could not be found. Very odd! very unaccountable! after the note I sent him this morning, and the message he returned, that he should certainly be at home till one."

"Donwell!" cried his wife.—"My dear Mr. E., you have not been to Donwell!—You mean the Crown; you come from the meeting at the Crown."

"No, no, that's to-morrow; and I particularly wanted to see Knightley to-day on that very account.—Such a dreadful broiling morning!—I went over the fields too—(speaking in a tone of great ill-usage,) which made it so much the worse. And then not to find him at home! I assure you I am not at all pleased. And no apology left, no message for me. The housekeeper declared she knew nothing of my being expected.—Very extraordinary!—And nobody knew at all which way he was gone. Perhaps to Hartfield, perhaps to the Abbey Mill, perhaps into his woods.—Miss Woodhouse, this is not like our friend Knightley!—Can you explain it?"

Emma amused herself by protesting that it was very extraordinary, indeed, and that she had not a syllable to say for him.

"I cannot imagine," said Mrs. Elton, (feeling the indignity as a wife ought to do), "I cannot imagine how he could do such a thing by you, of all people in the world! The very last person whom one should expect to be forgotten!—My dear Mr. E., he must have left a message for you, I am sure he must.—Not even Knightley could be so very eccentric;—and his servants forgot it. Depend upon it, that was the case: and very likely to happen with the Donwell servants, who are all, I have often observed, extremely awkward and remiss.—I am sure I would not have such a creature as his Harry stand at our sideboard for any consideration. And as for Mrs. Hodges, Wright holds her very cheap indeed.—She promised Wright a receipt, and never sent it."

"I met William Larkins," continued Mr. Elton, "as I got near the house, and he told me I should not find his master at home, but I did not believe him.—William seemed rather out of humour. He did not know what was come to his master lately, he said, but he could hardly ever get the speech of him. I have nothing to do with William's wants, but it really is of very great importance that *I* should see Knightley to-day; and it becomes a matter, therefore, of very serious inconvenience that I should have had this hot walk to no purpose."

Emma felt that she could not do better than go home directly. In all probability she was at this very time waited for there; and Mr. Knightley might be preserved from sinking deeper in aggression towards Mr. Elton, if not towards William Larkins.

She was pleased, on taking leave, to find Miss Fairfax determined to attend her out of the room, to go with her even downstairs; it gave her an opportunity which she immediately made use of, to say,

"It is as well, perhaps, that I have not had the possibility. Had you not been surrounded by other friends, I might have been tempted to introduce a subject, to ask questions, to speak more openly than might have been strictly correct.—I feel that I should certainly have been impertinent."

"Oh!" cried Jane, with a blush and an hesitation which Emma thought infinitely more becoming to her than all the elegance of all her usual composure—"there would have been no danger. The danger would have been of my wearying you. You could not have gratified me more than by expressing an interest—. Indeed, Miss Woodhouse, (speaking more collectedly,) with the consciousness which I have of misconduct, very great misconduct, it is particularly consoling to me to know that those of my friends, whose good opinion is most worth preserving, are not disgusted to such a degree as to—I have not time for half that I could wish to say. I long to make apologies, excuses, to urge something for myself. I feel it so very due. But, unfortunately—in short, if your compassion does not stand my friend—"

"Oh! you are too scrupulous, indeed you are," cried Emma warmly, and taking her hand. "You owe me no apologies; and every body to whom you might be supposed to owe them, is so perfectly satisfied, so delighted even—"

"You are very kind, but I know what my manners were to you.—So cold and artificial!—I had always a part to act.—It was a life of deceit!—I know that I must have disgusted you."

"Pray say no more. I feel that all the apologies should be on my side. Let us forgive each other at once. We must do whatever is to be done quickest, and I think our feelings will lose no time there. I hope you have pleasant accounts from Windsor?"

"Very."

"And the next news, I suppose, will be, that we are to lose you—just as I begin to know you."

"Oh! as to all that, of course nothing can be thought of yet. I am here till claimed by Colonel and Mrs. Campbell."

"Nothing can be actually settled yet, perhaps," replied Emma, smiling—"but, excuse me, it must be thought of."

The smile was returned as Jane answered,

"You are very right; it has been thought of. And I will own to you, (I am sure it will be safe), that so far as our living with Mr. Churchill at Enscombe, it is settled. There must be three months, at least, of deep mourning; but when they are over, I imagine there will be nothing more to wait for."

"Thank you, thank you.—This is just what I wanted to be assured of.—Oh! if you knew how much I love every thing that is decided and open!—Good-bye, good-bye."

CHAPTER XVII

Mrs. Weston's friends were all made happy by her safety; and if the satisfaction of her well-doing could be increased to Emma, it was by knowing her to be the mother of a little girl. She had been decided in wishing for a Miss Weston. She would not acknowledge that it was with any view of making a match for her, hereafter, with either of Isabella's sons; but she was convinced that a daughter would suit both father and mother best. It would be a great comfort to Mr. Weston, as he grew older—and even Mr. Weston might be growing older ten years hence—to have his fireside enlivened by the sports and the nonsense, the freaks and the fancies of a child never banished from home; and Mrs. Weston—no one could doubt that a daughter would be most to her; and it would be quite a pity that any one who so well knew how to teach, should not have their powers in exercise again.

"She has had the advantage, you know, of practising on me," she continued—"like La Baronne d'Almane on La Comtesse d'Ostalis, in Madame de Genlis' *Adelaide and Theodore*, and we shall now see her own little Adelaide educated on a more perfect plan."

"That is," replied Mr. Knightley, "she will indulge her even more than she did you, and believe that she does not indulge her at all. It will be the only difference."

"Poor child!" cried Emma; "at that rate, what will become of her?"

"Nothing very bad.—The fate of thousands. She will be disagreeable in infancy, and correct herself as she grows older. I am losing all my bitterness against spoilt children, my dearest Emma. I, who am owing all my happiness to *you*, would not it be horrible ingratitude in me to be severe on them?"

Emma laughed, and replied: "But I had the assistance of all your endeavours to counteract the indulgence of other people. I doubt whether my own sense would have corrected me without it."

"Do you?—I have no doubt. Nature gave you understanding:—Miss Taylor gave you principles. You must have done well. My interference was quite as likely to do harm as good. It was very natural for you to say, what right has he to lecture me?—and I am afraid very natural for you to feel that it was done in a disagreeable manner. I do not believe I did you any good. The good was all to myself, by making you an object of the tenderest affection to me. I could not think about you so much without doating on you, faults and all; and by dint of fancying so many errors, have been in love with you ever since you were thirteen at least."

"I am sure you were of use to me," cried Emma. "I was very often influenced rightly by you—oftener than I would own at the time. I am very sure you did me good. And if poor little Anna Weston is to be spoiled, it will be the greatest humanity in you to do as much for her as you have done for me, except falling in love with her when she is thirteen."

"How often, when you were a girl, have you said to me, with one of your saucy looks—'Mr. Knightley, I am going to do so-and-so; papa says I may, or I have Miss Taylor's leave'—something which, you knew, I did not approve. In such cases my interference was giving you two bad feelings instead of one."

"What an amiable creature I was!—No wonder you should hold my speeches in such affectionate remembrance."

"'Mr. Knightley.'—You always called me, 'Mr. Knightley;' and, from habit, it has not so very formal a sound.—And yet it is formal. I want you to call me something else, but I do not know what."

"I remember once calling you 'George,' in one of my amiable fits, about ten years ago. I did it because I thought it would offend you; but, as you made no objection, I never did it again."

"And cannot you call me 'George' now?"

"Impossible!—I never can call you any thing but 'Mr. Knightley.' I will not promise even to equal the elegant terseness of Mrs. Elton, by calling you Mr. K.—But I will promise," she added presently, laughing and blushing—"I will promise to call you once by your Christian name. I do not say when, but perhaps you may guess where;—in the building in which N. takes M. for better, for worse."

Emma grieved that she could not be more openly just to one important service which his better sense would have rendered her, to the advice which would have saved her from the worst of all her womanly follies—her wilful intimacy with Harriet Smith; but it was too tender a subject.—She could not enter on it.—Harriet was very seldom mentioned between them. This, on his side, might merely proceed from her not being thought of; but Emma was rather inclined to attribute it to delicacy, and a suspicion, from some appearances, that their friendship were declining. She was aware herself, that, parting under any other circumstances, they certainly should have corresponded more, and that her intelligence would not have rested, as it now almost wholly did, on Isabella's letters. He might observe that it was so. The pain of being obliged to practise concealment towards him, was very little inferior to the pain of having made Harriet unhappy.

Isabella sent quite as good an account of her visitor as could be expected; on her first arrival she had thought her out of spirits, which appeared perfectly natural, as there was a dentist to be consulted; but, since that business had been over, she did not appear to find Harriet different from what she had known her before.—Isabella, to be sure, was no very quick observer; yet if Harriet had not been equal to playing with the children, it would not have escaped her. Emma's comforts and hopes were most agreeably carried on, by Harriet's being to stay longer; her fortnight was likely to be a month at least. Mr. and Mrs. John Knightley were to come down in August, and she was invited to remain till they could bring her back.

"John does not even mention your friend," said Mr. Knightley. "Here is his answer, if you like to see it."

It was the answer to the communication of his intended marriage. Emma accepted it with a very eager hand, with an impatience all alive to know what he would say about it, and not at all checked by hearing that her friend was unmentioned.

"John enters like a brother into my happiness," continued Mr. Knightley, "but he is no complimenter; and though I well know him to have, likewise, a most brotherly affection for you, he is so far from making flourishes, that any other young woman might think him rather cool in her praise. But I am not afraid of your seeing what he writes."

"He writes like a sensible man," replied Emma, when she had read the letter. "I honour his sincerity. It is very plain that he considers the good fortune of the engagement as all on my side, but that he is not without hope of my growing, in time, as worthy of your affection, as you think me already. Had he said any thing to bear a different construction, I should not have believed him."

"My Emma, he means no such thing. He only means—"

"He and I should differ very little in our estimation of the two," interrupted she, with a sort of serious smile—"much less, perhaps, than he is aware of, if we could enter without ceremony or reserve on the subject."

"Emma, my dear Emma—"

"Oh!" she cried with more thorough gaiety, "if you fancy your brother does not do me justice, only wait till my dear father is in the secret, and hear his opinion. Depend upon it, he will be much farther from doing *you* justice. He will think all the happiness, all the advantage, on your side of the question; all the merit on mine. I wish I may not sink into 'poor Emma' with him at once.—His tender compassion towards oppressed worth can go no farther."

"Ah!" he cried, "I wish your father might be half as easily convinced as John will be, of our having every right that equal worth can give, to be happy together. I am amused by one part of John's letter—did you notice it?—where he says, that my information did not take him wholly by surprize, that he was rather in expectation of hearing something of the kind."

"If I understand your brother, he only means so far as your having some thoughts of marrying. He had no idea of me. He seems perfectly unprepared for that."

"Yes, yes—but I am amused that he should have seen so far into my feelings. What has he been judging by?—I am not conscious of any difference in my spirits or conversation that could prepare him at this time for my marrying any more than at another.—But it was so, I suppose. I dare say there was a difference when I was staying with them the other day. I believe I did not play with the children quite so much as usual. I remember one evening the poor boys saying, 'Uncle seems always tired now.'"

The time was coming when the news must spread farther, and other persons' reception of it tried. As soon as Mrs. Weston was sufficiently recovered to admit Mr. Woodhouse's visits, Emma having it in view that her gentle reasonings should be employed in the cause, resolved first to announce it at home, and then at Randalls.—But how to break it to her father at last!—She had bound herself to do it, in such an hour of Mr. Knightley's absence, or when it came to the point her heart would have failed her, and she must have put it off; but Mr. Knightley was to come at such a time, and follow up the beginning she was to make.—She was forced to speak, and to speak cheerfully too. She must not make it a more decided subject of misery to him, by a melancholy tone herself.

She must not appear to think it a misfortune.—With all the spirits she could command, she prepared him first for something strange, and then, in a few words, said, that if his consent and approbation could be obtained—which, she trusted, would be attended with no difficulty, since it was a plan to promote the happiness of all—she and Mr. Knightley meant to marry; by which means Hartfield would receive the constant addition of that person's company whom she knew he loved, next to his daughters and Mrs. Weston, best in the world.

Poor man!—it was at first a considerable shock to him, and he tried earnestly to dissuade her from it. She was reminded, more than once, of having always said she would never marry, and assured that it would be a great deal better for her to remain single; and told of poor Isabella, and poor Miss Taylor.—But it would not do. Emma hung about him affectionately, and smiled, and said it must be so; and that he must not class her with Isabella and Mrs. Weston, whose marriages taking them from Hartfield, had, indeed, made a melancholy change: but she was not going from Hartfield; she should be always there; she was introducing no change in their numbers or their comforts but for the better; and she was very sure that he would be a great deal the happier for having Mr. Knightley always at hand, when he were once got used to the idea.—Did he not love Mr. Knightley very much?—He would not deny that he did, she was sure.—Whom did he ever want to consult on business but Mr. Knightley?—Who was so useful to him, who so ready to write his letters, who so glad to assist him?—Who so cheerful, so attentive, so attached to him?—Would not he like to have him always on the spot?—Yes. That was all very true. Mr. Knightley could not be there too often; he should be glad to see him every day;—but they did see him every day as it was.—Why could not they go on as they had done?

Mr. Woodhouse could not be soon reconciled; but the worst was overcome, the idea was given; time and continual repetition must do the rest.—To Emma's entreaties and assurances succeeded Mr. Knightley's, whose fond praise of her gave the subject even a kind of welcome; and he was soon used to be talked to by each, on every fair occasion.—They had all the assistance which Isabella could give, by letters of the strongest approbation; and Mrs. Weston was ready, on the first meeting, to consider the subject in the most serviceable light—first, as a settled, and, secondly, as a good one—well aware of the nearly equal importance of the two recommendations to Mr. Woodhouse's mind.—

It was agreed upon, as what was to be; and every body by whom he was used to be guided assuring him that it would be for his happiness; and having some feelings himself which almost admitted it, he began to think that some time or other—in another year or two, perhaps—it might not be so very bad if the marriage did take place.

Mrs. Weston was acting no part, feigning no feelings in all that she said to him in favour of the event.—She had been extremely surprized, never more so, than when Emma first opened the affair to her; but she saw in it only increase of happiness to all, and had no scruple in urging him to the utmost.—She had such a regard for Mr. Knightley, as to think he deserved even her dearest Emma; and it was in every respect so proper, suitable, and unexceptionable a connexion, and in one respect, one point of the highest importance, so peculiarly eligible, so singularly fortunate, that now it seemed as if Emma could not safely have attached herself to any other creature, and that she had herself been the stupidest of beings in not having thought of it, and wished it long ago.—How very few of those men in a rank of life to address Emma would have renounced their own home for Hartfield! And who but Mr. Knightley could know and bear with Mr. Woodhouse, so as to make such an arrangement desirable!—The difficulty of disposing of poor Mr. Woodhouse had been always felt in her husband's plans and her own, for a marriage between Frank and Emma. How to settle the claims of Enscombe and Hartfield had been a continual impediment—less acknowledged by Mr. Weston than by herself—but even he had never been able to finish the subject better than by saying—"Those matters will take care of themselves; the young people will find a way." But here there was nothing to be shifted off in a wild speculation on the future. It was all right, all open, all equal. No sacrifice on any side worth the name. It was a union of the highest promise of felicity in itself, and without one real, rational difficulty to oppose or delay it.

Mrs. Weston, with her baby on her knee, indulging in such reflections as these, was one of the happiest women in the world. If any thing could increase her delight, it was perceiving that the baby would soon have outgrown its first set of caps.

The news was universally a surprize wherever it spread; and Mr. Weston had his five minutes' share of it; but five minutes were enough to familiarise the idea to his quickness of mind.—He saw the advantages of the match, and rejoiced in them with all the constancy of his wife;

but the wonder of it was very soon nothing; and by the end of an hour he was not far from believing that he had always foreseen it.

"It is to be a secret, I conclude," said he. "These matters are always a secret, till it is found out that every body knows them. Only let me be told when I may speak out.—I wonder whether Jane has any suspicion."

He went to Highbury the next morning, and satisfied himself on that point. He told her the news. Was not she like a daughter, his eldest daughter?—he must tell her; and Miss Bates being present, it passed, of course, to Mrs. Cole, Mrs. Perry, and Mrs. Elton, immediately afterwards. It was no more than the principals were prepared for; they had calculated from the time of its being known at Randalls, how soon it would be over Highbury; and were thinking of themselves, as the evening wonder in many a family circle, with great sagacity.

In general, it was a very well approved match. Some might think him, and others might think her, the most in luck. One set might recommend their all removing to Donwell, and leaving Hartfield for the John Knightleys; and another might predict disagreements among their servants; but yet, upon the whole, there was no serious objection raised, except in one habitation, the Vicarage.—There, the surprize was not softened by any satisfaction. Mr. Elton cared little about it, compared with his wife; he only hoped "the young lady's pride would now be contented;" and supposed "she had always meant to catch Knightley if she could;" and, on the point of living at Hartfield, could daringly exclaim, "Rather he than I!"—But Mrs. Elton was very much discomposed indeed.—"Poor Knightley! poor fellow!—sad business for him.—She was extremely concerned; for, though very eccentric, he had a thousand good qualities.—How could he be so taken in?—Did not think him at all in love—not in the least.—Poor Knightley!—There would be an end of all pleasant intercourse with him.—How happy he had been to come and dine with them whenever they asked him! But that would be all over now.—Poor fellow!—No more exploring parties to Donwell made for *her*. Oh! no; there would be a Mrs. Knightley to throw cold water on every thing.—Extremely disagreeable! But she was not at all sorry that she had abused the housekeeper the other day.—Shocking plan, living together. It would never do. She knew a family near Maple Grove who had tried it, and been obliged to separate before the end of the first quarter.

CHAPTER XVIII

Time passed on. A few more to-morrows, and the party from London would be arriving. It was an alarming change; and Emma was thinking of it one morning, as what must bring a great deal to agitate and grieve her, when Mr. Knightley came in, and distressing thoughts were put by. After the first chat of pleasure he was silent; and then, in a graver tone, began with,

"I have something to tell you, Emma; some news."

"Good or bad?" said she, quickly, looking up in his face.

"I do not know which it ought to be called."

"Oh! good I am sure.—I see it in your countenance. You are trying not to smile."

"I am afraid," said he, composing his features, "I am very much afraid, my dear Emma, that you will not smile when you hear it."

"Indeed! but why so?—I can hardly imagine that any thing which pleases or amuses you, should not please and amuse me too."

"There is one subject," he replied, "I hope but one, on which we do not think alike." He paused a moment, again smiling, with his eyes fixed on her face. "Does nothing occur to you?—Do not you recollect?—Harriet Smith."

Her cheeks flushed at the name, and she felt afraid of something, though she knew not what.

"Have you heard from her yourself this morning?" cried he. "You have, I believe, and know the whole."

"No, I have not; I know nothing; pray tell me."

"You are prepared for the worst, I see—and very bad it is. Harriet Smith marries Robert Martin."

Emma gave a start, which did not seem like being prepared—and her eyes, in eager gaze, said, "No, this is impossible!" but her lips were closed.

"It is so, indeed," continued Mr. Knightley; "I have it from Robert Martin himself. He left me not half an hour ago."

She was still looking at him with the most speaking amazement.

"You like it, my Emma, as little as I feared.—I wish our opinions were the same. But in time they will. Time, you may be sure, will make one or the other of us think differently; and, in the meanwhile, we need not talk much on the subject."

"You mistake me, you quite mistake me," she replied, exerting herself. "It is not that such a circumstance would now make me unhappy, but I cannot believe it. It seems an impossibility!—You cannot mean to say, that Harriet Smith has accepted Robert Martin. You cannot mean that he has even proposed to her again—yet. You only mean, that he intends it."

"I mean that he has done it," answered Mr. Knightley, with smiling but determined decision, "and been accepted."

"Good God!" she cried.—"Well!"—Then having recourse to her workbasket, in excuse for leaning down her face, and concealing all the exquisite feelings of delight and entertainment which she knew she must be expressing, she added, "Well, now tell me every thing; make this intelligible to me. How, where, when?—Let me know it all. I never was more surprized—but it does not make me unhappy, I assure you.—How—how has it been possible?"

"It is a very simple story. He went to town on business three days ago, and I got him to take charge of some papers which I was wanting to send to John.—He delivered these papers to John, at his chambers, and was asked by him to join their party the same evening to Astley's. They were going to take the two eldest boys to Astley's. The party was to be our brother and sister, Henry, John—and Miss Smith. My friend Robert could not resist. They called for him in their way; were all extremely amused; and my brother asked him to dine with them the next day—which he did—and in the course of that visit (as I understand) he found an opportunity of speaking to Harriet; and certainly did not speak in vain.—She made him, by her acceptance, as happy even as he is deserving. He came down by yesterday's coach, and was with me this morning immediately after breakfast, to report his proceedings, first on my affairs, and then on his own. This is all that I can relate of the how, where, and when. Your friend Harriet will make a much longer history when you see her.—She will give you all the minute particulars, which only woman's language can make interesting.—In our communications we deal only in the great.—However, I must say, that Robert Martin's heart seemed for *him*, and to *me*, very overflowing; and that he did mention, without its being much to the purpose, that on quitting their box at Astley's, my brother took charge of Mrs. John

Knightley and little John, and he followed with Miss Smith and Henry; and that at one time they were in such a crowd, as to make Miss Smith rather uneasy."

He stopped.—Emma dared not attempt any immediate reply. To speak, she was sure would be to betray a most unreasonable degree of happiness. She must wait a moment, or he would think her mad. Her silence disturbed him; and after observing her a little while, he added,

"Emma, my love, you said that this circumstance would not now make you unhappy; but I am afraid it gives you more pain than you expected. His situation is an evil—but you must consider it as what satisfies your friend; and I will answer for your thinking better and better of him as you know him more. His good sense and good principles would delight you.—As far as the man is concerned, you could not wish your friend in better hands. His rank in society I would alter if I could, which is saying a great deal I assure you, Emma.—You laugh at me about William Larkins; but I could quite as ill spare Robert Martin."

He wanted her to look up and smile; and having now brought herself not to smile too broadly—she did—cheerfully answering,

"You need not be at any pains to reconcile me to the match. I think Harriet is doing extremely well. *Her* connexions may be worse than *his*. In respectability of character, there can be no doubt that they are. I have been silent from surprize merely, excessive surprize. You cannot imagine how suddenly it has come on me! how peculiarly unprepared I was!—for I had reason to believe her very lately more determined against him, much more, than she was before."

"You ought to know your friend best," replied Mr. Knightley; "but I should say she was a good-tempered, soft-hearted girl, not likely to be very, very determined against any young man who told her he loved her."

Emma could not help laughing as she answered, "Upon my word, I believe you know her quite as well as I do.—But, Mr. Knightley, are you perfectly sure that she has absolutely and downright *accepted* him? I could suppose she might in time—but can she already?—Did not you misunderstand him?—You were both talking of other things; of business, shows of cattle, or new drills—and might not you, in the confusion of so many subjects, mistake him?—It was not Harriet's hand that he was certain of—it was the dimensions of some famous ox."

The contrast between the countenance and air of Mr. Knightley and Robert Martin was, at this moment, so strong to Emma's feelings, and so strong was the recollection of all that had so recently passed on Harriet's side, so fresh the sound of those words, spoken with such emphasis, "No, I hope I know better than to think of Robert Martin," that she was really expecting the intelligence to prove, in some measure, premature. It could not be otherwise.

"Do you dare say this?" cried Mr. Knightley. "Do you dare to suppose me so great a blockhead, as not to know what a man is talking of?—What do you deserve?"

"Oh! I always deserve the best treatment, because I never put up with any other; and, therefore, you must give me a plain, direct answer. Are you quite sure that you understand the terms on which Mr. Martin and Harriet now are?"

"I am quite sure," he replied, speaking very distinctly, "that he told me she had accepted him; and that there was no obscurity, nothing doubtful, in the words he used; and I think I can give you a proof that it must be so. He asked my opinion as to what he was now to do. He knew of no one but Mrs. Goddard to whom he could apply for information of her relations or friends. Could I mention any thing more fit to be done, than to go to Mrs. Goddard? I assured him that I could not. Then, he said, he would endeavour to see her in the course of this day."

"I am perfectly satisfied," replied Emma, with the brightest smiles, "and most sincerely wish them happy."

"You are materially changed since we talked on this subject before."

"I hope so—for at that time I was a fool."

"And I am changed also; for I am now very willing to grant you all Harriet's good qualities. I have taken some pains for your sake, and for Robert Martin's sake, (whom I have always had reason to believe as much in love with her as ever), to get acquainted with her. I have often talked to her a good deal. You must have seen that I did. Sometimes, indeed, I have thought you were half suspecting me of pleading poor Martin's cause, which was never the case; but, from all my observations, I am convinced of her being an artless, amiable girl, with very good notions, very seriously good principles, and placing her happiness in the affections and utility of domestic life.—Much of this, I have no doubt, she may thank you for."

"Me!" cried Emma, shaking her head.—"Ah! poor Harriet!"

She checked herself, however, and submitted quietly to a little more praise than she deserved.

Their conversation was soon afterwards closed by the entrance of her father. She was not sorry. She wanted to be alone. Her mind was in a state of flutter and wonder, which made it impossible for her to be collected. She was in dancing, singing, exclaiming spirits; and till she had moved about, and talked to herself, and laughed and reflected, she could be fit for nothing rational.

Her father's business was to announce James's being gone out to put the horses to, preparatory to their now daily drive to Randalls; and she had, therefore, an immediate excuse for disappearing.

The joy, the gratitude, the exquisite delight of her sensations may be imagined. The sole grievance and alloy thus removed in the prospect of Harriet's welfare, she was really in danger of becoming too happy for security.—What had she to wish for? Nothing, but to grow more worthy of him, whose intentions and judgment had been ever so superior to her own. Nothing, but that the lessons of her past folly might teach her humility and circumspection in future.

Serious she was, very serious in her thankfulness, and in her resolutions; and yet there was no preventing a laugh, sometimes in the very midst of them. She must laugh at such a close! Such an end of the doleful disappointment of five weeks back! Such a heart—such a Harriet!

Now there would be pleasure in her returning—Every thing would be a pleasure. It would be a great pleasure to know Robert Martin.

High in the rank of her most serious and heartfelt felicities, was the reflection that all necessity of concealment from Mr. Knightley would soon be over. The disguise, equivocation, mystery, so hateful to her to practise, might soon be over. She could now look forward to giving him that full and perfect confidence which her disposition was most ready to welcome as a duty.

In the gayest and happiest spirits she set forward with her father; not always listening, but always agreeing to what he said; and, whether in speech or silence, conniving at the comfortable persuasion of his being obliged to go to Randalls every day, or poor Mrs. Weston would be disappointed.

They arrived.—Mrs. Weston was alone in the drawing-room:—but hardly had they been told of the baby, and Mr. Woodhouse received the thanks for coming, which he asked for, when a glimpse was caught through the blind, of two figures passing near the window.

"It is Frank and Miss Fairfax," said Mrs. Weston. "I was just going to tell you of our agreeable surprize in seeing him arrive this morning. He stays till to-morrow, and Miss Fairfax has been persuaded to spend the day with us.—They are coming in, I hope."

In half a minute they were in the room. Emma was extremely glad to see him—but there was a degree of confusion—a number of embarrassing recollections on each side. They met readily and smiling, but with a consciousness which at first allowed little to be said; and having all sat down again, there was for some time such a blank in the circle, that Emma began to doubt whether the wish now indulged, which she had long felt, of seeing Frank Churchill once more, and of seeing him with Jane, would yield its proportion of pleasure. When Mr. Weston joined the party, however, and when the baby was fetched, there was no longer a want of subject or animation—or of courage and opportunity for Frank Churchill to draw near her and say,

"I have to thank you, Miss Woodhouse, for a very kind forgiving message in one of Mrs. Weston's letters. I hope time has not made you less willing to pardon. I hope you do not retract what you then said."

"No, indeed," cried Emma, most happy to begin, "not in the least. I am particularly glad to see and shake hands with you—and to give you joy in person."

He thanked her with all his heart, and continued some time to speak with serious feeling of his gratitude and happiness.

"Is not she looking well?" said he, turning his eyes towards Jane. "Better than she ever used to do?—You see how my father and Mrs. Weston doat upon her."

But his spirits were soon rising again, and with laughing eyes, after mentioning the expected return of the Campbells, he named the name of Dixon.—Emma blushed, and forbade its being pronounced in her hearing.

"I can never think of it," she cried, "without extreme shame."

"The shame," he answered, "is all mine, or ought to be. But is it possible that you had no suspicion?—I mean of late. Early, I know, you had none."

"I never had the smallest, I assure you."

"That appears quite wonderful. I was once very near—and I wish

I had—it would have been better. But though I was always doing wrong things, they were very bad wrong things, and such as did me no service.—It would have been a much better transgression had I broken the bond of secrecy and told you every thing."

"It is not now worth a regret," said Emma.

"I have some hope," resumed he, "of my uncle's being persuaded to pay a visit at Randalls; he wants to be introduced to her. When the Campbells are returned, we shall meet them in London, and continue there, I trust, till we may carry her northward.—But now, I am at such a distance from her—is not it hard, Miss Woodhouse?—Till this morning, we have not once met since the day of reconciliation. Do not you pity me?"

Emma spoke her pity so very kindly, that with a sudden accession of gay thought, he cried,

"Ah! by the bye," then sinking his voice, and looking demure for the moment—"I hope Mr. Knightley is well?" He paused.—She coloured and laughed.—"I know you saw my letter, and think you may remember my wish in your favour. Let me return your congratulations.—I assure you that I have heard the news with the warmest interest and satisfaction.—He is a man whom I cannot presume to praise."

Emma was delighted, and only wanted him to go on in the same style; but his mind was the next moment in his own concerns and with his own Jane, and his next words were,

"Did you ever see such a skin?—such smoothness! such delicacy!—and yet without being actually fair.—One cannot call her fair. It is a most uncommon complexion, with her dark eye-lashes and hair—a most distinguishing complexion! So peculiarly the lady in it.—Just colour enough for beauty."

"I have always admired her complexion," replied Emma, archly; "but do not I remember the time when you found fault with her for being so pale?—When we first began to talk of her.—Have you quite forgotten?"

"Oh! no—what an impudent dog I was!—How could I dare—"

But he laughed so heartily at the recollection, that Emma could not help saying,

"I do suspect that in the midst of your perplexities at that time, you had very great amusement in tricking us all.—I am sure you had.—I am sure it was a consolation to you."

"Oh! no, no, no—how can you suspect me of such a thing? I was the most miserable wretch!"

"Not quite so miserable as to be insensible to mirth. I am sure it was a source of high entertainment to you, to feel that you were taking us all in.—Perhaps I am the readier to suspect, because, to tell you the truth, I think it might have been some amusement to myself in the same situation. I think there is a little likeness between us."

He bowed.

"If not in our dispositions," she presently added, with a look of true sensibility, "there is a likeness in our destiny; the destiny which bids fair to connect us with two characters so much superior to our own."

"True, true," he answered, warmly. "No, not true on your side. You can have no superior, but most true on mine.—She is a complete angel. Look at her. Is not she an angel in every gesture? Observe the turn of her throat. Observe her eyes, as she is looking up at my father.—You will be glad to hear (inclining his head, and whispering seriously) that my uncle means to give her all my aunt's jewels. They are to be new set. I am resolved to have some in an ornament for the head. Will not it be beautiful in her dark hair?"

"Very beautiful, indeed," replied Emma; and she spoke so kindly, that he gratefully burst out,

"How delighted I am to see you again! and to see you in such excellent looks!—I would not have missed this meeting for the world. I should certainly have called at Hartfield, had you failed to come."

The others had been talking of the child, Mrs. Weston giving an account of a little alarm she had been under, the evening before, from the infant's appearing not quite well. She believed she had been foolish, but it had alarmed her, and she had been within half a minute of sending for Mr. Perry. Perhaps she ought to be ashamed, but Mr. Weston had been almost as uneasy as herself.—In ten minutes, however, the child had been perfectly well again. This was her history; and particularly interesting it was to Mr. Woodhouse, who commended her very much for thinking of sending for Perry, and only regretted that she had not done it. "She should always send for Perry, if the child appeared in the slightest degree disordered, were it only for a moment. She could not be too soon alarmed, nor send for Perry too often. It was a pity, perhaps, that he had not come last night; for, though the child seemed well now, very well considering, it would probably have been better if Perry had seen it."

Frank Churchill caught the name.

"Perry!" said he to Emma, and trying, as he spoke, to catch Miss Fairfax's eye. "My friend Mr. Perry! What are they saying about Mr. Perry?—Has he been here this morning?—And how does he travel now?—Has he set up his carriage?"

Emma soon recollected, and understood him; and while she joined in the laugh, it was evident from Jane's countenance that she too was really hearing him, though trying to seem deaf.

"Such an extraordinary dream of mine!" he cried. "I can never think of it without laughing.—She hears us, she hears us, Miss Woodhouse. I see it in her cheek, her smile, her vain attempt to frown. Look at her. Do not you see that, at this instant, the very passage of her own letter, which sent me the report, is passing under her eye—that the whole blunder is spread before her—that she can attend to nothing else, though pretending to listen to the others?"

Jane was forced to smile completely, for a moment; and the smile partly remained as she turned towards him, and said in a conscious, low, yet steady voice,

"How you can bear such recollections, is astonishing to me!—They *will* sometimes obtrude—but how you can court them!"

He had a great deal to say in return, and very entertainingly; but Emma's feelings were chiefly with Jane, in the argument; and on leaving Randalls, and falling naturally into a comparison of the two men, she felt, that pleased as she had been to see Frank Churchill, and really regarding him as she did with friendship, she had never been more sensible of Mr. Knightley's high superiority of character. The happiness of this most happy day, received its completion, in the animated contemplation of his worth which this comparison produced.

CHAPTER XIX

If Emma had still, at intervals, an anxious feeling for Harriet, a momentary doubt of its being possible for her to be really cured of her attachment to Mr. Knightley, and really able to accept another man from unbiased inclination, it was not long that she had to suffer from the recurrence of any such uncertainty. A very few days brought the party from London, and she had no sooner an opportunity of being one hour alone with Harriet, than she became perfectly satisfied—unaccountable as it was!—that Robert Martin had thoroughly supplanted Mr. Knightley, and was now forming all her views of happiness.

Harriet was a little distressed—did look a little foolish at first: but having once owned that she had been presumptuous and silly, and self-deceived, before, her pain and confusion seemed to die away with the words, and leave her without a care for the past, and with the fullest exultation in the present and future; for, as to her friend's approbation, Emma had instantly removed every fear of that nature, by meeting her with the most unqualified congratulations.—Harriet was most happy to give every particular of the evening at Astley's, and the dinner the next day; she could dwell on it all with the utmost delight. But what did such particulars explain?—The fact was, as Emma could now acknowledge, that Harriet had always liked Robert Martin; and that his continuing to love her had been irresistible.—Beyond this, it must ever be unintelligible to Emma.

The event, however, was most joyful; and every day was giving her fresh reason for thinking so.—Harriet's parentage became known. She proved to be the daughter of a tradesman, rich enough to afford her the comfortable maintenance which had ever been hers, and decent enough to have always wished for concealment.—Such was the blood of gentility which Emma had formerly been so ready to vouch for!—It was likely to be as untainted, perhaps, as the blood of many a gentleman: but what a connexion had she been preparing for Mr. Knightley—or for the Churchills—or even for Mr. Elton!—The stain of illegitimacy, unbleached by nobility or wealth, would have been a stain indeed.

No objection was raised on the father's side; the young man was treated liberally; it was all as it should be: and as Emma became acquainted with Robert Martin, who was now introduced at Hartfield, she fully acknowledged in him all the appearance of sense and worth which could bid fairest for her little friend. She had no doubt of Harriet's happiness with any good-tempered man; but with him, and in the home he offered, there would be the hope of more, of security, stability, and improvement. She would be placed in the midst of those who loved her, and who had better sense than herself; retired enough for safety, and occupied enough for cheerfulness. She would be never led into temptation, nor left for it to find her out. She would be respectable and happy; and Emma admitted her to be the luckiest creature in the world, to have created so steady and persevering an affection in such a man;—or, if not quite the luckiest, to yield only to herself.

Harriet, necessarily drawn away by her engagements with the Martins, was less and less at Hartfield; which was not to be regretted.—The intimacy between her and Emma must sink; their friendship must change into a calmer sort of good-will; and, fortunately, what ought to be, and must be, seemed already beginning, and in the most gradual, natural manner.

Before the end of September, Emma attended Harriet to church, and saw her hand bestowed on Robert Martin with so complete a satisfaction, as no remembrances, even connected with Mr. Elton as he stood before them, could impair.—Perhaps, indeed, at that time she scarcely saw Mr. Elton, but as the clergyman whose blessing at the altar might next fall on herself.—Robert Martin and Harriet Smith, the latest couple engaged of the three, were the first to be married.

Jane Fairfax had already quitted Highbury, and was restored to the comforts of her beloved home with the Campbells.—The Mr. Churchills were also in town; and they were only waiting for November.

The intermediate month was the one fixed on, as far as they dared, by Emma and Mr. Knightley.—They had determined that their marriage ought to be concluded while John and Isabella were still at Hartfield, to allow them the fortnight's absence in a tour to the seaside, which was the plan.—John and Isabella, and every other friend, were agreed in approving it. But Mr. Woodhouse—how was Mr. Woodhouse to be induced to consent?—he, who had never yet alluded to their marriage but as a distant event.

When first sounded on the subject, he was so miserable, that they were almost hopeless.—A second allusion, indeed, gave less pain.—He began to think it was to be, and that he could not prevent it—a very promising step of the mind on its way to resignation. Still, however, he was not happy. Nay, he appeared so much otherwise, that his daughter's courage failed. She could not bear to see him suffering, to know him fancying himself neglected; and though her understanding almost acquiesced in the assurance of both the Mr. Knightleys, that when once the event were over, his distress would be soon over too, she hesitated—she could not proceed.

In this state of suspense they were befriended, not by any sudden illumination of Mr. Woodhouse's mind, or any wonderful change of his nervous system, but by the operation of the same system in another way.—Mrs. Weston's poultry-house was robbed one night of all her turkeys—evidently by the ingenuity of man. Other poultry-yards in the neighbourhood also suffered.—Pilfering was *housebreaking* to Mr. Woodhouse's fears.—He was very uneasy; and but for the sense of his son-in-law's protection, would have been under wretched alarm every night of his life. The strength, resolution, and presence of mind of the Mr. Knightleys, commanded his fullest dependence. While either of them protected him and his, Hartfield was safe.—But Mr. John Knightley must be in London again by the end of the first week in November.

The result of this distress was, that, with a much more voluntary, cheerful consent than his daughter had ever presumed to hope for at the moment, she was able to fix her wedding-day—and Mr. Elton was called on, within a month from the marriage of Mr. and Mrs. Robert Martin, to join the hands of Mr. Knightley and Miss Woodhouse.

The wedding was very much like other weddings, where the parties have no taste for finery or parade; and Mrs. Elton, from the particulars detailed by her husband, thought it all extremely shabby, and very inferior to her own.—"Very little white satin, very few lace veils; a most pitiful business!—Selina would stare when she heard of it."—But, in spite of these deficiencies, the wishes, the hopes, the confidence, the predictions of the small band of true friends who witnessed the ceremony, were fully answered in the perfect happiness of the union.

Pride and Prejudice

Word Cloud Classics

A Christmas Carol and Other Holiday Treasures

Adventures of Huckleberry Finn

The Adventures of Sherlock Holmes

Aesop's Fables

The Age of Innocence

Anna Karenina

Anne of Green Gables

The Art of War

The Brothers Grimm: 101 Fairy Tales

The Brothers Grimm Volume II: 110 Grimmer Fairy Tales

Common Sense and Selected Works of Thomas Paine

The Count of Monte Cristo

Don Quixote

Dracula

Emma

Frankenstein

Great Expectations

Inferno

Jane Eyre

Lady Chatterley's Lover

Les Misérables

Little Women

Madame Bovary

Moby-Dick

Narrative of the Life of Frederick Douglass and Other Works

Persuasion

The Picture of Dorian Gray

The Prince and Other Writings

The Red Badge of Courage and Other Stories

The Scarlet Letter

The Secret Garden

Sense and Sensibility

The Three Musketeers

Twenty Thousand Leagues Under the Sea

Uncle Tom's Cabin

Walden and Civil Disobedience

The Wizard of Oz

Pride and Prejudice

Jane Austen

CANTERBURY CLASSICS
San Diego

All correspondence concerning the content of this book should be addressed to: Canterbury Classics
10350 Barnes Canyon Road, Suite 100
San Diego, CA 92121

Publisher: Peter Norton
Publishing Team: Lori Asbury, Ana Parker
Director Editorial and Production: JoAnn Padgett

Library of Congress Cataloging-in-Publication Data

Austen, Jane, 1775-1817.
Pride and prejudice / Jane Austen.
p. cm. -- (Canterbury classics)
ISBN-13: 978-1-60710-554-1
ISBN-10: 1-60710-554-3
1. England--Social life and customs--19th century--Fiction. 2. Young women--England--Fiction. 3. Courtship--England--Fiction. 4. Families--England--Fiction. I. Title.

PR4034.P7 2012
823'.7--dc23

2011049592

PRINTED IN CHINA

5 6 7 8 9 19 18 17 16 15

CHAPTER I

It is a truth universally acknowledged, that a single man in possession of a good fortune, must be in want of a wife.

However little known the feelings or views of such a man may be on his first entering a neighbourhood, this truth is so well fixed in the minds of the surrounding families, that he is considered the rightful property of some one or other of their daughters.

"My dear Mr. Bennet," said his lady to him one day, "have you heard that Netherfield Park is let at last?"

Mr. Bennet replied that he had not.

"But it is," returned she; "for Mrs. Long has just been here, and she told me all about it."

Mr. Bennet made no answer.

"Do you not want to know who has taken it?" cried his wife impatiently.

"*You* want to tell me, and I have no objection to hearing it."

This was invitation enough.

"Why, my dear, you must know, Mrs. Long says that Netherfield is taken by a young man of large fortune from the north of England; that he came down on Monday in a chaise and four to see the place, and was so much delighted with it, that he agreed with Mr. Morris immediately; that he is to take possession before Michaelmas, and some of his servants are to be in the house by the end of next week."

"What is his name?"

"Bingley."

"Is he married or single?"

"Oh! Single, my dear, to be sure! A single man of large fortune; four or five thousand a year. What a fine thing for our girls!"

"How so? How can it affect them?"

"My dear Mr. Bennet," replied his wife, "how can you be so tiresome! You must know that I am thinking of his marrying one of them."

"Is that his design in settling here?"

"Design! Nonsense, how can you talk so! But it is very likely that he *may* fall in love with one of them, and therefore you must visit him as soon as he comes."

"I see no occasion for that. You and the girls may go, or you may send them by themselves, which perhaps will be still better, for as you are as handsome as any of them, Mr. Bingley may like you the best of the party."

"My dear, you flatter me. I certainly *have* had my share of beauty, but I do not pretend to be anything extraordinary now. When a woman has five grown-up daughters, she ought to give over thinking of her own beauty."

"In such cases, a woman has not often much beauty to think of."

"But, my dear, you must indeed go and see Mr. Bingley when he comes into the neighbourhood."

"It is more than I engage for, I assure you."

"But consider your daughters. Only think what an establishment it would be for one of them. Sir William and Lady Lucas are determined to go, merely on that account, for in general, you know, they visit no newcomers. Indeed you must go, for it will be impossible for *us* to visit him if you do not."

"You are over-scrupulous, surely. I dare say Mr. Bingley will be very glad to see you; and I will send a few lines by you to assure him of my hearty consent to his marrying whichever he chooses of the girls; though I must throw in a good word for my little Lizzy."

"I desire you will do no such thing. Lizzy is not a bit better than the others; and I am sure she is not half so handsome as Jane, nor half so good-humoured as Lydia. But you are always giving *her* the preference."

"They have none of them much to recommend them," replied he; "they are all silly and ignorant like other girls; but Lizzy has something more of quickness than her sisters."

"Mr. Bennet, how *can* you abuse your own children in such a way? You take delight in vexing me. You have no compassion for my poor nerves."

"You mistake me, my dear. I have a high respect for your nerves. They are my old friends. I have heard you mention them with consideration these last twenty years at least."

"Ah, you do not know what I suffer."

"But I hope you will get over it, and live to see many young men of four thousand a year come into the neighbourhood."

"It will be no use to us, if twenty such should come, since you will not visit them."

"Depend upon it, my dear, that when there are twenty, I will visit them all."

Mr. Bennet was so odd a mixture of quick parts, sarcastic humour, reserve, and caprice, that the experience of three-and-twenty years had been insufficient to make his wife understand his character. *Her* mind was less difficult to develop. She was a woman of mean understanding, little information, and uncertain temper. When she was discontented, she fancied herself nervous. The business of her life was to get her daughters married; its solace was visiting and news.

CHAPTER II

Mr. Bennet was among the earliest of those who waited on Mr. Bingley. He had always intended to visit him, though to the last always assuring his wife that he should not go; and till the evening after the visit was paid she had no knowledge of it. It was then disclosed in the following manner. Observing his second daughter employed in trimming a hat, he suddenly addressed her with:

"I hope Mr. Bingley will like it, Lizzy."

"We are not in a way to know *what* Mr. Bingley likes," said her mother resentfully, "since we are not to visit."

"But you forget, mamma," said Elizabeth, "that we shall meet him at the assemblies, and that Mrs. Long promised to introduce him."

"I do not believe Mrs. Long will do any such thing. She has two nieces of her own. She is a selfish, hypocritical woman, and I have no opinion of her."

"No more have I," said Mr. Bennet; "and I am glad to find that you do not depend on her serving you."

Mrs. Bennet deigned not to make any reply, but, unable to contain herself, began scolding one of her daughters.

"Don't keep coughing so, Kitty, for Heaven's sake! Have a little compassion on my nerves. You tear them to pieces."

"Kitty has no discretion in her coughs," said her father; "she times them ill."

"I do not cough for my own amusement," replied Kitty fretfully. "When is your next ball to be, Lizzy?"

"To-morrow fortnight."

"Aye, so it is," cried her mother, "and Mrs. Long does not come back till the day before; so it will be impossible for her to introduce him, for she will not know him herself."

"Then, my dear, you may have the advantage of your friend, and introduce Mr. Bingley to *her*."

"Impossible, Mr. Bennet, impossible, when I am not acquainted with him myself; how can you be so teasing?"

"I honour your circumspection. A fortnight's acquaintance is certainly very little. One cannot know what a man really is by the end of a fortnight. But if *we* do not venture somebody else will; and after all, Mrs. Long and her daughters must stand their chance; and, therefore, as she will think it an act of kindness, if you decline the office, I will take it on myself."

The girls stared at their father. Mrs. Bennet said only, "Nonsense, nonsense!"

"What can be the meaning of that emphatic exclamation?" cried he. "Do you consider the forms of introduction, and the stress that is laid on them, as nonsense? I cannot quite agree with you *there*. What say you, Mary? For you are a young lady of deep reflection, I know, and read great books and make extracts."

Mary wished to say something sensible, but knew not how.

"While Mary is adjusting her ideas," he continued, "let us return to Mr. Bingley."

"I am sick of Mr. Bingley," cried his wife.

"I am sorry to hear *that*; but why did not you tell me that before? If I had known as much this morning I certainly would not have called on him. It is very unlucky; but as I have actually paid the visit, we cannot escape the acquaintance now."

The astonishment of the ladies was just what he wished; that of Mrs. Bennet perhaps surpassing the rest; though, when the first tumult of joy was over, she began to declare that it was what she had expected all the while.

"How good it was in you, my dear Mr. Bennet! But I knew I should persuade you at last. I was sure you loved your girls too well to neglect such an acquaintance. Well, how pleased I am! and it is such a good joke, too, that you should have gone this morning and never said a word about it till now."

"Now, Kitty, you may cough as much as you choose," said Mr. Bennet; and, as he spoke, he left the room, fatigued with the raptures of his wife.

"What an excellent father you have, girls!" said she, when the door was shut. "I do not know how you will ever make him amends for his kindness; or me, either, for that matter. At our time of life it is not so pleasant, I can tell you, to be making new acquaintances every day; but for your sakes, we would do anything. Lydia, my love, though you *are* the youngest, I dare say Mr. Bingley will dance with you at the next ball."

"Oh!" said Lydia stoutly, "I am not afraid; for though I *am* the youngest, I'm the tallest."

The rest of the evening was spent in conjecturing how soon he would return Mr. Bennet's visit, and determining when they should ask him to dinner.

CHAPTER III

Not all that Mrs. Bennet, however, with the assistance of her five daughters, could ask on the subject, was sufficient to draw from her husband any satisfactory description of Mr. Bingley. They attacked him in various ways—with barefaced questions, ingenious suppositions, and distant surmises; but he eluded the skill of them all, and they were at last obliged to accept the second-hand intelligence of their neighbour, Lady Lucas. Her report was highly favourable. Sir William had been delighted with him. He was quite young, wonderfully handsome, extremely agreeable, and, to crown the whole, he meant to be at the next assembly with a large party. Nothing could be more delightful! To be fond of dancing was a certain step towards falling in love; and very lively hopes of Mr. Bingley's heart were entertained.

"If I can but see one of my daughters happily settled at Netherfield," said Mrs. Bennet to her husband, "and all the others equally well married, I shall have nothing to wish for."

In a few days Mr. Bingley returned Mr. Bennet's visit, and sat about ten minutes with him in his library. He had entertained hopes of being admitted to a sight of the young ladies, of whose beauty he had heard much; but he saw only the father. The ladies were somewhat more fortunate, for they had the advantage of ascertaining from an upper window that he wore a blue coat, and rode a black horse.

An invitation to dinner was soon afterwards dispatched; and already had Mrs. Bennet planned the courses that were to do credit to her housekeeping, when an answer arrived which deferred it all. Mr. Bingley was obliged to be in town the following day, and, consequently, unable to accept the honour of their invitation, etc. Mrs. Bennet was quite disconcerted. She could not imagine what business he could have in town so soon after his arrival in Hertfordshire; and she began to fear that he might be always flying about from one place to another, and never settled at Netherfield as he ought to be. Lady Lucas quieted her fears a little by starting the idea of his being gone to London only to get a large party for the ball; and a report soon followed that Mr. Bingley was to bring twelve ladies and seven gentlemen with him to the assembly. The girls grieved over such a number of ladies, but were comforted the day before the ball by hearing, that instead of twelve he brought only six with him from London—his five sisters and a cousin. And when the party entered the assembly room it consisted of only five altogether—Mr. Bingley, his two sisters, the husband of the eldest, and another young man.

Mr. Bingley was good-looking and gentlemanlike; he had a pleasant countenance, and easy, unaffected manners. His sisters were fine women, with an air of decided fashion. His brother-in-law, Mr. Hurst, merely looked the gentleman; but his friend Mr. Darcy soon drew the attention of the room by his fine, tall person, handsome features, noble mien, and the report which was in general circulation within five minutes after his entrance, of his having ten thousand a year. The gentlemen pronounced him to be a fine figure of a man, the ladies declared he was much handsomer than Mr. Bingley, and he was looked at with great admiration for about half the evening, till his manners gave a disgust which turned the tide of his popularity; for he was discovered to be proud; to be above his company, and above being pleased; and not all his large estate in Derbyshire could then save him from having a most forbidding, disagreeable countenance, and being unworthy to be compared with his friend.

Mr. Bingley had soon made himself acquainted with all the principal people in the room; he was lively and unreserved, danced every dance, was angry that the ball closed so early, and talked of giving one himself at Netherfield. Such amiable qualities must speak for themselves. What a contrast between him and his friend! Mr. Darcy danced only once with Mrs. Hurst and once with Miss Bingley, declined being introduced to any other lady, and spent the rest of the evening in walking about the room, speaking occasionally to one of his own party. His character was decided. He was the proudest, most disagreeable man in the world, and everybody hoped that he would never come there again. Amongst the most violent against him was Mrs. Bennet, whose dislike of his general behaviour was sharpened into particular resentment by his having slighted one of her daughters.

Elizabeth Bennet had been obliged, by the scarcity of gentlemen, to sit down for two dances; and during part of that time, Mr. Darcy had been standing near enough for her to hear a conversation between him and Mr. Bingley, who came from the dance for a few minutes, to press his friend to join it.

"Come, Darcy," said he, "I must have you dance. I hate to see you standing about by yourself in this stupid manner. You had much better dance."

"I certainly shall not. You know how I detest it, unless I am particularly acquainted with my partner. At such an assembly as this it would be insupportable. Your sisters are engaged, and there is not another woman in the room whom it would not be a punishment to me to stand up with."

"I would not be so fastidious as you are," cried Mr. Bingley, "for a kingdom! Upon my honour, I never met with so many pleasant girls in my life as I have this evening; and there are several of them you see uncommonly pretty."

"*You* are dancing with the only handsome girl in the room," said Mr. Darcy, looking at the eldest Miss Bennet.

"Oh! She is the most beautiful creature I ever beheld! But there is one of her sisters sitting down just behind you, who is very pretty, and I dare say very agreeable. Do let me ask my partner to introduce you."

"Which do you mean?" and turning round he looked for a moment at Elizabeth, till catching her eye, he withdrew his own and coldly said: "She is tolerable, but not handsome enough to tempt *me*; I am in no humour at present to give consequence to young ladies who are slighted by other men. You had better return to your partner and enjoy her smiles, for you are wasting your time with me."

Mr. Bingley followed his advice. Mr. Darcy walked off; and Elizabeth remained with no very cordial feelings toward him. She told the story, however, with great spirit among her friends; for she had a lively, playful disposition, which delighted in anything ridiculous.

The evening altogether passed off pleasantly to the whole family. Mrs. Bennet had seen her eldest daughter much admired by the Netherfield party. Mr. Bingley had danced with her twice, and she had been distinguished by his sisters. Jane was as much gratified by this as her mother could be, though in a quieter way. Elizabeth felt Jane's pleasure. Mary had heard herself mentioned to Miss Bingley as the most accomplished girl in the neighbourhood; and Catherine and Lydia had been fortunate enough never to be without partners, which was all that they had yet learnt to care for at a ball. They returned, therefore, in good spirits to Longbourn, the village where they lived, and of which they were the principal inhabitants. They found Mr. Bennet still up.

With a book he was regardless of time; and on the present occasion he had a good deal of curiosity as to the events of an evening which had raised such splendid expectations. He had rather hoped that his wife's views on the stranger would be disappointed; but he soon found out that he had a different story to hear.

"Oh! my dear Mr. Bennet," as she entered the room, "we have had a most delightful evening, a most excellent ball. I wish you had been there. Jane was so admired, nothing could be like it. Everybody said how well she looked; and Mr. Bingley thought her quite beautiful, and danced with her twice! Only think of *that*, my dear; he actually danced with her twice! and she was the only creature in the room that he asked a second time. First of all, he asked Miss Lucas. I was so vexed to see him stand up with her! But, however, he did not admire her at all; indeed, nobody can, you know; and he seemed quite struck with Jane as she was going down the dance. So he inquired who she was, and got introduced, and asked her for the two next. Then the two third he danced with Miss King, and the two fourth with Maria Lucas, and the two fifth with Jane again, and the two sixth with Lizzy, and the *Boulanger*—"

"If he had had any compassion for *me*," cried her husband impatiently, "he would not have danced half so much! For God's sake, say no more of his partners. O that he had sprained his ankle in the first dance!"

"Oh! my dear, I am quite delighted with him. He is so excessively handsome! And his sisters are charming women. I never in my life saw anything more elegant than their dresses. I dare say the lace upon Mrs. Hurst's gown—"

Here she was interrupted again. Mr. Bennet protested against any description of finery. She was therefore obliged to seek another branch of the subject, and related, with much bitterness of spirit and some exaggeration, the shocking rudeness of Mr. Darcy.

"But I can assure you," she added, "that Lizzy does not lose much by not suiting *his* fancy; for he is a most disagreeable, horrid man, not at all worth pleasing. So high and so conceited that there was no enduring him! He walked here, and he walked there, fancying himself so very great! Not handsome enough to dance with! I wish you had been there, my dear, to have given him one of your set-downs. I quite detest the man."

CHAPTER IV

When Jane and Elizabeth were alone, the former, who had been cautious in her praise of Mr. Bingley before, expressed to her sister just how very much she admired him.

"He is just what a young man ought to be," said she, "sensible, good-humoured, lively; and I never saw such happy manners!—so much ease, with such perfect good breeding!"

"He is also handsome," replied Elizabeth, "which a young man ought likewise to be, if he possibly can. His character is thereby complete."

"I was very much flattered by his asking me to dance a second time. I did not expect such a compliment."

"Did not you? I did for you. But that is one great difference between us. Compliments always take *you* by surprise, and *me* never. What could be more natural than his asking you again? He could not help seeing that you were about five times as pretty as every other woman in the room. No thanks to his gallantry for that. Well, he certainly is very agreeable, and I give you leave to like him. You have liked many a stupider person."

"Dear Lizzy!"

"Oh! you are a great deal too apt, you know, to like people in general. You never see a fault in anybody. All the world are good and agreeable in your eyes. I never heard you speak ill of a human being in your life."

"I would not wish to be hasty in censuring anyone; but I always speak what I think."

"I know you do; and it is *that* which makes the wonder. With *your* good sense, to be so honestly blind to the follies and nonsense of others! Affectation of candour is common enough—one meets with it everywhere. But to be candid without ostentation or design—to take the good of everybody's character and make it still better, and say nothing of the bad—belongs to you alone. And so you like this man's sisters, too, do you? Their manners are not equal to his."

"Certainly not—at first. But they are very pleasing women when you converse with them. Miss Bingley is to live with her brother, and keep his house; and I am much mistaken if we shall not find a very charming neighbour in her."

Elizabeth listened in silence, but was not convinced; their behaviour at the assembly had not been calculated to please in general; and with more quickness of observation and less pliancy of temper than her sister, and with a judgement too unassailed by any attention to herself, she was very little disposed to approve them. They were in fact very fine ladies; not deficient in good humour when they were pleased, nor in the power of making themselves agreeable when they chose it, but proud and conceited. They were rather handsome, had been educated in one of the first private seminaries in town, had a fortune of twenty thousand pounds, were in the habit of spending more than they ought, and of associating with people of rank, and were therefore in every respect entitled to think well of themselves, and meanly of others. They were of a respectable family in the north of England; a circumstance more deeply impressed on their memories than that their brother's fortune and their own had been acquired by trade.

Mr. Bingley inherited property to the amount of nearly a hundred thousand pounds from his father, who had intended to purchase an estate, but did not live to do it. Mr. Bingley intended it likewise, and sometimes made choice of his county; but as he was now provided with a good house and the liberty of a manor, it was doubtful to many of those who best knew the easiness of his temper, whether he might not spend the remainder of his days at Netherfield, and leave the next generation to purchase.

His sisters were anxious for his having an estate of his own; but, though he was now only established as a tenant, Miss Bingley was by no means unwilling to preside at his table—nor was Mrs. Hurst, who had married a man of more fashion than fortune, less disposed to consider his house as her home when it suited her. Mr. Bingley had not been of age two years, when he was tempted by an accidental recommendation to look at Netherfield House. He did look at it, and into it for half-an-hour—was pleased with the situation and the principal rooms, satisfied with what the owner said in its praise, and took it immediately.

Between him and Darcy there was a very steady friendship, in spite of great opposition of character. Bingley was endeared to Darcy by the easiness, openness, and ductility of his temper, though no disposition could offer a greater contrast to his own, and though with his own he never appeared dissatisfied. On the strength of Darcy's regard, Bingley had the firmest reliance, and of his judgement the highest opinion.

In understanding, Darcy was the superior. Bingley was by no means deficient, but Darcy was clever. He was at the same time haughty, reserved, and fastidious, and his manners, though well-bred, were not inviting. In that respect his friend had greatly the advantage. Bingley was sure of being liked wherever he appeared, Darcy was continually giving offense.

The manner in which they spoke of the Meryton assembly was sufficiently characteristic. Bingley had never met with more pleasant people or prettier girls in his life; everybody had been most kind and attentive to him; there had been no formality, no stiffness; he had soon felt acquainted with all the room; and, as to Miss Bennet, he could not conceive an angel more beautiful. Darcy, on the contrary, had seen a collection of people in whom there was little beauty and no fashion, for none of whom he had felt the smallest interest, and from none received either attention or pleasure. Miss Bennet he acknowledged to be pretty, but she smiled too much.

Mrs. Hurst and her sister allowed it to be so—but still they admired her and liked her, and pronounced her to be a sweet girl, and one whom they would not object to know more of. Miss Bennet was therefore established as a sweet girl, and their brother felt authorized by such commendation to think of her as he chose.

CHAPTER V

Within a short walk of Longbourn lived a family with whom the Bennets were particularly intimate. Sir William Lucas had been formerly in trade in Meryton, where he had made a tolerable fortune, and risen to the honour of knighthood by an address to the king during his mayoralty. The distinction had perhaps been felt too strongly. It had given him a disgust to his business, and to his residence in a small market town; and, in quitting them both, he had removed with his family to a house about a mile from Meryton, denominated from that period Lucas Lodge, where he could think with pleasure of his own importance, and, unshackled by business, occupy himself solely in being civil to all the world. For, though elated by his rank, it did not render him supercilious; on the contrary, he was all attention to everybody. By nature inoffensive, friendly, and obliging, his presentation at St. James's had made him courteous.

Lady Lucas was a very good kind of woman, not too clever to be a valuable neighbour to Mrs. Bennet. They had several children. The eldest of them, a sensible, intelligent young woman, about twenty-seven, was Elizabeth's intimate friend.

That the Miss Lucases and the Miss Bennets should meet to talk over a ball was absolutely necessary; and the morning after the assembly brought the former to Longbourn to hear and to communicate.

"*You* began the evening well, Charlotte," said Mrs. Bennet with civil self-command to Miss Lucas. "*You* were Mr. Bingley's first choice."

"Yes; but he seemed to like his second better."

"Oh! you mean Jane, I suppose, because he danced with her twice. To be sure that *did* seem as if he admired her—indeed I rather believe he *did*—I heard something about it—but I hardly know what—something about Mr. Robinson."

"Perhaps you mean what I overheard between him and Mr. Robinson; did not I mention it to you? Mr. Robinson's asking him how he liked our Meryton assemblies, and whether he did not think there were a great many pretty women in the room, and *which* he thought the prettiest? and his answering immediately to the last question: 'Oh! the eldest Miss Bennet, beyond a doubt; there cannot be two opinions on that point.' "

"Upon my word! Well, that is very decided indeed—that does seem as if—but, however, it may all come to nothing, you know."

"*My* overhearings were more to the purpose than *yours*, Eliza," said Charlotte. "Mr. Darcy is not so well worth listening to as his friend, is he?—poor Eliza!—to be only just *tolerable*."

"I beg you would not put it into Lizzy's head to be vexed by his ill-treatment, for he is such a disagreeable man, that it would be quite a misfortune to be liked by him. Mrs. Long told me last night that he sat close to her for half-an-hour without once opening his lips."

"Are you quite sure, ma'am?—is not there a little mistake?" said Jane. "I certainly saw Mr. Darcy speaking to her."

"Aye—because she asked him at last how he liked Netherfield, and he could not help answering her; but she said he seemed quite angry at being spoke to."

"Miss Bingley told me," said Jane, "that he never speaks much, unless among his intimate acquaintances. With *them* he is remarkably agreeable."

"I do not believe a word of it, my dear. If he had been so very agreeable, he would have talked to Mrs. Long. But I can guess how it was; everybody says that he is eat up with pride, and I dare say he had heard somehow that Mrs. Long does not keep a carriage, and had come to the ball in a hack chaise."

"I do not mind his not talking to Mrs. Long," said Miss Lucas, "but I wish he had danced with Eliza."

"Another time, Lizzy," said her mother, "I would not dance with *him*, if I were you."

"I believe, ma'am, I may safely promise you *never* to dance with him."

"His pride," said Miss Lucas, "does not offend *me* so much as pride often does, because there is an excuse for it. One cannot wonder that so very fine a young man, with family, fortune, everything in his favour, should think highly of himself. If I may so express it, he has a *right* to be proud."

"That is very true," replied Elizabeth, "and I could easily forgive *his* pride, if he had not mortified *mine*."

"Pride," observed Mary, who piqued herself upon the solidity of her reflections, "is a very common failing, I believe. By all that I have ever read, I am convinced that it is very common indeed; that human nature is particularly prone to it, and that there are very few of us who do not cherish a feeling of self-complacency on the score of some quality or other, real or imaginary. Vanity and pride are different things, though the words are often used synonymously. A person may be proud without being vain. Pride relates more to our opinion of ourselves, vanity to what we would have others think of us."

"If I were as rich as Mr. Darcy," cried a young Lucas, who came with his sisters, "I should not care how proud I was. I would keep a pack of foxhounds, and drink a bottle of wine a day."

"Then you would drink a great deal more than you ought," said Mrs. Bennet; "and if I were to see you at it, I should take away your bottle directly."

The boy protested that she should not; she continued to declare that she would, and the argument ended only with the visit.

CHAPTER VI

The ladies of Longbourn soon waited on those of Netherfield. The visit was soon returned in due form. Miss Bennet's pleasing manners grew on the goodwill of Mrs. Hurst and Miss Bingley; and though the mother was found to be intolerable, and the younger sisters not worth speaking to, a wish of being better acquainted with *them* was expressed towards the two eldest. By Jane, this attention was received with the greatest pleasure, but Elizabeth still saw superciliousness in their treatment of everybody, hardly excepting even her sister, and could not like them; though their kindness to Jane, such as it was, had a value as arising in all probability from the influence of their brother's admiration. It was generally evident whenever they met, that he *did* admire her and to *her* it was equally evident that Jane was yielding to the preference which she had begun to entertain for him from the first, and was in a way to be very much in love; but she considered with pleasure that it was not likely to be discovered by the world in general, since Jane united, with great strength of feeling, a composure of temper and a uniform cheerfulness of manner which would guard her from the suspicions of the impertinent. She mentioned this to her friend Miss Lucas.

"It may perhaps be pleasant," replied Charlotte, "to be able to impose on the public in such a case; but it is sometimes a disadvantage to be so very guarded. If a woman conceals her affection with the same skill from the object of it, she may lose the opportunity of fixing him; and it will then be but poor consolation to believe the world equally in the dark. There is so much of gratitude or vanity in almost every attachment, that it is not safe to leave any to itself. We can all *begin* freely—a slight preference is natural enough; but there are very few of us who have heart enough to be really in love without encouragement. In nine cases out of ten a women had better show *more* affection than she feels. Bingley likes your sister undoubtedly; but he may never do more than like her, if she does not help him on."

"But she does help him on, as much as her nature will allow. If I can perceive her regard for him, he must be a simpleton, indeed, not to discover it too."

"Remember, Eliza, that he does not know Jane's disposition as you do."

"But if a woman is partial to a man, and does not endeavour to conceal it, he must find it out."

"Perhaps he must, if he sees enough of her. But, though Bingley and Jane meet tolerably often, it is never for many hours together; and, as they always see each other in large mixed parties, it is impossible that every moment should be employed in conversing together. Jane should therefore make the most of every half-hour in which she can command his attention. When she is secure of him, there will be more leisure for falling in love as much as she chooses."

"Your plan is a good one," replied Elizabeth, "where nothing is in question but the desire of being well married, and if I were determined to get a rich husband, or any husband, I dare say I should adopt it. But these are not Jane's feelings; she is not acting by design. As yet, she cannot even be certain of the degree of her own regard nor of its reasonableness. She has known him only a fortnight. She danced four dances with him at Meryton; she saw him one morning at his own house, and has since dined with him in company four times. This is not quite enough to make her understand his character."

"Not as you represent it. Had she merely *dined* with him, she might only have discovered whether he had a good appetite; but you must remember that four evenings have also been spent together—and four evenings may do a great deal."

"Yes; these four evenings have enabled them to ascertain that they both like Vingt-un better than Commerce; but with respect to any other leading characteristic, I do not imagine that much has been unfolded."

"Well," said Charlotte, "I wish Jane success with all my heart; and if she were married to him to-morrow, I should think she had as good a chance of happiness as if she were to be studying his character for a twelvemonth. Happiness in marriage is entirely a matter of chance. If the dispositions of the parties are ever so well known to each other or ever so similar beforehand, it does not advance their felicity in the least. They always continue to grow sufficiently unlike afterwards to have their share of vexation; and it is better to know as little as possible of the defects of the person with whom you are to pass your life."

"You make me laugh, Charlotte; but it is not sound. You know it is not sound, and that you would never act in this way yourself."

Occupied in observing Mr. Bingley's attentions to her sister, Elizabeth was far from suspecting that she was herself becoming an object of some interest in the eyes of his friend. Mr. Darcy had at first scarcely allowed her to be pretty; he had looked at her without admiration at the ball; and when they next met, he looked at her only to criticise. But no sooner had he made it clear to himself and his friends that she hardly had a good feature in her face, than he began to find it was rendered uncommonly intelligent by the beautiful expression of her dark eyes. To this discovery succeeded some others equally mortifying. Though he had detected with a critical eye more than one failure of perfect symmetry in her form, he was forced to acknowledge her figure to be light and pleasing; and in spite of his asserting that her manners were not those of the fashionable world, he was caught by their easy playfulness. Of this she was perfectly unaware; to her he was only the man who made himself agreeable nowhere, and who had not thought her handsome enough to dance with.

He began to wish to know more of her, and as a step towards conversing with her himself, attended to her conversation with others. His doing so drew her notice. It was at Sir William Lucas's, where a large party were assembled.

"What does Mr. Darcy mean," said she to Charlotte, "by listening to my conversation with Colonel Forster?"

"That is a question which Mr. Darcy only can answer."

"But if he does it any more I shall certainly let him know that I see what he is about. He has a very satirical eye, and if I do not begin by being impertinent myself, I shall soon grow afraid of him."

On his approaching them soon afterwards, though without seeming to have any intention of speaking, Miss Lucas defied her friend to mention such a subject to him; which immediately provoking Elizabeth to do it, she turned to him and said:

"Did you not think, Mr. Darcy, that I expressed myself uncommonly well just now, when I was teasing Colonel Forster to give us a ball at Meryton?"

"With great energy; but it is always a subject which makes a lady energetic."

"You are severe on us."

"It will be *her* turn soon to be teased," said Miss Lucas. "I am going to open the instrument, Eliza, and you know what follows."

"You are a very strange creature by way of a friend!—always wanting me to play and sing before anybody and everybody! If my vanity had taken a musical turn, you would have been invaluable; but as it is, I would really rather not sit down before those who must be in the habit of hearing the very best performers." On Miss Lucas's persevering, however, she added, "Very well, if it must be so, it must." And gravely glancing at Mr. Darcy, "There is a fine old saying, which everybody here is of course familiar with: 'Keep your breath to cool your porridge'; and I shall keep mine to swell my song."

Her performance was pleasing, though by no means capital. After a song or two, and before she could reply to the entreaties of several that she would sing again, she was eagerly succeeded at the instrument by her sister Mary, who having, in consequence of being the only plain one in the family, worked hard for knowledge and accomplishments, was always impatient for display.

Mary had neither genius nor taste; and though vanity had given her application, it had given her likewise a pedantic air and conceited manner, which would have injured a higher degree of excellence than she had reached. Elizabeth, easy and unaffected, had been listened to with much more pleasure, though not playing half so well; and Mary, at the end of a long concerto, was glad to purchase praise and gratitude by Scotch and Irish airs, at the request of her younger sisters, who, with some of the Lucases, and two or three officers, joined eagerly in dancing at one end of the room.

Mr. Darcy stood near them in silent indignation at such a mode of passing the evening, to the exclusion of all conversation, and was too much engrossed by his thoughts to perceive that Sir William Lucas was his neighbour, till Sir William thus began:

"What a charming amusement for young people this is, Mr. Darcy! There is nothing like dancing after all. I consider it as one of the first refinements of polished society."

"Certainly, sir; and it has the advantage also of being in vogue amongst the less polished societies of the world. Every savage can dance."

Sir William only smiled. "Your friend performs delightfully," he continued after a pause, on seeing Bingley join the group; "and I doubt not that you are an adept in the science yourself, Mr. Darcy."

"You saw me dance at Meryton, I believe, sir."

"Yes, indeed, and received no inconsiderable pleasure from the sight. Do you often dance at St. James's?"

"Never, sir."

"Do you not think it would be a proper compliment to the place?"

"It is a compliment which I never pay to any place if I can avoid it."

"You have a house in town, I conclude?"

Mr. Darcy bowed.

"I had once had some thought of fixing in town myself—for I am fond of superior society; but I did not feel quite certain that the air of London would agree with Lady Lucas."

He paused in hopes of an answer; but his companion was not disposed to make any; and Elizabeth at that instant moving towards them, he was struck with the action of doing a very gallant thing, and called out to her:

"My dear Miss Eliza, why are you not dancing? Mr. Darcy, you must allow me to present this young lady to you as a very desirable partner. You cannot refuse to dance, I am sure when so much beauty is before you." And, taking her hand, he would have given it to Mr. Darcy who, though extremely surprised, was not unwilling to receive it, when she instantly drew back, and said with some discomposure to Sir William:

"Indeed, sir, I have not the least intention of dancing. I entreat you not to suppose that I moved this way in order to beg for a partner."

Mr. Darcy, with grave propriety, requested to be allowed the honour of her hand, but in vain. Elizabeth was determined; nor did Sir William at all shake her purpose by his attempt at persuasion.

"You excel so much in the dance, Miss Eliza, that it is cruel to deny me the happiness of seeing you; and though this gentleman dislikes the amusement in general, he can have no objection, I am sure, to oblige us for one half-hour."

"Mr. Darcy is all politeness," said Elizabeth, smiling.

"He is, indeed; but, considering the inducement, my dear Miss Eliza, we cannot wonder at his complaisance—for who would object to such a partner?"

Elizabeth looked archly, and turned away. Her resistance had not injured her with the gentleman, and he was thinking of her with some complacency, when thus accosted by Miss Bingley:

"I can guess the subject of your reverie."

"I should imagine not."

"You are considering how insupportable it would be to pass many evenings in this manner—in such society; and indeed I am quite of your opinion. I was never more annoyed! The insipidity, and yet the noise—the nothingness, and yet the self-importance of all those people! What would I give to hear your strictures on them!"

"Your conjecture is totally wrong, I assure you. My mind was more agreeably engaged. I have been meditating on the very great pleasure which a pair of fine eyes in the face of a pretty woman can bestow."

Miss Bingley immediately fixed her eyes on his face, and desired he would tell her what lady had the credit of inspiring such reflections. Mr. Darcy replied with great intrepidity:

"Miss Elizabeth Bennet."

"Miss Elizabeth Bennet!" repeated Miss Bingley. "I am all astonishment. How long has she been such a favourite?—and pray, when am I to wish you joy?"

"That is exactly the question which I expected you to ask. A lady's imagination is very rapid; it jumps from admiration to love, from love to matrimony, in a moment. I knew you would be wishing me joy."

"Nay, if you are serious about it, I shall consider the matter is absolutely settled. You will be having a charming mother-in-law, indeed; and, of course, she will always be at Pemberley with you."

He listened to her with perfect indifference while she chose to entertain herself in this manner; and as his composure convinced her that all was safe, her wit flowed long.

CHAPTER VII

Mr. Bennet's property consisted almost entirely in an estate of two thousand a year, which, unfortunately for his daughters, was entailed, in default of heirs male, on a distant relation; and their mother's fortune, though ample for her situation in life, could but ill supply the deficiency of his. Her father had been an attorney in Meryton, and had left her four thousand pounds.

She had a sister married to a Mr. Phillips, who had been a clerk to their father and succeeded him in the business, and a brother settled in London in a respectable line of trade.

The village of Longbourn was only one mile from Meryton; a most convenient distance for the young ladies, who were usually tempted thither three or four times a week, to pay their duty to their aunt and to a milliner's shop just over the way. The two youngest of the family, Catherine and Lydia, were particularly frequent in these attentions; their minds were more vacant than their sisters', and when nothing better offered, a walk to Meryton was necessary to amuse their morning hours and furnish conversation for the evening; and however bare of news the country in general might be, they always contrived to learn some from their aunt. At present, indeed, they were well supplied both with news and happiness by the recent arrival of a militia regiment in the neighbourhood; it was to remain the whole winter, and Meryton was the headquarters.

Their visits to Mrs. Phillips were now productive of the most interesting intelligence. Every day added something to their knowledge of the officers' names and connections. Their lodgings were not long a secret, and at length they began to know the officers themselves. Mr. Phillips visited them all, and this opened to his nieces a store of felicity unknown before. They could talk of nothing but officers; and Mr. Bingley's large fortune, the mention of which gave animation to their mother, was worthless in their eyes when opposed to the regimentals of an ensign.

After listening one morning to their effusions on this subject, Mr. Bennet coolly observed:

"From all that I can collect by your manner of talking, you must be two of the silliest girls in the country. I have suspected it some time, but I am now convinced."

Catherine was disconcerted, and made no answer; but Lydia, with perfect indifference, continued to express her admiration of Captain Carter, and her hope of seeing him in the course of the day, as he was going the next morning to London.

"I am astonished, my dear," said Mrs. Bennet, "that you should be so ready to think your own children silly. If I wished to think slightingly of anybody's children, it should not be of my own, however."

"If my children are silly, I must hope to be always sensible of it."

"Yes—but as it happens, they are all of them very clever."

"This is the only point, I flatter myself, on which we do not agree. I had hoped that our sentiments coincided in every particular, but I must so far differ from you as to think our two youngest daughters uncommonly foolish."

"My dear Mr. Bennet, you must not expect such girls to have the sense of their father and mother. When they get to our age, I dare say they will not think about officers any more than we do. I remember the time when I liked a red coat myself very well—and, indeed, so I do still at my heart; and if a smart young colonel, with five or six thousand a year, should want one of my girls I shall not say nay to him; and I thought Colonel Forster looked very becoming the other night at Sir William's in his regimentals."

"Mamma," cried Lydia, "my aunt says that Colonel Forster and Captain Carter do not go so often to Miss Watson's as they did when they first came; she sees them now very often standing in Clarke's library."

Mrs. Bennet was prevented replying by the entrance of the footman with a note for Miss Bennet; it came from Netherfield, and the servant waited for an answer. Mrs. Bennet's eyes sparkled with pleasure, and she was eagerly calling out, while her daughter read,

"Well, Jane, who is it from? What is it about? What does he say? Well, Jane, make haste and tell us; make haste, my love."

"It is from Miss Bingley," said Jane, and then read it aloud.

"MY DEAR FRIEND,—

"If you are not so compassionate as to dine to-day with Louisa and me, we shall be in danger of hating each other

> for the rest of our lives, for a whole day's tete-a-tete between two women can never end without a quarrel. Come as soon as you can on receipt of this. My brother and the gentlemen are to dine with the officers.—Yours ever,
>
> "CAROLINE BINGLEY"

"With the officers!" cried Lydia. "I wonder my aunt did not tell us of *that*."

"Dining out," said Mrs. Bennet, "that is very unlucky."

"Can I have the carriage?" said Jane.

"No, my dear, you had better go on horseback, because it seems likely to rain; and then you must stay all night."

"That would be a good scheme," said Elizabeth, "if you were sure that they would not offer to send her home."

"Oh! but the gentlemen will have Mr. Bingley's chaise to go to Meryton, and the Hursts have no horses to theirs."

"I had much rather go in the coach."

"But, my dear, your father cannot spare the horses, I am sure. They are wanted in the farm, Mr. Bennet, are they not?"

"They are wanted in the farm much oftener than I can get them."

"But if you have got them to-day," said Elizabeth, "my mother's purpose will be answered."

She did at last extort from her father an acknowledgment that the horses were engaged. Jane was therefore obliged to go on horseback, and her mother attended her to the door with many cheerful prognostics of a bad day. Her hopes were answered; Jane had not been gone long before it rained hard. Her sisters were uneasy for her, but her mother was delighted. The rain continued the whole evening without intermission; Jane certainly could not come back.

"This was a lucky idea of mine, indeed!" said Mrs. Bennet more than once, as if the credit of making it rain were all her own. Till the next morning, however, she was not aware of all the felicity of her contrivance. Breakfast was scarcely over when a servant from Netherfield brought the following note for Elizabeth:

"MY DEAREST LIZZY,—

"I find myself very unwell this morning, which, I suppose, is to be imputed to my getting wet through yesterday. My kind friends will not hear of my returning till I am better. They insist also on my seeing Mr. Jones—therefore do not be alarmed if you should hear of his having been to me—and, excepting a sore throat and headache, there is not much the matter with me.—Yours, etc."

"Well, my dear," said Mr. Bennet, when Elizabeth had read the note aloud, "if your daughter should have a dangerous fit of illness—if she should die, it would be a comfort to know that it was all in pursuit of Mr. Bingley, and under your orders."

"Oh! I am not afraid of her dying. People do not die of little trifling colds. She will be taken good care of. As long as she stays there, it is all very well. I would go and see her if I could have the carriage."

Elizabeth, feeling really anxious, was determined to go to her, though the carriage was not to be had; and as she was no horsewoman, walking was her only alternative. She declared her resolution.

"How can you be so silly," cried her mother, "as to think of such a thing, in all this dirt! You will not be fit to be seen when you get there."

"I shall be very fit to see Jane—which is all I want."

"Is this a hint to me, Lizzy," said her father, "to send for the horses?"

"No, indeed, I do not wish to avoid the walk. The distance is nothing when one has a motive; only three miles. I shall be back by dinner."

"I admire the activity of your benevolence," observed Mary, "but every impulse of feeling should be guided by reason; and, in my opinion, exertion should always be in proportion to what is required."

"We will go as far as Meryton with you," said Catherine and Lydia. Elizabeth accepted their company, and the three young ladies set off together.

"If we make haste," said Lydia, as they walked along, "perhaps we may see something of Captain Carter before he goes."

In Meryton they parted; the two youngest repaired to the lodgings of one of the officers' wives, and Elizabeth continued her walk alone, crossing field after field at a quick pace, jumping over stiles and springing over puddles with impatient activity, and finding herself at last within view of the house, with weary ankles, dirty stockings, and a face glowing with the warmth of exercise.

She was shown into the breakfast-parlour, where all but Jane were assembled, and where her appearance created a great deal of surprise. That she should have walked three miles so early in the day, in such dirty weather, and by herself, was almost incredible to Mrs. Hurst and Miss Bingley; and Elizabeth was convinced that they held her in contempt for it. She was received, however, very politely by them; and in their brother's manners there was something better than politeness; there was good humour and kindness. Mr. Darcy said very little, and Mr. Hurst nothing at all. The former was divided between admiration of the brilliancy which exercise had given to her complexion, and doubt as to the occasion's justifying her coming so far alone. The latter was thinking only of his breakfast.

Her inquiries after her sister were not very favourably answered. Miss Bennet had slept ill, and though up, was very feverish, and not well enough to leave her room. Elizabeth was glad to be taken to her immediately; and Jane, who had only been withheld by the fear of giving alarm or inconvenience from expressing in her note how much she longed for such a visit, was delighted at her entrance. She was not equal, however, to much conversation, and when Miss Bingley left them together, could attempt little besides expressions of gratitude for the extraordinary kindness she was treated with. Elizabeth silently attended her.

When breakfast was over they were joined by the sisters; and Elizabeth began to like them herself, when she saw how much affection and solicitude they showed for Jane. The apothecary came, and having examined his patient, said, as might be supposed, that she had caught a violent cold, and that they must endeavour to get the better of it; advised her to return to bed, and promised her some draughts. The advice was followed readily, for the feverish symptoms increased, and her head ached acutely. Elizabeth did not quit her room for a moment; nor were the other ladies often absent; the gentlemen being out, they had, in fact, nothing to do elsewhere.

When the clock struck three, Elizabeth felt that she must go, and very unwillingly said so. Miss Bingley offered her the carriage, and she only wanted a little pressing to accept it, when Jane testified such concern in parting with her, that Miss Bingley was obliged to convert the offer of the chaise to an invitation to remain at Netherfield for the present. Elizabeth most thankfully consented, and a servant was dispatched to Longbourn to acquaint the family with her stay and bring back a supply of clothes.

CHAPTER VIII

At five o'clock the two ladies retired to dress, and at half-past six Elizabeth was summoned to dinner. To the civil inquiries which then poured in, and amongst which she had the pleasure of distinguishing the much superior solicitude of Mr. Bingley's, she could not make a very favourable answer. Jane was by no means better. The sisters, on hearing this, repeated three or four times how much they were grieved, how shocking it was to have a bad cold, and how excessively they disliked being ill themselves; and then thought no more of the matter: and their indifference towards Jane when not immediately before them restored Elizabeth to the enjoyment of all her former dislike.

Their brother, indeed, was the only one of the party whom she could regard with any complacency. His anxiety for Jane was evident, and his attentions to herself most pleasing, and they prevented her feeling herself so much an intruder as she believed she was considered by the others. She had very little notice from any but him. Miss Bingley was engrossed by Mr. Darcy, her sister scarcely less so; and as for Mr. Hurst, by whom Elizabeth sat, he was an indolent man, who lived only to eat, drink, and play at cards; who, when he found her to prefer a plain dish to a ragout, had nothing to say to her.

When dinner was over, she returned directly to Jane, and Miss Bingley began abusing her as soon as she was out of the room. Her manners were pronounced to be very bad indeed, a mixture of pride and impertinence; she had no conversation, no style, no beauty. Mrs. Hurst thought the same, and added:

"She has nothing, in short, to recommend her, but being an excellent walker. I shall never forget her appearance this morning. She really looked almost wild."

"She did, indeed, Louisa. I could hardly keep my countenance. Very nonsensical to come at all! Why must *she* be scampering about the country, because her sister had a cold? Her hair, so untidy, so blowsy!"

"Yes, and her petticoat; I hope you saw her petticoat, six inches deep in mud, I am absolutely certain; and the gown which had been let down to hide it not doing its office."

"Your picture may be very exact, Louisa," said Bingley; "but this was all lost upon me. I thought Miss Elizabeth Bennet looked remarkably well when she came into the room this morning. Her dirty petticoat quite escaped my notice."

"*You* observed it, Mr. Darcy, I am sure," said Miss Bingley; "and I am inclined to think that you would not wish to see *your* sister make such an exhibition."

"Certainly not."

"To walk three miles, or four miles, or five miles, or whatever it is, above her ankles in dirt, and alone, quite alone! What could she mean by it? It seems to me to show an abominable sort of conceited independence, a most country-town indifference to decorum."

"It shows an affection for her sister that is very pleasing," said Bingley.

"I am afraid, Mr. Darcy," observed Miss Bingley in a half whisper, "that this adventure has rather affected your admiration of her fine eyes."

"Not at all," he replied; "they were brightened by the exercise." A short pause followed this speech, and Mrs. Hurst began again:

"I have an excessive regard for Miss Jane Bennet, she is really a very sweet girl, and I wish with all my heart she were well settled. But with such a father and mother, and such low connections, I am afraid there is no chance of it."

"I think I have heard you say that their uncle is an attorney on Meryton."

"Yes; and they have another, who lives somewhere near Cheapside."

"That is capital," added her sister, and they both laughed heartily.

"If they had uncles enough to fill *all* Cheapside," cried Bingley, "it would not make them one jot less agreeable."

"But it must very materially lessen their chance of marrying men of any consideration in the world," replied Darcy.

To this speech Bingley made no answer; but his sisters gave it their hearty assent, and indulged their mirth for some time at the expense of their dear friend's vulgar relations.

With a renewal of tenderness, however, they returned to her room on leaving the dining-parlour, and sat with her till summoned to coffee. She was still very poorly, and Elizabeth would not quit her at all, till late in the evening, when she had the comfort of seeing her sleep, and when it seemed to her rather right than pleasant that she should go downstairs herself. On entering the drawing-room she found the whole party at loo, and was immediately invited to join them; but suspecting them to be playing high she declined it, and making her sister the excuse, said she would amuse herself for the short time she could stay below, with a book. Mr. Hurst looked at her with astonishment.

"Do you prefer reading to cards?" said he; "that is rather singular."

"Miss Eliza Bennet," said Miss Bingley, "despises cards. She is a great reader, and has no pleasure in anything else."

"I deserve neither such praise nor such censure," cried Elizabeth; "I am *not* a great reader, and I have pleasure in many things."

"In nursing your sister I am sure you have pleasure," said Bingley; "and I hope it will be soon increased by seeing her quite well."

Elizabeth thanked him from her heart, and then walked towards the table where a few books were lying. He immediately offered to fetch her others—all that his library afforded.

"And I wish my collection were larger for your benefit and my own credit; but I am an idle fellow, and though I have not many, I have more than I ever looked into."

Elizabeth assured him that she could suit herself perfectly with those in the room.

"I am astonished," said Miss Bingley, "that my father should have left so small a collection of books. What a delightful library you have at Pemberley, Mr. Darcy!"

"It ought to be good," he replied, "it has been the work of many generations."

"And then you have added so much to it yourself, you are always buying books."

"I cannot comprehend the neglect of a family library in such days as these."

"Neglect! I am sure you neglect nothing that can add to the beauties of that noble place. Charles, when you build *your* house, I wish it may be half as delightful as Pemberley."

"I wish it may."

"But I would really advise you to make your purchase in that neighbourhood, and take Pemberley for a kind of model. There is not a finer county in England than Derbyshire."

"With all my heart; I will buy Pemberley itself if Darcy will sell it."

"I am talking of possibilities, Charles."

"Upon my word, Caroline, I should think it more possible to get Pemberley by purchase than by imitation."

Elizabeth was so much caught with what passed, as to leave her very little attention for her book; and soon laying it wholly aside, she drew near the card-table, and stationed herself between Mr. Bingley and his eldest sister, to observe the game.

"Is Miss Darcy much grown since the spring?" said Miss Bingley; "will she be as tall as I am?"

"I think she will. She is now about Miss Elizabeth Bennet's height, or rather taller."

"How I long to see her again! I never met with anybody who delighted me so much. Such a countenance, such manners! And so extremely accomplished for her age! Her performance on the pianoforte is exquisite."

"It is amazing to me," said Bingley, "how young ladies can have patience to be so very accomplished as they all are."

"All young ladies accomplished! My dear Charles, what do you mean?"

"Yes, all of them, I think. They all paint tables, cover screens, and net purses. I scarcely know anyone who cannot do all this, and I am sure I never heard a young lady spoken of for the first time, without being informed that she was very accomplished."

"Your list of the common extent of accomplishments," said Darcy, "has too much truth. The word is applied to many a woman who deserves it no otherwise than by netting a purse or covering a screen. But I am very far from agreeing with you in your estimation of ladies in general. I cannot boast of knowing more than half-a-dozen, in the whole range of my acquaintance, that are really accomplished."

"Nor I, I am sure," said Miss Bingley.

"Then," observed Elizabeth, "you must comprehend a great deal in your idea of an accomplished woman."

"Yes, I do comprehend a great deal in it."

"Oh! certainly," cried his faithful assistant, "no one can be really esteemed accomplished who does not greatly surpass what is usually met with. A woman must have a thorough knowledge of music, singing, drawing, dancing, and the modern languages, to deserve the word; and besides all this, she must possess a certain something in her air and manner of walking, the tone of her voice, her address and expressions, or the word will be but half-deserved."

"All this she must possess," added Darcy, "and to all this she must yet add something more substantial, in the improvement of her mind by extensive reading."

"I am no longer surprised at your knowing *only* six accomplished women. I rather wonder now at your knowing *any*."

"Are you so severe upon your own sex as to doubt the possibility of all this?"

"I never saw such a woman. I never saw such capacity, and taste, and application, and elegance, as you describe united."

Mrs. Hurst and Miss Bingley both cried out against the injustice of her implied doubt, and were both protesting that they knew many women who answered this description, when Mr. Hurst called them to order, with bitter complaints of their inattention to what was going forward. As all conversation was thereby at an end, Elizabeth soon afterwards left the room.

"Elizabeth Bennet," said Miss Bingley, when the door was closed on her, "is one of those young ladies who seek to recommend themselves to the other sex by undervaluing their own; and with many men, I dare say, it succeeds. But, in my opinion, it is a paltry device, a very mean art."

"Undoubtedly," replied Darcy, to whom this remark was chiefly addressed, "there is a meanness in *all* the arts which ladies sometimes condescend to employ for captivation. Whatever bears affinity to cunning is despicable."

Miss Bingley was not so entirely satisfied with this reply as to continue the subject.

Elizabeth joined them again only to say that her sister was worse, and that she could not leave her. Bingley urged Mr. Jones being sent for immediately; while his sisters, convinced that no country advice could be of any service, recommended an express to town for one of the most eminent physicians. This she would not hear of; but she was not so unwilling to comply with their brother's proposal; and it was settled that Mr. Jones should be sent for early in the morning, if Miss Bennet were not decidedly better. Bingley was quite uncomfortable; his sisters declared that they were miserable. They solaced their wretchedness, however, by duets after supper, while he could find no better relief to his feelings than by giving his housekeeper directions that every attention might be paid to the sick lady and her sister.

CHAPTER IX

Elizabeth passed the chief of the night in her sister's room, and in the morning had the pleasure of being able to send a tolerable answer to the inquiries which she very early received from Mr. Bingley by a housemaid, and some time afterwards from the two elegant ladies who waited on his sisters. In spite of this amendment, however, she requested to have a note sent to Longbourn, desiring her mother to visit Jane, and form her own judgement of her situation. The note was immediately dispatched, and its contents as quickly complied with. Mrs. Bennet, accompanied by her two youngest girls, reached Netherfield soon after the family breakfast.

Had she found Jane in any apparent danger, Mrs. Bennet would have been very miserable; but being satisfied on seeing her that her illness was not alarming, she had no wish of her recovering immediately, as her restoration to health would probably remove her from Netherfield. She would not listen, therefore, to her daughter's proposal of being carried home; neither did the apothecary, who arrived about the same time, think it at all advisable. After sitting a little while with Jane, on Miss Bingley's appearance and invitation, the mother and three daughters all attended her into the breakfast parlour. Bingley met them with hopes that Mrs. Bennet had not found Miss Bennet worse than she expected.

"Indeed I have, sir," was her answer. "She is a great deal too ill to be moved. Mr. Jones says we must not think of moving her. We must trespass a little longer on your kindness."

"Removed!" cried Bingley. "It must not be thought of. My sister, I am sure, will not hear of her removal."

"You may depend upon it, Madam," said Miss Bingley, with cold civility, "that Miss Bennet will receive every possible attention while she remains with us."

Mrs. Bennet was profuse in her acknowledgments.

"I am sure," she added, "if it was not for such good friends I do not know what would become of her, for she is very ill indeed, and suffers a vast deal, though with the greatest patience in the world, which is always the way with her, for she has, without exception, the sweetest temper I have ever met with. I often tell my other girls they are nothing to *her*. You have a sweet room here, Mr. Bingley, and a charming prospect over the gravel walk. I do not know a place in the country that is equal to Netherfield. You will not think of quitting it in a hurry, I hope, though you have but a short lease."

"Whatever I do is done in a hurry," replied he; "and therefore if I should resolve to quit Netherfield, I should probably be off in five minutes. At present, however, I consider myself as quite fixed here."

"That is exactly what I should have supposed of you," said Elizabeth.

"You begin to comprehend me, do you?" cried he, turning towards her.

"Oh! yes—I understand you perfectly."

"I wish I might take this for a compliment; but to be so easily seen through I am afraid is pitiful."

"That is as it happens. It does not follow that a deep, intricate character is more or less estimable than such a one as yours."

"Lizzy," cried her mother, "remember where you are, and do not run on in the wild manner that you are suffered to do at home."

"I did not know before," continued Bingley immediately, "that you were a studier of character. It must be an amusing study."

"Yes, but intricate characters are the *most* amusing. They have at least that advantage."

"The country," said Darcy, "can in general supply but a few subjects for such a study. In a country neighbourhood you move in a very confined and unvarying society."

"But people themselves alter so much, that there is something new to be observed in them for ever."

"Yes, indeed," cried Mrs. Bennet, offended by his manner of mentioning a country neighbourhood. "I assure you there is quite as much of *that* going on in the country as in town."

Everybody was surprised, and Darcy, after looking at her for a moment, turned silently away. Mrs. Bennet, who fancied she had gained a complete victory over him, continued her triumph.

"I cannot see that London has any great advantage over the country, for my part, except the shops and public places. The country is a vast deal pleasanter, is it not, Mr. Bingley?"

"When I am in the country," he replied, "I never wish to leave it; and when I am in town it is pretty much the same. They have each their advantages, and I can be equally happy in either."

"Aye—that is because you have the right disposition. But that gentleman," looking at Darcy, "seemed to think the country was nothing at all."

"Indeed, Mamma, you are mistaken," said Elizabeth, blushing for her mother. "You quite mistook Mr. Darcy. He only meant that there was not such a variety of people to be met with in the country as in the town, which you must acknowledge to be true."

"Certainly, my dear, nobody said there were; but as to not meeting with many people in this neighbourhood, I believe there are few neighbourhoods larger. I know we dine with four-and-twenty families."

Nothing but concern for Elizabeth could enable Bingley to keep his countenance. His sister was less delicate, and directed her eyes towards Mr. Darcy with a very expressive smile. Elizabeth, for the sake of saying something that might turn her mother's thoughts, now asked her if Charlotte Lucas had been at Longbourn since *her* coming away.

"Yes, she called yesterday with her father. What an agreeable man Sir William is, Mr. Bingley, is not he? So much the man of fashion! So genteel and easy! He had always something to say to everybody. *That* is my idea of good breeding; and those persons who fancy themselves very important, and never open their mouths, quite mistake the matter."

"Did Charlotte dine with you?"

"No, she would go home. I fancy she was wanted about the mince-pies. For my part, Mr. Bingley, I always keep servants that can do their own work; *my* daughters are brought up very differently. But everybody is to judge for themselves, and the Lucases are a very good sort of girls, I assure you. It is a pity they are not handsome! Not that I think Charlotte so *very* plain—but then she is our particular friend."

"She seems a very pleasant young woman."

"Oh! dear, yes; but you must own she is very plain. Lady Lucas herself has often said so, and envied me Jane's beauty. I do not like to boast of my own child, but to be sure, Jane—one does not often see anybody better looking. It is what everybody says. I do not trust my own partiality. When she was only fifteen, there was a man at my brother Gardiner's in town so much in love with her that my sister-in-law was sure he would make her an offer before we came away. But, however, he did not. Perhaps he thought her too young. However, he wrote some verses on her, and very pretty they were."

"And so ended his affection," said Elizabeth impatiently. "There has been many a one, I fancy, overcome in the same way. I wonder who first discovered the efficacy of poetry in driving away love!"

"I have been used to consider poetry as the *food* of love," said Darcy.

"Of a fine, stout, healthy love it may. Everything nourishes what is strong already. But if it be only a slight, thin sort of inclination, I am convinced that one good sonnet will starve it entirely away."

Darcy only smiled; and the general pause which ensued made Elizabeth tremble lest her mother should be exposing herself again. She longed to speak, but could think of nothing to say; and after a short silence Mrs. Bennet began repeating her thanks to Mr. Bingley for his kindness to Jane, with an apology for troubling him also with Lizzy. Mr. Bingley was unaffectedly civil in his answer, and forced his younger sister to be civil also, and say what the occasion required. She performed her part indeed without much graciousness, but Mrs. Bennet was satisfied, and soon afterwards ordered her carriage. Upon this signal, the youngest of her daughters put herself forward. The two girls had been whispering to each other during the whole visit, and the result of it was, that the youngest should tax Mr. Bingley with having promised on his first coming into the country to give a ball at Netherfield.

Lydia was a stout, well-grown girl of fifteen, with a fine complexion and good-humoured countenance; a favourite with her mother, whose affection had brought her into public at an early age. She had high animal spirits, and a sort of natural self-consequence, which the attention of the officers, to whom her uncle's good dinners, and her own easy manners recommended her, had increased into assurance. She was very equal, therefore, to address Mr. Bingley on the subject of the ball, and abruptly reminded him of his promise; adding, that it would be the most shameful thing in the world if he did not keep it. His answer to this sudden attack was delightful to their mother's ear:

"I am perfectly ready, I assure you, to keep my engagement; and when your sister is recovered, you shall, if you please, name the very day of the ball. But you would not wish to be dancing when she is ill."

Lydia declared herself satisfied. "Oh! yes—it would be much better to wait till Jane was well, and by that time most likely Captain Carter would be at Meryton again. And when you have given *your* ball," she added, "I shall insist on their giving one also. I shall tell Colonel Forster it will be quite a shame if he does not."

Mrs. Bennet and her daughters then departed, and Elizabeth returned instantly to Jane, leaving her own and her relations' behaviour to the remarks of the two ladies and Mr. Darcy; the latter of whom, however, could not be prevailed on to join in their censure of *her*, in spite of all Miss Bingley's witticisms on *fine eyes*.

CHAPTER X

The day passed much as the day before had done. Mrs. Hurst and Miss Bingley had spent some hours of the morning with the invalid, who continued, though slowly, to mend; and in the evening Elizabeth joined their party in the drawing-room. The loo-table, however, did not appear. Mr. Darcy was writing, and Miss Bingley, seated near him, was watching the progress of his letter and repeatedly calling off his attention by messages to his sister. Mr. Hurst and Mr. Bingley were at piquet, and Mrs. Hurst was observing their game.

Elizabeth took up some needlework, and was sufficiently amused in attending to what passed between Darcy and his companion. The perpetual commendations of the lady, either on his handwriting, or on the evenness of his lines, or on the length of his letter, with the perfect unconcern with which her praises were received, formed a curious dialogue, and was exactly in union with her opinion of each.

"How delighted Miss Darcy will be to receive such a letter!"

He made no answer.

"You write uncommonly fast."

"You are mistaken. I write rather slowly."

"How many letters you must have occasion to write in the course of a year! Letters of business, too! How odious I should think them!"

"It is fortunate, then, that they fall to my lot instead of yours."

"Pray tell your sister that I long to see her."

"I have already told her so once, by your desire."

"I am afraid you do not like your pen. Let me mend it for you. I mend pens remarkably well."

"Thank you—but I always mend my own."

"How can you contrive to write so even?"

He was silent.

"Tell your sister I am delighted to hear of her improvement on the harp; and pray let her know that I am quite in raptures with her beautiful little design for a table, and I think it infinitely superior to Miss Grantley's."

"Will you give me leave to defer your raptures till I write again? At present I have not room to do them justice."

"Oh! it is of no consequence. I shall see her in January. But do you always write such charming long letters to her, Mr. Darcy?"

"They are generally long; but whether always charming it is not for me to determine."

"It is a rule with me, that a person who can write a long letter with ease, cannot write ill."

"That will not do for a compliment to Darcy, Caroline," cried her brother, "because he does *not* write with ease. He studies too much for words of four syllables. Do not you, Darcy?"

"My style of writing is very different from yours."

"Oh!" cried Miss Bingley, "Charles writes in the most careless way imaginable. He leaves out half his words, and blots the rest."

"My ideas flow so rapidly that I have not time to express them—by which means my letters sometimes convey no ideas at all to my correspondents."

"Your humility, Mr. Bingley," said Elizabeth, "must disarm reproof."

"Nothing is more deceitful," said Darcy, "than the appearance of humility. It is often only carelessness of opinion, and sometimes an indirect boast."

"And which of the two do you call *my* little recent piece of modesty?"

"The indirect boast; for you are really proud of your defects in writing, because you consider them as proceeding from a rapidity of thought and carelessness of execution, which, if not estimable, you think at least highly interesting. The power of doing anything with quickness is always prized much by the possessor, and often without any attention to the imperfection of the performance. When you told Mrs. Bennet this morning that if you ever resolved upon quitting Netherfield you should be gone in five minutes, you meant it to be a sort of panegyric, of compliment to yourself—and yet what is there so very laudable in a precipitance which must leave very necessary business undone, and can be of no real advantage to yourself or anyone else?"

"Nay," cried Bingley, "this is too much, to remember at night all the foolish things that were said in the morning. And yet, upon my honour, I believe what I said of myself to be true, and I believe it at this moment. At least, therefore, I did not assume the character of needless precipitance merely to show off before the ladies."

"I dare say you believed it; but I am by no means convinced that you would be gone with such celerity. Your conduct would be quite as dependent on chance as that of any man I know; and if, as you were mounting your horse, a friend were to say, 'Bingley, you had better stay till next week,' you would probably do it, you would probably not go—and at another word, might stay a month."

"You have only proved by this," cried Elizabeth, "that Mr. Bingley did not do justice to his own disposition. You have shown him off now much more than he did himself."

"I am exceedingly gratified," said Bingley, "by your converting what my friend says into a compliment on the sweetness of my temper. But I am afraid you are giving it a turn which that gentleman did by no means intend; for he would certainly think better of me, if under such a circumstance I were to give a flat denial, and ride off as fast as I could."

"Would Mr. Darcy then consider the rashness of your original intentions as atoned for by your obstinacy in adhering to it?"

"Upon my word, I cannot exactly explain the matter; Darcy must speak for himself."

"You expect me to account for opinions which you choose to call mine, but which I have never acknowledged. Allowing the case, however, to stand according to your representation, you must remember, Miss Bennet, that the friend who is supposed to desire his return to the house, and the delay of his plan, has merely desired it, asked it without offering one argument in favour of its propriety."

"To yield readily—easily—to the *persuasion* of a friend is no merit with you."

"To yield without conviction is no compliment to the understanding of either."

"You appear to me, Mr. Darcy, to allow nothing for the influence of friendship and affection. A regard for the requester would often make one readily yield to a request, without waiting for arguments to reason one into it. I am not particularly speaking of such a case as you have supposed about Mr. Bingley. We may as well wait, perhaps, till the circumstance occurs before we discuss the discretion of his behaviour thereupon. But in general and ordinary cases between friend and friend, where one of them is desired by the other to change a resolution of no very great moment, should you think ill of that person for complying with the desire, without waiting to be argued into it?"

"Will it not be advisable, before we proceed on this subject, to arrange with rather more precision the degree of importance which is to appertain to this request, as well as the degree of intimacy subsisting between the parties?"

"By all means," cried Bingley; "let us hear all the particulars, not forgetting their comparative height and size; for that will have more weight in the argument, Miss Bennet, than you may be aware of. I assure you, that if Darcy were not such a great tall fellow, in comparison with myself, I should not pay him half so much deference. I declare I do not know a more awful object than Darcy, on particular occasions, and in particular places; at his own house especially, and of a Sunday evening, when he has nothing to do."

Mr. Darcy smiled; but Elizabeth thought she could perceive that he was rather offended, and therefore checked her laugh. Miss Bingley warmly resented the indignity he had received, in an expostulation with her brother for talking such nonsense.

"I see your design, Bingley," said his friend. "You dislike an argument, and want to silence this."

"Perhaps I do. Arguments are too much like disputes. If you and Miss Bennet will defer yours till I am out of the room, I shall be very thankful; and then you may say whatever you like of me."

"What you ask," said Elizabeth, "is no sacrifice on my side; and Mr. Darcy had much better finish his letter."

Mr. Darcy took her advice, and did finish his letter.

When that business was over, he applied to Miss Bingley and Elizabeth for an indulgence of some music. Miss Bingley moved with some alacrity to the pianoforte; and, after a polite request that Elizabeth would lead the way which the other as politely and more earnestly negatived, she seated herself.

Mrs. Hurst sang with her sister, and while they were thus employed, Elizabeth could not help observing, as she turned over some music-books that lay on the instrument, how frequently Mr. Darcy's eyes were fixed on her. She hardly knew how to suppose that she could be an object of admiration to so great a man; and yet that he should look at her because he disliked her, was still more strange. She could only imagine, however, at last that she drew his notice because there was something more wrong and reprehensible, according to his ideas of right, than in any other person present. The supposition did not pain her. She liked him too little to care for his approbation.

After playing some Italian songs, Miss Bingley varied the charm by a lively Scotch air; and soon afterwards Mr. Darcy, drawing near Elizabeth, said to her:

"Do not you feel a great inclination, Miss Bennet, to seize such an opportunity of dancing a reel?"

She smiled, but made no answer. He repeated the question, with some surprise at her silence.

"Oh!" said she, "I heard you before, but I could not immediately determine what to say in reply. You wanted me, I know, to say 'Yes,' that you might have the pleasure of despising my taste; but I always delight in overthrowing those kind of schemes, and cheating a person of their premeditated contempt. I have, therefore, made up my mind to tell you, that I do not want to dance a reel at all—and now despise me if you dare."

"Indeed I do not dare."

Elizabeth, having rather expected to affront him, was amazed at his gallantry; but there was a mixture of sweetness and archness in her manner which made it difficult for her to affront anybody; and Darcy had never been so bewitched by any woman as he was by her. He really believed, that were it not for the inferiority of her connections, he should be in some danger.

Miss Bingley saw, or suspected enough to be jealous; and her great anxiety for the recovery of her dear friend Jane received some assistance from her desire of getting rid of Elizabeth.

She often tried to provoke Darcy into disliking her guest, by talking of their supposed marriage, and planning his happiness in such an alliance.

"I hope," said she, as they were walking together in the shrubbery the next day, "you will give your mother-in-law a few hints, when this desirable event takes place, as to the advantage of holding her tongue; and if you can compass it, do cure the younger girls of running after officers. And, if I may mention so delicate a subject, endeavour to check that little something, bordering on conceit and impertinence, which your lady possesses."

"Have you anything else to propose for my domestic felicity?"

"Oh! yes. Do let the portraits of your uncle and aunt Phillips be placed in the gallery at Pemberley. Put them next to your great-uncle the judge. They are in the same profession, you know, only in different lines. As for your Elizabeth's picture, you must not have it taken, for what painter could do justice to those beautiful eyes?"

"It would not be easy, indeed, to catch their expression, but their colour and shape, and the eyelashes, so remarkably fine, might be copied."

At that moment they were met from another walk by Mrs. Hurst and Elizabeth herself.

"I did not know that you intended to walk," said Miss Bingley, in some confusion, lest they had been overheard.

"You used us abominably ill," answered Mrs. Hurst, "running away without telling us that you were coming out."

Then taking the disengaged arm of Mr. Darcy, she left Elizabeth to walk by herself. The path just admitted three. Mr. Darcy felt their rudeness, and immediately said:

"This walk is not wide enough for our party. We had better go into the avenue."

But Elizabeth, who had not the least inclination to remain with them, laughingly answered:

"No, no; stay where you are. You are charmingly grouped, and appear to uncommon advantage. The picturesque would be spoilt by admitting a fourth. Good-bye."

She then ran gaily off, rejoicing as she rambled about, in the hope of being at home again in a day or two. Jane was already so much recovered as to intend leaving her room for a couple of hours that evening.

CHAPTER XI

When the ladies removed after dinner, Elizabeth ran up to her sister, and seeing her well guarded from cold, attended her into the drawing-room, where she was welcomed by her two friends with many professions of pleasure; and Elizabeth had never seen them so agreeable as they were during the hour which passed before the gentlemen appeared. Their powers of conversation were considerable. They could describe an entertainment with accuracy, relate an anecdote with humour, and laugh at their acquaintance with spirit.

But when the gentlemen entered, Jane was no longer the first object; Miss Bingley's eyes were instantly turned toward Darcy, and she had something to say to him before he had advanced many steps. He addressed himself to Miss Bennet, with a polite congratulation; Mr. Hurst also made her a slight bow, and said he was "very glad;" but diffuseness and warmth remained for Bingley's salutation. He was full of joy and attention. The first half-hour was spent in piling up the fire, lest she should suffer from the change of room; and she removed at his desire to the other side of the fireplace, that she might be further from the door. He then sat down by her, and talked scarcely to anyone else. Elizabeth, at work in the opposite corner, saw it all with great delight.

When tea was over, Mr. Hurst reminded his sister-in-law of the card-table—but in vain. She had obtained private intelligence that Mr. Darcy did not wish for cards; and Mr. Hurst soon found even his open petition rejected. She assured him that no one intended to play, and the silence of the whole party on the subject seemed to justify her. Mr. Hurst had therefore nothing to do, but to stretch himself on one of the sofas and go to sleep. Darcy took up a book; Miss Bingley did the same; and Mrs. Hurst, principally occupied in playing with her bracelets and rings, joined now and then in her brother's conversation with Miss Bennet.

Miss Bingley's attention was quite as much engaged in watching Mr. Darcy's progress through *his* book, as in reading her own; and she was perpetually either making some inquiry, or looking at his page. She could not win him, however, to any conversation; he merely answered her question, and read on. At length, quite exhausted by the attempt to be amused with her own book, which she had only chosen because it was the second volume of his, she gave a great yawn and said, "How pleasant it is to spend an evening in this way! I declare after all there is no enjoyment like reading! How much sooner one tires of anything than of a book! When I have a house of my own, I shall be miserable if I have not an excellent library."

No one made any reply. She then yawned again, threw aside her book, and cast her eyes round the room in quest for some amusement; when hearing her brother mentioning a ball to Miss Bennet, she turned suddenly towards him and said:

"By the bye, Charles, are you really serious in meditating a dance at Netherfield? I would advise you, before you determine on it, to consult the wishes of the present party; I am much mistaken if there are not some among us to whom a ball would be rather a punishment than a pleasure."

"If you mean Darcy," cried her brother, "he may go to bed, if he chooses, before it begins—but as for the ball, it is quite a settled thing; and as soon as Nicholls has made white soup enough, I shall send round my cards."

"I should like balls infinitely better," she replied, "if they were carried on in a different manner; but there is something insufferably tedious in the usual process of such a meeting. It would surely be much more rational if conversation instead of dancing were made the order of the day."

"Much more rational, my dear Caroline, I dare say, but it would not be near so much like a ball."

Miss Bingley made no answer, and soon afterwards she got up and walked about the room. Her figure was elegant, and she walked well; but Darcy, at whom it was all aimed, was still inflexibly studious. In the desperation of her feelings, she resolved on one effort more, and, turning to Elizabeth, said:

"Miss Eliza Bennet, let me persuade you to follow my example, and take a turn about the room. I assure you it is very refreshing after sitting so long in one attitude."

Elizabeth was surprised, but agreed to it immediately. Miss Bingley succeeded no less in the real object of her civility; Mr. Darcy looked up. He was as much awake to the novelty of attention in that quarter as Elizabeth herself could be, and unconsciously closed his book. He was directly invited to join their party, but he declined it, observing that he could imagine but two motives for their choosing to walk up and down the room together, with either of which motives his joining them would interfere. "What could he mean? She was dying to know what could be his meaning?"—and asked Elizabeth whether she could at all understand him?

"Not at all," was her answer; "but depend upon it, he means to be severe on us, and our surest way of disappointing him will be to ask nothing about it."

Miss Bingley, however, was incapable of disappointing Mr. Darcy in anything, and persevered therefore in requiring an explanation of his two motives.

"I have not the smallest objection to explaining them," said he, as soon as she allowed him to speak. "You either choose this method of passing the evening because you are in each other's confidence, and have secret affairs to discuss, or because you are conscious that your figures appear to the greatest advantage in walking; if the first, I would be completely in your way, and if the second, I can admire you much better as I sit by the fire."

"Oh! shocking!" cried Miss Bingley. "I never heard anything so abominable. How shall we punish him for such a speech?"

"Nothing so easy, if you have but the inclination," said Elizabeth. "We can all plague and punish one another. Tease him—laugh at him. Intimate as you are, you must know how it is to be done."

"But upon my honour, I do *not*. I do assure you that my intimacy has not yet taught me *that*. Tease calmness of manner and presence of mind! No, no—feel he may defy us there. And as to laughter, we will not expose ourselves, if you please, by attempting to laugh without a subject. Mr. Darcy may hug himself."

"Mr. Darcy is not to be laughed at!" cried Elizabeth. "That is an uncommon advantage, and uncommon I hope it will continue, for it would be a great loss to *me* to have many such acquaintances. I dearly love a laugh."

"Miss Bingley," said he, "has given me more credit than can be. The wisest and the best of men—nay, the wisest and best of their actions—may be rendered ridiculous by a person whose first object in life is a joke."

"Certainly," replied Elizabeth—"there are such people, but I hope

I am not one of *them*. I hope I never ridicule what is wise and good. Follies and nonsense, whims and inconsistencies, *do* divert me, I own, and I laugh at them whenever I can. But these, I suppose, are precisely what you are without."

"Perhaps that is not possible for anyone. But it has been the study of my life to avoid those weaknesses which often expose a strong understanding to ridicule."

"Such as vanity and pride."

"Yes, vanity is a weakness indeed. But pride—where there is a real superiority of mind, pride will be always under good regulation."

Elizabeth turned away to hide a smile.

"Your examination of Mr. Darcy is over, I presume," said Miss Bingley; "and pray what is the result?"

"I am perfectly convinced by it that Mr. Darcy has no defect. He owns it himself without disguise."

"No," said Darcy, "I have made no such pretension. I have faults enough, but they are not, I hope, of understanding. My temper I dare not vouch for. It is, I believe, too little yielding—certainly too little for the convenience of the world. I cannot forget the follies and vices of other so soon as I ought, nor their offenses against myself. My feelings are not puffed about with every attempt to move them. My temper would perhaps be called resentful. My good opinion once lost, is lost forever."

"*That* is a failing indeed!" cried Elizabeth. "Implacable resentment *is* a shade in a character. But you have chosen your fault well. I really cannot *laugh* at it. You are safe from me."

"There is, I believe, in every disposition a tendency to some particular evil—a natural defect, which not even the best education can overcome."

"And *your* defect is to hate everybody."

"And yours," he replied with a smile, "is willfully to misunderstand them."

"Do let us have a little music," cried Miss Bingley, tired of a conversation in which she had no share. "Louisa, you will not mind my waking Mr. Hurst?"

Her sister had not the smallest objection, and the pianoforte was opened; and Darcy, after a few moments' recollection, was not sorry for it. He began to feel the danger of paying Elizabeth too much attention.

CHAPTER XII

In consequence of an agreement between the sisters, Elizabeth wrote the next morning to their mother, to beg that the carriage might be sent for them in the course of the day. But Mrs. Bennet, who had calculated on her daughters remaining at Netherfield till the following Tuesday, which would exactly finish Jane's week, could not bring herself to receive them with pleasure before. Her answer, therefore, was not propitious, at least not to Elizabeth's wishes, for she was impatient to get home. Mrs. Bennet sent them word that they could not possibly have the carriage before Tuesday; and in her postscript it was added, that if Mr. Bingley and his sister pressed them to stay longer, she could spare them very well. Against staying longer, however, Elizabeth was positively resolved—nor did she much expect it would be asked; and fearful, on the contrary, as being considered as intruding themselves needlessly long, she urged Jane to borrow Mr. Bingley's carriage immediately, and at length it was settled that their original design of leaving Netherfield that morning should be mentioned, and the request made.

The communication excited many professions of concern; and enough was said of wishing them to stay at least till the following day to work on Jane; and till the morrow their going was deferred. Miss Bingley was then sorry that she had proposed the delay, for her jealousy and dislike of one sister much exceeded her affection for the other.

The master of the house heard with real sorrow that they were to go so soon, and repeatedly tried to persuade Miss Bennet that it would not be safe for her—that she was not enough recovered; but Jane was firm where she felt herself to be right.

To Mr. Darcy it was welcome intelligence—Elizabeth had been at Netherfield long enough. She attracted him more than he liked—and Miss Bingley was uncivil to *her*, and more teasing than usual to himself. He wisely resolved to be particularly careful that no sign of admiration should *now* escape him, nothing that could elevate her with the hope of influencing his felicity; sensible that if such an idea had been suggested, his behaviour during the last day must have material weight in confirming or crushing it. Steady to his purpose, he scarcely spoke ten words to her through the whole of Saturday, and though they were at one time left by themselves for half-an-hour, he adhered most conscientiously to his book, and would not even look at her.

On Sunday, after morning service, the separation, so agreeable to almost all, took place. Miss Bingley's civility to Elizabeth increased at last very rapidly, as well as her affection for Jane; and when they parted, after assuring the latter of the pleasure it would always give her to see her either at Longbourn or Netherfield, and embracing her most tenderly, she even shook hands with the former. Elizabeth took leave of the whole party in the liveliest of spirits.

They were not welcomed home very cordially by their mother. Mrs. Bennet wondered at their coming, and thought them very wrong to give so much trouble, and was sure Jane would have caught cold again. But their father, though very laconic in his expressions of pleasure, was really glad to see them; he had felt their importance in the family circle. The evening conversation, when they were all assembled, had lost much of its animation, and almost all its sense by the absence of Jane and Elizabeth.

They found Mary, as usual, deep in the study of thorough-bass and human nature; and had some extracts to admire, and some new observations of threadbare morality to listen to. Catherine and Lydia had information for them of a different sort. Much had been done and much had been said in the regiment since the preceding Wednesday; several of the officers had dined lately with their uncle, a private had been flogged, and it had actually been hinted that Colonel Forster was going to be married.

CHAPTER XIII

"I hope, my dear," said Mr. Bennet to his wife, as they were at breakfast the next morning, "that you have ordered a good dinner to-day, because I have reason to expect an addition to our family party."

"Who do you mean, my dear? I know of nobody that is coming, I am sure, unless Charlotte Lucas should happen to call in—and I hope *my* dinners are good enough for her. I do not believe she often sees such at home."

"The person of whom I speak is a gentleman, and a stranger."

Mrs. Bennet's eyes sparkled. "A gentleman and a stranger! It is Mr. Bingley, I am sure! Well, I am sure I shall be extremely glad to see Mr. Bingley. But—good Lord! how unlucky! There is not a bit of fish to be got to-day. Lydia, my love, ring the bell—I must speak to Hill this moment."

"It is *not* Mr. Bingley," said her husband; "it is a person whom I never saw in the whole course of my life."

This roused a general astonishment; and he had the pleasure of being eagerly questioned by his wife and his five daughters at once.

After amusing himself some time with their curiosity, he thus explained:

"About a month ago I received this letter; and about a fortnight ago I answered it, for I thought it a case of some delicacy, and requiring early attention. It is from my cousin, Mr. Collins, who, when I am dead, may turn you all out of this house as soon as he pleases."

"Oh! my dear," cried his wife, "I cannot bear to hear that mentioned. Pray do not talk of that odious man. I do think it is the hardest thing in the world, that your estate should be entailed away from your own children; and I am sure, if I had been you, I should have tried long ago to do something or other about it."

Jane and Elizabeth tried to explain to her the nature of an entail. They had often attempted to do it before, but it was a subject on which Mrs. Bennet was beyond the reach of reason, and she continued to rail bitterly against the cruelty of settling an estate away from a family of five daughters, in favour of a man whom nobody cared anything about.

"It certainly is a most iniquitous affair," said Mr. Bennet, "and nothing can clear Mr. Collins from the guilt of inheriting Longbourn. But if you will listen to his letter, you may perhaps be a little softened by his manner of expressing himself."

"No, that I am sure I shall not; and I think it is very impertinent of him to write to you at all, and very hypocritical. I hate such false friends. Why could he not keep on quarreling with you, as his father did before him?"

"Why, indeed; he does seem to have had some filial scruples on that head, as you will hear."

"Hunsford, near Westerham, Kent, 15th October.

"Dear Sir,—

"The disagreement subsisting between yourself and my late honoured father always gave me much uneasiness, and since I have had the misfortune to lose him, I have frequently wished to heal the breach; but for some time I was kept back by my own doubts, fearing lest it might seem disrespectful to his memory for me to be on good terms with anyone with whom it had always pleased him to be at variance.—'There, Mrs. Bennet.'—My mind, however, is now made up on the subject, for having received ordination at Easter, I have been so fortunate as to be distinguished by the patronage of the Right Honourable Lady Catherine de Bourgh, widow of Sir Lewis de Bourgh, whose bounty and beneficence has preferred me to the valuable rectory of this parish, where it shall be my earnest endeavour to demean myself with grateful respect towards her ladyship, and be ever ready to perform those rites and ceremonies which are instituted by the Church of England. As a clergyman, moreover, I feel it my duty to promote and establish the blessing of peace in all families within the reach of my influence; and on these grounds I flatter myself that my present overtures are highly commendable, and that the circumstance of my being next in the entail of Longbourn estate will be kindly overlooked on your side, and not lead you to reject the offered olive-branch. I cannot be otherwise than concerned at being the means of injuring your amiable daughters, and beg leave to apologise for it, as well as to assure you of my readiness to make them every possible amends—but of this hereafter. If you should have no objection to receive me into your house, I propose myself the satisfaction of waiting on you and your family, Monday, November 18th, by four o'clock, and shall probably trespass on your hospitality till the Saturday se'nnight following, which I can do without any inconvenience, as Lady Catherine is far from objecting to my occasional absence on a Sunday, provided that some other clergyman is engaged to do the duty of the day.—I remain, dear sir, with respectful compliments to your lady and daughters, your well-wisher and friend,

"WILLIAM COLLINS"

"At four o'clock, therefore, we may expect this peace-making gentleman," said Mr. Bennet, as he folded up the letter. "He seems to be a most conscientious and polite young man, upon my word, and I doubt not will prove a valuable acquaintance, especially if Lady Catherine should be so indulgent as to let him come to us again."

"There is some sense in what he says about the girls, however, and if he is disposed to make them any amends, I shall not be the person to discourage him."

"Though it is difficult," said Jane, "to guess in what way he can mean to make us the atonement he thinks our due, the wish is certainly to his credit."

Elizabeth was chiefly struck by his extraordinary deference for Lady Catherine, and his kind intention of christening, marrying, and burying his parishioners whenever it were required.

"He must be an oddity, I think," said she. "I cannot make him out.—There is something very pompous in his style.—And what can he mean by apologising for being next in the entail?—We cannot suppose he would help it if he could.—Could he be a sensible man, sir?"

"No, my dear, I think not. I have great hopes of finding him quite the reverse. There is a mixture of servility and self-importance in his letter, which promises well. I am impatient to see him."

"In point of composition," said Mary, "the letter does not seem defective. The idea of the olive-branch perhaps is not wholly new, yet I think it is well expressed."

To Catherine and Lydia, neither the letter nor its writer were in any degree interesting. It was next to impossible that their cousin should come in a scarlet coat, and it was now some weeks since they had received pleasure from the society of a man in any other colour. As for their mother, Mr. Collins's letter had done away much of her ill-will, and she was preparing to see him with a degree of composure which astonished her husband and daughters.

Mr. Collins was punctual to his time, and was received with great politeness by the whole family. Mr. Bennet indeed said little; but the ladies were ready enough to talk, and Mr. Collins seemed neither in need of encouragement, nor inclined to be silent himself. He was a tall, heavy-looking young man of five-and-twenty. His air was grave and stately, and his manners were very formal. He had not been long seated before he complimented Mrs. Bennet on having so fine a family of daughters; said he had heard much of their beauty, but that in this instance fame had fallen short of the truth; and added, that he did not doubt her seeing them all in due time disposed of in marriage. This gallantry was not much to the taste of some of his hearers; but Mrs. Bennet, who quarreled with no compliments, answered most readily.

"You are very kind, I am sure; and I wish with all my heart it may prove so, for else they will be destitute enough. Things are settled so oddly."

"You allude, perhaps, to the entail of this estate."

"Ah! sir, I do indeed. It is a grievous affair to my poor girls, you must confess. Not that I mean to find fault with *you*, for such things I know are all chance in this world. There is no knowing how estates will go when once they come to be entailed."

"I am very sensible, madam, of the hardship to my fair cousins, and could say much on the subject, but that I am cautious of appearing forward and precipitate. But I can assure the young ladies that I come prepared to admire them. At present I will not say more; but, perhaps, when we are better acquainted—"

He was interrupted by a summons to dinner; and the girls smiled on each other. They were not the only objects of Mr. Collins's admiration. The hall, the dining-room, and all its furniture, were examined and praised; and his commendation of everything would have touched Mrs. Bennet's heart, but for the mortifying supposition of his viewing it all as his own future property. The dinner too in its turn was highly admired; and he begged to know to which of his fair cousins the excellency of its cooking was owing. But he was set right there by Mrs. Bennet, who assured him with some asperity that they were very well able to keep a good cook, and that her daughters had nothing to do in the kitchen. He begged pardon for having displeased her. In a softened tone she declared herself not at all offended; but he continued to apologise for about a quarter of an hour.

CHAPTER XIV

During dinner, Mr. Bennet scarcely spoke at all; but when the servants were withdrawn, he thought it time to have some conversation with his guest, and therefore started a subject in which he expected him to shine, by observing that he seemed very fortunate in his patroness. Lady Catherine de Bourgh's attention to his wishes, and consideration for his comfort, appeared very remarkable. Mr. Bennet could not have chosen better. Mr. Collins was eloquent in her praise. The subject elevated him to more than usual solemnity of manner, and with a most important aspect he protested that "he had never in his life witnessed such behaviour in a person of rank—such affability and condescension, as he had himself experienced from Lady Catherine. She had been graciously pleased to approve of both of the discourses which he had already had the honour of preaching before her. She had also asked him twice to dine at Rosings, and had sent for him only the Saturday before, to make up her pool of quadrille in the evening. Lady Catherine was reckoned proud by many people he knew, but *he* had never seen anything but affability in her. She had always spoken to him as she would to any other gentleman; she made not the smallest objection to his joining in the society of the neighbourhood nor to his leaving the parish occasionally for a week or two, to visit his relations. She had even condescended to advise him to marry as soon as he could, provided he chose with discretion; and had once paid him a visit in his humble parsonage, where she had perfectly approved all the alterations he had been making, and had even vouchsafed to suggest some herself—some shelves in the closet upstairs."

"That is all very proper and civil, I am sure," said Mrs. Bennet, "and I dare say she is a very agreeable woman. It is a pity that great ladies in general are not more like her. Does she live near you, sir?"

"The garden in which stands my humble abode is separated only by a lane from Rosings Park, her ladyship's residence."

"I think you said she was a widow, sir? Has she any family?"

"She has only one daughter, the heiress of Rosings, and of very extensive property."

"Ah!" said Mrs. Bennet, shaking her head, "then she is better off than many girls. And what sort of young lady is she? Is she handsome?"

"She is a most charming young lady indeed. Lady Catherine herself says that, in point of true beauty, Miss de Bourgh is far superior to the handsomest of her sex, because there is that in her features which marks the young lady of distinguished birth. She is unfortunately of a sickly constitution, which has prevented her from making that progress in many accomplishments which she could not have otherwise failed of, as I am informed by the lady who superintended her education, and who still resides with them. But she is perfectly amiable, and often condescends to drive by my humble abode in her little phaeton and ponies."

"Has she been presented? I do not remember her name among the ladies at court."

"Her indifferent state of health unhappily prevents her being in town; and by that means, as I told Lady Catherine one day, has deprived the British court of its brightest ornaments. Her ladyship seemed pleased with the idea; and you may imagine that I am happy on every occasion to offer those little delicate compliments which are always acceptable to ladies. I have more than once observed to Lady Catherine, that her charming daughter seemed born to be a duchess, and that the most elevated rank, instead of giving her consequence, would be adorned by her. These are the kind of little things which please her ladyship, and it is a sort of attention which I conceive myself peculiarly bound to pay."

"You judge very properly," said Mr. Bennet, "and it is happy for you that you possess the talent of flattering with delicacy. May I ask whether these pleasing attentions proceed from the impulse of the moment, or are the result of previous study?"

"They arise chiefly from what is passing at the time, and though I sometimes amuse myself with suggesting and arranging such little elegant compliments as may be adapted to ordinary occasions, I always wish to give them as unstudied an air as possible."

Mr. Bennet's expectations were fully answered. His cousin was as absurd as he had hoped, and he listened to him with the keenest enjoyment, maintaining at the same time the most resolute composure of countenance, and, except in an occasional glance at Elizabeth, requiring no partner in his pleasure.

By tea-time, however, the dose had been enough, and Mr. Bennet was glad to take his guest into the drawing-room again, and, when tea was over, glad to invite him to read aloud to the ladies. Mr. Collins readily assented, and a book was produced; but, on beholding it (for everything announced it to be from a circulating library), he started back, and begging pardon, protested that he never read novels. Kitty stared at him, and Lydia exclaimed. Other books were produced, and after some deliberation he chose Fordyce's Sermons. Lydia gaped as he opened the volume, and before he had, with very monotonous solemnity, read three pages, she interrupted him with:

"Do you know, mamma, that my uncle Phillips talks of turning away Richard; and if he does, Colonel Forster will hire him. My aunt told me so herself on Saturday. I shall walk to Meryton to-morrow to hear more about it, and to ask when Mr. Denny comes back from town."

Lydia was bid by her two eldest sisters to hold her tongue; but Mr. Collins, much offended, laid aside his book, and said:

"I have often observed how little young ladies are interested by books of a serious stamp, though written solely for their benefit. It amazes me, I confess; for, certainly, there can be nothing so advantageous to them as instruction. But I will no longer importune my young cousin."

Then turning to Mr. Bennet, he offered himself as his antagonist at backgammon. Mr. Bennet accepted the challenge, observing that he acted very wisely in leaving the girls to their own trifling amusements. Mrs. Bennet and her daughters apologised most civilly for Lydia's interruption, and promised that it should not occur again, if he would resume his book; but Mr. Collins, after assuring them that he bore his young cousin no ill-will, and should never resent her behaviour as any affront, seated himself at another table with Mr. Bennet, and prepared for backgammon.

CHAPTER XV

Mr. Collins was not a sensible man, and the deficiency of nature had been but little assisted by education or society; the greatest part of his life having been spent under the guidance of an illiterate and miserly father; and though he belonged to one of the universities, he had merely kept the necessary terms, without forming at it any useful acquaintance. The subjection in which his father had brought him up had given him originally great humility of manner; but it was now a good deal counteracted by the self-conceit of a weak head, living in retirement, and the consequential feelings of early and unexpected prosperity. A fortunate chance had recommended him to Lady Catherine de Bourgh when the living of Hunsford was vacant; and the respect which he felt for her high rank, and his veneration for her as his patroness, mingling with a very good opinion of himself, of his authority as a clergyman, and his right as a rector, made him altogether a mixture of pride and obsequiousness, self-importance and humility.

Having now a good house and a very sufficient income, he intended to marry; and in seeking a reconciliation with the Longbourn family he had a wife in view, as he meant to choose one of the daughters, if he found them as handsome and amiable as they were represented by common report. This was his plan of amends—of atonement—for inheriting their father's estate; and he thought it an excellent one, full of eligibility and suitableness, and excessively generous and disinterested on his own part.

His plan did not vary on seeing them. Miss Bennet's lovely face confirmed his views, and established all his strictest notions of what was due to seniority; and for the first evening *she* was his settled choice. The next morning, however, made an alteration; for in a quarter of an hour's tete-a-tete with Mrs. Bennet before breakfast, a conversation beginning with his parsonage-house, and leading naturally to the avowal of his hopes, that a mistress might be found for it at Longbourn, produced from her, amid very complaisant smiles and general encouragement, a caution against the very Jane he had fixed on. "As to her *younger* daughters, she could not take upon her to say—she could not positively answer—but she did not *know* of any prepossession; her *eldest* daughter, she must just mention—she felt it incumbent on her to hint, was likely to be very soon engaged."

Mr. Collins had only to change from Jane to Elizabeth—and it was soon done—done while Mrs. Bennet was stirring the fire. Elizabeth, equally next to Jane in birth and beauty, succeeded her of course.

Mrs. Bennet treasured up the hint, and trusted that she might soon have two daughters married; and the man whom she could not bear to speak of the day before was now high in her good graces.

Lydia's intention of walking to Meryton was not forgotten; every sister except Mary agreed to go with her; and Mr. Collins was to attend them, at the request of Mr. Bennet, who was most anxious to get rid of him, and have his library to himself; for thither Mr. Collins had followed him after breakfast; and there he would continue, nominally engaged with one of the largest folios in the collection, but really talking to Mr. Bennet, with little cessation, of his house and garden at Hunsford. Such doings discomposed Mr. Bennet exceedingly. In his library he had been always sure of leisure and tranquillity; and though prepared, as he told Elizabeth, to meet with folly and conceit in every other room of the house, he was used to be free from them there; his civility, therefore, was most prompt in inviting Mr. Collins to join his daughters in their walk; and Mr. Collins, being in fact much better fitted for a walker than a reader, was extremely pleased to close his large book, and go.

In pompous nothings on his side, and civil assents on that of his cousins, their time passed till they entered Meryton. The attention of the younger ones was then no longer to be gained by him. Their eyes were immediately wandering up in the street in quest of the officers, and nothing less than a very smart bonnet indeed, or a really new muslin in a shop window, could recall them.

But the attention of every lady was soon caught by a young man, whom they had never seen before, of most gentlemanlike appearance, walking with another officer on the other side of the way. The officer was the very Mr. Denny concerning whose return from London Lydia came to inquire, and he bowed as they passed. All were struck with the stranger's air, all wondered who he could be; and Kitty and Lydia, determined if possible to find out, led the way across the street, under pretense of wanting something in an opposite shop, and fortunately had just gained the pavement when the two gentlemen, turning back, had reached the same spot. Mr. Denny addressed them directly, and entreated permission to introduce his friend, Mr. Wickham, who had returned with him the day before from town, and he was happy to say had accepted a commission in their corps. This was exactly as it should be; for the young man wanted only regimentals to make him completely charming. His appearance was greatly in his favour; he had all the best part of beauty, a fine countenance, a good figure, and very pleasing address. The introduction was followed up on his side by a happy readiness of conversation—a readiness at the same time perfectly correct and unassuming; and the whole party were still standing and talking together very agreeably, when the sound of horses drew their notice, and Darcy and Bingley were seen riding down the street. On distinguishing the ladies of the group, the two gentlemen came directly towards them, and began the usual civilities. Bingley was the principal spokesman, and Miss Bennet the principal object. He was then, he said, on his way to Longbourn on purpose to inquire after her. Mr. Darcy corroborated it with a bow, and was beginning to determine not to fix his eyes on Elizabeth, when they were suddenly arrested by the sight of the stranger, and Elizabeth happening to see the countenance of both as they looked at each other, was all astonishment at the effect of the meeting. Both changed colour, one looked white, the other red. Mr. Wickham, after a few moments, touched his hat—a salutation which Mr. Darcy just deigned to return. What could be the meaning of it? It was impossible to imagine; it was impossible not to long to know.

In another minute, Mr. Bingley, but without seeming to have noticed what passed, took leave and rode on with his friend.

Mr. Denny and Mr. Wickham walked with the young ladies to the door of Mr. Phillips's house, and then made their bows, in spite of Miss Lydia's pressing entreaties that they should come in, and even in spite of Mrs. Phillips's throwing up the parlour window and loudly seconding the invitation.

Mrs. Phillips was always glad to see her nieces; and the two eldest, from their recent absence, were particularly welcome, and she was eagerly expressing her surprise at their sudden return home, which, as their own carriage had not fetched them, she should have known nothing about, if she had not happened to see Mr. Jones's shop-boy in the street, who had told her that they were not to send any more draughts to Netherfield because the Miss Bennets were come away, when her civility was claimed towards Mr. Collins by Jane's introduction of him. She received him with her very best politeness, which he returned with as much more, apologising for his intrusion, without any previous acquaintance with her, which he could not help flattering himself, however, might be justified by his relationship to the young ladies who introduced him to her notice. Mrs. Phillips was quite awed by such an excess of good breeding; but her contemplation of one stranger was soon put to an end by exclamations and inquiries about the other; of whom, however, she could only tell her nieces what they already knew, that Mr. Denny had brought him from London, and that he was to have a lieutenant's commission in the ——shire. She had been watching him the last hour, she said, as he walked up and down the street, and had Mr. Wickham appeared, Kitty and Lydia would certainly have continued the occupation, but unluckily no one passed windows now except a few of the officers, who, in comparison with the stranger, were become "stupid, disagreeable fellows." Some of them were to dine with the Phillipses the next day, and their aunt promised to make her husband call on Mr. Wickham, and give him an invitation also, if the family from Longbourn would come in the evening. This was agreed to, and Mrs. Phillips protested that they would have a nice comfortable noisy game of lottery tickets, and a little bit of hot supper afterwards. The prospect of such delights was very cheering, and they parted in mutual good spirits. Mr. Collins repeated his apologies in quitting the room, and was assured with unwearying civility that they were perfectly needless.

As they walked home, Elizabeth related to Jane what she had seen pass between the two gentlemen; but though Jane would have defended either or both, had they appeared to be in the wrong, she could no more explain such behaviour than her sister.

Mr. Collins on his return highly gratified Mrs. Bennet by admiring Mrs. Phillips's manners and politeness. He protested that, except Lady Catherine and her daughter, he had never seen a more elegant woman; for she had not only received him with the utmost civility, but even pointedly included him in her invitation for the next evening, although utterly unknown to her before. Something, he supposed, might be attributed to his connection with them, but yet he had never met with so much attention in the whole course of his life.

CHAPTER XVI

As no objection was made to the young people's engagement with their aunt, and all Mr. Collins's scruples of leaving Mr. and Mrs. Bennet for a single evening during his visit were most steadily resisted, the coach conveyed him and his five cousins at a suitable hour to Meryton; and the girls had the pleasure of hearing, as they entered the drawing-room, that Mr. Wickham had accepted their uncle's invitation, and was then in the house.

When this information was given, and they had all taken their seats, Mr. Collins was at leisure to look around him and admire, and he was so much struck with the size and furniture of the apartment, that he declared he might almost have supposed himself in the small summer breakfast parlour at Rosings; a comparison that did not at first convey much gratification; but when Mrs. Phillips understood from him what Rosings was, and who was its proprietor—when she had listened to the description of only one of Lady Catherine's drawing-rooms, and found that the chimney-piece alone had cost eight hundred pounds, she felt all the force of the compliment, and would hardly have resented a comparison with the housekeeper's room.

In describing to her all the grandeur of Lady Catherine and her mansion, with occasional digressions in praise of his own humble abode, and the improvements it was receiving, he was happily employed until the gentlemen joined them; and he found in Mrs. Phillips a very attentive listener, whose opinion of his consequence increased with what she heard, and who was resolving to retail it all among her neighbours as soon as she could. To the girls, who could not listen to their cousin, and who had nothing to do but to wish for an instrument, and examine their own indifferent imitations of china on the mantelpiece, the interval of waiting appeared very long. It was over at last, however. The gentlemen did approach, and when Mr. Wickham walked into the room, Elizabeth felt that she had neither been seeing him before, nor thinking of him since, with the smallest degree of unreasonable admiration. The officers of the ——shire were in general a very creditable, gentlemanlike set, and the best of them were of the present party; but Mr. Wickham was as far beyond them all in person, countenance, air, and walk, as *they* were superior to the broad-faced, stuffy uncle Phillips, breathing port wine, who followed them into the room.

Mr. Wickham was the happy man towards whom almost every female eye was turned, and Elizabeth was the happy woman by whom he finally seated himself; and the agreeable manner in which he immediately fell into conversation, though it was only on its being a wet night, made her feel that the commonest, dullest, most threadbare topic might be rendered interesting by the skill of the speaker.

With such rivals for the notice of the fair as Mr. Wickham and the officers, Mr. Collins seemed to sink into insignificance; to the young ladies he certainly was nothing; but he had still at intervals a kind listener in Mrs. Phillips, and was by her watchfulness, most abundantly supplied with coffee and muffin. When the card-tables were placed, he had the opportunity of obliging her in turn, by sitting down to whist.

"I know little of the game at present," said he, "but I shall be glad to improve myself, for in my situation in life—" Mrs. Phillips was very glad for his compliance, but could not wait for his reason.

Mr. Wickham did not play at whist, and with ready delight was he received at the other table between Elizabeth and Lydia. At first there seemed danger of Lydia's engrossing him entirely, for she was a most determined talker; but being likewise extremely fond of lottery tickets, she soon grew too much interested in the game, too eager in making bets and exclaiming after prizes to have attention for anyone in particular. Allowing for the common demands of the game, Mr. Wickham was therefore at leisure to talk to Elizabeth, and she was very willing to hear him, though what she chiefly wished to hear she could not hope to be told—the history of his acquaintance with Mr. Darcy. She dared not even mention that gentleman. Her curiosity, however, was unexpectedly relieved. Mr. Wickham began the subject himself. He inquired how far Netherfield was from Meryton; and, after receiving her answer, asked in a hesitating manner how long Mr. Darcy had been staying there.

"About a month," said Elizabeth; and then, unwilling to let the subject drop, added, "He is a man of very large property in Derbyshire, I understand."

"Yes," replied Mr. Wickham; "his estate there is a noble one. A clear ten thousand per annum. You could not have met with a person more capable of giving you certain information on that head than myself, for I have been connected with his family in a particular manner from my infancy."

Elizabeth could not but look surprised.

"You may well be surprised, Miss Bennet, at such an assertion, after seeing, as you probably might, the very cold manner of our meeting yesterday. Are you much acquainted with Mr. Darcy?"

"As much as I ever wish to be," cried Elizabeth very warmly. "I have spent four days in the same house with him, and I think him very disagreeable."

"I have no right to give *my* opinion," said Wickham, "as to his being agreeable or otherwise. I am not qualified to form one. I have known him too long and too well to be a fair judge. It is impossible for *me* to be impartial. But I believe your opinion of him would in general astonish—and perhaps you would not express it quite so strongly anywhere else. Here you are in your own family."

"Upon my word, I say no more *here* than I might say in any house in the neighbourhood, except Netherfield. He is not at all liked in Hertfordshire. Everybody is disgusted with his pride. You will not find him more favourably spoken of by anyone."

"I cannot pretend to be sorry," said Wickham, after a short interruption, "that he or that any man should not be estimated beyond their deserts; but with *him* I believe it does not often happen. The world is blinded by his fortune and consequence, or frightened by his high and imposing manners, and sees him only as he chooses to be seen."

"I should take him, even on *my* slight acquaintance, to be an ill-tempered man." Wickham only shook his head.

"I wonder," said he, at the next opportunity of speaking, "whether he is likely to be in this country much longer."

"I do not at all know; but I *heard* nothing of his going away when I was at Netherfield. I hope your plans in favour of the ——shire will not be affected by his being in the neighbourhood."

"Oh! no—it is not for *me* to be driven away by Mr. Darcy. If *he* wishes to avoid seeing *me*, he must go. We are not on friendly terms, and it always gives me pain to meet him, but I have no reason for avoiding *him* but what I might proclaim before all the world, a sense of very great ill-usage, and most painful regrets at his being what he is. His father, Miss Bennet, the late Mr. Darcy, was one of the best men that ever breathed, and the truest friend I ever had; and I can never be in company with this Mr. Darcy without being grieved to the soul by a thousand tender recollections. His behaviour to myself has been scandalous; but I verily believe I could forgive him anything and everything, rather than his disappointing the hopes and disgracing the memory of his father."

Elizabeth found the interest of the subject increase, and listened with all her heart; but the delicacy of it prevented further inquiry.

Mr. Wickham began to speak on more general topics, Meryton, the neighbourhood, the society, appearing highly pleased with all that he had yet seen, and speaking of the latter with gentle but very intelligible gallantry.

"It was the prospect of constant society, and good society," he added, "which was my chief inducement to enter the ——shire. I knew it to be a most respectable, agreeable corps, and my friend Denny tempted me further by his account of their present quarters, and the very great attentions and excellent acquaintances Meryton had procured them. Society, I own, is necessary to me. I have been a disappointed man, and my spirits will not bear solitude. I *must* have employment and society. A military life is not what I was intended for, but circumstances have now made it eligible. The church *ought* to have been my profession—I was brought up for the church, and I should at this time have been in possession of a most valuable living, had it pleased the gentleman we were speaking of just now."

"Indeed!"

"Yes—the late Mr. Darcy bequeathed me the next presentation of the best living in his gift. He was my godfather, and excessively attached to me. I cannot do justice to his kindness. He meant to provide for me amply, and thought he had done it; but when the living fell, it was given elsewhere."

"Good heavens!" cried Elizabeth; "but how could *that* be? How could his will be disregarded? Why did you not seek legal redress?"

"There was just such an informality in the terms of the bequest as to give me no hope from law. A man of honour could not have doubted the intention, but Mr. Darcy chose to doubt it—or to treat it as a merely conditional recommendation, and to assert that I had forfeited all claim to it by extravagance, imprudence—in short anything or nothing. Certain it is, that the living became vacant two years ago, exactly as

I was of an age to hold it, and that it was given to another man; and no less certain is it, that I cannot accuse myself of having really done anything to deserve to lose it. I have a warm, unguarded temper, and I may have spoken my opinion *of* him, and *to* him, too freely. I can recall nothing worse. But the fact is, that we are very different sort of men, and that he hates me."

"This is quite shocking! He deserves to be publicly disgraced."

"Some time or other he *will* be—but it shall not be by *me*. Till I can forget his father, I can never defy or expose *him*."

Elizabeth honoured him for such feelings, and thought him handsomer than ever as he expressed them.

"But what," said she, after a pause, "can have been his motive? What can have induced him to behave so cruelly?"

"A thorough, determined dislike of me—a dislike which I cannot but attribute in some measure to jealousy. Had the late Mr. Darcy liked me less, his son might have borne with me better; but his father's uncommon attachment to me irritated him, I believe, very early in life. He had not a temper to bear the sort of competition in which we stood—the sort of preference which was often given me."

"I had not thought Mr. Darcy so bad as this—though I have never liked him. I had not thought so very ill of him. I had supposed him to be despising his fellow-creatures in general, but did not suspect him of descending to such malicious revenge, such injustice, such inhumanity as this."

After a few minutes' reflection, however, she continued, "I *do* remember his boasting one day, at Netherfield, of the implacability of his resentments, of his having an unforgiving temper. His disposition must be dreadful."

"I will not trust myself on the subject," replied Wickham; "I can hardly be just to him."

Elizabeth was again deep in thought, and after a time exclaimed, "To treat in such a manner the godson, the friend, the favourite of his father!" She could have added, "A young man, too, like *you*, whose very countenance may vouch for your being amiable"—but she contented herself with, "and one, too, who had probably been his companion from childhood, connected together, as I think you said, in the closest manner!"

"We were born in the same parish, within the same park; the greatest part of our youth was passed together; inmates of the same house, sharing the same amusements, objects of the same parental care. *My* father began life in the profession which your uncle, Mr. Phillips, appears to do so much credit to—but he gave up everything to be of use to the late Mr. Darcy and devoted all his time to the care of the Pemberley property. He was most highly esteemed by Mr. Darcy, a most intimate, confidential friend. Mr. Darcy often acknowledged himself to be under the greatest obligations to my father's active superintendence, and when, immediately before my father's death, Mr. Darcy gave him a voluntary promise of providing for me, I am convinced that he felt it to be as much a debt of gratitude to *him*, as of his affection to myself."

"How strange!" cried Elizabeth. "How abominable! I wonder that the very pride of this Mr. Darcy has not made him just to you! If from no better motive, that he should not have been too proud to be dishonest—for dishonesty I must call it."

"It *is* wonderful," replied Wickham, "for almost all his actions may be traced to pride; and pride had often been his best friend. It has connected him nearer with virtue than with any other feeling. But we are none of us consistent, and in his behaviour to me there were stronger impulses even than pride."

"Can such abominable pride as his have ever done him good?"

"Yes. It has often led him to be liberal and generous, to give his money freely, to display hospitality, to assist his tenants, and relieve the poor. Family pride, and *filial* pride—for he is very proud of what his father was—have done this. Not to appear to disgrace his family, to degenerate from the popular qualities, or lose the influence of the Pemberley House, is a powerful motive. He has also *brotherly* pride, which, with *some* brotherly affection, makes him a very kind and careful guardian of his sister, and you will hear him generally cried up as the most attentive and best of brothers."

"What sort of girl is Miss Darcy?"

He shook his head. "I wish I could call her amiable. It gives me pain to speak ill of a Darcy. But she is too much like her brother—very, very proud. As a child, she was affectionate and pleasing, and extremely fond of me; and I have devoted hours and hours to her amusement. But she is nothing to me now. She is a handsome girl, about fifteen or sixteen, and, I understand, highly accomplished. Since her father's death, her home has been London, where a lady lives with her, and superintends her education."

After many pauses and many trials of other subjects, Elizabeth could not help reverting once more to the first, and saying:

"I am astonished at his intimacy with Mr. Bingley! How can Mr. Bingley, who seems good humour itself, and is, I really believe, truly amiable, be in friendship with such a man? How can they suit each other? Do you know Mr. Bingley?"

"Not at all."

"He is a sweet-tempered, amiable, charming man. He cannot know what Mr. Darcy is."

"Probably not; but Mr. Darcy can please where he chooses. He does not want abilities. He can be a conversible companion if he thinks it worth his while. Among those who are at all his equals in consequence, he is a very different man from what he is to the less prosperous. His pride never deserts him; but with the rich he is liberal-minded, just, sincere, rational, honourable, and perhaps agreeable—allowing something for fortune and figure."

The whist party soon afterwards breaking up, the players gathered round the other table and Mr. Collins took his station between his cousin Elizabeth and Mrs. Phillips. The usual inquiries as to his success was made by the latter. It had not been very great; he had lost every point; but when Mrs. Phillips began to express her concern thereupon, he assured her with much earnest gravity that it was not of the least importance, that he considered the money as a mere trifle, and begged that she would not make herself uneasy.

"I know very well, madam," said he, "that when persons sit down to a card-table, they must take their chances of these things, and happily I am not in such circumstances as to make five shillings any object. There are undoubtedly many who could not say the same, but thanks to Lady Catherine de Bourgh, I am removed far beyond the necessity of regarding little matters."

Mr. Wickham's attention was caught; and after observing Mr. Collins for a few moments, he asked Elizabeth in a low voice whether her relation was very intimately acquainted with the family of de Bourgh.

"Lady Catherine de Bourgh," she replied, "has very lately given him a living. I hardly know how Mr. Collins was first introduced to her notice, but he certainly has not known her long."

"You know of course that Lady Catherine de Bourgh and Lady

Anne Darcy were sisters; consequently that she is aunt to the present Mr. Darcy."

"No, indeed, I did not. I knew nothing at all of Lady Catherine's connections. I never heard of her existence till the day before yesterday."

"Her daughter, Miss de Bourgh, will have a very large fortune, and it is believed that she and her cousin will unite the two estates."

This information made Elizabeth smile, as she thought of poor Miss Bingley. Vain indeed must be all her attentions, vain and useless her affection for his sister and her praise of himself, if he were already self-destined for another.

"Mr. Collins," said she, "speaks highly both of Lady Catherine and her daughter; but from some particulars that he has related of her ladyship, I suspect his gratitude misleads him, and that in spite of her being his patroness, she is an arrogant, conceited woman."

"I believe her to be both in a great degree," replied Wickham; "I have not seen her for many years, but I very well remember that I never liked her, and that her manners were dictatorial and insolent. She has the reputation of being remarkably sensible and clever; but I rather believe she derives part of her abilities from her rank and fortune, part from her authoritative manner, and the rest from the pride for her nephew, who chooses that everyone connected with him should have an understanding of the first class."

Elizabeth allowed that he had given a very rational account of it, and they continued talking together, with mutual satisfaction till supper put an end to cards, and gave the rest of the ladies their share of Mr. Wickham's attentions. There could be no conversation in the noise of Mrs. Phillips's supper party, but his manners recommended him to everybody. Whatever he said, was said well; and whatever he did, done gracefully. Elizabeth went away with her head full of him. She could think of nothing but of Mr. Wickham, and of what he had told her, all the way home; but there was not time for her even to mention his name as they went, for neither Lydia nor Mr. Collins were once silent. Lydia talked incessantly of lottery tickets, of the fish she had lost and the fish she had won; and Mr. Collins in describing the civility of Mr. and Mrs. Phillips, protesting that he did not in the least regard his losses at whist, enumerating all the dishes at supper, and repeatedly fearing that he crowded his cousins, had more to say than he could well manage before the carriage stopped at Longbourn House.

CHAPTER XVII

Elizabeth related to Jane the next day what had passed between Mr. Wickham and herself. Jane listened with astonishment and concern; she knew not how to believe that Mr. Darcy could be so unworthy of Mr. Bingley's regard; and yet, it was not in her nature to question the veracity of a young man of such amiable appearance as Wickham. The possibility of his having endured such unkindness, was enough to interest all her tender feelings; and nothing remained therefore to be done, but to think well of them both, to defend the conduct of each, and throw into the account of accident or mistake whatever could not be otherwise explained.

"They have both," said she, "been deceived, I dare say, in some way or other, of which we can form no idea. Interested people have perhaps misrepresented each to the other. It is, in short, impossible for us to conjecture the causes or circumstances which may have alienated them, without actual blame on either side."

"Very true, indeed; and now, my dear Jane, what have you got to say on behalf of the interested people who have probably been concerned in the business? Do clear *them* too, or we shall be obliged to think ill of somebody."

"Laugh as much as you choose, but you will not laugh me out of my opinion. My dearest Lizzy, do but consider in what a disgraceful light it places Mr. Darcy, to be treating his father's favourite in such a manner, one whom his father had promised to provide for. It is impossible. No man of common humanity, no man who had any value for his character, could be capable of it. Can his most intimate friends be so excessively deceived in him? Oh! no."

"I can much more easily believe Mr. Bingley's being imposed on, than that Mr. Wickham should invent such a history of himself as he gave me last night; names, facts, everything mentioned without ceremony. If it be not so, let Mr. Darcy contradict it. Besides, there was truth in his looks."

"It is difficult indeed—it is distressing. One does not know what to think."

"I beg your pardon; one knows exactly what to think."

But Jane could think with certainty on only one point—that Mr. Bingley, if he *had* been imposed on, would have much to suffer when the affair became public.

The two young ladies were summoned from the shrubbery, where this conversation passed, by the arrival of the very persons of whom they had been speaking; Mr. Bingley and his sisters came to give their personal invitation for the long-expected ball at Netherfield, which was fixed for the following Tuesday. The two ladies were delighted to see their dear friend again, called it an age since they had met, and repeatedly asked what she had been doing with herself since their separation. To the rest of the family they paid little attention; avoiding Mrs. Bennet as much as possible, saying not much to Elizabeth, and nothing at all to the others. They were soon gone again, rising from their seats with an activity which took their brother by surprise, and hurrying off as if eager to escape from Mrs. Bennet's civilities.

The prospect of the Netherfield ball was extremely agreeable to every female of the family. Mrs. Bennet chose to consider it as given in compliment to her eldest daughter, and was particularly flattered by receiving the invitation from Mr. Bingley himself, instead of a ceremonious card. Jane pictured to herself a happy evening in the society of her two friends, and the attentions of their brother; and Elizabeth thought with pleasure of dancing a great deal with Mr. Wickham, and of seeing a confirmation of everything in Mr. Darcy's look and behaviour. The happiness anticipated by Catherine and Lydia depended less on any single event, or any particular person, for though they each, like Elizabeth, meant to dance half the evening with Mr. Wickham, he was by no means the only partner who could satisfy them, and a ball was, at any rate, a ball. And even Mary could assure her family that she had no disinclination for it.

"While I can have my mornings to myself," said she, "it is enough—I think it is no sacrifice to join occasionally in evening engagements. Society has claims on us all; and I profess myself one of those who consider intervals of recreation and amusement as desirable for everybody."

Elizabeth's spirits were so high on this occasion, that though she did not often speak unnecessarily to Mr. Collins, she could not help asking him whether he intended to accept Mr. Bingley's invitation, and if he did, whether he would think it proper to join in the evening's amusement; and she was rather surprised to find that he entertained no scruple whatever on that head, and was very far from dreading a rebuke either from the Archbishop, or Lady Catherine de Bourgh, by venturing to dance.

"I am by no means of the opinion, I assure you," said he, "that a ball of this kind, given by a young man of character, to respectable people, can have any evil tendency; and I am so far from objecting to dancing myself, that I shall hope to be honoured with the hands of all my fair cousins in the course of the evening; and I take this opportunity of soliciting yours, Miss Elizabeth, for the two first dances especially, a preference which I trust my cousin Jane will attribute to the right cause, and not to any disrespect for her."

Elizabeth felt herself completely taken in. She had fully proposed being engaged by Mr. Wickham for those very dances; and to have Mr. Collins instead! her liveliness had never been worse timed. There was no help for it, however. Mr. Wickham's happiness and her own were perforce delayed a little longer, and Mr. Collins's proposal accepted with as good a grace as she could. She was not the better pleased with his gallantry from the idea it suggested of something more. It now first struck her, that *she* was selected from among her sisters as worthy of being mistress of Hunsford Parsonage, and of assisting to form a quadrille table at Rosings, in the absence of more eligible visitors. The idea soon reached to conviction, as she observed his increasing civilities toward herself, and heard his frequent attempt at a compliment on her wit and vivacity; and though more astonished than gratified herself by this effect of her charms, it was not long before her mother gave her to understand that the probability of their marriage was extremely agreeable to *her*. Elizabeth, however, did not choose to take the hint, being well aware that a serious dispute must be the consequence of any reply. Mr. Collins might never make the offer, and till he did, it was useless to quarrel about him.

If there had not been a Netherfield ball to prepare for and talk of, the younger Miss Bennets would have been in a very pitiable state at this time, for from the day of the invitation, to the day of the ball, there was such a succession of rain as prevented their walking to Meryton once. No aunt, no officers, no news could be sought after—the very shoe-roses for Netherfield were got by proxy. Even Elizabeth might have found some trial of her patience in weather which totally suspended the improvement of her acquaintance with Mr. Wickham; and nothing less than a dance on Tuesday, could have made such a Friday, Saturday, Sunday, and Monday endurable to Kitty and Lydia.

CHAPTER XVIII

Till Elizabeth entered the drawing-room at Netherfield, and looked in vain for Mr. Wickham among the cluster of red coats there assembled, a doubt of his being present had never occurred to her. The certainty of meeting him had not been checked by any of those recollections that might not unreasonably have alarmed her. She had dressed with more than usual care, and prepared in the highest spirits for the conquest of all that remained unsubdued of his heart, trusting that it was not more than might be won in the course of the evening. But in an instant arose the dreadful suspicion of his being purposely omitted for Mr. Darcy's pleasure in the Bingleys' invitation to the officers; and though this was not exactly the case, the absolute fact of his absence was pronounced by his friend Denny, to whom Lydia eagerly applied, and who told them that Wickham had been obliged to go to town on business the day before, and was not yet returned; adding, with a significant smile, "I do not imagine his business would have called him away just now, if he had not wanted to avoid a certain gentleman here."

This part of his intelligence, though unheard by Lydia, was caught by Elizabeth, and, as it assured her that Darcy was not less answerable for Wickham's absence than if her first surmise had been just, every feeling of displeasure against the former was so sharpened by immediate disappointment, that she could hardly reply with tolerable civility to the polite inquiries which he directly afterwards approached to make. Attendance, forbearance, patience with Darcy, was injury to Wickham. She was resolved against any sort of conversation with him, and turned away with a degree of ill-humour which she could not wholly surmount even in speaking to Mr. Bingley, whose blind partiality provoked her.

But Elizabeth was not formed for ill-humour; and though every prospect of her own was destroyed for the evening, it could not dwell long on her spirits; and having told all her griefs to Charlotte Lucas, whom she had not seen for a week, she was soon able to make a voluntary transition to the oddities of her cousin, and to point him out to her particular notice. The first two dances, however, brought a return of distress; they were dances of mortification. Mr. Collins, awkward and solemn, apologising instead of attending, and often moving wrong without being aware of it, gave her all the shame and misery which a disagreeable partner for a couple of dances can give. The moment of her release from him was ecstasy.

She danced next with an officer, and had the refreshment of talking of Wickham, and of hearing that he was universally liked. When those dances were over, she returned to Charlotte Lucas, and was in conversation with her, when she found herself suddenly addressed by Mr. Darcy who took her so much by surprise in his application for her hand, that, without knowing what she did, she accepted him. He walked away again immediately, and she was left to fret over her own want of presence of mind; Charlotte tried to console her:

"I dare say you will find him very agreeable."

"Heaven forbid! *That* would be the greatest misfortune of all! To find a man agreeable whom one is determined to hate! Do not wish me such an evil."

When the dancing recommenced, however, and Darcy approached to claim her hand, Charlotte could not help cautioning her in a whisper, not to be a simpleton, and allow her fancy for Wickham to make her appear unpleasant in the eyes of a man ten times his consequence. Elizabeth made no answer, and took her place in the set, amazed at the dignity to which she was arrived in being allowed to stand opposite to Mr. Darcy, and reading in her neighbours' looks, their equal amazement in beholding it. They stood for some time without speaking a word; and she began to imagine that their silence was to last through the two dances, and at first was resolved not to break it; till suddenly fancying that it would be the greater punishment to her partner to oblige him to talk, she made some slight observation on the dance. He replied, and was again silent. After a pause of some minutes, she addressed him a second time with:—"It is *your* turn to say something now, Mr. Darcy. I talked about the dance, and *you* ought to make some sort of remark on the size of the room, or the number of couples."

He smiled, and assured her that whatever she wished him to say should be said.

"Very well. That reply will do for the present. Perhaps by and by I may observe that private balls are much pleasanter than public ones. But *now* we may be silent."

"Do you talk by rule, then, while you are dancing?"

"Sometimes. One must speak a little, you know. It would look odd to be entirely silent for half an hour together; and yet for the advantage of *some*, conversation ought to be so arranged, as that they may have the trouble of saying as little as possible."

"Are you consulting your own feelings in the present case, or do you imagine that you are gratifying mine?"

"Both," replied Elizabeth archly; "for I have always seen a great similarity in the turn of our minds. We are each of an unsocial, taciturn disposition, unwilling to speak, unless we expect to say something that will amaze the whole room, and be handed down to posterity with all the eclat of a proverb."

"This is no very striking resemblance of your own character, I am sure," said he. "How near it may be to *mine*, I cannot pretend to say. *You* think it a faithful portrait undoubtedly."

"I must not decide on my own performance."

He made no answer, and they were again silent till they had gone down the dance, when he asked her if she and her sisters did not very often walk to Meryton. She answered in the affirmative, and, unable to resist the temptation, added, "When you met us there the other day, we had just been forming a new acquaintance."

The effect was immediate. A deeper shade of *hauteur* overspread his features, but he said not a word, and Elizabeth, though blaming herself for her own weakness, could not go on. At length Darcy spoke, and in a constrained manner said, "Mr. Wickham is blessed with such happy manners as may ensure his *making* friends—whether he may be equally capable of *retaining* them, is less certain."

"He has been so unlucky as to lose *your* friendship," replied Elizabeth with emphasis, "and in a manner which he is likely to suffer from all his life."

Darcy made no answer, and seemed desirous of changing the subject. At that moment, Sir William Lucas appeared close to them, meaning to pass through the set to the other side of the room; but on perceiving Mr. Darcy, he stopped with a bow of superior courtesy to compliment him on his dancing and his partner.

"I have been most highly gratified indeed, my dear sir. Such very superior dancing is not often seen. It is evident that you belong to the first circles. Allow me to say, however, that your fair partner does not disgrace you, and that I must hope to have this pleasure often repeated, especially when a certain desirable event, my dear Eliza (glancing at her sister and Bingley) shall take place. What congratulations will then flow in! I appeal to Mr. Darcy:—but let me not interrupt you, sir. You will not thank me for detaining you from the bewitching converse of that young lady, whose bright eyes are also upbraiding me."

The latter part of this address was scarcely heard by Darcy; but Sir William's allusion to his friend seemed to strike him forcibly, and his eyes were directed with a very serious expression towards Bingley and Jane, who were dancing together. Recovering himself, however, shortly, he turned to his partner, and said, "Sir William's interruption has made me forget what we were talking of."

"I do not think we were speaking at all. Sir William could not have interrupted two people in the room who had less to say for themselves. We have tried two or three subjects already without success, and what we are to talk of next I cannot imagine."

"What think you of books?" said he, smiling.

"Books—oh! no. I am sure we never read the same, or not with the same feelings."

"I am sorry you think so; but if that be the case, there can at least be no want of subject. We may compare our different opinions."

"No—I cannot talk of books in a ball-room; my head is always full of something else."

"The *present* always occupies you in such scenes—does it?" said he, with a look of doubt.

"Yes, always," she replied, without knowing what she said, for her thoughts had wandered far from the subject, as soon afterwards appeared by her suddenly exclaiming, "I remember hearing you once say, Mr. Darcy, that you hardly ever forgave, that your resentment once created was unappeasable. You are very cautious, I suppose, as to its *being created*."

"I am," said he, with a firm voice.

"And never allow yourself to be blinded by prejudice?"

"I hope not."

"It is particularly incumbent on those who never change their opinion, to be secure of judging properly at first."

"May I ask to what these questions tend?"

"Merely to the illustration of *your* character," said she, endeavouring to shake off her gravity. "I am trying to make it out."

"And what is your success?"

She shook her head. "I do not get on at all. I hear such different accounts of you as puzzle me exceedingly."

"I can readily believe," answered he gravely, "that reports may vary greatly with respect to me; and I could wish, Miss Bennet, that you were not to sketch my character at the present moment, as there is reason to fear that the performance would reflect no credit on either."

"But if I do not take your likeness now, I may never have another opportunity."

"I would by no means suspend any pleasure of yours," he coldly replied. She said no more, and they went down the other dance and parted in silence; and on each side dissatisfied, though not to an equal degree, for in Darcy's breast there was a tolerable powerful feeling towards her, which soon procured her pardon, and directed all his anger against another.

They had not long separated, when Miss Bingley came towards her, and with an expression of civil disdain accosted her:

"So, Miss Eliza, I hear you are quite delighted with George Wickham! Your sister has been talking to me about him, and asking me a thousand questions; and I find that the young man quite forgot to tell you, among his other communication, that he was the son of old Wickham, the late Mr. Darcy's steward. Let me recommend you, however, as a friend, not to give implicit confidence to all his assertions; for as to Mr. Darcy's using him ill, it is perfectly false; for, on the contrary, he has always been remarkably kind to him, though George Wickham has treated Mr. Darcy in a most infamous manner. I do not know the particulars, but I know very well that Mr. Darcy is not in the least to blame, that he cannot bear to hear George Wickham mentioned, and that though my brother thought that he could not well avoid including him in his invitation to the officers, he was excessively glad to find that he had taken himself out of the way. His coming into the country at all is a most insolent thing, indeed, and I wonder how he could presume to do it. I pity you, Miss Eliza, for this discovery of your favourite's guilt; but really, considering his descent, one could not expect much better."

"His guilt and his descent appear by your account to be the same," said Elizabeth angrily; "for I have heard you accuse him of nothing worse than of being the son of Mr. Darcy's steward, and of *that*, I can assure you, he informed me himself."

"I beg your pardon," replied Miss Bingley, turning away with a sneer. "Excuse my interference—it was kindly meant."

"Insolent girl!" said Elizabeth to herself. "You are much mistaken if you expect to influence me by such a paltry attack as this. I see nothing in it but your own wilful ignorance and the malice of Mr. Darcy." She then sought her eldest sister, who had undertaken to make inquiries on the same subject of Bingley. Jane met her with a smile of such sweet complacency, a glow of such happy expression, as sufficiently marked how well she was satisfied with the occurrences of the evening. Elizabeth instantly read her feelings, and at that moment solicitude for Wickham, resentment against his enemies, and everything else, gave way before the hope of Jane's being in the fairest way for happiness.

"I want to know," said she, with a countenance no less smiling than her sister's, "what you have learnt about Mr. Wickham. But perhaps you have been too pleasantly engaged to think of any third person; in which case you may be sure of my pardon."

"No," replied Jane, "I have not forgotten him; but I have nothing satisfactory to tell you. Mr. Bingley does not know the whole of his history, and is quite ignorant of the circumstances which have principally offended Mr. Darcy; but he will vouch for the good conduct, the probity, and honour of his friend, and is perfectly convinced that Mr. Wickham has deserved much less attention from Mr. Darcy than he has received; and I am sorry to say by his account as well as his sister's, Mr. Wickham is by no means a respectable young man. I am afraid he has been very imprudent, and has deserved to lose Mr. Darcy's regard."

"Mr. Bingley does not know Mr. Wickham himself?"

"No; he never saw him till the other morning at Meryton."

"This account then is what he has received from Mr. Darcy. I am satisfied. But what does he say of the living?"

"He does not exactly recollect the circumstances, though he has heard them from Mr. Darcy more than once, but he believes that it was left to him *conditionally* only."

"I have not a doubt of Mr. Bingley's sincerity," said Elizabeth warmly; "but you must excuse my not being convinced by assurances only. Mr. Bingley's defense of his friend was a very able one, I dare say; but since he is unacquainted with several parts of the story, and has learnt the rest from that friend himself, I shall venture to still think of both gentlemen as I did before."

She then changed the discourse to one more gratifying to each, and on which there could be no difference of sentiment. Elizabeth listened with delight to the happy, though modest hopes which Jane entertained of Mr. Bingley's regard, and said all in her power to heighten her confidence in it. On their being joined by Mr. Bingley himself, Elizabeth withdrew to Miss Lucas; to whose inquiry after the pleasantness of her last partner she had scarcely replied, before Mr. Collins came up to them, and told her with great exultation that he had just been so fortunate as to make a most important discovery.

"I have found out," said he, "by a singular accident, that there is now in the room a near relation of my patroness. I happened to overhear the gentleman himself mentioning to the young lady who does the honours of the house the names of his cousin Miss de Bourgh, and of her mother Lady Catherine. How wonderfully these sort of things occur! Who would have thought of my meeting with, perhaps, a nephew of Lady Catherine de Bourgh in this assembly! I am most thankful that the discovery is made in time for me to pay my respects to him, which I am now going to do, and trust he will excuse my not having done it before. My total ignorance of the connection must plead my apology."

"You are not going to introduce yourself to Mr. Darcy!"

"Indeed I am. I shall entreat his pardon for not having done it earlier. I believe him to be Lady Catherine's *nephew*. It will be in my power to assure him that her ladyship was quite well yesterday se'nnight."

Elizabeth tried hard to dissuade him from such a scheme, assuring him that Mr. Darcy would consider his addressing him without introduction as an impertinent freedom, rather than a compliment to his aunt; that it was not in the least necessary there should be any notice on either side; and that if it were, it must belong to Mr. Darcy, the superior in consequence, to begin the acquaintance. Mr. Collins listened to her with the determined air of following his own inclination, and, when she ceased speaking, replied thus:

"My dear Miss Elizabeth, I have the highest opinion in the world in your excellent judgement in all matters within the scope of your understanding; but permit me to say, that there must be a wide difference between the established forms of ceremony amongst the laity, and those which regulate the clergy; for, give me leave to observe that I consider the clerical office as equal in point of dignity with the highest rank in the kingdom—provided that a proper humility of behaviour is at the same time maintained. You must therefore allow me to follow the dictates of my conscience on this occasion, which leads me to perform what I look on as a point of duty. Pardon me for neglecting to profit by your advice, which on every other subject shall be my constant guide, though in the case before us I consider myself more fitted by education and habitual study to decide on what is right than a young lady like yourself." And with a low bow he left her to attack Mr. Darcy, whose reception of his advances she eagerly watched, and whose astonishment at being so addressed was very evident. Her cousin prefaced his speech with a solemn bow and though she could not hear a word of it, she felt as if hearing it all, and saw in the motion of his lips the words "apology," "Hunsford," and "Lady Catherine de Bourgh." It vexed her to see him expose himself to such a man. Mr. Darcy was eyeing him with unrestrained wonder, and when at last Mr. Collins allowed him time to speak, replied with an air of distant civility. Mr. Collins, however, was not discouraged from speaking again, and Mr. Darcy's contempt seemed abundantly increasing with the length of his second speech, and at the end of it he only made him a slight bow, and moved another way. Mr. Collins then returned to Elizabeth.

"I have no reason, I assure you," said he, "to be dissatisfied with my reception. Mr. Darcy seemed much pleased with the attention. He answered me with the utmost civility, and even paid me the compliment of saying that he was so well convinced of Lady Catherine's discernment as to be certain she could never bestow a favour unworthily. It was really a very handsome thought. Upon the whole, I am much pleased with him."

As Elizabeth had no longer any interest of her own to pursue, she turned her attention almost entirely on her sister and Mr. Bingley; and the train of agreeable reflections which her observations gave birth to, made her perhaps almost as happy as Jane. She saw her in idea settled in that very house, in all the felicity which a marriage of true affection could bestow; and she felt capable, under such circumstances, of endeavouring even to like Bingley's two sisters. Her mother's thoughts she plainly saw were bent the same way, and she determined not to venture near her, lest she might hear too much. When they sat down to supper, therefore, she considered it a most unlucky perverseness which placed them within one of each other; and deeply was she vexed to find that her mother was talking to that one person (Lady Lucas) freely, openly, and of nothing else but her expectation that Jane would soon be married to Mr. Bingley. It was an animating subject, and Mrs. Bennet seemed incapable of fatigue while enumerating the advantages of the match. His being such a charming young man, and so rich, and living but three miles from them, were the first points of self-gratulation; and then it was such a comfort to think how fond the two sisters were of Jane, and to be certain that they must desire the connection as much as she could do. It was, moreover, such a promising thing for her younger daughters, as Jane's marrying so greatly must throw them in the way of other rich men; and lastly, it was so pleasant at her time of life to be able to consign her single daughters to the care of their sister, that she might not be obliged to go into company more than she liked. It was necessary to make this circumstance a matter of pleasure, because on such occasions it is the etiquette; but no one was less likely than Mrs. Bennet to find comfort in staying home at any period of her life. She concluded with many good wishes that Lady Lucas might soon be equally fortunate, though evidently and triumphantly believing there was no chance of it.

In vain did Elizabeth endeavour to check the rapidity of her mother's words, or persuade her to describe her felicity in a less audible whisper; for, to her inexpressible vexation, she could perceive that the chief of it was overheard by Mr. Darcy, who sat opposite to them. Her mother only scolded her for being nonsensical.

"What is Mr. Darcy to me, pray, that I should be afraid of him? I am sure we owe him no such particular civility as to be obliged to say nothing *he* may not like to hear."

"For heaven's sake, madam, speak lower. What advantage can it be for you to offend Mr. Darcy? You will never recommend yourself to his friend by so doing!"

Nothing that she could say, however, had any influence. Her mother would talk of her views in the same intelligible tone. Elizabeth blushed and blushed again with shame and vexation. She could not help frequently glancing her eye at Mr. Darcy, though every glance convinced her of what she dreaded; for though he was not always looking at her mother, she was convinced that his attention was invariably fixed by her. The expression of his face changed gradually from indignant contempt to a composed and steady gravity.

At length, however, Mrs. Bennet had no more to say; and Lady

Lucas, who had been long yawning at the repetition of delights which she saw no likelihood of sharing, was left to the comforts of cold ham and chicken. Elizabeth now began to revive. But not long was the interval of tranquillity; for, when supper was over, singing was talked of, and she had the mortification of seeing Mary, after very little entreaty, preparing to oblige the company. By many significant looks and silent entreaties, did she endeavour to prevent such a proof of complaisance, but in vain; Mary would not understand them; such an opportunity of exhibiting was delightful to her, and she began her song. Elizabeth's eyes were fixed on her with most painful sensations, and she watched her progress through the several stanzas with an impatience which was very ill rewarded at their close; for Mary, on receiving, amongst the thanks of the table, the hint of a hope that she might be prevailed on to favour them again, after the pause of half a minute began another. Mary's powers were by no means fitted for such a display; her voice was weak, and her manner affected. Elizabeth was in agonies. She looked at Jane, to see how she bore it; but Jane was very composedly talking to Bingley. She looked at his two sisters, and saw them making signs of derision at each other, and at Darcy, who continued, however, imperturbably grave. She looked at her father to entreat his interference, lest Mary should be singing all night. He took the hint, and when Mary had finished her second song, said aloud, "That will do extremely well, child. You have delighted us long enough. Let the other young ladies have time to exhibit."

Mary, though pretending not to hear, was somewhat disconcerted; and Elizabeth, sorry for her, and sorry for her father's speech, was afraid her anxiety had done no good. Others of the party were now applied to.

"If I," said Mr. Collins, "were so fortunate as to be able to sing, I should have great pleasure, I am sure, in obliging the company with an air; for I consider music as a very innocent diversion, and perfectly compatible with the profession of a clergyman. I do not mean, however, to assert that we can be justified in devoting too much of our time to music, for there are certainly other things to be attended to. The rector of a parish has much to do. In the first place, he must make such an agreement for tithes as may be beneficial to himself and not offensive to his patron. He must write his own sermons; and the time that remains will not be too much for his parish duties, and the care and improvement of his dwelling, which he cannot be excused from making as comfortable as possible. And I do not think it of light importance that he should have attentive and conciliatory manner towards everybody, especially towards those to whom he owes his preferment. I cannot acquit him of that duty; nor could I think well of the man who should omit an occasion of testifying his respect towards anybody connected with the family." And with a bow to Mr. Darcy, he concluded his speech, which had been spoken so loud as to be heard by half the room. Many stared—many smiled; but no one looked more amused than Mr. Bennet himself, while his wife seriously commended Mr. Collins for having spoken so sensibly, and observed in a half-whisper to Lady Lucas, that he was a remarkably clever, good kind of young man.

To Elizabeth it appeared that, had her family made an agreement to expose themselves as much as they could during the evening, it would have been impossible for them to play their parts with more spirit or finer success; and happy did she think it for Bingley and her sister that some of the exhibition had escaped his notice, and that his feelings were not of a sort to be much distressed by the folly which he must have witnessed. That his two sisters and Mr. Darcy, however, should have such an opportunity of ridiculing her relations, was bad enough, and she could not determine whether the silent contempt of the gentleman, or the insolent smiles of the ladies, were more intolerable.

The rest of the evening brought her little amusement. She was teased by Mr. Collins, who continued most perseveringly by her side, and though he could not prevail on her to dance with him again, put it out of her power to dance with others. In vain did she entreat him to stand up with somebody else, and offer to introduce him to any young lady in the room. He assured her, that as to dancing, he was perfectly indifferent to it; that his chief object was by delicate attentions to recommend himself to her and that he should therefore make a point of remaining close to her the whole evening. There was no arguing upon such a project. She owed her greatest relief to her friend Miss Lucas, who often joined them, and good-naturedly engaged Mr. Collins's conversation to herself.

She was at least free from the offense of Mr. Darcy's further notice; though often standing within a very short distance of her, quite disengaged, he never came near enough to speak. She felt it to be the probable consequence of her allusions to Mr. Wickham, and rejoiced in it.

The Longbourn party were the last of all the company to depart, and, by a manoeuvre of Mrs. Bennet, had to wait for their carriage a quarter of an hour after everybody else was gone, which gave them time to see how heartily they were wished away by some of the family. Mrs. Hurst and her sister scarcely opened their mouths, except to complain of fatigue, and were evidently impatient to have the house to themselves. They repulsed every attempt of Mrs. Bennet at conversation, and by so doing threw a languor over the whole party, which was very little relieved by the long speeches of Mr. Collins, who was complimenting Mr. Bingley and his sisters on the elegance of their entertainment, and the hospitality and politeness which had marked their behaviour to their guests. Darcy said nothing at all. Mr. Bennet, in equal silence, was enjoying the scene. Mr. Bingley and Jane were standing together, a little detached from the rest, and talked only to each other. Elizabeth preserved as steady a silence as either Mrs. Hurst or Miss Bingley; and even Lydia was too much fatigued to utter more than the occasional exclamation of "Lord, how tired I am!" accompanied by a violent yawn.

When at length they arose to take leave, Mrs. Bennet was most pressingly civil in her hope of seeing the whole family soon at Longbourn, and addressed herself especially to Mr. Bingley, to assure him how happy he would make them by eating a family dinner with them at any time, without the ceremony of a formal invitation. Bingley was all grateful pleasure, and he readily engaged for taking the earliest opportunity of waiting on her, after his return from London, whither he was obliged to go the next day for a short time.

Mrs. Bennet was perfectly satisfied, and quitted the house under the delightful persuasion that, allowing for the necessary preparations of settlements, new carriages, and wedding clothes, she should undoubtedly see her daughter settled at Netherfield in the course of three or four months. Of having another daughter married to Mr. Collins, she thought with equal certainty, and with considerable, though not equal, pleasure. Elizabeth was the least dear to her of all her children; and though the man and the match were quite good enough for *her*, the worth of each was eclipsed by Mr. Bingley and Netherfield.

CHAPTER XIX

The next day opened a new scene at Longbourn. Mr. Collins made his declaration in form. Having resolved to do it without loss of time, as his leave of absence extended only to the following Saturday, and having no feelings of diffidence to make it distressing to himself even at the moment, he set about it in a very orderly manner, with all the observances, which he supposed a regular part of the business. On finding Mrs. Bennet, Elizabeth, and one of the younger girls together, soon after breakfast, he addressed the mother in these words:

"May I hope, madam, for your interest with your fair daughter Elizabeth, when I solicit for the honour of a private audience with her in the course of this morning?"

Before Elizabeth had time for anything but a blush of surprise, Mrs. Bennet answered instantly, "Oh dear!—yes—certainly. I am sure Lizzy will be very happy—I am sure she can have no objection. Come, Kitty, I want you upstairs." And, gathering her work together, she was hastening away, when Elizabeth called out:

"Dear madam, do not go. I beg you will not go. Mr. Collins must excuse me. He can have nothing to say to me that anybody need not hear. I am going away myself."

"No, no, nonsense, Lizzy. I desire you to stay where you are." And upon Elizabeth's seeming really, with vexed and embarrassed looks, about to escape, she added: "Lizzy, I *insist* upon your staying and hearing Mr. Collins."

Elizabeth would not oppose such an injunction—and a moment's consideration making her also sensible that it would be wisest to get it over as soon and as quietly as possible, she sat down again and tried to conceal, by incessant employment the feelings which were divided between distress and diversion. Mrs. Bennet and Kitty walked off, and as soon as they were gone, Mr. Collins began.

"Believe me, my dear Miss Elizabeth, that your modesty, so far from doing you any disservice, rather adds to your other perfections. You would have been less amiable in my eyes had there *not* been this little unwillingness; but allow me to assure you, that I have your respected mother's permission for this address. You can hardly doubt the purport of my discourse, however your natural delicacy may lead you to dissemble; my attentions have been too marked to be mistaken. Almost as soon as I entered the house, I singled you out as the companion of my future life. But before I am run away with by my feelings on this subject, perhaps it would be advisable for me to state my reasons for marrying—and, moreover, for coming into Hertfordshire with the design of selecting a wife, as I certainly did."

The idea of Mr. Collins, with all his solemn composure, being run away with by his feelings, made Elizabeth so near laughing, that she could not use the short pause he allowed in any attempt to stop him further, and he continued:

"My reasons for marrying are, first, that I think it a right thing for every clergyman in easy circumstances (like myself) to set the example of matrimony in his parish; secondly, that I am convinced that it will add very greatly to my happiness; and thirdly—which perhaps I ought to have mentioned earlier, that it is the particular advice and recommendation of the very noble lady whom I have the honour of calling patroness. Twice has she condescended to give me her opinion (unasked too!) on this subject; and it was but the very Saturday night before I left Hunsford—between our pools at quadrille, while Mrs. Jenkinson was arranging Miss de Bourgh's footstool, that she said, 'Mr. Collins, you must marry. A clergyman like you must marry. Choose properly, choose a gentlewoman for *my* sake; and for your *own*, let her be an active, useful sort of person, not brought up high, but able to make a small income go a good way. This is my advice. Find such a woman as soon as you can, bring her to Hunsford, and I will visit her.' Allow me, by the way, to observe, my fair cousin, that I do not reckon the notice and kindness of Lady Catherine de Bourgh as among the least of the advantages in my power to offer. You will find her manners beyond anything I can describe; and your wit and vivacity, I think, must be acceptable to her, especially when tempered with the silence and respect which her rank will inevitably excite. Thus much for my general intention in favour of matrimony; it remains to be told why my views were directed towards Longbourn instead of my own neighbourhood, where I can assure you there are many amiable young women. But the fact is, that being, as I am, to inherit this estate after the death of your honoured father (who, however, may live many years longer), I could not satisfy myself without resolving to choose a wife from among his daughters, that the loss to them might be as little as possible, when the melancholy event takes place—which, however, as I have already said, may not be for several years. This has been my motive, my fair cousin, and I flatter myself it will not sink me in your esteem. And now nothing remains for me but to assure you in the most animated language of the violence of my affection. To fortune I am perfectly indifferent, and shall make no demand of that nature on your father, since I am well aware that it could not be complied with; and that one thousand pounds in the four per cents, which will not be yours till after your mother's decease, is all that you may ever be entitled to. On that head, therefore, I shall be uniformly silent; and you may assure yourself that no ungenerous reproach shall ever pass my lips when we are married."

It was absolutely necessary to interrupt him now.

"You are too hasty, sir," she cried. "You forget that I have made no answer. Let me do it without further loss of time. Accept my thanks for the compliment you are paying me. I am very sensible of the honour of your proposals, but it is impossible for me to do otherwise than to decline them."

"I am not now to learn," replied Mr. Collins, with a formal wave of the hand, "that it is usual with young ladies to reject the addresses of the man whom they secretly mean to accept, when he first applies for their favour; and that sometimes the refusal is repeated a second, or even a third time. I am therefore by no means discouraged by what you have just said, and shall hope to lead you to the altar ere long."

"Upon my word, sir," cried Elizabeth, "your hope is a rather extraordinary one after my declaration. I do assure you that I am not one of those young ladies (if such young ladies there are) who are so daring as to risk their happiness on the chance of being asked a second time. I am perfectly serious in my refusal. You could not make *me* happy, and I am convinced that I am the last woman in the world who could make you so. Nay, were your friend Lady Catherine to know me, I am persuaded she would find me in every respect ill qualified for the situation."

"Were it certain that Lady Catherine would think so," said Mr. Collins very gravely—"but I cannot imagine that her ladyship would at all disapprove of you. And you may be certain when I have the honour of seeing her again, I shall speak in the very highest terms of your modesty, economy, and other amiable qualification."

"Indeed, Mr. Collins, all praise of me will be unnecessary. You must give me leave to judge for myself, and pay me the compliment of believing what I say. I wish you very happy and very rich, and by refusing your hand, do all in my power to prevent your being otherwise. In making me the offer, you must have satisfied the delicacy of your feelings with regard to my family, and may take possession of Longbourn estate whenever it falls, without any self-reproach. This matter may be considered, therefore, as finally settled." And rising as she thus spoke, she would have quitted the room, had Mr. Collins not thus addressed her:

"When I do myself the honour of speaking to you next on the subject, I shall hope to receive a more favourable answer than you have now given me; though I am far from accusing you of cruelty at present, because I know it to be the established custom of your sex to reject a man on the first application, and perhaps you have even now said as much to encourage my suit as would be consistent with the true delicacy of the female character."

"Really, Mr. Collins," cried Elizabeth with some warmth, "you puzzle me exceedingly. If what I have hitherto said can appear to you in the form of encouragement, I know not how to express my refusal in such a way as to convince you of its being one."

"You must give me leave to flatter myself, my dear cousin, that your refusal of my addresses is merely words of course. My reasons for believing it are briefly these: It does not appear to me that my hand is unworthy your acceptance, or that the establishment I can offer would be any other than highly desirable. My situation in life, my connections with the family of de Bourgh, and my relationship to your own, are circumstances highly in my favour; and you should take it into further consideration, that in spite of your manifold attractions, it is by no means certain that another offer of marriage may ever be made you. Your portion is unhappily so small that it will in all likelihood undo the effects of your loveliness and amiable qualifications. As I must therefore conclude that you are not serious in your rejection of me, I shall choose to attribute it to your wish of increasing my love by suspense, according to the usual practice of elegant females."

"I do assure you, sir, that I have no pretensions whatever to that kind of elegance which consists in tormenting a respectable man. I would rather be paid the compliment of being believed sincere. I thank you again and again for the honour you have done me in your proposals, but to accept them is absolutely impossible. My feelings in every respect forbid it. Can I speak plainer? Do not consider me now as an elegant female, intending to plague you, but as a rational creature, speaking the truth from her heart."

"You are uniformly charming!" cried he, with an air of awkward gallantry; "and I am persuaded that when sanctioned by the express authority of both your excellent parents, my proposals will not fail of being acceptable."

To such perseverance in wilful self-deception Elizabeth would make no reply, and immediately and in silence withdrew; determined, if he persisted in considering her repeated refusals as flattering encouragement, to apply to her father, whose negative might be uttered in such a manner as to be decisive, and whose behaviour at least could not be mistaken for the affectation and coquetry of an elegant female.

CHAPTER XX

Mr. Collins was not left long to the silent contemplation of his successful love; for Mrs. Bennet, having dawdled about in the vestibule to watch for the end of the conference, no sooner saw Elizabeth open the door and with quick step pass her towards the staircase, than she entered the breakfast-room, and congratulated both him and herself in warm terms on the happy prospect of their nearer connection. Mr. Collins received and returned these felicitations with equal pleasure, and then proceeded to relate the particulars of their interview, with the result of which he trusted he had every reason to be satisfied, since the refusal which his cousin had steadfastly given him would naturally flow from her bashful modesty and the genuine delicacy of her character.

This information, however, startled Mrs. Bennet; she would have been glad to be equally satisfied that her daughter had meant to encourage him by protesting against his proposals, but she dared not believe it, and could not help saying so.

"But, depend upon it, Mr. Collins," she added, "that Lizzy shall be brought to reason. I will speak to her about it directly. She is a very headstrong, foolish girl, and does not know her own interest but I will *make* her know it."

"Pardon me for interrupting you, madam," cried Mr. Collins; "but if she is really headstrong and foolish, I know not whether she would altogether be a very desirable wife to a man in my situation, who naturally looks for happiness in the marriage state. If therefore she actually persists in rejecting my suit, perhaps it were better not to force her into accepting me, because if liable to such defects of temper, she could not contribute much to my felicity."

"Sir, you quite misunderstand me," said Mrs. Bennet, alarmed. "Lizzy is only headstrong in such matters as these. In everything else she is as good-natured a girl as ever lived. I will go directly to Mr. Bennet, and we shall very soon settle it with her, I am sure."

She would not give him time to reply, but hurrying instantly to her husband, called out as she entered the library, "Oh! Mr. Bennet, you are wanted immediately; we are all in an uproar. You must come and make

Lizzy marry Mr. Collins, for she vows she will not have him, and if you do not make haste he will change his mind and not have *her*."

Mr. Bennet raised his eyes from his book as she entered, and fixed them on her face with a calm unconcern which was not in the least altered by her communication.

"I have not the pleasure of understanding you," said he, when she had finished her speech. "Of what are you talking?"

"Of Mr. Collins and Lizzy. Lizzy declares she will not have Mr. Collins, and Mr. Collins begins to say that he will not have Lizzy."

"And what am I to do on the occasion? It seems an hopeless business."

"Speak to Lizzy about it yourself. Tell her that you insist upon her marrying him."

"Let her be called down. She shall hear my opinion."

Mrs. Bennet rang the bell, and Miss Elizabeth was summoned to the library.

"Come here, child," cried her father as she appeared. "I have sent for you on an affair of importance. I understand that Mr. Collins has made you an offer of marriage. Is it true?" Elizabeth replied that it was. "Very well—and this offer of marriage you have refused?"

"I have, sir."

"Very well. We now come to the point. Your mother insists upon your accepting it. Is it not so, Mrs. Bennet?"

"Yes, or I will never see her again."

"An unhappy alternative is before you, Elizabeth. From this day you must be a stranger to one of your parents. Your mother will never see you again if you do *not* marry Mr. Collins, and I will never see you again if you *do*."

Elizabeth could not but smile at such a conclusion of such a beginning, but Mrs. Bennet, who had persuaded herself that her husband regarded the affair as she wished, was excessively disappointed.

"What do you mean, Mr. Bennet, in talking this way? You promised me to *insist* upon her marrying him."

"My dear," replied her husband, "I have two small favours to request. First, that you will allow me the free use of my understanding on the present occasion; and secondly, of my room. I shall be glad to have the library to myself as soon as may be."

Not yet, however, in spite of her disappointment in her husband, did

Mrs. Bennet give up the point. She talked to Elizabeth again and again; coaxed and threatened her by turns. She endeavoured to secure Jane in her interest; but Jane, with all possible mildness, declined interfering; and Elizabeth, sometimes with real earnestness, and sometimes with playful gaiety, replied to her attacks. Though her manner varied, however, her determination never did.

Mr. Collins, meanwhile, was meditating in solitude on what had passed. He thought too well of himself to comprehend on what motives his cousin could refuse him; and though his pride was hurt, he suffered in no other way. His regard for her was quite imaginary; and the possibility of her deserving her mother's reproach prevented his feeling any regret.

While the family were in this confusion, Charlotte Lucas came to spend the day with them. She was met in the vestibule by Lydia, who, flying to her, cried in a half whisper, "I am glad you are come, for there is such fun here! What do you think has happened this morning? Mr. Collins has made an offer to Lizzy, and she will not have him."

Charlotte hardly had time to answer, before they were joined by Kitty, who came to tell the same news; and no sooner had they entered the breakfast-room, where Mrs. Bennet was alone, than she likewise began on the subject, calling on Miss Lucas for her compassion, and entreating her to persuade her friend Lizzy to comply with the wishes of all her family. "Pray do, my dear Miss Lucas," she added in a melancholy tone, "for nobody is on my side, nobody takes part with me. I am cruelly used, nobody feels for my poor nerves."

Charlotte's reply was spared by the entrance of Jane and Elizabeth.

"Aye, there she comes," continued Mrs. Bennet, "looking as unconcerned as may be, and caring no more for us than if we were at York, provided she can have her own way. But I tell you, Miss Lizzy—if you take it into your head to go on refusing every offer of marriage in this way, you will never get a husband at all—and I am sure I do not know who is to maintain you when your father is dead. I shall not be able to keep you—and so I warn you. I have done with you from this very day. I told you in the library, you know, that I should never speak to you again, and you will find me as good as my word. I have no pleasure in talking to undutiful children. Not that I have much pleasure, indeed, in talking to anybody. People who suffer as I do from nervous complaints can have no great inclination for talking. Nobody can tell what I suffer! But it is always so. Those who do not complain are never pitied."

Her daughters listened in silence to this effusion, sensible that any attempt to reason with her or soothe her would only increase the irritation. She talked on, therefore, without interruption from any of them, till they were joined by Mr. Collins, who entered the room with an air more stately than usual, and on perceiving whom, she said to the girls, "Now, I do insist upon it, that you, all of you, hold your tongues, and let me and Mr. Collins have a little conversation together."

Elizabeth passed quietly out of the room, Jane and Kitty followed, but Lydia stood her ground, determined to hear all she could; and Charlotte, detained first by the civility of Mr. Collins, whose inquiries after herself and all her family were very minute, and then by a little curiosity, satisfied herself with walking to the window and pretending not to hear. In a doleful voice Mrs. Bennet began the projected conversation: "Oh! Mr. Collins!"

"My dear madam," replied he, "let us be for ever silent on this point. Far be it from me," he presently continued, in a voice that marked his displeasure, "to resent the behaviour of your daughter. Resignation to inevitable evils is the evil duty of us all; the peculiar duty of a young man who has been so fortunate as I have been in early preferment; and I trust I am resigned. Perhaps not the less so from feeling a doubt of my positive happiness had my fair cousin honoured me with her hand; for I have often observed that resignation is never so perfect as when the blessing denied begins to lose somewhat of its value in our estimation. You will not, I hope, consider me as showing any disrespect to your family, my dear madam, by thus withdrawing my pretensions to your daughter's favour, without having paid yourself and Mr. Bennet the compliment of requesting you to interpose your authority in my behalf. My conduct may, I fear, be objectionable in having accepted my dismission from your daughter's lips instead of your own. But we are all liable to error. I have certainly meant well through the whole affair. My object has been to secure an amiable companion for myself, with due consideration for the advantage of all your family, and if my *manner* has been at all reprehensible, I here beg leave to apologise."

CHAPTER XXI

The discussion of Mr. Collins's offer was now nearly at an end, and Elizabeth had only to suffer from the uncomfortable feelings necessarily attending it, and occasionally from some peevish allusions of her mother. As for the gentleman himself, *his* feelings were chiefly expressed, not by embarrassment or dejection, or by trying to avoid her, but by stiffness of manner and resentful silence. He scarcely ever spoke to her, and the assiduous attentions which he had been so sensible of himself were transferred for the rest of the day to Miss Lucas, whose civility in listening to him was a seasonable relief to them all, and especially to her friend.

The morrow produced no abatement of Mrs. Bennet's ill-humour or ill health. Mr. Collins was also in the same state of angry pride. Elizabeth had hoped that his resentment might shorten his visit, but his plan did not appear in the least affected by it. He was always to have gone on Saturday, and to Saturday he meant to stay.

After breakfast, the girls walked to Meryton to inquire if Mr. Wickham were returned, and to lament over his absence from the Netherfield ball. He joined them on their entering the town, and attended them to their aunt's where his regret and vexation, and the concern of everybody, was well talked over. To Elizabeth, however, he voluntarily acknowledged that the necessity of his absence *had* been self-imposed.

"I found," said he, "as the time drew near that I had better not meet Mr. Darcy; that to be in the same room, the same party with him for so many hours together, might be more than I could bear, and that scenes might arise unpleasant to more than myself."

She highly approved his forbearance, and they had leisure for a full discussion of it, and for all the commendation which they civilly bestowed on each other, as Wickham and another officer walked back with them to Longbourn, and during the walk he particularly attended to her. His accompanying them was a double advantage; she felt all the compliment it offered to herself, and it was most acceptable as an occasion of introducing him to her father and mother.

Soon after their return, a letter was delivered to Miss Bennet; it came from Netherfield. The envelope contained a sheet of elegant, little, hot-pressed paper, well covered with a lady's fair, flowing hand; and Elizabeth saw her sister's countenance change as she read it, and saw her dwelling intently on some particular passages. Jane recollected herself soon, and putting the letter away, tried to join with her usual cheerfulness in the general conversation; but Elizabeth felt an anxiety on the subject which drew off her attention even from Wickham; and no sooner had he and his companion taken leave, than a glance from Jane invited her to follow her upstairs. When they had gained their own room, Jane, taking out the letter, said:

"This is from Caroline Bingley; what it contains has surprised me a good deal. The whole party have left Netherfield by this time, and are on their way to town—and without any intention of coming back again. You shall hear what she says."

She then read the first sentence aloud, which comprised the information of their having just resolved to follow their brother to town directly, and of their meaning to dine in Grosvenor Street, where Mr. Hurst had a house. The next was in these words: "I do not pretend to regret anything I shall leave in Hertfordshire, except your society, my dearest friend; but we will hope, at some future period, to enjoy many returns of that delightful intercourse we have known, and in the meanwhile may lessen the pain of separation by a very frequent and most unreserved correspondence. I depend on you for that." To these highflown expressions Elizabeth listened with all the insensibility of distrust; and though the suddenness of their removal surprised her, she saw nothing in it really to lament; it was not to be supposed that their absence from Netherfield would prevent Mr. Bingley's being there; and as to the loss of their society, she was persuaded that Jane must cease to regard it, in the enjoyment of his.

"It is unlucky," said she, after a short pause, "that you should not be able to see your friends before they leave the country. But may we not hope that the period of future happiness to which Miss Bingley looks forward may arrive earlier than she is aware, and that the delightful intercourse you have known as friends will be renewed with yet greater satisfaction as sisters? Mr. Bingley will not be detained in London by them."

"Caroline decidedly says that none of the party will return into Hertfordshire this winter. I will read it to you:"

"When my brother left us yesterday, he imagined that the business which took him to London might be concluded in three or four days; but as we are certain it cannot be so, and at the same time convinced that when Charles gets to town he will be in no hurry to leave it again, we have determined on following him thither, that he may not be obliged to spend his vacant hours in a comfortless hotel. Many of my acquaintances are already there for the winter; I wish that I could hear that you, my dearest friend, had any intention of making one of the crowd—but of that I despair. I sincerely hope your Christmas in Hertfordshire may abound in the gaieties which that season generally brings, and that your beaux will be so numerous as to prevent your feeling the loss of the three of whom we shall deprive you."

"It is evident by this," added Jane, "that he comes back no more this winter."

"It is only evident that Miss Bingley does not mean that he *should*."

"Why will you think so? It must be his own doing. He is his own master. But you do not know *all*. I *will* read you the passage which particularly hurts me. I will have no reserves from *you*."

"Mr. Darcy is impatient to see his sister; and, to confess the truth, *we* are scarcely less eager to meet her again. I really do not think Georgiana Darcy has her equal for beauty, elegance, and accomplishments; and the affection she inspires in Louisa and myself is heightened into something still more interesting, from the hope we dare entertain of her being hereafter our sister. I do not know whether I ever before mentioned to you my feelings on this subject; but I will not leave the country without confiding them, and I trust you will not esteem them unreasonable. My brother admires her greatly already; he will have frequent opportunity now of seeing her on the most intimate footing; her relations all wish the connection as much as his own; and a sister's partiality is not misleading me, I think, when I call Charles most capable of engaging any woman's heart. With all these circumstances to favour an attachment, and nothing to prevent it, am I wrong, my dearest Jane, in indulging the hope of an event which will secure the happiness of so many?"

"What do you think of *this* sentence, my dear Lizzy?" said Jane as she finished it. "Is it not clear enough? Does it not expressly declare that Caroline neither expects nor wishes me to be her sister; that she is perfectly convinced of her brother's indifference; and that if she suspects the nature of my feelings for him, she means (most kindly!) to put me on my guard? Can there be any other opinion on the subject?"

"Yes, there can; for mine is totally different. Will you hear it?"

"Most willingly."

"You shall have it in a few words. Miss Bingley sees that her brother is in love with you, and wants him to marry Miss Darcy. She follows him to town in hope of keeping him there, and tries to persuade you that he does not care about you."

Jane shook her head.

"Indeed, Jane, you ought to believe me. No one who has ever seen you together can doubt his affection. Miss Bingley, I am sure, cannot. She is not such a simpleton. Could she have seen half as much love in Mr. Darcy for herself, she would have ordered her wedding clothes. But the case is this: We are not rich enough or grand enough for them; and she is the more anxious to get Miss Darcy for her brother, from the notion that when there has been *one* intermarriage, she may have less trouble in achieving a second; in which there is certainly some ingenuity, and I dare say it would succeed, if Miss de Bourgh were out of the way. But, my dearest Jane, you cannot seriously imagine that because Miss Bingley tells you her brother greatly admires Miss Darcy, he is in the smallest degree less sensible of *your* merit than when he took leave of you on Tuesday, or that it will be in her power to persuade him that, instead of being in love with you, he is very much in love with her friend."

"If we thought alike of Miss Bingley," replied Jane, "your representation of all this might make me quite easy. But I know the foundation is unjust. Caroline is incapable of wilfully deceiving anyone; and all that I can hope in this case is that she is deceiving herself."

"That is right. You could not have started a more happy idea, since you will not take comfort in mine. Believe her to be deceived, by all means. You have now done your duty by her, and must fret no longer."

"But, my dear sister, can I be happy, even supposing the best, in accepting a man whose sisters and friends are all wishing him to marry elsewhere?"

"You must decide for yourself," said Elizabeth; "and if, upon mature deliberation, you find that the misery of disobliging his two sisters is more than equivalent to the happiness of being his wife, I advise you by all means to refuse him."

"How can you talk so?" said Jane, faintly smiling. "You must know that though I should be exceedingly grieved at their disapprobation, I could not hesitate."

"I did not think you would; and that being the case, I cannot consider your situation with much compassion."

"But if he returns no more this winter, my choice will never be required. A thousand things may arise in six months!"

The idea of his returning no more Elizabeth treated with the utmost contempt. It appeared to her merely the suggestion of Caroline's interested wishes, and she could not for a moment suppose that those wishes, however openly or artfully spoken, could influence a young man so totally independent of everyone.

She represented to her sister as forcibly as possible what she felt on the subject, and had soon the pleasure of seeing its happy effect. Jane's temper was not desponding, and she was gradually led to hope, though the diffidence of affection sometimes overcame the hope, that Bingley would return to Netherfield and answer every wish of her heart.

They agreed that Mrs. Bennet should only hear of the departure of the family, without being alarmed on the score of the gentleman's conduct; but even this partial communication gave her a great deal of concern, and she bewailed it as exceedingly unlucky that the ladies should happen to go away just as they were all getting so intimate together. After lamenting it, however, at some length, she had the consolation that Mr. Bingley would be soon down again and soon dining at Longbourn, and the conclusion of all was the comfortable declaration, that though he had been invited only to a family dinner, she would take care to have two full courses.

CHAPTER XXII

The Bennets were engaged to dine with the Lucases and again during the chief of the day was Miss Lucas so kind as to listen to Mr. Collins. Elizabeth took an opportunity of thanking her. "It keeps him in good humour," said she, "and I am more obliged to you than I can express." Charlotte assured her friend of her satisfaction in being useful, and that it amply repaid her for the little sacrifice of her time. This was very amiable, but Charlotte's kindness extended farther than Elizabeth had any conception of; its object was nothing else than to secure her from any return of Mr. Collins's addresses, by engaging them towards herself. Such was Miss Lucas's scheme; and appearances were so favourable, that when they parted at night, she would have felt almost secure of success if he had not been to leave Hertfordshire so very soon. But here she did injustice to the fire and independence of his character, for it led him to escape out of Longbourn House the next morning with admirable slyness, and hasten to Lucas Lodge to throw himself at her feet. He was anxious to avoid the notice of his cousins, from a conviction that if they saw him depart, they could not fail to conjecture his design, and he was not willing to have the attempt known till its success might be known likewise; for though feeling almost secure, and with reason, for Charlotte had been tolerably encouraging, he was comparatively diffident since the adventure of Wednesday. His reception, however, was of the most flattering kind. Miss Lucas perceived him from an upper window as he walked towards the house, and instantly set out to meet him accidentally in the lane. But little had she dared to hope that so much love and eloquence awaited her there.

In as short a time as Mr. Collins's long speeches would allow, everything was settled between them to the satisfaction of both; and as they entered the house he earnestly entreated her to name the day that was to make him the happiest of men; and though such a solicitation must be waived for the present, the lady felt no inclination to trifle with his happiness. The stupidity with which he was favoured by nature must guard his courtship from any charm that could make a woman wish for its continuance; and Miss Lucas, who accepted him solely from the pure and disinterested desire of an establishment, cared not how soon that establishment were gained.

Sir William and Lady Lucas were speedily applied to for their consent; and it was bestowed with a most joyful alacrity. Mr. Collins's present circumstances made it a most eligible match for their daughter, to whom they could give little fortune; and his prospects of future wealth were exceedingly fair. Lady Lucas began directly to calculate, with more interest than the matter had ever excited before, how many years longer Mr. Bennet was likely to live; and Sir William gave it as his decided opinion, that whenever Mr. Collins should be in possession of the Longbourn estate, it would be highly expedient that both he and his wife should make their appearance at St. James's. The whole family, in short, were properly overjoyed on the occasion. The younger girls formed hopes of *coming out* a year or two sooner than they might otherwise have done; and the boys were relieved from their apprehension of Charlotte's dying an old maid. Charlotte herself was tolerably composed. She had gained her point, and had time to consider of it. Her reflections were in general satisfactory. Mr. Collins, to be sure, was neither sensible nor agreeable; his society was irksome, and his attachment to her must be imaginary. But still he would be her husband. Without thinking highly either of men or matrimony, marriage had always been her object; it was the only provision for well-educated young women of small fortune, and however uncertain of giving happiness, must be their pleasantest preservative from want. This preservative she had now obtained; and at the age of twenty-seven, without having ever been handsome, she felt all the good luck of it. The least agreeable circumstance in the business was the surprise it must occasion to Elizabeth Bennet, whose friendship she valued beyond that of any other person. Elizabeth would wonder, and probably would blame her; and though her resolution was not to be shaken, her feelings must be hurt by such a disapprobation. She resolved to give her the information herself, and therefore charged Mr. Collins, when he returned to Longbourn to dinner, to drop no hint of what had passed before any of the family. A promise of secrecy was of course very dutifully given, but it could not be kept without difficulty; for the curiosity excited by his long absence burst forth in such very direct questions on his return as required some ingenuity to evade, and he was at the same time exercising great self-denial, for he was longing to publish his prosperous love.

As he was to begin his journey too early on the morrow to see any of the family, the ceremony of leave-taking was performed when the ladies moved for the night; and Mrs. Bennet, with great politeness and cordiality, said how happy they should be to see him at Longbourn again, whenever his engagements might allow him to visit them.

"My dear madam," he replied, "this invitation is particularly gratifying, because it is what I have been hoping to receive; and you may be very certain that I shall avail myself of it as soon as possible."

They were all astonished; and Mr. Bennet, who could by no means wish for so speedy a return, immediately said:

"But is there not danger of Lady Catherine's disapprobation here, my good sir? You had better neglect your relations than run the risk of offending your patroness."

"My dear sir," replied Mr. Collins, "I am particularly obliged to you for this friendly caution, and you may depend upon my not taking so material a step without her ladyship's concurrence."

"You cannot be too much upon your guard. Risk anything rather than her displeasure; and if you find it likely to be raised by your coming to us again, which I should think exceedingly probable, stay quietly at home, and be satisfied that *we* shall take no offence."

"Believe me, my dear sir, my gratitude is warmly excited by such affectionate attention; and depend upon it, you will speedily receive from me a letter of thanks for this, and for every other mark of your regard during my stay in Hertfordshire. As for my fair cousins, though my absence may not be long enough to render it necessary, I shall now take the liberty of wishing them health and happiness, not excepting my cousin Elizabeth."

With proper civilities the ladies then withdrew; all of them equally surprised that he meditated a quick return. Mrs. Bennet wished to understand by it that he thought of paying his addresses to one of her younger girls, and Mary might have been prevailed on to accept him. She rated his abilities much higher than any of the others; there was a solidity in his reflections which often struck her, and though by no means so clever as herself, she thought that if encouraged to read and improve himself by such an example as hers, he might become a very agreeable companion. But on the following morning, every hope of this kind was done away. Miss Lucas called soon after breakfast, and in a private conference with Elizabeth related the event of the day before.

The possibility of Mr. Collins's fancying himself in love with her friend had once occurred to Elizabeth within the last day or two; but that Charlotte could encourage him seemed almost as far from possibility as she could encourage him herself, and her astonishment was consequently so great as to overcome at first the bounds of decorum, and she could not help crying out:

"Engaged to Mr. Collins! My dear Charlotte—impossible!"

The steady countenance which Miss Lucas had commanded in telling her story, gave way to a momentary confusion here on receiving so direct a reproach; though, as it was no more than she expected, she soon regained her composure, and calmly replied:

"Why should you be surprised, my dear Eliza? Do you think it incredible that Mr. Collins should be able to procure any woman's good opinion, because he was not so happy as to succeed with you?"

But Elizabeth had now recollected herself, and making a strong effort for it, was able to assure with tolerable firmness that the prospect of their relationship was highly grateful to her, and that she wished her all imaginable happiness.

"I see what you are feeling," replied Charlotte. "You must be surprised, very much surprised—so lately as Mr. Collins was wishing to marry you. But when you have had time to think it over, I hope you will be satisfied with what I have done. I am not romantic, you know; I never was. I ask only a comfortable home; and considering Mr. Collins's character, connection, and situation in life, I am convinced that my chance of happiness with him is as fair as most people can boast on entering the marriage state."

Elizabeth quietly answered "Undoubtedly;" and after an awkward pause, they returned to the rest of the family. Charlotte did not stay much longer, and Elizabeth was then left to reflect on what she had heard. It was a long time before she became at all reconciled to the idea of so unsuitable a match. The strangeness of Mr. Collins's making two offers of marriage within three days was nothing in comparison of his being now accepted. She had always felt that Charlotte's opinion of matrimony was not exactly like her own, but she had not supposed it to be possible that, when called into action, she would have sacrificed every better feeling to worldly advantage. Charlotte the wife of Mr. Collins was a most humiliating picture! And to the pang of a friend disgracing herself and sunk in her esteem, was added the distressing conviction that it was impossible for that friend to be tolerably happy in the lot she had chosen.

CHAPTER XXIII

Elizabeth was sitting with her mother and sisters, reflecting on what she had heard, and doubting whether she was authorised to mention it, when Sir William Lucas himself appeared, sent by his daughter, to announce her engagement to the family. With many compliments to them, and much self-gratulation on the prospect of a connection between the houses, he unfolded the matter—to an audience not merely wondering, but incredulous; for Mrs. Bennet, with more perseverance than politeness, protested he must be entirely mistaken; and Lydia, always unguarded and often uncivil, boisterously exclaimed:

"Good Lord! Sir William, how can you tell such a story? Do not you know that Mr. Collins wants to marry Lizzy?"

Nothing less than the complaisance of a courtier could have borne without anger such treatment; but Sir William's good breeding carried him through it all; and though he begged leave to be positive as to the truth of his information, he listened to all their impertinence with the most forbearing courtesy.

Elizabeth, feeling it incumbent on her to relieve him from so unpleasant a situation, now put herself forward to confirm his account, by mentioning her prior knowledge of it from Charlotte herself; and endeavoured to put a stop to the exclamations of her mother and sisters by the earnestness of her congratulations to Sir William, in which she was readily joined by Jane, and by making a variety of remarks on the happiness that might be expected from the match, the excellent character of Mr. Collins, and the convenient distance of Hunsford from London.

Mrs. Bennet was in fact too much overpowered to say a great deal while Sir William remained; but no sooner had he left them than her feelings found a rapid vent. In the first place, she persisted in disbelieving the whole of the matter; secondly, she was very sure that Mr. Collins had been taken in; thirdly, she trusted that they would never be happy together; and fourthly, that the match might be broken off. Two inferences, however, were plainly deduced from the whole: one, that Elizabeth was the real cause of the mischief; and the other that she herself had been barbarously misused by them all; and on these two points she principally dwelt during the rest of the day. Nothing could console and nothing could appease her. Nor did that day wear out her resentment. A week elapsed before she could see Elizabeth without scolding her, a month passed away before she could speak to Sir William or Lady Lucas without being rude, and many months were gone before she could at all forgive their daughter.

Mr. Bennet's emotions were much more tranquil on the occasion, and such as he did experience he pronounced to be of a most agreeable sort; for it gratified him, he said, to discover that Charlotte Lucas, whom he had been used to think tolerably sensible, was as foolish as his wife, and more foolish than his daughter!

Jane confessed herself a little surprised at the match; but she said less of her astonishment than of her earnest desire for their happiness; nor could Elizabeth persuade her to consider it as improbable. Kitty and Lydia were far from envying Miss Lucas, for Mr. Collins was only a clergyman; and it affected them in no other way than as a piece of news to spread at Meryton.

Lady Lucas could not be insensible of triumph on being able to retort on Mrs. Bennet the comfort of having a daughter well married; and she called at Longbourn rather oftener than usual to say how happy she was, though Mrs. Bennet's sour looks and ill-natured remarks might have been enough to drive happiness away.

Between Elizabeth and Charlotte there was a restraint which kept them mutually silent on the subject; and Elizabeth felt persuaded that no real confidence could ever subsist between them again. Her disappointment in Charlotte made her turn with fonder regard to her sister, of whose rectitude and delicacy she was sure her opinion could never be shaken, and for whose happiness she grew daily more anxious, as Bingley had now been gone a week and nothing more was heard of his return.

Jane had sent Caroline an early answer to her letter, and was counting the days till she might reasonably hope to hear again. The promised letter of thanks from Mr. Collins arrived on Tuesday, addressed to their father, and written with all the solemnity of gratitude which a twelvemonth's abode in the family might have prompted. After discharging his conscience on that head, he proceeded to inform them, with many rapturous expressions, of his happiness in having obtained the affection of their amiable neighbour, Miss Lucas, and then explained that it was merely with the view of enjoying her society that he had been so ready to close with their kind wish of seeing him again at Longbourn, whither he hoped to be able to return on Monday fortnight; for Lady Catherine, he added, so heartily approved his marriage, that she wished it to take place as soon as possible, which he trusted would be an unanswerable argument with his amiable Charlotte to name an early day for making him the happiest of men.

Mr. Collins's return into Hertfordshire was no longer a matter of pleasure to Mrs. Bennet. On the contrary, she was as much disposed to complain of it as her husband. It was very strange that he should come to Longbourn instead of to Lucas Lodge; it was also very inconvenient and exceedingly troublesome. She hated having visitors in the house while her health was so indifferent, and lovers were of all people the most disagreeable. Such were the gentle murmurs of Mrs. Bennet, and they gave way only to the greater distress of Mr. Bingley's continued absence.

Neither Jane nor Elizabeth were comfortable on this subject. Day after day passed away without bringing any other tidings of him than the report which shortly prevailed in Meryton of his coming no more to Netherfield the whole winter; a report which highly incensed Mrs. Bennet, and which she never failed to contradict as a most scandalous falsehood.

Even Elizabeth began to fear—not that Bingley was indifferent—but that his sisters would be successful in keeping him away. Unwilling as she was to admit an idea so destructive of Jane's happiness, and so dishonorable to the stability of her lover, she could not prevent its frequently occurring. The united efforts of his two unfeeling sisters and of his overpowering friend, assisted by the attractions of Miss Darcy and the amusements of London might be too much, she feared, for the strength of his attachment.

As for Jane, *her* anxiety under this suspense was, of course, more painful than Elizabeth's, but whatever she felt she was desirous of concealing, and between herself and Elizabeth, therefore, the subject was never alluded to. But as no such delicacy restrained her mother, an hour seldom passed in which she did not talk of Bingley, express her impatience for his arrival, or even require Jane to confess that if he did not come back she would think herself very ill used. It needed all Jane's steady mildness to bear these attacks with tolerable tranquillity.

Mr. Collins returned most punctually on Monday fortnight, but his reception at Longbourn was not quite so gracious as it had been on his first introduction. He was too happy, however, to need much attention; and luckily for the others, the business of love-making relieved them from a great deal of his company. The chief of every day was spent by him at Lucas Lodge, and he sometimes returned to Longbourn only in time to make an apology for his absence before the family went to bed.

Mrs. Bennet was really in a most pitiable state. The very mention of anything concerning the match threw her into an agony of ill-humour, and wherever she went she was sure of hearing it talked of. The sight of Miss Lucas was odious to her. As her successor in that house, she regarded her with jealous abhorrence. Whenever Charlotte came to see them, she concluded her to be anticipating the hour of possession; and whenever she spoke in a low voice to Mr. Collins, was convinced that they were talking of the Longbourn estate, and resolving to turn herself and her daughters out of the house, as soon as Mr. Bennet were dead. She complained bitterly of all this to her husband.

"Indeed, Mr. Bennet," said she, "it is very hard to think that Charlotte Lucas should ever be mistress of this house, that I should be forced to make way for *her*, and live to see her take her place in it!"

"My dear, do not give way to such gloomy thoughts. Let us hope for better things. Let us flatter ourselves that I may be the survivor."

This was not very consoling to Mrs. Bennet, and therefore, instead of making any answer, she went on as before.

"I cannot bear to think that they should have all this estate. If it was not for the entail, I should not mind it."

"What should not you mind?"

"I should not mind anything at all."

"Let us be thankful that you are preserved from a state of such insensibility."

"I never can be thankful, Mr. Bennet, for anything about the entail. How anyone could have the conscience to entail away an estate from one's own daughters, I cannot understand; and all for the sake of Mr. Collins too! Why should *he* have it more than anybody else?"

"I leave it to yourself to determine," said Mr. Bennet.

CHAPTER XXIV

Miss Bingley's letter arrived, and put an end to doubt. The very first sentence conveyed the assurance of their being all settled in London for the winter, and concluded with her brother's regret at not having had time to pay his respects to his friends in Hertfordshire before he left the country.

Hope was over, entirely over; and when Jane could attend to the rest of the letter, she found little, except the professed affection of the writer, that could give her any comfort. Miss Darcy's praise occupied the chief of it. Her many attractions were again dwelt on, and Caroline boasted joyfully of their increasing intimacy, and ventured to predict the accomplishment of the wishes which had been unfolded in her former letter. She wrote also with great pleasure of her brother's being an inmate of Mr. Darcy's house, and mentioned with raptures some plans of the latter with regard to new furniture.

Elizabeth, to whom Jane very soon communicated the chief of all this, heard it in silent indignation. Her heart was divided between concern for her sister, and resentment against all others. To Caroline's assertion of her brother's being partial to Miss Darcy she paid no credit. That he was really fond of Jane, she doubted no more than she had ever done; and much as she had always been disposed to like him, she could not think without anger, hardly without contempt, on that easiness of temper, that want of proper resolution, which now made him the slave of his designing friends, and led him to sacrifice of his own happiness to the caprice of their inclination. Had his own happiness, however, been the only sacrifice, he might have been allowed to sport with it in whatever manner he thought best, but her sister's was involved in it, as she thought he must be sensible himself. It was a subject, in short, on which reflection would be long indulged, and must be unavailing. She could think of nothing else; and yet whether Bingley's regard had really died away, or were suppressed by his friends' interference; whether he had been aware of Jane's attachment, or whether it had escaped his observation; whatever were the case, though her opinion of him must be materially affected by the difference, her sister's situation remained the same, her peace equally wounded.

A day or two passed before Jane had courage to speak of her feelings to Elizabeth; but at last, on Mrs. Bennet's leaving them together, after a longer irritation than usual about Netherfield and its master, she could not help saying:

"Oh, that my dear mother had more command over herself! She can have no idea of the pain she gives me by her continual reflections on him. But I will not repine. It cannot last long. He will be forgot, and we shall all be as we were before."

Elizabeth looked at her sister with incredulous solicitude, but said nothing.

"You doubt me," cried Jane, slightly colouring; "indeed, you have no reason. He may live in my memory as the most amiable man of my acquaintance, but that is all. I have nothing either to hope or fear, and nothing to reproach him with. Thank God! I have not *that* pain. A little time, therefore—I shall certainly try to get the better."

With a stronger voice she soon added, "I have this comfort immediately, that it has not been more than an error of fancy on my side, and that it has done no harm to anyone but myself."

"My dear Jane!" exclaimed Elizabeth, "you are too good. Your sweetness and disinterestedness are really angelic; I do not know what to say to you. I feel as if I had never done you justice, or loved you as you deserve."

Miss Bennet eagerly disclaimed all extraordinary merit, and threw back the praise on her sister's warm affection.

"Nay," said Elizabeth, "this is not fair. *You* wish to think all the world respectable, and are hurt if I speak ill of anybody. I only want to think *you* perfect, and you set yourself against it. Do not be afraid of my running into any excess, of my encroaching on your privilege of universal good-will. You need not. There are few people whom I really love, and still fewer of whom I think well. The more I see of the world, the more am I dissatisfied with it; and every day confirms my belief of the inconsistency of all human characters, and of the little dependence that can be placed on the appearance of merit or sense. I have met with two instances lately, one I will not mention; the other is Charlotte's marriage. It is unaccountable! In every view it is unaccountable!"

"My dear Lizzy, do not give way to such feelings as these. They will ruin your happiness. You do not make allowance enough for difference of situation and temper. Consider Mr. Collins's respectability, and

Charlotte's steady, prudent character. Remember that she is one of a large family; that as to fortune, it is a most eligible match; and be ready to believe, for everybody's sake, that she may feel something like regard and esteem for our cousin."

"To oblige you, I would try to believe almost anything, but no one else could be benefited by such a belief as this; for were I persuaded that Charlotte had any regard for him, I should only think worse of her understanding than I now do of her heart. My dear Jane, Mr. Collins is a conceited, pompous, narrow-minded, silly man; you know he is, as well as I do; and you must feel, as well as I do, that the woman who married him cannot have a proper way of thinking. You shall not defend her, though it is Charlotte Lucas. You shall not, for the sake of one individual, change the meaning of principle and integrity, nor endeavour to persuade yourself or me, that selfishness is prudence, and insensibility of danger security for happiness."

"I must think your language too strong in speaking of both," replied Jane; "and I hope you will be convinced of it by seeing them happy together. But enough of this. You alluded to something else. You mentioned *two* instances. I cannot misunderstand you, but I entreat you, dear Lizzy, not to pain me by thinking *that person* to blame, and saying your opinion of him is sunk. We must not be so ready to fancy ourselves intentionally injured. We must not expect a lively young man to be always so guarded and circumspect. It is very often nothing but our own vanity that deceives us. Women fancy admiration means more than it does."

"And men take care that they should."

"If it is designedly done, they cannot be justified; but I have no idea of there being so much design in the world as some persons imagine."

"I am far from attributing any part of Mr. Bingley's conduct to design," said Elizabeth; "but without scheming to do wrong, or to make others unhappy, there may be error, and there may be misery. Thoughtlessness, want of attention to other people's feelings, and want of resolution, will do the business."

"And do you impute it to either of those?"

"Yes; to the last. But if I go on, I shall displease you by saying what I think of persons you esteem. Stop me whilst you can."

"You persist, then, in supposing his sisters influence him?"

"Yes, in conjunction with his friend."

"I cannot believe it. Why should they try to influence him? They can only wish his happiness; and if he is attached to me, no other woman can secure it."

"Your first position is false. They may wish many things besides his happiness; they may wish his increase of wealth and consequence; they may wish him to marry a girl who has all the importance of money, great connections, and pride."

"Beyond a doubt, they *do* wish him to choose Miss Darcy," replied Jane; "but this may be from better feelings than you are supposing. They have known her much longer than they have known me; no wonder if they love her better. But, whatever may be their own wishes, it is very unlikely they should have opposed their brother's. What sister would think herself at liberty to do it, unless there were something very objectionable? If they believed him attached to me, they would not try to part us; if he were so, they could not succeed. By supposing such an affection, you make everybody acting unnaturally and wrong, and me most unhappy. Do not distress me by the idea. I am not ashamed of having been mistaken—or, at least, it is light, it is nothing in comparison of what I should feel in thinking ill of him or his sisters. Let me take it in the best light, in the light in which it may be understood."

Elizabeth could not oppose such a wish; and from this time Mr. Bingley's name was scarcely ever mentioned between them.

Mrs. Bennet still continued to wonder and repine at his returning no more, and though a day seldom passed in which Elizabeth did not account for it clearly, there was little chance of her ever considering it with less perplexity. Her daughter endeavoured to convince her of what she did not believe herself, that his attentions to Jane had been merely the effect of a common and transient liking, which ceased when he saw her no more; but though the probability of the statement was admitted at the time, she had the same story to repeat every day. Mrs. Bennet's best comfort was that Mr. Bingley must be down again in the summer.

Mr. Bennet treated the matter differently. "So, Lizzy," said he one day, "your sister is crossed in love, I find. I congratulate her. Next to being married, a girl likes to be crossed a little in love now and then. It is something to think of, and it gives her a sort of distinction among her companions. When is your turn to come? You will hardly bear to be long outdone by Jane. Now is your time. Here are officers enough in

Meryton to disappoint all the young ladies in the country. Let Wickham be *your* man. He is a pleasant fellow, and would jilt you creditably."

"Thank you, sir, but a less agreeable man would satisfy me. We must not all expect Jane's good fortune."

"True," said Mr. Bennet, "but it is a comfort to think that whatever of that kind may befall you, you have an affectionate mother who will make the most of it."

Mr. Wickham's society was of material service in dispelling the gloom which the late perverse occurrences had thrown on many of the Longbourn family. They saw him often, and to his other recommendations was now added that of general unreserve. The whole of what Elizabeth had already heard, his claims on Mr. Darcy, and all that he had suffered from him, was now openly acknowledged and publicly canvassed; and everybody was pleased to know how much they had always disliked Mr. Darcy before they had known anything of the matter.

Miss Bennet was the only creature who could suppose there might be any extenuating circumstances in the case, unknown to the society of Hertfordshire; her mild and steady candour always pleaded for allowances, and urged the possibility of mistakes—but by everybody else Mr. Darcy was condemned as the worst of men.

CHAPTER XXV

After a week spent in professions of love and schemes of felicity, Mr. Collins was called from his amiable Charlotte by the arrival of Saturday. The pain of separation, however, might be alleviated on his side, by preparations for the reception of his bride; as he had reason to hope, that shortly after his return into Hertfordshire, the day would be fixed that was to make him the happiest of men. He took leave of his relations at Longbourn with as much solemnity as before; wished his fair cousins health and happiness again, and promised their father another letter of thanks.

On the following Monday, Mrs. Bennet had the pleasure of receiving her brother and his wife, who came as usual to spend the Christmas at Longbourn. Mr. Gardiner was a sensible, gentlemanlike man, greatly superior to his sister, as well by nature as education. The Netherfield ladies would have had difficulty in believing that a man who lived by trade, and within view of his own warehouses, could have been so well-bred and agreeable. Mrs. Gardiner, who was several years younger than Mrs. Bennet and Mrs. Phillips, was an amiable, intelligent, elegant woman, and a great favourite with all her Longbourn nieces. Between the two eldest and herself especially, there subsisted a particular regard. They had frequently been staying with her in town.

The first part of Mrs. Gardiner's business on her arrival was to distribute her presents and describe the newest fashions. When this was done she had a less active part to play. It became her turn to listen. Mrs. Bennet had many grievances to relate, and much to complain of. They had all been very ill-used since she last saw her sister. Two of her girls had been upon the point of marriage, and after all there was nothing in it.

"I do not blame Jane," she continued, "for Jane would have got Mr. Bingley if she could. But Lizzy! Oh, sister! It is very hard to think that she might have been Mr. Collins's wife by this time, had it not been for her own perverseness. He made her an offer in this very room, and she refused him. The consequence of it is, that Lady Lucas will have a daughter married before I have, and that the Longbourn estate is just as much entailed as ever. The Lucases are very artful people indeed, sister. They are all for what they can get. I am sorry to say it of them, but so it is. It makes me very nervous and poorly, to be thwarted so in my own family, and to have neighbours who think of themselves before anybody else. However, your coming just at this time is the greatest of comforts, and I am very glad to hear what you tell us, of long sleeves."

Mrs. Gardiner, to whom the chief of this news had been given before, in the course of Jane and Elizabeth's correspondence with her, made her sister a slight answer, and, in compassion to her nieces, turned the conversation.

When alone with Elizabeth afterwards, she spoke more on the subject. "It seems likely to have been a desirable match for Jane," said she. "I am sorry it went off. But these things happen so often! A young man, such as you describe Mr. Bingley, so easily falls in love with a pretty girl for a few weeks, and when accident separates them, so easily forgets her, that these sort of inconsistencies are very frequent."

"An excellent consolation in its way," said Elizabeth, "but it will not do for *us*. We do not suffer by *accident*. It does not often happen that the interference of friends will persuade a young man of independent fortune to think no more of a girl whom he was violently in love with only a few days before."

"But that expression of 'violently in love' is so hackneyed, so doubtful, so indefinite, that it gives me very little idea. It is as often applied to feelings which arise from a half-hour's acquaintance, as to a real, strong attachment. Pray, how *violent was* Mr. Bingley's love?"

"I never saw a more promising inclination; he was growing quite inattentive to other people, and wholly engrossed by her. Every time they met, it was more decided and remarkable. At his own ball he offended two or three young ladies, by not asking them to dance; and I spoke to him twice myself, without receiving an answer. Could there be finer symptoms? Is not general incivility the very essence of love?"

"Oh, yes!—of that kind of love which I suppose him to have felt. Poor Jane! I am sorry for her, because, with her disposition, she may not get over it immediately. It had better have happened to *you*, Lizzy; you would have laughed yourself out of it sooner. But do you think she would be prevailed upon to go back with us? Change of scene might be of service—and perhaps a little relief from home may be as useful as anything."

Elizabeth was exceedingly pleased with this proposal, and felt persuaded of her sister's ready acquiescence.

"I hope," added Mrs. Gardiner, "that no consideration with regard to this young man will influence her. We live in so different a part of town, all our connections are so different, and, as you well know, we go out so little, that it is very improbable that they should meet at all, unless he really comes to see her."

"And *that* is quite impossible; for he is now in the custody of his friend, and Mr. Darcy would no more suffer him to call on Jane in such a part of London! My dear aunt, how could you think of it? Mr. Darcy may perhaps have *heard* of such a place as Gracechurch Street, but he would hardly think a month's ablution enough to cleanse him from its impurities, were he once to enter it; and depend upon it, Mr. Bingley never stirs without him."

"So much the better. I hope they will not meet at all. But does not Jane correspond with his sister? *She* will not be able to help calling."

"She will drop the acquaintance entirely."

But in spite of the certainty in which Elizabeth affected to place this point, as well as the still more interesting one of Bingley's being withheld from seeing Jane, she felt a solicitude on the subject which convinced her, on examination, that she did not consider it entirely hopeless. It was possible, and sometimes she thought it probable, that his affection might be reanimated, and the influence of his friends successfully combated by the more natural influence of Jane's attractions.

Miss Bennet accepted her aunt's invitation with pleasure; and the Bingleys were no otherwise in her thoughts at the same time, than as she hoped by Caroline's not living in the same house with her brother, she might occasionally spend a morning with her, without any danger of seeing him.

The Gardiners stayed a week at Longbourn; and what with the Phillipses, the Lucases, and the officers, there was not a day without its engagement. Mrs. Bennet had so carefully provided for the entertainment of her brother and sister, that they did not once sit down to a family dinner. When the engagement was for home, some of the officers always made part of it—of which officers Mr. Wickham was sure to be one; and on these occasions, Mrs. Gardiner, rendered suspicious by Elizabeth's warm commendation, narrowly observed them both. Without supposing them, from what she saw, to be very seriously in love, their preference of each other was plain enough to make her a little uneasy; and she resolved to speak to Elizabeth on the subject before she left Hertfordshire, and represent to her the imprudence of encouraging such an attachment.

To Mrs. Gardiner, Wickham had one means of affording pleasure, unconnected with his general powers. About ten or a dozen years ago, before her marriage, she had spent a considerable time in that very part of Derbyshire to which he belonged. They had, therefore, many acquaintances in common; and though Wickham had been little there since the death of Darcy's father, it was yet in his power to give her fresher intelligence of her former friends than she had been in the way of procuring.

Mrs. Gardiner had seen Pemberley, and known the late Mr. Darcy by character perfectly well. Here consequently was an inexhaustible subject of discourse. In comparing her recollection of Pemberley with the minute description which Wickham could give, and in bestowing her tribute of praise on the character of its late possessor, she was delighting both him and herself. On being made acquainted with the present Mr. Darcy's treatment of him, she tried to remember something of that gentleman's reputed disposition when quite a lad which might agree with it, and was confident at last that she recollected having heard Mr. Fitzwilliam Darcy formerly spoken of as a very proud, ill-natured boy.

CHAPTER XXVI

Mrs. Gardiner's caution to Elizabeth was punctually and kindly given on the first favourable opportunity of speaking to her alone; after honestly telling her what she thought, she thus went on:

"You are too sensible a girl, Lizzy, to fall in love merely because you are warned against it; and, therefore, I am not afraid of speaking openly. Seriously, I would have you be on your guard. Do not involve yourself or endeavour to involve him in an affection which the want of fortune would make so very imprudent. I have nothing to say against *him*; he is a most interesting young man; and if he had the fortune he ought to have, I should think you could not do better. But as it is, you must not let your fancy run away with you. You have sense, and we all expect you to use it. Your father would depend on *your* resolution and good conduct, I am sure. You must not disappoint your father."

"My dear aunt, this is being serious indeed."

"Yes, and I hope to engage you to be serious likewise."

"Well, then, you need not be under any alarm. I will take care of myself, and of Mr. Wickham too. He shall not be in love with me, if I can prevent it."

"Elizabeth, you are not serious now."

"I beg your pardon, I will try again. At present I am not in love with Mr. Wickham; no, I certainly am not. But he is, beyond all comparison, the most agreeable man I ever saw—and if he becomes really attached to me—I believe it will be better that he should not. I see the imprudence of it. Oh! *that* abominable Mr. Darcy! My father's opinion of me does me the greatest honour, and I should be miserable to forfeit it. My father, however, is partial to Mr. Wickham. In short, my dear aunt, I should be very sorry to be the means of making any of you unhappy; but since we see every day that where there is affection, young people are seldom withheld by immediate want of fortune from entering into engagements with each other, how can I promise to be wiser than so many of my fellow-creatures if I am tempted, or how am I even to know that it would be wisdom to resist? All that I can promise you, therefore, is not to be in a hurry. I will not be in a hurry to believe myself his first object. When I am in company with him, I will not be wishing. In short, I will do my best."

"Perhaps it will be as well if you discourage his coming here so very often. At least, you should not *remind* your mother of inviting him."

"As I did the other day," said Elizabeth with a conscious smile: "very true, it will be wise in me to refrain from *that*. But do not imagine that he is always here so often. It is on your account that he has been so frequently invited this week. You know my mother's ideas as to the necessity of constant company for her friends. But really, and upon my honour, I will try to do what I think to be the wisest; and now I hope you are satisfied."

Her aunt assured her that she was, and Elizabeth having thanked her for the kindness of her hints, they parted; a wonderful instance of advice being given on such a point, without being resented.

Mr. Collins returned into Hertfordshire soon after it had been quitted by the Gardiners and Jane; but as he took up his abode with the Lucases, his arrival was no great inconvenience to Mrs. Bennet. His marriage was now fast approaching, and she was at length so far resigned as to think it inevitable, and even repeatedly to say, in an ill-natured tone, that she "*wished* they might be happy." Thursday was to be the wedding day, and on Wednesday Miss Lucas paid her farewell visit; and when she rose to take leave, Elizabeth, ashamed of her mother's ungracious and reluctant good wishes, and sincerely affected herself, accompanied her out of the room. As they went downstairs together, Charlotte said:

"I shall depend on hearing from you very often, Eliza."

"*That* you certainly shall."

"And I have another favour to ask you. Will you come and see me?"

"We shall often meet, I hope, in Hertfordshire."

"I am not likely to leave Kent for some time. Promise me, therefore, to come to Hunsford."

Elizabeth could not refuse, though she foresaw little pleasure in the visit.

"My father and Maria are coming to me in March," added Charlotte, "and I hope you will consent to be of the party. Indeed, Eliza, you will be as welcome as either of them."

The wedding took place; the bride and bridegroom set off for Kent from the church door, and everybody had as much to say, or to hear, on the subject as usual. Elizabeth soon heard from her friend; and their correspondence was as regular and frequent as it had ever been; that it should be equally unreserved was impossible. Elizabeth could never address her without feeling that all the comfort of intimacy was over, and though determined not to slacken as a correspondent, it was for the sake of what had been, rather than what was. Charlotte's first letters were received with a good deal of eagerness; there could not but be curiosity to know how she would speak of her new home, how she would like Lady Catherine, and how happy she would dare pronounce herself to be; though, when the letters were read, Elizabeth felt that Charlotte expressed herself on every point exactly as she might have foreseen. She wrote cheerfully, seemed surrounded with comforts, and mentioned nothing which she could not praise. The house, furniture, neighbourhood, and roads, were all to her taste, and Lady Catherine's behaviour was most friendly and obliging. It was Mr. Collins's picture of Hunsford and Rosings rationally softened; and Elizabeth perceived that she must wait for her own visit there to know the rest.

Jane had already written a few lines to her sister to announce their safe arrival in London; and when she wrote again, Elizabeth hoped it would be in her power to say something of the Bingleys.

Her impatience for this second letter was as well rewarded as impatience generally is. Jane had been a week in town without either seeing or hearing from Caroline. She accounted for it, however, by supposing that her last letter to her friend from Longbourn had by some accident been lost.

"My aunt," she continued, "is going to-morrow into that part of the town, and I shall take the opportunity of calling in Grosvenor Street."

She wrote again when the visit was paid, and she had seen Miss Bingley. "I did not think Caroline in spirits," were her words, "but she was very glad to see me, and reproached me for giving her no notice of my coming to London. I was right, therefore, my last letter had never reached her. I inquired after their brother, of course. He was well, but so much engaged with Mr. Darcy that they scarcely ever saw him. I found that Miss Darcy was expected to dinner. I wish I could see her. My visit was not long, as Caroline and Mrs. Hurst were going out. I dare say I shall see them soon here."

Elizabeth shook her head over this letter. It convinced her that accident only could discover to Mr. Bingley her sister's being in town.

Four weeks passed away, and Jane saw nothing of him. She endeavoured to persuade herself that she did not regret it; but she could no longer be blind to Miss Bingley's inattention. After waiting at home every morning for a fortnight, and inventing every evening a fresh excuse for her, the visitor did at last appear; but the shortness of her stay, and yet more, the alteration of her manner would allow Jane to deceive herself no longer. The letter which she wrote on this occasion to her sister will prove what she felt.

"My dearest Lizzy will, I am sure, be incapable of triumphing in her better judgement, at my expense, when I confess myself to have been entirely deceived in Miss Bingley's regard for me. But, my dear sister, though the event has proved you right, do not think me obstinate if I still assert that, considering what her behaviour was, my confidence was as natural as your suspicion. I do not at all comprehend her reason for wishing to be intimate with me; but if the same circumstances were to happen again, I am sure I should be deceived again. Caroline did not return my visit till yesterday; and not a note, not a line, did I receive in the meantime. When she did come, it was very evident that she had no pleasure in it; she made a slight, formal apology, for not calling before, said not a word of wishing to see me again, and was in every respect so altered a creature, that when she went away I was perfectly resolved to continue the acquaintance no longer. I pity, though I cannot help blaming her. She was very wrong in singling me out as she did; I can safely say that every advance to intimacy began on her side. But I pity her, because she must feel that she has been acting wrong, and because I am very sure that anxiety for her brother is the cause of it. I need not explain myself farther; and though *we* know this anxiety to be quite needless, yet if she feels it, it will easily account for her behaviour to me; and so deservedly dear as he is to his sister, whatever anxiety she must feel on his behalf is natural and amiable. I cannot but wonder, however, at her having any such fears now, because, if he had at all cared about me, we must have met, long ago. He knows of my being in town, I am certain, from something she said herself; and yet it would seem, by her manner of talking, as if she wanted to persuade herself that he is really partial to Miss Darcy. I cannot understand it. If I were not afraid of judging harshly, I should be almost tempted to say that there is a strong appearance of duplicity in all this. But I will endeavour to banish every painful thought, and think only of what will make me happy—your affection, and the invariable kindness of my dear uncle and aunt. Let me hear from you very soon. Miss Bingley said something of his never returning to Netherfield again, of giving up the house, but not with any certainty. We had better not mention it. I am extremely glad that you have such pleasant accounts from our friends at Hunsford. Pray go to see them, with Sir William and Maria. I am sure you will be very comfortable there.—Yours, etc."

This letter gave Elizabeth some pain; but her spirits returned as she considered that Jane would no longer be duped, by the sister at least. All expectation from the brother was now absolutely over. She would not even wish for a renewal of his attentions. His character sunk on every review of it; and as a punishment for him, as well as a possible advantage to Jane, she seriously hoped he might really soon marry Mr. Darcy's sister, as by Wickham's account, she would make him abundantly regret what he had thrown away.

Mrs. Gardiner about this time reminded Elizabeth of her promise concerning that gentleman, and required information; and Elizabeth had such to send as might rather give contentment to her aunt than to herself. His apparent partiality had subsided, his attentions were over, he was the admirer of some one else. Elizabeth was watchful enough to see it all, but she could see it and write of it without material pain. Her heart had been but slightly touched, and her vanity was satisfied with believing that *she* would have been his only choice, had fortune permitted it. The sudden acquisition of ten thousand pounds was the most remarkable charm of the young lady to whom he was now rendering himself agreeable; but Elizabeth, less clear-sighted perhaps in this case than in Charlotte's, did not quarrel with him for his wish of independence. Nothing, on the contrary, could be more natural; and while able to suppose that it cost him a few struggles to relinquish her, she was ready to allow it a wise and desirable measure for both, and could very sincerely wish him happy.

All this was acknowledged to Mrs. Gardiner; and after relating the circumstances, she thus went on: "I am now convinced, my dear aunt, that I have never been much in love; for had I really experienced that pure and elevating passion, I should at present detest his very name, and wish him all manner of evil. But my feelings are not only cordial towards *him*; they are even impartial towards Miss King. I cannot find out that I hate her at all, or that I am in the least unwilling to think her a very good sort of girl. There can be no love in all this. My watchfulness has been effectual; and though I certainly should be a more interesting object to all my acquaintances were I distractedly in love with him, I cannot say that I regret my comparative insignificance. Importance may sometimes be purchased too dearly. Kitty and Lydia take his defection much more to heart than I do. They are young in the ways of the world, and not yet open to the mortifying conviction that handsome young men must have something to live on as well as the plain."

CHAPTER XXVII

With no greater events than these in the Longbourn family, and otherwise diversified by little beyond the walks to Meryton, sometimes dirty and sometimes cold, did January and February pass away. March was to take Elizabeth to Hunsford. She had not at first thought very seriously of going thither; but Charlotte, she soon found, was depending on the plan and she gradually learned to consider it herself with greater pleasure as well as greater certainty. Absence had increased her desire of seeing Charlotte again, and weakened her disgust of Mr. Collins. There was novelty in the scheme, and as, with such a mother and such uncompanionable sisters, home could not be faultless, a little change was not unwelcome for its own sake. The journey would moreover give her a peep at Jane; and, in short, as the time drew near, she would have been very sorry for any delay. Everything, however, went on smoothly, and was finally settled according to Charlotte's first sketch. She was to accompany Sir William and his second daughter. The improvement of spending a night in London was added in time, and the plan became perfect as plan could be.

The only pain was in leaving her father, who would certainly miss her, and who, when it came to the point, so little liked her going, that he told her to write to him, and almost promised to answer her letter.

The farewell between herself and Mr. Wickham was perfectly friendly; on his side even more. His present pursuit could not make him forget that Elizabeth had been the first to excite and to deserve his attention, the first to listen and to pity, the first to be admired; and in his manner of bidding her adieu, wishing her every enjoyment, reminding her of what she was to expect in Lady Catherine de Bourgh, and trusting their opinion of her—their opinion of everybody—would always coincide, there was a solicitude, an interest which she felt must ever attach her to him with a most sincere regard; and she parted from him convinced that, whether married or single, he must always be her model of the amiable and pleasing.

Her fellow-travellers the next day were not of a kind to make her think him less agreeable. Sir William Lucas, and his daughter Maria, a good-humoured girl, but as empty-headed as himself, had nothing to say that could be worth hearing, and were listened to with about as much delight as the rattle of the chaise. Elizabeth loved absurdities, but she had known Sir William's too long. He could tell her nothing new of the wonders of his presentation and knighthood; and his civilities were worn out, like his information.

It was a journey of only twenty-four miles, and they began it so early as to be in Gracechurch Street by noon. As they drove to Mr. Gardiner's door, Jane was at a drawing-room window watching their arrival; when they entered the passage she was there to welcome them, and Elizabeth, looking earnestly in her face, was pleased to see it healthful and lovely as ever. On the stairs were a troop of little boys and girls, whose eagerness for their cousin's appearance would not allow them to wait in the drawing-room, and whose shyness, as they had not seen her for a twelvemonth, prevented their coming lower. All was joy and kindness. The day passed most pleasantly away; the morning in bustle and shopping, and the evening at one of the theatres.

Elizabeth then contrived to sit by her aunt. Their first object was her sister; and she was more grieved than astonished to hear, in reply to her minute inquiries, that though Jane always struggled to support her spirits, there were periods of dejection. It was reasonable, however, to hope that they would not continue long. Mrs. Gardiner gave her the particulars also of Miss Bingley's visit in Gracechurch Street, and repeated conversations occurring at different times between Jane and herself, which proved that the former had, from her heart, given up the acquaintance.

Mrs. Gardiner then rallied her niece on Wickham's desertion, and complimented her on bearing it so well.

"But my dear Elizabeth," she added, "what sort of girl is Miss King? I should be sorry to think our friend mercenary."

"Pray, my dear aunt, what is the difference in matrimonial affairs, between the mercenary and the prudent motive? Where does discretion end, and avarice begin? Last Christmas you were afraid of his marrying me, because it would be imprudent; and now, because he is trying to get a girl with only ten thousand pounds, you want to find out that he is mercenary."

"If you will only tell me what sort of girl Miss King is, I shall know what to think."

"She is a very good kind of girl, I believe. I know no harm of her."

"But he paid her not the smallest attention till her grandfather's death made her mistress of this fortune."

"No—what should he? If it were not allowable for him to gain *my* affections because I had no money, what occasion could there be for making love to a girl whom he did not care about, and who was equally poor?"

"But there seems an indelicacy in directing his attentions towards her so soon after this event."

"A man in distressed circumstances has not time for all those elegant decorums which other people may observe. If *she* does not object to it, why should *we*?"

"*Her* not objecting does not justify *him*. It only shows her being deficient in something herself—sense or feeling."

"Well," cried Elizabeth, "have it as you choose. *He* shall be mercenary, and *she* shall be foolish."

"No, Lizzy, that is what I do *not* choose. I should be sorry, you know, to think ill of a young man who has lived so long in Derbyshire."

"Oh! if that is all, I have a very poor opinion of young men who live in Derbyshire; and their intimate friends who live in Hertfordshire are not much better. I am sick of them all. Thank Heaven! I am going to-morrow where I shall find a man who has not one agreeable quality, who has neither manner nor sense to recommend him. Stupid men are the only ones worth knowing, after all."

"Take care, Lizzy; that speech savours strongly of disappointment."

Before they were separated by the conclusion of the play, she had the unexpected happiness of an invitation to accompany her uncle and aunt in a tour of pleasure which they proposed taking in the summer.

"We have not determined how far it shall carry us," said Mrs. Gardiner, "but, perhaps, to the Lakes."

No scheme could have been more agreeable to Elizabeth, and her acceptance of the invitation was most ready and grateful. "Oh, my dear, dear aunt," she rapturously cried, "what delight! what felicity! You give me fresh life and vigour. Adieu to disappointment and spleen. What are young men to rocks and mountains? Oh! what hours of transport we shall spend! And when we *do* return, it shall not be like other travellers, without being able to give one accurate idea of anything. We *will* know where we have gone—we *will* recollect what we have seen. Lakes, mountains, and rivers shall not be jumbled together in our imaginations; nor when we attempt to describe any particular scene, will we begin quarreling about its relative situation. Let *our* first effusions be less insupportable than those of the generality of travellers."

CHAPTER XXVIII

Every object in the next day's journey was new and interesting to Elizabeth; and her spirits were in a state of enjoyment; for she had seen her sister looking so well as to banish all fear for her health, and the prospect of her northern tour was a constant source of delight.

When they left the high road for the lane to Hunsford, every eye was in search of the Parsonage, and every turning expected to bring it in view. The palings of Rosings Park was their boundary on one side. Elizabeth smiled at the recollection of all that she had heard of its inhabitants.

At length the Parsonage was discernible. The garden sloping to the road, the house standing in it, the green pales, and the laurel hedge, everything declared they were arriving. Mr. Collins and Charlotte appeared at the door, and the carriage stopped at the small gate which led by a short gravel walk to the house, amidst the nods and smiles of the whole party. In a moment they were all out of the chaise, rejoicing at the sight of each other. Mrs. Collins welcomed her friend with the liveliest pleasure, and Elizabeth was more and more satisfied with coming when she found herself so affectionately received. She saw instantly that her cousin's manners were not altered by his marriage; his formal civility was just what it had been, and he detained her some minutes at the gate to hear and satisfy his inquiries after all her family. They were then, with no other delay than his pointing out the neatness of the entrance, taken into the house; and as soon as they were in the parlour, he welcomed them a second time, with ostentatious formality to his humble abode, and punctually repeated all his wife's offers of refreshment.

Elizabeth was prepared to see him in his glory; and she could not help in fancying that in displaying the good proportion of the room, its aspect and its furniture, he addressed himself particularly to her, as if wishing to make her feel what she had lost in refusing him. But though everything seemed neat and comfortable, she was not able to gratify him by any sigh of repentance, and rather looked with wonder at her friend that she could have so cheerful an air with such a companion. When Mr. Collins said anything of which his wife might reasonably be ashamed, which certainly was not unseldom, she involuntarily turned her eye on Charlotte. Once or twice she could discern a faint blush; but in general Charlotte wisely did not hear. After sitting long enough to admire every article of furniture in the room, from the sideboard to the fender, to give an account of their journey, and of all that had happened in London, Mr. Collins invited them to take a stroll in the garden, which was large and well laid out, and to the cultivation of which he attended himself. To work in this garden was one of his most respectable pleasures; and Elizabeth admired the command of countenance with which Charlotte talked of the healthfulness of the exercise, and owned she encouraged it as much as possible. Here, leading the way through every walk and cross walk, and scarcely allowing them an interval to utter the praises he asked for, every view was pointed out with a minuteness which left beauty entirely behind. He could number the fields in every direction, and could tell how many trees there were in the most distant clump. But of all the views which his garden, or which the country or kingdom could boast, none were to be compared with the prospect of Rosings, afforded by an opening in the trees that bordered the park nearly opposite the front of his house. It was a handsome modern building, well situated on rising ground.

From his garden, Mr. Collins would have led them round his two meadows; but the ladies, not having shoes to encounter the remains of a white frost, turned back; and while Sir William accompanied him, Charlotte took her sister and friend over the house, extremely well pleased, probably, to have the opportunity of showing it without her husband's help. It was rather small, but well built and convenient; and everything was fitted up and arranged with a neatness and consistency of which Elizabeth gave Charlotte all the credit. When Mr. Collins could be forgotten, there was really an air of great comfort throughout, and by Charlotte's evident enjoyment of it, Elizabeth supposed he must be often forgotten.

She had already learnt that Lady Catherine was still in the country. It was spoken of again while they were at dinner, when Mr. Collins joining in, observed:

"Yes, Miss Elizabeth, you will have the honour of seeing Lady Catherine de Bourgh on the ensuing Sunday at church, and I need not say you will be delighted with her. She is all affability and condescension, and I doubt not but you will be honoured with some portion of her notice when service is over. I have scarcely any hesitation in saying she will include you and my sister Maria in every invitation with which she honours us during your stay here. Her behaviour to my dear Charlotte is charming. We dine at Rosings twice every week, and are never allowed to walk home. Her ladyship's carriage is regularly ordered for us. I *should* say, one of her ladyship's carriages, for she has several."

"Lady Catherine is a very respectable, sensible woman indeed," added Charlotte, "and a most attentive neighbour."

"Very true, my dear, that is exactly what I say. She is the sort of woman whom one cannot regard with too much deference."

The evening was spent chiefly in talking over Hertfordshire news, and telling again what had already been written; and when it closed, Elizabeth, in the solitude of her chamber, had to meditate upon Charlotte's degree of contentment, to understand her address in guiding, and composure in bearing with, her husband, and to acknowledge that it was all done very well. She had also to anticipate how her visit would pass, the quiet tenor of their usual employments, the vexatious interruptions of Mr. Collins, and the gaieties of their intercourse with Rosings. A lively imagination soon settled it all.

About the middle of the next day, as she was in her room getting ready for a walk, a sudden noise below seemed to speak the whole house in confusion; and, after listening a moment, she heard somebody running upstairs in a violent hurry, and calling loudly after her. She opened the door and met Maria in the landing place, who, breathless with agitation, cried out—

"Oh, my dear Eliza! pray make haste and come into the dining-room, for there is such a sight to be seen! I will not tell you what it is. Make haste, and come down this moment."

Elizabeth asked questions in vain; Maria would tell her nothing more, and down they ran into the dining-room, which fronted the lane, in quest of this wonder; It was two ladies stopping in a low phaeton at the garden gate.

"And is this all?" cried Elizabeth. "I expected at least that the pigs were got into the garden, and here is nothing but Lady Catherine and her daughter."

"La! my dear," said Maria, quite shocked at the mistake, "it is not Lady Catherine. The old lady is Mrs. Jenkinson, who lives with them;

the other is Miss de Bourgh. Only look at her. She is quite a little creature. Who would have thought that she could be so thin and small?"

"She is abominably rude to keep Charlotte out of doors in all this wind. Why does she not come in?"

"Oh, Charlotte says she hardly ever does. It is the greatest of favours when Miss de Bourgh comes in."

"I like her appearance," said Elizabeth, struck with other ideas. "She looks sickly and cross. Yes, she will do for him very well. She will make him a very proper wife."

Mr. Collins and Charlotte were both standing at the gate in conversation with the ladies; and Sir William, to Elizabeth's high diversion, was stationed in the doorway, in earnest contemplation of the greatness before him, and constantly bowing whenever Miss de Bourgh looked that way.

At length there was nothing more to be said; the ladies drove on, and the others returned into the house. Mr. Collins no sooner saw the two girls than he began to congratulate them on their good fortune, which Charlotte explained by letting them know that the whole party was asked to dine at Rosings the next day.

CHAPTER XXIX

Mr. Collins's triumph, in consequence of this invitation, was complete. The power of displaying the grandeur of his patroness to his wondering visitors, and of letting them see her civility towards himself and his wife, was exactly what he had wished for; and that an opportunity of doing it should be given so soon, was such an instance of Lady Catherine's condescension, as he knew not how to admire enough.

"I confess," said he, "that I should not have been at all surprised by her ladyship's asking us on Sunday to drink tea and spend the evening at Rosings. I rather expected, from my knowledge of her affability, that it would happen. But who could have foreseen such an attention as this? Who could have imagined that we should receive an invitation to dine there (an invitation, moreover, including the whole party) so immediately after your arrival!"

"I am the less surprised at what has happened," replied Sir William, "from that knowledge of what the manners of the great really are, which my situation in life has allowed me to acquire. About the court, such instances of elegant breeding are not uncommon."

Scarcely anything was talked of the whole day or next morning but their visit to Rosings. Mr. Collins was carefully instructing them in what they were to expect, that the sight of such rooms, so many servants, and so splendid a dinner, might not wholly overpower them.

When the ladies were separating for the toilette, he said to Elizabeth—

"Do not make yourself uneasy, my dear cousin, about your apparel. Lady Catherine is far from requiring that elegance of dress in us which becomes herself and her daughter. I would advise you merely to put on whatever of your clothes is superior to the rest—there is no occasion for anything more. Lady Catherine will not think the worse of you for being simply dressed. She likes to have the distinction of rank preserved."

While they were dressing, he came two or three times to their different doors, to recommend their being quick, as Lady Catherine very much objected to be kept waiting for her dinner. Such formidable accounts of her ladyship, and her manner of living, quite frightened

Maria Lucas who had been little used to company, and she looked forward to her introduction at Rosings with as much apprehension as her father had done to his presentation at St. James's.

As the weather was fine, they had a pleasant walk of about half a mile across the park. Every park has its beauty and its prospects; and Elizabeth saw much to be pleased with, though she could not be in such raptures as Mr. Collins expected the scene to inspire, and was but slightly affected by his enumeration of the windows in front of the house, and his relation of what the glazing altogether had originally cost Sir Lewis de Bourgh.

When they ascended the steps to the hall, Maria's alarm was every moment increasing, and even Sir William did not look perfectly calm. Elizabeth's courage did not fail her. She had heard nothing of Lady Catherine that spoke her awful from any extraordinary talents or miraculous virtue, and the mere stateliness of money or rank she thought she could witness without trepidation.

From the entrance-hall, of which Mr. Collins pointed out, with a rapturous air, the fine proportion and the finished ornaments, they followed the servants through an ante-chamber, to the room where Lady Catherine, her daughter, and Mrs. Jenkinson were sitting. Her ladyship, with great condescension, arose to receive them; and as Mrs. Collins had settled it with her husband that the office of introduction should be hers, it was performed in a proper manner, without any of those apologies and thanks which he would have thought necessary.

In spite of having been at St. James's Sir William was so completely awed by the grandeur surrounding him, that he had but just courage enough to make a very low bow, and take his seat without saying a word; and his daughter, frightened almost out of her senses, sat on the edge of her chair, not knowing which way to look. Elizabeth found herself quite equal to the scene, and could observe the three ladies before her composedly. Lady Catherine was a tall, large woman, with strongly-marked features, which might once have been handsome. Her air was not conciliating, nor was her manner of receiving them such as to make her visitors forget their inferior rank. She was not rendered formidable by silence; but whatever she said was spoken in so authoritative a tone, as marked her self-importance, and brought Mr. Wickham immediately to Elizabeth's mind; and from the observation of the day altogether, she believed Lady Catherine to be exactly what he represented.

When, after examining the mother, in whose countenance and deportment she soon found some resemblance of Mr. Darcy, she turned her eyes on the daughter, she could almost have joined in Maria's astonishment at her being so thin and so small. There was neither in figure nor face any likeness between the ladies. Miss de Bourgh was pale and sickly; her features, though not plain, were insignificant; and she spoke very little, except in a low voice, to Mrs. Jenkinson, in whose appearance there was nothing remarkable, and who was entirely engaged in listening to what she said, and placing a screen in the proper direction before her eyes.

After sitting a few minutes, they were all sent to one of the windows to admire the view, Mr. Collins attending them to point out its beauties, and Lady Catherine kindly informing them that it was much better worth looking at in the summer.

The dinner was exceedingly handsome, and there were all the servants and all the articles of plate which Mr. Collins had promised; and, as he had likewise foretold, he took his seat at the bottom of the table, by her ladyship's desire, and looked as if he felt that life could furnish nothing greater. He carved, and ate, and praised with delighted alacrity; and every dish was commended, first by him and then by Sir William, who was now enough recovered to echo whatever his son-in-law said, in a manner which Elizabeth wondered Lady Catherine could bear. But Lady Catherine seemed gratified by their excessive admiration, and gave most gracious smiles, especially when any dish on the table proved a novelty to them. The party did not supply much conversation. Elizabeth was ready to speak whenever there was an opening, but she was seated between Charlotte and Miss de Bourgh—the former of whom was engaged in listening to Lady Catherine, and the latter said not a word to her all dinner-time. Mrs. Jenkinson was chiefly employed in watching how little Miss de Bourgh ate, pressing her to try some other dish, and fearing she was indisposed. Maria thought speaking out of the question, and the gentlemen did nothing but eat and admire.

When the ladies returned to the drawing-room, there was little to be done but to hear Lady Catherine talk, which she did without any intermission till coffee came in, delivering her opinion on every subject in so decisive a manner, as proved that she was not used to have her judgement controverted. She inquired into Charlotte's domestic concerns familiarly and minutely, gave her a great deal of advice as to the management of them all; told her how everything ought to be regulated in so small a family as hers, and instructed her as to the care of her cows and her poultry. Elizabeth found that nothing was beneath this great lady's attention, which could furnish her with an occasion of dictating to others. In the intervals of her discourse with Mrs. Collins, she addressed a variety of questions to Maria and Elizabeth, but especially to the latter, of whose connections she knew the least, and who she observed to Mrs. Collins was a very genteel, pretty kind of girl. She asked her, at different times, how many sisters she had, whether they were older or younger than herself, whether any of them were likely to be married, whether they were handsome, where they had been educated, what carriage her father kept, and what had been her mother's maiden name? Elizabeth felt all the impertinence of her questions but answered them very composedly. Lady Catherine then observed,

"Your father's estate is entailed on Mr. Collins, I think. For your sake," turning to Charlotte, "I am glad of it; but otherwise I see no occasion for entailing estates from the female line. It was not thought necessary in Sir Lewis de Bourgh's family. Do you play and sing, Miss Bennet?"

"A little."

"Oh! then—some time or other we shall be happy to hear you. Our instrument is a capital one, probably superior to—You shall try it some day. Do your sisters play and sing?"

"One of them does."

"Why did not you all learn? You ought all to have learned. The Miss Webbs all play, and their father has not so good an income as yours. Do you draw?"

"No, not at all."

"What, none of you?"

"Not one."

"That is very strange. But I suppose you had no opportunity. Your mother should have taken you to town every spring for the benefit of masters."

"My mother would have had no objection, but my father hates London."

"Has your governess left you?"

"We never had any governess."

"No governess! How was that possible? Five daughters brought up at home without a governess! I never heard of such a thing. Your mother must have been quite a slave to your education."

Elizabeth could hardly help smiling as she assured her that had not been the case.

"Then, who taught you? who attended to you? Without a governess, you must have been neglected."

"Compared with some families, I believe we were; but such of us as wished to learn never wanted the means. We were always encouraged to read, and had all the masters that were necessary. Those who chose to be idle, certainly might."

"Aye, no doubt; but that is what a governess will prevent, and if I had known your mother, I should have advised her most strenuously to engage one. I always say that nothing is to be done in education without steady and regular instruction, and nobody but a governess can give it. It is wonderful how many families I have been the means of supplying in that way. I am always glad to get a young person well placed out. Four nieces of Mrs. Jenkinson are most delightfully situated through my means; and it was but the other day that I recommended another young person, who was merely accidentally mentioned to me, and the family are quite delighted with her. Mrs. Collins, did I tell you of Lady Metcalf's calling yesterday to thank me? She finds Miss Pope a treasure. 'Lady Catherine,' said she, 'you have given me a treasure.' Are any of your younger sisters out, Miss Bennet?"

"Yes, ma'am, all."

"All! What, all five out at once? Very odd! And you only the second. The younger ones out before the elder ones are married! Your younger sisters must be very young?"

"Yes, my youngest is not sixteen. Perhaps *she* is full young to be much in company. But really, ma'am, I think it would be very hard upon younger sisters, that they should not have their share of society and amusement, because the elder may not have the means or inclination to marry early. The last-born has as good a right to the pleasures of youth as the first. And to be kept back on *such* a motive! I think it would not be very likely to promote sisterly affection or delicacy of mind."

"Upon my word," said her ladyship, "you give your opinion very decidedly for so young a person. Pray, what is your age?"

"With three younger sisters grown up," replied Elizabeth, smiling, "your ladyship can hardly expect me to own it."

Lady Catherine seemed quite astonished at not receiving a direct answer; and Elizabeth suspected herself to be the first creature who had ever dared to trifle with so much dignified impertinence.

"You cannot be more than twenty, I am sure, therefore you need not conceal your age."

"I am not one-and-twenty."

When the gentlemen had joined them, and tea was over, the card-tables were placed. Lady Catherine, Sir William, and Mr. and Mrs. Collins sat down to quadrille; and as Miss de Bourgh chose to play at cassino, the two girls had the honour of assisting Mrs. Jenkinson to make up her party. Their table was superlatively stupid. Scarcely a syllable was uttered that did not relate to the game, except when Mrs. Jenkinson expressed her fears of Miss de Bourgh's being too hot or too cold, or having too much or too little light. A great deal more passed at the other table. Lady Catherine was generally speaking—stating the mistakes of the three others, or relating some anecdote of herself. Mr. Collins was employed in agreeing to everything her ladyship said, thanking her for every fish he won, and apologising if he thought he won too many. Sir William did not say much. He was storing his memory with anecdotes and noble names.

When Lady Catherine and her daughter had played as long as they chose, the tables were broken up, the carriage was offered to Mrs. Collins, gratefully accepted and immediately ordered. The party then gathered round the fire to hear Lady Catherine determine what weather they were to have on the morrow. From these instructions they were summoned by the arrival of the coach; and with many speeches of thankfulness on Mr. Collins's side and as many bows on Sir William's they departed. As soon as they had driven from the door, Elizabeth was called on by her cousin to give her opinion of all that she had seen at Rosings, which, for Charlotte's sake, she made more favourable than it really was. But her commendation, though costing her some trouble, could by no means satisfy Mr. Collins, and he was very soon obliged to take her ladyship's praise into his own hands.

CHAPTER XXX

Sir William stayed only a week at Hunsford, but his visit was long enough to convince him of his daughter's being most comfortably settled, and of her possessing such a husband and such a neighbour as were not often met with. While Sir William was with them, Mr. Collins devoted his morning to driving him out in his gig, and showing him the country; but when he went away, the whole family returned to their usual employments, and Elizabeth was thankful to find that they did not see more of her cousin by the alteration, for the chief of the time between breakfast and dinner was now passed by him either at work in the garden or in reading and writing, and looking out of the window in his own book-room, which fronted the road. The room in which the ladies sat was backwards. Elizabeth had at first rather wondered that Charlotte should not prefer the dining-parlour for common use; it was a better sized room, and had a more pleasant aspect; but she soon saw that her friend had an excellent reason for what she did, for Mr. Collins would undoubtedly have been much less in his own apartment, had they sat in one equally lively; and she gave Charlotte credit for the arrangement.

From the drawing-room they could distinguish nothing in the lane, and were indebted to Mr. Collins for the knowledge of what carriages went along, and how often especially Miss de Bourgh drove by in her phaeton, which he never failed coming to inform them of, though it happened almost every day. She not unfrequently stopped at the Parsonage, and had a few minutes' conversation with Charlotte, but was scarcely ever prevailed upon to get out.

Very few days passed in which Mr. Collins did not walk to Rosings, and not many in which his wife did not think it necessary to go likewise; and till Elizabeth recollected that there might be other family livings to be disposed of, she could not understand the sacrifice of so many hours. Now and then they were honoured with a call from her ladyship, and nothing escaped her observation that was passing in the room during these visits. She examined into their employments, looked at their work, and advised them to do it differently; found fault with the arrangement of the furniture; or detected the housemaid in negligence; and if she accepted any refreshment, seemed to do it only for the sake of finding out that Mrs. Collins's joints of meat were too large for her family.

Elizabeth soon perceived, that though this great lady was not in commission of the peace of the county, she was a most active magistrate in her own parish, the minutest concerns of which were carried to her by Mr. Collins; and whenever any of the cottagers were disposed to be quarrelsome, discontented, or too poor, she sallied forth into the village to settle their differences, silence their complaints, and scold them into harmony and plenty.

The entertainment of dining at Rosings was repeated about twice a week; and, allowing for the loss of Sir William, and there being only one card-table in the evening, every such entertainment was the counterpart of the first. Their other engagements were few, as the style of living in the neighbourhood in general was beyond Mr. Collins's reach. This, however, was no evil to Elizabeth, and upon the whole she spent her time comfortably enough; there were half-hours of pleasant conversation with Charlotte, and the weather was so fine for the time of year that she had often great enjoyment out of doors. Her favourite walk, and where she frequently went while the others were calling on Lady Catherine, was along the open grove which edged that side of the park, where there was a nice sheltered path, which no one seemed to value but herself, and where she felt beyond the reach of Lady Catherine's curiosity.

In this quiet way, the first fortnight of her visit soon passed away. Easter was approaching, and the week preceding it was to bring an addition to the family at Rosings, which in so small a circle must be important. Elizabeth had heard soon after her arrival that Mr. Darcy was expected there in the course of a few weeks, and though there were not many of her acquaintances whom she did not prefer, his coming would furnish one comparatively new to look at in their Rosings parties, and she might be amused in seeing how hopeless Miss Bingley's designs on him were, by his behaviour to his cousin, for whom he was evidently destined by Lady Catherine, who talked of his coming with the greatest satisfaction, spoke of him in terms of the highest admiration, and seemed almost angry to find that he had already been frequently seen by Miss Lucas and herself.

His arrival was soon known at the Parsonage; for Mr. Collins was walking the whole morning within view of the lodges opening into

Hunsford Lane, in order to have the earliest assurance of it, and after making his bow as the carriage turned into the Park, hurried home with the great intelligence. On the following morning he hastened to Rosings to pay his respects. There were two nephews of Lady Catherine to require them, for Mr. Darcy had brought with him a Colonel Fitzwilliam, the younger son of his uncle Lord ——, and, to the great surprise of all the party, when Mr. Collins returned, the gentlemen accompanied him. Charlotte had seen them from her husband's room, crossing the road, and immediately running into the other, told the girls what an honour they might expect, adding:

"I may thank you, Eliza, for this piece of civility. Mr. Darcy would never have come so soon to wait upon me."

Elizabeth had scarcely time to disclaim all right to the compliment, before their approach was announced by the door-bell, and shortly afterwards the three gentlemen entered the room. Colonel Fitzwilliam, who led the way, was about thirty, not handsome, but in person and address most truly the gentleman. Mr. Darcy looked just as he had been used to look in Hertfordshire—paid his compliments, with his usual reserve, to Mrs. Collins, and whatever might be his feelings toward her friend, met her with every appearance of composure. Elizabeth merely curtseyed to him without saying a word.

Colonel Fitzwilliam entered into conversation directly with the readiness and ease of a well-bred man, and talked very pleasantly; but his cousin, after having addressed a slight observation on the house and garden to Mrs. Collins, sat for some time without speaking to anybody. At length, however, his civility was so far awakened as to inquire of Elizabeth after the health of her family. She answered him in the usual way, and after a moment's pause, added:

"My eldest sister has been in town these three months. Have you never happened to see her there?"

She was perfectly sensible that he never had; but she wished to see whether he would betray any consciousness of what had passed between the Bingleys and Jane, and she thought he looked a little confused as he answered that he had never been so fortunate as to meet Miss Bennet. The subject was pursued no farther, and the gentlemen soon afterwards went away.

CHAPTER XXXI

Colonel Fitzwilliam's manners were very much admired at the Parsonage, and the ladies all felt that he must add considerably to the pleasures of their engagements at Rosings. It was some days, however, before they received any invitation thither—for while there were visitors in the house, they could not be necessary; and it was not till Easter-day, almost a week after the gentlemen's arrival, that they were honoured by such an attention, and then they were merely asked on leaving church to come there in the evening. For the last week they had seen very little of Lady Catherine or her daughter. Colonel Fitzwilliam had called at the Parsonage more than once during the time, but Mr. Darcy they had seen only at church.

The invitation was accepted of course, and at a proper hour they joined the party in Lady Catherine's drawing-room. Her ladyship received them civilly, but it was plain that their company was by no means so acceptable as when she could get nobody else; and she was, in fact, almost engrossed by her nephews, speaking to them, especially to Darcy, much more than to any other person in the room.

Colonel Fitzwilliam seemed really glad to see them; anything was a welcome relief to him at Rosings; and Mrs. Collins's pretty friend had moreover caught his fancy very much. He now seated himself by her, and talked so agreeably of Kent and Hertfordshire, of travelling and staying at home, of new books and music, that Elizabeth had never been half so well entertained in that room before; and they conversed with so much spirit and flow, as to draw the attention of Lady Catherine herself, as well as of Mr. Darcy. *His* eyes had been soon and repeatedly turned towards them with a look of curiosity; and that her ladyship, after a while, shared the feeling, was more openly acknowledged, for she did not scruple to call out:

"What is that you are saying, Fitzwilliam? What is it you are talking of? What are you telling Miss Bennet? Let me hear what it is."

"We are speaking of music, madam," said he, when no longer able to avoid a reply.

"Of music! Then pray speak aloud. It is of all subjects my delight. I must have my share in the conversation if you are speaking of music.

There are few people in England, I suppose, who have more true enjoyment of music than myself, or a better natural taste. If I had ever learnt, I should have been a great proficient. And so would Anne, if her health had allowed her to apply. I am confident that she would have performed delightfully. How does Georgiana get on, Darcy?"

Mr. Darcy spoke with affectionate praise of his sister's proficiency.

"I am very glad to hear such a good account of her," said Lady Catherine; "and pray tell her from me, that she cannot expect to excel if she does not practice a good deal."

"I assure you, madam," he replied, "that she does not need such advice. She practises very constantly."

"So much the better. It cannot be done too much; and when I next write to her, I shall charge her not to neglect it on any account. I often tell young ladies that no excellence in music is to be acquired without constant practice. I have told Miss Bennet several times, that she will never play really well unless she practises more; and though Mrs. Collins has no instrument, she is very welcome, as I have often told her, to come to Rosings every day, and play on the pianoforte in Mrs. Jenkinson's room. She would be in nobody's way, you know, in that part of the house."

Mr. Darcy looked a little ashamed of his aunt's ill-breeding, and made no answer.

When coffee was over, Colonel Fitzwilliam reminded Elizabeth of having promised to play to him; and she sat down directly to the instrument. He drew a chair near her. Lady Catherine listened to half a song, and then talked, as before, to her other nephew; till the latter walked away from her, and making with his usual deliberation towards the pianoforte stationed himself so as to command a full view of the fair performer's countenance. Elizabeth saw what he was doing, and at the first convenient pause, turned to him with an arch smile, and said:

"You mean to frighten me, Mr. Darcy, by coming in all this state to hear me? I will not be alarmed though your sister *does* play so well. There is a stubbornness about me that never can bear to be frightened at the will of others. My courage always rises at every attempt to intimidate me."

"I shall not say you are mistaken," he replied, "because you could not really believe me to entertain any design of alarming you; and I have had the pleasure of your acquaintance long enough to know that you find great enjoyment in occasionally professing opinions which in fact are not your own."

Elizabeth laughed heartily at this picture of herself, and said to Colonel Fitzwilliam, "Your cousin will give you a very pretty notion of me, and teach you not to believe a word I say. I am particularly unlucky in meeting with a person so able to expose my real character, in a part of the world where I had hoped to pass myself off with some degree of credit. Indeed, Mr. Darcy, it is very ungenerous in you to mention all that you knew to my disadvantage in Hertfordshire—and, give me leave to say, very impolitic too—for it is provoking me to retaliate, and such things may come out as will shock your relations to hear."

"I am not afraid of you," said he, smilingly.

"Pray let me hear what you have to accuse him of," cried Colonel Fitzwilliam. "I should like to know how he behaves among strangers."

"You shall hear then—but prepare yourself for something very dreadful. The first time of my ever seeing him in Hertfordshire, you must know, was at a ball—and at this ball, what do you think he did? He danced only four dances, though gentlemen were scarce; and, to my certain knowledge, more than one young lady was sitting down in want of a partner. Mr. Darcy, you cannot deny the fact."

"I had not at that time the honour of knowing any lady in the assembly beyond my own party."

"True; and nobody can ever be introduced in a ball-room. Well, Colonel Fitzwilliam, what do I play next? My fingers wait your orders."

"Perhaps," said Darcy, "I should have judged better, had I sought an introduction; but I am ill-qualified to recommend myself to strangers."

"Shall we ask your cousin the reason of this?" said Elizabeth, still addressing Colonel Fitzwilliam. "Shall we ask him why a man of sense and education, and who has lived in the world, is ill qualified to recommend himself to strangers?"

"I can answer your question," said Fitzwilliam, "without applying to him. It is because he will not give himself the trouble."

"I certainly have not the talent which some people possess," said Darcy, "of conversing easily with those I have never seen before. I cannot catch their tone of conversation, or appear interested in their concerns, as I often see done."

"My fingers," said Elizabeth, "do not move over this instrument in the masterly manner which I see so many women's do. They have not the same force or rapidity, and do not produce the same expression. But then I have always supposed it to be my own fault—because I will not take the trouble of practising. It is not that I do not believe *my* fingers as capable as any other woman's of superior execution."

Darcy smiled and said, "You are perfectly right. You have employed your time much better. No one admitted to the privilege of hearing you can think anything wanting. We neither of us perform to strangers."

Here they were interrupted by Lady Catherine, who called out to know what they were talking of. Elizabeth immediately began playing again. Lady Catherine approached, and, after listening for a few minutes, said to Darcy:

"Miss Bennet would not play at all amiss if she practised more, and could have the advantage of a London master. She has a very good notion of fingering, though her taste is not equal to Anne's. Anne would have been a delightful performer, had her health allowed her to learn."

Elizabeth looked at Darcy to see how cordially he assented to his cousin's praise; but neither at that moment nor at any other could she discern any symptom of love; and from the whole of his behaviour to Miss de Bourgh she derived this comfort for Miss Bingley, that he might have been just as likely to marry *her*, had she been his relation.

Lady Catherine continued her remarks on Elizabeth's performance, mixing with them many instructions on execution and taste. Elizabeth received them with all the forbearance of civility, and, at the request of the gentlemen, remained at the instrument till her ladyship's carriage was ready to take them all home.

CHAPTER XXXII

Elizabeth was sitting by herself the next morning, and writing to Jane while Mrs. Collins and Maria were gone on business into the village, when she was startled by a ring at the door, the certain signal of a visitor. As she had heard no carriage, she thought it not unlikely to be Lady Catherine, and under that apprehension was putting away her half-finished letter that she might escape all impertinent questions, when the door opened, and, to her very great surprise, Mr. Darcy, and Mr. Darcy only, entered the room.

He seemed astonished too on finding her alone, and apologised for his intrusion by letting her know that he had understood all the ladies were to be within.

They then sat down, and when her inquiries after Rosings were made, seemed in danger of sinking into total silence. It was absolutely necessary, therefore, to think of something, and in this emergence recollecting *when* she had seen him last in Hertfordshire, and feeling curious to know what he would say on the subject of their hasty departure, she observed:

"How very suddenly you all quitted Netherfield last November, Mr. Darcy! It must have been a most agreeable surprise to Mr. Bingley to see you all after him so soon; for, if I recollect right, he went but the day before. He and his sisters were well, I hope, when you left London?"

"Perfectly so, I thank you."

She found that she was to receive no other answer, and, after a short pause added:

"I think I have understood that Mr. Bingley has not much idea of ever returning to Netherfield again?"

"I have never heard him say so; but it is probable that he may spend very little of his time there in the future. He has many friends, and is at a time of life when friends and engagements are continually increasing."

"If he means to be but little at Netherfield, it would be better for the neighbourhood that he should give up the place entirely, for then we might possibly get a settled family there. But, perhaps, Mr. Bingley did not take the house so much for the convenience of the neighbourhood as for his own, and we must expect him to keep it or quit it on the same principle."

"I should not be surprised," said Darcy, "if he were to give it up as soon as any eligible purchase offers."

Elizabeth made no answer. She was afraid of talking longer of his friend; and, having nothing else to say, was now determined to leave the trouble of finding a subject to him.

He took the hint, and soon began with, "This seems a very comfortable house. Lady Catherine, I believe, did a great deal to it when Mr. Collins first came to Hunsford."

"I believe she did—and I am sure she could not have bestowed her kindness on a more grateful object."

"Mr. Collins appears to be very fortunate in his choice of a wife."

"Yes, indeed, his friends may well rejoice in his having met with one of the very few sensible women who would have accepted him, or have made him happy if they had. My friend has an excellent understanding—though I am not certain that I consider her marrying Mr. Collins as the wisest thing she ever did. She seems perfectly happy, however, and in a prudential light it is certainly a very good match for her."

"It must be very agreeable for her to be settled within so easy a distance of her own family and friends."

"An easy distance, do you call it? It is nearly fifty miles."

"And what is fifty miles of good road? Little more than half a day's journey. Yes, I call it a *very* easy distance."

"I should never have considered the distance as one of the *advantages* of the match," cried Elizabeth. "I should never have said Mrs. Collins was settled *near* her family."

"It is a proof of your own attachment to Hertfordshire. Anything beyond the very neighbourhood of Longbourn, I suppose, would appear far."

As he spoke there was a sort of smile which Elizabeth fancied she understood; he must be supposing her to be thinking of Jane and Netherfield, and she blushed as she answered:

"I do not mean to say that a woman may not be settled too near her family. The far and the near must be relative, and depend on many varying circumstances. Where there is fortune to make the expenses of travelling unimportant, distance becomes no evil. But that is not the case *here*. Mr. and Mrs. Collins have a comfortable income, but not such a one as will allow of frequent journeys—and I am persuaded my friend would not call herself *near* her family under less than *half* the present distance."

Mr. Darcy drew his chair a little towards her, and said, "*You* cannot have a right to such very strong local attachment. *You* cannot have been always at Longbourn."

Elizabeth looked surprised. The gentleman experienced some change of feeling; he drew back his chair, took a newspaper from the table, and glancing over it, said, in a colder voice:

"Are you pleased with Kent?"

A short dialogue on the subject of the country ensued, on either side calm and concise—and soon put an end to by the entrance of Charlotte and her sister, just returned from her walk. The tete-a-tete surprised them. Mr. Darcy related the mistake which had occasioned his intruding on Miss Bennet, and after sitting a few minutes longer without saying much to anybody, went away.

"What can be the meaning of this?" said Charlotte, as soon as he was gone. "My dear, Eliza, he must be in love with you, or he would never have called us in this familiar way."

But when Elizabeth told of his silence; it did not seem very likely, even to Charlotte's wishes, to be the case; and after various conjectures, they could at last only suppose his visit to proceed from the difficulty of finding anything to do, which was the more probable from the time of year. All field sports were over. Within doors there was Lady Catherine, books, and a billiard-table, but gentlemen cannot always be within doors; and in the nearness of the Parsonage, or the pleasantness of the walk to it, or of the people who lived in it, the two cousins found a temptation from this period of walking thither almost every day. They called at various times of the morning, sometimes separately, sometimes together, and now and then accompanied by their aunt. It was plain to them all that Colonel Fitzwilliam came because he had pleasure in their society, a persuasion which of course recommended him still more; and Elizabeth was reminded by her own satisfaction in being with him, as well as by his evident admiration of her, of her former favourite George Wickham; and though, in comparing them, she saw there was less captivating softness in Colonel Fitzwilliam's manners, she believed he might have the best informed mind.

But why Mr. Darcy came so often to the Parsonage, it was more difficult to understand. It could not be for society, as he frequently sat there ten minutes together without opening his lips; and when he did speak, it seemed the effect of necessity rather than of choice—a sacrifice to propriety, not a pleasure to himself. He seldom appeared really animated. Mrs. Collins knew not what to make of him. Colonel Fitzwilliam's occasionally laughing at his stupidity, proved that he was generally different, which her own knowledge of him could not have told her; and as she would liked to have believed this change the effect of love, and the object of that love her friend Eliza, she set herself seriously to work to find it out. She watched him whenever they were at Rosings, and whenever he came to Hunsford; but without much success. He certainly looked at her friend a great deal, but the expression of that look was disputable. It was an earnest, steadfast gaze, but she often doubted whether there were much admiration in it, and sometimes it seemed nothing but absence of mind.

She had once or twice suggested to Elizabeth the possibility of his being partial to her, but Elizabeth always laughed at the idea; and Mrs. Collins did not think it right to press the subject, from the danger of raising expectations which might only end in disappointment; for in her opinion it admitted not of a doubt, that all her friend's dislike would vanish, if she could suppose him to be in her power.

In her kind schemes for Elizabeth, she sometimes planned her marrying Colonel Fitzwilliam. He was beyond comparison the most pleasant man; he certainly admired her, and his situation in life was most eligible; but, to counterbalance these advantages, Mr. Darcy had considerable patronage in the church, and his cousin could have none at all.

CHAPTER XXXIII

More than once did Elizabeth, in her ramble within the park, unexpectedly meet Mr. Darcy. She felt all the perverseness of the mischance that should bring him where no one else was brought, and, to prevent its ever happening again, took care to inform him at first that it was a favourite haunt of hers. How it could occur a second time, therefore, was very odd! Yet it did, and even a third. It seemed like wilful ill-nature, or a voluntary penance, for on these occasions it was not merely a few formal inquiries and an awkward pause and then away, but he actually thought it necessary to turn back and walk with her. He never said a great deal, nor did she give herself the trouble of talking or of listening much; but it struck her in the course of their third rencontre that he was asking some odd unconnected questions—about her pleasure in being at Hunsford, her love of solitary walks, and her opinion of Mr. and Mrs. Collins's happiness; and that in speaking of Rosings and her not perfectly understanding the house, he seemed to expect that whenever she came into Kent again she would be staying *there* too. His words seemed to imply it. Could he have Colonel Fitzwilliam in his thoughts? She supposed, if he meant anything, he must mean an allusion to what might arise in that quarter. It distressed her a little, and she was quite glad to find herself at the gate in the pales opposite the Parsonage.

She was engaged one day as she walked, in perusing Jane's last letter, and dwelling on some passages which proved that Jane had not written in spirits, when, instead of being again surprised by Mr. Darcy, she saw on looking up that Colonel Fitzwilliam was meeting her. Putting away the letter immediately and forcing a smile, she said:

"I did not know before that you ever walked this way."

"I have been making the tour of the park," he replied, "as I generally do every year, and intend to close it with a call at the Parsonage. Are you going much farther?"

"No, I should have turned in a moment."

And accordingly she did turn, and they walked towards the Parsonage together.

"Do you certainly leave Kent on Saturday?" said she.

"Yes—if Darcy does not put it off again. But I am at his disposal. He arranges the business just as he pleases."

"And if not able to please himself in the arrangement, he has at least pleasure in the great power of choice. I do not know anybody who seems more to enjoy the power of doing what he likes than Mr. Darcy."

"He likes to have his own way very well," replied Colonel Fitzwilliam. "But so we all do. It is only that he has better means of having it than many others, because he is rich, and many others are poor. I speak feelingly. A younger son, you know, must be inured to self-denial and dependence."

"In my opinion, the younger son of an earl can know very little of either. Now seriously, what have you ever known of self-denial and dependence? When have you been prevented by want of money from going wherever you chose, or procuring anything you had a fancy for?"

"These are home questions—and perhaps I cannot say that I have experienced many hardships of that nature. But in matters of greater weight, I may suffer from want of money. Younger sons cannot marry where they like."

"Unless where they like women of fortune, which I think they very often do."

"Our habits of expense make us too dependent, and there are not many in my rank of life who can afford to marry without some attention to money."

"Is this," thought Elizabeth, "meant for me?" and she coloured at the idea; but, recovering herself, said in a lively tone, "And pray, what is the usual price of an earl's younger son? Unless the elder brother is very sickly, I suppose you would not ask above fifty thousand pounds."

He answered her in the same style, and the subject dropped. To interrupt a silence which might make him fancy her affected with what had passed, she soon afterwards said:

"I imagine your cousin brought you down with him chiefly for the sake of having someone at his disposal. I wonder he does not marry, to secure a lasting convenience of that kind. But, perhaps, his sister does as well for the present, and, as she is under his sole care, he may do what he likes with her."

"No," said Colonel Fitzwilliam, "that is an advantage which he must divide with me. I am joined with him in the guardianship of Miss Darcy."

"Are you indeed? And pray what sort of guardians do you make?

Does your charge give you much trouble? Young ladies of her age are sometimes a little difficult to manage, and if she has the true Darcy spirit, she may like to have her own way."

As she spoke she observed him looking at her earnestly; and the manner in which he immediately asked her why she supposed Miss Darcy likely to give them any uneasiness, convinced her that she had somehow or other got pretty near the truth. She directly replied:

"You need not be frightened. I never heard any harm of her; and I dare say she is one of the most tractable creatures in the world. She is a very great favourite with some ladies of my acquaintance, Mrs. Hurst and Miss Bingley. I think I have heard you say that you know them."

"I know them a little. Their brother is a pleasant gentlemanlike man—he is a great friend of Darcy's."

"Oh! yes," said Elizabeth drily; "Mr. Darcy is uncommonly kind to Mr. Bingley, and takes a prodigious deal of care of him."

"Care of him! Yes, I really believe Darcy *does* take care of him in those points where he most wants care. From something that he told me in our journey hither, I have reason to think Bingley very much indebted to him. But I ought to beg his pardon, for I have no right to suppose that Bingley was the person meant. It was all conjecture."

"What is it you mean?"

"It is a circumstance which Darcy could not wish to be generally known, because if it were to get round to the lady's family, it would be an unpleasant thing."

"You may depend upon my not mentioning it."

"And remember that I have not much reason for supposing it to be Bingley. What he told me was merely this: that he congratulated himself on having lately saved a friend from the inconveniences of a most imprudent marriage, but without mentioning names or any other particulars, and I only suspected it to be Bingley from believing him the kind of young man to get into a scrape of that sort, and from knowing them to have been together the whole of last summer."

"Did Mr. Darcy give you reasons for this interference?"

"I understood that there were some very strong objections against the lady."

"And what arts did he use to separate them?"

"He did not talk to me of his own arts," said Fitzwilliam, smiling. "He only told me what I have now told you."

Elizabeth made no answer, and walked on, her heart swelling with indignation. After watching her a little, Fitzwilliam asked her why she was so thoughtful.

"I am thinking of what you have been telling me," said she. "Your cousin's conduct does not suit my feelings. Why was he to be the judge?"

"You are rather disposed to call his interference officious?"

"I do not see what right Mr. Darcy had to decide on the propriety of his friend's inclination, or why, upon his own judgement alone, he was to determine and direct in what manner his friend was to be happy. But," she continued, recollecting herself, "as we know none of the particulars, it is not fair to condemn him. It is not to be supposed that there was much affection in the case."

"That is not an unnatural surmise," said Fitzwilliam, "but it is a lessening of the honour of my cousin's triumph very sadly."

This was spoken jestingly; but it appeared to her so just a picture of Mr. Darcy, that she would not trust herself with an answer, and therefore, abruptly changing the conversation talked on indifferent matters until they reached the Parsonage. There, shut into her own room, as soon as their visitor left them, she could think without interruption of all that she had heard. It was not to be supposed that any other people could be meant than those with whom she was connected. There could not exist in the world *two* men over whom Mr. Darcy could have such boundless influence. That he had been concerned in the measures taken to separate Bingley and Jane she had never doubted; but she had always attributed to Miss Bingley the principal design and arrangement of them. If his own vanity, however, did not mislead him, *he* was the cause, his pride and caprice were the cause, of all that Jane had suffered, and still continued to suffer. He had ruined for a while every hope of happiness for the most affectionate, generous heart in the world; and no one could say how lasting an evil he might have inflicted.

"There were some very strong objections against the lady," were Colonel Fitzwilliam's words; and those strong objections probably were, her having one uncle who was a country attorney, and another who was in business in London.

"To Jane herself," she exclaimed, "there could be no possibility of objection; all loveliness and goodness as she is!—her understanding excellent, her mind improved, and her manners captivating. Neither could anything be urged against my father, who, though with some peculiarities, has abilities Mr. Darcy himself need not disdain, and respectability which he will probably never reach." When she thought of her mother, her confidence gave way a little; but she would not allow that any objections *there* had material weight with Mr. Darcy, whose pride, she was convinced, would receive a deeper wound from the want of importance in his friend's connections, than from their want of sense; and she was quite decided, at last, that he had been partly governed by this worst kind of pride, and partly by the wish of retaining Mr. Bingley for his sister.

The agitation and tears which the subject occasioned, brought on a headache; and it grew so much worse towards the evening, that, added to her unwillingness to see Mr. Darcy, it determined her not to attend her cousins to Rosings, where they were engaged to drink tea. Mrs. Collins, seeing that she was really unwell, did not press her to go and as much as possible prevented her husband from pressing her; but Mr. Collins could not conceal his apprehension of Lady Catherine's being rather displeased by her staying at home.

CHAPTER XXXIV

When they were gone, Elizabeth, as if intending to exasperate herself as much as possible against Mr. Darcy, chose for her employment the examination of all the letters which Jane had written to her since her being in Kent. They contained no actual complaint, nor was there any revival of past occurrences, or any communication of present suffering. But in all, and in almost every line of each, there was a want of that cheerfulness which had been used to characterise her style, and which, proceeding from the serenity of a mind at ease with itself and kindly disposed towards everyone, had been scarcely ever clouded. Elizabeth noticed every sentence conveying the idea of uneasiness, with an attention which it had hardly received on the first perusal. Mr. Darcy's shameful boast of what misery he had been able to inflict, gave her a keener sense of her sister's sufferings. It was some consolation to think that his visit to Rosings was to end on the day after the next—and, a still greater, that in less than a fortnight she should herself be with Jane again, and enabled to contribute to the recovery of her spirits, by all that affection could do.

She could not think of Darcy's leaving Kent without remembering that his cousin was to go with him; but Colonel Fitzwilliam had made it clear that he had no intentions at all, and agreeable as he was, she did not mean to be unhappy about him.

While settling this point, she was suddenly roused by the sound of the door-bell, and her spirits were a little fluttered by the idea of its being Colonel Fitzwilliam himself, who had once before called late in the evening, and might now come to inquire particularly after her. But this idea was soon banished, and her spirits were very differently affected, when, to her utter amazement, she saw Mr. Darcy walk into the room. In an hurried manner he immediately began an inquiry after her health, imputing his visit to a wish of hearing that she were better. She answered him with cold civility. He sat down for a few moments, and then getting up, walked about the room. Elizabeth was surprised, but said not a word. After a silence of several minutes, he came towards her in an agitated manner, and thus began:

"In vain I have struggled. It will not do. My feelings will not be repressed. You must allow me to tell you how ardently I admire and love you."

Elizabeth's astonishment was beyond expression. She stared, coloured, doubted, and was silent. This he considered sufficient encouragement; and the avowal of all that he felt, and had long felt for her, immediately followed. He spoke well; but there were feelings besides those of the heart to be detailed; and he was not more eloquent on the subject of tenderness than of pride. His sense of her inferiority—of its being a degradation—of the family obstacles which had always opposed to inclination, were dwelt on with a warmth which seemed due to the consequence he was wounding, but was very unlikely to recommend his suit.

In spite of her deeply-rooted dislike, she could not be insensible to the compliment of such a man's affection, and though her intentions did not vary for an instant, she was at first sorry for the pain he was to receive; till, roused to resentment by his subsequent language, she lost all compassion in anger. She tried, however, to compose herself to answer him with patience, when he should have done. He concluded with representing to her the strength of that attachment which, in spite of all his endeavours, he had found impossible to conquer; and with expressing his hope that it would now be rewarded by her acceptance of his hand. As he said this, she could easily see that he had no doubt of a favourable answer. He *spoke* of apprehension and anxiety, but his countenance expressed real security. Such a circumstance could only exasperate farther, and, when he ceased, the colour rose into her cheeks, and she said:

"In such cases as this, it is, I believe, the established mode to express a sense of obligation for the sentiments avowed, however unequally they may be returned. It is natural that obligation should be felt, and if I could *feel* gratitude, I would now thank you. But I cannot—I have never desired your good opinion, and you have certainly bestowed it most unwillingly. I am sorry to have occasioned pain to anyone. It has been most unconsciously done, however, and I hope will be of short duration. The feelings which, you tell me, have long prevented the acknowledgment of your regard, can have little difficulty in overcoming it after this explanation."

Mr. Darcy, who was leaning against the mantelpiece with his eyes fixed on her face, seemed to catch her words with no less resentment than surprise. His complexion became pale with anger, and the disturbance of his mind was visible in every feature. He was struggling for the appearance of composure, and would not open his lips till he believed himself to have attained it. The pause was to Elizabeth's feelings dreadful. At length, with a voice of forced calmness, he said:

"And this is all the reply which I am to have the honour of expecting! I might, perhaps, wish to be informed why, with so little *endeavour* at civility, I am thus rejected. But it is of small importance."

"I might as well inquire," replied she, "why with so evident a desire of offending and insulting me, you chose to tell me that you liked me against your will, against your reason, and even against your character? Was not this some excuse for incivility, if I *was* uncivil? But I have other provocations. You know I have. Had not my feelings decided against you—had they been indifferent, or had they even been favourable, do you think that any consideration would tempt me to accept the man who has been the means of ruining, perhaps for ever, the happiness of a most beloved sister?"

As she pronounced these words, Mr. Darcy changed colour; but the emotion was short, and he listened without attempting to interrupt her while she continued:

"I have every reason in the world to think ill of you. No motive can excuse the unjust and ungenerous part you acted *there*. You dare not, you cannot deny, that you have been the principal, if not the only means of dividing them from each other—of exposing one to the censure of the world for caprice and instability, and the other to its derision for disappointed hopes, and involving them both in misery of the acutest kind."

She paused, and saw with no slight indignation that he was listening with an air which proved him wholly unmoved by any feeling of remorse. He even looked at her with a smile of affected incredulity.

"Can you deny that you have done it?" she repeated.

With assumed tranquillity he then replied: "I have no wish of denying that I did everything in my power to separate my friend from your sister, or that I rejoice in my success. Towards *him* I have been kinder than towards myself."

Elizabeth disdained the appearance of noticing this civil reflection, but its meaning did not escape, nor was it likely to conciliate her.

"But it is not merely this affair," she continued, "on which my dislike is founded. Long before it had taken place my opinion of you was decided. Your character was unfolded in the recital which I received many months ago from Mr. Wickham. On this subject, what can you have to say? In what imaginary act of friendship can you here defend yourself? or under what misrepresentation can you here impose upon others?"

"You take an eager interest in that gentleman's concerns," said Darcy, in a less tranquil tone, and with a heightened colour.

"Who that knows what his misfortunes have been, can help feeling an interest in him?"

"His misfortunes!" repeated Darcy contemptuously; "yes, his misfortunes have been great indeed."

"And of your infliction," cried Elizabeth with energy. "You have reduced him to his present state of poverty—comparative poverty. You have withheld the advantages which you must know to have been designed for him. You have deprived the best years of his life of that independence which was no less his due than his desert. You have done all this! and yet you can treat the mention of his misfortune with contempt and ridicule."

"And this," cried Darcy, as he walked with quick steps across the room, "is your opinion of me! This is the estimation in which you hold me! I thank you for explaining it so fully. My faults, according to this calculation, are heavy indeed! But perhaps," added he, stopping in his walk, and turning towards her, "these offenses might have been overlooked, had not your pride been hurt by my honest confession of the scruples that had long prevented my forming any serious design. These bitter accusations might have been suppressed, had I, with greater policy, concealed my struggles, and flattered you into the belief of my being impelled by unqualified, unalloyed inclination; by reason, by reflection, by everything. But disguise of every sort is my abhorrence. Nor am I ashamed of the feelings I related. They were natural and just. Could you expect me to rejoice in the inferiority of your connections?—to congratulate myself on the hope of relations, whose condition in life is so decidedly beneath my own?"

Elizabeth felt herself growing more angry every moment; yet she tried to the utmost to speak with composure when she said:

"You are mistaken, Mr. Darcy, if you suppose that the mode of your declaration affected me in any other way, than as it spared the concern which I might have felt in refusing you, had you behaved in a more gentlemanlike manner."

She saw him start at this, but he said nothing, and she continued:

"You could not have made the offer of your hand in any possible way that would have tempted me to accept it."

Again his astonishment was obvious; and he looked at her with an expression of mingled incredulity and mortification. She went on:

"From the very beginning—from the first moment, I may almost say—of my acquaintance with you, your manners, impressing me with the fullest belief of your arrogance, your conceit, and your selfish disdain of the feelings of others, were such as to form the groundwork of disapprobation on which succeeding events have built so immovable a dislike; and I had not known you a month before I felt that you were the last man in the world whom I could ever be prevailed on to marry."

"You have said quite enough, madam. I perfectly comprehend your feelings, and have now only to be ashamed of what my own have been. Forgive me for having taken up so much of your time, and accept my best wishes for your health and happiness."

And with these words he hastily left the room, and Elizabeth heard him the next moment open the front door and quit the house.

The tumult of her mind, was now painfully great. She knew not how to support herself, and from actual weakness sat down and cried for half-an-hour. Her astonishment, as she reflected on what had passed, was increased by every review of it. That she should receive an offer of marriage from Mr. Darcy! That he should have been in love with her for so many months! So much in love as to wish to marry her in spite of all the objections which had made him prevent his friend's marrying her sister, and which must appear at least with equal force in his own case—was almost incredible! It was gratifying to have inspired unconsciously so strong an affection. But his pride, his abominable pride—his shameless avowal of what he had done with respect to Jane—his unpardonable assurance in acknowledging, though he could not justify it, and the unfeeling manner in which he had mentioned Mr. Wickham, his cruelty towards whom he had not attempted to deny, soon overcame the pity which the consideration of his attachment had for a moment excited. She continued in very agitated reflections till the sound of Lady Catherine's carriage made her feel how unequal she was to encounter Charlotte's observation, and hurried her away to her room.

CHAPTER XXXV

Elizabeth awoke the next morning to the same thoughts and meditations which had at length closed her eyes. She could not yet recover from the surprise of what had happened; it was impossible to think of anything else; and, totally indisposed for employment, she resolved, soon after breakfast, to indulge herself in air and exercise. She was proceeding directly to her favourite walk, when the recollection of Mr. Darcy's sometimes coming there stopped her, and instead of entering the park, she turned up the lane, which led farther from the turnpike-road. The park paling was still the boundary on one side, and she soon passed one of the gates into the ground.

After walking two or three times along that part of the lane, she was tempted, by the pleasantness of the morning, to stop at the gates and look into the park. The five weeks which she had now passed in Kent had made a great difference in the country, and every day was adding to the verdure of the early trees. She was on the point of continuing her walk, when she caught a glimpse of a gentleman within the sort of grove which edged the park; he was moving that way; and, fearful of its being Mr. Darcy, she was directly retreating. But the person who advanced was now near enough to see her, and stepping forward with eagerness, pronounced her name. She had turned away; but on hearing herself called, though in a voice which proved it to be Mr. Darcy, she moved again towards the gate. He had by that time reached it also, and, holding out a letter, which she instinctively took, said, with a look of haughty composure, "I have been walking in the grove some time in the hope of meeting you. Will you do me the honour of reading that letter?" And then, with a slight bow, turned again into the plantation, and was soon out of sight.

With no expectation of pleasure, but with the strongest curiosity, Elizabeth opened the letter, and, to her still increasing wonder, perceived an envelope containing two sheets of letter-paper, written quite through, in a very close hand. The envelope itself was likewise full. Pursuing her way along the lane, she then began it. It was dated from Rosings, at eight o'clock in the morning, and was as follows:—

"Be not alarmed, madam, on receiving this letter, by the apprehension of its containing any repetition of those sentiments or renewal of those offers which were last night so disgusting to you. I write without any intention of paining you, or humbling myself, by dwelling on wishes which, for the happiness of both, cannot be too soon forgotten; and the effort which the formation and the perusal of this letter must occasion, should have been spared, had not my character required it to be written and read. You must, therefore, pardon the freedom with which I demand your attention; your feelings, I know, will bestow it unwillingly, but I demand it of your justice.

"Two offenses of a very different nature, and by no means of equal magnitude, you last night laid to my charge. The first mentioned was, that, regardless of the sentiments of either, I had detached Mr. Bingley from your sister, and the other, that I had, in defiance of various claims, in defiance of honour and humanity, ruined the immediate prosperity and blasted the prospects of Mr. Wickham. Wilfully and wantonly to have thrown off the companion of my youth, the acknowledged favourite of my father, a young man who had scarcely any other dependence than on our patronage, and who had been brought up to expect its exertion, would be a depravity, to which the separation of two young persons, whose affection could be the growth of only a few weeks, could bear no comparison. But from the severity of that blame which was last night so liberally bestowed, respecting each circumstance, I shall hope to be in the future secured, when the following account of my actions and their motives has been read. If, in the explanation of them, which is due to myself, I am under the necessity of relating feelings which may be offensive to yours, I can only say that I am sorry. The necessity must be obeyed, and further apology would be absurd.

"I had not been long in Hertfordshire, before I saw, in common with others, that Bingley preferred your elder sister to any other young woman in the country. But it was not till the evening of the dance at Netherfield that I had any apprehension of his feeling a serious attachment. I had often seen him in love before. At that ball, while I had the honour of dancing with you, I was first made acquainted, by Sir William Lucas's accidental information, that Bingley's attentions to your sister had given rise to a general expectation of their marriage. He spoke of it as a certain event, of which the time alone could be undecided. From that moment I observed my friend's behaviour attentively; and I could then perceive that his partiality for Miss Bennet was beyond what I had ever witnessed in him. Your sister I also watched. Her look and manners were open, cheerful, and engaging as ever, but without any symptom of peculiar regard, and I remained convinced from the evening's scrutiny, that though she received his attentions with pleasure, she did not invite them by any participation of sentiment. If *you* have not been mistaken here, *I* must have been in error. Your superior knowledge of your sister must make the latter probable. If it be so, if I have been misled by such error to inflict pain on her, your resentment has not been unreasonable. But I shall not scruple to assert, that the serenity of your sister's countenance and air was such as might have given the most acute observer a conviction that, however amiable her temper, her heart was not likely to be easily touched. That I was desirous of believing her indifferent is certain—but I will venture to say that my investigation and decisions are not usually influenced by my hopes or fears. I did not believe her to be indifferent because I wished it; I believed it on impartial conviction, as truly as I wished it in reason. My objections to the marriage were not merely those which I last night acknowledged to have the utmost force of passion to put aside, in my own case; the want of connection could not be so great an evil to my friend as to me. But there were other causes of repugnance; causes which, though still existing, and existing to an equal degree in both instances, I had myself endeavoured to forget, because they were not immediately before me. These causes must be stated, though briefly. The situation of your mother's family, though objectionable, was nothing in comparison to that total want of propriety so frequently, so almost uniformly betrayed by herself, by your three younger sisters, and occasionally even by your father. Pardon me. It pains me to offend you. But amidst your concern for the defects of your nearest relations, and your displeasure at this representation of them, let it give you consolation to consider that, to have conducted yourselves so as to avoid any share of the like censure, is praise no less generally bestowed on you and your elder sister, than it is honourable to the sense and disposition of both. I will only say farther that from what passed that evening, my opinion of all parties was confirmed, and every inducement heightened which could have led me before, to preserve my friend from what I esteemed a most unhappy connection. He left Netherfield for London, on the day following, as you, I am certain, remember, with the design of soon returning.

"The part which I acted is now to be explained. His sisters' uneasiness had been equally excited with my own; our coincidence of feeling was soon discovered, and, alike sensible that no time was to be lost in detaching their brother, we shortly resolved on joining him directly in London. We accordingly went—and there I readily engaged in the office of pointing out to my friend the certain evils of such a choice. I described, and enforced them earnestly. But, however this remonstrance might have staggered or delayed his determination, I do not suppose that it would ultimately have prevented the marriage, had it not been seconded by the assurance that I hesitated not in giving, of your sister's indifference. He had before believed her to return his affection with sincere, if not with equal regard. But Bingley has great natural modesty, with a stronger dependence on my judgement than on his own. To convince him, therefore, that he had deceived himself, was no very difficult point. To persuade him against returning into Hertfordshire, when that conviction had been given, was scarcely the work of a moment. I cannot blame myself for having done thus much. There is but one part of my conduct in the whole affair on which I do not reflect with satisfaction;

it is that I condescended to adopt the measures of art so far as to conceal from him your sister's being in town. I knew it myself, as it was known to Miss Bingley; but her brother is even yet ignorant of it. That they might have met without ill consequence is perhaps probable; but his regard did not appear to me enough extinguished for him to see her without some danger. Perhaps this concealment, this disguise was beneath me; it is done, however, and it was done for the best. On this subject I have nothing more to say, no other apology to offer. If I have wounded your sister's feelings, it was unknowingly done and though the motives which governed me may to you very naturally appear insufficient, I have not yet learnt to condemn them.

"With respect to that other, more weighty accusation, of having injured Mr. Wickham, I can only refute it by laying before you the whole of his connection with my family. Of what he has *particularly* accused me I am ignorant; but of the truth of what I shall relate, I can summon more than one witness of undoubted veracity.

"Mr. Wickham is the son of a very respectable man, who had for many years the management of all the Pemberley estates, and whose good conduct in the discharge of his trust naturally inclined my father to be of service to him; and on George Wickham, who was his godson, his kindness was therefore liberally bestowed. My father supported him at school, and afterwards at Cambridge—most important assistance, as his own father, always poor from the extravagance of his wife, would have been unable to give him a gentleman's education. My father was not only fond of this young man's society, whose manners were always engaging; he had also the highest opinion of him, and hoping the church would be his profession, intended to provide for him in it. As for myself, it is many, many years since I first began to think of him in a very different manner. The vicious propensities—the want of principle, which he was careful to guard from the knowledge of his best friend, could not escape the observation of a young man of nearly the same age with himself, and who had opportunities of seeing him in unguarded moments, which Mr. Darcy could not have. Here again I shall give you pain—to what degree you only can tell. But whatever may be the sentiments which Mr. Wickham has created, a suspicion of their nature shall not prevent me from unfolding his real character—it adds even another motive.

"My excellent father died about five years ago; and his attachment to Mr. Wickham was to the last so steady, that in his will he particularly recommended it to me, to promote his advancement in the best manner that his profession might allow—and if he took orders, desired that a valuable family living might be his as soon as it became vacant. There was also a legacy of one thousand pounds. His own father did not long survive mine, and within half a year from these events, Mr. Wickham wrote to inform me that, having finally resolved against taking orders, he hoped I should not think it unreasonable for him to expect some more immediate pecuniary advantage, in lieu of the preferment, by which he could not be benefited. He had some intention, he added, of studying law, and I must be aware that the interest of one thousand pounds would be a very insufficient support therein. I rather wished, than believed him to be sincere; but, at any rate, was perfectly ready to accede to his proposal. I knew that Mr. Wickham ought not to be a clergyman; the business was therefore soon settled—he resigned all claim to assistance in the church, were it possible that he could ever be in a situation to receive it, and accepted in return three thousand pounds. All connection between us seemed now dissolved. I thought too ill of him to invite him to Pemberley, or admit his society in town. In town I believe he chiefly lived, but his studying the law was a mere pretence, and being now free from all restraint, his life was a life of idleness and dissipation. For about three years I heard little of him; but on the decease of the incumbent of the living which had been designed for him, he applied to me again by letter for the presentation. His circumstances, he assured me, and I had no difficulty in believing it, were exceedingly bad. He had found the law a most unprofitable study, and was now absolutely resolved on being ordained, if I would present him to the living in question—of which he trusted there could be little doubt, as he was well assured that I had no other person to provide for, and I could not have forgotten my revered father's intentions. You will hardly blame me for refusing to comply with this entreaty, or for resisting every repetition to it. His resentment was in proportion to the distress of his circumstances—and he was doubtless as violent in his abuse of me to others as in his reproaches to myself. After this period every appearance of acquaintance was dropped. How he lived I know not. But last summer he was again most painfully obtruded on my notice.

"I must now mention a circumstance which I would wish to forget myself, and which no obligation less than the present should induce me to unfold to any human being. Having said thus much, I feel no doubt of your secrecy. My sister, who is more than ten years my junior, was left to the guardianship of my mother's nephew, Colonel Fitzwilliam, and myself. About a year ago, she was taken from school, and an establishment formed for her in London; and last summer she went with the lady who presided over it, to Ramsgate; and thither also went Mr. Wickham, undoubtedly by design; for there proved to have been a prior acquaintance between him and Mrs. Younge, in whose character we were most unhappily deceived; and by her connivance and aid, he so far recommended himself to Georgiana, whose affectionate heart retained a strong impression of his kindness to her as a child, that she was persuaded to believe herself in love, and to consent to an elopement. She was then but fifteen, which must be her excuse; and after stating her imprudence, I am happy to add, that I owed the knowledge of it to herself. I joined them unexpectedly a day or two before the intended elopement, and then Georgiana, unable to support the idea of grieving and offending a brother whom she almost looked up to as a father, acknowledged the whole to me. You may imagine what I felt and how I acted. Regard for my sister's credit and feelings prevented any public exposure; but I wrote to Mr. Wickham, who left the place immediately, and Mrs. Younge was of course removed from her charge. Mr. Wickham's chief object was unquestionably my sister's fortune, which is thirty thousand pounds; but I cannot help supposing that the hope of revenging himself on me was a strong inducement. His revenge would have been complete indeed.

"This, madam, is a faithful narrative of every event in which we have been concerned together; and if you do not absolutely reject it as false, you will, I hope, acquit me henceforth of cruelty towards Mr. Wickham. I know not in what manner, under what form of falsehood he had imposed on you; but his success is not perhaps to be wondered at. Ignorant as you previously were of everything concerning either, detection could not be in your power, and suspicion certainly not in your inclination.

"You may possibly wonder why all this was not told you last night; but I was not then master enough of myself to know what could or ought to be revealed. For the truth of everything here related, I can appeal more particularly to the testimony of Colonel Fitzwilliam, who, from our near relationship and constant intimacy, and, still more, as one of the executors of my father's will, has been unavoidably acquainted with every particular of these transactions. If your abhorrence of *me* should make *my* assertions valueless, you cannot be prevented by the same cause from confiding in my cousin; and that there may be the possibility of consulting him, I shall endeavour to find some opportunity of putting this letter in your hands in the course of the morning. I will only add, God bless you.

"FITZWILLIAM DARCY"

CHAPTER XXXVI

If Elizabeth, when Mr. Darcy gave her the letter, did not expect it to contain a renewal of his offers, she had formed no expectation at all of its contents. But such as they were, it may well be supposed how eagerly she went through them, and what a contrariety of emotion they excited. Her feelings as she read were scarcely to be defined. With amazement did she first understand that he believed any apology to be in his power; and steadfastly was she persuaded, that he could have no explanation to give, which a just sense of shame would not conceal. With a strong prejudice against everything he might say, she began his account of what had happened at Netherfield. She read with an eagerness which hardly left her power of comprehension, and from impatience of knowing what the next sentence might bring, was incapable of attending to the sense of the one before her eyes. His belief of her sister's insensibility she instantly resolved to be false; and his account of the real, the worst objections to the match, made her too angry to have any wish of doing him justice. He expressed no regret for what he had done which satisfied her; his style was not penitent, but haughty. It was all pride and insolence.

But when this subject was succeeded by his account of Mr. Wickham—when she read with somewhat clearer attention a relation of events which, if true, must overthrow every cherished opinion of his worth, and which bore so alarming an affinity to his own history of himself—her feelings were yet more acutely painful and more difficult of definition. Astonishment, apprehension, and even horror, oppressed her. She wished to discredit it entirely, repeatedly exclaiming, "This must be false! This cannot be! This must be the grossest falsehood!"—and when she had gone through the whole letter, though scarcely knowing anything of the last page or two, put it hastily away, protesting that she would not regard it, that she would never look in it again.

In this perturbed state of mind, with thoughts that could rest on nothing, she walked on; but it would not do; in half a minute the letter was unfolded again, and collecting herself as well as she could, she again began the mortifying perusal of all that related to Wickham, and commanded herself so far as to examine the meaning of every sentence.

The account of his connection with the Pemberley family was exactly what he had related himself; and the kindness of the late Mr. Darcy, though she had not before known its extent, agreed equally well with his own words. So far each recital confirmed the other; but when she came to the will, the difference was great. What Wickham had said of the living was fresh in her memory, and as she recalled his very words, it was impossible not to feel that there was gross duplicity on one side or the other; and, for a few moments, she flattered herself that her wishes did not err. But when she read and re-read with the closest attention, the particulars immediately following of Wickham's resigning all pretensions to the living, of his receiving in lieu so considerable a sum as three thousand pounds, again was she forced to hesitate. She put down the letter, weighed every circumstance with what she meant to be impartiality—deliberated on the probability of each statement—but with little success. On both sides it was only assertion. Again she read on; but every line proved more clearly that the affair, which she had believed it impossible that any contrivance could so represent as to render Mr. Darcy's conduct in it less than infamous, was capable of a turn which must make him entirely blameless throughout the whole.

The extravagance and general profligacy which he scrupled not to lay at Mr. Wickham's charge, exceedingly shocked her; the more so, as she could bring no proof of its injustice. She had never heard of him before his entrance into the ——shire Militia, in which he had engaged at the persuasion of the young man who, on meeting him accidentally in town, had there renewed a slight acquaintance. Of his former way of life nothing had been known in Hertfordshire but what he told himself. As to his real character, had information been in her power, she had never felt a wish of inquiring. His countenance, voice, and manner had established him at once in the possession of every virtue. She tried to recollect some instance of goodness, some distinguished trait of integrity or benevolence, that might rescue him from the attacks of Mr. Darcy; or at least, by the predominance of virtue, atone for those casual errors under which she would endeavour to class what Mr. Darcy had described as the idleness and vice of many years' continuance. But no such recollection befriended her. She could see him instantly before her, in every charm of air and address; but she could remember no more substantial good than the general approbation of the neighbourhood, and the regard which his social powers had gained him in the mess.

After pausing on this point a considerable while, she once more continued to read. But, alas! the story which followed, of his designs on Miss Darcy, received some confirmation from what had passed between Colonel Fitzwilliam and herself only the morning before; and at last she was referred for the truth of every particular to Colonel Fitzwilliam himself—from whom she had previously received the information of his near concern in all his cousin's affairs, and whose character she had no reason to question. At one time she had almost resolved on applying to him, but the idea was checked by the awkwardness of the application, and at length wholly banished by the conviction that Mr. Darcy would never have hazarded such a proposal, if he had not been well assured of his cousin's corroboration.

She perfectly remembered everything that had passed in conversation between Wickham and herself, in their first evening at Mr. Phillips's. Many of his expressions were still fresh in her memory. She was *now* struck with the impropriety of such communications to a stranger, and wondered it had escaped her before. She saw the indelicacy of putting himself forward as he had done, and the inconsistency of his professions with his conduct. She remembered that he had boasted of having no fear of seeing Mr. Darcy—that Mr. Darcy might leave the country, but that *he* should stand his ground; yet he had avoided the Netherfield ball the very next week. She remembered also that, till the Netherfield family had quitted the country, he had told his story to no one but herself; but that after their removal it had been everywhere discussed; that he had then no reserves, no scruples in sinking Mr. Darcy's character, though he had assured her that respect for the father would always prevent his exposing the son.

How differently did everything now appear in which he was concerned! His attentions to Miss King were now the consequence of views solely and hatefully mercenary; and the mediocrity of her fortune proved no longer the moderation of his wishes, but his eagerness to grasp at anything. His behaviour to herself could now have had no tolerable motive; he had either been deceived with regard to her fortune, or had been gratifying his vanity by encouraging the preference which she believed she had most incautiously shown. Every lingering struggle in his favour grew fainter and fainter; and in farther justification of Mr. Darcy, she could not but allow Mr. Bingley, when questioned by Jane, had long ago asserted his blamelessness in the affair; that proud and repulsive as were his manners, she had never, in the whole course of their acquaintance—an acquaintance which had latterly brought them much together, and given her a sort of intimacy with his ways—seen anything that betrayed him to be unprincipled or unjust—anything that spoke him of irreligious or immoral habits; that among his own connections he was esteemed and valued—that even Wickham had allowed him merit as a brother, and that she had often heard him speak so affectionately of his sister as to prove him capable of *some* amiable feeling; that had his actions been what Mr. Wickham represented them, so gross a violation of everything right could hardly have been concealed from the world; and that friendship between a person capable of it, and such an amiable man as Mr. Bingley, was incomprehensible.

She grew absolutely ashamed of herself. Of neither Darcy nor Wickham could she think without feeling she had been blind, partial, prejudiced, absurd.

"How despicably I have acted!" she cried; "I, who have prided myself on my discernment! I, who have valued myself on my abilities! who have often disdained the generous candour of my sister, and gratified my vanity in useless or blameable mistrust! How humiliating is this discovery! Yet, how just a humiliation! Had I been in love, I could not have been more wretchedly blind! But vanity, not love, has been my folly. Pleased with the preference of one, and offended by the neglect of the other, on the very beginning of our acquaintance, I have courted prepossession and ignorance, and driven reason away, where either were concerned. Till this moment I never knew myself."

From herself to Jane—from Jane to Bingley, her thoughts were in a line which soon brought to her recollection that Mr. Darcy's explanation *there* had appeared very insufficient, and she read it again. Widely different was the effect of a second perusal. How could she deny that credit to his assertions in one instance, which she had been obliged to give in the other? He declared himself to be totally unsuspicious of her sister's attachment; and she could not help remembering what Charlotte's opinion had always been. Neither could she deny the justice of his description of Jane. She felt that Jane's feelings, though fervent, were little displayed, and that there was a constant complacency in her air and manner not often united with great sensibility.

When she came to that part of the letter in which her family were mentioned in terms of such mortifying, yet merited reproach, her sense of shame was severe. The justice of the charge struck her too forcibly for denial, and the circumstances to which he particularly alluded as having passed at the Netherfield ball, and as confirming all his first disapprobation, could not have made a stronger impression on his mind than on hers.

The compliment to herself and her sister was not unfelt. It soothed, but it could not console her for the contempt which had thus been self-attracted by the rest of her family; and as she considered that Jane's disappointment had in fact been the work of her nearest relations, and reflected how materially the credit of both must be hurt by such impropriety of conduct, she felt depressed beyond anything she had ever known before.

After wandering along the lane for two hours, giving way to every variety of thought—re-considering events, determining probabilities, and reconciling herself, as well as she could, to a change so sudden and so important, fatigue, and a recollection of her long absence, made her at length return home; and she entered the house with the wish of appearing cheerful as usual, and the resolution of repressing such reflections as must make her unfit for conversation.

She was immediately told that the two gentlemen from Rosings had each called during her absence; Mr. Darcy, only for a few minutes, to take leave—but that Colonel Fitzwilliam had been sitting with them at least an hour, hoping for her return, and almost resolving to walk after her till she could be found. Elizabeth could but just *affect* concern in missing him; she really rejoiced at it. Colonel Fitzwilliam was no longer an object; she could think only of her letter.

CHAPTER XXXVII

The two gentlemen left Rosings the next morning, and Mr. Collins having been in waiting near the lodges, to make them his parting obeisance, was able to bring home the pleasing intelligence, of their appearing in very good health, and in as tolerable spirits as could be expected, after the melancholy scene so lately gone through at Rosings. To Rosings he then hastened, to console Lady Catherine and her daughter; and on his return brought back, with great satisfaction, a message from her ladyship, importing that she felt herself so dull as to make her very desirous of having them all to dine with her.

Elizabeth could not see Lady Catherine without recollecting that, had she chosen it, she might by this time have been presented to her as her future niece; nor could she think, without a smile, of what her ladyship's indignation would have been. "What would she have said? how would she have behaved?" were questions with which she amused herself.

Their first subject was the diminution of the Rosings party. "I assure you, I feel it exceedingly," said Lady Catherine; "I believe no one feels the loss of friends so much as I do. But I am particularly attached to these young men, and know them to be so much attached to me! They were excessively sorry to go! But so they always are. The dear Colonel rallied his spirits tolerably till just at last; but Darcy seemed to feel it most acutely, more, I think, than last year. His attachment to Rosings certainly increases."

Mr. Collins had a compliment, and an allusion to throw in here, which were kindly smiled on by the mother and daughter.

Lady Catherine observed, after dinner, that Miss Bennet seemed out of spirits, and immediately accounting for it by herself, by supposing that she did not like to go home again so soon, she added:

"But if that is the case, you must write to your mother and beg that you may stay a little longer. Mrs. Collins will be very glad of your company, I am sure."

"I am much obliged to your ladyship for your kind invitation," replied Elizabeth, "but it is not in my power to accept it. I must be in town next Saturday."

"Why, at that rate, you will have been here only six weeks. I expected you to stay two months. I told Mrs. Collins so before you came. There can be no occasion for your going so soon. Mrs. Bennet could certainly spare you for another fortnight."

"But my father cannot. He wrote last week to hurry my return."

"Oh! your father of course may spare you, if your mother can. Daughters are never of so much consequence to a father. And if you will stay another *month* complete, it will be in my power to take one of you as far as London, for I am going there early in June, for a week; and as Dawson does not object to the barouche-box, there will be very good room for one of you—and indeed, if the weather should happen to be cool, I should not object to taking you both, as you are neither of you large."

"You are all kindness, madam; but I believe we must abide by our original plan."

Lady Catherine seemed resigned. "Mrs. Collins, you must send a servant with them. You know I always speak my mind, and I cannot bear the idea of two young women travelling post by themselves. It is highly improper. You must contrive to send somebody. I have the greatest dislike in the world to that sort of thing. Young women should always be properly guarded and attended, according to their situation in life. When my niece Georgiana went to Ramsgate last summer, I made a point of her having two men-servants go with her. Miss Darcy, the daughter of Mr. Darcy, of Pemberley, and Lady Anne, could not have appeared with propriety in a different manner. I am excessively attentive to all those things. You must send John with the young ladies, Mrs. Collins. I am glad it occurred to me to mention it; for it would really be discreditable to *you* to let them go alone."

"My uncle is to send a servant for us."

"Oh! Your uncle! He keeps a man-servant, does he? I am very glad you have somebody who thinks of these things. Where shall you change horses? Oh! Bromley, of course. If you mention my name at the Bell, you will be attended to."

Lady Catherine had many other questions to ask respecting their journey, and as she did not answer them all herself, attention was necessary, which Elizabeth believed to be lucky for her; or, with a mind so occupied, she might have forgotten where she was. Reflection must be reserved for solitary hours; whenever she was alone, she gave way to it as the greatest relief; and not a day went by without a solitary walk, in which she might indulge in all the delight of unpleasant recollections.

Mr. Darcy's letter she was in a fair way of soon knowing by heart. She studied every sentence; and her feelings towards its writer were at times widely different. When she remembered the style of his address, she was still full of indignation; but when she considered how unjustly she had condemned and upbraided him, her anger was turned against herself; and his disappointed feelings became the object of compassion. His attachment excited gratitude, his general character respect; but she could not approve him; nor could she for a moment repent her refusal, or feel the slightest inclination ever to see him again. In her own past behaviour, there was a constant source of vexation and regret; and in the unhappy defects of her family, a subject of yet heavier chagrin. They were hopeless of remedy. Her father, contented with laughing at them, would never exert himself to restrain the wild giddiness of his youngest daughters; and her mother, with manners so far from right herself, was entirely insensible of the evil. Elizabeth had frequently united with Jane in an endeavour to check the imprudence of Catherine and Lydia; but while they were supported by their mother's indulgence, what chance could there be of improvement? Catherine, weak-spirited, irritable, and completely under Lydia's guidance, had been always affronted by their advice; and Lydia, self-willed and careless, would scarcely give them a hearing. They were ignorant, idle, and vain. While there was an officer in Meryton, they would flirt with him; and while Meryton was within a walk of Longbourn, they would be going there for ever.

Anxiety on Jane's behalf was another prevailing concern; and Mr. Darcy's explanation, by restoring Bingley to all her former good opinion, heightened the sense of what Jane had lost. His affection was proved to have been sincere, and his conduct cleared of all blame, unless any could attach to the implicitness of his confidence in his friend. How grievous then was the thought that, of a situation so desirable in every respect, so replete with advantage, so promising for happiness, Jane had been deprived, by the folly and indecorum of her own family!

When to these recollections was added the development of Wickham's character, it may be easily believed that the happy spirits which had seldom been depressed before, were now so much affected as to make it almost impossible for her to appear tolerably cheerful.

Their engagements at Rosings were as frequent during the last week of her stay as they had been at first. The very last evening was spent there; and her ladyship again inquired minutely into the particulars of their journey, gave them directions as to the best method of packing, and was so urgent on the necessity of placing gowns in the only right way, that Maria thought herself obliged, on her return, to undo all the work of the morning, and pack her trunk afresh.

When they parted, Lady Catherine, with great condescension, wished them a good journey, and invited them to come to Hunsford again next year; and Miss de Bourgh exerted herself so far as to curtsey and hold out her hand to both.

CHAPTER XXXVIII

On Saturday morning Elizabeth and Mr. Collins met for breakfast a few minutes before the others appeared; and he took the opportunity of paying the parting civilities which he deemed indispensably necessary.

"I know not, Miss Elizabeth," said he, "whether Mrs. Collins has yet expressed her sense of your kindness in coming to us; but I am very certain you will not leave the house without receiving her thanks for it. The favor of your company has been much felt, I assure you. We know how little there is to tempt anyone to our humble abode. Our plain manner of living, our small rooms and few domestics, and the little we see of the world, must make Hunsford extremely dull to a young lady like yourself; but I hope you will believe us grateful for the condescension, and that we have done everything in our power to prevent your spending your time unpleasantly."

Elizabeth was eager with her thanks and assurances of happiness. She had spent six weeks with great enjoyment; and the pleasure of being with Charlotte, and the kind attentions she had received, must make *her* feel the obliged. Mr. Collins was gratified, and with a more smiling solemnity replied:

"It gives me great pleasure to hear that you have passed your time not disagreeably. We have certainly done our best; and most fortunately having it in our power to introduce you to very superior society, and, from our connection with Rosings, the frequent means of varying the humble home scene, I think we may flatter ourselves that your Hunsford visit cannot have been entirely irksome. Our situation with regard to Lady Catherine's family is indeed the sort of extraordinary advantage and blessing which few can boast. You see on what a footing we are. You see how continually we are engaged there. In truth I must acknowledge that, with all the disadvantages of this humble parsonage, I should not think anyone abiding in it an object of compassion, while they are sharers of our intimacy at Rosings."

Words were insufficient for the elevation of his feelings; and he was obliged to walk about the room, while Elizabeth tried to unite civility and truth in a few short sentences.

"You may, in fact, carry a very favourable report of us into Hertfordshire, my dear cousin. I flatter myself at least that you will be able to do so. Lady Catherine's great attentions to Mrs. Collins you have been a daily witness of; and altogether I trust it does not appear that your friend has drawn an unfortunate—but on this point it will be as well to be silent. Only let me assure you, my dear Miss Elizabeth, that I can from my heart most cordially wish you equal felicity in marriage. My dear Charlotte and I have but one mind and one way of thinking. There is in everything a most remarkable resemblance of character and ideas between us. We seem to have been designed for each other."

Elizabeth could safely say that it was a great happiness where that was the case, and with equal sincerity could add, that she firmly believed and rejoiced in his domestic comforts. She was not sorry, however, to have the recital of them interrupted by the lady from whom they sprang. Poor Charlotte! it was melancholy to leave her to such society! But she had chosen it with her eyes open; and though evidently regretting that her visitors were to go, she did not seem to ask for compassion. Her home and her housekeeping, her parish and her poultry, and all their dependent concerns, had not yet lost their charms.

At length the chaise arrived, the trunks were fastened on, the parcels placed within, and it was pronounced to be ready. After an affectionate parting between the friends, Elizabeth was attended to the carriage by Mr. Collins, and as they walked down the garden he was commissioning her with his best respects to all her family, not forgetting his thanks for the kindness he had received at Longbourn in the winter, and his compliments to Mr. and Mrs. Gardiner, though unknown. He then handed her in, Maria followed, and the door was on the point of being closed, when he suddenly reminded them, with some consternation, that they had hitherto forgotten to leave any message for the ladies at Rosings.

"But," he added, "you will of course wish to have your humble respects delivered to them, with your grateful thanks for their kindness to you while you have been here."

Elizabeth made no objection; the door was then allowed to be shut, and the carriage drove off.

"Good gracious!" cried Maria, after a few minutes' silence, "it seems but a day or two since we first came! and yet how many things have happened!"

"A great many indeed," said her companion with a sigh.

"We have dined nine times at Rosings, besides drinking tea there twice! How much I shall have to tell!"

Elizabeth added privately, "And how much I shall have to conceal!"

Their journey was performed without much conversation, or any alarm; and within four hours of their leaving Hunsford they reached Mr. Gardiner's house, where they were to remain a few days.

Jane looked well, and Elizabeth had little opportunity of studying her spirits, amidst the various engagements which the kindness of her aunt had reserved for them. But Jane was to go home with her, and at Longbourn there would be leisure enough for observation.

It was not without an effort, meanwhile, that she could wait even for Longbourn, before she told her sister of Mr. Darcy's proposals. To know that she had the power of revealing what would so exceedingly astonish Jane, and must, at the same time, so highly gratify whatever of her own vanity she had not yet been able to reason away, was such a temptation to openness as nothing could have conquered but the state of indecision in which she remained as to the extent of what she should communicate; and her fear, if she once entered on the subject, of being hurried into repeating something of Bingley which might only grieve her sister further.

CHAPTER XXXIX

It was the second week in May, in which the three young ladies set out together from Gracechurch Street for the town of ——, in Hertfordshire; and, as they drew near the appointed inn where Mr. Bennet's carriage was to meet them, they quickly perceived, in token of the coachman's punctuality, both Kitty and Lydia looking out of a dining-room upstairs. These two girls had been above an hour in the place, happily employed in visiting an opposite milliner, watching the sentinel on guard, and dressing a salad and cucumber.

After welcoming their sisters, they triumphantly displayed a table set out with such cold meat as an inn larder usually affords, exclaiming, "Is not this nice? Is not this an agreeable surprise?"

"And we mean to treat you all," added Lydia, "but you must lend us the money, for we have just spent ours at the shop out there." Then, showing her purchases—"Look here, I have bought this bonnet. I do not think it is very pretty; but I thought I might as well buy it as not. I shall pull it to pieces as soon as I get home, and see if I can make it up any better."

And when her sisters abused it as ugly, she added, with perfect unconcern, "Oh! but there were two or three much uglier in the shop; and when I have bought some prettier-coloured satin to trim it with fresh, I think it will be very tolerable. Besides, it will not much signify what one wears this summer, after the ——shire have left Meryton, and they are going in a fortnight."

"Are they indeed!" cried Elizabeth, with the greatest satisfaction.

"They are going to be encamped near Brighton; and I do so want papa to take us all there for the summer! It would be such a delicious scheme; and I dare say would hardly cost anything at all. Mamma would like to go too of all things! Only think what a miserable summer else we shall have!"

"Yes," thought Elizabeth, "*that* would be a delightful scheme indeed, and completely do for us at once. Good Heaven! Brighton, and a whole campful of soldiers, to us, who have been overset already by one poor regiment of militia, and the monthly balls of Meryton!"

"Now I have got some news for you," said Lydia, as they sat down at table. "What do you think? It is excellent news—capital news—and about a certain person we all like!"

Jane and Elizabeth looked at each other, and the waiter was told he need not stay. Lydia laughed, and said:

"Aye, that is just like your formality and discretion. You thought the waiter must not hear, as if he cared! I dare say he often hears worse things said than I am going to say. But he is an ugly fellow! I am glad he is gone. I never saw such a long chin in my life. Well, but now for my news; it is about dear Wickham; too good for the waiter, is it not? There is no danger of Wickham's marrying Mary King. There's for you! She is gone down to her uncle at Liverpool: gone to stay. Wickham is safe."

"And Mary King is safe!" added Elizabeth; "safe from a connection imprudent as to fortune."

"She is a great fool for going away, if she liked him."

"But I hope there is no strong attachment on either side," said Jane.

"I am sure there is not on *his*. I will answer for it, he never cared three straws about her—who could about such a nasty little freckled thing?"

Elizabeth was shocked to think that, however incapable of such coarseness of *expression* herself, the coarseness of the *sentiment* was little other than her own breast had harboured and fancied liberal!

As soon as all had ate, and the elder ones paid, the carriage was ordered; and after some contrivance, the whole party, with all their boxes, work-bags, and parcels, and the unwelcome addition of Kitty's and Lydia's purchases, were seated in it.

"How nicely we are all crammed in," cried Lydia. "I am glad I bought my bonnet, if it is only for the fun of having another bandbox! Well, now let us be quite comfortable and snug, and talk and laugh all the way home. And in the first place, let us hear what has happened to you all since you went away. Have you seen any pleasant men? Have you had any flirting? I was in great hopes that one of you would have got a husband before you came back. Jane will be quite an old maid soon, I declare. She is almost three-and-twenty! Lord, how ashamed I should be of not being married before three-and-twenty! My aunt Phillips wants you so to get husbands, you can't think. She says Lizzy had better have taken Mr. Collins; but *I* do not think there would have been any fun in it. Lord! how I should like to be married before any of you; and then I would chaperon you about to all the balls. Dear me! we had such a good piece of fun the other day at Colonel Forster's. Kitty and me were to spend the day there, and Mrs. Forster promised to have a little dance in the evening; (by the bye, Mrs. Forster and me are *such* friends!) and so she asked the two Harringtons to come, but Harriet was ill, and so Pen was forced to come by herself; and then, what do you think we did? We dressed up Chamberlayne in woman's clothes on purpose to pass for a lady, only think what fun! Not a soul knew of it, but Colonel and Mrs. Forster, and Kitty and me, except my aunt, for we were forced to borrow one of her gowns; and you cannot imagine how well he looked! When Denny, and Wickham, and Pratt, and two or three more of the men came in, they did not know him in the least. Lord! how I laughed! and so did Mrs. Forster. I thought I should have died. And *that* made the men suspect something, and then they soon found out what was the matter."

With such kinds of histories of their parties and good jokes, did Lydia, assisted by Kitty's hints and additions, endeavour to amuse her companions all the way to Longbourn. Elizabeth listened as little as she could, but there was no escaping the frequent mention of Wickham's name.

Their reception at home was most kind. Mrs. Bennet rejoiced to see Jane in undiminished beauty; and more than once during dinner did Mr. Bennet say voluntarily to Elizabeth:

"I am glad you are come back, Lizzy."

Their party in the dining-room was large, for almost all the Lucases came to meet Maria and hear the news; and various were the subjects that occupied them: Lady Lucas was inquiring of Maria, after the welfare and poultry of her eldest daughter; Mrs. Bennet was doubly engaged, on one hand collecting an account of the present fashions from Jane, who sat some way below her, and, on the other, retailing them all to the younger Lucases; and Lydia, in a voice rather louder than any other person's, was enumerating the various pleasures of the morning to anybody who would hear her.

"Oh! Mary," said she, "I wish you had gone with us, for we had such fun! As we went along, Kitty and I drew up the blinds, and pretended there was nobody in the coach; and I should have gone so all the way, if Kitty had not been sick; and when we got to the George, I do think we behaved very handsomely, for we treated the other three with the nicest cold luncheon in the world, and if you would have gone, we would have treated you too. And then when we came away it was such fun! I thought we never should have got into the coach. I was ready to die of laughter. And then we were so merry all the way home! we talked and laughed so loud, that anybody might have heard us ten miles off!"

To this Mary very gravely replied, "Far be it from me, my dear sister, to depreciate such pleasures! They would doubtless be congenial with the generality of female minds. But I confess they would have no charms for *me*—I should infinitely prefer a book."

But of this answer Lydia heard not a word. She seldom listened to anybody for more than half a minute, and never attended to Mary at all.

In the afternoon Lydia was urgent with the rest of the girls to walk to Meryton, and to see how everybody went on; but Elizabeth steadily opposed the scheme. It should not be said that the Miss Bennets could not be at home half a day before they were in pursuit of the officers. There was another reason too for her opposition. She dreaded seeing Mr. Wickham again, and was resolved to avoid it as long as possible. The comfort to *her* of the regiment's approaching removal was indeed beyond expression. In a fortnight they were to go—and once gone, she hoped there could be nothing more to plague her on his account.

She had not been many hours at home before she found that the Brighton scheme, of which Lydia had given them a hint at the inn, was under frequent discussion between her parents. Elizabeth saw directly that her father had not the smallest intention of yielding; but his answers were at the same time so vague and equivocal, that her mother, though often disheartened, had never yet despaired of succeeding at last.

CHAPTER XL

Elizabeth's impatience to acquaint Jane with what had happened could no longer be overcome; and at length, resolving to suppress every particular in which her sister was concerned, and preparing her to be surprised, she related to her the next morning the chief of the scene between Mr. Darcy and herself.

Miss Bennet's astonishment was soon lessened by the strong sisterly partiality which made any admiration of Elizabeth appear perfectly natural; and all surprise was shortly lost in other feelings. She was sorry that Mr. Darcy should have delivered his sentiments in a manner so little suited to recommend them; but still more was she grieved for the unhappiness which her sister's refusal must have given him.

"His being so sure of succeeding was wrong," said she, "and certainly ought not to have appeared; but consider how much it must increase his disappointment!"

"Indeed," replied Elizabeth, "I am heartily sorry for him; but he has other feelings, which will probably soon drive away his regard for me. You do not blame me, however, for refusing him?"

"Blame you! Oh, no."

"But you blame me for having spoken so warmly of Wickham?"

"No—I do not know that you were wrong in saying what you did."

"But you *will* know it, when I tell you what happened the very next day."

She then spoke of the letter, repeating the whole of its contents as far as they concerned George Wickham. What a stroke was this for poor Jane! who would willingly have gone through the world without believing that so much wickedness existed in the whole race of mankind, as was here collected in one individual. Nor was Darcy's vindication, though grateful to her feelings, capable of consoling her for such discovery. Most earnestly did she labour to prove the probability of error, and seek to clear the one without involving the other.

"This will not do," said Elizabeth; "you never will be able to make both of them good for anything. Take your choice, but you must be satisfied with only one. There is but such a quantity of merit between them; just enough to make one good sort of man; and of late it has been shifting about pretty much. For my part, I am inclined to believe it all Darcy's; but you shall do as you choose."

It was some time, however, before a smile could be extorted from Jane.

"I do not know when I have been more shocked," said she. "Wickham so very bad! It is almost past belief. And poor Mr. Darcy! Dear Lizzy, only consider what he must have suffered. Such a disappointment! and with the knowledge of your ill opinion, too! and having to relate such a thing of his sister! It is really too distressing. I am sure you must feel it so."

"Oh! no, my regret and compassion are all done away by seeing you so full of both. I know you will do him such ample justice, that I am growing every moment more unconcerned and indifferent. Your profusion makes me saving; and if you lament over him much longer, my heart will be as light as a feather."

"Poor Wickham! there is such an expression of goodness in his countenance! such an openness and gentleness in his manner!"

"There certainly was some great mismanagement in the education of those two young men. One has got all the goodness, and the other all the appearance of it."

"I never thought Mr. Darcy so deficient in the *appearance* of it as you used to do."

"And yet I meant to be uncommonly clever in taking so decided a dislike to him, without any reason. It is such a spur to one's genius, such an opening for wit, to have a dislike of that kind. One may be continually abusive without saying anything just; but one cannot always be laughing at a man without now and then stumbling on something witty."

"Lizzy, when you first read that letter, I am sure you could not treat the matter as you do now."

"Indeed, I could not. I was uncomfortable enough, I may say unhappy. And with no one to speak to about what I felt, no Jane to comfort me and say that I had not been so very weak and vain and nonsensical as I knew I had! Oh! how I wanted you!"

"How unfortunate that you should have used such very strong expressions in speaking of Wickham to Mr. Darcy, for now they *do* appear wholly undeserved."

"Certainly. But the misfortune of speaking with bitterness is a most natural consequence of the prejudices I had been encouraging. There is one point on which I want your advice. I want to be told whether I ought, or ought not, to make our acquaintances in general understand Wickham's character."

Miss Bennet paused a little, and then replied, "Surely there can be no occasion for exposing him so dreadfully. What is your opinion?"

"That it ought not to be attempted. Mr. Darcy has not authorised me to make his communication public. On the contrary, every particular relative to his sister was meant to be kept as much as possible to myself; and if I endeavour to undeceive people as to the rest of his conduct, who will believe me? The general prejudice against Mr. Darcy is so violent, that it would be the death of half the good people in Meryton to attempt to place him in an amiable light. I am not equal to it. Wickham will soon be gone; and therefore it will not signify to anyone here what he really is. Some time hence it will be all found out, and then we may laugh at their stupidity in not knowing it before. At present I will say nothing about it."

"You are quite right. To have his errors made public might ruin him for ever. He is now, perhaps, sorry for what he has done, and anxious to re-establish a character. We must not make him desperate."

The tumult of Elizabeth's mind was allayed by this conversation. She had got rid of two of the secrets which had weighed on her for a fortnight, and was certain of a willing listener in Jane, whenever she might wish to talk again of either. But there was still something lurking behind, of which prudence forbade the disclosure. She dared not relate the other half of Mr. Darcy's letter, nor explain to her sister how sincerely she had been valued by her friend. Here was knowledge in which no one could partake; and she was sensible that nothing less than a perfect understanding between the parties could justify her in throwing off this last encumbrance of mystery. "And then," said she, "if that very improbable event should ever take place, I shall merely be able to tell what Bingley may tell in a much more agreeable manner himself. The liberty of communication cannot be mine till it has lost all its value!"

She was now, on being settled at home, at leisure to observe the real state of her sister's spirits. Jane was not happy. She still cherished a very tender affection for Bingley. Having never even fancied herself in love before, her regard had all the warmth of first attachment, and, from her age and disposition, greater steadiness than most first attachments often boast; and so fervently did she value his remembrance, and prefer him to every other man, that all her good sense, and all her attention to the feelings of her friends, were requisite to check the indulgence of those regrets which must have been injurious to her own health and their tranquillity.

"Well, Lizzy," said Mrs. Bennet one day, "what is your opinion *now* of this sad business of Jane's? For my part, I am determined never to speak of it again to anybody. I told my sister Phillips so the other day. But I cannot find out that Jane saw anything of him in London. Well, he is a very undeserving young man—and I do not suppose there's the least chance in the world of her ever getting him now. There is no talk of his coming to Netherfield again in the summer; and I have inquired of everybody, too, who is likely to know."

"I do not believe he will ever live at Netherfield any more."

"Oh well! it is just as he chooses. Nobody wants him to come. Though I shall always say he used my daughter extremely ill; and if I was her, I would not have put up with it. Well, my comfort is, I am sure Jane will die of a broken heart; and then he will be sorry for what he has done."

But as Elizabeth could not receive comfort from any such expectation, she made no answer.

"Well, Lizzy," continued her mother, soon afterwards, "and so the Collinses live very comfortable, do they? Well, well, I only hope it will last. And what sort of table do they keep? Charlotte is an excellent manager, I dare say. If she is half as sharp as her mother, she is saving enough. There is nothing extravagant in *their* housekeeping, I dare say."

"No, nothing at all."

"A great deal of good management, depend upon it. Yes, yes. *they* will take care not to outrun their income. *They* will never be distressed for money. Well, much good may it do them! And so, I suppose, they often talk of having Longbourn when your father is dead. They look upon it as quite their own, I dare say, whenever that happens."

"It was a subject which they could not mention before me."

"No; it would have been strange if they had; but I make no doubt they often talk of it between themselves. Well, if they can be easy with an estate that is not lawfully their own, so much the better. I should be ashamed of having one that was only entailed on me."

CHAPTER XLI

The first week of their return was soon gone. The second began. It was the last of the regiment's stay in Meryton, and all the young ladies in the neighbourhood were drooping apace. The dejection was almost universal. The elder Miss Bennets alone were still able to eat, drink, and sleep, and pursue the usual course of their employments. Very frequently were they reproached for this insensibility by Kitty and Lydia, whose own misery was extreme, and who could not comprehend such hard-heartedness in any of the family.

"Good Heaven! what is to become of us? What are we to do?" would they often exclaim in the bitterness of woe. "How can you be smiling so, Lizzy?"

Their affectionate mother shared all their grief; she remembered what she had herself endured on a similar occasion, five-and-twenty years ago.

"I am sure," said she, "I cried for two days together when Colonel Miller's regiment went away. I thought I should have broken my heart."

"I am sure I shall break *mine*," said Lydia.

"If one could but go to Brighton!" observed Mrs. Bennet.

"Oh, yes!—if one could but go to Brighton! But papa is so disagreeable."

"A little sea-bathing would set me up forever."

"And my aunt Phillips is sure it would do *me* a great deal of good," added Kitty.

Such were the kind of lamentations resounding perpetually through Longbourn House. Elizabeth tried to be diverted by them; but all sense of pleasure was lost in shame. She felt anew the justice of Mr. Darcy's objections; and never had she been so much disposed to pardon his interference in the views of his friend.

But the gloom of Lydia's prospect was shortly cleared away; for she received an invitation from Mrs. Forster, the wife of the colonel of the regiment, to accompany her to Brighton. This invaluable friend was a very young woman, and very lately married. A resemblance in good humour and good spirits had recommended her and Lydia to each other, and out of their *three* months' acquaintance they had been intimate *two*.

The rapture of Lydia on this occasion, her adoration of Mrs. Forster, the delight of Mrs. Bennet, and the mortification of Kitty, are scarcely to be described. Wholly inattentive to her sister's feelings, Lydia flew about the house in restless ecstasy, calling for everyone's congratulations, and laughing and talking with more violence than ever; whilst the luckless Kitty continued in the parlour repined at her fate in terms as unreasonable as her accent was peevish.

"I cannot see why Mrs. Forster should not ask *me* as well as Lydia," said she, "Though I am *not* her particular friend. I have just as much right to be asked as she has, and more too, for I am two years older."

In vain did Elizabeth attempt to make her reasonable, and Jane to make her resigned. As for Elizabeth herself, this invitation was so far from exciting in her the same feelings as in her mother and Lydia, that she considered it as the death warrant of all possibility of common sense for the latter; and detestable as such a step must make her were it known, she could not help secretly advising her father not to let her go. She represented to him all the improprieties of Lydia's general behaviour, the little advantage she could derive from the friendship of such a woman as Mrs. Forster, and the probability of her being yet more imprudent with such a companion at Brighton, where the temptations must be greater than at home. He heard her attentively, and then said:

"Lydia will never be easy until she has exposed herself in some public place or other, and we can never expect her to do it with so little expense or inconvenience to her family as under the present circumstances."

"If you were aware," said Elizabeth, "of the very great disadvantage to us all which must arise from the public notice of Lydia's unguarded and imprudent manner—nay, which has already arisen from it, I am sure you would judge differently in the affair."

"Already arisen?" repeated Mr. Bennet. "What, has she frightened away some of your lovers? Poor little Lizzy! But do not be cast down. Such squeamish youths as cannot bear to be connected with a little absurdity are not worth a regret. Come, let me see the list of pitiful fellows who have been kept aloof by Lydia's folly."

"Indeed you are mistaken. I have no such injuries to resent. It is not of particular, but of general evils, which I am now complaining. Our importance, our respectability in the world must be affected by the wild volatility, the assurance and disdain of all restraint which mark Lydia's character. Excuse me, for I must speak plainly. If you, my dear father, will not take the trouble of checking her exuberant spirits, and of teaching her that her present pursuits are not to be the business of her life, she will soon be beyond the reach of amendment. Her character will be fixed, and she will, at sixteen, be the most determined flirt that ever made herself or her family ridiculous; a flirt, too, in the worst and meanest degree of flirtation; without any attraction beyond youth and a tolerable person; and, from the ignorance and emptiness of her mind, wholly unable to ward off any portion of that universal contempt which her rage for admiration will excite. In this danger Kitty also is comprehended. She will follow wherever Lydia leads. Vain, ignorant, idle, and absolutely uncontrolled! Oh! my dear father, can you suppose it possible that they will not be censured and despised wherever they are known, and that their sisters will not be often involved in the disgrace?"

Mr. Bennet saw that her whole heart was in the subject, and affectionately taking her hand said in reply:

"Do not make yourself uneasy, my love. Wherever you and Jane are known you must be respected and valued; and you will not appear to less advantage for having a couple of—or I may say, three—very silly sisters. We shall have no peace at Longbourn if Lydia does not go to Brighton. Let her go, then. Colonel Forster is a sensible man, and will keep her out of any real mischief; and she is luckily too poor to be an object of prey to anybody. At Brighton she will be of less importance even as a common flirt than she has been here. The officers will find women better worth their notice. Let us hope, therefore, that her being there may teach her her own insignificance. At any rate, she cannot grow many degrees worse, without authorising us to lock her up for the rest of her life."

With this answer Elizabeth was forced to be content; but her own opinion continued the same, and she left him disappointed and sorry. It was not in her nature, however, to increase her vexations by dwelling on them. She was confident of having performed her duty, and to fret over unavoidable evils, or augment them by anxiety, was no part of her disposition.

Had Lydia and her mother known the substance of her conference with her father, their indignation would hardly have found expression in their united volubility. In Lydia's imagination, a visit to Brighton comprised every possibility of earthly happiness. She saw, with the creative eye of fancy, the streets of that gay bathing-place covered with officers. She saw herself the object of attention, to tens and to scores of them at present unknown. She saw all the glories of the camp—its tents stretched forth in beauteous uniformity of lines, crowded with the young and the gay, and dazzling with scarlet; and, to complete the view, she saw herself seated beneath a tent, tenderly flirting with at least six officers at once.

Had she known her sister sought to tear her from such prospects and such realities as these, what would have been her sensations? They could have been understood only by her mother, who might have felt nearly the same. Lydia's going to Brighton was all that consoled her for her melancholy conviction of her husband's never intending to go there himself.

But they were entirely ignorant of what had passed; and their raptures continued, with little intermission, to the very day of Lydia's leaving home.

Elizabeth was now to see Mr. Wickham for the last time. Having been frequently in company with him since her return, agitation was pretty well over; the agitations of formal partiality entirely so. She had even learnt to detect, in the very gentleness which had first delighted her, an affectation and a sameness to disgust and weary. In his present behaviour to herself, moreover, she had a fresh source of displeasure, for the inclination he soon testified of renewing those intentions which had marked the early part of their acquaintance could only serve, after what had since passed, to provoke her. She lost all concern for him in finding herself thus selected as the object of such idle and frivolous gallantry; and while she steadily repressed it, could not but feel the reproof contained in his believing, that however long, and for whatever cause, his attentions had been withdrawn, her vanity would be gratified, and her preference secured at any time by their renewal.

On the very last day of the regiment's remaining at Meryton, he dined, with other of the officers, at Longbourn; and so little was Elizabeth disposed to part from him in good humour, that on his making some inquiry as to the manner in which her time had passed at Hunsford, she mentioned Colonel Fitzwilliam's and Mr. Darcy's having both spent three weeks at Rosings, and asked him, if he was acquainted with the former.

He looked surprised, displeased, alarmed; but with a moment's recollection and a returning smile, replied, that he had formerly seen him often; and, after observing that he was a very gentlemanlike man, asked her how she had liked him. Her answer was warmly in his favour. With an air of indifference he soon afterwards added:

"How long did you say he was at Rosings?"

"Nearly three weeks."

"And you saw him frequently?"

"Yes, almost every day."

"His manners are very different from his cousin's."

"Yes, very different. But I think Mr. Darcy improves upon acquaintance."

"Indeed!" cried Mr. Wickham with a look which did not escape her. "And pray, may I ask?—" But checking himself, he added, in a gayer tone, "Is it in address that he improves? Has he deigned to add aught of civility to his ordinary style?—for I dare not hope," he continued in a lower and more serious tone, "that he is improved in essentials."

"Oh, no!" said Elizabeth. "In essentials, I believe, he is very much what he ever was."

While she spoke, Wickham looked as if scarcely knowing whether to rejoice over her words, or to distrust their meaning. There was a something in her countenance which made him listen with an apprehensive and anxious attention, while she added:

"When I said that he improved on acquaintance, I did not mean that his mind or his manners were in a state of improvement, but that, from knowing him better, his disposition was better understood."

Wickham's alarm now appeared in a heightened complexion and agitated look; for a few minutes he was silent, till, shaking off his embarrassment, he turned to her again, and said in the gentlest of accents:

"You, who so well know my feeling towards Mr. Darcy, will readily comprehend how sincerely I must rejoice that he is wise enough to assume even the *appearance* of what is right. His pride, in that direction, may be of service, if not to himself, to many others, for it must only deter him from such foul misconduct as I have suffered by. I only fear that the sort of cautiousness to which you, I imagine, have been alluding, is merely adopted on his visits to his aunt, of whose good opinion and judgement he stands much in awe. His fear of her has always operated, I know, when they were together; and a good deal is to be imputed to his wish of forwarding the match with Miss de Bourgh, which I am certain he has very much at heart."

Elizabeth could not repress a smile at this, but she answered only by a slight inclination of the head. She saw that he wanted to engage her on the old subject of his grievances, and she was in no humour to indulge him. The rest of the evening passed with the *appearance*, on his side, of usual cheerfulness, but with no further attempt to distinguish Elizabeth; and they parted at last with mutual civility, and possibly a mutual desire of never meeting again.

When the party broke up, Lydia returned with Mrs. Forster to Meryton, from whence they were to set out early the next morning. The separation between her and her family was rather noisy than pathetic. Kitty was the only one who shed tears; but she did weep from vexation and envy. Mrs. Bennet was diffuse in her good wishes for the felicity of her daughter, and impressive in her injunctions that she should not miss the opportunity of enjoying herself as much as possible—advice which there was every reason to believe would be well attended to; and in the clamorous happiness of Lydia herself in bidding farewell, the more gentle adieus of her sisters were uttered without being heard.

CHAPTER XLII

Had Elizabeth's opinion been all drawn from her own family, she could not have formed a very pleasing opinion of conjugal felicity or domestic comfort. Her father, captivated by youth and beauty, and that appearance of good humour which youth and beauty generally give, had married a woman whose weak understanding and illiberal mind had very early in their marriage put an end to all real affection for her. Respect, esteem, and confidence had vanished for ever; and all his views of domestic happiness were overthrown. But Mr. Bennet was not of a disposition to seek comfort for the disappointment which his own imprudence had brought on, in any of those pleasures which too often console the unfortunate for their folly or their vice. He was fond of the country and of books; and from these tastes had arisen his principal enjoyments. To his wife he was very little otherwise indebted, than as her ignorance and folly had contributed to his amusement. This is not the sort of happiness which a man would in general wish to owe to his wife; but where other powers of entertainment are wanting, the true philosopher will derive benefit from such as are given.

Elizabeth, however, had never been blind to the impropriety of her father's behaviour as a husband. She had always seen it with pain; but respecting his abilities, and grateful for his affectionate treatment of herself, she endeavoured to forget what she could not overlook, and to banish from her thoughts that continual breach of conjugal obligation and decorum which, in exposing his wife to the contempt of her own children, was so highly reprehensible. But she had never felt so strongly as now the disadvantages which must attend the children of so unsuitable a marriage, nor ever been so fully aware of the evils arising from so ill-judged a direction of talents; talents, which, rightly used, might at least have preserved the respectability of his daughters, even if incapable of enlarging the mind of his wife.

When Elizabeth had rejoiced over Wickham's departure she found little other cause for satisfaction in the loss of the regiment. Their parties abroad were less varied than before, and at home she had a mother and sister whose constant repinings at the dullness of everything around them threw a real gloom over their domestic circle; and, though Kitty might in time regain her natural degree of sense, since the disturbers of her brain were removed, her other sister, from whose disposition greater evil might be apprehended, was likely to be hardened in all her folly and assurance by a situation of such double danger as a watering-place and a camp. Upon the whole, therefore, she found, what has been sometimes found before, that an event to which she had been looking with impatient desire did not, in taking place, bring all the satisfaction she had promised herself. It was consequently necessary to name some other period for the commencement of actual felicity—to have some other point on which her wishes and hopes might be fixed, and by again enjoying the pleasure of anticipation, console herself for the present, and prepare for another disappointment. Her tour to the Lakes was now the object of her happiest thoughts; it was her best consolation for all the uncomfortable hours which the discontentedness of her mother and Kitty made inevitable; and could she have included Jane in the scheme, every part of it would have been perfect.

"But it is fortunate," thought she, "that I have something to wish for. Were the whole arrangement complete, my disappointment would be certain. But here, by carrying with me one ceaseless source of regret in my sister's absence, I may reasonably hope to have all my expectations of pleasure realised. A scheme of which every part promises delight can never be successful; and general disappointment is only warded off by the defence of some little peculiar vexation."

When Lydia went away she promised to write very often and very minutely to her mother and Kitty; but her letters were always long expected, and always very short. Those to her mother contained little else than that they were just returned from the library, where such and such officers had attended them, and where she had seen such beautiful ornaments as made her quite wild; that she had a new gown, or a new parasol, which she would have described more fully, but was obliged to leave off in a violent hurry, as Mrs. Forster called her, and they were going off to the camp; and from her correspondence with her sister, there was still less to be learnt—for her letters to Kitty, though rather longer, were much too full of lines under the words to be made public.

After the first fortnight or three weeks of her absence, health, good humour, and cheerfulness began to reappear at Longbourn. Everything wore a happier aspect. The families who had been in town for the winter came back again, and summer finery and summer engagements arose. Mrs. Bennet was restored to her usual querulous serenity; and, by the middle of June, Kitty was so much recovered as to be able to enter Meryton without tears; an event of such happy promise as to make Elizabeth hope that by the following Christmas she might be so tolerably reasonable as not to mention an officer above once a day, unless, by some cruel and malicious arrangement at the War Office, another regiment should be quartered in Meryton.

The time fixed for the beginning of their northern tour was now fast approaching, and a fortnight only was wanting of it, when a letter arrived from Mrs. Gardiner, which at once delayed its commencement and curtailed its extent. Mr. Gardiner would be prevented by business from setting out till a fortnight later in July, and must be in London again within a month, and as that left too short a period for them to go so far, and see so much as they had proposed, or at least to see it with the leisure and comfort they had built on, they were obliged to give up the Lakes, and substitute a more contracted tour, and, according to the present plan, were to go no farther northwards than Derbyshire. In that county there was enough to be seen to occupy the chief of their three weeks; and to Mrs. Gardiner it had a peculiarly strong attraction. The town where she had formerly passed some years of her life, and where they were now to spend a few days, was probably as great an object of her curiosity as all the celebrated beauties of Matlock, Chatsworth, Dovedale, or the Peak.

Elizabeth was excessively disappointed; she had set her heart on seeing the Lakes, and still thought there might have been time enough. But it was her business to be satisfied—and certainly her temper to be happy; and all was soon right again.

With the mention of Derbyshire there were many ideas connected. It was impossible for her to see the word without thinking of Pemberley and its owner. "But surely," said she, "I may enter his county without impunity, and rob it of a few petrified spars without his perceiving me."

The period of expectation was now doubled. Four weeks were to pass away before her uncle and aunt's arrival. But they did pass away, and Mr. and Mrs. Gardiner, with their four children, did at length appear at Longbourn. The children, two girls of six and eight years old, and two younger boys, were to be left under the particular care of their cousin Jane, who was the general favourite, and whose steady sense and sweetness of temper exactly adapted her for attending to them in every way—teaching them, playing with them, and loving them.

The Gardiners stayed only one night at Longbourn, and set off the next morning with Elizabeth in pursuit of novelty and amusement. One enjoyment was certain—that of suitableness of companions; a suitableness which comprehended health and temper to bear inconveniences—cheerfulness to enhance every pleasure—and affection and intelligence, which might supply it among themselves if there were disappointments abroad.

It is not the object of this work to give a description of Derbyshire, nor of any of the remarkable places through which their route thither lay; Oxford, Blenheim, Warwick, Kenilworth, Birmingham, etc. are sufficiently known. A small part of Derbyshire is all the present concern. To the little town of Lambton, the scene of Mrs. Gardiner's former residence, and where she had lately learned some acquaintance still remained, they bent their steps, after having seen all the principal wonders of the country; and within five miles of Lambton, Elizabeth found from her aunt that Pemberley was situated. It was not in their direct road, nor more than a mile or two out of it. In talking over their route the evening before, Mrs. Gardiner expressed an inclination to see the place again. Mr. Gardiner declared his willingness, and Elizabeth was applied to for her approbation.

"My love, should not you like to see a place of which you have heard so much?" said her aunt; "a place, too, with which so many of your acquaintances are connected. Wickham passed all his youth there, you know."

Elizabeth was distressed. She felt that she had no business at Pemberley, and was obliged to assume a disinclination for seeing it. She must own that she was tired of seeing great houses; after going over so many, she really had no pleasure in fine carpets or satin curtains.

Mrs. Gardiner abused her stupidity. "If it were merely a fine house richly furnished," said she, "I should not care about it myself; but the grounds are delightful. They have some of the finest woods in the country."

Elizabeth said no more—but her mind could not acquiesce. The possibility of meeting Mr. Darcy, while viewing the place, instantly occurred. It would be dreadful! She blushed at the very idea, and thought it would be better to speak openly to her aunt than to run such a risk. But against this there were objections; and she finally resolved that it could be the last resource, if her private inquiries to the absence of the family were unfavourably answered.

Accordingly, when she retired at night, she asked the chambermaid whether Pemberley were not a very fine place? what was the name of its proprietor? and, with no little alarm, whether the family were down for the summer? A most welcome negative followed the last question—and her alarms now being removed, she was at leisure to feel a great deal of curiosity to see the house herself; and when the subject was revived the next morning, and she was again applied to, could readily answer, and with a proper air of indifference, that she had not really any dislike to the scheme. To Pemberley, therefore, they were to go.

CHAPTER XLIII

Elizabeth, as they drove along, watched for the first appearance of Pemberley Woods with some perturbation; and when at length they turned in at the lodge, her spirits were in a high flutter.

The park was very large, and contained great variety of ground. They entered it in one of its lowest points, and drove for some time through a beautiful wood stretching over a wide extent.

Elizabeth's mind was too full for conversation, but she saw and admired every remarkable spot and point of view. They gradually ascended for half-a-mile, and then found themselves at the top of a considerable eminence, where the wood ceased, and the eye was instantly caught by Pemberley House, situated on the opposite side of a valley, into which the road with some abruptness wound. It was a large, handsome stone building, standing well on rising ground, and backed by a ridge of high woody hills; and in front, a stream of some natural importance was swelled into greater, but without any artificial appearance. Its banks were neither formal nor falsely adorned. Elizabeth was delighted. She had never seen a place for which nature had done more, or where natural beauty had been so little counteracted by an awkward taste. They were all of them warm in their admiration; and at that moment she felt that to be mistress of Pemberley might be something!

They descended the hill, crossed the bridge, and drove to the door; and, while examining the nearer aspect of the house, all her apprehension of meeting its owner returned. She dreaded lest the chambermaid had been mistaken. On applying to see the place, they were admitted into the hall; and Elizabeth, as they waited for the housekeeper, had leisure to wonder at her being where she was.

The housekeeper came; a respectable-looking elderly woman, much less fine, and more civil, than she had any notion of finding her. They followed her into the dining-parlour. It was a large, well proportioned room, handsomely fitted up. Elizabeth, after slightly surveying it, went to a window to enjoy its prospect. The hill, crowned with wood, which they had descended, receiving increased abruptness from the distance, was a beautiful object. Every disposition of the ground was good; and she looked on the whole scene, the river, the trees scattered on its banks and the winding of the valley, as far as she could trace it, with delight. As they passed into other rooms these objects were taking different positions; but from every window there were beauties to be seen. The rooms were lofty and handsome, and their furniture suitable to the fortune of its proprietor; but Elizabeth saw, with admiration of his taste, that it was neither gaudy nor uselessly fine; with less of splendour, and more real elegance, than the furniture of Rosings.

"And of this place," thought she, "I might have been mistress! With these rooms I might now have been familiarly acquainted! Instead of viewing them as a stranger, I might have rejoiced in them as my own, and welcomed to them as visitors my uncle and aunt. But no,"—recollecting herself—"that could never be; my uncle and aunt would have been lost to me; I should not have been allowed to invite them."

This was a lucky recollection—it saved her from something very like regret.

She longed to inquire of the housekeeper whether her master was really absent, but had not the courage for it. At length however, the question was asked by her uncle; and she turned away with alarm, while Mrs. Reynolds replied that he was, adding, "But we expect him to-morrow, with a large party of friends." How rejoiced was Elizabeth that their own journey had not by any circumstance been delayed a day!

Her aunt now called her to look at a picture. She approached and saw the likeness of Mr. Wickham, suspended, amongst several other miniatures, over the mantelpiece. Her aunt asked her, smilingly, how she liked it. The housekeeper came forward, and told them it was a picture of a young gentleman, the son of her late master's steward, who had been brought up by him at his own expense. "He is now gone into the army," she added; "but I am afraid he has turned out very wild."

Mrs. Gardiner looked at her niece with a smile, but Elizabeth could not return it.

"And that," said Mrs. Reynolds, pointing to another of the miniatures, "is my master—and very like him. It was drawn at the same time as the other—about eight years ago."

"I have heard much of your master's fine person," said Mrs. Gardiner, looking at the picture; "it is a handsome face. But, Lizzy, you can tell us whether it is like or not."

Mrs. Reynolds's respect for Elizabeth seemed to increase on this intimation of her knowing her master.

"Does that young lady know Mr. Darcy?"

Elizabeth coloured, and said: "A little."

"And do not you think him a very handsome gentleman, ma'am?"

"Yes, very handsome."

"I am sure I know none so handsome; but in the gallery upstairs you will see a finer, larger picture of him than this. This room was my late master's favourite room, and these miniatures are just as they used to be then. He was very fond of them."

This accounted to Elizabeth for Mr. Wickham's being among them.

Mrs. Reynolds then directed their attention to one of Miss Darcy, drawn when she was only eight years old.

"And is Miss Darcy as handsome as her brother?" said Mrs. Gardiner.

"Oh! yes—the handsomest young lady that ever was seen; and so accomplished!—She plays and sings all day long. In the next room is a new instrument just come down for her—a present from my master; she comes here to-morrow with him."

Mr. Gardiner, whose manners were very easy and pleasant, encouraged her communicativeness by his questions and remarks; Mrs. Reynolds, either by pride or attachment, had evidently great pleasure in talking of her master and his sister.

"Is your master much at Pemberley in the course of the year?"

"Not so much as I could wish, sir; but I dare say he may spend half his time here; and Miss Darcy is always down for the summer months."

"Except," thought Elizabeth, "when she goes to Ramsgate."

"If your master would marry, you might see more of him."

"Yes, sir; but I do not know when *that* will be. I do not know who is good enough for him."

Mr. and Mrs. Gardiner smiled. Elizabeth could not help saying, "It is very much to his credit, I am sure, that you should think so."

"I say no more than the truth, and everybody will say that knows him," replied the other. Elizabeth thought this was going pretty far; and she listened with increasing astonishment as the housekeeper added, "I have never known a cross word from him in my life, and I have known him ever since he was four years old."

This was praise, of all others most extraordinary, most opposite to her ideas. That he was not a good-tempered man had been her firmest opinion. Her keenest attention was awakened; she longed to hear more, and was grateful to her uncle for saying:

"There are very few people of whom so much can be said. You are lucky in having such a master."

"Yes, sir, I know I am. If I were to go through the world, I could not meet with a better. But I have always observed, that they who are good-natured when children, are good-natured when they grow up; and he was always the sweetest-tempered, most generous-hearted boy in the world."

Elizabeth almost stared at her. "Can this be Mr. Darcy?" thought she.

"His father was an excellent man," said Mrs. Gardiner.

"Yes, ma'am, that he was indeed; and his son will be just like him—just as affable to the poor."

Elizabeth listened, wondered, doubted, and was impatient for more. Mrs. Reynolds could interest her on no other point. She related the subjects of the pictures, the dimensions of the rooms, and the price of the furniture, in vain. Mr. Gardiner, highly amused by the kind of family prejudice to which he attributed her excessive commendation of her master, soon led again to the subject; and she dwelt with energy on his many merits as they proceeded together up the great staircase.

"He is the best landlord, and the best master," said she, "that ever lived; not like the wild young men nowadays, who think of nothing but themselves. There is not one of his tenants or servants but will give him a good name. Some people call him proud; but I am sure I never saw anything of it. To my fancy, it is only because he does not rattle away like other young men."

"In what an amiable light does this place him!" thought Elizabeth.

"This fine account of him," whispered her aunt as they walked, "is not quite consistent with his behaviour to our poor friend."

"Perhaps we might be deceived."

"That is not very likely; our authority was too good."

On reaching the spacious lobby above they were shown into a very pretty sitting-room, lately fitted up with greater elegance and lightness than the apartments below; and were informed that it was but just done to give pleasure to Miss Darcy, who had taken a liking to the room when last at Pemberley.

"He is certainly a good brother," said Elizabeth, as she walked towards one of the windows.

Mrs. Reynolds anticipated Miss Darcy's delight, when she should enter the room. "And this is always the way with him," she added.

"Whatever can give his sister any pleasure is sure to be done in a moment. There is nothing he would not do for her."

The picture-gallery, and two or three of the principal bedrooms, were all that remained to be shown. In the former were many good paintings; but Elizabeth knew nothing of the art; and from such as had been already visible below, she had willingly turned to look at some drawings of Miss Darcy's, in crayons, whose subjects were usually more interesting, and also more intelligible.

In the gallery there were many family portraits, but they could have little to fix the attention of a stranger. Elizabeth walked in quest of the only face whose features would be known to her. At last it arrested her—and she beheld a striking resemblance to Mr. Darcy, with such a smile over the face as she remembered to have sometimes seen when he looked at her. She stood several minutes before the picture, in earnest contemplation, and returned to it again before they quitted the gallery. Mrs. Reynolds informed them that it had been taken in his father's lifetime.

There was certainly at this moment, in Elizabeth's mind, a more gentle sensation towards the original than she had ever felt at the height of their acquaintance. The commendation bestowed on him by Mrs. Reynolds was of no trifling nature. What praise is more valuable than the praise of an intelligent servant? As a brother, a landlord, a master, she considered how many people's happiness were in his guardianship!—how much of pleasure or pain was it in his power to bestow!—how much of good or evil must be done by him! Every idea that had been brought forward by the housekeeper was favourable to his character, and as she stood before the canvas on which he was represented, and fixed his eyes upon herself, she thought of his regard with a deeper sentiment of gratitude than it had ever raised before; she remembered its warmth, and softened its impropriety of expression.

When all of the house that was open to general inspection had been seen, they returned downstairs, and, taking leave of the housekeeper, were consigned over to the gardener, who met them at the hall-door.

As they walked across the hall towards the river, Elizabeth turned back to look again; her uncle and aunt stopped also, and while the former was conjecturing as to the date of the building, the owner of it himself suddenly came forward from the road, which led behind it to the stables.

They were within twenty yards of each other, and so abrupt was his appearance, that it was impossible to avoid his sight. Their eyes instantly met, and the cheeks of both were overspread with the deepest blush. He absolutely started, and for a moment seemed immovable from surprise; but shortly recovering himself, advanced towards the party, and spoke to Elizabeth, if not in terms of perfect composure, at least of perfect civility.

She had instinctively turned away; but stopping on his approach, received his compliments with an embarrassment impossible to be overcome. Had his first appearance, or his resemblance to the picture they had just been examining, been insufficient to assure the other two that they now saw Mr. Darcy, the gardener's expression of surprise, on beholding his master, must immediately have told it. They stood a little aloof while he was talking to their niece, who, astonished and confused, scarcely dared lift her eyes to his face, and knew not what answer she returned to his civil inquiries after her family. Amazed at the alteration of his manner since they last parted, every sentence that he uttered was increasing her embarrassment; and every idea of the impropriety of her being found there recurring to her mind, the few minutes in which they continued were some of the most uncomfortable in her life. Nor did he seem much more at ease; when he spoke, his accent had none of its usual sedateness; and he repeated his inquiries as to the time of her having left Longbourn, and of her having stayed in Derbyshire, so often, and in so hurried a way, as plainly spoke the distraction of his thoughts.

At length every idea seemed to fail him; and, after standing a few moments without saying a word, he suddenly recollected himself, and took leave.

The others then joined her, and expressed admiration of his figure; but Elizabeth heard not a word, and wholly engrossed by her own feelings, followed them in silence. She was overpowered by shame and vexation. Her coming there was the most unfortunate, the most ill-judged thing in the world! How strange it must appear to him! In what a disgraceful light might it not strike so vain a man! It might seem as if she had purposely thrown herself in his way again! Oh! why did she come? Or, why did he thus come a day before he was expected? Had they been only ten minutes sooner, they should have been beyond the reach of his discrimination; for it was plain that he was that moment arrived—that moment alighted from his horse or his carriage. She blushed again and again over the perverseness of the meeting. And his behaviour, so strikingly altered—what could it mean? That he should even speak to her was amazing!—but to speak with such civility, to inquire after her family! Never in her life had she seen his manners so little dignified, never had he spoken with such gentleness as on this unexpected meeting. What a contrast did it offer to his last address in Rosings Park, when he put his letter into her hand! She knew not what to think, or how to account for it.

They had now entered a beautiful walk by the side of the water, and every step was bringing forward a nobler fall of ground, or a finer reach of the woods to which they were approaching; but it was some time before Elizabeth was sensible of any of it; and, though she answered mechanically to the repeated appeals of her uncle and aunt, and seemed to direct her eyes to such objects as they pointed out, she distinguished no part of the scene. Her thoughts were all fixed on that one spot of Pemberley House, whichever it might be, where Mr. Darcy then was. She longed to know what at the moment was passing in his mind—in what manner he thought of her, and whether, in defiance of everything, she was still dear to him. Perhaps he had been civil only because he felt himself at ease; yet there had been *that* in his voice which was not like ease. Whether he had felt more of pain or of pleasure in seeing her she could not tell, but he certainly had not seen her with composure.

At length, however, the remarks of her companions on her absence of mind aroused her, and she felt the necessity of appearing more like herself.

They entered the woods, and bidding adieu to the river for a while, ascended some of the higher grounds; when, in spots where the opening of the trees gave the eye power to wander, were many charming views of the valley, the opposite hills, with the long range of woods overspreading many, and occasionally part of the stream. Mr. Gardiner expressed a wish of going round the whole park, but feared it might be beyond a walk. With a triumphant smile they were told that it was ten miles round. It settled the matter; and they pursued the accustomed circuit; which brought them again, after some time, in a descent among hanging woods, to the edge of the water, and one of its narrowest parts. They crossed it by a simple bridge, in character with the general air of the scene; it was a spot less adorned than any they had yet visited; and the valley, here contracted into a glen, allowed room only for the stream, and a narrow walk amidst the rough coppice-wood which bordered it. Elizabeth longed to explore its windings; but when they had crossed the bridge, and perceived their distance from the house, Mrs. Gardiner, who was not a great walker, could go no farther, and thought only of returning to the carriage as quickly as possible. Her niece was, therefore, obliged to submit, and they took their way towards the house on the opposite side of the river, in the nearest direction; but their progress was slow, for Mr. Gardiner, though seldom able to indulge the taste, was very fond of fishing, and was so much engaged in watching the occasional appearance of some trout in the water, and talking to the man about them, that he advanced but little. Whilst wandering on in this slow manner, they were again surprised, and Elizabeth's astonishment was quite equal to what it had been at first, by the sight of Mr. Darcy approaching them, and at no great distance. The walk being here less sheltered than on the other side, allowed them to see him before they met. Elizabeth, however astonished, was at least more prepared for an interview than before, and resolved to appear and to speak with calmness, if he really intended to meet them. For a few moments, indeed, she felt that he would probably strike into some other path. The idea lasted while a turning in the walk concealed him from their view; the turning past, he was immediately before them. With a glance, she saw that he had lost none of his recent civility; and, to imitate his politeness, she began, as they met, to admire the beauty of the place; but she had not got beyond the words "delightful," and "charming," when some unlucky recollections obtruded, and she fancied that praise of Pemberley from her might be mischievously construed. Her colour changed, and she said no more.

Mrs. Gardiner was standing a little behind; and on her pausing, he asked her if she would do him the honour of introducing him to her friends. This was a stroke of civility for which she was quite unprepared; and she could hardly suppress a smile at his being now seeking the acquaintance of some of those very people against whom his pride had revolted in his offer to herself. "What will be his surprise," thought she, "when he knows who they are? He takes them now for people of fashion."

The introduction, however, was immediately made; and as she named their relationship to herself, she stole a sly look at him, to see how he bore it, and was not without the expectation of his decamping as fast as he could from such disgraceful companions. That he was *surprised* by the connection was evident; he sustained it, however, with fortitude, and so far from going away, turned his back with them, and entered into conversation with Mr. Gardiner. Elizabeth could not but be pleased, could not but triumph. It was consoling that he should know she had some relations for whom there was no need to blush. She listened most attentively to all that passed between them, and gloried in every expression, every sentence of her uncle, which marked his intelligence, his taste, or his good manners.

The conversation soon turned upon fishing; and she heard Mr. Darcy invite him, with the greatest civility, to fish there as often as he chose while he continued in the neighbourhood, offering at the same time to supply him with fishing tackle, and pointing out those parts of the stream where there was usually most sport. Mrs. Gardiner, who was walking arm-in-arm with Elizabeth, gave her a look expressive of wonder. Elizabeth said nothing, but it gratified her exceedingly; the compliment must be all for herself. Her astonishment, however, was extreme, and continually was she repeating, "Why is he so altered? From what can it proceed? It cannot be for *me*—it cannot be for *my* sake that his manners are thus softened. My reproofs at Hunsford could not work such a change as this. It is impossible that he should still love me."

After walking some time in this way, the two ladies in front, the two gentlemen behind, on resuming their places, after descending to the brink of the river for the better inspection of some curious water-plant, there chanced to be a little alteration. It originated in Mrs. Gardiner, who, fatigued by the exercise of the morning, found Elizabeth's arm inadequate to her support, and consequently preferred her husband's. Mr. Darcy took her place by her niece, and they walked on together. After a short silence, the lady first spoke. She wished him to know that she had been assured of his absence before she came to the place, and accordingly began by observing, that his arrival had been very unexpected—"for your housekeeper," she added, "informed us that you would certainly not be here till to-morrow; and indeed, before we left Bakewell, we understood that you were not immediately expected in the country." He acknowledged the truth of it all, and said that business with his steward had occasioned his coming forward a few hours before the rest of the party with whom he had been travelling. "They will join me early to-morrow," he continued, "and among them are some who will claim an acquaintance with you—Mr. Bingley and his sisters."

Elizabeth answered only by a slight bow. Her thoughts were instantly driven back to the time when Mr. Bingley's name had been the last mentioned between them; and, if she might judge by his complexion, *his* mind was not very differently engaged.

"There is also one other person in the party," he continued after a pause, "who more particularly wishes to be known to you. Will you allow me, or do I ask too much, to introduce my sister to your acquaintance during your stay at Lambton?"

The surprise of such an application was great indeed; it was too great for her to know in what manner she acceded to it. She immediately felt that whatever desire Miss Darcy might have of being acquainted with her must be the work of her brother, and, without looking farther, it was satisfactory; it was gratifying to know that his resentment had not made him think really ill of her.

They now walked on in silence, each of them deep in thought. Elizabeth was not comfortable; that was impossible; but she was flattered and pleased. His wish of introducing his sister to her was a compliment of the highest kind. They soon outstripped the others, and when they had reached the carriage, Mr. and Mrs. Gardiner were half a quarter of a mile behind.

He then asked her to walk into the house—but she declared herself not tired, and they stood together on the lawn. At such a time much might have been said, and silence was very awkward. She wanted to talk, but there seemed to be an embargo on every subject. At last she recollected that she had been travelling, and they talked of Matlock and Dove Dale with great perseverance. Yet time and her aunt moved slowly—and her patience and her ideas were nearly worn out before the tete-a-tete was over. On Mr. and Mrs. Gardiner's coming up they were all pressed to go into the house and take some refreshment; but this was declined, and they parted on each side with utmost politeness. Mr. Darcy handed the ladies into the carriage; and when it drove off, Elizabeth saw him walking slowly towards the house.

The observations of her uncle and aunt now began; and each of them pronounced him to be infinitely superior to anything they had expected. "He is perfectly well behaved, polite, and unassuming," said her uncle.

"There *is* something a little stately in him, to be sure," replied her aunt, "but it is confined to his air, and is not unbecoming. I can now say with the housekeeper, that though some people may call him proud, I have seen nothing of it."

"I was never more surprised than by his behaviour to us. It was more than civil; it was really attentive; and there was no necessity for such attention. His acquaintance with Elizabeth was very trifling."

"To be sure, Lizzy," said her aunt, "he is not so handsome as Wickham; or, rather, he has not Wickham's countenance, for his features are perfectly good. But how came you to tell me that he was so disagreeable?"

Elizabeth excused herself as well as she could; said that she had liked him better when they had met in Kent than before, and that she had never seen him so pleasant as this morning.

"But perhaps he may be a little whimsical in his civilities," replied her uncle. "Your great men often are; and therefore I shall not take him at his word, as he might change his mind another day, and warn me off his grounds."

Elizabeth felt that they had entirely misunderstood his character, but said nothing.

"From what we have seen of him," continued Mrs. Gardiner, "I really should not have thought that he could have behaved in so cruel a way by anybody as he has done by poor Wickham. He has not an ill-natured look. On the contrary, there is something pleasing about his mouth when he speaks. And there is something of dignity in his countenance that would not give one an unfavourable idea of his heart. But, to be sure, the good lady who showed us his house did give him a most flaming character! I could hardly help laughing aloud sometimes. But he is a liberal master, I suppose, and *that* in the eye of a servant comprehends every virtue."

Elizabeth here felt herself called on to say something in vindication of his behaviour to Wickham; and therefore gave them to understand, in as guarded a manner as she could, that by what she had heard from his relations in Kent, his actions were capable of a very different construction; and that his character was by no means so faulty, nor Wickham's so amiable, as they had been considered in Hertfordshire. In confirmation of this, she related the particulars of all the pecuniary transactions in which they had been connected, without actually naming her authority, but stating it to be such as might be relied on.

Mrs. Gardiner was surprised and concerned; but as they were now approaching the scene of her former pleasures, every idea gave way to the charm of recollection; and she was too much engaged in pointing out to her husband all the interesting spots in its environs to think of anything else. Fatigued as she had been by the morning's walk they had no sooner dined than she set off again in quest of her former acquaintance, and the evening was spent in the satisfactions of an intercourse renewed after many years' discontinuance.

The occurrences of the day were too full of interest to leave Elizabeth much attention for any of these new friends; and she could do nothing but think, and think with wonder, of Mr. Darcy's civility, and, above all, of his wishing her to be acquainted with his sister.

CHAPTER XLIV

Elizabeth had settled it that Mr. Darcy would bring his sister to visit her the very day after her reaching Pemberley; and was consequently resolved not to be out of sight of the inn the whole of that morning. But her conclusion was false; for on the very morning after their arrival at Lambton, these visitors came. They had been walking about the place with some of their new friends, and were just returning to the inn to dress themselves for dining with the same family, when the sound of a carriage drew them to a window, and they saw a gentleman and a lady in a curricle driving up the street. Elizabeth immediately recognizing the livery, guessed what it meant, and imparted no small degree of her surprise to her relations by acquainting them with the honour which she expected. Her uncle and aunt were all amazement; and the embarrassment of her manner as she spoke, joined to the circumstance itself, and many of the circumstances of the preceding day, opened to them a new idea on the business. Nothing had ever suggested it before, but they felt that there was no other way of accounting for such attentions from such a quarter than by supposing a partiality for their niece. While these newly-born notions were passing in their heads, the perturbation of Elizabeth's feelings was at every moment increasing. She was quite amazed at her own discomposure; but amongst other causes of disquiet, she dreaded lest the partiality of the brother should have said too much in her favour; and, more than commonly anxious to please, she naturally suspected that every power of pleasing would fail her.

She retreated from the window, fearful of being seen; and as she walked up and down the room, endeavouring to compose herself, saw such looks of inquiring surprise in her uncle and aunt as made everything worse.

Miss Darcy and her brother appeared, and this formidable introduction took place. With astonishment did Elizabeth see that her new acquaintance was at least as much embarrassed as herself. Since her being at Lambton, she had heard that Miss Darcy was exceedingly proud; but the observation of a very few minutes convinced her that she was only exceedingly shy. She found it difficult to obtain even a word from her beyond a monosyllable.

Miss Darcy was tall, and on a larger scale than Elizabeth; and, though little more than sixteen, her figure was formed, and her appearance womanly and graceful. She was less handsome than her brother; but there was sense and good humour in her face, and her manners were perfectly unassuming and gentle. Elizabeth, who had expected to find in her as acute and unembarrassed an observer as ever Mr. Darcy had been, was much relieved by discerning such different feelings.

They had not long been together before Mr. Darcy told her that Bingley was also coming to wait on her; and she had barely time to express her satisfaction, and prepare for such a visitor, when Bingley's quick step was heard on the stairs, and in a moment he entered the room. All Elizabeth's anger against him had been long done away; but had she still felt any, it could hardly have stood its ground against the unaffected cordiality with which he expressed himself on seeing her again. He inquired in a friendly, though general way, after her family, and looked and spoke with the same good-humoured ease that he had ever done.

To Mr. and Mrs. Gardiner he was scarcely a less interesting personage than to herself. They had long wished to see him. The whole party before them, indeed, excited a lively attention. The suspicions which had just arisen of Mr. Darcy and their niece directed their observation towards each with an earnest though guarded inquiry; and they soon drew from those inquiries the full conviction that one of them at least knew what it was to love. Of the lady's sensations they remained a little in doubt; but that the gentleman was overflowing with admiration was evident enough.

Elizabeth, on her side, had much to do. She wanted to ascertain the feelings of each of her visitors; she wanted to compose her own, and to make herself agreeable to all; and in the latter object, where she feared most to fail, she was most sure of success, for those to whom she endeavoured to give pleasure were prepossessed in her favour. Bingley was ready, Georgiana was eager, and Darcy determined, to be pleased.

In seeing Bingley, her thoughts naturally flew to her sister; and, oh! how ardently did she long to know whether any of his were directed in a like manner. Sometimes she could fancy that he talked less than on former occasions, and once or twice pleased herself with the notion that, as he looked at her, he was trying to trace a resemblance. But, though this might be imaginary, she could not be deceived as to his behaviour to Miss Darcy, who had been set up as a rival to Jane. No look appeared on either side that spoke particular regard. Nothing occurred between them that could justify the hopes of his sister. On this point she was soon satisfied; and two or three little circumstances occurred ere they parted, which, in her anxious interpretation, denoted a recollection of Jane not untinctured by tenderness, and a wish of saying more that might lead to the mention of her, had he dared. He observed to her, at a moment when the others were talking together, and in a tone which had something of real regret, that it "was a very long time since he had had the pleasure of seeing her;" and, before she could reply, he added, "It is above eight months. We have not met since the 26th of November, when we were all dancing together at Netherfield."

Elizabeth was pleased to find his memory so exact; and he afterwards took occasion to ask her, when unattended to by any of the rest, whether *all* her sisters were at Longbourn. There was not much in the question, nor in the preceding remark; but there was a look and a manner which gave them meaning.

It was not often that she could turn her eyes on Mr. Darcy himself; but, whenever she did catch a glimpse, she saw an expression of general complaisance, and in all that he said she heard an accent so removed from *hauteur* or disdain of his companions, as convinced her that the improvement of manners which she had yesterday witnessed however temporary its existence might prove, had at least outlived one day. When she saw him thus seeking the acquaintance and courting the good opinion of people with whom any intercourse a few months ago would have been a disgrace—when she saw him thus civil, not only to herself, but to the very relations whom he had openly disdained, and recollected their last lively scene in Hunsford Parsonage—the difference, the change was so great, and struck so forcibly on her mind, that she could hardly restrain her astonishment from being visible. Never, even in the company of his dear friends at Netherfield, or his dignified relations at Rosings, had she seen him so desirous to please, so free from self-consequence or unbending reserve, as now, when no importance could result from the success of his endeavours, and when even the acquaintance of those to whom his attentions were addressed would draw down the ridicule and censure of the ladies both of Netherfield and Rosings.

Their visitors stayed with them above half-an-hour; and when they arose to depart, Mr. Darcy called on his sister to join him in expressing their wish of seeing Mr. and Mrs. Gardiner, and Miss Bennet, to dinner at Pemberley, before they left the country. Miss Darcy, though with a diffidence which marked her little in the habit of giving invitations, readily obeyed. Mrs. Gardiner looked at her niece, desirous of knowing how *she*, whom the invitation most concerned, felt disposed as to its acceptance, but Elizabeth had turned away her head. Presuming however, that this studied avoidance spoke rather a momentary embarrassment than any dislike of the proposal, and seeing in her husband, who was fond of society, a perfect willingness to accept it, she ventured to engage for her attendance, and the day after the next was fixed on.

Bingley expressed great pleasure in the certainty of seeing Elizabeth again, having still a great deal to say to her, and many inquiries to make after all their Hertfordshire friends. Elizabeth, construing all this into a wish of hearing her speak of her sister, was pleased, and on this account, as well as some others, found herself, when their visitors left them, capable of considering the last half-hour with some satisfaction, though while it was passing, the enjoyment of it had been little. Eager to be alone, and fearful of inquiries or hints from her uncle and aunt, she stayed with them only long enough to hear their favourable opinion of Bingley, and then hurried away to dress.

But she had no reason to fear Mr. and Mrs. Gardiner's curiosity; it was not their wish to force her communication. It was evident that she was much better acquainted with Mr. Darcy than they had before any idea of; it was evident that he was very much in love with her. They saw much to interest, but nothing to justify inquiry.

Of Mr. Darcy it was now a matter of anxiety to think well; and, as far as their acquaintance reached, there was no fault to find. They could not be untouched by his politeness; and had they drawn his character from their own feelings and his servant's report, without any reference to any other account, the circle in Hertfordshire to which he was known would not have recognized it for Mr. Darcy. There was now an interest, however, in believing the housekeeper; and they soon became sensible that the authority of a servant who had known him since he was four years old, and whose own manners indicated respectability, was not to be hastily rejected. Neither had anything occurred in the intelligence of their Lambton friends that could materially lessen its weight. They had nothing to accuse him of but pride; pride he probably had, and if not, it would certainly be imputed by the inhabitants of a small market-town where the family did not visit. It was acknowledged, however, that he was a liberal man, and did much good among the poor.

With respect to Wickham, the travellers soon found that he was not held there in much estimation; for though the chief of his concerns with the son of his patron were imperfectly understood, it was yet a well-known fact that, on his quitting Derbyshire, he had left many debts behind him, which Mr. Darcy afterwards discharged.

As for Elizabeth, her thoughts were at Pemberley this evening more than the last; and the evening, though as it passed it seemed long, was not long enough to determine her feelings towards *one* in that mansion; and she lay awake two whole hours endeavouring to make them out. She certainly did not hate him. No; hatred had vanished long ago, and she had almost as long been ashamed of ever feeling a dislike against him, that could be so called. The respect created by the conviction of his valuable qualities, though at first unwillingly admitted, had for some time ceased to be repugnant to her feeling; and it was now heightened into somewhat of a friendlier nature, by the testimony so highly in his favour, and bringing forward his disposition in so amiable a light, which yesterday had produced. But above all, above respect and esteem, there was a motive within her of goodwill which could not be overlooked. It was gratitude; gratitude, not merely for having once loved her, but for loving her still well enough to forgive all the petulance and acrimony of her manner in rejecting him, and all the unjust accusations accompanying her rejection. He who, she had been persuaded, would avoid her as his greatest enemy, seemed, on this accidental meeting, most eager to preserve the acquaintance, and without any indelicate display of regard, or any peculiarity of manner, where their two selves only were concerned, was soliciting the good opinion of her friends, and bent on making her known to his sister. Such a change in a man of so much pride exciting not only astonishment but gratitude—for to love, ardent love, it must be attributed; and as such its impression on her was of a sort to be encouraged, as by no means unpleasing, though it could not be exactly defined. She respected, she esteemed, she was grateful to him, she felt a real interest in his welfare; and she only wanted to know how far she wished that welfare to depend upon herself, and how far it would be for the happiness of both that she should employ the power, which her fancy told her she still possessed, of bringing on her the renewal of his addresses.

It had been settled in the evening between the aunt and the niece, that such a striking civility as Miss Darcy's in coming to see them on the very day of her arrival at Pemberley, for she had reached it only to a late breakfast, ought to be imitated, though it could not be equalled, by some exertion of politeness on their side; and, consequently, that it would be highly expedient to wait on her at Pemberley the following morning. They were, therefore, to go. Elizabeth was pleased; though when she asked herself the reason, she had very little to say in reply.

Mr. Gardiner left them soon after breakfast. The fishing scheme had been renewed the day before, and a positive engagement made of his meeting some of the gentlemen at Pemberley before noon.

CHAPTER XLV

Convinced as Elizabeth now was that Miss Bingley's dislike of her had originated in jealousy, she could not help feeling how unwelcome her appearance at Pemberley must be to her, and was curious to know with how much civility on that lady's side the acquaintance would now be renewed.

On reaching the house, they were shown through the hall into the saloon, whose northern aspect rendered it delightful for summer. Its windows opening to the ground, admitted a most refreshing view of the high woody hills behind the house, and of the beautiful oaks and Spanish chestnuts which were scattered over the intermediate lawn.

In this house they were received by Miss Darcy, who was sitting there with Mrs. Hurst and Miss Bingley, and the lady with whom she lived in London. Georgiana's reception of them was very civil, but attended with all the embarrassment which, though proceeding from shyness and the fear of doing wrong, would easily give to those who felt themselves inferior the belief of her being proud and reserved. Mrs. Gardiner and her niece, however, did her justice, and pitied her.

By Mrs. Hurst and Miss Bingley they were noticed only by a curtsey; and, on their being seated, a pause, awkward as such pauses must always be, succeeded for a few moments. It was first broken by Mrs. Annesley, a genteel, agreeable-looking woman, whose endeavour to introduce some kind of discourse proved her to be more truly well-bred than either of the others; and between her and Mrs. Gardiner, with occasional help from Elizabeth, the conversation was carried on. Miss Darcy looked as if she wished for courage enough to join in it; and sometimes did venture a short sentence when there was least danger of its being heard.

Elizabeth soon saw that she was herself closely watched by Miss Bingley, and that she could not speak a word, especially to Miss Darcy, without calling her attention. This observation would not have prevented her from trying to talk to the latter, had they not been seated at an inconvenient distance; but she was not sorry to be spared the necessity of saying much. Her own thoughts were employing her. She expected every moment that some of the gentlemen would enter the room. She wished, she feared that the master of the house might be amongst them; and whether she wished or feared it most, she could scarcely determine. After sitting in this manner a quarter of an hour without hearing Miss Bingley's voice, Elizabeth was roused by receiving from her a cold inquiry after the health of her family. She answered with equal indifference and brevity, and the others said no more.

The next variation which their visit afforded was produced by the entrance of servants with cold meat, cake, and a variety of all the finest fruits in season; but this did not take place till after many a significant look and smile from Mrs. Annesley to Miss Darcy had been given, to remind her of her post. There was now employment for the whole party—for though they could not all talk, they could all eat; and the beautiful pyramids of grapes, nectarines, and peaches soon collected them round the table.

While thus engaged, Elizabeth had a fair opportunity of deciding whether she most feared or wished for the appearance of Mr. Darcy, by the feelings which prevailed on his entering the room; and then, though but a moment before she had believed her wishes to predominate, she began to regret that he came.

He had been some time with Mr. Gardiner, who, with two or three other gentlemen from the house, was engaged by the river, and had left him only on learning that the ladies of the family intended a visit to Georgiana that morning. No sooner did he appear than Elizabeth wisely resolved to be perfectly easy and unembarrassed; a resolution the more necessary to be made, but perhaps not the more easily kept, because she saw that the suspicions of the whole party were awakened against them, and that there was scarcely an eye which did not watch his behaviour when he first came into the room. In no countenance was attentive curiosity so strongly marked as in Miss Bingley's, in spite of the smiles which overspread her face whenever she spoke to one of its objects; for jealousy had not yet made her desperate, and her attentions to Mr. Darcy were by no means over. Miss Darcy, on her brother's entrance, exerted herself much more to talk, and Elizabeth saw that he was anxious for his sister and herself to get acquainted, and forwarded as much as possible, every attempt at conversation on either side. Miss Bingley saw all this likewise; and, in the imprudence of anger, took the first opportunity of saying, with sneering civility:

"Pray, Miss Eliza, are not the ——shire Militia removed from Meryton? They must be a great loss to *your* family."

In Darcy's presence she dared not mention Wickham's name; but Elizabeth instantly comprehended that he was uppermost in her thoughts; and the various recollections connected with him gave her a moment's distress; but exerting herself vigorously to repel the ill-natured attack, she presently answered the question in a tolerably detached tone. While she spoke, an involuntary glance showed her Darcy, with a heightened complexion, earnestly looking at her, and his sister overcome with confusion, and unable to lift up her eyes. Had Miss Bingley known what pain she was then giving her beloved friend, she undoubtedly would have refrained from the hint; but she had merely intended to discompose Elizabeth by bringing forward the idea of a man to whom she believed her partial, to make her betray a sensibility which might injure her in Darcy's opinion, and, perhaps, to remind the latter of all the follies and absurdities by which some part of her family were connected with that corps. Not a syllable had ever reached her of Miss Darcy's meditated elopement. To no creature had it been revealed, where secrecy was possible, except to Elizabeth; and from all Bingley's connections her brother was particularly anxious to conceal it, from the very wish which Elizabeth had long ago attributed to him, of their becoming hereafter her own. He had certainly formed such a plan, and without meaning that it should effect his endeavour to separate him from Miss Bennet, it is probable that it might add something to his lively concern for the welfare of his friend.

Elizabeth's collected behaviour, however, soon quieted his emotion; and as Miss Bingley, vexed and disappointed, dared not approach nearer to Wickham, Georgiana also recovered in time, though not enough to be able to speak any more. Her brother, whose eye she feared to meet, scarcely recollected her interest in the affair, and the very circumstance which had been designed to turn his thoughts from Elizabeth seemed to have fixed them on her more and more cheerfully.

Their visit did not continue long after the question and answer above mentioned; and while Mr. Darcy was attending them to their carriage Miss Bingley was venting her feelings in criticisms on Elizabeth's person, behaviour, and dress. But Georgiana would not join her. Her brother's recommendation was enough to ensure her favour; his judgement could not err. And he had spoken in such terms of Elizabeth as to leave Georgiana without the power of finding her otherwise than lovely and amiable. When Darcy returned to the saloon, Miss Bingley could not help repeating to him some part of what she had been saying to his sister.

"How very ill Miss Eliza Bennet looks this morning, Mr. Darcy," she cried; "I never in my life saw anyone so much altered as she is since the winter. She is grown so brown and coarse! Louisa and I were agreeing that we should not have known her again."

However little Mr. Darcy might have liked such an address, he contented himself with coolly replying that he perceived no other alteration than her being rather tanned, no miraculous consequence of travelling in the summer.

"For my own part," she rejoined, "I must confess that I never could see any beauty in her. Her face is too thin; her complexion has no brilliancy; and her features are not at all handsome. Her nose wants character—there is nothing marked in its lines. Her teeth are tolerable, but not out of the common way; and as for her eyes, which have sometimes been called so fine, I could never see anything extraordinary in them. They have a sharp, shrewish look, which I do not like at all; and in her air altogether there is a self-sufficiency without fashion, which is intolerable."

Persuaded as Miss Bingley was that Darcy admired Elizabeth, this was not the best method of recommending herself; but angry people are not always wise; and in seeing him at last look somewhat nettled, she had all the success she expected. He was resolutely silent, however, and, from a determination of making him speak, she continued:

"I remember, when we first knew her in Hertfordshire, how amazed we all were to find that she was a reputed beauty; and I particularly recollect your saying one night, after they had been dining at Netherfield, '*She* a beauty!—I should as soon call her mother a wit.' But afterwards she seemed to improve on you, and I believe you thought her rather pretty at one time."

"Yes," replied Darcy, who could contain himself no longer, "but *that* was only when I first saw her, for it is many months since I have considered her as one of the handsomest women of my acquaintance."

He then went away, and Miss Bingley was left to all the satisfaction of having forced him to say what gave no one any pain but herself.

Mrs. Gardiner and Elizabeth talked of all that had occurred during their visit, as they returned, except what had particularly interested them both. The look and behaviour of everybody they had seen were discussed, except of the person who had mostly engaged their attention. They talked of his sister, his friends, his house, his fruit—of everything but himself; yet Elizabeth was longing to know what Mrs. Gardiner thought of him, and Mrs. Gardiner would have been highly gratified by her niece's beginning the subject.

CHAPTER XLVI

Elizabeth had been a good deal disappointed in not finding a letter from Jane on their first arrival at Lambton; and this disappointment had been renewed on each of the mornings that had now been spent there; but on the third her repining was over, and her sister justified, by the receipt of two letters from her at once, on one of which was marked that it had been missent elsewhere. Elizabeth was not surprised at it, as Jane had written the direction remarkably ill.

They had just been preparing to walk as the letters came in; and her uncle and aunt, leaving her to enjoy them in quiet, set off by themselves. The one missent must first be attended to; it had been written five days ago. The beginning contained an account of all their little parties and engagements, with such news as the country afforded; but the latter half, which was dated a day later, and written in evident agitation, gave more important intelligence. It was to this effect:

"Since writing the above, dearest Lizzy, something has occurred of a most unexpected and serious nature; but I am afraid of alarming you—be assured that we are all well. What I have to say relates to poor Lydia. An express came at twelve last night, just as we were all gone to bed, from Colonel Forster, to inform us that she was gone off to Scotland with one of his officers; to own the truth, with Wickham! Imagine our surprise. To Kitty, however, it does not seem so wholly unexpected. I am very, very sorry. So imprudent a match on both sides! But I am willing to hope the best, and that his character has been misunderstood. Thoughtless and indiscreet I can easily believe him, but this step (and let us rejoice over it) marks nothing bad at heart. His choice is disinterested at least, for he must know my father can give her nothing. Our poor mother is sadly grieved. My father bears it better. How thankful am I that we never let them know what has been said against him; we must forget it ourselves. They were off Saturday night about twelve, as is conjectured, but were not missed till yesterday morning at eight. The express was sent off directly. My dear Lizzy, they must have passed within ten miles of us. Colonel Forster gives us reason to expect him here soon. Lydia left a few lines for his wife, informing her of their intention. I must conclude, for I cannot be long from my poor mother.

I am afraid you will not be able to make it out, but I hardly know what I have written."

Without allowing herself time for consideration, and scarcely knowing what she felt, Elizabeth on finishing this letter instantly seized the other, and opening it with the utmost impatience, read as follows: it had been written a day later than the conclusion of the first.

"By this time, my dearest sister, you have received my hurried letter; I wish this may be more intelligible, but though not confined for time, my head is so bewildered that I cannot answer for being coherent. Dearest Lizzy, I hardly know what I would write, but I have bad news for you, and it cannot be delayed. Imprudent as the marriage between Mr. Wickham and our poor Lydia would be, we are now anxious to be assured it has taken place, for there is but too much reason to fear they are not gone to Scotland. Colonel Forster came yesterday, having left Brighton the day before, not many hours after the express. Though Lydia's short letter to Mrs. F. gave them to understand that they were going to Gretna Green, something was dropped by Denny expressing his belief that W. never intended to go there, or to marry Lydia at all, which was repeated to Colonel F., who, instantly taking the alarm, set off from B. intending to trace their route. He did trace them easily to Clapham, but no further; for on entering that place, they removed into a hackney coach, and dismissed the chaise that brought them from Epsom. All that is known after this is, that they were seen to continue the London road. I know not what to think. After making every possible inquiry on that side London, Colonel F. came on into Hertfordshire, anxiously renewing them at all the turnpikes, and at the inns in Barnet and Hatfield, but without any success—no such people had been seen to pass through. With the kindest concern he came on to Longbourn, and broke his apprehensions to us in a manner most creditable to his heart. I am sincerely grieved for him and Mrs. F., but no one can throw any blame on them. Our distress, my dear Lizzy, is very great. My father and mother believe the worst, but I cannot think so ill of him. Many circumstances might make it more eligible for them to be married privately in town than to pursue their first plan; and even if *he* could form such a design against a young woman of Lydia's connections, which is not likely, can I suppose her so lost to everything? Impossible! I grieve to find, however, that Colonel F. is not disposed to depend upon their marriage; he shook his head when I expressed my hopes, and said he feared W. was not a man to be trusted. My poor mother is really ill, and keeps her room. Could she exert herself, it would be better; but this is not to be expected. And as to my father, I never in my life saw him so affected. Poor Kitty has anger for having concealed their attachment; but as it was a matter of confidence, one cannot wonder. I am truly glad, dearest Lizzy, that you have been spared something of these distressing scenes; but now, as the first shock is over, shall I own that I long for your return? I am not so selfish, however, as to press for it, if inconvenient. Adieu! I take up my pen again to do what I have just told you I would not; but circumstances are such that I cannot help earnestly begging you all to come here as soon as possible. I know my dear uncle and aunt so well, that I am not afraid of requesting it, though I have still something more to ask of the former. My father is going to London with Colonel Forster instantly, to try to discover her. What he means to do I am sure I know not; but his excessive distress will not allow him to pursue any measure in the best and safest way, and Colonel Forster is obliged to be at Brighton again to-morrow evening. In such an exigence, my uncle's advice and assistance would be everything in the world; he will immediately comprehend what I must feel, and I rely upon his goodness."

"Oh! where, where is my uncle?" cried Elizabeth, darting from her seat as she finished the letter, in eagerness to follow him, without losing a moment of the time so precious; but as she reached the door it was opened by a servant, and Mr. Darcy appeared. Her pale face and impetuous manner made him start, and before he could recover himself to speak, she, in whose mind every idea was superseded by Lydia's situation, hastily exclaimed, "I beg your pardon, but I must leave you. I must find Mr. Gardiner this moment, on business that cannot be delayed; I have not an instant to lose."

"Good God! what is the matter?" cried he, with more feeling than politeness; then recollecting himself, "I will not detain you a minute; but let me, or let the servant go after Mr. and Mrs. Gardiner. You are not well enough; you cannot go yourself."

Elizabeth hesitated, but her knees trembled under her and she felt how little would be gained by her attempting to pursue them. Calling back the servant, therefore, she commissioned him, though in so breathless an accent as made her almost unintelligible, to fetch his master and mistress home instantly.

On his quitting the room she sat down, unable to support herself, and looking so miserably ill, that it was impossible for Darcy to leave her, or to refrain from saying, in a tone of gentleness and commiseration, "Let me call your maid. Is there nothing you could take to give you present relief? A glass of wine; shall I get you one? You are very ill."

"No, I thank you," she replied, endeavouring to recover herself. "There is nothing the matter with me. I am quite well; I am only distressed by some dreadful news which I have just received from Longbourn."

She burst into tears as she alluded to it, and for a few minutes could not speak another word. Darcy, in wretched suspense, could only say something indistinctly of his concern, and observe her in compassionate silence. At length she spoke again. "I have just had a letter from Jane, with such dreadful news. It cannot be concealed from anyone. My younger sister has left all her friends—has eloped; has thrown herself into the power of—of Mr. Wickham. They are gone off together from Brighton. *You* know him too well to doubt the rest. She has no money, no connections, nothing that can tempt him to—she is lost for ever."

Darcy was fixed in astonishment. "When I consider," she added in a yet more agitated voice, "that I might have prevented it! I, who knew what he was. Had I but explained some part of it only—some part of what I learnt, to my own family! Had his character been known, this could not have happened. But it is all—all too late now."

"I am grieved indeed," cried Darcy; "grieved—shocked. But is it certain—absolutely certain?"

"Oh, yes! They left Brighton together on Sunday night, and were traced almost to London, but not beyond; they are certainly not gone to Scotland."

"And what has been done, what has been attempted, to recover her?"

"My father is gone to London, and Jane has written to beg my uncle's immediate assistance; and we shall be off, I hope, in half-an-hour. But nothing can be done—I know very well that nothing can be done. How is such a man to be worked on? How are they even to be discovered? I have not the smallest hope. It is every way horrible!"

Darcy shook his head in silent acquiescence.

"When *my* eyes were opened to his real character—Oh! had I known what I ought, what I dared to do! But I knew not—I was afraid of doing too much. Wretched, wretched mistake!"

Darcy made no answer. He seemed scarcely to hear her, and was walking up and down the room in earnest meditation, his brow contracted, his air gloomy. Elizabeth soon observed, and instantly understood it. Her power was sinking; everything *must* sink under such a proof of family weakness, such an assurance of the deepest disgrace. She could neither wonder nor condemn, but the belief of his self-conquest brought nothing consolatory to her bosom, afforded no palliation of her distress. It was, on the contrary, exactly calculated to make her understand her own wishes; and never had she so honestly felt that she could have loved him, as now, when all love must be vain.

But self, though it would intrude, could not engross her. Lydia—the humiliation, the misery she was bringing on them all, soon swallowed up every private care; and covering her face with her handkerchief, Elizabeth was soon lost to everything else; and, after a pause of several minutes, was only recalled to a sense of her situation by the voice of her companion, who, in a manner which, though it spoke compassion, spoke likewise restraint, said, "I am afraid you have been long desiring my absence, nor have I anything to plead in excuse of my stay, but real, though unavailing concern. Would to Heaven that anything could be either said or done on my part that might offer consolation to such distress! But I will not torment you with vain wishes, which may seem purposely to ask for your thanks. This unfortunate affair will, I fear, prevent my sister's having the pleasure of seeing you at Pemberley to-day."

"Oh, yes. Be so kind as to apologise for us to Miss Darcy. Say that urgent business calls us home immediately. Conceal the unhappy truth as long as it is possible, I know it cannot be long."

He readily assured her of his secrecy; again expressed his sorrow for her distress, wished it a happier conclusion than there was at present reason to hope, and leaving his compliments for her relations, with only one serious, parting look, went away.

As he quitted the room, Elizabeth felt how improbable it was that they should ever see each other again on such terms of cordiality as had marked their several meetings in Derbyshire; and as she threw a retrospective glance over the whole of their acquaintance, so full of contradictions and varieties, sighed at the perverseness of those feelings which would now have promoted its continuance, and would formerly have rejoiced in its termination.

If gratitude and esteem are good foundations of affection, Elizabeth's change of sentiment will be neither improbable nor faulty. But if otherwise—if regard springing from such sources is unreasonable or unnatural, in comparison of what is so often described as arising on a first interview with its object, and even before two words have been exchanged, nothing can be said in her defence, except that she had given somewhat of a trial to the latter method in her partiality for Wickham, and that its ill success might, perhaps, authorise her to seek the other less interesting mode of attachment. Be that as it may, she saw him go with regret; and in this early example of what Lydia's infamy must produce, found additional anguish as she reflected on that wretched business. Never, since reading Jane's second letter, had she entertained a hope of Wickham's meaning to marry her. No one but Jane, she thought, could flatter herself with such an expectation. Surprise was the least of her feelings on this development. While the contents of the first letter remained in her mind, she was all surprise—all astonishment that Wickham should marry a girl whom it was impossible he could marry for money; and how Lydia could ever have attached him had appeared incomprehensible. But now it was all too natural. For such an attachment as this she might have sufficient charms; and though she did not suppose Lydia to be deliberately engaging in an elopement without the intention of marriage, she had no difficulty in believing that neither her virtue nor her understanding would preserve her from falling an easy prey.

She had never perceived, while the regiment was in Hertfordshire, that Lydia had any partiality for him; but she was convinced that Lydia wanted only encouragement to attach herself to anybody. Sometimes one officer, sometimes another, had been her favourite, as their attentions raised them in her opinion. Her affections had continually been fluctuating but never without an object. The mischief of neglect and mistaken indulgence towards such a girl—oh! how acutely did she now feel it!

She was wild to be at home—to hear, to see, to be upon the spot to share with Jane in the cares that must now fall wholly upon her, in a family so deranged, a father absent, a mother incapable of exertion, and requiring constant attendance; and though almost persuaded that nothing could be done for Lydia, her uncle's interference seemed of the utmost importance, and till he entered the room her impatience was severe. Mr. and Mrs. Gardiner had hurried back in alarm, supposing by the servant's account that their niece was taken suddenly ill; but satisfying them instantly on that head, she eagerly communicated the cause of their summons, reading the two letters aloud, and dwelling on the postscript of the last with trembling energy, though Lydia had never been a favourite with them, Mr. and Mrs. Gardiner could not but be deeply afflicted. Not Lydia only, but all were concerned in it; and after the first exclamations of surprise and horror, Mr. Gardiner promised every assistance in his power. Elizabeth, though expecting no less, thanked him with tears of gratitude; and all three being actuated by one spirit, everything relating to their journey was speedily settled. They were to be off as soon as possible. "But what is to be done about Pemberley?" cried Mrs. Gardiner. "John told us Mr. Darcy was here when you sent for us; was it so?"

"Yes; and I told him we should not be able to keep our engagement. *That* is all settled."

"What is all settled?" repeated the other, as she ran into her room to prepare. "And are they upon such terms as for her to disclose the real truth? Oh, that I knew how it was!"

But wishes were vain, or at least could only serve to amuse her in the hurry and confusion of the following hour. Had Elizabeth been at leisure to be idle, she would have remained certain that all employment was impossible to one so wretched as herself; but she had her share of business as well as her aunt, and amongst the rest there were notes to be written to all their friends at Lambton, with false excuses for their sudden departure. An hour, however, saw the whole completed; and Mr. Gardiner meanwhile having settled his account at the inn, nothing remained to be done but to go; and Elizabeth, after all the misery of the morning, found herself, in a shorter space of time than she could have supposed, seated in the carriage, and on the road to Longbourn.

CHAPTER XLVII

"I have been thinking it over again, Elizabeth," said her uncle, as they drove from the town; "and really, upon serious consideration, I am much more inclined than I was to judge as your eldest sister does on the matter. It appears to me so very unlikely that any young man should form such a design against a girl who is by no means unprotected or friendless, and who was actually staying in his colonel's family, that I am strongly inclined to hope the best. Could he expect that her friends would not step forward? Could he expect to be noticed again by the regiment, after such an affront to Colonel Forster? His temptation is not adequate to the risk!"

"Do you really think so?" cried Elizabeth, brightening up for a moment.

"Upon my word," said Mrs. Gardiner, "I begin to be of your uncle's opinion. It is really too great a violation of decency, honour, and interest, for him to be guilty of. I cannot think so very ill of Wickham. Can you yourself, Lizzy, so wholly give him up, as to believe him capable of it?"

"Not, perhaps, of neglecting his own interest; but of every other neglect I can believe him capable. If, indeed, it should be so! But I dare not hope it. Why should they not go on to Scotland if that had been the case?"

"In the first place," replied Mr. Gardiner, "there is no absolute proof that they are not gone to Scotland."

"Oh! but their removing from the chaise into a hackney coach is such a presumption! And, besides, no traces of them were to be found on the Barnet road."

"Well, then—supposing them to be in London. They may be there, though for the purpose of concealment, for no more exceptional purpose. It is not likely that money should be very abundant on either side; and it might strike them that they could be more economically, though less expeditiously, married in London than in Scotland."

"But why all this secrecy? Why any fear of detection? Why must their marriage be private? Oh, no, no—this is not likely. His most particular friend, you see by Jane's account, was persuaded of his never intending to marry her. Wickham will never marry a woman without some money. He cannot afford it. And what claims has Lydia—what attraction has she beyond youth, health, and good humour that could make him, for her sake, forego every chance of benefiting himself by marrying well? As to what restraint the apprehensions of disgrace in the corps might throw on a dishonourable elopement with her, I am not able to judge; for I know nothing of the effects that such a step might produce. But as to your other objection, I am afraid it will hardly hold good. Lydia has no brothers to step forward; and he might imagine, from my father's behaviour, from his indolence and the little attention he has ever seemed to give to what was going forward in his family, that *he* would do as little, and think as little about it, as any father could do, in such a matter."

"But can you think that Lydia is so lost to everything but love of him as to consent to live with him on any terms other than marriage?"

"It does seem, and it is most shocking indeed," replied Elizabeth, with tears in her eyes, "that a sister's sense of decency and virtue in such a point should admit of doubt. But, really, I know not what to say. Perhaps I am not doing her justice. But she is very young; she has never been taught to think on serious subjects; and for the last half-year, nay, for a twelvemonth—she has been given up to nothing but amusement and vanity. She has been allowed to dispose of her time in the most idle and frivolous manner, and to adopt any opinions that came in her way. Since the ——shire were first quartered in Meryton, nothing but love, flirtation, and officers have been in her head. She has been doing everything in her power by thinking and talking on the subject, to give greater—what shall I call it? susceptibility to her feelings; which are naturally lively enough. And we all know that Wickham has every charm of person and address that can captivate a woman."

"But you see that Jane," said her aunt, "does not think so very ill of Wickham as to believe him capable of the attempt."

"Of whom does Jane ever think ill? And who is there, whatever might be their former conduct, that she would think capable of such an attempt, till it were proved against them? But Jane knows, as well as I do, what Wickham really is. We both know that he has been profligate in every sense of the word; that he has neither integrity nor honour; that he is as false and deceitful as he is insinuating."

"And do you really know all this?" cried Mrs. Gardiner, whose curiosity as to the mode of her intelligence was all alive.

"I do indeed," replied Elizabeth, colouring. "I told you, the other day, of his infamous behaviour to Mr. Darcy; and you yourself, when last at Longbourn, heard in what manner he spoke of the man who had behaved with such forbearance and liberality towards him. And there are other circumstances which I am not at liberty—which it is not worth while to relate; but his lies about the whole Pemberley family are endless. From what he said of Miss Darcy I was thoroughly prepared to see a proud, reserved, disagreeable girl. Yet he knew to the contrary himself. He must know that she was as amiable and unpretending as we have found her."

"But does Lydia know nothing of this? can she be ignorant of what you and Jane seem so well to understand?"

"Oh, yes!—that, that is the worst of all. Till I was in Kent, and saw so much both of Mr. Darcy and his relation Colonel Fitzwilliam, I was ignorant of the truth myself. And when I returned home, the ——shire was to leave Meryton in a week or fortnight's time. As that was the case, neither Jane, to whom I related the whole, nor I, thought it necessary to make our knowledge public; for of what use could it apparently be to any one, that the good opinion which all the neighbourhood had of him should then be overthrown? And even when it was settled that Lydia should go with Mrs. Forster, the necessity of opening her eyes to his character never occurred to me. That *she* could be in any danger from the deception never entered my head. That such a consequence as *this* could ensue, you may easily believe, was far enough from my thoughts."

"When they all removed to Brighton, therefore, you had no reason, I suppose, to believe them fond of each other?"

"Not the slightest. I can remember no symptom of affection on either side; and had anything of the kind been perceptible, you must be aware that ours is not a family on which it could be thrown away. When first he entered the corps, she was ready enough to admire him; but so we all were. Every girl in or near Meryton was out of her senses about him for the first two months; but he never distinguished *her* by any particular attention; and, consequently, after a moderate period of extravagant and wild admiration, her fancy for him gave way, and others of the regiment, who treated her with more distinction, again became her favourites."

*****

It may be easily believed, that however little of novelty could be added to their fears, hopes, and conjectures, on this interesting subject, by its repeated discussion, no other could detain them from it long, during the whole of the journey. From Elizabeth's thoughts it was never absent. Fixed there by the keenest of all anguish, self-reproach, she could find no interval of ease or forgetfulness.

They travelled as expeditiously as possible, and, sleeping one night on the road, reached Longbourn by dinner time the next day. It was a comfort to Elizabeth to consider that Jane could not have been wearied by long expectations.

The little Gardiners, attracted by the sight of a chaise, were standing on the steps of the house as they entered the paddock; and, when the carriage drove up to the door, the joyful surprise that lighted up their faces, and displayed itself over their whole bodies, in a variety of capers and frisks, was the first pleasing earnest of their welcome.

Elizabeth jumped out; and, after giving each of them a hasty kiss, hurried into the vestibule, where Jane, who came running down from her mother's apartment, immediately met her.

Elizabeth, as she affectionately embraced her, whilst tears filled the eyes of both, lost not a moment in asking whether anything had been heard of the fugitives.

"Not yet," replied Jane. "But now that my dear uncle is come, I hope everything will be well."

"Is my father in town?"

"Yes, he went on Tuesday, as I wrote you word."

"And have you heard from him often?"

"We have heard only twice. He wrote me a few lines on Wednesday to say that he had arrived in safety, and to give me his directions, which I particularly begged him to do. He merely added that he should not write again till he had something of importance to mention."

"And my mother—how is she? How are you all?"

"My mother is tolerably well, I trust; though her spirits are greatly shaken. She is upstairs and will have great satisfaction in seeing you all. She does not yet leave her dressing-room. Mary and Kitty, thank Heaven, are quite well."

"But you—how are you?" cried Elizabeth. "You look pale. How much you must have gone through!"

Her sister, however, assured her of her being perfectly well;

and their conversation, which had been passing while Mr. and Mrs. Gardiner were engaged with their children, was now put an end to by the approach of the whole party. Jane ran to her uncle and aunt, and welcomed and thanked them both, with alternate smiles and tears.

When they were all in the drawing-room, the questions which Elizabeth had already asked were of course repeated by the others, and they soon found that Jane had no intelligence to give. The sanguine hope of good, however, which the benevolence of her heart suggested had not yet deserted her; she still expected that it would all end well, and that every morning would bring some letter, either from Lydia or her father, to explain their proceedings, and, perhaps, announce their marriage.

Mrs. Bennet, to whose apartment they all repaired, after a few minutes' conversation together, received them exactly as might be expected; with tears and lamentations of regret, invectives against the villainous conduct of Wickham, and complaints of her own sufferings and ill-usage; blaming everybody but the person to whose ill-judging indulgence the errors of her daughter must principally be owing.

"If I had been able," said she, "to carry my point in going to Brighton, with all my family, *this* would not have happened; but poor dear Lydia had nobody to take care of her. Why did the Forsters ever let her go out of their sight? I am sure there was some great neglect or other on their side, for she is not the kind of girl to do such a thing if she had been well looked after. I always thought they were very unfit to have the charge of her; but I was overruled, as I always am. Poor dear child! And now here's Mr. Bennet gone away, and I know he will fight Wickham, wherever he meets him and then he will be killed, and what is to become of us all? The Collinses will turn us out before he is cold in his grave, and if you are not kind to us, brother, I do not know what we shall do."

They all exclaimed against such terrific ideas; and Mr. Gardiner, after general assurances of his affection for her and all her family, told her that he meant to be in London the very next day, and would assist Mr. Bennet in every endeavour for recovering Lydia.

"Do not give way to useless alarm," added he; "though it is right to be prepared for the worst, there is no occasion to look on it as certain. It is not quite a week since they left Brighton. In a few days more we may gain some news of them; and till we know that they are not married, and have no design of marrying, do not let us give the matter over as lost. As soon as I get to town I shall go to my brother, and make him come home with me to Gracechurch Street; and then we may consult together as to what is to be done."

"Oh! my dear brother," replied Mrs. Bennet, "that is exactly what I could most wish for. And now do, when you get to town, find them out, wherever they may be; and if they are not married already, *make* them marry. And as for wedding clothes, do not let them wait for that, but tell Lydia she shall have as much money as she chooses to buy them, after they are married. And, above all, keep Mr. Bennet from fighting. Tell him what a dreadful state I am in, that I am frighted out of my wits—and have such tremblings, such flutterings, all over me—such spasms in my side and pains in my head, and such beatings at heart, that I can get no rest by night nor by day. And tell my dear Lydia not to give any directions about her clothes till she has seen me, for she does not know which are the best warehouses. Oh, brother, how kind you are! I know you will contrive it all."

But Mr. Gardiner, though he assured her again of his earnest endeavours in the cause, could not avoid recommending moderation to her, as well in her hopes as her fears; and after talking with her in this manner till dinner was on the table, they all left her to vent all her feelings on the housekeeper, who attended in the absence of her daughters.

Though her brother and sister were persuaded that there was no real occasion for such a seclusion from the family, they did not attempt to oppose it, for they knew that she had not prudence enough to hold her tongue before the servants, while they waited at table, and judged it better that *one* only of the household, and the one whom they could most trust should comprehend all her fears and solicitude on the subject.

In the dining-room they were soon joined by Mary and Kitty, who had been too busily engaged in their separate apartments to make their appearance before. One came from her books, and the other from her toilette. The faces of both, however, were tolerably calm; and no change was visible in either, except that the loss of her favourite sister, or the anger which she had herself incurred in this business, had given more of fretfulness than usual to the accents of Kitty. As for Mary, she was mistress enough of herself to whisper to Elizabeth, with a countenance of grave reflection, soon after they were seated at table:

"This is a most unfortunate affair, and will probably be much talked of. But we must stem the tide of malice, and pour into the wounded bosoms of each other the balm of sisterly consolation."

Then, perceiving in Elizabeth no inclination of replying, she added, "Unhappy as the event must be for Lydia, we may draw from it this useful lesson: that loss of virtue in a female is irretrievable; that one false step involves her in endless ruin; that her reputation is no less brittle than it is beautiful; and that she cannot be too much guarded in her behaviour towards the undeserving of the other sex."

Elizabeth lifted up her eyes in amazement, but was too much oppressed to make any reply. Mary, however, continued to console herself with such kind of moral extractions from the evil before them.

In the afternoon, the two elder Miss Bennets were able to be for half-an-hour by themselves; and Elizabeth instantly availed herself of the opportunity of making any inquiries, which Jane was equally eager to satisfy. After joining in general lamentations over the dreadful sequel of this event, which Elizabeth considered as all but certain, and Miss Bennet could not assert to be wholly impossible, the former continued the subject, by saying, "But tell me all and everything about it which I have not already heard. Give me further particulars. What did Colonel Forster say? Had they no apprehension of anything before the elopement took place? They must have seen them together for ever."

"Colonel Forster did own that he had often suspected some partiality, especially on Lydia's side, but nothing to give him any alarm. I am so grieved for him! His behaviour was attentive and kind to the utmost. He *was* coming to us, in order to assure us of his concern, before he had any idea of their not being gone to Scotland: when that apprehension first got abroad, it hastened his journey."

"And was Denny convinced that Wickham would not marry? Did he know of their intending to go off? Had Colonel Forster seen Denny himself?"

"Yes; but, when questioned by *him*, Denny denied knowing anything of their plans, and would not give his real opinion about it. He did not repeat his persuasion of their not marrying—and from *that*, I am inclined to hope, he might have been misunderstood before."

"And till Colonel Forster came himself, not one of you entertained a doubt, I suppose, of their being really married?"

"How was it possible that such an idea should enter our brains? I felt a little uneasy—a little fearful of my sister's happiness with him in marriage, because I knew that his conduct had not been always quite right. My father and mother knew nothing of that; they only felt how imprudent a match it must be. Kitty then owned, with a very natural triumph on knowing more than the rest of us, that in Lydia's last letter she had prepared her for such a step. She had known, it seems, of their being in love with each other, many weeks."

"But not before they went to Brighton?"

"No, I believe not."

"And did Colonel Forster appear to think well of Wickham himself? Does he know his real character?"

"I must confess that he did not speak so well of Wickham as he formerly did. He believed him to be imprudent and extravagant. And since this sad affair has taken place, it is said that he left Meryton greatly in debt; but I hope this may be false."

"Oh, Jane, had we been less secret, had we told what we knew of him, this could not have happened!"

"Perhaps it would have been better," replied her sister. "But to expose the former faults of any person without knowing what their present feelings were, seemed unjustifiable. We acted with the best intentions."

"Could Colonel Forster repeat the particulars of Lydia's note to his wife?"

"He brought it with him for us to see."

Jane then took it from her pocket-book, and gave it to Elizabeth. These were the contents:

"MY DEAR HARRIET,

"You will laugh when you know where I am gone, and I cannot help laughing myself at your surprise to-morrow morning, as soon as I am missed. I am going to Gretna Green, and if you cannot guess with who, I shall think you a simpleton, for there is but one man in the world I love, and he is an angel. I should never be happy without him, so think it no harm to be off. You need not send them word at Longbourn of my going, if you do not like it, for it will make the surprise the greater, when I write to them and sign my name 'Lydia Wickham.' What a good joke it will be! I can hardly write for laughing. Pray make my excuses to Pratt for not keeping my engagement, and dancing with him to-night. Tell him I hope he will excuse me when he knows all; and tell him I will dance with him at the next ball we meet, with great pleasure. I shall send for my clothes when I get to Longbourn; but I wish you would tell Sally to mend a great slit in my worked muslin gown before they are packed up. Good-bye. Give my love to Colonel Forster. I hope you will drink to our good journey.

"Your affectionate friend,

"LYDIA BENNET."

"Oh! thoughtless, thoughtless Lydia!" cried Elizabeth when she had finished it. "What a letter is this, to be written at such a moment! But at least it shows that *she* was serious on the subject of their journey. Whatever he might afterwards persuade her to, it was not on her side a *scheme* of infamy. My poor father! how he must have felt it!"

"I never saw anyone so shocked. He could not speak a word for full ten minutes. My mother was taken ill immediately, and the whole house in such confusion!"

"Oh! Jane," cried Elizabeth, "was there a servant belonging to it who did not know the whole story before the end of the day?"

"I do not know. I hope there was. But to be guarded at such a time is very difficult. My mother was in hysterics, and though I endeavoured to give her every assistance in my power, I am afraid I did not do so much as I might have done! But the horror of what might possibly happen almost took from me my faculties."

"Your attendance upon her has been too much for you. You do not look well. Oh that I had been with you! you have had every care and anxiety upon yourself alone."

"Mary and Kitty have been very kind, and would have shared in every fatigue, I am sure; but I did not think it right for either of them. Kitty is slight and delicate; and Mary studies so much, that her hours of repose should not be broken in on. My aunt Phillips came to Longbourn on Tuesday, after my father went away; and was so good as to stay till Thursday with me. She was of great use and comfort to us all. And Lady

Lucas has been very kind; she walked here on Wednesday morning to condole with us, and offered her services, or any of her daughters', if they should be of use to us."

"She had better have stayed at home," cried Elizabeth; "perhaps she *meant* well, but, under such a misfortune as this, one cannot see too little of one's neighbours. Assistance is impossible; condolence insufferable. Let them triumph over us at a distance, and be satisfied."

She then proceeded to inquire into the measures which her father had intended to pursue, while in town, for the recovery of his daughter.

"He meant I believe," replied Jane, "to go to Epsom, the place where they last changed horses, see the postilions and try if anything could be made out from them. His principal object must be to discover the number of the hackney coach which took them from Clapham. It had come with a fare from London; and as he thought that the circumstance of a gentleman and lady's removing from one carriage into another might be remarked he meant to make inquiries at Clapham. If he could anyhow discover at what house the coachman had before set down his fare, he determined to make inquiries there, and hoped it might not be impossible to find out the stand and number of the coach. I do not know of any other designs that he had formed; but he was in such a hurry to be gone, and his spirits so greatly discomposed, that I had difficulty in finding out even so much as this."

CHAPTER XLVIII

The whole party were in hopes of a letter from Mr. Bennet the next morning, but the post came in without bringing a single line from him. His family knew him to be, on all common occasions, a most negligent and dilatory correspondent; but at such a time they had hoped for exertion. They were forced to conclude that he had no pleasing intelligence to send; but even of *that* they would have been glad to be certain. Mr. Gardiner had waited only for the letters before he set off.

When he was gone, they were certain at least of receiving constant information of what was going on, and their uncle promised, at parting, to prevail on Mr. Bennet to return to Longbourn, as soon as he could, to the great consolation of his sister, who considered it as the only security for her husband's not being killed in a duel.

Mrs. Gardiner and the children were to remain in Hertfordshire a few days longer, as the former thought her presence might be serviceable to her nieces. She shared in their attendance on Mrs. Bennet, and was a great comfort to them in their hours of freedom. Their other aunt also visited them frequently, and always, as she said, with the design of cheering and heartening them up—though, as she never came without reporting some fresh instance of Wickham's extravagance or irregularity, she seldom went away without leaving them more dispirited than she found them.

All Meryton seemed striving to blacken the man who, but three months before, had been almost an angel of light. He was declared to be in debt to every tradesman in the place, and his intrigues, all honoured with the title of seduction, had been extended into every tradesman's family. Everybody declared that he was the wickedest young man in the world; and everybody began to find out that they had always distrusted the appearance of his goodness. Elizabeth, though she did not credit above half of what was said, believed enough to make her former assurance of her sister's ruin more certain; and even Jane, who believed still less of it, became almost hopeless, more especially as the time was now come when, if they had gone to Scotland, which she had never before entirely despaired of, they must in all probability have gained some news of them.

Mr. Gardiner left Longbourn on Sunday; on Tuesday his wife received a letter from him; it told them that, on his arrival, he had immediately found out his brother, and persuaded him to come to Gracechurch Street; that Mr. Bennet had been to Epsom and Clapham, before his arrival, but without gaining any satisfactory information; and that he was now determined to inquire at all the principal hotels in town, as Mr. Bennet thought it possible they might have gone to one of them, on their first coming to London, before they procured lodgings. Mr. Gardiner himself did not expect any success from this measure, but as his brother was eager in it, he meant to assist him in pursuing it. He added that Mr. Bennet seemed wholly disinclined at present to leave London and promised to write again very soon. There was also a postscript to this effect:

"I have written to Colonel Forster to desire him to find out, if possible, from some of the young man's intimates in the regiment, whether Wickham has any relations or connections who would be likely to know in what part of town he has now concealed himself. If there were anyone that one could apply to with a probability of gaining such a clue as that, it might be of essential consequence. At present we have nothing to guide us. Colonel Forster will, I dare say, do everything in his power to satisfy us on this head. But, on second thoughts, perhaps, Lizzy could tell us what relations he has now living, better than any other person."

Elizabeth was at no loss to understand from whence this deference to her authority proceeded; but it was not in her power to give any information of so satisfactory a nature as the compliment deserved. She had never heard of his having had any relations, except a father and mother, both of whom had been dead many years. It was possible, however, that some of his companions in the ——shire might be able to give more information; and though she was not very sanguine in expecting it, the application was a something to look forward to.

Every day at Longbourn was now a day of anxiety; but the most anxious part of each was when the post was expected. The arrival of letters was the grand object of every morning's impatience. Through letters, whatever of good or bad was to be told would be communicated, and every succeeding day was expected to bring some news of importance.

But before they heard again from Mr. Gardiner, a letter arrived for their father, from a different quarter, from Mr. Collins; which, as Jane had received directions to open all that came for him in his absence, she accordingly read; and Elizabeth, who knew what curiosities his letters always were, looked over her, and read it likewise. It was as follows:

"MY DEAR SIR,

"I feel myself called upon, by our relationship, and my situation in life, to condole with you on the grievous affliction you are now suffering under, of which we were yesterday informed by a letter from Hertfordshire. Be assured, my dear sir, that Mrs. Collins and myself sincerely sympathise with you and all your respectable family, in your present distress, which must be of the bitterest kind, because proceeding from a cause which no time can remove. No arguments shall be wanting on my part that can alleviate so severe a misfortune—or that may comfort you, under a circumstance that must be of all others the most afflicting to a parent's mind. The death of your daughter would have been a blessing in comparison of this. And it is the more to be lamented, because there is reason to suppose as my dear Charlotte informs me, that this licentiousness of behaviour in your daughter has proceeded from a faulty degree of indulgence; though, at the same time, for the consolation of yourself and Mrs. Bennet, I am inclined to think that her own disposition must be naturally bad, or she could not be guilty of such an enormity, at so early an age. Howsoever that may be, you are grievously to be pitied; in which opinion I am not only joined by Mrs. Collins, but likewise by Lady Catherine and her daughter, to whom I have related the affair. They agree with me in apprehending that this false step in one daughter will be injurious to the fortunes of all the others; for who, as Lady Catherine herself condescendingly says, will connect themselves with such a family? And this consideration leads me moreover to reflect, with augmented satisfaction, on a certain event of last November; for had it been otherwise, I must have been involved in all your sorrow and disgrace. Let me then advise you, dear sir, to console yourself as much as possible, to throw off your unworthy child from your affection for ever, and leave her to reap the fruits of her own heinous offense.

"I am, dear sir, etc., etc."

Mr. Gardiner did not write again till he had received an answer from Colonel Forster; and then he had nothing of a pleasant nature to send. It was not known that Wickham had a single relationship with whom he kept up any connection, and it was certain that he had no near one living. His former acquaintances had been numerous; but since he had been in the militia, it did not appear that he was on terms of particular friendship with any of them. There was no one, therefore, who could be pointed out as likely to give any news of him. And in the wretched state of his own finances, there was a very powerful motive for secrecy, in addition to his fear of discovery by Lydia's relations, for it had just transpired that he had left gaming debts behind him to a very considerable amount. Colonel Forster believed that more than a thousand pounds would be necessary to clear his expenses at Brighton. He owed a good deal in town, but his debts of honour were still more formidable. Mr. Gardiner did not attempt to conceal these particulars from the Longbourn family. Jane heard them with horror. "A gamester!" she cried. "This is wholly unexpected. I had not an idea of it."

Mr. Gardiner added in his letter, that they might expect to see their father at home on the following day, which was Saturday. Rendered spiritless by the ill-success of all their endeavours, he had yielded to his brother-in-law's entreaty that he would return to his family, and leave it to him to do whatever occasion might suggest to be advisable for continuing their pursuit. When Mrs. Bennet was told of this, she did not express so much satisfaction as her children expected, considering what her anxiety for his life had been before.

"What, is he coming home, and without poor Lydia?" she cried. "Sure he will not leave London before he has found them. Who is to fight Wickham, and make him marry her, if he comes away?"

As Mrs. Gardiner began to wish to be at home, it was settled that she and the children should go to London, at the same time that Mr. Bennet came from it. The coach, therefore, took them the first stage of their journey, and brought its master back to Longbourn.

Mrs. Gardiner went away in all the perplexity about Elizabeth and her Derbyshire friend that had attended her from that part of the world. His name had never been voluntarily mentioned before them by her niece; and the kind of half-expectation which Mrs. Gardiner had formed, of their being followed by a letter from him, had ended in nothing. Elizabeth had received none since her return that could come from Pemberley.

The present unhappy state of the family rendered any other excuse for the lowness of her spirits unnecessary; nothing, therefore, could be fairly conjectured from *that*, though Elizabeth, who was by this time tolerably well acquainted with her own feelings, was perfectly aware that, had she known nothing of Darcy, she could have borne the dread of Lydia's infamy somewhat better. It would have spared her, she thought, one sleepless night out of two.

When Mr. Bennet arrived, he had all the appearance of his usual philosophic composure. He said as little as he had ever been in the habit of saying; made no mention of the business that had taken him away, and it was some time before his daughters had courage to speak of it.

It was not till the afternoon, when he had joined them at tea, that Elizabeth ventured to introduce the subject; and then, on her briefly expressing her sorrow for what he must have endured, he replied, "Say nothing of that. Who should suffer but myself? It has been my own doing, and I ought to feel it."

"You must not be too severe upon yourself," replied Elizabeth.

"You may well warn me against such an evil. Human nature is so prone to fall into it! No, Lizzy, let me once in my life feel how much I have been to blame. I am not afraid of being overpowered by the impression. It will pass away soon enough."

"Do you suppose them to be in London?"

"Yes; where else can they be so well concealed?"

"And Lydia used to want to go to London," added Kitty.

"She is happy then," said her father drily; "and her residence there will probably be of some duration."

Then after a short silence he continued:

"Lizzy, I bear you no ill-will for being justified in your advice to me last May, which, considering the event, shows some greatness of mind."

They were interrupted by Miss Bennet, who came to fetch her mother's tea.

"This is a parade," he cried, "which does one good; it gives such an elegance to misfortune! Another day I will do the same; I will sit in my library, in my nightcap and powdering gown, and give as much trouble as I can; or, perhaps, I may defer it till Kitty runs away."

"I am not going to run away, papa," said Kitty fretfully. "If I should ever go to Brighton, I would behave better than Lydia."

"*You* go to Brighton. I would not trust you so near it as Eastbourne for fifty pounds! No, Kitty, I have at last learnt to be cautious, and you will feel the effects of it. No officer is ever to enter into my house again, nor even to pass through the village. Balls will be absolutely prohibited, unless you stand up with one of your sisters. And you are never to stir out of doors till you can prove that you have spent ten minutes of every day in a rational manner."

Kitty, who took all these threats in a serious light, began to cry.

"Well, well," said he, "do not make yourself unhappy. If you are a good girl for the next ten years, I will take you to a review at the end of them."

CHAPTER XLIX

Two days after Mr. Bennet's return, as Jane and Elizabeth were walking together in the shrubbery behind the house, they saw the housekeeper coming towards them, and, concluding that she came to call them to their mother, went forward to meet her; but, instead of the expected summons, when they approached her, she said to Miss Bennet, "I beg your pardon, madam, for interrupting you, but I was in hopes you might have got some good news from town, so I took the liberty of coming to ask."

"What do you mean, Hill? We have heard nothing from town."

"Dear madam," cried Mrs. Hill, in great astonishment, "don't you know there is an express come for master from Mr. Gardiner? He has been here this half-hour, and master has had a letter."

Away ran the girls, too eager to get in to have time for speech. They ran through the vestibule into the breakfast-room; from thence to the library; their father was in neither; and they were on the point of seeking him upstairs with their mother, when they were met by the butler, who said:

"If you are looking for my master, ma'am, he is walking towards the little copse."

Upon this information, they instantly passed through the hall once more, and ran across the lawn after their father, who was deliberately pursuing his way towards a small wood on one side of the paddock.

Jane, who was not so light nor so much in the habit of running as Elizabeth, soon lagged behind, while her sister, panting for breath, came up with him, and eagerly cried out:

"Oh, papa, what news—what news? Have you heard from my uncle?"

"Yes I have had a letter from him by express."

"Well, and what news does it bring—good or bad?"

"What is there of good to be expected?" said he, taking the letter from his pocket. "But perhaps you would like to read it."

Elizabeth impatiently caught it from his hand. Jane now came up.

"Read it aloud," said their father, "for I hardly know myself what it is about."

"Gracechurch Street, Monday, August 2.

"MY DEAR BROTHER,

"At last I am able to send you some tidings of my niece, and such as, upon the whole, I hope it will give you satisfaction. Soon after you left me on Saturday, I was fortunate enough to find out in what part of London they were. The particulars I reserve till we meet; it is enough to know they are discovered. I have seen them both—"

"Then it is as I always hoped," cried Jane; "they are married!"

Elizabeth read on:

"I have seen them both. They are not married, nor can I find there was any intention of being so; but if you are willing to perform the engagements which I have ventured to make on your side, I hope it will not be long before they are. All that is required of you is, to assure to your daughter, by settlement, her equal share of the five thousand pounds secured among your children after the decease of yourself and my sister; and, moreover, to enter into an engagement of allowing her, during your life, one hundred pounds per annum. These are conditions which, considering everything, I had no hesitation in complying with, as far as I thought myself privileged, for you. I shall send this by express, that no time may be lost in bringing me your answer. You will easily comprehend, from these particulars, that Mr. Wickham's circumstances are not so hopeless as they are generally believed to be. The world has been deceived in that respect; and I am happy to say there will be some little money, even when all his debts are discharged, to settle on my niece, in addition to her own fortune. If, as I conclude will be the case, you send me full powers to act in your name throughout the whole of this business, I will immediately give directions to Haggerston for preparing a proper settlement. There will not be the smallest occasion for your coming to town again; therefore stay quiet at Longbourn, and depend on my diligence and care. Send back your answer as fast as you can, and be careful to write explicitly. We have judged it best that my niece should be married from this house, of which I hope you will approve. She comes to us to-day. I shall write again as soon as anything more is determined on. Yours, etc.,

"EDW. GARDINER."

"Is it possible?" cried Elizabeth, when she had finished. "Can it be possible that he will marry her?"

"Wickham is not so undeserving, then, as we thought him," said her sister. "My dear father, I congratulate you."

"And have you answered the letter?" cried Elizabeth.

"No; but it must be done soon."

Most earnestly did she then entreaty him to lose no more time before he wrote.

"Oh! my dear father," she cried, "come back and write immediately. Consider how important every moment is in such a case."

"Let me write for you," said Jane, "if you dislike the trouble yourself."

"I dislike it very much," he replied; "but it must be done."

And so saying, he turned back with them, and walked towards the house.

"And may I ask—" said Elizabeth; "but the terms, I suppose, must be complied with."

"Complied with! I am only ashamed of his asking so little."

"And they *must* marry! Yet he is *such* a man!"

"Yes, yes, they must marry. There is nothing else to be done. But there are two things that I want very much to know; one is, how much money your uncle has laid down to bring it about; and the other, how am I ever to pay him."

"Money! My uncle!" cried Jane, "what do you mean, sir?"

"I mean, that no man in his senses would marry Lydia on so slight a temptation as one hundred a year during my life, and fifty after I am gone."

"That is very true," said Elizabeth; "though it had not occurred to me before. His debts to be discharged, and something still to remain!

Oh! it must be my uncle's doings! Generous, good man, I am afraid he has distressed himself. A small sum could not do all this."

"No," said her father; "Wickham's a fool if he takes her with a farthing less than ten thousand pounds. I should be sorry to think so ill of him, in the very beginning of our relationship."

"Ten thousand pounds! Heaven forbid! How is half such a sum to be repaid?"

Mr. Bennet made no answer, and each of them, deep in thought, continued silent till they reached the house. Their father then went on to the library to write, and the girls walked into the breakfast-room.

"And they are really to be married!" cried Elizabeth, as soon as they were by themselves. "How strange this is! And for *this* we are to be thankful. That they should marry, small as is their chance of happiness, and wretched as is his character, we are forced to rejoice. Oh, Lydia!"

"I comfort myself with thinking," replied Jane, "that he certainly would not marry Lydia if he had not a real regard for her. Though our kind uncle has done something towards clearing him, I cannot believe that ten thousand pounds, or anything like it, has been advanced. He has children of his own, and may have more. How could he spare half ten thousand pounds?"

"If he were ever able to learn what Wickham's debts have been," said Elizabeth, "and how much is settled on his side on our sister, we shall exactly know what Mr. Gardiner has done for them, because Wickham has not sixpence of his own. The kindness of my uncle and aunt can never be requited. Their taking her home, and affording her their personal protection and countenance, is such a sacrifice to her advantage as years of gratitude cannot enough acknowledge. By this time she is actually with them! If such goodness does not make her miserable now, she will never deserve to be happy! What a meeting for her, when she first sees my aunt!"

"We must endeavour to forget all that has passed on either side," said Jane: "I hope and trust they will yet be happy. His consenting to marry her is a proof, I will believe, that he is come to a right way of thinking. Their mutual affection will steady them; and I flatter myself they will settle so quietly, and live in so rational a manner, as may in time make their past imprudence forgotten."

"Their conduct has been such," replied Elizabeth, "as neither you, nor I, nor anybody can ever forget. It is useless to talk of it."

It now occurred to the girls that their mother was in all likelihood perfectly ignorant of what had happened. They went to the library, therefore, and asked their father whether he would not wish them to make it known to her. He was writing and, without raising his head, coolly replied:

"Just as you please."

"May we take my uncle's letter to read to her?"

"Take whatever you like, and get away."

Elizabeth took the letter from his writing-table, and they went upstairs together. Mary and Kitty were both with Mrs. Bennet: one communication would, therefore, do for all. After a slight preparation for good news, the letter was read aloud. Mrs. Bennet could hardly contain herself. As soon as Jane had read Mr. Gardiner's hope of Lydia's being soon married, her joy burst forth, and every following sentence added to its exuberance. She was now in an irritation as violent from delight, as she had ever been fidgety from alarm and vexation. To know that her daughter would be married was enough. She was disturbed by no fear for her felicity, nor humbled by any remembrance of her misconduct.

"My dear, dear Lydia!" she cried. "This is delightful indeed! She will be married! I shall see her again! She will be married at sixteen! My good, kind brother! I knew how it would be. I knew he would manage everything! How I long to see her! and to see dear Wickham too! But the clothes, the wedding clothes! I will write to my sister Gardiner about them directly. Lizzy, my dear, run down to your father, and ask him how much he will give her. Stay, stay, I will go myself. Ring the bell, Kitty, for Hill. I will put on my things in a moment. My dear, dear Lydia! How merry we shall be together when we meet!"

Her eldest daughter endeavoured to give some relief to the violence of these transports, by leading her thoughts to the obligations which Mr. Gardiner's behaviour laid them all under.

"For we must attribute this happy conclusion," she added, "in a great measure to his kindness. We are persuaded that he has pledged himself to assist Mr. Wickham with money."

"Well," cried her mother, "it is all very right; who should do it but her own uncle? If he had not had a family of his own, I and my children must have had all his money, you know; and it is the first time we have ever had anything from him, except a few presents. Well! I am so happy!

In a short time I shall have a daughter married. Mrs. Wickham! How well it sounds! And she was only sixteen last June. My dear Jane, I am in such a flutter, that I am sure I can't write; so I will dictate, and you write for me. We will settle with your father about the money afterwards; but the things should be ordered immediately."

She was then proceeding to all the particulars of calico, muslin, and cambric, and would shortly have dictated some very plentiful orders, had not Jane, though with some difficulty, persuaded her to wait till her father was at leisure to be consulted. One day's delay, she observed, would be of small importance; and her mother was too happy to be quite so obstinate as usual. Other schemes, too, came into her head.

"I will go to Meryton," said she, "as soon as I am dressed, and tell the good, good news to my sister Philips. And as I come back, I can call on Lady Lucas and Mrs. Long. Kitty, run down and order the carriage. An airing would do me a great deal of good, I am sure. Girls, can I do anything for you in Meryton? Oh! Here comes Hill! My dear Hill, have you heard the good news? Miss Lydia is going to be married; and you shall all have a bowl of punch to make merry at her wedding."

Mrs. Hill began instantly to express her joy. Elizabeth received her congratulations amongst the rest, and then, sick of this folly, took refuge in her own room, that she might think with freedom.

Poor Lydia's situation must, at best, be bad enough; but that it was no worse, she had need to be thankful. She felt it so; and though, in looking forward, neither rational happiness nor worldly prosperity could be justly expected for her sister, in looking back to what they had feared, only two hours ago, she felt all the advantages of what they had gained.

CHAPTER L

Mr. Bennet had very often wished before this period of his life that, instead of spending his whole income, he had laid by an annual sum for the better provision of his children, and of his wife, if she survived him. He now wished it more than ever. Had he done his duty in that respect, Lydia need not have been indebted to her uncle for whatever of honour or credit could now be purchased for her. The satisfaction of prevailing on one of the most worthless young men in Great Britain to be her husband might then have rested in its proper place.

He was seriously concerned that a cause of so little advantage to anyone should be forwarded at the sole expense of his brother-in-law, and he was determined, if possible, to find out the extent of his assistance, and to discharge the obligation as soon as he could.

When first Mr. Bennet had married, economy was held to be perfectly useless, for, of course, they were to have a son. The son was to join in cutting off the entail, as soon as he should be of age, and the widow and younger children would by that means be provided for. Five daughters successively entered the world, but yet the son was to come; and Mrs. Bennet, for many years after Lydia's birth, had been certain that he would. This event had at last been despaired of, but it was then too late to be saving. Mrs. Bennet had no turn for economy, and her husband's love of independence had alone prevented their exceeding their income.

Five thousand pounds was settled by marriage articles on Mrs. Bennet and the children. But in what proportions it should be divided amongst the latter depended on the will of the parents. This was one point, with regard to Lydia, at least, which was now to be settled, and Mr. Bennet could have no hesitation in acceding to the proposal before him. In terms of grateful acknowledgment for the kindness of his brother, though expressed most concisely, he then delivered on paper his perfect approbation of all that was done, and his willingness to fulfil the engagements that had been made for him. He had never before supposed that, could Wickham be prevailed on to marry his daughter, it would be done with so little inconvenience to himself as by the present arrangement. He would scarcely be ten pounds a year the loser by the hundred that was to be paid them; for, what with her board and pocket allowance, and the continual presents in money which passed to her through her mother's hands, Lydia's expenses had been very little within that sum.

That it would be done with such trifling exertion on his side, too, was another very welcome surprise; for his wish at present was to have as little trouble in the business as possible. When the first transports of rage which had produced his activity in seeking her were over, he naturally returned to all his former indolence. His letter was soon dispatched; for, though dilatory in undertaking business, he was quick in its execution. He begged to know further particulars of what he was indebted to his brother, but was too angry with Lydia to send any message to her.

The good news spread quickly through the house, and with proportionate speed through the neighbourhood. It was borne in the latter with decent philosophy. To be sure, it would have been more for the advantage of conversation had Miss Lydia Bennet come upon the town; or, as the happiest alternative, been secluded from the world, in some distant farmhouse. But there was much to be talked of in marrying her; and the good-natured wishes for her well-doing which had proceeded before from all the spiteful old ladies in Meryton lost but a little of their spirit in this change of circumstances, because with such an husband her misery was considered certain.

It was a fortnight since Mrs. Bennet had been downstairs; but on this happy day she again took her seat at the head of her table, and in spirits oppressively high. No sentiment of shame gave a damp to her triumph. The marriage of a daughter, which had been the first object of her wishes since Jane was sixteen, was now on the point of accomplishment, and her thoughts and her words ran wholly on those attendants of elegant nuptials, fine muslins, new carriages, and servants. She was busily searching through the neighbourhood for a proper situation for her daughter, and, without knowing or considering what their income might be, rejected many as deficient in size and importance.

"Haye Park might do," said she, "if the Gouldings could quit it—or the great house at Stoke, if the drawing-room were larger; but Ashworth is too far off! I could not bear to have her ten miles from me; and as for Pulvis Lodge, the attics are dreadful."

Her husband allowed her to talk on without interruption while the servants remained. But when they had withdrawn, he said to her: "Mrs. Bennet, before you take any or all of these houses for your son and daughter, let us come to a right understanding. Into *one* house in this neighbourhood they shall never have admittance. I will not encourage the impudence of either, by receiving them at Longbourn."

A long dispute followed this declaration; but Mr. Bennet was firm. It soon led to another; and Mrs. Bennet found, with amazement and horror, that her husband would not advance a guinea to buy clothes for his daughter. He protested that she should receive from him no mark of affection whatever on the occasion. Mrs. Bennet could hardly comprehend it. That his anger could be carried to such a point of inconceivable resentment as to refuse his daughter a privilege without which her marriage would scarcely seem valid, exceeded all she could believe possible. She was more alive to the disgrace which her want of new clothes must reflect on her daughter's nuptials, than to any sense of shame at her eloping and living with Wickham a fortnight before they took place.

Elizabeth was now most heartily sorry that she had, from the distress of the moment, been led to make Mr. Darcy acquainted with their fears for her sister; for since her marriage would so shortly give the proper termination to the elopement, they might hope to conceal its unfavourable beginning from all those who were not immediately on the spot.

She had no fear of its spreading farther through his means. There were few people on whose secrecy she would have more confidently depended; but, at the same time, there was no one whose knowledge of a sister's frailty would have mortified her so much—not, however, from any fear of disadvantage from it individually to herself, for, at any rate, there seemed a gulf impassable between them. Had Lydia's marriage been concluded on the most honourable terms, it was not to be supposed that Mr. Darcy would connect himself with a family where, to every other objection, would now be added an alliance and relationship of the nearest kind with a man whom he so justly scorned.

From such a connection she could not wonder that he would shrink. The wish of procuring her regard, which she had assured herself of his feeling in Derbyshire, could not in rational expectation survive such a blow as this. She was humbled, she was grieved; she repented, though she hardly knew of what. She became jealous of his esteem, when she could no longer hope to be benefited by it. She wanted to hear of him, when there seemed the least chance of gaining intelligence. She was convinced that she could have been happy with him, when it was no longer likely they should meet.

What a triumph for him, as she often thought, could he know that the proposals which she had proudly spurned only four months ago, would now have been most gladly and gratefully received! He was as generous, she doubted not, as the most generous of his sex; but while he was mortal, there must be a triumph.

She began now to comprehend that he was exactly the man who, in disposition and talents, would most suit her. His understanding and temper, though unlike her own, would have answered all her wishes. It was an union that must have been to the advantage of both; by her ease and liveliness, his mind might have been softened, his manners improved; and from his judgement, information, and knowledge of the world, she must have received benefit of greater importance.

But no such happy marriage could now teach the admiring multitude what connubial felicity really was. An union of a different tendency, and precluding the possibility of the other, was soon to be formed in their family.

How Wickham and Lydia were to be supported in tolerable independence, she could not imagine. But how little of permanent happiness could belong to a couple who were only brought together because their passions were stronger than their virtue, she could easily conjecture.

* * * * *

Mr. Gardiner soon wrote again to his brother. To Mr. Bennet's acknowledgments he briefly replied, with assurance of his eagerness to promote the welfare of any of his family; and concluded with entreaties that the subject might never be mentioned to him again. The principal purport of his letter was to inform them that Mr. Wickham had resolved on quitting the militia.

> "It was greatly my wish that he should do so," he added, "as soon as his marriage was fixed on. And I think you will agree with me, in considering the removal from that corps

as highly advisable, both on his account and my niece's. It is Mr. Wickham's intention to go into the regulars; and among his former friends, there are still some who are able and willing to assist him in the army. He has the promise of an ensigncy in General ——'s regiment, now quartered in the North. It is an advantage to have it so far from this part of the kingdom. He promises fairly; and I hope among different people, where they may each have a character to preserve, they will both be more prudent. I have written to Colonel Forster, to inform him of our present arrangements, and to request that he will satisfy the various creditors of Mr. Wickham in and near Brighton, with assurances of speedy payment, for which I have pledged myself. And will you give yourself the trouble of carrying similar assurances to his creditors in Meryton, of whom I shall subjoin a list according to his information? He has given in all his debts; I hope at least he has not deceived us. Haggerston has our directions, and all will be completed in a week. They will then join his regiment, unless they are first invited to Longbourn; and I understand from Mrs. Gardiner, that my niece is very desirous of seeing you all before she leaves the South. She is well, and begs to be dutifully remembered to you and your mother.—Yours, etc.,

"E. GARDINER."

Mr. Bennet and his daughters saw all the advantages of Wickham's removal from the ——shire as clearly as Mr. Gardiner could do. But Mrs. Bennet was not so well pleased with it. Lydia's being settled in the North, just when she had expected most pleasure and pride in her company, for she had by no means given up her plan of their residing in Hertfordshire, was a severe disappointment; and, besides, it was such a pity that Lydia should be taken from a regiment where she was acquainted with everybody, and had so many favourites.

"She is so fond of Mrs. Forster," said she, "it will be quite shocking to send her away! And there are several of the young men, too, that she likes very much. The officers may not be so pleasant in General ——'s regiment."

His daughter's request, for such it might be considered, of being admitted into her family again before she set off for the North, received at first an absolute negative. But Jane and Elizabeth, who agreed in wishing, for the sake of their sister's feelings and consequence, that she should be noticed on her marriage by her parents, urged him so earnestly yet so rationally and so mildly, to receive her and her husband at Longbourn, as soon as they were married, that he was prevailed on to think as they thought, and act as they wished. And their mother had the satisfaction of knowing that she would be able to show her married daughter in the neighbourhood before she was banished to the North. When Mr. Bennet wrote again to his brother, therefore, he sent his permission for them to come; and it was settled, that as soon as the ceremony was over, they should proceed to Longbourn. Elizabeth was surprised, however, that Wickham should consent to such a scheme, and had she consulted only her own inclination, any meeting with him would have been the last object of her wishes.

CHAPTER LI

Their sister's wedding day arrived; and Jane and Elizabeth felt for her probably more than she felt for herself. The carriage was sent to meet them at ——, and they were to return in it by dinner-time. Their arrival was dreaded by the elder Miss Bennets, and Jane more especially, who gave Lydia the feelings which would have attended herself, had she been the culprit, and was wretched in the thought of what her sister must endure.

They came. The family were assembled in the breakfast room to receive them. Smiles decked the face of Mrs. Bennet as the carriage drove up to the door; her husband looked impenetrably grave; her daughters, alarmed, anxious, uneasy.

Lydia's voice was heard in the vestibule; the door was thrown open, and she ran into the room. Her mother stepped forwards, embraced her, and welcomed her with rapture; gave her hand, with an affectionate smile, to Wickham, who followed his lady; and wished them both joy with an alacrity which shewed no doubt of their happiness.

Their reception from Mr. Bennet, to whom they then turned, was not quite so cordial. His countenance rather gained in austerity; and he scarcely opened his lips. The easy assurance of the young couple, indeed, was enough to provoke him. Elizabeth was disgusted, and even Miss Bennet was shocked. Lydia was Lydia still; untamed, unabashed, wild, noisy, and fearless. She turned from sister to sister, demanding their congratulations; and when at length they all sat down, looked eagerly round the room, took notice of some little alteration in it, and observed, with a laugh, that it was a great while since she had been there.

Wickham was not at all more distressed than herself, but his manners were always so pleasing, that had his character and his marriage been exactly what they ought, his smiles and his easy address, while he claimed their relationship, would have delighted them all. Elizabeth had not before believed him quite equal to such assurance; but she sat down, resolving within herself to draw no limits in future to the impudence of an impudent man. She blushed, and Jane blushed; but the cheeks of the two who caused their confusion suffered no variation of colour.

There was no want of discourse. The bride and her mother could neither of them talk fast enough; and Wickham, who happened to sit near Elizabeth, began inquiring after his acquaintance in that neighbourhood, with a good humoured ease which she felt very unable to equal in her replies. They seemed each of them to have the happiest memories in the world. Nothing of the past was recollected with pain; and Lydia led voluntarily to subjects which her sisters would not have alluded to for the world.

"Only think of its being three months," she cried, "since I went away; it seems but a fortnight I declare; and yet there have been things enough happened in the time. Good gracious! when I went away, I am sure I had no more idea of being married till I came back again! though I thought it would be very good fun if I was."

Her father lifted up his eyes. Jane was distressed. Elizabeth looked expressively at Lydia; but she, who never heard nor saw anything of which she chose to be insensible, gaily continued, "Oh! mamma, do the people hereabouts know I am married to-day? I was afraid they might not; and we overtook William Goulding in his curricle, so I was determined he should know it, and so I let down the side-glass next to him, and took off my glove, and let my hand just rest upon the window frame, so that he might see the ring, and then I bowed and smiled like anything."

Elizabeth could bear it no longer. She got up, and ran out of the room; and returned no more, till she heard them passing through the hall to the dining parlour. She then joined them soon enough to see Lydia, with anxious parade, walk up to her mother's right hand, and hear her say to her eldest sister, "Ah! Jane, I take your place now, and you must go lower, because I am a married woman."

It was not to be supposed that time would give Lydia that embarrassment from which she had been so wholly free at first. Her ease and good spirits increased. She longed to see Mrs. Phillips, the Lucases, and all their other neighbours, and to hear herself called "Mrs. Wickham" by each of them; and in the mean time, she went after dinner to show her ring, and boast of being married, to Mrs. Hill and the two housemaids.

"Well, mamma," said she, when they were all returned to the breakfast room, "and what do you think of my husband? Is not he a charming man? I am sure my sisters must all envy me. I only hope they may have half my good luck. They must all go to Brighton. That is the place to get husbands. What a pity it is, mamma, we did not all go."

"Very true; and if I had my will, we should. But my dear Lydia, I don't at all like your going such a way off. Must it be so?"

"Oh, lord! yes;—there is nothing in that. I shall like it of all things. You and papa, and my sisters, must come down and see us. We shall be at Newcastle all the winter, and I dare say there will be some balls, and I will take care to get good partners for them all."

"I should like it beyond anything!" said her mother.

"And then when you go away, you may leave one or two of my sisters behind you; and I dare say I shall get husbands for them before the winter is over."

"I thank you for my share of the favour," said Elizabeth; "but I do not particularly like your way of getting husbands."

Their visitors were not to remain above ten days with them. Mr. Wickham had received his commission before he left London, and he was to join his regiment at the end of a fortnight.

No one but Mrs. Bennet regretted that their stay would be so short; and she made the most of the time by visiting about with her daughter, and having very frequent parties at home. These parties were acceptable to all; to avoid a family circle was even more desirable to such as did think, than such as did not.

Wickham's affection for Lydia was just what Elizabeth had expected to find it; not equal to Lydia's for him. She had scarcely needed her present observation to be satisfied, from the reason of things, that their elopement had been brought on by the strength of her love, rather than by his; and she would have wondered why, without violently caring for her, he chose to elope with her at all, had she not felt certain that his flight was rendered necessary by distress of circumstances; and if that were the case, he was not the young man to resist an opportunity of having a companion.

Lydia was exceedingly fond of him. He was her dear Wickham on every occasion; no one was to be put in competition with him. He did every thing best in the world; and she was sure he would kill more birds on the first of September, than any body else in the country.

One morning, soon after their arrival, as she was sitting with her two elder sisters, she said to Elizabeth:

"Lizzy, I never gave *you* an account of my wedding, I believe. You were not by, when I told mamma and the others all about it. Are not you curious to hear how it was managed?"

"No really," replied Elizabeth; "I think there cannot be too little said on the subject."

"La! You are so strange! But I must tell you how it went off. We were married, you know, at St. Clement's, because Wickham's lodgings were in that parish. And it was settled that we should all be there by eleven o'clock. My uncle and aunt and I were to go together; and the others were to meet us at the church. Well, Monday morning came, and I was in such a fuss! I was so afraid, you know, that something would happen to put it off, and then I should have gone quite distracted. And there was my aunt, all the time I was dressing, preaching and talking away just as if she was reading a sermon. However, I did not hear above one word in ten, for I was thinking, you may suppose, of my dear Wickham. I longed to know whether he would be married in his blue coat."

"Well, and so we breakfasted at ten as usual; I thought it would never be over; for, by the bye, you are to understand, that my uncle and aunt were horrid unpleasant all the time I was with them. If you'll believe me, I did not once put my foot out of doors, though I was there a fortnight. Not one party, or scheme, or anything. To be sure London was rather thin, but, however, the Little Theatre was open. Well, and so just as the carriage came to the door, my uncle was called away upon business to that horrid man Mr. Stone. And then, you know, when once they get together, there is no end of it. Well, I was so frightened I did not know what to do, for my uncle was to give me away; and if we were beyond the hour, we could not be married all day. But, luckily, he came back again in ten minutes' time, and then we all set out. However, I recollected afterwards that if he had been prevented going, the wedding need not be put off, for Mr. Darcy might have done as well."

"Mr. Darcy!" repeated Elizabeth, in utter amazement.

"Oh, yes!—he was to come there with Wickham, you know. But gracious me! I quite forgot! I ought not to have said a word about it. I promised them so faithfully! What will Wickham say? It was to be such a secret!"

"If it was to be secret," said Jane, "say not another word on the subject. You may depend upon my seeking no further."

"Oh! certainly," said Elizabeth, though burning with curiosity; "we will ask you no questions."

"Thank you," said Lydia, "for if you did, I should certainly tell you all, and then Wickham would be angry."

On such encouragement to ask, Elizabeth was forced to put it out of her power, by running away.

But to live in ignorance on such a point was impossible; or at least it was impossible not to try for information. Mr. Darcy had been at her sister's wedding. It was exactly a scene, and exactly among people, where he had apparently least to do, and least temptation to go. Conjectures as to the meaning of it, rapid and wild, hurried into her brain; but she was satisfied with none. Those that best pleased her, as placing his conduct in the noblest light, seemed most improbable. She could not bear such suspense; and hastily seizing a sheet of paper, wrote a short letter to her aunt, to request an explanation of what Lydia had dropt, if it were compatible with the secrecy which had been intended.

"You may readily comprehend," she added, "what my curiosity must be to know how a person unconnected with any of us, and (comparatively speaking) a stranger to our family, should have been amongst you at such a time. Pray write instantly, and let me understand it—unless it is, for very cogent reasons, to remain in the secrecy which Lydia seems to think necessary; and then I must endeavour to be satisfied with ignorance."

"Not that I *shall*, though," she added to herself, as she finished the letter; "and my dear aunt, if you do not tell me in an honourable manner, I shall certainly be reduced to tricks and stratagems to find it out."

Jane's delicate sense of honour would not allow her to speak to Elizabeth privately of what Lydia had let fall; Elizabeth was glad of it;—till it appeared whether her inquiries would receive any satisfaction, she had rather be without a confidante.

CHAPTER LII

Elizabeth had the satisfaction of receiving an answer to her letter as soon as she possibly could. She was no sooner in possession of it than, hurrying into the little copse, where she was least likely to be interrupted, she sat down on one of the benches and prepared to be happy; for the length of the letter convinced her that it did not contain a denial.

"Gracechurch street, Sept. 6.

"MY DEAR NIECE,

"I have just received your letter, and shall devote this whole morning to answering it, as I foresee that a *little* writing will not comprise what I have to tell you. I must confess myself surprised by your application; I did not expect it from *you*. Don't think me angry, however, for I only mean to let you know that I had not imagined such inquiries to be necessary on *your* side. If you do not choose to understand me, forgive my impertinence. Your uncle is as much surprised as I am—and nothing but the belief of your being a party concerned would have allowed him to act as he has done. But if you are really innocent and ignorant, I must be more explicit.

"On the very day of my coming home from Longbourn, your uncle had a most unexpected visitor. Mr. Darcy called, and was shut up with him several hours. It was all over before I arrived; so my curiosity was not so dreadfully racked as *yours* seems to have been. He came to tell Mr. Gardiner that he had found out where your sister and Mr. Wickham were, and that he had seen and talked with them both; Wickham repeatedly, Lydia once. From what I can collect, he left Derbyshire only one day after ourselves, and came to town with the resolution of hunting for them. The motive professed was his conviction of its being owing to himself that Wickham's worthlessness had not been so well known as to make it impossible for any young woman of character to love or confide in him. He generously imputed the whole to his mistaken pride, and confessed that he had before thought it beneath him to lay his private actions open to the world. His character was to speak for itself. He called it, therefore, his duty to step forward, and endeavour to remedy an evil which had been brought on by himself. If he *had another* motive, I am sure it would never disgrace him. He had been some days in town, before he was able to discover them; but he had something to direct his search, which was more than *we* had; and the consciousness of this was another reason for his resolving to follow us.

"There is a lady, it seems, a Mrs. Younge, who was some time ago governess to Miss Darcy, and was dismissed from her charge on some cause of disapprobation, though he did not say what. She then took a large house in Edward-street, and has since maintained herself by letting lodgings. This Mrs. Younge was, he knew, intimately acquainted with Wickham; and he went to her for intelligence of him as soon as he got to town. But it was two or three days before he could get from her what he wanted. She would not betray her trust, I suppose, without bribery and corruption, for she really did know where her friend was to be found. Wickham indeed had gone to her on their first arrival in London, and had she been able to receive them into her house, they would have taken up their abode with her. At length, however, our kind friend procured the wished-for direction. They were in —— street. He saw Wickham, and afterwards insisted on seeing Lydia. His first object with her, he acknowledged, had been to persuade her to quit her present disgraceful situation, and return to her friends as soon as they could be prevailed on to receive her, offering his assistance, as far as it would go. But he found Lydia absolutely resolved on remaining where she was. She cared for none of her friends; she wanted no help of his; she would not hear of leaving Wickham. She was sure they should be married some time or other, and it did not much signify when. Since such were her feelings, it only remained, he thought, to secure and expedite a marriage, which, in his very first conversation with Wickham, he easily learnt had never been *his* design. He confessed himself obliged to leave the regiment, on account of some debts of honour, which were very pressing; and scrupled not to lay all the ill-consequences of Lydia's flight on her own folly alone. He meant to resign his commission immediately; and as to his future situation, he could conjecture very little about it. He must go somewhere, but he did not know where, and he knew he should have nothing to live on.

"Mr. Darcy asked him why he had not married your sister at once. Though Mr. Bennet was not imagined to be very rich, he would have been able to do something for him, and his situation must have been benefited by marriage. But he found, in reply to this question, that Wickham still cherished the hope of more effectually making his fortune by marriage in some other country. Under such circumstances, however, he was not likely to be proof against the temptation of immediate relief.

"They met several times, for there was much to be discussed. Wickham of course wanted more than he could get; but at length was reduced to be reasonable.

"Every thing being settled between *them*, Mr. Darcy's next step was to make your uncle acquainted with it, and he first called in Gracechurch street the evening before I came home. But Mr. Gardiner could not be seen, and Mr. Darcy found, on further inquiry, that your father was still with him, but would quit town the next morning. He did not judge your father to be a person whom he could so properly consult as your uncle, and therefore readily postponed seeing him till after the departure of the former. He did not leave his name, and till the next day it was only known that a gentleman had called on business.

"On Saturday he came again. Your father was gone, your uncle at home, and, as I said before, they had a great deal of talk together.

"They met again on Sunday, and then *I* saw him too. It was not all settled before Monday: as soon as it was, the express was sent off to Longbourn. But our visitor was very obstinate. I fancy, Lizzy, that obstinacy is the real defect of his character, after all. He has been accused of many faults at different times, but *this* is the true one. Nothing was to be done that he did not do himself; though I am sure (and I do not speak it to be thanked, therefore say nothing about it), your uncle would most readily have settled the whole.

"They battled it together for a long time, which was more than either the gentleman or lady concerned in it deserved. But at last your uncle was forced to yield, and instead of being allowed to be of use to his niece, was forced to put up with only having the probable credit of it, which went sorely against the grain; and I really believe your letter this morning gave him great pleasure, because it required an explanation that would rob him of his borrowed feathers, and give the praise where it was due. But, Lizzy, this must go no farther than yourself, or Jane at most.

"You know pretty well, I suppose, what has been done for the young people. His debts are to be paid, amounting, I believe, to considerably more than a thousand pounds, another thousand in addition to her own settled upon *her*, and his commission purchased. The reason why all this was to be done by him alone, was such as I have given above. It was owing to him, to his reserve and want of proper consideration, that Wickham's character had been so misunderstood, and consequently that he had been received and noticed as he was. Perhaps there was some truth in *this*; though I doubt whether *his* reserve, or *anybody's* reserve, can be answerable for the event. But in spite of all this fine talking, my dear Lizzy, you may rest perfectly assured that your uncle would never have yielded, if we had not given him credit for *another interest* in the affair.

"When all this was resolved on, he returned again to his friends, who were still staying at Pemberley; but it was agreed that he should be in London once more when the wedding took place, and all money matters were then to receive the last finish.

"I believe I have now told you every thing. It is a relation which you tell me is to give you great surprise; I hope at least it will not afford you any displeasure. Lydia came to us; and Wickham had constant admission to the house. *He* was exactly what he had been, when I knew him in Hertfordshire; but I would not tell you how little I was satisfied with her behaviour while she staid with us, if I had not perceived, by Jane's letter last Wednesday, that her conduct on coming home was exactly of a piece with it, and therefore what I now tell you can give you no fresh pain. I talked to her repeatedly in the most serious manner, representing to her all the wickedness of what she had done, and all the unhappiness she had brought on her family. If she heard me, it was by good luck, for I am sure she did not listen. I was sometimes quite provoked, but then I recollected my dear Elizabeth and Jane, and for their sakes had patience with her.

"Mr. Darcy was punctual in his return, and as Lydia informed you, attended the wedding. He dined with us the next day, and was to leave town again on Wednesday or Thursday. Will you be very angry with me, my dear Lizzy, if I take this opportunity of saying (what I was never bold enough to say before) how much I like him. His behaviour to us has, in every respect, been as pleasing as when we were in Derbyshire. His understanding and opinions all please me; he wants nothing but a little more liveliness, and *that*, if he marry *prudently*, his wife may teach him. I thought him very sly;—he hardly ever mentioned your name. But slyness seems the fashion.

"Pray forgive me if I have been very presuming, or at least do not punish me so far as to exclude me from P. I shall never be quite happy till I have been all round the park. A low phaeton, with a nice little pair of ponies, would be the very thing.

"But I must write no more. The children have been wanting me this half hour.

"Yours, very sincerely,

"M. GARDINER."

The contents of this letter threw Elizabeth into a flutter of spirits, in which it was difficult to determine whether pleasure or pain bore the greatest share. The vague and unsettled suspicions which uncertainty had produced of what Mr. Darcy might have been doing to forward her sister's match, which she had feared to encourage as an exertion of goodness too great to be probable, and at the same time dreaded to be just, from the pain of obligation, were proved beyond their greatest extent to be true! He had followed them purposely to town, he had taken on himself all the trouble and mortification attendant on such a research; in which supplication had been necessary to a woman whom he must abominate and despise, and where he was reduced to meet, frequently meet, reason with, persuade, and finally bribe, the man whom he always most wished to avoid, and whose very name it was punishment to him to pronounce. He had done all this for a girl whom he could neither regard nor esteem. Her heart did whisper that he had done it for her. But it was a hope shortly checked by other considerations, and she soon felt that even her vanity was insufficient, when required to depend on his affection for her—for a woman who had already refused him—as able to overcome a sentiment so natural as abhorrence against relationship with Wickham. Brother-in-law of Wickham! Every kind of pride must revolt from the connection. He had, to be sure, done much. She was ashamed to think how much. But he had given a reason for his interference, which asked no extraordinary stretch of belief. It was reasonable that he should feel he had been wrong; he had liberality, and he had the means of exercising it; and though she would not place herself as his principal inducement, she could, perhaps, believe that remaining partiality for her might assist his endeavours in a cause where her peace of mind must be materially concerned. It was painful, exceedingly painful, to know that they were under obligations to a person who could never receive a return. They owed the restoration of Lydia, her character, every thing, to him. Oh! how heartily did she grieve over every ungracious sensation she had ever encouraged, every saucy speech she had ever directed towards him. For herself she was humbled; but she was proud of him. Proud that in a cause of compassion and honour, he had been able to get the better of himself. She read over her aunt's commendation of him again and again. It was hardly enough; but it pleased her. She was even sensible of some pleasure, though mixed with regret, on finding how steadfastly both she and her uncle had been persuaded that affection and confidence subsisted between Mr. Darcy and herself.

She was roused from her seat, and her reflections, by some one's approach; and before she could strike into another path, she was overtaken by Wickham.

"I am afraid I interrupt your solitary ramble, my dear sister?" said he, as he joined her.

"You certainly do," she replied with a smile; "but it does not follow that the interruption must be unwelcome."

"I should be sorry indeed, if it were. We were always good friends; and now we are better."

"True. Are the others coming out?"

"I do not know. Mrs. Bennet and Lydia are going in the carriage to Meryton. And so, my dear sister, I find, from our uncle and aunt, that you have actually seen Pemberley."

She replied in the affirmative.

"I almost envy you the pleasure, and yet I believe it would be too much for me, or else I could take it in my way to Newcastle. And you saw the old housekeeper, I suppose? Poor Reynolds, she was always very fond of me. But of course she did not mention my name to you."

"Yes, she did."

"And what did she say?"

"That you were gone into the army, and she was afraid had—not turned out well. At such a distance as *that*, you know, things are strangely misrepresented."

"Certainly," he replied, biting his lips. Elizabeth hoped she had silenced him; but he soon afterwards said:

"I was surprised to see Darcy in town last month. We passed each other several times. I wonder what he can be doing there."

"Perhaps preparing for his marriage with Miss de Bourgh," said Elizabeth. "It must be something particular, to take him there at this time of year."

"Undoubtedly. Did you see him while you were at Lambton? I thought I understood from the Gardiners that you had."

"Yes; he introduced us to his sister."

"And do you like her?"

"Very much."

"I have heard, indeed, that she is uncommonly improved within this year or two. When I last saw her, she was not very promising. I am very glad you liked her. I hope she will turn out well."

"I dare say she will; she has got over the most trying age."

"Did you go by the village of Kympton?"

"I do not recollect that we did."

"I mention it, because it is the living which I ought to have had. A most delightful place!—Excellent Parsonage House! It would have suited me in every respect."

"How should you have liked making sermons?"

"Exceedingly well. I should have considered it as part of my duty, and the exertion would soon have been nothing. One ought not to repine;—but, to be sure, it would have been such a thing for me! The quiet, the retirement of such a life would have answered all my ideas of happiness! But it was not to be. Did you ever hear Darcy mention the circumstance, when you were in Kent?"

"I have heard from authority, which I thought *as good*, that it was left you conditionally only, and at the will of the present patron."

"You have. Yes, there was something in *that*; I told you so from the first, you may remember."

"I *did* hear, too, that there was a time, when sermon-making was not so palatable to you as it seems to be at present; that you actually declared your resolution of never taking orders, and that the business had been compromised accordingly."

"You did! and it was not wholly without foundation. You may remember what I told you on that point, when first we talked of it."

They were now almost at the door of the house, for she had walked fast to get rid of him; and unwilling, for her sister's sake, to provoke him, she only said in reply, with a good-humoured smile:

"Come, Mr. Wickham, we are brother and sister, you know. Do not let us quarrel about the past. In future, I hope we shall be always of one mind."

She held out her hand; he kissed it with affectionate gallantry, though he hardly knew how to look, and they entered the house.

CHAPTER LIII

Mr. Wickham was so perfectly satisfied with this conversation that he never again distressed himself, or provoked his dear sister Elizabeth, by introducing the subject of it; and she was pleased to find that she had said enough to keep him quiet.

The day of his and Lydia's departure soon came, and Mrs. Bennet was forced to submit to a separation, which, as her husband by no means entered into her scheme of their all going to Newcastle, was likely to continue at least a twelvemonth.

"Oh! my dear Lydia," she cried, "when shall we meet again?"

"Oh, lord! I don't know. Not these two or three years, perhaps."

"Write to me very often, my dear."

"As often as I can. But you know married women have never much time for writing. My sisters may write to *me*. They will have nothing else to do."

Mr. Wickham's adieus were much more affectionate than his wife's. He smiled, looked handsome, and said many pretty things.

"He is as fine a fellow," said Mr. Bennet, as soon as they were out of the house, "as ever I saw. He simpers, and smirks, and makes love to us all. I am prodigiously proud of him. I defy even Sir William Lucas himself to produce a more valuable son-in-law."

The loss of her daughter made Mrs. Bennet very dull for several days.

"I often think," said she, "that there is nothing so bad as parting with one's friends. One seems so forlorn without them."

"This is the consequence, you see, Madam, of marrying a daughter," said Elizabeth. "It must make you better satisfied that your other four are single."

"It is no such thing. Lydia does not leave me because she is married, but only because her husband's regiment happens to be so far off. If that had been nearer, she would not have gone so soon."

But the spiritless condition which this event threw her into was shortly relieved, and her mind opened again to the agitation of hope, by an article of news which then began to be in circulation. The housekeeper at Netherfield had received orders to prepare for the arrival of her master, who was coming down in a day or two, to shoot there for several weeks. Mrs. Bennet was quite in the fidgets. She looked at Jane, and smiled and shook her head by turns.

"Well, well, and so Mr. Bingley is coming down, sister," (for Mrs. Phillips first brought her the news). "Well, so much the better. Not that I care about it, though. He is nothing to us, you know, and I am sure *I* never want to see him again. But, however, he is very welcome to come to Netherfield, if he likes it. And who knows what *may* happen? But that is nothing to us. You know, sister, we agreed long ago never to mention a word about it. And so, is it quite certain he is coming?"

"You may depend on it," replied the other, "for Mrs. Nicholls was in Meryton last night; I saw her passing by, and went out myself on purpose to know the truth of it; and she told me that it was certain true. He comes down on Thursday at the latest, very likely on Wednesday. She was going to the butcher's, she told me, on purpose to order in some meat on Wednesday, and she has got three couple of ducks just fit to be killed."

Miss Bennet had not been able to hear of his coming without changing colour. It was many months since she had mentioned his name to Elizabeth; but now, as soon as they were alone together, she said:

"I saw you look at me to-day, Lizzy, when my aunt told us of the present report; and I know I appeared distressed. But don't imagine it was from any silly cause. I was only confused for the moment, because I felt that I *should* be looked at. I do assure you that the news does not affect me either with pleasure or pain. I am glad of one thing, that he comes alone; because we shall see the less of him. Not that I am afraid of *myself*, but I dread other people's remarks."

Elizabeth did not know what to make of it. Had she not seen him in Derbyshire, she might have supposed him capable of coming there with no other view than what was acknowledged; but she still thought him partial to Jane, and she wavered as to the greater probability of his coming there *with* his friend's permission, or being bold enough to come without it.

"Yet it is hard," she sometimes thought, "that this poor man cannot come to a house which he has legally hired, without raising all this speculation! I *will* leave him to himself."

In spite of what her sister declared, and really believed to be her feelings in the expectation of his arrival, Elizabeth could easily perceive that her spirits were affected by it. They were more disturbed, more unequal, than she had often seen them.

The subject which had been so warmly canvassed between their parents, about a twelvemonth ago, was now brought forward again.

"As soon as ever Mr. Bingley comes, my dear," said Mrs. Bennet, "you will wait on him of course."

"No, no. You forced me into visiting him last year, and promised, if I went to see him, he should marry one of my daughters. But it ended in nothing, and I will not be sent on a fool's errand again."

His wife represented to him how absolutely necessary such an attention would be from all the neighbouring gentlemen, on his returning to Netherfield.

" 'Tis an etiquette I despise," said he. "If he wants our society, let him seek it. He knows where we live. I will not spend my hours in running after my neighbours every time they go away and come back again."

"Well, all I know is, that it will be abominably rude if you do not wait on him. But, however, that shan't prevent my asking him to dine here, I am determined. We must have Mrs. Long and the Gouldings soon. That will make thirteen with ourselves, so there will be just room at table for him."

Consoled by this resolution, she was the better able to bear her husband's incivility; though it was very mortifying to know that her neighbours might all see Mr. Bingley, in consequence of it, before *they* did. As the day of his arrival drew near:

"I begin to be sorry that he comes at all," said Jane to her sister. "It would be nothing; I could see him with perfect indifference, but I can hardly bear to hear it thus perpetually talked of. My mother means well; but she does not know, no one can know, how much I suffer from what she says. Happy shall I be, when his stay at Netherfield is over!"

"I wish I could say anything to comfort you," replied Elizabeth; "but it is wholly out of my power. You must feel it; and the usual satisfaction of preaching patience to a sufferer is denied me, because you have always so much."

Mr. Bingley arrived. Mrs. Bennet, through the assistance of servants, contrived to have the earliest tidings of it, that the period of anxiety and fretfulness on her side might be as long as it could. She counted the days that must intervene before their invitation could be sent; hopeless of seeing him before. But on the third morning after his arrival in Hertfordshire, she saw him, from her dressing-room window, enter the paddock and ride towards the house.

Her daughters were eagerly called to partake of her joy. Jane resolutely kept her place at the table; but Elizabeth, to satisfy her mother, went to the window—she looked,—she saw Mr. Darcy with him, and sat down again by her sister.

"There is a gentleman with him, mamma," said Kitty; "who can it be?"

"Some acquaintance or other, my dear, I suppose; I am sure I do not know."

"La!" replied Kitty, "it looks just like that man that used to be with him before. Mr. what's-his-name. That tall, proud man."

"Good gracious! Mr. Darcy!—and so it does, I vow. Well, any friend of Mr. Bingley's will always be welcome here, to be sure; but else I must say that I hate the very sight of him."

Jane looked at Elizabeth with surprise and concern. She knew but little of their meeting in Derbyshire, and therefore felt for the awkwardness which must attend her sister, in seeing him almost for the first time after receiving his explanatory letter. Both sisters were uncomfortable enough. Each felt for the other, and of course for themselves; and their mother talked on, of her dislike of Mr. Darcy, and her resolution to be civil to him only as Mr. Bingley's friend, without being heard by either of them. But Elizabeth had sources of uneasiness which could not be suspected by Jane, to whom she had never yet had courage to shew Mrs. Gardiner's letter, or to relate her own change of sentiment towards him. To Jane, he could be only a man whose proposals she had refused, and whose merit she had undervalued; but to her own more extensive information, he was the person to whom the whole family were indebted for the first of benefits, and whom she regarded herself with an interest, if not quite so tender, at least as reasonable and just as what Jane felt for Bingley. Her astonishment at his coming—at his coming to Netherfield, to Longbourn, and voluntarily seeking her again, was almost equal to what she had known on first witnessing his altered behaviour in Derbyshire.

The colour which had been driven from her face, returned for half a minute with an additional glow, and a smile of delight added lustre to her eyes, as she thought for that space of time that his affection and wishes must still be unshaken. But she would not be secure.

"Let me first see how he behaves," said she; "it will then be early enough for expectation."

She sat intently at work, striving to be composed, and without daring to lift up her eyes, till anxious curiosity carried them to the face of her sister as the servant was approaching the door. Jane looked a little paler than usual, but more sedate than Elizabeth had expected. On the gentlemen's appearing, her colour increased; yet she received them with tolerable ease, and with a propriety of behaviour equally free from any symptom of resentment or any unnecessary complaisance.

Elizabeth said as little to either as civility would allow, and sat down again to her work, with an eagerness which it did not often command. She had ventured only one glance at Darcy. He looked serious, as usual; and, she thought, more as he had been used to look in Hertfordshire, than as she had seen him at Pemberley. But, perhaps he could not in her mother's presence be what he was before her uncle and aunt. It was a painful, but not an improbable, conjecture.

Bingley, she had likewise seen for an instant, and in that short period saw him looking both pleased and embarrassed. He was received by Mrs. Bennet with a degree of civility which made her two daughters ashamed, especially when contrasted with the cold and ceremonious politeness of her curtsey and address to his friend.

Elizabeth, particularly, who knew that her mother owed to the latter the preservation of her favourite daughter from irremediable infamy, was hurt and distressed to a most painful degree by a distinction so ill applied.

Darcy, after inquiring of her how Mr. and Mrs. Gardiner did, a question which she could not answer without confusion, said scarcely anything. He was not seated by her; perhaps that was the reason of his silence; but it had not been so in Derbyshire. There he had talked to her friends, when he could not to herself. But now several minutes elapsed without bringing the sound of his voice; and when occasionally, unable to resist the impulse of curiosity, she raised her eyes to his face, she as often found him looking at Jane as at herself, and frequently on no object but the ground. More thoughtfulness and less anxiety to please, than when they last met, were plainly expressed. She was disappointed, and angry with herself for being so.

"Could I expect it to be otherwise!" said she. "Yet why did he come?"

She was in no humour for conversation with anyone but himself; and to him she had hardly courage to speak.

She inquired after his sister, but could do no more.

"It is a long time, Mr. Bingley, since you went away," said Mrs. Bennet.

He readily agreed to it.

"I began to be afraid you would never come back again. People *did* say you meant to quit the place entirely at Michaelmas; but, however, I hope it is not true. A great many changes have happened in the neighbourhood, since you went away. Miss Lucas is married and settled. And one of my own daughters. I suppose you have heard of it; indeed, you must have seen it in the papers. It was in The Times and The Courier, I know; though it was not put in as it ought to be. It was only said, 'Lately, George Wickham, Esq. to Miss Lydia Bennet,' without there being a syllable said of her father, or the place where she lived, or anything. It was my brother Gardiner's drawing up too, and I wonder how he came to make such an awkward business of it. Did you see it?"

Bingley replied that he did, and made his congratulations. Elizabeth dared not lift up her eyes. How Mr. Darcy looked, therefore, she could not tell.

"It is a delightful thing, to be sure, to have a daughter well married," continued her mother, "but at the same time, Mr. Bingley, it is very hard to have her taken such a way from me. They are gone down to Newcastle, a place quite northward, it seems, and there they are to stay I do not know how long. His regiment is there; for I suppose you have heard of his leaving the ——shire, and of his being gone into the regulars. Thank Heaven! he has *some* friends, though perhaps not so many as he deserves."

Elizabeth, who knew this to be levelled at Mr. Darcy, was in such misery of shame, that she could hardly keep her seat. It drew from her, however, the exertion of speaking, which nothing else had so effectually done before; and she asked Bingley whether he meant to make any stay in the country at present. A few weeks, he believed.

"When you have killed all your own birds, Mr. Bingley," said her mother, "I beg you will come here, and shoot as many as you please on

Mr. Bennet's manor. I am sure he will be vastly happy to oblige you, and will save all the best of the covies for you."

Elizabeth's misery increased, at such unnecessary, such officious attention! Were the same fair prospect to arise at present as had flattered them a year ago, every thing, she was persuaded, would be hastening to the same vexatious conclusion. At that instant, she felt that years of happiness could not make Jane or herself amends for moments of such painful confusion.

"The first wish of my heart," said she to herself, "is never more to be in company with either of them. Their society can afford no pleasure that will atone for such wretchedness as this! Let me never see either one or the other again!"

Yet the misery, for which years of happiness were to offer no compensation, received soon afterwards material relief, from observing how much the beauty of her sister re-kindled the admiration of her former lover. When first he came in, he had spoken to her but little; but every five minutes seemed to be giving her more of his attention. He found her as handsome as she had been last year; as good natured, and as unaffected, though not quite so chatty. Jane was anxious that no difference should be perceived in her at all, and was really persuaded that she talked as much as ever. But her mind was so busily engaged, that she did not always know when she was silent.

When the gentlemen rose to go away, Mrs. Bennet was mindful of her intended civility, and they were invited and engaged to dine at Longbourn in a few days time.

"You are quite a visit in my debt, Mr. Bingley," she added, "for when you went to town last winter, you promised to take a family dinner with us, as soon as you returned. I have not forgot, you see; and I assure you, I was very much disappointed that you did not come back and keep your engagement."

Bingley looked a little silly at this reflection, and said something of his concern at having been prevented by business. They then went away.

Mrs. Bennet had been strongly inclined to ask them to stay and dine there that day; but, though she always kept a very good table, she did not think anything less than two courses could be good enough for a man on whom she had such anxious designs, or satisfy the appetite and pride of one who had ten thousand a year.

CHAPTER LIV

As soon as they were gone, Elizabeth walked out to recover her spirits; or in other words, to dwell without interruption on those subjects that must deaden them more. Mr. Darcy's behaviour astonished and vexed her.

"Why, if he came only to be silent, grave, and indifferent," said she, "did he come at all?"

She could settle it in no way that gave her pleasure.

"He could be still amiable, still pleasing, to my uncle and aunt, when he was in town; and why not to me? If he fears me, why come hither? If he no longer cares for me, why silent? Teasing, teasing, man! I will think no more about him."

Her resolution was for a short time involuntarily kept by the approach of her sister, who joined her with a cheerful look, which showed her better satisfied with their visitors, than Elizabeth.

"Now," said she, "that this first meeting is over, I feel perfectly easy. I know my own strength, and I shall never be embarrassed again by his coming. I am glad he dines here on Tuesday. It will then be publicly seen that, on both sides, we meet only as common and indifferent acquaintance."

"Yes, very indifferent indeed," said Elizabeth, laughingly. "Oh, Jane, take care."

"My dear Lizzy, you cannot think me so weak, as to be in danger now?"

"I think you are in very great danger of making him as much in love with you as ever."

*****

They did not see the gentlemen again till Tuesday; and Mrs. Bennet, in the meanwhile, was giving way to all the happy schemes, which the good humour and common politeness of Bingley, in half an hour's visit, had revived.

On Tuesday there was a large party assembled at Longbourn; and the two who were most anxiously expected, to the credit of their punctuality as sportsmen, were in very good time. When they repaired to the dining-room, Elizabeth eagerly watched to see whether Bingley would take the place, which, in all their former parties, had belonged to him, by her sister. Her prudent mother, occupied by the same ideas, forbore to invite him to sit by herself. On entering the room, he seemed to hesitate; but Jane happened to look round, and happened to smile: it was decided. He placed himself by her.

Elizabeth, with a triumphant sensation, looked towards his friend. He bore it with noble indifference, and she would have imagined that Bingley had received his sanction to be happy, had she not seen his eyes likewise turned towards Mr. Darcy, with an expression of half-laughing alarm.

His behaviour to her sister was such, during dinner time, as showed an admiration of her, which, though more guarded than formerly, persuaded Elizabeth, that if left wholly to himself, Jane's happiness, and his own, would be speedily secured. Though she dared not depend upon the consequence, she yet received pleasure from observing his behaviour. It gave her all the animation that her spirits could boast; for she was in no cheerful humour. Mr. Darcy was almost as far from her as the table could divide them. He was on one side of her mother. She knew how little such a situation would give pleasure to either, or make either appear to advantage. She was not near enough to hear any of their discourse, but she could see how seldom they spoke to each other, and how formal and cold was their manner whenever they did. Her mother's ungraciousness, made the sense of what they owed him more painful to Elizabeth's mind; and she would, at times, have given anything to be privileged to tell him that his kindness was neither unknown nor unfelt by the whole of the family.

She was in hopes that the evening would afford some opportunity of bringing them together; that the whole of the visit would not pass away without enabling them to enter into something more of conversation than the mere ceremonious salutation attending his entrance. Anxious and uneasy, the period which passed in the drawing-room, before the gentlemen came, was wearisome and dull to a degree that almost made her uncivil. She looked forward to their entrance as the point on which all her chance of pleasure for the evening must depend.

"If he does not come to me, *then*," said she, "I shall give him up for ever."

The gentlemen came; and she thought he looked as if he would have answered her hopes; but, alas! the ladies had crowded round the table, where Miss Bennet was making tea, and Elizabeth pouring out the coffee, in so close a confederacy that there was not a single vacancy near her which would admit of a chair. And on the gentlemen's approaching, one of the girls moved closer to her than ever, and said, in a whisper:

"The men shan't come and part us, I am determined. We want none of them; do we?"

Darcy had walked away to another part of the room. She followed him with her eyes, envied everyone to whom he spoke, had scarcely patience enough to help anybody to coffee; and then was enraged against herself for being so silly!

"A man who has once been refused! How could I ever be foolish enough to expect a renewal of his love? Is there one among the sex, who would not protest against such a weakness as a second proposal to the same woman? There is no indignity so abhorrent to their feelings!"

She was a little revived, however, by his bringing back his coffee cup himself; and she seized the opportunity of saying:

"Is your sister at Pemberley still?"

"Yes, she will remain there till Christmas."

"And quite alone? Have all her friends left her?"

"Mrs. Annesley is with her. The others have been gone on to Scarborough, these three weeks."

She could think of nothing more to say; but if he wished to converse with her, he might have better success. He stood by her, however, for some minutes, in silence; and, at last, on the young lady's whispering to Elizabeth again, he walked away.

When the tea-things were removed, and the card-tables placed, the ladies all rose, and Elizabeth was then hoping to be soon joined by him, when all her views were overthrown by seeing him fall a victim to her mother's rapacity for whist players, and in a few moments after seated with the rest of the party. She now lost every expectation of pleasure. They were confined for the evening at different tables, and she had nothing to hope, but that his eyes were so often turned towards her side of the room, as to make him play as unsuccessfully as herself.

Mrs. Bennet had designed to keep the two Netherfield gentlemen to supper; but their carriage was unluckily ordered before any of the others, and she had no opportunity of detaining them.

"Well girls," said she, as soon as they were left to themselves, "What say you to the day? I think every thing has passed off uncommonly well, I assure you. The dinner was as well dressed as any I ever saw. The venison was roasted to a turn—and everybody said they never saw so fat a haunch. The soup was fifty times better than what we had at the Lucases' last week; and even Mr. Darcy acknowledged, that the partridges were remarkably well done; and I suppose he has two or three French cooks at least. And, my dear Jane, I never saw you look in greater beauty. Mrs. Long said so too, for I asked her whether you did not. And what do you think she said besides? 'Ah! Mrs. Bennet, we shall have her at Netherfield at last.' She did indeed. I do think Mrs. Long is as good a creature as ever lived—and her nieces are very pretty behaved girls, and not at all handsome: I like them prodigiously."

Mrs. Bennet, in short, was in very great spirits; she had seen enough of Bingley's behaviour to Jane, to be convinced that she would get him at last; and her expectations of advantage to her family, when in a happy humour, were so far beyond reason, that she was quite disappointed at not seeing him there again the next day, to make his proposals.

"It has been a very agreeable day," said Miss Bennet to Elizabeth. "The party seemed so well selected, so suitable one with the other. I hope we may often meet again."

Elizabeth smiled.

"Lizzy, you must not do so. You must not suspect me. It mortifies me. I assure you that I have now learnt to enjoy his conversation as an agreeable and sensible young man, without having a wish beyond it. I am perfectly satisfied, from what his manners now are, that he never had any design of engaging my affection. It is only that he is blessed with greater sweetness of address, and a stronger desire of generally pleasing, than any other man."

"You are very cruel," said her sister, "you will not let me smile, and are provoking me to it every moment."

"How hard it is in some cases to be believed!"

"And how impossible in others!"

"But why should you wish to persuade me that I feel more than I acknowledge?"

"That is a question which I hardly know how to answer. We all love to instruct, though we can teach only what is not worth knowing. Forgive me; and if you persist in indifference, do not make me your confidante."

CHAPTER LV

A few days after this visit, Mr. Bingley called again, and alone. His friend had left him that morning for London, but was to return home in ten days time. He sat with them above an hour, and was in remarkably good spirits. Mrs. Bennet invited him to dine with them; but, with many expressions of concern, he confessed himself engaged elsewhere.

"Next time you call," said she, "I hope we shall be more lucky."

He should be particularly happy at any time, etc. etc.; and if she would give him leave, would take an early opportunity of waiting on them.

"Can you come to-morrow?"

Yes, he had no engagement at all for to-morrow; and her invitation was accepted with alacrity.

He came, and in such very good time that the ladies were none of them dressed. In ran Mrs. Bennet to her daughter's room, in her dressing gown, and with her hair half finished, crying out:

"My dear Jane, make haste and hurry down. He is come—Mr. Bingley is come. He is, indeed. Make haste, make haste. Here, Sarah, come to Miss Bennet this moment, and help her on with her gown. Never mind Miss Lizzy's hair."

"We will be down as soon as we can," said Jane; "but I dare say Kitty is forwarder than either of us, for she went up stairs half an hour ago."

"Oh! hang Kitty! what has she to do with it? Come be quick, be quick! Where is your sash, my dear?"

But when her mother was gone, Jane would not be prevailed on to go down without one of her sisters.

The same anxiety to get them by themselves was visible again in the evening. After tea, Mr. Bennet retired to the library, as was his custom, and Mary went up stairs to her instrument. Two obstacles of the five being thus removed, Mrs. Bennet sat looking and winking at Elizabeth and Catherine for a considerable time, without making any impression on them. Elizabeth would not observe her; and when at last Kitty did, she very innocently said, "What is the matter mamma? What do you keep winking at me for? What am I to do?"

"Nothing child, nothing. I did not wink at you." She then sat still five minutes longer; but unable to waste such a precious occasion, she suddenly got up, and saying to Kitty, "Come here, my love, I want to speak to you," took her out of the room. Jane instantly gave a look at Elizabeth which spoke her distress at such premeditation, and her entreaty that *she* would not give in to it. In a few minutes, Mrs. Bennet half-opened the door and called out:

"Lizzy, my dear, I want to speak with you."

Elizabeth was forced to go.

"We may as well leave them by themselves you know;" said her mother, as soon as she was in the hall. "Kitty and I are going upstairs to sit in my dressing-room."

Elizabeth made no attempt to reason with her mother, but remained quietly in the hall, till she and Kitty were out of sight, then returned into the drawing-room.

Mrs. Bennet's schemes for this day were ineffectual. Bingley was every thing that was charming, except the professed lover of her daughter. His ease and cheerfulness rendered him a most agreeable addition to their evening party; and he bore with the ill-judged officiousness of the mother, and heard all her silly remarks with a forbearance and command of countenance particularly grateful to the daughter.

He scarcely needed an invitation to stay supper; and before he went away, an engagement was formed, chiefly through his own and Mrs. Bennet's means, for his coming next morning to shoot with her husband.

After this day, Jane said no more of her indifference. Not a word passed between the sisters concerning Bingley; but Elizabeth went to bed in the happy belief that all must speedily be concluded, unless Mr. Darcy returned within the stated time. Seriously, however, she felt tolerably persuaded that all this must have taken place with that gentleman's concurrence.

Bingley was punctual to his appointment; and he and Mr. Bennet spent the morning together, as had been agreed on. The latter was much more agreeable than his companion expected. There was nothing of presumption or folly in Bingley that could provoke his ridicule, or disgust him into silence; and he was more communicative, and less eccentric, than the other had ever seen him. Bingley of course returned with him to dinner; and in the evening Mrs. Bennet's invention was again at work to get every body away from him and her daughter. Elizabeth, who had a letter to write, went into the breakfast-room for that purpose soon after tea; for as the others were all going to sit down to cards, she could not be wanted to counteract her mother's schemes.

But on returning to the drawing-room, when her letter was finished, she saw, to her infinite surprise, there was reason to fear that her mother had been too ingenious for her. On opening the door, she perceived her sister and Bingley standing together over the hearth, as if engaged in earnest conversation; and had this led to no suspicion, the faces of both, as they hastily turned round and moved away from each other, would have told it all. Their situation was awkward enough; but *hers* she thought was still worse. Not a syllable was uttered by either; and Elizabeth was on the point of going away again, when Bingley, who as well as the other had sat down, suddenly rose, and whispering a few words to her sister, ran out of the room.

Jane could have no reserves from Elizabeth, where confidence would give pleasure; and instantly embracing her, acknowledged, with the liveliest emotion, that she was the happiest creature in the world.

" 'Tis too much!" she added, "by far too much. I do not deserve it. Oh! why is not everybody as happy?"

Elizabeth's congratulations were given with a sincerity, a warmth, a delight, which words could but poorly express. Every sentence of kindness was a fresh source of happiness to Jane. But she would not allow herself to stay with her sister, or say half that remained to be said for the present.

"I must go instantly to my mother;" she cried. "I would not on any account trifle with her affectionate solicitude; or allow her to hear it from anyone but myself. He is gone to my father already. Oh! Lizzy, to know that what I have to relate will give such pleasure to all my dear family! how shall I bear so much happiness!"

She then hastened away to her mother, who had purposely broken up the card party, and was sitting up stairs with Kitty.

Elizabeth, who was left by herself, now smiled at the rapidity and ease with which an affair was finally settled, that had given them so many previous months of suspense and vexation.

"And this," said she, "is the end of all his friend's anxious circumspection! of all his sister's falsehood and contrivance! the happiest, wisest, most reasonable end!"

In a few minutes she was joined by Bingley, whose conference with her father had been short and to the purpose.

"Where is your sister?" said he hastily, as he opened the door.

"With my mother up stairs. She will be down in a moment, I dare say."

He then shut the door, and, coming up to her, claimed the good wishes and affection of a sister. Elizabeth honestly and heartily expressed her delight in the prospect of their relationship. They shook hands with great cordiality; and then, till her sister came down, she had to listen to all he had to say of his own happiness, and of Jane's perfections; and in spite of his being a lover, Elizabeth really believed all his expectations of felicity to be rationally founded, because they had for basis the excellent understanding, and super-excellent disposition of Jane, and a general similarity of feeling and taste between her and himself.

It was an evening of no common delight to them all; the satisfaction of Miss Bennet's mind gave a glow of such sweet animation to her face, as made her look handsomer than ever. Kitty simpered and smiled, and hoped her turn was coming soon. Mrs. Bennet could not give her consent or speak her approbation in terms warm enough to satisfy her feelings, though she talked to Bingley of nothing else for half an hour; and when Mr. Bennet joined them at supper, his voice and manner plainly showed how really happy he was.

Not a word, however, passed his lips in allusion to it, till their visitor took his leave for the night; but as soon as he was gone, he turned to his daughter, and said:

"Jane, I congratulate you. You will be a very happy woman."

Jane went to him instantly, kissed him, and thanked him for his goodness.

"You are a good girl;" he replied, "and I have great pleasure in thinking you will be so happily settled. I have not a doubt of your doing very well together. Your tempers are by no means unlike. You are each of you so complying, that nothing will ever be resolved on; so easy, that every servant will cheat you; and so generous, that you will always exceed your income."

"I hope not so. Imprudence or thoughtlessness in money matters would be unpardonable in me."

"Exceed their income! My dear Mr. Bennet," cried his wife, "what are you talking of? Why, he has four or five thousand a year, and very likely more." Then addressing her daughter, "Oh! my dear, dear Jane,

I am so happy! I am sure I shan't get a wink of sleep all night. I knew how it would be. I always said it must be so, at last. I was sure you could not be so beautiful for nothing! I remember, as soon as ever I saw him, when he first came into Hertfordshire last year, I thought how likely it was that you should come together. Oh! he is the handsomest young man that ever was seen!"

Wickham, Lydia, were all forgotten. Jane was beyond competition her favourite child. At that moment, she cared for no other. Her younger sisters soon began to make interest with her for objects of happiness which she might in future be able to dispense.

Mary petitioned for the use of the library at Netherfield; and Kitty begged very hard for a few balls there every winter.

Bingley, from this time, was of course a daily visitor at Longbourn; coming frequently before breakfast, and always remaining till after supper; unless when some barbarous neighbour, who could not be enough detested, had given him an invitation to dinner which he thought himself obliged to accept.

Elizabeth had now but little time for conversation with her sister; for while he was present, Jane had no attention to bestow on anyone else; but she found herself considerably useful to both of them in those hours of separation that must sometimes occur. In the absence of Jane, he always attached himself to Elizabeth, for the pleasure of talking of her; and when Bingley was gone, Jane constantly sought the same means of relief.

"He has made me so happy," said she, one evening, "by telling me that he was totally ignorant of my being in town last spring! I had not believed it possible."

"I suspected as much," replied Elizabeth. "But how did he account for it?"

"It must have been his sisters' doing. They were certainly no friends to his acquaintance with me, which I cannot wonder at, since he might have chosen so much more advantageously in many respects. But when they see, as I trust they will, that their brother is happy with me, they will learn to be contented, and we shall be on good terms again; though we can never be what we once were to each other."

"That is the most unforgiving speech," said Elizabeth, "that I ever heard you utter. Good girl! It would vex me, indeed, to see you again the dupe of Miss Bingley's pretended regard."

"Would you believe it, Lizzy, that when he went to town last November, he really loved me, and nothing but a persuasion of *my* being indifferent would have prevented his coming down again!"

"He made a little mistake to be sure; but it is to the credit of his modesty."

This naturally introduced a panegyric from Jane on his diffidence, and the little value he put on his own good qualities. Elizabeth was pleased to find that he had not betrayed the interference of his friend; for, though Jane had the most generous and forgiving heart in the world, she knew it was a circumstance which must prejudice her against him.

"I am certainly the most fortunate creature that ever existed!" cried Jane. "Oh! Lizzy, why am I thus singled from my family, and blessed above them all! If I could but see *you* as happy! If there *were* but such another man for you!"

"If you were to give me forty such men, I never could be so happy as you. Till I have your disposition, your goodness, I never can have your happiness. No, no, let me shift for myself; and, perhaps, if I have very good luck, I may meet with another Mr. Collins in time."

The situation of affairs in the Longbourn family could not be long a secret. Mrs. Bennet was privileged to whisper it to Mrs. Phillips, and she ventured, without any permission, to do the same by all her neighbours in Meryton.

The Bennets were speedily pronounced to be the luckiest family in the world, though only a few weeks before, when Lydia had first run away, they had been generally proved to be marked out for misfortune.

CHAPTER LVI

One morning, about a week after Bingley's engagement with Jane had been formed, as he and the females of the family were sitting together in the dining-room, their attention was suddenly drawn to the window, by the sound of a carriage; and they perceived a chaise and four driving up the lawn. It was too early in the morning for visitors, and besides, the equipage did not answer to that of any of their neighbours. The horses were post; and neither the carriage, nor the livery of the servant who preceded it, were familiar to them. As it was certain, however, that somebody was coming, Bingley instantly prevailed on Miss Bennet to avoid the confinement of such an intrusion, and walk away with him into the shrubbery. They both set off, and the conjectures of the remaining three continued, though with little satisfaction, till the door was thrown open and their visitor entered. It was Lady Catherine de Bourgh.

They were of course all intending to be surprised; but their astonishment was beyond their expectation; and on the part of Mrs. Bennet and Kitty, though she was perfectly unknown to them, even inferior to what Elizabeth felt.

She entered the room with an air more than usually ungracious, made no other reply to Elizabeth's salutation than a slight inclination of the head, and sat down without saying a word. Elizabeth had mentioned her name to her mother on her ladyship's entrance, though no request of introduction had been made.

Mrs. Bennet, all amazement, though flattered by having a guest of such high importance, received her with the utmost politeness. After sitting for a moment in silence, she said very stiffly to Elizabeth,

"I hope you are well, Miss Bennet. That lady, I suppose, is your mother."

Elizabeth replied very concisely that she was.

"And *that* I suppose is one of your sisters."

"Yes, madam," said Mrs. Bennet, delighted to speak to Lady Catherine. "She is my youngest girl but one. My youngest of all is lately married, and my eldest is somewhere about the grounds, walking with a young man who, I believe, will soon become a part of the family."

"You have a very small park here," returned Lady Catherine after a short silence.

"It is nothing in comparison of Rosings, my lady, I dare say; but I assure you it is much larger than Sir William Lucas's."

"This must be a most inconvenient sitting room for the evening, in summer; the windows are full west."

Mrs. Bennet assured her that they never sat there after dinner, and then added:

"May I take the liberty of asking your ladyship whether you left Mr. and Mrs. Collins well."

"Yes, very well. I saw them the night before last."

Elizabeth now expected that she would produce a letter for her from Charlotte, as it seemed the only probable motive for her calling. But no letter appeared, and she was completely puzzled.

Mrs. Bennet, with great civility, begged her ladyship to take some refreshment; but Lady Catherine very resolutely, and not very politely, declined eating anything; and then, rising up, said to Elizabeth,

"Miss Bennet, there seemed to be a prettyish kind of a little wilderness on one side of your lawn. I should be glad to take a turn in it, if you will favour me with your company."

"Go, my dear," cried her mother, "and show her ladyship about the different walks. I think she will be pleased with the hermitage."

Elizabeth obeyed, and running into her own room for her parasol, attended her noble guest downstairs. As they passed through the hall, Lady Catherine opened the doors into the dining-parlour and drawing-room, and pronouncing them, after a short survey, to be decent looking rooms, walked on.

Her carriage remained at the door, and Elizabeth saw that her waiting-woman was in it. They proceeded in silence along the gravel walk that led to the copse; Elizabeth was determined to make no effort for conversation with a woman who was now more than usually insolent and disagreeable.

"How could I ever think her like her nephew?" said she, as she looked in her face.

As soon as they entered the copse, Lady Catherine began in the following manner:—

"You can be at no loss, Miss Bennet, to understand the reason of my journey hither. Your own heart, your own conscience, must tell you why I come."

Elizabeth looked with unaffected astonishment.

"Indeed, you are mistaken, Madam. I have not been at all able to account for the honour of seeing you here."

"Miss Bennet," replied her ladyship, in an angry tone, "you ought to know, that I am not to be trifled with. But however insincere *you* may choose to be, you shall not find *me* so. My character has ever been celebrated for its sincerity and frankness, and in a cause of such moment as this, I shall certainly not depart from it. A report of a most alarming nature reached me two days ago. I was told that not only your sister was on the point of being most advantageously married, but that you, that Miss Elizabeth Bennet, would, in all likelihood, be soon afterwards united to my nephew, my own nephew, Mr. Darcy. Though I *know* it must be a scandalous falsehood, though I would not injure him so much as to suppose the truth of it possible, I instantly resolved on setting off for this place, that I might make my sentiments known to you."

"If you believed it impossible to be true," said Elizabeth, colouring with astonishment and disdain, "I wonder you took the trouble of coming so far. What could your ladyship propose by it?"

"At once to insist upon having such a report universally contradicted."

"Your coming to Longbourn, to see me and my family," said Elizabeth coolly, "will be rather a confirmation of it; if, indeed, such a report is in existence."

"If! Do you then pretend to be ignorant of it? Has it not been industriously circulated by yourselves? Do you not know that such a report is spread abroad?"

"I never heard that it was."

"And can you likewise declare, that there is no foundation for it?"

"I do not pretend to possess equal frankness with your ladyship. You may ask questions which I shall not choose to answer."

"This is not to be borne. Miss Bennet, I insist on being satisfied. Has he, has my nephew, made you an offer of marriage?"

"Your ladyship has declared it to be impossible."

"It ought to be so; it must be so, while he retains the use of his reason. But your arts and allurements may, in a moment of infatuation, have made him forget what he owes to himself and to all his family. You may have drawn him in."

"If I have, I shall be the last person to confess it."

"Miss Bennet, do you know who I am? I have not been accustomed to such language as this. I am almost the nearest relation he has in the world, and am entitled to know all his dearest concerns."

"But you are not entitled to know mine; nor will such behaviour as this, ever induce me to be explicit."

"Let me be rightly understood. This match, to which you have the presumption to aspire, can never take place. No, never. Mr. Darcy is engaged to my daughter. Now what have you to say?"

"Only this; that if he is so, you can have no reason to suppose he will make an offer to me."

Lady Catherine hesitated for a moment, and then replied:

"The engagement between them is of a peculiar kind. From their infancy, they have been intended for each other. It was the favourite wish of *his* mother, as well as of hers. While in their cradles, we planned the union: and now, at the moment when the wishes of both sisters would be accomplished in their marriage, to be prevented by a young woman of inferior birth, of no importance in the world, and wholly unallied to the family! Do you pay no regard to the wishes of his friends? To his tacit engagement with Miss de Bourgh? Are you lost to every feeling of propriety and delicacy? Have you not heard me say that from his earliest hours he was destined for his cousin?"

"Yes, and I had heard it before. But what is that to me? If there is no other objection to my marrying your nephew, I shall certainly not be kept from it by knowing that his mother and aunt wished him to marry Miss de Bourgh. You both did as much as you could in planning the marriage. Its completion depended on others. If Mr. Darcy is neither by honour nor inclination confined to his cousin, why is not he to make another choice? And if I am that choice, why may not I accept him?"

"Because honour, decorum, prudence, nay, interest, forbid it. Yes, Miss Bennet, interest; for do not expect to be noticed by his family or friends, if you wilfully act against the inclinations of all. You will be censured, slighted, and despised, by everyone connected with him. Your alliance will be a disgrace; your name will never even be mentioned by any of us."

"These are heavy misfortunes," replied Elizabeth. "But the wife of Mr. Darcy must have such extraordinary sources of happiness necessarily attached to her situation, that she could, upon the whole, have no cause to repine."

"Obstinate, headstrong girl! I am ashamed of you! Is this your gratitude for my attentions to you last spring? Is nothing due to me on that score? Let us sit down. You are to understand, Miss Bennet, that I came here with the determined resolution of carrying my purpose; nor will I be dissuaded from it. I have not been used to submit to any person's whims. I have not been in the habit of brooking disappointment."

"*That* will make your ladyship's situation at present more pitiable; but it will have no effect on me."

"I will not be interrupted. Hear me in silence. My daughter and my nephew are formed for each other. They are descended, on the maternal side, from the same noble line; and, on the father's, from respectable, honourable, and ancient—though untitled—families. Their fortune on both sides is splendid. They are destined for each other by the voice of every member of their respective houses; and what is to divide them? The upstart pretensions of a young woman without family, connections, or fortune. Is this to be endured! But it must not, shall not be. If you were sensible of your own good, you would not wish to quit the sphere in which you have been brought up."

"In marrying your nephew, I should not consider myself as quitting that sphere. He is a gentleman; I am a gentleman's daughter; so far we are equal."

"True. You *are* a gentleman's daughter. But who was your mother? Who are your uncles and aunts? Do not imagine me ignorant of their condition."

"Whatever my connections may be," said Elizabeth, "if your nephew does not object to them, they can be nothing to *you*."

"Tell me once for all, are you engaged to him?"

Though Elizabeth would not, for the mere purpose of obliging Lady Catherine, have answered this question, she could not but say, after a moment's deliberation:

"I am not."

Lady Catherine seemed pleased.

"And will you promise me, never to enter into such an engagement?"

"I will make no promise of the kind."

"Miss Bennet I am shocked and astonished. I expected to find a more reasonable young woman. But do not deceive yourself into a belief that I will ever recede. I shall not go away till you have given me the assurance I require."

"And I certainly *never* shall give it. I am not to be intimidated into anything so wholly unreasonable. Your ladyship wants Mr. Darcy to marry your daughter; but would my giving you the wished-for promise make their marriage at all more probable? Supposing him to be attached to me, would my refusing to accept his hand make him wish to bestow it on his cousin? Allow me to say, Lady Catherine, that the arguments with which you have supported this extraordinary application have been as frivolous as the application was ill-judged. You have widely mistaken my character, if you think I can be worked on by such persuasions as these. How far your nephew might approve of your interference in his affairs, I cannot tell; but you have certainly no right to concern yourself in mine. I must beg, therefore, to be importuned no farther on the subject."

"Not so hasty, if you please. I have by no means done. To all the objections I have already urged, I have still another to add. I am no stranger to the particulars of your youngest sister's infamous elopement. I know it all; that the young man's marrying her was a patched-up business, at the expence of your father and uncles. And is such a girl to be my nephew's sister? Is her husband, is the son of his late father's steward, to be his brother? Heaven and earth!—of what are you thinking? Are the shades of Pemberley to be thus polluted?"

"You can now have nothing further to say," she resentfully answered. "You have insulted me in every possible method. I must beg to return to the house."

And she rose as she spoke. Lady Catherine rose also, and they turned back. Her ladyship was highly incensed.

"You have no regard, then, for the honour and credit of my nephew! Unfeeling, selfish girl! Do you not consider that a connection with you must disgrace him in the eyes of everybody?"

"Lady Catherine, I have nothing further to say. You know my sentiments."

"You are then resolved to have him?"

"I have said no such thing. I am only resolved to act in that manner, which will, in my own opinion, constitute my happiness, without reference to *you*, or to any person so wholly unconnected with me."

"It is well. You refuse, then, to oblige me. You refuse to obey the claims of duty, honour, and gratitude. You are determined to ruin him in the opinion of all his friends, and make him the contempt of the world."

"Neither duty, nor honour, nor gratitude," replied Elizabeth, "have any possible claim on me, in the present instance. No principle of either would be violated by my marriage with Mr. Darcy. And with regard to the resentment of his family, or the indignation of the world, if the former *were* excited by his marrying me, it would not give me one moment's concern—and the world in general would have too much sense to join in the scorn."

"And this is your real opinion! This is your final resolve! Very well. I shall now know how to act. Do not imagine, Miss Bennet, that your ambition will ever be gratified. I came to try you. I hoped to find you reasonable; but, depend upon it, I will carry my point."

In this manner Lady Catherine talked on, till they were at the door of the carriage, when, turning hastily round, she added, "I take no leave of you, Miss Bennet. I send no compliments to your mother. You deserve no such attention. I am most seriously displeased."

Elizabeth made no answer; and without attempting to persuade her ladyship to return into the house, walked quietly into it herself. She heard the carriage drive away as she proceeded up stairs. Her mother impatiently met her at the door of the dressing-room, to ask why Lady Catherine would not come in again and rest herself.

"She did not choose it," said her daughter, "she would go."

"She is a very fine-looking woman! and her calling here was prodigiously civil! for she only came, I suppose, to tell us the Collinses were well. She is on her road somewhere, I dare say, and so, passing through Meryton, thought she might as well call on you. I suppose she had nothing particular to say to you, Lizzy?"

Elizabeth was forced to give into a little falsehood here; for to acknowledge the substance of their conversation was impossible.

CHAPTER LVII

The discomposure of spirits which this extraordinary visit threw Elizabeth into, could not be easily overcome; nor could she, for many hours, learn to think of it less than incessantly. Lady Catherine, it appeared, had actually taken the trouble of this journey from Rosings, for the sole purpose of breaking off her supposed engagement with Mr. Darcy. It was a rational scheme, to be sure! but from what the report of their engagement could originate, Elizabeth was at a loss to imagine; till she recollected that *his* being the intimate friend of Bingley, and *her* being the sister of Jane, was enough, at a time when the expectation of one wedding made everybody eager for another, to supply the idea. She had not herself forgotten to feel that the marriage of her sister must bring them more frequently together. And her neighbours at Lucas Lodge, therefore (for through their communication with the Collinses, the report, she concluded, had reached Lady Catherine), had only set that down as almost certain and immediate, which she had looked forward to as possible at some future time.

In revolving Lady Catherine's expressions, however, she could not help feeling some uneasiness as to the possible consequence of her persisting in this interference. From what she had said of her resolution to prevent their marriage, it occurred to Elizabeth that she must meditate an application to her nephew; and how *he* might take a similar representation of the evils attached to a connection with her, she dared not pronounce. She knew not the exact degree of his affection for his aunt, or his dependence on her judgment, but it was natural to suppose that he thought much higher of her ladyship than *she* could do; and it was certain that, in enumerating the miseries of a marriage with *one*, whose immediate connections were so unequal to his own, his aunt would address him on his weakest side. With his notions of dignity, he would probably feel that the arguments, which to Elizabeth had appeared weak and ridiculous, contained much good sense and solid reasoning.

If he had been wavering before as to what he should do, which had often seemed likely, the advice and entreaty of so near a relation might settle every doubt, and determine him at once to be as happy as dignity unblemished could make him. In that case he would return no more. Lady Catherine might see him in her way through town; and his engagement to Bingley of coming again to Netherfield must give way.

"If, therefore, an excuse for not keeping his promise should come to his friend within a few days," she added, "I shall know how to understand it. I shall then give over every expectation, every wish of his constancy. If he is satisfied with only regretting me, when he might have obtained my affections and hand, I shall soon cease to regret him at all."

*****

The surprise of the rest of the family, on hearing who their visitor had been, was very great; but they obligingly satisfied it, with the same kind of supposition which had appeased Mrs. Bennet's curiosity; and Elizabeth was spared from much teasing on the subject.

The next morning, as she was going downstairs, she was met by her father, who came out of his library with a letter in his hand.

"Lizzy," said he, "I was going to look for you; come into my room."

She followed him thither; and her curiosity to know what he had to tell her was heightened by the supposition of its being in some manner connected with the letter he held. It suddenly struck her that it might be from Lady Catherine; and she anticipated with dismay all the consequent explanations.

She followed her father to the fire place, and they both sat down. He then said,

"I have received a letter this morning that has astonished me exceedingly. As it principally concerns yourself, you ought to know its contents. I did not know before, that I had two daughters on the brink of matrimony. Let me congratulate you on a very important conquest."

The colour now rushed into Elizabeth's cheeks in the instantaneous conviction of its being a letter from the nephew, instead of the aunt; and she was undetermined whether most to be pleased that he explained himself at all, or offended that his letter was not rather addressed to herself; when her father continued:

"You look conscious. Young ladies have great penetration in such matters as these; but I think I may defy even *your* sagacity, to discover the name of your admirer. This letter is from Mr. Collins."

"From Mr. Collins! and what can *he* have to say?"

"Something very much to the purpose of course. He begins with congratulations on the approaching nuptials of my eldest daughter, of which, it seems, he has been told by some of the good-natured, gossiping Lucases. I shall not sport with your impatience, by reading what he says on that point. What relates to yourself, is as follows: 'Having thus offered you the sincere congratulations of Mrs. Collins and myself on this happy event, let me now add a short hint on the subject of another; of which we have been advertised by the same authority. Your daughter Elizabeth, it is presumed, will not long bear the name of Bennet, after her elder sister has resigned it, and the chosen partner of her fate may be reasonably looked up to as one of the most illustrious personages in this land.'

"Can you possibly guess, Lizzy, who is meant by this? 'This young gentleman is blessed, in a peculiar way, with every thing the heart of mortal can most desire,—splendid property, noble kindred, and extensive patronage. Yet in spite of all these temptations, let me warn my cousin Elizabeth, and yourself, of what evils you may incur by a precipitate closure with this gentleman's proposals, which, of course, you will be inclined to take immediate advantage of.'

"Have you any idea, Lizzy, who this gentleman is? But now it comes out:

"'My motive for cautioning you is as follows. We have reason to imagine that his aunt, Lady Catherine de Bourgh, does not look on the match with a friendly eye.'

"*Mr. Darcy*, you see, is the man! Now, Lizzy, I think I *have* surprised you. Could he, or the Lucases, have pitched on any man within the circle of our acquaintance, whose name would have given the lie more effectually to what they related? Mr. Darcy, who never looks at any woman but to see a blemish, and who probably never looked at you in his life! It is admirable!"

Elizabeth tried to join in her father's pleasantry, but could only force one most reluctant smile. Never had his wit been directed in a manner so little agreeable to her.

"Are you not diverted?"

"Oh! yes. Pray read on."

"'After mentioning the likelihood of this marriage to her ladyship last night, she immediately, with her usual condescension, expressed what she felt on the occasion; when it became apparent, that on the score of some family objections on the part of my cousin, she would never give her consent to what she termed so disgraceful a match. I thought it my duty to give the speediest intelligence of this to my cousin, that she and her noble admirer may be aware of what they are about, and not run hastily into a marriage which has not been properly sanctioned.' Mr. Collins moreover adds, 'I am truly rejoiced that my cousin Lydia's sad business has been so well hushed up, and am only concerned that their living together before the marriage took place should be so generally known. I must not, however, neglect the duties of my station, or refrain from declaring my amazement at hearing that you received the young couple into your house as soon as they were married. It was an encouragement of vice; and had I been the rector of Longbourn, I should very strenuously have opposed it. You ought certainly to forgive them, as a Christian, but never to admit them in your sight, or allow their names to be mentioned in your hearing.' That is his notion of Christian forgiveness! The rest of his letter is only about his dear Charlotte's situation, and his expectation of a young olive-branch. But, Lizzy, you look as if you did not enjoy it. You are not going to be *missish*, I hope, and pretend to be affronted at an idle report. For what do we live, but to make sport for our neighbours, and laugh at them in our turn?"

"Oh!" cried Elizabeth, "I am excessively diverted. But it is so strange!"

"Yes—*that* is what makes it amusing. Had they fixed on any other man it would have been nothing; but *his* perfect indifference, and *your* pointed dislike, make it so delightfully absurd! Much as I abominate writing, I would not give up Mr. Collins's correspondence for any consideration. Nay, when I read a letter of his, I cannot help giving him the preference even over Wickham, much as I value the impudence and hypocrisy of my son-in-law. And pray, Lizzy, what said Lady Catherine about this report? Did she call to refuse her consent?"

To this question his daughter replied only with a laugh; and as it had been asked without the least suspicion, she was not distressed by his repeating it. Elizabeth had never been more at a loss to make her feelings appear what they were not. It was necessary to laugh, when she would rather have cried. Her father had most cruelly mortified her, by what he said of Mr. Darcy's indifference, and she could do nothing but wonder at such a want of penetration, or fear that perhaps, instead of his seeing too little, she might have fancied too much.

CHAPTER LVIII

Instead of receiving any such letter of excuse from his friend, as Elizabeth half expected Mr. Bingley to do, he was able to bring Darcy with him to Longbourn before many days had passed after Lady Catherine's visit. The gentlemen arrived early; and, before Mrs. Bennet had time to tell him of their having seen his aunt, of which her daughter sat in momentary dread, Bingley, who wanted to be alone with Jane, proposed their all walking out. It was agreed to. Mrs. Bennet was not in the habit of walking; Mary could never spare time; but the remaining five set off together. Bingley and Jane, however, soon allowed the others to outstrip them. They lagged behind, while Elizabeth, Kitty, and Darcy were to entertain each other. Very little was said by either; Kitty was too much afraid of him to talk; Elizabeth was secretly forming a desperate resolution; and perhaps he might be doing the same.

They walked towards the Lucases, because Kitty wished to call upon Maria; and as Elizabeth saw no occasion for making it a general concern, when Kitty left them she went boldly on with him alone. Now was the moment for her resolution to be executed, and, while her courage was high, she immediately said:

"Mr. Darcy, I am a very selfish creature; and, for the sake of giving relief to my own feelings, care not how much I may be wounding yours. I can no longer help thanking you for your unexampled kindness to my poor sister. Ever since I have known it, I have been most anxious to acknowledge to you how gratefully I feel it. Were it known to the rest of my family, I should not have merely my own gratitude to express."

"I am sorry, exceedingly sorry," replied Darcy, in a tone of surprise and emotion, "that you have ever been informed of what may, in a mistaken light, have given you uneasiness. I did not think Mrs. Gardiner was so little to be trusted."

"You must not blame my aunt. Lydia's thoughtlessness first betrayed to me that you had been concerned in the matter; and, of course, I could not rest till I knew the particulars. Let me thank you again and again, in the name of all my family, for that generous compassion which induced you to take so much trouble, and bear so many mortifications, for the sake of discovering them."

"If you *will* thank me," he replied, "let it be for yourself alone. That the wish of giving happiness to you might add force to the other inducements which led me on, I shall not attempt to deny. But your *family* owe me nothing. Much as I respect them, I believe I thought only of *you*."

Elizabeth was too much embarrassed to say a word. After a short pause, her companion added, "You are too generous to trifle with me. If your feelings are still what they were last April, tell me so at once. *My* affections and wishes are unchanged, but one word from you will silence me on this subject for ever."

Elizabeth, feeling all the more than common awkwardness and anxiety of his situation, now forced herself to speak; and immediately, though not very fluently, gave him to understand that her sentiments had undergone so material a change, since the period to which he alluded, as to make her receive with gratitude and pleasure his present assurances. The happiness which this reply produced, was such as he had probably never felt before; and he expressed himself on the occasion as sensibly and as warmly as a man violently in love can be supposed to do. Had Elizabeth been able to encounter his eye, she might have seen how well the expression of heartfelt delight, diffused over his face, became him; but, though she could not look, she could listen, and he told her of feelings, which, in proving of what importance she was to him, made his affection every moment more valuable.

They walked on, without knowing in what direction. There was too much to be thought, and felt, and said, for attention to any other objects. She soon learnt that they were indebted for their present good understanding to the efforts of his aunt, who did call on him in her return through London, and there relate her journey to Longbourn, its motive, and the substance of her conversation with Elizabeth; dwelling emphatically on every expression of the latter which, in her ladyship's apprehension, peculiarly denoted her perverseness and assurance; in the belief that such a relation must assist her endeavours to obtain that promise from her nephew which she had refused to give. But, unluckily for her ladyship, its effect had been exactly contrariwise.

"It taught me to hope," said he, "as I had scarcely ever allowed myself to hope before. I knew enough of your disposition to be certain that, had you been absolutely, irrevocably decided against me, you would have acknowledged it to Lady Catherine, frankly and openly."

Elizabeth coloured and laughed as she replied, "Yes, you know enough of my frankness to believe me capable of *that*. After abusing you so abominably to your face, I could have no scruple in abusing you to all your relations."

"What did you say of me, that I did not deserve? For, though your accusations were ill-founded, formed on mistaken premises, my behaviour to you at the time had merited the severest reproof. It was unpardonable. I cannot think of it without abhorrence."

"We will not quarrel for the greater share of blame annexed to that evening," said Elizabeth. "The conduct of neither, if strictly examined, will be irreproachable; but since then, we have both, I hope, improved in civility."

"I cannot be so easily reconciled to myself. The recollection of what I then said, of my conduct, my manners, my expressions during the whole of it, is now, and has been many months, inexpressibly painful to me. Your reproof, so well applied, I shall never forget: 'had you behaved in a more gentlemanlike manner.' Those were your words. You know not, you can scarcely conceive, how they have tortured me;—though it was some time, I confess, before I was reasonable enough to allow their justice."

"I was certainly very far from expecting them to make so strong an impression. I had not the smallest idea of their being ever felt in such a way."

"I can easily believe it. You thought me then devoid of every proper feeling, I am sure you did. The turn of your countenance I shall never forget, as you said that I could not have addressed you in any possible way that would induce you to accept me."

"Oh! do not repeat what I then said. These recollections will not do at all. I assure you that I have long been most heartily ashamed of it."

Darcy mentioned his letter. "Did it," said he, "did it soon make you think better of me? Did you, on reading it, give any credit to its contents?"

She explained what its effect on her had been, and how gradually all her former prejudices had been removed.

"I knew," said he, "that what I wrote must give you pain, but it was necessary. I hope you have destroyed the letter. There was one part especially, the opening of it, which I should dread your having the power of reading again. I can remember some expressions which might justly make you hate me."

"The letter shall certainly be burnt, if you believe it essential to the preservation of my regard; but, though we have both reason to think my opinions not entirely unalterable, they are not, I hope, quite so easily changed as that implies."

"When I wrote that letter," replied Darcy, "I believed myself perfectly calm and cool, but I am since convinced that it was written in a dreadful bitterness of spirit."

"The letter, perhaps, began in bitterness, but it did not end so. The adieu is charity itself. But think no more of the letter. The feelings of the person who wrote, and the person who received it, are now so widely different from what they were then, that every unpleasant circumstance attending it ought to be forgotten. You must learn some of my philosophy. Think only of the past as its remembrance gives you pleasure."

"I cannot give you credit for any philosophy of the kind. Your retrospections must be so totally void of reproach, that the contentment arising from them is not of philosophy, but, what is much better, of innocence. But with me, it is not so. Painful recollections will intrude which cannot, which ought not, to be repelled. I have been a selfish being all my life, in practice, though not in principle. As a child I was taught what was right, but I was not taught to correct my temper. I was given good principles, but left to follow them in pride and conceit. Unfortunately an only son (for many years an only child), I was spoilt by my parents, who, though good themselves (my father, particularly, all that was benevolent and amiable), allowed, encouraged, almost taught me to be selfish and overbearing; to care for none beyond my own family circle; to think meanly of all the rest of the world; to wish at least to think meanly of their sense and worth compared with my own. Such I was, from eight to eight and twenty; and such I might still have been but for you, dearest, loveliest Elizabeth! What do I not owe you! You taught me a lesson, hard indeed at first, but most advantageous. By you, I was properly humbled. I came to you without a doubt of my reception. You showed me how insufficient were all my pretensions to please a woman worthy of being pleased."

"Had you then persuaded yourself that I should?"

"Indeed I had. What will you think of my vanity? I believed you to be wishing, expecting my addresses."

"My manners must have been in fault, but not intentionally, I assure you. I never meant to deceive you, but my spirits might often lead me wrong. How you must have hated me after *that* evening?"

"Hate you! I was angry perhaps at first, but my anger soon began to take a proper direction."

"I am almost afraid of asking what you thought of me, when we met at Pemberley. You blamed me for coming?"

"No indeed; I felt nothing but surprise."

"Your surprise could not be greater than *mine* in being noticed by you. My conscience told me that I deserved no extraordinary politeness, and I confess that I did not expect to receive *more* than my due."

"My object then," replied Darcy, "was to show you, by every civility in my power, that I was not so mean as to resent the past; and I hoped to obtain your forgiveness, to lessen your ill opinion, by letting you see that your reproofs had been attended to. How soon any other wishes introduced themselves I can hardly tell, but I believe in about half an hour after I had seen you."

He then told her of Georgiana's delight in her acquaintance, and of her disappointment at its sudden interruption; which naturally leading to the cause of that interruption, she soon learnt that his resolution of following her from Derbyshire in quest of her sister had been formed before he quitted the inn, and that his gravity and thoughtfulness there had arisen from no other struggles than what such a purpose must comprehend.

She expressed her gratitude again, but it was too painful a subject to each, to be dwelt on farther.

After walking several miles in a leisurely manner, and too busy to know anything about it, they found at last, on examining their watches, that it was time to be at home.

"What could become of Mr. Bingley and Jane!" was a wonder which introduced the discussion of their affairs. Darcy was delighted with their engagement; his friend had given him the earliest information of it.

"I must ask whether you were surprised?" said Elizabeth.

"Not at all. When I went away, I felt that it would soon happen."

"That is to say, you had given your permission. I guessed as much." And though he exclaimed at the term, she found that it had been pretty much the case.

"On the evening before my going to London," said he, "I made a confession to him, which I believe I ought to have made long ago. I told him of all that had occurred to make my former interference in his affairs absurd and impertinent. His surprise was great. He had never had the slightest suspicion. I told him, moreover, that I believed myself mistaken in supposing, as I had done, that your sister was indifferent to him; and as I could easily perceive that his attachment to her was unabated, I felt no doubt of their happiness together."

Elizabeth could not help smiling at his easy manner of directing his friend.

"Did you speak from your own observation," said she, "when you told him that my sister loved him, or merely from my information last spring?"

"From the former. I had narrowly observed her during the two visits which I had lately made here; and I was convinced of her affection."

"And your assurance of it, I suppose, carried immediate conviction to him."

"It did. Bingley is most unaffectedly modest. His diffidence had prevented his depending on his own judgment in so anxious a case, but his reliance on mine made every thing easy. I was obliged to confess one thing, which for a time, and not unjustly, offended him. I could not allow myself to conceal that your sister had been in town three months last winter, that I had known it, and purposely kept it from him. He was angry. But his anger, I am persuaded, lasted no longer than he remained in any doubt of your sister's sentiments. He has heartily forgiven me now."

Elizabeth longed to observe that Mr. Bingley had been a most delightful friend; so easily guided that his worth was invaluable; but she checked herself. She remembered that he had yet to learn to be laughed at, and it was rather too early to begin. In anticipating the happiness of Bingley, which of course was to be inferior only to his own, he continued the conversation till they reached the house. In the hall they parted.

CHAPTER LIX

"My dear Lizzy, where can you have been walking to?" was a question which Elizabeth received from Jane as soon as she entered their room, and from all the others when they sat down to table. She had only to say in reply, that they had wandered about, till she was beyond her own knowledge. She coloured as she spoke; but neither that, nor anything else, awakened a suspicion of the truth.

The evening passed quietly, unmarked by anything extraordinary. The acknowledged lovers talked and laughed, the unacknowledged were silent. Darcy was not of a disposition in which happiness overflows in mirth; and Elizabeth, agitated and confused, rather *knew* that she was happy than *felt* herself to be so; for, besides the immediate embarrassment, there were other evils before her. She anticipated what would be felt in the family when her situation became known; she was aware that no one liked him but Jane; and even feared that with the others it was a dislike which not all his fortune and consequence might do away.

At night she opened her heart to Jane. Though suspicion was very far from Miss Bennet's general habits, she was absolutely incredulous here.

"You are joking, Lizzy. This cannot be!—engaged to Mr. Darcy! No, no, you shall not deceive me. I know it to be impossible."

"This is a wretched beginning indeed! My sole dependence was on you; and I am sure nobody else will believe me, if you do not. Yet, indeed, I am in earnest. I speak nothing but the truth. He still loves me, and we are engaged."

Jane looked at her doubtingly. "Oh, Lizzy! it cannot be. I know how much you dislike him."

"You know nothing of the matter. *That* is all to be forgot. Perhaps I did not always love him so well as I do now. But in such cases as these, a good memory is unpardonable. This is the last time I shall ever remember it myself."

Miss Bennet still looked all amazement. Elizabeth again, and more seriously assured her of its truth.

"Good Heaven! can it be really so! Yet now I must believe you," cried Jane. "My dear, dear Lizzy, I would—I do congratulate you—but are you certain? forgive the question—are you quite certain that you can be happy with him?"

"There can be no doubt of that. It is settled between us already, that we are to be the happiest couple in the world. But are you pleased, Jane? Shall you like to have such a brother?"

"Very, very much. Nothing could give either Bingley or myself more delight. But we considered it, we talked of it as impossible. And do you really love him quite well enough? Oh, Lizzy! do anything rather than marry without affection. Are you quite sure that you feel what you ought to do?"

"Oh, yes! You will only think I feel *more* than I ought to do, when I tell you all."

"What do you mean?"

"Why, I must confess that I love him better than I do Bingley. I am afraid you will be angry."

"My dearest sister, now *be* serious. I want to talk very seriously. Let me know every thing that I am to know, without delay. Will you tell me how long you have loved him?"

"It has been coming on so gradually, that I hardly know when it began. But I believe I must date it from my first seeing his beautiful grounds at Pemberley."

Another entreaty that she would be serious, however, produced the desired effect; and she soon satisfied Jane by her solemn assurances of attachment. When convinced on that article, Miss Bennet had nothing further to wish.

"Now I am quite happy," said she, "for you will be as happy as myself. I always had a value for him. Were it for nothing but his love of you, I must always have esteemed him; but now, as Bingley's friend and your husband, there can be only Bingley and yourself more dear to me. But Lizzy, you have been very sly, very reserved with me. How little did you tell me of what passed at Pemberley and Lambton! I owe all that I know of it to another, not to you."

Elizabeth told her the motives of her secrecy. She had been unwilling to mention Bingley; and the unsettled state of her own feelings had made her equally avoid the name of his friend. But now she would no longer conceal from her his share in Lydia's marriage. All was acknowledged, and half the night spent in conversation.

* * * * *

"Good gracious!" cried Mrs. Bennet, as she stood at a window the next morning, "if that disagreeable Mr. Darcy is not coming here again with our dear Bingley! What can he mean by being so tiresome as to be always coming here? I had no notion but he would go a-shooting, or something or other, and not disturb us with his company. What shall we do with him? Lizzy, you must walk out with him again, that he may not be in Bingley's way."

Elizabeth could hardly help laughing at so convenient a proposal; yet was really vexed that her mother should be always giving him such an epithet.

As soon as they entered, Bingley looked at her so expressively, and shook hands with such warmth, as left no doubt of his good information; and he soon afterwards said aloud, "Mrs. Bennet, have you no more lanes hereabouts in which Lizzy may lose her way again to-day?"

"I advise Mr. Darcy, and Lizzy, and Kitty," said Mrs. Bennet, "to walk to Oakham Mount this morning. It is a nice long walk, and Mr. Darcy has never seen the view."

"It may do very well for the others," replied Mr. Bingley; "but I am sure it will be too much for Kitty. Won't it, Kitty?" Kitty owned that she had rather stay at home. Darcy professed a great curiosity to see the view from the Mount, and Elizabeth silently consented. As she went up stairs to get ready, Mrs. Bennet followed her, saying:

"I am quite sorry, Lizzy, that you should be forced to have that disagreeable man all to yourself. But I hope you will not mind it: it is all for Jane's sake, you know; and there is no occasion for talking to him, except just now and then. So, do not put yourself to inconvenience."

During their walk, it was resolved that Mr. Bennet's consent should be asked in the course of the evening. Elizabeth reserved to herself the application for her mother's. She could not determine how her mother would take it; sometimes doubting whether all his wealth and grandeur would be enough to overcome her abhorrence of the man. But whether she were violently set against the match, or violently delighted with it, it was certain that her manner would be equally ill adapted to do credit to her sense; and she could no more bear that Mr. Darcy should hear the first raptures of her joy, than the first vehemence of her disapprobation.

*****

In the evening, soon after Mr. Bennet withdrew to the library, she saw Mr. Darcy rise also and follow him, and her agitation on seeing it was extreme. She did not fear her father's opposition, but he was going to be made unhappy; and that it should be through her means—that *she*, his favourite child, should be distressing him by her choice, should be filling him with fears and regrets in disposing of her—was a wretched reflection, and she sat in misery till Mr. Darcy appeared again, when, looking at him, she was a little relieved by his smile. In a few minutes he approached the table where she was sitting with Kitty; and, while pretending to admire her work said in a whisper, "Go to your father, he wants you in the library." She was gone directly.

Her father was walking about the room, looking grave and anxious. "Lizzy," said he, "what are you doing? Are you out of your senses, to be accepting this man? Have not you always hated him?"

How earnestly did she then wish that her former opinions had been more reasonable, her expressions more moderate! It would have spared her from explanations and professions which it was exceedingly awkward to give; but they were now necessary, and she assured him, with some confusion, of her attachment to Mr. Darcy.

"Or, in other words, you are determined to have him. He is rich, to be sure, and you may have more fine clothes and fine carriages than Jane. But will they make you happy?"

"Have you any other objection," said Elizabeth, "than your belief of my indifference?"

"None at all. We all know him to be a proud, unpleasant sort of man; but this would be nothing if you really liked him."

"I do, I do like him," she replied, with tears in her eyes, "I love him. Indeed he has no improper pride. He is perfectly amiable. You do not know what he really is; then pray do not pain me by speaking of him in such terms."

"Lizzy," said her father, "I have given him my consent. He is the kind of man, indeed, to whom I should never dare refuse anything, which he condescended to ask. I now give it to *you*, if you are resolved on having him. But let me advise you to think better of it. I know your disposition, Lizzy. I know that you could be neither happy nor respectable, unless you truly esteemed your husband; unless you looked up to him as a superior. Your lively talents would place you in the greatest danger in an unequal marriage. You could scarcely escape discredit and misery. My child, let me not have the grief of seeing *you* unable to respect your partner in life. You know not what you are about."

Elizabeth, still more affected, was earnest and solemn in her reply; and at length, by repeated assurances that Mr. Darcy was really the object of her choice, by explaining the gradual change which her estimation of him had undergone, relating her absolute certainty that his affection was not the work of a day, but had stood the test of many months' suspense, and enumerating with energy all his good qualities, she did conquer her father's incredulity, and reconcile him to the match.

"Well, my dear," said he, when she ceased speaking, "I have no more to say. If this be the case, he deserves you. I could not have parted with you, my Lizzy, to anyone less worthy."

To complete the favourable impression, she then told him what Mr. Darcy had voluntarily done for Lydia. He heard her with astonishment.

"This is an evening of wonders, indeed! And so, Darcy did every thing; made up the match, gave the money, paid the fellow's debts, and got him his commission! So much the better. It will save me a world of trouble and economy. Had it been your uncle's doing, I must and *would* have paid him; but these violent young lovers carry every thing their own way. I shall offer to pay him to-morrow; he will rant and storm about his love for you, and there will be an end of the matter."

He then recollected her embarrassment a few days before, on his reading Mr. Collins's letter; and after laughing at her some time, allowed her at last to go—saying, as she quitted the room, "If any young men come for Mary or Kitty, send them in, for I am quite at leisure."

Elizabeth's mind was now relieved from a very heavy weight; and, after half an hour's quiet reflection in her own room, she was able to join the others with tolerable composure. Every thing was too recent for gaiety, but the evening passed tranquilly away; there was no longer anything material to be dreaded, and the comfort of ease and familiarity would come in time.

When her mother went up to her dressing-room at night, she followed her, and made the important communication. Its effect was most extraordinary; for on first hearing it, Mrs. Bennet sat quite still, and unable to utter a syllable. Nor was it under many, many minutes that she could comprehend what she heard; though not in general backward to credit what was for the advantage of her family, or that came in the shape of a lover to any of them. She began at length to recover, to fidget about in her chair, get up, sit down again, wonder, and bless herself.

"Good gracious! Lord bless me! only think! dear me! Mr. Darcy! Who would have thought it! And is it really true? Oh! my sweetest Lizzy! how rich and how great you will be! What pin-money, what jewels, what carriages you will have! Jane's is nothing to it—nothing at all. I am so pleased—so happy. Such a charming man!—so handsome! so tall!—Oh, my dear Lizzy! pray apologise for my having disliked him so much before. I hope he will overlook it. Dear, dear Lizzy. A house in town! Every thing that is charming! Three daughters married! Ten thousand a year! Oh, Lord! What will become of me. I shall go distracted."

This was enough to prove that her approbation need not be doubted: and Elizabeth, rejoicing that such an effusion was heard only by herself, soon went away. But before she had been three minutes in her own room, her mother followed her.

"My dearest child," she cried, "I can think of nothing else! Ten thousand a year, and very likely more! 'Tis as good as a Lord! And a special licence. You must and shall be married by a special licence. But my dearest love, tell me what dish Mr. Darcy is particularly fond of, that I may have it to-morrow."

This was a sad omen of what her mother's behaviour to the gentleman himself might be; and Elizabeth found that, though in the certain possession of his warmest affection, and secure of her relations' consent, there was still something to be wished for. But the morrow passed off much better than she expected; for Mrs. Bennet luckily stood in such awe of her intended son-in-law that she ventured not to speak to him, unless it was in her power to offer him any attention, or mark her deference for his opinion.

Elizabeth had the satisfaction of seeing her father taking pains to get acquainted with him; and Mr. Bennet soon assured her that he was rising every hour in his esteem.

"I admire all my three sons-in-law highly," said he. "Wickham, perhaps, is my favourite; but I think I shall like *your* husband quite as well as Jane's."

CHAPTER LX

Elizabeth's spirits soon rising to playfulness again, she wanted Mr. Darcy to account for his having ever fallen in love with her. "How could you begin?" said she. "I can comprehend your going on charmingly, when you had once made a beginning; but what could set you off in the first place?"

"I cannot fix on the hour, or the spot, or the look, or the words, which laid the foundation. It is too long ago. I was in the middle before I knew that I *had* begun."

"My beauty you had early withstood, and as for my manners—my behaviour to *you* was at least always bordering on the uncivil, and I never spoke to you without rather wishing to give you pain than not. Now be sincere; did you admire me for my impertinence?"

"For the liveliness of your mind, I did."

"You may as well call it impertinence at once. It was very little less. The fact is, that you were sick of civility, of deference, of officious attention. You were disgusted with the women who were always speaking, and looking, and thinking for *your* approbation alone. I roused, and interested you, because I was so unlike *them*. Had you not been really amiable, you would have hated me for it; but in spite of the pains you took to disguise yourself, your feelings were always noble and just; and in your heart, you thoroughly despised the persons who so assiduously courted you. There—I have saved you the trouble of accounting for it; and really, all things considered, I begin to think it perfectly reasonable. To be sure, you knew no actual good of me—but nobody thinks of *that* when they fall in love."

"Was there no good in your affectionate behaviour to Jane while she was ill at Netherfield?"

"Dearest Jane! who could have done less for her? But make a virtue of it by all means. My good qualities are under your protection, and you are to exaggerate them as much as possible; and, in return, it belongs to me to find occasions for teasing and quarrelling with you as often as may be; and I shall begin directly by asking you what made you so unwilling to come to the point at last. What made you so shy of me, when you first called, and afterwards dined here? Why, especially, when you called, did you look as if you did not care about me?"

"Because you were grave and silent, and gave me no encouragement."

"But I was embarrassed."

"And so was I."

"You might have talked to me more when you came to dinner."

"A man who had felt less, might."

"How unlucky that you should have a reasonable answer to give, and that I should be so reasonable as to admit it! But I wonder how long you *would* have gone on, if you had been left to yourself. I wonder when you *would* have spoken, if I had not asked you! My resolution of thanking you for your kindness to Lydia had certainly great effect. *Too much*, I am afraid; for what becomes of the moral, if our comfort springs from a breach of promise? for I ought not to have mentioned the subject. This will never do."

"You need not distress yourself. The moral will be perfectly fair. Lady Catherine's unjustifiable endeavours to separate us were the means of removing all my doubts. I am not indebted for my present happiness to your eager desire of expressing your gratitude. I was not in a humour to wait for any opening of yours. My aunt's intelligence had given me hope, and I was determined at once to know every thing."

"Lady Catherine has been of infinite use, which ought to make her happy, for she loves to be of use. But tell me, what did you come down to Netherfield for? Was it merely to ride to Longbourn and be embarrassed? or had you intended any more serious consequence?"

"My real purpose was to see *you*, and to judge, if I could, whether I might ever hope to make you love me. My avowed one, or what I avowed to myself, was to see whether your sister were still partial to Bingley, and if she were, to make the confession to him which I have since made."

"Shall you ever have courage to announce to Lady Catherine what is to befall her?"

"I am more likely to want more time than courage, Elizabeth. But it ought to be done, and if you will give me a sheet of paper, it shall be done directly."

"And if I had not a letter to write myself, I might sit by you and admire the evenness of your writing, as another young lady once did. But I have an aunt, too, who must not be longer neglected."

From an unwillingness to confess how much her intimacy with Mr. Darcy had been over-rated, Elizabeth had never yet answered Mrs. Gardiner's long letter; but now, having *that* to communicate which she knew would be most welcome, she was almost ashamed to find that her uncle and aunt had already lost three days of happiness, and immediately wrote as follows:

"I would have thanked you before, my dear aunt, as I ought to have done, for your long, kind, satisfactory, detail of particulars; but to say the truth, I was too cross to write. You supposed more than really existed. But *now* suppose as much as you choose; give a loose rein to your fancy, indulge your imagination in every possible flight which the subject will afford, and unless you believe me actually married, you cannot greatly err. You must write again very soon, and praise him a great deal more than you did in your last. I thank you, again and again, for not going to the Lakes. How could I be so silly as to wish it! Your idea of the ponies is delightful. We will go round the Park every day. I am the happiest creature in the world. Perhaps other people have said so before, but not one with such justice. I am happier even than Jane; she only smiles, I laugh. Mr. Darcy sends you all the love in the world that he can spare from me. You are all to come to Pemberley at Christmas. Yours, etc."

Mr. Darcy's letter to Lady Catherine was in a different style; and still different from either was what Mr. Bennet sent to Mr. Collins, in reply to his last.

"DEAR SIR,

"I must trouble you once more for congratulations. Elizabeth will soon be the wife of Mr. Darcy. Console Lady Catherine as well as you can. But, if I were you, I would stand by the nephew. He has more to give.

"Yours sincerely, etc."

Miss Bingley's congratulations to her brother, on his approaching marriage, were all that was affectionate and insincere. She wrote even to Jane on the occasion, to express her delight, and repeat all her former professions of regard. Jane was not deceived, but she was affected; and though feeling no reliance on her, could not help writing her a much kinder answer than she knew was deserved.

The joy which Miss Darcy expressed on receiving similar information, was as sincere as her brother's in sending it. Four sides of paper were insufficient to contain all her delight, and all her earnest desire of being loved by her sister.

Before any answer could arrive from Mr. Collins, or any congratulations to Elizabeth from his wife, the Longbourn family heard that the Collinses were come themselves to Lucas Lodge. The reason of this sudden removal was soon evident. Lady Catherine had been rendered so exceedingly angry by the contents of her nephew's letter, that Charlotte, really rejoicing in the match, was anxious to get away till the storm was blown over. At such a moment, the arrival of her friend was a sincere pleasure to Elizabeth, though in the course of their meetings she must sometimes think the pleasure dearly bought, when she saw Mr. Darcy exposed to all the parading and obsequious civility of her husband. He bore it, however, with admirable calmness. He could even listen to Sir William Lucas, when he complimented him on carrying away the brightest jewel of the country, and expressed his hopes of their all meeting frequently at St. James's, with very decent composure. If he did shrug his shoulders, it was not till Sir William was out of sight.

Mrs. Phillips's vulgarity was another, and perhaps a greater, tax on his forbearance; and though Mrs. Phillips, as well as her sister, stood in too much awe of him to speak with the familiarity which Bingley's good humour encouraged, yet, whenever she *did* speak, she must be vulgar. Nor was her respect for him, though it made her more quiet, at all likely to make her more elegant. Elizabeth did all she could to shield him from the frequent notice of either, and was ever anxious to keep him to herself, and to those of her family with whom he might converse without mortification; and though the uncomfortable feelings arising from all this took from the season of courtship much of its pleasure, it added to the hope of the future; and she looked forward with delight to the time when they should be removed from society so little pleasing to either, to all the comfort and elegance of their family party at Pemberley.

CHAPTER LXI

Happy for all her maternal feelings was the day on which Mrs. Bennet got rid of her two most deserving daughters. With what delighted pride she afterwards visited Mrs. Bingley, and talked of Mrs. Darcy, may be guessed. I wish I could say, for the sake of her family, that the accomplishment of her earnest desire in the establishment of so many of her children produced so happy an effect as to make her a sensible, amiable, well-informed woman for the rest of her life; though perhaps it was lucky for her husband, who might not have relished domestic felicity in so unusual a form, that she still was occasionally nervous and invariably silly.

Mr. Bennet missed his second daughter exceedingly; his affection for her drew him oftener from home than anything else could do. He delighted in going to Pemberley, especially when he was least expected.

Mr. Bingley and Jane remained at Netherfield only a twelvemonth. So near a vicinity to her mother and Meryton relations was not desirable even to *his* easy temper, or *her* affectionate heart. The darling wish of his sisters was then gratified; he bought an estate in a neighbouring county to Derbyshire, and Jane and Elizabeth, in addition to every other source of happiness, were within thirty miles of each other.

Kitty, to her very material advantage, spent the chief of her time with her two elder sisters. In society so superior to what she had generally known, her improvement was great. She was not of so ungovernable a temper as Lydia; and, removed from the influence of Lydia's example, she became, by proper attention and management, less irritable, less ignorant, and less insipid. From the further disadvantage of Lydia's society she was of course carefully kept, and though Mrs. Wickham frequently invited her to come and stay with her, with the promise of balls and young men, her father would never consent to her going.

Mary was the only daughter who remained at home; and she was necessarily drawn from the pursuit of accomplishments by Mrs. Bennet's being quite unable to sit alone. Mary was obliged to mix more with the world, but she could still moralize over every morning visit; and as she was no longer mortified by comparisons between her sisters' beauty and her own, it was suspected by her father that she submitted to the change without much reluctance.

As for Wickham and Lydia, their characters suffered no revolution from the marriage of her sisters. He bore with philosophy the conviction that Elizabeth must now become acquainted with whatever of his ingratitude and falsehood had before been unknown to her; and in spite of every thing, was not wholly without hope that Darcy might yet be prevailed on to make his fortune. The congratulatory letter which Elizabeth received from Lydia on her marriage, explained to her that, by his wife at least, if not by himself, such a hope was cherished. The letter was to this effect:

"MY DEAR LIZZY,

"I wish you joy. If you love Mr. Darcy half as well as I do my dear Wickham, you must be very happy. It is a great comfort to have you so rich, and when you have nothing else to do, I hope you will think of us. I am sure Wickham would like a place at court very much, and I do not think we shall have quite money enough to live upon without some help. Any place would do, of about three or four hundred a year; but however, do not speak to Mr. Darcy about it, if you had rather not.

"Yours, etc."

As it happened that Elizabeth had *much* rather not, she endeavoured in her answer to put an end to every entreaty and expectation of the kind. Such relief, however, as it was in her power to afford, by the practice of what might be called economy in her own private expenses, she frequently sent them. It had always been evident to her that such an income as theirs, under the direction of two persons so extravagant in their wants, and heedless of the future, must be very insufficient to their support; and whenever they changed their quarters, either Jane or herself were sure of being applied to for some little assistance towards discharging their bills. Their manner of living, even when the restoration of peace dismissed them to a home, was unsettled in the extreme. They were always moving from place to place in quest of a cheap situation, and always spending more than they ought. His affection for her soon sunk into indifference; hers lasted a little longer; and in spite of her youth and her manners, she retained all the claims to reputation which her marriage had given her.

Though Darcy could never receive *him* at Pemberley, yet, for Elizabeth's sake, he assisted him further in his profession. Lydia was occasionally a visitor there, when her husband was gone to enjoy himself in London or Bath; and with the Bingleys they both of them frequently staid so long, that even Bingley's good humour was overcome, and he proceeded so far as to talk of giving them a hint to be gone.

Miss Bingley was very deeply mortified by Darcy's marriage; but as she thought it advisable to retain the right of visiting at Pemberley, she dropt all her resentment; was fonder than ever of Georgiana, almost as attentive to Darcy as heretofore, and paid off every arrear of civility to Elizabeth.

Pemberley was now Georgiana's home; and the attachment of the sisters was exactly what Darcy had hoped to see. They were able to love each other even as well as they intended. Georgiana had the highest opinion in the world of Elizabeth; though at first she often listened with an astonishment bordering on alarm at her lively, sportive, manner of talking to her brother. He, who had always inspired in herself a respect which almost overcame her affection, she now saw the object of open pleasantry. Her mind received knowledge which had never before fallen in her way. By Elizabeth's instructions, she began to comprehend that a woman may take liberties with her husband which a brother will not always allow in a sister more than ten years younger than himself.

Lady Catherine was extremely indignant on the marriage of her nephew; and as she gave way to all the genuine frankness of her character in her reply to the letter which announced its arrangement, she sent him language so very abusive, especially of Elizabeth, that for some time all intercourse was at an end. But at length, by Elizabeth's persuasion, he was prevailed on to overlook the offence, and seek a reconciliation; and, after a little further resistance on the part of his aunt, her resentment gave way, either to her affection for him, or her curiosity to see how his wife conducted herself; and she condescended to wait on them at Pemberley, in spite of that pollution which its woods had received, not merely from the presence of such a mistress, but the visits of her uncle and aunt from the city.

With the Gardiners, they were always on the most intimate terms. Darcy, as well as Elizabeth, really loved them; and they were both ever sensible of the warmest gratitude towards the persons who, by bringing her into Derbyshire, had been the means of uniting them.

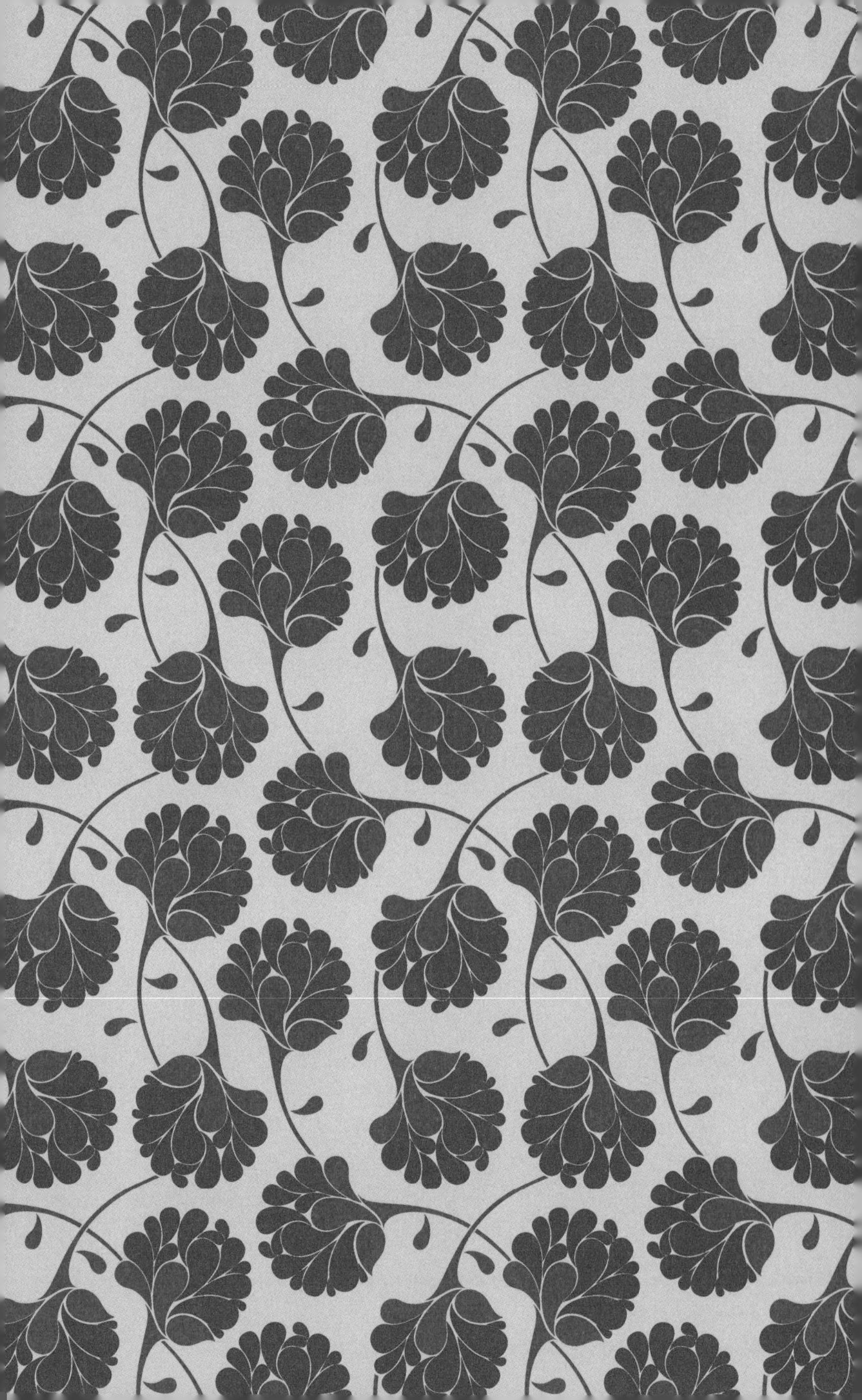

Persuasion

Persuasion

JANE AUSTEN

CANTERBURY CLASSICS
San Diego

All correspondence concerning the content of this book should be addressed to: Canterbury Classics
10350 Barnes Canyon Road, Suite 100
San Diego, CA 92121

Publisher: Peter Norton
Publishing Team: Lori Asbury, Ana Parker
Director Editorial and Production: JoAnn Padgett
Editor: Dan Mansfield

Library of Congress Cataloging-in-Publication Data

Austen, Jane, 1775-1817.
Persuasion / Jane Austen.
p. cm.
ISBN-13: 978-1-60710-735-4 (alk. paper)
ISBN-10: 1-60710-735-X (alk. paper)
1. Young women--England--Fiction. 2. Rejection (Psychology)--Fiction. 3. Motherless families--Fiction. 4. Ship captains--Fiction. 5. England--Social life and customs--19th century--Fiction. 6. Love stories. 7. Regency fiction. I. Title.

PR4034.P4 2013b
823'.7--dc23

2012037811

PRINTED IN CHINA

3 4 5 6 7 19 18 17 16 15

CHAPTER 1

Sir Walter Elliot, of Kellynch Hall, in Somersetshire, was a man who, for his own amusement, never took up any book but the Baronetage; there he found occupation for an idle hour, and consolation in a distressed one; there his faculties were roused into admiration and respect, by contemplating the limited remnant of the earliest patents; there any unwelcome sensations, arising from domestic affairs changed naturally into pity and contempt as he turned over the almost endless creations of the last century; and there, if every other leaf were powerless, he could read his own history with an interest which never failed. This was the page at which the favourite volume always opened:

> "ELLIOT OF KELLYNCH HALL.
>
> "Walter Elliot, born March 1, 1760, married, July 15, 1784, Elizabeth, daughter of James Stevenson, Esq. of South Park, in the county of Gloucester, by which lady (who died 1800) he has issue Elizabeth, born June 1, 1785; Anne, born August 9, 1787; a still-born son, November 5, 1789; Mary, born November 20, 1791."

Precisely such had the paragraph originally stood from the printer's hands; but Sir Walter had improved it by adding, for the information of himself and his family, these words, after the date of Mary's birth—"Married, December 16, 1810, Charles, son and heir of Charles Musgrove, Esq. of Uppercross, in the county of Somerset," and by inserting most accurately the day of the month on which he had lost his wife.

Then followed the history and rise of the ancient and respectable family, in the usual terms; how it had been first settled in Cheshire; how mentioned in Dugdale, serving the office of high sheriff, representing a borough in three successive parliaments, exertions of loyalty, and dignity of baronet, in the first year of Charles II, with all the Marys and Elizabeths they had married; forming altogether two handsome duodecimo pages, and concluding with the arms and motto: "Principal seat, Kellynch Hall, in the county of Somerset," and Sir Walter's handwriting again in this finale:

"Heir presumptive, William Walter Elliot, Esq., great grandson of the second Sir Walter."

Vanity was the beginning and the end of Sir Walter Elliot's character; vanity of person and of situation. He had been remarkably handsome in his youth; and, at fifty-four, was still a very fine man. Few women could think more of their personal appearance than he did, nor could the valet of any new made lord be more delighted with the place he held in society. He considered the blessing of beauty as inferior only to the blessing of a baronetcy; and the Sir Walter Elliot, who united these gifts, was the constant object of his warmest respect and devotion.

His good looks and his rank had one fair claim on his attachment; since to them he must have owed a wife of very superior character to any thing deserved by his own. Lady Elliot had been an excellent woman, sensible and amiable; whose judgement and conduct, if they might be pardoned the youthful infatuation, which made her Lady Elliot, had never required indulgence afterwards. She had humoured, or softened, or concealed his failings, and promoted his real respectability for seventeen years; and though not the very happiest being in the world herself, had found enough in her duties, her friends, and her children, to attach her to life, and make it no matter of indifference to her when she was called on to quit them. Three girls, the two eldest sixteen and fourteen, was an awful legacy for a mother to bequeath, an awful charge rather, to confide to the authority and guidance of a conceited, silly father. She had, however, one very intimate friend, a sensible, deserving woman, who had been brought, by strong attachment to herself, to settle close by her, in the village of Kellynch; and on her kindness and advice, Lady Elliot mainly relied for the best help and maintenance of the good principles and instruction which she had been anxiously giving her daughters.

This friend, and Sir Walter, did not marry, whatever might have been anticipated on that head by their acquaintance. Thirteen years had passed away since Lady Elliot's death, and they were still near neighbours and intimate friends, and one remained a widower, the other a widow.

That Lady Russell, of steady age and character, and extremely well provided for, should have no thought of a second marriage, needs no apology to the public, which is rather apt to be unreasonably discontented when a woman does marry again, than when she does not; but Sir Walter's continuing in singleness requires explanation. Be it known then, that Sir Walter, like a good father, (having met with one or two private disappointments in very unreasonable applications), prided himself on remaining single for his dear daughters' sake. For one daughter, his eldest, he would really have given up any thing, which he had not been very much tempted to do. Elizabeth had succeeded, at sixteen, to all that was possible, of her mother's rights and consequence; and being very handsome, and very like himself, her influence had always been great, and they had gone on together most happily. His two other children were of very inferior value. Mary had acquired a little artificial importance, by becoming Mrs. Charles Musgrove; but Anne, with an elegance of mind and sweetness of character, which must have placed her high with any people of real understanding, was nobody with either father or sister; her word had no weight, her convenience was always to give way—she was only Anne.

To Lady Russell, indeed, she was a most dear and highly valued goddaughter, favourite, and friend. Lady Russell loved them all; but it was only in Anne that she could fancy the mother to revive again. A few years before, Anne Elliot had been a very pretty girl, but her bloom had vanished early; and as even in its height, her father had found little to admire in her, (so totally different were her delicate features and mild dark eyes from his own), there could be nothing in them, now that she was faded and thin, to excite his esteem. He had never indulged much hope; he had now none, of ever reading her name in any other page of his favourite work. All equality of alliance must rest with Elizabeth, for Mary had merely connected herself with an old country family of respectability and large fortune, and had therefore given all the honour and received none: Elizabeth would, one day or other, marry suitably.

It sometimes happens that a woman is handsomer at twenty-nine than she was ten years before; and, generally speaking, if there has been neither ill health nor anxiety, it is a time of life at which scarcely any charm is lost. It was so with Elizabeth, still the same handsome Miss Elliot that she had begun to be thirteen years ago, and Sir Walter might be excused, therefore, in forgetting her age, or, at least, be deemed only half a fool, for thinking himself and Elizabeth as blooming as ever, amidst the wreck of the good looks of everybody else; for he could plainly see how old all the rest of his family and acquaintance were growing. Anne haggard, Mary coarse, every face in the neighbourhood worsting, and the rapid increase of the crow's foot about Lady Russell's temples had long been a distress to him.

Elizabeth did not quite equal her father in personal contentment. Thirteen years had seen her mistress of Kellynch Hall, presiding and directing with a self-possession and decision that could never have given the idea of her being younger than she was. For thirteen years had she been doing the honours, and laying down the domestic law at home, and leading the way to the chaise and four, and walking immediately after Lady Russell out of all the drawing-rooms and dining-rooms in the country. Thirteen winters' revolving frosts had seen her opening every ball of credit that a scanty neighbourhood afforded, and thirteen springs shown their blossoms, as she travelled up to London with her father, for a few weeks' annual enjoyment of the great world. She had the remembrance of all this, she had the consciousness of being nine-and-twenty to give her some regrets and some apprehensions; she was fully satisfied of being still quite as handsome as ever, but she felt her approach to the years of danger, and would have rejoiced to be certain of being properly solicited by baronet-blood within the next twelvemonth or two. Then might she again take up the book of books with as much enjoyment as in her early youth, but now she liked it not. Always to be presented with the date of her own birth and see no marriage follow but that of a youngest sister, made the book an evil; and more than once, when her father had left it open on the table near her, had she closed it, with averted eyes, and pushed it away.

She had had a disappointment, moreover, which that book, and especially the history of her own family, must ever present the remembrance of. The heir presumptive, the very William Walter Elliot, Esq., whose rights had been so generously supported by her father, had disappointed her.

She had, while a very young girl, as soon as she had known him to be, in the event of her having no brother, the future baronet, meant to marry him, and her father had always meant that she should. He had not been known to them as a boy; but soon after Lady Elliot's death, Sir Walter had sought the acquaintance, and though his overtures had not been met with any warmth, he had persevered in seeking it, making allowance for the modest drawing-back of youth; and, in one of their spring excursions to London, when Elizabeth was in her first bloom, Mr. Elliot had been forced into the introduction. He was at that time a very young man, just engaged in the study of the law; and Elizabeth found him extremely agreeable, and every plan in his favour was confirmed. He was invited to Kellynch Hall; he was talked of and expected all the rest of the year; but he never came. The following spring he was seen again in town, found equally agreeable, again encouraged, invited, and expected, and again he did not come; and the next tidings were that he was married. Instead of pushing his fortune in the line marked out for the heir of the house of Elliot, he had purchased independence by uniting himself to a rich woman of inferior birth.

Sir Walter has resented it. As the head of the house, he felt that he ought to have been consulted, especially after taking the young man so publicly by the hand; "For they must have been seen together," he observed, "once at Tattersall's, and twice in the lobby of the House of Commons." His disapprobation was expressed, but apparently very little regarded. Mr. Elliot had attempted no apology, and shown himself as unsolicitous of being longer noticed by the family, as Sir Walter considered him unworthy of it: all acquaintance between them had ceased.

This very awkward history of Mr. Elliot was still, after an interval of several years, felt with anger by Elizabeth, who had liked the man for himself, and still more for being her father's heir, and whose strong family pride could see only in him a proper match for Sir Walter Elliot's eldest daughter. There was not a baronet from A to Z whom her feelings could have so willingly acknowledged as an equal. Yet so miserably had he conducted himself, that though she was at this present time (the summer of 1814) wearing black ribbons for his wife, she could not admit him to be worth thinking of again. The disgrace of his first marriage might, perhaps, as there was no reason to suppose it perpetuated by offspring, have been got over, had he not done worse; but he had, as by the accustomary intervention of kind friends, they had been informed, spoken most disrespectfully of them all, most slightingly and contemptuously of the very blood he belonged to, and the honours which were hereafter to be his own. This could not be pardoned.

Such were Elizabeth Elliot's sentiments and sensations; such the cares to alloy, the agitations to vary, the sameness and the elegance, the prosperity and the nothingness of her scene of life; such the feelings to give interest to a long, uneventful residence in one country circle, to fill the vacancies which there were no habits of utility abroad, no talents or accomplishments for home, to occupy.

But now, another occupation and solicitude of mind was beginning to be added to these. Her father was growing distressed for money. She knew, that when he now took up the Baronetage, it was to drive the heavy bills of his tradespeople, and the unwelcome hints of Mr. Shepherd, his agent, from his thoughts. The Kellynch property was good, but not equal to Sir Walter's apprehension of the state required in its possessor. While Lady Elliot lived, there had been method, moderation, and economy, which had just kept him within his income; but with her had died all such right-mindedness, and from that period he had been constantly exceeding it. It had not been possible for him to spend less; he had done nothing but what Sir Walter Elliot was imperiously called on to do; but blameless as he was, he was not only growing dreadfully in debt, but was hearing of it so often, that it became vain to attempt concealing it longer, even partially, from his daughter. He had given her some hints of it the last spring in town; he had gone so far even as to say, "Can we retrench? Does it occur to you that there is any one article in which we can retrench?" and Elizabeth, to do her justice, had, in the first ardour of female alarm, set seriously to think what could be done, and had finally proposed these two branches of economy, to cut off some unnecessary charities, and to refrain from new furnishing the drawing-room; to which expedients she afterwards added the happy thought of their taking no present down to Anne, as had been the usual yearly custom. But these measures, however good in themselves, were insufficient for the real extent of the evil, the whole of which Sir Walter found himself obliged to confess to her soon afterwards. Elizabeth had nothing to propose of deeper efficacy. She felt herself ill-used and unfortunate, as did her father; and they were neither of them able to devise any means of lessening their expenses without compromising their dignity, or relinquishing their comforts in a way not to be borne.

There was only a small part of his estate that Sir Walter could dispose of; but had every acre been alienable, it would have made no difference. He had condescended to mortgage as far as he had the power, but he would never condescend to sell. No; he would never disgrace his name so far. The Kellynch estate should be transmitted whole and entire, as he had received it.

Their two confidential friends, Mr. Shepherd, who lived in the neighbouring market town, and Lady Russell, were called to advise them; and both father and daughter seemed to expect that something should be struck out by one or the other to remove their embarrassments and reduce their expenditure, without involving the loss of any indulgence of taste or pride.

CHAPTER 2

Mr. Shepherd, a civil, cautious lawyer, who, whatever might be his hold or his views on Sir Walter, would rather have the disagreeable prompted by anybody else, excused himself from offering the slightest hint, and only begged leave to recommend an implicit reference to the excellent judgement of Lady Russell, from whose known good sense he fully expected to have just such resolute measures advised as he meant to see finally adopted.

Lady Russell was most anxiously zealous on the subject, and gave it much serious consideration. She was a woman rather of sound than of quick abilities, whose difficulties in coming to any decision in this instance were great, from the opposition of two leading principles. She was of strict integrity herself, with a delicate sense of honour; but she was as desirous of saving Sir Walter's feelings, as solicitous for the credit of the family, as aristocratic in her ideas of what was due to them, as anybody of sense and honesty could well be. She was a benevolent, charitable, good woman, and capable of strong attachments, most correct in her conduct, strict in her notions of decorum, and with manners that were held a standard of good breeding. She had a cultivated mind, and was, generally speaking, rational and consistent; but she had prejudices on the side of ancestry; she had a value for rank and consequence, which blinded her a little to the faults of those who possessed them. Herself the widow of only a knight, she gave the dignity of a baronet all its due; and Sir Walter, independent of his claims as an old acquaintance, an attentive neighbour, an obliging landlord, the husband of her very dear friend, the father of Anne and her sisters, was, as being Sir Walter, in her apprehension, entitled to a great deal of compassion and consideration under his present difficulties.

They must retrench; that did not admit of a doubt. But she was very anxious to have it done with the least possible pain to him and Elizabeth. She drew up plans of economy, she made exact calculations, and she did what nobody else thought of doing: she consulted Anne, who never seemed considered by the others as having any interest in the question. She consulted, and in a degree was influenced by her in marking out the scheme of retrenchment, which was at last submitted to Sir Walter. Every emendation of Anne's had been on the side of honesty against importance. She wanted more vigorous measures, a more complete reformation, a quicker release from debt, a much higher tone of indifference for everything but justice and equity.

"If we can persuade your father to all this," said Lady Russell, looking over her paper, "much may be done. If he will adopt these regulations, in seven years he will be clear; and I hope we may be able to convince him and Elizabeth, that Kellynch Hall has a respectability in itself which cannot be affected by these reductions; and that the true dignity of Sir Walter Elliot will be very far from lessened in the eyes of sensible people, by acting like a man of principle. What will he be doing, in fact, but what very many of our first families have done, or ought to do? There will be nothing singular in his case; and it is singularity that often makes the worst part of our suffering, as it always does of our conduct. I have great hope of prevailing. We must be serious and decided; for after all, the person who has contracted debts must pay them; and though a great deal is due to the feelings of the gentleman, and the head of a house, like your father, there is still more due to the character of an honest man."

This was the principle on which Anne wanted her father to be proceeding, his friends to be urging him. She considered it as an act of indispensable duty to clear away the claims of creditors with all the expedition which the most comprehensive retrenchments could secure, and saw no dignity in anything short of it. She wanted it to be prescribed, and felt as a duty. She rated Lady Russell's influence highly; and as to the severe degree of self-denial which her own conscience prompted, she believed there might be little more difficulty in persuading them to a complete, than to half a reformation. Her knowledge of her father and Elizabeth inclined her to think that the sacrifice of one pair of horses would be hardly less painful than of both, and so on, through the whole list of Lady Russell's too gentle reductions.

How Anne's more rigid requisitions might have been taken is of little consequence. Lady Russell's had no success at all: could not be put up with, were not to be borne. "What! Every comfort of life knocked off! Journeys, London, servants, horses, table—contractions and restrictions everywhere! To live no longer with the decencies even of a private gentleman! No, he would sooner quit Kellynch Hall at once, than remain in it on such disgraceful terms."

"Quit Kellynch Hall." The hint was immediately taken up by Mr. Shepherd, whose interest was involved in the reality of Sir Walter's retrenching, and who was perfectly persuaded that nothing would be done without a change of abode. "Since the idea had been started in the very quarter which ought to dictate, he had no scruple," he said, "in confessing his judgement to be entirely on that side. It did not appear to him that Sir Walter could materially alter his style of living in a house that had such a character of hospitality and ancient dignity to support. In any other place Sir Walter might judge for himself; and would be looked up to, as regulating the modes of life in whatever way he might choose to model his household."

Sir Walter would quit Kellynch Hall; and after a very few days more of doubt and indecision, the great question of whither he should go was settled, and the first outline of this important change made out.

There had been three alternatives, London, Bath, or another house in the country. All Anne's wishes had been for the latter. A small house in their own neighbourhood, where they might still have Lady Russell's society, still be near Mary, and still have the pleasure of sometimes seeing the lawns and groves of Kellynch, was the object of her ambition. But the usual fate of Anne attended her, in having something very opposite from her inclination fixed on. She disliked Bath, and did not think it agreed with her; and Bath was to be her home.

Sir Walter had at first thought more of London; but Mr. Shepherd felt that he could not be trusted in London, and had been skilful enough to dissuade him from it, and make Bath preferred. It was a much safer place for a gentleman in his predicament: he might there be important at comparatively little expense. Two material advantages of Bath over London had of course been given all their weight: its more convenient distance from Kellynch, only fifty miles, and Lady Russell's spending some part of every winter there; and to the very great satisfaction of Lady Russell, whose first views on the projected change had been for Bath, Sir Walter and Elizabeth were induced to believe that they should lose neither consequence nor enjoyment by settling there.

Lady Russell felt obliged to oppose her dear Anne's known wishes. It would be too much to expect Sir Walter to descend into a small house in his own neighbourhood. Anne herself would have found the mortifications of it more than she foresaw, and to Sir Walter's feelings they must have been dreadful. And with regard to Anne's dislike of Bath, she considered it as a prejudice and mistake arising, first, from the circumstance of her having been three years at school there, after her mother's death; and secondly, from her happening to be not in perfectly good spirits the only winter which she had afterwards spent there with herself.

Lady Russell was fond of Bath, in short, and disposed to think it must suit them all; and as to her young friend's health, by passing all the warm months with her at Kellynch Lodge, every danger would be avoided; and it was in fact, a change that must do both health and spirits good. Anne had been too little from home, too little seen. Her spirits were not high. A larger society would improve them. She wanted her to be more known.

The undesirableness of any other house in the same neighbourhood for Sir Walter was certainly much strengthened by one part, and a very material part of the scheme, which had been happily engrafted on the beginning. He was not only to quit his home, but to see it in the hands of others; a trial of fortitude, which stronger heads than Sir Walter's have found too much. Kellynch Hall was to be let. This, however, was a profound secret, not to be breathed beyond their own circle.

Sir Walter could not have borne the degradation of being known to design letting his house. Mr. Shepherd had once mentioned the word "advertise," but never dared approach it again. Sir Walter spurned the idea of its being offered in any manner; forbad the slightest hint being dropped of his having such an intention; and it was only on the supposition of his being spontaneously solicited by some most unexceptionable applicant, on his own terms, and as a great favour, that he would let it at all.

How quick come the reasons for approving what we like! Lady Russell had another excellent one at hand, for being extremely glad that Sir Walter and his family were to remove from the country. Elizabeth had been lately forming an intimacy, which she wished to see interrupted. It was with the daughter of Mr. Shepherd, who had returned, after an unprosperous marriage, to her father's house, with the additional burden of two children. She was a clever young woman, who understood the art of pleasing—the art of pleasing, at least, at Kellynch Hall; and who had made herself so acceptable to Miss Elliot, as to have been already staying there more than once, in spite of all that Lady Russell, who thought it a friendship quite out of place, could hint of caution and reserve.

Lady Russell, indeed, had scarcely any influence with Elizabeth, and seemed to love her, rather because she would love her, than because Elizabeth deserved it. She had never received from her more than outward attention, nothing beyond the observances of complaisance; had never succeeded in any point that she wanted to carry, against previous inclination. She had been repeatedly very earnest in trying to get Anne included in the visit to London, sensibly open to all the injustice and all the discredit of the selfish arrangements which shut her out, and on many lesser occasions had endeavoured to give Elizabeth the advantage of her own better judgement and experience; but always in vain: Elizabeth would go her own way; and never had she pursued it in more decided opposition to Lady Russell than in this selection of Mrs. Clay; turning from the society of so deserving a sister, to bestow her affection and confidence on one who ought to have been nothing to her but the object of distant civility.

From situation, Mrs. Clay was, in Lady Russell's estimate, a very unequal, and in her character she believed a very dangerous companion; and a removal that would leave Mrs. Clay behind, and bring a choice of more suitable intimates within Miss Elliot's reach, was therefore an object of first-rate importance.

CHAPTER 3

"I must take leave to observe, Sir Walter," said Mr. Shepherd one morning at Kellynch Hall, as he laid down the newspaper, "that the present juncture is much in our favour. This peace will be turning all our rich naval officers ashore. They will all be wanting a home. Could not be a better time, Sir Walter, for having a choice of tenants, very responsible tenants. Many a noble fortune has been made during the war. If a rich admiral were to come in our way, Sir Walter—"

"He would be a very lucky man, Shepherd," replied Sir Walter; "that's all I have to remark. A prize indeed would Kellynch Hall be to him; rather the greatest prize of all, let him have taken ever so many before; hey, Shepherd?"

Mr. Shepherd laughed, as he knew he must, at this wit, and then added, "I presume to observe, Sir Walter, that, in the way of business, gentlemen of the navy are well to deal with. I have had a little knowledge of their methods of doing business; and I am free to confess that they have very liberal notions, and are as likely to make desirable tenants as any set of people one should meet with. Therefore, Sir Walter, what I would take leave to suggest is, that if in consequence of any rumours getting abroad of your intention; which must be contemplated as a possible thing, because we know how difficult it is to keep the actions and designs of one part of the world from the notice and curiosity of the other; consequence has its tax; I, John Shepherd, might conceal any family-matters that I chose, for nobody would think it worth their while to observe me; but Sir Walter Elliot has eyes upon him which it may be very difficult to elude; and therefore, thus much I venture upon, that it will not greatly surprise me if, with all our caution, some rumour of the truth should get abroad; in the supposition of which, as I was going to observe, since applications will unquestionably follow, I should think any from our wealthy naval commanders particularly worth attending to; and beg leave to add, that two hours will bring me over at any time, to save you the trouble of replying."

Sir Walter only nodded. But soon afterwards, rising and pacing the room, he observed sarcastically, "There are few among the gentlemen of the navy, I imagine, who would not be surprised to find themselves in a house of this description."

"They would look around them, no doubt, and bless their good fortune," said Mrs. Clay, for Mrs. Clay was present: her father had driven her over, nothing being of so much use to Mrs. Clay's health as a drive to Kellynch: "but I quite agree with my father in thinking a sailor might be a very desirable tenant. I have known a good deal of the profession; and besides their liberality, they are so neat and careful in all their ways! These valuable pictures of yours, Sir Walter, if you chose to leave them, would be perfectly safe. Everything in and about the house would be taken such excellent care of! The gardens and shrubberies would be kept in almost as high order as they are now. You need not be afraid, Miss Elliot, of your own sweet flower gardens being neglected."

"As to all that," rejoined Sir Walter coolly, "supposing I were induced to let my house, I have by no means made up my mind as to the privileges to be annexed to it. I am not particularly disposed to favour a tenant. The park would be open to him of course, and few navy officers, or men of any other description, can have had such a range; but what restrictions I might impose on the use of the pleasure-grounds, is another thing. I am not fond of the idea of my shrubberies being always approachable; and I should recommend Miss Elliot to be on her guard with respect to her flower garden. I am very little disposed to grant a tenant of Kellynch Hall any extraordinary favour, I assure you, be he sailor or soldier."

After a short pause, Mr. Shepherd presumed to say, "In all these cases, there are established usages which make everything plain and easy between landlord and tenant. Your interest, Sir Walter, is in pretty safe hands. Depend upon me for taking care that no tenant has more than his just rights. I venture to hint, that Sir Walter Elliot cannot be half so jealous for his own, as John Shepherd will be for him."

Here Anne spoke, "The navy, I think, who have done so much for us, have at least an equal claim with any other set of men, for all the comforts and all the privileges which any home can give. Sailors work hard enough for their comforts, we must all allow."

"Very true, very true. What Miss Anne says, is very true," was Mr. Shepherd's rejoinder, and "Oh! Certainly," was his daughter's; but Sir Walter's remark was, soon afterwards, "The profession has its utility, but I should be sorry to see any friend of mine belonging to it."

"Indeed!" was the reply, and with a look of surprise.

"Yes; it is in two points offensive to me; I have two strong grounds of objection to it. First, as being the means of bringing persons of obscure birth into undue distinction, and raising men to honours which their fathers and grandfathers never dreamt of; and secondly, as it cuts up a man's youth and vigour most horribly; a sailor grows old sooner than any other man. I have observed it all my life. A man is in greater danger in the navy of being insulted by the rise of one whose father, his father might have disdained to speak to, and of becoming prematurely an object of disgust himself, than in any other line. One day last spring, in town, I was in company with two men, striking instances of what I am talking of; Lord St Ives, whose father we all know to have been a country curate, without bread to eat; I was to give place to Lord St Ives, and a certain Admiral Baldwin, the most deplorable-looking personage you can imagine; his face the colour of mahogany, rough and rugged to the last degree; all lines and wrinkles, nine grey hairs of a side, and nothing but a dab of powder at top. 'In the name of heaven, who is that old fellow?' said I to a friend of mine who was standing near, (Sir Basil Morley). 'Old fellow!' cried Sir Basil, 'it is Admiral Baldwin. What do you take his age to be?' 'Sixty,' said I, 'or perhaps sixty-two.' 'Forty,' replied Sir Basil, 'forty, and no more.' Picture to yourselves my amazement; I shall not easily forget Admiral Baldwin. I never saw quite so wretched an example of what a sea-faring life can do; but to a degree, I know it is the same with them all: they are all knocked about, and exposed to every climate, and every weather, till they are not fit to be seen. It is a pity they are not knocked on the head at once, before they reach Admiral Baldwin's age."

"Nay, Sir Walter," cried Mrs. Clay, "this is being severe indeed. Have a little mercy on the poor men. We are not all born to be handsome. The sea is no beautifier, certainly; sailors do grow old betimes; I have observed it; they soon lose the look of youth. But then, is not it the same with many other professions, perhaps most other? Soldiers, in active service, are not at all better off: and even in the quieter professions, there is a toil and a labour of the mind, if not of the body, which seldom leaves a man's looks to the natural effect of time. The lawyer plods, quite care-worn; the physician is up at all hours, and travelling in all weather; and even the clergyman—" she stopped a moment to consider what might do for the clergyman. "—and even the clergyman, you know is obliged to go into infected rooms, and expose his health and looks to all the injury of a poisonous atmosphere. In fact, as I have long been convinced, though every profession is necessary and honourable in its turn, it is only the lot of those who are not obliged to follow any, who can live in a regular way, in the country, choosing their own hours, following their own pursuits, and living on their own property, without the torment of trying for more; it is only their lot, I say, to hold the blessings of health and a good appearance to the utmost: I know no other set of men but what lose something of their personableness when they cease to be quite young."

It seemed as if Mr. Shepherd, in this anxiety to bespeak Sir Walter's goodwill towards a naval officer as tenant, had been gifted with foresight; for the very first application for the house was from an Admiral Croft, with whom he shortly afterwards fell into company in attending the quarter sessions at Taunton; and indeed, he had received a hint of the Admiral from a London correspondent. By the report which he hastened over to Kellynch to make, Admiral Croft was a native of Somersetshire, who having acquired a very handsome fortune, was wishing to settle in his own country, and had come down to Taunton in order to look at some advertised places in that immediate neighbourhood, which, however, had not suited him; that accidentally hearing—(it was just as he had foretold, Mr. Shepherd observed, Sir Walter's concerns could not be kept a secret)—accidentally hearing of the possibility of Kellynch Hall being to let, and understanding his (Mr. Shepherd's) connection with the owner, he had introduced himself to him in order to make particular inquiries, and had, in the course of a pretty long conference, expressed as strong an inclination for the place as a man who knew it only by description could feel; and given Mr. Shepherd, in his explicit account of himself, every proof of his being a most responsible, eligible tenant.

"And who is Admiral Croft?" was Sir Walter's cold suspicious inquiry.

Mr. Shepherd answered for his being of a gentleman's family, and mentioned a place; and Anne, after the little pause that followed, added, "He is a rear admiral of the white. He was in the Trafalgar action, and has been in the East Indies since; he was stationed there, I believe, several years."

"Then I take it for granted," observed Sir Walter, "that his face is about as orange as the cuffs and capes of my livery."

Mr. Shepherd hastened to assure him, that Admiral Croft was a very hale, hearty, well-looking man, a little weather-beaten, to be sure, but not much, and quite the gentleman in all his notions and behaviour; not likely to make the smallest difficulty about terms, only wanted a comfortable home, and to get into it as soon as possible; knew he must pay for his convenience; knew what rent a ready-furnished house of that consequence might fetch; should not have been surprised if Sir Walter had asked more; had inquired about the manor; would be glad of the deputation, certainly, but made no great point of it; said he sometimes took out a gun, but never killed; quite the gentleman.

Mr. Shepherd was eloquent on the subject, pointing out all the circumstances of the Admiral's family, which made him peculiarly desirable as a tenant. He was a married man, and without children, the very state to be wished for. A house was never taken good care of, Mr. Shepherd observed, without a lady: he did not know, whether furniture might not be in danger of suffering as much where there was no lady, as where there were many children. A lady, without a family, was the very best preserver of furniture in the world. He had seen Mrs. Croft, too; she was at Taunton with the admiral, and had been present almost all the time they were talking the matter over.

"And a very well-spoken, genteel, shrewd lady, she seemed to be," continued he; "asked more questions about the house, and terms, and taxes, than the Admiral himself, and seemed more conversant with business; and moreover, Sir Walter, I found she was not quite unconnected in this country, any more than her husband; that is to say, she is sister to a gentleman who did live amongst us once; she told me so herself: sister to the gentleman who lived a few years back at Monkford. Bless me! What was his name? At this moment I cannot recollect his name, though I have heard it so lately. Penelope, my dear, can you help me to the name of the gentleman who lived at Monkford: Mrs. Croft's brother?"

But Mrs. Clay was talking so eagerly with Miss Elliot, that she did not hear the appeal.

"I have no conception whom you can mean, Shepherd; I remember no gentleman resident at Monkford since the time of old Governor Trent."

"Bless me! How very odd! I shall forget my own name soon, I suppose. A name that I am so very well acquainted with; knew the gentleman so well by sight; seen him a hundred times; came to consult me once, I remember, about a trespass of one of his neighbours; farmer's man breaking into his orchard; wall torn down; apples stolen; caught in the fact; and afterwards, contrary to my judgement, submitted to an amicable compromise. Very odd indeed!"

After waiting another moment, "You mean Mr. Wentworth, I suppose?" said Anne.

Mr. Shepherd was all gratitude.

"Wentworth was the very name! Mr. Wentworth was the very man. He had the curacy of Monkford, you know, Sir Walter, some time back, for two or three years. Came there about the year —-5, I take it. You remember him, I am sure."

"Wentworth? Oh! Ay, Mr. Wentworth, the curate of Monkford. You misled me by the term gentleman. I thought you were speaking of some man of property: Mr. Wentworth was nobody, I remember; quite unconnected, nothing to do with the Strafford family. One wonders how the names of many of our nobility become so common."

As Mr. Shepherd perceived that this connexion of the Crofts did them no service with Sir Walter, he mentioned it no more; returning, with all his zeal, to dwell on the circumstances more indisputably in their favour; their age, and number, and fortune; the high idea they had formed of Kellynch Hall, and extreme solicitude for the advantage of renting it; making it appear as if they ranked nothing beyond the happiness of being the tenants of Sir Walter Elliot: an extraordinary taste, certainly, could they have been supposed in the secret of Sir Walter's estimate of the dues of a tenant.

It succeeded, however; and though Sir Walter must ever look with an evil eye on anyone intending to inhabit that house, and think them infinitely too well off in being permitted to rent it on the highest terms, he was talked into allowing Mr. Shepherd to proceed in the treaty, and authorising him to wait on Admiral Croft, who still remained at Taunton, and fix a day for the house being seen.

Sir Walter was not very wise; but still he had experience enough of the world to feel, that a more unobjectionable tenant, in all essentials, than Admiral Croft bid fair to be, could hardly offer. So far went his understanding; and his vanity supplied a little additional soothing, in the Admiral's situation in life, which was just high enough, and not too high. "I have let my house to Admiral Croft," would sound extremely well; much better than to any mere Mr.—; a Mr. (save, perhaps, some half dozen in the nation,) always needs a note of explanation. An admiral speaks his own consequence, and, at the same time, can never make a baronet look small. In all their dealings and intercourse, Sir Walter Elliot must ever have the precedence.

Nothing could be done without a reference to Elizabeth: but her inclination was growing so strong for a removal, that she was happy to have it fixed and expedited by a tenant at hand; and not a word to suspend decision was uttered by her.

Mr. Shepherd was completely empowered to act; and no sooner had such an end been reached, than Anne, who had been a most attentive listener to the whole, left the room, to seek the comfort of cool air for her flushed cheeks; and as she walked along a favourite grove, said, with a gentle sigh, "A few months more, and he, perhaps, may be walking here."

CHAPTER 4

He was not Mr. Wentworth, the former curate of Monkford, however suspicious appearances may be, but a Captain Frederick Wentworth, his brother, who being made commander in consequence of the action off St Domingo, and not immediately employed, had come into Somersetshire, in the summer of 1806; and having no parent living, found a home for half a year at Monkford. He was, at that time, a remarkably fine young man, with a great deal of intelligence, spirit, and brilliancy; and Anne an extremely pretty girl, with gentleness, modesty, taste, and feeling. Half the sum of attraction, on either side, might have been enough, for he had nothing to do, and she had hardly anybody to love; but the encounter of such lavish recommendations could not fail. They were gradually acquainted, and when acquainted, rapidly and deeply in love. It would be difficult to say which had seen highest perfection in the other, or which had been the happiest: she, in receiving his declarations and proposals, or he in having them accepted.

A short period of exquisite felicity followed, and but a short one. Troubles soon arose. Sir Walter, on being applied to, without actually withholding his consent, or saying it should never be, gave it all the negative of great astonishment, great coldness, great silence, and a professed resolution of doing nothing for his daughter. He thought it a very degrading alliance; and Lady Russell, though with more tempered and pardonable pride, received it as a most unfortunate one.

Anne Elliot, with all her claims of birth, beauty, and mind, to throw herself away at nineteen; involve herself at nineteen in an engagement with a young man, who had nothing but himself to recommend him, and no hopes of attaining affluence, but in the chances of a most uncertain profession, and no connexions to secure even his farther rise in the profession, would be, indeed, a throwing away, which she grieved to think of! Anne Elliot, so young; known to so few, to be snatched off by a stranger without alliance or fortune; or rather sunk by him into a state of most wearing, anxious, youth-killing dependence! It must not be, if by any fair interference of friendship, any representations from one who had almost a mother's love, and mother's rights, it would be prevented.

Captain Wentworth had no fortune. He had been lucky in his profession; but spending freely, what had come freely, had realized nothing. But he was confident that he should soon be rich: full of life and ardour, he knew that he should soon have a ship, and soon be on a station that would lead to everything he wanted. He had always been lucky; he knew he should be so still. Such confidence, powerful in its own warmth, and bewitching in the wit that often expressed it, must have been enough for Anne; but Lady Russell saw it very differently. His sanguine temper, and fearlessness of mind, operated very differently on her. She saw in it but an aggravation of the evil. It only added a dangerous character to himself. He was brilliant; he was headstrong. Lady Russell had little taste for wit, and of anything approaching to imprudence a horror. She deprecated the connexion in every light.

Such opposition, as these feelings produced, was more than Anne could combat. Young and gentle as she was, it might yet have been possible to withstand her father's ill-will, though unsoftened by one kind word or look on the part of her sister; but Lady Russell, whom she had always loved and relied on, could not, with such steadiness of opinion, and such tenderness of manner, be continually advising her in vain. She was persuaded to believe the engagement a wrong thing: indiscreet, improper, hardly capable of success, and not deserving it. But it was not a merely selfish caution, under which she acted, in putting an end to it. Had she not imagined herself consulting his good, even more than her own, she could hardly have given him up. The belief of being prudent, and self-denying, principally for his advantage, was her chief consolation, under the misery of a parting, a final parting; and every consolation was required, for she had to encounter all the additional pain of opinions, on his side, totally unconvinced and unbending, and of his feeling himself ill used by so forced a relinquishment. He had left the country in consequence.

A few months had seen the beginning and the end of their acquaintance; but not with a few months ended Anne's share of suffering from it. Her attachment and regrets had, for a long time, clouded every enjoyment of youth, and an early loss of bloom and spirits had been their lasting effect.

More than seven years were gone since this little history of sorrowful interest had reached its close; and time had softened down much, perhaps nearly all of peculiar attachment to him, but she had been too dependent on time alone; no aid had been given in change of place (except in one visit to Bath soon after the rupture), or in any novelty or enlargement of society. No one had ever come within the Kellynch circle that could bear a comparison with Frederick Wentworth, as he stood in her memory. No second attachment, the only thoroughly natural, happy, and sufficient cure, at her time of life, had been possible to the nice tone of her mind, the fastidiousness of her taste, in the small limits of the society around them. She had been solicited, when about two-and-twenty, to change her name, by the young man, who not long afterwards found a more willing mind in her younger sister; and Lady Russell had lamented her refusal; for Charles Musgrove was the eldest son of a man, whose landed property and general importance were second in that country, only to Sir Walter's, and of good character and appearance; and however Lady Russell might have asked yet for something more, while Anne was nineteen, she would have rejoiced to see her at twenty-two so respectably removed from the partialities and injustice of her father's house, and settled so permanently near herself. But in this case, Anne had left nothing for advice to do; and though Lady Russell, as satisfied as ever with her own discretion, never wished the past undone, she began now to have the anxiety which borders on hopelessness for Anne's being tempted, by some man of talents and independence, to enter a state for which she held her to be peculiarly fitted by her warm affections and domestic habits.

They knew not each other's opinion, either its constancy or its change, on the one leading point of Anne's conduct, for the subject was never alluded to; but Anne, at seven-and-twenty, thought very differently from what she had been made to think at nineteen. She did not blame Lady Russell, she did not blame herself for having been guided by her; but she felt that were any young person, in similar circumstances, to apply to her for counsel, they would never receive any of such certain immediate wretchedness, such uncertain future good. She was persuaded that under every disadvantage of disapprobation at home, and every anxiety attending his profession, all their probable fears, delays, and disappointments, she should yet have been a happier woman in maintaining the engagement, than she had been in the sacrifice of it; and this, she fully believed, had the usual share, had even more than the usual share of all such solicitudes and suspense been theirs, without reference to the actual results of their case, which, as it happened, would have bestowed earlier prosperity than could be reasonably calculated on. All his sanguine expectations, all his confidence had been justified. His genius and ardour had seemed to foresee and to command his prosperous path. He had, very soon after their engagement ceased, got employ: and all that he had told her would follow, had taken place. He had distinguished himself, and early gained the other step in rank, and must now, by successive captures, have made a handsome fortune. She had only navy lists and newspapers for her authority, but she could not doubt his being rich; and, in favour of his constancy, she had no reason to believe him married.

How eloquent could Anne Elliot have been! How eloquent, at least, were her wishes on the side of early warm attachment, and a cheerful confidence in futurity, against that over-anxious caution which seems to insult exertion and distrust Providence! She had been forced into prudence in her youth, she learned romance as she grew older: the natural sequel of an unnatural beginning.

With all these circumstances, recollections and feelings, she could not hear that Captain Wentworth's sister was likely to live at Kellynch without a revival of former pain; and many a stroll, and many a sigh, was necessary to dispel the agitation of the idea. She often told herself it was folly, before she could harden her nerves sufficiently to feel the continual discussion of the Crofts and their business no evil. She was assisted, however, by that perfect indifference and apparent unconsciousness, among the only three of her own friends in the secret of the past, which seemed almost to deny any recollection of it. She could do justice to the superiority of Lady Russell's motives in this, over those of her father and Elizabeth; she could honour all the better feelings of her calmness; but the general air of oblivion among them was highly important from whatever it sprung; and in the event of Admiral Croft's really taking Kellynch Hall, she rejoiced anew over the conviction which had always been most grateful to her, of the past being known to those three only among her connexions, by whom no syllable, she believed, would ever be whispered, and in the trust that among his, the brother only with whom he had been residing, had received any information of their short-lived engagement. That brother had been long removed from the country and being a sensible man—

and, moreover, a single man at the time—she had a fond dependence on no human creature's having heard of it from him.

The sister, Mrs. Croft, had then been out of England, accompanying her husband on a foreign station, and her own sister, Mary, had been at school while it all occurred; and never admitted by the pride of some, and the delicacy of others, to the smallest knowledge of it afterwards.

With these supports, she hoped that the acquaintance between herself and the Crofts, which, with Lady Russell still resident in Kellynch and Mary fixed only three miles off, must be anticipated, need not involve any particular awkwardness.

CHAPTER 5

On the morning appointed for Admiral and Mrs. Croft's seeing Kellynch Hall, Anne found it most natural to take her almost daily walk to Lady Russell's, and keep out of the way till all was over; when she found it most natural to be sorry that she had missed the opportunity of seeing them.

This meeting of the two parties proved highly satisfactory, and decided the whole business at once. Each lady was previously well disposed for an agreement, and saw nothing, therefore, but good manners in the other; and with regard to the gentlemen, there was such an hearty good humour, such an open, trusting liberality on the Admiral's side, as could not but influence Sir Walter, who had besides been flattered into his very best and most polished behaviour by Mr. Shepherd's assurances of his being known, by report, to the Admiral, as a model of good breeding.

The house and grounds, and furniture, were approved, the Crofts were approved, terms, time, every thing, and every body, was right; and Mr. Shepherd's clerks were set to work, without there having been a single preliminary difference to modify of all that "This indenture showeth."

Sir Walter, without hesitation, declared the Admiral to be the best-looking sailor he had ever met with, and went so far as to say, that if his own man might have had the arranging of his hair, he should not be ashamed of being seen with him anywhere; and the Admiral, with sympathetic cordiality, observed to his wife as they drove back through the park, "I thought we should soon come to a deal, my dear, in spite of what they told us at Taunton. The Baronet will never set the Thames on fire, but there seems to be no harm in him." Reciprocal compliments, which would have been esteemed about equal.

The Crofts were to have possession at Michaelmas; and as Sir Walter proposed removing to Bath in the course of the preceding month, there was no time to be lost in making every dependent arrangement.

Lady Russell, convinced that Anne would not be allowed to be of any use, or any importance, in the choice of the house which they were going to secure, was very unwilling to have her hurried away so soon, and wanted to make it possible for her to stay behind till she might convey her to Bath herself after Christmas; but having engagements of her own which must take her from Kellynch for several weeks, she was unable to give the full invitation she wished, and Anne though dreading the possible heats of September in all the white glare of Bath, and grieving to forego all the influence so sweet and so sad of the autumnal months in the country, did not think that, everything considered, she wished to remain. It would be most right, and most wise, and, therefore must involve least suffering to go with the others.

Something occurred, however, to give her a different duty. Mary, often a little unwell, and always thinking a great deal of her own complaints, and always in the habit of claiming Anne when anything was the matter, was indisposed; and foreseeing that she should not have a day's health all the autumn, entreated, or rather required her, for it was hardly entreaty, to come to Uppercross Cottage, and bear her company as long as she should want her, instead of going to Bath. "I cannot possibly do without Anne," was Mary's reasoning; and Elizabeth's reply was, "Then I am sure Anne had better stay, for nobody will want her in Bath."

To be claimed as a good, though in an improper style, is at least better than being rejected as no good at all; and Anne, glad to be thought of some use, glad to have anything marked out as a duty, and certainly not sorry to have the scene of it in the country, and her own dear country, readily agreed to stay.

This invitation of Mary's removed all Lady Russell's difficulties, and it was consequently soon settled that Anne should not go to Bath till Lady Russell took her, and that all the intervening time should be divided between Uppercross Cottage and Kellynch Lodge.

So far all was perfectly right; but Lady Russell was almost startled by the wrong of one part of the Kellynch Hall plan, when it burst on her, which was, Mrs. Clay's being engaged to go to Bath with Sir Walter and Elizabeth, as a most important and valuable assistant to the latter in all the business before her.

Lady Russell was extremely sorry that such a measure should have been resorted to at all, wondered, grieved, and feared; and the affront it contained to Anne, in Mrs. Clay's being of so much use, while Anne could be of none, was a very sore aggravation.

Anne herself was become hardened to such affronts; but she felt the imprudence of the arrangement quite as keenly as Lady Russell. With a great deal of quiet observation, and a knowledge, which she often wished less, of her father's character, she was sensible that results the most serious to his family from the intimacy were more than possible. She did not imagine that her father had at present an idea of the kind. Mrs. Clay had freckles, and a projecting tooth, and a clumsy wrist, which he was continually making severe remarks upon, in her absence; but she was young, and certainly altogether well-looking, and possessed, in an acute mind and assiduous pleasing manners, infinitely more dangerous attractions than any merely personal might have been. Anne was so impressed by the degree of their danger, that she could not excuse herself from trying to make it perceptible to her sister. She had little hope of success; but Elizabeth, who in the event of such a reverse would be so much more to be pitied than herself, should never, she thought, have reason to reproach her for giving no warning.

She spoke, and seemed only to offend. Elizabeth could not conceive how such an absurd suspicion should occur to her, and indignantly answered for each party's perfectly knowing their situation.

"Mrs. Clay," said she, warmly, "never forgets who she is; and as I am rather better acquainted with her sentiments than you can be, I can assure you, that upon the subject of marriage they are particularly nice, and that she reprobates all inequality of condition and rank more strongly than most people. And as to my father, I really should not have thought that he, who has kept himself single so long for our sakes, need be suspected now. If Mrs. Clay were a very beautiful woman, I grant you, it might be wrong to have her so much with me; not that anything in the world, I am sure, would induce my father to make a degrading match, but he might be rendered unhappy. But poor Mrs. Clay who, with all her merits, can never have been reckoned tolerably pretty, I really think poor Mrs. Clay may be staying here in perfect safety. One would imagine you had never heard my father speak of her personal misfortunes, though I know you must fifty times. That tooth of hers and those freckles. Freckles do not disgust me so very much as they do him. I have known a face not materially disfigured by a few, but he abominates them. You must have heard him notice Mrs. Clay's freckles."

"There is hardly any personal defect," replied Anne, "which an agreeable manner might not gradually reconcile one to."

"I think very differently," answered Elizabeth, shortly; "an agreeable manner may set off handsome features, but can never alter plain ones. However, at any rate, as I have a great deal more at stake on this point than anybody else can have, I think it rather unnecessary in you to be advising me."

Anne had done; glad that it was over, and not absolutely hopeless of doing good.

Elizabeth, though resenting the suspicion, might yet be made observant by it.

The last office of the four carriage-horses was to draw Sir Walter, Miss Elliot, and Mrs. Clay to Bath. The party drove off in very good spirits; Sir Walter prepared with condescending bows for all the afflicted tenantry and cottagers who might have had a hint to show themselves, and Anne walked up at the same time, in a sort of desolate tranquillity, to the Lodge, where she was to spend the first week.

Her friend was not in better spirits than herself. Lady Russell felt this break-up of the family exceedingly. Their respectability was as dear to her as her own, and a daily intercourse had become precious by habit. It was painful to look upon their deserted grounds, and still worse to anticipate the new hands they were to fall into; and to escape the solitariness and the melancholy of so altered a village, and be out of the way when Admiral and Mrs. Croft first arrived, she had determined to make her own absence from home begin when she must give up Anne. Accordingly their removal was made together, and Anne was set down at Uppercross Cottage, in the first stage of Lady Russell's journey.

Uppercross was a moderate-sized village, which a few years back had been completely in the old English style, containing only two houses superior in appearance to those of the yeomen and labourers; the mansion of the squire, with its high walls, great gates, and old trees, substantial and unmodernized, and the compact, tight parsonage, enclosed in its own neat garden, with a vine and a pear-tree trained round its casements; but upon the marriage of the young 'squire, it had received the improvement of a farm-house elevated into a cottage, for his residence, and Uppercross Cottage, with its veranda, French windows, and other prettiness, was quite as likely to catch the traveller's eye as the more consistent and considerable aspect and premises of the Great House, about a quarter of a mile farther on.

Here Anne had often been staying. She knew the ways of Uppercross as well as those of Kellynch. The two families were so continually meeting, so much in the habit of running in and out of each other's house at all hours, that it was rather a surprise to her to find Mary alone; but being alone, her being unwell and out of spirits was almost a matter of course. Though better endowed than the elder sister, Mary had not Anne's understanding nor temper. While well, and happy, and properly attended to, she had great good humour and excellent spirits; but any indisposition sunk her completely. She had no resources for solitude; and inheriting a considerable share of the Elliot self-importance, was very prone to add to every other distress that of fancying herself neglected and ill-used. In person, she was inferior to both sisters, and had, even in her bloom, only reached the dignity of being "a fine girl." She was now lying on the faded sofa of the pretty little drawing-room, the once elegant furniture of which had been gradually growing shabby, under the influence of four summers and two children; and, on Anne's appearing, greeted her with—

"So, you are come at last! I began to think I should never see you. I am so ill I can hardly speak. I have not seen a creature the whole morning!"

"I am sorry to find you unwell," replied Anne. "You sent me such a good account of yourself on Thursday!"

"Yes, I made the best of it; I always do: but I was very far from well at the time; and I do not think I ever was so ill in my life as I have been all this morning: very unfit to be left alone, I am sure. Suppose I were to be seized of a sudden in some dreadful way, and not able to ring the bell! So, Lady Russell would not get out. I do not think she has been in this house three times this summer."

Anne said what was proper, and enquired after her husband. "Oh! Charles is out shooting. I have not seen him since seven o'clock. He would go, though I told him how ill I was. He said he should not stay out long; but he has never come back, and now it is almost one. I assure you, I have not seen a soul this whole long morning."

"You have had your little boys with you?"

"Yes, as long as I could bear their noise; but they are so unmanageable that they do me more harm than good. Little Charles does not mind a word I say, and Walter is growing quite as bad."

"Well, you will soon be better now," replied Anne, cheerfully. "You know I always cure you when I come. How are your neighbours at the Great House?"

"I can give you no account of them. I have not seen one of them today, except Mr. Musgrove, who just stopped and spoke through the window, but without getting off his horse; and though I told him how ill I was, not one of them have been near me. It did not happen to suit the Miss Musgroves, I suppose, and they never put themselves out of their way."

"You will see them yet, perhaps, before the morning is gone. It is early."

"I never want them, I assure you. They talk and laugh a great deal too much for me. Oh! Anne, I am so very unwell! It was quite unkind of you not to come on Thursday."

"My dear Mary, recollect what a comfortable account you sent me of yourself! You wrote in the cheerfullest manner, and said you were perfectly well, and in no hurry for me; and that being the case, you must be aware that my wish would be to remain with Lady Russell to the last: and besides what I felt on her account, I have really been so busy, have had so much to do, that I could not very conveniently have left Kellynch sooner."

"Dear me! What can you possibly have to do?"

"A great many things, I assure you. More than I can recollect in a moment; but I can tell you some. I have been making a duplicate of the catalogue of my father's books and pictures. I have been several times in the garden with Mackenzie, trying to understand, and make him understand, which of Elizabeth's plants are for Lady Russell. I have had all my own little concerns to arrange, books and music to divide, and all my trunks to repack, from not having understood in time what was intended as to the waggons: and one thing I have had to do, Mary, of a more trying nature: going to almost every house in the parish, as a sort of take-leave. I was told that they wished it. But all these things took up a great deal of time."

"Oh! Well!" and after a moment's pause, "but you have never asked me one word about our dinner at the Pooles yesterday."

"Did you go then? I have made no enquiries, because I concluded you must have been obliged to give up the party."

"Oh yes! I went. I was very well yesterday. Nothing at all the matter with me till this morning. It would have been strange if I had not gone."

"I am very glad you were well enough, and I hope you had a pleasant party."

"Nothing remarkable. One always knows beforehand what the dinner will be, and who will be there; and it is so very uncomfortable not having a carriage of one's own. Mr. and Mrs. Musgrove took me, and we were so crowded! They are both so very large, and take up so much room; and Mr. Musgrove always sits forward. So, there was I, crowded into the back seat with Henrietta and Louise; and I think it very likely that my illness today may be owing to it."

A little further perseverance in patience and forced cheerfulness on Anne's side produced nearly a cure on Mary's. She could soon sit upright on the sofa, and began to hope she might be able to leave it by dinnertime. Then, forgetting to think of it, she was at the other end of the room, beautifying a nosegay; then, she ate her cold meat; and then she was well enough to propose a little walk.

"Where shall we go?" said she, when they were ready. "I suppose you will not like to call at the Great House before they have been to see you?"

"I have not the smallest objection on that account," replied Anne. "I should never think of standing on such ceremony with people I know so well as Mrs. and the Miss Musgroves."

"Oh! But they ought to call upon you as soon as possible. They ought to feel what is due to you as my sister. However, we may as well go and sit with them a little while, and when we have that over, we can enjoy our walk."

Anne had always thought such a style of intercourse highly imprudent; but she had ceased to endeavour to check it, from believing that, though there were on each side continual subjects of offence, neither family could now do without it.

To the Great House accordingly they went, to sit the full half hour in the old-fashioned square parlour, with a small carpet and shining floor, to which the present daughters of the house were gradually giving the proper air of confusion by a grand pianoforte and a harp, flower-stands and little tables placed in every direction. Oh! Could the originals of the portraits against the wainscot, could the gentlemen in brown velvet and the ladies in blue satin have seen what was going on, have been conscious of such an overthrow of all order and neatness! The portraits themselves seemed to be staring in astonishment.

The Musgroves, like their houses, were in a state of alteration, perhaps of improvement. The father and mother were in the old English style, and the young people in the new. Mr. and Mrs. Musgrove were a very good sort of people; friendly and hospitable, not much educated, and not at all elegant. Their children had more modern minds and manners. There was a numerous family; but the only two grown up, excepting Charles, were Henrietta and Louisa, young ladies of nineteen and twenty, who had brought from school at Exeter all the usual stock of accomplishments, and were now like thousands of other young ladies, living to be fashionable, happy, and merry. Their dress had every advantage, their faces were rather pretty, their spirits extremely good, their manner unembarrassed and pleasant; they were of consequence at home, and favourites abroad. Anne always contemplated them as some of the happiest creatures of her acquaintance; but still, saved as we all are, by some comfortable feeling of superiority from wishing for the possibility of exchange, she would not have given up her own more elegant and cultivated mind for all their enjoyments; and envied them nothing but that seemingly perfect good understanding and agreement together, that goodhumoured mutual affection, of which she had known so little herself with either of her sisters.

They were received with great cordiality. Nothing seemed amiss on the side of the Great House family, which was generally, as Anne very well knew, the least to blame. The half hour was chatted away pleasantly enough; and she was not at all surprised at the end of it, to have their walking party joined by both the Miss Musgroves, at Mary's particular invitation.

CHAPTER 6

Anne had not wanted this visit to Uppercross, to learn that a removal from one set of people to another, though at a distance of only three miles, will often include a total change of conversation, opinion, and idea. She had never been staying there before, without being struck by it, or without wishing that other Elliots could have her advantage in seeing how unknown, or unconsidered there, were the affairs which at Kellynch Hall were treated as of such general publicity and pervading interest; yet, with all this experience, she believed she must now submit to feel that another lesson, in the art of knowing our own nothingness beyond our own circle, was become necessary for her; for certainly, coming as she did, with a heart full of the subject which had been completely occupying both houses in Kellynch for many weeks, she had expected rather more curiosity and sympathy than she found in the separate but very similar remark of Mr. and Mrs. Musgrove: "So, Miss Anne, Sir Walter and your sister are gone; and what part of Bath do you think they will settle in?" and this, without much waiting for an answer; or in the young ladies' addition of, "I hope we shall be in Bath in the winter; but remember, papa, if we do go, we must be in a good situation: none of your Queen Squares for us!" or in the anxious supplement from Mary, of "Upon my word, I shall be pretty well off, when you are all gone away to be happy at Bath!"

She could only resolve to avoid such self-delusion in future, and think with heightened gratitude of the extraordinary blessing of having one such truly sympathising friend as Lady Russell.

The Mr. Musgroves had their own game to guard, and to destroy, their own horses, dogs, and newspapers to engage them, and the females were fully occupied in all the other common subjects of housekeeping, neighbours, dress, dancing, and music. She acknowledged it to be very fitting, that every little social commonwealth should dictate its own matters of discourse; and hoped, ere long, to become a not unworthy member of the one she was now transplanted into. With the prospect of spending at least two months at Uppercross, it was highly incumbent on her to clothe her imagination, her memory, and all her ideas in as much of Uppercross as possible.

She had no dread of these two months. Mary was not so repulsive and unsisterly as Elizabeth, nor so inaccessible to all influence of hers; neither was there anything among the other component parts of the cottage inimical to comfort. She was always on friendly terms with her brother-in-law; and in the children, who loved her nearly as well, and respected her a great deal more than their mother, she had an object of interest, amusement, and wholesome exertion.

Charles Musgrove was civil and agreeable; in sense and temper he was undoubtedly superior to his wife, but not of powers, or conversation, or grace, to make the past, as they were connected together, at all a dangerous contemplation; though, at the same time, Anne could believe, with Lady Russell, that a more equal match might have greatly improved him; and that a woman of real understanding might have given more consequence to his character, and more usefulness, rationality, and elegance to his habits and pursuits. As it was, he did nothing with much zeal, but sport; and his time was otherwise trifled away, without benefit from books or anything else. He had very good spirits, which never seemed much affected by his wife's occasional lowness, bore with her unreasonableness sometimes to Anne's admiration, and upon the whole, though there was very often a little disagreement (in which she had sometimes more share than she wished, being appealed to by both parties), they might pass for a happy couple. They were always perfectly agreed in the want of more money, and a strong inclination for a handsome present from his father; but here, as on most topics, he had the superiority, for while Mary thought it a great shame that such a present was not made, he always contended for his father's having many other uses for his money, and a right to spend it as he liked.

As to the management of their children, his theory was much better than his wife's, and his practice not so bad. "I could manage them very well, if it were not for Mary's interference," was what Anne often heard him say, and had a good deal of faith in; but when listening in turn to Mary's reproach of "Charles spoils the children so that I cannot get them into any order," she never had the smallest temptation to say, "Very true."

One of the least agreeable circumstances of her residence there was her being treated with too much confidence by all parties, and being too much in the secret of the complaints of each house. Known to have some influence with her sister, she was continually requested, or at least receiving hints to exert it, beyond what was practicable. "I wish you could persuade Mary not to be always fancying herself ill," was Charles's language; and, in an unhappy mood, thus spoke Mary: "I do believe if Charles were to see me dying, he would not think there was anything the matter with me. I am sure, Anne, if you would, you might persuade him that I really am very ill—a great deal worse than I ever own."

Mary's declaration was, "I hate sending the children to the Great House, though their grandmamma is always wanting to see them, for she humours and indulges them to such a degree, and gives them so much trash and sweet things, that they are sure to come back sick and cross for the rest of the day." And Mrs. Musgrove took the first opportunity of being alone with Anne, to say, "Oh! Miss Anne, I cannot help wishing Mrs. Charles had a little of your method with those children. They are quite different creatures with you! But to be sure, in general they are so spoilt! It is a pity you cannot put your sister in the way of managing them. They are as fine healthy children as ever were seen, poor little dears! Without partiality; but Mrs. Charles knows no more how they should be treated! Bless me! How troublesome they are sometimes. I assure you, Miss Anne, it prevents my wishing to see them at our house so often as I otherwise should. I believe Mrs. Charles is not quite pleased with my not inviting them oftener; but you know it is very bad to have children with one that one is obligated to be checking every moment; 'don't do this,' and 'don't do that;' or that one can only keep in tolerable order by more cake than is good for them."

She had this communication, moreover, from Mary. "Mrs. Musgrove thinks all her servants so steady, that it would be high treason to call it in question; but I am sure, without exaggeration, that her upper housemaid and laundrymaid, instead of being in their business, are gadding about the village, all day long. I meet them wherever I go; and I declare, I never go twice into my nursery without seeing something of them. If Jemima were not the trustiest, steadiest creature in the world, it would be enough to spoil her; for she tells me, they are always tempting her to take a walk with them." And on Mrs. Musgrove's side, it was, "I make a rule of never interfering in any of my daughter-in-law's concerns, for I know it would not do; but I shall tell you, Miss Anne, because you may be able to set things to rights, that I have no very good opinion of Mrs. Charles's nursery-maid: I hear strange stories of her; she is always upon the gad; and from my own knowledge, I can declare, she is such a fine-dressing lady, that she is enough to ruin any servants she comes near. Mrs. Charles quite swears by her, I know; but I just give you this hint, that you may be upon the watch; because, if you see anything amiss, you need not be afraid of mentioning it."

Again, it was Mary's complaint, that Mrs. Musgrove was very apt not to give her the precedence that was her due, when they dined at the Great House with other families; and she did not see any reason why she was to be considered so much at home as to lose her place. And one day when Anne was walking with only the Musgroves, one of them after talking of rank, people of rank, and jealousy of rank, said, "I have no scruple of observing to you, how nonsensical some persons are about their place, because all the world knows how easy and indifferent you are about it; but I wish anybody could give Mary a hint that it would be a great deal better if she were not so very tenacious, especially if she would not be always putting herself forward to take place of mamma. Nobody doubts her right to have precedence of mamma, but it would be more becoming in her not to be always insisting on it. It is not that mamma cares about it the least in the world, but I know it is taken notice of by many persons."

How was Anne to set all these matters to rights? She could do little more than listen patiently, soften every grievance, and excuse each to the other; give them all hints of the forbearance necessary between such near neighbours, and make those hints broadest which were meant for her sister's benefit.

In all other respects, her visit began and proceeded very well. Her own spirits improved by change of place and subject, by being removed three miles from Kellynch; Mary's ailments lessened by having a constant companion, and their daily intercourse with the other family, since there was neither superior affection, confidence, nor employment in the cottage, to be interrupted by it, was rather an advantage. It was certainly carried nearly as far as possible, for they met every morning, and hardly ever spent an evening asunder; but she believed they should not have done so well without the sight of Mr. and Mrs. Musgrove's respectable forms in the usual places, or without the talking, laughing, and singing of their daughters.

She played a great deal better than either of the Miss Musgroves, but having no voice, no knowledge of the harp, and no fond parents, to sit by and fancy themselves delighted, her performance was little thought of, only out of civility, or to refresh the others, as she was well aware. She knew that when she played she was giving pleasure only to herself; but this was no new sensation. Excepting one short period of her life, she had never, since the age of fourteen, never since the loss of her dear mother, known the happiness of being listened to, or encouraged by any just appreciation or real taste. In music she had been always used to feel alone in the world; and Mr. and Mrs. Musgrove's fond partiality for their own daughters' performance, and total indifference to any other person's, gave her much more pleasure for their sakes, than mortification for her own.

The party at the Great House was sometimes increased by other company. The neighbourhood was not large, but the Musgroves were visited by everybody, and had more dinner-parties, and more callers, more visitors by invitation and by chance, than any other family. There were more completely popular.

The girls were wild for dancing; and the evenings ended, occasionally, in an unpremeditated little ball. There was a family of cousins within a walk of Uppercross, in less affluent circumstances, who depended on the Musgroves for all their pleasures: they would come at any time, and help play at anything, or dance anywhere; and Anne, very much preferring the office of musician to a more active post, played country dances to them by the hour together; a kindness which always recommended her musical powers to the notice of Mr. and Mrs. Musgrove more than anything else, and often drew this compliment: "Well done, Miss Anne! Very well done indeed! Lord bless me! How those little fingers of yours fly about!"

So passed the first three weeks. Michaelmas came; and now Anne's heart must be in Kellynch again. A beloved home made over to others; all the precious rooms and furniture, groves, and prospects, beginning to own other eyes and other limbs! She could not think of much else on the 29th of September; and she had this sympathetic touch in the evening from Mary, who, on having occasion to note down the day of the month, exclaimed, "Dear me, is not this the day the Crofts were to come to Kellynch? I am glad I did not think of it before. How low it makes me!"

The Crofts took possession with true naval alertness, and were to be visited.

Mary deplored the necessity for herself. "Nobody knew how much she should suffer. She should put it off as long as she could;" but was not easy till she had talked Charles into driving her over on an early day, and was in a very animated, comfortable state of imaginary agitation, when she came back. Anne had very sincerely rejoiced in there being no means of her going. She wished, however to see the Crofts, and was glad to be within when the visit was returned. They came: the master of the house was not at home, but the two sisters were together; and as it chanced that Mrs. Croft fell to the share of Anne, while the Admiral sat by Mary, and made himself very agreeable by his goodhumoured notice of her little boys, she was well able to watch for a likeness, and if it failed her in the features, to catch it in the voice, or in the turn of sentiment and expression.

Mrs. Croft, though neither tall nor fat, had a squareness, uprightness, and vigour of form, which gave importance to her person. She had bright dark eyes, good teeth, and altogether an agreeable face; though her reddened and weather-beaten complexion, the consequence of her having been almost as much at sea as her husband, made her seem to have lived some years longer in the world than her real eight-and-thirty. Her manners were open, easy, and decided, like one who had no distrust of herself, and no doubts of what to do; without any approach to coarseness, however, or any want of good humour. Anne gave her credit, indeed, for feelings of great consideration towards herself, in all that related to Kellynch, and it pleased her: especially, as she had satisfied herself in the very first half minute, in the instant even of introduction, that there was not the smallest symptom of any knowledge or suspicion on Mrs. Croft's side, to give a bias of any sort. She was quite easy on that head, and consequently full of strength and courage, till for a moment electrified by Mrs. Croft's suddenly saying, "It was you, and not your sister, I find, that my brother had the pleasure of being acquainted with, when he was in this country."

Anne hoped she had outlived the age of blushing; but the age of emotion she certainly had not.

"Perhaps you may not have heard that he is married?" added Mrs. Croft.

She could now answer as she ought; and was happy to feel, when

Mrs. Croft's next words explained it to be Mr. Wentworth of whom she spoke, that she had said nothing which might not do for either brother. She immediately felt how reasonable it was, that Mrs. Croft should be thinking and speaking of Edward, and not of Frederick; and with shame at her own forgetfulness applied herself to the knowledge of their former neighbour's present state with proper interest.

The rest was all tranquillity; till, just as they were moving, she heard the Admiral say to Mary, "We are expecting a brother of Mrs. Croft's here soon; I dare say you know him by name."

He was cut short by the eager attacks of the little boys, clinging to him like an old friend, and declaring he should not go; and being too much engrossed by proposals of carrying them away in his coat pockets, &c., to have another moment for finishing or recollecting what he had begun, Anne was left to persuade herself, as well as she could, that the same brother must still be in question.

She could not, however, reach such a degree of certainty, as not to be anxious to hear whether anything had been said on the subject at the other house, where the Crofts had previously been calling.

The folks of the Great House were to spend the evening of this day at the Cottage; and it being now too late in the year for such visits to be made on foot, the coach was beginning to be listened for, when the youngest Miss Musgrove walked in. That she was coming to apologize, and that they should have to spend the evening by themselves, was the first black idea; and Mary was quite ready to be affronted, when Louisa made all right by saying, that she only came on foot, to leave more room for the harp, which was bringing in the carriage.

"And I will tell you our reason," she added, "and all about it. I am come on to give you notice, that papa and mamma are out of spirits this evening, especially mamma; she is thinking so much of poor Richard! And we agreed it would be best to have the harp, for it seems to amuse her more than the piano-forte. I will tell you why she is out of spirits. When the Crofts called this morning, (they called here afterwards, did not they?), they happened to say, that her brother, Captain Wentworth, is just returned to England, or paid off, or something, and is coming to see them almost directly; and most unluckily it came into mamma's head, when they were gone, that Wentworth, or something very like it, was the name of poor Richard's captain at one time; I do not know when or where, but a great while before he died, poor fellow! And upon looking over his letters and things, she found it was so, and is perfectly sure that this must be the very man, and her head is quite full of it, and of poor Richard! So we must be as merry as we can, that she may not be dwelling upon such gloomy things."

The real circumstances of this pathetic piece of family history were, that the Musgroves had had the ill fortune of a very troublesome, hopeless son; and the good fortune to lose him before he reached his twentieth year; that he had been sent to sea because he was stupid and unmanageable on shore; that he had been very little cared for at any time by his family, though quite as much as he deserved; seldom heard of, and scarcely at all regretted, when the intelligence of his death abroad had worked its way to Uppercross, two years before.

He had, in fact, though his sisters were now doing all they could for him, by calling him "poor Richard," been nothing better than a thick-headed, unfeeling, unprofitable Dick Musgrove, who had never done anything to entitle himself to more than the abbreviation of his name, living or dead.

He had been several years at sea, and had, in the course of those removals to which all midshipmen are liable, and especially such midshipmen as every captain wishes to get rid of, been six months on board Captain Frederick Wentworth's frigate, the Laconia; and from the Laconia he had, under the influence of his captain, written the only two letters which his father and mother had ever received from him during the whole of his absence; that is to say, the only two disinterested letters; all the rest had been mere applications for money.

In each letter he had spoken well of his captain; but yet, so little were they in the habit of attending to such matters, so unobservant and incurious were they as to the names of men or ships, that it had made scarcely any impression at the time; and that Mrs. Musgrove should have been suddenly struck, this very day, with a recollection of the name of Wentworth, as connected with her son, seemed one of those extraordinary bursts of mind which do sometimes occur.

She had gone to her letters, and found it all as she supposed; and the re-perusal of these letters, after so long an interval, her poor son gone for ever, and all the strength of his faults forgotten, had affected her spirits exceedingly, and thrown her into greater grief for him than she had known on first hearing of his death. Mr. Musgrove was, in a lesser degree, affected likewise; and when they reached the cottage, they were evidently in want, first, of being listened to anew on this subject, and afterwards, of all the relief which cheerful companions could give them.

To hear them talking so much of Captain Wentworth, repeating his name so often, puzzling over past years, and at last ascertaining that it might, that it probably would, turn out to be the very same Captain Wentworth whom they recollected meeting, once or twice, after their coming back from Clifton—a very fine young man—but they could not say whether it was seven or eight years ago, was a new sort of trial to Anne's nerves. She found, however, that it was one to which she must inure herself. Since he actually was expected in the country, she must teach herself to be insensible on such points. And not only did it appear that he was expected, and speedily, but the Musgroves, in their warm gratitude for the kindness he had shown poor Dick, and very high respect for his character, stamped as it was by poor Dick's having been six months under his care, and mentioning him in strong, though not perfectly well-spelt praise, as "a fine dashing felow, only two perticular about the schoolmaster," were bent on introducing themselves, and seeking his acquaintance, as soon as they could hear of his arrival.

The resolution of doing so helped to form the comfort of their evening.

CHAPTER 7

A very few days more, and Captain Wentworth was known to be at Kellynch, and Mr. Musgrove had called on him, and come back warm in his praise, and he was engaged with the Crofts to dine at Uppercross, by the end of another week. It had been a great disappointment to Mr. Musgrove to find that no earlier day could be fixed, so impatient was he to show his gratitude, by seeing Captain Wentworth under his own roof, and welcoming him to all that was strongest and best in his cellars.

But a week must pass; only a week, in Anne's reckoning, and then, she supposed, they must meet; and soon she began to wish that she could feel secure even for a week.

Captain Wentworth made a very early return to Mr. Musgrove's civility, and she was all but calling there in the same half hour. She and Mary were actually setting forward for the Great House, where, as she afterwards learnt, they must inevitably have found him, when they were stopped by the eldest boy's being at that moment brought home in consequence of a bad fall. The child's situation put the visit entirely aside; but she could not hear of her escape with indifference, even in the midst of the serious anxiety, which they afterwards felt on his account.

His collarbone was found to be dislocated, and such injury received in the back, as roused the most alarming ideas. It was an afternoon of distress, and Anne had every thing to do at once; the apothecary to send for, the father to have pursued and informed, the mother to support and keep from hysterics, the servants to control, the youngest child to banish, and the poor suffering one to attend and soothe; besides sending, as soon as she recollected it, proper notice to the other house, which brought her an accession rather of frightened, enquiring companions, than of very useful assistants.

Her brother's return was the first comfort; he could take best care of his wife; and the second blessing was the arrival of the apothecary. Till he came and had examined the child, their apprehensions were the worse for being vague; they suspected great injury, but knew not where; but now the collar-bone was soon replaced, and though Mr. Robinson felt and felt, and rubbed, and looked grave, and spoke low words both to the father and the aunt, still they were all to hope the best, and to be able to part and eat their dinner in tolerable ease of mind; and then it was, just before they parted, that the two young aunts were able so far to digress from their nephew's state, as to give the information of Captain Wentworth's visit; staying five minutes behind their father and mother, to endeavour to express how perfectly delighted they were with him, how much handsomer, how infinitely more agreeable they thought him than any individual among their male acquaintance, who had been at all a favourite before. How glad they had been to hear papa invite him to stay dinner, how sorry when he said it was quite out of his power, and how glad again when he had promised in reply to papa and mamma's farther pressing invitations to come and dine with them on the morrow—actually on the morrow; and he had promised it in so pleasant a manner, as if he felt all the motive of their attention just as he ought. And in short, he had looked and said everything with such exquisite grace, that they could assure them all, their heads were both turned by him; and off they ran, quite as full of glee as of love, and apparently more full of Captain Wentworth than of little Charles.

The same story and the same raptures were repeated, when the two girls came with their father, through the gloom of the evening, to make enquiries; and Mr. Musgrove, no longer under the first uneasiness about his heir, could add his confirmation and praise, and hope there would be now no occasion for putting Captain Wentworth off, and only be sorry to think that the cottage party, probably, would not like to leave the little boy, to give him the meeting. "Oh no; as to leaving the little boy," both father and mother were in much too strong and recent alarm to bear the thought; and Anne, in the joy of the escape, could not help adding her warm protestations to theirs.

Charles Musgrove, indeed, afterwards, showed more of inclination; "the child was going on so well, and he wished so much to be introduced to Captain Wentworth, that, perhaps, he might join them in the evening; he would not dine from home, but he might walk in for half an hour." But in this he was eagerly opposed by his wife, with "Oh! No, indeed, Charles, I cannot bear to have you go away. Only think if anything should happen?"

The child had a good night, and was going on well the next day. It must be a work of time to ascertain that no injury had been done to the spine; but Mr. Robinson found nothing to increase alarm, and Charles Musgrove began, consequently, to feel no necessity for longer confinement. The child was to be kept in bed and amused as quietly as possible; but what was there for a father to do? This was quite a female case, and it would be highly absurd in him, who could be of no use at home, to shut himself up. His father very much wished him to meet Captain Wentworth, and there being no sufficient reason against it, he ought to go; and it ended in his making a bold, public declaration, when he came in from shooting, of his meaning to dress directly, and dine at the other house.

"Nothing can be going on better than the child," said he; "so I told my father, just now, that I would come, and he thought me quite right. Your sister being with you, my love, I have no scruple at all. You would not like to leave him yourself, but you see I can be of no use. Anne will send for me if anything is the matter."

Husbands and wives generally understand when opposition will be vain. Mary knew, from Charles's manner of speaking, that he was quite determined on going, and that it would be of no use to teaze him. She said nothing, therefore, till he was out of the room, but as soon as there was only Anne to hear—

"So you and I are to be left to shift by ourselves, with this poor sick child; and not a creature coming near us all the evening! I knew how it would be. This is always my luck. If there is anything disagreeable going on men are always sure to get out of it, and Charles is as bad as any of them. Very unfeeling! I must say it is very unfeeling of him to be running away from his poor little boy. Talks of his being going on so well! How does he know that he is going on well, or that there may not be a sudden change half an hour hence? I did not think Charles would have been so unfeeling. So here he is to go away and enjoy himself, and because I am the poor mother, I am not to be allowed to stir; and yet, I am sure, I am more unfit than anybody else to be about the child. My being the mother is the very reason why my feelings should not be tried. I am not at all equal to it. You saw how hysterical I was yesterday."

"But that was only the effect of the suddenness of your alarm—of the shock. You will not be hysterical again. I dare say we shall have nothing to distress us. I perfectly understand Mr. Robinson's directions, and have no fears; and indeed, Mary, I cannot wonder at your husband.

Nursing does not belong to a man; it is not his province. A sick child is always the mother's property: her own feelings generally make it so."

"I hope I am as fond of my child as any mother, but I do not know that I am of any more use in the sick-room than Charles, for I cannot be always scolding and teazing the poor child when it is ill; and you saw, this morning, that if I told him to keep quiet, he was sure to begin kicking about. I have not nerves for the sort of thing."

"But, could you be comfortable yourself, to be spending the whole evening away from the poor boy?"

"Yes; you see his papa can, and why should not I? Jemima is so careful; and she could send us word every hour how he was. I really think Charles might as well have told his father we would all come. I am not more alarmed about little Charles now than he is. I was dreadfully alarmed yesterday, but the case is very different today."

"Well, if you do not think it too late to give notice for yourself, suppose you were to go, as well as your husband. Leave little Charles to my care. Mr. and Mrs. Musgrove cannot think it wrong while I remain with him."

"Are you serious?" cried Mary, her eyes brightening. "Dear me! that's a very good thought, very good, indeed. To be sure, I may just as well go as not, for I am of no use at home—am I? and it only harasses me. You, who have not a mother's feelings, are a great deal the properest person. You can make little Charles do anything; he always minds you at a word. It will be a great deal better than leaving him only with Jemima. Oh! I shall certainly go; I am sure I ought if I can, quite as much as Charles, for they want me excessively to be acquainted with Captain Wentworth, and I know you do not mind being left alone.

An excellent thought of yours, indeed, Anne. I will go and tell Charles, and get ready directly. You can send for us, you know, at a moment's notice, if anything is the matter; but I dare say there will be nothing to alarm you. I should not go, you may be sure, if I did not feel quite at ease about my dear child."

The next moment she was tapping at her husband's dressing-room door, and as Anne followed her up stairs, she was in time for the whole conversation, which began with Mary's saying, in a tone of great exultation, "I mean to go with you, Charles, for I am of no more use at home than you are.

If I were to shut myself up for ever with the child, I should not be able to persuade him to do anything he did not like. Anne will stay; Anne undertakes to stay at home and take care of him. It is Anne's own proposal, and so I shall go with you, which will be a great deal better, for I have not dined at the other house since Tuesday."

"This is very kind of Anne," was her husband's answer, "and I should be very glad to have you go; but it seems rather hard that she should be left at home by herself, to nurse our sick child."

Anne was now at hand to take up her own cause, and the sincerity of her manner being soon sufficient to convince him, where conviction was at least very agreeable, he had no farther scruples as to her being left to dine alone, though he still wanted her to join them in the evening, when the child might be at rest for the night, and kindly urged her to let him come and fetch her, but she was quite unpersuadable; and this being the case, she had ere long the pleasure of seeing them set off together in high spirits. They were gone, she hoped, to be happy, however oddly constructed such happiness might seem; as for herself, she was left with as many sensations of comfort, as were, perhaps, ever likely to be hers. She knew herself to be of the first utility to the child; and what was it to her if Frederick Wentworth were only half a mile distant, making himself agreeable to others? She would have liked to know how he felt as to a meeting. Perhaps indifferent, if indifference could exist under such circumstances. He must be either indifferent or unwilling. Had he wished ever to see her again, he need not have waited till this time; he would have done what she could not but believe that in his place she should have done long ago, when events had been early giving him the independence which alone had been wanting.

Her brother and sister came back delighted with their new acquaintance, and their visit in general. There had been music, singing, talking, laughing, all that was most agreeable; charming manners in Captain Wentworth, no shyness or reserve; they seemed all to know each other perfectly, and he was coming the very next morning to shoot with Charles. He was to come to breakfast, but not at the Cottage, though that had been proposed at first; but then he had been pressed to come to the Great House instead, and he seemed afraid of being in Mrs. Charles Musgrove's way, on account of the child, and therefore, somehow, they hardly knew how, it ended in Charles's being to meet him to breakfast at his father's.

Anne understood it. He wished to avoid seeing her. He had inquired after her, she found, slightly, as might suit a former slight acquaintance, seeming to acknowledge such as she had acknowledged, actuated, perhaps, by the same view of escaping introduction when they were to meet.

The morning hours of the Cottage were always later than those of the other house, and on the morrow the difference was so great that Mary and Anne were not more than beginning breakfast when Charles came in to say that they were just setting off, that he was come for his dogs, that his sisters were following with Captain Wentworth; his sisters meaning to visit Mary and the child, and Captain Wentworth proposing also to wait on her for a few minutes if not inconvenient; and though Charles had answered for the child's being in no such state as could make it inconvenient, Captain Wentworth would not be satisfied without his running on to give notice.

Mary, very much gratified by this attention, was delighted to receive him, while a thousand feelings rushed on Anne, of which this was the most consoling, that it would soon be over. And it was soon over. In two minutes after Charles's preparation, the others appeared; they were in the drawing-room. Her eye half met Captain Wentworth's, a bow, a curtsey passed; she heard his voice; he talked to Mary, said all that was right, said something to the Miss Musgroves, enough to mark an easy footing; the room seemed full, full of persons and voices, but a few minutes ended it. Charles showed himself at the window, all was ready, their visitor had bowed and was gone, the Miss Musgroves were gone too, suddenly resolving to walk to the end of the village with the sportsmen: the room was cleared, and Anne might finish her breakfast as she could.

"It is over! It is over!" she repeated to herself again and again, in nervous gratitude. "The worst is over!"

Mary talked, but she could not attend. She had seen him. They had met. They had been once more in the same room.

Soon, however, she began to reason with herself, and try to be feeling less.

Eight years, almost eight years had passed, since all had been given up. How absurd to be resuming the agitation which such an interval had banished into distance and indistinctness! What might not eight years do? Events of every description, changes, alienations, removals—all, all must be comprised in it, and oblivion of the past— how natural, how certain too! It included nearly a third part of her own life.

Alas! With all her reasoning, she found, that to retentive feelings eight years may be little more than nothing.

Now, how were his sentiments to be read? Was this like wishing to avoid her? And the next moment she was hating herself for the folly which asked the question.

On one other question, which perhaps her utmost wisdom might not have prevented, she was soon spared all suspense; for, after the Miss Musgroves had returned and finished their visit at the Cottage she had this spontaneous information from Mary, "Captain Wentworth is not very gallant by you, Anne, though he was so attentive to me. Henrietta asked him what he thought of you, when they went away, and he said, 'You were so altered he should not have known you again.'"

Mary had no feelings to make her respect her sister's in a common way, but she was perfectly unsuspicious of being inflicting any peculiar wound.

"Altered beyond his knowledge." Anne fully submitted, in silent, deep mortification. Doubtless it was so, and she could take no revenge, for he was not altered, or not for the worse. She had already acknowledged it to herself, and she could not think differently, let him think of her as he would. No: the years which had destroyed her youth and bloom had only given him a more glowing, manly, open look, in no respect lessening his personal advantages. She had seen the same Frederick Wentworth.

"So altered that he should not have known her again!" These were words, which could not but dwell with her. Yet she soon began to rejoice that she had heard them. They were of sobering tendency; they allayed agitation; they composed, and consequently must make her happier.

Frederick Wentworth had used such words, or something like them, but without an idea that they would be carried round to her. He had thought her wretchedly altered, and in the first moment of appeal, had spoken as he felt. He had not forgiven Anne Elliot. She had used him ill, deserted and disappointed him; and worse, she had shown a feebleness of character in doing so, which his own decided, confident temper could not endure. She had given him up to oblige others. It had been the effect of over-persuasion. It had been weakness and timidity.

He had been most warmly attached to her, and had never seen a woman since whom he thought her equal; but, except from some natural sensation of curiosity, he had no desire of meeting her again. Her power with him was gone forever.

It was now his object to marry. He was rich, and being turned on shore, fully intended to settle as soon as he could be properly tempted; actually looking round, ready to fall in love with all the speed which a clear head and a quick taste could allow. He had a heart for either of the Miss Musgroves, if they could catch it; a heart, in short, for any pleasing young woman who came in his way, excepting Anne Elliot. This was his only secret exception, when he said to his sister, in answer to her suppositions, "Yes, here I am, Sophia, quite ready to make a foolish match. Anybody between fifteen and thirty may have me for asking. A little beauty, and a few smiles, and a few compliments to the navy, and I am a lost man. Should not this be enough for a sailor, who has had no society among women to make him nice?"

He said it, she knew, to be contradicted. His bright proud eye spoke the conviction that he was nice; and Anne Elliot was not out of his thoughts, when he more seriously described the woman he should wish to meet with. "A strong mind, with sweetness of manner," made the first and the last of the description.

"That is the woman I want," said he. "Something a little inferior I shall of course put up with, but it must not be much. If I am a fool, I shall be a fool indeed, for I have thought on the subject more than most men."

CHAPTER 8

From this time Captain Wentworth and Anne Elliot were repeatedly in the same circle. They were soon dining in company together at Mr. Musgrove's, for the little boy's state could no longer supply his aunt with a pretence for absenting herself; and this was but the beginning of other dinings and other meetings.

Whether former feelings were to be renewed must be brought to the proof; former times must undoubtedly be brought to the recollection of each; they could not but be reverted to; the year of their engagement could not but be named by him, in the little narratives or descriptions which conversation called forth. His profession qualified him, his disposition lead him, to talk; and "That was in the year six;" "That happened before I went to sea in the year six," occurred in the course of the first evening they spent together: and though his voice did not falter, and though she had no reason to suppose his eye wandering towards her while he spoke, Anne felt the utter impossibility, from her knowledge of his mind, that he could be unvisited by remembrance any more than herself. There must be the same immediate association of thought, though she was very far from conceiving it to be of equal pain.

They had no conversation together, no intercourse but what the commonest civility required. Once so much to each other! Now nothing! There had been a time, when of all the large party now filling the drawing room at Uppercross, they would have found it most difficult to cease to speak to one another. With the exception, perhaps, of Admiral and Mrs. Croft, who seemed particularly attached and happy, (Anne could allow no other exceptions even among the married couples), there could have been no two hearts so open, no tastes so similar, no feelings so in unison, no countenances so beloved. Now they were as strangers; nay, worse than strangers, for they could never become acquainted. It was a perpetual estrangement.

When he talked, she heard the same voice, and discerned the same mind. There was a very general ignorance of all naval matters throughout the party; and he was very much questioned, and especially by the two Miss Musgroves, who seemed hardly to have any eyes but for him, as to the manner of living on board, daily regulations, food, hours, &c., and their surprise at his accounts, at learning the degree of accommodation and arrangement which was practicable, drew from him some pleasant ridicule, which reminded Anne of the early days when she too had been ignorant, and she too had been accused of supposing sailors to be living on board without anything to eat, or any cook to dress it if there were, or any servant to wait, or any knife and fork to use.

From thus listening and thinking, she was roused by a whisper of Mrs. Musgrove's who, overcome by fond regrets, could not help saying, "Ah! Miss Anne, if it had pleased Heaven to spare my poor son, I dare say he would have been just such another by this time."

Anne suppressed a smile, and listened kindly, while Mrs. Musgrove relieved her heart a little more; and for a few minutes, therefore, could not keep pace with the conversation of the others.

When she could let her attention take its natural course again, she found the Miss Musgroves just fetching the Navy List (their own navy list, the first that had ever been at Uppercross), and sitting down together to pore over it, with the professed view of finding out the ships that Captain Wentworth had commanded.

"Your first was the Asp, I remember; we will look for the Asp."

"You will not find her there. Quite worn out and broken up. I was the last man who commanded her. Hardly fit for service then. Reported fit for home service for a year or two, and so I was sent off to the West Indies."

The girls looked all in amazement.

"The Admiralty," he continued, "entertain themselves now and then, with sending a few hundred men to sea, in a ship not fit to be employed. But they have a great many to provide for; and among the thousands that may just as well go to the bottom as not, it is impossible for them to distinguish the very set who may be least missed."

"Phoo! Phoo!" cried the Admiral, "What stuff these young fellows talk! Never was a better sloop than the Asp in her day. For an old built sloop, you would not see her equal. Lucky fellow to get her! He knows there must have been twenty better men than himself applying for her at the same time. Lucky fellow to get anything so soon, with no more interest than his."

"I felt my luck, Admiral, I assure you;" replied Captain Wentworth, seriously.

"I was as well satisfied with my appointment as you can desire. It was a great object with me at that time to be at sea; a very great object, I wanted to be doing something."

"To be sure you did. What should a young fellow like you do ashore for half a year together? If a man had not a wife, he soon wants to be afloat again."

"But, Captain Wentworth," cried Louisa, "how vexed you must have been when you came to the Asp, to see what an old thing they had given you."

"I knew pretty well what she was before that day;" said he, smiling. "I had no more discoveries to make than you would have as to the fashion and strength of any old pelisse, which you had seen lent about among half your acquaintance ever since you could remember, and which at last, on some very wet day, is lent to yourself. Ah! She was a dear old Asp to me. She did all that I wanted. I knew she would. I knew that we should either go to the bottom together, or that she would be the making of me; and I never had two days of foul weather all the time I was at sea in her; and after taking privateers enough to be very entertaining, I had the good luck in my passage home the next autumn, to fall in with the very French frigate I wanted. I brought her into Plymouth; and here another instance of luck. We had not been six hours in the Sound, when a gale came on, which lasted four days and nights, and which would have done for poor old Asp in half the time; our touch with the Great Nation not having much improved our condition. Four-and-twenty hours later, and I should only have been a gallant Captain Wentworth, in a small paragraph at one corner of the newspapers; and being lost in only a sloop, nobody would have thought about me." Anne's shudderings were to herself alone; but the Miss Musgroves could be as open as they were sincere, in their exclamations of pity and horror.

"And so then, I suppose," said Mrs. Musgrove, in a low voice, as if thinking aloud, "so then he went away to the Laconia, and there he met with our poor boy."

"Charles, my dear," (beckoning him to her), "do ask Captain Wentworth where it was he first met with your poor brother. I always forgot."

"It was at Gibraltar, mother, I know. Dick had been left ill at Gibraltar, with a recommendation from his former captain to Captain Wentworth."

"Oh! But, Charles, tell Captain Wentworth, he need not be afraid of mentioning poor Dick before me, for it would be rather a pleasure to hear him talked of by such a good friend."

Charles, being somewhat more mindful of the probabilities of the case, only nodded in reply, and walked away.

The girls were now hunting for the Laconia; and Captain Wentworth could not deny himself the pleasure of taking the precious volume into his own hands to save them the trouble, and once more read aloud the little statement of her name and rate, and present non-commissioned class, observing over it that she too had been one of the best friends man ever had.

"Ah! Those were pleasant days when I had the Laconia! How fast I made money in her. A friend of mine and I had such a lovely cruise together off the Western Islands. Poor Harville, sister! You know how much he wanted money: worse than myself. He had a wife. Excellent fellow. I shall never forget his happiness. He felt it all, so much for her sake. I wished for him again the next summer, when I had still the same luck in the Mediterranean."

"And I am sure, Sir," said Mrs. Musgrove, "it was a lucky day for us, when you were put captain into that ship. We shall never forget what you did."

Her feelings made her speak low; and Captain Wentworth, hearing only in part, and probably not having Dick Musgrove at all near his thoughts, looked rather in suspense, and as if waiting for more.

"My brother," whispered one of the girls. "Mamma is thinking of poor Richard."

"Poor dear fellow!" continued Mrs. Musgrove; "He was grown so steady, and such an excellent correspondent, while he was under your care! Ah! It would have been a happy thing, if he had never left you. I assure you, Captain Wentworth, we are very sorry he ever left you."

There was a momentary expression in Captain Wentworth's face at this speech, a certain glance of his bright eye, and curl of his handsome mouth, which convinced Anne, that instead of sharing in Mrs. Musgrove's kind wishes, as to her son, he had probably been at some pains to get rid of him; but it was too transient an indulgence of self-amusement to be detected by any who understood him less than herself; in another moment he was perfectly collected and serious, and almost instantly afterwards coming up to the sofa, on which she and

Mrs. Musgrove were sitting, took a place by the latter, and entered into conversation with her, in a low voice, about her son, doing it with so much sympathy and natural grace, as showed the kindest consideration for all that was real and unabsurd in the parent's feelings.

They were actually on the same sofa, for Mrs. Musgrove had most readily made room for him; they were divided only by Mrs. Musgrove. It was no insignificant barrier, indeed. Mrs. Musgrove was of a comfortable, substantial size, infinitely more fitted by nature to express good cheer and good humour, than tenderness and sentiment; and while the agitations of Anne's slender form, and pensive face, may be considered as very completely screened, Captain Wentworth should be allowed some credit for the self-command with which he attended to her large fat sighings over the destiny of a son, whom alive nobody had cared for.

Personal size and mental sorrow have certainly no necessary proportions. A large bulky figure has as good a right to be in deep affliction, as the most graceful set of limbs in the world. But, fair or not fair, there are unbecoming conjunctions, which reason will patronize in vain, which taste cannot tolerate, which ridicule will seize.

The Admiral, after taking two or three refreshing turns about the room with his hands behind him, being called to order by his wife, now came up to Captain Wentworth, and without any observation of what he might be interrupting, thinking only of his own thoughts, began with, "If you had been a week later at Lisbon, last spring, Frederick, you would have been asked to give a passage to Lady Mary Grierson and her daughters."

"Should I? I am glad I was not a week later then."

The Admiral abused him for his want of gallantry. He defended himself; though professing that he would never willingly admit any ladies on board a ship of his, excepting for a ball, or a visit, which a few hours might comprehend.

"But, if I know myself," said he, "this is from no want of gallantry towards them. It is rather from feeling how impossible it is, with all one's efforts, and all one's sacrifices, to make the accommodations on board such as women ought to have. There can be no want of gallantry, Admiral, in rating the claims of women to every personal comfort high, and this is what I do. I hate to hear of women on board, or to see them on board; and no ship under my command shall ever convey a family of ladies anywhere, if I can help it."

This brought his sister upon him.

"Oh! Frederick! But I cannot believe it of you. All idle refinement! Women may be as comfortable on board, as in the best house in England. I believe I have lived as much on board as most women, and I know nothing superior to the accommodations of a man-of-war. I declare I have not a comfort or an indulgence about me, even at Kellynch Hall," (with a kind bow to Anne), "beyond what I always had in most of the ships I have lived in; and they have been five altogether."

"Nothing to the purpose," replied her brother. "You were living with your husband, and were the only woman on board."

"But you, yourself, brought Mrs. Harville, her sister, her cousin, and three children, round from Portsmouth to Plymouth. Where was this superfine, extraordinary sort of gallantry of yours then?"

"All merged in my friendship, Sophia. I would assist any brother officer's wife that I could, and I would bring anything of Harville's from the world's end, if he wanted it. But do not imagine that I did not feel it an evil in itself."

"Depend upon it, they were all perfectly comfortable."

"I might not like them the better for that perhaps. Such a number of women and children have no right to be comfortable on board."

"My dear Frederick, you are talking quite idly. Pray, what would become of us poor sailors' wives, who often want to be conveyed to one port or another, after our husbands, if everybody had your feelings?"

"My feelings, you see, did not prevent my taking Mrs. Harville and all her family to Plymouth."

"But I hate to hear you talking so like a fine gentleman, and as if women were all fine ladies, instead of rational creatures. We none of us expect to be in smooth water all our days."

"Ah! my dear," said the Admiral, "when he had got a wife, he will sing a different tune. When he is married, if we have the good luck to live to another war, we shall see him do as you and I, and a great many others, have done. We shall have him very thankful to anybody that will bring him his wife."

"Ay, that we shall."

"Now I have done," cried Captain Wentworth. "When once married people begin to attack me with,—'Oh! you will think very differently, when you are married.' I can only say, 'No, I shall not;' and then they say again, 'Yes, you will,' and there is an end of it."

He got up and moved away.

"What a great traveller you must have been, ma'am!" said Mrs. Musgrove to Mrs. Croft.

"Pretty well, ma'am in the fifteen years of my marriage; though many women have done more. I have crossed the Atlantic four times, and have been once to the East Indies, and back again, and only once; besides being in different places about home: Cork, and Lisbon, and Gibraltar. But I never went beyond the Streights, and never was in the West Indies. We do not call Bermuda or Bahama, you know, the West Indies."

Mrs. Musgrove had not a word to say in dissent; she could not accuse herself of having ever called them anything in the whole course of her life.

"And I do assure you, ma'am," pursued Mrs. Croft, "that nothing can exceed the accommodations of a man-of-war; I speak, you know, of the higher rates. When you come to a frigate, of course, you are more confined; though any reasonable woman may be perfectly happy in one of them; and I can safely say, that the happiest part of my life has been spent on board a ship. While we were together, you know, there was nothing to be feared. Thank God! I have always been blessed with excellent health, and no climate disagrees with me. A little disordered always the first twenty-four hours of going to sea, but never knew what sickness was afterwards. The only time I ever really suffered in body or mind, the only time that I ever fancied myself unwell, or had any ideas of danger, was the winter that I passed by myself at Deal, when the Admiral (Captain Croft then) was in the North Seas. I lived in perpetual fright at that time, and had all manner of imaginary complaints from not knowing what to do with myself, or when I should hear from him next; but as long as we could be together, nothing ever ailed me, and I never met with the smallest inconvenience."

"Aye, to be sure. Yes, indeed, oh yes! I am quite of your opinion, Mrs. Croft," was Mrs. Musgrove's hearty answer. "There is nothing so bad as a separation. I am quite of your opinion. I know what it is, for Mr. Musgrove always attends the assizes, and I am so glad when they are over, and he is safe back again."

The evening ended with dancing. On its being proposed, Anne offered her services, as usual; and though her eyes would sometimes fill with tears as she sat at the instrument, she was extremely glad to be employed, and desired nothing in return but to be unobserved.

It was a merry, joyous party, and no one seemed in higher spirits than Captain Wentworth. She felt that he had every thing to elevate him which general attention and deference, and especially the attention of all the young women, could do. The Miss Hayters, the females of the family of cousins already mentioned, were apparently admitted to the honour of being in love with him; and as for Henrietta and Louisa, they both seemed so entirely occupied by him, that nothing but the continued appearance of the most perfect goodwill between themselves could have made it credible that they were not decided rivals. If he were a little spoilt by such universal, such eager admiration, who could wonder?

These were some of the thoughts that occupied Anne, while her fingers were mechanically at work, proceeding for half an hour together, equally without error, and without consciousness. Once she felt that he was looking at herself, observing her altered features, perhaps, trying to trace in them the ruins of the face which had once charmed him; and once she knew that he must have spoken of her; she was hardly aware of it, till she heard the answer; but then she was sure of his having asked his partner whether Miss Elliot never danced? The answer was, "Oh, no; never; she has quite given up dancing. She had rather play.

She is never tired of playing." Once, too, he spoke to her. She had left the instrument on the dancing being over, and he had sat down to try to make out an air, which he wished to give the Miss Musgroves an idea of. Unintentionally she returned to that part of the room; he saw her, and, instantly rising, said, with studied politeness. "I beg your pardon, madam, this is your seat;" and though she immediately drew back with a decided negative, he was not to be induced to sit down again.

Anne did not wish for more of such looks and speeches. His cold politeness—his ceremonious grace—was worse than anything.

CHAPTER 9

Captain Wentworth was come to Kellynch as to a home, to stay as long as he liked, being as thoroughly the object of the Admiral's fraternal kindness as of his wife's. He had intended, on first arriving, to proceed very soon into Shropshire, and visit the brother settled in that country, but the attractions of Uppercross induced him to put this off. There was so much of friendliness, and of flattery, and of everything most bewitching in his reception there; the old were so hospitable, the young so agreeable, that he could not but resolve to remain where he was, and take all the charms and perfections of Edward's wife upon credit a little longer.

It was soon Uppercross with him almost every day. The Musgroves could hardly be more ready to invite than he to come, particularly in the morning, when he had no companion at home, for the Admiral and Mrs. Croft were generally out of doors together, interesting themselves in their new possessions, their grass, and their sheep, and dawdling about in a way not endurable to a third person, or driving out in a gig, lately added to their establishment.

Hitherto there had been but one opinion of Captain Wentworth among the Musgroves and their dependencies. It was unvarying, warm admiration everywhere; but this intimate footing was not more than established, when a certain Charles Hayter returned among them, to be a good deal disturbed by it, and to think Captain Wentworth very much in the way.

Charles Hayter was the eldest of all the cousins, and a very amiable, pleasing young man, between whom and Henrietta there had been a considerable appearance of attachment previous to Captain Wentworth's introduction. He was in orders; and having a curacy in the neighbourhood, where residence was not required, lived at his father's house, only two miles from Uppercross. A short absence from home had left his fair one unguarded by his attentions at this critical period, and when he came back he had the pain of finding very altered manners, and of seeing Captain Wentworth.

Mrs. Musgrove and Mrs. Hayter were sisters. They had each had money, but their marriages had made a material difference in their degree of consequence. Mr. Hayter had some property of his own, but it was insignificant compared with Mr. Musgrove's; and while the Musgroves were in the first class of society in the country, the young Hayters would, from their parents' inferior, retired, and unpolished way of living, and their own defective education, have been hardly in any class at all, but for their connexion with Uppercross, this eldest son of course excepted, who had chosen to be a scholar and a gentleman, and who was very superior in cultivation and manners to all the rest.

The two families had always been on excellent terms, there being no pride on one side, and no envy on the other, and only such a consciousness of superiority in the Miss Musgroves, as made them pleased to improve their cousins. Charles's attentions to Henrietta had been observed by her father and mother without any disapprobation. "It would not be a great match for her; but if Henrietta liked him,"— and Henrietta did seem to like him.

Henrietta fully thought so herself, before Captain Wentworth came; but from that time Cousin Charles had been very much forgotten.

Which of the two sisters was preferred by Captain Wentworth was as yet quite doubtful, as far as Anne's observation reached. Henrietta was perhaps the prettiest, Louisa had the higher spirits; and she knew not now, whether the more gentle or the more lively character were most likely to attract him.

Mr. and Mrs. Musgrove, either from seeing little, or from an entire confidence in the discretion of both their daughters, and of all the young men who came near them, seemed to leave everything to take its chance. There was not the smallest appearance of solicitude or remark about them in the Mansion-house; but it was different at the Cottage: the young couple there were more disposed to speculate and wonder; and Captain Wentworth had not been above four or five times in the Miss Musgroves' company, and Charles Hayter had but just reappeared, when Anne had to listen to the opinions of her brother and sister, as to which was the one liked best. Charles gave it for Louisa, Mary for Henrietta, but quite agreeing that to have him marry either could be extremely delightful.

Charles "had never seen a pleasanter man in his life; and from what he had once heard Captain Wentworth himself say, was very sure that he had not made less than twenty thousand pounds by the war. Here was a fortune at once; besides which, there would be the chance of what might be done in any future war; and he was sure Captain Wentworth was as likely a man to distinguish himself as any officer in the navy. Oh! it would be a capital match for either of his sisters."

"Upon my word it would," replied Mary. "Dear me! If he should rise to any very great honours! If he should ever be made a baronet! 'Lady Wentworth' sounds very well. That would be a noble thing, indeed, for Henrietta! She would take place of me then, and Henrietta would not dislike that. Sir Frederick and Lady Wentworth! It would be but a new creation, however, and I never think much of your new creations."

It suited Mary best to think Henrietta the one preferred on the very account of Charles Hayter, whose pretensions she wished to see put an end to. She looked down very decidedly upon the Hayters, and thought it would be quite a misfortune to have the existing connection between the families renewed—very sad for herself and her children.

"You know," said she, "I cannot think him at all a fit match for Henrietta; and considering the alliances which the Musgroves have made, she has no right to throw herself away. I do not think any young woman has a right to make a choice that may be disagreeable and inconvenient to the principal part of her family, and be giving bad connections to those who have not been used to them. And, pray, who is Charles Hayter? Nothing but a country curate. A most improper match for Miss Musgrove of Uppercross."

Her husband, however, would not agree with her here; for besides having a regard for his cousin, Charles Hayter was an eldest son, and he saw things as an eldest son himself.

"Now you are talking nonsense, Mary," was therefore his answer. "It would not be a great match for Henrietta, but Charles has a very fair chance, through the Spicers, of getting something from the Bishop in the course of a year or two; and you will please to remember, that he is the eldest son; whenever my uncle dies, he steps into very pretty property. The estate at Winthrop is not less than two hundred and fifty acres, besides the farm near Taunton, which is some of the best land in the country. I grant you, that any of them but Charles would be a very shocking match for Henrietta, and indeed it could not be; he is the only one that could be possible; but he is a very goodnatured, good sort of a fellow; and whenever Winthrop comes into his hands, he will make a different sort of place of it, and live in a very different sort of way; and with that property, he will never be a contemptible man—good, freehold property. No, no; Henrietta might do worse than marry Charles Hayter; and if she has him, and Louisa can get Captain Wentworth, I shall be very well satisfied."

"Charles may say what he pleases," cried Mary to Anne, as soon as he was out of the room, "but it would be shocking to have Henrietta marry Charles Hayter; a very bad thing for her, and still worse for me; and therefore it is very much to be wished that Captain Wentworth may soon put him quite out of her head, and I have very little doubt that he has. She took hardly any notice of Charles Hayter yesterday. I wish you had been there to see her behaviour. And as to Captain Wentworth's liking Louisa as well as Henrietta, it is nonsense to say so; for he certainly does like Henrietta a great deal the best. But Charles is so positive! I wish you had been with us yesterday, for then you might have decided between us; and I am sure you would have thought as I did, unless you had been determined to give it against me."

A dinner at Mr. Musgrove's had been the occasion when all these things should have been seen by Anne; but she had staid at home, under the mixed plea of a headache of her own, and some return of indisposition in little Charles. She had thought only of avoiding Captain Wentworth; but an escape from being appealed to as umpire was now added to the advantages of a quiet evening.

As to Captain Wentworth's views, she deemed it of more consequence that he should know his own mind early enough not to be endangering the happiness of either sister, or impeaching his own honour, than that he should prefer Henrietta to Louisa, or Louisa to Henrietta. Either of them would, in all probability, make him an affectionate, goodhumoured wife. With regard to Charles Hayter, she had delicacy which must be pained by any lightness of conduct in a well-meaning young woman, and a heart to sympathize in any of the sufferings it occasioned; but if Henrietta found herself mistaken in the nature of her feelings, the alternation could not be understood too soon.

Charles Hayter had met with much to disquiet and mortify him in his cousin's behaviour. She had too old a regard for him to be so wholly estranged as might in two meetings extinguish every past hope, and leave him nothing to do but to keep away from Uppercross: but there was such a change as became very alarming, when such a man as Captain Wentworth was to be regarded as the probable cause.

He had been absent only two Sundays, and when they parted, had left her interested, even to the height of his wishes, in his prospect of soon quitting his present curacy, and obtaining that of Uppercross instead. It had then seemed the object nearest her heart, that Dr. Shirley, the rector, who for more than forty years had been zealously discharging all the duties of his office, but was now growing too infirm for many of them, should be quite fixed on engaging a curate; should make his curacy quite as good as he could afford, and should give Charles Hayter the promise of it. The advantage of his having to come only to Uppercross, instead of going six miles another way; of his having, in every respect, a better curacy; of his belonging to their dear Dr. Shirley, and of dear, good Dr. Shirley's being relieved from the duty which he could no longer get through without most injurious fatigue, had been a great deal, even to Louisa, but had been almost everything to Henrietta. When he came back, alas! the zeal of the business was gone by. Louisa could not listen at all to his account of a conversation which he had just held with Dr. Shirley: she was at a window, looking out for Captain Wentworth; and even Henrietta had at best only a divided attention to give, and seemed to have forgotten all the former doubt and solicitude of the negotiation.

"Well, I am very glad indeed: but I always thought you would have it; I always thought you sure. It did not appear to me that—in short, you know, Dr. Shirley must have a curate, and you had secured his promise. Is he coming, Louisa?"

One morning, very soon after the dinner at the Musgroves, at which Anne had not been present, Captain Wentworth walked into the drawing-room at the Cottage, where were only herself and the little invalid Charles, who was lying on the sofa.

The surprise of finding himself almost alone with Anne Elliot, deprived his manners of their usual composure: he started, and could only say, "I thought the Miss Musgroves had been here: Mrs. Musgrove told me I should find them here," before he walked to the window to recollect himself, and feel how he ought to behave.

"They are up stairs with my sister: they will be down in a few moments, I dare say," had been Anne's reply, in all the confusion that was natural; and if the child had not called her to come and do something for him, she would have been out of the room the next moment, and released Captain Wentworth as well as herself.

He continued at the window; and after calmly and politely saying, "I hope the little boy is better," was silent.

She was obliged to kneel down by the sofa, and remain there to satisfy her patient; and thus they continued a few minutes, when, to her very great satisfaction, she heard some other person crossing the little vestibule. She hoped, on turning her head, to see the master of the house; but it proved to be one much less calculated for making matters easy—Charles Hayter, probably not at all better pleased by the sight of Captain Wentworth than Captain Wentworth had been by the sight of Anne.

She only attempted to say, "How do you do? Will you not sit down? The others will be here presently."

Captain Wentworth, however, came from his window, apparently not ill-disposed for conversation; but Charles Hayter soon put an end to his attempts by seating himself near the table, and taking up the newspaper; and Captain Wentworth returned to his window.

Another minute brought another addition. The younger boy, a remarkable stout, forward child, of two years old, having got the door opened for him by some one without, made his determined appearance among them, and went straight to the sofa to see what was going on, and put in his claim to anything good that might be giving away.

There being nothing to eat, he could only have some play; and as his aunt would not let him tease his sick brother, he began to fasten himself upon her, as she knelt, in such a way that, busy as she was about Charles, she could not shake him off. She spoke to him, ordered, entreated, and insisted in vain. Once she did contrive to push him away, but the boy had the greater pleasure in getting upon her back again directly.

"Walter," said she, "get down this moment. You are extremely troublesome. I am very angry with you."

"Walter," cried Charles Hayter, "why do you not do as you are bid? Do not you hear your aunt speak? Come to me, Walter, come to cousin Charles."

But not a bit did Walter stir.

In another moment, however, she found herself in the state of being released from him; some one was taking him from her, though he had bent down her head so much, that his little sturdy hands were unfastened from around her neck, and he was resolutely borne away, before she knew that Captain Wentworth had done it.

Her sensations on the discovery made her perfectly speechless. She could not even thank him. She could only hang over little Charles, with most disordered feelings. His kindness in stepping forward to her relief, the manner, the silence in which it had passed, the little particulars of the circumstance, with the conviction soon forced on her by the noise he was studiously making with the child, that he meant to avoid hearing her thanks, and rather sought to testify that her conversation was the last of his wants, produced such a confusion of varying, but very painful agitation, as she could not recover from, till enabled by the entrance of Mary and the Miss Musgroves to make over her little patient to their cares, and leave the room. She could not stay. It might have been an opportunity of watching the loves and jealousies of the four—they were now altogether; but she could stay for none of it. It was evident that Charles Hayter was not well inclined towards Captain Wentworth. She had a strong impression of his having said, in a vext tone of voice, after Captain Wentworth's interference, "You ought to have minded me, Walter; I told you not to teaze your aunt;" and could comprehend his regretting that Captain Wentworth should do what he ought to have done himself. But neither Charles Hayter's feelings, nor anybody's feelings, could interest her, till she had a little better arranged her own. She was ashamed of herself, quite ashamed of being so nervous, so overcome by such a trifle; but so it was, and it required a long application of solitude and reflection to recover her.

CHAPTER 10

Other opportunities of making her observations could not fail to occur. Anne had soon been in company with all the four together often enough to have an opinion, though too wise to acknowledge as much at home, where she knew it would have satisfied neither husband nor wife; for while she considered Louisa to be rather the favourite, she could not but think, as far as she might dare to judge from memory and experience, that Captain Wentworth was not in love with either. They were more in love with him; yet there it was not love. It was a little fever of admiration; but it might, probably must, end in love with some. Charles Hayter seemed aware of being slighted, and yet Henrietta had sometimes the air of being divided between them. Anne longed for the power of representing to them all what they were about, and of pointing out some of the evils they were exposing themselves to. She did not attribute guile to any. It was the highest satisfaction to her to believe Captain Wentworth not in the least aware of the pain he was occasioning. There was no triumph, no pitiful triumph in his manner.

He had, probably, never heard, and never thought of any claims of Charles Hayter. He was only wrong in accepting the attentions (for accepting must be the word) of two young women at once.

After a short struggle, however, Charles Hayter seemed to quit the field. Three days had passed without his coming once to Uppercross; a most decided change. He had even refused one regular invitation to dinner; and having been found on the occasion by Mr. Musgrove with some large books before him, Mr. and Mrs. Musgrove were sure all could not be right, and talked, with grave faces, of his studying himself to death. It was Mary's hope and belief that he had received a positive dismissal from Henrietta, and her husband lived under the constant dependence of seeing him to-morrow. Anne could only feel that Charles Hayter was wise.

One morning, about this time Charles Musgrove and Captain Wentworth being gone a-shooting together, as the sisters in the Cottage were sitting quietly at work, they were visited at the window by the sisters from the Mansion-house.

It was a very fine November day, and the Miss Musgroves came through the little grounds, and stopped for no other purpose than to say, that they were going to take a *long* walk, and therefore concluded Mary could not like to go with them; and when Mary immediately replied, with some jealousy at not being supposed a good walker, "Oh, yes, I should like to join you very much, I am very fond of a long walk;" Anne felt persuaded, by the looks of the two girls, that it was precisely what they did not wish, and admired again the sort of necessity which the family habits seemed to produce, of everything being to be communicated, and everything being to be done together, however undesired and inconvenient. She tried to dissuade Mary from going, but in vain; and that being the case, thought it best to accept the Miss Musgroves's much more cordial invitation to herself to go likewise, as she might be useful in turning back with her sister, and lessening the interference in any plan of their own.

"I cannot imagine why they should suppose I should not like a long walk," said Mary, as she went upstairs. "Everybody is always supposing that I am not a good walker; and yet they would not have been pleased, if we had refused to join them. When people come in this manner on purpose to ask us, how can one say no?"

Just as they were setting off, the gentlemen returned. They had taken out a young dog, who had spoilt their sport, and sent them back early. Their time and strength, and spirits, were, therefore, exactly ready for this walk, and they entered into it with pleasure. Could Anne have foreseen such a junction, she would have stayed at home; but, from some feelings of interest and curiosity, she fancied now that it was too late to retract, and the whole six set forward together in the direction chosen by the Miss Musgroves, who evidently considered the walk as under their guidance.

Anne's object was, not to be in the way of anybody; and where the narrow paths across the fields made many separations necessary, to keep with her brother and sister. Her *pleasure* in the walk must arise from the exercise and the day, from the view of the last smiles of the year upon the tawny leaves, and withered hedges, and from repeating to herself some few of the thousand poetical descriptions extant of autumn, that season of peculiar and inexhaustible influence on the mind of taste and tenderness, that season which had drawn from every poet, worthy of being read, some attempt at description, or some lines of feeling. She occupied her mind as much as possible in such like musings and quotations; but it was not possible, that when within reach of Captain Wentworth's conversation with either of the Miss Musgroves, she should not try to hear it; yet she caught little very remarkable. It was mere lively chat, such as any young persons, on an intimate footing, might fall into. He was more engaged with Louisa than with Henrietta. Louisa certainly put more forward for his notice than her sister. This distinction appeared to increase, and there was one speech of Louisa's that struck her. After one of the many praises of the day, which were continually bursting forth, Captain Wentworth added, "What glorious weather for the Admiral and my sister! They meant to take a long drive this morning; perhaps we may hail them from some of these hills. They talked of coming into this side of the country. I wonder whereabouts they will upset today. Oh! It does happen very often, I assure you; but my sister makes nothing of it; she would as willingly be tossed out as not."

"Ah! You make the most of it, I know," cried Louisa, "but if it were really so, I should do just the same in her place. If I loved a man, as she loves the Admiral, I would always be with him, nothing should ever separate us, and I would rather be overturned by him, than driven safely by anybody else."

It was spoken with enthusiasm.

"Had you?" cried he, catching the same tone; "I honour you!" And there was silence between them for a little while.

Anne could not immediately fall into a quotation again. The sweet scenes of autumn were for a while put by, unless some tender sonnet, fraught with the apt analogy of the declining year, with declining happiness, and the images of youth and hope, and spring, all gone together, blessed her memory. She roused herself to say, as they struck by order into another path, "Is not this one of the ways to Winthrop?" But nobody heard, or, at least, nobody answered her.

Winthrop, however, or its environs—for young men are, sometimes, to be met with, strolling about near home—was their destination; and after another half mile of gradual ascent through large enclosures, where the ploughs at work and the fresh-made path spoke the farmer, counteracting the sweets of poetical despondence, and meaning to have spring again, they gained the summit of the most considerable hill, which parted Uppercross and Winthrop, and soon commanded a full view of the latter, at the foot of the hill on the other side.

Winthrop, without beauty and without dignity, was stretched before them: an indifferent house, standing low, and hemmed in by the barns and buildings of a farmyard.

Mary exclaimed, "Bless me! Here is Winthrop. I declare I had no idea! Well now, I think we had better turn back; I am excessively tired."

Henrietta, conscious and ashamed, and seeing no cousin Charles walking along any path, or leaning against any gate, was ready to do as Mary wished; but "No!" said Charles Musgrove, and "No, no!" cried Louisa more eagerly, and taking her sister aside, seemed to be arguing the matter warmly.

Charles, in the meanwhile, was very decidedly declaring his resolution of calling on his aunt, now that he was so near; and very evidently, though more fearfully, trying to induce his wife to go too. But this was one of the points on which the lady showed her strength; and when he recommended the advantage of resting herself a quarter of an hour at Winthrop, as she felt so tired, she resolutely answered, "Oh! No, indeed! Walking up that hill again would do her more harm than any sitting down could do her good;" and, in short, her look and manner declared, that go she would not.

After a little succession of these sort of debates and consultations, it was settled between Charles and his two sisters, that he and Henrietta should just run down for a few minutes, to see their aunt and cousins, while the rest of the party waited for them at the top of the hill. Louisa seemed the principal arranger of the plan; and, as she went a little way with them, down the hill, still talking to Henrietta, Mary took the opportunity of looking scornfully around her, and saying to Captain Wentworth, "It is very unpleasant, having such connexions! But, I assure you, I have never been in the house above twice in my life."

She received no other answer, than an artificial, assenting smile, followed by a contemptuous glance, as he turned away, which Anne perfectly knew the meaning of.

The brow of the hill, where they remained, was a cheerful spot; Louisa returned; and Mary, finding a comfortable seat for herself on the step of a stile, was very well satisfied so long as the others all stood about her; but when Louisa drew Captain Wentworth away, to try for a gleaning of nuts in an adjoining hedgerow, and they were gone by degrees quite out of sight and sound, Mary was happy no longer; she quarrelled with her own seat, was sure Louisa had got a much better somewhere, and nothing could prevent her from going to look for a better also. She turned through the same gate, but could not see them. Anne found a nice seat for her, on a dry sunny bank, under the hedgerow, in which she had no doubt of their still being, in some spot or other. Mary sat down for a moment, but it would not do; she was sure Louisa had found a better seat somewhere else, and she would go on till she overtook her.

Anne, really tired herself, was glad to sit down; and she very soon heard Captain Wentworth and Louisa in the hedgerow, behind her, as if making their way back along the rough, wild sort of channel, down the centre. They were speaking as they drew near. Louisa's voice was the first distinguished. She seemed to be in the middle of some eager speech. What Anne first heard was, "And so, I made her go. I could not bear that she should be frightened from the visit by such nonsense. What! Would I be turned back from doing a thing that I had determined to do, and that I knew to be right, by the airs and interference of such a person, or of any person I may say? No, I have no idea of being so easily persuaded. When I have made up my mind, I have made it; and Henrietta seemed entirely to have made up hers to call at Winthrop today; and yet, she was as near giving it up, out of nonsensical complaisance!"

"She would have turned back then, but for you?"

"She would indeed. I am almost ashamed to say it."

"Happy for her, to have such a mind as yours at hand! After the hints you gave just now, which did but confirm my own observations, the last time I was in company with him, I need not affect to have no comprehension of what is going on. I see that more than a mere dutiful morning visit to your aunt was in question; and woe betide him, and her too, when it comes to things of consequence, when they are placed in circumstances requiring fortitude and strength of mind, if she have not resolution enough to resist idle interference in such a trifle as this. Your sister is an amiable creature; but *yours* is the character of decision and firmness, I see. If you value her conduct or happiness, infuse as much of your own spirit into her as you can. But this, no doubt, you have been always doing. It is the worst evil of too yielding and indecisive a character, that no influence over it can be depended on. You are never sure of a good impression being durable; everybody may sway it. Let those who would be happy be firm. Here is a nut," said he, catching one down from an upper bough, "to exemplify: a beautiful glossy nut, which, blessed with original strength, has outlived all the storms of autumn. Not a puncture, not a weak spot anywhere. This nut," he continued, with playful solemnity, "while so many of his brethren have fallen and been trodden underfoot, is still in possession of all the happiness that a hazelnut can be supposed capable of." Then returning to his former earnest tone, "My first wish for all whom I am interested in, is that they should be firm. If Louisa Musgrove would be beautiful and happy in her November of life, she will cherish all her present powers of mind."

He had done, and was unanswered. It would have surprised Anne if Louisa could have readily answered such a speech: words of such interest, spoken with such serious warmth! She could imagine what Louisa was feeling. For herself, she feared to move, lest she should be seen. While she remained, a bush of low rambling holly protected her, and they were moving on. Before they were beyond her hearing, however, Louisa spoke again.

"Mary is good-natured enough in many respects," said she; "but she does sometimes provoke me excessively, by her nonsense and pride—the Elliot pride. She has a great deal too much of the Elliot pride. We do so wish that Charles had married Anne instead. I suppose you know he wanted to marry Anne?"

After a moment's pause, Captain Wentworth said, "Do you mean that she refused him?"

"Oh! Yes, certainly."

"When did that happen?"

"I do not exactly know, for Henrietta and I were at school at the time; but I believe about a year before he married Mary. I wish she had accepted him. We should all have liked her a great deal better; and papa and mamma always think it was her great friend Lady Russell's doing, that she did not. They think Charles might not be learned and bookish enough to please Lady Russell, and that therefore, she persuaded Anne to refuse him."

The sounds were retreating, and Anne distinguished no more. Her own emotions still kept her fixed. She had much to recover from, before she could move. The listener's proverbial fate was not absolutely hers; she had heard no evil of herself, but she had heard a great deal of very painful import. She saw how her own character was considered by Captain Wentworth, and there had been just that degree of feeling and curiosity about her in his manner which must give her extreme agitation.

As soon as she could, she went after Mary, and having found, and walked back with her to their former station, by the stile, felt some comfort in their whole party being immediately afterwards collected, and once more in motion together.

Her spirits wanted the solitude and silence which only numbers could give.

Charles and Henrietta returned, bringing, as may be conjectured, Charles Hayter with them. The minutiae of the business Anne could not attempt to understand; even Captain Wentworth did not seem admitted to perfect confidence here; but that there had been a withdrawing on the gentleman's side, and a relenting on the lady's, and that they were now very glad to be together again, did not admit a doubt. Henrietta looked a little ashamed, but very well pleased; Charles Hayter exceedingly happy, and they were devoted to each other almost from the first instant of their all setting forward for Uppercross.

Everything now marked out Louisa for Captain Wentworth; nothing could be plainer; and where many divisions were necessary, or even where they were not, they walked side by side nearly as much as the other two. In a long strip of meadowland, where there was ample space for all, they were thus divided, forming three distinct parties; and to that party of the three, which boasted least animation, and least complaisance, Anne necessarily belonged. She joined Charles and Mary, and was tired enough to be very glad of Charles's other arm; but Charles, though in very good humour with her, was out of temper with his wife. Mary had shown herself disobliging to him, and was now to reap the consequence, which consequence was his dropping her arm almost every moment to cut off the heads of some nettles in the hedge with his switch; and when Mary began to complain of it, and lament her being ill-used, according to custom, in being on the hedge side, while Anne was never incommoded on the other, he dropped the arms of both to hunt after a weasel which he had a momentary glance of, and they could hardly get him along at all.

This long meadow bordered a lane, which their footpath, at the end of it, was to cross, and when the party had all reached the gate of exit, the carriage advancing in the same direction, which had been some time heard, was just coming up, and proved to be Admiral Croft's gig. He and his wife had taken their intended drive, and were returning home. Upon hearing how long a walk the young people had engaged in, they kindly offered a seat to any lady who might be particularly tired; it would save her a full mile, and they were going through Uppercross. The invitation was general, and generally declined. The Miss Musgroves were not at all tired, and Mary was either offended by not being asked before any of the others, or—what Louisa called the Elliot pride—could not endure to make a third in a one horse chaise.

The walking party had crossed the lane, and was surmounting an opposite stile, and the Admiral was putting his horse in motion again, when Captain Wentworth cleared the hedge in a moment to say something to his sister. The something might be guessed by its effects.

"Miss Elliot, I am sure *you* are tired," cried Mrs. Croft. "Do let us have the pleasure of taking you home. Here is excellent room for three, I assure you. If we were all like you, I believe we might sit four. You must, indeed, you must."

Anne was still in the lane; and though instinctively beginning to decline, she was not allowed to proceed. The Admiral's kind urgency came in support of his wife's; they would not be refused; they compressed themselves into the smallest possible space to leave her a corner, and Captain Wentworth, without saying a word, turned to her, and quietly obliged her to be assisted into the carriage.

Yes, he had done it. She was in the carriage, and felt that he had placed her there, that his will and his hands had done it, that she owed it to his perception of her fatigue, and his resolution to give her rest. She was very much affected by the view of his disposition towards her, which all these things made apparent. This little circumstance seemed the completion of all that had gone before. She understood him. He could not forgive her, but he could not be unfeeling. Though condemning her for the past, and considering it with high and unjust resentment, though perfectly careless of her, and though becoming attached to another, still he could not see her suffer, without the desire of giving her relief. It was a remainder of former sentiment; it was an impulse of pure, though unacknowledged friendship; it was a proof of his own warm and amiable heart, which she could not contemplate without emotions so compounded of pleasure and pain that she knew not which prevailed.

Her answers to the kindness and the remarks of her companions were at first unconsciously given. They had travelled half their way along the rough lane, before she was quite awake to what they said. She then found them talking of "Frederick."

"He certainly means to have one or other of those two girls, Sophy," said the Admiral; "but there is no saying which. He has been running after them, too, long enough, one would think, to make up his mind. Ay, this comes of the peace. If it were war now, he would have settled it long ago. We sailors, Miss Elliot, cannot afford to make long courtships in time of war. How many days was it, my dear, between the first time of my seeing you and our sitting down together in our lodgings at North Yarmouth?"

"We had better not talk about it, my dear," replied Mrs. Croft, pleasantly; "for if Miss Elliot were to hear how soon we came to an understanding, she would never be persuaded that we could be happy together. I had known you by character, however, long before."

"Well, and I had heard of you as a very pretty girl, and what were we to wait for besides? I do not like having such things so long in hand. I wish Frederick would spread a little more canvas, and bring us home one of these young ladies to Kellynch. Then there would always be company for us. And very nice young ladies they both are; I hardly know one from the other."

"Very good humoured, unaffected girls, indeed," said Mrs. Croft, in a tone of calmer praise, such as made Anne suspect that her keener powers might not consider either of them as quite worthy of her brother; "and a very respectable family. One could not be connected with better people. My dear Admiral, that post! We shall certainly take that post."

But by coolly giving the reins a better direction herself they happily passed the danger; and by once afterwards judiciously putting out her hand they neither fell into a rut, nor ran foul of a dung-cart; and Anne, with some amusement at their style of driving, which she imagined no bad representation of the general guidance of their affairs, found herself safely deposited by them at the Cottage.

CHAPTER 11

The time now approached for Lady Russell's return: the day was even fixed; and Anne, being engaged to join her as soon as she was resettled, was looking forward to an early removal to Kellynch, and beginning to think how her own comfort was likely to be affected by it.

It would place her in the same village with Captain Wentworth, within half a mile of him; they would have to frequent the same church, and there must be intercourse between the two families. This was against her; but on the other hand, he spent so much of his time at Uppercross, that in removing thence she might be considered rather as leaving him behind, than as going towards him; and, upon the whole, she believed she must, on this interesting question, be the gainer, almost as certainly as in her change of domestic society, in leaving poor Mary for Lady Russell.

She wished it might be possible for her to avoid ever seeing Captain Wentworth at the Hall: those rooms had witnessed former meetings which would be brought too painfully before her; but she was yet more anxious for the possibility of Lady Russell and Captain Wentworth never meeting anywhere. They did not like each other, and no renewal of acquaintance now could do any good; and were Lady Russell to see them together, she might think that he had too much self-possession, and she too little.

These points formed her chief solicitude in anticipating her removal from Uppercross, where she felt she had been stationed quite long enough. Her usefulness to little Charles would always give some sweetness to the memory of her two months' visit there, but he was gaining strength apace, and she had nothing else to stay for.

The conclusion of her visit, however, was diversified in a way that she had not at all imagined. Captain Wentworth, after being unseen and unheard of at Uppercross for two whole days, appeared again among them to justify himself by a relation of what had kept him away.

A letter from his friend, Captain Harville, having found him out at last, had brought intelligence of Captain Harville's being settled with his family at Lyme for the winter; of their being therefore, quite unknowingly, within twenty miles of each other. Captain Harville had never been in good health since a severe wound which he received two years before, and Captain Wentworth's anxiety to see him had determined him to go immediately to Lyme. He had been there for four-and-twenty hours. His acquittal was complete, his friendship warmly honoured, a lively interest excited for his friend, and his description of the fine country about Lyme so feelingly attended to by the party, that an earnest desire to see Lyme themselves, and a project for going thither was the consequence.

The young people were all wild to see Lyme. Captain Wentworth talked of going there again himself, it was only seventeen miles from Uppercross; though November, the weather was by no means bad; and, in short, Louisa, who was the most eager of the eager, having formed the resolution to go, and besides the pleasure of doing as she liked, being now armed with the idea of merit in maintaining her own way, bore down all the wishes of her father and mother for putting it off till summer; and to Lyme they were to go—Charles, Mary, Anne, Henrietta, Louisa, and Captain Wentworth.

The first heedless scheme had been to go in the morning and return at night; but to this Mr. Musgrove, for the sake of his horses, would not consent; and when it came to be rationally considered, a day in the middle of November would not leave much time for seeing a new place, after deducting seven hours, as the nature of the country required, for going and returning. They were, consequently, to stay the night there, and not to be expected back till the next day's dinner. This was felt to be a considerable amendment; and though they all met at the Great House at rather an early breakfast hour, and set off very punctually, it was so much past noon before the two carriages, Mr. Musgrove's coach containing the four ladies, and Charles's curricle, in which he drove Captain Wentworth, were descending the long hill into Lyme, and entering upon the still steeper street of the town itself, that it was very evident they would not have more than time for looking about them, before the light and warmth of the day were gone.

After securing accommodations, and ordering a dinner at one of the inns, the next thing to be done was unquestionably to walk directly down to the sea. They were come too late in the year for any amusement or variety, which Lyme, as a public place, might offer. The rooms were shut up, the lodgers almost all gone, scarcely any family but of the residents left; and, as there is nothing to admire in the buildings themselves, the remarkable situation of the town, the principal street almost hurrying into the water, the walk to the Cobb, skirting round the pleasant little bay, which, in the season, is animated with bathing machines and company, the Cobb itself, its old wonders and new improvements, with the very beautiful line of cliffs stretching out to the east of the town, are what the stranger's eye will seek; and a very strange stranger it must be, who does not see charms in the immediate environs of Lyme, to make him wish to know it better. The scenes in its neighbourhood, Charmouth, with its high grounds and extensive sweeps of country, and still more, its sweet, retired bay, backed by dark cliffs, where fragments of low rock among the sands make it the happiest spot for watching the flow of the tide, for sitting in unwearied contemplation; the woody varieties of the cheerful village of Up Lyme; and, above all, Pinny, with its green chasms between romantic rocks, where the scattered forest trees and orchards of luxuriant growth declare that many a generation must have passed away since the first partial falling of the cliff prepared the ground for such a state, where a scene so wonderful and so lovely is exhibited, as may more than equal any of the resembling scenes of the far-famed Isle of Wight: these places must be visited, and visited again, to make the worth of Lyme understood.

The party from Uppercross passing down by the now deserted and melancholy looking rooms, and still descending, soon found themselves on the seashore; and lingering only, as all must linger and gaze on a first return to the sea, whoever deserved to look on it at all, proceeded towards the Cobb, equally their object in itself and on Captain Wentworth's account: for in a small house, near the foot of an old pier of unknown date, were the Harvilles settled. Captain Wentworth turned in to call on his friend; the others walked on, and he was to join them on the Cobb.

They were by no means tired of wondering and admiring; and not even Louisa seemed to feel that they had parted with Captain Wentworth long, when they saw him coming after them, with three companions, all well known already, by description, to be Captain and Mrs. Harville, and a Captain Benwick, who was staying with them.

Captain Benwick had some time ago been first lieutenant of the *Laconia*; and the account which Captain Wentworth had given of him, on his return from Lyme before, his warm praise of him as an excellent young man and an officer, whom he had always valued highly, which must have stamped him well in the esteem of every listener, had been followed by a little history of his private life, which rendered him perfectly interesting in the eyes of all the ladies. He had been engaged to Captain Harville's sister, and was now mourning her loss. They had been a year or two waiting for fortune and promotion. Fortune came, his prize-money as lieutenant being great; promotion, too, came at *last*; but Fanny Harville did not live to know it. She had died the preceding summer while he was at sea. Captain Wentworth believed it impossible for man to be more attached to woman than poor Benwick had been to Fanny Harville, or to be more deeply afflicted under the dreadful change. He considered his disposition as of the sort that must suffer heavily, uniting very strong feelings with quiet, serious, and retiring manners, and a decided taste for reading, and sedentary pursuits. To finish the interest of the story, the friendship between him and the Harvilles seemed, if possible, augmented by the event, which closed all their views of alliance, and Captain Benwick was now living with them entirely.

Captain Harville had taken his present house for half a year; his taste, and his health, and his fortune, all directing him to a residence inexpensive, and by the sea; and the grandeur of the country, and the retirement of Lyme in the winter, appeared exactly adapted to Captain Benwick's state of mind. The sympathy and goodwill excited towards Captain Benwick was very great.

"And yet," said Anne to herself, as they now moved forward to meet the party, "he has not, perhaps, a more sorrowing heart than I have. I cannot believe his prospects so blighted forever. He is younger than I am; younger in feeling, if not in fact; younger as a man. He will rally again, and be happy with another."

They all met, and were introduced. Captain Harville was a tall, dark man, with a sensible, benevolent countenance; a little lame; and from strong features and want of health, looking much older than Captain Wentworth. Captain Benwick looked, and was, the youngest of the three, and, compared with either of them, a little man. He had a pleasing face and a melancholy air, just as he ought to have, and drew back from conversation.

Captain Harville, though not equalling Captain Wentworth in

manners, was a perfect gentleman, unaffected, warm, and obliging. Mrs. Harville, a degree less polished than her husband, seemed, however, to have the same good feelings; and nothing could be more pleasant than their desire of considering the whole party as friends of their own, because the friends of Captain Wentworth, or more kindly hospitable than their entreaties for their all promising to dine with them. The dinner, already ordered at the inn, was at last, though unwillingly, accepted as an excuse; but they seemed almost hurt that Captain Wentworth should have brought any such party to Lyme, without considering it as a thing of course that they should dine with them.

There was so much attachment to Captain Wentworth in all this, and such a bewitching charm in a degree of hospitality so uncommon, so unlike the usual style of give-and-take invitations, and dinners of formality and display, that Anne felt her spirits not likely to be benefited by an increasing acquaintance among his brother-officers. "These would have been all my friends," was her thought; and she had to struggle against a great tendency to lowness.

On quitting the Cobb, they all went indoors with their new friends, and found rooms so small as none but those who invite from the heart could think capable of accommodating so many. Anne had a moment's astonishment on the subject herself; but it was soon lost in the pleasanter feelings which sprang from the sight of all the ingenious contrivances and nice arrangements of Captain Harville, to turn the actual space to the best account, to supply the deficiencies of lodging-house furniture, and defend the windows and doors against the winter storms to be expected. The varieties in the fitting-up of the rooms, where the common necessaries provided by the owner, in the common indifferent plight, were contrasted with some few articles of a rare species of wood, excellently worked up, and with something curious and valuable from all the distant countries Captain Harville had visited, were more than amusing to Anne; connected as it all was with his profession, the fruit of its labours, the effect of its influence on his habits, the picture of repose and domestic happiness it presented, made it to her a something more, or less, than gratification.

Captain Harville was no reader; but he had contrived excellent accommodations, and fashioned very pretty shelves, for a tolerable collection of well-bound volumes, the property of Captain Benwick.

His lameness prevented him from taking much exercise; but a mind of usefulness and ingenuity seemed to furnish him with constant employment within. He drew, he varnished, he carpentered, he glued; he made toys for the children; he fashioned new netting-needles and pins with improvements; and if everything else was done, sat down to his large fishing-net at one corner of the room.

Anne thought she left great happiness behind her when they quitted the house; and Louisa, by whom she found herself walking, burst forth into raptures of admiration and delight on the character of the navy; their friendliness, their brotherliness, their openness, their uprightness; protesting that she was convinced of sailors having more worth and warmth than any other set of men in England; that they only knew how to live, and they only deserved to be respected and loved.

They went back to dress and dine; and so well had the scheme answered already, that nothing was found amiss; though its being "so entirely out of season," and the "no thoroughfare of Lyme," and the "no expectation of company," had brought many apologies from the heads of the inn.

Anne found herself by this time growing so much more hardened to being in Captain Wentworth's company than she had at first imagined could ever be, that the sitting down to the same table with him now, and the interchange of the common civilities attending on it (they never got beyond), was become a mere nothing.

The nights were too dark for the ladies to meet again till the morrow, but Captain Harville had promised them a visit in the evening; and he came, bringing his friend also, which was more than had been expected, it having been agreed that Captain Benwick had all the appearance of being oppressed by the presence of so many strangers. He ventured among them again, however, though his spirits certainly did not seem fit for the mirth of the party in general.

While Captains Wentworth and Harville led the talk on one side of the room, and by recurring to former days, supplied anecdotes in abundance to occupy and entertain the others, it fell to Anne's lot to be placed rather apart with Captain Benwick; and a very good impulse of her nature obliged her to begin an acquaintance with him. He was shy, and disposed to abstraction; but the engaging mildness of her countenance, and gentleness of her manners, soon had their effect; and Anne was well repaid the first trouble of exertion. He was evidently a young man of considerable taste in reading, though principally in poetry; and besides the persuasion of having given him at least an evening's indulgence in the discussion of subjects, which his usual companions had probably no concern in, she had the hope of being of real use to him in some suggestions as to the duty and benefit of struggling against affliction, which had naturally grown out of their conversation. For, though shy, he did not seem reserved; it had rather the appearance of feelings glad to burst their usual restraints; and having talked of poetry, the richness of the present age, and gone through a brief comparison of opinion as to the first-rate poets, trying to ascertain whether *Marmion* or *The Lady of the Lake* were to be preferred, and how ranked the *Giaour* and *The Bride of Abydos*; and moreover, how the *Giaour* was to be pronounced, he showed himself so intimately acquainted with all the tenderest songs of the one poet, and all the impassioned descriptions of hopeless agony of the other; he repeated, with such tremulous feeling, the various lines which imaged a broken heart, or a mind destroyed by wretchedness, and looked so entirely as if he meant to be understood, that she ventured to hope he did not always read only poetry, and to say, that she thought it was the misfortune of poetry to be seldom safely enjoyed by those who enjoyed it completely; and that the strong feelings which alone could estimate it truly were the very feelings which ought to taste it but sparingly.

His looks showing him not pained, but pleased with this allusion to his situation, she was emboldened to go on; and feeling in herself the right of seniority of mind, she ventured to recommend a larger allowance of prose in his daily study; and on being requested to particularize, mentioned such works of our best moralists, such collections of the finest letters, such memoirs of characters of worth and suffering, as occurred to her at the moment as calculated to rouse and fortify the mind by the highest precepts, and the strongest examples of moral and religious endurances.

Captain Benwick listened attentively, and seemed grateful for the interest implied; and though with a shake of the head, and sighs which declared his little faith in the efficacy of any books on grief like his, noted down the names of those she recommended, and promised to procure and read them.

When the evening was over, Anne could not but be amused at the idea of her coming to Lyme to preach patience and resignation to a young man whom she had never seen before; nor could she help fearing, on more serious reflection, that, like many other great moralists and preachers, she had been eloquent on a point in which her own conduct would ill bear examination.

CHAPTER 12

Anne and Henrietta, finding themselves the earliest of the party the next morning, agreed to stroll down to the sea before breakfast. They went to the sands, to watch the flowing of the tide, which a fine southeasterly breeze was bringing in with all the grandeur that so flat a shore admitted. They praised the morning; gloried in the sea; sympathized in the delight of the fresh-feeling breeze—and were silent; till Henrietta suddenly began again with, "Oh! Yes, I am quite convinced that, with very few exceptions, the sea-air always does good. There can be no doubt of its having been of the greatest service to Dr. Shirley, after his illness, last spring twelvemonth. He declares himself, that coming to Lyme for a month did him more good than all the medicine he took; and, that being by the sea, always makes him feel young again. Now, I cannot help thinking it a pity that he does not live entirely by the sea. I do think he had better leave Uppercross entirely, and fix at Lyme. Do not you, Anne? Do not you agree with me, that it is the best thing he could do, both for himself and Mrs. Shirley? She has cousins here, you know, and many acquaintance, which would make it cheerful for her, and I am sure she would be glad to get to a place where she could have medical attendance at hand, in case of his having another seizure. Indeed I think it quite melancholy to have such excellent people as Dr. and Mrs. Shirley, who have been doing good all their lives, wearing out their last days in a place like Uppercross, where, excepting our family, they seem shut out from all the world. I wish his friends would propose it to him. I really think they ought. And, as to procuring a dispensation, there could be no difficulty at his time of life, and with his character. My only doubt is, whether anything could persuade him to leave his parish. He is so very strict and scrupulous in his notions; over-scrupulous I must say. Do not you think, Anne, it is being over-scrupulous? Do not you think it is quite a mistaken point of conscience, when a clergyman sacrifices his health for the sake of duties, which may be just as well performed by another person? And at Lyme too, only seventeen miles off, he would be near enough to hear, if people thought there was anything to complain of."

Anne smiled more than once to herself during this speech, and entered into the subject, as ready to do good by entering into the feelings of a young lady as of a young man, though here it was good of a lower standard, for what could be offered but general acquiescence? She said all that was reasonable and proper on the business; felt the claims of Dr. Shirley to repose as she ought; saw how very desirable it was that he should have some active, respectable young man, as a resident curate, and was even courteous enough to hint at the advantage of such resident curate's being married.

"I wish," said Henrietta, very well pleased with her companion, "I wish Lady Russell lived at Uppercross, and were intimate with Dr. Shirley. I have always heard of Lady Russell as a woman of the greatest influence with everybody! I always look upon her as able to persuade a person to anything! I am afraid of her, as I have told you before, quite afraid of her, because she is so very clever; but I respect her amazingly, and wish we had such a neighbour at Uppercross."

Anne was amused by Henrietta's manner of being grateful, and amused also that the course of events and the new interests of Henrietta's views should have placed her friend at all in favour with any of the Musgrove family; she had only time, however, for a general answer, and a wish that such another woman were at Uppercross, before all subjects suddenly ceased, on seeing Louisa and Captain Wentworth coming towards them. They came also for a stroll till breakfast was likely to be ready; but Louisa recollecting, immediately afterwards, that she had something to procure at a shop, invited them all to go back with her into the town. They were all at her disposal.

When they came to the steps, leading upwards from the beach, a gentleman, at the same moment preparing to come down, politely drew back, and stopped to give them way. They ascended and passed him; and as they passed, Anne's face caught his eye, and he looked at her with a degree of earnest admiration, which she could not be insensible of. She was looking remarkably well; her very regular, very pretty features, having the bloom and freshness of youth restored by the fine wind, which had been blowing on her complexion, and by the animation of eye, which it had also produced. It was evident that the gentleman, (completely a gentleman in manner) admired her exceedingly. Captain Wentworth looked round at her instantly in a way which showed his noticing of it. He gave her a momentary glance, a glance of brightness, which seemed to say, "That man is struck with you, and even I, at this moment, see something like Anne Elliot again."

After attending Louisa through her business, and loitering about a little longer, they returned to the inn; and Anne, in passing afterwards quickly from her own chamber to their dining room, had nearly run against the very same gentleman, as he came out of an adjoining apartment. She had before conjectured him to be a stranger like themselves, and determined that a well-looking groom, who was strolling about near the two inns as they came back, should be his servant. Both master and man being in mourning assisted the idea. It was now proved that he belonged to the same inn as themselves; and this second meeting, short as it was, also proved again by the gentleman's looks, that he thought hers very lovely, and by the readiness and propriety of his apologies, that he was a man of exceedingly good manners. He seemed about thirty, and though not handsome, had an agreeable person. Anne felt that she should like to know who he was.

They had nearly done breakfast, when the sound of a carriage, (almost the first they had heard since entering Lyme) drew half the party to the window. It was a gentleman's carriage, a curricle, but only coming round from the stable-yard to the front door; somebody must be going away. It was driven by a servant in mourning.

The word curricle made Charles Musgrove jump up that he might compare it with his own, the servant in mourning roused Anne's curiosity, and the whole six were collected to look, by the time the owner of the curricle was to be seen issuing from the door amidst the bows and civilities of the household, and taking his seat, to drive off.

"Ah!" cried Captain Wentworth, instantly, and with half a glance at Anne, "it is the very man we passed."

The Miss Musgroves agreed to it; and having all kindly watched him as far up the hill as they could, they returned to the breakfast table. The waiter came into the room soon afterwards.

"Pray," said Captain Wentworth, immediately, "can you tell us the name of the gentleman who is just gone away?"

"Yes, sir, a Mr. Elliot, a gentleman of large fortune, came in last night from Sidmouth. Dare say you heard the carriage, sir, while you were at dinner; and going on now for Crewkherne, in his way to Bath and London."

"Elliot!" Many had looked on each other, and many had repeated the name, before all this had been got through, even by the smart rapidity of a waiter.

"Bless me!" cried Mary, "It must be our cousin; it must be our Mr. Elliot, it must, indeed! Charles, Anne, must not it? In mourning, you see, just as our Mr. Elliot must be. How very extraordinary! In the very same inn with us! Anne, must not it be our Mr. Elliot? My father's next heir? Pray sir," turning to the waiter, "did not you hear, did not his servant say whether he belonged to the Kellynch family?"

"No, ma'am, he did not mention no particular family; but he said his master was a very rich gentleman, and would be a baronight some day."

"There! You see!" cried Mary in an ecstasy. "Just as I said! Heir to Sir Walter Elliot! I was sure that would come out, if it was so. Depend upon it, that is a circumstance that his servants take care to publish, wherever he goes. But, Anne, only conceive how extraordinary! I wish I had looked at him more. I wish we had been aware in time, who it was, that he might have been introduced to us. What a pity that we should not have been introduced to each other! Do you think he had the Elliot countenance? I hardly looked at him, I was looking at the horses; but I think he had something of the Elliot countenance. I wonder the arms did not strike me! Oh! The greatcoat was hanging over the panel, and hid the arms, so it did; otherwise, I am sure, I should have observed them, and the livery too; if the servant had not been in mourning, one should have known him by the livery."

"Putting all these very extraordinary circumstances together," said Captain Wentworth, "we must consider it to be the arrangement of Providence, that you should not be introduced to your cousin."

When she could command Mary's attention, Anne quietly tried to convince her that their father and Mr. Elliot had not, for many years, been on such terms as to make the power of attempting an introduction at all desirable.

At the same time, however, it was a secret gratification to herself to have seen her cousin, and to know that the future owner of Kellynch was undoubtedly a gentleman, and had an air of good sense. She would not, upon any account, mention her having met with him the second time; luckily Mary did not much attend to their having passed close by him in their earlier walk, but she would have felt quite ill-used by Anne's having actually run against him in the passage, and received his very polite excuses, while she had never been near him at all; no, that cousinly little interview must remain a perfect secret.

"Of course," said Mary, "you will mention our seeing Mr. Elliot, the next time you write to Bath. I think my father certainly ought to hear of it; do mention all about him."

Anne avoided a direct reply, but it was just the circumstance which she considered as not merely unnecessary to be communicated, but as what ought to be suppressed. The offence which had been given her father, many years back, she knew; Elizabeth's particular share in it she suspected; and that Mr. Elliot's idea always produced irritation in both was beyond a doubt. Mary never wrote to Bath herself; all the toil of keeping up a slow and unsatisfactory correspondence with Elizabeth fell on Anne.

Breakfast had not been long over, when they were joined by Captain and Mrs. Harville and Captain Benwick, with whom they had appointed to take their last walk about Lyme. They ought to be setting off for Uppercross by one, and in the meanwhile were to be all together, and out of doors as long as they could.

Anne found Captain Benwick getting near her, as soon as they were all fairly in the street. Their conversation the preceding evening did not disincline him to seek her again; and they walked together some time, talking as before of Mr. Scott and Lord Byron, and still as unable as before, and as unable as any other two readers, to think exactly alike of the merits of either, till something occasioned an almost general change amongst their party, and instead of Captain Benwick, she had Captain Harville by her side.

"Miss Elliot," said he, speaking rather low, "you have done a good deed in making that poor fellow talk so much. I wish he could have such company oftener. It is bad for him, I know, to be shut up as he is; but what can we do? We cannot part."

"No," said Anne, "that I can easily believe to be impossible; but in time, perhaps—we know what time does in every case of affliction, and you must remember, Captain Harville, that your friend may yet be called a young mourner—only last summer, I understand."

"Ay, true enough," (with a deep sigh) "only June."

"And not known to him, perhaps, so soon."

"Not till the first week of August, when he came home from the Cape, just made into the *Grappler*. I was at Plymouth dreading to hear of him; he sent in letters, but the *Grappler* was under orders for Portsmouth. There the news must follow him, but who was to tell it? Not I. I would as soon have been run up to the yardarm. Nobody could do it, but that good fellow" (pointing to Captain Wentworth.) "The *Laconia* had come into Plymouth the week before; no danger of her being sent to sea again. He stood his chance for the rest: wrote up for leave of absence, but without waiting the return, travelled night and day till he got to Portsmouth, rowed off to the *Grappler* that instant, and never left the poor fellow for a week. That's what he did, and nobody else could have saved poor James. You may think, Miss Elliot, whether he is dear to us!"

Anne did think on the question with perfect decision, and said as much in reply as her own feeling could accomplish, or as his seemed able to bear, for he was too much affected to renew the subject, and when he spoke again, it was of something totally different.

Mrs. Harville's giving it as her opinion that her husband would have quite walking enough by the time he reached home, determined the direction of all the party in what was to be their last walk; they would accompany them to their door, and then return and set off themselves. By all their calculations there was just time for this; but as they drew near the Cobb, there was such a general wish to walk along it once more, all were so inclined, and Louisa soon grew so determined, that the difference of a quarter of an hour, it was found, would be no difference at all; so with all the kind leave-taking, and all the kind interchange of invitations and promises which may be imagined, they parted from Captain and Mrs. Harville at their own door, and still accompanied by Captain Benwick, who seemed to cling to them to the last, proceeded to make the proper adieus to the Cobb.

Anne found Captain Benwick again drawing near her. Lord Byron's "dark blue seas" could not fail of being brought forward by their present view, and she gladly gave him all her attention as long as attention was possible. It was soon drawn, perforce another way.

There was too much wind to make the high part of the new Cobb pleasant for the ladies, and they agreed to get down the steps to the lower, and all were contented to pass quietly and carefully down the steep flight, excepting Louisa; she must be jumped down them by Captain Wentworth. In all their walks, he had had to jump her from the stiles; the sensation was delightful to her. The hardness of the pavement for her feet, made him less willing upon the present occasion; he did it, however. She was safely down, and instantly, to show her enjoyment, ran up the steps to be jumped down again. He advised her against it, thought the jar too great; but no, he reasoned and talked in vain; she smiled and said, "I am determined I will:" he put out his hands; she was too precipitate by half a second, she fell on the pavement on the Lower Cobb, and was taken up lifeless!

There was no wound, no blood, no visible bruise; but her eyes were closed, she breathed not, her face was like death. The horror of the moment to all who stood around!

Captain Wentworth, who had caught her up, knelt with her in his arms, looking on her with a face as pallid as her own, in an agony of silence. "She is dead! She is dead!" screamed Mary, catching hold of her husband, and contributing with his own horror to make him immoveable; and in another moment, Henrietta, sinking under the conviction, lost her senses too, and would have fallen on the steps, but for Captain Benwick and Anne, who caught and supported her between them.

"Is there no one to help me?" were the first words which burst from Captain Wentworth, in a tone of despair, and as if all his own strength were gone.

"Go to him, go to him," cried Anne, "for heaven's sake go to him. I can support her myself. Leave me, and go to him. Rub her hands, rub her temples; here are salts; take them, take them."

Captain Benwick obeyed, and Charles at the same moment, disengaging himself from his wife, they were both with him; and Louisa was raised up and supported more firmly between them, and everything was done that Anne had prompted, but in vain; while Captain Wentworth, staggering against the wall for his support, exclaimed in the bitterest agony, "Oh God! Her father and mother!"

"A surgeon!" said Anne.

He caught the word; it seemed to rouse him at once, and saying only, "True, true, a surgeon this instant," was darting away, when Anne eagerly suggested, "Captain Benwick, would not it be better for Captain Benwick? He knows where a surgeon is to be found."

Everyone capable of thinking felt the advantage of the idea, and in a moment (it was all done in rapid moments) Captain Benwick had resigned the poor corpse-like figure entirely to the brother's care, and was off for the town with the utmost rapidity.

As to the wretched party left behind, it could scarcely be said which of the three, who were completely rational, was suffering most: Captain Wentworth, Anne, or Charles, who, really a very affectionate brother, hung over Louisa with sobs of grief, and could only turn his eyes from one sister, to see the other in a state as insensible, or to witness the hysterical agitations of his wife, calling on him for help which he could not give.

Anne, attending with all the strength and zeal, and thought, which instinct supplied, to Henrietta, still tried, at intervals, to suggest comfort to the others, tried to quiet Mary, to animate Charles, to assuage the feelings of Captain Wentworth. Both seemed to look to her for directions.

"Anne, Anne," cried Charles, "What is to be done next? What, in heaven's name, is to be done next?"

Captain Wentworth's eyes were also turned towards her.

"Had not she better be carried to the inn? Yes, I am sure: carry her gently to the inn."

"Yes, yes, to the inn," repeated Captain Wentworth, comparatively collected, and eager to be doing something. "I will carry her myself. Musgrove, take care of the others."

By this time the report of the accident had spread among the workmen and boatmen about the Cobb, and many were collected near them, to be useful if wanted, at any rate, to enjoy the sight of a dead young lady, nay, two dead young ladies, for it proved twice as fine as the first report. To some of the best-looking of these good people Henrietta was consigned, for, though partially revived, she was quite helpless; and in this manner, Anne walking by her side, and Charles attending to his wife, they set forward, treading back with feelings unutterable, the ground, which so lately, so very lately, and so light of heart, they had passed along.

They were not off the Cobb, before the Harvilles met them. Captain Benwick had been seen flying by their house, with a countenance that showed something to be wrong; and they had set off immediately, informed and directed as they passed, towards the spot. Shocked as Captain Harville was, he brought senses and nerves that could be instantly useful; and a look between him and his wife decided what was to be done. She must be taken to their house; all must go to their house; and await the surgeon's arrival there. They would not listen to scruples:

he was obeyed; they were all beneath his roof; and while Louisa, under Mrs. Harville's direction, was conveyed upstairs, and given possession of her own bed, assistance, cordials, restoratives were supplied by her husband to all who needed them.

Louisa had once opened her eyes, but soon closed them again, without apparent consciousness. This had been a proof of life, however, of service to her sister; and Henrietta, though perfectly incapable of being in the same room with Louisa, was kept, by the agitation of hope and fear, from a return of her own insensibility. Mary, too, was growing calmer.

The surgeon was with them almost before it had seemed possible. They were sick with horror, while he examined; but he was not hopeless. The head had received a severe contusion, but he had seen greater injuries recovered from: he was by no means hopeless; he spoke cheerfully.

That he did not regard it as a desperate case, that he did not say a few hours must end it, was at first felt, beyond the hope of most; and the ecstasy of such a reprieve, the rejoicing, deep and silent, after a few fervent ejaculations of gratitude to Heaven had been offered, may be conceived.

The tone, the look, with which "Thank God!" was uttered by Captain Wentworth, Anne was sure could never be forgotten by her; nor the sight of him afterwards, as he sat near a table, leaning over it with folded arms and face concealed, as if overpowered by the various feelings of his soul, and trying by prayer and reflection to calm them.

Louisa's limbs had escaped. There was no injury but to the head.

It now became necessary for the party to consider what was best to be done, as to their general situation. They were now able to speak to each other and consult. That Louisa must remain where she was, however distressing to her friends to be involving the Harvilles in such trouble, did not admit a doubt. Her removal was impossible. The Harvilles silenced all scruples; and, as much as they could, all gratitude. They had looked forward and arranged everything before the others began to reflect. Captain Benwick must give up his room to them, and get another bed elsewhere; and the whole was settled. They were only concerned that the house could accommodate no more; and yet perhaps, by "putting the children away in the maid's room, or swinging a cot somewhere," they could hardly bear to think of not finding room for two or three besides, supposing they might wish to stay; though, with regard to any attendance on Miss Musgrove, there need not be the least uneasiness in leaving her to Mrs. Harville's care entirely. Mrs. Harville was a very experienced nurse, and her nurserymaid, who had lived with her long, and gone about with her everywhere, was just such another. Between these two, she could want no possible attendance by day or night. And all this was said with a truth and sincerity of feeling irresistible.

Charles, Henrietta, and Captain Wentworth were the three in consultation, and for a little while it was only an interchange of perplexity and terror. "Uppercross, the necessity of someone's going to Uppercross; the news to be conveyed; how it could be broken to Mr. and Mrs. Musgrove; the lateness of the morning; an hour already gone since they ought to have been off; the impossibility of being in tolerable time."

At first, they were capable of nothing more to the purpose than such exclamations; but, after a while, Captain Wentworth, exerting himself, said, "We must be decided, and without the loss of another minute. Every minute is valuable. Someone must resolve on being off for Uppercross instantly. Musgrove, either you or I must go."

Charles agreed, but declared his resolution of not going away. He would be as little encumbrance as possible to Captain and Mrs. Harville; but as to leaving his sister in such a state, he neither ought, nor would. So far it was decided; and Henrietta at first declared the same. She, however, was soon persuaded to think differently. The usefulness of her staying! She who had not been able to remain in Louisa's room, or to look at her, without sufferings which made her worse than helpless! She was forced to acknowledge that she could do no good, yet was still unwilling to be away, till touched by the thought of her father and mother, she gave it up; she consented, she was anxious to be at home.

The plan had reached this point, when Anne, coming quietly down from Louisa's room, could not but hear what followed, for the parlour door was open.

"Then it is settled, Musgrove," cried Captain Wentworth, "that you stay, and that I take care of your sister home. But as to the rest, as to the others, if one stays to assist Mrs. Harville, I think it need be only one. Mrs. Charles Musgrove will, of course, wish to get back to her children; but if Anne will stay, no one so proper, so capable as Anne."

She paused a moment to recover from the emotion of hearing

herself so spoken of. The other two warmly agreed with what he said, and she then appeared.

"You will stay, I am sure; you will stay and nurse her;" cried he, turning to her and speaking with a glow, and yet a gentleness, which seemed almost restoring the past. She coloured deeply, and he recollected himself, and moved away. She expressed herself most willing, ready, happy to remain. "It was what she had been thinking of, and wishing to be allowed to do. A bed on the floor in Louisa's room would be sufficient for her, if Mrs. Harville would but think so."

One thing more, and all seemed arranged. Though it was rather desirable that Mr. and Mrs. Musgrove should be previously alarmed by some share of delay; yet the time required by the Uppercross horses to take them back, would be a dreadful extension of suspense; and Captain Wentworth proposed, and Charles Musgrove agreed, that it would be much better for him to take a chaise from the inn, and leave Mr. Musgrove's carriage and horses to be sent home the next morning early, when there would be the farther advantage of sending an account of Louisa's night.

Captain Wentworth now hurried off to get everything ready on his part, and to be soon followed by the two ladies. When the plan was made known to Mary, however, there was an end of all peace in it. She was so wretched and so vehement, complained so much of injustice in being expected to go away instead of Anne; Anne, who was nothing to Louisa, while she was her sister, and had the best right to stay in Henrietta's stead! Why was not she to be as useful as Anne? And to go home without Charles, too, without her husband! No, it was too unkind. And in short, she said more than her husband could long withstand, and as none of the others could oppose when he gave way, there was no help for it; the change of Mary for Anne was inevitable.

Anne had never submitted more reluctantly to the jealous and ill-judging claims of Mary; but so it must be, and they set off for the town, Charles taking care of his sister, and Captain Benwick attending to her. She gave a moment's recollection, as they hurried along, to the little circumstances which the same spots had witnessed earlier in the morning. There she had listened to Henrietta's schemes for Dr. Shirley's leaving Uppercross; farther on, she had first seen Mr. Elliot; a moment seemed all that could now be given to anyone but Louisa, or those who were wrapped up in her welfare.

Captain Benwick was most considerately attentive to her; and, united as they all seemed by the distress of the day, she felt an increasing degree of goodwill towards him, and a pleasure even in thinking that it might, perhaps, be the occasion of continuing their acquaintance.

Captain Wentworth was on the watch for them, and a chaise and four in waiting, stationed for their convenience in the lowest part of the street; but his evident surprise and vexation at the substitution of one sister for the other, the change in his countenance, the astonishment, the expressions begun and suppressed, with which Charles was listened to, made but a mortifying reception of Anne; or must at least convince her that she was valued only as she could be useful to Louisa.

She endeavoured to be composed, and to be just. Without emulating the feelings of an Emma towards her Henry, she would have attended on Louisa with a zeal above the common claims of regard, for his sake; and she hoped he would not long be so unjust as to suppose she would shrink unnecessarily from the office of a friend.

In the meanwhile she was in the carriage. He had handed them both in, and placed himself between them; and in this manner, under these circumstances, full of astonishment and emotion to Anne, she quitted Lyme. How the long stage would pass; how it was to affect their manners; what was to be their sort of intercourse, she could not foresee. It was all quite natural, however. He was devoted to Henrietta; always turning towards her; and when he spoke at all, always with the view of supporting her hopes and raising her spirits. In general, his voice and manner were studiously calm. To spare Henrietta from agitation seemed the governing principle. Once only, when she had been grieving over the last ill-judged, ill-fated walk to the Cobb, bitterly lamenting that it ever had been thought of, he burst forth, as if wholly overcome—

"Don't talk of it, don't talk of it," he cried. "Oh God! That I had not given way to her at the fatal moment! Had I done as I ought! But so eager and so resolute! Dear, sweet Louisa!"

Anne wondered whether it ever occurred to him now, to question the justness of his own previous opinion as to the universal felicity and advantage of firmness of character; and whether it might not strike him that, like all other qualities of the mind, it should have its proportions and limits. She thought it could scarcely escape him to feel that a persuadable temper might sometimes be as much in favour of happiness as a very resolute character.

They got on fast. Anne was astonished to recognise the same hills and the same objects so soon. Their actual speed, heightened by some dread of the conclusion, made the road appear but half as long as on the day before. It was growing quite dusk, however, before they were in the neighbourhood of Uppercross, and there had been total silence among them for some time, Henrietta leaning back in the corner, with a shawl over her face, giving the hope of her having cried herself to sleep; when, as they were going up their last hill, Anne found herself all at once addressed by Captain Wentworth. In a low, cautious voice, he said:

"I have been considering what we had best do. She must not appear at first. She could not stand it. I have been thinking whether you had not better remain in the carriage with her, while I go in and break it to Mr. and Mrs. Musgrove. Do you think this is a good plan?"

She did: he was satisfied, and said no more. But the remembrance of the appeal remained a pleasure to her, as a proof of friendship, and of deference for her judgement, a great pleasure; and when it became a sort of parting proof; its value did not lessen.

When the distressing communication at Uppercross was over, and he had seen the father and mother quite as composed as could be hoped, and the daughter all the better for being with them, he announced his intention of returning in the same carriage to Lyme; and when the horses were baited, he was off.

CHAPTER 13

The remainder of Anne's time at Uppercross, comprehending only two days, was spent entirely at the Mansion House; and she had the satisfaction of knowing herself extremely useful there, both as an immediate companion, and as assisting in all those arrangements for the future, which, in Mr. and Mrs. Musgrove's distressed state of spirits, would have been difficulties.

They had an early account from Lyme the next morning. Louisa was much the same. No symptoms worse than before had appeared. Charles came a few hours afterwards, to bring a later and more particular account. He was tolerably cheerful. A speedy cure must not be hoped, but everything was going on as well as the nature of the case admitted. In speaking of the Harvilles, he seemed unable to satisfy his own sense of their kindness, especially of Mrs. Harville's exertions as a nurse. "She really left nothing for Mary to do. He and Mary had been persuaded to go early to their inn last night. Mary had been hysterical again this morning. When he came away, she was going to walk out with Captain Benwick, which, he hoped, would do her good. He almost wished she had been prevailed on to come home the day before; but the truth was, that Mrs. Harville left nothing for anybody to do."

Charles was to return to Lyme the same afternoon, and his father had at first half a mind to go with him, but the ladies could not consent. It would be going only to multiply trouble to the others, and increase his own distress; and a much better scheme followed and was acted upon. A chaise was sent for from Crewkherne, and Charles conveyed back a far more useful person in the old nurserymaid of the family, one who having brought up all the children, and seen the very last, the lingering and long-petted Master Harry, sent to school after his brothers, was now living in her deserted nursery to mend stockings and dress all the blains and bruises she could get near her, and who, consequently, was only too happy in being allowed to go and help nurse dear Miss Louisa. Vague wishes of getting Sarah thither, had occurred before to Mrs. Musgrove and Henrietta; but without Anne, it would hardly have been resolved on, and found practicable so soon.

They were indebted, the next day, to Charles Hayter, for all the minute knowledge of Louisa, which it was so essential to obtain every twenty-four hours. He made it his business to go to Lyme, and his account was still encouraging. The intervals of sense and consciousness were believed to be stronger. Every report agreed in Captain Wentworth's appearing fixed in Lyme.

Anne was to leave them on the morrow, an event that they all dreaded. "What should they do without her? They were wretched comforters for one another." And so much was said in this way, that Anne thought she could not do better than impart among them the general inclination to which she was privy, and persuaded them all to go to Lyme at once. She had little difficulty; it was soon determined that they would go; go tomorrow, fix themselves at the inn, or get into lodgings, as it suited, and there remain till dear Louisa could be moved.

They must be taking off some trouble from the good people she was with; they might at least relieve Mrs. Harville from the care of her own children; and in short, they were so happy in the decision, that Anne was delighted with what she had done, and felt that she could not spend her last morning at Uppercross better than in assisting their preparations, and sending them off at an early hour, though her being left to the solitary range of the house was the consequence.

She was the last, excepting the little boys at the cottage, she was the very last, the only remaining one of all that had filled and animated both houses, of all that had given Uppercross its cheerful character. A few days had made a change indeed! If Louisa recovered, it would all be well again. More than former happiness would be restored. There could not be a doubt, to her mind there was none, of what would follow her recovery. A few months hence, and the room now so deserted, occupied but by her silent, pensive self, might be filled again with all that was happy and gay, all that was glowing and bright in prosperous love, all that was most unlike Anne Elliot! An hour's complete leisure for such reflections as these, on a dark November day, a small thick rain almost blotting out the very few objects ever to be discerned from the windows, was enough to make the sound of Lady Russell's carriage exceedingly welcome; and yet, though desirous to be gone, she could not quit the Mansion House, or look an adieu to the Cottage, with its black, dripping and comfortless veranda, or even notice through the misty glasses the last humble tenements of the village, without a saddened heart. Scenes had passed in Uppercross which made it precious. It stood the record of many sensations of pain, once severe, but now softened; and of some instances of relenting feeling, some breathings of friendship and reconciliation, which could never be looked for again, and which could never cease to be dear. She left it all behind her, all but the recollection that such things had been.

Anne had never entered Kellynch since her quitting Lady Russell's house in September. It had not been necessary, and the few occasions of its being possible for her to go to the Hall she had contrived to evade and escape from. Her first return was to resume her place in the modern and elegant apartments of the Lodge, and to gladden the eyes of its mistress.

There was some anxiety mixed with Lady Russell's joy in meeting her. She knew who had been frequenting Uppercross. But happily, either Anne was improved in plumpness and looks, or Lady Russell fancied her so; and Anne, in receiving her compliments on the occasion, had the amusement of connecting them with the silent admiration of her cousin, and of hoping that she was to be blessed with a second spring of youth and beauty.

When they came to converse, she was soon sensible of some mental change. The subjects of which her heart had been full on leaving Kellynch, and which she had felt slighted, and been compelled to smother among the Musgroves, were now become but of secondary interest. She had lately lost sight even of her father and sister and Bath. Their concerns had been sunk under those of Uppercross; and when Lady Russell reverted to their former hopes and fears, and spoke her satisfaction in the house in Camden Place, which had been taken, and her regret that Mrs. Clay should still be with them, Anne would have been ashamed to have it known how much more she was thinking of Lyme and Louisa Musgrove, and all her acquaintance there; how much more interesting to her was the home and the friendship of the Harvilles and Captain Benwick, than her own father's house in Camden Place, or her own sister's intimacy with Mrs. Clay. She was actually forced to exert herself to meet Lady Russell with anything like the appearance of equal solicitude, on topics, which had by nature the first claim on her.

There was a little awkwardness at first in their discourse on another subject. They must speak of the accident at Lyme. Lady Russell had not been arrived five minutes the day before, when a full account of the whole had burst on her; but still it must be talked of, she must make enquiries, she must regret the imprudence, lament the result, and Captain Wentworth's name must be mentioned by both. Anne was conscious of not doing it so well as Lady Russell. She could not speak the name, and look straight forward to Lady Russell's eye, till she had adopted the expedient of telling her briefly what she thought of the attachment between him and Louisa. When this was told, his name distressed her no longer.

Lady Russell had only to listen composedly, and wish them happy, but internally her heart revelled in angry pleasure, in pleased contempt, that the man who at twenty-three had seemed to understand somewhat of the value of an Anne Elliot, should, eight years afterwards, be charmed by a Louisa Musgrove.

The first three or four days passed most quietly, with no circumstance to mark them excepting the receipt of a note or two from Lyme, which found their way to Anne, she could not tell how, and brought a rather improving account of Louisa. At the end of that period, Lady Russell's politeness could repose no longer, and the fainter self-threatenings of the past became in a decided tone, "I must call on Mrs. Croft; I really must call upon her soon. Anne, have you courage to go with me, and pay a visit in that house? It will be some trial to us both."

Anne did not shrink from it; on the contrary, she truly felt as she said, in observing—

"I think you are very likely to suffer the most of the two; your feelings are less reconciled to the change than mine. By remaining in the neighbourhood, I am become inured to it."

She could have said more on the subject; for she had in fact so high an opinion of the Crofts, and considered her father so very fortunate in his tenants, felt the parish to be so sure of a good example, and the poor of the best attention and relief, that however sorry and ashamed for the necessity of the removal, she could not but in conscience feel that they were gone who deserved not to stay, and that Kellynch Hall had passed into better hands than its owners'. These convictions must unquestionably have their own pain, and severe was its kind; but they precluded that pain which Lady Russell would suffer in entering the house again, and returning through the well-known apartments.

In such moments Anne had no power of saying to herself, "These rooms ought to belong only to us. Oh, how fallen in their destination!

How unworthily occupied! An ancient family to be so driven away! Strangers filling their place!" No, except when she thought of her mother, and remembered where she had been used to sit and preside, she had no sigh of that description to heave.

Mrs. Croft always met her with a kindness, which gave her the pleasure of fancying herself a favourite, and on the present occasion, receiving her in that house, there was particular attention.

The sad accident at Lyme was soon the prevailing topic, and on comparing their latest accounts of the invalid, it appeared that each lady dated her intelligence from the same hour of yestermorn; that Captain Wentworth had been in Kellynch yesterday (the first time since the accident), had brought Anne the last note, which she had not been able to trace the exact steps of; had stayed a few hours and then returned again to Lyme, and without any present intention of quitting it any more. He had enquired after her, she found, particularly; had expressed his hope of Miss Elliot's not being the worse for her exertions, and had spoken of those exertions as great. This was handsome, and gave her more pleasure than almost anything else could have done.

As to the sad catastrophe itself, it could be canvassed only in one style by a couple of steady, sensible women, whose judgements had to work on ascertained events; and it was perfectly decided that it had been the consequence of much thoughtlessness and much imprudence; that its effects were most alarming, and that it was frightful to think, how long Miss Musgrove's recovery might yet be doubtful, and how liable she would still remain to suffer from the concussion hereafter!

The Admiral wound it up summarily by exclaiming, "Ay, a very bad business indeed. A new sort of way this, for a young fellow to be making love, by breaking his mistress's head, is not it, Miss Elliot? This is breaking a head and giving a plaster, truly!"

Admiral Croft's manners were not quite of the tone to suit Lady Russell, but they delighted Anne. His goodness of heart and simplicity of character were irresistible.

"Now, this must be very bad for you," said he, suddenly rousing from a little reverie, "to be coming and finding us here. I had not recollected it before, I declare, but it must be very bad. But now, do not stand upon ceremony. Get up and go over all the rooms in the house if you like it."

"Another time, sir, I thank you, not now."

"Well, whenever it suits you. You can slip in from the shrubbery at any time; and there you will find we keep our umbrellas hanging up by that door. A good place, is not it? But," (checking himself), "you will not think it a good place, for yours were always kept in the butler's room. Ay, so it always is, I believe. One man's ways may be as good as another's, but we all like our own best. And so you must judge for yourself, whether it would be better for you to go about the house or not."

Anne, finding she might decline it, did so, very gratefully.

"We have made very few changes either," continued the Admiral, after thinking a moment. "Very few. We told you about the laundry-door, at Uppercross. That has been a very great improvement. The wonder was, how any family upon earth could bear with the inconvenience of its opening as it did, so long! You will tell Sir Walter what we have done, and that Mr. Shepherd thinks it the greatest improvement the house ever had. Indeed, I must do ourselves the justice to say, that the few alterations we have made have been all very much for the better. My wife should have the credit of them, however. I have done very little besides sending away some of the large looking glasses from my dressing room, which was your father's. A very good man, and very much the gentleman I am sure; but I should think, Miss Elliot," (looking with serious reflection), "I should think he must be rather a dressy man for his time of life. Such a number of looking glasses! Oh Lord! There was no getting away from one's self. So I got Sophy to lend me a hand, and we soon shifted their quarters; and now I am quite snug, with my little shaving glass in one corner, and another great thing that I never go near."

Anne, amused in spite of herself, was rather distressed for an answer, and the Admiral, fearing he might not have been civil enough, took up the subject again, to say, "The next time you write to your good father, Miss Elliot, pray give him my compliments and Mrs. Croft's, and say that we are settled here quite to our liking, and have no fault at all to find with the place. The breakfast-room chimney smokes a little, I grant you, but it is only when the wind is due north and blows hard, which may not happen three times a winter. And take it altogether, now that we have been into most of the houses hereabouts and can judge, there is not one that we like better than this. Pray say so, with my compliments. He will be glad to hear it."

Lady Russell and Mrs. Croft were very well pleased with each other; but the acquaintance which this visit began was fated not to proceed far at present; for when it was returned, the Crofts announced themselves to be going away for a few weeks, to visit their connexions in the north of the county, and probably might not be at home again before Lady Russell would be removing to Bath.

So ended all danger to Anne of meeting Captain Wentworth at Kellynch Hall, or of seeing him in company with her friend. Everything was safe enough, and she smiled over the many anxious feelings she had wasted on the subject.

CHAPTER 14

Though Charles and Mary had remained at Lyme much longer after Mr. and Mrs. Musgrove's going than Anne conceived they could have been at all wanted, they were yet the first of the family to be at home again; and as soon as possible after their return to Uppercross they drove over to the Lodge. They had left Louisa beginning to sit up; but her head, though clear, was exceedingly weak, and her nerves susceptible to the highest extreme of tenderness; and though she might be pronounced to be altogether doing very well, it was still impossible to say when she might be able to bear the removal home; and her father and mother, who must return in time to receive their younger children for the Christmas holidays, had hardly a hope of being allowed to bring her with them.

They had been all in lodgings together. Mrs. Musgrove had got Mrs. Harville's children away as much as she could, every possible supply from Uppercross had been furnished, to lighten the inconvenience to the Harvilles, while the Harvilles had been wanting them to come to dinner every day; and in short, it seemed to have been only a struggle on each side as to which should be most disinterested and hospitable.

Mary had had her evils; but upon the whole, as was evident by her staying so long, she had found more to enjoy than to suffer. Charles Hayter had been at Lyme oftener than suited her; and when they dined with the Harvilles there had been only a maidservant to wait, and at first Mrs. Harville had always given Mrs. Musgrove precedence; but then, she had received so very handsome an apology from her on finding out whose daughter she was, and there had been so much going on every day, there had been so many walks between their lodgings and the Harvilles, and she had got books from the library, and changed them so often, that the balance had certainly been much in favour of Lyme. She had been taken to Charmouth too, and she had bathed, and she had gone to church, and there were a great many more people to look at in the church at Lyme than at Uppercross; and all this, joined to the sense of being so very useful, had made really an agreeable fortnight.

Anne enquired after Captain Benwick; Mary's face was clouded directly. Charles laughed.

"Oh! Captain Benwick is very well, I believe, but he is a very odd young man. I do not know what he would be at. We asked him to come home with us for a day or two; Charles undertook to give him some shooting, and he seemed quite delighted, and, for my part, I thought it was all settled; when behold! On Tuesday night, he made a very awkward sort of excuse; 'he never shot' and he had 'been quite misunderstood,' and he had promised this and he had promised that, and the end of it was, I found, that he did not mean to come. I suppose he was afraid of finding it dull; but upon my word I should have thought we were lively enough at the Cottage for such a heartbroken man as Captain Benwick."

Charles laughed again and said, "Now Mary, you know very well how it really was. It was all your doing," (turning to Anne.) "He fancied that if he went with us, he should find you close by; he fancied everybody to be living in Uppercross; and when he discovered that Lady Russell lived three miles off, his heart failed him, and he had not courage to come. That is the fact, upon my honour, Mary knows it is."

But Mary did not give into it very graciously, whether from not considering Captain Benwick entitled by birth and situation to be in love with an Elliot, or from not wanting to believe Anne a greater attraction to Uppercross than herself, must be left to be guessed. Anne's goodwill, however, was not to be lessened by what she heard. She boldly acknowledged herself flattered, and continued her enquiries.

"Oh! He talks of you," cried Charles, "in such terms—"

Mary interrupted him. "I declare, Charles, I never heard him mention Anne twice all the time I was there. I declare, Anne, he never talks of you at all."

"No," admitted Charles, "I do not know that he ever does, in a general way; but however, it is a very clear thing that he admires you exceedingly. His head is full of some books that he is reading upon your recommendation, and he wants to talk to you about them; he has found out something or other in one of them that he thinks—oh! I cannot pretend to remember it, but it was something very fine—I overheard him telling Henrietta all about it; and then 'Miss Elliot' was spoken of in the highest terms! Now Mary, I declare it was so, I heard it myself, and you were in the other room. 'Elegance, sweetness, beauty.' Oh! There was no end of Miss Elliot's charms."

"And I am sure," cried Mary, warmly, "it was very little to his credit, if he did. Miss Harville only died last June. Such a heart is very little worth having; is it, Lady Russell? I am sure you will agree with me."

"I must see Captain Benwick before I decide," said Lady Russell, smiling.

"And that you are very likely to do very soon, I can tell you, ma'am," said Charles. "Though he had not nerves for coming away with us, and setting off again afterwards to pay a formal visit here, he will make his way over to Kellynch one day by himself, you may depend on it. I told him the distance and the road, and I told him of the church's being so very well worth seeing; for as he has a taste for those sort of things, I thought that would be a good excuse, and he listened with all his understanding and soul; and I am sure from his manner that you will have him calling here soon. So, I give you notice, Lady Russell."

"Any acquaintance of Anne's will always be welcome to me," was Lady Russell's kind answer.

"Oh! As to being Anne's acquaintance," said Mary, "I think he is rather my acquaintance, for I have been seeing him every day this last fortnight."

"Well, as your joint acquaintance, then, I shall be very happy to see Captain Benwick."

"You will not find anything very agreeable in him, I assure you, ma'am. He is one of the dullest young men that ever lived. He has walked with me, sometimes, from one end of the sands to the other, without saying a word. He is not at all a well-bred young man. I am sure you will not like him."

"There we differ, Mary," said Anne. "I think Lady Russell would like him. I think she would be so much pleased with his mind, that she would very soon see no deficiency in his manner."

"So do I, Anne," said Charles. "I am sure Lady Russell would like him. He is just Lady Russell's sort. Give him a book, and he will read all day long."

"Yes, that he will!" exclaimed Mary, tauntingly. "He will sit poring over his book, and not know when a person speaks to him, or when one drop's one's scissors, or anything that happens. Do you think Lady Russell would like that?"

Lady Russell could not help laughing. "Upon my word," said she, "I should not have supposed that my opinion of anyone could have admitted of such difference of conjecture, steady and matter of fact as I may call myself. I have really a curiosity to see the person who can give occasion to such directly opposite notions. I wish he may be induced to call here. And when he does, Mary, you may depend upon hearing my opinion; but I am determined not to judge him beforehand."

"You will not like him, I will answer for it."

Lady Russell began talking of something else. Mary spoke with animation of their meeting with, or rather missing, Mr. Elliot so extraordinarily.

"He is a man," said Lady Russell, "whom I have no wish to see. His declining to be on cordial terms with the head of his family, has left a very strong impression in his disfavour with me."

This decision checked Mary's eagerness, and stopped her short in the midst of the Elliot countenance.

With regard to Captain Wentworth, though Anne hazarded no enquiries, there was voluntary communication sufficient. His spirits had been greatly recovering lately as might be expected. As Louisa improved, he had improved, and he was now quite a different creature from what he had been the first week. He had not seen Louisa; and was so extremely fearful of any ill consequence to her from an interview, that he did not press for it at all; and, on the contrary, seemed to have a plan of going away for a week or ten days, till her head was stronger. He had talked of going down to Plymouth for a week, and wanted to persuade Captain Benwick to go with him; but, as Charles maintained to the last, Captain Benwick seemed much more disposed to ride over to Kellynch.

There can be no doubt that Lady Russell and Anne were both occasionally thinking of Captain Benwick, from this time. Lady Russell could not hear the doorbell without feeling that it might be his herald; nor could Anne return from any stroll of solitary indulgence in her father's grounds, or any visit of charity in the village, without wondering whether she might see him or hear of him.

Captain Benwick came not, however. He was either less disposed for it than Charles had imagined, or he was too shy; and after giving him a week's indulgence, Lady Russell determined him to be unworthy of the interest which he had been beginning to excite.

The Musgroves came back to receive their happy boys and girls from school, bringing with them Mrs. Harville's little children, to improve the noise of Uppercross, and lessen that of Lyme. Henrietta remained with Louisa; but all the rest of the family was again in their usual quarters.

Lady Russell and Anne paid their compliments to them once, when Anne could not but feel that Uppercross was already quite alive again. Though neither Henrietta, nor Louisa, nor Charles Hayter, nor Captain Wentworth were there, the room presented as strong a contrast as could be wished to the last state she had seen it in.

Immediately surrounding Mrs. Musgrove were the little Harvilles, whom she was sedulously guarding from the tyranny of the two children from the Cottage, expressly arrived to amuse them. On one side was a table occupied by some chattering girls, cutting up silk and gold paper; and on the other were tressels and trays, bending under the weight of brawn and cold pies, where riotous boys were holding high revel; the whole completed by a roaring Christmas fire, which seemed determined to be heard, in spite of all the noise of the others. Charles and Mary also came in, of course, during their visit, and Mr. Musgrove made a point of paying his respects to Lady Russell, and sat down close to her for ten minutes, talking with a very raised voice, but from the clamour of the children on his knees, generally in vain. It was a fine family piece.

Anne, judging from her own temperament, would have deemed such a domestic hurricane a bad restorative of the nerves, which Louisa's illness must have so greatly shaken. But Mrs. Musgrove, who got Anne near her on purpose to thank her most cordially, again and again, for all her attentions to them, concluded a short recapitulation of what she had suffered herself by observing, with a happy glance round the room, that after all she had gone through, nothing was so likely to do her good as a little quiet cheerfulness at home.

Louisa was now recovering apace. Her mother could even think of her being able to join their party at home, before her brothers and sisters went to school again. The Harvilles had promised to come with her and stay at Uppercross, whenever she returned. Captain Wentworth was gone, for the present, to see his brother in Shropshire.

"I hope I shall remember, in future," said Lady Russell, as soon as they were reseated in the carriage, "not to call at Uppercross in the Christmas holidays."

Everybody has their taste in noises as well as in other matters; and sounds are quite innoxious, or most distressing, by their sort rather than their quantity. When Lady Russell, not long afterwards, was entering Bath on a wet afternoon, and driving through the long course of streets from the Old Bridge to Camden Place, amidst the dash of other carriages, the heavy rumble of carts and drays, the bawling of newspapermen, muffin-men and milkmen, and the ceaseless clink of pattens, she made no complaint. No, these were noises which belonged to the winter pleasures; her spirits rose under their influence; and like Mrs. Musgrove, she was feeling, though not saying, that after being long in the country, nothing could be so good for her as a little quiet cheerfulness.

Anne did not share these feelings. She persisted in a very determined, though very silent disinclination for Bath; caught the first dim view of the extensive buildings, smoking in rain, without any wish of seeing them better; felt their progress through the streets to be, however disagreeable, yet too rapid; for who would be glad to see her when she arrived? And looked back, with fond regret, to the bustles of Uppercross and the seclusion of Kellynch.

Elizabeth's last letter had communicated a piece of news of some interest. Mr. Elliot was in Bath. He had called in Camden Place; had called a second time, a third; had been pointedly attentive: if Elizabeth and her father did not deceive themselves, had been taking many pains to seek the acquaintance, and proclaim the value of the connection, as he had formerly taken pains to show neglect.

This was very wonderful if it were true; and Lady Russell was in a state of very agreeable curiosity and perplexity about Mr. Elliot, already recanting the sentiment she had so lately expressed to Mary, of his being "a man whom she had no wish to see." She had a great wish to see him. If he really sought to reconcile himself like a dutiful branch, he must be forgiven for having dismembered himself from the paternal tree.

Anne was not animated to an equal pitch by the circumstance, but she felt that she would rather see Mr. Elliot again than not, which was more than she could say for many other persons in Bath.

She was put down in Camden Place; and Lady Russell then drove to her own lodgings, in Rivers Street.

CHAPTER 15

Sir Walter had taken a very good house in Camden Place, a lofty dignified situation, such as becomes a man of consequence; and both he and Elizabeth were settled there, much to their satisfaction.

Anne entered it with a sinking heart, anticipating an imprisonment of many months, and anxiously saying to herself, "Oh! When shall I leave you again?" A degree of unexpected cordiality, however, in the welcome she received, did her good. Her father and sister were glad to see her, for the sake of showing her the house and furniture, and met her with kindness. Her making a fourth, when they sat down to dinner, was noticed as an advantage.

Mrs. Clay was very pleasant, and very smiling, but her courtesies and smiles were more a matter of course. Anne had always felt that she would pretend what was proper on her arrival, but the complaisance of the others was unlooked for. They were evidently in excellent spirits, and she was soon to listen to the causes.

They had no inclination to listen to her. After laying out for some compliments of being deeply regretted in their old neighbourhood, which Anne could not pay, they had only a few faint enquiries to make, before the talk must be all their own. Uppercross excited no interest, Kellynch very little: it was all Bath.

They had the pleasure of assuring her that Bath more than answered their expectations in every respect. Their house was undoubtedly the best in Camden Place; their drawing rooms had many decided advantages over all the others, which they had either seen or heard of, and the superiority was not less in the style of the fitting-up, or the taste of the furniture. Their acquaintance was exceedingly sought after. Everybody was wanting to visit them. They had drawn back from many introductions, and still were perpetually having cards left by people of whom they knew nothing.

Here were funds of enjoyment. Could Anne wonder that her father and sister were happy? She might not wonder, but she must sigh that her father should feel no degradation in his change, should see nothing to regret in the duties and dignity of the resident landholder, should find so much to be vain of in the littlenesses of a town; and she must sigh, and smile, and wonder too, as Elizabeth threw open the folding-doors and walked with exultation from one drawing room to the other, boasting of their space; at the possibility of that woman, who had been mistress of Kellynch Hall, finding extent to be proud of between two walls, perhaps thirty feet asunder.

But this was not all that they had to make them happy. They had Mr. Elliot too.

Anne had a great deal to hear of Mr. Elliot. He was not only pardoned, they were delighted with him. He had been in Bath about a fortnight; (he had passed through Bath in November, in his way to London, when the intelligence of Sir Walter's being settled there had of course reached him, though only twenty-four hours in the place, but he had not been able to avail himself of it;) but he had now been a fortnight in Bath, and his first object on arriving, had been to leave his card in Camden Place, following it up by such assiduous endeavours to meet, and when they did meet, by such great openness of conduct, such readiness to apologize for the past, such solicitude to be received as a relation again, that their former good understanding was completely reestablished.

They had not a fault to find in him. He had explained away all the appearance of neglect on his own side. It had originated in misapprehension entirely. He had never had an idea of throwing himself off; he had feared that he was thrown off, but knew not why, and delicacy had kept him silent. Upon the hint of having spoken disrespectfully or carelessly of the family and the family honours, he was quite indignant. He, who had ever boasted of being an Elliot, and whose feelings, as to connection, were only too strict to suit the unfeudal tone of the present day. He was astonished, indeed, but his character and general conduct must refute it. He could refer Sir Walter to all who knew him; and certainly, the pains he had been taking on this, the first opportunity of reconciliation, to be restored to the footing of a relation and heir-presumptive, was a strong proof of his opinions on the subject.

The circumstances of his marriage, too, were found to admit of much extenuation. This was an article not to be entered on by himself; but a very intimate friend of his, a Colonel Wallis, a highly respectable man, perfectly the gentleman, (and not an ill-looking man, Sir Walter added), who was living in very good style in Marlborough Buildings, and had, at his own particular request, been admitted to their acquaintance through Mr. Elliot, had mentioned one or two things relative to the marriage, which made a material difference in the discredit of it.

Colonel Wallis had known Mr. Elliot long, had been well acquainted also with his wife, had perfectly understood the whole story. She was certainly not a woman of family, but well educated, accomplished, rich, and excessively in love with his friend. There had been the charm. She had sought him. Without that attraction, not all her money would have tempted Elliot, and Sir Walter was, moreover, assured of her having been a very fine woman. Here was a great deal to soften the business. A very fine woman with a large fortune, in love with him! Sir Walter seemed to admit it as complete apology; and though Elizabeth could not see the circumstance in quite so favourable a light, she allowed it be a great extenuation.

Mr. Elliot had called repeatedly, had dined with them once, evidently delighted by the distinction of being asked, for they gave no dinners in general; delighted, in short, by every proof of cousinly notice, and placing his whole happiness in being on intimate terms in Camden Place.

Anne listened, but without quite understanding it. Allowances, large allowances, she knew, must be made for the ideas of those who spoke. She heard it all under embellishment. All that sounded extravagant or irrational in the progress of the reconciliation might have no origin but in the language of the relators. Still, however, she had the sensation of there being something more than immediately appeared, in Mr. Elliot's wishing, after an interval of so many years, to be well received by them. In a worldly view, he had nothing to gain by being on terms with Sir Walter; nothing to risk by a state of variance. In all probability he was already the richer of the two, and the Kellynch estate would as surely be his hereafter as the title. A sensible man, and he had looked like a *very* sensible man, why should it be an object to him? She could only offer one solution; it was, perhaps, for Elizabeth's sake. There might really have been a liking formerly, though convenience and accident had drawn him a different way; and now that he could afford to please himself, he might mean to pay his addresses to her. Elizabeth was certainly very handsome, with well-bred, elegant manners, and her character might never have been penetrated by Mr. Elliot, knowing her but in public, and when very young himself. How her temper and understanding might bear the investigation of his present keener time of life was another concern and rather a fearful one. Most earnestly did she wish that he might not be too nice, or too observant, if Elizabeth were his object; and that Elizabeth was disposed to believe herself so, and that her friend Mrs. Clay was encouraging the idea, seemed apparent by a glance or two between them, while Mr. Elliot's frequent visits were talked of.

Anne mentioned the glimpses she had had of him at Lyme, but without being much attended to. "Oh! Yes, perhaps, it had been Mr. Elliot. They did not know. It might be him, perhaps." They could not listen to her description of him. They were describing him themselves; Sir Walter especially. He did justice to his very gentlemanlike appearance, his air of elegance and fashion, his good shaped face, his sensible eye; but, at the same time, "must lament his being very much under-hung, a defect which time seemed to have increased; nor could he pretend to say that ten years had not altered almost every feature for the worse. Mr. Elliot appeared to think that he (Sir Walter) was looking exactly as he had done when they last parted;" but Sir Walter had "not been able to return the compliment entirely, which had embarrassed him. He did not mean to complain, however. Mr. Elliot was better to look at than most men, and he had no objection to being seen with him anywhere."

Mr. Elliot, and his friends in Marlborough Buildings, were talked of the whole evening. "Colonel Wallis had been so impatient to be introduced to them! And Mr. Elliot so anxious that he should!" and there was a Mrs. Wallis, at present known only to them by description, as she was in daily expectation of her confinement; but Mr. Elliot spoke of her as "a most charming woman, quite worthy of being known in Camden Place," and as soon as she recovered they were to be acquainted.

Sir Walter thought much of Mrs. Wallis; she was said to be an excessively pretty woman, beautiful. "He longed to see her. He hoped she might make some amends for the many very plain faces he was continually passing in the streets. The worst of Bath was the number of its plain women. He did not mean to say that there were no pretty women, but the number of the plain was out of all proportion. He had frequently observed, as he walked, that one handsome face would be followed by thirty, or five-and-thirty frights; and once, as he had stood in a shop on Bond Street, he had counted eighty-seven women go by, one after another, without there being a tolerable face among them. It had been a frosty morning, to be sure, a sharp frost, which hardly one woman in a thousand could stand the test of. But still, there certainly were a dreadful multitude of ugly women in Bath; and as for the men! They were infinitely worse. Such scarecrows as the streets were full of! It was evident how little the women were used to the sight of anything tolerable, by the effect that a man of decent appearance produced. He had never walked anywhere arm-in-arm with Colonel Wallis (who was a fine military figure, though sandy-haired) without observing that every woman's eye was upon him; every woman's eye was sure to be upon Colonel Wallis." Modest Sir Walter! He was not allowed to escape, however. His daughter and Mrs. Clay united in hinting that Colonel Wallis's companion might have as good a figure as Colonel Wallis, and certainly was not sandy-haired.

"How is Mary looking?" said Sir Walter, in the height of his good humour. "The last time I saw her she had a red nose, but I hope that may not happen every day."

"Oh! No, that must have been quite accidental. In general she has been in very good health and very good looks since Michaelmas."

"If I thought it would not tempt her to go out in sharp winds, and grow coarse, I would send her a new hat and pelisse."

Anne was considering whether she should venture to suggest that a gown, or a cap, would not be liable to any such misuse, when a knock at the door suspended everything. "A knock at the door! And so late! It was ten o'clock. Could it be Mr. Elliot? They knew he was to dine in Lansdown Crescent. It was possible that he might stop in his way home to ask them how they did. They could think of no one else. Mrs. Clay decidedly thought it Mr. Elliot's knock. Mrs. Clay was right. With all the state that a butler and footboy could give, Mr. Elliot was ushered into the room.

It was the same, the very same man, with no difference but of dress. Anne drew a little back, while the others received his compliments, and her sister his apologies for calling at so unusual an hour, but "he could not be so near without wishing to know that neither she nor her friend had taken cold the day before," etc. etc; which was all as politely done, and as politely taken, as possible, but her part must follow then. Sir Walter talked of his youngest daughter; "Mr. Elliot must give him leave to present him to his youngest daughter" (there was no occasion for remembering Mary); and Anne, smiling and blushing, very becomingly showed to Mr. Elliot the pretty features which he had by no means forgotten, and instantly saw, with amusement at his little start of surprise, that he had not been at all aware of who she was. He looked completely astonished, but not more astonished than pleased; his eyes brightened! And with the most perfect alacrity he welcomed the relationship, alluded to the past, and entreated to be received as an acquaintance already. He was quite as good-looking as he had appeared at Lyme, his countenance improved by speaking, and his manners were so exactly what they ought to be, so polished, so easy, so particularly agreeable, that she could compare them in excellence to only one person's manners. They were not the same, but they were, perhaps, equally good.

He sat down with them, and improved their conversation very much. There could be no doubt of his being a sensible man. Ten minutes were enough to certify that. His tone, his expressions, his choice of subject, his knowing where to stop; it was all the operation of a sensible, discerning mind. As soon as he could, he began to talk to her of Lyme, wanting to compare opinions respecting the place, but especially wanting to speak of the circumstance of their happening to be guests in the same inn at the same time; to give his own route, understand something of hers, and regret that he should have lost such an opportunity of paying his respects to her. She gave him a short account of her party and business at Lyme. His regret increased as he listened. He had spent his whole solitary evening in the room adjoining theirs; had heard voices, mirth continually; thought they must be a most delightful set of people, longed to be with them, but certainly without the smallest suspicion of his possessing the shadow of a right to introduce himself. If he had but asked who the party were! The name of Musgrove would have told him enough. "Well, it would serve to cure him of an absurd practice of never asking a question at an inn, which he had adopted, when quite a young man, on the principal of its being very ungenteel to be curious."

"The notions of a young man of one or two and twenty," said he, "as to what is necessary in manners to make him quite the thing, are more absurd, I believe, than those of any other set of beings in the world. The folly of the means they often employ is only to be equalled by the folly of what they have in view."

But he must not be addressing his reflections to Anne alone: he knew it; he was soon diffused again among the others, and it was only at intervals that he could return to Lyme.

His enquiries, however, produced at length an account of the scene she had been engaged in there, soon after his leaving the place. Having alluded to "an accident," he must hear the whole. When he questioned, Sir Walter and Elizabeth began to question also, but the difference in their manner of doing it could not be unfelt. She could only compare Mr. Elliot to Lady Russell, in the wish of really comprehending what had passed, and in the degree of concern for what she must have suffered in witnessing it.

He stayed an hour with them. The elegant little clock on the mantelpiece had struck "eleven with its silver sounds," and the watchman was beginning to be heard at a distance telling the same tale, before Mr. Elliot or any of them seemed to feel that he had been there long.

Anne could not have supposed it possible that her first evening in Camden Place could have passed so well!

CHAPTER 16

There was one point which Anne, on returning to her family, would have been more thankful to ascertain even than Mr. Elliot's being in love with Elizabeth, which was, her father's not being in love with Mrs. Clay; and she was very far from easy about it, when she had been at home a few hours. On going down to breakfast the next morning, she found there had just been a decent pretence on the lady's side of meaning to leave them. She could imagine Mrs. Clay to have said, that "now Miss Anne was come, she could not suppose herself at all wanted;" for Elizabeth was replying in a sort of whisper, "That must not be any reason, indeed. I assure you I feel it none. She is nothing to me, compared with you;" and she was in full time to hear her father say, "My dear madam, this must not be. As yet, you have seen nothing of Bath. You have been here only to be useful. You must not run away from us now. You must stay to be acquainted with Mrs. Wallis, the beautiful Mrs. Wallis. To your fine mind, I well know the sight of beauty is a real gratification."

He spoke and looked so much in earnest, that Anne was not surprised to see Mrs. Clay stealing a glance at Elizabeth and herself. Her countenance, perhaps, might express some watchfulness; but the praise of the fine mind did not appear to excite a thought in her sister. The lady could not but yield to such joint entreaties, and promise to stay.

In the course of the same morning, Anne and her father chancing to be alone together, he began to compliment her on her improved looks; he thought her "less thin in her person, in her cheeks; her skin, her complexion, greatly improved: clearer, fresher. Had she been using anything in particular?" "No, nothing." "Merely Gowland," he supposed. "No, nothing at all." "Ha! He was surprised at that;" and added, "certainly you cannot do better than to continue as you are; you cannot be better than well; or I should recommend Gowland, the constant use of Gowland, during the spring months. Mrs. Clay has been using it at my recommendation, and you see what it has done for her. You see how it has carried away her freckles."

If Elizabeth could but have heard this! Such personal praise might have struck her, especially as it did not appear to Anne that the freckles were at all lessened. But everything must take its chance. The evil of a marriage would be much diminished, if Elizabeth were also to marry. As for herself, she might always command a home with Lady Russell.

Lady Russell's composed mind and polite manners were put to some trial on this point, in her intercourse in Camden Place. The sight of Mrs. Clay in such favour, and of Anne so overlooked, was a perpetual provocation to her there; and vexed her as much when she was away, as a person in Bath who drinks the water, gets all the new publications, and has a very large acquaintance, has time to be vexed.

As Mr. Elliot became known to her, she grew more charitable, or more indifferent, towards the others. His manners were an immediate recommendation; and on conversing with him she found the solid so fully supporting the superficial, that she was at first, as she told Anne, almost ready to exclaim, "Can this be Mr. Elliot?" and could not seriously picture to herself a more agreeable or estimable man. Everything united in him; good understanding, correct opinions, knowledge of the world, and a warm heart. He had strong feelings of family attachment and family honour, without pride or weakness; he lived with the liberality of a man of fortune, without display; he judged for himself in everything essential, without defying public opinion in any point of worldly decorum. He was steady, observant, moderate, candid; never run away with by spirits or by selfishness, which fancied itself strong feeling; and yet, with a sensibility to what was amiable and lovely, and a value for all the felicities of domestic life, which characters of fancied enthusiasm and violent agitation seldom really possess. She was sure that he had not been happy in marriage.

Colonel Wallis said it, and Lady Russell saw it; but it had been no unhappiness to sour his mind, nor (she began pretty soon to suspect) to prevent his thinking of a second choice. Her satisfaction in Mr. Elliot outweighed all the plague of Mrs. Clay.

It was now some years since Anne had begun to learn that she and her excellent friend could sometimes think differently; and it did not surprise her, therefore, that Lady Russell should see nothing suspicious or inconsistent, nothing to require more motives than appeared, in Mr. Elliot's great desire of a reconciliation. In Lady Russell's view, it was perfectly natural that Mr. Elliot, at a mature time of life, should feel it a most desirable object, and what would very generally recommend him among all sensible people, to be on good terms with the head of his family; the simplest process in the world of time upon a head naturally clear, and only erring in the heyday of youth. Anne presumed, however, still to smile about it, and at last to mention "Elizabeth." Lady Russell listened, and looked, and made only this cautious reply: "Elizabeth! Very well; time will explain."

It was a reference to the future, which Anne, after a little observation, felt she must submit to. She could determine nothing at present. In that house Elizabeth must be first; and she was in the habit of such general observance as "Miss Elliot," that any particularity of attention seemed almost impossible. Mr. Elliot, too, it must be remembered, had not been a widower seven months. A little delay on his side might be very excusable. In fact, Anne could never see the crape round his hat, without fearing that she was the inexcusable one, in attributing to him such imaginations; for though his marriage had not been very happy, still it had existed so many years that she could not comprehend a very rapid recovery from the awful impression of its being dissolved.

However it might end, he was without any question their pleasantest acquaintance in Bath: she saw nobody equal to him; and it was a great indulgence now and then to talk to him about Lyme, which he seemed to have as lively a wish to see again, and to see more of, as herself. They went through the particulars of their first meeting a great many times. He gave her to understand that he had looked at her with some earnestness. She knew it well; and she remembered another person's look also.

They did not always think alike. His value for rank and connexion she perceived was greater than hers. It was not merely complaisance, it must be a liking to the cause, which made him enter warmly into her father and sister's solicitudes on a subject which she thought unworthy to excite them. The Bath paper one morning announced the arrival of the Dowager Viscountess Dalrymple, and her daughter, the Honourable Miss Carteret; and all the comfort of No. —, Camden Place, was swept away for many days; for the Dalrymples (in Anne's opinion, most unfortunately) were cousins of the Elliots; and the agony was how to introduce themselves properly.

Anne had never seen her father and sister before in contact with nobility, and she must acknowledge herself disappointed. She had hoped better things from their high ideas of their own situation in life, and was reduced to form a wish that she had never foreseen; a wish that they had more pride; for "our cousins Lady Dalrymple and Miss Carteret;" "our cousins, the Dalrymples," sounded in her ears all day long.

Sir Walter had once been in company with the late viscount, but had never seen any of the rest of the family; and the difficulties of the case arose from there having been a suspension of all intercourse by letters of ceremony, ever since the death of that said late viscount, when, in consequence of a dangerous illness of Sir Walter's at the same time, there had been an unlucky omission at Kellynch. No letter of condolence had been sent to Ireland. The neglect had been visited on the head of the sinner; for when poor Lady Elliot died herself, no letter of condolence was received at Kellynch, and, consequently, there was but too much reason to apprehend that the Dalrymples considered the relationship as closed. How to have this anxious business set to rights, and be admitted as cousins again, was the question: and it was a question which, in a more rational manner, neither Lady Russell nor Mr. Elliot thought unimportant. "Family connexions were always worth preserving, good company always worth seeking; Lady Dalrymple had taken a house, for three months, in Laura Place, and would be living in style. She had been at Bath the year before, and Lady Russell had heard her spoken of as a charming woman. It was very desirable that the connexion should be renewed, if it could be done, without any compromise of propriety on the side of the Elliots."

Sir Walter, however, would choose his own means, and at last wrote a very fine letter of ample explanation, regret, and entreaty, to his right honourable cousin. Neither Lady Russell nor Mr. Elliot could admire the letter; but it did all that was wanted, in bringing three lines of scrawl from the Dowager Viscountess. "She was very much honoured, and should be happy in their acquaintance." The toils of the business were over, the sweets began. They visited in Laura Place, they had the cards of Dowager Viscountess Dalrymple, and the Honourable Miss Carteret, to be arranged wherever they might be most visible: and "Our cousins in Laura Place,"—"Our cousin, Lady Dalrymple and Miss Carteret," were talked of to everybody.

Anne was ashamed. Had Lady Dalrymple and her daughter even been very agreeable, she would still have been ashamed of the agitation they created, but they were nothing. There was no superiority of manner, accomplishment, or understanding.

Lady Dalrymple had acquired the name of "a charming woman," because she had a smile and a civil answer for everybody. Miss Carteret, with still less to say, was so plain and so awkward, that she would never have been tolerated in Camden Place but for her birth.

Lady Russell confessed she had expected something better; but yet "it was an acquaintance worth having;" and when Anne ventured to speak her opinion of them to Mr. Elliot, he agreed to their being nothing in themselves, but still maintained that, as a family connexion, as good company, as those who would collect good company around them, they had their value. Anne smiled and said, "My idea of good company, Mr. Elliot, is the company of clever, well-informed people, who have a great deal of conversation; that is what I call good company."

"You are mistaken," said he gently, "that is not good company; that is the best. Good company requires only birth, education, and manners, and with regard to education is not very nice. Birth and good manners are essential; but a little learning is by no means a dangerous thing in good company; on the contrary, it will do very well. My cousin Anne shakes her head. She is not satisfied. She is fastidious. My dear cousin," (sitting down by her), "you have a better right to be fastidious than almost any other woman I know; but will it answer? Will it make you happy? Will it not be wiser to accept the society of those good ladies in Laura Place, and enjoy all the advantages of the connexion as far as possible? You may depend upon it, that they will move in the first set in Bath this winter, and as rank is rank, your being known to be related to them will have its use in fixing your family (our family let me say) in that degree of consideration which we must all wish for."

"Yes," sighed Anne, "we shall, indeed, be known to be related to them!" then recollecting herself, and not wishing to be answered, she added, "I certainly do think there has been by far too much trouble taken to procure the acquaintance. I suppose" (smiling) "I have more pride than any of you; but I confess it does vex me, that we should be so solicitous to have the relationship acknowledged, which we may be very sure is a matter of perfect indifference to them."

"Pardon me, dear cousin, you are unjust in your own claims. In London, perhaps, in your present quiet style of living, it might be as you say; but in Bath, Sir Walter Elliot and his family will always be worth knowing, always acceptable as acquaintance."

"Well," said Anne, "I certainly am proud, too proud to enjoy a welcome which depends so entirely upon place."

"I love your indignation," said he; "it is very natural. But here you are in Bath, and the object is to be established here with all the credit and dignity which ought to belong to Sir Walter Elliot. You talk of being proud; I am called proud, I know, and I shall not wish to believe myself otherwise; for our pride, if investigated, would have the same object, I have no doubt, though the kind may seem a little different. In one point, I am sure, my dear cousin," (he continued, speaking lower, though there was no one else in the room) "in one point, I am sure, we must feel alike. We must feel that every addition to your father's society, among his equals or superiors, may be of use in diverting his thoughts from those who are beneath him."

He looked, as he spoke, to the seat which Mrs. Clay had been lately occupying: a sufficient explanation of what he particularly meant; and though Anne could not believe in their having the same sort of pride, she was pleased with him for not liking Mrs. Clay; and her conscience admitted that his wishing to promote her father's getting great acquaintance was more than excusable in the view of defeating her.

CHAPTER 17

While Sir Walter and Elizabeth were assiduously pushing their good fortune in Laura Place, Anne was renewing an acquaintance of a very different description.

She had called on her former governess, and had heard from her of there being an old schoolfellow in Bath, who had the two strong claims on her attention of past kindness and present suffering. Miss Hamilton, now Mrs. Smith, had shown her kindness in one of those periods of her life when it had been most valuable.

Anne had gone unhappy to school, grieving for the loss of a mother whom she had dearly loved, feeling her separation from home, and suffering as a girl of fourteen, of strong sensibility and not high spirits, must suffer at such a time; and Miss Hamilton, three years older than herself, but still from the want of near relations and a settled home, remaining another year at school, had been useful and good to her in a way which had considerably lessened her misery, and could never be remembered with indifference.

Miss Hamilton had left school, had married not long afterwards, was said to have married a man of fortune, and this was all that Anne had known of her, till now that their governess's account brought her situation forward in a more decided but very different form.

She was a widow and poor. Her husband had been extravagant; and at his death, about two years before, had left his affairs dreadfully involved. She had had difficulties of every sort to contend with, and in addition to these distresses had been afflicted with a severe rheumatic fever, which, finally settling in her legs, had made her for the present a cripple. She had come to Bath on that account, and was now in lodgings near the hot baths, living in a very humble way, unable even to afford herself the comfort of a servant, and of course almost excluded from society.

Their mutual friend answered for the satisfaction that a visit from Miss Elliot would give Mrs. Smith, and Anne therefore lost no time in going. She mentioned nothing of what she had heard, or what she intended, at home. It would excite no proper interest there. She only consulted Lady Russell, who entered thoroughly into her sentiments, and was most happy to convey her as near to Mrs. Smith's lodgings in Westgate Buildings, as Anne chose to be taken.

The visit was paid, their acquaintance reestablished, their interest in each other more than rekindled. The first ten minutes had its awkwardness and its emotion. Twelve years were gone since they had parted, and each presented a somewhat different person from what the other had imagined. Twelve years had changed Anne from the blooming, silent, unformed girl of fifteen, to the elegant little woman of seven-and-twenty, with every beauty except bloom, and with manners as consciously right as they were invariably gentle; and twelve years had transformed the fine-looking, well-grown Miss Hamilton, in all the glow of health and confidence of superiority, into a poor, infirm, helpless widow, receiving the visit of her former protégée as a favour; but all that was uncomfortable in the meeting had soon passed away, and left only the interesting charm of remembering former partialities and talking over old times.

Anne found in Mrs. Smith the good sense and agreeable manners which she had almost ventured to depend on, and a disposition to converse and be cheerful beyond her expectation. Neither the dissipations of the past—and she had lived very much in the world—nor the restrictions of the present, neither sickness nor sorrow seemed to have closed her heart or ruined her spirits.

In the course of a second visit she talked with great openness, and Anne's astonishment increased. She could scarcely imagine a more cheerless situation in itself than Mrs. Smith's. She had been very fond of her husband: she had buried him. She had been used to affluence: it was gone. She had no child to connect her with life and happiness again, no relations to assist in the arrangement of perplexed affairs, no health to make all the rest supportable. Her accommodations were limited to a noisy parlour, and a dark bedroom behind, with no possibility of moving from one to the other without assistance, which there was only one servant in the house to afford, and she never quitted the house but to be conveyed into the warm bath. Yet, in spite of all this, Anne had reason to believe that she had moments only of languor and depression, to hours of occupation and enjoyment. How could it be? She watched, observed, reflected, and finally determined that this was not a case of fortitude or of resignation only.

A submissive spirit might be patient, a strong understanding would supply resolution, but here was something more; here was that elasticity of mind, that disposition to be comforted, that power of turning readily from evil to good, and of finding employment which carried her out of herself, which was from nature alone. It was the choicest gift of Heaven; and Anne viewed her friend as one of those instances in which, by a merciful appointment, it seems designed to counterbalance almost every other want.

There had been a time, Mrs. Smith told her, when her spirits had nearly failed. She could not call herself an invalid now, compared with her state on first reaching Bath. Then she had, indeed, been a pitiable object; for she had caught cold on the journey, and had hardly taken possession of her lodgings before she was again confined to her bed and suffering under severe and constant pain; and all this among strangers, with the absolute necessity of having a regular nurse, and finances at that moment particularly unfit to meet any extraordinary expense. She had weathered it, however, and could truly say that it had done her good. It had increased her comforts by making her feel herself to be in good hands. She had seen too much of the world, to expect sudden or disinterested attachment anywhere, but her illness had proved to her that her landlady had a character to preserve, and would not use her ill; and she had been particularly fortunate in her nurse, as a sister of her landlady, a nurse by profession, and who had always a home in that house when unemployed, chanced to be at liberty just in time to attend her. "And she," said Mrs. Smith, "besides nursing me most admirably, has really proved an invaluable acquaintance. As soon as I could use my hands she taught me to knit, which has been a great amusement; and she put me in the way of making these little thread-cases, pincushions and card-racks, which you always find me so busy about, and which supply me with the means of doing a little good to one or two very poor families in this neighbourhood. She had a large acquaintance, of course professionally, among those who can afford to buy, and she disposes of my merchandise. She always takes the right time for applying. Everybody's heart is open, you know, when they have recently escaped from severe pain, or are recovering the blessing of health, and Nurse Rooke thoroughly understands when to speak. She is a shrewd, intelligent, sensible woman. Hers is a line for seeing human nature; and she has a fund of good sense and observation, which, as a companion, make her infinitely superior to thousands of those who having only received 'the best education in the world,' know nothing worth attending to. Call it gossip, if you will, but when Nurse Rooke has half an hour's leisure to bestow on me, she is sure to have something to relate that is entertaining and profitable, something that makes one know one's species better. One likes to hear what is going on, to be au fait as to the newest modes of being trifling and silly. To me, who live so much alone, her conversation, I assure you, is a treat."

Anne, far from wishing to cavil at the pleasure, replied, "I can easily believe it. Women of that class have great opportunities, and if they are intelligent may be well worth listening to. Such varieties of human nature as they are in the habit of witnessing! And it is not merely in its follies, that they are well read; for they see it occasionally under every circumstance that can be most interesting or affecting. What instances must pass before them of ardent, disinterested, self-denying attachment, of heroism, fortitude, patience, resignation: of all the conflicts and all the sacrifices that ennoble us most. A sick chamber may often furnish the worth of volumes."

"Yes," said Mrs. Smith more doubtingly, "sometimes it may, though I fear its lessons are not often in the elevated style you describe. Here and there, human nature may be great in times of trial; but generally speaking, it is its weakness and not its strength that appears in a sick chamber: it is selfishness and impatience rather than generosity and fortitude, that one hears of. There is so little real friendship in the world! And unfortunately" (speaking low and tremulously) "there are so many who forget to think seriously till it is almost too late."

Anne saw the misery of such feelings. The husband had not been what he ought, and the wife had been led among that part of mankind, which made her think worse of the world than she hoped it deserved. It was but a passing emotion however with Mrs. Smith, she shook it off, and soon added in a different tone, "I do not suppose the situation my friend Mrs. Rooke is in at present, will furnish much either to interest or edify me. She is only nursing Mrs. Wallis of Marlborough Buildings; a mere pretty, silly, expensive, fashionable woman, I believe; and of course will have nothing to report but of lace and finery. I mean to make my profit of Mrs. Wallis, however. She has plenty of money, and I intend she shall buy all the high-priced things I have in hand now."

Anne had called several times on her friend, before the existence of such a person was known in Camden Place. At last, it became necessary to speak of her.

Sir Walter, Elizabeth, and Mrs. Clay returned one morning from Laura Place, with a sudden invitation from Lady Dalrymple for the same evening, and Anne was already engaged, to spend that evening in Westgate Buildings. She was not sorry for the excuse. They were only asked, she was sure, because Lady Dalrymple being kept at home by a bad cold, was glad to make use of the relationship which had been so pressed on her; and she declined on her own account with great alacrity—"She was engaged to spend the evening with an old schoolfellow." They were not much interested in anything relative to Anne; but still there were questions enough asked, to make it understood what this old schoolfellow was; and Elizabeth was disdainful, and Sir Walter severe.

"Westgate Buildings!" said he, "and who is Miss Anne Elliot to be visiting in Westgate Buildings? A Mrs. Smith. A widow Mrs. Smith; and who was her husband? One of five thousand Mr. Smiths whose names are to be met with everywhere. And what is her attraction? That she is old and sickly. Upon my word, Miss Anne Elliot, you have the most extraordinary taste! Everything that revolts other people, low company, paltry rooms, foul air, disgusting associations are inviting to you. But surely you may put off this old lady till tomorrow: she is not so near her end, I presume, but that she may hope to see another day. What is her age? Forty?"

"No, sir, she is not one-and-thirty; but I do not think I can put off my engagement, because it is the only evening for some time which will at once suit her and myself. She goes into the warm bath tomorrow, and for the rest of the week, you know, we are engaged."

"But what does Lady Russell think of this acquaintance?" asked Elizabeth.

"She sees nothing to blame in it," replied Anne; "on the contrary, she approves it, and has generally taken me when I have called on Mrs. Smith."

"Westgate Buildings must have been rather surprised by the appearance of a carriage drawn up near its pavement," observed Sir Walter. "Sir Henry Russell's widow, indeed, has no honours to distinguish her arms, but still it is a handsome equipage, and no doubt is well known to convey a Miss Elliot. A widow Mrs. Smith lodging in

Westgate Buildings! A poor widow barely able to live, between thirty and forty; a mere Mrs. Smith, an everyday Mrs. Smith, of all people and all names in the world, to be the chosen friend of Miss Anne Elliot, and to be preferred by her to her own family connections among the nobility of England and Ireland! Mrs. Smith! Such a name!"

Mrs. Clay, who had been present while all this passed, now thought it advisable to leave the room, and Anne could have said much, and did long to say a little in defence of *her* friend's not very dissimilar claims to theirs, but her sense of personal respect to her father prevented her. She made no reply. She left it to himself to recollect, that Mrs. Smith was not the only widow in Bath between thirty and forty, with little to live on, and no surname of dignity.

Anne kept her appointment; the others kept theirs, and of course she heard the next morning that they had had a delightful evening. She had been the only one of the set absent, for Sir Walter and Elizabeth had not only been quite at her ladyship's service themselves, but had actually been happy to be employed by her in collecting others, and had been at the trouble of inviting both Lady Russell and Mr. Elliot; and Mr. Elliot had made a point of leaving Colonel Wallis early, and Lady Russell had fresh arranged all her evening engagements in order to wait on her. Anne had the whole history of all that such an evening could supply from Lady Russell. To her, its greatest interest must be, in having been very much talked of between her friend and Mr. Elliot; in having been wished for, regretted, and at the same time honoured for staying away in such a cause. Her kind, compassionate visits to this old schoolfellow, sick and reduced, seemed to have quite delighted Mr. Elliot. He thought her a most extraordinary young woman; in her temper, manners, mind, a model of female excellence. He could meet even Lady Russell in a discussion of her merits; and Anne could not be given to understand so much by her friend, could not know herself to be so highly rated by a sensible man, without many of those agreeable sensations which her friend meant to create.

Lady Russell was now perfectly decided in her opinion of Mr. Elliot. She was as much convinced of his meaning to gain Anne in time as of his deserving her, and was beginning to calculate the number of weeks which would free him from all the remaining restraints of widowhood, and leave him at liberty to exert his most open powers of pleasing. She would not speak to Anne with half the certainty she felt on the subject;

she would venture on little more than hints of what might be hereafter, of a possible attachment on his side, of the desirableness of the alliance, supposing such attachment to be real and returned. Anne heard her, and made no violent exclamations; she only smiled, blushed, and gently shook her head.

"I am no matchmaker, as you well know," said Lady Russell, "being much too well aware of the uncertainty of all human events and calculations. I only mean that if Mr. Elliot should some time hence pay his addresses to you, and if you should be disposed to accept him, I think there would be every possibility of your being happy together. A most suitable connection everybody must consider it, but I think it might be a very happy one."

"Mr. Elliot is an exceedingly agreeable man, and in many respects I think highly of him," said Anne; "but we should not suit."

Lady Russell let this pass, and only said in rejoinder, "I own that to be able to regard you as the future mistress of Kellynch, the future Lady Elliot, to look forward and see you occupying your dear mother's place, succeeding to all her rights, and all her popularity, as well as to all her virtues, would be the highest possible gratification to me. You are your mother's self in countenance and disposition; and if I might be allowed to fancy you such as she was, in situation and name, and home, presiding and blessing in the same spot, and only superior to her in being more highly valued! My dearest Anne, it would give me more delight than is often felt at my time of life!"

Anne was obliged to turn away, to rise, to walk to a distant table, and, leaning there in pretended employment, try to subdue the feelings this picture excited. For a few moments her imagination and her heart were bewitched. The idea of becoming what her mother had been; of having the precious name of "Lady Elliot" first revived in herself; of being restored to Kellynch, calling it her home again, her home forever, was a charm that she could not immediately resist.

Lady Russell said not another word, willing to leave the matter to its own operation; and believing that, could Mr. Elliot at that moment with propriety have spoken for himself, she believed, in short, what Anne did not believe. The same image of Mr. Elliot speaking for himself brought Anne to composure again. The charm of Kellynch and of "Lady Elliot" all faded away. She never could accept him. And it was not only that her feelings were still adverse to any man save one;

her judgement, on a serious consideration of the possibilities of such a case, was against Mr. Elliot.

Though they had now been acquainted a month, she could not be satisfied that she really knew his character. That he was a sensible man, an agreeable man, that he talked well, professed good opinions, seemed to judge properly and as a man of principle, this was all clear enough. He certainly knew what was right, nor could she fix on any one article of moral duty evidently transgressed; but yet she would have been afraid to answer for his conduct. She distrusted the past, if not the present. The names which occasionally dropped of former associates, the allusions to former practices and pursuits, suggested suspicions not favourable of what he had been. She saw that there had been bad habits; that Sunday travelling had been a common thing; that there had been a period of his life (and probably not a short one) when he had been, at least, careless in all serious matters; and, though he might now think very differently, who could answer for the true sentiments of a clever, cautious man, grown old enough to appreciate a fair character? How could it ever be ascertained that his mind was truly cleansed?

Mr. Elliot was rational, discreet, polished, but he was not open. There was never any burst of feeling, any warmth of indignation or delight, at the evil or good of others. This, to Anne, was a decided imperfection. Her early impressions were incurable. She prized the frank, the openhearted, eager character beyond all others. Warmth and enthusiasm did captivate her still. She felt that she could so much more depend upon the sincerity of those who sometimes looked or said a careless or a hasty thing, than of those whose presence of mind never varied, whose tongue never slipped.

Mr. Elliot was too generally agreeable. Various as were the tempers in her father's house, he pleased them all. He endured too well, stood too well with everybody. He had spoken to her with some degree of openness of Mrs. Clay; had appeared completely to see what Mrs. Clay was about, and to hold her in contempt; and yet Mrs. Clay found him as agreeable as anybody.

Lady Russell saw either less or more than her young friend, for she saw nothing to excite distrust. She could not imagine a man more exactly what he ought to be than Mr. Elliot; nor did she ever enjoy a sweeter feeling than the hope of seeing him receive the hand of her beloved Anne in Kellynch church, in the course of the following autumn.

CHAPTER 18

It was the beginning of February; and Anne, having been a month in Bath, was growing very eager for news from Uppercross and Lyme. She wanted to hear much more than Mary had communicated. It was three weeks since she had heard at all. She only knew that Henrietta was at home again; and that Louisa, though considered to be recovering fast, was still in Lyme; and she was thinking of them all very intently one evening, when a thicker letter than usual from Mary was delivered to her; and, to quicken the pleasure and surprise, with Admiral and Mrs. Croft's compliments.

The Crofts must be in Bath! A circumstance to interest her. They were people whom her heart turned to very naturally.

"What is this?" cried Sir Walter. "The Crofts have arrived in Bath? The Crofts who rent Kellynch? What have they brought you?"

"A letter from Uppercross Cottage, sir."

"Oh! Those letters are convenient passports. They secure an introduction. I should have visited Admiral Croft, however, at any rate. I know what is due to my tenant."

Anne could listen no longer; she could not even have told how the poor Admiral's complexion escaped; her letter engrossed her. It had been begun several days back.

> February 1st.
>
> My dear Anne,
>
> I make no apology for my silence, because I know how little people think of letters in such a place as Bath. You must be a great deal too happy to care for Uppercross, which, as you well know, affords little to write about. We have had a very dull Christmas; Mr. and Mrs. Musgrove have not had one dinner party all the holidays. I do not reckon the Hayters as anybody. The holidays, however, are over at last: I believe no children ever had such long ones. I am sure I had not. The house was cleared yesterday, except of the little Harvilles; but you will be surprised to hear they have never gone home. Mrs. Harville must be an odd mother to part with them so

long. I do not understand it. They are not at all nice children, in my opinion; but Mrs. Musgrove seems to like them quite as well, if not better, than her grandchildren. What dreadful weather we have had! It may not be felt in Bath, with your nice pavements; but in the country it is of some consequence. I have not had a creature call on me since the second week in January, except Charles Hayter, who had been calling much oftener than was welcome. Between ourselves, I think it a great pity Henrietta did not remain at Lyme as long as Louisa; it would have kept her a little out of his way. The carriage is gone today, to bring Louisa and the Harvilles tomorrow. We are not asked to dine with them, however, till the day after, Mrs. Musgrove is so afraid of her being fatigued by the journey, which is not very likely, considering the care that will be taken of her; and it would be much more convenient to me to dine there tomorrow. I am glad you find Mr. Elliot so agreeable, and wish I could be acquainted with him too; but I have my usual luck: I am always out of the way when anything desirable is going on; always the last of my family to be noticed. What an immense time Mrs. Clay has been staying with Elizabeth! Does she never mean to go away? But perhaps if she were to leave the room vacant, we might not be invited. Let me know what you think of this. I do not expect my children to be asked, you know. I can leave them at the Great House very well, for a month or six weeks. I have this moment heard that the Crofts are going to Bath almost immediately; they think the Admiral gouty. Charles heard it quite by chance; they have not had the civility to give me any notice, or of offering to take anything. I do not think they improve at all as neighbours. We see nothing of them, and this is really an instance of gross inattention. Charles joins me in love, and everything proper. Yours affectionately,

Mary M.

I am sorry to say that I am very far from well; and Jemima has just told me that the butcher says there is a bad sore throat very much about. I dare say I shall catch it; and my sore throats, you know, are always worse than anybody's.

So ended the first part, which had been afterwards put into an envelope, containing nearly as much more.

I kept my letter open, that I might send you word how Louisa bore her journey, and now I am extremely glad I did, having a great deal to add. In the first place, I had a note from Mrs. Croft yesterday, offering to convey anything to you; a very kind, friendly note indeed, addressed to me, just as it ought; I shall therefore be able to make my letter as long as I like. The Admiral does not seem very ill, and I sincerely hope Bath will do him all the good he wants. I shall be truly glad to have them back again. Our neighbourhood cannot spare such a pleasant family. But now for Louisa. I have something to communicate that will astonish you not a little. She and the Harvilles came on Tuesday very safely, and in the evening we went to ask her how she did, when we were rather surprised not to find Captain Benwick of the party, for he had been invited as well as the Harvilles; and what do you think was the reason? Neither more nor less than his being in love with Louisa, and not choosing to venture to Uppercross till he had had an answer from Mr. Musgrove; for it was all settled between him and her before she came away, and he had written to her father by Captain Harville. True, upon my honour! Are not you astonished? I shall be surprised at least if you ever received a hint of it, for I never did. Mrs. Musgrove protests solemnly that she knew nothing of the matter. We are all very well pleased, however, for though it is not equal to her marrying Captain Wentworth, it is infinitely better than Charles Hayter; and Mr. Musgrove has written his consent, and Captain Benwick is expected today. Mrs. Harville says her husband feels a good deal on his poor sister's account; but, however, Louisa is a great favourite with both. Indeed, Mrs. Harville and I quite agree that we love her the better for having nursed her. Charles wonders what Captain Wentworth will say; but if you remember, I never thought him attached to Louisa; I never could see anything of it. And this is the end, you see, of Captain Benwick's being supposed to be an admirer of yours. How Charles could take such a thing into his head was always incomprehensible to me. I hope he will be more agreeable now. Certainly not a great match for Louisa Musgrove, but a million times better than marrying among the Hayters.

Mary need not have feared her sister's being in any degree prepared for the news. She had never in her life been more astonished. Captain

Benwick and Louisa Musgrove! It was almost too wonderful for belief, and it was with the greatest effort that she could remain in the room, preserve an air of calmness, and answer the common questions of the moment. Happily for her, they were not many.

Sir Walter wanted to know whether the Crofts travelled with four horses, and whether they were likely to be situated in such a part of Bath as it might suit Miss Elliot and himself to visit in; but had little curiosity beyond.

"How is Mary?" said Elizabeth; and without waiting for an answer, "And pray what brings the Crofts to Bath?"

"They come on the Admiral's account. He is thought to be gouty."

"Gout and decrepitude!" said Sir Walter. "Poor old gentleman."

"Have they any acquaintance here?" asked Elizabeth.

"I do not know; but I can hardly suppose that, at Admiral Croft's time of life, and in his profession, he should not have many acquaintance in such a place as this."

"I suspect," said Sir Walter coolly, "that Admiral Croft will be best known in Bath as the renter of Kellynch Hall. Elizabeth, may we venture to present him and his wife in Laura Place?"

"Oh, no! I think not. Situated as we are with Lady Dalrymple, cousins, we ought to be very careful not to embarrass her with acquaintance she might not approve. If we were not related, it would not signify; but as cousins, she would feel scrupulous as to any proposal of ours. We had better leave the Crofts to find their own level. There are several odd-looking men walking about here, who, I am told, are sailors. The Crofts will associate with them."

This was Sir Walter and Elizabeth's share of interest in the letter; when Mrs. Clay had paid her tribute of more decent attention, in an enquiry after Mrs. Charles Musgrove, and her fine little boys, Anne was at liberty.

In her own room, she tried to comprehend it. Well might Charles wonder how Captain Wentworth would feel! Perhaps he had quitted the field, had given Louisa up, had ceased to love, had found he did not love her. She could not endure the idea of treachery or levity, or anything akin to ill usage between him and his friend. She could not endure that such a friendship as theirs should be severed unfairly.

Captain Benwick and Louisa Musgrove! The high-spirited, joyous-talking Louisa Musgrove, and the dejected, thinking, feeling, reading

Captain Benwick, seemed each of them everything that would not suit the other. Their minds most dissimilar! Where could have been the attraction? The answer soon presented itself. It had been in situation. They had been thrown together several weeks; they had been living in the same small family party: since Henrietta's coming away, they must have been depending almost entirely on each other, and Louisa, just recovering from illness, had been in an interesting state, and Captain Benwick was not inconsolable. That was a point that Anne had not been able to avoid suspecting before; and instead of drawing the same conclusion as Mary, from the present course of events, they served only to confirm the idea of his having felt some dawning of tenderness toward herself. She did not mean, however, to derive much more from it to gratify her vanity, than Mary might have allowed. She was persuaded that any tolerably pleasing young woman who had listened and seemed to feel for him would have received the same compliment. He had an affectionate heart. He must love somebody.

She saw no reason against their being happy. Louisa had fine naval fervour to begin with, and they would soon grow more alike. He would gain cheerfulness, and she would learn to be an enthusiast for Scott and Lord Byron; nay, that was probably learnt already; of course they had fallen in love over poetry. The idea of Louisa Musgrove turned into a person of literary taste, and sentimental reflection, was amusing, but she had no doubt of its being so. The day at Lyme, the fall from the Cobb, might influence her health, her nerves, her courage, her character to the end of her life, as thoroughly as it appeared to have influenced her fate.

The conclusion of the whole was, that if the woman who had been sensible of Captain Wentworth's merits could be allowed to prefer another man, there was nothing in the engagement to excite lasting wonder; and if Captain Wentworth lost no friend by it, certainly nothing to be regretted. No, it was not regret which made Anne's heart beat in spite of herself, and brought the colour into her cheeks when she thought of Captain Wentworth unshackled and free. She had some feelings that she was ashamed to investigate. They were too much like joy, senseless joy! She longed to see the Crofts; but when the meeting took place, it was evident that no rumour of the news had yet reached them. The visit of ceremony was paid and returned; and Louisa Musgrove was mentioned, and Captain Benwick, too, without even half a smile.

The Crofts had placed themselves in lodgings in Gay Street, perfectly to Sir Walter's satisfaction. He was not at all ashamed of the acquaintance, and did, in fact, think and talk a great deal more about the Admiral, than the Admiral ever thought or talked about him.

The Crofts knew quite as many people in Bath as they wished for, and considered their intercourse with the Elliots as a mere matter of form, and not in the least likely to afford them any pleasure. They brought with them their country habit of being almost always together. He was ordered to walk to keep off the gout, and Mrs. Croft seemed to go shares with him in everything, and to walk for her life to do him good. Anne saw them wherever she went. Lady Russell took her out in her carriage almost every morning, and she never failed to think of them, and never failed to see them. Knowing their feelings as she did, it was a most attractive picture of happiness to her. She always watched them as long as she could, delighted to fancy she understood what they might be talking of, as they walked along in happy independence, or equally delighted to see the Admiral's hearty shake of the hand when he encountered an old friend, and observe their eagerness of conversation when occasionally forming into a little knot of the navy, Mrs. Croft looking as intelligent and keen as any of the officers around her.

Anne was too much engaged with Lady Russell to be often walking herself; but it so happened that one morning, about a week or ten days after the Crofts' arrival, it suited her best to leave her friend, or her friend's carriage, in the lower part of the town, and return alone to Camden Place, and in walking up Milsom Street she had the good fortune to meet with the Admiral. He was standing by himself at a printshop window, with his hands behind him, in earnest contemplation of some print, and she not only might have passed him unseen, but was obliged to touch as well as address him before she could catch his notice.

When he did perceive and acknowledge her, however, it was done with all his usual frankness and good humour. "Ha! Is it you? Thank you, thank you. This is treating me like a friend. Here I am, you see, staring at a picture. I can never get by this shop without stopping. But what a thing here is, by way of a boat! Do look at it. Did you ever see the like? What queer fellows your fine painters must be, to think that anybody would venture their lives in such a shapeless old cockleshell as that? And yet here are two gentlemen stuck up in it mightily at their ease, and looking about them at the rocks and mountains, as if they were not to be upset the next moment, which they certainly must be. I wonder where that boat was built!" (laughing heartily); "I would not venture over a horsepond in it. Well," (turning away), "now, where are you bound? Can I go anywhere for you, or with you? Can I be of any use?"

"None, I thank you, unless you will give me the pleasure of your company the little way our road lies together. I am going home."

"That I will, with all my heart, and farther, too. Yes, yes, we will have a snug walk together, and I have something to tell you as we go along. There, take my arm; that's right; I do not feel comfortable if I have not a woman there. Lord! What a boat it is!" taking a last look at the picture, as they began to be in motion.

"Did you say that you had something to tell me, sir?"

"Yes, I have, presently. But here comes a friend, Captain Brigden; I shall only say, 'How d'ye do?' as we pass, however. I shall not stop. 'How d'ye do?' Brigden stares to see anybody with me but my wife. She, poor soul, is tied by the leg. She has a blister on one of her heels, as large as a three-shilling piece. If you look across the street, you will see Admiral Brand coming down and his brother. Shabby fellows, both of them! I am glad they are not on this side of the way. Sophy cannot bear them. They played me a pitiful trick once: got away with some of my best men. I will tell you the whole story another time. There comes old Sir Archibald Drew and his grandson. Look, he sees us; he kisses his hand to you; he takes you for my wife. Ah! The peace has come too soon for that younker. Poor old Sir Archibald! How do you like Bath, Miss Elliot? It suits us very well. We are always meeting with some old friend or other; the streets full of them every morning; sure to have plenty of chat; and then we get away from them all, and shut ourselves in our lodgings, and draw in our chairs, and are snug as if we were at Kellynch, ay, or as we used to be even at North Yarmouth and Deal. We do not like our lodgings here the worse, I can tell you, for putting us in mind of those we first had at North Yarmouth. The wind blows through one of the cupboards just in the same way."

When they were got a little farther, Anne ventured to press again for what he had to communicate. She hoped when clear of Milsom Street to have her curiosity gratified; but she was still obliged to wait, for the Admiral had made up his mind not to begin till they had gained the greater space and quiet of Belmont; and as she was not really Mrs.

Croft, she must let him have his own way. As soon as they were fairly ascending Belmont, he began—

"Well, now you shall hear something that will surprise you. But first of all, you must tell me the name of the young lady I am going to talk about. That young lady, you know, that we have all been so concerned for. The Miss Musgrove, that all this has been happening to. Her Christian name: I always forget her Christian name."

Anne had been ashamed to appear to comprehend so soon as she really did; but now she could safely suggest the name of "Louisa."

"Ay, ay, Miss Louisa Musgrove, that is the name. I wish young ladies had not such a number of fine Christian names. I should never be out if they were all Sophys, or something of that sort. Well, this Miss Louisa, we all thought, you know, was to marry Frederick. He was courting her week after week. The only wonder was, what they could be waiting for, till the business at Lyme came; then, indeed, it was clear enough that they must wait till her brain was set to right. But even then there was something odd in their way of going on. Instead of staying at Lyme, he went off to Plymouth, and then he went off to see Edward. When we came back from Minehead he was gone down to Edward's, and there he has been ever since. We have seen nothing of him since November. Even Sophy could not understand it. But now, the matter has taken the strangest turn of all; for this young lady, the same Miss Musgrove, instead of being to marry Frederick, is to marry James Benwick. You know James Benwick."

"A little. I am a little acquainted with Captain Benwick."

"Well, she is to marry him. Nay, most likely they are married already, for I do not know what they should wait for."

"I thought Captain Benwick a very pleasing young man," said Anne, "and I understand that he bears an excellent character."

"Oh! Yes, yes, there is not a word to be said against James Benwick. He is only a commander, it is true, made last summer, and these are bad times for getting on, but he has not another fault that I know of. An excellent, good-hearted fellow, I assure you; a very active, zealous officer too, which is more than you would think for, perhaps, for that soft sort of manner does not do him justice."

"Indeed you are mistaken there, sir; I should never augur want of spirit from Captain Benwick's manners. I thought them particularly pleasing, and I will answer for it, they would generally please."

"Well, well, ladies are the best judges; but James Benwick is rather too piano for me; and though very likely it is all our partiality, Sophy and I cannot help thinking Frederick's manners better than his. There is something about Frederick more to our taste."

Anne was caught. She had only meant to oppose the too common idea of spirit and gentleness being incompatible with each other, not at all to represent Captain Benwick's manners as the very best that could possibly be; and, after a little hesitation, she was beginning to say, "I was not entering into any comparison of the two friends," but the Admiral interrupted her with—

"And the thing is certainly true. It is not a mere bit of gossip. We have it from Frederick himself. His sister had a letter from him yesterday, in which he tells us of it, and he had just had it in a letter from Harville, written upon the spot, from Uppercross. I fancy they are all at Uppercross."

This was an opportunity that Anne could not resist; she said, therefore, "I hope, Admiral, I hope there is nothing in the style of Captain Wentworth's letter to make you and Mrs. Croft particularly uneasy. It did seem, last autumn, as if there were an attachment between him and Louisa Musgrove; but I hope it may be understood to have worn out on each side equally, and without violence. I hope his letter does not breathe the spirit of an ill-used man."

"Not at all, not at all; there is not an oath or a murmur from beginning to end."

Anne looked down to hide her smile.

"No, no; Frederick is not a man to whine and complain; he has too much spirit for that. If the girl likes another man better, it is very fit she should have him."

"Certainly. But what I mean is, that I hope there is nothing in Captain Wentworth's manner of writing to make you suppose he thinks himself ill-used by his friend, which might appear, you know, without its being absolutely said. I should be very sorry that such a friendship as has subsisted between him and Captain Benwick should be destroyed, or even wounded, by a circumstance of this sort."

"Yes, yes, I understand you. But there is nothing at all of that nature in the letter. He does not give the least fling at Benwick; does not so much as say, 'I wonder at it, I have a reason of my own for wondering at it.' No, you would not guess, from his way of writing, that he had ever thought of this Miss (what's her name?) for himself. He very handsomely hopes they will be happy together; and there is nothing very unforgiving in that, I think."

Anne did not receive the perfect conviction that the Admiral meant to convey, but it would have been useless to press the enquiry farther. She therefore satisfied herself with commonplace remarks or quiet attention, and the Admiral had it all his own way.

"Poor Frederick!" said he at last. "Now he must begin all over again with somebody else. I think we must get him to Bath. Sophy must write, and beg him to come to Bath. Here are pretty girls enough, I am sure. It would be of no use to go to Uppercross again, for that other Miss Musgrove, I find, is bespoke by her cousin, the young parson. Do not you think, Miss Elliot, we had better try to get him to Bath?"

CHAPTER 19

While Admiral Croft was taking this walk with Anne, and expressing his wish of getting Captain Wentworth to Bath, Captain Wentworth was already on his way thither. Before Mrs. Croft had written, he was arrived, and the very next time Anne walked out, she saw him.

Mr. Elliot was attending his two cousins and Mrs. Clay. They were in Milsom Street. It began to rain, not much, but enough to make shelter desirable for women, and quite enough to make it very desirable for Miss Elliot to have the advantage of being conveyed home in Lady Dalrymple's carriage, which was seen waiting at a little distance; she, Anne, and Mrs. Clay, therefore, turned into Molland's, while Mr. Elliot stepped to Lady Dalrymple, to request her assistance. He soon joined them again, successful, of course; Lady Dalrymple would be most happy to take them home, and would call for them in a few minutes.

Her ladyship's carriage was a barouche, and did not hold more than four with any comfort. Miss Carteret was with her mother; consequently it was not reasonable to expect accommodation for all the three Camden Place ladies. There could be no doubt as to Miss Elliot. Whoever suffered inconvenience, she must suffer none, but it occupied a little time to settle the point of civility between the other two. The rain was a mere trifle, and Anne was most sincere in preferring a walk with Mr. Elliot. But the rain was also a mere trifle to Mrs. Clay; she would hardly allow it even to drop at all, and her boots were so thick!—much thicker than Miss Anne's; and, in short, her civility rendered her quite as anxious to be left to walk with Mr. Elliot as Anne could be, and it was discussed between them with a generosity so polite and so determined, that the others were obliged to settle it for them; Miss Elliot maintaining that Mrs. Clay had a little cold already, and Mr. Elliot deciding on appeal, that his cousin Anne's boots were rather the thickest.

It was fixed accordingly, that Mrs. Clay should be of the party in the carriage; and they had just reached this point, when Anne, as she sat near the window, descried, most decidedly and distinctly, Captain Wentworth walking down the street.

Her start was perceptible only to herself; but she instantly felt that she was the greatest simpleton in the world, the most unaccountable and absurd! For a few minutes she saw nothing before her; it was all confusion. She was lost, and when she had scolded back her senses, she found the others still waiting for the carriage, and Mr. Elliot (always obliging) just setting off for Union Street on a commission of Mrs. Clay's.

She now felt a great inclination to go to the outer door; she wanted to see if it rained. Why was she to suspect herself of another motive? Captain Wentworth must be out of sight. She left her seat, she would go; one half of her should not be always so much wiser than the other half, or always suspecting the other of being worse than it was. She would see if it rained. She was sent back, however, in a moment by the entrance of Captain Wentworth himself, among a party of gentlemen and ladies, evidently his acquaintance, and whom he must have joined a little below Milsom Street. He was more obviously struck and confused by the sight of her than she had ever observed before; he looked quite red. For the first time, since their renewed acquaintance, she felt that she was betraying the least sensibility of the two. She had the advantage of him in the preparation of the last few moments. All the overpowering, blinding, bewildering, first effects of strong surprise were over with her. Still, however, she had enough to feel! It was agitation, pain, pleasure, a something between delight and misery.

He spoke to her, and then turned away. The character of his manner was embarrassment. She could not have called it either cold or friendly, or anything so certainly as embarrassed.

After a short interval, however, he came towards her, and spoke again. Mutual enquiries on common subjects passed: neither of them, probably, much the wiser for what they heard, and Anne continuing fully sensible of his being less at ease than formerly. They had by dint of being so very much together, got to speak to each other with a considerable portion of apparent indifference and calmness; but he could not do it now. Time had changed him, or Louisa had changed him. There was consciousness of some sort or other. He looked very well, not as if he had been suffering in health or spirits, and he talked of Uppercross, of the Musgroves, nay, even of Louisa, and had even a momentary look of his own arch significance as he named her; but yet it was Captain Wentworth not comfortable, not easy, not able to feign that he was.

It did not surprise, but it grieved Anne to observe that Elizabeth would not know him. She saw that he saw Elizabeth, that Elizabeth saw him, that there was complete internal recognition on each side; she was convinced that he was ready to be acknowledged as an acquaintance, expecting it, and she had the pain of seeing her sister turn away with unalterable coldness.

Lady Dalrymple's carriage, for which Miss Elliot was growing very impatient, now drew up; the servant came in to announce it. It was beginning to rain again, and altogether there was a delay, and a bustle, and a talking, which must make all the little crowd in the shop understand that Lady Dalrymple was calling to convey Miss Elliot. At last Miss Elliot and her friend, unattended but by the servant, (for there was no cousin returned), were walking off; and Captain Wentworth, watching them, turned again to Anne, and by manner, rather than words, was offering his services to her.

"I am much obliged to you," was her answer, "but I am not going with them. The carriage would not accommodate so many. I walk; I prefer walking."

"But it rains."

"Oh! Very little. Nothing that I regard."

After a moment's pause he said: "Though I came only yesterday, I have equipped myself properly for Bath already, you see," (pointing to a new umbrella); "I wish you would make use of it, if you are determined to walk; though I think it would be more prudent to let me get you a chair."

She was very much obliged to him, but declined it all, repeating her conviction, that the rain would come to nothing at present, and adding, "I am only waiting for Mr. Elliot. He will be here in a moment, I am sure."

She had hardly spoken the words, when Mr. Elliot walked in. Captain Wentworth recollected him perfectly. There was no difference between him and the man who had stood on the steps at Lyme, admiring Anne as she passed, except in the air and look and manner of the privileged relation and friend. He came in with eagerness, appeared to see and think only of her, apologised for his stay, was grieved to have kept her waiting, and anxious to get her away without further loss of time and before the rain increased; and in another moment they walked off together, her arm under his, a gentle and embarrassed glance, and a

"Good morning to you!" being all that she had time for, as she passed away.

As soon as they were out of sight, the ladies of Captain Wentworth's party began talking of them.

"Mr. Elliot does not dislike his cousin, I fancy?"

"Oh! No, that is clear enough. One can guess what will happen there. He is always with them; half lives in the family, I believe. What a very good-looking man!"

"Yes, and Miss Atkinson, who dined with him once at the Wallises, says he is the most agreeable man she ever was in company with."

"She is pretty, I think; Anne Elliot; very pretty, when one comes to look at her. It is not the fashion to say so, but I confess I admire her more than her sister."

"Oh! So do I."

"And so do I. No comparison. But the men are all wild after Miss Elliot. Anne is too delicate for them."

Anne would have been particularly obliged to her cousin, if he would have walked by her side all the way to Camden Place, without saying a word. She had never found it so difficult to listen to him, though nothing could exceed his solicitude and care, and though his subjects were principally such as were wont to be always interesting: praise—warm, just, and discriminating—of Lady Russell, and insinuations highly rational against Mrs. Clay. But just now she could think only of Captain Wentworth. She could not understand his present feelings, whether he were really suffering much from disappointment or not; and till that point were settled, she could not be quite herself.

She hoped to be wise and reasonable in time; but alas! Alas! She must confess to herself that she was not wise yet.

Another circumstance very essential for her to know was how long he meant to be in Bath; he had not mentioned it, or she could not recollect it. He might be only passing through. But it was more probable that he should be come to stay.

In that case, so liable as everybody was to meet everybody in Bath, Lady Russell would in all likelihood see him somewhere. Would she recollect him? How would it all be? She had already been obliged to tell Lady Russell that Louisa Musgrove was to marry Captain Benwick. It had cost her something to encounter Lady Russell's surprise; and now, if she were by any chance to be thrown into company with Captain

Wentworth, her imperfect knowledge of the matter might add another shade of prejudice against him.

The following morning Anne was out with her friend, and for the first hour, in an incessant and fearful sort of watch for him in vain; but at last, in returning down Pulteney Street, she distinguished him on the right hand pavement at such a distance as to have him in view the greater part of the street. There were many other men about him, many groups walking the same way, but there was no mistaking him. She looked instinctively at Lady Russell, but not from any mad idea of her recognising him so soon as she did herself. No, it was not to be supposed that Lady Russell would perceive him till they were nearly opposite.

She looked at her however, from time to time, anxiously; and when the moment approached which must point him out, though not daring to look again (for her own countenance she knew was unfit to be seen), she was yet perfectly conscious of Lady Russell's eyes being turned exactly in the direction for him—of her being, in short, intently observing him. She could thoroughly comprehend the sort of fascination he must possess over Lady Russell's mind, the difficulty it must be for her to withdraw her eyes, the astonishment she must be feeling that eight or nine years should have passed over him, and in foreign climes and in active service too, without robbing him of one personal grace! At last, Lady Russell drew back her head. "Now, how would she speak of him?"

"You will wonder," said she, "what has been fixing my eye so long; but I was looking after some window curtains, which Lady Alicia and Mrs. Frankland were telling me of last night. They described the drawing room window curtains of one of the houses on this side of the way, and this part of the street, as being the handsomest and best hung of any in Bath, but could not recollect the exact number, and I have been trying to find out which it could be; but I confess I can see no curtains hereabouts that answer their description."

Anne sighed and blushed and smiled, in pity and disdain, either at her friend or herself. The part that provoked her most, was that in all this waste of foresight and caution, she should have lost the right moment for seeing whether he saw them.

A day or two passed without producing anything. The theatre or the rooms, where he was most likely to be, were not fashionable enough for the Elliots, whose evening amusements were solely in the elegant stupidity of private parties, in which they were getting more and more engaged; and Anne, wearied of such a state of stagnation, sick of knowing nothing, and fancying herself stronger because her strength was not tried, was quite impatient for the concert evening. It was a concert for the benefit of a person patronised by Lady Dalrymple. Of course they must attend. It was really expected to be a good one, and Captain Wentworth was very fond of music. If she could only have a few minutes conversation with him again, she fancied she should be satisfied; and as to the power of addressing him, she felt all over courage if the opportunity occurred. Elizabeth had turned from him, Lady Russell overlooked him; her nerves were strengthened by these circumstances; she felt that she owed him attention.

She had once partly promised Mrs. Smith to spend the evening with her; but in a short hurried call she excused herself and put it off, with the more decided promise of a longer visit on the morrow. Mrs. Smith gave a most good-humoured acquiescence.

"By all means," said she; "only tell me all about it, when you do come. Who is your party?"

Anne named them all. Mrs. Smith made no reply; but when she was leaving her, said, and with an expression half serious, half arch, "Well, I heartily wish your concert may answer; and do not fail me tomorrow if you can come; for I begin to have a foreboding that I may not have many more visits from you."

Anne was startled and confused; but after standing in a moment's suspense, was obliged, and not sorry to be obliged, to hurry away.

CHAPTER 20

Sir Walter, his two daughters, and Mrs. Clay, were the earliest of all their party at the rooms in the evening; and as Lady Dalrymple must be waited for, they took their station by one of the fires in the Octagon Room. But hardly were they so settled, when the door opened again, and Captain Wentworth walked in alone. Anne was the nearest to him, and making yet a little advance, she instantly spoke. He was preparing only to bow and pass on, but her gentle "How do you do?" brought him out of the straight line to stand near her, and make enquiries in return, in spite of the formidable father and sister in the background. Their being in the background was a support to Anne; she knew nothing of their looks, and felt equal to everything that she believed right to be done.

While they were speaking, a whispering between her father and Elizabeth caught her ear. She could not distinguish, but she must guess the subject; and on Captain Wentworth's making a distant bow, she comprehended that her father had judged so well as to give him that simple acknowledgement of acquaintance, and she was just in time by a side glance to see a slight curtsey from Elizabeth herself. This, though late, and reluctant, and ungracious, was yet better than nothing, and her spirits improved.

After talking, however, of the weather, and Bath, and the concert, their conversation began to flag, and so little was said at last, that she was expecting him to go every moment, but he did not; he seemed in no hurry to leave her; and presently with renewed spirit, with a little smile, a little glow, he said—

"I have hardly seen you since our day at Lyme. I am afraid you must have suffered from the shock, and the more from its not overpowering you at the time."

She assured him that she had not.

"It was a frightful hour," said he, "a frightful day!" and he passed his hand across his eyes, as if the remembrance were still too painful, but in a moment, half smiling again, added, "The day has produced some effects however, has had some consequences which must be considered as the very reverse of frightful. When you had the presence of mind to suggest that Benwick would be the properest person to fetch a surgeon, you could have little idea of his being eventually one of those most concerned in her recovery."

"Certainly I could have none. But it appears—I should hope it would be a very happy match. There are on both sides good principles and good temper."

"Yes," said he, looking not exactly forward; "but there, I think, ends the resemblance. With all my soul I wish them happy, and rejoice over every circumstance in favour of it. They have no difficulties to contend with at home, no opposition, no caprice, no delays. The Musgroves are behaving like themselves, most honourably and kindly, only anxious with true parental hearts to promote their daughter's comfort. All this is much, very much in favour of their happiness; more than perhaps—"

He stopped. A sudden recollection seemed to occur, and to give him some taste of that emotion which was reddening Anne's cheeks and fixing her eyes on the ground. After clearing his throat, however, he proceeded thus, "I confess that I do think there is a disparity, too great a disparity, and in a point no less essential than mind. I regard Louisa Musgrove as a very amiable, sweet-tempered girl, and not deficient in understanding, but Benwick is something more. He is a clever man, a reading man; and I confess, that I do consider his attaching himself to her with some surprise. Had it been the effect of gratitude, had he learnt to love her, because he believed her to prefer him, it would have been another thing. But I have no reason to suppose it so. It seems, on the contrary, to have been a perfectly spontaneous, untaught feeling on his side, and this surprises me. A man like him, in his situation! With a heart pierced, wounded, almost broken! Fanny Harville was a very superior creature, and his attachment to her was indeed attachment. A man does not recover from such a devotion of the heart to such a woman. He ought not; he does not."

Either from the consciousness, however, that his friend had recovered, or from some other consciousness, he went no farther; and Anne, who, in spite of the agitated voice in which the latter part had been uttered, and in spite of all the various noises of the room, the almost ceaseless slam of the door, and ceaseless buzz of persons walking through, had distinguished every word, was struck, gratified, confused, and beginning to breathe very quick, and feel an hundred things in a moment. It was impossible for her to enter on such a subject; and yet, after a pause, feeling the necessity of speaking, and having not the smallest wish for a total change, she only deviated so far as to say, "You were a good while at Lyme, I think?"

"About a fortnight. I could not leave it till Louisa's doing well was quite ascertained. I had been too deeply concerned in the mischief to be soon at peace. It had been my doing, solely mine. She would not have been obstinate if I had not been weak. The country round Lyme is very fine. I walked and rode a great deal; and the more I saw, the more I found to admire."

"I should very much like to see Lyme again," said Anne.

"Indeed! I should not have supposed that you could have found anything in Lyme to inspire such a feeling. The horror and distress you were involved in, the stretch of mind, the wear of spirits! I should have thought your last impressions of Lyme must have been strong disgust."

"The last hours were certainly very painful," replied Anne; "but when pain is over, the remembrance of it often becomes a pleasure. One does not love a place the less for having suffered in it, unless it has been all suffering, nothing but suffering, which was by no means the case at Lyme. We were only in anxiety and distress during the last two hours, and previously there had been a great deal of enjoyment. So much novelty and beauty! I have travelled so little, that every fresh place would be interesting to me; but there is real beauty at Lyme; and in short" (with a faint blush at some recollections), "altogether my impressions of the place are very agreeable."

As she ceased, the entrance door opened again, and the very party appeared for whom they were waiting. "Lady Dalrymple, Lady Dalrymple," was the rejoicing sound; and with all the eagerness compatible with anxious elegance, Sir Walter and his two ladies stepped forward to meet her. Lady Dalrymple and Miss Carteret, escorted by Mr. Elliot and Colonel Wallis, who had happened to arrive nearly at the same instant, advanced into the room. The others joined them, and it was a group in which Anne found herself also necessarily included. She was divided from Captain Wentworth. Their interesting, almost too interesting conversation must be broken up for a time, but slight was the penance compared with the happiness which brought it on!

She had learnt, in the last ten minutes, more of his feelings towards Louisa, more of all his feelings than she dared to think of; and she gave herself up to the demands of the party, to the needful civilities of the moment, with exquisite, though agitated sensations. She was in good humour with all. She had received ideas which disposed her to be courteous and kind to all, and to pity everyone, as being less happy than herself.

The delightful emotions were a little subdued when, on stepping back from the group, to be joined again by Captain Wentworth, she saw that he was gone. She was just in time to see him turn into the Concert Room. He was gone; he had disappeared; she felt a moment's regret. But "they should meet again. He would look for her, he would find her out before the evening was over, and at present, perhaps, it was as well to be asunder. She was in need of a little interval for recollection."

Upon Lady Russell's appearance soon afterwards, the whole party was collected, and all that remained was to marshal themselves, and proceed into the Concert Room; and be of all the consequence in their power, draw as many eyes, excite as many whispers, and disturb as many people as they could.

Very, very happy were both Elizabeth and Anne Elliot as they walked in. Elizabeth arm in arm with Miss Carteret, and looking on the broad back of the dowager Viscountess Dalrymple before her, had nothing to wish for which did not seem within her reach; and Anne—but it would be an insult to the nature of Anne's felicity, to draw any comparison between it and her sister's; the origin of one all selfish vanity, of the other all generous attachment.

Anne saw nothing, thought nothing of the brilliancy of the room. Her happiness was from within. Her eyes were bright and her cheeks glowed; but she knew nothing about it. She was thinking only of the last half hour, and as they passed to their seats, her mind took a hasty range over it. His choice of subjects, his expressions, and still more his manner and look, had been such as she could see in only one light. His opinion of Louisa Musgrove's inferiority, an opinion which he had seemed solicitous to give, his wonder at Captain Benwick, his feelings as to a first, strong attachment—sentences begun which he could not finish, his half averted eyes and more than half expressive glance—all, all declared that he had a heart returning to her at least; that anger, resentment, avoidance, were no more; and that they were succeeded, not merely by friendship and regard, but by the tenderness of the past. Yes, some share of the tenderness of the past. She could not contemplate the change as implying less.

He must love her.

These were thoughts, with their attendant visions, which occupied and flurried her too much to leave her any power of observation; and she passed along the room without having a glimpse of him, without even trying to discern him. When their places were determined on, and they were all properly arranged, she looked round to see if he should happen to be in the same part of the room, but he was not; her eye could not reach him; and the concert being just opening, she must consent for a time to be happy in a humbler way.

The party was divided and disposed of on two contiguous benches: Anne was among those on the foremost, and Mr. Elliot had manoeuvred so well, with the assistance of his friend Colonel Wallis, as to have a seat by her. Miss Elliot, surrounded by her cousins, and the principal object of Colonel Wallis's gallantry, was quite contented.

Anne's mind was in a most favourable state for the entertainment of the evening; it was just occupation enough: she had feelings for the tender, spirits for the gay, attention for the scientific, and patience for the wearisome; and had never liked a concert better, at least during the first act. Towards the close of it, in the interval succeeding an Italian song, she explained the words of the song to Mr. Elliot. They had a concert bill between them.

"This," said she, "is nearly the sense, or rather the meaning of the words, for certainly the sense of an Italian love song must not be talked of, but it is as nearly the meaning as I can give; for I do not pretend to understand the language. I am a very poor Italian scholar."

"Yes, yes, I see you are. I see you know nothing of the matter. You have only knowledge enough of the language to translate at sight these inverted, transposed, curtailed Italian lines, into clear, comprehensible, elegant English. You need not say anything more of your ignorance. Here is complete proof."

"I will not oppose such kind politeness; but I should be sorry to be examined by a real proficient."

"I have not had the pleasure of visiting in Camden Place so long," replied he, "without knowing something of Miss Anne Elliot; and I do regard her as one who is too modest for the world in general to be aware of half her accomplishments, and too highly accomplished for modesty to be natural in any other woman."

"For shame! For shame! This is too much flattery. I forget what we are to have next," turning to the bill.

"Perhaps," said Mr. Elliot, speaking low, "I have had a longer acquaintance with your character than you are aware of."

"Indeed! How so? You can have been acquainted with it only since I came to Bath, excepting as you might hear me previously spoken of in my own family."

"I knew you by report long before you came to Bath. I had heard you described by those who knew you intimately. I have been acquainted with you by character many years. Your person, your disposition, accomplishments, manner; they were all present to me."

Mr. Elliot was not disappointed in the interest he hoped to raise. No one can withstand the charm of such a mystery. To have been described long ago to a recent acquaintance, by nameless people, is irresistible; and Anne was all curiosity. She wondered, and questioned him eagerly, but in vain. He delighted in being asked, but he would not tell.

"No, no, some time or other, perhaps, but not now. He would mention no names now; but such, he could assure her, had been the fact. He had many years ago received such a description of Miss Anne Elliot as had inspired him with the highest idea of her merit, and excited the warmest curiosity to know her."

Anne could think of no one so likely to have spoken with partiality of her many years ago as the Mr. Wentworth of Monkford, Captain Wentworth's brother. He might have been in Mr. Elliot's company, but she had not courage to ask the question.

"The name of Anne Elliot," said he, "has long had an interesting sound to me. Very long has it possessed a charm over my fancy; and, if I dared, I would breathe my wishes that the name might never change."

Such, she believed, were his words; but scarcely had she received their sound, than her attention was caught by other sounds immediately behind her, which rendered everything else trivial. Her father and Lady Dalrymple were speaking.

"A well-looking man," said Sir Walter, "a very well-looking man."

"A very fine young man indeed!" said Lady Dalrymple. "More air than one often sees in Bath. Irish, I dare say."

"No, I just know his name. A bowing acquaintance. Wentworth;

Captain Wentworth of the navy. His sister married my tenant in Somersetshire, the Croft, who rents Kellynch."

Before Sir Walter had reached this point, Anne's eyes had caught the right direction, and distinguished Captain Wentworth standing among a cluster of men at a little distance. As her eyes fell on him, his seemed to be withdrawn from her. It had that appearance. It seemed as if she had been one moment too late; and as long as she dared observe, he did not look again: but the performance was recommencing, and she was forced to seem to restore her attention to the orchestra and look straight forward.

When she could give another glance, he had moved away. He could not have come nearer to her if he would; she was so surrounded and shut in: but she would rather have caught his eye.

Mr. Elliot's speech, too, distressed her. She had no longer any inclination to talk to him. She wished him not so near her.

The first act was over. Now she hoped for some beneficial change; and, after a period of nothing saying amongst the party, some of them did decide on going in quest of tea. Anne was one of the few who did not choose to move. She remained in her seat, and so did Lady Russell; but she had the pleasure of getting rid of Mr. Elliot; and she did not mean, whatever she might feel on Lady Russell's account, to shrink from conversation with Captain Wentworth, if he gave her the opportunity. She was persuaded by Lady Russell's countenance that she had seen him.

He did not come however. Anne sometimes fancied she discerned him at a distance, but he never came. The anxious interval wore away unproductively. The others returned, the room filled again, benches were reclaimed and repossessed, and another hour of pleasure or of penance was to be sat out, another hour of music was to give delight or the gapes, as real or affected taste for it prevailed. To Anne, it chiefly wore the prospect of an hour of agitation. She could not quit that room in peace without seeing Captain Wentworth once more, without the interchange of one friendly look.

In re-settling themselves there were now many changes, the result of which was favourable for her. Colonel Wallis declined sitting down again, and Mr. Elliot was invited by Elizabeth and Miss Carteret, in a manner not to be refused, to sit between them; and by some other removals, and a little scheming of her own, Anne was enabled to place herself much nearer the end of the bench than she had been before, much more within reach of a passerby. She could not do so without comparing herself with Miss Larolles, the inimitable Miss Larolles; but still she did it, and not with much happier effect; though by what seemed prosperity in the shape of an early abdication in her next neighbours, she found herself at the very end of the bench before the concert closed.

Such was her situation, with a vacant space at hand, when Captain Wentworth was again in sight. She saw him not far off. He saw her too; yet he looked grave, and seemed irresolute, and only by very slow degrees came at last near enough to speak to her. She felt that something must be the matter. The change was indubitable. The difference between his present air and what it had been in the Octagon Room was strikingly great. Why was it? She thought of her father, of Lady Russell. Could there have been any unpleasant glances? He began by speaking of the concert gravely, more like the Captain Wentworth of Uppercross; owned himself disappointed, had expected singing; and in short, must confess that he should not be sorry when it was over. Anne replied, and spoke in defence of the performance so well, and yet in allowance for his feelings so pleasantly, that his countenance improved, and he replied again with almost a smile. They talked for a few minutes more; the improvement held; he even looked down towards the bench, as if he saw a place on it well worth occupying; when at that moment a touch on her shoulder obliged Anne to turn round. It came from Mr. Elliot. He begged her pardon, but she must be applied to, to explain Italian again. Miss Carteret was very anxious to have a general idea of what was next to be sung. Anne could not refuse; but never had she sacrificed to politeness with a more suffering spirit.

A few minutes, though as few as possible, were inevitably consumed; and when her own mistress again, when able to turn and look as she had done before, she found herself accosted by Captain Wentworth, in a reserved yet hurried sort of farewell. "He must wish her good night; he was going; he should get home as fast as he could."

"Is not this song worth staying for?" said Anne, suddenly struck by an idea which made her yet more anxious to be encouraging.

"No!" he replied impressively, "there is nothing worth my staying for;" and he was gone directly.

Jealousy of Mr. Elliot! It was the only intelligible motive. Captain

Wentworth jealous of her affection! Could she have believed it a week ago—three hours ago! For a moment the gratification was exquisite. But, alas! There were very different thoughts to succeed. How was such jealousy to be quieted? How was the truth to reach him? How, in all the peculiar disadvantages of their respective situations, would he ever learn of her real sentiments? It was misery to think of Mr. Elliot's attentions. Their evil was incalculable.

CHAPTER 21

Anne recollected with pleasure the next morning her promise of going to Mrs. Smith, meaning that it should engage her from home at the time when Mr. Elliot would be most likely to call; for to avoid Mr. Elliot was almost a first object.

She felt a great deal of goodwill towards him. In spite of the mischief of his attentions, she owed him gratitude and regard, perhaps compassion. She could not help thinking much of the extraordinary circumstances attending their acquaintance, of the right that he seemed to have to interest her, by everything in situation, by his own sentiments, by his early prepossession. It was altogether very extraordinary; flattering, but painful. There was much to regret. How she might have felt had there been no Captain Wentworth in the case was not worth enquiry; for there was a Captain Wentworth; and be the conclusion of the present suspense good or bad, her affection would be his forever. Their union, she believed, could not divide her more from other men, than their final separation.

Prettier musings of high-wrought love and eternal constancy could never have passed along the streets of Bath, than Anne was sporting with from Camden Place to Westgate Buildings. It was almost enough to spread purification and perfume all the way.

She was sure of a pleasant reception; and her friend seemed this morning particularly obliged to her for coming, seemed hardly to have expected her, though it had been an appointment.

An account of the concert was immediately claimed; and Anne's recollections of the concert were quite happy enough to animate her features and make her rejoice to talk of it. All that she could tell she told most gladly, but the all was little for one who had been there, and unsatisfactory for such an enquirer as Mrs. Smith, who had already heard, through the shortcut of a laundress and a waiter, rather more of the general success and produce of the evening than Anne could relate, and who now asked in vain for several particulars of the company. Everybody of any consequence or notoriety in Bath was well known by name to Mrs. Smith.

"The little Durands were there, I conclude," said she, "with their mouths open to catch the music, like unfledged sparrows ready to be fed. They never miss a concert."

"Yes; I did not see them myself, but I heard Mr. Elliot say they were in the room."

"The Ibbotsons, were they there? And the two new beauties, with the tall Irish officer, who is talked of for one of them."

"I do not know. I do not think they were."

"Old Lady Mary Maclean? I need not ask after her. She never misses, I know; and you must have seen her. She must have been in your own circle; for as you went with Lady Dalrymple, you were in the seats of grandeur, round the orchestra, of course."

"No, that was what I dreaded. It would have been very unpleasant to me in every respect. But happily Lady Dalrymple always chooses to be farther off; and we were exceedingly well placed, that is, for hearing; I must not say for seeing, because I appear to have seen very little."

"Oh! You saw enough for your own amusement. I can understand. There is a sort of domestic enjoyment to be known even in a crowd, and this you had. You were a large party in yourselves, and you wanted nothing beyond."

"But I ought to have looked about me more," said Anne, conscious while she spoke that there had in fact been no want of looking about, that the object only had been deficient.

"No, no; you were better employed. You need not tell me that you had a pleasant evening. I see it in your eye. I perfectly see how the hours passed, that you had always something agreeable to listen to. In the intervals of the concert it was conversation."

Anne half smiled and said, "Do you see that in my eye?"

"Yes, I do. Your countenance perfectly informs me that you were in company last night with the person whom you think the most agreeable in the world, the person who interests you at this present time more than all the rest of the world put together."

A blush overspread Anne's cheeks. She could say nothing.

"And such being the case," continued Mrs. Smith, after a short pause, "I hope you believe that I do know how to value your kindness in coming to me this morning. It is really very good of you to come and sit with me, when you must have so many pleasanter demands upon your time."

Anne heard nothing of this. She was still in the astonishment and confusion excited by her friend's penetration, unable to imagine how any report of Captain Wentworth could have reached her. After another short silence, "Pray," said Mrs. Smith, "is Mr. Elliot aware of your acquaintance with me? Does he know that I am in Bath?"

"Mr. Elliot!" repeated Anne, looking up surprised. A moment's reflection showed her the mistake she had been under. She caught it instantaneously; and recovering her courage with the feeling of safety, soon added, more composedly, "Are you acquainted with Mr. Elliot?"

"I have been a good deal acquainted with him," replied Mrs. Smith, gravely, "but it seems worn out now. It is a great while since we met."

"I was not at all aware of this. You never mentioned it before. Had I known it, I would have had the pleasure of talking to him about you."

"To confess the truth," said Mrs. Smith, assuming her usual air of cheerfulness, "that is exactly the pleasure I want you to have. I want you to talk about me to Mr. Elliot. I want your interest with him. He can be of essential service to me; and if you would have the goodness, my dear Miss Elliot, to make it an object to yourself, of course it is done."

"I should be extremely happy; I hope you cannot doubt my willingness to be of even the slightest use to you," replied Anne; "but I suspect that you are considering me as having a higher claim on Mr. Elliot, a greater right to influence him, than is really the case. I am sure you have, somehow or other, imbibed such a notion. You must consider me only as Mr. Elliot's relation. If in that light there is anything which you suppose his cousin might fairly ask of him, I beg you would not hesitate to employ me."

Mrs. Smith gave her a penetrating glance, and then, smiling, said, "I have been a little premature, I perceive; I beg your pardon. I ought to have waited for official information. But now, my dear Miss Elliot, as an old friend, do give me a hint as to when I may speak. Next week? To be sure by next week I may be allowed to think it all settled, and build my own selfish schemes on Mr. Elliot's good fortune."

"No," replied Anne, "nor next week, nor next, nor next. I assure you that nothing of the sort you are thinking of will be settled any week. I am not going to marry Mr. Elliot. I should like to know why you imagine I am?"

Mrs. Smith looked at her again, looked earnestly, smiled, shook her head, and exclaimed—

"Now, how I do wish I understood you! How I do wish I knew what you were at! I have a great idea that you do not design to be cruel, when the right moment occurs. Till it does come, you know, we women never mean to have anybody. It is a thing of course among us, that every man is refused, till he offers. But why should you be cruel? Let me plead for my—present friend I cannot call him, but for my former friend. Where can you look for a more suitable match? Where could you expect a more gentlemanlike, agreeable man? Let me recommend Mr. Elliot. I am sure you hear nothing but good of him from Colonel Wallis; and who can know him better than Colonel Wallis?"

"My dear Mrs. Smith, Mr. Elliot's wife has not been dead much above half a year. He ought not to be supposed to be paying his addresses to anyone."

"Oh! If these are your only objections," cried Mrs. Smith, archly, "Mr. Elliot is safe, and I shall give myself no more trouble about him. Do not forget me when you are married, that's all. Let him know me to be a friend of yours, and then he will think little of the trouble required, which it is very natural for him now, with so many affairs and engagements of his own, to avoid and get rid of as he can; very natural, perhaps. Ninety-nine out of a hundred would do the same. Of course, he cannot be aware of the importance to me. Well, my dear Miss Elliot, I hope and trust you will be very happy. Mr. Elliot has sense to understand the value of such a woman. Your peace will not be shipwrecked as mine has been. You are safe in all worldly matters, and safe in his character. He will not be led astray; he will not be misled by others to his ruin."

"No," said Anne, "I can readily believe all that of my cousin. He seems to have a calm, decided temper, not at all open to dangerous impressions. I consider him with great respect. I have no reason, from anything that has fallen within my observation, to do otherwise. But I have not known him long; and he is not a man, I think, to be known intimately soon. Will not this manner of speaking of him, Mrs. Smith, convince you that he is nothing to me? Surely this must be calm enough. And, upon my word, he is nothing to me. Should he ever propose to me (which I have very little reason to imagine he has any thought of doing), I shall not accept him. I assure you I shall not. I assure you Mr. Elliot had not the share which you have been supposing, in whatever pleasure the concert of last night might afford: not Mr. Elliot; it is not Mr. Elliot that—"

She stopped, regretting with a deep blush that she had implied so much; but less would hardly have been sufficient. Mrs. Smith would hardly have believed so soon in Mr. Elliot's failure, but from the perception of there being a somebody else.

As it was, she instantly submitted, and with all the semblance of seeing nothing beyond; and Anne, eager to escape farther notice, was impatient to know why Mrs. Smith should have fancied she was to marry Mr. Elliot; where she could have received the idea, or from whom she could have heard it.

"Do tell me how it first came into your head."

"It first came into my head," replied Mrs. Smith, "upon finding how much you were together, and feeling it to be the most probable thing in the world to be wished for by everybody belonging to either of you; and you may depend upon it that all your acquaintance have disposed of you in the same way. But I never heard it spoken of till two days ago."

"And has it indeed been spoken of?"

"Did you observe the woman who opened the door to you when you called yesterday?"

"No. Was not it Mrs. Speed, as usual, or the maid? I observed no one in particular."

"It was my friend Mrs. Rooke; Nurse Rooke; who, by the by, had a great curiosity to see you, and was delighted to be in the way to let you in. She came away from Marlborough Buildings only on Sunday; and she it was who told me you were to marry Mr. Elliot. She had had it from Mrs. Wallis herself, which did not seem bad authority. She sat an hour with me on Monday evening, and gave me the whole history."

"The whole history," repeated Anne, laughing. "She could not make a very long history, I think, of one such little article of unfounded news."

Mrs. Smith said nothing.

"But," continued Anne, presently, "though there is no truth in my having this claim on Mr. Elliot, I should be extremely happy to be of use to you in any way that I could. Shall I mention to him your being in Bath? Shall I take any message?"

"No, I thank you: no, certainly not. In the warmth of the moment, and under a mistaken impression, I might, perhaps, have endeavoured to interest you in some circumstances, but not now. No, I thank you, I have nothing to trouble you with."

"I think you spoke of having known Mr. Elliot many years?"

"I did."

"Not before he was married, I suppose?"

"Yes; he was not married when I knew him first."

"And—were you much acquainted?"

"Intimately."

"Indeed! Then do tell me what he was at that time of life. I have a great curiosity to know what Mr. Elliot was as a very young man. Was he at all such as he appears now?"

"I have not seen Mr. Elliot these three years," was Mrs. Smith's answer, given so gravely that it was impossible to pursue the subject farther; and Anne felt that she had gained nothing but an increase of curiosity. They were both silent: Mrs. Smith very thoughtful. At last—

"I beg your pardon, my dear Miss Elliot," she cried, in her natural tone of cordiality, "I beg your pardon for the short answers I have been giving you, but I have been uncertain what I ought to do. I have been doubting and considering as to what I ought to tell you. There were many things to be taken into the account. One hates to be officious, to be giving bad impressions, making mischief. Even the smooth surface of family union seems worth preserving, though there may be nothing durable beneath. However, I have determined; I think I am right; I think you ought to be made acquainted with Mr. Elliot's real character. Though I fully believe that, at present, you have not the smallest intention of accepting him, there is no saying what may happen. You might, some time or other, be differently affected towards him. Hear the truth, therefore, now, while you are unprejudiced. Mr. Elliot is a man without heart or conscience; a designing, wary, cold-blooded being, who thinks only of himself; whom for his own interest or ease, would be guilty of any cruelty, or any treachery, that could be perpetrated without risk of his general character. He has no feeling for others. Those whom he has been the chief cause of leading into ruin, he can neglect and desert without the smallest compunction. He is totally beyond the reach of any sentiment of justice or compassion. Oh! He is black at heart, hollow and black!"

Anne's astonished air, and exclamation of wonder, made her pause, and in a calmer manner, she added, "My expressions startle you. You must allow for an injured, angry woman. But I will try to command myself. I will not abuse him. I will only tell you what I have found him. Facts shall speak. He was the intimate friend of my dear husband, who trusted and loved him, and thought him as good as himself. The intimacy had been formed before our marriage. I found them most intimate friends; and I, too, became excessively pleased with Mr. Elliot, and entertained the highest opinion of him. At nineteen, you know, one does not think very seriously; but Mr. Elliot appeared to me quite as good as others, and much more agreeable than most others, and we were almost always together. We were principally in town, living in very good style. He was then the inferior in circumstances; he was then the poor one; he had chambers in the Temple, and it was as much as he could do to support the appearance of a gentleman. He had always a home with us whenever he chose it; he was always welcome; he was like a brother. My poor Charles, who had the finest, most generous spirit in the world, would have divided his last farthing with him; and I know that his purse was open to him; I know that he often assisted him."

"This must have been about that very period of Mr. Elliot's life," said Anne, "which has always excited my particular curiosity. It must have been about the same time that he became known to my father and sister. I never knew him myself; I only heard of him; but there was a something in his conduct then, with regard to my father and sister, and afterwards in the circumstances of his marriage, which I never could quite reconcile with present times. It seemed to announce a different sort of man."

"I know it all, I know it all," cried Mrs. Smith. "He had been introduced to Sir Walter and your sister before I was acquainted with him, but I heard him speak of them forever. I know he was invited and encouraged, and I know he did not choose to go. I can satisfy you, perhaps, on points that you would little expect; and as to his marriage, I knew all about it at the time. I was privy to all the fors and againsts; I was the friend to whom he confided his hopes and plans; and though I did not know his wife previously (her inferior situation in society, indeed, rendered that impossible) yet I knew her all her life afterwards, or at least till within the last two years of her life, and can answer any question you may wish to put."

"Nay," said Anne, "I have no particular enquiry to make about her. I have always understood they were not a happy couple. But I should like to know why, at that time of his life, he should slight my father's acquaintance as he did. My father was certainly disposed to take very kind and proper notice of him. Why did Mr. Elliot draw back?"

"Mr. Elliot," replied Mrs. Smith, "at that period of his life, had one object in view: to make his fortune, and by a rather quicker process than the law. He was determined to make it by marriage. He was determined, at least, not to mar it by an imprudent marriage; and I know it was his belief (whether justly or not, of course I cannot decide), that your father and sister, in their civilities and invitations, were designing a match between the heir and the young lady, and it was impossible that such a match should have answered his ideas of wealth and independence. That was his motive for drawing back, I can assure you. He told me the whole story. He had no concealments with me. It was curious, that having just left you behind me in Bath, my first and principal acquaintance on marrying should be your cousin; and that, through him, I should be continually hearing of your father and sister. He described one Miss Elliot, and I thought very affectionately of the other."

"Perhaps," cried Anne, struck by a sudden idea, "you sometimes spoke of me to Mr. Elliot?"

"To be sure I did; very often. I used to boast of my own Anne Elliot, and vouch for your being a very different creature from—"

She checked herself just in time.

"This accounts for something which Mr. Elliot said last night," cried Anne. "This explains it. I found he had been used to hear of me. I could not comprehend how. What wild imaginations one forms where dear self is concerned! How sure to be mistaken! But I beg your pardon; I have interrupted you. Mr. Elliot married, then, completely for money? The circumstances, probably, which first opened your eyes to his character."

Mrs. Smith hesitated a little here. "Oh! Those things are too common. When one lives in the world, a man or woman's marrying for money is too common to strike one as it ought. I was very young, and associated only with the young, and we were a thoughtless, gay set, without any strict rules of conduct. We lived for enjoyment. I think differently now; time and sickness and sorrow have given me other notions; but at that period I must own I saw nothing reprehensible in what Mr. Elliot was doing. 'To do the best for himself,' passed as a duty."

"But was not she a very low woman?"

"Yes; which I objected to, but he would not regard. Money, money, was all that he wanted. Her father was a grazier, her grandfather had been a butcher, but that was all nothing. She was a fine woman, had had a decent education, was brought forward by some cousins, thrown by chance into Mr. Elliot's company, and fell in love with him; and not a difficulty or a scruple was there on his side, with respect to her birth. All his caution was spent in being secured of the real amount of her fortune, before he committed himself. Depend upon it, whatever esteem Mr. Elliot may have for his own situation in life now, as a young man he had not the smallest value for it. His chance for the Kellynch estate was something, but all the honour of the family he held as cheap as dirt. I have often heard him declare, that if baronetcies were saleable, anybody should have his for fifty pounds, arms and motto, name and livery included; but I will not pretend to repeat half that I used to hear him say on that subject. It would not be fair; and yet you ought to have proof, for what is all this but assertion, and you shall have proof."

"Indeed, my dear Mrs. Smith, I want none," cried Anne. "You have asserted nothing contradictory to what Mr. Elliot appeared to be some years ago. This is all in confirmation, rather, of what we used to hear and believe. I am more curious to know why he should be so different now."

"But for my satisfaction, if you will have the goodness to ring for Mary—stay: I am sure you will have the still greater goodness of going yourself into my bedroom, and bringing me the small inlaid box which you will find on the upper shelf of the closet."

Anne, seeing her friend to be earnestly bent on it, did as she was desired. The box was brought and placed before her, and Mrs. Smith, sighing over it as she unlocked it, said, "This is full of papers belonging to him, to my husband; a small portion only of what I had to look over when I lost him. The letter I am looking for was one written by Mr. Elliot to him before our marriage, and happened to be saved; why, one can hardly imagine. But he was careless and immethodical, like other men, about those things; and when I came to examine his papers, I found it with others still more trivial, from different people scattered here and there, while many letters and memorandums of real importance had been destroyed. Here it is; I would not burn it, because being even then very little satisfied with Mr. Elliot, I was determined to preserve every document of former intimacy. I have now another motive for being glad that I can produce it."

This was the letter, directed to "Charles Smith, Esq. Tunbridge Wells," and dated from London, as far back as July, 1803:

> Dear Smith,
>
> I have received yours. Your kindness almost overpowers me. I wish nature had made such hearts as yours more common, but I have lived three-and-twenty years in the world, and have seen none like it. At present, believe me, I have no need of your services, being in cash again. Give me joy: I have got rid of Sir Walter and Miss. They are gone back to Kellynch, and almost made me swear to visit them this summer; but my first visit to Kellynch will be with a surveyor, to tell me how to bring it with best advantage to the hammer. The baronet, nevertheless, is not unlikely to marry again; he is quite fool enough. If he does, however, they will leave me in peace, which may be a decent equivalent for the reversion. He is worse than last year. I wish I had any name but Elliot. I am sick of it. The name of Walter I can drop, thank God! And I desire you will never insult me with my second W. again, meaning, for the rest of my life, to be only yours truly,
>
> Wm. Elliot.

Such a letter could not be read without putting Anne in a glow; and Mrs. Smith, observing the high colour in her face, said, "The language, I know, is highly disrespectful. Though I have forgot the exact terms, I have a perfect impression of the general meaning. But it shows you the man. Mark his professions to my poor husband. Can anything be stronger?"

Anne could not immediately get over the shock and mortification of finding such words applied to her father. She was obliged to recollect that her seeing the letter was a violation of the laws of honour, that no one ought to be judged or to be known by such testimonies, that no private correspondence could bear the eye of others, before she could recover calmness enough to return the letter which she had been meditating over, and say, "Thank you. This is full proof undoubtedly proof of everything you were saying. But why be acquainted with us now?"

"I can explain this too," cried Mrs. Smith, smiling.

"Can you really?"

"Yes. I have shown you Mr. Elliot as he was a dozen years ago, and

I will show him as he is now. I cannot produce written proof again, but I can give as authentic oral testimony as you can desire, of what he is now wanting, and what he is now doing. He is no hypocrite now. He truly wants to marry you. His present attentions to your family are very sincere, quite from the heart. I will give you my authority: his friend Colonel Wallis."

"Colonel Wallis! You are acquainted with him?"

"No. It does not come to me in quite so direct a line as that; it takes a bend or two, but nothing of consequence. The stream is as good as at first; the little rubbish it collects in the turnings is easily moved away. Mr. Elliot talks unreservedly to Colonel Wallis of his views on you, which said Colonel Wallis, I imagine to be, in himself, a sensible, careful, discerning sort of character; but Colonel Wallis has a very pretty silly wife, to whom he tells things which he had better not, and he repeats it all to her. She, in the overflowing spirits of her recovery, repeats it all to her nurse; and the nurse knowing my acquaintance with you, very naturally brings it all to me. On Monday evening, my good friend Mrs. Rooke let me thus much into the secrets of Marlborough Buildings. When I talked of a whole history, therefore, you see I was not romancing so much as you supposed."

"My dear Mrs. Smith, your authority is deficient. This will not do. Mr. Elliot's having any views on me will not in the least account for the efforts he made towards a reconciliation with my father. That was all prior to my coming to Bath. I found them on the most friendly terms when I arrived."

"I know you did; I know it all perfectly, but—"

"Indeed, Mrs. Smith, we must not expect to get real information in such a line. Facts or opinions which are to pass through the hands of so many, to be misconceived by folly in one, and ignorance in another, can hardly have much truth left."

"Only give me a hearing. You will soon be able to judge of the general credit due, by listening to some particulars, which you can yourself immediately contradict or confirm. Nobody supposes that you were his first inducement. He had seen you indeed, before he came to Bath, and admired you, but without knowing it to be you. So says my historian, at least. Is this true? Did he see you last summer or autumn, 'somewhere down in the west,' to use her own words, without knowing it to be you?"

"He certainly did. So far it is very true. At Lyme. I happened to be at Lyme."

"Well," continued Mrs. Smith, triumphantly, "grant my friend the credit due to the establishment of the first point asserted. He saw you then at Lyme, and liked you so well as to be exceedingly pleased to meet with you again in Camden Place, as Miss Anne Elliot, and from that moment, I have no doubt, had a double motive in his visits there. But there was another, and an earlier, which I will now explain. If there is anything in my story which you know to be either false or improbable, stop me. My account states, that your sister's friend, the lady now staying with you, whom I have heard you mention, came to Bath with Miss Elliot and Sir Walter as long ago as September (in short when they first came themselves), and has been staying there ever since; that she is a clever, insinuating, handsome woman, poor and plausible, and altogether such in situation and manner, as to give a general idea, among Sir Walter's acquaintance, of her meaning to be Lady Elliot, and as general a surprise that Miss Elliot should be, apparently, blind to the danger."

Here Mrs. Smith paused a moment; but Anne had not a word to say, and she continued, "This was the light in which it appeared to those who knew the family, long before you returned to it; and Colonel Wallis had his eye upon your father enough to be sensible of it, though he did not then visit in Camden Place; but his regard for Mr. Elliot gave him an interest in watching all that was going on there, and when Mr. Elliot came to Bath for a day or two, as he happened to do a little before Christmas, Colonel Wallis made him acquainted with the appearance of things, and the reports beginning to prevail. Now you are to understand, that time had worked a very material change in Mr. Elliot's opinions as to the value of a baronetcy. Upon all points of blood and connexion, he is a completely altered man. Having long had as much money as he could spend, nothing to wish for on the side of avarice or indulgence, he has been gradually learning to pin his happiness upon the consequence he is heir to. I thought it coming on before our acquaintance ceased, but it is now a confirmed feeling. He cannot bear the idea of not being Sir William. You may guess, therefore, that the news he heard from his friend could not be very agreeable, and you may guess what it produced; the resolution of coming back to Bath as soon as possible, and of fixing himself here for a time, with the view of renewing his former acquaintance, and recovering such a footing in the family as might give him the means of ascertaining the degree of his danger, and of circumventing the lady if he found it material. This was agreed upon between the two friends as the only thing to be done; and Colonel Wallis was to assist in every way that he could. He was to be introduced, and Mrs. Wallis was to be introduced, and everybody was to be introduced. Mr. Elliot came back accordingly; and on application was forgiven, as you know, and re-admitted into the family; and there it was his constant object, and his only object (till your arrival added another motive), to watch Sir Walter and Mrs. Clay. He omitted no opportunity of being with them, threw himself in their way, called at all hours; but I need not be particular on this subject. You can imagine what an artful man would do; and with this guide, perhaps, may recollect what you have seen him do."

"Yes," said Anne, "you tell me nothing which does not accord with what I have known, or could imagine. There is always something offensive in the details of cunning. The manoeuvres of selfishness and duplicity must ever be revolting, but I have heard nothing which really surprises me. I know those who would be shocked by such a representation of Mr. Elliot, who would have difficulty in believing it; but I have never been satisfied. I have always wanted some other motive for his conduct than appeared. I should like to know his present opinion, as to the probability of the event he has been in dread of; whether he considers the danger to be lessening or not."

"Lessening, I understand," replied Mrs. Smith. "He thinks Mrs. Clay afraid of him, aware that he sees through her, and not daring to proceed as she might do in his absence. But since he must be absent some time or other, I do not perceive how he can ever be secure while she holds her present influence. Mrs. Wallis has an amusing idea, as nurse tells me, that it is to be put into the marriage articles when you and Mr. Elliot marry, that your father is not to marry Mrs. Clay. A scheme, worthy of Mrs. Wallis's understanding, by all accounts; but my sensible nurse Rooke sees the absurdity of it. 'Why, to be sure, ma'am,' said she, 'it would not prevent his marrying anybody else.' And, indeed, to own the truth, I do not think nurse, in her heart, is a very strenuous opposer of Sir Walter's making a second match. She must be allowed to be a favourer of matrimony, you know; and (since self will intrude) who can say that she may not have some flying visions of attending the next Lady Elliot, through Mrs. Wallis's recommendation?"

"I am very glad to know all this," said Anne, after a little thoughtfulness. "It will be more painful to me in some respects to be in company with him, but I shall know better what to do. My line of conduct will be more direct. Mr. Elliot is evidently a disingenuous, artificial, worldly man, who has never had any better principle to guide him than selfishness."

But Mr. Elliot was not done with. Mrs. Smith had been carried away from her first direction, and Anne had forgotten, in the interest of her own family concerns, how much had been originally implied against him; but her attention was now called to the explanation of those first hints, and she listened to a recital which, if it did not perfectly justify the unqualified bitterness of Mrs. Smith, proved him to have been very unfeeling in his conduct towards her, very deficient both in justice and compassion.

She learned that (the intimacy between them continuing unimpaired by Mr. Elliot's marriage) they had been as before always together, and Mr. Elliot had led his friend into expenses much beyond his fortune. Mrs. Smith did not want to take blame to herself, and was most tender of throwing any on her husband; but Anne could collect that their income had never been equal to their style of living, and that from the first, there had been a great deal of general and joint extravagance. From his wife's account of him she could discern Mr. Smith to have been a man of warm feelings, easy temper, careless habits, and not strong understanding, much more amiable than his friend, and very unlike him, led by him, and probably despised by him. Mr. Elliot, raised by his marriage to great affluence, and disposed to every gratification of pleasure and vanity which could be commanded without involving himself, (for with all his self-indulgence he had become a prudent man), and beginning to be rich, just as his friend ought to have found himself to be poor, seemed to have had no concern at all for that friend's probable finances, but, on the contrary, had been prompting and encouraging expenses which could end only in ruin; and the Smiths accordingly had been ruined.

The husband had died just in time to be spared the full knowledge of it. They had previously known embarrassments enough to try the friendship of their friends, and to prove that Mr. Elliot's had better not be tried; but it was not till his death that the wretched state of his affairs was fully known. With a confidence in Mr. Elliot's regard, more creditable to his feelings than his judgement, Mr. Smith had appointed him the executor of his will; but Mr. Elliot would not act, and the difficulties and distress which this refusal had heaped on her, in addition to the inevitable sufferings of her situation, had been such as could not be related without anguish of spirit, or listened to without corresponding indignation.

Anne was shown some letters of his on the occasion, answers to urgent applications from Mrs. Smith, which all breathed the same stern resolution of not engaging in a fruitless trouble, and, under a cold civility, the same hard-hearted indifference to any of the evils it might bring on her. It was a dreadful picture of ingratitude and inhumanity; and Anne felt, at some moments, that no flagrant open crime could have been worse. She had a great deal to listen to; all the particulars of past sad scenes, all the minutiae of distress upon distress, which in former conversations had been merely hinted at, were dwelt on now with a natural indulgence. Anne could perfectly comprehend the exquisite relief, and was only the more inclined to wonder at the composure of her friend's usual state of mind.

There was one circumstance in the history of her grievances of particular irritation. She had good reason to believe that some property of her husband in the West Indies, which had been for many years under a sort of sequestration for the payment of its own incumbrances, might be recoverable by proper measures; and this property, though not large, would be enough to make her comparatively rich. But there was nobody to stir in it. Mr. Elliot would do nothing, and she could do nothing herself, equally disabled from personal exertion by her state of bodily weakness, and from employing others by her want of money. She had no natural connexions to assist her even with their counsel, and she could not afford to purchase the assistance of the law. This was a cruel aggravation of actually straitened means. To feel that she ought to be in better circumstances, that a little trouble in the right place might do it, and to fear that delay might be even weakening her claims, was hard to bear.

It was on this point that she had hoped to engage Anne's good offices with Mr. Elliot. She had previously, in the anticipation of their marriage, been very apprehensive of losing her friend by it; but on being assured that he could have made no attempt of that nature, since he did not even know her to be in Bath, it immediately occurred, that something might be done in her favour by the influence of the woman he loved, and she had been hastily preparing to interest Anne's feelings, as far as the observances due to Mr. Elliot's character would allow, when Anne's refutation of the supposed engagement changed the face of everything; and while it took from her the new-formed hope of succeeding in the object of her first anxiety, left her at least the comfort of telling the whole story her own way.

After listening to this full description of Mr. Elliot, Anne could not but express some surprise at Mrs. Smith's having spoken of him so favourably in the beginning of their conversation. "She had seemed to recommend and praise him!"

"My dear," was Mrs. Smith's reply, "there was nothing else to be done. I considered your marrying him as certain, though he might not yet have made the offer, and I could no more speak the truth of him, than if he had been your husband. My heart bled for you, as I talked of happiness; and yet he is sensible, he is agreeable, and with such a woman as you, it was not absolutely hopeless. He was very unkind to his first wife. They were wretched together. But she was too ignorant and giddy for respect, and he had never loved her. I was willing to hope that you must fare better."

Anne could just acknowledge within herself such a possibility of having been induced to marry him, as made her shudder at the idea of the misery which must have followed. It was just possible that she might have been persuaded by Lady Russell! And under such a supposition, which would have been most miserable, when time had disclosed all, too late?

It was very desirable that Lady Russell should be no longer deceived; and one of the concluding arrangements of this important conference, which carried them through the greater part of the morning, was that Anne had full liberty to communicate to her friend everything relative to Mrs. Smith, in which his conduct was involved.

CHAPTER 22

Anne went home to think over all that she had heard. In one point, her feelings were relieved by this knowledge of Mr. Elliot. There was no longer anything of tenderness due to him. He stood as opposed to Captain Wentworth, in all his own unwelcome obtrusiveness; and the evil of his attentions last night, the irremediable mischief he might have done, was considered with sensations unqualified, unperplexed. Pity for him was all over. But this was the only point of relief. In every other respect, in looking around her, or penetrating forward, she saw more to distrust and to apprehend. She was concerned for the disappointment and pain Lady Russell would be feeling, for the mortifications which must be hanging over her father and sister, and had all the distress of foreseeing many evils, without knowing how to avert any one of them. She was most thankful for her own knowledge of him. She had never considered herself as entitled to reward for not slighting an old friend like Mrs. Smith, but here was a reward indeed springing from it! Mrs. Smith had been able to tell her what no one else could have done. Could the knowledge have been extended through her family? But this was a vain idea. She must talk to Lady Russell, tell her, consult with her, and having done her best, wait the event with as much composure as possible; and after all, her greatest want of composure would be in that quarter of the mind which could not be opened to Lady Russell, in that flow of anxieties and fears which must be all to herself.

She found, on reaching home, that she had, as she intended, escaped seeing Mr. Elliot; that he had called and paid them a long morning visit; but hardly had she congratulated herself, and felt safe, when she heard that he was coming again in the evening.

"I had not the smallest intention of asking him," said Elizabeth, with affected carelessness, "but he gave so many hints; so Mrs. Clay says, at least."

"Indeed, I do say it. I never saw anybody in my life spell harder for an invitation. Poor man! I was really in pain for him; for your hard-hearted sister, Miss Anne, seems bent on cruelty."

"Oh!" cried Elizabeth, "I have been rather too much used to the game to be soon overcome by a gentleman's hints. However, when I found how excessively he was regretting that he should miss my father this morning, I gave way immediately, for I would never really omit an opportunity of bringing him and Sir Walter together. They appear to so much advantage in company with each other. Each behaving so pleasantly. Mr. Elliot looking up with so much respect."

"Quite delightful!" cried Mrs. Clay, not daring, however, to turn her eyes towards Anne. "Exactly like father and son! Dear Miss Elliot, may I not say father and son?"

"Oh! I lay no embargo on anybody's words. If you will have such ideas! But, upon my word, I am scarcely sensible of his attentions being beyond those of other men."

"My dear Miss Elliot!" exclaimed Mrs. Clay, lifting her hands and eyes, and sinking all the rest of her astonishment in a convenient silence.

"Well, my dear Penelope, you need not be so alarmed about him. I did invite him, you know. I sent him away with smiles. When I found he was really going to his friends at Thornberry Park for the whole day tomorrow, I had compassion on him."

Anne admired the good acting of the friend, in being able to show such pleasure as she did, in the expectation and in the actual arrival of the very person whose presence must really be interfering with her prime object. It was impossible but that Mrs. Clay must hate the sight of Mr. Elliot; and yet she could assume a most obliging, placid look, and appear quite satisfied with the curtailed license of devoting herself only half as much to Sir Walter as she would have done otherwise.

To Anne herself it was most distressing to see Mr. Elliot enter the room; and quite painful to have him approach and speak to her. She had been used before to feel that he could not be always quite sincere, but now she saw insincerity in everything. His attentive deference to her father, contrasted with his former language, was odious; and when she thought of his cruel conduct towards Mrs. Smith, she could hardly bear the sight of his present smiles and mildness, or the sound of his artificial good sentiments.

She meant to avoid any such alteration of manners as might provoke a remonstrance on his side. It was a great object to her to escape all enquiry or éclat; but it was her intention to be as decidedly cool to him as might be compatible with their relationship; and to retrace, as quietly as she could, the few steps of unnecessary intimacy she had been gradually led along. She was accordingly more guarded, and more cool, than she had been the night before.

He wanted to animate her curiosity again as to how and where he could have heard her formerly praised; wanted very much to be gratified by more solicitation; but the charm was broken: he found that the heat and animation of a public room was necessary to kindle his modest cousin's vanity; he found, at least, that it was not to be done now, by any of those attempts which he could hazard among the too-commanding claims of the others. He little surmised that it was a subject acting now exactly against his interest, bringing immediately into her thoughts all those parts of his conduct which were least excusable.

She had some satisfaction in finding that he was really going out of Bath the next morning, going early, and that he would be gone the greater part of two days. He was invited again to Camden Place the very evening of his return; but from Thursday to Saturday evening his absence was certain. It was bad enough that a Mrs. Clay should be always before her; but that a deeper hypocrite should be added to their party, seemed the destruction of everything like peace and comfort. It was so humiliating to reflect on the constant deception practised on her father and Elizabeth; to consider the various sources of mortification preparing for them! Mrs. Clay's selfishness was not so complicate nor so revolting as his; and Anne would have compounded for the marriage at once, with all its evils, to be clear of Mr. Elliot's subtleties in endeavouring to prevent it.

On Friday morning she meant to go very early to Lady Russell, and accomplish the necessary communication; and she would have gone directly after breakfast, but that Mrs. Clay was also going out on some obliging purpose of saving her sister trouble, which determined her to wait till she might be safe from such a companion. She saw Mrs. Clay fairly off, therefore, before she began to talk of spending the morning in Rivers Street.

"Very well," said Elizabeth, "I have nothing to send but my love. Oh! You may as well take back that tiresome book she would lend me, and pretend I have read it through. I really cannot be plaguing myself forever with all the new poems and states of the nation that come out. Lady Russell quite bores one with her new publications. You need not tell her so, but I thought her dress hideous the other night. I used to think she had some taste in dress, but I was ashamed of her at the concert. Something so formal and *arrangé* in her air! And she sits so upright! My best love, of course."

"And mine," added Sir Walter. "Kindest regards. And you may say, that I mean to call upon her soon. Make a civil message; but I shall only leave my card. Morning visits are never fair by women at her time of life, who make themselves up so little. If she would only wear rouge she would not be afraid of being seen; but last time I called, I observed the blinds were let down immediately."

While her father spoke, there was a knock at the door. Who could it be? Anne, remembering the preconcerted visits, at all hours, of Mr. Elliot, would have expected him, but for his known engagement seven miles off. After the usual period of suspense, the usual sounds of approach were heard, and "Mr. and Mrs. Charles Musgrove" were ushered into the room.

Surprise was the strongest emotion raised by their appearance; but Anne was really glad to see them; and the others were not so sorry but that they could put on a decent air of welcome; and as soon as it became clear that these, their nearest relations, were not arrived with any views of accommodation in that house, Sir Walter and Elizabeth were able to rise in cordiality, and do the honours of it very well. They were come to Bath for a few days with Mrs. Musgrove, and were at the White Hart. So much was pretty soon understood; but till Sir Walter and Elizabeth were walking Mary into the other drawing room, and regaling themselves with her admiration, Anne could not draw upon Charles's brain for a regular history of their coming, or an explanation of some smiling hints of particular business, which had been ostentatiously dropped by Mary, as well as of some apparent confusion as to whom their party consisted of.

She then found that it consisted of Mrs. Musgrove, Henrietta, and Captain Harville, beside their two selves. He gave her a very plain, intelligible account of the whole; a narration in which she saw a great deal of most characteristic proceeding. The scheme had received its first impulse by Captain Harville's wanting to come to Bath on business. He had begun to talk of it a week ago; and by way of doing something, as shooting was over, Charles had proposed coming with him, and Mrs. Harville had seemed to like the idea of it very much, as an advantage to her husband; but Mary could not bear to be left, and had made herself so unhappy about it, that for a day or two everything seemed to be in suspense, or at an end. But then, it had been taken up by his father and mother. His mother had some old friends in Bath whom she wanted to see; it was thought a good opportunity for Henrietta to come and buy wedding clothes for herself and her sister; and, in short, it ended in being his mother's party, that everything might be comfortable and easy to Captain Harville; and he and Mary were included in it by way of general convenience.

They had arrived late the night before. Mrs. Harville, her children, and Captain Benwick, remained with Mr. Musgrove and Louisa at Uppercross.

Anne's only surprise was, that affairs should be in forwardness enough for Henrietta's wedding clothes to be talked of. She had imagined such difficulties of fortune to exist there as must prevent the marriage from being near at hand; but she learned from Charles that, very recently, (since Mary's last letter to herself), Charles Hayter had been applied to by a friend to hold a living for a youth who could not possibly claim it under many years; and that on the strength of his present income, with almost a certainty of something more permanent long before the term in question, the two families had consented to the young people's wishes, and that their marriage was likely to take place in a few months, quite as soon as Louisa's. "And a very good living it was," Charles added: "only five-and-twenty miles from Uppercross, and in a very fine country, fine part of Dorsetshire. In the centre of some of the best preserves in the kingdom, surrounded by three great proprietors, each more careful and jealous than the other, and to two of the three at least, Charles Hayter might get a special recommendation. Not that he will value it as he ought," he observed, "Charles is too cool about sporting. That's the worst of him."

"I am extremely glad, indeed," cried Anne, "particularly glad that this should happen; and that of two sisters, who both deserve equally well, and who have always been such good friends, the pleasant prospect of one should not be dimming those of the other—that they should be so equal in their prosperity and comfort. I hope your father and mother are quite happy with regard to both."

"Oh! Yes. My father would be well pleased if the gentlemen were richer, but he has no other fault to find. Money, you know, coming down with money—two daughters at once—it cannot be a very agreeable operation, and it straitens him as to many things. However, I do not mean to say they have not a right to it. It is very fit they should have daughters' shares; and I am sure he has always been a very kind, liberal father to me. Mary does not above half like Henrietta's match. She never did, you know. But she does not do him justice, nor think enough about Winthrop. I cannot make her attend to the value of the property. It is a very fair match, as times go; and I have liked Charles Hayter all my life, and I shall not leave off now."

"Such excellent parents as Mr. and Mrs. Musgrove," exclaimed Anne, "should be happy in their children's marriages. They do everything to confer happiness, I am sure. What a blessing to young people to be in such hands! Your father and mother seem so totally free from all those ambitious feelings which have led to so much misconduct and misery, both in young and old. I hope you think Louisa perfectly recovered now?"

He answered rather hesitatingly, "Yes, I believe I do; very much recovered; but she is altered; there is no running or jumping about, no laughing or dancing; it is quite different. If one happens only to shut the door a little hard, she starts and wriggles like a young dabchick in the water; and Benwick sits at her elbow, reading verses, or whispering to her, all day long."

Anne could not help laughing. "That cannot be much to your taste, I know," said she; "but I do believe him to be an excellent young man."

"To be sure he is. Nobody doubts it; and I hope you do not think I am so illiberal as to want every man to have the same objects and pleasures as myself. I have a great value for Benwick; and when one can but get him to talk, he has plenty to say. His reading has done him no harm, for he has fought as well as read. He is a brave fellow. I got more acquainted with him last Monday than ever I did before. We had a famous set-to at rat-hunting all the morning in my father's great barns; and he played his part so well that I have liked him the better ever since."

Here they were interrupted by the absolute necessity of Charles's following the others to admire mirrors and china; but Anne had heard enough to understand the present state of Uppercross, and rejoice in its happiness; and though she sighed as she rejoiced, her sigh had none of the ill will of envy in it. She would certainly have risen to their blessings if she could, but she did not want to lessen theirs.

The visit passed off altogether in high good humour. Mary was in excellent spirits, enjoying the gaiety and the change, and so well satisfied with the journey in her mother-in-law's carriage with four horses, and with her own complete independence of Camden Place, that she was exactly in a temper to admire everything as she ought, and enter most readily into all the superiorities of the house, as they were detailed to her. She had no demands on her father or sister, and her consequence was just enough increased by their handsome drawing rooms.

Elizabeth was, for a short time, suffering a good deal. She felt that Mrs. Musgrove and all her party ought to be asked to dine with them; but she could not bear to have the difference of style, the reduction of servants, which a dinner must betray, witnessed by those who had been always so inferior to the Elliots of Kellynch. It was a struggle between propriety and vanity; but vanity got the better, and then Elizabeth was happy again. These were her internal persuasions: "Old fashioned notions; country hospitality; we do not profess to give dinners; few people in Bath do; Lady Alicia never does; did not even ask her own sister's family, though they were here a month: and I dare say it would be very inconvenient to Mrs. Musgrove; put her quite out of her way. I am sure she would rather not come; she cannot feel easy with us. I will ask them all for an evening; that will be much better; that will be a novelty and a treat. They have not seen two such drawing rooms before. They will be delighted to come tomorrow evening. It shall be a regular party, small, but most elegant." And this satisfied Elizabeth: and when the invitation was given to the two present, and promised for the absent, Mary was as completely satisfied. She was particularly asked to meet Mr. Elliot, and be introduced to Lady Dalrymple and Miss Carteret, who were fortunately already engaged to come; and she could not have received a more gratifying attention. Miss Elliot was to have the honour of calling on Mrs. Musgrove in the course of the morning; and Anne walked off with Charles and Mary, to go and see her and Henrietta directly.

Her plan of sitting with Lady Russell must give way for the present. They all three called in Rivers Street for a couple of minutes; but Anne convinced herself that a day's delay of the intended communication could be of no consequence, and hastened forward to the White Hart, to see again the friends and companions of the last autumn, with an eagerness of goodwill which many associations contributed to form.

They found Mrs. Musgrove and her daughter within, and by

themselves, and Anne had the kindest welcome from each. Henrietta was exactly in that state of recently-improved views, of fresh-formed happiness, which made her full of regard and interest for everybody she had ever liked before at all; and Mrs. Musgrove's real affection had been won by her usefulness when they were in distress. It was a heartiness, and a warmth, and a sincerity that Anne delighted in the more, from the sad want of such blessings at home. She was entreated to give them as much of her time as possible, invited for every day and all day long, or rather claimed as part of the family; and, in return, she naturally fell into all her wonted ways of attention and assistance, and on Charles's leaving them together, was listening to Mrs. Musgrove's history of Louisa, and to Henrietta's of herself, giving opinions on business, and recommendations to shops; with intervals of every help which Mary required, from altering her ribbon to settling her accounts, from finding her keys, and assorting her trinkets, to trying to convince her that she was not ill-used by anybody; which Mary, well amused as she generally was, in her station at a window overlooking the entrance to the Pump Room, could not but have her moments of imagining.

A morning of thorough confusion was to be expected. A large party in a hotel ensured a quick-changing, unsettled scene. One five minutes brought a note, the next a parcel; and Anne had not been there half an hour, when their dining room, spacious as it was, seemed more than half filled: a party of steady old friends were seated around Mrs. Musgrove, and Charles came back with Captains Harville and Wentworth. The appearance of the latter could not be more than the surprise of the moment. It was impossible for her to have forgotten to feel that this arrival of their common friends must be soon bringing them together again. Their last meeting had been most important in opening his feelings; she had derived from it a delightful conviction; but she feared from his looks, that the same unfortunate persuasion, which had hastened him away from the Concert Room, still governed. He did not seem to want to be near enough for conversation.

She tried to be calm, and leave things to take their course, and tried to dwell much on this argument of rational dependence: "Surely, if there be constant attachment on each side, our hearts must understand each other ere long. We are not boy and girl, to be captiously irritable, misled by every moment's inadvertence, and wantonly playing with our own happiness." And yet, a few minutes afterwards, she felt as if their being in company with each other, under their present circumstances, could only be exposing them to inadvertencies and misconstructions of the most mischievous kind.

"Anne," cried Mary, still at her window, "there is Mrs. Clay, I am sure, standing under the colonnade, and a gentleman with her. I saw them turn the corner from Bath Street just now. They seemed deep in talk. Who is it? Come, and tell me. Good heavens! I recollect. It is Mr. Elliot himself."

"No," cried Anne, quickly, "it cannot be Mr. Elliot, I assure you. He was to leave Bath at nine this morning, and does not come back till tomorrow."

As she spoke, she felt that Captain Wentworth was looking at her, the consciousness of which vexed and embarrassed her, and made her regret that she had said so much, simple as it was.

Mary, resenting that she should be supposed not to know her own cousin, began talking very warmly about the family features, and protesting still more positively that it was Mr. Elliot, calling again upon Anne to come and look for herself, but Anne did not mean to stir, and tried to be cool and unconcerned.

Her distress returned, however, on perceiving smiles and intelligent glances pass between two or three of the lady visitors, as if they believed themselves quite in the secret. It was evident that the report concerning her had spread, and a short pause succeeded, which seemed to ensure that it would now spread farther.

"Do come, Anne," cried Mary, "come and look yourself. You will be too late if you do not make haste. They are parting; they are shaking hands. He is turning away. Not know Mr. Elliot, indeed! You seem to have forgot all about Lyme."

To pacify Mary, and perhaps screen her own embarrassment, Anne did move quietly to the window. She was just in time to ascertain that it really was Mr. Elliot, which she had never believed, before he disappeared on one side, as Mrs. Clay walked quickly off on the other; and checking the surprise which she could not but feel at such an appearance of friendly conference between two persons of totally opposite interest, she calmly said, "Yes, it is Mr. Elliot, certainly. He has changed his hour of going, I suppose, that is all; or I may be mistaken; I might not attend;" and walked back to her chair, recomposed, and with the comfortable hope of having acquitted herself well.

The visitors took their leave; and Charles, having civilly seen them off, and then made a face at them, and abused them for coming, began with, "Well, mother, I have done something for you that you will like. I have been to the theatre, and secured a box for tomorrow night. A'n't I a good boy? I know you love a play; and there is room for us all. It holds nine. I have engaged Captain Wentworth. Anne will not be sorry to join us, I am sure. We all like a play. Have not I done well, mother?"

Mrs. Musgrove was good-humouredly beginning to express her perfect readiness for the play, if Henrietta and all the others liked it, when Mary eagerly interrupted her by exclaiming—

"Good heavens, Charles! How can you think of such a thing? Take a box for tomorrow night! Have you forgot that we are engaged to Camden Place tomorrow night? And that we were most particularly asked to meet Lady Dalrymple and her daughter, and Mr. Elliot, and all the principal family connexions, on purpose to be introduced to them? How can you be so forgetful?"

"Phoo! Phoo!" replied Charles, "What's an evening party? Never worth remembering. Your father might have asked us to dinner, I think, if he had wanted to see us. You may do as you like, but I shall go to the play."

"Oh! Charles, I declare it will be too abominable if you do, when you promised to go."

"No, I did not promise. I only smirked and bowed, and said the word 'happy.' There was no promise."

"But you must go, Charles. It would be unpardonable to fail. We were asked on purpose to be introduced. There was always such a great connexion between the Dalrymples and ourselves. Nothing ever happened on either side that was not announced immediately. We are quite near relations, you know; and Mr. Elliot too, whom you ought so particularly to be acquainted with! Every attention is due to Mr. Elliot. Consider, my father's heir: the future representative of the family."

"Don't talk to me about heirs and representatives," cried Charles. "I am not one of those who neglect the reigning power to bow to the rising sun. If I would not go for the sake of your father, I should think it scandalous to go for the sake of his heir. What is Mr. Elliot to me?"

The careless expression was life to Anne, who saw that Captain Wentworth was all attention, looking and listening with his whole soul;

and that the last words brought his enquiring eyes from Charles to herself.

Charles and Mary still talked on in the same style; he, half serious and half jesting, maintaining the scheme for the play, and she, invariably serious, most warmly opposing it, and not omitting to make it known that, however determined to go to Camden Place herself, she should not think herself very well used, if they went to the play without her. Mrs. Musgrove interposed.

"We had better put it off. Charles, you had much better go back and change the box for Tuesday. It would be a pity to be divided, and we should be losing Miss Anne, too, if there is a party at her father's; and I am sure neither Henrietta nor I should care at all for the play, if Miss Anne could not be with us."

Anne felt truly obliged to her for such kindness; and quite as much so for the opportunity it gave her of decidedly saying, "If it depended only on my inclination, ma'am, the party at home (excepting on Mary's account) would not be the smallest impediment. I have no pleasure in the sort of meeting, and should be too happy to change it for a play, and with you. But, it had better not be attempted, perhaps." She had spoken it; but she trembled when it was done, conscious that her words were listened to, and daring not even to try to observe their effect.

It was soon generally agreed that Tuesday should be the day; Charles only reserving the advantage of still teasing his wife, by persisting that he would go to the play tomorrow if nobody else would.

Captain Wentworth left his seat, and walked to the fireplace; probably for the sake of walking away from it soon afterwards, and taking a station, with less barefaced design, by Anne.

"You have not been long enough in Bath," said he, "to enjoy the evening parties of the place."

"Oh! No. The usual character of them has nothing for me. I am no cardplayer."

"You were not formerly, I know. You did not use to like cards; but time makes many changes."

"I am not yet so much changed," cried Anne, and stopped, fearing she hardly knew what misconstruction. After waiting a few moments he said, and as if it were the result of immediate feeling, "It is a period, indeed! Eight years and a half is a period."

Whether he would have proceeded farther was left to Anne's

imagination to ponder over in a calmer hour; for while still hearing the sounds he had uttered, she was startled to other subjects by Henrietta, eager to make use of the present leisure for getting out, and calling on her companions to lose no time, lest somebody else should come in.

They were obliged to move. Anne talked of being perfectly ready, and tried to look it; but she felt that could Henrietta have known the regret and reluctance of her heart in quitting that chair, in preparing to quit the room, she would have found, in all her own sensations for her cousin, in the very security of his affection, wherewith to pity her.

Their preparations, however, were stopped short. Alarming sounds were heard; other visitors approached, and the door was thrown open for Sir Walter and Miss Elliot, whose entrance seemed to give a general chill. Anne felt an instant oppression, and wherever she looked saw symptoms of the same. The comfort, the freedom, the gaiety of the room was over, hushed into cold composure, determined silence, or insipid talk, to meet the heartless elegance of her father and sister. How mortifying to feel that it was so! Her jealous eye was satisfied in one particular. Captain Wentworth was acknowledged again by each, by Elizabeth more graciously than before. She even addressed him once, and looked at him more than once. Elizabeth was, in fact, revolving a great measure. The sequel explained it. After the waste of a few minutes in saying the proper nothings, she began to give the invitation that was to comprise all the remaining dues of the Musgroves. "Tomorrow evening, to meet a few friends: no formal party." It was all said very gracefully, and the cards with which she had provided herself, the "Miss Elliot at home," were laid on the table, with a courteous, comprehensive smile to all, and one smile and one card more decidedly for Captain Wentworth. The truth was, that Elizabeth had been long enough in Bath to understand the importance of a man of such an air and appearance as his. The past was nothing. The present was that Captain Wentworth would move about well in her drawing room. The card was pointedly given, and Sir Walter and Elizabeth arose and disappeared.

The interruption had been short, though severe, and ease and animation returned to most of those they left as the door shut them out, but not to Anne. She could think only of the invitation she had with such astonishment witnessed, and of the manner in which it had been received; a manner of doubtful meaning, of surprise rather than gratification, of polite acknowledgement rather than acceptance. She knew him; she saw disdain in his eye, and could not venture to believe that he had determined to accept such an offering, as an atonement for all the insolence of the past. Her spirits sank. He held the card in his hand after they were gone, as if deeply considering it.

"Only think of Elizabeth's including everybody!" whispered Mary very audibly. "I do not wonder Captain Wentworth is delighted! You see he cannot put the card out of his hand."

Anne caught his eye, saw his cheeks glow, and his mouth form itself into a momentary expression of contempt, and turned away, that she might neither see nor hear more to vex her.

The party separated. The gentlemen had their own pursuits, the ladies proceeded on their own business, and they met no more while Anne belonged to them. She was earnestly begged to return and dine, and give them all the rest of the day, but her spirits had been so long exerted that at present she felt unequal to more, and fit only for home, where she might be sure of being as silent as she chose.

Promising to be with them the whole of the following morning, therefore, she closed the fatigues of the present by a toilsome walk to Camden Place, there to spend the evening chiefly in listening to the busy arrangements of Elizabeth and Mrs. Clay for the morrow's party, the frequent enumeration of the persons invited, and the continually improving detail of all the embellishments which were to make it the most completely elegant of its kind in Bath, while harassing herself with the never-ending question, of whether Captain Wentworth would come or not? They were reckoning him as certain, but with her it was a gnawing solicitude never appeased for five minutes together. She generally thought he would come, because she generally thought he ought; but it was a case which she could not so shape into any positive act of duty or discretion, as inevitably to defy the suggestions of very opposite feelings.

She only roused herself from the broodings of this restless agitation, to let Mrs. Clay know that she had been seen with Mr. Elliot three hours after his being supposed to be out of Bath; for having watched in vain for some intimation of the interview from the lady herself, she determined to mention it, and it seemed to her there was guilt in Mrs. Clay's face as she listened. It was transient: cleared away in an instant; but Anne could imagine she read there the consciousness of having, by some complication of mutual trick, or some overbearing authority of his, been obliged to attend (perhaps for half an hour) to his lectures and restrictions on her designs on Sir Walter. She exclaimed, however, with a very tolerable imitation of nature:

"Oh dear! Very true. Only think, Miss Elliot, to my great surprise I met with Mr. Elliot in Bath Street. I was never more astonished. He turned back and walked with me to the Pump Yard. He had been prevented setting off for Thornberry, but I really forget by what; for I was in a hurry, and could not much attend, and I can only answer for his being determined not to be delayed in his return. He wanted to know how early he might be admitted tomorrow. He was full of 'tomorrow,' and it is very evident that I have been full of it too, ever since I entered the house, and learnt the extension of your plan and all that had happened, or my seeing him could never have gone so entirely out of my head."

CHAPTER 23

One day only had passed since Anne's conversation with Mrs. Smith; but a keener interest had succeeded, and she was now so little touched by Mr. Elliot's conduct, except by its effects in one quarter, that it became a matter of course the next morning, still to defer her explanatory visit in Rivers Street. She had promised to be with the Musgroves from breakfast to dinner. Her faith was plighted, and Mr. Elliot's character, like the Sultaness Scheherazade's head, must live another day.

She could not keep her appointment punctually, however; the weather was unfavourable, and she had grieved over the rain on her friends' account, and felt it very much on her own, before she was able to attempt the walk. When she reached the White Hart, and made her way to the proper apartment, she found herself neither arriving quite in time, nor the first to arrive. The party before her were Mrs. Musgrove, talking to Mrs. Croft, and Captain Harville to Captain Wentworth; and she immediately heard that Mary and Henrietta, too impatient to wait, had gone out the moment it had cleared, but would be back again soon, and that the strictest injunctions had been left with Mrs. Musgrove to keep her there till they returned. She had only to submit, sit down, be outwardly composed, and feel herself plunged at once in all the agitations which she had merely laid her account of tasting a little before the morning closed.

There was no delay, no waste of time. She was deep in the happiness of such misery, or the misery of such happiness, instantly. Two minutes after her entering the room, Captain Wentworth said, "We will write the letter we were talking of, Harville, now, if you will give me materials."

Materials were at hand, on a separate table; he went to it, and nearly turning his back to them all, was engrossed by writing.

Mrs. Musgrove was giving Mrs. Croft the history of her eldest daughter's engagement, and just in that inconvenient tone of voice, which was perfectly audible while it pretended to be a whisper. Anne felt that she did not belong to the conversation, and yet, as Captain Harville seemed thoughtful and not disposed to talk, she could not avoid hearing many undesirable particulars; such as "how Mr. Musgrove and my brother Hayter had met again and again to talk it over; what my brother Hayter had said one day, and what Mr. Musgrove had proposed the next, and what had occurred to my sister Hayter, and what the young people had wished, and what I said at first I never could consent to, but was afterwards persuaded to think might do very well," and a great deal in the same style of openhearted communication: minutiae which, even with every advantage of taste and delicacy, which good Mrs. Musgrove could not give, could be properly interesting only to the principals. Mrs. Croft was attending with great good humour, and whenever she spoke at all, it was very sensibly. Anne hoped the gentlemen might each be too much self-occupied to hear.

"And so, ma'am, all these thing considered," said Mrs. Musgrove, in her powerful whisper, "though we could have wished it different, yet altogether, we did not think it fair to stand out any longer, for Charles Hayter was quite wild about it, and Henrietta was pretty near as bad; and so we thought they had better marry at once, and make the best of it, as many others have done before them. At any rate, said I, it will be better than a long engagement."

"That is precisely what I was going to observe," cried Mrs. Croft. "I would rather have young people settle on a small income at once, and have to struggle with a few difficulties together, than be involved in a long engagement. I always think that no mutual—"

"Oh! Dear Mrs. Croft," cried Mrs. Musgrove, unable to let her finish her speech, "there is nothing I so abominate for young people as a long engagement. It is what I always protested against for my children. It is all very well, I used to say, for young people to be engaged, if there is a certainty of their being able to marry in six months, or even in twelve; but a long engagement—"

"Yes, dear ma'am," said Mrs. Croft, "or an uncertain engagement, an engagement which may be long. To begin without knowing that at such a time there will be the means of marrying, I hold to be very unsafe and unwise, and what I think all parents should prevent as far as they can."

Anne found an unexpected interest here. She felt its application to herself, felt it in a nervous thrill all over her; and at the same moment that her eyes instinctively glanced towards the distant table, Captain Wentworth's pen ceased to move, his head was raised, pausing, listening, and he turned round the next instant to give a look, one quick, conscious look at her.

The two ladies continued to talk, to re-urge the same admitted truths, and enforce them with such examples of the ill effect of a contrary practice as had fallen within their observation, but Anne heard nothing distinctly; it was only a buzz of words in her ear, her mind was in confusion.

Captain Harville, who had in truth been hearing none of it, now left his seat, and moved to a window; and Anne seeming to watch him, though it was from thorough absence of mind, became gradually sensible that he was inviting her to join him where he stood. He looked at her with a smile, and a little motion of the head, which expressed, "Come to me, I have something to say;" and the unaffected, easy kindness of manner which denoted the feelings of an older acquaintance than he really was, strongly enforced the invitation. She roused herself and went to him. The window at which he stood was at the other end of the room from where the two ladies were sitting, and though nearer to Captain Wentworth's table, not very near. As she joined him, Captain Harville's countenance reassumed the serious, thoughtful expression, which seemed its natural character.

"Look here," said he, unfolding a parcel in his hand, and displaying a small miniature painting, "do you know who that is?"

"Certainly: Captain Benwick."

"Yes, and you may guess who it is for. But," (in a deep tone,) "it was not done for her. Miss Elliot, do you remember our walking together at Lyme, and grieving for him? I little thought then—but no matter. This was drawn at the Cape. He met with a clever young German artist at the Cape, and in compliance with a promise to my poor sister, sat to him, and was bringing it home for her; and I have now the charge of getting it properly set for another! It was a commission to me! But who else was there to employ? I hope I can allow for him. I am not sorry, indeed, to make it over to another. He undertakes it;" (looking towards Captain Wentworth,) "he is writing about it now." And with a quivering lip he wound up the whole by adding, "Poor Fanny! She would not have forgotten him so soon!"

"No," replied Anne, in a low, feeling voice. "That I can easily believe."

"It was not in her nature. She doted on him."

"It would not be the nature of any woman who truly loved."

Captain Harville smiled, as much as to say, "Do you claim that for your sex?" and she answered the question, smiling also, "Yes. We certainly do not forget you as soon as you forget us. It is, perhaps, our fate rather than our merit. We cannot help ourselves. We live at home, quiet, confined, and our feelings prey upon us. You are forced on exertion. You have always a profession, pursuits, business of some sort or other, to take you back into the world immediately, and continual occupation and change soon weaken impressions."

"Granting your assertion that the world does all this so soon for men (which, however, I do not think I shall grant), it does not apply to Benwick. He has not been forced upon any exertion. The peace turned him on shore at the very moment, and he has been living with us, in our little family circle, ever since."

"True," said Anne, "very true; I did not recollect; but what shall we say now, Captain Harville? If the change be not from outward circumstances, it must be from within; it must be nature, man's nature, which has done the business for Captain Benwick."

"No, no, it is not man's nature. I will not allow it to be more man's nature than woman's to be inconstant and forget those they do love, or have loved. I believe the reverse. I believe in a true analogy between our bodily frames and our mental; and that as our bodies are the strongest, so are our feelings; capable of bearing most rough usage, and riding out the heaviest weather."

"Your feelings may be the strongest," replied Anne, "but the same spirit of analogy will authorise me to assert that ours are the most tender. Man is more robust than woman, but he is not longer lived; which exactly explains my view of the nature of their attachments. Nay, it would be too hard upon you, if it were otherwise. You have difficulties, and privations, and dangers enough to struggle with. You are always labouring and toiling, exposed to every risk and hardship. Your home, country, friends, all quitted. Neither time, nor health, nor life, to be called your own. It would be too hard, indeed" (with a faltering voice), "if woman's feelings were to be added to all this."

"We shall never agree upon this question," Captain Harville was beginning to say, when a slight noise called their attention to Captain Wentworth's hitherto perfectly quiet division of the room. It was nothing more than that his pen had fallen down; but Anne was startled at finding him nearer than she had supposed, and half inclined to suspect that the pen had only fallen because he had been occupied by them, striving to catch sounds, which yet she did not think he could have caught.

"Have you finished your letter?" said Captain Harville.

"Not quite, a few lines more. I shall have done in five minutes."

"There is no hurry on my side. I am only ready whenever you are. I am in very good anchorage here," (smiling at Anne,) "well supplied, and want for nothing. No hurry for a signal at all. Well, Miss Elliot," (lowering his voice,) "as I was saying we shall never agree, I suppose, upon this point. No man and woman would, probably. But let me observe that all histories are against you—all stories, prose and verse. If I had such a memory as Benwick, I could bring you fifty quotations in a moment on my side the argument, and I do not think I ever opened a book in my life which had not something to say upon woman's inconstancy. Songs and proverbs, all talk of woman's fickleness. But perhaps you will say, these were all written by men."

"Perhaps I shall. Yes, yes, if you please, no reference to examples in books. Men have had every advantage of us in telling their own story. Education has been theirs in so much higher a degree; the pen has been in their hands. I will not allow books to prove anything."

"But how shall we prove anything?"

"We never shall. We never can expect to prove anything upon such a point. It is a difference of opinion, which does not admit of proof. We each begin, probably, with a little bias towards our own sex; and upon that bias build every circumstance in favour of it which has occurred within our own circle; many of which circumstances (perhaps those very cases which strike us the most) may be precisely such as cannot be brought forward without betraying a confidence, or in some respect saying what should not be said."

"Ah!" cried Captain Harville, in a tone of strong feeling, "if I could but make you comprehend what a man suffers when he takes a last look at his wife and children, and watches the boat that he has sent them off in, as long as it is in sight, and then turns away and says, 'God knows whether we ever meet again!' And then, if I could convey to you the glow of his soul when he does see them again; when, coming back after a twelvemonth's absence, perhaps, and obliged to put into another port, he calculates how soon it be possible to get them there, pretending to deceive himself, and saying, 'They cannot be here till such a day,' but all the while hoping for them twelve hours sooner, and seeing them arrive at last, as if Heaven had given them wings, by many hours sooner still! If I could explain to you all this, and all that a man can bear and do, and glories to do, for the sake of these treasures of his existence! I speak, you know, only of such men as have hearts!" pressing his own with emotion.

"Oh!" cried Anne eagerly. "I hope I do justice to all that is felt by you, and by those who resemble you. God forbid that I should undervalue the warm and faithful feelings of any of my fellow-creatures! I should deserve utter contempt if I dared to suppose that true attachment and constancy were known only by woman. No, I believe you capable of everything great and good in your married lives. I believe you equal to every important exertion, and to every domestic forbearance, so long as—if I may be allowed the expression—so long as you have an object. I mean while the woman you love lives, and lives for you. All the privilege I claim for my own sex (it is not a very enviable one; you need not covet it), is that of loving longest, when existence or when hope is gone."

She could not immediately have uttered another sentence; her heart was too full, her breath too much oppressed.

"You are a good soul," cried Captain Harville, putting his hand on her arm, quite affectionately. "There is no quarrelling with you. And when I think of Benwick, my tongue is tied."

Their attention was called towards the others. Mrs. Croft was taking leave.

"Here, Frederick, you and I part company, I believe," said she. "I am going home, and you have an engagement with your friend. Tonight we may have the pleasure of all meeting again at your party," (turning to Anne.) "We had your sister's card yesterday, and I understood Frederick had a card too, though I did not see it; and you are disengaged, Frederick, are you not, as well as ourselves?"

Captain Wentworth was folding up a letter in great haste, and either could not or would not answer fully.

"Yes," said he, "very true; here we separate, but Harville and I shall soon be after you; that is, Harville, if you are ready, I am in half a minute. I know you will not be sorry to be off. I shall be at your service in half a minute."

Mrs. Croft left them, and Captain Wentworth, having sealed his letter with great rapidity, was indeed ready, and had even a hurried, agitated air, which showed impatience to be gone. Anne knew not how to understand it. She had the kindest "Good morning, God bless you!" from Captain Harville, but from him not a word, nor a look! He had passed out of the room without a look!

She had only time, however, to move closer to the table where he had been writing, when footsteps were heard returning; the door opened, it was himself. He begged their pardon, but he had forgotten his gloves, and instantly crossing the room to the writing table, he drew out a letter from under the scattered paper, placed it before Anne with eyes of glowing entreaty fixed on her for a time, and hastily collecting his gloves, was again out of the room, almost before Mrs. Musgrove was aware of his being in it: the work of an instant!

The revolution, which one instant had made in Anne, was almost beyond expression. The letter, with a direction hardly legible, to "Miss A. E.," was evidently the one that he had been folding so hastily. While supposed to be writing only to Captain Benwick, he had been also addressing her! On the contents of that letter depended all which this world could do for her. Anything was possible, anything might be defied rather than suspense. Mrs. Musgrove had little arrangements of her own at her own table; to their protection she must trust, and sinking into the chair which he had occupied, succeeding to the very spot where he had leaned and written, her eyes devoured the following words:

> I can listen no longer in silence. I must speak to you by such means as are within my reach. You pierce my soul. I am half agony, half hope. Tell me not that I am too late, that such precious feelings are gone forever. I offer myself to you again with a heart even more your own than when you almost broke it, eight years and a half ago. Dare not say that man forgets sooner than woman, that his love has an earlier death. I have loved none but you. Unjust I may have been, weak and resentful I have been, but never inconstant. You alone have brought me to Bath. For you alone, I think and plan. Have you not seen this? Can you fail to have understood my wishes? I had not waited even these ten days, could I have read your feelings, as I think you must have penetrated mine. I can hardly write. I am every instant

> hearing something which overpowers me. You sink your voice, but I can distinguish the tones of that voice when they would be lost on others. Too good, too excellent creature! You do us justice, indeed. You do believe that there is true attachment and constancy among men. Believe it to be most fervent, most undeviating, in
>
> F. W.
>
> I must go, uncertain of my fate; but I shall return hither, or follow your party, as soon as possible. A word, a look, will be enough to decide whether I enter your father's house this evening or never.

Such a letter was not to be soon recovered from. Half an hour's solitude and reflection might have tranquillized her; but the ten minutes only which now passed before she was interrupted, with all the restraints of her situation, could do nothing towards tranquillity. Every moment rather brought fresh agitation. It was overpowering happiness. And before she was beyond the first stage of full sensation, Charles, Mary, and Henrietta all came in.

The absolute necessity of seeming like herself produced then an immediate struggle, but after a while she could do no more. She began not to understand a word they said, and was obliged to plead indisposition and excuse herself. They could then see that she looked very ill, were shocked and concerned, and would not stir without her for the world. This was dreadful. Would they only have gone away, and left her in the quiet possession of that room it would have been her cure; but to have them all standing or waiting around her was distracting, and in desperation, she said she would go home.

"By all means, my dear," cried Mrs. Musgrove, "go home directly, and take care of yourself, that you may be fit for the evening. I wish Sarah was here to doctor you, but I am no doctor myself. Charles, ring and order a chair. She must not walk."

But the chair would never do. Worse than all! To lose the possibility of speaking two words to Captain Wentworth in the course of her quiet, solitary progress up the town (and she felt almost certain of meeting him) could not be borne. The chair was earnestly protested against, and Mrs. Musgrove, who thought only of one sort of illness, having assured herself with some anxiety, that there had been no fall in the case; that Anne had not at any time lately slipped down, and got a blow on her head; that she was perfectly convinced of having had no fall; could part with her cheerfully, and depend on finding her better at night.

Anxious to omit no possible precaution, Anne struggled, and said, "I am afraid, ma'am, that it is not perfectly understood. Pray be so good as to mention to the other gentlemen that we hope to see your whole party this evening. I am afraid there had been some mistake; and I wish you particularly to assure Captain Harville and Captain Wentworth, that we hope to see them both."

"Oh! My dear, it is quite understood, I give you my word. Captain Harville has no thought but of going."

"Do you think so? But I am afraid; and I should be so very sorry. Will you promise me to mention it, when you see them again? You will see them both this morning, I dare say. Do promise me."

"To be sure I will, if you wish it. Charles, if you see Captain Harville anywhere, remember to give Miss Anne's message. But indeed, my dear, you need not be uneasy. Captain Harville holds himself quite engaged, I'll answer for it; and Captain Wentworth the same, I dare say."

Anne could do no more; but her heart prophesied some mischance to damp the perfection of her felicity. It could not be very lasting, however. Even if he did not come to Camden Place himself, it would be in her power to send an intelligible sentence by Captain Harville. Another momentary vexation occurred.

Charles, in his real concern and good nature, would go home with her; there was no preventing him. This was almost cruel. But she could not be long ungrateful; he was sacrificing an engagement at a gunsmith's, to be of use to her; and she set off with him, with no feeling but gratitude apparent.

They were on Union Street, when a quicker step behind, a something of familiar sound, gave her two moments' preparation for the sight of Captain Wentworth. He joined them; but, as if irresolute whether to join or to pass on, said nothing, only looked. Anne could command herself enough to receive that look, and not repulsively. The cheeks, which had been pale, now glowed, and the movements, which had hesitated, were decided. He walked by her side. Presently, struck by a sudden thought, Charles said, "Captain Wentworth, which way are you going? Only to Gay Street, or farther up the town?"

"I hardly know," replied Captain Wentworth, surprised.

"Are you going as high as Belmont? Are you going near Camden Place? Because, if you are, I shall have no scruple in asking you to take my place, and give Anne your arm to her father's door. She is rather done for this morning, and must not go so far without help, and I ought to be at that fellow's in the market place. He promised me the sight of a capital gun he is just going to send off; said he would keep it unpacked to the last possible moment, that I might see it; and if I do not turn back now, I have no chance. By his description, a good deal like the second size double-barrel of mine, which you shot with one day round Winthrop."

There could not be an objection. There could be only the most proper alacrity, a most obliging compliance for public view; and smiles reined in and spirits dancing in private rapture. In half a minute Charles was at the bottom of Union Street again, and the other two proceeding together; and soon words enough had passed between them to decide their direction towards the comparatively quiet and retired gravel walk, where the power of conversation would make the present hour a blessing indeed, and prepare it for all the immortality which the happiest recollections of their own future lives could bestow. There they exchanged again those feelings and those promises which had once before seemed to secure everything, but which had been followed by so many, many years of division and estrangement. There they returned again into the past, more exquisitely happy, perhaps, in their reunion, than when it had been first projected; more tender, more tried, more fixed in a knowledge of each other's character, truth, and attachment; more equal to act, more justified in acting.

And there, as they slowly paced the gradual ascent, heedless of every group around them, seeing neither sauntering politicians, bustling housekeepers, flirting girls, nor nurserymaids and children, they could indulge in those retrospections and acknowledgements, and especially in those explanations of what had directly preceded the present moment, which were so poignant and so ceaseless in interest. All the little variations of the last week were gone through; and of yesterday and today there could scarcely be an end.

She had not mistaken him. Jealousy of Mr. Elliot had been the retarding weight, the doubt, the torment. That had begun to operate in the very hour of first meeting her in Bath; that had returned, after a short suspension, to ruin the concert; and that had influenced him in everything he had said and done, or omitted to say and do, in the last four-and-twenty hours. It had been gradually yielding to the better hopes which her looks, or words, or actions occasionally encouraged; it had been vanquished at last by those sentiments and those tones which had reached him while she talked with Captain Harville; and under the irresistible governance of which he had seized a sheet of paper, and poured out his feelings.

Of what he had then written, nothing was to be retracted or qualified. He persisted in having loved none but her. She had never been supplanted. He never even believed himself to see her equal. Thus much indeed he was obliged to acknowledge: that he had been constant unconsciously, nay unintentionally; that he had meant to forget her, and believed it to be done. He had imagined himself indifferent, when he had only been angry; and he had been unjust to her merits, because he had been a sufferer from them. Her character was now fixed on his mind as perfection itself, maintaining the loveliest medium of fortitude and gentleness; but he was obliged to acknowledge that only at Uppercross had he learnt to do her justice, and only at Lyme had he begun to understand himself.

At Lyme, he had received lessons of more than one sort. The passing admiration of Mr. Elliot had at least roused him, and the scenes on the Cobb and at Captain Harville's had fixed her superiority.

In his preceding attempts to attach himself to Louisa Musgrove (the attempts of angry pride), he protested that he had forever felt it to be impossible; that he had not cared, could not care, for Louisa; though till that day, till the leisure for reflection which followed it, he had not understood the perfect excellence of the mind with which Louisa's could so ill bear a comparison, or the perfect unrivalled hold it possessed over his own. There, he had learnt to distinguish between the steadiness of principle and the obstinacy of self-will, between the darings of heedlessness and the resolution of a collected mind.

There he had seen everything to exalt in his estimation the woman he had lost; and there begun to deplore the pride, the folly, the madness of resentment, which had kept him from trying to regain her when thrown in his way.

From that period his penance had become severe. He had no sooner been free from the horror and remorse attending the first few days of Louisa's accident, no sooner begun to feel himself alive again, than he had begun to feel himself, though alive, not at liberty.

"I found," said he, "that I was considered by Harville an engaged man! That neither Harville nor his wife entertained a doubt of our mutual attachment. I was startled and shocked. To a degree, I could contradict this instantly; but when I began to reflect that others might have felt the same—her own family, nay, perhaps herself—I was no longer at my own disposal. I was hers in honour if she wished it. I had been unguarded. I had not thought seriously on this subject before. I had not considered that my excessive intimacy must have its danger of ill consequence in many ways; and that I had no right to be trying whether I could attach myself to either of the girls, at the risk of raising even an unpleasant report, were there no other ill effects. I had been grossly wrong, and must abide the consequences."

He found too late, in short, that he had entangled himself; and that precisely as he became fully satisfied of his not caring for Louisa at all, he must regard himself as bound to her, if her sentiments for him were what the Harvilles supposed. It determined him to leave Lyme, and await her complete recovery elsewhere. He would gladly weaken, by any fair means, whatever feelings or speculations concerning him might exist; and he went, therefore, to his brother's, meaning after a while to return to Kellynch, and act as circumstances might require.

"I was six weeks with Edward," said he, "and saw him happy. I could have no other pleasure. I deserved none. He enquired after you very particularly; asked even if you were personally altered, little suspecting that to my eye you could never alter."

Anne smiled, and let it pass. It was too pleasing a blunder for a reproach. It is something for a woman to be assured, in her eight-and-twentieth year, that she has not lost one charm of earlier youth; but the value of such homage was inexpressibly increased to Anne, by comparing it with former words, and feeling it to be the result, not the cause of a revival of his warm attachment.

He had remained in Shropshire, lamenting the blindness of his own pride, and the blunders of his own calculations, till at once released from Louisa by the astonishing and felicitous intelligence of her engagement with Benwick.

"Here," said he, "ended the worst of my state; for now I could at least put myself in the way of happiness; I could exert myself; I could do something. But to be waiting so long in inaction, and waiting only for evil, had been dreadful. Within the first five minutes I said, 'I will be at Bath on Wednesday,' and I was. Was it unpardonable to think it worth my while to come? And to arrive with some degree of hope? You were single. It was possible that you might retain the feelings of the past, as I did; and one encouragement happened to be mine. I could never doubt that you would be loved and sought by others, but I knew to a certainty that you had refused one man, at least, of better pretensions than myself; and I could not help often saying, 'Was this for me?'"

Their first meeting in Milsom Street afforded much to be said, but the concert still more. That evening seemed to be made up of exquisite moments. The moment of her stepping forward in the Octagon Room to speak to him, the moment of Mr. Elliot's appearing and tearing her away, and one or two subsequent moments, marked by returning hope or increasing despondency, were dwelt on with energy.

"To see you," cried he, "in the midst of those who could not be my well-wishers; to see your cousin close by you, conversing and smiling, and feel all the horrible eligibilities and proprieties of the match! To consider it as the certain wish of every being who could hope to influence you! Even if your own feelings were reluctant or indifferent, to consider what powerful supports would be his! Was it not enough to make the fool of me that I appeared? How could I look on without agony? Was not the very sight of the friend who sat behind you, was not the recollection of what had been, the knowledge of her influence, the indelible, immoveable impression of what persuasion had once done—was it not all against me?"

"You should have distinguished," replied Anne. "You should not have suspected me now; the case is so different, and my age is so different. If I was wrong in yielding to persuasion once, remember that it was to persuasion exerted on the side of safety, not of risk. When I yielded, I thought it was to duty, but no duty could be called in aid here. In marrying a man indifferent to me, all risk would have been incurred, and all duty violated."

"Perhaps I ought to have reasoned thus," he replied, "but I could not. I could not derive benefit from the late knowledge I had acquired of your character. I could not bring it into play; it was overwhelmed, buried, lost in those earlier feelings, which I had been smarting under year after year. I could think of you only as one who had yielded, who had given me up, who had been influenced by anyone rather than by me. I saw you with the very person who had guided you in that year of misery. I had no reason to believe her of less authority now. The force of habit was to be added."

"I should have thought," said Anne, "that my manner to yourself might have spared you much or all of this."

"No, no! Your manner might be only the ease that your engagement to another man would give. I left you in this belief; and yet, I was determined to see you again. My spirits rallied with the morning, and I felt that I had still a motive for remaining here."

At last Anne was at home again, and happier than anyone in that house could have conceived. All the surprise and suspense, and every other painful part of the morning dissipated by this conversation, she reentered the house so happy as to be obliged to find an alloy in some momentary apprehensions of its being impossible to last. An interval of meditation, serious and grateful, was the best corrective of everything dangerous in such high-wrought felicity; and she went to her room, and grew steadfast and fearless in the thankfulness of her enjoyment.

The evening came, the drawing rooms were lighted up, the company assembled. It was but a card party, it was but a mixture of those who had never met before, and those who met too often; a commonplace business, too numerous for intimacy, too small for variety; but Anne had never found an evening shorter. Glowing and lovely in sensibility and happiness, and more generally admired than she thought about or cared for, she had cheerful or forbearing feelings for every creature around her. Mr. Elliot was there; she avoided, but she could pity him. The Wallises, she had amusement in understanding them. Lady Dalrymple and Miss Carteret, they would soon be innoxious cousins to her. She cared not for Mrs. Clay, and had nothing to blush for in the public manners of her father and sister. With the Musgroves, there was the happy chat of perfect ease; with Captain Harville, the kindhearted intercourse of brother and sister; with Lady Russell, attempts at conversation, which a delicious consciousness cut short; with Admiral and Mrs. Croft, everything of peculiar cordiality and fervent interest, which the same consciousness sought to conceal; and with Captain Wentworth, some moments of communications continually occurring, and always the hope of more, and always the knowledge of his being there.

It was in one of these short meetings, each apparently occupied in admiring a fine display of greenhouse plants, that she said, "I have been thinking over the past, and trying impartially to judge of the right and wrong, I mean with regard to myself; and I must believe that I was right, much as I suffered from it, that I was perfectly right in being guided by the friend whom you will love better than you do now. To me, she was in the place of a parent. Do not mistake me, however. I am not saying that she did not err in her advice. It was, perhaps, one of those cases in which advice is good or bad only as the event decides; and for myself, I certainly never should, in any circumstance of tolerable similarity, give such advice. But I mean, that I was right in submitting to her, and that if I had done otherwise, I should have suffered more in continuing the engagement than I did even in giving it up, because I should have suffered in my conscience. I have now, as far as such a sentiment is allowable in human nature, nothing to reproach myself with; and if I mistake not, a strong sense of duty is no bad part of a woman's portion."

He looked at her, looked at Lady Russell, and looking again at her, replied, as if in cool deliberation, "Not yet. But there are hopes of her being forgiven in time. I trust to being in charity with her soon. But I too have been thinking over the past, and a question has suggested itself, whether there may not have been one person more my enemy even than that lady? My own self. Tell me if, when I returned to England in the year eight, with a few thousand pounds, and was posted into the *Laconia*, if I had then written to you, would you have answered my letter? Would you, in short, have renewed the engagement then?"

"Would I!" was all her answer; but the accent was decisive enough.

"Good God!" he cried, "you would! It is not that I did not think of it, or desire it, as what could alone crown all my other success; but I was proud, too proud to ask again. I did not understand you. I shut my eyes, and would not understand you, or do you justice. This is a recollection which ought to make me forgive everyone sooner than myself. Six years of separation and suffering might have been spared. It is a sort of pain, too, which is new to me. I have been used to the gratification of believing myself to earn every blessing that I enjoyed. I have valued myself on honourable toils and just rewards. Like other great men under reverses," he added, with a smile. "I must endeavour to subdue my mind to my fortune. I must learn to brook being happier than I deserve."

CHAPTER 24

Who can be in doubt of what followed? When any two young people take it into their heads to marry, they are pretty sure by perseverance to carry their point, be they ever so poor, or ever so imprudent, or ever so little likely to be necessary to each other's ultimate comfort. This may be bad morality to conclude with, but I believe it to be truth; and if such parties succeed, how should a Captain Wentworth and an Anne Elliot, with the advantage of maturity of mind, consciousness of right, and one independent fortune between them, fail of bearing down every opposition? They might in fact have borne down a great deal more than they met with, for there was little to distress them beyond the want of graciousness and warmth. Sir Walter made no objection, and Elizabeth did nothing worse than look cold and unconcerned. Captain Wentworth, with five-and-twenty thousand pounds, and as high in his profession as merit and activity could place him, was no longer nobody. He was now esteemed quite worthy to address the daughter of a foolish, spendthrift baronet, who had not had principle or sense enough to maintain himself in the situation in which Providence had placed him, and who could give his daughter at present but a small part of the share of ten thousand pounds which must be hers hereafter.

Sir Walter, indeed, though he had no affection for Anne, and no vanity flattered, to make him really happy on the occasion, was very far from thinking it a bad match for her. On the contrary, when he saw more of Captain Wentworth, saw him repeatedly by daylight, and eyed him well, he was very much struck by his personal claims, and felt that his superiority of appearance might be not unfairly balanced against her superiority of rank; and all this, assisted by his well-sounding name, enabled Sir Walter at last to prepare his pen, with a very good grace, for the insertion of the marriage in the volume of honour.

The only one among them, whose opposition of feeling could excite any serious anxiety was Lady Russell. Anne knew that Lady Russell must be suffering some pain in understanding and relinquishing Mr. Elliot, and be making some struggles to become truly acquainted with, and do justice to Captain Wentworth. This however was what

Lady Russell had now to do. She must learn to feel that she had been mistaken with regard to both; that she had been unfairly influenced by appearances in each; that because Captain Wentworth's manners had not suited her own ideas, she had been too quick in suspecting them to indicate a character of dangerous impetuosity; and that because Mr. Elliot's manners had precisely pleased her in their propriety and correctness, their general politeness and suavity, she had been too quick in receiving them as the certain result of the most correct opinions and well-regulated mind. There was nothing less for Lady Russell to do, than to admit that she had been pretty completely wrong, and to take up a new set of opinions and of hopes.

There is a quickness of perception in some, a nicety in the discernment of character, a natural penetration, in short, which no experience in others can equal, and Lady Russell had been less gifted in this part of understanding than her young friend. But she was a very good woman, and if her second object was to be sensible and well-judging, her first was to see Anne happy. She loved Anne better than she loved her own abilities, and when the awkwardness of the beginning was over, found little hardship in attaching herself as a mother to the man who was securing the happiness of her other child.

Of all the family, Mary was probably the one most immediately gratified by the circumstance. It was creditable to have a sister married, and she might flatter herself with having been greatly instrumental to the connexion, by keeping Anne with her in the autumn; and as her own sister must be better than her husband's sisters, it was very agreeable that Captain Wentworth should be a richer man than either Captain Benwick or Charles Hayter. She had something to suffer, perhaps, when they came into contact again, in seeing Anne restored to the rights of seniority, and the mistress of a very pretty landaulette; but she had a future to look forward to, of powerful consolation. Anne had no Uppercross Hall before her, no landed estate, no headship of a family; and if they could but keep Captain Wentworth from being made a baronet, she would not change situations with Anne.

It would be well for the eldest sister if she were equally satisfied with her situation, for a change is not very probable there. She had soon the mortification of seeing Mr. Elliot withdraw, and no one of proper condition has since presented himself to raise even the unfounded hopes that sunk with him.

The news of his cousin Anne's engagement burst on Mr. Elliot most unexpectedly. It deranged his best plan of domestic happiness, his best hope of keeping Sir Walter single by the watchfulness which a son-in-law's rights would have given.

But, though discomfited and disappointed, he could still do something for his own interest and his own enjoyment. He soon quitted Bath; and on Mrs. Clay's quitting it soon afterwards, and being next heard of as established under his protection in London, it was evident how double a game he had been playing, and how determined he was to save himself from being cut out by one artful woman, at least.

Mrs. Clay's affections had overpowered her interest, and she had sacrificed, for the young man's sake, the possibility of scheming longer for Sir Walter. She has abilities, however, as well as affections; and it is now a doubtful point whether his cunning, or hers, may finally carry the day; whether, after preventing her from being the wife of Sir Walter, he may not be wheedled and caressed at last into making her the wife of Sir William.

It cannot be doubted that Sir Walter and Elizabeth were shocked and mortified by the loss of their companion, and the discovery of their deception in her. They had their great cousins, to be sure, to resort to for comfort; but they must long feel that to flatter and follow others, without being flattered and followed in turn, is but a state of half enjoyment.

Anne, satisfied at a very early period of Lady Russell's meaning to love Captain Wentworth as she ought, had no other alloy to the happiness of her prospects than what arose from the consciousness of having no relations to bestow on him which a man of sense could value. There she felt her own inferiority very keenly. The disproportion in their fortune was nothing; it did not give her a moment's regret; but to have no family to receive and estimate him properly, nothing of respectability, of harmony, of goodwill to offer in return for all the worth and all the prompt welcome which met her in his brothers and sisters, was a source of as lively pain as her mind could well be sensible of under circumstances of otherwise strong felicity. She had but two friends in the world to add to his list, Lady Russell and Mrs. Smith. To those, however, he was very well disposed to attach himself. Lady Russell, in spite of all her former transgressions, he could now value from his heart. While he was not obliged to say that he believed her to have been right in originally dividing them, he was ready to say almost everything else in her favour, and as for Mrs. Smith, she had claims of various kinds to recommend her quickly and permanently.

Her recent good offices by Anne had been enough in themselves, and their marriage, instead of depriving her of one friend, secured her two. She was their earliest visitor in their settled life; and Captain Wentworth, by putting her in the way of recovering her husband's property in the West Indies, by writing for her, acting for her, and seeing her through all the petty difficulties of the case with the activity and exertion of a fearless man and a determined friend, fully requited the services which she had rendered, or ever meant to render, to his wife.

Mrs. Smith's enjoyments were not spoiled by this improvement of income, with some improvement of health, and the acquisition of such friends to be often with, for her cheerfulness and mental alacrity did not fail her; and while these prime supplies of good remained, she might have bid defiance even to greater accessions of worldly prosperity. She might have been absolutely rich and perfectly healthy, and yet be happy. Her spring of felicity was in the glow of her spirits, as her friend Anne's was in the warmth of her heart. Anne was tenderness itself, and she had the full worth of it in Captain Wentworth's affection. His profession was all that could ever make her friends wish that tenderness less, the dread of a future war all that could dim her sunshine. She gloried in being a sailor's wife, but she must pay the tax of quick alarm for belonging to that profession which is, if possible, more distinguished in its domestic virtues than in its national importance.

Word Cloud Classics

A Christmas Carol and Other Holiday Treasures

Adventures of Huckleberry Finn

The Adventures of Sherlock Holmes

Aesop's Fables

Anna Karenina

Anne of Green Gables

The Art of War

Black Beauty

The Brothers Grimm 101 Fairy Tales

The Brothers Grimm Volume II: 110 Grimmer Fairy Tales

Common Sense and Selected Works of Thomas Paine

The Count of Monte Cristo

Don Quixote

Dr. Jekyll and Mr. Hyde & Other Stories

Dracula

Frankenstein

Great Expectations

Hans Christian Andersen Tales

Inferno

The Jungle Book

Lady Chatterley's Lover

Jane Eyre

Les Misérables

Little Women

Madame Bovary

Moby-Dick

Narrative of the Life of Frederick Douglass and Other Works

Persuasion

The Picture of Dorian Gray

Pride and Prejudice

The Prince and Other Writings

The Red Badge of Courage and Other Stories

The Scarlet Letter

The Secret Garden

Sense and Sensibility

The Three Musketeers

Treasure Island

Twenty Thousand Leagues Under the Sea

Uncle Tom's Cabin

Walden and Civil Disobedience

The Wizard of Oz

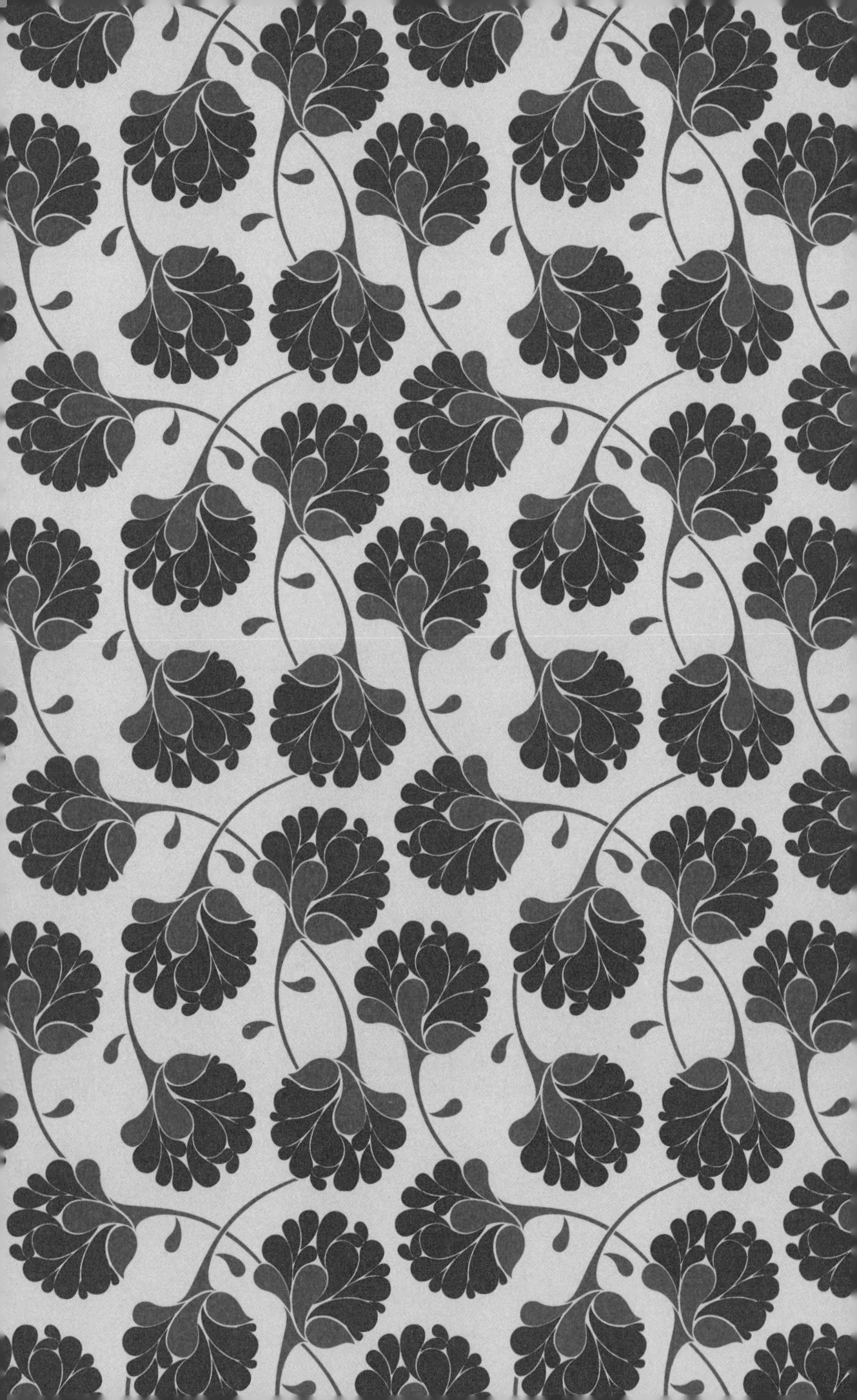

Sense and Sensibility

Word Cloud Classics

A Christmas Carol and Other Holiday Treasures

Adventures of Huckleberry Finn

The Adventures of Sherlock Holmes

Aesop's Fables

The Age of Innocence

Anna Karenina

Anne of Green Gables

The Art of War

The Brothers Grimm: 101 Fairy Tales

The Brothers Grimm Volume II: 110 Grimmer Fairy Tales

Common Sense and Selected Works of Thomas Paine

The Count of Monte Cristo

Don Quixote

Dracula

Emma

Frankenstein

Great Expectations

Inferno

Jane Eyre

Lady Chatterley's Lover

Les Misérables

Little Women

Madame Bovary

Moby-Dick

Narrative of the Life of Frederick Douglass and Other Works

Persuasion

The Picture of Dorian Gray

Pride and Prejudice

The Prince and Other Writings

The Red Badge of Courage and Other Stories

The Scarlet Letter

The Secret Garden

The Three Musketeers

Twenty Thousand Leagues Under the Sea

Uncle Tom's Cabin

Walden and Civil Disobedience

The Wizard of Oz

Sense and Sensibility

Jane Austen

CANTERBURY CLASSICS
San Diego

All correspondence concerning the content of this book should be addressed to: Canterbury Classics
10350 Barnes Canyon Road, Suite 100
San Diego, CA 92121

Publisher: Peter Norton
Publishing Team: Lori Asbury, Ana Parker
Director Editorial and Production: JoAnn Padgett
Editor: Melinda Allman

Library of Congress Cataloging-in-Publication Data

Austen, Jane, 1775-1817.
Sense and sensibility / Jane Austen.
p. cm. -- (Canterbury classics)
ISBN-13: 978-1-60710-555-8
ISBN-10: 1-60710-555-1
1. Inheritance and succession--Fiction. 2. Social classes--Fiction.
3. Young women--Fiction. 4. Sisters--Fiction. 5. England--Fiction.
I. Title.

PR4034.S4 2012
823'.7--dc23

2011049593

PRINTED IN CHINA

5 6 7 8 9 19 18 17 16 15

CHAPTER I

The family of Dashwood had long been settled in Sussex. Their estate was large, and their residence was at Norland Park, in the centre of their property, where, for many generations, they had lived in so respectable a manner as to engage the general good opinion of their surrounding acquaintance. The late owner of this estate was a single man, who lived to a very advanced age, and who for many years of his life, had a constant companion and housekeeper in his sister. But her death, which happened ten years before his own, produced a great alteration in his home; for to supply her loss, he invited and received into his house the family of his nephew Mr. Henry Dashwood, the legal inheritor of the Norland estate, and the person to whom he intended to bequeath it. In the society of his nephew and niece, and their children, the old gentleman's days were comfortably spent. His attachment to them all increased. The constant attention of Mr. and Mrs. Henry Dashwood to his wishes, which proceeded not merely from interest, but from goodness of heart, gave him every degree of solid comfort which his age could receive; and the cheerfulness of the children added a relish to his existence.

By a former marriage, Mr. Henry Dashwood had one son; by his present lady, three daughters. The son, a steady respectable young man, was amply provided for by the fortune of his mother, which had been large, and half of which devolved on him on his coming of age. By his own marriage, likewise, which happened soon afterwards, he added to his wealth. To him therefore the succession to the Norland estate was not so really important as to his sisters; for their fortune, independent of what might arise to them from their father's inheriting that property, could be but small. Their mother had nothing, and their father only seven thousand pounds in his own disposal; for the remaining moiety of his first wife's fortune was also secured to her child, and he had only a life-interest in it.

The old gentleman died: his will was read, and like almost every other will, gave as much disappointment as pleasure. He was neither so unjust, nor so ungrateful, as to leave his estate from his nephew—but he left it to him on such terms as destroyed half the value of the bequest. Mr. Dashwood had wished for it more for the sake of his wife and daughters than for himself or his son—but to his son, and his son's son, a child of four years old, it was secured, in such a way, as to leave to himself no power of providing for those who were most dear to him, and who most needed a provision by any charge on the estate, or by any sale of its valuable woods. The whole was tied up for the benefit of this child, who, in occasional visits with his father and mother at Norland, had so far gained on the affections of his uncle, by such attractions as are by no means unusual in children of two or three years old: an imperfect articulation, an earnest desire of having his own way, many cunning tricks, and a great deal of noise, as to outweigh all the value of all the attention which, for years, he had received from his niece and her daughters. He meant not to be unkind, however, and, as a mark of his affection for the three girls, he left them a thousand pounds a-piece.

Mr. Dashwood's disappointment was, at first, severe; but his temper was cheerful and sanguine, and he might reasonably hope to live many years, and by living economically, lay by a considerable sum from the produce of an estate already large, and capable of almost immediate improvement. But the fortune, which had been so tardy in coming, was his only one twelvemonth. He survived his uncle no longer; and ten thousand pounds, including the late legacies, was all that remained for his widow and daughters.

His son was sent for as soon as his danger was known, and to him Mr. Dashwood recommended, with all the strength and urgency which illness could command, the interest of his mother-in-law and sisters.

Mr. John Dashwood had not the strong feelings of the rest of the family; but he was affected by a recommendation of such a nature at such a time, and he promised to do every thing in his power to make them comfortable. His father was rendered easy by such an assurance, and Mr. John Dashwood had then leisure to consider how much there might prudently be in his power to do for them.

He was not an ill-disposed young man, unless to be rather cold hearted and rather selfish is to be ill-disposed: but he was, in general, well respected, for he conducted himself with propriety in the discharge of his ordinary duties. Had he married a more amiable woman, he might have been made still more respectable than he was—he might even have been made amiable himself; for he was very young when he married, and very fond of his wife. But Mrs. John Dashwood was a strong caricature of himself—more narrow-minded and selfish.

When he gave his promise to his father, he meditated within himself to increase the fortunes of his sisters by the present of a thousand pounds a-piece. He then really thought himself equal to it. The prospect of four thousand a-year, in addition to his present income, besides the remaining half of his own mother's fortune, warmed his heart, and made him feel capable of generosity. "Yes, he would give them three thousand pounds: it would be liberal and handsome! It would be enough to make them completely easy. Three thousand pounds! He could spare so considerable a sum with little inconvenience." He thought of it all day long, and for many days successively, and he did not repent.

No sooner was his father's funeral over, than Mrs. John Dashwood, without sending any notice of her intention to her mother-in-law, arrived with her child and their attendants. No one could dispute her right to come; the house was her husband's from the moment of his father's decease; but the indelicacy of her conduct was so much the greater, and to a woman in Mrs. Dashwood's situation, with only common feelings, must have been highly unpleasing—but in *her* mind there was a sense of honor so keen, a generosity so romantic, that any offence of the kind, by whomsoever given or received, was to her a source of immoveable disgust. Mrs. John Dashwood had never been a favourite with any of her husband's family; but she had had no opportunity, till the present, of shewing them with how little attention to the comfort of other people she could act when occasion required it.

So acutely did Mrs. Dashwood feel this ungracious behaviour, and so earnestly did she despise her daughter-in-law for it, that, on the arrival of the latter, she would have quitted the house for ever, had not the entreaty of her eldest girl induced her first to reflect on the propriety of going, and her own tender love for all her three children determined her afterwards to stay, and for their sakes avoid a breach with their brother.

Elinor, this eldest daughter, whose advice was so effectual, possessed a strength of understanding, and coolness of judgment, which qualified her, though only nineteen, to be the counsellor of her mother, and enabled her frequently to counteract, to the advantage of them all, that eagerness of mind in Mrs. Dashwood which must generally have led to imprudence. She had an excellent heart—her disposition was affectionate, and her feelings were strong; but she knew how to govern them: it was a knowledge which her mother had yet to learn; and which one of her sisters had resolved never to be taught.

Marianne's abilities were, in many respects, quite equal to Elinor's. She was sensible and clever; but eager in everything; her sorrows, her joys, could have no moderation. She was generous, amiable, interesting: she was everything but prudent. The resemblance between her and her mother was strikingly great.

Elinor saw, with concern, the excess of her sister's sensibility; but by Mrs. Dashwood it was valued and cherished. They encouraged each other now in the violence of their affliction. The agony of grief which overpowered them at first, was voluntarily renewed, was sought for, was created again and again. They gave themselves up wholly to their sorrow, seeking increase of wretchedness in every reflection that could afford it, and resolved against ever admitting consolation in future. Elinor, too, was deeply afflicted; but still she could struggle, she could exert herself. She could consult with her brother, could receive her sister-in-law on her arrival, and treat her with proper attention; and could strive to rouse her mother to similar exertion, and encourage her to similar forbearance.

Margaret, the other sister, was a good-humored, well-disposed girl; but as she had already imbibed a good deal of Marianne's romance, without having much of her sense, she did not, at thirteen, bid fair to equal her sisters at a more advanced period of life.

CHAPTER II

Mrs. John Dashwood now installed herself mistress of Norland, and her mother and sisters-in-law were degraded to the condition of visitors. As such, however, they were treated by her with quiet civility; and by her husband with as much kindness as he could feel towards anybody beyond himself, his wife, and their child. He really pressed them, with some earnestness, to consider Norland as their home; and, as no plan appeared so eligible to Mrs. Dashwood as remaining there till she could accommodate herself with a house in the neighbourhood, his invitation was accepted.

A continuance in a place where everything reminded her of former delight, was exactly what suited her mind. In seasons of cheerfulness, no temper could be more cheerful than hers, or possess, in a greater degree, that sanguine expectation of happiness which is happiness itself. But in sorrow she must be equally carried away by her fancy, and as far beyond consolation as in pleasure she was beyond alloy.

Mrs. John Dashwood did not at all approve of what her husband intended to do for his sisters. To take three thousand pounds from the fortune of their dear little boy would be impoverishing him to the most dreadful degree. She begged him to think again on the subject. How could he answer it to himself to rob his child, and his only child too, of so large a sum? And what possible claim could the Miss Dashwoods, who were related to him only by half blood, which she considered as no relationship at all, have on his generosity to so large an amount. It was very well known that no affection was ever supposed to exist between the children of any man by different marriages; and why was he to ruin himself, and their poor little Harry, by giving away all his money to his half sisters?

"It was my father's last request to me," replied her husband, "that I should assist his widow and daughters."

"He did not know what he was talking of, I dare say; ten to one but he was light-headed at the time. Had he been in his right senses, he could not have thought of such a thing as begging you to give away half your fortune from your own child."

"He did not stipulate for any particular sum, my dear Fanny; he only requested me, in general terms, to assist them, and make their situation more comfortable than it was in his power to do. Perhaps it would have been as well if he had left it wholly to myself. He could hardly suppose I should neglect them. But as he required the promise, I could not do less than give it; at least I thought so at the time. The promise, therefore, was given, and must be performed. Something must be done for them whenever they leave Norland and settle in a new home."

"Well, then, *let* something be done for them; but *that* something need not be three thousand pounds. Consider," she added, "that when the money is once parted with, it never can return. Your sisters will marry, and it will be gone for ever. If, indeed, it could be restored to our poor little boy—"

"Why, to be sure," said her husband, very gravely, "that would make great difference. The time may come when Harry will regret that so large a sum was parted with. If he should have a numerous family, for instance, it would be a very convenient addition."

"To be sure it would."

"Perhaps, then, it would be better for all parties, if the sum were diminished one half. Five hundred pounds would be a prodigious increase to their fortunes!"

"Oh! Beyond anything great! What brother on earth would do half so much for his sisters, even if *really* his sisters! And as it is—only half blood! But you have such a generous spirit!"

"I would not wish to do any thing mean," he replied. "One had rather, on such occasions, do too much than too little. No one, at least, can think I have not done enough for them: even themselves, they can hardly expect more."

"There is no knowing what *they* may expect," said the lady, "but we are not to think of their expectations: the question is, what you can afford to do."

"Certainly—and I think I may afford to give them five hundred pounds a-piece. As it is, without any addition of mine, they will each have about three thousand pounds on their mother's death—a very comfortable fortune for any young woman."

"To be sure it is; and, indeed, it strikes me that they can want no addition at all. They will have ten thousand pounds divided amongst them. If they marry, they will be sure of doing well, and if they do not, they may all live very comfortably together on the interest of ten thousand pounds."

"That is very true, and, therefore, I do not know whether, upon the whole, it would not be more advisable to do something for their mother while she lives, rather than for them—something of the annuity kind I mean. My sisters would feel the good effects of it as well as herself. A hundred a year would make them all perfectly comfortable."

His wife hesitated a little, however, in giving her consent to this plan.

"To be sure," said she, "it is better than parting with fifteen hundred pounds at once. But, then, if Mrs. Dashwood should live fifteen years we shall be completely taken in."

"Fifteen years! My dear Fanny; her life cannot be worth half that purchase."

"Certainly not; but if you observe, people always live for ever when there is an annuity to be paid them; and she is very stout and healthy, and hardly forty. An annuity is a very serious business; it comes over and over every year, and there is no getting rid of it. You are not aware of what you are doing. I have known a great deal of the trouble of annuities; for my mother was clogged with the payment of three to old superannuated servants by my father's will, and it is amazing how disagreeable she found it. Twice every year these annuities were to be paid; and then there was the trouble of getting it to them; and then one of them was said to have died, and afterwards it turned out to be no such thing. My mother was quite sick of it. Her income was not her own, she said, with such perpetual claims on it; and it was the more unkind in my father, because, otherwise, the money would have been entirely at my mother's disposal, without any restriction whatever. It has given me such an abhorrence of annuities, that I am sure I would not pin myself down to the payment of one for all the world."

"It is certainly an unpleasant thing," replied Mr. Dashwood, "to have those kind of yearly drains on one's income. One's fortune, as your mother justly says, is *not* one's own. To be tied down to the regular payment of such a sum, on every rent day, is by no means desirable: it takes away one's independence."

"Undoubtedly; and after all you have no thanks for it. They think themselves secure, you do no more than what is expected, and it raises no gratitude at all. If I were you, whatever I did should be done at my own discretion entirely. I would not bind myself to allow them any thing yearly. It may be very inconvenient some years to spare a hundred, or even fifty pounds from our own expenses."

"I believe you are right, my love; it will be better that there should be no annuity in the case; whatever I may give them occasionally will be of far greater assistance than a yearly allowance, because they would only enlarge their style of living if they felt sure of a larger income, and would not be sixpence the richer for it at the end of the year. It will certainly be much the best way. A present of fifty pounds, now and then, will prevent their ever being distressed for money, and will, I think, be amply discharging my promise to my father."

"To be sure it will. Indeed, to say the truth, I am convinced within myself that your father had no idea of your giving them any money at all. The assistance he thought of, I dare say, was only such as might be reasonably expected of you; for instance, such as looking out for a comfortable small house for them, helping them to move their things, and sending them presents of fish and game, and so forth, whenever they are in season. I'll lay my life that he meant nothing farther; indeed, it would be very strange and unreasonable if he did. Do but consider, my dear Mr. Dashwood, how excessively comfortable your mother-in-law and her daughters may live on the interest of seven thousand pounds, besides the thousand pounds belonging to each of the girls, which brings them in fifty pounds a year a-piece, and, of course, they will pay their mother for their board out of it. Altogether, they will have five hundred a-year amongst them, and what on earth can four women want for more than that? They will live so cheap! Their housekeeping will be nothing at all. They will have no carriage, no horses, and hardly any servants; they will keep no company, and can have no expenses of any kind! Only conceive how comfortable they will be! Five hundred a year! I am sure I cannot imagine how they will spend half of it; and as to your giving them more, it is quite absurd to think of it. They will be much more able to give *you* something."

"Upon my word," said Mr. Dashwood, "I believe you are perfectly right. My father certainly could mean nothing more by his request to me than what you say. I clearly understand it now, and I will strictly fulfil my engagement by such acts of assistance and kindness to them as you have described. When my mother removes into another house my services shall be readily given to accommodate her as far as I can. Some little present of furniture too may be acceptable then."

"Certainly," returned Mrs. John Dashwood. "But, however, *one* thing must be considered. When your father and mother moved to Norland, though the furniture of Stanhill was sold, all the china, plate, and linen was saved, and is now left to your mother. Her house will therefore be almost completely fitted up as soon as she takes it."

"That is a material consideration undoubtedly. A valuable legacy indeed! And yet some of the plate would have been a very pleasant addition to our own stock here."

"Yes; and the set of breakfast china is twice as handsome as what belongs to this house. A great deal too handsome, in my opinion, for any place *they* can ever afford to live in. But, however, so it is. Your father thought only of *them*. And I must say this: that you owe no particular gratitude to him, nor attention to his wishes; for we very well know that if he could, he would have left almost everything in the world to *them*."

This argument was irresistible. It gave to his intentions whatever of decision was wanting before; and he finally resolved, that it would be absolutely unnecessary, if not highly indecorous, to do more for the widow and children of his father, than such kind of neighbourly acts as his own wife pointed out.

CHAPTER III

Mrs. Dashwood remained at Norland several months; not from any disinclination to move when the sight of every well-known spot ceased to raise the violent emotion which it produced for a while; for when her spirits began to revive, and her mind became capable of some other exertion than that of heightening its affliction by melancholy remembrances, she was impatient to be gone, and indefatigable in her inquiries for a suitable dwelling in the neighbourhood of Norland; for to remove far from that beloved spot was impossible. But she could hear of no situation that at once answered her notions of comfort and ease, and suited the prudence of her eldest daughter, whose steadier judgment rejected several houses as too large for their income, which her mother would have approved.

Mrs. Dashwood had been informed by her husband of the solemn promise on the part of his son in their favour, which gave comfort to his last earthly reflections. She doubted the sincerity of this assurance no more than he had doubted it himself, and she thought of it for her daughters' sake with satisfaction, though as for herself she was persuaded that a much smaller provision than 7000£ would support her in affluence. For their brother's sake, too, for the sake of his own heart, she rejoiced; and she reproached herself for being unjust to his merit before, in believing him incapable of generosity. His attentive behaviour to herself and his sisters convinced her that their welfare was dear to him, and, for a long time, she firmly relied on the liberality of his intentions.

The contempt which she had, very early in their acquaintance, felt for her daughter-in-law, was very much increased by the farther knowledge of her character, which half a year's residence in her family afforded; and perhaps in spite of every consideration of politeness or maternal affection on the side of the former, the two ladies might have found it impossible to have lived together so long, had not a particular circumstance occurred to give still greater eligibility, according to the opinions of Mrs. Dashwood, to her daughters' continuance at Norland.

This circumstance was a growing attachment between her eldest girl and the brother of Mrs. John Dashwood, a gentleman-like and pleasing young man, who was introduced to their acquaintance soon after his sister's establishment at Norland, and who had since spent the greatest part of his time there.

Some mothers might have encouraged the intimacy from motives of interest, for Edward Ferrars was the eldest son of a man who had died very rich; and some might have repressed it from motives of prudence, for, except a trifling sum, the whole of his fortune depended on the will of his mother. But Mrs. Dashwood was alike uninfluenced by either consideration. It was enough for her that he appeared to be amiable, that he loved her daughter, and that Elinor returned the partiality. It was contrary to every doctrine of her's that difference of fortune should keep any couple asunder who were attracted by resemblance of disposition; and that Elinor's merit should not be acknowledged by every one who knew her, was to her comprehension impossible.

Edward Ferrars was not recommended to their good opinion by any peculiar graces of person or address. He was not handsome, and his manners required intimacy to make them pleasing. He was too diffident to do justice to himself; but when his natural shyness was overcome, his behaviour gave every indication of an open, affectionate heart. His understanding was good, and his education had given it solid improvement. But he was neither fitted by abilities nor disposition to answer the wishes of his mother and sister, who longed to see him distinguished—as—they hardly knew what. They wanted him to make a fine figure in the world in some manner or other. His mother wished to interest him in political concerns, to get him into parliament, or to see him connected with some of the great men of the day. Mrs. John Dashwood wished it likewise; but in the mean while, till one of these superior blessings could be attained, it would have quieted her ambition to see him driving a barouche. But Edward had no turn for great men or barouches. All his wishes centered in domestic comfort and the quiet of private life. Fortunately he had a younger brother who was more promising.

Edward had been staying several weeks in the house before he engaged much of Mrs. Dashwood's attention; for she was, at that time, in such affliction as rendered her careless of surrounding objects. She saw only that he was quiet and unobtrusive, and she liked him for it. He did not disturb the wretchedness of her mind by ill-timed conversation. She was first called to observe and approve him farther, by a reflection which Elinor chanced one day to make on the difference between him and his sister. It was a contrast which recommended him most forcibly to her mother.

"It is enough," said she; "to say that he is unlike Fanny is enough. It implies everything amiable. I love him already."

"I think you will like him," said Elinor, "when you know more of him."

"Like him!" replied her mother with a smile. "I feel no sentiment of approbation inferior to love."

"You may esteem him."

"I have never yet known what it was to separate esteem and love."

Mrs. Dashwood now took pains to get acquainted with him. Her manners were attaching, and soon banished his reserve. She speedily comprehended all his merits; the persuasion of his regard for Elinor perhaps assisted her penetration; but she really felt assured of his worth: and even that quietness of manner, which militated against all her established ideas of what a young man's address ought to be, was no longer uninteresting when she knew his heart to be warm and his temper affectionate.

No sooner did she perceive any symptom of love in his behaviour to Elinor, than she considered their serious attachment as certain, and looked forward to their marriage as rapidly approaching.

"In a few months, my dear Marianne," said she, "Elinor will, in all probability be settled for life. We shall miss her; but *she* will be happy."

"Oh! Mamma, how shall we do without her?"

"My love, it will be scarcely a separation. We shall live within a few miles of each other, and shall meet every day of our lives. You will gain a brother, a real, affectionate brother. I have the highest opinion in the world of Edward's heart. But you look grave, Marianne; do you disapprove your sister's choice?"

"Perhaps," said Marianne, "I may consider it with some surprise. Edward is very amiable, and I love him tenderly. But yet—he is not the kind of young man—there is something wanting—his figure is not striking; it has none of that grace which I should expect in the man who could seriously attach my sister. His eyes want all that spirit, that fire, which at once announce virtue and intelligence. And besides all this, I am afraid, Mamma, he has no real taste. Music seems scarcely to attract him, and though he admires Elinor's drawings very much, it is not the admiration of a person who can understand their worth. It is evident, in spite of his frequent attention to her while she draws, that in fact he knows nothing of the matter. He admires as a lover, not as a connoisseur. To satisfy me, those characters must be united. I could not be happy with a man whose taste did not in every point coincide with my own. He must enter into all my feelings; the same books, the same music must charm us both. Oh! Mama, how spiritless, how tame was Edward's manner in reading to us last night! I felt for my sister most severely. Yet she bore it with so much composure, she seemed scarcely to notice it. I could hardly keep my seat. To hear those beautiful lines which have frequently almost driven me wild, pronounced with such impenetrable calmness, such dreadful indifference!"

"He would certainly have done more justice to simple and elegant prose. I thought so at the time; but you *would* give him Cowper."

"Nay, Mamma, if he is not to be animated by Cowper! But we must allow for difference of taste. Elinor has not my feelings, and therefore she may overlook it, and be happy with him. But it would have broke *my* heart, had I loved him, to hear him read with so little sensibility. Mama, the more I know of the world, the more am I convinced that I shall never see a man whom I can really love. I require so much! He must have all Edward's virtues, and his person and manners must ornament his goodness with every possible charm."

"Remember, my love, that you are not seventeen. It is yet too early in life to despair of such a happiness. Why should you be less fortunate than your mother? In one circumstance only, my Marianne, may your destiny be different from hers!"

CHAPTER IV

"What a pity it is, Elinor," said Marianne, "that Edward should have no taste for drawing."

"No taste for drawing!" replied Elinor, "why should you think so? He does not draw himself, indeed, but he has great pleasure in seeing the performances of other people, and I assure you he is by no means deficient in natural taste, though he has not had opportunities of improving it. Had he ever been in the way of learning, I think he would have drawn very well. He distrusts his own judgment in such matters so much, that he is always unwilling to give his opinion on any picture; but he has an innate propriety and simplicity of taste, which in general direct him perfectly right."

Marianne was afraid of offending, and said no more on the subject; but the kind of approbation which Elinor described as excited in him by the drawings of other people, was very far from that rapturous delight, which, in her opinion, could alone be called taste. Yet, though smiling within herself at the mistake, she honoured her sister for that blind partiality to Edward which produced it.

"I hope, Marianne," continued Elinor, "you do not consider him as deficient in general taste. Indeed, I think I may say that you cannot, for your behaviour to him is perfectly cordial, and if *that* were your opinion, I am sure you could never be civil to him."

Marianne hardly knew what to say. She would not wound the feelings of her sister on any account, and yet to say what she did not believe was impossible. At length she replied:

"Do not be offended, Elinor, if my praise of him is not in every thing equal to your sense of his merits. I have not had so many opportunities of estimating the minuter propensities of his mind, his inclinations and tastes, as you have; but I have the highest opinion in the world of his goodness and sense. I think him every thing that is worthy and amiable."

"I am sure," replied Elinor, with a smile, "that his dearest friends could not be dissatisfied with such commendation as that. I do not perceive how you could express yourself more warmly."

Marianne was rejoiced to find her sister so easily pleased.

"Of his sense and his goodness," continued Elinor, "no one can, I think, be in doubt, who has seen him often enough to engage him in unreserved conversation. The excellence of his understanding and his principles can be concealed only by that shyness which too often keeps him silent. You know enough of him to do justice to his solid worth. But of his minuter propensities, as you call them you have from peculiar circumstances been kept more ignorant than myself. He and I have been at times thrown a good deal together, while you have been wholly engrossed on the most affectionate principle by my mother. I have seen a great deal of him, have studied his sentiments and heard his opinion on subjects of literature and taste; and, upon the whole, I venture to pronounce that his mind is well-informed, enjoyment of books exceedingly great, his imagination lively, his observation just and correct, and his taste delicate and pure. His abilities in every respect improve as much upon acquaintance as his manners and person. At first sight, his address is certainly not striking; and his person can hardly be called handsome, till the expression of his eyes, which are uncommonly good, and the general sweetness of his countenance, is perceived. At present, I know him so well, that I think him really handsome; or at least, almost so. What say you, Marianne?"

"I shall very soon think him handsome, Elinor, if I do not now. When you tell me to love him as a brother, I shall no more see imperfection in his face, than I now do in his heart."

Elinor started at this declaration, and was sorry for the warmth she had been betrayed into, in speaking of him. She felt that Edward stood very high in her opinion. She believed the regard to be mutual; but she required greater certainty of it to make Marianne's conviction of their attachment agreeable to her. She knew that what Marianne and her mother conjectured one moment, they believed the next—that with them, to wish was to hope, and to hope was to expect. She tried to explain the real state of the case to her sister.

"I do not attempt to deny," said she, "that I think very highly of him—that I greatly esteem, that I like him."

Marianne here burst forth with indignation—

"Esteem him! Like him! Cold-hearted Elinor! Oh! Worse than cold-hearted! Ashamed of being otherwise. Use those words again, and I will leave the room this moment."

Elinor could not help laughing. "Excuse me," said she; "and be assured that I meant no offence to you, by speaking, in so quiet a way, of my own feelings. Believe them to be stronger than I have declared; believe them, in short, to be such as his merit, and the suspicion—the hope of his affection for me may warrant, without imprudence or folly. But farther than this you must not believe. I am by no means assured of his regard for me. There are moments when the extent of it seems doubtful; and till his sentiments are fully known, you cannot wonder at my wishing to avoid any encouragement of my own partiality, by believing or calling it more than it is. In my heart I feel little—scarcely any doubt of his preference. But there are other points to be considered besides his inclination. He is very far from being independent. What his mother really is we cannot know; but, from Fanny's occasional mention of her conduct and opinions, we have never been disposed to think her amiable; and I am very much mistaken if Edward is not himself aware that there would be many difficulties in his way, if he were to wish to marry a woman who had not either a great fortune or high rank."

Marianne was astonished to find how much the imagination of her mother and herself had outstripped the truth.

"And you really are not engaged to him!" said she. "Yet it certainly soon will happen. But two advantages will proceed from this delay. I shall not lose you so soon, and Edward will have greater opportunity of improving that natural taste for your favourite pursuit which must be so indispensably necessary to your future felicity. Oh! If he should be so far stimulated by your genius as to learn to draw himself, how delightful it would be!"

Elinor had given her real opinion to her sister. She could not consider her partiality for Edward in so prosperous a state as Marianne had believed it. There was, at times, a want of spirits about him which, if it did not denote indifference, spoke of something almost as unpromising. A doubt of her regard, supposing him to feel it, need not give him more than inquietude. It would not be likely to produce that dejection of mind which frequently attended him. A more reasonable cause might be found in the dependent situation which forbade the indulgence of his affection. She knew that his mother neither behaved to him so as to make his home comfortable at present, nor to give him any assurance that he might form a home for himself, without strictly attending to her views for his aggrandizement. With such a knowledge as this, it was impossible for Elinor to feel easy on the subject. She was far from depending on that result of his preference of her, which her mother and sister still considered as certain. Nay, the longer they were together the more doubtful seemed the nature of his regard; and sometimes, for a few painful minutes, she believed it to be no more than friendship.

But, whatever might really be its limits, it was enough, when perceived by his sister, to make her uneasy, and at the same time, (which was still more common) to make her uncivil. She took the first opportunity of affronting her mother-in-law on the occasion, talking to her so expressively of her brother's great expectations, of Mrs. Ferrars's resolution that both her sons should marry well, and of the danger attending any young woman who attempted to *draw him in*; that Mrs. Dashwood could neither pretend to be unconscious, nor endeavor to be calm. She gave her an answer which marked her contempt, and instantly left the room, resolving that, whatever might be the inconvenience or expense of so sudden a removal, her beloved Elinor should not be exposed another week to such insinuations.

In this state of her spirits, a letter was delivered to her from the post, which contained a proposal particularly well timed. It was the offer of a small house, on very easy terms, belonging to a relation of her own, a gentleman of consequence and property in Devonshire. The letter was from this gentleman himself, and written in the true spirit of friendly accommodation. He understood that she was in need of a dwelling; and though the house he now offered her was merely a cottage, he assured her that everything should be done to it which she might think necessary, if the situation pleased her. He earnestly pressed her, after giving the particulars of the house and garden, to come with her daughters to Barton Park, the place of his own residence, from whence she might judge, herself, whether Barton Cottage, for the houses were in the same parish, could, by any alteration, be made comfortable to her. He seemed really anxious to accommodate them and the whole of his letter was written in so friendly a style as could not fail of giving pleasure to his cousin; more especially at a moment when she was suffering under the cold and unfeeling behaviour of her nearer connections. She needed no time for deliberation or inquiry. Her resolution was formed as she read. The situation of Barton, in a county so far distant from Sussex as Devonshire, which, but a few hours before, would have been a sufficient objection to outweigh every possible advantage belonging to the place, was now its first recommendation. To quit the neighbourhood of Norland was no longer an evil; it was an object of desire; it was a blessing, in comparison of the misery of continuing her daughter-in-law's guest; and to remove for ever from that beloved place would be less painful than to inhabit or visit it while such a woman was its mistress. She instantly wrote Sir John Middleton her acknowledgment of his kindness, and her acceptance of his proposal; and then hastened to shew both letters to her daughters, that she might be secure of their approbation before her answer were sent.

Elinor had always thought it would be more prudent for them to settle at some distance from Norland, than immediately amongst their present acquaintance. On *that* head, therefore, it was not for her to oppose her mother's intention of removing into Devonshire. The house, too, as described by Sir John, was on so simple a scale, and the rent so uncommonly moderate, as to leave her no right of objection on either point; and, therefore, though it was not a plan which brought any charm to her fancy, though it was a removal from the vicinity of Norland beyond her wishes, she made no attempt to dissuade her mother from sending a letter of acquiescence.

CHAPTER V

No sooner was her answer dispatched, than Mrs. Dashwood indulged herself in the pleasure of announcing to her son-in-law and his wife that she was provided with a house, and should incommode them no longer than till every thing were ready for her inhabiting it. They heard her with surprise. Mrs. John Dashwood said nothing; but her husband civilly hoped that she would not be settled far from Norland. She had great satisfaction in replying that she was going into Devonshire. Edward turned hastily towards her, on hearing this, and, in a voice of surprise and concern, which required no explanation to her, repeated, "Devonshire! Are you, indeed, going there? So far from hence! And to what part of it?" She explained the situation. It was within four miles northward of Exeter.

"It is but a cottage," she continued, "but I hope to see many of my friends in it. A room or two can easily be added; and if my friends find no difficulty in travelling so far to see me, I am sure I will find none in accommodating them."

She concluded with a very kind invitation to Mr. and Mrs. John Dashwood to visit her at Barton; and to Edward she gave one with still greater affection. Though her late conversation with her daughter-in-law had made her resolve on remaining at Norland no longer than was unavoidable, it had not produced the smallest effect on her in that point to which it principally tended. To separate Edward and Elinor was as far from being her object as ever; and she wished to show Mrs. John Dashwood, by this pointed invitation to her brother, how totally she disregarded her disapprobation of the match.

Mr. John Dashwood told his mother again and again how exceedingly sorry he was that she had taken a house at such a distance from Norland as to prevent his being of any service to her in removing her furniture. He really felt conscientiously vexed on the occasion; for the very exertion to which he had limited the performance of his promise to his father was by this arrangement rendered impracticable. The furniture was all sent around by water. It chiefly consisted of household linen, plate, china, and books, with a handsome pianoforte of Marianne's. Mrs. John Dashwood saw the packages depart with a sigh: she could not help feeling it hard that as Mrs. Dashwood's income would be so trifling in comparison with their own, she should have any handsome article of furniture.

Mrs. Dashwood took the house for a twelvemonth; it was ready furnished, and she might have immediate possession. No difficulty arose on either side in the agreement; and she waited only for the disposal of her effects at Norland, and to determine her future household, before she set off for the west; and this, as she was exceedingly rapid in the performance of everything that interested her, was soon done. The horses which were left her by her husband had been sold soon after his death, and an opportunity now offering of disposing of her carriage, she agreed to sell that likewise at the earnest advice of her eldest daughter. For the comfort of her children, had she consulted only her own wishes, she would have kept it; but the discretion of Elinor prevailed. *Her* wisdom too limited the number of their servants to three; two maids and a man, with whom they were speedily provided from amongst those who had formed their establishment at Norland.

The man and one of the maids were sent off immediately into Devonshire, to prepare the house for their mistress's arrival; for as Lady Middleton was entirely unknown to Mrs. Dashwood, she preferred going directly to the cottage to being a visitor at Barton Park; and she relied so undoubtingly on Sir John's description of the house, as to feel no curiosity to examine it herself till she entered it as her own. Her eagerness to be gone from Norland was preserved from diminution by the evident satisfaction of her daughter-in-law in the prospect of her removal; a satisfaction which was but feebly attempted to be concealed under a cold invitation to her to defer her departure. Now was the time when her son-in-law's promise to his father might with particular propriety be fulfilled. Since he had neglected to do it on first coming to the estate, their quitting his house might be looked on as the most suitable period for its accomplishment. But Mrs. Dashwood began shortly to give over every hope of the kind, and to be convinced, from the general drift of his discourse, that his assistance extended no farther than their maintenance for six months at Norland. He so frequently talked of the increasing expenses of housekeeping, and of the perpetual demands upon his purse, which a man of any consequence in the world was beyond calculation exposed to, that he seemed rather to stand in need of more money himself than to have any design of giving money away.

In a very few weeks from the day which brought Sir John Middleton's first letter to Norland, every thing was so far settled in their future abode as to enable Mrs. Dashwood and her daughters to begin their journey.

Many were the tears shed by them in their last adieus to a place so much beloved. "Dear, dear Norland!" said Marianne, as she wandered alone before the house, on the last evening of their being there; "when shall I cease to regret you! When learn to feel a home elsewhere! Oh! Happy house, could you know what I suffer in now viewing you from this spot, from whence perhaps I may view you no more! And you, ye well-known trees! But you will continue the same. No leaf will decay because we are removed, nor any branch become motionless although we can observe you no longer! No; you will continue the same; unconscious of the pleasure or the regret you occasion, and insensible of any change in those who walk under your shade! But who will remain to enjoy you?"

CHAPTER VI

The first part of their journey was performed in too melancholy a disposition to be otherwise than tedious and unpleasant. But as they drew towards the end of it, their interest in the appearance of a country which they were to inhabit overcame their dejection, and a view of Barton Valley as they entered it gave them cheerfulness. It was a pleasant fertile spot, well wooded, and rich in pasture. After winding along it for more than a mile, they reached their own house. A small green court was the whole of its demesne in front; and a neat wicket gate admitted them into it.

As a house, Barton Cottage, though small, was comfortable and compact; but as a cottage it was defective, for the building was regular, the roof was tiled, the window shutters were not painted green, nor were the walls covered with honeysuckles. A narrow passage led directly through the house into the garden behind. On each side of the entrance was a sitting room, about sixteen feet square; and beyond them were the offices and the stairs. Four bed-rooms and two garrets formed the rest of the house. It had not been built many years and was in good repair. In comparison of Norland, it was poor and small indeed! But the tears which recollection called forth as they entered the house were soon dried away. They were cheered by the joy of the servants on their arrival, and each for the sake of the others resolved to appear happy. It was very early in September; the season was fine, and from first seeing the place under the advantage of good weather, they received an impression in its favour which was of material service in recommending it to their lasting approbation.

The situation of the house was good. High hills rose immediately behind, and at no great distance on each side; some of which were open downs, the others cultivated and woody. The village of Barton was chiefly on one of these hills, and formed a pleasant view from the cottage windows. The prospect in front was more extensive; it commanded the whole of the valley, and reached into the country beyond. The hills which surrounded the cottage terminated the valley in that direction; under another name, and in another course, it branched out again between two of the steepest of them.

With the size and furniture of the house Mrs. Dashwood was upon the whole well satisfied; for though her former style of life rendered many additions to the latter indispensable, yet to add and improve was a delight to her; and she had at this time ready money enough to supply all that was wanted of greater elegance to the apartments. "As for the house itself, to be sure," said she, "it is too small for our family, but we will make ourselves tolerably comfortable for the present, as it is too late in the year for improvements. Perhaps in the spring, if I have plenty of money, as I dare say I shall, we may think about building. These parlors are both too small for such parties of our friends as I hope to see often collected here; and I have some thoughts of throwing the passage into one of them with perhaps a part of the other, and so leave the remainder of that other for an entrance; this, with a new drawing room which may be easily added, and a bed-chamber and garret above, will make it a very snug little cottage. I could wish the stairs were handsome. But one must not expect every thing; though I suppose it would be no difficult matter to widen them. I shall see how much I am before-hand with the world in the spring, and we will plan our improvements accordingly."

In the mean time, till all these alterations could be made from the savings of an income of five hundred a-year by a woman who never saved in her life, they were wise enough to be contented with the house as it was; and each of them was busy in arranging their particular concerns, and endeavoring, by placing around them books and other possessions, to form themselves a home. Marianne's pianoforte was unpacked and properly disposed of; and Elinor's drawings were affixed to the walls of their sitting room.

In such employments as these they were interrupted soon after breakfast the next day by the entrance of their landlord, who called to welcome them to Barton, and to offer them every accommodation from his own house and garden in which theirs might at present be deficient. Sir John Middleton was a good looking man about forty. He had formerly visited at Stanhill, but it was too long for his young cousins to remember him. His countenance was thoroughly good-humoured; and his manners were as friendly as the style of his letter. Their arrival seemed to afford him real satisfaction, and their comfort to be an object of real solicitude to him. He said much of his earnest desire of their living in the most sociable terms with his family, and pressed them so cordially to dine at Barton Park every day till they were better settled at home, that, though his entreaties were carried to a point of perseverance beyond civility, they could not give offence. His kindness was not confined to words; for within an hour after he left them, a large basket full of garden stuff and fruit arrived from the park, which was followed before the end of the day by a present of game. He insisted, moreover, on conveying all their letters to and from the post for them, and would not be denied the satisfaction of sending them his newspaper every day.

Lady Middleton had sent a very civil message by him, denoting her intention of waiting on Mrs. Dashwood as soon as she could be assured that her visit would be no inconvenience; and as this message was answered by an invitation equally polite, her ladyship was introduced to them the next day.

They were, of course, very anxious to see a person on whom so much of their comfort at Barton must depend; and the elegance of her appearance was favourable to their wishes. Lady Middleton was not more than six or seven and twenty; her face was handsome, her figure tall and striking, and her address graceful. Her manners had all the elegance which her husband's wanted. But they would have been improved by some share of his frankness and warmth; and her visit was long enough to detract something from their first admiration, by shewing that, though perfectly well-bred, she was reserved, cold, and had nothing to say for herself beyond the most common-place inquiry or remark.

Conversation however was not wanted, for Sir John was very chatty, and Lady Middleton had taken the wise precaution of bringing with her their eldest child, a fine little boy about six years old, by which means there was one subject always to be recurred to by the ladies in case of extremity, for they had to enquire his name and age, admire his beauty, and ask him questions which his mother answered for him, while he hung about her and held down his head, to the great surprise of her ladyship, who wondered at his being so shy before company, as he could make noise enough at home. On every formal visit a child ought to be of the party, by way of provision for discourse. In the present case it took up ten minutes to determine whether the boy were most like his father or mother, and in what particular he resembled either, for of course every body differed, and every body was astonished at the opinion of the others.

An opportunity was soon to be given to the Dashwoods of debating on the rest of the children, as Sir John would not leave the house without securing their promise of dining at the park the next day.

CHAPTER VII

Barton Park was about half a mile from the cottage. The ladies had passed near it in their way along the valley, but it was screened from their view at home by the projection of a hill. The house was large and handsome; and the Middletons lived in a style of equal hospitality and elegance. The former was for Sir John's gratification, the latter for that of his lady. They were scarcely ever without some friends staying with them in the house, and they kept more company of every kind than any other family in the neighbourhood. It was necessary to the happiness of both; for however dissimilar in temper and outward behaviour, they strongly resembled each other in that total want of talent and taste which confined their employments, unconnected with such as society produced, within a very narrow compass. Sir John was a sportsman, Lady Middleton a mother. He hunted and shot, and she humoured her children; and these were their only resources. Lady Middleton had the advantage of being able to spoil her children all the year round, while Sir John's independent employments were in existence only half the time. Continual engagements at home and abroad, however, supplied all the deficiencies of nature and education; supported the good spirits of Sir John, and gave exercise to the good breeding of his wife.

Lady Middleton piqued herself upon the elegance of her table, and of all her domestic arrangements; and from this kind of vanity was her greatest enjoyment in any of their parties. But Sir John's satisfaction in society was much more real; he delighted in collecting about him more young people than his house would hold, and the noisier they were the better was he pleased. He was a blessing to all the juvenile part of the neighbourhood, for in summer he was for ever forming parties to eat cold ham and chicken out of doors, and in winter his private balls were numerous enough for any young lady who was not suffering under the unsatiable appetite of fifteen.

The arrival of a new family in the country was always a matter of joy to him, and in every point of view he was charmed with the inhabitants he had now procured for his cottage at Barton. The Miss Dashwoods were young, pretty, and unaffected. It was enough to secure his good opinion; for to be unaffected was all that a pretty girl could want to make her mind as captivating as her person. The friendliness of his disposition made him happy in accommodating those, whose situation might be considered, in comparison with the past, as unfortunate. In showing kindness to his cousins therefore he had the real satisfaction of a good heart; and in settling a family of females only in his cottage, he had all the satisfaction of a sportsman; for a sportsman, though he esteems only those of his sex who are sportsmen likewise, is not often desirous of encouraging their taste by admitting them to a residence within his own manor.

Mrs. Dashwood and her daughters were met at the door of the house by Sir John, who welcomed them to Barton Park with unaffected sincerity; and as he attended them to the drawing room repeated to the young ladies the concern which the same subject had drawn from him the day before, at being unable to get any smart young men to meet them. They would see, he said, only one gentleman there besides himself; a particular friend who was staying at the park, but who was neither very young nor very gay. He hoped they would all excuse the smallness of the party, and could assure them it should never happen so again. He had been to several families that morning in hopes of procuring some addition to their number, but it was moonlight and every body was full of engagements. Luckily Lady Middleton's mother had arrived at Barton within the last hour, and as she was a very cheerful agreeable woman, he hoped the young ladies would not find it so very dull as they might imagine. The young ladies, as well as their mother, were perfectly satisfied with having two entire strangers of the party, and wished for no more.

Mrs. Jennings, Lady Middleton's mother, was a good-humoured, merry, fat, elderly woman, who talked a great deal, seemed very happy, and rather vulgar. She was full of jokes and laughter, and before dinner was over had said many witty things on the subject of lovers and husbands; hoped they had not left their hearts behind them in Sussex, and pretended to see them blush whether they did or not. Marianne was vexed at it for her sister's sake, and turned her eyes towards Elinor to see how she bore these attacks, with an earnestness which gave Elinor far more pain than could arise from such common-place raillery as Mrs. Jennings's.

Colonel Brandon, the friend of Sir John, seemed no more adapted by resemblance of manner to be his friend, than Lady Middleton was to be his wife, or Mrs. Jennings to be Lady Middleton's mother. He was silent and grave. His appearance however was not unpleasing, in spite of his being in the opinion of Marianne and Margaret an absolute old bachelor, for he was on the wrong side of five and thirty; but though his face was not handsome, his countenance was sensible, and his address was particularly gentlemanlike.

There was nothing in any of the party which could recommend them as companions to the Dashwoods; but the cold insipidity of Lady Middleton was so particularly repulsive, that in comparison of it the gravity of Colonel Brandon, and even the boisterous mirth of Sir John and his mother-in-law was interesting. Lady Middleton seemed to be roused to enjoyment only by the entrance of her four noisy children after dinner, who pulled her about, tore her clothes, and put an end to every kind of discourse except what related to themselves.

In the evening, as Marianne was discovered to be musical, she was invited to play. The instrument was unlocked, every body prepared to be charmed, and Marianne, who sang very well, at their request went through the chief of the songs which Lady Middleton had brought into the family on her marriage, and which perhaps had lain ever since in the same position on the pianoforte, for her ladyship had celebrated that event by giving up music, although by her mother's account, she had played extremely well, and by her own was very fond of it.

Marianne's performance was highly applauded. Sir John was loud in his admiration at the end of every song, and as loud in his conversation with the others while every song lasted. Lady Middleton frequently called him to order, wondered how any one's attention could be diverted from music for a moment, and asked Marianne to sing a particular song which Marianne had just finished. Colonel Brandon alone, of all the party, heard her without being in raptures. He paid her only the compliment of attention; and she felt a respect for him on the occasion, which the others had reasonably forfeited by their shameless want of taste. His pleasure in music, though it amounted not to that ecstatic delight which alone could sympathize with her own, was estimable when contrasted against the horrible insensibility of the others; and she was reasonable enough to allow that a man of five and thirty might well have outlived all acuteness of feeling and every exquisite power of enjoyment. She was perfectly disposed to make every allowance for the colonel's advanced state of life which humanity required.

CHAPTER VIII

Mrs. Jennings was a widow with an ample jointure. She had only two daughters, both of whom she had lived to see respectably married, and she had now therefore nothing to do but to marry all the rest of the world. In the promotion of this object she was zealously active, as far as her ability reached; and missed no opportunity of projecting weddings among all the young people of her acquaintance. She was remarkably quick in the discovery of attachments, and had enjoyed the advantage of raising the blushes and the vanity of many a young lady by insinuations of her power over such a young man; and this kind of discernment enabled her soon after her arrival at Barton decisively to pronounce that Colonel Brandon was very much in love with Marianne Dashwood. She rather suspected it to be so, on the very first evening of their being together, from his listening so attentively while she sang to them; and when the visit was returned by the Middletons' dining at the cottage, the fact was ascertained by his listening to her again. It must be so. She was perfectly convinced of it. It would be an excellent match, for *he* was rich, and *she* was handsome. Mrs. Jennings had been anxious to see Colonel Brandon well married, ever since her connection with Sir John first brought him to her knowledge; and she was always anxious to get a good husband for every pretty girl.

The immediate advantage to herself was by no means inconsiderable, for it supplied her with endless jokes against them both. At the park she laughed at the colonel, and in the cottage at Marianne. To the former her raillery was probably, as far as it regarded only himself, perfectly indifferent; but to the latter it was at first incomprehensible; and when its object was understood, she hardly knew whether most to laugh at its absurdity, or censure its impertinence, for she considered it as an unfeeling reflection on the colonel's advanced years, and on his forlorn condition as an old bachelor.

Mrs. Dashwood, who could not think a man five years younger than herself, so exceedingly ancient as he appeared to the youthful fancy of her daughter, ventured to clear Mrs. Jennings from the probability of wishing to throw ridicule on his age.

"But at least, Mamma, you cannot deny the absurdity of the accusation, though you may not think it intentionally ill-natured. Colonel Brandon is certainly younger than Mrs. Jennings, but he is old enough to be *my* father; and if he were ever animated enough to be in love, must have long outlived every sensation of the kind. It is too ridiculous! When is a man to be safe from such wit, if age and infirmity will not protect him?"

"Infirmity!" said Elinor, "Do you call Colonel Brandon infirm? I can easily suppose that his age may appear much greater to you than to my mother; but you can hardly deceive yourself as to his having the use of his limbs!"

"Did not you hear him complain of the rheumatism? And is not that the commonest infirmity of declining life?"

"My dearest child," said her mother, laughing, "at this rate you must be in continual terror of *my* decay; and it must seem to you a miracle that my life has been extended to the advanced age of forty."

"Mamma, you are not doing me justice. I know very well that Colonel Brandon is not old enough to make his friends yet apprehensive of losing him in the course of nature. He may live twenty years longer. But thirty-five has nothing to do with matrimony."

"Perhaps," said Elinor, "thirty-five and seventeen had better not have any thing to do with matrimony together. But if there should by any chance happen to be a woman who is single at seven and twenty, I should not think Colonel Brandon's being thirty-five any objection to his marrying *her*."

"A woman of seven and twenty," said Marianne, after pausing a moment, "can never hope to feel or inspire affection again, and if her home be uncomfortable, or her fortune small, I can suppose that she might bring herself to submit to the offices of a nurse, for the sake of the provision and security of a wife. In his marrying such a woman therefore there would be nothing unsuitable. It would be a compact of convenience, and the world would be satisfied. In my eyes it would be no marriage at all, but that would be nothing. To me it would seem only a commercial exchange, in which each wished to be benefited at the expense of the other."

"It would be impossible, I know," replied Elinor, "to convince you that a woman of seven and twenty could feel for a man of thirty-five anything near enough to love, to make him a desirable companion to her. But I must object to your dooming Colonel Brandon and his wife to the constant confinement of a sick chamber, merely because he chanced to complain yesterday (a very cold damp day) of a slight rheumatic feel in one of his shoulders."

"But he talked of flannel waistcoats," said Marianne; "and with me a flannel waistcoat is invariably connected with aches, cramps, rheumatisms, and every species of ailment that can afflict the old and the feeble."

"Had he been only in a violent fever, you would not have despised him half so much. Confess, Marianne, is not there something interesting to you in the flushed cheek, hollow eye, and quick pulse of a fever?"

Soon after this, upon Elinor's leaving the room, "Mamma," said Marianne, "I have an alarm on the subject of illness which I cannot conceal from you. I am sure Edward Ferrars is not well. We have now been here almost a fortnight, and yet he does not come. Nothing but real indisposition could occasion this extraordinary delay. What else can detain him at Norland?"

"Had you any idea of his coming so soon?" said Mrs. Dashwood. "I had none. On the contrary, if I have felt any anxiety at all on the subject, it has been in recollecting that he sometimes showed a want of pleasure and readiness in accepting my invitation, when I talked of his coming to Barton. Does Elinor expect him already?"

"I have never mentioned it to her, but of course she must."

"I rather think you are mistaken, for when I was talking to her yesterday of getting a new grate for the spare bedchamber, she observed that there was no immediate hurry for it, as it was not likely that the room would be wanted for some time."

"How strange this is! What can be the meaning of it! But the whole of their behaviour to each other has been unaccountable! How cold, how composed were their last adieus! How languid their conversation the last evening of their being together! In Edward's farewell there was no distinction between Elinor and me: it was the good wishes of an affectionate brother to both. Twice did I leave them purposely together in the course of the last morning, and each time did he most unaccountably follow me out of the room. And Elinor, in quitting Norland and Edward, cried not as I did. Even now her self-command is invariable. When is she dejected or melancholy? When does she try to avoid society, or appear restless and dissatisfied in it?"

CHAPTER IX

The Dashwoods were now settled at Barton with tolerable comfort to themselves. The house and the garden, with all the objects surrounding them, were now become familiar, and the ordinary pursuits which had given to Norland half its charms were engaged in again with far greater enjoyment than Norland had been able to afford, since the loss of their father. Sir John Middleton, who called on them every day for the first fortnight, and who was not in the habit of seeing much occupation at home, could not conceal his amazement on finding them always employed.

Their visitors, except those from Barton Park, were not many; for, in spite of Sir John's urgent entreaties that they would mix more in the neighbourhood, and repeated assurances of his carriage being always at their service, the independence of Mrs. Dashwood's spirit overcame the wish of society for her children; and she was resolute in declining to visit any family beyond the distance of a walk. There were but few who could be so classed; and it was not all of them that were attainable. About a mile and a half from the cottage, along the narrow winding valley of Allenham, which issued from that of Barton, as formerly described, the girls had, in one of their earliest walks, discovered an ancient respectable looking mansion which, by reminding them a little of Norland, interested their imagination and made them wish to be better acquainted with it. But they learnt, on enquiry, that its possessor, an elderly lady of very good character, was unfortunately too infirm to mix with the world, and never stirred from home.

The whole country about them abounded in beautiful walks. The high downs which invited them from almost every window of the cottage to seek the exquisite enjoyment of air on their summits, were a happy alternative when the dirt of the valleys beneath shut up their superior beauties; and towards one of these hills did Marianne and Margaret one memorable morning direct their steps, attracted by the partial sunshine of a showery sky, and unable longer to bear the confinement which the settled rain of the two preceding days had occasioned. The weather was not tempting enough to draw the two others from their pencil and their book, in spite of Marianne's declaration that the day would be lastingly fair, and that every threatening cloud would be drawn off from their hills; and the two girls set off together.

They gaily ascended the downs, rejoicing in their own penetration at every glimpse of blue sky; and when they caught in their faces the animating gales of a high south-westerly wind, they pitied the fears which had prevented their mother and Elinor from sharing such delightful sensations.

"Is there a felicity in the world," said Marianne, "superior to this? Margaret, we will walk here at least two hours."

Margaret agreed, and they pursued their way against the wind, resisting it with laughing delight for about twenty minutes longer, when suddenly the clouds united over their heads, and a driving rain set full in their face. Chagrined and surprised, they were obliged, though unwillingly, to turn back, for no shelter was nearer than their own house. One consolation however remained for them, to which the exigence of the moment gave more than usual propriety; it was that of running with all possible speed down the steep side of the hill which led immediately to their garden gate.

They set off. Marianne had at first the advantage, but a false step brought her suddenly to the ground; and Margaret, unable to stop herself to assist her, was involuntarily hurried along, and reached the bottom in safety.

A gentleman carrying a gun, with two pointers playing round him, was passing up the hill and within a few yards of Marianne, when her accident happened. He put down his gun and ran to her assistance. She had raised herself from the ground, but her foot had been twisted in her fall, and she was scarcely able to stand. The gentleman offered his services; and perceiving that her modesty declined what her situation rendered necessary, took her up in his arms without farther delay, and carried her down the hill. Then passing through the garden, the gate of which had been left open by Margaret, he bore her directly into the house, whither Margaret was just arrived, and quitted not his hold till he had seated her in a chair in the parlour.

Elinor and her mother rose up in amazement at their entrance, and while the eyes of both were fixed on him with an evident wonder and a secret admiration which equally sprung from his appearance, he apologized for his intrusion by relating its cause, in a manner so frank and so graceful that his person, which was uncommonly handsome, received additional charms from his voice and expression. Had he been even old, ugly, and vulgar, the gratitude and kindness of Mrs. Dashwood would have been secured by any act of attention to her child; but the influence of youth, beauty, and elegance, gave an interest to the action which came home to her feelings.

She thanked him again and again; and, with a sweetness of address which always attended her, invited him to be seated. But this he declined, as he was dirty and wet. Mrs. Dashwood then begged to know to whom she was obliged. His name, he replied, was Willoughby, and his present home was at Allenham, from whence he hoped she would allow him the honour of calling tomorrow to enquire after Miss Dashwood. The honour was readily granted, and he then departed, to make himself still more interesting, in the midst of a heavy rain.

His manly beauty and more than common gracefulness were instantly the theme of general admiration, and the laugh which his gallantry raised against Marianne received particular spirit from his exterior attractions. Marianne herself had seen less of his person that the rest, for the confusion which crimsoned over her face, on his lifting her up, had robbed her of the power of regarding him after their entering the house. But she had seen enough of him to join in all the admiration of the others, and with an energy which always adorned her praise. His person and air were equal to what her fancy had ever drawn for the hero of a favourite story; and in his carrying her into the house with so little previous formality, there was a rapidity of thought which particularly recommended the action to her. Every circumstance belonging to him was interesting. His name was good, his residence was in their favourite village, and she soon found out that of all manly dresses a shooting-jacket was the most becoming. Her imagination was busy, her reflections were pleasant, and the pain of a sprained ankle was disregarded.

Sir John called on them as soon as the next interval of fair weather that morning allowed him to get out of doors; and Marianne's accident being related to him, he was eagerly asked whether he knew any gentleman of the name of Willoughby at Allenham.

"Willoughby!" cried Sir John; "what, is *he* in the country? That is good news however; I will ride over tomorrow, and ask him to dinner on Thursday."

"You know him then," said Mrs. Dashwood.

"Know him! to be sure I do. Why, he is down here every year."

"And what sort of a young man is he?"

"As good a kind of fellow as ever lived, I assure you. A very decent shot, and there is not a bolder rider in England."

"And is that all you can say for him?" cried Marianne, indignantly. "But what are his manners on more intimate acquaintance? What his pursuits, his talents, and genius?"

Sir John was rather puzzled.

"Upon my soul," said he, "I do not know much about him as to all *that*. But he is a pleasant, good humoured fellow, and has got the nicest little black bitch of a pointer I ever saw. Was she out with him today?"

But Marianne could no more satisfy him as to the colour of Mr. Willoughby's pointer, than he could describe to her the shades of his mind.

"But who is he?" said Elinor. "Where does he come from? Has he a house at Allenham?"

On this point Sir John could give more certain intelligence; and he told them that Mr. Willoughby had no property of his own in the country; that he resided there only while he was visiting the old lady at Allenham Court, to whom he was related, and whose possessions he was to inherit; adding, "Yes, yes, he is very well worth catching I can tell you, Miss Dashwood; he has a pretty little estate of his own in Somersetshire besides; and if I were you, I would not give him up to my younger sister, in spite of all this tumbling down hills. Miss Marianne must not expect to have all the men to herself. Brandon will be jealous, if she does not take care."

"I do not believe," said Mrs. Dashwood, with a good humoured smile, "that Mr. Willoughby will be incommoded by the attempts of either of *my* daughters towards what you call *catching* him. It is not an employment to which they have been brought up. Men are very safe with us, let them be ever so rich. I am glad to find, however, from what you say, that he is a respectable young man, and one whose acquaintance will not be ineligible."

"He is as good a sort of fellow, I believe, as ever lived," repeated Sir John. "I remember last Christmas at a little hop at the park, he danced from eight o'clock till four, without once sitting down."

"Did he indeed?" cried Marianne with sparkling eyes, "and with elegance, with spirit?"

"Yes; and he was up again at eight to ride to covert."

"That is what I like; that is what a young man ought to be. Whatever be his pursuits, his eagerness in them should know no moderation, and leave him no sense of fatigue."

"Aye, aye, I see how it will be," said Sir John, "I see how it will be. You will be setting your cap at him now, and never think of poor Brandon."

"That is an expression, Sir John," said Marianne, warmly, "which I particularly dislike. I abhor every common-place phrase by which wit is intended; and 'setting one's cap at a man,' or 'making a conquest,' are the most odious of all. Their tendency is gross and illiberal; and if their construction could ever be deemed clever, time has long ago destroyed all its ingenuity."

Sir John did not much understand this reproof; but he laughed as heartily as if he did, and then replied,

"Ay, you will make conquests enough, I dare say, one way or other. Poor Brandon! He is quite smitten already, and he is very well worth setting your cap at, I can tell you, in spite of all this tumbling about and spraining of ankles."

CHAPTER X

Marianne's preserver, as Margaret, with more elegance than precision, styled Willoughby, called at the cottage early the next morning to make his personal enquiries. He was received by Mrs. Dashwood with more than politeness; with a kindness which Sir John's account of him and her own gratitude prompted; and every thing that passed during the visit tended to assure him of the sense, elegance, mutual affection, and domestic comfort of the family to whom accident had now introduced him. Of their personal charms he had not required a second interview to be convinced.

Miss Dashwood had a delicate complexion, regular features, and a remarkably pretty figure. Marianne was still handsomer. Her form, though not so correct as her sister's, in having the advantage of height, was more striking; and her face was so lovely, that when in the common cant of praise, she was called a beautiful girl, truth was less violently outraged than usually happens. Her skin was very brown, but, from its transparency, her complexion was uncommonly brilliant; her features were all good; her smile was sweet and attractive; and in her eyes, which were very dark, there was a life, a spirit, an eagerness, which could hardily be seen without delight. From Willoughby their expression was at first held back, by the embarrassment which the remembrance of his assistance created. But when this passed away, when her spirits became collected, when she saw that to the perfect good-breeding of the gentleman, he united frankness and vivacity, and above all, when she heard him declare, that of music and dancing he was passionately fond, she gave him such a look of approbation as secured the largest share of his discourse to herself for the rest of his stay.

It was only necessary to mention any favourite amusement to engage her to talk. She could not be silent when such points were introduced, and she had neither shyness nor reserve in their discussion. They speedily discovered that their enjoyment of dancing and music was mutual, and that it arose from a general conformity of judgment in all that related to either. Encouraged by this to a further examination of his opinions, she proceeded to question him on the subject of books; her favourite authors were brought forward and dwelt upon with so rapturous a delight, that any young man of five and twenty must have been insensible indeed, not to become an immediate convert to the excellence of such works, however disregarded before. Their taste was strikingly alike. The same books, the same passages were idolized by each—or if any difference appeared, any objection arose, it lasted no longer than till the force of her arguments and the brightness of her eyes could be displayed. He acquiesced in all her decisions, caught all her enthusiasm; and long before his visit concluded, they conversed with the familiarity of a long-established acquaintance.

"Well, Marianne," said Elinor, as soon as he had left them, "for *one* morning I think you have done pretty well. You have already ascertained Mr. Willoughby's opinion in almost every matter of importance. You know what he thinks of Cowper and Scott; you are certain of his estimating their beauties as he ought, and you have received every assurance of his admiring Pope no more than is proper. But how is your acquaintance to be long supported, under such extraordinary despatch of every subject for discourse? You will soon have exhausted each favourite topic. Another meeting will suffice to explain his sentiments on picturesque beauty, and second marriages, and then you can have nothing farther to ask."

"Elinor," cried Marianne, "is this fair? Is this just? Are my ideas so scanty? But I see what you mean. I have been too much at my ease, too happy, too frank. I have erred against every common-place notion of decorum; I have been open and sincere where I ought to have been reserved, spiritless, dull, and deceitful—had I talked only of the weather and the roads, and had I spoken only once in ten minutes, this reproach would have been spared."

"My love," said her mother, "you must not be offended with Elinor—she was only in jest. I should scold her myself, if she were capable of wishing to check the delight of your conversation with our new friend." Marianne was softened in a moment.

Willoughby, on his side, gave every proof of his pleasure in their acquaintance, which an evident wish of improving it could offer. He came to them every day. To enquire after Marianne was at first his excuse; but the encouragement of his reception, to which every day gave greater kindness, made such an excuse unnecessary before it had ceased to be possible, by Marianne's perfect recovery. She was confined for some days to the house; but never had any confinement been less irksome. Willoughby was a young man of good abilities, quick imagination, lively spirits, and open, affectionate manners. He was exactly formed to engage Marianne's heart, for with all this, he joined not only a captivating person, but a natural ardour of mind which was now roused and increased by the example of her own, and which recommended him to her affection beyond everything else.

His society became gradually her most exquisite enjoyment. They read, they talked, they sang together; his musical talents were considerable; and he read with all the sensibility and spirit which Edward had unfortunately wanted.

In Mrs. Dashwood's estimation he was as faultless as in Marianne's; and Elinor saw nothing to censure in him but a propensity, in which he strongly resembled and peculiarly delighted her sister, of saying too much what he thought on every occasion, without attention to persons or circumstances. In hastily forming and giving his opinion of other people, in sacrificing general politeness to the enjoyment of undivided attention where his heart was engaged, and in slighting too easily the forms of worldly propriety, he displayed a want of caution which Elinor could not approve, in spite of all that he and Marianne could say in its support.

Marianne began now to perceive that the desperation which had seized her at sixteen and a half, of ever seeing a man who could satisfy her ideas of perfection, had been rash and unjustifiable. Willoughby was all that her fancy had delineated in that unhappy hour and in every brighter period, as capable of attaching her; and his behaviour declared his wishes to be in that respect as earnest, as his abilities were strong.

Her mother too, in whose mind not one speculative thought of their marriage had been raised, by his prospect of riches, was led before the end of a week to hope and expect it; and secretly to congratulate herself on having gained two such sons-in-law as Edward and Willoughby.

Colonel Brandon's partiality for Marianne, which had so early been discovered by his friends, now first became perceptible to Elinor, when it ceased to be noticed by them. Their attention and wit were drawn off to his more fortunate rival; and the raillery which the other had incurred before any partiality arose, was removed when his feelings began really to call for the ridicule so justly annexed to sensibility. Elinor was obliged, though unwillingly, to believe that the sentiments which Mrs. Jennings had assigned him for her own satisfaction, were now actually excited by her sister; and that however a general resemblance of disposition between the parties might forward the affection of Mr. Willoughby, an equally striking opposition of character was no hindrance to the regard of Colonel Brandon. She saw it with concern; for what could a silent man of five and thirty hope, when opposed to a very lively one of five and twenty? And as she could not even wish him successful, she heartily wished him indifferent. She liked him—in spite of his gravity and reserve, she beheld in him an object of interest. His manners, though serious, were mild; and his reserve appeared rather the result of some oppression of spirits than of any natural gloominess of temper. Sir John had dropped hints of past injuries and disappointments, which justified her belief of his being an unfortunate man, and she regarded him with respect and compassion.

Perhaps she pitied and esteemed him the more because he was slighted by Willoughby and Marianne, who, prejudiced against him for being neither lively nor young, seemed resolved to undervalue his merits.

"Brandon is just the kind of man," said Willoughby one day, when they were talking of him together, "whom every body speaks well of, and nobody cares about; whom all are delighted to see, and nobody remembers to talk to."

"That is exactly what I think of him," cried Marianne.

"Do not boast of it, however," said Elinor, "for it is injustice in both of you. He is highly esteemed by all the family at the park, and I never see him myself without taking pains to converse with him."

"That he is patronised by *you*," replied Willoughby, "is certainly in his favour; but as for the esteem of the others, it is a reproach in itself. Who would submit to the indignity of being approved by such a woman as Lady Middleton and Mrs. Jennings, that could command the indifference of anybody else?"

"But perhaps the abuse of such people as yourself and Marianne will make amends for the regard of Lady Middleton and her mother. If their praise is censure, your censure may be praise, for they are not more undiscerning, than you are prejudiced and unjust."

"In defence of your protege you can even be saucy."

"My protege, as you call him, is a sensible man; and sense will always have attractions for me. Yes, Marianne, even in a man between thirty and forty. He has seen a great deal of the world; has been abroad, has read, and has a thinking mind. I have found him capable of giving me much information on various subjects; and he has always answered my inquiries with readiness of good-breeding and good nature."

"That is to say," cried Marianne contemptuously, "he has told you, that in the East Indies the climate is hot, and the mosquitoes are troublesome."

"He *would* have told me so, I doubt not, had I made any such inquiries, but they happened to be points on which I had been previously informed."

"Perhaps," said Willoughby, "his observations may have extended to the existence of nabobs, gold mohrs, and palanquins."

"I may venture to say that *his* observations have stretched much further than your candour. But why should you dislike him?"

"I do not dislike him. I consider him, on the contrary, as a very respectable man, who has everybody's good word, and nobody's notice; who, has more money than he can spend, more time than he knows how to employ, and two new coats every year."

"Add to which," cried Marianne, "that he has neither genius, taste, nor spirit. That his understanding has no brilliancy, his feelings no ardour, and his voice no expression."

"You decide on his imperfections so much in the mass," replied Elinor, "and so much on the strength of your own imagination, that the commendation I am able to give of him is comparatively cold and insipid. I can only pronounce him to be a sensible man, well-bred, well-informed, of gentle address, and, I believe, possessing an amiable heart."

"Miss Dashwood," cried Willoughby, "you are now using me unkindly. You are endeavouring to disarm me by reason, and to convince me against my will. But it will not do. You shall find me as stubborn as you can be artful. I have three unanswerable reasons for disliking Colonel Brandon; he threatened me with rain when I wanted it to be fine; he has found fault with the hanging of my curricle, and I cannot persuade him to buy my brown mare. If it will be any satisfaction to you, however, to be told, that I believe his character to be in other respects irreproachable, I am ready to confess it. And in return for an acknowledgment, which must give me some pain, you cannot deny me the privilege of disliking him as much as ever."

CHAPTER XI

Little had Mrs. Dashwood or her daughters imagined when they first came into Devonshire, that so many engagements would arise to occupy their time as shortly presented themselves, or that they should have such frequent invitations and such constant visitors as to leave them little leisure for serious employment. Yet such was the case. When Marianne was recovered, the schemes of amusement at home and abroad, which Sir John had been previously forming, were put into execution. The private balls at the park then began; and parties on the water were made and accomplished as often as a showery October would allow. In every meeting of the kind Willoughby was included; and the ease and familiarity which naturally attended these parties were exactly calculated to give increasing intimacy to his acquaintance with the Dashwoods, to afford him opportunity of witnessing the excellencies of Marianne, of marking his animated admiration of her, and of receiving, in her behaviour to himself, the most pointed assurance of her affection.

Elinor could not be surprised at their attachment. She only wished that it were less openly shewn; and once or twice did venture to suggest the propriety of some self-command to Marianne. But Marianne abhorred all concealment where no real disgrace could attend unreserve; and to aim at the restraint of sentiments which were not in themselves illaudable, appeared to her not merely an unnecessary effort, but a disgraceful subjection of reason to common-place and mistaken notions. Willoughby thought the same; and their behaviour at all times, was an illustration of their opinions.

When he was present she had no eyes for any one else. Everything he did, was right. Every thing he said, was clever. If their evenings at the park were concluded with cards, he cheated himself and all the rest of the party to get her a good hand. If dancing formed the amusement of the night, they were partners for half the time; and when obliged to separate for a couple of dances, were careful to stand together and scarcely spoke a word to any body else. Such conduct made them of course most exceedingly laughed at; but ridicule could not shame, and seemed hardly to provoke them.

Mrs. Dashwood entered into all their feelings with a warmth which left her no inclination for checking this excessive display of them. To her it was but the natural consequence of a strong affection in a young and ardent mind.

This was the season of happiness to Marianne. Her heart was devoted to Willoughby, and the fond attachment to Norland, which she brought with her from Sussex, was more likely to be softened than she had thought it possible before, by the charms which his society bestowed on her present home.

Elinor's happiness was not so great. Her heart was not so much at ease, nor her satisfaction in their amusements so pure. They afforded her no companion that could make amends for what she had left behind, nor that could teach her to think of Norland with less regret than ever. Neither Lady Middleton nor Mrs. Jennings could supply to her the conversation she missed; although the latter was an everlasting talker, and from the first had regarded her with a kindness which ensured her a large share of her discourse. She had already repeated her own history to Elinor three or four times; and had Elinor's memory been equal to her means of improvement, she might have known very early in their acquaintance all the particulars of Mr. Jenning's last illness, and what he said to his wife a few minutes before he died. Lady Middleton was more agreeable than her mother only in being more silent. Elinor needed little observation to perceive that her reserve was a mere calmness of manner with which sense had nothing to do. Towards her husband and mother she was the same as to them; and intimacy was therefore neither to be looked for nor desired. She had nothing to say one day that she had not said the day before. Her insipidity was invariable, for even her spirits were always the same; and though she did not oppose the parties arranged by her husband, provided every thing were conducted in style and her two eldest children attended her, she never appeared to receive more enjoyment from them than she might have experienced in sitting at home—and so little did her presence add to the pleasure of the others, by any share in their conversation, that they were sometimes only reminded of her being amongst them by her solicitude about her troublesome boys.

In Colonel Brandon alone, of all her new acquaintance, did Elinor find a person who could in any degree claim the respect of abilities, excite the interest of friendship, or give pleasure as a companion.

Willoughby was out of the question. Her admiration and regard, even her sisterly regard, was all his own; but he was a lover; his attentions were wholly Marianne's, and a far less agreeable man might have been more generally pleasing. Colonel Brandon, unfortunately for himself, had no such encouragement to think only of Marianne, and in conversing with Elinor he found the greatest consolation for the indifference of her sister.

Elinor's compassion for him increased, as she had reason to suspect that the misery of disappointed love had already been known to him. This suspicion was given by some words which accidently dropped from him one evening at the park, when they were sitting down together by mutual consent, while the others were dancing. His eyes were fixed on Marianne, and, after a silence of some minutes, he said, with a faint smile, "Your sister, I understand, does not approve of second attachments."

"No," replied Elinor, "her opinions are all romantic."

"Or rather, as I believe, she considers them impossible to exist."

"I believe she does. But how she contrives it without reflecting on the character of her own father, who had himself two wives, I know not. A few years however will settle her opinions on the reasonable basis of common sense and observation; and then they may be more easy to define and to justify than they now are, by anybody but herself."

"This will probably be the case," he replied; "and yet there is something so amiable in the prejudices of a young mind, that one is sorry to see them give way to the reception of more general opinions."

"I cannot agree with you there," said Elinor. "There are inconveniences attending such feelings as Marianne's, which all the charms of enthusiasm and ignorance of the world cannot atone for. Her systems have all the unfortunate tendency of setting propriety at nought; and a better acquaintance with the world is what I look forward to as her greatest possible advantage."

After a short pause he resumed the conversation by saying,

"Does your sister make no distinction in her objections against a second attachment? or is it equally criminal in every body? Are those who have been disappointed in their first choice, whether from the inconstancy of its object, or the perverseness of circumstances, to be equally indifferent during the rest of their lives?"

"Upon my word, I am not acquainted with the minutiae of her

principles. I only know that I never yet heard her admit any instance of a second attachment's being pardonable."

"This," said he, "cannot hold; but a change, a total change of sentiments—no, no, do not desire it; for when the romantic refinements of a young mind are obliged to give way, how frequently are they succeeded by such opinions as are but too common, and too dangerous! I speak from experience. I once knew a lady who in temper and mind greatly resembled your sister, who thought and judged like her, but who from an inforced change—from a series of unfortunate circumstances"—here he stopt suddenly; appeared to think that he had said too much, and by his countenance gave rise to conjectures, which might not otherwise have entered Elinor's head. The lady would probably have passed without suspicion, had he not convinced Miss Dashwood that what concerned her ought not to escape his lips. As it was, it required but a slight effort of fancy to connect his emotion with the tender recollection of past regard. Elinor attempted no more. But Marianne, in her place, would not have done so little. The whole story would have been speedily formed under her active imagination; and every thing established in the most melancholy order of disastrous love.

CHAPTER XII

As Elinor and Marianne were walking together the next morning the latter communicated a piece of news to her sister, which in spite of all that she knew before of Marianne's imprudence and want of thought, surprised her by its extravagant testimony of both. Marianne told her, with the greatest delight, that Willoughby had given her a horse, one that he had bred himself on his estate in Somersetshire, and which was exactly calculated to carry a woman. Without considering that it was not in her mother's plan to keep any horse, that if she were to alter her resolution in favour of this gift, she must buy another for the servant, and keep a servant to ride it, and after all, build a stable to receive them, she had accepted the present without hesitation, and told her sister of it in raptures.

"He intends to send his groom into Somersetshire immediately for it," she added, "and when it arrives we will ride every day. You shall share its use with me. Imagine to yourself, my dear Elinor, the delight of a gallop on some of these downs."

Most unwilling was she to awaken from such a dream of felicity to comprehend all the unhappy truths which attended the affair; and for some time she refused to submit to them. As to an additional servant, the expense would be a trifle; Mamma she was sure would never object to it; and any horse would do for *him*; he might always get one at the park; as to a stable, the merest shed would be sufficient. Elinor then ventured to doubt the propriety of her receiving such a present from a man so little, or at least so lately known to her. This was too much.

"You are mistaken, Elinor," said she warmly, "in supposing I know very little of Willoughby. I have not known him long indeed, but I am much better acquainted with him, than I am with any other creature in the world, except yourself and mama. It is not time or opportunity that is to determine intimacy—it is disposition alone. Seven years would be insufficient to make some people acquainted with each other, and seven days are more than enough for others. I should hold myself guilty of greater impropriety in accepting a horse from my brother, than from Willoughby. Of John I know very little, though we have lived together for years; but of Willoughby my judgment has long been formed."

Elinor thought it wisest to touch that point no more. She knew her sister's temper. Opposition on so tender a subject would only attach her the more to her own opinion. But by an appeal to her affection for her mother, by representing the inconveniences which that indulgent mother must draw on herself, if (as would probably be the case) she consented to this increase of establishment, Marianne was shortly subdued; and she promised not to tempt her mother to such imprudent kindness by mentioning the offer, and to tell Willoughby when she saw him next, that it must be declined.

She was faithful to her word; and when Willoughby called at the cottage, the same day, Elinor heard her express her disappointment to him in a low voice, on being obliged to forego the acceptance of his present. The reasons for this alteration were at the same time related, and they were such as to make further entreaty on his side impossible. His concern however was very apparent; and after expressing it with earnestness, he added, in the same low voice, "But, Marianne, the horse is still yours, though you cannot use it now. I shall keep it only till you can claim it. When you leave Barton to form your own establishment in a more lasting home, Queen Mab shall receive you."

This was all overheard by Miss Dashwood; and in the whole of the sentence, in his manner of pronouncing it, and in his addressing her sister by her Christian name alone, she instantly saw an intimacy so decided, a meaning so direct, as marked a perfect agreement between them. From that moment she doubted not of their being engaged to each other; and the belief of it created no other surprise than that she, or any of their friends, should be left by tempers so frank, to discover it by accident.

Margaret related something to her the next day, which placed this matter in a still clearer light. Willoughby had spent the preceding evening with them, and Margaret, by being left some time in the parlour with only him and Marianne, had had opportunity for observations, which, with a most important face, she communicated to her eldest sister, when they were next by themselves.

"Oh, Elinor!" she cried, "I have such a secret to tell you about Marianne. I am sure she will be married to Mr. Willoughby very soon."

"You have said so," replied Elinor, "almost every day since they first met on High-church Down; and they had not known each other a week, I believe, before you were certain that Marianne wore his picture round her neck; but it turned out to be only the miniature of our great uncle."

"But indeed this is quite another thing. I am sure they will be married very soon, for he has got a lock of her hair."

"Take care, Margaret. It may be only the hair of some great uncle of *his*."

"But, indeed, Elinor, it is Marianne's. I am almost sure it is, for I saw him cut it off. Last night after tea, when you and mama went out of the room, they were whispering and talking together as fast as could be, and he seemed to be begging something of her, and presently he took up her scissors and cut off a long lock of her hair, for it was all tumbled down her back; and he kissed it, and folded it up in a piece of white paper; and put it into his pocket-book."

For such particulars, stated on such authority, Elinor could not withhold her credit; nor was she disposed to it, for the circumstance was in perfect unison with what she had heard and seen herself.

Margaret's sagacity was not always displayed in a way so satisfactory to her sister. When Mrs. Jennings attacked her one evening at the park, to give the name of the young man who was Elinor's particular favourite, which had been long a matter of great curiosity to her, Margaret answered by looking at her sister, and saying, "I must not tell, may I, Elinor?"

This of course made everybody laugh; and Elinor tried to laugh too. But the effort was painful. She was convinced that Margaret had fixed on a person whose name she could not bear with composure to become a standing joke with Mrs. Jennings.

Marianne felt for her most sincerely; but she did more harm than good to the cause, by turning very red and saying in an angry manner to Margaret,

"Remember that whatever your conjectures may be, you have no right to repeat them."

"I never had any conjectures about it," replied Margaret; "it was you who told me of it yourself."

This increased the mirth of the company, and Margaret was eagerly pressed to say something more.

"Oh! Pray, Miss Margaret, let us know all about it," said Mrs. Jennings. "What is the gentleman's name?"

"I must not tell, ma'am. But I know very well what it is; and I know where he is too."

"Yes, yes, we can guess where he is; at his own house at Norland to be sure. He is the curate of the parish I dare say."

"No, *that* he is not. He is of no profession at all."

"Margaret," said Marianne with great warmth, "you know that all this is an invention of your own, and that there is no such person in existence."

"Well, then, he is lately dead, Marianne, for I am sure there was such a man once, and his name begins with an F."

Most grateful did Elinor feel to Lady Middleton for observing, at this moment, "that it rained very hard," though she believed the interruption to proceed less from any attention to her, than from her ladyship's great dislike of all such inelegant subjects of raillery as delighted her husband and mother. The idea however started by her, was immediately pursued by Colonel Brandon, who was on every occasion mindful of the feelings of others; and much was said on the subject of rain by both of them. Willoughby opened the piano-forte, and asked Marianne to sit down to it; and thus amidst the various endeavours of different people to quit the topic, it fell to the ground. But not so easily did Elinor recover from the alarm into which it had thrown her.

A party was formed this evening for going on the following day to see a very fine place about twelve miles from Barton, belonging to a brother-in-law of Colonel Brandon, without whose interest it could not be seen, as the proprietor, who was then abroad, had left strict orders on that head. The grounds were declared to be highly beautiful, and Sir John, who was particularly warm in their praise, might be allowed to be a tolerable judge, for he had formed parties to visit them, at least, twice every summer for the last ten years. They contained a noble piece of water; a sail on which was to a form a great part of the morning's amusement; cold provisions were to be taken, open carriages only to be employed, and every thing conducted in the usual style of a complete party of pleasure.

To some few of the company it appeared rather a bold undertaking, considering the time of year, and that it had rained every day for the last fortnight—and Mrs. Dashwood, who had already a cold, was persuaded by Elinor to stay at home.

CHAPTER XIII

Their intended excursion to Whitwell turned out very different from what Elinor had expected. She was prepared to be wet through, fatigued, and frightened; but the event was still more unfortunate, for they did not go at all.

By ten o'clock the whole party was assembled at the park, where they were to breakfast. The morning was rather favourable, though it had rained all night, as the clouds were then dispersing across the sky, and the sun frequently appeared. They were all in high spirits and good humour, eager to be happy, and determined to submit to the greatest inconveniences and hardships rather than be otherwise.

While they were at breakfast the letters were brought in. Among the rest there was one for Colonel Brandon—he took it, looked at the direction, changed colour, and immediately left the room.

"What is the matter with Brandon?" said Sir John.

Nobody could tell.

"I hope he has had no bad news," said Lady Middleton. "It must be something extraordinary that could make Colonel Brandon leave my breakfast table so suddenly."

In about five minutes he returned.

"No bad news, Colonel, I hope," said Mrs. Jennings, as soon as he entered the room.

"None at all, ma'am, I thank you."

"Was it from Avignon? I hope it is not to say that your sister is worse."

"No, ma'am. It came from town, and is merely a letter of business."

"But how came the hand to discompose you so much, if it was only a letter of business? Come, come, this won't do, Colonel; so let us hear the truth of it."

"My dear madam," said Lady Middleton, "recollect what you are saying."

"Perhaps it is to tell you that your cousin Fanny is married?" said Mrs. Jennings, without attending to her daughter's reproof.

"No, indeed, it is not."

"Well, then, I know who it is from, Colonel. And I hope she is well."

"Whom do you mean, ma'am?" said he, colouring a little.

"Oh! You know who I mean."

"I am particularly sorry, ma'am," said he, addressing Lady Middleton, "that I should receive this letter today, for it is on business which requires my immediate attendance in town."

"In town!" cried Mrs. Jennings. "What can you have to do in town at this time of year?"

"My own loss is great," he continued, "in being obliged to leave so agreeable a party; but I am the more concerned, as I fear my presence is necessary to gain your admittance at Whitwell."

What a blow upon them all was this!

"But if you write a note to the housekeeper, Mr. Brandon," said Marianne, eagerly, "will it not be sufficient?"

He shook his head.

"We must go," said Sir John. "It shall not be put off when we are so near it. You cannot go to town till tomorrow, Brandon, that is all."

"I wish it could be so easily settled. But it is not in my power to delay my journey for one day!"

"If you would but let us know what your business is," said Mrs. Jennings, "we might see whether it could be put off or not."

"You would not be six hours later," said Willoughby, "if you were to defer your journey till our return."

"I cannot afford to lose *one* hour."

Elinor then heard Willoughby say, in a low voice to Marianne, "There are some people who cannot bear a party of pleasure. Brandon is one of them. He was afraid of catching cold I dare say, and invented this trick for getting out of it. I would lay fifty guineas the letter was of his own writing."

"I have no doubt of it," replied Marianne.

"There is no persuading you to change your mind, Brandon, I know of old," said Sir John, "when once you are determined on anything. But, however, I hope you will think better of it. Consider, here are the two Miss Careys come over from Newton, the three Miss Dashwoods walked up from the cottage, and Mr. Willoughby got up two hours before his usual time, on purpose to go to Whitwell."

Colonel Brandon again repeated his sorrow at being the cause of disappointing the party; but at the same time declared it to be unavoidable.

"Well, then, when will you come back again?"

"I hope we shall see you at Barton," added her ladyship, "as soon as you can conveniently leave town; and we must put off the party to Whitwell till you return."

"You are very obliging. But it is so uncertain, when I may have it in my power to return, that I dare not engage for it at all."

"Oh! He must and shall come back," cried Sir John. "If he is not here by the end of the week, I shall go after him."

"Ay, so do, Sir John," cried Mrs. Jennings, "and then perhaps you may find out what his business is."

"I do not want to pry into other men's concerns. I suppose it is something he is ashamed of."

Colonel Brandon's horses were announced.

"You do not go to town on horseback, do you?" added Sir John.

"No. Only to Honiton. I shall then go post."

"Well, as you are resolved to go, I wish you a good journey. But you had better change your mind."

"I assure you it is not in my power."

He then took leave of the whole party.

"Is there no chance of my seeing you and your sisters in town this winter, Miss Dashwood?"

"I am afraid, none at all."

"Then I must bid you farewell for a longer time than I should wish to do."

To Marianne, he merely bowed and said nothing.

"Come Colonel," said Mrs. Jennings, "before you go, do let us know what you are going about."

He wished her a good morning, and, attended by Sir John, left the room.

The complaints and lamentations which politeness had hitherto restrained, now burst forth universally; and they all agreed again and again how provoking it was to be so disappointed.

"I can guess what his business is, however," said Mrs. Jennings exultingly.

"Can you, ma'am?" said almost everybody.

"Yes; it is about Miss Williams, I am sure."

"And who is Miss Williams?" asked Marianne.

"What! Do not you know who Miss Williams is? I am sure you must have heard of her before. She is a relation of the Colonel's, my dear; a very near relation. We will not say how near, for fear of shocking the young ladies." Then, lowering her voice a little, she said to Elinor, "She is his natural daughter."

"Indeed!"

"Oh, yes; and as like him as she can stare. I dare say the Colonel will leave her all his fortune."

When Sir John returned, he joined most heartily in the general regret on so unfortunate an event; concluding however by observing, that as they were all got together, they must do something by way of being happy; and after some consultation it was agreed, that although happiness could only be enjoyed at Whitwell, they might procure a tolerable composure of mind by driving about the country. The carriages were then ordered; Willoughby's was first, and Marianne never looked happier than when she got into it. He drove through the park very fast, and they were soon out of sight; and nothing more of them was seen till their return, which did not happen till after the return of all the rest. They both seemed delighted with their drive; but said only in general terms that they had kept in the lanes, while the others went on the downs.

It was settled that there should be a dance in the evening, and that everybody should be extremely merry all day long. Some more of the Careys came to dinner, and they had the pleasure of sitting down nearly twenty to table, which Sir John observed with great contentment. Willoughby took his usual place between the two elder Miss Dashwoods. Mrs. Jennings sat on Elinor's right hand; and they had not been long seated, before she leant behind her and Willoughby, and said to Marianne, loud enough for them both to hear, "I have found you out in spite of all your tricks. I know where you spent the morning."

Marianne coloured, and replied very hastily, "Where, pray?"

"Did not you know," said Willoughby, "that we had been out in my curricle?"

"Yes, yes, Mr. Impudence, I know that very well, and I was determined to find out *where* you had been to. I hope you like your house, Miss Marianne. It is a very large one, I know; and when I come to see you, I hope you will have new-furnished it, for it wanted it very much when I was there six years ago."

Marianne turned away in great confusion. Mrs. Jennings laughed heartily; and Elinor found that in her resolution to know where they had been, she had actually made her own woman enquire of Mr. Willoughby's groom; and that she had by that method been informed that they had gone to Allenham, and spent a considerable time there in walking about the garden and going all over the house.

Elinor could hardly believe this to be true, as it seemed very unlikely that Willoughby should propose, or Marianne consent, to enter the house while Mrs. Smith was in it, with whom Marianne had not the smallest acquaintance.

As soon as they left the dining-room, Elinor enquired of her about it; and great was her surprise when she found that every circumstance related by Mrs. Jennings was perfectly true. Marianne was quite angry with her for doubting it.

"Why should you imagine, Elinor, that we did not go there, or that we did not see the house? Is not it what you have often wished to do yourself?"

"Yes, Marianne, but I would not go while Mrs. Smith was there, and with no other companion than Mr. Willoughby."

"Mr. Willoughby however is the only person who can have a right to shew that house; and as he went in an open carriage, it was impossible to have any other companion. I never spent a pleasanter morning in my life."

"I am afraid," replied Elinor, "that the pleasantness of an employment does not always evince its propriety."

"On the contrary, nothing can be a stronger proof of it, Elinor; for if there had been any real impropriety in what I did, I should have been sensible of it at the time, for we always know when we are acting wrong, and with such a conviction I could have had no pleasure."

"But, my dear Marianne, as it has already exposed you to some very impertinent remarks, do you not now begin to doubt the discretion of your own conduct?"

"If the impertinent remarks of Mrs. Jennings are to be the proof of impropriety in conduct, we are all offending every moment of our lives. I value not her censure any more than I should do her commendation. I am not sensible of having done anything wrong in walking over Mrs. Smith's grounds, or in seeing her house. They will one day be Mr. Willoughby's, and—"

"If they were one day to be your own, Marianne, you would not be justified in what you have done."

She blushed at this hint; but it was even visibly gratifying to her; and after a ten minutes' interval of earnest thought, she came to her sister again, and said with great good humour, "Perhaps, Elinor, it *was* rather ill-judged in me to go to Allenham; but Mr. Willoughby wanted particularly to shew me the place; and it is a charming house, I assure you. There is one remarkably pretty sitting room up stairs; of a nice comfortable size for constant use, and with modern furniture it would be delightful. It is a corner room, and has windows on two sides. On one side you look across the bowling-green, behind the house, to a beautiful hanging wood, and on the other you have a view of the church and village, and, beyond them, of those fine bold hills that we have so often admired. I did not see it to advantage, for nothing could be more forlorn than the furniture, but if it were newly fitted up—a couple of hundred pounds, Willoughby says, would make it one of the pleasantest summer-rooms in England."

Could Elinor have listened to her without interruption from the others, she would have described every room in the house with equal delight.

CHAPTER XIV

The sudden termination of Colonel Brandon's visit at the park, with his steadiness in concealing its cause, filled the mind, and raised the wonder of Mrs. Jennings for two or three days; she was a great wonderer, as every one must be who takes a very lively interest in all the comings and goings of all their acquaintance. She wondered, with little intermission what could be the reason of it; was sure there must be some bad news, and thought over every kind of distress that could have befallen him, with a fixed determination that he should not escape them all.

"Something very melancholy must be the matter, I am sure," said she. "I could see it in his face. Poor man! I am afraid his circumstances may be bad. The estate at Delaford was never reckoned more than two thousand a year, and his brother left everything sadly involved. I do think he must have been sent for about money matters, for what else can it be? I wonder whether it is so. I would give anything to know the truth of it. Perhaps it is about Miss Williams and, by the bye, I dare say it is, because he looked so conscious when I mentioned her. May be she is ill in town; nothing in the world more likely, for I have a notion she is always rather sickly. I would lay any wager it is about Miss Williams. It is not so very likely he should be distressed in his circumstances *now*, for he is a very prudent man, and to be sure must have cleared the estate by this time. I wonder what it can be! May be his sister is worse at Avignon, and has sent for him over. His setting off in such a hurry seems very like it. Well, I wish him out of all his trouble with all my heart, and a good wife into the bargain."

So wondered, so talked Mrs. Jennings. Her opinion varying with every fresh conjecture, and all seeming equally probable as they arose. Elinor, though she felt really interested in the welfare of Colonel Brandon, could not bestow all the wonder on his going so suddenly away, which Mrs. Jennings was desirous of her feeling; for besides that the circumstance did not in her opinion justify such lasting amazement or variety of speculation, her wonder was otherwise disposed of. It was engrossed by the extraordinary silence of her sister and Willoughby on the subject, which they must know to be peculiarly interesting to them all. As this silence continued, every day made it appear more strange and more incompatible with the disposition of both. Why they should not openly acknowledge to her mother and herself, what their constant behaviour to each other declared to have taken place, Elinor could not imagine.

She could easily conceive that marriage might not be immediately in their power; for though Willoughby was independent, there was no reason to believe him rich. His estate had been rated by Sir John at about six or seven hundred a year; but he lived at an expense to which that income could hardly be equal, and he had himself often complained of his poverty. But for this strange kind of secrecy maintained by them relative to their engagement, which in fact concealed nothing at all, she could not account; and it was so wholly contradictory to their general opinions and practice, that a doubt sometimes entered her mind of their being really engaged, and this doubt was enough to prevent her making any inquiry of Marianne.

Nothing could be more expressive of attachment to them all, than Willoughby's behaviour. To Marianne it had all the distinguishing tenderness which a lover's heart could give, and to the rest of the family it was the affectionate attention of a son and a brother. The cottage seemed to be considered and loved by him as his home; many more of his hours were spent there than at Allenham; and if no general engagement collected them at the park, the exercise which called him out in the morning was almost certain of ending there, where the rest of the day was spent by himself at the side of Marianne, and by his favourite pointer at her feet.

One evening in particular, about a week after Colonel Brandon left the country, his heart seemed more than usually open to every feeling of attachment to the objects around him; and on Mrs. Dashwood's happening to mention her design of improving the cottage in the spring, he warmly opposed every alteration of a place which affection had established as perfect with him.

"What!" he exclaimed—"Improve this dear cottage! No. *That* I will never consent to. Not a stone must be added to its walls, not an inch to its size, if my feelings are regarded."

"Do not be alarmed," said Miss Dashwood, "nothing of the kind will be done; for my mother will never have money enough to attempt it."

"I am heartily glad of it," he cried. "May she always be poor, if she can employ her riches no better."

"Thank you, Willoughby. But you may be assured that I would not sacrifice one sentiment of local attachment of yours, or of any one whom I loved, for all the improvements in the world. Depend upon it that whatever unemployed sum may remain, when I make up my accounts in the spring, I would even rather lay it uselessly by than dispose of it in a manner so painful to you. But are you really so attached to this place as to see no defect in it?"

"I am," said he. "To me it is faultless. Nay, more, I consider it as the only form of building in which happiness is attainable, and were I rich enough I would instantly pull Combe down, and build it up again in the exact plan of this cottage."

"With dark narrow stairs and a kitchen that smokes, I suppose," said Elinor.

"Yes," cried he in the same eager tone, "with all and every thing belonging to it—in no one convenience or INconvenience about it, should the least variation be perceptible. Then, and then only, under such a roof, I might perhaps be as happy at Combe as I have been at Barton."

"I flatter myself," replied Elinor, "that even under the disadvantage of better rooms and a broader staircase, you will hereafter find your own house as faultless as you now do this."

"There certainly are circumstances," said Willoughby, "which might greatly endear it to me; but this place will always have one claim of my affection, which no other can possibly share."

Mrs. Dashwood looked with pleasure at Marianne, whose fine eyes were fixed so expressively on Willoughby, as plainly denoted how well she understood him.

"How often did I wish," added he, "when I was at Allenham this time twelvemonth, that Barton cottage were inhabited! I never passed within view of it without admiring its situation, and grieving that no one should live in it. How little did I then think that the very first news I should hear from Mrs. Smith, when I next came into the country, would be that Barton cottage was taken: and I felt an immediate satisfaction and interest in the event, which nothing but a kind of prescience of what happiness I should experience from it, can account for. Must it not have been so, Marianne?" speaking to her in a lowered voice. Then continuing his former tone, he said, "And yet this house you would spoil, Mrs. Dashwood? You would rob it of its simplicity by imaginary improvement! And this dear parlour in which our acquaintance first began, and in which so many happy hours have been since spent by us together, you would degrade to the condition of a common entrance, and everybody would be eager to pass through the room which has hitherto contained within itself more real accommodation and comfort than any other apartment of the handsomest dimensions in the world could possibly afford."

Mrs. Dashwood again assured him that no alteration of the kind should be attempted.

"You are a good woman," he warmly replied. "Your promise makes me easy. Extend it a little farther, and it will make me happy. Tell me that not only your house will remain the same, but that I shall ever find you and yours as unchanged as your dwelling; and that you will always consider me with the kindness which has made everything belonging to you so dear to me."

The promise was readily given, and Willoughby's behaviour during the whole of the evening declared at once his affection and happiness.

"Shall we see you tomorrow to dinner?" said Mrs. Dashwood, when he was leaving them. "I do not ask you to come in the morning, for we must walk to the park, to call on Lady Middleton."

He engaged to be with them by four o'clock.

CHAPTER XV

Mrs. Dashwood's visit to Lady Middleton took place the next day, and two of her daughters went with her; but Marianne excused herself from being of the party, under some trifling pretext of employment; and her mother, who concluded that a promise had been made by Willoughby the night before of calling on her while they were absent, was perfectly satisfied with her remaining at home.

On their return from the park they found Willoughby's curricle and servant in waiting at the cottage, and Mrs. Dashwood was convinced that her conjecture had been just. So far it was all as she had foreseen; but on entering the house she beheld what no foresight had taught her to expect. They were no sooner in the passage than Marianne came hastily out of the parlour apparently in violent affliction, with her handkerchief at her eyes; and without noticing them ran up stairs. Surprised and alarmed they proceeded directly into the room she had just quitted, where they found only Willoughby, who was leaning against the mantel-piece with his back towards them. He turned round on their coming in, and his countenance shewed that he strongly partook of the emotion which over-powered Marianne.

"Is anything the matter with her?" cried Mrs. Dashwood as she entered—"is she ill?"

"I hope not," he replied, trying to look cheerful; and with a forced smile presently added, "It is I who may rather expect to be ill—for I am now suffering under a very heavy disappointment!"

"Disappointment?"

"Yes, for I am unable to keep my engagement with you. Mrs. Smith has this morning exercised the privilege of riches upon a poor dependent cousin, by sending me on business to London. I have just received my dispatches, and taken my farewell of Allenham; and by way of exhilaration I am now come to take my farewell of you."

"To London! And are you going this morning?"

"Almost this moment."

"This is very unfortunate. But Mrs. Smith must be obliged—and her business will not detain you from us long I hope."

He coloured as he replied, "You are very kind, but I have no idea of returning into Devonshire immediately. My visits to Mrs. Smith are never repeated within the twelvemonth."

"And is Mrs. Smith your only friend? Is Allenham the only house in the neighbourhood to which you will be welcome? For shame, Willoughby, can you wait for an invitation here?"

His colour increased; and with his eyes fixed on the ground he only replied, "You are too good."

Mrs. Dashwood looked at Elinor with surprise. Elinor felt equal amazement. For a few moments every one was silent. Mrs. Dashwood first spoke.

"I have only to add, my dear Willoughby, that at Barton cottage you will always be welcome; for I will not press you to return here immediately, because you only can judge how far *that* might be pleasing to Mrs. Smith; and on this head I shall be no more disposed to question your judgment than to doubt your inclination."

"My engagements at present," replied Willoughby, confusedly, "are of such a nature—that—I dare not flatter myself—"

He stopt. Mrs. Dashwood was too much astonished to speak, and another pause succeeded. This was broken by Willoughby, who said with a faint smile, "It is folly to linger in this manner. I will not torment myself any longer by remaining among friends whose society it is impossible for me now to enjoy."

He then hastily took leave of them all and left the room. They saw him step into his carriage, and in a minute it was out of sight.

Mrs. Dashwood felt too much for speech, and instantly quitted the parlour to give way in solitude to the concern and alarm which this sudden departure occasioned.

Elinor's uneasiness was at least equal to her mother's. She thought of what had just passed with anxiety and distrust. Willoughby's behaviour in taking leave of them, his embarrassment, and affectation of cheerfulness, and, above all, his unwillingness to accept her mother's invitation, a backwardness so unlike a lover, so unlike himself, greatly disturbed her. One moment she feared that no serious design had ever been formed on his side; and the next that some unfortunate quarrel had taken place between him and her sister—the distress in which Marianne had quitted the room was such as a serious quarrel could most reasonably account for, though when she considered what Marianne's love for him was, a quarrel seemed almost impossible.

But whatever might be the particulars of their separation, her sister's affliction was indubitable; and she thought with the tenderest compassion of that violent sorrow which Marianne was in all probability not merely giving way to as a relief, but feeding and encouraging as a duty.

In about half an hour her mother returned, and though her eyes were red, her countenance was not uncheerful.

"Our dear Willoughby is now some miles from Barton, Elinor," said she, as she sat down to work, "and with how heavy a heart does he travel?"

"It is all very strange. So suddenly to be gone! It seems but the work of a moment. And last night he was with us so happy, so cheerful, so affectionate? And now, after only ten minutes notice—gone too without intending to return! Something more than what he owned to us must have happened. He did not speak, he did not behave like himself. *You* must have seen the difference as well as I. What can it be? Can they have quarrelled? Why else should he have shewn such unwillingness to accept your invitation here?"

"It was not inclination that he wanted, Elinor; I could plainly see *that*. He had not the power of accepting it. I have thought it all over I assure you, and I can perfectly account for every thing that at first seemed strange to me as well as to you."

"Can you, indeed!"

"Yes. I have explained it to myself in the most satisfactory way—but you, Elinor, who love to doubt where you can—it will not satisfy *you*, I know; but you shall not talk *me* out of my trust in it. I am persuaded that Mrs. Smith suspects his regard for Marianne, disapproves of it, (perhaps because she has other views for him,) and on that account is eager to get him away—and that the business which she sends him off to transact is invented as an excuse to dismiss him. This is what I believe to have happened. He is, moreover, aware that she *does* disapprove the connection, he dares not therefore at present confess to her his engagement with Marianne, and he feels himself obliged, from his dependent situation, to give into her schemes, and absent himself from Devonshire for a while. You will tell me, I know, that this may or may *not* have happened; but I will listen to no cavil, unless you can point out any other method of understanding the affair as satisfactory at this. And now, Elinor, what have you to say?"

"Nothing, for you have anticipated my answer."

"Then you would have told me, that it might or might not have happened. Oh, Elinor, how incomprehensible are your feelings! You had rather take evil upon credit than good. You had rather look out for misery for Marianne, and guilt for poor Willoughby, than an apology for the latter. You are resolved to think him blameable, because he took leave of us with less affection than his usual behaviour has shewn. And is no allowance to be made for inadvertence, or for spirits depressed by recent disappointment? Are no probabilities to be accepted, merely because they are not certainties? Is nothing due to the man whom we have all such reason to love, and no reason in the world to think ill of? To the possibility of motives unanswerable in themselves, though unavoidably secret for a while? And, after all, what is it you suspect him of?"

"I can hardly tell myself. But suspicion of something unpleasant is the inevitable consequence of such an alteration as we just witnessed in him. There is great truth, however, in what you have now urged of the allowances which ought to be made for him, and it is my wish to be candid in my judgment of everybody. Willoughby may undoubtedly have very sufficient reasons for his conduct, and I will hope that he has. But it would have been more like Willoughby to acknowledge them at once. Secrecy may be advisable; but still I cannot help wondering at its being practiced by him."

"Do not blame him, however, for departing from his character, where the deviation is necessary. But you really do admit the justice of what I have said in his defence? I am happy—and he is acquitted."

"Not entirely. It may be proper to conceal their engagement (if they *are* engaged) from Mrs. Smith—and if that is the case, it must be highly expedient for Willoughby to be but little in Devonshire at present. But this is no excuse for their concealing it from us."

"Concealing it from us! My dear child, do you accuse Willoughby and Marianne of concealment? This is strange indeed, when your eyes have been reproaching them every day for incautiousness."

"I want no proof of their affection," said Elinor; "but of their engagement I do."

"I am perfectly satisfied of both."

"Yet not a syllable has been said to you on the subject, by either of them."

"I have not wanted syllables where actions have spoken so plainly.

Has not his behaviour to Marianne and to all of us, for at least the last fortnight, declared that he loved and considered her as his future wife, and that he felt for us the attachment of the nearest relation? Have we not perfectly understood each other? Has not my consent been daily asked by his looks, his manner, his attentive and affectionate respect? My Elinor, is it possible to doubt their engagement? How could such a thought occur to you? How is it to be supposed that Willoughby, persuaded as he must be of your sister's love, should leave her, and leave her perhaps for months, without telling her of his affection—that they should part without a mutual exchange of confidence?"

"I confess," replied Elinor, "that every circumstance except *one* is in favour of their engagement; but that *one* is the total silence of both on the subject, and with me it almost outweighs every other."

"How strange this is! You must think wretchedly indeed of Willoughby, if, after all that has openly passed between them, you can doubt the nature of the terms on which they are together. Has he been acting a part in his behaviour to your sister all this time? Do you suppose him really indifferent to her?"

"No, I cannot think that. He must and does love her I am sure."

"But with a strange kind of tenderness, if he can leave her with such indifference, such carelessness of the future, as you attribute to him."

"You must remember, my dear mother, that I have never considered this matter as certain. I have had my doubts, I confess; but they are fainter than they were, and they may soon be entirely done away. If we find they correspond, every fear of mine will be removed."

"A mighty concession indeed! If you were to see them at the altar, you would suppose they were going to be married. Ungracious girl! But I require no such proof. Nothing in my opinion has ever passed to justify doubt; no secrecy has been attempted; all has been uniformly open and unreserved. You cannot doubt your sister's wishes. It must be Willoughby therefore whom you suspect. But why? Is he not a man of honour and feeling? Has there been any inconsistency on his side to create alarm? Can he be deceitful?"

"I hope not, I believe not," cried Elinor. "I love Willoughby, sincerely love him; and suspicion of his integrity cannot be more painful to yourself than to me. It has been involuntary, and I will not encourage it. I was startled, I confess, by the alteration in his manners this morning—he did not speak like himself, and did not return your kindness with any cordiality. But all this may be explained by such a situation of his affairs as you have supposed. He had just parted from my sister, had seen her leave him in the greatest affliction; and if he felt obliged, from a fear of offending Mrs. Smith, to resist the temptation of returning here soon, and yet aware that by declining your invitation, by saying that he was going away for some time, he should seem to act an ungenerous, a suspicious part by our family, he might well be embarrassed and disturbed. In such a case, a plain and open avowal of his difficulties would have been more to his honour I think, as well as more consistent with his general character—but I will not raise objections against any one's conduct on so illiberal a foundation, as a difference in judgment from myself, or a deviation from what I may think right and consistent."

"You speak very properly. Willoughby certainly does not deserve to be suspected. Though *we* have not known him long, he is no stranger in this part of the world; and who has ever spoken to his disadvantage? Had he been in a situation to act independently and marry immediately, it might have been odd that he should leave us without acknowledging everything to me at once: but this is not the case. It is an engagement in some respects not prosperously begun, for their marriage must be at a very uncertain distance; and even secrecy, as far as it can be observed, may now be very advisable."

They were interrupted by the entrance of Margaret; and Elinor was then at liberty to think over the representations of her mother, to acknowledge the probability of many, and hope for the justice of all.

They saw nothing of Marianne till dinner time, when she entered the room and took her place at the table without saying a word. Her eyes were red and swollen; and it seemed as if her tears were even then restrained with difficulty. She avoided the looks of them all, could neither eat nor speak, and after some time, on her mother's silently pressing her hand with tender compassion, her small degree of fortitude was quite overcome, she burst into tears and left the room.

This violent oppression of spirits continued the whole evening. She was without any power, because she was without any desire of command over herself. The slightest mention of anything relative to Willoughby overpowered her in an instant; and though her family were most anxiously attentive to her comfort, it was impossible for them, if they spoke at all, to keep clear of every subject which her feelings connected with him.

CHAPTER XVI

Marianne would have thought herself very inexcusable had she been able to sleep at all the first night after parting from Willoughby. She would have been ashamed to look her family in the face the next morning, had she not risen from her bed in more need of repose than when she lay down in it. But the feelings which made such composure a disgrace, left her in no danger of incurring it. She was awake the whole night, and she wept the greatest part of it. She got up with a headache, was unable to talk, and unwilling to take any nourishment; giving pain every moment to her mother and sisters, and forbidding all attempt at consolation from either. Her sensibility was potent enough!

When breakfast was over she walked out by herself, and wandered about the village of Allenham, indulging the recollection of past enjoyment and crying over the present reverse for the chief of the morning.

The evening passed off in the equal indulgence of feeling. She played over every favourite song that she had been used to play to Willoughby, every air in which their voices had been oftenest joined, and sat at the instrument gazing on every line of music that he had written out for her, till her heart was so heavy that no farther sadness could be gained; and this nourishment of grief was every day applied. She spent whole hours at the pianoforte alternately singing and crying; her voice often totally suspended by her tears. In books too, as well as in music, she courted the misery which a contrast between the past and present was certain of giving. She read nothing but what they had been used to read together.

Such violence of affliction indeed could not be supported for ever; it sunk within a few days into a calmer melancholy; but these employments, to which she daily recurred, her solitary walks and silent meditations, still produced occasional effusions of sorrow as lively as ever.

No letter from Willoughby came; and none seemed expected by Marianne. Her mother was surprised, and Elinor again became uneasy. But Mrs. Dashwood could find explanations whenever she wanted them, which at least satisfied herself.

"Remember, Elinor," said she, "how very often Sir John fetches our letters himself from the post, and carries them to it. We have already agreed that secrecy may be necessary, and we must acknowledge that it could not be maintained if their correspondence were to pass through Sir John's hands."

Elinor could not deny the truth of this, and she tried to find in it a motive sufficient for their silence. But there was one method so direct, so simple, and in her opinion so eligible of knowing the real state of the affair, and of instantly removing all mystery, that she could not help suggesting it to her mother.

"Why do you not ask Marianne at once," said she, "whether she is or she is not engaged to Willoughby? From you, her mother, and so kind, so indulgent a mother, the question could not give offence. It would be the natural result of your affection for her. She used to be all unreserve, and to you more especially."

"I would not ask such a question for the world. Supposing it possible that they are not engaged, what distress would not such an enquiry inflict! At any rate it would be most ungenerous. I should never deserve her confidence again, after forcing from her a confession of what is meant at present to be unacknowledged to any one. I know Marianne's heart: I know that she dearly loves me, and that I shall not be the last to whom the affair is made known, when circumstances make the revealment of it eligible. I would not attempt to force the confidence of any one; of a child much less; because a sense of duty would prevent the denial which her wishes might direct."

Elinor thought this generosity overstrained, considering her sister's youth, and urged the matter farther, but in vain; common sense, common care, common prudence, were all sunk in Mrs. Dashwood's romantic delicacy.

It was several days before Willoughby's name was mentioned before Marianne by any of her family; Sir John and Mrs. Jennings, indeed, were not so nice; their witticisms added pain to many a painful hour—but one evening, Mrs. Dashwood, accidentally taking up a volume of Shakespeare, exclaimed,

"We have never finished Hamlet, Marianne; our dear Willoughby went away before we could get through it. We will put it by, that when he comes again . . . But it may be months, perhaps, before *that* happens."

"Months!" cried Marianne, with strong surprise. "No—nor many weeks."

Mrs. Dashwood was sorry for what she had said; but it gave Elinor pleasure, as it produced a reply from Marianne so expressive of confidence in Willoughby and knowledge of his intentions.

One morning, about a week after his leaving the country, Marianne was prevailed on to join her sisters in their usual walk, instead of wandering away by herself. Hitherto she had carefully avoided every companion in her rambles. If her sisters intended to walk on the downs, she directly stole away towards the lanes; if they talked of the valley, she was as speedy in climbing the hills, and could never be found when the others set off. But at length she was secured by the exertions of Elinor, who greatly disapproved such continual seclusion. They walked along the road through the valley, and chiefly in silence, for Marianne's *mind* could not be controlled, and Elinor, satisfied with gaining one point, would not then attempt more. Beyond the entrance of the valley, where the country, though still rich, was less wild and more open, a long stretch of the road which they had travelled on first coming to Barton, lay before them; and on reaching that point, they stopped to look around them, and examine a prospect which formed the distance of their view from the cottage, from a spot which they had never happened to reach in any of their walks before.

Amongst the objects in the scene, they soon discovered an animated one; it was a man on horseback riding towards them. In a few minutes they could distinguish him to be a gentleman; and in a moment afterwards Marianne rapturously exclaimed,

"It is he; it is indeed—I know it is!"—and was hastening to meet him, when Elinor cried out,

"Indeed, Marianne, I think you are mistaken. It is not Willoughby. The person is not tall enough for him, and has not his air."

"He has, he has," cried Marianne, "I am sure he has. His air, his coat, his horse. I knew how soon he would come."

She walked eagerly on as she spoke; and Elinor, to screen Marianne from particularity, as she felt almost certain of its not being Willoughby, quickened her pace and kept up with her. They were soon within thirty yards of the gentleman. Marianne looked again; her heart sunk within her; and abruptly turning round, she was hurrying back, when the voices of both her sisters were raised to detain her; a third, almost as well known as Willoughby's, joined them in begging her to stop, and she turned round with surprise to see and welcome Edward Ferrars.

He was the only person in the world who could at that moment be forgiven for not being Willoughby; the only one who could have gained a smile from her; but she dispersed her tears to smile on *him*, and in her sister's happiness forgot for a time her own disappointment.

He dismounted, and giving his horse to his servant, walked back with them to Barton, whither he was purposely coming to visit them.

He was welcomed by them all with great cordiality, but especially by Marianne, who showed more warmth of regard in her reception of him than even Elinor herself. To Marianne, indeed, the meeting between Edward and her sister was but a continuation of that unaccountable coldness which she had often observed at Norland in their mutual behaviour. On Edward's side, more particularly, there was a deficiency of all that a lover ought to look and say on such an occasion. He was confused, seemed scarcely sensible of pleasure in seeing them, looked neither rapturous nor gay, said little but what was forced from him by questions, and distinguished Elinor by no mark of affection. Marianne saw and listened with increasing surprise. She began almost to feel a dislike of Edward; and it ended, as every feeling must end with her, by carrying back her thoughts to Willoughby, whose manners formed a contrast sufficiently striking to those of his brother elect.

After a short silence which succeeded the first surprise and enquiries of meeting, Marianne asked Edward if he came directly from London. No, he had been in Devonshire a fortnight.

"A fortnight!" she repeated, surprised at his being so long in the same county with Elinor without seeing her before.

He looked rather distressed as he added, that he had been staying with some friends near Plymouth.

"Have you been lately in Sussex?" said Elinor.

"I was at Norland about a month ago."

"And how does dear, dear Norland look?" cried Marianne.

"Dear, dear Norland," said Elinor, "probably looks much as it always does at this time of the year. The woods and walks thickly covered with dead leaves."

"Oh," cried Marianne, "with what transporting sensation have I formerly seen them fall! How have I delighted, as I walked, to see them driven in showers about me by the wind! What feelings have they, the season, the air altogether inspired! Now there is no one to regard them. They are seen only as a nuisance, swept hastily off, and driven as much as possible from the sight."

"It is not every one," said Elinor, "who has your passion for dead leaves."

"No; my feelings are not often shared, not often understood. But *sometimes* they are." As she said this, she sunk into a reverie for a few moments—but rousing herself again, "Now, Edward," said she, calling his attention to the prospect, "here is Barton valley. Look up to it, and be tranquil if you can. Look at those hills! Did you ever see their equals? To the left is Barton park, amongst those woods and plantations. You may see the end of the house. And there, beneath that farthest hill, which rises with such grandeur, is our cottage."

"It is a beautiful country," he replied; "but these bottoms must be dirty in winter."

"How can you think of dirt, with such objects before you?"

"Because," replied he, smiling, "among the rest of the objects before me, I see a very dirty lane."

"How strange!" said Marianne to herself as she walked on.

"Have you an agreeable neighbourhood here? Are the Middletons pleasant people?"

"No, not all," answered Marianne; "we could not be more unfortunately situated."

"Marianne," cried her sister, "how can you say so? How can you be so unjust? They are a very respectable family, Mr. Ferrars; and towards us have behaved in the friendliest manner. Have you forgot, Marianne, how many pleasant days we have owed to them?"

"No," said Marianne, in a low voice, "nor how many painful moments."

Elinor took no notice of this; and directing her attention to their visitor, endeavoured to support something like discourse with him, by talking of their present residence, its conveniences, &c. extorting from him occasional questions and remarks. His coldness and reserve mortified her severely; she was vexed and half angry; but resolving to regulate her behaviour to him by the past rather than the present, she avoided every appearance of resentment or displeasure, and treated him as she thought he ought to be treated from the family connection.

CHAPTER XVII

Mrs. Dashwood was surprised only for a moment at seeing him; for his coming to Barton was, in her opinion, of all things the most natural. Her joy and expression of regard long outlived her wonder. He received the kindest welcome from her; and shyness, coldness, reserve could not stand against such a reception. They had begun to fail him before he entered the house, and they were quite overcome by the captivating manners of Mrs. Dashwood. Indeed a man could not very well be in love with either of her daughters, without extending the passion to her; and Elinor had the satisfaction of seeing him soon become more like himself. His affections seemed to reanimate towards them all, and his interest in their welfare again became perceptible. He was not in spirits, however; he praised their house, admired its prospect, was attentive, and kind; but still he was not in spirits. The whole family perceived it, and Mrs. Dashwood, attributing it to some want of liberality in his mother, sat down to table indignant against all selfish parents.

"What are Mrs. Ferrars's views for you at present, Edward?" said she, when dinner was over and they had drawn round the fire; "are you still to be a great orator in spite of yourself?"

"No. I hope my mother is now convinced that I have no more talents than inclination for a public life!"

"But how is your fame to be established? For famous you must be to satisfy all your family; and with no inclination for expense, no affection for strangers, no profession, and no assurance, you may find it a difficult matter."

"I shall not attempt it. I have no wish to be distinguished; and have every reason to hope I never shall. Thank Heaven! I cannot be forced into genius and eloquence."

"You have no ambition, I well know. Your wishes are all moderate."

"As moderate as those of the rest of the world, I believe. I wish as well as every body else to be perfectly happy; but, like everybody else it must be in my own way. Greatness will not make me so."

"Strange that it would!" cried Marianne. "What have wealth or grandeur to do with happiness?"

"Grandeur has but little," said Elinor, "but wealth has much to do with it."

"Elinor, for shame!" said Marianne, "money can only give happiness where there is nothing else to give it. Beyond a competence, it can afford no real satisfaction, as far as mere self is concerned."

"Perhaps," said Elinor, smiling, "we may come to the same point. *Your* competence and *my* wealth are very much alike, I dare say; and without them, as the world goes now, we shall both agree that every kind of external comfort must be wanting. Your ideas are only more noble than mine. Come, what is your competence?"

"About eighteen hundred or two thousand a year; not more than *that*."

Elinor laughed. "*Two* thousand a year! *One* is my wealth! I guessed how it would end."

"And yet two thousand a-year is a very moderate income," said Marianne. "A family cannot well be maintained on a smaller. I am sure I am not extravagant in my demands. A proper establishment of servants, a carriage, perhaps two, and hunters, cannot be supported on less."

Elinor smiled again, to hear her sister describing so accurately their future expenses at Combe Magna.

"Hunters!" repeated Edward—"but why must you have hunters? Every body does not hunt."

Marianne coloured as she replied, "But most people do."

"I wish," said Margaret, striking out a novel thought, "that somebody would give us all a large fortune apiece!"

"Oh that they would!" cried Marianne, her eyes sparkling with animation, and her cheeks glowing with the delight of such imaginary happiness.

"We are all unanimous in that wish, I suppose," said Elinor, "in spite of the insufficiency of wealth."

"Oh dear!" cried Margaret, "how happy I should be! I wonder what I should do with it!"

Marianne looked as if she had no doubt on that point.

"I should be puzzled to spend so large a fortune myself," said Mrs. Dashwood, "if my children were all to be rich without my help."

"You must begin your improvements on this house," observed Elinor, "and your difficulties will soon vanish."

"What magnificent orders would travel from this family to London," said Edward, "in such an event! What a happy day for booksellers, music-sellers, and print-shops! You, Miss Dashwood, would give a general commission for every new print of merit to be sent you—and as for Marianne, I know her greatness of soul, there would not be music enough in London to content her. And books! Thomson, Cowper, Scott—she would buy them all over and over again: she would buy up every copy, I believe, to prevent their falling into unworthy hands; and she would have every book that tells her how to admire an old twisted tree. Should not you, Marianne? Forgive me, if I am very saucy. But I was willing to shew you that I had not forgot our old disputes."

"I love to be reminded of the past, Edward—whether it be melancholy or gay, I love to recall it—and you will never offend me by talking of former times. You are very right in supposing how my money would be spent—some of it, at least—my loose cash would certainly be employed in improving my collection of music and books."

"And the bulk of your fortune would be laid out in annuities on the authors or their heirs."

"No, Edward, I should have something else to do with it."

"Perhaps, then, you would bestow it as a reward on that person who wrote the ablest defence of your favourite maxim, that no one can ever be in love more than once in their life—your opinion on that point is unchanged, I presume?"

"Undoubtedly. At my time of life opinions are tolerably fixed. It is not likely that I should now see or hear any thing to change them."

"Marianne is as steadfast as ever, you see," said Elinor, "she is not at all altered."

"She is only grown a little more grave than she was."

"Nay, Edward," said Marianne, "you need not reproach me. You are not very gay yourself."

"Why should you think so!" replied he, with a sigh. "But gaiety never was a part of *my* character."

"Nor do I think it a part of Marianne's," said Elinor; "I should hardly call her a lively girl—she is very earnest, very eager in all she does—sometimes talks a great deal and always with animation—but she is not often really merry."

"I believe you are right," he replied, "and yet I have always set her down as a lively girl."

"I have frequently detected myself in such kind of mistakes," said

Elinor, "in a total misapprehension of character in some point or other: fancying people so much more gay or grave, or ingenious or stupid than they really are, and I can hardly tell why or in what the deception originated. Sometimes one is guided by what they say of themselves, and very frequently by what other people say of them, without giving oneself time to deliberate and judge."

"But I thought it was right, Elinor," said Marianne, "to be guided wholly by the opinion of other people. I thought our judgments were given us merely to be subservient to those of neighbours. This has always been your doctrine, I am sure."

"No, Marianne, never. My doctrine has never aimed at the subjection of the understanding. All I have ever attempted to influence has been the behaviour. You must not confound my meaning. I am guilty, I confess, of having often wished you to treat our acquaintance in general with greater attention; but when have I advised you to adopt their sentiments or to conform to their judgment in serious matters?"

"You have not been able to bring your sister over to your plan of general civility," said Edward to Elinor. "Do you gain no ground?"

"Quite the contrary," replied Elinor, looking expressively at Marianne.

"My judgment," he returned, "is all on your side of the question; but I am afraid my practice is much more on your sister's. I never wish to offend, but I am so foolishly shy, that I often seem negligent, when I am only kept back by my natural awkwardness. I have frequently thought that I must have been intended by nature to be fond of low company, I am so little at my ease among strangers of gentility!"

"Marianne has not shyness to excuse any inattention of hers," said Elinor.

"She knows her own worth too well for false shame," replied Edward. "Shyness is only the effect of a sense of inferiority in some way or other. If I could persuade myself that my manners were perfectly easy and graceful, I should not be shy."

"But you would still be reserved," said Marianne, "and that is worse."

Edward started—"Reserved! Am I reserved, Marianne?"

"Yes, very."

"I do not understand you," replied he, colouring. "Reserved! How, in what manner? What am I to tell you? What can you suppose?"

Elinor looked surprised at his emotion; but trying to laugh off the subject, she said to him, "Do not you know my sister well enough to understand what she means? Do not you know she calls every one reserved who does not talk as fast, and admire what she admires as rapturously as herself?"

Edward made no answer. His gravity and thoughtfulness returned on him in their fullest extent—and he sat for some time silent and dull.

CHAPTER XVIII

Elinor saw, with great uneasiness the low spirits of her friend. His visit afforded her but a very partial satisfaction, while his own enjoyment in it appeared so imperfect. It was evident that he was unhappy; she wished it were equally evident that he still distinguished her by the same affection which once she had felt no doubt of inspiring; but hitherto the continuance of his preference seemed very uncertain; and the reservedness of his manner towards her contradicted one moment what a more animated look had intimated the preceding one.

He joined her and Marianne in the breakfast-room the next morning before the others were down; and Marianne, who was always eager to promote their happiness as far as she could, soon left them to themselves. But before she was half way upstairs she heard the parlour door open, and, turning round, was astonished to see Edward himself come out.

"I am going into the village to see my horses," said he, "as you are not yet ready for breakfast; I shall be back again presently."

*****

Edward returned to them with fresh admiration of the surrounding country; in his walk to the village, he had seen many parts of the valley to advantage; and the village itself, in a much higher situation than the cottage, afforded a general view of the whole, which had exceedingly pleased him. This was a subject which ensured Marianne's attention, and she was beginning to describe her own admiration of these scenes, and to question him more minutely on the objects that had particularly struck him, when Edward interrupted her by saying, "You must not enquire too far, Marianne—remember I have no knowledge in the picturesque, and I shall offend you by my ignorance and want of taste if we come to particulars. I shall call hills steep, which ought to be bold; surfaces strange and uncouth, which ought to be irregular and rugged; and distant objects out of sight, which ought only to be indistinct through the soft medium of a hazy atmosphere. You must be satisfied with such admiration as I can honestly give. I call it a very fine country—the hills are steep, the woods seem full of fine timber, and the valley looks comfortable and snug—with rich meadows and several neat farm houses scattered here and there. It exactly answers my idea of a fine country, because it unites beauty with utility—and I dare say it is a picturesque one too, because you admire it; I can easily believe it to be full of rocks and promontories, grey moss and brush wood, but these are all lost on me. I know nothing of the picturesque."

"I am afraid it is but too true," said Marianne; "but why should you boast of it?"

"I suspect," said Elinor, "that to avoid one kind of affectation, Edward here falls into another. Because he believes many people pretend to more admiration of the beauties of nature than they really feel, and is disgusted with such pretensions, he affects greater indifference and less discrimination in viewing them himself than he possesses. He is fastidious and will have an affectation of his own."

"It is very true," said Marianne, "that admiration of landscape scenery is become a mere jargon. Everybody pretends to feel and tries to describe with the taste and elegance of him who first defined what picturesque beauty was. I detest jargon of every kind, and sometimes I have kept my feelings to myself, because I could find no language to describe them in but what was worn and hackneyed out of all sense and meaning."

"I am convinced," said Edward, "that you really feel all the delight in a fine prospect which you profess to feel. But, in return, your sister must allow me to feel no more than I profess. I like a fine prospect, but not on picturesque principles. I do not like crooked, twisted, blasted trees. I admire them much more if they are tall, straight, and flourishing. I do not like ruined, tattered cottages. I am not fond of nettles or thistles, or heath blossoms. I have more pleasure in a snug farm-house than a watch-tower—and a troop of tidy, happy villagers please me better than the finest banditti in the world."

Marianne looked with amazement at Edward, with compassion at her sister. Elinor only laughed.

The subject was continued no farther; and Marianne remained thoughtfully silent, till a new object suddenly engaged her attention. She was sitting by Edward, and in taking his tea from Mrs. Dashwood, his hand passed so directly before her, as to make a ring, with a plait of hair in the centre, very conspicuous on one of his fingers.

"I never saw you wear a ring before, Edward," she cried. "Is that

Fanny's hair? I remember her promising to give you some. But I should have thought her hair had been darker."

Marianne spoke inconsiderately what she really felt—but when she saw how much she had pained Edward, her own vexation at her want of thought could not be surpassed by his. He coloured very deeply, and giving a momentary glance at Elinor, replied, "Yes; it is my sister's hair. The setting always casts a different shade on it, you know."

Elinor had met his eye, and looked conscious likewise. That the hair was her own, she instantaneously felt as well satisfied as Marianne; the only difference in their conclusions was, that what Marianne considered as a free gift from her sister, Elinor was conscious must have been procured by some theft or contrivance unknown to herself. She was not in a humour, however, to regard it as an affront, and affecting to take no notice of what passed, by instantly talking of something else, she internally resolved henceforward to catch every opportunity of eyeing the hair and of satisfying herself, beyond all doubt, that it was exactly the shade of her own.

Edward's embarrassment lasted some time, and it ended in an absence of mind still more settled. He was particularly grave the whole morning. Marianne severely censured herself for what she had said; but her own forgiveness might have been more speedy, had she known how little offence it had given her sister.

Before the middle of the day, they were visited by Sir John and Mrs. Jennings, who, having heard of the arrival of a gentleman at the cottage, came to take a survey of the guest. With the assistance of his mother-in-law, Sir John was not long in discovering that the name of Ferrars began with an F. and this prepared a future mine of raillery against the devoted Elinor, which nothing but the newness of their acquaintance with Edward could have prevented from being immediately sprung. But, as it was, she only learned, from some very significant looks, how far their penetration, founded on Margaret's instructions, extended.

Sir John never came to the Dashwoods without either inviting them to dine at the park the next day, or to drink tea with them that evening. On the present occasion, for the better entertainment of their visitor, towards whose amusement he felt himself bound to contribute, he wished to engage them for both.

"You *must* drink tea with us to night," said he, "for we shall be quite alone—and tomorrow you must absolutely dine with us, for we shall be a large party."

Mrs. Jennings enforced the necessity. "And who knows but you may raise a dance," said she. "And that will tempt *you*, Miss Marianne."

"A dance!" cried Marianne. "Impossible! Who is to dance?"

"Who! Why yourselves, and the Careys, and Whitakers to be sure. What! You thought nobody could dance because a certain person that shall be nameless is gone!"

"I wish with all my soul," cried Sir John, "that Willoughby were among us again."

This, and Marianne's blushing, gave new suspicions to Edward. "And who is Willoughby?" said he, in a low voice, to Miss Dashwood, by whom he was sitting.

She gave him a brief reply. Marianne's countenance was more communicative. Edward saw enough to comprehend, not only the meaning of others, but such of Marianne's expressions as had puzzled him before; and when their visitors left them, he went immediately round her, and said, in a whisper, "I have been guessing. Shall I tell you my guess?"

"What do you mean?"

"Shall I tell you?"

"Certainly."

"Well then; I guess that Mr. Willoughby hunts."

Marianne was surprised and confused, yet she could not help smiling at the quiet archness of his manner, and after a moment's silence, said,

"Oh, Edward! How can you? But the time will come I hope . . . I am sure you will like him."

"I do not doubt it," replied he, rather astonished at her earnestness and warmth; for had he not imagined it to be a joke for the good of her acquaintance in general, founded only on a something or a nothing between Mr. Willoughby and herself, he would not have ventured to mention it.

CHAPTER XIX

Edward remained a week at the cottage; he was earnestly pressed by Mrs. Dashwood to stay longer; but, as if he were bent only on self-mortification, he seemed resolved to be gone when his enjoyment among his friends was at the height. His spirits, during the last two or three days, though still very unequal, were greatly improved—he grew more and more partial to the house and environs—never spoke of going away without a sigh—declared his time to be wholly disengaged—even doubted to what place he should go when he left them—but still, go he must. Never had any week passed so quickly—he could hardly believe it to be gone. He said so repeatedly; other things he said too, which marked the turn of his feelings and gave the lie to his actions. He had no pleasure at Norland; he detested being in town; but either to Norland or London, he must go. He valued their kindness beyond any thing, and his greatest happiness was in being with them. Yet, he must leave them at the end of a week, in spite of their wishes and his own, and without any restraint on his time.

Elinor placed all that was astonishing in this way of acting to his mother's account; and it was happy for her that he had a mother whose character was so imperfectly known to her, as to be the general excuse for every thing strange on the part of her son. Disappointed, however, and vexed as she was, and sometimes displeased with his uncertain behaviour to herself, she was very well disposed on the whole to regard his actions with all the candid allowances and generous qualifications, which had been rather more painfully extorted from her, for Willoughby's service, by her mother. His want of spirits, of openness, and of consistency, were most usually attributed to his want of independence, and his better knowledge of Mrs. Ferrars's disposition and designs. The shortness of his visit, the steadiness of his purpose in leaving them, originated in the same fettered inclination, the same inevitable necessity of temporizing with his mother. The old well-established grievance of duty against will, parent against child, was the cause of all. She would have been glad to know when these difficulties were to cease, this opposition was to yield, when Mrs. Ferrars would be reformed, and her son be at liberty to be happy. But from such vain wishes she was forced to turn for comfort to the renewal of her confidence in Edward's affection, to the remembrance of every mark of regard in look or word which fell from him while at Barton, and above all to that flattering proof of it which he constantly wore round his finger.

"I think, Edward," said Mrs. Dashwood, as they were at breakfast the last morning, "you would be a happier man if you had any profession to engage your time and give an interest to your plans and actions. Some inconvenience to your friends, indeed, might result from it—you would not be able to give them so much of your time. But (with a smile) you would be materially benefited in one particular at least—you would know where to go when you left them."

"I do assure you," he replied, "that I have long thought on this point, as you think now. It has been, and is, and probably will always be a heavy misfortune to me, that I have had no necessary business to engage me, no profession to give me employment, or afford me any thing like independence. But unfortunately my own nicety, and the nicety of my friends, have made me what I am, an idle, helpless being. We never could agree in our choice of a profession. I always preferred the church, as I still do. But that was not smart enough for my family. They recommended the army. That was a great deal too smart for me. The law was allowed to be genteel enough; many young men, who had chambers in the Temple, made a very good appearance in the first circles, and drove about town in very knowing gigs. But I had no inclination for the law, even in this less abstruse study of it, which my family approved. As for the navy, it had fashion on its side, but I was too old when the subject was first started to enter it—and, at length, as there was no necessity for my having any profession at all, as I might be as dashing and expensive without a red coat on my back as with one, idleness was pronounced on the whole to be most advantageous and honourable, and a young man of eighteen is not in general so earnestly bent on being busy as to resist the solicitations of his friends to do nothing. I was therefore entered at Oxford and have been properly idle ever since."

"The consequence of which, I suppose, will be," said Mrs. Dashwood, "since leisure has not promoted your own happiness, that your sons will be brought up to as many pursuits, employments, professions, and trades as Columella's."

"They will be brought up," said he, in a serious accent, "to be as unlike myself as is possible. In feeling, in action, in condition, in every thing."

"Come, come; this is all an effusion of immediate want of spirits, Edward. You are in a melancholy humour, and fancy that any one unlike yourself must be happy. But remember that the pain of parting from friends will be felt by every body at times, whatever be their education or state. Know your own happiness. You want nothing but patience—or give it a more fascinating name, call it hope. Your mother will secure to you, in time, that independence you are so anxious for; it is her duty, and it will, it must ere long become her happiness to prevent your whole youth from being wasted in discontent. How much may not a few months do?"

"I think," replied Edward, "that I may defy many months to produce any good to me."

This desponding turn of mind, though it could not be communicated to Mrs. Dashwood, gave additional pain to them all in the parting, which shortly took place, and left an uncomfortable impression on Elinor's feelings especially, which required some trouble and time to subdue. But as it was her determination to subdue it, and to prevent herself from appearing to suffer more than what all her family suffered on his going away, she did not adopt the method so judiciously employed by Marianne, on a similar occasion, to augment and fix her sorrow, by seeking silence, solitude and idleness. Their means were as different as their objects, and equally suited to the advancement of each.

Elinor sat down to her drawing-table as soon as he was out of the house, busily employed herself the whole day, neither sought nor avoided the mention of his name, appeared to interest herself almost as much as ever in the general concerns of the family, and if, by this conduct, she did not lessen her own grief, it was at least prevented from unnecessary increase, and her mother and sisters were spared much solicitude on her account.

Such behaviour as this, so exactly the reverse of her own, appeared no more meritorious to Marianne, than her own had seemed faulty to her. The business of self-command she settled very easily—with strong affections it was impossible, with calm ones it could have no merit. That her sister's affections *were* calm, she dared not deny, though she blushed to acknowledge it; and of the strength of her own, she gave a very striking proof, by still loving and respecting that sister, in spite of this mortifying conviction.

Without shutting herself up from her family, or leaving the house in determined solitude to avoid them, or lying awake the whole night to indulge meditation, Elinor found every day afforded her leisure enough to think of Edward, and of Edward's behaviour, in every possible variety which the different state of her spirits at different times could produce, with tenderness, pity, approbation, censure, and doubt. There were moments in abundance, when, if not by the absence of her mother and sisters, at least by the nature of their employments, conversation was forbidden among them, and every effect of solitude was produced. Her mind was inevitably at liberty; her thoughts could not be chained elsewhere; and the past and the future, on a subject so interesting, must be before her, must force her attention, and engross her memory, her reflection, and her fancy.

From a reverie of this kind, as she sat at her drawing-table, she was roused one morning, soon after Edward's leaving them, by the arrival of company. She happened to be quite alone. The closing of the little gate, at the entrance of the green court in front of the house, drew her eyes to the window, and she saw a large party walking up to the door. Amongst them were Sir John and Lady Middleton and Mrs. Jennings, but there were two others, a gentleman and lady, who were quite unknown to her. She was sitting near the window, and as soon as Sir John perceived her, he left the rest of the party to the ceremony of knocking at the door, and stepping across the turf, obliged her to open the casement to speak to him, though the space was so short between the door and the window, as to make it hardly possible to speak at one without being heard at the other.

"Well," said he, "we have brought you some strangers. How do you like them?"

"Hush! They will hear you."

"Never mind if they do. It is only the Palmers. Charlotte is very pretty, I can tell you. You may see her if you look this way."

As Elinor was certain of seeing her in a couple of minutes, without taking that liberty, she begged to be excused.

"Where is Marianne? Has she run away because we are come? I see her instrument is open."

"She is walking, I believe."

They were now joined by Mrs. Jennings, who had not patience enough to wait till the door was opened before she told *her* story. She came hallooing to the window, "How do you do, my dear? How does Mrs. Dashwood do? And where are your sisters? What! all alone! You will be glad of a little company to sit with you. I have brought my other son and daughter to see you. Only think of their coming so suddenly! I thought I heard a carriage last night, while we were drinking our tea, but it never entered my head that it could be them. I thought of nothing but whether it might not be Colonel Brandon come back again; so I said to Sir John, I do think I hear a carriage; perhaps it is Colonel Brandon come back again—"

Elinor was obliged to turn from her, in the middle of her story, to receive the rest of the party; Lady Middleton introduced the two strangers; Mrs. Dashwood and Margaret came down stairs at the same time, and they all sat down to look at one another, while Mrs. Jennings continued her story as she walked through the passage into the parlour, attended by Sir John.

Mrs. Palmer was several years younger than Lady Middleton, and totally unlike her in every respect. She was short and plump, had a very pretty face, and the finest expression of good humour in it that could possibly be. Her manners were by no means so elegant as her sister's, but they were much more prepossessing. She came in with a smile, smiled all the time of her visit, except when she laughed, and smiled when she went away. Her husband was a grave looking young man of five or six and twenty, with an air of more fashion and sense than his wife, but of less willingness to please or be pleased. He entered the room with a look of self-consequence, slightly bowed to the ladies, without speaking a word, and, after briefly surveying them and their apartments, took up a newspaper from the table, and continued to read it as long as he staid.

Mrs. Palmer, on the contrary, who was strongly endowed by nature with a turn for being uniformly civil and happy, was hardly seated before her admiration of the parlour and every thing in it burst forth.

"Well! What a delightful room this is! I never saw anything so charming! Only think, Mamma, how it is improved since I was here last! I always thought it such a sweet place, ma'am! (turning to Mrs. Dashwood) but you have made it so charming! Only look, sister, how delightful every thing is! How I should like such a house for myself! Should not you, Mr. Palmer?"

Mr. Palmer made her no answer, and did not even raise his eyes from the newspaper.

"Mr. Palmer does not hear me," said she, laughing; "he never does sometimes. It is so ridiculous!"

This was quite a new idea to Mrs. Dashwood; she had never been used to find wit in the inattention of any one, and could not help looking with surprise at them both.

Mrs. Jennings, in the meantime, talked on as loud as she could, and continued her account of their surprise, the evening before, on seeing their friends, without ceasing till every thing was told. Mrs. Palmer laughed heartily at the recollection of their astonishment, and every body agreed, two or three times over, that it had been quite an agreeable surprise.

"You may believe how glad we all were to see them," added Mrs. Jennings, leaning forward towards Elinor, and speaking in a low voice as if she meant to be heard by no one else, though they were seated on different sides of the room; "but, however, I can't help wishing they had not travelled quite so fast, nor made such a long journey of it, for they came all round by London upon account of some business, for you know (nodding significantly and pointing to her daughter) it was wrong in her situation. I wanted her to stay at home and rest this morning, but she would come with us; she longed so much to see you all!"

Mrs. Palmer laughed, and said it would not do her any harm.

"She expects to be confined in February," continued Mrs. Jennings.

Lady Middleton could no longer endure such a conversation, and therefore exerted herself to ask Mr. Palmer if there was any news in the paper.

"No, none at all," he replied, and read on.

"Here comes Marianne," cried Sir John. "Now, Palmer, you shall see a monstrous pretty girl."

He immediately went into the passage, opened the front door, and ushered her in himself. Mrs. Jennings asked her, as soon as she appeared, if she had not been to Allenham; and Mrs. Palmer laughed so heartily at the question, as to show she understood it. Mr. Palmer looked up on her entering the room, stared at her some minutes, and then returned to his newspaper. Mrs. Palmer's eye was now caught by the drawings which hung round the room. She got up to examine them.

"Oh! Dear, how beautiful these are! Well! How delightful! Do but look, mama, how sweet! I declare they are quite charming; I could look at them for ever." And then sitting down again, she very soon forgot that there were any such things in the room.

When Lady Middleton rose to go away, Mr. Palmer rose also, laid down the newspaper, stretched himself and looked at them all around.

"My love, have you been asleep?" said his wife, laughing.

He made her no answer; and only observed, after again examining the room, that it was very low pitched, and that the ceiling was crooked. He then made his bow, and departed with the rest.

Sir John had been very urgent with them all to spend the next day at the park. Mrs. Dashwood, who did not chuse to dine with them oftener than they dined at the cottage, absolutely refused on her own account; her daughters might do as they pleased. But they had no curiosity to see how Mr. and Mrs. Palmer ate their dinner, and no expectation of pleasure from them in any other way. They attempted, therefore, likewise, to excuse themselves; the weather was uncertain, and not likely to be good. But Sir John would not be satisfied—the carriage should be sent for them and they must come. Lady Middleton too, though she did not press their mother, pressed them. Mrs. Jennings and Mrs. Palmer joined their entreaties, all seemed equally anxious to avoid a family party; and the young ladies were obliged to yield.

"Why should they ask us?" said Marianne, as soon as they were gone. "The rent of this cottage is said to be low; but we have it on very hard terms, if we are to dine at the park whenever any one is staying either with them, or with us."

"They mean no less to be civil and kind to us now," said Elinor, "by these frequent invitations, than by those which we received from them a few weeks ago. The alteration is not in them, if their parties are grown tedious and dull. We must look for the change elsewhere."

CHAPTER XX

As the Miss Dashwoods entered the drawing-room of the park the next day, at one door, Mrs. Palmer came running in at the other, looking as good humoured and merry as before. She took them all most affectionately by the hand, and expressed great delight in seeing them again.

"I am so glad to see you!" said she, seating herself between Elinor and Marianne, "for it is so bad a day I was afraid you might not come, which would be a shocking thing, as we go away again tomorrow. We must go, for the Westons come to us next week you know. It was quite a sudden thing our coming at all, and I knew nothing of it till the carriage was coming to the door, and then Mr. Palmer asked me if I would go with him to Barton. He is so droll! He never tells me any thing! I am so sorry we cannot stay longer; however we shall meet again in town very soon, I hope."

They were obliged to put an end to such an expectation.

"Not go to town!" cried Mrs. Palmer, with a laugh, "I shall be quite disappointed if you do not. I could get the nicest house in world for you, next door to ours, in Hanover-square. You must come, indeed. I am sure I shall be very happy to chaperon you at any time till I am confined, if Mrs. Dashwood should not like to go into public."

They thanked her; but were obliged to resist all her entreaties.

"Oh, my love," cried Mrs. Palmer to her husband, who just then entered the room—"you must help me to persuade the Miss Dashwoods to go to town this winter."

Her love made no answer; and after slightly bowing to the ladies, began complaining of the weather.

"How horrid all this is!" said he. "Such weather makes every thing and every body disgusting. Dullness is as much produced within doors as without, by rain. It makes one detest all one's acquaintance. What the devil does Sir John mean by not having a billiard room in his house? How few people know what comfort is! Sir John is as stupid as the weather."

The rest of the company soon dropt in.

"I am afraid, Miss Marianne," said Sir John, "you have not been able to take your usual walk to Allenham today."

Marianne looked very grave and said nothing.

"Oh, don't be so sly before us," said Mrs. Palmer; "for we know all about it, I assure you; and I admire your taste very much, for I think he is extremely handsome. We do not live a great way from him in the country, you know. Not above ten miles, I dare say."

"Much nearer thirty," said her husband.

"Ah, well! There is not much difference. I never was at his house; but they say it is a sweet pretty place."

"As vile a spot as I ever saw in my life," said Mr. Palmer.

Marianne remained perfectly silent, though her countenance betrayed her interest in what was said.

"Is it very ugly?" continued Mrs. Palmer—"then it must be some other place that is so pretty I suppose."

When they were seated in the dining room, Sir John observed with regret that they were only eight all together.

"My dear," said he to his lady, "it is very provoking that we should be so few. Why did not you ask the Gilberts to come to us today?"

"Did not I tell you, Sir John, when you spoke to me about it before, that it could not be done? They dined with us last."

"You and I, Sir John," said Mrs. Jennings, "should not stand upon such ceremony."

"Then you would be very ill-bred," cried Mr. Palmer.

"My love you contradict everybody," said his wife with her usual laugh. "Do you know that you are quite rude?"

"I did not know I contradicted anybody in calling your mother ill-bred."

"Ay, you may abuse me as you please," said the good-natured old lady, "you have taken Charlotte off my hands, and cannot give her back again. So there I have the whip hand of you."

Charlotte laughed heartily to think that her husband could not get rid of her; and exultingly said, she did not care how cross he was to her, as they must live together. It was impossible for any one to be more thoroughly good-natured, or more determined to be happy than Mrs. Palmer. The studied indifference, insolence, and discontent of her husband gave her no pain; and when he scolded or abused her, she was highly diverted.

"Mr. Palmer is so droll!" said she, in a whisper, to Elinor. "He is always out of humour."

Elinor was not inclined, after a little observation, to give him credit for being so genuinely and unaffectedly ill-natured or ill-bred as he wished to appear. His temper might perhaps be a little soured by finding, like many others of his sex, that through some unaccountable bias in favour of beauty, he was the husband of a very silly woman, but she knew that this kind of blunder was too common for any sensible man to be lastingly hurt by it. It was rather a wish of distinction, she believed, which produced his contemptuous treatment of everybody, and his general abuse of every thing before him. It was the desire of appearing superior to other people. The motive was too common to be wondered at; but the means, however they might succeed by establishing his superiority in ill-breeding, were not likely to attach any one to him except his wife.

"Oh, my dear Miss Dashwood," said Mrs. Palmer soon afterwards, "I have got such a favour to ask of you and your sister. Will you come and spend some time at Cleveland this Christmas? Now, pray do, and come while the Westons are with us. You cannot think how happy I shall be! It will be quite delightful! My love," applying to her husband, "don't you long to have the Miss Dashwoods come to Cleveland?"

"Certainly," he replied, with a sneer—"I came into Devonshire with no other view."

"There now," said his lady, "you see Mr. Palmer expects you; so you cannot refuse to come."

They both eagerly and resolutely declined her invitation.

"But indeed you must and shall come. I am sure you will like it of all things. The Westons will be with us, and it will be quite delightful. You cannot think what a sweet place Cleveland is; and we are so gay now, for Mr. Palmer is always going about the country canvassing against the election; and so many people came to dine with us that I never saw before, it is quite charming! But, poor fellow! It is very fatiguing to him! for he is forced to make everybody like him."

Elinor could hardly keep her countenance as she assented to the hardship of such an obligation.

"How charming it will be," said Charlotte, "when he is in Parliament! Won't it? How I shall laugh! It will be so ridiculous to see all his letters directed to him with an M.P. But do you know, he says, he will never frank for me? He declares he won't. Don't you, Mr. Palmer?"

Mr. Palmer took no notice of her.

"He cannot bear writing, you know," she continued—"he says it is quite shocking."

"No," said he, "I never said any thing so irrational. Don't palm all your abuses of languages upon me."

"There now; you see how droll he is. This is always the way with him! Sometimes he won't speak to me for half a day together, and then he comes out with something so droll—all about anything in the world."

She surprised Elinor very much as they returned into the drawing-room, by asking her whether she did not like Mr. Palmer excessively.

"Certainly," said Elinor; "he seems very agreeable."

"Well—I am so glad you do. I thought you would, he is so pleasant; and Mr. Palmer is excessively pleased with you and your sisters I can tell you, and you can't think how disappointed he will be if you don't come to Cleveland. I can't imagine why you should object to it."

Elinor was again obliged to decline her invitation; and by changing the subject, put a stop to her entreaties. She thought it probable that as they lived in the same county, Mrs. Palmer might be able to give some more particular account of Willoughby's general character, than could be gathered from the Middletons' partial acquaintance with him; and she was eager to gain from any one, such a confirmation of his merits as might remove the possibility of fear from Marianne. She began by inquiring if they saw much of Mr. Willoughby at Cleveland, and whether they were intimately acquainted with him.

"Oh dear, yes; I know him extremely well," replied Mrs. Palmer—"Not that I ever spoke to him, indeed; but I have seen him for ever in town. Somehow or other I never happened to be staying at Barton while he was at Allenham. Mama saw him here once before—but I was with my uncle at Weymouth. However, I dare say we should have seen a great deal of him in Somersetshire, if it had not happened very unluckily that we should never have been in the country together. He is very little at Combe, I believe; but if he were ever so much there, I do not think Mr. Palmer would visit him, for he is in the opposition, you know, and besides it is such a way off. I know why you inquire about him, very well; your sister is to marry him. I am monstrous glad of it, for then I shall have her for a neighbour you know."

"Upon my word," replied Elinor, "you know much more of the matter than I do, if you have any reason to expect such a match."

"Don't pretend to deny it, because you know it is what everybody talks of. I assure you I heard of it in my way through town."

"My dear Mrs. Palmer!"

"Upon my honour I did. I met Colonel Brandon Monday morning in Bond-street, just before we left town, and he told me of it directly."

"You surprise me very much. Colonel Brandon tell you of it! Surely you must be mistaken. To give such intelligence to a person who could not be interested in it, even if it were true, is not what I should expect Colonel Brandon to do."

"But I do assure you it was so, for all that, and I will tell you how it happened. When we met him, he turned back and walked with us; and so we began talking of my brother and sister, and one thing and another, and I said to him, 'So, Colonel, there is a new family come to Barton Cottage, I hear, and mama sends me word they are very pretty, and that one of them is going to be married to Mr. Willoughby of Combe Magna. Is it true, pray? for of course you must know, as you have been in Devonshire so lately.' "

"And what did the Colonel say?"

"Oh—he did not say much; but he looked as if he knew it to be true, so from that moment I set it down as certain. It will be quite delightful, I declare! When is it to take place?"

"Mr. Brandon was very well I hope?"

"Oh! Yes, quite well; and so full of your praises, he did nothing but say fine things of you."

"I am flattered by his commendation. He seems an excellent man; and I think him uncommonly pleasing."

"So do I. He is such a charming man, that it is quite a pity he should be so grave and so dull. Mamma says *he* was in love with your sister too. I assure you it was a great compliment if he was, for he hardly ever falls in love with any body."

"Is Mr. Willoughby much known in your part of Somersetshire?" said Elinor.

"Oh! Yes, extremely well; that is, I do not believe many people are acquainted with him, because Combe Magna is so far off; but they all think him extremely agreeable I assure you. Nobody is more liked than Mr. Willoughby wherever he goes, and so you may tell your sister. She is a monstrous lucky girl to get him, upon my honour; not but that he is much more lucky in getting her, because she is so very handsome and agreeable, that nothing can be good enough for her. However, I don't think her hardly at all handsomer than you, I assure you; for I think you both excessively pretty, and so does Mr. Palmer too I am sure, though we could not get him to own it last night."

Mrs. Palmer's information respecting Willoughby was not very material; but any testimony in his favour, however small, was pleasing to her.

"I am so glad we are got acquainted at last," continued Charlotte. "And now I hope we shall always be great friends. You can't think how much I longed to see you! It is so delightful that you should live at the cottage! Nothing can be like it, to be sure! And I am so glad your sister is going to be well married! I hope you will be a great deal at Combe Magna. It is a sweet place, by all accounts."

"You have been long acquainted with Colonel Brandon, have not you?"

"Yes, a great while; ever since my sister married. He was a particular friend of Sir John's. I believe," she added in a low voice, "he would have been very glad to have had me, if he could. Sir John and Lady Middleton wished it very much. But mama did not think the match good enough for me, otherwise Sir John would have mentioned it to the Colonel, and we should have been married immediately."

"Did not Colonel Brandon know of Sir John's proposal to your mother before it was made? Had he never owned his affection to yourself?"

"Oh, no; but if mama had not objected to it, I dare say he would have liked it of all things. He had not seen me then above twice, for it was before I left school. However, I am much happier as I am. Mr. Palmer is the kind of man I like."

CHAPTER XXI

The Palmers returned to Cleveland the next day, and the two families at Barton were again left to entertain each other. But this did not last long; Elinor had hardly got their last visitors out of her head, had hardly done wondering at Charlotte's being so happy without a cause, at Mr. Palmer's acting so simply, with good abilities, and at the strange unsuitableness which often existed between husband and wife, before Sir John's and Mrs. Jennings's active zeal in the cause of society, procured her some other new acquaintance to see and observe.

In a morning's excursion to Exeter, they had met with two young ladies, whom Mrs. Jennings had the satisfaction of discovering to be her relations, and this was enough for Sir John to invite them directly to the Park, as soon as their present engagements at Exeter were over. Their engagements at Exeter instantly gave way before such an invitation, and Lady Middleton was thrown into no little alarm on the return of Sir John, by hearing that she was very soon to receive a visit from two girls whom she had never seen in her life, and of whose elegance, whose tolerable gentility even, she could have no proof; for the assurances of her husband and mother on that subject went for nothing at all. Their being her relations too made it so much the worse; and Mrs. Jennings's attempts at consolation were therefore unfortunately founded, when she advised her daughter not to care about their being so fashionable; because they were all cousins and must put up with one another. As it was impossible, however, now to prevent their coming, Lady Middleton resigned herself to the idea of it, with all the philosophy of a well-bred woman, contenting herself with merely giving her husband a gentle reprimand on the subject five or six times every day.

The young ladies arrived: their appearance was by no means ungenteel or unfashionable. Their dress was very smart, their manners very civil, they were delighted with the house, and in raptures with the furniture, and they happened to be so doatingly fond of children that Lady Middleton's good opinion was engaged in their favour before they had been an hour at the Park. She declared them to be very agreeable girls indeed, which for her ladyship was enthusiastic admiration. Sir John's confidence in his own judgment rose with this animated praise, and he set off directly for the cottage to tell the Miss Dashwoods of the Miss Steeles' arrival, and to assure them of their being the sweetest girls in the world. From such commendation as this, however, there was not much to be learned; Elinor well knew that the sweetest girls in the world were to be met with in every part of England, under every possible variation of form, face, temper and understanding. Sir John wanted the whole family to walk to the Park directly and look at his guests. Benevolent, philanthropic man! It was painful to him even to keep a third cousin to himself.

"Do come now," said he—"pray come—you must come—I declare you shall come—you can't think how you will like them. Lucy is monstrous pretty, and so good humoured and agreeable! The children are all hanging about her already, as if she was an old acquaintance. And they both long to see you of all things, for they have heard at Exeter that you are the most beautiful creatures in the world; and I have told them it is all very true, and a great deal more. You will be delighted with them I am sure. They have brought the whole coach full of playthings for the children. How can you be so cross as not to come? Why they are your cousins, you know, after a fashion. *You* are my cousins, and they are my wife's, so you must be related."

But Sir John could not prevail. He could only obtain a promise of their calling at the Park within a day or two, and then left them in amazement at their indifference, to walk home and boast anew of their attractions to the Miss Steeles, as he had been already boasting of the Miss Steeles to them.

When their promised visit to the Park and consequent introduction to these young ladies took place, they found in the appearance of the eldest, who was nearly thirty, with a very plain and not a sensible face, nothing to admire; but in the other, who was not more than two or three and twenty, they acknowledged considerable beauty; her features were pretty, and she had a sharp quick eye, and a smartness of air, which though it did not give actual elegance or grace, gave distinction to her person. Their manners were particularly civil, and Elinor soon allowed them credit for some kind of sense, when she saw with what constant and judicious attention they were making themselves agreeable to Lady Middleton. With her children they were in continual raptures, extolling their beauty, courting their notice, and humouring their whims; and such of their time as could be spared from the importunate demands which this politeness made on it, was spent in admiration of whatever her ladyship was doing, if she happened to be doing anything, or in taking patterns of some elegant new dress, in which her appearance the day before had thrown them into unceasing delight. Fortunately for those who pay their court through such foibles, a fond mother, though, in pursuit of praise for her children, the most rapacious of human beings, is likewise the most credulous; her demands are exorbitant; but she will swallow any thing; and the excessive affection and endurance of the Miss Steeles towards her offspring were viewed therefore by Lady Middleton without the smallest surprise or distrust. She saw with maternal complacency all the impertinent encroachments and mischievous tricks to which her cousins submitted. She saw their sashes untied, their hair pulled about their ears, their work-bags searched, and their knives and scissors stolen away, and felt no doubt of its being a reciprocal enjoyment. It suggested no other surprise than that Elinor and Marianne should sit so composedly by, without claiming a share in what was passing.

"John is in such spirits today!" said she, on his taking Miss Steeles's pocket handkerchief, and throwing it out of window—"He is full of monkey tricks."

And soon afterwards, on the second boy's violently pinching one of the same lady's fingers, she fondly observed, "How playful William is!"

"And here is my sweet little Annamaria," she added, tenderly caressing a little girl of three years old, who had not made a noise for the last two minutes; "And she is always so gentle and quiet—Never was there such a quiet little thing!"

But unfortunately in bestowing these embraces, a pin in her ladyship's head dress slightly scratching the child's neck, produced from this pattern of gentleness such violent screams, as could hardly be outdone by any creature professedly noisy. The mother's consternation was excessive; but it could not surpass the alarm of the Miss Steeles, and every thing was done by all three, in so critical an emergency, which affection could suggest as likely to assuage the agonies of the little sufferer. She was seated in her mother's lap, covered with kisses, her wound bathed with lavender-water, by one of the Miss Steeles, who was on her knees to attend her, and her mouth stuffed with sugar plums by the other. With such a reward for her tears, the child was too wise to cease crying. She still screamed and sobbed lustily, kicked her two brothers for offering to touch her, and all their united soothings were ineffectual till Lady Middleton luckily remembering that in a scene of similar distress last week, some apricot marmalade had been successfully applied for a bruised temple, the same remedy was eagerly proposed for this unfortunate scratch, and a slight intermission of screams in the young lady on hearing it, gave them reason to hope that it would not be rejected. She was carried out of the room therefore in her mother's arms, in quest of this medicine, and as the two boys chose to follow, though earnestly entreated by their mother to stay behind, the four young ladies were left in a quietness which the room had not known for many hours.

"Poor little creatures!" said Miss Steele, as soon as they were gone. "It might have been a very sad accident."

"Yet I hardly know how," cried Marianne, "unless it had been under totally different circumstances. But this is the usual way of heightening alarm, where there is nothing to be alarmed at in reality."

"What a sweet woman Lady Middleton is!" said Lucy Steele.

Marianne was silent; it was impossible for her to say what she did not feel, however trivial the occasion; and upon Elinor therefore the whole task of telling lies when politeness required it, always fell. She did her best when thus called on, by speaking of Lady Middleton with more warmth than she felt, though with far less than Miss Lucy.

"And Sir John too," cried the elder sister, "what a charming man he is!"

Here too, Miss Dashwood's commendation, being only simple and just, came in without any *éclat*. She merely observed that he was perfectly good humoured and friendly.

"And what a charming little family they have! I never saw such fine children in my life. I declare I quite doat upon them already, and indeed I am always distractedly fond of children."

"I should guess so," said Elinor, with a smile, "from what I have witnessed this morning."

"I have a notion," said Lucy, "you think the little Middletons rather too much indulged; perhaps they may be the outside of enough; but it is so natural in Lady Middleton; and for my part, I love to see children full of life and spirits; I cannot bear them if they are tame and quiet."

"I confess," replied Elinor, "that while I am at Barton Park, I never think of tame and quiet children with any abhorrence."

A short pause succeeded this speech, which was first broken by Miss Steele, who seemed very much disposed for conversation, and who now said rather abruptly, "And how do you like Devonshire, Miss Dashwood? I suppose you were very sorry to leave Sussex."

In some surprise at the familiarity of this question, or at least of the manner in which it was spoken, Elinor replied that she was.

"Norland is a prodigious beautiful place, is not it?" added Miss Steele.

"We have heard Sir John admire it excessively," said Lucy, who seemed to think some apology necessary for the freedom of her sister.

"I think every one *must* admire it," replied Elinor, "who ever saw the place; though it is not to be supposed that any one can estimate its beauties as we do."

"And had you a great many smart beaux there? I suppose you have not so many in this part of the world; for my part, I think they are a vast addition always."

"But why should you think," said Lucy, looking ashamed of her sister, "that there are not as many genteel young men in Devonshire as Sussex?"

"Nay, my dear, I'm sure I don't pretend to say that there a'n't. I'm sure there's a vast many smart beaux in Exeter; but you know, how could I tell what smart beaux there might be about Norland; and I was only afraid the Miss Dashwoods might find it dull at Barton, if they had not so many as they used to have. But perhaps you young ladies may not care about the beaux, and had as lief be without them as with them. For my part, I think they are vastly agreeable, provided they dress smart and behave civil. But I can't bear to see them dirty and nasty. Now there's Mr. Rose at Exeter, a prodigious smart young man, quite a beau, clerk to Mr. Simpson, you know, and yet if you do but meet him of a morning, he is not fit to be seen. I suppose your brother was quite a beau, Miss Dashwood, before he married, as he was so rich?"

"Upon my word," replied Elinor, "I cannot tell you, for I do not perfectly comprehend the meaning of the word. But this I can say, that if he ever was a beau before he married, he is one still for there is not the smallest alteration in him."

"Oh! Dear! one never thinks of married men's being beaux—they have something else to do."

"Lord! Anne," cried her sister, "you can talk of nothing but beaux—you will make Miss Dashwood believe you think of nothing else." And then to turn the discourse, she began admiring the house and the furniture.

This specimen of the Miss Steeles was enough. The vulgar freedom and folly of the eldest left her no recommendation, and as Elinor was not blinded by the beauty, or the shrewd look of the youngest, to her want of real elegance and artlessness, she left the house without any wish of knowing them better.

Not so the Miss Steeles. They came from Exeter, well provided with admiration for the use of Sir John Middleton, his family, and all his relations, and no niggardly proportion was now dealt out to his fair cousins, whom they declared to be the most beautiful, elegant, accomplished, and agreeable girls they had ever beheld, and with whom they were particularly anxious to be better acquainted. And to be better acquainted therefore, Elinor soon found was their inevitable lot, for as Sir John was entirely on the side of the Miss Steeles, their party would be too strong for opposition, and that kind of intimacy must be submitted to, which consists of sitting an hour or two together in the same room almost every day. Sir John could do no more; but he did not know that any more was required: to be together was, in his opinion, to be intimate, and while his continual schemes for their meeting were effectual, he had not a doubt of their being established friends.

To do him justice, he did every thing in his power to promote their unreserve, by making the Miss Steeles acquainted with whatever he knew or supposed of his cousins' situations in the most delicate particulars, and Elinor had not seen them more than twice, before the eldest of them wished her joy on her sister's having been so lucky as to make a conquest of a very smart beau since she came to Barton.

"'Twill be a fine thing to have her married so young to be sure," said she, "and I hear he is quite a beau, and prodigious handsome. And I hope you may have as good luck yourself soon, but perhaps you may have a friend in the corner already."

Elinor could not suppose that Sir John would be more nice in proclaiming his suspicions of her regard for Edward, than he had been with respect to Marianne; indeed it was rather his favourite joke of the two, as being somewhat newer and more conjectural; and since Edward's visit, they had never dined together without his drinking to her best affections with so much significancy and so many nods and winks, as to excite general attention. The letter F had been likewise invariably brought forward, and found productive of such countless jokes, that its character as the wittiest letter in the alphabet had been long established with Elinor.

The Miss Steeles, as she expected, had now all the benefit of these jokes, and in the eldest of them they raised a curiosity to know the name of the gentleman alluded to, which, though often impertinently expressed, was perfectly of a piece with her general inquisitiveness into the concerns of their family. But Sir John did not sport long with the curiosity which he delighted to raise, for he had at least as much pleasure in telling the name, as Miss Steele had in hearing it.

"His name is Ferrars," said he, in a very audible whisper; "but pray do not tell it, for it's a great secret."

"Ferrars!" repeated Miss Steele; "Mr. Ferrars is the happy man, is he? What! Your sister-in-law's brother, Miss Dashwood? a very agreeable young man to be sure; I know him very well."

"How can you say so, Anne?" cried Lucy, who generally made an amendment to all her sister's assertions. "Though we have seen him once or twice at my uncle's, it is rather too much to pretend to know him very well."

Elinor heard all this with attention and surprise. "And who was this uncle? Where did he live? How came they acquainted?" She wished very much to have the subject continued, though she did not chuse to join in it herself; but nothing more of it was said, and for the first time in her life, she thought Mrs. Jennings deficient either in curiosity after petty information, or in a disposition to communicate it. The manner in which Miss Steele had spoken of Edward, increased her curiosity; for it struck her as being rather ill-natured, and suggested the suspicion of that lady's knowing, or fancying herself to know something to his disadvantage. But her curiosity was unavailing, for no farther notice was taken of Mr. Ferrars's name by Miss Steele when alluded to, or even openly mentioned by Sir John.

CHAPTER XXII

Marianne, who had never much toleration for anything like impertinence, vulgarity, inferiority of parts, or even difference of taste from herself, was at this time particularly ill-disposed, from the state of her spirits, to be pleased with the Miss Steeles, or to encourage their advances; and to the invariable coldness of her behaviour towards them, which checked every endeavour at intimacy on their side, Elinor principally attributed that preference of herself which soon became evident in the manners of both, but especially of Lucy, who missed no opportunity of engaging her in conversation, or of striving to improve their acquaintance by an easy and frank communication of her sentiments.

Lucy was naturally clever; her remarks were often just and amusing; and as a companion for half an hour Elinor frequently found her agreeable; but her powers had received no aid from education: she was ignorant and illiterate; and her deficiency of all mental improvement, her want of information in the most common particulars, could not be concealed from Miss Dashwood, in spite of her constant endeavour to appear to advantage. Elinor saw, and pitied her for, the neglect of abilities which education might have rendered so respectable; but she saw, with less tenderness of feeling, the thorough want of delicacy, of rectitude, and integrity of mind, which her attentions, her assiduities, her flatteries at the Park betrayed; and she could have no lasting satisfaction in the company of a person who joined insincerity with ignorance; whose want of instruction prevented their meeting in conversation on terms of equality, and whose conduct toward others made every shew of attention and deference towards herself perfectly valueless.

"You will think my question an odd one, I dare say," said Lucy to her one day, as they were walking together from the park to the cottage—"but pray, are you personally acquainted with your sister-in-law's mother, Mrs. Ferrars?"

Elinor *did* think the question a very odd one, and her countenance expressed it, as she answered that she had never seen Mrs. Ferrars.

"Indeed!" replied Lucy; "I wonder at that, for I thought you must have seen her at Norland sometimes. Then, perhaps, you cannot tell me what sort of a woman she is?"

"No," returned Elinor, cautious of giving her real opinion of Edward's mother, and not very desirous of satisfying what seemed impertinent curiosity—"I know nothing of her."

"I am sure you think me very strange, for enquiring about her in such a way," said Lucy, eyeing Elinor attentively as she spoke; "but perhaps there may be reasons—I wish I might venture; but however I hope you will do me the justice of believing that I do not mean to be impertinent."

Elinor made her a civil reply, and they walked on for a few minutes in silence. It was broken by Lucy, who renewed the subject again by saying, with some hesitation,

"I cannot bear to have you think me impertinently curious. I am sure I would rather do any thing in the world than be thought so by a person whose good opinion is so well worth having as yours. And I am sure I should not have the smallest fear of trusting *you*; indeed, I should be very glad of your advice how to manage in such an uncomfortable situation as I am; but, however, there is no occasion to trouble *you*. I am sorry you do not happen to know Mrs. Ferrars."

"I am sorry I do *not*," said Elinor, in great astonishment, "if it could be of any use to *you* to know my opinion of her. But really I never understood that you were at all connected with that family, and therefore I am a little surprised, I confess, at so serious an inquiry into her character."

"I dare say you are, and I am sure I do not at all wonder at it. But if I dared tell you all, you would not be so much surprised. Mrs. Ferrars is certainly nothing to me at present—but the time *may* come—how soon it will come must depend upon herself—when we may be very intimately connected."

She looked down as she said this, amiably bashful, with only one side glance at her companion to observe its effect on her.

"Good heavens!" cried Elinor, "What do you mean? Are you acquainted with Mr. Robert Ferrars? Can you be?" And she did not feel much delighted with the idea of such a sister-in-law.

"No," replied Lucy, "not to Mr. *Robert* Ferrars—I never saw him in my life; but," fixing her eyes upon Elinor, "to his eldest brother."

What felt Elinor at that moment? Astonishment, that would have been as painful as it was strong, had not an immediate disbelief of the assertion attended it. She turned towards Lucy in silent amazement, unable to divine the reason or object of such a declaration; and though her complexion varied, she stood firm in incredulity, and felt in no danger of an hysterical fit, or a swoon.

"You may well be surprised," continued Lucy; "for to be sure you could have had no idea of it before; for I dare say he never dropped the smallest hint of it to you or any of your family; because it was always meant to be a great secret, and I am sure has been faithfully kept so by me to this hour. Not a soul of all my relations know of it but Anne, and I never should have mentioned it to you, if I had not felt the greatest dependence in the world upon your secrecy; and I really thought my behaviour in asking so many questions about Mrs. Ferrars must seem so odd, that it ought to be explained. And I do not think Mr. Ferrars can be displeased, when he knows I have trusted you, because I know he has the highest opinion in the world of all your family, and looks upon yourself and the other Miss Dashwoods quite as his own sisters."—She paused.

Elinor for a few moments remained silent. Her astonishment at what she heard was at first too great for words; but at length forcing herself to speak, and to speak cautiously, she said, with calmness of manner, which tolerably well concealed her surprise and solicitude—"May I ask if your engagement is of long standing?"

"We have been engaged these four years."

"Four years!"

"Yes."

Elinor, though greatly shocked, still felt unable to believe it.

"I did not know," said she, "that you were even acquainted till the other day."

"Our acquaintance, however, is of many years date. He was under my uncle's care, you know, a considerable while."

"Your uncle!"

"Yes; Mr. Pratt. Did you never hear him talk of Mr. Pratt?"

"I think I have," replied Elinor, with an exertion of spirits, which increased with her increase of emotion.

"He was four years with my uncle, who lives at Longstaple, near Plymouth. It was there our acquaintance begun, for my sister and me was often staying with my uncle, and it was there our engagement was formed, though not till a year after he had quitted as a pupil; but he was almost always with us afterwards. I was very unwilling to enter into it, as you may imagine, without the knowledge and approbation of his mother; but I was too young, and loved him too well, to be so prudent as I ought to have been. Though you do not know him so well as me, Miss Dashwood, you must have seen enough of him to be sensible he is very capable of making a woman sincerely attached to him."

"Certainly," answered Elinor, without knowing what she said; but after a moment's reflection, she added, with revived security of Edward's honour and love, and her companion's falsehood—"Engaged to Mr. Edward Ferrars! I confess myself so totally surprised at what you tell me, that really—I beg your pardon; but surely there must be some mistake of person or name. We cannot mean the same Mr. Ferrars."

"We can mean no other," cried Lucy, smiling. "Mr. Edward Ferrars, the eldest son of Mrs. Ferrars, of Park Street, and brother of your sister-in-law, Mrs. John Dashwood, is the person I mean; you must allow that I am not likely to be deceived as to the name of the man on who all my happiness depends."

"It is strange," replied Elinor, in a most painful perplexity, "that I should never have heard him even mention your name."

"No; considering our situation, it was not strange. Our first care has been to keep the matter secret. You knew nothing of me, or my family, and, therefore, there could be no *occasion* for ever mentioning my name to you; and, as he was always particularly afraid of his sister's suspecting any thing, *that* was reason enough for his not mentioning it."

She was silent. Elinor's security sunk; but her self-command did not sink with it.

"Four years you have been engaged," said she with a firm voice.

"Yes; and heaven knows how much longer we may have to wait. Poor Edward! It puts him quite out of heart." Then taking a small miniature from her pocket, she added, "To prevent the possibility of mistake, be so good as to look at this face. It does not do him justice, to be sure, but yet I think you cannot be deceived as to the person it was drew for. I have had it above these three years."

She put it into her hands as she spoke; and when Elinor saw the painting, whatever other doubts her fear of a too hasty decision, or her wish of detecting falsehood might suffer to linger in her mind, she could have none of its being Edward's face. She returned it almost instantly, acknowledging the likeness.

"I have never been able," continued Lucy, "to give him my picture in return, which I am very much vexed at, for he has been always so anxious to get it! But I am determined to set for it the very first opportunity."

"You are quite in the right," replied Elinor calmly. They then proceeded a few paces in silence. Lucy spoke first.

"I am sure," said she, "I have no doubt in the world of your faithfully keeping this secret, because you must know of what importance it is to us, not to have it reach his mother; for she would never approve of it, I dare say. I shall have no fortune, and I fancy she is an exceeding proud woman."

"I certainly did not seek your confidence," said Elinor; "but you do me no more than justice in imagining that I may be depended on. Your secret is safe with me; but pardon me if I express some surprise at so unnecessary a communication. You must at least have felt that my being acquainted with it could not add to its safety."

As she said this, she looked earnestly at Lucy, hoping to discover something in her countenance; perhaps the falsehood of the greatest part of what she had been saying; but Lucy's countenance suffered no change.

"I was afraid you would think I was taking a great liberty with you," said she, "in telling you all this. I have not known you long to be sure, personally at least, but I have known you and all your family by description a great while; and as soon as I saw you, I felt almost as if you was an old acquaintance. Besides in the present case, I really thought some explanation was due to you after my making such particular inquiries about Edward's mother; and I am so unfortunate, that I have not a creature whose advice I can ask. Anne is the only person that knows of it, and she has no judgment at all; indeed, she does me a great deal more harm than good, for I am in constant fear of her betraying me. She does not know how to hold her tongue, as you must perceive, and I am sure I was in the greatest fright in the world t'other day, when Edward's name was mentioned by Sir John, lest she should out with it all. You can't think how much I go through in my mind from it altogether. I only wonder that I am alive after what I have suffered for Edward's sake these last four years. Everything in such suspense and uncertainty; and seeing him so seldom—we can hardly meet above twice a-year. I am sure I wonder my heart is not quite broke."

Here she took out her handkerchief; but Elinor did not feel very compassionate.

"Sometimes." continued Lucy, after wiping her eyes, "I think whether it would not be better for us both to break off the matter entirely." As she said this, she looked directly at her companion. "But then at other times I have not resolution enough for it. I cannot bear the thoughts of making him so miserable, as I know the very mention of such a thing would do. And on my own account too—so dear as he is to me—I don't think I could be equal to it. What would you advise me to do in such a case, Miss Dashwood? What would you do yourself?"

"Pardon me," replied Elinor, startled by the question; "but I can give you no advice under such circumstances. Your own judgment must direct you."

"To be sure," continued Lucy, after a few minutes silence on both sides, "his mother must provide for him sometime or other; but poor Edward is so cast down by it! Did you not think him dreadful low-spirited when he was at Barton? He was so miserable when he left us at Longstaple, to go to you, that I was afraid you would think him quite ill."

"Did he come from your uncle's, then, when he visited us?"

"Oh, yes; he had been staying a fortnight with us. Did you think he came directly from town?"

"No," replied Elinor, most feelingly sensible of every fresh circumstance in favour of Lucy's veracity; "I remember he told us, that he had been staying a fortnight with some friends near Plymouth." She remembered too, her own surprise at the time, at his mentioning nothing farther of those friends, at his total silence with respect even to their names.

"Did not you think him sadly out of spirits?" repeated Lucy.

"We did, indeed, particularly so when he first arrived."

"I begged him to exert himself for fear you should suspect what was the matter; but it made him so melancholy, not being able to stay more than a fortnight with us, and seeing me so much affected. Poor fellow! I am afraid it is just the same with him now; for he writes in wretched spirits. I heard from him just before I left Exeter"; taking a letter from her pocket and carelessly showing the direction to Elinor. "You know his hand, I dare say, a charming one it is; but that is not written so well as usual. He was tired, I dare say, for he had just filled the sheet to me as full as possible."

Elinor saw that it *was* his hand, and she could doubt no longer. This picture, she had allowed herself to believe, might have been accidentally obtained; it might not have been Edward's gift; but a correspondence between them by letter, could subsist only under a positive engagement, could be authorised by nothing else; for a few moments, she was almost overcome—her heart sunk within her, and she could hardly stand; but exertion was indispensably necessary; and she struggled so resolutely against the oppression of her feelings, that her success was speedy, and for the time complete.

"Writing to each other," said Lucy, returning the letter into her pocket, "is the only comfort we have in such long separations. Yes, I have one other comfort in his picture, but poor Edward has not even *that*. If he had but my picture, he says he should be easy. I gave him a lock of my hair set in a ring when he was at Longstaple last, and that was some comfort to him, he said, but not equal to a picture. Perhaps you might notice the ring when you saw him?"

"I did," said Elinor, with a composure of voice, under which was concealed an emotion and distress beyond any thing she had ever felt before. She was mortified, shocked, confounded.

Fortunately for her, they had now reached the cottage, and the conversation could be continued no farther. After sitting with them a few minutes, the Miss Steeles returned to the Park, and Elinor was then at liberty to think and be wretched.

CHAPTER XXIII

However small Elinor's general dependence on Lucy's veracity might be, it was impossible for her on serious reflection to suspect it in the present case, where no temptation could be answerable to the folly of inventing a falsehood of such a description. What Lucy had asserted to be true, therefore, Elinor could not, dared not longer doubt; supported as it was too on every side by such probabilities and proofs, and contradicted by nothing but her own wishes. Their opportunity of acquaintance in the house of Mr. Pratt was a foundation for the rest, at once indisputable and alarming; and Edward's visit near Plymouth, his melancholy state of mind, his dissatisfaction at his own prospects, his uncertain behaviour towards herself, the intimate knowledge of the Miss Steeles as to Norland and their family connections, which had often surprised her, the picture, the letter, the ring, formed altogether such a body of evidence, as overcame every fear of condemning him unfairly, and established as a fact, which no partiality could set aside, his ill-treatment of herself. Her resentment of such behaviour, her indignation at having been its dupe, for a short time made her feel only for herself; but other ideas, other considerations, soon arose. Had Edward been intentionally deceiving her? Had he feigned a regard for her which he did not feel? Was his engagement to Lucy an engagement of the heart? No; whatever it might once have been, she could not believe it such at present. His affection was all her own. She could not be deceived in that. Her mother, sisters, Fanny, all had been conscious of his regard for her at Norland; it was not an illusion of her own vanity. He certainly loved her. What a softener of the heart was this persuasion! How much could it not tempt her to forgive! He had been blamable, highly blamable, in remaining at Norland after he first felt her influence over him to be more than it ought to be. In that, he could not be defended; but if he had injured her, how much more had he injured himself; if her case were pitiable, his was hopeless. His imprudence had made her miserable for a while; but it seemed to have deprived himself of all chance of ever being otherwise. She might in time regain tranquillity; but *he*, what had he to look forward to? Could he ever be tolerably happy with Lucy Steele; could he, were his affection for herself out of the question, with his integrity, his delicacy, and well-informed mind, be satisfied with a wife like her—illiterate, artful, and selfish?

The youthful infatuation of nineteen would naturally blind him to everything but her beauty and good nature; but the four succeeding years—years, which if rationally spent, give such improvement to the understanding, must have opened his eyes to her defects of education, while the same period of time, spent on her side in inferior society and more frivolous pursuits, had perhaps robbed her of that simplicity which might once have given an interesting character to her beauty.

If in the supposition of his seeking to marry herself, his difficulties from his mother had seemed great, how much greater were they now likely to be, when the object of his engagement was undoubtedly inferior in connections, and probably inferior in fortune to herself. These difficulties, indeed, with a heart so alienated from Lucy, might not press very hard upon his patience; but melancholy was the state of the person by whom the expectation of family opposition and unkindness, could be felt as a relief!

As these considerations occurred to her in painful succession, she wept for him, more than for herself. Supported by the conviction of having done nothing to merit her present unhappiness, and consoled by the belief that Edward had done nothing to forfeit her esteem, she thought she could even now, under the first smart of the heavy blow, command herself enough to guard every suspicion of the truth from her mother and sisters. And so well was she able to answer her own expectations, that when she joined them at dinner only two hours after she had first suffered the extinction of all her dearest hopes, no one would have supposed from the appearance of the sisters, that Elinor was mourning in secret over obstacles which must divide her forever from the object of her love, and that Marianne was internally dwelling on the perfections of a man, of whose whole heart she felt thoroughly possessed, and whom she expected to see in every carriage which drove near their house.

The necessity of concealing from her mother and Marianne, what had been entrusted in confidence to herself, though it obliged her to unceasing exertion, was no aggravation of Elinor's distress. On the contrary it was a relief to her, to be spared the communication of what would give such affliction to them, and to be saved likewise from hearing that condemnation of Edward, which would probably flow from the excess of their partial affection for herself, and which was more than she felt equal to support.

From their counsel, or their conversation, she knew she could receive no assistance, their tenderness and sorrow must add to her distress, while her self-command would neither receive encouragement from their example nor from their praise. She was stronger alone, and her own good sense so well supported her, that her firmness was as unshaken, her appearance of cheerfulness as invariable, as with regrets so poignant and so fresh, it was possible for them to be.

Much as she had suffered from her first conversation with Lucy on the subject, she soon felt an earnest wish of renewing it; and this for more reasons than one. She wanted to hear many particulars of their engagement repeated again, she wanted more clearly to understand what Lucy really felt for Edward, whether there were any sincerity in her declaration of tender regard for him, and she particularly wanted to convince Lucy, by her readiness to enter on the matter again, and her calmness in conversing on it, that she was no otherwise interested in it than as a friend, which she very much feared her involuntary agitation, in their morning discourse, must have left at least doubtful. That Lucy was disposed to be jealous of her appeared very probable: it was plain that Edward had always spoken highly in her praise, not merely from Lucy's assertion, but from her venturing to trust her on so short a personal acquaintance, with a secret so confessedly and evidently important. And even Sir John's joking intelligence must have had some weight. But indeed, while Elinor remained so well assured within herself of being really beloved by Edward, it required no other consideration of probabilities to make it natural that Lucy should be jealous; and that she was so, her very confidence was a proof. What other reason for the disclosure of the affair could there be, but that Elinor might be informed by it of Lucy's superior claims on Edward, and be taught to avoid him in future? She had little difficulty in understanding thus much of her rival's intentions, and while she was firmly resolved to act by her as every principle of honour and honesty directed, to combat her own affection for Edward and to see him as little as possible; she could not deny herself the comfort of endeavouring to convince Lucy that her heart was unwounded. And as she could now have nothing more painful to hear on the subject than had already been told, she did not mistrust her own ability of going through a repetition of particulars with composure.

But it was not immediately that an opportunity of doing so could be commanded, though Lucy was as well disposed as herself to take advantage of any that occurred; for the weather was not often fine enough to allow of their joining in a walk, where they might most easily separate themselves from the others; and though they met at least every other evening either at the park or cottage, and chiefly at the former, they could not be supposed to meet for the sake of conversation. Such a thought would never enter either Sir John or Lady Middleton's head; and therefore very little leisure was ever given for a general chat, and none at all for particular discourse. They met for the sake of eating, drinking, and laughing together, playing at cards, or consequences, or any other game that was sufficiently noisy.

One or two meetings of this kind had taken place, without affording Elinor any chance of engaging Lucy in private, when Sir John called at the cottage one morning, to beg, in the name of charity, that they would all dine with Lady Middleton that day, as he was obliged to attend the club at Exeter, and she would otherwise be quite alone, except her mother and the two Miss Steeles. Elinor, who foresaw a fairer opening for the point she had in view, in such a party as this was likely to be, more at liberty among themselves under the tranquil and well-bred direction of Lady Middleton than when her husband united them together in one noisy purpose, immediately accepted the invitation; Margaret, with her mother's permission, was equally compliant, and Marianne, though always unwilling to join any of their parties, was persuaded by her mother, who could not bear to have her seclude herself from any chance of amusement, to go likewise.

The young ladies went, and Lady Middleton was happily preserved from the frightful solitude which had threatened her. The insipidity of the meeting was exactly such as Elinor had expected; it produced not one novelty of thought or expression, and nothing could be less interesting than the whole of their discourse both in the dining parlour and drawing room: to the latter, the children accompanied them, and while they remained there, she was too well convinced of the impossibility of engaging Lucy's attention to attempt it. They quitted it only with the removal of the tea-things. The card-table was then placed, and Elinor began to wonder at herself for having ever entertained a hope of finding time for conversation at the park. They all rose up in preparation for a round game.

"I am glad," said Lady Middleton to Lucy, "you are not going to finish poor little Annamaria's basket this evening; for I am sure it must hurt your eyes to work filigree by candlelight. And we will make the dear little love some amends for her disappointment to-morrow, and then I hope she will not much mind it."

This hint was enough, Lucy recollected herself instantly and replied, "Indeed you are very much mistaken, Lady Middleton; I am only waiting to know whether you can make your party without me, or I should have been at my filigree already. I would not disappoint the little angel for all the world: and if you want me at the card-table now, I am resolved to finish the basket after supper."

"You are very good, I hope it won't hurt your eyes—will you ring the bell for some working candles? My poor little girl would be sadly disappointed, I know, if the basket was not finished tomorrow, for though I told her it certainly would not, I am sure she depends upon having it done."

Lucy directly drew her work table near her and reseated herself with an alacrity and cheerfulness which seemed to infer that she could taste no greater delight than in making a filigree basket for a spoilt child.

Lady Middleton proposed a rubber of cassino to the others. No one made any objection but Marianne, who with her usual inattention to the forms of general civility, exclaimed, "Your Ladyship will have the goodness to excuse *me*—you know I detest cards. I shall go to the piano-forte; I have not touched it since it was tuned." And without farther ceremony, she turned away and walked to the instrument.

Lady Middleton looked as if she thanked heaven that *she* had never made so rude a speech.

"Marianne can never keep long from that instrument you know, ma'am," said Elinor, endeavouring to smooth away the offence; "and I do not much wonder at it; for it is the very best toned piano-forte I ever heard."

The remaining five were now to draw their cards.

"Perhaps," continued Elinor, "if I should happen to cut out, I may be of some use to Miss Lucy Steele, in rolling her papers for her; and there is so much still to be done to the basket, that it must be impossible I think for her labour singly, to finish it this evening. I should like the work exceedingly, if she would allow me a share in it."

"Indeed I shall be very much obliged to you for your help," cried

Lucy, "for I find there is more to be done to it than I thought there was; and it would be a shocking thing to disappoint dear Annamaria after all."

"Oh! that would be terrible, indeed," said Miss Steele—"Dear little soul, how I do love her!"

"You are very kind," said Lady Middleton to Elinor; "and as you really like the work, perhaps you will be as well pleased not to cut in till another rubber, or will you take your chance now?"

Elinor joyfully profited by the first of these proposals, and thus by a little of that address which Marianne could never condescend to practise, gained her own end, and pleased Lady Middleton at the same time. Lucy made room for her with ready attention, and the two fair rivals were thus seated side by side at the same table, and, with the utmost harmony, engaged in forwarding the same work. The pianoforte at which Marianne, wrapped up in her own music and her own thoughts, had by this time forgotten that any body was in the room besides herself, was luckily so near them that Miss Dashwood now judged she might safely, under the shelter of its noise, introduce the interesting subject, without any risk of being heard at the card-table.

CHAPTER XXIV

In a firm, though cautious tone, Elinor thus began.

"I should be undeserving of the confidence you have honoured me with, if I felt no desire for its continuance, or no farther curiosity on its subject. I will not apologize therefore for bringing it forward again."

"Thank you," cried Lucy warmly, "for breaking the ice; you have set my heart at ease by it; for I was somehow or other afraid I had offended you by what I told you that Monday."

"Offended me! How could you suppose so? Believe me," and Elinor spoke it with the truest sincerity, "nothing could be farther from my intention than to give you such an idea. Could you have a motive for the trust, that was not honourable and flattering to me?"

"And yet I do assure you," replied Lucy, her little sharp eyes full of meaning, "there seemed to me to be a coldness and displeasure in your manner that made me quite uncomfortable. I felt sure that you was angry with me; and have been quarrelling with myself ever since, for having took such a liberty as to trouble you with my affairs. But I am very glad to find it was only my own fancy, and that you really do not blame me. If you knew what a consolation it was to me to relieve my heart speaking to you of what I am always thinking of every moment of my life, your compassion would make you overlook everything else I am sure."

"Indeed, I can easily believe that it was a very great relief to you, to acknowledge your situation to me, and be assured that you shall never have reason to repent it. Your case is a very unfortunate one; you seem to me to be surrounded with difficulties, and you will have need of all your mutual affection to support you under them. Mr. Ferrars, I believe, is entirely dependent on his mother."

"He has only two thousand pounds of his own; it would be madness to marry upon that, though for my own part, I could give up every prospect of more without a sigh. I have been always used to a very small income, and could struggle with any poverty for him; but I love him too well to be the selfish means of robbing him, perhaps, of all that his mother might give him if he married to please her. We must wait, it may be for many years. With almost every other man in the world, it would be an alarming prospect; but Edward's affection and constancy nothing can deprive me of I know."

"That conviction must be every thing to you; and he is undoubtedly supported by the same trust in yours. If the strength of your reciprocal attachment had failed, as between many people, and under many circumstances it naturally would during a four years' engagement, your situation would have been pitiable, indeed."

Lucy here looked up; but Elinor was careful in guarding her countenance from every expression that could give her words a suspicious tendency.

"Edward's love for me," said Lucy, "has been pretty well put to the test, by our long, very long absence since we were first engaged, and it has stood the trial so well, that I should be unpardonable to doubt it now. I can safely say that he has never gave me one moment's alarm on that account from the first."

Elinor hardly knew whether to smile or sigh at this assertion.

Lucy went on. "I am rather of a jealous temper too by nature, and from our different situations in life, from his being so much more in the world than me, and our continual separation, I was enough inclined for suspicion, to have found out the truth in an instant, if there had been the slightest alteration in his behaviour to me when we met, or any lowness of spirits that I could not account for, or if he had talked more of one lady than another, or seemed in any respect less happy at Longstaple than he used to be. I do not mean to say that I am particularly observant or quick-sighted in general, but in such a case I am sure I could not be deceived."

"All this," thought Elinor, "is very pretty; but it can impose upon neither of us."

"But what," said she after a short silence, "are your views? Or have you none but that of waiting for Mrs. Ferrars's death, which is a melancholy and shocking extremity? Is her son determined to submit to this, and to all the tediousness of the many years of suspense in which it may involve you, rather than run the risk of her displeasure for a while by owning the truth?"

"If we could be certain that it would be only for a while! But Mrs. Ferrars is a very headstrong proud woman, and in her first fit of anger upon hearing it, would very likely secure every thing to Robert, and the idea of that, for Edward's sake, frightens away all my inclination for hasty measures."

"And for your own sake too, or you are carrying your disinterestedness beyond reason."

Lucy looked at Elinor again, and was silent.

"Do you know Mr. Robert Ferrars?" asked Elinor.

"Not at all—I never saw him; but I fancy he is very unlike his brother—silly and a great coxcomb."

"A great coxcomb!" repeated Miss Steele, whose ear had caught those words by a sudden pause in Marianne's music. "Oh, they are talking of their favourite beaux, I dare say."

"No sister," cried Lucy, "you are mistaken there, our favourite beaux are *not* great coxcombs."

"I can answer for it that Miss Dashwood's is not," said Mrs. Jennings, laughing heartily; "for he is one of the modestest, prettiest behaved young men I ever saw; but as for Lucy, she is such a sly little creature, there is no finding out who *she* likes."

"Oh," cried Miss Steele, looking significantly round at them, "I dare say Lucy's beau is quite as modest and pretty behaved as Miss Dashwood's."

Elinor blushed in spite of herself. Lucy bit her lip, and looked angrily at her sister. A mutual silence took place for some time. Lucy first put an end to it by saying in a lower tone, though Marianne was then giving them the powerful protection of a very magnificent concerto—

"I will honestly tell you of one scheme which has lately come into my head, for bringing matters to bear; indeed I am bound to let you into the secret, for you are a party concerned. I dare say you have seen enough of Edward to know that he would prefer the church to every other profession; now my plan is that he should take orders as soon as he can, and then through your interest, which I am sure you would be kind enough to use out of friendship for him, and I hope out of some regard to me, your brother might be persuaded to give him Norland living; which I understand is a very good one, and the present incumbent not likely to live a great while. That would be enough for us to marry upon, and we might trust to time and chance for the rest."

"I should always be happy," replied Elinor, "to show any mark of my esteem and friendship for Mr. Ferrars; but do you not perceive that my interest on such an occasion would be perfectly unnecessary? He is brother to Mrs. John Dashwood—*that* must be recommendation enough to her husband."

"But Mrs. John Dashwood would not much approve of Edward's going into orders."

"Then I rather suspect that my interest would do very little."

They were again silent for many minutes. At length Lucy exclaimed with a deep sigh—

"I believe it would be the wisest way to put an end to the business at once by dissolving the engagement. We seem so beset with difficulties on every side, that though it would make us miserable for a time, we should be happier perhaps in the end. But you will not give me your advice, Miss Dashwood?"

"No," answered Elinor, with a smile, which concealed very agitated feelings, "on such a subject I certainly will not. You know very well that my opinion would have no weight with you, unless it were on the side of your wishes."

"Indeed you wrong me," replied Lucy, with great solemnity; "I know nobody of whose judgment I think so highly as I do of yours; and I do really believe, that if you was to say to me, 'I advise you by all means to put an end to your engagement with Edward Ferrars, it will be more for the happiness of both of you,' I should resolve upon doing it immediately."

Elinor blushed for the insincerity of Edward's future wife, and replied, "This compliment would effectually frighten me from giving any opinion on the subject had I formed one. It raises my influence much too high; the power of dividing two people so tenderly attached is too much for an indifferent person."

"'Tis because you are an indifferent person," said Lucy, with some pique, and laying a particular stress on those words, "that your judgment might justly have such weight with me. If you could be supposed to be biased in any respect by your own feelings, your opinion would not be worth having."

Elinor thought it wisest to make no answer to this, lest they might provoke each other to an unsuitable increase of ease and unreserve; and was even partly determined never to mention the subject again. Another pause therefore of many minutes' duration, succeeded this speech, and Lucy was still the first to end it.

"Shall you be in town this winter, Miss Dashwood?" said she with all her accustomary complacency.

"Certainly not."

"I am sorry for that," returned the other, while her eyes brightened at the information, "it would have gave me such pleasure to meet you there! But I dare say you will go for all that. To be sure, your brother and sister will ask you to come to them."

"It will not be in my power to accept their invitation if they do."

"How unlucky that is! I had quite depended upon meeting you there. Anne and me are to go the latter end of January to some relations who have been wanting us to visit them these several years! But I only go for the sake of seeing Edward. He will be there in February, otherwise London would have no charms for me; I have not spirits for it."

Elinor was soon called to the card-table by the conclusion of the first rubber, and the confidential discourse of the two ladies was therefore at an end, to which both of them submitted without any reluctance, for nothing had been said on either side to make them dislike each other less than they had done before; and Elinor sat down to the card table with the melancholy persuasion that Edward was not only without affection for the person who was to be his wife; but that he had not even the chance of being tolerably happy in marriage, which sincere affection on *her* side would have given, for self-interest alone could induce a woman to keep a man to an engagement, of which she seemed so thoroughly aware that he was weary.

From this time the subject was never revived by Elinor, and when entered on by Lucy, who seldom missed an opportunity of introducing it, and was particularly careful to inform her confidante, of her happiness whenever she received a letter from Edward, it was treated by the former with calmness and caution, and dismissed as soon as civility would allow; for she felt such conversations to be an indulgence which Lucy did not deserve, and which were dangerous to herself.

The visit of the Miss Steeles at Barton Park was lengthened far beyond what the first invitation implied. Their favour increased; they could not be spared; Sir John would not hear of their going; and in spite of their numerous and long arranged engagements in Exeter, in spite of the absolute necessity of returning to fulfill them immediately, which was in full force at the end of every week, they were prevailed on to stay nearly two months at the park, and to assist in the due celebration of that festival which requires a more than ordinary share of private balls and large dinners to proclaim its importance.

CHAPTER XXV

Though Mrs. Jennings was in the habit of spending a large portion of the year at the houses of her children and friends, she was not without a settled habitation of her own. Since the death of her husband, who had traded with success in a less elegant part of the town, she had resided every winter in a house in one of the streets near Portman Square. Towards this home, she began on the approach of January to turn her thoughts, and thither she one day abruptly, and very unexpectedly by them, asked the elder Misses Dashwood to accompany her. Elinor, without observing the varying complexion of her sister, and the animated look which spoke no indifference to the plan, immediately gave a grateful but absolute denial for both, in which she believed herself to be speaking their united inclinations. The reason alleged was their determined resolution of not leaving their mother at that time of the year. Mrs. Jennings received the refusal with some surprise, and repeated her invitation immediately.

"Oh, Lord! I am sure your mother can spare you very well, and I *do* beg you will favour me with your company, for I've quite set my heart upon it. Don't fancy that you will be any inconvenience to me, for I shan't put myself at all out of my way for you. It will only be sending Betty by the coach, and I hope I can afford *that*. We three shall be able to go very well in my chaise; and when we are in town, if you do not like to go wherever I do, well and good, you may always go with one of my daughters. I am sure your mother will not object to it; for I have had such good luck in getting my own children off my hands that she will think me a very fit person to have the charge of you; and if I don't get one of you at least well married before I have done with you, it shall not be my fault. I shall speak a good word for you to all the young men, you may depend upon it."

"I have a notion," said Sir John, "that Miss Marianne would not object to such a scheme, if her elder sister would come into it. It is very hard indeed that she should not have a little pleasure, because Miss Dashwood does not wish it. So I would advise you two, to set off for town, when you are tired of Barton, without saying a word to Miss Dashwood about it."

"Nay," cried Mrs. Jennings, "I am sure I shall be monstrous glad of Miss Marianne's company, whether Miss Dashwood will go or not, only the more the merrier say I, and I thought it would be more comfortable for them to be together; because, if they got tired of me, they might talk to one another, and laugh at my old ways behind my back. But one or the other, if not both of them, I must have. Lord bless me! How do you think I can live poking by myself, I who have been always used till this winter to have Charlotte with me. Come, Miss Marianne, let us strike hands upon the bargain, and if Miss Dashwood will change her mind by and bye, why so much the better."

"I thank you, ma'am, sincerely thank you," said Marianne, with warmth; "your invitation has insured my gratitude for ever, and it would give me such happiness, yes, almost the greatest happiness I am capable of, to be able to accept it. But my mother, my dearest, kindest mother, I feel the justice of what Elinor has urged, and if she were to be made less happy, less comfortable by our absence—Oh! No, nothing should tempt me to leave her. It should not, must not be a struggle."

Mrs. Jennings repeated her assurance that Mrs. Dashwood could spare them perfectly well; and Elinor, who now understood her sister, and saw to what indifference to almost every thing else she was carried by her eagerness to be with Willoughby again, made no farther direct opposition to the plan, and merely referred it to her mother's decision, from whom however she scarcely expected to receive any support in her endeavour to prevent a visit, which she could not approve of for Marianne, and which on her own account she had particular reasons to avoid. Whatever Marianne was desirous of, her mother would be eager to promote—she could not expect to influence the latter to cautiousness of conduct in an affair respecting which she had never been able to inspire her with distrust; and she dared not explain the motive of her own disinclination for going to London. That Marianne, fastidious as she was, thoroughly acquainted with Mrs. Jennings's manners, and invariably disgusted by them, should overlook every inconvenience of that kind, should disregard whatever must be most wounding to her irritable feelings, in her pursuit of one object, was such a proof, so strong, so full, of the importance of that object to her, as Elinor, in spite of all that had passed, was not prepared to witness.

On being informed of the invitation, Mrs. Dashwood, persuaded that such an excursion would be productive of much amusement to both her daughters, and perceiving through all her affectionate attention to herself, how much the heart of Marianne was in it, would not hear of their declining the offer upon *her* account; insisted on their both accepting it directly; and then began to foresee, with her usual cheerfulness, a variety of advantages that would accrue to them all, from this separation.

"I am delighted with the plan," she cried, "it is exactly what I could wish. Margaret and I shall be as much benefited by it as yourselves. When you and the Middletons are gone, we shall go on so quietly and happily together with our books and our music! You will find Margaret so improved when you come back again! I have a little plan of alteration for your bedrooms too, which may now be performed without any inconvenience to any one. It is very right that you *should* go to town; I would have every young woman of your condition in life acquainted with the manners and amusements of London. You will be under the care of a motherly good sort of woman, of whose kindness to you I can have no doubt. And in all probability you will see your brother, and whatever may be his faults, or the faults of his wife, when I consider whose son he is, I cannot bear to have you so wholly estranged from each other."

"Though with your usual anxiety for our happiness," said Elinor, "you have been obviating every impediment to the present scheme which occurred to you, there is still one objection which, in my opinion, cannot be so easily removed."

Marianne's countenance sunk.

"And what," said Mrs. Dashwood, "is my dear prudent Elinor going to suggest? What formidable obstacle is she now to bring forward? Do let me hear a word about the expense of it."

"My objection is this; though I think very well of Mrs. Jennings's heart, she is not a woman whose society can afford us pleasure, or whose protection will give us consequence."

"That is very true," replied her mother, "but of her society, separately from that of other people, you will scarcely have any thing at all, and you will almost always appear in public with Lady Middleton."

"If Elinor is frightened away by her dislike of Mrs. Jennings," said Marianne, "at least it need not prevent *my* accepting her invitation. I have no such scruples, and I am sure I could put up with every unpleasantness of that kind with very little effort."

Elinor could not help smiling at this display of indifference towards the manners of a person, to whom she had often had difficulty in persuading Marianne to behave with tolerable politeness; and resolved within herself, that if her sister persisted in going, she would go likewise, as she did not think it proper that Marianne should be left to the sole guidance of her own judgment, or that Mrs. Jennings should be abandoned to the mercy of Marianne for all the comfort of her domestic hours. To this determination she was the more easily reconciled, by recollecting that Edward Ferrars, by Lucy's account, was not to be in town before February; and that their visit, without any unreasonable abridgement, might be previously finished.

"I will have you *both* go," said Mrs. Dashwood; "these objections are nonsensical. You will have much pleasure in being in London, and especially in being together; and if Elinor would ever condescend to anticipate enjoyment, she would foresee it there from a variety of sources; she would, perhaps, expect some from improving her acquaintance with her sister-in-law's family."

Elinor had often wished for an opportunity of attempting to weaken her mother's dependence on the attachment of Edward and herself, that the shock might be less when the whole truth were revealed, and now on this attack, though almost hopeless of success, she forced herself to begin her design by saying, as calmly as she could, "I like Edward Ferrars very much, and shall always be glad to see him; but as to the rest of the family, it is a matter of perfect indifference to me, whether I am ever known to them or not."

Mrs. Dashwood smiled, and said nothing. Marianne lifted up her eyes in astonishment, and Elinor conjectured that she might as well have held her tongue.

After very little farther discourse, it was finally settled that the invitation should be fully accepted. Mrs. Jennings received the information with a great deal of joy, and many assurances of kindness and care; nor was it a matter of pleasure merely to her. Sir John was delighted; for to a man, whose prevailing anxiety was the dread of being alone, the acquisition of two, to the number of inhabitants in London, was something. Even Lady Middleton took the trouble of being delighted, which was putting herself rather out of her way; and as for the Miss Steeles, especially Lucy, they had never been so happy in their lives as this intelligence made them.

Elinor submitted to the arrangement which counteracted her wishes with less reluctance than she had expected to feel. With regard to herself, it was now a matter of unconcern whether she went to town or not, and when she saw her mother so thoroughly pleased with the plan, and her sister exhilarated by it in look, voice, and manner, restored to all her usual animation, and elevated to more than her usual gaiety, she could not be dissatisfied with the cause, and would hardly allow herself to distrust the consequence.

Marianne's joy was almost a degree beyond happiness, so great was the perturbation of her spirits and her impatience to be gone. Her unwillingness to quit her mother was her only restorative to calmness; and at the moment of parting her grief on that score was excessive. Her mother's affliction was hardly less, and Elinor was the only one of the three, who seemed to consider the separation as anything short of eternal.

Their departure took place in the first week in January. The Middletons were to follow in about a week. The Miss Steeles kept their station at the park, and were to quit it only with the rest of the family.

CHAPTER XXVI

Elinor could not find herself in the carriage with Mrs. Jennings, and beginning a journey to London under her protection, and as her guest, without wondering at her own situation, so short had their acquaintance with that lady been, so wholly unsuited were they in age and disposition, and so many had been her objections against such a measure only a few days before! But these objections had all, with that happy ardour of youth which Marianne and her mother equally shared, been overcome or overlooked; and Elinor, in spite of every occasional doubt of Willoughby's constancy, could not witness the rapture of delightful expectation which filled the whole soul and beamed in the eyes of Marianne, without feeling how blank was her own prospect, how cheerless her own state of mind in the comparison, and how gladly she would engage in the solicitude of Marianne's situation to have the same animating object in view, the same possibility of hope. A short, a very short time however must now decide what Willoughby's intentions were; in all probability he was already in town. Marianne's eagerness to be gone declared her dependence on finding him there; and Elinor was resolved not only upon gaining every new light as to his character which her own observation or the intelligence of others could give her, but likewise upon watching his behaviour to her sister with such zealous attention, as to ascertain what he was and what he meant, before many meetings had taken place. Should the result of her observations be unfavourable, she was determined at all events to open the eyes of her sister; should it be otherwise, her exertions would be of a different nature—she must then learn to avoid every selfish comparison, and banish every regret which might lessen her satisfaction in the happiness of Marianne.

They were three days on their journey, and Marianne's behaviour as they travelled was a happy specimen of what future complaisance and companionableness to Mrs. Jennings might be expected to be. She sat in silence almost all the way, wrapt in her own meditations, and scarcely ever voluntarily speaking, except when any object of picturesque beauty within their view drew from her an exclamation of delight exclusively addressed to her sister. To atone for this conduct therefore, Elinor took immediate possession of the post of civility which she had assigned herself, behaved with the greatest attention to Mrs. Jennings, talked with her, laughed with her, and listened to her whenever she could; and Mrs. Jennings on her side treated them both with all possible kindness, was solicitous on every occasion for their ease and enjoyment, and only disturbed that she could not make them choose their own dinners at the inn, nor extort a confession of their preferring salmon to cod, or boiled fowls to veal cutlets. They reached town by three o'clock the third day, glad to be released, after such a journey, from the confinement of a carriage, and ready to enjoy all the luxury of a good fire.

The house was handsome, and handsomely fitted up, and the young ladies were immediately put in possession of a very comfortable apartment. It had formerly been Charlotte's, and over the mantelpiece still hung a landscape in coloured silks of her performance, in proof of her having spent seven years at a great school in town to some effect.

As dinner was not to be ready in less than two hours from their arrival, Elinor determined to employ the interval in writing to her mother, and sat down for that purpose. In a few moments Marianne did the same. "I am writing home, Marianne," said Elinor; "had not you better defer your letter for a day or two?"

"I am *not* going to write to my mother," replied Marianne, hastily, and as if wishing to avoid any farther inquiry. Elinor said no more; it immediately struck her that she must then be writing to Willoughby; and the conclusion which as instantly followed was, that, however mysteriously they might wish to conduct the affair, they must be engaged. This conviction, though not entirely satisfactory, gave her pleasure, and she continued her letter with greater alacrity. Marianne's was finished in a very few minutes; in length it could be no more than a note; it was then folded up, sealed, and directed with eager rapidity. Elinor thought she could distinguish a large W in the direction; and no sooner was it complete than Marianne, ringing the bell, requested the footman who answered it to get that letter conveyed for her to the two-penny post. This decided the matter at once.

Her spirits still continued very high; but there was a flutter in them which prevented their giving much pleasure to her sister, and this agitation increased as the evening drew on. She could scarcely eat any dinner, and when they afterwards returned to the drawing room, seemed anxiously listening to the sound of every carriage.

It was a great satisfaction to Elinor that Mrs. Jennings, by being much engaged in her own room, could see little of what was passing. The tea things were brought in, and already had Marianne been disappointed more than once by a rap at a neighbouring door, when a loud one was suddenly heard which could not be mistaken for one at any other house, Elinor felt secure of its announcing Willoughby's approach, and Marianne, starting up, moved towards the door. Every thing was silent; this could not be borne many seconds; she opened the door, advanced a few steps towards the stairs, and after listening half a minute, returned into the room in all the agitation which a conviction of having heard him would naturally produce; in the ecstasy of her feelings at that instant she could not help exclaiming, "Oh, Elinor, it is Willoughby, indeed it is!" and seemed almost ready to throw herself into his arms, when Colonel Brandon appeared.

It was too great a shock to be borne with calmness, and she immediately left the room. Elinor was disappointed too; but at the same time her regard for Colonel Brandon ensured his welcome with her; and she felt particularly hurt that a man so partial to her sister should perceive that she experienced nothing but grief and disappointment in seeing him. She instantly saw that it was not unnoticed by him, that he even observed Marianne as she quitted the room, with such astonishment and concern, as hardly left him the recollection of what civility demanded towards herself.

"Is your sister ill?" said he.

Elinor answered in some distress that she was, and then talked of head-aches, low spirits, and over fatigues; and of every thing to which she could decently attribute her sister's behaviour.

He heard her with the most earnest attention, but seeming to recollect himself, said no more on the subject, and began directly to speak of his pleasure at seeing them in London, making the usual inquiries about their journey, and the friends they had left behind.

In this calm kind of way, with very little interest on either side, they continued to talk, both of them out of spirits, and the thoughts of both engaged elsewhere. Elinor wished very much to ask whether Willoughby were then in town, but she was afraid of giving him pain by any enquiry after his rival; and at length, by way of saying something, she asked if he had been in London ever since she had seen him last. "Yes," he replied, with some embarrassment, "almost ever since; I have been once or twice at Delaford for a few days, but it has never been in my power to return to Barton."

This, and the manner in which it was said, immediately brought back to her remembrance all the circumstances of his quitting that place, with the uneasiness and suspicions they had caused to Mrs. Jennings, and she was fearful that her question had implied much more curiosity on the subject than she had ever felt.

Mrs. Jennings soon came in. "Oh! Colonel," said she, with her usual noisy cheerfulness, "I am monstrous glad to see you—sorry I could not come before—beg your pardon, but I have been forced to look about me a little, and settle my matters; for it is a long while since I have been at home, and you know one has always a world of little odd things to do after one has been away for any time; and then I have had Cartwright to settle with—Lord, I have been as busy as a bee ever since dinner! But pray, Colonel, how came you to conjure out that I should be in town today?"

"I had the pleasure of hearing it at Mr. Palmer's, where I have been dining."

"Oh, you did; well, and how do they all do at their house? How does Charlotte do? I warrant you she is a fine size by this time."

"Mrs. Palmer appeared quite well, and I am commissioned to tell you, that you will certainly see her to-morrow."

"Ay, to be sure, I thought as much. Well, Colonel, I have brought two young ladies with me, you see—that is, you see but one of them now, but there is another somewhere. Your friend, Miss Marianne, too—which you will not be sorry to hear. I do not know what you and Mr. Willoughby will do between you about her. Ay, it is a fine thing to be young and handsome. Well! I was young once, but I never was very handsome—worse luck for me. However, I got a very good husband, and I don't know what the greatest beauty can do more. Ah! Poor man! he has been dead these eight years and better. But Colonel, where have you been to since we parted? And how does your business go on? Come, come, let's have no secrets among friends."

He replied with his accustomary mildness to all her inquiries, but without satisfying her in any. Elinor now began to make the tea, and Marianne was obliged to appear again.

After her entrance, Colonel Brandon became more thoughtful and silent than he had been before, and Mrs. Jennings could not prevail on him to stay long. No other visitor appeared that evening, and the ladies were unanimous in agreeing to go early to bed.

Marianne rose the next morning with recovered spirits and happy looks. The disappointment of the evening before seemed forgotten in the expectation of what was to happen that day. They had not long finished their breakfast before Mrs. Palmer's barouche stopped at the door, and in a few minutes she came laughing into the room; so delighted to see them all, that it was hard to say whether she received most pleasure from meeting her mother or the Miss Dashwoods again. So surprised at their coming to town, though it was what she had rather expected all along; so angry at their accepting her mother's invitation after having declined her own, though at the same time she would never have forgiven them if they had not come!

"Mr. Palmer will be so happy to see you," said she; "What do you think he said when he heard of your coming with Mamma? I forget what it was now, but it was something so droll!"

After an hour or two spent in what her mother called comfortable chat, or in other words, in every variety of inquiry concerning all their acquaintance on Mrs. Jennings's side, and in laughter without cause on Mrs. Palmer's, it was proposed by the latter that they should all accompany her to some shops where she had business that morning, to which Mrs. Jennings and Elinor readily consented, as having likewise some purchases to make themselves; and Marianne, though declining it at first was induced to go likewise.

Wherever they went, she was evidently always on the watch. In Bond Street especially, where much of their business lay, her eyes were in constant inquiry; and in whatever shop the party were engaged, her mind was equally abstracted from every thing actually before them, from all that interested and occupied the others. Restless and dissatisfied every where, her sister could never obtain her opinion of any article of purchase, however it might equally concern them both; she received no pleasure from anything; was only impatient to be at home again, and could with difficulty govern her vexation at the tediousness of Mrs. Palmer, whose eye was caught by every thing pretty, expensive, or new; who was wild to buy all, could determine on none, and dawdled away her time in rapture and indecision.

It was late in the morning before they returned home; and no sooner had they entered the house than Marianne flew eagerly up stairs, and when Elinor followed, she found her turning from the table with a sorrowful countenance, which declared that no Willoughby had been there.

"Has no letter been left here for me since we went out?" said she to the footman who then entered with the parcels. She was answered in the negative. "Are you quite sure of it?" she replied. "Are you certain that no servant, no porter has left any letter or note?"

The man replied that none had.

"How very odd!" said she, in a low and disappointed voice, as she turned away to the window.

"How odd, indeed!" repeated Elinor within herself, regarding her sister with uneasiness. "If she had not known him to be in town she would not have written to him, as she did; she would have written to Combe Magna; and if he is in town, how odd that he should neither come nor write! Oh! My dear mother, you must be wrong in permitting an engagement between a daughter so young, a man so little known, to be carried on in so doubtful, so mysterious a manner! I long to inquire; and how will *my* interference be borne."

She determined, after some consideration, that if appearances continued many days longer as unpleasant as they now were, she would represent in the strongest manner to her mother the necessity of some serious enquiry into the affair.

Mrs. Palmer and two elderly ladies of Mrs. Jennings's intimate acquaintance, whom she had met and invited in the morning, dined with them. The former left them soon after tea to fulfill her evening engagements; and Elinor was obliged to assist in making a whist table for the others. Marianne was of no use on these occasions, as she would never learn the game; but though her time was therefore at her own disposal, the evening was by no means more productive of pleasure to her than to Elinor, for it was spent in all the anxiety of expectation and the pain of disappointment. She sometimes endeavoured for a few minutes to read; but the book was soon thrown aside, and she returned to the more interesting employment of walking backwards and forwards across the room, pausing for a moment whenever she came to the window, in hopes of distinguishing the long-expected rap.

CHAPTER XXVII

"If this open weather holds much longer," said Mrs. Jennings, when they met at breakfast the following morning, "Sir John will not like leaving Barton next week; 'tis a sad thing for sportsmen to lose a day's pleasure. Poor souls! I always pity them when they do; they seem to take it so much to heart."

"That is true," cried Marianne, in a cheerful voice, and walking to the window as she spoke, to examine the day. "I had not thought of that. This weather will keep many sportsmen in the country."

It was a lucky recollection, all her good spirits were restored by it. "It is charming weather for *them* indeed," she continued, as she sat down to the breakfast table with a happy countenance. "How much they must enjoy it! But," (with a little return of anxiety) "it cannot be expected to last long. At this time of the year, and after such a series of rain, we shall certainly have very little more of it. Frosts will soon set in, and in all probability with severity. In another day or two perhaps; this extreme mildness can hardly last longer—nay, perhaps it may freeze tonight!"

"At any rate," said Elinor, wishing to prevent Mrs. Jennings from seeing her sister's thoughts as clearly as she did, "I dare say we shall have Sir John and Lady Middleton in town by the end of next week."

"Ay, my dear, I'll warrant you we do. Mary always has her own way."

"And now," silently conjectured Elinor, "she will write to Combe by this day's post."

But if she *did*, the letter was written and sent away with a privacy which eluded all her watchfulness to ascertain the fact. Whatever the truth of it might be, and far as Elinor was from feeling thorough contentment about it, yet while she saw Marianne in spirits, she could not be very uncomfortable herself. And Marianne was in spirits; happy in the mildness of the weather, and still happier in her expectation of a frost.

The morning was chiefly spent in leaving cards at the houses of Mrs. Jennings's acquaintance to inform them of her being in town; and Marianne was all the time busy in observing the direction of the wind, watching the variations of the sky and imagining an alteration in the air.

"Don't you find it colder than it was in the morning, Elinor? There seems to me a very decided difference. I can hardly keep my hands warm even in my muff. It was not so yesterday, I think. The clouds seem parting too, the sun will be out in a moment, and we shall have a clear afternoon."

Elinor was alternately diverted and pained; but Marianne persevered, and saw every night in the brightness of the fire, and every morning in the appearance of the atmosphere, the certain symptoms of approaching frost.

The Miss Dashwoods had no greater reason to be dissatisfied with Mrs. Jennings's style of living, and set of acquaintance, than with her behaviour to themselves, which was invariably kind. Every thing in her household arrangements was conducted on the most liberal plan, and excepting a few old city friends, whom, to Lady Middleton's regret, she had never dropped, she visited no one to whom an introduction could at all discompose the feelings of her young companions. Pleased to find herself more comfortably situated in that particular than she had expected, Elinor was very willing to compound for the want of much real enjoyment from any of their evening parties, which, whether at home or abroad, formed only for cards, could have little to amuse her.

Colonel Brandon, who had a general invitation to the house, was with them almost every day; he came to look at Marianne and talk to Elinor, who often derived more satisfaction from conversing with him than from any other daily occurrence, but who saw at the same time with much concern his continued regard for her sister. She feared it was a strengthening regard. It grieved her to see the earnestness with which he often watched Marianne, and his spirits were certainly worse than when at Barton.

About a week after their arrival, it became certain that Willoughby was also arrived. His card was on the table when they came in from the morning's drive.

"Good God!" cried Marianne, "he has been here while we were out." Elinor, rejoiced to be assured of his being in London, now ventured to say, "Depend upon it, he will call again tomorrow." But Marianne seemed hardly to hear her, and on Mrs. Jennings's entrance, escaped with the precious card.

This event, while it raised the spirits of Elinor, restored to those of her sister all, and more than all, their former agitation. From this moment her mind was never quiet; the expectation of seeing him every hour of the day, made her unfit for any thing. She insisted on being left behind, the next morning, when the others went out.

Elinor's thoughts were full of what might be passing in Berkeley Street during their absence; but a moment's glance at her sister when they returned was enough to inform her, that Willoughby had paid no second visit there. A note was just then brought in, and laid on the table.

"For me!" cried Marianne, stepping hastily forward.

"No, ma'am, for my mistress."

But Marianne, not convinced, took it instantly up.

"It is indeed for Mrs. Jennings; how provoking!"

"You are expecting a letter, then?" said Elinor, unable to be longer silent.

"Yes, a little—not much."

After a short pause. "You have no confidence in me, Marianne."

"Nay, Elinor, this reproach from *you*—you who have confidence in no one!"

"Me!" returned Elinor in some confusion; "Indeed, Marianne, I have nothing to tell."

"Nor I," answered Marianne with energy, "our situations then are alike. We have neither of us any thing to tell; you, because you do not communicate, and I, because I conceal nothing."

Elinor, distressed by this charge of reserve in herself, which she was not at liberty to do away, knew not how, under such circumstances, to press for greater openness in Marianne.

Mrs. Jennings soon appeared, and the note being given her, she read it aloud. It was from Lady Middleton, announcing their arrival in Conduit Street the night before, and requesting the company of her mother and cousins the following evening. Business on Sir John's part, and a violent cold on her own, prevented their calling in Berkeley Street. The invitation was accepted; but when the hour of appointment drew near, necessary as it was in common civility to Mrs. Jennings, that they should both attend her on such a visit, Elinor had some difficulty in persuading her sister to go, for still she had seen nothing of Willoughby; and therefore was not more indisposed for amusement abroad, than unwilling to run the risk of his calling again in her absence.

Elinor found, when the evening was over, that disposition is not materially altered by a change of abode, for although scarcely settled in town, Sir John had contrived to collect around him, nearly twenty young people, and to amuse them with a ball. This was an affair, however, of which Lady Middleton did not approve. In the country, an unpremeditated dance was very allowable; but in London, where the reputation of elegance was more important and less easily attained, it was risking too much for the gratification of a few girls, to have it known that Lady Middleton had given a small dance of eight or nine couple, with two violins, and a mere side-board collation.

Mr. and Mrs. Palmer were of the party; from the former, whom they had not seen before since their arrival in town, as he was careful to avoid the appearance of any attention to his mother-in-law, and therefore never came near her, they received no mark of recognition on their entrance. He looked at them slightly, without seeming to know who they were, and merely nodded to Mrs. Jennings from the other side of the room. Marianne gave one glance round the apartment as she entered: it was enough—*he* was not there—and she sat down, equally ill-disposed to receive or communicate pleasure. After they had been assembled about an hour, Mr. Palmer sauntered towards the Miss Dashwoods to express his surprise on seeing them in town, though Colonel Brandon had been first informed of their arrival at his house, and he had himself said something very droll on hearing that they were to come.

"I thought you were both in Devonshire," said he.

"Did you?" replied Elinor.

"When do you go back again?"

"I do not know." And thus ended their discourse.

Never had Marianne been so unwilling to dance in her life, as she was that evening, and never so much fatigued by the exercise. She complained of it as they returned to Berkeley Street.

"Aye, aye," said Mrs. Jennings, "we know the reason of all that very well; if a certain person who shall be nameless, had been there, you would not have been a bit tired: and to say the truth it was not very pretty of him not to give you the meeting when he was invited."

"Invited!" cried Marianne.

"So my daughter Middleton told me, for it seems Sir John met him somewhere in the street this morning." Marianne said no more, but looked exceedingly hurt. Impatient in this situation to be doing something that might lead to her sister's relief, Elinor resolved to write the next morning to her mother, and hoped by awakening her fears for the health of Marianne, to procure those inquiries which had been so long delayed; and she was still more eagerly bent on this measure by perceiving after breakfast on the morrow, that Marianne was again writing to Willoughby, for she could not suppose it to be to any other person.

About the middle of the day, Mrs. Jennings went out by herself on business, and Elinor began her letter directly, while Marianne, too restless for employment, too anxious for conversation, walked from one window to the other, or sat down by the fire in melancholy meditation. Elinor was very earnest in her application to her mother, relating all that had passed, her suspicions of Willoughby's inconstancy, urging her by every plea of duty and affection to demand from Marianne an account of her real situation with respect to him.

Her letter was scarcely finished, when a rap foretold a visitor, and Colonel Brandon was announced. Marianne, who had seen him from the window, and who hated company of any kind, left the room before he entered it. He looked more than usually grave, and though expressing satisfaction at finding Miss Dashwood alone, as if he had somewhat in particular to tell her, sat for some time without saying a word. Elinor, persuaded that he had some communication to make in which her sister was concerned, impatiently expected its opening. It was not the first time of her feeling the same kind of conviction; for, more than once before, beginning with the observation of "your sister looks unwell to-day," or "your sister seems out of spirits," he had appeared on the point, either of disclosing, or of inquiring, something particular about her. After a pause of several minutes, their silence was broken, by his asking her in a voice of some agitation, when he was to congratulate her on the acquisition of a brother? Elinor was not prepared for such a question, and having no answer ready, was obliged to adopt the simple and common expedient, of asking what he meant? He tried to smile as he replied, "your sister's engagement to Mr. Willoughby is very generally known."

"It cannot be generally known," returned Elinor, "for her own family do not know it."

He looked surprised and said, "I beg your pardon, I am afraid my inquiry has been impertinent; but I had not supposed any secrecy intended, as they openly correspond, and their marriage is universally talked of."

"How can that be? By whom can you have heard it mentioned?"

"By many—by some of whom you know nothing, by others with whom you are most intimate, Mrs. Jennings, Mrs. Palmer, and the Middletons. But still I might not have believed it, for where the mind is perhaps rather unwilling to be convinced, it will always find something to support its doubts, if I had not, when the servant let me in today, accidentally seen a letter in his hand, directed to Mr. Willoughby in your sister's writing. I came to inquire, but I was convinced before I could ask the question. Is every thing finally settled? Is it impossible to—? But I have no right, and I could have no chance of succeeding. Excuse me, Miss Dashwood. I believe I have been wrong in saying so much, but I hardly know what to do, and on your prudence I have the strongest dependence. Tell me that it is all absolutely resolved on, that any attempt, that in short concealment, if concealment be possible, is all that remains."

These words, which conveyed to Elinor a direct avowal of his love for her sister, affected her very much. She was not immediately able to say anything, and even when her spirits were recovered, she debated for a short time, on the answer it would be most proper to give. The real state of things between Willoughby and her sister was so little known to herself, that in endeavouring to explain it, she might be as liable to say too much as too little. Yet as she was convinced that Marianne's affection for Willoughby, could leave no hope of Colonel Brandon's success, whatever the event of that affection might be, and at the same time wished to shield her conduct from censure, she thought it most prudent and kind, after some consideration, to say more than she really knew or believed. She acknowledged, therefore, that though she had never been informed by themselves of the terms on which they stood with each other, of their mutual affection she had no doubt, and of their correspondence she was not astonished to hear.

He listened to her with silent attention, and on her ceasing to speak, rose directly from his seat, and after saying in a voice of emotion, "to your sister I wish all imaginable happiness; to Willoughby that he may endeavour to deserve her," took leave, and went away.

Elinor derived no comfortable feelings from this conversation, to lessen the uneasiness of her mind on other points; she was left, on the contrary, with a melancholy impression of Colonel Brandon's unhappiness, and was prevented even from wishing it removed, by her anxiety for the very event that must confirm it.

CHAPTER XXVIII

Nothing occurred during the next three or four days, to make Elinor regret what she had done, in applying to her mother; for Willoughby neither came nor wrote. They were engaged about the end of that time to attend Lady Middleton to a party, from which Mrs. Jennings was kept away by the indisposition of her youngest daughter; and for this party, Marianne, wholly dispirited, careless of her appearance, and seeming equally indifferent whether she went or staid, prepared, without one look of hope or one expression of pleasure. She sat by the drawing-room fire after tea, till the moment of Lady Middleton's arrival, without once stirring from her seat, or altering her attitude, lost in her own thoughts, and insensible of her sister's presence; and when at last they were told that Lady Middleton waited for them at the door, she started as if she had forgotten that any one was expected.

They arrived in due time at the place of destination, and as soon as the string of carriages before them would allow, alighted, ascended the stairs, heard their names announced from one landing-place to another in an audible voice, and entered a room splendidly lit up, quite full of company, and insufferably hot. When they had paid their tribute of politeness by curtsying to the lady of the house, they were permitted to mingle in the crowd, and take their share of the heat and inconvenience, to which their arrival must necessarily add. After some time spent in saying little or doing less, Lady Middleton sat down to cassino, and as Marianne was not in spirits for moving about, she and Elinor luckily succeeding to chairs, placed themselves at no great distance from the table.

They had not remained in this manner long, before Elinor perceived Willoughby, standing within a few yards of them, in earnest conversation with a very fashionable looking young woman. She soon caught his eye, and he immediately bowed, but without attempting to speak to her, or to approach Marianne, though he could not but see her; and then continued his discourse with the same lady. Elinor turned involuntarily to Marianne, to see whether it could be unobserved by her. At that moment she first perceived him, and her whole countenance glowing with sudden delight, she would have moved towards him instantly, had not her sister caught hold of her.

"Good heavens!" she exclaimed, "he is there—he is there—Oh! Why does he not look at me? why cannot I speak to him?"

"Pray, pray be composed," cried Elinor, "and do not betray what you feel to every body present. Perhaps he has not observed you yet."

This however was more than she could believe herself; and to be composed at such a moment was not only beyond the reach of Marianne, it was beyond her wish. She sat in an agony of impatience which affected every feature.

At last he turned round again, and regarded them both; she started up, and pronouncing his name in a tone of affection, held out her hand to him. He approached, and addressing himself rather to Elinor than Marianne, as if wishing to avoid her eye, and determined not to observe her attitude, inquired in a hurried manner after Mrs. Dashwood, and asked how long they had been in town. Elinor was robbed of all presence of mind by such an address, and was unable to say a word. But the feelings of her sister were instantly expressed. Her face was crimsoned over, and she exclaimed, in a voice of the greatest emotion, "Good God! Willoughby, what is the meaning of this? Have you not received my letters? Will you not shake hands with me?"

He could not then avoid it, but her touch seemed painful to him, and he held her hand only for a moment. During all this time he was evidently struggling for composure. Elinor watched his countenance and saw its expression becoming more tranquil. After a moment's pause, he spoke with calmness.

"I did myself the honour of calling in Berkeley Street last Tuesday, and very much regretted that I was not fortunate enough to find yourselves and Mrs. Jennings at home. My card was not lost, I hope."

"But have you not received my notes?" cried Marianne in the wildest anxiety. "Here is some mistake I am sure—some dreadful mistake. What can be the meaning of it? Tell me, Willoughby; for heaven's sake tell me, what is the matter?"

He made no reply; his complexion changed and all his embarrassment returned; but as if, on catching the eye of the young lady with whom he had been previously talking, he felt the necessity of instant exertion, he recovered himself again, and after saying, "Yes, I had the pleasure of receiving the information of your arrival in town, which you were so good as to send me," turned hastily away with a slight bow and joined his friend.

Marianne, now looking dreadfully white, and unable to stand, sunk into her chair, and Elinor, expecting every moment to see her faint, tried to screen her from the observation of others, while reviving her with lavender water.

"Go to him, Elinor," she cried, as soon as she could speak, "and force him to come to me. Tell him I must see him again—must speak to him instantly. I cannot rest—I shall not have a moment's peace till this is explained—some dreadful misapprehension or other. Oh go to him this moment."

"How can that be done? No, my dearest Marianne, you must wait. This is not the place for explanations. Wait only till tomorrow."

With difficulty however could she prevent her from following him herself; and to persuade her to check her agitation, to wait, at least, with the appearance of composure, till she might speak to him with more privacy and more effect, was impossible; for Marianne continued incessantly to give way in a low voice to the misery of her feelings, by exclamations of wretchedness. In a short time Elinor saw Willoughby quit the room by the door towards the staircase, and telling Marianne that he was gone, urged the impossibility of speaking to him again that evening, as a fresh argument for her to be calm. She instantly begged her sister would entreat Lady Middleton to take them home, as she was too miserable to stay a minute longer.

Lady Middleton, though in the middle of a rubber, on being informed that Marianne was unwell, was too polite to object for a moment to her wish of going away, and making over her cards to a friend, they departed as soon as the carriage could be found. Scarcely a word was spoken during their return to Berkeley Street. Marianne was in a silent agony, too much oppressed even for tears; but as Mrs. Jennings was luckily not come home, they could go directly to their own room, where hartshorn restored her a little to herself. She was soon undressed and in bed, and as she seemed desirous of being alone, her sister then left her, and while she waited the return of Mrs. Jennings, had leisure enough for thinking over the past.

That some kind of engagement had subsisted between Willoughby and Marianne she could not doubt, and that Willoughby was weary of it, seemed equally clear; for however Marianne might still feed her own wishes, *she* could not attribute such behaviour to mistake or misapprehension of any kind. Nothing but a thorough change of sentiment could account for it. Her indignation would have been still stronger than it was, had she not witnessed that embarrassment which seemed to speak a consciousness of his own misconduct, and prevented her from believing him so unprincipled as to have been sporting with the affections of her sister from the first, without any design that would bear investigation. Absence might have weakened his regard, and convenience might have determined him to overcome it, but that such a regard had formerly existed she could not bring herself to doubt.

As for Marianne, on the pangs which so unhappy a meeting must already have given her, and on those still more severe which might await her in its probable consequence, she could not reflect without the deepest concern. Her own situation gained in the comparison; for while she could *esteem* Edward as much as ever, however they might be divided in future, her mind might be always supported. But every circumstance that could embitter such an evil seemed uniting to heighten the misery of Marianne in a final separation from Willoughby—in an immediate and irreconcilable rupture with him.

CHAPTER XXIX

Before the house-maid had lit their fire the next day, or the sun gained any power over a cold, gloomy morning in January, Marianne, only half dressed, was kneeling against one of the window-seats for the sake of all the little light she could command from it, and writing as fast as a continual flow of tears would permit her. In this situation, Elinor, roused from sleep by her agitation and sobs, first perceived her; and after observing her for a few moments with silent anxiety, said, in a tone of the most considerate gentleness,

"Marianne, may I ask—?"

"No, Elinor," she replied, "ask nothing; you will soon know all."

The sort of desperate calmness with which this was said, lasted no longer than while she spoke, and was immediately followed by a return of the same excessive affliction. It was some minutes before she could go on with her letter, and the frequent bursts of grief which still obliged her, at intervals, to withhold her pen, were proofs enough of her feeling how more than probable it was that she was writing for the last time to Willoughby.

Elinor paid her every quiet and unobtrusive attention in her power; and she would have tried to sooth and tranquilize her still more, had not Marianne entreated her, with all the eagerness of the most nervous irritability, not to speak to her for the world. In such circumstances, it was better for both that they should not be long together; and the restless state of Marianne's mind not only prevented her from remaining in the room a moment after she was dressed, but requiring at once solitude and continual change of place, made her wander about the house till breakfast time, avoiding the sight of everybody.

At breakfast she neither ate, nor attempted to eat any thing; and Elinor's attention was then all employed, not in urging her, not in pitying her, nor in appearing to regard her, but in endeavouring to engage Mrs. Jennings's notice entirely to herself.

As this was a favourite meal with Mrs. Jennings, it lasted a considerable time, and they were just setting themselves, after it, round the common working table, when a letter was delivered to Marianne, which she eagerly caught from the servant, and, turning of a death-like paleness, instantly ran out of the room. Elinor, who saw as plainly by this, as if she had seen the direction, that it must come from Willoughby, felt immediately such a sickness at heart as made her hardly able to hold up her head, and sat in such a general tremour as made her fear it impossible to escape Mrs. Jennings's notice. That good lady, however, saw only that Marianne had received a letter from Willoughby, which appeared to her a very good joke, and which she treated accordingly, by hoping, with a laugh, that she would find it to her liking. Of Elinor's distress, she was too busily employed in measuring lengths of worsted for her rug, to see anything at all; and calmly continuing her talk, as soon as Marianne disappeared, she said,

"Upon my word, I never saw a young woman so desperately in love in my life! *My* girls were nothing to her, and yet they used to be foolish enough; but as for Miss Marianne, she is quite an altered creature. I hope, from the bottom of my heart, he won't keep her waiting much longer, for it is quite grievous to see her look so ill and forlorn. Pray, when are they to be married?"

Elinor, though never less disposed to speak than at that moment, obliged herself to answer such an attack as this, and, therefore, trying to smile, replied, "And have you really, Ma'am, talked yourself into a persuasion of my sister's being engaged to Mr. Willoughby? I thought it had been only a joke, but so serious a question seems to imply more; and I must beg, therefore, that you will not deceive yourself any longer. I do assure you that nothing would surprise me more than to hear of their being going to be married."

"For shame, for shame, Miss Dashwood! How can you talk so? Don't we all know that it must be a match, that they were over head and ears in love with each other from the first moment they met? Did not I see them together in Devonshire every day, and all day long; and did not I know that your sister came to town with me on purpose to buy wedding clothes? Come, come, this won't do. Because you are so sly about it yourself, you think nobody else has any senses; but it is no such thing, I can tell you, for it has been known all over town this ever so long. I tell everybody of it and so does Charlotte."

"Indeed, Ma'am," said Elinor, very seriously, "you are mistaken. Indeed, you are doing a very unkind thing in spreading the report, and you will find that you have though you will not believe me now."

Mrs. Jennings laughed again, but Elinor had not spirits to say more, and eager at all events to know what Willoughby had written, hurried away to their room, where, on opening the door, she saw Marianne stretched on the bed, almost choked by grief, one letter in her hand, and two or three others laying by her. Elinor drew near, but without saying a word; and seating herself on the bed, took her hand, kissed her affectionately several times, and then gave way to a burst of tears, which at first was scarcely less violent than Marianne's. The latter, though unable to speak, seemed to feel all the tenderness of this behaviour, and after some time thus spent in joint affliction, she put all the letters into Elinor's hands; and then covering her face with her handkerchief, almost screamed with agony. Elinor, who knew that such grief, shocking as it was to witness it, must have its course, watched by her till this excess of suffering had somewhat spent itself, and then turning eagerly to Willoughby's letter, read as follows:

"Bond Street, January.

"My Dear Madam,

"I have just had the honour of receiving your letter, for which I beg to return my sincere acknowledgments. I am much concerned to find there was anything in my behaviour last night that did not meet your approbation; and though I am quite at a loss to discover in what point I could be so unfortunate as to offend you, I entreat your forgiveness of what I can assure you to have been perfectly unintentional. I shall never reflect on my former acquaintance with your family in Devonshire without the most grateful pleasure, and flatter myself it will not be broken by any mistake or misapprehension of my actions. My esteem for your whole family is very sincere; but if I have been so unfortunate as to give rise to a belief of more than I felt, or meant to express, I shall reproach myself for not having been more guarded in my professions of that esteem. That I should ever have meant more you will allow to be impossible, when you understand that my affections have been long engaged elsewhere, and it will not be many weeks, I believe, before this engagement is fulfilled. It is with great regret that I obey your commands in returning the letters with which I have been honoured from you, and the lock of hair, which you so obligingly bestowed on me.

"I am, dear Madam,
"Your most obedient
"humble servant,

"JOHN WILLOUGHBY."

With what indignation such a letter as this must be read by Miss Dashwood, may be imagined. Though aware, before she began it, that it must bring a confession of his inconstancy, and confirm their separation for ever, she was not aware that such language could be suffered to announce it; nor could she have supposed Willoughby capable of departing so far from the appearance of every honourable and delicate feeling—so far from the common decorum of a gentleman, as to send a letter so impudently cruel: a letter which, instead of bringing with his desire of a release any professions of regret, acknowledged no breach of faith, denied all peculiar affection whatever—a letter of which every line was an insult, and which proclaimed its writer to be deep in hardened villainy.

She paused over it for some time with indignant astonishment; then read it again and again; but every perusal only served to increase her abhorrence of the man, and so bitter were her feelings against him, that she dared not trust herself to speak, lest she might wound Marianne still deeper by treating their disengagement, not as a loss to her of any possible good but as an escape from the worst and most irremediable of all evils, a connection, for life, with an unprincipled man, as a deliverance the most real, a blessing the most important.

In her earnest meditations on the contents of the letter, on the depravity of that mind which could dictate it, and probably, on the very different mind of a very different person, who had no other connection whatever with the affair than what her heart gave him with everything that passed, Elinor forgot the immediate distress of her sister, forgot that she had three letters on her lap yet unread, and so entirely forgot how long she had been in the room, that when on hearing a carriage drive up to the door, she went to the window to see who could be coming so unreasonably early, she was all astonishment to perceive Mrs. Jennings's chariot, which she knew had not been ordered till one. Determined not to quit Marianne, though hopeless of contributing, at present, to her ease, she hurried away to excuse herself from attending Mrs. Jennings, on account of her sister being indisposed. Mrs. Jennings, with a thoroughly good-humoured concern for its cause, admitted the excuse most readily, and Elinor, after seeing her safe off, returned to Marianne, whom she found attempting to rise from the bed, and whom she reached just in time to prevent her from falling on the floor, faint and giddy from a long want of proper rest and food; for it was many days since she had any appetite, and many nights since she had really slept; and now, when her mind was no longer supported by the fever of suspense, the consequence of all this was felt in an aching head, a weakened stomach, and a general nervous faintness. A glass of wine, which Elinor procured for her directly, made her more comfortable, and she was at last able to express some sense of her kindness, by saying,

"Poor Elinor! How unhappy I make you!"

"I only wish," replied her sister, "there were any thing I *could* do, which might be of comfort to you."

This, as every thing else would have been, was too much for Marianne, who could only exclaim, in the anguish of her heart, "Oh! Elinor, I am miserable, indeed," before her voice was entirely lost in sobs.

Elinor could no longer witness this torrent of unresisted grief in silence.

"Exert yourself, dear Marianne," she cried, "if you would not kill yourself and all who love you. Think of your mother; think of her misery while *you* suffer: for her sake you must exert yourself."

"I cannot, I cannot," cried Marianne; "leave me, leave me, if I distress you; leave me, hate me, forget me! But do not torture me so. Oh! How easy for those, who have no sorrow of their own to talk of exertion! Happy, happy Elinor, *you* cannot have an idea of what I suffer."

"Do you call *me* happy, Marianne? Ah! If you knew! And can you believe me to be so, while I see you so wretched!"

"Forgive me, forgive me," throwing her arms round her sister's neck; "I know you feel for me; I know what a heart you have; but yet you are—you must be happy; Edward loves you—what, oh what, can do away such happiness as that?"

"Many, many circumstances," said Elinor, solemnly.

"No, no, no," cried Marianne wildly, "he loves you, and only you. You *can* have no grief."

"I can have no pleasure while I see you in this state."

"And you will never see me otherwise. Mine is a misery which nothing can do away."

"You must not talk so, Marianne. Have you no comforts? No friends? Is your loss such as leaves no opening for consolation? Much as you suffer now, think of what you would have suffered if the discovery of his character had been delayed to a later period—if your engagement had been carried on for months and months, as it might have been, before he chose to put an end to it. Every additional day of unhappy confidence, on your side, would have made the blow more dreadful."

"Engagement!" cried Marianne, "There has been no engagement."

"No engagement!"

"No, he is not so unworthy as you believe him. He has broken no faith with me."

"But he told you that he loved you."

"Yes—no—never absolutely. It was every day implied, but never professedly declared. Sometimes I thought it had been—but it never was."

"Yet you wrote to him?"

"Yes—could that be wrong after all that had passed? But I cannot talk."

Elinor said no more, and turning again to the three letters which now raised a much stronger curiosity than before, directly ran over the contents of all. The first, which was what her sister had sent him on their arrival in town, was to this effect.

Berkeley Street, January.

> "How surprised you will be, Willoughby, on receiving this; and I think you will feel something more than surprise, when you know that I am in town. An opportunity of coming hither, though with Mrs. Jennings, was a temptation we could not resist. I wish you may receive this in time to come here to-night, but I will not depend on it. At any rate I shall expect you to-morrow. For the present, adieu.
>
> "M.D."

Her second note, which had been written on the morning after the dance at the Middletons', was in these words:

> "I cannot express my disappointment in having missed you the day before yesterday, nor my astonishment at not having received any answer to a note which I sent you above a week ago. I have been expecting to hear from you, and

still more to see you, every hour of the day. Pray call again as soon as possible, and explain the reason of my having expected this in vain. You had better come earlier another time, because we are generally out by one. We were last night at Lady Middleton's, where there was a dance. I have been told that you were asked to be of the party. But could it be so? You must be very much altered indeed since we parted, if that could be the case, and you not there. But I will not suppose this possible, and I hope very soon to receive your personal assurance of its being otherwise.

"M.D."

The contents of her last note to him were these:

"What am I to imagine, Willoughby, by your behaviour last night? Again I demand an explanation of it. I was prepared to meet you with the pleasure which our separation naturally produced, with the familiarity which our intimacy at Barton appeared to me to justify. I was repulsed indeed! I have passed a wretched night in endeavouring to excuse a conduct which can scarcely be called less than insulting; but though I have not yet been able to form any reasonable apology for your behaviour, I am perfectly ready to hear your justification of it. You have perhaps been misinformed, or purposely deceived, in something concerning me, which may have lowered me in your opinion. Tell me what it is, explain the grounds on which you acted, and I shall be satisfied, in being able to satisfy you. It would grieve me indeed to be obliged to think ill of you; but if I am to do it, if I am to learn that you are not what we have hitherto believed you, that your regard for us all was insincere, that your behaviour to me was intended only to deceive, let it be told as soon as possible. My feelings are at present in a state of dreadful indecision; I wish to acquit you, but certainty on either side will be ease to what I now suffer. If your sentiments are no longer what they were, you will return my notes, and the lock of my hair which is in your possession.

"M.D."

That such letters, so full of affection and confidence, could have been so answered, Elinor, for Willoughby's sake, would have been unwilling to believe. But her condemnation of him did not blind her to the impropriety of their having been written at all; and she was silently grieving over the imprudence which had hazarded such unsolicited proofs of tenderness, not warranted by anything preceding, and most severely condemned by the event, when Marianne, perceiving that she had finished the letters, observed to her that they contained nothing but what any one would have written in the same situation.

"I felt myself," she added, "to be as solemnly engaged to him, as if the strictest legal covenant had bound us to each other."

"I can believe it," said Elinor; "but unfortunately he did not feel the same."

"He *did* feel the same, Elinor—for weeks and weeks he felt it. I know he did. Whatever may have changed him now, (and nothing but the blackest art employed against me can have done it), I was once as dear to him as my own soul could wish. This lock of hair, which now he can so readily give up, was begged of me with the most earnest supplication. Had you seen his look, his manner, had you heard his voice at that moment! Have you forgot the last evening of our being together at Barton? The morning that we parted too! When he told me that it might be many weeks before we met again—his distress—can I ever forget his distress?"

For a moment or two she could say no more; but when this emotion had passed away, she added, in a firmer tone,

"Elinor, I have been cruelly used; but not by Willoughby."

"Dearest Marianne, who but himself? By whom can he have been instigated?"

"By all the world, rather than by his own heart. I could rather believe every creature of my acquaintance leagued together to ruin me in his opinion, than believe his nature capable of such cruelty. This woman of whom he writes—whoever she be—or any one, in short, but your own dear self, mama, and Edward, may have been so barbarous to bely me. Beyond you three, is there a creature in the world whom I would not rather suspect of evil than Willoughby, whose heart I know so well?"

Elinor would not contend, and only replied, "Whoever may have been so detestably your enemy, let them be cheated of their malignant triumph, my dear sister, by seeing how nobly the consciousness of your own innocence and good intentions supports your spirits. It is a reasonable and laudable pride which resists such malevolence."

"No, no," cried Marianne, "misery such as mine has no pride. I care not who knows that I am wretched. The triumph of seeing me so may be open to all the world. Elinor, Elinor, they who suffer little may be proud and independent as they like—may resist insult, or return mortification—but I cannot. I must feel—I must be wretched—and they are welcome to enjoy the consciousness of it that can."

"But for my mother's sake and mine—"

"I would do more than for my own. But to appear happy when I am so miserable—Oh! Who can require it?"

Again they were both silent. Elinor was employed in walking thoughtfully from the fire to the window, from the window to the fire, without knowing that she received warmth from one, or discerning objects through the other; and Marianne, seated at the foot of the bed, with her head leaning against one of its posts, again took up Willoughby's letter, and, after shuddering over every sentence, exclaimed—

"It is too much! Oh, Willoughby, Willoughby, could this be yours! Cruel, cruel—nothing can acquit you. Elinor, nothing can. Whatever he might have heard against me—ought he not to have suspended his belief? Ought he not to have told me of it, to have given me the power of clearing myself? 'The lock of hair, (repeating it from the letter,) which you so obligingly bestowed on me'—that is unpardonable. Willoughby, where was your heart when you wrote those words? Oh, barbarously insolent! Elinor, can he be justified?"

"No, Marianne, in no possible way."

"And yet this woman—who knows what her art may have been? How long it may have been premeditated, and how deeply contrived by her! Who is she? Who can she be? Whom did I ever hear him talk of as young and attractive among his female acquaintance? Oh! No one, no one—he talked to me only of myself."

Another pause ensued; Marianne was greatly agitated, and it ended thus.

"Elinor, I must go home. I must go and comfort mama. Can not we be gone to-morrow?"

"To-morrow, Marianne!"

"Yes, why should I stay here? I came only for Willoughby's sake—and now who cares for me? Who regards me?"

"It would be impossible to go to-morrow. We owe Mrs. Jennings much more than civility; and civility of the commonest kind must prevent such a hasty removal as that."

"Well then, another day or two, perhaps; but I cannot stay here long, I cannot stay to endure the questions and remarks of all these people. The Middletons and Palmers—how am I to bear their pity? The pity of such a woman as Lady Middleton! Oh, what would *he* say to that!"

Elinor advised her to lie down again, and for a moment she did so; but no attitude could give her ease; and in restless pain of mind and body she moved from one posture to another, till growing more and more hysterical, her sister could with difficulty keep her on the bed at all, and for some time was fearful of being constrained to call for assistance. Some lavender drops, however, which she was at length persuaded to take, were of use; and from that time till Mrs. Jennings returned, she continued on the bed quiet and motionless.

CHAPTER XXX

Mrs. Jennings came immediately to their room on her return, and without waiting to have her request of admittance answered, opened the door and walked in with a look of real concern.

"How do you do my dear?" said she in a voice of great compassion to Marianne, who turned away her face without attempting to answer.

"How is she, Miss Dashwood? Poor thing! She looks very bad. No wonder. Ay, it is but too true. He is to be married very soon—a good-for-nothing fellow! I have no patience with him. Mrs. Taylor told me of it half an hour ago, and she was told it by a particular friend of Miss Grey herself, else I am sure I should not have believed it; and I was almost ready to sink as it was. Well, said I, all I can say is, that if this be true, he has used a young lady of my acquaintance abominably ill, and I wish with all my soul his wife may plague his heart out. And so I shall always say, my dear, you may depend on it. I have no notion of men's going on in this way; and if ever I meet him again, I will give him such a dressing as he has not had this many a day. But there is one comfort, my dear Miss Marianne; he is not the only young man in the world worth having; and with your pretty face you will never want admirers. Well, poor thing! I won't disturb her any longer, for she had better have her cry out at once and have done with. The Parrys and Sandersons luckily are coming tonight you know, and that will amuse her."

She then went away, walking on tiptoe out of the room, as if she supposed her young friend's affliction could be increased by noise.

Marianne, to the surprise of her sister, determined on dining with them. Elinor even advised her against it. But "No, she would go down; she could bear it very well, and the bustle about her would be less." Elinor, pleased to have her governed for a moment by such a motive, though believing it hardly possible that she could sit out the dinner, said no more; and adjusting her dress for her as well as she could, while Marianne still remained on the bed, was ready to assist her into the dining room as soon as they were summoned to it.

When there, though looking most wretchedly, she ate more and was calmer than her sister had expected. Had she tried to speak, or had she been conscious of half Mrs. Jennings's well-meant but ill-judged attentions to her, this calmness could not have been maintained; but not a syllable escaped her lips; and the abstraction of her thoughts preserved her in ignorance of everything that was passing before her.

Elinor, who did justice to Mrs. Jennings's kindness, though its effusions were often distressing, and sometimes almost ridiculous, made her those acknowledgments, and returned her those civilities, which her sister could not make or return for herself. Their good friend saw that Marianne was unhappy, and felt that everything was due to her which might make her at all less so. She treated her therefore, with all the indulgent fondness of a parent towards a favourite child on the last day of its holidays. Marianne was to have the best place by the fire, was to be tempted to eat by every delicacy in the house, and to be amused by the relation of all the news of the day. Had not Elinor, in the sad countenance of her sister, seen a check to all mirth, she could have been entertained by Mrs. Jennings's endeavours to cure a disappointment in love, by a variety of sweetmeats and olives, and a good fire. As soon, however, as the consciousness of all this was forced by continual repetition on Marianne, she could stay no longer. With a hasty exclamation of Misery, and a sign to her sister not to follow her, she directly got up and hurried out of the room.

"Poor soul!" cried Mrs. Jennings, as soon as she was gone, "How it grieves me to see her! And I declare if she is not gone away without finishing her wine! And the dried cherries too! Lord! Nothing seems to do her any good. I am sure if I knew of anything she would like, I would send all over the town for it. Well, it is the oddest thing to me, that a man should use such a pretty girl so ill! But when there is plenty of money on one side, and next to none on the other, Lord bless you! they care no more about such things!"

"The lady then—Miss Grey I think you called her—is very rich?"

"Fifty thousand pounds, my dear. Did you ever see her? A smart, stylish girl they say, but not handsome. I remember her aunt very well, Biddy Henshawe; she married a very wealthy man. But the family are all rich together. Fifty thousand pounds! And by all accounts, it won't come before it's wanted; for they say he is all to pieces. No wonder! Dashing about with his curricle and hunters! Well, it don't signify talking; but when a young man, be who he will, comes and makes love to a pretty girl, and promises marriage, he has no business to fly off from his word only because he grows poor, and a richer girl is ready to have him. Why don't he, in such a case, sell his horses, let his house, turn off his servants, and make a thorough reform at once? I warrant you, Miss Marianne would have been ready to wait till matters came round. But that won't do now-a-days; nothing in the way of pleasure can ever be given up by the young men of this age."

"Do you know what kind of a girl Miss Grey is? Is she said to be amiable?"

"I never heard any harm of her; indeed I hardly ever heard her mentioned; except that Mrs. Taylor did say this morning, that one day Miss Walker hinted to her, that she believed Mr. and Mrs. Ellison would not be sorry to have Miss Grey married, for she and Mrs. Ellison could never agree."

"And who are the Ellisons?"

"Her guardians, my dear. But now she is of age and may choose for herself; and a pretty choice she has made! What now," after pausing a moment—"your poor sister is gone to her own room, I suppose, to moan by herself. Is there nothing one can get to comfort her? Poor dear, it seems quite cruel to let her be alone. Well, by-and-by we shall have a few friends, and that will amuse her a little. What shall we play at? She hates whist I know; but is there no round game she cares for?"

"Dear ma'am, this kindness is quite unnecessary. Marianne, I dare say, will not leave her room again this evening. I shall persuade her if I can to go early to bed, for I am sure she wants rest."

"Aye, I believe that will be best for her. Let her name her own supper, and go to bed. Lord! No wonder she has been looking so bad and so cast down this last week or two, for this matter I suppose has been hanging over her head as long as that. And so the letter that came today finished it! Poor soul! I am sure if I had had a notion of it, I would not have joked her about it for all my money. But then you know, how should I guess such a thing? I made sure of its being nothing but a common love letter, and you know young people like to be laughed at about them. Lord! How concerned Sir John and my daughters will be when they hear it! If I had my senses about me I might have called in Conduit Street in my way home, and told them of it. But I shall see them tomorrow."

"It would be unnecessary I am sure, for you to caution Mrs. Palmer and Sir John against ever naming Mr. Willoughby, or making the slightest allusion to what has passed, before my sister. Their own good-nature must point out to them the real cruelty of appearing to know any thing about it when she is present; and the less that may ever be said to myself on the subject, the more my feelings will be spared, as you my dear madam will easily believe."

"Oh! Lord! Yes, that I do indeed. It must be terrible for you to hear it talked of; and as for your sister, I am sure I would not mention a word about it to her for the world. You saw I did not all dinner time. No more would Sir John, nor my daughters, for they are all very thoughtful and considerate; especially if I give them a hint, as I certainly will. For my part, I think the less that is said about such things, the better, the sooner 'tis blown over and forgot. And what does talking ever do you know?"

"In this affair it can only do harm; more so perhaps than in many cases of a similar kind, for it has been attended by circumstances which, for the sake of everyone concerned in it, make it unfit to become the public conversation. I must do *this* justice to Mr. Willoughby—he has broken no positive engagement with my sister."

"Law, my dear! Don't pretend to defend him. No positive engagement indeed! After taking her all over Allenham House, and fixing on the very rooms they were to live in hereafter!"

Elinor, for her sister's sake, could not press the subject farther, and she hoped it was not required of her for Willoughby's; since, though Marianne might lose much, he could gain very little by the enforcement of the real truth. After a short silence on both sides, Mrs. Jennings, with all her natural hilarity, burst forth again.

"Well, my dear, 'tis a true saying about an ill-wind, for it will be all the better for Colonel Brandon. He will have her at last; aye, that he will. Mind me, now, if they an't married by Mid-summer. Lord! how he'll chuckle over this news! I hope he will come tonight. It will be all to one a better match for your sister. Two thousand a year without debt or drawback—except the little love-child, indeed; aye, I had forgot her; but she may be 'prenticed out at a small cost, and then what does it signify? Delaford is a nice place, I can tell you; exactly what I call a nice old fashioned place, full of comforts and conveniences; quite shut in with great garden walls that are covered with the best fruit-trees in the country; and such a mulberry tree in one corner! Lord! How Charlotte and I did stuff the only time we were there! Then, there is a dove-cote, some delightful stew-ponds, and a very pretty canal; and every thing, in short, that one could wish for; and, moreover, it is close to the church, and only a quarter of a mile from the turnpike-road, so 'tis never dull, for if you only go and sit up in an old yew arbour behind the house, you may see all the carriages that pass along. Oh! 'tis a nice place! A butcher hard by in the village, and the parsonage-house within a stone's throw. To my fancy, a thousand times prettier than Barton Park, where they are forced to send three miles for their meat, and have not a neighbour nearer than your mother. Well, I shall spirit up the Colonel as soon as I can. One shoulder of mutton, you know, drives another down. If we *can* but put Willoughby out of her head!"

"Ay, if we can do *that*, Ma'am," said Elinor, "we shall do very well with or without Colonel Brandon." And then rising, she went away to join Marianne, whom she found, as she expected, in her own room, leaning, in silent misery, over the small remains of a fire, which, till Elinor's entrance, had been her only light.

"You had better leave me," was all the notice that her sister received from her.

"I will leave you," said Elinor, "if you will go to bed." But this, from the momentary perverseness of impatient suffering, she at first refused to do. Her sister's earnest, though gentle persuasion, however, soon softened her to compliance, and Elinor saw her lay her aching head on the pillow, and as she hoped, in a way to get some quiet rest before she left her.

In the drawing-room, whither she then repaired, she was soon joined by Mrs. Jennings, with a wine-glass, full of something, in her hand.

"My dear," said she, entering, "I have just recollected that I have some of the finest old Constantia wine in the house that ever was tasted, so I have brought a glass of it for your sister. My poor husband! How fond he was of it! Whenever he had a touch of his old colicky gout, he said it did him more good than any thing else in the world. Do take it to your sister."

"Dear Ma'am," replied Elinor, smiling at the difference of the complaints for which it was recommended, "how good you are! But I have just left Marianne in bed, and, I hope, almost asleep; and as I think nothing will be of so much service to her as rest, if you will give me leave, I will drink the wine myself."

Mrs. Jennings, though regretting that she had not been five minutes earlier, was satisfied with the compromise; and Elinor, as she swallowed the chief of it, reflected, that though its effects on a colicky gout were, at present, of little importance to her, its healing powers, on a disappointed heart might be as reasonably tried on herself as on her sister.

Colonel Brandon came in while the party were at tea, and by his manner of looking round the room for Marianne, Elinor immediately fancied that he neither expected nor wished to see her there, and, in short, that he was already aware of what occasioned her absence. Mrs. Jennings was not struck by the same thought; for soon after his entrance, she walked across the room to the tea-table where Elinor presided, and whispered—"The Colonel looks as grave as ever you see. He knows nothing of it; do tell him, my dear."

He shortly afterwards drew a chair close to hers, and, with a look which perfectly assured her of his good information, inquired after her sister.

"Marianne is not well," said she. "She has been indisposed all day, and we have persuaded her to go to bed."

"Perhaps, then," he hesitatingly replied, "what I heard this morning may be—there may be more truth in it than I could believe possible at first."

"What did you hear?"

"That a gentleman, whom I had reason to think—in short, that a man, whom I *knew* to be engaged—but how shall I tell you? If you know it already, as surely you must, I may be spared."

"You mean," answered Elinor, with forced calmness, "Mr. Willoughby's marriage with Miss Grey. Yes, we *do* know it all. This seems to have been a day of general elucidation, for this very morning first unfolded it to us. Mr. Willoughby is unfathomable! Where did you hear it?"

"In a stationer's shop in Pall Mall, where I had business. Two ladies were waiting for their carriage, and one of them was giving the other an account of the intended match, in a voice so little attempting concealment, that it was impossible for me not to hear all. The name of Willoughby, John Willoughby, frequently repeated, first caught my attention; and what followed was a positive assertion that everything was now finally settled respecting his marriage with Miss Grey—it was no longer to be a secret—it would take place even within a few weeks, with many particulars of preparations and other matters. One thing, especially, I remember, because it served to identify the man still more—as soon as the ceremony was over, they were to go to Combe Magna, his seat in Somersetshire. My astonishment! But it would be impossible to describe what I felt. The communicative lady I learnt, on inquiry, for I stayed in the shop till they were gone, was a Mrs. Ellison, and that, as I have been since informed, is the name of Miss Grey's guardian."

"It is. But have you likewise heard that Miss Grey has fifty thousand pounds? In that, if in any thing, we may find an explanation."

"It may be so; but Willoughby is capable—at least I think"—he stopped a moment; then added in a voice which seemed to distrust itself, "And your sister—how did she—"

"Her sufferings have been very severe. I have only to hope that they may be proportionately short. It has been, it is a most cruel affliction. Till yesterday, I believe, she never doubted his regard; and even now, perhaps—but I am almost convinced that he never was really attached to her. He has been very deceitful! And, in some points, there seems a hardness of heart about him."

"Ah!" said Colonel Brandon, "there is, indeed! But your sister does not—I think you said so—she does not consider quite as you do?"

"You know her disposition, and may believe how eagerly she would still justify him if she could."

He made no answer; and soon afterwards, by the removal of the tea-things, and the arrangement of the card parties, the subject was necessarily dropped. Mrs. Jennings, who had watched them with pleasure while they were talking, and who expected to see the effect of Miss Dashwood's communication, in such an instantaneous gaiety on Colonel Brandon's side, as might have become a man in the bloom of youth, of hope and happiness, saw him, with amazement, remain the whole evening more serious and thoughtful than usual.

CHAPTER XXXI

From a night of more sleep than she had expected, Marianne awoke the next morning to the same consciousness of misery in which she had closed her eyes.

Elinor encouraged her as much as possible to talk of what she felt; and before breakfast was ready, they had gone through the subject again and again; and with the same steady conviction and affectionate counsel on Elinor's side, the same impetuous feelings and varying opinions on Marianne's, as before. Sometimes she could believe Willoughby to be as unfortunate and as innocent as herself, and at others, lost every consolation in the impossibility of acquitting him. At one moment she was absolutely indifferent to the observation of all the world, at another she would seclude herself from it for ever, and at a third could resist it with energy. In one thing, however, she was uniform, when it came to the point, in avoiding, where it was possible, the presence of Mrs. Jennings, and in a determined silence when obliged to endure it. Her heart was hardened against the belief of Mrs. Jennings's entering into her sorrows with any compassion.

"No, no, no, it cannot be," she cried; "she cannot feel. Her kindness is not sympathy; her good-nature is not tenderness. All that she wants is gossip, and she only likes me now because I supply it."

Elinor had not needed this to be assured of the injustice to which her sister was often led in her opinion of others, by the irritable refinement of her own mind, and the too great importance placed by her on the delicacies of a strong sensibility, and the graces of a polished manner. Like half the rest of the world, if more than half there be that are clever and good, Marianne, with excellent abilities and an excellent disposition, was neither reasonable nor candid. She expected from other people the same opinions and feelings as her own, and she judged of their motives by the immediate effect of their actions on herself. Thus a circumstance occurred, while the sisters were together in their own room after breakfast, which sunk the heart of Mrs. Jennings still lower in her estimation; because, through her own weakness, it chanced to prove a source of fresh pain to herself, though Mrs. Jennings was governed in it by an impulse of the utmost goodwill.

With a letter in her outstretched hand, and countenance gaily smiling, from the persuasion of bringing comfort, she entered their room, saying—

"Now, my dear, I bring you something that I am sure will do you good."

Marianne heard enough. In one moment her imagination placed before her a letter from Willoughby, full of tenderness and contrition, explanatory of all that had passed, satisfactory, convincing; and instantly followed by Willoughby himself, rushing eagerly into the room to inforce, at her feet, by the eloquence of his eyes, the assurances of his letter. The work of one moment was destroyed by the next. The hand writing of her mother, never till then unwelcome, was before her; and, in the acuteness of the disappointment which followed such an ecstasy of more than hope, she felt as if, till that instant, she had never suffered.

The cruelty of Mrs. Jennings no language, within her reach in her moments of happiest eloquence, could have expressed; and now she could reproach her only by the tears which streamed from her eyes with passionate violence—a reproach, however, so entirely lost on its object, that after many expressions of pity, she withdrew, still referring her to the letter of comfort. But the letter, when she was calm enough to read it, brought little comfort. Willoughby filled every page. Her mother, still confident of their engagement, and relying as warmly as ever on his constancy, had only been roused by Elinor's application, to intreat from Marianne greater openness towards them both; and this, with such tenderness towards her, such affection for Willoughby, and such a conviction of their future happiness in each other, that she wept with agony through the whole of it.

All her impatience to be at home again now returned; her mother was dearer to her than ever; dearer through the very excess of her mistaken confidence in Willoughby, and she was wildly urgent to be gone. Elinor, unable herself to determine whether it were better for Marianne to be in London or at Barton, offered no counsel of her own except of patience till their mother's wishes could be known; and at length she obtained her sister's consent to wait for that knowledge.

Mrs. Jennings left them earlier than usual; for she could not be easy till the Middletons and Palmers were able to grieve as much as herself; and positively refusing Elinor's offered attendance, went out alone for the rest of the morning. Elinor, with a very heavy heart, aware of the pain she was going to communicate, and perceiving, by Marianne's letter, how ill she had succeeded in laying any foundation for it, then sat down to write her mother an account of what had passed, and entreat her directions for the future; while Marianne, who came into the drawing-room on Mrs. Jennings's going away, remained fixed at the table where Elinor wrote, watching the advancement of her pen, grieving over her for the hardship of such a task, and grieving still more fondly over its effect on her mother.

In this manner they had continued about a quarter of an hour, when Marianne, whose nerves could not then bear any sudden noise, was startled by a rap at the door.

"Who can this be?" cried Elinor. "So early too! I thought we *had* been safe."

Marianne moved to the window.

"It is Colonel Brandon!" said she, with vexation. "We are never safe from *him*."

"He will not come in, as Mrs. Jennings is from home."

"I will not trust to *that*," retreating to her own room. "A man who has nothing to do with his own time has no conscience in his intrusion on that of others."

The event proved her conjecture right, though it was founded on injustice and error; for Colonel Brandon *did* come in; and Elinor, who was convinced that solicitude for Marianne brought him thither, and who saw *that* solicitude in his disturbed and melancholy look, and in his anxious though brief inquiry after her, could not forgive her sister for esteeming him so lightly.

"I met Mrs. Jennings in Bond Street," said he, after the first salutation, "and she encouraged me to come on; and I was the more easily encouraged, because I thought it probable that I might find you alone, which I was very desirous of doing. My object—my wish—my sole wish in desiring it—I hope, I believe it is—is to be a means of giving comfort—no, I must not say comfort—not present comfort—but conviction, lasting conviction to your sister's mind. My regard for her, for yourself, for your mother—will you allow me to prove it, by relating some circumstances which nothing but a *very* sincere regard—nothing but an earnest desire of being useful—I think I am justified—though where so many hours have been spent in convincing myself that I am right, is there not some reason to fear I may be wrong?" He stopped.

"I understand you," said Elinor. "You have something to tell me of Mr. Willoughby, that will open his character farther. Your telling it will be the greatest act of friendship that can be shewn Marianne. *my* gratitude will be insured immediately by any information tending to that end, and *hers* must be gained by it in time. Pray, pray let me hear it."

"You shall; and, to be brief, when I quitted Barton last October, but this will give you no idea—I must go farther back. You will find me a very awkward narrator, Miss Dashwood; I hardly know where to begin. A short account of myself, I believe, will be necessary, and it *shall* be a short one. On such a subject," sighing heavily, "can I have little temptation to be diffuse."

He stopt a moment for recollection, and then, with another sigh, went on.

"You have probably entirely forgotten a conversation—(it is not to be supposed that it could make any impression on you)—a conversation between us one evening at Barton Park—it was the evening of a dance—in which I alluded to a lady I had once known, as resembling, in some measure, your sister Marianne."

"Indeed," answered Elinor, "I have *not* forgotten it." He looked pleased by this remembrance, and added,

"If I am not deceived by the uncertainty, the partiality of tender recollection, there is a very strong resemblance between them, as well in mind as person. The same warmth of heart, the same eagerness of fancy and spirits. This lady was one of my nearest relations, an orphan from her infancy, and under the guardianship of my father. Our ages were nearly the same, and from our earliest years we were playfellows and friends. I cannot remember the time when I did not love Eliza; and my affection for her, as we grew up, was such, as perhaps, judging from my present forlorn and cheerless gravity, you might think me incapable of having ever felt. Hers, for me, was, I believe, fervent as the attachment of your sister to Mr. Willoughby and it was, though from a different cause, no less unfortunate. At seventeen she was lost to me for ever. She was married—married against her inclination to my brother. Her fortune was large, and our family estate much encumbered. And this, I fear, is all that can be said for the conduct of one, who was at once her uncle and guardian. My brother did not deserve her; he did not even love her. I had hoped that her regard for me would support her under any difficulty, and for some time it did; but at last the misery of her situation, for she experienced great unkindness, overcame all her resolution, and though she had promised me that nothing—but how blindly I relate! I have never told you how this was brought on. We were within a few hours of eloping together for Scotland. The treachery, or the folly, of my cousin's maid betrayed us. I was banished to the house of a relation far distant, and she was allowed no liberty, no society, no amusement, till my father's point was gained. I had depended on her fortitude too far, and the blow was a severe one—but had her marriage been happy, so young as I then was, a few months must have reconciled me to it, or at least I should not have now to lament it. This however was not the case. My brother had no regard for her; his pleasures were not what they ought to have been, and from the first he treated her unkindly. The consequence of this, upon a mind so young, so lively, so inexperienced as Mrs. Brandon's, was but too natural. She resigned herself at first to all the misery of her situation; and happy had it been if she had not lived to overcome those regrets which the remembrance of me occasioned. But can we wonder that, with such a husband to provoke inconstancy, and without a friend to advise or restrain her (for my father lived only a few months after their marriage, and I was with my regiment in the East Indies) she should fall? Had I remained in England, perhaps—but I meant to promote the happiness of both by removing from her for years, and for that purpose had procured my exchange. The shock which her marriage had given me," he continued, in a voice of great agitation, "was of trifling weight—was nothing to what I felt when I heard, about two years afterwards, of her divorce. It was *that* which threw this gloom, even now the recollection of what I suffered—"

He could say no more, and rising hastily walked for a few minutes about the room. Elinor, affected by his relation, and still more by his distress, could not speak. He saw her concern, and coming to her, took her hand, pressed it, and kissed it with grateful respect. A few minutes more of silent exertion enabled him to proceed with composure.

"It was nearly three years after this unhappy period before I returned to England. My first care, when I *did* arrive, was of course to seek for her; but the search was as fruitless as it was melancholy. I could not trace her beyond her first seducer, and there was every reason to fear that she had removed from him only to sink deeper in a life of sin. Her legal allowance was not adequate to her fortune, nor sufficient for her comfortable maintenance, and I learnt from my brother that the power of receiving it had been made over some months before to another person. He imagined, and calmly could he imagine it, that her extravagance, and consequent distress, had obliged her to dispose of it for some immediate relief. At last, however, and after I had been six months in England, I *did* find her. Regard for a former servant of my own, who had since fallen into misfortune, carried me to visit him in a spunging-house, where he was confined for debt; and there, the same house, under a similar confinement, was my unfortunate sister. So altered—so faded—worn down by acute suffering of every kind! hardly could I believe the melancholy and sickly figure before me, to be the remains of the lovely, blooming, healthful girl, on whom I had once doted. What I endured in so beholding her—but I have no right to wound your feelings by attempting to describe it—I have pained you too much already. That she was, to all appearance, in the last stage of a consumption, was—yes, in such a situation it was my greatest comfort. Life could do nothing for her, beyond giving time for a better preparation for death; and that was given. I saw her placed in comfortable lodgings, and under proper attendants; I visited her every day during the rest of her short life: I was with her in her last moments."

Again he stopped to recover himself; and Elinor spoke her feelings in an exclamation of tender concern, at the fate of his unfortunate friend.

"Your sister, I hope, cannot be offended," said he, "by the resemblance I have fancied between her and my poor disgraced relation. Their fates, their fortunes, cannot be the same; and had the natural sweet disposition of the one been guarded by a firmer mind, or a happier marriage, she might have been all that you will live to see the other be. But to what does all this lead? I seem to have been distressing you for nothing. Ah! Miss Dashwood—a subject such as this—untouched for fourteen years—it is dangerous to handle it at all! I *will* be more collected—more concise. She left to my care her only child, a little girl, the offspring of her first guilty connection, who was then about three years old. She loved the child, and had always kept it with her. It was a valued, a precious trust to me; and gladly would I have discharged it in the strictest sense, by watching over her education myself, had the nature of our situations allowed it; but I had no family, no home; and my little Eliza was therefore placed at school. I saw her there whenever I could, and after the death of my brother, (which happened about five years ago, and which left to me the possession of the family property) she visited me at Delaford. I called her a distant relation; but I am well aware that I have in general been suspected of a much nearer connection with her. It is now three years ago (she had just reached her fourteenth year) that I removed her from school, to place her under the care of a very respectable woman, residing in Dorsetshire, who had the charge of four or five other girls of about the same time of life; and for two years I had every reason to be pleased with her situation. But last February, almost a twelvemonth back, she suddenly disappeared. I had allowed her, (imprudently, as it has since turned out) at her earnest desire, to go to Bath with one of her young friends, who was attending her father there for his health. I knew him to be a very good sort of man, and I thought well of his daughter—better than she deserved, for, with a most obstinate and ill-judged secrecy, she would tell nothing, would give no clue, though she certainly knew all. He, her father, a well-meaning, but not a quick-sighted man, could really, I believe, give no information; for he had been generally confined to the house, while the girls were ranging over the town and making what acquaintance they chose; and he tried to convince me, as thoroughly as he was convinced himself, of his daughter's being entirely unconcerned in the business. In short, I could learn nothing but that she was gone; all the rest, for eight long months, was left to conjecture. What I thought, what I feared, may be imagined; and what I suffered too."

"Good heavens!" cried Elinor, "could it be—could Willoughby—"

"The first news that reached me of her," he continued, "came in a letter from herself, last October. It was forwarded to me from Delaford, and I received it on the very morning of our intended party to Whitwell; and this was the reason of my leaving Barton so suddenly, which I am sure must at the time have appeared strange to everybody, and which I believe gave offence to some. Little did Mr. Willoughby imagine, I suppose, when his looks censured me for incivility in breaking up the party, that I was called away to the relief of one whom he had made poor and miserable; but *had* he known it, what would it have availed? Would he have been less gay or less happy in the smiles of your sister? No, he had already done that, which no man who *can* feel for another would do. He had left the girl whose youth and innocence he had seduced, in a situation of the utmost distress, with no creditable home, no help, no friends, ignorant of his address! He had left her, promising to return; he neither returned, nor wrote, nor relieved her."

"This is beyond everything!" exclaimed Elinor.

"His character is now before you; expensive, dissipated, and worse than both. Knowing all this, as I have now known it many weeks, guess what I must have felt on seeing your sister as fond of him as ever, and on being assured that she was to marry him: guess what I must have felt for all your sakes. When I came to you last week and found you alone, I came determined to know the truth; though irresolute what to do when it *was* known. My behaviour must have seemed strange to you then; but now you will comprehend it. To suffer you all to be so deceived; to see your sister—but what could I do? I had no hope of interfering with success; and sometimes I thought your sister's influence might yet reclaim him. But now, after such dishonorable usage, who can tell what were his designs on her. Whatever they may have been, however, she may now, and hereafter doubtless *will* turn with gratitude towards her own condition, when she compares it with that of my poor Eliza, when she considers the wretched and hopeless situation of this poor girl, and pictures her to herself, with an affection for him so strong, still as strong as her own, and with a mind tormented by self-reproach, which must attend her through life. Surely this comparison must have its use with her. She will feel her own sufferings to be nothing. They proceed from no misconduct, and can bring no disgrace. On the contrary, every friend must be made still more her friend by them. Concern for her unhappiness, and respect for her fortitude under it, must strengthen every attachment. Use your own discretion, however, in communicating to her what I have told you. You must know best what will be its effect; but had I not seriously, and from my heart believed it might be of service, might lessen her regrets, I would not have suffered myself to trouble you with this account of my family afflictions, with a recital which may seem to have been intended to raise myself at the expense of others."

Elinor's thanks followed this speech with grateful earnestness; attended too with the assurance of her expecting material advantage to Marianne, from the communication of what had passed.

"I have been more pained," said she, "by her endeavors to acquit him than by all the rest; for it irritates her mind more than the most perfect conviction of his unworthiness can do. Now, though at first she will suffer much, I am sure she will soon become easier. Have you," she continued, after a short silence, "ever seen Mr. Willoughby since you left him at Barton?"

"Yes," he replied gravely, "once I have. One meeting was unavoidable."

Elinor, startled by his manner, looked at him anxiously, saying,

"What? Have you met him to—"

"I could meet him no other way. Eliza had confessed to me, though most reluctantly, the name of her lover; and when he returned to town, which was within a fortnight after myself, we met by appointment, he to defend, I to punish his conduct. We returned unwounded, and the meeting, therefore, never got abroad."

Elinor sighed over the fancied necessity of this; but to a man and a soldier she presumed not to censure it.

"Such," said Colonel Brandon, after a pause, "has been the unhappy resemblance between the fate of mother and daughter! And so imperfectly have I discharged my trust!"

"Is she still in town?"

"No; as soon as she recovered from her lying-in, for I found her near her delivery, I removed her and her child into the country, and there she remains."

Recollecting, soon afterwards, that he was probably dividing Elinor from her sister, he put an end to his visit, receiving from her again the same grateful acknowledgments, and leaving her full of compassion and esteem for him.

CHAPTER XXXII

When the particulars of this conversation were repeated by Miss Dashwood to her sister, as they very soon were, the effect on her was not entirely such as the former had hoped to see. Not that Marianne appeared to distrust the truth of any part of it, for she listened to it all with the most steady and submissive attention, made neither objection nor remark, attempted no vindication of Willoughby, and seemed to shew by her tears that she felt it to be impossible. But though this behaviour assured Elinor that the conviction of this guilt *was* carried home to her mind, though she saw with satisfaction the effect of it, in her no longer avoiding Colonel Brandon when he called, in her speaking to him, even voluntarily speaking, with a kind of compassionate respect, and though she saw her spirits less violently irritated than before, she did not see her less wretched. Her mind did become settled, but it was settled in a gloomy dejection. She felt the loss of Willoughby's character yet more heavily than she had felt the loss of his heart; his seduction and desertion of Miss Williams, the misery of that poor girl, and the doubt of what his designs might *once* have been on herself, preyed altogether so much on her spirits, that she could not bring herself to speak of what she felt even to Elinor; and, brooding over her sorrows in silence, gave more pain to her sister than could have been communicated by the most open and most frequent confession of them.

To give the feelings or the language of Mrs. Dashwood on receiving and answering Elinor's letter would be only to give a repetition of what her daughters had already felt and said; of a disappointment hardly less painful than Marianne's, and an indignation even greater than Elinor's. Long letters from her, quickly succeeding each other, arrived to tell all that she suffered and thought; to express her anxious solicitude for Marianne, and entreat she would bear up with fortitude under this misfortune. Bad indeed must the nature of Marianne's affliction be, when her mother could talk of fortitude! Mortifying and humiliating must be the origin of those regrets, which *she* could wish her not to indulge!

Against the interest of her own individual comfort, Mrs. Dashwood had determined that it would be better for Marianne to be any where, at that time, than at Barton, where everything within her view would be bringing back the past in the strongest and most afflicting manner, by constantly placing Willoughby before her, such as she had always seen him there. She recommended it to her daughters, therefore, by all means not to shorten their visit to Mrs. Jennings; the length of which, though never exactly fixed, had been expected by all to comprise at least five or six weeks. A variety of occupations, of objects, and of company, which could not be procured at Barton, would be inevitable there, and might yet, she hoped, cheat Marianne, at times, into some interest beyond herself, and even into some amusement, much as the ideas of both might now be spurned by her.

From all danger of seeing Willoughby again, her mother considered her to be at least equally safe in town as in the country, since his acquaintance must now be dropped by all who called themselves her friends. Design could never bring them in each other's way: negligence could never leave them exposed to a surprise; and chance had less in its favour in the crowd of London than even in the retirement of Barton, where it might force him before her while paying that visit at Allenham on his marriage, which Mrs. Dashwood, from foreseeing at first as a probable event, had brought herself to expect as a certain one.

She had yet another reason for wishing her children to remain where they were; a letter from her son-in-law had told her that he and his wife were to be in town before the middle of February, and she judged it right that they should sometimes see their brother.

Marianne had promised to be guided by her mother's opinion, and she submitted to it therefore without opposition, though it proved perfectly different from what she wished and expected, though she felt it to be entirely wrong, formed on mistaken grounds, and that by requiring her longer continuance in London it deprived her of the only possible alleviation of her wretchedness, the personal sympathy of her mother, and doomed her to such society and such scenes as must prevent her ever knowing a moment's rest.

But it was a matter of great consolation to her, that what brought evil to herself would bring good to her sister; and Elinor, on the other hand, suspecting that it would not be in her power to avoid Edward entirely, comforted herself by thinking, that though their longer stay would therefore militate against her own happiness, it would be better for Marianne than an immediate return into Devonshire.

Her carefulness in guarding her sister from ever hearing

Willoughby's name mentioned, was not thrown away. Marianne, though without knowing it herself, reaped all its advantage; for neither Mrs. Jennings, nor Sir John, nor even Mrs. Palmer herself, ever spoke of him before her. Elinor wished that the same forbearance could have extended towards herself, but that was impossible, and she was obliged to listen day after day to the indignation of them all.

Sir John could not have thought it possible. "A man of whom he had always had such reason to think well! Such a good-natured fellow! He did not believe there was a bolder rider in England! It was an unaccountable business. He wished him at the devil with all his heart. He would not speak another word to him, meet him where he might, for all the world! No, not if it were to be by the side of Barton covert, and they were kept watching for two hours together. Such a scoundrel of a fellow! such a deceitful dog! It was only the last time they met that he had offered him one of Folly's puppies! And this was the end of it!"

Mrs. Palmer, in her way, was equally angry. "She was determined to drop his acquaintance immediately, and she was very thankful that she had never been acquainted with him at all. She wished with all her heart Combe Magna was not so near Cleveland; but it did not signify, for it was a great deal too far off to visit; she hated him so much that she was resolved never to mention his name again, and she should tell everybody she saw, how good-for-nothing he was."

The rest of Mrs. Palmer's sympathy was shewn in procuring all the particulars in her power of the approaching marriage, and communicating them to Elinor. She could soon tell at what coachmaker's the new carriage was building, by what painter Mr. Willoughby's portrait was drawn, and at what warehouse Miss Grey's clothes might be seen.

The calm and polite unconcern of Lady Middleton on the occasion was a happy relief to Elinor's spirits, oppressed as they often were by the clamorous kindness of the others. It was a great comfort to her to be sure of exciting no interest in *one* person at least among their circle of friends: a great comfort to know that there was *one* who would meet her without feeling any curiosity after particulars, or any anxiety for her sister's health.

Every qualification is raised at times, by the circumstances of the moment, to more than its real value; and she was sometimes worried down by officious condolence to rate good-breeding as more indispensable to comfort than good-nature.

Lady Middleton expressed her sense of the affair about once every day, or twice, if the subject occurred very often, by saying, "It is very shocking, indeed!" and by the means of this continual though gentle vent, was able not only to see the Miss Dashwoods from the first without the smallest emotion, but very soon to see them without recollecting a word of the matter; and having thus supported the dignity of her own sex, and spoken her decided censure of what was wrong in the other, she thought herself at liberty to attend to the interest of her own assemblies, and therefore determined (though rather against the opinion of Sir John) that as Mrs. Willoughby would at once be a woman of elegance and fortune, to leave her card with her as soon as she married.

Colonel Brandon's delicate, unobtrusive enquiries were never unwelcome to Miss Dashwood. He had abundantly earned the privilege of intimate discussion of her sister's disappointment, by the friendly zeal with which he had endeavoured to soften it, and they always conversed with confidence. His chief reward for the painful exertion of disclosing past sorrows and present humiliations, was given in the pitying eye with which Marianne sometimes observed him, and the gentleness of her voice whenever (though it did not often happen) she was obliged, or could oblige herself to speak to him. *These* assured him that his exertion had produced an increase of good-will towards himself, and *these* gave Elinor hopes of its being farther augmented hereafter; but Mrs. Jennings, who knew nothing of all this, who knew only that the Colonel continued as grave as ever, and that she could neither prevail on him to make the offer himself, nor commission her to make it for him, began, at the end of two days, to think that, instead of Midsummer, they would not be married till Michaelmas, and by the end of a week that it would not be a match at all. The good understanding between the Colonel and Miss Dashwood seemed rather to declare that the honours of the mulberry-tree, the canal, and the yew arbour, would all be made over to *her*; and Mrs. Jennings had, for some time ceased to think at all of Mrs. Ferrars.

Early in February, within a fortnight from the receipt of Willoughby's letter, Elinor had the painful office of informing her sister that he was married. She had taken care to have the intelligence conveyed to herself, as soon as it was known that the ceremony was over, as she was desirous that Marianne should not receive the first notice of it from the public papers, which she saw her eagerly examining every morning.

She received the news with resolute composure; made no observation on it, and at first shed no tears; but after a short time they would burst out, and for the rest of the day, she was in a state hardly less pitiable than when she first learnt to expect the event.

The Willoughbys left town as soon as they were married; and Elinor now hoped, as there could be no danger of her seeing either of them, to prevail on her sister, who had never yet left the house since the blow first fell, to go out again by degrees as she had done before.

About this time the two Miss Steeles, lately arrived at their cousin's house in Bartlett's Buildings, Holburn, presented themselves again before their more grand relations in Conduit and Berkeley Streets; and were welcomed by them all with great cordiality.

Elinor only was sorry to see them. Their presence always gave her pain, and she hardly knew how to make a very gracious return to the overpowering delight of Lucy in finding her *still* in town.

"I should have been quite disappointed if I had not found you here *still*," said she repeatedly, with a strong emphasis on the word. "But I always thought I *should*. I was almost sure you would not leave London yet awhile; though you *told* me, you know, at Barton, that you should not stay above a *month*. But I thought, at the time, that you would most likely change your mind when it came to the point. It would have been such a great pity to have went away before your brother and sister came. And now to be sure you will be in no hurry to be gone. I am amazingly glad you did not keep to *your word*."

Elinor perfectly understood her, and was forced to use all her self-command to make it appear that she did *not*.

"Well, my dear," said Mrs. Jennings, "and how did you travel?"

"Not in the stage, I assure you," replied Miss Steele, with quick exultation; "we came post all the way, and had a very smart beau to attend us. Dr. Davies was coming to town, and so we thought we'd join him in a post-chaise; and he behaved very genteelly, and paid ten or twelve shillings more than we did."

"Oh, oh!" cried Mrs. Jennings; "very pretty, indeed! And the Doctor is a single man, I warrant you."

"There now," said Miss Steele, affectedly simpering, "everybody laughs at me so about the Doctor, and I cannot think why. My cousins say they are sure I have made a conquest; but for my part I declare I never think about him from one hour's end to another. 'Lord! here comes your beau, Nancy,' my cousin said t'other day, when she saw him crossing the street to the house. My beau, indeed! Said I—I cannot think who you mean. The Doctor is no beau of mine."

"Aye, aye, that is very pretty talking—but it won't do—the Doctor is the man, I see."

"No, indeed!" replied her cousin, with affected earnestness, "and I beg you will contradict it, if you ever hear it talked of."

Mrs. Jennings directly gave her the gratifying assurance that she certainly would *not*, and Miss Steele was made completely happy.

"I suppose you will go and stay with your brother and sister, Miss Dashwood, when they come to town," said Lucy, returning, after a cessation of hostile hints, to the charge.

"No, I do not think we shall."

"Oh, yes, I dare say you will."

Elinor would not humour her by farther opposition.

"What a charming thing it is that Mrs. Dashwood can spare you both for so long a time together!"

"Long a time, indeed!" interposed Mrs. Jennings. "Why, their visit is but just begun!"

Lucy was silenced.

"I am sorry we cannot see your sister, Miss Dashwood," said Miss Steele. "I am sorry she is not well—" for Marianne had left the room on their arrival.

"You are very good. My sister will be equally sorry to miss the pleasure of seeing you; but she has been very much plagued lately with nervous head-aches, which make her unfit for company or conversation."

"Oh, dear, that is a great pity! But such old friends as Lucy and me! I think she might see *us*; and I am sure we would not speak a word."

Elinor, with great civility, declined the proposal. Her sister was perhaps laid down upon the bed, or in her dressing gown, and therefore not able to come to them.

"Oh, if that's all," cried Miss Steele, "we can just as well go and see *her*."

Elinor began to find this impertinence too much for her temper; but she was saved the trouble of checking it, by Lucy's sharp reprimand, which now, as on many occasions, though it did not give much sweetness to the manners of one sister, was of advantage in governing those of the other.

CHAPTER XXXIII

After some opposition, Marianne yielded to her sister's entreaties, and consented to go out with her and Mrs. Jennings one morning for half an hour. She expressly conditioned, however, for paying no visits, and would do no more than accompany them to Gray's in Sackville Street, where Elinor was carrying on a negotiation for the exchange of a few old-fashioned jewels of her mother.

When they stopped at the door, Mrs. Jennings recollected that there was a lady at the other end of the street on whom she ought to call; and as she had no business at Gray's, it was resolved, that while her young friends transacted theirs, she should pay her visit and return for them.

On ascending the stairs, the Miss Dashwoods found so many people before them in the room, that there was not a person at liberty to tend to their orders; and they were obliged to wait. All that could be done was, to sit down at that end of the counter which seemed to promise the quickest succession; one gentleman only was standing there, and it is probable that Elinor was not without hope of exciting his politeness to a quicker despatch. But the correctness of his eye, and the delicacy of his taste, proved to be beyond his politeness. He was giving orders for a toothpick-case for himself, and till its size, shape, and ornaments were determined, all of which, after examining and debating for a quarter of an hour over every toothpick-case in the shop, were finally arranged by his own inventive fancy, he had no leisure to bestow any other attention on the two ladies, than what was comprised in three or four very broad stares; a kind of notice which served to imprint on Elinor the remembrance of a person and face, of strong, natural, sterling insignificance, though adorned in the first style of fashion.

Marianne was spared from the troublesome feelings of contempt and resentment, on this impertinent examination of their features, and on the puppyism of his manner in deciding on all the different horrors of the different toothpick-cases presented to his inspection, by remaining unconscious of it all; for she was as well able to collect her thoughts within herself, and be as ignorant of what was passing around her, in Mr. Gray's shop, as in her own bedroom.

At last the affair was decided. The ivory, the gold, and the pearls, all received their appointment, and the gentleman having named the last day on which his existence could be continued without the possession of the toothpick-case, drew on his gloves with leisurely care, and bestowing another glance on the Miss Dashwoods, but such a one as seemed rather to demand than express admiration, walked off with a happy air of real conceit and affected indifference.

Elinor lost no time in bringing her business forward, was on the point of concluding it, when another gentleman presented himself at her side. She turned her eyes towards his face, and found him with some surprise to be her brother.

Their affection and pleasure in meeting was just enough to make a very creditable appearance in Mr. Gray's shop. John Dashwood was really far from being sorry to see his sisters again; it rather gave them satisfaction; and his inquiries after their mother were respectful and attentive.

Elinor found that he and Fanny had been in town two days.

"I wished very much to call upon you yesterday," said he, "but it was impossible, for we were obliged to take Harry to see the wild beasts at Exeter Exchange; and we spent the rest of the day with Mrs. Ferrars. Harry was vastly pleased. *This* morning I had fully intended to call on you, if I could possibly find a spare half hour, but one has always so much to do on first coming to town. I am come here to bespeak Fanny a seal. But tomorrow I think I shall certainly be able to call in Berkeley Street, and be introduced to your friend Mrs. Jennings. I understand she is a woman of very good fortune. And the Middletons too, you must introduce me to *them*. As my mother-in-law's relations, I shall be happy to show them every respect. They are excellent neighbours to you in the country, I understand."

"Excellent indeed. Their attention to our comfort, their friendliness in every particular, is more than I can express."

"I am extremely glad to hear it, upon my word; extremely glad indeed. But so it ought to be; they are people of large fortune, they are related to you, and every civility and accommodation that can serve to make your situation pleasant might be reasonably expected. And so you are most comfortably settled in your little cottage and want for nothing! Edward brought us a most charming account of the place: the most complete thing of its kind, he said, that ever was, and you all seemed to enjoy it beyond anything. It was a great satisfaction to us to hear it, I assure you."

Elinor did feel a little ashamed of her brother; and was not sorry to be spared the necessity of answering him, by the arrival of Mrs. Jennings's servant, who came to tell her that his mistress waited for them at the door.

Mr. Dashwood attended them down stairs, was introduced to Mrs. Jennings at the door of her carriage, and repeating his hope of being able to call on them the next day, took leave.

His visit was duly paid. He came with a pretence at an apology from their sister-in-law, for not coming too; "but she was so much engaged with her mother, that really she had no leisure for going any where." Mrs. Jennings, however, assured him directly, that she should not stand upon ceremony, for they were all cousins, or something like it, and she should certainly wait on Mrs. John Dashwood very soon, and bring her sisters to see her. His manners to *them*, though calm, were perfectly kind; to Mrs. Jennings, most attentively civil; and on Colonel Brandon's coming in soon after himself, he eyed him with a curiosity which seemed to say, that he only wanted to know him to be rich, to be equally civil to *him*.

After staying with them half an hour, he asked Elinor to walk with him to Conduit Street, and introduce him to Sir John and Lady Middleton. The weather was remarkably fine, and she readily consented. As soon as they were out of the house, his enquiries began.

"Who is Colonel Brandon? Is he a man of fortune?"

"Yes; he has very good property in Dorsetshire."

"I am glad of it. He seems a most gentlemanlike man; and I think, Elinor, I may congratulate you on the prospect of a very respectable establishment in life."

"Me, brother! What do you mean?"

"He likes you. I observed him narrowly, and am convinced of it. What is the amount of his fortune?"

"I believe about two thousand a year."

"Two thousand a year"; and then working himself up to a pitch of enthusiastic generosity, he added, "Elinor, I wish with all my heart it were *twice* as much, for your sake."

"Indeed I believe you," replied Elinor; "but I am very sure that Colonel Brandon has not the smallest wish of marrying *me*."

"You are mistaken, Elinor; you are very much mistaken. A very little trouble on your side secures him. Perhaps just at present he may be undecided; the smallness of your fortune may make him hang back; his friends may all advise him against it. But some of those little attentions and encouragements which ladies can so easily give will fix him, in spite of himself. And there can be no reason why you should not try for him. It is not to be supposed that any prior attachment on your side—in short, you know as to an attachment of that kind, it is quite out of the question, the objections are insurmountable—you have too much sense not to see all that. Colonel Brandon must be the man; and no civility shall be wanting on my part to make him pleased with you and your family. It is a match that must give universal satisfaction. In short, it is a kind of thing that"—lowering his voice to an important whisper—"will be exceedingly welcome to *all parties*." Recollecting himself, however, he added, "That is, I mean to say—your friends are all truly anxious to see you well settled; Fanny particularly, for she has your interest very much at heart, I assure you. And her mother too, Mrs. Ferrars, a very good-natured woman, I am sure it would give her great pleasure; she said as much the other day."

Elinor would not vouchsafe any answer.

"It would be something remarkable, now," he continued, "something droll, if Fanny should have a brother and I a sister settling at the same time. And yet it is not very unlikely."

"Is Mr. Edward Ferrars," said Elinor, with resolution, "going to be married?"

"It is not actually settled, but there is such a thing in agitation. He has a most excellent mother. Mrs. Ferrars, with the utmost liberality, will come forward, and settle on him a thousand a year, if the match takes place. The lady is the Hon. Miss Morton, only daughter of the late Lord Morton, with thirty thousand pounds. A very desirable connection on both sides, and I have not a doubt of its taking place in time. A thousand a-year is a great deal for a mother to give away, to make over for ever; but Mrs. Ferrars has a noble spirit. To give you another instance of her liberality—The other day, as soon as we came to town, aware that money could not be very plenty with us just now, she put bank-notes into Fanny's hands to the amount of two hundred pounds. And extremely acceptable it is, for we must live at a great expense while we are here."

He paused for her assent and compassion; and she forced herself to say:

"Your expenses both in town and country must certainly be considerable; but your income is a large one."

"Not so large, I dare say, as many people suppose. I do not mean to complain, however; it is undoubtedly a comfortable one, and I hope will in time be better. The enclosure of Norland Common, now carrying on, is a most serious drain. And then I have made a little purchase within this half year; East Kingham Farm, you must remember the place, where old Gibson used to live. The land was so very desirable for me in every respect, so immediately adjoining my own property, that I felt it my duty to buy it. I could not have answered it to my conscience to let it fall into any other hands. A man must pay for his convenience; and it *has* cost me a vast deal of money."

"More than you think it really and intrinsically worth."

"Why, I hope not that. I might have sold it again, the next day, for more than I gave: but, with regard to the purchase-money, I might have been very unfortunate indeed; for the stocks were at that time so low, that if I had not happened to have the necessary sum in my banker's hands, I must have sold out to very great loss."

Elinor could only smile.

"Other great and inevitable expenses too we have had on first coming to Norland. Our respected father, as you well know, bequeathed all the Stanhill effects that remained at Norland (and very valuable they were) to your mother. Far be it from me to repine at his doing so; he had an undoubted right to dispose of his own property as he chose, but, in consequence of it, we have been obliged to make large purchases of linen, china, &c. to supply the place of what was taken away. You may guess, after all these expenses, how very far we must be from being rich, and how acceptable Mrs. Ferrars's kindness is."

"Certainly," said Elinor; "and assisted by her liberality, I hope you may yet live to be in easy circumstances."

"Another year or two may do much towards it," he gravely replied; "but however there is still a great deal to be done. There is not a stone laid of Fanny's green-house, and nothing but the plan of the flower-garden marked out."

"Where is the green-house to be?"

"Upon the knoll behind the house. The old walnut trees are all come down to make room for it. It will be a very fine object from many parts of the park, and the flower-garden will slope down just before it, and be exceedingly pretty. We have cleared away all the old thorns that grew in patches over the brow."

Elinor kept her concern and her censure to herself; and was very thankful that Marianne was not present, to share the provocation.

Having now said enough to make his poverty clear, and to do away the necessity of buying a pair of ear-rings for each of his sisters, in his next visit at Gray's his thoughts took a cheerfuller turn, and he began to congratulate Elinor on having such a friend as Mrs. Jennings.

"She seems a most valuable woman indeed—Her house, her style of living, all bespeak an exceeding good income; and it is an acquaintance that has not only been of great use to you hitherto, but in the end may prove materially advantageous. Her inviting you to town is certainly a vast thing in your favour; and indeed, it speaks altogether so great a regard for you, that in all probability when she dies you will not be forgotten. She must have a great deal to leave."

"Nothing at all, I should rather suppose; for she has only her jointure, which will descend to her children."

"But it is not to be imagined that she lives up to her income. Few people of common prudence will do *that*; and whatever she saves, she will be able to dispose of."

"And do you not think it more likely that she should leave it to her daughters, than to us?"

"Her daughters are both exceedingly well married, and therefore I cannot perceive the necessity of her remembering them farther. Whereas, in my opinion, by her taking so much notice of you, and treating you in this kind of way, she has given you a sort of claim on her future consideration, which a conscientious woman would not disregard. Nothing can be kinder than her behaviour; and she can hardly do all this, without being aware of the expectation it raises."

"But she raises none in those most concerned. Indeed, brother, your anxiety for our welfare and prosperity carries you too far."

"Why, to be sure," said he, seeming to recollect himself, "people have little, have very little in their power. But, my dear Elinor, what is the matter with Marianne? She looks very unwell, has lost her colour, and is grown quite thin. Is she ill?"

"She is not well, she has had a nervous complaint on her for several weeks."

"I am sorry for that. At her time of life, any thing of an illness destroys the bloom for ever! Hers has been a very short one! She was as handsome a girl last September, as I ever saw; and as likely to attract the man. There was something in her style of beauty, to please them particularly. I remember Fanny used to say that she would marry sooner and better than you did; not but what she is exceedingly fond of *you*, but so it happened to strike her. She will be mistaken, however. I question whether Marianne *now*, will marry a man worth more than five or six hundred a-year, at the utmost, and I am very much deceived if *you* do not do better. Dorsetshire! I know very little of Dorsetshire; but, my dear Elinor, I shall be exceedingly glad to know more of it; and I think I can answer for your having Fanny and myself among the earliest and best pleased of your visitors."

Elinor tried very seriously to convince him that there was no likelihood of her marrying Colonel Brandon; but it was an expectation of too much pleasure to himself to be relinquished, and he was really resolved on seeking an intimacy with that gentleman, and promoting the marriage by every possible attention. He had just compunction enough for having done nothing for his sisters himself, to be exceedingly anxious that everybody else should do a great deal; and an offer from Colonel Brandon, or a legacy from Mrs. Jennings, was the easiest means of atoning for his own neglect.

They were lucky enough to find Lady Middleton at home, and Sir John came in before their visit ended. Abundance of civilities passed on all sides. Sir John was ready to like anybody, and though Mr. Dashwood did not seem to know much about horses, he soon set him down as a very good-natured fellow: while Lady Middleton saw enough of fashion in his appearance to think his acquaintance worth having; and Mr. Dashwood went away delighted with both.

"I shall have a charming account to carry to Fanny," said he, as he walked back with his sister. "Lady Middleton is really a most elegant woman! Such a woman as I am sure Fanny will be glad to know. And Mrs. Jennings too, an exceedingly well-behaved woman, though not so elegant as her daughter. Your sister need not have any scruple even of visiting *her*, which, to say the truth, has been a little the case, and very naturally; for we only knew that Mrs. Jennings was the widow of a man who had got all his money in a low way; and Fanny and Mrs. Ferrars were both strongly prepossessed, that neither she nor her daughters were such kind of women as Fanny would like to associate with. But now I can carry her a most satisfactory account of both."

CHAPTER XXXIV

Mrs. John Dashwood had so much confidence in her husband's judgment, that she waited the very next day both on Mrs. Jennings and her daughter; and her confidence was rewarded by finding even the former, even the woman with whom her sisters were staying, by no means unworthy her notice; and as for Lady Middleton, she found her one of the most charming women in the world!

Lady Middleton was equally pleased with Mrs. Dashwood. There was a kind of cold hearted selfishness on both sides, which mutually attracted them; and they sympathised with each other in an insipid propriety of demeanor, and a general want of understanding.

The same manners, however, which recommended Mrs. John Dashwood to the good opinion of Lady Middleton did not suit the fancy of Mrs. Jennings, and to *her* she appeared nothing more than a little proud-looking woman of uncordial address, who met her husband's sisters without any affection, and almost without having anything to say to them; for of the quarter of an hour bestowed on Berkeley Street, she sat at least seven minutes and a half in silence.

Elinor wanted very much to know, though she did not choose to ask, whether Edward was then in town; but nothing would have induced Fanny voluntarily to mention his name before her, till able to tell her that his marriage with Miss Morton was resolved on, or till her husband's expectations on Colonel Brandon were answered; because she believed them still so very much attached to each other, that they could not be too sedulously divided in word and deed on every occasion. The intelligence however, which *she* would not give, soon flowed from another quarter. Lucy came very shortly to claim Elinor's compassion on being unable to see Edward, though he had arrived in town with Mr. and Mrs. Dashwood. He dared not come to Bartlett's Buildings for fear of detection, and though their mutual impatience to meet, was not to be told, they could do nothing at present but write.

Edward assured them himself of his being in town, within a very short time, by twice calling in Berkeley Street. Twice was his card found on the table, when they returned from their morning's engagements.

Elinor was pleased that he had called; and still more pleased that she had missed him.

The Dashwoods were so prodigiously delighted with the Middletons, that, though not much in the habit of giving anything, they determined to give them—a dinner; and soon after their acquaintance began, invited them to dine in Harley Street, where they had taken a very good house for three months. Their sisters and Mrs. Jennings were invited likewise, and John Dashwood was careful to secure Colonel Brandon, who, always glad to be where the Miss Dashwoods were, received his eager civilities with some surprise, but much more pleasure. They were to meet Mrs. Ferrars; but Elinor could not learn whether her sons were to be of the party. The expectation of seeing *her*, however, was enough to make her interested in the engagement; for though she could now meet Edward's mother without that strong anxiety which had once promised to attend such an introduction, though she could now see her with perfect indifference as to her opinion of herself, her desire of being in company with Mrs. Ferrars, her curiosity to know what she was like, was as lively as ever.

The interest with which she thus anticipated the party, was soon afterwards increased, more powerfully than pleasantly, by her hearing that the Miss Steeles were also to be at it.

So well had they recommended themselves to Lady Middleton, so agreeable had their assiduities made them to her, that though Lucy was certainly not so elegant, and her sister not even genteel, she was as ready as Sir John to ask them to spend a week or two in Conduit Street; and it happened to be particularly convenient to the Miss Steeles, as soon as the Dashwoods' invitation was known, that their visit should begin a few days before the party took place.

Their claims to the notice of Mrs. John Dashwood, as the nieces of the gentleman who for many years had had the care of her brother, might not have done much, however, towards procuring them seats at her table; but as Lady Middleton's guests they must be welcome; and Lucy, who had long wanted to be personally known to the family, to have a nearer view of their characters and her own difficulties, and to have an opportunity of endeavouring to please them, had seldom been happier in her life, than she was on receiving Mrs. John Dashwood's card.

On Elinor its effect was very different. She began immediately to determine, that Edward who lived with his mother, must be asked as his mother was, to a party given by his sister; and to see him for the first time, after all that passed, in the company of Lucy! She hardly knew how she could bear it!

These apprehensions, perhaps, were not founded entirely on reason, and certainly not at all on truth. They were relieved however, not by her own recollection, but by the good will of Lucy, who believed herself to be inflicting a severe disappointment when she told her that Edward certainly would not be in Harley Street on Tuesday, and even hoped to be carrying the pain still farther by persuading her that he was kept away by the extreme affection for herself, which he could not conceal when they were together.

The important Tuesday came that was to introduce the two young ladies to this formidable mother-in-law.

"Pity me, dear Miss Dashwood!" said Lucy, as they walked up the stairs together—for the Middletons arrived so directly after Mrs. Jennings, that they all followed the servant at the same time—"There is nobody here but you, that can feel for me. I declare I can hardly stand. Good gracious! In a moment I shall see the person that all my happiness depends on—that is to be my mother!"

Elinor could have given her immediate relief by suggesting the possibility of its being Miss Morton's mother, rather than her own, whom they were about to behold; but instead of doing that, she assured her, and with great sincerity, that she did pity her—to the utter amazement of Lucy, who, though really uncomfortable herself, hoped at least to be an object of irrepressible envy to Elinor.

Mrs. Ferrars was a little, thin woman, upright, even to formality, in her figure, and serious, even to sourness, in her aspect. Her complexion was sallow; and her features small, without beauty, and naturally without expression; but a lucky contraction of the brow had rescued her countenance from the disgrace of insipidity, by giving it the strong characters of pride and ill nature. She was not a woman of many words; for, unlike people in general, she proportioned them to the number of her ideas; and of the few syllables that did escape her, not one fell to the share of Miss Dashwood, whom she eyed with the spirited determination of disliking her at all events.

Elinor could not *now* be made unhappy by this behaviour. A few months ago it would have hurt her exceedingly; but it was not in Mrs.

Ferrars's power to distress her by it now—and the difference of her manners to the Miss Steeles, a difference which seemed purposely made to humble her more, only amused her. She could not but smile to see the graciousness of both mother and daughter towards the very person—for Lucy was particularly distinguished—whom of all others, had they known as much as she did, they would have been most anxious to mortify; while she herself, who had comparatively no power to wound them, sat pointedly slighted by both. But while she smiled at a graciousness so misapplied, she could not reflect on the mean-spirited folly from which it sprung, nor observe the studied attentions with which the Miss Steeles courted its continuance, without thoroughly despising them all four.

Lucy was all exultation on being so honorably distinguished; and Miss Steele wanted only to be teazed about Dr. Davies to be perfectly happy.

The dinner was a grand one, the servants were numerous, and every thing bespoke the Mistress's inclination for show, and the Master's ability to support it. In spite of the improvements and additions which were making to the Norland estate, and in spite of its owner having once been within some thousand pounds of being obliged to sell out at a loss, nothing gave any symptom of that indigence which he had tried to infer from it—no poverty of any kind, except of conversation, appeared—but there, the deficiency was considerable. John Dashwood had not much to say for himself that was worth hearing, and his wife had still less. But there was no peculiar disgrace in this; for it was very much the case with the chief of their visitors, who almost all laboured under one or other of these disqualifications for being agreeable—Want of sense, either natural or improved—want of elegance—want of spirits—or want of temper.

When the ladies withdrew to the drawing-room after dinner, this poverty was particularly evident, for the gentlemen *had* supplied the discourse with some variety—the variety of politics, inclosing land, and breaking horses—but then it was all over; and one subject only engaged the ladies till coffee came in, which was the comparative heights of Harry Dashwood, and Lady Middleton's second son William, who were nearly of the same age.

Had both the children been there, the affair might have been determined too easily by measuring them at once; but as Harry only was present, it was all conjectural assertion on both sides; and every body had a right to be equally positive in their opinion, and to repeat it over and over again as often as they liked.

The parties stood thus:

The two mothers, though each really convinced that her own son was the tallest, politely decided in favour of the other.

The two grandmothers, with not less partiality, but more sincerity, were equally earnest in support of their own descendant.

Lucy, who was hardly less anxious to please one parent than the other, thought the boys were both remarkably tall for their age, and could not conceive that there could be the smallest difference in the world between them; and Miss Steele, with yet greater address gave it, as fast as she could, in favour of each.

Elinor, having once delivered her opinion on William's side, by which she offended Mrs. Ferrars and Fanny still more, did not see the necessity of enforcing it by any farther assertion; and Marianne, when called on for hers, offended them all, by declaring that she had no opinion to give, as she had never thought about it.

Before her removing from Norland, Elinor had painted a very pretty pair of screens for her sister-in-law, which being now just mounted and brought home, ornamented her present drawing room; and these screens, catching the eye of John Dashwood on his following the other gentlemen into the room, were officiously handed by him to Colonel Brandon for his admiration.

"These are done by my eldest sister," said he; "and you, as a man of taste, will, I dare say, be pleased with them. I do not know whether you have ever happened to see any of her performances before, but she is in general reckoned to draw extremely well."

The Colonel, though disclaiming all pretensions to connoisseurship, warmly admired the screens, as he would have done anything painted by Miss Dashwood; and on the curiosity of the others being of course excited, they were handed round for general inspection. Mrs. Ferrars, not aware of their being Elinor's work, particularly requested to look at them; and after they had received gratifying testimony of Lady Middleton's approbation, Fanny presented them to her mother, considerately informing her, at the same time, that they were done by Miss Dashwood.

"Hum"—said Mrs. Ferrars—"very pretty"—and without regarding them at all, returned them to her daughter.

Perhaps Fanny thought for a moment that her mother had been quite rude enough, for, colouring a little, she immediately said,

"They are very pretty, ma'am—an't they?" But then again, the dread of having been too civil, too encouraging herself, probably came over her, for she presently added,

"Do you not think they are something in Miss Morton's style of painting, Ma'am? She *does* paint most delightfully! How beautifully her last landscape is done!"

"Beautifully indeed! But *she* does every thing well."

Marianne could not bear this. She was already greatly displeased with Mrs. Ferrars; and such ill-timed praise of another, at Elinor's expense, though she had not any notion of what was principally meant by it, provoked her immediately to say with warmth,

"This is admiration of a very particular kind! What is Miss Morton to us? Who knows, or who cares, for her? It is Elinor of whom *we* think and speak."

And so saying, she took the screens out of her sister-in-law's hands, to admire them herself as they ought to be admired.

Mrs. Ferrars looked exceedingly angry, and drawing herself up more stiffly than ever, pronounced in retort this bitter philippic, "Miss Morton is Lord Morton's daughter."

Fanny looked very angry too, and her husband was all in a fright at his sister's audacity. Elinor was much more hurt by Marianne's warmth than she had been by what produced it; but Colonel Brandon's eyes, as they were fixed on Marianne, declared that he noticed only what was amiable in it, the affectionate heart which could not bear to see a sister slighted in the smallest point.

Marianne's feelings did not stop here. The cold insolence of Mrs. Ferrars's general behaviour to her sister, seemed, to her, to foretell such difficulties and distresses to Elinor, as her own wounded heart taught her to think of with horror; and urged by a strong impulse of affectionate sensibility, she moved after a moment, to her sister's chair, and putting one arm round her neck, and one cheek close to hers, said in a low, but eager, voice,

"Dear, dear Elinor, don't mind them. Don't let them make *you* unhappy."

She could say no more; her spirits were quite overcome, and hiding her face on Elinor's shoulder, she burst into tears. Everybody's attention was called, and almost every body was concerned. Colonel Brandon rose up and went to them without knowing what he did. Mrs. Jennings, with a very intelligent "Ah! Poor dear," immediately gave her her salts; and Sir John felt so desperately enraged against the author of this nervous distress, that he instantly changed his seat to one close by Lucy Steele, and gave her, in a whisper, a brief account of the whole shocking affair.

In a few minutes, however, Marianne was recovered enough to put an end to the bustle, and sit down among the rest; though her spirits retained the impression of what had passed, the whole evening.

"Poor Marianne!" said her brother to Colonel Brandon, in a low voice, as soon as he could secure his attention, "She has not such good health as her sister, she is very nervous, she has not Elinor's constitution—and one must allow that there is something very trying to a young woman who *has been* a beauty in the loss of her personal attractions. You would not think it perhaps, but Marianne *was* remarkably handsome a few months ago; quite as handsome as Elinor. Now you see it is all gone."

CHAPTER XXXV

Elinor's curiosity to see Mrs. Ferrars was satisfied. She had found in her every thing that could tend to make a farther connection between the families undesirable. She had seen enough of her pride, her meanness, and her determined prejudice against herself, to comprehend all the difficulties that must have perplexed the engagement, and retarded the marriage, of Edward and herself, had he been otherwise free—and she had seen almost enough to be thankful for her *own* sake, that one greater obstacle preserved her from suffering under any other of Mrs. Ferrars's creation, preserved her from all dependence upon her caprice, or any solicitude for her good opinion. Or at least, if she did not bring herself quite to rejoice in Edward's being fettered to Lucy, she determined, that had Lucy been more amiable, she *ought* to have rejoiced.

She wondered that Lucy's spirits could be so very much elevated by the civility of Mrs. Ferrars—that her interest and her vanity should so very much blind her as to make the attention which seemed only paid her because she was *not Elinor*, appear a compliment to herself—or to allow her to derive encouragement from a preference only given her, because her real situation was unknown. But that it was so, had not only been declared by Lucy's eyes at the time, but was declared over again the next morning more openly, for at her particular desire, Lady Middleton set her down in Berkeley Street on the chance of seeing Elinor alone, to tell her how happy she was.

The chance proved a lucky one, for a message from Mrs. Palmer soon after she arrived, carried Mrs. Jennings away.

"My dear friend," cried Lucy, as soon as they were by themselves, "I come to talk to you of my happiness. Could anything be so flattering as Mrs. Ferrars's way of treating me yesterday? So exceeding affable as she was! You know how I dreaded the thoughts of seeing her—but the very moment I was introduced, there was such an affability in her behaviour as really should seem to say, she had quite took a fancy to me. Now was not it so? You saw it all; and was not you quite struck with it?"

"She was certainly very civil to you."

"Civil! Did you see nothing but only civility? I saw a vast deal more. Such kindness as fell to the share of nobody but me! No pride, no hauteur, and your sister just the same—all sweetness and affability!"

Elinor wished to talk of something else, but Lucy still pressed her to own that she had reason for her happiness; and Elinor was obliged to go on.

"Undoubtedly, if they had known your engagement," said she, "nothing could be more flattering than their treatment of you—but as that was not the case—"

"I guessed you would say so"—replied Lucy quickly—"but there was no reason in the world why Mrs. Ferrars should seem to like me, if she did not, and her liking me is every thing. You shan't talk me out of my satisfaction. I am sure it will all end well, and there will be no difficulties at all, to what I used to think. Mrs. Ferrars is a charming woman, and so is your sister. They are both delightful women, indeed! I wonder I should never hear you say how agreeable Mrs. Dashwood was!"

To this Elinor had no answer to make, and did not attempt any.

"Are you ill, Miss Dashwood? You seem low—you don't speak—sure you an't well."

"I never was in better health."

"I am glad of it with all my heart; but really you did not look it. I should be sorry to have *you* ill; you, that have been the greatest comfort to me in the world! Heaven knows what I should have done without your friendship."

Elinor tried to make a civil answer, though doubting her own success. But it seemed to satisfy Lucy, for she directly replied,

"Indeed I am perfectly convinced of your regard for me, and next to Edward's love, it is the greatest comfort I have. Poor Edward! But now there is one good thing, we shall be able to meet, and meet pretty often, for Lady Middleton's delighted with Mrs. Dashwood, so we shall be a good deal in Harley Street, I dare say, and Edward spends half his time with his sister—besides, Lady Middleton and Mrs. Ferrars will visit now—and Mrs. Ferrars and your sister were both so good to say more than once, they should always be glad to see me. They are such charming women! I am sure if ever you tell your sister what I think of her, you cannot speak too high."

But Elinor would not give her any encouragement to hope that she *should* tell her sister. Lucy continued.

"I am sure I should have seen it in a moment, if Mrs. Ferrars had took a dislike to me. If she had only made me a formal courtesy, for instance, without saying a word, and never after had took any notice of me, and never looked at me in a pleasant way—you know what I mean—if I had been treated in that forbidding sort of way, I should have gave it all up in despair. I could not have stood it. For where she *does* dislike, I know it is most violent."

Elinor was prevented from making any reply to this civil triumph, by the door's being thrown open, the servant's announcing Mr. Ferrars, and Edward's immediately walking in.

It was a very awkward moment; and the countenance of each shewed that it was so. They all looked exceedingly foolish; and Edward seemed to have as great an inclination to walk out of the room again, as to advance farther into it. The very circumstance, in its unpleasantest form, which they would each have been most anxious to avoid, had fallen on them. They were not only all three together, but were together without the relief of any other person. The ladies recovered themselves first. It was not Lucy's business to put herself forward, and the appearance of secrecy must still be kept up. She could therefore only *look* her tenderness, and after slightly addressing him, said no more.

But Elinor had more to do; and so anxious was she, for his sake and her own, to do it well, that she forced herself, after a moment's recollection, to welcome him, with a look and manner that were almost easy, and almost open; and another struggle, another effort still improved them. She would not allow the presence of Lucy, nor the consciousness of some injustice towards herself, to deter her from saying that she was happy to see him, and that she had very much regretted being from home, when he called before in Berkeley Street. She would not be frightened from paying him those attentions which, as a friend and almost a relation, were his due, by the observant eyes of Lucy, though she soon perceived them to be narrowly watching her.

Her manners gave some re-assurance to Edward, and he had courage enough to sit down; but his embarrassment still exceeded that of the ladies in a proportion, which the case rendered reasonable, though his sex might make it rare; for his heart had not the indifference of Lucy's, nor could his conscience have quite the ease of Elinor's.

Lucy, with a demure and settled air, seemed determined to make no contribution to the comfort of the others, and would not say a word; and almost every thing that *was* said, proceeded from Elinor, who was obliged to volunteer all the information about her mother's health, their coming to town, &c. which Edward ought to have inquired about, but never did.

Her exertions did not stop here; for she soon afterwards felt herself so heroically disposed as to determine, under pretence of fetching Marianne, to leave the others by themselves; and she really did it, and *that* in the handsomest manner, for she loitered away several minutes on the landing-place, with the most high-minded fortitude, before she went to her sister. When that was once done, however, it was time for the raptures of Edward to cease; for Marianne's joy hurried her into the drawing-room immediately. Her pleasure in seeing him was like every other of her feelings, strong in itself, and strongly spoken. She met him with a hand that would be taken, and a voice that expressed the affection of a sister.

"Dear Edward!" she cried, "This is a moment of great happiness! This would almost make amends for everything!"

Edward tried to return her kindness as it deserved, but before such witnesses he dared not say half what he really felt. Again they all sat down, and for a moment or two all were silent; while Marianne was looking with the most speaking tenderness, sometimes at Edward and sometimes at Elinor, regretting only that their delight in each other should be checked by Lucy's unwelcome presence. Edward was the first to speak, and it was to notice Marianne's altered looks, and express his fear of her not finding London agree with her.

"Oh, don't think of me!" she replied with spirited earnestness, though her eyes were filled with tears as she spoke, "Don't think of *my* health. Elinor is well, you see. That must be enough for us both."

This remark was not calculated to make Edward or Elinor more easy, nor to conciliate the good will of Lucy, who looked up at Marianne with no very benignant expression.

"Do you like London?" said Edward, willing to say any thing that might introduce another subject.

"Not at all. I expected much pleasure in it, but I have found none. The sight of you, Edward, is the only comfort it has afforded; and thank Heaven! You are what you always were!"

She paused—no one spoke.

"I think, Elinor," she presently added, "we must employ Edward to take care of us in our return to Barton. In a week or two, I suppose, we shall be going; and, I trust, Edward will not be very unwilling to accept the charge."

Poor Edward muttered something, but what it was, nobody knew, not even himself. But Marianne, who saw his agitation, and could easily trace it to whatever cause best pleased herself, was perfectly satisfied, and soon talked of something else.

"We spent such a day, Edward, in Harley Street yesterday! So dull, so wretchedly dull! But I have much to say to you on that head, which cannot be said now."

And with this admirable discretion did she defer the assurance of her finding their mutual relatives more disagreeable than ever, and of her being particularly disgusted with his mother, till they were more in private.

"But why were you not there, Edward? Why did you not come?"

"I was engaged elsewhere."

"Engaged! But what was that, when such friends were to be met?"

"Perhaps, Miss Marianne," cried Lucy, eager to take some revenge on her, "you think young men never stand upon engagements, if they have no mind to keep them, little as well as great."

Elinor was very angry, but Marianne seemed entirely insensible of the sting; for she calmly replied,

"Not so, indeed; for, seriously speaking, I am very sure that conscience only kept Edward from Harley Street. And I really believe he *has* the most delicate conscience in the world; the most scrupulous in performing every engagement, however minute, and however it may make against his interest or pleasure. He is the most fearful of giving pain, of wounding expectation, and the most incapable of being selfish, of any body I ever saw. Edward, it is so, and I will say it. What! Are you never to hear yourself praised! Then you must be no friend of mine; for those who will accept of my love and esteem, must submit to my open commendation."

The nature of her commendation, in the present case, however, happened to be particularly ill-suited to the feelings of two thirds of her auditors, and was so very unexhilarating to Edward, that he very soon got up to go away.

"Going so soon!" said Marianne; "my dear Edward, this must not be."

And drawing him a little aside, she whispered her persuasion that Lucy could not stay much longer. But even this encouragement failed, for he would go; and Lucy, who would have outstaid him, had his visit lasted two hours, soon afterwards went away.

"What can bring her here so often?" said Marianne, on her leaving them. "Could not she see that we wanted her gone! How teasing to Edward!"

"Why so? We were all his friends, and Lucy has been the longest known to him of any. It is but natural that he should like to see her as well as ourselves."

Marianne looked at her steadily, and said, "You know, Elinor, that this is a kind of talking which I cannot bear. If you only hope to have your assertion contradicted, as I must suppose to be the case, you ought to recollect that I am the last person in the world to do it. I cannot descend to be tricked out of assurances, that are not really wanted."

She then left the room; and Elinor dared not follow her to say more, for bound as she was by her promise of secrecy to Lucy, she could give no information that would convince Marianne; and painful as the consequences of her still continuing in an error might be, she was obliged to submit to it. All that she could hope, was that Edward would not often expose her or himself to the distress of hearing Marianne's mistaken warmth, nor to the repetition of any other part of the pain that had attended their recent meeting—and this she had every reason to expect.

CHAPTER XXXVI

Within a few days after this meeting, the newspapers announced to the world, that the lady of Thomas Palmer, Esq. was safely delivered of a son and heir; a very interesting and satisfactory paragraph, at least to all those intimate connections who knew it before.

This event, highly important to Mrs. Jennings's happiness, produced a temporary alteration in the disposal of her time, and influenced, in a like degree, the engagements of her young friends; for as she wished to be as much as possible with Charlotte, she went thither every morning as soon as she was dressed, and did not return till late in the evening; and the Miss Dashwoods, at the particular request of the Middletons, spent the whole of every day, in every day in Conduit Street. For their own comfort they would much rather have remained, at least all the morning, in Mrs. Jennings's house; but it was not a thing to be urged against the wishes of everybody. Their hours were therefore made over to Lady Middleton and the two Miss Steeles, by whom their company, in fact was as little valued, as it was professedly sought.

They had too much sense to be desirable companions to the former; and by the latter they were considered with a jealous eye, as intruding on *their* ground, and sharing the kindness which they wanted to monopolize. Though nothing could be more polite than Lady Middleton's behaviour to Elinor and Marianne, she did not really like them at all. Because they neither flattered herself nor her children, she could not believe them good-natured; and because they were fond of reading, she fancied them satirical: perhaps without exactly knowing what it was to be satirical; but *that* did not signify. It was censure in common use, and easily given.

Their presence was a restraint both on her and on Lucy. It checked the idleness of one, and the business of the other. Lady Middleton was ashamed of doing nothing before them, and the flattery which Lucy was proud to think of and administer at other times, she feared they would despise her for offering. Miss Steele was the least discomposed of the three, by their presence; and it was in their power to reconcile her to it entirely. Would either of them only have given her a full and minute account of the whole affair between Marianne and Mr. Willoughby, she would have thought herself amply rewarded for the sacrifice of the best place by the fire after dinner, which their arrival occasioned. But this conciliation was not granted; for though she often threw out expressions of pity for her sister to Elinor, and more than once dropped a reflection on the inconstancy of beaux before Marianne, no effect was produced, but a look of indifference from the former, or of disgust in the latter. An effort even yet lighter might have made her their friend. Would they only have laughed at her about the Doctor! But so little were they, anymore than the others, inclined to oblige her, that if Sir John dined from home, she might spend a whole day without hearing any other raillery on the subject, than what she was kind enough to bestow on herself.

All these jealousies and discontents, however, were so totally unsuspected by Mrs. Jennings, that she thought it a delightful thing for the girls to be together; and generally congratulated her young friends every night, on having escaped the company of a stupid old woman so long. She joined them sometimes at Sir John's, sometimes at her own house; but wherever it was, she always came in excellent spirits, full of delight and importance, attributing Charlotte's well doing to her own care, and ready to give so exact, so minute a detail of her situation, as only Miss Steele had curiosity enough to desire. One thing *did* disturb her; and of that she made her daily complaint. Mr. Palmer maintained the common, but unfatherly opinion among his sex, of all infants being alike; and though she could plainly perceive, at different times, the most striking resemblance between this baby and every one of his relations on both sides, there was no convincing his father of it; no persuading him to believe that it was not exactly like every other baby of the same age; nor could he even be brought to acknowledge the simple proposition of its being the finest child in the world.

I come now to the relation of a misfortune, which about this time befell Mrs. John Dashwood. It so happened that while her two sisters with Mrs. Jennings were first calling on her in Harley Street, another of her acquaintance had dropped in—a circumstance in itself not apparently likely to produce evil to her. But while the imaginations of other people will carry them away to form wrong judgments of our conduct, and to decide on it by slight appearances, one's happiness must in some measure be always at the mercy of chance. In the present instance, this last-arrived lady allowed her fancy to so far outrun truth and probability, that on merely hearing the name of the Miss Dashwoods, and understanding them to be Mr. Dashwood's sisters, she immediately concluded them to be staying in Harley Street; and this misconstruction produced within a day or two afterwards, cards of invitation for them as well as for their brother and sister, to a small musical party at her house. The consequence of which was, that Mrs. John Dashwood was obliged to submit not only to the exceedingly great inconvenience of sending her carriage for the Miss Dashwoods, but, what was still worse, must be subject to all the unpleasantness of appearing to treat them with attention: and who could tell that they might not expect to go out with her a second time? The power of disappointing them, it was true, must always be hers. But that was not enough; for when people are determined on a mode of conduct which they know to be wrong, they feel injured by the expectation of any thing better from them.

Marianne had now been brought by degrees, so much into the habit of going out every day, that it was become a matter of indifference to her, whether she went or not: and she prepared quietly and mechanically for every evening's engagement, though without expecting the smallest amusement from any, and very often without knowing, till the last moment, where it was to take her.

To her dress and appearance she was grown so perfectly indifferent, as not to bestow half the consideration on it, during the whole of her toilet, which it received from Miss Steele in the first five minutes of their being together, when it was finished. Nothing escaped *her* minute observation and general curiosity; she saw everything, and asked everything; was never easy till she knew the price of every part of Marianne's dress; could have guessed the number of her gowns altogether with better judgment than Marianne herself, and was not without hopes of finding out before they parted, how much her washing cost per week, and how much she had every year to spend upon herself. The impertinence of these kind of scrutinies, moreover, was generally concluded with a compliment, which though meant as its douceur, was considered by Marianne as the greatest impertinence of all; for after undergoing an examination into the value and make of her gown, the colour of her shoes, and the arrangement of her hair, she was almost sure of being told that upon "her word she looked vastly smart, and she dared to say she would make a great many conquests."

With such encouragement as this, was she dismissed on the present occasion, to her brother's carriage; which they were ready to enter five minutes after it stopped at the door, a punctuality not very agreeable to their sister-in-law, who had preceded them to the house of her acquaintance, and was there hoping for some delay on their part that might inconvenience either herself or her coachman.

The events of this evening were not very remarkable. The party, like other musical parties, comprehended a great many people who had real taste for the performance, and a great many more who had none at all; and the performers themselves were, as usual, in their own estimation, and that of their immediate friends, the first private performers in England.

As Elinor was neither musical, nor affecting to be so, she made no scruple of turning her eyes from the grand pianoforte, whenever it suited her, and unrestrained even by the presence of a harp, and violoncello, would fix them at pleasure on any other object in the room. In one of these excursive glances she perceived among a group of young men, the very he, who had given them a lecture on toothpick-cases at Gray's. She perceived him soon afterwards looking at herself, and speaking familiarly to her brother; and had just determined to find out his name from the latter, when they both came towards her, and Mr. Dashwood introduced him to her as Mr. Robert Ferrars.

He addressed her with easy civility, and twisted his head into a bow which assured her as plainly as words could have done, that he was exactly the coxcomb she had heard him described to be by Lucy. Happy had it been for her, if her regard for Edward had depended less on his own merit, than on the merit of his nearest relations! For then his brother's bow must have given the finishing stroke to what the ill-humour of his mother and sister would have begun. But while she wondered at the difference of the two young men, she did not find that the emptiness of conceit of the one, put her out of all charity with the modesty and worth of the other. Why they *were* different, Robert exclaimed to her himself in the course of a quarter of an hour's conversation; for, talking of his brother, and lamenting the extreme *gaucherie* which he really believed kept him from mixing in proper society, he candidly and generously attributed it much less to any natural deficiency, than to the misfortune of a private education; while he himself, though probably without any particular, any material superiority by nature, merely from the advantage of a public school, was as well fitted to mix in the world as any other man.

"Upon my soul," he added, "I believe it is nothing more; and so I often tell my mother, when she is grieving about it. 'My dear Madam,' I always say to her, 'you must make yourself easy. The evil is now irremediable, and it has been entirely your own doing. Why would you be persuaded by my uncle, Sir Robert, against your own judgment, to place Edward under private tuition, at the most critical time of his life? If you had only sent him to Westminster as well as myself, instead of sending him to Mr. Pratt's, all this would have been prevented.' This is the way in which I always consider the matter, and my mother is perfectly convinced of her error."

Elinor would not oppose his opinion, because, whatever might be her general estimation of the advantage of a public school, she could not think of Edward's abode in Mr. Pratt's family, with any satisfaction.

"You reside in Devonshire, I think"—was his next observation—"in a cottage near Dawlish."

Elinor set him right as to its situation; and it seemed rather surprising to him that anybody could live in Devonshire, without living near Dawlish. He bestowed his hearty approbation however on their species of house.

"For my own part," said he, "I am excessively fond of a cottage; there is always so much comfort, so much elegance about them. And I protest, if I had any money to spare, I should buy a little land and build one myself, within a short distance of London, where I might drive myself down at any time, and collect a few friends about me, and be happy. I advise every body who is going to build, to build a cottage. My friend Lord Courtland came to me the other day on purpose to ask my advice, and laid before me three different plans of Bonomi's. I was to decide on the best of them. 'My dear Courtland,' said I, immediately throwing them all into the fire, 'do not adopt either of them, but by all means build a cottage.' And that I fancy, will be the end of it.

"Some people imagine that there can be no accommodations, no space in a cottage; but this is all a mistake. I was last month at my friend Elliott's, near Dartford. Lady Elliott wished to give a dance. 'But how can it be done?' said she; 'my dear Ferrars, do tell me how it is to be managed. There is not a room in this cottage that will hold ten couple, and where can the supper be?' I immediately saw that there could be no difficulty in it, so I said, 'My dear Lady Elliott, do not be uneasy. The dining parlour will admit eighteen couple with ease; card-tables may be placed in the drawing-room; the library may be open for tea and other refreshments; and let the supper be set out in the saloon.' Lady Elliott was delighted with the thought. We measured the dining-room, and found it would hold exactly eighteen couple, and the affair was arranged precisely after my plan. So that, in fact, you see, if people do but know how to set about it, every comfort may be as well enjoyed in a cottage as in the most spacious dwelling."

Elinor agreed to it all, for she did not think he deserved the compliment of rational opposition.

As John Dashwood had no more pleasure in music than his eldest sister, his mind was equally at liberty to fix on anything else; and a thought struck him during the evening, which he communicated to his wife, for her approbation, when they got home. The consideration of Mrs. Dennison's mistake, in supposing his sisters their guests, had suggested the propriety of their being really invited to become such, while Mrs. Jennings's engagements kept her from home. The expense would be nothing, the inconvenience not more; and it was altogether an attention which the delicacy of his conscience pointed out to be requisite to its complete enfranchisement from his promise to his father. Fanny was startled at the proposal.

"I do not see how it can be done," said she, "without affronting Lady Middleton, for they spend every day with her; otherwise I should be exceedingly glad to do it. You know I am always ready to pay them any attention in my power, as my taking them out this evening shews. But they are Lady Middleton's visitors. How can I ask them away from her?"

Her husband, but with great humility, did not see the force of her objection. "They had already spent a week in this manner in Conduit Street, and Lady Middleton could not be displeased at their giving the same number of days to such near relations."

Fanny paused a moment, and then, with fresh vigor, said,

"My love I would ask them with all my heart, if it was in my power. But I had just settled within myself to ask the Miss Steeles to spend a few days with us. They are very well behaved, good kind of girls; and I think the attention is due to them, as their uncle did so very well by Edward. We can ask your sisters some other year, you know; but the Miss Steeles may not be in town any more. I am sure you will like them;

indeed, you *do* like them, you know, very much already, and so does my mother; and they are such favourites with Harry!"

Mr. Dashwood was convinced. He saw the necessity of inviting the Miss Steeles immediately, and his conscience was pacified by the resolution of inviting his sisters another year; at the same time, however, slyly suspecting that another year would make the invitation needless, by bringing Elinor to town as Colonel Brandon's wife, and Marianne as *their* visitor.

Fanny, rejoicing in her escape, and proud of the ready wit that had procured it, wrote the next morning to Lucy, to request her company and her sister's, for some days, in Harley Street, as soon as Lady Middleton could spare them. This was enough to make Lucy really and reasonably happy. Mrs. Dashwood seemed actually working for her, herself; cherishing all her hopes, and promoting all her views! Such an opportunity of being with Edward and his family was, above all things, the most material to her interest, and such an invitation the most gratifying to her feelings! It was an advantage that could not be too gratefully acknowledged, nor too speedily made use of; and the visit to Lady Middleton, which had not before had any precise limits, was instantly discovered to have been always meant to end in two days' time.

When the note was shown to Elinor, as it was within ten minutes after its arrival, it gave her, for the first time, some share in the expectations of Lucy; for such a mark of uncommon kindness, vouchsafed on so short an acquaintance, seemed to declare that the good-will towards her arose from something more than merely malice against herself; and might be brought, by time and address, to do every thing that Lucy wished. Her flattery had already subdued the pride of Lady Middleton, and made an entry into the close heart of Mrs. John Dashwood; and these were effects that laid open the probability of greater.

The Miss Steeles removed to Harley Street, and all that reached Elinor of their influence there, strengthened her expectation of the event. Sir John, who called on them more than once, brought home such accounts of the favour they were in, as must be universally striking. Mrs. Dashwood had never been so much pleased with any young women in her life, as she was with them; had given each of them a needle book made by some emigrant; called Lucy by her Christian name; and did not know whether she should ever be able to part with them.

CHAPTER XXXVII

Mrs. Palmer was so well at the end of a fortnight, that her mother felt it no longer necessary to give up the whole of her time to her; and, contenting herself with visiting her once or twice a day, returned from that period to her own home, and her own habits, in which she found the Miss Dashwoods very ready to resume their former share.

About the third or fourth morning after their being thus resettled in Berkeley Street, Mrs. Jennings, on returning from her ordinary visit to Mrs. Palmer, entered the drawing-room, where Elinor was sitting by herself, with an air of such hurrying importance as prepared her to hear something wonderful; and giving her time only to form that idea, began directly to justify it, by saying—

"Lord! My dear Miss Dashwood! Have you heard the news?"

"No, ma'am. What is it?"

"Something so strange! But you shall hear it all. When I got to Mr. Palmer's, I found Charlotte quite in a fuss about the child. She was sure it was very ill—it cried, and fretted, and was all over pimples. So I looked at it directly, and, 'Lord! My dear,' says I, 'it is nothing in the world, but the red gum—' and nurse said just the same. But Charlotte, she would not be satisfied, so Mr. Donavan was sent for; and luckily he happened to just come in from Harley Street, so he stepped over directly, and as soon as ever he saw the child, be said just as we did, that it was nothing in the world but the red gum, and then Charlotte was easy. And so, just as he was going away again, it came into my head, I am sure I do not know how I happened to think of it, but it came into my head to ask him if there was any news. So upon that, he smirked, and simpered, and looked grave, and seemed to know something or other, and at last he said in a whisper, 'For fear any unpleasant report should reach the young ladies under your care as to their sister's indisposition, I think it advisable to say, that I believe there is no great reason for alarm; I hope Mrs. Dashwood will do very well.' "

"What! Is Fanny ill?"

"That is exactly what I said, my dear. 'Lord!' says I, 'is Mrs. Dashwood ill?' So then it all came out; and the long and the short of the matter, by all I can learn, seems to be this. Mr. Edward Ferrars, the very young man I used to joke with you about (but however, as it turns out, I am monstrous glad there was never any thing in it), Mr. Edward Ferrars, it seems, has been engaged above this twelvemonth to my cousin Lucy! There's for you, my dear! And not a creature knowing a syllable of the matter, except Nancy! Could you have believed such a thing possible? There is no great wonder in their liking one another; but that matters should be brought so forward between them, and nobody suspect it! *That* is strange! I never happened to see them together, or I am sure I should have found it out directly. Well, and so this was kept a great secret, for fear of Mrs. Ferrars, and neither she nor your brother or sister suspected a word of the matter—till this very morning, poor Nancy, who, you know, is a well-meaning creature, but no conjurer, popt it all out. 'Lord!' thinks she to herself, 'they are all so fond of Lucy, to be sure they will make no difficulty about it;' and so, away she went to your sister, who was sitting all alone at her carpet-work, little suspecting what was to come—for she had just been saying to your brother, only five minutes before, that she thought to make a match between Edward and some Lord's daughter or other, I forget who. So you may think what a blow it was to all her vanity and pride. She fell into violent hysterics immediately, with such screams as reached your brother's ears, as he was sitting in his own dressing-room down stairs, thinking about writing a letter to his steward in the country. So up he flew directly, and a terrible scene took place, for Lucy was come to them by that time, little dreaming what was going on. Poor soul! I pity *her*. And I must say, I think she was used very hardly; for your sister scolded like any fury, and soon drove her into a fainting fit. Nancy, she fell upon her knees, and cried bitterly; and your brother, he walked about the room, and said he did not know what to do. Mrs. Dashwood declared they should not stay a minute longer in the house, and your brother was forced to go down upon *his* knees too, to persuade her to let them stay till they had packed up their clothes. *Then* she fell into hysterics again, and he was so frightened that he would send for Mr. Donavan, and Mr. Donavan found the house in all this uproar. The carriage was at the door ready to take my poor cousins away, and they were just stepping in as he came off; poor Lucy in such a condition, he says, she could hardly walk; and Nancy, she was almost as bad. I declare, I have no patience with your sister; and I hope, with all my heart, it will be a match in spite of her. Lord! What a taking poor Mr. Edward will be in when he hears of it! To have his love used so scornfully! for they say he is monstrous fond of her, as well he may. I should not wonder, if he was to be in the greatest passion! And Mr. Donavan thinks just the same. He and I had a great deal of talk about it; and the best of all is, that he is gone back again to Harley Street, that he may be within call when Mrs. Ferrars is told of it, for she was sent for as soon as ever my cousins left the house, for your sister was sure *she* would be in hysterics too; and so she may, for what I care. I have no pity for either of them. I have no notion of people's making such a to-do about money and greatness. There is no reason on earth why Mr. Edward and Lucy should not marry; for I am sure Mrs. Ferrars may afford to do very well by her son, and though Lucy has next to nothing herself, she knows better than any body how to make the most of every thing; I dare say, if Mrs. Ferrars would only allow him five hundred a-year, she would make as good an appearance with it as any body else would with eight. Lord! How snug they might live in such another cottage as yours—or a little bigger—with two maids, and two men; and I believe I could help them to a housemaid, for my Betty has a sister out of place, that would fit them exactly."

Here Mrs. Jennings ceased, and as Elinor had had time enough to collect her thoughts, she was able to give such an answer, and make such observations, as the subject might naturally be supposed to produce. Happy to find that she was not suspected of any extraordinary interest in it; that Mrs. Jennings (as she had of late often hoped might be the case) had ceased to imagine her at all attached to Edward; and happy above all the rest, in the absence of Marianne, she felt very well able to speak of the affair without embarrassment, and to give her judgment, as she believed, with impartiality on the conduct of every one concerned in it.

She could hardly determine what her own expectation of its event really was; though she earnestly tried to drive away the notion of its being possible to end otherwise at last, than in the marriage of Edward and Lucy. What Mrs. Ferrars would say and do, though there could not be a doubt of its nature, she was anxious to hear; and still more anxious to know how Edward would conduct himself. For *him* she felt much compassion—for Lucy very little—and it cost her some pains to procure that little—for the rest of the party none at all.

As Mrs. Jennings could talk on no other subject, Elinor soon saw the necessity of preparing Marianne for its discussion. No time was to be lost in undeceiving her, in making her acquainted with the real truth, and in endeavouring to bring her to hear it talked of by others, without betraying that she felt any uneasiness for her sister, or any resentment against Edward.

Elinor's office was a painful one. She was going to remove what she really believed to be her sister's chief consolation, to give such particulars of Edward as she feared would ruin him for ever in her good opinion, and to make Marianne, by a resemblance in their situations, which to *her* fancy would seem strong, feel all her own disappointment over again. But unwelcome as such a task must be, it was necessary to be done, and Elinor therefore hastened to perform it.

She was very far from wishing to dwell on her own feelings, or to represent herself as suffering much, any otherwise than as the self-command she had practised since her first knowledge of Edward's engagement, might suggest a hint of what was practicable to Marianne. Her narration was clear and simple; and though it could not be given without emotion, it was not accompanied by violent agitation, nor impetuous grief. *That* belonged rather to the hearer, for Marianne listened with horror, and cried excessively. Elinor was to be the comforter of others in her own distresses, no less than in theirs; and all the comfort that could be given by assurances of her own composure of mind, and a very earnest vindication of Edward from every charge but of imprudence, was readily offered.

But Marianne for some time would give credit to neither. Edward seemed a second Willoughby; and acknowledging as Elinor did, that she *had* loved him most sincerely, could she feel less than herself! As for Lucy Steele, she considered her so totally unamiable, so absolutely incapable of attaching a sensible man, that she could not be persuaded at first to believe, and afterwards to pardon, any former affection of Edward for her. She would not even admit it to have been natural; and Elinor left her to be convinced that it was so, by that which only could convince her, a better knowledge of mankind.

Her first communication had reached no farther than to state the fact of the engagement, and the length of time it had existed. Marianne's feelings had then broken in, and put an end to all regularity of detail; and for some time all that could be done was to soothe her distress, lessen her alarms, and combat her resentment. The first question on her side, which led to farther particulars, was—

"How long has this been known to you, Elinor? Has he written to you?"

"I have known it these four months. When Lucy first came to Barton Park last November, she told me in confidence of her engagement."

At these words, Marianne's eyes expressed the astonishment which her lips could not utter. After a pause of wonder, she exclaimed—

"Four months! Have you known of this four months?"

Elinor confirmed it.

"What! While attending me in all my misery, has this been on your heart? And I have reproached you for being happy!"

"It was not fit that you should then know how much I was the reverse!"

"Four months!" cried Marianne again. "So calm! So cheerful! How have you been supported?"

"By feeling that I was doing my duty. My promise to Lucy, obliged me to be secret. I owed it to her, therefore, to avoid giving any hint of the truth; and I owed it to my family and friends, not to create in them a solicitude about me, which it could not be in my power to satisfy."

Marianne seemed much struck.

"I have very often wished to undeceive yourself and my mother," added Elinor; "and once or twice I have attempted it—but without betraying my trust, I never could have convinced you."

"Four months! And yet you loved him!"

"Yes. But I did not love only him—and while the comfort of others was dear to me, I was glad to spare them from knowing how much I felt. Now, I can think and speak of it with little emotion. I would not have you suffer on my account; for I assure you I no longer suffer materially myself. I have many things to support me. I am not conscious of having provoked the disappointment by any imprudence of my own, I have borne it as much as possible without spreading it farther. I acquit Edward of essential misconduct. I wish him very happy; and I am so sure of his always doing his duty, that though now he may harbour some regret, in the end he must become so. Lucy does not want sense, and that is the foundation on which every thing good may be built. And after all, Marianne, after all that is bewitching in the idea of a single and constant attachment, and all that can be said of one's happiness depending entirely on any particular person, it is not meant—it is not fit—it is not possible that it should be so. Edward will marry Lucy; he will marry a woman superior in person and understanding to half her sex; and time and habit will teach him to forget that he ever thought another superior to *her*."

"If such is your way of thinking," said Marianne, "if the loss of what is most valued is so easily to be made up by something else, your resolution, your self-command, are, perhaps, a little less to be wondered at. They are brought more within my comprehension."

"I understand you. You do not suppose that I have ever felt much. For four months, Marianne, I have had all this hanging on my mind, without being at liberty to speak of it to a single creature; knowing that it would make you and my mother most unhappy whenever it were explained to you, yet unable to prepare you for it in the least. It was told me, it was in a manner forced on me by the very person herself, whose prior engagement ruined all my prospects; and told me, as I thought, with triumph. This person's suspicions, therefore, I have had to oppose, by endeavouring to appear indifferent where I have been most deeply interested—and it has not been only once—I have had her hopes and exultation to listen to again and again. I have known myself to be divided from Edward for ever, without hearing one circumstance that could make me less desire the connection. Nothing has proved him unworthy; nor has anything declared him indifferent to me. I have had to contend against the unkindness of his sister, and the insolence of his mother; and have suffered the punishment of an attachment, without enjoying its advantages. And all this has been going on at a time, when, as you know too well, it has not been my only unhappiness. If you can think me capable of ever feeling—surely you may suppose that I have suffered *now*. The composure of mind with which I have brought myself at present to consider the matter, the consolation that I have been willing to admit, have been the effect of constant and painful exertion—they did not spring up of themselves—they did not occur to relieve my spirits at first. No, Marianne. *Then*, if I had not been bound to silence, perhaps nothing could have kept me entirely—not even what I owed to my dearest friends—from openly shewing that I was *very* unhappy."

Marianne was quite subdued.

"Oh! Elinor," she cried, "you have made me hate myself for ever. How barbarous have I been to you! You, who have been my only comfort, who have borne with me in all my misery, who have seemed to be only suffering for me! Is this my gratitude? Is this the only return

I can make you? Because your merit cries out upon myself, I have been trying to do it away."

The tenderest caresses followed this confession. In such a frame of mind as she was now in, Elinor had no difficulty in obtaining from her whatever promise she required; and at her request, Marianne engaged never to speak of the affair to any one with the least appearance of bitterness—to meet Lucy without betraying the smallest increase of dislike to her—and even to see Edward himself, if chance should bring them together, without any diminution of her usual cordiality. These were great concessions—but where Marianne felt that she had injured, no reparation could be too much for her to make.

She performed her promise of being discreet, to admiration. She attended to all that Mrs. Jennings had to say upon the subject, with an unchanging complexion, dissented from her in nothing, and was heard three times to say, "Yes, ma'am." She listened to her praise of Lucy with only moving from one chair to another, and when Mrs. Jennings talked of Edward's affection, it cost her only a spasm in her throat. Such advances towards heroism in her sister, made Elinor feel equal to any thing herself.

The next morning brought a farther trial of it, in a visit from their brother, who came with a most serious aspect to talk over the dreadful affair, and bring them news of his wife.

"You have heard, I suppose," said he with great solemnity, as soon as he was seated, "of the very shocking discovery that took place under our roof yesterday."

They all looked their assent; it seemed too awful a moment for speech.

"Your sister," he continued, "has suffered dreadfully. Mrs. Ferrars too—in short it has been a scene of such complicated distress—but I will hope that the storm may be weathered without our being any of us quite overcome. Poor Fanny! She was in hysterics all yesterday. But I would not alarm you too much. Donavan says there is nothing materially to be apprehended; her constitution is a good one, and her resolution equal to any thing. She has borne it all, with the fortitude of an angel! She says she never shall think well of anybody again; and one cannot wonder at it, after being so deceived! Meeting with such ingratitude, where so much kindness had been shewn, so much confidence had been placed! It was quite out of the benevolence of her heart, that she had asked these young women to her house; merely because she thought they deserved some attention, were harmless, well-behaved girls, and would be pleasant companions; for otherwise we both wished very much to have invited you and Marianne to be with us, while your kind friend there, was attending her daughter. And now to be so rewarded! 'I wish, with all my heart,' says poor Fanny in her affectionate way, 'that we had asked your sisters instead of them.' "

Here he stopped to be thanked; which being done, he went on.

"What poor Mrs. Ferrars suffered, when first Fanny broke it to her, is not to be described. While she with the truest affection had been planning a most eligible connection for him, was it to be supposed that he could be all the time secretly engaged to another person! Such a suspicion could never have entered her head! If she suspected *any* prepossession elsewhere, it could not be in *that* quarter. '*There*, to be sure,' said she, 'I might have thought myself safe.' She was quite in an agony. We consulted together, however, as to what should be done, and at last she determined to send for Edward. He came. But I am sorry to relate what ensued. All that Mrs. Ferrars could say to make him put an end to the engagement, assisted too as you may well suppose by my arguments, and Fanny's entreaties, was of no avail. Duty, affection, every thing was disregarded. I never thought Edward so stubborn, so unfeeling before. His mother explained to him her liberal designs, in case of his marrying Miss Morton; told him she would settle on him the Norfolk estate, which, clear of land-tax, brings in a good thousand a-year; offered even, when matters grew desperate, to make it twelve hundred; and in opposition to this, if he still persisted in this low connection, represented to him the certain penury that must attend the match. His own two thousand pounds she protested should be his all; she would never see him again; and so far would she be from affording him the smallest assistance, that if he were to enter into any profession with a view of better support, she would do all in her power to prevent him advancing in it."

Here Marianne, in an ecstasy of indignation, clapped her hands together, and cried, "Gracious God! Can this be possible!"

"Well may you wonder, Marianne," replied her brother, "at the obstinacy which could resist such arguments as these. Your exclamation is very natural."

Marianne was going to retort, but she remembered her promises, and forbore.

"All this, however," he continued, "was urged in vain. Edward said very little; but what he did say, was in the most determined manner. Nothing should prevail on him to give up his engagement. He would stand to it, cost him what it might."

"Then," cried Mrs. Jennings with blunt sincerity, no longer able to be silent, "he has acted like an honest man! I beg your pardon, Mr. Dashwood, but if he had done otherwise, I should have thought him a rascal. I have some little concern in the business, as well as yourself, for Lucy Steele is my cousin, and I believe there is not a better kind of girl in the world, nor one who more deserves a good husband."

John Dashwood was greatly astonished; but his nature was calm, not open to provocation, and he never wished to offend anybody, especially anybody of good fortune. He therefore replied, without any resentment,

"I would by no means speak disrespectfully of any relation of yours, madam. Miss Lucy Steele is, I dare say, a very deserving young woman, but in the present case you know, the connection must be impossible. And to have entered into a secret engagement with a young man under her uncle's care, the son of a woman especially of such very large fortune as Mrs. Ferrars, is perhaps, altogether a little extraordinary. In short, I do not mean to reflect upon the behaviour of any person whom you have a regard for, Mrs. Jennings. We all wish her extremely happy; and Mrs. Ferrars's conduct throughout the whole, has been such as every conscientious, good mother, in like circumstances, would adopt. It has been dignified and liberal. Edward has drawn his own lot, and I fear it will be a bad one."

Marianne sighed out her similar apprehension; and Elinor's heart wrung for the feelings of Edward, while braving his mother's threats, for a woman who could not reward him.

"Well, sir," said Mrs. Jennings, "and how did it end?"

"I am sorry to say, ma'am, in a most unhappy rupture: Edward is dismissed for ever from his mother's notice. He left her house yesterday, but where he is gone, or whether he is still in town, I do not know; for *we* of course can make no inquiry."

"Poor young man! And what is to become of him?"

"What, indeed, ma'am! It is a melancholy consideration. Born to the prospect of such affluence! I cannot conceive a situation more deplorable. The interest of two thousand pounds—how can a man live on it? And when to that is added the recollection, that he might, but for his own folly, within three months have been in the receipt of two thousand, five hundred a-year (for Miss Morton has thirty thousand pounds), I cannot picture to myself a more wretched condition. We must all feel for him; and the more so, because it is totally out of our power to assist him."

"Poor young man!" cried Mrs. Jennings, "I am sure he should be very welcome to bed and board at my house; and so I would tell him if I could see him. It is not fit that he should be living about at his own charge now, at lodgings and taverns."

Elinor's heart thanked her for such kindness towards Edward, though she could not forbear smiling at the form of it.

"If he would only have done as well by himself," said John Dashwood, "as all his friends were disposed to do by him, he might now have been in his proper situation, and would have wanted for nothing. But as it is, it must be out of anybody's power to assist him. And there is one thing more preparing against him, which must be worse than all—his mother has determined, with a very natural kind of spirit, to settle *that* estate upon Robert immediately, which might have been Edward's, on proper conditions. I left her this morning with her lawyer, talking over the business."

"Well!" said Mrs. Jennings, "that is *her* revenge. Everybody has a way of their own. But I don't think mine would be, to make one son independent, because another had plagued me."

Marianne got up and walked about the room.

"Can anything be more galling to the spirit of a man," continued John, "than to see his younger brother in possession of an estate which might have been his own? Poor Edward! I feel for him sincerely."

A few minutes more spent in the same kind of effusion, concluded his visit; and with repeated assurances to his sisters that he really believed there was no material danger in Fanny's indisposition, and that they need not therefore be very uneasy about it, he went away; leaving the three ladies unanimous in their sentiments on the present occasion, as far at least as it regarded Mrs. Ferrars's conduct, the Dashwoods', and Edward's.

Marianne's indignation burst forth as soon as he quitted the room; and as her vehemence made reserve impossible in Elinor, and unnecessary in Mrs. Jennings, they all joined in a very spirited critique upon the party.

CHAPTER XXXVIII

Mrs. Jennings was very warm in her praise of Edward's conduct, but only Elinor and Marianne understood its true merit. *They* only knew how little he had had to tempt him to be disobedient, and how small was the consolation, beyond the consciousness of doing right, that could remain to him in the loss of friends and fortune. Elinor gloried in his integrity; and Marianne forgave all his offences in compassion for his punishment. But though confidence between them was, by this public discovery, restored to its proper state, it was not a subject on which either of them were fond of dwelling when alone. Elinor avoided it upon principle, as tending to fix still more upon her thoughts, by the too warm, too positive assurances of Marianne, that belief of Edward's continued affection for herself which she rather wished to do away; and Marianne's courage soon failed her, in trying to converse upon a topic which always left her more dissatisfied with herself than ever, by the comparison it necessarily produced between Elinor's conduct and her own.

She felt all the force of that comparison; but not as her sister had hoped, to urge her to exertion now; she felt it with all the pain of continual self-reproach, regretted most bitterly that she had never exerted herself before; but it brought only the torture of penitence, without the hope of amendment. Her mind was so much weakened that she still fancied present exertion impossible, and therefore it only dispirited her more.

Nothing new was heard by them, for a day or two afterwards, of affairs in Harley Street, or Bartlett's Buildings. But though so much of the matter was known to them already, that Mrs. Jennings might have had enough to do in spreading that knowledge farther, without seeking after more, she had resolved from the first to pay a visit of comfort and inquiry to her cousins as soon as she could; and nothing but the hindrance of more visitors than usual, had prevented her going to them within that time.

The third day succeeding their knowledge of the particulars, was so fine, so beautiful a Sunday as to draw many to Kensington Gardens, though it was only the second week in March. Mrs. Jennings and Elinor were of the number; but Marianne, who knew that the Willoughbys were again in town, and had a constant dread of meeting them, chose rather to stay at home, than venture into so public a place.

An intimate acquaintance of Mrs. Jennings joined them soon after they entered the Gardens, and Elinor was not sorry that by her continuing with them, and engaging all Mrs. Jennings's conversation, she was herself left to quiet reflection. She saw nothing of the Willoughbys, nothing of Edward, and for some time nothing of anybody who could by any chance whether grave or gay, be interesting to her. But at last she found herself with some surprise, accosted by Miss Steele, who, though looking rather shy, expressed great satisfaction in meeting them, and on receiving encouragement from the particular kindness of Mrs. Jennings, left her own party for a short time, to join their's. Mrs. Jennings immediately whispered to Elinor,

"Get it all out of her, my dear. She will tell you any thing if you ask. You see I cannot leave Mrs. Clarke."

It was lucky, however, for Mrs. Jennings's curiosity and Elinor's too, that she would tell any thing *without* being asked; for nothing would otherwise have been learnt.

"I am so glad to meet you," said Miss Steele, taking her familiarly by the arm—"for I wanted to see you of all things in the world." And then lowering her voice, "I suppose Mrs. Jennings has heard all about it. Is she angry?"

"Not at all, I believe, with you."

"That is a good thing. And Lady Middleton, is *she* angry?"

"I cannot suppose it possible that she should."

"I am monstrous glad of it. Good gracious! I have had such a time of it! I never saw Lucy in such a rage in my life. She vowed at first she would never trim me up a new bonnet, nor do any thing else for me again, so long as she lived; but now she is quite come to, and we are as good friends as ever. Look, she made me this bow to my hat, and put in the feather last night. There now, *you* are going to laugh at me too. But why should not I wear pink ribbons? I do not care if it *is* the Doctor's favourite colour. I am sure, for my part, I should never have known he *did* like it better than any other colour, if he had not happened to say so. My cousins have been so plaguing me! I declare sometimes I do not know which way to look before them."

She had wandered away to a subject on which Elinor had nothing to say, and therefore soon judged it expedient to find her way back again to the first.

"Well, but Miss Dashwood," speaking triumphantly, "people may say what they choose about Mr. Ferrars's declaring he would not have Lucy, for it is no such thing I can tell you; and it is quite a shame for such ill-natured reports to be spread abroad. Whatever Lucy might think about it herself, you know, it was no business of other people to set it down for certain."

"I never heard any thing of the kind hinted at before, I assure you," said Elinor.

"Oh, did not you? But it *was* said, I know, very well, and by more than one; for Miss Godby told Miss Sparks, that nobody in their senses could expect Mr. Ferrars to give up a woman like Miss Morton, with thirty thousand pounds to her fortune, for Lucy Steele that had nothing at all; and I had it from Miss Sparks myself. And besides that, my cousin Richard said himself, that when it came to the point he was afraid Mr. Ferrars would be off; and when Edward did not come near us for three days, I could not tell what to think myself; and I believe in my heart Lucy gave it up all for lost; for we came away from your brother's Wednesday, and we saw nothing of him not all Thursday, Friday, and Saturday, and did not know what was become of him. Once Lucy thought to write to him, but then her spirits rose against that. However this morning he came just as we came home from church; and then it all came out, how he had been sent for Wednesday to Harley Street, and been talked to by his mother and all of them, and how he had declared before them all that he loved nobody but Lucy, and nobody but Lucy would he have. And how he had been so worried by what passed, that as soon as he had went away from his mother's house, he had got upon his horse, and rid into the country, some where or other; and how he had stayed about at an inn all Thursday and Friday, on purpose to get the better of it. And after thinking it all over and over again, he said, it seemed to him as if, now he had no fortune, and no nothing at all, it would be quite unkind to keep her on to the engagement, because it must be for her loss, for he had nothing but two thousand pounds, and no hope of any thing else; and if he was to go into orders, as he had some thoughts, he could get nothing but a curacy, and how was they to live upon that? He could not bear to think of her doing no better, and so he begged, if she had the least mind for it, to put an end to the matter directly, and leave him shift for himself. I heard him say all this as plain as could possibly be. And it was entirely for *her* sake, and upon *her* account, that he said a word about being off, and not upon his own. I will take my oath he never dropt a syllable of being tired of her, or of wishing to marry Miss Morton, or any thing like it. But, to be sure, Lucy would not give ear to such kind of talking; so she told him directly (with a great deal about sweet and love, you know, and all that—Oh, la! one can't repeat such kind of things you know)—she told him directly, she had not the least mind in the world to be off, for she could live with him upon a trifle, and how little so ever he might have, she should be very glad to have it all, you know, or something of the kind. So then he was monstrous happy, and talked on some time about what they should do, and they agreed he should take orders directly, and they must wait to be married till he got a living. And just then I could not hear any more, for my cousin called from below to tell me Mrs. Richardson was come in her coach, and would take one of us to Kensington Gardens; so I was forced to go into the room and interrupt them, to ask Lucy if she would like to go, but she did not care to leave Edward; so I just run up stairs and put on a pair of silk stockings and came off with the Richardsons."

"I do not understand what you mean by interrupting them," said Elinor; "you were all in the same room together, were not you?"

"No, indeed, not us. La! Miss Dashwood, do you think people make love when any body else is by? Oh, for shame! To be sure you must know better than that. (Laughing affectedly.)—No, no; they were shut up in the drawing-room together, and all I heard was only by listening at the door."

"How!" cried Elinor; "have you been repeating to me what you only learnt yourself by listening at the door? I am sorry I did not know it before; for I certainly would not have suffered you to give me particulars of a conversation which you ought not to have known yourself. How could you behave so unfairly by your sister?"

"Oh, la! There is nothing in *that*. I only stood at the door, and heard what I could. And I am sure Lucy would have done just the same by me; for a year or two back, when Martha Sharpe and I had so many secrets together, she never made any bones of hiding in a closet, or behind a chimney-board, on purpose to hear what we said."

Elinor tried to talk of something else; but Miss Steele could not be kept beyond a couple of minutes, from what was uppermost in her mind.

"Edward talks of going to Oxford soon," said she; "but now he is lodging at No. —, Pall Mall. What an ill-natured woman his mother is, an't she? And your brother and sister were not very kind! However, I shan't say anything against them to *you*; and to be sure they did send us home in their own chariot, which was more than I looked for. And for my part, I was all in a fright for fear your sister should ask us for the huswifes she had gave us a day or two before; but, however, nothing was said about them, and I took care to keep mine out of sight. Edward have got some business at Oxford, he says; so he must go there for a time; and after *that*, as soon as he can light upon a Bishop, he will be ordained. I wonder what curacy he will get! Good gracious! (giggling as she spoke) I'd lay my life I know what my cousins will say, when they hear of it. They will tell me I should write to the Doctor, to get Edward the curacy of his new living. I know they will; but I am sure I would not do such a thing for all the world. 'La!' I shall say directly, 'I wonder how you could think of such a thing? I write to the Doctor, indeed!' "

"Well," said Elinor, "it is a comfort to be prepared against the worst. You have got your answer ready."

Miss Steele was going to reply on the same subject, but the approach of her own party made another more necessary.

"Oh, la! Here come the Richardsons. I had a vast deal more to say to you, but I must not stay away from them any longer. I assure you they are very genteel people. He makes a monstrous deal of money, and they keep their own coach. I have not time to speak to Mrs. Jennings about it myself, but pray tell her I am quite happy to hear she is not in anger against us, and Lady Middleton the same; and if anything should happen to take you and your sister away, and Mrs. Jennings should want company, I am sure we should be very glad to come and stay with her for as long a time as she likes. I suppose Lady Middleton won't ask us any more this bout. Good-by; I am sorry Miss Marianne was not here. Remember me kindly to her. La! If you have not got your spotted muslin on! I wonder you was not afraid of its being torn."

Such was her parting concern; for after this, she had time only to pay her farewell compliments to Mrs. Jennings, before her company was claimed by Mrs. Richardson; and Elinor was left in possession of knowledge which might feed her powers of reflection some time, though she had learnt very little more than what had been already foreseen and foreplanned in her own mind. Edward's marriage with Lucy was as firmly determined on, and the time of its taking place remained as absolutely uncertain, as she had concluded it would be—every thing depended, exactly after her expectation, on his getting that preferment, of which, at present, there seemed not the smallest chance.

As soon as they returned to the carriage, Mrs. Jennings was eager for information; but as Elinor wished to spread as little as possible intelligence that had in the first place been so unfairly obtained, she confined herself to the brief repetition of such simple particulars, as she felt assured that Lucy, for the sake of her own consequence, would choose to have known. The continuance of their engagement, and the means that were able to be taken for promoting its end, was all her communication; and this produced from Mrs. Jennings the following natural remark.

"Wait for his having a living! Ay, we all know how *that* will end—they will wait a twelvemonth, and finding no good comes of it, will set down upon a curacy of fifty pounds a-year, with the interest of his two thousand pounds, and what little matter Mr. Steele and Mr. Pratt can give her. Then they will have a child every year! And Lord help 'em! how poor they will be! I must see what I can give them towards furnishing their house. Two maids and two men, indeed! As I talked of t'other day. No, no, they must get a stout girl of all works. Betty's sister would never do for them *now*."

The next morning brought Elinor a letter by the two-penny post from Lucy herself. It was as follows:

"Bartlett's Building, March.

"I hope my dear Miss Dashwood will excuse the liberty I take of writing to her; but I know your friendship for me will make you pleased to hear such a good account of myself and my dear Edward, after all the troubles we have went through lately, therefore will make no more apologies, but proceed to say that, thank God! Though we have suffered dreadfully, we are both quite well now, and as happy as we must always be in one another's love. We have had great trials, and great persecutions, but however, at the same time, gratefully acknowledge many friends, yourself not the least among them, whose great kindness I shall always thankfully remember, as will Edward too, who I have told of it. I am sure you will be glad to hear, as likewise dear Mrs. Jennings, I spent two happy hours with him yesterday afternoon, he would not hear of our parting, though earnestly did I, as I thought my duty required, urge him to it for prudence sake, and would have parted for ever on the spot, would he consent to it; but he said it should never be, he did not regard his mother's anger, while he could have my affections; our prospects are not very bright, to be sure, but we must wait, and hope for the best; he will be ordained shortly; and should it ever be in your power to recommend him to any body that has a living to bestow, am very sure you will not forget us, and dear Mrs. Jennings too, trust she will speak a good word for us to Sir John, or Mr. Palmer, or any friend that may be able to assist us. Poor Anne was much to blame for what she did, but she did it for the best, so I say nothing; hope Mrs. Jennings won't think it too much trouble to give us a call, should she come this way any morning, 'twould be a great kindness, and my cousins would be proud to know her. My paper reminds me to conclude; and begging to be most gratefully and respectfully remembered to her, and to Sir John, and Lady Middleton, and the dear children, when you chance to see them, and love to Miss Marianne,

"I am, &c."

As soon as Elinor had finished it, she performed what she concluded to be its writer's real design, by placing it in the hands of Mrs. Jennings, who read it aloud with many comments of satisfaction and praise.

"Very well indeed! How prettily she writes! Aye, that was quite proper to let him be off if he would. That was just like Lucy. Poor soul! I wish I *could* get him a living, with all my heart. She calls me dear Mrs. Jennings, you see. She is a good-hearted girl as ever lived. Very well upon my word. That sentence is very prettily turned. Yes, yes, I will go and see her, sure enough. How attentive she is, to think of everybody! Thank you, my dear, for shewing it me. It is as pretty a letter as ever I saw, and does Lucy's head and heart great credit."

CHAPTER XXXIX

The Miss Dashwoods had now been rather more than two months in town, and Marianne's impatience to be gone increased every day. She sighed for the air, the liberty, the quiet of the country; and fancied that if any place could give her ease, Barton must do it. Elinor was hardly less anxious than herself for their removal, and only so much less bent on its being effected immediately, as that she was conscious of the difficulties of so long a journey, which Marianne could not be brought to acknowledge. She began, however, seriously to turn her thoughts towards its accomplishment, and had already mentioned their wishes to their kind hostess, who resisted them with all the eloquence of her good-will, when a plan was suggested, which, though detaining them from home yet a few weeks longer, appeared to Elinor altogether much more eligible than any other. The Palmers were to remove to Cleveland about the end of March, for the Easter holidays; and Mrs. Jennings, with both her friends, received a very warm invitation from Charlotte to go with them. This would not, in itself, have been sufficient for the delicacy of Miss Dashwood—but it was inforced with so much real politeness by Mr. Palmer himself, as, joined to the very great amendment of his manners towards them since her sister had been known to be unhappy, induced her to accept it with pleasure.

When she told Marianne what she had done, however, her first reply was not very auspicious.

"Cleveland!" she cried, with great agitation. "No, I cannot go to Cleveland."

"You forget," said Elinor gently, "that its situation is not . . . that it is not in the neighbourhood of . . ."

"But it is in Somersetshire. I cannot go into Somersetshire. There, where I looked forward to going . . . No, Elinor, you cannot expect me to go there."

Elinor would not argue upon the propriety of overcoming such feelings—she only endeavoured to counteract them by working on others—represented it, therefore, as a measure which would fix the time of her returning to that dear mother, whom she so much wished to see, in a more eligible, more comfortable manner, than any other plan could do, and perhaps without any greater delay. From Cleveland, which was within a few miles of Bristol, the distance to Barton was not beyond one day, though a long day's journey; and their mother's servant might easily come there to attend them down; and as there could be no occasion of their staying above a week at Cleveland, they might now be at home in little more than three weeks' time. As Marianne's affection for her mother was sincere, it must triumph with little difficulty, over the imaginary evils she had started.

Mrs. Jennings was so far from being weary of her guests, that she pressed them very earnestly to return with her again from Cleveland. Elinor was grateful for the attention, but it could not alter her design; and their mother's concurrence being readily gained, everything relative to their return was arranged as far as it could be—and Marianne found some relief in drawing up a statement of the hours that were yet to divide her from Barton.

"Ah! Colonel, I do not know what you and I shall do without the Miss Dashwoods"—was Mrs. Jennings's address to him when he first called on her, after their leaving her was settled—"for they are quite resolved upon going home from the Palmers—and how forlorn we shall be, when I come back! Lord! We shall sit and gape at one another as dull as two cats."

Perhaps Mrs. Jennings was in hopes, by this vigorous sketch of their future *ennui*, to provoke him to make that offer, which might give himself an escape from it—and if so, she had soon afterwards good reason to think her object gained; for, on Elinor's moving to the window to take more expeditiously the dimensions of a print, which she was going to copy for her friend, he followed her to it with a look of particular meaning, and conversed with her there for several minutes. The effect of his discourse on the lady too, could not escape her observation, for though she was too honorable to listen, and had even changed her seat, on purpose that she might *not* hear, to one close by the pianoforte on which Marianne was playing, she could not keep herself from seeing that Elinor changed colour, attended with agitation, and was too intent on what he said to pursue her employment. Still farther in confirmation of her hopes, in the interval of Marianne's turning from one lesson to another, some words of the Colonel's inevitably reached her ear, in which he seemed to be apologising for the badness of his house. This set the matter beyond a doubt. She wondered, indeed, at his thinking it necessary to do so; but supposed it to be the proper etiquette. What Elinor said in reply she could not distinguish, but judged from the motion of her lips, that she did not think *that* any material objection—and Mrs. Jennings commended her in her heart for being so honest. They then talked on for a few minutes longer without her catching a syllable, when another lucky stop in Marianne's performance brought her these words in the Colonel's calm voice,

"I am afraid it cannot take place very soon."

Astonished and shocked at so unlover-like a speech, she was almost ready to cry out, "Lord! what should hinder it?" but checking her desire, confined herself to this silent ejaculation.

"This is very strange! Sure he need not wait to be older."

This delay on the Colonel's side, however, did not seem to offend or mortify his fair companion in the least, for on their breaking up the conference soon afterwards, and moving different ways, Mrs. Jennings very plainly heard Elinor say, and with a voice which shewed her to feel what she said—

"I shall always think myself very much obliged to you."

Mrs. Jennings was delighted with her gratitude, and only wondered that after hearing such a sentence, the Colonel should be able to take leave of them, as he immediately did, with the utmost sang-froid, and go away without making her any reply! She had not thought her old friend could have made so indifferent a suitor.

What had really passed between them was to this effect.

"I have heard," said he, with great compassion, "of the injustice your friend Mr. Ferrars has suffered from his family; for if I understand the matter right, he has been entirely cast off by them for persevering in his engagement with a very deserving young woman. Have I been rightly informed? Is it so?"

Elinor told him that it was.

"The cruelty, the impolitic cruelty," he replied, with great feeling, "of dividing, or attempting to divide, two young people long attached to each other, is terrible. Mrs. Ferrars does not know what she may be doing—what she may drive her son to. I have seen Mr. Ferrars two or three times in Harley Street, and am much pleased with him. He is not a young man with whom one can be intimately acquainted in a short time, but I have seen enough of him to wish him well for his own sake, and as a friend of yours, I wish it still more. I understand that he intends to take orders. Will you be so good as to tell him that the living of Delaford, now just vacant, as I am informed by this day's post, is his, if he think it worth his acceptance—but *that*, perhaps, so unfortunately circumstanced as he is now, it may be nonsense to appear to doubt; I only wish it were more valuable. It is a rectory, but a small one; the late incumbent, I believe, did not make more than 200 pounds per annum, and though it is certainly capable of improvement, I fear, not to such an amount as to afford him a very comfortable income. Such as it is, however, my pleasure in presenting him to it, will be very great. Pray assure him of it."

Elinor's astonishment at this commission could hardly have been greater, had the Colonel been really making her an offer of his hand. The preferment, which only two days before she had considered as hopeless for Edward, was already provided to enable him to marry—and *she*, of all people in the world, was fixed on to bestow it! Her emotion was such as Mrs. Jennings had attributed to a very different cause—but whatever minor feelings less pure, less pleasing, might have a share in that emotion, her esteem for the general benevolence, and her gratitude for the particular friendship, which together prompted Colonel Brandon to this act, were strongly felt, and warmly expressed. She thanked him for it with all her heart, spoke of Edward's principles and disposition with that praise which she knew them to deserve; and promised to undertake the commission with pleasure, if it were really his wish to put off so agreeable an office to another. But at the same time, she could not help thinking that no one could so well perform it as himself. It was an office in short, from which, unwilling to give Edward the pain of receiving an obligation from *her*, she would have been very glad to be spared herself—but Colonel Brandon, on motives of equal delicacy, declining it likewise, still seemed so desirous of its being given through her means, that she would not on any account make farther opposition. Edward, she believed, was still in town, and fortunately she had heard his address from Miss Steele. She could undertake therefore to inform him of it, in the course of the day. After this had been settled, Colonel Brandon began to talk of his own advantage in securing so respectable and agreeable a neighbour, and *then* it was that he mentioned with regret, that the house was small and indifferent—an evil which Elinor, as

Mrs. Jennings had supposed her to do, made very light of, at least as far as regarded its size.

"The smallness of the house," said she, "I cannot imagine any inconvenience to them, for it will be in proportion to their family and income."

By which the Colonel was surprised to find that *she* was considering Mr. Ferrars's marriage as the certain consequence of the presentation; for he did not suppose it possible that Delaford living could supply such an income, as anybody in his style of life would venture to settle on—and he said so.

"This little rectory *can* do no more than make Mr. Ferrars comfortable as a bachelor; it cannot enable him to marry. I am sorry to say that my patronage ends with this; and my interest is hardly more extensive. If, however, by an unforeseen chance it should be in my power to serve him farther, I must think very differently of him from what I now do, if I am not as ready to be useful to him then as I sincerely wish I could be at present. What I am now doing indeed, seems nothing at all, since it can advance him so little towards what must be his principal, his only object of happiness. His marriage must still be a distant good—at least, I am afraid it cannot take place very soon."

Such was the sentence which, when misunderstood, so justly offended the delicate feelings of Mrs. Jennings; but after this narration of what really passed between Colonel Brandon and Elinor, while they stood at the window, the gratitude expressed by the latter on their parting, may perhaps appear in general, not less reasonably excited, nor less properly worded than if it had arisen from an offer of marriage.

CHAPTER XL

"Well, Miss Dashwood," said Mrs. Jennings, sagaciously smiling, as soon as the gentleman had withdrawn, "I do not ask you what the Colonel has been saying to you; for though, upon my honour, I *tried* to keep out of hearing, I could not help catching enough to understand his business. And I assure you I never was better pleased in my life, and I wish you joy of it with all my heart."

"Thank you, ma'am," said Elinor. "It is a matter of great joy to me; and I feel the goodness of Colonel Brandon most sensibly. There are not many men who would act as he has done. Few people who have so compassionate a heart! I never was more astonished in my life."

"Lord! My dear, you are very modest. I a'n't the least astonished at it in the world, for I have often thought of late, there was nothing more likely to happen."

"You judged from your knowledge of the Colonel's general benevolence; but at least you could not foresee that the opportunity would so very soon occur."

"Opportunity!" repeated Mrs. Jennings—"Oh! As to that, when a man has once made up his mind to such a thing, somehow or other he will soon find an opportunity. Well, my dear, I wish you joy of it again and again; and if ever there was a happy couple in the world, I think I shall soon know where to look for them."

"You mean to go to Delaford after them I suppose," said Elinor, with a faint smile.

"Aye, my dear, that I do, indeed. And as to the house being a bad one, I do not know what the Colonel would be at, for it is as good a one as ever I saw."

"He spoke of its being out of repair."

"Well, and whose fault is that? Why don't he repair it? Who should do it but himself?"

They were interrupted by the servant's coming in to announce the carriage being at the door; and Mrs. Jennings immediately preparing to go, said—

"Well, my dear, I must be gone before I have had half my talk out. But, however, we may have it all over in the evening; for we shall be quite alone. I do not ask you to go with me, for I dare say your mind is too full of the matter to care for company; and besides, you must long to tell your sister all about it."

Marianne had left the room before the conversation began.

"Certainly, ma'am, I shall tell Marianne of it; but I shall not mention it at present to anybody else."

"Oh! Very well," said Mrs. Jennings rather disappointed. "Then you would not have me tell it to Lucy, for I think of going as far as Holborn to-day."

"No, ma'am, not even Lucy if you please. One day's delay will not be very material; and till I have written to Mr. Ferrars, I think it ought not to be mentioned to anybody else. I shall do *that* directly. It is of importance that no time should be lost with him, for he will of course have much to do relative to his ordination."

This speech at first puzzled Mrs. Jennings exceedingly. Why Mr. Ferrars was to have been written to about it in such a hurry, she could not immediately comprehend. A few moments' reflection, however, produced a very happy idea, and she exclaimed—

"Oh, ho! I understand you. Mr. Ferrars is to be the man. Well, so much the better for him. Ay, to be sure, he must be ordained in readiness; and I am very glad to find things are so forward between you. But, my dear, is not this rather out of character? Should not the Colonel write himself? Sure, he is the proper person."

Elinor did not quite understand the beginning of Mrs. Jennings's speech, neither did she think it worth inquiring into; and therefore only replied to its conclusion.

"Colonel Brandon is so delicate a man, that he rather wished any one to announce his intentions to Mr. Ferrars than himself."

"And so *you* are forced to do it. Well *that* is an odd kind of delicacy! However, I will not disturb you (seeing her preparing to write). You know your own concerns best. So goodby, my dear. I have not heard of any thing to please me so well since Charlotte was brought to bed."

And away she went; but returning again in a moment—

"I have just been thinking of Betty's sister, my dear. I should be very glad to get her so good a mistress. But whether she would do for a lady's maid, I am sure I can't tell. She is an excellent housemaid, and works very well at her needle. However, you will think of all that at your leisure."

"Certainly, ma'am," replied Elinor, not hearing much of what she said, and more anxious to be alone, than to be mistress of the subject.

How she should begin—how she should express herself in her note to Edward, was now all her concern. The particular circumstances between them made a difficulty of that which to any other person would have been the easiest thing in the world; but she equally feared to say too much or too little, and sat deliberating over her paper, with the pen in her hand, till broken in on by the entrance of Edward himself.

He had met Mrs. Jennings at the door in her way to the carriage, as he came to leave his farewell card; and she, after apologising for not returning herself, had obliged him to enter, by saying that Miss Dashwood was above, and wanted to speak with him on very particular business.

Elinor had just been congratulating herself, in the midst of her perplexity, that however difficult it might be to express herself properly by letter, it was at least preferable to giving the information by word of mouth, when her visitor entered, to force her upon this greatest exertion of all. Her astonishment and confusion were very great on his so sudden appearance. She had not seen him before since his engagement became public, and therefore not since his knowing her to be acquainted with it; which, with the consciousness of what she had been thinking of, and what she had to tell him, made her feel particularly uncomfortable for some minutes. He too was much distressed; and they sat down together in a most promising state of embarrassment. Whether he had asked her pardon for his intrusion on first coming into the room, he could not recollect; but determining to be on the safe side, he made his apology in form as soon as he could say any thing, after taking a chair.

"Mrs. Jennings told me," said he, "that you wished to speak with me, at least I understood her so—or I certainly should not have intruded on you in such a manner; though at the same time, I should have been extremely sorry to leave London without seeing you and your sister; especially as it will most likely be some time—it is not probable that I should soon have the pleasure of meeting you again. I go to Oxford tomorrow."

"You would not have gone, however," said Elinor, recovering herself, and determined to get over what she so much dreaded as soon as possible, "without receiving our good wishes, even if we had not been able to give them in person. Mrs. Jennings was quite right in what she said. I have something of consequence to inform you of, which I was on the point of communicating by paper. I am charged with a most agreeable office (breathing rather faster than usual as she spoke.) Colonel Brandon, who was here only ten minutes ago, has desired me to say, that understanding you mean to take orders, he has great pleasure in offering you the living of Delaford now just vacant, and only wishes it were more valuable. Allow me to congratulate you on having so respectable and well-judging a friend, and to join in his wish that the living—it is about two hundred a-year—were much more considerable, and such as might better enable you to—as might be more than a temporary accommodation to yourself—such, in short, as might establish all your views of happiness."

What Edward felt, as he could not say it himself, it cannot be expected that anyone else should say for him. He *looked* all the astonishment which such unexpected, such unthought-of information could not fail of exciting; but he said only these two words—

"Colonel Brandon!"

"Yes," continued Elinor, gathering more resolution, as some of the worst was over, "Colonel Brandon means it as a testimony of his concern for what has lately passed—for the cruel situation in which the unjustifiable conduct of your family has placed you—a concern which I am sure Marianne, myself, and all your friends, must share; and likewise as a proof of his high esteem for your general character, and his particular approbation of your behaviour on the present occasion."

"Colonel Brandon give *me* a living! Can it be possible?"

"The unkindness of your own relations has made you astonished to find friendship any where."

"No," replied he, with sudden consciousness, "not to find it in *you*; for I cannot be ignorant that to you, to your goodness, I owe it all. I feel it—I would express it if I could—but, as you well know, I am no orator."

"You are very much mistaken. I do assure you that you owe it entirely, at least almost entirely, to your own merit, and Colonel Brandon's discernment of it. I have had no hand in it. I did not even know, till I understood his design, that the living was vacant; nor had it ever occurred to me that he might have had such a living in his gift.

As a friend of mine, of my family, he may, perhaps—indeed I know he *has*, still greater pleasure in bestowing it; but, upon my word, you owe nothing to my solicitation."

Truth obliged her to acknowledge some small share in the action, but she was at the same time so unwilling to appear as the benefactress of Edward, that she acknowledged it with hesitation; which probably contributed to fix that suspicion in his mind which had recently entered it. For a short time he sat deep in thought, after Elinor had ceased to speak—at last, and as if it were rather an effort, he said,

"Colonel Brandon seems a man of great worth and respectability. I have always heard him spoken of as such, and your brother I know esteems him highly. He is undoubtedly a sensible man, and in his manners perfectly the gentleman."

"Indeed," replied Elinor, "I believe that you will find him, on farther acquaintance, all that you have heard him to be, and as you will be such very near neighbours (for I understand the parsonage is almost close to the mansion-house), it is particularly important that he *should* be all this."

Edward made no answer; but when she had turned away her head, gave her a look so serious, so earnest, so uncheerful, as seemed to say, that he might hereafter wish the distance between the parsonage and the mansion-house much greater.

"Colonel Brandon, I think, lodges in St. James Street," said he, soon afterwards, rising from his chair.

Elinor told him the number of the house.

"I must hurry away then, to give him those thanks which you will not allow me to give *you*; to assure him that he has made me a very—an exceedingly happy man."

Elinor did not offer to detain him; and they parted, with a very earnest assurance on *her* side of her unceasing good wishes for his happiness in every change of situation that might befall him; on *his*, with rather an attempt to return the same good will, than the power of expressing it.

"When I see him again," said Elinor to herself, as the door shut him out, "I shall see him the husband of Lucy."

And with this pleasing anticipation, she sat down to reconsider the past, recall the words and endeavour to comprehend all the feelings of Edward; and, of course, to reflect on her own with discontent.

When Mrs. Jennings came home, though she returned from seeing people whom she had never seen before, and of whom therefore she must have a great deal to say, her mind was so much more occupied by the important secret in her possession, than by anything else, that she reverted to it again as soon as Elinor appeared.

"Well, my dear," she cried, "I sent you up to the young man. Did not I do right? And I suppose you had no great difficulty—you did not find him very unwilling to accept your proposal?"

"No, ma'am; *that* was not very likely."

"Well, and how soon will he be ready? For it seems all to depend upon that."

"Really," said Elinor, "I know so little of these kind of forms, that I can hardly even conjecture as to the time, or the preparation necessary; but I suppose two or three months will complete his ordination."

"Two or three months!" cried Mrs. Jennings; "Lord! My dear, how calmly you talk of it; and can the Colonel wait two or three months! Lord bless me! I am sure it would put *me* quite out of patience! And though one would be very glad to do a kindness by poor Mr. Ferrars, I do think it is not worth while to wait two or three months for him. Sure somebody else might be found that would do as well; somebody that is in orders already."

"My dear ma'am," said Elinor, "what can you be thinking of? Why, Colonel Brandon's only object is to be of use to Mr. Ferrars."

"Lord bless you, my dear! Sure you do not mean to persuade me that the Colonel only marries you for the sake of giving ten guineas to Mr. Ferrars!"

The deception could not continue after this; and an explanation immediately took place, by which both gained considerable amusement for the moment, without any material loss of happiness to either, for Mrs. Jennings only exchanged one form of delight for another, and still without forfeiting her expectation of the first.

"Aye, aye, the parsonage is but a small one," said she, after the first ebullition of surprise and satisfaction was over, "and very likely *may* be out of repair; but to hear a man apologising, as I thought, for a house that to my knowledge has five sitting rooms on the ground-floor, and I think the housekeeper told me could make up fifteen beds! And to you too, that had been used to live in Barton cottage! It seems quite ridiculous. But, my dear, we must touch up the Colonel to do some thing to the parsonage, and make it comfortable for them, before Lucy goes to it."

"But Colonel Brandon does not seem to have any idea of the living's being enough to allow them to marry."

"The Colonel is a ninny, my dear; because he has two thousand a-year himself, he thinks that nobody else can marry on less. Take my word for it, that, if I am alive, I shall be paying a visit at Delaford Parsonage before Michaelmas; and I am sure I shan't go if Lucy an't there."

Elinor was quite of her opinion, as to the probability of their not waiting for any thing more.

CHAPTER XLI

Edward, having carried his thanks to Colonel Brandon, proceeded with his happiness to Lucy; and such was the excess of it by the time he reached Bartlett's Buildings, that she was able to assure Mrs. Jennings, who called on her again the next day with her congratulations, that she had never seen him in such spirits before in her life.

Her own happiness, and her own spirits, were at least very certain; and she joined Mrs. Jennings most heartily in her expectation of their being all comfortably together in Delaford Parsonage before Michaelmas. So far was she, at the same time, from any backwardness to give Elinor that credit which Edward *would* give her, that she spoke of her friendship for them both with the most grateful warmth, was ready to own all their obligation to her, and openly declared that no exertion for their good on Miss Dashwood's part, either present or future, would ever surprise her, for she believed her capable of doing any thing in the world for those she really valued. As for Colonel Brandon, she was not only ready to worship him as a saint, but was moreover truly anxious that he should be treated as one in all worldly concerns; anxious that his tithes should be raised to the utmost; and scarcely resolved to avail herself, at Delaford, as far as she possibly could, of his servants, his carriage, his cows, and his poultry.

It was now above a week since John Dashwood had called in Berkeley Street, and as since that time no notice had been taken by them of his wife's indisposition, beyond one verbal enquiry, Elinor began to feel it necessary to pay her a visit. This was an obligation, however, which not only opposed her own inclination, but which had not the assistance of any encouragement from her companions. Marianne, not contented with absolutely refusing to go herself, was very urgent to prevent her sister's going at all; and Mrs. Jennings, though her carriage was always at Elinor's service, so very much disliked Mrs. John Dashwood, that not even her curiosity to see how she looked after the late discovery, nor her strong desire to affront her by taking Edward's part, could overcome her unwillingness to be in her company again. The consequence was, that Elinor set out by herself to pay a visit, for which no one could really have less inclination, and to run the risk of a *tête-à-tête* with a woman, whom neither of the others had so much reason to dislike.

Mrs. Dashwood was denied; but before the carriage could turn from the house, her husband accidentally came out. He expressed great pleasure in meeting Elinor, told her that he had been just going to call in Berkeley Street, and, assuring her that Fanny would be very glad to see her, invited her to come in.

They walked up stairs in to the drawing-room. Nobody was there.

"Fanny is in her own room, I suppose," said he; "I will go to her presently, for I am sure she will not have the least objection in the world to seeing *you*. Very far from it, indeed. *Now* especially there cannot be—but however, you and Marianne were always great favourites. Why would not Marianne come?"

Elinor made what excuse she could for her.

"I am not sorry to see you alone," he replied, "for I have a good deal to say to you. This living of Colonel Brandon's—can it be true? Has he really given it to Edward? I heard it yesterday by chance, and was coming to you on purpose to enquire farther about it."

"It is perfectly true. Colonel Brandon has given the living of Delaford to Edward."

"Really! Well, this is very astonishing! No relationship! No connection between them! And now that livings fetch such a price! What was the value of this?"

"About two hundred a year."

"Very well—and for the next presentation to a living of that value—supposing the late incumbent to have been old and sickly, and likely to vacate it soon—he might have got I dare say—fourteen hundred pounds. And how came he not to have settled that matter before this person's death? *Now* indeed it would be too late to sell it, but a man of Colonel Brandon's sense! I wonder he should be so improvident in a point of such common, such natural, concern! Well, I am convinced that there is a vast deal of inconsistency in almost every human character. I suppose, however—on recollection—that the case may probably be *this*. Edward is only to hold the living till the person to whom the Colonel has really sold the presentation, is old enough to take it. Aye, aye, that is the fact, depend upon it."

Elinor contradicted it, however, very positively; and by relating that she had herself been employed in conveying the offer from Colonel

Brandon to Edward, and, therefore, must understand the terms on which it was given, obliged him to submit to her authority.

"It is truly astonishing!" he cried, after hearing what she said—"what could be the Colonel's motive?"

"A very simple one—to be of use to Mr. Ferrars."

"Well, well; whatever Colonel Brandon may be, Edward is a very lucky man. You will not mention the matter to Fanny, however, for though I have broke it to her, and she bears it vastly well, she will not like to hear it much talked of."

Elinor had some difficulty here to refrain from observing, that she thought Fanny might have borne with composure, an acquisition of wealth to her brother, by which neither she nor her child could be possibly impoverished.

"Mrs. Ferrars," added he, lowering his voice to the tone becoming so important a subject, "knows nothing about it at present, and I believe it will be best to keep it entirely concealed from her as long as may be. When the marriage takes place, I fear she must hear of it all."

"But why should such precaution be used? Though it is not to be supposed that Mrs. Ferrars can have the smallest satisfaction in knowing that her son has money enough to live upon, for *that* must be quite out of the question; yet why, upon her late behaviour, is she supposed to feel at all? She has done with her son, she cast him off for ever, and has made all those over whom she had any influence, cast him off likewise. Surely, after doing so, she cannot be imagined liable to any impression of sorrow or of joy on his account—she cannot be interested in any thing that befalls him. She would not be so weak as to throw away the comfort of a child, and yet retain the anxiety of a parent!"

"Ah! Elinor," said John, "your reasoning is very good, but it is founded on ignorance of human nature. When Edward's unhappy match takes place, depend upon it his mother will feel as much as if she had never discarded him; and, therefore every circumstance that may accelerate that dreadful event, must be concealed from her as much as possible. Mrs. Ferrars can never forget that Edward is her son."

"You surprise me; I should think it must nearly have escaped her memory by *this* time."

"You wrong her exceedingly. Mrs. Ferrars is one of the most affectionate mothers in the world."

Elinor was silent.

"We think *now*," said Mr. Dashwood, after a short pause, "of *Robert's* marrying Miss Morton."

Elinor, smiling at the grave and decisive importance of her brother's tone, calmly replied,

"The lady, I suppose, has no choice in the affair."

"Choice! How do you mean?"

"I only mean that I suppose, from your manner of speaking, it must be the same to Miss Morton whether she marry Edward or Robert."

"Certainly, there can be no difference; for Robert will now to all intents and purposes be considered as the eldest son—and as to any thing else, they are both very agreeable young men: I do not know that one is superior to the other."

Elinor said no more, and John was also for a short time silent. His reflections ended thus.

"Of *one* thing, my dear sister," kindly taking her hand, and speaking in an awful whisper, "I may assure you—and I *will* do it, because I know it must gratify you. I have good reason to think—indeed I have it from the best authority, or I should not repeat it, for otherwise it would be very wrong to say any thing about it—but I have it from the very best authority—not that I ever precisely heard Mrs. Ferrars say it herself—but her daughter *did*, and I have it from her—That in short, whatever objections there might be against a certain—a certain connection—you understand me—it would have been far preferable to her, it would not have given her half the vexation that *this* does. I was exceedingly pleased to hear that Mrs. Ferrars considered it in that light—a very gratifying circumstance you know to us all. 'It would have been beyond comparison,' she said, 'the least evil of the two, and she would be glad to compound *now* for nothing worse.' But however, all that is quite out of the question—not to be thought of or mentioned—as to any attachment you know—it never could be—all that is gone by. But I thought I would just tell you of this, because I knew how much it must please you. Not that you have any reason to regret, my dear Elinor. There is no doubt of your doing exceedingly well—quite as well, or better, perhaps, all things considered. Has Colonel Brandon been with you lately?"

Elinor had heard enough, if not to gratify her vanity, and raise her self-importance, to agitate her nerves and fill her mind—and she was therefore glad to be spared from the necessity of saying much in reply herself, and from the danger of hearing any thing more from her brother, by the entrance of Mr. Robert Ferrars. After a few moments' chat, John Dashwood, recollecting that Fanny was yet uninformed of her sister's being there, quitted the room in quest of her; and Elinor was left to improve her acquaintance with Robert, who, by the gay unconcern, the happy self-complacency of his manner while enjoying so unfair a division of his mother's love and liberality, to the prejudice of his banished brother, earned only by his own dissipated course of life, and that brother's integrity, was confirming her most unfavourable opinion of his head and heart.

They had scarcely been two minutes by themselves, before he began to speak of Edward; for he, too, had heard of the living, and was very inquisitive on the subject. Elinor repeated the particulars of it, as she had given them to John; and their effect on Robert, though very different, was not less striking than it had been on *him*. He laughed most immoderately. The idea of Edward's being a clergyman, and living in a small parsonage-house, diverted him beyond measure—and when to that was added the fanciful imagery of Edward reading prayers in a white surplice, and publishing the banns of marriage between John Smith and Mary Brown, he could conceive nothing more ridiculous.

Elinor, while she waited in silence and immovable gravity, the conclusion of such folly, could not restrain her eyes from being fixed on him with a look that spoke all the contempt it excited. It was a look, however, very well bestowed, for it relieved her own feelings, and gave no intelligence to him. He was recalled from wit to wisdom, not by any reproof of her's, but by his own sensibility.

"We may treat it as a joke," said he, at last, recovering from the affected laugh which had considerably lengthened out the genuine gaiety of the moment—"but, upon my soul, it is a most serious business. Poor Edward! He is ruined for ever. I am extremely sorry for it—for I know him to be a very good-hearted creature; as well-meaning a fellow perhaps, as any in the world. You must not judge of him, Miss Dashwood, from *your* slight acquaintance. Poor Edward! His manners are certainly not the happiest in nature. But we are not all born, you know, with the same powers, the same address. Poor fellow! To see him in a circle of strangers! To be sure it was pitiable enough! But upon my soul, I believe he has as good a heart as any in the kingdom; and I declare and protest to you I never was so shocked in my life, as when it all burst forth. I could not believe it. My mother was the first person who told me of it; and I, feeling myself called on to act with resolution, immediately said to her, 'My dear madam, I do not know what you may intend to do on the occasion, but as for myself, I must say, that if Edward does marry this young woman, I never will see him again.' That was what I said immediately. I was most uncommonly shocked, indeed! Poor Edward! He has done for himself completely—shut himself out for ever from all decent society! But, as I directly said to my mother, I am not in the least surprised at it; from his style of education, it was always to be expected. My poor mother was half frantic."

"Have you ever seen the lady?"

"Yes; once, while she was staying in this house, I happened to drop in for ten minutes; and I saw quite enough of her. The merest awkward country girl, without style, or elegance, and almost without beauty. I remember her perfectly. Just the kind of girl I should suppose likely to captivate poor Edward. I offered immediately, as soon as my mother related the affair to me, to talk to him myself, and dissuade him from the match; but it was too late *then*, I found, to do any thing, for unluckily, I was not in the way at first, and knew nothing of it till after the breach had taken place, when it was not for me, you know, to interfere. But had I been informed of it a few hours earlier—I think it is most probable—that something might have been hit on. I certainly should have represented it to Edward in a very strong light. 'My dear fellow,' I should have said, 'consider what you are doing. You are making a most disgraceful connection, and such a one as your family are unanimous in disapproving.' I cannot help thinking, in short, that means might have been found. But now it is all too late. He must be starved, you know—that is certain; absolutely starved."

He had just settled this point with great composure, when the entrance of Mrs. John Dashwood put an end to the subject. But though *she* never spoke of it out of her own family, Elinor could see its influence on her mind, in the something like confusion of countenance with which she entered, and an attempt at cordiality in her behaviour to herself. She even proceeded so far as to be concerned to find that Elinor and her sister were so soon to leave town, as she had hoped to see more of them—an exertion in which her husband, who attended her into the room, and hung enamoured over her accents, seemed to distinguish everything that was most affectionate and graceful.

CHAPTER XLII

One other short call in Harley Street, in which Elinor received her brother's congratulations on their travelling so far towards Barton without any expense, and on Colonel Brandon's being to follow them to Cleveland in a day or two, completed the intercourse of the brother and sisters in town—and a faint invitation from Fanny, to come to Norland whenever it should happen to be in their way, which of all things was the most unlikely to occur, with a more warm, though less public, assurance, from John to Elinor, of the promptitude with which he should come to see her at Delaford, was all that foretold any meeting in the country.

It amused her to observe that all her friends seemed determined to send her to Delaford—a place, in which, of all others, she would now least chuse to visit, or wish to reside; for not only was it considered as her future home by her brother and Mrs. Jennings, but even Lucy, when they parted, gave her a pressing invitation to visit her there.

Very early in April, and tolerably early in the day, the two parties from Hanover Square and Berkeley Street set out from their respective homes, to meet, by appointment, on the road. For the convenience of Charlotte and her child, they were to be more than two days on their journey, and Mr. Palmer, travelling more expeditiously with Colonel Brandon, was to join them at Cleveland soon after their arrival.

Marianne, few as had been her hours of comfort in London, and eager as she had long been to quit it, could not, when it came to the point, bid adieu to the house in which she had for the last time enjoyed those hopes, and that confidence, in Willoughby, which were now extinguished for ever, without great pain. Nor could she leave the place in which Willoughby remained, busy in new engagements, and new schemes, in which *she* could have no share, without shedding many tears.

Elinor's satisfaction, at the moment of removal, was more positive. She had no such object for her lingering thoughts to fix on, she left no creature behind, from whom it would give her a moment's regret to be divided for ever, she was pleased to be free herself from the persecution of Lucy's friendship, she was grateful for bringing her sister away unseen by Willoughby since his marriage, and she looked forward with hope to what a few months of tranquility at Barton might do towards restoring Marianne's peace of mind, and confirming her own.

Their journey was safely performed. The second day brought them into the cherished, or the prohibited, county of Somerset, for as such was it dwelt on by turns in Marianne's imagination; and in the forenoon of the third they drove up to Cleveland.

Cleveland was a spacious, modern-built house, situated on a sloping lawn. It had no park, but the pleasure-grounds were tolerably extensive; and like every other place of the same degree of importance, it had its open shrubbery, and closer wood walk, a road of smooth gravel winding round a plantation, led to the front, the lawn was dotted over with timber, the house itself was under the guardianship of the fir, the mountain-ash, and the acacia, and a thick screen of them altogether, interspersed with tall Lombardy poplars, shut out the offices.

Marianne entered the house with a heart swelling with emotion from the consciousness of being only eighty miles from Barton, and not thirty from Combe Magna; and before she had been five minutes within its walls, while the others were busily helping Charlotte to show her child to the housekeeper, she quitted it again, stealing away through the winding shrubberies, now just beginning to be in beauty, to gain a distant eminence; where, from its Grecian temple, her eye, wandering over a wide tract of country to the south-east, could fondly rest on the farthest ridge of hills in the horizon, and fancy that from their summits Combe Magna might be seen.

In such moments of precious, invaluable misery, she rejoiced in tears of agony to be at Cleveland; and as she returned by a different circuit to the house, feeling all the happy privilege of country liberty, of wandering from place to place in free and luxurious solitude, she resolved to spend almost every hour of every day while she remained with the Palmers, in the indulgence of such solitary rambles.

She returned just in time to join the others as they quitted the house, on an excursion through its more immediate premises; and the rest of the morning was easily whiled away, in lounging round the kitchen garden, examining the bloom upon its walls, and listening to the gardener's lamentations upon blights, in dawdling through the green-house, where the loss of her favourite plants, unwarily exposed, and nipped by the lingering frost, raised the laughter of Charlotte, and in visiting her poultry-yard, where, in the disappointed hopes of her dairy-maid, by hens forsaking their nests, or being stolen by a fox, or in the rapid decrease of a promising young brood, she found fresh sources of merriment.

The morning was fine and dry, and Marianne, in her plan of employment abroad, had not calculated for any change of weather during their stay at Cleveland. With great surprise therefore, did she find herself prevented by a settled rain from going out again after dinner. She had depended on a twilight walk to the Grecian temple, and perhaps all over the grounds, and an evening merely cold or damp would not have deterred her from it; but a heavy and settled rain even *she* could not fancy dry or pleasant weather for walking.

Their party was small, and the hours passed quietly away. Mrs. Palmer had her child, and Mrs. Jennings her carpet-work; they talked of the friends they had left behind, arranged Lady Middleton's engagements, and wondered whether Mr. Palmer and Colonel Brandon would get farther than Reading that night. Elinor, however little concerned in it, joined in their discourse; and Marianne, who had the knack of finding her way in every house to the library, however it might be avoided by the family in general, soon procured herself a book.

Nothing was wanting on Mrs. Palmer's side that constant and friendly good humour could do, to make them feel themselves welcome. The openness and heartiness of her manner more than atoned for that want of recollection and elegance which made her often deficient in the forms of politeness; her kindness, recommended by so pretty a face, was engaging; her folly, though evident was not disgusting, because it was not conceited; and Elinor could have forgiven everything but her laugh.

The two gentlemen arrived the next day to a very late dinner, affording a pleasant enlargement of the party, and a very welcome variety to their conversation, which a long morning of the same continued rain had reduced very low.

Elinor had seen so little of Mr. Palmer, and in that little had seen so much variety in his address to her sister and herself, that she knew not what to expect to find him in his own family. She found him, however, perfectly the gentleman in his behaviour to all his visitors, and only occasionally rude to his wife and her mother; she found him very capable of being a pleasant companion, and only prevented from being so always, by too great an aptitude to fancy himself as much superior to people in general, as he must feel himself to be to Mrs. Jennings and Charlotte. For the rest of his character and habits, they were marked, as far as Elinor could perceive, with no traits at all unusual in his sex and time of life. He was nice in his eating, uncertain in his hours; fond of his child, though affecting to slight it; and idled away the mornings at billiards, which ought to have been devoted to business. She liked him, however, upon the whole, much better than she had expected, and in her heart was not sorry that she could like him no more—not sorry to be driven by the observation of his Epicurism, his selfishness, and his conceit, to rest with complacency on the remembrance of Edward's generous temper, simple taste, and diffident feelings.

Of Edward, or at least of some of his concerns, she now received intelligence from Colonel Brandon, who had been into Dorsetshire lately; and who, treating her at once as the disinterested friend of Mr. Ferrars, and the kind of confidant of himself, talked to her a great deal of the parsonage at Delaford, described its deficiencies, and told her what he meant to do himself towards removing them. His behaviour to her in this, as well as in every other particular, his open pleasure in meeting her after an absence of only ten days, his readiness to converse with her, and his deference for her opinion, might very well justify Mrs. Jennings's persuasion of his attachment, and would have been enough, perhaps, had not Elinor still, as from the first, believed Marianne his real favourite, to make her suspect it herself. But as it was, such a notion had scarcely ever entered her head, except by Mrs. Jennings's suggestion; and she could not help believing herself the nicest observer of the two—she watched his eyes, while Mrs. Jennings thought only of his behaviour—and while his looks of anxious solicitude on Marianne's feeling, in her head and throat, the beginning of a heavy cold, because unexpressed by words, entirely escaped the latter lady's observation—*she* could discover in them the quick feelings, and needless alarm of a lover.

Two delightful twilight walks on the third and fourth evenings of her being there, not merely on the dry gravel of the shrubbery, but all over the grounds, and especially in the most distant parts of them, where there was something more of wildness than in the rest, where the trees were the oldest, and the grass was the longest and wettest, had—assisted by the still greater imprudence of sitting in her wet shoes and stockings—given Marianne a cold so violent as, though for a day or two trifled with or denied, would force itself by increasing ailments on the concern of everybody, and the notice of herself. Prescriptions poured in from all quarters, and as usual, were all declined. Though heavy and feverish, with a pain in her limbs, and a cough, and a sore throat, a good night's rest was to cure her entirely; and it was with difficulty that Elinor prevailed on her, when she went to bed, to try one or two of the simplest of the remedies.

CHAPTER XLIII

Marianne got up the next morning at her usual time; to every inquiry replied that she was better, and tried to prove herself so, by engaging in her accustomary employments. But a day spent in sitting shivering over the fire with a book in her hand, which she was unable to read, or in lying, weary and languid, on a sofa, did not speak much in favour of her amendment; and when, at last, she went early to bed, more and more indisposed, Colonel Brandon was only astonished at her sister's composure, who, though attending and nursing her the whole day, against Marianne's inclination, and forcing proper medicines on her at night, trusted, like Marianne, to the certainty and efficacy of sleep, and felt no real alarm.

A very restless and feverish night, however, disappointed the expectation of both; and when Marianne, after persisting in rising, confessed herself unable to sit up, and returned voluntarily to her bed, Elinor was very ready to adopt Mrs. Jennings's advice, of sending for the Palmers' apothecary.

He came, examined his patient, and though encouraging Miss Dashwood to expect that a very few days would restore her sister to health, yet, by pronouncing her disorder to have a putrid tendency, and allowing the word "infection" to pass his lips, gave instant alarm to Mrs. Palmer, on her baby's account. Mrs. Jennings, who had been inclined from the first to think Marianne's complaint more serious than Elinor, now looked very grave on Mr. Harris's report, and confirming Charlotte's fears and caution, urged the necessity of her immediate removal with her infant; and Mr. Palmer, though treating their apprehensions as idle, found the anxiety and importunity of his wife too great to be withstood. Her departure, therefore, was fixed on; and within an hour after Mr. Harris's arrival, she set off, with her little boy and his nurse, for the house of a near relation of Mr. Palmer's, who lived a few miles on the other side of Bath; whither her husband promised, at her earnest entreaty, to join her in a day or two; and whither she was almost equally urgent with her mother to accompany her. Mrs. Jennings, however, with a kindness of heart which made Elinor really love her, declared her resolution of not stirring from

Cleveland as long as Marianne remained ill, and of endeavouring, by her own attentive care, to supply to her the place of the mother she had taken her from; and Elinor found her on every occasion a most willing and active helpmate, desirous to share in all her fatigues, and often by her better experience in nursing, of material use.

Poor Marianne, languid and low from the nature of her malady, and feeling herself universally ill, could no longer hope that tomorrow would find her recovered; and the idea of what tomorrow would have produced, but for this unlucky illness, made every ailment severe; for on that day they were to have begun their journey home; and, attended the whole way by a servant of Mrs. Jennings, were to have taken their mother by surprise on the following forenoon. The little she said was all in lamentation of this inevitable delay; though Elinor tried to raise her spirits, and make her believe, as she *then* really believed herself, that it would be a very short one.

The next day produced little or no alteration in the state of the patient; she certainly was not better, and, except that there was no amendment, did not appear worse. Their party was now farther reduced; for Mr. Palmer, though very unwilling to go as well from real humanity and good-nature, as from a dislike of appearing to be frightened away by his wife, was persuaded at last by Colonel Brandon to perform his promise of following her; and while he was preparing to go, Colonel Brandon himself, with a much greater exertion, began to talk of going likewise. Here, however, the kindness of Mrs. Jennings interposed most acceptably; for to send the Colonel away while his love was in so much uneasiness on her sister's account, would be to deprive them both, she thought, of every comfort; and therefore telling him at once that his stay at Cleveland was necessary to herself, that she should want him to play at piquet of an evening, while Miss Dashwood was above with her sister, &c. she urged him so strongly to remain, that he, who was gratifying the first wish of his own heart by a compliance, could not long even affect to demur; especially as Mrs. Jennings's entreaty was warmly seconded by Mr. Palmer, who seemed to feel a relief to himself, in leaving behind him a person so well able to assist or advise Miss Dashwood in any emergence.

Marianne was, of course, kept in ignorance of all these arrangements. She knew not that she had been the means of sending the owners of Cleveland away, in about seven days from the time of their arrival. It gave her no surprise that she saw nothing of Mrs. Palmer; and as it gave her likewise no concern, she never mentioned her name.

Two days passed away from the time of Mr. Palmer's departure, and her situation continued, with little variation, the same. Mr. Harris, who attended her every day, still talked boldly of a speedy recovery, and Miss Dashwood was equally sanguine; but the expectation of the others was by no means so cheerful. Mrs. Jennings had determined very early in the seizure that Marianne would never get over it, and Colonel Brandon, who was chiefly of use in listening to Mrs. Jennings's forebodings, was not in a state of mind to resist their influence. He tried to reason himself out of fears, which the different judgment of the apothecary seemed to render absurd; but the many hours of each day in which he was left entirely alone, were but too favourable for the admission of every melancholy idea, and he could not expel from his mind the persuasion that he should see Marianne no more.

On the morning of the third day however, the gloomy anticipations of both were almost done away; for when Mr. Harris arrived, he declared his patient materially better. Her pulse was much stronger, and every symptom more favourable than on the preceding visit. Elinor, confirmed in every pleasant hope, was all cheerfulness; rejoicing that in her letters to her mother, she had pursued her own judgment rather than her friend's, in making very light of the indisposition which delayed them at Cleveland; and almost fixing on the time when Marianne would be able to travel.

But the day did not close so auspiciously as it began. Towards the evening Marianne became ill again, growing more heavy, restless, and uncomfortable than before. Her sister, however, still sanguine, was willing to attribute the change to nothing more than the fatigue of having sat up to have her bed made; and carefully administering the cordials prescribed, saw her, with satisfaction, sink at last into a slumber, from which she expected the most beneficial effects. Her sleep, though not so quiet as Elinor wished to see it, lasted a considerable time; and anxious to observe the result of it herself, she resolved to sit with her during the whole of it. Mrs. Jennings, knowing nothing of any change in the patient, went unusually early to bed; her maid, who was one of the principal nurses, was recreating herself in the housekeeper's room, and Elinor remained alone with Marianne.

The repose of the latter became more and more disturbed; and her sister, who watched, with unremitting attention her continual change of posture, and heard the frequent but inarticulate sounds of complaint which passed her lips, was almost wishing to rouse her from so painful a slumber, when Marianne, suddenly awakened by some accidental noise in the house, started hastily up, and, with feverish wildness, cried out,

"Is mama coming?"

"Not yet," cried the other, concealing her terror, and assisting Marianne to lie down again, "but she will be here, I hope, before it is long. It is a great way, you know, from hence to Barton."

"But she must not go round by London," cried Marianne, in the same hurried manner. "I shall never see her, if she goes by London."

Elinor perceived with alarm that she was not quite herself, and, while attempting to soothe her, eagerly felt her pulse. It was lower and quicker than ever! And Marianne, still talking wildly of mama, her alarm increased so rapidly, as to determine her on sending instantly for Mr. Harris, and despatching a messenger to Barton for her mother. To consult with Colonel Brandon on the best means of effecting the latter, was a thought which immediately followed the resolution of its performance; and as soon she had rung up the maid to take her place by her sister, she hastened down to the drawing-room, where she knew he was generally to be found at a much later hour than the present.

It was no time for hesitation. Her fears and her difficulties were immediately before him. Her fears, he had no courage, no confidence to attempt the removal of—he listened to them in silent despondence—but her difficulties were instantly obviated, for with a readiness that seemed to speak the occasion, and the service pre-arranged in his mind, he offered himself as the messenger who should fetch Mrs. Dashwood. Elinor made no resistance that was not easily overcome. She thanked him with brief, though fervent gratitude, and while he went to hurry off his servant with a message to Mr. Harris, and an order for post-horses directly, she wrote a few lines to her mother.

The comfort of such a friend at that moment as Colonel Brandon—or such a companion for her mother, how gratefully was it felt! A companion whose judgment would guide, whose attendance must relieve, and whose friendship might soothe her! As far as the shock of such a summons *could* be lessened to her, his presence, his manners, his assistance, would lessen it.

He, meanwhile, whatever he might feel, acted with all the firmness of a collected mind, made every necessary arrangement with the utmost despatch, and calculated with exactness the time in which she might look for his return. Not a moment was lost in delay of any kind. The horses arrived, even before they were expected, and Colonel Brandon only pressing her hand with a look of solemnity, and a few words spoken too low to reach her ear, hurried into the carriage. It was then about twelve o'clock, and she returned to her sister's apartment to wait for the arrival of the apothecary, and to watch by her the rest of the night. It was a night of almost equal suffering to both. Hour after hour passed away in sleepless pain and delirium on Marianne's side, and in the most cruel anxiety on Elinor's, before Mr. Harris appeared. Her apprehensions once raised, paid by their excess for all her former security; and the servant who sat up with her, for she would not allow Mrs. Jennings to be called, only tortured her more, by hints of what her mistress had always thought.

Marianne's ideas were still, at intervals, fixed incoherently on her mother, and whenever she mentioned her name, it gave a pang to the heart of poor Elinor, who, reproaching herself for having trifled with so many days of illness, and wretched for some immediate relief, fancied that all relief might soon be in vain, that every thing had been delayed too long, and pictured to herself her suffering mother arriving too late to see this darling child, or to see her rational.

She was on the point of sending again for Mr. Harris, or if *he* could not come, for some other advice, when the former—but not till after five o'clock—arrived. His opinion, however, made some little amends for his delay, for though acknowledging a very unexpected and unpleasant alteration in his patient, he would not allow the danger to be material, and talked of the relief which a fresh mode of treatment must procure, with a confidence which, in a lesser degree, was communicated to Elinor. He promised to call again in the course of three or four hours, and left both the patient and her anxious attendant more composed than he had found them.

With strong concern, and with many reproaches for not being called to their aid, did Mrs. Jennings hear in the morning of what had passed. Her former apprehensions, now with greater reason restored, left her no doubt of the event; and though trying to speak comfort to Elinor, her conviction of her sister's danger would not allow her to offer the comfort of hope. Her heart was really grieved. The rapid decay, the early death of a girl so young, so lovely as Marianne, must have struck a less interested person with concern. On Mrs. Jennings's compassion she had other claims. She had been for three months her companion, was still under her care, and she was known to have been greatly injured, and long unhappy. The distress of her sister too, particularly a favourite, was before her—and as for their mother, when Mrs. Jennings considered that Marianne might probably be to *her* what Charlotte was to herself, her sympathy in *her* sufferings was very sincere.

Mr. Harris was punctual in his second visit—but he came to be disappointed in his hopes of what the last would produce. His medicines had failed—the fever was unabated; and Marianne only more quiet—not more herself—remained in a heavy stupor. Elinor, catching all, and more than all, his fears in a moment, proposed to call in further advice. But he judged it unnecessary: he had still something more to try, some more fresh application, of whose success he was as confident as the last, and his visit concluded with encouraging assurances which reached the ear, but could not enter the heart of Miss Dashwood. She was calm, except when she thought of her mother; but she was almost hopeless; and in this state she continued till noon, scarcely stirring from her sister's bed, her thoughts wandering from one image of grief, one suffering friend to another, and her spirits oppressed to the utmost by the conversation of Mrs. Jennings, who scrupled not to attribute the severity and danger of this attack to the many weeks of previous indisposition which Marianne's disappointment had brought on. Elinor felt all the reasonableness of the idea, and it gave fresh misery to her reflections.

About noon, however, she began—but with a caution—a dread of disappointment which for some time kept her silent, even to her friend—to fancy, to hope she could perceive a slight amendment in her sister's pulse—she waited, watched, and examined it again and again—and at last, with an agitation more difficult to bury under exterior calmness, than all her foregoing distress, ventured to communicate her hopes. Mrs. Jennings, though forced, on examination, to acknowledge a temporary revival, tried to keep her young friend from indulging a thought of its continuance—and Elinor, conning over every injunction of distrust, told herself likewise not to hope. But it was too late. Hope had already entered; and feeling all its anxious flutter, she bent over her sister to watch—she hardly knew for what. Half an hour passed away, and the favourable symptom yet blessed her. Others even arose to confirm it. Her breath, her skin, her lips, all flattered Elinor with signs of amendment; and Marianne fixed her eyes on her with a rational, though languid, gaze. Anxiety and hope now oppressed her in equal degrees, and left her no moment of tranquillity till the arrival of Mr. Harris at four o'clock—when his assurances, his felicitations on a recovery in her sister even surpassing his expectation, gave her confidence, comfort, and tears of joy.

Marianne was in every respect materially better, and he declared her entirely out of danger. Mrs. Jennings, perhaps satisfied with the partial justification of her forebodings which had been found in their late alarm, allowed herself to trust in his judgment, and admitted, with unfeigned joy, and soon with unequivocal cheerfulness, the probability of an entire recovery.

Elinor could not be cheerful. Her joy was of a different kind, and led to any thing rather than to gaiety. Marianne restored to life, health, friends, and to her doting mother, was an idea to fill her heart with sensations of exquisite comfort, and expand it in fervent gratitude—but it lead to no outward demonstrations of joy, no words, no smiles. All within Elinor's breast was satisfaction, silent and strong.

She continued by the side of her sister, with little intermission the whole afternoon, calming every fear, satisfying every inquiry of her enfeebled spirits, supplying every succour, and watching almost every look and every breath. The possibility of a relapse would of course, in some moments, occur to remind her of what anxiety was—but when she saw, on her frequent and minute examination, that every symptom of recovery continued, and saw Marianne at six o'clock sink into a quiet, steady, and to all appearance comfortable, sleep, she silenced every doubt.

The time was now drawing on, when Colonel Brandon might be expected back. At ten o'clock, she trusted, or at least not much later her mother would be relieved from the dreadful suspense in which she must now be travelling towards them. The Colonel, too! Perhaps scarcely less an object of pity! Oh! How slow was the progress of time which yet kept them in ignorance!

At seven o'clock, leaving Marianne still sweetly asleep, she joined Mrs. Jennings in the drawing-room to tea. Of breakfast she had been kept by her fears, and of dinner by their sudden reverse, from eating much—and the present refreshment, therefore, with such feelings of content as she brought to it, was particularly welcome. Mrs. Jennings would have persuaded her, at its conclusion, to take some rest before her mother's arrival, and allow *her* to take her place by Marianne; but Elinor had no sense of fatigue, no capability of sleep at that moment about her, and she was not to be kept away from her sister an unnecessary instant. Mrs. Jennings therefore attending her up stairs into the sick chamber, to satisfy herself that all continued right, left her there again to her charge and her thoughts, and retired to her own room to write letters and sleep.

The night was cold and stormy. The wind roared round the house, and the rain beat against the windows; but Elinor, all happiness within, regarded it not. Marianne slept through every blast; and the travellers—they had a rich reward in store, for every present inconvenience.

The clock struck eight. Had it been ten, Elinor would have been convinced that at that moment she heard a carriage driving up to the house; and so strong was the persuasion that she *did*, in spite of the *almost* impossibility of their being already come, that she moved into the adjoining dressing-closet and opened a window shutter, to be satisfied of the truth. She instantly saw that her ears had not deceived her. The flaring lamps of a carriage were immediately in view. By their uncertain light she thought she could discern it to be drawn by four horses; and this, while it told the excess of her poor mother's alarm, gave some explanation to such unexpected rapidity.

Never in her life had Elinor found it so difficult to be calm, as at that moment. The knowledge of what her mother must be feeling as the carriage stopt at the door—of her doubt—her dread—perhaps her despair! And of what *she* had to tell! With such knowledge it was impossible to be calm. All that remained to be done was to be speedy; and, therefore staying only till she could leave Mrs. Jennings's maid with her sister, she hurried down stairs.

The bustle in the vestibule, as she passed along an inner lobby, assured her that they were already in the house. She rushed to the drawing-room, she entered it, and saw only Willoughby.

CHAPTER XLIV

Elinor, starting back with a look of horror at the sight of him, obeyed the first impulse of her heart in turning instantly to quit the room, and her hand was already on the lock, when its action was suspended by his hastily advancing, and saying, in a voice rather of command than supplication,

"Miss Dashwood, for half an hour—for ten minutes—I entreat you to stay."

"No, sir," she replied with firmness, "I shall *not* stay. Your business cannot be with *me*. The servants, I suppose, forgot to tell you that Mr. Palmer was not in the house."

"Had they told me," he cried with vehemence, "that Mr. Palmer and all his relations were at the devil, it would not have turned me from the door. My business is with you, and only you."

"With me!"—in the utmost amazement—"well, sir, be quick—and if you can—less violent."

"Sit down, and I will be both."

She hesitated; she knew not what to do. The possibility of Colonel Brandon's arriving and finding her there, came across her. But she had promised to hear him, and her curiosity no less than her honor was engaged. After a moment's recollection, therefore, concluding that prudence required dispatch, and that her acquiescence would best promote it, she walked silently towards the table, and sat down. He took the opposite chair, and for half a minute not a word was said by either.

"Pray be quick, sir," said Elinor, impatiently—"I have no time to spare."

He was sitting in an attitude of deep meditation, and seemed not to hear her.

"Your sister," said he, with abruptness, a moment afterwards—"is out of danger. I heard it from the servant. God be praised! But is it true? is it really true?"

Elinor would not speak. He repeated the inquiry with yet greater eagerness.

"For God's sake tell me, is she out of danger, or is she not?"

"We hope she is."

He rose up, and walked across the room.

"Had I known as much half an hour ago—But since I *am* here"—speaking with a forced vivacity as he returned to his seat—"what does it signify? For once, Miss Dashwood—it will be the last time, perhaps—let us be cheerful together. I am in a fine mood for gaiety. Tell me honestly"—a deeper glow overspreading his cheeks—"do you think me most a knave or a fool?"

Elinor looked at him with greater astonishment than ever. She began to think that he must be in liquor—the strangeness of such a visit, and of such manners, seemed no otherwise intelligible; and with this impression she immediately rose, saying—

"Mr. Willoughby, I advise you at present to return to Combe—I am not at leisure to remain with you longer. Whatever your business may be with me, will it be better recollected and explained to-morrow."

"I understand you," he replied, with an expressive smile, and a voice perfectly calm; "yes, I am very drunk. A pint of porter with my cold beef at Marlborough was enough to over-set me."

"At Marlborough!" cried Elinor, more and more at a loss to understand what he would be at.

"Yes, I left London this morning at eight o'clock, and the only ten minutes I have spent out of my chaise since that time procured me a nuncheon at Marlborough."

The steadiness of his manner, and the intelligence of his eye as he spoke, convincing Elinor, that whatever other unpardonable folly might bring him to Cleveland, he was not brought there by intoxication, she said, after a moment's recollection—

"Mr. Willoughby, you *ought* to feel, and I certainly DO—that after what has passed—your coming here in this manner, and forcing yourself upon my notice, requires a very particular excuse. What is it, that you mean by it?"

"I mean," said he, with serious energy—"if I can, to make you hate me one degree less than you do *now*. I mean to offer some kind of explanation, some kind of apology, for the past; to open my whole heart to you, and by convincing you, that though I have been always a blockhead, I have not been always a rascal, to obtain something like forgiveness from Ma—from your sister."

"Is this the real reason of your coming?"

"Upon my soul it is," was his answer, with a warmth which brought all the former Willoughby to her remembrance, and in spite of herself made her think him sincere.

"If that is all, you may be satisfied already, for Marianne *does*—she has *long* forgiven you."

"Has she?" he cried, in the same eager tone. "Then she has forgiven me before she ought to have done it. But she shall forgive me again, and on more reasonable grounds. *Now* will you listen to me?"

Elinor bowed her assent.

"I do not know," said he, after a pause of expectation on her side, and thoughtfulness on his own, "how *you* may have accounted for my behaviour to your sister, or what diabolical motive you may have imputed to me. Perhaps you will hardly think the better of me, it is worth the trial however, and you shall hear every thing. When I first became intimate in your family, I had no other intention, no other view in the acquaintance than to pass my time pleasantly while I was obliged to remain in Devonshire, more pleasantly than I had ever done before. Your sister's lovely person and interesting manners could not but please me; and her behaviour to me almost from the first, was of a kind—it is astonishing, when I reflect on what it was, and what *she* was, that my heart should have been so insensible! But at first I must confess, my vanity only was elevated by it. Careless of her happiness, thinking only of my own amusement, giving way to feelings which I had always been too much in the habit of indulging, I endeavoured, by every means in my power, to make myself pleasing to her, without any design of returning her affection."

Miss Dashwood, at this point, turning her eyes on him with the most angry contempt, stopped him, by saying,

"It is hardly worth while, Mr. Willoughby, for you to relate, or for me to listen any longer. Such a beginning as this cannot be followed by any thing. Do not let me be pained by hearing any thing more on the subject."

"I insist on you hearing the whole of it," he replied, "My fortune was never large, and I had always been expensive, always in the habit of associating with people of better income than myself. Every year since my coming of age, or even before, I believe, had added to my debts; and though the death of my old cousin, Mrs. Smith, was to set me free; yet that event being uncertain, and possibly far distant, it had been for some time my intention to re-establish my circumstances by marrying a woman of fortune. To attach myself to your sister, therefore, was not a thing to be thought of—and with a meanness, selfishness, cruelty—which no indignant, no contemptuous look, even of yours, Miss Dashwood, can ever reprobate too much—I was acting in this manner, trying to engage her regard, without a thought of returning it. But one thing may be said for me: even in that horrid state of selfish vanity, I did not know the extent of the injury I meditated, because I did not *then* know what it was to love. But have I ever known it? Well may it be doubted; for, had I really loved, could I have sacrificed my feelings to vanity, to avarice? Or, what is more, could I have sacrificed hers? But I have done it. To avoid a comparative poverty, which her affection and her society would have deprived of all its horrors, I have, by raising myself to affluence, lost every thing that could make it a blessing."

"You did then," said Elinor, a little softened, "believe yourself at one time attached to her?"

"To have resisted such attractions, to have withstood such tenderness! Is there a man on earth who could have done it? Yes, I found myself, by insensible degrees, sincerely fond of her; and the happiest hours of my life were what I spent with her when I felt my intentions were strictly honourable, and my feelings blameless. Even *then*, however, when fully determined on paying my addresses to her, I allowed myself most improperly to put off, from day to day, the moment of doing it, from an unwillingness to enter into an engagement while my circumstances were so greatly embarrassed. I will not reason here—nor will I stop for *you* to expatiate on the absurdity, and the worse than absurdity, of scrupling to engage my faith where my honour was already bound. The event has proved, that I was a cunning fool, providing with great circumspection for a possible opportunity of making myself contemptible and wretched for ever. At last, however, my resolution was taken, and I had determined, as soon as I could engage her alone, to justify the attentions I had so invariably paid her, and openly assure her of an affection which I had already taken such pains to display. But in the interim—in the interim of the very few hours that were to pass, before I could have an opportunity of speaking with her in private—a circumstance occurred—an unlucky circumstance, to ruin all my resolution, and with it all my comfort. A discovery took place"—here he hesitated and looked down. "Mrs. Smith had somehow or other been informed, I imagine by some distant relation, whose interest it was to deprive me of her favour, of an affair, a connection—but I need not explain myself farther," he added, looking at her with an heightened colour and an enquiring eye—"your particular intimacy—you have probably heard the whole story long ago."

"I have," returned Elinor, colouring likewise, and hardening her heart anew against any compassion for him, "I have heard it all. And how you will explain away any part of your guilt in that dreadful business, I confess is beyond my comprehension."

"Remember," cried Willoughby, "from whom you received the account. Could it be an impartial one? I acknowledge that her situation and her character ought to have been respected by me. I do not mean to justify myself, but at the same time cannot leave you to suppose that I have nothing to urge—that because she was injured she was irreproachable, and because I was a libertine, *she* must be a saint. If the violence of her passions, the weakness of her understanding—I do not mean, however, to defend myself. Her affection for me deserved better treatment, and I often, with great self-reproach, recall the tenderness which, for a very short time, had the power of creating any return. I wish—I heartily wish it had never been. But I have injured more than herself; and I have injured one, whose affection for me—(may I say it?) was scarcely less warm than hers; and whose mind—Oh! How infinitely superior!"—

"Your indifference, however, towards that unfortunate girl—I must say it, unpleasant to me as the discussion of such a subject may well be—your indifference is no apology for your cruel neglect of her. Do not think yourself excused by any weakness, any natural defect of understanding on her side, in the wanton cruelty so evident on yours. You must have known, that while you were enjoying yourself in Devonshire pursuing fresh schemes, always gay, always happy, she was reduced to the extremest indigence."

"But, upon my soul, I did *not* know it," he warmly replied; "I did not recollect that I had omitted to give her my direction; and common sense might have told her how to find it out."

"Well, sir, and what said Mrs. Smith?"

"She taxed me with the offence at once, and my confusion may be guessed. The purity of her life, the formality of her notions, her ignorance of the world—everything was against me. The matter itself

I could not deny, and vain was every endeavour to soften it. She was previously disposed, I believe, to doubt the morality of my conduct in general, and was moreover discontented with the very little attention, the very little portion of my time that I had bestowed on her, in my present visit. In short, it ended in a total breach. By one measure I might have saved myself. In the height of her morality, good woman! she offered to forgive the past, if I would marry Eliza. That could not be—and I was formally dismissed from her favour and her house. The night following this affair—I was to go the next morning—was spent by me in deliberating on what my future conduct should be. The struggle was great—but it ended too soon. My affection for Marianne, my thorough conviction of her attachment to me—it was all insufficient to outweigh that dread of poverty, or get the better of those false ideas of the necessity of riches, which I was naturally inclined to feel, and expensive society had increased. I had reason to believe myself secure of my present wife, if I chose to address her, and I persuaded myself to think that nothing else in common prudence remained for me to do. A heavy scene however awaited me, before I could leave Devonshire—I was engaged to dine with you on that very day; some apology was therefore necessary for my breaking this engagement. But whether I should write this apology, or deliver it in person, was a point of long debate. To see Marianne, I felt, would be dreadful, and I even doubted whether I could see her again, and keep to my resolution. In that point, however, I undervalued my own magnanimity, as the event declared; for I went, I saw her, and saw her miserable, and left her miserable—and left her hoping never to see her again."

"Why did you call, Mr. Willoughby?" said Elinor, reproachfully; "a note would have answered every purpose. Why was it necessary to call?"

"It was necessary to my own pride. I could not bear to leave the country in a manner that might lead you, or the rest of the neighbourhood, to suspect any part of what had really passed between Mrs. Smith and myself—and I resolved therefore on calling at the cottage, in my way to Honiton. The sight of your dear sister, however, was really dreadful; and, to heighten the matter, I found her alone. You were all gone I do not know where. I had left her only the evening before, so fully, so firmly resolved within my self on doing right! A few hours were to have engaged her to me forever; and I remember how happy, how gay were my spirits, as I walked from the cottage to Allenham, satisfied with myself, delighted with every body! But in this, our last interview of friendship, I approached her with a sense of guilt that almost took from me the power of dissembling. Her sorrow, her disappointment, her deep regret, when I told her that I was obliged to leave Devonshire so immediately—I never shall forget it—united too with such reliance, such confidence in me! Oh, God! What a hard-hearted rascal I was!"

They were both silent for a few moments. Elinor first spoke.

"Did you tell her that you should soon return?"

"I do not know what I told her," he replied, impatiently; "less than was due to the past, beyond a doubt, and in all likelihood much more than was justified by the future. I cannot think of it. It won't do. Then came your dear mother to torture me farther, with all her kindness and confidence. Thank Heaven! It *did* torture me. I was miserable. Miss Dashwood, you cannot have an idea of the comfort it gives me to look back on my own misery. I owe such a grudge to myself for the stupid, rascally folly of my own heart, that all my past sufferings under it are only triumph and exultation to me now. Well, I went, left all that I loved, and went to those to whom, at best, I was only indifferent. My journey to town—travelling with my own horses, and therefore so tediously—no creature to speak to—my own reflections so cheerful—when I looked forward every thing so inviting! When I looked back at Barton, the picture so soothing! Oh, it was a blessed journey!"

He stopped.

"Well, sir," said Elinor, who, though pitying him, grew impatient for his departure, "and this is all?"

"Ah! No, have you forgot what passed in town? That infamous letter—did she shew it you?"

"Yes, I saw every note that passed."

"When the first of hers reached me (as it immediately did, for I was in town the whole time), what I felt is—in the common phrase, not to be expressed; in a more simple one—perhaps too simple to raise any emotion—my feelings were very, very painful. Every line, every word was—in the hackneyed metaphor which their dear writer, were she here, would forbid—a dagger to my heart. To know that Marianne was in town was—in the same language—a thunderbolt. Thunderbolts and daggers! What a reproof would she have given me! Her taste, her opinions—I believe they are better known to me than my own, and I am sure they are dearer."

Elinor's heart, which had undergone many changes in the course of this extraordinary conversation, was now softened again—yet she felt it her duty to check such ideas in her companion as the last.

"This is not right, Mr. Willoughby. Remember that you are married. Relate only what in your conscience you think necessary for me to hear."

"Marianne's note, by assuring me that I was still as dear to her as in former days, that in spite of the many, many weeks we had been separated, she was as constant in her own feelings, and as full of faith in the constancy of mine as ever, awakened all my remorse. I say awakened, because time and London, business and dissipation, had in some measure quieted it, and I had been growing a fine hardened villain, fancying myself indifferent to her, and chusing to fancy that she too must have become indifferent to me; talking to myself of our past attachment as a mere idle, trifling business, shrugging up my shoulders in proof of its being so, and silencing every reproach, overcoming every scruple, by secretly saying now and then, 'I shall be heartily glad to hear she is well married.' But this note made me know myself better. I felt that she was infinitely dearer to me than any other woman in the world, and that I was using her infamously. But every thing was then just settled between Miss Grey and me. To retreat was impossible. All that I had to do, was to avoid you both. I sent no answer to Marianne, intending by that to preserve myself from her farther notice; and for some time I was even determined not to call in Berkeley Street—but at last, judging it wiser to affect the air of a cool, common acquaintance than anything else, I watched you all safely out of the house one morning, and left my name."

"Watched us out of the house!"

"Even so. You would be surprised to hear how often I watched you, how often I was on the point of falling in with you. I have entered many a shop to avoid your sight, as the carriage drove by. Lodging as I did in Bond Street, there was hardly a day in which I did not catch a glimpse of one or other of you; and nothing but the most constant watchfulness on my side, a most invariably prevailing desire to keep out of your sight, could have separated us so long. I avoided the Middletons as much as possible, as well as everybody else who was likely to prove an acquaintance in common. Not aware of their being in town, however, I blundered on Sir John, I believe, the first day of his coming, and the day after I had called at Mrs. Jennings's. He asked me to a party, a dance at his house in the evening. Had he *not* told me as an inducement that you and your sister were to be there, I should have felt it too certain a thing, to trust myself near him. The next morning brought another short note from Marianne—still affectionate, open, artless, confiding—everything that could make *my* conduct most hateful. I could not answer it. I tried—but could not frame a sentence. But I thought of her, I believe, every moment of the day. If you *can* pity me, Miss Dashwood, pity my situation as it was *then*. With my head and heart full of your sister, I was forced to play the happy lover to another woman! Those three or four weeks were worse than all. Well, at last, as I need not tell you, you were forced on me; and what a sweet figure I cut! What an evening of agony it was! Marianne, beautiful as an angel on one side, calling me Willoughby in such a tone! Oh, God! Holding out her hand to me, asking me for an explanation, with those bewitching eyes fixed in such speaking solicitude on my face! And Sophia, jealous as the devil on the other hand, looking all that was—well, it does not signify; it is over now. Such an evening! I ran away from you all as soon as I could; but not before I had seen Marianne's sweet face as white as death. *That* was the last, last look I ever had of her—the last manner in which she appeared to me. It was a horrid sight! Yet when I thought of her to-day as really dying, it was a kind of comfort to me to imagine that I knew exactly how she would appear to those, who saw her last in this world. She was before me, constantly before me, as I travelled, in the same look and hue."

A short pause of mutual thoughtfulness succeeded. Willoughby first rousing himself, broke it thus:

"Well, let me make haste and be gone. Your sister is certainly better, certainly out of danger?"

"We are assured of it."

"Your poor mother, too! Doting on Marianne."

"But the letter, Mr. Willoughby, your own letter; have you any thing to say about that?"

"Yes, yes, *that* in particular. Your sister wrote to me again, you know, the very next morning. You saw what she said. I was breakfasting at the Ellisons, and her letter, with some others, was brought to me there from my lodgings. It happened to catch Sophia's eye before it caught mine—and its size, the elegance of the paper, the hand-writing altogether, immediately gave her a suspicion. Some vague report had reached her before of my attachment to some young lady in Devonshire, and what had passed within her observation the preceding evening had marked who the young lady was, and made her more jealous than ever. Affecting that air of playfulness, therefore, which is delightful in a woman one loves, she opened the letter directly, and read its contents. She was well paid for her impudence. She read what made her wretched. Her wretchedness I could have borne, but her passion—her malice—at all events it must be appeased. And, in short—what do you think of my wife's style of letter-writing? Delicate—tender—truly feminine—was it not?"

"Your wife! The letter was in your own hand-writing."

"Yes, but I had only the credit of servilely copying such sentences as I was ashamed to put my name to. The original was all her own—her own happy thoughts and gentle diction. But what could I do! We were engaged, every thing in preparation, the day almost fixed—But I am talking like a fool. Preparation day! In honest words, her money was necessary to me, and in a situation like mine, anything was to be done to prevent a rupture. And after all, what did it signify to my character in the opinion of Marianne and her friends, in what language my answer was couched? It must have been only to one end. My business was to declare myself a scoundrel, and whether I did it with a bow or a bluster was of little importance. 'I am ruined for ever in their opinion'—said I to myself—'I am shut out for ever from their society, they already think me an unprincipled fellow, this letter will only make them think me a blackguard one.' Such were my reasonings, as, in a sort of desperate carelessness, I copied my wife's words, and parted with the last relics of Marianne. Her three notes—unluckily they were all in my pocketbook, or I should have denied their existence, and hoarded them for ever—I was forced to put them up, and could not even kiss them. And the lock of hair—that too I had always carried about me in the same pocket-book, which was now searched by Madam with the most ingratiating virulence, the dear lock—all, every memento was torn from me."

"You are very wrong, Mr. Willoughby, very blamable," said Elinor, while her voice, in spite of herself, betrayed her compassionate emotion; "you ought not to speak in this way, either of Mrs. Willoughby or my sister. You had made your own choice. It was not forced on you. Your wife has a claim to your politeness, to your respect, at least. She must be attached to you, or she would not have married you. To treat her with unkindness, to speak of her slightingly is no atonement to Marianne—nor can I suppose it a relief to your own conscience."

"Do not talk to me of my wife," said he with a heavy sigh. "She does not deserve your compassion. She knew I had no regard for her when we married. Well, married we were, and came down to Combe Magna to be happy, and afterwards returned to town to be gay. And now do you pity me, Miss Dashwood? Or have I said all this to no purpose? Am I—be it only one degree—am I less guilty in your opinion than I was before? My intentions were not always wrong. Have I explained away any part of my guilt?"

"Yes, you have certainly removed something—a little. You have proved yourself, on the whole, less faulty than I had believed you. You have proved your heart less wicked, much less wicked. But I hardly know—the misery that you have inflicted—I hardly know what could have made it worse."

"Will you repeat to your sister when she is recovered, what I have been telling you? Let me be a little lightened too in her opinion as well as in yours. You tell me that she has forgiven me already. Let me be able to fancy that a better knowledge of my heart, and of my present feelings, will draw from her a more spontaneous, more natural, more gentle, less dignified, forgiveness. Tell her of my misery and my penitence—tell her that my heart was never inconstant to her, and if you will, that at this moment she is dearer to me than ever."

"I will tell her all that is necessary to what may comparatively be called, your justification. But you have not explained to me the particular reason of your coming now, nor how you heard of her illness."

"Last night, in Drury Lane lobby, I ran against Sir John Middleton, and when he saw who I was—for the first time these two months—he spoke to me. That he had cut me ever since my marriage, I had seen without surprise or resentment. Now, however, his good-natured, honest, stupid soul, full of indignation against me, and concern for your sister, could not resist the temptation of telling me what he knew ought to—though probably he did not think it *would*—vex me horridly. As bluntly as he could speak it, therefore, he told me that Marianne Dashwood was dying of a putrid fever at Cleveland—a letter that morning received from Mrs. Jennings declared her danger most imminent—the Palmers are all gone off in a fright, &c. I was too much shocked to be able to pass myself off as insensible even to the undiscerning Sir John. His heart was softened in seeing mine suffer; and so much of his ill-will was done away, that when we parted, he almost shook me by the hand while he reminded me of an old promise about a pointer puppy. What I felt on hearing that your sister was dying—and dying too, believing me the greatest villain upon earth, scorning, hating me in her latest moments—for how could I tell what horrid projects might not have been imputed? *One* person I was sure would represent me as capable of any thing—what I felt was dreadful! My resolution was soon made, and at eight o'clock this morning I was in my carriage. Now you know all."

Elinor made no answer. Her thoughts were silently fixed on the irreparable injury which too early an independence and its consequent habits of idleness, dissipation, and luxury, had made in the mind, the character, the happiness, of a man who, to every advantage of person and talents, united a disposition naturally open and honest, and a feeling, affectionate temper. The world had made him extravagant and vain—extravagance and vanity had made him cold-hearted and selfish. Vanity, while seeking its own guilty triumph at the expense of another, had involved him in a real attachment, which extravagance, or at least its offspring, necessity, had required to be sacrificed. Each faulty propensity in leading him to evil, had led him likewise to punishment. The attachment, from which against honour, against feeling, against every better interest he had outwardly torn himself, now, when no longer allowable, governed every thought; and the connection, for the sake of which he had, with little scruple, left her sister to misery, was likely to prove a source of unhappiness to himself of a far more incurable nature. From a reverie of this kind she was recalled at the end of some minutes by Willoughby, who, rousing himself from a reverie at least equally painful, started up in preparation for going, and said—

"There is no use in staying here; I must be off."

"Are you going back to town?"

"No—to Combe Magna. I have business there; from thence to town in a day or two. Good bye."

He held out his hand. She could not refuse to give him hers—he pressed it with affection.

"And you *do* think something better of me than you did?" said he, letting it fall, and leaning against the mantel-piece as if forgetting he was to go.

Elinor assured him that she did—that she forgave, pitied, wished him well—was even interested in his happiness—and added some gentle counsel as to the behaviour most likely to promote it. His answer was not very encouraging.

"As to that," said he, "I must rub through the world as well as I can. Domestic happiness is out of the question. If, however, I am allowed to think that you and yours feel an interest in my fate and actions, it may be the means—it may put me on my guard—at least, it may be something to live for. Marianne to be sure is lost to me for ever. Were I even by any blessed chance at liberty again—"

Elinor stopped him with a reproof.

"Well," he replied, "once more good bye. I shall now go away and live in dread of one event."

"What do you mean?"

"Your sister's marriage."

"You are very wrong. She can never be more lost to you than she is now."

"But she will be gained by some one else. And if that some one should be the very he whom, of all others, I could least bear—but I will not stay to rob myself of all your compassionate goodwill, by shewing that where I have most injured I can least forgive. Good bye, God bless you!"

And with these words, he almost ran out of the room.

CHAPTER XLV

Elinor, for some time after he left her, for some time even after the sound of his carriage had died away, remained too much oppressed by a crowd of ideas, widely differing in themselves, but of which sadness was the general result, to think even of her sister.

Willoughby, he, whom only half an hour ago she had abhorred as the most worthless of men, Willoughby, in spite of all his faults, excited a degree of commiseration for the sufferings produced by them, which made her think of him as now separated for ever from her family, with a tenderness, a regret, rather in proportion, as she soon acknowledged within herself—to his wishes than to his merits. She felt that his influence over her mind was heightened by circumstances which ought not in reason to have weight; by that person of uncommon attraction, that open, affectionate, and lively manner which it was no merit to possess; and by that still ardent love for Marianne, which it was not even innocent to indulge. But she felt that it was so, long, long before she could feel his influence less.

When at last she returned to the unconscious Marianne, she found her just awaking, refreshed by so long and sweet a sleep to the extent of her hopes. Elinor's heart was full. The past, the present, the future, Willoughby's visit, Marianne's safety, and her mother's expected arrival, threw her altogether into an agitation of spirits which kept off every indication of fatigue, and made her only fearful of betraying herself to her sister. Short was the time, however, in which that fear could affect her, for within half an hour after Willoughby's leaving the house, she was again called down stairs by the sound of another carriage. Eager to save her mother from every unnecessary moment's horrible suspense, she ran immediately into the hall, and reached the outward door just in time to receive and support her as she entered it.

Mrs. Dashwood, whose terror as they drew near the house had produced almost the conviction of Marianne's being no more, had no voice to inquire after her, no voice even for Elinor; but *she*, waiting neither for salutation nor inquiry, instantly gave the joyful relief—and her mother, catching it with all her usual warmth, was in a moment as much overcome by her happiness, as she had been before by her fears.

She was supported into the drawing-room between her daughter and her friend—and there, shedding tears of joy, though still unable to speak, embraced Elinor again and again, turning from her at intervals to press Colonel Brandon's hand, with a look which spoke at once her gratitude, and her conviction of his sharing with herself in the bliss of the moment. He shared it, however, in a silence even greater than her own.

As soon as Mrs. Dashwood had recovered herself, to see Marianne was her first desire; and in two minutes she was with her beloved child, rendered dearer to her than ever by absence, unhappiness, and danger. Elinor's delight, as she saw what each felt in the meeting, was only checked by an apprehension of its robbing Marianne of farther sleep—but Mrs. Dashwood could be calm, could be even prudent, when the life of a child was at stake, and Marianne, satisfied in knowing her mother was near her, and conscious of being too weak for conversation, submitted readily to the silence and quiet prescribed by every nurse around her. Mrs. Dashwood *would* sit up with her all night; and Elinor, in compliance with her mother's entreaty, went to bed. But the rest, which one night entirely sleepless, and many hours of the most wearing anxiety seemed to make requisite, was kept off by irritation of spirits. Willoughby, "poor Willoughby," as she now allowed herself to call him, was constantly in her thoughts; she would not but have heard his vindication for the world, and now blamed, now acquitted herself for having judged him so harshly before. But her promise of relating it to her sister was invariably painful. She dreaded the performance of it, dreaded what its effect on Marianne might be; doubted whether after such an explanation she could ever be happy with another; and for a moment wished Willoughby a widower. Then, remembering Colonel Brandon, reproved herself, felt that to *his* sufferings and his constancy far more than to his rival's, the reward of her sister was due, and wished any thing rather than Mrs. Willoughby's death.

The shock of Colonel Brandon's errand at Barton had been much softened to Mrs. Dashwood by her own previous alarm; for so great was her uneasiness about Marianne, that she had already determined to set out for Cleveland on that very day, without waiting for any further intelligence, and had so far settled her journey before his arrival, that the Careys were then expected every moment to fetch Margaret away, as her mother was unwilling to take her where there might be infection.

Marianne continued to mend every day, and the brilliant cheerfulness of Mrs. Dashwood's looks and spirits proved her to be, as she repeatedly declared herself, one of the happiest women in the world. Elinor could not hear the declaration, nor witness its proofs without sometimes wondering whether her mother ever recollected Edward. But Mrs. Dashwood, trusting to the temperate account of her own disappointment which Elinor had sent her, was led away by the exuberance of her joy to think only of what would increase it. Marianne was restored to her from a danger in which, as she now began to feel, her own mistaken judgment in encouraging the unfortunate attachment to Willoughby, had contributed to place her—and in her recovery she had yet another source of joy unthought of by Elinor. It was thus imparted to her, as soon as any opportunity of private conference between them occurred.

"At last we are alone. My Elinor, you do not yet know all my happiness. Colonel Brandon loves Marianne. He has told me so himself."

Her daughter, feeling by turns both pleased and pained, surprised and not surprised, was all silent attention.

"You are never like me, dear Elinor, or I should wonder at your composure now. Had I sat down to wish for any possible good to my family, I should have fixed on Colonel Brandon's marrying one of you as the object most desirable. And I believe Marianne will be the most happy with him of the two."

Elinor was half inclined to ask her reason for thinking so, because satisfied that none founded on an impartial consideration of their age, characters, or feelings, could be given—but her mother must always be carried away by her imagination on any interesting subject, and therefore instead of an inquiry, she passed it off with a smile.

"He opened his whole heart to me yesterday as we travelled. It came out quite unawares, quite undesignedly. I, you may well believe, could talk of nothing but my child—he could not conceal his distress; I saw that it equalled my own, and he perhaps, thinking that mere friendship, as the world now goes, would not justify so warm a sympathy—or rather, not thinking at all, I suppose—giving way to irresistible feelings, made me acquainted with his earnest, tender, constant, affection for Marianne. He has loved her, my Elinor, ever since the first moment of seeing her."

Here, however, Elinor perceived, not the language, not the

professions of Colonel Brandon, but the natural embellishments of her mother's active fancy, which fashioned every thing delightful to her as it chose.

"His regard for her, infinitely surpassing anything that Willoughby ever felt or feigned, as much more warm, as more sincere or constant—which ever we are to call it—has subsisted through all the knowledge of dear Marianne's unhappy prepossession for that worthless young man! And without selfishness—without encouraging a hope! Could he have seen her happy with another—such a noble mind! Such openness, such sincerity! No one can be deceived in *him*."

"Colonel Brandon's character," said Elinor, "as an excellent man, is well established."

"I know it is," replied her mother seriously, "or after such a warning, I should be the last to encourage such affection, or even to be pleased by it. But his coming for me as he did, with such active, such ready friendship, is enough to prove him one of the worthiest of men."

"His character, however," answered Elinor, "does not rest on *one* act of kindness, to which his affection for Marianne, were humanity out of the case, would have prompted him. To Mrs. Jennings, to the Middletons, he has been long and intimately known; they equally love and respect him; and even my own knowledge of him, though lately acquired, is very considerable; and so highly do I value and esteem him, that if Marianne can be happy with him, I shall be as ready as yourself to think our connection the greatest blessing to us in the world. What answer did you give him? Did you allow him to hope?"

"Oh! My love, I could not then talk of hope to him or to myself. Marianne might at that moment be dying. But he did not ask for hope or encouragement. His was an involuntary confidence, an irrepressible effusion to a soothing friend—not an application to a parent. Yet after a time I *did* say, for at first I was quite overcome—that if she lived, as I trusted she might, my greatest happiness would lie in promoting their marriage; and since our arrival, since our delightful security, I have repeated it to him more fully, have given him every encouragement in my power. Time, a very little time, I tell him, will do everything—Marianne's heart is not to be wasted for ever on such a man as Willoughby. His own merits must soon secure it."

"To judge from the Colonel's spirits, however, you have not yet made him equally sanguine."

"No. He thinks Marianne's affection too deeply rooted for any change in it under a great length of time, and even supposing her heart again free, is too diffident of himself to believe, that with such a difference of age and disposition he could ever attach her. There, however, he is quite mistaken. His age is only so much beyond hers as to be an advantage, as to make his character and principles fixed—and his disposition, I am well convinced, is exactly the very one to make your sister happy. And his person, his manners too, are all in his favour. My partiality does not blind me; he certainly is not so handsome as Willoughby—but at the same time, there is something much more pleasing in his countenance. There was always a something, if you remember, in Willoughby's eyes at times, which I did not like."

Elinor could *not* remember it—but her mother, without waiting for her assent, continued,

"And his manners, the Colonel's manners are not only more pleasing to me than Willoughby's ever were, but they are of a kind I well know to be more solidly attaching to Marianne. Their gentleness, their genuine attention to other people, and their manly unstudied simplicity is much more accordant with her real disposition, than the liveliness—often artificial, and often ill-timed of the other. I am very sure myself, that had Willoughby turned out as really amiable, as he has proved himself the contrary, Marianne would yet never have been so happy with *him*, as she will be with Colonel Brandon."

She paused. Her daughter could not quite agree with her, but her dissent was not heard, and therefore gave no offence.

"At Delaford, she will be within an easy distance of me," added Mrs. Dashwood, "even if I remain at Barton; and in all probability, for I hear it is a large village, indeed there certainly *must* be some small house or cottage close by, that would suit us quite as well as our present situation."

Poor Elinor! Here was a new scheme for getting her to Delaford! But her spirit was stubborn.

"His fortune too! For at my time of life you know, everybody cares about *that*—and though I neither know nor desire to know, what it really is, I am sure it must be a good one."

Here they were interrupted by the entrance of a third person, and Elinor withdrew to think it all over in private, to wish success to her friend, and yet in wishing it, to feel a pang for Willoughby.

CHAPTER XLVI

Marianne's illness, though weakening in its kind, had not been long enough to make her recovery slow; and with youth, natural strength, and her mother's presence in aid, it proceeded so smoothly as to enable her to remove, within four days after the arrival of the latter, into Mrs. Palmer's dressing-room. When there, at her own particular request, for she was impatient to pour forth her thanks to him for fetching her mother, Colonel Brandon was invited to visit her.

His emotion on entering the room, in seeing her altered looks, and in receiving the pale hand which she immediately held out to him, was such, as, in Elinor's conjecture, must arise from something more than his affection for Marianne, or the consciousness of its being known to others; and she soon discovered in his melancholy eye and varying complexion as he looked at her sister, the probable recurrence of many past scenes of misery to his mind, brought back by that resemblance between Marianne and Eliza already acknowledged, and now strengthened by the hollow eye, the sickly skin, the posture of reclining weakness, and the warm acknowledgment of peculiar obligation.

Mrs. Dashwood, not less watchful of what passed than her daughter, but with a mind very differently influenced, and therefore watching to very different effect, saw nothing in the Colonel's behaviour but what arose from the most simple and self-evident sensations, while in the actions and words of Marianne she persuaded herself to think that something more than gratitude already dawned.

At the end of another day or two, Marianne growing visibly stronger every twelve hours, Mrs. Dashwood, urged equally by her own and her daughter's wishes, began to talk of removing to Barton. On *her* measures depended those of her two friends; Mrs. Jennings could not quit Cleveland during the Dashwoods' stay; and Colonel Brandon was soon brought, by their united request, to consider his own abode there as equally determinate, if not equally indispensable. At his and Mrs. Jennings's united request in return, Mrs. Dashwood was prevailed on to accept the use of his carriage on her journey back, for the better accommodation of her sick child; and the Colonel, at the joint invitation of Mrs. Dashwood and Mrs. Jennings, whose active good-nature made her friendly and hospitable for other people as well as herself, engaged with pleasure to redeem it by a visit at the cottage, in the course of a few weeks.

The day of separation and departure arrived; and Marianne, after taking so particular and lengthened a leave of Mrs. Jennings, one so earnestly grateful, so full of respect and kind wishes as seemed due to her own heart from a secret acknowledgment of past inattention, and bidding Colonel Brandon farewell with a cordiality of a friend, was carefully assisted by him into the carriage, of which he seemed anxious that she should engross at least half. Mrs. Dashwood and Elinor then followed, and the others were left by themselves, to talk of the travellers, and feel their own dullness, till Mrs. Jennings was summoned to her chaise to take comfort in the gossip of her maid for the loss of her two young companions; and Colonel Brandon immediately afterwards took his solitary way to Delaford.

The Dashwoods were two days on the road, and Marianne bore her journey on both, without essential fatigue. Every thing that the most zealous affection, the most solicitous care could do to render her comfortable, was the office of each watchful companion, and each found their reward in her bodily ease, and her calmness of spirits. To Elinor, the observation of the latter was particularly grateful. She, who had seen her week after week so constantly suffering, oppressed by anguish of heart which she had neither courage to speak of, nor fortitude to conceal, now saw with a joy, which no other could equally share, an apparent composure of mind, which, in being the result as she trusted of serious reflection, must eventually lead her to contentment and cheerfulness.

As they approached Barton, indeed, and entered on scenes of which every field and every tree brought some peculiar, some painful recollection, she grew silent and thoughtful, and turning away her face from their notice, sat earnestly gazing through the window. But here, Elinor could neither wonder nor blame; and when she saw, as she assisted Marianne from the carriage, that she had been crying, she saw only an emotion too natural in itself to raise any thing less tender than pity, and in its unobtrusiveness entitled to praise. In the whole of her subsequent manner, she traced the direction of a mind awakened to reasonable exertion; for no sooner had they entered their common sitting-room, than Marianne turned her eyes around it with a look of resolute firmness, as if determined at once to accustom herself to the sight of every object with which the remembrance of Willoughby could be connected. She said little, but every sentence aimed at cheerfulness, and though a sigh sometimes escaped her, it never passed away without the atonement of a smile. After dinner she would try her piano-forte. She went to it; but the music on which her eye first rested was an opera, procured for her by Willoughby, containing some of their favourite duets, and bearing on its outward leaf her own name in his handwriting. That would not do. She shook her head, put the music aside, and after running over the keys for a minute, complained of feebleness in her fingers, and closed the instrument again; declaring however with firmness as she did so, that she should in future practice much.

The next morning produced no abatement in these happy symptoms. On the contrary, with a mind and body alike strengthened by rest, she looked and spoke with more genuine spirit, anticipating the pleasure of Margaret's return, and talking of the dear family party which would then be restored, of their mutual pursuits and cheerful society, as the only happiness worth a wish.

"When the weather is settled, and I have recovered my strength," said she, "we will take long walks together every day. We will walk to the farm at the edge of the down, and see how the children go on; we will walk to Sir John's new plantations at Barton Cross, and the Abbeyland; and we will often go the old ruins of the Priory, and try to trace its foundations as far as we are told they once reached. I know we shall be happy. I know the summer will pass happily away. I mean never to be later in rising than six, and from that time till dinner I shall divide every moment between music and reading. I have formed my plan, and am determined to enter on a course of serious study. Our own library is too well known to me, to be resorted to for anything beyond mere amusement. But there are many works well worth reading at the Park; and there are others of more modern production which I know I can borrow of Colonel Brandon. By reading only six hours a-day, I shall gain in the course of a twelve-month a great deal of instruction which I now feel myself to want."

Elinor honoured her for a plan which originated so nobly as this; though smiling to see the same eager fancy which had been leading her to the extreme of languid indolence and selfish repining, now at work in introducing excess into a scheme of such rational employment and virtuous self-control. Her smile however changed to a sigh when she remembered that promise to Willoughby was yet unfulfilled, and feared she had that to communicate which might again unsettle the mind of Marianne, and ruin at least for a time this fair prospect of busy tranquillity. Willing therefore to delay the evil hour, she resolved to wait till her sister's health were more secure, before she appointed it. But the resolution was made only to be broken.

Marianne had been two or three days at home, before the weather was fine enough for an invalid like herself to venture out. But at last a soft, genial morning appeared; such as might tempt the daughter's wishes and the mother's confidence; and Marianne, leaning on Elinor's arm, was authorised to walk as long as she could without fatigue, in the lane before the house.

The sisters set out at a pace, slow as the feebleness of Marianne in an exercise hitherto untried since her illness required—and they had advanced only so far beyond the house as to admit a full view of the hill, the important hill behind, when pausing with her eyes turned towards it, Marianne calmly said,

"There, exactly there"—pointing with one hand—"on that projecting mound, there I fell; and there I first saw Willoughby."

Her voice sunk with the word, but presently reviving she added,

"I am thankful to find that I can look with so little pain on the spot! Shall we ever talk on that subject, Elinor?" Hesitatingly it was said. "Or will it be wrong? I can talk of it now, I hope, as I ought to do."

Elinor tenderly invited her to be open.

"As for regret," said Marianne, "I have done with that, as far as *he* is concerned. I do not mean to talk to you of what my feelings have been for him, but what they are *now*. At present, if I could be satisfied on one point, if I could be allowed to think that he was not *always* acting a part, not *always* deceiving me—but above all, if I could be assured that he never was so *very* wicked as my fears have sometimes fancied him, since the story of that unfortunate girl"

She stopped. Elinor joyfully treasured her words as she answered,

"If you could be assured of that, you think you should be easy."

"Yes. My peace of mind is doubly involved in it—for not only is it horrible to suspect a person, who has been what *he* has been to *me*, of such designs, but what must it make me appear to myself? What in a situation like mine, but a most shamefully unguarded affection could expose me to—"

"How then," asked her sister, "would you account for his behaviour?"

"I would suppose him, Oh, how gladly would I suppose him, only fickle, very, very fickle."

Elinor said no more. She was debating within herself on the eligibility of beginning her story directly, or postponing it till Marianne were in stronger health—and they crept on for a few minutes in silence.

"I am not wishing him too much good," said Marianne at last with a sigh, "when I wish his secret reflections may be no more unpleasant than my own. He will suffer enough in them."

"Do you compare your conduct with his?"

"No. I compare it with what it ought to have been; I compare it with yours."

"Our situations have borne little resemblance."

"They have borne more than our conduct. Do not, my dearest Elinor, let your kindness defend what I know your judgment must censure. My illness has made me think—it has given me leisure and calmness for serious recollection. Long before I was enough recovered to talk, I was perfectly able to reflect. I considered the past: I saw in my own behaviour, since the beginning of our acquaintance with him last autumn, nothing but a series of imprudence towards myself, and want of kindness to others. I saw that my own feelings had prepared my sufferings, and that my want of fortitude under them had almost led me to the grave. My illness, I well knew, had been entirely brought on by myself by such negligence of my own health, as I had felt even at the time to be wrong. Had I died, it would have been self-destruction. I did not know my danger till the danger was removed; but with such feelings as these reflections gave me, I wonder at my recovery, wonder that the very eagerness of my desire to live, to have time for atonement to my God, and to you all, did not kill me at once. Had I died, in what peculiar misery should I have left you, my nurse, my friend, my sister! You, who had seen all the fretful selfishness of my latter days; who had known all the murmurings of my heart! How should I have lived in *your* remembrance! My mother too! How could you have consoled her! I cannot express my own abhorrence of myself. Whenever I looked towards the past, I saw some duty neglected, or some failing indulged. Everybody seemed injured by me. The kindness, the unceasing kindness of Mrs. Jennings, I had repaid with ungrateful contempt. To the

Middletons, to the Palmers, the Steeles, to every common acquaintance even, I had been insolent and unjust; with a heart hardened against their merits, and a temper irritated by their very attention. To John, to Fanny, yes, even to them, little as they deserve, I had given less than their due. But you, you above all, above my mother, had been wronged by me. I, and only I, knew your heart and its sorrows; yet to what did it influence me? Not to any compassion that could benefit you or myself. Your example was before me; but to what avail? Was I more considerate of you and your comfort? Did I imitate your forbearance, or lessen your restraints, by taking any part in those offices of general complaisance or particular gratitude which you had hitherto been left to discharge alone? No—not less when I knew you to be unhappy, than when I had believed you at ease, did I turn away from every exertion of duty or friendship; scarcely allowing sorrow to exist but with me, regretting only *that* heart which had deserted and wronged me, and leaving you, for whom I professed an unbounded affection, to be miserable for my sake."

Here ceased the rapid flow of her self-reproving spirit; and Elinor, impatient to soothe, though too honest to flatter, gave her instantly that praise and support which her frankness and her contrition so well deserved. Marianne pressed her hand and replied—

"You are very good. The future must be my proof. I have laid down my plan, and if I am capable of adhering to it—my feelings shall be governed and my temper improved. They shall no longer worry others, nor torture myself. I shall now live solely for my family. You, my mother, and Margaret, must henceforth be all the world to me; you will share my affections entirely between you. From you, from my home, I shall never again have the smallest incitement to move; and if I do mix in other society, it will be only to shew that my spirit is humbled, my heart amended, and that I can practise the civilities, the lesser duties of life, with gentleness and forbearance. As for Willoughby—to say that I shall soon or that I shall ever forget him, would be idle. His remembrance can be overcome by no change of circumstances or opinions. But it shall be regulated, it shall be checked by religion, by reason, by constant employment."

She paused—and added in a low voice, "If I could but know *his* heart, everything would become easy."

Elinor, who had now been for some time reflecting on the propriety or impropriety of speedily hazarding her narration, without feeling at all nearer decision than at first, heard this; and perceiving that as reflection did nothing, resolution must do all, soon found herself leading to the fact.

She managed the recital, as she hoped, with address; prepared her anxious listener with caution; related simply and honestly the chief points on which Willoughby grounded his apology; did justice to his repentance, and softened only his protestations of present regard. Marianne said not a word. She trembled, her eyes were fixed on the ground, and her lips became whiter than even sickness had left them. A thousand inquiries sprung up from her heart, but she dared not urge one. She caught every syllable with panting eagerness; her hand, unknowingly to herself, closely pressed her sister's, and tears covered her cheeks.

Elinor, dreading her being tired, led her towards home; and till they reached the door of the cottage, easily conjecturing what her curiosity must be though no question was suffered to speak it, talked of nothing but Willoughby, and their conversation together; and was carefully minute in every particular of speech and look, where minuteness could be safely indulged. As soon as they entered the house, Marianne with a kiss of gratitude and these two words just articulate through her tears, "Tell mama," withdrew from her sister and walked slowly up stairs. Elinor would not attempt to disturb a solitude so reasonable as what she now sought; and with a mind anxiously pre-arranging its result, and a resolution of reviving the subject again, should Marianne fail to do it, she turned into the parlour to fulfill her parting injunction.

CHAPTER XLVII

Mrs. Dashwood did not hear unmoved the vindication of her former favourite. She rejoiced in his being cleared from some part of his imputed guilt—she was sorry for him—she wished him happy. But the feelings of the past could not be recalled. Nothing could restore him with a faith unbroken—a character unblemished, to Marianne. Nothing could do away the knowledge of what the latter had suffered through his means, nor remove the guilt of his conduct towards Eliza. Nothing could replace him, therefore, in her former esteem, nor injure the interests of Colonel Brandon.

Had Mrs. Dashwood, like her daughter, heard Willoughby's story from himself—had she witnessed his distress, and been under the influence of his countenance and his manner, it is probable that her compassion would have been greater. But it was neither in Elinor's power, nor in her wish, to rouse such feelings in another, by her retailed explanation, as had at first been called forth in herself. Reflection had given calmness to her judgment, and sobered her own opinion of Willoughby's deserts—she wished, therefore, to declare only the simple truth, and lay open such facts as were really due to his character, without any embellishment of tenderness to lead the fancy astray.

In the evening, when they were all three together, Marianne began voluntarily to speak of him again—but that it was not without an effort, the restless, unquiet thoughtfulness in which she had been for some time previously sitting—her rising colour, as she spoke, and her unsteady voice, plainly shewed.

"I wish to assure you both," said she, "that I see every thing—as you can desire me to do."

Mrs. Dashwood would have interrupted her instantly with soothing tenderness, had not Elinor, who really wished to hear her sister's unbiased opinion, by an eager sign, engaged her silence. Marianne slowly continued—

"It is a great relief to me—what Elinor told me this morning—I have now heard exactly what I wished to hear." For some moments her voice was lost; but recovering herself, she added, and with greater calmness than before—"I am now perfectly satisfied, I wish for no change. I never could have been happy with him, after knowing, as sooner or later I must have known, all this. I should have had no confidence, no esteem. Nothing could have done it away to my feelings."

"I know it—I know it," cried her mother. "Happy with a man of libertine practices! With one who so injured the peace of the dearest of our friends, and the best of men! No—my Marianne has not a heart to be made happy with such a man! Her conscience, her sensitive conscience, would have felt all that the conscience of her husband ought to have felt."

Marianne sighed, and repeated, "I wish for no change."

"You consider the matter," said Elinor, "exactly as a good mind and a sound understanding must consider it; and I dare say you perceive, as well as myself, not only in this, but in many other circumstances, reason enough to be convinced that your marriage must have involved you in many certain troubles and disappointments, in which you would have been poorly supported by an affection, on his side, much less certain. Had you married, you must have been always poor. His expensiveness is acknowledged even by himself, and his whole conduct declares that self-denial is a word hardly understood by him. His demands and your inexperience together, on a small, very small income, must have brought on distresses which would not be the *less* grievous to you, from having been entirely unknown and unthought of before. *Your* sense of honour and honesty would have led you, I know, when aware of your situation, to attempt all the economy that would appear to you possible: and, perhaps, as long as your frugality retrenched only on your own comfort, you might have been suffered to practice it, but beyond that—and how little could the utmost of your single management do to stop the ruin which had begun before your marriage? Beyond *that*, had you endeavoured, however reasonably, to abridge *his* enjoyments, is it not to be feared, that instead of prevailing on feelings so selfish to consent to it, you would have lessened your own influence on his heart, and made him regret the connection which had involved him in such difficulties?"

Marianne's lips quivered, and she repeated the word "Selfish?" in a tone that implied—"Do you really think him selfish?"

"The whole of his behaviour," replied Elinor, "from the beginning to the end of the affair, has been grounded on selfishness. It was selfishness which first made him sport with your affections; which afterwards, when his own were engaged, made him delay the confession of it, and which finally carried him from Barton. His own enjoyment, or his own ease, was, in every particular, his ruling principle."

"It is very true. *My* happiness never was his object."

"At present," continued Elinor, "he regrets what he has done. And why does he regret it? Because he finds it has not answered towards himself. It has not made him happy. His circumstances are now unembarrassed—he suffers from no evil of that kind; and he thinks only that he has married a woman of a less amiable temper than yourself. But does it follow that had he married you, he would have been happy? The inconveniences would have been different. He would then have suffered under the pecuniary distresses which, because they are removed, he now reckons as nothing. He would have had a wife of whose temper he could make no complaint, but he would have been always necessitous—always poor; and probably would soon have learned to rank the innumerable comforts of a clear estate and good income as of far more importance, even to domestic happiness, than the mere temper of a wife."

"I have not a doubt of it," said Marianne; "and I have nothing to regret—nothing but my own folly."

"Rather say your mother's imprudence, my child," said Mrs. Dashwood; "*she* must be answerable."

Marianne would not let her proceed—and Elinor, satisfied that each felt their own error, wished to avoid any survey of the past that might weaken her sister's spirits; she, therefore, pursuing the first subject, immediately continued—

"One observation may, I think, be fairly drawn from the whole of the story—that all Willoughby's difficulties have arisen from the first offence against virtue, in his behaviour to Eliza Williams. That crime has been the origin of every lesser one, and of all his present discontents."

Marianne assented most feelingly to the remark; and her mother was led by it to an enumeration of Colonel Brandon's injuries and merits, warm as friendship and design could unitedly dictate. Her daughter did not look, however, as if much of it were heard by her.

Elinor, according to her expectation, saw on the two or three following days, that Marianne did not continue to gain strength as she had done; but while her resolution was unsubdued, and she still tried to appear cheerful and easy, her sister could safely trust to the effect of time upon her health.

Margaret returned, and the family were again all restored to each other, again quietly settled at the cottage; and if not pursuing their usual studies with quite so much vigour as when they first came to Barton, at least planning a vigorous prosecution of them in future.

Elinor grew impatient for some tidings of Edward. She had heard nothing of him since her leaving London, nothing new of his plans, nothing certain even of his present abode. Some letters had passed between her and her brother, in consequence of Marianne's illness; and in the first of John's, there had been this sentence: "We know nothing of our unfortunate Edward, and can make no enquiries on so prohibited a subject, but conclude him to be still at Oxford"; which was all the intelligence of Edward afforded her by the correspondence, for his name was not even mentioned in any of the succeeding letters. She was not doomed, however, to be long in ignorance of his measures.

Their man-servant had been sent one morning to Exeter on business; and when, as he waited at table, he had satisfied the inquiries of his mistress as to the event of his errand, this was his voluntary communication—

"I suppose you know, ma'am, that Mr. Ferrars is married."

Marianne gave a violent start, fixed her eyes upon Elinor, saw her turning pale, and fell back in her chair in hysterics. Mrs. Dashwood, whose eyes, as she answered the servant's inquiry, had intuitively taken the same direction, was shocked to perceive by Elinor's countenance how much she really suffered, and a moment afterwards, alike distressed by Marianne's situation, knew not on which child to bestow her principal attention.

The servant, who saw only that Miss Marianne was taken ill, had sense enough to call one of the maids, who, with Mrs. Dashwood's assistance, supported her into the other room. By that time, Marianne was rather better, and her mother leaving her to the care of Margaret and the maid, returned to Elinor, who, though still much disordered, had so far recovered the use of her reason and voice as to be just beginning an inquiry of Thomas, as to the source of his intelligence. Mrs. Dashwood immediately took all that trouble on herself; and Elinor had the benefit of the information without the exertion of seeking it.

"Who told you that Mr. Ferrars was married, Thomas?"

"I see Mr. Ferrars myself, ma'am, this morning in Exeter, and his lady too, Miss Steele as was. They was stopping in a chaise at the door of the New London Inn, as I went there with a message from Sally at the Park to her brother, who is one of the post-boys. I happened to look up as I went by the chaise, and so I see directly it was the youngest Miss Steele; so I took off my hat, and she knew me and called to me, and inquired after you, ma'am, and the young ladies, especially Miss Marianne, and bid me I should give her compliments and Mr. Ferrars's, their best compliments and service, and how sorry they was they had not time to come on and see you, but they was in a great hurry to go forwards, for they was going further down for a little while, but howsever, when they come back, they'd make sure to come and see you."

"But did she tell you she was married, Thomas?"

"Yes, ma'am. She smiled, and said how she had changed her name since she was in these parts. She was always a very affable and free-spoken young lady, and very civil behaved. So, I made free to wish her joy."

"Was Mr. Ferrars in the carriage with her?"

"Yes, ma'am, I just see him leaning back in it, but he did not look up—he never was a gentleman much for talking."

Elinor's heart could easily account for his not putting himself forward; and Mrs. Dashwood probably found the same explanation.

"Was there no one else in the carriage?"

"No, ma'am, only they two."

"Do you know where they came from?"

"They come straight from town, as Miss Lucy—Mrs. Ferrars told me."

"And are they going farther westward?"

"Yes, ma'am—but not to bide long. They will soon be back again, and then they'd be sure and call here."

Mrs. Dashwood now looked at her daughter; but Elinor knew better than to expect them. She recognised the whole of Lucy in the message, and was very confident that Edward would never come near them. She observed in a low voice, to her mother, that they were probably going down to Mr. Pratt's, near Plymouth.

Thomas's intelligence seemed over. Elinor looked as if she wished to hear more.

"Did you see them off, before you came away?"

"No, ma'am—the horses were just coming out, but I could not bide any longer; I was afraid of being late."

"Did Mrs. Ferrars look well?"

"Yes, ma'am, she said how she was very well; and to my mind she was always a very handsome young lady—and she seemed vastly contented."

Mrs. Dashwood could think of no other question, and Thomas and the tablecloth, now alike needless, were soon afterwards dismissed. Marianne had already sent to say, that she should eat nothing more. Mrs. Dashwood's and Elinor's appetites were equally lost, and Margaret might think herself very well off, that with so much uneasiness as both her sisters had lately experienced, so much reason as they had often had to be careless of their meals, she had never been obliged to go without her dinner before.

When the dessert and the wine were arranged, and Mrs. Dashwood and Elinor were left by themselves, they remained long together in a similarity of thoughtfulness and silence. Mrs. Dashwood feared to hazard any remark, and ventured not to offer consolation. She now found that she had erred in relying on Elinor's representation of herself; and justly concluded that everything had been expressly softened at the time, to spare her from an increase of unhappiness, suffering as she then had suffered for Marianne. She found that she had been misled by the careful, the considerate attention of her daughter, to think the attachment, which once she had so well understood, much slighter in reality, than she had been wont to believe, or than it was now proved to be. She feared that under this persuasion she had been unjust, inattentive, nay, almost unkind, to her Elinor—that Marianne's affliction, because more acknowledged, more immediately before her, had too much engrossed her tenderness, and led her away to forget that in Elinor she might have a daughter suffering almost as much, certainly with less self-provocation, and greater fortitude.

CHAPTER XLVIII

Elinor now found the difference between the expectation of an unpleasant event, however certain the mind may be told to consider it, and certainty itself. She now found, that in spite of herself, she had always admitted a hope, while Edward remained single, that something would occur to prevent his marrying Lucy; that some resolution of his own, some mediation of friends, or some more eligible opportunity of establishment for the lady, would arise to assist the happiness of all. But he was now married; and she condemned her heart for the lurking flattery, which so much heightened the pain of the intelligence.

That he should be married soon, before (as she imagined) he could be in orders, and consequently before he could be in possession of the living, surprised her a little at first. But she soon saw how likely it was that Lucy, in her self-provident care, in her haste to secure him, should overlook every thing but the risk of delay. They were married, married in town, and now hastening down to her uncle's. What had Edward felt on being within four miles from Barton, on seeing her mother's servant, on hearing Lucy's message!

They would soon, she supposed, be settled at Delaford. Delaford, that place in which so much conspired to give her an interest; which she wished to be acquainted with, and yet desired to avoid. She saw them in an instant in their parsonage-house; saw in Lucy, the active, contriving manager, uniting at once a desire of smart appearance with the utmost frugality, and ashamed to be suspected of half her economical practices—pursuing her own interest in every thought, courting the favour of Colonel Brandon, of Mrs. Jennings, and of every wealthy friend. In Edward—she knew not what she saw, nor what she wished to see—happy or unhappy, nothing pleased her; she turned away her head from every sketch of him.

Elinor flattered herself that some one of their connections in London would write to them to announce the event, and give farther particulars, but day after day passed off, and brought no letter, no tidings. Though uncertain that any one were to blame, she found fault with every absent friend. They were all thoughtless or indolent.

"When do you write to Colonel Brandon, ma'am?" was an inquiry which sprung from the impatience of her mind to have something going on.

"I wrote to him, my love, last week, and rather expect to see, than to hear from him again. I earnestly pressed his coming to us, and should not be surprised to see him walk in today or tomorrow, or any day."

This was gaining something, something to look forward to. Colonel Brandon must have some information to give.

Scarcely had she so determined it, when the figure of a man on horseback drew her eyes to the window. He stopt at their gate. It was a gentleman, it was Colonel Brandon himself. Now she could hear more; and she trembled in expectation of it. But—it was *not* Colonel Brandon—neither his air—nor his height. Were it possible, she must say it must be Edward. She looked again. He had just dismounted—she could not be mistaken, it *was* Edward. She moved away and sat down. "He comes from Mr. Pratt's purposely to see us. I *will* be calm; I *will* be mistress of myself."

In a moment she perceived that the others were likewise aware of the mistake. She saw her mother and Marianne change colour; saw them look at herself, and whisper a few sentences to each other. She would have given the world to be able to speak—and to make them understand that she hoped no coolness, no slight, would appear in their behaviour to him—but she had no utterance, and was obliged to leave all to their own discretion.

Not a syllable passed aloud. They all waited in silence for the appearance of their visitor. His footsteps were heard along the gravel path; in a moment he was in the passage, and in another he was before them.

His countenance, as he entered the room, was not too happy, even for Elinor. His complexion was white with agitation, and he looked as if fearful of his reception, and conscious that he merited no kind one. Mrs. Dashwood, however, conforming, as she trusted, to the wishes of that daughter, by whom she then meant in the warmth of her heart to be guided in every thing, met with a look of forced complacency, gave him her hand, and wished him joy.

He coloured, and stammered out an unintelligible reply. Elinor's lips had moved with her mother's, and, when the moment of action was over, she wished that she had shaken hands with him too. But it was then too late, and with a countenance meaning to be open, she sat down again and talked of the weather.

Marianne had retreated as much as possible out of sight, to conceal her distress; and Margaret, understanding some part, but not the whole of the case, thought it incumbent on her to be dignified, and therefore took a seat as far from him as she could, and maintained a strict silence.

When Elinor had ceased to rejoice in the dryness of the season, a very awful pause took place. It was put an end to by Mrs. Dashwood, who felt obliged to hope that he had left Mrs. Ferrars very well. In a hurried manner, he replied in the affirmative.

Another pause.

Elinor resolving to exert herself, though fearing the sound of her own voice, now said,

"Is Mrs. Ferrars at Longstaple?"

"At Longstaple!" he replied, with an air of surprise. "No, my mother is in town."

"I meant," said Elinor, taking up some work from the table, "to inquire for Mrs. *Edward* Ferrars."

She dared not look up—but her mother and Marianne both turned their eyes on him. He coloured, seemed perplexed, looked doubtingly, and, after some hesitation, said—

"Perhaps you mean—my brother—you mean Mrs. *Robert* Ferrars."

"Mrs. Robert Ferrars!" was repeated by Marianne and her mother in an accent of the utmost amazement—and though Elinor could not speak, even *her* eyes were fixed on him with the same impatient wonder. He rose from his seat, and walked to the window, apparently from not knowing what to do; took up a pair of scissors that lay there, and while spoiling both them and their sheath by cutting the latter to pieces as he spoke, said, in a hurried voice—

"Perhaps you do not know—you may not have heard that my brother is lately married to—to the youngest—to Miss Lucy Steele."

His words were echoed with unspeakable astonishment by all but Elinor, who sat with her head leaning over her work, in a state of such agitation as made her hardly know where she was.

"Yes," said he, "they were married last week, and are now at Dawlish."

Elinor could sit it no longer. She almost ran out of the room, and as soon as the door was closed, burst into tears of joy, which at first she thought would never cease. Edward, who had till then looked any where, rather than at her, saw her hurry away, and perhaps saw—or even heard, her emotion; for immediately afterwards he fell into a reverie, which no remarks, no inquiries, no affectionate address of Mrs. Dashwood could penetrate, and at last, without saying a word, quitted the room, and walked out towards the village—leaving the others in the greatest astonishment and perplexity on a change in his situation, so wonderful and so sudden—a perplexity which they had no means of lessening but by their own conjectures.

CHAPTER XLIX

Unaccountable, however, as the circumstances of his release might appear to the whole family, it was certain that Edward was free; and to what purpose that freedom would be employed was easily pre-determined by all—for after experiencing the blessings of *one* imprudent engagement, contracted without his mother's consent, as he had already done for more than four years, nothing less could be expected of him in the failure of *that*, than the immediate contraction of another.

His errand at Barton, in fact, was a simple one. It was only to ask Elinor to marry him—and considering that he was not altogether inexperienced in such a question, it might be strange that he should feel so uncomfortable in the present case as he really did, so much in need of encouragement and fresh air.

How soon he had walked himself into the proper resolution, however, how soon an opportunity of exercising it occurred, in what manner he expressed himself, and how he was received, need not be particularly told. This only need be said—that when they all sat down to table at four o'clock, about three hours after his arrival, he had secured his lady, engaged her mother's consent, and was not only in the rapturous profession of the lover, but, in the reality of reason and truth, one of the happiest of men. His situation indeed was more than commonly joyful. He had more than the ordinary triumph of accepted love to swell his heart, and raise his spirits. He was released without any reproach to himself, from an entanglement which had long formed his misery, from a woman whom he had long ceased to love—and elevated at once to that security with another, which he must have thought of almost with despair, as soon as he had learnt to consider it with desire. He was brought, not from doubt or suspense, but from misery to happiness—and the change was openly spoken in such a genuine, flowing, grateful cheerfulness, as his friends had never witnessed in him before.

His heart was now open to Elinor, all its weaknesses, all its errors confessed, and his first boyish attachment to Lucy treated with all the philosophic dignity of twenty-four.

"It was a foolish, idle inclination on my side," said he, "the consequence of ignorance of the world—and want of employment. Had my brother given me some active profession when I was removed at eighteen from the care of Mr. Pratt, I think—nay, I am sure, it would never have happened; for though I left Longstaple with what I thought, at the time, a most unconquerable preference for his niece, yet had I then had any pursuit, any object to engage my time and keep me at a distance from her for a few months, I should very soon have outgrown the fancied attachment, especially by mixing more with the world, as in such case I must have done. But instead of having any thing to do, instead of having any profession chosen for me, or being allowed to chuse any myself, I returned home to be completely idle; and for the first twelvemonth afterwards I had not even the nominal employment, which belonging to the university would have given me; for I was not entered at Oxford till I was nineteen. I had therefore nothing in the world to do, but to fancy myself in love; and as my mother did not make my home in every respect comfortable, as I had no friend, no companion in my brother, and disliked new acquaintance, it was not unnatural for me to be very often at Longstaple, where I always felt myself at home, and was always sure of a welcome; and accordingly I spent the greatest part of my time there from eighteen to nineteen: Lucy appeared everything that was amiable and obliging. She was pretty too—at least I thought so *then*; and I had seen so little of other women, that I could make no comparisons, and see no defects. Considering everything, therefore, I hope, foolish as our engagement was, foolish as it has since in every way been proved, it was not at the time an unnatural or an inexcusable piece of folly."

The change which a few hours had wrought in the minds and the happiness of the Dashwoods, was such—so great—as promised them all, the satisfaction of a sleepless night. Mrs. Dashwood, too happy to be comfortable, knew not how to love Edward, nor praise Elinor enough, how to be enough thankful for his release without wounding his delicacy, nor how at once to give them leisure for unrestrained conversation together, and yet enjoy, as she wished, the sight and society of both.

Marianne could speak *her* happiness only by tears. Comparisons would occur—regrets would arise—and her joy, though sincere as her love for her sister, was of a kind to give her neither spirits nor language.

But Elinor—how are *her* feelings to be described? From the moment of learning that Lucy was married to another, that Edward was free, to the moment of his justifying the hopes which had so instantly followed, she was everything by turns but tranquil. But when the second moment had passed, when she found every doubt, every solicitude removed, compared her situation with what so lately it had been, saw him honourably released from his former engagement, saw him instantly profiting by the release, to address herself and declare an affection as tender, as constant as she had ever supposed it to be, she was oppressed, she was overcome by her own felicity—and happily disposed as is the human mind to be easily familiarized with any change for the better, it required several hours to give sedateness to her spirits, or any degree of tranquillity to her heart.

Edward was now fixed at the cottage at least for a week—for whatever other claims might be made on him, it was impossible that less than a week should be given up to the enjoyment of Elinor's company, or suffice to say half that was to be said of the past, the present, and the future—for though a very few hours spent in the hard labor of incessant talking will despatch more subjects than can really be in common between any two rational creatures, yet with lovers it is different. Between *them* no subject is finished, no communication is even made, till it has been made at least twenty times over.

Lucy's marriage, the unceasing and reasonable wonder among them all, formed of course one of the earliest discussions of the lovers—and Elinor's particular knowledge of each party made it appear to her in every view, as one of the most extraordinary and unaccountable circumstances she had ever heard. How they could be thrown together, and by what attraction Robert could be drawn on to marry a girl, of whose beauty she had herself heard him speak without any admiration, a girl too already engaged to his brother, and on whose account that brother had been thrown off by his family—it was beyond her comprehension to make out. To her own heart it was a delightful affair, to her imagination it was even a ridiculous one, but to her reason, her judgment, it was completely a puzzle.

Edward could only attempt an explanation by supposing, that, perhaps, at first accidentally meeting, the vanity of the one had been so worked on by the flattery of the other, as to lead by degrees to all the rest. Elinor remembered what Robert had told her in Harley Street, of his opinion of what his own mediation in his brother's affairs might have done, if applied to in time. She repeated it to Edward.

"*That* was exactly like Robert," was his immediate observation. "And *that*," he presently added, "might perhaps be in *his* head when the acquaintance between them first began. And Lucy perhaps at first might think only of procuring his good offices in my favour. Other designs might afterward arise."

How long it had been carrying on between them, however, he was equally at a loss with herself to make out; for at Oxford, where he had remained for choice ever since his quitting London, he had had no means of hearing of her but from herself, and her letters to the very last were neither less frequent, nor less affectionate than usual. Not the smallest suspicion, therefore, had ever occurred to prepare him for what followed—and when at last it burst on him in a letter from Lucy herself, he had been for some time, he believed, half stupified between the wonder, the horror, and the joy of such a deliverance. He put the letter into Elinor's hands.

"Dear Sir,

"Being very sure I have long lost your affections, I have thought myself at liberty to bestow my own on another, and have no doubt of being as happy with him as I once used to think I might be with you; but I scorn to accept a hand while the heart was another's. Sincerely wish you happy in your choice, and it shall not be my fault if we are not always good friends, as our near relationship now makes proper. I can safely say I owe you no ill-will, and am sure you will be too generous to do us any ill offices. Your brother has gained my affections entirely, and as we could not live without one another, we are just returned from the altar, and are now on our way to Dawlish for a few weeks, which place your dear brother has great curiosity to see, but thought I would first trouble you with these few lines, and shall always remain,

"Your sincere well-wisher, friend, and sister,

"Lucy Ferrars.

"I have burnt all your letters, and will return your picture the first opportunity. Please to destroy my scrawls—but the ring with my hair you are very welcome to keep."

Elinor read and returned it without any comment.

"I will not ask your opinion of it as a composition," said Edward. "For worlds would not I have had a letter of hers seen by *you* in former days. In a sister it is bad enough, but in a wife! How I have blushed over the pages of her writing! And I believe I may say that since the first half year of our foolish—business—this is the only letter I ever received from her, of which the substance made me any amends for the defect of the style."

"However it may have come about," said Elinor, after a pause, "they are certainly married. And your mother has brought on herself a most appropriate punishment. The independence she settled on Robert, through resentment against you, has put it in his power to make his own choice; and she has actually been bribing one son with a thousand a-year, to do the very deed which she disinherited the other for intending to do. She will hardly be less hurt, I suppose, by Robert's marrying Lucy, than she would have been by your marrying her."

"She will be more hurt by it, for Robert always was her favourite. She will be more hurt by it, and on the same principle will forgive him much sooner."

In what state the affair stood at present between them, Edward knew not, for no communication with any of his family had yet been attempted by him. He had quitted Oxford within four and twenty hours after Lucy's letter arrived, and with only one object before him, the nearest road to Barton, had had no leisure to form any scheme of conduct, with which that road did not hold the most intimate connection. He could do nothing till he were assured of his fate with Miss Dashwood; and by his rapidity in seeking *that* fate, it is to be supposed, in spite of the jealousy with which he had once thought of Colonel Brandon, in spite of the modesty with which he rated his own deserts, and the politeness with which he talked of his doubts, he did not, upon the whole, expect a very cruel reception. It was his business, however, to say that he *did*, and he said it very prettily. What he might say on the subject a twelvemonth after, must be referred to the imagination of husbands and wives.

That Lucy had certainly meant to deceive, to go off with a flourish of malice against him in her message by Thomas, was perfectly clear to Elinor; and Edward himself, now thoroughly enlightened on her character, had no scruple in believing her capable of the utmost meanness of wanton ill-nature. Though his eyes had been long opened, even before his acquaintance with Elinor began, to her ignorance and a want of liberality in some of her opinions—they had been equally imputed, by him, to her want of education; and till her last letter reached him, he had always believed her to be a well-disposed, good-hearted girl, and thoroughly attached to himself. Nothing but such a persuasion could have prevented his putting an end to an engagement, which, long before the discovery of it laid him open to his mother's anger, had been a continual source of disquiet and regret to him.

"I thought it my duty," said he, "independent of my feelings, to give her the option of continuing the engagement or not, when I was renounced by my mother, and stood to all appearance without a friend in the world to assist me. In such a situation as that, where there seemed nothing to tempt the avarice or the vanity of any living creature, how could I suppose, when she so earnestly, so warmly insisted on sharing my fate, whatever it might be, that anything but the most disinterested affection was her inducement? And even now, I cannot comprehend on what motive she acted, or what fancied advantage it could be to her, to be fettered to a man for whom she had not the smallest regard, and who had only two thousand pounds in the world. She could not foresee that Colonel Brandon would give me a living."

"No; but she might suppose that something would occur in your favour; that your own family might in time relent. And at any rate, she lost nothing by continuing the engagement, for she has proved that it fettered neither her inclination nor her actions. The connection was certainly a respectable one, and probably gained her consideration among her friends; and, if nothing more advantageous occurred, it would be better for her to marry *you* than be single."

Edward was, of course, immediately convinced that nothing could have been more natural than Lucy's conduct, nor more self-evident than the motive of it.

Elinor scolded him, harshly as ladies always scold the imprudence which compliments themselves, for having spent so much time with them at Norland, when he must have felt his own inconstancy.

"Your behaviour was certainly very wrong," said she; "because—to say nothing of my own conviction, our relations were all led away by it to fancy and expect *what*, as you were *then* situated, could never be."

He could only plead an ignorance of his own heart, and a mistaken confidence in the force of his engagement.

"I was simple enough to think, that because my *faith* was plighted to another, there could be no danger in my being with you; and that the consciousness of my engagement was to keep my heart as safe and sacred as my honour. I felt that I admired you, but I told myself it was only friendship; and till I began to make comparisons between yourself and Lucy, I did not know how far I was got. After that, I suppose, I *was* wrong in remaining so much in Sussex, and the arguments with which I reconciled myself to the expediency of it, were no better than these: The danger is my own; I am doing no injury to anybody but myself."

Elinor smiled, and shook her head.

Edward heard with pleasure of Colonel Brandon's being expected at the Cottage, as he really wished not only to be better acquainted with him, but to have an opportunity of convincing him that he no longer resented his giving him the living of Delaford—"Which, at present," said he, "after thanks so ungraciously delivered as mine were on the occasion, he must think I have never forgiven him for offering."

Now he felt astonished himself that he had never yet been to the place. But so little interest had he taken in the matter, that he owed all his knowledge of the house, garden, and glebe, extent of the parish, condition of the land, and rate of the tithes, to Elinor herself, who had heard so much of it from Colonel Brandon, and heard it with so much attention, as to be entirely mistress of the subject.

One question after this only remained undecided, between them, one difficulty only was to be overcome. They were brought together by mutual affection, with the warmest approbation of their real friends; their intimate knowledge of each other seemed to make their happiness certain—and they only wanted something to live upon. Edward had two thousand pounds, and Elinor one, which, with Delaford living, was all that they could call their own; for it was impossible that Mrs. Dashwood should advance anything; and they were neither of them quite enough in love to think that three hundred and fifty pounds a-year would supply them with the comforts of life.

Edward was not entirely without hopes of some favourable change in his mother towards him; and on *that* he rested for the residue of their income. But Elinor had no such dependence; for since Edward would still be unable to marry Miss Morton, and his chusing herself had been spoken of in Mrs. Ferrars's flattering language as only a lesser evil than his chusing Lucy Steele, she feared that Robert's offence would serve no other purpose than to enrich Fanny.

About four days after Edward's arrival Colonel Brandon appeared, to complete Mrs. Dashwood's satisfaction, and to give her the dignity of having, for the first time since her living at Barton, more company with her than her house would hold. Edward was allowed to retain the privilege of first comer, and Colonel Brandon therefore walked every night to his old quarters at the Park; from whence he usually returned in the morning, early enough to interrupt the lovers' first *tête-à-tête* before breakfast.

A three weeks' residence at Delaford, where, in his evening hours at least, he had little to do but to calculate the disproportion between thirty-six and seventeen, brought him to Barton in a temper of mind which needed all the improvement in Marianne's looks, all the kindness of her welcome, and all the encouragement of her mother's language, to make it cheerful. Among such friends, however, and such flattery, he did revive. No rumour of Lucy's marriage had yet reached him—he knew nothing of what had passed; and the first hours of his visit were consequently spent in hearing and in wondering. Every thing was explained to him by Mrs. Dashwood, and he found fresh reason to rejoice in what he had done for Mr. Ferrars, since eventually it promoted the interest of Elinor.

It would be needless to say, that the gentlemen advanced in the good opinion of each other, as they advanced in each other's acquaintance, for it could not be otherwise. Their resemblance in good principles and good sense, in disposition and manner of thinking, would probably have been sufficient to unite them in friendship, without any other attraction; but their being in love with two sisters, and two sisters fond of each other, made that mutual regard inevitable and immediate, which might otherwise have waited the effect of time and judgment.

The letters from town, which a few days before would have made every nerve in Elinor's body thrill with transport, now arrived to be read with less emotion than mirth. Mrs. Jennings wrote to tell the wonderful tale, to vent her honest indignation against the jilting girl, and pour forth her compassion towards poor Mr. Edward, who, she was sure, had quite doted upon the worthless hussy, and was now, by all accounts, almost broken-hearted, at Oxford. "I do think," she continued, "nothing was ever carried on so sly; for it was but two days before Lucy called and sat a couple of hours with me. Not a soul suspected anything of the matter, not even Nancy, who, poor soul, came crying to me the day after, in a great fright for fear of Mrs. Ferrars, as well as not knowing how to get to Plymouth; for Lucy it seems borrowed all her money before she went off to be married, on purpose we suppose to make a show with, and poor Nancy had not seven shillings in the world—so I was very glad to give her five guineas to take her down to Exeter, where she thinks of staying three or four weeks with Mrs. Burgess, in hopes, as I tell her, to fall in with the Doctor again. And I must say that Lucy's crossness not to take them along with them in the chaise is worse than all. Poor Mr. Edward! I cannot get him out of my head, but you must send for him to Barton, and Miss Marianne must try to comfort him."

Mr. Dashwood's strains were more solemn. Mrs. Ferrars was the most unfortunate of women—poor Fanny had suffered agonies of sensibility—and he considered the existence of each, under such a blow, with grateful wonder. Robert's offence was unpardonable, but Lucy's was infinitely worse. Neither of them were ever again to be mentioned to Mrs. Ferrars; and even, if she might hereafter be induced to forgive her son, his wife should never be acknowledged as her daughter, nor be permitted to appear in her presence. The secrecy with which everything had been carried on between them, was rationally treated as enormously heightening the crime, because, had any suspicion of it occurred to the others, proper measures would have been taken to prevent the marriage; and he called on Elinor to join with him in regretting that Lucy's engagement with Edward had not rather been fulfilled, than that she should thus be the means of spreading misery farther in the family. He thus continued:

"Mrs. Ferrars has never yet mentioned Edward's name, which does not surprise us; but, to our great astonishment, not a line has been received from him on the occasion. Perhaps, however, he is kept silent by his fear of offending, and I shall, therefore, give him a hint, by a line to Oxford, that his sister and I both think a letter of proper submission from him, addressed perhaps to Fanny, and by her shewn to her mother, might not be taken amiss; for we all know the tenderness of Mrs. Ferrars's heart, and that she wishes for nothing so much as to be on good terms with her children."

This paragraph was of some importance to the prospects and conduct of Edward. It determined him to attempt a reconciliation, though not exactly in the manner pointed out by their brother and sister.

"A letter of proper submission!" repeated he; "would they have me beg my mother's pardon for Robert's ingratitude to *her*, and breach of honour to *me*? I can make no submission—I am grown neither humble nor penitent by what has passed. I am grown very happy; but that would not interest. I know of no submission that *is* proper for me to make."

"You may certainly ask to be forgiven," said Elinor, "because you have offended—and I should think you might *now* venture so far as to profess some concern for having ever formed the engagement which drew on you your mother's anger."

He agreed that he might.

"And when she has forgiven you, perhaps a little humility may be convenient while acknowledging a second engagement, almost as imprudent in *her* eyes as the first."

He had nothing to urge against it, but still resisted the idea of a letter of proper submission; and therefore, to make it easier to him, as he declared a much greater willingness to make mean concessions by word of mouth than on paper, it was resolved that, instead of writing to Fanny, he should go to London, and personally intreat her good offices in his favour. "And if they really *do* interest themselves," said Marianne, in her new character of candour, "in bringing about a reconciliation, I shall think that even John and Fanny are not entirely without merit."

After a visit on Colonel Brandon's side of only three or four days, the two gentlemen quitted Barton together. They were to go immediately to Delaford, that Edward might have some personal knowledge of his future home, and assist his patron and friend in deciding on what improvements were needed to it; and from thence, after staying there a couple of nights, he was to proceed on his journey to town.

CHAPTER L

After a proper resistance on the part of Mrs. Ferrars, just so violent and so steady as to preserve her from that reproach which she always seemed fearful of incurring, the reproach of being too amiable, Edward was admitted to her presence, and pronounced to be again her son.

Her family had of late been exceedingly fluctuating. For many years of her life she had had two sons; but the crime and annihilation of Edward a few weeks ago, had robbed her of one; the similar annihilation of Robert had left her for a fortnight without any; and now, by the resuscitation of Edward, she had one again.

In spite of his being allowed once more to live, however, he did not feel the continuance of his existence secure, till he had revealed his present engagement; for the publication of that circumstance, he feared, might give a sudden turn to his constitution, and carry him off as rapidly as before. With apprehensive caution therefore it was revealed, and he was listened to with unexpected calmness. Mrs. Ferrars at first reasonably endeavoured to dissuade him from marrying Miss Dashwood, by every argument in her power—told him, that in Miss Morton he would have a woman of higher rank and larger fortune—and enforced the assertion, by observing that Miss Morton was the daughter of a nobleman with thirty thousand pounds, while Miss Dashwood was only the daughter of a private gentleman with no more than *three*; but when she found that, though perfectly admitting the truth of her representation, he was by no means inclined to be guided by it, she judged it wisest, from the experience of the past, to submit—and therefore, after such an ungracious delay as she owed to her own dignity, and as served to prevent every suspicion of good-will, she issued her decree of consent to the marriage of Edward and Elinor.

What she would engage to do towards augmenting their income was next to be considered; and here it plainly appeared, that though Edward was now her only son, he was by no means her eldest; for while Robert was inevitably endowed with a thousand pounds a-year, not the smallest objection was made against Edward's taking orders for the sake of two hundred and fifty at the utmost; nor was anything promised either for the present or in future, beyond the ten thousand pounds, which had been given with Fanny.

It was as much, however, as was desired, and more than was expected, by Edward and Elinor; and Mrs. Ferrars herself, by her shuffling excuses, seemed the only person surprised at her not giving more.

With an income quite sufficient to their wants thus secured to them, they had nothing to wait for after Edward was in possession of the living, but the readiness of the house, to which Colonel Brandon, with an eager desire for the accommodation of Elinor, was making considerable improvements; and after waiting some time for their completion, after experiencing, as usual, a thousand disappointments and delays from the unaccountable dilatoriness of the workmen, Elinor, as usual, broke through the first positive resolution of not marrying till every thing was ready, and the ceremony took place in Barton church early in the autumn.

The first month after their marriage was spent with their friend at the Mansion-house; from whence they could superintend the progress of the Parsonage, and direct every thing as they liked on the spot—could chuse papers, project shrubberies, and invent a sweep. Mrs. Jennings's prophecies, though rather jumbled together, were chiefly fulfilled; for she was able to visit Edward and his wife in their Parsonage by Michaelmas, and she found in Elinor and her husband, as she really believed, one of the happiest couples in the world. They had in fact nothing to wish for, but the marriage of Colonel Brandon and Marianne, and rather better pasturage for their cows.

They were visited on their first settling by almost all their relations and friends. Mrs. Ferrars came to inspect the happiness which she was almost ashamed of having authorised; and even the Dashwoods were at the expense of a journey from Sussex to do them honour.

"I will not say that I am disappointed, my dear sister," said John, as they were walking together one morning before the gates of Delaford House, "*that* would be saying too much, for certainly you have been one of the most fortunate young women in the world, as it is. But, I confess, it would give me great pleasure to call Colonel Brandon brother. His property here, his place, his house, everything is in such respectable and excellent condition! And his woods! I have not seen such timber any where in Dorsetshire, as there is now standing in Delaford Hanger! And though, perhaps, Marianne may not seem exactly the person to attract him—yet I think it would altogether be advisable for you to have them now frequently staying with you, for as Colonel Brandon seems a great deal at home, nobody can tell what may happen—for, when people are much thrown together, and see little of anybody else—and it will always be in your power to set her off to advantage, and so forth—in short, you may as well give her a chance—you understand me."

But though Mrs. Ferrars *did* come to see them, and always treated them with the make-believe of decent affection, they were never insulted by her real favour and preference. *That* was due to the folly of Robert, and the cunning of his wife; and it was earned by them before many months had passed away. The selfish sagacity of the latter, which had at first drawn Robert into the scrape, was the principal instrument of his deliverance from it; for her respectful humility, assiduous attentions, and endless flatteries, as soon as the smallest opening was given for their exercise, reconciled Mrs. Ferrars to his choice, and re-established him completely in her favour.

The whole of Lucy's behaviour in the affair, and the prosperity which crowned it, therefore, may be held forth as a most encouraging instance of what an earnest, an unceasing attention to self-interest, however its progress may be apparently obstructed, will do in securing every advantage of fortune, with no other sacrifice than that of time and conscience. When Robert first sought her acquaintance, and privately visited her in Bartlett's Buildings, it was only with the view imputed to him by his brother. He merely meant to persuade her to give up the engagement; and as there could be nothing to overcome but the affection of both, he naturally expected that one or two interviews would settle the matter. In that point, however, and that only, he erred—for though Lucy soon gave him hopes that his eloquence would convince her in *time*, another visit, another conversation, was always wanted to produce this conviction. Some doubts always lingered in her mind when they parted, which could only be removed by another half hour's discourse with himself. His attendance was by this means secured, and the rest followed in course. Instead of talking of Edward, they came gradually to talk only of Robert, a subject on which he had always more to say than on any other, and in which she soon betrayed an interest even equal to his own; and in short, it became speedily evident to both, that he had entirely supplanted his brother. He was proud of his conquest, proud of tricking Edward, and very proud of marrying privately without his mother's consent. What immediately followed is known. They passed some months in great happiness at Dawlish; for she had many relations and old acquaintances to cut—and he drew several plans for magnificent cottages—and from thence returning to town, procured the forgiveness of Mrs. Ferrars, by the simple expedient of asking it, which, at Lucy's instigation, was adopted. The forgiveness, at first, indeed, as was reasonable, comprehended only Robert; and Lucy, who had owed his mother no duty and therefore could have transgressed none, still remained some weeks longer unpardoned. But perseverance in humility of conduct and messages, in self-condemnation for Robert's offence, and gratitude for the unkindness she was treated with, procured her in time the haughty notice which overcame her by its graciousness, and led soon afterwards, by rapid degrees, to the highest state of affection and influence. Lucy became as necessary to Mrs. Ferrars, as either Robert or Fanny; and while Edward was never cordially forgiven for having once intended to marry her, and Elinor, though superior to her in fortune and birth, was spoken of as an intruder, *she* was in everything considered, and always openly acknowledged, to be a favourite child. They settled in town, received very liberal assistance from Mrs. Ferrars, were on the best terms imaginable with the Dashwoods; and setting aside the jealousies and ill-will continually subsisting between Fanny and Lucy, in which their husbands of course took a part, as well as the frequent domestic disagreements between Robert and Lucy themselves, nothing could exceed the harmony in which they all lived together.

What Edward had done to forfeit the right of eldest son, might have puzzled many people to find out; and what Robert had done to succeed to it, might have puzzled them still more. It was an arrangement, however, justified in its effects, if not in its cause; for nothing ever appeared in Robert's style of living or of talking to give a suspicion of his regretting the extent of his income, as either leaving his brother too little, or bringing himself too much—and if Edward might be judged from the ready discharge of his duties in every particular, from an increasing attachment to his wife and his home, and from the regular cheerfulness of his spirits, he might be supposed no less contented with his lot, no less free from every wish of an exchange.

Elinor's marriage divided her as little from her family as could well be contrived, without rendering the cottage at Barton entirely useless, for her mother and sisters spent much more than half their time with her. Mrs. Dashwood was acting on motives of policy as well as pleasure in the frequency of her visits at Delaford; for her wish of bringing Marianne and Colonel Brandon together was hardly less earnest, though rather more liberal than what John had expressed. It was now her darling object. Precious as was the company of her daughter to her, she desired nothing so much as to give up its constant enjoyment to her valued friend; and to see Marianne settled at the mansion-house was equally the wish of Edward and Elinor. They each felt his sorrows, and their own obligations, and Marianne, by general consent, was to be the reward of all.

With such a confederacy against her—with a knowledge so intimate of his goodness—with a conviction of his fond attachment to herself, which at last, though long after it was observable to everybody else—burst on her—what could she do?

Marianne Dashwood was born to an extraordinary fate. She was born to discover the falsehood of her own opinions, and to counteract, by her conduct, her most favourite maxims. She was born to overcome an affection formed so late in life as at seventeen, and with no sentiment superior to strong esteem and lively friendship, voluntarily to give her hand to another! And *that* other, a man who had suffered no less than herself under the event of a former attachment, whom, two years before, she had considered too old to be married, and who still sought the constitutional safeguard of a flannel waistcoat!

But so it was. Instead of falling a sacrifice to an irresistible passion, as once she had fondly flattered herself with expecting, instead of remaining even for ever with her mother, and finding her only pleasures in retirement and study, as afterwards in her more calm and sober judgment she had determined on, she found herself at nineteen, submitting to new attachments, entering on new duties, placed in a new home, a wife, the mistress of a family, and the patroness of a village.

Colonel Brandon was now as happy, as all those who best loved him, believed he deserved to be—in Marianne he was consoled for every past affliction—her regard and her society restored his mind to animation, and his spirits to cheerfulness; and that Marianne found her own happiness in forming his, was equally the persuasion and delight of each observing friend. Marianne could never love by halves; and her whole heart became, in time, as much devoted to her husband, as it had once been to Willoughby.

Willoughby could not hear of her marriage without a pang; and his punishment was soon afterwards complete in the voluntary forgiveness of Mrs. Smith, who, by stating his marriage with a woman of character, as the source of her clemency, gave him reason for believing that had he behaved with honour towards Marianne, he might at once have been happy and rich. That his repentance of misconduct, which thus brought its own punishment, was sincere, need not be doubted—nor that he long thought of Colonel Brandon with envy, and of Marianne with regret. But that he was for ever inconsolable, that he fled from society, or contracted an habitual gloom of temper, or died of a broken heart, must not be depended on—for he did neither. He lived to exert, and frequently to enjoy himself. His wife was not always out of humour, nor his home always uncomfortable; and in his breed of horses and dogs, and in sporting of every kind, he found no inconsiderable degree of domestic felicity.

For Marianne, however—in spite of his incivility in surviving her loss—he always retained that decided regard which interested him in every thing that befell her, and made her his secret standard of perfection in woman—and many a rising beauty would be slighted by him in after-days as bearing no comparison with Mrs. Brandon.

Mrs. Dashwood was prudent enough to remain at the cottage, without attempting a removal to Delaford; and fortunately for Sir John and Mrs. Jennings, when Marianne was taken from them, Margaret had reached an age highly suitable for dancing, and not very ineligible for being supposed to have a lover.

Between Barton and Delaford, there was that constant communication which strong family affection would naturally dictate—and among the merits and the happiness of Elinor and Marianne, let it not be ranked as the least considerable, that though sisters, and living almost within sight of each other, they could live without disagreement between themselves, or producing coolness between their husbands.

THE END

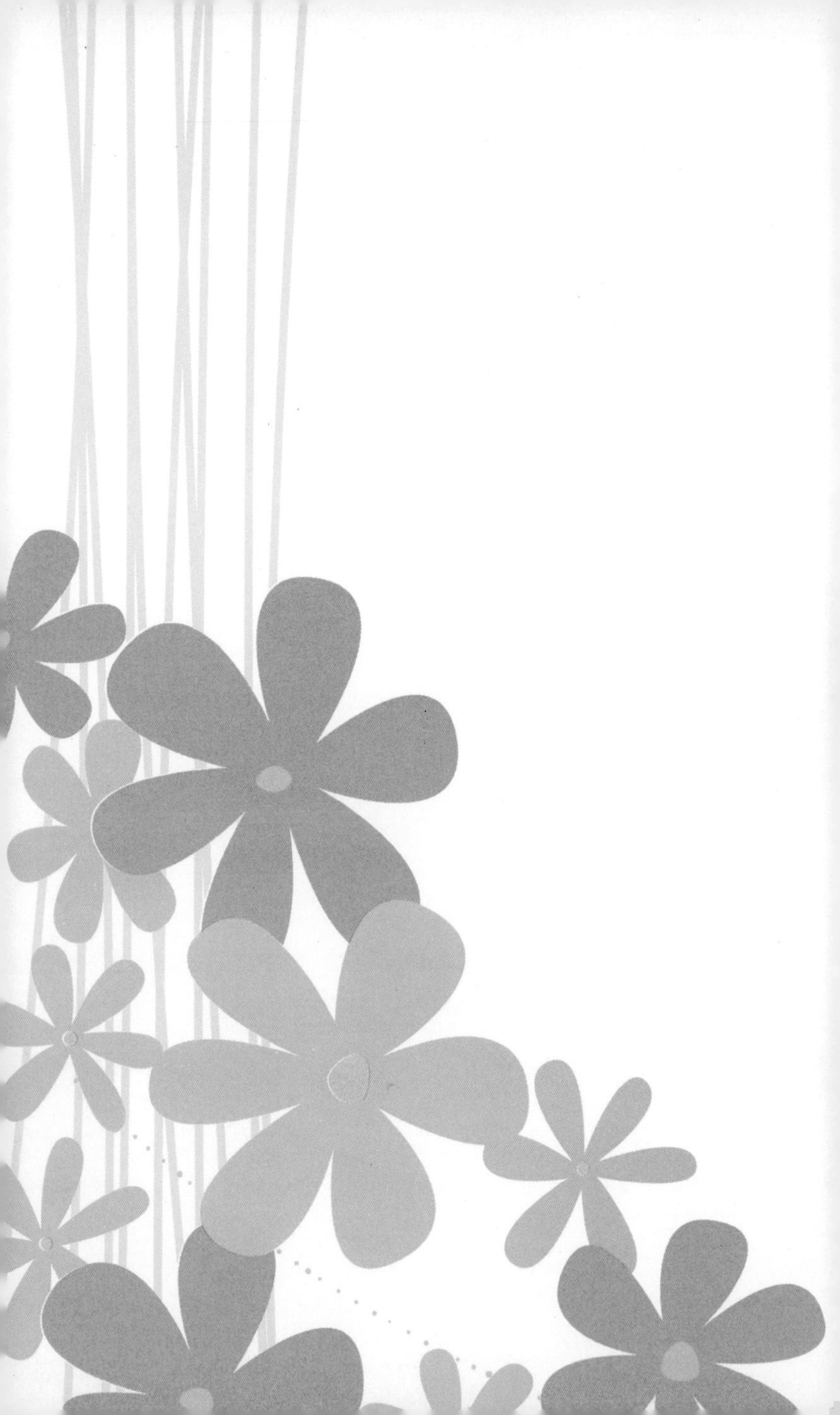

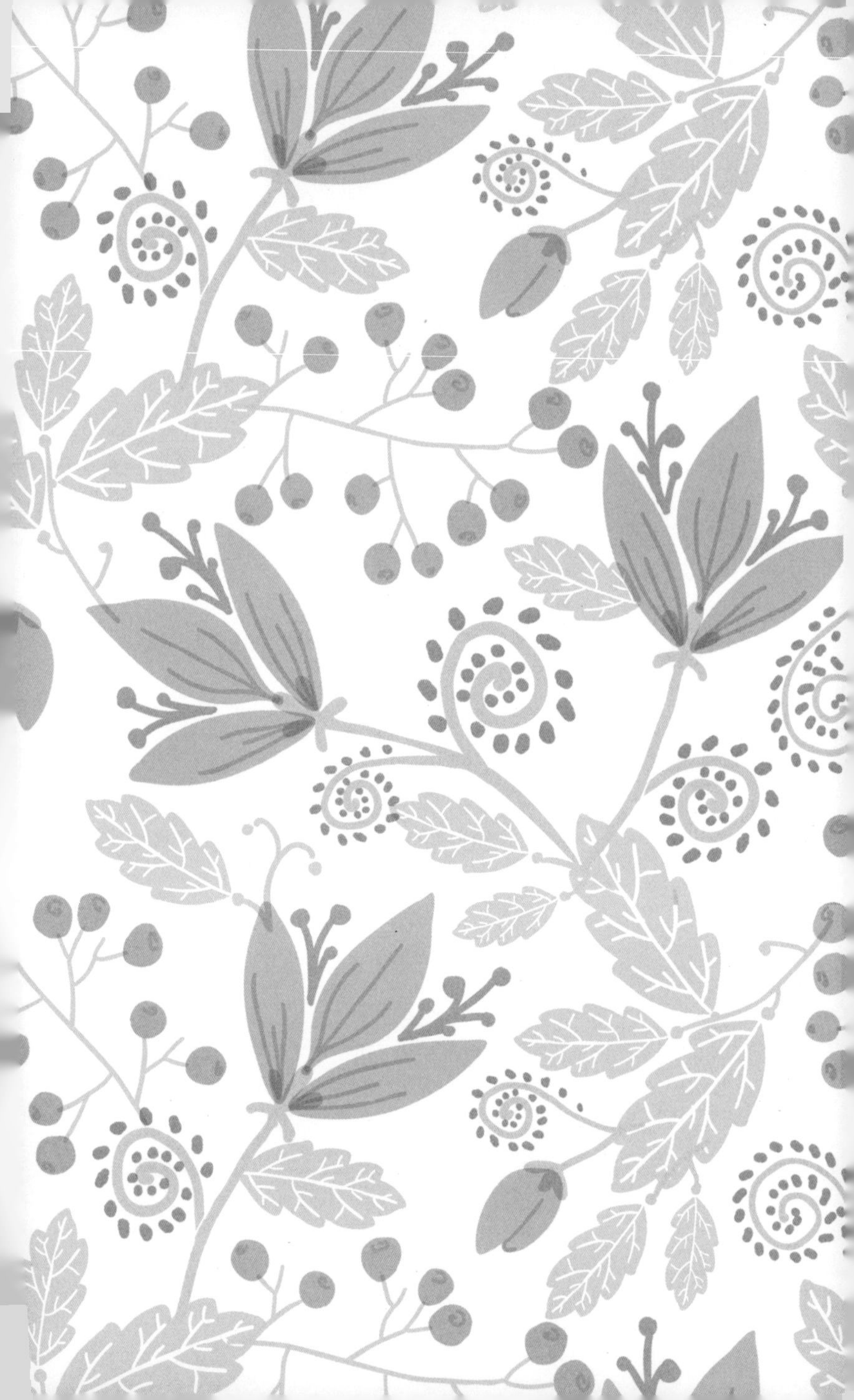

Jane Eyre

Jane Eyre

Charlotte Brontë

CC

CANTERBURY CLASSICS
San Diego

All correspondence concerning the content of this book should be addressed to: Canterbury Classics
10350 Barnes Canyon Road, Suite 100
San Diego, CA 92121

Publisher: Peter Norton
Publishing Team: Lori Asbury, Ana Parker
Director Editorial and Production: JoAnn Padgett
Editor: Melinda Allman

Library of Congress Cataloging-in-Publication Data

Brontë, Charlotte, 1816-1855.
Jane Eyre / Charlotte Bronte.
p. cm.
ISBN-13: 978-1-60710-553-4
ISBN-10: 1-60710-553-5
1. Governesses--England--Fiction. 2. Young women--England--Fiction.

PR4167.J3 2012
823'.8--dc23

2011047467

PRINTED IN CHINA

4 5 6 7 8 19 18 17 16 15

PREFACE

A preface to the first edition of *Jane Eyre* being unnecessary, I gave none: this second edition demands a few words both of acknowledgment and miscellaneous remark.

My thanks are due in three quarters.

To the Public, for the indulgent ear it has inclined to a plain tale with few pretensions.

To the Press, for the fair field its honest suffrage has opened to an obscure aspirant.

To my Publishers, for the aid their tact, their energy, their practical sense and frank liberality have afforded an unknown and unrecommended Author.

The Press and the Public are but vague personifications for me, and I must thank them in vague terms; but my Publishers are definite: so are certain generous critics who have encouraged me as only large-hearted and high-minded men know how to encourage a struggling stranger; to them, *i.e.*, to my Publishers and the select Reviewers, I say cordially, Gentlemen, I thank you from my heart.

Having thus acknowledged what I owe those who have aided and approved me, I turn to another class; a small one, so far as I know, but not, therefore, to be overlooked. I mean the timorous or carping few who doubt the tendency of such books as *Jane Eyre*: in whose eyes whatever is unusual is wrong; whose ears detect in each protest against bigotry—that parent of crime—an insult to piety, that regent of God on earth. I would suggest to such doubters certain obvious distinctions; I would remind them of certain simple truths.

Conventionality is not morality. Self-righteousness is not religion. To attack the first is not to assail the last. To pluck the mask from the face of the Pharisee, is not to lift an impious hand to the Crown of Thorns.

These things and deeds are diametrically opposed: they are as distinct as is vice from virtue. Men too often confound them: they should not be confounded: appearance should not be mistaken for truth; narrow human doctrines, that only tend to elate and magnify a few, should not be substituted for the world-redeeming creed of Christ. There is—I repeat it—a difference; and it is a good, and not a bad action to mark broadly and clearly the line of separation between them.

The world may not like to see these ideas dissevered, for it has been accustomed to blend them; finding it convenient to make external show pass for sterling worth—to let white-washed walls vouch for clean shrines. It may hate him who dares to scrutinise and expose—to rase the gilding, and show base metal under it—to penetrate the sepulchre, and reveal charnel relics: but hate as it will, it is indebted to him.

Ahab did not like Micaiah, because he never prophesied good concerning him, but evil; probably he liked the sycophant son of Chenaanah better; yet might Ahab have escaped a bloody death, had he but stopped his ears to flattery, and opened them to faithful counsel.

There is a man in our own days whose words are not framed to tickle delicate ears: who, to my thinking, comes before the great ones of society, much as the son of Imlah came before the throned Kings of Judah and Israel; and who speaks truth as deep, with a power as prophet-like and as vital—a mien as dauntless and as daring. Is the satirist of *Vanity Fair* admired in high places? I cannot tell; but I think if some of those amongst whom he hurls the Greek fire of his sarcasm, and over whom he flashes the levin-brand of his denunciation, were to take his warnings in time—they or their seed might yet escape a fatal Ramoth-Gilead.

Why have I alluded to this man? I have alluded to him, Reader, because I think I see in him an intellect profounder and more unique than his contemporaries have yet recognised; because I regard him as the first social regenerator of the day—as the very master of that working corps who would restore to rectitude the warped system of things; because I think no commentator on his writings has yet found the comparison that suits him, the terms which rightly characterise his talent. They say he is like Fielding: they talk of his wit, humour, comic powers. He resembles Fielding as an eagle does a vulture: Fielding could stoop on carrion, but Thackeray never does. His wit is bright, his humour attractive, but both bear the same relation to his serious genius that the mere lambent sheet-lightning playing under the edge of the summer-cloud does to the electric death-spark hid in its womb. Finally, I have alluded to Mr. Thackeray, because to him—if he will accept the tribute of a total stranger—I have dedicated this second edition of *Jane Eyre*.

CURRER BELL.
DECEMBER 21ST, 1847.

Note to the Third Edition

I avail myself of the opportunity which a third edition of *Jane Eyre* affords me, of again addressing a word to the Public, to explain that my claim to the title of novelist rests on this one work alone. If, therefore, the authorship of other works of fiction has been attributed to me, an honour is awarded where it is not merited; and consequently, denied where it is justly due.

This explanation will serve to rectify mistakes which may already have been made, and to prevent future errors.

Currer Bell.
April 13th, 1848.

CHAPTER I

There was no possibility of taking a walk that day. We had been wandering, indeed, in the leafless shrubbery an hour in the morning; but since dinner (Mrs. Reed, when there was no company, dined early) the cold winter wind had brought with it clouds so sombre, and a rain so penetrating, that further outdoor exercise was now out of the question.

I was glad of it: I never liked long walks, especially on chilly afternoons: dreadful to me was the coming home in the raw twilight, with nipped fingers and toes, and a heart saddened by the chidings of Bessie, the nurse, and humbled by the consciousness of my physical inferiority to Eliza, John, and Georgiana Reed.

The said Eliza, John, and Georgiana were now clustered round their mama in the drawing-room: she lay reclined on a sofa by the fireside, and with her darlings about her (for the time neither quarrelling nor crying) looked perfectly happy. Me, she had dispensed from joining the group; saying, "She regretted to be under the necessity of keeping me at a distance; but that until she heard from Bessie, and could discover by her own observation, that I was endeavouring in good earnest to acquire a more sociable and childlike disposition, a more attractive and sprightly manner—something lighter, franker, more natural, as it were—she really must exclude me from privileges intended only for contented, happy, little children."

"What does Bessie say I have done?" I asked.

"Jane, I don't like cavillers or questioners; besides, there is something truly forbidding in a child taking up her elders in that manner. Be seated somewhere; and until you can speak pleasantly, remain silent."

A breakfast-room adjoined the drawing-room. I slipped in there. It contained a bookcase: I soon possessed myself of a volume, taking care that it should be one stored with pictures. I mounted into the window-seat: gathering up my feet, I sat cross-legged, like a Turk; and, having drawn the red moreen curtain nearly close, I was shrined in double retirement.

Folds of scarlet drapery shut in my view to the right hand; to the left were the clear panes of glass, protecting, but not separating me from the drear November day. At intervals, while turning over the leaves of my book, I studied the aspect of that winter afternoon. Afar, it offered a pale blank of mist and cloud; near a scene of wet lawn and storm-beat shrub, with ceaseless rain sweeping away wildly before a long and lamentable blast.

I returned to my book—Bewick's *History of British Birds*: the letter-press thereof I cared little for, generally speaking; and yet there were certain introductory pages that, child as I was, I could not pass quite as a blank. They were those which treat of the haunts of sea-fowl; of "the solitary rocks and promontories" by them only inhabited; of the coast of Norway, studded with isles from its southern extremity, the Lindeness, or Naze, to the North Cape—

> "Where the Northern Ocean, in vast whirls,
> Boils round the naked, melancholy isles
> Of farthest Thule; and the Atlantic surge
> Pours in among the stormy Hebrides."

Nor could I pass unnoticed the suggestion of the bleak shores of Lapland, Siberia, Spitzbergen, Nova Zembla, Iceland, Greenland, with "the vast sweep of the Arctic Zone, and those forlorn regions of dreary space—that reservoir of frost and snow, where firm fields of ice, the accumulation of centuries of winters, glazed in Alpine heights above heights, surround the pole, and concentre the multiplied rigours of extreme cold." Of these death-white realms I formed an idea of my own: shadowy, like all the half-comprehended notions that float dim through children's brains, but strangely impressive. The words in these introductory pages connected themselves with the succeeding vignettes, and gave significance to the rock standing up alone in a sea of billow and spray; to the broken boat stranded on a desolate coast; to the cold and ghastly moon glancing through bars of cloud at a wreck just sinking.

I cannot tell what sentiment haunted the quite solitary churchyard, with its inscribed headstone; its gate, its two trees, its low horizon, girdled by a broken wall, and its newly-risen crescent, attesting the hour of eventide.

The two ships becalmed on a torpid sea, I believed to be marine phantoms.

The fiend pinning down the thief's pack behind him, I passed over quickly: it was an object of terror.

So was the black horned thing seated aloof on a rock, surveying a distant crowd surrounding a gallows.

Each picture told a story; mysterious often to my undeveloped understanding and imperfect feelings, yet ever profoundly interesting: as interesting as the tales Bessie sometimes narrated on winter evenings, when she chanced to be in good humour; and when, having brought her ironing-table to the nursery hearth, she allowed us to sit about it, and while she got up Mrs. Reed's lace frills, and crimped her nightcap borders, fed our eager attention with passages of love and adventure taken from old fairy tales and other ballads; or (as at a later period I discovered) from the pages of *Pamela*, and *Henry, Earl of Moreland*.

With Bewick on my knee, I was then happy: happy at least in my way. I feared nothing but interruption, and that came too soon. The breakfast-room door opened.

"Boh! Madam Mope!" cried the voice of John Reed; then he paused: he found the room apparently empty.

"Where the dickens is she!" he continued. "Lizzy! Georgy!"—calling to his sisters—"Joan is not here: tell mama she is run out into the rain—bad animal!"

"It is well I drew the curtain," thought I; and I wished fervently he might not discover my hiding-place: nor would John Reed have found it out himself; he was not quick either of vision or conception; but Eliza just put her head in at the door, and said at once—

"She is in the window-seat, to be sure, Jack."

And I came out immediately, for I trembled at the idea of being dragged forth by the said Jack.

"What do you want?" I asked, with awkward diffidence.

"Say, 'What do you want, Master Reed?' " was the answer. "I want you to come here"; and seating himself in an arm-chair, he intimated by a gesture that I was to approach and stand before him.

John Reed was a schoolboy of fourteen years old; four years older than I, for I was but ten: large and stout for his age, with a dingy and unwholesome skin; thick lineaments in a spacious visage, heavy limbs and large extremities. He gorged himself habitually at table, which made him bilious, and gave him a dim and bleared eye and flabby cheeks. He ought now to have been at school; but his mama had taken him home for a month or two, "on account of his delicate health." Mr. Miles, the master, affirmed that he would do very well if he had fewer cakes and sweetmeats sent him from home; but the mother's heart turned from an opinion so harsh, and inclined rather to the more refined idea that John's sallowness was owing to over-application and, perhaps, to pining after home.

John had not much affection for his mother and sisters, and an antipathy to me. He bullied and punished me; not two or three times in the week, nor once or twice in the day, but continually: every nerve I had feared him, and every morsel of flesh in my bones shrank when he came near. There were moments when I was bewildered by the terror he inspired, because I had no appeal whatever against either his menaces or his inflictions; the servants did not like to offend their young master by taking my part against him, and Mrs. Reed was blind and deaf on the subject: she never saw him strike or heard him abuse me, though he did both now and then in her very presence, more frequently, however, behind her back.

Habitually obedient to John, I came up to his chair: he spent some three minutes in thrusting out his tongue at me as far as he could without damaging the roots: I knew he would soon strike, and while dreading the blow, I mused on the disgusting and ugly appearance of him who would presently deal it. I wonder if he read that notion in my face; for, all at once, without speaking, he struck suddenly and strongly. I tottered, and on regaining my equilibrium retired back a step or two from his chair.

"That is for your impudence in answering mama awhile since," said he, "and for your sneaking way of getting behind curtains, and for the look you had in your eyes two minutes since, you rat!"

Accustomed to John Reed's abuse, I never had an idea of replying to it; my care was how to endure the blow which would certainly follow the insult.

"What were you doing behind the curtain?" he asked.

"I was reading."

"Show the book."

I returned to the window and fetched it thence.

"You have no business to take our books; you are a dependent, mama says; you have no money; your father left you none; you ought to beg, and not to live here with gentlemen's children like us, and eat the same meals we do, and wear clothes at our mama's expense. Now, I'll teach you to rummage my bookshelves: for they *are* mine; all the house belongs to me, or will do in a few years. Go and stand by the door, out of the way of the mirror and the windows."

I did so, not at first aware what was his intention; but when I saw him lift and poise the book and stand in act to hurl it, I instinctively started aside with a cry of alarm: not soon enough, however; the volume was flung, it hit me, and I fell, striking my head against the door and cutting it. The cut bled, the pain was sharp: my terror had passed its climax; other feelings succeeded.

"Wicked and cruel boy!" I said. "You are like a murderer—you are like a slave-driver—you are like the Roman emperors!"

I had read Goldsmith's *History of Rome*, and had formed my opinion of Nero, Caligula, etc. Also I had drawn parallels in silence, which I never thought thus to have declared aloud.

"What! What!" he cried. "Did she say that to me? Did you hear her, Eliza and Georgiana? Won't I tell mama? but first—"

He ran headlong at me: I felt him grasp my hair and my shoulder: he had closed with a desperate thing. I really saw in him a tyrant, a murderer. I felt a drop or two of blood from my head trickle down my neck, and was sensible of somewhat pungent suffering: these sensations for the time predominated over fear, and I received him in frantic sort. I don't very well know what I did with my hands, but he called me "Rat! Rat!" and bellowed out aloud. Aid was near him: Eliza and Georgiana had run for Mrs. Reed, who was gone upstairs: she now came upon the scene, followed by Bessie and her maid Abbot. We were parted: I heard the words—

"Dear! Dear! What a fury to fly at Master John!"

"Did ever anybody see such a picture of passion!"

Then Mrs. Reed subjoined—

"Take her away to the red-room, and lock her in there." Four hands were immediately laid upon me, and I was borne upstairs.

CHAPTER II

I resisted all the way: a new thing for me, and a circumstance which greatly strengthened the bad opinion Bessie and Miss Abbot were disposed to entertain of me. The fact is, I was a trifle beside myself; or rather *out* of myself, as the French would say: I was conscious that a moment's mutiny had already rendered me liable to strange penalties, and, like any other rebel slave, I felt resolved, in my desperation, to go all lengths.

"Hold her arms, Miss Abbot: she's like a mad cat."

"For shame! For shame!" cried the lady's-maid. "What shocking conduct, Miss Eyre, to strike a young gentleman, your benefactress's son! Your young master."

"Master! How is he my master? Am I a servant?"

"No; you are less than a servant, for you do nothing for your keep. There, sit down, and think over your wickedness."

They had got me by this time into the apartment indicated by Mrs. Reed, and had thrust me upon a stool: my impulse was to rise from it like a spring; their two pair of hands arrested me instantly.

"If you don't sit still, you must be tied down," said Bessie. "Miss Abbot, lend me your garters; she would break mine directly."

Miss Abbot turned to divest a stout leg of the necessary ligature. This preparation for bonds, and the additional ignominy it inferred, took a little of the excitement out of me.

"Don't take them off," I cried; "I will not stir."

In guarantee whereof, I attached myself to my seat by my hands.

"Mind you don't," said Bessie; and when she had ascertained that I was really subsiding, she loosened her hold of me; then she and Miss Abbot stood with folded arms, looking darkly and doubtfully on my face, as incredulous of my sanity.

"She never did so before," at last said Bessie, turning to the Abigail.

"But it was always in her," was the reply. "I've told Missis often my opinion about the child, and Missis agreed with me. She's an underhand little thing: I never saw a girl of her age with so much cover."

Bessie answered not; but ere long, addressing me, she said, "You ought to be aware, Miss, that you are under obligations to Mrs. Reed: she keeps you: if she were to turn you off, you would have to go to the poorhouse."

I had nothing to say to these words: they were not new to me: my very first recollections of existence included hints of the same kind. This reproach of my dependence had become a vague sing-song in my ear: very painful and crushing, but only half intelligible. Miss Abbot joined in—

"And you ought not to think yourself on an equality with the Misses Reed and Master Reed, because Missis kindly allows you to be brought up with them. They will have a great deal of money, and you will have none: it is your place to be humble, and to try to make yourself agreeable to them."

"What we tell you is for your good," added Bessie, in no harsh voice. "You should try to be useful and pleasant, then, perhaps, you would have a home here; but if you become passionate and rude, Missis will send you away, I am sure."

"Besides," said Miss Abbot, "God will punish her: He might strike her dead in the midst of her tantrums, and then where would she go? Come, Bessie, we will leave her: I wouldn't have her heart for anything. Say your prayers, Miss Eyre, when you are by yourself; for if you don't repent, something bad might be permitted to come down the chimney and fetch you away."

They went, shutting the door, and locking it behind them.

The red-room was a square chamber, very seldom slept in, I might say never, indeed, unless when a chance influx of visitors at Gateshead Hall rendered it necessary to turn to account all the accommodation it contained: yet it was one of the largest and stateliest chambers in the mansion. A bed supported on massive pillars of mahogany, hung with curtains of deep red damask, stood out like a tabernacle in the centre; the two large windows, with their blinds always drawn down, were half shrouded in festoons and falls of similar drapery; the carpet was red; the table at the foot of the bed was covered with a crimson cloth; the walls were a soft fawn colour with a blush of pink in it; the wardrobe, the toilet-table, the chairs were of darkly polished old mahogany. Out of these deep surrounding shades rose high, and glared white, the piled-up mattresses and pillows of the bed, spread with a snowy Marseilles counterpane. Scarcely less prominent was an ample cushioned easy-chair near the head of the bed, also white, with a footstool before it; and looking, as I thought, like a pale throne.

This room was chill, because it seldom had a fire; it was silent, because remote from the nursery and kitchen; solemn, because it was known to be so seldom entered. The house-maid alone came here on Saturdays, to wipe from the mirrors and the furniture a week's quiet dust: and Mrs. Reed herself, at far intervals, visited it to review the contents of a certain secret drawer in the wardrobe, where were stored divers parchments, her jewel-casket, and a miniature of her deceased husband; and in those last words lies the secret of the red-room—the spell which kept it so lonely in spite of its grandeur.

Mr. Reed had been dead nine years: it was in this chamber he breathed his last; here he lay in state; hence his coffin was borne by the undertaker's men; and, since that day, a sense of dreary consecration had guarded it from frequent intrusion.

My seat, to which Bessie and the bitter Miss Abbot had left me riveted, was a low ottoman near the marble chimney-piece; the bed rose before me; to my right hand there was the high, dark wardrobe, with subdued, broken reflections varying the gloss of its panels; to my left were the muffled windows; a great looking-glass between them repeated the vacant majesty of the bed and room. I was not quite sure whether they had locked the door; and when I dared move, I got up and went to see. Alas! Yes: no jail was ever more secure. Returning, I had to cross before the looking-glass; my fascinated glance involuntarily explored the depth it revealed. All looked colder and darker in that visionary hollow than in reality: and the strange little figure there gazing at me, with a white face and arms specking the gloom, and glittering eyes of fear moving where all else was still, had the effect of a real spirit: I thought it like one of the tiny phantoms, half fairy, half imp, Bessie's evening stories represented as coming out of lone, ferny dells in moors, and appearing before the eyes of belated travellers. I returned to my stool.

Superstition was with me at that moment; but it was not yet her hour for complete victory: my blood was still warm; the mood of the revolted slave was still bracing me with its bitter vigour; I had to stem a rapid rush of retrospective thought before I quailed to the dismal present.

All John Reed's violent tyrannies, all his sisters' proud indifference, all his mother's aversion, all the servants' partiality, turned up in my disturbed mind like a dark deposit in a turbid well. Why was I always suffering, always browbeaten, always accused, for ever condemned? Why could I never please? Why was it useless to try to win any one's favour? Eliza, who was headstrong and selfish, was respected. Georgiana, who had a spoiled temper, a very acrid spite, a captious and insolent carriage, was universally indulged. Her beauty, her pink cheeks and golden curls, seemed to give delight to all who looked at her, and to purchase indemnity for every fault. John no one thwarted, much less punished; though he twisted the necks of the pigeons, killed the little pea-chicks, set the dogs at the sheep, stripped the hothouse vines of their fruit, and broke the buds off the choicest plants in the conservatory: he called his mother "old girl," too; sometimes reviled her for her dark skin, similar to his own; bluntly disregarded her wishes; not unfrequently tore and spoiled her silk attire; and he was still "her own darling." I dared commit no fault: I strove to fulfil every duty; and I was termed naughty and tiresome, sullen and sneaking, from morning to noon, and from noon to night.

My head still ached and bled with the blow and fall I had received: no one had reproved John for wantonly striking me; and because I had turned against him to avert farther irrational violence, I was loaded with general opprobrium.

"Unjust—unjust!" said my reason, forced by the agonising stimulus into precocious though transitory power: and Resolve, equally wrought up, instigated some strange expedient to achieve escape from insupportable oppression—as running away, or, if that could not be effected, never eating or drinking more, and letting myself die.

What a consternation of soul was mine that dreary afternoon! How all my brain was in tumult, and all my heart in insurrection! Yet in what darkness, what dense ignorance, was the mental battle fought! I could not answer the ceaseless inward question—*why* I thus suffered; now, at the distance of—I will not say how many years, I see it clearly.

I was a discord in Gateshead Hall: I was like nobody there; I had nothing in harmony with Mrs. Reed or her children, or her chosen vassalage. If they did not love me, in fact, as little did I love them. They were not bound to regard with affection a thing that could not sympathise with one amongst them; a heterogeneous thing, opposed to them in temperament, in capacity, in propensities; a useless thing, incapable of serving their interest, or adding to their pleasure; a noxious thing, cherishing the germs of indignation at their treatment, of contempt of their judgment. I know that had I been a sanguine, brilliant, careless, exacting, handsome, romping child—though equally dependent and friendless—Mrs. Reed would have endured my presence more complacently; her children would have entertained for me more of the cordiality of fellow-feeling; the servants would have been less prone to make me the scapegoat of the nursery.

Daylight began to forsake the red-room; it was past four o'clock, and the beclouded afternoon was tending to drear twilight. I heard the rain still beating continuously on the staircase window, and the wind howling in the grove behind the hall; I grew by degrees cold as a stone, and then my courage sank. My habitual mood of humiliation, self-doubt, forlorn depression, fell damp on the embers of my decaying ire. All said I was wicked, and perhaps I might be so; what thought had I been but just conceiving of starving myself to death? That certainly was a crime: and was I fit to die? Or was the vault under the chancel of Gateshead Church an inviting bourne? In such vault I had been told did Mr. Reed lie buried; and led by this thought to recall his idea, I dwelt on it with gathering dread. I could not remember him; but I knew that he was my own uncle—my mother's brother—that he had taken me when a parentless infant to his house; and that in his last moments he had required a promise of Mrs. Reed that she would rear and maintain me as one of her own children. Mrs. Reed probably considered she had kept this promise; and so she had, I dare say, as well as her nature would permit her; but how could she really like an interloper not of her race, and unconnected with her, after her husband's death, by any tie? It must have been most irksome to find herself bound by a hard-wrung pledge to stand in the stead of a parent to a strange child she could not love, and to see an uncongenial alien permanently intruded on her own family group.

A singular notion dawned upon me. I doubted not—never doubted—that if Mr. Reed had been alive he would have treated me kindly; and now, as I sat looking at the white bed and overshadowed walls—occasionally also turning a fascinated eye towards the dimly gleaning mirror—I began to recall what I had heard of dead men, troubled in their graves by the violation of their last wishes, revisiting the earth to punish the perjured and avenge the oppressed; and I thought Mr. Reed's spirit, harassed by the wrongs of his sister's child, might quit its abode—whether in the church vault or in the unknown world of the departed—and rise before me in this chamber. I wiped my tears and hushed my sobs, fearful lest any sign of violent grief might waken a preternatural voice to comfort me, or elicit from the gloom some haloed face, bending over me with strange pity. This idea, consolatory in theory, I felt would be terrible if realised: with all my might I endeavoured to stifle it—I endeavoured to be firm. Shaking my hair from my eyes, I lifted my head and tried to look boldly round the dark room; at this moment a light gleamed on the wall. Was it, I asked myself, a ray from the moon penetrating some aperture in the blind? No; moonlight was still, and this stirred; while I gazed, it glided up to the ceiling and quivered over my head. I can now conjecture readily that this streak of light was, in all likelihood, a gleam from a lantern carried by some one across the lawn: but then, prepared as my mind was for horror, shaken as my nerves were by agitation, I thought the swift darting beam was a herald of some coming vision from another world. My heart beat thick, my head grew hot; a sound filled my ears, which I deemed the rushing of wings; something seemed near me; I was oppressed, suffocated: endurance broke down; I rushed to the door and shook the lock in desperate effort. Steps came running along the outer passage; the key turned, Bessie and Abbot entered.

"Miss Eyre, are you ill?" said Bessie.

"What a dreadful noise! It went quite through me!" exclaimed Abbot.

"Take me out! Let me go into the nursery!" was my cry.

"What for? Are you hurt? Have you seen something?" again demanded Bessie.

"Oh! I saw a light, and I thought a ghost would come." I had now got hold of Bessie's hand, and she did not snatch it from me.

"She has screamed out on purpose," declared Abbot, in some disgust. "And what a scream! If she had been in great pain one would have excused it, but she only wanted to bring us all here: I know her naughty tricks."

"What is all this?" demanded another voice peremptorily; and Mrs. Reed came along the corridor, her cap flying wide, her gown rustling stormily. "Abbot and Bessie, I believe I gave orders that Jane Eyre should be left in the red-room till I came to her myself."

"Miss Jane screamed so loud, ma'am," pleaded Bessie.

"Let her go," was the only answer. "Loose Bessie's hand, child: you cannot succeed in getting out by these means, be assured. I abhor artifice, particularly in children; it is my duty to show you that tricks will not answer: you will now stay here an hour longer, and it is only on condition of perfect submission and stillness that I shall liberate you then."

"O aunt! Have pity! Forgive me! I cannot endure it—let me be punished some other way! I shall be killed if—"

"Silence! This violence is all most repulsive"; and so, no doubt, she felt it. I was a precocious actress in her eyes; she sincerely looked on me as a compound of virulent passions, mean spirit, and dangerous duplicity.

Bessie and Abbot having retreated, Mrs. Reed, impatient of my now frantic anguish and wild sobs, abruptly thrust me back and locked me in, without farther parley. I heard her sweeping away; and soon after she was gone, I suppose I had a species of fit: unconsciousness closed the scene.

CHAPTER III

The next thing I remember is, waking up with a feeling as if I had had a frightful nightmare, and seeing before me a terrible red glare, crossed with thick black bars. I heard voices, too, speaking with a hollow sound, and as if muffled by a rush of wind or water: agitation, uncertainty, and an all-predominating sense of terror confused my faculties. Ere long, I became aware that some one was handling me; lifting me up and supporting me in a sitting posture, and that more tenderly than I had ever been raised or upheld before. I rested my head against a pillow or an arm, and felt easy.

In five minutes more the cloud of bewilderment dissolved: I knew quite well that I was in my own bed, and that the red glare was the nursery fire. It was night: a candle burnt on the table; Bessie stood at the bed-foot with a basin in her hand, and a gentleman sat in a chair near my pillow, leaning over me.

I felt an inexpressible relief, a soothing conviction of protection and security, when I knew that there was a stranger in the room, an individual not belonging to Gateshead, and not related to Mrs. Reed. Turning from Bessie (though her presence was far less obnoxious to me than that of Abbot, for instance, would have been), I scrutinised the face of the gentleman: I knew him; it was Mr. Lloyd, an apothecary, sometimes called in by Mrs. Reed when the servants were ailing: for herself and the children she employed a physician.

"Well, who am I?" he asked.

I pronounced his name, offering him at the same time my hand: he took it, smiling and saying, "We shall do very well by-and-by." Then he laid me down, and addressing Bessie, charged her to be very careful that I was not disturbed during the night. Having given some further directions, and intimates that he should call again the next day, he departed; to my grief: I felt so sheltered and befriended while he sat in the chair near my pillow; and as he closed the door after him, all the room darkened and my heart again sank: inexpressible sadness weighed it down.

"Do you feel as if you should sleep, Miss?" asked Bessie, rather softly.

Scarcely dared I answer her; for I feared the next sentence might be rough. "I will try."

"Would you like to drink, or could you eat anything?"

"No, thank you, Bessie."

"Then I think I shall go to bed, for it is past twelve o'clock; but you may call me if you want anything in the night."

Wonderful civility this! It emboldened me to ask a question.

"Bessie, what is the matter with me? Am I ill?"

"You fell sick, I suppose, in the red-room with crying; you'll be better soon, no doubt."

Bessie went into the housemaid's apartment, which was near. I heard her say—

"Sarah, come and sleep with me in the nursery; I daren't for my life be alone with that poor child tonight: she might die; it's such a strange thing she should have that fit: I wonder if she saw anything. Missis was rather too hard."

Sarah came back with her; they both went to bed; they were whispering together for half-an-hour before they fell asleep. I caught scraps of their conversation, from which I was able only too distinctly to infer the main subject discussed.

"Something passed her, all dressed in white, and vanished"—"A great black dog behind him"—"Three loud raps on the chamber door"—"A light in the churchyard just over his grave," etc., etc.

At last both slept: the fire and the candle went out. For me, the watches of that long night passed in ghastly wakefulness; strained by dread: such dread as children only can feel.

No severe or prolonged bodily illness followed this incident of the red-room; it only gave my nerves a shock of which I feel the reverberation to this day. Yes, Mrs. Reed, to you I owe some fearful pangs of mental suffering, but I ought to forgive you, for you knew not what you did: while rending my heart-strings, you thought you were only uprooting my bad propensities.

Next day, by noon, I was up and dressed, and sat wrapped in a shawl by the nursery hearth. I felt physically weak and broken down: but my worse ailment was an unutterable wretchedness of mind: a wretchedness which kept drawing from me silent tears; no sooner had I wiped one salt drop from my cheek than another followed. Yet, I thought, I ought to have been happy, for none of the Reeds were there, they were all gone out in the carriage with their mama. Abbot, too, was sewing in another room, and Bessie, as she moved hither and thither, putting away toys and arranging drawers, addressed to me every now and then a word of unwonted kindness. This state of things should have been to me a paradise of peace, accustomed as I was to a life of ceaseless reprimand and thankless fagging; but, in fact, my racked nerves were now in such a state that no calm could soothe, and no pleasure excite them agreeably.

Bessie had been down into the kitchen, and she brought up with her a tart on a certain brightly painted china plate, whose bird of paradise, nestling in a wreath of convolvuli and rosebuds, had been wont to stir in me a most enthusiastic sense of admiration; and which plate I had often petitioned to be allowed to take in my hand in order to examine it more closely, but had always hitherto been deemed unworthy of such a privilege. This precious vessel was now placed on my knee, and I was cordially invited to eat the circlet of delicate pastry upon it. Vain favour! Coming, like most other favours long deferred and often wished for, too late! I could not eat the tart; and the plumage of the bird, the tints of the flowers, seemed strangely faded: I put both plate and tart away. Bessie asked if I would have a book: the word *book* acted as a transient stimulus, and I begged her to fetch *Gulliver's Travels* from the library. This book I had again and again perused with delight. I considered it a narrative of facts, and discovered in it a vein of interest deeper than what I found in fairy tales: for as to the elves, having sought them in vain among foxglove leaves and bells, under mushrooms and beneath the ground-ivy mantling old wall-nooks, I had at length made up my mind to the sad truth, that they were all gone out of England to some savage country where the woods were wilder and thicker, and the population more scant; whereas, Lilliput and Brobdignag being, in my creed, solid parts of the earth's surface, I doubted not that I might one day, by taking a long voyage, see with my own eyes the little fields, houses, and trees, the diminutive people, the tiny cows, sheep, and birds of the one realm; and the corn-fields forest-high, the mighty mastiffs, the monster cats, the tower-like men and women, of the other. Yet, when this cherished volume was now placed in my hand—when I turned over its leaves, and sought in its marvellous pictures the charm I had, till now, never failed to find—all was eerie and dreary; the giants were gaunt goblins, the pigmies malevolent and fearful imps, Gulliver a most desolate wanderer in most dread and dangerous regions. I closed the book, which I dared no longer peruse, and put it on the table, beside the untasted tart.

Bessie had now finished dusting and tidying the room, and having washed her hands, she opened a certain little drawer, full of splendid shreds of silk and satin, and began making a new bonnet for Georgiana's doll. Meantime she sang: her song was—

"In the days when we went gipsying,
A long time ago."

I had often heard the song before, and always with lively delight; for Bessie had a sweet voice—at least, I thought so. But now, though her voice was still sweet, I found in its melody an indescribable sadness. Sometimes, preoccupied with her work, she sang the refrain very low, very lingeringly; "A long time ago" came out like the saddest cadence of a funeral hymn. She passed into another ballad, this time a really doleful one.

"My feet they are sore, and my limbs they are weary;
Long is the way, and the mountains are wild;
Soon will the twilight close moonless and dreary
Over the path of the poor orphan child.

"Why did they send me so far and so lonely,
Up where the moors spread and grey rocks are piled?
Men are hard-hearted, and kind angels only
Watch o'er the steps of a poor orphan child.

"Yet distant and soft the night breeze is blowing,
Clouds there are none, and clear stars beam mild.
God, in His mercy, protection is showing,
Comfort and hope to the poor orphan child.

"Ev'n should I fall o'er the broken bridge passing,
Or stray in the marshes, by false lights beguiled,
Still will my Father, with promise and blessing,
Take to His bosom the poor orphan child.

"There is a thought that for strength should avail me,
Though both of shelter and kindred despoiled;
Heaven is a home, and a rest will not fail me;
God is a friend to the poor orphan child."

"Come, Miss Jane, don't cry," said Bessie as she finished. She might as well have said to the fire, "Don't burn!" but how could she divine the morbid suffering to which I was a prey? In the course of the morning Mr. Lloyd came again.

"What, already up!" said he, as he entered the nursery. "Well, nurse, how is she?"

Bessie answered that I was doing very well.

"Then she ought to look more cheerful. Come here, Miss Jane: your name is Jane, is it not?"

"Yes, sir, Jane Eyre."

"Well, you have been crying, Miss Jane Eyre; can you tell me what about? Have you any pain?"

"No, sir."

"Oh! I daresay she is crying because she could not go out with Missis in the carriage," interposed Bessie.

"Surely not! Why, she is too old for such pettishness."

I thought so too; and my self-esteem being wounded by the false charge, I answered promptly, "I never cried for such a thing in my life: I hate going out in the carriage. I cry because I am miserable."

"Oh fie, Miss!" said Bessie.

The good apothecary appeared a little puzzled. I was standing before him; he fixed his eyes on me very steadily: his eyes were small and grey; not very bright, but I dare say I should think them shrewd now: he had a hard-featured yet good-natured looking face. Having considered me at leisure, he said—

"What made you ill yesterday?"

"She had a fall," said Bessie, again putting in her word.

"Fall! Why, that is like a baby again! Can't she manage to walk at her age? She must be eight or nine years old."

"I was knocked down," was the blunt explanation, jerked out of me by another pang of mortified pride; "but that did not make me ill," I added; while Mr. Lloyd helped himself to a pinch of snuff.

As he was returning the box to his waistcoat pocket, a loud bell rang for the servants' dinner; he knew what it was. "That's for you, nurse," said he; "you can go down; I'll give Miss Jane a lecture till you come back."

Bessie would rather have stayed, but she was obliged to go, because punctuality at meals was rigidly enforced at Gateshead Hall.

"The fall did not make you ill; what did, then?" pursued Mr. Lloyd when Bessie was gone.

"I was shut up in a room where there is a ghost till after dark."

I saw Mr. Lloyd smile and frown at the same time.

"Ghost! What, you are a baby after all! You are afraid of ghosts?"

"Of Mr. Reed's ghost I am: he died in that room, and was laid out there. Neither Bessie nor any one else will go into it at night, if they can help it; and it was cruel to shut me up alone without a candle—so cruel that I think I shall never forget it."

"Nonsense! And is it that makes you so miserable? Are you afraid now in daylight?"

"No: but night will come again before long: and besides—I am unhappy—very unhappy, for other things."

"What other things? Can you tell me some of them?"

How much I wished to reply fully to this question! How difficult it was to frame any answer! Children can feel, but they cannot analyse their feelings; and if the analysis is partially effected in thought, they know not how to express the result of the process in words. Fearful, however, of losing this first and only opportunity of relieving my grief by imparting it, I, after a disturbed pause, contrived to frame a meagre, though, as far as it went, true response.

"For one thing, I have no father or mother, brothers or sisters."

"You have a kind aunt and cousins."

Again I paused; then bunglingly enounced—

"But John Reed knocked me down, and my aunt shut me up in the red-room."

Mr. Lloyd a second time produced his snuff-box.

"Don't you think Gateshead Hall a very beautiful house?" asked he. "Are you not very thankful to have such a fine place to live at?"

"It is not my house, sir; and Abbot says I have less right to be here than a servant."

"Pooh! You can't be silly enough to wish to leave such a splendid place?"

"If I had anywhere else to go, I should be glad to leave it; but I can never get away from Gateshead till I am a woman."

"Perhaps you may—who knows? Have you any relations besides Mrs. Reed?"

"I think not, sir."

"None belonging to your father?"

"I don't know. I asked Aunt Reed once, and she said possibly I might have some poor, low relations called Eyre, but she knew nothing about them."

"If you had such, would you like to go to them?"

I reflected. Poverty looks grim to grown people; still more so to children: they have not much idea of industrious, working, respectable poverty; they think of the word only as connected with ragged clothes, scanty food, fireless grates, rude manners, and debasing vices: poverty for me was synonymous with degradation.

"No; I should not like to belong to poor people," was my reply.

"Not even if they were kind to you?"

I shook my head: I could not see how poor people had the means of being kind; and then to learn to speak like them, to adopt their manners, to be uneducated, to grow up like one of the poor women I saw sometimes nursing their children or washing their clothes at the cottage doors of the village of Gateshead: no, I was not heroic enough to purchase liberty at the price of caste.

"But are your relatives so very poor? Are they working people?"

"I cannot tell; Aunt Reed says if I have any, they must be a beggarly set: I should not like to go a begging."

"Would you like to go to school?"

Again I reflected: I scarcely knew what school was: Bessie sometimes spoke of it as a place where young ladies sat in the stocks, wore backboards, and were expected to be exceedingly genteel and precise: John Reed hated his school, and abused his master; but John Reed's tastes were no rule for mine, and if Bessie's accounts of school-discipline (gathered from the young ladies of a family where she had lived before coming to Gateshead) were somewhat appalling, her details of certain accomplishments attained by these same young ladies were, I thought, equally attractive. She boasted of beautiful paintings of landscapes and flowers by them executed; of songs they could sing and pieces they could play, of purses they could net, of French books they could translate; till my spirit was moved to emulation as I listened. Besides, school would be a complete change: it implied a long journey, an entire separation from Gateshead, an entrance into a new life.

"I should indeed like to go to school," was the audible conclusion of my musings.

"Well, well! Who knows what may happen?" said Mr. Lloyd, as he got up. "The child ought to have change of air and scene," he added, speaking to himself; "nerves not in a good state."

Bessie now returned; at the same moment the carriage was heard rolling up the gravel-walk.

"Is that your mistress, nurse?" asked Mr. Lloyd. "I should like to speak to her before I go."

Bessie invited him to walk into the breakfast-room, and led the way out. In the interview which followed between him and Mrs. Reed, I presume, from after-occurrences, that the apothecary ventured to recommend my being sent to school; and the recommendation was no doubt readily enough adopted; for as Abbot said, in discussing the subject with Bessie when both sat sewing in the nursery one night, after I was in bed, and, as they thought, asleep, "Missis was, she dared say, glad enough to get rid of such a tiresome, ill-conditioned child, who always looked as if she were watching everybody, and scheming plots underhand." Abbot, I think, gave me credit for being a sort of infantine Guy Fawkes.

On that same occasion I learned, for the first time, from Miss Abbot's communications to Bessie, that my father had been a poor clergyman; that my mother had married him against the wishes of her friends, who considered the match beneath her; that my grandfather Reed was so irritated at her disobedience, he cut her off without a shilling; that after my mother and father had been married a year, the latter caught the typhus fever while visiting among the poor of a large manufacturing town where his curacy was situated, and where that disease was then prevalent: that my mother took the infection from him, and both died within a month of each other.

Bessie, when she heard this narrative, sighed and said, "Poor Miss Jane is to be pitied, too, Abbot."

"Yes," responded Abbot; "if she were a nice, pretty child, one might compassionate her forlornness; but one really cannot care for such a little toad as that."

"Not a great deal, to be sure," agreed Bessie. "At any rate, a beauty like Miss Georgiana would be more moving in the same condition."

"Yes, I doat on Miss Georgiana!" cried the fervent Abbot. "Little darling! With her long curls and her blue eyes, and such a sweet colour as she has; just as if she were painted! Bessie, I could fancy a Welsh rabbit for supper."

"So could I—with a roast onion. Come, we'll go down." They went.

CHAPTER IV

From my discourse with Mr. Lloyd, and from the above reported conference between Bessie and Abbot, I gathered enough of hope to suffice as a motive for wishing to get well: a change seemed near—I desired and waited it in silence. It tarried, however: days and weeks passed: I had regained my normal state of health, but no new allusion was made to the subject over which I brooded. Mrs. Reed surveyed me at times with a severe eye, but seldom addressed me: since my illness, she had drawn a more marked line of separation than ever between me and her own children; appointing me a small closet to sleep in by myself, condemning me to take my meals alone, and pass all my time in the nursery, while my cousins were constantly in the drawing-room. Not a hint, however, did she drop about sending me to school: still I felt an instinctive certainty that she would not long endure me under the same roof with her; for her glance, now more than ever, when turned on me, expressed an insuperable and rooted aversion.

Eliza and Georgiana, evidently acting according to orders, spoke to me as little as possible: John thrust his tongue in his cheek whenever he saw me, and once attempted chastisement; but as I instantly turned against him, roused by the same sentiment of deep ire and desperate revolt which had stirred my corruption before, he thought it better to desist, and ran from me tittering execrations, and vowing I had burst his nose. I had indeed levelled at that prominent feature as hard a blow as my knuckles could inflict; and when I saw that either that or my look daunted him, I had the greatest inclination to follow up my advantage to purpose; but he was already with his mama. I heard him in a blubbering tone commence the tale of how "that nasty Jane Eyre" had flown at him like a mad cat: he was stopped rather harshly—

"Don't talk to me about her, John: I told you not to go near her; she is not worthy of notice; I do not choose that either you or your sisters should associate with her."

Here, leaning over the banister, I cried out suddenly, and without at all deliberating on my words—

"They are not fit to associate with me."

Mrs. Reed was rather a stout woman; but, on hearing this strange and audacious declaration, she ran nimbly up the stair, swept me like a whirlwind into the nursery, and crushing me down on the edge of my crib, dared me in an emphatic voice to rise from that place, or utter one syllable during the remainder of the day.

"What would Uncle Reed say to you, if he were alive?" was my scarcely voluntary demand. I say scarcely voluntary, for it seemed as if my tongue pronounced words without my will consenting to their utterance: something spoke out of me over which I had no control.

"What?" said Mrs. Reed under her breath: her usually cold composed grey eye became troubled with a look like fear; she took her hand from my arm, and gazed at me as if she really did not know whether I were child or fiend. I was now in for it.

"My Uncle Reed is in heaven, and can see all you do and think; and so can papa and mama: they know how you shut me up all day long, and how you wish me dead."

Mrs. Reed soon rallied her spirits: she shook me most soundly, she boxed both my ears, and then left me without a word. Bessie supplied the hiatus by a homily of an hour's length, in which she proved beyond a doubt that I was the most wicked and abandoned child ever reared under a roof. I half believed her; for I felt indeed only bad feelings surging in my breast.

November, December, and half of January passed away. Christmas and the New Year had been celebrated at Gateshead with the usual festive cheer; presents had been interchanged, dinners and evening parties given. From every enjoyment I was, of course, excluded: my share of the gaiety consisted in witnessing the daily apparelling of Eliza and Georgiana, and seeing them descend to the drawing-room, dressed out in thin muslin frocks and scarlet sashes, with hair elaborately ringletted; and afterwards, in listening to the sound of the piano or the harp played below, to the passing to and fro of the butler and footman, to the jingling of glass and china as refreshments were handed, to the broken hum of conversation as the drawing-room door opened and closed. When tired of this occupation, I would retire from the stairhead to the solitary and silent nursery: there, though somewhat sad, I was not miserable. To speak truth, I had not the least wish to go into company, for in company I was very rarely noticed; and if Bessie had but been kind and companionable, I should have deemed it a treat to spend the evenings quietly with her, instead of passing them under the formidable eye of Mrs. Reed, in a room full of ladies and gentlemen. But Bessie, as soon as she had dressed her young ladies, used to take herself off to the lively regions of the kitchen and housekeeper's room, generally bearing the candle along with her. I then sat with my doll on my knee till the fire got low, glancing round occasionally to make sure that nothing worse than myself haunted the shadowy room; and when the embers sank to a dull red, I undressed hastily, tugging at knots and strings as I best might, and sought shelter from cold and darkness in my crib. To this crib I always took my doll; human beings must love something, and, in the dearth of worthier objects of affection, I contrived to find a pleasure in loving and cherishing a faded graven image, shabby as a miniature scarecrow. It puzzles me now to remember with what absurd sincerity I doated on this little toy, half fancying it alive and capable of sensation. I could not sleep unless it was folded in my night-gown; and when it lay there safe and warm, I was comparatively happy, believing it to be happy likewise.

Long did the hours seem while I waited the departure of the company, and listened for the sound of Bessie's step on the stairs: sometimes she would come up in the interval to seek her thimble or her scissors, or perhaps to bring me something by way of supper—a bun or a cheese-cake—then she would sit on the bed while I ate it, and when I had finished, she would tuck the clothes round me, and twice she kissed me, and said, "Good night, Miss Jane." When thus gentle, Bessie seemed to me the best, prettiest, kindest being in the world; and I wished most intensely that she would always be so pleasant and amiable, and never push me about, or scold, or task me unreasonably, as she was too often wont to do. Bessie Lee must, I think, have been a girl of good natural capacity, for she was smart in all she did, and had a remarkable knack of narrative; so, at least, I judge from the impression made on me by her nursery tales. She was pretty too, if my recollections of her face and person are correct. I remember her as a slim young woman, with black hair, dark eyes, very nice features, and good, clear complexion; but she had a capricious and hasty temper, and indifferent ideas of principle or justice: still, such as she was, I preferred her to any one else at Gateshead Hall.

It was the fifteenth of January, about nine o'clock in the morning: Bessie was gone down to breakfast; my cousins had not yet been summoned to their mama; Eliza was putting on her bonnet and warm garden-coat to go and feed her poultry, an occupation of which she was fond: and not less so of selling the eggs to the housekeeper and hoarding up the money she thus obtained. She had a turn for traffic, and a marked propensity for saving; shown not only in the vending of eggs and chickens, but also in driving hard bargains with the gardener about flower-roots, seeds, and slips of plants; that functionary having orders from Mrs. Reed to buy of his young lady all the products of her parterre she wished to sell: and Eliza would have sold the hair off her head if she could have made a handsome profit thereby. As to her money, she first secreted it in odd corners, wrapped in a rag or an old curl-paper; but some of these hoards having been discovered by the housemaid, Eliza, fearful of one day losing her valued treasure, consented to intrust it to her mother, at a usurious rate of interest—fifty or sixty percent; which interest she exacted every quarter, keeping her accounts in a little book with anxious accuracy.

Georgiana sat on a high stool, dressing her hair at the glass, and interweaving her curls with artificial flowers and faded feathers, of which she had found a store in a drawer in the attic. I was making my bed, having received strict orders from Bessie to get it arranged before she returned (for Bessie now frequently employed me as a sort of under-nurserymaid, to tidy the room, dust the chairs, etc.). Having spread the quilt and folded my night-dress, I went to the window-seat to put in order some picture-books and doll's house furniture scattered there; an abrupt command from Georgiana to let her playthings alone (for the tiny chairs and mirrors, the fairy plates and cups, were her property) stopped my proceedings; and then, for lack of other occupation, I fell to breathing on the frost-flowers with which the window was fretted, and thus clearing a space in the glass through which I might look out on the grounds, where all was still and petrified under the influence of a hard frost.

From this window were visible the porter's lodge and the carriage-road, and just as I had dissolved so much of the silver-white foliage veiling the panes as left room to look out, I saw the gates thrown open and a carriage roll through. I watched it ascending the drive with indifference; carriages often came to Gateshead, but none ever brought visitors in whom I was interested; it stopped in front of the house, the door-bell rang loudly, the new-comer was admitted. All this being nothing to me, my vacant attention soon found livelier attraction in the spectacle of a little hungry robin, which came and chirruped on the twigs of the leafless cherry-tree nailed against the wall near the casement. The remains of my breakfast of bread and milk stood on the table, and having crumbled a morsel of roll, I was tugging at the sash to put out the crumbs on the window-sill, when Bessie came running upstairs into the nursery.

"Miss Jane, take off your pinafore; what are you doing there? Have you washed your hands and face this morning?" I gave another tug before I answered, for I wanted the bird to be secure of its bread: the sash yielded; I scattered the crumbs, some on the stone sill, some on the cherry-tree bough, then, closing the window, I replied—

"No, Bessie; I have only just finished dusting."

"Troublesome, careless child! And what are you doing now? You look quite red, as if you had been about some mischief: what were you opening the window for?"

I was spared the trouble of answering, for Bessie seemed in too great a hurry to listen to explanations; she hauled me to the washstand, inflicted a merciless, but happily brief scrub on my face and hands with soap, water, and a coarse towel; disciplined my head with a bristly brush, denuded me of my pinafore, and then hurrying me to the top of the stairs, bid me go down directly, as I was wanted in the breakfast-room.

I would have asked who wanted me: I would have demanded if Mrs. Reed was there; but Bessie was already gone, and had closed the nursery-door upon me. I slowly descended. For nearly three months, I had never been called to Mrs. Reed's presence; restricted so long to the nursery, the breakfast, dining, and drawing-rooms were become for me awful regions, on which it dismayed me to intrude.

I now stood in the empty hall; before me was the breakfast-room door, and I stopped, intimidated and trembling. What a miserable little poltroon had fear, engendered of unjust punishment, made of me in those days! I feared to return to the nursery, and feared to go forward to the parlour; ten minutes I stood in agitated hesitation; the vehement ringing of the breakfast-room bell decided me; I *must* enter.

"Who could want me?" I asked inwardly, as with both hands I turned the stiff door-handle, which, for a second or two, resisted my efforts. "What should I see besides Aunt Reed in the apartment? A man or a woman?" The handle turned, the door unclosed, and passing through and curtseying low, I looked up at—a black pillar!—such, at least, appeared to me, at first sight, the straight, narrow, sable-clad shape standing erect on the rug: the grim face at the top was like a carved mask, placed above the shaft by way of capital.

Mrs. Reed occupied her usual seat by the fireside; she made a signal to me to approach; I did so, and she introduced me to the stony stranger with the words: "This is the little girl respecting whom I applied to you."

He, for it was a man, turned his head slowly towards where I stood, and having examined me with the two inquisitive-looking grey eyes which twinkled under a pair of bushy brows, said solemnly, and in a bass voice, "Her size is small: what is her age?"

"Ten years."

"So much?" was the doubtful answer; and he prolonged his scrutiny for some minutes. Presently he addressed me: "Your name, little girl?"

"Jane Eyre, sir."

In uttering these words I looked up: he seemed to me a tall gentleman; but then I was very little; his features were large, and they and all the lines of his frame were equally harsh and prim.

"Well, Jane Eyre, and are you a good child?"

Impossible to reply to this in the affirmative: my little world held a contrary opinion: I was silent. Mrs. Reed answered for me by an expressive shake of the head, adding soon, "Perhaps the less said on that subject the better, Mr. Brocklehurst."

"Sorry indeed to hear it! She and I must have some talk"; and bending from the perpendicular, he installed his person in the arm-chair opposite Mrs. Reed's. "Come here," he said.

I stepped across the rug; he placed me square and straight before him. What a face he had, now that it was almost on a level with mine! What a great nose! And what a mouth! And what large prominent teeth!

"No sight so sad as that of a naughty child," he began, "especially a naughty little girl. Do you know where the wicked go after death?"

"They go to hell," was my ready and orthodox answer.

"And what is hell? Can you tell me that?"

"A pit full of fire."

"And should you like to fall into that pit, and to be burning there for ever?"

"No, sir."

"What must you do to avoid it?"

I deliberated a moment; my answer, when it did come, was objectionable: "I must keep in good health, and not die."

"How can you keep in good health? Children younger than you die daily. I buried a little child of five years old only a day or two since—a good little child, whose soul is now in heaven. It is to be feared the same could not be said of you were you to be called hence."

Not being in a condition to remove his doubt, I only cast my eyes down on the two large feet planted on the rug, and sighed, wishing myself far enough away.

"I hope that sigh is from the heart, and that you repent of ever having been the occasion of discomfort to your excellent benefactress."

"Benefactress! Benefactress!" said I inwardly: "They all call Mrs. Reed my benefactress; if so, a benefactress is a disagreeable thing."

"Do you say your prayers night and morning?" continued my interrogator.

"Yes, sir."

"Do you read your Bible?"

"Sometimes."

"With pleasure? Are you fond of it?"

"I like Revelations, and the book of Daniel, and Genesis and Samuel, and a little bit of Exodus, and some parts of Kings and Chronicles, and Job and Jonah."

"And the Psalms? I hope you like them?"

"No, sir."

"No? Oh, shocking! I have a little boy, younger than you, who knows six Psalms by heart: and when you ask him which he would rather have, a gingerbread-nut to eat or a verse of a Psalm to learn, he says: 'Oh! The verse of a Psalm! Angels sing Psalms'; says he, 'I wish to be a little angel here below'; he then gets two nuts in recompense for his infant piety."

"Psalms are not interesting," I remarked.

"That proves you have a wicked heart; and you must pray to God to change it: to give you a new and clean one: to take away your heart of stone and give you a heart of flesh."

I was about to propound a question, touching the manner in which that operation of changing my heart was to be performed, when Mrs.

Reed interposed, telling me to sit down; she then proceeded to carry on the conversation herself.

"Mr. Brocklehurst, I believe I intimated in the letter which I wrote to you three weeks ago, that this little girl has not quite the character and disposition I could wish: should you admit her into Lowood school, I should be glad if the superintendent and teachers were requested to keep a strict eye on her, and, above all, to guard against her worst fault, a tendency to deceit. I mention this in your hearing, Jane, that you may not attempt to impose on Mr. Brocklehurst."

Well might I dread, well might I dislike Mrs. Reed; for it was her nature to wound me cruelly; never was I happy in her presence; however carefully I obeyed, however strenuously I strove to please her, my efforts were still repulsed and repaid by such sentences as the above. Now, uttered before a stranger, the accusation cut me to the heart; I dimly perceived that she was already obliterating hope from the new phase of existence which she destined me to enter; I felt, though I could not have expressed the feeling, that she was sowing aversion and unkindness along my future path; I saw myself transformed under Mr. Brocklehurst's eye into an artful, noxious child, and what could I do to remedy the injury?

"Nothing, indeed," thought I, as I struggled to repress a sob, and hastily wiped away some tears, the impotent evidences of my anguish.

"Deceit is, indeed, a sad fault in a child," said Mr. Brocklehurst; "it is akin to falsehood, and all liars will have their portion in the lake burning with fire and brimstone; she shall, however, be watched, Mrs. Reed. I will speak to Miss Temple and the teachers."

"I should wish her to be brought up in a manner suiting her prospects," continued my benefactress; "to be made useful, to be kept humble: as for the vacations, she will, with your permission, spend them always at Lowood."

"Your decisions are perfectly judicious, madam," returned Mr. Brocklehurst. "Humility is a Christian grace, and one peculiarly appropriate to the pupils of Lowood; I, therefore, direct that especial care shall be bestowed on its cultivation amongst them. I have studied how best to mortify in them the worldly sentiment of pride; and, only the other day, I had a pleasing proof of my success. My second daughter, Augusta, went with her mama to visit the school, and on her return she exclaimed: 'Oh, dear papa, how quiet and plain all the girls at

Lowood look, with their hair combed behind their ears, and their long pinafores, and those little holland pockets outside their frocks—they are almost like poor people's children! And,' said she, 'they looked at my dress and mama's, as if they had never seen a silk gown before.' "

"This is the state of things I quite approve," returned Mrs. Reed. "Had I sought all England over, I could scarcely have found a system more exactly fitting a child like Jane Eyre. Consistency, my dear Mr. Brocklehurst; I advocate consistency in all things."

"Consistency, madam, is the first of Christian duties; and it has been observed in every arrangement connected with the establishment of Lowood: plain fare, simple attire, unsophisticated accommodations, hardy and active habits; such is the order of the day in the house and its inhabitants."

"Quite right, sir. I may then depend upon this child being received as a pupil at Lowood, and there being trained in conformity to her position and prospects?"

"Madam, you may: she shall be placed in that nursery of chosen plants, and I trust she will show herself grateful for the inestimable privilege of her election."

"I will send her, then, as soon as possible, Mr. Brocklehurst; for, I assure you, I feel anxious to be relieved of a responsibility that was becoming too irksome."

"No doubt, no doubt, madam; and now I wish you good morning. I shall return to Brocklehurst Hall in the course of a week or two: my good friend, the Archdeacon, will not permit me to leave him sooner. I shall send Miss Temple notice that she is to expect a new girl, so that there will be no difficulty about receiving her. Good-bye."

"Good-bye, Mr. Brocklehurst; remember me to Mrs. and Miss Brocklehurst, and to Augusta and Theodore, and Master Broughton Brocklehurst."

"I will, madam. Little girl, here is a book entitled the 'Child's Guide,' read it with prayer, especially that part containing 'An account of the awfully sudden death of Martha G—, a naughty child addicted to falsehood and deceit.' "

With these words Mr. Brocklehurst put into my hand a thin pamphlet sewn in a cover, and having rung for his carriage, he departed.

Mrs. Reed and I were left alone: some minutes passed in silence; she was sewing, I was watching her. Mrs. Reed might be at that time some six or seven and thirty; she was a woman of robust frame, square-shouldered and strong-limbed, not tall, and, though stout, not obese: she had a somewhat large face, the under jaw being much developed and very solid; her brow was low, her chin large and prominent, mouth and nose sufficiently regular; under her light eyebrows glimmered an eye devoid of ruth; her skin was dark and opaque, her hair nearly flaxen; her constitution was sound as a bell—illness never came near her; she was an exact, clever manager; her household and tenantry were thoroughly under her control; her children only at times defied her authority and laughed it to scorn; she dressed well, and had a presence and port calculated to set off handsome attire.

Sitting on a low stool, a few yards from her arm-chair, I examined her figure; I perused her features. In my hand I held the tract containing the sudden death of the Liar, to which narrative my attention had been pointed as to an appropriate warning. What had just passed; what Mrs. Reed had said concerning me to Mr. Brocklehurst; the whole tenor of their conversation, was recent, raw, and stinging in my mind; I had felt every word as acutely as I had heard it plainly, and a passion of resentment fomented now within me.

Mrs. Reed looked up from her work; her eye settled on mine, her fingers at the same time suspended their nimble movements.

"Go out of the room; return to the nursery," was her mandate. My look or something else must have struck her as offensive, for she spoke with extreme though suppressed irritation. I got up, I went to the door; I came back again; I walked to the window, across the room, then close up to her.

Speak I must: I had been trodden on severely, and *must* turn: but how? What strength had I to dart retaliation at my antagonist? I gathered my energies and launched them in this blunt sentence—

"I am not deceitful: if I were, I should say I loved you; but I declare I do not love you: I dislike you the worst of anybody in the world except John Reed; and this book about the liar, you may give to your girl, Georgiana, for it is she who tells lies, and not I."

Mrs. Reed's hands still lay on her work inactive: her eye of ice continued to dwell freezingly on mine.

"What more have you to say?" she asked, rather in the tone in which a person might address an opponent of adult age than such as is ordinarily used to a child.

That eye of hers, that voice stirred every antipathy I had. Shaking from head to foot, thrilled with ungovernable excitement, I continued—

"I am glad you are no relation of mine: I will never call you aunt again as long as I live. I will never come to see you when I am grown up; and if any one asks me how I liked you, and how you treated me, I will say the very thought of you makes me sick, and that you treated me with miserable cruelty."

"How dare you affirm that, Jane Eyre?"

"How dare I, Mrs. Reed? How dare I? Because it is the *truth*. You think I have no feelings, and that I can do without one bit of love or kindness; but I cannot live so: and you have no pity. I shall remember how you thrust me back—roughly and violently thrust me back—into the red-room, and locked me up there, to my dying day; though I was in agony; though I cried out, while suffocating with distress, 'Have mercy! Have mercy, Aunt Reed!' And that punishment you made me suffer because your wicked boy struck me—knocked me down for nothing. I will tell anybody who asks me questions, this exact tale. People think you a good woman, but you are bad, hard-hearted. *You* are deceitful!"

Ere I had finished this reply, my soul began to expand, to exult, with the strangest sense of freedom, of triumph, I ever felt. It seemed as if an invisible bond had burst, and that I had struggled out into unhoped-for liberty. Not without cause was this sentiment: Mrs. Reed looked frightened; her work had slipped from her knee; she was lifting up her hands, rocking herself to and fro, and even twisting her face as if she would cry.

"Jane, you are under a mistake: what is the matter with you? Why do you tremble so violently? Would you like to drink some water?"

"No, Mrs. Reed."

"Is there anything else you wish for, Jane? I assure you, I desire to be your friend."

"Not you. You told Mr. Brocklehurst I had a bad character, a deceitful disposition; and I'll let everybody at Lowood know what you are, and what you have done."

"Jane, you don't understand these things: children must be corrected for their faults."

"Deceit is not my fault!" I cried out in a savage, high voice.

"But you are passionate, Jane, that you must allow: and now return to the nursery—there's a dear—and lie down a little."

"I am not your dear; I cannot lie down: send me to school soon, Mrs. Reed, for I hate to live here."

"I will indeed send her to school soon," murmured Mrs. Reed *sotto voce*; and gathering up her work, she abruptly quitted the apartment.

I was left there alone—winner of the field. It was the hardest battle I had fought, and the first victory I had gained: I stood awhile on the rug, where Mr. Brocklehurst had stood, and I enjoyed my conqueror's solitude. First, I smiled to myself and felt elate; but this fierce pleasure subsided in me as fast as did the accelerated throb of my pulses. A child cannot quarrel with its elders, as I had done; cannot give its furious feelings uncontrolled play, as I had given mine, without experiencing afterwards the pang of remorse and the chill of reaction. A ridge of lighted heath, alive, glancing, devouring, would have been a meet emblem of my mind when I accused and menaced Mrs. Reed: the same ridge, black and blasted after the flames are dead, would have represented as meetly my subsequent condition, when half-an-hour's silence and reflection had shown me the madness of my conduct, and the dreariness of my hated and hating position.

Something of vengeance I had tasted for the first time; as aromatic wine it seemed, on swallowing, warm and racy: its after-flavour, metallic and corroding, gave me a sensation as if I had been poisoned. Willingly would I now have gone and asked Mrs. Reed's pardon; but I knew, partly from experience and partly from instinct, that was the way to make her repulse me with double scorn, thereby re-exciting every turbulent impulse of my nature.

I would fain exercise some better faculty than that of fierce speaking; fain find nourishment for some less fiendish feeling than that of sombre indignation. I took a book—some Arabian tales; I sat down and endeavoured to read. I could make no sense of the subject; my own thoughts swam always between me and the page I had usually found fascinating. I opened the glass-door in the breakfast-room: the shrubbery was quite still: the black frost reigned, unbroken by sun or breeze, through the grounds. I covered my head and arms with the skirt of my frock, and went out to walk in a part of the plantation which was quite sequestrated; but I found no pleasure in the silent trees, the falling fir-cones, the congealed relics of autumn, russet leaves, swept by past winds in heaps, and now stiffened together. I leaned against a gate, and looked into an empty field where no sheep were feeding, where the short grass was nipped and blanched. It was a very grey day; a most opaque sky, "onding on snaw," canopied all; thence flakes felt it intervals, which settled on the hard path and on the hoary lea without melting. I stood, a wretched child enough, whispering to myself over and over again, "What shall I do? What shall I do?"

All at once I heard a clear voice call, "Miss Jane! Where are you? Come to lunch!"

It was Bessie, I knew well enough; but I did not stir; her light step came tripping down the path.

"You naughty little thing!" she said. "Why don't you come when you are called?"

Bessie's presence, compared with the thoughts over which I had been brooding, seemed cheerful; even though, as usual, she was somewhat cross. The fact is, after my conflict with and victory over Mrs. Reed, I was not disposed to care much for the nursemaid's transitory anger; and I *was* disposed to bask in her youthful lightness of heart. I just put my two arms round her and said, "Come, Bessie! Don't scold."

The action was more frank and fearless than any I was habituated to indulge in: somehow it pleased her.

"You are a strange child, Miss Jane," she said, as she looked down at me; "a little roving, solitary thing: and you are going to school, I suppose?"

I nodded.

"And won't you be sorry to leave poor Bessie?"

"What does Bessie care for me? She is always scolding me."

"Because you're such a queer, frightened, shy little thing. You should be bolder."

"What! To get more knocks?"

"Nonsense! But you are rather put upon, that's certain. My mother said, when she came to see me last week, that she would not like a little one of her own to be in your place. Now, come in, and I've some good news for you."

"I don't think you have, Bessie."

"Child! What do you mean? What sorrowful eyes you fix on me! Well, but Missis and the young ladies and Master John are going out to tea this afternoon, and you shall have tea with me. I'll ask cook to bake you a little cake, and then you shall help me to look over your drawers; for I am soon to pack your trunk. Missis intends you to leave Gateshead in a day or two, and you shall choose what toys you like to take with you."

"Bessie, you must promise not to scold me any more till I go."

"Well, I will; but mind you are a very good girl, and don't be afraid of me. Don't start when I chance to speak rather sharply; it's so provoking."

"I don't think I shall ever be afraid of you again, Bessie, because I have got used to you, and I shall soon have another set of people to dread."

"If you dread them they'll dislike you."

"As you do, Bessie?"

"I don't dislike you, Miss; I believe I am fonder of you than of all the others."

"You don't show it."

"You little sharp thing! You've got quite a new way of talking. What makes you so venturesome and hardy?"

"Why, I shall soon be away from you, and besides"—I was going to say something about what had passed between me and Mrs. Reed, but on second thoughts I considered it better to remain silent on that head.

"And so you're glad to leave me?"

"Not at all, Bessie; indeed, just now I'm rather sorry."

"Just now! And rather! How coolly my little lady says it! I dare say now if I were to ask you for a kiss you wouldn't give it me: you'd say you'd *rather* not."

"I'll kiss you and welcome: bend your head down." Bessie stooped; we mutually embraced, and I followed her into the house quite comforted. That afternoon lapsed in peace and harmony; and in the evening Bessie told me some of her most enchanting stories, and sang me some of her sweetest songs. Even for me life had its gleams of sunshine.

CHAPTER V

Five o'clock had hardly struck on the morning of the 19th of January, when Bessie brought a candle into my closet and found me already up and nearly dressed. I had risen half-an-hour before her entrance, and had washed my face, and put on my clothes by the light of a half-moon just setting, whose rays streamed through the narrow window near my crib. I was to leave Gateshead that day by a coach which passed the lodge gates at six a.m. Bessie was the only person yet risen; she had lit a fire in the nursery, where she now proceeded to make my breakfast. Few children can eat when excited with the thoughts of a journey; nor could I. Bessie, having pressed me in vain to take a few spoonfuls of the boiled milk and bread she had prepared for me, wrapped up some biscuits in a paper and put them into my bag; then she helped me on with my pelisse and bonnet, and wrapping herself in a shawl, she and I left the nursery. As we passed Mrs. Reed's bedroom, she said, "Will you go in and bid Missis good-bye?"

"No, Bessie: she came to my crib last night when you were gone down to supper, and said I need not disturb her in the morning, or my cousins either; and she told me to remember that she had always been my best friend, and to speak of her and be grateful to her accordingly."

"What did you say, Miss?"

"Nothing: I covered my face with the bedclothes, and turned from her to the wall."

"That was wrong, Miss Jane."

"It was quite right, Bessie. Your Missis has not been my friend: she has been my foe."

"O Miss Jane! Don't say so!"

"Good-bye to Gateshead!" cried I, as we passed through the hall and went out at the front door.

The moon was set, and it was very dark; Bessie carried a lantern, whose light glanced on wet steps and gravel road sodden by a recent thaw. Raw and chill was the winter morning: my teeth chattered as I hastened down the drive. There was a light in the porter's lodge: when we reached it, we found the porter's wife just kindling her fire: my trunk, which had been carried down the evening before, stood corded at the door. It wanted but a few minutes of six, and shortly after that hour had struck, the distant roll of wheels announced the coming coach; I went to the door and watched its lamps approach rapidly through the gloom.

"Is she going by herself?" asked the porter's wife.

"Yes."

"And how far is it?"

"Fifty miles."

"What a long way! I wonder Mrs. Reed is not afraid to trust her so far alone."

The coach drew up; there it was at the gates with its four horses and its top laden with passengers: the guard and coachman loudly urged haste; my trunk was hoisted up; I was taken from Bessie's neck, to which I clung with kisses.

"Be sure and take good care of her," cried she to the guard, as he lifted me into the inside.

"Ay, ay!" was the answer: the door was slapped to, a voice exclaimed "All right," and on we drove. Thus was I severed from Bessie and Gateshead; thus whirled away to unknown, and, as I then deemed, remote and mysterious regions.

I remember but little of the journey; I only know that the day seemed to me of a preternatural length, and that we appeared to travel over hundreds of miles of road. We passed through several towns, and in one, a very large one, the coach stopped; the horses were taken out, and the passengers alighted to dine. I was carried into an inn, where the guard wanted me to have some dinner; but, as I had no appetite, he left me in an immense room with a fireplace at each end, a chandelier pendent from the ceiling, and a little red gallery high up against the wall filled with musical instruments. Here I walked about for a long time, feeling very strange, and mortally apprehensive of some one coming in and kidnapping me; for I believed in kidnappers, their exploits having frequently figured in Bessie's fireside chronicles. At last the guard returned; once more I was stowed away in the coach, my protector mounted his own seat, sounded his hollow horn, and away we rattled over the "stony street" of L——.

The afternoon came on wet and somewhat misty: as it waned into dusk, I began to feel that we were getting very far indeed from

Gateshead: we ceased to pass through towns; the country changed; great grey hills heaved up round the horizon: as twilight deepened, we descended a valley, dark with wood, and long after night had overclouded the prospect, I heard a wild wind rushing amongst trees.

Lulled by the sound, I at last dropped asleep; I had not long slumbered when the sudden cessation of motion awoke me; the coach-door was open, and a person like a servant was standing at it: I saw her face and dress by the light of the lamps.

"Is there a little girl called Jane Eyre here?" she asked. I answered "Yes," and was then lifted out; my trunk was handed down, and the coach instantly drove away.

I was stiff with long sitting, and bewildered with the noise and motion of the coach: Gathering my faculties, I looked about me. Rain, wind, and darkness filled the air; nevertheless, I dimly discerned a wall before me and a door open in it; through this door I passed with my new guide: she shut and locked it behind her. There was now visible a house or houses—for the building spread far—with many windows, and lights burning in some; we went up a broad pebbly path, splashing wet, and were admitted at a door; then the servant led me through a passage into a room with a fire, where she left me alone.

I stood and warmed my numbed fingers over the blaze, then I looked round; there was no candle, but the uncertain light from the hearth showed, by intervals, papered walls, carpet, curtains, shining mahogany furniture: it was a parlour, not so spacious or splendid as the drawing-room at Gateshead, but comfortable enough. I was puzzling to make out the subject of a picture on the wall, when the door opened, and an individual carrying a light entered; another followed close behind.

The first was a tall lady with dark hair, dark eyes, and a pale and large forehead; her figure was partly enveloped in a shawl, her countenance was grave, her bearing erect.

"The child is very young to be sent alone," said she, putting her candle down on the table. She considered me attentively for a minute or two, then further added—

"She had better be put to bed soon; she looks tired: are you tired?" she asked, placing her hand on my shoulder.

"A little, ma'am."

"And hungry too, no doubt: let her have some supper before she goes to bed, Miss Miller. Is this the first time you have left your parents to come to school, my little girl?"

I explained to her that I had no parents. She inquired how long they had been dead: then how old I was, what was my name, whether I could read, write, and sew a little: then she touched my cheek gently with her forefinger, and saying, "She hoped I should be a good child," dismissed me along with Miss Miller.

The lady I had left might be about twenty-nine; the one who went with me appeared some years younger: the first impressed me by her voice, look, and air. Miss Miller was more ordinary; ruddy in complexion, though of a careworn countenance; hurried in gait and action, like one who had always a multiplicity of tasks on hand: she looked, indeed, what I afterwards found she really was, an under-teacher. Led by her, I passed from compartment to compartment, from passage to passage, of a large and irregular building; till, emerging from the total and somewhat dreary silence pervading that portion of the house we had traversed, we came upon the hum of many voices, and presently entered a wide, long room, with great deal tables, two at each end, on each of which burnt a pair of candles, and seated all round on benches, a congregation of girls of every age, from nine or ten to twenty. Seen by the dim light of the dips, their number to me appeared countless, though not in reality exceeding eighty; they were uniformly dressed in brown stuff frocks of quaint fashion, and long holland pinafores. It was the hour of study; they were engaged in conning over their tomorrow's task, and the hum I had heard was the combined result of their whispered repetitions.

Miss Miller signed to me to sit on a bench near the door, then walking up to the top of the long room she cried out—

"Monitors, collect the lesson-books and put them away!"

Four tall girls arose from different tables, and going round, gathered the books and removed them. Miss Miller again gave the word of command—

"Monitors, fetch the supper-trays!"

The tall girls went out and returned presently, each bearing a tray, with portions of something, I knew not what, arranged thereon, and a pitcher of water and mug in the middle of each tray. The portions were handed round; those who liked took a draught of the water, the mug being common to all. When it came to my turn, I drank, for I was thirsty, but did not touch the food, excitement and fatigue rendering me incapable of eating: I now saw, however, that it was a thin oaten cake shared into fragments.

The meal over, prayers were read by Miss Miller, and the classes filed off, two and two, upstairs. Overpowered by this time with weariness, I scarcely noticed what sort of a place the bedroom was, except that, like the schoolroom, I saw it was very long. Tonight I was to be Miss Miller's bed-fellow; she helped me to undress: when laid down I glanced at the long rows of beds, each of which was quickly filled with two occupants; in ten minutes the single light was extinguished, and amidst silence and complete darkness I fell asleep.

The night passed rapidly. I was too tired even to dream; I only once awoke to hear the wind rave in furious gusts, and the rain fall in torrents, and to be sensible that Miss Miller had taken her place by my side. When I again unclosed my eyes, a loud bell was ringing; the girls were up and dressing; day had not yet begun to dawn, and a rushlight or two burned in the room. I too rose reluctantly; it was bitter cold, and I dressed as well as I could for shivering, and washed when there was a basin at liberty, which did not occur soon, as there was but one basin to six girls, on the stands down the middle of the room. Again the bell rang: all formed in file, two and two, and in that order descended the stairs and entered the cold and dimly lit schoolroom: here prayers were read by Miss Miller; afterwards she called out—

"Form classes!"

A great tumult succeeded for some minutes, during which Miss Miller repeatedly exclaimed, "Silence!" and "Order!" When it subsided, I saw them all drawn up in four semicircles, before four chairs, placed at the four tables; all held books in their hands, and a great book, like a Bible, lay on each table, before the vacant seat. A pause of some seconds succeeded, filled up by the low, vague hum of numbers; Miss Miller walked from class to class, hushing this indefinite sound.

A distant bell tinkled: immediately three ladies entered the room, each walked to a table and took her seat. Miss Miller assumed the fourth vacant chair, which was that nearest the door, and around which the smallest of the children were assembled: to this inferior class I was called, and placed at the bottom of it.

Business now began, the day's Collect was repeated, then certain texts of Scripture were said, and to these succeeded a protracted reading of chapters in the Bible, which lasted an hour. By the time that exercise was terminated, day had fully dawned. The indefatigable bell now sounded for the fourth time: the classes were marshalled and marched into another room to breakfast: how glad I was to behold a prospect of getting something to eat! I was now nearly sick from inanition, having taken so little the day before.

The refectory was a great, low-ceiled, gloomy room; on two long tables smoked basins of something hot, which, however, to my dismay, sent forth an odour far from inviting. I saw a universal manifestation of discontent when the fumes of the repast met the nostrils of those destined to swallow it; from the van of the procession, the tall girls of the first class, rose the whispered words—

"Disgusting! The porridge is burnt again!"

"Silence!" ejaculated a voice; not that of Miss Miller, but one of the upper teachers, a little and dark personage, smartly dressed, but of somewhat morose aspect, who installed herself at the top of one table, while a more buxom lady presided at the other. I looked in vain for her I had first seen the night before; she was not visible: Miss Miller occupied the foot of the table where I sat, and a strange, foreign-looking, elderly lady, the French teacher, as I afterwards found, took the corresponding seat at the other board. A long grace was said and a hymn sung; then a servant brought in some tea for the teachers, and the meal began.

Ravenous, and now very faint, I devoured a spoonful or two of my portion without thinking of its taste; but the first edge of hunger blunted, I perceived I had got in hand a nauseous mess; burnt porridge is almost as bad as rotten potatoes; famine itself soon sickens over it. The spoons were moved slowly: I saw each girl taste her food and try to swallow it; but in most cases the effort was soon relinquished. Breakfast was over, and none had breakfasted. Thanks being returned for what we had not got, and a second hymn chanted, the refectory was evacuated for the schoolroom. I was one of the last to go out, and in passing the tables, I saw one teacher take a basin of the porridge and taste it; she looked at the others; all their countenances expressed displeasure, and one of them, the stout one, whispered—

"Abominable stuff! How shameful!"

A quarter of an hour passed before lessons again began, during which the schoolroom was in a glorious tumult; for that space of time it seemed to be permitted to talk loud and more freely, and they used their privilege. The whole conversation ran on the breakfast, which one and all abused roundly. Poor things! It was the sole consolation they had. Miss Miller was now the only teacher in the room: a group of great girls standing about her spoke with serious and sullen gestures. I heard the name of Mr. Brocklehurst pronounced by some lips; at which Miss Miller shook her head disapprovingly; but she made no great effort to check the general wrath; doubtless she shared in it.

A clock in the schoolroom struck nine; Miss Miller left her circle, and standing in the middle of the room, cried—

"Silence! To your seats!"

Discipline prevailed: in five minutes the confused throng was resolved into order, and comparative silence quelled the Babel clamour of tongues. The upper teachers now punctually resumed their posts: but still, all seemed to wait. Ranged on benches down the sides of the room, the eighty girls sat motionless and erect; a quaint assemblage they appeared, all with plain locks combed from their faces, not a curl visible; in brown dresses, made high and surrounded by a narrow tucker about the throat, with little pockets of holland (shaped something like a Highlander's purse) tied in front of their frocks, and destined to serve the purpose of a work-bag: all, too, wearing woollen stockings and country-made shoes, fastened with brass buckles. Above twenty of those clad in this costume were full-grown girls, or rather young women; it suited them ill, and gave an air of oddity even to the prettiest.

I was still looking at them, and also at intervals examining the teachers—none of whom precisely pleased me; for the stout one was a little coarse, the dark one not a little fierce, the foreigner harsh and grotesque, and Miss Miller—poor thing!—looked purple, weather-beaten, and over-worked—when, as my eye wandered from face to face, the whole school rose simultaneously, as if moved by a common spring.

What was the matter? I had heard no order given: I was puzzled. Ere I had gathered my wits, the classes were again seated: but as all eyes were now turned to one point, mine followed the general direction, and encountered the personage who had received me last night. She stood at the bottom of the long room, on the hearth; for there was a fire at each end; she surveyed the two rows of girls silently and gravely. Miss Miller approaching, seemed to ask her a question, and having received her answer, went back to her place, and said aloud—

"Monitor of the first class, fetch the globes!"

While the direction was being executed, the lady consulted moved slowly up the room. I suppose I have a considerable organ of veneration, for I retain yet the sense of admiring awe with which my eyes traced her steps. Seen now, in broad daylight, she looked tall, fair, and shapely; brown eyes with a benignant light in their irids, and a fine pencilling of long lashes round, relieved the whiteness of her large front; on each of her temples her hair, of a very dark brown, was clustered in round curls, according to the fashion of those times, when neither smooth bands nor long ringlets were in vogue; her dress, also in the mode of the day, was of purple cloth, relieved by a sort of Spanish trimming of black velvet; a gold watch (watches were not so common then as now) shone at her girdle. Let the reader add, to complete the picture, refined features; a complexion, if pale, clear; and a stately air and carriage, and he will have, at least, as clearly as words can give it, a correct idea of the exterior of Miss Temple—Maria Temple, as I afterwards saw the name written in a prayer-book intrusted to me to carry to church.

The superintendent of Lowood (for such was this lady) having taken her seat before a pair of globes placed on one of the tables, summoned the first class round her, and commenced giving a lesson on geography; the lower classes were called by the teachers: repetitions in history, grammar, etc., went on for an hour; writing and arithmetic succeeded, and music lessons were given by Miss Temple to some of the elder girls. The duration of each lesson was measured by the clock, which at last struck twelve. The superintendent rose—

"I have a word to address to the pupils," said she.

The tumult of cessation from lessons was already breaking forth, but it sank at her voice. She went on—

"You had this morning a breakfast which you could not eat; you must be hungry: I have ordered that a lunch of bread and cheese shall be served to all."

The teachers looked at her with a sort of surprise.

"It is to be done on my responsibility," she added, in an explanatory tone to them, and immediately afterwards left the room.

The bread and cheese was presently brought in and distributed, to the high delight and refreshment of the whole school. The order was now given "To the garden!" Each put on a coarse straw bonnet, with strings of coloured calico, and a cloak of grey frieze. I was similarly equipped, and, following the stream, I made my way into the open air.

The garden was a wide inclosure, surrounded with walls so high as to exclude every glimpse of prospect; a covered verandah ran down one side, and broad walks bordered a middle space divided into scores of little beds: these beds were assigned as gardens for the pupils to cultivate, and each bed had an owner. When full of flowers they would doubtless look pretty; but now, at the latter end of January, all was wintry blight and brown decay. I shuddered as I stood and looked round me: it was an inclement day for outdoor exercise; not positively rainy, but darkened by a drizzling yellow fog; all under foot was still soaking wet with the floods of yesterday. The stronger among the girls ran about and engaged in active games, but sundry pale and thin ones herded together for shelter and warmth in the verandah; and amongst these, as the dense mist penetrated to their shivering frames, I heard frequently the sound of a hollow cough.

As yet I had spoken to no one, nor did anybody seem to take notice of me; I stood lonely enough: but to that feeling of isolation I was accustomed; it did not oppress me much. I leant against a pillar of the verandah, drew my grey mantle close about me, and, trying to forget the cold which nipped me without, and the unsatisfied hunger which gnawed me within, delivered myself up to the employment of watching and thinking. My reflections were too undefined and fragmentary to merit record: I hardly yet knew where I was; Gateshead and my past life seemed floated away to an immeasurable distance; the present was vague and strange, and of the future I could form no conjecture. I looked round the convent-like garden, and then up at the house—a large building, half of which seemed grey and old, the other half quite new. The new part, containing the schoolroom and dormitory, was lit by mullioned and latticed windows, which gave it a church-like aspect; a stone tablet over the door bore this inscription:

Lowood Institution. This portion was rebuilt A.D. —, by Naomi Brocklehurst, of Brocklehurst Hall, in this county.

"Let your light so shine before men, that they may see your good works, and glorify your Father which is in heaven." —St. Matt. v. 16.

I read these words over and over again: I felt that an explanation belonged to them, and was unable fully to penetrate their import. I was still pondering the signification of "Institution," and endeavouring to make out a connection between the first words and the verse of Scripture, when the sound of a cough close behind me made me turn my head. I saw a girl sitting on a stone bench near; she was bent over a book, on the perusal of which she seemed intent: from where I stood I could see the title—it was "Rasselas"; a name that struck me as strange, and consequently attractive. In turning a leaf she happened to look up, and I said to her directly—

"Is your book interesting?" I had already formed the intention of asking her to lend it to me some day.

"I like it," she answered, after a pause of a second or two, during which she examined me.

"What is it about?" I continued. I hardly know where I found the hardihood thus to open a conversation with a stranger; the step was contrary to my nature and habits: but I think her occupation touched a chord of sympathy somewhere; for I too liked reading, though of a frivolous and childish kind; I could not digest or comprehend the serious or substantial.

"You may look at it," replied the girl, offering me the book.

I did so; a brief examination convinced me that the contents were less taking than the title: "Rasselas" looked dull to my trifling taste; I saw nothing about fairies, nothing about genii; no bright variety seemed spread over the closely-printed pages. I returned it to her; she received it quietly, and without saying anything she was about to relapse into her former studious mood: again I ventured to disturb her—

"Can you tell me what the writing on that stone over the door means? What is Lowood Institution?"

"This house where you are come to live."

"And why do they call it Institution? Is it in any way different from other schools?"

"It is partly a charity-school: you and I, and all the rest of us, are charity-children. I suppose you are an orphan: are not either your father or your mother dead?"

"Both died before I can remember."

"Well, all the girls here have lost either one or both parents, and this is called an institution for educating orphans."

"Do we pay no money? Do they keep us for nothing?"

"We pay, or our friends pay, fifteen pounds a year for each."

"Then why do they call us charity-children?"

"Because fifteen pounds is not enough for board and teaching, and the deficiency is supplied by subscription."

"Who subscribes?"

"Different benevolent-minded ladies and gentlemen in this neighbourhood and in London."

"Who was Naomi Brocklehurst?"

"The lady who built the new part of this house as that tablet records, and whose son overlooks and directs everything here."

"Why?"

"Because he is treasurer and manager of the establishment."

"Then this house does not belong to that tall lady who wears a watch, and who said we were to have some bread and cheese?"

"To Miss Temple? Oh, no! I wish it did: she has to answer to Mr. Brocklehurst for all she does. Mr. Brocklehurst buys all our food and all our clothes."

"Does he live here?"

"No—two miles off, at a large hall."

"Is he a good man?"

"He is a clergyman, and is said to do a great deal of good."

"Did you say that tall lady was called Miss Temple?"

"Yes."

"And what are the other teachers called?"

"The one with red cheeks is called Miss Smith; she attends to the work, and cuts out—for we make our own clothes, our frocks, and pelisses, and everything; the little one with black hair is Miss Scatcherd; she teaches history and grammar, and hears the second class repetitions; and the one who wears a shawl, and has a pocket-handkerchief tied to her side with a yellow ribband, is Madame Pierrot: she comes from Lisle, in France, and teaches French."

"Do you like the teachers?"

"Well enough."

"Do you like the little black one, and the Madame ——? I cannot pronounce her name as you do."

"Miss Scatcherd is hasty—you must take care not to offend her; Madame Pierrot is not a bad sort of person."

"But Miss Temple is the best—isn't she?"

"Miss Temple is very good and very clever; she is above the rest, because she knows far more than they do."

"Have you been long here?"

"Two years."

"Are you an orphan?"

"My mother is dead."

"Are you happy here?"

"You ask rather too many questions. I have given you answers enough for the present: now I want to read."

But at that moment the summons sounded for dinner; all re-entered the house. The odour which now filled the refectory was scarcely more appetising than that which had regaled our nostrils at breakfast: the dinner was served in two huge tin-plated vessels, whence rose a strong steam redolent of rancid fat. I found the mess to consist of indifferent potatoes and strange shreds of rusty meat, mixed and cooked together. Of this preparation a tolerably abundant plateful was apportioned to each pupil. I ate what I could, and wondered within myself whether every day's fare would be like this.

After dinner, we immediately adjourned to the schoolroom: lessons recommenced, and were continued till five o'clock.

The only marked event of the afternoon was, that I saw the girl with whom I had conversed in the verandah dismissed in disgrace by Miss Scatcherd from a history class, and sent to stand in the middle of the large schoolroom. The punishment seemed to me in a high degree ignominious, especially for so great a girl—she looked thirteen or upwards. I expected she would show signs of great distress and shame; but to my surprise she neither wept nor blushed: composed, though grave, she stood, the central mark of all eyes. "How can she bear it so quietly—so firmly?" I asked of myself. "Were I in her place, it seems to me I should wish the earth to open and swallow me up. She looks as if she were thinking of something beyond her punishment—beyond her situation: of something not round her nor before her. I have heard of day-dreams—is she in a day-dream now? Her eyes are fixed on the floor, but I am sure they do not see it—her sight seems turned in, gone down into her heart: she is looking at what she can remember, I believe; not at what is really present. I wonder what sort of a girl she is—whether good or naughty."

Soon after five p.m. we had another meal, consisting of a small mug of coffee, and half-a-slice of brown bread. I devoured my bread and drank my coffee with relish; but I should have been glad of as much more—I was still hungry. Half-an-hour's recreation succeeded, then study; then the glass of water and the piece of oat-cake, prayers, and bed. Such was my first day at Lowood.

CHAPTER VI

The next day commenced as before, getting up and dressing by rushlight; but this morning we were obliged to dispense with the ceremony of washing; the water in the pitchers was frozen. A change had taken place in the weather the preceding evening, and a keen north-east wind, whistling through the crevices of our bedroom windows all night long, had made us shiver in our beds, and turned the contents of the ewers to ice.

Before the long hour and a half of prayers and Bible-reading was over, I felt ready to perish with cold. Breakfast-time came at last, and this morning the porridge was not burnt; the quality was eatable, the quantity small. How small my portion seemed! I wished it had been doubled.

In the course of the day I was enrolled a member of the fourth class, and regular tasks and occupations were assigned me: hitherto, I had only been a spectator of the proceedings at Lowood; I was now to become an actor therein. At first, being little accustomed to learn by heart, the lessons appeared to me both long and difficult; the frequent change from task to task, too, bewildered me; and I was glad when, about three o'clock in the afternoon, Miss Smith put into my hands a border of muslin two yards long, together with needle, thimble, etc., and sent me to sit in a quiet corner of the schoolroom, with directions to hem the same. At that hour most of the others were sewing likewise; but one class still stood round Miss Scatcherd's chair reading, and as all was quiet, the subject of their lessons could be heard, together with the manner in which each girl acquitted herself, and the animadversions or commendations of Miss Scatcherd on the performance. It was English history: among the readers I observed my acquaintance of the verandah: at the commencement of the lesson, her place had been at the top of the class, but for some error of pronunciation, or some inattention to stops, she was suddenly sent to the very bottom. Even in that obscure position, Miss Scatcherd continued to make her an object of constant notice: she was continually addressing to her such phrases as the following:

"Burns" (such it seems was her name: the girls here were all called by their surnames, as boys are elsewhere), "Burns, you are standing on the side of your shoe; turn your toes out immediately." "Burns, you poke your chin most unpleasantly; draw it in." "Burns, I insist on your holding your head up; I will not have you before me in that attitude," etc., etc.

A chapter having been read through twice, the books were closed and the girls examined. The lesson had comprised part of the reign of Charles I, and there were sundry questions about tonnage and poundage and ship-money, which most of them appeared unable to answer; still, every little difficulty was solved instantly when it reached Burns: her memory seemed to have retained the substance of the whole lesson, and she was ready with answers on every point. I kept expecting that Miss Scatcherd would praise her attention; but, instead of that, she suddenly cried out—

"You dirty, disagreeable girl! You have never cleaned your nails this morning!"

Burns made no answer: I wondered at her silence. "Why," thought I, "does she not explain that she could neither clean her nails nor wash her face, as the water was frozen?"

My attention was now called off by Miss Smith desiring me to hold a skein of thread: while she was winding it, she talked to me from time to time, asking whether I had ever been at school before, whether I could mark, stitch, knit, etc.; till she dismissed me, I could not pursue my observations on Miss Scatcherd's movements. When I returned to my seat, that lady was just delivering an order of which I did not catch the import; but Burns immediately left the class, and going into the small inner room where the books were kept, returned in half a minute, carrying in her hand a bundle of twigs tied together at one end. This ominous tool she presented to Miss Scatcherd with a respectful curtesy; then she quietly, and without being told, unloosed her pinafore, and the teacher instantly and sharply inflicted on her neck a dozen strokes with the bunch of twigs. Not a tear rose to Burns's eye; and, while I paused from my sewing, because my fingers quivered at this spectacle with a sentiment of unavailing and impotent anger, not a feature of her pensive face altered its ordinary expression.

"Hardened girl!" exclaimed Miss Scatcherd. "Nothing can correct you of your slatternly habits: carry the rod away."

Burns obeyed: I looked at her narrowly as she emerged from the book-closet; she was just putting back her handkerchief into her pocket, and the trace of a tear glistened on her thin cheek.

The play-hour in the evening I thought the pleasantest fraction of the day at Lowood: the bit of bread, the draught of coffee swallowed at five o'clock had revived vitality, if it had not satisfied hunger: the long restraint of the day was slackened; the schoolroom felt warmer than in the morning—its fires being allowed to burn a little more brightly, to supply, in some measure, the place of candles, not yet introduced: the ruddy gloaming, the licensed uproar, the confusion of many voices gave one a welcome sense of liberty.

On the evening of the day on which I had seen Miss Scatcherd flog her pupil, Burns, I wandered as usual among the forms and tables and laughing groups without a companion, yet not feeling lonely: when I passed the windows, I now and then lifted a blind, and looked out; it snowed fast, a drift was already forming against the lower panes; putting my ear close to the window, I could distinguish from the gleeful tumult within, the disconsolate moan of the wind outside.

Probably, if I had lately left a good home and kind parents, this would have been the hour when I should most keenly have regretted the separation; that wind would then have saddened my heart; this obscure chaos would have disturbed my peace! As it was, I derived from both a strange excitement, and reckless and feverish, I wished the wind to howl more wildly, the gloom to deepen to darkness, and the confusion to rise to clamour.

Jumping over forms, and creeping under tables, I made my way to one of the fire-places; there, kneeling by the high wire fender, I found Burns, absorbed, silent, abstracted from all round her by the companionship of a book, which she read by the dim glare of the embers.

"Is it still 'Rasselas'?" I asked, coming behind her.

"Yes," she said, "and I have just finished it."

And in five minutes more she shut it up. I was glad of this. "Now," thought I, "I can perhaps get her to talk." I sat down by her on the floor.

"What is your name besides Burns?"

"Helen."

"Do you come a long way from here?"

"I come from a place farther north, quite on the borders of Scotland."

"Will you ever go back?"

"I hope so; but nobody can be sure of the future."

"You must wish to leave Lowood?"

"No! Why should I? I was sent to Lowood to get an education; and it would be of no use going away until I have attained that object."

"But that teacher, Miss Scatcherd, is so cruel to you?"

"Cruel? Not at all! She is severe: she dislikes my faults."

"And if I were in your place I should dislike her; I should resist her. If she struck me with that rod, I should get it from her hand; I should break it under her nose."

"Probably you would do nothing of the sort: but if you did, Mr. Brocklehurst would expel you from the school; that would be a great grief to your relations. It is far better to endure patiently a smart which nobody feels but yourself, than to commit a hasty action whose evil consequences will extend to all connected with you; and besides, the Bible bids us return good for evil."

"But then it seems disgraceful to be flogged, and to be sent to stand in the middle of a room full of people; and you are such a great girl: I am far younger than you, and I could not bear it."

"Yet it would be your duty to bear it, if you could not avoid it: it is weak and silly to say you *cannot bear* what it is your fate to be required to bear."

I heard her with wonder: I could not comprehend this doctrine of endurance; and still less could I understand or sympathise with the forbearance she expressed for her chastiser. Still I felt that Helen Burns considered things by a light invisible to my eyes. I suspected she might be right and I wrong; but I would not ponder the matter deeply; like Felix, I put it off to a more convenient season.

"You say you have faults, Helen: what are they? To me you seem very good."

"Then learn from me, not to judge by appearances: I am, as Miss Scatcherd said, slatternly; I seldom put, and never keep, things, in order; I am careless; I forget rules; I read when I should learn my lessons; I have no method; and sometimes I say, like you, I cannot *bear* to be subjected to systematic arrangements. This is all very provoking to Miss Scatcherd, who is naturally neat, punctual, and particular."

"And cross and cruel," I added; but Helen Burns would not admit my addition: she kept silence.

"Is Miss Temple as severe to you as Miss Scatcherd?"

At the utterance of Miss Temple's name, a soft smile flitted over her grave face.

"Miss Temple is full of goodness; it pains her to be severe to any one, even the worst in the school: she sees my errors, and tells me of them gently; and, if I do anything worthy of praise, she gives me my meed liberally. One strong proof of my wretchedly defective nature is, that even her expostulations, so mild, so rational, have not influence to cure me of my faults; and even her praise, though I value it most highly, cannot stimulate me to continued care and foresight."

"That is curious," said I, "it is so easy to be careful."

"For *you* I have no doubt it is. I observed you in your class this morning, and saw you were closely attentive: your thoughts never seemed to wander while Miss Miller explained the lesson and questioned you. Now, mine continually rove away; when I should be listening to Miss Scatcherd, and collecting all she says with assiduity, often I lose the very sound of her voice; I fall into a sort of dream. Sometimes I think I am in Northumberland, and that the noises I hear round me are the bubbling of a little brook which runs through Deepden, near our house—then, when it comes to my turn to reply, I have to be awakened; and having heard nothing of what was read for listening to the visionary brook, I have no answer ready."

"Yet how well you replied this afternoon."

"It was mere chance; the subject on which we had been reading had interested me. This afternoon, instead of dreaming of Deepden, I was wondering how a man who wished to do right could act so unjustly and unwisely as Charles the First sometimes did; and I thought what a pity it was that, with his integrity and conscientiousness, he could see no farther than the prerogatives of the crown. If he had but been able to look to a distance, and see how what they call the spirit of the age was tending! Still, I like Charles—I respect him—I pity him, poor murdered king! Yes, his enemies were the worst: they shed blood they had no right to shed. How dared they kill him!"

Helen was talking to herself now: she had forgotten I could not very well understand her—that I was ignorant, or nearly so, of the subject she discussed. I recalled her to my level.

"And when Miss Temple teaches you, do your thoughts wander then?"

"No, certainly, not often; because Miss Temple has generally something to say which is newer than my own reflections; her language is singularly agreeable to me, and the information she communicates is often just what I wished to gain."

"Well, then, with Miss Temple you are good?"

"Yes, in a passive way: I make no effort; I follow as inclination guides me. There is no merit in such goodness."

"A great deal: you are good to those who are good to you. It is all I ever desire to be. If people were always kind and obedient to those who are cruel and unjust, the wicked people would have it all their own way: they would never feel afraid, and so they would never alter, but would grow worse and worse. When we are struck at without a reason, we should strike back again very hard; I am sure we should—so hard as to teach the person who struck us never to do it again."

"You will change your mind, I hope, when you grow older: as yet you are but a little untaught girl."

"But I feel this, Helen; I must dislike those who, whatever I do to please them, persist in disliking me; I must resist those who punish me unjustly. It is as natural as that I should love those who show me affection, or submit to punishment when I feel it is deserved."

"Heathens and savage tribes hold that doctrine, but Christians and civilised nations disown it."

"How? I don't understand."

"It is not violence that best overcomes hate—nor vengeance that most certainly heals injury."

"What then?"

"Read the New Testament, and observe what Christ says, and how He acts; make His word your rule, and His conduct your example."

"What does He say?"

"Love your enemies; bless them that curse you; do good to them that hate you and despitefully use you."

"Then I should love Mrs. Reed, which I cannot do; I should bless her son John, which is impossible."

In her turn, Helen Burns asked me to explain, and I proceeded forthwith to pour out, in my own way, the tale of my sufferings and resentments. Bitter and truculent when excited, I spoke as I felt, without reserve or softening.

Helen heard me patiently to the end: I expected she would then make a remark, but she said nothing.

"Well," I asked impatiently, "is not Mrs. Reed a hard-hearted, bad woman?"

"She has been unkind to you, no doubt; because you see, she dislikes your cast of character, as Miss Scatcherd does mine; but how minutely you remember all she has done and said to you! What a singularly deep impression her injustice seems to have made on your heart! No ill-usage so brands its record on my feelings. Would you not be happier if you tried to forget her severity, together with the passionate emotions it excited? Life appears to me too short to be spent in nursing animosity or registering wrongs. We are, and must be, one and all, burdened with faults in this world: but the time will soon come when, I trust, we shall put them off in putting off our corruptible bodies; when debasement and sin will fall from us with this cumbrous frame of flesh, and only the spark of the spirit will remain—the impalpable principle of light and thought, pure as when it left the Creator to inspire the creature: whence it came it will return; perhaps again to be communicated to some being higher than man—perhaps to pass through gradations of glory, from the pale human soul to brighten to the seraph! Surely it will never, on the contrary, be suffered to degenerate from man to fiend? No; I cannot believe that: I hold another creed: which no one ever taught me, and which I seldom mention; but in which I delight, and to which I cling: for it extends hope to all: it makes Eternity a rest—a mighty home, not a terror and an abyss. Besides, with this creed, I can so clearly distinguish between the criminal and his crime; I can so sincerely forgive the first while I abhor the last: with this creed revenge never worries my heart, degradation never too deeply disgusts me, injustice never crushes me too low: I live in calm, looking to the end."

Helen's head, always drooping, sank a little lower as she finished this sentence. I saw by her look she wished no longer to talk to me, but rather to converse with her own thoughts. She was not allowed much time for meditation: a monitor, a great rough girl, presently came up, exclaiming in a strong Cumberland accent—

"Helen Burns, if you don't go and put your drawer in order, and fold up your work this minute, I'll tell Miss Scatcherd to come and look at it!"

Helen sighed as her reverie fled, and getting up, obeyed the monitor without reply as without delay.

CHAPTER VII

My first quarter at Lowood seemed an age; and not the golden age either; it comprised an irksome struggle with difficulties in habituating myself to new rules and unwonted tasks. The fear of failure in these points harassed me worse than the physical hardships of my lot; though these were no trifles.

During January, February, and part of March, the deep snows, and, after their melting, the almost impassable roads, prevented our stirring beyond the garden walls, except to go to church; but within these limits we had to pass an hour every day in the open air. Our clothing was insufficient to protect us from the severe cold: we had no boots, the snow got into our shoes and melted there: our ungloved hands became numbed and covered with chilblains, as were our feet: I remember well the distracting irritation I endured from this cause every evening, when my feet inflamed; and the torture of thrusting the swelled, raw, and stiff toes into my shoes in the morning. Then the scanty supply of food was distressing: with the keen appetites of growing children, we had scarcely sufficient to keep alive a delicate invalid. From this deficiency of nourishment resulted an abuse, which pressed hardly on the younger pupils: whenever the famished great girls had an opportunity, they would coax or menace the little ones out of their portion. Many a time I have shared between two claimants the precious morsel of brown bread distributed at tea-time; and after relinquishing to a third half the contents of my mug of coffee, I have swallowed the remainder with an accompaniment of secret tears, forced from me by the exigency of hunger.

Sundays were dreary days in that wintry season. We had to walk two miles to Brocklebridge Church, where our patron officiated. We set out cold, we arrived at church colder: during the morning service we became almost paralysed. It was too far to return to dinner, and an allowance of cold meat and bread, in the same penurious proportion observed in our ordinary meals, was served round between the services.

At the close of the afternoon service we returned by an exposed and hilly road, where the bitter winter wind, blowing over a range of snowy summits to the north, almost flayed the skin from our faces.

I can remember Miss Temple walking lightly and rapidly along our drooping line, her plaid cloak, which the frosty wind fluttered, gathered close about her, and encouraging us, by precept and example, to keep up our spirits, and march forward, as she said, "like stalwart soldiers." The other teachers, poor things, were generally themselves too much dejected to attempt the task of cheering others.

How we longed for the light and heat of a blazing fire when we got back! But, to the little ones at least, this was denied: each hearth in the schoolroom was immediately surrounded by a double row of great girls, and behind them the younger children crouched in groups, wrapping their starved arms in their pinafores.

A little solace came at tea-time, in the shape of a double ration of bread—a whole, instead of a half, slice—with the delicious addition of a thin scrape of butter: it was the hebdomadal treat to which we all looked forward from Sabbath to Sabbath. I generally contrived to reserve a moiety of this bounteous repast for myself; but the remainder I was invariably obliged to part with.

The Sunday evening was spent in repeating, by heart, the Church Catechism, and the fifth, sixth, and seventh chapters of St. Matthew; and in listening to a long sermon, read by Miss Miller, whose irrepressible yawns attested her weariness. A frequent interlude of these performances was the enactment of the part of Eutychus by some half-dozen of little girls, who, overpowered with sleep, would fall down, if not out of the third loft, yet off the fourth form, and be taken up half dead. The remedy was, to thrust them forward into the centre of the schoolroom, and oblige them to stand there till the sermon was finished. Sometimes their feet failed them, and they sank together in a heap; they were then propped up with the monitors' high stools.

I have not yet alluded to the visits of Mr. Brocklehurst; and indeed that gentleman was from home during the greater part of the first month after my arrival; perhaps prolonging his stay with his friend the archdeacon: his absence was a relief to me. I need not say that I had my own reasons for dreading his coming: but come he did at last.

One afternoon (I had then been three weeks at Lowood), as I was sitting with a slate in my hand, puzzling over a sum in long division, my eyes, raised in abstraction to the window, caught sight of a figure just passing: I recognised almost instinctively that gaunt outline; and when, two minutes after, all the school, teachers included, rose *en masse*, it was not necessary for me to look up in order to ascertain whose entrance they thus greeted. A long stride measured the schoolroom, and presently beside Miss Temple, who herself had risen, stood the same black column which had frowned on me so ominously from the hearthrug of Gateshead. I now glanced sideways at this piece of architecture. Yes, I was right: it was Mr. Brocklehurst, buttoned up in a surtout, and looking longer, narrower, and more rigid than ever.

I had my own reasons for being dismayed at this apparition; too well I remembered the perfidious hints given by Mrs. Reed about my disposition, etc.; the promise pledged by Mr. Brocklehurst to apprise Miss Temple and the teachers of my vicious nature. All along I had been dreading the fulfilment of this promise—I had been looking out daily for the "Coming Man," whose information respecting my past life and conversation was to brand me as a bad child for ever: now there he was.

He stood at Miss Temple's side; he was speaking low in her ear: I did not doubt he was making disclosures of my villainy; and I watched her eye with painful anxiety, expecting every moment to see its dark orb turn on me a glance of repugnance and contempt. I listened too; and as I happened to be seated quite at the top of the room, I caught most of what he said: its import relieved me from immediate apprehension.

"I suppose, Miss Temple, the thread I bought at Lowton will do; it struck me that it would be just of the quality for the calico chemises, and I sorted the needles to match. You may tell Miss Smith that I forgot to make a memorandum of the darning needles, but she shall have some papers sent in next week; and she is not, on any account, to give out more than one at a time to each pupil: if they have more, they are apt to be careless and lose them. And, O ma'am! I wish the woollen stockings were better looked to! When I was here last, I went into the kitchen-garden and examined the clothes drying on the line; there was a quantity of black hose in a very bad state of repair: from the size of the holes in them I was sure they had not been well mended from time to time."

He paused.

"Your directions shall be attended to, sir," said Miss Temple.

"And, ma'am," he continued, "the laundress tells me some of the girls have two clean tuckers in the week: it is too much; the rules limit them to one."

"I think I can explain that circumstance, sir. Agnes and Catherine Johnstone were invited to take tea with some friends at Lowton last Thursday, and I gave them leave to put on clean tuckers for the occasion."

Mr. Brocklehurst nodded.

"Well, for once it may pass; but please not to let the circumstance occur too often. And there is another thing which surprised me; I find, in settling accounts with the housekeeper, that a lunch, consisting of bread and cheese, has twice been served out to the girls during the past fortnight. How is this? I looked over the regulations, and I find no such meal as lunch mentioned. Who introduced this innovation? And by what authority?"

"I must be responsible for the circumstance, sir," replied Miss Temple. "The breakfast was so ill prepared that the pupils could not possibly eat it; and I dared not allow them to remain fasting till dinner-time."

"Madam, allow me an instant. You are aware that my plan in bringing up these girls is, not to accustom them to habits of luxury and indulgence, but to render them hardy, patient, self-denying. Should any little accidental disappointment of the appetite occur, such as the spoiling of a meal, the under or the over dressing of a dish, the incident ought not to be neutralised by replacing with something more delicate the comfort lost, thus pampering the body and obviating the aim of this institution; it ought to be improved to the spiritual edification of the pupils, by encouraging them to evince fortitude under temporary privation. A brief address on those occasions would not be mistimed, wherein a judicious instructor would take the opportunity of referring to the sufferings of the primitive Christians; to the torments of martyrs; to the exhortations of our blessed Lord Himself, calling upon His disciples to take up their cross and follow Him; to His warnings that man shall not live by bread alone, but by every word that proceedeth out of the mouth of God; to His divine consolations, 'If ye suffer hunger or thirst for My sake, happy are ye.' Oh, madam, when you put bread and cheese, instead of burnt porridge, into these children's mouths, you may indeed feed their vile bodies, but you little think how you starve their immortal souls!"

Mr. Brocklehurst again paused—perhaps overcome by his feelings. Miss Temple had looked down when he first began to speak to her; but she now gazed straight before her, and her face, naturally pale as marble, appeared to be assuming also the coldness and fixity of that material; especially her mouth, closed as if it would have required a sculptor's chisel to open it, and her brow settled gradually into petrified severity.

Meantime, Mr. Brocklehurst, standing on the hearth with his hands behind his back, majestically surveyed the whole school. Suddenly his eye gave a blink, as if it had met something that either dazzled or shocked its pupil; turning, he said in more rapid accents than he had hitherto used—

"Miss Temple, Miss Temple, what—*what* is that girl with curled hair? Red hair, ma'am, curled—curled all over?" And extending his cane he pointed to the awful object, his hand shaking as he did so.

"It is Julia Severn," replied Miss Temple, very quietly.

"Julia Severn, ma'am! And why has she, or any other, curled hair? Why, in defiance of every precept and principle of this house, does she conform to the world so openly—here in an evangelical, charitable establishment—as to wear her hair one mass of curls?"

"Julia's hair curls naturally," returned Miss Temple, still more quietly.

"Naturally! Yes, but we are not to conform to nature; I wish these girls to be the children of Grace: and why that abundance? I have again and again intimated that I desire the hair to be arranged closely, modestly, plainly. Miss Temple, that girl's hair must be cut off entirely; I will send a barber tomorrow: and I see others who have far too much of the excrescence—that tall girl, tell her to turn round. Tell all the first form to rise up and direct their faces to the wall."

Miss Temple passed her handkerchief over her lips, as if to smooth away the involuntary smile that curled them; she gave the order, however, and when the first class could take in what was required of them, they obeyed. Leaning a little back on my bench, I could see the looks and grimaces with which they commented on this manoeuvre: it was a pity Mr. Brocklehurst could not see them too; he would perhaps have felt that, whatever he might do with the outside of the cup and platter, the inside was further beyond his interference than he imagined.

He scrutinised the reverse of these living medals some five minutes, then pronounced sentence. These words fell like the knell of doom—

"All those top-knots must be cut off."

Miss Temple seemed to remonstrate.

"Madam," he pursued, "I have a Master to serve whose kingdom is not of this world: my mission is to mortify in these girls the lusts of the flesh; to teach them to clothe themselves with shame-facedness and sobriety, not with braided hair and costly apparel; and each of the young persons before us has a string of hair twisted in plaits which vanity itself might have woven; these, I repeat, must be cut off; think of the time wasted, of—"

Mr. Brocklehurst was here interrupted: three other visitors, ladies, now entered the room. They ought to have come a little sooner to have heard his lecture on dress, for they were splendidly attired in velvet, silk, and furs. The two younger of the trio (fine girls of sixteen and seventeen) had grey beaver hats, then in fashion, shaded with ostrich plumes, and from under the brim of this graceful head-dress fell a profusion of light tresses, elaborately curled; the elder lady was enveloped in a costly velvet shawl, trimmed with ermine, and she wore a false front of French curls.

These ladies were deferentially received by Miss Temple, as Mrs. and the Misses Brocklehurst, and conducted to seats of honour at the top of the room. It seems they had come in the carriage with their reverend relative, and had been conducting a rummaging scrutiny of the room upstairs, while he transacted business with the housekeeper, questioned the laundress, and lectured the superintendent. They now proceeded to address divers remarks and reproofs to Miss Smith, who was charged with the care of the linen and the inspection of the dormitories: but I had no time to listen to what they said; other matters called off and enchanted my attention.

Hitherto, while gathering up the discourse of Mr. Brocklehurst and Miss Temple, I had not, at the same time, neglected precautions to secure my personal safety; which I thought would be effected, if I could only elude observation. To this end, I had sat well back on the form, and while seeming to be busy with my sum, had held my slate in such a manner as to conceal my face: I might have escaped notice, had not my treacherous slate somehow happened to slip from my hand, and falling with an obtrusive crash, directly drawn every eye upon me; I knew it was all over now, and, as I stooped to pick up the two fragments of slate, I rallied my forces for the worst. It came.

"A careless girl!" said Mr. Brocklehurst, and immediately after: "It is the new pupil, I perceive." And before I could draw breath: "I must not forget I have a word to say respecting her." Then aloud—how loud it seemed to me! "Let the child who broke her slate come forward!"

Of my own accord I could not have stirred; I was paralysed: but the two great girls who sit on each side of me, set me on my legs and pushed me towards the dread judge, and then Miss Temple gently assisted me to his very feet, and I caught her whispered counsel—

"Don't be afraid, Jane, I saw it was an accident; you shall not be punished."

The kind whisper went to my heart like a dagger.

"Another minute, and she will despise me for a hypocrite," thought I; and an impulse of fury against Reed, Brocklehurst, and Co. bounded in my pulses at the conviction. I was no Helen Burns.

"Fetch that stool," said Mr. Brocklehurst, pointing to a very high one from which a monitor had just risen: it was brought.

"Place the child upon it."

And I was placed there, by whom I don't know: I was in no condition to note particulars; I was only aware that they had hoisted me up to the height of Mr. Brocklehurst's nose, that he was within a yard of me, and that a spread of shot orange and purple silk pelisses and a cloud of silvery plumage extended and waved below me.

Mr. Brocklehurst hemmed.

"Ladies," said he, turning to his family, "Miss Temple, teachers, and children, you all see this girl?"

Of course they did; for I felt their eyes directed like burning-glasses against my scorched skin.

"You see she is yet young; you observe she possesses the ordinary form of childhood; God has graciously given her the shape that He has given to all of us; no signal deformity points her out as a marked character. Who would think that the Evil One had already found a servant and agent in her? Yet such, I grieve to say, is the case."

A pause—in which I began to steady the palsy of my nerves, and to feel that the Rubicon was passed; and that the trial, no longer to be shirked, must be firmly sustained.

"My dear children," pursued the black marble clergyman, with pathos, "this is a sad, a melancholy occasion; for it becomes my duty to warn you, that this girl, who might be one of God's own lambs, is a little castaway: not a member of the true flock, but evidently an interloper and an alien. You must be on your guard against her; you must shun her example; if necessary, avoid her company, exclude her from your sports, and shut her out from your converse. Teachers, you must watch her: keep your eyes on her movements, weigh well her words, scrutinise her actions, punish her body to save her soul: if, indeed, such salvation be possible, for (my tongue falters while I tell it) this girl, this child, the native of a Christian land, worse than many a little heathen who says its prayers to Brahma and kneels before Juggernaut—this girl is—a liar!"

Now came a pause of ten minutes, during which I, by this time in perfect possession of my wits, observed all the female Brocklehursts produce their pocket-handkerchiefs and apply them to their optics, while the elderly lady swayed herself to and fro, and the two younger ones whispered, "How shocking!"

Mr. Brocklehurst resumed.

"This I learned from her benefactress; from the pious and charitable lady who adopted her in her orphan state, reared her as her own daughter, and whose kindness, whose generosity the unhappy girl repaid by an ingratitude so bad, so dreadful, that at last her excellent patroness was obliged to separate her from her own young ones, fearful lest her vicious example should contaminate their purity: she has sent her here to be healed, even as the Jews of old sent their diseased to the troubled pool of Bethesda; and, teachers, superintendent, I beg of you not to allow the waters to stagnate round her."

With this sublime conclusion, Mr. Brocklehurst adjusted the top button of his surtout, muttered something to his family, who rose, bowed to Miss Temple, and then all the great people sailed in state from the room. Turning at the door, my judge said—

"Let her stand half-an-hour longer on that stool, and let no one speak to her during the remainder of the day."

There was I, then, mounted aloft; I, who had said I could not bear the shame of standing on my natural feet in the middle of the room, was now exposed to general view on a pedestal of infamy. What my sensations were no language can describe; but just as they all rose, stifling my breath and constricting my throat, a girl came up and passed me: in passing, she lifted her eyes. What a strange light inspired them! What an extraordinary sensation that ray sent through me! How the new feeling bore me up! It was as if a martyr, a hero, had passed a slave or victim, and imparted strength in the transit. I mastered the rising hysteria, lifted up my head, and took a firm stand on the stool. Helen Burns asked some slight question about her work of Miss Smith, was chidden for the triviality of the inquiry, returned to her place, and smiled at me as she again went by. What a smile! I remember it now, and I know that it was the effluence of fine intellect, of true courage; it lit up her marked lineaments, her thin face, her sunken grey eye, like a reflection from the aspect of an angel. Yet at that moment Helen Burns wore on her arm "the untidy badge"; scarcely an hour ago I had heard her condemned by Miss Scatcherd to a dinner of bread and water on the morrow because she had blotted an exercise in copying it out. Such is the imperfect nature of man! Such spots are there on the disc of the clearest planet; and eyes like Miss Scatcherd's can only see those minute defects, and are blind to the full brightness of the orb.

CHAPTER VIII

Ere the half-hour ended, five o'clock struck; school was dismissed, and all were gone into the refectory to tea. I now ventured to descend: it was deep dusk; I retired into a corner and sat down on the floor. The spell by which I had been so far supported began to dissolve; reaction took place, and soon, so overwhelming was the grief that seized me, I sank prostrate with my face to the ground. Now I wept: Helen Burns was not here; nothing sustained me; left to myself I abandoned myself, and my tears watered the boards. I had meant to be so good, and to do so much at Lowood: to make so many friends, to earn respect and win affection. Already I had made visible progress: that very morning I had reached the head of my class; Miss Miller had praised me warmly; Miss Temple had smiled approbation; she had promised to teach me drawing, and to let me learn French, if I continued to make similar improvement two months longer: and then I was well received by my fellow-pupils; treated as an equal by those of my own age, and not molested by any; now, here I lay again crushed and trodden on; and could I ever rise more?

"Never," I thought; and ardently I wished to die. While sobbing out this wish in broken accents, some one approached: I started up—again Helen Burns was near me; the fading fires just showed her coming up the long, vacant room; she brought my coffee and bread.

"Come, eat something," she said; but I put both away from me, feeling as if a drop or a crumb would have choked me in my present condition. Helen regarded me, probably with surprise: I could not now abate my agitation, though I tried hard; I continued to weep aloud. She sat down on the ground near me, embraced her knees with her arms, and rested her head upon them; in that attitude she remained silent as an Indian. I was the first who spoke—

"Helen, why do you stay with a girl whom everybody believes to be a liar?"

"Everybody, Jane? Why, there are only eighty people who have heard you called so, and the world contains hundreds of millions."

"But what have I to do with millions? The eighty, I know, despise me."

"Jane, you are mistaken: probably not one in the school either despises or dislikes you: many, I am sure, pity you much."

"How can they pity me after what Mr. Brocklehurst has said?"

"Mr. Brocklehurst is not a god: nor is he even a great and admired man: he is little liked here; he never took steps to make himself liked. Had he treated you as an especial favourite, you would have found enemies, declared or covert, all around you; as it is, the greater number would offer you sympathy if they dared. Teachers and pupils may look coldly on you for a day or two, but friendly feelings are concealed in their hearts; and if you persevere in doing well, these feelings will ere long appear so much the more evidently for their temporary suppression. Besides, Jane"—she paused.

"Well, Helen?" said I, putting my hand into hers: she chafed my fingers gently to warm them, and went on—

"If all the world hated you, and believed you wicked, while your own conscience approved you, and absolved you from guilt, you would not be without friends."

"No; I know I should think well of myself; but that is not enough: if others don't love me I would rather die than live—I cannot bear to be solitary and hated, Helen. Look here; to gain some real affection from you, or Miss Temple, or any other whom I truly love, I would willingly submit to have the bone of my arm broken, or to let a bull toss me, or to stand behind a kicking horse, and let it dash its hoof at my chest—"

"Hush, Jane! You think too much of the love of human beings; you are too impulsive, too vehement; the sovereign hand that created your frame, and put life into it, has provided you with other resources than your feeble self, or than creatures feeble as you. Besides this earth, and besides the race of men, there is an invisible world and a kingdom of spirits: that world is round us, for it is everywhere; and those spirits watch us, for they are commissioned to guard us; and if we were dying in pain and shame, if scorn smote us on all sides, and hatred crushed us, angels see our tortures, recognise our innocence (if innocent we be: as I know you are of this charge which Mr. Brocklehurst has weakly and pompously repeated at second-hand from Mrs. Reed; for I read a sincere nature in your ardent eyes and on your clear front), and God waits only the separation of spirit from flesh to crown us with a full reward. Why, then, should we ever sink overwhelmed with distress, when life is so soon over, and death is so certain an entrance to happiness—to glory?"

I was silent; Helen had calmed me; but in the tranquillity she imparted there was an alloy of inexpressible sadness. I felt the impression of woe as she spoke, but I could not tell whence it came; and when, having done speaking, she breathed a little fast and coughed a short cough, I momentarily forgot my own sorrows to yield to a vague concern for her.

Resting my head on Helen's shoulder, I put my arms round her waist; she drew me to her, and we reposed in silence. We had not sat long thus, when another person came in. Some heavy clouds, swept from the sky by a rising wind, had left the moon bare; and her light, streaming in through a window near, shone full both on us and on the approaching figure, which we at once recognised as Miss Temple.

"I came on purpose to find you, Jane Eyre," said she; "I want you in my room; and as Helen Burns is with you, she may come too."

We went; following the superintendent's guidance, we had to thread some intricate passages, and mount a staircase before we reached her apartment; it contained a good fire, and looked cheerful. Miss Temple told Helen Burns to be seated in a low arm-chair on one side of the hearth, and herself taking another, she called me to her side.

"Is it all over?" she asked, looking down at my face. "Have you cried your grief away?"

"I am afraid I never shall do that."

"Why?"

"Because I have been wrongly accused; and you, ma'am, and everybody else, will now think me wicked."

"We shall think you what you prove yourself to be, my child. Continue to act as a good girl, and you will satisfy us."

"Shall I, Miss Temple?"

"You will," said she, passing her arm round me. "And now tell me who is the lady whom Mr. Brocklehurst called your benefactress?"

"Mrs. Reed, my uncle's wife. My uncle is dead, and he left me to her care."

"Did she not, then, adopt you of her own accord?"

"No, ma'am; she was sorry to have to do it: but my uncle, as I have often heard the servants say, got her to promise before he died that she would always keep me."

"Well now, Jane, you know, or at least I will tell you, that when a criminal is accused, he is always allowed to speak in his own defence.

You have been charged with falsehood; defend yourself to me as well as you can. Say whatever your memory suggests is true; but add nothing and exaggerate nothing."

I resolved, in the depth of my heart, that I would be most moderate—most correct; and, having reflected a few minutes in order to arrange coherently what I had to say, I told her all the story of my sad childhood. Exhausted by emotion, my language was more subdued than it generally was when it developed that sad theme; and mindful of Helen's warnings against the indulgence of resentment, I infused into the narrative far less of gall and wormwood than ordinary. Thus restrained and simplified, it sounded more credible: I felt as I went on that Miss Temple fully believed me.

In the course of the tale I had mentioned Mr. Lloyd as having come to see me after the fit: for I never forgot the, to me, frightful episode of the red-room: in detailing which, my excitement was sure, in some degree, to break bounds; for nothing could soften in my recollection the spasm of agony which clutched my heart when Mrs. Reed spurned my wild supplication for pardon, and locked me a second time in the dark and haunted chamber.

I had finished: Miss Temple regarded me a few minutes in silence; she then said—

"I know something of Mr. Lloyd; I shall write to him; if his reply agrees with your statement, you shall be publicly cleared from every imputation; to me, Jane, you are clear now."

She kissed me, and still keeping me at her side (where I was well contented to stand, for I derived a child's pleasure from the contemplation of her face, her dress, her one or two ornaments, her white forehead, her clustered and shining curls, and beaming dark eyes), she proceeded to address Helen Burns.

"How are you tonight, Helen? Have you coughed much today?"

"Not quite so much, I think, ma'am."

"And the pain in your chest?"

"It is a little better."

Miss Temple got up, took her hand and examined her pulse; then she returned to her own seat: as she resumed it, I heard her sigh low. She was pensive a few minutes, then rousing herself, she said cheerfully—

"But you two are my visitors tonight; I must treat you as such." She rang her bell.

"Barbara," she said to the servant who answered it, "I have not yet had tea; bring the tray and place cups for these two young ladies."

And a tray was soon brought. How pretty, to my eyes, did the china cups and bright teapot look, placed on the little round table near the fire! How fragrant was the steam of the beverage, and the scent of the toast! Of which, however, I, to my dismay (for I was beginning to be hungry) discerned only a very small portion: Miss Temple discerned it too.

"Barbara," said she, "can you not bring a little more bread and butter? There is not enough for three."

Barbara went out: she returned soon—

"Madam, Mrs. Harden says she has sent up the usual quantity."

Mrs. Harden, be it observed, was the housekeeper: a woman after Mr. Brocklehurst's own heart, made up of equal parts of whalebone and iron.

"Oh, very well!" returned Miss Temple. "We must make it do, Barbara, I suppose." And as the girl withdrew she added, smiling, "Fortunately, I have it in my power to supply deficiencies for this once."

Having invited Helen and me to approach the table, and placed before each of us a cup of tea with one delicious but thin morsel of toast, she got up, unlocked a drawer, and taking from it a parcel wrapped in paper, disclosed presently to our eyes a good-sized seed-cake.

"I meant to give each of you some of this to take with you," said she, "but as there is so little toast, you must have it now," and she proceeded to cut slices with a generous hand.

We feasted that evening as on nectar and ambrosia; and not the least delight of the entertainment was the smile of gratification with which our hostess regarded us, as we satisfied our famished appetites on the delicate fare she liberally supplied.

Tea over and the tray removed, she again summoned us to the fire; we sat one on each side of her, and now a conversation followed between her and Helen, which it was indeed a privilege to be admitted to hear.

Miss Temple had always something of serenity in her air, of state in her mien, of refined propriety in her language, which precluded deviation into the ardent, the excited, the eager: something which chastened the pleasure of those who looked on her and listened to her, by a controlling sense of awe; and such was my feeling now: but as to Helen Burns, I was struck with wonder.

The refreshing meal, the brilliant fire, the presence and kindness of her beloved instructress, or, perhaps, more than all these, something in her own unique mind, had roused her powers within her. They woke, they kindled: first, they glowed in the bright tint of her cheek, which till this hour I had never seen but pale and bloodless; then they shone in the liquid lustre of her eyes, which had suddenly acquired a beauty more singular than that of Miss Temple's—a beauty neither of fine colour nor long eyelash, nor pencilled brow, but of meaning, of movement, of radiance. Then her soul sat on her lips, and language flowed, from what source I cannot tell. Has a girl of fourteen a heart large enough, vigorous enough, to hold the swelling spring of pure, full, fervid eloquence? Such was the characteristic of Helen's discourse on that, to me, memorable evening; her spirit seemed hastening to live within a very brief span as much as many live during a protracted existence.

They conversed of things I had never heard of; of nations and times past; of countries far away; of secrets of nature discovered or guessed at: they spoke of books: how many they had read! What stores of knowledge they possessed! Then they seemed so familiar with French names and French authors: but my amazement reached its climax when Miss Temple asked Helen if she sometimes snatched a moment to recall the Latin her father had taught her, and taking a book from a shelf, bade her read and construe a page of Virgil; and Helen obeyed, my organ of veneration expanding at every sounding line. She had scarcely finished ere the bell announced bedtime! No delay could be admitted; Miss Temple embraced us both, saying, as she drew us to her heart—

"God bless you, my children!"

Helen she held a little longer than me: she let her go more reluctantly; it was Helen her eye followed to the door; it was for her she a second time breathed a sad sigh; for her she wiped a tear from her cheek.

On reaching the bedroom, we heard the voice of Miss Scatcherd: she was examining drawers; she had just pulled out Helen Burns's, and when we entered Helen was greeted with a sharp reprimand, and told that tomorrow she should have half-a-dozen of untidily folded articles pinned to her shoulder.

"My things were indeed in shameful disorder," murmured Helen to me, in a low voice: "I intended to have arranged them, but I forgot."

Next morning, Miss Scatcherd wrote in conspicuous characters on a piece of pasteboard the word "Slattern," and bound it like a phylactery round Helen's large, mild, intelligent, and benign-looking forehead.

She wore it till evening, patient, unresentful, regarding it as a deserved punishment. The moment Miss Scatcherd withdrew after afternoon school, I ran to Helen, tore it off, and thrust it into the fire: the fury of which she was incapable had been burning in my soul all day, and tears, hot and large, had continually been scalding my cheek; for the spectacle of her sad resignation gave me an intolerable pain at the heart.

About a week subsequently to the incidents above narrated, Miss Temple, who had written to Mr. Lloyd, received his answer: it appeared that what he said went to corroborate my account. Miss Temple, having assembled the whole school, announced that inquiry had been made into the charges alleged against Jane Eyre, and that she was most happy to be able to pronounce her completely cleared from every imputation. The teachers then shook hands with me and kissed me, and a murmur of pleasure ran through the ranks of my companions.

Thus relieved of a grievous load, I from that hour set to work afresh, resolved to pioneer my way through every difficulty: I toiled hard, and my success was proportionate to my efforts; my memory, not naturally tenacious, improved with practice; exercise sharpened my wits; in a few weeks I was promoted to a higher class; in less than two months I was allowed to commence French and drawing. I learned the first two tenses of the verb *etre*, and sketched my first cottage (whose walls, by-the-by, outrivalled in slope those of the leaning tower of Pisa), on the same day. That night, on going to bed, I forgot to prepare in imagination the Barmecide supper of hot roast potatoes, or white bread and new milk, with which I was wont to amuse my inward cravings: I feasted instead on the spectacle of ideal drawings, which I saw in the dark; all the work of my own hands: freely pencilled houses and trees, picturesque rocks and ruins, Cuyp-like groups of cattle, sweet paintings of butterflies hovering over unblown roses, of birds picking at ripe cherries, of wren's nests enclosing pearl-like eggs, wreathed about with young ivy sprays. I examined, too, in thought, the possibility of my ever being able to translate currently a certain little French story which Madame Pierrot had that day shown me; nor was that problem solved to my satisfaction ere I fell sweetly asleep.

Well has Solomon said: "Better is a dinner of herbs where love is, than a stalled ox and hatred therewith."

I would not now have exchanged Lowood with all its privations for Gateshead and its daily luxuries.

CHAPTER IX

But the privations, or rather the hardships, of Lowood lessened. Spring drew on: she was indeed already come; the frosts of winter had ceased; its snows were melted, its cutting winds ameliorated. My wretched feet, flayed and swollen to lameness by the sharp air of January, began to heal and subside under the gentler breathings of April; the nights and mornings no longer by their Canadian temperature froze the very blood in our veins; we could now endure the play-hour passed in the garden: sometimes on a sunny day it began even to be pleasant and genial, and a greenness grew over those brown beds, which, freshening daily, suggested the thought that Hope traversed them at night, and left each morning brighter traces of her steps. Flowers peeped out amongst the leaves; snow-drops, crocuses, purple auriculas, and golden-eyed pansies. On Thursday afternoons (half-holidays) we now took walks, and found still sweeter flowers opening by the wayside, under the hedges.

I discovered, too, that a great pleasure, an enjoyment which the horizon only bounded, lay all outside the high and spike-guarded walls of our garden: this pleasure consisted in prospect of noble summits girdling a great hill-hollow, rich in verdure and shadow; in a bright beck, full of dark stones and sparkling eddies. How different had this scene looked when I viewed it laid out beneath the iron sky of winter, stiffened in frost, shrouded with snow! When mists as chill as death wandered to the impulse of east winds along those purple peaks, and rolled down "ing" and holm till they blended with the frozen fog of the beck! That beck itself was then a torrent, turbid and curbless: it tore asunder the wood, and sent a raving sound through the air, often thickened with wild rain or whirling sleet; and for the forest on its banks, *that* showed only ranks of skeletons.

April advanced to May: a bright serene May it was; days of blue sky, placid sunshine, and soft western or southern gales filled up its duration. And now vegetation matured with vigour; Lowood shook loose its tresses; it became all green, all flowery; its great elm, ash, and oak skeletons were restored to majestic life; woodland plants sprang up profusely in its recesses; unnumbered varieties of moss filled its hollows, and it made a strange ground-sunshine out of the wealth of its wild primrose plants: I have seen their pale gold gleam in overshadowed spots like scatterings of the sweetest lustre. All this I enjoyed often and fully, free, unwatched, and almost alone: for this unwonted liberty and pleasure there was a cause, to which it now becomes my task to advert.

Have I not described a pleasant site for a dwelling, when I speak of it as bosomed in hill and wood, and rising from the verge of a stream? Assuredly, pleasant enough: but whether healthy or not is another question.

That forest-dell, where Lowood lay, was the cradle of fog and fog-bred pestilence; which, quickening with the quickening spring, crept into the Orphan Asylum, breathed typhus through its crowded schoolroom and dormitory, and, ere May arrived, transformed the seminary into an hospital.

Semi-starvation and neglected colds had predisposed most of the pupils to receive infection: forty-five out of the eighty girls lay ill at one time. Classes were broken up, rules relaxed. The few who continued well were allowed almost unlimited license; because the medical attendant insisted on the necessity of frequent exercise to keep them in health: and had it been otherwise, no one had leisure to watch or restrain them. Miss Temple's whole attention was absorbed by the patients: she lived in the sick-room, never quitting it except to snatch a few hours' rest at night. The teachers were fully occupied with packing up and making other necessary preparations for the departure of those girls who were fortunate enough to have friends and relations able and willing to remove them from the seat of contagion. Many, already smitten, went home only to die: some died at the school, and were buried quietly and quickly, the nature of the malady forbidding delay.

While disease had thus become an inhabitant of Lowood, and death its frequent visitor; while there was gloom and fear within its walls; while its rooms and passages steamed with hospital smells, the drug and the pastille striving vainly to overcome the effluvia of mortality, that bright May shone unclouded over the bold hills and beautiful woodland out of doors. Its garden, too, glowed with flowers: hollyhocks had sprung up tall as trees, lilies had opened, tulips and roses were in bloom; the borders of the little beds were gay with pink thrift and crimson double daisies; the sweetbriars gave out, morning and evening, their scent of spice and apples; and these fragrant treasures were all useless for most of the inmates of Lowood, except to furnish now and then a handful of herbs and blossoms to put in a coffin.

But I, and the rest who continued well, enjoyed fully the beauties of the scene and season; they let us ramble in the wood, like gipsies, from morning till night; we did what we liked, went where we liked: we lived better too. Mr. Brocklehurst and his family never came near Lowood now: household matters were not scrutinised into; the cross housekeeper was gone, driven away by the fear of infection; her successor, who had been matron at the Lowton Dispensary, unused to the ways of her new abode, provided with comparative liberality. Besides, there were fewer to feed; the sick could eat little; our breakfast-basins were better filled; when there was no time to prepare a regular dinner, which often happened, she would give us a large piece of cold pie, or a thick slice of bread and cheese, and this we carried away with us to the wood, where we each chose the spot we liked best, and dined sumptuously.

My favourite seat was a smooth and broad stone, rising white and dry from the very middle of the beck, and only to be got at by wading through the water; a feat I accomplished barefoot. The stone was just broad enough to accommodate, comfortably, another girl and me, at that time my chosen comrade—one Mary Ann Wilson; a shrewd, observant personage, whose society I took pleasure in, partly because she was witty and original, and partly because she had a manner which set me at my ease. Some years older than I, she knew more of the world, and could tell me many things I liked to hear: with her my curiosity found gratification: to my faults also she gave ample indulgence, never imposing curb or rein on anything I said. She had a turn for narrative, I for analysis; she liked to inform, I to question; so we got on swimmingly together, deriving much entertainment, if not much improvement, from our mutual intercourse.

And where, meantime, was Helen Burns? Why did I not spend these sweet days of liberty with her? Had I forgotten her? Or was I so worthless as to have grown tired of her pure society? Surely the Mary Ann Wilson I have mentioned was inferior to my first acquaintance: she could only tell me amusing stories, and reciprocate any racy and pungent gossip I chose to indulge in; while, if I have spoken truth of Helen, she was qualified to give those who enjoyed the privilege of her converse a taste of far higher things.

True, reader; and I knew and felt this: and though I am a defective being, with many faults and few redeeming points, yet I never tired of Helen Burns; nor ever ceased to cherish for her a sentiment of attachment, as strong, tender, and respectful as any that ever animated my heart. How could it be otherwise, when Helen, at all times and under all circumstances, evinced for me a quiet and faithful friendship, which ill-humour never soured, nor irritation never troubled? But Helen was ill at present: for some weeks she had been removed from my sight to I knew not what room upstairs. She was not, I was told, in the hospital portion of the house with the fever patients; for her complaint was consumption, not typhus: and by consumption I, in my ignorance, understood something mild, which time and care would be sure to alleviate.

I was confirmed in this idea by the fact of her once or twice coming downstairs on very warm sunny afternoons, and being taken by Miss Temple into the garden; but, on these occasions, I was not allowed to go and speak to her; I only saw her from the schoolroom window, and then not distinctly; for she was much wrapped up, and sat at a distance under the verandah.

One evening, in the beginning of June, I had stayed out very late with Mary Ann in the wood; we had, as usual, separated ourselves from the others, and had wandered far; so far that we lost our way, and had to ask it at a lonely cottage, where a man and woman lived, who looked after a herd of half-wild swine that fed on the mast in the wood. When we got back, it was after moonrise: a pony, which we knew to be the surgeon's, was standing at the garden door. Mary Ann remarked that she supposed some one must be very ill, as Mr. Bates had been sent for at that time of the evening. She went into the house; I stayed behind a few minutes to plant in my garden a handful of roots I had dug up in the forest, and which I feared would wither if I left them till the morning. This done, I lingered yet a little longer: the flowers smelt so sweet as the dew fell; it was such a pleasant evening, so serene, so warm; the still glowing west promised so fairly another fine day on the morrow; the moon rose with such majesty in the grave east. I was noting these things and enjoying them as a child might, when it entered my mind as it had never done before:

"How sad to be lying now on a sick bed, and to be in danger of dying! This world is pleasant—it would be dreary to be called from it, and to have to go who knows where?"

And then my mind made its first earnest effort to comprehend what had been infused into it concerning heaven and hell; and for the first time it recoiled, baffled; and for the first time glancing behind, on each side, and before it, it saw all round an unfathomed gulf: it felt the one point where it stood—the present; all the rest was formless cloud and vacant depth; and it shuddered at the thought of tottering, and plunging amid that chaos. While pondering this new idea, I heard the front door open; Mr. Bates came out, and with him was a nurse. After she had seen him mount his horse and depart, she was about to close the door, but I ran up to her.

"How is Helen Burns?"

"Very poorly," was the answer.

"Is it her Mr. Bates has been to see?"

"Yes."

"And what does he say about her?"

"He says she'll not be here long."

This phrase, uttered in my hearing yesterday, would have only conveyed the notion that she was about to be removed to Northumberland, to her own home. I should not have suspected that it meant she was dying; but I knew instantly now! It opened clear on my comprehension that Helen Burns was numbering her last days in this world, and that she was going to be taken to the region of spirits, if such region there were. I experienced a shock of horror, then a strong thrill of grief, then a desire—a necessity to see her; and I asked in what room she lay.

"She is in Miss Temple's room," said the nurse.

"May I go up and speak to her?"

"Oh no, child! It is not likely; and now it is time for you to come in; you'll catch the fever if you stop out when the dew is falling."

The nurse closed the front door; I went in by the side entrance which led to the schoolroom: I was just in time; it was nine o'clock, and Miss Miller was calling the pupils to go to bed.

It might be two hours later, probably near eleven, when I—not having been able to fall asleep, and deeming, from the perfect silence of the dormitory, that my companions were all wrapt in profound repose—rose softly, put on my frock over my night-dress, and, without shoes, crept from the apartment, and set off in quest of Miss Temple's room. It was quite at the other end of the house; but I knew my way;

and the light of the unclouded summer moon, entering here and there at passage windows, enabled me to find it without difficulty. An odour of camphor and burnt vinegar warned me when I came near the fever room: and I passed its door quickly, fearful lest the nurse who sat up all night should hear me. I dreaded being discovered and sent back; for I *must* see Helen—I must embrace her before she died—I must give her one last kiss, exchange with her one last word.

Having descended a staircase, traversed a portion of the house below, and succeeded in opening and shutting, without noise, two doors, I reached another flight of steps; these I mounted, and then just opposite to me was Miss Temple's room. A light shone through the keyhole and from under the door; a profound stillness pervaded the vicinity. Coming near, I found the door slightly ajar; probably to admit some fresh air into the close abode of sickness. Indisposed to hesitate, and full of impatient impulses—soul and senses quivering with keen throes—I put it back and looked in. My eye sought Helen, and feared to find death.

Close by Miss Temple's bed, and half covered with its white curtains, there stood a little crib. I saw the outline of a form under the clothes, but the face was hid by the hangings: the nurse I had spoken to in the garden sat in an easy-chair asleep; an unsnuffed candle burnt dimly on the table. Miss Temple was not to be seen: I knew afterwards that she had been called to a delirious patient in the fever-room. I advanced; then paused by the crib side: my hand was on the curtain, but I preferred speaking before I withdrew it. I still recoiled at the dread of seeing a corpse.

"Helen!" I whispered softly. "Are you awake?"

She stirred herself, put back the curtain, and I saw her face, pale, wasted, but quite composed: she looked so little changed that my fear was instantly dissipated.

"Can it be you, Jane?" she asked, in her own gentle voice.

"Oh," I thought, "she is not going to die; they are mistaken: she could not speak and look so calmly if she were."

I got on to her crib and kissed her: her forehead was cold, and her cheek both cold and thin, and so were her hand and wrist; but she smiled as of old.

"Why are you come here, Jane? It is past eleven o'clock: I heard it strike some minutes since."

"I came to see you, Helen: I heard you were very ill, and I could not sleep till I had spoken to you."

"You came to bid me good-bye, then: you are just in time probably."

"Are you going somewhere, Helen? Are you going home?"

"Yes; to my long home—my last home."

"No, no, Helen!" I stopped, distressed. While I tried to devour my tears, a fit of coughing seized Helen; it did not, however, wake the nurse; when it was over, she lay some minutes exhausted; then she whispered—

"Jane, your little feet are bare; lie down and cover yourself with my quilt."

I did so: she put her arm over me, and I nestled close to her. After a long silence, she resumed, still whispering—

"I am very happy, Jane; and when you hear that I am dead, you must be sure and not grieve: there is nothing to grieve about. We all must die one day, and the illness which is removing me is not painful; it is gentle and gradual: my mind is at rest. I leave no one to regret me much: I have only a father; and he is lately married, and will not miss me. By dying young, I shall escape great sufferings. I had not qualities or talents to make my way very well in the world: I should have been continually at fault."

"But where are you going to, Helen? Can you see? Do you know?"

"I believe; I have faith: I am going to God."

"Where is God? What is God?"

"My Maker and yours, who will never destroy what He created. I rely implicitly on His power, and confide wholly in His goodness: I count the hours till that eventful one arrives which shall restore me to Him, reveal Him to me."

"You are sure, then, Helen, that there is such a place as heaven, and that our souls can get to it when we die?"

"I am sure there is a future state; I believe God is good; I can resign my immortal part to Him without any misgiving. God is my father; God is my friend: I love Him; I believe He loves me."

"And shall I see you again, Helen, when I die?"

"You will come to the same region of happiness: be received by the same mighty, universal Parent, no doubt, dear Jane."

Again I questioned, but this time only in thought. "Where is that region? Does it exist?" And I clasped my arms closer round Helen; she seemed dearer to me than ever; I felt as if I could not let her go; I lay with my face hidden on her neck. Presently she said, in the sweetest tone—

"How comfortable I am! That last fit of coughing has tired me a little; I feel as if I could sleep: but don't leave me, Jane; I like to have you near me."

"I'll stay with you, *dear* Helen: no one shall take me away."

"Are you warm, darling?"

"Yes."

"Good-night, Jane."

"Good-night, Helen."

She kissed me, and I her, and we both soon slumbered.

When I awoke it was day: an unusual movement roused me; I looked up; I was in somebody's arms; the nurse held me; she was carrying me through the passage back to the dormitory. I was not reprimanded for leaving my bed; people had something else to think about; no explanation was afforded then to my many questions; but a day or two afterwards I learned that Miss Temple, on returning to her own room at dawn, had found me laid in the little crib; my face against Helen Burns's shoulder, my arms round her neck. I was asleep, and Helen was—dead.

Her grave is in Brocklebridge churchyard: for fifteen years after her death it was only covered by a grassy mound; but now a grey marble tablet marks the spot, inscribed with her name, and the word "Resurgam."

CHAPTER X

Hitherto I have recorded in detail the events of my insignificant existence: to the first ten years of my life I have given almost as many chapters. But this is not to be a regular autobiography. I am only bound to invoke Memory where I know her responses will possess some degree of interest; therefore I now pass a space of eight years almost in silence: a few lines only are necessary to keep up the links of connection.

When the typhus fever had fulfilled its mission of devastation at Lowood, it gradually disappeared from thence; but not till its virulence and the number of its victims had drawn public attention on the school. Inquiry was made into the origin of the scourge, and by degrees various facts came out which excited public indignation in a high degree. The unhealthy nature of the site; the quantity and quality of the children's food; the brackish, fetid water used in its preparation; the pupils' wretched clothing and accommodations—all these things were discovered, and the discovery produced a result mortifying to Mr. Brocklehurst, but beneficial to the institution.

Several wealthy and benevolent individuals in the county subscribed largely for the erection of a more convenient building in a better situation; new regulations were made; improvements in diet and clothing introduced; the funds of the school were intrusted to the management of a committee. Mr. Brocklehurst, who, from his wealth and family connections, could not be overlooked, still retained the post of treasurer; but he was aided in the discharge of his duties by gentlemen of rather more enlarged and sympathising minds: his office of inspector, too, was shared by those who knew how to combine reason with strictness, comfort with economy, compassion with uprightness. The school, thus improved, became in time a truly useful and noble institution. I remained an inmate of its walls, after its regeneration, for eight years: six as pupil, and two as teacher; and in both capacities I bear my testimony to its value and importance.

During these eight years my life was uniform: but not unhappy, because it was not inactive. I had the means of an excellent education placed within my reach; a fondness for some of my studies, and a desire to excel in all, together with a great delight in pleasing my teachers, especially such as I loved, urged me on: I availed myself fully of the advantages offered me. In time I rose to be the first girl of the first class; then I was invested with the office of teacher; which I discharged with zeal for two years: but at the end of that time I altered.

Miss Temple, through all changes, had thus far continued superintendent of the seminary: to her instruction I owed the best part of my acquirements; her friendship and society had been my continual solace; she had stood me in the stead of mother, governess, and, latterly, companion. At this period she married, removed with her husband (a clergyman, an excellent man, almost worthy of such a wife) to a distant county, and consequently was lost to me.

From the day she left I was no longer the same: with her was gone every settled feeling, every association that had made Lowood in some degree a home to me. I had imbibed from her something of her nature and much of her habits: more harmonious thoughts: what seemed better regulated feelings had become the inmates of my mind. I had given in allegiance to duty and order; I was quiet; I believed I was content: to the eyes of others, usually even to my own, I appeared a disciplined and subdued character.

But destiny, in the shape of the Rev. Mr. Nasmyth, came between me and Miss Temple: I saw her in her travelling dress step into a post-chaise, shortly after the marriage ceremony; I watched the chaise mount the hill and disappear beyond its brow; and then retired to my own room, and there spent in solitude the greatest part of the half-holiday granted in honour of the occasion.

I walked about the chamber most of the time. I imagined myself only to be regretting my loss, and thinking how to repair it; but when my reflections were concluded, and I looked up and found that the afternoon was gone, and evening far advanced, another discovery dawned on me, namely, that in the interval I had undergone a transforming process; that my mind had put off all it had borrowed of Miss Temple—or rather that she had taken with her the serene atmosphere I had been breathing in her vicinity—and that now I was left in my natural element, and beginning to feel the stirring of old emotions. It did not seem as if a prop were withdrawn, but rather as if a motive were gone: it was not the power to be tranquil which had failed me, but the reason for tranquillity was no more. My world had for some years been in Lowood: my experience had been of its rules and systems; now I remembered that the real world was wide, and that a varied field of hopes and fears, of sensations and excitements, awaited those who had courage to go forth into its expanse, to seek real knowledge of life amidst its perils.

I went to my window, opened it, and looked out. There were the two wings of the building; there was the garden; there were the skirts of Lowood; there was the hilly horizon. My eye passed all other objects to rest on those most remote, the blue peaks; it was those I longed to surmount; all within their boundary of rock and heath seemed prison-ground, exile limits. I traced the white road winding round the base of one mountain, and vanishing in a gorge between two; how I longed to follow it farther! I recalled the time when I had travelled that very road in a coach; I remembered descending that hill at twilight; an age seemed to have elapsed since the day which brought me first to Lowood, and I had never quitted it since. My vacations had all been spent at school: Mrs. Reed had never sent for me to Gateshead; neither she nor any of her family had ever been to visit me. I had had no communication by letter or message with the outer world: school-rules, school-duties, school-habits and notions, and voices, and faces, and phrases, and costumes, and preferences, and antipathies—such was what I knew of existence. And now I felt that it was not enough; I tired of the routine of eight years in one afternoon. I desired liberty; for liberty I gasped; for liberty I uttered a prayer; it seemed scattered on the wind then faintly blowing. I abandoned it and framed a humbler supplication; for change, stimulus: that petition, too, seemed swept off into vague space: "Then," I cried, half desperate, "grant me at least a new servitude!"

Here a bell, ringing the hour of supper, called me downstairs.

I was not free to resume the interrupted chain of my reflections till bedtime: even then a teacher who occupied the same room with me kept me from the subject to which I longed to recur, by a prolonged effusion of small talk. How I wished sleep would silence her. It seemed as if, could I but go back to the idea which had last entered my mind as I stood at the window, some inventive suggestion would rise for my relief.

Miss Gryce snored at last; she was a heavy Welshwoman, and till now her habitual nasal strains had never been regarded by me in any other light than as a nuisance; tonight I hailed the first deep notes with satisfaction; I was debarrassed of interruption; my half-effaced thought instantly revived.

"A new servitude! There is something in that," I soliloquised (mentally, be it understood; I did not talk aloud), "I know there is, because it does not sound too sweet; it is not like such words as Liberty, Excitement, Enjoyment: delightful sounds truly; but no more than sounds for me; and so hollow and fleeting that it is mere waste of time to listen to them. But Servitude! That must be matter of fact. Any one may serve: I have served here eight years; now all I want is to serve elsewhere. Can I not get so much of my own will? Is not the thing feasible? Yes—yes—the end is not so difficult; if I had only a brain active enough to ferret out the means of attaining it."

I sat up in bed by way of arousing this said brain: it was a chilly night; I covered my shoulders with a shawl, and then I proceeded *to think* again with all my might.

"What do I want? A new place, in a new house, amongst new faces, under new circumstances: I want this because it is of no use wanting anything better. How do people do to get a new place? They apply to friends, I suppose: I have no friends. There are many others who have no friends, who must look about for themselves and be their own helpers; and what is their resource?"

I could not tell: nothing answered me; I then ordered my brain to find a response, and quickly. It worked and worked faster: I felt the pulses throb in my head and temples; but for nearly an hour it worked in chaos; and no result came of its efforts. Feverish with vain labour, I got up and took a turn in the room; undrew the curtain, noted a star or two, shivered with cold, and again crept to bed.

A kind fairy, in my absence, had surely dropped the required suggestion on my pillow; for as I lay down, it came quietly and naturally to my mind. "Those who want situations advertise; you must advertise in the *——shire Herald*."

"How? I know nothing about advertising."

Replies rose smooth and prompt now:

"You must enclose the advertisement and the money to pay for it under a cover directed to the editor of the *Herald*; you must put it, the first opportunity you have, into the post at Lowton; answers must be addressed to J.E., at the post-office there; you can go and inquire in about a week after you send your letter, if any are come, and act accordingly."

This scheme I went over twice, thrice; it was then digested in my mind; I had it in a clear practical form: I felt satisfied, and fell asleep.

With earliest day, I was up: I had my advertisement written, enclosed, and directed before the bell rang to rouse the school; it ran thus:

"A young lady accustomed to tuition" (had I not been a teacher two years?) "is desirous of meeting with a situation in a private family where the children are under fourteen (I thought that as I was barely eighteen, it would not do to undertake the guidance of pupils nearer my own age). She is qualified to teach the usual branches of a good English education, together with French, Drawing, and Music" (in those days, reader, this now narrow catalogue of accomplishments would have been held tolerably comprehensive). "Address, J.E., Post-office, Lowton, ——shire."

This document remained locked in my drawer all day: after tea, I asked leave of the new superintendent to go to Lowton, in order to perform some small commissions for myself and one or two of my fellow-teachers; permission was readily granted; I went. It was a walk of two miles, and the evening was wet, but the days were still long; I visited a shop or two, slipped the letter into the post-office, and came back through heavy rain, with streaming garments, but with a relieved heart.

The succeeding week seemed long: it came to an end at last, however, like all sublunary things, and once more, towards the close of a pleasant autumn day, I found myself afoot on the road to Lowton. A picturesque track it was, by the way; lying along the side of the beck and through the sweetest curves of the dale: but that day I thought more of the letters, that might or might not be awaiting me at the little burgh whither I was bound, than of the charms of lea and water.

My ostensible errand on this occasion was to get measured for a pair of shoes; so I discharged that business first, and when it was done, I stepped across the clean and quiet little street from the shoemaker's to the post-office: it was kept by an old dame, who wore horn spectacles on her nose, and black mittens on her hands.

"Are there any letters for J.E.?" I asked.

She peered at me over her spectacles, and then she opened a drawer and fumbled among its contents for a long time, so long that my hopes began to falter. At last, having held a document before her glasses for nearly five minutes, she presented it across the counter, accompanying the act by another inquisitive and mistrustful glance—it was for J.E.

"Is there only one?" I demanded.

"There are no more," said she; and I put it in my pocket and turned my face homeward: I could not open it then; rules obliged me to be back by eight, and it was already half-past seven.

Various duties awaited me on my arrival. I had to sit with the girls during their hour of study; then it was my turn to read prayers; to see them to bed: afterwards I supped with the other teachers. Even when we finally retired for the night, the inevitable Miss Gryce was still my companion: we had only a short end of candle in our candlestick, and I dreaded lest she should talk till it was all burnt out; fortunately, however, the heavy supper she had eaten produced a soporific effect: she was already snoring before I had finished undressing. There still remained an inch of candle: I now took out my letter; the seal was an initial F.; I broke it; the contents were brief.

"If J.E., who advertised in the ——*shire Herald* of last Thursday, possesses the acquirements mentioned, and if she is in a position to give satisfactory references as to character and competency, a situation can be offered her where there is but one pupil, a little girl, under ten years of age; and where the salary is thirty pounds per annum. J.E. is requested to send references, name, address, and all particulars to the direction:

"Mrs. Fairfax, Thornfield, near Millcote, ——shire."

I examined the document long: the writing was old-fashioned and rather uncertain, like that of an elderly lady. This circumstance was satisfactory: a private fear had haunted me, that in thus acting for myself, and by my own guidance, I ran the risk of getting into some scrape; and, above all things, I wished the result of my endeavours to be respectable, proper, *en règle*. I now felt that an elderly lady was no bad ingredient in the business I had on hand. Mrs. Fairfax! I saw her in a black gown and widow's cap; frigid, perhaps, but not uncivil: a model of elderly English respectability. Thornfield! That, doubtless, was the name of her house: a neat orderly spot, I was sure; though I failed in my efforts to conceive a correct plan of the premises. Millcote, ——shire; I brushed up my recollections of the map of England, yes, I saw it; both the shire and the town. ——shire was seventy miles nearer London than the remote county where I now resided: that was a recommendation to me. I longed to go where there was life and movement: Millcote was a large manufacturing town on the banks of the A——; a busy place enough, doubtless: so much the better; it would be a complete change at least. Not that my fancy was much captivated by the idea of long chimneys and clouds of smoke. "But," I argued, "Thornfield will, probably, be a good way from the town."

Here the socket of the candle dropped, and the wick went out.

Next day new steps were to be taken; my plans could no longer be confined to my own breast; I must impart them in order to achieve their success. Having sought and obtained an audience of the superintendent during the noontide recreation, I told her I had a prospect of getting a new situation where the salary would be double what I now received (for at Lowood I only got £15 per annum); and requested she would break the matter for me to Mr. Brocklehurst, or some of the committee, and ascertain whether they would permit me to mention them as references. She obligingly consented to act as mediatrix in the matter. The next day she laid the affair before Mr. Brocklehurst, who said that Mrs. Reed must be written to, as she was my natural guardian. A note was accordingly addressed to that lady, who returned for answer, that "I might do as I pleased: she had long relinquished all interference in my affairs." This note went the round of the committee, and at last, after what appeared to me most tedious delay, formal leave was given me to better my condition if I could; and an assurance added, that as I had always conducted myself well, both as teacher and pupil, at Lowood, a testimonial of character and capacity, signed by the inspectors of that institution, should forthwith be furnished me.

This testimonial I accordingly received in about a month, forwarded a copy of it to Mrs. Fairfax, and got that lady's reply, stating that she was satisfied, and fixing that day fortnight as the period for my assuming the post of governess in her house.

I now busied myself in preparations: the fortnight passed rapidly. I had not a very large wardrobe, though it was adequate to my wants; and the last day sufficed to pack my trunk—the same I had brought with me eight years ago from Gateshead.

The box was corded, the card nailed on. In half-an-hour the carrier was to call for it to take it to Lowton, whither I myself was to repair at an early hour the next morning to meet the coach. I had brushed my black stuff travelling-dress, prepared my bonnet, gloves, and muff; sought in all my drawers to see that no article was left behind; and now having nothing more to do, I sat down and tried to rest. I could not; though I had been on foot all day, I could not now repose an instant; I was too much excited. A phase of my life was closing tonight, a new one opening tomorrow: impossible to slumber in the interval; I must watch feverishly while the change was being accomplished.

"Miss," said a servant who met me in the lobby, where I was wandering like a troubled spirit, "a person below wishes to see you."

"The carrier, no doubt," I thought, and ran downstairs without inquiry. I was passing the back-parlour or teachers' sitting-room, the door of which was half open, to go to the kitchen, when some one ran out—

"It's her, I am sure! I could have told her anywhere!" cried the individual who stopped my progress and took my hand.

I looked: I saw a woman attired like a well-dressed servant, matronly, yet still young; very good-looking, with black hair and eyes, and lively complexion.

"Well, who is it?" she asked, in a voice and with a smile I half recognised; "you've not quite forgotten me, I think, Miss Jane?"

In another second I was embracing and kissing her rapturously: "Bessie! Bessie! Bessie!" that was all I said; whereat she half laughed, half cried, and we both went into the parlour. By the fire stood a little fellow of three years old, in plaid frock and trousers.

"That is my little boy," said Bessie directly.

"Then you are married, Bessie?"

"Yes; nearly five years since to Robert Leaven, the coachman; and I've a little girl besides Bobby there, that I've christened Jane."

"And you don't live at Gateshead?"

"I live at the lodge: the old porter has left."

"Well, and how do they all get on? Tell me everything about them, Bessie: but sit down first; and, Bobby, come and sit on my knee, will you?" but Bobby preferred sidling over to his mother.

"You're not grown so very tall, Miss Jane, nor so very stout," continued Mrs. Leaven. "I dare say they've not kept you too well at school: Miss Reed is the head and shoulders taller than you are; and Miss Georgiana would make two of you in breadth."

"Georgiana is handsome, I suppose, Bessie?"

"Very. She went up to London last winter with her mama, and there everybody admired her, and a young lord fell in love with her: but his relations were against the match; and—what do you think?—he and Miss Georgiana made it up to run away; but they were found out and stopped. It was Miss Reed that found them out: I believe she was envious; and now she and her sister lead a cat and dog life together; they are always quarrelling—"

"Well, and what of John Reed?"

"Oh, he is not doing so well as his mama could wish. He went to college, and he got—plucked, I think they call it: and then his uncles wanted him to be a barrister, and study the law: but he is such a dissipated young man, they will never make much of him, I think."

"What does he look like?"

"He is very tall: some people call him a fine-looking young man; but he has such thick lips."

"And Mrs. Reed?"

"Missis looks stout and well enough in the face, but I think she's not quite easy in her mind: Mr. John's conduct does not please her—he spends a deal of money."

"Did she send you here, Bessie?"

"No, indeed: but I have long wanted to see you, and when I heard that there had been a letter from you, and that you were going to another part of the country, I thought I'd just set off, and get a look at you before you were quite out of my reach."

"I am afraid you are disappointed in me, Bessie." I said this laughing: I perceived that Bessie's glance, though it expressed regard, did in no shape denote admiration.

"No, Miss Jane, not exactly: you are genteel enough; you look like a lady, and it is as much as ever I expected of you: you were no beauty as a child."

I smiled at Bessie's frank answer: I felt that it was correct, but I confess I was not quite indifferent to its import: at eighteen most people wish to please, and the conviction that they have not an exterior likely to second that desire brings anything but gratification.

"I dare say you are clever, though," continued Bessie, by way of solace. "What can you do? Can you play on the piano?"

"A little."

There was one in the room; Bessie went and opened it, and then asked me to sit down and give her a tune: I played a waltz or two, and she was charmed.

"The Miss Reeds could not play as well!" said she exultingly. "I always said you would surpass them in learning: and can you draw?"

"That is one of my paintings over the chimney-piece." It was a landscape in water colours, of which I had made a present to the superintendent, in acknowledgment of her obliging mediation with the committee on my behalf, and which she had framed and glazed.

"Well, that is beautiful, Miss Jane! It is as fine a picture as any Miss Reed's drawing-master could paint, let alone the young ladies themselves, who could not come near it: and have you learnt French?"

"Yes, Bessie, I can both read it and speak it."

"And you can work on muslin and canvas?"

"I can."

"Oh, you are quite a lady, Miss Jane! I knew you would be: you will get on whether your relations notice you or not. There was something I wanted to ask you. Have you ever heard anything from your father's kinsfolk, the Eyres?"

"Never in my life."

"Well, you know Missis always said they were poor and quite despicable: and they may be poor; but I believe they are as much gentry as the Reeds are; for one day, nearly seven years ago, a Mr. Eyre came to Gateshead and wanted to see you; Missis said you were at school fifty miles off; he seemed so much disappointed, for he could not stay: he was going on a voyage to a foreign country, and the ship was to sail from London in a day or two. He looked quite a gentleman, and I believe he was your father's brother."

"What foreign country was he going to, Bessie?"

"An island thousands of miles off, where they make wine—the butler did tell me—"

"Madeira?" I suggested.

"Yes, that is it—that is the very word."

"So he went?"

"Yes; he did not stay many minutes in the house: Missis was very high with him; she called him afterwards a 'sneaking tradesman.' My Robert believes he was a wine-merchant."

"Very likely," I returned; "or perhaps clerk or agent to a wine-merchant."

Bessie and I conversed about old times an hour longer, and then she was obliged to leave me: I saw her again for a few minutes the next morning at Lowton, while I was waiting for the coach. We parted finally at the door of the Brocklehurst Arms there: each went her separate way; she set off for the brow of Lowood Fell to meet the conveyance which was to take her back to Gateshead, I mounted the vehicle which was to bear me to new duties and a new life in the unknown environs of Millcote.

CHAPTER XI

A new chapter in a novel is something like a new scene in a play; and when I draw up the curtain this time, reader, you must fancy you see a room in the George Inn at Millcote, with such large figured papering on the walls as inn rooms have; such a carpet, such furniture, such ornaments on the mantelpiece, such prints, including a portrait of George the Third, and another of the Prince of Wales, and a representation of the death of Wolfe. All this is visible to you by the light of an oil lamp hanging from the ceiling, and by that of an excellent fire, near which I sit in my cloak and bonnet; my muff and umbrella lie on the table, and I am warming away the numbness and chill contracted by sixteen hours' exposure to the rawness of an October day: I left Lowton at four o'clock a.m., and the Millcote town clock is now just striking eight.

Reader, though I look comfortably accommodated, I am not very tranquil in my mind. I thought when the coach stopped here there would be some one to meet me; I looked anxiously round as I descended the wooden steps the "boots" placed for my convenience, expecting to hear my name pronounced, and to see some description of carriage waiting to convey me to Thornfield. Nothing of the sort was visible; and when I asked a waiter if any one had been to inquire after a Miss Eyre, I was answered in the negative: so I had no resource but to request to be shown into a private room: and here I am waiting, while all sorts of doubts and fears are troubling my thoughts.

It is a very strange sensation to inexperienced youth to feel itself quite alone in the world, cut adrift from every connection, uncertain whether the port to which it is bound can be reached, and prevented by many impediments from returning to that it has quitted. The charm of adventure sweetens that sensation, the glow of pride warms it; but then the throb of fear disturbs it; and fear with me became predominant when half-an-hour elapsed and still I was alone. I bethought myself to ring the bell.

"Is there a place in this neighbourhood called Thornfield?" I asked of the waiter who answered the summons.

"Thornfield? I don't know, ma'am; I'll inquire at the bar." He vanished, but reappeared instantly—

"Is your name Eyre, Miss?"

"Yes."

"Person here waiting for you."

I jumped up, took my muff and umbrella, and hastened into the inn-passage: a man was standing by the open door, and in the lamp-lit street I dimly saw a one-horse conveyance.

"This will be your luggage, I suppose?" said the man rather abruptly when he saw me, pointing to my trunk in the passage.

"Yes." He hoisted it on to the vehicle, which was a sort of car, and then I got in; before he shut me up, I asked him how far it was to Thornfield.

"A matter of six miles."

"How long shall we be before we get there?"

"Happen an hour and a half."

He fastened the car door, climbed to his own seat outside, and we set off. Our progress was leisurely, and gave me ample time to reflect; I was content to be at length so near the end of my journey; and as I leaned back in the comfortable though not elegant conveyance, I meditated much at my ease.

"I suppose," thought I, "judging from the plainness of the servant and carriage, Mrs. Fairfax is not a very dashing person: so much the better; I never lived amongst fine people but once, and I was very miserable with them. I wonder if she lives alone except this little girl; if so, and if she is in any degree amiable, I shall surely be able to get on with her; I will do my best; it is a pity that doing one's best does not always answer. At Lowood, indeed, I took that resolution, kept it, and succeeded in pleasing; but with Mrs. Reed, I remember my best was always spurned with scorn. I pray God Mrs. Fairfax may not turn out a second Mrs. Reed; but if she does, I am not bound to stay with her! Let the worst come to the worst, I can advertise again. How far are we on our road now, I wonder?"

I let down the window and looked out; Millcote was behind us; judging by the number of its lights, it seemed a place of considerable magnitude, much larger than Lowton. We were now, as far as I could see, on a sort of common; but there were houses scattered all over the district; I felt we were in a different region to Lowood, more populous, less picturesque; more stirring, less romantic.

The roads were heavy, the night misty; my conductor let his horse walk all the way, and the hour and a half extended, I verily believe, to two hours; at last he turned in his seat and said—

"You're noan so far fro' Thornfield now."

Again I looked out: we were passing a church; I saw its low broad tower against the sky, and its bell was tolling a quarter; I saw a narrow galaxy of lights too, on a hillside, marking a village or hamlet. About ten minutes after, the driver got down and opened a pair of gates: we passed through, and they clashed to behind us. We now slowly ascended a drive, and came upon the long front of a house: candlelight gleamed from one curtained bow-window; all the rest were dark. The car stopped at the front door; it was opened by a maid-servant; I alighted and went in.

"Will you walk this way, ma'am?" said the girl; and I followed her across a square hall with high doors all round: she ushered me into a room whose double illumination of fire and candle at first dazzled me, contrasting as it did with the darkness to which my eyes had been for two hours inured; when I could see, however, a cosy and agreeable picture presented itself to my view.

A snug small room; a round table by a cheerful fire; an arm-chair high-backed and old-fashioned, wherein sat the neatest imaginable little elderly lady, in widow's cap, black silk gown, and snowy muslin apron; exactly like what I had fancied Mrs. Fairfax, only less stately and milder looking. She was occupied in knitting; a large cat sat demurely at her feet; nothing in short was wanting to complete the beau-ideal of domestic comfort. A more reassuring introduction for a new governess could scarcely be conceived; there was no grandeur to overwhelm, no stateliness to embarrass; and then, as I entered, the old lady got up and promptly and kindly came forward to meet me.

"How do you do, my dear? I am afraid you have had a tedious ride; John drives so slowly; you must be cold, come to the fire."

"Mrs. Fairfax, I suppose?" said I.

"Yes, you are right: do sit down."

She conducted me to her own chair, and then began to remove my shawl and untie my bonnet-strings; I begged she would not give herself so much trouble.

"Oh, it is no trouble; I dare say your own hands are almost numbed with cold. Leah, make a little hot negus and cut a sandwich or two: here are the keys of the storeroom."

And she produced from her pocket a most housewifely bunch of keys, and delivered them to the servant.

"Now, then, draw nearer to the fire," she continued. "You've brought your luggage with you, haven't you, my dear?"

"Yes, ma'am."

"I'll see it carried into your room," she said, and bustled out.

"She treats me like a visitor," thought I. "I little expected such a reception; I anticipated only coldness and stiffness: this is not like what I have heard of the treatment of governesses; but I must not exult too soon."

She returned; with her own hands cleared her knitting apparatus and a book or two from the table, to make room for the tray which Leah now brought, and then herself handed me the refreshments. I felt rather confused at being the object of more attention than I had ever before received, and, that too, shown by my employer and superior; but as she did not herself seem to consider she was doing anything out of her place, I thought it better to take her civilities quietly.

"Shall I have the pleasure of seeing Miss Fairfax tonight?" I asked, when I had partaken of what she offered me.

"What did you say, my dear? I am a little deaf," returned the good lady, approaching her ear to my mouth.

I repeated the question more distinctly.

"Miss Fairfax? Oh, you mean Miss Varens! Varens is the name of your future pupil."

"Indeed! Then she is not your daughter?"

"No—I have no family."

I should have followed up my first inquiry, by asking in what way Miss Varens was connected with her; but I recollected it was not polite to ask too many questions: besides, I was sure to hear in time.

"I am so glad," she continued, as she sat down opposite to me, and took the cat on her knee; "I am so glad you are come; it will be quite pleasant living here now with a companion. To be sure it is pleasant at any time; for Thornfield is a fine old hall, rather neglected of late years perhaps, but still it is a respectable place; yet you know in winter-time one feels dreary quite alone in the best quarters. I say alone—Leah is a nice girl to be sure, and John and his wife are very decent people; but then you see they are only servants, and one can't converse with them on terms of equality: one must keep them at due distance, for fear of losing one's authority. I'm sure last winter (it was a very severe one, if you recollect, and when it did not snow, it rained and blew), not a creature but the butcher and postman came to the house, from November till February; and I really got quite melancholy with sitting night after night alone; I had Leah in to read to me sometimes; but I don't think the poor girl liked the task much: she felt it confining. In spring and summer one got on better: sunshine and long days make such a difference; and then, just at the commencement of this autumn, little Adela Varens came and her nurse: a child makes a house alive all at once; and now you are here I shall be quite gay."

My heart really warmed to the worthy lady as I heard her talk; and I drew my chair a little nearer to her, and expressed my sincere wish that she might find my company as agreeable as she anticipated.

"But I'll not keep you sitting up late tonight," said she; "it is on the stroke of twelve now, and you have been travelling all day: you must feel tired. If you have got your feet well warmed, I'll show you your bedroom. I've had the room next to mine prepared for you; it is only a small apartment, but I thought you would like it better than one of the large front chambers: to be sure they have finer furniture, but they are so dreary and solitary, I never sleep in them myself."

I thanked her for her considerate choice, and as I really felt fatigued with my long journey, expressed my readiness to retire. She took her candle, and I followed her from the room. First she went to see if the hall-door was fastened; having taken the key from the lock, she led the way upstairs. The steps and banisters were of oak; the staircase window was high and latticed; both it and the long gallery into which the bedroom doors opened looked as if they belonged to a church rather than a house. A very chill and vault-like air pervaded the stairs and gallery, suggesting cheerless ideas of space and solitude; and I was glad, when finally ushered into my chamber, to find it of small dimensions, and furnished in ordinary, modern style.

When Mrs. Fairfax had bidden me a kind good-night, and I had fastened my door, gazed leisurely round, and in some measure effaced the eerie impression made by that wide hall, that dark and spacious staircase, and that long, cold gallery, by the livelier aspect of my little room, I remembered that, after a day of bodily fatigue and mental anxiety, I was now at last in safe haven. The impulse of gratitude swelled my heart, and I knelt down at the bedside, and offered up thanks where thanks were due; not forgetting, ere I rose, to implore aid on my further path, and the power of meriting the kindness which seemed so frankly offered me before it was earned. My couch had no thorns in it that night; my solitary room no fears. At once weary and content, I slept soon and soundly: when I awoke it was broad day.

The chamber looked such a bright little place to me as the sun shone in between the gay blue chintz window curtains, showing papered walls and a carpeted floor, so unlike the bare planks and stained plaster of Lowood, that my spirits rose at the view. Externals have a great effect on the young: I thought that a fairer era of life was beginning for me, one that was to have its flowers and pleasures, as well as its thorns and toils. My faculties, roused by the change of scene, the new field offered to hope, seemed all astir. I cannot precisely define what they expected, but it was something pleasant: not perhaps that day or that month, but at an indefinite future period.

I rose; I dressed myself with care: obliged to be plain—for I had no article of attire that was not made with extreme simplicity—I was still by nature solicitous to be neat. It was not my habit to be disregardful of appearance or careless of the impression I made: on the contrary, I ever wished to look as well as I could, and to please as much as my want of beauty would permit. I sometimes regretted that I was not handsomer; I sometimes wished to have rosy cheeks, a straight nose, and small cherry mouth; I desired to be tall, stately, and finely developed in figure; I felt it a misfortune that I was so little, so pale, and had features so irregular and so marked. And why had I these aspirations and these regrets? It would be difficult to say: I could not then distinctly say it to myself; yet I had a reason, and a logical, natural reason too. However, when I had brushed my hair very smooth, and put on my black frock—which, Quakerlike as it was, at least had the merit of fitting to a nicety—and adjusted my clean white tucker, I thought I should do respectably enough to appear before Mrs. Fairfax, and that my new pupil would not at least recoil from me with antipathy. Having opened my chamber window, and seen that I left all things straight and neat on the toilet table, I ventured forth.

Traversing the long and matted gallery, I descended the slippery steps of oak; then I gained the hall: I halted there a minute; I looked at some pictures on the walls (one, I remember, represented a grim man in a cuirass, and one a lady with powdered hair and a pearl necklace), at a bronze lamp pendent from the ceiling, at a great clock whose case was of oak curiously carved, and ebon black with time and rubbing. Everything appeared very stately and imposing to me; but then I was so little accustomed to grandeur. The hall-door, which was half of glass, stood open; I stepped over the threshold. It was a fine autumn morning; the early sun shone serenely on embrowned groves and still green fields; advancing on to the lawn, I looked up and surveyed the front of the mansion. It was three storeys high, of proportions not vast, though considerable: a gentleman's manor-house, not a nobleman's seat: battlements round the top gave it a picturesque look. Its grey front stood out well from the background of a rookery, whose cawing tenants were now on the wing: they flew over the lawn and grounds to alight in a great meadow, from which these were separated by a sunk fence, and where an array of mighty old thorn trees, strong, knotty, and broad as oaks, at once explained the etymology of the mansion's designation. Farther off were hills: not so lofty as those round Lowood, nor so craggy, nor so like barriers of separation from the living world; but yet quiet and lonely hills enough, and seeming to embrace Thornfield with a seclusion I had not expected to find existent so near the stirring locality of Millcote. A little hamlet, whose roofs were blent with trees, straggled up the side of one of these hills; the church of the district stood nearer Thornfield: its old tower-top looked over a knoll between the house and gates.

I was yet enjoying the calm prospect and pleasant fresh air, yet listening with delight to the cawing of the rooks, yet surveying the wide, hoary front of the hall, and thinking what a great place it was for one lonely little dame like Mrs. Fairfax to inhabit, when that lady appeared at the door.

"What! Out already?" said she. "I see you are an early riser." I went up to her, and was received with an affable kiss and shake of the hand.

"How do you like Thornfield?" she asked. I told her I liked it very much.

"Yes," she said, "it is a pretty place; but I fear it will be getting out of order, unless Mr. Rochester should take it into his head to come and reside here permanently; or, at least, visit it rather oftener: great houses and fine grounds require the presence of the proprietor."

"Mr. Rochester!" I exclaimed. "Who is he?"

"The owner of Thornfield," she responded quietly. "Did you not know he was called Rochester?"

Of course I did not—I had never heard of him before; but the old lady seemed to regard his existence as a universally understood fact, with which everybody must be acquainted by instinct.

"I thought," I continued, "Thornfield belonged to you."

"To me? Bless you, child; what an idea! To me! I am only the housekeeper—the manager. To be sure I am distantly related to the Rochesters by the mother's side, or at least my husband was; he was a clergyman, incumbent of Hay—that little village yonder on the hill—and that church near the gates was his. The present Mr. Rochester's mother was a Fairfax, and second cousin to my husband: but I never presume on the connection—in fact, it is nothing to me; I consider myself quite in the light of an ordinary housekeeper: my employer is always civil, and I expect nothing more."

"And the little girl—my pupil!"

"She is Mr. Rochester's ward; he commissioned me to find a governess for her. He intended to have her brought up in ——shire, I believe. Here she comes, with her 'bonne,' as she calls her nurse." The enigma then was explained: this affable and kind little widow was no great dame; but a dependent like myself. I did not like her the worse for that; on the contrary, I felt better pleased than ever. The equality between her and me was real; not the mere result of condescension on her part: so much the better—my position was all the freer.

As I was meditating on this discovery, a little girl, followed by her attendant, came running up the lawn. I looked at my pupil, who did not at first appear to notice me: she was quite a child, perhaps seven or eight years old, slightly built, with a pale, small-featured face, and a redundancy of hair falling in curls to her waist.

"Good morning, Miss Adela," said Mrs. Fairfax. "Come and speak to the lady who is to teach you, and to make you a clever woman some day." She approached.

"C'est là ma gouverante!" said she, pointing to me, and addressing her nurse; who answered—

"Mais oui, certainement."

"Are they foreigners?" I inquired, amazed at hearing the French language.

"The nurse is a foreigner, and Adela was born on the Continent; and, I believe, never left it till within six months ago. When she first came here she could speak no English; now she can make shift to talk it a little: I don't understand her, she mixes it so with French; but you will make out her meaning very well, I dare say."

Fortunately I had had the advantage of being taught French by a French lady; and as I had always made a point of conversing with Madame Pierrot as often as I could, and had besides, during the last seven years, learnt a portion of French by heart daily—applying myself to take pains with my accent, and imitating as closely as possible the pronunciation of my teacher, I had acquired a certain degree of readiness and correctness in the language, and was not likely to be much at a loss with Mademoiselle Adela. She came and shook hand with me when she heard that I was her governess; and as I led her in to breakfast, I addressed some phrases to her in her own tongue: she replied briefly at first, but after we were seated at the table, and she had examined me some ten minutes with her large hazel eyes, she suddenly commenced chattering fluently.

"Ah!" cried she, in French. "You speak my language as well as Mr. Rochester does: I can talk to you as I can to him, and so can Sophie. She will be glad: nobody here understands her: Madame Fairfax is all English. Sophie is my nurse; she came with me over the sea in a great ship with a chimney that smoked—how it did smoke!—and I was sick, and so was Sophie, and so was Mr. Rochester. Mr. Rochester lay down on a sofa in a pretty room called the salon, and Sophie and I had little beds in another place. I nearly fell out of mine; it was like a shelf. And Mademoiselle—what is your name?"

"Eyre—Jane Eyre."

"Aire? Bah! I cannot say it. Well, our ship stopped in the morning, before it was quite daylight, at a great city—a huge city, with very dark houses and all smoky; not at all like the pretty clean town I came from; and Mr. Rochester carried me in his arms over a plank to the land, and Sophie came after, and we all got into a coach, which took us to a beautiful large house, larger than this and finer, called an hotel. We stayed there nearly a week: I and Sophie used to walk every day in a great green place full of trees, called the Park; and there were many children there besides me, and a pond with beautiful birds in it, that I fed with crumbs."

"Can you understand her when she runs on so fast?" asked Mrs. Fairfax.

I understood her very well, for I had been accustomed to the fluent tongue of Madame Pierrot.

"I wish," continued the good lady, "you would ask her a question or two about her parents: I wonder if she remembers them?"

"Adèle," I inquired, "with whom did you live when you were in that pretty clean town you spoke of?"

"I lived long ago with mama; but she is gone to the Holy Virgin. Mama used to teach me to dance and sing, and to say verses. A great many gentlemen and ladies came to see mama, and I used to dance before them, or to sit on their knees and sing to them: I liked it. Shall I let you hear me sing now?"

She had finished her breakfast, so I permitted her to give a specimen of her accomplishments. Descending from her chair, she came and placed herself on my knee; then, folding her little hands demurely before her, shaking back her curls and lifting her eyes to the ceiling, she commenced singing a song from some opera. It was the strain of a forsaken lady, who, after bewailing the perfidy of her lover, calls pride to her aid; desires her attendant to deck her in her brightest jewels and richest robes, and resolves to meet the false one that night at a ball, and prove to him, by the gaiety of her demeanour, how little his desertion has affected her.

The subject seemed strangely chosen for an infant singer; but I suppose the point of the exhibition lay in hearing the notes of love and jealousy warbled with the lisp of childhood; and in very bad taste that point was: at least I thought so.

Adèle sang the canzonette tunefully enough, and with the *naïveté* of her age. This achieved, she jumped from my knee and said, "Now, Mademoiselle, I will repeat you some poetry."

Assuming an attitude, she began, "La Ligue des Rats: fable de La Fontaine." She then declaimed the little piece with an attention to punctuation and emphasis, a flexibility of voice and an appropriateness of gesture, very unusual indeed at her age, and which proved she had been carefully trained.

"Was it your mama who taught you that piece?" I asked.

"Yes, and she just used to say it in this way: 'Qu'avez vous donc? Lui dit un de ces rats; parlez!' She made me lift my hand—so—to remind me to raise my voice at the question. Now shall I dance for you?"

"No, that will do: but after your mama went to the Holy Virgin, as you say, with whom did you live then?"

"With Madame Fréderic and her husband: she took care of me, but she is nothing related to me. I think she is poor, for she had not so fine a house as mama. I was not long there. Mr. Rochester asked me if I would like to go and live with him in England, and I said yes; for I knew Mr. Rochester before I knew Madame Fréderic, and he was always kind to me and gave me pretty dresses and toys: but you see he has not kept his word, for he has brought me to England, and now he is gone back again himself, and I never see him."

After breakfast, Adèle and I withdrew to the library, which room, it appears, Mr. Rochester had directed should be used as the schoolroom. Most of the books were locked up behind glass doors; but there was one bookcase left open containing everything that could be needed in the way of elementary works, and several volumes of light literature, poetry, biography, travels, a few romances, etc. I suppose he had considered that these were all the governess would require for her private perusal; and, indeed, they contented me amply for the present; compared with the scanty pickings I had now and then been able to glean at Lowood, they seemed to offer an abundant harvest of entertainment and information. In this room, too, there was a cabinet piano, quite new and of superior tone; also an easel for painting and a pair of globes.

I found my pupil sufficiently docile, though disinclined to apply: she had not been used to regular occupation of any kind. I felt it would be injudicious to confine her too much at first; so, when I had talked to her a great deal, and got her to learn a little, and when the morning had advanced to noon, I allowed her to return to her nurse. I then proposed to occupy myself till dinner-time in drawing some little sketches for her use.

As I was going upstairs to fetch my portfolio and pencils, Mrs. Fairfax called to me: "Your morning school-hours are over now, I suppose," said she. She was in a room the folding-doors of which stood open: I went in when she addressed me. It was a large, stately apartment, with purple chairs and curtains, a Turkey carpet, walnut-panelled walls, one vast window rich in slanted glass, and a lofty ceiling, nobly moulded. Mrs. Fairfax was dusting some vases of fine purple spar, which stood on a sideboard.

"What a beautiful room!" I exclaimed, as I looked round; for I had never before seen any half so imposing.

"Yes; this is the dining-room. I have just opened the window, to let in a little air and sunshine; for everything gets so damp in apartments that are seldom inhabited; the drawing-room yonder feels like a vault."

She pointed to a wide arch corresponding to the window, and hung like it with a Tyrian-dyed curtain, now looped up. Mounting to it by two broad steps, and looking through, I thought I caught a glimpse of a fairy place, so bright to my novice-eyes appeared the view beyond. Yet it was merely a very pretty drawing-room, and within it a boudoir, both spread with white carpets, on which seemed laid brilliant garlands of flowers; both ceiled with snowy mouldings of white grapes and vine-leaves, beneath which glowed in rich contrast crimson couches and ottomans; while the ornaments on the pale Parian mantelpiece were of sparkling Bohemian glass, ruby red; and between the windows large mirrors repeated the general blending of snow and fire.

"In what order you keep these rooms, Mrs. Fairfax!" said I. "No dust, no canvas coverings: except that the air feels chilly, one would think they were inhabited daily."

"Why, Miss Eyre, though Mr. Rochester's visits here are rare, they are always sudden and unexpected; and as I observed that it put him out to find everything swathed up, and to have a bustle of arrangement on his arrival, I thought it best to keep the rooms in readiness."

"Is Mr. Rochester an exacting, fastidious sort of man?"

"Not particularly so; but he has a gentleman's tastes and habits, and he expects to have things managed in conformity to them."

"Do you like him? Is he generally liked?"

"Oh, yes; the family have always been respected here. Almost all the land in this neighbourhood, as far as you can see, has belonged to the Rochesters time out of mind."

"Well, but, leaving his land out of the question, do you like him? Is he liked for himself?"

"I have no cause to do otherwise than like him; and I believe he is considered a just and liberal landlord by his tenants: but he has never lived much amongst them."

"But has he no peculiarities? What, in short, is his character?"

"Oh! His character is unimpeachable, I suppose. He is rather peculiar, perhaps: he has travelled a great deal, and seen a great deal of the world, I should think. I dare say he is clever, but I never had much conversation with him."

"In what way is he peculiar?"

"I don't know—it is not easy to describe—nothing striking, but you feel it when he speaks to you; you cannot be always sure whether he is in jest or earnest, whether he is pleased or the contrary; you don't thoroughly understand him, in short—at least, I don't: but it is of no consequence, he is a very good master."

This was all the account I got from Mrs. Fairfax of her employer and mine. There are people who seem to have no notion of sketching a character, or observing and describing salient points, either in persons or things: the good lady evidently belonged to this class; my queries puzzled, but did not draw her out. Mr. Rochester was Mr. Rochester in her eyes; a gentleman, a landed proprietor—nothing more: she inquired and searched no further, and evidently wondered at my wish to gain a more definite notion of his identity.

When we left the dining-room, she proposed to show me over the rest of the house; and I followed her upstairs and downstairs, admiring as I went; for all was well arranged and handsome. The large front chambers I thought especially grand: and some of the third-storey rooms, though dark and low, were interesting from their air of antiquity. The furniture once appropriated to the lower apartments had from time to time been removed here, as fashions changed: and the imperfect light entering by their narrow casement showed bedsteads of a hundred years old; chests in oak or walnut, looking, with their strange carvings of palm branches and cherubs' heads, like types of the Hebrew ark; rows of venerable chairs, high-backed and narrow; stools still more antiquated, on whose cushioned tops were yet apparent traces of half-effaced embroideries, wrought by fingers that for two generations had been coffin-dust. All these relics gave to the third storey of Thornfield Hall the aspect of a home of the past: a shrine of memory. I liked the hush, the gloom, the quaintness of these retreats in the day; but I by no means coveted a night's repose on one of those wide and heavy beds: shut in, some of them, with doors of oak; shaded, others, with wrought old English hangings crusted with thick work, portraying effigies of strange flowers, and stranger birds, and strangest human beings—all which would have looked strange, indeed, by the pallid gleam of moonlight.

"Do the servants sleep in these rooms?" I asked.

"No; they occupy a range of smaller apartments to the back; no one ever sleeps here: one would almost say that, if there were a ghost at Thornfield Hall, this would be its haunt."

"So I think: you have no ghost, then?"

"None that I ever heard of," returned Mrs. Fairfax, smiling.

"Nor any traditions of one? No legends or ghost stories?"

"I believe not. And yet it is said the Rochesters have been rather a violent than a quiet race in their time: perhaps, though, that is the reason they rest tranquilly in their graves now."

"Yes—'after life's fitful fever they sleep well,' " I muttered. "Where are you going now, Mrs. Fairfax?" for she was moving away.

"On to the leads; will you come and see the view from thence?" I followed still, up a very narrow staircase to the attics, and thence by a ladder and through a trap-door to the roof of the hall. I was now on a level with the crow colony, and could see into their nests. Leaning over the battlements and looking far down, I surveyed the grounds laid out like a map: the bright and velvet lawn closely girdling the grey base of the mansion; the field, wide as a park, dotted with its ancient timber; the wood, dun and sere, divided by a path visibly overgrown, greener with moss than the trees were with foliage; the church at the gates, the road, the tranquil hills, all reposing in the autumn day's sun; the horizon bounded by a propitious sky, azure, marbled with pearly white. No feature in the scene was extraordinary, but all was pleasing. When I turned from it and repassed the trap-door, I could scarcely see my way down the ladder; the attic seemed black as a vault compared with that arch of blue air to which I had been looking up, and to that sunlit scene of grove, pasture, and green hill, of which the hall was the centre, and over which I had been gazing with delight.

Mrs. Fairfax stayed behind a moment to fasten the trap-door; I, by drift of groping, found the outlet from the attic, and proceeded to descend the narrow garret staircase. I lingered in the long passage to which this led, separating the front and back rooms of the third storey: narrow, low, and dim, with only one little window at the far end, and looking, with its two rows of small black doors all shut, like a corridor in some Bluebeard's castle.

While I paced softly on, the last sound I expected to hear in so still a region, a laugh, struck my ear. It was a curious laugh; distinct, formal, mirthless. I stopped: the sound ceased, only for an instant; it began again, louder: for at first, though distinct, it was very low. It passed off in a clamorous peal that seemed to wake an echo in every lonely chamber; though it originated but in one, and I could have pointed out the door whence the accents issued.

"Mrs. Fairfax!" I called out: for I now heard her descending the great stairs. "Did you hear that loud laugh? Who is it?"

"Some of the servants, very likely," she answered: "perhaps Grace Poole."

"Did you hear it?" I again inquired.

"Yes, plainly: I often hear her: she sews in one of these rooms. Sometimes Leah is with her; they are frequently noisy together."

The laugh was repeated in its low, syllabic tone, and terminated in an odd murmur.

"Grace!" exclaimed Mrs. Fairfax.

I really did not expect any Grace to answer; for the laugh was as tragic, as preternatural a laugh as any I ever heard; and, but that it was high noon, and that no circumstance of ghostliness accompanied the curious cachinnation; but that neither scene nor season favoured fear, I should have been superstitiously afraid. However, the event showed me I was a fool for entertaining a sense even of surprise.

The door nearest me opened, and a servant came out—a woman of between thirty and forty; a set, square-made figure, red-haired, and with a hard, plain face: any apparition less romantic or less ghostly could scarcely be conceived.

"Too much noise, Grace," said Mrs. Fairfax. "Remember directions!" Grace curtseyed silently and went in.

"She is a person we have to sew and assist Leah in her housemaid's work," continued the widow; "not altogether unobjectionable in some points, but she does well enough. By-the-by, how have you got on with your new pupil this morning?"

The conversation, thus turned on Adèle, continued till we reached the light and cheerful region below. Adèle came running to meet us in the hall, exclaiming—

"Mesdames, vous êtes servies!" adding, "J'ai bien faim, moi!"

We found dinner ready, and waiting for us in Mrs. Fairfax's room.

CHAPTER XII

The promise of a smooth career, which my first calm introduction to Thornfield Hall seemed to pledge, was not belied on a longer acquaintance with the place and its inmates. Mrs. Fairfax turned out to be what she appeared, a placid-tempered, kind-natured woman, of competent education and average intelligence. My pupil was a lively child, who had been spoilt and indulged, and therefore was sometimes wayward; but as she was committed entirely to my care, and no injudicious interference from any quarter ever thwarted my plans for her improvement, she soon forgot her little freaks, and became obedient and teachable. She had no great talents, no marked traits of character, no peculiar development of feeling or taste which raised her one inch above the ordinary level of childhood; but neither had she any deficiency or vice which sunk her below it. She made reasonable progress, entertained for me a vivacious, though perhaps not very profound, affection; and by her simplicity, gay prattle, and efforts to please, inspired me, in return, with a degree of attachment sufficient to make us both content in each other's society.

This, *par parenthèse*, will be thought cool language by persons who entertain solemn doctrines about the angelic nature of children, and the duty of those charged with their education to conceive for them an idolatrous devotion: but I am not writing to flatter parental egotism, to echo cant, or prop up humbug; I am merely telling the truth. I felt a conscientious solicitude for Adèle's welfare and progress, and a quiet liking for her little self: just as I cherished towards Mrs. Fairfax a thankfulness for her kindness, and a pleasure in her society proportionate to the tranquil regard she had for me, and the moderation of her mind and character.

Anybody may blame me who likes, when I add further, that, now and then, when I took a walk by myself in the grounds; when I went down to the gates and looked through them along the road; or when, while Adèle played with her nurse, and Mrs. Fairfax made jellies in the storeroom, I climbed the three staircases, raised the trap-door of the attic, and having reached the leads, looked out afar over sequestered field and hill, and along dim sky-line—that then I longed for a power of vision which might overpass that limit; which might reach the busy world, towns, regions full of life I had heard of but never seen—that then I desired more of practical experience than I possessed; more of intercourse with my kind, of acquaintance with variety of character, than was here within my reach. I valued what was good in Mrs. Fairfax, and what was good in Adèle; but I believed in the existence of other and more vivid kinds of goodness, and what I believed in I wished to behold.

Who blames me? Many, no doubt; and I shall be called discontented. I could not help it: the restlessness was in my nature; it agitated me to pain sometimes. Then my sole relief was to walk along the corridor of the third storey, backwards and forwards, safe in the silence and solitude of the spot, and allow my mind's eye to dwell on whatever bright visions rose before it—and, certainly, they were many and glowing; to let my heart be heaved by the exultant movement, which, while it swelled it in trouble, expanded it with life; and, best of all, to open my inward ear to a tale that was never ended—a tale my imagination created, and narrated continuously; quickened with all of incident, life, fire, feeling, that I desired and had not in my actual existence.

It is in vain to say human beings ought to be satisfied with tranquillity: they must have action; and they will make it if they cannot find it. Millions are condemned to a stiller doom than mine, and millions are in silent revolt against their lot. Nobody knows how many rebellions besides political rebellions ferment in the masses of life which people earth. Women are supposed to be very calm generally: but women feel just as men feel; they need exercise for their faculties, and a field for their efforts, as much as their brothers do; they suffer from too rigid a restraint, too absolute a stagnation, precisely as men would suffer; and it is narrow-minded in their more privileged fellow-creatures to say that they ought to confine themselves to making puddings and knitting stockings, to playing on the piano and embroidering bags. It is thoughtless to condemn them, or laugh at them, if they seek to do more or learn more than custom has pronounced necessary for their sex.

When thus alone, I not unfrequently heard Grace Poole's laugh: the same peal, the same low, slow *ha! ha!* which, when first heard, had thrilled me: I heard, too, her eccentric murmurs; stranger than her laugh. There were days when she was quite silent; but there were others when I could not account for the sounds she made. Sometimes I saw her: she would come out of her room with a basin, or a plate, or a tray in her hand, go down to the kitchen and shortly return, generally (oh, romantic reader, forgive me for telling the plain truth!) bearing a pot of porter. Her appearance always acted as a damper to the curiosity raised by her oral oddities: hard-featured and staid, she had no point to which interest could attach. I made some attempts to draw her into conversation, but she seemed a person of few words: a monosyllabic reply usually cut short every effort of that sort.

The other members of the household, viz., John and his wife, Leah the housemaid, and Sophie the French nurse, were decent people; but in no respect remarkable; with Sophie I used to talk French, and sometimes I asked her questions about her native country; but she was not of a descriptive or narrative turn, and generally gave such vapid and confused answers as were calculated rather to check than encourage inquiry.

October, November, December passed away. One afternoon in January, Mrs. Fairfax had begged a holiday for Adèle, because she had a cold; and, as Adèle seconded the request with an ardour that reminded me how precious occasional holidays had been to me in my own childhood, I accorded it, deeming that I did well in showing pliability on the point. It was a fine, calm day, though very cold; I was tired of sitting still in the library through a whole long morning: Mrs. Fairfax had just written a letter which was waiting to be posted, so I put on my bonnet and cloak and volunteered to carry it to Hay; the distance, two miles, would be a pleasant winter afternoon walk. Having seen Adèle comfortably seated in her little chair by Mrs. Fairfax's parlour fireside, and given her her best wax doll (which I usually kept enveloped in silver paper in a drawer) to play with, and a story-book for change of amusement; and having replied to her "Revenez bientôt, ma bonne amie, ma chère Mdlle. Jeannette," with a kiss I set out.

The ground was hard, the air was still, my road was lonely; I walked fast till I got warm, and then I walked slowly to enjoy and analyse the species of pleasure brooding for me in the hour and situation. It was three o'clock; the church bell tolled as I passed under the belfry: the charm of the hour lay in its approaching dimness, in the low-gliding and pale-beaming sun. I was a mile from Thornfield, in a lane noted for wild roses in summer, for nuts and blackberries in autumn, and even now possessing a few coral treasures in hips and haws, but whose best winter delight lay in its utter solitude and leafless repose. If a breath of air stirred, it made no sound here; for there was not a holly, not an evergreen to rustle, and the stripped hawthorn and hazel bushes were as still as the white, worn stones which causewayed the middle of the path. Far and wide, on each side, there were only fields, where no cattle now browsed; and the little brown birds, which stirred occasionally in the hedge, looked like single russet leaves that had forgotten to drop.

This lane inclined up-hill all the way to Hay; having reached the middle, I sat down on a stile which led thence into a field. Gathering my mantle about me, and sheltering my hands in my muff, I did not feel the cold, though it froze keenly; as was attested by a sheet of ice covering the causeway, where a little brooklet, now congealed, had overflowed after a rapid thaw some days since. From my seat I could look down on Thornfield: the grey and battlemented hall was the principal object in the vale below me; its woods and dark rookery rose against the west. I lingered till the sun went down amongst the trees, and sank crimson and clear behind them. I then turned eastward.

On the hill-top above me sat the rising moon; pale yet as a cloud, but brightening momentarily, she looked over Hay, which, half lost in trees, sent up a blue smoke from its few chimneys: it was yet a mile distant, but in the absolute hush I could hear plainly its thin murmurs of life. My ear, too, felt the flow of currents; in what dales and depths I could not tell: but there were many hills beyond Hay, and doubtless many becks threading their passes. That evening calm betrayed alike the tinkle of the nearest streams, the sough of the most remote.

A rude noise broke on these fine ripplings and whisperings, at once so far away and so clear: a positive tramp, tramp, a metallic clatter, which effaced the soft wave-wanderings; as, in a picture, the solid mass of a crag, or the rough boles of a great oak, drawn in dark and strong on the foreground, efface the aërial distance of azure hill, sunny horizon, and blended clouds where tint melts into tint.

The din was on the causeway: a horse was coming; the windings of the lane yet hid it, but it approached. I was just leaving the stile; yet, as the path was narrow, I sat still to let it go by. In those days I was young, and all sorts of fancies bright and dark tenanted my mind: the memories of nursery stories were there amongst other rubbish; and when they recurred, maturing youth added to them a vigour and vividness beyond what childhood could give. As this horse approached, and as I watched for it to appear through the dusk, I remembered certain of Bessie's tales, wherein figured a North-of-England spirit called a "Gytrash," which, in the form of horse, mule, or large dog, haunted solitary ways, and sometimes came upon belated travellers, as this horse was now coming upon me.

It was very near, but not yet in sight; when, in addition to the tramp, tramp, I heard a rush under the hedge, and close down by the hazel stems glided a great dog, whose black and white colour made him a distinct object against the trees. It was exactly one form of Bessie's Gytrash—a lion-like creature with long hair and a huge head: it passed me, however, quietly enough; not staying to look up, with strange pretercanine eyes, in my face, as I half expected it would. The horse followed—a tall steed, and on its back a rider. The man, the human being, broke the spell at once. Nothing ever rode the Gytrash: it was always alone; and goblins, to my notions, though they might tenant the dumb carcasses of beasts, could scarce covet shelter in the commonplace human form. No Gytrash was this—only a traveller taking the short cut to Millcote. He passed, and I went on; a few steps, and I turned: a sliding sound and an exclamation of "What the deuce is to do now?" and a clattering tumble, arrested my attention. Man and horse were down; they had slipped on the sheet of ice which glazed the causeway. The dog came bounding back, and seeing his master in a predicament, and hearing the horse groan, barked till the evening hills echoed the sound, which was deep in proportion to his magnitude. He snuffed round the prostrate group, and then he ran up to me; it was all he could do—there was no other help at hand to summon. I obeyed him, and walked down to the traveller, by this time struggling himself free of his steed. His efforts were so vigorous, I thought he could not be much hurt; but I asked him the question—

"Are you injured, sir?"

I think he was swearing, but am not certain; however, he was pronouncing some formula which prevented him from replying to me directly.

"Can I do anything?" I asked again.

"You must just stand on one side," he answered as he rose, first to his knees, and then to his feet. I did; whereupon began a heaving, stamping, clattering process, accompanied by a barking and baying which removed me effectually some yards' distance; but I would not be driven quite away till I saw the event. This was finally fortunate; the horse was re-established, and the dog was silenced with a "Down, Pilot!" The traveller now, stooping, felt his foot and leg, as if trying whether they were sound; apparently something ailed them, for he halted to the stile whence I had just risen, and sat down.

I was in the mood for being useful, or at least officious, I think, for I now drew near him again.

"If you are hurt, and want help, sir, I can fetch some one either from Thornfield Hall or from Hay."

"Thank you: I shall do: I have no broken bones—only a sprain"; and again he stood up and tried his foot, but the result extorted an involuntary "Ugh!"

Something of daylight still lingered, and the moon was waxing bright: I could see him plainly. His figure was enveloped in a riding cloak, fur collared and steel clasped; its details were not apparent, but I traced the general points of middle height and considerable breadth of chest. He had a dark face, with stern features and a heavy brow; his eyes and gathered eyebrows looked ireful and thwarted just now; he was past youth, but had not reached middle-age; perhaps he might be thirty-five. I felt no fear of him, and but little shyness. Had he been a handsome, heroic-looking young gentleman, I should not have dared to stand thus questioning him against his will, and offering my services unasked. I had hardly ever seen a handsome youth; never in my life spoken to one. I had a theoretical reverence and homage for beauty, elegance, gallantry, fascination; but had I met those qualities incarnate in masculine shape, I should have known instinctively that they neither had nor could have sympathy with anything in me, and should have shunned them as one would fire, lightning, or anything else that is bright but antipathetic.

If even this stranger had smiled and been good-humoured to me when I addressed him; if he had put off my offer of assistance gaily and with thanks, I should have gone on my way and not felt any vocation to renew inquiries: but the frown, the roughness of the traveller, set me at my ease: I retained my station when he waved to me to go, and announced—

"I cannot think of leaving you, sir, at so late an hour, in this solitary lane, till I see you are fit to mount your horse."

He looked at me when I said this; he had hardly turned his eyes in my direction before.

"I should think you ought to be at home yourself," said he, "if you have a home in this neighbourhood: where do you come from?"

"From just below; and I am not at all afraid of being out late when it is moonlight: I will run over to Hay for you with pleasure, if you wish it: indeed, I am going there to post a letter."

"You live just below—do you mean at that house with the battlements?" pointing to Thornfield Hall, on which the moon cast a hoary gleam, bringing it out distinct and pale from the woods that, by contrast with the western sky, now seemed one mass of shadow.

"Yes, sir."

"Whose house is it?"

"Mr. Rochester's."

"Do you know Mr. Rochester?"

"No, I have never seen him."

"He is not resident, then?"

"No."

"Can you tell me where he is?"

"I cannot."

"You are not a servant at the hall, of course. You are—" He stopped, ran his eye over my dress, which, as usual, was quite simple: a black merino cloak, a black beaver bonnet; neither of them half fine enough for a lady's-maid. He seemed puzzled to decide what I was; I helped him.

"I am the governess."

"Ah, the governess!" he repeated. "Deuce take me, if I had not forgotten! The governess!" And again my raiment underwent scrutiny. In two minutes he rose from the stile: his face expressed pain when he tried to move.

"I cannot commission you to fetch help," he said, "but you may help me a little yourself, if you will be so kind."

"Yes, sir."

"You have not an umbrella that I can use as a stick?"

"No."

"Try to get hold of my horse's bridle and lead him to me: you are not afraid?"

I should have been afraid to touch a horse when alone, but when told to do it, I was disposed to obey. I put down my muff on the stile, and went up to the tall steed; I endeavoured to catch the bridle, but it was a spirited thing, and would not let me come near its head; I made effort on effort, though in vain: meantime, I was mortally afraid of its trampling fore-feet. The traveller waited and watched for some time, and at last he laughed.

"I see," he said, "the mountain will never be brought to Mahomet, so all you can do is to aid Mahomet to go to the mountain; I must beg of you to come here."

I came. "Excuse me," he continued: "necessity compels me to make you useful." He laid a heavy hand on my shoulder, and leaning on me with some stress, limped to his horse. Having once caught the bridle, he mastered it directly and sprang to his saddle; grimacing grimly as he made the effort, for it wrenched his sprain.

"Now," said he, releasing his under lip from a hard bite, "just hand me my whip; it lies there under the hedge."

I sought it and found it.

"Thank you; now make haste with the letter to Hay, and return as fast as you can."

A touch of a spurred heel made his horse first start and rear, and then bound away; the dog rushed in his traces; all three vanished,

> "Like heath that, in the wilderness,
> The wild wind whirls away."

I took up my muff and walked on. The incident had occurred and was gone for me: it *was* an incident of no moment, no romance, no interest in a sense; yet it marked with change one single hour of a monotonous life. My help had been needed and claimed; I had given it: I was pleased to have done something; trivial, transitory though the deed was, it was yet an active thing, and I was weary of an existence all passive. The new face, too, was like a new picture introduced to the gallery of memory; and it was dissimilar to all the others hanging there: firstly, because it was masculine; and, secondly, because it was dark, strong, and stern. I had it still before me when I entered Hay, and slipped the letter into the post-office; I saw it as I walked fast down-hill all the way home. When I came to the stile, I stopped a minute, looked round and listened, with an idea that a horse's hoofs might ring on the causeway again, and that a rider in a cloak, and a Gytrash-like Newfoundland dog, might be again apparent: I saw only the hedge and a pollard willow before me, rising up still and straight to meet the moonbeams; I heard only the faintest waft of wind roaming fitful among the trees round Thornfield, a mile distant; and when I glanced down in the direction of the murmur, my eye, traversing the hall-front, caught a light kindling in a window: it reminded me that I was late, and I hurried on.

I did not like re-entering Thornfield. To pass its threshold was to return to stagnation; to cross the silent hall, to ascend the darksome staircase, to seek my own lonely little room, and then to meet tranquil Mrs. Fairfax, and spend the long winter evening with her, and her only, was to quell wholly the faint excitement wakened by my walk—to slip again over my faculties the viewless fetters of an uniform and too still existence; of an existence whose very privileges of security and ease I was becoming incapable of appreciating. What good it would have done me at that time to have been tossed in the storms of an uncertain struggling life, and to have been taught by rough and bitter experience to long for the calm amidst which I now repined! Yes, just as much good as it would do a man tired of sitting still in a "too easy chair" to take a long walk: and just as natural was the wish to stir, under my circumstances, as it would be under his.

I lingered at the gates; I lingered on the lawn; I paced backwards and forwards on the pavement; the shutters of the glass door were closed; I could not see into the interior; and both my eyes and spirit seemed drawn from the gloomy house—from the grey-hollow filled with rayless cells, as it appeared to me—to that sky expanded before me—a blue sea absolved from taint of cloud; the moon ascending it in solemn march; her orb seeming to look up as she left the hill-tops, from behind which she had come, far and farther below her, and aspired to the zenith, midnight dark in its fathomless depth and measureless distance; and for those trembling stars that followed her course; they made my heart tremble, my veins glow when I viewed them. Little things recall us to earth; the clock struck in the hall; that sufficed; I turned from moon and stars, opened a side-door, and went in.

The hall was not dark, nor yet was it lit, only by the high-hung bronze lamp; a warm glow suffused both it and the lower steps of the oak staircase. This ruddy shine issued from the great dining-room, whose two-leaved door stood open, and showed a genial fire in the grate, glancing on marble hearth and brass fire-irons, and revealing purple draperies and polished furniture, in the most pleasant radiance. It revealed, too, a group near the mantelpiece: I had scarcely caught it, and scarcely become aware of a cheerful mingling of voices, amongst which I seemed to distinguish the tones of Adèle, when the door closed.

I hastened to Mrs. Fairfax's room; there was a fire there too, but no candle, and no Mrs. Fairfax. Instead, all alone, sitting upright on the rug, and gazing with gravity at the blaze, I beheld a great black and white long-haired dog, just like the Gytrash of the lane. It was so like it that I went forward and said—

"Pilot," and the thing got up and came to me and snuffed me. I caressed him, and he wagged his great tail; but he looked an eerie creature to be alone with, and I could not tell whence he had come. I rang the bell, for I wanted a candle; and I wanted, too, to get an account of this visitant. Leah entered.

"What dog is this?"

"He came with master."

"With whom?"

"With master—Mr. Rochester—he is just arrived."

"Indeed! And is Mrs. Fairfax with him?"

"Yes, and Miss Adèle; they are in the dining-room, and John is gone for a surgeon; for master has had an accident; his horse fell and his ankle is sprained."

"Did the horse fall in Hay Lane?"

"Yes, coming down-hill; it slipped on some ice."

"Ah! Bring me a candle, will you, Leah?"

Leah brought it; she entered, followed by Mrs. Fairfax, who repeated the news; adding that Mr. Carter the surgeon was come, and was now with Mr. Rochester: then she hurried out to give orders about tea, and I went upstairs to take off my things.

CHAPTER XIII

Mr. Rochester, it seems, by the surgeon's orders, went to bed early that night; nor did he rise soon next morning. When he did come down, it was to attend to business: his agent and some of his tenants were arrived, and waiting to speak with him.

Adèle and I had now to vacate the library: it would be in daily requisition as a reception-room for callers. A fire was lit in an apartment upstairs, and there I carried our books, and arranged it for the future schoolroom. I discerned in the course of the morning that Thornfield Hall was a changed place: no longer silent as a church, it echoed every hour or two to a knock at the door, or a clang of the bell; steps, too, often traversed the hall, and new voices spoke in different keys below; a rill from the outer world was flowing through it; it had a master: for my part, I liked it better.

Adèle was not easy to teach that day; she could not apply: she kept running to the door and looking over the banisters to see if she could get a glimpse of Mr. Rochester; then she coined pretexts to go downstairs, in order, as I shrewdly suspected, to visit the library, where I knew she was not wanted; then, when I got a little angry, and made her sit still, she continued to talk incessantly of her "ami, Monsieur Edouard Fairfax *de* Rochester," as she dubbed him (I had not before heard his prenomens), and to conjecture what presents he had brought her: for it appears he had intimated the night before, that when his luggage came from Millcote, there would be found amongst it a little box in whose contents she had an interest.

"Et cela doit signifier," said she, "qu'il y aura là dedans un cadeau pour moi, et peut-être pour vous aussi, mademoiselle. Monsieur a parlé de vous: il m'a demandé le nom de ma gouvernante, et si elle n'était pas une petite personne, assez mince et un peu pâle. J'ai dit qu'oui: car c'est vrai, n'est-ce pas, mademoiselle?"

I and my pupil dined as usual in Mrs. Fairfax's parlour; the afternoon was wild and snowy, and we passed it in the schoolroom. At dark I allowed Adèle to put away books and work, and to run downstairs; for, from the comparative silence below, and from the cessation of appeals to the door-bell, I conjectured that Mr. Rochester was now at liberty. Left alone, I walked to the window; but nothing was to be seen thence: twilight and snowflakes together thickened the air, and hid the very shrubs on the lawn. I let down the curtain and went back to the fireside.

In the clear embers I was tracing a view, not unlike a picture I remembered to have seen of the castle of Heidelberg, on the Rhine, when Mrs. Fairfax came in, breaking up by her entrance the fiery mosaic I had been piercing together, and scattering too some heavy unwelcome thoughts that were beginning to throng on my solitude.

"Mr. Rochester would be glad if you and your pupil would take tea with him in the drawing-room this evening," said she: "he has been so much engaged all day that he could not ask to see you before."

"When is his tea-time?" I inquired.

"Oh, at six o'clock: he keeps early hours in the country. You had better change your frock now; I will go with you and fasten it. Here is a candle."

"Is it necessary to change my frock?"

"Yes, you had better: I always dress for the evening when Mr. Rochester is here."

This additional ceremony seemed somewhat stately; however, I repaired to my room, and, with Mrs. Fairfax's aid, replaced my black stuff dress by one of black silk; the best and the only additional one I had, except one of light grey, which, in my Lowood notions of the toilette, I thought too fine to be worn, except on first-rate occasions.

"You want a brooch," said Mrs. Fairfax. I had a single little pearl ornament which Miss Temple gave me as a parting keepsake: I put it on, and then we went downstairs. Unused as I was to strangers, it was rather a trial to appear thus formally summoned in Mr. Rochester's presence. I let Mrs. Fairfax precede me into the dining-room, and kept in her shade as we crossed that apartment; and, passing the arch, whose curtain was now dropped, entered the elegant recess beyond.

Two wax candles stood lighted on the table, and two on the mantelpiece; basking in the light and heat of a superb fire, lay Pilot—Adèle knelt near him. Half reclined on a couch appeared Mr. Rochester, his foot supported by the cushion; he was looking at Adèle and the dog: the fire shone full on his face. I knew my traveller with his broad and jetty eyebrows; his square forehead, made squarer by the horizontal sweep of his black hair. I recognised his decisive nose, more remarkable for character than beauty; his full nostrils, denoting, I thought, choler; his grim mouth, chin, and jaw—yes, all three were very grim, and no mistake. His shape, now divested of cloak, I perceived harmonised in squareness with his physiognomy: I suppose it was a good figure in the athletic sense of the term—broad chested and thin flanked, though neither tall nor graceful.

Mr. Rochester must have been aware of the entrance of Mrs. Fairfax and myself; but it appeared he was not in the mood to notice us, for he never lifted his head as we approached.

"Here is Miss Eyre, sir," said Mrs. Fairfax, in her quiet way. He bowed, still not taking his eyes from the group of the dog and child.

"Let Miss Eyre be seated," said he: and there was something in the forced stiff bow, in the impatient yet formal tone, which seemed further to express, "What the deuce is it to me whether Miss Eyre be there or not? At this moment I am not disposed to accost her."

I sat down quite disembarrassed. A reception of finished politeness would probably have confused me: I could not have returned or repaid it by answering grace and elegance on my part; but harsh caprice laid me under no obligation; on the contrary, a decent quiescence, under the freak of manner, gave me the advantage. Besides, the eccentricity of the proceeding was piquant: I felt interested to see how he would go on.

He went on as a statue would, that is, he neither spoke nor moved. Mrs. Fairfax seemed to think it necessary that some one should be amiable, and she began to talk. Kindly, as usual—and, as usual, rather trite—she condoled with him on the pressure of business he had had all day; on the annoyance it must have been to him with that painful sprain: then she commended his patience and perseverance in going through with it.

"Madam, I should like some tea," was the sole rejoinder she got. She hastened to ring the bell; and when the tray came, she proceeded to arrange the cups, spoons, etc., with assiduous celerity. I and Adèle went to the table; but the master did not leave his couch.

"Will you hand Mr. Rochester's cup?" said Mrs. Fairfax to me. "Adèle might perhaps spill it."

I did as requested. As he took the cup from my hand, Adèle, thinking the moment propitious for making a request in my favour, cried out—

"N'est-ce pas, monsieur, qu'il y a un cadeau pour Mademoiselle Eyre dans votre petit coffre?"

"Who talks of cadeaux?" said he gruffly. "Did you expect a present, Miss Eyre? Are you fond of presents?" And he searched my face with eyes that I saw were dark, irate, and piercing.

"I hardly know, sir; I have little experience of them: they are generally thought pleasant things."

"Generally thought? But what do *you* think?"

"I should be obliged to take time, sir, before I could give you an answer worthy of your acceptance: a present has many faces to it, has it not? And one should consider all, before pronouncing an opinion as to its nature."

"Miss Eyre, you are not so unsophisticated as Adèle: she demands a 'cadeau,' clamorously, the moment she sees me: you beat about the bush."

"Because I have less confidence in my deserts than Adèle has: she can prefer the claim of old acquaintance, and the right too of custom; for she says you have always been in the habit of giving her playthings; but if I had to make out a case I should be puzzled, since I am a stranger, and have done nothing to entitle me to an acknowledgment."

"Oh, don't fall back on over-modesty! I have examined Adèle, and find you have taken great pains with her: she is not bright, she has no talents; yet in a short time she has made much improvement."

"Sir, you have now given me my 'cadeau'; I am obliged to you: it is the meed teachers most covet—praise of their pupils' progress."

"Humph!" said Mr. Rochester, and he took his tea in silence.

"Come to the fire," said the master, when the tray was taken away, and Mrs. Fairfax had settled into a corner with her knitting; while Adèle was leading me by the hand round the room, showing me the beautiful books and ornaments on the consoles and chiffonnières. We obeyed, as in duty bound; Adèle wanted to take a seat on my knee, but she was ordered to amuse herself with Pilot.

"You have been resident in my house three months?"

"Yes, sir."

"And you came from—?"

"From Lowood school, in ——shire."

"Ah! A charitable concern. How long were you there?"

"Eight years."

"Eight years! You must be tenacious of life. I thought half the time in such a place would have done up any constitution! No wonder you have rather the look of another world. I marvelled where you had got that sort of face. When you came on me in Hay Lane last night, I thought unaccountably of fairy tales, and had half a mind to demand whether you had bewitched my horse: I am not sure yet. Who are your parents?"

"I have none."

"Nor ever had, I suppose: do you remember them?"

"No."

"I thought not. And so you were waiting for your people when you sat on that stile?"

"For whom, sir?"

"For the men in green: it was a proper moonlight evening for them. Did I break through one of your rings, that you spread that damned ice on the causeway?"

I shook my head. "The men in green all forsook England a hundred years ago," said I, speaking as seriously as he had done. "And not even in Hay Lane, or the fields about it, could you find a trace of them. I don't think either summer or harvest, or winter moon, will ever shine on their revels more."

Mrs. Fairfax had dropped her knitting, and, with raised eyebrows, seemed wondering what sort of talk this was.

"Well," resumed Mr. Rochester, "if you disown parents, you must have some sort of kinsfolk: uncles and aunts?"

"No; none that I ever saw."

"And your home?"

"I have none."

"Where do your brothers and sisters live?"

"I have no brothers or sisters."

"Who recommended you to come here?"

"I advertised, and Mrs. Fairfax answered my advertisement."

"Yes," said the good lady, who now knew what ground we were upon, "and I am daily thankful for the choice Providence led me to make. Miss Eyre has been an invaluable companion to me, and a kind and careful teacher to Adèle."

"Don't trouble yourself to give her a character," returned Mr. Rochester: "eulogiums will not bias me; I shall judge for myself. She began by felling my horse."

"Sir?" said Mrs. Fairfax.

"I have to thank her for this sprain."

The widow looked bewildered.

"Miss Eyre, have you ever lived in a town?"

"No, sir."

"Have you seen much society?"

"None but the pupils and teachers of Lowood, and now the inmates of Thornfield."

"Have you read much?"

"Only such books as came in my way; and they have not been numerous or very learned."

"You have lived the life of a nun: no doubt you are well drilled in religious forms; Brocklehurst, who I understand directs Lowood, is a parson, is he not?"

"Yes, sir."

"And you girls probably worshipped him, as a convent full of religieuses would worship their director."

"Oh, no."

"You are very cool! No! What! A novice not worship her priest! That sounds blasphemous."

"I disliked Mr. Brocklehurst; and I was not alone in the feeling. He is a harsh man; at once pompous and meddling; he cut off our hair; and for economy's sake bought us bad needles and thread, with which we could hardly sew."

"That was very false economy," remarked Mrs. Fairfax, who now again caught the drift of the dialogue.

"And was that the head and front of his offending?" demanded Mr. Rochester.

"He starved us when he had the sole superintendence of the provision department, before the committee was appointed; and he bored us with long lectures once a week, and with evening readings from books of his own inditing, about sudden deaths and judgments, which made us afraid to go to bed."

"What age were you when you went to Lowood?"

"About ten."

"And you stayed there eight years: you are now, then, eighteen?"

I assented.

"Arithmetic, you see, is useful; without its aid, I should hardly have been able to guess your age. It is a point difficult to fix where the features and countenance are so much at variance as in your case. And now what did you learn at Lowood? Can you play?"

"A little."

"Of course: that is the established answer. Go into the library—I mean, if you please. (Excuse my tone of command; I am used to say, 'Do this,' and it is done: I cannot alter my customary habits for one new inmate.) "Go, then, into the library; take a candle with you; leave the door open; sit down to the piano, and play a tune."

I departed, obeying his directions.

"Enough!" he called out in a few minutes. "You play *a little*, I see; like any other English school-girl; perhaps rather better than some, but not well."

I closed the piano and returned. Mr. Rochester continued.

"Adèle showed me some sketches this morning, which she said were yours. I don't know whether they were entirely of your doing; probably a master aided you?"

"No, indeed!" I interjected.

"Ah! That pricks pride. Well, fetch me your portfolio, if you can vouch for its contents being original; but don't pass your word unless you are certain: I can recognise patchwork."

"Then I will say nothing, and you shall judge for yourself, sir."

I brought the portfolio from the library.

"Approach the table," said he; and I wheeled it to his couch. Adèle and Mrs. Fairfax drew near to see the pictures.

"No crowding," said Mr. Rochester; "take the drawings from my hand as I finish with them; but don't push your faces up to mine."

He deliberately scrutinised each sketch and painting. Three he laid aside; the others, when he had examined them, he swept from him.

"Take them off to the other table, Mrs. Fairfax," said he, "and look at them with Adèle; you" (glancing at me) "resume your seat, and answer my questions. I perceive those pictures were done by one hand: was that hand yours?"

"Yes."

"And when did you find time to do them? They have taken much time, and some thought."

"I did them in the last two vacations I spent at Lowood, when I had no other occupation."

"Where did you get your copies?"

"Out of my head."

"That head I see now on your shoulders?"

"Yes, sir."

"Has it other furniture of the same kind within?"

"I should think it may have: I should hope—better."

He spread the pictures before him, and again surveyed them alternately.

While he is so occupied, I will tell you, reader, what they are: and first, I must premise that they are nothing wonderful. The subjects had, indeed, risen vividly on my mind. As I saw them with the spiritual eye, before I attempted to embody them, they were striking; but my hand would not second my fancy, and in each case it had wrought out but a pale portrait of the thing I had conceived.

These pictures were in water-colours. The first represented clouds low and livid, rolling over a swollen sea: all the distance was in eclipse; so, too, was the foreground; or rather, the nearest billows, for there was no land. One gleam of light lifted into relief a half-submerged mast, on which sat a cormorant, dark and large, with wings flecked with foam; its beak held a gold bracelet set with gems, that I had touched with as brilliant tints as my palette could yield, and as glittering distinctness as my pencil could impart. Sinking below the bird and mast, a drowned corpse glanced through the green water; a fair arm was the only limb clearly visible, whence the bracelet had been washed or torn.

The second picture contained for foreground only the dim peak of a hill, with grass and some leaves slanting as if by a breeze. Beyond and above spread an expanse of sky, dark blue as at twilight: rising into the sky was a woman's shape to the bust, portrayed in tints as dusk and soft as I could combine. The dim forehead was crowned with a star; the lineaments below were seen as through the suffusion of vapour; the eyes shone dark and wild; the hair streamed shadowy, like a beamless cloud torn by storm or by electric travail. On the neck lay a pale reflection like moonlight; the same faint lustre touched the train of thin clouds from which rose and bowed this vision of the Evening Star.

The third showed the pinnacle of an iceberg piercing a polar winter sky: a muster of northern lights reared their dim lances, close serried, along the horizon. Throwing these into distance, rose, in the foreground, a head—a colossal head, inclined towards the iceberg, and resting against it. Two thin hands, joined under the forehead, and supporting it, drew up before the lower features a sable veil, a brow quite bloodless, white as bone, and an eye hollow and fixed, blank of meaning but for the glassiness of despair, alone were visible. Above the temples, amidst wreathed turban folds of black drapery, vague in its character and consistency as cloud, gleamed a ring of white flame, gemmed with sparkles of a more lurid tinge. This pale crescent was "the likeness of a kingly crown"; what it diademed was "the shape which shape had none."

"Were you happy when you painted these pictures?" asked Mr. Rochester presently.

"I was absorbed, sir: yes, and I was happy. To paint them, in short, was to enjoy one of the keenest pleasures I have ever known."

"That is not saying much. Your pleasures, by your own account, have been few; but I daresay you did exist in a kind of artist's dreamland while you blent and arranged these strange tints. Did you sit at them long each day?"

"I had nothing else to do, because it was the vacation, and I sat at them from morning till noon, and from noon till night: the length of the midsummer days favoured my inclination to apply."

"And you felt self-satisfied with the result of your ardent labours?"

"Far from it. I was tormented by the contrast between my idea and my handiwork: in each case I had imagined something which I was quite powerless to realise."

"Not quite: you have secured the shadow of your thought; but no more, probably. You had not enough of the artist's skill and science to give it full being: yet the drawings are, for a school-girl, peculiar. As to the thoughts, they are elfish. These eyes in the Evening Star you must have seen in a dream. How could you make them look so clear, and yet not at all brilliant? For the planet above quells their rays. And what meaning is that in their solemn depth? And who taught you to paint wind? There is a high gale in that sky, and on this hill-top. Where did you see Latmos? For that is Latmos. There! Put the drawings away!"

I had scarce tied the strings of the portfolio, when, looking at his watch, he said abruptly—

"It is nine o'clock: what are you about, Miss Eyre, to let Adèle sit up so long? Take her to bed."

Adèle went to kiss him before quitting the room: he endured the caress, but scarcely seemed to relish it more than Pilot would have done, nor so much.

"I wish you all good-night, now," said he, making a movement of the hand towards the door, in token that he was tired of our company, and wished to dismiss us. Mrs. Fairfax folded up her knitting: I took my portfolio: we curtseyed to him, received a frigid bow in return, and so withdrew.

"You said Mr. Rochester was not strikingly peculiar, Mrs. Fairfax," I observed, when I rejoined her in her room, after putting Adèle to bed.

"Well, is he?"

"I think so: he is very changeful and abrupt."

"True: no doubt he may appear so to a stranger, but I am so accustomed to his manner, I never think of it; and then, if he has peculiarities of temper, allowance should be made."

"Why?"

"Partly because it is his nature—and we can none of us help our nature; and partly because he has painful thoughts, no doubt, to harass him, and make his spirits unequal."

"What about?"

"Family troubles, for one thing."

"But he has no family."

"Not now, but he has had—or, at least, relatives. He lost his elder brother a few years since."

"His *elder* brother?"

"Yes. The present Mr. Rochester has not been very long in possession of the property; only about nine years."

"Nine years is a tolerable time. Was he so very fond of his brother as to be still inconsolable for his loss?"

"Why, no, perhaps not. I believe there were some misunderstandings between them. Mr. Rowland Rochester was not quite just to Mr. Edward; and perhaps he prejudiced his father against him. The old gentleman was fond of money, and anxious to keep the family estate together. He did not like to diminish the property by division, and yet he was anxious that Mr. Edward should have wealth, too, to keep up the consequence of the name; and, soon after he was of age, some steps were taken that were not quite fair, and made a great deal of mischief. Old Mr. Rochester and Mr. Rowland combined to bring Mr. Edward into what he considered a painful position, for the sake of making his fortune: what the precise nature of that position was I never clearly knew, but his spirit could not brook what he had to suffer in it. He is not very forgiving: he broke with his family, and now for many years he has led an unsettled kind of life. I don't think he has ever been resident at Thornfield for a fortnight together, since the death of his brother without a will left him master of the estate; and, indeed, no wonder he shuns the old place."

"Why should he shun it?"

"Perhaps he thinks it gloomy."

The answer was evasive. I should have liked something clearer; but Mrs. Fairfax either could not, or would not, give me more explicit information of the origin and nature of Mr. Rochester's trials. She averred they were a mystery to herself, and that what she knew was chiefly from conjecture. It was evident, indeed, that she wished me to drop the subject, which I did accordingly.

CHAPTER XIV

For several subsequent days I saw little of Mr. Rochester. In the mornings he seemed much engaged with business, and, in the afternoon, gentlemen from Millcote or the neighbourhood called, and sometimes stayed to dine with him. When his sprain was well enough to admit of horse exercise, he rode out a good deal; probably to return these visits, as he generally did not come back till late at night.

During this interval, even Adèle was seldom sent for to his presence, and all my acquaintance with him was confined to an occasional rencontre in the hall, on the stairs, or in the gallery, when he would sometimes pass me haughtily and coldly, just acknowledging my presence by a distant nod or a cool glance, and sometimes bow and smile with gentlemanlike affability. His changes of mood did not offend me, because I saw that I had nothing to do with their alternation; the ebb and flow depended on causes quite disconnected with me.

One day he had had company to dinner, and had sent for my portfolio; in order, doubtless, to exhibit its contents: the gentlemen went away early, to attend a public meeting at Millcote, as Mrs. Fairfax informed me; but the night being wet and inclement, Mr. Rochester did not accompany them. Soon after they were gone he rang the bell: a message came that I and Adèle were to go downstairs. I brushed Adèle's hair and made her neat, and having ascertained that I was myself in my usual Quaker trim, where there was nothing to retouch—all being too close and plain, braided locks included, to admit of disarrangement—we descended, Adèle wondering whether the *petit coffre* was at length come; for, owing to some mistake, its arrival had hitherto been delayed. She was gratified: there it stood, a little carton, on the table when we entered the dining-room. She appeared to know it by instinct.

"Ma boite! Ma boite!" exclaimed she, running towards it.

"Yes, there is your 'boite' at last: take it into a corner, you genuine daughter of Paris, and amuse yourself with disembowelling it," said the deep and rather sarcastic voice of Mr. Rochester, proceeding from the depths of an immense easy-chair at the fireside. "And mind," he continued, "don't bother me with any details of the anatomical process, or any notice of the condition of the entrails: let your operation be conducted in silence: tiens-toi tranquille, enfant; comprends-tu?"

Adèle seemed scarcely to need the warning—she had already retired to a sofa with her treasure, and was busy untying the cord which secured the lid. Having removed this impediment, and lifted certain silvery envelopes of tissue paper, she merely exclaimed—

"Oh ciel! Que c'est beau!" and then remained absorbed in ecstatic contemplation.

"Is Miss Eyre there?" now demanded the master, half rising from his seat to look round to the door, near which I still stood.

"Ah! Well, come forward; be seated here." He drew a chair near his own. "I am not fond of the prattle of children," he continued; "for, old bachelor as I am, I have no pleasant associations connected with their lisp. It would be intolerable to me to pass a whole evening *tête-à-tête* with a brat. Don't draw that chair farther off, Miss Eyre; sit down exactly where I placed it—if you please, that is. Confound these civilities! I continually forget them. Nor do I particularly affect simple-minded old ladies. By-the-by, I must have mine in mind; it won't do to neglect her; she is a Fairfax, or wed to one; and blood is said to be thicker than water."

He rang, and despatched an invitation to Mrs. Fairfax, who soon arrived, knitting-basket in hand.

"Good evening, madam; I sent to you for a charitable purpose. I have forbidden Adèle to talk to me about her presents, and she is bursting with repletion: have the goodness to serve her as auditress and interlocutrice; it will be one of the most benevolent acts you ever performed."

Adèle, indeed, no sooner saw Mrs. Fairfax, than she summoned her to her sofa, and there quickly filled her lap with the porcelain, the ivory, the waxen contents of her "boite"; pouring out, meantime, explanations and raptures in such broken English as she was mistress of.

"Now I have performed the part of a good host," pursued Mr. Rochester, "put my guests into the way of amusing each other, I ought to be at liberty to attend to my own pleasure. Miss Eyre, draw your chair still a little farther forward: you are yet too far back; I cannot see you without disturbing my position in this comfortable chair, which I have no mind to do."

I did as I was bid, though I would much rather have remained somewhat in the shade; but Mr. Rochester had such a direct way of giving orders, it seemed a matter of course to obey him promptly.

We were, as I have said, in the dining-room: the lustre, which had been lit for dinner, filled the room with a festal breadth of light; the large fire was all red and clear; the purple curtains hung rich and ample before the lofty window and loftier arch; everything was still, save the subdued chat of Adèle (she dared not speak loud), and, filling up each pause, the beating of winter rain against the panes.

Mr. Rochester, as he sat in his damask-covered chair, looked different to what I had seen him look before; not quite so stern—much less gloomy. There was a smile on his lips, and his eyes sparkled, whether with wine or not, I am not sure; but I think it very probable. He was, in short, in his after-dinner mood; more expanded and genial, and also more self-indulgent than the frigid and rigid temper of the morning; still he looked preciously grim, cushioning his massive head against the swelling back of his chair, and receiving the light of the fire on his granite-hewn features, and in his great, dark eyes; for he had great, dark eyes, and very fine eyes, too—not without a certain change in their depths sometimes, which, if it was not softness, reminded you, at least, of that feeling.

He had been looking two minutes at the fire, and I had been looking the same length of time at him, when, turning suddenly, he caught my gaze fastened on his physiognomy.

"You examine me, Miss Eyre," said he. "Do you think me handsome?"

I should, if I had deliberated, have replied to this question by something conventionally vague and polite; but the answer somehow slipped from my tongue before I was aware: "No, sir."

"Ah! By my word! There is something singular about you," said he. "You have the air of a little *nonnette*; quaint, quiet, grave, and simple, as you sit with your hands before you, and your eyes generally bent on the carpet (except, by-the-by, when they are directed piercingly to my face; as just now, for instance); and when one asks you a question, or makes a remark to which you are obliged to reply, you rap out a round rejoinder, which, if not blunt, is at least brusque. What do you mean by it?"

"Sir, I was too plain; I beg your pardon. I ought to have replied that it was not easy to give an impromptu answer to a question about appearances; that tastes mostly differ; and that beauty is of little consequence, or something of that sort."

"You ought to have replied no such thing. Beauty of little consequence, indeed! And so, under pretence of softening the previous outrage, of stroking and soothing me into placidity, you stick a sly penknife under my ear! Go on: what fault do you find with me, pray? I suppose I have all my limbs and all my features like any other man?"

"Mr. Rochester, allow me to disown my first answer: I intended no pointed repartee: it was only a blunder."

"Just so: I think so: and you shall be answerable for it. Criticise me: does my forehead not please you?"

He lifted up the sable waves of hair which lay horizontally over his brow, and showed a solid enough mass of intellectual organs, but an abrupt deficiency where the suave sign of benevolence should have risen.

"Now, ma'am, am I a fool?"

"Far from it, sir. You would, perhaps, think me rude if I inquired in return whether you are a philanthropist?"

"There again! Another stick of the penknife, when she pretended to pat my head: and that is because I said I did not like the society of children and old women (low be it spoken!). No, young lady, I am not a general philanthropist; but I bear a conscience"; and he pointed to the prominences which are said to indicate that faculty, and which, fortunately for him, were sufficiently conspicuous; giving, indeed, a marked breadth to the upper part of his head: "and, besides, I once had a kind of rude tenderness of heart. When I was as old as you, I was a feeling fellow enough, partial to the unfledged, unfostered, and unlucky; but Fortune has knocked me about since: she has even kneaded me with her knuckles, and now I flatter myself I am hard and tough as an India-rubber ball; pervious, though, through a chink or two still, and with one sentient point in the middle of the lump. Yes: does that leave hope for me?"

"Hope of what, sir?"

"Of my final re-transformation from India-rubber back to flesh?"

"Decidedly he has had too much wine," I thought; and I did not know what answer to make to his queer question: how could I tell whether he was capable of being re-transformed?

"You looked very much puzzled, Miss Eyre; and though you are not pretty any more than I am handsome, yet a puzzled air becomes you; besides, it is convenient, for it keeps those searching eyes of yours away from my physiognomy, and busies them with the worsted flowers of the rug; so puzzle on. Young lady, I am disposed to be gregarious and communicative tonight."

With this announcement he rose from his chair, and stood, leaning his arm on the marble mantelpiece: in that attitude his shape was seen plainly as well as his face; his unusual breadth of chest, disproportionate almost to his length of limb. I am sure most people would have thought him an ugly man; yet there was so much unconscious pride in his port; so much ease in his demeanour; such a look of complete indifference to his own external appearance; so haughty a reliance on the power of other qualities, intrinsic or adventitious, to atone for the lack of mere personal attractiveness, that, in looking at him, one inevitably shared the indifference, and, even in a blind, imperfect sense, put faith in the confidence.

"I am disposed to be gregarious and communicative tonight," he repeated, "and that is why I sent for you: the fire and the chandelier were not sufficient company for me; nor would Pilot have been, for none of these can talk. Adèle is a degree better, but still far below the mark; Mrs. Fairfax ditto; you, I am persuaded, can suit me if you will: you puzzled me the first evening I invited you down here. I have almost forgotten you since: other ideas have driven yours from my head; but tonight I am resolved to be at ease; to dismiss what importunes, and recall what pleases. It would please me now to draw you out—to learn more of you—therefore speak."

Instead of speaking, I smiled; and not a very complacent or submissive smile either.

"Speak," he urged.

"What about, sir?"

"Whatever you like. I leave both the choice of subject and the manner of treating it entirely to yourself."

Accordingly I sat and said nothing: "If he expects me to talk for the mere sake of talking and showing off, he will find he has addressed himself to the wrong person," I thought.

"You are dumb, Miss Eyre."

I was dumb still. He bent his head a little towards me, and with a single hasty glance seemed to dive into my eyes.

"Stubborn?" he said, "and annoyed. Ah! It is consistent. I put my request in an absurd, almost insolent form. Miss Eyre, I beg your pardon.

The fact is, once for all, I don't wish to treat you like an inferior: that is" (correcting himself), "I claim only such superiority as must result from twenty years' difference in age and a century's advance in experience. This is legitimate, *et j'y tiens*, as Adèle would say; and it is by virtue of this superiority, and this alone, that I desire you to have the goodness to talk to me a little now, and divert my thoughts, which are galled with dwelling on one point—cankering as a rusty nail."

He had deigned an explanation, almost an apology, and I did not feel insensible to his condescension, and would not seem so.

"I am willing to amuse you, if I can, sir—quite willing; but I cannot introduce a topic, because how do I know what will interest you? Ask me questions, and I will do my best to answer them."

"Then, in the first place, do you agree with me that I have a right to be a little masterful, abrupt, perhaps exacting, sometimes, on the grounds I stated, namely, that I am old enough to be your father, and that I have battled through a varied experience with many men of many nations, and roamed over half the globe, while you have lived quietly with one set of people in one house?"

"Do as you please, sir."

"That is no answer; or rather it is a very irritating, because a very evasive one. Reply clearly."

"I don't think, sir, you have a right to command me, merely because you are older than I, or because you have seen more of the world than I have; your claim to superiority depends on the use you have made of your time and experience."

"Humph! Promptly spoken. But I won't allow that, seeing that it would never suit my case, as I have made an indifferent, not to say a bad, use of both advantages. Leaving superiority out of the question, then, you must still agree to receive my orders now and then, without being piqued or hurt by the tone of command. Will you?"

I smiled: I thought to myself Mr. Rochester *is* peculiar—he seems to forget that he pays me £30 per annum for receiving his orders.

"The smile is very well," said he, catching instantly the passing expression; "but speak too."

"I was thinking, sir, that very few masters would trouble themselves to inquire whether or not their paid subordinates were piqued and hurt by their orders."

"Paid subordinates! What! You are my paid subordinate, are you?

Oh yes, I had forgotten the salary! Well then, on that mercenary ground, will you agree to let me hector a little?"

"No, sir, not on that ground; but, on the ground that you did forget it, and that you care whether or not a dependent is comfortable in his dependency, I agree heartily."

"And will you consent to dispense with a great many conventional forms and phrases, without thinking that the omission arises from insolence?"

"I am sure, sir, I should never mistake informality for insolence: one I rather like, the other nothing free-born would submit to, even for a salary."

"Humbug! Most things free-born will submit to anything for a salary; therefore, keep to yourself, and don't venture on generalities of which you are intensely ignorant. However, I mentally shake hands with you for your answer, despite its inaccuracy; and as much for the manner in which it was said, as for the substance of the speech; the manner was frank and sincere; one does not often see such a manner: no, on the contrary, affectation, or coldness, or stupid, coarse-minded misapprehension of one's meaning are the usual rewards of candour. Not three in three thousand raw school-girl-governesses would have answered me as you have just done. But I don't mean to flatter you: if you are cast in a different mould to the majority, it is no merit of yours: Nature did it. And then, after all, I go too fast in my conclusions: for what I yet know, you may be no better than the rest; you may have intolerable defects to counterbalance your few good points."

"And so may you," I thought. My eye met his as the idea crossed my mind: he seemed to read the glance, answering as if its import had been spoken as well as imagined—

"Yes, yes, you are right," said he; "I have plenty of faults of my own: I know it, and I don't wish to palliate them, I assure you. God wot I need not be too severe about others; I have a past existence, a series of deeds, a colour of life to contemplate within my own breast, which might well call my sneers and censures from my neighbours to myself. I started, or rather (for like other defaulters, I like to lay half the blame on ill fortune and adverse circumstances) was thrust on to a wrong tack at the age of one-and-twenty, and have never recovered the right course since: but I might have been very different; I might have been as good as you—wiser—almost as stainless. I envy you your peace of mind, your clean conscience, your unpolluted memory. Little girl, a memory without blot or contamination must be an exquisite treasure—an inexhaustible source of pure refreshment: is it not?"

"How was your memory when you were eighteen, sir?"

"All right then; limpid, salubrious: no gush of bilge water had turned it to fetid puddle. I was your equal at eighteen—quite your equal. Nature meant me to be, on the whole, a good man, Miss Eyre; one of the better kind, and you see I am not so. You would say you don't see it; at least I flatter myself I read as much in your eye (beware, by-the-by, what you express with that organ; I am quick at interpreting its language). Then take my word for it—I am not a villain: you are not to suppose that—not to attribute to me any such bad eminence; but, owing, I verily believe, rather to circumstances than to my natural bent, I am a trite commonplace sinner, hackneyed in all the poor petty dissipations with which the rich and worthless try to put on life. Do you wonder that I avow this to you? Know, that in the course of your future life you will often find yourself elected the involuntary confidant of your acquaintances' secrets: people will instinctively find out, as I have done, that it is not your forte to tell of yourself, but to listen while others talk of themselves; they will feel, too, that you listen with no malevolent scorn of their indiscretion, but with a kind of innate sympathy; not the less comforting and encouraging because it is very unobtrusive in its manifestations."

"How do you know? How can you guess all this, sir?"

"I know it well; therefore I proceed almost as freely as if I were writing my thoughts in a diary. You would say, I should have been superior to circumstances; so I should—so I should; but you see I was not. When fate wronged me, I had not the wisdom to remain cool: I turned desperate; then I degenerated. Now, when any vicious simpleton excites my disgust by his paltry ribaldry, I cannot flatter myself that I am better than he: I am forced to confess that he and I are on a level. I wish I had stood firm—God knows I do! Dread remorse when you are tempted to err, Miss Eyre; remorse is the poison of life."

"Repentance is said to be its cure, sir."

"It is not its cure. Reformation may be its cure; and I could reform—I have strength yet for that—if—but where is the use of thinking of it, hampered, burdened, cursed as I am? Besides, since happiness is irrevocably denied me, I have a right to get pleasure out of life: and I *will* get it, cost what it may."

"Then you will degenerate still more, sir."

"Possibly: yet why should I, if I can get sweet, fresh pleasure? And I may get it as sweet and fresh as the wild honey the bee gathers on the moor."

"It will sting—it will taste bitter, sir."

"How do you know? You never tried it. How very serious—how very solemn you look: and you are as ignorant of the matter as this cameo head" (taking one from the mantelpiece). "You have no right to preach to me, you neophyte, that have not passed the porch of life, and are absolutely unacquainted with its mysteries."

"I only remind you of your own words, sir: you said error brought remorse, and you pronounced remorse the poison of existence."

"And who talks of error now? I scarcely think the notion that flittered across my brain was an error. I believe it was an inspiration rather than a temptation: it was very genial, very soothing—I know that. Here it comes again! It is no devil, I assure you; or if it be, it has put on the robes of an angel of light. I think I must admit so fair a guest when it asks entrance to my heart."

"Distrust it, sir; it is not a true angel."

"Once more, how do you know? By what instinct do you pretend to distinguish between a fallen seraph of the abyss and a messenger from the eternal throne—between a guide and a seducer?"

"I judged by your countenance, sir, which was troubled when you said the suggestion had returned upon you. I feel sure it will work you more misery if you listen to it."

"Not at all—it bears the most gracious message in the world: for the rest, you are not my conscience-keeper, so don't make yourself uneasy. Here, come in, bonny wanderer!"

He said this as if he spoke to a vision, viewless to any eye but his own; then, folding his arms, which he had half extended, on his chest, he seemed to enclose in their embrace the invisible being.

"Now," he continued, again addressing me, "I have received the pilgrim—a disguised deity, as I verily believe. Already it has done me good: my heart was a sort of charnel; it will now be a shrine."

"To speak truth, sir, I don't understand you at all: I cannot keep up the conversation, because it has got out of my depth. Only one thing, I know: you said you were not as good as you should like to be, and that you regretted your own imperfection; one thing I can comprehend:

you intimated that to have a sullied memory was a perpetual bane. It seems to me, that if you tried hard, you would in time find it possible to become what you yourself would approve; and that if from this day you began with resolution to correct your thoughts and actions, you would in a few years have laid up a new and stainless store of recollections, to which you might revert with pleasure."

"Justly thought; rightly said, Miss Eyre; and, at this moment, I am paving hell with energy."

"Sir?"

"I am laying down good intentions, which I believe durable as flint. Certainly, my associates and pursuits shall be other than they have been."

"And better?"

"And better—so much better as pure ore is than foul dross. You seem to doubt me; I don't doubt myself: I know what my aim is, what my motives are; and at this moment I pass a law, unalterable as that of the Medes and Persians, that both are right."

"They cannot be, sir, if they require a new statute to legalise them."

"They are, Miss Eyre, though they absolutely require a new statute: unheard-of combinations of circumstances demand unheard-of rules."

"That sounds a dangerous maxim, sir; because one can see at once that it is liable to abuse."

"Sententious sage! So it is: but I swear by my household gods not to abuse it."

"You are human and fallible."

"I am: so are you—what then?"

"The human and fallible should not arrogate a power with which the divine and perfect alone can be safely intrusted."

"What power?"

"That of saying of any strange, unsanctioned line of action: 'Let it be right.'"

"'Let it be right'—the very words: you have pronounced them."

"*May* it be right then," I said, as I rose, deeming it useless to continue a discourse which was all darkness to me; and, besides, sensible that the character of my interlocutor was beyond my penetration; at least, beyond its present reach; and feeling the uncertainty, the vague sense of insecurity, which accompanies a conviction of ignorance.

"Where are you going?"

"To put Adèle to bed: it is past her bedtime."

"You are afraid of me, because I talk like a Sphynx."

"Your language is enigmatical, sir: but though I am bewildered, I am certainly not afraid."

"You *are* afraid—your self-love dreads a blunder."

"In that sense I do feel apprehensive—I have no wish to talk nonsense."

"If you did, it would be in such a grave, quiet manner, I should mistake it for sense. Do you never laugh, Miss Eyre? Don't trouble yourself to answer—I see you laugh rarely; but you can laugh very merrily: believe me, you are not naturally austere, any more than I am naturally vicious. The Lowood constraint still clings to you somewhat; controlling your features, muffling your voice, and restricting your limbs; and you fear in the presence of a man and a brother—or father, or master, or what you will—to smile too gaily, speak too freely, or move too quickly: but, in time, I think you will learn to be natural with me, as I find it impossible to be conventional with you; and then your looks and movements will have more vivacity and variety than they dare offer now. I see at intervals the glance of a curious sort of bird through the close-set bars of a cage: a vivid, restless, resolute captive is there; were it but free, it would soar cloud-high. You are still bent on going?"

"It has struck nine, sir."

"Never mind—wait a minute: Adèle is not ready to go to bed yet. My position, Miss Eyre, with my back to the fire, and my face to the room, favours observation. While talking to you, I have also occasionally watched Adèle (I have my own reasons for thinking her a curious study—reasons that I may, nay, that I shall, impart to you some day). She pulled out of her box, about ten minutes ago, a little pink silk frock; rapture lit her face as she unfolded it; coquetry runs in her blood, blends with her brains, and seasons the marrow of her bones. 'Il faut que je l'essaie!' cried she. 'Et à l'instant même!' and she rushed out of the room. She is now with Sophie, undergoing a robing process: in a few minutes she will re-enter; and I know what I shall see—a miniature of Céline Varens, as she used to appear on the boards at the rising of ——. But never mind that. However, my tenderest feelings are about to receive a shock: such is my presentiment; stay now, to see whether it will be realised."

Ere long, Adèle's little foot was heard tripping across the hall. She entered, transformed as her guardian had predicted. A dress of rose-coloured satin, very short, and as full in the skirt as it could be gathered, replaced the brown frock she had previously worn; a wreath of rosebuds circled her forehead; her feet were dressed in silk stockings and small white satin sandals.

"Est-ce que ma robe va bien?" cried she, bounding forwards. "Et mes souliers? Et mes bas? Tenez, je crois que je vais danser!"

And spreading out her dress, she chasséed across the room till, having reached Mr. Rochester, she wheeled lightly round before him on tip-toe, then dropped on one knee at his feet, exclaiming—

"Monsieur, je vous remercie mille fois de votre bonté." Then rising, she added, "C'est comme cela que maman faisait, n'est-ce pas, monsieur?"

"Pre-cise-ly!" was the answer. "And, 'comme cela,' she charmed my English gold out of my British breeches' pocket. I have been green, too, Miss Eyre—ay, grass green: not a more vernal tint freshens you now than once freshened me. My Spring is gone, however, but it has left me that French floweret on my hands, which, in some moods, I would fain be rid of. Not valuing now the root whence it sprang; having found that it was of a sort which nothing but gold dust could manure, I have but half a liking to the blossom, especially when it looks so artificial as just now. I keep it and rear it rather on the Roman Catholic principle of expiating numerous sins, great or small, by one good work. I'll explain all this some day. Good-night."

CHAPTER XV

Mr. Rochester did, on a future occasion, explain it. It was one afternoon, when he chanced to meet me and Adèle in the grounds: and while she played with Pilot and her shuttlecock, he asked me to walk up and down a long beech avenue within sight of her.

He then said that she was the daughter of a French opera-dancer, Céline Varens, towards whom he had once cherished what he called a "*grande passion.*" This passion Céline had professed to return with even superior ardour. He thought himself her idol, ugly as he was: he believed, as he said, that she preferred his "*taille d'athlète*" to the elegance of the Apollo Belvidere.

"And, Miss Eyre, so much was I flattered by this preference of the Gallic sylph for her British gnome, that I installed her in an hotel; gave her a complete establishment of servants, a carriage, cashmeres, diamonds, dentelles, etc. In short, I began the process of ruining myself in the received style, like any other spoony. I had not, it seems, the originality to chalk out a new road to shame and destruction, but trode the old track with stupid exactness not to deviate an inch from the beaten centre. I had—as I deserved to have—the fate of all other spoonies. Happening to call one evening when Céline did not expect me, I found her out; but it was a warm night, and I was tired with strolling through Paris, so I sat down in her boudoir; happy to breathe the air consecrated so lately by her presence. No—I exaggerate; I never thought there was any consecrating virtue about her: it was rather a sort of pastille perfume she had left; a scent of musk and amber, than an odour of sanctity. I was just beginning to stifle with the fumes of conservatory flowers and sprinkled essences, when I bethought myself to open the window and step out on to the balcony. It was moonlight and gaslight besides, and very still and serene. The balcony was furnished with a chair or two; I sat down, and took out a cigar—I will take one now, if you will excuse me."

Here ensued a pause, filled up by the producing and lighting of a cigar; having placed it to his lips and breathed a trail of Havannah incense on the freezing and sunless air, he went on—

"I liked bonbons too in those days, Miss Eyre, and I was *croquant*—

(overlook the barbarism)—*croquant* chocolate comfits, and smoking alternately, watching meantime the equipages that rolled along the fashionable streets towards the neighbouring opera-house, when in an elegant close carriage drawn by a beautiful pair of English horses, and distinctly seen in the brilliant city-night, I recognised the 'voiture' I had given Céline. She was returning: of course my heart thumped with impatience against the iron rails I leant upon. The carriage stopped, as I had expected, at the hotel door; my flame (that is the very word for an opera inamorata) alighted: though muffed in a cloak—an unnecessary encumbrance, by-the-by, on so warm a June evening—I knew her instantly by her little foot, seen peeping from the skirt of her dress, as she skipped from the carriage-step. Bending over the balcony, I was about to murmur 'Mon ange'—in a tone, of course, which should be audible to the ear of love alone—when a figure jumped from the carriage after her; cloaked also; but that was a spurred heel which had rung on the pavement, and that was a hatted head which now passed under the arched *porte cochère* of the hotel.

"You never felt jealousy, did you, Miss Eyre? Of course not: I need not ask you; because you never felt love. You have both sentiments yet to experience: your soul sleeps; the shock is yet to be given which shall waken it. You think all existence lapses in as quiet a flow as that in which your youth has hitherto slid away. Floating on with closed eyes and muffled ears, you neither see the rocks bristling not far off in the bed of the flood, nor hear the breakers boil at their base. But I tell you—and you may mark my words—you will come some day to a craggy pass in the channel, where the whole of life's stream will be broken up into whirl and tumult, foam and noise: either you will be dashed to atoms on crag points, or lifted up and borne on by some master-wave into a calmer current—as I am now.

"I like this day; I like that sky of steel; I like the sternness and stillness of the world under this frost. I like Thornfield, its antiquity, its retirement, its old crow-trees and thorn-trees, its grey façade, and lines of dark windows reflecting that metal welkin: and yet how long have I abhorred the very thought of it, shunned it like a great plague-house? How I do still abhor—"

He ground his teeth and was silent: he arrested his step and struck his boot against the hard ground. Some hated thought seemed to have him in its grip, and to hold him so tightly that he could not advance.

We were ascending the avenue when he thus paused; the hall was before us. Lifting his eye to its battlements, he cast over them a glare such as I never saw before or since. Pain, shame, ire, impatience, disgust, detestation, seemed momentarily to hold a quivering conflict in the large pupil dilating under his ebon eyebrow. Wild was the wrestle which should be paramount; but another feeling rose and triumphed: something hard and cynical: self-willed and resolute: it settled his passion and petrified his countenance: he went on—

"During the moment I was silent, Miss Eyre, I was arranging a point with my destiny. She stood there, by that beech-trunk—a hag like one of those who appeared to Macbeth on the heath of Forres. 'You like Thornfield?' she said, lifting her finger; and then she wrote in the air a memento, which ran in lurid hieroglyphics all along the house-front, between the upper and lower row of windows, 'Like it if you can! Like it if you dare!'

" 'I will like it,' said I; 'I dare like it'; and" (he subjoined moodily) "I will keep my word; I will break obstacles to happiness, to goodness—yes, goodness. I wish to be a better man than I have been, than I am; as Job's leviathan broke the spear, the dart, and the habergeon, hindrances which others count as iron and brass, I will esteem but straw and rotten wood."

Adèle here ran before him with her shuttlecock. "Away!" he cried harshly; "keep at a distance, child; or go in to Sophie!" Continuing then to pursue his walk in silence, I ventured to recall him to the point whence he had abruptly diverged—

"Did you leave the balcony, sir," I asked, "when Mdlle. Varens entered?"

I almost expected a rebuff for this hardly well-timed question, but, on the contrary, waking out of his scowling abstraction, he turned his eyes towards me, and the shade seemed to clear off his brow. "Oh, I had forgotten Céline! Well, to resume. When I saw my charmer thus come in accompanied by a cavalier, I seemed to hear a hiss, and the green snake of jealousy, rising on undulating coils from the moonlit balcony, glided within my waistcoat, and ate its way in two minutes to my heart's core. Strange!" he exclaimed, suddenly starting again from the point. "Strange that I should choose you for the confidant of all this, young lady; passing strange that you should listen to me quietly, as if it were the most usual thing in the world for a man like me to tell stories of his opera-mistresses to a quaint, inexperienced girl like you! But the last singularity explains the first, as I intimated once before: you, with your gravity, considerateness, and caution were made to be the recipient of secrets. Besides, I know what sort of a mind I have placed in communication with my own: I know it is one not liable to take infection: it is a peculiar mind: it is a unique one. Happily I do not mean to harm it: but, if I did, it would not take harm from me. The more you and I converse, the better; for while I cannot blight you, you may refresh me." After this digression he proceeded—

"I remained in the balcony. 'They will come to her boudoir, no doubt,' thought I; 'let me prepare an ambush.' So putting my hand in through the open window, I drew the curtain over it, leaving only an opening through which I could take observations; then I closed the casement, all but a chink just wide enough to furnish an outlet to lovers' whispered vows: then I stole back to my chair; and as I resumed it the pair came in. My eye was quickly at the aperture. Céline's chambermaid entered, lit a lamp, left it on the table, and withdrew. The couple were thus revealed to me clearly: both removed their cloaks, and there was 'the Varens,' shining in satin and jewels—my gifts of course—and there was her companion in an officer's uniform; and I knew him for a young roué of a vicomte—a brainless and vicious youth whom I had sometimes met in society, and had never thought of hating because I despised him so absolutely. On recognising him, the fang of the snake Jealousy was instantly broken; because at the same moment my love for Céline sank under an extinguisher. A woman who could betray me for such a rival was not worth contending for; she deserved only scorn; less, however, than I, who had been her dupe.

"They began to talk; their conversation eased me completely: frivolous, mercenary, heartless, and senseless, it was rather calculated to weary than enrage a listener. A card of mine lay on the table; this being perceived, brought my name under discussion. Neither of them possessed energy or wit to belabour me soundly, but they insulted me as coarsely as they could in their little way: especially Céline, who even waxed rather brilliant on my personal defects—deformities she termed them. Now it had been her custom to launch out into fervent admiration of what she called my '*beauté mâle*': wherein she differed diametrically from you, who told me point-blank, at the second interview, that you did not think me handsome. The contrast struck me at the time and—"

Adèle here came running up again.

"Monsieur, John has just been to say that your agent has called and wishes to see you."

"Ah! In that case I must abridge. Opening the window, I walked in upon them; liberated Céline from my protection; gave her notice to vacate her hotel; offered her a purse for immediate exigencies; disregarded screams, hysterics, prayers, protestations, convulsions; made an appointment with the vicomte for a meeting at the Bois de Boulogne. Next morning I had the pleasure of encountering him; left a bullet in one of his poor etiolated arms, feeble as the wing of a chicken in the pip, and then thought I had done with the whole crew. But unluckily the Varens, six months before, had given me this filette Adèle, who, she affirmed, was my daughter; and perhaps she may be, though I see no proofs of such grim paternity written in her countenance: Pilot is more like me than she. Some years after I had broken with the mother, she abandoned her child, and ran away to Italy with a musician or singer. I acknowledged no natural claim on Adèle's part to be supported by me, nor do I now acknowledge any, for I am not her father; but hearing that she was quite destitute, I e'en took the poor thing out of the slime and mud of Paris, and transplanted it here, to grow up clean in the wholesome soil of an English country garden. Mrs. Fairfax found you to train it; but now you know that it is the illegitimate offspring of a French opera-girl, you will perhaps think differently of your post and protégée: you will be coming to me some day with notice that you have found another place—that you beg me to look out for a new governess, etc. Eh?"

"No: Adèle is not answerable for either her mother's faults or yours: I have a regard for her; and now that I know she is, in a sense, parentless—forsaken by her mother and disowned by you, sir—I shall cling closer to her than before. How could I possibly prefer the spoilt pet of a wealthy family, who would hate her governess as a nuisance, to a lonely little orphan, who leans towards her as a friend?"

"Oh, that is the light in which you view it! Well, I must go in now; and you too: it darkens."

But I stayed out a few minutes longer with Adèle and Pilot—ran a race with her, and played a game of battledore and shuttlecock. When we went in, and I had removed her bonnet and coat, I took her on my knee; kept her there an hour, allowing her to prattle as she liked: not rebuking even some little freedoms and trivialities into which she was apt to stray when much noticed, and which betrayed in her a superficiality of character, inherited probably from her mother, hardly congenial to an English mind. Still she had her merits; and I was disposed to appreciate all that was good in her to the utmost. I sought in her countenance and features a likeness to Mr. Rochester, but found none: no trait, no turn of expression announced relationship. It was a pity: if she could but have been proved to resemble him, he would have thought more of her.

It was not till after I had withdrawn to my own chamber for the night, that I steadily reviewed the tale Mr. Rochester had told me. As he had said, there was probably nothing at all extraordinary in the substance of the narrative itself: a wealthy Englishman's passion for a French dancer, and her treachery to him, were every-day matters enough, no doubt, in society; but there was something decidedly strange in the paroxysm of emotion which had suddenly seized him when he was in the act of expressing the present contentment of his mood, and his newly revived pleasure in the old hall and its environs. I meditated wonderingly on this incident; but gradually quitting it, as I found it for the present inexplicable, I turned to the consideration of my master's manner to myself. The confidence he had thought fit to repose in me seemed a tribute to my discretion: I regarded and accepted it as such. His deportment had now for some weeks been more uniform towards me than at the first. I never seemed in his way; he did not take fits of chilling hauteur: when he met me unexpectedly, the encounter seemed welcome; he had always a word and sometimes a smile for me: when summoned by formal invitation to his presence, I was honoured by a cordiality of reception that made me feel I really possessed the power to amuse him, and that these evening conferences were sought as much for his pleasure as for my benefit.

I, indeed, talked comparatively little, but I heard him talk with relish. It was his nature to be communicative; he liked to open to a mind unacquainted with the world glimpses of its scenes and ways (I do not mean its corrupt scenes and wicked ways, but such as derived their interest from the great scale on which they were acted, the strange novelty by which they were characterised); and I had a keen delight in receiving the new ideas he offered, in imagining the new pictures he portrayed, and following him in thought through the new regions he disclosed, never startled or troubled by one noxious allusion.

The ease of his manner freed me from painful restraint: the friendly frankness, as correct as cordial, with which he treated me, drew me to him. I felt at times as if he were my relation rather than my master: yet he was imperious sometimes still; but I did not mind that; I saw it was his way. So happy, so gratified did I become with this new interest added to life, that I ceased to pine after kindred: my thin crescent-destiny seemed to enlarge; the blanks of existence were filled up; my bodily health improved; I gathered flesh and strength.

And was Mr. Rochester now ugly in my eyes? No, reader: gratitude, and many associations, all pleasurable and genial, made his face the object I best liked to see; his presence in a room was more cheering than the brightest fire. Yet I had not forgotten his faults; indeed, I could not, for he brought them frequently before me. He was proud, sardonic, harsh to inferiority of every description: in my secret soul I knew that his great kindness to me was balanced by unjust severity to many others. He was moody, too; unaccountably so; I more than once, when sent for to read to him, found him sitting in his library alone, with his head bent on his folded arms; and, when he looked up, a morose, almost a malignant, scowl blackened his features. But I believed that his moodiness, his harshness, and his former faults of morality (I say *former*, for now he seemed corrected of them) had their source in some cruel cross of fate. I believed he was naturally a man of better tendencies, higher principles, and purer tastes than such as circumstances had developed, education instilled, or destiny encouraged. I thought there were excellent materials in him; though for the present they hung together somewhat spoiled and tangled. I cannot deny that I grieved for his grief, whatever that was, and would have given much to assuage it.

Though I had now extinguished my candle and was laid down in bed, I could not sleep for thinking of his look when he paused in the avenue, and told how his destiny had risen up before him, and dared him to be happy at Thornfield.

"Why not?" I asked myself. "What alienates him from the house? Will he leave it again soon? Mrs. Fairfax said he seldom stayed here longer than a fortnight at a time; and he has now been resident eight weeks. If he does go, the change will be doleful. Suppose he should be absent spring, summer, and autumn: how joyless sunshine and fine days will seem!"

I hardly know whether I had slept or not after this musing; at any rate, I started wide awake on hearing a vague murmur, peculiar and lugubrious, which sounded, I thought, just above me. I wished I had kept my candle burning: the night was drearily dark; my spirits were depressed. I rose and sat up in bed, listening. The sound was hushed.

I tried again to sleep; but my heart beat anxiously: my inward tranquillity was broken. The clock, far down in the hall, struck two. Just then it seemed my chamber-door was touched; as if fingers had swept the panels in groping a way along the dark gallery outside. I said, "Who is there?" Nothing answered. I was chilled with fear.

All at once I remembered that it might be Pilot, who, when the kitchen-door chanced to be left open, not unfrequently found his way up to the threshold of Mr. Rochester's chamber: I had seen him lying there myself in the mornings. The idea calmed me somewhat: I lay down. Silence composes the nerves; and as an unbroken hush now reigned again through the whole house, I began to feel the return of slumber. But it was not fated that I should sleep that night. A dream had scarcely approached my ear, when it fled affrighted, scared by a marrow-freezing incident enough.

This was a demoniac laugh—low, suppressed, and deep—uttered, as it seemed, at the very keyhole of my chamber door. The head of my bed was near the door, and I thought at first the goblin-laugher stood at my bedside—or rather, crouched by my pillow: but I rose, looked round, and could see nothing; while, as I still gazed, the unnatural sound was reiterated: and I knew it came from behind the panels. My first impulse was to rise and fasten the bolt; my next, again to cry out, "Who is there?"

Something gurgled and moaned. Ere long, steps retreated up the gallery towards the third-storey staircase: a door had lately been made to shut in that staircase; I heard it open and close, and all was still.

"Was that Grace Poole? And is she possessed with a devil?" thought I. Impossible now to remain longer by myself: I must go to Mrs. Fairfax. I hurried on my frock and a shawl; I withdrew the bolt and opened the door with a trembling hand. There was a candle burning just outside, and on the matting in the gallery. I was surprised at this circumstance: but still more was I amazed to perceive the air quite dim, as if filled with smoke; and, while looking to the right hand and left, to find whence these blue wreaths issued, I became further aware of a strong smell of burning.

Something creaked: it was a door ajar; and that door was Mr. Rochester's, and the smoke rushed in a cloud from thence. I thought no more of Mrs. Fairfax; I thought no more of Grace Poole, or the laugh: in an instant, I was within the chamber. Tongues of flame darted round the bed: the curtains were on fire. In the midst of blaze and vapour, Mr. Rochester lay stretched motionless, in deep sleep.

"Wake! Wake!" I cried. I shook him, but he only murmured and turned: the smoke had stupefied him. Not a moment could be lost: the very sheets were kindling, I rushed to his basin and ewer; fortunately, one was wide and the other deep, and both were filled with water. I heaved them up, deluged the bed and its occupant, flew back to my own room, brought my own water-jug, baptized the couch afresh, and, by God's aid, succeeded in extinguishing the flames which were devouring it.

The hiss of the quenched element, the breakage of a pitcher which I flung from my hand when I had emptied it, and, above all, the splash of the shower-bath I had liberally bestowed, roused Mr. Rochester at last. Though it was now dark, I knew he was awake; because I heard him fulminating strange anathemas at finding himself lying in a pool of water.

"Is there a flood?" he cried.

"No, sir," I answered; "but there has been a fire: get up, do; you are quenched now; I will fetch you a candle."

"In the name of all the elves in Christendom, is that Jane Eyre?" he demanded. "What have you done with me, witch, sorceress? Who is in the room besides you? Have you plotted to drown me?"

"I will fetch you a candle, sir; and, in Heaven's name, get up. Somebody has plotted something: you cannot too soon find out who and what it is."

"There! I am up now; but at your peril you fetch a candle yet: wait two minutes till I get into some dry garments, if any dry there be—yes, here is my dressing-gown. Now run!"

I did run; I brought the candle which still remained in the gallery. He took it from my hand, held it up, and surveyed the bed, all blackened and scorched, the sheets drenched, the carpet round swimming in water.

"What is it? And who did it?" he asked. I briefly related to him what had transpired: the strange laugh I had heard in the gallery: the step ascending to the third storey; the smoke—the smell of fire which had conducted me to his room; in what state I had found matters there, and how I had deluged him with all the water I could lay hands on.

He listened very gravely; his face, as I went on, expressed more concern than astonishment; he did not immediately speak when I had concluded.

"Shall I call Mrs. Fairfax?" I asked.

"Mrs. Fairfax? No; what the deuce would you call her for? What can she do? Let her sleep unmolested."

"Then I will fetch Leah, and wake John and his wife."

"Not at all: just be still. You have a shawl on. If you are not warm enough, you may take my cloak yonder; wrap it about you, and sit down in the arm-chair: there—I will put it on. Now place your feet on the stool, to keep them out of the wet. I am going to leave you a few minutes. I shall take the candle. Remain where you are till I return; be as still as a mouse. I must pay a visit to the second storey. Don't move, remember, or call any one."

He went: I watched the light withdraw. He passed up the gallery very softly, unclosed the staircase door with as little noise as possible, shut it after him, and the last ray vanished. I was left in total darkness. I listened for some noise, but heard nothing. A very long time elapsed. I grew weary: it was cold, in spite of the cloak; and then I did not see the use of staying, as I was not to rouse the house. I was on the point of risking Mr. Rochester's displeasure by disobeying his orders, when the light once more gleamed dimly on the gallery wall, and I heard his unshod feet tread the matting. "I hope it is he," thought I, "and not something worse."

He re-entered, pale and very gloomy. "I have found it all out," said he, setting his candle down on the washstand; "it is as I thought."

"How, sir?"

He made no reply, but stood with his arms folded, looking on the ground. At the end of a few minutes he inquired in rather a peculiar tone—

"I forget whether you said you saw anything when you opened your chamber door."

"No, sir, only the candlestick on the ground."

"But you heard an odd laugh? You have heard that laugh before, I should think, or something like it?"

"Yes, sir: there is a woman who sews here, called Grace Poole—she laughs in that way. She is a singular person."

"Just so. Grace Poole—you have guessed it. She is, as you say, singular—very. Well, I shall reflect on the subject. Meantime, I am glad that you are the only person, besides myself, acquainted with the precise details of tonight's incident. You are no talking fool: say nothing about it. I will account for this state of affairs" (pointing to the bed), "and now return to your own room. I shall do very well on the sofa in the library for the rest of the night. It is near four—in two hours the servants will be up."

"Good-night, then, sir," said I, departing.

He seemed surprised—very inconsistently so, as he had just told me to go.

"What!" he exclaimed. "Are you quitting me already, and in that way?"

"You said I might go, sir."

"But not without taking leave; not without a word or two of acknowledgment and good-will: not, in short, in that brief, dry fashion. Why, you have saved my life! Snatched me from a horrible and excruciating death! And you walk past me as if we were mutual strangers! At least shake hands."

He held out his hand; I gave him mine: he took it first in one, then in both his own.

"You have saved my life: I have a pleasure in owing you so immense a debt. I cannot say more. Nothing else that has being would have been tolerable to me in the character of creditor for such an obligation: but you: it is different—I feel your benefits no burden, Jane."

He paused; gazed at me: words almost visible trembled on his lips—but his voice was checked.

"Good-night again, sir. There is no debt, benefit, burden, obligation, in the case."

"I knew," he continued, "you would do me good in some way, at some time; I saw it in your eyes when I first beheld you: their expression and smile did not"—(again he stopped)—"did not" (he proceeded hastily) "strike delight to my very inmost heart so for nothing. People talk of natural sympathies; I have heard of good genii: there are grains of truth in the wildest fable. My cherished preserver, goodnight!"

Strange energy was in his voice, strange fire in his look.

"I am glad I happened to be awake," I said: and then I was going.

"What! You *will* go?"

"I am cold, sir."

"Cold? Yes—and standing in a pool! Go, then, Jane; go!" But he still retained my hand, and I could not free it. I bethought myself of an expedient.

"I think I hear Mrs. Fairfax move, sir," said I.

"Well, leave me"; he relaxed his fingers, and I was gone.

I regained my couch, but never thought of sleep. Till morning dawned I was tossed on a buoyant but unquiet sea, where billows of trouble rolled under surges of joy. I thought sometimes I saw beyond its wild waters a shore, sweet as the hills of Beulah; and now and then a freshening gale, wakened by hope, bore my spirit triumphantly towards the bourne: but I could not reach it, even in fancy—a counteracting breeze blew off land, and continually drove me back. Sense would resist delirium: judgment would warn passion. Too feverish to rest, I rose as soon as day dawned.

CHAPTER XVI

I both wished and feared to see Mr. Rochester on the day which followed this sleepless night: I wanted to hear his voice again, yet feared to meet his eye. During the early part of the morning, I momentarily expected his coming; he was not in the frequent habit of entering the schoolroom, but he did step in for a few minutes sometimes, and I had the impression that he was sure to visit it that day.

But the morning passed just as usual: nothing happened to interrupt the quiet course of Adèle's studies; only soon after breakfast, I heard some bustle in the neighbourhood of Mr. Rochester's chamber, Mrs. Fairfax's voice, and Leah's, and the cook's—that is, John's wife—and even John's own gruff tones. There were exclamations of "What a mercy master was not burnt in his bed!" "It is always dangerous to keep a candle lit at night." "How providential that he had presence of mind to think of the water-jug!" "I wonder he waked nobody!" "It is to be hoped he will not take cold with sleeping on the library sofa," etc.

To much confabulation succeeded a sound of scrubbing and setting to rights; and when I passed the room, in going downstairs to dinner, I saw through the open door that all was again restored to complete order; only the bed was stripped of its hangings. Leah stood up in the window-seat, rubbing the panes of glass dimmed with smoke. I was about to address her, for I wished to know what account had been given of the affair: but, on advancing, I saw a second person in the chamber—a woman sitting on a chair by the bedside, and sewing rings to new curtains. That woman was no other than Grace Poole.

There she sat, staid and taciturn-looking, as usual, in her brown stuff gown, her check apron, white handkerchief, and cap. She was intent on her work, in which her whole thoughts seemed absorbed: on her hard forehead, and in her commonplace features, was nothing either of the paleness or desperation one would have expected to see marking the countenance of a woman who had attempted murder, and whose intended victim had followed her last night to her lair, and (as I believed), charged her with the crime she wished to perpetrate. I was amazed—confounded. She looked up, while I still gazed at her: no start, no increase or failure of colour betrayed emotion, consciousness of guilt, or fear of detection. She said "Good morning, Miss," in her usual phlegmatic and brief manner; and taking up another ring and more tape, went on with her sewing.

"I will put her to some test," thought I. "Such absolute impenetrability is past comprehension."

"Good morning, Grace," I said. "Has anything happened here? I thought I heard the servants all talking together a while ago."

"Only master had been reading in his bed last night; he fell asleep with his candle lit, and the curtains got on fire; but, fortunately, he awoke before the bed-clothes or the wood-work caught, and contrived to quench the flames with the water in the ewer."

"A strange affair!" I said, in a low voice: then, looking at her fixedly—"Did Mr. Rochester wake nobody? Did no one hear him move?"

She again raised her eyes to me, and this time there was something of consciousness in their expression. She seemed to examine me warily; then she answered—

"The servants sleep so far off, you know, Miss, they would not be likely to hear. Mrs. Fairfax's room and yours are the nearest to master's; but Mrs. Fairfax said she heard nothing: when people get elderly, they often sleep heavy." She paused, and then added, with a sort of assumed indifference, but still in a marked and significant tone, "But you are young, Miss; and I should say a light sleeper: perhaps you may have heard a noise?"

"I did," said I, dropping my voice, so that Leah, who was still polishing the panes, could not hear me, "and at first I thought it was Pilot: but Pilot cannot laugh; and I am certain I heard a laugh, and a strange one."

She took a new needleful of thread, waxed it carefully, threaded her needle with a steady hand, and then observed, with perfect composure—

"It is hardly likely master would laugh, I should think, Miss, when he was in such danger: You must have been dreaming."

"I was not dreaming," I said, with some warmth, for her brazen coolness provoked me. Again she looked at me; and with the same scrutinising and conscious eye.

"Have you told master that you heard a laugh?" she inquired.

"I have not had the opportunity of speaking to him this morning."

"You did not think of opening your door and looking out into the gallery?" she further asked.

She appeared to be cross-questioning me, attempting to draw from me information unawares. The idea struck me that if she discovered I knew or suspected her guilt, she would be playing of some of her malignant pranks on me; I thought it advisable to be on my guard.

"On the contrary," said I, "I bolted my door."

"Then you are not in the habit of bolting your door every night before you get into bed?"

"Fiend! She wants to know my habits, that she may lay her plans accordingly!" Indignation again prevailed over prudence: I replied sharply, "Hitherto I have often omitted to fasten the bolt: I did not think it necessary. I was not aware any danger or annoyance was to be dreaded at Thornfield Hall: but in future" (and I laid marked stress on the words) "I shall take good care to make all secure before I venture to lie down."

"It will be wise so to do," was her answer; "this neighbourhood is as quiet as any I know, and I never heard of the hall being attempted by robbers since it was a house; though there are hundreds of pounds' worth of plate in the plate-closet, as is well known. And you see, for such a large house, there are very few servants, because master has never lived here much; and when he does come, being a bachelor, he needs little waiting on: but I always think it best to err on the safe side; a door is soon fastened, and it is as well to have a drawn bolt between one and any mischief that may be about. A deal of people, Miss, are for trusting all to Providence; but I say Providence will not dispense with the means, though He often blesses them when they are used discreetly." And here she closed her harangue: a long one for her, and uttered with the demureness of a Quakeress.

I still stood absolutely dumfoundered at what appeared to me her miraculous self-possession and most inscrutable hypocrisy, when the cook entered.

"Mrs. Poole," said she, addressing Grace, "the servants' dinner will soon be ready: will you come down?"

"No; just put my pint of porter and bit of pudding on a tray, and I'll carry it upstairs."

"You'll have some meat?"

"Just a morsel, and a taste of cheese, that's all."

"And the sago?"

"Never mind it at present: I shall be coming down before teatime: I'll make it myself."

The cook here turned to me, saying that Mrs. Fairfax was waiting for me: so I departed.

I hardly heard Mrs. Fairfax's account of the curtain conflagration during dinner, so much was I occupied in puzzling my brains over the enigmatical character of Grace Poole, and still more in pondering the problem of her position at Thornfield and questioning why she had not been given into custody that morning, or, at the very least, dismissed from her master's service. He had almost as much as declared his conviction of her criminality last night: what mysterious cause withheld him from accusing her? Why had he enjoined me, too, to secrecy? It was strange: a bold, vindictive, and haughty gentleman seemed somehow in the power of one of the meanest of his dependents; so much in her power, that even when she lifted her hand against his life, he dared not openly charge her with the attempt, much less punish her for it.

Had Grace been young and handsome, I should have been tempted to think that tenderer feelings than prudence or fear influenced Mr. Rochester in her behalf; but, hard-favoured and matronly as she was, the idea could not be admitted. "Yet," I reflected, "she has been young once; her youth would be contemporary with her master's: Mrs. Fairfax told me once, she had lived here many years. I don't think she can ever have been pretty; but, for aught I know, she may possess originality and strength of character to compensate for the want of personal advantages. Mr. Rochester is an amateur of the decided and eccentric: Grace is eccentric at least. What if a former caprice (a freak very possible to a nature so sudden and headstrong as his) has delivered him into her power, and she now exercises over his actions a secret influence, the result of his own indiscretion, which he cannot shake off, and dare not disregard?" But, having reached this point of conjecture, Mrs. Poole's square, flat figure, and uncomely, dry, even coarse face, recurred so distinctly to my mind's eye, that I thought, "No; impossible! My supposition cannot be correct. Yet," suggested the secret voice which talks to us in our own hearts, "you are not beautiful either, and perhaps Mr. Rochester approves you: at any rate, you have often felt as if he did; and last night—remember his words; remember his look; remember his voice!"

I well remembered all; language, glance, and tone seemed at the moment vividly renewed. I was now in the schoolroom; Adèle was drawing; I bent over her and directed her pencil. She looked up with a sort of start.

"Qu'avez-vous, mademoiselle?" said she. "Vos doigts tremblent comme la feuille, et vos joues sont rouges: mais, rouges comme des cerises!"

"I am hot, Adèle, with stooping!" She went on sketching; I went on thinking.

I hastened to drive from my mind the hateful notion I had been conceiving respecting Grace Poole; it disgusted me. I compared myself with her, and found we were different. Bessie Leaven had said I was quite a lady; and she spoke truth—I was a lady. And now I looked much better than I did when Bessie saw me; I had more colour and more flesh, more life, more vivacity, because I had brighter hopes and keener enjoyments.

"Evening approaches," said I, as I looked towards the window. "I have never heard Mr. Rochester's voice or step in the house today; but surely I shall see him before night: I feared the meeting in the morning; now I desire it, because expectation has been so long baffled that it is grown impatient."

When dusk actually closed, and when Adèle left me to go and play in the nursery with Sophie, I did most keenly desire it. I listened for the bell to ring below; I listened for Leah coming up with a message; I fancied sometimes I heard Mr. Rochester's own tread, and I turned to the door, expecting it to open and admit him. The door remained shut; darkness only came in through the window. Still it was not late; he often sent for me at seven and eight o'clock, and it was yet but six. Surely I should not be wholly disappointed tonight, when I had so many things to say to him! I wanted again to introduce the subject of Grace Poole, and to hear what he would answer; I wanted to ask him plainly if he really believed it was she who had made last night's hideous attempt; and if so, why he kept her wickedness a secret. It little mattered whether my curiosity irritated him; I knew the pleasure of vexing and soothing him by turns; it was one I chiefly delighted in, and a sure instinct always prevented me from going too far; beyond the verge of provocation I never ventured; on the extreme brink I liked well to try my skill. Retaining every minute form of respect, every propriety of my station,

I could still meet him in argument without fear or uneasy restraint; this suited both him and me.

A tread creaked on the stairs at last. Leah made her appearance; but it was only to intimate that tea was ready in Mrs. Fairfax's room. Thither I repaired, glad at least to go downstairs; for that brought me, I imagined, nearer to Mr. Rochester's presence.

"You must want your tea," said the good lady, as I joined her; "you ate so little at dinner. I am afraid," she continued, "you are not well today: you look flushed and feverish."

"Oh, quite well! I never felt better."

"Then you must prove it by evincing a good appetite; will you fill the teapot while I knit off this needle?" Having completed her task, she rose to draw down the blind, which she had hitherto kept up, by way, I suppose, of making the most of daylight, though dusk was now fast deepening into total obscurity.

"It is fair tonight," said she, as she looked through the panes, "though not starlight; Mr. Rochester has, on the whole, had a favourable day for his journey."

"Journey! Is Mr. Rochester gone anywhere? I did not know he was out."

"Oh, he set off the moment he had breakfasted! He is gone to the Leas, Mr. Eshton's place, ten miles on the other side Millcote. I believe there is quite a party assembled there; Lord Ingram, Sir George Lynn, Colonel Dent, and others."

"Do you expect him back tonight?"

"No—nor tomorrow either; I should think he is very likely to stay a week or more: when these fine, fashionable people get together, they are so surrounded by elegance and gaiety, so well provided with all that can please and entertain, they are in no hurry to separate. Gentlemen especially are often in request on such occasions; and Mr. Rochester is so talented and so lively in society, that I believe he is a general favourite: the ladies are very fond of him; though you would not think his appearance calculated to recommend him particularly in their eyes: but I suppose his acquirements and abilities, perhaps his wealth and good blood, make amends for any little fault of look."

"Are there ladies at the Leas?"

"There are Mrs. Eshton and her three daughters—very elegant young ladies indeed; and there are the Honourable Blanche and Mary

Ingram, most beautiful women, I suppose: indeed I have seen Blanche, six or seven years since, when she was a girl of eighteen. She came here to a Christmas ball and party Mr. Rochester gave. You should have seen the dining-room that day—how richly it was decorated, how brilliantly lit up! I should think there were fifty ladies and gentlemen present—all of the first county families; and Miss Ingram was considered the belle of the evening."

"You saw her, you say, Mrs. Fairfax: what was she like?"

"Yes, I saw her. The dining-room doors were thrown open; and, as it was Christmas-time, the servants were allowed to assemble in the hall, to hear some of the ladies sing and play. Mr. Rochester would have me to come in, and I sat down in a quiet corner and watched them. I never saw a more splendid scene: the ladies were magnificently dressed; most of them—at least most of the younger ones—looked handsome; but Miss Ingram was certainly the queen."

"And what was she like?"

"Tall, fine bust, sloping shoulders; long, graceful neck: olive complexion, dark and clear; noble features; eyes rather like Mr. Rochester's: large and black, and as brilliant as her jewels. And then she had such a fine head of hair; raven-black and so becomingly arranged: a crown of thick plaits behind, and in front the longest, the glossiest curls I ever saw. She was dressed in pure white; an amber-coloured scarf was passed over her shoulder and across her breast, tied at the side, and descending in long, fringed ends below her knee. She wore an amber-coloured flower, too, in her hair: it contrasted well with the jetty mass of her curls."

"She was greatly admired, of course?"

"Yes, indeed: and not only for her beauty, but for her accomplishments. She was one of the ladies who sang: a gentleman accompanied her on the piano. She and Mr. Rochester sang a duet."

"Mr. Rochester? I was not aware he could sing."

"Oh! He has a fine bass voice, and an excellent taste for music."

"And Miss Ingram: what sort of a voice had she?"

"A very rich and powerful one: she sang delightfully; it was a treat to listen to her—and she played afterwards. I am no judge of music, but Mr. Rochester is; and I heard him say her execution was remarkably good."

"And this beautiful and accomplished lady, she is not yet married?"

"It appears not: I fancy neither she nor her sister have very large fortunes. Old Lord Ingram's estates were chiefly entailed, and the eldest son came in for everything almost."

"But I wonder no wealthy nobleman or gentleman has taken a fancy to her: Mr. Rochester, for instance. He is rich, is he not?"

"Oh! Yes. But you see there is a considerable difference in age: Mr. Rochester is nearly forty; she is but twenty-five."

"What of that? More unequal matches are made every day."

"True: yet I should scarcely fancy Mr. Rochester would entertain an idea of the sort. But you eat nothing: you have scarcely tasted since you began tea."

"No: I am too thirsty to eat. Will you let me have another cup?"

I was about again to revert to the probability of a union between Mr. Rochester and the beautiful Blanche; but Adèle came in, and the conversation was turned into another channel.

When once more alone, I reviewed the information I had got; looked into my heart, examined its thoughts and feelings, and endeavoured to bring back with a strict hand such as had been straying through imagination's boundless and trackless waste, into the safe fold of common sense.

Arraigned at my own bar, Memory having given her evidence of the hopes, wishes, sentiments I had been cherishing since last night—of the general state of mind in which I had indulged for nearly a fortnight past; Reason having come forward and told, in her own quiet way a plain, unvarnished tale, showing how I had rejected the real, and rabidly devoured the ideal—I pronounced judgment to this effect:

That a greater fool than Jane Eyre had never breathed the breath of life; that a more fantastic idiot had never surfeited herself on sweet lies, and swallowed poison as if it were nectar.

"*You*," I said, "a favourite with Mr. Rochester? *You* gifted with the power of pleasing him? *You* of importance to him in any way? Go! Your folly sickens me. And you have derived pleasure from occasional tokens of preference—equivocal tokens shown by a gentleman of family and a man of the world to a dependent and a novice. How dared you? Poor stupid dupe! Could not even self-interest make you wiser? You repeated to yourself this morning the brief scene of last night? Cover your face and be ashamed! He said something in praise of your eyes, did he? Blind puppy! Open their bleared lids and look on your own accursed senselessness! It does good to no woman to be flattered by her superior, who cannot possibly intend to marry her; and it is madness in all women to let a secret love kindle within them, which, if unreturned and unknown, must devour the life that feeds it; and, if discovered and responded to, must lead, *ignis-fatus*-like, into miry wilds whence there is no extrication.

"Listen, then, Jane Eyre, to your sentence: tomorrow, place the glass before you, and draw in chalk your own picture, faithfully, without softening one defect; omit no harsh line, smooth away no displeasing irregularity; write under it, 'Portrait of a Governess, disconnected, poor, and plain.'

"Afterwards, take a piece of smooth ivory—you have one prepared in your drawing-box: take your palette, mix your freshest, finest, clearest tints; choose your most delicate camel-hair pencils; delineate carefully the loveliest face you can imagine; paint it in your softest shades and sweetest lines, according to the description given by Mrs. Fairfax of Blanche Ingram; remember the raven ringlets, the oriental eye: What! You revert to Mr. Rochester as a model! Order! No snivel! No sentiment! No regret! I will endure only sense and resolution. Recall the august yet harmonious lineaments, the Grecian neck and bust; let the round and dazzling arm be visible, and the delicate hand; omit neither diamond ring nor gold bracelet; portray faithfully the attire, aërial lace and glistening satin, graceful scarf and golden rose; call it 'Blanche, an accomplished lady of rank.'

"Whenever, in future, you should chance to fancy Mr. Rochester thinks well of you, take out these two pictures and compare them: say, 'Mr. Rochester might probably win that noble lady's love, if he chose to strive for it; is it likely he would waste a serious thought on this indigent and insignificant plebeian?'

"I'll do it," I resolved: and having framed this determination, I grew calm, and fell asleep.

I kept my word. An hour or two sufficed to sketch my own portrait in crayons; and in less than a fortnight I had completed an ivory miniature of an imaginary Blanche Ingram. It looked a lovely face enough, and when compared with the real head in chalk, the contrast was as great as self-control could desire. I derived benefit from the task: it had kept my head and hands employed, and had given force and fixedness to the new impressions I wished to stamp indelibly on my heart.

Ere long, I had reason to congratulate myself on the course of wholesome discipline to which I had thus forced my feelings to submit. Thanks to it, I was able to meet subsequent occurrences with a decent calm, which, had they found me unprepared, I should probably have been unequal to maintain, even externally.

CHAPTER XVII

A week passed, and no news arrived of Mr. Rochester: ten days, and still he did not come. Mrs. Fairfax said she should not be surprised if he were to go straight from the Leas to London, and thence to the Continent, and not show his face again at Thornfield for a year to come; he had not unfrequently quitted it in a manner quite as abrupt and unexpected. When I heard this, I was beginning to feel a strange chill and failing at the heart. I was actually permitting myself to experience a sickening sense of disappointment; but rallying my wits, and recollecting my principles, I at once called my sensations to order; and it was wonderful how I got over the temporary blunder—how I cleared up the mistake of supposing Mr. Rochester's movements a matter in which I had any cause to take a vital interest. Not that I humbled myself by a slavish notion of inferiority: on the contrary, I just said—

"You have nothing to do with the master of Thornfield, further than to receive the salary he gives you for teaching his protégée, and to be grateful for such respectful and kind treatment as, if you do your duty, you have a right to expect at his hands. Be sure that is the only tie he seriously acknowledges between you and him; so don't make him the object of your fine feelings, your raptures, agonies, and so forth. He is not of your order: keep to your caste, and be too self-respecting to lavish the love of the whole heart, soul, and strength, where such a gift is not wanted and would be despised."

I went on with my day's business tranquilly; but ever and anon vague suggestions kept wandering across my brain of reasons why I should quit Thornfield; and I kept involuntarily framing advertisements and pondering conjectures about new situations: these thoughts I did not think to check; they might germinate and bear fruit if they could.

Mr. Rochester had been absent upwards of a fortnight, when the post brought Mrs. Fairfax a letter.

"It is from the master," said she, as she looked at the direction. "Now I suppose we shall know whether we are to expect his return or not."

And while she broke the seal and perused the document, I went on taking my coffee (we were at breakfast): it was hot, and I attributed to that circumstance a fiery glow which suddenly rose to my face. Why my hand shook, and why I involuntarily spilt half the contents of my cup into my saucer, I did not choose to consider.

"Well, I sometimes think we are too quiet; but we run a chance of being busy enough now: for a little while at least," said Mrs. Fairfax, still holding the note before her spectacles.

Ere I permitted myself to request an explanation, I tied the string of Adèle's pinafore, which happened to be loose: having helped her also to another bun and refilled her mug with milk, I said, nonchalantly—

"Mr. Rochester is not likely to return soon, I suppose?"

"Indeed he is—in three days, he says: that will be next Thursday; and not alone either. I don't know how many of the fine people at the Leas are coming with him: he sends directions for all the best bedrooms to be prepared; and the library and drawing-rooms are to be cleaned out; I am to get more kitchen hands from the George Inn, at Millcote, and from wherever else I can; and the ladies will bring their maids and the gentlemen their valets: so we shall have a full house of it." And Mrs. Fairfax swallowed her breakfast and hastened away to commence operations.

The three days were, as she had foretold, busy enough. I had thought all the rooms at Thornfield beautifully clean and well arranged; but it appears I was mistaken. Three women were got to help; and such scrubbing, such brushing, such washing of paint and beating of carpets, such taking down and putting up of pictures, such polishing of mirrors and lustres, such lighting of fires in bedrooms, such airing of sheets and feather-beds on hearths, I never beheld, either before or since. Adèle ran quite wild in the midst of it: the preparations for company and the prospect of their arrival seemed to throw her into ecstasies. She would have Sophie to look over all her "toilettes," as she called frocks; to furbish up any that were "*passées*," and to air and arrange the new. For herself, she did nothing but caper about in the front chambers, jump on and off the bedsteads, and lie on the mattresses and piled-up bolsters and pillows before the enormous fires roaring in the chimneys. From school duties she was exonerated: Mrs. Fairfax had pressed me into her service, and I was all day in the storeroom, helping (or hindering) her and the cook; learning to make custards and cheese-cakes and French pastry, to truss game and garnish dessert-dishes.

The party were expected to arrive on Thursday afternoon, in

time for dinner at six. During the intervening period I had no time to nurse chimeras; and I believe I was as active and gay as anybody—Adèle excepted. Still, now and then, I received a damping check to my cheerfulness; and was, in spite of myself, thrown back on the region of doubts and portents, and dark conjectures. This was when I chanced to see the third-storey staircase door (which of late had always been kept locked) open slowly, and give passage to the form of Grace Poole, in prim cap, white apron, and handkerchief; when I watched her glide along the gallery, her quiet tread muffled in a list slipper; when I saw her look into the bustling, topsy-turvy bedrooms—just say a word, perhaps, to the charwoman about the proper way to polish a grate, or clean a marble mantelpiece, or take stains from papered walls, and then pass on. She would thus descend to the kitchen once a day, eat her dinner, smoke a moderate pipe on the hearth, and go back, carrying her pot of porter with her, for her private solace, in her own gloomy, upper haunt. Only one hour in the twenty-four did she pass with her fellow-servants below; all the rest of her time was spent in some low-ceiled, oaken chamber of the second storey: there she sat and sewed—and probably laughed drearily to herself—as companionless as a prisoner in his dungeon.

The strangest thing of all was, that not a soul in the house, except me, noticed her habits, or seemed to marvel at them: no one discussed her position or employment; no one pitied her solitude or isolation. I once, indeed, overheard part of a dialogue between Leah and one of the charwomen, of which Grace formed the subject. Leah had been saying something I had not caught, and the charwoman remarked—

"She gets good wages, I guess?"

"Yes," said Leah; "I wish I had as good; not that mine are to complain of—there's no stinginess at Thornfield; but they're not one fifth of the sum Mrs. Poole receives. And she is laying by: she goes every quarter to the bank at Millcote. I should not wonder but she has saved enough to keep her independent if she liked to leave; but I suppose she's got used to the place; and then she's not forty yet, and strong and able for anything. It is too soon for her to give up business."

"She is a good hand, I daresay," said the charwoman.

"Ah! She understands what she has to do—nobody better," rejoined Leah significantly; "and it is not every one could fill her shoes—not for all the money she gets."

"That it is not!" was the reply. "I wonder whether the master—"

The charwoman was going on; but here Leah turned and perceived me, and she instantly gave her companion a nudge.

"Doesn't she know?" I heard the woman whisper.

Leah shook her head, and the conversation was of course dropped. All I had gathered from it amounted to this—that there was a mystery at Thornfield; and that from participation in that mystery I was purposely excluded.

Thursday came: all work had been completed the previous evening; carpets were laid down, bed-hangings festooned, radiant white counterpanes spread, toilet tables arranged, furniture rubbed, flowers piled in vases: both chambers and saloons looked as fresh and bright as hands could make them. The hall, too, was scoured; and the great carved clock, as well as the steps and banisters of the staircase, were polished to the brightness of glass; in the dining-room, the sideboard flashed resplendent with plate; in the drawing-room and boudoir, vases of exotics bloomed on all sides.

Afternoon arrived: Mrs. Fairfax assumed her best black satin gown, her gloves, and her gold watch; for it was her part to receive the company—to conduct the ladies to their rooms, etc. Adèle, too, would be dressed: though I thought she had little chance of being introduced to the party that day at least. However, to please her, I allowed Sophie to apparel her in one of her short, full muslin frocks. For myself, I had no need to make any change; I should not be called upon to quit my sanctum of the schoolroom; for a sanctum it was now become to me—"a very pleasant refuge in time of trouble."

It had been a mild, serene spring day—one of those days which, towards the end of March or the beginning of April, rise shining over the earth as heralds of summer. It was drawing to an end now; but the evening was even warm, and I sat at work in the schoolroom with the window open.

"It gets late," said Mrs. Fairfax, entering in rustling state. "I am glad I ordered dinner an hour after the time Mr. Rochester mentioned; for it is past six now. I have sent John down to the gates to see if there is anything on the road: one can see a long way from thence in the direction of Millcote." She went to the window. "Here he is!" said she. "Well, John" (leaning out), "any news?"

"They're coming, ma'am," was the answer. "They'll be here in ten minutes."

Adèle flew to the window. I followed, taking care to stand on one side, so that, screened by the curtain, I could see without being seen.

The ten minutes John had given seemed very long, but at last wheels were heard; four equestrians galloped up the drive, and after them came two open carriages. Fluttering veils and waving plumes filled the vehicles; two of the cavaliers were young, dashing-looking gentlemen; the third was Mr. Rochester, on his black horse, Mesrour, Pilot bounding before him; at his side rode a lady, and he and she were the first of the party. Her purple riding-habit almost swept the ground, her veil streamed long on the breeze; mingling with its transparent folds, and gleaming through them, shone rich raven ringlets.

"Miss Ingram!" exclaimed Mrs. Fairfax, and away she hurried to her post below.

The cavalcade, following the sweep of the drive, quickly turned the angle of the house, and I lost sight of it. Adèle now petitioned to go down; but I took her on my knee, and gave her to understand that she must not on any account think of venturing in sight of the ladies, either now or at any other time, unless expressly sent for: that Mr. Rochester would be very angry, etc. "Some natural tears she shed" on being told this; but as I began to look very grave, she consented at last to wipe them.

A joyous stir was now audible in the hall: gentlemen's deep tones and ladies' silvery accents blent harmoniously together, and distinguishable above all, though not loud, was the sonorous voice of the master of Thornfield Hall, welcoming his fair and gallant guests under its roof. Then light steps ascended the stairs; and there was a tripping through the gallery, and soft cheerful laughs, and opening and closing doors, and, for a time, a hush.

"Elles changent de toilettes," said Adèle; who, listening attentively, had followed every movement; and she sighed.

"Chez maman," said she, "quand il y avait du monde, je le suivais partout, au salon et à leurs chambres; souvent je regardais les femmes de chambre coiffer et habiller les dames, et c'était si amusant: comme cela on apprend."

"Don't you feel hungry, Adèle?"

"Mais oui, mademoiselle: voilà cinq ou six heures que nous n'avons pas mangé."

"Well now, while the ladies are in their rooms, I will venture down and get you something to eat."

And issuing from my asylum with precaution, I sought a back-stairs which conducted directly to the kitchen. All in that region was fire and commotion; the soup and fish were in the last stage of projection, and the cook hung over her crucibles in a frame of mind and body threatening spontaneous combustion. In the servants' hall two coachmen and three gentlemen's gentlemen stood or sat round the fire; the abigails, I suppose, were upstairs with their mistresses; the new servants, that had been hired from Millcote, were bustling about everywhere. Threading this chaos, I at last reached the larder; there I took possession of a cold chicken, a roll of bread, some tarts, a plate or two and a knife and fork: with this booty I made a hasty retreat. I had regained the gallery, and was just shutting the back-door behind me, when an accelerated hum warned me that the ladies were about to issue from their chambers. I could not proceed to the schoolroom without passing some of their doors, and running the risk of being surprised with my cargo of victualage; so I stood still at this end, which, being windowless, was dark: quite dark now, for the sun was set and twilight gathering.

Presently the chambers gave up their fair tenants one after another: each came out gaily and airily, with dress that gleamed lustrous through the dusk. For a moment they stood grouped together at the other extremity of the gallery, conversing in a key of sweet subdued vivacity: they then descended the staircase almost as noiselessly as a bright mist rolls down a hill. Their collective appearance had left on me an impression of high-born elegance, such as I had never before received.

I found Adèle peeping through the schoolroom door, which she held ajar. "What beautiful ladies!" cried she in English. "Oh, I wish I might go to them! Do you think Mr. Rochester will send for us by-and-by, after dinner?"

"No, indeed, I don't; Mr. Rochester has something else to think about. Never mind the ladies tonight; perhaps you will see them tomorrow: here is your dinner."

She was really hungry, so the chicken and tarts served to divert her attention for a time. It was well I secured this forage, or both she, I, and Sophie, to whom I conveyed a share of our repast, would have run a chance of getting no dinner at all: every one downstairs was too much engaged to think of us. The dessert was not carried out till after nine and at ten footmen were still running to and fro with trays and coffee-cups. I allowed Adèle to sit up much later than usual; for she declared she could not possibly go to sleep while the doors kept opening and shutting below, and people bustling about. Besides, she added, a message might possibly come from Mr. Rochester when she was undressed; "et alors quel dommage!"

I told her stories as long as she would listen to them; and then for a change I took her out into the gallery. The hall lamp was now lit, and it amused her to look over the balustrade and watch the servants passing backwards and forwards. When the evening was far advanced, a sound of music issued from the drawing-room, whither the piano had been removed; Adèle and I sat down on the top step of the stairs to listen. Presently a voice blent with the rich tones of the instrument; it was a lady who sang, and very sweet her notes were. The solo over, a duet followed, and then a glee: a joyous conversational murmur filled up the intervals. I listened long: suddenly I discovered that my ear was wholly intent on analysing the mingled sounds, and trying to discriminate amidst the confusion of accents those of Mr. Rochester; and when it caught them, which it soon did, it found a further task in framing the tones, rendered by distance inarticulate, into words.

The clock struck eleven. I looked at Adèle, whose head leant against my shoulder; her eyes were waxing heavy, so I took her up in my arms and carried her off to bed. It was near one before the gentlemen and ladies sought their chambers.

The next day was as fine as its predecessor: it was devoted by the party to an excursion to some site in the neighbourhood. They set out early in the forenoon, some on horseback, the rest in carriages; I witnessed both the departure and the return. Miss Ingram, as before, was the only lady equestrian; and, as before, Mr. Rochester galloped at her side; the two rode a little apart from the rest. I pointed out this circumstance to Mrs. Fairfax, who was standing at the window with me—

"You said it was not likely they should think of being married," said I, "but you see Mr. Rochester evidently prefers her to any of the other ladies."

"Yes, I daresay: no doubt he admires her."

"And she him," I added. "Look how she leans her head towards him as if she were conversing confidentially; I wish I could see her face; I have never had a glimpse of it yet."

"You will see her this evening," answered Mrs. Fairfax. "I happened to remark to Mr. Rochester how much Adèle wished to be introduced to the ladies, and he said: 'Oh! Let her come into the drawing-room after dinner; and request Miss Eyre to accompany her.'"

"Yes; he said that from mere politeness: I need not go, I am sure," I answered.

"Well, I observed to him that as you were unused to company, I did not think you would like appearing before so gay a party—all strangers; and he replied, in his quick way: 'Nonsense! If she objects, tell her it is my particular wish; and if she resists, say I shall come and fetch her in case of contumacy.' "

"I will not give him that trouble," I answered. "I will go, if no better may be; but I don't like it. Shall you be there, Mrs. Fairfax?"

"No; I pleaded off, and he admitted my plea. I'll tell you how to manage so as to avoid the embarrassment of making a formal entrance, which is the most disagreeable part of the business. You must go into the drawing-room while it is empty, before the ladies leave the dinner-table; choose your seat in any quiet nook you like; you need not stay long after the gentlemen come in, unless you please: just let Mr. Rochester see you are there and then slip away—nobody will notice you."

"Will these people remain long, do you think?"

"Perhaps two or three weeks, certainly not more. After the Easter recess, Sir George Lynn, who was lately elected member for Millcote, will have to go up to town and take his seat; I daresay Mr. Rochester will accompany him: it surprises me that he has already made so protracted a stay at Thornfield."

It was with some trepidation that I perceived the hour approach when I was to repair with my charge to the drawing-room. Adèle had been in a state of ecstasy all day, after hearing she was to be presented to the ladies in the evening; and it was not till Sophie commenced the operation of dressing her that she sobered down. Then the importance of the process quickly steadied her, and by the time she had her curls arranged in well-smoothed, drooping clusters, her pink satin frock put on, her long sash tied, and her lace mittens adjusted, she looked as grave as any judge. No need to warn her not to disarrange her attire: when she was dressed, she sat demurely down in her little chair, taking care previously to lift up the satin skirt for fear she should crease it, and assured me she would not stir thence till I was ready. This I quickly was: my best dress (the silver-grey one, purchased for Miss Temple's wedding, and never worn since) was soon put on; my hair was soon smoothed; my sole ornament, the pearl brooch, soon assumed. We descended.

Fortunately there was another entrance to the drawing-room than that through the saloon where they were all seated at dinner. We found the apartment vacant; a large fire burning silently on the marble hearth, and wax candles shining in bright solitude, amid the exquisite flowers with which the tables were adorned. The crimson curtain hung before the arch: slight as was the separation this drapery formed from the party in the adjoining saloon, they spoke in so low a key that nothing of their conversation could be distinguished beyond a soothing murmur.

Adèle, who appeared to be still under the influence of a most solemnising impression, sat down, without a word, on the footstool I pointed out to her. I retired to a window-seat, and taking a book from a table near, endeavoured to read. Adèle brought her stool to my feet; ere long she touched my knee.

"What is it, Adèle?"

"Est-ce que je ne puis pas prendrie une seule de ces fleurs magnifiques, mademoiselle? Seulement pour completer ma toilette."

"You think too much of your 'toilette,' Adèle: but you may have a flower." And I took a rose from a vase and fastened it in her sash. She sighed a sigh of ineffable satisfaction, as if her cup of happiness were now full. I turned my face away to conceal a smile I could not suppress: there was something ludicrous as well as painful in the little Parisienne's earnest and innate devotion to matters of dress.

A soft sound of rising now became audible; the curtain was swept back from the arch; through it appeared the dining-room, with its lit lustre pouring down light on the silver and glass of a magnificent dessert-service covering a long table; a band of ladies stood in the opening; they entered, and the curtain fell behind them.

There were but eight; yet, somehow, as they flocked in, they gave the impression of a much larger number. Some of them were very tall; many were dressed in white; and all had a sweeping amplitude of array that seemed to magnify their persons as a mist magnifies the moon. I rose and curtseyed to them: one or two bent their heads in return, the others only stared at me.

They dispersed about the room, reminding me, by the lightness and buoyancy of their movements, of a flock of white plumy birds. Some of them threw themselves in half-reclining positions on the sofas and ottomans: some bent over the tables and examined the flowers and books: the rest gathered in a group round the fire: all talked in a low but clear tone which seemed habitual to them. I knew their names afterwards, and may as well mention them now.

First, there was Mrs. Eshton and two of her daughters. She had evidently been a handsome woman, and was well preserved still. Of her daughters, the eldest, Amy, was rather little: naive, and child-like in face and manner, and piquant in form; her white muslin dress and blue sash became her well. The second, Louisa, was taller and more elegant in figure; with a very pretty face, of that order the French term *minois chiffoné*: both sisters were fair as lilies.

Lady Lynn was a large and stout personage of about forty, very erect, very haughty-looking, richly dressed in a satin robe of changeful sheen: her dark hair shone glossily under the shade of an azure plume, and within the circlet of a band of gems.

Mrs. Colonel Dent was less showy; but, I thought, more lady-like. She had a slight figure, a pale, gentle face, and fair hair. Her black satin dress, her scarf of rich foreign lace, and her pearl ornaments, pleased me better than the rainbow radiance of the titled dame.

But the three most distinguished—partly, perhaps, because the tallest figures of the band—were the Dowager Lady Ingram and her daughters, Blanche and Mary. They were all three of the loftiest stature of women. The Dowager might be between forty and fifty: her shape was still fine; her hair (by candle-light at least) still black; her teeth, too, were still apparently perfect. Most people would have termed her a splendid woman of her age: and so she was, no doubt, physically speaking; but then there was an expression of almost insupportable haughtiness in her bearing and countenance. She had Roman features and a double chin, disappearing into a throat like a pillar: these features appeared to me not only inflated and darkened, but even furrowed with pride; and the chin was sustained by the same principle, in a position of almost preternatural erectness. She had, likewise, a fierce and a hard eye: it reminded me of Mrs. Reed's; she mouthed her words in speaking; her voice was deep, its inflections very pompous, very dogmatical—very intolerable, in short. A crimson velvet robe, and a shawl turban of some gold-wrought Indian fabric, invested her (I suppose she thought) with a truly imperial dignity.

Blanche and Mary were of equal stature—straight and tall as poplars. Mary was too slim for her height, but Blanche was moulded like a Dian. I regarded her, of course, with special interest. First, I wished to see whether her appearance accorded with Mrs. Fairfax's description; secondly, whether it at all resembled the fancy miniature I had painted of her; and thirdly—it will out!—whether it were such as I should fancy likely to suit Mr. Rochester's taste.

As far as person went, she answered point for point, both to my picture and Mrs. Fairfax's description. The noble bust, the sloping shoulders, the graceful neck, the dark eyes and black ringlets were all there—but her face? Her face was like her mother's; a youthful unfurrowed likeness: the same low brow, the same high features, the same pride. It was not, however, so saturnine a pride! She laughed continually; her laugh was satirical, and so was the habitual expression of her arched and haughty lip.

Genius is said to be self-conscious. I cannot tell whether Miss Ingram was a genius, but she was self-conscious—remarkably self-conscious indeed. She entered into a discourse on botany with the gentle Mrs. Dent. It seemed Mrs. Dent had not studied that science: though, as she said, she liked flowers, "especially wild ones"; Miss Ingram had, and she ran over its vocabulary with an air. I presently perceived she was (what is vernacularly termed) *trailing* Mrs. Dent; that is, playing on her ignorance—her *trail* might be clever, but it was decidedly not good-natured. She played: her execution was brilliant; she sang: her voice was fine; she talked French apart to her mamma; and she talked it well, with fluency and with a good accent.

Mary had a milder and more open countenance than Blanche; softer features too, and a skin some shades fairer (Miss Ingram was dark as a Spaniard)—but Mary was deficient in life: her face lacked expression, her eye lustre; she had nothing to say, and having once taken her seat, remained fixed like a statue in its niche. The sisters were both attired in spotless white.

And did I now think Miss Ingram such a choice as Mr. Rochester would be likely to make? I could not tell—I did not know his taste in female beauty. If he liked the majestic, she was the very type of majesty: then she was accomplished, sprightly. Most gentlemen would admire her, I thought; and that he *did* admire her, I already seemed to have obtained proof: to remove the last shade of doubt, it remained but to see them together.

You are not to suppose, reader, that Adèle has all this time been sitting motionless on the stool at my feet: no; when the ladies entered, she rose, advanced to meet them, made a stately reverence, and said with gravity—

"Bon jour, mesdames."

And Miss Ingram had looked down at her with a mocking air, and exclaimed, "Oh, what a little puppet!"

Lady Lynn had remarked, "It is Mr. Rochester's ward, I suppose—the little French girl he was speaking of."

Mrs. Dent had kindly taken her hand, and given her a kiss.

Amy and Louisa Eshton had cried out simultaneously: "What a love of a child!"

And then they had called her to a sofa, where she now sat, ensconced between them, chattering alternately in French and broken English; absorbing not only the young ladies' attention, but that of Mrs. Eshton and Lady Lynn, and getting spoilt to her heart's content.

At last coffee is brought in, and the gentlemen are summoned. I sit in the shade—if any shade there be in this brilliantly-lit apartment; the window-curtain half hides me. Again the arch yawns; they come. The collective appearance of the gentlemen, like that of the ladies, is very imposing: they are all costumed in black; most of them are tall, some young. Henry and Frederick Lynn are very dashing sparks indeed; and Colonel Dent is a fine soldierly man. Mr. Eshton, the magistrate of the district, is gentleman-like: his hair is quite white, his eyebrows and whiskers still dark, which gives him something of the appearance of a "père noble de théâtre." Lord Ingram, like his sisters, is very tall; like them, also, he is handsome; but he shares Mary's apathetic and listless look: he seems to have more length of limb than vivacity of blood or vigour of brain.

And where is Mr. Rochester?

He comes in last: I am not looking at the arch, yet I see him enter. I try to concentrate my attention on those netting-needles, on the meshes of the purse I am forming—I wish to think only of the work I have in my hands, to see only the silver beads and silk threads that lie in my lap; whereas, I distinctly behold his figure, and I inevitably recall the moment when I last saw it; just after I had rendered him, what he deemed, an essential service, and he, holding my hand, and looking down on my face, surveyed me with eyes that revealed a heart full and eager to overflow; in whose emotions I had a part. How near had I approached him at that moment! What had occurred since, calculated to change his and my relative positions? Yet now, how distant, how far estranged we were! So far estranged, that I did not expect him to come and speak to me. I did not wonder, when, without looking at me, he took a seat at the other side of the room, and began conversing with some of the ladies.

No sooner did I see that his attention was riveted on them, and that I might gaze without being observed, than my eyes were drawn involuntarily to his face; I could not keep their lids under control: they would rise, and the irids would fix on him. I looked, and had an acute pleasure in looking—a precious yet poignant pleasure; pure gold, with a steely point of agony: a pleasure like what the thirst-perishing man might feel who knows the well to which he has crept is poisoned, yet stoops and drinks divine draughts nevertheless.

Most true is it that "beauty is in the eye of the gazer." My master's colourless, olive face, square, massive brow, broad and jetty eyebrows, deep eyes, strong features, firm, grim mouth—all energy, decision, will—were not beautiful, according to rule; but they were more than beautiful to me; they were full of an interest, an influence that quite mastered me—that took my feelings from my own power and fettered them in his. I had not intended to love him; the reader knows I had wrought hard to extirpate from my soul the germs of love there detected; and now, at the first renewed view of him, they spontaneously arrived, green and strong! He made me love him without looking at me.

I compared him with his guests. What was the gallant grace of the Lynns, the languid elegance of Lord Ingram—even the military distinction of Colonel Dent, contrasted with his look of native pith and genuine power? I had no sympathy in their appearance, their expression: yet I could imagine that most observers would call them attractive, handsome, imposing; while they would pronounce Mr. Rochester at once harsh-featured and melancholy-looking. I saw them smile, laugh—it was nothing; the light of the candles had as much soul in it as their smile; the tinkle of the bell as much significance as their laugh. I saw Mr. Rochester smile: his stern features softened; his eye grew both brilliant and gentle, its ray both searching and sweet. He was talking, at the moment, to Louisa and Amy Eshton. I wondered to see them receive with calm that look which seemed to me so penetrating: I expected their eyes to fall, their colour to rise under it; yet I was glad when I found they were in no sense moved. "He is not to them what he is to me," I thought: "he is not of their kind. I believe he is of mine—I am sure he is—I feel akin to him—I understand the language of his countenance and movements: though rank and wealth sever us widely, I have something in my brain and heart, in my blood and nerves, that assimilates me mentally to him. Did I say, a few days since, that I had nothing to do with him but to receive my salary at his hands? Did I forbid myself to think of him in any other light than as a paymaster? Blasphemy against nature! Every good, true, vigorous feeling I have gathers impulsively round him. I know I must conceal my sentiments: I must smother hope; I must remember that he cannot care much for me. For when I say that I am of his kind, I do not mean that I have his force to influence, and his spell to attract; I mean only that I have certain tastes and feelings in common with him. I must, then, repeat continually that we are for ever sundered—and yet, while I breathe and think, I must love him."

Coffee is handed. The ladies, since the gentlemen entered, have become lively as larks; conversation waxes brisk and merry. Colonel Dent and Mr. Eshton argue on politics; their wives listen. The two proud dowagers, Lady Lynn and Lady Ingram, confabulate together. Sir George—whom, by-the-by, I have forgotten to describe—a very big, and very fresh-looking country gentleman, stands before their sofa, coffee-cup in hand, and occasionally puts in a word. Mr. Frederick Lynn has taken a seat beside Mary Ingram, and is showing her the engravings of a splendid volume: she looks, smiles now and then, but apparently says little. The tall and phlegmatic Lord Ingram leans with folded arms on the chair-back of the little and lively Amy Eshton; she glances up at him, and chatters like a wren: she likes him better than she does Mr. Rochester. Henry Lynn has taken possession of an ottoman at the feet of Louisa: Adèle shares it with him: he is trying to talk French with her, and Louisa laughs at his blunders. With whom will Blanche Ingram pair? She is standing alone at the table, bending gracefully over an album. She seems waiting to be sought; but she will not wait too long: she herself selects a mate.

Mr. Rochester, having quitted the Eshtons, stands on the hearth as solitary as she stands by the table: she confronts him, taking her station on the opposite side of the mantelpiece.

"Mr. Rochester, I thought you were not fond of children?"

"Nor am I."

"Then, what induced you to take charge of such a little doll as that?" (pointing to Adèle). "Where did you pick her up?"

"I did not pick her up; she was left on my hands."

"You should have sent her to school."

"I could not afford it: schools are so dear."

"Why, I suppose you have a governess for her: I saw a person with her just now—is she gone? Oh, no! There she is still, behind the window-curtain. You pay her, of course; I should think it quite as expensive—more so; for you have them both to keep in addition."

I feared—or should I say, hoped?—the allusion to me would make Mr. Rochester glance my way; and I involuntarily shrank farther into the shade: but he never turned his eyes.

"I have not considered the subject," said he indifferently, looking straight before him.

"No, you men never do consider economy and common sense. You should hear mama on the chapter of governesses: Mary and I have had, I should think, a dozen at least in our day; half of them detestable and the rest ridiculous, and all incubi—were they not, mama?"

"Did you speak, my own?"

The young lady thus claimed as the dowager's special property, reiterated her question with an explanation.

"My dearest, don't mention governesses; the word makes me nervous. I have suffered a martyrdom from their incompetency and caprice. I thank Heaven I have now done with them!"

Mrs. Dent here bent over to the pious lady and whispered something in her ear; I suppose, from the answer elicited, it was a reminder that one of the anathematised race was present.

"Tant pis!" said her Ladyship, "I hope it may do her good!" Then, in a lower tone, but still loud enough for me to hear, "I noticed her; I am a judge of physiognomy, and in hers I see all the faults of her class."

"What are they, madam?" inquired Mr. Rochester aloud.

"I will tell you in your private ear," replied she, wagging her turban three times with portentous significancy.

"But my curiosity will be past its appetite; it craves food now."

"Ask Blanche; she is nearer you than I."

"Oh, don't refer him to me, mama! I have just one word to say of the whole tribe; they are a nuisance. Not that I ever suffered much from them; I took care to turn the tables. What tricks Theodore and I used to play on our Miss Wilsons, and Mrs. Greys, and Madame Jouberts! Mary was always too sleepy to join in a plot with spirit. The best fun was with Madame Joubert: Miss Wilson was a poor sickly thing, lachrymose and low-spirited, not worth the trouble of vanquishing, in short; and Mrs. Grey was coarse and insensible; no blow took effect on her. But poor Madame Joubert! I see her yet in her raging passions, when we had driven her to extremities—spilt our tea, crumbled our bread and butter, tossed our books up to the ceiling, and played a charivari with the ruler and desk, the fender and fire-irons. Theodore, do you remember those merry days?"

"Yaas, to be sure I do," drawled Lord Ingram; "and the poor old stick used to cry out 'Oh you villains childs!'—and then we sermonised her on the presumption of attempting to teach such clever blades as we were, when she was herself so ignorant."

"We did; and, Tedo, you know, I helped you in prosecuting (or persecuting) your tutor, whey-faced Mr. Vining—the parson in the pip, as we used to call him. He and Miss Wilson took the liberty of falling in love with each other—at least Tedo and I thought so; we surprised sundry tender glances and sighs which we interpreted as tokens of 'la belle passion,' and I promise you the public soon had the benefit of our discovery; we employed it as a sort of lever to hoist our dead-weights from the house. Dear mama, there, as soon as she got an inkling of the business, found out that it was of an immoral tendency. Did you not, my lady-mother?"

"Certainly, my best. And I was quite right: depend on that: there are a thousand reasons why liaisons between governesses and tutors should never be tolerated a moment in any well-regulated house; firstly—"

"Oh, gracious, mama! Spare us the enumeration! *Au reste*, we all know them: danger of bad example to innocence of childhood; distractions and consequent neglect of duty on the part of the attached—mutual alliance and reliance; confidence thence resulting—insolence accompanying—mutiny and general blow-up. Am I right, Baroness Ingram, of Ingram Park?"

"My lily-flower, you are right now, as always."

"Then no more need be said: change the subject."

Amy Eshton, not hearing or not heeding this dictum, joined in with her soft, infantine tone: "Louisa and I used to quiz our governess too; but she was such a good creature, she would bear anything: nothing put her out. She was never cross with us; was she, Louisa?"

"No, never: we might do what we pleased; ransack her desk and her workbox, and turn her drawers inside out; and she was so good-natured, she would give us anything we asked for."

"I suppose, now," said Miss Ingram, curling her lip sarcastically, "we shall have an abstract of the memoirs of all the governesses extant: in order to avert such a visitation, I again move the introduction of a new topic. Mr. Rochester, do you second my motion?"

"Madam, I support you on this point, as on every other."

"Then on me be the onus of bringing it forward. Signior Eduardo, are you in voice tonight?"

"Donna Bianca, if you command it, I will be."

"Then, signior, I lay on you my sovereign behest to furbish up your lungs and other vocal organs, as they will be wanted on my royal service."

"Who would not be the Rizzio of so divine a Mary?"

"A fig for Rizzio!" cried she, tossing her head with all its curls, as she moved to the piano. "It is my opinion the fiddler David must have been an insipid sort of fellow; I like black Bothwell better: to my mind a man is nothing without a spice of the devil in him; and history may say what it will of James Hepburn, but I have a notion, he was just the sort of wild, fierce, bandit hero whom I could have consented to gift with my hand."

"Gentlemen, you hear! Now which of you most resembles Bothwell?" cried Mr. Rochester.

"I should say the preference lies with you," responded Colonel Dent.

"On my honour, I am much obliged to you," was the reply.

Miss Ingram, who had now seated herself with proud grace at the piano, spreading out her snowy robes in queenly amplitude, commenced a brilliant prelude; talking meantime. She appeared to be on her high horse tonight; both her words and her air seemed intended to excite not only the admiration, but the amazement of her auditors: she was evidently bent on striking them as something very dashing and daring indeed.

"Oh, I am so sick of the young men of the present day!" exclaimed she, rattling away at the instrument. "Poor, puny things, not fit to stir a step beyond papa's park gates: nor to go even so far without mama's permission and guardianship! Creatures so absorbed in care about their pretty faces, and their white hands, and their small feet; as if a man had anything to do with beauty! As if loveliness were not the special prerogative of woman—her legitimate appanage and heritage! I grant an ugly *woman* is a blot on the fair face of creation; but as to the *gentlemen*, let them be solicitous to possess only strength and valour: let their motto be: Hunt, shoot, and fight; the rest is not worth a fillip. Such should be my device, were I a man.

"Whenever I marry," she continued after a pause which none interrupted, "I am resolved my husband shall not be a rival, but a foil to me. I will suffer no competitor near the throne; I shall exact an undivided homage: his devotions shall not be shared between me and the shape he sees in his mirror. Mr. Rochester, now sing, and I will play for you."

"I am all obedience," was the response.

"Here then is a Corsair-song. Know that I doat on Corsairs; and for that reason, sing it *con spirito*."

"Commands from Miss Ingram's lips would put spirit into a mug of milk and water."

"Take care, then: if you don't please me, I will shame you by showing how such things *should* be done."

"That is offering a premium on incapacity: I shall now endeavour to fail."

"Gardez-vous en bien! If you err wilfully, I shall devise a proportionate punishment."

"Miss Ingram ought to be clement, for she has it in her power to inflict a chastisement beyond mortal endurance."

"Ha! Explain!" commanded the lady.

"Pardon me, madam: no need of explanation; your own fine sense must inform you that one of your frowns would be a sufficient substitute for capital punishment."

"Sing!" said she, and again touching the piano, she commenced an accompaniment in spirited style.

"Now is my time to slip away," thought I: but the tones that then severed the air arrested me. Mrs. Fairfax had said Mr. Rochester possessed a fine voice: he did—a mellow, powerful bass, into which he threw his own feeling, his own force; finding a way through the ear to the heart, and there waking sensation strangely. I waited till the last deep and full vibration had expired—till the tide of talk, checked an instant, had resumed its flow; I then quitted my sheltered corner and made my exit by the side-door, which was fortunately near. Thence a narrow passage led into the hall: in crossing it, I perceived my sandal was loose; I stopped to tie it, kneeling down for that purpose on the mat at the foot of the staircase. I heard the dining-room door unclose; a gentleman came out; rising hastily, I stood face to face with him: it was Mr. Rochester.

"How do you do?" he asked.

"I am very well, sir."

"Why did you not come and speak to me in the room?"

I thought I might have retorted the question on him who put it: but I would not take that freedom. I answered—

"I did not wish to disturb you, as you seemed engaged, sir."

"What have you been doing during my absence?"

"Nothing particular; teaching Adèle as usual."

"And getting a good deal paler than you were—as I saw at first sight. What is the matter?"

"Nothing at all, sir."

"Did you take any cold that night you half drowned me?"

"Not the least."

"Return to the drawing-room: you are deserting too early."

"I am tired, sir."

He looked at me for a minute.

"And a little depressed," he said. "What about? Tell me."

"Nothing—nothing, sir. I am not depressed."

"But I affirm that you are: so much depressed that a few more words would bring tears to your eyes—indeed, they are there now, shining and swimming; and a bead has slipped from the lash and fallen on to the flag. If I had time, and was not in mortal dread of some prating prig of a servant passing, I would know what all this means. Well, tonight I excuse you; but understand that so long as my visitors stay, I expect you to appear in the drawing-room every evening; it is my wish, don't neglect it. Now go, and send Sophie for Adèle. Good-night, my—" He stopped, bit his lip, and abruptly left me.

CHAPTER XVIII

Merry days were these at Thornfield Hall; and busy days too: how different from the first three months of stillness, monotony, and solitude I had passed beneath its roof! All sad feelings seemed now driven from the house, all gloomy associations forgotten: there was life everywhere, movement all day long. You could not now traverse the gallery, once so hushed, nor enter the front chambers, once so tenantless, without encountering a smart lady's-maid or a dandy valet.

The kitchen, the butler's pantry, the servants' hall, the entrance hall, were equally alive; and the saloons were only left void and still when the blue sky and halcyon sunshine of the genial spring weather called their occupants out into the grounds. Even when that weather was broken, and continuous rain set in for some days, no damp seemed cast over enjoyment: indoor amusements only became more lively and varied, in consequence of the stop put to outdoor gaiety.

I wondered what they were going to do the first evening a change of entertainment was proposed: they spoke of "playing charades," but in my ignorance I did not understand the term. The servants were called in, the dining-room tables wheeled away, the lights otherwise disposed, the chairs placed in a semicircle opposite the arch. While Mr. Rochester and the other gentlemen directed these alterations, the ladies were running up and down stairs ringing for their maids. Mrs. Fairfax was summoned to give information respecting the resources of the house in shawls, dresses, draperies of any kind; and certain wardrobes of the third storey were ransacked, and their contents, in the shape of brocaded and hooped petticoats, satin sacques, black modes, lace lappets, etc., were brought down in armfuls by the abigails; then a selection was made, and such things as were chosen were carried to the boudoir within the drawing-room.

Meantime, Mr. Rochester had again summoned the ladies round him, and was selecting certain of their number to be of his party. "Miss Ingram is mine, of course," said he: afterwards he named the two Misses Eshton, and Mrs. Dent. He looked at me: I happened to be near him, as I had been fastening the clasp of Mrs. Dent's bracelet, which had got loose.

"Will you play?" he asked. I shook my head. He did not insist, which I rather feared he would have done; he allowed me to return quietly to my usual seat.

He and his aids now withdrew behind the curtain: the other party, which was headed by Colonel Dent, sat down on the crescent of chairs. One of the gentlemen, Mr. Eshton, observing me, seemed to propose that I should be asked to join them; but Lady Ingram instantly negatived the notion.

"No," I heard her say; "she looks too stupid for any game of the sort."

Ere long a bell tinkled, and the curtain drew up. Within the arch, the bulky figure of Sir George Lynn, whom Mr. Rochester had likewise chosen, was seen enveloped in a white sheet: before him, on a table, lay open a large book; and at his side stood Amy Eshton, draped in Mr. Rochester's cloak, and holding a book in her hand. Somebody, unseen, rang the bell merrily; then Adèle (who had insisted on being one of her guardian's party), bounded forward, scattering round her the contents of a basket of flowers she carried on her arm. Then appeared the magnificent figure of Miss Ingram, clad in white, a long veil on her head, and a wreath of roses round her brow; by her side walked Mr. Rochester, and together they drew near the table. They knelt; while Mrs. Dent and Louisa Eshton, dressed also in white, took up their stations behind them. A ceremony followed, in dumb show, in which it was easy to recognise the pantomime of a marriage. At its termination, Colonel Dent and his party consulted in whispers for two minutes, then the Colonel called out—

"Bride!" Mr. Rochester bowed, and the curtain fell.

A considerable interval elapsed before it again rose. Its second rising displayed a more elaborately prepared scene than the last. The drawing-room, as I have before observed, was raised two steps above the dining-room, and on the top of the upper step, placed a yard or two back within the room, appeared a large marble basin—which I recognised as an ornament of the conservatory—where it usually stood, surrounded by exotics, and tenanted by gold fish—and whence it must have been transported with some trouble, on account of its size and weight.

Seated on the carpet, by the side of this basin, was seen Mr. Rochester, costumed in shawls, with a turban on his head. His dark eyes and swarthy skin and Paynim features suited the costume exactly: he looked the very model of an Eastern emir, an agent or a victim of the bowstring. Presently advanced into view Miss Ingram. She, too, was attired in oriental fashion: a crimson scarf tied sash-like round the waist: an embroidered handkerchief knotted about her temples; her beautifully-moulded arms bare, one of them upraised in the act of supporting a pitcher, poised gracefully on her head. Both her cast of form and feature, her complexion and her general air, suggested the idea of some Israelitish princess of the patriarchal days; and such was doubtless the character she intended to represent.

She approached the basin, and bent over it as if to fill her pitcher; she again lifted it to her head. The personage on the well-brink now seemed to accost her; to make some request: "She hasted, let down her pitcher on her hand, and gave him to drink." From the bosom of his robe he then produced a casket, opened it and showed magnificent bracelets and earrings; she acted astonishment and admiration; kneeling, he laid the treasure at her feet; incredulity and delight were expressed by her looks and gestures; the stranger fastened the bracelets on her arms and the rings in her ears. It was Eliezer and Rebecca: the camels only were wanting.

The divining party again laid their heads together: apparently they could not agree about the word or syllable the scene illustrated. Colonel Dent, their spokesman, demanded "the tableau of the whole," whereupon the curtain again descended.

On its third rising only a portion of the drawing-room was disclosed; the rest being concealed by a screen, hung with some sort of dark and coarse drapery. The marble basin was removed; in its place stood a deal table and a kitchen chair: these objects were visible by a very dim light proceeding from a horn lantern, the wax candles being all extinguished.

Amidst this sordid scene sat a man with his clenched hands resting on his knees, and his eyes bent on the ground. I knew Mr. Rochester; though the begrimed face, the disordered dress (his coat hanging loose from one arm, as if it had been almost torn from his back in a scuffle), the desperate and scowling countenance, the rough, bristling hair might well have disguised him. As he moved, a chain clanked; to his wrists were attached fetters.

"Bridewell!" exclaimed Colonel Dent, and the charade was solved.

A sufficient interval having elapsed for the performers to resume their ordinary costume, they re-entered the dining-room. Mr. Rochester led in Miss Ingram; she was complimenting him on his acting.

"Do you know," said she, "that, of the three characters, I liked you in the last best? Oh, had you but lived a few years earlier, what a gallant gentleman-highwayman you would have made!"

"Is all the soot washed from my face?" he asked, turning it towards her.

"Alas! Yes: the more 's the pity! Nothing could be more becoming to your complexion than that ruffian's rouge."

"You would like a hero of the road then?"

"An English hero of the road would be the next best thing to an Italian bandit; and that could only be surpassed by a Levantine pirate."

"Well, whatever I am, remember you are my wife; we were married an hour since, in the presence of all these witnesses." She giggled, and her colour rose.

"Now, Dent," continued Mr. Rochester, "it is your turn." And as the other party withdrew, he and his band took the vacated seats. Miss Ingram placed herself at her leader's right hand; the other diviners filled the chairs on each side of him and her. I did not now watch the actors; I no longer waited with interest for the curtain to rise; my attention was absorbed by the spectators; my eyes, erewhile fixed on the arch, were now irresistibly attracted to the semicircle of chairs. What charade Colonel Dent and his party played, what word they chose, how they acquitted themselves, I no longer remember; but I still see the consultation which followed each scene: I see Mr. Rochester turn to Miss Ingram, and Miss Ingram to him; I see her incline her head towards him, till the jetty curls almost touch his shoulder and wave against his cheek; I hear their mutual whisperings; I recall their interchanged glances; and something even of the feeling roused by the spectacle returns in memory at this moment.

I have told you, reader, that I had learnt to love Mr. Rochester: I could not unlove him now, merely because I found that he had ceased to notice me—because I might pass hours in his presence, and he would never once turn his eyes in my direction—because I saw all his attentions appropriated by a great lady, who scorned to touch me with the hem of her robes as she passed; who, if ever her dark and imperious eye fell on me by chance, would withdraw it instantly as from an object too mean to merit observation. I could not unlove him, because I felt sure he would soon marry this very lady—because I read daily in her a proud security in his intentions respecting her—because I witnessed hourly in him a style of courtship which, if careless and choosing rather to be sought than to seek, was yet, in its very carelessness, captivating, and in its very pride, irresistible.

There was nothing to cool or banish love in these circumstances, though much to create despair. Much too, you will think, reader, to engender jealousy: if a woman, in my position, could presume to be jealous of a woman in Miss Ingram's. But I was not jealous: or very rarely—the nature of the pain I suffered could not be explained by that word. Miss Ingram was a mark beneath jealousy: she was too inferior to excite the feeling. Pardon the seeming paradox; I mean what I say. She was very showy, but she was not genuine: she had a fine person, many brilliant attainments; but her mind was poor, her heart barren by nature: nothing bloomed spontaneously on that soil; no unforced natural fruit delighted by its freshness. She was not good; she was not original: she used to repeat sounding phrases from books: she never offered, nor had, an opinion of her own. She advocated a high tone of sentiment; but she did not know the sensations of sympathy and pity; tenderness and truth were not in her. Too often she betrayed this, by the undue vent she gave to a spiteful antipathy she had conceived against little Adèle: pushing her away with some contumelious epithet if she happened to approach her; sometimes ordering her from the room, and always treating her with coldness and acrimony. Other eyes besides mine watched these manifestations of character—watched them closely, keenly, shrewdly. Yes; the future bridegroom, Mr. Rochester himself, exercised over his intended a ceaseless surveillance; and it was from this sagacity—this guardedness of his—this perfect, clear consciousness of his fair one's defects—this obvious absence of passion in his sentiments towards her, that my ever-torturing pain arose.

I saw he was going to marry her, for family, perhaps political reasons, because her rank and connections suited him; I felt he had not given her his love, and that her qualifications were ill adapted to win from him that treasure. This was the point—this was where the nerve was touched and teased—this was where the fever was sustained and fed: *she could not charm him.*

If she had managed the victory at once, and he had yielded and sincerely laid his heart at her feet, I should have covered my face, turned to the wall, and (figuratively) have died to them. If Miss Ingram had been a good and noble woman, endowed with force, fervour, kindness, sense, I should have had one vital struggle with two tigers—jealousy and despair: then, my heart torn out and devoured, I should have admired her—acknowledged her excellence, and been quiet for the rest of my days: and the more absolute her superiority, the deeper would have been my admiration—the more truly tranquil my quiescence. But as matters really stood, to watch Miss Ingram's efforts at fascinating Mr. Rochester, to witness their repeated failure—herself unconscious that they did fail; vainly fancying that each shaft launched hit the mark, and infatuatedly pluming herself on success, when her pride and self-complacency repelled further and further what she wished to allure—to witness *this*, was to be at once under ceaseless excitation and ruthless restraint.

Because, when she failed, I saw how she might have succeeded. Arrows that continually glanced off from Mr. Rochester's breast and fell harmless at his feet, might, I knew, if shot by a surer hand, have quivered keen in his proud heart—have called love into his stern eye, and softness into his sardonic face; or, better still, without weapons a silent conquest might have been won.

"Why can she not influence him more, when she is privileged to draw so near to him?" I asked myself. "Surely she cannot truly like him, or not like him with true affection! If she did, she need not coin her smiles so lavishly, flash her glances so unremittingly, manufacture airs so elaborate, graces so multitudinous. It seems to me that she might, by merely sitting quietly at his side, saying little and looking less, get nigher his heart. I have seen in his face a far different expression from that which hardens it now while she is so vivaciously accosting him; but then it came of itself: it was not elicited by meretricious arts and calculated manoeuvres; and one had but to accept it—to answer what he asked without pretension, to address him when needful without grimace—and it increased and grew kinder and more genial, and warmed one like a fostering sunbeam. How will she manage to please him when they are married? I do not think she will manage it; and yet it might be managed; and his wife might, I verily believe, be the very happiest woman the sun shines on."

I have not yet said anything condemnatory of Mr. Rochester's project of marrying for interest and connections. It surprised me when I first discovered that such was his intention: I had thought him a man unlikely to be influenced by motives so commonplace in his choice of a wife; but the longer I considered the position, education, etc., of the parties, the less I felt justified in judging and blaming either him or Miss Ingram for acting in conformity to ideas and principles instilled into them, doubtless, from their childhood. All their class held these principles: I supposed, then, they had reasons for holding them such as I could not fathom. It seemed to me that, were I a gentleman like him, I would take to my bosom only such a wife as I could love; but the very obviousness of the advantages to the husband's own happiness offered by this plan convinced me that there must be arguments against its general adoption of which I was quite ignorant: otherwise I felt sure all the world would act as I wished to act.

But in other points, as well as this, I was growing very lenient to my master: I was forgetting all his faults, for which I had once kept a sharp look-out. It had formerly been my endeavour to study all sides of his character: to take the bad with the good; and from the just weighing of both, to form an equitable judgment. Now I saw no bad. The sarcasm that had repelled, the harshness that had startled me once, were only like keen condiments in a choice dish: their presence was pungent, but their absence would be felt as comparatively insipid. And as for the vague something—was it a sinister or a sorrowful, a designing or a desponding expression?—that opened upon a careful observer, now and then, in his eye, and closed again before one could fathom the strange depth partially disclosed; that something which used to make me fear and shrink, as if I had been wandering amongst volcanic-looking hills, and had suddenly felt the ground quiver and seen it gape: that something, I, at intervals, beheld still; and with throbbing heart, but not with palsied nerves. Instead of wishing to shun, I longed only to dare—to divine it; and I thought Miss Ingram happy, because one day she might look into the abyss at her leisure, explore its secrets and analyse their nature.

Meantime, while I thought only of my master and his future bride—saw only them, heard only their discourse, and considered only their movements of importance—the rest of the party were occupied with their own separate interests and pleasures. The Ladies Lynn and Ingram continued to consort in solemn conferences, where they nodded their two turbans at each other, and held up their four hands in confronting gestures of surprise, or mystery, or horror, according to the theme on which their gossip ran, like a pair of magnified puppets. Mild Mrs. Dent talked with good-natured Mrs. Eshton; and the two sometimes bestowed a courteous word or smile on me. Sir George Lynn, Colonel Dent, and Mr. Eshton discussed politics, or county affairs, or justice business. Lord Ingram flirted with Amy Eshton; Louisa played and sang to and with one of the Messrs. Lynn; and Mary Ingram listened languidly to the gallant speeches of the other. Sometimes all, as with one consent, suspended their by-play to observe and listen to the principal actors: for, after all, Mr. Rochester and—because closely connected with him—Miss Ingram were the life and soul of the party. If he was absent from the room an hour, a perceptible dulness seemed to steal over the spirits of his guests; and his re-entrance was sure to give a fresh impulse to the vivacity of conversation.

The want of his animating influence appeared to be peculiarly felt one day that he had been summoned to Millcote on business, and was not likely to return till late. The afternoon was wet: a walk the party had proposed to take to see a gipsy camp, lately pitched on a common beyond Hay, was consequently deferred. Some of the gentlemen were gone to the stables: the younger ones, together with the younger ladies, were playing billiards in the billiard-room. The dowagers Ingram and Lynn sought solace in a quiet game at cards. Blanche Ingram, after having repelled, by supercilious taciturnity, some efforts of Mrs. Dent and Mrs. Eshton to draw her into conversation, had first murmured over some sentimental tunes and airs on the piano, and then, having fetched a novel from the library, had flung herself in haughty listlessness on a sofa, and prepared to beguile, by the spell of fiction, the tedious hours of absence. The room and the house were silent: only now and then the merriment of the billiard-players was heard from above.

It was verging on dusk, and the clock had already given warning of the hour to dress for dinner, when little Adèle, who knelt by me in the drawing-room window-seat, suddenly exclaimed—

"Voilà, Monsieur Rochester, qui revient!"

I turned, and Miss Ingram darted forwards from her sofa: the others, too, looked up from their several occupations; for at the same time a crunching of wheels and a splashing tramp of horse-hoofs became audible on the wet gravel. A post-chaise was approaching.

"What can possess him to come home in that style?" said Miss

Ingram. "He rode Mesrour (the black horse), did he not, when he went out? And Pilot was with him—what has he done with the animals?"

As she said this, she approached her tall person and ample garments so near the window, that I was obliged to bend back almost to the breaking of my spine: in her eagerness she did not observe me at first, but when she did, she curled her lip and moved to another casement. The post-chaise stopped; the driver rang the door-bell, and a gentleman alighted attired in travelling garb; but it was not Mr. Rochester; it was a tall, fashionable-looking man, a stranger.

"How provoking!" exclaimed Miss Ingram. "You tiresome monkey!" (Apostrophising Adèle), "Who perched you up in the window to give false intelligence?" And she cast on me an angry glance, as if I were in fault.

Some parleying was audible in the hall, and soon the new-comer entered. He bowed to Lady Ingram, as deeming her the eldest lady present.

"It appears I come at an inopportune time, madam," said he, "when my friend, Mr. Rochester, is from home; but I arrive from a very long journey, and I think I may presume so far on old and intimate acquaintance as to instal myself here till he returns."

His manner was polite; his accent, in speaking, struck me as being somewhat unusual—not precisely foreign, but still not altogether English: his age might be about Mr. Rochester's—between thirty and forty; his complexion was singularly sallow: otherwise he was a fine-looking man, at first sight especially. On closer examination, you detected something in his face that displeased, or rather that failed to please. His features were regular, but too relaxed: his eye was large and well cut, but the life looking out of it was a tame, vacant life—at least so I thought.

The sound of the dressing-bell dispersed the party. It was not till after dinner that I saw him again: he then seemed quite at his ease. But I liked his physiognomy even less than before: it struck me as being at the same time unsettled and inanimate. His eye wandered, and had no meaning in its wandering: this gave him an odd look, such as I never remembered to have seen. For a handsome and not an unamiable-looking man, he repelled me exceedingly: there was no power in that smooth-skinned face of a full oval shape: no firmness in that aquiline nose and small cherry mouth; there was no thought on the low, even forehead; no command in that blank, brown eye.

As I sat in my usual nook, and looked at him with the light of the girandoles on the mantelpiece beaming full over him—for he occupied an arm-chair drawn close to the fire, and kept shrinking still nearer, as if he were cold, I compared him with Mr. Rochester. I think (with deference be it spoken) the contrast could not be much greater between a sleek gander and a fierce falcon: between a meek sheep and the rough-coated keen-eyed dog, its guardian.

He had spoken of Mr. Rochester as an old friend. A curious friendship theirs must have been: a pointed illustration, indeed, of the old adage that "extremes meet."

Two or three of the gentlemen sat near him, and I caught at times scraps of their conversation across the room. At first I could not make much sense of what I heard; for the discourse of Louisa Eshton and Mary Ingram, who sat nearer to me, confused the fragmentary sentences that reached me at intervals. These last were discussing the stranger; they both called him "a beautiful man." Louisa said he was "a love of a creature," and she "adored him"; and Mary instanced his "pretty little mouth, and nice nose," as her ideal of the charming.

"And what a sweet-tempered forehead he has!" cried Louisa. "So smooth—none of those frowning irregularities I dislike so much; and such a placid eye and smile!"

And then, to my great relief, Mr. Henry Lynn summoned them to the other side of the room, to settle some point about the deferred excursion to Hay Common.

I was now able to concentrate my attention on the group by the fire, and I presently gathered that the new-comer was called Mr. Mason; then I learned that he was but just arrived in England, and that he came from some hot country: which was the reason, doubtless, his face was so sallow, and that he sat so near the hearth, and wore a surtout in the house. Presently the words Jamaica, Kingston, Spanish Town, indicated the West Indies as his residence; and it was with no little surprise I gathered, ere long, that he had there first seen and become acquainted with Mr. Rochester. He spoke of his friend's dislike of the burning heats, the hurricanes, and rainy seasons of that region. I knew Mr. Rochester had been a traveller: Mrs. Fairfax had said so; but I thought the continent of Europe had bounded his wanderings; till now I had never heard a hint given of visits to more distant shores.

I was pondering these things, when an incident, and a somewhat unexpected one, broke the thread of my musings. Mr. Mason, shivering as some one chanced to open the door, asked for more coal to be put on the fire, which had burnt out its flame, though its mass of cinder still shone hot and red. The footman who brought the coal, in going out, stopped near Mr. Eshton's chair, and said something to him in a low voice, of which I heard only the words "old woman"—"quite troublesome."

"Tell her she shall be put in the stocks if she does not take herself off," replied the magistrate.

"No—stop!" interrupted Colonel Dent. "Don't send her away, Eshton; we might turn the thing to account; better consult the ladies." And speaking aloud, he continued, "Ladies, you talked of going to Hay Common to visit the gipsy camp; Sam here says that one of the old Mother Bunches is in the servants' hall at this moment, and insists upon being brought in before 'the quality,' to tell them their fortunes. Would you like to see her?"

"Surely, colonel," cried Lady Ingram, "you would not encourage such a low impostor? Dismiss her, by all means, at once!"

"But I cannot persuade her to go away, my lady," said the footman; "nor can any of the servants: Mrs. Fairfax is with her just now, entreating her to be gone; but she has taken a chair in the chimney-corner, and says nothing shall stir her from it till she gets leave to come in here."

"What does she want?" asked Mrs. Eshton.

" 'To tell the gentry their fortunes,' she says, ma'am; and she swears she must and will do it."

"What is she like?" inquired the Misses Eshton, in a breath.

"A shockingly ugly old creature, miss; almost as black as a crock."

"Why, she's a real sorceress!" cried Frederick Lynn. "Let us have her in, of course."

"To be sure," rejoined his brother; "it would be a thousand pities to throw away such a chance of fun."

"My dear boys, what are you thinking about?" exclaimed Mrs. Lynn.

"I cannot possibly countenance any such inconsistent proceeding," chimed in the Dowager Ingram.

"Indeed, mama, but you can—and will," pronounced the haughty voice of Blanche, as she turned round on the piano-stool; where till now she had sat silent, apparently examining sundry sheets of music. "I have a curiosity to hear my fortune told: therefore, Sam, order the beldame forward."

"My darling Blanche! Recollect—"

"I do—I recollect all you can suggest; and I must have my will—quick, Sam!"

"Yes—yes—yes!" cried all the juveniles, both ladies and gentlemen. "Let her come—it will be excellent sport!"

The footman still lingered. "She looks such a rough one," said he.

"Go!" ejaculated Miss Ingram, and the man went.

Excitement instantly seized the whole party: a running fire of raillery and jests was proceeding when Sam returned.

"She won't come now," said he. "She says it's not her mission to appear before the 'vulgar herd' (them's her words). I must show her into a room by herself, and then those who wish to consult her must go to her one by one."

"You see now, my queenly Blanche," began Lady Ingram, "she encroaches. Be advised, my angel girl—and—"

"Show her into the library, of course," cut in the "angel girl." "It is not my mission to listen to her before the vulgar herd either: I mean to have her all to myself. Is there a fire in the library?"

"Yes, ma'am—but she looks such a tinkler."

"Cease that chatter, blockhead! And do my bidding."

Again Sam vanished; and mystery, animation, expectation rose to full flow once more.

"She's ready now," said the footman, as he reappeared. "She wishes to know who will be her first visitor."

"I think I had better just look in upon her before any of the ladies go," said Colonel Dent.

"Tell her, Sam, a gentleman is coming."

Sam went and returned.

"She says, sir, that she'll have no gentlemen; they need not trouble themselves to come near her; nor," he added, with difficulty suppressing a titter, "any ladies either, except the young, and single."

"By Jove, she has taste!" exclaimed Henry Lynn.

Miss Ingram rose solemnly: "I go first," she said, in a tone which might have befitted the leader of a forlorn hope, mounting a breach in the van of his men.

"Oh, my best! Oh, my dearest! Pause—reflect!" was her mama's cry; but she swept past her in stately silence, passed through the door which Colonel Dent held open, and we heard her enter the library.

A comparative silence ensued. Lady Ingram thought it "le cas" to wring her hands: which she did accordingly. Miss Mary declared she felt, for her part, she never dared venture. Amy and Louisa Eshton tittered under their breath, and looked a little frightened.

The minutes passed very slowly: fifteen were counted before the library-door again opened. Miss Ingram returned to us through the arch.

Would she laugh? Would she take it as a joke? All eyes met her with a glance of eager curiosity, and she met all eyes with one of rebuff and coldness; she looked neither flurried nor merry: she walked stiffly to her seat, and took it in silence.

"Well, Blanche?" said Lord Ingram.

"What did she say, sister?" asked Mary.

"What did you think? How do you feel? Is she a real fortune-teller?" demanded the Misses Eshton.

"Now, now, good people," returned Miss Ingram, "don't press upon me. Really your organs of wonder and credulity are easily excited: you seem, by the importance of you all—my good mama included—ascribe to this matter, absolutely to believe we have a genuine witch in the house, who is in close alliance with the old gentleman. I have seen a gipsy vagabond; she has practised in hackneyed fashion the science of palmistry and told me what such people usually tell. My whim is gratified; and now I think Mr. Eshton will do well to put the hag in the stocks tomorrow morning, as he threatened."

Miss Ingram took a book, leant back in her chair, and so declined further conversation. I watched her for nearly half-an-hour: during all that time she never turned a page, and her face grew momently darker, more dissatisfied, and more sourly expressive of disappointment. She had obviously not heard anything to her advantage: and it seemed to me, from her prolonged fit of gloom and taciturnity, that she herself, notwithstanding her professed indifference, attached undue importance to whatever revelations had been made her.

Meantime, Mary Ingram, Amy and Louisa Eshton, declared they dared not go alone; and yet they all wished to go. A negotiation was opened through the medium of the ambassador, Sam; and after much pacing to and fro, till, I think, the said Sam's calves must have ached with the exercise, permission was at last, with great difficulty, extorted from the rigorous Sibyl, for the three to wait upon her in a body.

Their visit was not so still as Miss Ingram's had been: we heard hysterical giggling and little shrieks proceeding from the library; and at the end of about twenty minutes they burst the door open, and came running across the hall, as if they were half-scared out of their wits.

"I am sure she is something not right!" they cried, one and all. "She told us such things! She knows all about us!" and they sank breathless into the various seats the gentlemen hastened to bring them.

Pressed for further explanation, they declared she had told them of things they had said and done when they were mere children; described books and ornaments they had in their boudoirs at home: keepsakes that different relations had presented to them. They affirmed that she had even divined their thoughts, and had whispered in the ear of each the name of the person she liked best in the world, and informed them of what they most wished for.

Here the gentlemen interposed with earnest petitions to be further enlightened on these two last-named points; but they got only blushes, ejaculations, tremors, and titters, in return for their importunity. The matrons, meantime, offered vinaigrettes and wielded fans; and again and again reiterated the expression of their concern that their warning had not been taken in time; and the elder gentlemen laughed, and the younger urged their services on the agitated fair ones.

In the midst of the tumult, and while my eyes and ears were fully engaged in the scene before me, I heard a hem close at my elbow: I turned, and saw Sam.

"If you please, miss, the gipsy declares that there is another young single lady in the room who has not been to her yet, and she swears she will not go till she has seen all. I thought it must be you: there is no one else for it. What shall I tell her?"

"Oh, I will go by all means," I answered: and I was glad of the unexpected opportunity to gratify my much-excited curiosity. I slipped out of the room, unobserved by any eye—for the company were gathered in one mass about the trembling trio just returned—and I closed the door quietly behind me.

"If you like, miss," said Sam, "I'll wait in the hall for you; and if she frightens you, just call and I'll come in."

"No, Sam, return to the kitchen: I am not in the least afraid." Nor was I; but I was a good deal interested and excited.

CHAPTER XIX

The library looked tranquil enough as I entered it, and the Sibyl—if Sibyl she were—was seated snugly enough in an easy-chair at the chimney-corner. She had on a red cloak and a black bonnet: or rather, a broad-brimmed gipsy hat, tied down with a striped handkerchief under her chin. An extinguished candle stood on the table; she was bending over the fire, and seemed reading in a little black book, like a prayer-book, by the light of the blaze: she muttered the words to herself, as most old women do, while she read; she did not desist immediately on my entrance: it appeared she wished to finish a paragraph.

I stood on the rug and warmed my hands, which were rather cold with sitting at a distance from the drawing-room fire. I felt now as composed as ever I did in my life: there was nothing indeed in the gipsy's appearance to trouble one's calm. She shut her book and slowly looked up; her hat-brim partially shaded her face, yet I could see, as she raised it, that it was a strange one. It looked all brown and black: elf-locks bristled out from beneath a white band which passed under her chin, and came half over her cheeks, or rather jaws: her eye confronted me at once, with a bold and direct gaze.

"Well, and you want your fortune told?" she said, in a voice as decided as her glance, as harsh as her features.

"I don't care about it, mother; you may please yourself: but I ought to warn you, I have no faith."

"It's like your impudence to say so: I expected it of you; I heard it in your step as you crossed the threshold."

"Did you? You've a quick ear."

"I have; and a quick eye and a quick brain."

"You need them all in your trade."

"I do; especially when I've customers like you to deal with. Why don't you tremble?"

"I'm not cold."

"Why don't you turn pale?"

"I am not sick."

"Why don't you consult my art?"

"I'm not silly."

The old crone "nichered" a laugh under her bonnet and bandage; she then drew out a short black pipe, and lighting it began to smoke. Having indulged a while in this sedative, she raised her bent body, took the pipe from her lips, and while gazing steadily at the fire, said very deliberately, "You are cold; you are sick; and you are silly."

"Prove it," I rejoined.

"I will, in few words. You are cold, because you are alone: no contact strikes the fire from you that is in you. You are sick; because the best of feelings, the highest and the sweetest given to man, keeps far away from you. You are silly, because, suffer as you may, you will not beckon it to approach, nor will you stir one step to meet it where it waits you."

She again put her short black pipe to her lips, and renewed her smoking with vigour.

"You might say all that to almost any one who you knew lived as a solitary dependent in a great house."

"I might say it to almost any one: but would it be true of almost any one?"

"In my circumstances."

"Yes; just so, in *your* circumstances: but find me another precisely placed as you are."

"It would be easy to find you thousands."

"You could scarcely find me one. If you knew it, you are peculiarly situated: very near happiness; yes, within reach of it. The materials are all prepared; there only wants a movement to combine them. Chance laid them somewhat apart; let them be once approached and bliss results."

"I don't understand enigmas. I never could guess a riddle in my life."

"If you wish me to speak more plainly, show me your palm."

"And I must cross it with silver, I suppose?"

"To be sure."

I gave her a shilling: she put it into an old stocking-foot which she took out of her pocket, and having tied it round and returned it, she told me to hold out my hand. I did. She approached her face to the palm, and pored over it without touching it.

"It is too fine," said she. "I can make nothing of such a hand as that; almost without lines: besides, what is in a palm? Destiny is not written there."

"I believe you," said I.

"No," she continued, "it is in the face: on the forehead, about the eyes, in the lines of the mouth. Kneel, and lift up your head."

"Ah! Now you are coming to reality," I said, as I obeyed her. "I shall begin to put some faith in you presently."

I knelt within half a yard of her. She stirred the fire, so that a ripple of light broke from the disturbed coal: the glare, however, as she sat, only threw her face into deeper shadow: mine, it illumined.

"I wonder with what feelings you came to me tonight," she said, when she had examined me a while. "I wonder what thoughts are busy in your heart during all the hours you sit in yonder room with the fine people flitting before you like shapes in a magic-lantern: just as little sympathetic communion passing between you and them as if they were really mere shadows of human forms, and not the actual substance."

"I feel tired often, sleepy sometimes, but seldom sad."

"Then you have some secret hope to buoy you up and please you with whispers of the future?"

"Not I. The utmost I hope is, to save money enough out of my earnings to set up a school some day in a little house rented by myself."

"A mean nutriment for the spirit to exist on: and sitting in that window-seat (you see I know your habits)—"

"You have learned them from the servants."

"Ah! You think yourself sharp. Well, perhaps I have: to speak truth, I have an acquaintance with one of them, Mrs. Poole—"

I started to my feet when I heard the name.

"You have—have you?" thought I. "There is diablerie in the business after all, then!"

"Don't be alarmed," continued the strange being; "she's a safe hand is Mrs. Poole: close and quiet; any one may repose confidence in her. But, as I was saying: sitting in that window-seat, do you think of nothing but your future school? Have you no present interest in any of the company who occupy the sofas and chairs before you? Is there not one face you study? One figure whose movements you follow with at least curiosity?"

"I like to observe all the faces and all the figures."

"But do you never single one from the rest—or it may be, two?"

"I do frequently; when the gestures or looks of a pair seem telling a tale: it amuses me to watch them."

"What tale do you like best to hear?"

"Oh, I have not much choice! They generally run on the same theme—courtship; and promise to end in the same catastrophe—marriage."

"And do you like that monotonous theme?"

"Positively, I don't care about it: it is nothing to me."

"Nothing to you? When a lady, young and full of life and health, charming with beauty and endowed with the gifts of rank and fortune, sits and smiles in the eyes of a gentleman you—"

"I what?"

"You know—and perhaps think well of."

"I don't know the gentlemen here. I have scarcely interchanged a syllable with one of them; and as to thinking well of them, I consider some respectable, and stately, and middle-aged, and others young, dashing, handsome, and lively: but certainly they are all at liberty to be the recipients of whose smiles they please, without my feeling disposed to consider the transaction of any moment to me."

"You don't know the gentlemen here? You have not exchanged a syllable with one of them? Will you say that of the master of the house?"

"He is not at home."

"A profound remark! A most ingenious quibble! He went to Millcote this morning, and will be back here tonight or tomorrow: does that circumstance exclude him from the list of your acquaintance—blot him, as it were, out of existence?"

"No; but I can scarcely see what Mr. Rochester has to do with the theme you had introduced."

"I was talking of ladies smiling in the eyes of gentlemen; and of late so many smiles have been shed into Mr. Rochester's eyes that they overflow like two cups filled above the brim: have you never remarked that?"

"Mr. Rochester has a right to enjoy the society of his guests."

"No question about his right: but have you never observed that, of all the tales told here about matrimony, Mr. Rochester has been favoured with the most lively and the most continuous?"

"The eagerness of a listener quickens the tongue of a narrator." I said this rather to myself than to the gipsy, whose strange talk, voice, manner, had by this time wrapped me in a kind of dream. One unexpected sentence came from her lips after another, till I got involved in a web of mystification; and wondered what unseen spirit had been sitting for weeks by my heart watching its workings and taking record of every pulse.

"Eagerness of a listener!" repeated she. "Yes; Mr. Rochester has sat by the hour, his ear inclined to the fascinating lips that took such delight in their task of communicating; and Mr. Rochester was so willing to receive and looked so grateful for the pastime given him; you have noticed this?"

"Grateful! I cannot remember detecting gratitude in his face."

"Detecting! You have analysed, then. And what did you detect, if not gratitude?"

I said nothing.

"You have seen love: have you not? And, looking forward, you have seen him married, and beheld his bride happy?"

"Humph! Not exactly. Your witch's skill is rather at fault sometimes."

"What the devil have you seen, then?"

"Never mind: I came here to inquire, not to confess. Is it known that Mr. Rochester is to be married?"

"Yes; and to the beautiful Miss Ingram."

"Shortly?"

"Appearances would warrant that conclusion: and, no doubt (though, with an audacity that wants chastising out of you, you seem to question it), they will be a superlatively happy pair. He must love such a handsome, noble, witty, accomplished lady; and probably she loves him, or, if not his person, at least his purse. I know she considers the Rochester estate eligible to the last degree; though (God pardon me!) I told her something on that point about an hour ago which made her look wondrous grave: the corners of her mouth fell half an inch. I would advise her black-avised suitor to look out: if another comes, with a longer or clearer rent-roll—he's dished—"

"But, mother, I did not come to hear Mr. Rochester's fortune: I came to hear my own; and you have told me nothing of it."

"Your fortune is yet doubtful: when I examined your face, one trait contradicted another. Chance has meted you a measure of happiness: that I know. I knew it before I came here this evening. She has laid it carefully on one side for you. I saw her do it. It depends on yourself to stretch out your hand, and take it up: but whether you will do so, is the problem I study. Kneel again on the rug."

"Don't keep me long; the fire scorches me."

I knelt. She did not stoop towards me, but only gazed, leaning back in her chair. She began muttering—

"The flame flickers in the eye; the eye shines like dew; it looks soft and full of feeling; it smiles at my jargon: it is susceptible; impression follows impression through its clear sphere; where it ceases to smile, it is sad; an unconscious lassitude weighs on the lid: that signifies melancholy resulting from loneliness. It turns from me; it will not suffer further scrutiny; it seems to deny, by a mocking glance, the truth of the discoveries I have already made—to disown the charge both of sensibility and chagrin: its pride and reserve only confirm me in my opinion. The eye is favourable.

"As to the mouth, it delights at times in laughter; it is disposed to impart all that the brain conceives; though I daresay it would be silent on much the heart experiences. Mobile and flexible, it was never intended to be compressed in the eternal silence of solitude: it is a mouth which should speak much and smile often, and have human affection for its interlocutor. That feature too is propitious.

"I see no enemy to a fortunate issue but in the brow; and that brow professes to say, 'I can live alone, if self-respect, and circumstances require me so to do. I need not sell my soul to buy bliss. I have an inward treasure born with me, which can keep me alive if all extraneous delights should be withheld, or offered only at a price I cannot afford to give.' The forehead declares, 'Reason sits firm and holds the reins, and she will not let the feelings burst away and hurry her to wild chasms. The passions may rage furiously, like true heathens, as they are; and the desires may imagine all sorts of vain things: but judgment shall still have the last word in every argument, and the casting vote in every decision. Strong wind, earthquake-shock, and fire may pass by: but I shall follow the guiding of that still small voice which interprets the dictates of conscience.'

"Well said, forehead; your declaration shall be respected. I have formed my plans—right plans I deem them—and in them I have attended to the claims of conscience, the counsels of reason. I know how soon youth would fade and bloom perish, if, in the cup of bliss offered, but one dreg of shame, or one flavour of remorse were detected; and I do not want sacrifice, sorrow, dissolution—such is not my taste. I wish to foster, not to blight—to earn gratitude, not to wring tears of blood—no, nor of brine: my harvest must be in smiles, in endearments, in sweet—that will do. I think I rave in a kind of exquisite delirium. I should wish now to protract this moment *ad infinitum*; but I dare not. So far I have governed myself thoroughly. I have acted as I inwardly swore I would act; but further might try me beyond my strength. Rise, Miss Eyre: leave me; 'the play is played out.' "

Where was I? Did I wake or sleep? Had I been dreaming? Did I dream still? The old woman's voice had changed: her accent, her gesture, and all were familiar to me as my own face in a glass—as the speech of my own tongue. I got up, but did not go. I looked; I stirred the fire, and I looked again: but she drew her bonnet and her bandage closer about her face, and again beckoned me to depart. The flame illuminated her hand stretched out: roused now, and on the alert for discoveries, I at once noticed that hand. It was no more the withered limb of eld than my own; it was a rounded supple member, with smooth fingers, symmetrically turned; a broad ring flashed on the little finger, and stooping forward, I looked at it, and saw a gem I had seen a hundred times before. Again I looked at the face, which was no longer turned from me—on the contrary, the bonnet was doffed, the bandage displaced, the head advanced.

"Well, Jane, do you know me?" asked the familiar voice.

"Only take off the red cloak, sir, and then—"

"But the string is in a knot—help me."

"Break it, sir."

"There, then—'Off, ye lendings!' " And Mr. Rochester stepped out of his disguise.

"Now, sir, what a strange idea!"

"But well carried out, eh? Don't you think so?"

"With the ladies you must have managed well."

"But not with you?"

"You did not act the character of a gipsy with me."

"What character did I act? My own?"

"No; some unaccountable one. In short, I believe you have been trying to draw me out—or in; you have been talking nonsense to make me talk nonsense. It is scarcely fair, sir."

"Do you forgive me, Jane?"

"I cannot tell till I have thought it all over. If, on reflection, I find I have fallen into no great absurdity, I shall try to forgive you; but it was not right."

"Oh, you have been very correct—very careful, very sensible."

I reflected, and thought, on the whole, I had. It was a comfort; but, indeed, I had been on my guard almost from the beginning of the interview. Something of masquerade I suspected. I knew gipsies and fortune-tellers did not express themselves as this seeming old woman had expressed herself; besides I had noted her feigned voice, her anxiety to conceal her features. But my mind had been running on Grace Poole—that living enigma, that mystery of mysteries, as I considered her. I had never thought of Mr. Rochester.

"Well," said he, "what are you musing about? What does that grave smile signify?"

"Wonder and self-congratulation, sir. I have your permission to retire now, I suppose?"

"No; stay a moment; and tell me what the people in the drawing-room yonder are doing."

"Discussing the gipsy, I daresay."

"Sit down! Let me hear what they said about me."

"I had better not stay long, sir; it must be near eleven o'clock. Oh, are you aware, Mr. Rochester, that a stranger has arrived here since you left this morning?"

"A stranger! No; who can it be? I expected no one; is he gone?"

"No; he said he had known you long, and that he could take the liberty of installing himself here till you returned."

"The devil he did! Did he give his name?"

"His name is Mason, sir; and he comes from the West Indies; from Spanish Town, in Jamaica, I think."

Mr. Rochester was standing near me; he had taken my hand, as if to lead me to a chair. As I spoke he gave my wrist a convulsive grip; the smile on his lips froze: apparently a spasm caught his breath.

"Mason! The West Indies!" he said, in the tone one might fancy a speaking automaton to enounce its single words; "Mason! The West Indies!" he reiterated; and he went over the syllables three times, growing, in the intervals of speaking, whiter than ashes: he hardly seemed to know what he was doing.

"Do you feel ill, sir?" I inquired.

"Jane, I've got a blow; I've got a blow, Jane!" He staggered.

"Oh, lean on me, sir."

"Jane, you offered me your shoulder once before; let me have it now."

"Yes, sir, yes; and my arm."

He sat down, and made me sit beside him. Holding my hand in both his own, he chafed it; gazing on me, at the same time, with the most troubled and dreary look.

"My little friend!" said he. "I wish I were in a quiet island with only you; and trouble, and danger, and hideous recollections removed from me."

"Can I help you, sir? I'd give my life to serve you."

"Jane, if aid is wanted, I'll seek it at your hands; I promise you that."

"Thank you, sir. Tell me what to do—I'll try, at least, to do it."

"Fetch me now, Jane, a glass of wine from the dining-room: they will be at supper there; and tell me if Mason is with them, and what he is doing."

I went. I found all the party in the dining-room at supper, as Mr. Rochester had said; they were not seated at table—the supper was arranged on the sideboard; each had taken what he chose, and they stood about here and there in groups, their plates and glasses in their hands. Every one seemed in high glee; laughter and conversation were general and animated. Mr. Mason stood near the fire, talking to Colonel and Mrs. Dent, and appeared as merry as any of them. I filled a wine-glass (I saw Miss Ingram watch me frowningly as I did so: she thought I was taking a liberty, I daresay), and I returned to the library.

Mr. Rochester's extreme pallor had disappeared, and he looked once more firm and stern. He took the glass from my hand.

"Here is to your health, ministrant spirit!" he said. He swallowed the contents and returned it to me. "What are they doing, Jane?"

"Laughing and talking, sir."

"They don't look grave and mysterious, as if they had heard something strange?"

"Not at all: they are full of jests and gaiety."

"And Mason?"

"He was laughing too."

"If all these people came in a body and spat at me, what would you do, Jane?"

"Turn them out of the room, sir, if I could."

He half smiled. "But if I were to go to them, and they only looked at me coldly, and whispered sneeringly amongst each other, and then dropped off and left me one by one, what then? Would you go with them?"

"I rather think not, sir: I should have more pleasure in staying with you."

"To comfort me?"

"Yes, sir, to comfort you, as well as I could."

"And if they laid you under a ban for adhering to me?"

"I, probably, should know nothing about their ban; and if I did, I should care nothing about it."

"Then, you could dare censure for my sake?"

"I could dare it for the sake of any friend who deserved my adherence; as you, I am sure, do."

"Go back now into the room; step quietly up to Mason, and whisper in his ear that Mr. Rochester is come and wishes to see him: show him in here and then leave me."

"Yes, sir."

I did his behest. The company all stared at me as I passed straight among them. I sought Mr. Mason, delivered the message, and preceded him from the room: I ushered him into the library, and then I went upstairs.

At a late hour, after I had been in bed some time, I heard the visitors repair to their chambers: I distinguished Mr. Rochester's voice, and heard him say, "This way, Mason; this is your room."

He spoke cheerfully: the gay tones set my heart at ease. I was soon asleep.

CHAPTER XX

I had forgotten to draw my curtain, which I usually did, and also to let down my window-blind. The consequence was, that when the moon, which was full and bright (for the night was fine), came in her course to that space in the sky opposite my casement, and looked in at me through the unveiled panes, her glorious gaze roused me. Awaking in the dead of night, I opened my eyes on her disk—silver-white and crystal clear. It was beautiful, but too solemn; I half rose, and stretched my arm to draw the curtain.

Good God! What a cry!

The night—its silence—its rest, was rent in twain by a savage, a sharp, a shrilly sound that ran from end to end of Thornfield Hall.

My pulse stopped: my heart stood still; my stretched arm was paralysed. The cry died, and was not renewed. Indeed, whatever being uttered that fearful shriek could not soon repeat it: not the widest-winged condor on the Andes could, twice in succession, send out such a yell from the cloud shrouding his eyrie. The thing delivering such utterance must rest ere it could repeat the effort.

It came out of the third storey; for it passed overhead. And overhead—yes, in the room just above my chamber-ceiling—I now heard a struggle: a deadly one it seemed from the noise; and a half-smothered voice shouted—

"Help! Help! Help!" three times rapidly.

"Will no one come?" it cried; and then, while the staggering and stamping went on wildly, I distinguished through plank and plaster—

"Rochester! Rochester! For God's sake, come!"

A chamber-door opened: some one ran, or rushed, along the gallery. Another step stamped on the flooring above and something fell; and there was silence.

I had put on some clothes, though horror shook all my limbs; I issued from my apartment. The sleepers were all aroused: ejaculations, terrified murmurs sounded in every room; door after door unclosed; one looked out and another looked out; the gallery filled. Gentlemen and ladies alike had quitted their beds; and "Oh! What is it?"—

"Who is hurt?"—"What has happened?"—"Fetch a light!"—"Is it fire?"—"Are there robbers?"—"Where shall we run?" was demanded confusedly on all hands. But for the moonlight they would have been in complete darkness. They ran to and fro; they crowded together: some sobbed, some stumbled: the confusion was inextricable.

"Where the devil is Rochester?" cried Colonel Dent. "I cannot find him in his bed."

"Here! Here!" was shouted in return. "Be composed, all of you: I'm coming."

And the door at the end of the gallery opened, and Mr. Rochester advanced with a candle: he had just descended from the upper storey. One of the ladies ran to him directly; she seized his arm: it was Miss Ingram.

"What awful event has taken place?" said she. "Speak! Let us know the worst at once!"

"But don't pull me down or strangle me," he replied: for the Misses Eshton were clinging about him now; and the two dowagers, in vast white wrappers, were bearing down on him like ships in full sail.

"All's right! All's right!" he cried. "It's a mere rehearsal of *Much Ado About Nothing*. Ladies, keep off, or I shall wax dangerous."

And dangerous he looked: his black eyes darted sparks. Calming himself by an effort, he added—

"A servant has had the nightmare; that is all. She's an excitable, nervous person: she construed her dream into an apparition, or something of that sort, no doubt; and has taken a fit with fright. Now, then, I must see you all back into your rooms; for, till the house is settled, she cannot be looked after. Gentlemen, have the goodness to set the ladies the example. Miss Ingram, I am sure you will not fail in evincing superiority to idle terrors. Amy and Louisa, return to your nests like a pair of doves, as you are. Mesdames" (to the dowagers), "you will take cold to a dead certainty, if you stay in this chill gallery any longer."

And so, by dint of alternate coaxing and commanding, he contrived to get them all once more enclosed in their separate dormitories. I did not wait to be ordered back to mine, but retreated unnoticed, as unnoticed I had left it.

Not, however, to go to bed: on the contrary, I began and dressed myself carefully. The sounds I had heard after the scream, and the words that had been uttered, had probably been heard only by me; for they had proceeded from the room above mine: but they assured me that it was not a servant's dream which had thus struck horror through the house; and that the explanation Mr. Rochester had given was merely an invention framed to pacify his guests. I dressed, then, to be ready for emergencies. When dressed, I sat a long time by the window looking out over the silent grounds and silvered fields and waiting for I knew not what. It seemed to me that some event must follow the strange cry, struggle, and call.

No: stillness returned: each murmur and movement ceased gradually, and in about an hour Thornfield Hall was again as hushed as a desert. It seemed that sleep and night had resumed their empire. Meantime the moon declined: she was about to set. Not liking to sit in the cold and darkness, I thought I would lie down on my bed, dressed as I was. I left the window, and moved with little noise across the carpet; as I stooped to take off my shoes, a cautious hand tapped low at the door.

"Am I wanted?" I asked.

"Are you up?" asked the voice I expected to hear, viz., my master's.

"Yes, sir."

"And dressed?"

"Yes."

"Come out, then, quietly."

I obeyed. Mr. Rochester stood in the gallery holding a light.

"I want you," he said. "Come this way: take your time, and make no noise."

My slippers were thin: I could walk the matted floor as softly as a cat. He glided up the gallery and up the stairs, and stopped in the dark, low corridor of the fateful third storey: I had followed and stood at his side.

"Have you a sponge in your room?" he asked in a whisper.

"Yes, sir."

"Have you any salts—volatile salts?"

"Yes."

"Go back and fetch both."

I returned, sought the sponge on the washstand, the salts in my drawer, and once more retraced my steps. He still waited; he held a key in his hand: approaching one of the small, black doors, he put it in the lock; he paused, and addressed me again.

"You don't turn sick at the sight of blood?"

"I think I shall not: I have never been tried yet."

I felt a thrill while I answered him; but no coldness, and no faintness.

"Just give me your hand," he said; "it will not do to risk a fainting fit."

I put my fingers into his. "Warm and steady," was his remark: he turned the key and opened the door.

I saw a room I remembered to have seen before, the day Mrs. Fairfax showed me over the house: it was hung with tapestry; but the tapestry was now looped up in one part, and there was a door apparent, which had then been concealed. This door was open; a light shone out of the room within: I heard thence a snarling, snatching sound, almost like a dog quarrelling. Mr. Rochester, putting down his candle, said to me, "Wait a minute," and he went forward to the inner apartment. A shout of laughter greeted his entrance; noisy at first, and terminating in Grace Poole's own goblin ha! ha! *She* then was there. He made some sort of arrangement without speaking, though I heard a low voice address him: he came out and closed the door behind him.

"Here, Jane!" he said; and I walked round to the other side of a large bed, which with its drawn curtains concealed a considerable portion of the chamber. An easy-chair was near the bed-head: a man sat in it, dressed with the exception of his coat; he was still; his head leant back; his eyes were closed. Mr. Rochester held the candle over him; I recognised in his pale and seemingly lifeless face—the stranger, Mason: I saw too that his linen on one side, and one arm, was almost soaked in blood.

"Hold the candle," said Mr. Rochester, and I took it: he fetched a basin of water from the washstand: "Hold that," said he. I obeyed. He took the sponge, dipped it in, and moistened the corpse-like face; he asked for my smelling-bottle, and applied it to the nostrils. Mr. Mason shortly unclosed his eyes; he groaned. Mr. Rochester opened the shirt of the wounded man, whose arm and shoulder were bandaged: he sponged away blood, trickling fast down.

"Is there immediate danger?" murmured Mr. Mason.

"Pooh! No—a mere scratch. Don't be so overcome, man: bear up! I'll fetch a surgeon for you now, myself: you'll be able to be removed by morning, I hope. Jane," he continued.

"Sir?"

"I shall have to leave you in this room with this gentleman, for an hour, or perhaps two hours: you will sponge the blood as I do when it returns: if he feels faint, you will put the glass of water on that stand to his lips, and your salts to his nose. You will not speak to him on any pretext—and—Richard, it will be at the peril of your life if you speak to her: open your lips—agitate yourself—and I'll not answer for the consequences."

Again the poor man groaned; he looked as if he dared not move; fear, either of death or of something else, appeared almost to paralyse him. Mr. Rochester put the now bloody sponge into my hand, and I proceeded to use it as he had done. He watched me a second, then saying, "Remember! No conversation," he left the room. I experienced a strange feeling as the key grated in the lock, and the sound of his retreating step ceased to be heard.

Here then I was in the third storey, fastened into one of its mystic cells; night around me; a pale and bloody spectacle under my eyes and hands; a murderess hardly separated from me by a single door: yes—that was appalling—the rest I could bear; but I shuddered at the thought of Grace Poole bursting out upon me.

I must keep to my post, however. I must watch this ghastly countenance—these blue, still lips forbidden to unclose—these eyes now shut, now opening, now wandering through the room, now fixing on me, and ever glazed with the dulness of horror. I must dip my hand again and again in the basin of blood and water, and wipe away the trickling gore. I must see the light of the unsnuffed candle wane on my employment; the shadows darken on the wrought, antique tapestry round me, and grow black under the hangings of the vast old bed, and quiver strangely over the doors of a great cabinet opposite—whose front, divided into twelve panels, bore, in grim design, the heads of the twelve apostles, each enclosed in its separate panel as in a frame; while above them at the top rose an ebon crucifix and a dying Christ.

According as the shifting obscurity and flickering gleam hovered here or glanced there, it was now the bearded physician, Luke, that bent his brow; now St. John's long hair that waved; and anon the devilish face of Judas, that grew out of the panel, and seemed gathering life and threatening a revelation of the arch-traitor—of Satan himself—in his subordinate's form.

Amidst all this, I had to listen as well as watch: to listen for the movements of the wild beast or the fiend in yonder side den. But since Mr. Rochester's visit it seemed spellbound: all the night I heard but three sounds at three long intervals—a step creak, a momentary renewal of the snarling, canine noise, and a deep human groan.

Then my own thoughts worried me. What crime was this that lived incarnate in this sequestered mansion, and could neither be expelled nor subdued by the owner? What mystery, that broke out now in fire and now in blood, at the deadest hours of night? What creature was it, that, masked in an ordinary woman's face and shape, uttered the voice, now of a mocking demon, and anon of a carrion-seeking bird of prey?

And this man I bent over—this commonplace, quiet stranger—how had he become involved in the web of horror? And why had the Fury flown at him? What made him seek this quarter of the house at an untimely season, when he should have been asleep in bed? I had heard Mr. Rochester assign him an apartment below—what brought him here? And why, now, was he so tame under the violence or treachery done him? Why did he so quietly submit to the concealment Mr. Rochester enforced? Why *did* Mr. Rochester enforce this concealment? His guest had been outraged, his own life on a former occasion had been hideously plotted against; and both attempts he smothered in secrecy and sank in oblivion! Lastly, I saw Mr. Mason was submissive to Mr. Rochester; that the impetuous will of the latter held complete sway over the inertness of the former: the few words which had passed between them assured me of this. It was evident that in their former intercourse, the passive disposition of the one had been habitually influenced by the active energy of the other: whence then had arisen Mr. Rochester's dismay when he heard of Mr. Mason's arrival? Why had the mere name of this unresisting individual—whom his word now sufficed to control like a child—fallen on him, a few hours since, as a thunderbolt might fall on an oak?

Oh! I could not forget his look and his paleness when he whispered: "Jane, I have got a blow—I have got a blow, Jane." I could not forget how the arm had trembled which he rested on my shoulder: and it was no light matter which could thus bow the resolute spirit and thrill the vigorous frame of Fairfax Rochester.

"When will he come? When will he come?" I cried inwardly, as the night lingered and lingered—as my bleeding patient drooped, moaned, sickened: and neither day nor aid arrived. I had, again and again, held the water to Mason's white lips; again and again offered him the stimulating salts: my efforts seemed ineffectual: either bodily or mental suffering, or loss of blood, or all three combined, were fast prostrating his strength. He moaned so, and looked so weak, wild, and lost, I feared he was dying; and I might not even speak to him.

The candle, wasted at last, went out; as it expired, I perceived streaks of grey light edging the window curtains: dawn was then approaching. Presently I heard Pilot bark far below, out of his distant kennel in the courtyard: hope revived. Nor was it unwarranted: in five minutes more the grating key, the yielding lock, warned me my watch was relieved. It could not have lasted more than two hours: many a week has seemed shorter.

Mr. Rochester entered, and with him the surgeon he had been to fetch.

"Now, Carter, be on the alert," he said to this last: "I give you but half-an-hour for dressing the wound, fastening the bandages, getting the patient downstairs and all."

"But is he fit to move, sir?"

"No doubt of it; it is nothing serious; he is nervous, his spirits must be kept up. Come, set to work."

Mr. Rochester drew back the thick curtain, drew up the holland blind, let in all the daylight he could; and I was surprised and cheered to see how far dawn was advanced: what rosy streaks were beginning to brighten the east. Then he approached Mason, whom the surgeon was already handling.

"Now, my good fellow, how are you?" he asked.

"She's done for me, I fear," was the faint reply.

"Not a whit! Courage! This day fortnight you'll hardly be a pin the worse of it: you've lost a little blood; that's all. Carter, assure him there's no danger."

"I can do that conscientiously," said Carter, who had now undone the bandages; "only I wish I could have got here sooner: he would not have bled so much—but how is this? The flesh on the shoulder is torn as well as cut. This wound was not done with a knife: there have been teeth here!"

"She bit me," he murmured. "She worried me like a tigress, when Rochester got the knife from her."

"You should not have yielded: you should have grappled with her at once," said Mr. Rochester.

"But under such circumstances, what could one do?" returned Mason. "Oh, it was frightful!" he added, shuddering. "And I did not expect it: she looked so quiet at first."

"I warned you," was his friend's answer; "I said—be on your guard when you go near her. Besides, you might have waited till tomorrow, and had me with you: it was mere folly to attempt the interview tonight, and alone."

"I thought I could have done some good."

"You thought! You thought! Yes, it makes me impatient to hear you: but, however, you have suffered, and are likely to suffer enough for not taking my advice; so I'll say no more. Carter—hurry! Hurry! The sun will soon rise, and I must have him off."

"Directly, sir; the shoulder is just bandaged. I must look to this other wound in the arm: she has had her teeth here too, I think."

"She sucked the blood: she said she'd drain my heart," said Mason.

I saw Mr. Rochester shudder: a singularly marked expression of disgust, horror, hatred, warped his countenance almost to distortion; but he only said—

"Come, be silent, Richard, and never mind her gibberish: don't repeat it."

"I wish I could forget it," was the answer.

"You will when you are out of the country: when you get back to Spanish Town, you may think of her as dead and buried—or rather, you need not think of her at all."

"Impossible to forget this night!"

"It is not impossible: have some energy, man. You thought you were as dead as a herring two hours since, and you are all alive and talking now. There! Carter has done with you or nearly so; I'll make you decent in a trice. Jane" (he turned to me for the first time since his re-entrance), "take this key: go down into my bedroom, and walk straight forward into my dressing-room: open the top drawer of the wardrobe and take out a clean shirt and neck-handkerchief: bring them here; and be nimble."

I went; sought the repository he had mentioned, found the articles named, and returned with them.

"Now," said he, "go to the other side of the bed while I order his toilet; but don't leave the room: you may be wanted again."

I retired as directed.

"Was anybody stirring below when you went down, Jane?" inquired Mr. Rochester presently.

"No, sir; all was very still."

"We shall get you off cannily, Dick: and it will be better, both for your sake, and for that of the poor creature in yonder. I have striven long to avoid exposure, and I should not like it to come at last. Here, Carter, help him on with his waist-coat. Where did you leave your furred cloak? You can't travel a mile without that, I know, in this damned cold climate. In your room? Jane, run down to Mr. Mason's room—the one next mine—and fetch a cloak you will see there."

Again I ran, and again returned, bearing an immense mantle lined and edged with fur.

"Now, I've another errand for you," said my untiring master. "You must away to my room again. What a mercy you are shod with velvet, Jane! A clod-hopping messenger would never do at this juncture. You must open the middle drawer of my toilet-table and take out a little phial and a little glass you will find there—quick!"

I flew thither and back, bringing the desired vessels.

"That's well! Now, doctor, I shall take the liberty of administering a dose myself, on my own responsibility. I got this cordial at Rome, of an Italian charlatan—a fellow you would have kicked, Carter. It is not a thing to be used indiscriminately, but it is good upon occasion: as now, for instance. Jane, a little water."

He held out the tiny glass, and I half filled it from the water-bottle on the washstand.

"That will do—now wet the lip of the phial."

I did so; he measured twelve drops of a crimson liquid, and presented it to Mason.

"Drink, Richard: it will give you the heart you lack, for an hour or so."

"But will it hurt me? Is it inflammatory?"

"Drink! Drink! Drink!"

Mr. Mason obeyed, because it was evidently useless to resist. He was dressed now: he still looked pale, but he was no longer gory and sullied. Mr. Rochester let him sit three minutes after he had swallowed the liquid; he then took his arm—

"Now I am sure you can get on your feet," he said. "Try."

The patient rose.

"Carter, take him under the other shoulder. Be of good cheer, Richard; step out—that's it!"

"I do feel better," remarked Mr. Mason.

"I am sure you do. Now, Jane, trip on before us away to the backstairs; unbolt the side-passage door, and tell the driver of the post-chaise you will see in the yard—or just outside, for I told him not to drive his rattling wheels over the pavement—to be ready; we are coming: and, Jane, if any one is about, come to the foot of the stairs and hem."

It was by this time half-past five, and the sun was on the point of rising; but I found the kitchen still dark and silent. The side-passage door was fastened; I opened it with as little noise as possible: all the yard was quiet; but the gates stood wide open, and there was a post-chaise, with horses ready harnessed, and driver seated on the box, stationed outside. I approached him, and said the gentlemen were coming; he nodded: then I looked carefully round and listened. The stillness of early morning slumbered everywhere; the curtains were yet drawn over the servants' chamber windows; little birds were just twittering in the blossom-blanched orchard trees, whose boughs drooped like white garlands over the wall enclosing one side of the yard; the carriage horses stamped from time to time in their closed stables: all else was still.

The gentlemen now appeared. Mason, supported by Mr. Rochester and the surgeon, seemed to walk with tolerable ease: they assisted him into the chaise; Carter followed.

"Take care of him," said Mr. Rochester to the latter, "and keep him at your house till he is quite well: I shall ride over in a day or two to see how he gets on. Richard, how is it with you?"

"The fresh air revives me, Fairfax."

"Leave the window open on his side, Carter; there is no wind—good-bye, Dick."

"Fairfax—"

"Well, what is it?"

"Let her be taken care of; let her be treated as tenderly as may be: let her—" he stopped and burst into tears.

"I do my best; and have done it, and will do it," was the answer: he shut up the chaise door, and the vehicle drove away.

"Yet would to God there was an end of all this!" added Mr. Rochester, as he closed and barred the heavy yard-gates. This done, he moved with slow step and abstracted air towards a door in the wall bordering the orchard. I, supposing he had done with me, prepared to return to the house; again, however, I heard him call "Jane!" He had opened the portal and stood at it, waiting for me.

"Come where there is some freshness, for a few moments," he said; "that house is a mere dungeon: don't you feel it so?"

"It seems to me a splendid mansion, sir."

"The glamour of inexperience is over your eyes," he answered; "and you see it through a charmed medium: you cannot discern that the gilding is slime and the silk draperies cobwebs; that the marble is sordid slate, and the polished woods mere refuse chips and scaly bark. Now *here*" (he pointed to the leafy enclosure we had entered) "all is real, sweet, and pure."

He strayed down a walk edged with box, with apple trees, pear trees, and cherry trees on one side, and a border on the other full of all sorts of old-fashioned flowers, stocks, sweet-williams, primroses, pansies, mingled with southernwood, sweet-briar, and various fragrant herbs. They were fresh now as a succession of April showers and gleams, followed by a lovely spring morning, could make them: the sun was just entering the dappled east, and his light illumined the wreathed and dewy orchard trees and shone down the quiet walks under them.

"Jane, will you have a flower?"

He gathered a half-blown rose, the first on the bush, and offered it to me.

"Thank you, sir."

"Do you like this sunrise, Jane? That sky with its high and light clouds which are sure to melt away as the day waxes warm—this placid and balmly atmosphere?"

"I do, very much."

"You have passed a strange night, Jane."

"Yes, sir."

"And it has made you look pale—were you afraid when I left you alone with Mason?"

"I was afraid of some one coming out of the inner room."

"But I had fastened the door—I had the key in my pocket: I should have been a careless shepherd if I had left a lamb—my pet lamb—so near a wolf's den, unguarded: you were safe."

"Will Grace Poole live here still, sir?"

"Oh yes! Don't trouble your head about her—put the thing out of your thoughts."

"Yet it seems to me your life is hardly secure while she stays."

"Never fear—I will take care of myself."

"Is the danger you apprehended last night gone by now, sir?"

"I cannot vouch for that till Mason is out of England: nor even then. To live, for me, Jane, is to stand on a crater-crust which may crack and spue fire any day."

"But Mr. Mason seems a man easily led. Your influence, sir, is evidently potent with him: he will never set you at defiance or wilfully injure you."

"Oh, no! Mason will not defy me; nor, knowing it, will he hurt me—but, unintentionally, he might in a moment, by one careless word, deprive me, if not of life, yet for ever of happiness."

"Tell him to be cautious, sir: let him know what you fear, and show him how to avert the danger."

He laughed sardonically, hastily took my hand, and as hastily threw it from him.

"If I could do that, simpleton, where would the danger be? Annihilated in a moment. Ever since I have known Mason, I have only had to say to him, 'Do that,' and the thing has been done. But I cannot give him orders in this case: I cannot say, 'Beware of harming me, Richard'; for it is imperative that I should keep him ignorant that harm to me is possible. Now you look puzzled; and I will puzzle you further. You are my little friend, are you not?"

"I like to serve you, sir, and to obey you in all that is right."

"Precisely: I see you do. I see genuine contentment in your gait and mien, your eye and face, when you are helping me and pleasing me—working for me, and with me, in, as you characteristically say, '*all that is right*': for if I bid you do what you thought wrong, there would be no light-footed running, no neat-handed alacrity, no lively glance and animated complexion. My friend would then turn to me, quiet and pale, and would say, 'No, sir; that is impossible: I cannot do it, because it is wrong,' and would become immutable as a fixed star. Well, you too have power over me, and may injure me: yet I dare not show you where I am vulnerable, lest, faithful and friendly as you are, you should transfix me at once."

"If you have no more to fear from Mr. Mason than you have from me, sir, you are very safe."

"God grant it may be so! Here, Jane, is an arbour; sit down."

The arbour was an arch in the wall, lined with ivy; it contained a rustic seat. Mr. Rochester took it, leaving room, however, for me: but I stood before him.

"Sit," he said; "the bench is long enough for two. You don't hesitate to take a place at my side, do you? Is that wrong, Jane?"

I answered him by assuming it: to refuse would, I felt, have been unwise.

"Now, my little friend, while the sun drinks the dew—while all the flowers in this old garden awake and expand, and the birds fetch their young ones' breakfast out of the Thornfield, and the early bees do their first spell of work—I'll put a case to you, which you must endeavour to suppose your own: but first, look at me, and tell me you are at ease, and not fearing that I err in detaining you, or that you err in staying."

"No, sir; I am content."

"Well then, Jane, call to aid your fancy: suppose you were no longer a girl well reared and disciplined, but a wild boy indulged from childhood upwards; imagine yourself in a remote foreign land; conceive that you there commit a capital error, no matter of what nature or from what motives, but one whose consequences must follow you through life and taint all your existence. Mind, I don't say a *crime*; I am not speaking of shedding of blood or any other guilty act, which might make the perpetrator amenable to the law: my word is *error*. The results of what you have done become in time to you utterly insupportable; you take measures to obtain relief: unusual measures, but neither unlawful nor culpable. Still you are miserable; for hope has quitted you on the very confines of life: your sun at noon darkens in an eclipse, which you feel will not leave it till the time of setting. Bitter and base associations have become the sole food of your memory: you wander here and there, seeking rest in exile: happiness in pleasure—I mean in heartless, sensual pleasure—such as dulls intellect and blights feeling. Heart-weary and soul-withered, you come home after years of voluntary banishment: you make a new acquaintance—how or where no matter: you find in this stranger much of the good and bright qualities which you have sought for twenty years, and never before encountered; and they are all fresh, healthy, without soil and without taint. Such society revives, regenerates: you feel better days come back—higher wishes, purer feelings; you desire to recommence your life, and to spend what remains to you of days in a way more worthy of an immortal being. To attain this end, are you justified in overleaping an obstacle of custom—a mere conventional impediment which neither your conscience sanctifies nor your judgment approves?"

He paused for an answer: and what was I to say? Oh, for some good spirit to suggest a judicious and satisfactory response! Vain aspiration! The west wind whispered in the ivy round me; but no gentle Ariel borrowed its breath as a medium of speech: the birds sang in the tree-tops; but their song, however sweet, was inarticulate.

Again Mr. Rochester propounded his query:

"Is the wandering and sinful, but now rest-seeking and repentant, man justified in daring the world's opinion, in order to attach to him for ever this gentle, gracious, genial stranger, thereby securing his own peace of mind and regeneration of life?"

"Sir," I answered, "a wanderer's repose or a sinner's reformation should never depend on a fellow-creature. Men and women die; philosophers falter in wisdom, and Christians in goodness: if any one you know has suffered and erred, let him look higher than his equals for strength to amend and solace to heal."

"But the instrument—the instrument! God, who does the work, ordains the instrument. I have myself—I tell it you without parable—been a worldly, dissipated, restless man; and I believe I have found the instrument for my cure in—"

He paused: the birds went on carolling, the leaves lightly rustling. I almost wondered they did not check their songs and whispers to catch the suspended revelation; but they would have had to wait many minutes—so long was the silence protracted. At last I looked up at the tardy speaker: he was looking eagerly at me.

"Little friend," said he, in quite a changed tone—while his face changed too, losing all its softness and gravity, and becoming harsh and sarcastic—"you have noticed my tender penchant for Miss Ingram: don't you think if I married her she would regenerate me with a vengeance?"

He got up instantly, went quite to the other end of the walk, and when he came back he was humming a tune.

"Jane, Jane," said he, stopping before me, "you are quite pale with your vigils: don't you curse me for disturbing your rest?"

"Curse you? No, sir."

"Shake hands in confirmation of the word. What cold fingers! They were warmer last night when I touched them at the door of the mysterious chamber. Jane, when will you watch with me again?"

"Whenever I can be useful, sir."

"For instance, the night before I am married! I am sure I shall not be able to sleep. Will you promise to sit up with me to bear me company? To you I can talk of my lovely one: for now you have seen her and know her."

"Yes, sir."

"She's a rare one, is she not, Jane?"

"Yes, sir."

"A strapper—a real strapper, Jane: big, brown, and buxom; with hair just such as the ladies of Carthage must have had. Bless me! There's Dent and Lynn in the stables! Go in by the shrubbery, through that wicket."

As I went one way, he went another, and I heard him in the yard, saying cheerfully—

"Mason got the start of you all this morning; he was gone before sunrise: I rose at four to see him off."

CHAPTER XXI

Presentiments are strange things! And so are sympathies; and so are signs; and the three combined make one mystery to which humanity has not yet found the key. I never laughed at presentiments in my life, because I have had strange ones of my own. Sympathies, I believe, exist (for instance, between far-distant, long-absent, wholly estranged relatives asserting, notwithstanding their alienation, the unity of the source to which each traces his origin) whose workings baffle mortal comprehension. And signs, for aught we know, may be but the sympathies of Nature with man.

When I was a little girl, only six years old, I one night heard Bessie Leaven say to Martha Abbot that she had been dreaming about a little child; and that to dream of children was a sure sign of trouble, either to one's self or one's kin. The saying might have worn out of my memory, had not a circumstance immediately followed which served indelibly to fix it there. The next day Bessie was sent for home to the deathbed of her little sister.

Of late I had often recalled this saying and this incident; for during the past week scarcely a night had gone over my couch that had not brought with it a dream of an infant, which I sometimes hushed in my arms, sometimes dandled on my knee, sometimes watched playing with daisies on a lawn, or again, dabbling its hands in running water. It was a wailing child this night, and a laughing one the next: now it nestled close to me, and now it ran from me; but whatever mood the apparition evinced, whatever aspect it wore, it failed not for seven successive nights to meet me the moment I entered the land of slumber.

I did not like this iteration of one idea—this strange recurrence of one image, and I grew nervous as bedtime approached and the hour of the vision drew near. It was from companionship with this baby-phantom I had been roused on that moonlight night when I heard the cry; and it was on the afternoon of the day following I was summoned downstairs by a message that some one wanted me in Mrs. Fairfax's room. On repairing thither, I found a man waiting for me, having the appearance of a gentleman's servant: he was dressed in deep mourning, and the hat he held in his hand was surrounded with a crape band.

"I daresay you hardly remember me, Miss," he said, rising as I entered; "but my name is Leaven: I lived coachman with Mrs. Reed when you were at Gateshead, eight or nine years since, and I live there still."

"Oh, Robert! How do you do? I remember you very well: you used to give me a ride sometimes on Miss Georgiana's bay pony. And how is Bessie? You are married to Bessie?"

"Yes, Miss: my wife is very hearty, thank you; she brought me another little one about two months since—we have three now—and both mother and child are thriving."

"And are the family well at the house, Robert?"

"I am sorry I can't give you better news of them, Miss: they are very badly at present—in great trouble."

"I hope no one is dead," I said, glancing at his black dress. He too looked down at the crape round his hat and replied—

"Mr. John died yesterday was a week, at his chambers in London."

"Mr. John?"

"Yes."

"And how does his mother bear it?"

"Why, you see, Miss Eyre, it is not a common mishap: his life has been very wild: these last three years he gave himself up to strange ways, and his death was shocking."

"I heard from Bessie he was not doing well."

"Doing well! He could not do worse: he ruined his health and his estate amongst the worst men and the worst women. He got into debt and into jail: his mother helped him out twice, but as soon as he was free he returned to his old companions and habits. His head was not strong: the knaves he lived amongst fooled him beyond anything I ever heard. He came down to Gateshead about three weeks ago and wanted missis to give up all to him. Missis refused: her means have long been much reduced by his extravagance; so he went back again, and the next news was that he was dead. How he died, God knows! They say he killed himself."

I was silent: the things were frightful. Robert Leaven resumed—

"Missis had been out of health herself for some time: she had got very stout, but was not strong with it; and the loss of money and fear of poverty were quite breaking her down. The information about Mr. John's death and the manner of it came too suddenly: it brought on a stroke. She was three days without speaking; but last Tuesday she seemed rather better: she appeared as if she wanted to say something, and kept making signs to my wife and mumbling. It was only yesterday morning, however, that Bessie understood she was pronouncing your name; and at last she made out the words, 'Bring Jane—fetch Jane Eyre: I want to speak to her.' Bessie is not sure whether she is in her right mind, or means anything by the words; but she told Miss Reed and Miss Georgiana, and advised them to send for you. The young ladies put it off at first; but their mother grew so restless, and said, 'Jane, Jane,' so many times, that at last they consented. I left Gateshead yesterday: and if you can get ready, Miss, I should like to take you back with me early tomorrow morning."

"Yes, Robert, I shall be ready: it seems to me that I ought to go."

"I think so too, Miss. Bessie said she was sure you would not refuse: but I suppose you will have to ask leave before you can get off?"

"Yes; and I will do it now"; and having directed him to the servants' hall, and recommended him to the care of John's wife, and the attentions of John himself, I went in search of Mr. Rochester.

He was not in any of the lower rooms; he was not in the yard, the stables, or the grounds. I asked Mrs. Fairfax if she had seen him—yes: she believed he was playing billiards with Miss Ingram. To the billiard-room I hastened: the click of balls and the hum of voices resounded thence; Mr. Rochester, Miss Ingram, the two Misses Eshton, and their admirers, were all busied in the game. It required some courage to disturb so interesting a party; my errand, however, was one I could not defer, so I approached the master where he stood at Miss Ingram's side. She turned as I drew near, and looked at me haughtily: her eyes seemed to demand, "What can the creeping creature want now?" and when I said, in a low voice, "Mr. Rochester," she made a movement as if tempted to order me away. I remember her appearance at the moment—it was very graceful and very striking: she wore a morning robe of sky-blue crape; a gauzy azure scarf was twisted in her hair. She had been all animation with the game, and irritated pride did not lower the expression of her haughty lineaments.

"Does that person want you?" she inquired of Mr. Rochester; and Mr. Rochester turned to see who the "person" was. He made a curious grimace—one of his strange and equivocal demonstrations—threw down his cue and followed me from the room.

"Well, Jane?" he said, as he rested his back against the schoolroom door, which he had shut.

"If you please, sir, I want leave of absence for a week or two."

"What to do? Where to go?"

"To see a sick lady who has sent for me."

"What sick lady? Where does she live?"

"At Gateshead; in ——shire."

"——shire? That is a hundred miles off! Who may she be that sends for people to see her that distance?"

"Her name is Reed, sir—Mrs. Reed."

"Reed of Gateshead? There was a Reed of Gateshead, a magistrate."

"It is his widow, sir."

"And what have you to do with her? How do you know her?"

"Mr. Reed was my uncle—my mother's brother."

"The deuce he was! You never told me that before: you always said you had no relations."

"None that would own me, sir. Mr. Reed is dead, and his wife cast me off."

"Why?"

"Because I was poor, and burdensome, and she disliked me."

"But Reed left children? You must have cousins? Sir George Lynn was talking of a Reed of Gateshead yesterday, who, he said, was one of the veriest rascals on town; and Ingram was mentioning a Georgiana Reed of the same place, who was much admired for her beauty a season or two ago in London."

"John Reed is dead, too, sir: he ruined himself and half-ruined his family, and is supposed to have committed suicide. The news so shocked his mother that it brought on an apoplectic attack."

"And what good can you do her? Nonsense, Jane! I would never think of running a hundred miles to see an old lady who will, perhaps, be dead before you reach her: besides, you say she cast you off."

"Yes, sir, but that is long ago; and when her circumstances were very different: I could not be easy to neglect her wishes now."

"How long will you stay?"

"As short a time as possible, sir."

"Promise me only to stay a week—"

"I had better not pass my word: I might be obliged to break it."

"At all events you *will* come back: you will not be induced under any pretext to take up a permanent residence with her?"

"Oh, no! I shall certainly return if all be well."

"And who goes with you? You don't travel a hundred miles alone."

"No, sir, she has sent her coachman."

"A person to be trusted?"

"Yes, sir, he has lived ten years in the family."

Mr. Rochester meditated. "When do you wish to go?"

"Early tomorrow morning, sir."

"Well, you must have some money; you can't travel without money, and I daresay you have not much: I have given you no salary yet. How much have you in the world, Jane?" he asked, smiling.

I drew out my purse; a meagre thing it was. "Five shillings, sir." He took the purse, poured the hoard into his palm, and chuckled over it as if its scantiness amused him. Soon he produced his pocket-book: "Here," said he, offering me a note; it was fifty pounds, and he owed me but fifteen. I told him I had no change.

"I don't want change; you know that. Take your wages."

I declined accepting more than was my due. He scowled at first; then, as if recollecting something, he said—

"Right, right! Better not give you all now: you would, perhaps, stay away three months if you had fifty pounds. There are ten; is it not plenty?"

"Yes, sir, but now you owe me five."

"Come back for it, then; I am your banker for forty pounds."

"Mr. Rochester, I may as well mention another matter of business to you while I have the opportunity."

"Matter of business? I am curious to hear it."

"You have as good as informed me, sir, that you are going shortly to be married?"

"Yes; what then?"

"In that case, sir, Adèle ought to go to school: I am sure you will perceive the necessity of it."

"To get her out of my bride's way, who might otherwise walk over her rather too emphatically? There's sense in the suggestion; not a doubt of it. Adèle, as you say, must go to school; and you, of course, must march straight to—the devil?"

"I hope not, sir; but I must seek another situation somewhere."

"In course!" he exclaimed, with a twang of voice and a distortion of features equally fantastic and ludicrous. He looked at me some minutes.

"And old Madam Reed, or the Misses, her daughters, will be solicited by you to seek a place, I suppose?"

"No, sir; I am not on such terms with my relatives as would justify me in asking favours of them—but I shall advertise."

"You shall walk up the pyramids of Egypt!" he growled. "At your peril you advertise! I wish I had only offered you a sovereign instead of ten pounds. Give me back nine pounds, Jane; I've a use for it."

"And so have I, sir," I returned, putting my hands and my purse behind me. "I could not spare the money on any account."

"Little niggard!" said he. "Refusing me a pecuniary request! Give me five pounds, Jane."

"Not five shillings, sir; nor five pence."

"Just let me look at the cash."

"No, sir; you are not to be trusted."

"Jane!"

"Sir?"

"Promise me one thing."

"I'll promise you anything, sir, that I think I am likely to perform."

"Not to advertise: and to trust this quest of a situation to me. I'll find you one in time."

"I shall be glad so to do, sir, if you, in your turn, will promise that I and Adèle shall be both safe out of the house before your bride enters it."

"Very well! Very well! I'll pledge my word on it. You go tomorrow, then?"

"Yes, sir; early."

"Shall you come down to the drawing-room after dinner?"

"No, sir, I must prepare for the journey."

"Then you and I must bid good-bye for a little while?"

"I suppose so, sir."

"And how do people perform that ceremony of parting, Jane? Teach me; I'm not quite up to it."

"They say, Farewell, or any other form they prefer."

"Then say it."

"Farewell, Mr. Rochester, for the present."

"What must I say?"

"The same, if you like, sir."

"Farewell, Miss Eyre, for the present; is that all?"

"Yes."

"It seems stingy, to my notions, and dry, and unfriendly. I should like something else: a little addition to the rite. If one shook hands, for instance; but no—that would not content me either. So you'll do no more than say Farewell, Jane?"

"It is enough, sir: as much good-will may be conveyed in one hearty word as in many."

"Very likely; but it is blank and cool—'farewell.' "

"How long is he going to stand with his back against that door?" I asked myself; "I want to commence my packing." The dinner-bell rang, and suddenly away he bolted, without another syllable: I saw him no more during the day, and was off before he had risen in the morning.

I reached the lodge at Gateshead about five o'clock in the afternoon of the first of May: I stepped in there before going up to the hall. It was very clean and neat: the ornamental windows were hung with little white curtains; the floor was spotless; the grate and fire-irons were burnished bright, and the fire burnt clear. Bessie sat on the hearth, nursing her last-born, and Robert and his sister played quietly in a corner.

"Bless you! I knew you would come!" exclaimed Mrs. Leaven, as I entered.

"Yes, Bessie," said I, after I had kissed her; "and I trust I am not too late. How is Mrs. Reed? Alive still, I hope."

"Yes, she is alive; and more sensible and collected than she was. The doctor says she may linger a week or two yet; but he hardly thinks she will finally recover."

"Has she mentioned me lately?"

"She was talking of you only this morning, and wishing you would come, but she is sleeping now, or was ten minutes ago, when I was up at the house. She generally lies in a kind of lethargy all the afternoon, and wakes up about six or seven. Will you rest yourself here an hour, Miss, and then I will go up with you?"

Robert here entered, and Bessie laid her sleeping child in the cradle and went to welcome him: afterwards she insisted on my taking off my bonnet and having some tea; for she said I looked pale and tired. I was glad to accept her hospitality; and I submitted to be relieved of my travelling garb just as passively as I used to let her undress me when a child.

Old times crowded fast back on me as I watched her bustling about—setting out the tea-tray with her best china, cutting bread and butter, toasting a tea-cake, and, between whiles, giving little Robert or Jane an occasional tap or push, just as she used to give me in former days. Bessie had retained her quick temper as well as her light foot and good looks.

Tea ready, I was going to approach the table; but she desired me to sit still, quite in her old peremptory tones. I must be served at the fireside, she said; and she placed before me a little round stand with my cup and a plate of toast, absolutely as she used to accommodate me with some privately purloined dainty on a nursery chair: and I smiled and obeyed her as in bygone days.

She wanted to know if I was happy at Thornfield Hall, and what sort of a person the mistress was; and when I told her there was only a master, whether he was a nice gentleman, and if I liked him. I told her he was rather an ugly man, but quite a gentleman; and that he treated me kindly, and I was content. Then I went on to describe to her the gay company that had lately been staying at the house; and to these details Bessie listened with interest: they were precisely of the kind she relished.

In such conversation an hour was soon gone: Bessie restored to me my bonnet, etc., and, accompanied by her, I quitted the lodge for the hall. It was also accompanied by her that I had, nearly nine years ago, walked down the path I was now ascending. On a dark, misty, raw morning in January, I had left a hostile roof with a desperate and embittered heart—a sense of outlawry and almost of reprobation—to seek the chilly harbourage of Lowood: that bourne so far away and unexplored. The same hostile roof now again rose before me: my prospects were doubtful yet; and I had yet an aching heart. I still felt as a wanderer on the face of the earth; but I experienced firmer trust in myself and my own powers, and less withering dread of oppression. The gaping wound of my wrongs, too, was now quite healed; and the flame of resentment extinguished.

"You shall go into the breakfast-room first," said Bessie, as she preceded me through the hall; "the young ladies will be there."

In another moment I was within that apartment. There was every article of furniture looking just as it did on the morning I was first introduced to Mr. Brocklehurst: the very rug he had stood upon still covered the hearth. Glancing at the bookcases, I thought I could distinguish the two volumes of Bewick's *British Birds* occupying their old place on the third shelf, and *Gulliver's Travels* and the *Arabian Nights* ranged just above. The inanimate objects were not changed; but the living things had altered past recognition.

Two young ladies appeared before me; one very tall, almost as tall as Miss Ingram—very thin too, with a sallow face and severe mien. There was something ascetic in her look, which was augmented by the extreme plainness of a straight-skirted, black, stuff dress, a starched linen collar, hair combed away from the temples, and the nun-like ornament of a string of ebony beads and a crucifix. This I felt sure was Eliza, though I could trace little resemblance to her former self in that elongated and colourless visage.

The other was as certainly Georgiana: but not the Georgiana I remembered—the slim and fairy-like girl of eleven. This was a full-blown, very plump damsel, fair as waxwork, with handsome and regular features, languishing blue eyes, and ringleted yellow hair. The hue of her dress was black too; but its fashion was so different from her sister's—so much more flowing and becoming—it looked as stylish as the other's looked puritanical.

In each of the sisters there was one trait of the mother—and only one; the thin and pallid elder daughter had her parent's Cairngorm eye: the blooming and luxuriant younger girl had her contour of jaw and chin—perhaps a little softened, but still imparting an indescribable hardness to the countenance otherwise so voluptuous and buxom.

Both ladies, as I advanced, rose to welcome me, and both addressed me by the name of "Miss Eyre." Eliza's greeting was delivered in a short, abrupt voice, without a smile; and then she sat down again, fixed her eyes on the fire, and seemed to forget me. Georgiana added to her "How d'ye do?" several commonplaces about my journey, the weather, and so on, uttered in rather a drawling tone: and accompanied by sundry side-glances that measured me from head to foot—now traversing the folds of my drab merino pelisse, and now lingering on the plain trimming of my cottage bonnet. Young ladies have a remarkable way of letting you know that they think you a "quiz" without actually saying the words. A certain superciliousness of look, coolness of manner, nonchalance of tone, express fully their sentiments on the point, without committing them by any positive rudeness in word or deed.

A sneer, however, whether covert or open, had now no longer that power over me it once possessed: as I sat between my cousins, I was surprised to find how easy I felt under the total neglect of the one and the semi-sarcastic attentions of the other—Eliza did not mortify, nor Georgiana ruffle me. The fact was, I had other things to think about; within the last few months feelings had been stirred in me so much more potent than any they could raise—pains and pleasures so much more acute and exquisite had been excited than any it was in their power to inflict or bestow—that their airs gave me no concern either for good or bad.

"How is Mrs. Reed?" I asked soon, looking calmly at Georgiana, who thought fit to bridle at the direct address, as if it were an unexpected liberty.

"Mrs. Reed? Ah! Mama, you mean; she is extremely poorly: I doubt if you can see her tonight."

"If," said I, "you would just step upstairs and tell her I am come, I should be much obliged to you."

Georgiana almost started, and she opened her blue eyes wild and wide. "I know she had a particular wish to see me," I added, "and I would not defer attending to her desire longer than is absolutely necessary."

"Mama dislikes being disturbed in an evening," remarked Eliza. I soon rose, quietly took off my bonnet and gloves, uninvited, and said I would just step out to Bessie—who was, I dared say, in the kitchen—and ask her to ascertain whether Mrs. Reed was disposed to receive me or not tonight. I went, and having found Bessie and despatched her on my errand, I proceeded to take further measures. It had heretofore been my habit always to shrink from arrogance: received as I had been today, I should, a year ago, have resolved to quit Gateshead the very next morning; now, it was disclosed to me all at once that that would be a foolish plan. I had taken a journey of a hundred miles to see my aunt, and I must stay with her till she was better—or dead: as to her daughters' pride or folly, I must put it on one side, make myself independent of it. So I addressed the housekeeper; asked her to show me a room, told her I should probably be a visitor here for a week or two, had my trunk conveyed to my chamber, and followed it thither myself: I met Bessie on the landing.

"Missis is awake," said she; "I have told her you are here: come and let us see if she will know you."

I did not need to be guided to the well-known room, to which I had so often been summoned for chastisement or reprimand in former days. I hastened before Bessie; I softly opened the door: a shaded light stood on the table, for it was now getting dark. There was the great four-post bed with amber hangings as of old; there the toilet-table, the armchair, and the footstool, at which I had a hundred times been sentenced to kneel, to ask pardon for offences by me uncommitted. I looked into a certain corner near, half-expecting to see the slim outline of a once dreaded switch which used to lurk there, waiting to leap out imp-like and lace my quivering palm or shrinking neck. I approached the bed; I opened the curtains and leant over the high-piled pillows.

Well did I remember Mrs. Reed's face, and I eagerly sought the familiar image. It is a happy thing that time quells the longings of vengeance and hushes the promptings of rage and aversion. I had left this woman in bitterness and hate, and I came back to her now with no other emotion than a sort of ruth for her great sufferings, and a strong yearning to forget and forgive all injuries—to be reconciled and clasp hands in amity.

The well-known face was there: stern, relentless as ever—there was that peculiar eye which nothing could melt, and the somewhat raised, imperious, despotic eyebrow. How often had it lowered on me menace and hate! And how the recollection of childhood's terrors and sorrows revived as I traced its harsh line now! And yet I stooped down and kissed her: she looked at me.

"Is this Jane Eyre?" she said.

"Yes, Aunt Reed. How are you, dear aunt?"

I had once vowed that I would never call her aunt again: I thought it no sin to forget and break that vow now. My fingers had fastened on her hand which lay outside the sheet: had she pressed mine kindly, I should at that moment have experienced true pleasure. But unimpressionable natures are not so soon softened, nor are natural antipathies so readily eradicated. Mrs. Reed took her hand away, and, turning her face rather from me, she remarked that the night was warm. Again she regarded me so icily, I felt at once that her opinion of me—her feeling towards me—was unchanged and unchangeable. I knew by her stony eye—opaque to tenderness, indissoluble to tears—that she was resolved to consider me bad to the last; because to believe me good would give her no generous pleasure: only a sense of mortification.

I felt pain, and then I felt ire; and then I felt a determination to subdue her—to be her mistress in spite both of her nature and her will. My tears had risen, just as in childhood: I ordered them back to their source. I brought a chair to the bed-head: I sat down and leaned over the pillow.

"You sent for me," I said, "and I am here; and it is my intention to stay till I see how you get on."

"Oh, of course! You have seen my daughters?"

"Yes."

"Well, you may tell them I wish you to stay till I can talk some things over with you I have on my mind: tonight it is too late, and I have a difficulty in recalling them. But there was something I wished to say—let me see—"

The wandering look and changed utterance told what wreck had taken place in her once-vigorous frame. Turning restlessly, she drew the bedclothes round her; my elbow, resting on a corner of the quilt, fixed it down: she was at once irritated.

"Sit up!" said she. "Don't annoy me with holding the clothes fast. Are you Jane Eyre?"

"I am Jane Eyre."

"I have had more trouble with that child than any one would believe. Such a burden to be left on my hands—and so much annoyance as she caused me, daily and hourly, with her incomprehensible disposition, and her sudden starts of temper, and her continual, unnatural watchings of one's movements! I declare she talked to me once like something mad, or like a fiend—no child ever spoke or looked as she did; I was glad to get her away from the house. What did they do with her at Lowood? The fever broke out there, and many of the pupils died. She, however, did not die: but I said she did—I wish she had died!"

"A strange wish, Mrs. Reed; why do you hate her so?"

"I had a dislike to her mother always; for she was my husband's only sister, and a great favourite with him: he opposed the family's disowning her when she made her low marriage; and when news came of her death, he wept like a simpleton. He would send for the baby; though I entreated him rather to put it out to nurse and pay for its maintenance. I hated it the first time I set my eyes on it—a sickly, whining, pining thing! It would wail in its cradle all night long—not screaming heartily like any other child, but whimpering and moaning. Reed pitied it; and he used to nurse it and notice it as if it had been his own: more, indeed, than he ever noticed his own at that age. He would try to make my children friendly to the little beggar: the darlings could not bear it, and he was angry with them when they showed their dislike. In his last illness, he had it brought continually to his bedside; and but an hour before he died, he bound me by vow to keep the creature. I would as soon have been charged with a pauper brat out of a workhouse: but he was weak, naturally weak. John does not at all resemble his father, and I am glad of it: John is like me and like my brothers—he is quite a Gibson. Oh, I wish he would cease tormenting me with letters for money! I have no more money to give him: we are getting poor. I must send away half the servants and shut up part of the house; or let it off. I can never submit to do that—yet how are we to get on? Two-thirds of my income goes in paying the interest of mortgages. John gambles dreadfully, and always loses—poor boy! He is beset by sharpers: John is sunk and degraded—his look is frightful—I feel ashamed for him when I see him."

She was getting much excited. "I think I had better leave her now," said I to Bessie, who stood on the other side of the bed.

"Perhaps you had, Miss: but she often talks in this way towards night—in the morning she is calmer."

I rose. "Stop!" exclaimed Mrs. Reed, "there is another thing I wished to say. He threatens me—he continually threatens me with his own death, or mine: and I dream sometimes that I see him laid out with a great wound in his throat, or with a swollen and blackened face. I am come to a strange pass: I have heavy troubles. What is to be done? How is the money to be had?"

Bessie now endeavoured to persuade her to take a sedative draught: she succeeded with difficulty. Soon after, Mrs. Reed grew more composed, and sank into a dozing state. I then left her.

More than ten days elapsed before I had again any conversation with her. She continued either delirious or lethargic; and the doctor forbade everything which could painfully excite her. Meantime, I got on as well as I could with Georgiana and Eliza. They were very cold, indeed, at first. Eliza would sit half the day sewing, reading, or writing, and scarcely utter a word either to me or her sister. Georgiana would chatter nonsense to her canary bird by the hour, and take no notice of me. But I was determined not to seem at a loss for occupation or amusement: I had brought my drawing materials with me, and they served me for both.

Provided with a case of pencils, and some sheets of paper, I used to take a seat apart from them, near the window, and busy myself in sketching fancy vignettes, representing any scene that happened momentarily to shape itself in the ever-shifting kaleidoscope of imagination: a glimpse of sea between two rocks; the rising moon, and a ship crossing its disk; a group of reeds and water-flags, and a naiad's head, crowned with lotus-flowers, rising out of them; an elf sitting in a hedge-sparrow's nest, under a wreath of hawthorn-bloom.

One morning I fell to sketching a face: what sort of a face it was to be, I did not care or know. I took a soft black pencil, gave it a broad point, and worked away. Soon I had traced on the paper a broad and prominent forehead and a square lower outline of visage: that contour gave me pleasure; my fingers proceeded actively to fill it with features. Strongly-marked horizontal eyebrows must be traced under that brow; then followed, naturally, a well-defined nose, with a straight ridge and full nostrils; then a flexible-looking mouth, by no means narrow; then a firm chin, with a decided cleft down the middle of it: of course, some black whiskers were wanted, and some jetty hair, tufted on the temples, and waved above the forehead. Now for the eyes: I had left them to the last, because they required the most careful working. I drew them large; I shaped them well: the eyelashes I traced long and sombre; the irids lustrous and large. "Good! But not quite the thing," I thought, as I surveyed the effect; "they want more force and spirit"; and I wrought the shades blacker, that the lights might flash more brilliantly—a happy touch or two secured success. There, I had a friend's face under my gaze; and what did it signify that those young ladies turned their backs on me? I looked at it; I smiled at the speaking likeness: I was absorbed and content.

"Is that a portrait of some one you know?" asked Eliza, who had approached me unnoticed. I responded that it was merely a fancy head, and hurried it beneath the other sheets. Of course, I lied: it was, in fact, a very faithful representation of Mr. Rochester. But what was that to her, or to any one but myself? Georgiana also advanced to look. The other drawings pleased her much, but she called that "an ugly man." They both seemed surprised at my skill. I offered to sketch their portraits; and each, in turn, sat for a pencil outline. Then Georgiana produced her album. I promised to contribute a water-colour drawing: this put her at once into good humour. She proposed a walk in the grounds. Before we had been out two hours, we were deep in a confidential conversation: she had favoured me with a description of the brilliant winter she had spent in London two seasons ago—of the admiration she had there excited—the attention she had received; and I even got hints of the titled conquest she had made. In the course of the afternoon and evening these hints were enlarged on: various soft conversations were reported, and sentimental scenes represented; and, in short, a volume of a novel of fashionable life was that day improvised by her for my benefit. The communications were renewed from day to day: they always ran on the same theme—herself, her loves, and woes. It was strange she never once adverted either to her mother's illness, or her brother's death, or the present gloomy state of the family prospects. Her mind seemed wholly taken up with reminiscences of past gaiety, and aspirations after dissipations to come. She passed about five minutes each day in her mother's sick-room, and no more.

Eliza still spoke little: she had evidently no time to talk. I never saw a busier person than she seemed to be; yet it was difficult to say what she did: or rather, to discover any result of her diligence. She had an alarm to call her up early. I know not how she occupied herself before breakfast, but after that meal she divided her time into regular portions, and each hour had its allotted task. Three times a day she studied a little book, which I found, on inspection, was a Common Prayer Book. I asked her once what was the great attraction of that volume, and she said, "the Rubric." Three hours she gave to stitching, with gold thread, the border of a square crimson cloth, almost large enough for a carpet. In answer to my inquiries after the use of this article, she informed me it was a covering for the altar of a new church lately erected near Gateshead. Two hours she devoted to her diary; two to working by herself in the kitchen-garden; and one to the regulation of her accounts. She seemed to want no company; no conversation. I believe she was happy in her way: this routine sufficed for her; and nothing annoyed her so much as the occurrence of any incident which forced her to vary its clockwork regularity.

She told me one evening, when more disposed to be communicative than usual, that John's conduct, and the threatened ruin of the family, had been a source of profound affliction to her: but she had now, she said, settled her mind, and formed her resolution. Her own fortune she had taken care to secure; and when her mother died—and it was wholly improbable, she tranquilly remarked, that she should either recover or linger long—she would execute a long-cherished project: seek a retirement where punctual habits would be permanently secured from disturbance, and place safe barriers between herself and a frivolous world. I asked if Georgiana would accompany her.

"Of course not. Georgiana and she had nothing in common: they never had had. She would not be burdened with her society for any consideration. Georgiana should take her own course; and she, Eliza, would take hers."

Georgiana, when not unburdening her heart to me, spent most of her time in lying on the sofa, fretting about the dulness of the house, and wishing over and over again that her aunt Gibson would send her an invitation up to town. "It would be so much better," she said, "if she could only get out of the way for a month or two, till all was over." I did not ask what she meant by "all being over," but I suppose she referred to the expected decease of her mother and the gloomy sequel of funeral rites. Eliza generally took no more notice of her sister's indolence and complaints than if no such murmuring, lounging object had been before her. One day, however, as she put away her account-book and unfolded her embroidery, she suddenly took her up thus—

"Georgiana, a more vain and absurd animal than you was certainly never allowed to cumber the earth. You had no right to be born, for you make no use of life. Instead of living for, in, and with yourself, as a reasonable being ought, you seek only to fasten your feebleness on some other person's strength: if no one can be found willing to burden her or himself with such a fat, weak, puffy, useless thing, you cry out that you are ill-treated, neglected, miserable. Then, too, existence for you must be a scene of continual change and excitement, or else the world is a dungeon: you must be admired, you must be courted, you must be flattered—you must have music, dancing, and society—or you languish, you die away. Have you no sense to devise a system which will make you independent of all efforts, and all wills, but your own? Take one day; share it into sections; to each section apportion its task: leave no stray unemployed quarters of an hour, ten minutes, five minutes—include all; do each piece of business in its turn with method, with rigid regularity. The day will close almost before you are aware it has begun; and you are indebted to no one for helping you to get rid of one vacant moment: you have had to seek no one's company, conversation, sympathy, forbearance; you have lived, in short, as an independent being ought to do. Take this advice: the first and last I shall offer you; then you will not want me or any one else, happen what may. Neglect it—go on as heretofore, craving, whining, and idling—and suffer the results of your idiocy, however bad and insuperable they may be. I tell you this plainly; and listen: for though I shall no more repeat what I am now about to say, I shall steadily act on it. After my mother's death, I wash my hands of you: from the day her coffin is carried to the vault in Gateshead Church, you and I will be as separate as if we had never known each other. You need not think that because we chanced to be born of the same parents, I shall suffer you to fasten me down by even the feeblest claim: I can tell you this—if the whole human race, ourselves excepted, were swept away, and we two stood alone on the earth, I would leave you in the old world, and betake myself to the new."

She closed her lips.

"You might have spared yourself the trouble of delivering that tirade," answered Georgiana. "Everybody knows you are the most selfish, heartless creature in existence: and *I* know your spiteful hatred towards me: I have had a specimen of it before in the trick you played me about Lord Edwin Vere: you could not bear me to be raised above you, to have a title, to be received into circles where you dare not show your face, and so you acted the spy and informer, and ruined my prospects for ever." Georgiana took out her handkerchief and blew her nose for an hour afterwards; Eliza sat cold, impassable, and assiduously industrious.

True, generous feeling is made small account of by some, but here were two natures rendered, the one intolerably acrid, the other despicably savourless for the want of it. Feeling without judgment is a washy draught indeed; but judgment untempered by feeling is too bitter and husky a morsel for human deglutition.

It was a wet and windy afternoon: Georgiana had fallen asleep on the sofa over the perusal of a novel; Eliza was gone to attend a saint's-day service at the new church—for in matters of religion she was a rigid formalist: no weather ever prevented the punctual discharge of what she considered her devotional duties; fair or foul, she went to church thrice every Sunday, and as often on week-days as there were prayers.

I bethought myself to go upstairs and see how the dying woman sped, who lay there almost unheeded: the very servants paid her but a remittent attention: the hired nurse, being little looked after, would slip out of the room whenever she could. Bessie was faithful; but she had her own family to mind, and could only come occasionally to the hall. I found the sick-room unwatched, as I had expected: no nurse was there; the patient lay still, and seemingly lethargic; her livid face sunk in the pillows: the fire was dying in the grate. I renewed the fuel, re-arranged the bedclothes, gazed awhile on her who could not now gaze on me, and then I moved away to the window.

The rain beat strongly against the panes, the wind blew tempestuously: "One lies there," I thought, "who will soon be beyond the war of earthly elements. Whither will that spirit—now struggling to quit its material tenement—flit when at length released?"

In pondering the great mystery, I thought of Helen Burns, recalled her dying words—her faith—her doctrine of the equality of disembodied souls. I was still listening in thought to her well-remembered tones—still picturing her pale and spiritual aspect, her wasted face and sublime gaze, as she lay on her placid deathbed, and whispered her longing to be restored to her divine Father's bosom—when a feeble voice murmured from the couch behind: "Who is that?"

I knew Mrs. Reed had not spoken for days: was she reviving? I went up to her.

"It is I, Aunt Reed."

"Who—I?" was her answer. "Who are you?" looking at me with surprise and a sort of alarm, but still not wildly. "You are quite a stranger to me—where is Bessie?"

"She is at the lodge, aunt."

"Aunt," she repeated. "Who calls me aunt? You are not one of the Gibsons; and yet I know you—that face, and the eyes and forehead, are quiet familiar to me: you are like—why, you are like Jane Eyre!"

I said nothing: I was afraid of occasioning some shock by declaring my identity.

"Yet," said she, "I am afraid it is a mistake: my thoughts deceive me. I wished to see Jane Eyre, and I fancy a likeness where none exists: besides, in eight years she must be so changed." I now gently assured her that I was the person she supposed and desired me to be: and seeing that I was understood, and that her senses were quite collected, I explained how Bessie had sent her husband to fetch me from Thornfield.

"I am very ill, I know," she said ere long. "I was trying to turn myself a few minutes since, and find I cannot move a limb. It is as well I should ease my mind before I die: what we think little of in health, burdens us at such an hour as the present is to me. Is the nurse here? Or is there no one in the room but you?"

I assured her we were alone.

"Well, I have twice done you a wrong which I regret now. One was in breaking the promise which I gave my husband to bring you up as my own child; the other—" she stopped. "After all, it is of no great importance, perhaps," she murmured to herself; "and then I may get better; and to humble myself so to her is painful."

She made an effort to alter her position, but failed: her face changed; she seemed to experience some inward sensation—the precursor, perhaps, of the last pang.

"Well, I must get it over. Eternity is before me: I had better tell her. Go to my dressing-case, open it, and take out a letter you will see there."

I obeyed her directions. "Read the letter," she said.

It was short, and thus conceived:

"Madam,

"Will you have the goodness to send me the address of my niece, Jane Eyre, and to tell me how she is? It is my intention to write shortly and desire her to come to me at Madeira. Providence has blessed my endeavours to secure a competency; and as I am unmarried and childless, I wish to adopt her during my life, and bequeath her at my death whatever I may have to leave.

"I am, Madam, etc., etc.,

"John Eyre, Madeira."

It was dated three years back.

"Why did I never hear of this?" I asked.

"Because I disliked you too fixedly and thoroughly ever to lend a hand in lifting you to prosperity. I could not forget your conduct to me, Jane—the fury with which you once turned on me; the tone in which you declared you abhorred me the worst of anybody in the world;

the unchildlike look and voice with which you affirmed that the very thought of me made you sick, and asserted that I had treated you with miserable cruelty. I could not forget my own sensations when you thus started up and poured out the venom of your mind: I felt fear as if an animal that I had struck or pushed had looked up at me with human eyes and cursed me in a man's voice. Bring me some water! Oh, make haste!"

"Dear Mrs. Reed," said I, as I offered her the draught she required, "think no more of all this, let it pass away from your mind. Forgive me for my passionate language: I was a child then; eight, nine years have passed since that day."

She heeded nothing of what I said; but when she had tasted the water and drawn breath, she went on thus—

"I tell you I could not forget it; and I took my revenge: for you to be adopted by your uncle, and placed in a state of ease and comfort, was what I could not endure. I wrote to him; I said I was sorry for his disappointment, but Jane Eyre was dead: she had died of typhus fever at Lowood. Now act as you please: write and contradict my assertion—expose my falsehood as soon as you like. You were born, I think, to be my torment: my last hour is racked by the recollection of a deed which, but for you, I should never have been tempted to commit."

"If you could but be persuaded to think no more of it, aunt, and to regard me with kindness and forgiveness—"

"You have a very bad disposition," said she, "and one to this day I feel it impossible to understand: how for nine years you could be patient and quiescent under any treatment, and in the tenth break out all fire and violence, I can never comprehend."

"My disposition is not so bad as you think: I am passionate, but not vindictive. Many a time, as a little child, I should have been glad to love you if you would have let me; and I long earnestly to be reconciled to you now: kiss me, aunt."

I approached my cheek to her lips: she would not touch it. She said I oppressed her by leaning over the bed, and again demanded water. As I laid her down—for I raised her and supported her on my arm while she drank—I covered her ice-cold and clammy hand with mine: the feeble fingers shrank from my touch—the glazing eyes shunned my gaze.

"Love me, then, or hate me, as you will," I said at last, "you have my full and free forgiveness: ask now for God's, and be at peace."

Poor, suffering woman! It was too late for her to make now the effort to change her habitual frame of mind: living, she had ever hated me—dying, she must hate me still.

The nurse now entered, and Bessie followed. I yet lingered half-an-hour longer, hoping to see some sign of amity: but she gave none. She was fast relapsing into stupor; nor did her mind again rally: at twelve o'clock that night she died. I was not present to close her eyes, nor were either of her daughters. They came to tell us the next morning that all was over. She was by that time laid out. Eliza and I went to look at her: Georgiana, who had burst out into loud weeping, said she dared not go. There was stretched Sarah Reed's once robust and active frame, rigid and still: her eye of flint was covered with its cold lid; her brow and strong traits wore yet the impress of her inexorable soul. A strange and solemn object was that corpse to me. I gazed on it with gloom and pain: nothing soft, nothing sweet, nothing pitying, or hopeful, or subduing did it inspire; only a grating anguish for *her* woes—not *my* loss—and a sombre tearless dismay at the fearfulness of death in such a form.

Eliza surveyed her parent calmly. After a silence of some minutes she observed—

"With her constitution she should have lived to a good old age: her life was shortened by trouble." And then a spasm constricted her mouth for an instant: as it passed away she turned and left the room, and so did I. Neither of us had dropt a tear.

CHAPTER XXII

Mr. Rochester had given me but one week's leave of absence: yet a month elapsed before I quitted Gateshead. I wished to leave immediately after the funeral, but Georgiana entreated me to stay till she could get off to London, whither she was now at last invited by her uncle, Mr. Gibson, who had come down to direct his sister's interment and settle the family affairs. Georgiana said she dreaded being left alone with Eliza; from her she got neither sympathy in her dejection, support in her fears, nor aid in her preparations; so I bore with her feeble-minded wailings and selfish lamentations as well as I could, and did my best in sewing for her and packing her dresses. It is true, that while I worked, she would idle; and I thought to myself, "If you and I were destined to live always together, cousin, we would commence matters on a different footing. I should not settle tamely down into being the forbearing party; I should assign you your share of labour, and compel you to accomplish it, or else it should be left undone: I should insist, also, on your keeping some of those drawling, half-insincere complaints hushed in your own breast. It is only because our connection happens to be very transitory, and comes at a peculiarly mournful season, that I consent thus to render it so patient and compliant on my part."

At last I saw Georgiana off; but now it was Eliza's turn to request me to stay another week. Her plans required all her time and attention, she said; she was about to depart for some unknown bourne; and all day long she stayed in her own room, her door bolted within, filling trunks, emptying drawers, burning papers, and holding no communication with any one. She wished me to look after the house, to see callers, and answer notes of condolence.

One morning she told me I was at liberty. "And," she added, "I am obliged to you for your valuable services and discreet conduct! There is some difference between living with such a one as you and with Georgiana: you perform your own part in life and burden no one. Tomorrow," she continued, "I set out for the Continent. I shall take up my abode in a religious house near Lisle—a nunnery you would call it; there I shall be quiet and unmolested. I shall devote myself for a time to the examination of the Roman Catholic dogmas, and to a careful study of the workings of their system: if I find it to be, as I half suspect it is, the one best calculated to ensure the doing of all things decently and in order, I shall embrace the tenets of Rome and probably take the veil."

I neither expressed surprise at this resolution nor attempted to dissuade her from it. "The vocation will fit you to a hair," I thought; "much good may it do you!"

When we parted, she said: "Good-bye, cousin Jane Eyre; I wish you well: you have some sense."

I then returned: "You are not without sense, cousin Eliza; but what you have, I suppose, in another year will be walled up alive in a French convent. However, it is not my business, and so it suits you, I don't much care."

"You are in the right," said she; and with these words we each went our separate way. As I shall not have occasion to refer either to her or her sister again, I may as well mention here, that Georgiana made an advantageous match with a wealthy worn-out man of fashion, and that Eliza actually took the veil, and is at this day superior of the convent where she passed the period of her novitiate, and which she endowed with her fortune.

How people feel when they are returning home from an absence, long or short, I did not know: I had never experienced the sensation. I had known what it was to come back to Gateshead when a child after a long walk, to be scolded for looking cold or gloomy; and later, what it was to come back from church to Lowood, to long for a plenteous meal and a good fire, and to be unable to get either. Neither of these returnings was very pleasant or desirable: no magnet drew me to a given point, increasing in its strength of attraction the nearer I came. The return to Thornfield was yet to be tried.

My journey seemed tedious—very tedious: fifty miles one day, a night spent at an inn; fifty miles the next day. During the first twelve hours I thought of Mrs. Reed in her last moments; I saw her disfigured and discoloured face, and heard her strangely altered voice. I mused on the funeral day, the coffin, the hearse, the black train of tenants and servants—few was the number of relatives—the gaping vault, the silent church, the solemn service. Then I thought of Eliza and Georgiana; I beheld one the cynosure of a ball-room, the other the inmate of a convent cell; and I dwelt on and analysed their separate peculiarities of person and character. The evening arrival at the great town of —— scattered these thoughts; night gave them quite another turn: laid down on my traveller's bed, I left reminiscence for anticipation.

I was going back to Thornfield: but how long was I to stay there? Not long; of that I was sure. I had heard from Mrs. Fairfax in the interim of my absence: the party at the hall was dispersed; Mr. Rochester had left for London three weeks ago, but he was then expected to return in a fortnight. Mrs. Fairfax surmised that he was gone to make arrangements for his wedding, as he had talked of purchasing a new carriage: she said the idea of his marrying Miss Ingram still seemed strange to her; but from what everybody said, and from what she had herself seen, she could no longer doubt that the event would shortly take place. "You would be strangely incredulous if you did doubt it," was my mental comment. "I don't doubt it."

The question followed, "Where was I to go?" I dreamt of Miss Ingram all the night: in a vivid morning dream I saw her closing the gates of Thornfield against me and pointing me out another road; and Mr. Rochester looked on with his arms folded—smiling sardonically, as it seemed, at both her and me.

I had not notified to Mrs. Fairfax the exact day of my return; for I did not wish either car or carriage to meet me at Millcote. I proposed to walk the distance quietly by myself; and very quietly, after leaving my box in the ostler's care, did I slip away from the George Inn, about six o'clock of a June evening, and take the old road to Thornfield: a road which lay chiefly through fields, and was now little frequented.

It was not a bright or splendid summer evening, though fair and soft: the haymakers were at work all along the road; and the sky, though far from cloudless, was such as promised well for the future: its blue—where blue was visible—was mild and settled, and its cloud strata high and thin. The west, too, was warm: no watery gleam chilled it—it seemed as if there was a fire lit, an altar burning behind its screen of marbled vapour, and out of apertures shone a golden redness.

I felt glad as the road shortened before me: so glad that I stopped once to ask myself what that joy meant: and to remind reason that it was not to my home I was going, or to a permanent resting-place, or to a place where fond friends looked out for me and waited my arrival. "Mrs. Fairfax will smile you a calm welcome, to be sure," said I; "and little Adèle will clap her hands and jump to see you: but you know very well you are thinking of another than they, and that he is not thinking of you."

But what is so headstrong as youth? What so blind as inexperience? These affirmed that it was pleasure enough to have the privilege of again looking on Mr. Rochester, whether he looked on me or not; and they added—"Hasten! Hasten! Be with him while you may: but a few more days or weeks, at most, and you are parted from him for ever!" And then I strangled a new-born agony—a deformed thing which I could not persuade myself to own and rear—and ran on.

They are making hay, too, in Thornfield meadows: or rather, the labourers are just quitting their work, and returning home with their rakes on their shoulders, now, at the hour I arrive. I have but a field or two to traverse, and then I shall cross the road and reach the gates. How full the hedges are of roses! But I have no time to gather any; I want to be at the house. I passed a tall briar, shooting leafy and flowery branches across the path; I see the narrow stile with stone steps; and I see—Mr. Rochester sitting there, a book and a pencil in his hand; he is writing.

Well, he is not a ghost; yet every nerve I have is unstrung: for a moment I am beyond my own mastery. What does it mean? I did not think I should tremble in this way when I saw him, or lose my voice or the power of motion in his presence. I will go back as soon as I can stir: I need not make an absolute fool of myself. I know another way to the house. It does not signify if I knew twenty ways; for he has seen me.

"Hillo!" he cries; and he puts up his book and his pencil. "There you are! Come on, if you please."

I suppose I do come on; though in what fashion I know not; being scarcely cognisant of my movements, and solicitous only to appear calm; and, above all, to control the working muscles of my face—which I feel rebel insolently against my will, and struggle to express what I had resolved to conceal. But I have a veil—it is down: I may make shift yet to behave with decent composure.

"And this is Jane Eyre? Are you coming from Millcote, and on foot? Yes—just one of your tricks: not to send for a carriage, and come clattering over street and road like a common mortal, but to steal into the vicinage of your home along with twilight, just as if you were a dream or a shade. What the deuce have you done with yourself this last month?"

"I have been with my aunt, sir, who is dead."

"A true Janian reply! Good angels be my guard! She comes from the other world—from the abode of people who are dead; and tells me so when she meets me alone here in the gloaming! If I dared, I'd touch you, to see if you are substance or shadow, you elf! But I'd as soon offer to take hold of a blue *ignis fatuus* light in a marsh. Truant! Truant!" he added, when he had paused an instant. "Absent from me a whole month, and forgetting me quite, I'll be sworn!"

I knew there would be pleasure in meeting my master again, even though broken by the fear that he was so soon to cease to be my master, and by the knowledge that I was nothing to him: but there was ever in Mr. Rochester (so at least I thought) such a wealth of the power of communicating happiness, that to taste but of the crumbs he scattered to stray and stranger birds like me, was to feast genially. His last words were balm: they seemed to imply that it imported something to him whether I forgot him or not. And he had spoken of Thornfield as my home—would that it were my home!

He did not leave the stile, and I hardly liked to ask to go by. I inquired soon if he had not been to London.

"Yes; I suppose you found that out by second-sight."

"Mrs. Fairfax told me in a letter."

"And did she inform you what I went to do?"

"Oh, yes, sir! Everybody knew your errand."

"You must see the carriage, Jane, and tell me if you don't think it will suit Mrs. Rochester exactly; and whether she won't look like Queen Boadicea, leaning back against those purple cushions. I wish, Jane, I were a trifle better adapted to match with her externally. Tell me now, fairy as you are—can't you give me a charm, or a philter, or something of that sort, to make me a handsome man?"

"It would be past the power of magic, sir." And, in thought, I added, "A loving eye is all the charm needed: to such you are handsome enough; or rather your sternness has a power beyond beauty."

Mr. Rochester had sometimes read my unspoken thoughts with an acumen to me incomprehensible: in the present instance he took no notice of my abrupt vocal response; but he smiled at me with a certain smile he had of his own, and which he used but on rare occasions. He seemed to think it too good for common purposes: it was the real sunshine of feeling—he shed it over me now.

"Pass, Janet," said he, making room for me to cross the stile; "go up home, and stay your weary little wandering feet at a friend's threshold."

All I had now to do was to obey him in silence: no need for me to colloquise further. I got over the stile without a word, and meant to leave him calmly. An impulse held me fast—a force turned me round. I said—or something in me said for me, and in spite of me—

"Thank you, Mr. Rochester, for your great kindness. I am strangely glad to get back again to you: and wherever you are is my home—my only home."

I walked on so fast that even he could hardly have overtaken me had he tried. Little Adèle was half wild with delight when she saw me. Mrs. Fairfax received me with her usual plain friendliness. Leah smiled, and even Sophie bid me "bon soir" with glee. This was very pleasant; there is no happiness like that of being loved by your fellow-creatures, and feeling that your presence is an addition to their comfort.

I that evening shut my eyes resolutely against the future: I stopped my ears against the voice that kept warning me of near separation and coming grief. When tea was over and Mrs. Fairfax had taken her knitting, and I had assumed a low seat near her, and Adèle, kneeling on the carpet, had nestled close up to me, and a sense of mutual affection seemed to surround us with a ring of golden peace, I uttered a silent prayer that we might not be parted far or soon; but when, as we thus sat, Mr. Rochester entered, unannounced, and looking at us, seemed to take pleasure in the spectacle of a group so amicable—when he said he supposed the old lady was all right now that she had got her adopted daughter back again, and added that he saw Adèle was "prête à croquer sa petite maman Anglaise"—I half ventured to hope that he would, even after his marriage, keep us together somewhere under the shelter of his protection, and not quite exiled from the sunshine of his presence.

A fortnight of dubious calm succeeded my return to Thornfield Hall. Nothing was said of the master's marriage, and I saw no preparation going on for such an event. Almost every day I asked Mrs. Fairfax if she had yet heard anything decided: her answer was always in the negative. Once she said she had actually put the question to Mr. Rochester as to when he was going to bring his bride home; but he had answered her only by a joke and one of his queer looks, and she could not tell what to make of him.

One thing specially surprised me, and that was, there were no journeyings backward and forward, no visits to Ingram Park: to be sure it was twenty miles off, on the borders of another county; but what was that distance to an ardent lover? To so practised and indefatigable a horseman as Mr. Rochester, it would be but a morning's ride. I began to cherish hopes I had no right to conceive: that the match was broken off; that rumour had been mistaken; that one or both parties had changed their minds. I used to look at my master's face to see if it were sad or fierce; but I could not remember the time when it had been so uniformly clear of clouds or evil feelings. If, in the moments I and my pupil spent with him, I lacked spirits and sank into inevitable dejection, he became even gay. Never had he called me more frequently to his presence; never been kinder to me when there—and, alas! Never had I loved him so well.

CHAPTER XXIII

A splendid Midsummer shone over England: skies so pure, suns so radiant as were then seen in long succession, seldom favour even singly, our wave-girt land. It was as if a band of Italian days had come from the South, like a flock of glorious passenger birds, and lighted to rest them on the cliffs of Albion. The hay was all got in; the fields round Thornfield were green and shorn; the roads white and baked; the trees were in their dark prime; hedge and wood, full-leaved and deeply tinted, contrasted well with the sunny hue of the cleared meadows between.

On Midsummer-eve, Adèle, weary with gathering wild strawberries in Hay Lane half the day, had gone to bed with the sun. I watched her drop asleep, and when I left her, I sought the garden.

It was now the sweetest hour of the twenty-four: "Day its fervid fires had wasted," and dew fell cool on panting plain and scorched summit. Where the sun had gone down in simple state—pure of the pomp of clouds—spread a solemn purple, burning with the light of red jewel and furnace flame at one point, on one hill-peak, and extending high and wide, soft and still softer, over half heaven. The east had its own charm or fine deep blue, and its own modest gem, a casino and solitary star: soon it would boast the moon; but she was yet beneath the horizon.

I walked a while on the pavement; but a subtle, well-known scent—that of a cigar—stole from some window; I saw the library casement open a handbreadth; I knew I might be watched thence; so I went apart into the orchard. No nook in the grounds more sheltered and more Eden-like; it was full of trees, it bloomed with flowers: a very high wall shut it out from the court, on one side; on the other, a beech avenue screened it from the lawn. At the bottom was a sunk fence; its sole separation from lonely fields: a winding walk, bordered with laurels and terminating in a giant horse-chestnut, circled at the base by a seat, led down to the fence. Here one could wander unseen. While such honey-dew fell, such silence reigned, such gloaming gathered, I felt as if I could haunt such shade for ever; but in threading the flower and fruit parterres at the upper part of the enclosure, enticed there by the light the now rising moon cast on this more open quarter, my step is stayed—not by sound, not by sight, but once more by a warning fragrance.

Sweet-briar and southernwood, jasmine, pink, and rose have long been yielding their evening sacrifice of incense: this new scent is neither of shrub nor flower; it is—I know it well—it is Mr. Rochester's cigar. I look round and I listen. I see trees laden with ripening fruit. I hear a nightingale warbling in a wood half a mile off; no moving form is visible, no coming step audible; but that perfume increases: I must flee. I make for the wicket leading to the shrubbery, and I see Mr. Rochester entering. I step aside into the ivy recess; he will not stay long: he will soon return whence he came, and if I sit still he will never see me.

But no—eventide is as pleasant to him as to me, and this antique garden as attractive; and he strolls on, now lifting the gooseberry-tree branches to look at the fruit, large as plums, with which they are laden; now taking a ripe cherry from the wall; now stooping towards a knot of flowers, either to inhale their fragrance or to admire the dew-beads on their petals. A great moth goes humming by me; it alights on a plant at Mr. Rochester's foot: he sees it, and bends to examine it.

"Now, he has his back towards me," thought I, "and he is occupied too; perhaps, if I walk softly, I can slip away unnoticed."

I trode on an edging of turf that the crackle of the pebbly gravel might not betray me: he was standing among the beds at a yard or two distant from where I had to pass; the moth apparently engaged him. "I shall get by very well," I meditated. As I crossed his shadow, thrown long over the garden by the moon, not yet risen high, he said quietly, without turning—

"Jane, come and look at this fellow."

I had made no noise: he had not eyes behind—could his shadow feel? I started at first, and then I approached him.

"Look at his wings," said he, "he reminds me rather of a West Indian insect; one does not often see so large and gay a night-rover in England; there! He is flown."

The moth roamed away. I was sheepishly retreating also; but Mr. Rochester followed me, and when we reached the wicket, he said—

"Turn back: on so lovely a night it is a shame to sit in the house; and surely no one can wish to go to bed while sunset is thus at meeting with moonrise."

It is one of my faults, that though my tongue is sometimes prompt enough at an answer, there are times when it sadly fails me in framing an excuse; and always the lapse occurs at some crisis, when a facile word or plausible pretext is specially wanted to get me out of painful embarrassment. I did not like to walk at this hour alone with Mr. Rochester in the shadowy orchard; but I could not find a reason to allege for leaving him. I followed with lagging step, and thoughts busily bent on discovering a means of extrication; but he himself looked so composed and so grave also, I became ashamed of feeling any confusion: the evil—if evil existent or prospective there was—seemed to lie with me only; his mind was unconscious and quiet.

"Jane," he recommenced, as we entered the laurel walk, and slowly strayed down in the direction of the sunk fence and the horse-chestnut, "Thornfield is a pleasant place in summer, is it not?"

"Yes, sir."

"You must have become in some degree attached to the house—you, who have an eye for natural beauties, and a good deal of the organ of Adhesiveness?"

"I am attached to it, indeed."

"And though I don't comprehend how it is, I perceive you have acquired a degree of regard for that foolish little child Adèle, too; and even for simple dame Fairfax?"

"Yes, sir; in different ways, I have an affection for both."

"And would be sorry to part with them?"

"Yes."

"Pity!" he said, and sighed and paused. "It is always the way of events in this life," he continued presently; "no sooner have you got settled in a pleasant resting-place, than a voice calls out to you to rise and move on, for the hour of repose is expired."

"Must I move on, sir?" I asked. "Must I leave Thornfield?"

"I believe you must, Jane. I am sorry, Janet, but I believe indeed you must."

This was a blow: but I did not let it prostrate me.

"Well, sir, I shall be ready when the order to march comes."

"It is come now—I must give it tonight."

"Then you *are* going to be married, sir?"

"Ex-act-ly—pre-cise-ly: with your usual acuteness, you have hit the nail straight on the head."

"Soon, sir?"

"Very soon, my—that is, Miss Eyre: and you'll remember, Jane, the first time I, or Rumour, plainly intimated to you that it was my intention to put my old bachelor's neck into the sacred noose, to enter into the holy estate of matrimony—to take Miss Ingram to my bosom, in short (she's an extensive armful: but that's not to the point—one can't have too much of such a very excellent thing as my beautiful Blanche): well, as I was saying—listen to me, Jane! You're not turning your head to look after more moths, are you? That was only a lady-clock, child, 'flying away home.' I wish to remind you that it was you who first said to me, with that discretion I respect in you—with that foresight, prudence, and humility which befit your responsible and dependent position—that in case I married Miss Ingram, both you and little Adèle had better trot forthwith. I pass over the sort of slur conveyed in this suggestion on the character of my beloved; indeed, when you are far away, Janet, I'll try to forget it: I shall notice only its wisdom; which is such that I have made it my law of action. Adèle must go to school; and you, Miss Eyre, must get a new situation."

"Yes, sir, I will advertise immediately: and meantime, I suppose—" I was going to say, "I suppose I may stay here, till I find another shelter to betake myself to"; but I stopped, feeling it would not do to risk a long sentence, for my voice was not quite under command.

"In about a month I hope to be a bridegroom," continued Mr. Rochester; "and in the interim, I shall myself look out for employment and an asylum for you."

"Thank you, sir; I am sorry to give—"

"Oh, no need to apologise! I consider that when a dependent does her duty as well as you have done yours, she has a sort of claim upon her employer for any little assistance he can conveniently render her; indeed I have already, through my future mother-in-law, heard of a place that I think will suit: it is to undertake the education of the five daughters of Mrs. Dionysius O'Gall of Bitternutt Lodge, Connaught, Ireland. You'll like Ireland, I think: they're such warm-hearted people there, they say."

"It is a long way off, sir."

"No matter—a girl of your sense will not object to the voyage or the distance."

"Not the voyage, but the distance: and then the sea is a barrier—"

"From what, Jane?"

"From England and from Thornfield: and—"

"Well?"

"From *you*, sir."

I said this almost involuntarily, and, with as little sanction of free will, my tears gushed out. I did not cry so as to be heard, however; I avoided sobbing. The thought of Mrs. O'Gall and Bitternutt Lodge struck cold to my heart; and colder the thought of all the brine and foam, destined, as it seemed, to rush between me and the master at whose side I now walked, and coldest the remembrance of the wider ocean—wealth, caste, custom intervened between me and what I naturally and inevitably loved.

"It is a long way," I again said.

"It is, to be sure; and when you get to Bitternutt Lodge, Connaught, Ireland, I shall never see you again, Jane: that's morally certain. I never go over to Ireland, not having myself much of a fancy for the country. We have been good friends, Jane; have we not?"

"Yes, sir."

"And when friends are on the eve of separation, they like to spend the little time that remains to them close to each other. Come! We'll talk over the voyage and the parting quietly half-an-hour or so, while the stars enter into their shining life up in heaven yonder: here is the chestnut tree: here is the bench at its old roots. Come, we will sit there in peace tonight, though we should never more be destined to sit there together." He seated me and himself.

"It is a long way to Ireland, Janet, and I am sorry to send my little friend on such weary travels: but if I can't do better, how is it to be helped? Are you anything akin to me, do you think, Jane?"

I could risk no sort of answer by this time: my heart was still.

"Because," he said, "I sometimes have a queer feeling with regard to you—especially when you are near me, as now: it is as if I had a string somewhere under my left ribs, tightly and inextricably knotted to a similar string situated in the corresponding quarter of your little frame. And if that boisterous Channel, and two hundred miles or so of land come broad between us, I am afraid that cord of communion will be snapt; and then I've a nervous notion I should take to bleeding inwardly. As for you—you'd forget me."

"That I *never* should, sir: you know—" Impossible to proceed.

"Jane, do you hear that nightingale singing in the wood? Listen!"

In listening, I sobbed convulsively; for I could repress what I endured no longer; I was obliged to yield, and I was shaken from head to foot with acute distress. When I did speak, it was only to express an impetuous wish that I had never been born, or never come to Thornfield.

"Because you are sorry to leave it?"

The vehemence of emotion, stirred by grief and love within me, was claiming mastery, and struggling for full sway, and asserting a right to predominate, to overcome, to live, rise, and reign at last: yes—and to speak.

"I grieve to leave Thornfield: I love Thornfield—I love it, because I have lived in it a full and delightful life—momentarily at least. I have not been trampled on. I have not been petrified. I have not been buried with inferior minds, and excluded from every glimpse of communion with what is bright and energetic and high. I have talked, face to face, with what I reverence, with what I delight in—with an original, a vigorous, an expanded mind. I have known you, Mr. Rochester; and it strikes me with terror and anguish to feel I absolutely must be torn from you for ever. I see the necessity of departure; and it is like looking on the necessity of death."

"Where do you see the necessity?" he asked suddenly.

"Where? You, sir, have placed it before me."

"In what shape?"

"In the shape of Miss Ingram; a noble and beautiful woman—your bride."

"My bride! What bride? I have no bride!"

"But you will have."

"Yes—I will! I will!" He set his teeth.

"Then I must go—you have said it yourself."

"No: you must stay! I swear it—and the oath shall be kept."

"I tell you I must go!" I retorted, roused to something like passion. "Do you think I can stay to become nothing to you? Do you think I am an automaton? A machine without feelings? And can bear to have my morsel of bread snatched from my lips, and my drop of living water dashed from my cup? Do you think, because I am poor, obscure, plain, and little, I am soulless and heartless? You think wrong! I have as much soul as you—and full as much heart! And if God had gifted me with some beauty and much wealth, I should have made it as hard for you to leave me, as it is now for me to leave you. I am not talking to you now through the medium of custom, conventionalities, nor even of mortal flesh—it is my spirit that addresses your spirit; just as if both had passed through the grave, and we stood at God's feet, equal—as we are!"

"As we are!" repeated Mr. Rochester. "So," he added, enclosing me in his arms. Gathering me to his breast, pressing his lips on my lips: "So, Jane!"

"Yes, so, sir," I rejoined; "and yet not so; for you are a married man—or as good as a married man, and wed to one inferior to you—to one with whom you have no sympathy—whom I do not believe you truly love; for I have seen and heard you sneer at her. I would scorn such a union: therefore I am better than you—let me go!"

"Where, Jane? To Ireland?"

"Yes—to Ireland. I have spoken my mind, and can go anywhere now."

"Jane, be still; don't struggle so, like a wild frantic bird that is rending its own plumage in its desperation."

"I am no bird; and no net ensnares me; I am a free human being with an independent will, which I now exert to leave you."

Another effort set me at liberty, and I stood erect before him.

"And your will shall decide your destiny," he said. "I offer you my hand, my heart, and a share of all my possessions."

"You play a farce, which I merely laugh at."

"I ask you to pass through life at my side—to be my second self, and best earthly companion."

"For that fate you have already made your choice, and must abide by it."

"Jane, be still a few moments: you are over-excited: I will be still too."

A waft of wind came sweeping down the laurel-walk, and trembled through the boughs of the chestnut: it wandered away—away—to an indefinite distance—it died. The nightingale's song was then the only voice of the hour: in listening to it, I again wept. Mr. Rochester sat quiet, looking at me gently and seriously. Some time passed before he spoke; he at last said—

"Come to my side, Jane, and let us explain and understand one another."

"I will never again come to your side: I am torn away now, and cannot return."

"But, Jane, I summon you as my wife: it is you only I intend to marry."

I was silent: I thought he mocked me.

"Come, Jane—come hither."

"Your bride stands between us."

He rose, and with a stride reached me.

"My bride is here," he said, again drawing me to him, "because my equal is here, and my likeness. Jane, will you marry me?"

Still I did not answer, and still I writhed myself from his grasp: for I was still incredulous.

"Do you doubt me, Jane?"

"Entirely."

"You have no faith in me?"

"Not a whit."

"Am I a liar in your eyes?" he asked passionately. "Little sceptic, you *shall* be convinced. What love have I for Miss Ingram? None: and that you know. What love has she for me? None: as I have taken pains to prove: I caused a rumour to reach her that my fortune was not a third of what was supposed, and after that I presented myself to see the result; it was coldness both from her and her mother. I would not—I could not—marry Miss Ingram. You—you strange, you almost unearthly thing! I love as my own flesh. You—poor and obscure, and small and plain as you are—I entreat to accept me as a husband."

"What, me!" I ejaculated, beginning in his earnestness—and especially in his incivility—to credit his sincerity. "Me, who have not a friend in the world but you—if you are my friend: not a shilling but what you have given me?"

"You, Jane, I must have you for my own—entirely my own. Will you be mine? Say yes, quickly."

"Mr. Rochester, let me look at your face: turn to the moonlight."

"Why?"

"Because I want to read your countenance—turn!"

"There! You will find it scarcely more legible than a crumpled, scratched page. Read on: only make haste, for I suffer."

His face was very much agitated and very much flushed, and there were strong workings in the features, and strange gleams in the eyes.

"Oh, Jane, you torture me!" he exclaimed. "With that searching and yet faithful and generous look, you torture me!"

"How can I do that? If you are true, and your offer real, my only feelings to you must be gratitude and devotion—they cannot torture."

"Gratitude!" he ejaculated; and added wildly: "Jane, accept me quickly. Say, Edward—give me my name—Edward—I will marry you."

"Are you in earnest? Do you truly love me? Do you sincerely wish me to be your wife?"

"I do; and if an oath is necessary to satisfy you, I swear it."

"Then, sir, I will marry you."

"Edward—my little wife!"

"Dear Edward!"

"Come to me—come to me entirely now," said he; and added, in his deepest tone, speaking in my ear as his cheek was laid on mine, "Make my happiness—I will make yours."

"God pardon me!" he subjoined ere long. "And man meddle not with me: I have her, and will hold her."

"There is no one to meddle, sir. I have no kindred to interfere."

"No—that is the best of it," he said. And if I had loved him less I should have thought his accent and look of exultation savage; but, sitting by him, roused from the nightmare of parting—called to the paradise of union—I thought only of the bliss given me to drink in so abundant a flow. Again and again he said, "Are you happy, Jane?" And again and again I answered, "Yes." After which he murmured, "It will atone—it will atone. Have I not found her friendless, and cold, and comfortless? Will I not guard, and cherish, and solace her? Is there not love in my heart, and constancy in my resolves? It will expiate at God's tribunal. I know my Maker sanctions what I do. For the world's judgment—I wash my hands thereof. For man's opinion—I defy it."

But what had befallen the night? The moon was not yet set, and we were all in shadow: I could scarcely see my master's face, near as I was. And what ailed the chestnut tree? It writhed and groaned; while wind roared in the laurel walk, and came sweeping over us.

"We must go in," said Mr. Rochester; "the weather changes. I could have sat with thee till morning, Jane."

"And so," thought I, "could I with you." I should have said so, perhaps, but a livid, vivid spark leapt out of a cloud at which I was looking, and there was a crack, a crash, and a close rattling peal; and I thought only of hiding my dazzled eyes against Mr. Rochester's shoulder.

The rain rushed down. He hurried me up the walk, through the grounds, and into the house; but we were quite wet before we could pass the threshold. He was taking off my shawl in the hall, and shaking the water out of my loosened hair, when Mrs. Fairfax emerged from her room. I did not observe her at first, nor did Mr. Rochester. The lamp was lit. The clock was on the stroke of twelve.

"Hasten to take off your wet things," said he; "and before you go, good-night—good-night, my darling!"

He kissed me repeatedly. When I looked up, on leaving his arms, there stood the widow, pale, grave, and amazed. I only smiled at her, and ran upstairs. "Explanation will do for another time," thought I. Still, when I reached my chamber, I felt a pang at the idea she should even temporarily misconstrue what she had seen. But joy soon effaced every other feeling; and loud as the wind blew, near and deep as the thunder crashed, fierce and frequent as the lightning gleamed, cataract-like as the rain fell during a storm of two hours' duration, I experienced no fear and little awe. Mr. Rochester came thrice to my door in the course of it, to ask if I was safe and tranquil: and that was comfort, that was strength for anything.

Before I left my bed in the morning, little Adèle came running in to tell me that the great horse-chestnut at the bottom of the orchard had been struck by lightning in the night, and half of it split away.

CHAPTER XXIV

As I rose and dressed, I thought over what had happened, and wondered if it were a dream. I could not be certain of the reality till I had seen Mr. Rochester again, and heard him renew his words of love and promise.

While arranging my hair, I looked at my face in the glass, and felt it was no longer plain: there was hope in its aspect and life in its colour; and my eyes seemed as if they had beheld the fount of fruition, and borrowed beams from the lustrous ripple. I had often been unwilling to look at my master, because I feared he could not be pleased at my look; but I was sure I might lift my face to his now, and not cool his affection by its expression. I took a plain but clean and light summer dress from my drawer and put it on: it seemed no attire had ever so well become me, because none had I ever worn in so blissful a mood.

I was not surprised, when I ran down into the hall, to see that a brilliant June morning had succeeded to the tempest of the night; and to feel, through the open glass door, the breathing of a fresh and fragrant breeze. Nature must be gladsome when I was so happy. A beggar-woman and her little boy—pale, ragged objects both—were coming up the walk, and I ran down and gave them all the money I happened to have in my purse—some three or four shillings: good or bad, they must partake of my jubilee. The rooks cawed, and blither birds sang; but nothing was so merry or so musical as my own rejoicing heart.

Mrs. Fairfax surprised me by looking out of the window with a sad countenance, and saying gravely, "Miss Eyre, will you come to breakfast?" During the meal she was quiet and cool: but I could not undeceive her then. I must wait for my master to give explanations; and so must she. I ate what I could, and then I hastened upstairs. I met Adèle leaving the schoolroom.

"Where are you going? It is time for lessons."

"Mr. Rochester has sent me away to the nursery."

"Where is he?"

"In there," pointing to the apartment she had left; and I went in, and there he stood.

"Come and bid me good-morning," said he. I gladly advanced; and it was not merely a cold word now, or even a shake of the hand that I received, but an embrace and a kiss. It seemed natural: it seemed genial to be so well loved, so caressed by him.

"Jane, you look blooming, and smiling, and pretty," said he; "truly pretty this morning. Is this my pale, little elf? Is this my mustard-seed? This little sunny-faced girl with the dimpled cheek and rosy lips; the satin-smooth hazel hair, and the radiant hazel eyes?" (I had green eyes, reader; but you must excuse the mistake: for him they were new-dyed, I suppose.)

"It is Jane Eyre, sir."

"Soon to be Jane Rochester," he added; "in four weeks, Janet; not a day more. Do you hear that?"

I did, and I could not quite comprehend it: it made me giddy. The feeling, the announcement sent through me, was something stronger than was consistent with joy—something that smote and stunned. It was, I think almost fear.

"You blushed, and now you are white, Jane: what is that for?"

"Because you gave me a new name—Jane Rochester; and it seems so strange."

"Yes, Mrs. Rochester," said he; "young Mrs. Rochester—Fairfax Rochester's girl-bride."

"It can never be, sir; it does not sound likely. Human beings never enjoy complete happiness in this world. I was not born for a different destiny to the rest of my species: to imagine such a lot befalling me is a fairy tale—a day-dream."

"Which I can and will realise. I shall begin today. This morning I wrote to my banker in London to send me certain jewels he has in his keeping—heirlooms for the ladies of Thornfield. In a day or two I hope to pour them into your lap: for every privilege, every attention shall be yours that I would accord a peer's daughter, if about to marry her."

"Oh, sir! Never rain jewels! I don't like to hear them spoken of. Jewels for Jane Eyre sounds unnatural and strange: I would rather not have them."

"I will myself put the diamond chain round your neck, and the circlet on your forehead—which it will become: for nature, at least, has stamped her patent of nobility on this brow, Jane; and I will clasp the bracelets on these fine wrists, and load these fairy-like fingers with rings."

"No, no, sir! Think of other subjects, and speak of other things, and in another strain. Don't address me as if I were a beauty; I am your plain, Quakerish governess."

"You are a beauty in my eyes, and a beauty just after the desire of my heart—delicate and aërial."

"Puny and insignificant, you mean. You are dreaming, sir—or you are sneering. For God's sake don't be ironical!"

"I will make the world acknowledge you a beauty, too," he went on, while I really became uneasy at the strain he had adopted, because I felt he was either deluding himself or trying to delude me. "I will attire my Jane in satin and lace, and she shall have roses in her hair; and I will cover the head I love best with a priceless veil."

"And then you won't know me, sir; and I shall not be your Jane Eyre any longer, but an ape in a harlequin's jacket—a jay in borrowed plumes. I would as soon see you, Mr. Rochester, tricked out in stage-trappings, as myself clad in a court-lady's robe; and I don't call you handsome, sir, though I love you most dearly: far too dearly to flatter you. Don't flatter me."

He pursued his theme, however, without noticing my deprecation. "This very day I shall take you in the carriage to Millcote, and you must choose some dresses for yourself. I told you we shall be married in four weeks. The wedding is to take place quietly, in the church down below yonder; and then I shall waft you away at once to town. After a brief stay there, I shall bear my treasure to regions nearer the sun: to French vineyards and Italian plains; and she shall see whatever is famous in old story and in modern record: she shall taste, too, of the life of cities; and she shall learn to value herself by just comparison with others."

"Shall I travel? And with you, sir?"

"You shall sojourn at Paris, Rome, and Naples: at Florence, Venice, and Vienna: all the ground I have wandered over shall be re-trodden by you: wherever I stamped my hoof, your sylph's foot shall step also. Ten years since, I flew through Europe half mad; with disgust, hate, and rage as my companions: now I shall revisit it healed and cleansed, with a very angel as my comforter."

I laughed at him as he said this. "I am not an angel," I asserted; "and I will not be one till I die: I will be myself. Mr. Rochester, you must neither expect nor exact anything celestial of me—for you will not get it, any more than I shall get it of you: which I do not at all anticipate."

"What do you anticipate of me?"

"For a little while you will perhaps be as you are now—a very little while; and then you will turn cool; and then you will be capricious; and then you will be stern, and I shall have much ado to please you: but when you get well used to me, you will perhaps like me again—*like* me, I say, not *love* me. I suppose your love will effervesce in six months, or less. I have observed in books written by men, that period assigned as the farthest to which a husband's ardour extends. Yet, after all, as a friend and companion, I hope never to become quite distasteful to my dear master."

"Distasteful! And like you again! I think I shall like you again, and yet again: and I will make you confess I do not only *like*, but *love* you—with truth, fervour, constancy."

"Yet are you not capricious, sir?"

"To women who please me only by their faces, I am the very devil when I find out they have neither souls nor hearts—when they open to me a perspective of flatness, triviality, and perhaps imbecility, coarseness, and ill-temper: but to the clear eye and eloquent tongue, to the soul made of fire, and the character that bends but does not break—at once supple and stable, tractable and consistent—I am ever tender and true."

"Had you ever experience of such a character, sir? Did you ever love such a one?"

"I love it now."

"But before me: if I, indeed, in any respect come up to your difficult standard?"

"I never met your likeness. Jane, you please me, and you master me—you seem to submit, and I like the sense of pliancy you impart; and while I am twining the soft, silken skein round my finger, it sends a thrill up my arm to my heart. I am influenced—conquered; and the influence is sweeter than I can express; and the conquest I undergo has a witchery beyond any triumph I can win. Why do you smile, Jane? What does that inexplicable, that uncanny turn of countenance mean?"

"I was thinking, sir (you will excuse the idea; it was involuntary), I was thinking of Hercules and Samson with their charmers—"

"You were, you little elfish—"

"Hush, sir! You don't talk very wisely just now; any more than those gentlemen acted very wisely. However, had they been married, they would no doubt by their severity as husbands have made up for their softness as suitors; and so will you, I fear. I wonder how you will answer me a year hence, should I ask a favour it does not suit your convenience or pleasure to grant."

"Ask me something now, Jane—the least thing: I desire to be entreated—"

"Indeed I will, sir; I have my petition all ready."

"Speak! But if you look up and smile with that countenance, I shall swear concession before I know to what, and that will make a fool of me."

"Not at all, sir; I ask only this: don't send for the jewels, and don't crown me with roses: you might as well put a border of gold lace round that plain pocket handkerchief you have there."

"I might as well 'gild refined gold.' I know it: your request is granted then—for the time. I will remand the order I despatched to my banker. But you have not yet asked for anything; you have prayed a gift to be withdrawn: try again."

"Well then, sir, have the goodness to gratify my curiosity, which is much piqued on one point."

He looked disturbed. "What? What?" he said hastily. "Curiosity is a dangerous petition: it is well I have not taken a vow to accord every request—"

"But there can be no danger in complying with this, sir."

"Utter it, Jane: but I wish that instead of a mere inquiry into, perhaps, a secret, it was a wish for half my estate."

"Now, King Ahasuerus! What do I want with half your estate? Do you think I am a Jew-usurer, seeking good investment in land? I would much rather have all your confidence. You will not exclude me from your confidence if you admit me to your heart?"

"You are welcome to all my confidence that is worth having, Jane; but for God's sake, don't desire a useless burden! Don't long for poison—don't turn out a downright Eve on my hands!"

"Why not, sir? You have just been telling me how much you liked to be conquered, and how pleasant over-persuasion is to you. Don't you think I had better take advantage of the confession, and begin and coax and entreat—even cry and be sulky if necessary—for the sake of a mere essay of my power?"

"I dare you to any such experiment. Encroach, presume, and the game is up."

"Is it, sir? You soon give in. How stern you look now! Your eyebrows have become as thick as my finger, and your forehead resembles what, in some very astonishing poetry, I once saw styled 'a blue-piled thunderloft.' That will be your married look, sir, I suppose?"

"If that will be *your* married look, I, as a Christian, will soon give up the notion of consorting with a mere sprite or salamander. But what had you to ask, thing—out with it?"

"There, you are less than civil now; and I like rudeness a great deal better than flattery. I had rather be a *thing* than an angel. This is what I have to ask: Why did you take such pains to make me believe you wished to marry Miss Ingram?"

"Is that all? Thank God it is no worse!" And now he unknit his black brows; looked down, smiling at me, and stroked my hair, as if well pleased at seeing a danger averted. "I think I may confess," he continued, "even although I should make you a little indignant, Jane—and I have seen what a fire-spirit you can be when you are indignant. You glowed in the cool moonlight last night, when you mutinied against fate, and claimed your rank as my equal. Janet, by-the-by, it was you who made me the offer."

"Of course I did. But to the point if you please, sir—Miss Ingram?"

"Well, I feigned courtship of Miss Ingram, because I wished to render you as madly in love with me as I was with you; and I knew jealousy would be the best ally I could call in for the furtherance of that end."

"Excellent! Now you are small—not one whit bigger than the end of my little finger. It was a burning shame and a scandalous disgrace to act in that way. Did you think nothing of Miss Ingram's feelings, sir?"

"Her feelings are concentrated in one—pride; and that needs humbling. Were you jealous, Jane?"

"Never mind, Mr. Rochester: it is in no way interesting to you to know that. Answer me truly once more. Do you think Miss Ingram will not suffer from your dishonest coquetry? Won't she feel forsaken and deserted?"

"Impossible! When I told you how she, on the contrary, deserted me: the idea of my insolvency cooled, or rather extinguished, her flame in a moment."

"You have a curious, designing mind, Mr. Rochester. I am afraid your principles on some points are eccentric."

"My principles were never trained, Jane: they may have grown a little awry for want of attention."

"Once again, seriously; may I enjoy the great good that has been vouchsafed to me, without fearing that any one else is suffering the bitter pain I myself felt a while ago?"

"That you may, my good little girl: there is not another being in the world has the same pure love for me as yourself—for I lay that pleasant unction to my soul, Jane, a belief in your affection."

I turned my lips to the hand that lay on my shoulder. I loved him very much—more than I could trust myself to say—more than words had power to express.

"Ask something more," he said presently; "it is my delight to be entreated, and to yield."

I was again ready with my request. "Communicate your intentions to Mrs. Fairfax, sir: she saw me with you last night in the hall, and she was shocked. Give her some explanation before I see her again. It pains me to be misjudged by so good a woman."

"Go to your room, and put on your bonnet," he replied. "I mean you to accompany me to Millcote this morning; and while you prepare for the drive, I will enlighten the old lady's understanding. Did she think, Janet, you had given the world for love, and considered it well lost?"

"I believe she thought I had forgotten my station, and yours, sir."

"Station! Station! Your station is in my heart, and on the necks of those who would insult you, now or hereafter. Go."

I was soon dressed; and when I heard Mr. Rochester quit Mrs. Fairfax's parlour, I hurried down to it. The old lady had been reading her morning portion of Scripture—the Lesson for the day; her Bible lay open before her, and her spectacles were upon it. Her occupation, suspended by Mr. Rochester's announcement, seemed now forgotten: her eyes, fixed on the blank wall opposite, expressed the surprise of a quiet mind stirred by unwonted tidings. Seeing me, she roused herself: she made a sort of effort to smile, and framed a few words of congratulation; but the smile expired, and the sentence was abandoned unfinished. She put up her spectacles, shut the Bible, and pushed her chair back from the table.

"I feel so astonished," she began, "I hardly know what to say to you, Miss Eyre. I have surely not been dreaming, have I? Sometimes I half fall asleep when I am sitting alone and fancy things that have never happened. It has seemed to me more than once when I have been in a doze, that my dear husband, who died fifteen years since, has come in and sat down beside me; and that I have even heard him call me by my name, Alice, as he used to do. Now, can you tell me whether it is actually true that Mr. Rochester has asked you to marry him? Don't laugh at me. But I really thought he came in here five minutes ago, and said that in a month you would be his wife."

"He has said the same thing to me," I replied.

"He has! Do you believe him? Have you accepted him?"

"Yes."

She looked at me bewildered. "I could never have thought it. He is a proud man: all the Rochesters were proud: and his father, at least, liked money. He, too, has always been called careful. He means to marry you?"

"He tells me so."

She surveyed my whole person: in her eyes I read that they had there found no charm powerful enough to solve the enigma.

"It passes me!" she continued. "But no doubt, it is true since you say so. How it will answer, I cannot tell: I really don't know. Equality of position and fortune is often advisable in such cases; and there are twenty years of difference in your ages. He might almost be your father."

"No, indeed, Mrs. Fairfax!" exclaimed I, nettled. "He is nothing like my father! No one, who saw us together, would suppose it for an instant. Mr. Rochester looks as young, and is as young, as some men at five-and-twenty."

"Is it really for love he is going to marry you?" she asked.

I was so hurt by her coldness and scepticism, that the tears rose to my eyes.

"I am sorry to grieve you," pursued the widow; "but you are so young, and so little acquainted with men, I wished to put you on your guard. It is an old saying that 'all is not gold that glitters'; and in this case I do fear there will be something found to be different to what either you or I expect."

"Why? Am I a monster?" I said. "Is it impossible that Mr. Rochester should have a sincere affection for me?"

"No: you are very well; and much improved of late; and Mr. Rochester, I daresay, is fond of you. I have always noticed that you were a sort of pet of his. There are times when, for your sake, I have been a little uneasy at his marked preference, and have wished to put you on your guard: but I did not like to suggest even the possibility of wrong. I knew such an idea would shock, perhaps offend you; and you were so discreet, and so thoroughly modest and sensible, I hoped you might be trusted to protect yourself. Last night I cannot tell you what I suffered when I sought all over the house, and could find you nowhere, nor the master either; and then, at twelve o'clock, saw you come in with him."

"Well, never mind that now," I interrupted impatiently; "it is enough that all was right."

"I hope all will be right in the end," she said; "but believe me, you cannot be too careful. Try and keep Mr. Rochester at a distance: distrust yourself as well as him. Gentlemen in his station are not accustomed to marry their governesses."

I was growing truly irritated: happily, Adèle ran in.

"Let me go—let me go to Millcote too!" she cried. "Mr. Rochester won't: though there is so much room in the new carriage. Beg him to let me go, mademoiselle."

"That I will, Adèle"; and I hastened away with her, glad to quit my gloomy monitress. The carriage was ready: they were bringing it round to the front, and my master was pacing the pavement, Pilot following him backwards and forwards.

"Adèle may accompany us, may she not, sir?"

"I told her no. I'll have no brats! I'll have only you."

"Do let her go, Mr. Rochester, if you please: it would be better."

"Not it: she will be a restraint."

He was quite peremptory, both in look and voice. The chill of Mrs. Fairfax's warnings, and the damp of her doubts were upon me: something of unsubstantiality and uncertainty had beset my hopes. I half lost the sense of power over him. I was about mechanically to obey him, without further remonstrance; but as he helped me into the carriage, he looked at my face.

"What is the matter?" he asked. "All the sunshine is gone. Do you really wish the bairn to go? Will it annoy you if she is left behind?"

"I would far rather she went, sir."

"Then off for your bonnet, and back like a flash of lightning!" cried he to Adèle.

She obeyed him with what speed she might.

"After all, a single morning's interruption will not matter much," said he, "when I mean shortly to claim you—your thoughts, conversation, and company—for life."

Adèle, when lifted in, commenced kissing me, by way of expressing her gratitude for my intercession: she was instantly stowed away into a corner on the other side of him. She then peeped round to where I sat; so stern a neighbour was too restrictive to him, in his present fractious mood, she dared whisper no observations, nor ask of him any information.

"Let her come to me," I entreated; "she will, perhaps, trouble you, sir: there is plenty of room on this side."

He handed her over as if she had been a lapdog. "I'll send her to school yet," he said, but now he was smiling.

Adèle heard him, and asked if she was to go to school "sans mademoiselle?"

"Yes," he replied, "absolutely sans mademoiselle; for I am to take mademoiselle to the moon, and there I shall seek a cave in one of the white valleys among the volcano-tops, and mademoiselle shall live with me there, and only me."

"She will have nothing to eat: you will starve her," observed Adèle.

"I shall gather manna for her morning and night: the plains and hillsides in the moon are bleached with manna, Adèle."

"She will want to warm herself: what will she do for a fire?"

"Fire rises out of the lunar mountains: when she is cold, I'll carry her up to a peak, and lay her down on the edge of a crater."

"Oh, qu' elle y sera mal—peu comfortable! And her clothes, they will wear out: how can she get new ones?"

Mr. Rochester professed to be puzzled. "Hem!" said he. "What would you do, Adèle? Cudgel your brains for an expedient. How would a white or a pink cloud answer for a gown, do you think? And one could cut a pretty enough scarf out of a rainbow."

"She is far better as she is," concluded Adèle, after musing some time; "besides, she would get tired of living with only you in the moon. If I were mademoiselle, I would never consent to go with you."

"She has consented: she has pledged her word."

"But you can't get her there; there is no road to the moon: it is all air; and neither you nor she can fly."

"Adèle, look at that field." We were now outside Thornfield gates, and bowling lightly along the smooth road to Millcote, where the dust was well laid by the thunderstorm, and, where the low hedges and lofty timber trees on each side glistened green and rain-refreshed.

"In that field, Adèle, I was walking late one evening about a fortnight since—the evening of the day you helped me to make hay in the orchard meadows; and, as I was tired with raking swaths, I sat down to rest me on a stile; and there I took out a little book and a pencil, and began to write about a misfortune that befell me long ago, and a wish I had for happy days to come: I was writing away very fast, though daylight was fading from the leaf, when something came up the path and stopped two yards off me. I looked at it. It was a little thing with a veil of gossamer on its head. I beckoned it to come near me; it stood soon at my knee. I never spoke to it, and it never spoke to me, in words; but I read its eyes, and it read mine; and our speechless colloquy was to this effect—

"It was a fairy, and come from Elf-land, it said; and its errand was to make me happy: I must go with it out of the common world to a lonely place—such as the moon, for instance—and it nodded its head towards her horn, rising over Hay-hill: it told me of the alabaster cave and silver vale where we might live. I said I should like to go; but reminded it, as you did me, that I had no wings to fly.

" 'Oh,' returned the fairy, 'that does not signify! Here is a talisman will remove all difficulties'; and she held out a pretty gold ring. 'Put it,' she said, 'on the fourth finger of my left hand, and I am yours, and you are mine; and we shall leave earth, and make our own heaven yonder.' She nodded again at the moon. The ring, Adèle, is in my breeches-pocket, under the disguise of a sovereign: but I mean soon to change it to a ring again."

"But what has mademoiselle to do with it? I don't care for the fairy: you said it was mademoiselle you would take to the moon?"

"Mademoiselle is a fairy," he said, whispering mysteriously. Whereupon I told her not to mind his badinage; and she, on her part, evinced a fund of genuine French scepticism: denominating Mr. Rochester "un vrai menteur," and assuring him that she made no account whatever of his "contes de fée," and that "du reste, il n'y avait pas de fées, et quand même il y en avait": she was sure they would never appear to him, nor ever give him rings, or offer to live with him in the moon.

The hour spent at Millcote was a somewhat harassing one to me. Mr. Rochester obliged me to go to a certain silk warehouse: there I was ordered to choose half-a-dozen dresses. I hated the business, I begged leave to defer it: no—it should be gone through with now. By dint of entreaties expressed in energetic whispers, I reduced the half-dozen to two: these however, he vowed he would select himself. With anxiety I watched his eye rove over the gay stores: he fixed on a rich silk of the most brilliant amethyst dye, and a superb pink satin. I told him in a new series of whispers, that he might as well buy me a gold gown and a silver bonnet at once: I should certainly never venture to wear his choice. With infinite difficulty, for he was stubborn as a stone, I persuaded him to make an exchange in favour of a sober black satin and pearl-grey silk. "It might pass for the present," he said; "but he would yet see me glittering like a parterre."

Glad was I to get him out of the silk warehouse, and then out of a jewellers shop: the more he bought me, the more my cheek burned with a sense of annoyance and degradation. As we re-entered the carriage, and I sat back feverish and fagged, I remembered what, in the hurry of events, dark and bright, I had wholly forgotten—the letter of my uncle, John Eyre, to Mrs. Reed: his intention to adopt me and make me his legatee. "It would, indeed, be a relief," I thought, "if I had ever so small an independency; I never can bear being dressed like a doll by Mr. Rochester, or sitting like a second Danae with the golden shower falling daily round me. I will write to Madeira the moment I get home, and tell my uncle John I am going to be married, and to whom: if I had but a prospect of one day bringing Mr. Rochester an accession of fortune, I could better endure to be kept by him now." And somewhat relieved by this idea (which I failed not to execute that day), I ventured once more to meet my master's and lover's eye, which most pertinaciously sought mine, though I averted both face and gaze. He smiled; and I thought his smile was such as a sultan might, in a blissful and fond moment, bestow on a slave his gold and gems had enriched: I crushed his hand, which was ever hunting mine, vigorously, and thrust it back to him red with the passionate pressure.

"You need not look in that way," I said; "if you do, I'll wear nothing but my old Lowood frocks to the end of the chapter. I'll be married in this lilac gingham: you may make a dressing-gown for yourself out of the pearl-grey silk, and an infinite series of waistcoats out of the black satin."

He chuckled; he rubbed his hands. "Oh, it is rich to see and hear her!" he exclaimed. "Is she original? Is she piquant? I would not exchange this one little English girl for the Grand Turk's whole seraglio, gazelle-eyes, houri forms, and all!"

The Eastern allusion bit me again. "I'll not stand you an inch in the stead of a seraglio," I said; "so don't consider me an equivalent for one. If you have a fancy for anything in that line, away with you, sir, to the bazaars of Stamboul without delay, and lay out in extensive slave-purchases some of that spare cash you seem at a loss to spend satisfactorily here."

"And what will you do, Janet, while I am bargaining for so many tons of flesh and such an assortment of black eyes?"

"I'll be preparing myself to go out as a missionary to preach liberty to them that are enslaved—your harem inmates amongst the rest. I'll get admitted there, and I'll stir up mutiny; and you, three-tailed bashaw as you are, sir, shall in a trice find yourself fettered amongst our hands: nor will I, for one, consent to cut your bonds till you have signed a charter, the most liberal that despot ever yet conferred."

"I would consent to be at your mercy, Jane."

"I would have no mercy, Mr. Rochester, if you supplicated for it with an eye like that. While you looked so, I should be certain that whatever charter you might grant under coercion, your first act, when released, would be to violate its conditions."

"Why, Jane, what would you have? I fear you will compel me to go through a private marriage ceremony, besides that performed at the altar. You will stipulate, I see, for peculiar terms—what will they be?"

"I only want an easy mind, sir; not crushed by crowded obligations. Do you remember what you said of Céline Varens? Of the diamonds, the cashmeres you gave her? I will not be your English Céline Varens. I shall continue to act as Adèle's governess; by that I shall earn my board and lodging, and thirty pounds a year besides. I'll furnish my own wardrobe out of that money, and you shall give me nothing but—"

"Well, but what?"

"Your regard; and if I give you mine in return, that debt will be quit."

"Well, for cool native impudence and pure innate pride, you haven't your equal," said he. We were now approaching Thornfield.

"Will it please you to dine with me today?" he asked, as we re-entered the gates.

"No, thank you, sir."

"And what for, 'no, thank you' if one may inquire?"

"I never have dined with you, sir: and I see no reason why I should now: till—"

"Till what? You delight in half-phrases."

"Till I can't help it."

"Do you suppose I eat like an ogre or a ghoul, that you dread being the companion of my repast?"

"I have formed no supposition on the subject, sir; but I want to go on as usual for another month."

"You will give up your governessing slavery at once."

"Indeed, begging your pardon, sir, I shall not. I shall just go on with it as usual. I shall keep out of your way all day, as I have been accustomed to do: you may send for me in the evening, when you feel disposed to see me, and I'll come then; but at no other time."

"I want a smoke, Jane, or a pinch of snuff, to comfort me under all this, 'pour me donner une contenance,' as Adèle would say; and unfortunately I have neither my cigar-case, nor my snuff-box. But listen—whisper. It is your time now, little tyrant, but it will be mine presently; and when once I have fairly seized you, to have and to hold, I'll just—figuratively speaking—attach you to a chain like this" (touching his watch-guard). "Yes, bonny wee thing, I'll wear you in my bosom, lest my jewel I should tyne."

He said this as he helped me to alight from the carriage, and while he afterwards lifted out Adèle, I entered the house, and made good my retreat upstairs.

He duly summoned me to his presence in the evening. I had prepared an occupation for him; for I was determined not to spend the whole time in a *tête-à-tête* conversation. I remembered his fine voice; I knew he liked to sing—good singers generally do. I was no vocalist myself, and, in his fastidious judgment, no musician, either; but I delighted in listening when the performance was good. No sooner had twilight, that hour of romance, began to lower her blue and starry banner over the lattice, than I rose, opened the piano, and entreated him, for the love of heaven, to give me a song. He said I was a capricious witch, and that he would rather sing another time; but I averred that no time was like the present.

"Did I like his voice?" he asked.

"Very much." I was not fond of pampering that susceptible vanity of his; but for once, and from motives of expediency, I would e'en soothe and stimulate it.

"Then, Jane, you must play the accompaniment."

"Very well, sir, I will try."

I did try, but was presently swept off the stool and denominated "a little bungler." Being pushed unceremoniously to one side—which was precisely what I wished—he usurped my place, and proceeded to accompany himself: for he could play as well as sing. I hied me to the window-recess. And while I sat there and looked out on the still trees and dim lawn, to a sweet air was sung in mellow tones the following strain:

The truest love that ever heart
Felt at its kindled core
Did through each vein, in quickened start,
The tide of being pour.

Her coming was my hope each day,
Her parting was my pain;
The chance that did her steps delay
Was ice in every vein.

I dreamed it would be nameless bliss,
As I loved, loved to be;
And to this object did I press
As blind as eagerly.

But wide as pathless was the space
That lay our lives between,
And dangerous as the foamy race
Of ocean-surges green.

And haunted as a robber-path
Through wilderness or wood;
For Might and Right, and Woe and Wrath,
Between our spirits stood.

I dangers dared; I hindrance scorned;
I omens did defy:
Whatever menaced, harassed, warned,
I passed impetuous by.

On sped my rainbow, fast as light;
I flew as in a dream;
For glorious rose upon my sight
That child of Shower and Gleam.

Still bright on clouds of suffering dim
Shines that soft, solemn joy;
Nor care I now, how dense and grim
Disasters gather nigh.

I care not in this moment sweet,
Though all I have rushed o'er
Should come on pinion, strong and fleet,
Proclaiming vengeance sore:

Though haughty Hate should strike me down,
Right, bar approach to me,
And grinding Might, with furious frown,
Swear endless enmity.

My love has placed her little hand
With noble faith in mine,
And vowed that wedlock's sacred band
Our nature shall entwine.

My love has sworn, with sealing kiss,
With me to live—to die;
I have at last my nameless bliss.
As I love—loved am I!

He rose and came towards me, and I saw his face all kindled, and his full falcon-eye flashing, and tenderness and passion in every lineament. I quailed momentarily—then I rallied. Soft scene, daring demonstration, I would not have; and I stood in peril of both: a weapon of defence must be prepared—I whetted my tongue: as he reached me, I asked with asperity, "whom he was going to marry now?"

"That was a strange question to be put by his darling Jane."

"Indeed! I considered it a very natural and necessary one: he had talked of his future wife dying with him. What did he mean by such a pagan idea? *I* had no intention of dying with him—he might depend on that."

"Oh, all he longed, all he prayed for, was that I might live with him! Death was not for such as I."

"Indeed it was: I had as good a right to die when my time came as he had: but I should bide that time, and not be hurried away in a suttee."

"Would I forgive him for the selfish idea, and prove my pardon by a reconciling kiss?"

"No: I would rather be excused."

Here I heard myself apostrophised as a "hard little thing"; and it was added, "any other woman would have been melted to marrow at hearing such stanzas crooned in her praise."

I assured him I was naturally hard—very flinty, and that he would often find me so; and that, moreover, I was determined to show him divers rugged points in my character before the ensuing four weeks elapsed: he should know fully what sort of a bargain he had made, while there was yet time to rescind it.

"Would I be quiet and talk rationally?"

"I would be quiet if he liked, and as to talking rationally, I flattered myself I was doing that now."

He fretted, pished, and pshawed. "Very good," I thought; "you may fume and fidget as you please: but this is the best plan to pursue with you, I am certain. I like you more than I can say; but I'll not sink into a bathos of sentiment: and with this needle of repartee I'll keep you from the edge of the gulf too; and, moreover, maintain by its pungent aid that distance between you and myself most conducive to our real mutual advantage."

From less to more, I worked him up to considerable irritation; then, after he had retired, in dudgeon, quite to the other end of the room, I got up, and saying, "I wish you good-night, sir," in my natural and wonted respectful manner, I slipped out by the side-door and got away.

The system thus entered on, I pursued during the whole season of probation; and with the best success. He was kept, to be sure, rather cross and crusty; but on the whole I could see he was excellently entertained, and that a lamb-like submission and turtle-dove sensibility, while fostering his despotism more, would have pleased his judgment, satisfied his common-sense, and even suited his taste less.

In other people's presence I was, as formerly, deferential and quiet; any other line of conduct being uncalled for: it was only in the evening conferences I thus thwarted and afflicted him. He continued to send for me punctually the moment the clock struck seven; though when I appeared before him now, he had no such honeyed terms as "love" and "darling" on his lips: the best words at my service were "provoking puppet," "malicious elf," "sprite," "changeling," etc. For caresses, too, I now got grimaces; for a pressure of the hand, a pinch on the arm; for a kiss on the cheek, a severe tweak of the ear. It was all right: at present I decidedly preferred these fierce favours to anything more tender. Mrs. Fairfax, I saw, approved me: her anxiety on my account vanished; therefore I was certain I did well. Meantime, Mr. Rochester affirmed I was wearing him to skin and bone, and threatened awful vengeance for my present conduct at some period fast coming. I laughed in my sleeve at his menaces. "I can keep you in reasonable check now," I reflected; "and I don't doubt to be able to do it hereafter: if one expedient loses its virtue, another must be devised."

Yet after all, my task was not an easy one; often I would rather have pleased than teased him. My future husband was becoming to me my whole world; and more than the world: almost my hope of heaven. He stood between me and every thought of religion, as an eclipse intervenes between man and the broad sun. I could not, in those days, see God for His creature: of whom I had made an idol.

CHAPTER XXV

The month of courtship had wasted: its very last hours were being numbered. There was no putting off the day that advanced—the bridal day; and all preparations for its arrival were complete. *I*, at least, had nothing more to do: there were my trunks, packed, locked, corded, ranged in a row along the wall of my little chamber; tomorrow, at this time, they would be far on their road to London: and so should I (D.V.)—or rather, not I, but one Jane Rochester, a person whom as yet I knew not. The cards of address alone remained to nail on: they lay, four little squares, in the drawer. Mr. Rochester had himself written the direction, "Mrs. Rochester, —— Hotel, London," on each: I could not persuade myself to affix them, or to have them affixed. Mrs. Rochester! She did not exist: she would not be born till tomorrow, some time after eight o'clock a.m.; and I would wait to be assured she had come into the world alive before I assigned to her all that property. It was enough that in yonder closet, opposite my dressing-table, garments said to be hers had already displaced my black stuff Lowood frock and straw bonnet: for not to me appertained that suit of wedding raiment; the pearl-coloured robe, the vapoury veil pendent from the usurped portmanteau. I shut the closet to conceal the strange, wraith-like apparel it contained; which, at this evening hour—nine o'clock—gave out certainly a most ghostly shimmer through the shadow of my apartment. "I will leave you by yourself, white dream," I said. "I am feverish: I hear the wind blowing: I will go out of doors and feel it."

It was not only the hurry of preparation that made me feverish; not only the anticipation of the great change—the new life which was to commence tomorrow: both these circumstances had their share, doubtless, in producing that restless, excited mood which hurried me forth at this late hour into the darkening grounds: but a third cause influenced my mind more than they.

I had at heart a strange and anxious thought. Something had happened which I could not comprehend; no one knew of or had seen the event but myself: it had taken place the preceding night. Mr. Rochester that night was absent from home; nor was he yet returned:

business had called him to a small estate of two or three farms he possessed thirty miles off—business it was requisite he should settle in person, previous to his meditated departure from England. I waited now his return; eager to disburthen my mind, and to seek of him the solution of the enigma that perplexed me. Stay till he comes, reader; and, when I disclose my secret to him, you shall share the confidence.

I sought the orchard, driven to its shelter by the wind, which all day had blown strong and full from the south, without, however, bringing a speck of rain. Instead of subsiding as night drew on, it seemed to augment its rush and deepen its roar: the trees blew steadfastly one way, never writhing round, and scarcely tossing back their boughs once in an hour; so continuous was the strain bending their branchy heads northward—the clouds drifted from pole to pole, fast following, mass on mass: no glimpse of blue sky had been visible that July day.

It was not without a certain wild pleasure I ran before the wind, delivering my trouble of mind to the measureless air-torrent thundering through space. Descending the laurel walk, I faced the wreck of the chestnut-tree; it stood up black and riven: the trunk, split down the centre, gasped ghastly. The cloven halves were not broken from each other, for the firm base and strong roots kept them unsundered below; though community of vitality was destroyed—the sap could flow no more: their great boughs on each side were dead, and next winter's tempests would be sure to fell one or both to earth: as yet, however, they might be said to form one tree—a ruin, but an entire ruin.

"You did right to hold fast to each other," I said: as if the monster-splinters were living things, and could hear me. "I think, scathed as you look, and charred and scorched, there must be a little sense of life in you yet, rising out of that adhesion at the faithful, honest roots: you will never have green leaves more—never more see birds making nests and singing idylls in your boughs; the time of pleasure and love is over with you: but you are not desolate: each of you has a comrade to sympathise with him in his decay." As I looked up at them, the moon appeared momentarily in that part of the sky which filled their fissure; her disk was blood-red and half overcast; she seemed to throw on me one bewildered, dreary glance, and buried herself again instantly in the deep drift of cloud. The wind fell, for a second, round Thornfield; but far away over wood and water, poured a wild, melancholy wail: it was sad to listen to, and I ran off again.

Here and there I strayed through the orchard, gathered up the apples with which the grass round the tree roots was thickly strewn; then I employed myself in dividing the ripe from the unripe; I carried them into the house and put them away in the store-room. Then I repaired to the library to ascertain whether the fire was lit, for, though summer, I knew on such a gloomy evening Mr. Rochester would like to see a cheerful hearth when he came in: yes, the fire had been kindled some time, and burnt well. I placed his arm-chair by the chimney-corner: I wheeled the table near it: I let down the curtain, and had the candles brought in ready for lighting. More restless than ever, when I had completed these arrangements I could not sit still, nor even remain in the house: a little time-piece in the room and the old clock in the hall simultaneously struck ten.

"How late it grows!" I said. "I will run down to the gates: it is moonlight at intervals; I can see a good way on the road. He may be coming now, and to meet him will save some minutes of suspense."

The wind roared high in the great trees which embowered the gates; but the road as far as I could see, to the right hand and the left, was all still and solitary: save for the shadows of clouds crossing it at intervals as the moon looked out, it was but a long pale line, unvaried by one moving speck.

A puerile tear dimmed my eye while I looked—a tear of disappointment and impatience; ashamed of it, I wiped it away. I lingered; the moon shut herself wholly within her chamber, and drew close her curtain of dense cloud: the night grew dark; rain came driving fast on the gale.

"I wish he would come! I wish he would come!" I exclaimed, seized with hypochondriac foreboding. I had expected his arrival before tea; now it was dark: what could keep him? Had an accident happened? The event of last night again recurred to me. I interpreted it as a warning of disaster. I feared my hopes were too bright to be realised; and I had enjoyed so much bliss lately that I imagined my fortune had passed its meridian, and must now decline.

"Well, I cannot return to the house," I thought. "I cannot sit by the fireside, while he is abroad in inclement weather: better tire my limbs than strain my heart; I will go forward and meet him."

I set out; I walked fast, but not far: ere I had measured a quarter of a mile, I heard the tramp of hoofs; a horseman came on, full gallop; a dog ran by his side. Away with evil presentiment! It was he: here he was, mounted on Mesrour, followed by Pilot. He saw me; for the moon had opened a blue field in the sky, and rode in it watery bright: he took his hat off, and waved it round his head. I now ran to meet him.

"There!" he exclaimed, as he stretched out his hand and bent from the saddle: "You can't do without me, that is evident. Step on my boot-toe; give me both hands: mount!"

I obeyed: joy made me agile: I sprang up before him. A hearty kissing I got for a welcome, and some boastful triumph, which I swallowed as well as I could. He checked himself in his exultation to demand, "But is there anything the matter, Janet, that you come to meet me at such an hour? Is there anything wrong?"

"No, but I thought you would never come. I could not bear to wait in the house for you, especially with this rain and wind."

"Rain and wind, indeed! Yes, you are dripping like a mermaid; pull my cloak round you: but I think you are feverish, Jane: both your cheek and hand are burning hot. I ask again, is there anything the matter?"

"Nothing now; I am neither afraid nor unhappy."

"Then you have been both?"

"Rather: but I'll tell you all about it by-and-by, sir; and I daresay you will only laugh at me for my pains."

"I'll laugh at you heartily when tomorrow is past; till then I dare not: my prize is not certain. This is you, who have been as slippery as an eel this last month, and as thorny as a briar-rose? I could not lay a finger anywhere but I was pricked; and now I seem to have gathered up a stray lamb in my arms. You wandered out of the fold to seek your shepherd, did you, Jane?"

"I wanted you: but don't boast. Here we are at Thornfield: now let me get down."

He landed me on the pavement. As John took his horse, and he followed me into the hall, he told me to make haste and put something dry on, and then return to him in the library; and he stopped me, as I made for the staircase, to extort a promise that I would not be long: nor was I long; in five minutes I rejoined him. I found him at supper.

"Take a seat and bear me company, Jane: please God, it is the last meal but one you will eat at Thornfield Hall for a long time."

I sat down near him, but told him I could not eat. "Is it because you have the prospect of a journey before you, Jane? Is it the thoughts of going to London that takes away your appetite?"

"I cannot see my prospects clearly tonight, sir; and I hardly know what thoughts I have in my head. Everything in life seems unreal."

"Except me: I am substantial enough—touch me."

"You, sir, are the most phantom-like of all: you are a mere dream."

He held out his hand, laughing. "Is that a dream?" said he, placing it close to my eyes. He had a rounded, muscular, and vigorous hand, as well as a long, strong arm.

"Yes; though I touch it, it is a dream," said I, as I put it down from before my face. "Sir, have you finished supper?"

"Yes, Jane."

I rang the bell and ordered away the tray. When we were again alone, I stirred the fire, and then took a low seat at my master's knee.

"It is near midnight," I said.

"Yes: but remember, Jane, you promised to wake with me the night before my wedding."

"I did; and I will keep my promise, for an hour or two at least: I have no wish to go to bed."

"Are all your arrangements complete?"

"All, sir."

"And on my part likewise," he returned, "I have settled everything; and we shall leave Thornfield tomorrow, within half-an-hour after our return from church."

"Very well, sir."

"With what an extraordinary smile you uttered that word—'very well,' Jane! What a bright spot of colour you have on each cheek! And how strangely your eyes glitter! Are you well?"

"I believe I am."

"Believe! What is the matter? Tell me what you feel."

"I could not, sir: no words could tell you what I feel. I wish this present hour would never end: who knows with what fate the next may come charged?"

"This is hypochondria, Jane. You have been over-excited, or over-fatigued."

"Do you, sir, feel calm and happy?"

"Calm? No: but happy—to the heart's core."

I looked up at him to read the signs of bliss in his face: it was ardent and flushed.

"Give me your confidence, Jane," he said. "Relieve your mind of any weight that oppresses it, by imparting it to me. What do you fear? That I shall not prove a good husband?"

"It is the idea farthest from my thoughts."

"Are you apprehensive of the new sphere you are about to enter? Of the new life into which you are passing?"

"No."

"You puzzle me, Jane: your look and tone of sorrowful audacity perplex and pain me. I want an explanation."

"Then, sir, listen. You were from home last night?"

"I was: I know that; and you hinted a while ago at something which had happened in my absence:—nothing, probably, of consequence; but, in short, it has disturbed you. Let me hear it. Mrs. Fairfax has said something, perhaps? Or you have overheard the servants talk? Your sensitive self-respect has been wounded?"

"No, sir." It struck twelve—I waited till the time-piece had concluded its silver chime, and the clock its hoarse, vibrating stroke, and then I proceeded.

"All day yesterday I was very busy, and very happy in my ceaseless bustle; for I am not, as you seem to think, troubled by any haunting fears about the new sphere, et cetera: I think it a glorious thing to have the hope of living with you, because I love you. No, sir, don't caress me now—let me talk undisturbed. Yesterday I trusted well in Providence, and believed that events were working together for your good and mine: it was a fine day, if you recollect—the calmness of the air and sky forbade apprehensions respecting your safety or comfort on your journey. I walked a little while on the pavement after tea, thinking of you; and I beheld you in imagination so near me, I scarcely missed your actual presence. I thought of the life that lay before me—*your* life, sir—an existence more expansive and stirring than my own: as much more so as the depths of the sea to which the brook runs are than the shallows of its own strait channel. I wondered why moralists call this world a dreary wilderness: for me it blossomed like a rose. Just at sunset, the air turned cold and the sky cloudy: I went in, Sophie called me upstairs to look at my wedding-dress, which they had just brought; and under it in the box I found your present—the veil which, in your princely extravagance, you sent for from London: resolved, I suppose, since I would not have jewels, to cheat me into accepting something as costly. I smiled as I unfolded it, and devised how I would tease you about your aristocratic tastes, and your efforts to masque your plebeian bride in the attributes of a peeress. I thought how I would carry down to you the square of unembroidered blond I had myself prepared as a covering for my low-born head, and ask if that was not good enough for a woman who could bring her husband neither fortune, beauty, nor connections. I saw plainly how you would look; and heard your impetuous republican answers, and your haughty disavowal of any necessity on your part to augment your wealth, or elevate your standing, by marrying either a purse or a coronet."

"How well you read me, you witch!" interposed Mr. Rochester. "But what did you find in the veil besides its embroidery? Did you find poison, or a dagger, that you look so mournful now?"

"No, no, sir; besides the delicacy and richness of the fabric, I found nothing save Fairfax Rochester's pride; and that did not scare me, because I am used to the sight of the demon. But, sir, as it grew dark, the wind rose: it blew yesterday evening, not as it blows now—wild and high—but 'with a sullen, moaning sound' far more eerie. I wished you were at home. I came into this room, and the sight of the empty chair and fireless hearth chilled me. For some time after I went to bed, I could not sleep—a sense of anxious excitement distressed me. The gale still rising, seemed to my ear to muffle a mournful under-sound; whether in the house or abroad I could not at first tell, but it recurred, doubtful yet doleful at every lull; at last I made out it must be some dog howling at a distance. I was glad when it ceased. On sleeping, I continued in dreams the idea of a dark and gusty night. I continued also the wish to be with you, and experienced a strange, regretful consciousness of some barrier dividing us. During all my first sleep, I was following the windings of an unknown road; total obscurity environed me; rain pelted me; I was burdened with the charge of a little child: a very small creature, too young and feeble to walk, and which shivered in my cold arms, and wailed piteously in my ear. I thought, sir, that you were on the road a long way before me; and I strained every nerve to overtake you, and made effort on effort to utter your name and entreat you to stop—but my movements were fettered, and my voice still died away inarticulate; while you, I felt, withdrew farther and farther every moment."

"And these dreams weigh on your spirits now, Jane, when I am close to you? Little nervous subject! Forget visionary woe, and think only of real happiness! You say you love me, Janet: yes—I will not forget that;

and you cannot deny it. *Those* words did not die inarticulate on your lips. I heard them clear and soft: a thought too solemn perhaps, but sweet as music—'I think it is a glorious thing to have the hope of living with you, Edward, because I love you.' Do you love me, Jane? Repeat it."

"I do, sir—I do, with my whole heart."

"Well," he said, after some minutes' silence, "it is strange; but that sentence has penetrated my breast painfully. Why? I think because you said it with such an earnest, religious energy, and because your upward gaze at me now is the very sublime of faith, truth, and devotion: it is too much as if some spirit were near me. Look wicked, Jane: as you know well how to look: coin one of your wild, shy, provoking smiles; tell me you hate me—tease me, vex me; do anything but move me: I would rather be incensed than saddened."

"I will tease you and vex you to your heart's content, when I have finished my tale: but hear me to the end."

"I thought, Jane, you had told me all. I thought I had found the source of your melancholy in a dream."

I shook my head. "What! Is there more? But I will not believe it to be anything important. I warn you of incredulity beforehand. Go on."

The disquietude of his air, the somewhat apprehensive impatience of his manner, surprised me: but I proceeded.

"I dreamt another dream, sir: that Thornfield Hall was a dreary ruin, the retreat of bats and owls. I thought that of all the stately front nothing remained but a shell-like wall, very high and very fragile-looking. I wandered, on a moonlight night, through the grass-grown enclosure within: here I stumbled over a marble hearth, and there over a fallen fragment of cornice. Wrapped up in a shawl, I still carried the unknown little child: I might not lay it down anywhere, however tired were my arms—however much its weight impeded my progress, I must retain it. I heard the gallop of a horse at a distance on the road; I was sure it was you; and you were departing for many years and for a distant country. I climbed the thin wall with frantic perilous haste, eager to catch one glimpse of you from the top: the stones rolled from under my feet, the ivy branches I grasped gave way, the child clung round my neck in terror, and almost strangled me; at last I gained the summit. I saw you like a speck on a white track, lessening every moment. The blast blew so strong I could not stand. I sat down on the narrow ledge; I hushed the scared infant in my lap: you turned an angle of the road:

I bent forward to take a last look; the wall crumbled; I was shaken; the child rolled from my knee, I lost my balance, fell, and woke."

"Now, Jane, that is all."

"All the preface, sir; the tale is yet to come. On waking, a gleam dazzled my eyes; I thought—oh, it is daylight! But I was mistaken; it was only candlelight. Sophie, I supposed, had come in. There was a light in the dressing-table, and the door of the closet, where, before going to bed, I had hung my wedding-dress and veil, stood open; I heard a rustling there. I asked, 'Sophie, what are you doing?' No one answered; but a form emerged from the closet; it took the light, held it aloft, and surveyed the garments pendent from the portmanteau. 'Sophie! Sophie!' I again cried: and still it was silent. I had risen up in bed, I bent forward: first surprise, then bewilderment, came over me; and then my blood crept cold through my veins. Mr. Rochester, this was not Sophie, it was not Leah, it was not Mrs. Fairfax: it was not—no, I was sure of it, and am still—it was not even that strange woman, Grace Poole."

"It must have been one of them," interrupted my master.

"No, sir, I solemnly assure you to the contrary. The shape standing before me had never crossed my eyes within the precincts of Thornfield Hall before; the height, the contour were new to me."

"Describe it, Jane."

"It seemed, sir, a woman, tall and large, with thick and dark hair hanging long down her back. I know not what dress she had on: it was white and straight; but whether gown, sheet, or shroud, I cannot tell."

"Did you see her face?"

"Not at first. But presently she took my veil from its place; she held it up, gazed at it long, and then she threw it over her own head, and turned to the mirror. At that moment I saw the reflection of the visage and features quite distinctly in the dark oblong glass."

"And how were they?"

"Fearful and ghastly to me—oh, sir, I never saw a face like it! It was a discoloured face—it was a savage face. I wish I could forget the roll of the red eyes and the fearful blackened inflation of the lineaments!"

"Ghosts are usually pale, Jane."

"This, sir, was purple: the lips were swelled and dark; the brow furrowed: the black eyebrows widely raised over the bloodshot eyes. Shall I tell you of what it reminded me?"

"You may."

"Of the foul German spectre—the Vampyre."

"Ah! What did it do?"

"Sir, it removed my veil from its gaunt head, rent it in two parts, and flinging both on the floor, trampled on them."

"Afterwards?"

"It drew aside the window-curtain and looked out; perhaps it saw dawn approaching, for, taking the candle, it retreated to the door. Just at my bedside, the figure stopped: the fiery eyes glared upon me—she thrust up her candle close to my face, and extinguished it under my eyes. I was aware her lurid visage flamed over mine, and I lost consciousness: for the second time in my life—only the second time—I became insensible from terror."

"Who was with you when you revived?"

"No one, sir, but the broad day. I rose, bathed my head and face in water, drank a long draught; felt that though enfeebled I was not ill, and determined that to none but you would I impart this vision. Now, sir, tell me who and what that woman was?"

"The creature of an over-stimulated brain; that is certain. I must be careful of you, my treasure: nerves like yours were not made for rough handling."

"Sir, depend on it, my nerves were not in fault; the thing was real: the transaction actually took place."

"And your previous dreams, were they real too? Is Thornfield Hall a ruin? Am I severed from you by insuperable obstacles? Am I leaving you without a tear—without a kiss—without a word?"

"Not yet."

"Am I about to do it? Why, the day is already commenced which is to bind us indissolubly; and when we are once united, there shall be no recurrence of these mental terrors: I guarantee that."

"Mental terrors, sir! I wish I could believe them to be only such: I wish it more now than ever; since even you cannot explain to me the mystery of that awful visitant."

"And since I cannot do it, Jane, it must have been unreal."

"But, sir, when I said so to myself on rising this morning, and when I looked round the room to gather courage and comfort from the cheerful aspect of each familiar object in full daylight, there—on the carpet—I saw what gave the distinct lie to my hypothesis—the veil, torn from top to bottom in two halves!"

I felt Mr. Rochester start and shudder; he hastily flung his arms round me. "Thank God!" he exclaimed, "That if anything malignant did come near you last night, it was only the veil that was harmed. Oh, to think what might have happened!"

He drew his breath short, and strained me so close to him, I could scarcely pant. After some minutes' silence, he continued, cheerily—

"Now, Janet, I'll explain to you all about it. It was half dream, half reality. A woman did, I doubt not, enter your room: and that woman was—must have been—Grace Poole. You call her a strange being yourself: from all you know, you have reason so to call her—what did she do to me? What to Mason? In a state between sleeping and waking, you noticed her entrance and her actions; but feverish, almost delirious as you were, you ascribed to her a goblin appearance different from her own: the long dishevelled hair, the swelled black face, the exaggerated stature, were figments of imagination; results of nightmare: the spiteful tearing of the veil was real: and it is like her. I see you would ask why I keep such a woman in my house: when we have been married a year and a day, I will tell you; but not now. Are you satisfied, Jane? Do you accept my solution of the mystery?"

I reflected, and in truth it appeared to me the only possible one: satisfied I was not, but to please him I endeavoured to appear so—relieved, I certainly did feel; so I answered him with a contented smile. And now, as it was long past one, I prepared to leave him.

"Does not Sophie sleep with Adèle in the nursery?" he asked, as I lit my candle.

"Yes, sir."

"And there is room enough in Adèle's little bed for you. You must share it with her tonight, Jane: it is no wonder that the incident you have related should make you nervous, and I would rather you did not sleep alone: promise me to go to the nursery."

"I shall be very glad to do so, sir."

"And fasten the door securely on the inside. Wake Sophie when you go upstairs, under pretence of requesting her to rouse you in good time tomorrow; for you must be dressed and have finished breakfast before eight. And now, no more sombre thoughts: chase dull care away, Janet. Don't you hear to what soft whispers the wind has fallen? and there is no more beating of rain against the window-panes: look here" (he lifted up the curtain)—"it is a lovely night!"

It was. Half heaven was pure and stainless: the clouds, now trooping before the wind, which had shifted to the west, were filing off eastward in long, silvered columns. The moon shone peacefully.

"Well," said Mr. Rochester, gazing inquiringly into my eyes, "how is my Janet now?"

"The night is serene, sir; and so am I."

"And you will not dream of separation and sorrow tonight; but of happy love and blissful union."

This prediction was but half fulfilled: I did not indeed dream of sorrow, but as little did I dream of joy; for I never slept at all. With little Adèle in my arms, I watched the slumber of childhood—so tranquil, so passionless, so innocent—and waited for the coming day: all my life was awake and astir in my frame: and as soon as the sun rose I rose too. I remember Adèle clung to me as I left her: I remember I kissed her as I loosened her little hands from my neck; and I cried over her with strange emotion, and quitted her because I feared my sobs would break her still sound repose. She seemed the emblem of my past life; and here I was now to array myself to meet, the dread, but adored, type of my unknown future day.

CHAPTER XXVI

Sophie came at seven to dress me: she was very long indeed in accomplishing her task; so long that Mr. Rochester, grown, I suppose, impatient of my delay, sent up to ask why I did not come. She was just fastening my veil (the plain square of blond after all) to my hair with a brooch; I hurried from under her hands as soon as I could.

"Stop!" she cried in French. "Look at yourself in the mirror: you have not taken one peep."

So I turned at the door: I saw a robed and veiled figure, so unlike my usual self that it seemed almost the image of a stranger. "Jane!" called a voice, and I hastened down. I was received at the foot of the stairs by Mr. Rochester.

"Lingerer!" he said. "My brain is on fire with impatience, and you tarry so long!"

He took me into the dining-room, surveyed me keenly all over, pronounced me "fair as a lily, and not only the pride of his life, but the desire of his eyes," and then telling me he would give me but ten minutes to eat some breakfast, he rang the bell. One of his lately hired servants, a footman, answered it.

"Is John getting the carriage ready?"

"Yes, sir."

"Is the luggage brought down?"

"They are bringing it down, sir."

"Go you to the church: see if Mr. Wood (the clergyman) and the clerk are there: return and tell me."

The church, as the reader knows, was but just beyond the gates; the footman soon returned.

"Mr. Wood is in the vestry, sir, putting on his surplice."

"And the carriage?"

"The horses are harnessing."

"We shall not want it to go to church; but it must be ready the moment we return: all the boxes and luggage arranged and strapped on, and the coachman in his seat."

"Yes, sir."

"Jane, are you ready?"

I rose. There were no groomsmen, no bridesmaids, no relatives to wait for or marshal: none but Mr. Rochester and I. Mrs. Fairfax stood in the hall as we passed. I would fain have spoken to her, but my hand was held by a grasp of iron: I was hurried along by a stride I could hardly follow; and to look at Mr. Rochester's face was to feel that not a second of delay would be tolerated for any purpose. I wonder what other bridegroom ever looked as he did—so bent up to a purpose, so grimly resolute: or who, under such steadfast brows, ever revealed such flaming and flashing eyes.

I know not whether the day was fair or foul; in descending the drive, I gazed neither on sky nor earth: my heart was with my eyes; and both seemed migrated into Mr. Rochester's frame. I wanted to see the invisible thing on which, as we went along, he appeared to fasten a glance fierce and fell. I wanted to feel the thoughts whose force he seemed breasting and resisting.

At the churchyard wicket he stopped: he discovered I was quite out of breath. "Am I cruel in my love?" he said. "Delay an instant: lean on me, Jane."

And now I can recall the picture of the grey old house of God rising calm before me, of a rook wheeling round the steeple, of a ruddy morning sky beyond. I remember something, too, of the green grave-mounds; and I have not forgotten, either, two figures of strangers straying amongst the low hillocks and reading the mementoes graven on the few mossy head-stones. I noticed them, because, as they saw us, they passed round to the back of the church; and I doubted not they were going to enter by the side-aisle door and witness the ceremony. By Mr. Rochester they were not observed; he was earnestly looking at my face from which the blood had, I daresay, momentarily fled: for I felt my forehead dewy, and my cheeks and lips cold. When I rallied, which I soon did, he walked gently with me up the path to the porch.

We entered the quiet and humble temple; the priest waited in his white surplice at the lowly altar, the clerk beside him. All was still: two shadows only moved in a remote corner. My conjecture had been correct: the strangers had slipped in before us, and they now stood by the vault of the Rochesters, their backs towards us, viewing through the rails the old time-stained marble tomb, where a kneeling angel guarded the remains of Damer de Rochester, slain at Marston Moor in the time of the civil wars, and of Elizabeth, his wife.

Our place was taken at the communion rails. Hearing a cautious step behind me, I glanced over my shoulder: one of the strangers—a gentleman, evidently—was advancing up the chancel. The service began. The explanation of the intent of matrimony was gone through; and then the clergyman came a step further forward, and, bending slightly towards Mr. Rochester, went on.

"I require and charge you both (as ye will answer at the dreadful day of judgment, when the secrets of all hearts shall be disclosed), that if either of you know any impediment why ye may not lawfully be joined together in matrimony, ye do now confess it; for be ye well assured that so many as are coupled together otherwise than God's Word doth allow, are not joined together by God, neither is their matrimony lawful."

He paused, as the custom is. When is the pause after that sentence ever broken by reply? Not, perhaps, once in a hundred years. And the clergyman, who had not lifted his eyes from his book, and had held his breath but for a moment, was proceeding: his hand was already stretched towards Mr. Rochester, as his lips unclosed to ask, "Wilt thou have this woman for thy wedded wife?" when a distinct and near voice said—

"The marriage cannot go on: I declare the existence of an impediment."

The clergyman looked up at the speaker and stood mute; the clerk did the same; Mr. Rochester moved slightly, as if an earthquake had rolled under his feet: taking a firmer footing, and not turning his head or eyes, he said, "Proceed."

Profound silence fell when he had uttered that word, with deep but low intonation. Presently Mr. Wood said—

"I cannot proceed without some investigation into what has been asserted, and evidence of its truth or falsehood."

"The ceremony is quite broken off," subjoined the voice behind us. "I am in a condition to prove my allegation: an insuperable impediment to this marriage exists."

Mr. Rochester heard, but heeded not: he stood stubborn and rigid, making no movement but to possess himself of my hand. What a hot and strong grasp he had! And how like quarried marble was his pale, firm, massive front at this moment! How his eye shone, still watchful, and yet wild beneath!

Mr. Wood seemed at a loss. "What is the nature of the impediment?" he asked. "Perhaps it may be got over—explained away?"

"Hardly," was the answer. "I have called it insuperable, and I speak advisedly."

The speaker came forward and leaned on the rails. He continued, uttering each word distinctly, calmly, steadily, but not loudly—

"It simply consists in the existence of a previous marriage. Mr. Rochester has a wife now living."

My nerves vibrated to those low-spoken words as they had never vibrated to thunder—my blood felt their subtle violence as it had never felt frost or fire; but I was collected, and in no danger of swooning. I looked at Mr. Rochester: I made him look at me. His whole face was colourless rock: his eye was both spark and flint. He disavowed nothing: he seemed as if he would defy all things. Without speaking, without smiling, without seeming to recognise in me a human being, he only twined my waist with his arm and riveted me to his side.

"Who are you?" he asked of the intruder.

"My name is Briggs, a solicitor of —— Street, London."

"And you would thrust on me a wife?"

"I would remind you of your lady's existence, sir, which the law recognises, if you do not."

"Favour me with an account of her—with her name, her parentage, her place of abode."

"Certainly." Mr. Briggs calmly took a paper from his pocket, and read out in a sort of official, nasal voice:

" 'I affirm and can prove that on the 20th of October A.D. —— (a date of fifteen years back), Edward Fairfax Rochester, of Thornfield Hall, in the county of ——, and of Ferndean Manor, in ——shire, England, was married to my sister, Bertha Antoinetta Mason, daughter of Jonas Mason, merchant, and of Antoinetta his wife, a Creole, at —— church, Spanish Town, Jamaica. The record of the marriage will be found in the register of that church—a copy of it is now in my possession. Signed, Richard Mason.' "

"That—if a genuine document—may prove I have been married, but it does not prove that the woman mentioned therein as my wife is still living."

"She was living three months ago," returned the lawyer.

"How do you know?"

"I have a witness to the fact, whose testimony even you, sir, will scarcely controvert."

"Produce him—or go to hell."

"I will produce him first—he is on the spot. Mr. Mason, have the goodness to step forward."

Mr. Rochester, on hearing the name, set his teeth; he experienced, too, a sort of strong convulsive quiver; near to him as I was, I felt the spasmodic movement of fury or despair run through his frame. The second stranger, who had hitherto lingered in the background, now drew near; a pale face looked over the solicitor's shoulder—yes, it was Mason himself. Mr. Rochester turned and glared at him. His eye, as I have often said, was a black eye: it had now a tawny, nay, a bloody light in its gloom; and his face flushed—olive cheek and hueless forehead received a glow as from spreading, ascending heart-fire: and he stirred, lifted his strong arm—he could have struck Mason, dashed him on the church-floor, shocked by ruthless blow the breath from his body—but Mason shrank away, and cried faintly, "Good God!" Contempt fell cool on Mr. Rochester—his passion died as if a blight had shrivelled it up: he only asked, "What have *you* to say?"

An inaudible reply escaped Mason's white lips.

"The devil is in it if you cannot answer distinctly. I again demand, what have you to say?"

"Sir—sir," interrupted the clergyman, "do not forget you are in a sacred place." Then addressing Mason, he inquired gently, "Are you aware, sir, whether or not this gentleman's wife is still living?"

"Courage," urged the lawyer; "speak out."

"She is now living at Thornfield Hall," said Mason, in more articulate tones: "I saw her there last April. I am her brother."

"At Thornfield Hall!" ejaculated the clergyman. "Impossible! I am an old resident in this neighbourhood, sir, and I never heard of a Mrs. Rochester at Thornfield Hall."

I saw a grim smile contort Mr. Rochester's lips, and he muttered—

"No, by God! I took care that none should hear of it—or of her under that name." He mused—for ten minutes he held counsel with himself: he formed his resolve, and announced it—

"Enough! All shall bolt out at once, like the bullet from the barrel. Wood, close your book and take off your surplice; John Green (to the clerk), leave the church: there will be no wedding today." The man obeyed.

Mr. Rochester continued, hardily and recklessly: "Bigamy is an ugly word! I meant, however, to be a bigamist; but fate has out-manoeuvred me, or Providence has checked me—perhaps the last. I am little better than a devil at this moment; and, as my pastor there would tell me, deserve no doubt the sternest judgments of God, even to the quenchless fire and deathless worm. Gentlemen, my plan is broken up—what this lawyer and his client say is true: I have been married, and the woman to whom I was married lives! You say you never heard of a Mrs. Rochester at the house up yonder, Wood; but I daresay you have many a time inclined your ear to gossip about the mysterious lunatic kept there under watch and ward. Some have whispered to you that she is my bastard half-sister: some, my cast-off mistress. I now inform you that she is my wife, whom I married fifteen years ago—Bertha Mason by name; sister of this resolute personage, who is now, with his quivering limbs and white cheeks, showing you what a stout heart men may bear. Cheer up, Dick! Never fear me! I'd almost as soon strike a woman as you. Bertha Mason is mad; and she came of a mad family; idiots and maniacs through three generations! Her mother, the Creole, was both a madwoman and a drunkard! As I found out after I had wed the daughter: for they were silent on family secrets before. Bertha, like a dutiful child, copied her parent in both points. I had a charming partner—pure, wise, modest: you can fancy I was a happy man. I went through rich scenes! Oh! My experience has been heavenly, if you only knew it! But I owe you no further explanation. Briggs, Wood, Mason, I invite you all to come up to the house and visit Mrs. Poole's patient, and *my wife*! You shall see what sort of a being I was cheated into espousing, and judge whether or not I had a right to break the compact, and seek sympathy with something at least human. This girl," he continued, looking at me, "knew no more than you, Wood, of the disgusting secret: she thought all was fair and legal and never dreamt she was going to be entrapped into a feigned union with a defrauded wretch, already bound to a bad, mad, and embruted partner! Come all of you—follow!"

Still holding me fast, he left the church: the three gentlemen came after. At the front door of the hall we found the carriage.

"Take it back to the coach-house, John," said Mr. Rochester coolly; "it will not be wanted today."

At our entrance, Mrs. Fairfax, Adèle, Sophie, Leah, advanced to meet and greet us.

"To the right-about—every soul!" cried the master. "Away with your congratulations! Who wants them? Not I! They are fifteen years too late!"

He passed on and ascended the stairs, still holding my hand, and still beckoning the gentlemen to follow him, which they did. We mounted the first staircase, passed up the gallery, proceeded to the third storey: the low, black door, opened by Mr. Rochester's master-key, admitted us to the tapestried room, with its great bed and its pictorial cabinet.

"You know this place, Mason," said our guide; "she bit and stabbed you here."

He lifted the hangings from the wall, uncovering the second door: this, too, he opened. In a room without a window, there burnt a fire guarded by a high and strong fender, and a lamp suspended from the ceiling by a chain. Grace Poole bent over the fire, apparently cooking something in a saucepan. In the deep shade, at the farther end of the room, a figure ran backwards and forwards. What it was, whether beast or human being, one could not, at first sight, tell: it grovelled, seemingly, on all fours; it snatched and growled like some strange wild animal: but it was covered with clothing, and a quantity of dark, grizzled hair, wild as a mane, hid its head and face.

"Good-morrow, Mrs. Poole!" said Mr. Rochester. "How are you? And how is your charge today?"

"We're tolerable, sir, I thank you," replied Grace, lifting the boiling mess carefully on to the hob. "Rather snappish, but not 'rageous."

A fierce cry seemed to give the lie to her favourable report: the clothed hyena rose up, and stood tall on its hind-feet.

"Ah! Sir, she sees you!" exclaimed Grace. "You'd better not stay."

"Only a few moments, Grace: you must allow me a few moments."

"Take care then, sir! For God's sake, take care!"

The maniac bellowed: she parted her shaggy locks from her visage, and gazed wildly at her visitors. I recognised well that purple face—those bloated features. Mrs. Poole advanced.

"Keep out of the way," said Mr. Rochester, thrusting her aside; "she has no knife now, I suppose, and I'm on my guard."

"One never knows what she has, sir: she is so cunning: it is not in mortal discretion to fathom her craft."

"We had better leave her," whispered Mason.

"Go to the devil!" was his brother-in-law's recommendation.

" 'Ware!" cried Grace. The three gentlemen retreated simultaneously. Mr. Rochester flung me behind him: the lunatic sprang and grappled his throat viciously, and laid her teeth to his cheek: they struggled. She was a big woman, in stature almost equalling her husband, and corpulent besides: she showed virile force in the contest—more than once she almost throttled him, athletic as he was. He could have settled her with a well-planted blow; but he would not strike: he would only wrestle. At last he mastered her arms; Grace Poole gave him a cord, and he pinioned them behind her: with more rope, which was at hand, he bound her to a chair. The operation was performed amidst the fiercest yells and the most convulsive plunges. Mr. Rochester then turned to the spectators: he looked at them with a smile both acrid and desolate.

"That is *my wife*," said he. "Such is the sole conjugal embrace I am ever to know—such are the endearments which are to solace my leisure hours! And *this* is what I wished to have" (laying his hand on my shoulder): "this young girl, who stands so grave and quiet at the mouth of hell, looking collectedly at the gambols of a demon, I wanted her just as a change after that fierce ragout. Wood and Briggs, look at the difference! Compare these clear eyes with the red balls yonder—this face with that mask—this form with that bulk; then judge me, priest of the gospel and man of the law, and remember with what judgment ye judge ye shall be judged! Off with you now. I must shut up my prize."

We all withdrew. Mr. Rochester stayed a moment behind us, to give some further order to Grace Poole. The solicitor addressed me as he descended the stair.

"You, madam," said he, "are cleared from all blame: your uncle will be glad to hear it—if, indeed, he should be still living—when Mr. Mason returns to Madeira."

"My uncle! What of him? Do you know him?"

"Mr. Mason does. Mr. Eyre has been the Funchal correspondent of his house for some years. When your uncle received your letter intimating the contemplated union between yourself and Mr. Rochester, Mr. Mason, who was staying at Madeira to recruit his health, on his way back to Jamaica, happened to be with him. Mr. Eyre mentioned the intelligence; for he knew that my client here was acquainted with a gentleman of the name of Rochester. Mr. Mason, astonished and distressed as you may suppose, revealed the real state of matters. Your uncle, I am sorry to say, is now on a sick bed; from which, considering the nature of his disease—decline—and the stage it has reached, it is unlikely he will ever rise. He could not then hasten to England himself, to extricate you from the snare into which you had fallen, but he implored Mr. Mason to lose no time in taking steps to prevent the false marriage. He referred him to me for assistance. I used all despatch, and am thankful I was not too late: as you, doubtless, must be also. Were I not morally certain that your uncle will be dead ere you reach Madeira, I would advise you to accompany Mr. Mason back; but as it is, I think you had better remain in England till you can hear further, either from or of Mr. Eyre. Have we anything else to stay for?" he inquired of Mr. Mason.

"No, no—let us be gone," was the anxious reply; and without waiting to take leave of Mr. Rochester, they made their exit at the hall door. The clergyman stayed to exchange a few sentences, either of admonition or reproof, with his haughty parishioner; this duty done, he too departed.

I heard him go as I stood at the half-open door of my own room, to which I had now withdrawn. The house cleared, I shut myself in, fastened the bolt that none might intrude, and proceeded—not to weep, not to mourn, I was yet too calm for that, but—mechanically to take off the wedding dress, and replace it by the stuff gown I had worn yesterday, as I thought, for the last time. I then sat down: I felt weak and tired. I leaned my arms on a table, and my head dropped on them. And now I thought: till now I had only heard, seen, moved—followed up and down where I was led or dragged—watched event rush on event, disclosure open beyond disclosure: but *now*, *I thought*.

The morning had been a quiet morning enough—all except the brief scene with the lunatic: the transaction in the church had not been noisy; there was no explosion of passion, no loud altercation, no dispute, no defiance or challenge, no tears, no sobs: a few words had been spoken, a calmly pronounced objection to the marriage made; some stern, short questions put by Mr. Rochester; answers, explanations given, evidence adduced; an open admission of the truth had been uttered by my master; then the living proof had been seen; the intruders were gone, and all was over.

I was in my own room as usual—just myself, without obvious change:

nothing had smitten me, or scathed me, or maimed me. And yet where was the Jane Eyre of yesterday? Where was her life? Where were her prospects?

Jane Eyre, who had been an ardent, expectant woman—almost a bride, was a cold, solitary girl again: her life was pale; her prospects were desolate. A Christmas frost had come at midsummer; a white December storm had whirled over June; ice glazed the ripe apples, drifts crushed the blowing roses; on hayfield and cornfield lay a frozen shroud: lanes which last night blushed full of flowers, today were pathless with untrodden snow; and the woods, which twelve hours since waved leafy and flagrant as groves between the tropics, now spread, waste, wild, and white as pine-forests in wintry Norway. My hopes were all dead—struck with a subtle doom, such as, in one night, fell on all the first-born in the land of Egypt. I looked on my cherished wishes, yesterday so blooming and glowing; they lay stark, chill, livid corpses that could never revive. I looked at my love: that feeling which was my master's—which he had created; it shivered in my heart, like a suffering child in a cold cradle; sickness and anguish had seized it; it could not seek Mr. Rochester's arms—it could not derive warmth from his breast. Oh, never more could it turn to him; for faith was blighted—confidence destroyed! Mr. Rochester was not to me what he had been; for he was not what I had thought him. I would not ascribe vice to him; I would not say he had betrayed me; but the attribute of stainless truth was gone from his idea, and from his presence I must go: *that* I perceived well. When—how—whither, I could not yet discern; but he himself, I doubted not, would hurry me from Thornfield. Real affection, it seemed, he could not have for me; it had been only fitful passion: that was balked; he would want me no more. I should fear even to cross his path now: my view must be hateful to him. Oh, how blind had been my eyes! How weak my conduct!

My eyes were covered and closed: eddying darkness seemed to swim round me, and reflection came in as black and confused a flow. Self-abandoned, relaxed, and effortless, I seemed to have laid me down in the dried-up bed of a great river; I heard a flood loosened in remote mountains, and felt the torrent come: to rise I had no will, to flee I had no strength. I lay faint, longing to be dead. One idea only still throbbed life-like within me—a remembrance of God: it begot an unuttered prayer: these words went wandering up and down in my rayless mind, as something that should be whispered, but no energy was found to express them—

"Be not far from me, for trouble is near: there is none to help."

It was near: and as I had lifted no petition to Heaven to avert it—as I had neither joined my hands, nor bent my knees, nor moved my lips—it came: in full heavy swing the torrent poured over me. The whole consciousness of my life lorn, my love lost, my hope quenched, my faith death-struck, swayed full and mighty above me in one sullen mass. That bitter hour cannot be described: in truth, "the waters came into my soul; I sank in deep mire: I felt no standing; I came into deep waters; the floods overflowed me."

CHAPTER XXVII

Some time in the afternoon I raised my head, and looking round and seeing the western sun gilding the sign of its decline on the wall, I asked, "What am I to do?"

But the answer my mind gave—"Leave Thornfield at once"—was so prompt, so dread, that I stopped my ears. I said I could not bear such words now. "That I am not Edward Rochester's bride is the least part of my woe," I alleged. "That I have wakened out of most glorious dreams, and found them all void and vain, is a horror I could bear and master; but that I must leave him decidedly, instantly, entirely, is intolerable. I cannot do it."

But, then, a voice within me averred that I could do it and foretold that I should do it. I wrestled with my own resolution: I wanted to be weak that I might avoid the awful passage of further suffering I saw laid out for me; and Conscience, turned tyrant, held Passion by the throat, told her tauntingly, she had yet but dipped her dainty foot in the slough, and swore that with that arm of iron he would thrust her down to unsounded depths of agony.

"Let me be torn away," then I cried. "Let another help me!"

"No; you shall tear yourself away, none shall help you: you shall yourself pluck out your right eye; yourself cut off your right hand: your heart shall be the victim, and you the priest to transfix it."

I rose up suddenly, terror-struck at the solitude which so ruthless a judge haunted—at the silence which so awful a voice filled. My head swam as I stood erect. I perceived that I was sickening from excitement and inanition; neither meat nor drink had passed my lips that day, for I had taken no breakfast. And, with a strange pang, I now reflected that, long as I had been shut up here, no message had been sent to ask how I was, or to invite me to come down: not even little Adèle had tapped at the door; not even Mrs. Fairfax had sought me. "Friends always forget those whom fortune forsakes," I murmured, as I undrew the bolt and passed out. I stumbled over an obstacle: my head was still dizzy, my sight was dim, and my limbs were feeble. I could not soon recover myself. I fell, but not on to the ground: an outstretched arm caught me. I looked up—I was supported by Mr. Rochester, who sat in a chair across my chamber threshold.

"You come out at last," he said. "Well, I have been waiting for you long, and listening: yet not one movement have I heard, nor one sob: five minutes more of that death-like hush, and I should have forced the lock like a burglar. So you shun me? You shut yourself up and grieve alone! I would rather you had come and upbraided me with vehemence. You are passionate. I expected a scene of some kind. I was prepared for the hot rain of tears; only I wanted them to be shed on my breast: now a senseless floor has received them, or your drenched handkerchief. But I err: you have not wept at all! I see a white cheek and a faded eye, but no trace of tears. I suppose, then, your heart has been weeping blood?

"Well, Jane! Not a word of reproach? Nothing bitter—nothing poignant? Nothing to cut a feeling or sting a passion? You sit quietly where I have placed you, and regard me with a weary, passive look.

"Jane, I never meant to wound you thus. If the man who had but one little ewe lamb that was dear to him as a daughter, that ate of his bread and drank of his cup, and lay in his bosom, had by some mistake slaughtered it at the shambles, he would not have rued his bloody blunder more than I now rue mine. Will you ever forgive me?"

Reader, I forgave him at the moment and on the spot. There was such deep remorse in his eye, such true pity in his tone, such manly energy in his manner; and besides, there was such unchanged love in his whole look and mien—I forgave him all: yet not in words, not outwardly; only at my heart's core.

"You know I am a scoundrel, Jane?" ere long he inquired wistfully—wondering, I suppose, at my continued silence and tameness, the result rather of weakness than of will.

"Yes, sir."

"Then tell me so roundly and sharply—don't spare me."

"I cannot: I am tired and sick. I want some water." He heaved a sort of shuddering sigh, and taking me in his arms, carried me downstairs. At first I did not know to what room he had borne me; all was cloudy to my glazed sight: presently I felt the reviving warmth of a fire; for, summer as it was, I had become icy cold in my chamber. He put wine to my lips; I tasted it and revived; then I ate something he offered me, and was soon myself. I was in the library—sitting in his chair—he was quite near. "If I could go out of life now, without too sharp a pang, it would be well for me," I thought; "then I should not have to make the effort of cracking my heart-strings in rending them from among Mr. Rochester's. I must leave him, it appears. I do not want to leave him—I cannot leave him."

"How are you now, Jane?"

"Much better, sir; I shall be well soon."

"Taste the wine again, Jane."

I obeyed him; then he put the glass on the table, stood before me, and looked at me attentively. Suddenly he turned away, with an inarticulate exclamation, full of passionate emotion of some kind; he walked fast through the room and came back; he stooped towards me as if to kiss me; but I remembered caresses were now forbidden. I turned my face away and put his aside.

"What! How is this?" he exclaimed hastily. "Oh, I know! You won't kiss the husband of Bertha Mason? You consider my arms filled and my embraces appropriated?"

"At any rate, there is neither room nor claim for me, sir."

"Why, Jane? I will spare you the trouble of much talking; I will answer for you—because I have a wife already, you would reply. I guess rightly?"

"Yes."

"If you think so, you must have a strange opinion of me; you must regard me as a plotting profligate—a base and low rake who has been simulating disinterested love in order to draw you into a snare deliberately laid, and strip you of honour and rob you of self-respect. What do you say to that? I see you can say nothing in the first place, you are faint still, and have enough to do to draw your breath; in the second place, you cannot yet accustom yourself to accuse and revile me, and besides, the flood-gates of tears are opened, and they would rush out if you spoke much; and you have no desire to expostulate, to upbraid, to make a scene: you are thinking how *to act—talking* you consider is of no use. I know you—I am on my guard."

"Sir, I do not wish to act against you," I said; and my unsteady voice warned me to curtail my sentence.

"Not in your sense of the word, but in mine you are scheming to destroy me. You have as good as said that I am a married man—as a married man you will shun me, keep out of my way: just now you have refused to kiss me. You intend to make yourself a complete stranger to me: to live under this roof only as Adèle's governess; if ever I say a friendly word to you, if ever a friendly feeling inclines you again to me, you will say—'That man had nearly made me his mistress: I must be ice and rock to him'; and ice and rock you will accordingly become."

I cleared and steadied my voice to reply: "All is changed about me, sir; I must change too—there is no doubt of that; and to avoid fluctuations of feeling, and continual combats with recollections and associations, there is only one way—Adèle must have a new governess, sir."

"Oh, Adèle will go to school—I have settled that already; nor do I mean to torment you with the hideous associations and recollections of Thornfield Hall—this accursed place—this tent of Achan—this insolent vault, offering the ghastliness of living death to the light of the open sky—this narrow stone hell, with its one real fiend, worse than a legion of such as we imagine. Jane, you shall not stay here, nor will I. I was wrong ever to bring you to Thornfield Hall, knowing as I did how it was haunted. I charged them to conceal from you, before I ever saw you, all knowledge of the curse of the place; merely because I feared Adèle never would have a governess to stay if she knew with what inmate she was housed, and my plans would not permit me to remove the maniac elsewhere—though I possess an old house, Ferndean Manor, even more retired and hidden than this, where I could have lodged her safely enough, had not a scruple about the unhealthiness of the situation, in the heart of a wood, made my conscience recoil from the arrangement. Probably those damp walls would soon have eased me of her charge: but to each villain his own vice; and mine is not a tendency to indirect assassination, even of what I most hate.

"Concealing the mad-woman's neighbourhood from you, however, was something like covering a child with a cloak and laying it down near a upas-tree: that demon's vicinage is poisoned, and always was. But I'll shut up Thornfield Hall: I'll nail up the front door and board the lower windows: I'll give Mrs. Poole two hundred a year to live here with *my wife*, as you term that fearful hag: Grace will do much for money, and she shall have her son, the keeper at Grimsby Retreat, to bear her company and be at hand to give her aid in the paroxysms, when *my wife* is prompted by her familiar to burn people in their beds at night, to stab them, to bite their flesh from their bones, and so on—"

"Sir," I interrupted him, "you are inexorable for that unfortunate lady: you speak of her with hate—with vindictive antipathy. It is cruel—she cannot help being mad."

"Jane, my little darling (so I will call you, for so you are), you don't know what you are talking about; you misjudge me again: it is not because she is mad I hate her. If you were mad, do you think I should hate you?"

"I do indeed, sir."

"Then you are mistaken, and you know nothing about me, and nothing about the sort of love of which I am capable. Every atom of your flesh is as dear to me as my own: in pain and sickness it would still be dear. Your mind is my treasure, and if it were broken, it would be my treasure still: if you raved, my arms should confine you, and not a strait waistcoat—your grasp, even in fury, would have a charm for me: if you flew at me as wildly as that woman did this morning, I should receive you in an embrace, at least as fond as it would be restrictive. I should not shrink from you with disgust as I did from her: in your quiet moments you should have no watcher and no nurse but me; and I could hang over you with untiring tenderness, though you gave me no smile in return; and never weary of gazing into your eyes, though they had no longer a ray of recognition for me. But why do I follow that train of ideas? I was talking of removing you from Thornfield. All, you know, is prepared for prompt departure: tomorrow you shall go. I only ask you to endure one more night under this roof, Jane; and then, farewell to its miseries and terrors for ever! I have a place to repair to, which will be a secure sanctuary from hateful reminiscences, from unwelcome intrusion—even from falsehood and slander."

"And take Adèle with you, sir," I interrupted; "she will be a companion for you."

"What do you mean, Jane? I told you I would send Adèle to school; and what do I want with a child for a companion, and not my own child—a French dancer's bastard? Why do you importune me about her! I say, why do you assign Adèle to me for a companion?"

"You spoke of a retirement, sir; and retirement and solitude are dull: too dull for you."

"Solitude! Solitude!" he reiterated with irritation. "I see I must come to an explanation. I don't know what sphynx-like expression is forming in your countenance. You are to share my solitude. Do you understand?"

I shook my head: it required a degree of courage, excited as he was becoming, even to risk that mute sign of dissent. He had been walking fast about the room, and he stopped, as if suddenly rooted to one spot. He looked at me long and hard: I turned my eyes from him, fixed them on the fire, and tried to assume and maintain a quiet, collected aspect.

"Now for the hitch in Jane's character," he said at last, speaking more calmly than from his look I had expected him to speak. "The reel of silk has run smoothly enough so far; but I always knew there would come a knot and a puzzle: here it is. Now for vexation, and exasperation, and endless trouble! By God! I long to exert a fraction of Samson's strength, and break the entanglement like tow!"

He recommenced his walk, but soon again stopped, and this time just before me.

"Jane! Will you hear reason?" He stooped and approached his lips to my ear. "Because, if you won't, I'll try violence." His voice was hoarse; his look that of a man who is just about to burst an insufferable bond and plunge headlong into wild license. I saw that in another moment, and with one impetus of frenzy more, I should be able to do nothing with him. The present—the passing second of time—was all I had in which to control and restrain him—a movement of repulsion, flight, fear would have sealed my doom—and his. But I was not afraid: not in the least. I felt an inward power; a sense of influence, which supported me. The crisis was perilous; but not without its charm: such as the Indian, perhaps, feels when he slips over the rapid in his canoe. I took hold of his clenched hand, loosened the contorted fingers, and said to him, soothingly—

"Sit down; I'll talk to you as long as you like, and hear all you have to say, whether reasonable or unreasonable."

He sat down: but he did not get leave to speak directly. I had been struggling with tears for some time: I had taken great pains to repress them, because I knew he would not like to see me weep. Now, however, I considered it well to let them flow as freely and as long as they liked. If the flood annoyed him, so much the better. So I gave way and cried heartily.

Soon I heard him earnestly entreating me to be composed. I said I could not while he was in such a passion.

"But I am not angry, Jane: I only love you too well; and you had steeled your little pale face with such a resolute, frozen look, I could not endure it. Hush, now, and wipe your eyes."

His softened voice announced that he was subdued; so I, in my turn, became calm. Now he made an effort to rest his head on my shoulder, but I would not permit it. Then he would draw me to him: no.

"Jane! Jane!" he said, in such an accent of bitter sadness it thrilled along every nerve I had. "You don't love me, then? It was only my station, and the rank of my wife, that you valued? Now that you think me disqualified to become your husband, you recoil from my touch as if I were some toad or ape."

These words cut me: yet what could I do or I say? I ought probably to have done or said nothing; but I was so tortured by a sense of remorse at thus hurting his feelings, I could not control the wish to drop balm where I had wounded.

"I *do* love you," I said, "more than ever: but I must not show or indulge the feeling: and this is the last time I must express it."

"The last time, Jane! What! Do you think you can live with me, and see me daily, and yet, if you still love me, be always cold and distant?"

"No, sir; that I am certain I could not; and therefore I see there is but one way: but you will be furious if I mention it."

"Oh, mention it! If I storm, you have the art of weeping."

"Mr. Rochester, I must leave you."

"For how long, Jane? For a few minutes, while you smooth your hair—which is somewhat dishevelled; and bathe your face—which looks feverish?"

"I must leave Adèle and Thornfield. I must part with you for my whole life: I must begin a new existence among strange faces and strange scenes."

"Of course: I told you you should. I pass over the madness about parting from me. You mean you must become a part of me. As to the new existence, it is all right: you shall yet be my wife: I am not married. You shall be Mrs. Rochester—both virtually and nominally. I shall keep only to you so long as you and I live. You shall go to a place I have in the south of France: a whitewashed villa on the shores of the Mediterranean. There you shall live a happy, and guarded, and most innocent life. Never fear that I wish to lure you into error—to make you my mistress. Why did you shake your head? Jane, you must be reasonable, or in truth I shall again become frantic."

His voice and hand quivered: his large nostrils dilated; his eye blazed: still I dared to speak.

"Sir, your wife is living: that is a fact acknowledged this morning by yourself. If I lived with you as you desire, I should then be your mistress: to say otherwise is sophistical—is false."

"Jane, I am not a gentle-tempered man—you forget that: I am not long-enduring; I am not cool and dispassionate. Out of pity to me and yourself, put your finger on my pulse, feel how it throbs, and—beware!"

He bared his wrist, and offered it to me: the blood was forsaking his cheek and lips, they were growing livid; I was distressed on all hands. To agitate him thus deeply, by a resistance he so abhorred, was cruel: to yield was out of the question. I did what human beings do instinctively when they are driven to utter extremity—looked for aid to one higher than man: the words "God help me!" burst involuntarily from my lips.

"I am a fool!" cried Mr. Rochester suddenly. "I keep telling her I am not married, and do not explain to her why. I forget she knows nothing of the character of that woman, or of the circumstances attending my infernal union with her. Oh, I am certain Jane will agree with me in opinion, when she knows all that I know! Just put your hand in mine, Janet—that I may have the evidence of touch as well as sight, to prove you are near me—and I will in a few words show you the real state of the case. Can you listen to me?"

"Yes, sir; for hours if you will."

"I ask only minutes. Jane, did you ever hear or know that I was not the eldest son of my house: that I had once a brother older than I?"

"I remember Mrs. Fairfax told me so once."

"And did you ever hear that my father was an avaricious, grasping man?"

"I have understood something to that effect."

"Well, Jane, being so, it was his resolution to keep the property together; he could not bear the idea of dividing his estate and leaving me a fair portion: all, he resolved, should go to my brother, Rowland. Yet as little could he endure that a son of his should be a poor man. I must be provided for by a wealthy marriage. He sought me a partner betimes. Mr. Mason, a West India planter and merchant, was his old acquaintance. He was certain his possessions were real and vast: he made inquiries. Mr. Mason, he found, had a son and daughter; and he learned from him that he could and would give the latter a fortune of thirty thousand pounds: that sufficed. When I left college, I was sent out to Jamaica, to espouse a bride already courted for me. My father said nothing about her money; but he told me Miss Mason was the boast of Spanish Town for her beauty: and this was no lie. I found her a fine woman, in the style of Blanche Ingram: tall, dark, and majestic. Her family wished to secure me because I was of a good race; and so did she. They showed her to me in parties, splendidly dressed. I seldom saw her alone, and had very little private conversation with her. She flattered me, and lavishly displayed for my pleasure her charms and accomplishments. All the men in her circle seemed to admire her and envy me. I was dazzled, stimulated: my senses were excited; and being ignorant, raw, and inexperienced, I thought I loved her. There is no folly so besotted that the idiotic rivalries of society, the prurience, the rashness, the blindness of youth, will not hurry a man to its commission. Her relatives encouraged me; competitors piqued me; she allured me: a marriage was achieved almost before I knew where I was. Oh, I have no respect for myself when I think of that act! An agony of inward contempt masters me. I never loved, I never esteemed, I did not even know her. I was not sure of the existence of one virtue in her nature: I had marked neither modesty, nor benevolence, nor candour, nor refinement in her mind or manners—and, I married her: gross, grovelling, mole-eyed blockhead that I was! With less sin I might have—but let me remember to whom I am speaking.

"My bride's mother I had never seen: I understood she was dead. The honeymoon over, I learned my mistake; she was only mad, and shut up in a lunatic asylum. There was a younger brother, too—a complete dumb idiot. The elder one, whom you have seen (and whom I cannot hate, whilst I abhor all his kindred, because he has some grains of affection in his feeble mind, shown in the continued interest he takes in his wretched sister, and also in a dog-like attachment he once bore me), will probably be in the same state one day. My father and my brother Rowland knew all this; but they thought only of the thirty thousand pounds, and joined in the plot against me.

"These were vile discoveries; but except for the treachery of concealment, I should have made them no subject of reproach to my wife, even when I found her nature wholly alien to mine, her tastes obnoxious to me, her cast of mind common, low, narrow, and singularly incapable of being led to anything higher, expanded to anything larger—when I found that I could not pass a single evening, nor even a single hour of the day with her in comfort; that kindly conversation could not be sustained between us, because whatever topic I started, immediately received from her a turn at once coarse and trite, perverse and imbecile—when I perceived that I should never have a quiet or settled household, because no servant would bear the continued outbreaks of her violent and unreasonable temper, or the vexations of her absurd, contradictory, exacting orders—even then I restrained myself: I eschewed upbraiding, I curtailed remonstrance; I tried to devour my repentance and disgust in secret; I repressed the deep antipathy I felt.

"Jane, I will not trouble you with abominable details: some strong words shall express what I have to say. I lived with that woman upstairs four years, and before that time she had tried me indeed: her character ripened and developed with frightful rapidity; her vices sprang up fast and rank: they were so strong, only cruelty could check them, and I would not use cruelty. What a pigmy intellect she had, and what giant propensities! How fearful were the curses those propensities entailed on me! Bertha Mason, the true daughter of an infamous mother, dragged me through all the hideous and degrading agonies which must attend a man bound to a wife at once intemperate and unchaste.

"My brother in the interval was dead, and at the end of the four years my father died too. I was rich enough now—yet poor to hideous indigence: a nature the most gross, impure, depraved I ever saw, was associated with mine, and called by the law and by society a part of me. And I could not rid myself of it by any legal proceedings: for the doctors now discovered that *my wife* was mad—her excesses had prematurely developed the germs of insanity. Jane, you don't like my narrative; you look almost sick—shall I defer the rest to another day?"

"No, sir, finish it now; I pity you—I do earnestly pity you."

"Pity, Jane, from some people is a noxious and insulting sort of tribute, which one is justified in hurling back in the teeth of those who offer it; but that is the sort of pity native to callous, selfish hearts; it is a hybrid, egotistical pain at hearing of woes, crossed with ignorant contempt for those who have endured them. But that is not your pity, Jane; it is not the feeling of which your whole face is full at this moment—with which your eyes are now almost overflowing—with which your heart is heaving—with which your hand is trembling in mine. Your pity, my darling, is the suffering mother of love: its anguish is the very natal pang of the divine passion. I accept it, Jane; let the daughter have free advent—my arms wait to receive her."

"Now, sir, proceed; what did you do when you found she was mad?"

"Jane, I approached the verge of despair; a remnant of self-respect was all that intervened between me and the gulf. In the eyes of the world, I was doubtless covered with grimy dishonour; but I resolved to be clean in my own sight—and to the last I repudiated the contamination of her crimes, and wrenched myself from connection with her mental defects. Still, society associated my name and person with hers; I yet saw her and heard her daily: something of her breath (faugh!) mixed with the air I breathed; and besides, I remembered I had once been her husband—that recollection was then, and is now, inexpressibly odious to me; moreover, I knew that while she lived I could never be the husband of another and better wife; and, though five years my senior (her family and her father had lied to me even in the particular of her age), she was likely to live as long as I, being as robust in frame as she was infirm in mind. Thus, at the age of twenty-six, I was hopeless.

"One night I had been awakened by her yells—(since the medical men had pronounced her mad, she had, of course, been shut up)—it was a fiery West Indian night; one of the description that frequently precede the hurricanes of those climates. Being unable to sleep in bed, I got up and opened the window. The air was like sulphur-steams—I could find no refreshment anywhere. Mosquitoes came buzzing in and hummed sullenly round the room; the sea, which I could hear from thence, rumbled dull like an earthquake—black clouds were casting up over it; the moon was setting in the waves, broad and red, like a hot cannon-ball—she threw her last bloody glance over a world quivering with the ferment of tempest. I was physically influenced by the atmosphere and scene, and my ears were filled with the curses the maniac still shrieked out; wherein she momentarily mingled my name with such a tone of demon-hate, with such language! No professed harlot ever had a fouler vocabulary than she: though two rooms off, I heard every word—the thin partitions of the West India house opposing but slight obstruction to her wolfish cries.

" 'This life,' said I at last, 'is hell: this is the air—those are the sounds of the bottomless pit! I have a right to deliver myself from it if I can. The sufferings of this mortal state will leave me with the heavy flesh that now cumbers my soul. Of the fanatic's burning eternity I have no fear: there is not a future state worse than this present one—let me break away, and go home to God!'

"I said this whilst I knelt down at, and unlocked a trunk which contained a brace of loaded pistols: I mean to shoot myself. I only entertained the intention for a moment; for, not being insane, the crisis of exquisite and unalloyed despair, which had originated the wish and design of self-destruction, was past in a second.

"A wind fresh from Europe blew over the ocean and rushed through the open casement: the storm broke, streamed, thundered, blazed, and the air grew pure. I then framed and fixed a resolution. While I walked under the dripping orange-trees of my wet garden, and amongst its drenched pomegranates and pine-apples, and while the refulgent dawn of the tropics kindled round me—I reasoned thus, Jane—and now listen; for it was true Wisdom that consoled me in that hour, and showed me the right path to follow.

"The sweet wind from Europe was still whispering in the refreshed leaves, and the Atlantic was thundering in glorious liberty; my heart, dried up and scorched for a long time, swelled to the tone, and filled with living blood—my being longed for renewal—my soul thirsted for a pure draught. I saw hope revive—and felt regeneration possible. From a flowery arch at the bottom of my garden I gazed over the sea—bluer than the sky: the old world was beyond; clear prospects opened thus:

" 'Go,' said Hope, 'and live again in Europe: there it is not known what a sullied name you bear, nor what a filthy burden is bound to you. You may take the maniac with you to England; confine her with due attendance and precautions at Thornfield: then travel yourself to what clime you will, and form what new tie you like. That woman, who has so abused your long-suffering, so sullied your name, so outraged your honour, so blighted your youth, is not your wife, nor are you her husband. See that she is cared for as her condition demands, and you have done all that God and humanity require of you. Let her identity, her connection with yourself, be buried in oblivion: you are bound to impart them to no living being. Place her in safety and comfort: shelter her degradation with secrecy, and leave her.'

"I acted precisely on this suggestion. My father and brother had not made my marriage known to their acquaintance; because, in the very first letter I wrote to apprise them of the union—having already begun to experience extreme disgust of its consequences, and, from the family character and constitution, seeing a hideous future opening to me—I added an urgent charge to keep it secret: and very soon the infamous conduct of the wife my father had selected for me was such as to make him blush to own her as his daughter-in-law. Far from desiring to publish the connection, he became as anxious to conceal it as myself.

"To England, then, I conveyed her; a fearful voyage I had with such a monster in the vessel. Glad was I when I at last got her to Thornfield, and saw her safely lodged in that third-storey room, of whose secret inner cabinet she has now for ten years made a wild beast's den—a goblin's cell. I had some trouble in finding an attendant for her, as it was necessary to select one on whose fidelity dependence could be placed; for her ravings would inevitably betray my secret: besides, she had lucid intervals of days—sometimes weeks—which she filled up with abuse of me. At last I hired Grace Poole from the Grimbsy Retreat. She and the surgeon, Carter (who dressed Mason's wounds that night he was stabbed and worried), are the only two I have ever admitted to my confidence. Mrs. Fairfax may indeed have suspected something, but she could have gained no precise knowledge as to facts. Grace has, on the whole, proved a good keeper; though, owing partly to a fault of her own, of which it appears nothing can cure her, and which is incident to her harassing profession, her vigilance has been more than once lulled and baffled. The lunatic is both cunning and malignant; she has never failed to take advantage of her guardian's temporary lapses; once to secrete the knife with which she stabbed her brother, and twice to possess herself of the key of her cell, and issue therefrom in the night-time. On the first of these occasions, she perpetrated the attempt to burn me in my bed; on the second, she paid that ghastly visit to you. I thank Providence, who watched over you, that she then spent her fury on your wedding apparel, which perhaps brought back vague reminiscences of her own bridal days: but on what might have happened, I cannot endure to reflect. When I think of the thing which flew at my throat this morning, hanging its black and scarlet visage over the nest of my dove, my blood curdles—"

"And what, sir," I asked, while he paused, "did you do when you had settled her here? Where did you go?"

"What did I do, Jane? I transformed myself into a will-o'-the-wisp. Where did I go? I pursued wanderings as wild as those of the March-spirit. I sought the Continent, and went devious through all its lands. My fixed desire was to seek and find a good and intelligent woman, whom I could love: a contrast to the fury I left at Thornfield—"

"But you could not marry, sir."

"I had determined and was convinced that I could and ought. It was not my original intention to deceive, as I have deceived you. I meant to tell my tale plainly, and make my proposals openly: and it appeared to me so absolutely rational that I should be considered free to love and be loved, I never doubted some woman might be found willing and able to understand my case and accept me, in spite of the curse with which I was burdened."

"Well, sir?"

"When you are inquisitive, Jane, you always make me smile. You open your eyes like an eager bird, and make every now and then a restless movement, as if answers in speech did not flow fast enough for you, and you wanted to read the tablet of one's heart. But before I go on, tell me what you mean by your 'Well, sir?' It is a small phrase very frequent with you; and which many a time has drawn me on and on through interminable talk: I don't very well know why."

"I mean—what next? How did you proceed? What came of such an event?"

"Precisely! And what do you wish to know now?"

"Whether you found any one you liked: whether you asked her to marry you; and what she said."

"I can tell you whether I found any one I liked, and whether I asked her to marry me: but what she said is yet to be recorded in the book of Fate. For ten long years I roved about, living first in one capital, then another: sometimes in St. Petersburg; oftener in Paris; occasionally in Rome, Naples, and Florence. Provided with plenty of money and the passport of an old name, I could choose my own society: no circles were closed against me. I sought my ideal of a woman amongst English ladies, French countesses, Italian signoras, and German gräfinnen. I could not find her. Sometimes, for a fleeting moment, I thought I caught a glance, heard a tone, beheld a form, which announced the realisation of my dream: but I was presently undeserved. You are not to suppose that I desired perfection, either of mind or person. I longed only for what suited me—for the antipodes of the Creole: and I longed vainly. Amongst them all I found not one whom, had I been ever so free, I—

warned as I was of the risks, the horrors, the loathings of incongruous unions—would have asked to marry me. Disappointment made me reckless. I tried dissipation—never debauchery: that I hated, and hate. That was my Indian Messalina's attribute: rooted disgust at it and her restrained me much, even in pleasure. Any enjoyment that bordered on riot seemed to approach me to her and her vices, and I eschewed it.

"Yet I could not live alone; so I tried the companionship of mistresses. The first I chose was Céline Varens—another of those steps which make a man spurn himself when he recalls them. You already know what she was, and how my liaison with her terminated. She had two successors: an Italian, Giacinta, and a German, Clara; both considered singularly handsome. What was their beauty to me in a few weeks? Giacinta was unprincipled and violent: I tired of her in three months. Clara was honest and quiet; but heavy, mindless, and unimpressible: not one whit to my taste. I was glad to give her a sufficient sum to set her up in a good line of business, and so get decently rid of her. But, Jane, I see by your face you are not forming a very favourable opinion of me just now. You think me an unfeeling, loose-principled rake: don't you?"

"I don't like you so well as I have done sometimes, indeed, sir. Did it not seem to you in the least wrong to live in that way, first with one mistress and then another? You talk of it as a mere matter of course."

"It was with me; and I did not like it. It was a grovelling fashion of existence: I should never like to return to it. Hiring a mistress is the next worse thing to buying a slave: both are often by nature, and always by position, inferior: and to live familiarly with inferiors is degrading. I now hate the recollection of the time I passed with Céline, Giacinta, and Clara."

I felt the truth of these words; and I drew from them the certain inference, that if I were so far to forget myself and all the teaching that had ever been instilled into me, as—under any pretext—with any justification—through any temptation—to become the successor of these poor girls, he would one day regard me with the same feeling which now in his mind desecrated their memory. I did not give utterance to this conviction: it was enough to feel it. I impressed it on my heart, that it might remain there to serve me as aid in the time of trial.

"Now, Jane, why don't you say 'Well, sir?' I have not done. You are looking grave. You disapprove of me still, I see. But let me come to the point. Last January, rid of all mistresses—in a harsh, bitter frame of mind, the result of a useless, roving, lonely life—corroded with disappointment, sourly disposed against all men, and especially against all womankind (for I began to regard the notion of an intellectual, faithful, loving woman as a mere dream), recalled by business, I came back to England.

"On a frosty winter afternoon, I rode in sight of Thornfield Hall. Abhorred spot! I expected no peace—no pleasure there. On a stile in Hay Lane I saw a quiet little figure sitting by itself. I passed it as negligently as I did the pollard willow opposite to it: I had no presentiment of what it would be to me; no inward warning that the arbitress of my life—my genius for good or evil—waited there in humble guise. I did not know it, even when, on the occasion of Mesrour's accident, it came up and gravely offered me help. Childish and slender creature! It seemed as if a linnet had hopped to my foot and proposed to bear me on its tiny wing. I was surly; but the thing would not go: it stood by me with strange perseverance, and looked and spoke with a sort of authority. I must be aided, and by that hand: and aided I was.

"When once I had pressed the frail shoulder, something new—a fresh sap and sense—stole into my frame. It was well I had learnt that this elf must return to me—that it belonged to my house down below—or I could not have felt it pass away from under my hand, and seen it vanish behind the dim hedge, without singular regret. I heard you come home that night, Jane, though probably you were not aware that I thought of you or watched for you. The next day I observed you—myself unseen—for half-an-hour, while you played with Adèle in the gallery. It was a snowy day, I recollect, and you could not go out of doors. I was in my room; the door was ajar: I could both listen and watch. Adèle claimed your outward attention for a while; yet I fancied your thoughts were elsewhere: but you were very patient with her, my little Jane; you talked to her and amused her a long time. When at last she left you, you lapsed at once into deep reverie: you betook yourself slowly to pace the gallery. Now and then, in passing a casement, you glanced out at the thick-falling snow; you listened to the sobbing wind, and again you paced gently on and dreamed. I think those day visions were not dark: there was a pleasurable illumination in your eye occasionally, a soft excitement in your aspect, which told of no bitter, bilious, hypochondriac brooding: your look revealed rather the sweet musings of youth when its spirit follows on willing wings the flight of

Hope up and on to an ideal heaven. The voice of Mrs. Fairfax, speaking to a servant in the hall, wakened you: and how curiously you smiled to and at yourself, Janet! There was much sense in your smile: it was very shrewd, and seemed to make light of your own abstraction. It seemed to say—'My fine visions are all very well, but I must not forget they are absolutely unreal. I have a rosy sky and a green flowery Eden in my brain; but without, I am perfectly aware, lies at my feet a rough tract to travel, and around me gather black tempests to encounter.' You ran downstairs and demanded of Mrs. Fairfax some occupation: the weekly house accounts to make up, or something of that sort, I think it was. I was vexed with you for getting out of my sight.

"Impatiently I waited for evening, when I might summon you to my presence. An unusual—to me—a perfectly new character I suspected was yours: I desired to search it deeper and know it better. You entered the room with a look and air at once shy and independent: you were quaintly dressed—much as you are now. I made you talk: ere long I found you full of strange contrasts. Your garb and manner were restricted by rule; your air was often diffident, and altogether that of one refined by nature, but absolutely unused to society, and a good deal afraid of making herself disadvantageously conspicuous by some solecism or blunder; yet when addressed, you lifted a keen, a daring, and a glowing eye to your interlocutor's face: there was penetration and power in each glance you gave; when plied by close questions, you found ready and round answers. Very soon you seemed to get used to me: I believe you felt the existence of sympathy between you and your grim and cross master, Jane; for it was astonishing to see how quickly a certain pleasant ease tranquillised your manner: snarl as I would, you showed no surprise, fear, annoyance, or displeasure at my moroseness; you watched me, and now and then smiled at me with a simple yet sagacious grace I cannot describe. I was at once content and stimulated with what I saw: I liked what I had seen, and wished to see more. Yet, for a long time, I treated you distantly, and sought your company rarely. I was an intellectual epicure, and wished to prolong the gratification of making this novel and piquant acquaintance: besides, I was for a while troubled with a haunting fear that if I handled the flower freely its bloom would fade—the sweet charm of freshness would leave it. I did not then know that it was no transitory blossom, but rather the radiant resemblance of one, cut in an indestructible gem. Moreover, I wished to see whether you would seek me if I shunned you—but you did not; you kept in the schoolroom as still as your own desk and easel; if by chance I met you, you passed me as soon, and with as little token of recognition, as was consistent with respect. Your habitual expression in those days, Jane, was a thoughtful look; not despondent, for you were not sickly; but not buoyant, for you had little hope, and no actual pleasure. I wondered what you thought of me, or if you ever thought of me, and resolved to find this out.

"I resumed my notice of you. There was something glad in your glance, and genial in your manner, when you conversed: I saw you had a social heart; it was the silent schoolroom—it was the tedium of your life—that made you mournful. I permitted myself the delight of being kind to you; kindness stirred emotion soon: your face became soft in expression, your tones gentle; I liked my name pronounced by your lips in a grateful happy accent. I used to enjoy a chance meeting with you, Jane, at this time: there was a curious hesitation in your manner: you glanced at me with a slight trouble—a hovering doubt: you did not know what my caprice might be—whether I was going to play the master and be stern, or the friend and be benignant. I was now too fond of you often to simulate the first whim; and, when I stretched my hand out cordially, such bloom and light and bliss rose to your young, wistful features, I had much ado often to avoid straining you then and there to my heart."

"Don't talk any more of those days, sir," I interrupted, furtively dashing away some tears from my eyes; his language was torture to me; for I knew what I must do—and do soon—and all these reminiscences, and these revelations of his feelings only made my work more difficult.

"No, Jane," he returned; "what necessity is there to dwell on the Past, when the Present is so much surer—the Future so much brighter?"

I shuddered to hear the infatuated assertion.

"You see now how the case stands—do you not?" he continued. "After a youth and manhood passed half in unutterable misery and half in dreary solitude, I have for the first time found what I can truly love—I have found you. You are my sympathy—my better self—my good angel. I am bound to you with a strong attachment. I think you good, gifted, lovely: a fervent, a solemn passion is conceived in my heart; it leans to you, draws you to my centre and spring of life, wraps my existence about you, and, kindling in pure, powerful flame, fuses you and me in one.

"It was because I felt and knew this, that I resolved to marry you. To tell me that I had already a wife is empty mockery: you know now that I had but a hideous demon. I was wrong to attempt to deceive you; but I feared a stubbornness that exists in your character. I feared early instilled prejudice: I wanted to have you safe before hazarding confidences. This was cowardly: I should have appealed to your nobleness and magnanimity at first, as I do now—opened to you plainly my life of agony—described to you my hunger and thirst after a higher and worthier existence—shown to you, not my *resolution* (that word is weak), but my resistless *bent* to love faithfully and well, where I am faithfully and well loved in return. Then I should have asked you to accept my pledge of fidelity and to give me yours. Jane—give it me now."

A pause.

"Why are you silent, Jane?"

I was experiencing an ordeal: a hand of fiery iron grasped my vitals. Terrible moment: full of struggle, blackness, burning! Not a human being that ever lived could wish to be loved better than I was loved; and him who thus loved me I absolutely worshipped: and I must renounce love and idol. One drear word comprised my intolerable duty—"Depart!"

"Jane, you understand what I want of you? Just this promise—'I will be yours, Mr. Rochester.'"

"Mr. Rochester, I will *not* be yours."

Another long silence.

"Jane!" recommenced he, with a gentleness that broke me down with grief, and turned me stone-cold with ominous terror—for this still voice was the pant of a lion rising—"Jane, do you mean to go one way in the world, and to let me go another?"

"I do."

"Jane" (bending towards and embracing me), "do you mean it now?"

"I do."

"And now?" softly kissing my forehead and cheek.

"I do," extricating myself from restraint rapidly and completely.

"Oh, Jane, this is bitter! This—this is wicked. It would not be wicked to love me."

"It would to obey you."

A wild look raised his brows—crossed his features: he rose; but he forebore yet. I laid my hand on the back of a chair for support: I shook, I feared—but I resolved.

"One instant, Jane. Give one glance to my horrible life when you are gone. All happiness will be torn away with you. What then is left? For a wife I have but the maniac upstairs: as well might you refer me to some corpse in yonder churchyard. What shall I do, Jane? Where turn for a companion and for some hope?"

"Do as I do: trust in God and yourself. Believe in heaven. Hope to meet again there."

"Then you will not yield?"

"No."

"Then you condemn me to live wretched and to die accursed?" His voice rose.

"I advise you to live sinless, and I wish you to die tranquil."

"Then you snatch love and innocence from me? You fling me back on lust for a passion—vice for an occupation?"

"Mr. Rochester, I no more assign this fate to you than I grasp at it for myself. We were born to strive and endure—you as well as I: do so. You will forget me before I forget you."

"You make me a liar by such language: you sully my honour. I declared I could not change: you tell me to my face I shall change soon. And what a distortion in your judgment, what a perversity in your ideas, is proved by your conduct! Is it better to drive a fellow-creature to despair than to transgress a mere human law, no man being injured by the breach? For you have neither relatives nor acquaintances whom you need fear to offend by living with me?"

This was true: and while he spoke my very conscience and reason turned traitors against me, and charged me with crime in resisting him. They spoke almost as loud as Feeling: and that clamoured wildly. "Oh, comply!" it said. "Think of his misery; think of his danger—look at his state when left alone; remember his headlong nature; consider the recklessness following on despair—soothe him; save him; love him; tell him you love him and will be his. Who in the world cares for *you*? Or who will be injured by what you do?"

Still indomitable was the reply—"*I* care for myself. The more solitary, the more friendless, the more unsustained I am, the more I will respect myself. I will keep the law given by God; sanctioned by man. I will hold to the principles received by me when I was sane, and not mad—as I am now. Laws and principles are not for the times when there is no temptation: they are for such moments as this, when body and soul rise in mutiny against their rigour; stringent are they; inviolate they shall be. If at my individual convenience I might break them, what would be their worth? They have a worth—so I have always believed; and if I cannot believe it now, it is because I am insane—quite insane: with my veins running fire, and my heart beating faster than I can count its throbs. Preconceived opinions, foregone determinations, are all I have at this hour to stand by: there I plant my foot."

I did. Mr. Rochester, reading my countenance, saw I had done so. His fury was wrought to the highest: he must yield to it for a moment, whatever followed; he crossed the floor and seized my arm and grasped my waist. He seemed to devour me with his flaming glance: physically, I felt, at the moment, powerless as stubble exposed to the draught and glow of a furnace: mentally, I still possessed my soul, and with it the certainty of ultimate safety. The soul, fortunately, has an interpreter—often an unconscious, but still a truthful interpreter—in the eye. My eye rose to his; and while I looked in his fierce face I gave an involuntary sigh; his gripe was painful, and my over-taxed strength almost exhausted.

"Never," said he, as he ground his teeth, "never was anything at once so frail and so indomitable. A mere reed she feels in my hand!" (And he shook me with the force of his hold.) "I could bend her with my finger and thumb: and what good would it do if I bent, if I uptore, if I crushed her? Consider that eye: consider the resolute, wild, free thing looking out of it, defying me, with more than courage—with a stern triumph. Whatever I do with its cage, I cannot get at it—the savage, beautiful creature! If I tear, if I rend the slight prison, my outrage will only let the captive loose. Conqueror I might be of the house; but the inmate would escape to heaven before I could call myself possessor of its clay dwelling-place. And it is you, spirit—with will and energy, and virtue and purity—that I want: not alone your brittle frame. Of yourself you could come with soft flight and nestle against my heart, if you would: seized against your will, you will elude the grasp like an essence—you will vanish ere I inhale your fragrance. Oh! Come, Jane, come!"

As he said this, he released me from his clutch, and only looked at me. The look was far worse to resist than the frantic strain: only an idiot, however, would have succumbed now. I had dared and baffled his fury; I must elude his sorrow: I retired to the door.

"You are going, Jane?"

"I am going, sir."

"You are leaving me?"

"Yes."

"You will not come? You will not be my comforter, my rescuer? My deep love, my wild woe, my frantic prayer, are all nothing to you?"

What unutterable pathos was in his voice! How hard it was to reiterate firmly, "I am going."

"Jane!"

"Mr. Rochester!"

"Withdraw, then—I consent; but remember, you leave me here in anguish. Go up to your own room; think over all I have said, and, Jane, cast a glance on my sufferings—think of me."

He turned away; he threw himself on his face on the sofa. "Oh, Jane! My hope—my love—my life!" broke in anguish from his lips. Then came a deep, strong sob.

I had already gained the door; but, reader, I walked back—walked back as determinedly as I had retreated. I knelt down by him; I turned his face from the cushion to me; I kissed his cheek; I smoothed his hair with my hand.

"God bless you, my dear master!" I said. "God keep you from harm and wrong—direct you, solace you—reward you well for your past kindness to me."

"Little Jane's love would have been my best reward," he answered; "without it, my heart is broken. But Jane will give me her love: yes—nobly, generously."

Up the blood rushed to his face; forth flashed the fire from his eyes; erect he sprang; he held his arms out; but I evaded the embrace, and at once quitted the room.

"Farewell!" was the cry of my heart as I left him. Despair added, "Farewell for ever!"

That night I never thought to sleep; but a slumber fell on me as soon as I lay down in bed. I was transported in thought to the scenes of childhood: I dreamt I lay in the red-room at Gateshead; that the night was dark, and my mind impressed with strange fears. The light that long ago had struck me into syncope, recalled in this vision, seemed glidingly to mount the wall, and tremblingly to pause in the centre of the obscured ceiling. I lifted up my head to look: the roof resolved to clouds, high and dim; the gleam was such as the moon imparts to vapours she is about to sever. I watched her come—watched with the strangest anticipation; as though some word of doom were to be written on her disk. She broke forth as never moon yet burst from cloud: a hand first penetrated the sable folds and waved them away; then, not a moon, but a white human form shone in the azure, inclining a glorious brow earthward. It gazed and gazed on me. It spoke to my spirit: immeasurably distant was the tone, yet so near, it whispered in my heart—

"My daughter, flee temptation."

"Mother, I will."

So I answered after I had waked from the trance-like dream. It was yet night, but July nights are short: soon after midnight, dawn comes. "It cannot be too early to commence the task I have to fulfil," thought I. I rose: I was dressed; for I had taken off nothing but my shoes. I knew where to find in my drawers some linen, a locket, a ring. In seeking these articles, I encountered the beads of a pearl necklace Mr. Rochester had forced me to accept a few days ago. I left that; it was not mine: it was the visionary bride's who had melted in air. The other articles I made up in a parcel; my purse, containing twenty shillings (it was all I had), I put in my pocket: I tied on my straw bonnet, pinned my shawl, took the parcel and my slippers, which I would not put on yet, and stole from my room.

"Farewell, kind Mrs. Fairfax!" I whispered, as I glided past her door. "Farewell, my darling Adèle!" I said, as I glanced towards the nursery. No thought could be admitted of entering to embrace her. I had to deceive a fine ear: for aught I knew it might now be listening.

I would have got past Mr. Rochester's chamber without a pause; but my heart momentarily stopping its beat at that threshold, my foot was forced to stop also. No sleep was there: the inmate was walking restlessly from wall to wall; and again and again he sighed while I listened. There was a heaven—a temporary heaven—in this room for me, if I chose: I had but to go in and to say—

"Mr. Rochester, I will love you and live with you through life till death," and a fount of rapture would spring to my lips. I thought of this.

That kind master, who could not sleep now, was waiting with impatience for day. He would send for me in the morning; I should be gone. He would have me sought for: vainly. He would feel himself forsaken; his love rejected: he would suffer; perhaps grow desperate. I thought of this too. My hand moved towards the lock: I caught it back, and glided on.

Drearily I wound my way downstairs: I knew what I had to do, and I did it mechanically. I sought the key of the side-door in the kitchen; I sought, too, a phial of oil and a feather; I oiled the key and the lock. I got some water, I got some bread: for perhaps I should have to walk far; and my strength, sorely shaken of late, must not break down. All this I did without one sound. I opened the door, passed out, shut it softly. Dim dawn glimmered in the yard. The great gates were closed and locked; but a wicket in one of them was only latched. Through that I departed: it, too, I shut; and now I was out of Thornfield.

A mile off, beyond the fields, lay a road which stretched in the contrary direction to Millcote; a road I had never travelled, but often noticed, and wondered where it led: thither I bent my steps. No reflection was to be allowed now: not one glance was to be cast back; not even one forward. Not one thought was to be given either to the past or the future. The first was a page so heavenly sweet—so deadly sad—that to read one line of it would dissolve my courage and break down my energy. The last was an awful blank: something like the world when the deluge was gone by.

I skirted fields, and hedges, and lanes till after sunrise. I believe it was a lovely summer morning: I know my shoes, which I had put on when I left the house, were soon wet with dew. But I looked neither to rising sun, nor smiling sky, nor wakening nature. He who is taken out to pass through a fair scene to the scaffold, thinks not of the flowers that smile on his road, but of the block and axe-edge; of the disseverment of bone and vein; of the grave gaping at the end: and I thought of drear flight and homeless wandering—and oh! With agony I thought of what I left. I could not help it. I thought of him now—in his room—watching the sunrise; hoping I should soon come to say I would stay with him and be his. I longed to be his; I panted to return: it was not too late; I could yet spare him the bitter pang of bereavement. As yet my flight, I was sure, was undiscovered. I could go back and be his comforter—his pride; his redeemer from misery, perhaps from ruin. Oh, that fear of his self-abandonment—far worse than my abandonment—how it goaded me! It was a barbed arrow-head in my breast; it tore me when I tried to extract it; it sickened me when remembrance thrust it farther in. Birds began singing in brake and copse: birds were faithful to their mates; birds were emblems of love. What was I? In the midst of my pain of heart and frantic effort of principle, I abhorred myself. I had no solace from self-approbation: none even from self-respect. I had injured—wounded—left my master. I was hateful in my own eyes. Still I could not turn, nor retrace one step. God must have led me on. As to my own will or conscience, impassioned grief had trampled one and stifled the other. I was weeping wildly as I walked along my solitary way: fast, fast I went like one delirious. A weakness, beginning inwardly, extending to the limbs, seized me, and I fell: I lay on the ground some minutes, pressing my face to the wet turf. I had some fear—or hope—that here I should die: but I was soon up; crawling forwards on my hands and knees, and then again raised to my feet—as eager and as determined as ever to reach the road.

When I got there, I was forced to sit to rest me under the hedge; and while I sat, I heard wheels, and saw a coach come on. I stood up and lifted my hand; it stopped. I asked where it was going: the driver named a place a long way off, and where I was sure Mr. Rochester had no connections. I asked for what sum he would take me there; he said thirty shillings; I answered I had but twenty; well, he would try to make it do. He further gave me leave to get into the inside, as the vehicle was empty: I entered, was shut in, and it rolled on its way.

Gentle reader, may you never feel what I then felt! May your eyes never shed such stormy, scalding, heart-wrung tears as poured from mine. May you never appeal to Heaven in prayers so hopeless and so agonised as in that hour left my lips; for never may you, like me, dread to be the instrument of evil to what you wholly love.

CHAPTER XXVIII

Two days are passed. It is a summer evening; the coachman has set me down at a place called Whitcross; he could take me no farther for the sum I had given, and I was not possessed of another shilling in the world. The coach is a mile off by this time; I am alone. At this moment I discover that I forgot to take my parcel out of the pocket of the coach, where I had placed it for safety; there it remains, there it must remain; and now, I am absolutely destitute.

Whitcross is no town, nor even a hamlet; it is but a stone pillar set up where four roads meet: whitewashed, I suppose, to be more obvious at a distance and in darkness. Four arms spring from its summit: the nearest town to which these point is, according to the inscription, distant ten miles; the farthest, above twenty. From the well-known names of these towns I learn in what county I have lighted; a north-midland shire, dusk with moorland, ridged with mountain: this I see. There are great moors behind and on each hand of me; there are waves of mountains far beyond that deep valley at my feet. The population here must be thin, and I see no passengers on these roads: they stretch out east, west, north, and south—white, broad, lonely; they are all cut in the moor, and the heather grows deep and wild to their very verge. Yet a chance traveller might pass by; and I wish no eye to see me now: strangers would wonder what I am doing, lingering here at the sign-post, evidently objectless and lost. I might be questioned: I could give no answer but what would sound incredible and excite suspicion. Not a tie holds me to human society at this moment—not a charm or hope calls me where my fellow-creatures are—none that saw me would have a kind thought or a good wish for me. I have no relative but the universal mother, Nature: I will seek her breast and ask repose.

I struck straight into the heath; I held on to a hollow I saw deeply furrowing the brown moorside; I waded knee-deep in its dark growth; I turned with its turnings, and finding a moss-blackened granite crag in a hidden angle, I sat down under it. High banks of moor were about me; the crag protected my head: the sky was over that.

Some time passed before I felt tranquil even here: I had a vague dread that wild cattle might be near, or that some sportsman or poacher might discover me. If a gust of wind swept the waste, I looked up, fearing it was the rush of a bull; if a plover whistled, I imagined it a man. Finding my apprehensions unfounded, however, and calmed by the deep silence that reigned as evening declined at nightfall, I took confidence. As yet I had not thought; I had only listened, watched, dreaded; now I regained the faculty of reflection.

What was I to do? Where to go? Oh, intolerable questions, when I could do nothing and go nowhere! When a long way must yet be measured by my weary, trembling limbs before I could reach human habitation—when cold charity must be entreated before I could get a lodging: reluctant sympathy importuned, almost certain repulse incurred, before my tale could be listened to, or one of my wants relieved!

I touched the heath: it was dry, and yet warm with the heat of the summer day. I looked at the sky; it was pure: a kindly star twinkled just above the chasm ridge. The dew fell, but with propitious softness; no breeze whispered. Nature seemed to me benign and good; I thought she loved me, outcast as I was; and I, who from man could anticipate only mistrust, rejection, insult, clung to her with filial fondness. Tonight, at least, I would be her guest, as I was her child: my mother would lodge me without money and without price. I had one morsel of bread yet: the remnant of a roll I had bought in a town we passed through at noon with a stray penny—my last coin. I saw ripe bilberries gleaming here and there, like jet beads in the heath: I gathered a handful and ate them with the bread. My hunger, sharp before, was, if not satisfied, appeased by this hermit's meal. I said my evening prayers at its conclusion, and then chose my couch.

Beside the crag the heath was very deep: when I lay down my feet were buried in it; rising high on each side, it left only a narrow space for the night-air to invade. I folded my shawl double, and spread it over me for a coverlet; a low, mossy swell was my pillow. Thus lodged, I was not, at least—at the commencement of the night, cold.

My rest might have been blissful enough, only a sad heart broke it. It plained of its gaping wounds, its inward bleeding, its riven chords. It trembled for Mr. Rochester and his doom; it bemoaned him with bitter pity; it demanded him with ceaseless longing; and, impotent as a bird with both wings broken, it still quivered its shattered pinions in vain attempts to seek him.

Worn out with this torture of thought, I rose to my knees. Night was come, and her planets were risen: a safe, still night: too serene for the companionship of fear. We know that God is everywhere; but certainly we feel His presence most when His works are on the grandest scale spread before us; and it is in the unclouded night-sky, where His worlds wheel their silent course, that we read clearest His infinitude, His omnipotence, His omnipresence. I had risen to my knees to pray for Mr. Rochester. Looking up, I, with tear-dimmed eyes, saw the mighty Milky-way. Remembering what it was—what countless systems there swept space like a soft trace of light—I felt the might and strength of God. Sure was I of His efficiency to save what He had made: convinced I grew that neither earth should perish, nor one of the souls it treasured. I turned my prayer to thanksgiving: the Source of Life was also the Saviour of spirits. Mr. Rochester was safe; he was God's, and by God would he be guarded. I again nestled to the breast of the hill; and ere long in sleep forgot sorrow.

But next day, Want came to me pale and bare. Long after the little birds had left their nests; long after bees had come in the sweet prime of day to gather the heath honey before the dew was dried—when the long morning shadows were curtailed, and the sun filled earth and sky—I got up, and I looked round me.

What a still, hot, perfect day! What a golden desert this spreading moor! Everywhere sunshine. I wished I could live in it and on it. I saw a lizard run over the crag; I saw a bee busy among the sweet bilberries. I would fain at the moment have become bee or lizard, that I might have found fitting nutriment, permanent shelter here. But I was a human being, and had a human being's wants: I must not linger where there was nothing to supply them. I rose; I looked back at the bed I had left. Hopeless of the future, I wished but this—that my Maker had that night thought good to require my soul of me while I slept; and that this weary frame, absolved by death from further conflict with fate, had now but to decay quietly, and mingle in peace with the soil of this wilderness. Life, however, was yet in my possession, with all its requirements, and pains, and responsibilities. The burden must be carried; the want provided for; the suffering endured; the responsibility fulfilled. I set out.

Whitcross regained, I followed a road which led from the sun, now fervent and high. By no other circumstance had I will to decide my choice. I walked a long time, and when I thought I had nearly done enough, and might conscientiously yield to the fatigue that almost overpowered me—might relax this forced action, and, sitting down on a stone I saw near, submit resistlessly to the apathy that clogged heart and limb—I heard a bell chime—a church bell.

I turned in the direction of the sound, and there, amongst the romantic hills, whose changes and aspect I had ceased to note an hour ago, I saw a hamlet and a spire. All the valley at my right hand was full of pasture-fields, and cornfields, and wood; and a glittering stream ran zig-zag through the varied shades of green, the mellowing grain, the sombre woodland, the clear and sunny lea. Recalled by the rumbling of wheels to the road before me, I saw a heavily-laden waggon labouring up the hill, and not far beyond were two cows and their drover. Human life and human labour were near. I must struggle on: strive to live and bend to toil like the rest.

About two o'clock p.m. I entered the village. At the bottom of its one street there was a little shop with some cakes of bread in the window. I coveted a cake of bread. With that refreshment I could perhaps regain a degree of energy: without it, it would be difficult to proceed. The wish to have some strength and some vigour returned to me as soon as I was amongst my fellow-beings. I felt it would be degrading to faint with hunger on the causeway of a hamlet. Had I nothing about me I could offer in exchange for one of these rolls? I considered. I had a small silk handkerchief tied round my throat; I had my gloves. I could hardly tell how men and women in extremities of destitution proceeded. I did not know whether either of these articles would be accepted: probably they would not; but I must try.

I entered the shop: a woman was there. Seeing a respectably-dressed person, a lady as she supposed, she came forward with civility. How could she serve me? I was seized with shame: my tongue would not utter the request I had prepared. I dared not offer her the half-worn gloves, the creased handkerchief: besides, I felt it would be absurd. I only begged permission to sit down a moment, as I was tired. Disappointed in the expectation of a customer, she coolly acceded to my request. She pointed to a seat; I sank into it. I felt sorely urged to weep; but conscious how unseasonable such a manifestation would be,

I restrained it. Soon I asked her "if there were any dressmaker or plain-workwoman in the village?"

"Yes; two or three. Quite as many as there was employment for."

I reflected. I was driven to the point now. I was brought face to face with Necessity. I stood in the position of one without a resource, without a friend, without a coin. I must do something. What? I must apply somewhere. Where?

"Did she know of any place in the neighbourhood where a servant was wanted?"

"Nay; she couldn't say."

"What was the chief trade in this place? What did most of the people do?"

"Some were farm labourers; a good deal worked at Mr. Oliver's needle-factory, and at the foundry."

"Did Mr. Oliver employ women?"

"Nay; it was men's work."

"And what do the women do?"

"I knawn't," was the answer. "Some does one thing, and some another. Poor folk mun get on as they can."

She seemed to be tired of my questions: and, indeed, what claim had I to importune her? A neighbour or two came in; my chair was evidently wanted. I took leave.

I passed up the street, looking as I went at all the houses to the right hand and to the left; but I could discover no pretext, nor see an inducement to enter any. I rambled round the hamlet, going sometimes to a little distance and returning again, for an hour or more. Much exhausted, and suffering greatly now for want of food, I turned aside into a lane and sat down under the hedge. Ere many minutes had elapsed, I was again on my feet, however, and again searching something—a resource, or at least an informant. A pretty little house stood at the top of the lane, with a garden before it, exquisitely neat and brilliantly blooming. I stopped at it. What business had I to approach the white door or touch the glittering knocker? In what way could it possibly be the interest of the inhabitants of that dwelling to serve me? Yet I drew near and knocked. A mild-looking, cleanly-attired young woman opened the door. In such a voice as might be expected from a hopeless heart and fainting frame—a voice wretchedly low and faltering—I asked if a servant was wanted here?

"No," said she; "we do not keep a servant."

"Can you tell me where I could get employment of any kind?" I continued. "I am a stranger, without acquaintance in this place. I want some work: no matter what."

But it was not her business to think for me, or to seek a place for me: besides, in her eyes, how doubtful must have appeared my character, position, tale. She shook her head, she "was sorry she could give me no information," and the white door closed, quite gently and civilly: but it shut me out. If she had held it open a little longer, I believe I should have begged a piece of bread; for I was now brought low.

I could not bear to return to the sordid village, where, besides, no prospect of aid was visible. I should have longed rather to deviate to a wood I saw not far off, which appeared in its thick shade to offer inviting shelter; but I was so sick, so weak, so gnawed with nature's cravings, instinct kept me roaming round abodes where there was a chance of food. Solitude would be no solitude—rest no rest—while the vulture, hunger, thus sank beak and talons in my side.

I drew near houses; I left them, and came back again, and again I wandered away: always repelled by the consciousness of having no claim to ask—no right to expect interest in my isolated lot. Meantime, the afternoon advanced, while I thus wandered about like a lost and starving dog. In crossing a field, I saw the church spire before me: I hastened towards it. Near the churchyard, and in the middle of a garden, stood a well-built though small house, which I had no doubt was the parsonage. I remembered that strangers who arrive at a place where they have no friends, and who want employment, sometimes apply to the clergyman for introduction and aid. It is the clergyman's function to help—at least with advice—those who wished to help themselves. I seemed to have something like a right to seek counsel here. Renewing then my courage, and gathering my feeble remains of strength, I pushed on. I reached the house, and knocked at the kitchen-door. An old woman opened: I asked was this the parsonage?

"Yes."

"Was the clergyman in?"

"No."

"Would he be in soon?"

"No, he was gone from home."

"To a distance?"

"Not so far—happen three mile. He had been called away by the sudden death of his father: he was at Marsh End now, and would very likely stay there a fortnight longer."

"Was there any lady of the house?"

"Nay, there was naught but her, and she was housekeeper"; and of her, reader, I could not bear to ask the relief for want of which I was sinking; I could not yet beg; and again I crawled away.

Once more I took off my handkerchief—once more I thought of the cakes of bread in the little shop. Oh, for but a crust! For but one mouthful to allay the pang of famine! Instinctively I turned my face again to the village; I found the shop again, and I went in; and though others were there besides the woman I ventured the request—"Would she give me a roll for this handkerchief?"

She looked at me with evident suspicion: "Nay, she never sold stuff i' that way."

Almost desperate, I asked for half a cake; she again refused. "How could she tell where I had got the handkerchief?" she said.

"Would she take my gloves?"

"No! What could she do with them?"

Reader, it is not pleasant to dwell on these details. Some say there is enjoyment in looking back to painful experience past; but at this day I can scarcely bear to review the times to which I allude: the moral degradation, blent with the physical suffering, form too distressing a recollection ever to be willingly dwelt on. I blamed none of those who repulsed me. I felt it was what was to be expected, and what could not be helped: an ordinary beggar is frequently an object of suspicion; a well-dressed beggar inevitably so. To be sure, what I begged was employment; but whose business was it to provide me with employment? Not, certainly, that of persons who saw me then for the first time, and who knew nothing about my character. And as to the woman who would not take my handkerchief in exchange for her bread, why, she was right, if the offer appeared to her sinister or the exchange unprofitable. Let me condense now. I am sick of the subject.

A little before dark I passed a farm-house, at the open door of which the farmer was sitting, eating his supper of bread and cheese. I stopped and said—

"Will you give me a piece of bread? For I am very hungry." He cast on me a glance of surprise; but without answering, he cut a thick slice from his loaf, and gave it to me. I imagine he did not think I was a beggar, but only an eccentric sort of lady, who had taken a fancy to his brown loaf. As soon as I was out of sight of his house, I sat down and ate it.

I could not hope to get a lodging under a roof, and sought it in the wood I have before alluded to. But my night was wretched, my rest broken: the ground was damp, the air cold: besides, intruders passed near me more than once, and I had again and again to change my quarters; no sense of safety or tranquillity befriended me. Towards morning it rained; the whole of the following day was wet. Do not ask me, reader, to give a minute account of that day; as before, I sought work; as before, I was repulsed; as before, I starved; but once did food pass my lips. At the door of a cottage I saw a little girl about to throw a mess of cold porridge into a pig trough. "Will you give me that?" I asked.

She stared at me. "Mother!" she exclaimed. "There is a woman wants me to give her these porridge."

"Well lass," replied a voice within, "give it her if she's a beggar. T' pig doesn't want it."

The girl emptied the stiffened mould into my hand, and I devoured it ravenously.

As the wet twilight deepened, I stopped in a solitary bridle-path, which I had been pursuing an hour or more.

"My strength is quite failing me," I said in a soliloquy. "I feel I cannot go much farther. Shall I be an outcast again this night? While the rain descends so, must I lay my head on the cold, drenched ground? I fear I cannot do otherwise: for who will receive me? But it will be very dreadful, with this feeling of hunger, faintness, chill, and this sense of desolation—this total prostration of hope. In all likelihood, though, I should die before morning. And why cannot I reconcile myself to the prospect of death? Why do I struggle to retain a valueless life? Because I know, or believe, Mr. Rochester is living: and then, to die of want and cold is a fate to which nature cannot submit passively. Oh, Providence! Sustain me a little longer! Aid! Direct me!"

My glazed eye wandered over the dim and misty landscape. I saw I had strayed far from the village: it was quite out of sight. The very cultivation surrounding it had disappeared. I had, by cross-ways and by-paths, once more drawn near the tract of moorland; and now, only a few fields, almost as wild and unproductive as the heath from which they were scarcely reclaimed, lay between me and the dusky hill.

"Well, I would rather die yonder than in a street or on a frequented road," I reflected. "And far better that crows and ravens—if any ravens there be in these regions—should pick my flesh from my bones, than that they should be prisoned in a workhouse coffin and moulder in a pauper's grave."

To the hill, then, I turned. I reached it. It remained now only to find a hollow where I could lie down, and feel at least hidden, if not secure. But all the surface of the waste looked level. It showed no variation but of tint: green, where rush and moss overgrew the marshes; black, where the dry soil bore only heath. Dark as it was getting, I could still see these changes, though but as mere alternations of light and shade; for colour had faded with the daylight.

My eye still roved over the sullen swell and along the moor-edge, vanishing amidst the wildest scenery, when at one dim point, far in among the marshes and the ridges, a light sprang up. "That is an *ignis fatuus*," was my first thought; and I expected it would soon vanish. It burnt on, however, quite steadily, neither receding nor advancing. "Is it, then, a bonfire just kindled?" I questioned. I watched to see whether it would spread: but no; as it did not diminish, so it did not enlarge. "It may be a candle in a house," I then conjectured; "but if so, I can never reach it. It is much too far away: and were it within a yard of me, what would it avail? I should but knock at the door to have it shut in my face."

And I sank down where I stood, and hid my face against the ground. I lay still a while: the night-wind swept over the hill and over me, and died moaning in the distance; the rain fell fast, wetting me afresh to the skin. Could I but have stiffened to the still frost—the friendly numbness of death—it might have pelted on; I should not have felt it; but my yet living flesh shuddered at its chilling influence. I rose ere long.

The light was yet there, shining dim but constant through the rain. I tried to walk again: I dragged my exhausted limbs slowly towards it. It led me aslant over the hill, through a wide bog, which would have been impassable in winter, and was splashy and shaking even now, in the height of summer. Here I fell twice; but as often I rose and rallied my faculties. This light was my forlorn hope: I must gain it.

Having crossed the marsh, I saw a trace of white over the moor. I approached it; it was a road or a track: it led straight up to the light, which now beamed from a sort of knoll, amidst a clump of trees—firs, apparently, from what I could distinguish of the character of their forms and foliage through the gloom. My star vanished as I drew near: some obstacle had intervened between me and it. I put out my hand to feel the dark mass before me: I discriminated the rough stones of a low wall—above it, something like palisades, and within, a high and prickly hedge. I groped on. Again a whitish object gleamed before me: it was a gate—a wicket; it moved on its hinges as I touched it. On each side stood a sable bush-holly or yew.

Entering the gate and passing the shrubs, the silhouette of a house rose to view, black, low, and rather long; but the guiding light shone nowhere. All was obscurity. Were the inmates retired to rest? I feared it must be so. In seeking the door, I turned an angle: there shot out the friendly gleam again, from the lozenged panes of a very small latticed window, within a foot of the ground, made still smaller by the growth of ivy or some other creeping plant, whose leaves clustered thick over the portion of the house wall in which it was set. The aperture was so screened and narrow, that curtain or shutter had been deemed unnecessary; and when I stooped down and put aside the spray of foliage shooting over it, I could see all within. I could see clearly a room with a sanded floor, clean scoured; a dresser of walnut, with pewter plates ranged in rows, reflecting the redness and radiance of a glowing peat-fire. I could see a clock, a white deal table, some chairs. The candle, whose ray had been my beacon, burnt on the table; and by its light an elderly woman, somewhat rough-looking, but scrupulously clean, like all about her, was knitting a stocking.

I noticed these objects cursorily only—in them there was nothing extraordinary. A group of more interest appeared near the hearth, sitting still amidst the rosy peace and warmth suffusing it. Two young, graceful women—ladies in every point—sat, one in a low rocking-chair, the other on a lower stool; both wore deep mourning of crape and bombazeen, which sombre garb singularly set off very fair necks and faces: a large old pointer dog rested its massive head on the knee of one girl—in the lap of the other was cushioned a black cat.

A strange place was this humble kitchen for such occupants! Who were they? They could not be the daughters of the elderly person at the table; for she looked like a rustic, and they were all delicacy and cultivation. I had nowhere seen such faces as theirs: and yet, as I gazed on them, I seemed intimate with every lineament. I cannot call them handsome—they were too pale and grave for the word: as they each bent over a book, they looked thoughtful almost to severity. A stand between them supported a second candle and two great volumes, to which they frequently referred, comparing them, seemingly, with the smaller books they held in their hands, like people consulting a dictionary to aid them in the task of translation. This scene was as silent as if all the figures had been shadows and the firelit apartment a picture: so hushed was it, I could hear the cinders fall from the grate, the clock tick in its obscure corner; and I even fancied I could distinguish the click-click of the woman's knitting-needles. When, therefore, a voice broke the strange stillness at last, it was audible enough to me.

"Listen, Diana," said one of the absorbed students; "Franz and old Daniel are together in the night-time, and Franz is telling a dream from which he has awakened in terror—listen!" And in a low voice she read something, of which not one word was intelligible to me; for it was in an unknown tongue—neither French nor Latin. Whether it were Greek or German I could not tell.

"That is strong," she said, when she had finished; "I relish it." The other girl, who had lifted her head to listen to her sister, repeated, while she gazed at the fire, a line of what had been read. At a later day, I knew the language and the book; therefore, I will here quote the line: though, when I first heard it, it was only like a stroke on sounding brass to me—conveying no meaning:

" 'Da trat hervor Einer, anzusehen wie die Sternen Nacht.' Good! Good!" she exclaimed, while her dark and deep eye sparkled. "There you have a dim and mighty archangel fitly set before you! The line is worth a hundred pages of fustian. 'Ich wäge die Gedanken in der Schale meines Zornes und die Werke mit dem Gewichte meines Grimms.' I like it!"

Both were again silent.

"Is there ony country where they talk i' that way?" asked the old woman, looking up from her knitting.

"Yes, Hannah—a far larger country than England, where they talk in no other way."

"Well, for sure case, I knawn't how they can understand t' one t'other: and if either o' ye went there, ye could tell what they said, I guess?"

"We could probably tell something of what they said, but not all—for we are not as clever as you think us, Hannah. We don't speak German, and we cannot read it without a dictionary to help us."

"And what good does it do you?"

"We mean to teach it some time—or at least the elements, as they say; and then we shall get more money than we do now."

"Varry like: but give ower studying; ye've done enough for tonight."

"I think we have: at least I'm tired. Mary, are you?"

"Mortally: after all, it's tough work fagging away at a language with no master but a lexicon."

"It is, especially such a language as this crabbed but glorious Deutsch. I wonder when St. John will come home."

"Surely he will not be long now: it is just ten (looking at a little gold watch she drew from her girdle). It rains fast, Hannah: will you have the goodness to look at the fire in the parlour?"

The woman rose: she opened a door, through which I dimly saw a passage: soon I heard her stir a fire in an inner room; she presently came back.

"Ah, childer!" said she. "It fair troubles me to go into yond' room now: it looks so lonesome wi' the chair empty and set back in a corner."

She wiped her eyes with her apron: the two girls, grave before, looked sad now.

"But he is in a better place," continued Hannah; "we shouldn't wish him here again. And then, nobody need to have a quieter death nor he had."

"You say he never mentioned us?" inquired one of the ladies.

"He hadn't time, bairn: he was gone in a minute, was your father. He had been a bit ailing like the day before, but naught to signify; and when Mr. St. John asked if he would like either o' ye to be sent for, he fair laughed at him. He began again with a bit of a heaviness in his head the next day—that is, a fortnight sin'—and he went to sleep and niver wakened: he wor a'most stark when your brother went into t' chamber and fand him. Ah, childer! That's t' last o' t' old stock—for ye and Mr. St. John is like of different soart to them 'at's gone; for all your mother wor mich i' your way, and a'most as book-learned. She wor the pictur' o' ye, Mary: Diana is more like your father."

I thought them so similar I could not tell where the old servant (for such I now concluded her to be) saw the difference. Both were fair complexioned and slenderly made; both possessed faces full of distinction and intelligence. One, to be sure, had hair a shade darker than the other, and there was a difference in their style of wearing it; Mary's pale brown locks were parted and braided smooth: Diana's duskier tresses covered her neck with thick curls. The clock struck ten.

"Ye'll want your supper, I am sure," observed Hannah; "and so will Mr. St. John when he comes in."

And she proceeded to prepare the meal. The ladies rose; they seemed about to withdraw to the parlour. Till this moment, I had been so intent on watching them, their appearance and conversation had excited in me so keen an interest, I had half-forgotten my own wretched position: now it recurred to me. More desolate, more desperate than ever, it seemed from contrast. And how impossible did it appear to touch the inmates of this house with concern on my behalf; to make them believe in the truth of my wants and woes—to induce them to vouchsafe a rest for my wanderings! As I groped out the door, and knocked at it hesitatingly, I felt that last idea to be a mere chimera. Hannah opened.

"What do you want?" she inquired, in a voice of surprise, as she surveyed me by the light of the candle she held.

"May I speak to your mistresses?" I said.

"You had better tell me what you have to say to them. Where do you come from?"

"I am a stranger."

"What is your business here at this hour?"

"I want a night's shelter in an out-house or anywhere, and a morsel of bread to eat."

Distrust, the very feeling I dreaded, appeared in Hannah's face. "I'll give you a piece of bread," she said, after a pause; "but we can't take in a vagrant to lodge. It isn't likely."

"Do let me speak to your mistresses."

"No, not I. What can they do for you? You should not be roving about now; it looks very ill."

"But where shall I go if you drive me away? What shall I do?"

"Oh, I'll warrant you know where to go and what to do. Mind you don't do wrong, that's all. Here is a penny; now go—"

"A penny cannot feed me, and I have no strength to go farther. Don't shut the door—oh, don't, for God's sake!"

"I must; the rain is driving in—"

"Tell the young ladies. Let me see them—"

"Indeed, I will not. You are not what you ought to be, or you wouldn't make such a noise. Move off."

"But I must die if I am turned away."

"Not you. I'm fear'd you have some ill plans agate, that bring you about folk's houses at this time o' night. If you've any followers—housebreakers or such like—anywhere near, you may tell them we are not by ourselves in the house; we have a gentleman, and dogs, and guns." Here the honest but inflexible servant clapped the door to and bolted it within.

This was the climax. A pang of exquisite suffering—a throe of true despair—rent and heaved my heart. Worn out, indeed, I was; not another step could I stir. I sank on the wet doorstep: I groaned—I wrung my hands—I wept in utter anguish. Oh, this spectre of death! Oh, this last hour, approaching in such horror! Alas, this isolation—this banishment from my kind! Not only the anchor of hope, but the footing of fortitude was gone—at least for a moment; but the last I soon endeavoured to regain.

"I can but die," I said, "and I believe in God. Let me try to wait His will in silence."

These words I not only thought, but uttered; and thrusting back all my misery into my heart, I made an effort to compel it to remain there—dumb and still.

"All men must die," said a voice quite close at hand; "but all are not condemned to meet a lingering and premature doom, such as yours would be if you perished here of want."

"Who or what speaks?" I asked, terrified at the unexpected sound, and incapable now of deriving from any occurrence a hope of aid. A form was near—what form, the pitch-dark night and my enfeebled vision prevented me from distinguishing. With a loud long knock, the new-comer appealed to the door.

"Is it you, Mr. St. John?" cried Hannah.

"Yes—yes; open quickly."

"Well, how wet and cold you must be, such a wild night as it is! Come in—your sisters are quite uneasy about you, and I believe there are bad folks about. There has been a beggar-woman—I declare she is not gone yet!—laid down there. Get up! For shame! Move off, I say!"

"Hush, Hannah! I have a word to say to the woman. You have done your duty in excluding, now let me do mine in admitting her. I was near, and listened to both you and her. I think this is a peculiar case—I must at least examine into it. Young woman, rise, and pass before me into the house."

With difficulty I obeyed him. Presently I stood within that clean, bright kitchen—on the very hearth—trembling, sickening; conscious of an aspect in the last degree ghastly, wild, and weather-beaten. The two ladies, their brother, Mr. St. John, the old servant, were all gazing at me.

"St. John, who is it?" I heard one ask.

"I cannot tell: I found her at the door," was the reply.

"She does look white," said Hannah.

"As white as clay or death," was responded. "She will fall: let her sit."

And indeed my head swam: I dropped, but a chair received me. I still possessed my senses, though just now I could not speak.

"Perhaps a little water would restore her. Hannah, fetch some. But she is worn to nothing. How very thin, and how very bloodless!"

"A mere spectre!"

"Is she ill, or only famished?"

"Famished, I think. Hannah, is that milk? Give it me, and a piece of bread."

Diana (I knew her by the long curls which I saw drooping between me and the fire as she bent over me) broke some bread, dipped it in milk, and put it to my lips. Her face was near mine: I saw there was pity in it, and I felt sympathy in her hurried breathing. In her simple words, too, the same balm-like emotion spoke: "Try to eat."

"Yes—try," repeated Mary gently; and Mary's hand removed my sodden bonnet and lifted my head. I tasted what they offered me: feebly at first, eagerly soon.

"Not too much at first—restrain her," said the brother; "she has had enough." And he withdrew the cup of milk and the plate of bread.

"A little more, St. John—look at the avidity in her eyes."

"No more at present, sister. Try if she can speak now—ask her her name."

I felt I could speak, and I answered—"My name is Jane Elliott." Anxious as ever to avoid discovery, I had before resolved to assume an alias.

"And where do you live? Where are your friends?"

I was silent.

"Can we send for any one you know?"

I shook my head.

"What account can you give of yourself?"

Somehow, now that I had once crossed the threshold of this house, and once was brought face to face with its owners, I felt no longer outcast, vagrant, and disowned by the wide world. I dared to put off the mendicant—to resume my natural manner and character. I began once more to know myself; and when Mr. St. John demanded an account—which at present I was far too weak to render—I said after a brief pause—

"Sir, I can give you no details tonight."

"But what, then," said he, "do you expect me to do for you?"

"Nothing," I replied. My strength sufficed for but short answers. Diana took the word—

"Do you mean," she asked, "that we have now given you what aid you require? And that we may dismiss you to the moor and the rainy night?"

I looked at her. She had, I thought, a remarkable countenance, instinct both with power and goodness. I took sudden courage. Answering her compassionate gaze with a smile, I said, "I will trust you. If I were a masterless and stray dog, I know that you would not turn me from your hearth tonight: as it is, I really have no fear. Do with me and for me as you like; but excuse me from much discourse—my breath is short—I feel a spasm when I speak." All three surveyed me, and all three were silent.

"Hannah," said Mr. St. John, at last, "let her sit there at present, and ask her no questions; in ten minutes more, give her the remainder of that milk and bread. Mary and Diana, let us go into the parlour and talk the matter over."

They withdrew. Very soon one of the ladies returned—I could not tell which. A kind of pleasant stupor was stealing over me as I sat by the genial fire. In an undertone she gave some directions to Hannah. Ere long, with the servant's aid, I contrived to mount a staircase; my dripping clothes were removed; soon a warm, dry bed received me. I thanked God—experienced amidst unutterable exhaustion a glow of grateful joy—and slept.

CHAPTER XXIX

The recollection of about three days and nights succeeding this is very dim in my mind. I can recall some sensations felt in that interval; but few thoughts framed, and no actions performed. I knew I was in a small room and in a narrow bed. To that bed I seemed to have grown; I lay on it motionless as a stone; and to have torn me from it would have been almost to kill me. I took no note of the lapse of time—of the change from morning to noon, from noon to evening. I observed when any one entered or left the apartment: I could even tell who they were; I could understand what was said when the speaker stood near to me; but I could not answer; to open my lips or move my limbs was equally impossible. Hannah, the servant, was my most frequent visitor. Her coming disturbed me. I had a feeling that she wished me away: that she did not understand me or my circumstances; that she was prejudiced against me. Diana and Mary appeared in the chamber once or twice a day. They would whisper sentences of this sort at my bedside—

"It is very well we took her in."

"Yes; she would certainly have been found dead at the door in the morning had she been left out all night. I wonder what she has gone through?"

"Strange hardships, I imagine—poor, emaciated, pallid wanderer?"

"She is not an uneducated person, I should think, by her manner of speaking; her accent was quite pure; and the clothes she took off, though splashed and wet, were little worn and fine."

"She has a peculiar face; fleshless and haggard as it is, I rather like it; and when in good health and animated, I can fancy her physiognomy would be agreeable."

Never once in their dialogues did I hear a syllable of regret at the hospitality they had extended to me, or of suspicion of, or aversion to, myself. I was comforted.

Mr. St. John came but once: he looked at me, and said my state of lethargy was the result of reaction from excessive and protracted fatigue. He pronounced it needless to send for a doctor: nature, he was sure, would manage best, left to herself. He said every nerve had been overstrained in some way, and the whole system must sleep torpid a while. There was no disease. He imagined my recovery would be rapid enough when once commenced. These opinions he delivered in a few words, in a quiet, low voice; and added, after a pause, in the tone of a man little accustomed to expansive comment, "Rather an unusual physiognomy; certainly, not indicative of vulgarity or degradation."

"Far otherwise," responded Diana. "To speak truth, St. John, my heart rather warms to the poor little soul. I wish we may be able to benefit her permanently."

"That is hardly likely," was the reply. "You will find she is some young lady who has had a misunderstanding with her friends, and has probably injudiciously left them. We may, perhaps, succeed in restoring her to them, if she is not obstinate: but I trace lines of force in her face which make me sceptical of her tractability." He stood considering me some minutes; then added, "She looks sensible, but not at all handsome."

"She is so ill, St. John."

"Ill or well, she would always be plain. The grace and harmony of beauty are quite wanting in those features."

On the third day I was better; on the fourth, I could speak, move, rise in bed, and turn. Hannah had brought me some gruel and dry toast, about, as I supposed, the dinner-hour. I had eaten with relish: the food was good—void of the feverish flavour which had hitherto poisoned what I had swallowed. When she left me, I felt comparatively strong and revived: ere long satiety of repose and desire for action stirred me. I wished to rise; but what could I put on? Only my damp and bemired apparel; in which I had slept on the ground and fallen in the marsh. I felt ashamed to appear before my benefactors so clad. I was spared the humiliation.

On a chair by the bedside were all my own things, clean and dry. My black silk frock hung against the wall. The traces of the bog were removed from it; the creases left by the wet smoothed out: it was quite decent. My very shoes and stockings were purified and rendered presentable. There were the means of washing in the room, and a comb and brush to smooth my hair. After a weary process, and resting every five minutes, I succeeded in dressing myself. My clothes hung loose on me; for I was much wasted, but I covered deficiencies with a shawl, and once more, clean and respectable looking—no speck of the dirt, no trace of the disorder I so hated, and which seemed so to degrade me, left—I crept down a stone staircase with the aid of the banisters, to a narrow low passage, and found my way presently to the kitchen.

It was full of the fragrance of new bread and the warmth of a generous fire. Hannah was baking. Prejudices, it is well known, are most difficult to eradicate from the heart whose soil has never been loosened or fertilised by education: they grow there, firm as weeds among stones. Hannah had been cold and stiff, indeed, at the first: latterly she had begun to relent a little; and when she saw me come in tidy and well-dressed, she even smiled.

"What, you have got up!" she said. "You are better, then. You may sit you down in my chair on the hearthstone, if you will."

She pointed to the rocking-chair: I took it. She bustled about, examining me every now and then with the corner of her eye. Turning to me, as she took some loaves from the oven, she asked bluntly—

"Did you ever go a-begging afore you came here?"

I was indignant for a moment; but remembering that anger was out of the question, and that I had indeed appeared as a beggar to her, I answered quietly, but still not without a certain marked firmness—

"You are mistaken in supposing me a beggar. I am no beggar; any more than yourself or your young ladies."

After a pause she said, "I dunnut understand that: you've like no house, nor no brass, I guess?"

"The want of house or brass (by which I suppose you mean money) does not make a beggar in your sense of the word."

"Are you book-learned?" she inquired presently.

"Yes, very."

"But you've never been to a boarding-school?"

"I was at a boarding-school eight years."

She opened her eyes wide. "Whatever cannot ye keep yourself for, then?"

"I have kept myself; and, I trust, shall keep myself again. What are you going to do with these gooseberries?" I inquired, as she brought out a basket of the fruit.

"Mak' 'em into pies."

"Give them to me and I'll pick them."

"Nay; I dunnut want ye to do nought."

"But I must do something. Let me have them."

She consented; and she even brought me a clean towel to spread over my dress, "lest," as she said, "I should mucky it."

"Ye've not been used to sarvant's wark, I see by your hands," she remarked. "Happen ye've been a dressmaker?"

"No, you are wrong. And now, never mind what I have been: don't trouble your head further about me; but tell me the name of the house where we are."

"Some calls it Marsh End, and some calls it Moor House."

"And the gentleman who lives here is called Mr. St. John?"

"Nay; he doesn't live here: he is only staying a while. When he is at home, he is in his own parish at Morton."

"That village a few miles off?

"Aye."

"And what is he?"

"He is a parson."

I remembered the answer of the old housekeeper at the parsonage, when I had asked to see the clergyman. "This, then, was his father's residence?"

"Aye; old Mr. Rivers lived here, and his father, and grandfather, and gurt (great) grandfather afore him."

"The name, then, of that gentleman, is Mr. St. John Rivers?"

"Aye; St. John is like his kirstened name."

"And his sisters are called Diana and Mary Rivers?"

"Yes."

"Their father is dead?"

"Dead three weeks sin' of a stroke."

"They have no mother?"

"The mistress has been dead this mony a year."

"Have you lived with the family long?"

"I've lived here thirty year. I nursed them all three."

"That proves you must have been an honest and faithful servant. I will say so much for you, though you have had the incivility to call me a beggar."

She again regarded me with a surprised stare. "I believe," she said, "I was quite mista'en in my thoughts of you: but there is so mony cheats goes about, you mun forgie me."

"And though," I continued, rather severely, "you wished to turn me from the door, on a night when you should not have shut out a dog."

"Well, it was hard: but what can a body do? I thought more o' th' childer nor of mysel: poor things! They've like nobody to tak' care on 'em but me. I'm like to look sharpish."

I maintained a grave silence for some minutes.

"You munnut think too hardly of me," she again remarked.

"But I do think hardly of you," I said; "and I'll tell you why—not so much because you refused to give me shelter, or regarded me as an impostor, as because you just now made it a species of reproach that I had no 'brass' and no house. Some of the best people that ever lived have been as destitute as I am; and if you are a Christian, you ought not to consider poverty a crime."

"No more I ought," said she; "Mr. St. John tells me so too; and I see I wor wrang—but I've clear a different notion on you now to what I had. You look a raight down dacent little crater."

"That will do—I forgive you now. Shake hands."

She put her floury and horny hand into mine; another and heartier smile illumined her rough face, and from that moment we were friends.

Hannah was evidently fond of talking. While I picked the fruit, and she made the paste for the pies, she proceeded to give me sundry details about her deceased master and mistress, and "the childer," as she called the young people.

Old Mr. Rivers, she said, was a plain man enough, but a gentleman, and of as ancient a family as could be found. Marsh End had belonged to the Rivers ever since it was a house: and it was, she affirmed, "aboon two hundred year old—for all it looked but a small, humble place, naught to compare wi' Mr. Oliver's grand hall down i' Morton Vale. But she could remember Bill Oliver's father a journeyman needlemaker; and th' Rivers wor gentry i' th' owd days o' th' Henrys, as onybody might see by looking into th' registers i' Morton Church vestry." Still, she allowed, "the owd maister was like other folk—naught mich out o' t' common way: stark mad o' shooting, and farming, and sich like." The mistress was different. She was a great reader, and studied a deal; and the "bairns" had taken after her. There was nothing like them in these parts, nor ever had been; they had liked learning, all three, almost from the time they could speak; and they had always been "of a mak' of their own." Mr. St. John, when he grew up, would go to college and be a parson; and the girls, as soon as they left school, would seek places as governesses: for they had told her their father had some years ago lost a great deal of money by a man he had trusted turning bankrupt; and as he was now not rich enough to give them fortunes, they must provide for themselves. They had lived very little at home for a long while, and were only come now to stay a few weeks on account of their father's death; but they did so like Marsh End and Morton, and all these moors and hills about. They had been in London, and many other grand towns; but they always said there was no place like home; and then they were so agreeable with each other—never fell out nor "threaped." She did not know where there was such a family for being united.

Having finished my task of gooseberry picking, I asked where the two ladies and their brother were now.

"Gone over to Morton for a walk; but they would be back in half-an-hour to tea."

They returned within the time Hannah had allotted them: they entered by the kitchen door. Mr. St. John, when he saw me, merely bowed and passed through; the two ladies stopped: Mary, in a few words, kindly and calmly expressed the pleasure she felt in seeing me well enough to be able to come down; Diana took my hand: she shook her head at me.

"You should have waited for my leave to descend," she said. "You still look very pale—and so thin! Poor child! Poor girl!"

Diana had a voice toned, to my ear, like the cooing of a dove. She possessed eyes whose gaze I delighted to encounter. Her whole face seemed to me full of charm. Mary's countenance was equally intelligent—her features equally pretty; but her expression was more reserved, and her manners, though gentle, more distant. Diana looked and spoke with a certain authority: she had a will, evidently. It was my nature to feel pleasure in yielding to an authority supported like hers, and to bend, where my conscience and self-respect permitted, to an active will.

"And what business have you here?" she continued. "It is not your place. Mary and I sit in the kitchen sometimes, because at home we like to be free, even to license—but you are a visitor, and must go into the parlour."

"I am very well here."

"Not at all, with Hannah bustling about and covering you with flour."

"Besides, the fire is too hot for you," interposed Mary.

"To be sure," added her sister. "Come, you must be obedient." And still holding my hand she made me rise, and led me into the inner room.

"Sit there," she said, placing me on the sofa, "while we take our things off and get the tea ready; it is another privilege we exercise in our little moorland home—to prepare our own meals when we are so inclined, or when Hannah is baking, brewing, washing, or ironing."

She closed the door, leaving me solus with Mr. St. John, who sat opposite, a book or newspaper in his hand. I examined, first, the parlour, and then its occupant.

The parlour was rather a small room, very plainly furnished, yet comfortable, because clean and neat. The old-fashioned chairs were very bright, and the walnut-wood table was like a looking-glass. A few strange, antique portraits of the men and women of other days decorated the stained walls; a cupboard with glass doors contained some books and an ancient set of china. There was no superfluous ornament in the room—not one modern piece of furniture, save a brace of workboxes and a lady's desk in rosewood, which stood on a side-table: everything—including the carpet and curtains—looked at once well worn and well saved.

Mr. St. John—sitting as still as one of the dusty pictures on the walls, keeping his eyes fixed on the page he perused, and his lips mutely sealed—was easy enough to examine. Had he been a statue instead of a man, he could not have been easier. He was young—perhaps from twenty-eight to thirty—tall, slender; his face riveted the eye; it was like a Greek face, very pure in outline: quite a straight, classic nose; quite an Athenian mouth and chin. It is seldom, indeed, an English face comes so near the antique models as did his. He might well be a little shocked at the irregularity of my lineaments, his own being so harmonious. His eyes were large and blue, with brown lashes; his high forehead, colourless as ivory, was partially streaked over by careless locks of fair hair.

This is a gentle delineation, is it not, reader? Yet he whom it describes scarcely impressed one with the idea of a gentle, a yielding, an impressible, or even of a placid nature. Quiescent as he now sat, there was something about his nostril, his mouth, his brow, which, to my perceptions, indicated elements within either restless, or hard, or eager. He did not speak to me one word, nor even direct to me one glance, till his sisters returned. Diana, as she passed in and out, in the course of preparing tea, brought me a little cake, baked on the top of the oven.

"Eat that now," she said; "you must be hungry. Hannah says you have had nothing but some gruel since breakfast."

I did not refuse it, for my appetite was awakened and keen. Mr. Rivers now closed his book, approached the table, and, as he took a seat, fixed his blue pictorial-looking eyes full on me. There was an unceremonious directness, a searching, decided steadfastness in his gaze now, which told that intention, and not diffidence, had hitherto kept it averted from the stranger.

"You are very hungry," he said.

"I am, sir." It is my way—it always was my way, by instinct—ever to meet the brief with brevity, the direct with plainness.

"It is well for you that a low fever has forced you to abstain for the last three days: there would have been danger in yielding to the cravings of your appetite at first. Now you may eat, though still not immoderately."

"I trust I shall not eat long at your expense, sir," was my very clumsily-contrived, unpolished answer.

"No," he said coolly; "when you have indicated to us the residence of your friends, we can write to them, and you may be restored to home."

"That, I must plainly tell you, is out of my power to do; being absolutely without home and friends."

The three looked at me, but not distrustfully; I felt there was no suspicion in their glances: there was more of curiosity. I speak particularly of the young ladies. St. John's eyes, though clear enough in a literal sense, in a figurative one were difficult to fathom. He seemed to use them rather as instruments to search other people's thoughts, than as agents to reveal his own: the which combination of keenness and reserve was considerably more calculated to embarrass than to encourage.

"Do you mean to say," he asked, "that you are completely isolated from every connection?"

"I do. Not a tie links me to any living thing: not a claim do I possess to admittance under any roof in England."

"A most singular position at your age!"

Here I saw his glance directed to my hands, which were folded on the table before me. I wondered what he sought there: his words soon explained the quest.

"You have never been married? You are a spinster?"

Diana laughed. "Why, she can't be above seventeen or eighteen years old, St. John," said she.

"I am near nineteen: but I am not married. No."

I felt a burning glow mount to my face; for bitter and agitating recollections were awakened by the allusion to marriage. They all saw the embarrassment and the emotion. Diana and Mary relieved me by turning their eyes elsewhere than to my crimsoned visage; but the colder and sterner brother continued to gaze, till the trouble he had excited forced out tears as well as colour.

"Where did you last reside?" he now asked.

"You are too inquisitive, St. John," murmured Mary in a low voice; but he leaned over the table and required an answer by a second firm and piercing look.

"The name of the place where, and of the person with whom I lived, is my secret," I replied concisely.

"Which, if you like, you have, in my opinion, a right to keep, both from St. John and every other questioner," remarked Diana.

"Yet if I know nothing about you or your history, I cannot help you," he said. "And you need help, do you not?"

"I need it, and I seek it so far, sir, that some true philanthropist will put me in the way of getting work which I can do, and the remuneration for which will keep me, if but in the barest necessaries of life."

"I know not whether I am a true philanthropist; yet I am willing to aid you to the utmost of my power in a purpose so honest. First, then, tell me what you have been accustomed to do, and what you *can* do."

I had now swallowed my tea. I was mightily refreshed by the beverage; as much so as a giant with wine: it gave new tone to my unstrung nerves, and enabled me to address this penetrating young judge steadily.

"Mr. Rivers," I said, turning to him, and looking at him, as he looked at me, openly and without diffidence, "you and your sisters have done me a great service—the greatest man can do his fellow-being; you have rescued me, by your noble hospitality, from death. This benefit conferred gives you an unlimited claim on my gratitude, and a claim, to a certain extent, on my confidence. I will tell you as much of the history of the wanderer you have harboured, as I can tell without compromising my own peace of mind—my own security, moral and physical, and that of others.

"I am an orphan, the daughter of a clergyman. My parents died before I could know them. I was brought up a dependent; educated in a charitable institution. I will even tell you the name of the establishment, where I passed six years as a pupil, and two as a teacher—Lowood Orphan Asylum, ——shire: you will have heard of it, Mr. Rivers? The Rev. Robert Brocklehurst is the treasurer."

"I have heard of Mr. Brocklehurst, and I have seen the school."

"I left Lowood nearly a year since to become a private governess. I obtained a good situation, and was happy. This place I was obliged to leave four days before I came here. The reason of my departure I cannot and ought not to explain: it would be useless, dangerous, and would sound incredible. No blame attached to me: I am as free from culpability as any one of you three. Miserable I am, and must be for a time; for the catastrophe which drove me from a house I had found a paradise was of a strange and direful nature. I observed but two points in planning my departure—speed, secrecy: to secure these, I had to leave behind me everything I possessed except a small parcel; which, in my hurry and trouble of mind, I forgot to take out of the coach that brought me to Whitcross. To this neighbourhood, then, I came, quite destitute. I slept two nights in the open air, and wandered about two days without crossing a threshold: but twice in that space of time did I taste food; and it was when brought by hunger, exhaustion, and despair almost to the last gasp, that you, Mr. Rivers, forbade me to perish of want at your door, and took me under the shelter of your roof. I know all your sisters have done for me since—for I have not been insensible during my seeming torpor—and I owe to their spontaneous, genuine, genial compassion as large a debt as to your evangelical charity."

"Don't make her talk any more now, St. John," said Diana, as I paused; "she is evidently not yet fit for excitement. Come to the sofa and sit down now, Miss Elliott."

I gave an involuntary half start at hearing the alias: I had forgotten my new name. Mr. Rivers, whom nothing seemed to escape, noticed it at once.

"You said your name was Jane Elliott?" he observed.

"I did say so; and it is the name by which I think it expedient to be called at present, but it is not my real name, and when I hear it, it sounds strange to me."

"Your real name you will not give?"

"No: I fear discovery above all things; and whatever disclosure would lead to it, I avoid."

"You are quite right, I am sure," said Diana. "Now do, brother, let her be at peace a while."

But when St. John had mused a few moments he recommenced as imperturbably and with as much acumen as ever.

"You would not like to be long dependent on our hospitality—you would wish, I see, to dispense as soon as may be with my sisters' compassion, and, above all, with my *charity* (I am quite sensible of the distinction drawn, nor do I resent it—it is just): you desire to be independent of us?"

"I do: I have already said so. Show me how to work, or how to seek work: that is all I now ask; then let me go, if it be but to the meanest cottage; but till then, allow me to stay here: I dread another essay of the horrors of homeless destitution."

"Indeed you *shall* stay here," said Diana, putting her white hand on my head. "You *shall*," repeated Mary, in the tone of undemonstrative sincerity which seemed natural to her.

"My sisters, you see, have a pleasure in keeping you," said Mr. St. John, "as they would have a pleasure in keeping and cherishing a half-frozen bird, some wintry wind might have driven through their casement. I feel more inclination to put you in the way of keeping yourself, and shall endeavour to do so; but observe, my sphere is narrow. I am but the incumbent of a poor country parish: my aid must be of the humblest sort. And if you are inclined to despise the day of small things, seek some more efficient succour than such as I can offer."

"She has already said that she is willing to do anything honest she can do," answered Diana for me; "and you know, St. John, she has no choice of helpers: she is forced to put up with such crusty people as you."

"I will be a dressmaker; I will be a plain-workwoman; I will be a servant, a nurse-girl, if I can be no better," I answered.

"Right," said Mr. St. John, quite coolly. "If such is your spirit, I promise to aid you, in my own time and way."

He now resumed the book with which he had been occupied before tea. I soon withdrew, for I had talked as much, and sat up as long, as my present strength would permit.

CHAPTER XXX

The more I knew of the inmates of Moor House, the better I liked them. In a few days I had so far recovered my health that I could sit up all day, and walk out sometimes. I could join with Diana and Mary in all their occupations, converse with them as much as they wished, and aid them when and where they would allow me. There was a reviving pleasure in this intercourse, of a kind now tasted by me for the first time—the pleasure arising from perfect congeniality of tastes, sentiments, and principles.

I liked to read what they liked to read; what they enjoyed, delighted me; what they approved, I reverenced. They loved their sequestered home. I, too, in the grey, small, antique structure, with its low roof, its latticed casements, its mouldering walls, its avenue of aged firs—all grown aslant under the stress of mountain winds; its garden, dark with yew and holly—and where no flowers but of the hardiest species would bloom—found a charm both potent and permanent. They clung to the purple moors behind and around their dwelling—to the hollow vale into which the pebbly bridle-path leading from their gate descended, and which wound between fern-banks first, and then amongst a few of the wildest little pasture-fields that ever bordered a wilderness of heath, or gave sustenance to a flock of grey moorland sheep, with their little mossy-faced lambs: they clung to this scene, I say, with a perfect enthusiasm of attachment. I could comprehend the feeling, and share both its strength and truth. I saw the fascination of the locality. I felt the consecration of its loneliness: my eye feasted on the outline of swell and sweep—on the wild colouring communicated to ridge and dell by moss, by heath-bell, by flower-sprinkled turf, by brilliant bracken, and mellow granite crag. These details were just to me what they were to them—so many pure and sweet sources of pleasure. The strong blast and the soft breeze; the rough and the halcyon day; the hours of sunrise and sunset; the moonlight and the clouded night, developed for me, in these regions, the same attraction as for them—wound round my faculties the same spell that entranced theirs.

Indoors we agreed equally well. They were both more accomplished and better read than I was; but with eagerness I followed in the path of knowledge they had trodden before me. I devoured the books they lent me: then it was full satisfaction to discuss with them in the evening what I had perused during the day. Thought fitted thought; opinion met opinion: we coincided, in short, perfectly.

If in our trio there was a superior and a leader, it was Diana. Physically, she far excelled me: she was handsome; she was vigorous. In her animal spirits there was an affluence of life and certainty of flow, such as excited my wonder, while it baffled my comprehension. I could talk a while when the evening commenced, but the first gush of vivacity and fluency gone, I was fain to sit on a stool at Diana's feet, to rest my head on her knee, and listen alternately to her and Mary, while they sounded thoroughly the topic on which I had but touched. Diana offered to teach me German. I liked to learn of her: I saw the part of instructress pleased and suited her; that of scholar pleased and suited me no less. Our natures dovetailed: mutual affection—of the strongest kind—was the result. They discovered I could draw: their pencils and colour-boxes were immediately at my service. My skill, greater in this one point than theirs, surprised and charmed them. Mary would sit and watch me by the hour together: then she would take lessons; and a docile, intelligent, assiduous pupil she made. Thus occupied, and mutually entertained, days passed like hours, and weeks like days.

As to Mr. St John, the intimacy which had arisen so naturally and rapidly between me and his sisters did not extend to him. One reason of the distance yet observed between us was, that he was comparatively seldom at home: a large proportion of his time appeared devoted to visiting the sick and poor among the scattered population of his parish.

No weather seemed to hinder him in these pastoral excursions: rain or fair, he would, when his hours of morning study were over, take his hat, and, followed by his father's old pointer, Carlo, go out on his mission of love or duty—I scarcely know in which light he regarded it. Sometimes, when the day was very unfavourable, his sisters would expostulate. He would then say, with a peculiar smile, more solemn than cheerful—

"And if I let a gust of wind or a sprinkling of rain turn me aside from these easy tasks, what preparation would such sloth be for the future I propose to myself?"

Diana and Mary's general answer to this question was a sigh, and some minutes of apparently mournful meditation.

But besides his frequent absences, there was another barrier to friendship with him: he seemed of a reserved, an abstracted, and even of a brooding nature. Zealous in his ministerial labours, blameless in his life and habits, he yet did not appear to enjoy that mental serenity, that inward content, which should be the reward of every sincere Christian and practical philanthropist. Often, of an evening, when he sat at the window, his desk and papers before him, he would cease reading or writing, rest his chin on his hand, and deliver himself up to I know not what course of thought; but that it was perturbed and exciting might be seen in the frequent flash and changeful dilation of his eye.

I think, moreover, that Nature was not to him that treasury of delight it was to his sisters. He expressed once, and but once in my hearing, a strong sense of the rugged charm of the hills, and an inborn affection for the dark roof and hoary walls he called his home; but there was more of gloom than pleasure in the tone and words in which the sentiment was manifested; and never did he seem to roam the moors for the sake of their soothing silence—never seek out or dwell upon the thousand peaceful delights they could yield.

Incommunicative as he was, some time elapsed before I had an opportunity of gauging his mind. I first got an idea of its calibre when I heard him preach in his own church at Morton. I wish I could describe that sermon: but it is past my power. I cannot even render faithfully the effect it produced on me.

It began calm—and indeed, as far as delivery and pitch of voice went, it was calm to the end: an earnestly felt, yet strictly restrained zeal breathed soon in the distinct accents, and prompted the nervous language. This grew to force—compressed, condensed, controlled. The heart was thrilled, the mind astonished, by the power of the preacher: neither were softened. Throughout there was a strange bitterness; an absence of consolatory gentleness; stern allusions to Calvinistic doctrines—election, predestination, reprobation—were frequent; and each reference to these points sounded like a sentence pronounced for doom. When he had done, instead of feeling better, calmer, more enlightened by his discourse, I experienced an inexpressible sadness; for it seemed to me—I know not whether equally so to others—that the eloquence to which I had been listening had sprung from a depth where lay turbid dregs of disappointment—where moved troubling impulses of insatiate yearnings and disquieting aspirations. I was sure St. John Rivers—pure-lived, conscientious, zealous as he was—had not yet found that peace of God which passeth all understanding: he had no more found it, I thought, than had I with my concealed and racking regrets for my broken idol and lost elysium—regrets to which I have latterly avoided referring, but which possessed me and tyrannised over me ruthlessly.

Meantime a month was gone. Diana and Mary were soon to leave Moor House, and return to the far different life and scene which awaited them, as governesses in a large, fashionable, south-of-England city, where each held a situation in families by whose wealthy and haughty members they were regarded only as humble dependents, and who neither knew nor sought out their innate excellences, and appreciated only their acquired accomplishments as they appreciated the skill of their cook or the taste of their waiting-woman. Mr. St. John had said nothing to me yet about the employment he had promised to obtain for me; yet it became urgent that I should have a vocation of some kind. One morning, being left alone with him a few minutes in the parlour, I ventured to approach the window-recess—which his table, chair, and desk consecrated as a kind of study—and I was going to speak, though not very well knowing in what words to frame my inquiry—for it is at all times difficult to break the ice of reserve glassing over such natures as his—when he saved me the trouble by being the first to commence a dialogue.

Looking up as I drew near—"You have a question to ask of me?" he said.

"Yes; I wish to know whether you have heard of any service I can offer myself to undertake?"

"I found or devised something for you three weeks ago; but as you seemed both useful and happy here—as my sisters had evidently become attached to you, and your society gave them unusual pleasure—I deemed it inexpedient to break in on your mutual comfort till their approaching departure from Marsh End should render yours necessary."

"And they will go in three days now?" I said.

"Yes; and when they go, I shall return to the parsonage at Morton: Hannah will accompany me; and this old house will be shut up."

I waited a few moments, expecting he would go on with the subject first broached: but he seemed to have entered another train of reflection: his look denoted abstraction from me and my business. I was obliged to recall him to a theme which was of necessity one of close and anxious interest to me.

"What is the employment you had in view, Mr. Rivers? I hope this delay will not have increased the difficulty of securing it."

"Oh, no; since it is an employment which depends only on me to give, and you to accept."

He again paused: there seemed a reluctance to continue. I grew impatient: a restless movement or two, and an eager and exacting glance fastened on his face, conveyed the feeling to him as effectually as words could have done, and with less trouble.

"You need be in no hurry to hear," he said. "Let me frankly tell you, I have nothing eligible or profitable to suggest. Before I explain, recall, if you please, my notice, clearly given, that if I helped you, it must be as the blind man would help the lame. I am poor; for I find that, when I have paid my father's debts, all the patrimony remaining to me will be this crumbling grange, the row of scathed firs behind, and the patch of moorish soil, with the yew-trees and holly-bushes in front. I am obscure: Rivers is an old name; but of the three sole descendants of the race, two earn the dependent's crust among strangers, and the third considers himself an alien from his native country—not only for life, but in death. Yes, and deems, and is bound to deem, himself honoured by the lot, and aspires but after the day when the cross of separation from fleshly ties shall be laid on his shoulders, and when the Head of that church-militant of whose humblest members he is one, shall give the word, 'Rise, follow Me!' "

St. John said these words as he pronounced his sermons, with a quiet, deep voice; with an unflushed cheek, and a coruscating radiance of glance. He resumed—

"And since I am myself poor and obscure, I can offer you but a service of poverty and obscurity. *You* may even think it degrading—for I see now your habits have been what the world calls refined: your tastes lean to the ideal, and your society has at least been amongst the educated; but *I* consider that no service degrades which can better our race. I hold that the more arid and unreclaimed the soil where the Christian labourer's task of tillage is appointed him—the scantier the meed his toil brings—the higher the honour. His, under such circumstances, is the destiny of the pioneer; and the first pioneers of the Gospel were the Apostles—their captain was Jesus, the Redeemer, Himself."

"Well?" I said, as he again paused. "Proceed."

He looked at me before he proceeded: indeed, he seemed leisurely to read my face, as if its features and lines were characters on a page. The conclusions drawn from this scrutiny he partially expressed in his succeeding observations.

"I believe you will accept the post I offer you," said he, "and hold it for a while: not permanently, though: any more than I could permanently keep the narrow and narrowing—the tranquil, hidden office of English country incumbent; for in your nature is an alloy as detrimental to repose as that in mine, though of a different kind."

"Do explain," I urged, when he halted once more.

"I will; and you shall hear how poor the proposal is—how trivial—how cramping. I shall not stay long at Morton, now that my father is dead, and that I am my own master. I shall leave the place probably in the course of a twelve-month; but while I do stay, I will exert myself to the utmost for its improvement. Morton, when I came to it two years ago, had no school: the children of the poor were excluded from every hope of progress. I established one for boys: I mean now to open a second school for girls. I have hired a building for the purpose, with a cottage of two rooms attached to it for the mistress's house. Her salary will be thirty pounds a year: her house is already furnished, very simply, but sufficiently, by the kindness of a lady, Miss Oliver; the only daughter of the sole rich man in my parish—Mr. Oliver, the proprietor of a needle-factory and iron-foundry in the valley. The same lady pays for the education and clothing of an orphan from the workhouse, on condition that she shall aid the mistress in such menial offices connected with her own house and the school as her occupation of teaching will prevent her having time to discharge in person. Will you be this mistress?"

He put the question rather hurriedly; he seemed half to expect an indignant, or at least a disdainful rejection of the offer: not knowing all my thoughts and feelings, though guessing some, he could not tell in what light the lot would appear to me. In truth it was humble—but then it was sheltered, and I wanted a safe asylum: it was plodding—but then, compared with that of a governess in a rich house, it was independent; and the fear of servitude with strangers entered my soul like iron: it was not ignoble—not unworthy—not mentally degrading, I made my decision.

"I thank you for the proposal, Mr. Rivers, and I accept it with all my heart."

"But you comprehend me?" he said. "It is a village school: your scholars will be only poor girls—cottagers' children—at the best, farmers' daughters. Knitting, sewing, reading, writing, ciphering, will be all you will have to teach. What will you do with your accomplishments? What, with the largest portion of your mind—sentiments—tastes?"

"Save them till they are wanted. They will keep."

"You know what you undertake, then?"

"I do."

He now smiled: and not a bitter or a sad smile, but one well pleased and deeply gratified.

"And when will you commence the exercise of your function?"

"I will go to my house tomorrow, and open the school, if you like, next week."

"Very well: so be it."

He rose and walked through the room. Standing still, he again looked at me. He shook his head.

"What do you disapprove of, Mr. Rivers?" I asked.

"You will not stay at Morton long: no, no!"

"Why? What is your reason for saying so?"

"I read it in your eye; it is not of that description which promises the maintenance of an even tenor in life."

"I am not ambitious."

He started at the word "ambitious." He repeated, "No. What made you think of ambition? Who is ambitious? I know I am: but how did you find it out?"

"I was speaking of myself."

"Well, if you are not ambitious, you are—" He paused.

"What?"

"I was going to say, impassioned: but perhaps you would have misunderstood the word, and been displeased. I mean, that human affections and sympathies have a most powerful hold on you. I am sure you cannot long be content to pass your leisure in solitude, and to devote your working hours to a monotonous labour wholly void of stimulus: any more than I can be content," he added, with emphasis, "to live here buried in morass, pent in with mountains—my nature, that God gave me, contravened; my faculties, heaven-bestowed, paralysed—made useless. You hear now how I contradict myself. I, who preached contentment with a humble lot, and justified the vocation even of hewers of wood and drawers of water in God's service—I, His ordained minister, almost rave in my restlessness. Well, propensities and principles must be reconciled by some means."

He left the room. In this brief hour I had learnt more of him than in the whole previous month: yet still he puzzled me.

Diana and Mary Rivers became more sad and silent as the day approached for leaving their brother and their home. They both tried to appear as usual; but the sorrow they had to struggle against was one that could not be entirely conquered or concealed. Diana intimated that this would be a different parting from any they had ever yet known. It would probably, as far as St. John was concerned, be a parting for years: it might be a parting for life.

"He will sacrifice all to his long-framed resolves," she said: "natural affection and feelings more potent still. St. John looks quiet, Jane; but he hides a fever in his vitals. You would think him gentle, yet in some things he is inexorable as death; and the worst of it is, my conscience will hardly permit me to dissuade him from his severe decision: certainly, I cannot for a moment blame him for it. It is right, noble, Christian: yet it breaks my heart!" And the tears gushed to her fine eyes. Mary bent her head low over her work.

"We are now without father: we shall soon be without home and brother," she murmured.

At that moment a little accident supervened, which seemed decreed by fate purposely to prove the truth of the adage, that "misfortunes never come singly," and to add to their distresses the vexing one of the slip between the cup and the lip. St. John passed the window reading a letter. He entered.

"Our uncle John is dead," said he.

Both the sisters seemed struck: not shocked or appalled; the tidings appeared in their eyes rather momentous than afflicting.

"Dead?" repeated Diana.

"Yes."

She riveted a searching gaze on her brother's face. "And what then?" she demanded, in a low voice.

"What then, Die?" he replied, maintaining a marble immobility of feature. "What then? Why—nothing. Read."

He threw the letter into her lap. She glanced over it, and handed it to Mary. Mary perused it in silence, and returned it to her brother. All three looked at each other, and all three smiled—a dreary, pensive smile enough.

"Amen! We can yet live," said Diana at last.

"At any rate, it makes us no worse off than we were before," remarked Mary.

"Only it forces rather strongly on the mind the picture of what *might have been*," said Mr. Rivers, "and contrasts it somewhat too vividly with what *is*."

He folded the letter, locked it in his desk, and again went out.

For some minutes no one spoke. Diana then turned to me.

"Jane, you will wonder at us and our mysteries," she said, "and think us hard-hearted beings not to be more moved at the death of so near a relation as an uncle; but we have never seen him or known him. He was my mother's brother. My father and he quarrelled long ago. It was by his advice that my father risked most of his property in the speculation that ruined him. Mutual recrimination passed between them: they parted in anger, and were never reconciled. My uncle engaged afterwards in more prosperous undertakings: it appears he realised a fortune of twenty thousand pounds. He was never married, and had no near kindred but ourselves and one other person, not more closely related than we. My father always cherished the idea that he would atone for his error by leaving his possessions to us; that letter informs us that he has bequeathed every penny to the other relation, with the exception of thirty guineas, to be divided between St. John, Diana, and Mary Rivers, for the purchase of three mourning rings. He had a right, of course, to do as he pleased: and yet a momentary damp is cast on the spirits by the receipt of such news. Mary and I would have esteemed ourselves rich with a thousand pounds each; and to St. John such a sum would have been valuable, for the good it would have enabled him to do."

This explanation given, the subject was dropped, and no further reference made to it by either Mr. Rivers or his sisters. The next day I left Marsh End for Morton. The day after, Diana and Mary quitted it for distant B——. In a week, Mr. Rivers and Hannah repaired to the parsonage: and so the old grange was abandoned.

CHAPTER XXXI

My home, then, when I at last find a home—is a cottage; a little room with whitewashed walls and a sanded floor, containing four painted chairs and a table, a clock, a cupboard, with two or three plates and dishes, and a set of tea-things in delf. Above, a chamber of the same dimensions as the kitchen, with a deal bedstead and chest of drawers; small, yet too large to be filled with my scanty wardrobe: though the kindness of my gentle and generous friends has increased that, by a modest stock of such things as are necessary.

It is evening. I have dismissed, with the fee of an orange, the little orphan who serves me as a handmaid. I am sitting alone on the hearth. This morning, the village school opened. I had twenty scholars. But three of the number can read: none write or cipher. Several knit, and a few sew a little. They speak with the broadest accent of the district. At present, they and I have a difficulty in understanding each other's language. Some of them are unmannered, rough, intractable, as well as ignorant; but others are docile, have a wish to learn, and evince a disposition that pleases me. I must not forget that these coarsely-clad little peasants are of flesh and blood as good as the scions of gentlest genealogy; and that the germs of native excellence, refinement, intelligence, kind feeling, are as likely to exist in their hearts as in those of the best-born. My duty will be to develop these germs: surely I shall find some happiness in discharging that office. Much enjoyment I do not expect in the life opening before me: yet it will, doubtless, if I regulate my mind, and exert my powers as I ought, yield me enough to live on from day to day.

Was I very gleeful, settled, content, during the hours I passed in yonder bare, humble schoolroom this morning and afternoon? Not to deceive myself, I must reply—No: I felt desolate to a degree. I felt—yes, idiot that I am—I felt degraded. I doubted I had taken a step which sank instead of raising me in the scale of social existence. I was weakly dismayed at the ignorance, the poverty, the coarseness of all I heard and saw round me. But let me not hate and despise myself too much for these feelings; I know them to be wrong—that is a great step gained; I shall strive to overcome them. Tomorrow, I trust, I shall get the better of them partially; and in a few weeks, perhaps, they will be quite subdued. In a few months, it is possible, the happiness of seeing progress, and a change for the better in my scholars may substitute gratification for disgust.

Meantime, let me ask myself one question: Which is better? To have surrendered to temptation; listened to passion; made no painful effort—no struggle—but to have sunk down in the silken snare; fallen asleep on the flowers covering it; wakened in a southern clime, amongst the luxuries of a pleasure villa: to have been now living in France, Mr. Rochester's mistress; delirious with his love half my time—for he would—oh, yes, he would have loved me well for a while. He *did* love me—no one will ever love me so again. I shall never more know the sweet homage given to beauty, youth, and grace—for never to any one else shall I seem to possess these charms. He was fond and proud of me—it is what no man besides will ever be. But where am I wandering, and what am I saying, and above all, feeling? Whether is it better, I ask, to be a slave in a fool's paradise at Marseilles—fevered with delusive bliss one hour—suffocating with the bitterest tears of remorse and shame the next—or to be a village-schoolmistress, free and honest, in a breezy mountain nook in the healthy heart of England?

Yes; I feel now that I was right when I adhered to principle and law, and scorned and crushed the insane promptings of a frenzied moment. God directed me to a correct choice: I thank His providence for the guidance!

Having brought my eventide musings to this point, I rose, went to my door, and looked at the sunset of the harvest-day, and at the quiet fields before my cottage, which, with the school, was distant half a mile from the village. The birds were singing their last strains—

"The air was mild, the dew was balm."

While I looked, I thought myself happy, and was surprised to find myself ere long weeping—and why? For the doom which had reft me from adhesion to my master: for him I was no more to see; for the desperate grief and fatal fury—consequences of my departure—which might now, perhaps, be dragging him from the path of right, too far to leave hope of ultimate restoration thither. At this thought, I turned my face aside from the lovely sky of eve and lonely vale of Morton—I say *lonely*, for in that bend of it visible to me there was no building apparent save the church and the parsonage, half-hid in trees, and, quite at the extremity, the roof of Vale Hall, where the rich Mr. Oliver and his daughter lived. I hid my eyes, and leant my head against the stone frame of my door; but soon a slight noise near the wicket which shut in my tiny garden from the meadow beyond it made me look up. A dog—old Carlo, Mr. Rivers' pointer, as I saw in a moment—was pushing the gate with his nose, and St. John himself leant upon it with folded arms; his brow knit, his gaze, grave almost to displeasure, fixed on me. I asked him to come in.

"No, I cannot stay; I have only brought you a little parcel my sisters left for you. I think it contains a colour-box, pencils, and paper."

I approached to take it: a welcome gift it was. He examined my face, I thought, with austerity, as I came near: the traces of tears were doubtless very visible upon it.

"Have you found your first day's work harder than you expected?" he asked.

"Oh, no! On the contrary, I think in time I shall get on with my scholars very well."

"But perhaps your accommodations—your cottage—your furniture—have disappointed your expectations? They are, in truth, scanty enough; but—" I interrupted—

"My cottage is clean and weather-proof; my furniture sufficient and commodious. All I see has made me thankful, not despondent. I am not absolutely such a fool and sensualist as to regret the absence of a carpet, a sofa, and silver plate; besides, five weeks ago I had nothing—I was an outcast, a beggar, a vagrant; now I have acquaintance, a home, a business. I wonder at the goodness of God; the generosity of my friends; the bounty of my lot. I do not repine."

"But you feel solitude an oppression? The little house there behind you is dark and empty."

"I have hardly had time yet to enjoy a sense of tranquillity, much less to grow impatient under one of loneliness."

"Very well; I hope you feel the content you express: at any rate, your good sense will tell you that it is too soon yet to yield to the vacillating fears of Lot's wife. What you had left before I saw you, of course I do not know; but I counsel you to resist firmly every temptation which would incline you to look back: pursue your present career steadily, for some months at least."

"It is what I mean to do," I answered. St. John continued—

"It is hard work to control the workings of inclination and turn the bent of nature; but that it may be done, I know from experience. God has given us, in a measure, the power to make our own fate; and when our energies seem to demand a sustenance they cannot get—when our will strains after a path we may not follow—we need neither starve from inanition, nor stand still in despair: we have but to seek another nourishment for the mind, as strong as the forbidden food it longed to taste—and perhaps purer; and to hew out for the adventurous foot a road as direct and broad as the one Fortune has blocked up against us, if rougher than it.

"A year ago I was myself intensely miserable, because I thought I had made a mistake in entering the ministry: its uniform duties wearied me to death. I burnt for the more active life of the world—for the more exciting toils of a literary career—for the destiny of an artist, author, orator; anything rather than that of a priest: yes, the heart of a politician, of a soldier, of a votary of glory, a lover of renown, a luster after power, beat under my curate's surplice. I considered; my life was so wretched, it must be changed, or I must die. After a season of darkness and struggling, light broke and relief fell: my cramped existence all at once spread out to a plain without bounds—my powers heard a call from heaven to rise, gather their full strength, spread their wings, and mount beyond ken. God had an errand for me; to bear which afar, to deliver it well, skill and strength, courage and eloquence, the best qualifications of soldier, statesman, and orator, were all needed: for these all centre in the good missionary.

"A missionary I resolved to be. From that moment my state of mind changed; the fetters dissolved and dropped from every faculty, leaving nothing of bondage but its galling soreness—which time only can heal. My father, indeed, imposed the determination, but since his death, I have not a legitimate obstacle to contend with; some affairs settled, a successor for Morton provided, an entanglement or two of the feelings broken through or cut asunder—a last conflict with human weakness, in which I know I shall overcome, because I have vowed that I *will* overcome—and I leave Europe for the East."

He said this, in his peculiar, subdued, yet emphatic voice; looking, when he had ceased speaking, not at me, but at the setting sun, at which I looked too. Both he and I had our backs towards the path leading up the field to the wicket. We had heard no step on that grass-grown track; the water running in the vale was the one lulling sound of the hour and scene; we might well then start when a gay voice, sweet as a silver bell, exclaimed—

"Good evening, Mr. Rivers. And good evening, old Carlo. Your dog is quicker to recognise his friends than you are, sir; he pricked his ears and wagged his tail when I was at the bottom of the field, and you have your back towards me now."

It was true. Though Mr. Rivers had started at the first of those musical accents, as if a thunderbolt had split a cloud over his head, he stood yet, at the close of the sentence, in the same attitude in which the speaker had surprised him—his arm resting on the gate, his face directed towards the west. He turned at last, with measured deliberation. A vision, as it seemed to me, had risen at his side. There appeared, within three feet of him, a form clad in pure white—a youthful, graceful form: full, yet fine in contour; and when, after bending to caress Carlo, it lifted up its head, and threw back a long veil, there bloomed under his glance a face of perfect beauty. Perfect beauty is a strong expression; but I do not retrace or qualify it: as sweet features as ever the temperate clime of Albion moulded; as pure hues of rose and lily as ever her humid gales and vapoury skies generated and screened, justified, in this instance, the term. No charm was wanting, no defect was perceptible; the young girl had regular and delicate lineaments; eyes shaped and coloured as we see them in lovely pictures, large, and dark, and full; the long and shadowy eyelash which encircles a fine eye with so soft a fascination; the pencilled brow which gives such clearness; the white smooth forehead, which adds such repose to the livelier beauties of tint and ray; the cheek oval, fresh, and smooth; the lips, fresh too, ruddy, healthy, sweetly formed; the even and gleaming teeth without flaw; the small dimpled chin; the ornament of rich, plenteous tresses—all advantages, in short, which, combined, realise the ideal of beauty, were fully hers. I wondered, as I looked at this fair creature: I admired her with my whole heart. Nature had surely formed her in a partial mood; and, forgetting her usual stinted step-mother dole of gifts, had endowed this, her darling, with a grand-dame's bounty.

What did St. John Rivers think of this earthly angel? I naturally asked myself that question as I saw him turn to her and look at her; and, as naturally, I sought the answer to the inquiry in his countenance.

He had already withdrawn his eye from the Peri, and was looking at a humble tuft of daisies which grew by the wicket.

"A lovely evening, but late for you to be out alone," he said, as he crushed the snowy heads of the closed flowers with his foot.

"Oh, I only came home from S——" (she mentioned the name of a large town some twenty miles distant) "this afternoon. Papa told me you had opened your school, and that the new mistress was come; and so I put on my bonnet after tea, and ran up the valley to see her: this is she?" pointing to me.

"It is," said St. John.

"Do you think you shall like Morton?" she asked of me, with a direct and naive simplicity of tone and manner, pleasing, if child-like.

"I hope I shall. I have many inducements to do so."

"Did you find your scholars as attentive as you expected?"

"Quite."

"Do you like your house?"

"Very much."

"Have I furnished it nicely?"

"Very nicely, indeed."

"And made a good choice of an attendant for you in Alice Wood?"

"You have indeed. She is teachable and handy." (This then, I thought, is Miss Oliver, the heiress; favoured, it seems, in the gifts of fortune, as well as in those of nature! What happy combination of the planets presided over her birth, I wonder?)

"I shall come up and help you to teach sometimes," she added. "It will be a change for me to visit you now and then; and I like a change. Mr. Rivers, I have been *so* gay during my stay at S——. Last night, or rather this morning, I was dancing till two o'clock. The ——th regiment are stationed there since the riots; and the officers are the most agreeable men in the world: they put all our young knife-grinders and scissor merchants to shame."

It seemed to me that Mr. St. John's under lip protruded, and his upper lip curled a moment. His mouth certainly looked a good deal compressed, and the lower part of his face unusually stern and square, as the laughing girl gave him this information. He lifted his gaze, too, from the daisies, and turned it on her. An unsmiling, a searching, a meaning gaze it was. She answered it with a second laugh, and laughter well became her youth, her roses, her dimples, her bright eyes.

As he stood, mute and grave, she again fell to caressing Carlo. "Poor Carlo loves me," said she. "*He* is not stern and distant to his friends; and if he could speak, he would not be silent."

As she patted the dog's head, bending with native grace before his young and austere master, I saw a glow rise to that master's face. I saw his solemn eye melt with sudden fire, and flicker with resistless emotion. Flushed and kindled thus, he looked nearly as beautiful for a man as she for a woman. His chest heaved once, as if his large heart, weary of despotic constriction, had expanded, despite the will, and made a vigorous bound for the attainment of liberty. But he curbed it, I think, as a resolute rider would curb a rearing steed. He responded neither by word nor movement to the gentle advances made him.

"Papa says you never come to see us now," continued Miss Oliver, looking up. "You are quite a stranger at Vale Hall. He is alone this evening, and not very well: will you return with me and visit him?"

"It is not a seasonable hour to intrude on Mr. Oliver," answered St. John.

"Not a seasonable hour! But I declare it is. It is just the hour when papa most wants company: when the works are closed and he has no business to occupy him. Now, Mr. Rivers, *do* come. Why are you so very shy, and so very sombre?" She filled up the hiatus his silence left by a reply of her own.

"I forgot!" she exclaimed, shaking her beautiful curled head, as if shocked at herself. "I am so giddy and thoughtless! *Do* excuse me. It had slipped my memory that you have good reasons to be indisposed for joining in my chatter. Diana and Mary have left you, and Moor House is shut up, and you are so lonely. I am sure I pity you. Do come and see papa."

"Not tonight, Miss Rosamond, not tonight."

Mr. St. John spoke almost like an automaton: himself only knew the effort it cost him thus to refuse.

"Well, if you are so obstinate, I will leave you; for I dare not stay any longer: the dew begins to fall. Good evening!"

She held out her hand. He just touched it. "Good evening!" he repeated, in a voice low and hollow as an echo. She turned, but in a moment returned.

"Are you well?" she asked. Well might she put the question: his face was blanched as her gown.

"Quite well," he enunciated; and, with a bow, he left the gate. She went one way; he another. She turned twice to gaze after him as she tripped fairy-like down the field; he, as he strode firmly across, never turned at all.

This spectacle of another's suffering and sacrifice rapt my thoughts from exclusive meditation on my own. Diana Rivers had designated her brother "inexorable as death." She had not exaggerated.

CHAPTER XXXII

I continued the labours of the village-school as actively and faithfully as I could. It was truly hard work at first. Some time elapsed before, with all my efforts, I could comprehend my scholars and their nature. Wholly untaught, with faculties quite torpid, they seemed to me hopelessly dull; and, at first sight, all dull alike: but I soon found I was mistaken. There was a difference amongst them as amongst the educated; and when I got to know them, and they me, this difference rapidly developed itself. Their amazement at me, my language, my rules, and ways, once subsided, I found some of these heavy-looking, gaping rustics wake up into sharp-witted girls enough. Many showed themselves obliging, and amiable too; and I discovered amongst them not a few examples of natural politeness, and innate self-respect, as well as of excellent capacity, that won both my goodwill and my admiration. These soon took a pleasure in doing their work well, in keeping their persons neat, in learning their tasks regularly, in acquiring quiet and orderly manners. The rapidity of their progress, in some instances, was even surprising; and an honest and happy pride I took in it: besides, I began personally to like some of the best girls; and they liked me. I had amongst my scholars several farmers' daughters: young women grown, almost. These could already read, write, and sew; and to them I taught the elements of grammar, geography, history, and the finer kinds of needlework. I found estimable characters amongst them—characters desirous of information and disposed for improvement—with whom I passed many a pleasant evening hour in their own homes. Their parents then (the farmer and his wife) loaded me with attentions. There was an enjoyment in accepting their simple kindness, and in repaying it by a consideration—a scrupulous regard to their feelings—to which they were not, perhaps, at all times accustomed, and which both charmed and benefited them; because, while it elevated them in their own eyes, it made them emulous to merit the deferential treatment they received.

I felt I became a favourite in the neighbourhood. Whenever I went out, I heard on all sides cordial salutations, and was welcomed with friendly smiles. To live amidst general regard, though it be but the regard of working people, is like "sitting in sunshine, calm and sweet"; serene inward feelings bud and bloom under the ray. At this period of my life, my heart far oftener swelled with thankfulness than sank with dejection: and yet, reader, to tell you all, in the midst of this calm, this useful existence—after a day passed in honourable exertion amongst my scholars, an evening spent in drawing or reading contentedly alone—I used to rush into strange dreams at night: dreams many-coloured, agitated, full of the ideal, the stirring, the stormy—dreams where, amidst unusual scenes, charged with adventure, with agitating risk and romantic chance, I still again and again met Mr. Rochester, always at some exciting crisis; and then the sense of being in his arms, hearing his voice, meeting his eye, touching his hand and cheek, loving him, being loved by him—the hope of passing a lifetime at his side, would be renewed, with all its first force and fire. Then I awoke. Then I recalled where I was, and how situated. Then I rose up on my curtainless bed, trembling and quivering; and then the still, dark night witnessed the convulsion of despair, and heard the burst of passion. By nine o'clock the next morning I was punctually opening the school; tranquil, settled, prepared for the steady duties of the day.

Rosamond Oliver kept her word in coming to visit me. Her call at the school was generally made in the course of her morning ride. She would canter up to the door on her pony, followed by a mounted livery servant. Anything more exquisite than her appearance, in her purple habit, with her Amazon's cap of black velvet placed gracefully above the long curls that kissed her cheek and floated to her shoulders, can scarcely be imagined: and it was thus she would enter the rustic building, and glide through the dazzled ranks of the village children. She generally came at the hour when Mr. Rivers was engaged in giving his daily catechising lesson. Keenly, I fear, did the eye of the visitress pierce the young pastor's heart. A sort of instinct seemed to warn him of her entrance, even when he did not see it; and when he was looking quite away from the door, if she appeared at it, his cheek would glow, and his marble-seeming features, though they refused to relax, changed indescribably, and in their very quiescence became expressive of a repressed fervour, stronger than working muscle or darting glance could indicate.

Of course, she knew her power: indeed, he did not, because he could not, conceal it from her. In spite of his Christian stoicism, when she went up and addressed him, and smiled gaily, encouragingly, even fondly in his face, his hand would tremble and his eye burn. He seemed to say, with his sad and resolute look, if he did not say it with his lips, "I love you, and I know you prefer me. It is not despair of success that keeps me dumb. If I offered my heart, I believe you would accept it. But that heart is already laid on a sacred altar: the fire is arranged round it. It will soon be no more than a sacrifice consumed."

And then she would pout like a disappointed child; a pensive cloud would soften her radiant vivacity; she would withdraw her hand hastily from his, and turn in transient petulance from his aspect, at once so heroic and so martyr-like. St. John, no doubt, would have given the world to follow, recall, retain her, when she thus left him; but he would not give one chance of heaven, nor relinquish, for the elysium of her love, one hope of the true, eternal Paradise. Besides, he could not bind all that he had in his nature—the rover, the aspirant, the poet, the priest—in the limits of a single passion. He could not—he would not—renounce his wild field of mission warfare for the parlours and the peace of Vale Hall. I learnt so much from himself in an inroad I once, despite his reserve, had the daring to make on his confidence.

Miss Oliver already honoured me with frequent visits to my cottage. I had learnt her whole character, which was without mystery or disguise: she was coquettish but not heartless; exacting, but not worthlessly selfish. She had been indulged from her birth, but was not absolutely spoilt. She was hasty, but good-humoured; vain (she could not help it, when every glance in the glass showed her such a flush of loveliness), but not affected; liberal-handed; innocent of the pride of wealth; ingenuous; sufficiently intelligent; gay, lively, and unthinking: she was very charming, in short, even to a cool observer of her own sex like me; but she was not profoundly interesting or thoroughly impressive. A very different sort of mind was hers from that, for instance, of the sisters of St. John. Still, I liked her almost as I liked my pupil Adèle; except that, for a child whom we have watched over and taught, a closer affection is engendered than we can give an equally attractive adult acquaintance.

She had taken an amiable caprice to me. She said I was like Mr. Rivers, only, certainly, she allowed, "not one-tenth so handsome, though I was a nice neat little soul enough, but he was an angel." I was, however, good, clever, composed, and firm, like him. I was a *lusus naturæ*, she affirmed, as a village schoolmistress: she was sure my previous history, if known, would make a delightful romance.

One evening, while, with her usual child-like activity, and thoughtless yet not offensive inquisitiveness, she was rummaging the cupboard and the table-drawer of my little kitchen, she discovered first two French books, a volume of Schiller, a German grammar and dictionary, and then my drawing-materials and some sketches, including a pencil-head of a pretty little cherub-like girl, one of my scholars, and sundry views from nature, taken in the Vale of Morton and on the surrounding moors. She was first transfixed with surprise, and then electrified with delight.

"Had I done these pictures? Did I know French and German? What a love—what a miracle I was! I drew better than her master in the first school in S——. Would I sketch a portrait of her, to show to papa?"

"With pleasure," I replied; and I felt a thrill of artist-delight at the idea of copying from so perfect and radiant a model. She had then on a dark-blue silk dress; her arms and her neck were bare; her only ornament was her chestnut tresses, which waved over her shoulders with all the wild grace of natural curls. I took a sheet of fine card-board, and drew a careful outline. I promised myself the pleasure of colouring it; and, as it was getting late then, I told her she must come and sit another day.

She made such a report of me to her father, that Mr. Oliver himself accompanied her next evening—a tall, massive-featured, middle-aged, and grey-headed man, at whose side his lovely daughter looked like a bright flower near a hoary turret. He appeared a taciturn, and perhaps a proud personage; but he was very kind to me. The sketch of Rosamond's portrait pleased him highly: he said I must make a finished picture of it. He insisted, too, on my coming the next day to spend the evening at Vale Hall.

I went. I found it a large, handsome residence, showing abundant evidences of wealth in the proprietor. Rosamond was full of glee and pleasure all the time I stayed. Her father was affable; and when he entered into conversation with me after tea, he expressed in strong terms his approbation of what I had done in Morton school, and said he only feared, from what he saw and heard, I was too good for the place, and would soon quit it for one more suitable.

"Indeed," cried Rosamond, "she is clever enough to be a governess in a high family, papa."

I thought I would far rather be where I am than in any high family in the land. Mr. Oliver spoke of Mr. Rivers—of the Rivers family—with great respect. He said it was a very old name in that neighbourhood; that the ancestors of the house were wealthy; that all Morton had once belonged to them; that even now he considered the representative of that house might, if he liked, make an alliance with the best. He accounted it a pity that so fine and talented a young man should have formed the design of going out as a missionary; it was quite throwing a valuable life away. It appeared, then, that her father would throw no obstacle in the way of Rosamond's union with St. John. Mr. Oliver evidently regarded the young clergyman's good birth, old name, and sacred profession as sufficient compensation for the want of fortune.

It was the 5th of November, and a holiday. My little servant, after helping me to clean my house, was gone, well satisfied with the fee of a penny for her aid. All about me was spotless and bright—scoured floor, polished grate, and well-rubbed chairs. I had also made myself neat, and had now the afternoon before me to spend as I would.

The translation of a few pages of German occupied an hour; then I got my palette and pencils, and fell to the more soothing, because easier occupation, of completing Rosamond Oliver's miniature. The head was finished already: there was but the background to tint and the drapery to shade off; a touch of carmine, too, to add to the ripe lips—a soft curl here and there to the tresses—a deeper tinge to the shadow of the lash under the azured eyelid. I was absorbed in the execution of these nice details, when, after one rapid tap, my door unclosed, admitting St. John Rivers.

"I am come to see how you are spending your holiday," he said. "Not, I hope, in thought? No, that is well: while you draw you will not feel lonely. You see, I mistrust you still, though you have borne up wonderfully so far. I have brought you a book for evening solace," and he laid on the table a new publication—a poem: one of those genuine productions so often vouchsafed to the fortunate public of those days—the golden age of modern literature. Alas! The readers of our era are less favoured. But courage! I will not pause either to accuse or repine. I know poetry is not dead, nor genius lost; nor has Mammon gained power over either, to bind or slay: they will both assert their existence, their presence, their liberty and strength again one day. Powerful angels, safe in heaven! They smile when sordid souls triumph, and feeble ones weep over their destruction. Poetry destroyed? Genius banished? No! Mediocrity, no: do not let envy prompt you to the thought. No; they not only live, but reign and redeem: and without their divine influence spread everywhere, you would be in hell—the hell of your own meanness.

While I was eagerly glancing at the bright pages of "Marmion" (for "Marmion" it was), St. John stooped to examine my drawing. His tall figure sprang erect again with a start: he said nothing. I looked up at him: he shunned my eye. I knew his thoughts well, and could read his heart plainly; at the moment I felt calmer and cooler than he: I had then temporarily the advantage of him, and I conceived an inclination to do him some good, if I could.

"With all his firmness and self-control," thought I, "he tasks himself too far: locks every feeling and pang within—expresses, confesses, imparts nothing. I am sure it would benefit him to talk a little about this sweet Rosamond, whom he thinks he ought not to marry: I will make him talk."

I said first, "Take a chair, Mr. Rivers." But he answered, as he always did, that he could not stay. "Very well," I responded, mentally, "stand if you like; but you shall not go just yet, I am determined: solitude is at least as bad for you as it is for me. I'll try if I cannot discover the secret spring of your confidence, and find an aperture in that marble breast through which I can shed one drop of the balm of sympathy."

"Is this portrait like?" I asked bluntly.

"Like! Like whom? I did not observe it closely."

"You did, Mr. Rivers."

He almost started at my sudden and strange abruptness: he looked at me astonished. "Oh, that is nothing yet," I muttered within. "I don't mean to be baffled by a little stiffness on your part; I'm prepared to go to considerable lengths." I continued, "You observed it closely and distinctly; but I have no objection to your looking at it again," and I rose and placed it in his hand.

"A well-executed picture," he said; "very soft, clear colouring; very graceful and correct drawing."

"Yes, yes; I know all that. But what of the resemblance? Who is it like?"

Mastering some hesitation, he answered, "Miss Oliver, I presume."

"Of course. And now, sir, to reward you for the accurate guess, I will promise to paint you a careful and faithful duplicate of this very picture, provided you admit that the gift would be acceptable to you. I don't wish to throw away my time and trouble on an offering you would deem worthless."

He continued to gaze at the picture: the longer he looked, the firmer he held it, the more he seemed to covet it. "It is like!" he murmured. "The eye is well managed: the colour, light, expression, are perfect. It smiles!"

"Would it comfort, or would it wound you to have a similar painting? Tell me that. When you are at Madagascar, or at the Cape, or in India, would it be a consolation to have that memento in your possession? Or would the sight of it bring recollections calculated to enervate and distress?"

He now furtively raised his eyes: he glanced at me, irresolute, disturbed: he again surveyed the picture.

"That I should like to have it is certain: whether it would be judicious or wise is another question."

Since I had ascertained that Rosamond really preferred him, and that her father was not likely to oppose the match, I—less exalted in my views than St. John—had been strongly disposed in my own heart to advocate their union. It seemed to me that, should he become the possessor of Mr. Oliver's large fortune, he might do as much good with it as if he went and laid his genius out to wither, and his strength to waste, under a tropical sun. With this persuasion I now answered—

"As far as I can see, it would be wiser and more judicious if you were to take to yourself the original at once."

By this time he had sat down: he had laid the picture on the table before him, and with his brow supported on both hands, hung fondly over it. I discerned he was now neither angry nor shocked at my audacity. I saw even that to be thus frankly addressed on a subject he had deemed unapproachable—to hear it thus freely handled—was beginning to be felt by him as a new pleasure—an unhoped-for relief. Reserved people often really need the frank discussion of their sentiments and griefs more than the expansive. The sternest-seeming stoic is human after all; and to "burst" with boldness and good-will into "the silent sea" of their souls is often to confer on them the first of obligations.

"She likes you, I am sure," said I, as I stood behind his chair, "and her father respects you. Moreover, she is a sweet girl—rather thoughtless;

but you would have sufficient thought for both yourself and her. You ought to marry her."

"*Does* she like me?" he asked.

"Certainly; better than she likes any one else. She talks of you continually: there is no subject she enjoys so much or touches upon so often."

"It is very pleasant to hear this," he said. "Very: go on for another quarter of an hour." And he actually took out his watch and laid it upon the table to measure the time.

"But where is the use of going on," I asked, "when you are probably preparing some iron blow of contradiction, or forging a fresh chain to fetter your heart?"

"Don't imagine such hard things. Fancy me yielding and melting, as I am doing: human love rising like a freshly opened fountain in my mind and overflowing with sweet inundation all the field I have so carefully and with such labour prepared—so assiduously sown with the seeds of good intentions, of self-denying plans. And now it is deluged with a nectarous flood—the young germs swamped—delicious poison cankering them: now I see myself stretched on an ottoman in the drawing-room at Vale Hall at my bride Rosamond Oliver's feet: she is talking to me with her sweet voice—gazing down on me with those eyes your skilful hand has copied so well—smiling at me with these coral lips. She is mine—I am hers—this present life and passing world suffice to me. Hush! Say nothing—my heart is full of delight—my senses are entranced—let the time I marked pass in peace."

I humoured him: the watch ticked on: he breathed fast and low: I stood silent. Amidst this hush the quartet sped; he replaced the watch, laid the picture down, rose, and stood on the hearth.

"Now," said he, "that little space was given to delirium and delusion. I rested my temples on the breast of temptation, and put my neck voluntarily under her yoke of flowers. I tasted her cup. The pillow was burning: there is an asp in the garland: the wine has a bitter taste: her promises are hollow—her offers false: I see and know all this."

I gazed at him in wonder.

"It is strange," pursued he, "that while I love Rosamond Oliver so wildly—with all the intensity, indeed, of a first passion, the object of which is exquisitely beautiful, graceful, fascinating—I experience at the same time a calm, unwarped consciousness that she would not make me a good wife; that she is not the partner suited to me; that I should discover this within a year after marriage; and that to twelve months' rapture would succeed a lifetime of regret. This I know."

"Strange indeed!" I could not help ejaculating.

"While something in me," he went on, "is acutely sensible to her charms, something else is as deeply impressed with her defects: they are such that she could sympathise in nothing I aspired to—co-operate in nothing I undertook. Rosamond a sufferer, a labourer, a female apostle? Rosamond a missionary's wife? No!"

"But you need not be a missionary. You might relinquish that scheme."

"Relinquish! What! My vocation? My great work? My foundation laid on earth for a mansion in heaven? My hopes of being numbered in the band who have merged all ambitions in the glorious one of bettering their race—of carrying knowledge into the realms of ignorance—of substituting peace for war—freedom for bondage—religion for superstition—the hope of heaven for the fear of hell? Must I relinquish that? It is dearer than the blood in my veins. It is what I have to look forward to, and to live for."

After a considerable pause, I said—"And Miss Oliver? Are her disappointment and sorrow of no interest to you?"

"Miss Oliver is ever surrounded by suitors and flatterers: in less than a month, my image will be effaced from her heart. She will forget me; and will marry, probably, some one who will make her far happier than I should do."

"You speak coolly enough; but you suffer in the conflict. You are wasting away."

"No. If I get a little thin, it is with anxiety about my prospects, yet unsettled—my departure, continually procrastinated. Only this morning, I received intelligence that the successor, whose arrival I have been so long expecting, cannot be ready to replace me for three months to come yet; and perhaps the three months may extend to six."

"You tremble and become flushed whenever Miss Oliver enters the schoolroom."

Again the surprised expression crossed his face. He had not imagined that a woman would dare to speak so to a man. For me, I felt at home in this sort of discourse. I could never rest in communication with strong, discreet, and refined minds, whether male or female, till I had passed the outworks of conventional reserve, and crossed the threshold of confidence, and won a place by their heart's very hearthstone.

"You are original," said he, "and not timid. There is something brave in your spirit, as well as penetrating in your eye; but allow me to assure you that you partially misinterpret my emotions. You think them more profound and potent than they are. You give me a larger allowance of sympathy than I have a just claim to. When I colour, and when I shade before Miss Oliver, I do not pity myself. I scorn the weakness. I know it is ignoble: a mere fever of the flesh: not, I declare, the convulsion of the soul. *That* is just as fixed as a rock, firm set in the depths of a restless sea. Know me to be what I am—a cold hard man."

I smiled incredulously.

"You have taken my confidence by storm," he continued, "and now it is much at your service. I am simply, in my original state—stripped of that blood-bleached robe with which Christianity covers human deformity—a cold, hard, ambitious man. Natural affection only, of all the sentiments, has permanent power over me. Reason, and not feeling, is my guide; my ambition is unlimited: my desire to rise higher, to do more than others, insatiable. I honour endurance, perseverance, industry, talent; because these are the means by which men achieve great ends and mount to lofty eminence. I watch your career with interest, because I consider you a specimen of a diligent, orderly, energetic woman: not because I deeply compassionate what you have gone through, or what you still suffer."

"You would describe yourself as a mere pagan philosopher," I said.

"No. There is this difference between me and deistic philosophers: I believe; and I believe the Gospel. You missed your epithet. I am not a pagan, but a Christian philosopher—a follower of the sect of Jesus. As His disciple I adopt His pure, His merciful, His benignant doctrines. I advocate them: I am sworn to spread them. Won in youth to religion, she has cultivated my original qualities thus: From the minute germ, natural affection, she has developed the overshadowing tree, philanthropy. From the wild stringy root of human uprightness, she has reared a due sense of the Divine justice. Of the ambition to win power and renown for my wretched self, she has formed the ambition to spread my Master's kingdom; to achieve victories for the standard of the cross. So much has religion done for me; turning the original materials to the best account; pruning and training nature. But she could not eradicate nature: nor will it be eradicated 'till this mortal shall put on immortality.' "

Having said this, he took his hat, which lay on the table beside my palette. Once more he looked at the portrait.

"She *is* lovely," he murmured. "She is well named the Rose of the World, indeed!"

"And may I not paint one like it for you?"

"*Cui bono*? No."

He drew over the picture the sheet of thin paper on which I was accustomed to rest my hand in painting, to prevent the cardboard from being sullied. What he suddenly saw on this blank paper, it was impossible for me to tell; but something had caught his eye. He took it up with a snatch; he looked at the edge; then shot a glance at me, inexpressibly peculiar, and quite incomprehensible: a glance that seemed to take and make note of every point in my shape, face, and dress; for it traversed all, quick, keen as lightning. His lips parted, as if to speak: but he checked the coming sentence, whatever it was.

"What is the matter?" I asked.

"Nothing in the world," was the reply; and, replacing the paper, I saw him dexterously tear a narrow slip from the margin. It disappeared in his glove; and, with one hasty nod and "good-afternoon," he vanished.

"Well!" I exclaimed, using an expression of the district, "that caps the globe, however!"

I, in my turn, scrutinised the paper; but saw nothing on it save a few dingy stains of paint where I had tried the tint in my pencil. I pondered the mystery a minute or two; but finding it insolvable, and being certain it could not be of much moment, I dismissed, and soon forgot it.

CHAPTER XXXIII

When Mr. St. John went, it was beginning to snow; the whirling storm continued all night. The next day a keen wind brought fresh and blinding falls; by twilight the valley was drifted up and almost impassable. I had closed my shutter, laid a mat to the door to prevent the snow from blowing in under it, trimmed my fire, and after sitting nearly an hour on the hearth listening to the muffled fury of the tempest, I lit a candle, took down "Marmion," and beginning—

"Day set on Norham's castled steep,
And Tweed's fair river broad and deep,
And Cheviot's mountains lone;
The massive towers, the donjon keep,
The flanking walls that round them sweep,
In yellow lustre shone."

I soon forgot storm in music.

I heard a noise: the wind, I thought, shook the door. No; it was St. John Rivers, who, lifting the latch, came in out of the frozen hurricane—the howling darkness—and stood before me: the cloak that covered his tall figure all white as a glacier. I was almost in consternation, so little had I expected any guest from the blocked-up vale that night.

"Any ill news?" I demanded. "Has anything happened?"

"No. How very easily alarmed you are!" he answered, removing his cloak and hanging it up against the door, towards which he again coolly pushed the mat which his entrance had deranged. He stamped the snow from his boots.

"I shall sully the purity of your floor," said he, "but you must excuse me for once." Then he approached the fire. "I have had hard work to get here, I assure you," he observed, as he warmed his hands over the flame. "One drift took me up to the waist; happily the snow is quite soft yet."

"But why are you come?" I could not forbear saying.

"Rather an inhospitable question to put to a visitor; but since you ask it, I answer simply to have a little talk with you; I got tired of my mute books and empty rooms. Besides, since yesterday I have experienced the excitement of a person to whom a tale has been half-told, and who is impatient to hear the sequel."

He sat down. I recalled his singular conduct of yesterday, and really I began to fear his wits were touched. If he were insane, however, his was a very cool and collected insanity: I had never seen that handsome-featured face of his look more like chiselled marble than it did just now, as he put aside his snow-wet hair from his forehead and let the firelight shine free on his pale brow and cheek as pale, where it grieved me to discover the hollow trace of care or sorrow now so plainly graved. I waited, expecting he would say something I could at least comprehend; but his hand was now at his chin, his finger on his lip: he was thinking. It struck me that his hand looked wasted like his face. A perhaps uncalled-for gush of pity came over my heart: I was moved to say—

"I wish Diana or Mary would come and live with you: it is too bad that you should be quite alone; and you are recklessly rash about your own health."

"Not at all," said he. "I care for myself when necessary. I am well now. What do you see amiss in me?"

This was said with a careless, abstracted indifference, which showed that my solicitude was, at least in his opinion, wholly superfluous. I was silenced.

He still slowly moved his finger over his upper lip, and still his eye dwelt dreamily on the glowing grate; thinking it urgent to say something, I asked him presently if he felt any cold draught from the door, which was behind him.

"No, no!" he responded shortly and somewhat testily.

"Well," I reflected, "if you won't talk, you may be still; I'll let you alone now, and return to my book."

So I snuffed the candle and resumed the perusal of "Marmion." He soon stirred; my eye was instantly drawn to his movements; he only took out a morocco pocket-book, thence produced a letter, which he read in silence, folded it, put it back, relapsed into meditation. It was vain to try to read with such an inscrutable fixture before me; nor could I, in impatience, consent to be dumb; he might rebuff me if he liked, but talk I would.

"Have you heard from Diana and Mary lately?"

"Not since the letter I showed you a week ago."

"There has not been any change made about your own arrangements? You will not be summoned to leave England sooner than you expected?"

"I fear not, indeed: such chance is too good to befall me." Baffled so far, I changed my ground. I bethought myself to talk about the school and my scholars.

"Mary Garrett's mother is better, and Mary came back to the school this morning, and I shall have four new girls next week from the Foundry Close—they would have come today but for the snow."

"Indeed!"

"Mr. Oliver pays for two."

"Does he?"

"He means to give the whole school a treat at Christmas."

"I know."

"Was it your suggestion?"

"No."

"Whose, then?"

"His daughter's, I think."

"It is like her: she is so good-natured."

"Yes."

Again came the blank of a pause: the clock struck eight strokes. It aroused him; he uncrossed his legs, sat erect, turned to me.

"Leave your book a moment, and come a little nearer the fire," he said.

Wondering, and of my wonder finding no end, I complied.

"Half-an-hour ago," he pursued, "I spoke of my impatience to hear the sequel of a tale: on reflection, I find the matter will be better managed by my assuming the narrator's part, and converting you into a listener. Before commencing, it is but fair to warn you that the story will sound somewhat hackneyed in your ears; but stale details often regain a degree of freshness when they pass through new lips. For the rest, whether trite or novel, it is short.

"Twenty years ago, a poor curate—never mind his name at this moment—fell in love with a rich man's daughter; she fell in love with him, and married him, against the advice of all her friends, who consequently disowned her immediately after the wedding. Before two years passed, the rash pair were both dead, and laid quietly side by side under one slab. (I have seen their grave; it formed part of the pavement of a huge churchyard surrounding the grim, soot-black old cathedral of an overgrown manufacturing town in ——shire.) They left a daughter, which, at its very birth, Charity received in her lap—cold as that of the snow-drift I almost stuck fast in tonight. Charity carried the friendless thing to the house of its rich maternal relations; it was reared by an aunt-in-law, called (I come to names now) Mrs. Reed of Gateshead. You start—did you hear a noise? I daresay it is only a rat scrambling along the rafters of the adjoining schoolroom: it was a barn before I had it repaired and altered, and barns are generally haunted by rats. To proceed. Mrs. Reed kept the orphan ten years: whether it was happy or not with her, I cannot say, never having been told; but at the end of that time she transferred it to a place you know—being no other than Lowood School, where you so long resided yourself. It seems her career there was very honourable: from a pupil, she became a teacher, like yourself—really it strikes me there are parallel points in her history and yours—she left it to be a governess: there, again, your fates were analogous; she undertook the education of the ward of a certain Mr. Rochester."

"Mr. Rivers!" I interrupted.

"I can guess your feelings," he said, "but restrain them for a while: I have nearly finished; hear me to the end. Of Mr. Rochester's character I know nothing, but the one fact that he professed to offer honourable marriage to this young girl, and that at the very altar she discovered he had a wife yet alive, though a lunatic. What his subsequent conduct and proposals were is a matter of pure conjecture; but when an event transpired which rendered inquiry after the governess necessary, it was discovered she was gone—no one could tell when, where, or how. She had left Thornfield Hall in the night; every research after her course had been vain: the country had been scoured far and wide; no vestige of information could be gathered respecting her. Yet that she should be found is become a matter of serious urgency: advertisements have been put in all the papers; I myself have received a letter from one Mr. Briggs, a solicitor, communicating the details I have just imparted. Is it not an odd tale?"

"Just tell me this," said I, "and since you know so much, you surely can tell it me—what of Mr. Rochester? How and where is he? What is he doing? Is he well?"

"I am ignorant of all concerning Mr. Rochester: the letter never mentions him but to narrate the fraudulent and illegal attempt I have adverted to. You should rather ask the name of the governess—the nature of the event which requires her appearance."

"Did no one go to Thornfield Hall, then? Did no one see Mr. Rochester?"

"I suppose not."

"But they wrote to him?"

"Of course."

"And what did he say? Who has his letters?"

"Mr. Briggs intimates that the answer to his application was not from Mr. Rochester, but from a lady: it is signed 'Alice Fairfax.' "

I felt cold and dismayed: my worst fears then were probably true: he had in all probability left England and rushed in reckless desperation to some former haunt on the Continent. And what opiate for his severe sufferings—what object for his strong passions—had he sought there? I dared not answer the question. Oh, my poor master—once almost my husband—whom I had often called "my dear Edward!"

"He must have been a bad man," observed Mr. Rivers.

"You don't know him—don't pronounce an opinion upon him," I said, with warmth.

"Very well," he answered quietly; "and indeed my head is otherwise occupied than with him: I have my tale to finish. Since you won't ask the governess's name, I must tell it of my own accord. Stay! I have it here—it is always more satisfactory to see important points written down, fairly committed to black and white."

And the pocket-book was again deliberately produced, opened, sought through; from one of its compartments was extracted a shabby slip of paper, hastily torn off: I recognised in its texture and its stains of ultra-marine, and lake, and vermillion, the ravished margin of the portrait-cover. He got up, held it close to my eyes: and I read, traced in Indian ink, in my own handwriting, the words "Jane Eyre"—the work doubtless of some moment of abstraction.

"Briggs wrote to me of a Jane Eyre," he said. "The advertisements demanded a Jane Eyre; I knew a Jane Elliott. I confess I had my suspicions, but it was only yesterday afternoon they were at once resolved into certainty. You own the name and renounce the alias?"

"Yes—yes; but where is Mr. Briggs? He perhaps knows more of Mr. Rochester than you do."

"Briggs is in London. I should doubt his knowing anything at all about Mr. Rochester; it is not in Mr. Rochester he is interested. Meantime, you forget essential points in pursuing trifles: you do not inquire why Mr. Briggs sought after you—what he wanted with you."

"Well, what did he want?"

"Merely to tell you that your uncle, Mr. Eyre of Madeira, is dead; that he has left you all his property, and that you are now rich—merely that—nothing more."

"I! Rich?"

"Yes, you, rich—quite an heiress."

Silence succeeded.

"You must prove your identity, of course," resumed St. John presently. "A step which will offer no difficulties; you can then enter on immediate possession. Your fortune is vested in the English funds; Briggs has the will and the necessary documents."

Here was a new card turned up! It is a fine thing, reader, to be lifted in a moment from indigence to wealth—a very fine thing; but not a matter one can comprehend, or consequently enjoy, all at once. And then there are other chances in life far more thrilling and rapture-giving: *this* is solid, an affair of the actual world, nothing ideal about it: all its associations are solid and sober, and its manifestations are the same. One does not jump, and spring, and shout *hurrah!* at hearing one has got a fortune; one begins to consider responsibilities, and to ponder business; on a base of steady satisfaction rise certain grave cares, and we contain ourselves, and brood over our bliss with a solemn brow.

Besides, the words Legacy, Bequest go side by side with the words Death, Funeral. My uncle I had heard was dead—my only relative; ever since being made aware of his existence, I had cherished the hope of one day seeing him: now, I never should. And then this money came only to me: not to me and a rejoicing family, but to my isolated self. It was a grand boon doubtless; and independence would be glorious—yes, I felt that—that thought swelled my heart.

"You unbend your forehead at last," said Mr. Rivers. "I thought Medusa had looked at you, and that you were turning to stone. Perhaps now you will ask how much you are worth?"

"How much am I worth?"

"Oh, a trifle! Nothing of course to speak of—twenty thousand pounds, I think they say—but what is that?"

"Twenty thousand pounds?"

Here was a new stunner—I had been calculating on four or five thousand. This news actually took my breath for a moment: Mr. St. John, whom I had never heard laugh before, laughed now.

"Well," said he, "if you had committed a murder, and I had told you your crime was discovered, you could scarcely look more aghast."

"It is a large sum—don't you think there is a mistake?"

"No mistake at all."

"Perhaps you have read the figures wrong—it may be two thousand!"

"It is written in letters, not figures—twenty thousand."

I again felt rather like an individual of but average gastronomical powers sitting down to feast alone at a table spread with provisions for a hundred. Mr. Rivers rose now and put his cloak on.

"If it were not such a very wild night," he said, "I would send Hannah down to keep you company: you look too desperately miserable to be left alone. But Hannah—poor woman!—could not stride the drifts so well as I: her legs are not quite so long: so I must e'en leave you to your sorrows. Good-night."

He was lifting the latch: a sudden thought occurred to me. "Stop one minute!" I cried.

"Well?"

"It puzzles me to know why Mr. Briggs wrote to you about me; or how he knew you, or could fancy that you, living in such an out-of-the-way place, had the power to aid in my discovery."

"Oh! I am a clergyman," he said; "and the clergy are often appealed to about odd matters." Again the latch rattled.

"No; that does not satisfy me!" I exclaimed: and indeed there was something in the hasty and unexplanatory reply which, instead of allaying, piqued my curiosity more than ever.

"It is a very strange piece of business," I added; "I must know more about it."

"Another time."

"No; tonight! Tonight!" and as he turned from the door, I placed myself between it and him. He looked rather embarrassed.

"You certainly shall not go till you have told me all," I said.

"I would rather not just now."

"You shall! You must!"

"I would rather Diana or Mary informed you."

Of course these objections wrought my eagerness to a climax: gratified it must be, and that without delay; and I told him so.

"But I apprised you that I was a hard man," said he, "difficult to persuade."

"And I am a hard woman—impossible to put off."

"And then," he pursued, "I am cold: no fervour infects me."

"Whereas I am hot, and fire dissolves ice. The blaze there has thawed all the snow from your cloak; by the same token, it has streamed on to my floor, and made it like a trampled street. As you hope ever to be forgiven, Mr. Rivers, the high crime and misdemeanour of spoiling a sanded kitchen, tell me what I wish to know."

"Well, then," he said, "I yield; if not to your earnestness, to your perseverance: as stone is worn by continual dropping. Besides, you must know some day—as well now as later. Your name is Jane Eyre?"

"Of course: that was all settled before."

"You are not, perhaps, aware that I am your namesake? That I was christened St. John Eyre Rivers?"

"No, indeed! I remember now seeing the letter E comprised in your initials written in books you have at different times lent me; but I never asked for what name it stood. But what then? Surely—"

I stopped: I could not trust myself to entertain, much less to express, the thought that rushed upon me—that embodied itself—that, in a second, stood out a strong, solid probability. Circumstances knit themselves, fitted themselves, shot into order: the chain that had been lying hitherto a formless lump of links was drawn out straight—every ring was perfect, the connection complete. I knew, by instinct, how the matter stood, before St. John had said another word; but I cannot expect the reader to have the same intuitive perception, so I must repeat his explanation.

"My mother's name was Eyre; she had two brothers; one a clergyman, who married Miss Jane Reed, of Gateshead; the other, John Eyre, Esq., merchant, late of Funchal, Madeira. Mr. Briggs, being Mr. Eyre's solicitor, wrote to us last August to inform us of our uncle's death, and to say that he had left his property to his brother the clergyman's orphan daughter, overlooking us, in consequence of a quarrel, never forgiven, between him and my father. He wrote again a few weeks since, to intimate that the heiress was lost, and asking if we knew anything of her. A name casually written on a slip of paper has enabled me to find her out. You know the rest." Again he was going, but I set my back against the door.

"Do let me speak," I said; "let me have one moment to draw breath and reflect." I paused—he stood before me, hat in hand, looking composed enough. I resumed—

"Your mother was my father's sister?"

"Yes."

"My aunt, consequently?"

He bowed.

"My uncle John was your uncle John? You, Diana, and Mary are his sister's children, as I am his brother's child?"

"Undeniably."

"You three, then, are my cousins; half our blood on each side flows from the same source?"

"We are cousins; yes."

I surveyed him. It seemed I had found a brother: one I could be proud of—one I could love; and two sisters, whose qualities were such, that, when I knew them but as mere strangers, they had inspired me with genuine affection and admiration. The two girls, on whom, kneeling down on the wet ground, and looking through the low, latticed window of Moor House kitchen, I had gazed with so bitter a mixture of interest and despair, were my near kinswomen; and the young and stately gentleman who had found me almost dying at his threshold was my blood relation. Glorious discovery to a lonely wretch! This was wealth indeed! Wealth to the heart! A mine of pure, genial affections. This was a blessing, bright, vivid, and exhilarating—not like the ponderous gift of gold: rich and welcome enough in its way, but sobering from its weight. I now clapped my hands in sudden joy—my pulse bounded, my veins thrilled.

"Oh, I am glad! I am glad!" I exclaimed.

St. John smiled. "Did I not say you neglected essential points to pursue trifles?" he asked. "You were serious when I told you you had got a fortune; and now, for a matter of no moment, you are excited."

"What can you mean? It may be of no moment to you; you have sisters and don't care for a cousin; but I had nobody; and now three relations—or two, if you don't choose to be counted—are born into my world full-grown. I say again, I am glad!"

I walked fast through the room: I stopped, half suffocated with the thoughts that rose faster than I could receive, comprehend, settle them: thoughts of what might, could, would, and should be, and that ere long. I looked at the blank wall: it seemed a sky thick with ascending stars—every one lit me to a purpose or delight. Those who had saved my life, whom, till this hour, I had loved barrenly, I could now benefit. They were under a yoke—I could free them: they were scattered—I could reunite them: the independence, the affluence which was mine, might be theirs too. Were we not four? Twenty thousand pounds shared equally would be five thousand each, justice—enough and to spare: justice would be done—mutual happiness secured. Now the wealth did not weigh on me: now it was not a mere bequest of coin—it was a legacy of life, hope, enjoyment.

How I looked while these ideas were taking my spirit by storm, I cannot tell; but I perceived soon that Mr. Rivers had placed a chair behind me, and was gently attempting to make me sit down on it. He also advised me to be composed; I scorned the insinuation of helplessness and distraction, shook off his hand, and began to walk about again.

"Write to Diana and Mary tomorrow," I said, "and tell them to come home directly. Diana said they would both consider themselves rich with a thousand pounds, so with five thousand they will do very well."

"Tell me where I can get you a glass of water," said St. John; "you must really make an effort to tranquillise your feelings."

"Nonsense! And what sort of an effect will the bequest have on you? Will it keep you in England, induce you to marry Miss Oliver, and settle down like an ordinary mortal?"

"You wander: your head becomes confused. I have been too abrupt in communicating the news; it has excited you beyond your strength."

"Mr. Rivers! You quite put me out of patience: I am rational enough; it is you who misunderstand, or rather who affect to misunderstand."

"Perhaps, if you explained yourself a little more fully, I should comprehend better."

"Explain! What is there to explain? You cannot fail to see that twenty thousand pounds, the sum in question, divided equally between the nephew and three nieces of our uncle, will give five thousand to each? What I want is, that you should write to your sisters and tell them of the fortune that has accrued to them."

"To you, you mean."

"I have intimated my view of the case: I am incapable of taking any other. I am not brutally selfish, blindly unjust, or fiendishly ungrateful. Besides, I am resolved I will have a home and connections. I like Moor House, and I will live at Moor House; I like Diana and Mary, and I will attach myself for life to Diana and Mary. It would please and benefit me to have five thousand pounds; it would torment and oppress me to have twenty thousand; which, moreover, could never be mine in justice, though it might in law. I abandon to you, then, what is absolutely superfluous to me. Let there be no opposition, and no discussion about it; let us agree amongst each other, and decide the point at once."

"This is acting on first impulses; you must take days to consider such a matter, ere your word can be regarded as valid."

"Oh! If all you doubt is my sincerity, I am easy: you see the justice of the case?"

"I *do* see a certain justice; but it is contrary to all custom. Besides, the entire fortune is your right: my uncle gained it by his own efforts; he was free to leave it to whom he would: he left it to you. After all, justice permits you to keep it: you may, with a clear conscience, consider it absolutely your own."

"With me," said I, "it is fully as much a matter of feeling as of conscience: I must indulge my feelings; I so seldom have had an opportunity of doing so. Were you to argue, object, and annoy me for a year, I could not forego the delicious pleasure of which I have caught a glimpse—that of repaying, in part, a mighty obligation, and winning to myself lifelong friends."

"You think so now," rejoined St. John, "because you do not know what it is to possess, nor consequently to enjoy wealth: you cannot form a notion of the importance twenty thousand pounds would give you; of the place it would enable you to take in society; of the prospects it would open to you: you cannot—"

"And you," I interrupted, "cannot at all imagine the craving I have for fraternal and sisterly love. I never had a home, I never had brothers or sisters; I must and will have them now: you are not reluctant to admit me and own me, are you?"

"Jane, I will be your brother—my sisters will be your sisters—without stipulating for this sacrifice of your just rights."

"Brother? Yes; at the distance of a thousand leagues! Sisters? Yes; slaving amongst strangers! I, wealthy—gorged with gold I never earned and do not merit! You, penniless! Famous equality and fraternisation! Close union! Intimate attachment!"

"But, Jane, your aspirations after family ties and domestic happiness may be realised otherwise than by the means you contemplate: you may marry."

"Nonsense, again! Marry! I don't want to marry, and never shall marry."

"That is saying too much: such hazardous affirmations are a proof of the excitement under which you labour."

"It is not saying too much: I know what I feel, and how averse are my inclinations to the bare thought of marriage. No one would take me for love; and I will not be regarded in the light of a mere money speculation. And I do not want a stranger—unsympathising, alien, different from me; I want my kindred: those with whom I have full fellow-feeling. Say again you will be my brother: when you uttered the words I was satisfied, happy; repeat them, if you can, repeat them sincerely."

"I think I can. I know I have always loved my own sisters; and I know on what my affection for them is grounded—respect for their worth and admiration of their talents. You too have principle and mind: your tastes and habits resemble Diana's and Mary's; your presence is always agreeable to me; in your conversation I have already for some time found a salutary solace. I feel I can easily and naturally make room in my heart for you, as my third and youngest sister."

"Thank you: that contents me for tonight. Now you had better go; for if you stay longer, you will perhaps irritate me afresh by some mistrustful scruple."

"And the school, Miss Eyre? It must now be shut up, I suppose?"

"No. I will retain my post of mistress till you get a substitute."

He smiled approbation: we shook hands, and he took leave.

I need not narrate in detail the further struggles I had, and arguments I used, to get matters regarding the legacy settled as I wished. My task was a very hard one; but, as I was absolutely resolved—as my cousins saw at length that my mind was really and immutably fixed on making a just division of the property—as they must in their own hearts have felt the equity of the intention; and must, besides, have been innately conscious that in my place they would have done precisely what I wished to do—they yielded at length so far as to consent to put the affair to arbitration. The judges chosen were Mr. Oliver and an able lawyer: both coincided in my opinion: I carried my point. The instruments of transfer were drawn out: St. John, Diana, Mary, and I, each became possessed of a competency.

CHAPTER XXXIV

It was near Christmas by the time all was settled: the season of general holiday approached. I now closed Morton school, taking care that the parting should not be barren on my side. Good fortune opens the hand as well as the heart wonderfully; and to give somewhat when we have largely received, is but to afford a vent to the unusual ebullition of the sensations. I had long felt with pleasure that many of my rustic scholars liked me, and when we parted, that consciousness was confirmed: they manifested their affection plainly and strongly. Deep was my gratification to find I had really a place in their unsophisticated hearts: I promised them that never a week should pass in future that I did not visit them, and give them an hour's teaching in their school.

Mr. Rivers came up as, having seen the classes, now numbering sixty girls, file out before me, and locked the door, I stood with the key in my hand, exchanging a few words of special farewell with some half-dozen of my best scholars: as decent, respectable, modest, and well-informed young women as could be found in the ranks of the British peasantry. And that is saying a great deal; for after all, the British peasantry are the best taught, best mannered, most self-respecting of any in Europe: since those days I have seen paysannes and Bäuerinnen; and the best of them seemed to me ignorant, coarse, and besotted, compared with my Morton girls.

"Do you consider you have got your reward for a season of exertion?" asked Mr. Rivers, when they were gone. "Does not the consciousness of having done some real good in your day and generation give pleasure?"

"Doubtless."

"And you have only toiled a few months! Would not a life devoted to the task of regenerating your race be well spent?"

"Yes," I said; "but I could not go on for ever so: I want to enjoy my own faculties as well as to cultivate those of other people. I must enjoy them now; don't recall either my mind or body to the school; I am out of it and disposed for full holiday."

He looked grave. "What now? What sudden eagerness is this you evince? What are you going to do?"

"To be active: as active as I can. And first I must beg you to set Hannah at liberty, and get somebody else to wait on you."

"Do you want her?"

"Yes, to go with me to Moor House. Diana and Mary will be at home in a week, and I want to have everything in order against their arrival."

"I understand. I thought you were for flying off on some excursion. It is better so: Hannah shall go with you."

"Tell her to be ready by tomorrow then; and here is the schoolroom key: I will give you the key of my cottage in the morning."

He took it. "You give it up very gleefully," said he; "I don't quite understand your light-heartedness, because I cannot tell what employment you propose to yourself as a substitute for the one you are relinquishing. What aim, what purpose, what ambition in life have you now?"

"My first aim will be to *clean down* (do you comprehend the full force of the expression?)—to *clean down* Moor House from chamber to cellar; my next to rub it up with bees-wax, oil, and an indefinite number of cloths, till it glitters again; my third, to arrange every chair, table, bed, carpet, with mathematical precision; afterwards I shall go near to ruin you in coals and peat to keep up good fires in every room; and lastly, the two days preceding that on which your sisters are expected will be devoted by Hannah and me to such a beating of eggs, sorting of currants, grating of spices, compounding of Christmas cakes, chopping up of materials for mince-pies, and solemnising of other culinary rites, as words can convey but an inadequate notion of to the uninitiated like you. My purpose, in short, is to have all things in an absolutely perfect state of readiness for Diana and Mary before next Thursday; and my ambition is to give them a beau-ideal of a welcome when they come."

St. John smiled slightly: still he was dissatisfied.

"It is all very well for the present," said he; "but seriously, I trust that when the first flush of vivacity is over, you will look a little higher than domestic endearments and household joys."

"The best things the world has!" I interrupted.

"No, Jane, no: this world is not the scene of fruition; do not attempt to make it so: nor of rest; do not turn slothful."

"I mean, on the contrary, to be busy."

"Jane, I excuse you for the present: two months' grace I allow you for the full enjoyment of your new position, and for pleasing yourself with this late-found charm of relationship; but *then*, I hope you will begin to look beyond Moor House and Morton, and sisterly society, and the selfish calm and sensual comfort of civilised affluence. I hope your energies will then once more trouble you with their strength."

I looked at him with surprise. "St. John," I said, "I think you are almost wicked to talk so. I am disposed to be as content as a queen, and you try to stir me up to restlessness! To what end?"

"To the end of turning to profit the talents which God has committed to your keeping; and of which He will surely one day demand a strict account. Jane, I shall watch you closely and anxiously—I warn you of that. And try to restrain the disproportionate fervour with which you throw yourself into commonplace home pleasures. Don't cling so tenaciously to ties of the flesh; save your constancy and ardour for an adequate cause; forbear to waste them on trite transient objects. Do you hear, Jane?"

"Yes; just as if you were speaking Greek. I feel I have adequate cause to be happy, and I *will* be happy. Goodbye!"

Happy at Moor House I was, and hard I worked; and so did Hannah: she was charmed to see how jovial I could be amidst the bustle of a house turned topsy-turvy—how I could brush, and dust, and clean, and cook. And really, after a day or two of confusion worse confounded, it was delightful by degrees to invoke order from the chaos ourselves had made. I had previously taken a journey to S—— to purchase some new furniture: my cousins having given me carte blanche to effect what alterations I pleased, and a sum having been set aside for that purpose. The ordinary sitting-room and bedrooms I left much as they were: for I knew Diana and Mary would derive more pleasure from seeing again the old homely tables, and chairs, and beds, than from the spectacle of the smartest innovations. Still some novelty was necessary, to give to their return the piquancy with which I wished it to be invested. Dark handsome new carpets and curtains, an arrangement of some carefully selected antique ornaments in porcelain and bronze, new coverings, and mirrors, and dressing-cases, for the toilet tables, answered the end: they looked fresh without being glaring. A spare parlour and bedroom I refurnished entirely, with old mahogany and crimson upholstery: I laid canvas on the passage, and carpets on the stairs. When all was finished,

I thought Moor House as complete a model of bright modest snugness within, as it was, at this season, a specimen of wintry waste and desert dreariness without.

The eventful Thursday at length came. They were expected about dark, and ere dusk fires were lit upstairs and below; the kitchen was in perfect trim; Hannah and I were dressed, and all was in readiness.

St. John arrived first. I had entreated him to keep quite clear of the house till everything was arranged: and, indeed, the bare idea of the commotion, at once sordid and trivial, going on within its walls sufficed to scare him to estrangement. He found me in the kitchen, watching the progress of certain cakes for tea, then baking. Approaching the hearth, he asked, "If I was at last satisfied with housemaid's work?" I answered by inviting him to accompany me on a general inspection of the result of my labours. With some difficulty, I got him to make the tour of the house. He just looked in at the doors I opened; and when he had wandered upstairs and downstairs, he said I must have gone through a great deal of fatigue and trouble to have effected such considerable changes in so short a time: but not a syllable did he utter indicating pleasure in the improved aspect of his abode.

This silence damped me. I thought perhaps the alterations had disturbed some old associations he valued. I inquired whether this was the case: no doubt in a somewhat crest-fallen tone.

"Not at all; he had, on the contrary, remarked that I had scrupulously respected every association: he feared, indeed, I must have bestowed more thought on the matter than it was worth. How many minutes, for instance, had I devoted to studying the arrangement of this very room? By-the-by, could I tell him where such a book was?"

I showed him the volume on the shelf: he took it down, and withdrawing to his accustomed window recess, he began to read it.

Now, I did not like this, reader. St. John was a good man; but I began to feel he had spoken truth of himself when he said he was hard and cold. The humanities and amenities of life had no attraction for him—its peaceful enjoyments no charm. Literally, he lived only to aspire—after what was good and great, certainly; but still he would never rest, nor approve of others resting round him. As I looked at his lofty forehead, still and pale as a white stone—at his fine lineaments fixed in study—I comprehended all at once that he would hardly make a good husband: that it would be a trying thing to be his wife. I understood, as by inspiration, the nature of his love for Miss Oliver; I agreed with him that it was but a love of the senses. I comprehended how he should despise himself for the feverish influence it exercised over him; how he should wish to stifle and destroy it; how he should mistrust its ever conducting permanently to his happiness or hers. I saw he was of the material from which nature hews her heroes—Christian and Pagan—her lawgivers, her statesmen, her conquerors: a steadfast bulwark for great interests to rest upon; but, at the fireside, too often a cold cumbrous column, gloomy and out of place.

"This parlour is not his sphere," I reflected; "the Himalayan ridge or Caffre bush, even the plague-cursed Guinea Coast swamp would suit him better. Well may he eschew the calm of domestic life; it is not his element: there his faculties stagnate—they cannot develop or appear to advantage. It is in scenes of strife and danger—where courage is proved, and energy exercised, and fortitude tasked—that he will speak and move, the leader and superior. A merry child would have the advantage of him on this hearth. He is right to choose a missionary's career—I see it now."

"They are coming! They are coming!" cried Hannah, throwing open the parlour door. At the same moment old Carlo barked joyfully. Out I ran. It was now dark; but a rumbling of wheels was audible. Hannah soon had a lantern lit. The vehicle had stopped at the wicket; the driver opened the door: first one well-known form, then another, stepped out. In a minute I had my face under their bonnets, in contact first with Mary's soft cheek, then with Diana's flowing curls. They laughed—kissed me—then Hannah: patted Carlo, who was half wild with delight; asked eagerly if all was well; and being assured in the affirmative, hastened into the house.

They were stiff with their long and jolting drive from Whitcross, and chilled with the frosty night air; but their pleasant countenances expanded to the cheerful firelight. While the driver and Hannah brought in the boxes, they demanded St. John. At this moment he advanced from the parlour. They both threw their arms round his neck at once. He gave each one quiet kiss, said in a low tone a few words of welcome, stood a while to be talked to, and then, intimating that he supposed they would soon rejoin him in the parlour, withdrew there as to a place of refuge.

I had lit their candles to go upstairs, but Diana had first to give hospitable orders respecting the driver; this done, both followed me. They were delighted with the renovation and decorations of their rooms; with the new drapery, and fresh carpets, and rich tinted china vases: they expressed their gratification ungrudgingly. I had the pleasure of feeling that my arrangements met their wishes exactly, and that what I had done added a vivid charm to their joyous return home.

Sweet was that evening. My cousins, full of exhilaration, were so eloquent in narrative and comment, that their fluency covered St. John's taciturnity: he was sincerely glad to see his sisters; but in their glow of fervour and flow of joy he could not sympathise. The event of the day—that is, the return of Diana and Mary—pleased him; but the accompaniments of that event, the glad tumult, the garrulous glee of reception irked him: I saw he wished the calmer morrow was come. In the very meridian of the night's enjoyment, about an hour after tea, a rap was heard at the door. Hannah entered with the intimation that "a poor lad was come, at that unlikely time, to fetch Mr. Rivers to see his mother, who was drawing away."

"Where does she live, Hannah?"

"Clear up at Whitcross Brow, almost four miles off, and moor and moss all the way."

"Tell him I will go."

"I'm sure, sir, you had better not. It's the worst road to travel after dark that can be: there's no track at all over the bog. And then it is such a bitter night—the keenest wind you ever felt. You had better send word, sir, that you will be there in the morning."

But he was already in the passage, putting on his cloak; and without one objection, one murmur, he departed. It was then nine o'clock: he did not return till midnight. Starved and tired enough he was: but he looked happier than when he set out. He had performed an act of duty; made an exertion; felt his own strength to do and deny, and was on better terms with himself.

I am afraid the whole of the ensuing week tried his patience. It was Christmas week: we took to no settled employment, but spent it in a sort of merry domestic dissipation. The air of the moors, the freedom of home, the dawn of prosperity, acted on Diana and Mary's spirits like some life-giving elixir: they were gay from morning till noon, and from noon till night. They could always talk; and their discourse, witty, pithy, original, had such charms for me, that I preferred listening to, and sharing in it, to doing anything else. St. John did not rebuke our vivacity; but he escaped from it: he was seldom in the house; his parish was large, the population scattered, and he found daily business in visiting the sick and poor in its different districts.

One morning at breakfast, Diana, after looking a little pensive for some minutes, asked him, "If his plans were yet unchanged."

"Unchanged and unchangeable," was the reply. And he proceeded to inform us that his departure from England was now definitively fixed for the ensuing year.

"And Rosamond Oliver?" suggested Mary, the words seeming to escape her lips involuntarily: for no sooner had she uttered them, than she made a gesture as if wishing to recall them. St. John had a book in his hand—it was his unsocial custom to read at meals—he closed it, and looked up.

"Rosamond Oliver," said he, "is about to be married to Mr. Granby, one of the best connected and most estimable residents in S——, grandson and heir to Sir Frederic Granby: I had the intelligence from her father yesterday."

His sisters looked at each other and at me; we all three looked at him: he was serene as glass.

"The match must have been got up hastily," said Diana; "they cannot have known each other long."

"But two months: they met in October at the county ball at S——. But where there are no obstacles to a union, as in the present case, where the connection is in every point desirable, delays are unnecessary: they will be married as soon as S—— Place, which Sir Frederic gives up to them, can he refitted for their reception."

The first time I found St. John alone after this communication, I felt tempted to inquire if the event distressed him: but he seemed so little to need sympathy, that, so far from venturing to offer him more, I experienced some shame at the recollection of what I had already hazarded. Besides, I was out of practice in talking to him: his reserve was again frozen over, and my frankness was congealed beneath it. He had not kept his promise of treating me like his sisters; he continually made little chilling differences between us, which did not at all tend to the development of cordiality: in short, now that I was acknowledged his kinswoman, and lived under the same roof with him, I felt the distance between us to be far greater than when he had known me only as the village schoolmistress. When I remembered how far I had once been admitted to his confidence, I could hardly comprehend his present frigidity.

Such being the case, I felt not a little surprised when he raised his head suddenly from the desk over which he was stooping, and said—

"You see, Jane, the battle is fought and the victory won."

Startled at being thus addressed, I did not immediately reply: after a moment's hesitation I answered—

"But are you sure you are not in the position of those conquerors whose triumphs have cost them too dear? Would not such another ruin you?"

"I think not; and if I were, it does not much signify; I shall never be called upon to contend for such another. The event of the conflict is decisive: my way is now clear; I thank God for it!" So saying, he returned to his papers and his silence.

As our mutual happiness (i.e., Diana's, Mary's, and mine) settled into a quieter character, and we resumed our usual habits and regular studies, St. John stayed more at home: he sat with us in the same room, sometimes for hours together. While Mary drew, Diana pursued a course of encyclopaedic reading she had (to my awe and amazement) undertaken, and I fagged away at German, he pondered a mystic lore of his own: that of some Eastern tongue, the acquisition of which he thought necessary to his plans.

Thus engaged, he appeared, sitting in his own recess, quiet and absorbed enough; but that blue eye of his had a habit of leaving the outlandish-looking grammar, and wandering over, and sometimes fixing upon us, his fellow-students, with a curious intensity of observation: if caught, it would be instantly withdrawn; yet ever and anon, it returned searchingly to our table. I wondered what it meant: I wondered, too, at the punctual satisfaction he never failed to exhibit on an occasion that seemed to me of small moment, namely, my weekly visit to Morton school; and still more was I puzzled when, if the day was unfavourable, if there was snow, or rain, or high wind, and his sisters urged me not to go, he would invariably make light of their solicitude, and encourage me to accomplish the task without regard to the elements.

"Jane is not such a weakling as you would make her," he would say; "she can bear a mountain blast, or a shower, or a few flakes of snow, as well as any of us. Her constitution is both sound and elastic—better calculated to endure variations of climate than many more robust."

And when I returned, sometimes a good deal tired, and not a little weather-beaten, I never dared complain, because I saw that to murmur would be to vex him: on all occasions fortitude pleased him; the reverse was a special annoyance.

One afternoon, however, I got leave to stay at home, because I really had a cold. His sisters were gone to Morton in my stead: I sat reading Schiller; he, deciphering his crabbed Oriental scrolls. As I exchanged a translation for an exercise, I happened to look his way: there I found myself under the influence of the ever-watchful blue eye. How long it had been searching me through and through, and over and over, I cannot tell: so keen was it, and yet so cold, I felt for the moment superstitious—as if I were sitting in the room with something uncanny.

"Jane, what are you doing?"

"Learning German."

"I want you to give up German and learn Hindostanee."

"You are not in earnest?"

"In such earnest that I must have it so: and I will tell you why."

He then went on to explain that Hindostanee was the language he was himself at present studying; that, as he advanced, he was apt to forget the commencement; that it would assist him greatly to have a pupil with whom he might again and again go over the elements, and so fix them thoroughly in his mind; that his choice had hovered for some time between me and his sisters; but that he had fixed on me because he saw I could sit at a task the longest of the three. Would I do him this favour? I should not, perhaps, have to make the sacrifice long, as it wanted now barely three months to his departure.

St. John was not a man to be lightly refused: you felt that every impression made on him, either for pain or pleasure, was deep-graved and permanent. I consented. When Diana and Mary returned, the former found her scholar transferred from her to her brother: she laughed, and both she and Mary agreed that St. John should never have persuaded them to such a step. He answered quietly—

"I know it."

I found him a very patient, very forbearing, and yet an exacting master: he expected me to do a great deal; and when I fulfilled his expectations, he, in his own way, fully testified his approbation. By degrees, he acquired a certain influence over me that took away my liberty of mind: his praise and notice were more restraining than his indifference. I could no longer talk or laugh freely when he was by, because a tiresomely importunate instinct reminded me that vivacity (at least in me) was distasteful to him. I was so fully aware that only serious moods and occupations were acceptable, that in his presence every effort to sustain or follow any other became vain: I fell under a freezing spell. When he said "go," I went; "come," I came; "do this," I did it. But I did not love my servitude: I wished, many a time, he had continued to neglect me.

One evening when, at bedtime, his sisters and I stood round him, bidding him good-night, he kissed each of them, as was his custom; and, as was equally his custom, he gave me his hand. Diana, who chanced to be in a frolicsome humour (*she* was not painfully controlled by his will; for hers, in another way, was as strong), exclaimed—

"St. John! You used to call Jane your third sister, but you don't treat her as such: you should kiss her too."

She pushed me towards him. I thought Diana very provoking, and felt uncomfortably confused; and while I was thus thinking and feeling, St. John bent his head; his Greek face was brought to a level with mine, his eyes questioned my eyes piercingly—he kissed me. There are no such things as marble kisses or ice kisses, or I should say my ecclesiastical cousin's salute belonged to one of these classes; but there may be experiment kisses, and his was an experiment kiss. When given, he viewed me to learn the result; it was not striking: I am sure I did not blush; perhaps I might have turned a little pale, for I felt as if this kiss were a seal affixed to my fetters. He never omitted the ceremony afterwards, and the gravity and quiescence with which I underwent it, seemed to invest it for him with a certain charm.

As for me, I daily wished more to please him; but to do so, I felt daily more and more that I must disown half my nature, stifle half my faculties, wrest my tastes from their original bent, force myself to the adoption of pursuits for which I had no natural vocation. He wanted to train me to an elevation I could never reach; it racked me hourly to aspire to the standard he uplifted. The thing was as impossible as to mould my irregular features to his correct and classic pattern, to give to my changeable green eyes the sea-blue tint and solemn lustre of his own.

Not his ascendancy alone, however, held me in thrall at present. Of late it had been easy enough for me to look sad: a cankering evil sat at my heart and drained my happiness at its source—the evil of suspense.

Perhaps you think I had forgotten Mr. Rochester, reader, amidst these changes of place and fortune. Not for a moment. His idea was still with me, because it was not a vapour sunshine could disperse, nor a sand-traced effigy storms could wash away; it was a name graven on a tablet, fated to last as long as the marble it inscribed. The craving to know what had become of him followed me everywhere; when I was at Morton, I re-entered my cottage every evening to think of that; and now at Moor House, I sought my bedroom each night to brood over it.

In the course of my necessary correspondence with Mr. Briggs about the will, I had inquired if he knew anything of Mr. Rochester's present residence and state of health; but, as St. John had conjectured, he was quite ignorant of all concerning him. I then wrote to Mrs. Fairfax, entreating information on the subject. I had calculated with certainty on this step answering my end: I felt sure it would elicit an early answer. I was astonished when a fortnight passed without reply; but when two months wore away, and day after day the post arrived and brought nothing for me, I fell a prey to the keenest anxiety.

I wrote again: there was a chance of my first letter having missed. Renewed hope followed renewed effort: it shone like the former for some weeks, then, like it, it faded, flickered: not a line, not a word reached me. When half a year wasted in vain expectancy, my hope died out, and then I felt dark indeed.

A fine spring shone round me, which I could not enjoy. Summer approached; Diana tried to cheer me: she said I looked ill, and wished to accompany me to the sea-side. This St. John opposed; he said I did not want dissipation, I wanted employment; my present life was too purposeless, I required an aim; and, I suppose, by way of supplying deficiencies, he prolonged still further my lessons in Hindostanee, and grew more urgent in requiring their accomplishment: and I, like a fool, never thought of resisting him—I could not resist him.

One day I had come to my studies in lower spirits than usual; the ebb was occasioned by a poignantly felt disappointment. Hannah had told me in the morning there was a letter for me, and when I went down to take it, almost certain that the long-looked for tidings were vouchsafed me at last, I found only an unimportant note from Mr. Briggs on business. The bitter check had wrung from me some tears; and now, as I sat poring over the crabbed characters and flourishing tropes of an Indian scribe, my eyes filled again.

St. John called me to his side to read; in attempting to do this my voice failed me: words were lost in sobs. He and I were the only occupants of the parlour: Diana was practising her music in the drawing-room, Mary was gardening—it was a very fine May day, clear, sunny, and breezy. My companion expressed no surprise at this emotion, nor did he question me as to its cause; he only said—

"We will wait a few minutes, Jane, till you are more composed." And while I smothered the paroxysm with all haste, he sat calm and patient, leaning on his desk, and looking like a physician watching with the eye of science an expected and fully understood crisis in a patient's malady. Having stifled my sobs, wiped my eyes, and muttered something about not being very well that morning, I resumed my task, and succeeded in completing it. St. John put away my books and his, locked his desk, and said—

"Now, Jane, you shall take a walk; and with me."

"I will call Diana and Mary."

"No; I want only one companion this morning, and that must be you. Put on your things; go out by the kitchen-door: take the road towards the head of Marsh Glen: I will join you in a moment."

I know no medium: I never in my life have known any medium in my dealings with positive, hard characters, antagonistic to my own, between absolute submission and determined revolt. I have always faithfully observed the one, up to the very moment of bursting, sometimes with volcanic vehemence, into the other; and as neither present circumstances warranted, nor my present mood inclined me to mutiny, I observed careful obedience to St. John's directions; and in ten minutes I was treading the wild track of the glen, side by side with him.

The breeze was from the west: it came over the hills, sweet with scents of heath and rush; the sky was of stainless blue; the stream descending the ravine, swelled with past spring rains, poured along plentiful and clear, catching golden gleams from the sun, and sapphire tints from the firmament. As we advanced and left the track, we trod a soft turf, mossy fine and emerald green, minutely enamelled with a tiny white flower, and spangled with a star-like yellow blossom: the hills, meantime, shut us quite in; for the glen, towards its head, wound to their very core.

"Let us rest here," said St. John, as we reached the first stragglers of a battalion of rocks, guarding a sort of pass, beyond which the beck rushed down a waterfall; and where, still a little farther, the mountain shook off turf and flower, had only heath for raiment and crag for gem—where it exaggerated the wild to the savage, and exchanged the fresh for the frowning—where it guarded the forlorn hope of solitude, and a last refuge for silence.

I took a seat: St. John stood near me. He looked up the pass and down the hollow; his glance wandered away with the stream, and returned to traverse the unclouded heaven which coloured it: he removed his hat, let the breeze stir his hair and kiss his brow. He seemed in communion with the genius of the haunt: with his eye he bade farewell to something.

"And I shall see it again," he said aloud, "in dreams when I sleep by the Ganges: and again in a more remote hour—when another slumber overcomes me—on the shore of a darker stream!"

Strange words of a strange love! An austere patriot's passion for his fatherland! He sat down; for half-an-hour we never spoke; neither he to me nor I to him: that interval past, he recommenced—

"Jane, I go in six weeks; I have taken my berth in an East Indiaman which sails on the 20th of June."

"God will protect you; for you have undertaken His work," I answered.

"Yes," said he, "there is my glory and joy. I am the servant of an infallible Master. I am not going out under human guidance, subject to the defective laws and erring control of my feeble fellow-worms: my king, my lawgiver, my captain, is the All-perfect. It seems strange to me that all round me do not burn to enlist under the same banner—to join in the same enterprise."

"All have not your powers, and it would be folly for the feeble to wish to march with the strong."

"I do not speak to the feeble, or think of them: I address only such as are worthy of the work, and competent to accomplish it."

"Those are few in number, and difficult to discover."

"You say truly; but when found, it is right to stir them up—to urge and exhort them to the effort—to show them what their gifts are, and why they were given—to speak Heaven's message in their ear—to offer them, direct from God, a place in the ranks of His chosen."

"If they are really qualified for the task, will not their own hearts be the first to inform them of it?"

I felt as if an awful charm was framing round and gathering over me: I trembled to hear some fatal word spoken which would at once declare and rivet the spell.

"And what does *your* heart say?" demanded St. John.

"My heart is mute—my heart is mute," I answered, struck and thrilled.

"Then I must speak for it," continued the deep, relentless voice. "Jane, come with me to India: come as my helpmeet and fellow-labourer."

The glen and sky spun round: the hills heaved! It was as if I had heard a summons from Heaven—as if a visionary messenger, like him of Macedonia, had enounced, "Come over and help us!" But I was no apostle—I could not behold the herald—I could not receive his call.

"Oh, St. John!" I cried. "Have some mercy!"

I appealed to one who, in the discharge of what he believed his duty, knew neither mercy nor remorse. He continued—

"God and nature intended you for a missionary's wife. It is not personal, but mental endowments they have given you: you are formed for labour, not for love. A missionary's wife you must—shall be. You shall be mine: I claim you—not for my pleasure, but for my Sovereign's service."

"I am not fit for it: I have no vocation," I said.

He had calculated on these first objections: he was not irritated by them. Indeed, as he leaned back against the crag behind him, folded his arms on his chest, and fixed his countenance, I saw he was prepared for a long and trying opposition, and had taken in a stock of patience to last him to its close—resolved, however, that that close should be conquest for him.

"Humility, Jane," said he, "is the groundwork of Christian virtues: you say right that you are not fit for the work. Who is fit for it? Or who, that ever was truly called, believed himself worthy of the summons? I, for instance, am but dust and ashes. With St. Paul, I acknowledge myself the chiefest of sinners; but I do not suffer this sense of my personal vileness to daunt me. I know my Leader: that He is just as well as mighty; and while He has chosen a feeble instrument to perform a great task, He will, from the boundless stores of His providence, supply the inadequacy of the means to the end. Think like me, Jane—trust like me. It is the Rock of Ages I ask you to lean on: do not doubt but it will bear the weight of your human weakness."

"I do not understand a missionary life: I have never studied missionary labours."

"There I, humble as I am, can give you the aid you want: I can set you your task from hour to hour; stand by you always; help you from moment to moment. This I could do in the beginning: soon (for I know your powers) you would be as strong and apt as myself, and would not require my help."

"But my powers—where are they for this undertaking? I do not feel them. Nothing speaks or stirs in me while you talk. I am sensible of no light kindling—no life quickening—no voice counselling or cheering. Oh, I wish I could make you see how much my mind is at this moment like a rayless dungeon, with one shrinking fear fettered in its depths—the fear of being persuaded by you to attempt what I cannot accomplish!"

"I have an answer for you—hear it. I have watched you ever since we first met: I have made you my study for ten months. I have proved you in that time by sundry tests: and what have I seen and elicited? In the village school I found you could perform well, punctually, uprightly, labour uncongenial to your habits and inclinations; I saw you could perform it with capacity and tact: you could win while you controlled. In the calm with which you learnt you had become suddenly rich, I read a mind clear of the vice of Demas: lucre had no undue power over you. In the resolute readiness with which you cut your wealth into four shares, keeping but one to yourself, and relinquishing the three others to the claim of abstract justice, I recognised a soul that revelled in the flame and excitement of sacrifice. In the tractability with which, at my wish, you forsook a study in which you were interested, and adopted another because it interested me; in the untiring assiduity with which you have since persevered in it—in the unflagging energy and unshaken temper with which you have met its difficulties—I acknowledge the complement of the qualities I seek. Jane, you are docile, diligent, disinterested, faithful, constant, and courageous; very gentle, and very heroic: cease to mistrust yourself—I can trust you unreservedly. As a conductress of Indian schools, and a helper amongst Indian women, your assistance will be to me invaluable."

My iron shroud contracted round me; persuasion advanced with slow sure step. Shut my eyes as I would, these last words of his succeeded in making the way, which had seemed blocked up, comparatively clear. My work, which had appeared so vague, so hopelessly diffuse, condensed itself as he proceeded, and assumed a definite form under his shaping hand. He waited for an answer. I demanded a quarter of an hour to think, before I again hazarded a reply.

"Very willingly," he rejoined; and rising, he strode a little distance up the pass, threw himself down on a swell of heath, and there lay still.

"I *can* do what he wants me to do: I am forced to see and acknowledge that," I meditated—"that is, if life be spared me. But I feel mine is not the existence to be long protracted under an Indian sun. What then? He does not care for that: when my time came to die, he would resign me, in all serenity and sanctity, to the God who gave me. The case is very plain before me. In leaving England, I should leave a loved but empty land—Mr. Rochester is not there; and if he were, what is, what can that ever be to me? My business is to live without him now: nothing so absurd, so weak as to drag on from day to day, as if I were waiting some impossible change in circumstances, which might reunite me to him. Of course (as St. John once said) I must seek another interest in life to replace the one lost: is not the occupation he now offers me truly the most glorious man can adopt or God assign? Is it not, by its noble cares and sublime results, the one best calculated to fill the void left by uptorn affections and demolished hopes? I believe I must say, Yes—and yet I shudder. Alas! If I join St. John, I abandon half myself: if I go to India, I go to premature death. And how will the interval between leaving England for India, and India for the grave, be filled? Oh, I know well! That, too, is very clear to my vision. By straining to satisfy St. John till my sinews ache, I *shall* satisfy him—to the finest central point and farthest outward circle of his expectations. If I *do* go with him—if I *do* make the sacrifice he urges, I will make it absolutely: I will throw all on the altar—heart, vitals, the entire victim. He will never love me; but he shall approve me; I will show him energies he has not yet seen, resources he has never suspected. Yes, I can work as hard as he can, and with as little grudging.

"Consent, then, to his demand is possible: but for one item—one dreadful item. It is—that he asks me to be his wife, and has no more of a husband's heart for me than that frowning giant of a rock, down which the stream is foaming in yonder gorge. He prizes me as a soldier would a good weapon; and that is all. Unmarried to him, this would never grieve me; but can I let him complete his calculations—coolly put into practice his plans—go through the wedding ceremony? Can I receive from him the bridal ring, endure all the forms of love (which I doubt not he would scrupulously observe) and know that the spirit was quite absent? Can I bear the consciousness that every endearment he bestows is a sacrifice made on principle? No: such a martyrdom would be monstrous. I will never undergo it. As his sister, I might accompany him—not as his wife: I will tell him so."

I looked towards the knoll: there he lay, still as a prostrate column; his face turned to me: his eye beaming watchful and keen. He started to his feet and approached me.

"I am ready to go to India, if I may go free."

"Your answer requires a commentary," he said; "it is not clear."

"You have hitherto been my adopted brother—I, your adopted sister: let us continue as such: you and I had better not marry."

He shook his head. "Adopted fraternity will not do in this case. If you were my real sister it would be different: I should take you, and seek no wife. But as it is, either our union must be consecrated and sealed by marriage, or it cannot exist: practical obstacles oppose themselves to any other plan. Do you not see it, Jane? Consider a moment—your strong sense will guide you."

I did consider; and still my sense, such as it was, directed me only to the fact that we did not love each other as man and wife should: and therefore it inferred we ought not to marry. I said so. "St. John," I returned, "I regard you as a brother—you, me as a sister: so let us continue."

"We cannot—we cannot," he answered, with short, sharp determination; "it would not do. You have said you will go with me to India: remember—you have said that."

"Conditionally."

"Well—well. To the main point—the departure with me from England, the co-operation with me in my future labours—you do not object. You have already as good as put your hand to the plough: you are too consistent to withdraw it. You have but one end to keep in view—how the work you have undertaken can best be done. Simplify your complicated interests, feelings, thoughts, wishes, aims; merge all considerations in one purpose: that of fulfilling with effect—with power—the mission of your great Master. To do so, you must have a coadjutor: not a brother—that is a loose tie—but a husband. I, too, do not want a sister: a sister might any day be taken from me. I want a wife: the sole helpmeet I can influence efficiently in life, and retain absolutely till death."

I shuddered as he spoke: I felt his influence in my marrow—his hold on my limbs.

"Seek one elsewhere than in me, St. John: seek one fitted to you."

"One fitted to my purpose, you mean—fitted to my vocation. Again I tell you it is not the insignificant private individual—the mere man, with the man's selfish senses—I wish to mate: it is the missionary."

"And I will give the missionary my energies—it is all he wants—but not myself: that would be only adding the husk and shell to the kernel. For them he has no use: I retain them."

"You cannot—you ought not. Do you think God will be satisfied with half an oblation? Will He accept a mutilated sacrifice? It is the cause of God I advocate: it is under His standard I enlist you. I cannot accept on His behalf a divided allegiance: it must be entire."

"Oh! I will give my heart to God," I said. "*You* do not want it."

I will not swear, reader, that there was not something of repressed sarcasm both in the tone in which I uttered this sentence, and in the feeling that accompanied it. I had silently feared St. John till now, because I had not understood him. He had held me in awe, because he had held me in doubt. How much of him was saint, how much mortal, I could not heretofore tell: but revelations were being made in this conference: the analysis of his nature was proceeding before my eyes. I saw his fallibilities: I comprehended them. I understood that, sitting there where I did, on the bank of heath, and with that handsome form before me, I sat at the feet of a man, caring as I. The veil fell from his hardness and despotism. Having felt in him the presence of these qualities, I felt his imperfection and took courage. I was with an equal—one with whom I might argue—one whom, if I saw good, I might resist.

He was silent after I had uttered the last sentence, and I presently risked an upward glance at his countenance.

His eye, bent on me, expressed at once stern surprise and keen inquiry. "Is she sarcastic, and sarcastic to *me*!" it seemed to say. "What does this signify?"

"Do not let us forget that this is a solemn matter," he said ere long; "one of which we may neither think nor talk lightly without sin. I trust, Jane, you are in earnest when you say you will serve your heart to God: it is all I want. Once wrench your heart from man, and fix it on your Maker, the advancement of that Maker's spiritual kingdom on earth will be your chief delight and endeavour; you will be ready to do at once whatever furthers that end. You will see what impetus would be given to your efforts and mine by our physical and mental union in marriage: the only union that gives a character of permanent conformity to the destinies and designs of human beings; and, passing over all minor caprices—all trivial difficulties and delicacies of feeling—all scruple about the degree, kind, strength or tenderness of mere personal inclination—you will hasten to enter into that union at once."

"Shall I?" I said briefly; and I looked at his features, beautiful in their harmony, but strangely formidable in their still severity; at his brow, commanding but not open; at his eyes, bright and deep and searching, but never soft; at his tall imposing figure; and fancied myself in idea *his wife*. Oh! It would never do! As his curate, his comrade, all would be right: I would cross oceans with him in that capacity; toil under Eastern suns, in Asian deserts with him in that office; admire and emulate his courage and devotion and vigour; accommodate quietly to his masterhood; smile undisturbed at his ineradicable ambition; discriminate the Christian from the man: profoundly esteem the one, and freely forgive the other. I should suffer often, no doubt, attached to him only in this capacity: my body would be under rather a stringent yoke, but my heart and mind would be free. I should still have my unblighted self to turn to: my natural unenslaved feelings with which to communicate in moments of loneliness. There would be recesses in my mind which would be only mine, to which he never came, and sentiments growing there fresh and sheltered which his austerity could never blight, nor his measured warrior-march trample down: but as his wife—at his side always, and always restrained, and always checked—forced to keep the fire of my nature continually low, to compel it to burn inwardly and never utter a cry, though the imprisoned flame consumed vital after vital—*this* would be unendurable.

"St. John!" I exclaimed, when I had got so far in my meditation.

"Well?" he answered icily.

"I repeat I freely consent to go with you as your fellow-missionary, but not as your wife; I cannot marry you and become part of you."

"A part of me you must become," he answered steadily; "otherwise the whole bargain is void. How can I, a man not yet thirty, take out with me to India a girl of nineteen, unless she be married to me? How can we be for ever together—sometimes in solitudes, sometimes amidst savage tribes—and unwed?"

"Very well," I said shortly; "under the circumstances, quite as well as if I were either your real sister, or a man and a clergyman like yourself."

"It is known that you are not my sister; I cannot introduce you as such: to attempt it would be to fasten injurious suspicions on us both. And for the rest, though you have a man's vigorous brain, you have a woman's heart and—it would not do."

"It would do," I affirmed with some disdain, "perfectly well. I have a woman's heart, but not where you are concerned; for you I have only a comrade's constancy; a fellow-soldier's frankness, fidelity, fraternity, if you like; a neophyte's respect and submission to his hierophant: nothing more—don't fear."

"It is what I want," he said, speaking to himself; "it is just what I want. And there are obstacles in the way: they must be hewn down. Jane, you would not repent marrying me—be certain of that; we *must* be married. I repeat it: there is no other way; and undoubtedly enough of love would follow upon marriage to render the union right even in your eyes."

"I scorn your idea of love," I could not help saying, as I rose up and stood before him, leaning my back against the rock. "I scorn the counterfeit sentiment you offer: yes, St. John, and I scorn you when you offer it."

He looked at me fixedly, compressing his well-cut lips while he did so. Whether he was incensed or surprised, or what, it was not easy to tell: he could command his countenance thoroughly.

"I scarcely expected to hear that expression from you," he said: "I think I have done and uttered nothing to deserve scorn."

I was touched by his gentle tone, and overawed by his high, calm mien.

"Forgive me the words, St. John; but it is your own fault that I have been roused to speak so unguardedly. You have introduced a topic on which our natures are at variance—a topic we should never discuss: the very name of love is an apple of discord between us. If the reality were required, what should we do? How should we feel? My dear cousin, abandon your scheme of marriage—forget it."

"No," said he; "it is a long-cherished scheme, and the only one which can secure my great end: but I shall urge you no further at present. Tomorrow, I leave home for Cambridge: I have many friends there to whom I should wish to say farewell. I shall be absent a fortnight—take that space of time to consider my offer: and do not forget that if you reject it, it is not me you deny, but God. Through my means, He opens to you a noble career; as my wife only can you enter upon it. Refuse to be my wife, and you limit yourself for ever to a track of selfish ease and barren obscurity. Tremble lest in that case you should be numbered with those who have denied the faith, and are worse than infidels!"

He had done. Turning from me, he once more

"Looked to river, looked to hill."

But this time his feelings were all pent in his heart: I was not worthy to hear them uttered. As I walked by his side homeward, I read well in his iron silence all he felt towards me: the disappointment of an austere and despotic nature, which has met resistance where it expected submission—the disapprobation of a cool, inflexible judgment, which has detected in another feelings and views in which it has no power to sympathise: in short, as a man, he would have wished to coerce me into obedience: it was only as a sincere Christian he bore so patiently with my perversity, and allowed so long a space for reflection and repentance.

That night, after he had kissed his sisters, he thought proper to forget even to shake hands with me, but left the room in silence. I—who, though I had no love, had much friendship for him—was hurt by the marked omission: so much hurt that tears started to my eyes.

"I see you and St. John have been quarrelling, Jane," said Diana, "during your walk on the moor. But go after him; he is now lingering in the passage expecting you—he will make it up."

I have not much pride under such circumstances: I would always rather be happy than dignified; and I ran after him—he stood at the foot of the stairs.

"Good-night, St. John," said I.

"Good-night, Jane," he replied calmly.

"Then shake hands," I added.

What a cold, loose touch, he impressed on my fingers! He was deeply displeased by what had occurred that day; cordiality would not warm, nor tears move him. No happy reconciliation was to be had with him—no cheering smile or generous word: but still the Christian was patient and placid; and when I asked him if he forgave me, he answered that he was not in the habit of cherishing the remembrance of vexation; that he had nothing to forgive, not having been offended.

And with that answer he left me. I would much rather he had knocked me down.

CHAPTER XXXV

He did not leave for Cambridge the next day, as he had said he would. He deferred his departure a whole week, and during that time he made me feel what severe punishment a good yet stern, a conscientious yet implacable man can inflict on one who has offended him. Without one overt act of hostility, one upbraiding word, he contrived to impress me momently with the conviction that I was put beyond the pale of his favour.

Not that St. John harboured a spirit of unchristian vindictiveness—not that he would have injured a hair of my head, if it had been fully in his power to do so. Both by nature and principle, he was superior to the mean gratification of vengeance: he had forgiven me for saying I scorned him and his love, but he had not forgotten the words; and as long as he and I lived he never would forget them. I saw by his look, when he turned to me, that they were always written on the air between me and him; whenever I spoke, they sounded in my voice to his ear, and their echo toned every answer he gave me.

He did not abstain from conversing with me: he even called me as usual each morning to join him at his desk; and I fear the corrupt man within him had a pleasure unimparted to, and unshared by, the pure Christian, in evincing with what skill he could, while acting and speaking apparently just as usual, extract from every deed and every phrase the spirit of interest and approval which had formerly communicated a certain austere charm to his language and manner. To me, he was in reality become no longer flesh, but marble; his eye was a cold, bright, blue gem; his tongue a speaking instrument—nothing more.

All this was torture to me—refined, lingering torture. It kept up a slow fire of indignation and a trembling trouble of grief, which harassed and crushed me altogether. I felt how—if I were his wife, this good man, pure as the deep sunless source, could soon kill me, without drawing from my veins a single drop of blood, or receiving on his own crystal conscience the faintest stain of crime. Especially I felt this when I made any attempt to propitiate him. No ruth met my ruth. *He* experienced no suffering from estrangement—no yearning after reconciliation; and though, more than once, my fast falling tears blistered the page over which we both bent, they produced no more effect on him than if his heart had been really a matter of stone or metal. To his sisters, meantime, he was somewhat kinder than usual: as if afraid that mere coldness would not sufficiently convince me how completely I was banished and banned, he added the force of contrast; and this I am sure he did not by force, but on principle.

The night before he left home, happening to see him walking in the garden about sunset, and remembering, as I looked at him, that this man, alienated as he now was, had once saved my life, and that we were near relations, I was moved to make a last attempt to regain his friendship. I went out and approached him as he stood leaning over the little gate; I spoke to the point at once.

"St. John, I am unhappy because you are still angry with me. Let us be friends."

"I hope we are friends," was the unmoved reply; while he still watched the rising of the moon, which he had been contemplating as I approached.

"No, St. John, we are not friends as we were. You know that."

"Are we not? That is wrong. For my part, I wish you no ill and all good."

"I believe you, St. John; for I am sure you are incapable of wishing any one ill; but, as I am your kinswoman, I should desire somewhat more of affection than that sort of general philanthropy you extend to mere strangers."

"Of course," he said. "Your wish is reasonable, and I am far from regarding you as a stranger."

This, spoken in a cool, tranquil tone, was mortifying and baffling enough. Had I attended to the suggestions of pride and ire, I should immediately have left him; but something worked within me more strongly than those feelings could. I deeply venerated my cousin's talent and principle. His friendship was of value to me: to lose it tried me severely. I would not so soon relinquish the attempt to reconquer it.

"Must we part in this way, St. John? And when you go to India, will you leave me so, without a kinder word than you have yet spoken?"

He now turned quite from the moon and faced me.

"When I go to India, Jane, will I leave you! What! Do you not go to India?"

"You said I could not unless I married you."

"And you will not marry me! You adhere to that resolution?"

Reader, do you know, as I do, what terror those cold people can put into the ice of their questions? How much of the fall of the avalanche is in their anger? Of the breaking up of the frozen sea in their displeasure?

"No. St. John, I will not marry you. I adhere to my resolution."

The avalanche had shaken and slid a little forward, but it did not yet crash down.

"Once more, why this refusal?" he asked.

"Formerly," I answered, "because you did not love me; now, I reply, because you almost hate me. If I were to marry you, you would kill me. You are killing me now."

His lips and cheeks turned white—quite white.

"*I should kill you—I am killing you*? Your words are such as ought not to be used: violent, unfeminine, and untrue. They betray an unfortunate state of mind: they merit severe reproof: they would seem inexcusable, but that it is the duty of man to forgive his fellow even until seventy-and-seven times."

I had finished the business now. While earnestly wishing to erase from his mind the trace of my former offence, I had stamped on that tenacious surface another and far deeper impression, I had burnt it in.

"Now you will indeed hate me," I said. "It is useless to attempt to conciliate you: I see I have made an eternal enemy of you."

A fresh wrong did these words inflict: the worse, because they touched on the truth. That bloodless lip quivered to a temporary spasm. I knew the steely ire I had whetted. I was heart-wrung.

"You utterly misinterpret my words," I said, at once seizing his hand: "I have no intention to grieve or pain you—indeed, I have not."

Most bitterly he smiled—most decidedly he withdrew his hand from mine. "And now you recall your promise, and will not go to India at all, I presume?" said he, after a considerable pause.

"Yes, I will, as your assistant," I answered.

A very long silence succeeded. What struggle there was in him between Nature and Grace in this interval, I cannot tell: only singular gleams scintillated in his eyes, and strange shadows passed over his face. He spoke at last.

"I before proved to you the absurdity of a single woman of your age proposing to accompany abroad a single man of mine. I proved it to you in such terms as, I should have thought, would have prevented your ever again alluding to the plan. That you have done so, I regret—for your sake."

I interrupted him. Anything like a tangible reproach gave me courage at once. "Keep to common sense, St. John: you are verging on nonsense. You pretend to be shocked by what I have said. You are not really shocked: for, with your superior mind, you cannot be either so dull or so conceited as to misunderstand my meaning. I say again, I will be your curate, if you like, but never your wife."

Again he turned lividly pale; but, as before, controlled his passion perfectly. He answered emphatically but calmly—

"A female curate, who is not my wife, would never suit me. With me, then, it seems, you cannot go: but if you are sincere in your offer, I will, while in town, speak to a married missionary, whose wife needs a coadjutor. Your own fortune will make you independent of the Society's aid; and thus you may still be spared the dishonour of breaking your promise and deserting the band you engaged to join."

Now I never had, as the reader knows, either given any formal promise or entered into any engagement; and this language was all much too hard and much too despotic for the occasion. I replied—

"There is no dishonour, no breach of promise, no desertion in the case. I am not under the slightest obligation to go to India, especially with strangers. With you I would have ventured much, because I admire, confide in, and, as a sister, I love you; but I am convinced that, go when and with whom I would, I should not live long in that climate."

"Ah! You are afraid of yourself," he said, curling his lip.

"I am. God did not give me my life to throw away; and to do as you wish me would, I begin to think, be almost equivalent to committing suicide. Moreover, before I definitively resolve on quitting England, I will know for certain whether I cannot be of greater use by remaining in it than by leaving it."

"What do you mean?"

"It would be fruitless to attempt to explain; but there is a point on which I have long endured painful doubt, and I can go nowhere till by some means that doubt is removed."

"I know where your heart turns and to what it clings. The interest you cherish is lawless and unconsecrated. Long since you ought to have crushed it: now you should blush to allude to it. You think of Mr. Rochester?"

It was true. I confessed it by silence.

"Are you going to seek Mr. Rochester?"

"I must find out what is become of him."

"It remains for me, then," he said, "to remember you in my prayers, and to entreat God for you, in all earnestness, that you may not indeed become a castaway. I had thought I recognised in you one of the chosen. But God sees not as man sees: *His* will be done—"

He opened the gate, passed through it, and strayed away down the glen. He was soon out of sight.

On re-entering the parlour, I found Diana standing at the window, looking very thoughtful. Diana was a great deal taller than I: she put her hand on my shoulder, and, stooping, examined my face.

"Jane," she said, "you are always agitated and pale now. I am sure there is something the matter. Tell me what business St. John and you have on hands. I have watched you this half hour from the window; you must forgive my being such a spy, but for a long time I have fancied I hardly know what. St. John is a strange being—"

She paused—I did not speak: soon she resumed—

"That brother of mine cherishes peculiar views of some sort respecting you, I am sure: he has long distinguished you by a notice and interest he never showed to any one else—to what end? I wish he loved you—does he, Jane?"

I put her cool hand to my hot forehead. "No, Die, not one whit."

"Then why does he follow you so with his eyes, and get you so frequently alone with him, and keep you so continually at his side? Mary and I had both concluded he wished you to marry him."

"He does—he has asked me to be his wife."

Diana clapped her hands. "That is just what we hoped and thought! And you will marry him, Jane, won't you? And then he will stay in England."

"Far from that, Diana; his sole idea in proposing to me is to procure a fitting fellow-labourer in his Indian toils."

"What! He wishes you to go to India?"

"Yes."

"Madness!" she exclaimed. "You would not live three months there, I am certain. You never shall go: you have not consented, have you, Jane?"

"I have refused to marry him—"

"And have consequently displeased him?" she suggested.

"Deeply: he will never forgive me, I fear: yet I offered to accompany him as his sister."

"It was frantic folly to do so, Jane. Think of the task you undertook—one of incessant fatigue, where fatigue kills even the strong, and you are weak. St. John—you know him—would urge you to impossibilities: with him there would be no permission to rest during the hot hours; and unfortunately, I have noticed, whatever he exacts, you force yourself to perform. I am astonished you found courage to refuse his hand. You do not love him then, Jane?"

"Not as a husband."

"Yet he is a handsome fellow."

"And I am so plain, you see, Die. We should never suit."

"Plain! You? Not at all. You are much too pretty, as well as too good, to be grilled alive in Calcutta." And again she earnestly conjured me to give up all thoughts of going out with her brother.

"I must indeed," I said; "for when just now I repeated the offer of serving him for a deacon, he expressed himself shocked at my want of decency. He seemed to think I had committed an impropriety in proposing to accompany him unmarried: as if I had not from the first hoped to find in him a brother, and habitually regarded him as such."

"What makes you say he does not love you, Jane?"

"You should hear himself on the subject. He has again and again explained that it is not himself, but his office he wishes to mate. He has told me I am formed for labour—not for love: which is true, no doubt. But, in my opinion, if I am not formed for love, it follows that I am not formed for marriage. Would it not be strange, Die, to be chained for life to a man who regarded one but as a useful tool?"

"Insupportable—unnatural—out of the question!"

"And then," I continued, "though I have only sisterly affection for him now, yet, if forced to be his wife, I can imagine the possibility of conceiving an inevitable, strange, torturing kind of love for him, because he is so talented; and there is often a certain heroic grandeur in his look, manner, and conversation. In that case, my lot would become unspeakably wretched. He would not want me to love him; and if I showed the feeling, he would make me sensible that it was a superfluity, unrequired by him, unbecoming in me. I know he would."

"And yet St. John is a good man," said Diana.

"He is a good and a great man; but he forgets, pitilessly, the feelings and claims of little people, in pursuing his own large views. It is better, therefore, for the insignificant to keep out of his way, lest, in his progress, he should trample them down. Here he comes! I will leave you, Diana." And I hastened upstairs as I saw him entering the garden.

But I was forced to meet him again at supper. During that meal he appeared just as composed as usual. I had thought he would hardly speak to me, and I was certain he had given up the pursuit of his matrimonial scheme: the sequel showed I was mistaken on both points. He addressed me precisely in his ordinary manner, or what had, of late, been his ordinary manner—one scrupulously polite. No doubt he had invoked the help of the Holy Spirit to subdue the anger I had roused in him, and now believed he had forgiven me once more.

For the evening reading before prayers, he selected the twenty-first chapter of Revelation. It was at all times pleasant to listen while from his lips fell the words of the Bible: never did his fine voice sound at once so sweet and full—never did his manner become so impressive in its noble simplicity, as when he delivered the oracles of God: and tonight that voice took a more solemn tone—that manner a more thrilling meaning—as he sat in the midst of his household circle (the May moon shining in through the uncurtained window, and rendering almost unnecessary the light of the candle on the table): as he sat there, bending over the great old Bible, and described from its page the vision of the new heaven and the new earth—told how God would come to dwell with men, how He would wipe away all tears from their eyes, and promised that there should be no more death, neither sorrow nor crying, nor any more pain, because the former things were passed away.

The succeeding words thrilled me strangely as he spoke them: especially as I felt, by the slight, indescribable alteration in sound, that in uttering them, his eye had turned on me.

"He that overcometh shall inherit all things; and I will be his God, and he shall be my son. But," was slowly, distinctly read, "the fearful, the unbelieving, etc., shall have their part in the lake which burneth with fire and brimstone, which is the second death."

Henceforward, I knew what fate St. John feared for me.

A calm, subdued triumph, blent with a longing earnestness, marked his enunciation of the last glorious verses of that chapter. The reader believed his name was already written in the Lamb's book of life, and he yearned after the hour which should admit him to the city to which the kings of the earth bring their glory and honour; which has no need of sun or moon to shine in it, because the glory of God lightens it, and the Lamb is the light thereof.

In the prayer following the chapter, all his energy gathered—all his stern zeal woke: he was in deep earnest, wrestling with God, and resolved on a conquest. He supplicated strength for the weak-hearted; guidance for wanderers from the fold: a return, even at the eleventh hour, for those whom the temptations of the world and the flesh were luring from the narrow path. He asked, he urged, he claimed the boon of a brand snatched from the burning. Earnestness is ever deeply solemn: first, as I listened to that prayer, I wondered at his; then, when it continued and rose, I was touched by it, and at last awed. He felt the greatness and goodness of his purpose so sincerely: others who heard him plead for it, could not but feel it too.

The prayer over, we took leave of him: he was to go at a very early hour in the morning. Diana and Mary having kissed him, left the room—in compliance, I think, with a whispered hint from him: I tendered my hand, and wished him a pleasant journey.

"Thank you, Jane. As I said, I shall return from Cambridge in a fortnight: that space, then, is yet left you for reflection. If I listened to human pride, I should say no more to you of marriage with me; but I listen to my duty, and keep steadily in view my first aim—to do all things to the glory of God. My Master was long-suffering: so will I be. I cannot give you up to perdition as a vessel of wrath: repent—resolve, while there is yet time. Remember, we are bid to work while it is day—warned that 'the night cometh when no man shall work.' Remember the fate of Dives, who had his good things in this life. God give you strength to choose that better part which shall not be taken from you!"

He laid his hand on my head as he uttered the last words. He had spoken earnestly, mildly: his look was not, indeed, that of a lover beholding his mistress, but it was that of a pastor recalling his wandering sheep—or better, of a guardian angel watching the soul for which he is responsible. All men of talent, whether they be men of feeling or not; whether they be zealots, or aspirants, or despots—provided only they be sincere—have their sublime moments, when they subdue and rule. I felt veneration for St. John—veneration so strong that its impetus thrust me at once to the point I had so long shunned. I was tempted to cease struggling with him—to rush down the torrent of his will into the gulf of his existence, and there lose my own. I was almost as hard beset by him now as I had been once before, in a different way, by another. I was a fool both times. To have yielded then would have been an error of principle; to have yielded now would have been an error of judgment. So I think at this hour, when I look back to the crisis through the quiet medium of time: I was unconscious of folly at the instant.

I stood motionless under my hierophant's touch. My refusals were forgotten—my fears overcome—my wrestlings paralysed. The Impossible—i.e., my marriage with St. John—was fast becoming the Possible. All was changing utterly with a sudden sweep. Religion called—Angels beckoned—God commanded—life rolled together like a scroll—death's gates opening, showed eternity beyond: it seemed, that for safety and bliss there, all here might be sacrificed in a second. The dim room was full of visions.

"Could you decide now?" asked the missionary. The inquiry was put in gentle tones: he drew me to him as gently. Oh, that gentleness! How far more potent is it than force! I could resist St. John's wrath: I grew pliant as a reed under his kindness. Yet I knew all the time, if I yielded now, I should not the less be made to repent, some day, of my former rebellion. His nature was not changed by one hour of solemn prayer: it was only elevated.

"I could decide if I were but certain," I answered; "were I but convinced that it is God's will I should marry you, I could vow to marry you here and now—come afterwards what would!"

"My prayers are heard!" ejaculated St. John. He pressed his hand firmer on my head, as if he claimed me: he surrounded me with his arm, *almost* as if he loved me (I say *almost*—I knew the difference—for I had felt what it was to be loved; but, like him, I had now put love out of the question, and thought only of duty). I contended with my inward dimness of vision, before which clouds yet rolled. I sincerely, deeply, fervently longed to do what was right; and only that. "Show me, show me the path!" I entreated of Heaven. I was excited more than I had ever been; and whether what followed was the effect of excitement the reader shall judge.

All the house was still; for I believe all, except St. John and myself, were now retired to rest. The one candle was dying out: the room was full of moonlight. My heart beat fast and thick: I heard its throb. Suddenly it stood still to an inexpressible feeling that thrilled it through, and passed at once to my head and extremities. The feeling was not like an electric shock, but it was quite as sharp, as strange, as startling: it acted on my senses as if their utmost activity hitherto had been but torpor, from which they were now summoned and forced to wake. They rose expectant: eye and ear waited while the flesh quivered on my bones.

"What have you heard? What do you see?" asked St. John. I saw nothing, but I heard a voice somewhere cry—

"Jane! Jane! Jane!"—nothing more.

"O God! What is it?" I gasped.

I might have said, "Where is it?" for it did not seem in the room—nor in the house—nor in the garden; it did not come out of the air—nor from under the earth—nor from overhead. I had heard it—where, or whence, for ever impossible to know! And it was the voice of a human being—a known, loved, well-remembered voice—that of Edward Fairfax Rochester; and it spoke in pain and woe, wildly, eerily, urgently.

"I am coming!" I cried. "Wait for me! Oh, I will come!" I flew to the door and looked into the passage: it was dark. I ran out into the garden: it was void.

"Where are you?" I exclaimed.

The hills beyond Marsh Glen sent the answer faintly back: "Where are you?" I listened. The wind sighed low in the firs: all was moorland loneliness and midnight hush.

"Down superstition!" I commented, as that spectre rose up black by the black yew at the gate. "This is not thy deception, nor thy witchcraft: it is the work of nature. She was roused, and did—no miracle—but her best."

I broke from St. John, who had followed, and would have detained me. It was *my* time to assume ascendency. *My* powers were in play and in force. I told him to forbear question or remark; I desired him to leave me: I must and would be alone. He obeyed at once. Where there is energy to command well enough, obedience never fails. I mounted to my chamber; locked myself in; fell on my knees; and prayed in my way—a different way to St. John's, but effective in its own fashion. I seemed to penetrate very near a Mighty Spirit; and my soul rushed out in gratitude at His feet. I rose from the thanksgiving—took a resolve—and lay down, unscared, enlightened—eager but for the daylight.

CHAPTER XXXVI

The daylight came. I rose at dawn. I busied myself for an hour or two with arranging my things in my chamber, drawers, and wardrobe, in the order wherein I should wish to leave them during a brief absence. Meantime, I heard St. John quit his room. He stopped at my door: I feared he would knock—no, but a slip of paper was passed under the door. I took it up. It bore these words—

"You left me too suddenly last night. Had you stayed but a little longer, you would have laid your hand on the Christian's cross and the angel's crown. I shall expect your clear decision when I return this day fortnight. Meantime, watch and pray that you enter not into temptation: the spirit, I trust, is willing, but the flesh, I see, is weak. I shall pray for you hourly. Yours, St. John."

"My spirit," I answered mentally, "is willing to do what is right; and my flesh, I hope, is strong enough to accomplish the will of Heaven, when once that will is distinctly known to me. At any rate, it shall be strong enough to search—inquire—to grope an outlet from this cloud of doubt, and find the open day of certainty."

It was the first of June; yet the morning was overcast and chilly: rain beat fast on my casement. I heard the front-door open, and St. John pass out. Looking through the window, I saw him traverse the garden. He took the way over the misty moors in the direction of Whitcross—there he would meet the coach.

"In a few more hours I shall succeed you in that track, cousin," thought I. "I too have a coach to meet at Whitcross. I too have some to see and ask after in England, before I depart for ever."

It wanted yet two hours of breakfast-time. I filled the interval in walking softly about my room, and pondering the visitation which had given my plans their present bent. I recalled that inward sensation I had experienced: for I could recall it, with all its unspeakable strangeness. I recalled the voice I had heard; again I questioned whence it came, as vainly as before: it seemed in *me*—not in the external world. I asked was it a mere nervous impression—a delusion? I could not conceive or believe: it was more like an inspiration. The wondrous shock of feeling had come like the earthquake which shook the foundations of Paul and Silas's prison; it had opened the doors of the soul's cell and loosed its bands—it had wakened it out of its sleep, whence it sprang trembling, listening, aghast; then vibrated thrice a cry on my startled ear, and in my quaking heart and through my spirit, which neither feared nor shook, but exulted as if in joy over the success of one effort it had been privileged to make, independent of the cumbrous body.

"Ere many days," I said, as I terminated my musings, "I will know something of him whose voice seemed last night to summon me. Letters have proved of no avail—personal inquiry shall replace them."

At breakfast I announced to Diana and Mary that I was going a journey, and should be absent at least four days.

"Alone, Jane?" they asked.

"Yes; it was to see or hear news of a friend about whom I had for some time been uneasy."

They might have said, as I have no doubt they thought, that they had believed me to be without any friends save them: for, indeed, I had often said so; but, with their true natural delicacy, they abstained from comment, except that Diana asked me if I was sure I was well enough to travel. I looked very pale, she observed. I replied, that nothing ailed me save anxiety of mind, which I hoped soon to alleviate.

It was easy to make my further arrangements; for I was troubled with no inquiries—no surmises. Having once explained to them that I could not now be explicit about my plans, they kindly and wisely acquiesced in the silence with which I pursued them, according to me the privilege of free action I should under similar circumstances have accorded them.

I left Moor House at three o'clock p.m., and soon after four I stood at the foot of the sign-post of Whitcross, waiting the arrival of the coach which was to take me to distant Thornfield. Amidst the silence of those solitary roads and desert hills, I heard it approach from a great distance. It was the same vehicle whence, a year ago, I had alighted one summer evening on this very spot—how desolate, and hopeless, and objectless! It stopped as I beckoned. I entered—not now obliged to part with my whole fortune as the price of its accommodation. Once more on the road to Thornfield, I felt like the messenger-pigeon flying home.

It was a journey of six-and-thirty hours. I had set out from Whitcross on a Tuesday afternoon, and early on the succeeding Thursday morning the coach stopped to water the horses at a wayside inn, situated in the midst of scenery whose green hedges and large fields and low pastoral hills (how mild of feature and verdant of hue compared with the stern North-Midland moors of Morton!) met my eye like the lineaments of a once familiar face. Yes, I knew the character of this landscape: I was sure we were near my bourne.

"How far is Thornfield Hall from here?" I asked of the ostler.

"Just two miles, ma'am, across the fields."

"My journey is closed," I thought to myself. I got out of the coach, gave a box I had into the ostler's charge, to be kept till I called for it; paid my fare; satisfied the coachman, and was going: the brightening day gleamed on the sign of the inn, and I read in gilt letters, "The Rochester Arms." My heart leapt up: I was already on my master's very lands. It fell again: the thought struck it:

"Your master himself may be beyond the British Channel, for aught you know: and then, if he is at Thornfield Hall, towards which you hasten, who besides him is there? His lunatic wife: and you have nothing to do with him: you dare not speak to him or seek his presence. You have lost your labour—you had better go no farther," urged the monitor. "Ask information of the people at the inn; they can give you all you seek: they can solve your doubts at once. Go up to that man, and inquire if Mr. Rochester be at home."

The suggestion was sensible, and yet I could not force myself to act on it. I so dreaded a reply that would crush me with despair. To prolong doubt was to prolong hope. I might yet once more see the Hall under the ray of her star. There was the stile before me—the very fields through which I had hurried, blind, deaf, distracted with a revengeful fury tracking and scourging me, on the morning I fled from Thornfield: ere I well knew what course I had resolved to take, I was in the midst of them. How fast I walked! How I ran sometimes! How I looked forward to catch the first view of the well-known woods! With what feelings I welcomed single trees I knew, and familiar glimpses of meadow and hill between them!

At last the woods rose; the rookery clustered dark; a loud cawing broke the morning stillness. Strange delight inspired me: on I hastened. Another field crossed—a lane threaded—and there were the courtyard walls—the back offices: the house itself, the rookery still hid. "My first view of it shall be in front," I determined, "where its bold battlements will strike the eye nobly at once, and where I can single out my master's very window: perhaps he will be standing at it—he rises early: perhaps he is now walking in the orchard, or on the pavement in front. Could I but see him! But a moment! Surely, in that case, I should not be so mad as to run to him? I cannot tell—I am not certain. And if I did—what then? God bless him! What then? Who would be hurt by my once more tasting the life his glance can give me? I rave: perhaps at this moment he is watching the sun rise over the Pyrenees, or on the tideless sea of the south."

I had coasted along the lower wall of the orchard—turned its angle: there was a gate just there, opening into the meadow, between two stone pillars crowned by stone balls. From behind one pillar I could peep round quietly at the full front of the mansion. I advanced my head with precaution, desirous to ascertain if any bedroom window-blinds were yet drawn up: battlements, windows, long front—all from this sheltered station were at my command.

The crows sailing overhead perhaps watched me while I took this survey. I wonder what they thought. They must have considered I was very careful and timid at first, and that gradually I grew very bold and reckless. A peep, and then a long stare; and then a departure from my niche and a straying out into the meadow; and a sudden stop full in front of the great mansion, and a protracted, hardy gaze towards it. "What affectation of diffidence was this at first?" they might have demanded. "What stupid regardlessness now?"

Hear an illustration, reader.

A lover finds his mistress asleep on a mossy bank; he wishes to catch a glimpse of her fair face without waking her. He steals softly over the grass, careful to make no sound; he pauses—fancying she has stirred: he withdraws: not for worlds would he be seen. All is still: he again advances: he bends above her; a light veil rests on her features: he lifts it, bends lower; now his eyes anticipate the vision of beauty—warm, and blooming, and lovely, in rest. How hurried was their first glance! But how they fix! How he starts! How he suddenly and vehemently clasps in both arms the form he dared not, a moment since, touch with his finger! How he calls aloud a name, and drops his burden, and gazes on it wildly! He thus grasps and cries, and gazes, because he no longer fears to waken by any sound he can utter—by any movement he can make. He thought his love slept sweetly: he finds she is stone dead.

I looked with timorous joy towards a stately house: I saw a blackened ruin.

No need to cower behind a gate-post, indeed! To peep up at chamber lattices, fearing life was astir behind them! No need to listen for doors opening—to fancy steps on the pavement or the gravel-walk! The lawn, the grounds were trodden and waste: the portal yawned void. The front was, as I had once seen it in a dream, but a well-like wall, very high and very fragile-looking, perforated with paneless windows: no roof, no battlements, no chimneys—all had crashed in.

And there was the silence of death about it: the solitude of a lonesome wild. No wonder that letters addressed to people here had never received an answer: as well despatch epistles to a vault in a church aisle. The grim blackness of the stones told by what fate the Hall had fallen—by conflagration: but how kindled? What story belonged to this disaster? What loss, besides mortar and marble and wood-work had followed upon it? Had life been wrecked as well as property? If so, whose? Dreadful question: there was no one here to answer it—not even dumb sign, mute token.

In wandering round the shattered walls and through the devastated interior, I gathered evidence that the calamity was not of late occurrence. Winter snows, I thought, had drifted through that void arch, winter rains beaten in at those hollow casements; for, amidst the drenched piles of rubbish, spring had cherished vegetation: grass and weed grew here and there between the stones and fallen rafters. And oh! Where meantime was the hapless owner of this wreck? In what land? Under what auspices? My eye involuntarily wandered to the grey church tower near the gates, and I asked, "Is he with Damer de Rochester, sharing the shelter of his narrow marble house?"

Some answer must be had to these questions. I could find it nowhere but at the inn, and thither, ere long, I returned. The host himself brought my breakfast into the parlour. I requested him to shut the door and sit down: I had some questions to ask him. But when he complied, I scarcely knew how to begin; such horror had I of the possible answers. And yet the spectacle of desolation I had just left prepared me in a measure for a tale of misery. The host was a respectable-looking, middle-aged man.

"You know Thornfield Hall, of course?" I managed to say at last.

"Yes, ma'am; I lived there once."

"Did you?" Not in my time, I thought: you are a stranger to me.

"I was the late Mr. Rochester's butler," he added.

The late! I seem to have received, with full force, the blow I had been trying to evade.

"The late!" I gasped. "Is he dead?"

"I mean the present gentleman, Mr. Edward's father," he explained. I breathed again: my blood resumed its flow. Fully assured by these words that Mr. Edward—*my* Mr. Rochester (God bless him, wherever he was!)—was at least alive: was, in short, "the present gentleman." Gladdening words! It seemed I could hear all that was to come—whatever the disclosures might be—with comparative tranquillity. Since he was not in the grave, I could bear, I thought, to learn that he was at the Antipodes.

"Is Mr. Rochester living at Thornfield Hall now?" I asked, knowing, of course, what the answer would be, but yet desirous of deferring the direct question as to where he really was.

"No, ma'am—oh, no! No one is living there. I suppose you are a stranger in these parts, or you would have heard what happened last autumn—Thornfield Hall is quite a ruin: it was burnt down just about harvest-time. A dreadful calamity! Such an immense quantity of valuable property destroyed: hardly any of the furniture could be saved. The fire broke out at dead of night, and before the engines arrived from Millcote, the building was one mass of flame. It was a terrible spectacle: I witnessed it myself."

"At dead of night!" I muttered. Yes, that was ever the hour of fatality at Thornfield. "Was it known how it originated?" I demanded.

"They guessed, ma'am: they guessed. Indeed, I should say it was ascertained beyond a doubt. You are not perhaps aware," he continued, edging his chair a little nearer the table, and speaking low, "that there was a lady—a—a lunatic, kept in the house?"

"I have heard something of it."

"She was kept in very close confinement, ma'am: people even for some years was not absolutely certain of her existence. No one saw her: they only knew by rumour that such a person was at the Hall; and who or what she was it was difficult to conjecture. They said Mr. Edward had brought her from abroad, and some believed she had been his mistress. But a queer thing happened a year since—a very queer thing."

I feared now to hear my own story. I endeavoured to recall him to the main fact.

"And this lady?"

"This lady, ma'am," he answered, "turned out to be Mr. Rochester's wife! The discovery was brought about in the strangest way. There was a young lady, a governess at the Hall, that Mr. Rochester fell in—"

"But the fire," I suggested.

"I'm coming to that, ma'am—that Mr. Edward fell in love with. The servants say they never saw anybody so much in love as he was: he was after her continually. They used to watch him—servants will, you know, ma'am—and he set store on her past everything: for all, nobody but him thought her so very handsome. She was a little small thing, they say, almost like a child. I never saw her myself; but I've heard Leah, the house-maid, tell of her. Leah liked her well enough. Mr. Rochester was about forty, and this governess not twenty; and you see, when gentlemen of his age fall in love with girls, they are often like as if they were bewitched. Well, he would marry her."

"You shall tell me this part of the story another time," I said; "but now I have a particular reason for wishing to hear all about the fire. Was it suspected that this lunatic, Mrs. Rochester, had any hand in it?"

"You've hit it, ma'am: it's quite certain that it was her, and nobody but her, that set it going. She had a woman to take care of her called Mrs. Poole—an able woman in her line, and very trustworthy, but for one fault—a fault common to a deal of them nurses and matrons—she *kept a private bottle of gin by her*, and now and then took a drop over-much. It is excusable, for she had a hard life of it: but still it was dangerous; for when Mrs. Poole was fast asleep after the gin and water, the mad lady, who was as cunning as a witch, would take the keys out of her pocket, let herself out of her chamber, and go roaming about the house, doing any wild mischief that came into her head. They say she had nearly burnt her husband in his bed once: but I don't know about that. However, on this night, she set fire first to the hangings of the room next her own, and then she got down to a lower storey, and made her way to the chamber that had been the governess's—(she was like as if she knew somehow how matters had gone on, and had a spite at her)—and she kindled the bed there; but there was nobody sleeping in it, fortunately. The governess had run away two months before; and for all Mr. Rochester sought her as if she had been the most precious thing he had in the world, he never could hear a word of her; and he grew savage—quite savage on his disappointment: he never was a wild man, but he got dangerous after he lost her. He would be alone, too. He sent Mrs. Fairfax, the housekeeper, away to her friends at a distance; but he did it handsomely, for he settled an annuity on her for life: and she deserved it—she was a very good woman. Miss Adèle, a ward he had, was put to school. He broke off acquaintance with all the gentry, and shut himself up like a hermit at the Hall."

"What! Did he not leave England?"

"Leave England? Bless you, no! He would not cross the door-stones of the house, except at night, when he walked just like a ghost about the grounds and in the orchard as if he had lost his senses—which it is my opinion he had; for a more spirited, bolder, keener gentleman than he was before that midge of a governess crossed him, you never saw, ma'am. He was not a man given to wine, or cards, or racing, as some are, and he was not so very handsome; but he had a courage and a will of his own, if ever man had. I knew him from a boy, you see: and for my part, I have often wished that Miss Eyre had been sunk in the sea before she came to Thornfield Hall."

"Then Mr. Rochester was at home when the fire broke out?"

"Yes, indeed was he; and he went up to the attics when all was burning above and below, and got the servants out of their beds and helped them down himself, and went back to get his mad wife out of her cell. And then they called out to him that she was on the roof, where she was standing, waving her arms, above the battlements, and shouting out till they could hear her a mile off: I saw her and heard her with my own eyes. She was a big woman, and had long black hair: we could see it streaming against the flames as she stood. I witnessed, and several more witnessed, Mr. Rochester ascend through the sky-light on to the roof; we heard him call 'Bertha!' We saw him approach her; and then, ma'am, she yelled and gave a spring, and the next minute she lay smashed on the pavement."

"Dead?"

"Dead! Ay, dead as the stones on which her brains and blood were scattered."

"Good God!"

"You may well say so, ma'am: it was frightful!"

He shuddered.

"And afterwards?" I urged.

"Well, ma'am, afterwards the house was burnt to the ground: there are only some bits of walls standing now."

"Were any other lives lost?"

"No—perhaps it would have been better if there had."

"What do you mean?"

"Poor Mr. Edward!" he ejaculated. "I little thought ever to have seen it! Some say it was a just judgment on him for keeping his first marriage secret, and wanting to take another wife while he had one living: but I pity him, for my part."

"You said he was alive?" I exclaimed.

"Yes, yes: he is alive; but many think he had better be dead."

"Why? How?" My blood was again running cold. "Where is he?" I demanded. "Is he in England?"

"Ay—ay—he's in England; he can't get out of England, I fancy—he's a fixture now."

What agony was this! And the man seemed resolved to protract it.

"He is stone-blind," he said at last. "Yes, he is stone-blind, is Mr. Edward."

I had dreaded worse. I had dreaded he was mad. I summoned strength to ask what had caused this calamity.

"It was all his own courage, and a body may say, his kindness, in a way, ma'am: he wouldn't leave the house till every one else was out before him. As he came down the great staircase at last, after Mrs. Rochester had flung herself from the battlements, there was a great crash—all fell. He was taken out from under the ruins, alive, but sadly hurt: a beam had fallen in such a way as to protect him partly; but one eye was knocked out, and one hand so crushed that Mr. Carter, the surgeon, had to amputate it directly. The other eye inflamed: he lost the sight of that also. He is now helpless, indeed—blind and a cripple."

"Where is he? Where does he now live?"

"At Ferndean, a manor-house on a farm he has, about thirty miles off: quite a desolate spot."

"Who is with him?"

"Old John and his wife: he would have none else. He is quite broken down, they say."

"Have you any sort of conveyance?"

"We have a chaise, ma'am, a very handsome chaise."

"Let it be got ready instantly; and if your post-boy can drive me to Ferndean before dark this day, I'll pay both you and him twice the hire you usually demand."

CHAPTER XXXVII

The manor-house of Ferndean was a building of considerable antiquity, moderate size, and no architectural pretensions, deep buried in a wood. I had heard of it before. Mr. Rochester often spoke of it, and sometimes went there. His father had purchased the estate for the sake of the game covers. He would have let the house, but could find no tenant, in consequence of its ineligible and insalubrious site. Ferndean then remained uninhabited and unfurnished, with the exception of some two or three rooms fitted up for the accommodation of the squire when he went there in the season to shoot.

To this house I came just ere dark on an evening marked by the characteristics of sad sky, cold gale, and continued small penetrating rain. The last mile I performed on foot, having dismissed the chaise and driver with the double remuneration I had promised. Even when within a very short distance of the manor-house, you could see nothing of it, so thick and dark grew the timber of the gloomy wood about it. Iron gates between granite pillars showed me where to enter, and passing through them, I found myself at once in the twilight of close-ranked trees. There was a grass-grown track descending the forest aisle between hoar and knotty shafts and under branched arches. I followed it, expecting soon to reach the dwelling; but it stretched on and on, it would far and farther: no sign of habitation or grounds was visible.

I thought I had taken a wrong direction and lost my way. The darkness of natural as well as of sylvan dusk gathered over me. I looked round in search of another road. There was none: all was interwoven stem, columnar trunk, dense summer foliage—no opening anywhere.

I proceeded: at last my way opened, the trees thinned a little; presently I beheld a railing, then the house—scarce, by this dim light, distinguishable from the trees; so dank and green were its decaying walls. Entering a portal, fastened only by a latch, I stood amidst a space of enclosed ground, from which the wood swept away in a semicircle. There were no flowers, no garden-beds; only a broad gravel-walk girdling a grass-plat, and this set in the heavy frame of the forest. The house presented two pointed gables in its front; the windows were latticed and narrow: the front door was narrow too, one step led up to it. The whole looked, as the host of the Rochester Arms had said, "quite a desolate spot." It was as still as a church on a week-day: the pattering rain on the forest leaves was the only sound audible in its vicinage.

"Can there be life here?" I asked.

Yes, life of some kind there was; for I heard a movement—that narrow front-door was unclosing, and some shape was about to issue from the grange.

It opened slowly: a figure came out into the twilight and stood on the step; a man without a hat: he stretched forth his hand as if to feel whether it rained. Dusk as it was, I had recognised him—it was my master, Edward Fairfax Rochester, and no other.

I stayed my step, almost my breath, and stood to watch him—to examine him, myself unseen, and alas! To him invisible. It was a sudden meeting, and one in which rapture was kept well in check by pain. I had no difficulty in restraining my voice from exclamation, my step from hasty advance.

His form was of the same strong and stalwart contour as ever: his port was still erect, his hair was still raven black; nor were his features altered or sunk: not in one year's space, by any sorrow, could his athletic strength be quelled or his vigorous prime blighted. But in his countenance I saw a change: that looked desperate and brooding—that reminded me of some wronged and fettered wild beast or bird, dangerous to approach in his sullen woe. The caged eagle, whose gold-ringed eyes cruelty has extinguished, might look as looked that sightless Samson.

And, reader, do you think I feared him in his blind ferocity? If you do, you little know me. A soft hope blest with my sorrow that soon I should dare to drop a kiss on that brow of rock, and on those lips so sternly sealed beneath it: but not yet. I would not accost him yet.

He descended the one step, and advanced slowly and gropingly towards the grass-plat. Where was his daring stride now? Then he paused, as if he knew not which way to turn. He lifted his hand and opened his eyelids; gazed blank, and with a straining effort, on the sky, and toward the amphitheatre of trees: one saw that all to him was void darkness. He stretched his right hand (the left arm, the mutilated one, he kept hidden in his bosom); he seemed to wish by touch to gain an idea of what lay around him: he met but vacancy still; for the trees were some yards off where he stood. He relinquished the endeavour, folded his arms, and stood quiet and mute in the rain, now falling fast on his uncovered head. At this moment John approached him from some quarter.

"Will you take my arm, sir?" he said. "There is a heavy shower coming on: had you not better go in?"

"Let me alone," was the answer.

John withdrew without having observed me. Mr. Rochester now tried to walk about: vainly—all was too uncertain. He groped his way back to the house, and, re-entering it, closed the door.

I now drew near and knocked: John's wife opened for me. "Mary," I said, "how are you?"

She started as if she had seen a ghost: I calmed her. To her hurried "Is it really you, miss, come at this late hour to this lonely place?" I answered by taking her hand; and then I followed her into the kitchen, where John now sat by a good fire. I explained to them, in few words, that I had heard all which had happened since I left Thornfield, and that I was come to see Mr. Rochester. I asked John to go down to the turnpike-house, where I had dismissed the chaise, and bring my trunk, which I had left there: and then, while I removed my bonnet and shawl, I questioned Mary as to whether I could be accommodated at the Manor House for the night; and finding that arrangements to that effect, though difficult, would not be impossible, I informed her I should stay. Just at this moment the parlour-bell rang.

"When you go in," said I, "tell your master that a person wishes to speak to him, but do not give my name."

"I don't think he will see you," she answered; "he refuses everybody."

When she returned, I inquired what he had said. "You are to send in your name and your business," she replied. She then proceeded to fill a glass with water, and place it on a tray, together with candles.

"Is that what he rang for?" I asked.

"Yes: he always has candles brought in at dark, though he is blind."

"Give the tray to me; I will carry it in."

I took it from her hand: she pointed me out the parlour door. The tray shook as I held it; the water spilt from the glass; my heart struck my ribs loud and fast. Mary opened the door for me, and shut it behind me.

This parlour looked gloomy: a neglected handful of fire burnt low in the grate; and, leaning over it, with his head supported against the high, old-fashioned mantelpiece, appeared the blind tenant of the room. His old dog, Pilot, lay on one side, removed out of the way, and coiled up as if afraid of being inadvertently trodden upon. Pilot pricked up his ears when I came in: then he jumped up with a yelp and a whine, and bounded towards me: he almost knocked the tray from my hands. I set it on the table; then patted him, and said softly, "Lie down!" Mr. Rochester turned mechanically to *see* what the commotion was: but as he *saw* nothing, he returned and sighed.

"Give me the water, Mary," he said.

I approached him with the now only half-filled glass; Pilot followed me, still excited.

"What is the matter?" he inquired.

"Down, Pilot!" I again said. He checked the water on its way to his lips, and seemed to listen: he drank, and put the glass down. "This is you, Mary, is it not?"

"Mary is in the kitchen," I answered.

He put out his hand with a quick gesture, but not seeing where I stood, he did not touch me. "Who is this? Who is this?" he demanded, trying, as it seemed, to *see* with those sightless eyes—unavailing and distressing attempt! "Answer me—speak again!" he ordered, imperiously and aloud.

"Will you have a little more water, sir? I spilt half of what was in the glass," I said.

"*Who* is it? *What* is it? Who speaks?"

"Pilot knows me, and John and Mary know I am here. I came only this evening," I answered.

"Great God! What delusion has come over me? What sweet madness has seized me?"

"No delusion—no madness: your mind, sir, is too strong for delusion, your health too sound for frenzy."

"And where is the speaker? Is it only a voice? Oh! I *cannot* see, but I must feel, or my heart will stop and my brain burst. Whatever—whoever you are—be perceptible to the touch or I cannot live!"

He groped; I arrested his wandering hand, and prisoned it in both mine.

"Her very fingers!" he cried. "Her small, slight fingers! If so there must be more of her."

The muscular hand broke from my custody; my arm was seized, my shoulder—neck—waist—I was entwined and gathered to him.

"Is it Jane? *What* is it? This is her shape—this is her size—"

"And this her voice," I added. "She is all here: her heart, too. God bless you, sir! I am glad to be so near you again."

"Jane Eyre! Jane Eyre," was all he said.

"My dear master," I answered, "I am Jane Eyre: I have found you out—I am come back to you."

"In truth? In the flesh? My living Jane?"

"You touch me, sir—you hold me, and fast enough: I am not cold like a corpse, nor vacant like air, am I?"

"My living darling! These are certainly her limbs, and these her features; but I cannot be so blest, after all my misery. It is a dream; such dreams as I have had at night when I have clasped her once more to my heart, as I do now; and kissed her, as thus—and felt that she loved me, and trusted that she would not leave me."

"Which I never will, sir, from this day."

"Never will, says the vision? But I always woke and found it an empty mockery; and I was desolate and abandoned—my life dark, lonely, hopeless—my soul athirst and forbidden to drink—my heart famished and never to be fed. Gentle, soft dream, nestling in my arms now, you will fly, too, as your sisters have all fled before you: but kiss me before you go—embrace me, Jane."

"There, sir—and there!"

I pressed my lips to his once brilliant and now rayless eyes—I swept his hair from his brow, and kissed that too. He suddenly seemed to arouse himself: the conviction of the reality of all this seized him.

"It is you—is it, Jane? You are come back to me then?"

"I am."

"And you do not lie dead in some ditch under some stream? And you are not a pining outcast amongst strangers?"

"No, sir! I am an independent woman now."

"Independent! What do you mean, Jane?"

"My uncle in Madeira is dead, and he left me five thousand pounds."

"Ah! This is practical—this is real!" he cried. "I should never dream that. Besides, there is that peculiar voice of hers, so animating and piquant, as well as soft: it cheers my withered heart; it puts life into it. What, Janet! Are you an independent woman? A rich woman?"

"If you won't let me live with you, I can build a house of my own close up to your door, and you may come and sit in my parlour when you want company of an evening."

"But as you are rich, Jane, you have now, no doubt, friends who will look after you, and not suffer you to devote yourself to a blind lameter like me?"

"I told you I am independent, sir, as well as rich: I am my own mistress."

"And you will stay with me?"

"Certainly—unless you object. I will be your neighbour, your nurse, your housekeeper. I find you lonely: I will be your companion—to read to you, to walk with you, to sit with you, to wait on you, to be eyes and hands to you. Cease to look so melancholy, my dear master; you shall not be left desolate, so long as I live."

He replied not: he seemed serious—abstracted; he sighed; he half-opened his lips as if to speak: he closed them again. I felt a little embarrassed. Perhaps I had too rashly over-leaped conventionalities; and he, like St. John, saw impropriety in my inconsiderateness. I had indeed made my proposal from the idea that he wished and would ask me to be his wife: an expectation, not the less certain because unexpressed, had buoyed me up, that he would claim me at once as his own. But no hint to that effect escaping him and his countenance becoming more overcast, I suddenly remembered that I might have been all wrong, and was perhaps playing the fool unwittingly; and I began gently to withdraw myself from his arms—but he eagerly snatched me closer.

"No—no—Jane; you must not go. No—I have touched you, heard you, felt the comfort of your presence—the sweetness of your consolation: I cannot give up these joys. I have little left in myself—I must have you. The world may laugh—may call me absurd, selfish—but it does not signify. My very soul demands you: it will be satisfied, or it will take deadly vengeance on its frame."

"Well, sir, I will stay with you: I have said so."

"Yes—but you understand one thing by staying with me; and I understand another. You, perhaps, could make up your mind to be about my hand and chair—to wait on me as a kind little nurse (for you have an affectionate heart and a generous spirit, which prompt you to make sacrifices for those you pity), and that ought to suffice for me no doubt. I suppose I should now entertain none but fatherly feelings for you: do you think so? Come—tell me."

"I will think what you like, sir: I am content to be only your nurse, if you think it better."

"But you cannot always be my nurse, Janet: you are young—you must marry one day."

"I don't care about being married."

"You should care, Janet: if I were what I once was, I would try to make you care—but—a sightless block!"

He relapsed again into gloom. I, on the contrary, became more cheerful, and took fresh courage: these last words gave me an insight as to where the difficulty lay; and as it was no difficulty with me, I felt quite relieved from my previous embarrassment. I resumed a livelier vein of conversation.

"It is time some one undertook to rehumanise you," said I, parting his thick and long uncut locks; "for I see you are being metamorphosed into a lion, or something of that sort. You have a 'faux air' of Nebuchadnezzar in the fields about you, that is certain: your hair reminds me of eagles' feathers; whether your nails are grown like birds' claws or not, I have not yet noticed."

"On this arm, I have neither hand nor nails," he said, drawing the mutilated limb from his breast, and showing it to me. "It is a mere stump—a ghastly sight! Don't you think so, Jane?"

"It is a pity to see it; and a pity to see your eyes—and the scar of fire on your forehead: and the worst of it is, one is in danger of loving you too well for all this; and making too much of you."

"I thought you would be revolted, Jane, when you saw my arm, and my cicatrised visage."

"Did you? Don't tell me so—lest I should say something disparaging to your judgment. Now, let me leave you an instant, to make a better fire, and have the hearth swept up. Can you tell when there is a good fire?"

"Yes; with the right eye I see a glow—a ruddy haze."

"And you see the candles?"

"Very dimly—each is a luminous cloud."

"Can you see me?"

"No, my fairy: but I am only too thankful to hear and feel you."

"When do you take supper?"

"I never take supper."

"But you shall have some tonight. I am hungry: so are you, I daresay, only you forget."

Summoning Mary, I soon had the room in more cheerful order: I prepared him, likewise, a comfortable repast. My spirits were excited, and with pleasure and ease I talked to him during supper, and for a long time after. There was no harassing restraint, no repressing of glee and vivacity with him; for with him I was at perfect ease, because I knew I suited him; all I said or did seemed either to console or revive him. Delightful consciousness! It brought to life and light my whole nature: in his presence I thoroughly lived; and he lived in mine. Blind as he was, smiles played over his face, joy dawned on his forehead: his lineaments softened and warmed.

After supper, he began to ask me many questions, of where I had been, what I had been doing, how I had found him out; but I gave him only very partial replies: it was too late to enter into particulars that night. Besides, I wished to touch no deep-thrilling chord—to open no fresh well of emotion in his heart: my sole present aim was to cheer him. Cheered, as I have said, he was: and yet but by fits. If a moment's silence broke the conversation, he would turn restless, touch me, then say, "Jane."

"You are altogether a human being, Jane? You are certain of that?"

"I conscientiously believe so, Mr. Rochester."

"Yet how, on this dark and doleful evening, could you so suddenly rise on my lone hearth? I stretched my hand to take a glass of water from a hireling, and it was given me by you: I asked a question, expecting John's wife to answer me, and your voice spoke at my ear."

"Because I had come in, in Mary's stead, with the tray."

"And there is enchantment in the very hour I am now spending with you. Who can tell what a dark, dreary, hopeless life I have dragged on for months past? Doing nothing, expecting nothing; merging night in day; feeling but the sensation of cold when I let the fire go out, of hunger when I forgot to eat: and then a ceaseless sorrow, and, at times, a very delirium of desire to behold my Jane again. Yes: for her restoration I longed, far more than for that of my lost sight. How can it be that Jane is with me, and says she loves me? Will she not depart as suddenly as she came? Tomorrow, I fear I shall find her no more."

A commonplace, practical reply, out of the train of his own disturbed ideas, was, I was sure, the best and most reassuring for him in this frame of mind. I passed my finger over his eyebrows, and remarked that they were scorched, and that I would apply something which would make them grow as broad and black as ever.

"Where is the use of doing me good in any way, beneficent spirit, when, at some fatal moment, you will again desert me—passing like a shadow, whither and how to me unknown, and for me remaining afterwards undiscoverable?"

"Have you a pocket-comb about you, sir?"

"What for, Jane?"

"Just to comb out this shaggy black mane. I find you rather alarming, when I examine you close at hand: you talk of my being a fairy, but I am sure, you are more like a brownie."

"Am I hideous, Jane?"

"Very, sir: you always were, you know."

"Humph! The wickedness has not been taken out of you, wherever you have sojourned."

"Yet I have been with good people; far better than you: a hundred times better people; possessed of ideas and views you never entertained in your life: quite more refined and exalted."

"Who the deuce have you been with?"

"If you twist in that way you will make me pull the hair out of your head; and then I think you will cease to entertain doubts of my substantiality."

"Who have you been with, Jane?"

"You shall not get it out of me tonight, sir; you must wait till tomorrow; to leave my tale half told, will, you know, be a sort of security that I shall appear at your breakfast table to finish it. By-the-by, I must mind not to rise on your hearth with only a glass of water then: I must bring an egg at the least, to say nothing of fried ham."

"You mocking changeling—fairy-born and human-bred! You make me feel as I have not felt these twelve months. If Saul could have had you for his David, the evil spirit would have been exorcised without the aid of the harp."

"There, sir, you are redd up and made decent. Now I'll leave you: I have been travelling these last three days, and I believe I am tired. Good night."

"Just one word, Jane: were there only ladies in the house where you have been?"

I laughed and made my escape, still laughing as I ran upstairs. "A good idea!" I thought with glee. "I see I have the means of fretting him out of his melancholy for some time to come."

Very early the next morning I heard him up and astir, wandering from one room to another. As soon as Mary came down I heard the question: "Is Miss Eyre here?" Then: "Which room did you put her into? Was it dry? Is she up? Go and ask if she wants anything; and when she will come down."

I came down as soon as I thought there was a prospect of breakfast. Entering the room very softly, I had a view of him before he discovered my presence. It was mournful, indeed, to witness the subjugation of that vigorous spirit to a corporeal infirmity. He sat in his chair—still, but not at rest: expectant evidently; the lines of now habitual sadness marking his strong features. His countenance reminded one of a lamp quenched, waiting to be re-lit—and alas! It was not himself that could now kindle the lustre of animated expression: he was dependent on another for that office! I had meant to be gay and careless, but the powerlessness of the strong man touched my heart to the quick: still I accosted him with what vivacity I could.

"It is a bright, sunny morning, sir," I said. "The rain is over and gone, and there is a tender shining after it: you shall have a walk soon."

I had wakened the glow: his features beamed.

"Oh, you are indeed there, my skylark! Come to me. You are not gone: not vanished? I heard one of your kind an hour ago, singing high over the wood: but its song had no music for me, any more than the rising sun had rays. All the melody on earth is concentrated in my Jane's tongue to my ear (I am glad it is not naturally a silent one): all the sunshine I can feel is in her presence."

The water stood in my eyes to hear this avowal of his dependence; just as if a royal eagle, chained to a perch, should be forced to entreat a sparrow to become its purveyor. But I would not be lachrymose: I dashed off the salt drops, and busied myself with preparing breakfast.

Most of the morning was spent in the open air. I led him out of the wet and wild wood into some cheerful fields: I described to him how brilliantly green they were; how the flowers and hedges looked refreshed; how sparklingly blue was the sky. I sought a seat for him in a hidden and lovely spot, a dry stump of a tree; nor did I refuse to let him, when seated, place me on his knee. Why should I, when both he and I were happier near than apart? Pilot lay beside us: all was quiet. He broke out suddenly while clasping me in his arms—

"Cruel, cruel deserter! Oh, Jane, what did I feel when I discovered you had fled from Thornfield, and when I could nowhere find you; and, after examining your apartment, ascertained that you had taken no money, nor anything which could serve as an equivalent! A pearl necklace I had given you lay untouched in its little casket; your trunks were left corded and locked as they had been prepared for the bridal tour. What could my darling do, I asked, left destitute and penniless? And what did she do? Let me hear now."

Thus urged, I began the narrative of my experience for the last year. I softened considerably what related to the three days of wandering and starvation, because to have told him all would have been to inflict unnecessary pain: the little I did say lacerated his faithful heart deeper than I wished.

I should not have left him thus, he said, without any means of making my way: I should have told him my intention. I should have confided in him: he would never have forced me to be his mistress. Violent as he had seemed in his despair, he, in truth, loved me far too well and too tenderly to constitute himself my tyrant: he would have given me half his fortune, without demanding so much as a kiss in return, rather than I should have flung myself friendless on the wide world. I had endured, he was certain, more than I had confessed to him.

"Well, whatever my sufferings had been, they were very short," I answered: and then I proceeded to tell him how I had been received at Moor House; how I had obtained the office of schoolmistress, etc. The accession of fortune, the discovery of my relations, followed in due order. Of course, St. John Rivers' name came in frequently in the progress of my tale. When I had done, that name was immediately taken up.

"This St. John, then, is your cousin?"

"Yes."

"You have spoken of him often: do you like him?"

"He was a very good man, sir; I could not help liking him."

"A good man. Does that mean a respectable well-conducted man of fifty? Or what does it mean?"

"St. John was only twenty-nine, sir."

" '*Jeune encore*,' as the French say. Is he a person of low stature, phlegmatic, and plain? A person whose goodness consists rather in his guiltlessness of vice, than in his prowess in virtue?"

"He is untiringly active. Great and exalted deeds are what he lives to perform."

"But his brain? That is probably rather soft? He means well: but you shrug your shoulders to hear him talk?"

"He talks little, sir: what he does say is ever to the point. His brain is first-rate, I should think not impressible, but vigorous."

"Is he an able man, then?"

"Truly able."

"A thoroughly educated man?"

"St. John is an accomplished and profound scholar."

"His manners, I think, you said are not to your taste? Priggish and parsonic?"

"I never mentioned his manners; but, unless I had a very bad taste, they must suit it; they are polished, calm, and gentlemanlike."

"His appearance—I forget what description you gave of his appearance—a sort of raw curate, half strangled with his white neckcloth, and stilted up on his thick-soled high-lows, eh?"

"St. John dresses well. He is a handsome man: tall, fair, with blue eyes, and a Grecian profile."

(Aside.) "Damn him!" (To me.) "Did you like him, Jane?"

"Yes, Mr. Rochester, I liked him: but you asked me that before."

I perceived, of course, the drift of my interlocutor. Jealousy had got hold of him: she stung him; but the sting was salutary: it gave him respite from the gnawing fang of melancholy. I would not, therefore, immediately charm the snake.

"Perhaps you would rather not sit any longer on my knee, Miss Eyre?" was the next somewhat unexpected observation.

"Why not, Mr. Rochester?"

"The picture you have just drawn is suggestive of a rather too overwhelming contrast. Your words have delineated very prettily a graceful Apollo: he is present to your imagination—tall, fair, blue-eyed, and with a Grecian profile. Your eyes dwell on a Vulcan—a real blacksmith, brown, broad-shouldered: and blind and lame into the bargain."

"I never thought of it, before; but you certainly are rather like Vulcan, sir."

"Well, you can leave me, ma'am: but before you go" (and he retained me by a firmer grasp than ever), "you will be pleased just to answer me a question or two." He paused.

"What questions, Mr. Rochester?"

Then followed this cross-examination.

"St. John made you schoolmistress of Morton before he knew you were his cousin?"

"Yes."

"You would often see him? He would visit the school sometimes?"

"Daily."

"He would approve of your plans, Jane? I know they would be clever, for you are a talented creature!"

"He approved of them—yes."

"He would discover many things in you he could not have expected to find? Some of your accomplishments are not ordinary."

"I don't know about that."

"You had a little cottage near the school, you say: did he ever come there to see you?"

"Now and then?"

"Of an evening?"

"Once or twice."

A pause.

"How long did you reside with him and his sisters after the cousinship was discovered?"

"Five months."

"Did Rivers spend much time with the ladies of his family?"

"Yes; the back parlour was both his study and ours: he sat near the window, and we by the table."

"Did he study much?"

"A good deal."

"What?"

"Hindostanee."

"And what did you do meantime?"

"I learnt German, at first."

"Did he teach you?"

"He did not understand German."

"Did he teach you nothing?"

"A little Hindostanee."

"Rivers taught you Hindostanee?"

"Yes, sir."

"And his sisters also?"

"No."

"Only you?"

"Only me."

"Did you ask to learn?"

"No."

"He wished to teach you?"

"Yes."

A second pause.

"Why did he wish it? Of what use could Hindostanee be to you?"

"He intended me to go with him to India."

"Ah! Here I reach the root of the matter. He wanted you to marry him?"

"He asked me to marry him."

"That is a fiction—an impudent invention to vex me."

"I beg your pardon, it is the literal truth: he asked me more than once, and was as stiff about urging his point as ever you could be."

"Miss Eyre, I repeat it, you can leave me. How often am I to say the same thing? Why do you remain pertinaciously perched on my knee, when I have given you notice to quit?"

"Because I am comfortable there."

"No, Jane, you are not comfortable there, because your heart is not with me: it is with this cousin—this St. John. Oh, till this moment, I thought my little Jane was all mine! I had a belief she loved me even when she left me: that was an atom of sweet in much bitter. Long as we have been parted, hot tears as I have wept over our separation, I never thought that while I was mourning her, she was loving another! But it is useless grieving. Jane, leave me: go and marry Rivers."

"Shake me off, then, sir—push me away, for I'll not leave you of my own accord."

"Jane, I ever like your tone of voice: it still renews hope, it sounds so truthful. When I hear it, it carries me back a year. I forget that you have formed a new tie. But I am not a fool—go—"

"Where must I go, sir?"

"Your own way—with the husband you have chosen."

"Who is that?"

"You know—this St. John Rivers."

"He is not my husband, nor ever will be. He does not love me: I do not love him. He loves (as he *can* love, and that is not as you love) a beautiful young lady called Rosamond. He wanted to marry me only because he thought I should make a suitable missionary's wife, which she would not have done. He is good and great, but severe; and, for me, cold as an iceberg. He is not like you, sir: I am not happy at his side, nor near him, nor with him. He has no indulgence for me—no fondness. He sees nothing attractive in me; not even youth—only a few useful mental points. Then I must leave you, sir, to go to him?"

I shuddered involuntarily, and clung instinctively closer to my blind but beloved master. He smiled.

"What, Jane! Is this true? Is such really the state of matters between you and Rivers?"

"Absolutely, sir! Oh, you need not be jealous! I wanted to tease you a little to make you less sad: I thought anger would be better than grief. But if you wish me to love you, could you but see how much I *do* love you, you would be proud and content. All my heart is yours, sir: it belongs to you; and with you it would remain, were fate to exile the rest of me from your presence for ever."

Again, as he kissed me, painful thoughts darkened his aspect.

"My seared vision! My crippled strength!" he murmured regretfully.

I caressed, in order to soothe him. I knew of what he was thinking, and wanted to speak for him, but dared not. As he turned aside his face a minute, I saw a tear slide from under the sealed eyelid, and trickle down the manly cheek. My heart swelled.

"I am no better than the old lightning-struck chestnut-tree in Thornfield orchard," he remarked ere long. "And what right would that ruin have to bid a budding woodbine cover its decay with freshness?"

"You are no ruin, sir—no lightning-struck tree: you are green and vigorous. Plants will grow about your roots, whether you ask them or not, because they take delight in your bountiful shadow; and as they grow they will lean towards you, and wind round you, because your strength offers them so safe a prop."

Again he smiled: I gave him comfort.

"You speak of friends, Jane?" he asked.

"Yes, of friends," I answered rather hesitatingly: for I knew I meant more than friends, but could not tell what other word to employ. He helped me.

"Ah! Jane. But I want a wife."

"Do you, sir?"

"Yes: is it news to you?"

"Of course: you said nothing about it before."

"Is it unwelcome news?"

"That depends on circumstances, sir—on your choice."

"Which you shall make for me, Jane. I will abide by your decision."

"Choose then, sir—*her who loves you best.*"

"I will at least choose—*her I love best.* Jane, will you marry me?"

"Yes, sir."

"A poor blind man, whom you will have to lead about by the hand?"

"Yes, sir."

"A crippled man, twenty years older than you, whom you will have to wait on?"

"Yes, sir."

"Truly, Jane?"

"Most truly, sir."

"Oh! My darling! God bless you and reward you!"

"Mr. Rochester, if ever I did a good deed in my life—if ever I thought a good thought—if ever I prayed a sincere and blameless prayer—if ever I wished a righteous wish—I am rewarded now. To be your wife is, for me, to be as happy as I can be on earth."

"Because you delight in sacrifice."

"Sacrifice! What do I sacrifice? Famine for food, expectation for content. To be privileged to put my arms round what I value—to press my lips to what I love—to repose on what I trust: is that to make a sacrifice? If so, then certainly I delight in sacrifice."

"And to bear with my infirmities, Jane: to overlook my deficiencies."

"Which are none, sir, to me. I love you better now, when I can really be useful to you, than I did in your state of proud independence, when you disdained every part but that of the giver and protector."

"Hitherto I have hated to be helped—to be led: henceforth, I feel I shall hate it no more. I did not like to put my hand into a hireling's, but it is pleasant to feel it circled by Jane's little fingers. I preferred utter loneliness to the constant attendance of servants; but Jane's soft ministry will be a perpetual joy. Jane suits me: do I suit her?"

"To the finest fibre of my nature, sir."

"The case being so, we have nothing in the world to wait for: we must be married instantly."

He looked and spoke with eagerness: his old impetuosity was rising.

"We must become one flesh without any delay, Jane: there is but the licence to get—then we marry."

"Mr. Rochester, I have just discovered the sun is far declined from its meridian, and Pilot is actually gone home to his dinner. Let me look at your watch."

"Fasten it into your girdle, Janet, and keep it henceforward: I have no use for it."

"It is nearly four o'clock in the afternoon, sir. Don't you feel hungry?"

"The third day from this must be our wedding-day, Jane. Never mind fine clothes and jewels, now: all that is not worth a fillip."

"The sun has dried up all the rain-drops, sir. The breeze is still: it is quite hot."

"Do you know, Jane, I have your little pearl necklace at this moment fastened round my bronze scrag under my cravat? I have worn it since the day I lost my only treasure, as a memento of her."

"We will go home through the wood: that will be the shadiest way."

He pursued his own thoughts without heeding me.

"Jane! You think me, I daresay, an irreligious dog: but my heart swells with gratitude to the beneficent God of this earth just now. He sees not as man sees, but far clearer: judges not as man judges, but far more wisely. I did wrong: I would have sullied my innocent flower—breathed guilt on its purity: the Omnipotent snatched it from me. I, in my stiff-necked rebellion, almost cursed the dispensation: instead of bending to the decree, I defied it. Divine justice pursued its course; disasters came thick on me: I was forced to pass through the valley of the shadow of death. *His* chastisements are mighty; and one smote me which has humbled me for ever. You know I was proud of my strength: but what is it now, when I must give it over to foreign guidance, as a child does its weakness? Of late, Jane—only—only of late—I began to see and acknowledge the hand of God in my doom. I began to experience remorse, repentance; the wish for reconcilement to my Maker. I began sometimes to pray: very brief prayers they were, but very sincere.

"Some days since: nay, I can number them—four; it was last Monday night, a singular mood came over me: one in which grief replaced frenzy—sorrow, sullenness. I had long had the impression that since I could nowhere find you, you must be dead. Late that night—perhaps it might be between eleven and twelve o'clock—ere I retired to my dreary rest, I supplicated God, that, if it seemed good to Him, I might soon be taken from this life, and admitted to that world to come, where there was still hope of rejoining Jane.

"I was in my own room, and sitting by the window, which was open: it soothed me to feel the balmy night-air; though I could see no stars and only by a vague, luminous haze, knew the presence of a moon. I longed for thee, Janet! Oh, I longed for thee both with soul and flesh! I asked of God, at once in anguish and humility, if I had not been long enough desolate, afflicted, tormented; and might not soon taste bliss and peace once more. That I merited all I endured, I acknowledged—that I could scarcely endure more, I pleaded; and the alpha and omega of my heart's wishes broke involuntarily from my lips in the words 'Jane! Jane! Jane!' "

"Did you speak these words aloud?"

"I did, Jane. If any listener had heard me, he would have thought me mad: I pronounced them with such frantic energy."

"And it was last Monday night, somewhere near midnight?"

"Yes; but the time is of no consequence: what followed is the strange point. You will think me superstitious—some superstition I have in my blood, and always had: nevertheless, this is true—true at least it is that I heard what I now relate.

"As I exclaimed 'Jane! Jane! Jane!' a voice—I cannot tell whence the voice came, but I know whose voice it was—replied, 'I am coming: wait for me'; and a moment after, went whispering on the wind the words 'Where are you?'

"I'll tell you, if I can, the idea, the picture these words opened to my mind: yet it is difficult to express what I want to express. Ferndean is buried, as you see, in a heavy wood, where sound falls dull, and dies unreverberating. 'Where are you?' seemed spoken amongst mountains; for I heard a hill-sent echo repeat the words. Cooler and fresher at the moment the gale seemed to visit my brow: I could have deemed that in some wild, lone scene, I and Jane were meeting. In spirit, I believe we must have met. You no doubt were, at that hour, in unconscious sleep, Jane: perhaps your soul wandered from its cell to comfort mine; for those were your accents—as certain as I live—they were yours!"

Reader, it was on Monday night—near midnight—that I too had received the mysterious summons: those were the very words by which I replied to it. I listened to Mr. Rochester's narrative, but made no disclosure in return. The coincidence struck me as too awful and inexplicable to be communicated or discussed. If I told anything, my tale would be such as must necessarily make a profound impression on the mind of my hearer: and that mind, yet from its sufferings too prone to gloom, needed not the deeper shade of the supernatural. I kept these things then, and pondered them in my heart.

"You cannot now wonder," continued my master, "that when you rose upon me so unexpectedly last night, I had difficulty in believing you any other than a mere voice and vision, something that would melt to silence and annihilation, as the midnight whisper and mountain echo had melted before. Now, I thank God! I know it to be otherwise. Yes, I thank God!"

He put me off his knee, rose, and reverently lifting his hat from his brow, and bending his sightless eyes to the earth, he stood in mute devotion. Only the last words of the worship were audible.

"I thank my Maker, that, in the midst of judgment, he has remembered mercy. I humbly entreat my Redeemer to give me strength to lead henceforth a purer life than I have done hitherto!"

Then he stretched his hand out to be led. I took that dear hand, held it a moment to my lips, then let it pass round my shoulder: being so much lower of stature than he, I served both for his prop and guide. We entered the wood, and wended homeward.

CHAPTER XXXVIII

CONCLUSION

Reader, I married him. A quiet wedding we had: he and I, the parson and clerk, were alone present. When we got back from church, I went into the kitchen of the manor-house, where Mary was cooking the dinner and John cleaning the knives, and I said—

"Mary, I have been married to Mr. Rochester this morning." The housekeeper and her husband were both of that decent phlegmatic order of people, to whom one may at any time safely communicate a remarkable piece of news without incurring the danger of having one's ears pierced by some shrill ejaculation, and subsequently stunned by a torrent of wordy wonderment. Mary did look up, and she did stare at me: the ladle with which she was basting a pair of chickens roasting at the fire, did for some three minutes hang suspended in air; and for the same space of time John's knives also had rest from the polishing process: but Mary, bending again over the roast, said only—

"Have you, Miss? Well, for sure!"

A short time after she pursued—"I seed you go out with the master, but I didn't know you were gone to church to be wed"; and she basted away. John, when I turned to him, was grinning from ear to ear.

"I telled Mary how it would be," he said. "I knew what Mr. Edward" (John was an old servant, and had known his master when he was the cadet of the house, therefore, he often gave him his Christian name)—"I knew what Mr. Edward would do; and I was certain he would not wait long neither: and he's done right, for aught I know. I wish you joy, Miss!" and he politely pulled his forelock.

"Thank you, John. Mr. Rochester told me to give you and Mary this." I put into his hand a five-pound note. Without waiting to hear more, I left the kitchen. In passing the door of that sanctum some time after, I caught the words—

"She'll happen do better for him nor ony o't' grand ladies." And again, "If she ben't one o' th' handsomest, she's noan faâl and varry good-natured; and i' his een she's fair beautiful, onybody may see that."

I wrote to Moor House and to Cambridge immediately, to say what

I had done: fully explaining also why I had thus acted. Diana and Mary approved the step unreservedly. Diana announced that she would just give me time to get over the honeymoon, and then she would come and see me.

"She had better not wait till then, Jane," said Mr. Rochester, when I read her letter to him; "if she does, she will be too late, for our honeymoon will shine our life long: its beams will only fade over your grave or mine."

How St. John received the news, I don't know: he never answered the letter in which I communicated it: yet six months after he wrote to me, without, however, mentioning Mr. Rochester's name or alluding to my marriage. His letter was then calm, and, though very serious, kind. He has maintained a regular, though not frequent, correspondence ever since: he hopes I am happy, and trusts I am not of those who live without God in the world, and only mind earthly things.

You have not quite forgotten little Adèle, have you, reader? I had not; I soon asked and obtained leave of Mr. Rochester, to go and see her at the school where he had placed her. Her frantic joy at beholding me again moved me much. She looked pale and thin: she said she was not happy. I found the rules of the establishment were too strict, its course of study too severe for a child of her age: I took her home with me. I meant to become her governess once more, but I soon found this impracticable; my time and cares were now required by another—my husband needed them all. So I sought out a school conducted on a more indulgent system, and near enough to permit of my visiting her often, and bringing her home sometimes. I took care she should never want for anything that could contribute to her comfort: she soon settled in her new abode, became very happy there, and made fair progress in her studies. As she grew up, a sound English education corrected in a great measure her French defects; and when she left school, I found in her a pleasing and obliging companion: docile, good-tempered, and well-principled. By her grateful attention to me and mine, she has long since well repaid any little kindness I ever had it in my power to offer her.

My tale draws to its close: one word respecting my experience of married life, and one brief glance at the fortunes of those whose names have most frequently recurred in this narrative, and I have done.

I have now been married ten years. I know what it is to live entirely for and with what I love best on earth. I hold myself supremely blest—blest beyond what language can express; because I am my husband's life as fully as he is mine. No woman was ever nearer to her mate than I am: ever more absolutely bone of his bone and flesh of his flesh. I know no weariness of my Edward's society: he knows none of mine, any more than we each do of the pulsation of the heart that beats in our separate bosoms; consequently, we are ever together. To be together is for us to be at once as free as in solitude, as gay as in company. We talk, I believe, all day long: to talk to each other is but a more animated and an audible thinking. All my confidence is bestowed on him, all his confidence is devoted to me; we are precisely suited in character—perfect concord is the result.

Mr. Rochester continued blind the first two years of our union; perhaps it was that circumstance that drew us so very near—that knit us so very close: for I was then his vision, as I am still his right hand. Literally, I was (what he often called me) the apple of his eye. He saw nature—he saw books through me; and never did I weary of gazing for his behalf, and of putting into words the effect of field, tree, town, river, cloud, sunbeam—of the landscape before us; of the weather round us—and impressing by sound on his ear what light could no longer stamp on his eye. Never did I weary of reading to him; never did I weary of conducting him where he wished to go: of doing for him what he wished to be done. And there was a pleasure in my services, most full, most exquisite, even though sad—because he claimed these services without painful shame or damping humiliation. He loved me so truly, that he knew no reluctance in profiting by my attendance: he felt I loved him so fondly, that to yield that attendance was to indulge my sweetest wishes.

One morning at the end of the two years, as I was writing a letter to his dictation, he came and bent over me, and said, "Jane, have you a glittering ornament round your neck?"

I had a gold watch-chain: I answered, "Yes."

"And have you a pale blue dress on?"

I had. He informed me then, that for some time he had fancied the obscurity clouding one eye was becoming less dense; and that now he was sure of it.

He and I went up to London. He had the advice of an eminent oculist; and he eventually recovered the sight of that one eye. He cannot now see very distinctly: he cannot read or write much; but he can find his way without being led by the hand: the sky is no longer a blank to him—the earth no longer a void. When his first-born was put into his arms, he could see that the boy had inherited his own eyes, as they once were—large, brilliant, and black. On that occasion, he again, with a full heart, acknowledged that God had tempered judgment with mercy.

My Edward and I, then, are happy: and the more so, because those we most love are happy likewise. Diana and Mary Rivers are both married: alternately, once every year, they come to see us, and we go to see them. Diana's husband is a captain in the navy, a gallant officer and a good man. Mary's is a clergyman, a college friend of her brother's, and, from his attainments and principles, worthy of the connection. Both Captain Fitzjames and Mr. Wharton love their wives, and are loved by them.

As to St. John Rivers, he left England: he went to India. He entered on the path he had marked for himself; he pursues it still. A more resolute, indefatigable pioneer never wrought amidst rocks and dangers. Firm, faithful, and devoted, full of energy, and zeal, and truth, he labours for his race; he clears their painful way to improvement; he hews down like a giant the prejudices of creed and caste that encumber it. He may be stern; he may be exacting; he may be ambitious yet; but his is the sternness of the warrior Greatheart, who guards his pilgrim convoy from the onslaught of Apollyon. His is the exaction of the apostle, who speaks but for Christ, when he says, "Whosoever will come after me, let him deny himself, and take up his cross and follow me." His is the ambition of the high master-spirit, which aims to fill a place in the first rank of those who are redeemed from the earth—who stand without fault before the throne of God, who share the last mighty victories of the Lamb, who are called, and chosen, and faithful.

St. John is unmarried: he never will marry now. Himself has hitherto sufficed to the toil, and the toil draws near its close: his glorious sun hastens to its setting. The last letter I received from him drew from my eyes human tears, and yet filled my heart with divine joy: he anticipated his sure reward, his incorruptible crown. I know that a stranger's hand will write to me next, to say that the good and faithful servant has been called at length into the joy of his Lord. And why weep for this? No fear of death will darken St. John's last hour: his mind will be unclouded, his heart will be undaunted, his hope will be sure, his faith steadfast. His own words are a pledge of this:

"My Master," he says, "has forewarned me. Daily He announces more distinctly, 'Surely I come quickly!' and hourly I more eagerly respond, 'Amen; even so come, Lord Jesus!' "

Word Cloud Classics

A Christmas Carol and Other Holiday Treasures

Adventures of Huckleberry Finn

The Adventures of Sherlock Holmes

Aesop's Fables

Anna Karenina

Anne of Green Gables

The Art of War

Black Beauty

The Brothers Grimm 101 Fairy Tales

The Brothers Grimm Volume II: 110 Grimmer Fairy Tales

Common Sense and Selected Works of Thomas Paine

The Count of Monte Cristo

Don Quixote

Dr. Jekyll and Mr. Hyde & Other Stories

Dracula

Frankenstein

Great Expectations

Hans Christian Andersen Tales

Inferno

The Jungle Book

Lady Chatterley's Lover

Jane Eyre

Les Misérables

Little Women

Madame Bovary

Moby-Dick

Narrative of the Life of Frederick Douglass and Other Works

Persuasion

The Picture of Dorian Gray

Pride and Prejudice

The Prince and Other Writings

The Red Badge of Courage and Other Stories

The Scarlet Letter

The Secret Garden

Sense and Sensibility

The Three Musketeers

Treasure Island

Twenty Thousand Leagues Under the Sea

Uncle Tom's Cabin

Walden and Civil Disobedience

The Wizard of Oz

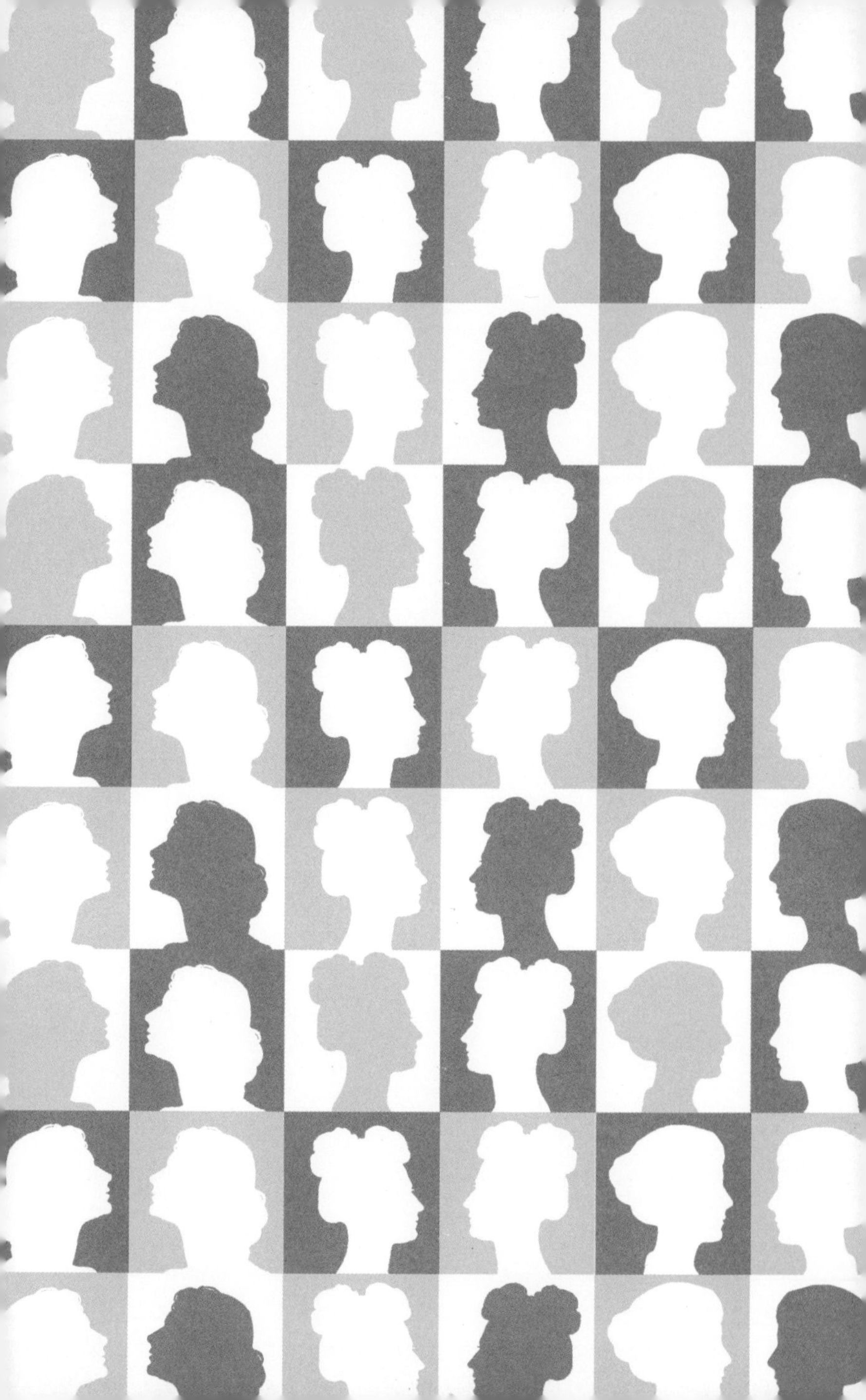

Little Women

Little Women

Louisa May Alcott

CANTERBURY CLASSICS
San Diego

All correspondence concerning the content of this book should be addressed to: Canterbury Classics
10350 Barnes Canyon Road, Suite 100
San Diego, CA 92121

Publisher: Peter Norton
Publishing Team: Lori Asbury, Ana Parker
Director Editorial and Production: JoAnn Padgett

Library of Congress Cataloging-in-Publication Data

Alcott, Louisa May, 1832-1888.
Little women / Louisa May Alcott.
p. cm.
ISBN 978-1-60710-548-0 -- ISBN 1-60710-548-9
1. March family (Fictitious characters)--Fiction. 2. Mothers and daughters--Fiction. 3. New England--Fiction. 4. Young women--Fiction. 5. Sisters--Fiction. 6. Domestic fiction. I. Title.

PS1017.L5 2012
813'.4--dc23

2012029711

PRINTED IN CHINA

4 5 6 7 8 19 18 17 16 15

CHAPTER I

PLAYING PILGRIMS

"Christmas won't be Christmas without any presents," grumbled Jo, lying on the rug.

"It's so dreadful to be poor!" sighed Meg, looking down at her old dress.

"I don't think it's fair for some girls to have plenty of pretty things, and other girls nothing at all," added little Amy, with an injured sniff.

"We've got Father and Mother, and each other," said Beth contentedly from her corner.

The four young faces on which the firelight shone brightened at the cheerful words, but darkened again as Jo said sadly, "We haven't got Father, and shall not have him for a long time." She didn't say "perhaps never," but each silently added it, thinking of Father far away, where the fighting was.

Nobody spoke for a minute; then Meg said in an altered tone, "You know the reason Mother proposed not having any presents this Christmas was because it is going to be a hard winter for everyone; and she thinks we ought not to spend money for pleasure, when our men are suffering so in the army. We can't do much, but we can make our little sacrifices, and ought to do it gladly. But I am afraid I don't," and Meg shook her head, as she thought regretfully of all the pretty things she wanted.

"But I don't think the little we should spend would do any good. We've each got a dollar, and the army wouldn't be much helped by our giving that. I agree not to expect anything from Mother or you, but I do want to buy *Undine and Sintran* for myself. I've wanted it so long," said Jo, who was a bookworm.

"I planned to spend mine in new music," said Beth, with a little sigh, which no one heard but the hearth brush and kettle-holder. "I shall get a nice box of Faber's drawing pencils; I really need them," said Amy decidedly.

"Mother didn't say anything about our money, and she won't wish us to give up everything. Let's each buy what we want, and have a little fun; I'm sure we work hard enough to earn it," cried Jo, examining the heels of her shoes in a gentlemanly manner.

"I know *I* do—teaching those tiresome children nearly all day, when I'm longing to enjoy myself at home," began Meg, in the complaining tone again.

"You don't have half such a hard time as I do," said Jo. "How would you like to be shut up for hours with a nervous, fussy old lady, who keeps you trotting, is never satisfied, and worries you till you're ready to fly out the window or cry?"

"It's naughty to fret, but I do think washing dishes and keeping things tidy is the worst work in the world. It makes me cross, and my hands get so stiff, I can't practice well at all." And Beth looked at her rough hands with a sigh that any one could hear that time.

"I don't believe any of you suffer as I do," cried Amy, "for you don't have to go to school with impertinent girls, who plague you if you don't know your lessons, and laugh at your dresses, and label your father if he isn't rich, and insult you when your nose isn't nice."

"If you mean *libel*, I'd say so, and not talk about *labels*, as if Papa was a pickle bottle," advised Jo, laughing.

"I know what I mean, and you needn't be *statirical* about it. It's proper to use good words, and improve your *vocabilary*," returned Amy, with dignity.

"Don't peck at one another, children. Don't you wish we had the money Papa lost when we were little, Jo? Dear me! How happy and good we'd be, if we had no worries!" said Meg, who could remember better times.

"You said the other day you thought we were a deal happier than the King children, for they were fighting and fretting all the time, in spite of their money."

"So I did, Beth. Well, I think we are. For though we do have to work, we make fun of ourselves, and are a pretty jolly set, as Jo would say."

"Jo does use such slang words!" observed Amy, with a reproving look at the long figure stretched on the rug. Jo immediately sat up, put her hands in her pockets, and began to whistle.

"Don't, Jo. It's so boyish!"

"That's why I do it."

"I detest rude, unladylike girls!"

"I hate affected, niminy-piminy chits!"

"Birds in their little nests agree," sang Beth, the peacemaker, with such a funny face that both sharp voices softened to a laugh, and the "pecking" ended for that time.

"Really, girls, you are both to be blamed," said Meg, beginning to lecture in her elder-sisterly fashion. "You are old enough to leave off boyish tricks, and to behave better, Josephine. It didn't matter so much when you were a little girl, but now you are so tall, and turn up your hair, you should remember that you are a young lady."

"I'm not! And if turning up my hair makes me one, I'll wear it in two tails till I'm twenty," cried Jo, pulling off her net, and shaking down a chestnut mane. "I hate to think I've got to grow up, and be Miss March, and wear long gowns, and look as prim as a China Aster! It's bad enough to be a girl, anyway, when I like boy's games and work and manners! I can't get over my disappointment in not being a boy. And it's worse than ever now, for I'm dying to go and fight with Papa. And I can only stay home and knit, like a poky old woman!" And Jo shook the blue army sock till the needles rattled like castanets, and her ball bounded across the room.

"Poor Jo! It's too bad, but it can't be helped. So you must try to be contented with making your name boyish, and playing brother to us girls," said Beth, stroking the rough head with a hand that all the dish washing and dusting in the world could not make ungentle in its touch.

"As for you, Amy," continued Meg, "you are altogether too particular and prim. Your airs are funny now, but you'll grow up an affected little goose, if you don't take care. I like your nice manners and refined ways of speaking, when you don't try to be elegant. But your absurd words are as bad as Jo's slang."

"If Jo is a tomboy and Amy a goose, what am I, please?" asked Beth, ready to share the lecture.

"You're a dear, and nothing else," answered Meg warmly, and no one contradicted her, for the 'Mouse' was the pet of the family.

As young readers like to know 'how people look', we will take this moment to give them a little sketch of the four sisters, who sat knitting away in the twilight, while the December snow fell quietly without, and the fire crackled cheerfully within. It was a comfortable room, though the carpet was faded and the furniture very plain, for a good picture or two hung on the walls, books filled the recesses, chrysanthemums and

Christmas roses bloomed in the windows, and a pleasant atmosphere of home peace pervaded it.

Margaret, the eldest of the four, was sixteen, and very pretty, being plump and fair, with large eyes, plenty of soft brown hair, a sweet mouth, and white hands, of which she was rather vain. Fifteen-year-old Jo was very tall, thin, and brown, and reminded one of a colt, for she never seemed to know what to do with her long limbs, which were very much in her way. She had a decided mouth, a comical nose, and sharp, gray eyes, which appeared to see everything, and were by turns fierce, funny, or thoughtful. Her long, thick hair was her one beauty, but it was usually bundled into a net, to be out of her way. Round shoulders had Jo, big hands and feet, a flyaway look to her clothes, and the uncomfortable appearance of a girl who was rapidly shooting up into a woman and didn't like it. Elizabeth, or Beth, as everyone called her, was a rosy, smooth-haired, bright-eyed girl of thirteen, with a shy manner, a timid voice, and a peaceful expression which was seldom disturbed. Her father called her "Little Miss Tranquility," and the name suited her excellently, for she seemed to live in a happy world of her own, only venturing out to meet the few whom she trusted and loved. Amy, though the youngest, was a most important person, in her own opinion at least. A regular snow maiden, with blue eyes, and yellow hair curling on her shoulders, pale and slender, and always carrying herself like a young lady mindful of her manners. What the characters of the four sisters were we will leave to be found out.

The clock struck six and, having swept up the hearth, Beth put a pair of slippers down to warm. Somehow the sight of the old shoes had a good effect upon the girls, for Mother was coming, and everyone brightened to welcome her. Meg stopped lecturing, and lighted the lamp, Amy got out of the easy chair without being asked, and Jo forgot how tired she was as she sat up to hold the slippers nearer to the blaze.

"They are quite worn out. Marmee must have a new pair."

"I thought I'd get her some with my dollar," said Beth.

"No, I shall!" cried Amy.

"I'm the oldest," began Meg, but Jo cut in with a decided—

"I'm the man of the family now Papa is away, and *I* shall provide the slippers, for he told me to take special care of Mother while he was gone."

"I'll tell you what we'll do," said Beth, "let's each get her something for Christmas, and not get anything for ourselves."

"That's like you, dear! What will we get?" exclaimed Jo.

Everyone thought soberly for a minute, then Meg announced, as if the idea was suggested by the sight of her own pretty hands, "I shall give her a nice pair of gloves."

"Army shoes, best to be had," cried Jo.

"Some handkerchiefs, all hemmed," said Beth.

"I'll get a little bottle of cologne. She likes it, and it won't cost much, so I'll have some left to buy my pencils," added Amy.

"How will we give the things?" asked Meg.

"Put them on the table, and bring her in and see her open the bundles. Don't you remember how we used to do on our birthdays?" answered Jo.

"I used to be so frightened when it was my turn to sit in the chair with the crown on, and see you all come marching round to give the presents, with a kiss. I liked the things and the kisses, but it was dreadful to have you sit looking at me while I opened the bundles," said Beth, who was toasting her face and the bread for tea at the same time.

"Let Marmee think we are getting things for ourselves, and then surprise her. We must go shopping tomorrow afternoon, Meg. There is so much to do about the play for Christmas night," said Jo, marching up and down, with her hands behind her back, and her nose in the air.

"I don't mean to act any more after this time. I'm getting too old for such things," observed Meg, who was as much a child as ever about "dressing-up" frolics.

"You won't stop, I know, as long as you can trail round in a white gown with your hair down, and wear gold-paper jewelry. You are the best actress we've got, and there'll be an end of everything if you quit the boards," said Jo. "We ought to rehearse tonight. Come here, Amy, and do the fainting scene, for you are as stiff as a poker in that."

"I can't help it. I never saw anyone faint, and I don't choose to make myself all black and blue, tumbling flat as you do. If I can go down easily, I'll drop. If I can't, I shall fall into a chair and be graceful. I don't care if Hugo does come at me with a pistol," returned Amy, who was not gifted with dramatic power, but was chosen because she was small enough to be borne out shrieking by the villain of the piece.

"Do it this way. Clasp your hands so, and stagger across the room, crying frantically, 'Roderigo! Save me! Save me!'"and away went Jo, with a melodramatic scream which was truly thrilling.

Amy followed, but she poked her hands out stiffly before her, and jerked herself along as if she went by machinery, and her "Ow!" was more suggestive of pins being run into her than of fear and anguish. Jo gave a despairing groan, and Meg laughed outright, while Beth let her bread burn as she watched the fun with interest.

"It's no use! Do the best you can when the time comes, and if the audience laughs, don't blame me. Come on, Meg."

Then things went smoothly, for Don Pedro defied the world in a speech of two pages without a single break. Hagar, the witch, chanted an awful incantation over her kettleful of simmering toads, with weird effect. Roderigo rent his chains asunder manfully, and Hugo died in agonies of remorse and arsenic, with a wild, "Ha! Ha!"

"It's the best we've had yet," said Meg, as the dead villain sat up and rubbed his elbows.

"I don't see how you can write and act such splendid things, Jo. You're a regular Shakespeare!" exclaimed Beth, who firmly believed that her sisters were gifted with wonderful genius in all things.

"Not quite," replied Jo modestly. "I do think *The Witches Curse, an Operatic Tragedy* is rather a nice thing, but I'd like to try *Macbeth*, if we only had a trapdoor for Banquo. I always wanted to do the killing part. 'Is that a dagger that I see before me?'" muttered Jo, rolling her eyes and clutching at the air, as she had seen a famous tragedian do.

"No, it's the toasting fork, with Mother's shoe on it instead of the bread. Beth's stage-struck!" cried Meg, and the rehearsal ended in a general burst of laughter.

"Glad to find you so merry, my girls," said a cheery voice at the door, and actors and audience turned to welcome a tall, motherly lady with a "can-I-help-you" look about her which was truly delightful. She was not elegantly dressed, but a noble-looking woman, and the girls thought the gray cloak and unfashionable bonnet covered the most splendid mother in the world.

"Well, dearies, how have you got on today? There was so much to do, getting the boxes ready to go tomorrow, that I didn't come home to dinner. Has anyone called, Beth? How is your cold, Meg? Jo, you look tired to death. Come and kiss me, baby."

While making these maternal inquiries Mrs. March got her wet things off, her warm slippers on, and sitting down in the easy chair, drew Amy to her lap, preparing to enjoy the happiest hour of her busy day. The girls flew about, trying to make things comfortable, each in her own way. Meg arranged the tea table, Jo brought wood and set chairs, dropping, over-turning, and clattering everything she touched. Beth trotted to and fro between parlor kitchen, quiet and busy, while Amy gave directions to everyone, as she sat with her hands folded.

As they gathered about the table, Mrs. March said, with a particularly happy face, "I've got a treat for you after supper."

A quick, bright smile went round like a streak of sunshine. Beth clapped her hands, regardless of the biscuit she held, and Jo tossed up her napkin, crying, "A letter! A letter! Three cheers for Father!"

"Yes, a nice long letter. He is well, and thinks he shall get through the cold season better than we feared. He sends all sorts of loving wishes for Christmas, and an especial message to you girls," said Mrs. March, patting her pocket as if she had got a treasure there.

"Hurry and get done! Don't stop to quirk your little finger and simper over your plate, Amy," cried Jo, choking on her tea and dropping her bread, butter side down, on the carpet in her haste to get at the treat.

Beth ate no more, but crept away to sit in her shadowy corner and brood over the delight to come, till the others were ready.

"I think it was so splendid in Father to go as chaplain when he was too old to be drafted, and not strong enough for a soldier," said Meg warmly.

"Don't I wish I could go as a drummer, a *vivan*—what's its name? Or a nurse, so I could be near him and help him," exclaimed Jo, with a groan.

"It must be very disagreeable to sleep in a tent, and eat all sorts of bad-tasting things, and drink out of a tin mug," sighed Amy.

"When will he come home, Marmee?" asked Beth, with a little quiver in her voice.

"Not for many months, dear, unless he is sick. He will stay and do his work faithfully as long as he can, and we won't ask for him back a minute sooner than he can be spared. Now come and hear the letter."

They all drew to the fire, Mother in the big chair with Beth at her feet, Meg and Amy perched on either arm of the chair, and Jo leaning on the back, where no one would see any sign of emotion if the letter should happen to be touching. Very few letters were written in those hard times that were not touching, especially those which fathers sent home. In this one little was said of the hardships endured, the dangers faced, or the homesickness conquered. It was a cheerful, hopeful letter, full of lively descriptions of camp life, marches, and military news, and only at the end did the writer's heart over-flow with fatherly love and longing for the little girls at home.

"Give them all of my dear love and a kiss. Tell them I think of them by day, pray for them by night, and find my best comfort in their affection at all times. A year seems very long to wait before I see them, but remind them that while we wait we may all work, so that these hard days need not be wasted. I know they will remember all I said to them, that they will be loving children to you, will do their duty faithfully, fight their bosom enemies bravely, and conquer themselves so beautifully that when I come back to them I may be fonder and prouder than ever of my little women."

Everybody sniffed when they came to that part. Jo wasn't ashamed of the great tear that dropped off the end of her nose, and Amy never minded the rumpling of her curls as she hid her face on her mother's shoulder and sobbed out, "I *am* a selfish girl! But I'll truly try to be better, so he mayn't be disappointed in me by-and-by."

"We all will," cried Meg. "I think too much of my looks and hate to work, but won't any more, if I can help it."

"I'll try and be what he loves to call me, 'a little woman,' and not be rough and wild, but do my duty here instead of wanting to be somewhere else," said Jo, thinking that keeping her temper at home was a much harder task than facing a rebel or two down South.

Beth said nothing, but wiped away her tears with the blue army sock and began to knit with all her might, losing no time in doing the duty that lay nearest her, while she resolved in her quiet little soul to be all that Father hoped to find her when the year brought round the happy coming home.

Mrs. March broke the silence that followed Jo's words, by saying in her cheery voice, "Do you remember how you used to play Pilgrims Progress when you were little things? Nothing delighted you more than to have me tie my piece bags on your backs for burdens, give you hats and sticks and rolls of paper, and let you travel through the house from the cellar, which was the City of Destruction, up, up, to the housetop, where you had all the lovely things you could collect to make a Celestial City."

"What fun it was, especially going by the lions, fighting Apollyon, and passing through the valley where the hob-goblins were," said Jo.

"I liked the place where the bundles fell off and tumbled downstairs," said Meg.

"My favorite part was when we came out on the flat roof where our flowers and arbors and pretty things were, and all stood and sung for joy up there in the sunshine," said Beth, smiling, as if that pleasant moment had come back to her.

"I don't remember much about it, except that I was afraid of the cellar and the dark entry, and always liked the cake and milk we had up at the top. If I wasn't too old for such things, I'd rather like to play it over again," said Amy, who began to talk of renouncing childish things at the mature age of twelve.

"We never are too old for this, my dear, because it is a play we are playing all the time in one way or another. Our burdens are here, our road is before us, and the longing for goodness and happiness is the guide that leads us through many troubles and mistakes to the peace which is a true Celestial City. Now, my little pilgrims, suppose you begin again, not in play, but in earnest, and see how far on you can get before Father comes home."

"Really, Mother? Where are our bundles?" asked Amy, who was a very literal young lady.

"Each of you told what your burden was just now, except Beth. I rather think she hasn't got any," said her mother.

"Yes, I have. Mine is dishes and dusters, and envying girls with nice pianos, and being afraid of people."

Beth's bundle was such a funny one that everybody wanted to laugh, but nobody did, for it would have hurt her feelings very much.

"Let us do it," said Meg thoughtfully. "It is only another name for trying to be good, and the story may help us, for though we do want to be good, it's hard work and we forget, and don't do our best."

"We were in the Slough of Despond tonight, and Mother came and pulled us out as Help did in the book. We ought to have our roll of directions, like Christian. What shall we do about that?" asked Jo, delighted with the fancy which lent a little romance to the very dull task of doing her duty.

"Look under your pillows Christmas morning, and you will find your guidebook," replied Mrs. March.

They talked over the new plan while old Hannah cleared the table, then out came the four little work baskets, and the needles flew as the girls made sheets for Aunt March. It was uninteresting sewing, but tonight no one grumbled. They adopted Jo's plan of dividing the long seams into four parts, and calling the quarters Europe, Asia, Africa, and America, and in that way got on capitally, especially when they talked about the different countries as they stitched their way through them.

At nine they stopped work, and sang, as usual, before they went to bed. No one but Beth could get much music out of the old piano, but she had a way of softly touching the yellow keys and making a pleasant accompaniment to the simple songs they sang. Meg had a voice like a flute, and she and her mother led the little choir. Amy chirped like a cricket, and Jo wandered through the airs at her own sweet will, always coming out at the wrong place with a croak or a quaver that spoiled the most pensive tune. They had always done this from the time they could lisp . . .

Crinkle, crinkle, 'ittle 'tar,

and it had become a household custom, for the mother was a born singer. The first sound in the morning was her voice as she went about the house singing like a lark, and the last sound at night was the same cheery sound, for the girls never grew too old for that familiar lullaby.

CHAPTER II

A MERRY CHRISTMAS

Jo was the first to wake in the gray dawn of Christmas morning. No stockings hung at the fireplace, and for a moment she felt as much disappointed as she did long ago, when her little sock fell down because it was crammed so full of goodies. Then she remembered her mother's promise and, slipping her hand under her pillow, drew out a little crimson-covered book. She knew it very well, for it was that beautiful old story of the best life ever lived, and Jo felt that it was a true guidebook for any pilgrim going on a long journey. She woke Meg with a "Merry Christmas," and bade her see what was under her pillow. A green-covered book appeared, with the same picture inside, and a few words written by their mother, which made their one present very precious in their eyes. Presently Beth and Amy woke to rummage and find their little books also, one dove-colored, the other blue, and all sat looking at and talking about them, while the east grew rosy with the coming day.

In spite of her small vanities, Margaret had a sweet and pious nature, which unconsciously influenced her sisters, especially Jo, who loved her very tenderly, and obeyed her because her advice was so gently given.

"Girls," said Meg seriously, looking from the tumbled head beside her to the two little night-capped ones in the room beyond, "Mother wants us to read and love and mind these books, and we must begin at once. We used to be faithful about it, but since Father went away and all this war trouble unsettled us, we have neglected many things. You can do as you please, but I shall keep my book on the table here and read a little every morning as soon as I wake, for I know it will do me good and help me through the day."

Then she opened her new book and began to read. Jo put her arm round her and, leaning cheek to cheek, read also, with the quiet expression so seldom seen on her restless face.

"How good Meg is! Come, Amy, let's do as they do. I'll help you with the hard words, and they'll explain things if we don't understand," whispered Beth, very much impressed by the pretty books and her sisters' example.

"I'm glad mine is blue," said Amy. and then the rooms were very still while the pages were softly turned, and the winter sunshine crept in to touch the bright heads and serious faces with a Christmas greeting.

"Where is Mother?" asked Meg, as she and Jo ran down to thank her for their gifts, half an hour later.

"Goodness only knows. Some poor creeter came a-beggin', and your ma went straight off to see what was needed. There never was such a woman for givin' away vittles and drink, clothes and firin'," replied Hannah, who had lived with the family since Meg was born, and was considered by them all more as a friend than a servant.

"She will be back soon, I think, so fry your cakes, and have everything ready," said Meg, looking over the presents which were collected in a basket and kept under the sofa, ready to be produced at the proper time. "Why, where is Amy's bottle of cologne?" she added, as the little flask did not appear.

"She took it out a minute ago, and went off with it to put a ribbon on it, or some such notion," replied Jo, dancing about the room to take the first stiffness off the new army slippers.

"How nice my handkerchiefs look, don't they? Hannah washed and ironed them for me, and I marked them all myself," said Beth, looking proudly at the somewhat uneven letters which had cost her such labor.

"Bless the child! She's gone and put 'Mother' on them instead of 'M. March.' How funny!" cried Jo, taking one up.

"Isn't that right? I thought it was better to do it so, because Meg's initials are M.M., and I don't want anyone to use these but Marmee," said Beth, looking troubled.

"It's all right, dear, and a very pretty idea, quite sensible too, for no one can ever mistake now. It will please her very much, I know," said Meg, with a frown for Jo and a smile for Beth.

"There's Mother. Hide the basket, quick!" cried Jo, as a door slammed and steps sounded in the hall.

Amy came in hastily, and looked rather abashed when she saw her sisters all waiting for her.

"Where have you been, and what are you hiding behind you?" asked Meg, surprised to see, by her hood and cloak, that lazy Amy had been out so early.

"Don't laugh at me, Jo! I didn't mean anyone should know till the time came. I only meant to change the little bottle for a big one, and I gave all my money to get it, and I'm truly trying not to be selfish any more."

As she spoke, Amy showed the handsome flask which replaced the cheap one, and looked so earnest and humble in her little effort to forget herself that Meg hugged her on the spot, and Jo pronounced her 'a trump,' while Beth ran to the window, and picked her finest rose to ornament the stately bottle.

"You see I felt ashamed of my present, after reading and talking about being good this morning, so I ran round the corner and changed it the minute I was up, and I'm so glad, for mine is the handsomest now."

Another bang of the street door sent the basket under the sofa, and the girls to the table, eager for breakfast.

"Merry Christmas, Marmee! Many of them! Thank you for our books. We read some, and mean to every day," they all cried in chorus.

"Merry Christmas, little daughters! I'm glad you began at once, and hope you will keep on. But I want to say one word before we sit down. Not far away from here lies a poor woman with a little newborn baby. Six children are huddled into one bed to keep from freezing, for they have no fire. There is nothing to eat over there, and the oldest boy came to tell me they were suffering hunger and cold. My girls, will you give them your breakfast as a Christmas present?"

They were all unusually hungry, having waited nearly an hour, and for a minute no one spoke, only a minute, for Jo exclaimed impetuously, "I'm so glad you came before we began!"

"May I go and help carry the things to the poor little children?" asked Beth eagerly.

"*I* shall take the cream and the muffins," added Amy, heroically giving up the article she most liked.

Meg was already covering the buckwheats, and piling the bread into one big plate.

"I thought you'd do it," said Mrs. March, smiling as if satisfied. "You shall all go and help me, and when we come back we will have bread and milk for breakfast, and make it up at dinnertime."

They were soon ready, and the procession set out. Fortunately it was early, and they went through back streets, so few people saw them, and no one laughed at the queer party.

A poor, bare, miserable room it was, with broken windows, no fire, ragged bedclothes, a sick mother, wailing baby, and a group of pale, hungry children cuddled under one old quilt, trying to keep warm.

How the big eyes stared and the blue lips smiled as the girls went in.

"*Ach, mein Gott!* It is good angels come to us!" said the poor woman, crying for joy.

"Funny angels in hoods and mittens," said Jo, and set them to laughing.

In a few minutes it really did seem as if kind spirits had been at work there. Hannah, who had carried wood, made a fire, and stopped up the broken panes with old hats and her own cloak. Mrs. March gave the mother tea and gruel, and comforted her with promises of help, while she dressed the little baby as tenderly as if it had been her own. The girls meantime spread the table, set the children round the fire, and fed them like so many hungry birds, laughing, talking, and trying to understand the funny broken English.

"*Das ist gut!*" "*Die Engel-kinder!*" cried the poor things as they ate and warmed their purple hands at the comfortable blaze.

The girls had never been called angel children before, and thought it very agreeable, especially Jo, who had been considered a "Sancho" ever since she was born. That was a very happy breakfast, though they didn't get any of it. And when they went away, leaving comfort behind, I think there were not in all the city four merrier people than the hungry little girls who gave away their breakfasts and contented themselves with bread and milk on Christmas morning.

"That's loving our neighbor better than ourselves, and I like it," said Meg, as they set out their presents while their mother was upstairs collecting clothes for the poor Hummels.

Not a very splendid show, but there was a great deal of love done up in the few little bundles, and the tall vase of red roses, white chrysanthemums, and trailing vines, which stood in the middle, gave quite an elegant air to the table.

"She's coming! Strike up, Beth! Open the door, Amy! Three cheers for Marmee!" cried Jo, prancing about while Meg went to conduct Mother to the seat of honor.

Beth played her gayest march, Amy threw open the door, and Meg enacted escort with great dignity. Mrs. March was both surprised and touched, and smiled with her eyes full as she examined her presents and read the little notes which accompanied them. The slippers went on at once, a new handkerchief was slipped into her pocket, well scented with Amy's cologne, the rose was fastened in her bosom, and the nice gloves were pronounced a perfect fit.

There was a good deal of laughing and kissing and explaining, in the simple, loving fashion which makes these home festivals so pleasant at the time, so sweet to remember long afterward, and then all fell to work.

The morning charities and ceremonies took so much time that the rest of the day was devoted to preparations for the evening festivities. Being still too young to go often to the theater, and not rich enough to afford any great outlay for private performances, the girls put their wits to work, and necessity being the mother of invention, made whatever they needed. Very clever were some of their productions, pasteboard guitars, antique lamps made of old-fashioned butter boats covered with silver paper, gorgeous robes of old cotton, glittering with tin spangles from a pickle factory, and armor covered with the same useful diamond shaped bits left in sheets when the lids of preserve pots were cut out. The big chamber was the scene of many innocent revels.

No gentleman were admitted, so Jo played male parts to her heart's content and took immense satisfaction in a pair of russet leather boots given her by a friend, who knew a lady who knew an actor. These boots, an old foil, and a slashed doublet once used by an artist for some picture, were Jo's chief treasures and appeared on all occasions. The smallness of the company made it necessary for the two principal actors to take several parts apiece, and they certainly deserved some credit for the hard work they did in learning three or four different parts, whisking in and out of various costumes, and managing the stage besides. It was excellent drill for their memories, a harmless amusement, and employed many hours which otherwise would have been idle, lonely, or spent in less profitable society.

On Christmas night, a dozen girls piled onto the bed which was the dress circle, and sat before the blue and yellow chintz curtains in a most flattering state of expectancy. There was a good deal of rustling and whispering behind the curtain, a trifle of lamp smoke, and an occasional giggle from Amy, who was apt to get hysterical in the excitement of the moment. Presently a bell sounded, the curtains flew apart, and the *Operatic Tragedy* began.

"A gloomy wood," according to the one playbill, was represented by a few shrubs in pots, green baize on the floor, and a cave in the distance. This cave was made with a clothes horse for a roof, bureaus for walls, and in it was a small furnace in full blast, with a black pot on it and an old witch bending over it. The stage was dark and the glow of the furnace had a fine effect, especially as real steam issued from the kettle when the witch took off the cover. A moment was allowed for the first thrill to subside, then Hugo, the villain, stalked in with a clanking sword at his side, a slouching hat, black beard, mysterious cloak, and the boots. After pacing to and fro in much agitation, he struck his forehead, and burst out in a wild strain, singing of his hatred for Roderigo, his love for Zara, and his pleasing resolution to kill the one and win the other. The gruff tones of Hugo's voice, with an occasional shout when his feelings overcame him, were very impressive, and the audience applauded the moment he paused for breath. Bowing with the air of one accustomed to public praise, he stole to the cavern and ordered Hagar to come forth with a commanding, "What ho, minion! I need thee!"

Out came Meg, with gray horsehair hanging about her face, a red and black robe, a staff, and cabalistic signs upon her cloak. Hugo demanded a potion to make Zara adore him, and one to destroy Roderigo. Hagar, in a fine dramatic melody, promised both, and proceeded to call up the spirit who would bring the love philter.

> Hither, hither, from thy home,
> Airy sprite, I bid thee come!
> Born of roses, fed on dew,
> Charms and potions canst thou brew?
> Bring me here, with elfin speed,
> The fragrant philter which I need;
> Make it sweet and swift and strong,
> Spirit, answer now my song!

A soft strain of music sounded, and then at the back of the cave appeared a little figure in cloudy white, with glittering wings, golden hair, and a garland of roses on its head. Waving a wand, it sang,

> Hither I come,
> From my airy home,
> Afar in the silver moon.

Take the magic spell,
And use it well,
Or its power will vanish soon!

And dropping a small, gilded bottle at the witch's feet, the spirit vanished. Another chant from Hagar produced another apparition, not a lovely one, for with a bang an ugly black imp appeared and, having croaked a reply, tossed a dark bottle at Hugo and disappeared with a mocking laugh. Having warbled his thanks and put the potions in his boots, Hugo departed, and Hagar informed the audience that as he had killed a few of her friends in times past, she had cursed him, and intends to thwart his plans, and be revenged on him. Then the curtain fell, and the audience reposed and ate candy while discussing the merits of the play.

A good deal of hammering went on before the curtain rose again, but when it became evident what a masterpiece of stage carpentery had been got up, no one murmured at the delay. It was truly superb. A tower rose to the ceiling, halfway up appeared a window with a lamp burning in it, and behind the white curtain appeared Zara in a lovely blue and silver dress, waiting for Roderigo. He came in gorgeous array, with plumed cap, red cloak, chestnut lovelocks, a guitar, and the boots, of course. Kneeling at the foot of the tower, he sang a serenade in melting tones. Zara replied and, after a musical dialogue, consented to fly. Then came the grand effect of the play. Roderigo produced a rope ladder, with five steps to it, threw up one end, and invited Zara to descend. Timidly she crept from her lattice, put her hand on Roderigo's shoulder, and was about to leap gracefully down when "Alas! Alas for Zara!" she forgot her train. It caught in the window, the tower tottered, leaned forward, fell with a crash, and buried the unhappy lovers in the ruins.

A universal shriek arose as the russet boots waved wildly from the wreck and a golden head emerged, exclaiming, "I told you so! I told you so!" With wonderful presence of mind, Don Pedro, the cruel sire, rushed in, dragged out his daughter, with a hasty aside—

"Don't laugh! Act as if it was all right!" —And, ordering Roderigo up, banished him from the kingdom with wrath and scorn. Though decidedly shaken by the fall from the tower upon him, Roderigo defied the old gentleman and refused to stir. This dauntless example fired

Zara. She also defied her sire, and he ordered them both to the deepest dungeons of the castle. A stout little retainer came in with chains and led them away, looking very much frightened and evidently forgetting the speech he ought to have made.

Act third was the castle hall, and here Hagar appeared, having come to free the lovers and finish Hugo. She hears him coming and hides, sees him put the potions into two cups of wine and bid the timid little servant, "Bear them to the captives in their cells, and tell them I shall come anon." The servant takes Hugo aside to tell him something, and Hagar changes the cups for two others which are harmless. Ferdinando, the "minion," carries them away, and Hagar puts back the cup which holds the poison meant for Roderigo. Hugo, getting thirsty after a long warble, drinks it, loses his wits, and after a good deal of clutching and stamping, falls flat and dies, while Hagar informs him what she has done in a song of exquisite power and melody.

This was a truly thrilling scene, though some persons might have thought that the sudden tumbling down of a quantity of long red hair rather marred the effect of the villain's death. He was called before the curtain, and with great propriety appeared, leading Hagar, whose singing was considered more wonderful than all the rest of the performance put together.

Act fourth displayed the despairing Roderigo on the point of stabbing himself because he has been told that Zara has deserted him. Just as the dagger is at his heart, a lovely song is sung under his window, informing him that Zara is true but in danger, and he can save her if he will. A key is thrown in, which unlocks the door, and in a spasm of rapture he tears off his chains and rushes away to find and rescue his lady love.

Act fifth opened with a stormy scene between Zara and Don Pedro. He wishes her to go into a convent, but she won't hear of it, and after a touching appeal, is about to faint when Roderigo dashes in and demands her hand. Don Pedro refuses, because he is not rich. They shout and gesticulate tremendously but cannot agree, and Rodrigo is about to bear away the exhausted Zara, when the timid servant enters with a letter and a bag from Hagar, who has mysteriously disappeared. The latter informs the party that she bequeaths untold wealth to the young pair and an awful doom to Don Pedro, if he doesn't make them happy. The bag is opened, and several quarts of tin money shower down upon the stage till it is quite glorified with the glitter. This entirely softens the stern sire. He consents without a murmur, all join in a joyful chorus, and the curtain falls upon the lovers kneeling to receive Don Pedro's blessing in attitudes of the most romantic grace.

Tumultuous applause followed but received an unexpected check, for the cot bed, on which the dress circle was built, suddenly shut up and extinguished the enthusiastic audience. Roderigo and Don Pedro flew to the rescue, and all were taken out unhurt, though many were speechless with laughter. The excitement had hardly subsided when Hannah appeared, with "Mrs. March's compliments, and would the ladies walk down to supper."

This was a surprise even to the actors, and when they saw the table, they looked at one another in rapturous amazement. It was like Marmee to get up a little treat for them, but anything so fine as this was unheard of since the departed days of plenty. There was ice cream—actually two dishes of it, pink and white—and cake and fruit and distracting French bonbons and, in the middle of the table, four great bouquets of hothouse flowers.

It quite took their breath away, and they stared first at the table and then at their mother, who looked as if she enjoyed it immensely.

"Is it fairies?" asked Amy.

"It's Santa Claus," said Beth.

"Mother did it." And Meg smiled her sweetest, in spite of her gray beard and white eyebrows.

"Aunt March had a good fit and sent the supper," cried Jo, with a sudden inspiration.

"All wrong. Old Mr. Laurence sent it," replied Mrs. March.

"The Laurence boy's grandfather! What in the world put such a thing into his head? We don't know him!" exclaimed Meg.

"Hannah told one of his servants about your breakfast party. He is an odd old gentleman, but that pleased him. He knew my father years ago, and he sent me a polite note this afternoon, saying he hoped I would allow him to express his friendly feeling toward my children by sending them a few trifles in honor of the day. I could not refuse, and so you have a little feast at night to make up for the bread-and-milk breakfast."

"That boy put it into his head, I know he did! He's a capital fellow, and I wish we could get acquainted. He looks as if he'd like to know us but he's bashful, and Meg is so prim she won't let me speak to him when we pass," said Jo, as the plates went round, and the ice began to melt out of sight, with ohs and ahs of satisfaction.

"You mean the people who live in the big house next door, don't you?" asked one of the girls. "My mother knows old Mr. Laurence, but says he's very proud and doesn't like to mix with his neighbors. He keeps his grandson shut up, when he isn't riding or walking with his tutor, and makes him study very hard. We invited him to our party, but he didn't come. Mother says he's very nice, though he never speaks to us girls."

"Our cat ran away once, and he brought her back, and we talked over the fence, and were getting on capitally—all about cricket, and so on—when he saw Meg coming, and walked off. I mean to know him some day, for he needs fun, I'm sure he does," said Jo decidedly.

"I like his manners, and he looks like a little gentleman, so I've no objection to your knowing him, if a proper opportunity comes. He brought the flowers himself, and I should have asked him in, if I had been sure what was going on upstairs. He looked so wistful as he went away, hearing the frolic and evidently having none of his own."

"It's a mercy you didn't, Mother!" laughed Jo, looking at her boots. "But we'll have another play sometime that he can see. Perhaps he'll help act. Wouldn't that be jolly?"

"I never had such a fine bouquet before! How pretty it is!" And Meg examined her flowers with great interest.

"They *are* lovely. But Beth's roses are sweeter to me," said Mrs. March, smelling the half-dead posy in her belt.

Beth nestled up to her, and whispered softly, "I wish I could send my bunch to Father. I'm afraid he isn't having such a merry Christmas as we are."

CHAPTER III

THE LAURENCE BOY

"Jo! Jo! Where are you?" cried Meg at the foot of the garret stairs.

"Here!" answered a husky voice from above, and, running up, Meg found her sister eating apples and crying over the *Heir of Redclyffe*, wrapped up in a comforter on an old three-legged sofa by the sunny window. This was Jo's favorite refuge, and here she loved to retire with half a dozen russets and a nice book, to enjoy the quiet and the society of a pet rat who lived near by and didn't mind her a particle. As Meg appeared, Scrabble whisked into his hole. Jo shook the tears off her cheeks and waited to hear the news.

"Such fun! Only see! A regular note of invitation from Mrs. Gardiner for tomorrow night!" cried Meg, waving the precious paper and then proceeding to read it with girlish delight.

"'Mrs. Gardiner would be happy to see Miss March and Miss Josephine at a little dance on New Year's Eve.' Marmee is willing we should go, now what *shall* we wear?"

"What's the use of asking that, when you know we shall wear our poplins, because we haven't got anything else?" answered Jo with her mouth full.

"If I only had a silk!" sighed Meg. "Mother says I may when I'm eighteen perhaps, but two years is an everlasting time to wait."

"I'm sure our pops look like silk, and they are nice enough for us. Yours is as good as new, but I forgot the burn and the tear in mine. Whatever shall I do? The burn shows badly, and I can't take any out."

"You must sit still all you can and keep your back out of sight. The front is all right. I shall have a new ribbon for my hair, and Marmee will lend me her little pearl pin, and my new slippers are lovely, and my gloves will do, though they aren't as nice as I'd like."

"Mine are spoiled with lemonade, and I can't get any new ones, so I shall have to go without," said Jo, who never troubled herself much about dress.

"You *must* have gloves, or I won't go," cried Meg decidedly. "Gloves are more important than anything else. You can't dance without them, and if you don't I should be so mortified."

"Then I'll stay still. I don't care much for company dancing. It's no fun to go sailing round. I like to fly about and cut capers."

"You can't ask Mother for new ones, they are so expensive, and you are so careless. She said when you spoiled the others that she shouldn't get you any more this winter. Can't you make them do?"

"I can hold them crumpled up in my hand, so no one will know how stained they are. That's all I can do. No! I'll tell you how we can manage—each wear one good one and carry a bad one. Don't you see?"

"Your hands are bigger than mine, and you will stretch my glove dreadfully," began Meg, whose gloves were a tender point with her.

"Then I'll go without. I don't care what people say!" cried Jo, taking up her book.

"You may have it, you may! Only don't stain it, and do behave nicely. Don't put your hands behind you, or stare, or say 'Christopher Columbus!' will you?"

"Don't worry about me. I'll be as prim as I can and not get into any scrapes, if I can help it. Now go and answer your note, and let me finish this splendid story."

So Meg went away to "accept with thanks," look over her dress, and sing blithely as she did up her one real lace frill, while Jo finished her story, her four apples, and had a game of romps with Scrabble.

On New Year's Eve the parlor was deserted, for the two younger girls played dressing maids and the two elder were absorbed in the all-important business of "getting ready for the party." Simple as the toilets were, there was a great deal of running up and down, laughing and talking, and at one time a strong smell of burned hair pervaded the house. Meg wanted a few curls about her face, and Jo undertook to pinch the papered locks with a pair of hot tongs.

"Ought they to smoke like that?" asked Beth from her perch on the bed.

"It's the dampness drying," replied Jo.

"What a queer smell! It's like burned feathers," observed Amy, smoothing her own pretty curls with a superior air.

"There, now I'll take off the papers and you'll see a cloud of little ringlets," said Jo, putting down the tongs.

She did take off the papers, but no cloud of ringlets appeared, for the hair came with the papers, and the horrified hairdresser laid a row of little scorched bundles on the bureau before her victim.

"Oh, oh, oh! What have you done? I'm spoiled! I can't go! My hair, oh, my hair!" wailed Meg, looking with despair at the uneven frizzle on her forehead.

"Just my luck! You shouldn't have asked me to do it. I always spoil everything. I'm so sorry, but the tongs were too hot, and so I've made a mess," groaned poor Jo, regarding the little black pancakes with tears of regret.

"It isn't spoiled; just frizzle it, and tie your ribbon so the ends come on your forehead a bit, and it will look like the last fashion. I've seen many girls do it so," said Amy consolingly.

"Serves me right for trying to be fine. I wish I'd let my hair alone," cried Meg petulantly.

"So do I, it was so smooth and pretty. But it will soon grow out again," said Beth, coming to kiss and comfort the shorn sheep.

After various lesser mishaps, Meg was finished at last, and by the united exertions of the entire family Jo's hair was got up and her dress on. They looked very well in their simple suits—Meg's in silvery drab, with a blue velvet snood, lace frills, and the pearl pin. Jo in maroon, with a stiff, gentlemanly linen collar, and a white chrysanthemum or two for her only ornament. Each put on one nice light glove, and carried one soiled one, and all pronounced the effect "quite easy and fine." Meg's high-heeled slippers were very tight and hurt her, though she would not own it, and Jo's nineteen hairpins all seemed stuck straight into her head, which was not exactly comfortable, but, dear me, let us be elegant or die.

"Have a good time, dearies!" said Mrs. March, as the sisters went daintily down the walk. "Don't eat much supper, and come away at eleven when I send Hannah for you." As the gate clashed behind them, a voice cried from a window—

"Girls, girls! *Have* you both got nice pocket handkerchiefs?"

"Yes, yes, spandy nice, and Meg has cologne on hers," cried Jo, adding with a laugh as they went on, "I do believe Marmee would ask that if we were all running away from an earthquake."

"It is one of her aristocratic tastes, and quite proper, for a real lady is always known by neat boots, gloves, and handkerchief," replied Meg, who had a good many little "aristocratic tastes" of her own.

"Now don't forget to keep the bad breadth out of sight, Jo. Is my sash right? And does my hair look very bad?" said Meg, as she turned from the glass in Mrs. Gardiner's dressing room after a prolonged prink.

"I know I shall forget. If you see me doing anything wrong, just remind me by a wink, will you?" returned Jo, giving her collar a twitch and her head a hasty brush.

"No, winking isn't ladylike. I'll lift my eyebrows if any thing is wrong, and nod if you are all right. Now hold your shoulder straight, and take short steps, and don't shake hands if you are introduced to anyone. It isn't the thing."

"How *do* you learn all the proper ways? I never can. Isn't that music gay?"

Down they went, feeling a trifle timid, for they seldom went to parties, and informal as this little gathering was, it was an event to them. Mrs. Gardiner, a stately old lady, greeted them kindly and handed them over to the eldest of her six daughters. Meg knew Sallie and was at her ease very soon, but Jo, who didn't care much for girls or girlish gossip, stood about, with her back carefully against the wall, and felt as much out of place as a colt in a flower garden. Half a dozen jovial lads were talking about skates in another part of the room, and she longed to go and join them, for skating was one of the joys of her life. She telegraphed her wish to Meg, but the eyebrows went up so alarmingly that she dared not stir. No one came to talk to her, and one by one the group dwindled away till she was left alone. She could not roam about and amuse herself, for the burned breadth would show, so she stared at people rather forlornly till the dancing began. Meg was asked at once, and the tight slippers tripped about so briskly that none would have guessed the pain their wearer suffered smilingly. Jo saw a big red headed youth approaching her corner, and fearing he meant to engage her, she slipped into a curtained recess, intending to peep and enjoy herself in peace. Unfortunately, another bashful person had chosen the same refuge, for, as the curtain fell behind her, she found herself face to face with the "Laurence boy."

"Dear me, I didn't know anyone was here!" stammered Jo, preparing to back out as speedily as she had bounced in.

But the boy laughed and said pleasantly, though he looked a little startled, "Don't mind me, stay if you like."

"Shan't I disturb you?"

"Not a bit. I only came here because I don't know many people and felt rather strange at first, you know."

"So did I. Don't go away, please, unless you'd rather."

The boy sat down again and looked at his pumps, till Jo said, trying to be polite and easy, "I think I've had the pleasure of seeing you before. You live near us, don't you?"

"Next door." And he looked up and laughed outright, for Jo's prim manner was rather funny when he remembered how they had chatted about cricket when he brought the cat home.

That put Jo at her ease and she laughed too, as she said, in her heartiest way, "We did have such a good time over your nice Christmas present."

"Grandpa sent it."

"But you put it into his head, didn't you, now?"

"How is your cat, Miss March?" asked the boy, trying to look sober while his black eyes shone with fun.

"Nicely, thank you, Mr. Laurence. But I am not Miss March, I'm only Jo," returned the young lady.

"I'm not Mr. Laurence, I'm only Laurie."

"Laurie Laurence—what an odd name."

"My first name is Theodore, but I don't like it, for the fellows called me Dora, so I made them say Laurie instead."

"I hate my name, too—so sentimental! I wish every one would say Jo instead of Josephine. How did you make the boys stop calling you Dora?"

"I thrashed 'em."

"I can't thrash Aunt March, so I suppose I shall have to bear it." And Jo resigned herself with a sigh.

"Don't you like to dance, Miss Jo?" asked Laurie, looking as if he thought the name suited her.

"I like it well enough if there is plenty of room, and everyone is lively. In a place like this I'm sure to upset something, tread on people's toes, or do something dreadful, so I keep out of mischief and let Meg sail about. Don't you dance?"

"Sometimes. You see I've been abroad a good many years, and haven't been into company enough yet to know how you do things here."

"Abroad!" cried Jo. "Oh, tell me about it! I love dearly to hear people describe their travels."

Laurie didn't seem to know where to begin, but Jo's eager questions soon set him going, and he told her how he had been at school in Vevay, where the boys never wore hats and had a fleet of boats on the lake, and for holiday fun went on walking trips about Switzerland with their teachers.

"Don't I wish I'd been there!" cried Jo. "Did you go to Paris?"

"We spent last winter there."

"Can you talk French?"

"We were not allowed to speak anything else at Vevay."

"Do say some! I can read it, but can't pronounce."

"*Quel nom a cette jeune demoiselle en les pantoufles jolis?*" said Laurie good-naturedly.

"How nicely you do it! Let me see—you said, 'Who is the young lady in the pretty slippers,' didn't you?"

"*Oui, mademoiselle.*"

"It's my sister Margaret, and you knew it was! Do you think she is pretty?"

"Yes, she makes me think of the German girls, she looks so fresh and quiet, and dances like a lady."

Jo quite glowed with pleasure at this boyish praise of her sister, and stored it up to repeat to Meg. Both peeped and criticized and chatted till they felt like old acquaintances. Laurie's bashfulness soon wore off, for Jo's gentlemanly demeanor amused and set him at his ease, and Jo was her merry self again, because her dress was forgotten and nobody lifted their eyebrows at her. She liked the "Laurence boy" better than ever and took several good looks at him, so that she might describe him to the girls, for they had no brothers, very few male cousins, and boys were almost unknown creatures to them.

"Curly black hair, brown skin, big black eyes, handsome nose, fine teeth, small hands and feet, taller than I am, very polite, for a boy, and altogether jolly. Wonder how old he is?"

It was on the tip of Jo's tongue to ask, but she checked herself in time and, with unusual tact, tried to find out in a round-about way.

"I suppose you are going to college soon? I see you pegging away at your books—no, I mean studying hard." And Jo blushed at the dreadful "pegging" which had escaped her.

Laurie smiled but didn't seem shocked, and answered with a shrug. "Not for a year or two. I won't go before seventeen, anyway."

"Aren't you but fifteen?" asked Jo, looking at the tall lad, whom she had imagined seventeen already.

"Sixteen, next month."

"How I wish I was going to college! You don't look as if you liked it."

"I hate it! Nothing but grinding or skylarking. And I don't like the way fellows do either, in this country."

"What do you like?"

"To live in Italy, and to enjoy myself in my own way."

Jo wanted very much to ask what his own way was, but his black brows looked rather threatening as he knit them, so she changed the subject by saying, as her foot kept time, "That's a splendid polka! Why don't you go and try it?"

"If you will come too," he answered, with a gallant little bow.

"I can't; for I told Meg I wouldn't, because—" There Jo stopped, and looked undecided whether to tell or to laugh.

"Because, what?"

"You won't tell?"

"Never!"

"Well, I have a bad trick of standing before the fire, and so I burn my frocks, and I scorched this one, and though it's nicely mended, it shows, and Meg told me to keep still so no one would see it. You may laugh, if you want to. It is funny, I know."

But Laurie didn't laugh. He only looked down a minute, and the expression of his face puzzled Jo when he said very gently, "Never mind that. I'll tell you how we can manage. There's a long hall out there, and we can dance grandly, and no one will see us. Please come."

Jo thanked him and gladly went, wishing she had two neat gloves when she saw the nice, pearl-colored ones her partner wore. The hall was empty, and they had a grand polka, for Laurie danced well, and taught her the German step, which delighted Jo, being full of swing and spring. When the music stopped, they sat down on the stairs to get their breath, and Laurie was in the midst of an account of a students' festival at Heidelberg when Meg appeared in search of her sister. She beckoned, and Jo reluctantly followed her into a side room, where she found her on a sofa, holding her foot, and looking pale.

"I've sprained my ankle. That stupid high heel turned and gave me a sad wrench. It aches so, I can hardly stand, and I don't know how I'm ever going to get home," she said, rocking to and fro in pain.

"I knew you'd hurt your feet with those silly shoes. I'm sorry. But I don't see what you can do, except get a carriage, or stay here all night," answered Jo, softly rubbing the poor ankle as she spoke.

"I can't have a carriage without its costing ever so much. I dare say I can't get one at all, for most people come in their own, and it's a long way to the stable, and no one to send."

"I'll go."

"No, indeed! It's past nine, and dark as Egypt. I can't stop here, for the house is full. Sallie has some girls staying with her. I'll rest till Hannah comes, and then do the best I can."

"I'll ask Laurie; he will go," said Jo, looking relieved as the idea occurred to her.

"Mercy, no! Don't ask or tell anyone. Get me my rubbers, and put these slippers with our things. I can't dance anymore, but as soon as supper is over, watch for Hannah and tell me the minute she comes."

"They are going out to supper now. I'll stay with you. I'd rather."

"No, dear, run along, and bring me some coffee. I'm so tired I can't stir."

So Meg reclined, with rubbers well hidden, and Jo went blundering away to the dining room, which she found after going into a china closet, and opening the door of a room where old Mr. Gardiner was taking a little private refreshment. Making a dart at the table, she secured the coffee, which she immediately spilled, thereby making the front of her dress as bad as the back.

"Oh, dear, what a blunderbuss I am!" exclaimed Jo, finishing Meg's glove by scrubbing her gown with it.

"Can I help you?" said a friendly voice. And there was Laurie, with a full cup in one hand and a plate of ice in the other.

"I was trying to get something for Meg, who is very tired, and someone shook me, and here I am in a nice state," answered Jo, glancing dismally from the stained skirt to the coffee-colored glove.

"Too bad! I was looking for someone to give this to. May I take it to your sister?"

"Oh, thank you! I'll show you where she is. I don't offer to take it myself, for I should only get into another scrape if I did."

Jo led the way, and as if used to waiting on ladies, Laurie drew up a little table, brought a second installment of coffee and ice for Jo, and was so obliging that even particular Meg pronounced him a "nice boy."

They had a merry time over the bonbons and mottoes, and were in the midst of a quiet game of "*Buzz*," with two or three other young people who had strayed in, when Hannah appeared. Meg forgot her foot and rose so quickly that she was forced to catch hold of Jo, with an exclamation of pain.

"Hush! Don't say anything," she whispered, adding aloud, "It's nothing. I turned my foot a little, that's all," and limped upstairs to put her things on.

Hannah scolded, Meg cried, and Jo was at her wits' end, till she decided to take things into her own hands. Slipping out, she ran down and, finding a servant, asked if he could get her a carriage. It happened to be a hired waiter who knew nothing about the neighborhood and Jo was looking round for help when Laurie, who had heard what she said, came up and offered his grandfather's carriage, which had just come for him, he said.

"It's so early! You can't mean to go yet?" began Jo, looking relieved but hesitating to accept the offer.

"I always go early—I do, truly! Please let me take you home. It's all on my way, you know, and it rains, they say."

That settled it, and telling him of Meg's mishap, Jo gratefully accepted and rushed up to bring down the rest of the party. Hannah hated rain as much as a cat does so she made no trouble, and they rolled away in the luxurious close carriage, feeling very festive and elegant. Laurie went on the box so Meg could keep her foot up, and the girls talked over their party in freedom.

"I had a capital time. Did you?" asked Jo, rumpling up her hair, and making herself comfortable.

"Yes, till I hurt myself. Sallie's friend, Annie Moffat, took a fancy to me, and asked me to come and spend a week with her when Sallie does. She is going in the spring when the opera comes, and it will be perfectly splendid, if Mother only lets me go," answered Meg, cheering up at the thought.

"I saw you dancing with the redheaded man I ran away from. Was he nice?"

"Oh, very! His hair is auburn, not red, and he was very polite, and I had a delicious redowa with him."

"He looked like a grasshopper in a fit when he did the new step. Laurie and I couldn't help laughing. Did you hear us?"

"No, but it was very rude. What were you about all that time, hidden away there?"

Jo told her adventures, and by the time she had finished they were at home. With many thanks, they said good night and crept in, hoping to disturb no one, but the instant their door creaked, two little nightcaps bobbed up, and two sleepy but eager voices cried out—

"Tell about the party! Tell about the party!"

With what Meg called "a great want of manners" Jo had saved some bonbons for the little girls, and they soon subsided, after hearing the most thrilling events of the evening.

"I declare, it really seems like being a fine young lady, to come home from the party in a carriage and sit in my dressing gown with a maid to wait on me," said Meg, as Jo bound up her foot with arnica and brushed her hair.

"I don't believe fine young ladies enjoy themselves a bit more than we do, in spite of our burned hair, old gowns, one glove apiece and tight slippers that sprain our ankles when we are silly enough to wear them." And I think Jo was quite right.

CHAPTER IV

BURDENS

"Oh, dear, how hard it does seem to take up our packs and go on," sighed Meg the morning after the party, for now the holidays were over, the week of merrymaking did not fit her for going on easily with the task she never liked.

"I wish it was Christmas or New Year's all the time. Wouldn't it be fun?" answered Jo, yawning dismally.

"We shouldn't enjoy ourselves half so much as we do now. But it does seem so nice to have little suppers and bouquets, and go to parties, and drive home, and read and rest, and not work. It's like other people, you know, and I always envy girls who do such things, I'm so fond of luxury," said Meg, trying to decide which of two shabby gowns was the least shabby.

"Well, we can't have it, so don't let us grumble but shoulder our bundles and trudge along as cheerfully as Marmee does. I'm sure Aunt March is a regular Old Man of the Sea to me, but I suppose when I've learned to carry her without complaining, she will tumble off, or get so light that I shan't mind her."

This idea tickled Jo's fancy and put her in good spirits, but Meg didn't brighten, for her burden, consisting of four spoiled children, seemed heavier than ever. She had not heart enough even to make herself pretty as usual by putting on a blue neck ribbon and dressing her hair in the most becoming way.

"Where's the use of looking nice, when no one sees me but those cross midgets, and no one cares whether I'm pretty or not?" she muttered, shutting her drawer with a jerk. "I shall have to toil and moil all my days, with only little bits of fun now and then, and get old and ugly and sour, because I'm poor and can't enjoy my life as other girls do. It's a shame!"

So Meg went down, wearing an injured look, and wasn't at all agreeable at breakfast time. Everyone seemed rather out of sorts and inclined to croak. Beth had a headache and lay on the sofa, trying to comfort herself with the cat and three kittens. Amy was fretting because her lessons were not learned, and she couldn't find her rubbers. Jo *would* whistle and make a great racket getting ready. Mrs. March was very busy trying to finish a letter, which must go at once, and Hannah had the grumps, for being up late didn't suit her.

"There never *was* such a cross family!" cried Jo, losing her temper when she had upset an inkstand, broken both boot lacings, and sat down upon her hat.

"You're the crossest person in it!" returned Amy, washing out the sum that was all wrong with the tears that had fallen on her slate.

"Beth, if you don't keep these horrid cats down cellar I'll have them drowned," exclaimed Meg angrily as she tried to get rid of the kitten which had scrambled up her back and stuck like a burr just out of reach.

Jo laughed, Meg scolded, Beth implored, and Amy wailed because she couldn't remember how much nine times twelve was.

"Girls, girls, do be quiet one minute! I *must* get this off by the early mail, and you drive me distracted with your worry," cried Mrs. March, crossing out the third spoiled sentence in her letter.

There was a momentary lull, broken by Hannah, who stalked in, laid two hot turnovers on the table, and stalked out again. These turnovers were an institution, and the girls called them "muffs," for they had no others and found the hot pies very comforting to their hands on cold mornings. Hannah never forgot to make them, no matter how busy or grumpy she might be, for the walk was long and bleak. The poor things got no other lunch and were seldom home before two.

"Cuddle your cats and get over your headache, Bethy. Goodbye, Marmee. We are a set of rascals this morning, but we'll come home regular angels. Now then, Meg!" And Jo tramped away, feeling that the pilgrims were not setting out as they ought to do.

They always looked back before turning the corner, for their mother was always at the window to nod and smile, and wave her hand to them. Somehow it seemed as if they couldn't have got through the day without that, for whatever their mood might be, the last glimpse of that motherly face was sure to affect them like sunshine.

"If Marmee shook her fist instead of kissing her hand to us, it would serve us right, for more ungrateful wretches than we are were never seen," cried Jo, taking a remorseful satisfaction in the snowy walk and bitter wind.

"Don't use such dreadful expressions," replied Meg from the depths of the veil in which she had shrouded herself like a nun sick of the world.

"I like good strong words that mean something," replied Jo, catching her hat as it took a leap off her head preparatory to flying away altogether.

"Call yourself any names you like, but *I* am neither a rascal nor a wretch and I don't choose to be called so."

"You're a blighted being, and decidedly cross today because you can't sit in the lap of luxury all the time. Poor dear, just wait till I make my fortune, and you shall revel in carriages and ice cream and high-heeled slippers, and posies, and red-headed boys to dance with."

"How ridiculous you are, Jo!" But Meg laughed at the nonsense and felt better in spite of herself.

"Lucky for you I am, for if I put on crushed airs and tried to be dismal, as you do, we should be in a nice state. Thank goodness, I can always find something funny to keep me up. Don't croak any more, but come home jolly, there's a dear."

Jo gave her sister an encouraging pat on the shoulder as they parted for the day, each going a different way, each hugging her little warm turnover, and each trying to be cheerful in spite of wintry weather, hard work, and the unsatisfied desires of pleasure-loving youth.

When Mr. March lost his property in trying to help an unfortunate friend, the two oldest girls begged to be allowed to do something toward their own support, at least. Believing that they could not begin too early to cultivate energy, industry, and independence, their parents consented, and both fell to work with the hearty good will which in spite of all obstacles is sure to succeed at last. Margaret found a place as nursery governess and felt rich with her small salary. As she said, she was "fond of luxury," and her chief trouble was poverty. She found it harder to bear than the others because she could remember a time when home was beautiful, life full of ease and pleasure, and want of any kind unknown. She tried not to be envious or discontented, but it was very natural that the young girl should long for pretty things, gay friends, accomplishments, and a happy life. At the Kings' she daily saw all she wanted, for the children's older sisters were just out, and Meg caught frequent glimpses of dainty ball dresses and bouquets, heard lively gossip about theaters, concerts, sleighing parties, and merrymakings of all kinds, and saw money lavished on trifles which would have been so precious to her. Poor Meg seldom complained, but a sense of injustice made her feel bitter toward everyone sometimes, for she had not yet learned to know how rich she was in the blessings which alone can make life happy.

Jo happened to suit Aunt March, who was lame and needed an active person to wait upon her. The childless old lady had offered to adopt one of the girls when the troubles came, and was much offended because her offer was declined. Other friends told the Marches that they had lost all chance of being remembered in the rich old lady's will, but the unworldly Marches only said—

"We can't give up our girls for a dozen fortunes. Rich or poor, we will keep together and be happy in one another."

The old lady wouldn't speak to them for a time, but happening to meet Jo at a friend's, something in her comical face and blunt manners struck the old lady's fancy, and she proposed to take her for a companion. This did not suit Jo at all, but she accepted the place since nothing better appeared and, to every one's surprise, got on remarkably well with her irascible relative. There was an occasional tempest, and once Jo marched home, declaring she couldn't bear it longer, but Aunt March always cleared up quickly, and sent for her to come back again with such urgency that she could not refuse, for in her heart she rather liked the peppery old lady.

I suspect that the real attraction was a large library of fine books, which was left to dust and spiders since Uncle March died. Jo remembered the kind old gentleman, who used to let her build railroads and bridges with his big dictionaries, tell her stories about queer pictures in his Latin books, and buy her cards of gingerbread whenever he met her in the street. The dim, dusty room, with the busts staring down from the tall bookcases, the cozy chairs, the globes, and best of all, the wilderness of books in which she could wander where she liked, made the library a region of bliss to her. The moment Aunt March took her nap, or was busy with company, Jo hurried to this quiet place, and curling herself up in the easy chair, devoured poetry, romance, history, travels, and pictures like a regular bookworm. But, like all happiness, it did not last long, for as sure as she had just reached the heart of the story, the sweetest verse of a song, or the most perilous adventure of her traveler, a shrill voice called, "Josy-phine! Josy-phine!" and she had to leave her paradise to wind yarn, wash the poodle, or read Belsham's *Essays* by the hour together.

Jo's ambition was to do something very splendid. What it was, she had no idea as yet, but left it for time to tell her, and meanwhile, found her greatest affliction in the fact that she couldn't read, run, and ride as much as she liked. A quick temper, sharp tongue, and restless spirit were always getting her into scrapes, and her life was a series of ups and downs, which were both comic and pathetic. But the training she received at Aunt March's was just what she needed, and the thought that she was doing something to support herself made her happy in spite of the perpetual "Josy-phine!"

Beth was too bashful to go to school. It had been tried, but she suffered so much that it was given up, and she did her lessons at home with her father. Even when he went away, and her mother was called to devote her skill and energy to Soldiers' Aid Societies, Beth went faithfully on by herself and did the best she could. She was a housewifely little creature, and helped Hannah keep home neat and comfortable for the workers, never thinking of any reward but to be loved. Long, quiet days she spent, not lonely nor idle, for her little world was peopled with imaginary friends, and she was by nature a busy bee. There were six dolls to be taken up and dressed every morning, for Beth was a child still and loved her pets as well as ever. Not one whole or handsome one among them, all were outcasts till Beth took them in, for when her sisters outgrew these idols, they passed to her because Amy would have nothing old or ugly. Beth cherished them all the more tenderly for that very reason, and set up a hospital for infirm dolls. No pins were ever stuck into their cotton vitals, no harsh words or blows were ever given them, no neglect ever saddened the heart of the most repulsive, but all were fed and clothed, nursed and caressed with an affection which never failed. One forlorn fragment of *dollanity* had belonged to Jo and, having led a tempestuous life, was left a wreck in the rag bag, from which dreary poorhouse it was rescued by Beth and taken to her refuge. Having no top to its head, she tied on a neat little cap, and as both arms and legs were gone, she hid these deficiencies by folding it in a blanket and devoting her best bed to this chronic invalid. If anyone had known the care lavished on that dolly, I think it would have touched their hearts, even while they laughed. She brought it bits of bouquets, she read to it, took it out to breathe fresh air, hidden under her coat, she sang it lullabies and never went to bed without kissing its dirty face and whispering tenderly, "I hope you'll have a good night, my poor dear."

Beth had her troubles as well as the others, and not being an angel but a very human little girl, she often "wept a little weep" as Jo said, because she couldn't take music lessons and have a fine piano. She loved music so dearly, tried so hard to learn, and practiced away so patiently at the jingling old instrument, that it did seem as if someone (not to hint Aunt March) ought to help her. Nobody did, however, and nobody saw Beth wipe the tears off the yellow keys, that wouldn't keep in tune, when she was all alone. She sang like a little lark about her work, never was too tired for Marmee and the girls, and day after day said hopefully to herself, "I know I'll get my music some time, if I'm good."

There are many Beths in the world, shy and quiet, sitting in corners till needed, and living for others so cheerfully that no one sees the sacrifices till the little cricket on the hearth stops chirping, and the sweet, sunshiny presence vanishes, leaving silence and shadow behind.

If anybody had asked Amy what the greatest trial of her life was, she would have answered at once, "My nose." When she was a baby, Jo had accidently dropped her into the coal hod, and Amy insisted that the fall had ruined her nose forever. It was not big nor red, like poor "Petrea's," it was only rather flat, and all the pinching in the world could not give it an aristocratic point. No one minded it but herself, and it was doing its best to grow, but Amy felt deeply the want of a Grecian nose, and drew whole sheets of handsome ones to console herself.

"Little Raphael," as her sisters called her, had a decided talent for drawing, and was never so happy as when copying flowers, designing fairies, or illustrating stories with queer specimens of art. Her teachers complained that instead of doing her sums she covered her slate with animals, the blank pages of her atlas were used to copy maps on, and caricatures of the most ludicrous description came fluttering out of all her books at unlucky moments. She got through her lessons as well as she could, and managed to escape reprimands by being a model of deportment. She was a great favorite with her mates, being good-tempered and possessing the happy art of pleasing without effort. Her little airs and graces were much admired, so were her accomplishments, for besides her drawing, she could play twelve tunes, crochet, and read French without mispronouncing more than two-thirds of the words. She had a plaintive way of saying, "When Papa was rich we did so-and-so," which was very touching, and her long words were considered "perfectly elegant" by the girls.

Amy was in a fair way to be spoiled, for everyone petted her, and her small vanities and selfishnesses were growing nicely. One thing, however, rather quenched the vanities. She had to wear her cousin's clothes. Now Florence's mama hadn't a particle of taste, and Amy suffered deeply at having to wear a red instead of a blue bonnet, unbecoming gowns, and fussy aprons that did not fit. Everything was good, well made, and little worn, but Amy's artistic eyes were much afflicted, especially this winter, when her school dress was a dull purple with yellow dots and no trimming.

"My only comfort," she said to Meg, with tears in her eyes, "is that Mother doesn't take tucks in my dresses whenever I'm naughty, as Maria Parks's mother does. My dear, it's really dreadful, for sometimes she is so bad her frock is up to her knees, and she can't come to school. When I think of this *deggerredation*, I feel that I can bear even my flat nose and purple gown with yellow sky-rockets on it."

Meg was Amy's confidant and monitor, and by some strange attraction of opposites Jo was gentle Beth's. To Jo alone did the shy child tell her thoughts, and over her big harum-scarum sister Beth unconsciously exercised more influence than anyone in the family. The two older girls were a great deal to one another, but each took one of the younger sisters into her keeping and watched over her in her own way—"playing mother" they called it, and put their sisters in the places of discarded dolls with the maternal instinct of little women.

"Has anybody got anything to tell? It's been such a dismal day I'm really dying for some amusement," said Meg, as they sat sewing together that evening.

"I had a queer time with Aunt today, and, as I got the best of it, I'll tell you about it," began Jo, who dearly loved to tell stories. "I was reading that everlasting Belsham, and droning away as I always do, for Aunt soon drops off, and then I take out some nice book, and read like fury till she wakes up. I actually made myself sleepy, and before she began to nod, I gave such a gape that she asked me what I meant by opening my mouth wide enough to take the whole book in at once."

"I wish I could, and be done with it," said I, trying not to be saucy.

"Then she gave me a long lecture on my sins, and told me to sit and think them over while she just 'lost' herself for a moment. She never finds herself very soon, so the minute her cap began to bob like a top-heavy dahlia, I whipped the *Vicar of Wakefield* out of my pocket, and read away, with one eye on him and one on Aunt. I'd just got to where they all tumbled into the water when I forgot and laughed out loud. Aunt woke up and, being more good-natured after her nap, told me to read a bit and show what frivolous work I preferred to the worthy and instructive Belsham. I did my very best, and she liked it, though she only said—

"'I don't understand what it's all about. Go back and begin it, child.'"

"Back I went, and made the Primroses as interesting as ever I could. Once I was wicked enough to stop in a thrilling place, and say meekly, 'I'm afraid it tires you, ma'am. Shan't I stop now?'"

"She caught up her knitting, which had dropped out of her hands, gave me a sharp look through her specs, and said, in her short way, 'Finish the chapter, and don't be impertinent, miss.'"

"Did she own she liked it?" asked Meg.

"Oh, bless you, no! But she let old Belsham rest, and when I ran back after my gloves this afternoon, there she was, so hard at the Vicar that she didn't hear me laugh as I danced a jig in the hall because of the good time coming. What a pleasant life she might have if only she chose! I don't envy her much, in spite of her money, for after all rich people have about as many worries as poor ones, I think," added Jo.

"That reminds me," said Meg, "that I've got something to tell. It isn't funny, like Jo's story, but I thought about it a good deal as I came home. At the Kings' today I found everybody in a flurry, and one of the children said that her oldest brother had done something dreadful, and Papa had sent him away. I heard Mrs. King crying and Mr. King talking very loud, and Grace and Ellen turned away their faces when they passed me, so I shouldn't see how red and swollen their eyes were. I didn't ask any questions, of course, but I felt so sorry for them and was rather glad I hadn't any wild brothers to do wicked things and disgrace the family."

"I think being disgraced in school is a great deal try*inger* than anything bad boys can do," said Amy, shaking her head, as if her experience of life had been a deep one. "Susie Perkins came to school today with a lovely red carnelian ring. I wanted it dreadfully, and wished I was her with all my might. Well, she drew a picture of Mr. Davis, with a monstrous nose and a hump, and the words, 'Young ladies, my eye is upon you!' coming out of his mouth in a balloon thing. We were laughing over it when all of a sudden his eye *was* on us, and he ordered Susie to bring up her slate. She was *parry*lized with fright, but she went, and oh, what *do* you think he did? He took her by the ear—the ear! Just fancy how horrid!—and led her to the recitation platform, and made her stand there half an hour, holding the slate so everyone could see."

"Didn't the girls laugh at the picture?" asked Jo, who relished the scrape.

"Laugh? Not one! They sat still as mice, and Susie cried quarts, I know she did. I didn't envy her then, for I felt that millions of carnelian rings wouldn't have made me happy after that. I never, never should have got over such a agonizing mortification." And Amy went on with her work, in the proud consciousness of virtue and the successful utterance of two long words in a breath.

"I saw something I liked this morning, and I meant to tell it at dinner, but I forgot," said Beth, putting Jo's topsy-turvy basket in order as she talked. "When I went to get some oysters for Hannah, Mr. Laurence was in the fish shop, but he didn't see me, for I kept behind the fish barrel, and he was busy with Mr. Cutter the fish-man. A poor woman came in with a pail and a mop, and asked Mr. Cutter if he would let her do some scrubbing for a bit of fish, because she hadn't any dinner for her children, and had been disappointed of a day's work. Mr. Cutter was in a hurry and said 'No,' rather crossly, so she was going away, looking hungry and sorry, when Mr. Laurence hooked up a big fish with the crooked end of his cane and held it out to her. She was so glad and surprised she took it right into her arms, and thanked him over and over. He told her to "go along and cook it," and she hurried off, so happy! Wasn't it good of him? Oh, she did look so funny, hugging the big, slippery fish, and hoping Mr. Laurence's bed in heaven would be 'aisy.'"

When they had laughed at Beth's story, they asked their mother for one, and after a moment's thought, she said soberly, "As I sat cutting out blue flannel jackets today at the rooms, I felt very anxious about Father, and thought how lonely and helpless we should be, if anything happened to him. It was not a wise thing to do, but I kept on worrying till an old man came in with an order for some clothes. He sat down near me, and I began to talk to him, for he looked poor and tired and anxious.

"'Have you sons in the army?' I asked, for the note he brought was not to me."

"Yes, ma'am. I had four, but two were killed, one is a prisoner, and I'm going to the other, who is very sick in a Washington hospital,' he answered quietly."

"'You have done a great deal for your country, sir,' I said, feeling respect now, instead of pity."

"'Not a mite more than I ought, ma'am. I'd go myself, if I was any use. As I ain't, I give my boys, and give 'em free.'"

"He spoke so cheerfully, looked so sincere, and seemed so glad to give his all, that I was ashamed of myself. I'd given one man and thought it too much, while he gave four without grudging them. I had all my girls to comfort me at home, and his last son was waiting, miles away, to say good-by to him, perhaps! I felt so rich, so happy thinking of my blessings, that I made him a nice bundle, gave him some money, and thanked him heartily for the lesson he had taught me."

"Tell another story, Mother—one with a moral to it, like this. I like to think about them afterward, if they are real and not too preachy," said Jo, after a minute's silence.

Mrs. March smiled and began at once, for she had told stories to this little audience for many years, and knew how to please them.

"Once upon a time, there were four girls, who had enough to eat and drink and wear, a good many comforts and pleasures, kind friends and parents who loved them dearly, and yet they were not contented." (Here the listeners stole sly looks at one another, and began to sew diligently.) "These girls were anxious to be good and made many excellent resolutions, but they did not keep them very well, and were constantly saying, 'If only we had this,' or 'If we could only do that,' quite forgetting how much they already had, and how many things they actually could do. So they asked an old woman what spell they could use to make them happy, and she said, 'When you feel discontented, think over your blessings, and be grateful.'" (Here Jo looked up quickly, as if about to speak, but changed her mind, seeing that the story was not done yet.)

"Being sensible girls, they decided to try her advice, and soon were surprised to see how well off they were. One discovered that money couldn't keep shame and sorrow out of rich people's houses, another that, though she was poor, she was a great deal happier, with her youth, health, and good spirits, than a certain fretful, feeble old lady who couldn't enjoy her comforts, a third that, disagreeable as it was to help get dinner, it was harder still to go begging for it and the fourth, that even carnelian rings were not so valuable as good behavior. So they agreed to stop complaining, to enjoy the blessings already possessed, and try to deserve them, lest they should be taken away entirely, instead of increased, and I believe they were never disappointed or sorry that they took the old woman's advice."

"Now, Marmee, that is very cunning of you to turn our own stories against us, and give us a sermon instead of a romance!" cried Meg.

"I like that kind of sermon. It's the sort Father used to tell us," said Beth thoughtfully, putting the needles straight on Jo's cushion.

"I don't complain near as much as the others do, and I shall be more careful than ever now, for I've had warning from Susie's downfall," said Amy morally.

"We needed that lesson, and we won't forget it. If we do so, you just say to us, as old Chloe did in *Uncle Tom*, 'Tink ob yer marcies, chillen! Tink ob yer marcies!'" added Jo, who could not, for the life of her, help getting a morsel of fun out of the little sermon, though she took it to heart as much as any of them.

CHAPTER V

BEING NEIGHBORLY

"What in the world are you going to do now, Jo?" asked Meg one snowy afternoon, as her sister came tramping through the hall, in rubber boots, old sack, and hood, with a broom in one hand and a shovel in the other.

"Going out for exercise," answered Jo with a mischievous twinkle in her eyes.

"I should think two long walks this morning would have been enough! It's cold and dull out, and I advise you to stay warm and dry by the fire, as I do," said Meg with a shiver.

"Never take advice! Can't keep still all day, and not being a pussycat, I don't like to doze by the fire. I like adventures, and I'm going to find some."

Meg went back to toast her feet and read *Ivanhoe*, and Jo began to dig paths with great energy. The snow was light, and with her broom she soon swept a path all round the garden, for Beth to walk in when the sun came out and the invalid dolls needed air. Now, the garden separated the Marches' house from that of Mr. Laurence. Both stood in a suburb of the city, which was still country-like, with groves and lawns, large gardens, and quiet streets. A low hedge parted the two estates. On one side was an old, brown house, looking rather bare and shabby, robbed of the vines that in summer covered its walls and the flowers, which then surrounded it. On the other side was a stately stone mansion, plainly betokening every sort of comfort and luxury, from the big coach house and well-kept grounds to the conservatory and the glimpses of lovely things one caught between the rich curtains. Yet it seemed a lonely, lifeless sort of house, for no children frolicked on the lawn, no motherly face ever smiled at the windows, and few people went in and out, except the old gentleman and his grandson.

To Jo's lively fancy, this fine house seemed a kind of enchanted palace, full of splendors and delights which no one enjoyed. She had long wanted to behold these hidden glories, and to know the Laurence boy, who looked as if he would like to be known, if he only knew how to begin. Since the party, she had been more eager than ever, and had planned many ways of making friends with him, but he had not been seen lately, and Jo began to think he had gone away, when she one day spied a brown face at an upper window, looking wistfully down into their garden, where Beth and Amy were snow-balling one another.

"That boy is suffering for society and fun," she said to herself. "His grandpa does not know what's good for him, and keeps him shut up all alone. He needs a party of jolly boys to play with, or somebody young and lively. I've a great mind to go over and tell the old gentleman so!"

The idea amused Jo, who liked to do daring things and was always scandalizing Meg by her queer performances. The plan of "going over" was not forgotten. And when the snowy afternoon came, Jo resolved to try what could be done. She saw Mr. Laurence drive off, and then sallied out to dig her way down to the hedge, where she paused and took a survey. All quiet—curtains down at the lower windows, servants out of sight, and nothing human visible but a curly black head leaning on a thin hand at the upper window.

"There he is," thought Jo, "Poor boy! All alone and sick this dismal day. It's a shame! I'll toss up a snowball and make him look out, and then say a kind word to him."

Up went a handful of soft snow, and the head turned at once, showing a face which lost its listless look in a minute, as the big eyes brightened and the mouth began to smile. Jo nodded and laughed, and flourished her broom as she called out—

"How do you do? Are you sick?"

Laurie opened the window, and croaked out as hoarsely as a raven—

"Better, thank you. I've had a bad cold, and been shut up a week."

"I'm sorry. What do you amuse yourself with?"

"Nothing. It's dull as tombs up here."

"Don't you read?"

"Not much. They won't let me."

"Can't somebody read to you?"

"Grandpa does sometimes, but my books don't interest him, and I hate to ask Brooke all the time."

"Have someone come and see you then."

"There isn't anyone I'd like to see. Boys make such a row, and my head is weak."

"Isn't there some nice girl who'd read and amuse you? Girls are quiet and like to play nurse."

"Don't know any."

"You know us," began Jo, then laughed and stopped.

"So I do! Will you come, please?" cried Laurie.

"I'm not quiet and nice, but I'll come, if Mother will let me. I'll go ask her. Shut the window, like a good boy, and wait till I come."

With that, Jo shouldered her broom and marched into the house, wondering what they would all say to her. Laurie was in a flutter of excitement at the idea of having company, and flew about to get ready, for as Mrs. March said, he was "a little gentleman," and did honor to the coming guest by brushing his curly pate, putting on a fresh color, and trying to tidy up the room, which in spite of half a dozen servants, was anything but neat. Presently there came a loud ring, than a decided voice, asking for "Mr. Laurie," and a surprised-looking servant came running up to announce a young lady.

"All right, show her up, it's Miss Jo," said Laurie, going to the door of his little parlor to meet Jo, who appeared, looking rosy and quite at her ease, with a covered dish in one hand and Beth's three kittens in the other.

"Here I am, bag and baggage," she said briskly. "Mother sent her love, and was glad if I could do anything for you. Meg wanted me to bring some of her blanc mange, she makes it very nicely, and Beth thought her cats would be comforting. I knew you'd laugh at them, but I couldn't refuse, she was so anxious to do something."

It so happened that Beth's funny loan was just the thing, for in laughing over the kits, Laurie forgot his bashfulness, and grew sociable at once.

"That looks too pretty to eat," he said, smiling with pleasure, as Jo uncovered the dish, and showed the blanc mange, surrounded by a garland of green leaves, and the scarlet flowers of Amy's pet geranium.

"It isn't anything, only they all felt kindly and wanted to show it. Tell the girl to put it away for your tea. It's so simple you can eat it, and being soft, it will slip down without hurting your sore throat. What a cozy room this is!"

"It might be if it was kept nice, but the maids are lazy, and I don't know how to make them mind. It worries me though."

"I'll right it up in two minutes, for it only needs to have the hearth brushed, so—and the things made straight on the mantelpiece, so—and the books put here, and the bottles there, and your sofa turned from the light, and the pillows plumped up a bit. Now then, you're fixed."

And so he was, for, as she laughed and talked, Jo had whisked things into place and given quite a different air to the room. Laurie watched her in respectful silence, and when she beckoned him to his sofa, he sat down with a sigh of satisfaction, saying gratefully—

"How kind you are! Yes, that's what it wanted. Now please take the big chair and let me do something to amuse my company."

"No, I came to amuse you. Shall I read aloud?" and Jo looked affectionately toward some inviting books near by.

"Thank you! I've read all those, and if you don't mind, I'd rather talk," answered Laurie.

"Not a bit. I'll talk all day if you'll only set me going. Beth says I never know when to stop."

"Is Beth the rosy one, who stays at home good deal and sometimes goes out with a little basket?" asked Laurie with interest.

"Yes, that's Beth. She's my girl, and a regular good one she is, too."

"The pretty one is Meg, and the curly-haired one is Amy, I believe?"

"How did you find that out?"

Laurie colored up, but answered frankly, "Why, you see I often hear you calling to one another, and when I'm alone up here, I can't help looking over at your house, you always seem to be having such good times. I beg your pardon for being so rude, but sometimes you forget to put down the curtain at the window where the flowers are. And when the lamps are lighted, it's like looking at a picture to see the fire, and you all around the table with your mother. Her face is right opposite, and it looks so sweet behind the flowers, I can't help watching it. I haven't got any mother, you know." And Laurie poked the fire to hide a little twitching of the lips that he could not control.

The solitary, hungry look in his eyes went straight to Jo's warm heart. She had been so simply taught that there was no nonsense in her head, and at fifteen she was as innocent and frank as any child. Laurie was sick and lonely, and feeling how rich she was in home and happiness, she gladly tried to share it with him. Her face was very friendly and her sharp voice unusually gentle as she said—

"We'll never draw that curtain any more, and I give you leave to look as much as you like. I just wish, though, instead of peeping, you'd come over and see us. Mother is so splendid, she'd do you heaps of good, and Beth would sing to you if *I* begged her to, and Amy would dance. Meg and I would make you laugh over our funny stage properties, and we'd have jolly times. Wouldn't your grandpa let you?"

"I think he would, if your mother asked him. He's very kind, though he does not look so, and he lets me do what I like, pretty much, only he's afraid I might be a bother to strangers," began Laurie, brightening more and more.

"We are not strangers, we are neighbors, and you needn't think you'd be a bother. We *want* to know you, and I've been trying to do it this ever so long. We haven't been here a great while, you know, but we have got acquainted with all our neighbors but you."

"You see, Grandpa lives among his books, and doesn't mind much what happens outside. Mr. Brooke, my tutor, doesn't stay here, you know, and I have no one to go about with me, so I just stop at home and get on as I can."

"That's bad. You ought to make an effort and go visiting everywhere you are asked, then you'll have plenty of friends, and pleasant places to go to. Never mind being bashful. It won't last long if you keep going."

Laurie turned red again, but wasn't offended at being accused of bashfulness, for there was so much good will in Jo it was impossible not to take her blunt speeches as kindly as they were meant.

"Do you like your school?" asked the boy, changing the subject, after a little pause, during which he stared at the fire and Jo looked about her, well pleased.

"Don't go to school, I'm a businessman—girl, I mean. I go to wait on my great-aunt, and a dear, cross old soul she is, too," answered Jo.

Laurie opened his mouth to ask another question, but remembering just in time that it wasn't manners to make too many inquiries into people's affairs, he shut it again, and looked uncomfortable. Jo liked his good breeding, and didn't mind having a laugh at Aunt March, so she gave him a lively description of the fidgety old lady, her fat poodle, the parrot that talked Spanish, and the library where she reveled. Laurie enjoyed that immensely, and when she told about the prim old gentleman who came once to woo Aunt March, and in the middle of a fine speech, how Poll had tweaked his wig off to his great dismay, the boy lay back and laughed till the tears ran down his cheeks, and a maid popped her head in to see what was the matter.

"Oh! That does me no end of good. Tell on, please," he said, taking his face out of the sofa cushion, red and shining with merriment.

Much elated with her success, Jo did "tell on," all about their plays and plans, their hopes and fears for Father, and the most interesting events of the little world in which the sisters lived. Then they got to talking about books, and to Jo's delight, she found that Laurie loved them as well as she did, and had read even more than herself.

"If you like them so much, come down and see ours. Grandfather is out, so you needn't be afraid," said Laurie, getting up.

"I'm not afraid of anything," returned Jo, with a toss of the head.

"I don't believe you are!" exclaimed the boy, looking at her with much admiration, though he privately thought she would have good reason to be a trifle afraid of the old gentleman, if she met him in some of his moods.

The atmosphere of the whole house being summerlike, Laurie led the way from room to room, letting Jo stop to examine whatever struck her fancy. And so, at last they came to the library, where she clapped her hands and pranced, as she always did when especially delighted. It was lined with books, and there were pictures and statues, and distracting little cabinets full of coins and curiosities, and Sleepy Hollow chairs, and queer tables, and bronzes, and best of all, a great open fireplace with quaint tiles all round it.

"What richness!" sighed Jo, sinking into the depth of a velour chair and gazing about her with an air of intense satisfaction. "Theodore Laurence, you ought to be the happiest boy in the world," she added impressively.

"A fellow can't live on books," said Laurie, shaking his head as he perched on a table opposite.

Before he could more, a bell rang, and Jo flew up, exclaiming with alarm, "Mercy me! It's your grandpa!"

"Well, what if it is? You are not afraid of anything, you know," returned the boy, looking wicked.

"I think I am a little bit afraid of him, but I don't know why I should be. Marmee said I might come, and I don't think you're any the worse for it," said Jo, composing herself, though she kept her eyes on the door.

"I'm a great deal better for it, and ever so much obliged. I'm only afraid you are very tired of talking to me. It was so pleasant, I couldn't bear to stop," said Laurie gratefully.

"The doctor to see you, sir," and the maid beckoned as she spoke.

"Would you mind if I left you for a minute? I suppose I must see him," said Laurie.

"Don't mind me. I'm happy as a cricket here," answered Jo.

Laurie went away, and his guest amused herself in her own way. She was standing before a fine portrait of the old gentleman when the door opened again, and without turning, she said decidedly, "I'm sure now that I shouldn't be afraid of him, for he's got kind eyes, though his mouth is grim, and he looks as if he had a tremendous will of his own. He isn't as handsome as *my* grandfather, but I like him."

"Thank you, ma'am," said a gruff voice behind her, and there, to her great dismay, stood old Mr. Laurence.

Poor Jo blushed till she couldn't blush any redder, and her heart began to beat uncomfortably fast as she thought what she had said. For a minute a wild desire to run away possessed her, but that was cowardly, and the girls would laugh at her, so she resolved to stay and get out of the scrape as she could. A second look showed her that the living eyes, under the bushy eyebrows, were kinder even than the painted ones, and there was a sly twinkle in them, which lessened her fear a good deal. The gruff voice was gruffer than ever, as the old gentleman said abruptly, after the dreadful pause, "So you're not afraid of me, hey?"

"Not much, sir."

"And you don't think me as handsome as your grandfather?"

"Not quite, sir."

"And I've got a tremendous will, have I?"

"I only said I thought so."

"But you like me in spite of it?"

"Yes, I do, sir."

That answer pleased the old gentleman. He gave a short laugh, shook hands with her, and, putting his finger under her chin, turned up her face, examined it gravely, and let it go, saying with a nod, "You've got your grandfather's spirit, if you haven't his face. He *was* a fine man, my dear, but what is better, he was a brave and an honest one, and I was proud to be his friend."

"Thank you, sir," And Jo was quite comfortable after that, for it suited her exactly.

"What have you been doing to this boy of mine, hey?" was the next question, sharply put.

"Only trying to be neighborly, sir." And Jo told how her visit came about.

"You think he needs cheering up a bit, do you?"

"Yes, sir, he seems a little lonely, and young folks would do him good perhaps. We are only girls, but we should be glad to help if we could, for we don't forget the splendid Christmas present you sent us," said Jo eagerly.

"Tut, tut, tut! That was the boy's affair. How is the poor woman?"

"Doing nicely, sir." And off went Jo, talking very fast, as she told all about the Hummels, in whom her mother had interested richer friends than they were.

"Just her father's way of doing good. I shall come and see your mother some fine day. Tell her so. There's the tea bell, we have it early on the boy's account. Come down and go on being neighborly."

"If you'd like to have me, sir."

"Shouldn't ask you, if I didn't." And Mr. Laurence offered her his arm with old-fashioned courtesy.

"What *would* Meg say to this?" thought Jo, as she was marched away, while her eyes danced with fun as she imagined herself telling the story at home.

"Hey! Why, what the dickens has come to the fellow?" said the old gentleman, as Laurie came running downstairs and brought up with a start of surprise at the astounding sight of Jo arm in arm with his redoubtable grandfather.

"I didn't know you'd come, sir," he began, as Jo gave him a triumphant little glance.

"That's evident, by the way you racket downstairs. Come to your tea, sir, and behave like a gentleman." And having pulled the boy's hair by way of a caress, Mr. Laurence walked on, while Laurie went through a series of comic evolutions behind their backs, which nearly produced an explosion of laughter from Jo.

The old gentleman did not say much as he drank his four cups of tea, but he watched the young people, who soon chatted away like old friends, and the change in his grandson did not escape him. There was color, light, and life in the boy's face now, vivacity in his manner, and genuine merriment in his laugh.

"She's right, the lad *is* lonely. I'll see what these little girls can do for him," thought Mr. Laurence, as he looked and listened. He liked Jo, for her odd, blunt ways suited him, and she seemed to understand the boy almost as well as if she had been one herself.

If the Laurences had been what Jo called "prim and poky," she would not have got on at all, for such people always made her shy and awkward. But finding them free and easy, she was so herself, and made a good impression. When they rose she proposed to go, but Laurie said he had something more to show her, and took her away to the conservatory, which had been lighted for her benefit. It seemed quite fairylike to Jo, as she went up and down the walks, enjoying the blooming walls on either side, the soft light, the damp sweet air, and the wonderful vines and trees that hung about her, while her new friend cut the finest flowers till his hands were full. Then he tied them up, saying, with the happy look Jo liked to see, "Please give these to your mother, and tell her I like the medicine she sent me very much."

They found Mr. Laurence standing before the fire in the great drawing room, but Jo's attention was entirely absorbed by a grand piano, which stood open.

"Do you play?" she asked, turning to Laurie with a respectful expression.

"Sometimes," he answered modestly.

"Please do now. I want to hear it, so I can tell Beth."

"Won't you first?"

"Don't know how. Too stupid to learn, but I love music dearly."

So Laurie played and Jo listened, with her nose luxuriously buried in heliotrope and tea roses. Her respect and regard for the "Laurence boy" increased very much, for he played remarkably well and didn't put on any airs. She wished Beth could hear him, but she did not say so, only praised him till he was quite abashed, and his grandfather came to his rescue. "That will do, that will do, young lady. Too many sugarplums are not good for him. His music isn't bad, but I hope he will do as well in more important things. Going? Well, I'm much obliged to you, and I hope you'll come again. My respects to your mother. Good night, Doctor Jo."

He shook hands kindly, but looked as if something did not please him. When they got into the hall, Jo asked Laurie if she had said something amiss. He shook his head.

"No, it was me. He doesn't like to hear me play."

"Why not?"

"I'll tell you some day. John is going home with you, as I can't."

"No need of that. I am not a young lady, and it's only a step. Take care of yourself, won't you?"

"Yes, but you will come again, I hope?"

"If you promise to come and see us after you are well."

"I will."

"Good night, Laurie!"

"Good night, Jo, good night!"

When all the afternoon's adventures had been told, the family felt inclined to go visiting in a body, for each found something very attractive in the big house on the other side of the hedge. Mrs. March wanted to talk of her father with the old man who had not forgotten him, Meg longed to walk in the conservatory, Beth sighed for the grand piano, and Amy was eager to see the fine pictures and statues.

"Mother, why didn't Mr. Laurence like to have Laurie play?" asked Jo, who was of an inquiring disposition.

"I am not sure, but I think it was because his son, Laurie's father, married an Italian lady, a musician, which displeased the old man, who is very proud. The lady was good and lovely and accomplished, but he did not like her, and never saw his son after he married. They both died when Laurie was a little child, and then his grandfather took him home. I fancy the boy, who was born in Italy, is not very strong, and the old man is afraid of losing him, which makes him so careful. Laurie comes naturally by his love of music, for he is like his mother, and I dare say his grandfather fears that he may want to be a musician. At any rate, his skill reminds him of the woman he did not like, and so he 'glowered' as Jo said."

"Dear me, how romantic!" exclaimed Meg.

"How silly!" said Jo. "Let him be a musician if he wants to, and not plague his life out sending him to college, when he hates to go."

"That's why he has such handsome black eyes and pretty manners, I suppose. Italians are always nice," said Meg, who was a little sentimental.

"What do you know about his eyes and his manners? You never spoke to him, hardly," cried Jo, who was *not* sentimental.

"I saw him at the party, and what you tell shows that he knows how to behave. That was a nice little speech about the medicine Mother sent him."

"He meant the blancmange, I suppose."

"How stupid you are, child! He meant you, of course."

"Did he?" And Jo opened her eyes as if it had never occurred to her before.

"I never saw such a girl! You don't know a compliment when you get it," said Meg, with the air of a young lady who knew all about the matter.

"I think they are great nonsense, and I'll thank you not to be silly and spoil my fun. Laurie's a nice boy and I like him, and I won't have any sentimental stuff about compliments and such rubbish. We'll all be good to him because he hasn't got any mother, and he may come over and see us, mayn't he, Marmee?"

"Yes, Jo, your little friend is very welcome, and I hope Meg will remember that children should be children as long as they can."

"I don't call myself a child, and I'm not in my teens yet," observed Amy. "What do you say, Beth?"

"I was thinking about our 'Pilgrim's Progress,'" answered Beth, who had not heard a word. "How we got out of the Slough and through the Wicket Gate by resolving to be good, and up the steep hill by trying, and that maybe the house over there, full of splendid things, is going to be our Palace Beautiful."

"We have got to get by the lions first," said Jo, as if she rather liked the prospect.

CHAPTER VI

BETH FINDS THE PALACE BEAUTIFUL

The big house did prove a Palace Beautiful, though it took some time for all to get in, and Beth found it very hard to pass the lions. Old Mr. Laurence was the biggest one, but after he had called, said something funny or kind to each one of the girls, and talked over old times with their mother, nobody felt much afraid of him, except timid Beth. The other lion was the fact that they were poor and Laurie rich, for this made them shy of accepting favors which they could not return. But, after a while, they found that he considered them the benefactors, and could not do enough to show how grateful he was for Mrs. March's motherly welcome, their cheerful society, and the comfort he took in that humble home of theirs. So they soon forgot their pride and interchanged kindnesses without stopping to think which was the greater.

All sorts of pleasant things happened about that time, for the new friendship flourished like grass in spring. Every one liked Laurie, and he privately informed his tutor that "the Marches were regularly splendid girls." With the delightful enthusiasm of youth, they took the solitary boy into their midst and made much of him, and he found something very charming in the innocent companionship of these simple-hearted girls. Never having known mother or sisters, he was quick to feel the influences they brought about him, and their busy, lively ways made him ashamed of the indolent life he led. He was tired of books, and found people so interesting now that Mr. Brooke was obliged to make very unsatisfactory reports, for Laurie was always playing truant and running over to the Marches'.

"Never mind, let him take a holiday, and make it up afterward," said the old gentleman. "The good lady next door says he is studying too hard and needs young society, amusement, and exercise. I suspect she is right, and that I've been coddling the fellow as if I'd been his grandmother. Let him do what he likes, as long as he is happy. He can't get into mischief in that little nunnery over there, and Mrs. March is doing more for him than we can."

What good times they had, to be sure. Such plays and tableaux, such sleigh rides and skating frolics, such pleasant evenings in the old parlor, and now and then such gay little parties at the great house. Meg could walk in the conservatory whenever she liked and revel in bouquets, Jo browsed over the new library voraciously, and convulsed the old gentleman with her criticisms, Amy copied pictures and enjoyed beauty to her heart's content, and Laurie played "lord of the manor" in the most delightful style.

But Beth, though yearning for the grand piano, could not pluck up courage to go to the "Mansion of Bliss," as Meg called it. She went once with Jo, but the old gentleman, not being aware of her infirmity, stared at her so hard from under his heavy eyebrows, and said "Hey!" so loud, that he frightened her so much her "feet chattered on the floor," she never told her mother, and she ran away, declaring she would never go there any more, not even for the dear piano. No persuasions or enticements could overcome her fear, till, the fact coming to Mr. Laurence's ear in some mysterious way, he set about mending matters. During one of the brief calls he made, he artfully led the conversation to music, and talked away about great singers whom he had seen, fine organs he had heard, and told such charming anecdotes that Beth found it impossible to stay in her distant corner, but crept nearer and nearer, as if fascinated. At the back of his chair she stopped and stood listening, with her great eyes wide open and her cheeks red with excitement of this unusual performance. Taking no more notice of her than if she had been a fly, Mr. Laurence talked on about Laurie's lessons and teachers. And presently, as if the idea had just occurred to him, he said to Mrs. March—

"The boy neglects his music now, and I'm glad of it, for he was getting too fond of it. But the piano suffers for want of use. Wouldn't some of your girls like to run over, and practice on it now and then, just to keep it in tune, you know, ma'am?"

Beth took a step forward, and pressed her hands tightly together to keep from clapping them, for this was an irresistible temptation, and the thought of practicing on that splendid instrument quite took her breath away. Before Mrs. March could reply, Mr. Laurence went on with an odd little nod and smile—

"They needn't see or speak to anyone, but run in at any time. For I'm shut up in my study at the other end of the house, Laurie is out a great deal, and the servants are never near the drawing room after nine o'clock."

Here he rose, as if going, and Beth made up her mind to speak, for that last arrangement left nothing to be desired. "Please, tell the young ladies what I say, and if they don't care to come, why, never mind." Here a little hand slipped into his, and Beth looked up at him with a face full of gratitude, as she said, in her earnest yet timid way—

"Oh sir, they do care, very very much!"

"Are you the musical girl?" he asked, without any startling "Hey!" as he looked down at her very kindly.

"I'm Beth. I love it dearly, and I'll come, if you are quite sure nobody will hear me—and be disturbed," she added, fearing to be rude, and trembling at her own boldness as she spoke.

"Not a soul, my dear. The house is empty half the day, so come and drum away as much as you like, and I shall be obliged to you."

"How kind you are, sir!"

Beth blushed like a rose under the friendly look he wore, but she was not frightened now, and gave the hand a grateful squeeze because she had no words to thank him for the precious gift he had given her. The old gentleman softly stroked the hair off her forehead, and, stooping down, he kissed her, saying, in a tone few people ever heard—

"I had a little girl once, with eyes like these. God bless you, my dear! Good day, madam." And away he went, in a great hurry.

Beth had a rapture with her mother, and then rushed up to impart the glorious news to her family of invalids, as the girls were not home. How blithely she sang that evening, and how they all laughed at her because she woke Amy in the night by playing the piano on her face in her sleep. Next day, having seen both the old and young gentleman out of the house, Beth, after two or three retreats, fairly got in at the side door, and made her way as noiselessly as any mouse to the drawing room where her idol stood. Quite by accident, of course, some pretty, easy music lay on the piano, and with trembling fingers and frequent stops to listen and look about, Beth at last touched the great instrument, and straightway forgot her fear, herself, and everything else but the unspeakable delight which the music gave her, for it was like the voice of a beloved friend.

She stayed till Hannah came to take her home to dinner, but she had no appetite, and could only sit and smile upon everyone in a general state of beatitude.

After that, the little brown hood slipped through the hedge nearly every day, and the great drawing room was haunted by a tuneful spirit that came and went unseen. She never knew that Mr. Laurence opened his study door to hear the old-fashioned airs he liked. She never saw Laurie mount guard in the hall to warn the servants away. She never suspected that the exercise books and new songs which she found in the rack were put there for her especial benefit, and when he talked to her about music at home, she only thought how kind he was to tell things that helped her so much. So she enjoyed herself heartily, and found, what isn't always the case, that her granted wish was all she had hoped. Perhaps it was because she was so grateful for this blessing that a greater was given her. At any rate she deserved both.

"Mother, I'm going to work Mr. Laurence a pair of slippers. He is so kind to me, I must thank him, and I don't know any other way. Can I do it?" asked Beth, a few weeks after that eventful call of his.

"Yes, dear. It will please him very much, and be a nice way of thanking him. The girls will help you about them, and I will pay for the making up," replied Mrs. March, who took peculiar pleasure in granting Beth's requests because she so seldom asked anything for herself.

After many serious discussions with Meg and Jo, the pattern was chosen, the materials bought, and the slippers begun. A cluster of grave yet cheerful pansies on a deeper purple ground was pronounced very appropriate and pretty, and Beth worked away early and late, with occasional lifts over hard parts. She was a nimble little needlewoman, and they were finished before anyone got tired of them. Then she wrote a short, simple note, and with Laurie's help, got them smuggled onto the study table one morning before the old gentleman was up.

When this excitement was over, Beth waited to see what would happen. All day passed and a part of the next before any acknowledgement arrived, and she was beginning to fear she had offended her crochety friend. On the afternoon of the second day, she went out to do an errand, and give poor Joanna, the invalid doll, her daily exercise. As she came up the street, on her return, she saw three, yes, four heads popping in and out of the parlor windows, and the moment they saw her, several hands were waved, and several joyful voices screamed—

"Here's a letter from the old gentleman! Come quick, and read it!"

"Oh, Beth, he's sent you—" began Amy, gesticulating with unseemly energy, but she got no further, for Jo quenched her by slamming down the window.

Beth hurried on in a flutter of suspense. At the door her sisters seized and bore her to the parlor in a triumphal procession, all pointing and all saying at once, "Look there! Look there!" Beth did look, and turned pale with delight and surprise, for there stood a little cabinet piano, with a letter lying on the glossy lid, directed like a sign board to "Miss Elizabeth March."

"For me?" gasped Beth, holding onto Jo and feeling as if she should tumble down, it was such an overwhelming thing altogether.

"Yes, all for you, my precious! Isn't it splendid of him? Don't you think he's the dearest old man in the world? Here's the key in the letter. We didn't open it, but we are dying to know what he says," cried Jo, hugging her sister and offering the note.

"You read it! I can't, I feel so queer! Oh, it is too lovely!" and Beth hid her face in Jo's apron, quite upset by her present.

Jo opened the paper and began to laugh, for the first words she saw were—

> "MISS MARCH:
> "*Dear Madam*—"

"How nice it sounds! I wish someone would write to me so!" said Amy, who thought the old-fashioned address very elegant.

> " 'I have had many pairs of slippers in my life, but I never had any that suited me so well as yours,' "

continued Jo.

> " 'Heartsease is my favorite flower, and these will always remind me of the gentle giver. I like to pay my debts, so I know you will allow 'the old gentleman' to send you something which once belonged to the little grand daughter he lost. With hearty thanks and best wishes, I remain
> " 'Your grateful friend and humble servant,
> " 'JAMES LAURENCE.' "

"There, Beth, that's an honor to be proud of, I'm sure! Laurie told me how fond Mr. Laurence used to be of the child who died, and how he kept all her little things carefully. Just think, he's given you her piano. That comes of having big blue eyes and loving music," said Jo, trying to soothe Beth, who trembled and looked more excited than she had ever been before.

"See the cunning brackets to hold candles, and the nice green silk, puckered up, with a gold rose in the middle, and the pretty rack and stool, all complete," added Meg, opening the instrument and displaying its beauties.

"'Your humble servant, James Laurence.' Only think of his writing that to you. I'll tell the girls. They'll think it's splendid," said Amy, much impressed by the note.

"Try it, honey. Let's hear the sound of the baby pianny," said Hannah, who always took a share in the family joys and sorrows.

So Beth tried it, and everyone pronounced it the most remarkable piano ever heard. It had evidently been newly tuned and put in apple-pie order, but, perfect as it was, I think the real charm lay in the happiest of all happy faces which leaned over it, as Beth lovingly touched the beautiful black and white keys and pressed the bright pedals.

"You'll have to go and thank him," said Jo, by way of a joke, for the idea of the child's really going never entered her head.

"Yes, I mean to. I guess I'll go now, before I get frightened thinking about it." And, to the utter amazement of the assembled family, Beth walked deliberately down the garden, through the hedge, and in at the Laurences' door.

"Well, I wish I may die if it ain't the queerest thing I ever see! The pianny has turned her head! She'd never have gone in her right mind," cried Hannah, staring after her, while the girls were rendered quite speechless by the miracle.

They would have been still more amazed if they had seen what Beth did afterward. If you will believe me, she went and knocked at the study door before she gave herself time to think, and when a gruff voice called out, "Come in!" she did go in, right up to Mr. Laurence, who looked quite taken aback, and held out her hand, saying, with only a small quaver in her voice, "I came to thank you, sir, for—" But she didn't finish, for he looked so friendly that she forgot her speech and, only remembering that he had lost the little girl he loved, she put both arms round his neck and kissed him.

If the roof of the house had suddenly flown off, the old gentleman wouldn't have been more astonished. But he liked it—oh, dear, yes, he liked it amazingly!—and was so touched and pleased by that confiding little kiss that all his crustiness vanished, and he just set her on his knee, and laid his wrinkled cheek against her rosy one, feeling as if he had got his own little granddaughter back again. Beth ceased to fear him from that moment, and sat there talking to him as cozily as if she had known him all her life, for love casts out fear, and gratitude can conquer pride.

When she went home, he walked with her to her own gate, shook hands cordially, and touched his hat as he marched back again, looking very stately and erect, like a handsome, soldierly old gentleman, as he was. When the girls saw that performance, Jo began to dance a jig, by way of expressing her satisfaction, Amy nearly fell out of the window in her surprise, and Meg exclaimed, with uplifted hands, "Well, I do believe the world is coming to an end."

CHAPTER VII

AMY'S VALLEY OF HUMILIATION

"That boy is a perfect cyclops, isn't he?" said Amy one day, as Laurie clattered by on horseback, with a flourish of his whip as he passed.

"How dare you say so, when he's got both his eyes? And very handsome ones they are, too," cried Jo, who resented any slighting remarks about her friend.

"I didn't say anything about his eyes, and I don't see why you need fire up when I admire his riding."

"Oh, my goodness! That little goose means a centaur, and she called him a Cyclops," exclaimed Jo, with a burst of laughter.

"You needn't be so rude, it's only a 'lapse of lingy,' as Mr. Davis says," retorted Amy, finishing Jo with her Latin. "I just wish I had a little of the money Laurie spends on that horse," she added, as if to herself, yet hoping her sisters would hear.

"Why?" asked Meg kindly, for Jo had gone off in another laugh at Amy's second blunder.

"I need it so much. I'm dreadfully in debt, and it won't be my turn to have the rag money for a month."

"In debt, Amy? What do you mean?" And Meg looked sober.

"Why, I owe at least a dozen pickled limes, and I can't pay them, you know, till I have money, for Marmee forbade my having anything charged at the shop."

"Tell me all about it. Are limes the fashion now? It used to be pricking bits of rubber to make balls." And Meg tried to keep her countenance, Amy looked so grave and important.

"Why, you see, the girls are always buying them, and unless you want to be thought mean, you must do it too. It's nothing but limes now, for everyone is sucking them in their desks in schooltime, and trading them off for pencils, bead rings, paper dolls, or something else, at recess. If one girl likes another, she gives her a lime. If she's mad with her, she eats one before her face, and doesn't offer even a suck. They treat by turns, and I've had ever so many but haven't returned them, and I ought for they are debts of honor, you know."

"How much will pay them off and restore your credit?" asked Meg, taking out her purse.

"A quarter would more than do it, and leave a few cents over for a treat for you. Don't you like limes?"

"Not much. You may have my share. Here's the money. Make it last as long as you can, for it isn't very plenty, you know."

"Oh, thank you! It must be so nice to have pocket money! I'll have a grand feast, for I haven't tasted a lime this week. I felt delicate about taking any, as I couldn't return them, and I'm actually suffering for one."

Next day Amy was rather late at school, but could not resist the temptation of displaying, with pardonable pride, a moist brown-paper parcel, before she consigned it to the inmost recesses of her desk. During the next few minutes the rumor that Amy March had got twenty-four delicious limes (she ate one on the way) and was going to treat circulated through her "set," and the attentions of her friends became quite overwhelming. Katy Brown invited her to her next party on the spot. Mary Kinglsey insisted on lending her her watch till recess, and Jenny Snow, a satirical young lady, who had basely twitted Amy upon her limeless state, promptly buried the hatchet and offered to furnish answers to certain appalling sums. But Amy had not forgotten Miss Snow's cutting remarks about "some persons whose noses were not too flat to smell other people's limes, and stuck-up people who were not too proud to ask for them," and she instantly crushed "that Snow girl's" hopes by the withering telegram, "You needn't be so polite all of a sudden, for you won't get any."

A distinguished personage happened to visit the school that morning, and Amy's beautifully drawn maps received praise, which honor to her foe rankled in the soul of Miss Snow, and caused Miss March to assume the airs of a studious young peacock. But, alas, alas! Pride goes before a fall, and the revengeful Snow turned the tables with disastrous success. No sooner had the guest paid the usual stale compliments and bowed himself out, than Jenny, under pretense of asking an important question, informed Mr. Davis, the teacher, that Amy March had pickled limes in her desk.

Now Mr. Davis had declared limes a contraband article, and

solemnly vowed to publicly ferrule the first person who was found breaking the law. This much-enduring man had succeeded in banishing chewing gum after a long and stormy war, had made a bonfire of the confiscated novels and newspapers, had suppressed a private post office, had forbidden distortions of the face, nicknames, and caricatures, and done all that one man could do to keep half a hundred rebellious girls in order. Boys are trying enough to human patience, goodness knows, but girls are infinitely more so, especially to nervous gentlemen with tyrannical tempers and no more talent for teaching than Dr. Blimber. Mr. Davis knew any quantity of Greek, Latin, algebra, and ologies of all sorts so he was called a fine teacher, and manners, morals, feelings, and examples were not considered of any particular importance. It was a most unfortunate moment for denouncing Amy, and Jenny knew it. Mr. Davis had evidently taken his coffee too strong that morning, there was an east wind, which always affected his neuralgia, and his pupils had not done him the credit which he felt he deserved. Therefore, to use the expressive, if not elegant, language of a schoolgirl, "He was as nervous as a witch and as cross as a bear." The word "limes" was like fire to powder, his yellow face flushed, and he rapped on his desk with an energy which made Jenny skip to her seat with unusual rapidity.

"Young ladies, attention, if you please!"

At the stern order the buzz ceased, and fifty pairs of blue, black, gray, and brown eyes were obediently fixed upon his awful countenance.

"Miss March, come to the desk."

Amy rose to comply with outward composure, but a secret fear oppressed her, for the limes weighed upon her conscience.

"Bring with you the limes you have in your desk," was the unexpected command which arrested her before she got out of her seat.

"Don't take all," whispered her neighbor, a young lady of great presence of mind.

Amy hastily shook out half a dozen and laid the rest down before Mr. Davis, feeling that any man possessing a human heart would relent when that delicious perfume met his nose. Unfortunately, Mr. Davis particularly detested the odor of the fashionable pickle, and disgust added to his wrath.

"Is that all?"

"Not quite," stammered Amy.

"Bring the rest immediately."

With a despairing glance at her set, she obeyed.

"You are sure there are no more?"

"I never lie, sir."

"So I see. Now take these disgusting things two by two, and throw them out of the window."

There was a simultaneous sigh, which created quite a little gust, as the last hope fled, and the treat was ravished from their longing lips. Scarlet with shame and anger, Amy went to and fro six dreadful times, and as each doomed couple—looking oh, so plump and juicy—fell from her reluctant hands, a shout from the street completed the anguish of the girls, for it told them that their feast was being exulted over by the little Irish children, who were their sworn foes. This—this was too much. All flashed indignant or appealing glances at the inexorable Davis, and one passionate lime lover burst into tears.

As Amy returned from her last trip, Mr. Davis gave a portentous "Hem!" and said, in his most impressive manner—

"Young ladies, you remember what I said to you a week ago. I am sorry this has happened, but I never allow my rules to be infringed, and I *never* break my word. Miss March, hold out your hand."

Amy started, and put both hands behind her, turning on him an imploring look which pleaded for her better than the words she could not utter. She was rather a favorite with "old Davis," as, of course, he was called, and it's my private belief that he *would* have broken his word if the indignation of one irrepressible young lady had not found vent in a hiss. That hiss, faint as it was, irritated the irascible gentleman, and sealed the culprit's fate.

"Your hand, Miss March!" was the only answer her mute appeal received, and too proud to cry or beseech, Amy set her teeth, threw back her head defiantly, and bore without flinching several tingling blows on her little palm. They were neither many nor heavy, but that made no difference to her. For the first time in her life she had been struck, and the disgrace, in her eyes, was as deep as if he had knocked her down.

"You will now stand on the platform till recess," said Mr. Davis, resolved to do the thing thoroughly, since he had begun.

That was dreadful. It would have been bad enough to go to her seat, and see the pitying faces of her friends, or the satisfied ones of her few enemies, but to face the whole school, with that shame fresh upon her, seemed impossible, and for a second she felt as if she could only drop down where she stood, and break her heart with crying. A bitter sense of wrong and the thought of Jenny Snow helped her to bear it, and, taking the ignominious place, she fixed her eyes on the stove funnel above what now seemed a sea of faces, and stood there, so motionless and white that the girls found it hard to study with that pathetic figure before them.

During the fifteen minutes that followed, the proud and sensitive little girl suffered a shame and pain which she never forgot. To others it might seem a ludicrous or trivial affair, but to her it was a hard experience, for during the twelve years of her life she had been governed by love alone, and a blow of that sort had never touched her before. The smart of her hand and the ache of her heart were forgotten in the sting of the thought, "I shall have to tell at home, and they will be so disappointed in me!"

The fifteen minutes seemed an hour, but they came to an end at last, and the word "Recess!" had never seemed so welcome to her before.

"You can go, Miss March," said Mr. Davis, looking, as he felt, uncomfortable.

He did not soon forget the reproachful glance Amy gave him, as she went, without a word to anyone, straight into the anteroom, snatched her things, and left the place "forever," as she passionately declared to herself. She was in a sad state when she got home, and when the older girls arrived, some time later, an indignation meeting was held at once. Mrs. March did not say much but looked disturbed, and comforted her afflicted little daughter in her tenderest manner. Meg bathed the insulted hand with glycerine and tears, Beth felt that even her beloved kittens would fail as a balm for griefs like this, Jo wrathfully proposed that Mr. Davis be arrested without delay, and Hannah shook her fist at the "villain" and pounded potatoes for dinner as if she had him under her pestle.

No notice was taken of Amy's flight, except by her mates; but the sharp-eyed demoiselles discovered that Mr. Davis was quite benignant in the afternoon, also unusually nervous. Just before school closed, Jo appeared, wearing a grim expression as she stalked up to the desk, and delivered a letter from her mother, then collected Amy's property, and departed, carefully scraping the mud from her boots on the door mat, as if she shook the dust of the place off her feet.

"Yes, you can have a vacation from school, but I want you to study a little every day with Beth," said Mrs. March that evening. "I don't approve of corporal punishment, especially for girls. I dislike Mr. Davis's manner of teaching and don't think the girls you associate with are doing you any good, so I shall ask your father's advice before I send you anywhere else."

"That's good! I wish all the girls would leave, and spoil his old school. It's perfectly maddening to think of those lovely limes," sighed Amy, with the air of a martyr.

"I am not sorry you lost them, for you broke the rules, and deserved some punishment for disobedience," was the severe reply, which rather disappointed the young lady, who expected nothing but sympathy.

"Do you mean you are glad I was disgraced before the whole school?" cried Amy.

"I should not have chosen that way of mending a fault," replied her mother, "but I'm not sure that it won't do you more good than a bolder method. You are getting to be rather conceited, my dear, and it is quite time you set about correcting it. You have a good many little gifts and virtues, but there is no need of parading them, for conceit spoils the finest genius. There is not much danger that real talent or goodness will be overlooked long, even if it is, the consciousness of possessing and using it well should satisfy one, and the great charm of all power is modesty."

"So it is!" cried Laurie, who was playing chess in a corner with Jo. "I knew a girl once, who had a really remarkable talent for music, and she didn't know it, never guessed what sweet little things she composed when she was alone, and wouldn't have believed it if anyone had told her."

"I wish I'd known that nice girl. Maybe she would have helped me, I'm so stupid," said Beth, who stood beside him, listening eagerly.

"You do know her, and she helps you better than anyone else could," answered Laurie, looking at her with such mischievous meaning in his merry black eyes that Beth suddenly turned very red, and hid her face in the sofa cushion, quite overcome by such an unexpected discovery.

Jo let Laurie win the game to pay for that praise of her Beth, who could not be prevailed upon to play for them after her compliment. So Laurie did his best, and sang delightfully, being in a particularly lively humor, for to the Marches he seldom showed the moody side of his character. When he was gone, Amy, who had been pensive all evening, said suddenly, as if busy over some new idea, "Is Laurie an accomplished boy?"

"Yes, he has had an excellent education, and has much talent. He will make a fine man, if not spoiled by petting," replied her mother.

"And he isn't conceited, is he?" asked Amy.

"Not in the least. That is why he is so charming and we all like him so much."

"I see. It's nice to have accomplishments and be elegant, but not to show off or get perked up," said Amy thoughtfully.

"These things are always seen and felt in a person's manner and conversations, if modestly used, but it is not necessary to display them," said Mrs. March.

"Any more than it's proper to wear all your bonnets and gowns and ribbons at once, that folks may know you've got them," added Jo, and the lecture ended in a laugh.

CHAPTER VIII

JO MEETS APOLLYON

"Girls, where are you going?" asked Amy, coming into their room one Saturday afternoon, and finding them getting ready to go out with an air of secrecy which excited her curiosity.

"Never mind. Little girls shouldn't ask questions," returned Jo sharply.

Now if there is anything mortifying to our feelings when we are young, it is to be told that, and to be bidden to "run away, dear" is still more trying to us. Amy bridled up at this insult, and determined to find out the secret, if she teased for an hour. Turning to Meg, who never refused her anything very long, she said coaxingly, "Do tell me! I should think you might let me go, too, for Beth is fussing over her piano, and I haven't got anything to do, and am so lonely."

"I can't, dear, because you aren't invited," began Meg, but Jo broke in impatiently, "Now, Meg, be quiet or you will spoil it all. You can't go, Amy, so don't be a baby and whine about it."

"You are going somewhere with Laurie, I know you are. You were whispering and laughing together on the sofa last night, and you stopped when I came in. Aren't you going with him?"

"Yes, we are. Now do be still, and stop bothering."

Amy held her tongue, but used her eyes, and saw Meg slip a fan into her pocket.

"I know! I know! You're going to the theater to see the *Seven Castles*!" she cried, adding resolutely, "and I *shall* go, for Mother said I might see it, and I've got my rag money, and it was mean not to tell me in time."

"Just listen to me a minute, and be a good child," said Meg soothingly. "Mother doesn't wish you to go this week, because your eyes are not well enough yet to bear the light of this fairy piece. Next week you can go with Beth and Hannah, and have a nice time."

"I don't like that half as well as going with you and Laurie. Please let me. I've been sick with this cold so long, and shut up, I'm dying for some fun. Do, Meg! I'll be ever so good," pleaded Amy, looking as pathetic as she could.

"Suppose we take her. I don't believe Mother would mind, if we bundle her up well," began Meg.

"If *she* goes I shan't, and if I don't, Laurie won't like it, and it will be very rude, after he invited only us, to go and drag in Amy. I should think she'd hate to poke herself where she isn't wanted," said Jo crossly, for she disliked the trouble of overseeing a fidgety child when she wanted to enjoy herself.

Her tone and manner angered Amy, who began to put her boots on, saying, in her most aggravating way, "I *shall* go. Meg says I may, and if I pay for myself, Laurie hasn't anything to do with it."

"You can't sit with us, for our seats are reserved, and you mustn't sit alone, so Laurie will give you his place, and that will spoil our pleasure. Or he'll get another seat for you, and that isn't proper when you weren't asked. You shan't stir a step, so you may just stay where you are," scolded Jo, crosser than ever, having just pricked her finger in her hurry.

Sitting on the floor with one boot on, Amy began to cry and Meg to reason with her, when Laurie called from below, and the two girls hurried down, leaving their sister wailing. For now and then she forgot her grown-up ways and acted like a spoiled child. Just as the party was setting out, Amy called over the banisters in a threatening tone, "You'll be sorry for this, Jo March, see if you ain't."

"Fiddlesticks!" returned Jo, slamming the door.

They had a charming time, for *The Seven Castles of the Diamond Lake* was as brilliant and wonderful as heart could wish. But in spite of the comical red imps, sparkling elves, and the gorgeous princes and princesses, Jo's pleasure had a drop of bitterness in it. The fairy queen's yellow curls reminded her of Amy, and between the acts she amused herself with wondering what her sister would do to make her "sorry for it." She and Amy had had many lively skirmishes in the course of their lives, for both had quick tempers and were apt to be violent when fairly roused. Amy teased Jo, and Jo irritated Amy, and semioccasional explosions occurred, of which both were much ashamed afterward. Although the oldest, Jo had the least self-control, and had hard times trying to curb the fiery spirit which was continually getting her into trouble. Her anger never lasted long, and having humbly confessed her fault, she sincerely repented and tried to do better. Her sisters used to say that they rather liked to get Jo into a fury because she was such an angel afterward. Poor Jo tried desperately to be good, but her bosom enemy was always ready to flame up and defeat her, and it took years of patient effort to subdue it.

When they got home, they found Amy reading in the parlor. She assumed an injured air as they came in, never lifted her eyes from her book, or asked a single question. Perhaps curiosity might have conquered resentment, if Beth had not been there to inquire and receive a glowing description of the play. On going up to put away her best hat, Jo's first look was toward the bureau, for in their last quarrel Amy had soothed her feelings by turning Jo's top drawer upside down on the floor. Everything was in its place, however, and after a hasty glance into her various closets, bags, and boxes, Jo decided that Amy had forgiven and forgotten her wrongs.

There Jo was mistaken, for next day she made a discovery which produced a tempest. Meg, Beth, and Amy were sitting together, late in the afternoon, when Jo burst into the room, looking excited and demanding breathlessly, "Has anyone taken my book?"

Meg and Beth said, "No," at once, and looked surprised. Amy poked the fire and said nothing. Jo saw her color rise and was down upon her in a minute.

"Amy, you've got it!"

"No, I haven't."

"You know where it is, then!"

"No, I don't."

"That's a fib!" cried Jo, taking her by the shoulders, and looking fierce enough to frighten a much braver child than Amy.

"It isn't. I haven't got it, don't know where it is now, and don't care."

"You know something about it, and you'd better tell at once, or I'll make you." And Jo gave her a slight shake.

"Scold as much as you like, you'll never see your silly old book again," cried Amy, getting excited in her turn.

"Why not?"

"I burned it up."

"What! My little book I was so fond of, and worked over, and meant to finish before Father got home? Have you really burned it?" said Jo, turning very pale, while her eyes kindled and her hands clutched Amy nervously.

"Yes, I did! I told you I'd make you pay for being so cross yesterday, and I have, so—"

Amy got no farther, for Jo's hot temper mastered her, and she shook Amy till her teeth chattered in her head, crying in a passion of grief and anger—

"You wicked, wicked girl! I never can write it again, and I'll never forgive you as long as I live."

Meg flew to rescue Amy, and Beth to pacify Jo, but Jo was quite beside herself, and with a parting box on her sister's ear, she rushed out of the room up to the old sofa in the garret, and finished her fight alone.

The storm cleared up below, for Mrs. March came home, and, having heard the story, soon brought Amy to a sense of the wrong she had done her sister. Jo's book was the pride of her heart, and was regarded by her family as a literary sprout of great promise. It was only half a dozen little fairy tales, but Jo had worked over them patiently, putting her whole heart into her work, hoping to make something good enough to print. She had just copied them with great care, and had destroyed the old manuscript, so that Amy's bonfire had consumed the loving work of several years. It seemed a small loss to others, but to Jo it was a dreadful calamity, and she felt that it never could be made up to her. Beth mourned as for a departed kitten, and Meg refused to defend her pet. Mrs. March looked grave and grieved, and Amy felt that no one would love her till she had asked pardon for the act which she now regretted more than any of them.

When the tea bell rang, Jo appeared, looking so grim and unapproachable that it took all Amy's courage to say meekly—

"Please forgive me, Jo. I'm very, very sorry."

"I never shall forgive you," was Jo's stern answer, and from that moment she ignored Amy entirely.

No one spoke of the great trouble—not even Mrs. March—for all had learned by experience that when Jo was in that mood words were wasted, and the wisest course was to wait till some little accident, or her own generous nature, softened Jo's resentment and healed the breach. It was not a happy evening, for though they sewed as usual, while their mother read aloud from Bremer, Scott, or Edgeworth, something was wanting, and the sweet home peace was disturbed. They felt this most when singing time came, for Beth could only play, Jo stood dumb as a stone, and Amy broke down, so Meg and Mother sang alone. But in spite of their efforts to be as cheery as larks, the flutelike voices did not seem to chord as well as usual, and all felt out of tune.

As Jo received her good-night kiss, Mrs. March whispered gently, "My dear, don't let the sun go down upon your anger. Forgive each other, help each other, and begin again tomorrow."

Jo wanted to lay her head down on that motherly bosom, and cry her grief and anger all away, but tears were an unmanly weakness, and she felt so deeply injured that she really *couldn't* quite forgive yet. So she winked hard, shook her head, and said gruffly because Amy was listening, "It was an abominable thing, and she doesn't deserve to be forgiven."

With that she marched off to bed, and there was no merry or confidential gossip that night.

Amy was much offended that her overtures of peace had been repulsed, and began to wish she had not humbled herself, to feel more injured than ever, and to plume herself on her superior virtue in a way which was particularly exasperating. Jo still looked like a thunder cloud, and nothing went well all day. It was bitter cold in the morning, she dropped her precious turnover in the gutter, Aunt March had an attack of the fidgets, Meg was sensitive, Beth *would* look grieved and wistful when she got home, and Amy kept making remarks about people who were always talking about being good and yet wouldn't even try when other people set them a virtuous example.

"Everybody is so hateful, I'll ask Laurie to go skating. He is always kind and jolly, and will put me to rights, I know," said Jo to herself, and off she went.

Amy heard the clash of skates, and looked out with an impatient exclamation.

"There! She promised I should go next time, for this is the last ice we shall have. But it's no use to ask such a crosspatch to take me."

"Don't say that. You *were* very naughty, and it *is* hard to forgive the loss of her precious little book, but I think she might do it now, and I guess she will, if you try her at the right minute," said Meg. "Go after them. Don't say anything till Jo has got good-natured with Laurie, then take a quiet minute and just kiss her, or do some kind thing, and I'm sure she'll be friends again with all her heart."

"I'll try," said Amy, for the advice suited her, and after a flurry to get ready, she ran after the friends, who were just disappearing over the hill.

It was not far to the river, but both were ready before Amy reached them. Jo saw her coming, and turned her back. Laurie did not see, for he was carefully skating along the shore, sounding the ice, for a warm spell had preceded the cold snap.

"I'll go on to the first bend, and see if it's all right before we begin to race," Amy heard him say, as he shot away, looking like a young Russian in his fur-trimmed coat and cap.

Jo heard Amy panting after her run, stamping her feet and blowing on her fingers as she tried to put her skates on, but Jo never turned and went slowly zigzagging down the river, taking a bitter, unhappy sort of satisfaction in her sister's troubles. She had cherished her anger till it grew strong and took possession of her, as evil thoughts and feelings always do unless cast out at once. As Laurie turned the bend, he shouted back—

"Keep near the shore. It isn't safe in the middle."

Jo heard, but Amy was struggling to her feet and did not catch a word. Jo glanced over her shoulder, and the little demon she was harboring said in her ear—

"No matter whether she heard or not, let her take care of herself."

Laurie had vanished round the bend, Jo was just at the turn, and Amy, far behind, striking out toward the smoother ice in the middle of the river. For a minute Jo stood still with a strange feeling in her heart; then she resolved to go on, but something held and turned her round, just in time to see Amy throw up her hands and go down, with a sudden crash of rotten ice, the splash of water, and a cry that made Jo's heart stand still with fear. She tried to call Laurie, but her voice was gone. She tried to rush forward, but her feet seemed to have no strength in them, and for a second, she could only stand motionless, staring with a terror-stricken face at the little blue hood above the black water. Something rushed swiftly by her, and Laurie's voice cried out—

"Bring a rail. Quick, quick!"

How she did it, she never knew, but for the next few minutes she worked as if possessed, blindly obeying Laurie, who was quite self-possessed, and lying flat, held Amy up by his arm and hockey stick till Jo dragged a rail from the fence, and together they got the child out, more frightened than hurt.

"Now then, we must walk her home as fast as we can. Pile our things on her, while I get off these confounded skates," cried Laurie, wrapping his coat round Amy, and tugging away at the straps which never seemed so intricate before.

Shivering, dripping, and crying, they got Amy home, and after an exciting time of it, she fell asleep, rolled in blankets before a hot fire. During the bustle Jo had scarcely spoken but flown about, looking pale and wild, with her things half off, her dress torn, and her hands cut and bruised by ice and rails and refractory buckles. When Amy was comfortably asleep, the house quiet, and Mrs. March sitting by the bed, she called Jo to her and began to bind up the hurt hands.

"Are you sure she is safe?" whispered Jo, looking remorsefully at the golden head, which might have been swept away from her sight forever under the treacherous ice.

"Quite safe, dear. She is not hurt, and won't even take cold, I think, you were so sensible in covering and getting her home quickly," replied her mother cheerfully.

"Laurie did it all. I only let her go. Mother, if she *should* die, it would be my fault." And Jo dropped down beside the bed in a passion of penitent tears, telling all that had happened, bitterly condemning her hardness of heart, and sobbing out her gratitude for being spared the heavy punishment which might have come upon her.

"It's my dreadful temper! I try to cure it, I think I have, and then it breaks out worse than ever. Oh, Mother, what shall I do? What shall I do?" cried poor Jo, in despair.

"Watch and pray, dear, never get tired of trying, and never think it is impossible to conquer your fault," said Mrs. March, drawing the blowzy head to her shoulder and kissing the wet cheek so tenderly that Jo cried even harder.

"You don't know, you can't guess how bad it is! It seems as if I could do anything when I'm in a passion. I get so savage, I could hurt anyone and enjoy it. I'm afraid I *shall* do something dreadful some day, and spoil my life, and make everybody hate me. Oh, Mother, help me, do help me!"

"I will, my child, I will. Don't cry so bitterly, but remember this day, and resolve with all your soul that you will never know another like it. Jo, dear, we all have our temptations, some far greater than yours, and it often takes us all our lives to conquer them. You think your temper is the worst in the world, but mine used to be just like it."

"Yours, Mother? Why, you are never angry!" And for the moment Jo forgot remorse in surprise.

"I've been trying to cure it for forty years, and have only succeeded in controlling it. I am angry nearly every day of my life, Jo, but I have learned not to show it, and I still hope to learn not to feel it, though it may take me another forty years to do so."

The patience and the humility of the face she loved so well was a better lesson to Jo than the wisest lecture, the sharpest reproof. She felt comforted at once by the sympathy and confidence given her. The knowledge that her mother had a fault like hers, and tried to mend it, made her own easier to bear and strengthened her resolution to cure it, though forty years seemed rather a long time to watch and pray to a girl of fifteen.

"Mother, are you angry when you fold your lips tight together and go out of the room sometimes, when Aunt March scolds or people worry you?" asked Jo, feeling nearer and dearer to her mother than ever before.

"Yes, I've learned to check the hasty words that rise to my lips, and when I feel that they mean to break out against my will, I just go away for a minute, and give myself a little shake for being so weak and wicked," answered Mrs. March with a sigh and a smile, as she smoothed and fastened up Jo's disheveled hair.

"How did you learn to keep still? That is what troubles me, for the sharp words fly out before I know what I'm about, and the more I say the worse I get, till it's a pleasure to hurt people's feelings and say dreadful things. Tell me how you do it, Marmee dear."

"My good mother used to help me—"

"As you do us—" interrupted Jo, with a grateful kiss.

"But I lost her when I was a little older than you are, and for years had to struggle on alone, for I was too proud to confess my weakness to anyone else. I had a hard time, Jo, and shed a good many bitter tears over my failures, for in spite of my efforts I never seemed to get on. Then your father came, and I was so happy that I found it easy to be good. But by-and-by, when I had four little daughters round me and we were poor, then the old trouble began again, for I am not patient by nature, and it tried me very much to see my children wanting anything."

"Poor Mother! What helped you then?"

"Your father, Jo. He never loses patience—never doubts or complains—but always hopes, and works and waits so cheerfully that one is ashamed to do otherwise before him. He helped and comforted me, and showed me that I must try to practice all the virtues I would have my little girls possess, for I was their example. It was easier to try for your sakes than for my own. A startled or surprised look from one of you when I spoke sharply rebuked me more than any words could have done, and the love, respect, and confidence of my children was the sweetest reward I could receive for my efforts to be the woman I would have them copy."

"Oh, Mother, if I'm ever half as good as you, I shall be satisfied," cried Jo, much touched.

"I hope you will be a great deal better, dear, but you must keep watch over your "bosom enemy," as father calls it, or it may sadden, if not spoil your life. You have had a warning. Remember it, and try with heart and soul to master this quick temper, before it brings you greater sorrow and regret than you have known today."

"I will try, Mother, I truly will. But you must help me, remind me, and keep me from flying out. I used to see Father sometimes put his finger on his lips, and look at you with a very kind but sober face, and you always folded your lips tight and went away. Was he reminding you then?" asked Jo softly.

"Yes. I asked him to help me so, and he never forgot it, but saved me from many a sharp word by that little gesture and kind look."

Jo saw that her mother's eyes filled and her lips trembled as she spoke, and fearing that she had said too much, she whispered anxiously, "Was it wrong to watch you and to speak of it? I didn't mean to be rude, but it's so comfortable to say all I think to you, and feel so safe and happy here."

"My Jo, you may say anything to your mother, for it is my greatest happiness and pride to feel that my girls confide in me and know how much I love them."

"I thought I'd grieved you."

"No, dear, but speaking of Father reminded me how much I miss him, how much I owe him, and how faithfully I should watch and work to keep his little daughters safe and good for him."

"Yet you told him to go, Mother, and didn't cry when he went, and never complain now, or seem as if you needed any help," said Jo, wondering.

"I gave my best to the country I love, and kept my tears till he was gone. Why should I complain, when we both have merely done our duty and will surely be the happier for it in the end? If I don't seem to need help, it is because I have a better friend, even than Father, to comfort and sustain me. My child, the troubles and temptations of your life are beginning and may be many, but you can overcome and outlive them all if you learn to feel the strength and tenderness of your Heavenly Father as you do that of your earthly one. The more you love and trust Him, the nearer you will feel to Him, and the less you will depend on human power and wisdom. His love and care never tire or change, can never be taken from you, but may become the source of lifelong peace, happiness, and strength. Believe this heartily, and go to God with all your little cares, and hopes, and sins, and sorrows, as freely and confidingly as you come to your mother."

Jo's only answer was to hold her mother close, and in the silence which followed the sincerest prayer she had ever prayed left her heart without words. For in that sad yet happy hour, she had learned not only the bitterness of remorse and despair, but the sweetness of self-denial and self-control, and led by her mother's hand, she had drawn nearer to the Friend who always welcomes every child with a love stronger than that of any father, tenderer than that of any mother.

Amy stirred and sighed in her sleep, and as if eager to begin at once to mend her fault, Jo looked up with an expression on her face which it had never worn before.

"I let the sun go down on my anger. I wouldn't forgive her, and today, if it hadn't been for Laurie, it might have been too late! How could I be so wicked?" said Jo, half aloud, as she leaned over her sister softly stroking the wet hair scattered on the pillow.

As if she heard, Amy opened her eyes, and held out her arms, with a smile that went straight to Jo's heart. Neither said a word, but they hugged one another close, in spite of the blankets, and everything was forgiven and forgotten in one hearty kiss.

CHAPTER IX

MEG GOES TO VANITY FAIR

"I do think it was the most fortunate thing in the world that those children should have the measles just now," said Meg, one April day, as she stood packing the "go abroady" trunk in her room, surrounded by her sisters.

"And so nice of Annie Moffat not to forget her promise. A whole fortnight of fun will be regularly splendid," replied Jo, looking like a windmill as she folded skirts with her long arms.

"And such lovely weather, I'm so glad of that," added Beth, tidily sorting neck and hair ribbons in her best box, lent for the great occasion.

"I wish I was going to have a fine time and wear all these nice things," said Amy with her mouth full of pins, as she artistically replenished her sister's cushion.

"I wish you were all going, but as you can't, I shall keep my adventures to tell you when I come back. I'm sure it's the least I can do when you have been so kind, lending me things and helping me get ready," said Meg, glancing round the room at the very simple outfit, which seemed nearly perfect in their eyes.

"What did Mother give you out of the treasure box?" asked Amy, who had not been present at the opening of a certain cedar chest in which Mrs. March kept a few relics of past splendor, as gifts for her girls when the proper time came.

"A pair of silk stockings, that pretty carved fan, and a lovely blue sash. I wanted the violet silk, but there isn't time to make it over, so I must be contented with my old tarlaton."

"It will look nice over my new muslin skirt, and the sash will set it off beautifully. I wish I hadn't smashed my coral bracelet, for you might have had it," said Jo, who loved to give and lend, but whose possessions were usually too dilapidated to be of much use.

"There is a lovely old-fashioned pearl set in the treasure chest, but Mother said real flowers were the prettiest ornament for a young girl, and Laurie promised to send me all I want," replied Meg. "Now, let me see, there's my new gray walking suit—just curl up the feather in my hat, Beth—then my poplin for Sunday and the small party—it looks heavy for spring, doesn't it? The violet silk would be so nice. Oh, dear!"

"Never mind, you've got the tarlaton for the big party, and you always look like an angel in white," said Amy, brooding over the little store of finery in which her soul delighted.

"It isn't low-necked, and it doesn't sweep enough, but it will have to do. My blue housedress looks so well, turned and freshly trimmed, that I feel as if I'd got a new one. My silk sacque isn't a bit the fashion, and my bonnet doesn't look like Sallie's. I didn't like to say anything, but I was sadly disappointed in my umbrella. I told Mother black with a white handle, but she forgot and bought a green one with a yellowish handle. It's strong and neat, so I ought not to complain, but I know I shall feel ashamed of it beside Annie's silk one with a gold top," sighed Meg, surveying the little umbrella with great disfavor.

"Change it," advised Jo.

"I won't be so silly, or hurt Marmee's feelings, when she took so much pains to get my things. It's a nonsensical notion of mine, and I'm not going to give up to it. My silk stockings and two pairs of new gloves are my comfort. You are a dear to lend me yours, Jo. I feel so rich and sort of elegant, with two new pairs, and the old ones cleaned up for common." And Meg took a refreshing peep at her glove box.

"Annie Moffat has blue and pink bows on her nightcaps. Would you put some on mine?" she asked, as Beth brought up a pile of snowy muslins, fresh from Hannah's hands.

"No, I wouldn't, for the smart caps won't match the plain gowns without any trimming on them. Poor folks shouldn't rig," said Jo decidedly.

"I wonder if I shall *ever* be happy enough to have real lace on my clothes and bows on my caps?" said Meg impatiently.

"You said the other day that you'd be perfectly happy if you could only go to Annie Moffat's," observed Beth in her quiet way.

"So I did! Well, I *am* happy, and I *won't* fret, but it does seem as if the more one gets the more one wants, doesn't it? There now, the trays are ready, and everything in but my ball dress, which I shall leave for Mother to pack," said Meg, cheering up, as she glanced from the half-filled trunk to the many times pressed and mended white tarlaton, which she called her "ball dress" with an important air.

The next day was fine, and Meg departed in style for a fortnight of novelty and pleasure. Mrs. March had consented to the visit rather reluctantly, fearing that Margaret would come back more discontented than she went. But she begged so hard, and Sallie had promised to take good care of her, and a little pleasure seemed so delightful after a winter of irksome work that the mother yielded, and the daughter went to take her first taste of fashionable life.

The Moffats *were* very fashionable, and simple Meg was rather daunted, at first, by the splendor of the house and the elegance of its occupants. But they were kindly people, in spite of the frivolous life they led, and soon put their guest at her ease. Perhaps Meg felt, without understanding why, that they were not particularly cultivated or intelligent people, and that all their gilding could not quite conceal the ordinary material of which they were made. It certainly was agreeable to fare sumptuously, drive in a fine carriage, wear her best frock every day, and do nothing but enjoy herself. It suited her exactly, and soon she began to imitate the manners and conversation of those about her, to put on little airs and graces, use French phrases, crimp her hair, take in her dresses, and talk about the fashions as well as she could. The more she saw of Annie Moffat's pretty things, the more she envied her and sighed to be rich. Home now looked bare and dismal as she thought of it, work grew harder than ever, and she felt that she was a very destitute and much-injured girl, in spite of the new gloves and silk stockings.

She had not much time for repining, however, for the three young girls were busily employed in "having a good time." They shopped, walked, rode, and called all day, went to theaters and operas or frolicked at home in the evening, for Annie had many friends and knew how to entertain them. Her older sisters were very fine young ladies, and one was engaged, which was extremely interesting and romantic, Meg thought. Mr. Moffat was a fat, jolly old gentleman, who knew her father, and Mrs. Moffat, a fat, jolly old lady, who took as great a fancy to Meg as her daughter had done. Everyone petted her, and "Daisy," as they called her, was in a fair way to have her head turned.

When the evening for the "small party" came, she found that the poplin wouldn't do at all, for the other girls were putting on thin dresses and making themselves very fine indeed. So out came the tarlatan, looking older, limper, and shabbier than ever beside Sallie's crisp new one. Meg saw the girls glance at it and then at one another, and her cheeks began to burn, for with all her gentleness she was very proud. No one said a word about it, but Sallie offered to dress her hair, and Annie to tie her sash, and Belle, the engaged sister, praised her white arms. But in their kindness Meg saw only pity for her poverty, and her heart felt very heavy as she stood by herself, while the others laughed, chattered, and flew about like gauzy butterflies. The hard, bitter feeling was getting pretty bad, when the maid brought in a box of flowers. Before she could speak, Annie had the cover off, and all were exclaiming at the lovely roses, heath, and fern within.

"It's for Belle, of course, George always sends her some, but these are altogether ravishing," cried Annie, with a great sniff.

"They are for Miss March, the man said. And here's a note," put in the maid, holding it to Meg.

"What fun! Who are they from? Didn't know you had a lover," cried the girls, fluttering about Meg in a high state of curiosity and surprise.

"The note is from Mother, and the flowers from Laurie," said Meg simply, yet much gratified that he had not forgotten her.

"Oh, indeed!" said Annie with a funny look, as Meg slipped the note into her pocket as a sort of talisman against envy, vanity, and false pride, for the few loving words had done her good, and the flowers cheered her up by their beauty.

Feeling almost happy again, she laid by a few ferns and roses for herself, and quickly made up the rest in dainty bouquets for the breasts, hair, or skirts of her friends, offering them so prettily that Clara, the elder sister, told her she was "the sweetest little thing she ever saw," and they looked quite charmed with her small attention. Somehow the kind act finished her despondency, and when all the rest went to show themselves to Mrs. Moffat, she saw a happy, bright-eyed face in the mirror, as she laid her ferns against her rippling hair and fastened the roses in the dress that didn't strike her as so *very* shabby now.

She enjoyed herself very much that evening, for she danced to her heart's content. Everyone was very kind, and she had three compliments. Annie made her sing, and some one said she had a remarkably fine voice. Major Lincoln asked who "the fresh little girl with the beautiful eyes" was, and Mr. Moffat insisted on dancing with her because she "didn't dawdle, but had some spring in her," as he gracefully expressed it. So altogether she had a very nice time, till she overheard a bit of conversation, which disturbed her extremely. She was sitting just inside the conservatory, waiting for her partner to bring her an ice, when she heard a voice ask on the other side of the flowery wall—

"How old is he?"

"Sixteen or seventeen, I should say," replied another voice.

"It would be a grand thing for one of those girls, wouldn't it? Sallie says they are very intimate now, and the old man quite dotes on them."

"Mrs. M. has made her plans, I dare say, and will play her cards well, early as it is. The girl evidently doesn't think of it yet," said Mrs. Moffat.

"She told that fib about her mamma, as if she did know, and colored up when the flowers came quite prettily. Poor thing! She'd be so nice if she was only got up in style. Do you think she'd be offended if we offered to lend her a dress for Thursday?" asked another voice.

"She's proud, but I don't believe she'd mind, for that dowdy tarlaton is all she has got. She may tear it tonight, and that will be a good excuse for offering a decent one."

"We'll see. I shall ask young Laurence, as a compliment to her, and we'll have fun about it afterward."

Here Meg's partner appeared, to find her looking much flushed and rather agitated. She *was* proud, and her pride was useful just then, for it helped her hide her mortification, anger, and disgust at what she had just heard. For, innocent and unsuspicious as she was, she could not help understanding the gossip of her friends. She tried to forget it, but could not, and kept repeating to herself, "Mrs. M. has made her plans," "that fib about her mamma," and "dowdy tarlaton," till she was ready to cry and rush home to tell her troubles and ask for advice. As that was impossible, she did her best to seem gay, and being rather excited, she succeeded so well that no one dreamed what an effort she was making. She was very glad when it was all over and she was quiet in her bed, where she could think and wonder and fume till her head ached and her hot cheeks were cooled by a few natural tears. Those foolish, yet well meant words, had opened a new world to Meg, and much disturbed the peace of the old one in which till now she had lived as happily as a child. Her innocent friendship with Laurie was spoiled by the silly speeches she had overheard. Her faith in her mother was a little shaken by the worldly plans attributed to her by Mrs. Moffat, who judged others by herself, and the sensible resolution to be contented with the simple wardrobe which suited a poor man's daughter was weakened by the unnecessary pity of girls who thought a shabby dress one of the greatest calamities under heaven.

Poor Meg had a restless night, and got up heavy-eyed, unhappy, half resentful toward her friends, and half ashamed of herself for not speaking out frankly and setting everything right. Everybody dawdled that morning, and it was noon before the girls found energy enough even to take up their worsted work. Something in the manner of her friends struck Meg at once. They treated her with more respect, she thought, took quite a tender interest in what she said, and looked at her with eyes that plainly betrayed curiosity. All this surprised and flattered her, though she did not understand it till Miss Belle looked up from her writing, and said, with a sentimental air—

"Daisy, dear, I've sent an invitation to your friend, Mr. Laurence, for Thursday. We should like to know him, and it's only a proper compliment to you."

Meg colored, but a mischievous fancy to tease the girls made her reply demurely, "You are very kind, but I'm afraid he won't come."

"Why not, *chérie?*" asked Miss Belle.

"He's too old."

"My child, what do you mean? What is his age, I beg to know!" cried Miss Clara.

"Nearly seventy, I believe," answered Meg, counting stitches to hide the merriment in her eyes.

"You sly creature! Of course we meant the young man," exclaimed Miss Belle, laughing.

"There isn't any, Laurie is only a little boy." And Meg laughed also at the queer look which the sisters exchanged as she thus described her supposed lover.

"About your age," Nan said.

"Nearer my sister Jo's; *I* am seventeen in August," returned Meg, tossing her head.

"It's very nice of him to send you flowers, isn't it?" said Annie, looking wise about nothing.

"Yes, he often does, to all of us, for their house is full, and we are so fond of them. My mother and old Mr. Laurence are friends, you know, so it is quite natural that we children should play together," and Meg hoped they would say no more.

"It's evident Daisy isn't out yet," said Miss Clara to Belle with a nod.

"Quite a pastoral state of innocence all round," returned Miss Belle with a shrug.

"I'm going out to get some little matters for my girls. Can I do anything for you, young ladies?" asked Mrs. Moffat, lumbering in like an elephant in silk and lace.

"No, thank you, ma'am," replied Sallie. "I've got my new pink silk for Thursday and don't want a thing."

"Nor I—" began Meg, but stopped because it occurred to her that she *did* want several things and could not have them.

"What shall you wear?" asked Sallie.

"My old white one again, if I can mend it fit to be seen, it got sadly torn last night," said Meg, trying to speak quite easily, but feeling very uncomfortable.

"Why don't you send home for another?" said Sallie, who was not an observing young lady.

"I haven't got any other." It cost Meg an effort to say that, but Sallie did not see it and exclaimed in amiable surprise, "Only that? How funny—" She did not finish her speech, for Belle shook her head at her and broke in, saying kindly—

"Not at all. Where is the use of having a lot of dresses when she isn't out yet? There's no need of sending home, Daisy, even if you had a dozen, for I've got a sweet blue silk laid away, which I've outgrown, and you shall wear it to please me, won't you, dear?"

"You are very kind, but I don't mind my old dress if you don't, it does well enough for a little girl like me," said Meg.

"Now do let me please myself by dressing you up in style. I admire to do it, and you'd be a regular little beauty with a touch here and there. I shan't let anyone see you till you are done, and then we'll burst upon them like Cinderella and her godmother going to the ball," said Belle in her persuasive tone.

Meg couldn't refuse the offer so kindly made, for a desire to see if she would be "a little beauty" after touching up caused her to accept and forget all her former uncomfortable feelings toward the Moffats.

On the Thursday evening, Belle shut herself up with her maid, and between them they turned Meg into a fine lady. They crimped and curled her hair, they polished her neck and arms with some fragrant powder, touched her lips with coralline salve to make them redder, and Hortense would have added "a *soupçon* of rouge," if Meg had not rebelled. They laced her into a sky-blue dress, which was so tight she could hardly breathe and so low in the neck that modest Meg blushed at herself in the mirror. A set of silver filagree was added, bracelets, necklace, brooch, and even earrings, for Hortense tied them on with a bit of pink silk which did not show. A cluster of tea-rose buds at the bosom, and a ruche, reconciled Meg to the display of her pretty, white shoulders, and a pair of high-heeled silk boots satisfied the last wish of her heart. A lace handkerchief, a plumy fan, and a bouquet in a shoulder holder finished her off, and Miss Belle surveyed her with the satisfaction of a little girl with a newly dressed doll.

"Mademoiselle is *charmante, très jolie*, is she not?" cried Hortense, clasping her hands in an affected rapture.

"Come and show yourself," said Miss Belle, leading the way to the room where the others were waiting.

As Meg went rustling after, with her long skirts trailing, her earrings tinkling, her curls waving, and her heart beating, she felt as if her fun had really begun at last, for the mirror had plainly told her that she *was* "a little beauty." Her friends repeated the pleasing phrase enthusiastically, and for several minutes she stood, like a jackdaw in the fable, enjoying her borrowed plumes, while the rest chattered like a party of magpies.

"While I dress, do you drill her, Nan, in the management of her skirt and those French heels, or she will trip herself up. Take your silver butterfly, and catch up that long curl on the left side of her head, Clara, and don't any of you disturb the charming work of my hands," said Belle, as she hurried away, looking well pleased with her success.

"You don't look a bit like yourself, but you are very nice. I'm nowhere beside you, for Belle has heaps of taste, and you're quite French, I assure you. Let your flowers hang, don't be so careful of them, and be sure you don't trip," returned Sallie, trying not to care that Meg was prettier than herself.

Keeping that warning carefully in mind, Margaret got safely down stairs and sailed into the drawing rooms where the Moffats and a few early guests were assembled. She very soon discovered that there is a charm about fine clothes which attracts a certain class of people and secures their respect. Several young ladies, who had taken no notice of her before, were very affectionate all of a sudden. Several young gentlemen, who had only stared at her at the other party, now not only stared, but asked to be introduced, and said all manner of foolish but agreeable things to her, and several old ladies, who sat on the sofas, and criticized the rest of the party, inquired who she was with an air of interest. She heard Mrs. Moffat reply to one of them.

"Daisy March—father a colonel in the army—one of our first families, but reverses of fortune, you know; intimate friends of the Laurences; sweet creature, I assure you; my Ned is quite wild about her."

"Dear me!" said the old lady, putting up her glass for another observation of Meg, who tried to look as if she had not heard and been rather shocked at Mrs. Moffat's fibs.

The "queer feeling" did not pass away, but she imagined herself acting the new part of fine lady and so got on pretty well, though the tight dress gave her a side-ache, the train kept getting under her feet, and she was in constant fear lest her earrings should fly off and get lost or broken. She was flirting her fan and laughing at the feeble jokes of a young gentleman who tried to be witty, when she suddenly stopped laughing and looked confused, for just opposite, she saw Laurie. He was staring at her with undisguised surprise, and disapproval also, she thought, for though he bowed and smiled, yet something in his honest eyes made her blush and wish she had her old dress on. To complete her confusion, she saw Belle nudge Annie, and both glance from her to Laurie, who, she was happy to see, looked unusually boyish and shy.

"Silly creatures, to put such thoughts into my head. I won't care for it, or let it change me a bit," thought Meg, and rustled across the room to shake hands with her friend.

"I'm glad you came, I was afraid you wouldn't," she said, with her most grown-up air.

"Jo wanted me to come, and tell her how you looked, so I did," answered Laurie, without turning his eyes upon her, though he half smiled at her maternal tone.

"What shall you tell her?" asked Meg, full of curiosity to know his opinion of her, yet feeling ill at ease with him for the first time.

"I shall say I didn't know you, for you look so grown-up and unlike yourself, I'm quite afraid of you," he said, fumbling at his glove button.

"How absurd of you! The girls dressed me up for fun, and I rather like it. Wouldn't Jo stare if she saw me?" said Meg, bent on making him say whether he thought her improved or not.

"Yes, I think she would," returned Laurie gravely.

"Don't you like me so?" asked Meg.

"No, I don't," was the blunt reply.

"Why not?" in an anxious tone.

He glanced at her frizzled head, bare shoulders, and fantastically trimmed dress with an expression that abashed her more than his answer, which had not a particle of his usual politeness in it.

"I don't like fuss and feathers."

That was altogether too much from a lad younger than herself, and Meg walked away, saying petulantly, "You are the rudest boy I ever saw."

Feeling very much ruffled, she went and stood at a quiet window to cool her cheeks, for the tight dress gave her an uncomfortably brilliant color. As she stood there, Major Lincoln passed by, and a minute after she heard him saying to his mother—

"They are making a fool of that little girl. I wanted you to see her, but they have spoiled her entirely. She's nothing but a doll tonight."

"Oh, dear!" sighed Meg. "I wish I'd been sensible and worn my own things, then I should not have disgusted other people, or felt so uncomfortable and ashamed of myself."

She leaned her forehead on the cool pane, and stood half hidden by the curtains, never minding that her favorite waltz had begun, till some one touched her, and turning, she saw Laurie, looking penitent, as he said, with his very best bow and his hand out—

"Please forgive my rudeness, and come and dance with me."

"I'm afraid it will be too disagreeable to you," said Meg, trying to look offended and failing entirely.

"Not a bit of it, I'm dying to do it. Come, I'll be good. I don't like your gown, but I do think you are just splendid." And he waved his hands, as if words failed to express his admiration.

Meg smiled and relented, and whispered as they stood waiting to catch the time, "Take care my skirt doesn't trip you up. It's the plague of my life and I was a goose to wear it."

"Pin it round your neck, and then it will be useful," said Laurie, looking down at the little blue boots, which he evidently approved of.

Away they went fleetly and gracefully, for having practiced at home, they were well matched, and the blithe young couple were a pleasant sight to see, as they twirled merrily round and round, feeling more friendly than ever after their small tiff.

"Laurie, I want you to do me a favor, will you?" said Meg, as he stood fanning her when her breath gave out, which it did very soon though she would not own why.

"Won't I!" said Laurie, with alacrity.

"Please don't tell them at home about my dress tonight. They won't understand the joke, and it will worry Mother."

"Then why did you do it?" said Laurie's eyes, so plainly that Meg hastily added—

"I shall tell them myself all about it, and 'fess' to Mother how silly I've been. But I'd rather do it myself. So you'll not tell, will you?"

"I give you my word I won't, only what shall I say when they ask me?"

"Just say I looked pretty well and was having a good time."

"I'll say the first with all my heart, but how about the other? You don't look as if you were having a good time. Are you?" And Laurie looked at her with an expression which made her answer in a whisper—

"No, not just now. Don't think I'm horrid. I only wanted a little fun, but this sort doesn't pay, I find, and I'm getting tired of it."

"Here comes Ned Moffat. What does he want?" said Laurie, knitting his black brows as if he did not regard his young host in the light of a pleasant addition to the party.

"He put his name down for three dances, and I suppose he's coming for them. What a bore!" said Meg, assuming a languid air which amused Laurie immensely.

He did not speak to her again till suppertime, when he saw her drinking champagne with Ned and his friend Fisher, who were behaving "like a pair of fools," as Laurie said to himself, for he felt a brotherly sort of right to watch over the Marches and fight their battles whenever a defender was needed.

"You'll have a splitting headache tomorrow, if you drink much of that. I wouldn't, Meg, your mother doesn't like it, you know," he whispered, leaning over her chair, as Ned turned to refill her glass and Fisher stooped to pick up her fan.

"I'm not Meg tonight, I'm 'a doll' who does all sorts of crazy things. Tomorrow I shall put away my 'fuss and feathers' and be desperately good again," she answered with an affected little laugh.

"Wish tomorrow was here, then," muttered Laurie, walking off, ill-pleased at the change he saw in her.

Meg danced and flirted, chattered and giggled, as the other girls did. After supper she undertook the German, and blundered through it, nearly upsetting her partner with her long skirt, and romping in a way that scandalized Laurie, who looked on and meditated a lecture. But he got no chance to deliver it, for Meg kept away from him till he came to say good night.

"Remember!" she said, trying to smile, for the splitting headache had already begun.

"*Silence à la mort*," replied Laurie, with a melodramatic flourish, as he went away.

This little bit of byplay excited Annie's curiosity, but Meg was too tired for gossip and went to bed, feeling as if she had been to a masquerade and hadn't enjoyed herself as much as she expected. She was sick all the next day, and on Saturday went home, quite used up with her fortnight's fun and feeling that she had "sat in the lap of luxury" long enough.

"It does seem pleasant to be quiet, and not have company manners on all the time. Home *is* a nice place, though it isn't splendid," said Meg, looking about her with a restful expression, as she sat with her mother and Jo on the Sunday evening.

"I'm glad to hear you say so, dear, for I was afraid home would seem dull and poor to you after your fine quarters," replied her mother, who had given her many anxious looks that day. For motherly eyes are quick to see any change in children's faces.

Meg had told her adventures gayly and said over and over what a charming time she had had, but something still seemed to weigh upon her spirits, and when the younger girls were gone to bed, she sat thoughtfully staring at the fire, saying little and looking worried. As the clock struck nine and Jo proposed bed, Meg suddenly left her chair and, taking Beth's stool, leaned her elbows on her mother's knee, saying bravely—

"Marmee, I want to 'fess.'"

"I thought so; what is it, dear?"

"Shall I go away?" asked Jo discreetly.

"Of course not. Don't I always tell you everything? I was ashamed to speak of it before the younger children, but I want you to know all the dreadful things I did at the Moffats'."

"We are prepared," said Mrs. March, smiling but looking a little anxious.

"I told you they dressed me up, but I didn't tell you that they powdered and squeezed and frizzled, and made me look like a fashion-plate. Laurie thought I wasn't proper. I know he did, though he didn't say so, and one man called me 'a doll.' I knew it was silly, but they flattered me and said I was a beauty, and quantities of nonsense, so I let them make a fool of me."

"Is that all?" asked Jo, as Mrs. March looked silently at the downcast face of her pretty daughter, and could not find it in her heart to blame her little follies.

"No, I drank champagne and romped and tried to flirt, and was altogether abominable," said Meg self-reproachfully.

"There is something more, I think." And Mrs. March smoothed the soft cheek, which suddenly grew rosy as Meg answered slowly—

"Yes. It's very silly, but I want to tell it, because I hate to have people say and think such things about us and Laurie."

Then she told the various bits of gossip she had heard at the Moffats', and as she spoke, Jo saw her mother fold her lips tightly, as if ill pleased that such ideas should be put into Meg's innocent mind.

"Well, if that isn't the greatest rubbish I ever heard," cried Jo indignantly. "Why didn't you pop out and tell them so on the spot?"

"I couldn't, it was so embarrassing for me. I couldn't help hearing at first, and then I was so angry and ashamed, I didn't remember that I ought to go away."

"Just wait till *I* see Annie Moffat, and I'll show you how to settle such ridiculous stuff. The idea of having 'plans' and being kind to Laurie because he's rich and may marry us by-and-by! Won't he shout when I tell him what those silly things say about us poor children?" And Jo laughed, as if on second thoughts the thing struck her as a good joke.

"If you tell Laurie, I'll never forgive you! She mustn't, must she, Mother?" said Meg, looking distressed.

"No, never repeat that foolish gossip, and forget it as soon as you can," said Mrs. March gravely. "I was very unwise to let you go among people of whom I know so little—kind, I dare say, but worldly, ill-bred, and full of these vulgar ideas about young people. I am more sorry than I can express for the mischief this visit may have done you, Meg."

"Don't be sorry, I won't let it hurt me. I'll forget all the bad and remember only the good, for I did enjoy a great deal, and thank you very much for letting me go. I'll not be sentimental or dissatisfied,

Mother. I know I'm a silly little girl, and I'll stay with you till I'm fit to take care of myself. But it *is* nice to be praised and admired, and I can't help saying I like it," said Meg, looking half ashamed of the confession.

"That is perfectly natural, and quite harmless, if the liking does not become a passion and lead one to do foolish or unmaidenly things. Learn to know and value the praise which is worth having, and to excite the admiration of excellent people by being modest as well as pretty, Meg."

Margaret sat thinking a moment, while Jo stood with her hands behind her, looking both interested and a little perplexed, for it was a new thing to see Meg blushing and talking about admiration, lovers, and things of that sort. And Jo felt as if during that fortnight her sister had grown up amazingly, and was drifting away from her into a world where she could not follow.

"Mother, do you have 'plans,' as Mrs. Moffat said?" asked Meg bashfully.

"Yes, my dear, I have a great many, all mothers do, but mine differ somewhat from Mrs. Moffat's, I suspect. I will tell you some of them, for the time has come when a word may set this romantic little head and heart of yours right, on a very serious subject. You are young, Meg, but not too young to understand me, and mothers' lips are the fittest to speak of such things to girls like you. Jo, your turn will come in time, perhaps, so listen to my 'plans' and help me carry them out, if they are good."

Jo went and sat on one arm of the chair, looking as if she thought they were about to join in some very solemn affair. Holding a hand of each, and watching the two young faces wistfully, Mrs. March said, in her serious yet cheery way—

"I want my daughters to be beautiful, accomplished, and good. To be admired, loved, and respected. To have a happy youth, to be well and wisely married, and to lead useful, pleasant lives, with as little care and sorrow to try them as God sees fit to send. To be loved and chosen by a good man is the best and sweetest thing which can happen to a woman, and I sincerely hope my girls may know this beautiful experience. It is natural to think of it, Meg, right to hope and wait for it, and wise to prepare for it, so that when the happy time comes, you may feel ready for the duties and worthy of the joy. My dear girls, I *am* ambitious for you, but not to have you make a dash in the world—

marry rich men merely because they are rich, or have splendid houses, which are not homes because love is wanting. Money is a needful and precious thing—and when well used, a noble thing—but I never want you to think it is the first or only prize to strive for. I'd rather see you poor men's wives, if you were happy, beloved, contented, than queens on thrones, without self-respect and peace."

"Poor girls don't stand any chance, Belle says, unless they put themselves forward," sighed Meg.

"Then we'll be old maids," said Jo stoutly.

"Right, Jo. Better be happy old maids than unhappy wives, or unmaidenly girls, running about to find husbands," said Mrs. March decidedly. "Don't be troubled, Meg, poverty seldom daunts a sincere lover. Some of the best and most honored women I know were poor girls, but so love-worthy that they were not allowed to be old maids. Leave these things to time. Make this home happy, so that you may be fit for homes of your own, if they are offered you, and contented here if they are not. One thing remember, my girls. Mother is always ready to be your confidant, Father to be your friend, and both of us hope and trust that our daughters, whether married or single, will be the pride and comfort of our lives."

"We will, Marmee, we will!" cried both, with all their hearts, as she bade them good night.

CHAPTER X

THE P.C. AND P.O.

As spring came on, a new set of amusements became the fashion, and the lengthening days gave long afternoons for work and play of all sorts. The garden had to be put in order, and each sister had a quarter of the little plot to do what she liked with. Hannah used to say, "I'd know which each of them gardings belonged to, ef I see 'em in Chiny," and so she might, for the girls' tastes differed as much as their characters. Meg's had roses and heliotrope, myrtle, and a little orange tree in it. Jo's bed was never alike two seasons, for she was always trying experiments. This year it was to be a plantation of sunflowers, the seeds of which cheerful land aspiring plant were to feed Aunt Cockle-top and her family of chicks. Beth had old-fashioned fragrant flowers in her garden—sweet peas and mignonette, larkspur, pinks, pansies, and southernwood, with chickweed for the birds and catnip for the pussies. Amy had a bower in hers—rather small and earwiggy, but very pretty to look at—with honeysuckle and morning-glories hanging their colored horns and bells in graceful wreaths all over it, tall white lilies, delicate ferns, and as many brilliant, picturesque plants as would consent to blossom there.

Gardening, walks, rows on the river, and flower hunts employed the fine days, and for rainy ones, they had house diversions—some old, some new—all more or less original. One of these was the "P.C.," for as secret societies were the fashion, it was thought proper to have one, and as all of the girls admired Dickens, they called themselves the Pickwick Club. With a few interruptions, they had kept this up for a year, and met every Saturday evening in the big garret, on which occasions the ceremonies were as follows: Three chairs were arranged in a row before a table on which was a lamp, also four white badges, with a big "P.C." in different colors on each, and the weekly newspaper called, The Pickwick Portfolio, to which all contributed something, while Jo, who reveled in pens and ink, was the editor. At seven o'clock, the four members ascended to the clubroom, tied their badges round their heads, and took their seats with great solemnity. Meg, as the eldest, was Samuel Pickwick, Jo, being of a literary turn, Augustus Snodgrass, Beth, because she was round and rosy, Tracy Tupman, and Amy, who was always trying to do what she couldn't, was Nathaniel Winkle. Pickwick, the president, read the paper, which was filled with original tales, poetry, local news, funny advertisements, and hints, in which they good-naturedly reminded each other of their faults and shortcomings. On one occasion, Mr. Pickwick put on a pair of spectacles without any glass, rapped upon the table, hemmed, and having stared hard at Mr. Snodgrass, who was tilting back in his chair, till he arranged himself properly, began to read:

"The Pickwick Portfolio"

MAY 20, 18—

POET'S CORNER

ANNIVERSARY ODE

Again we meet to celebrate
With badge and solemn rite,
Our fifty-second anniversary,
In Pickwick Hall, tonight.

We all are here in perfect health,
None gone from our small band:
Again we see each well-known face,
And press each friendly hand.

Our Pickwick, always at his post,
With reverence we greet,
As, spectacles on nose, he reads
Our well-filled weekly sheet.

Although he suffers from a cold,
We joy to hear him speak,
For words of wisdom from him fall,
In spite of croak or squeak.

Old six-foot Snodgrass looms on high,
With elephantine grace,
And beams upon the company,
With brown and jovial face.

Poetic fire lights up his eye,
He struggles 'gainst his lot.
Behold ambition on his brow,
And on his nose, a blot.

Next our peaceful Tupman comes,
So rosy, plump, and sweet,
Who chokes with laughter at the puns,
And tumbles off his seat.

Prim little Winkle too is here,
With every hair in place,
A model of propriety,
Though he hates to wash his face.

The year is gone, we still unite
To joke and laugh and read,
And tread the path of literature
That doth to glory lead.

Long may our paper prosper well,
Our club unbroken be,
And coming years their blessings pour
On the useful, gay "P. C."

A. SNODGRASS

*****

THE MASKED MARRIAGE
(A TALE OF VENICE)

Gondola after gondola swept up to the marble steps, and left its lovely load to swell the brilliant throng that filled the stately halls of Count Adelon. Knights and ladies, elves and pages, monks and flower girls, all mingled gaily in the dance.

Sweet voices and rich melody filled the air, and so with mirth and music the masquerade went on.

"Has your Highness seen the Lady Viola tonight?" asked a gallant troubadour of the fairy queen who floated down the hall upon his arm.

"Yes, is she not lovely, though so sad! Her dress is well chosen, too, for in a week she weds Count Antonio, whom she passionately hates."

"By my faith, I envy him. Yonder he comes, arrayed like a bridegroom, except the black mask. When that is off we shall see how he regards the fair maid whose heart he cannot win, though her stern father bestows her hand," returned the troubadour.

"'Tis whispered that she loves the young English artist who haunts her steps, and is spurned by the old Count," said the lady, as they joined the dance.

The revel was at its height when a priest appeared, and withdrawing the young pair to an alcove, hung with purple velvet, he motioned them to kneel. Instant silence fell on the gay throng, and not a sound, but the dash of fountains or the rustle of orange groves sleeping in the moonlight, broke the hush, as Count de Adelon spoke thus:

"My lords and ladies, pardon the ruse by which I have gathered you here to witness the marriage of my daughter. Father, we wait your services."

All eyes turned toward the bridal party, and a murmur of amazement went through the throng, for neither bride nor groom removed their masks. Curiosity and wonder possessed all hearts, but respect restrained all tongues till the holy rite was over. Then the eager spectators gathered round the count, demanding an explanation.

"Gladly would I give it if I could, but I only know that it was the whim of my timid Viola, and I yielded to it. Now, my children, let the play end. Unmask and receive my blessing."

But neither bent the knee, for the young bridegroom replied in a tone that startled all listeners as the mask fell, disclosing the noble face of Ferdinand Devereux, the artist lover, and leaning on the breast where now flashed the star of an English earl was the lovely Viola, radiant with joy and beauty.

"My lord, you scornfully bade me claim your daughter when I could boast as high a name and vast a fortune as the Count Antonio. I can do more, for even your ambitious soul cannot refuse the Earl of Devereux and De Vere, when he gives his ancient name and boundless wealth in return for the beloved hand of this fair lady, now my wife."

The count stood like one changed to stone, and turning to the bewildered crowd, Ferdinand added, with a gay smile of triumph, "To you, my gallant friends, I can only wish that your wooing may prosper as mine has done, and that you may all win as fair a bride as I have by this masked marriage."

S. PICKWICK

* * * * *

Why is the P. C. like the Tower of Babel? It is full of unruly members.

* * * * *

THE HISTORY OF A SQUASH

Once upon a time a farmer planted a little seed in his garden, and after a while it sprouted and became a vine and bore many squashes. One day in October, when they were ripe, he picked one and took it to market. A grocerman bought and put it in his shop. That same morning, a little girl in a brown hat and blue dress, with a round face and snub nose, went and bought it for her mother. She lugged it home, cut it up, and boiled it in the big pot, mashed some of it with salt and butter, for dinner. And to the rest she added a pint of milk, two eggs, four spoons of sugar, nutmeg, and some crackers, put it in a deep dish, and baked it till it was brown and nice, and next day it was eaten by a family named March.

T. TUPMAN

* * * * *

MR. PICKWICK, *SIR*:—

I address you upon the subject of sin the sinner I mean is a man named Winkle who makes trouble in his club by laughing and sometimes won't write his piece in this fine paper I hope you will pardon his badness and let him send a French fable because he can't write out of his head as he has so many lessons to do and no brains in future I will try to take time by the fetlock and prepare some work which will be all *commy la fo* that means all right I am in haste as it is nearly school time.

Yours respectably,
N. WINKLE

[The above is a manly and handsome acknowledgment of past misdemeanors. If our young friend studied punctuation, it would be well.]

*****

A SAD ACCIDENT

On Friday last, we were startled by a violent shock in our basement, followed by cries of distress. On rushing in a body to the cellar, we discovered our beloved President prostrate upon the floor, having tripped and fallen while getting wood for domestic purposes. A perfect scene of ruin met our eyes, for in his fall Mr. Pickwick had plunged his head and shoulders into a tub of water, upset a keg of soft soap upon his manly form, and torn his garments badly. On being removed from this perilous situation, it was discovered that he had suffered no injury but several bruises, and we are happy to add, is now doing well.

ED.

*****

THE PUBLIC BEREAVEMENT

It is our painful duty to record the sudden and mysterious disappearance of our cherished friend, Mrs. Snowball Pat Paw. This lovely and beloved cat was the pet of a large circle of warm and admiring friends; for her beauty attracted all eyes, her graces and virtues endeared her to all hearts, and her loss is deeply felt by the whole community.

When last seen, she was sitting at the gate, watching the butcher's cart, and it is feared that some villain, tempted by her charms, basely stole her. Weeks have passed, but no trace of her has been discovered, and we relinquish all hope, tie a black ribbon to her basket, set aside her dish, and weep for her as one lost to us forever.

*****

A sympathizing friend sends the following gem:

A LAMENT
(FOR S.B. PAT PAW)

We mourn the loss of our little pet,
And sigh o'er her hapless fate,
For never more by the fire she'll sit,
Nor play by the old green gate.

The little grave where her infant sleeps
Is 'neath the chestnut tree.
But o'er *her* grave we may not weep,
We know not where it may be.

Her empty bed, her idle ball,
Will never see her more;
No gentle tap, no loving purr
Is heard at the parlor door.

Another cat comes after her mice,
A cat with a dirty face,
But she does not hunt as our darling did,
Nor play with her airy grace.

Her stealthy paws tread the very hall
Where Snowball used to play,
But she only spits at the dogs our pet
So gallantly drove away.

She is useful and mild, and does her best,
But she is not fair to see,
And we cannot give her your place dear,
Nor worship her as we worship thee.

A.S.

*****

ADVERTISEMENTS

Miss Oranthy Bluggage, the accomplished strong-minded lecturer, will deliver her famous lecture on "WOMAN AND HER POSITION" at Pickwick Hall, next Saturday Evening, after the usual performances.

A Weekly Meeting will be held at Kitchen Place, to teach young ladies how to cook. Hannah Brown will preside, and all are invited to attend.

The Dustpan Society will meet on Wednesday next, and parade in the upper story of the Club House. All members to appear in uniform and shoulder their brooms at nine precisely.

Mrs. Beth Bouncer will open her new assortment of Doll's Millinery next week. The latest Paris fashions have arrived, and orders are respectfully solicited.

A New Play will appear at the Barnville Theatre, in the course of a few weeks, which will surpass anything ever seen on the American stage. "The Greek Slave, or Constantine the Avenger," is the name of this thrilling drama!!!

*****

HINTS

If S.P. didn't use so much soap on his hands, he wouldn't always be late at breakfast. A.S. is requested not to whistle in the street. T.T. please don't forget Amy's napkin. N.W. must not fret because his dress has not nine tucks.

*****

WEEKLY REPORT

Meg—Good.
Jo—Bad.
Beth—Very Good.
Amy—Middling.

As the President finished reading the paper (which I beg leave to assure my readers is a *bona fide* copy of one written by *bona fide* girls once upon a time), a round of applause followed, and then Mr. Snodgrass rose to make a proposition.

"Mr. President and gentlemen," he began, assuming a parliamentary attitude and tone, "I wish to propose the admission of a new member—one who highly deserves the honor, would be deeply grateful for it, and would add immensely to the spirit of the club, the literary value of the paper, and be no end jolly and nice. I propose Mr. Theodore Laurence as an honorary member of the P. C. Come now, do have him."

Jo's sudden change of tone made the girls laugh, but all looked rather anxious, and no one said a word as Snodgrass took his seat.

"We'll put it to a vote," said the President. "All in favor of this motion please to manifest it by saying, 'Aye.'"

A loud response from Snodgrass, followed, to everybody's surprise, by a timid one from Beth.

"Contrary-minded say, 'No.'"

Meg and Amy were contrary-minded, and Mr. Winkle rose to say with great elegance, "We don't wish any boys, they only joke and bounce about. This is a ladies' club, and we wish to be private and proper."

"I'm afraid he'll laugh at our paper, and make fun of us afterward," observed Pickwick, pulling the little curl on her forehead, as she always did when doubtful.

Up rose Snodgrass, very much in earnest. "Sir, I give you my word as a gentleman, Laurie won't do anything of the sort. He likes to write, and he'll give a tone to our contributions and keep us from being sentimental, don't you see? We can do so little for him, and he does so much for us, I think the least we can do is to offer him a place here, and make him welcome if he comes."

This artful allusion to benefits conferred brought Tupman to his feet, looking as if he had quite made up his mind.

"Yes, we ought to do it, even if we *are* afraid. I say he *may* come, and his grandpa, too, if he likes."

This spirited burst from Beth electrified the club, and Jo left her seat to shake hands approvingly. "Now then, vote again. Everybody remember it's our Laurie, and say, 'Aye!'" cried Snodgrass excitedly.

"Aye! Aye! Aye!" replied three voices at once.

"Good! Bless you! Now, as there's nothing like 'taking time by the *fetlock*,' as Winkle characteristically observes, allow me to present the new member." And, to the dismay of the rest of the club, Jo threw open the door of the closet, and displayed Laurie sitting on a rag bag, flushed and twinkling with suppressed laughter.

"You rogue! You traitor! Jo, how could you?" cried the three girls, as Snodgrass led her friend triumphantly forth, and producing both a chair and a badge, installed him in a jiffy.

"The coolness of you two rascals is amazing," began Mr. Pickwick, trying to get up an awful frown and only succeeding in producing an amiable smile. But the new member was equal to the occasion, and rising, with a grateful salutation to the Chair, said in the most engaging manner, "Mr. President and ladies—I beg pardon, gentlemen—allow me to introduce myself as Sam Weller, the very humble servant of the club."

"Good! Good!" cried Jo, pounding with the handle of the old warming pan on which she leaned.

"My faithful friend and noble patron," continued Laurie with a wave of the hand, "who has so flatteringly presented me, is not to be blamed for the base stratagem of tonight. I planned it, and she only gave in after lots of teasing."

"Come now, don't lay it all on yourself. You know I proposed the cupboard," broke in Snodgrass, who was enjoying the joke amazingly.

"Never you mind what she says. I'm the wretch that did it, sir," said the new member, with a Welleresque nod to Mr. Pickwick. "But on my honor, I never will do so again, and henceforth *devote* myself to the interest of this immortal club."

"Hear! Hear!" cried Jo, clashing the lid of the warming pan like a cymbal.

"Go on, go on!" added Winkle and Tupman, while the President bowed benignly.

"I merely wish to say, that as a slight token of my gratitude for the honor done me, and as a means of promoting friendly relations between adjoining nations, I have set up a post office in the hedge in the lower corner of the garden, a fine, spacious building with padlocks on the doors and every convenience for the mails—also the females, if I may be allowed the expression. It's the old martin house, but I've stopped up the door and made the roof open, so it will hold all sorts of things, and save our valuable time. Letters, manuscripts, books, and bundles can be passed in there, and as each nation has a key, it will be uncommonly nice, I fancy. Allow me to present the club key, and with many thanks for your favor, take my seat."

Great applause as Mr. Weller deposited a little key on the table and subsided, the warming pan clashed and waved wildly, and it was some time before order could be restored. A long discussion followed, and everyone came out surprising, for everyone did her best. So it was an unusually lively meeting, and did not adjourn till a late hour, when it broke up with three shrill cheers for the new member. No one ever regretted the admittance of Sam Weller, for a more devoted, well-behaved, and jovial member no club could have. He certainly did add "spirit" to the meetings, and "a tone" to the paper, for his orations convulsed his hearers and his contributions were excellent, being patriotic, classical, comical, or dramatic, but never sentimental. Jo regarded them as worthy of Bacon, Milton, or Shakespeare, and remodeled her own works with good effect, she thought.

The P. O. was a capital little institution, and flourished wonderfully, for nearly as many queer things passed through it as through the real post office. Tragedies and cravats, poetry and pickles, garden seeds and long letters, music and gingerbread, rubbers, invitations, scoldings, and puppies. The old gentleman liked the fun, and amused himself by sending odd bundles, mysterious messages, and funny telegrams, and his gardener, who was smitten with Hannah's charms, actually sent a love letter to Jo's care. How they laughed when the secret came out, never dreaming how many love letters that little post office would hold in the years to come!

CHAPTER XI

EXPERIMENTS

"The first of June! The Kings are off to the seashore tomorrow, and I'm free. Three months' vacation—how I shall enjoy it!" exclaimed Meg, coming home one warm day to find Jo laid upon the sofa in an unusual state of exhaustion, while Beth took off her dusty boots, and Amy made lemonade for the refreshment of the whole party.

"Aunt March went today, for which, oh, be joyful!" said Jo. "I was mortally afraid she'd ask me to go with her. If she had, I should have felt as if I ought to do it, but Plumfield is about as gay as a churchyard, you know, and I'd rather be excused. We had a flurry getting the old lady off, and I had a fright every time she spoke to me, for I was in such a hurry to be through that I was uncommonly helpful and sweet, and feared she'd find it impossible to part from me. I quaked till she was fairly in the carriage, and had a final fright, for as it drove of, she popped out her head, saying, 'Josyphine, won't you—?' I didn't hear any more, for I basely turned and fled. I did actually run, and whisked round the corner where I felt safe."

"Poor old Jo! She came in looking as if bears were after her," said Beth, as she cuddled her sister's feet with a motherly air.

"Aunt March is a regular samphire, is she not?" observed Amy, tasting her mixture critically.

"She means *vampire*, not seaweed, but it doesn't matter. It's too warm to be particular about one's parts of speech," murmured Jo.

"What shall you do all your vacation?" asked Amy, changing the subject with tact.

"I shall lie abed late, and do nothing," replied Meg, from the depths of the rocking chair. "I've been routed up early all winter and had to spend my days working for other people, so now I'm going to rest and revel to my heart's content."

"No," said Jo, "that dozy way wouldn't suit me. I've laid in a heap of books, and I'm going to improve my shining hours reading on my perch in the old apple tree, when I'm not having l—"

"Don't say 'larks!'" implored Amy, as a return snub for the "samphire" correction.

"I'll say 'nightingales' then, with Laurie; that's proper and appropriate, since he's a warbler."

"Don't let us do any lessons, Beth, for a while, but play all the time and rest, as the girls mean to," proposed Amy.

"Well, I will, if Mother doesn't mind. I want to learn some new songs, and my children need fitting up for the summer. They are dreadfully out of order and really suffering for clothes."

"May we, Mother?" asked Meg, turning to Mrs. March, who sat sewing in what they called "Marmee's corner."

"You may try your experiment for a week and see how you like it. I think by Saturday night you will find that all play and no work is as bad as all work and no play."

"Oh, dear, no! It will be delicious, I'm sure," said Meg complacently.

"I now propose a toast, as my 'friend and pardner, Sairy Gamp,' says. Fun forever, and no grubbing!" cried Jo, rising, glass in hand, as the lemonade went round.

They all drank it merrily, and began the experiment by lounging for the rest of the day. Next morning, Meg did not appear till ten o'clock. Her solitary breakfast did not taste good, and the room seemed lonely and untidy, for Jo had not filled the vases, Beth had not dusted, and Amy's books lay scattered about. Nothing was neat and pleasant but "Marmee's corner," which looked as usual. And there Meg sat, to "rest and read," which meant to yawn and imagine what pretty summer dresses she would get with her salary. Jo spent the morning on the river with Laurie and the afternoon reading and crying over *The Wide, Wide World*, up in the apple tree. Beth began by rummaging everything out of the big closet where her family resided, but getting tired before half done, she left her establishment topsy-turvy and went to her music, rejoicing that she had no dishes to wash. Amy arranged her bower, put on her best white frock, smoothed her curls, and sat down to draw under the honeysuckle, hoping someone would see and inquire who the young artist was. As no one appeared but an inquisitive daddy-longlegs, who examined her work with interest, she went to walk, got caught in a shower, and came home dripping.

At teatime they compared notes, and all agreed that it had been a delightful, though unusually long day. Meg, who went shopping in the afternoon and got a "sweet blue muslin," had discovered, after she had cut the breadths off, that it wouldn't wash, which mishap made her slightly cross. Jo had burned the skin off her nose boating, and got a raging headache by reading too long. Beth was worried by the confusion of her closet and the difficulty of learning three or four songs at once, and Amy deeply regretted the damage done her frock, for Katy Brown's party was to be the next day and now like Flora McFlimsey, she had "nothing to wear." But these were mere trifles, and they assured their mother that the experiment was working finely. She smiled, said nothing, and with Hannah's help did their neglected work, keeping home pleasant and the domestic machinery running smoothly. It was astonishing what a peculiar and uncomfortable state of things was produced by the "resting and reveling" process. The days kept getting longer and longer, the weather was unusually variable and so were tempers; an unsettled feeling possessed everyone, and Satan found plenty of mischief for the idle hands to do. As the height of luxury, Meg put out some of her sewing, and then found time hang so heavily, that she fell to snipping and spoiling her clothes in her attempts to furbish them up a la Moffat. Jo read till her eyes gave out and she was sick of books, got so fidgety that even good-natured Laurie had a quarrel with her, and so reduced in spirits that she desperately wished she had gone with Aunt March. Beth got on pretty well, for she was constantly forgetting that it was to be *all play and no work*, and fell back into her old ways now and then. But something in the air affected her, and more than once her tranquility was much disturbed—so much so that on one occasion she actually shook poor dear Joanna and told her she was "a fright." Amy fared worst of all, for her resources were small, and when her sisters left her to amuse herself, she soon found that accomplished and important little self a great burden. She didn't like dolls, fairy tales were childish, and one couldn't draw all the time. Tea parties didn't amount to much, neither did picnics, unless very well conducted. "If one could have a fine house, full of nice girls, or go traveling, the summer would be delightful, but to stay at home with three selfish sisters and a grown-up boy was enough to try the patience of a Boaz," complained Miss Malaprop, after several days devoted to pleasure, fretting, and ennui.

No one would own that they were tired of the experiment, but by Friday night each acknowledged to herself that she was glad the week was nearly done. Hoping to impress the lesson more deeply, Mrs. March, who had a good deal of humor, resolved to finish off the trial in an appropriate manner, so she gave Hannah a holiday and let the girls enjoy the full effect of the play system.

When they got up on Saturday morning, there was no fire in the kitchen, no breakfast in the dining room, and no mother anywhere to be seen.

"Mercy on us! What *has* happened?" cried Jo, staring about her in dismay.

Meg ran upstairs and soon came back again, looking relieved but rather bewildered, and a little ashamed.

"Mother isn't sick, only very tired, and she says she is going to stay quietly in her room all day and let us do the best we can. It's a very queer thing for her to do, she doesn't act a bit like herself. But she says it has been a hard week for her, so we mustn't grumble but take care of ourselves."

"That's easy enough, and I like the idea, I'm aching for something to do— that is, some new amusement, you know," added Jo quickly.

In fact it *was* an immense relief to them all to have a little work, and they took hold with a will, but soon realized the truth of Hannah's saying, "Housekeeping ain't no joke." There was plenty of food in the larder, and while Beth and Amy set the table, Meg and Jo got breakfast, wondering as they did why servants ever talked about hard work.

"I shall take some up to Mother, though she said we were not to think of her, for she'd take care of herself," said Meg, who presided and felt quite matronly behind the teapot.

So a tray was fitted out before anyone began, and taken up with the cook's compliments. The boiled tea was very bitter, the omelet scorched, and the biscuits speckled with saleratus, but Mrs. March received her repast with thanks and laughed heartily over it after Jo was gone.

"Poor little souls, they will have a hard time, I'm afraid, but they won't suffer, and it will do them good," she said, producing the more palatable viands with which she had provided herself, and disposing of the bad breakfast, so that their feelings might not be hurt, a motherly little deception for which they were grateful.

Many were the complaints below, and great the chagrin of the head cook at her failures. "Never mind, I'll get the dinner and be servant, you be mistress, keep your hands nice, see company, and give orders," said Jo, who knew still less than Meg about culinary affairs.

This obliging offer was gladly accepted, and Margaret retired to the parlor, which she hastily put in order by whisking the litter under the sofa and shutting the blinds to save the trouble of dusting. Jo, with perfect faith in her own powers and a friendly desire to make up the quarrel, immediately put a note in the office, inviting Laurie to dinner.

"You'd better see what you have got before you think of having company," said Meg, when informed of the hospitable but rash act.

"Oh, there's corned beef and plenty of potatoes, and I shall get some asparagus and a lobster, 'for a relish,' as Hannah says. We'll have lettuce and make a salad. I don't know how, but the book tells. I'll have blanc mange and strawberries for dessert, and coffee too, if you want to be elegant."

"Don't try too many messes, Jo, for you can't make anything but gingerbread and molasses candy fit to eat. I wash my hands of the dinner party, and since you have asked Laurie on your own responsibility, you may just take care of him."

"I don't want you to do anything but be civil to him and help to the pudding. You'll give me your advice if I get in a muddle, won't you?" asked Jo, rather hurt.

"Yes, but I don't know much, except about bread and a few trifles. You had better ask Mother's leave before you order anything," returned Meg prudently.

"Of course I shall. I'm not a fool." And Jo went off in a huff at the doubts expressed of her powers.

"Get what you like, and don't disturb me. I'm going out to dinner and can't worry about things at home," said Mrs. March, when Jo spoke to her. "I never enjoyed housekeeping, and I'm going to take a vacation today, and read, write, go visiting, and amuse myself."

The unusual spectacle of her busy mother rocking comfortably and reading early in the morning made Jo feel as if some unnatural phenomenon had occurred, for an eclipse, an earthquake, or a volcanic eruption would hardly have seemed stranger.

"Everything is out of sorts, somehow," she said to herself, going downstairs. "There's Beth crying, that's a sure sign that something is wrong in this family. If Amy is bothering, I'll shake her."

Feeling very much out of sorts herself, Jo hurried into the parlor to find Beth sobbing over Pip, the canary, who lay dead in the cage with his little claws pathetically extended, as if imploring the food for want of which he had died.

"It's all my fault—I forgot him—there isn't a seed or a drop left. Oh, Pip! Oh, Pip! How could I be so cruel to you?" cried Beth, taking the poor thing in her hands and trying to restore him.

Jo peeped into his half-open eye, felt his little heart, and finding him stiff and cold, shook her head, and offered her domino box for a coffin.

"Put him in the oven, and maybe he will get warm and revive," said Amy hopefully.

"He's been starved, and he shan't be baked now he's dead. I'll make him a shroud, and he shall be buried in the garden, and I'll never have another bird, never, my Pip! for I am too bad to own one," murmured Beth, sitting on the floor with her pet folded in her hands.

"The funeral shall be this afternoon, and we will all go. Now, don't cry, Bethy. It's a pity, but nothing goes right this week, and Pip has had the worst of the experiment. Make the shroud, and lay him in my box, and after the dinner party, we'll have a nice little funeral," said Jo, beginning to feel as if she had undertaken a good deal.

Leaving the others to console Beth, she departed to the kitchen, which was in a most discouraging state of confusion. Putting on a big apron, she fell to work and got the dishes piled up ready for washing, when she discovered that the fire was out.

"Here's a sweet prospect!" muttered Jo, slamming the stove door open, and poking vigorously among the cinders.

Having rekindled the fire, she thought she would go to market while the water heated. The walk revived her spirits, and flattering herself that she had made good bargains, she trudged home again, after buying a very young lobster, some very old asparagus, and two boxes of acid strawberries. By the time she got cleared up, the dinner arrived and the stove was red-hot. Hannah had left a pan of bread to rise, Meg had worked it up early, set it on the hearth for a second rising, and forgotten it. Meg was entertaining Sallie Gardiner in the parlor, when the door flew open and a floury, crocky, flushed, and disheveled figure appeared, demanding tartly—

"I say, isn't bread 'riz' enough when it runs over the pans?"

Sallie began to laugh, but Meg nodded and lifted her eyebrows as high as they would go, which caused the apparition to vanish and put the sour bread into the oven without further delay. Mrs. March went out, after peeping here and there to see how matters went, also saying a word of comfort to Beth, who sat making a winding sheet, while the dear departed lay in state in the domino box. A strange sense of helplessness fell upon the girls as the gray bonnet vanished round the corner, and despair seized them when a few minutes later Miss Crocker appeared, and said she'd come to dinner. Now this lady was a thin, yellow spinster, with a sharp nose and inquisitive eyes, who saw everything and gossiped about all she saw. They disliked her, but had been taught to be kind to her, simply because she was old and poor and had few friends. So Meg gave her the easy chair and tried to entertain her, while she asked questions, criticized everything, and told stories of the people whom she knew.

Language cannot describe the anxieties, experiences, and exertions which Jo underwent that morning, and the dinner she served up became a standing joke. Fearing to ask any more advice, she did her best alone, and discovered that something more than energy and good will is necessary to make a cook. She boiled the asparagus for an hour and was grieved to find the heads cooked off and the stalks harder than ever. The bread burned black; for the salad dressing so aggravated her that she let everything else go till she had convinced herself that she could not make it fit to eat. The lobster was a scarlet mystery to her, but she hammered and poked till it was unshelled and its meager proportions concealed in a grove of lettuce leaves. The potatoes had to be hurried, not to keep the asparagus waiting, and were not done at the last. The blancmange was lumpy, and the strawberries not as ripe as they looked, having been skilfully "deaconed."

"Well, they can eat beef and bread and butter, if they are hungry, only it's mortifying to have to spend your whole morning for nothing," thought Jo, as she rang the bell half an hour later than usual, and stood, hot, tired, and dispirited, surveying the feast spread before Laurie, accustomed to all sorts of elegance, and Miss Crocker, whose tattling tongue would report them far and wide.

Poor Jo would gladly have gone under the table, as one thing after another was tasted and left, while Amy giggled, Meg looked distressed, Miss Crocker pursed her lips, and Laurie talked and laughed with all his might to give a cheerful tone to the festive scene. Jo's one strong point was the fruit, for she had sugared it well, and had a pitcher of rich cream to eat with it. Her hot cheeks cooled a trifle, and she drew a long breath as the pretty glass plates went round, and everyone looked graciously at the little rosy islands floating in a sea of cream. Miss Crocker tasted first, made a wry face, and drank some water hastily. Jo, who refused, thinking there might not be enough, for they dwindled sadly after the picking over, glanced at Laurie, but he was eating away manfully, though there was a slight pucker about his mouth and he kept his eye fixed on his plate. Amy, who was fond of delicate fare, took a heaping spoonful, choked, hid her face in her napkin, and left the table precipitately.

"Oh, what is it?" exclaimed Jo, trembling.

"Salt instead of sugar, and the cream is sour," replied Meg with a tragic gesture.

Jo uttered a groan and fell back in her chair, remembering that she had given a last hasty powdering to the berries out of one of the two boxes on the kitchen table, and had neglected to put the milk in the refrigerator. She turned scarlet and was on the verge of crying, when she met Laurie's eyes, which *would* look merry in spite of his heroic efforts. The comical side of the affair suddenly struck her, and she laughed till the tears ran down her cheeks. So did everyone else, even "Croaker," as the girls called the old lady, and the unfortunate dinner ended gaily, with bread and butter, olives and fun.

"I haven't strength of mind enough to clear up now, so we will sober ourselves with a funeral," said Jo, as they rose, and Miss Crocker made ready to go, being eager to tell the new story at another friend's dinner table.

They did sober themselves for Beth's sake. Laurie dug a grave under the ferns in the grove, little Pip was laid in, with many tears by his tender-hearted mistress, and covered with moss, while a wreath of violets and chickweed was hung on the stone which bore his epitaph, composed by Jo while she struggled with the dinner:

> Here lies Pip March,
> Who died the 7th of June;
> Loved and lamented sore,
> And not forgotten soon.

At the conclusion of the ceremonies, Beth retired to her room, overcome with emotion and lobster, but there was no place of repose, for the beds were not made, and she found her grief much assuaged by beating up the pillows and putting things in order. Meg helped Jo clear away the remains of the feast, which took half the afternoon and left them so tired that they agreed to be contented with tea and toast for supper. Laurie took Amy to drive, which was a deed of charity, for the sour cream seemed to have had a bad effect upon her temper. Mrs. March came home to find the three older girls hard at work in the middle of the afternoon, and a glance at the closet gave her an idea of the success of one part of the experiment.

Before the housewives could rest, several people called, and there was a scramble to get ready to see them. Then tea must be got, errands done, and one or two necessary bits of sewing neglected until the last minute. As twilight fell, dewy and still, one by one they gathered on the porch where the June roses were budding beautifully, and each groaned or sighed as she sat down, as if tired or troubled.

"What a dreadful day this has been!" began Jo, usually the first to speak.

"It has seemed shorter than usual, but so uncomfortable," said Meg.

"Not a bit like home," added Amy.

"It can't seem so without Marmee and little Pip," sighed Beth, glancing with full eyes at the empty cage above her head.

"Here's Mother, dear, and you shall have another bird tomorrow, if you want it."

As she spoke, Mrs. March came and took her place among them, looking as if her holiday had not been much pleasanter than theirs.

"Are you satisfied with your experiment, girls, or do you want another week of it?" she asked, as Beth nestled up to her and the rest turned toward her with brightening faces, as flowers turn toward the sun.

"I don't!" cried Jo decidedly.

"Nor I," echoed the others.

"You think then, that it is better to have a few duties and live a little for others, do you?"

"Lounging and larking doesn't pay," observed Jo, shaking her head. "I'm tired of it and mean to go to work at something right off."

"Suppose you learn plain cooking. That's a useful accomplishment, which no woman should be without," said Mrs. March, laughing inaudibly at the recollection of Jo's dinner party, for she had met Miss Crocker and heard her account of it.

"Mother, did you go away and let everything be, just to see how we'd get on?" cried Meg, who had had suspicions all day.

"Yes, I wanted you to see how the comfort of all depends on each doing her share faithfully. While Hannah and I did your work, you got on pretty well, though I don't think you were very happy or amiable. So I thought, as a little lesson, I would show you what happens when everyone thinks only of herself. Don't you feel that it is pleasanter to help one another, to have daily duties which make leisure sweet when it comes, and to bear and forbear, that home may be comfortable and lovely to us all?"

"We do, Mother, we do!" cried the girls.

"Then let me advise you to take up your little burdens again, for though they seem heavy sometimes, they are good for us, and lighten as we learn to carry them. Work is wholesome, and there is plenty for everyone. It keeps us from ennui and mischief, is good for health and spirits, and gives us a sense of power and independence better than money or fashion."

"We'll work like bees, and love it too, see if we don't," said Jo. "I'll learn plain cooking for my holiday task, and the next dinner party I have shall be a success."

"I'll make the set of shirts for father, instead of letting you do it, Marmee. I can and I will, though I'm not fond of sewing. That will be better than fussing over my own things, which are plenty nice enough as they are," said Meg.

"I'll do my lessons every day, and not spend so much time with my music and dolls. I am a stupid thing, and ought to be studying, not playing," was Beth's resolution, while Amy followed their example by heroically declaring, "I shall learn to make buttonholes, and attend to my parts of speech."

"Very good! Then I am quite satisfied with the experiment, and fancy that we shall not have to repeat it, only don't go to the other extreme and delve like slaves. Have regular hours for work and play, make each day both useful and pleasant, and prove that you understand the worth of time by employing it well. Then youth will be delightful, old age will bring few regrets, and life become a beautiful success, in spite of poverty."

"We'll remember, Mother!" And they did.

CHAPTER XII

CAMP LAURENCE

Beth was postmistress, for, being most at home, she could attend to it regularly, and dearly liked the daily task of unlocking the little door and distributing the mail. One July day she came in with her hands full, and went about the house leaving letters and parcels like the penny post.

"Here's your posy, Mother! Laurie never forgets that," she said, putting the fresh nosegay in the vase that stood in "Marmee's corner," and was kept supplied by the affectionate boy.

"Miss Meg March, one letter and a glove," continued Beth, delivering the articles to her sister, who sat near her mother, stitching wristbands.

"Why, I left a pair over there, and here is only one," said Meg, looking at the gray cotton glove. "Didn't you drop the other in the garden?"

"No, I'm sure I didn't, for there was only one in the office."

"I hate to have odd gloves! Never mind, the other may be found. My letter is only a translation of the German song I wanted. I think Mr. Brooke did it, for this isn't Laurie's writing."

Mrs. March glanced at Meg, who was looking very pretty in her gingham morning gown, with the little curls blowing about her forehead, and very womanly, as she sat sewing at her little worktable, full of tidy white rolls, so unconscious of the thought in her mother's mind as she sewed and sang, while her fingers flew and her thoughts were busied with girlish fancies as innocent and fresh as the pansies in her belt, that Mrs. March smiled and was satisfied.

"Two letters for Doctor Jo, a book, and a funny old hat, which covered the whole post office and stuck outside," said Beth, laughing as she went into the study where Jo sat writing.

"What a sly fellow Laurie is! I said I wished bigger hats were the fashion, because I burn my face every hot day. He said, 'Why mind the fashion? Wear a big hat, and be comfortable!' I said I would if I had one, and he has sent me this, to try me. I'll wear it for fun, and show him I don't care for the fashion." And hanging the antique broad-brim on a bust of Plato, Jo read her letters.

One from her mother made her cheeks glow and her eyes fill, for it said to her—

> MY DEAR:
>
> I write a little word to tell you with how much satisfaction I watch your efforts to control your temper. You say nothing about your trials, failures, or successes, and think, perhaps, that no one sees them but the Friend whose help you daily ask, if I may trust the well-worn cover of your guidebook. I, too, have seen them all, and heartily believe in the sincerity of your resolution, since it begins to bear fruit. Go on, dear, patiently and bravely, and always believe that no one sympathizes more tenderly with you than your loving
>
> MOTHER.

"That does me good! That's worth millions of money and pecks of praise. Oh, Marmee, I do try! I will keep on trying, and not get tired, since I have you to help me."

Laying her head on her arms, Jo wet her little romance with a few happy tears, for she *had* thought that no one saw and appreciated her efforts to be good, and this assurance was doubly precious, doubly encouraging, because unexpected and from the person whose commendation she most valued. Feeling stronger than ever to meet and subdue her Apollyon, she pinned the note inside her frock, as a shield and a reminder, lest she be taken unaware, and proceeded to open her other letter, quite ready for either good or bad news. In a big, dashing hand, Laurie wrote—

> DEAR JO,
>
> What ho!
>
> Some English girls and boys are coming to see me tomorrow and I want to have a jolly time. If it's fine, I'm going to pitch my tent in Longmeadow, and row up the whole crew to lunch and croquet—have a fire, make messes, gypsy fashion, and all sorts of larks. They are nice people, and like such things. Brooke will go to keep us boys steady, and Kate Vaughn will play propriety for the girls. I want you all to come, can't let Beth off at any price, and nobody shall worry her. Don't bother about rations—I'll see to that and everything else—only do come, there's a good fellow!

In a tearing hurry,
Yours ever,
LAURIE.

"Here's richness!" cried Jo, flying in to tell the news to Meg.

"Of course we can go, Mother? It will be such a help to Laurie, for I can row, and Meg see to the lunch, and the children be useful in some way."

"I hope the Vaughns are not fine grown-up people. Do you know anything about them, Jo?" asked Meg.

"Only that there are four of them. Kate is older than you, Fred and Frank (twins) about my age, and a little girl (Grace), who is nine or ten. Laurie knew them abroad, and liked the boys. I fancied, from the way he primmed up his mouth in speaking of her, that he didn't admire Kate much."

"I'm so glad my French print is clean, it's just the thing and so becoming!" observed Meg complacently. "Have you anything decent, Jo?"

"Scarlet and gray boating suit, good enough for me. I shall row and tramp about, so I don't want any starch to think of. You'll come, Betty?"

"If you won't let any boys talk to me."

"Not a boy!"

"I like to please Laurie, and I'm not afraid of Mr. Brooke, he is so kind. But I don't want to play, or sing, or say anything. I'll work hard and not trouble anyone, and you'll take care of me, Jo, so I'll go."

"That's my good girl. You do try to fight off your shyness, and I love you for it. Fighting faults isn't easy, as I know, and a cheery word kind of gives a lift. Thank you, Mother," And Jo gave the thin cheek a grateful kiss, more precious to Mrs. March than if it had given back the rosy roundness of her youth.

"I had a box of chocolate drops, and the picture I wanted to copy," said Amy, showing her mail.

"And I got a note from Mr. Laurence, asking me to come over and play to him tonight, before the lamps are lighted, and I shall go," added Beth, whose friendship with the old gentleman prospered finely.

"Now let's fly round, and do double duty today, so that we can play tomorrow with free minds," said Jo, preparing to replace her pen with a broom.

When the sun peeped into the girls' room early next morning to promise them a fine day, he saw a comical sight. Each had made such preparation for the fete as seemed necessary and proper. Meg had an extra row of little curlpapers across her forehead, Jo had copiously anointed her afflicted face with cold cream, Beth had taken Joanna to bed with her to atone for the approaching separation, and Amy had capped the climax by putting a clothespin on her nose to uplift the offending feature. It was one of the kind artists use to hold the paper on their drawing boards, therefore quite appropriate and effective for the purpose it was now being put. This funny spectacle appeared to amuse the sun, for he burst out with such radiance that Jo woke up and roused her sisters by a hearty laugh at Amy's ornament.

Sunshine and laughter were good omens for a pleasure party, and soon a lively bustle began in both houses. Beth, who was ready first, kept reporting what went on next door, and enlivened her sisters' toilets by frequent telegrams from the window.

"There goes the man with the tent! I see Mrs. Barker doing up the lunch in a hamper and a great basket. Now Mr. Laurence is looking up at the sky and the weathercock. I wish he would go—too. There's Laurie, looking like a sailor—nice boy! Oh, mercy me! Here's a carriage full of people—a tall lady, a little girl, and two dreadful boys. One is lame, poor thing, he's got a crutch. Laurie didn't tell us that. Be quick, girls! It's getting late. Why, there is Ned Moffat, I do declare. Meg, isn't that the man who bowed to you one day when we were shopping?"

"So it is. How queer that he should come. I thought he was at the mountains. There is Sallie. I'm glad she got back in time. Am I all right, Jo?" cried Meg in a flutter.

"A regular daisy. Hold up your dress and put your hat on straight, it looks sentimental tipped that way and will fly off at the first puff. Now then, come on!"

"Oh, Jo, you are not going to wear that awful hat? It's too absurd! You shall *not* make a guy of yourself," remonstrated Meg, as Jo tied down with a red ribbon the broad-brimmed, old-fashioned leghorn Laurie had sent for a joke.

"I just will, though, for it's capital—so shady, light, and big. It will make fun, and I don't mind being a guy if I'm comfortable." With that Jo marched straight away and the rest followed, a bright little band of sisters, all looking their best in summer suits, with happy faces under the jaunty hatbrims.

Laurie ran to meet and present them to his friends in the most cordial manner. The lawn was the reception room, and for several minutes a lively scene was enacted there. Meg was grateful to see that Miss Kate, though twenty, was dressed with a simplicity which American girls would do well to imitate, and who was much flattered by Mr. Ned's assurances that he came especially to see her. Jo understood why Laurie "primmed up his mouth" when speaking of Kate, for that young lady had a stand-off-don't-touch-me air, which contrasted strongly with the free and easy demeanor of the other girls. Beth took an observation of the new boys and decided that the lame one was not "dreadful," but gentle and feeble, and she would be kind to him on that account. Amy found Grace a well-mannered, merry, little person, and after staring dumbly at one another for a few minutes, they suddenly became very good friends.

Tents, lunch, and croquet utensils having been sent on beforehand, the party was soon embarked, and the two boats pushed off together, leaving Mr. Laurence waving his hat on the shore. Laurie and Jo rowed one boat, Mr. Brooke and Ned the other, while Fred Vaughn, the riotous twin, did his best to upset both by paddling about in a wherry like a disturbed water bug. Jo's funny hat deserved a vote of thanks, for it was of general utility. It broke the ice in the beginning by producing a laugh, it created quite a refreshing breeze, flapping to and fro as she rowed, and would make an excellent umbrella for the whole party, if a shower came up, she said. Miss Kate decided that she was "odd, but rather clever," and smiled upon her from afar.

Meg, in the other boat, was delightfully situated, face to face with the rowers, who both admired the prospect and feathered their oars with uncommon "skill and dexterity." Mr. Brooke was a grave, silent young man, with handsome brown eyes and a pleasant voice. Meg liked his quiet manners and considered him a walking encyclopedia of useful knowledge. He never talked to her much, but he looked at her a good deal, and she felt sure that he did not regard her with aversion. Ned, being in college, of course put on all the airs which freshmen think it their bounden duty to assume. He was not very wise, but very good-natured, and altogether an excellent person to carry on a picnic. Sallie Gardiner was absorbed in keeping her white pique dress clean and chattering with the ubiquitous Fred, who kept Beth in constant terror by his pranks.

It was not far to Longmeadow, but the tent was pitched and the wickets down by the time they arrived. A pleasant green field, with three wide-spreading oaks in the middle and a smooth strip of turf for croquet.

"Welcome to Camp Laurence!" said the young host, as they landed with exclamations of delight.

"Brooke is commander in chief, I am commissary general, the other fellows are staff officers, and you, ladies, are company. The tent is for your especial benefit and that oak is your drawing room, this is the messroom and the third is the camp kitchen. Now, let's have a game before it gets hot, and then we'll see about dinner."

Frank, Beth, Amy, and Grace sat down to watch the game played by the other eight. Mr. Brooke chose Meg, Kate, and Fred. Laurie took Sallie, Jo, and Ned. The English played well, but the Americans played better, and contested every inch of the ground as strongly as if the spirit of '76 inspired them. Jo and Fred had several skirmishes and once narrowly escaped high words. Jo was through the last wicket and had missed the stroke, which failure ruffled her a good deal. Fred was close behind her and his turn came before hers. He gave a stroke, his ball hit the wicket, and stopped an inch on the wrong side. No one was very near, and running up to examine, he gave it a sly nudge with his toe, which put it just an inch on the right side.

"I'm through! Now, Miss Jo, I'll settle you, and get in first," cried the young gentleman, swinging his mallet for another blow.

"You pushed it. I saw you. It's my turn now," said Jo sharply.

"Upon my word, I didn't move it. It rolled a bit, perhaps, but that is allowed. So, stand off please, and let me have a go at the stake."

"We don't cheat in America, but you can, if you choose," said Jo angrily.

"Yankees are a deal the most tricky, everybody knows. There you go!" returned Fred, croqueting her ball far away.

Jo opened her lips to say something rude, but checked herself in time, colored up to her forehead and stood a minute, hammering down a wicket with all her might, while Fred hit the stake and declared himself out with much exultation. She went off to get her ball, and was a long time finding it among the bushes, but she came back, looking cool and quiet, and waited her turn patiently. It took several strokes to regain the place she had lost, and when she got there, the other side had nearly won, for Kate's ball was the last but one and lay near the stake.

"By George, it's all up with us! Goodbye, Kate. Miss Jo owes me one, so you are finished," cried Fred excitedly, as they all drew near to see the finish.

"Yankees have a trick of being generous to their enemies," said Jo, with a look that made the lad redden, "especially when they beat them," she added, as, leaving Kate's ball untouched, she won the game by a clever stroke.

Laurie threw up his hat, then remembered that it wouldn't do to exult over the defeat of his guests, and stopped in the middle of the cheer to whisper to his friend, "Good for you, Jo! He did cheat, I saw him. We can't tell him so, but he won't do it again, take my word for it."

Meg drew her aside, under pretense of pinning up a loose braid, and said approvingly, "It was dreadfully provoking, but you kept your temper, and I'm so glad, Jo."

"Don't praise me, Meg, for I could box his ears this minute. I should certainly have boiled over if I hadn't stayed among the nettles till I got my rage under control enough to hold my tongue. It's simmering now, so I hope he'll keep out of my way," returned Jo, biting her lips as she glowered at Fred from under her big hat.

"Time for lunch," said Mr. Brooke, looking at his watch. "Commissary general, will you make the fire and get water, while Miss March, Miss Sallie, and I spread the table? Who can make good coffee?"

"Jo can," said Meg, glad to recommend her sister. So Jo, feeling that her late lessons in cookery were to do her honor, went to preside over the coffeepot, while the children collected dry sticks, and the boys made a fire and got water from a spring near by. Miss Kate sketched and Frank talked to Beth, who was making little mats of braided rushes to serve as plates.

The commander in chief and his aides soon spread the tablecloth with an inviting array of eatables and drinkables, prettily decorated with green leaves. Jo announced that the coffee was ready, and everyone settled themselves to a hearty meal, for youth is seldom dyspeptic, and exercise develops wholesome appetites. A very merry lunch it was, for everything seemed fresh and funny, and frequent peals of laughter startled a venerable horse who fed near by. There was a pleasing inequality in the table, which produced many mishaps to cups and plates, acorns dropped in the milk, little black ants partook of the refreshments without being invited, and fuzzy caterpillars swung down from the tree to see what was going on. Three white-headed children peeped over the fence, and an objectionable dog barked at them from the other side of the river with all his might and main.

"There's salt here," said Laurie, as he handed Jo a saucer of berries.

"Thank you, I prefer spiders," she replied, fishing up two unwary little ones who had gone to a creamy death. "How dare you remind me of that horrid dinner party, when yours is so nice in every way?" added Jo, as they both laughed and ate out of one plate, the china having run short.

"I had an uncommonly good time that day, and haven't got over it yet. This is no credit to me, you know, I don't do anything. It's you and Meg and Brooke who make it all go, and I'm no end obliged to you. What shall we do when we can't eat anymore?" asked Laurie, feeling that his trump card had been played when lunch was over.

"Have games till it's cooler. I brought Authors, and I dare say Miss Kate knows something new and nice. Go and ask her. She's company, and you ought to stay with her more."

"Aren't you company too? I thought she'd suit Brooke, but he keeps talking to Meg, and Kate just stares at them through that ridiculous glass of hers. I'm going, so you needn't try to preach propriety, for you can't do it, Jo."

Miss Kate did know several new games, and as the girls would not, and the boys could not, eat any more, they all adjourned to the drawing room to play Rig-marole.

"One person begins a story, any nonsense you like, and tells as long as he pleases, only taking care to stop short at some exciting point, when the next takes it up and does the same. It's very funny when well done, and makes a perfect jumble of tragical comical stuff to laugh over. Please start it, Mr. Brooke," said Kate, with a commanding air, which surprised Meg, who treated the tutor with as much respect as any other gentleman.

Lying on the grass at the feet of the two young ladies, Mr. Brooke obediently began the story, with the handsome brown eyes steadily fixed upon the sunshiny river.

"Once on a time, a knight went out into the world to seek his fortune, for he had nothing but his sword and his shield. He traveled a long while, nearly eight-and-twenty years, and had a hard time of it, till he came to the palace of a good old king, who had offered a reward to anyone who could tame and train a fine but unbroken colt, of which he was very fond. The knight agreed to try, and got on slowly but surely, for the colt was a gallant fellow, and soon learned to love his new master, though he was freakish and wild. Every day, when he gave his lessons to this pet of the king's, the knight rode him through the city, and as he rode, he looked everywhere for a certain beautiful face, which he had seen many times in his dreams, but never found. One day, as he went prancing down a quiet street, he saw at the window of a ruinous castle the lovely face. He was delighted, inquired who lived in this old castle, and was told that several captive princesses were kept there by a spell, and spun all day to lay up money to buy their liberty. The knight wished intensely that he could free them, but he was poor and could only go by each day, watching for the sweet face and longing to see it out in the sunshine. At last he resolved to get into the castle and ask how he could help them. He went and knocked. The great door flew open, and he beheld—"

"A ravishingly lovely lady, who exclaimed, with a cry of rapture, 'At last! At last!'" continued Kate, who had read French novels, and admired the style. "'Tis she!' cried Count Gustave, and fell at her feet in an ecstasy of joy. 'Oh, rise!' she said, extending a hand of marble fairness. 'Never! Till you tell me how I may rescue you,' swore the knight, still kneeling. 'Alas, my cruel fate condemns me to remain here till my tyrant is destroyed.' 'Where is the villain?' 'In the mauve salon. Go, brave heart, and save me from despair.' 'I obey, and return victorious or dead!' With these thrilling words he rushed away, and flinging open the door of the mauve salon, was about to enter, when he received—"

"A stunning blow from the big Greek lexicon, which an old fellow in a black gown fired at him," said Ned. "Instantly, Sir What's-his-name recovered himself, pitched the tyrant out of the window, and turned to join the lady, victorious, but with a bump on his brow; found the door locked, tore up the curtains, made a rope ladder, got halfway down when the ladder broke, and he went headfirst into the moat, sixty feet below. Could swim like a duck, paddled round the castle till he came to a little door guarded by two stout fellows, knocked their heads together till they cracked like a couple of nuts, then, by a trifling exertion of his prodigious strength, he smashed in the door, went up a pair of stone steps covered with dust a foot thick, toads as big as your fist, and spiders that would frighten you into hysterics, Miss March. At the top of these steps he came plump upon a sight that took his breath away and chilled his blood—"

"A tall figure, all in white with a veil over its face and a lamp in its wasted hand," went on Meg. "It beckoned, gliding noiselessly before him down a corridor as dark and cold as any tomb. Shadowy effigies in armor stood on either side, a dead silence reigned, the lamp burned blue, and the ghostly figure ever and anon turned its face toward him, showing the glitter of awful eyes through its white veil. They reached a curtained door, behind which sounded lovely music. He sprang forward to enter, but the specter plucked him back, and waved threateningly before him a—"

"Snuffbox," said Jo, in a sepulchral tone, which convulsed the audience. "'Thankee,' said the knight politely, as he took a pinch and sneezed seven times so violently that his head fell off. 'Ha! Ha!' laughed the ghost, and having peeped through the keyhole at the princesses spinning away for dear life, the evil spirit picked up her victim and put him in a large tin box, where there were eleven other knights packed together without their heads, like sardines, who all rose and began to—"

"Dance a hornpipe," cut in Fred, as Jo paused for breath, "and, as they danced, the rubbishy old castle turned to a man-of-war in full sail. 'Up with the jib, reef the tops'l halliards, helm hard alee, and man the guns!' roared the captain, as a Portuguese pirate hove in sight, with a flag black as ink flying from her foremast. 'Go in and win, my hearties!' says the captain, and a tremendous fight began. Of course the British beat—they always do."

"No, they don't!" cried Jo, aside.

"Having taken the pirate captain prisoner, sailed slap over the schooner, whose decks were piled high with dead and whose lee scuppers ran blood, for the order had been 'Cutlasses, and die hard!' 'Bosun's mate, take a bight of the flying-jib sheet, and start this villain if he doesn't confess his sins double quick,' said the British captain. The Portuguese held his tongue like a brick, and walked the plank, while the jolly tars cheered like mad. But the sly dog dived, came up under the man-of-war, scuttled her, and down she went, with all sail set, 'To the bottom of the sea, sea, sea' where—"

"Oh, gracious! What *shall* I say?" cried Sallie, as Fred ended his rigmarole, in which he had jumbled together pell-mell nautical phrases and facts out of one of his favorite books. "Well, they went to the bottom, and a nice mermaid welcomed them, but was much grieved on finding the box of headless knights, and kindly pickled them in brine, hoping to discover the mystery about them, for being a woman, she was curious. By-and-by a diver came down, and the mermaid said, 'I'll give you a box of pearls if you can take it up,' for she wanted to restore the poor things to life, and couldn't raise the heavy load herself. So the diver hoisted it up, and was much disappointed on opening it to find no pearls. He left it in a great lonely field, where it was found by a—"

"Little goosegirl, who kept a hundred fat geese in the field," said Amy, when Sallie's invention gave out. "The little girl was sorry for them, and asked an old woman what she should do to help them. 'Your geese will tell you, they know everything,' said the old woman. So she asked what she should use for new heads, since the old ones were lost, and all the geese opened their hundred mouths and screamed—"

"'Cabbages!'" continued Laurie promptly. "'Just the thing,' said the girl, and ran to get twelve fine ones from her garden. She put them on, the knights revived at once, thanked her, and went on their way rejoicing, never knowing the difference, for there were so many other heads like them in the world that no one thought anything of it. The knight in whom I'm interested went back to find the pretty face, and learned that the princesses had spun themselves free and all gone and married, but one. He was in a great state of mind at that, and mounting the colt, who stood by him through thick and thin, rushed to the castle to see which was left. Peeping over the hedge, he saw the queen of his affections picking flowers in her garden. 'Will you give me a rose?' said he. 'You must come and get it. I can't come to you, it isn't proper,' said she, as sweet as honey. He tried to climb over the hedge, but it seemed to grow higher and higher. Then he tried to push through, but it grew thicker and thicker, and he was in despair. So he patiently broke twig after twig till he had made a little hole through which he peeped, saying imploringly, 'Let me in! Let me in!' But the pretty princess did not seem to understand, for she picked her roses quietly, and left him to fight his way in. Whether he did or not, Frank will tell you."

"I can't. I'm not playing, I never do," said Frank, dismayed at the sentimental predicament out of which he was to rescue the absurd couple. Beth had disappeared behind Jo, and Grace was asleep.

"So the poor knight is to be left sticking in the hedge, is he?" asked Mr. Brooke, still watching the river, and playing with the wild rose in his buttonhole.

"I guess the princess gave him a posy, and opened the gate after a while," said Laurie, smiling to himself, as he threw acorns at his tutor.

"What a piece of nonsense we have made! With practice we might do something quite clever. Do you know Truth?"

"I hope so," said Meg soberly.

"The game, I mean?"

"What is it?" said Fred.

"Why, you pile up your hands, choose a number, and draw out in turn, and the person who draws at the number has to answer truly any question put by the rest. It's great fun."

"Let's try it," said Jo, who liked new experiments.

Miss Kate and Mr. Brooke, Meg, and Ned declined, but Fred, Sallie, Jo, and Laurie piled and drew, and the lot fell to Laurie.

"Who are your heroes?" asked Jo.

"Grandfather and Napoleon."

"Which lady here do you think prettiest?" said Sallie.

"Margaret."

"Which do you like best?" from Fred.

"Jo, of course."

"What silly questions you ask!" And Jo gave a disdainful shrug as the rest laughed at Laurie's matter-of-fact tone.

"Try again. Truth isn't a bad game," said Fred.

"It's a very good one for you," retorted Jo in a low voice.

Her turn came next.

"What is your greatest fault?" asked Fred, by way of testing in her the virtue he lacked himself.

"A quick temper."

"What do you most wish for?" said Laurie.

"A pair of boot lacings," returned Jo, guessing and defeating his purpose.

"Not a true answer. You must say what you really do want most."

"Genius. Don't you wish you could give it to me, Laurie?" and she slyly smiled in his disappointed face.

"What virtues do you most admire in a man?" asked Sallie.

"Courage and honesty."

"Now my turn," said Fred, as his hand came last.

"Let's give it to him," whispered Laurie to Jo, who nodded and asked at once—

"Didn't you cheat at croquet?"

"Well, yes, a little bit."

"Good! Didn't you take your story out of *The Sea Lion*?" said Laurie.

"Rather."

"Don't you think the English nation perfect in every respect?" asked Sallie.

"I should be ashamed of myself if I didn't."

"He's a true John Bull. Now, Miss Sallie, you shall have a chance without waiting to draw. I'll harrrow up your feelings first by asking if you don't think you are something of a flirt," said Laurie, as Jo nodded to Fred as a sign that peace was declared.

"You impertinent boy! Of course I'm not," exclaimed Sallie, with an air that proved the contrary.

"What do you hate most?" asked Fred.

"Spiders and rice pudding."

"What do you like best?" asked Jo.

"Dancing and French gloves."

"Well, *I* think Truth is a very silly play. Let's have a sensible game of Authors to refresh our minds," proposed Jo.

Ned, Frank, and the little girls joined in this, and while it went on, the three elders sat apart, talking. Miss Kate took out her sketch again, and Margaret watched her, while Mr. Brooke lay on the grass with a book, which he did not read.

"How beautifully you do it! I wish I could draw," said Meg, with mingled admiration and regret in her voice.

"Why don't you learn? I should think you had taste and talent for it," replied Miss Kate graciously.

"I haven't time."

"Your mamma prefers other accomplishments, I fancy. So did mine, but I proved to her that I had talent by taking a few lessons privately, and then she was quite willing I should go on. Can't you do the same with your governess?"

"I have none."

"I forgot young ladies in America go to school more than with us.

Very fine schools they are, too, Papa says. You go to a private one, I suppose?"

"I don't go at all. I am a governess myself."

"Oh, indeed!" said Miss Kate, but she might as well have said, "Dear me, how dreadful!" for her tone implied it, and something in her face made Meg color, and wish she had not been so frank.

Mr. Brooke looked up and said quickly, "Young ladies in America love independence as much as their ancestors did, and are admired and respected for supporting themselves."

"Oh, yes, of course it's very nice and proper in them to do so. We have many most respectable and worthy young women who do the same and are employed by the nobility, because, being the daughters of gentlemen, they are both well bred and accomplished, you know," said Miss Kate in a patronizing tone that hurt Meg's pride, and made her work seem not only more distasteful, but degrading.

"Did the German song suit, Miss March?" inquired Mr. Brooke, breaking an awkward pause.

"Oh, yes! It was very sweet, and I'm much obliged to whoever translated it for me." And Meg's downcast face brightened as she spoke.

"Don't you read German?" asked Miss Kate with a look of surprise.

"Not very well. My father, who taught me, is away, and I don't get on very fast alone, for I've no one to correct my pronunciation."

"Try a little now. Here is Schiller's *Mary Stuart* and a tutor who loves to teach." And Mr. Brooke laid his book on her lap with an inviting smile.

"It's so hard I'm afraid to try," said Meg, grateful, but bashful in the presence of the accomplished young lady beside her.

"I'll read a bit to encourage you." And Miss Kate read one of the most beautiful passages in a perfectly correct but perfectly expressionless manner.

Mr. Brooke made no comment as she returned the book to Meg, who said innocently, "I thought it was poetry."

"Some of it is. Try this passage."

There was a queer smile about Mr. Brooke's mouth as he opened at poor Mary's lament.

Meg obediently following the long grass-blade which her new tutor used to point with, read slowly and timidly, unconsciously making poetry of the hard words by the soft intonation of her musical voice.

Down the page went the green guide, and presently, forgetting her listener in the beauty of the sad scene, Meg read as if alone, giving a little touch of tragedy to the words of the unhappy queen. If she had seen the brown eyes then, she would have stopped short, but she never looked up, and the lesson was not spoiled for her.

"Very well indeed!" said Mr. Brooke, as she paused, quite ignoring her many mistakes, and looking as if he did indeed "love to teach."

Miss Kate put up her glass, and, having taken a survey of the little tableau before her, shut her sketch book, saying with condescension, "You've a nice accent and in time will be a clever reader. I advise you to learn, for German is a valuable accomplishment to teachers. I must look after Grace, she is romping." And Miss Kate strolled away, adding to herself with a shrug, "I didn't come to chaperone a governess, though she is young and pretty. What odd people these Yankees are. I'm afraid Laurie will be quite spoiled among them."

"I forgot that English people rather turn up their noses at governesses and don't treat them as we do," said Meg, looking after the retreating figure with an annoyed expression.

"Tutors also have rather a hard time of it there, as I know to my sorrow. There's no place like America for us workers, Miss Margaret." And Mr. Brooke looked so contented and cheerful that Meg was ashamed to lament her hard lot.

"I'm glad I live in it then. I don't like my work, but I get a good deal of satisfaction out of it after all, so I won't complain. I only wished I liked teaching as you do."

"I think you would if you had Laurie for a pupil. I shall be very sorry to lose him next year," said Mr. Brooke, busily punching holes in the turf.

"Going to college, I suppose?" Meg's lips asked the question, but her eyes added, "And what becomes of you?"

"Yes, it's high time he went, for he is ready, and as soon as he is off, I shall turn soldier. I am needed."

"I am glad of that!" exclaimed Meg. "I should think every young man would want to go, though it is hard for the mothers and sisters who stay at home," she added sorrowfully.

"I have neither, and very few friends to care whether I live or die," said Mr. Brooke rather bitterly as he absently put the dead rose in the hole he had made and covered it up, like a little grave.

"Laurie and his grandfather would care a great deal, and we should all be very sorry to have any harm happen to you," said Meg heartily.

"Thank you, that sounds pleasant," began Mr. Brooke, looking cheerful again, but before he could finish his speech, Ned, mounted on the old horse, came lumbering up to display his equestrian skill before the young ladies, and there was no more quiet that day.

"Don't you love to ride?" asked Grace of Amy, as they stood resting after a race round the field with the others, led by Ned.

"I dote upon it. My sister, Meg, used to ride when Papa was rich, but we don't keep any horses now, except Ellen Tree," added Amy, laughing.

"Tell me about Ellen Tree. Is it a donkey?" asked Grace curiously.

"Why, you see, Jo is crazy about horses and so am I, but we've only got an old sidesaddle and no horse. Out in our garden is an apple tree that has a nice low branch, so Jo put the saddle on it, fixed some reins on the part that turns up, and we bounce away on Ellen Tree whenever we like."

"How funny!" laughed Grace. "I have a pony at home, and ride nearly every day in the park with Fred and Kate. It's very nice, for my friends go too, and the Row is full of ladies and gentlemen."

"Dear, how charming! I hope I shall go abroad some day, but I'd rather go to Rome than the Row," said Amy, who had not the remotest idea what the Row was and wouldn't have asked for the world.

Frank, sitting just behind the little girls, heard what they were saying, and pushed his crutch away from him with an impatient gesture as he watched the active lads going through all sorts of comical gymnastics. Beth, who was collecting the scattered Author cards, looked up and said, in her shy yet friendly way, "I'm afraid you are tired. Can I do anything for you?"

"Talk to me, please. It's dull, sitting by myself," answered Frank, who had evidently been used to being made much of at home.

If he asked her to deliver a Latin oration, it would not have seemed a more impossible task to bashful Beth, but there was no place to run to, no Jo to hide behind now, and the poor boy looked so wistfully at her that she bravely resolved to try.

"What do you like to talk about?" she asked, fumbling over the cards and dropping half as she tried to tie them up.

"Well, I like to hear about cricket and boating and hunting," said Frank, who had not yet learned to suit his amusements to his strength.

"My heart! What shall I do? I don't know anything about them, thought Beth, and forgetting the boy's misfortune in her flurry, she said, hoping to make him talk, "I never saw any hunting, but I suppose you know all about it."

"I did once, but I can never hunt again, for I got hurt leaping a confounded five-barred gate, so there are no more horses and hounds for me," said Frank with a sigh that made Beth hate herself for her innocent blunder.

"Your deer are much prettier than our ugly buffaloes," she said, turning to the prairies for help and feeling glad that she had read one of the boys' books in which Jo delighted.

Buffaloes proved soothing and satisfactory, and in her eagerness to amuse another, Beth forgot herself, and was quite unconscious of her sisters' surprise and delight at the unusual spectacle of Beth talking away to one of the dreadful boys, against whom she had begged protection.

"Bless her heart! She pities him, so she is good to him," said Jo, beaming at her from the croquet ground.

"I always said she was a little saint," added Meg, as if there could be no further doubt of it.

"I haven't heard Frank laugh so much for ever so long," said Grace to Amy, as they sat discussing dolls and making tea sets out of the acorn cups.

"My sister Beth is a very *fastidious* girl, when she likes to be," said Amy, well pleased at Beth's success. She meant "fascinating," but as Grace didn't know the exact meaning of either word, "fastidious" sounded well and made a good impression.

An impromptu circus, fox and geese, and an amicable game of croquet finished the afternoon. At sunset the tent was struck, hampers packed, wickets pulled up, boats loaded, and the whole party floated down the river, singing at the tops of their voices. Ned, getting sentimental, warbled a serenade with the pensive refrain—

> Alone, alone, ah! Woe, alone,

and at the lines—

> We each are young, we each have a heart,
> Oh, why should we stand thus coldly apart?

he looked at Meg with such a lackadaisical expression that she laughed outright and spoiled his song.

"How can you be so cruel to me?" he whispered, under cover of a lively chorus. "You've kept close to that starched-up Englishwoman all day, and now you snub me."

"I didn't mean to, but you looked so funny I really couldn't help it," replied Meg, passing over the first part of his reproach, for it was quite true that she *had* shunned him, remembering the Moffat party and the talk after it.

Ned was offended and turned to Sallie for consolation, saying to her rather pettishly, "There isn't a bit of flirt in that girl, is there?"

"Not a particle, but she's a dear," returned Sallie, defending her friend even while confessing her shortcomings.

"She's not a stricken deer anyway," said Ned, trying to be witty, and succeeding as well as very young gentlemen usually do.

On the lawn where it had gathered, the little party separated with cordial good nights and good-byes, for the Vaughns were going to Canada. As the four sisters went home through the garden, Miss Kate looked after them, saying, without the patronizing tone in her voice, "In spite of their demonstrative manners, American girls are very nice when one knows them."

"I quite agree with you," said Mr. Brooke.

CHAPTER XIII

CASTLES IN THE AIR

Laurie lay luxuriously swinging to and fro in his hammock one warm September afternoon, wondering what his neighbors were about, but too lazy to go and find out. He was in one of his moods, for the day had been both unprofitable and unsatisfactory, and he was wishing he could live it over again. The hot weather made him indolent, and he had shirked his studies, tried Mr. Brooke's patience to the utmost, displeased his grandfather by practicing half the afternoon, frightened the maidservants half out of their wits by mischievously hinting that one of his dogs was going mad, and, after high words with the stableman about some fancied neglect of his horse, he had flung himself into his hammock to fume over the stupidity of the world in general, till the peace of the lovely day quieted him in spite of himself. Staring up into the green gloom of the horse-chestnut trees above him, he dreamed dreams of all sorts, and was just imagining himself tossing on the ocean in a voyage round the world, when the sound of voices brought him ashore in a flash. Peeping through the meshes of the hammock, he saw the Marches coming out, as if bound on some expedition.

"What in the world are those girls about now?" thought Laurie, opening his sleepy eyes to take a good look, for there was something rather peculiar in the appearance of his neighbors. Each wore a large, flapping hat, a brown linen pouch slung over one shoulder, and carried a long staff. Meg had a cushion, Jo a book, Beth a basket, and Amy a portfolio. All walked quietly through the garden, out at the little back gate, and began to climb the hill that lay between the house and river.

"Well, that's cool," said Laurie to himself, "to have a picnic and never ask me! They can't be going in the boat, for they haven't got the key. Perhaps they forgot it. I'll take it to them, and see what's going on."

Though possessed of half a dozen hats, it took him some time to find one, then there was a hunt for the key, which was at last discovered in his pocket, so that the girls were quite out of sight when he leaped the fence and ran after them. Taking the shortest way to the boathouse, he waited for them to appear, but no one came, and he went up the hill to take an observation. A grove of pines covered one part of it, and from the heart of this green spot came a clearer sound than the soft sigh of the pines or the drowsy chirp of the crickets.

"Here's a landscape!" thought Laurie, peeping through the bushes, and looking wide-awake and good-natured already.

It *was* a rather pretty little picture, for the sisters sat together in the shady nook, with sun and shadow flickering over them, the aromatic wind lifting their hair and cooling their hot cheeks, and all the little wood people going on with their affairs as if these were no strangers but old friends. Meg sat upon her cushion, sewing daintily with her white hands, and looking as fresh and sweet as a rose in her pink dress among the green. Beth was sorting the cones that lay thick under the hemlock near by, for she made pretty things with them. Amy was sketching a group of ferns, and Jo was knitting as she read aloud. A shadow passed over the boy's face as he watched them, feeling that he ought to go away because uninvited; yet lingering because home seemed very lonely and this quiet party in the woods most attractive to his restless spirit. He stood so still that a squirrel, busy with its harvesting, ran down a pine close beside him, saw him suddenly and skipped back, scolding so shrilly that Beth looked up, espied the wistful face behind the birches, and beckoned with a reassuring smile.

"May I come in, please? Or shall I be a bother?" he asked, advancing slowly.

Meg lifted her eyebrows, but Jo scowled at her defiantly and said at once, "Of course you may. We should have asked you before, only we thought you wouldn't care for such a girl's game as this."

"I always like your games, but if Meg doesn't want me, I'll go away."

"I've no objection, if you do something. It's against the rules to be idle here," replied Meg gravely but graciously.

"Much obliged. I'll do anything if you'll let me stop a bit, for it's as dull as the Desert of Sahara down there. Shall I sew, read, cone, draw, or do all at once? Bring on your bears. I'm ready." And Laurie sat down with a submissive expression delightful to behold.

"Finish this story while I set my heel," said Jo, handing him the book.

"Yes'm," was the meek answer, as he began, doing his best to prove his gratitude for the favor of admission into the "Busy Bee Society."

The story was not a long one, and when it was finished, he ventured to ask a few questions as a reward of merit.

"Please, ma'am, could I inquire if this highly instructive and charming institution is a new one?"

"Would you tell him?" asked Meg of her sisters.

"He'll laugh," said Amy warningly.

"Who cares?" said Jo.

"I guess he'll like it," added Beth.

"Of course I shall! I give you my word I won't laugh. Tell away, Jo, and don't be afraid."

"The idea of being afraid of you! Well, you see we used to play Pilgrim's Progress, and we have been going on with it in earnest, all winter and summer."

"Yes, I know," said Laurie, nodding wisely.

"Who told you?" demanded Jo.

"Spirits."

"No, I did. I wanted to amuse him one night when you were all away, and he was rather dismal. He did like it, so don't scold, Jo," said Beth meekly.

"You can't keep a secret. Never mind, it saves trouble now."

"Go on, please," said Laurie, as Jo became absorbed in her work, looking a trifle displeased.

"Oh, didn't she tell you about this new plan of ours? Well, we have tried not to waste our holiday, but each has had a task and worked at it with a will. The vacation is nearly over, the stints are all done, and we are ever so glad that we didn't dawdle."

"Yes, I should think so," and Laurie thought regretfully of his own idle days.

"Mother likes to have us out-of-doors as much as possible, so we bring our work here and have nice times. For the fun of it we bring our things in these bags, wear the old hats, use poles to climb the hill, and play pilgrims, as we used to do years ago. We call this hill the Delectable Mountain, for we can look far away and see the country where we hope to live some time."

Jo pointed, and Laurie sat up to examine, for through an opening in the wood one could look cross the wide, blue river, the meadows on the other side, far over the outskirts of the great city, to the green hills that rose to meet the sky. The sun was low, and the heavens glowed with the splendor of an autumn sunset. Gold and purple clouds lay on the hilltops, and rising high into the ruddy light were silvery white peaks that shone like the airy spires of some Celestial City.

"How beautiful that is!" said Laurie softly, for he was quick to see and feel beauty of any kind.

"It's often so, and we like to watch it, for it is never the same, but always splendid," replied Amy, wishing she could paint it.

"Jo talks about the country where we hope to live sometime—the real country, she means, with pigs and chickens and haymaking. It would be nice, but I wish the beautiful country up there was real, and we could ever go to it," said Beth musingly.

"There is a lovelier country even than that, where we shall go, by-and-by, when we are good enough," answered Meg with her sweetest voice.

"It seems so long to wait, so hard to do. I want to fly away at once, as those swallows fly, and go in at that splendid gate."

"You'll get there, Beth, sooner or later, no fear of that," said Jo. "I'm the one that will have to fight and work, and climb and wait, and maybe never get in after all."

"You'll have me for company, if that's any comfort. I shall have to do a deal of traveling before I come in sight of your Celestial City. If I arrive late, you'll say a good word for me, won't you, Beth?"

Something in the boy's face troubled his little friend, but she said cheerfully, with her quiet eyes on the changing clouds, "If people really want to go, and really try all their lives, I think they will get in, for I don't believe there are any locks on that door or any guards at the gate. I always imagine it is as it is in the picture, where the shining ones stretch out their hands to welcome poor Christian as he comes up from the river."

"Wouldn't it be fun if all the castles in the air which we make could come true, and we could live in them?" said Jo, after a little pause.

"I've made such quantities it would be hard to choose which I'd have," said Laurie, lying flat and throwing cones at the squirrel who had betrayed him.

"You'd have to take your favorite one. What is it?" asked Meg.

"If I tell mine, will you tell yours?"

"Yes, if the girls will too."

"We will. Now, Laurie."

"After I'd seen as much of the world as I want to, I'd like to settle in Germany and have just as much music as I choose. I'm to be a famous musician myself, and all creation is to rush to hear me. And I'm never to be bothered about money or business, but just enjoy myself and live for what I like. That's my favorite castle. What's yours, Meg?"

Margaret seemed to find it a little hard to tell hers, and waved a brake before her face, as if to disperse imaginary gnats, while she said slowly, "I should like a lovely house, full of all sorts of luxurious things—nice food, pretty clothes, handsome furniture, pleasant people, and heaps of money. I am to be mistress of it, and manage it as I like, with plenty of servants, so I never need work a bit. How I should enjoy it! For I wouldn't be idle, but do good, and make everyone love me dearly."

"Wouldn't you have a master for your castle in the air?" asked Laurie slyly.

"I said 'pleasant people,' you know," and Meg carefully tied up her shoe as she spoke, so that no one saw her face.

"Why don't you say you'd have a splendid, wise, good husband and some angelic little children? You know your castle wouldn't be perfect without," said blunt Jo, who had no tender fancies yet, and rather scorned romance, except in books.

"You'd have nothing but horses, inkstands, and novels in yours," answered Meg petulantly.

"Wouldn't I though? I'd have a stable full of Arabian steeds, rooms piled high with books, and I'd write out of a magic inkstand, so that my works should be as famous as Laurie's music. I want to do something splendid before I go into my castle, something heroic or wonderful that won't be forgotten after I'm dead. I don't know what, but I'm on the watch for it, and mean to astonish you all some day. I think I shall write books, and get rich and famous, that would suit me, so that is my favorite dream."

"Mine is to stay at home safe with Father and Mother, and help take care of the family," said Beth contentedly.

"Don't you wish for anything else?" asked Laurie.

"Since I had my little piano, I am perfectly satisfied. I only wish we may all keep well and be together, nothing else."

"I have ever so many wishes, but the pet one is to be an artist, and go to Rome, and do fine pictures, and be the best artist in the whole world," was Amy's modest desire.

"We're an ambitious set, aren't we? Every one of us, but Beth, wants to be rich and famous, and gorgeous in every respect. I do wonder if any of us will ever get our wishes," said Laurie, chewing grass like a meditative calf.

"I've got the key to my castle in the air, but whether I can unlock the door remains to be seen," observed Jo mysteriously.

"I've got the key to mine, but I'm not allowed to try it. Hang college!" muttered Laurie with an impatient sigh.

"Here's mine!" and Amy waved her pencil.

"I haven't got any," said Meg forlornly.

"Yes, you have," said Laurie at once.

"Where?"

"In your face."

"Nonsense, that's of no use."

"Wait and see if it doesn't bring you something worth having," replied the boy, laughing at the thought of a charming little secret which he fancied he knew.

Meg colored behind the brake, but asked no questions and looked across the river with the same expectant expression which Mr. Brooke had worn when he told the story of the knight.

"If we are all alive ten years hence, let's meet, and see how many of us have got our wishes, or how much nearer we are then than now," said Jo, always ready with a plan.

"Bless me! How old I shall be—twenty-seven!" exclaimed Meg, who felt grown up already, having just reached seventeen.

"You and I will be twenty-six, Teddy, Beth twenty-four, and Amy twenty-two. What a venerable party!" said Jo.

"I hope I shall have done something to be proud of by that time, but I'm such a lazy dog, I'm afraid I shall dawdle, Jo."

"You need a motive, Mother says, and when you get it, she is sure you'll work splendidly."

"Is she? By Jupiter, I will, if I only get the chance!" cried Laurie, sitting up with sudden energy. "I ought to be satisfied to please Grandfather, and I do try, but it's working against the grain, you see, and comes hard. He wants me to be an India merchant, as he was, and I'd rather be shot. I hate tea and silk and spices, and every sort of rubbish his old ships bring, and I don't care how soon they go to the bottom when I own them. Going to college ought to satisfy him, for if

I give him four years he ought to let me off from the business. But he's set, and I've got to do just as he did, unless I break away and please myself, as my father did. If there was anyone left to stay with the old gentleman, I'd do it tomorrow."

Laurie spoke excitedly, and looked ready to carry his threat into execution on the slightest provocation, for he was growing up very fast and, in spite of his indolent ways, had a young man's hatred of subjection, a young man's restless longing to try the world for himself.

"I advise you to sail away in one of your ships, and never come home again till you have tried your own way," said Jo, whose imagination was fired by the thought of such a daring exploit, and whose sympathy was excited by what she called "Teddy's Wrongs."

"That's not right, Jo; you mustn't talk in that way, and Laurie mustn't take your bad advice. You should do just what your grandfather wishes, my dear boy," said Meg in her most maternal tone. "Do your best at college, and when he sees that you try to please him, I'm sure he won't be hard on you or unjust to you. As you say, there is no one else to stay with and love him, and you'd never forgive yourself if you left him without his permission. Don't be dismal or fret, but do your duty and you'll get your reward, as good Mr. Brooke has, by being respected and loved."

"What do you know about him?" asked Laurie, grateful for the good advice, but objecting to the lecture, and glad to turn the conversation from himself after his unusual outbreak.

"Only what your grandpa told us about him—how he took good care of his own mother till she died, and wouldn't go abroad as tutor to some nice person because he wouldn't leave her. And how he provides now for an old woman who nursed his mother, and never tells anyone, but is just as generous and patient and good as he can be."

"So he is, dear old fellow!" said Laurie heartily, as Meg paused, looking flushed and earnest with her story. "It's like Grandpa to find out all about him without letting him know, and to tell all his goodness to others, so that they might like him. Brooke couldn't understand why your mother was so kind to him, asking him over with me and treating him in her beautiful friendly way. He thought she was just perfect, and talked about it for days and days, and went on about you all in flaming style. If ever I do get my wish, you see what I'll do for Brooke."

"Begin to do something now by not plaguing his life out," said Meg sharply.

"How do you know I do, Miss?"

"I can always tell by his face when he goes away. If you have been good, he looks satisfied and walks briskly. If you have plagued him, he's sober and walks slowly, as if he wanted to go back and do his work better."

"Well, I like that? So you keep an account of my good and bad marks in Brooke's face, do you? I see him bow and smile as he passes your window, but I didn't know you'd got up a telegraph."

"We haven't. Don't be angry, and oh, don't tell him I said anything! It was only to show that I cared how you get on, and what is said here is said in confidence, you know," cried Meg, much alarmed at the thought of what might follow from her careless speech.

"I don't tell tales," replied Laurie, with his "high and mighty" air, as Jo called a certain expression which he occasionally wore. "Only if Brooke is going to be a thermometer, I must mind and have fair weather for him to report."

"Please don't be offended. I didn't mean to preach or tell tales or be silly. I only thought Jo was encouraging you in a feeling which you'd be sorry for by-and-by. You are so kind to us, we feel as if you were our brother and say just what we think. Forgive me, I meant it kindly." And Meg offered her hand with a gesture both affectionate and timid.

Ashamed of his momentary pique, Laurie squeezed the kind little hand, and said frankly, "I'm the one to be forgiven. I'm cross and have been out of sorts all day. I like to have you tell me my faults and be sisterly, so don't mind if I am grumpy sometimes. I thank you all the same."

Bent on showing that he was not offended, he made himself as agreeable as possible, wound cotton for Meg, recited poetry to please Jo, shook down cones for Beth, and helped Amy with her ferns, proving himself a fit person to belong to the "Busy Bee Society." In the midst of an animated discussion on the domestic habits of turtles (one of those amiable creatures having strolled up from the river), the faint sound of a bell warned them that Hannah had put the tea "to draw," and they would just have time to get home to supper.

"May I come again?" asked Laurie.

"Yes, if you are good, and love your book, as the boys in the primer are told to do," said Meg, smiling.

"I'll try."

"Then you may come, and I'll teach you to knit as the Scotchmen do. There's a demand for socks just now," added Jo, waving hers like a big blue worsted banner as they parted at the gate.

That night, when Beth played to Mr. Laurence in the twilight, Laurie, standing in the shadow of the curtain, listened to the little David, whose simple music always quieted his moody spirit, and watched the old man, who sat with his gray head on his hand, thinking tender thoughts of the dead child he had loved so much. Remembering the conversation of the afternoon, the boy said to himself, with the resolve to make the sacrifice cheerfully, "I'll let my castle go, and stay with the dear old gentleman while he needs me, for I am all he has."

CHAPTER XIV

SECRETS

Jo was very busy in the garret, for the October days began to grow chilly, and the afternoons were short. For two or three hours the sun lay warmly in the high window, showing Jo seated on the old sofa, writing busily, with her papers spread out upon a trunk before her, while Scrabble, the pet rat, promenaded the beams overhead, accompanied by his oldest son, a fine young fellow, who was evidently very proud of his whiskers. Quite absorbed in her work, Jo scribbled away till the last page was filled, when she signed her name with a flourish and threw down her pen, exclaiming—

"There, I've done my best! If this won't suit I shall have to wait till I can do better."

Lying back on the sofa, she read the manuscript carefully through, making dashes here and there, and putting in many exclamation points, which looked like little balloons. Then she tied it up with a smart red ribbon, and sat a minute looking at it with a sober, wistful expression, which plainly showed how earnest her work had been. Jo's desk up here was an old tin kitchen which hung against the wall. In it she kept her papers, and a few books, safely shut away from Scrabble, who, being likewise of a literary turn, was fond of making a circulating library of such books as were left in his way by eating the leaves. From this tin receptacle Jo produced another manuscript, and putting both in her pocket, crept quietly downstairs, leaving her friends to nibble on her pens and taste her ink.

She put on her hat and jacket as noiselessly as possible, and going to the back entry window, got out upon the roof of a low porch, swung herself down to the grassy bank, and took a roundabout way to the road. Once there, she composed herself, hailed a passing omnibus, and rolled away to town, looking very merry and mysterious.

If anyone had been watching her, he would have thought her movements decidedly peculiar, for on alighting, she went off at a great pace till she reached a certain number in a certain busy street. Having found the place with some difficulty, she went into the doorway, looked up the dirty stairs, and after standing stock still a minute, suddenly dived into the street and walked away as rapidly as she came. This maneuver she repeated several times, to the great amusement of a black-eyed young gentleman lounging in the window of a building opposite. On returning for the third time, Jo gave herself a shake, pulled her hat over her eyes, and walked up the stairs, looking as if she were going to have all her teeth out.

There was a dentist's sign, among others, which adorned the entrance, and after staring a moment at the pair of artificial jaws which slowly opened and shut to draw attention to a fine set of teeth, the young gentleman put on his coat, took his hat, and went down to post himself in the opposite doorway, saying with a smile and a shiver, "It's like her to come alone, but if she has a bad time she'll need someone to help her home."

In ten minutes Jo came running downstairs with a very red face and the general appearance of a person who had just passed through a trying ordeal of some sort. When she saw the young gentleman she looked anything but pleased, and passed him with a nod. But he followed, asking with an air of sympathy, "Did you have a bad time?"

"Not very."

"You got through quickly."

"Yes, thank goodness!"

"Why did you go alone?"

"Didn't want anyone to know."

"You're the oddest fellow I ever saw. How many did you have out?"

Jo looked at her friend as if she did not understand him, then began to laugh as if mightily amused at something.

"There are two which I want to have come out, but I must wait a week."

"What are you laughing at? You are up to some mischief, Jo," said Laurie, looking mystified.

"So are you. What were you doing, sir, up in that billiard saloon?"

"Begging your pardon, ma'am, it wasn't a billiard saloon, but a gymnasium, and I was taking a lesson in fencing."

"I'm glad of that."

"Why?"

"You can teach me, and then when we play *Hamlet*, you can be Laertes, and we'll make a fine thing of the fencing scene."

Laurie burst out with a hearty boy's laugh, which made several passers-by smile in spite of themselves.

"I'll teach you whether we play *Hamlet* or not. It's grand fun and will straighten you up capitally. But I don't believe that was your only reason for saying 'I'm glad' in that decided way, was it now?"

"No, I was glad that you were not in the saloon, because I hope you never go to such places. Do you?"

"Not often."

"I wish you wouldn't."

"It's no harm, Jo. I have billiards at home, but it's no fun unless you have good players, so, as I'm fond of it, I come sometimes and have a game with Ned Moffat or some of the other fellows."

"Oh dear, I'm so sorry, for you'll get to liking it better and better, and will waste time and money, and grow like those dreadful boys. I did hope you'd stay respectable and be a satisfaction to your friends," said Jo, shaking her head.

"Can't a fellow take a little innocent amusement now and then without losing his respectability?" asked Laurie, looking nettled.

"That depends upon how and where he takes it. I don't like Ned and his set, and wish you'd keep out of it. Mother won't let us have him at our house, though he wants to come. And if you grow like him she won't be willing to have us frolic together as we do now."

"Won't she?" asked Laurie anxiously.

"No, she can't bear fashionable young men, and she'd shut us all up in bandboxes rather than have us associate with them."

"Well, she needn't get out her bandboxes yet. I'm not a fashionable party and don't mean to be, but I do like harmless larks now and then, don't you?"

"Yes, nobody minds them, so lark away, but don't get wild, will you? Or there will be an end of all our good times."

"I'll be a double distilled saint."

"I can't bear saints. Just be a simple, honest, respectable boy, and we'll never desert you. I don't know what I *should* do if you acted like Mr. King's son. He had plenty of money, but didn't know how to spend it, and got tipsy and gambled, and ran away, and forged his father's name, I believe, and was altogether horrid."

"You think I'm likely to do the same? Much obliged."

"No, I don't—oh, *dear*, no!—but I hear people talking about money being such a temptation, and I sometimes wish you were poor. I shouldn't worry then."

"Do you worry about me, Jo?"

"A little, when you look moody and discontented, as you sometimes do; for you've got such a strong will, if you once get started wrong, I'm afraid it would be hard to stop you."

Laurie walked in silence a few minutes, and Jo watched him, wishing she had held her tongue, for his eyes looked angry, though his lips smiled as if at her warnings.

"Are you going to deliver lectures all the way home?" he asked presently.

"Of course not. Why?"

"Because if you are, I'll take a bus. If you're not, I'd like to walk with you and tell you something very interesting."

"I won't preach any more, and I'd like to hear the news immensely."

"Very well, then, come on. It's a secret, and if I tell you, you must tell me yours."

"I haven't got any," began Jo, but stopped suddenly, remembering that she had.

"You know you have—you can't hide anything, so up and 'fess, or I won't tell," cried Laurie.

"Is your secret a nice one?"

"Oh, isn't it! All about people you know, and such fun! You ought to hear it, and I've been aching to tell it this long time. Come, you begin."

"You'll not say anything about it at home, will you?"

"Not a word."

"And you won't tease me in private?"

"I never tease."

"Yes, you do. You get everything you want out of people. I don't know how you do it, but you are a born wheedler."

"Thank you. Fire away."

"Well, I've left two stories with a newspaperman, and he's to give his answer next week," whispered Jo, in her confidant's ear.

"Hurrah for Miss March, the celebrated American authoress!" cried Laurie, throwing up his hat and catching it again, to the great delight of two ducks, four cats, five hens, and half a dozen Irish children, for they were out of the city now.

"Hush! It won't come to anything, I dare say, but I couldn't rest till I had tried, and I said nothing about it because I didn't want anyone else to be disappointed."

"It won't fail. Why, Jo, your stories are works of Shakespeare compared to half the rubbish that is published every day. Won't it be fun to see them in print, and shan't we feel proud of our authoress?"

Jo's eyes sparkled, for it is always pleasant to be believed in, and a friend's praise is always sweeter than a dozen newspaper puffs.

"Where's *your* secret? Play fair, Teddy, or I'll never believe you again," she said, trying to extinguish the brilliant hopes that blazed up at a word of encouragement.

"I may get into a scrape for telling, but I didn't promise not to, so I will, for I never feel easy in my mind till I've told you any plummy bit of news I get. I know where Meg's glove is."

"Is that all?" said Jo, looking disappointed, as Laurie nodded and twinkled with a face full of mysterious intelligence.

"It's quite enough for the present, as you'll agree when I tell you where it is."

"Tell, then."

Laurie bent, and whispered three words in Jo's ear, which produced a comical change. She stood and stared at him for a minute, looking both surprised and displeased, then walked on, saying sharply, "How do you know?"

"Saw it."

"Where?"

"Pocket."

"All this time?"

"Yes, isn't that romantic?"

"No, it's horrid."

"Don't you like it?"

"Of course I don't. It's ridiculous, it won't be allowed. My patience! What would Meg say?"

"You are not to tell anyone. Mind that."

"I didn't promise."

"That was understood, and I trusted you."

"Well, I won't for the present, anyway, but I'm disgusted, and wish you hadn't told me."

"I thought you'd be pleased."

"At the idea of anybody coming to take Meg away? No, thank you."

"You'll feel better about it when somebody comes to take you away."

"I'd like to see anyone try it," cried Jo fiercely.

"So should I!" and Laurie chuckled at the idea.

"I don't think secrets agree with me, I feel rumpled up in my mind since you told me that," said Jo rather ungratefully.

"Race down this hill with me, and you'll be all right," suggested Laurie.

No one was in sight, the smooth road sloped invitingly before her, and finding the temptation irresistible, Jo darted away, soon leaving hat and comb behind her and scattering hairpins as she ran. Laurie reached the goal first and was quite satisfied with the success of his treatment, for his Atlanta came panting up with flying hair, bright eyes, ruddy cheeks, and no signs of dissatisfaction in her face.

"I wish I was a horse, then I could run for miles in this splendid air, and not lose my breath. It was capital, but see what a guy it's made me. Go, pick up my things, like a cherub, as you are," said Jo, dropping down under a maple tree, which was carpeting the bank with crimson leaves.

Laurie leisurely departed to recover the lost property, and Jo bundled up her braids, hoping no one would pass by till she was tidy again. But someone did pass, and who should it be but Meg, looking particularly ladylike in her state and festival suit, for she had been making calls.

"What in the world are you doing here?" she asked, regarding her disheveled sister with well-bred surprise.

"Getting leaves," meekly answered Jo, sorting the rosy handful she had just swept up.

"And hairpins," added Laurie, throwing half a dozen into Jo's lap. "They grow on this road, Meg, so do combs and brown straw hats."

"You have been running, Jo. How could you? When will you stop such romping ways?" said Meg reprovingly, as she settled her cuffs and smoothed her hair, with which the wind had taken liberties.

"Never till I'm stiff and old and have to use a crutch. Don't try to make me grow up before my time, Meg. It's hard enough to have you change all of a sudden. Let me be a little girl as long as I can."

As she spoke, Jo bent over the leaves to hide the trembling of her lips, for lately she had felt that Margaret was fast getting to be a woman, and Laurie's secret made her dread the separation which must surely come some time and now seemed very near. He saw the trouble in her face and drew Meg's attention from it by asking quickly, "Where have you been calling, all so fine?"

"At the Gardiners', and Sallie has been telling me all about Belle Moffat's wedding. It was very splendid, and they have gone to spend the winter in Paris. Just think how delightful that must be!"

"Do you envy her, Meg?" said Laurie.

"I'm afraid I do."

"I'm glad of it!" muttered Jo, tying on her hat with a jerk.

"Why?" asked Meg, looking surprised.

"Because if you care much about riches, you will never go and marry a poor man," said Jo, frowning at Laurie, who was mutely warning her to mind what she said.

"I shall never 'go and marry' anyone," observed Meg, walking on with great dignity while the others followed, laughing, whispering, skipping stones, and "behaving like children," as Meg said to herself, though she might have been tempted to join them if she had not had her best dress on.

For a week or two, Jo behaved so queerly that her sisters were quite bewildered. She rushed to the door when the postman rang, was rude to Mr. Brooke whenever they met, would sit looking at Meg with a woe-begone face, occasionally jumping up to shake and then kiss her in a very mysterious manner. Laurie and she were always making signs to one another, and talking about "Spread Eagles" till the girls declared they had both lost their wits. On the second Saturday after Jo got out of the window, Meg, as she sat sewing at her window, was scandalized by the sight of Laurie chasing Jo all over the garden and finally capturing her in Amy's bower. What went on there, Meg could not see, but shrieks of laughter were heard, followed by the murmur of voices and a great flapping of newspapers.

"What shall we do with that girl? She never *will* behave like a young lady," sighed Meg, as she watched the race with a disapproving face.

"I hope she won't. She is so funny and dear as she is," said Beth, who had never betrayed that she was a little hurt at Jo's having secrets with anyone but her.

"It's very trying, but we never can make her *commy la fo*," added Amy, who sat making some new frills for herself, with her curls tied up in a very becoming way, two agreeable things that made her feel unusually elegant and ladylike.

In a few minutes Jo bounced in, laid herself on the sofa, and affected to read.

"Have you anything interesting there?" asked Meg, with condescension.

"Nothing but a story, won't amount to much, I guess," returned Jo, carefully keeping the name of the paper out of sight.

"You'd better read it aloud. That will amuse us and keep you out of mischief," said Amy in her most grown-up tone.

"What's the name?" asked Beth, wondering why Jo kept her face behind the sheet.

"The Rival Painters."

"That sounds well. Read it," said Meg.

With a loud "Hem!" and a long breath, Jo began to read very fast. The girls listened with interest, for the tale was romantic, and somewhat pathetic, as most of the characters died in the end.

"I like that about the splendid picture," was Amy's approving remark, as Jo paused.

"I prefer the lovering part. Viola and Angelo are two of our favorite names, isn't that queer?" said Meg, wiping her eyes, for the lovering part was tragical.

"Who wrote it?" asked Beth, who had caught a glimpse of Jo's face.

The reader suddenly sat up, cast away the paper, displaying a flushed countenance, and with a funny mixture of solemnity and excitement replied in a loud voice, "Your sister."

"You?" cried Meg, dropping her work.

"It's very good," said Amy critically.

"I knew it! I knew it! Oh, my Jo, I *am* so proud!" and Beth ran to hug her sister and exult over this splendid success.

Dear me, how delighted they all were, to be sure! How Meg wouldn't believe it till she saw the words. "Miss Josephine March," actually printed in the paper. How graciously Amy criticized the artistic parts of the story, and offered hints for a sequel, which unfortunately couldn't be carried out, as the hero and heroine were dead. How Beth got excited, and skipped and sang with joy. How Hannah came in to exclaim, "Sakes alive, well I never!" in great astonishment at "that Jo's doin's." How proud Mrs. March was when she knew it. How Jo laughed, with tears in her eyes, as she declared she might as well be a peacock and done with it, and how the "Spread Eagle" might be said to flap his wings triumphantly over the House of March, as the paper passed from hand to hand.

"Tell us about it." "When did it come?" "How much did you get for it?" "What will Father say?" "Won't Laurie laugh?" cried the family, all in one breath as they clustered about Jo, for these foolish, affectionate people made a jubilee of every little household joy.

"Stop jabbering, girls, and I'll tell you everything," said Jo, wondering if Miss Burney felt any grander over her *Evelina* than she did over her "Rival Painters." Having told how she disposed of her tales, Jo added, "And when I went to get my answer, the man said he liked them both, but didn't pay beginners, only let them print in his paper, and noticed the stories. It was good practice, he said, and when the beginners improved, anyone would pay. So I let him have the two stories, and today this was sent to me, and Laurie caught me with it and insisted on seeing it, so I let him. And he said it was good, and I shall write more, and he's going to get the next paid for, and I *am* so happy, for in time I may be able to support myself and help the girls."

Jo's breath gave out here, and wrapping her head in the paper, she bedewed her little story with a few natural tears, for to be independent and earn the praise of those she loved were the dearest wishes of her heart, and this seemed to be the first step toward that happy end.

CHAPTER XV

A TELEGRAM

"November is the most disagreeable month in the whole year," said Margaret, standing at the window one dull afternoon, looking out at the frostbitten garden.

"That's the reason I was born in it," observed Jo pensively, quite unconscious of the blot on her nose.

"If something very pleasant should happen now, we should think it a delightful month," said Beth, who took a hopeful view of everything, even November.

"I dare say, but nothing pleasant ever does happen in this family," said Meg, who was out of sorts. "We go grubbing along day after day, without a bit of change, and very little fun. We might as well be in a treadmill."

"My patience, how blue we are!" cried Jo. "I don't much wonder, poor dear, for you see other girls having splendid times, while you grind, grind, year in and year out. Oh, don't I wish I could manage things for you as I do for my heroines! You're pretty enough and good enough already, so I'd have some rich relation leave you a fortune unexpectedly. Then you'd dash out as an heiress, scorn everyone who has slighted you, go abroad, and come home my Lady Something in a blaze of splendor and elegance."

"People don't have fortunes left them in that style nowadays, men have to work and women marry for money. It's a dreadfully unjust world," said Meg bitterly.

"Jo and I are going to make fortunes for you all. Just wait ten years, and see if we don't," said Amy, who sat in a corner making mud pies, as Hannah called her little clay models of birds, fruit, and faces.

"Can't wait, and I'm afraid I haven't much faith in ink and dirt, though I'm grateful for your good intentions."

Meg sighed, and turned to the frostbitten garden again. Jo groaned and leaned both elbows on the table in a despondent attitude, but Amy spatted away energetically, and Beth, who sat at the other window, said, smiling, "Two pleasant things are going to happen right away. Marmee is coming down the street, and Laurie is tramping through the garden as if he had something nice to tell."

In they both came, Mrs. March with her usual question, "Any letter from Father, girls?" and Laurie to say in his persuasive way, "Won't some of you come for a drive? I've been working away at mathematics till my head is in a muddle, and I'm going to freshen my wits by a brisk turn. It's a dull day, but the air isn't bad, and I'm going to take Brooke home, so it will be gay inside, if it isn't out. Come, Jo, you and Beth will go, won't you?"

"Of course we will."

"Much obliged, but I'm busy." And Meg whisked out her workbasket, for she had agreed with her mother that it was best, for her at least, not to drive too often with the young gentleman.

"We three will be ready in a minute," cried Amy, running away to wash her hands.

"Can I do anything for you, Madam Mother?" asked Laurie, leaning over Mrs. March's chair with the affectionate look and tone he always gave her.

"No, thank you, except call at the office, if you'll be so kind, dear. It's our day for a letter, and the postman hasn't been. Father is as regular as the sun, but there's some delay on the way, perhaps."

A sharp ring interrupted her, and a minute after Hannah came in with a letter.

"It's one of them horrid telegraph things, mum," she said, handling it as if she was afraid it would explode and do some damage.

At the word "telegraph," Mrs. March snatched it, read the two lines it contained, and dropped back into her chair as white as if the little paper had sent a bullet to her heart. Laurie dashed downstairs for water, while Meg and Hannah supported her, and Jo read aloud, in a frightened voice—

> MRS. MARCH:
> Your husband is very ill. Come at once.
> S. HALE
> Blank Hospital, Washington.

How still the room was as they listened breathlessly, how strangely the day darkened outside, and how suddenly the whole world seemed to change, as the girls gathered about their mother, feeling as if all the happiness and support of their lives was about to be taken from them. Mrs. March was herself again directly, read the message over, and stretched out her arms to her daughters, saying, in a tone they never forgot, "I shall go at once, but it may be too late. Oh, children, children, help me to bear it!"

For several minutes there was nothing but the sound of sobbing in the room, mingled with broken words of comfort, tender assurances of help, and hopeful whispers that died away in tears. Poor Hannah was the first to recover, and with unconscious wisdom she set all the rest a good example, for with her, work was panacea for most afflictions.

"The Lord keep the dear man! I won't waste no time a-cryin', but git your things ready right away, mum," she said heartily, as she wiped her face on her apron, gave her mistress a warm shake of the hand with her own hard one, and went away to work like three women in one.

"She's right, there's no time for tears now. Be calm, girls, and let me think."

They tried to be calm, poor things, as their mother sat up, looking pale but steady, and put away her grief to think and plan for them.

"Where's Laurie?" she asked presently, when she had collected her thoughts and decided on the first duties to be done.

"Here, ma'am. Oh, let me do something!" cried the boy, hurrying from the next room whither he had withdrawn, feeling that their first sorrow was too sacred for even his friendly eyes to see.

"Send a telegram saying I will come at once. The next train goes early in the morning. I'll take that."

"What else? The horses are ready. I can go anywhere, do anything," he said, looking ready to fly to the ends of the earth.

"Leave a note at Aunt March's. Jo, give me that pen and paper."

Tearing off the blank side of one of her newly copied pages, Jo drew the table before her mother, well knowing that money for the long, sad journey must be borrowed, and feeling as if she could do anything to add a little to the sum for her father.

"Now go, dear, but don't kill yourself driving at a desperate pace. There is no need of that."

Mrs. March's warning was evidently thrown away, for five minutes later Laurie tore by the window on his own fleet horse, riding as if for his life.

"Jo, run to the rooms, and tell Mrs. King that I can't come. On the way get these things. I'll put them down, they'll be needed and I must go prepared for nursing. Hospital stores are not always good. Beth, go and ask Mr. Laurence for a couple of bottles of old wine. I'm not too proud to beg for Father. He shall have the best of everything. Amy, tell Hannah to get down the black trunk, and Meg, come and help me find my things, for I'm half bewildered."

Writing, thinking, and directing all at once might well bewilder the poor lady, and Meg begged her to sit quietly in her room for a little while, and let them work. Everyone scattered like leaves before a gust of wind, and the quiet, happy household was broken up as suddenly as if the paper had been an evil spell.

Mr. Laurence came hurrying back with Beth, bringing every comfort the kind old gentleman could think of for the invalid, and friendliest promises of protection for the girls during the mother's absence, which comforted her very much. There was nothing he didn't offer, from his own dressing gown to himself as escort. But the last was impossible. Mrs. March would not hear of the old gentleman's undertaking the long journey, yet an expression of relief was visible when he spoke of it, for anxiety ill fits one for traveling. He saw the look, knit his heavy eyebrows, rubbed his hands, and marched abruptly away, saying he'd be back directly. No one had time to think of him again till, as Meg ran through the entry, with a pair of rubbers in one hand and a cup of tea in the other, she came suddenly upon Mr. Brooke.

"I'm very sorry to hear of this, Miss March," he said, in the kind, quiet tone which sounded very pleasantly to her perturbed spirit. "I came to offer myself as escort to your mother. Mr. Laurence has commissions for me in Washington, and it will give me real satisfaction to be of service to her there."

Down dropped the rubbers, and the tea was very near following, as Meg put out her hand, with a face so full of gratitude that Mr. Brooke would have felt repaid for a much greater sacrifice than the trifling one of time and comfort which he was about to take.

"How kind you all are! Mother will accept, I'm sure, and it will be such a relief to know that she has someone to take care of her. Thank you very, very much!"

Meg spoke earnestly, and forgot herself entirely till something in the brown eyes looking down at her made her remember the cooling tea, and lead the way into the parlor, saying she would call her mother.

Everything was arranged by the time Laurie returned with a note from Aunt March, enclosing the desired sum, and a few lines repeating what she had often said before, that she had always told them it was absurd for March to go into the army, always predicted that no good would come of it, and she hoped they would take her advice the next time. Mrs. March put the note in the fire, the money in her purse, and went on with her preparations, with her lips folded tightly in a way which Jo would have understood if she had been there.

The short afternoon wore away. All other errands were done, and Meg and her mother busy at some necessary needlework, while Beth and Amy got tea, and Hannah finished her ironing with what she called a "slap and a bang," but still Jo did not come. They began to get anxious, and Laurie went off to find her, for no one knew what freak Jo might take into her head. He missed her, however, and she came walking in with a very queer expression of countenance, for there was a mixture of fun and fear, satisfaction and regret in it, which puzzled the family as much as did the roll of bills she laid before her mother, saying with a little choke in her voice, "That's my contribution toward making Father comfortable and bringing him home!"

"My dear, where did you get it? Twenty-five dollars! Jo, I hope you haven't done anything rash?"

"No, it's mine honestly. I didn't beg, borrow, or steal it. I earned it, and I don't think you'll blame me, for I only sold what was my own."

As she spoke, Jo took off her bonnet, and a general outcry arose, for all her abundant hair was cut short.

"Your hair! Your beautiful hair!" "Oh, Jo, how could you? Your one beauty." "My dear girl, there was no need of this." "She doesn't look like my Jo any more, but I love her dearly for it!"

As everyone exclaimed, and Beth hugged the cropped head tenderly, Jo assumed an indifferent air, which did not deceive anyone a particle, and said, rumpling up the brown bush and trying to look as if she liked it, "It doesn't affect the fate of the nation, so don't wail, Beth. It will be good for my vanity, I was getting too proud of my wig. It will do my brains good to have that mop taken off. My head feels deliciously light and cool, and the barber said I could soon have a curly crop, which will be boyish, becoming, and easy to keep in order. I'm satisfied, so please take the money and let's have supper."

"Tell me all about it, Jo. *I* am not quite satisfied, but I can't blame you, for I know how willingly you sacrificed your vanity, as you call it, to your love. But, my dear, it was not necessary, and I'm afraid you will regret it one of these days," said Mrs. March.

"No, I won't!" returned Jo stoutly, feeling much relieved that her prank was not entirely condemned.

"What made you do it?" asked Amy, who would as soon have thought of cutting off her head as her pretty hair.

"Well, I was wild to do something for Father," replied Jo, as they gathered about the table, for healthy young people can eat even in the midst of trouble. "I hate to borrow as much as Mother does, and I knew Aunt March would croak, she always does, if you ask for a ninepence. Meg gave all her quarterly salary toward the rent, and I only got some clothes with mine, so I felt wicked, and was bound to have some money, if I sold the nose off my face to get it."

"You needn't feel wicked, my child! You had no winter things and got the simplest with your own hard earnings," said Mrs. March with a look that warmed Jo's heart.

"I hadn't the least idea of selling my hair at first, but as I went along I kept thinking what I could do, and feeling as if I'd like to dive into some of the rich stores and help myself. In a barber's window I saw tails of hair with the prices marked, and one black tail, not so thick as mine, was forty dollars. It came to me all of a sudden that I had one thing to make money out of, and without stopping to think, I walked in, asked if they bought hair, and what they would give for mine."

"I don't see how you dared to do it," said Beth in a tone of awe.

"Oh, he was a little man who looked as if he merely lived to oil his hair. He rather stared at first, as if he wasn't used to having girls bounce into his shop and ask him to buy their hair. He said he didn't care about mine, it wasn't the fashionable color, and he never paid much for it in the first place. The work put into it made it dear, and so on. It was getting late, and I was afraid if it wasn't done right away that I shouldn't have it done at all, and you know when I start to do a thing, I hate to give it up. So I begged him to take it, and told him why I was in such a hurry. It was silly, I dare say, but it changed his mind, for I got rather excited, and told the story in my topsy-turvy way, and his wife heard, and said so kindly, 'Take it, Thomas, and oblige the young lady. I'd do as much for our Jimmy any day if I had a spire of hair worth selling.'"

"Who was Jimmy?" asked Amy, who liked to have things explained as they went along.

"Her son, she said, who was in the army. How friendly such things make strangers feel, don't they? She talked away all the time the man clipped, and diverted my mind nicely."

"Didn't you feel dreadfully when the first cut came?" asked Meg, with a shiver.

"I took a last look at my hair while the man got his things, and that was the end of it. I never snivel over trifles like that. I will confess, though, I felt queer when I saw the dear old hair laid out on the table, and felt only the short rough ends of my head. It almost seemed as if I'd an arm or leg off. The woman saw me look at it, and picked out a long lock for me to keep. I'll give it to you, Marmee, just to remember past glories by, for a crop is so comfortable I don't think I shall ever have a mane again."

Mrs. March folded the wavy chestnut lock, and laid it away with a short gray one in her desk. She only said, "Thank you, deary," but something in her face made the girls change the subject, and talk as cheerfully as they could about Mr. Brooke's kindness, the prospect of a fine day tomorrow, and the happy times they would have when Father came home to be nursed.

No one wanted to go to bed when at ten o'clock Mrs. March put by the last finished job, and said, "Come girls." Beth went to the piano and played the father's favorite hymn. All began bravely, but broke down one by one till Beth was left alone, singing with all her heart, for to her music was always a sweet consoler.

"Go to bed and don't talk, for we must be up early and shall need all the sleep we can get. Good night, my darlings," said Mrs. March, as the hymn ended, for no one cared to try another.

They kissed her quietly, and went to bed as silently as if the dear invalid lay in the next room. Beth and Amy soon fell asleep in spite of the great trouble, but Meg lay awake, thinking the most serious thoughts she had ever known in her short life. Jo lay motionless, and her sister fancied that she was asleep, till a stifled sob made her exclaim, as she touched a wet cheek—

"Jo, dear, what is it? Are you crying about father?"

"No, not now."

"What then?"

"My—hair!" burst out poor Jo, trying vainly to smother her emotion in the pillow.

It did not seem at all comical to Meg, who kissed and caressed the afflicted heroine in the tenderest manner.

"I'm not sorry," protested Jo, with a choke. "I'd do it again tomorrow, if I could. It's only the vain part of me that goes and cries in this silly way. Don't tell anyone, it's all over now. I thought you were asleep, so I just made a little private moan for my one beauty. How came you to be awake?"

"I can't sleep, I'm so anxious," said Meg.

"Think about something pleasant, and you'll soon drop off."

"I tried it, but felt wider awake than ever."

"What did you think of?"

"Handsome faces—eyes particularly," answered Meg, smiling to herself in the dark.

"What color do you like best?"

"Brown, that is, sometimes. Blue are lovely."

Jo laughed, and Meg sharply ordered her not to talk, then amiably promised to make her hair curl, and fell asleep to dream of living in her castle in the air.

The clocks were striking midnight and the rooms were very still as a figure glided quietly from bed to bed, smoothing a coverlet here, settling a pillow there, and pausing to look long and tenderly at each unconscious face, to kiss each with lips that mutely blessed, and to pray the fervent prayers which only mothers utter. As she lifted the curtain to look out into the dreary night, the moon broke suddenly from behind the clouds and shone upon her like a bright, benignant face, which seemed to whisper in the silence, "Be comforted, dear soul! There is always light behind the clouds."

CHAPTER XVI

LETTERS

In the cold gray dawn the sisters lit their lamp and read their chapter with an earnestness never felt before. For now the shadow of a real trouble had come, the little books were full of help and comfort, and as they dressed, they agreed to say goodbye cheerfully and hopefully, and send their mother on her anxious journey unsaddened by tears or complaints from them. Everything seemed very strange when they went down—so dim and still outside, so full of light and bustle within. Breakfast at that early hour seemed odd, and even Hannah's familiar face looked unnatural as she flew about her kitchen with her nightcap on. The big trunk stood ready in the hall, Mother's cloak and bonnet lay on the sofa, and Mother herself sat trying to eat, but looking so pale and worn with sleeplessness and anxiety that the girls found it very hard to keep their resolution. Meg's eyes kept filling in spite of herself, Jo was obliged to hide her face in the kitchen roller more than once, and the little girls wore a grave, troubled expression, as if sorrow was a new experience to them.

Nobody talked much, but as the time drew very near and they sat waiting for the carriage, Mrs. March said to the girls, who were all busied about her, one folding her shawl, another smoothing out the strings of her bonnet, a third putting on her overshoes, and a fourth fastening up her travelling bag—

"Children, I leave you to Hannah's care and Mr. Laurence's protection. Hannah is faithfulness itself, and our good neighbor will guard you as if you were his own. I have no fears for you, yet I am anxious that you should take this trouble rightly. Don't grieve and fret when I am gone, or think that you can be idle and comfort yourselves by being idle and trying to forget. Go on with your work as usual, for work is a blessed solace. Hope and keep busy, and whatever happens, remember that you never can be fatherless."

"Yes, Mother."

"Meg, dear, be prudent, watch over your sisters, consult Hannah, and in any perplexity, go to Mr. Laurence. Be patient, Jo, don't get despondent or do rash things, write to me often, and be my brave girl, ready to help and cheer all. Beth, comfort yourself with your music, and be faithful to the little home duties, and you, Amy, help all you can, be obedient, and keep happy safe at home."

"We will, Mother! We will!"

The rattle of an approaching carriage made them all start and listen. That was the hard minute, but the girls stood it well. No one cried, no one ran away or uttered a lamentation, though their hearts were very heavy as they sent loving messages to Father, remembering, as they spoke that it might be too late to deliver them. They kissed their mother quietly, clung about her tenderly, and tried to wave their hands cheerfully when she drove away.

Laurie and his grandfather came over to see her off, and Mr. Brooke looked so strong and sensible and kind that the girls christened him "Mr. Greatheart" on the spot.

"Good-by, my darlings! God bless and keep us all!" whispered Mrs. March, as she kissed one dear little face after the other, and hurried into the carriage.

As she rolled away, the sun came out, and looking back, she saw it shining on the group at the gate like a good omen. They saw it also, and smiled and waved their hands, and the last thing she beheld as she turned the corner was the four bright faces, and behind them like a bodyguard, old Mr. Laurence, faithful Hannah, and devoted Laurie.

"How kind everyone is to us!" she said, turning to find fresh proof of it in the respectful sympathy of the young man's face.

"I don't see how they can help it," returned Mr. Brooke, laughing so infectiously that Mrs. March could not help smiling. And so the journey began with the good omens of sunshine, smiles, and cheerful words.

"I feel as if there had been an earthquake," said Jo, as their neighbors went home to breakfast, leaving them to rest and refresh themselves.

"It seems as if half the house was gone," added Meg forlornly.

Beth opened her lips to say something, but could only point to the pile of nicely mended hose which lay on Mother's table, showing that even in her last hurried moments she had thought and worked for them. It was a little thing, but it went straight to their hearts, and in spite of their brave resolutions, they all broke down and cried bitterly.

Hannah wisely allowed them to relieve their feelings, and when the shower showed signs of clearing up, she came to the rescue, armed with a coffeepot.

"Now, my dear young ladies, remember what your ma said, and don't fret. Come and have a cup of coffee all round, and then let's fall to work and be a credit to the family."

Coffee was a treat, and Hannah showed great tact in making it that morning. No one could resist her persuasive nods, or the fragrant invitation issuing from the nose of the coffee pot. They drew up to the table, exchanged their handkerchiefs for napkins, and in ten minutes were all right again.

"'Hope and keep busy,' that's the motto for us, so let's see who will remember it best. I shall go to Aunt March, as usual. Oh, won't she lecture though!" said Jo, as she sipped with returning spirit.

"I shall go to my Kings, though I'd much rather stay at home and attend to things here," said Meg, wishing she hadn't made her eyes so red.

"No need of that. Beth and I can keep house perfectly well," put in Amy, with an important air.

"Hannah will tell us what to do, and we'll have everything nice when you come home," added Beth, getting out her mop and dish tub without delay.

"I think anxiety is very interesting," observed Amy, eating sugar pensively.

The girls couldn't help laughing, and felt better for it, though Meg shook her head at the young lady who could find consolation in a sugar bowl.

The sight of the turnovers made Jo sober again; and when the two went out to their daily tasks, they looked sorrowfully back at the window where they were accustomed to see their mother's face. It was gone, but Beth had remembered the little household ceremony, and there she was, nodding away at them like a rosyfaced mandarin.

"That's so like my Beth!" said Jo, waving her hat, with a grateful face. "Goodbye, Meggy, I hope the Kings won't strain today. Don't fret about Father, dear," she added, as they parted.

"And I hope Aunt March won't croak. Your hair is becoming, and it looks very boyish and nice," returned Meg, trying not to smile at the curly head, which looked comically small on her tall sister's shoulders.

"That's my only comfort." And, touching her hat a la Laurie, away went Jo, feeling like a shorn sheep on a wintry day.

News from their father comforted the girls very much, for though dangerously ill, the presence of the best and tenderest of nurses had already done him good. Mr. Brooke sent a bulletin every day, and as the head of the family, Meg insisted on reading the dispatches, which grew more cheerful as the week passed. At first, everyone was eager to write, and plump envelopes were carefully poked into the letter box by one or other of the sisters, who felt rather important with their Washington correspondence. As one of these packets contained characteristic notes from the party, we will rob an imaginary mail, and read them.

My dearest Mother,

It is impossible to tell you how happy your last letter made us, for the news was so good we couldn't help laughing and crying over it. How very kind Mr. Brooke is, and how fortunate that Mr. Laurence's business detains him near you so long, since he is so useful to you and Father. The girls are all as good as gold. Jo helps me with the sewing, and insists on doing all sorts of hard jobs. I should be afraid she might overdo, if I didn't know her 'moral fit' wouldn't last long. Beth is as regular about her tasks as a clock, and never forgets what you told her. She grieves about Father, and looks sober except when she is at her little piano. Amy minds me nicely, and I take great care of her. She does her own hair, and I am teaching her to make buttonholes and mend her stockings. She tries very hard, and I know you will be pleased with her improvement when you come. Mr. Laurence watches over us like a motherly old hen, as Jo says, and Laurie is very kind and neighborly. He and Jo keep us merry, for we get pretty blue sometimes, and feel like orphans, with you so far away. Hannah is a perfect saint. She does not scold at all, and always calls me Miss Margaret, which is quite proper, you know, and treats me with respect. We are all well and busy, but we long, day and night, to have you back. Give my dearest love to Father, and believe me, ever your own

Meg.

This note, prettily written on scented paper, was a great contrast to the next, which was scribbled on a big sheet of thin foreign paper, ornamented with blots and all manner of flourishes and curly-tailed letters.

My precious Marmee,

Three cheers for dear Father! Brooke was a trump to telegraph right off, and let us know the minute he was better. I rushed up garret when the letter came, and tried to thank God for being so good to us, but I could only cry, and say, "I'm glad! I'm glad!" Didn't that do as well as a regular prayer? For I felt a great many in my heart. We have such funny times, and now I can enjoy them, for everyone is so desperately good, it's like living in a nest of turtledoves. You'd laugh to see Meg head the table and try to be motherish. She gets prettier every day, and I'm in love with her sometimes. The children are regular archangels, and I—well, I'm Jo, and never shall be anything else. Oh, I must tell you that I came near having a quarrel with Laurie. I freed my mind about a silly little thing, and he was offended. I was right, but didn't speak as I ought, and he marched home, saying he wouldn't come again till I begged pardon. I declared I wouldn't and got mad. It lasted all day. I felt bad and wanted you very much. Laurie and I are both so proud, it's hard to beg pardon. But I thought he'd come to it, for I *was* in the right. He didn't come, and just at night I remembered what you said when Amy fell into the river. I read my little book, felt better, resolved not to let the sun set on my anger, and ran over to tell Laurie I was sorry. I met him at the gate, coming for the same thing. We both laughed, begged each other's pardon, and felt all good and comfortable again.

I made a "pome" yesterday, when I was helping Hannah wash, and as Father likes my silly little things, I put it in to amuse him. Give him my lovingest hug that ever was, and kiss yourself a dozen times for your

Topsy-Turvy Jo.

A SONG FROM THE SUDS

Queen of my tub, I merrily sing,
While the white foam rises high;
And sturdily wash and rinse and wring,
And fasten the clothes to dry;
Then out in the free fresh air they swing,
Under the sunny sky.

I wish we could wash from our hearts and souls
The stains of the week away,
And let water and air by their magic make
Ourselves as pure as they.
Then on the earth there would be indeed,
A glorious washing-day!

Along the path of a useful life,
Will heartsease ever bloom.
The busy mind has no time to think
Of sorrow or care or gloom.
And anxious thoughts may be swept away,
As we bravely wield a broom.

I am glad a task to me is given,
To labor at day by day,
For it brings me health and strength and hope,
And I cheerfully learn to say,
"Head, you may think, Heart, you may feel,
But, Hand, you shall work alway!"

Dear Mother,

There is only room for me to send my love, and some pressed pansies from the root I have been keeping safe in the house for Father to see. I read every morning, try to be good all day, and sing myself to sleep with Father's tune. I can't sing "Land of the Leal" now, it makes me cry. Everyone is very kind, and we are as happy as we can be without you. Amy wants the rest of the page, so I must stop. I didn't forget to cover the holders, and I wind the clock and air the rooms every day.

Kiss dear Father on the cheek he calls mine. Oh, do come soon to your loving

Little Beth.

Ma Chere Mamma,

We are all well I do my lessons always and never corroberate the girls—Meg says I mean contradick so I put in both words and you can take the properest. Meg is a great comfort to me and lets me have jelly every night at tea its so good for me Jo says because it keeps me sweet tempered.

Laurie is not as respeckful as he ought to be now I am almost in my teens, he calls me Chick and hurts my feelings by talking French to me very fast when I say Merci or Bon jour as Hattie King does. The sleeves of my blue dress were all worn out, and Meg put in new ones, but the full front came wrong and they are more blue than the dress. I felt bad but did not fret I bear my troubles well but I do wish Hannah would put more starch in my aprons and have buckwheats every day. Can't she? Didn't I make that interrigation point nice? Meg says my punchtuation and spelling are disgraceful and I am mortyfied but dear me I have so many things to do, I can't stop. Adieu, I send heaps of love to Papa.

Your affectionate daughter
AMY CURTIS MARCH

DEAR MIS MARCH,

I jes drop a line to say we git on fust rate. The girls is clever and fly round right smart. Miss Meg is going to make a proper good housekeeper. She hes the liking for it, and gits the hang of things surprisin quick. Jo doos beat all for goin ahead, but she don't stop to cal'k'late fust, and you never know where she's like to bring up. She done out a tub of clothes on Monday, but she starched 'em afore they was wrenched, and blued a pink calico dress till I thought I should a died a laughin. Beth is the best of little creeters, and a sight of help to me, bein so forehanded and dependable. She tries to learn everything, and really goes to market beyond her years, likewise keeps accounts, with my help, quite wonderful. We have got on very economical so fur. I don't let the girls hev coffee only once a week, accordin to your wish, and keep em on plain wholesome vittles. Amy does well without frettin, wearin her best clothes and eatin sweet stuff. Mr. Laurie is as full of didoes as usual, and turns the house upside down frequent, but he heartens the girls, so I let em hev full swing. The old gentleman sends heaps of things, and is rather wearin, but means wal, and it aint my place to say nothin. My bread is riz, so no more at this time. I send my duty to Mr. March, and hope he's seen the last of his Pewmonia.

Yours respectful,
HANNAH MULLET

Head Nurse of Ward No. 2,

All serene on the Rappahannock, troops in fine condition, commisary department well conducted, the Home Guard under Colonel Teddy always on duty, Commander in Chief General Laurence reviews the army daily, Quartermaster Mullet keeps order in camp, and Major Lion does picket duty at night. A salute of twenty-four guns was fired on receipt of good news from Washington, and a dress parade took place at headquarters. Commander in chief sends best wishes, in which he is heartily joined by

Colonel Teddy.

Dear Madam,

The little girls are all well. Beth and my boy report daily. Hannah is a model servant, and guards pretty Meg like a dragon. Glad the fine weather holds. Pray make Brooke useful, and draw on me for funds if expenses exceed your estimate. Don't let your husband want anything. Thank God he is mending.

Your sincere friend and servant,
James Laurence.

CHAPTER XVII

LITTLE FAITHFUL

For a week the amount of virtue in the old house would have supplied the neighborhood. It was really amazing, for everyone seemed in a heavenly frame of mind, and self-denial was all the fashion. Relieved of their first anxiety about their father, the girls insensibly relaxed their praiseworthy efforts a little, and began to fall back into old ways. They did not forget their motto, but hoping and keeping busy seemed to grow easier, and after such tremendous exertions, they felt that Endeavor deserved a holiday, and gave it a good many.

Jo caught a bad cold through neglect to cover the shorn head enough, and was ordered to stay at home till she was better, for Aunt March didn't like to hear people read with colds in their heads. Jo liked this, and after an energetic rummage from garret to cellar, subsided on the sofa to nurse her cold with arsenicum and books. Amy found that housework and art did not go well together, and returned to her mud pies. Meg went daily to her pupils, and sewed, or thought she did, at home, but much time was spent in writing long letters to her mother, or reading the Washington dispatches over and over. Beth kept on, with only slight relapses into idleness or grieving.

All the little duties were faithfully done each day, and many of her sisters' also, for they were forgetful, and the house seemed like a clock whose pendulum was gone a-visiting. When her heart got heavy with longings for Mother or fears for Father, she went away into a certain closet, hid her face in the folds of a dear old gown, and made her little moan and prayed her little prayer quietly by herself. Nobody knew what cheered her up after a sober fit, but everyone felt how sweet and helpful Beth was, and fell into a way of going to her for comfort or advice in their small affairs.

All were unconscious that this experience was a test of character, and when the first excitement was over, felt that they had done well and deserved praise. So they did, but their mistake was in ceasing to do well, and they learned this lesson through much anxiety and regret.

"Meg, I wish you'd go and see the Hummels. You know Mother told us not to forget them," said Beth, ten days after Mrs. March's departure.

"I'm too tired to go this afternoon," replied Meg, rocking comfortably as she sewed.

"Can't you, Jo?" asked Beth.

"Too stormy for me with my cold."

"I thought it was almost well."

"It's well enough for me to go out with Laurie, but not well enough to go to the Hummels'," said Jo, laughing, but looking a little ashamed of her inconsistency.

"Why don't you go yourself?" asked Meg.

"I *have* been every day, but the baby is sick, and I don't know what to do for it. Mrs. Hummel goes away to work, and Lottchen takes care of it. But it gets sicker and sicker, and I think you or Hannah ought to go."

Beth spoke earnestly, and Meg promised she would go tomorrow.

"Ask Hannah for some nice little mess, and take it round, Beth, the air will do you good," said Jo, adding apologetically, "I'd go but I want to finish my writing."

"My head aches and I'm tired, so I thought maybe some of you would go," said Beth.

"Amy will be in presently, and she will run down for us," suggested Meg.

"Well, I'll rest a little and wait for her."

So Beth lay down on the sofa, the others returned to their work, and the Hummels were forgotten. An hour passed. Amy did not come, Meg went to her room to try on a new dress, Jo was absorbed in her story, and Hannah was sound asleep before the kitchen fire, when Beth quietly put on her hood, filled her basket with odds and ends for the poor children, and went out into the chilly air with a heavy head and a grieved look in her patient eyes. It was late when she came back, and no one saw her creep upstairs and shut herself into her mother's room. Half an hour after, Jo went to "Mother's closet" for something, and there found little Beth sitting on the medicine chest, looking very grave, with red eyes and a camphor bottle in her hand.

"Christopher Columbus! What's the matter?" cried Jo, as Beth put out her hand as if to warn her off, and asked quickly, "You've had the scarlet fever, haven't you?"

"Years ago, when Meg did. Why?"

"Then I'll tell you. Oh, Jo, the baby's dead!"

"What baby?"

"Mrs. Hummel's. It died in my lap before she got home," cried Beth with a sob.

"My poor dear, how dreadful for you! I ought to have gone," said Jo, taking her sister in her arms as she sat down in her mother's big chair, with a remorseful face.

"It wasn't dreadful, Jo, only so sad! I saw in a minute it was sicker, but Lottchen said her mother had gone for a doctor, so I took Baby and let Lotty rest. It seemed asleep, but all of a sudden if gave a little cry and trembled, and then lay very still. I tried to warm its feet, and Lotty gave it some milk, but it didn't stir, and I knew it was dead."

"Don't cry, dear! What did you do?"

"I just sat and held it softly till Mrs. Hummel came with the doctor. He said it was dead, and looked at Heinrich and Minna, who have sore throats. 'Scarlet fever, ma'am. Ought to have called me before,' he said crossly. Mrs. Hummel told him she was poor, and had tried to cure Baby herself, but now it was too late, and she could only ask him to help the others and trust to charity for his pay. He smiled then, and was kinder, but it was very sad, and I cried with them till he turned round all of a sudden, and told me to go home and take belladonna right away, or I'd have the fever."

"No, you won't!" cried Jo, hugging her close, with a frightened look. "Oh, Beth, if you should be sick I never could forgive myself! What shall we do?"

"Don't be frightened, I guess I shan't have it badly. I looked in Mother's book, and saw that it begins with headache, sore throat, and queer feelings like mine, so I did take some belladonna, and I feel better," said Beth, laying her cold hands on her hot forehead and trying to look well.

"If Mother was only at home!" exclaimed Jo, seizing the book, and feeling that Washington was an immense way off. She read a page, looked at Beth, felt her head, peeped into her throat, and then said gravely, "You've been over the baby every day for more than a week, and among the others who are going to have it, so I'm afraid you are going to have it, Beth. I'll call Hannah, she knows all about sickness."

"Don't let Amy come. She never had it, and I should hate to give it to her. Can't you and Meg have it over again?" asked Beth, anxiously.

"I guess not. Don't care if I do. Serve me right, selfish pig, to let you go, and stay writing rubbish myself!" muttered Jo, as she went to consult Hannah.

The good soul was wide awake in a minute, and took the lead at once, assuring that there was no need to worry; every one had scarlet fever, and if rightly treated, nobody died—all of which Jo believed, and felt much relieved as they went up to call Meg.

"Now I'll tell you what we'll do," said Hannah, when she had examined and questioned Beth, "we will have Dr. Bangs, just to take a look at you, dear, and see that we start right. Then we'll send Amy off to Aunt March's for a spell, to keep her out of harm's way, and one of you girls can stay at home and amuse Beth for a day or two."

"I shall stay, of course, I'm oldest," began Meg, looking anxious and self-reproachful.

"I shall, because it's my fault she is sick. I told Mother I'd do the errands, and I haven't," said Jo decidedly.

"Which will you have, Beth? There ain't no need of but one," said Hannah.

"Jo, please." And Beth leaned her head against her sister with a contented look, which effectually settled that point.

"I'll go and tell Amy," said Meg, feeling a little hurt, yet rather relieved on the whole, for she did not like nursing, and Jo did.

Amy rebelled outright, and passionately declared that she had rather have the fever than go to Aunt March. Meg reasoned, pleaded, and commanded, all in vain. Amy protested that she would *not* go, and Meg left her in despair to ask Hannah what should be done. Before she came back, Laurie walked into the parlor to find Amy sobbing, with her head in the sofa cushions. She told her story, expecting to be consoled, but Laurie only put his hands in his pockets and walked about the room, whistling softly, as he knit his brows in deep thought. Presently he sat down beside her, and said, in his most wheedlesome tone, "Now be a sensible little woman, and do as they say. No, don't cry, but hear what a jolly plan I've got. You go to Aunt March's, and I'll come and take you out every day, driving or walking, and we'll have capital times. Won't that be better than moping here?"

"I don't wish to be sent off as if I was in the way," began Amy, in an injured voice.

"Bless your heart, child, it's to keep you well. You don't want to be sick, do you?"

"No, I'm sure I don't, but I dare say I shall be, for I've been with Beth all the time."

"That's the very reason you ought to go away at once, so that you may escape it. Change of air and care will keep you well, I dare say, or if it does not entirely, you will have the fever more lightly. I advise you to be off as soon as you can, for scarlet fever is no joke, miss."

"But it's dull at Aunt March's, and she is so cross," said Amy, looking rather frightened.

"It won't be dull with me popping in every day to tell you how Beth is, and take you out gallivanting. The old lady likes me, and I'll be as sweet as possible to her, so she won't peck at us, whatever we do."

"Will you take me out in the trotting wagon with Puck?"

"On my honor as a gentleman."

"And come every single day?"

"See if I don't!"

"And bring me back the minute Beth is well?"

"The identical minute."

"And go to the theater, truly?"

"A dozen theaters, if we may."

"Well—I guess I will," said Amy slowly.

"Good girl! Call Meg, and tell her you'll give in," said Laurie, with an approving pat, which annoyed Amy more than the "giving in."

Meg and Jo came running down to behold the miracle which had been wrought, and Amy, feeling very precious and self-sacrificing, promised to go, if the doctor said Beth was going to be ill.

"How is the little dear?" asked Laurie, for Beth was his especial pet, and he felt more anxious about her than he liked to show.

"She is lying down on Mother's bed, and feels better. The baby's death troubled her, but I dare say she has only got cold. Hannah says she thinks so, but she *looks* worried, and that makes me fidgety," answered Meg.

"What a trying world it is!" said Jo, rumpling up her hair in a fretful way. "No sooner do we get out of one trouble than down comes another. There doesn't seem to be anything to hold on to when Mother's gone, so I'm all at sea."

"Well, don't make a porcupine of yourself, it isn't becoming. Settle your wig, Jo, and tell me if I shall telegraph to your mother, or do anything?" asked Laurie, who never had been reconciled to the loss of his friend's one beauty.

"That is what troubles me," said Meg. "I think we ought to tell her if Beth is really ill, but Hannah says we mustn't, for Mother can't leave Father, and it will only make them anxious. Beth won't be sick long, and Hannah knows just what to do, and Mother said we were to mind her, so I suppose we must, but it doesn't seem quite right to me."

"Hum, well, I can't say. Suppose you ask Grandfather after the doctor has been."

"We will. Jo, go and get Dr. Bangs at once," commanded Meg. "We can't decide anything till he has been."

"Stay where you are, Jo. I'm errand boy to this establishment," said Laurie, taking up his cap.

"I'm afraid you are busy," began Meg.

"No, I've done my lessons for the day."

"Do you study in vacation time?" asked Jo.

"I follow the good example my neighbors set me," was Laurie's answer, as he swung himself out of the room.

"I have great hopes for my boy," observed Jo, watching him fly over the fence with an approving smile.

"He does very well—for a boy," was Meg's somewhat ungracious answer, for the subject did not interest her.

Dr. Bangs came, said Beth had symptoms of the fever, but he thought she would have it lightly, though he looked sober over the Hummel story. Amy was ordered off at once, and provided with something to ward off danger, she departed in great state, with Jo and Laurie as escort.

Aunt March received them with her usual hospitality.

"What do you want now?" she asked, looking sharply over her spectacles, while the parrot, sitting on the back of her chair, called out—

"Go away. No boys allowed here."

Laurie retired to the window, and Jo told her story.

"No more than I expected, if you are allowed to go poking about among poor folks. Amy can stay and make herself useful if she isn't sick, which I've no doubt she will be—looks like it now. Don't cry, child, it worries me to hear people sniff."

Amy *was* on the point of crying, but Laurie slyly pulled the parrot's tail, which caused Polly to utter an astonished croak and call out, "Bless my boots!" in such a funny way, that she laughed instead.

"What do you hear from your mother?" asked the old lady gruffly.

"Father is much better," replied Jo, trying to keep sober.

"Oh, is he? Well, that won't last long, I fancy. March never had any stamina," was the cheerful reply.

"Ha, ha! Never say die, take a pinch of snuff, goodbye, goodbye!" squalled Polly, dancing on her perch, and clawing at the old lady's cap as Laurie tweaked him in the rear.

"Hold your tongue, you disrespectful old bird! And, Jo, you'd better go at once. It isn't proper to be gadding about so late with a rattlepated boy like—"

"Hold your tongue, you disrespectful old bird!" cried Polly, tumbling off the chair with a bounce, and running to peck the "rattlepated" boy, who was shaking with laughter at the last speech.

"I don't think I *can* bear it, but I'll try," thought Amy, as she was left alone with Aunt March.

"Get along, you fright!" screamed Polly, and at that rude speech Amy could not restrain a sniff.

CHAPTER XVIII

DARK DAYS

Beth did have the fever, and was much sicker than anyone but Hannah and the doctor suspected. The girls knew nothing about illness, and Mr. Laurence was not allowed to see her, so Hannah had everything her own way, and busy Dr. Bangs did his best, but left a good deal to the excellent nurse. Meg stayed at home, lest she should infect the Kings, and kept house, feeling very anxious and a little guilty when she wrote letters in which no mention was made of Beth's illness. She could not think it right to deceive her mother, but she had been bidden to mind Hannah, and Hannah wouldn't hear of "Mrs. March bein' told, and worried just for sech a trifle." Jo devoted herself to Beth day and night—not a hard task, for Beth was very patient, and bore her pain uncomplainingly as long as she could control herself. But there came a time when during the fever fits she began to talk in a hoarse, broken voice, to play on the coverlet as if on her beloved little piano, and try to sing with a throat so swollen that there was no music left, a time when she did not know the familiar faces around her, but addressed them by wrong names, and called imploringly for her mother. Then Jo grew frightened, Meg begged to be allowed to write the truth, and even Hannah said she "would think of it, though there was no danger *yet*." A letter from Washington added to their trouble, for Mr. March had had a relapse, and could not think of coming home for a long while.

How dark the days seemed now, how sad and lonely the house, and how heavy were the hearts of the sisters as they worked and waited, while the shadow of death hovered over the once happy home. Then it was that Margaret, sitting alone with tears dropping often on her work, felt how rich she had been in things more precious than any luxuries money could buy—in love, protection, peace, and health, the real blessings of life. Then it was that Jo, living in the darkened room, with that suffering little sister always before her eyes and that pathetic voice sounding in her ears, learned to see the beauty and the sweetness of Beth's nature, to feel how deep and tender a place she filled in all hearts, and to acknowledge the worth of Beth's unselfish ambition to live for others, and make home happy by that exercise of those simple virtues which all may possess, and which all should love and value more than talent, wealth, or beauty. And Amy, in her exile, longed eagerly to be at home, that she might work for Beth, feeling now that no service would be hard or irksome, and remembering, with regretful grief, how many neglected tasks those willing hands had done for her. Laurie haunted the house like a restless ghost, and Mr. Laurence locked the grand piano, because he could not bear to be reminded of the young neighbor who used to make the twilight pleasant for him. Everyone missed Beth. The milkman, baker, grocer, and butcher inquired how she did, poor Mrs. Hummel came to beg pardon for her thoughtlessness and to get a shroud for Minna, the neighbors sent all sorts of comforts and good wishes, and even those who knew her best were surprised to find how many friends shy little Beth had made.

Meanwhile she lay on her bed with old Joanna at her side, for even in her wanderings she did not forget her forlorn protege. She longed for her cats, but would not have them brought, lest they should get sick, and in her quiet hours she was full of anxiety about Jo. She sent loving messages to Amy, bade them tell her mother that she would write soon, and often begged for pencil and paper to try to say a word, that Father might not think she had neglected him. But soon even these intervals of consciousness ended, and she lay hour after hour, tossing to and fro, with incoherent words on her lips, or sank into a heavy sleep which brought her no refreshment. Dr. Bangs came twice a day, Hannah sat up at night, Meg kept a telegram in her desk all ready to send off at any minute, and Jo never stirred from Beth's side.

The first of December was a wintry day indeed to them, for a bitter wind blew, snow fell fast, and the year seemed getting ready for its death. When Dr. Bangs came that morning, he looked long at Beth, held the hot hand in both his own for a minute, and laid it gently down, saying, in a low voice to Hannah, "If Mrs. March *can* leave her husband she'd better be sent for."

Hannah nodded without speaking, for her lips twitched nervously, Meg dropped down into a chair as the strength seemed to go out of her limbs at the sound of those words, and Jo, standing with a pale face for a minute, ran to the parlor, snatched up the telegram, and throwing on her things, rushed out into the storm. She was soon back, and while noiselessly taking off her cloak, Laurie came in with a letter, saying that Mr. March was mending again. Jo read it thankfully, but the heavy weight did not seem lifted off her heart, and her face was so full of misery that Laurie asked quickly, "What is it? Is Beth worse?"

"I've sent for Mother," said Jo, tugging at her rubber boots with a tragic expression.

"Good for you, Jo! Did you do it on your own responsibility?" asked Laurie, as he seated her in the hall chair and took off the rebellious boots, seeing how her hands shook.

"No; the doctor told us to."

"Oh, Jo, it's not so bad as that?" cried Laurie, with a startled face.

"Yes, it is. She doesn't know us, she doesn't even talk about the flocks of green doves, as she calls the vine leaves on the wall. She doesn't look like my Beth, and there's nobody to help us bear it. Mother and Father both gone, and God seems so far away I can't find Him."

As the tears streamed fast down poor Jo's cheeks, she stretched out her hand in a helpless sort of way, as if groping in the dark, and Laurie took it in his, whispering as well as he could with a lump in his throat, "I'm here. Hold on to me, Jo, dear!"

She could not speak, but she did "hold on" and the warm grasp of the friendly human hand comforted her sore heart, and seemed to lead her nearer to the Divine arm which alone could uphold her in her trouble. Laurie longed to say something tender and comfortable, but no fitting words came to him, so he stood silent, gently stroking her bent head as her mother used to do. It was the best thing he could have done, far more soothing than the most eloquent words, for Jo felt the unspoken sympathy, and in the silence learned the sweet solace which affection administers to sorrow. Soon she dried the tears which had relieved her, and looked up with a grateful face.

"Thank you, Teddy, I'm better now. I don't feel so forlorn, and will try to bear it if it comes."

"Keep hoping for the best, that will help you, Jo. Soon your mother will be here, and then everything will be all right."

"I'm so glad Father is better. Now she won't feel so bad about leaving him. Oh, me! It does seem as if all the troubles came in a heap, and I got the heaviest part on my shoulders," sighed Jo, spreading her wet handkerchief over her knees to dry.

"Doesn't Meg pull fair?" asked Laurie, looking indignant.

"Oh, yes, she tries to, but she can't love Bethy as I do, and she won't miss her as I shall. Beth is my conscience, and I *can't* give her up. I can't! I can't!"

Down went Jo's face into the wet handkerchief, and she cried despairingly, for she had kept up bravely till now and never shed a tear. Laurie drew his hand across his eyes, but could not speak till he had subdued the choky feeling in his throat and steadied his lips. It might be unmanly, but he couldn't help it, and I am glad of it. Presently, as Jo's sobs quieted, he said hopefully, "I don't think she will die. She's so good, and we all love her so much, I don't believe God will take her away yet."

"The good and dear people always do die," groaned Jo, but she stopped crying, for her friend's words cheered her up in spite of her own doubts and fears.

"Poor girl, you're worn out. It isn't like you to be forlorn. Stop a bit. I'll hearten you up in a jiffy."

Laurie went off two stairs at a time, and Jo laid her wearied head down on Beth's little brown hood, which no one had thought of moving from the table where she left it. It must have possessed some magic, for the submissive spirit of its gentle owner seemed to enter into Jo, and when Laurie came running down with a glass of wine, she took it with a smile, and said bravely, "I drink—Health to my Beth! You are a good doctor, Teddy, and *such* a comfortable friend. How can I ever pay you?" she added, as the wine refreshed her body, as the kind words had done her troubled mind.

"I'll send my bill, by-and-by, and tonight I'll give you something that will warm the cockles of your heart better than quarts of wine," said Laurie, beaming at her with a face of suppressed satisfaction at something.

"What is it?" cried Jo, forgetting her woes for a minute in her wonder.

"I telegraphed to your mother yesterday, and Brooke answered she'd come at once, and she'll be here tonight, and everything will be all right. Aren't you glad I did it?"

Laurie spoke very fast, and turned red and excited all in a minute, for he had kept his plot a secret, for fear of disappointing the girls or harming Beth. Jo grew quite white, flew out of her chair, and the moment he stopped speaking she electrified him by throwing her arms round his neck, and crying out, with a joyful cry, "Oh, Laurie! Oh,

Mother! I *am* so glad!" She did not weep again, but laughed hysterically, and trembled and clung to her friend as if she was a little bewildered by the sudden news.

Laurie, though decidedly amazed, behaved with great presence of mind. He patted her back soothingly, and finding that she was recovering, followed it up by a bashful kiss or two, which brought Jo round at once. Holding on to the banisters, she put him gently away, saying breathlessly, "Oh, don't! I didn't mean to, it was dreadful of me, but you were such a dear to go and do it in spite of Hannah that I couldn't help flying at you. Tell me all about it, and don't give me wine again, it makes me act so."

"I don't mind," laughed Laurie, as he settled his tie. "Why, you see I got fidgety, and so did Grandpa. We thought Hannah was overdoing the authority business, and your mother ought to know. She'd never forgive us if Beth—well, if anything happened, you know. So I got grandpa to say it was high time we did something, and off I pelted to the office yesterday, for the doctor looked sober, and Hannah most took my head off when I proposed a telegram. I never can bear to be 'lorded over,' so that settled my mind, and I did it. Your mother will come, I know, and the late train is in at two A.M. I shall go for her, and you've only got to bottle up your rapture, and keep Beth quiet till that blessed lady gets here."

"Laurie, you're an angel! How shall I ever thank you?"

"Fly at me again. I rather liked it," said Laurie, looking mischievous—a thing he had not done for a fortnight.

"No, thank you. I'll do it by proxy, when your grandpa comes. Don't tease, but go home and rest, for you'll be up half the night. Bless you, Teddy, bless you!"

Jo had backed into a corner, and as she finished her speech, she vanished precipitately into the kitchen, where she sat down upon a dresser and told the assembled cats that she was "happy, oh, *so* happy!" while Laurie departed, feeling that he had made a rather neat thing of it.

"That's the interferingest chap I ever see, but I forgive him and do hope Mrs. March is coming right away," said Hannah, with an air of relief, when Jo told the good news.

Meg had a quiet rapture, and then brooded over the letter, while Jo set the sickroom in order, and Hannah "knocked up a couple of pies in case of company unexpected." A breath of fresh air seemed to blow through the house, and something better than sunshine brightened the quiet rooms. Everything appeared to feel the hopeful change. Beth's bird began to chirp again, and a half-blown rose was discovered on Amy's bush in the window. The fires seemed to burn with unusual cheeriness, and every time the girls met, their pale faces broke into smiles as they hugged one another, whispering encouragingly, "Mother's coming, dear! Mother's coming!" Every one rejoiced but Beth. She lay in that heavy stupor, alike unconscious of hope and joy, doubt and danger. It was a piteous sight—the once rosy face so changed and vacant, the once busy hands so weak and wasted, the once smiling lips quite dumb, and the once pretty, well-kept hair scattered rough and tangled on the pillow. All day she lay so, only rousing now and then to mutter, "Water!" with lips so parched they could hardly shape the word. All day Jo and Meg hovered over her, watching, waiting, hoping, and trusting in God and Mother, and all day the snow fell, the bitter wind raged, and the hours dragged slowly by. But night came at last, and every time the clock struck, the sisters, still sitting on either side of the bed, looked at each other with brightening eyes, for each hour brought help nearer. The doctor had been in to say that some change, for better or worse, would probably take place about midnight, at which time he would return.

Hannah, quite worn out, lay down on the sofa at the bed's foot and fell fast asleep, Mr. Laurence marched to and fro in the parlor, feeling that he would rather face a rebel battery than Mrs. March's countenance as she entered. Laurie lay on the rug, pretending to rest, but staring into the fire with the thoughtful look which made his black eyes beautifully soft and clear.

The girls never forgot that night, for no sleep came to them as they kept their watch, with that dreadful sense of powerlessness which comes to us in hours like those.

"If God spares Beth, I never will complain again," whispered Meg earnestly.

"If God spares Beth, I'll try to love and serve Him all my life," answered Jo, with equal fervor.

"I wish I had no heart, it aches so," sighed Meg, after a pause.

"If life is often as hard as this, I don't see how we ever shall get through it," added her sister despondently.

Here the clock struck twelve, and both forgot themselves in watching Beth, for they fancied a change passed over her wan face. The house was still as death, and nothing but the wailing of the wind broke the deep hush. Weary Hannah slept on, and no one but the sisters saw the pale shadow which seemed to fall upon the little bed. An hour went by, and nothing happened except Laurie's quiet departure for the station. Another hour—still no one came, and anxious fears of delay in the storm, or accidents by the way, or, worst of all, a great grief at Washington, haunted the girls.

It was past two, when Jo, who stood at the window thinking how dreary the world looked in its winding sheet of snow, heard a movement by the bed, and turning quickly, saw Meg kneeling before their mother's easy chair with her face hidden. A dreadful fear passed coldly over Jo, as she thought, "Beth is dead, and Meg is afraid to tell me."

She was back at her post in an instant, and to her excited eyes a great change seemed to have taken place. The fever flush and the look of pain were gone, and the beloved little face looked so pale and peaceful in its utter repose that Jo felt no desire to weep or to lament. Leaning low over this dearest of her sisters, she kissed the damp forehead with her heart on her lips, and softly whispered, "Good-by, my Beth. Good-by!"

As if awaked by the stir, Hannah started out of her sleep, hurried to the bed, looked at Beth, felt her hands, listened at her lips, and then, throwing her apron over her head, sat down to rock to and fro, exclaiming, under her breath, "The fever's turned, she's sleepin' nat'ral, her skin's damp, and she breathes easy. Praise be given! Oh, my goodness me!"

Before the girls could believe the happy truth, the doctor came to confirm it. He was a homely man, but they thought his face quite heavenly when he smiled and said, with a fatherly look at them, "Yes, my dears, I think the little girl will pull through this time. Keep the house quiet, let her sleep, and when she wakes, give her—"

What they were to give, neither heard, for both crept into the dark hall, and, sitting on the stairs, held each other close, rejoicing with hearts too full for words. When they went back to be kissed and cuddled by faithful Hannah, they found Beth lying, as she used to do, with her cheek pillowed on her hand, the dreadful pallor gone, and breathing quietly, as if just fallen asleep.

"If Mother would only come now!" said Jo, as the winter night began to wane.

"See," said Meg, coming up with a white, half-opened rose, "I thought this would hardly be ready to lay in Beth's hand tomorrow if she—went away from us. But it has blossomed in the night, and now I mean to put it in my vase here, so that when the darling wakes, the first thing she sees will be the little rose, and Mother's face."

Never had the sun risen so beautifully, and never had the world seemed so lovely as it did to the heavy eyes of Meg and Jo, as they looked out in the early morning, when their long, sad vigil was done.

"It looks like a fairy world," said Meg, smiling to herself, as she stood behind the curtain, watching the dazzling sight.

"Hark!" cried Jo, starting to her feet.

Yes, there was a sound of bells at the door below, a cry from Hannah, and then Laurie's voice saying in a joyful whisper, "Girls, she's come! She's come!"

CHAPTER XIX

AMY'S WILL

While these things were happening at home, Amy was having hard times at Aunt March's. She felt her exile deeply, and for the first time in her life, realized how much she was beloved and petted at home. Aunt March never petted any one; she did not approve of it, but she meant to be kind, for the well-behaved little girl pleased her very much, and Aunt March had a soft place in her old heart for her nephew's children, though she didn't think it proper to confess it. She really did her best to make Amy happy, but, dear me, what mistakes she made. Some old people keep young at heart in spite of wrinkles and gray hairs, can sympathize with children's little cares and joys, make them feel at home, and can hide wise lessons under pleasant plays, giving and receiving friendship in the sweetest way. But Aunt March had not this gift, and she worried Amy very much with her rules and orders, her prim ways, and long, prosy talks. Finding the child more docile and amiable than her sister, the old lady felt it her duty to try and counteract, as far as possible, the bad effects of home freedom and indulgence. So she took Amy by the hand, and taught her as she herself had been taught sixty years ago—a process which carried dismay to Amy's soul, and made her feel like a fly in the web of a very strict spider.

She had to wash the cups every morning, and polish up the old-fashioned spoons, the fat silver teapot, and the glasses till they shone. Then she must dust the room, and what a trying job that was. Not a speck escaped Aunt March's eye, and all the furniture had claw legs and much carving, which was never dusted to suit. Then Polly had to be fed, the lap dog combed, and a dozen trips upstairs and down to get things or deliver orders, for the old lady was very lame and seldom left her big chair. After these tiresome labors, she must do her lessons, which was a daily trial of every virtue she possessed. Then she was allowed one hour for exercise or play, and didn't she enjoy it? Laurie came every day, and wheedled Aunt March till Amy was allowed to go out with him, when they walked and rode and had capital times. After dinner, she had to read aloud, and sit still while the old lady slept, which she usually did for an hour, as she dropped off over the first page. Then patchwork or towels appeared, and Amy sewed with outward meekness and inward rebellion till dusk, when she was allowed to amuse herself as she liked till teatime. The evenings were the worst of all, for Aunt March fell to telling long stories about her youth, which were so unutterably dull that Amy was always ready to go to bed, intending to cry over her hard fate, but usually going to sleep before she had squeezed out more than a tear or two.

If it had not been for Laurie, and old Esther, the maid, she felt that she never could have got through that dreadful time. The parrot alone was enough to drive her distracted, for he soon felt that she did not admire him, and revenged himself by being as mischievous as possible. He pulled her hair whenever she came near him, upset his bread and milk to plague her when she had newly cleaned his cage, made Mop bark by pecking at him while Madam dozed, called her names before company, and behaved in all respects like a reprehensible old bird. Then she could not endure the dog—a fat, cross beast who snarled and yelped at her when she made his toilet, and who lay on his back with all his legs in the air and a most idiotic expression of countenance when he wanted something to eat, which was about a dozen times a day. The cook was bad-tempered, the old coachman was deaf, and Esther the only one who ever took any notice of the young lady.

Esther was a Frenchwoman, who had lived with "Madame," as she called her mistress, for many years, and who rather tyrannized over the old lady, who could not get along without her. Her real name was Estelle, but Aunt March ordered her to change it, and she obeyed, on condition that she was never asked to change her religion. She took a fancy to Mademoiselle, and amused her very much with odd stories of her life in France, when Amy sat with her while she got up Madame's laces. She also allowed her to roam about the great house, and examine the curious and pretty things stored away in the big wardrobes and the ancient chests, for Aunt March hoarded like a magpie. Amy's chief delight was an Indian cabinet, full of queer drawers, little pigeonholes, and secret places, in which were kept all sorts of ornaments, some precious, some merely curious, all more or less antique. To examine and arrange these things gave Amy great satisfaction, especially the jewel cases, in which on velvet cushions reposed the ornaments which had adorned a belle forty years ago. There was the garnet set which Aunt March wore when she came out, the pearls her father gave her on her wedding day, her lover's diamonds, the jet mourning rings and pins, the queer lockets, with portraits of dead friends and weeping willows made of hair inside, the baby bracelets her one little daughter had worn, Uncle March's big watch, with the red seal so many childish hands had played with, and in a box all by itself lay Aunt March's wedding ring, too small now for her fat finger, but put carefully away like the most precious jewel of them all.

"Which would Mademoiselle choose if she had her will?" asked Esther, who always sat near to watch over and lock up the valuables.

"I like the diamonds best, but there is no necklace among them, and I'm fond of necklaces, they are so becoming. I should choose this if I might," replied Amy, looking with great admiration at a string of gold and ebony beads from which hung a heavy cross of the same.

"I, too, covet that, but not as a necklace. Ah, no! To me it is a rosary, and as such I should use it like a good catholic," said Esther, eyeing the handsome thing wistfully.

"Is it meant to use as you use the string of good-smelling wooden beads hanging over your glass?" asked Amy.

"Truly, yes, to pray with. It would be pleasing to the saints if one used so fine a rosary as this, instead of wearing it as a vain bijou."

"You seem to take a great deal of comfort in your prayers, Esther, and always come down looking quiet and satisfied. I wish I could."

"If Mademoiselle was a Catholic, she would find true comfort, but as that is not to be, it would be well if you went apart each day to meditate and pray, as did the good mistress whom I served before Madame. She had a little chapel, and in it found solacement for much trouble."

"Would it be right for me to do so too?" asked Amy, who in her loneliness felt the need of help of some sort, and found that she was apt to forget her little book, now that Beth was not there to remind her of it.

"It would be excellent and charming, and I shall gladly arrange the little dressing room for you if you like it. Say nothing to Madame, but when she sleeps go you and sit alone a while to think good thoughts, and pray the dear God preserve your sister."

Esther was truly pious, and quite sincere in her advice, for she had an affectionate heart, and felt much for the sisters in their anxiety. Amy liked the idea, and gave her leave to arrange the light closet next her room, hoping it would do her good.

"I wish I knew where all these pretty things would go when Aunt March dies," she said, as she slowly replaced the shining rosary and shut the jewel cases one by one.

"To you and your sisters. I know it, Madame confides in me. I witnessed her will, and it is to be so," whispered Esther smiling.

"How nice! But I wish she'd let us have them now. Procrastination is not agreeable," observed Amy, taking a last look at the diamonds.

"It is too soon yet for the young ladies to wear these things. The first one who is affianced will have the pearls, Madame has said it, and I have a fancy that the little turquoise ring will be given to you when you go, for Madame approves your good behavior and charming manners."

"Do you think so? Oh, I'll be a lamb, if I can only have that lovely ring! It's ever so much prettier than Kitty Bryant's. I do like Aunt March after all." And Amy tried on the blue ring with a delighted face and a firm resolve to earn it.

From that day she was a model of obedience, and the old lady complacently admired the success of her training. Esther fitted up the closet with a little table, placed a footstool before it, and over it a picture taken from one of the shut-up rooms. She thought it was of no great value, but, being appropriate, she borrowed it, well knowing that Madame would never know it, nor care if she did. It was, however, a very valuable copy of one of the famous pictures of the world, and Amy's beauty-loving eyes were never tired of looking up at the sweet face of the Divine Mother, while her tender thoughts of her own were busy at her heart. On the table she laid her little testament and hymnbook, kept a vase always full of the best flowers Laurie brought her, and came every day to "sit alone thinking good thoughts, and praying the dear God to preserve her sister." Esther had given her a rosary of black beads with a silver cross, but Amy hung it up and did not use it, feeling doubtful as to its fitness for Protestant prayers.

The little girl was very sincere in all this, for being left alone outside the safe home nest, she felt the need of some kind hand to hold by so sorely that she instinctively turned to the strong and tender Friend, whose fatherly love most closely surrounds His little children. She missed her mother's help to understand and rule herself, but having been taught where to look, she did her best to find the way and walk in it confidingly. But, Amy was a young pilgrim, and just now her burden seemed very heavy. She tried to forget herself, to keep cheerful, and be satisfied with doing right, though no one saw or praised her for it. In her first effort at being very, very good, she decided to make her will, as Aunt March had done, so that if she *did* fall ill and die, her possessions might be justly and generously divided. It cost her a pang even to think of giving up the little treasures which in her eyes were as precious as the old lady's jewels.

During one of her play hours she wrote out the important document as well as she could, with some help from Esther as to certain legal terms, and when the good-natured Frenchwoman had signed her name, Amy felt relieved and laid it by to show Laurie, whom she wanted as a second witness. As it was a rainy day, she went upstairs to amuse herself in one of the large chambers, and took Polly with her for company. In this room there was a wardrobe full of old-fashioned costumes with which Esther allowed her to play, and it was her favorite amusement to array herself in the faded brocades, and parade up and down before the long mirror, making stately curtsies, and sweeping her train about with a rustle which delighted her ears. So busy was she on this day that she did not hear Laurie's ring nor see his face peeping in at her as she gravely promenaded to and fro, flirting her fan and tossing her head, on which she wore a great pink turban, contrasting oddly with her blue brocade dress and yellow quilted petticoat. She was obliged to walk carefully, for she had on high-heeled shoes, and, as Laurie told Jo afterward, it was a comical sight to see her mince along in her gay suit, with Polly sidling and bridling just behind her, imitating her as well as he could, and occasionally stopping to laugh or exclaim, "Ain't we fine? Get along, you fright! Hold your tongue! Kiss me, dear! Ha! Ha!"

Having with difficulty restrained an explosion of merriment, lest it should offend her majesty, Laurie tapped and was graciously received.

"Sit down and rest while I put these things away, then I want to consult you about a very serious matter," said Amy, when she had shown her splendor and driven Polly into a corner. "That bird is the trial of my life," she continued, removing the pink mountain from her head, while Laurie seated himself astride a chair. "Yesterday, when Aunt was asleep and I was trying to be as still as a mouse, Polly began to squall and flap about in his cage, so I went to let him out, and found a big spider there. I poked it out, and it ran under the bookcase. Polly marched straight after it, stooped down and peeped under the bookcase, saying, in his funny way, with a cock of his eye, 'Come out and take a walk, my dear.' I couldn't help laughing, which made Poll swear, and Aunt woke up and scolded us both."

"Did the spider accept the old fellow's invitation?" asked Laurie, yawning.

"Yes, out it came, and away ran Polly, frightened to death, and scrambled up on Aunt's chair, calling out, 'Catch her! Catch her! Catch her!' as I chased the spider."

"That's a lie! Oh, lor!" cried the parrot, pecking at Laurie's toes.

"I'd wring your neck if you were mine, you old torment," cried Laurie, shaking his fist at the bird, who put his head on one side and gravely croaked, "Allyluyer! bless your buttons, dear!"

"Now I'm ready," said Amy, shutting the wardrobe and taking a piece of paper out of her pocket. "I want you to read that, please, and tell me if it is legal and right. I felt I ought to do it, for life is uncertain and I don't want any ill feeling over my tomb."

Laurie bit his lips, and turning a little from the pensive speaker, read the following document, with praiseworthy gravity, considering the spelling:

MY LAST WILL AND TESTIMENT.

> I, Amy Curtis March, being in my sane mind, go give and bequeethe all my earthly property—viz. to wit:—namely
>
> To my father, my best pictures, sketches, maps, and works of art, including frames. Also my $100, to do what he likes with.
>
> To my mother, all my clothes, except the blue apron with pockets—also my likeness, and my medal, with much love.
>
> To my dear sister Margaret, I give my turkquoise ring (if I get it), also my green box with the doves on it, also my piece of real lace for her neck, and my sketch of her as a memorial of her "little girl."
>
> To Jo I leave my breastpin, the one mended with sealing wax, also my bronze inkstand—she lost the cover—and my most precious plaster rabbit, because I am sorry I burned up her story.

To Beth (if she lives after me) I give my dolls and the little bureau, my fan, my linen collars and my new slippers if she can wear them being thin when she gets well. And I herewith also leave her my regret that I ever made fun of old Joanna.

To my friend and neighbor Theodore Laurence I bequeethe my paper mashay portfolio, my clay model of a horse though he did say it hadn't any neck. Also in return for his great kindness in the hour of affliction any one of my artistic works he likes, Noter Dame is the best.

To our venerable benefactor Mr. Laurence I leave my purple box with a looking glass in the cover which will be nice for his pens and remind him of the departed girl who thanks him for his favors to her family, especially Beth.

I wish my favorite playmate Kitty Bryant to have the blue silk apron and my gold-bead ring with a kiss.

To Hannah I give the bandbox she wanted and all the patchwork I leave hoping she "will remember me, when it you see."

And now having disposed of my most valuable property I hope all will be satisfied and not blame the dead. I forgive everyone, and trust we may all meet when the trump shall sound. Amen.

To this will and testiment I set my hand and seal on this 20th day of Nov. Anni Domino 1861.

AMY CURTIS MARCH

Witnesses:
ESTELLE VALNOR,
THEODORE LAURENCE.

The last name was written in pencil, and Amy explained that he was to rewrite it in ink and seal it up for her properly.

"What put it into your head? Did anyone tell you about Beth's giving away her things?" asked Laurie soberly, as Amy laid a bit of red tape, with sealing wax, a taper, and a standish before him.

She explained and then asked anxiously, "What about Beth?"

"I'm sorry I spoke, but as I did, I'll tell you. She felt so ill one day that she told Jo she wanted to give her piano to Meg, her cats to you, and the poor old doll to Jo, who would love it for her sake. She was sorry she had so little to give, and left locks of hair to the rest of us, and her best love to Grandpa. *She* never thought of a will."

Laurie was signing and sealing as he spoke, and did not look up till a great tear dropped on the paper. Amy's face was full of trouble, but she only said, "Don't people put sort of postscripts to their wills, sometimes?"

"Yes, 'codicils,' they call them."

"Put one in mine then—that I wish *all* my curls cut off, and given round to my friends. I forgot it, but I want it done though it will spoil my looks."

Laurie added it, smiling at Amy's last and greatest sacrifice. Then he amused her for an hour, and was much interested in all her trials. But when he came to go, Amy held him back to whisper with trembling lips, "Is there really any danger about Beth?"

"I'm afraid there is, but we must hope for the best, so don't cry, dear." And Laurie put his arm about her with a brotherly gesture which was very comforting.

When he had gone, she went to her little chapel, and sitting in the twilight, prayed for Beth, with streaming tears and an aching heart, feeling that a million turquoise rings would not console her for the loss of her gentle little sister.

CHAPTER XX

CONFIDENTIAL

I don't think I have any words in which to tell the meeting of the mother and daughters. Such hours are beautiful to live, but very hard to describe, so I will leave it to the imagination of my readers, merely saying that the house was full of genuine happiness, and that Meg's tender hope was realized, for when Beth woke from that long, healing sleep, the first objects on which her eyes fell were the little rose and Mother's face. Too weak to wonder at anything, she only smiled and nestled close in the loving arms about her, feeling that the hungry longing was satisfied at last. Then she slept again, and the girls waited upon their mother, for she would not unclasp the thin hand which clung to hers even in sleep.

Hannah had "dished up" an astonishing breakfast for the traveler, finding it impossible to vent her excitement in any other way, and Meg and Jo fed their mother like dutiful young storks, while they listened to her whispered account of Father's state, Mr. Brooke's promise to stay and nurse him, the delays which the storm occasioned on the homeward journey, and the unspeakable comfort Laurie's hopeful face had given her when she arrived, worn out with fatigue, anxiety, and cold.

What a strange yet pleasant day that was. So brilliant and gay without, for all the world seemed abroad to welcome the first snow. So quiet and reposeful within, for everyone slept, spent with watching, and a Sabbath stillness reigned through the house, while nodding Hannah mounted guard at the door. With a blissful sense of burdens lifted off, Meg and Jo closed their weary eyes, and lay at rest, like storm-beaten boats safe at anchor in a quiet harbor. Mrs. March would not leave Beth's side, but rested in the big chair, waking often to look at, touch, and brood over her child, like a miser over some recovered treasure.

Laurie meanwhile posted off to comfort Amy, and told his story so well that Aunt March actually "sniffed" herself, and never once said "I told you so." Amy came out so strong on this occasion that I think the good thoughts in the little chapel really began to bear fruit. She dried her tears quickly, restrained her impatience to see her mother, and never even thought of the turquoise ring, when the old lady heartily agreed in Laurie's opinion, that she behaved "like a capital little woman." Even Polly seemed impressed, for he called her a good girl, blessed her buttons, and begged her to "come and take a walk, dear", in his most affable tone. She would very gladly have gone out to enjoy the bright wintry weather, but discovering that Laurie was dropping with sleep in spite of manful efforts to conceal the fact, she persuaded him to rest on the sofa, while she wrote a note to her mother. She was a long time about it, and when she returned, he was stretched out with both arms under his head, sound asleep, while Aunt March had pulled down the curtains and sat doing nothing in an unusual fit of benignity.

After a while, they began to think he was not going to wake up till night, and I'm not sure that he would, had he not been effectually roused by Amy's cry of joy at sight of her mother. There probably were a good many happy little girls in and about the city that day, but it is my private opinion that Amy was the happiest of all, when she sat in her mother's lap and told her trials, receiving consolation and compensation in the shape of approving smiles and fond caresses. They were alone together in the chapel, to which her mother did not object when its purpose was explained to her.

"On the contrary, I like it very much, dear," looking from the dusty rosary to the well-worn little book, and the lovely picture with its garland of evergreen. "It is an excellent plan to have some place where we can go to be quiet, when things vex or grieve us. There are a good many hard times in this life of ours, but we can always bear them if we ask help in the right way. I think my little girl is learning this."

"Yes, Mother, and when I go home I mean to have a corner in the big closet to put my books and the copy of that picture which I've tried to make. The woman's face is not good, it's too beautiful for me to draw, but the baby is done better, and I love it very much. I like to think He was a little child once, for then I don't seem so far away, and that helps me."

As Amy pointed to the smiling Christ child on his Mother's knee, Mrs. March saw something on the lifted hand that made her smile. She said nothing, but Amy understood the look, and after a minute's pause, she added gravely, "I wanted to speak to you about this, but I forgot it. Aunt gave me the ring today. She called me to her and kissed me, and put it on my finger, and said I was a credit to her, and she'd like to keep me always. She gave that funny guard to keep the turquoise on, as it's too big. I'd like to wear them Mother, can I?"

"They are very pretty, but I think you're rather too young for such ornaments, Amy," said Mrs. March, looking at the plump little hand, with the band of sky-blue stones on the forefinger, and the quaint guard formed of two tiny golden hands clasped together.

"I'll try not to be vain," said Amy. "I don't think I like it only because it's so pretty, but I want to wear it as the girl in the story wore her bracelet, to remind me of something."

"Do you mean Aunt March?" asked her mother, laughing.

"No, to remind me not to be selfish." Amy looked so earnest and sincere about it that her mother stopped laughing, and listened respectfully to the little plan.

"I've thought a great deal lately about my 'bundle of naughties,' and being selfish is the largest one in it, so I'm going to try hard to cure it, if I can. Beth isn't selfish, and that's the reason everyone loves her and feels so bad at the thoughts of losing her. People wouldn't feel so bad about me if I was sick, and I don't deserve to have them, but I'd like to be loved and missed by a great many friends, so I'm going to try and be like Beth all I can. I'm apt to forget my resolutions, but if I had something always about me to remind me, I guess I should do better. May we try this way?"

"Yes, but I have more faith in the corner of the big closet. Wear your ring, dear, and do your best. I think you will prosper, for the sincere wish to be good is half the battle. Now I must go back to Beth. Keep up your heart, little daughter, and we will soon have you home again."

That evening while Meg was writing to her father to report the traveler's safe arrival, Jo slipped upstairs into Beth's room, and finding her mother in her usual place, stood a minute twisting her fingers in her hair, with a worried gesture and an undecided look.

"What is it, deary?" asked Mrs. March, holding out her hand, with a face which invited confidence.

"I want to tell you something, Mother."

"About Meg?"

"How quickly you guessed! Yes, it's about her, and though it's a little thing, it fidgets me."

"Beth is asleep. Speak low, and tell me all about it. That Moffat hasn't been here, I hope?" asked Mrs. March rather sharply.

"No. I should have shut the door in his face if he had," said Jo, settling herself on the floor at her mother's feet. "Last summer Meg left a pair of gloves over at the Laurences' and only one was returned. We forgot about it, till Teddy told me that Mr. Brooke owned that he liked Meg but didn't dare say so, she was so young and he so poor. Now, isn't it a *dreadful* state of things?"

"Do you think Meg cares for him?" asked Mrs. March, with an anxious look.

"Mercy me! I don't know anything about love and such nonsense!" cried Jo, with a funny mixture of interest and contempt. "In novels, the girls show it by starting and blushing, fainting away, growing thin, and acting like fools. Now Meg does not do anything of the sort. She eats and drinks and sleeps like a sensible creature, she looks straight in my face when I talk about that man, and only blushes a little bit when Teddy jokes about lovers. I forbid him to do it, but he doesn't mind me as he ought."

"Then you fancy that Meg is not interested in John?"

"Who?" cried Jo, staring.

"Mr. Brooke. I call him 'John' now. We fell into the way of doing so at the hospital, and he likes it."

"Oh, dear! I know you'll take his part. He's been good to Father, and you won't send him away, but let Meg marry him, if she wants to. Mean thing! To go petting Papa and helping you, just to wheedle you into liking him." And Jo pulled her hair again with a wrathful tweak.

"My dear, don't get angry about it, and I will tell you how it happened. John went with me at Mr. Laurence's request, and was so devoted to poor Father that we couldn't help getting fond of him. He was perfectly open and honorable about Meg, for he told us he loved her, but would earn a comfortable home before he asked her to marry him. He only wanted our leave to love her and work for her, and the right to make her love him if he could. He is a truly excellent young man, and we could not refuse to listen to him, but I will not consent to Meg's engaging herself so young."

"Of course not. It would be idiotic! I knew there was mischief brewing. I felt it, and now it's worse than I imagined. I just wish I could marry Meg myself, and keep her safe in the family."

This odd arrangement made Mrs. March smile, but she said gravely, "Jo, I confide in you and don't wish you to say anything to Meg yet. When John comes back, and I see them together, I can judge better of her feelings toward him."

"She'll see his in those handsome eyes that she talks about, and then it will be all up with her. She's got such a soft heart, it will melt like butter in the sun if anyone looks sentimentally at her. She read the short reports he sent more than she did your letters, and pinched me when I spoke of it, and likes brown eyes, and doesn't think John an ugly name, and she'll go and fall in love, and there's an end of peace and fun, and cozy times together. I see it all! They'll go lovering around the house, and we shall have to dodge. Meg will be absorbed and no good to me any more. Brooke will scratch up a fortune somehow, carry her off, and make a hole in the family, and I shall break my heart, and everything will be abominably uncomfortable. Oh, dear me! Why weren't we all boys, then there wouldn't be any bother."

Jo leaned her chin on her knees in a disconsolate attitude and shook her fist at the reprehensible John. Mrs. March sighed, and Jo looked up with an air of relief.

"You don't like it, Mother? I'm glad of it. Let's send him about his business, and not tell Meg a word of it, but all be happy together as we always have been."

"I did wrong to sigh, Jo. It is natural and right you should all go to homes of your own in time, but I do want to keep my girls as long as I can, and I am sorry that this happened so soon, for Meg is only seventeen and it will be some years before John can make a home for her. Your father and I have agreed that she shall not bind herself in any way, nor be married, before twenty. If she and John love one another, they can wait, and test the love by doing so. She is conscientious, and I have no fear of her treating him unkindly. My pretty, tenderhearted girl! I hope things will go happily with her."

"Hadn't you rather have her marry a rich man?" asked Jo, as her mother's voice faltered a little over the last words.

"Money is a good and useful thing, Jo, and I hope my girls will never feel the need of it too bitterly, nor be tempted by too much. I should like to know that John was firmly established in some good business, which gave him an income large enough to keep free from debt and make Meg comfortable. I'm not ambitious for a splendid fortune, a fashionable position, or a great name for my girls. If rank and money come with love and virtue, also, I should accept them gratefully, and enjoy your good fortune, but I know, by experience, how much genuine happiness can be had in a plain little house, where the daily bread is earned, and some privations give sweetness to the few pleasures. I am content to see Meg begin humbly, for if I am not mistaken, she will be rich in the possession of a good man's heart, and that is better than a fortune."

"I understand, Mother, and quite agree, but I'm disappointed about Meg, for I'd planned to have her marry Teddy by-and-by and sit in the lap of luxury all her days. Wouldn't it be nice?" asked Jo, looking up with a brighter face.

"He is younger than she, you know," began Mrs. March, but Jo broke in—

"Only a little, he's old for his age, and tall, and can be quite grown-up in his manners if he likes. Then he's rich and generous and good, and loves us all, and *I* say it's a pity my plan is spoiled."

"I'm afraid Laurie is hardly grown-up enough for Meg, and altogether too much of a weathercock just now for anyone to depend on. Don't make plans, Jo, but let time and their own hearts mate your friends. We can't meddle safely in such matters, and had better not get 'romantic rubbish' as you call it, into our heads, lest it spoil our friendship."

"Well, I won't, but I hate to see things going all crisscross and getting snarled up, when a pull here and a snip there would straighten it out. I wish wearing flatirons on our heads would keep us from growing up. But buds will be roses, and kittens cats, more's the pity!"

"What's that about flatirons and cats?" asked Meg, as she crept into the room with the finished letter in her hand.

"Only one of my stupid speeches. I'm going to bed. Come, Peggy," said Jo, unfolding herself like an animated puzzle.

"Quite right, and beautifully written. Please add that I send my love to John," said Mrs. March, as she glanced over the letter and gave it back.

"Do you call him 'John'?" asked Meg, smiling, with her innocent eyes looking down into her mother's.

"Yes, he has been like a son to us, and we are very fond of him," replied Mrs. March, returning the look with a keen one.

"I'm glad of that, he is so lonely. Good night, Mother, dear. It is so inexpressibly comfortable to have you here," was Meg's answer.

The kiss her mother gave her was a very tender one, and as she went away, Mrs. March said, with a mixture of satisfaction and regret, "She does not love John yet, but will soon learn to."

CHAPTER XXI

LAURIE MAKES MISCHIEF, AND JO MAKES PEACE

Jo's face was a study next day, for the secret rather weighed upon her, and she found it hard not to look mysterious and important. Meg observed it, but did not trouble herself to make inquiries, for she had learned that the best way to manage Jo was by the law of contraries, so she felt sure of being told everything if she did not ask. She was rather surprised, therefore, when the silence remained unbroken, and Jo assumed a patronizing air, which decidedly aggravated Meg, who in turn assumed an air of dignified reserve and devoted herself to her mother. This left Jo to her own devices, for Mrs. March had taken her place as nurse, and bade her rest, exercise, and amuse herself after her long confinement. Amy being gone, Laurie was her only refuge, and much as she enjoyed his society, she rather dreaded him just then, for he was an incorrigible tease, and she feared he would coax the secret from her.

She was quite right, for the mischief-loving lad no sooner suspected a mystery than he set himself to find it out, and led Jo a trying life of it. He wheedled, bribed, ridiculed, threatened, and scolded; affected indifference, that he might surprise the truth from her; declared he knew, then that he didn't care; and at last, by dint of perseverance, he satisfied himself that it concerned Meg and Mr. Brooke. Feeling indignant that he was not taken into his tutor's confidence, he set his wits to work to devise some proper retaliation for the slight.

Meg meanwhile had apparently forgotten the matter and was absorbed in preparations for her father's return, but all of a sudden a change seemed to come over her, and, for a day or two, she was quite unlike herself. She started when spoken to, blushed when looked at, was very quiet, and sat over her sewing, with a timid, troubled look on her face. To her mother's inquiries she answered that she was quite well, and Jo's she silenced by begging to be let alone.

"She feels it in the air—love, I mean—and she's going very fast.

She's got most of the symptoms—is twittery and cross, doesn't eat, lies awake, and mopes in corners. I caught her singing that song he gave her, and once she said 'John,' as you do, and then turned as red as a poppy. Whatever shall we do?" said Jo, looking ready for any measures, however violent.

"Nothing but wait. Let her alone, be kind and patient, and Father's coming will settle everything," replied her mother.

"Here's a note to you, Meg, all sealed up. How odd! Teddy never seals mine," said Jo next day, as she distributed the contents of the little post office.

Mrs. March and Jo were deep in their own affairs, when a sound from Meg made them look up to see her staring at her note with a frightened face.

"My child, what is it?" cried her mother, running to her, while Jo tried to take the paper which had done the mischief.

"It's all a mistake, he didn't send it. Oh, Jo, how could you do it?" and Meg hid her face in her hands, crying as if her heart were quite broken.

"Me! I've done nothing! What's she talking about?" cried Jo, bewildered.

Meg's mild eyes kindled with anger as she pulled a crumpled note from her pocket and threw it at Jo, saying reproachfully, "You wrote it, and that bad boy helped you. How could you be so rude, so mean, and cruel to us both?"

Jo hardly heard her, for she and her mother were reading the note, which was written in a peculiar hand.

> "My Dearest Margaret—
>
> "I can no longer restrain my passion, and must know my fate before I return. I dare not tell your parents yet, but I think they would consent if they knew that we adored one another. Mr. Laurence will help me to some good place, and then, my sweet girl, you will make me happy. I implore you to say nothing to your family yet, but to send one word of hope through Laurie to
>
> "Your devoted John."

"Oh, the little villain! That's the way he meant to pay me for keeping my word to Mother. I'll give him a hearty scolding and bring him over to beg pardon," cried Jo, burning to execute immediate justice. But her mother held her back, saying, with a look she seldom wore—

"Stop, Jo, you must clear yourself first. You have played so many pranks that I am afraid you have had a hand in this."

"On my word, Mother, I haven't! I never saw that note before, and don't know anything about it, as true as I live!" said Jo, so earnestly that they believed her. "If I *had* taken part in it I'd have done it better than this, and have written a sensible note. I should think you'd have known Mr. Brooke wouldn't write such stuff as that," she added, scornfully tossing down the paper.

"It's like his writing," faltered Meg, comparing it with the note in her hand.

"Oh, Meg, you didn't answer it?" cried Mrs. March quickly.

"Yes, I did!" and Meg hid her face again, overcome with shame.

"Here's a scrape! *Do* let me bring that wicked boy over to explain and be lectured. I can't rest till I get hold of him." And Jo made for the door again.

"Hush! Let me handle this, for it is worse than I thought. Margaret, tell me the whole story," commanded Mrs. March, sitting down by Meg, yet keeping hold of Jo, lest she should fly off.

"I received the first letter from Laurie, who didn't look as if he knew anything about it," began Meg, without looking up. "I was worried at first and meant to tell you, then I remembered how you liked Mr. Brooke, so I thought you wouldn't mind if I kept my little secret for a few days. I'm so silly that I liked to think no one knew, and while I was deciding what to say, I felt like the girls in books, who have such things to do. Forgive me, Mother, I'm paid for my silliness now. I never can look him in the face again."

"What did you say to him?" asked Mrs. March.

"I only said I was too young to do anything about it yet, that I didn't wish to have secrets from you, and he must speak to father. I was very grateful for his kindness, and would be his friend, but nothing more, for a long while."

Mrs. March smiled, as if well pleased, and Jo clapped her hands, exclaiming, with a laugh, "You are almost equal to Caroline Percy, who was a pattern of prudence! Tell on, Meg. What did he say to that?"

"He writes in a different way entirely, telling me that he never sent any love letter at all, and is very sorry that my roguish sister, Jo, should take liberties with our names. It's very kind and respectful, but think how dreadful for me!"

Meg leaned against her mother, looking the image of despair, and Jo tramped about the room, calling Laurie names. All of a sudden she stopped, caught up the two notes, and after looking at them closely, said decidedly, "I don't believe Brooke ever saw either of these letters. Teddy wrote both, and keeps yours to crow over me with because I wouldn't tell him my secret."

"Don't have any secrets, Jo. Tell it to Mother and keep out of trouble, as I should have done," said Meg warningly.

"Bless you, child! Mother told me."

"That will do, Jo. I'll comfort Meg while you go and get Laurie. I shall sift the matter to the bottom, and put a stop to such pranks at once."

Away ran Jo, and Mrs. March gently told Meg Mr. Brooke's real feelings. "Now, dear, what are your own? Do you love him enough to wait till he can make a home for you, or will you keep yourself quite free for the present?"

"I've been so scared and worried, I don't want to have anything to do with lovers for a long while, perhaps never," answered Meg petulantly. "If John doesn't know anything about this nonsense, don't tell him, and make Jo and Laurie hold their tongues. I won't be deceived and plagued and made a fool of. It's a shame!"

Seeing Meg's usually gentle temper was roused and her pride hurt by this mischievous joke, Mrs. March soothed her by promises of entire silence and great discretion for the future. The instant Laurie's step was heard in the hall, Meg fled into the study, and Mrs. March received the culprit alone. Jo had not told him why he was wanted, fearing he wouldn't come, but he knew the minute he saw Mrs. March's face, and stood twirling his hat with a guilty air which convicted him at once. Jo was dismissed, but chose to march up and down the hall like a sentinel, having some fear that the prisoner might bolt. The sound of voices in the parlor rose and fell for half an hour, but what happened during that interview the girls never knew.

When they were called in, Laurie was standing by their mother with such a penitent face that Jo forgave him on the spot, but did not think it wise to betray the fact. Meg received his humble apology, and was much comforted by the assurance that Brooke knew nothing of the joke.

"I'll never tell him to my dying day—wild horses shan't drag it out of me, so you'll forgive me, Meg, and I'll do anything to show how out-and-out sorry I am," he added, looking very much ashamed of himself.

"I'll try, but it was a very ungentlemanly thing to do, I didn't think you could be so sly and malicious, Laurie," replied Meg, trying to hide her maidenly confusion under a gravely reproachful air.

"It was altogether abominable, and I don't deserve to be spoken to for a month, but you will, though, won't you?" And Laurie folded his hands together with such and imploring gesture, as he spoke in his irresistibly persuasive tone, that it was impossible to frown upon him in spite of his scandalous behavior. Meg pardoned him, and Mrs. March's grave face relaxed, in spite of her efforts to keep sober, when she heard him declare that he would atone for his sins by all sorts of penances, and abase himself like a worm before the injured damsel.

Jo stood aloof; meanwhile, trying to harden her heart against him, and succeeding only in primming up her face into an expression of entire disapprobation. Laurie looked at her once or twice, but as she showed no sign of relenting, he felt injured, and turned his back on her till the others were done with him, when he made her a low bow and walked off without a word.

As soon as he had gone, she wished she had been more forgiving, and when Meg and her mother went upstairs, she felt lonely and longed for Teddy. After resisting for some time, she yielded to the impulse, and armed with a book to return, went over to the big house.

"Is Mr. Laurence in?" asked Jo, of a housemaid, who was coming downstairs.

"Yes, Miss, but I don't believe he's seeable just yet."

"Why not? Is he ill?"

"La, no Miss, but he's had a scene with Mr. Laurie, who is in one of his tantrums about something, which vexes the old gentleman, so I dursn't go nigh him."

"Where is Laurie?"

"Shut up in his room, and he won't answer, though I've been a-tapping. I don't know what's to become of the dinner, for it's ready, and there's no one to eat it."

"I'll go and see what the matter is. I'm not afraid of either of them."

Up went Jo, and knocked smartly on the door of Laurie's little study.

"Stop that, or I'll open the door and make you!" called out the young gentleman in a threatening tone.

Jo immediately knocked again. The door flew open, and in she bounced before Laurie could recover from his surprise. Seeing that he really *was* out of temper, Jo, who knew how to manage him, assumed a contrite expression, and going artistically down upon her knees, said meekly, "Please forgive me for being so cross. I came to make it up, and can't go away till I have."

"It's all right. Get up, and don't be a goose, Jo," was the cavalier reply to her petition.

"Thank you, I will. Could I ask what's the matter? You don't look exactly easy in your mind."

"I've been shaken, and I won't bear it!" growled Laurie indignantly.

"Who did it?" demanded Jo.

"Grandfather. If it had been anyone else I'd have—" And the injured youth finished his sentence by an energetic gesture of the right arm.

"That's nothing. I often shake you, and you don't mind," said Jo soothingly.

"Pooh! You're a girl, and it's fun, but I'll allow no man to shake me!"

"I don't think anyone would care to try it, if you looked as much like a thundercloud as you do now. Why were you treated so?"

"Just because I wouldn't say what your mother wanted me for. I'd promised not to tell, and of course I wasn't going to break my word."

"Couldn't you satisfy your grandpa in any other way?"

"No, he *would* have the truth, the whole truth, and nothing but the truth. I'd have told my part of the scrape, if I could without bringing Meg in. As I couldn't, I held my tongue, and bore the scolding till the old gentleman collared me. Then I bolted, for fear I should forget myself."

"It wasn't nice, but he's sorry, I know, so go down and make up. I'll help you."

"Hanged if I do! I'm not going to be lectured and pummelled by everyone, just for a bit of a frolic. I was sorry about Meg, and begged pardon like a man, but I won't do it again, when I wasn't in the wrong."

"He didn't know that."

"He ought to trust me, and not act as if I was a baby. It's no use, Jo, he's got to learn that I'm able to take care of myself, and don't need anyone's apron string to hold on by."

"What pepper pots you are!" sighed Jo. "How do you mean to settle this affair?"

"Well, he ought to beg pardon, and believe me when I say I can't tell him what the fuss's about."

"Bless you! He won't do that."

"I won't go down till he does."

"Now, Teddy, be sensible. Let it pass, and I'll explain what I can. You can't stay here, so what's the use of being melodramatic?"

"I don't intend to stay here long, anyway. I'll slip off and take a journey somewhere, and when Grandpa misses me he'll come round fast enough."

"I dare say, but you ought not to go and worry him."

"Don't preach. I'll go to Washington and see Brooke. It's gay there, and I'll enjoy myself after the troubles."

"What fun you'd have! I wish I could run off too," said Jo, forgetting her part of mentor in lively visions of martial life at the capital.

"Come on, then! Why not? You go and surprise your father, and I'll stir up old Brooke. It would be a glorious joke. Let's do it, Jo. We'll leave a letter saying we are all right, and trot off at once. I've got money enough. It will do you good, and no harm, as you go to your father."

For a moment Jo looked as if she would agree, for wild as the plan was, it just suited her. She was tired of care and confinement, longed for change, and thoughts of her father blended temptingly with the novel charms of camps and hospitals, liberty and fun. Her eyes kindled as they turned wistfully toward the window, but they fell on the old house opposite, and she shook her head with sorrowful decision.

"If I was a boy, we'd run away together, and have a capital time, but as I'm a miserable girl, I must be proper and stop at home. Don't tempt me, Teddy, it's a crazy plan."

"That's the fun of it," began Laurie, who had got a willful fit on him and was possessed to break out of bounds in some way.

"Hold your tongue!" cried Jo, covering her ears. "'Prunes and prisms' are my doom, and I may as well make up my mind to it. I came here to moralize, not to hear things that make me skip to think of."

"I know Meg would wet-blanket such a proposal, but I thought you had more spirit," began Laurie insinuatingly.

"Bad boy, be quiet! Sit down and think of your own sins, don't go making me add to mine. If I get your grandpa to apologize for the shaking, will you give up running away?" asked Jo seriously.

"Yes, but you won't do it," answered Laurie, who wished to make up, but felt that his outraged dignity must be appeased first.

"If I can manage the young one, I can the old one," muttered Jo, as she walked away, leaving Laurie bent over a railroad map with his head propped up on both hands.

"Come in!" and Mr. Laurence's gruff voice sounded gruffer than ever, as Jo tapped at his door.

"It's only me, Sir, come to return a book," she said blandly, as she entered.

"Want any more?" asked the old gentleman, looking grim and vexed, but trying not to show it.

"Yes, please. I like old Sam so well, I think I'll try the second volume," returned Jo, hoping to propitiate him by accepting a second dose of Boswell's *Johnson*, as he had recommended that lively work.

The shaggy eyebrows unbent a little as he rolled the steps toward the shelf where the Johnsonian literature was placed. Jo skipped up, and sitting on the top step, affected to be searching for her book, but was really wondering how best to introduce the dangerous object of her visit. Mr. Laurence seemed to suspect that something was brewing in her mind, for after taking several brisk turns about the room, he faced round on her, speaking so abruptly that *Rasselas* tumbled face downward on the floor.

"What has that boy been about? Don't try to shield him. I know he has been in mischief by the way he acted when he came home. I can't get a word from him, and when I threatened to shake the truth out of him he bolted upstairs and locked himself into his room."

"He did wrong, but we forgave him, and all promised not to say a word to anyone," began Jo reluctantly.

"That won't do. He shall not shelter himself behind a promise from you softhearted girls. If he's done anything amiss, he shall confess, beg pardon, and be punished. Out with it, Jo. I won't be kept in the dark."

Mr. Laurence looked so alarming and spoke so sharply that Jo would have gladly run away, if she could, but she was perched aloft on the steps, and he stood at the foot, a lion in the path, so she had to stay and brave it out.

"Indeed, Sir, I cannot tell. Mother forbade it. Laurie has confessed, asked pardon, and been punished quite enough. We don't keep silence to shield him, but someone else, and it will make more trouble if you interfere. Please don't. It was partly my fault, but it's all right now. So let's forget it, and talk about the *Rambler* or something pleasant."

"Hang the *Rambler*! Come down and give me your word that this harum-scarum boy of mine hasn't done anything ungrateful or impertinent. If he has, after all your kindness to him, I'll thrash him with my own hands."

The threat sounded awful, but did not alarm Jo, for she knew the irascible old gentleman would never lift a finger against his grandson, whatever he might say to the contrary. She obediently descended, and made as light of the prank as she could without betraying Meg or forgetting the truth.

"Hum—ha—well, if the boy held his tongue because he promised, and not from obstinacy, I'll forgive him. He's a stubborn fellow and hard to manage," said Mr. Laurence, rubbing up his hair till it looked as if he had been out in a gale, and smoothing the frown from his brow with an air of relief.

"So am I, but a kind word will govern me when all the king's horses and all the king's men couldn't," said Jo, trying to say a kind word for her friend, who seemed to get out of one scrape only to fall into another.

"You think I'm not kind to him, hey?" was the sharp answer.

"Oh, dear no, Sir. You are rather too kind sometimes, and then just a trifle hasty when he tries your patience. Don't you think you are?"

Jo was determined to have it out now, and tried to look quite placid, though she quaked a little after her bold speech. To her great relief and surprise, the old gentleman only threw his spectacles onto the table with a rattle and exclaimed frankly—

"You're right, girl, I am! I love the boy, but he tries my patience past bearing, and I know how it will end, if we go on so."

"I'll tell you, he'll run away." Jo was sorry for that speech the minute it was made. She meant to warn him that Laurie would not bear much restraint, and hoped he would be more forebearing with the lad.

Mr. Laurence's ruddy face changed suddenly, and he sat down, with a troubled glance at the picture of a handsome man, which hung over his table. It was Laurie's father, who had run away in his youth, and married against the imperious old man's will. Jo fancied he remembered and regretted the past, and she wished she had held her tongue.

"He won't do it unless he is very much worried, and only threatens it sometimes, when he gets tired of studying. I often think I should like to, especially since my hair was cut, so if you ever miss us, you may advertise for two boys and look among the ships bound for India."

She laughed as she spoke, and Mr. Laurence looked relieved, evidently taking the whole as a joke.

"You hussy, how dare you talk in that way? Where's your respect for me, and your proper bringing up? Bless the boys and girls! What torments they are, yet we can't do without them," he said, pinching her cheeks good-humoredly. "Go and bring that boy down to his dinner, tell him it's all right, and advise him not to put on tragedy airs with his grandfather. I won't bear it."

"He won't come, Sir. He feels badly because you didn't believe him when he said he couldn't tell. I think the shaking hurt his feelings very much."

Jo tried to look pathetic but must have failed, for Mr. Laurence began to laugh, and she knew the day was won.

"I'm sorry for that, and ought to thank him for not shaking me, I suppose. What the dickens does the fellow expect?" and the old gentleman looked a trifle ashamed of his own testiness.

"If I were you, I'd write him an apology, Sir. He says he won't come down till he has one, and talks about Washington, and goes on in an absurd way. A formal apology will make him see how foolish he is, and bring him down quite amiable. Try it. He likes fun, and this way is better than talking. I'll carry it up, and teach him his duty."

Mr. Laurence gave her a sharp look, and put on his spectacles, saying slowly, "You're a sly puss, but I don't mind being managed by you and Beth. Here, give me a bit of paper, and let us have done with this nonsense."

The note was written in the terms which one gentleman would use to another after offering some deep insult. Jo dropped a kiss on the top of Mr. Laurence's bald head, and ran up to slip the apology under Laurie's door, advising him through the keyhole to be submissive, decorous, and a few other agreeable impossibilities. Finding the door locked again, she left the note to do its work, and was going quietly away, when the young gentleman slid down the banisters, and waited for her at the bottom, saying, with his most virtuous expression of countenance, "What a good fellow you are, Jo! Did you get blown up?" he added, laughing.

"No, he was pretty mild, on the whole."

"Ah! I got it all round. Even you cast me off over there, and I felt just ready to go to the deuce," he began apologetically.

"Don't talk that way, turn over a new leaf and begin again, Teddy, my son." "I keep turning over new leaves, and spoiling them, as I used to spoil my copybooks, and I make so many beginnings there never will be an end," he said dolefully.

"Go and eat your dinner, you'll feel better after it. Men always croak when they are hungry," and Jo whisked out at the front door after that.

"That's a 'label' on my 'sect,'" answered Laurie, quoting Amy, as he went to partake of humble pie dutifully with his grandfather, who was quite saintly in temper and overwhelmingly respectful in manner all the rest of the day.

Everyone thought the matter ended and the little cloud blown over, but the mischief was done, for though others forgot it, Meg remembered. She never alluded to a certain person, but she thought of him a good deal, dreamed dreams more than ever, and once Jo, rummaging her sister's desk for stamps, found a bit of paper scribbled over with the words, "Mrs. John Brooke," whereat she groaned tragically and cast it into the fire, feeling that Laurie's prank had hastened the evil day for her.

CHAPTER XXII

PLEASANT MEADOWS

Like sunshine after a storm were the peaceful weeks which followed. The invalids improved rapidly, and Mr. March began to talk of returning early in the new year. Beth was soon able to lie on the study sofa all day, amusing herself with the well-beloved cats at first, and in time with doll's sewing, which had fallen sadly behind-hand. Her once active limbs were so stiff and feeble that Jo took her for a daily airing about the house in her strong arms. Meg cheerfully blackened and burned her white hands cooking delicate messes for "the dear," while Amy, a loyal slave of the ring, celebrated her return by giving away as many of her treasures as she could prevail on her sisters to accept.

As Christmas approached, the usual mysteries began to haunt the house, and Jo frequently convulsed the family by proposing utterly impossible or magnificently absurd ceremonies, in honor of this unusually merry Christmas. Laurie was equally impracticable, and would have had bonfires, skyrockets, and triumphal arches, if he had had his own way. After many skirmishes and snubbings, the ambitious pair were considered effectually quenched and went about with forlorn faces, which were rather belied by explosions of laughter when the two got together.

Several days of unusually mild weather fitly ushered in a splendid Christmas Day. Hannah "felt in her bones" that it was going to be an unusually fine day, and she proved herself a true prophetess, for everybody and everything seemed bound to produce a grand success. To begin with, Mr. March wrote that he should soon be with them, then Beth felt uncommonly well that morning, and, being dressed in her mother's gift—a soft crimson merino wrapper—was borne in high triumph to the window to behold the offering of Jo and Laurie. The Unquenchables had done their best to be worthy of the name, for like elves they had worked by night and conjured up a comical surprise. Out in the garden stood a stately snow maiden, crowned with holly, bearing a basket of fruit and flowers in one hand, a great roll of music in the other, a perfect rainbow of an Afghan round her chilly shoulders, and a Christmas carol issuing from her lips on a pink paper streamer:

THE JUNGFRAU TO BETH

God bless you, dear Queen Bess!
May nothing you dismay,
But health and peace and happiness
Be yours, this Christmas day.

Here's fruit to feed our busy bee,
And flowers for her nose;
Here's music for her pianee,
An afghan for her toes,

A portrait of Joanna, see,
By Raphael No. 2,
Who labored with great industry
To make it fair and true.

Accept a ribbon red, I beg,
For Madam Purrer's tail;
And ice cream made by lovely Peg,—
A Mont Blanc in a pail.

Their dearest love my makers laid
Within my breast of snow:
Accept it, and the Alpine maid,
From Laurie and from Jo.

How Beth laughed when she saw it, how Laurie ran up and down to bring in the gifts, and what ridiculous speeches Jo made as she presented them!

"I'm so full of happiness, that if Father was only here, I couldn't hold one drop more," said Beth, quite sighing with contentment as Jo carried her off to the study to rest after the excitement, and to refresh herself with some of the delicious grapes the "Jungfrau" had sent her.

"So am I," added Jo, slapping the pocket wherein reposed the long-desired *Undine and Sintram*.

"I'm sure I am," echoed Amy, poring over the engraved copy of the Madonna and Child, which her mother had given her in a pretty frame.

"Of course I am!" cried Meg, smoothing the silvery folds of her first silk dress, for Mr. Laurence had insisted on giving it.

"How can *I* be otherwise?" said Mrs. March gratefully, as her eyes went from her husband's letter to Beth's smiling face, and her hand carressed the brooch made of gray and golden, chestnut and dark brown hair, which the girls had just fastened on her breast.

Now and then, in this workaday world, things do happen in the delightful storybook fashion, and what a comfort it is. Half an hour after everyone had said they were so happy they could only hold one drop more, the drop came. Laurie opened the parlor door and popped his head in very quietly. He might just as well have turned a somersault and uttered an Indian war whoop, for his face was so full of suppressed excitement and his voice so treacherously joyful that everyone jumped up, though he only said, in a queer, breathless voice, "Here's another Christmas present for the March family."

Before the words were well out of his mouth, he was whisked away somehow, and in his place appeared a tall man, muffled up to the eyes, leaning on the arm of another tall man, who tried to say something and couldn't. Of course there was a general stampede, and for several minutes everybody seemed to lose their wits, for the strangest things were done, and no one said a word. Mr. March became invisible in the embrace of four pairs of loving arms. Jo disgraced herself by nearly fainting away, and had to be doctored by Laurie in the china closet. Mr. Brooke kissed Meg entirely by mistake, as he somewhat incoherently explained. And Amy, the dignified, tumbled over a stool, and never stopping to get up, hugged and cried over her father's boots in the most touching manner. Mrs. March was the first to recover herself, and held up her hand with a warning, "Hush! Remember Beth!"

But it was too late. The study door flew open, the little red wrapper appeared on the threshold—joy put strength into the feeble limbs—and Beth ran straight into her father's arms. Never mind what happened just after that, for the full hearts overflowed, washing away the bitterness of the past and leaving only the sweetness of the present.

It was not at all romantic, but a hearty laugh set everybody straight again, for Hannah was discovered behind the door, sobbing over the fat turkey, which she had forgotten to put down when she rushed up from the kitchen. As the laugh subsided, Mrs. March began to thank Mr. Brooke for his faithful care of her husband, at which Mr. Brooke suddenly remembered that Mr. March needed rest, and seizing Laurie, he precipitately retired. Then the two invalids were ordered to repose, which they did, by both sitting in one big chair and talking hard.

Mr. March told how he had longed to surprise them, and how, when the fine weather came, he had been allowed by his doctor to take advantage of it, how devoted Brooke had been, and how he was altogether a most estimable and upright young man. Why Mr. March paused a minute just there, and after a glance at Meg, who was violently poking the fire, looked at his wife with an inquiring lift of the eyebrows, I leave you to imagine. Also why Mrs. March gently nodded her head and asked, rather abruptly, if he wouldn't like to have something to eat. Jo saw and understood the look, and she stalked grimly away to get wine and beef tea, muttering to herself as she slammed the door, "I hate estimable young men with brown eyes!"

There never *was* such a Christmas dinner as they had that day. The fat turkey was a sight to behold, when Hannah sent him up, stuffed, browned, and decorated. So was the plum pudding, which melted in one's mouth, likewise the jellies, in which Amy reveled like a fly in a honeypot. Everything turned out well, which was a mercy, Hannah said, "For my mind was that flustered, Mum, that it's a merrycle I didn't roast the pudding, and stuff the turkey with raisins, let alone bilin' of it in a cloth."

Mr. Laurence and his grandson dined with them, also Mr. Brooke—at whom Jo glowered darkly, to Laurie's infinite amusement. Two easy chairs stood side by side at the head of the table, in which sat Beth and her father, feasting modestly on chicken and a little fruit. They drank healths, told stories, sang songs, "reminisced," as the old folks say, and had a thoroughly good time. A sleigh ride had been planned, but the girls would not leave their father, so the guests departed early, and as twilight gathered, the happy family sat together round the fire.

"Just a year ago we were groaning over the dismal Christmas we expected to have. Do you remember?" asked Jo, breaking a short pause which had followed a long conversation about many things.

"Rather a pleasant year on the whole!" said Meg, smiling at the fire, and congratulating herself on having treated Mr. Brooke with dignity.

"I think it's been a pretty hard one," observed Amy, watching the light shine on her ring with thoughtful eyes.

"I'm glad it's over, because we've got you back," whispered Beth, who sat on her father's knee.

"Rather a rough road for you to travel, my little pilgrims,

especially the latter part of it. But you have got on bravely, and I think the burdens are in a fair way to tumble off very soon," said Mr. March, looking with fatherly satisfaction at the four young faces gathered round him.

"How do you know? Did Mother tell you?" asked Jo.

"Not much. Straws show which way the wind blows, and I've made several discoveries today."

"Oh, tell us what they are!" cried Meg, who sat beside him.

"Here is one." And taking up the hand which lay on the arm of his chair, he pointed to the roughened forefinger, a burn on the back, and two or three little hard spots on the palm. "I remember a time when this hand was white and smooth, and your first care was to keep it so. It was very pretty then, but to me it is much prettier now—for in this seeming blemishes I read a little history. A burnt offering has been made to vanity, this hardened palm has earned something better than blisters, and I'm sure the sewing done by these pricked fingers will last a long time, so much good will went into the stitches. Meg, my dear, I value the womanly skill which keeps home happy more than white hands or fashionable accomplishments. I'm proud to shake this good, industrious little hand, and hope I shall not soon be asked to give it away."

If Meg had wanted a reward for hours of patient labor, she received it in the hearty pressure of her father's hand and the approving smile he gave her.

"What about Jo? Please say something nice, for she has tried so hard and been so very, very good to me," said Beth in her father's ear.

He laughed and looked across at the tall girl who sat opposite, with an unusually mild expression in her face.

"In spite of the curly crop, I don't see the 'son Jo' whom I left a year ago," said Mr. March. "I see a young lady who pins her collar straight, laces her boots neatly, and neither whistles, talks slang, nor lies on the rug as she used to do. Her face is rather thin and pale just now, with watching and anxiety, but I like to look at it, for it has grown gentler, and her voice is lower. She doesn't bounce, but moves quietly, and takes care of a certain little person in a motherly way which delights me. I rather miss my wild girl, but if I get a strong, helpful, tenderhearted woman in her place, I shall feel quite satisfied. I don't know whether the shearing sobered our black sheep, but I do know that in all Washington

I couldn't find anything beautiful enough to be bought with the five-and-twenty dollars my good girl sent me."

Jo's keen eyes were rather dim for a minute, and her thin face grew rosy in the firelight as she received her father's praise, feeling that she did deserve a portion of it.

"Now, Beth," said Amy, longing for her turn, but ready to wait.

"There's so little of her, I'm afraid to say much, for fear she will slip away altogether, though she is not so shy as she used to be," began their father cheerfully. But recollecting how nearly he *had* lost her, he held her close, saying tenderly, with her cheek against his own, "I've got you safe, my Beth, and I'll keep you so, please God."

After a minute's silence, he looked down at Amy, who sat on the cricket at his feet, and said, with a caress of the shining hair—

"I observed that Amy took drumsticks at dinner, ran errands for her mother all the afternoon, gave Meg her place tonight, and has waited on every one with patience and good humor. I also observe that she does not fret much nor look in the glass, and has not even mentioned a very pretty ring which she wears, so I conclude that she has learned to think of other people more and of herself less, and has decided to try and mold her character as carefully as she molds her little clay figures. I am glad of this, for though I should be very proud of a graceful statue made by her, I shall be infinitely prouder of a lovable daughter with a talent for making life beautiful to herself and others."

"What are you thinking of, Beth?" asked Jo, when Amy had thanked her father and told about her ring.

"I read in *Pilgrim's Progress* today how, after many troubles, Christian and Hopeful came to a pleasant green meadow where lilies bloomed all year round, and there they rested happily, as we do now, before they went on to their journey's end," answered Beth, adding, as she slipped out of her father's arms and went to the instrument, "It's singing time now, and I want to be in my old place. I'll try to sing the song of the shepherd boy which the Pilgrims heard. I made the music for Father, because he likes the verses."

So, sitting at the dear little piano, Beth softly touched the keys, and in the sweet voice they had never thought to hear again, sang to her own accompaniment the quaint hymn, which was a singularly fitting song for her:

He that is down need fear no fall,
He that is low no pride.
He that is humble ever shall
Have God to be his guide.

I am content with what I have,
Little be it, or much;
And, Lord! Contentment still I crave,
Because Thou savest such.

Fulness to them a burden is,
That go on pilgrimage;
Here little, and hereafter bliss,
Is best from age to age!

CHAPTER XXIII

AUNT MARCH SETTLES THE QUESTION

Like bees swarming after their queen, mother and daughters hovered about Mr. March the next day, neglecting everything to look at, wait upon, and listen to the new invalid, who was in a fair way to be killed by kindness. As he sat propped up in a big chair by Beth's sofa, with the other three close by, and Hannah popping in her head now and then "to peek at the dear man," nothing seemed needed to complete their happiness. But something was needed, and the elder ones felt it, though none confessed the fact. Mr. and Mrs. March looked at one another with an anxious expression, as their eyes followed Meg. Jo had sudden fits of sobriety, and was seen to shake her fist at Mr. Brooke's umbrella, which had been left in the hall. Meg was absent-minded, shy, and silent, started when the bell rang, and colored when John's name was mentioned. Amy said, "Everyone seemed waiting for something, and couldn't settle down, which was queer, since Father was safe at home," and Beth innocently wondered why their neighbors didn't run over as usual.

Laurie went by in the afternoon, and seeing Meg at the window, seemed suddenly possessed with a melodramatic fit, for he fell down on one knee in the snow, beat his breast, tore his hair, and clasped his hands imploringly, as if begging some boon. And when Meg told him to behave himself and go away, he wrung imaginary tears out of his handkerchief, and staggered round the corner as if in utter despair.

"What does the goose mean?" said Meg, laughing and trying to look unconscious.

"He's showing you how your John will go on by-and-by. Touching, isn't it?" answered Jo scornfully.

"Don't say *my John*, it isn't proper or true," but Meg's voice lingered over the words as if they sounded pleasant to her. "Please don't plague me, Jo, I've told you I don't care much about him, and there isn't to be anything said, but we are all to be friendly, and go on as before."

"We can't, for something *has* been said, and Laurie's mischief has spoiled you for me. I see it, and so does Mother. You are not like your old self a bit, and seem ever so far away from me. I don't mean to plague you and will bear it like a man, but I do wish it was all settled. I hate to wait, so if you mean ever to do it, make haste and have it over quickly," said Jo pettishly.

"*I* can't say anything till he speaks, and he won't, because Father said I was too young," began Meg, bending over her work with a queer little smile, which suggested that she did not quite agree with her father on that point.

"If he did speak, you wouldn't know what to say, but would cry or blush, or let him have his own way, instead of giving a good, decided no."

"I'm not so silly and weak as you think. I know just what I should say, for I've planned it all, so I needn't be taken unawares. There's no knowing what may happen, and I wished to be prepared."

Jo couldn't help smiling at the important air which Meg had unconsciously assumed and which was as becoming as the pretty color varying in her cheeks.

"Would you mind telling me what you'd say?" asked Jo more respectfully.

"Not at all. You are sixteen now, quite old enough to be my confidante, and my experience will be useful to you by-and-by, perhaps, in your own affairs of this sort."

"Don't mean to have any. It's fun to watch other people philander, but I should feel like a fool doing it myself," said Jo, looking alarmed at the thought.

"I think not, if you liked anyone very much, and he liked you." Meg spoke as if to herself, and glanced out at the lane where she had often seen lovers walking together in the summer twilight.

"I thought you were going to tell your speech to that man," said Jo, rudely shortening her sister's little reverie.

"Oh, I should merely say, quite calmly and decidedly, 'Thank you, Mr. Brooke, you are very kind, but I agree with Father that I am too young to enter into any engagement at present, so please say no more, but let us be friends as we were.'"

"Hum, that's stiff and cool enough! I don't believe you'll ever say it, and I know he won't be satisfied if you do. If he goes on like the rejected lovers in books, you'll give in, rather than hurt his feelings."

"No, I won't. I shall tell him I've made up my mind, and shall walk out of the room with dignity."

Meg rose as she spoke, and was just going to rehearse the dignified exit, when a step in the hall made her fly into her seat and begin to sew as fast as if her life depended on finishing that particular seam in a given time. Jo smothered a laugh at the sudden change, and when someone gave a modest tap, opened the door with a grim aspect which was anything but hospitable.

"Good afternoon. I came to get my umbrella—that is, to see how your father finds himself today," said Mr. Brooke, getting a trifle confused as his eyes went from one telltale face to the other.

"It's very well, he's in the rack. I'll get him, and tell it you are here." And having jumbled her father and the umbrella well together in her reply, Jo slipped out of the room to give Meg a chance to make her speech and air her dignity. But the instant she vanished, Meg began to sidle toward the door, murmuring—

"Mother will like to see you. Pray sit down, I'll call her."

"Don't go. Are you afraid of me, Margaret?" And Mr. Brooke looked so hurt that Meg thought she must have done something very rude. She blushed up to the little curls on her forehead, for he had never called her Margaret before, and she was surprised to find how natural and sweet it seemed to hear him say it. Anxious to appear friendly and at her ease, she put out her hand with a confiding gesture, and said gratefully—

"How can I be afraid when you have been so kind to Father? I only wish I could thank you for it."

"Shall I tell you how?" asked Mr. Brooke, holding the small hand fast in both his own, and looking down at Meg with so much love in the brown eyes that her heart began to flutter, and she both longed to run away and to stop and listen.

"Oh no, please don't—I'd rather not," she said, trying to withdraw her hand, and looking frightened in spite of her denial.

"I won't trouble you. I only want to know if you care for me a little, Meg. I love you so much, dear," added Mr. Brooke tenderly.

This was the moment for the calm, proper speech, but Meg didn't make it. She forgot every word of it, hung her head, and answered, "I don't know," so softly that John had to stoop down to catch the foolish little reply.

He seemed to think it was worth the trouble, for he smiled to himself as if quite satisfied, pressed the plump hand gratefully, and said in his most persuasive tone, "Will you try and find out? I want to know so much, for I can't go to work with any heart until I learn whether I am to have my reward in the end or not."

"I'm too young," faltered Meg, wondering why she was so fluttered, yet rather enjoying it.

"I'll wait, and in the meantime, you could be learning to like me. Would it be a very hard lesson, dear?"

"Not if I chose to learn it, but. . ."

"Please choose to learn, Meg. I love to teach, and this is easier than German," broke in John, getting possession of the other hand, so that she had no way of hiding her face as he bent to look into it.

His tone was properly beseeching, but stealing a shy look at him, Meg saw that his eyes were merry as well as tender, and that he wore the satisfied smile of one who had no doubt of his success. This nettled her. Annie Moffat's foolish lessons in coquetry came into her mind, and the love of power, which sleeps in the bosoms of the best of little women, woke up all of a sudden and took possession of her. She felt excited and strange, and not knowing what else to do, followed a capricious impulse, and, withdrawing her hands, said petulantly, "I *don't* choose. Please go away and let me be!"

Poor Mr. Brooke looked as if his lovely castle in the air was tumbling about his ears, for he had never seen Meg in such a mood before, and it rather bewildered him.

"Do you really mean that?" he asked anxiously, following her as she walked away.

"Yes, I do. I don't want to be worried about such things. Father says I needn't, it's too soon and I'd rather not."

"Mayn't I hope you'll change your mind by-and-by? I'll wait and say nothing till you have had more time. Don't play with me, Meg. I didn't think that of you."

"Don't think of me at all. I'd rather you wouldn't," said Meg, taking a naughty satisfaction in trying her lover's patience and her own power.

He was grave and pale now, and looked decidedly more like the novel heroes whom she admired, but he neither slapped his forehead nor tramped about the room as they did. He just stood looking at her so wistfully, so tenderly, that she found her heart relenting in spite of herself. What would have happened next I cannot say, if Aunt March had not come hobbling in at this interesting minute.

The old lady couldn't resist her longing to see her nephew, for she had met Laurie as she took her airing, and hearing of Mr. March's arrival, drove straight out to see him. The family were all busy in the back part of the house, and she had made her way quietly in, hoping to surprise them. She did surprise two of them so much that Meg started as if she had seen a ghost, and Mr. Brooke vanished into the study.

"Bless me, what's all this?" cried the old lady with a rap of her cane as she glanced from the pale young gentleman to the scarlet young lady.

"It's Father's friend. I'm so surprised to see you!" stammered Meg, feeling that she was in for a lecture now.

"That's evident," returned Aunt March, sitting down. "But what is Father's friend saying to make you look like a peony? There's mischief going on, and I insist upon knowing what it is," with another rap.

"We were only talking. Mr. Brooke came for his umbrella," began Meg, wishing that Mr. Brooke and the umbrella were safely out of the house.

"Brooke? That boy's tutor? Ah! I understand now. I know all about it. Jo blundered into a wrong message in one of your Father's letters, and I made her tell me. You haven't gone and accepted him, child?" cried Aunt March, looking scandalized.

"Hush! He'll hear. Shan't I call Mother?" said Meg, much troubled.

"Not yet. I've something to say to you, and I must free my mind at once. Tell me, do you mean to marry this Cook? If you do, not one penny of my money ever goes to you. Remember that, and be a sensible girl," said the old lady impressively.

Now Aunt March possessed in perfection the art of rousing the spirit of opposition in the gentlest people, and enjoyed doing it. The best of us have a spice of perversity in us, especially when we are young and in love. If Aunt March had begged Meg to accept John Brooke, she would probably have declared she couldn't think of it, but as she was preemptorily ordered not to like him, she immediately made up her mind that she would. Inclination as well as perversity made the decision easy, and being already much excited, Meg opposed the old lady with unusual spirit.

"I shall marry whom I please, Aunt March, and you can leave your money to anyone you like," she said, nodding her head with a resolute air.

"Highty-tighty! Is that the way you take my advice, Miss? You'll be sorry for it by-and-by, when you've tried love in a cottage and found it a failure."

"It can't be a worse one than some people find in big houses," retorted Meg.

Aunt March put on her glasses and took a look at the girl, for she did not know her in this new mood. Meg hardly knew herself, she felt so brave and independent, so glad to defend John and assert her right to love him, if she liked. Aunt March saw that she had begun wrong, and after a little pause, made a fresh start, saying as mildly as she could, "Now, Meg, my dear, be reasonable and take my advice. I mean it kindly, and don't want you to spoil your whole life by making a mistake at the beginning. You ought to marry well and help your family. It's your duty to make a rich match and it ought to be impressed upon you."

"Father and Mother don't think so. They like John though he is poor."

"Your parents, my dear, have no more worldly wisdom than a pair of babies."

"I'm glad of it," cried Meg stoutly.

Aunt March took no notice, but went on with her lecture. "This Rook is poor and hasn't got any rich relations, has he?"

"No, but he has many warm friends."

"You can't live on friends, try it and see how cool they'll grow. He hasn't any business, has he?"

"Not yet. Mr. Laurence is going to help him."

"That won't last long. James Laurence is a crotchety old fellow and not to be depended on. So you intend to marry a man without money, position, or business, and go on working harder than you do now, when you might be comfortable all your days by minding me and doing better? I thought you had more sense, Meg."

"I couldn't do better if I waited half my life! John is good and wise, he's got heaps of talent, he's willing to work and sure to get on, he's so energetic and brave. Everyone likes and respects him, and I'm proud to think he cares for me, though I'm so poor and young and silly," said Meg, looking prettier than ever in her earnestness.

"He knows *you* have got rich relations, child. That's the secret of his liking, I suspect."

"Aunt March, how dare you say such a thing? John is above such meanness, and I won't listen to you a minute if you talk so," cried Meg indignantly, forgetting everything but the injustice of the old lady's suspicions. "My John wouldn't marry for money, any more than I would. We are willing to work and we mean to wait. I'm not afraid of being poor, for I've been happy so far, and I know I shall be with him because he loves me, and I—"

Meg stopped there, remembering all of a sudden that she hadn't made up her mind, that she had told "her John" to go away, and that he might be overhearing her inconsistent remarks.

Aunt March was very angry, for she had set her heart on having her pretty niece make a fine match, and something in the girl's happy young face made the lonely old woman feel both sad and sour.

"Well, I wash my hands of the whole affair! You are a willful child, and you've lost more than you know by this piece of folly. No, I won't stop. I'm disappointed in you, and haven't spirits to see your father now. Don't expect anything from me when you are married. Your Mr. Brooke's friends must take care of you. I'm done with you forever."

And slamming the door in Meg's face, Aunt March drove off in high dudgeon. She seemed to take all the girl's courage with her, for when left alone, Meg stood for a moment, undecided whether to laugh or cry. Before she could make up her mind, she was taken possession of by Mr. Brooke, who said all in one breath, "I couldn't help hearing, Meg. Thank you for defending me, and Aunt March for proving that you do care for me a little bit."

"I didn't know how much till she abused you," began Meg.

"And I needn't go away, but may stay and be happy, may I, dear?"

Here was another fine chance to make the crushing speech and the stately exit, but Meg never thought of doing either, and disgraced herself forever in Jo's eyes by meekly whispering, "Yes, John," and hiding her face on Mr. Brooke's waistcoat.

Fifteen minutes after Aunt March's departure, Jo came softly downstairs, paused an instant at the parlor door, and hearing no sound within, nodded and smiled with a satisfied expression, saying to herself, "She has seen him away as we planned, and that affair is settled. I'll go and hear the fun, and have a good laugh over it."

But poor Jo never got her laugh, for she was transfixed upon the threshold by a spectacle which held her there, staring with her mouth nearly as wide open as her eyes. Going in to exult over a fallen enemy and to praise a strong-minded sister for the banishment of an objectionable lover, it certainly was a shock to behold the aforesaid enemy serenely sitting on the sofa, with the strongminded sister enthroned upon his knee and wearing an expression of the most abject submission. Jo gave a sort of gasp, as if a cold shower bath had suddenly fallen upon her, for such an unexpected turning of the tables actually took her breath away. At the odd sound the lovers turned and saw her. Meg jumped up, looking both proud and shy, but "that man," as Jo called him, actually laughed and said coolly, as he kissed the astonished newcomer, "Sister Jo, congratulate us!"

That was adding insult to injury—it was altogether too much—and making some wild demonstration with her hands, Jo vanished without a word. Rushing upstairs, she startled the invalids by exclaiming tragically as she burst into the room, "Oh, *do* somebody go down quick! John Brooke is acting dreadfully, and Meg likes it!"

Mr. and Mrs. March left the room with speed, and casting herself upon the bed, Jo cried and scolded tempestuously as she told the awful news to Beth and Amy. The little girls, however, considered it a most agreeable and interesting event, and Jo got little comfort from them, so she went up to her refuge in the garret, and confided her troubles to the rats.

Nobody ever knew what went on in the parlor that afternoon, but a great deal of talking was done, and quiet Mr. Brooke astonished his friends by the eloquence and spirit with which he pleaded his suit, told his plans, and persuaded them to arrange everything just as he wanted it.

The tea bell rang before he had finished describing the paradise which he meant to earn for Meg, and he proudly took her in to supper, both looking so happy that Jo hadn't the heart to be jealous or dismal. Amy was very much impressed by John's devotion and Meg's dignity, Beth beamed at them from a distance, while Mr. and Mrs. March surveyed the young couple with such tender satisfaction that it was perfectly evident Aunt March was right in calling them as "unworldly as a pair of babies." No one ate much, but everyone looked very happy, and the old room seemed to brighten up amazingly when the first romance of the family began there.

"You can't say nothing pleasant ever happens now, can you, Meg?" said Amy, trying to decide how she would group the lovers in a sketch she was planning to make.

"No, I'm sure I can't. How much has happened since I said that! It seems a year ago," answered Meg, who was in a blissful dream lifted far above such common things as bread and butter.

"The joys come close upon the sorrows this time, and I rather think the changes have begun," said Mrs. March. "In most families there comes, now and then, a year full of events. This has been such a one, but it ends well, after all."

"Hope the next will end better," muttered Jo, who found it very hard to see Meg absorbed in a stranger before her face, for Jo loved a few persons very dearly and dreaded to have their affection lost or lessened in any way.

"I hope the third year from this will end better. I mean it shall, if I live to work out my plans," said Mr. Brooke, smiling at Meg, as if everything had become possible to him now.

"Doesn't it seem very long to wait?" asked Amy, who was in a hurry for the wedding.

"I've got so much to learn before I shall be ready, it seems a short time to me," answered Meg, with a sweet gravity in her face never seen there before.

"You have only to wait, I am to do the work," said John beginning his labors by picking up Meg's napkin, with an expression which caused Jo to shake her head, and then say to herself with an air of relief as the front door banged, "Here comes Laurie. Now we shall have some sensible conversation."

But Jo was mistaken, for Laurie came prancing in, overflowing with good spirits, bearing a great bridal-looking bouquet for "Mrs. John Brooke," and evidently laboring under the delusion that the whole affair had been brought about by his excellent management.

"I knew Brooke would have it all his own way, he always does, for when he makes up his mind to accomplish anything, it's done though the sky falls," said Laurie, when he had presented his offering and his congratulations.

"Much obliged for that recommendation. I take it as a good omen for the future and invite you to my wedding on the spot," answered Mr. Brooke, who felt at peace with all mankind, even his mischievous pupil.

"I'll come if I'm at the ends of the earth, for the sight of Jo's face alone on that occasion would be worth a long journey. You don't look festive, ma'am, what's the matter?" asked Laurie, following her into a corner of the parlor, whither all had adjourned to greet Mr. Laurence.

"I don't approve of the match, but I've made up my mind to bear it, and shall not say a word against it," said Jo solemnly. "You can't know how hard it is for me to give up Meg," she continued with a little quiver in her voice.

"You don't give her up. You only go halves," said Laurie consolingly.

"It can never be the same again. I've lost my dearest friend," sighed Jo.

"You've got me, anyhow. I'm not good for much, I know, but I'll stand by you, Jo, all the days of my life. Upon my word I will!" and Laurie meant what he said.

"I know you will, and I'm ever so much obliged. You are always a great comfort to me, Teddy," returned Jo, gratefully shaking hands.

"Well, now, don't be dismal, there's a good fellow. It's all right you see. Meg is happy, Brooke will fly round and get settled immediately, Grandpa will attend to him, and it will be very jolly to see Meg in her own little house. We'll have capital times after she is gone, for I shall be through college before long, and then we'll go abroad on some nice trip or other. Wouldn't that console you?"

"I rather think it would, but there's no knowing what may happen in three years," said Jo thoughtfully.

"That's true. Don't you wish you could take a look forward and see where we shall all be then? I do," returned Laurie.

"I think not, for I might see something sad, and everyone looks so happy now, I don't believe they could be much improved." And Jo's eyes went slowly round the room, brightening as they looked, for the prospect was a pleasant one.

Father and Mother sat together, quietly reliving the first chapter of the romance which for them began some twenty years ago. Amy was drawing the lovers, who sat apart in a beautiful world of their own, the light of which touched their faces with a grace the little artist could not copy. Beth lay on her sofa, talking cheerily with her old friend, who held her little hand as if he felt that it possessed the power to lead him along the peaceful way she walked. Jo lounged in her favorite low seat, with the grave quiet look which best became her, and Laurie, leaning on the back of her chair, his chin on a level with her curly head, smiled with his friendliest aspect, and nodded at her in the long glass which reflected them both.

So grouped, the curtain falls upon Meg, Jo, Beth, and Amy. Whether it ever rises again, depends upon the reception given the first act of the domestic drama called *Little Women.*

CHAPTER XXIV

GOSSIP

In order that we may start afresh and go to Meg's wedding with free minds, it will be well to begin with a little gossip about the Marches. And here let me premise that if any of the elders think there is too much "lovering" in the story, as I fear they may (I'm not afraid the young folks will make that objection), I can only say with Mrs. March, "What *can* you expect when I have four gay girls in the house, and a dashing young neighbor over the way?"

The three years that have passed have brought but few changes to the quiet family. The war is over, and Mr. March safely at home, busy with his books and the small parish which found in him a minister by nature as by grace—a quiet, studious man, rich in the wisdom that is better than learning, the charity which calls all mankind "brother," the piety that blossoms into character, making it august and lovely.

These attributes, in spite of poverty and the strict integrity which shut him out from the more worldly successes, attracted to him many admirable persons, as naturally as sweet herbs draw bees, and as naturally he gave them the honey into which fifty years of hard experience had distilled no bitter drop. Earnest young men found the gray-headed scholar as young at heart as they; thoughtful or troubled women instinctively brought their doubts to him, sure of finding the gentlest sympathy, the wisest counsel. Sinners told their sins to the pure-hearted old man and were both rebuked and saved. Gifted men found a companion in him. Ambitious men caught glimpses of nobler ambitions than their own, and even worldlings confessed that his beliefs were beautiful and true, although "they wouldn't pay."

To outsiders the five energetic women seemed to rule the house, and so they did in many things, but the quiet scholar, sitting among his books, was still the head of the family, the household conscience, anchor, and comforter, for to him the busy, anxious women always turned in troublous times, finding him, in the truest sense of those sacred words, husband and father.

The girls gave their hearts into their mother's keeping, their souls into their father's, and to both parents, who lived and labored so faithfully for them, they gave a love that grew with their growth and bound them tenderly together by the sweetest tie which blesses life and outlives death.

Mrs. March is as brisk and cheery, though rather grayer, than when we saw her last, and just now so absorbed in Meg's affairs that the hospitals and homes still full of wounded "boys" and soldiers' widows, decidedly miss the motherly missionary's visits.

John Brooke did his duty manfully for a year, got wounded, was sent home, and not allowed to return. He received no stars or bars, but he deserved them, for he cheerfully risked all he had, and life and love are very precious when both are in full bloom. Perfectly resigned to his discharge, he devoted himself to getting well, preparing for business, and earning a home for Meg. With the good sense and sturdy independence that characterized him, he refused Mr. Laurence's more generous offers, and accepted the place of bookkeeper, feeling better satisfied to begin with an honestly earned salary than by running any risks with borrowed money.

Meg had spent the time in working as well as waiting, growing womanly in character, wise in housewifely arts, and prettier than ever, for love is a great beautifier. She had her girlish ambitions and hopes, and felt some disappointment at the humble way in which the new life must begin. Ned Moffat had just married Sallie Gardiner, and Meg couldn't help contrasting their fine house and carriage, many gifts, and splendid outfit with her own, and secretly wishing she could have the same. But somehow envy and discontent soon vanished when she thought of all the patient love and labor John had put into the little home awaiting her, and when they sat together in the twilight, talking over their small plans, the future always grew so beautiful and bright that she forgot Sallie's splendor and felt herself the richest, happiest girl in Christendom.

Jo never went back to Aunt March, for the old lady took such a fancy to Amy that she bribed her with the offer of drawing lessons from one of the best teachers going, and for the sake of this advantage, Amy would have served a far harder mistress. So she gave her mornings to duty, her afternoons to pleasure, and prospered finely. Jo meantime devoted herself to literature and Beth, who remained delicate long after the fever was a thing of the past. Not an invalid exactly, but never again the rosy, healthy creature she had been, yet always hopeful, happy, and serene, and busy with the quiet duties she loved, everyone's friend, and an angel in the house, long before those who loved her most had learned to know it.

As long as *The Spread Eagle* paid her a dollar a column for her "rubbish," as she called it, Jo felt herself a woman of means, and spun her little romances diligently. But great plans fermented in her busy brain and ambitious mind, and the old tin kitchen in the garret held a slowly increasing pile of blotted manuscript, which was one day to place the name of March upon the roll of fame.

Laurie, having dutifully gone to college to please his grandfather, was now getting through it in the easiest possible manner to please himself. A universal favorite, thanks to money, manners, much talent, and the kindest heart that ever got its owner into scrapes by trying to get other people out of them, he stood in great danger of being spoiled, and probably would have been, like many another promising boy, if he had not possessed a talisman against evil in the memory of the kind old man who was bound up in his success, the motherly friend who watched over him as if he were her son, and last, but not least by any means, the knowledge that four innocent girls loved, admired, and believed in him with all their hearts.

Being only "a glorious human boy," of course he frolicked and flirted, grew dandified, aquatic, sentimental, or gymnastic, as college fashions ordained, hazed and was hazed, talked slang, and more than once came perilously near suspension and expulsion. But as high spirits and the love of fun were the causes of these pranks, he always managed to save himself by frank confession, honorable atonement, or the irresistible power of persuasion which he possessed in perfection. In fact, he rather prided himself on his narrow escapes, and liked to thrill the girls with graphic accounts of his triumphs over wrathful tutors, dignified professors, and vanquished enemies. The "men of my class," were heroes in the eyes of the girls, who never wearied of the exploits of "our fellows," and were frequently allowed to bask in the smiles of these great creatures, when Laurie brought them home with him.

Amy especially enjoyed this high honor, and became quite a belle among them, for her ladyship early felt and learned to use the gift of fascination with which she was endowed. Meg was too much absorbed in her private and particular John to care for any other lords of creation, and Beth too shy to do more than peep at them and wonder how Amy dared to order them about so, but Jo felt quite in her own element, and found it very difficult to refrain from imitating the gentlemanly attitudes, phrases, and feats, which seemed more natural to her than the decorums prescribed for young ladies. They all liked Jo immensely, but never fell in love with her, though very few escaped without paying the tribute of a sentimental sigh or two at Amy's shrine. And speaking of sentiment brings us very naturally to the "Dovecote."

That was the name of the little brown house Mr. Brooke had prepared for Meg's first home. Laurie had christened it, saying it was highly appropriate to the gentle lovers who "went on together like a pair of turtledoves, with first a bill and then a coo." It was a tiny house, with a little garden behind and a lawn about as big as a pocket handkerchief in the front. Here Meg meant to have a fountain, shrubbery, and a profusion of lovely flowers, though just at present the fountain was represented by a weather-beaten urn, very like a dilapidated slopbowl, the shrubbery consisted of several young larches, undecided whether to live or die, and the profusion of flowers was merely hinted by regiments of sticks to show where seeds were planted. But inside, it was altogether charming, and the happy bride saw no fault from garret to cellar. To be sure, the hall was so narrow it was fortunate that they had no piano, for one never could have been got in whole, the dining room was so small that six people were a tight fit, and the kitchen stairs seemed built for the express purpose of precipitating both servants and china pell-mell into the coalbin. But once get used to these slight blemishes and nothing could be more complete, for good sense and good taste had presided over the furnishing, and the result was highly satisfactory. There were no marble-topped tables, long mirrors, or lace curtains in the little parlor, but simple furniture, plenty of books, a fine picture or two, a stand of flowers in the bay window, and, scattered all about, the pretty gifts which came from friendly hands and were the fairer for the loving messages they brought.

I don't think the Parian Psyche Laurie gave lost any of its beauty because John put up the bracket it stood upon, that any upholsterer could have draped the plain muslin curtains more gracefully than Amy's artistic hand, or that any store-room was ever better provided with good wishes, merry words, and happy hopes than that in which Jo and her mother put away Meg's few boxes, barrels, and bundles, and

I am morally certain that the spandy new kitchen never could have looked so cozy and neat if Hannah had not arranged every pot and pan a dozen times over, and laid the fire all ready for lighting the minute "Mis. Brooke came home." I also doubt if any young matron ever began life with so rich a supply of dusters, holders, and piece bags, for Beth made enough to last till the silver wedding came round, and invented three different kinds of dishcloths for the express service of the bridal china.

People who hire all these things done for them never know what they lose, for the homeliest tasks get beautified if loving hands do them, and Meg found so many proofs of this that everything in her small nest, from the kitchen roller to the silver vase on her parlor table, was eloquent of home love and tender forethought.

What happy times they had planning together, what solemn shopping excursions, what funny mistakes they made, and what shouts of laughter arose over Laurie's ridiculous bargains. In his love of jokes, this young gentleman, though nearly through college, was as much of a boy as ever. His last whim had been to bring with him on his weekly visits some new, useful, and ingenious article for the young housekeeper. Now a bag of remarkable clothespins, next, a wonderful nutmeg grater which fell to pieces at the first trial, a knife cleaner that spoiled all the knives, or a sweeper that picked the nap neatly off the carpet and left the dirt, labor-saving soap that took the skin off one's hands, infallible cements which stuck firmly to nothing but the fingers of the deluded buyer, and every kind of tinware, from a toy savings bank for odd pennies, to a wonderful boiler which would wash articles in its own steam with every prospect of exploding in the process.

In vain Meg begged him to stop. John laughed at him, and Jo called him "Mr. Toodles." He was possessed with a mania for patronizing Yankee ingenuity, and seeing his friends fitly furnished forth. So each week beheld some fresh absurdity.

Everything was done at last, even to Amy's arranging different colored soaps to match the different colored rooms, and Beth's setting the table for the first meal.

"Are you satisfied? Does it seem like home, and do you feel as if you should be happy here?" asked Mrs. March, as she and her daughter went through the new kingdom arm in arm, for just then they seemed to cling together more tenderly than ever.

"Yes, Mother, perfectly satisfied, thanks to you all, and so happy that I can't talk about it," with a look that was far better than words.

"If she only had a servant or two it would be all right," said Amy, coming out of the parlor, where she had been trying to decide whether the bronze Mercury looked best on the whatnot or the mantlepiece.

"Mother and I have talked that over, and I have made up my mind to try her way first. There will be so little to do that with Lotty to run my errands and help me here and there, I shall only have enough work to keep me from getting lazy or homesick," answered Meg tranquilly.

"Sallie Moffat has four," began Amy.

"If Meg had four, the house wouldn't hold them, and master and missis would have to camp in the garden," broke in Jo, who, enveloped in a big blue pinafore, was giving the last polish to the door handles.

"Sallie isn't a poor man's wife, and many maids are in keeping with her fine establishment. Meg and John begin humbly, but I have a feeling that there will be quite as much happiness in the little house as in the big one. It's a great mistake for young girls like Meg to leave themselves nothing to do but dress, give orders, and gossip. When I was first married, I used to long for my new clothes to wear out or get torn, so that I might have the pleasure of mending them, for I got heartily sick of doing fancywork and tending my pocket handkerchief."

"Why didn't you go into the kitchen and make messes, as Sallie says she does to amuse herself, though they never turn out well and the servants laugh at her," said Meg.

"I did after a while, not to 'mess' but to learn of Hannah how things should be done, that my servants need not laugh at me. It was play then, but there came a time when I was truly grateful that I not only possessed the will but the power to cook wholesome food for my little girls, and help myself when I could no longer afford to hire help. You begin at the other end, Meg, dear, but the lessons you learn now will be of use to you by-and-by when John is a richer man, for the mistress of a house, however splendid, should know how work ought to be done, if she wishes to be well and honestly served."

"Yes, Mother, I'm sure of that," said Meg, listening respectfully to the little lecture, for the best of women will hold forth upon the all absorbing subject of housekeeping. "Do you know I like this room most of all in my baby house," added Meg, a minute after, as they went upstairs and she looked into her well-stored linen closet.

Beth was there, laying the snowy piles smoothly on the shelves and exulting over the goodly array. All three laughed as Meg spoke, for that linen closet was a joke. You see, having said that if Meg married "that Brooke" she shouldn't have a cent of her money, Aunt March was rather in a quandary when time had appeased her wrath and made her repent her vow. She never broke her word, and was much exercised in her mind how to get round it, and at last devised a plan whereby she could satisfy herself. Mrs. Carrol, Florence's mamma, was ordered to buy, have made, and marked a generous supply of house and table linen, and send it as *her* present, all of which was faithfully done, but the secret leaked out, and was greatly enjoyed by the family, for Aunt March tried to look utterly unconscious, and insisted that she could give nothing but the old-fashioned pearls long promised to the first bride.

"That's a housewifely taste which I am glad to see. I had a young friend who set up housekeeping with six sheets, but she had finger bowls for company and that satisfied her," said Mrs. March, patting the damask tablecloths, with a truly feminine appreciation of their fineness.

"I haven't a single finger bowl, but this is a setout that will last me all my days, Hannah says." And Meg looked quite contented, as well she might.

"Toodles is coming," cried Jo from below, and they all went down to meet Laurie, whose weekly visit was an important event in their quiet lives.

A tall, broad-shouldered young fellow, with a cropped head, a felt basin of a hat, and a flyaway coat, came tramping down the road at a great pace, walked over the low fence without stopping to open the gate, straight up to Mrs. March, with both hands out and a hearty—

"Here I am, Mother! Yes, it's all right."

The last words were in answer to the look the elder lady gave him, a kindly questioning look which the handsome eyes met so frankly that the little ceremony closed, as usual, with a motherly kiss.

"For Mrs. John Brooke, with the maker's congratulations and compliments. Bless you, Beth! What a refreshing spectacle you are, Jo. Amy, you are getting altogether too handsome for a single lady."

As Laurie spoke, he delivered a brown paper parcel to Meg, pulled Beth's hair ribbon, stared at Jo's big pinafore, and fell into an attitude of mock rapture before Amy, then shook hands all round, and everyone began to talk.

"Where is John?" asked Meg anxiously.

"Stopped to get the license for tomorrow, ma'am."

"Which side won the last match, Teddy?" inquired Jo, who persisted in feeling an interest in manly sports despite her nineteen years.

"Ours, of course. Wish you'd been there to see."

"How is the lovely Miss Randal?" asked Amy with a significant smile.

"More cruel than ever. Don't you see how I'm pining away?" and Laurie gave his broad chest a sounding slap and heaved a melodramatic sigh.

"What's the last joke? Undo the bundle and see, Meg," said Beth, eying the knobby parcel with curiosity.

"It's a useful thing to have in the house in case of fire or thieves," observed Laurie, as a watchman's rattle appeared, amid the laughter of the girls.

"Any time when John is away and you get frightened, Mrs. Meg, just swing that out of the front window, and it will rouse the neighborhood in a jiffy. Nice thing, isn't it?" and Laurie gave them a sample of its powers that made them cover up their ears.

"There's gratitude for you! And speaking of gratitude reminds me to mention that you may thank Hannah for saving your wedding cake from destruction. I saw it going into your house as I came by, and if she hadn't defended it manfully I'd have had a pick at it, for it looked like a remarkably plummy one."

"I wonder if you will ever grow up, Laurie," said Meg in a matronly tone.

"I'm doing my best, ma'am, but can't get much higher, I'm afraid, as six feet is about all men can do in these degenerate days," responded the young gentleman, whose head was about level with the little chandelier.

"I suppose it would be profanation to eat anything in this spick-and-span bower, so as I'm tremendously hungry, I propose an adjournment," he added presently.

"Mother and I are going to wait for John. There are some last things to settle," said Meg, bustling away.

"Beth and I are going over to Kitty Bryant's to get more flowers for tomorrow," added Amy, tying a picturesque hat over her picturesque curls, and enjoying the effect as much as anybody.

"Come, Jo, don't desert a fellow. I'm in such a state of exhaustion I can't get home without help. Don't take off your apron, whatever you do, it's peculiarly becoming," said Laurie, as Jo bestowed his especial aversion in her capacious pocket and offered her arm to support his feeble steps.

"Now, Teddy, I want to talk seriously to you about tomorrow," began Jo, as they strolled away together. "You must promise to behave well, and not cut up any pranks, and spoil our plans."

"Not a prank."

"And don't say funny things when we ought to be sober."

"I never do. You are the one for that."

"And I implore you not to look at me during the ceremony. I shall certainly laugh if you do."

"You won't see me, you'll be crying so hard that the thick fog round you will obscure the prospect."

"I never cry unless for some great affliction."

"Such as fellows going to college, hey?" cut in Laurie, with suggestive laugh.

"Don't be a peacock. I only moaned a trifle to keep the girls company."

"Exactly. I say, Jo, how is Grandpa this week? Pretty amiable?"

"Very. Why, have you got into a scrape and want to know how he'll take it?" asked Jo rather sharply.

"Now, Jo, do you think I'd look your mother in the face and say 'All right,' if it wasn't?" and Laurie stopped short, with an injured air.

"No, I don't."

"Then don't go and be suspicious. I only want some money," said Laurie, walking on again, appeased by her hearty tone.

"You spend a great deal, Teddy."

"Bless you, *I* don't spend it, it spends itself somehow, and is gone before I know it."

"You are so generous and kind-hearted that you let people borrow, and can't say 'No' to anyone. We heard about Henshaw and all you did for him. If you always spent money in that way, no one would blame you," said Jo warmly.

"Oh, he made a mountain out of a molehill. You wouldn't have me let that fine fellow work himself to death just for want of a little help, when he is worth a dozen of us lazy chaps, would you?"

"Of course not, but I don't see the use of your having seventeen waistcoats, endless neckties, and a new hat every time you come home. I thought you'd got over the dandy period, but every now and then it breaks out in a new spot. Just now it's the fashion to be hideous, to make your head look like a scrubbing brush, wear a strait jacket, orange gloves, and clumping square-toed boots. If it was cheap ugliness, I'd say nothing, but it costs as much as the other, and I don't get any satisfaction out of it."

Laurie threw back his head, and laughed so heartily at this attack, that the felt hat fell off, and Jo walked on it, which insult only afforded him an opportunity for expatiating on the advantages of a rough-and-ready costume, as he folded up the maltreated hat, and stuffed it into his pocket.

"Don't lecture any more, there's a good soul! I have enough all through the week, and like to enjoy myself when I come home. I'll get myself up regardless of expense tomorrow and be a satisfaction to my friends."

"I'll leave you in peace if you'll *only* let your hair grow. I'm not aristocratic, but I do object to being seen with a person who looks like a young prize fighter," observed Jo severely.

"This unassuming style promotes study, that's why we adopt it," returned Laurie, who certainly could not be accused of vanity, having voluntarily sacrificed a handsome curly crop to the demand for quarter-inch-long stubble.

"By the way, Jo, I think that little Parker is really getting desperate about Amy. He talks of her constantly, writes poetry, and moons about in a most suspicious manner. He'd better nip his little passion in the bud, hadn't he?" added Laurie, in a confidential, elder brotherly tone, after a minute's silence.

"Of course he had. We don't want any more marrying in this family for years to come. Mercy on us, what are the children thinking of?" and Jo looked as much scandalized as if Amy and little Parker were not yet in their teens.

"It's a fast age, and I don't know what we are coming to, ma'am. You are a mere infant, but you'll go next, Jo, and we'll be left lamenting," said Laurie, shaking his head over the degeneracy of the times.

"Don't be alarmed. I'm not one of the agreeable sort. Nobody will want me, and it's a mercy, for there should always be one old maid in a family."

"You won't give anyone a chance," said Laurie, with a sidelong glance and a little more color than before in his sunburned face. "You won't show the soft side of your character, and if a fellow gets a peep at it by accident and can't help showing that he likes it, you treat him as Mrs. Gummidge did her sweetheart, throw cold water over him, and get so thorny no one dares touch or look at you."

"I don't like that sort of thing. I'm too busy to be worried with nonsense, and I think it's dreadful to break up families so. Now don't say any more about it. Meg's wedding has turned all our heads, and we talk of nothing but lovers and such absurdities. I don't wish to get cross, so let's change the subject." And Jo looked quite ready to fling cold water on the slightest provocation.

Whatever his feelings might have been, Laurie found a vent for them in a long low whistle and the fearful prediction as they parted at the gate, "Mark my words, Jo, you'll go next."

CHAPTER XXV

THE FIRST WEDDING

The June roses over the porch were awake bright and early on that morning, rejoicing with all their hearts in the cloudless sunshine, like friendly little neighbors, as they were. Quite flushed with excitement were their ruddy faces, as they swung in the wind, whispering to one another what they had seen, for some peeped in at the dining room windows where the feast was spread, some climbed up to nod and smile at the sisters as they dressed the bride, others waved a welcome to those who came and went on various errands in garden, porch, and hall, and all, from the rosiest full-blown flower to the palest baby bud, offered their tribute of beauty and fragrance to the gentle mistress who had loved and tended them so long.

Meg looked very like a rose herself, for all that was best and sweetest in heart and soul seemed to bloom into her face that day, making it fair and tender, with a charm more beautiful than beauty. Neither silk, lace, nor orange flowers would she have. "I don't want a fashionable wedding, but only those about me whom I love, and to them I wish to look and be my familiar self."

So she made her wedding gown herself, sewing into it the tender hopes and innocent romances of a girlish heart. Her sisters braided up her pretty hair, and the only ornaments she wore were the lilies of the valley, which "her John" liked best of all the flowers that grew.

"You *do* look just like our own dear Meg, only so very sweet and lovely that I should hug you if it wouldn't crumple your dress," cried Amy, surveying her with delight when all was done.

"Then I am satisfied. But please hug and kiss me, everyone, and don't mind my dress. I want a great many crumples of this sort put into it today," and Meg opened her arms to her sisters, who clung about her with April faces for a minute, feeling that the new love had not changed the old.

"Now I'm going to tie John's cravat for him, and then to stay a few minutes with Father quietly in the study," and Meg ran down to perform these little ceremonies, and then to follow her mother wherever she went, conscious that in spite of the smiles on the motherly face, there was a secret sorrow hid in the motherly heart at the flight of the first bird from the nest.

As the younger girls stand together, giving the last touches to their simple toilet, it may be a good time to tell of a few changes which three years have wrought in their appearance, for all are looking their best just now.

Jo's angles are much softened, she has learned to carry herself with ease, if not grace. The curly crop has lengthened into a thick coil, more becoming to the small head atop of the tall figure. There is a fresh color in her brown cheeks, a soft shine in her eyes, and only gentle words fall from her sharp tongue today.

Beth has grown slender, pale, and more quiet than ever. The beautiful, kind eyes are larger, and in them lies an expression that saddens one, although it is not sad itself. It is the shadow of pain which touches the young face with such pathetic patience, but Beth seldom complains and always speaks hopefully of "being better soon."

Amy is with truth considered "the flower of the family," for at sixteen she has the air and bearing of a full-grown woman—not beautiful, but possessed of that indescribable charm called grace. One saw it in the lines of her figure, the make and motion of her hands, the flow of her dress, the droop of her hair, unconscious yet harmonious, and as attractive to many as beauty itself. Amy's nose still afflicted her, for it never would grow Grecian, so did her mouth, being too wide, and having a decided chin. These offending features gave character to her whole face, but she never could see it, and consoled herself with her wonderfully fair complexion, keen blue eyes, and curls more golden and abundant than ever.

All three wore suits of thin silver gray (their best gowns for the summer), with blush roses in hair and bosom, and all three looked just what they were—fresh-faced, happy-hearted girls, pausing a moment in their busy lives to read with wistful eyes the sweetest chapter in the romance of womanhood.

There were to be no ceremonious performances, everything was to be as natural and homelike as possible, so when Aunt March arrived, she was scandalized to see the bride come running to welcome and lead her in, to find the bridegroom fastening up a garland that had fallen down, and to catch a glimpse of the paternal minister marching upstairs with a grave countenance and a wine bottle under each arm.

"Upon my word, here's a state of things!" cried the old lady, taking the seat of honor prepared for her, and settling the folds of her lavender moire with a great rustle. "You oughtn't to be seen till the last minute, child."

"I'm not a show, Aunty, and no one is coming to stare at me, to criticize my dress, or count the cost of my luncheon. I'm too happy to care what anyone says or thinks, and I'm going to have my little wedding just as I like it. John, dear, here's your hammer." And away went Meg to help "that man" in his highly improper employment.

Mr. Brooke didn't even say, "Thank you," but as he stooped for the unromantic tool, he kissed his little bride behind the folding door, with a look that made Aunt March whisk out her pocket handkerchief with a sudden dew in her sharp old eyes.

A crash, a cry, and a laugh from Laurie, accompanied by the indecorous exclamation, "Jupiter Ammon! Jo's upset the cake again!" caused a momentary flurry, which was hardly over when a flock of cousins arrived, and "the party came in," as Beth used to say when a child.

"Don't let that young giant come near me, he worries me worse than mosquitoes," whispered the old lady to Amy, as the rooms filled and Laurie's black head towered above the rest.

"He has promised to be very good today, and he can be perfectly elegant if he likes," returned Amy, and gliding away to warn Hercules to beware of the dragon, which warning caused him to haunt the old lady with a devotion that nearly distracted her.

There was no bridal procession, but a sudden silence fell upon the room as Mr. March and the young couple took their places under the green arch. Mother and sisters gathered close, as if loath to give Meg up. The fatherly voice broke more than once, which only seemed to make the service more beautiful and solemn. The bridegroom's hand trembled visibly, and no one heard his replies. But Meg looked straight up in her husband's eyes, and said, "I will!" with such tender trust in her own face and voice that her mother's heart rejoiced and Aunt March sniffed audibly.

Jo did *not* cry, though she was very near it once, and was only saved from a demonstration by the consciousness that Laurie was staring fixedly at her, with a comical mixture of merriment and emotion in his wicked black eyes. Beth kept her face hidden on her mother's shoulder, but Amy stood like a graceful statue, with a most becoming ray of sunshine touching her white forehead and the flower in her hair.

It wasn't at all the thing, I'm afraid, but the minute she was fairly married, Meg cried, "The first kiss for Marmee!" and, turning, gave it with her heart on her lips. During the next fifteen minutes she looked more like a rose than ever, for everyone availed themselves of their privileges to the fullest extent, from Mr. Laurence to old Hannah, who, adorned with a headdress fearfully and wonderfully made, fell upon her in the hall, crying with a sob and a chuckle, "Bless you, deary, a hundred times! The cake ain't hurt a mite, and everything looks lovely."

Everybody cleared up after that, and said something brilliant, or tried to, which did just as well, for laughter is ready when hearts are light. There was no display of gifts, for they were already in the little house, nor was there an elaborate breakfast, but a plentiful lunch of cake and fruit, dressed with flowers. Mr. Laurence and Aunt March shrugged and smiled at one another when water, lemonade, and coffee were found to be the only sorts of nectar which the three Hebes carried round. No one said anything, till Laurie, who insisted on serving the bride, appeared before her, with a loaded salver in his hand and a puzzled expression on his face.

"Has Jo smashed all the bottles by accident?" he whispered, "or am I merely laboring under a delusion that I saw some lying about loose this morning?"

"No, your grandfather kindly offered us his best, and Aunt March actually sent some, but Father put away a little for Beth, and dispatched the rest to the Soldier's Home. You know he thinks that wine should be used only in illness, and Mother says that neither she nor her daughters will ever offer it to any young man under her roof."

Meg spoke seriously and expected to see Laurie frown or laugh, but he did neither, for after a quick look at her, he said, in his impetuous way, "I like that! For I've seen enough harm done to wish other women would think as you do."

"You are not made wise by experience, I hope?" and there was an anxious accent in Meg's voice.

"No. I give you my word for it. Don't think too well of me, either, this is not one of my temptations. Being brought up where wine is as common as water and almost as harmless, I don't care for it, but when a pretty girl offers it, one doesn't like to refuse, you see."

"But you will, for the sake of others, if not for your own. Come, Laurie, promise, and give me one more reason to call this the happiest day of my life."

A demand so sudden and so serious made the young man hesitate a moment, for ridicule is often harder to bear than self-denial. Meg knew that if he gave the promise he would keep it at all costs, and feeling her power, used it as a woman may for her friend's good. She did not speak, but she looked up at him with a face made very eloquent by happiness, and a smile which said, "No one can refuse me anything today." Laurie certainly could not, and with an answering smile, he gave her his hand, saying heartily, "I promise, Mrs. Brooke!"

"I thank you, very, very much."

"And I drink 'long life to your resolution,' Teddy," cried Jo, baptizing him with a splash of lemonade, as she waved her glass and beamed approvingly upon him.

So the toast was drunk, the pledge made and loyally kept in spite of many temptations, for with instinctive wisdom, the girls seized a happy moment to do their friend a service, for which he thanked them all his life.

After lunch, people strolled about, by twos and threes, through the house and garden, enjoying the sunshine without and within. Meg and John happened to be standing together in the middle of the grass plot, when Laurie was seized with an inspiration which put the finishing touch to this unfashionable wedding.

"All the married people take hands and dance round the new-made husband and wife, as the Germans do, while we bachelors and spinsters prance in couples outside!" cried Laurie, promenading down the path with Amy, with such infectious spirit and skill that everyone else followed their example without a murmur. Mr. and Mrs. March, Aunt and Uncle Carrol began it, others rapidly joined in, even Sallie Moffat, after a moment's hesitation, threw her train over her arm and whisked Ned into the ring. But the crowning joke was Mr. Laurence and Aunt March, for when the stately old gentleman chasséd solemnly up to the old lady, she just tucked her cane under her arm, and hopped briskly away to join hands with the rest and dance about the bridal pair, while the young folks pervaded the garden like butterflies on a midsummer day.

Want of breath brought the impromptu ball to a close, and then people began to go.

"I wish you well, my dear, I heartily wish you well, but I think you'll be sorry for it," said Aunt March to Meg, adding to the bridegroom, as he led her to the carriage, "You've got a treasure, young man, see that you deserve it."

"That is the prettiest wedding I've been to for an age, Ned, and I don't see why, for there wasn't a bit of style about it," observed Mrs. Moffat to her husband, as they drove away.

"Laurie, my lad, if you ever want to indulge in this sort of thing, get one of those little girls to help you, and I shall be perfectly satisfied," said Mr. Laurence, settling himself in his easy chair to rest after the excitement of the morning.

"I'll do my best to gratify you, Sir," was Laurie's unusually dutiful reply, as he carefully unpinned the posy Jo had put in his buttonhole.

The little house was not far away, and the only bridal journey Meg had was the quiet walk with John from the old home to the new. When she came down, looking like a pretty Quakeress in her dove-colored suit and straw bonnet tied with white, they all gathered about her to say 'good-by, as tenderly as if she had been going to make the grand tour.

"Don't feel that I am separated from you, Marmee dear, or that I love you any the less for loving John so much," she said, clinging to her mother, with full eyes for a moment. "I shall come every day, Father, and expect to keep my old place in all your hearts, though I am married. Beth is going to be with me a great deal, and the other girls will drop in now and then to laugh at my housekeeping struggles. Thank you all for my happy wedding day. Good-by, good-by!"

They stood watching her, with faces full of love and hope and tender pride as she walked away, leaning on her husband's arm, with her hands full of flowers and the June sunshine brightening her happy face—and so Meg's married life began.

CHAPTER XXVI

ARTISTIC ATTEMPTS

It takes people a long time to learn the difference between talent and genius, especially ambitious young men and women. Amy was learning this distinction through much tribulation, for mistaking enthusiasm for inspiration, she attempted every branch of art with youthful audacity. For a long time there was a lull in the "mud-pie" business, and she devoted herself to the finest pen-and-ink drawing, in which she showed such taste and skill that her graceful handiwork proved both pleasant and profitable. But over-strained eyes caused pen and ink to be laid aside for a bold attempt at poker-sketching.

While this attack lasted, the family lived in constant fear of a conflagration, for the odor of burning wood pervaded the house at all hours, smoke issued from attic and shed with alarming frequency, red-hot pokers lay about promiscuously, and Hannah never went to bed without a pail of water and the dinner bell at her door in case of fire. Raphael's face was found boldly executed on the underside of the moulding board, and Bacchus on the head of a beer barrel. A chanting cherub adorned the cover of the sugar bucket, and attempts to portray Romeo and Juliet supplied kindling for some time.

From fire to oil was a natural transition for burned fingers, and Amy fell to painting with undiminished ardor. An artist friend fitted her out with his castoff palettes, brushes, and colors, and she daubed away, producing pastoral and marine views such as were never seen on land or sea. Her monstrosities in the way of cattle would have taken prizes at an agricultural fair, and the perilous pitching of her vessels would have produced seasickness in the most nautical observer, if the utter disregard to all known rules of shipbuilding and rigging had not convulsed him with laughter at the first glance. Swarthy boys and dark-eyed Madonnas, staring at you from one corner of the studio, suggested Murillo; oily brown shadows of faces with a lurid streak in the wrong place, meant Rembrandt; buxom ladies and dropiscal infants, Rubens; and Turner appeared in tempests of blue thunder, orange lightning, brown rain, and purple clouds, with a tomato-colored splash in the middle, which might be the sun or a bouy, a sailor's shirt or a king's robe, as the spectator pleased.

Charcoal portraits came next, and the entire family hung in a row, looking as wild and crocky as if just evoked from a coalbin. Softened into crayon sketches, they did better, for the likenesses were good, and Amy's hair, Jo's nose, Meg's mouth, and Laurie's eyes were pronounced "wonderfully fine." A return to clay and plaster followed, and ghostly casts of her acquaintances haunted corners of the house, or tumbled off closet shelves onto people's heads. Children were enticed in as models, till their incoherent accounts of her mysterious doings caused Miss Amy to be regarded in the light of a young ogress. Her efforts in this line, however, were brought to an abrupt close by an untoward accident, which quenched her ardor. Other models failing her for a time, she undertook to cast her own pretty foot, and the family were one day alarmed by an unearthly bumping and screaming and running to the rescue, found the young enthusiast hopping wildly about the shed with her foot held fast in a pan full of plaster, which had hardened with unexpected rapidity. With much difficulty and some danger she was dug out, for Jo was so overcome with laughter while she excavated that her knife went too far, cut the poor foot, and left a lasting memorial of one artistic attempt, at least.

After this Amy subsided, till a mania for sketching from nature set her to haunting river, field, and wood, for picturesque studies, and sighing for ruins to copy. She caught endless colds sitting on damp grass to book "a delicious bit," composed of a stone, a stump, one mushroom, and a broken mullein stalk, or "a heavenly mass of clouds," that looked like a choice display of featherbeds when done. She sacrificed her complexion floating on the river in the midsummer sun to study light and shade, and got a wrinkle over her nose trying after "points of sight," or whatever the squint-and-string performance is called.

If "genius is eternal patience," as Michelangelo affirms, Amy had some claim to the divine attribute, for she persevered in spite of all obstacles, failures, and discouragements, firmly believing that in time she should do something worthy to be called "high art."

She was learning, doing, and enjoying other things, meanwhile, for she had resolved to be an attractive and accomplished woman, even if she never became a great artist. Here she succeeded better, for she was one of those happily created beings who please without effort, make friends everywhere, and take life so gracefully and easily that less fortunate souls are tempted to believe that such are born under a lucky star. Everybody liked her, for among her good gifts was tact. She had an instinctive sense of what was pleasing and proper, always said the right thing to the right person, did just what suited the time and place, and was so self-possessed that her sisters used to say, "If Amy went to court without any rehearsal beforehand, she'd know exactly what to do."

One of her weaknesses was a desire to move in "our best society," without being quite sure what the *best* really was. Money, position, fashionable accomplishments, and elegant manners were most desirable things in her eyes, and she liked to associate with those who possessed them, often mistaking the false for the true, and admiring what was not admirable. Never forgetting that by birth she was a gentlewoman, she cultivated her aristocratic tastes and feelings, so that when the opportunity came she might be ready to take the place from which poverty now excluded her.

"My lady," as her friends called her, sincerely desired to be a genuine lady, and was so at heart, but had yet to learn that money cannot buy refinement of nature, that rank does not always confer nobility, and that true breeding makes itself felt in spite of external drawbacks.

"I want to ask a favor of you, Mamma," Amy said, coming in with an important air one day.

"Well, little girl, what is it?" replied her mother, in whose eyes the stately young lady still remained "the baby."

"Our drawing class breaks up next week, and before the girls separate for the summer, I want to ask them out here for a day. They are wild to see the river, sketch the broken bridge, and copy some of the things they admire in my book. They have been very kind to me in many ways, and I am grateful, for they are all rich and I know I am poor, yet they never made any difference."

"Why should they?" and Mrs. March put the question with what the girls called her "Maria Theresa air."

"You know as well as I that it *does* make a difference with nearly everyone, so don't ruffle up like a dear, motherly hen, when your chickens get pecked by smarter birds. The ugly duckling turned out a swan, you know." And Amy smiled without bitterness, for she possessed a happy temper and hopeful spirit.

Mrs. March laughed, and smoothed down her maternal pride as she asked, "Well, my swan, what is your plan?"

"I should like to ask the girls out to lunch next week, to take them for a drive to the places they want to see, a row on the river, perhaps, and make a little artistic fete for them."

"That looks feasible. What do you want for lunch? Cake, sandwiches, fruit, and coffee will be all that is necessary, I suppose?"

"Oh, dear, no! We must have cold tongue and chicken, French chocolate and ice cream, besides. The girls are used to such things, and I want my lunch to be proper and elegant, though I *do* work for my living."

"How many young ladies are there?" asked her mother, beginning to look sober.

"Twelve or fourteen in the class, but I dare say they won't all come."

"Bless me, child, you will have to charter an omnibus to carry them about."

"Why, Mother, how can you think of such a thing? Not more than six or eight will probably come, so I shall hire a beach wagon and borrow Mr. Laurence's cherry-bounce." (Hannah's pronunciation of charabanc.)

"All of this will be expensive, Amy."

"Not very. I've calculated the cost, and I'll pay for it myself."

"Don't you think, dear, that as these girls are used to such things, and the best we can do will be nothing new, that some simpler plan would be pleasanter to them, as a change if nothing more, and much better for us than buying or borrowing what we don't need, and attempting a style not in keeping with our circumstances?"

"If I can't have it as I like, I don't care to have it at all. I know that I can carry it out perfectly well, if you and the girls will help a little, and I don't see why I can't if I'm willing to pay for it," said Amy, with the decision which opposition was apt to change into obstinacy.

Mrs. March knew that experience was an excellent teacher, and when it was possible she left her children to learn alone the lessons which she would gladly have made easier, if they had not objected to taking advice as much as they did salts and senna.

"Very well, Amy, if your heart is set upon it, and you see your way through without too great an outlay of money, time, and temper, I'll say no more. Talk it over with the girls, and whichever way you decide, I'll do my best to help you."

"Thanks, Mother, you are always *so* kind." and away went Amy to lay her plan before her sisters.

Meg agreed at once, and promised her aid, gladly offering anything she possessed, from her little house itself to her very best saltspoons. But Jo frowned upon the whole project and would have nothing to do with it at first.

"Why in the world should you spend your money, worry your family, and turn the house upside down for a parcel of girls who don't care a sixpence for you? I thought you had too much pride and sense to truckle to any mortal woman just because she wears French boots and rides in a coupe," said Jo, who, being called from the tragic climax of her novel, was not in the best mood for social enterprises.

"I *don't* truckle, and I hate being patronized as much as you do!" returned Amy indignantly, for the two still jangled when such questions arose. "The girls do care for me, and I for them, and there's a great deal of kindness and sense and talent among them, in spite of what you call fashionable nonsense. You don't care to make people like you, to go into good society, and cultivate your manners and tastes. I do, and I mean to make the most of every chance that comes. You can go through the world with your elbows out and your nose in the air, and call it independence, if you like. That's not my way."

When Amy had whetted her tongue and freed her mind she usually got the best of it, for she seldom failed to have common sense on her side, while Jo carried her love of liberty and hate of conventionalities to such an unlimited extent that she naturally found herself worsted in an argument. Amy's definition of Jo's idea of independence was such a good hit that both burst out laughing, and the discussion took a more amiable turn. Much against her will, Jo at length consented to sacrifice a day to Mrs. Grundy, and help her sister through what she regarded as "a nonsensical business."

The invitations were sent, nearly all accepted, and the following Monday was set apart for the grand event. Hannah was out of humor because her week's work was deranged, and prophesied that "ef the washin' and ironin' warn't done reg'lar, nothin' would go well anywheres." This hitch in the mainspring of the domestic machinery had a bad effect upon the whole concern, but Amy's motto was "*Nil desperandum*," and having made up her mind what to do, she proceeded to do it in spite of all obstacles. To begin with, Hannah's cooking didn't turn out well. The chicken was tough, the tongue too salty, and the chocolate wouldn't froth properly. Then the cake and ice cost more than Amy expected, so did the wagon, and various other expenses, which seemed trifling at the outset, counted up rather alarmingly afterward. Beth got a cold and took to her bed. Meg had an unusual number of callers to keep her at home, and Jo was in such a divided state of mind that her breakages, accidents, and mistakes were uncommonly numerous, serious, and trying.

"If it hadn't been for Mother I never should have got through," as Amy declared afterward, and gratefully remembered when "the best joke of the season," was entirely forgotten by everybody else.

If it was not fair on Monday, the young ladies were to come on Tuesday—an arrangement which aggravated Jo and Hannah to the last degree. On Monday morning the weather was in that undecided state which is more exasperating than a steady pour. It drizzled a little, shone a little, blew a little, and didn't make up its mind till it was too late for anyone else to make up theirs. Amy was up at dawn, hustling people out of their beds and through their breakfasts, that the house might be got in order. The parlor struck her as looking uncommonly shabby, but without stopping to sigh for what she had not, she skillfully made the best of what she had, arranging chairs over the worn places in the carpet, covering stains on the walls with pictures framed in ivy, and filling up empty corners with homemade statuary, which gave an artistic air to the room, as did the lovely vases of flowers Jo scattered about.

The lunch looked charming, and as she surveyed it, she sincerely hoped it would taste well, and that the borrowed glass, china, and silver would get safely home again. The carriages were promised, Meg and Mother were all ready to do the honors, Beth was able to help Hannah behind the scenes, Jo had engaged to be as lively and amiable as an absent mind, and aching head, and a very decided disapproval of everybody and everything would allow, and as she wearily dressed, Amy cheered herself with anticipations of the happy moment when, lunch safely over, she should drive away with her friends for an afternoon of artistic delights, for the "cherry-bounce" and the broken bridge were her strong points.

Then came the hours of suspense, during which she vibrated from parlor to porch, while public opinion varied like the weathercock. A smart shower at eleven had evidently quenched the enthusiasm of the young ladies who were to arrive at twelve, for nobody came, and at two the exhausted family sat down in a blaze of sunshine to consume the perishable portions of the feast, that nothing might be lost.

"No doubt about the weather today, they will certainly come, so we must fly round and be ready for them," said Amy, as the sun woke her next morning. She spoke briskly, but in her secret soul she wished she had said nothing about Tuesday, for her interest like her cake was getting a little stale.

"I can't get any lobsters, so you will have to do without salad today," said Mr. March, coming in half an hour later, with an expression of placid despair.

"Use the chicken then, the toughness won't matter in a salad," advised his wife.

"Hannah left it on the kitchen table a minute, and the kittens got at it. I'm very sorry, Amy," added Beth, who was still a patroness of cats.

"Then I *must* have a lobster, for tongue alone won't do," said Amy decidedly.

"Shall I rush into town and demand one?" asked Jo, with the magnanimity of a martyr.

"You'd come bringing it home under your arm without any paper, just to try me. I'll go myself," answered Amy, whose temper was beginning to fail.

Shrouded in a thick veil and armed with a genteel traveling basket, she departed, feeling that a cool drive would soothe her ruffled spirit and fit her for the labors of the day. After some delay, the object of her desire was procured, likewise a bottle of dressing to prevent further loss of time at home, and off she drove again, well pleased with her own forethought.

As the omnibus contained only one other passenger, a sleepy old lady, Amy pocketed her veil and beguiled the tedium of the way by trying to find out where all her money had gone to. So busy was she with her card full of refractory figures that she did not observe a newcomer, who entered without stopping the vehicle, till a masculine voice said, "Good morning, Miss March," and, looking up, she beheld one of Laurie's most elegant college friends. Fervently hoping that he would get out before she did, Amy utterly ignored the basket at her feet, and congratulating herself that she had on her new traveling dress, returned the young man's greeting with her usual suavity and spirit.

They got on excellently, for Amy's chief care was soon set at rest by learning that the gentleman would leave first, and she was chatting away in a peculiarly lofty strain, when the old lady got out. In stumbling to the door, she upset the basket, and—oh horror!—the lobster, in all its vulgar size and brilliancy, was revealed to the highborn eyes of a Tudor!

"By Jove, she's forgotten her dinner!" cried the unconscious youth, poking the scarlet monster into its place with his cane, and preparing to hand out the basket after the old lady.

"Please don't—it's—it's mine," murmured Amy, with a face nearly as red as her fish.

"Oh, really, I beg pardon. It's an uncommonly fine one, isn't it?" said Tudor, with great presence of mind, and an air of sober interest that did credit to his breeding.

Amy recovered herself in a breath, set her basket boldly on the seat, and said, laughing, "Don't you wish you were to have some of the salad he's going to make, and to see the charming young ladies who are to eat it?"

Now that was tact, for two of the ruling foibles of the masculine mind were touched. The lobster was instantly surrounded by a halo of pleasing reminiscences, and curiosity about "the charming young ladies" diverted his mind from the comical mishap.

"I suppose he'll laugh and joke over it with Laurie, but I shan't see them, that's a comfort," thought Amy, as Tudor bowed and departed.

She did not mention this meeting at home (though she discovered that, thanks to the upset, her new dress was much damaged by the rivulets of dressing that meandered down the skirt), but went through with the preparations which now seemed more irksome than before, and at twelve o'clock all was ready again. Feeling that the neighbors were interested in her movements, she wished to efface the memory of yesterday's failure by a grand success today, so she ordered the "cherry-bounce," and drove away in state to meet and escort her guests to the banquet.

"There's the rumble, they're coming! I'll go onto the porch and meet them. It looks hospitable, and I want the poor child to have a good time after all her trouble," said Mrs. March, suiting the action to the word.

But after one glance, she retired, with an indescribable expression, for looking quite lost in the big carriage, sat Amy and one young lady.

"Run, Beth, and help Hannah clear half the things off the table. It will be too absurd to put a luncheon for twelve before a single girl," cried Jo, hurrying away to the lower regions, too excited to stop even for a laugh.

In came Amy, quite calm and delightfully cordial to the one guest who had kept her promise. The rest of the family, being of a dramatic turn, played their parts equally well, and Miss Eliott found them a most hilarious set, for it was impossible to control entirely the merriment which possessed them. The remodeled lunch being gaily partaken of, the studio and garden visited, and art discussed with enthusiasm, Amy ordered a buggy (alas for the elegant cherry-bounce), and drove her friend quietly about the neighborhood till sunset, when "the party went out."

As she came walking in, looking very tired but as composed as ever, she observed that every vestige of the unfortunate fete had disappeared, except a suspicious pucker about the corners of Jo's mouth.

"You've had a loverly afternoon for your drive, dear," said her mother, as respectfully as if the whole twelve had come.

"Miss Eliott is a very sweet girl, and seemed to enjoy herself, I thought," observed Beth, with unusual warmth.

"Could you spare me some of your cake? I really need some, I have so much company, and I can't make such delicious stuff as yours," asked Meg soberly.

"Take it all. I'm the only one here who likes sweet things, and it will mold before I can dispose of it," answered Amy, thinking with a sigh of the generous store she had laid in for such an end as this.

"It's a pity Laurie isn't here to help us," began Jo, as they sat down to ice cream and salad for the second time in two days.

A warning look from her mother checked any further remarks, and the whole family ate in heroic silence, till Mr. March mildly observed, "salad was one of the favorite dishes of the ancients, and Evelyn" — here a general explosion of laughter cut short the "history of salads," to the great surprise of the learned gentleman.

"Bundle everything into a basket and send it to the Hummels. Germans like messes. I'm sick of the sight of this, and there's no reason you should all die of a surfeit because I've been a fool," cried Amy, wiping her eyes.

"I thought I *should* have died when I saw you two girls rattling about in the what-you-call-it, like two little kernels in a very big nutshell, and Mother waiting in state to receive the throng," sighed Jo, quite spent with laughter.

"I'm very sorry you were disappointed, dear, but we all did our best to satisfy you," said Mrs. March, in a tone full of motherly regret.

"I *am* satisfied. I've done what I undertook, and it's not my fault that it failed. I comfort myself with that," said Amy with a little quiver in her voice. "I thank you all very much for helping me, and I'll thank you still more if you won't allude to it for a month, at least."

No one did for several months, but the word "fete" always produced a general smile, and Laurie's birthday gift to Amy was a tiny coral lobster in the shape of a charm for her watch guard.

CHAPTER XXVII

LITERARY LESSONS

Fortune suddenly smiled upon Jo, and dropped a good luck penny in her path. Not a golden penny, exactly, but I doubt if half a million would have given more real happiness than did the little sum that came to her in this wise.

Every few weeks she would shut herself up in her room, put on her scribbling suit, and "fall into a vortex," as she expressed it, writing away at her novel with all her heart and soul, for till that was finished she could find no peace. Her "scribbling suit" consisted of a black woolen pinafore on which she could wipe her pen at will, and a cap of the same material, adorned with a cheerful red bow, into which she bundled her hair when the decks were cleared for action. This cap was a beacon to the inquiring eyes of her family, who during these periods kept their distance, merely popping in their heads semi-occasionally to ask, with interest, "Does genius burn, Jo?" They did not always venture even to ask this question, but took an observation of the cap, and judged accordingly. If this expressive article of dress was drawn low upon the forehead, it was a sign that hard work was going on, in exciting moments it was pushed rakishly askew, and when despair seized the author it was plucked wholly off, and cast upon the floor. At such times the intruder silently withdrew, and not until the red bow was seen gaily erect upon the gifted brow, did anyone dare address Jo.

She did not think herself a genius by any means, but when the writing fit came on, she gave herself up to it with entire abandon, and led a blissful life, unconscious of want, care, or bad weather, while she sat safe and happy in an imaginary world, full of friends almost as real and dear to her as any in the flesh. Sleep forsook her eyes, meals stood untasted, day and night were all too short to enjoy the happiness which blessed her only at such times, and made these hours worth living, even if they bore no other fruit. The devine afflatus usually lasted a week or two, and then she emerged from her "vortex" hungry, sleepy, cross, or despondent.

She was just recovering from one of these attacks when she was prevailed upon to escort Miss Crocker to a lecture, and in return for her virtue was rewarded with a new idea. It was a People's Course, the lecture on the Pyramids, and Jo rather wondered at the choice of such a subject for such an audience, but took it for granted that some great social evil would be remedied or some great want supplied by unfolding the glories of the Pharaohs to an audience whose thoughts were busy with the price of coal and flour, and whose lives were spent in trying to solve harder riddles than that of the Sphinx.

They were early, and while Miss Crocker set the heel of her stocking, Jo amused herself by examining the faces of the people who occupied the seat with them. On her left were two matrons, with massive foreheads and bonnets to match, discussing Women's Rights and making tatting. Beyond sat a pair of humble lovers, artlessly holding each other by the hand, a somber spinster eating peppermints out of a paper bag, and an old gentleman taking his preparatory nap behind a yellow bandanna. On her right, her only neighbor was a studious looking lad absorbed in a newspaper.

It was a pictorial sheet, and Jo examined the work of art nearest her, idly wondering what fortuitous concatenation of circumstances needed the melodramatic illustration of an Indian in full war costume, tumbling over a precipice with a wolf at his throat, while two infuriated young gentlemen, with unnaturally small feet and big eyes, were stabbing each other close by, and a disheveled female was flying away in the background with her mouth wide open. Pausing to turn a page, the lad saw her looking and, with boyish good nature offered half his paper, saying bluntly, "Want to read it? That's a first-rate story."

Jo accepted it with a smile, for she had never outgrown her liking for lads, and soon found herself involved in the usual labyrinth of love, mystery, and murder, for the story belonged to that class of light literature in which the passions have a holiday, and when the author's invention fails, a grand catastrophe clears the stage of one half the dramatis personae, leaving the other half to exult over their downfall.

"Prime, isn't it?" asked the boy, as her eye went down the last paragraph of her portion.

"I think you and I could do as well as that if we tried," returned Jo, amused at his admiration of the trash.

"I should think I was a pretty lucky chap if I could. She makes a good living out of such stories, they say." and he pointed to the name of Mrs. S.L.A.N.G. Northbury, under the title of the tale.

"Do you know her?" asked Jo, with sudden interest.

"No, but I read all her pieces, and I know a fellow who works in the office where this paper is printed."

"Do you say she makes a good living out of stories like this?" and Jo looked more respectfully at the agitated group and thickly sprinkled exclamation points that adorned the page.

"Guess she does! She knows just what folks like, and gets paid well for writing it."

Here the lecture began, but Jo heard very little of it, for while Professor Sands was prosing away about Belzoni, Cheops, scarabei, and hieroglyphics, she was covertly taking down the address of the paper, and boldly resolving to try for the hundred-dollar prize offered in its columns for a sensational story. By the time the lecture ended and the audience awoke, she had built up a splendid fortune for herself (not the first founded on paper), and was already deep in the concoction of her story, being unable to decide whether the duel should come before the elopement or after the murder.

She said nothing of her plan at home, but fell to work next day, much to the disquiet of her mother, who always looked a little anxious when "genius took to burning." Jo had never tried this style before, contenting herself with very mild romances for *The Spread Eagle*. Her experience and miscellaneous reading were of service now, for they gave her some idea of dramatic effect, and supplied plot, language, and costumes. Her story was as full of desperation and despair as her limited acquaintance with those uncomfortable emotions enabled her to make it, and having located it in Lisbon, she wound up with an earthquake, as a striking and appropriate denouement. The manuscript was privately dispatched, accompanied by a note, modestly saying that if the tale didn't get the prize, which the writer hardly dared expect, she would be very glad to receive any sum it might be considered worth.

Six weeks is a long time to wait, and a still longer time for a girl to keep a secret, but Jo did both, and was just beginning to give up all hope of ever seeing her manuscript again, when a letter arrived which almost took her breath away, for on opening it, a check for a hundred dollars fell into her lap. For a minute she stared at it as if it had been a snake, then she read her letter and began to cry. If the amiable gentleman who wrote that kindly note could have known what intense happiness he was giving a fellow creature, I think he would devote his leisure hours, if he has any, to that amusement, for Jo valued the letter more than the money, because it was encouraging, and after years of effort it was so pleasant to find that she had learned to do something, though it was only to write a sensation story.

A prouder young woman was seldom seen than she, when, having composed herself, she electrified the family by appearing before them with the letter in one hand, the check in the other, announcing that she had won the prize. Of course there was a great jubilee, and when the story came everyone read and praised it, though after her father had told her that the language was good, the romance fresh and hearty, and the tragedy quite thrilling, he shook his head, and said in his unworldly way—

"You can do better than this, Jo. Aim at the highest, and never mind the money."

"*I* think the money is the best part of it. What will you do with such a fortune?" asked Amy, regarding the magic slip of paper with a reverential eye.

"Send Beth and Mother to the seaside for a month or two," answered Jo promptly.

"Oh, how splendid! No, I can't do it, dear, it would be selfish," cried Beth, who had clapped her thin hands and taken a long breath, as if pining for fresh ocean breeze, then stopped herself and motioned away the check which her sister waved before her.

"Ah, but you shall go, I've set my heart on it. That's what I tried for, and that's why I succeeded. I never get on when I think of myself along, so it will help me to work for you don't you see? Besides, Marmee needs the change and she won't leave you, so you *must* go. Won't it be fun to see you come home plump and rosy again? Hurrah for Dr. Jo, who always cures her patients!"

To the seaside they went, after much discussion, and though Beth didn't come home as plump and rosy as could be desired, she was much better, while Mrs. March declared she felt ten years younger. So Jo was satisfied with the investment of her prize money, and fell to work with a cheery spirit, bent on earning more of those delightful checks. She did earn several that year, and began to feel herself a power in the house, for by the magic of a pen, her "rubbish" turned into comforts for them all. *The Duke's Daughter* paid the butcher's bill, *A Phantom Hand* put down a new carpet, and the *Curse of the Coventrys* proved the blessing of the Marches in the way of groceries and gowns.

Wealth is certainly a most desirable thing, but poverty has its sunny side, and one of the sweet uses of adversity is the genuine satisfaction which comes from hearty work of head or hand, and to the inspiration of necessity, we owe half the wise, beautiful, and useful blessings of the world. Jo enjoyed a taste of this satisfaction, and ceased to envy richer girls, taking great comfort in the knowledge that she could supply her own wants, and need ask no one for a penny.

Little notice was taken of her stories, but they found a market, and encouraged by this fact, she resolved to make a bold stroke for fame and fortune. Having copied her novel for the fourth time, read it to all her confidential friends, and submitted it with fear and trembling to three publishers, she at last disposed of it, on condition that she would cut it down one third, and omit all the parts which she particularly admired.

"Now I must either bundle it back in to my tin kitchen to mold, pay for printing it myself, or chop it up to suit purchasers and get what I can for it. Fame is a very good thing to have in the house, but cash is more convenient, so I wish to take the sense of the meeting on this important subject," said Jo, calling a family council.

"Don't spoil your book, my girl, for there is more in it than you know, and the idea is well worked out. Let it wait and ripen," was her father's advice, and he practiced what he preached, having waited patiently thirty years for fruit of his own to ripen, and being in no haste to gather it even now when it was sweet and mellow.

"It seems to me that Jo will profit more by taking the trial than by waiting," said Mrs. March. "Criticism is the best test of such work, for it will show her both unsuspected merits and faults, and help her to do better next time. We are too partial, but the praise and blame of outsiders will prove useful, even if she gets but little money."

"Yes," said Jo, knitting her brows, "that's just it. I've been fussing over the thing so long, I really don't know whether it's good, bad, or indifferent. It will be a great help to have cool, impartial persons take a look at it, and tell me what they think of it."

"I wouldn't leave a word out of it. You'll spoil it if you do, for the interest of the story is more in the minds than in the actions of the people, and it will be all a muddle if you don't explain as you go on," said Meg, who firmly believed that this book was the most remarkable novel ever written.

"But Mr. Allen says, 'Leave out the explanations, make it brief and dramatic, and let the characters tell the story,'" interrupted Jo, turning to the publisher's note.

"Do as he tells you. He knows what will sell, and we don't. Make a good, popular book, and get as much money as you can. By-and-by, when you've got a name, you can afford to digress, and have philosophical and metaphysical people in your novels," said Amy, who took a strictly practical view of the subject.

"Well," said Jo, laughing, "if my people *are* 'philosophical and metaphysical,' it isn't my fault, for I know nothing about such things, except what I hear father say, sometimes. If I've got some of his wise ideas jumbled up with my romance, so much the better for me. Now, Beth, what do you say?"

"I should so like to see it printed *soon*," was all Beth said, and smiled in saying it. But there was an unconscious emphasis on the last word, and a wistful look in the eyes that never lost their childlike candor, which chilled Jo's heart for a minute with a forboding fear, and decided her to make her little venture "soon."

So, with Spartan firmness, the young authoress laid her first-born on her table, and chopped it up as ruthlessly as any ogre. In the hope of pleasing everyone, she took everyone's advice, and like the old man and his donkey in the fable suited nobody.

Her father liked the metaphysical streak which had unconsciously got into it, so that was allowed to remain though she had her doubts about it. Her mother thought that there was a trifle too much description. Out, therefore it came, and with it many necessary links in the story. Meg admired the tragedy, so Jo piled up the agony to suit her, while Amy objected to the fun, and, with the best intentions in life, Jo quenched the sprightly scenes which relieved the somber character of the story. Then, to complicate the ruin, she cut it down one third, and confidingly sent the poor little romance, like a picked robin, out into the big, busy world to try its fate.

Well, it was printed, and she got three hundred dollars for it, likewise plenty of praise and blame, both so much greater than she expected that she was thrown into a state of bewilderment from which it took her some time to recover.

"You said, Mother, that criticism would help me. But how can it, when it's so contradictory that I don't know whether I've written a promising book or broken all the ten commandments?" cried poor Jo, turning over a heap of notices, the perusal of which filled her with pride and joy one minute, wrath and dismay the next. "This man says, 'An exquisite book, full of truth, beauty, and earnestness; all is sweet, pure, and healthy,'" continued the perplexed authoress. "The next, 'The theory of the book is bad, full of morbid fancies, spiritualistic ideas, and unnatural characters.' Now, as I had no theory of any kind, don't believe in Spiritualism, and copied my characters from life, I don't see how this critic can be right. Another says, 'It's one of the best American novels which has appeared for years.' (I know better than that), and the next asserts that 'Though it is original, and written with great force and feeling, it is a dangerous book.' 'Tisn't! Some make fun of it, some overpraise, and nearly all insist that I had a deep theory to expound, when I only wrote it for the pleasure and the money. I wish I'd printed the whole or not at all, for I do hate to be so misjudged."

Her family and friends administered comfort and commendation liberally. Yet it was a hard time for sensitive, high-spirited Jo, who meant so well and had apparently done so ill. But it did her good, for those whose opinion had real value gave her the criticism which is an author's best education, and when the first soreness was over, she could laugh at her poor little book, yet believe in it still, and feel herself the wiser and stronger for the buffeting she had received.

"Not being a genius, like Keats, it won't kill me," she said stoutly, "and I've got the joke on my side, after all, for the parts that were taken straight out of real life are denounced as impossible and absurd, and the scenes that I made up out of my own silly head are pronounced 'charmingly natural, tender, and true.' So I'll comfort myself with that, and when I'm ready, I'll up again and take another."

CHAPTER XXVIII

DOMESTIC EXPERIENCES

Like most other young matrons, Meg began her married life with the determination to be a model housekeeper. John should find home a paradise, he should always see a smiling face, should fare sumptuously every day, and never know the loss of a button. She brought so much love, energy, and cheerfulness to the work that she could not but succeed, in spite of some obstacles. Her paradise was not a tranquil one, for the little woman fussed, was over-anxious to please, and bustled about like a true Martha, cumbered with many cares. She was too tired, sometimes, even to smile, John grew dyspeptic after a course of dainty dishes and ungratefully demanded plain fare. As for buttons, she soon learned to wonder where they went, to shake her head over the carelessness of men, and to threaten to make him sew them on himself, and see if *his* work would stand impatient and clumsy fingers any better than hers.

They were very happy, even after they discovered that they couldn't live on love alone. John did not find Meg's beauty diminished, though she beamed at him from behind the familiar coffee pot. Nor did Meg miss any of the romance from the daily parting, when her husband followed up his kiss with the tender inquiry, "Shall I send some veal or mutton for dinner, darling?" The little house ceased to be a glorified bower, but it became a home, and the young couple soon felt that it was a change for the better. At first they played keep-house, and frolicked over it like children. Then John took steadily to business, feeling the cares of the head of a family upon his shoulders, and Meg laid by her cambric wrappers, put on a big apron, and fell to work, as before said, with more energy than discretion.

While the cooking mania lasted she went through Mrs. Cornelius's Receipt Book as if it were a mathematical exercise, working out the problems with patience and care. Sometimes her family were invited in to help eat up a too bounteous feast of successes, or Lotty would be privately dispatched with a batch of failures, which were to be concealed from all eyes in the convenient stomachs of the little Hummels. An evening with John over the account books usually produced a temporary lull in the culinary enthusiasm, and a frugal fit would ensue, during which the poor man was put through a course of bread pudding, hash, and warmed-over coffee, which tried his soul, although he bore it with praiseworthy fortitude. Before the golden mean was found, however, Meg added to her domestic possessions what young couples seldom get on long without—a family jar.

Fired with a housewifely wish to see her storeroom stocked with homemade preserves, she undertook to put up her own currant jelly. John was requested to order home a dozen or so of little pots and an extra quantity of sugar, for their own currants were ripe and were to be attended to at once. As John firmly believed that "my wife" was equal to anything, and took a natural pride in her skill, he resolved that she should be gratified, and their only crop of fruit laid by in a most pleasing form for winter use. Home came four dozen delightful little pots, half a barrel of sugar, and a small boy to pick the currants for her. With her pretty hair tucked into a little cap, arms bared to the elbow, and a checked apron which had a coquettish look in spite of the bib, the young housewife fell to work, feeling no doubts about her success, for hadn't she seen Hannah do it hundreds of times? The array of pots rather amazed her at first, but John was so fond of jelly, and the nice little jars would look so well on the top shelf, that Meg resolved to fill them all, and spent a long day picking, boiling, straining, and fussing over her jelly. She did her best, she asked advice of Mrs. Cornelius, she racked her brain to remember what Hannah did that she left undone, she reboiled, resugared, and restrained, but that dreadful stuff wouldn't "jell."

She longed to run home, bib and all, and ask Mother to lend her a hand, but John and she had agreed that they would never annoy anyone with their private worries, experiments, or quarrels. They had laughed over that last word as if the idea it suggested was a most preposterous one, but they had held to their resolve, and whenever they could get on without help they did so, and no one interfered, for Mrs. March had advised the plan. So Meg wrestled alone with the refractory sweetmeats all that hot summer day, and at five o'clock sat down in her topsy-turvey kitchen, wrung her bedaubed hands, lifted up her voice and wept.

Now, in the first flush of the new life, she had often said, "My husband shall always feel free to bring a friend home whenever he likes.

I shall always be prepared. There shall be no flurry, no scolding, no discomfort, but a neat house, a cheerful wife, and a good dinner. John, dear, never stop to ask my leave, invite whom you please, and be sure of a welcome from me."

How charming that was, to be sure! John quite glowed with pride to hear her say it, and felt what a blessed thing it was to have a superior wife. But, although they had had company from time to time, it never happened to be unexpected, and Meg had never had an opportunity to distinguish herself till now. It always happens so in this vale of tears, there is an inevitability about such things which we can only wonder at, deplore, and bear as we best can.

If John had not forgotten all about the jelly, it really would have been unpardonable in him to choose that day, of all the days in the year, to bring a friend home to dinner unexpectedly. Congratulating himself that a handsome repast had been ordered that morning, feeling sure that it would be ready to the minute, and indulging in pleasant anticipations of the charming effect it would produce, when his pretty wife came running out to meet him, he escorted his friend to his mansion, with the irrepressible satisfaction of a young host and husband.

It is a world of disappointments, as John discovered when he reached the Dovecote. The front door usually stood hospitably open. Now it was not only shut, but locked, and yesterday's mud still adorned the steps. The parlor windows were closed and curtained, no picture of the pretty wife sewing on the piazza, in white, with a distracting little bow in her hair, or a bright-eyed hostess, smiling a shy welcome as she greeted her guest. Nothing of the sort, for not a soul appeared but a sanginary-looking boy asleep under the current bushes.

"I'm afraid something has happened. Step into the garden, Scott, while I look up Mrs. Brooke," said John, alarmed at the silence and solitude.

Round the house he hurried, led by a pungent smell of burned sugar, and Mr. Scott strolled after him, with a queer look on his face. He paused discreetly at a distance when Brooke disappeared, but he could both see and hear, and being a bachelor, enjoyed the prospect mightily.

In the kitchen reigned confusion and despair. One edition of jelly was trickled from pot to pot, another lay upon the floor, and a third was burning gaily on the stove. Lotty, with Teutonic phlegm, was calmly eating bread and currant wine, for the jelly was still in a hopelessly liquid state, while Mrs. Brooke, with her apron over her head, sat sobbing dismally.

"My dearest girl, what is the matter?" cried John, rushing in, with awful visions of scalded hands, sudden news of affliction, and secret consternation at the thought of the guest in the garden.

"Oh, John, I *am* so tired and hot and cross and worried! I've been at it till I'm all worn out. Do come and help me or I *shall* die!" and the exhausted housewife cast herself upon his breast, giving him a sweet welcome in every sense of the word, for her pinafore had been baptized at the same time as the floor.

"What worries you dear? Has anything dreadful happened?" asked the anxious John, tenderly kissing the crown of the little cap, which was all askew.

"Yes," sobbed Meg despairingly.

"Tell me quick, then. Don't cry. I can bear anything better than that. Out with it, love."

"The—the jelly won't jell and I don't know what to do!"

John Brooke laughed then as he never dared to laugh afterward, and the derisive Scott smiled involuntarily as he heard the hearty peal, which put the finishing stroke to poor Meg's woe.

"Is that all? Fling it out of the window, and don't bother any more about it. I'll buy you quarts if you want it, but for heaven's sake don't have hysterics, for I've brought Jack Scott home to dinner, and—"

John got no further, for Meg cast him off, and clasped her hands with a tragic gesture as she fell into a chair, exclaiming in a tone of mingled indignation, reproach, and dismay—

"A man to dinner, and everything in a mess! John Brooke, how *could* you do such a thing?"

"Hush, he's in the garden! I forgot the confounded jelly, but it can't be helped now," said John, surveying the prospect with an anxious eye.

"You ought to have sent word, or told me this morning, and you ought to have remembered how busy I was," continued Meg petulantly, for even turtledoves will peck when ruffled.

"I didn't know it this morning, and there was no time to send word, for I met him on the way out. I never thought of asking leave, when you have always told me to do as I liked. I never tried it before, and hang me if I ever do again!" added John, with an aggrieved air.

"I should hope not! Take him away at once. I can't see him, and there isn't any dinner."

"Well, I like that! Where's the beef and vegetables I sent home, and the pudding you promised?" cried John, rushing to the larder.

"I hadn't time to cook anything. I meant to dine at Mother's. I'm sorry, but I was *so* busy," and Meg's tears began again.

John was a mild man, but he was human, and after a long day's work to come home tired, hungry, and hopeful, to find a chaotic house, an empty table, and a cross wife was not exactly conducive to repose of mind or manner. He restrained himself however, and the little squall would have blown over, but for one unlucky word.

"It's a scrape, I acknowledge, but if you will lend a hand, we'll pull through and have a good time yet. Don't cry, dear, but just exert yourself a bit, and fix us up something to eat. We're both as hungry as hunters, so we shan't mind what it is. Give us the cold meat, and bread and cheese. We won't ask for jelly."

He meant it to be a good-natured joke, but that one word sealed his fate. Meg thought it was *too* cruel to hint about her sad failure, and the last atom of patience vanished as he spoke.

"You must get yourself out of the scrape as you can. I'm too used up to 'exert' myself for anyone. It's like a man to propose a bone and vulgar bread and cheese for company. I won't have anything of the sort in my house. Take that Scott up to Mother's, and tell him I'm away, sick, dead—anything. I won't see him, and you two can laugh at me and my jelly as much as you like. You won't have anything else here." and having delivered her defiance all on one breath, Meg cast away her pinafore and precipitately left the field to bemoan herself in her own room.

What those two creatures did in her absence, she never knew, but Mr. Scott was not taken "up to Mother's," and when Meg descended, after they had strolled away together, she found traces of a promiscuous lunch which filled her with horror. Lotty reported that they had eaten "a much, and greatly laughed, and the master bid her throw away all the sweet stuff, and hide the pots."

Meg longed to go and tell Mother, but a sense of shame at her own short-comings, of loyalty to John, "who might be cruel, but nobody should know it," restrained her, and after a summary cleaning up, she dressed herself prettily, and sat down to wait for John to come and be forgiven.

Unfortunately, John didn't come, not seeing the matter in that light. He had carried it off as a good joke with Scott, excused his little wife as well as he could, and played the host so hospitably that his friend enjoyed the impromptu dinner, and promised to come again, but John was angry, though he did not show it, he felt that Meg had deserted him in his hour of need. "It wasn't fair to tell a man to bring folks home any time, with perfect freedom, and when he took you at your word, to flame up and blame him, and leave him in the lurch, to be laughed at or pitied. No, by George, it wasn't! And Meg must know it." He had fumed inwardly during the feast, but when the flurry was over and he strolled home after seeing Scott off, a milder mood came over him. "Poor little thing! It was hard upon her when she tried so heartily to please me. She was wrong, of course, but then she was young. I must be patient and teach her." He hoped she had not gone home—he hated gossip and interference. For a minute he was ruffled again at the mere thought of it, and then the fear that Meg would cry herself sick softened his heart, and sent him on at a quicker pace, resolving to be calm and kind, but firm, quite firm, and show her where she had failed in her duty to her spouse.

Meg likewise resolved to be "calm and kind, but firm," and show *him* his duty. She longed to run to meet him, and beg pardon, and be kissed and comforted, as she was sure of being, but, of course, she did nothing of the sort, and when she saw John coming, began to hum quite naturally, as she rocked and sewed, like a lady of leisure in her best parlor.

John was a little disappointed not to find a tender Niobe, but feeling that his dignity demanded the first apology, he made none, only came leisurely in and laid himself upon the sofa with the singularly relevant remark, "We are going to have a new moon, my dear."

"I've no objection," was Meg's equally soothing remark.

A few other topics of general interest were introduced by Mr. Brooke and wet-blanketed by Mrs. Brooke, and conversation languished. John went to one window, unfolded his paper, and wrapped himself in it, figuratively speaking. Meg went to the other window, and sewed as if new rosettes for slippers were among the necessaries of life. Neither spoke. Both looked quite "calm and firm," and both felt desperately uncomfortable.

"Oh, dear," thought Meg, "married life is very trying, and does need infinite patience as well as love, as Mother says." The word "Mother" suggested other maternal counsels given long ago, and received with unbelieving protests.

"John is a good man, but he has his faults, and you must learn to see and bear with them, remembering your own. He is very decided, but never will be obstinate, if you reason kindly, not oppose impatiently. He is very accurate, and particular about the truth—a good trait, though you call him 'fussy.' Never deceive him by look or word, Meg, and he will give you the confidence you deserve, the support you need. He has a temper, not like ours—one flash and then all over—but the white, still anger that is seldom stirred, but once kindled is hard to quench. Be careful, be very careful, not to wake his anger against yourself, for peace and happiness depend on keeping his respect. Watch yourself, be the first to ask pardon if you both err, and guard against the little piques, misunderstandings, and hasty words that often pave the way for bitter sorrow and regret."

These words came back to Meg, as she sat sewing in the sunset, especially the last. This was the first serious disagreement, her own hasty speeches sounded both silly and unkind, as she recalled them, her own anger looked childish now, and thoughts of poor John coming home to such a scene quite melted her heart. She glanced at him with tears in her eyes, but he did not see them. She put down her work and got up, thinking, "I *will* be the first to say, 'Forgive me,'" but he did not seem to hear her. She went very slowly across the room, for pride was hard to swallow, and stood by him, but he did not turn his head. For a minute she felt as if she really couldn't do it, then came the thought, "This is the beginning. I'll do my part, and have nothing to reproach myself with," and stooping down, she softly kissed her husband on the forehead. Of course that settled it. The penitent kiss was better than a world of words, and John had her on his knee in a minute, saying tenderly:

"It was too bad to laugh at the poor little jelly pots. Forgive me, dear. I never will again!"

But he did, oh bless you, yes, hundreds of times, and so did Meg, both declaring that it was the sweetest jelly they ever made, for family peace was preserved in that little family jar.

After this, Meg had Mr. Scott to dinner by special invitation, and served him up a pleasant feast without a cooked wife for the first course, on which occasion she was so gay and gracious, and made everything go off so charmingly, that Mr. Scott told John he was a lucky fellow, and shook his head over the hardships of bachelorhood all the way home.

In the autumn, new trials and experiences came to Meg. Sallie Moffat renewed her friendship, was always running out for a dish of gossip at the little house, or inviting "that poor dear" to come in and spend the day at the big house. It was pleasant, for in dull weather Meg often felt lonely. All were busy at home, John absent till night, and nothing to do but sew, or read, or potter about. So it naturally fell out that Meg got into the way of gadding and gossiping with her friend. Seeing Sallie's pretty things made her long for such, and pity herself because she had not got them. Sallie was very kind, and often offered her the coveted trifles, but Meg declined them, knowing that John wouldn't like it, and then this foolish little woman went and did what John disliked even worse.

She knew her husband's income, and she loved to feel that he trusted her, not only with his happiness, but what some men seem to value more—his money. She knew where it was, was free to take what she liked, and all he asked was that she should keep account of every penny, pay bills once a month, and remember that she was a poor man's wife. Till now she had done well, been prudent and exact, kept her little account books neatly, and showed them to him monthly without fear. But that autumn the serpent got into Meg's paradise, and tempted her like many a modern Eve, not with apples, but with dress. Meg didn't like to be pitied and made to feel poor. It irritated her, but she was ashamed to confess it, and now and then she tried to console herself by buying something pretty, so that Sallie needn't think she had to economize. She always felt wicked after it, for the pretty things were seldom necessaries, but then they cost so little, it wasn't worth worrying about, so the trifles increased unconsciously, and in the shopping excursions she was no longer a passive looker-on.

But the trifles cost more than one would imagine, and when she cast up her accounts at the end of the month the sum total rather scared her. John was busy that month and left the bills to her, the next month he was absent, but the third he had a grand quarterly settling up, and Meg never forgot it. A few days before she had done a dreadful thing, and it weighed upon her conscience. Sallie had been buying silks, and Meg longed for a new one, just a handsome light one for parties, her black silk was so common, and thin things for evening wear were only proper for girls. Aunt March usually gave the sisters a present of twenty-five dollars apiece at New Year's. That was only a month to wait, and here was a lovely violet silk going at a bargain, and she had the money, if she only dared to take it. John always said what was his was hers, but would he think it right to spend not only the prospective five-and-twenty, but another five-and-twenty out of the household fund? That was the question. Sallie had urged her to do it, had offered to lend the money, and with the best intentions in life had tempted Meg beyond her strength. In an evil moment the shopman held up the lovely, shimmering folds, and said, "A bargain, I assure, you, ma'am." She answered, "I'll take it," and it was cut off and paid for, and Sallie had exulted, and she had laughed as if it were a thing of no consequence, and driven away, feeling as if she had stolen something, and the police were after her.

When she got home, she tried to assuage the pangs of remorse by spreading forth the lovely silk, but it looked less silvery now, didn't become her, after all, and the words "fifty dollars" seemed stamped like a pattern down each breadth. She put it away, but it haunted her, not delightfully as a new dress should, but dreadfully like the ghost of a folly that was not easily laid. When John got out his books that night, Meg's heart sank, and for the first time in her married life, she was afraid of her husband. The kind, brown eyes looked as if they could be stern, and though he was unusually merry, she fancied he had found her out, but didn't mean to let her know it. The house bills were all paid, the books all in order. John had praised her, and was undoing the old pocketbook which they called the "bank," when Meg, knowing that it was quite empty, stopped his hand, saying nervously—

"You haven't seen my private expense book yet."

John never asked to see it, but she always insisted on his doing so, and used to enjoy his masculine amazement at the queer things women wanted, and made him guess what piping was, demand fiercely the meaning of a "hug-me-tight," or wonder how a little thing composed of three rosebuds, a bit of velvet, and a pair of strings, could possibly be a bonnet, and cost six dollars. That night he looked as if he would like the fun of quizzing her figures and pretending to be horrified at her extravagance, as he often did, being particularly proud of his prudent wife.

The little book was brought slowly out and laid down before him. Meg got behind his chair under pretense of smoothing the wrinkles out of his tired forehead, and standing there, she said, with her panic increasing with every word—

"John, dear, I'm ashamed to show you my book, for I've really been dreadfully extravagant lately. I go about so much I must have things, you know, and Sallie advised my getting it, so I did, and my New Year's money will partly pay for it: but I was sorry after I had done it, for I knew you'd think it wrong in me."

John laughed, and drew her round beside him, saying good-humoredly, "Don't go and hide. I won't beat you if you *have* got a pair of killing boots. I'm rather proud of my wife's feet, and don't mind if she does pay eight or nine dollars for her boots, if they are good ones."

That had been one of her last "trifles," and John's eye had fallen on it as he spoke. "Oh, what *will* he say when he comes to that awful fifty dollars!" thought Meg, with a shiver.

"It's worse than boots, it's a silk dress," she said, with the calmness of desperation, for she wanted the worst over.

"Well, dear, what is the 'dem'd total,' as Mr. Mantalini says?"

That didn't sound like John, and she knew he was looking up at her with the straightforward look that she had always been ready to meet and answer with one as frank till now. She turned the page and her head at the same time, pointing to the sum which would have been bad enough without the fifty, but which was appalling to her with that added. For a minute the room was very still, then John said slowly—but she could feel it cost him an effort to express no displeasure—

"Well, I don't know that fifty is much for a dress, with all the furbelows and notions you have to have to finish it off these days."

"It isn't made or trimmed," sighed Meg, faintly, for a sudden recollection of the cost still to be incurred quite overwhelmed her.

"Twenty-five yards of silk seems a good deal to cover one small woman, but I've no doubt my wife will look as fine as Ned Moffat's when she gets it on," said John dryly.

"I know you are angry, John, but I can't help it. I don't mean to waste your money, and I didn't think those little things would count up so. I can't resist them when I see Sallie buying all she wants, and pitying me because I don't. I try to be contented, but it is hard, and I'm tired of being poor."

The last words were spoken so low she thought he did not hear them, but he did, and they wounded him deeply, for he had denied himself many pleasures for Meg's sake. She could have bitten her tongue out the minute she had said it, for John pushed the books away and got up, saying with a little quiver in his voice, "I was afraid of this. I do my best, Meg." If he had scolded her, or even shaken her, it would not have broken her heart like those few words. She ran to him and held him close, crying, with repentant tears, "Oh, John, my dear, kind, hard-working boy. I didn't mean it! It was so wicked, so untrue and ungrateful, how could I say it! Oh, how could I say it!"

He was very kind, forgave her readily, and did not utter one reproach, but Meg knew that she had done and said a thing which would not be forgotten soon, although he might never allude to it again. She had promised to love him for better or worse, and then she, his wife, had reproached him with his poverty, after spending his earnings recklessly. It was dreadful, and the worst of it was John went on so quietly afterward, just as if nothing had happened, except that he stayed in town later, and worked at night when she had gone to cry herself to sleep. A week of remorse nearly made Meg sick, and the discovery that John had countermanded the order for his new greatcoat reduced her to a state of despair which was pathetic to behold. He had simply said, in answer to her surprised inquiries as to the change, "I can't afford it, my dear."

Meg said no more, but a few minutes after he found her in the hall with her face buried in the old greatcoat, crying as if her heart would break.

They had a long talk that night, and Meg learned to love her husband better for his poverty, because it seemed to have made a man of him, given him the strength and courage to fight his own way, and taught him a tender patience with which to bear and comfort the natural longings and failures of those he loved.

Next day she put her pride in her pocket, went to Sallie, told the truth, and asked her to buy the silk as a favor. The good-natured Mrs. Moffat willingly did so, and had the delicacy not to make her a present of it immediately afterward. Then Meg ordered home the greatcoat, and when John arrived, she put it on, and asked him how he liked her new silk gown. One can imagine what answer he made, how he received his present, and what a blissful state of things ensued. John came home early, Meg gadded no more, and that greatcoat was put on in the morning by a very happy husband, and taken off at night by a most devoted little wife. So the year rolled round, and at midsummer there came to Meg a new experience—the deepest and tenderest of a woman's life.

Laurie came sneaking into the kitchen of the Dovecote one Saturday, with an excited face, and was received with the clash of cymbals, for Hannah clapped her hands with a saucepan in one and the cover in the other.

"How's the little mamma? Where is everybody? Why didn't you tell me before I came home?" began Laurie in a loud whisper.

"Happy as a queen, the dear! Every soul of 'em is upstairs a worshipin'. We didn't want no hurrycanes round. Now you go into the parlor, and I'll send 'em down to you," with which somewhat involved reply Hannah vanished, chuckling ecstatically.

Presently Jo appeared, proudly bearing a flannel bundle laid forth upon a large pillow. Jo's face was very sober, but her eyes twinkled, and there was an odd sound in her voice of repressed emotion of some sort.

"Shut your eyes and hold out your arms," she said invitingly.

Laurie backed precipitately into a corner, and put his hands behind him with an imploring gesture. "No, thank you. I'd rather not. I shall drop it or smash it, as sure as fate."

"Then you shan't see your nevvy," said Jo decidedly, turning as if to go.

"I will, I will! Only you must be responsible for damages." and obeying orders, Laurie heroically shut his eyes while something was put into his arms. A peal of laughter from Jo, Amy, Mrs. March, Hannah, and John caused him to open them the next minute, to find himself invested with two babies instead of one.

No wonder they laughed, for the expression of his face was droll enough to convulse a Quaker, as he stood and stared wildly from the unconscious innocents to the hilarious spectators with such dismay that Jo sat down on the floor and screamed.

"Twins, by Jupiter!" was all he said for a minute, then turning to the women with an appealing look that was comically piteous, he added, "Take 'em quick, somebody! I'm going to laugh, and I shall drop 'em."

Jo rescued his babies, and marched up and down, with one on each arm, as if already initiated into the mysteries of babytending, while Laurie laughed till the tears ran down his cheeks.

"It's the best joke of the season, isn't it? I wouldn't have told you, for I set my heart on surprising you, and I flatter myself I've done it," said Jo, when she got her breath.

"I never was more staggered in my life. Isn't it fun? Are they boys? What are you going to name them? Let's have another look. Hold me up, Jo, for upon my life it's one too many for me," returned Laurie, regarding the infants with the air of a big, benevolent Newfoundland looking at a pair of infantile kittens.

"Boy and girl. Aren't they beauties?" said the proud papa, beaming upon the little red squirmers as if they were unfledged angels.

"Most remarkable children I ever saw. Which is which?" and Laurie bent like a well-sweep to examine the prodigies.

"Amy put a blue ribbon on the boy and a pink on the girl, French fashion, so you can always tell. Besides, one has blue eyes and one brown. Kiss them, Uncle Teddy," said wicked Jo.

"I'm afraid they mightn't like it," began Laurie, with unusual timidity in such matters.

"Of course they will, they are used to it now. Do it this minute, sir!" commanded Jo, fearing he might propose a proxy.

Laurie screwed up his face and obeyed with a gingerly peck at each little cheek that produced another laugh, and made the babies squeal.

"There, I knew they didn't like it! That's the boy, see him kick, he hits out with his fists like a good one. Now then, young Brooke, pitch into a man of your own size, will you?" cried Laurie, delighted with a poke in the face from a tiny fist, flapping aimlessly about.

"He's to be named John Laurence, and the girl Margaret, after mother and grandmother. We shall call her Daisey, so as not to have two Megs, and I suppose the mannie will be Jack, unless we find a better name," said Amy, with aunt-like interest.

"Name him Demijohn, and call him Demi for short," said Laurie.

"Daisy and Demi, just the thing! I *knew* Teddy would do it," cried Jo clapping her hands.

Teddy certainly had done it that time, for the babies were "Daisy" and "Demi" to the end of the chapter.

CHAPTER XXIX

CALLS

"Come, Jo, it's time."

"For what?"

"You don't mean to say you have forgotten that you promised to make half a dozen calls with me today?"

"I've done a good many rash and foolish things in my life, but I don't think I ever was mad enough to say I'd make six calls in one day, when a single one upsets me for a week."

"Yes, you did, it was a bargain between us. I was to finish the crayon of Beth for you, and you were to go properly with me, and return our neighbors' visits."

"If it was fair, that was in the bond, and I stand to the letter of my bond, Shylock. There is a pile of clouds in the east, it's *not* fair, and I don't go."

"Now, that's shirking. It's a lovely day, no prospect of rain, and you pride yourself on keeping promises, so be honorable, come and do your duty, and then be at peace for another six months."

At that minute Jo was particularly absorbed in dressmaking, for she was mantua-maker general to the family, and took especial credit to herself because she could use a needle as well as a pen. It was very provoking to be arrested in the act of a first trying-on, and ordered out to make calls in her best array on a warm July day. She hated calls of the formal sort, and never made any till Amy compelled her with a bargain, bribe, or promise. In the present instance there was no escape, and having clashed her scissors rebelliously, while protesting that she smelled thunder, she gave in, put away her work, and taking up her hat and gloves with an air of resignation, told Amy the victim was ready.

"Jo March, you are perverse enough to provoke a saint! You don't intend to make calls in that state, I hope," cried Amy, surveying her with amazement.

"Why not? I'm neat and cool and comfortable, quite proper for a dusty walk on a warm day. If people care more for my clothes than they do for me, I don't wish to see them. You can dress for both, and be as elegant as you please. It pays for you to be fine. It doesn't for me, and furbelows only worry me."

"Oh, dear!" sighed Amy, "now she's in a contrary fit, and will drive me distracted before I can get her properly ready. I'm sure it's no pleasure to me to go today, but it's a debt we owe society, and there's no one to pay it but you and me. I'll do anything for you, Jo, if you'll only dress yourself nicely, and come and help me do the civil. You can talk so well, look so aristocratic in your best things, and behave so beautifully, if you try, that I'm proud of you. I'm afraid to go alone, do come and take care of me."

"You're an artful little puss to flatter and wheedle your cross old sister in that way. The idea of my being aristocratic and well-bred, and your being afraid to go anywhere alone! I don't know which is the most absurd. Well, I'll go if I must, and do my best. You shall be commander of the expedition, and I'll obey blindly, will that satisfy you?" said Jo, with a sudden change from perversity to lamblike submission.

"You're a perfect cherub! Now put on all your best things, and I'll tell you how to behave at each place, so that you will make a good impression. I want people to like you, and they would if you'd only try to be a little more agreeable. Do your hair the pretty way, and put the pink rose in your bonnet. It's becoming, and you look too sober in your plain suit. Take your light gloves and the embroidered handkerchief. We'll stop at Meg's, and borrow her white sunshade, and then you can have my dove-colored one."

While Amy dressed, she issued her orders, and Jo obeyed them, not without entering her protest, however, for she sighed as she rustled into her new organdie, frowned darkly at herself as she tied her bonnet strings in an irreproachable bow, wrestled viciously with pins as she put on her collar, wrinkled up her features generally as she shook out the handkerchief, whose embroidery was as irritating to her nose as the present mission was to her feelings, and when she had squeezed her hands into tight gloves with three buttons and a tassel, as the last touch of elegance, she turned to Amy with an imbecile expression of countenance, saying meekly—

"I'm perfectly miserable, but if you consider me presentable, I die happy."

"You're highly satisfactory. Turn slowly round, and let me get a careful view." Jo revolved, and Amy gave a touch here and there, then fell back, with her head on one side, observing graciously, "Yes, you'll do. Your head is all I could ask, for that white bonnet *with* the rose is quite ravishing. Hold back your shoulders, and carry your hands easily, no matter if your gloves do pinch. There's one thing you can do well, Jo, that is, wear a shawl. I can't, but it's very nice to see you, and I'm so glad Aunt March gave you that lovely one. It's simple, but handsome, and those folds over the arm are really artistic. Is the point of my mantle in the middle, and have I looped my dress evenly? I like to show my boots, for my feet are pretty, though my nose isn't."

"You are a thing of beauty and a joy forever," said Jo, looking through her hand with the air of a connoisseur at the blue feather against the golden hair. "Am I to drag my best dress through the dust, or loop it up, please, ma'am?"

"Hold it up when you walk, but drop it in the house. The sweeping style suits you best, and you must learn to trail your skirts gracefully. You haven't half buttoned one cuff, do it at once. You'll never look finished if you are not careful about the little details, for they make up the pleasing whole."

Jo sighed, and proceeded to burst the buttons off her glove, in doing up her cuff, but at last both were ready, and sailed away, looking as "pretty as picters," Hannah said, as she hung out of the upper window to watch them.

"Now, Jo dear, the Chesters consider themselves very elegant people, so I want you to put on your best deportment. Don't make any of your abrupt remarks, or do anything odd, will you? Just be calm, cool, and quiet—that's safe and ladylike, and you can easily do it for fifteen minutes," said Amy, as they approached the first place, having borrowed the white parasol and been inspected by Meg, with a baby on each arm.

"Let me see. 'Calm, cool, and quiet'—yes, I think I can promise that. I've played the part of a prim young lady on the stage, and I'll try it off. My powers are great, as you shall see, so be easy in your mind, my child."

Amy looked relieved, but naughty Jo took her at her word, for during the first call she sat with every limb gracefully composed, every fold correctly draped, calm as a summer sea, cool as a snow-bank, and as silent as the sphinx. In vain Mrs. Chester alluded to her "charming novel," and the Misses Chester introduced parties, picnics, the opera, and the fashions. Each and all were answered by a smile, a bow, and a demure "Yes" or "No" with the chill on. In vain Amy telegraphed the word 'talk', tried to draw her out, and administered covert pokes with her foot. Jo sat as if blandly unconscious of it all, with deportment like Maud's face, "icily regular, splendidly null."

"What a haughty, uninteresting creature that oldest Miss March is!" was the unfortunately audible remark of one of the ladies, as the door closed upon their guests. Jo laughed noiselessly all through the hall, but Amy looked disgusted at the failure of her instructions, and very naturally laid the blame upon Jo.

"How could you mistake me so? I merely meant you to be properly dignified and composed, and you made yourself a perfect stock and stone. Try to be sociable at the Lambs'. Gossip as other girls do, and be interested in dress and flirtations and whatever nonsense comes up. They move in the best society, are valuable persons for us to know, and I wouldn't fail to make a good impression there for anything."

"I'll be agreeable. I'll gossip and giggle, and have horrors and raptures over any trifle you like. I rather enjoy this, and now I'll imitate what is called 'a charming girl.' I can do it, for I have May Chester as a model, and I'll improve upon her. See if the Lambs don't say, 'What a lively, nice creature that Jo March is!'"

Amy felt anxious, as well she might, for when Jo turned freakish there was no knowing where she would stop. Amy's face was a study when she saw her sister skim into the next drawing room, kiss all the young ladies with effusion, beam graciously upon the young gentlemen, and join in the chat with a spirit which amazed the beholder. Amy was taken possession of by Mrs. Lamb, with whom she was a favorite, and forced to hear a long account of Lucretia's last attack, while three delightful young gentlemen hovered near, waiting for a pause when they might rush in and rescue her. So situated, she was powerless to check Jo, who seemed possessed by a spirit of mischief, and talked away as volubly as the lady. A knot of heads gathered about her, and Amy strained her ears to hear what was going on, for broken sentences filled her with curiosity, and frequent peals of laughter made her wild to share the fun. One may imagine her suffering on overhearing fragments of this sort of conversation.

"She rides splendidly. Who taught her?"

"No one. She used to practice mounting, holding the reins, and sitting straight on an old saddle in a tree. Now she rides anything, for she doesn't know what fear is, and the stableman lets her have horses cheap because she trains them to carry ladies so well. She has such a passion for it, I often tell her if everything else fails, she can be a horsebreaker, and get her living so."

At this awful speech Amy contained herself with difficulty, for the impression was being given that she was rather a fast young lady, which was her especial aversion. But what could she do? For the old lady was in the middle of her story, and long before it was done, Jo was off again, making more droll revelations and committing still more fearful blunders.

"Yes, Amy was in despair that day, for all the good beasts were gone, and of three left, one was lame, one blind, and the other so balky that you had to put dirt in his mouth before he would start. Nice animal for a pleasure party, wasn't it?"

"Which did she choose?" asked one of the laughing gentlemen, who enjoyed the subject.

"None of them. She heard of a young horse at the farm house over the river, and though a lady had never ridden him, she resolved to try, because he was handsome and spirited. Her struggles were really pathetic. There was no one to bring the horse to the saddle, so she took the saddle to the horse. My dear creature, she actually rowed it over the river, put it on her head, and marched up to the barn to the utter amazement of the old man!"

"Did she ride the horse?"

"Of course she did, and had a capital time. I expected to see her brought home in fragments, but she managed him perfectly, and was the life of the party."

"Well, I call that plucky!" and young Mr. Lamb turned an approving glance upon Amy, wondering what his mother could be saying to make the girl look so red and uncomfortable.

She was still redder and more uncomfortable a moment after, when a sudden turn in the conversation introduced the subject of dress. One of the young ladies asked Jo where she got the pretty drab hat she wore to the picnic and stupid Jo, instead of mentioning the place where it was bought two years ago, must needs answer with unnecessary frankness, "Oh, Amy painted it. You can't buy those soft shades, so we paint ours any color we like. It's a great comfort to have an artistic sister."

"Isn't that an original idea?" cried Miss Lamb, who found Jo great fun.

"That's nothing compared to some of her brilliant performances. There's nothing the child can't do. Why, she wanted a pair of blue boots for Sallie's party, so she just painted her soiled white ones the loveliest shade of sky blue you ever saw, and they looked exactly like satin," added Jo, with an air of pride in her sister's accomplishments that exasperated Amy till she felt that it would be a relief to throw her cardcase at her.

"We read a story of yours the other day, and enjoyed it very much," observed the elder Miss Lamb, wishing to compliment the literary lady, who did not look the character just then, it must be confessed.

Any mention of her "works" always had a bad effect upon Jo, who either grew rigid and looked offended, or changed the subject with a brusque remark, as now. "Sorry you could find nothing better to read. I write that rubbish because it sells, and ordinary people like it. Are you going to New York this winter?"

As Miss Lamb had "enjoyed" the story, this speech was not exactly grateful or complimentary. The minute it was made Jo saw her mistake, but fearing to make the matter worse, suddenly remembered that it was for her to make the first move toward departure, and did so with an abruptness that left three people with half-finished sentences in their mouths.

"Amy, we *must* go. *Good*-by, dear, *do* come and see us. We are *pining* for a visit. I don't dare to ask *you*, Mr. Lamb, but if you *should* come, I don't think I shall have the heart to send you away."

Jo said this with such a droll imitation of May Chester's gushing style that Amy got out of the room as rapidly as possible, feeling a strong desire to laugh and cry at the same time.

"Didn't I do well?" asked Jo, with a satisfied air as they walked away.

"Nothing could have been worse," was Amy's crushing reply. "What possessed you to tell those stories about my saddle, and the hats and boots, and all the rest of it?"

"Why, it's funny, and amuses people. They know we are poor, so it's no use pretending that we have grooms, buy three or four hats a season, and have things as easy and fine as they do."

"You needn't go and tell them all our little shifts, and expose our poverty in that perfectly unnecessary way. You haven't a bit of proper pride, and never will learn when to hold your tongue and when to speak," said Amy despairingly.

Poor Jo looked abashed, and silently chafed the end of her nose with the stiff handkerchief, as if performing a penance for her misdemeanors.

"How shall I behave here?" she asked, as they approached the third mansion.

"Just as you please. I wash my hands of you," was Amy's short answer.

"Then I'll enjoy myself. The boys are at home, and we'll have a comfortable time. Goodness knows I need a little change, for elegance has a bad effect upon my constitution," returned Jo gruffly, being disturbed by her failure to suit.

An enthusiastic welcome from three big boys and several pretty children speedily soothed her ruffled feelings, and leaving Amy to entertain the hostess and Mr. Tudor, who happened to be calling likewise, Jo devoted herself to the young folks and found the change refreshing. She listened to college stories with deep interest, caressed pointers and poodles without a murmur, agreed heartily that "Tom Brown was a brick," regardless of the improper form of praise, and when one lad proposed a visit to his turtle tank, she went with an alacrity which caused Mamma to smile upon her, as that motherly lady settled the cap which was left in a ruinous condition by filial hugs, bearlike but affectionate, and dearer to her than the most faultless coiffure from the hands of an inspired Frenchwoman.

Leaving her sister to her own devices, Amy proceeded to enjoy herself to her heart's content. Mr. Tudor's uncle had married an English lady who was third cousin to a living lord, and Amy regarded the whole family with great respect, for in spite of her American birth and breeding, she possessed that reverence for titles which haunts the best of us—that unacknowledged loyalty to the early faith in kings which set the most democratic nation under the sun in ferment at the coming of a royal yellow-haired laddie, some years ago, and which still has something to do with the love the young country bears the old, like that of a big son for an imperious little mother, who held him while she could, and let him go with a farewell scolding when he rebelled. But even the satisfaction of talking with a distant connection of the British nobility did not render Amy forgetful of time, and when the proper number of minutes had passed, she reluctantly tore herself from this aristocratic society, and looked about for Jo, fervently hoping that her incorrigible sister would not be found in any position which should bring disgrace upon the name of March.

It might have been worse, but Amy considered it bad. For Jo sat on the grass, with an encampment of boys about her, and a dirty-footed dog reposing on the skirt of her state and festival dress, as she related one of Laurie's pranks to her admiring audience. One small child was poking turtles with Amy's cherished parasol, a second was eating gingerbread over Jo's best bonnet, and a third playing ball with her gloves, but all were enjoying themselves, and when Jo collected her damaged property to go, her escort accompanied her, begging her to come again, "It was such fun to hear about Laurie's larks."

"Capital boys, aren't they? I feel quite young and brisk again after that." said Jo, strolling along with her hands behind her, partly from habit, partly to conceal the bespattered parasol.

"Why do you always avoid Mr. Tudor?" asked Amy, wisely refraining from any comment upon Jo's dilapidated appearance.

"Don't like him, he puts on airs, snubs his sisters, worries his father, and doesn't speak respectfully of his mother. Laurie says he is fast, and I don't consider him a desirable acquaintance, so I let him alone."

"You might treat him civilly, at least. You gave him a cool nod, and just now you bowed and smiled in the politest way to Tommy Chamberlain, whose father keeps a grocery store. If you had just reversed the nod and the bow, it would have been right," said Amy reprovingly.

"No, it wouldn't," returned Jo, "I neither like, respect, nor admire Tudor, though his grandfather's uncle's nephew's niece *was* a third cousin to a lord. Tommy is poor and bashful and good and very clever. I think well of him, and like to show that I do, for he *is* a gentleman in spite of the brown paper parcels."

"It's no use trying to argue with you," began Amy.

"Not the least, my dear," interrupted Jo, "so let us look amiable, and drop a card here, as the Kings are evidently out, for which I'm deeply grateful."

The family cardcase having done its duty the girls walked on, and Jo uttered another thanksgiving on reaching the fifth house, and being told that the young ladies were engaged.

"Now let us go home, and never mind Aunt March today. We can run down there any time, and it's really a pity to trail through the dust in our best bibs and tuckers, when we are tired and cross."

"Speak for yourself, if you please. Aunt March likes to have us pay her the compliment of coming in style, and making a formal call. It's a little thing to do, but it gives her pleasure, and I don't believe it will hurt your things half so much as letting dirty dogs and clumping boys spoil them. Stoop down, and let me take the crumbs off of your bonnet."

"What a good girl you are, Amy!" said Jo, with a repentant glance from her own damaged costume to that of her sister, which was fresh and spotless still. "I wish it was as easy for me to do little things to please people as it is for you. I think of them, but it takes too much time to do them, so I wait for a chance to confer a great favor, and let the small ones slip, but they tell best in the end, I fancy."

Amy smiled and was mollified at once, saying with a maternal air, "Women should learn to be agreeable, particularly poor ones, for they have no other way of repaying the kindnesses they receive. If you'd remember that, and practice it, you'd be better liked than I am, because there is more of you."

"I'm a crotchety old thing, and always shall be, but I'm willing to own that you are right, only it's easier for me to risk my life for a person than to be pleasant to him when I don't feel like it. It's a great misfortune to have such strong likes and dislikes, isn't it?"

"It's a greater not to be able to hide them. I don't mind saying that I don't approve of Tudor any more than you do, but I'm not called upon to tell him so. Neither are you, and there is no use in making yourself disagreeable because he is."

"But I think girls ought to show when they disapprove of young men, and how can they do it except by their manners? Preaching does not do any good, as I know to my sorrow, since I've had Teddy to manage. But there are many little ways in which I can influence him without a word, and I say we *ought* to do it to others if we can."

"Teddy is a remarkable boy, and can't be taken as a sample of other boys," said Amy, in a tone of solemn conviction, which would have convulsed the "remarkable boy" if he had heard it. "If we were belles, or women of wealth and position, we might do something, perhaps, but for us to frown at one set of young gentlemen because we don't approve of them, and smile upon another set because we do, wouldn't have a particle of effect, and we should only be considered odd and puritanical."

"So we are to countenance things and people which we detest, merely because we are not belles and millionaires, are we? That's a nice sort of morality."

"I can't argue about it, I only know that it's the way of the world, and people who set themselves against it only get laughed at for their pains. I don't like reformers, and I hope you never try to be one."

"I do like them, and I shall be one if I can, for in spite of the laughing the world would never get on without them. We can't agree about that, for you belong to the old set, and I to the new. You will get on the best, but I shall have the liveliest time of it. I should rather enjoy the brickbats and hooting, I think."

"Well, compose yourself now, and don't worry Aunt with your new ideas."

"I'll try not to, but I'm always possessed to burst out with some particularly blunt speech or revolutionary sentiment before her. It's my doom, and I can't help it."

They found Aunt Carrol with the old lady, both absorbed in some very interesting subject, but they dropped it as the girls came in, with a conscious look which betrayed that they had been talking about their nieces. Jo was not in a good humor, and the perverse fit returned, but Amy, who had virtuously done her duty, kept her temper and pleased everybody, was in a most angelic frame of mind. This amiable spirit was felt at once, and both aunts "my deared" her affectionately, looking what they afterward said emphatically, "That child improves every day."

"Are you going to help about the fair, dear?" asked Mrs. Carrol, as Amy sat down beside her with the confiding air elderly people like so well in the young.

"Yes, Aunt. Mrs. Chester asked me if I would, and I offered to tend a table, as I have nothing but my time to give."

"I'm not," put in Jo decidedly. "I hate to be patronized, and the Chesters think it's a great favor to allow us to help with their highly connected fair. I wonder you consented, Amy, they only want you to work."

"I am willing to work. It's for the freedmen as well as the Chesters, and I think it very kind of them to let me share the labor and the fun. Patronage does not trouble me when it is well meant."

"Quite right and proper. I like your grateful spirit, my dear. It's a pleasure to help people who appreciate our efforts. Some do not, and that is trying," observed Aunt March, looking over her spectacles at Jo, who sat apart, rocking herself, with a somewhat morose expression.

If Jo had only known what a great happiness was wavering in the balance for one of them, she would have turned dove-like in a minute, but unfortunately, we don't have windows in our breasts, and cannot see what goes on in the minds of our friends. Better for us that we cannot as a general thing, but now and then it would be such a comfort, such a saving of time and temper. By her next speech, Jo deprived herself of several years of pleasure, and received a timely lesson in the art of holding her tongue.

"I don't like favors, they oppress and make me feel like a slave. I'd rather do everything for myself, and be perfectly independent."

"Ahem!" coughed Aunt Carrol softly, with a look at Aunt March.

"I told you so," said Aunt March, with a decided nod to Aunt Carrol.

Mercifully unconscious of what she had done, Jo sat with her nose in the air, and a revolutionary aspect which was anything but inviting.

"Do you speak French, dear?" asked Mrs. Carrol, laying a hand on Amy's.

"Pretty well, thanks to Aunt March, who lets Esther talk to me as often as I like," replied Amy, with a grateful look, which caused the old lady to smile affably.

"How are you about languages?" asked Mrs. Carrol of Jo.

"Don't know a word. I'm very stupid about studying anything, can't bear French, it's such a slippery, silly sort of language," was the brusque reply.

Another look passed between the ladies, and Aunt March said to Amy, "You are quite strong and well now, dear, I believe? Eyes don't trouble you any more, do they?"

"Not at all, thank you, ma'am. I'm very well, and mean to do great things next winter, so that I may be ready for Rome, whenever that joyful time arrives."

"Good girl! You deserve to go, and I'm sure you will some day," said Aunt March, with an approving pat on the head, as Amy picked up her ball for her.

Crosspatch, draw the latch,
Sit by the fire and spin,

squalled Polly, bending down from his perch on the back of her chair to peep into Jo's face, with such a comical air of impertinent inquiry that it was impossible to help laughing.

"Most observing bird," said the old lady.

"Come and take a walk, my dear?" cried Polly, hopping toward the china closet, with a look suggestive of a lump of sugar.

"Thank you, I will. Come Amy." And Jo brought the visit to an end, feeling more strongly than ever that calls did have a bad effect upon her constitution. She shook hands in a gentlemanly manner, but Amy kissed both the aunts, and the girls departed, leaving behind them the impression of shadow and sunshine, which impression caused Aunt March to say, as they vanished—

"You'd better do it, Mary. I'll supply the money," and Aunt Carrol to reply decidedly, "I certainly will, if her father and mother consent."

CHAPTER XXX

CONSEQUENCES

Mrs. Chester's fair was so very elegant and select that it was considered a great honor by the young ladies of the neighborhood to be invited to take a table, and everyone was much interested in the matter. Amy was asked, but Jo was not, which was fortunate for all parties, as her elbows were decidedly akimbo at this period of her life, and it took a good many hard knocks to teach her how to get on easily. The "haughty, uninteresting creature" was let severely alone, but Amy's talent and taste were duly complimented by the offer of the art table, and she exerted herself to prepare and secure appropriate and valuable contributions to it.

Everything went on smoothly till the day before the fair opened, then there occurred one of the little skirmishes which it is almost impossible to avoid, when some five-and-twenty women, old and young, with all their private piques and prejudices, try to work together.

May Chester was rather jealous of Amy because the latter was a greater favorite than herself, and just at this time several trifling circumstances occurred to increase the feeling. Amy's dainty pen-and-ink work entirely eclipsed May's painted vases—that was one thorn. Then the all conquering Tudor had danced four times with Amy at a late party and only once with May—that was thorn number two. But the chief grievance that rankled in her soul, and gave an excuse for her unfriendly conduct, was a rumor which some obliging gossip had whispered to her, that the March girls had made fun of her at the Lambs'. All the blame of this should have fallen upon Jo, for her naughty imitation had been too lifelike to escape detection, and the frolicsome Lambs had permitted the joke to escape. No hint of this had reached the culprits, however, and Amy's dismay can be imagined, when, the very evening before the fair, as she was putting the last touches to her pretty table, Mrs. Chester, who, of course, resented the supposed ridicule of her daughter, said, in a bland tone, but with a cold look—

"I find, dear, that there is some feeling among the young ladies about my giving this table to anyone but my girls. As this is the most prominent, and some say the most attractive table of all, and they are the chief getters-up of the fair, it is thought best for them to take this place. I'm sorry, but I know you are too sincerely interested in the cause to mind a little personal disappointment, and you shall have another table if you like."

Mrs. Chester fancied beforehand that it would be easy to deliver this little speech, but when the time came, she found it rather difficult to utter it naturally, with Amy's unsuspicious eyes looking straight at her full of surprise and trouble.

Amy felt that there was something behind this, but could not guess what, and said quietly, feeling hurt, and showing that she did, "Perhaps you had rather I took no table at all?"

"Now, my dear, don't have any ill feeling, I beg. It's merely a matter of expediency, you see, my girls will naturally take the lead, and this table is considered their proper place. I think it very appropriate to you, and feel very grateful for your efforts to make it so pretty, but we must give up our private wishes, of course, and I will see that you have a good place elsewhere. Wouldn't you like the flower table? The little girls undertook it, but they are discouraged. You could make a charming thing of it, and the flower table is always attractive you know."

"Especially to gentlemen," added May, with a look which enlightened Amy as to one cause of her sudden fall from favor. She colored angrily, but took no other notice of that girlish sarcasm, and answered with unexpected amiability—

"It shall be as you please, Mrs. Chester. I'll give up my place here at once, and attend to the flowers, if you like."

"You can put your own things on your own table, if you prefer," began May, feeling a little conscience-stricken, as she looked at the pretty racks, the painted shells, and quaint illuminations Amy had so carefully made and so gracefully arranged. She meant it kindly, but Amy mistook her meaning, and said quickly—

"Oh, certainly, if they are in your way," and sweeping her contributions into her apron, pell-mell, she walked off, feeling that herself and her works of art had been insulted past forgiveness.

"Now she's mad. Oh, dear, I wish I hadn't asked you to speak, Mama," said May, looking disconsolately at the empty spaces on her table.

"Girls' quarrels are soon over," returned her mother, feeling a trifle ashamed of her own part in this one, as well she might.

The little girls hailed Amy and her treasures with delight, which cordial reception somewhat soothed her perturbed spirit, and she fell to work, determined to succeed florally, if she could not artistically. But everything seemed against her. It was late, and she was tired. Everyone was too busy with their own affairs to help her, and the little girls were only hindrances, for the dears fussed and chattered like so many magpies, making a great deal of confusion in their artless efforts to preserve the most perfect order. The evergreen arch wouldn't stay firm after she got it up, but wiggled and threatened to tumble down on her head when the hanging baskets were filled. Her best tile got a splash of water, which left a sepia tear on the Cupid's cheek. She bruised her hands with hammering, and got cold working in a draft, which last affliction filled her with apprehensions for the morrow. Any girl reader who has suffered like afflictions will sympathize with poor Amy and wish her well through her task.

There was great indignation at home when she told her story that evening. Her mother said it was a shame, but told her she had done right. Beth declared she wouldn't go to the fair at all, and Jo demanded why she didn't take all her pretty things and leave those mean people to get on without her.

"Because they are mean is no reason why I should be. I hate such things, and though I think I've a right to be hurt, I don't intend to show it. They will feel that more than angry speeches or huffy actions, won't they, Marmee?"

"That's the right spirit, my dear. A kiss for a blow is always best, though it's not very easy to give it sometimes," said her mother, with the air of one who had learned the difference between preaching and practicing.

In spite of various very natural temptations to resent and retaliate, Amy adhered to her resolution all the next day, bent on conquering her enemy by kindness. She began well, thanks to a silent reminder that came to her unexpectedly, but most opportunely. As she arranged her table that morning, while the little girls were in the anteroom filling the baskets, she took up her pet production—a little book, the antique cover of which her father had found among his treasures, and in which on leaves of vellum she had beautifully illuminated different texts. As she turned the pages rich in dainty devices with very pardonable pride, her eye fell upon one verse that made her stop and think. Framed in a brilliant scrollwork of scarlet, blue and gold, with little spirits of good will helping one another up and down among the thorns and flowers, were the words, "Thou shalt love thy neighbor as thyself."

"I ought, but I don't," thought Amy, as her eye went from the bright page to May's discontented face behind the big vases, that could not hide the vacancies her pretty work had once filled. Amy stood a minute, turning the leaves in her hand, reading on each some sweet rebuke for all heartburnings and uncharitableness of spirit. Many wise and true sermons are preached us every day by unconscious ministers in street, school, office, or home. Even a fair table may become a pulpit, if it can offer the good and helpful words which are never out of season. Amy's conscience preached her a little sermon from that text, then and there, and she did what many of us do not always do—took the sermon to heart, and straightway put it in practice.

A group of girls were standing about May's table, admiring the pretty things, and talking over the change of saleswomen. They dropped their voices, but Amy knew they were speaking of her, hearing one side of the story and judging accordingly. It was not pleasant, but a better spirit had come over her, and presently a chance offered for proving it. She heard May say sorrowfully—

"It's too bad, for there is no time to make other things, and I don't want to fill up with odds and ends. The table was just complete then. Now it's spoiled."

"I dare say she'd put them back if you asked her," suggested someone.

"How could I after all the fuss?" began May, but she did not finish, for Amy's voice came across the hall, saying pleasantly —

"You may have them, and welcome, without asking, if you want them. I was just thinking I'd offer to put them back, for they belong to your table rather than mine. Here they are, please take them, and forgive me if I was hasty in carrying them away last night."

As she spoke, Amy returned her contribution, with a nod and a smile, and hurried away again, feeling that it was easier to do a friendly thing than it was to stay and be thanked for it.

"Now, I call that lovely of her, don't you?" cried one girl.

May's answer was inaudible, but another young lady, whose temper was evidently a little soured by making lemonade, added, with a disagreeable laugh, "Very lovely, for she knew she wouldn't sell them at her own table."

Now, that was hard. When we make little sacrifices we like to have them appreciated, at least, and for a minute Amy was sorry she had done it, feeling that virtue was not always its own reward. But it is, as she presently discovered, for her spirits began to rise, and her table to blossom under her skillful hands, the girls were very kind, and that one little act seemed to have cleared the atmosphere amazingly.

It was a very long day and a hard one for Amy, as she sat behind her table, often quite alone, for the little girls deserted very soon. Few cared to buy flowers in summer, and her bouquets began to droop long before night.

The art table was the most attractive in the room. There was a crowd about it all day long, and the tenders were constantly flying to and fro with important faces and rattling money boxes. Amy often looked wistfully across, longing to be there, where she felt at home and happy, instead of in a corner with nothing to do. It might seem no hardship to some of us, but to a pretty, blithe young girl, it was not only tedious, but very trying, and the thought of Laurie and his friends made it a real martyrdom.

She did not go home till night, and then she looked so pale and quiet that they knew the day had been a hard one, though she made no complaint, and did not even tell what she had done. Her mother gave her an extra cordial cup of tea. Beth helped her dress, and made a charming little wreath for her hair, while Jo astonished her family by getting herself up with unusual care, and hinting darkly that the tables were about to be turned.

"Don't do anything rude, pray Jo; I won't have any fuss made, so let it all pass and behave yourself," begged Amy, as she departed early, hoping to find a reinforcement of flowers to refresh her poor little table.

"I merely intend to make myself entrancingly agreeable to every one I know, and to keep them in your corner as long as possible. Teddy and his boys will lend a hand, and we'll have a good time yet," returned Jo, leaning over the gate to watch for Laurie. Presently the familiar tramp was heard in the dusk, and she ran out to meet him.

"Is that my boy?"

"As sure as this is my girl!" and Laurie tucked her hand under his arm with the air of a man whose every wish was gratified.

"Oh, Teddy, such doings!" and Jo told Amy's wrongs with sisterly zeal.

"A flock of our fellows are going to drive over by-and-by, and I'll be hanged if I don't make them buy every flower she's got, and camp down before her table afterward," said Laurie, espousing her cause with warmth.

"The flowers are not at all nice, Amy says, and the fresh ones may not arrive in time. I don't wish to be unjust or suspicious, but I shouldn't wonder if they never came at all. When people do one mean thing they are very likely to do another," observed Jo in a disgusted tone.

"Didn't Hayes give you the best out of our gardens? I told him to."

"I didn't know that, he forgot, I suppose, and, as your grandpa was poorly, I didn't like to worry him by asking, though I did want some."

"Now, Jo, how could you think there was any need of asking? They are just as much yours as mine. Don't we always go halves in everything?" began Laurie, in the tone that always made Jo turn thorny.

"Gracious, I hope not! Half of some of your things wouldn't suit me at all. But we mustn't stand philandering here. I've got to help Amy, so you go and make yourself splendid, and if you'll be so very kind as to let Hayes take a few nice flowers up to the Hall, I'll bless you forever."

"Couldn't you do it now?" asked Laurie, so suggestively that Jo shut the gate in his face with inhospitable haste, and called through the bars, "Go away, Teddy, I'm busy."

Thanks to the conspirators, the tables were turned that night, for Hayes sent up a wilderness of flowers, with a loverly basket arranged in his best manner for a centerpiece. Then the March family turned out en masse, and Jo exerted herself to some purpose, for people not only came, but stayed, laughing at her nonsense, admiring Amy's taste, and apparently enjoying themselves very much. Laurie and his friends gallantly threw themselves into the breach, bought up the bouquets, encamped before the table, and made that corner the liveliest spot in the room. Amy was in her element now, and out of gratitude, if nothing more, was as sprightly and gracious as possible—coming to the conclusion, about that time, that virtue was its own reward, after all.

Jo behaved herself with exemplary propriety, and when Amy was happily surrounded by her guard of honor, Jo circulated about the Hall, picking up various bits of gossip, which enlightened her upon the subject of the Chester change of base. She reproached herself for her share of the ill feeling and resolved to exonerate Amy as soon as possible. She also discovered what Amy had done about the things in the morning, and considered her a model of magnanimity. As she passed the art table, she glanced over it for her sister's things, but saw no sign of them. "Tucked away out of sight, I dare say," thought Jo, who could forgive her own wrongs, but hotly resented any insult offered her family.

"Good evening, Miss Jo. How does Amy get on?" asked May with a conciliatory air, for she wanted to show that she also could be generous.

"She has sold everything she had that was worth selling, and now she is enjoying herself. The flower table is always attractive, you know, 'especially to gentlemen.'"

Jo *couldn't* resist giving that little slap, but May took it so meekly she regretted it a minute after, and fell to praising the great vases, which still remained unsold.

"Is Amy's illumination anywhere about? I took a fancy to buy that for Father," said Jo, very anxious to learn the fate of her sister's work.

"Everything of Amy's sold long ago. I took care that the right people saw them, and they made a nice little sum of money for us," returned May, who had overcome sundry small temptations, as well as Amy had, that day.

Much gratified, Jo rushed back to tell the good news, and Amy looked both touched and surprised by the report of May's word and manner.

"Now, gentlemen, I want you to go and do your duty by the other tables as generously as you have by mine, especially the art table," she said, ordering out "Teddy's own," as the girls called the college friends.

"'Charge, Chester, charge!' is the motto for that table, but do your duty like men, and you'll get your money's worth of *art* in every sense of the word," said the irrepressible Jo, as the devoted phalanx prepared to take the field.

"To hear is to obey, but March is fairer far than May," said little Parker, making a frantic effort to be both witty and tender, and getting promptly quenched by Laurie, who said, "Very well, my son, for a small boy!" and walked him off, with a paternal pat on the head.

"Buy the vases," whispered Amy to Laurie, as a final heaping of coals of fire on her enemy's head.

To May's great delight, Mr. Laurence not only bought the vases, but pervaded the hall with one under each arm. The other gentlemen speculated with equal rashness in all sorts of frail trifles, and wandered helplessly about afterward, burdened with wax flowers, painted fans, filigree portfolios, and other useful and appropriate purchases.

Aunt Carrol was there, heard the story, looked pleased, and said something to Mrs. March in a corner, which made the latter lady beam with satisfaction, and watch Amy with a face full of mingled pride and anxiety, though she did not betray the cause of her pleasure till several days later.

The fair was pronounced a success, and when May bade Amy goodnight, she did not gush as usual, but gave her an affectionate kiss, and a look which said 'forgive and forget.' That satisfied Amy, and when she got home she found the vases paraded on the parlor chimney piece with a great bouquet in each. "The reward of merit for a magnanimous March," as Laurie announced with a flourish.

"You've a deal more principle and generosity and nobleness of character than I ever gave you credit for, Amy. You've behaved sweetly, and I respect you with all my heart," said Jo warmly, as they brushed their hair together late that night.

"Yes, we all do, and love her for being so ready to forgive. It must have been dreadfully hard, after working so long and setting your heart on selling your own pretty things. I don't believe I could have done it as kindly as you did," added Beth from her pillow.

"Why, girls, you needn't praise me so. I only did as I'd be done by. You laugh at me when I say I want to be a lady, but I mean a true gentlewoman in mind and manners, and I try to do it as far as I know how. I can't explain exactly, but I want to be above the little meannesses and follies and faults that spoil so many women. I'm far from it now, but I do my best, and hope in time to be what Mother is."

Amy spoke earnestly, and Jo said, with a cordial hug, "I understand now what you mean, and I'll never laugh at you again. You are getting on faster than you think, and I'll take lessons of you in true politeness, for you've learned the secret, I believe. Try away, deary, you'll get your reward some day, and no one will be more delighted than I shall."

A week later Amy did get her reward, and poor Jo found it hard to be delighted. A letter came from Aunt Carrol, and Mrs. March's face was illuminated to such a degree when she read it that Jo and Beth, who were with her, demanded what the glad tidings were.

"Aunt Carrol is going abroad next month, and wants—"

"Me to go with her!" burst in Jo, flying out of her chair in an uncontrollable rapture.

"No, dear, not you. It's Amy."

"Oh, Mother! She's too young, it's my turn first. I've wanted it so long. It would do me so much good, and be so altogether splendid—I *must* go!"

"I'm afraid it's impossible, Jo. Aunt says Amy, decidedly, and it is not for us to dictate when she offers such a favor."

"It's always so. Amy has all the fun and I have all the work. It isn't fair, oh, it isn't fair!" cried Jo passionately.

"I'm afraid it's partly your own fault, dear. When Aunt spoke to me the other day, she regretted your blunt manners and too independent spirit, and here she writes, as if quoting something you had said—'I planned at first to ask Jo, but as 'favors burden her,' and she 'hates French,' I think I won't venture to invite her. Amy is more docile, will make a good companion for Flo, and receive gratefully any help the trip may give her."

"Oh, my tongue, my abominable tongue! Why can't I learn to keep it quiet?" groaned Jo, remembering words which had been her undoing. When she had heard the explanation of the quoted phrases, Mrs. March said sorrowfully—

"I wish you could have gone, but there is no hope of it this time, so try to bear it cheerfully, and don't sadden Amy's pleasure by reproaches or regrets."

"I'll try," said Jo, winking hard as she knelt down to pick up the basket she had joyfully upset. "I'll take a leaf out of her book, and try not only to seem glad, but to be so, and not grudge her one minute of happiness. But it won't be easy, for it is a dreadful disappointment," and poor Jo bedewed the little fat pincushion she held with several very bitter tears.

"Jo, dear, I'm very selfish, but I couldn't spare you, and I'm glad you are not going quite yet," whispered Beth, embracing her, basket and all, with such a clinging touch and loving face that Jo felt comforted in spite of the sharp regret that made her want to box her own ears, and humbly beg Aunt Carrol to burden her with this favor, and see how gratefully she would bear it.

By the time Amy came in, Jo was able to take her part in the family jubilation, not quite as heartily as usual, perhaps, but without repinings at Amy's good fortune. The young lady herself received the news as tidings of great joy, went about in a solemn sort of rapture, and began to sort her colors and pack her pencils that evening, leaving such trifles as clothes, money, and passports to those less absorbed in visions of art than herself.

"It isn't a mere pleasure trip to me, girls," she said impressively, as she scraped her best palette. "It will decide my career, for if I have any genius, I shall find it out in Rome, and will do something to prove it."

"Suppose you haven't?" said Jo, sewing away, with red eyes, at the new collars which were to be handed over to Amy.

"Then I shall come home and teach drawing for my living," replied the aspirant for fame, with philosophic composure. But she made a wry face at the prospect, and scratched away at her palette as if bent on vigorous measures before she gave up her hopes.

"No, you won't. You hate hard work, and you'll marry some rich man, and come home to sit in the lap of luxury all your days," said Jo.

"Your predictions sometimes come to pass, but I don't believe that one will. I'm sure I wish it would, for if I can't be an artist myself, I should like to be able to help those who are," said Amy, smiling, as if the part of Lady Bountiful would suit her better than that of a poor drawing teacher.

"Hum!" said Jo, with a sigh. "If you wish it you'll have it, for your wishes are always granted—mine never."

"Would you like to go?" asked Amy, thoughtfully patting her nose with her knife.

"Rather!"

"Well, in a year or two I'll send for you, and we'll dig in the Forum for relics, and carry out all the plans we've made so many times."

"Thank you. I'll remind you of your promise when that joyful day comes, if it ever does," returned Jo, accepting the vague but magnificent offer as gratefully as she could.

There was not much time for preparation, and the house was in a ferment till Amy was off. Jo bore up very well till the last flutter of blue ribbon vanished, when she retired to her refuge, the garret, and cried till she couldn't cry any more. Amy likewise bore up stoutly till the steamer sailed. Then just as the gangway was about to be withdrawn, it suddenly came over her that a whole ocean was soon to roll between her and those who loved her best, and she clung to Laurie, the last lingerer, saying with a sob—

"Oh, take care of them for me, and if anything should happen—"

"I will, dear, I will, and if anything happens, I'll come and comfort you," whispered Laurie, little dreaming that he would be called upon to keep his word.

So Amy sailed away to find the Old World, which is always new and beautiful to young eyes, while her father and friend watched her from the shore, fervently hoping that none but gentle fortunes would befall the happy-hearted girl, who waved her hand to them till they could see nothing but the summer sunshine dazzling on the sea.

CHAPTER XXXI

OUR FOREIGN CORRESPONDENT

London

Dearest People,

Here I really sit at a front window of the Bath Hotel, Piccadilly. It's not a fashionable place, but Uncle stopped here years ago, and won't go anywhere else. However, we don't mean to stay long, so it's no great matter. Oh, I can't begin to tell you how I enjoy it all! I never can, so I'll only give you bits out of my notebook, for I've done nothing but sketch and scribble since I started.

I sent a line from Halifax, when I felt pretty miserable, but after that I got on delightfully, seldom ill, on deck all day, with plenty of pleasant people to amuse me. Everyone was very kind to me, especially the officers. Don't laugh, Jo, gentlemen really are very necessary aboard ship, to hold on to, or to wait upon one, and as they have nothing to do, it's a mercy to make them useful, otherwise they would smoke themselves to death, I'm afraid.

Aunt and Flo were poorly all the way, and liked to be let alone, so when I had done what I could for them, I went and enjoyed myself. Such walks on deck, such sunsets, such splendid air and waves! It was almost as exciting as riding a fast horse, when we went rushing on so grandly. I wish Beth could have come, it would have done her so much good. As for Jo, she would have gone up and sat on the maintop jib, or whatever the high thing is called, made friends with the engineers, and tooted on the captain's speaking trumpet, she'd have been in such a state of rapture.

It was all heavenly, but I was glad to see the Irish coast, and found it very lovely, so green and sunny, with brown cabins here and there, ruins on some of the hills, and gentlemen's countryseats in the valleys, with deer feeding in the parks. It was early in the morning, but I didn't regret getting up to see it, for the bay was full of little boats, the shore so picturesque, and a rosy sky overhead. I never shall forget it.

At Queenstown one of my new acquaintances left us—Mr.

Lennox—and when I said something about the Lakes of Killarney, he sighed, and sung, with a look at me—

"Oh, have you e'er heard of Kate Kearney?
She lives on the banks of Killarney;
From the glance of her eye,
Shun danger and fly,
For fatal's the glance of Kate Kearney."

Wasn't that nonsensical?

We only stopped at Liverpool a few hours. It's a dirty, noisy place, and I was glad to leave it. Uncle rushed out and bought a pair of dogskin gloves, some ugly, thick shoes, and an umbrella, and got shaved à la mutton chop, the first thing. Then he flattered himself that he looked like a true Briton, but the first time he had the mud cleaned off his shoes, the little bootblack knew that an American stood in them, and said, with a grin, "There yer har, sir. I've given 'em the latest Yankee shine." It amused Uncle immensely. Oh, I *must* tell you what that absurd Lennox did! He got his friend Ward, who came on with us, to order a bouquet for me, and the first thing I saw in my room was a lovely one, with "Robert Lennox's compliments," on the card. Wasn't that fun, girls? I like traveling.

I never *shall* get to London if I don't hurry. The trip was like riding through a long picture gallery, full of lovely landscapes. The farmhouses were my delight, with thatched roofs, ivy up to the eaves, latticed windows, and stout women with rosy children at the doors. The very cattle looked more tranquil than ours, as they stood knee-deep in clover, and the hens had a contented cluck, as if they never got nervous like Yankee biddies. Such perfect color I never saw—the grass so green, sky so blue, grain so yellow, woods so dark—I was in a rapture all the way. So was Flo, and we kept bouncing from one side to the other, trying to see everything while we were whisking along at the rate of sixty miles an hour. Aunt was tired and went to sleep, but Uncle read his guidebook, and wouldn't be astonished at anything. This is the way we went on. Amy, flying up—"Oh, that must be Kenilworth, that gray place among the trees!" Flo, darting to my window—"How sweet! We must go there sometime, won't we Papa?" Uncle, calmly admiring his boots—"No, my dear, not unless you want beer, that's a brewery."

A pause—then Flo cried out, "Bless me, there's a gallows and a man going up." "Where, where?" shrieks Amy, staring out at two tall posts with a crossbeam and some dangling chains. "A colliery," remarks Uncle, with a twinkle of the eye. "Here's a lovely flock of lambs all lying down," says Amy. "See, Papa, aren't they pretty?" added Flo sentimentally. "Geese, young ladies," returns Uncle, in a tone that keeps us quiet till Flo settles down to enjoy *The Flirtations of Captain Cavendish*, and I have the scenery all to myself.

Of course it rained when we got to London, and there was nothing to be seen but fog and umbrellas. We rested, unpacked, and shopped a little between the showers. Aunt Mary got me some new things, for I came off in such a hurry I wasn't half ready. A white hat and blue feather, a muslin dress to match, and the loveliest mantle you ever saw. Shopping in Regent Street is perfectly splendid. Things seem so cheap, nice ribbons only sixpence a yard. I laid in a stock, but shall get my gloves in Paris. Doesn't that sound sort of elegant and rich?

Flo and I, for the fun of it, ordered a hansom cab, while Aunt and Uncle were out, and went for a drive, though we learned afterward that it wasn't the thing for young ladies to ride in them alone. It was so droll! For when we were shut in by the wooden apron, the man drove so fast that Flo was frightened, and told me to stop him, but he was up outside behind somewhere, and I couldn't get at him. He didn't hear me call, nor see me flap my parasol in front, and there we were, quite helpless, rattling away, and whirling around corners at a breakneck pace. At last, in my despair, I saw a little door in the roof, and on poking it open, a red eye appeared, and a beery voice said—

"Now, then, mum?"

I gave my order as soberly as I could, and slamming down the door, with an "Aye, aye, mum," the man made his horse walk, as if going to a funeral. I poked again and said, "A little faster," then off he went, helter-skelter as before, and we resigned ourselves to our fate.

Today was fair, and we went to Hyde Park, close by, for we are more aristocratic than we look. The Duke of Devonshire lives near. I often see his footmen lounging at the back gate, and the Duke of Wellington's house is not far off. Such sights as I saw, my dear! It was as good as Punch, for there were fat dowagers rolling about in their red and yellow coaches, with gorgeous Jeameses in silk stockings and velvet coats, up behind, and powdered coachmen in front. Smart maids, with the rosiest children I ever saw, handsome girls, looking half asleep, dandies in queer English hats and lavender kids lounging about, and tall soldiers, in short red jackets and muffin caps stuck on one side, looking so funny I longed to sketch them.

Rotten Row means "*Route de Roi*," or the king's way, but now it's more like a riding school than anything else. The horses are splendid, and the men, especially the grooms, ride well, but the women are stiff, and bounce, which isn't according to our rules. I longed to show them a tearing American gallop, for they trotted solemnly up and down, in their scant habits and high hats, looking like the women in a toy Noah's Ark. Everyone rides—old men, stout ladies, little children—and the young folks do a deal of flirting here, I saw a pair exchange rose buds, for it's the thing to wear one in the button-hole, and I thought it rather a nice little idea.

In the P.M. to Westminster Abbey, but don't expect me to describe it, that's impossible, so I'll only say it was sublime! This evening we are going to see Fechter, which will be an appropriate end to the happiest day of my life.

MIDNIGHT

It's very late, but I can't let my letter go in the morning without telling you what happened last evening. Who do you think came in, as we were at tea? Laurie's English friends, Fred and Frank Vaughn! I was so surprised, for I shouldn't have known them but for the cards. Both are tall fellows with whiskers, Fred handsome in the English style, and Frank much better, for he only limps slightly, and uses no crutches. They had heard from Laurie where we were to be, and came to ask us to their house, but Uncle won't go, so we shall return the call, and see them as we can. They went to the theater with us, and we did have such a good time, for Frank devoted himself to Flo, and Fred and I talked over past, present, and future fun as if we had known each other all our days. Tell Beth Frank asked for her, and was sorry to hear of her ill health. Fred laughed when I spoke of Jo, and sent his "respectful compliments to the big hat." Neither of them had forgotten Camp Laurence, or the fun we had there. What ages ago it seems, doesn't it?

Aunt is tapping on the wall for the third time, so I *must* stop. I really feel like a dissipated London fine lady, writing here so late, with my room full of pretty things, and my head a jumble of parks, theaters, new gowns, and gallant creatures who say "Ah!" and twirl their blond mustaches with the true English lordliness. I long to see you all, and in spite of my nonsense am, as ever, your loving

AMY

PARIS

DEAR GIRLS,

In my last I told you about our London visit—how kind the Vaughns were, and what pleasant parties they made for us. I enjoyed the trips to Hampton Court and the Kensington Museum more than anything else, for at Hampton I saw Raphael's cartoons, and at the Museum, rooms full of pictures by Turner, Lawrence, Reynolds, Hogarth, and the other great creatures. The day in Richmond Park was charming, for we had a regular English picnic, and I had more splendid oaks and groups of deer than I could copy, also heard a nightingale, and saw larks go up. We 'did' London to our heart's content, thanks to Fred and Frank, and were sorry to go away, for though English people are slow to take you in, when they once make up their minds to do it they cannot be outdone in hospitality, I think. The Vaughns hope to meet us in Rome next winter, and I shall be dreadfully disappointed if they don't, for Grace and I are great friends, and the boys very nice fellows—especially Fred.

Well, we were hardly settled here, when he turned up again, saying he had come for a holiday, and was going to Switzerland. Aunt looked sober at first, but he was so cool about it she couldn't say a word. And now we get on nicely, and are very glad he came, for he speaks French like a native, and I don't know what we should do without him. Uncle doesn't know ten words, and insists on talking English very loud, as if it would make people understand him. Aunt's pronunciation is old-fashioned, and Flo and I, though we flattered ourselves that we knew a good deal, find we don't, and are very grateful to have Fred do the "*parley vooing,*" as Uncle calls it.

Such delightful times as we are having! Sight-seeing from morning till night, stopping for nice lunches in the gay cafés, and meeting with all sorts of droll adventures. Rainy days I spend in the Louvre, revelling in pictures. Jo would turn up her naughty nose at some of the finest, because she has no soul for art, but I have, and I'm cultivating eye and taste as fast as I can. She would like the relics of great people better, for I've seen her Napoleon's cocked hat and gray coat, his baby's cradle and his old toothbrush, also Marie Antoinette's little shoe, the ring of

Saint Denis, Charlemagne's sword, and many other interesting things. I'll talk for hours about them when I come, but haven't time to write.

The Palais Royale is a heavenly place, so full of *bijouterie* and lovely things that I'm nearly distracted because I can't buy them. Fred wanted to get me some, but of course I didn't allow it. Then the Bois and Champs Elysées are *très magnifique*. I've seen the imperial family several times—the emperor an ugly, hard-looking man, the empress pale and pretty, but dressed in bad taste, I thought—purple dress, green hat, and yellow gloves. Little Nap is a handsome boy, who sits chatting to his tutor, and kisses his hand to the people as he passes in his four-horse barouche, with postilions in red satin jackets and a mounted guard before and behind.

We often walk in the Tuileries Gardens, for they are lovely, though the antique Luxembourg Gardens suit me better. Père la Chaise is very curious, for many of the tombs are like small rooms, and looking in, one sees a table, with images or pictures of the dead, and chairs for the mourners to sit in when they come to lament. That is so Frenchy.

Our rooms are on the Rue de Rivoli, and sitting on the balcony, we look up and down the long, brilliant street. It is so pleasant that we spend our evenings talking there when too tired with our day's work to go out. Fred is very entertaining, and is altogether the most agreeable young man I ever knew—except Laurie, whose manners are more charming. I wish Fred was dark, for I don't fancy light men, however, the Vaughns are very rich and come of an excellent family, so I won't find fault with their yellow hair, as my own is yellower.

Next week we are off to Germany and Switzerland, and as we shall travel fast, I shall only be able to give you hasty letters. I keep my diary, and try to "remember correctly and describe clearly all that I see and admire," as Father advised. It is good practice for me, and with my sketchbook will give you a better idea of my tour than these scribbles.

Adieu, I embrace you tenderly.

VOTRE AMIE.

HEIDELBERG

MY DEAR MAMMA,

Having a quiet hour before we leave for Berne, I'll try to tell you what has happened, for some of it is very important, as you will see.

The sail up the Rhine was perfect, and I just sat and enjoyed it with all my might. Get Father's old guidebooks and read about it. I haven't words beautiful enough to describe it. At Coblentz we had a lovely time, for some students from Bonn, with whom Fred got acquainted on the boat, gave us a serenade. It was a moonlight night, and about one o'clock Flo and I were waked by the most delicious music under our windows. We flew up, and hid behind the curtains, but sly peeps showed us Fred and the students singing away down below. It was the most romantic thing I ever saw—the river, the bridge of boats, the great fortress opposite, moonlight everywhere, and music fit to melt a heart of stone.

When they were done we threw down some flowers, and saw them scramble for them, kiss their hands to the invisible ladies, and go laughing away, to smoke and drink beer, I suppose. Next morning Fred showed me one of the crumpled flowers in his vest pocket, and looked very sentimental. I laughed at him, and said I didn't throw it, but Flo, which seemed to disgust him, for he tossed it out of the window, and turned sensible again. I'm afraid I'm going to have trouble with that boy, it begins to look like it.

The baths at Nassau were very gay, so was Baden-Baden, where Fred lost some money, and I scolded him. He needs someone to look after him when Frank is not with him. Kate said once she hoped he'd marry soon, and I quite agree with her that it would be well for him. Frankfurt was delightful. I saw Goethe's house, Schiller's statue, and Dannecker's famous *Ariadne*. It was very lovely, but I should have enjoyed it more if I had known the story better. I didn't like to ask, as everyone knew it or pretended they did. I wish Jo would tell me all about it. I ought to have read more, for I find I don't know anything, and it mortifies me.

Now comes the serious part—for it happened here, and Fred has just gone. He has been so kind and jolly that we all got quite fond of him. I never thought of anything but a traveling friendship till the serenade night. Since then I've begun to feel that the moonlight walks, balcony talks, and daily adventures were something more to him than fun. I haven't flirted, Mother, truly, but remembered what you said to me, and have done my very best. I can't help it if people like me. I don't try to make them, and it worries me if I don't care for them, though Jo says I haven't got any heart. Now I know Mother will shake her head, and the girls say, "Oh, the mercenary little wretch!" but I've made up my mind, and if Fred asks me, I shall accept him, though I'm not madly in love. I like him, and we get on comfortably together. He is handsome, young, clever enough, and very rich—ever so much richer than the Laurences. I don't think his family would object, and I should be very happy, for they are all kind, well-bred, generous people, and they like me. Fred, as the eldest twin, will have the estate, I suppose, and such a splendid one it is! A city house in a fashionable street, not so showy as our big houses, but twice as comfortable and full of solid luxury, such as English people believe in. I like it, for it's genuine. I've seen the plate, the family jewels, the old servants, and pictures of the country place, with its park, great house, lovely grounds, and fine horses. Oh, it would be all I should ask! And I'd rather have it than any title such as girls snap up so readily, and find nothing behind. I may be mercenary, but I hate poverty, and don't mean to bear it a minute longer than I can help. One of us *must* marry well. Meg didn't, Jo won't, Beth can't yet, so I shall, and make everything okay all round. I wouldn't marry a man I hated or despised. You may be sure of that, and though Fred is not my model hero, he does very well, and in time I should get fond enough of him if he was very fond of me, and let me do just as I liked. So I've been turning the matter over in my mind the last week, for it was impossible to help seeing that Fred liked me. He said nothing, but little things showed it. He never goes with Flo, always gets on my side of the carriage, table, or promenade, looks sentimental when we are alone, and frowns at anyone else who ventures to speak to me. Yesterday at dinner, when an Austrian officer stared at us and then said something to his friend—a rakish-looking baron—about "*ein wonderschönes Blöndchen,*" Fred looked as fierce as a lion, and cut his meat so savagely it nearly flew off his plate. He isn't one of the cool, stiff Englishmen, but is rather peppery, for he has Scotch blood in him, as one might guess from his bonnie blue eyes.

Well, last evening we went up to the castle about sunset—at least all of us but Fred, who was to meet us there after going to the Post Restante for letters. We had a charming time poking about the ruins, the vaults where the monster tun is, and the beautiful gardens made by the elector long ago for his English wife. I liked the great terrace best, for the view was divine, so while the rest went to see the rooms inside, I sat there trying to sketch the gray stone lion's head on the wall, with scarlet woodbine sprays hanging round it. I felt as if I'd got into a romance, sitting there, watching the Neckar rolling through the valley, listening to the music of the Austrian band below, and waiting for my lover, like a real storybook girl. I had a feeling that something was going to happen and I was ready for it. I didn't feel blushy or quakey, but quite cool and only a little excited.

By-and-by I heard Fred's voice, and then he came hurrying through the great arch to find me. He looked so troubled that I forgot all about myself, and asked what the matter was. He said he'd just got a letter begging him to come home, for Frank was very ill. So he was going at once on the night train and only had time to say good-by. I was very sorry for him, and disappointed for myself, but only for a minute because he said, as he shook hands—and said it in a way that I could not mistake—"I shall soon come back, you won't forget me, Amy?"

I didn't promise, but I looked at him, and he seemed satisfied, and there was no time for anything but messages and good-byes, for he was off in an hour, and we all miss him very much. I know he wanted to speak, but I think, from something he once hinted, that he had promised his father not to do anything of the sort yet a while, for he is a rash boy, and the old gentleman dreads a foreign daughter-in-law. We shall soon meet in Rome, and then, if I don't change my mind, I'll say "Yes, thank you," when he says "Will you, please?"

Of course this is all *very private*, but I wished you to know what was going on. Don't be anxious about me, remember I am your 'prudent Amy,' and be sure I will do nothing rashly. Send me as much advice as you like. I'll use it if I can. I wish I could see you for a good talk, Marmee. Love and trust me.

Ever your

Amy

CHAPTER XXXII

TENDER TROUBLES

"Jo, I'm anxious about Beth."

"Why, Mother, she has seemed unusually well since the babies came."

"It's not her health that troubles me now, it's her spirits. I'm sure there is something on her mind, and I want you to discover what it is."

"What makes you think so, Mother?"

"She sits alone a good deal, and doesn't talk to her father as much as she used. I found her crying over the babies the other day. When she sings, the songs are always sad ones, and now and then I see a look in her face that I don't understand. This isn't like Beth, and it worries me."

"Have you asked her about it?"

"I have tried once or twice, but she either evaded my questions or looked so distressed that I stopped. I never force my children's confidence, and I seldom have to wait for long."

Mrs. March glanced at Jo as she spoke, but the face opposite seemed quite unconscious of any secret disquietude but Beth's, and after sewing thoughtfully for a minute, Jo said, "I think she is growing up, and so begins to dream dreams, and have hopes and fears and fidgets, without knowing why or being able to explain them. Why, Mother, Beth's eighteen, but we don't realize it, and treat her like a child, forgetting she's a woman."

"So she is. Dear heart, how fast you do grow up," returned her mother with a sigh and a smile.

"Can't be helped, Marmee, so you must resign yourself to all sorts of worries, and let your birds hop out of the nest, one by one. I promise never to hop very far, if that is any comfort to you."

"It's a great comfort, Jo. I always feel strong when you are at home, now Meg is gone. Beth is too feeble and Amy too young to depend upon, but when the tug comes, you are always ready."

"Why, you know I don't mind hard jobs much, and there must always be one scrub in a family. Amy is splendid in fine works and I'm not, but I feel in my element when all the carpets are to be taken up, or half the family fall sick at once. Amy is distinguishing herself abroad, but if anything is amiss at home, I'm your man."

"I leave Beth to your hands, then, for she will open her tender little heart to her Jo sooner than to anyone else. Be very kind, and don't let her think anyone watches or talks about her. If she only would get quite strong and cheerful again, I shouldn't have a wish in the world."

"Happy woman! I've got heaps."

"My dear, what are they?"

"I'll settle Bethy's troubles, and then I'll tell you mine. They are not very wearing, so they'll keep." And Jo stitched away, with a wise nod which set her mother's heart at rest about her for the present at least.

While apparently absorbed in her own affairs, Jo watched Beth, and after many conflicting conjectures, finally settled upon one which seemed to explain the change in her. A slight incident gave Jo the clue to the mystery, she thought, and lively fancy, loving heart did the rest. She was affecting to write busily one Saturday afternoon, when she and Beth were alone together. Yet as she scribbled, she kept her eye on her sister, who seemed unusually quiet. Sitting at the window, Beth's work often dropped into her lap, and she leaned her head upon her hand, in a dejected attitude, while her eyes rested on the dull, autumnal landscape. Suddenly some one passed below, whistling like an operatic blackbird, and a voice called out, "All serene! Coming in tonight."

Beth started, leaned forward, smiled and nodded, watched the passer-by till his quick tramp died away, then said softly as if to herself, "How strong and well and happy that dear boy looks."

"Hum!" said Jo, still intent upon her sister's face, for the bright color faded as quickly as it came, the smile vanished, and presently a tear lay shining on the window ledge. Beth whisked it off and glanced apprehensively at Jo; but she was scratching away at a tremendous rate, apparently engrossed in *Olympia's Oath*. The instant Beth Turned, Jo began her watch again, saw Beth's hand go quietly to her eyes more than once, and in her half-averted face read a tender sorrow that made her own eyes fill. Fearing to betray herself, she slipped away, murmuring something about needing more paper.

"Mercy on me, Beth loves Laurie!" she said, sitting down in her own room, pale with the shock of the discovery which she believed she had just made. "I never dreamed of such a thing. What *will* Mother say? I wonder if he—" There Jo stopped and turned scarlet with a sudden thought. "If he shouldn't love back again, how dreadful it would be. He must. I'll make him!" and she shook her head threateningly at the picture of the mischievous-looking boy laughing at her from the wall. "Oh dear, we are growing up with a vengeance. Here's Meg married and a mamma, Amy flourishing away at Paris, and Beth in love. I'm the only one that has sense enough to keep out of mischief." Jo thought intently for a minute with her eyes fixed on the picture, then she smoothed out her wrinkled forehead and said, with a decided nod at the face opposite, "No thank you, sir, you're very charming, but you've no more stability than a weathercock. So you needn't write touching notes and smile in that insinuating way, for it won't do a bit of good, and I won't have it."

Then she sighed, and fell into a reverie from which she did not wake till the early twilight sent her down to take new observations, which only confirmed her suspicion. Though Laurie flirted with Amy and joked with Jo, his manner to Beth had always been peculiarly kind and gentle, but so was everybody's. Therefore, no one thought of imagining that he cared more for her than for the others. Indeed, a general impression had prevailed in the family of late that "our boy" was getting fonder than ever of Jo, who, however, wouldn't hear a word upon the subject and scolded violently if anyone dared to suggest it. If they had known the various tender passages which had been nipped in the bud, they would have had the immense satisfaction of saying, "I told you so." But Jo hated "philandering," and wouldn't allow it, always having a joke or a smile ready at the least sign of impending danger.

When Laurie first went to college, he fell in love about once a month, but these small flames were as brief as ardent, did no damage, and much amused Jo, who took great interest in the alternations of hope, despair, and resignation, which were confided to her in their weekly conferences. But there came a time when Laurie ceased to worship at many shrines, hinted darkly at one all-absorbing passion, and indulged occasionally in Byronic fits of gloom. Then he avoided the tender subject altogether, wrote philosophical notes to Jo, turned studious, and gave out that he was going to "dig," intending to graduate in a blaze of glory. This suited the young lady better than twilight confidences, tender pressures of the hand, and eloquent glances of the eye, for with Jo, brain developed earlier than heart, and she preferred imaginary heroes to real ones, because when tired of them, the former could be shut up in the tin kitchen till called for, and the latter were less manageable.

Things were in this state when the grand discovery was made, and Jo watched Laurie that night as she had never done before. If she had not got the new idea into her head, she would have seen nothing unusual in the fact that Beth was very quiet, and Laurie very kind to her. But having given the rein to her lively fancy, it galloped away with her at a great pace, and common sense, being rather weakened by a long course of romance writing, did not come to the rescue. As usual Beth lay on the sofa and Laurie sat in a low chair close by, amusing her with all sorts of gossip, for she depended on her weekly "spin," and he never disappointed her. But that evening Jo fancied that Beth's eyes rested on the lively, dark face beside her with peculiar pleasure, and that she listened with intense interest to an account of some exciting cricket match, though the phrases, "caught off a tice," "stumped off his ground," and "the leg hit for three," were as intelligible to her as Sanskrit. She also fancied, having set her heart upon seeing it, that she saw a certain increase of gentleness in Laurie's manner, that he dropped his voice now and then, laughed less than usual, was a little absent-minded, and settled the afghan over Beth's feet with an assiduity that was really almost tender.

"Who knows? Stranger things have happened," thought Jo, as she fussed about the room. "She will make quite an angel of him, and he will make life delightfully easy and pleasant for the dear, if they only love each other. I don't see how he can help it, and I do believe he would if the rest of us were out of the way."

As everyone *was* out of the way but herself, Jo began to feel that she ought to dispose of herself with all speed. But where should she go? And burning to lay herself upon the shrine of sisterly devotion, she sat down to settle that point.

Now, the old sofa was a regular patriarch of a sofa—long, broad, well-cushioned, and low, a trifle shabby, as well it might be, for the girls had slept and sprawled on it as babies, fished over the back, rode on the arms, and had menageries under it as children, and rested tired heads, dreamed dreams, and listened to tender talk on it as young women. They all loved it, for it was a family refuge, and one corner had always been Jo's favorite lounging place. Among the many pillows that adorned the venerable couch was one, hard, round, covered with prickly horsehair, and furnished with a knobby button at each end. This repulsive pillow was her especial property, being used as a weapon of defense, a barricade, or a stern preventive of too much slumber.

Laurie knew this pillow well, and had cause to regard it with deep aversion, having been unmercifully pummeled with it in former days when romping was allowed, and now frequently debarred by it from the seat he most coveted next to Jo in the sofa corner. If "the sausage" as they called it, stood on end, it was a sign that he might approach and repose, but if it lay flat across the sofa, woe to man, woman, or child who dared disturb it! That evening Jo forgot to barricade her corner, and had not been in her seat five minutes, before a massive form appeared beside her, and with both arms spread over the sofa back, both long legs stretched out before him, Laurie exclaimed, with a sigh of satisfaction—

"Now, this is filling at the price."

"No slang," snapped Jo, slamming down the pillow. But it was too late, there was no room for it, and coasting onto the floor, it disappeared in a most mysterious manner.

"Come, Jo, don't be thorny. After studying himself to a skeleton all the week, a fellow deserves petting and ought to get it."

"Beth will pet you. I'm busy."

"No, she's not to be bothered with me, but you like that sort of thing, unless you've suddenly lost your taste for it. Have you? Do you hate your boy, and want to fire pillows at him?"

Anything more wheedlesome than that touching appeal was seldom heard, but Jo quenched "her boy" by turning on him with a stern query, "How many bouquets have you sent Miss Randal this week?"

"Not one, upon my word. She's engaged. Now then."

"I'm glad of it, that's one of your foolish extravagances—sending flowers and things to girls for whom you don't care two pins," continued Jo reprovingly.

"Sensible girls for whom I do care whole papers of pins won't let me send them 'flowers and things,' so what can I do? My feelings must have a *went*."

"Mother doesn't approve of flirting even in fun, and you do flirt desperately, Teddy."

"I'd give anything if I could answer, 'So do you.' As I can't, I'll merely say that I don't see any harm in that pleasant little game, if all parties understand that it's only play."

"Well, it does look pleasant, but I can't learn how it's done. I've tried, because one feels awkward in company not to do as everybody else is doing, but I don't seem to get on," said Jo, forgetting to play mentor.

"Take lessons of Amy, she has a regular talent for it."

"Yes, she does it very prettily, and never seems to go too far. I suppose it's natural to some people to please without trying, and others to always say and do the wrong thing in the wrong place."

"I'm glad you can't flirt. It's really refreshing to see a sensible, straightforward girl, who can be jolly and kind without making a fool of herself. Between ourselves, Jo, some of the girls I know really do go on at such a rate I'm ashamed of them. They don't mean any harm, I'm sure, but if they knew how we fellows talked about them afterward, they'd mend their ways, I fancy."

"They do the same, and as their tongues are the sharpest, you fellows get the worst of it, for you are as silly as they, every bit. If you behaved properly, they would, but knowing you like their nonsense, they keep it up, and then you blame them."

"Much you know about it, ma'am," said Laurie in a superior tone. "We don't like romps and flirts, though we may act as if we did sometimes. The pretty, modest girls are never talked about, except respectfully, among gentleman. Bless your innocent soul! If you could be in my place for a month you'd see things that would astonish you a trifle. Upon my word, when I see one of those harum-scarum girls, I always want to say with our friend Cock Robin—

> "Out upon you, fie upon you,
> Bold-faced jig!"

It was impossible to help laughing at the funny conflict between Laurie's chivalrous reluctance to speak ill of womankind, and his very natural dislike of the unfeminine folly of which fashionable society showed him many samples. Jo knew that "young Laurence" was regarded as a most eligible *parti* by worldly mamas, was much smiled upon by their daughters, and flattered enough by ladies of all ages to make a coxcomb of him, so she watched him rather jealously, fearing he would be spoiled, and rejoiced more than she confessed to find that he still believed in modest girls. Returning suddenly to her admonitory tone, she said, dropping her voice, "If you *must* have a 'went,' Teddy, go and devote yourself to one of the 'pretty, modest girls' whom you do respect, and not waste your time with the silly ones."

"You really advise it?" and Laurie looked at her with an odd mixture of anxiety and merriment in his face.

"Yes, I do, but you'd better wait till you are through college, on the whole, and be fitting yourself for the place meantime. You're not half good enough for—well, whoever the modest girl may be." And Jo looked a little queer likewise, for a name had almost escaped her.

"That I'm not!" acquiesced Laurie, with an expression of humility quite new to him, as he dropped his eyes and absently wound Jo's apron tassel round his finger.

"Mercy on us, this will never do," thought Jo, adding aloud, "Go and sing to me. I'm dying for some music, and always like yours."

"I'd rather stay here, thank you."

"Well, you can't, there isn't room. Go and make yourself useful, since you are too big to be ornamental. I thought you hated to be tied to a woman's apron string?" retorted Jo, quoting certain rebellious words of his own.

"Ah, that depends on who wears the apron!" And Laurie gave an audacious tweak at the tassel.

"Are you going?" demanded Jo, diving for the pillow.

He fled at once, and the minute it was well, "Up with the bonnets of bonnie Dundee," she slipped away to return no more till the young gentleman departed in high dudgeon.

Jo lay long awake that night, and was just dropping off when the sound of a stifled sob made her fly to Beth's bedside, with the anxious inquiry, "What is it, dear?"

"I thought you were asleep," sobbed Beth.

"Is it the old pain, my precious?"

"No, it's a new one, but I can bear it," and Beth tried to check her tears.

"Tell me all about it, and let me cure it as I often did the other."

"You can't, there is no cure." There Beth's voice gave way, and clinging to her sister, she cried so despairingly that Jo was frightened.

"Where is it? Shall I call Mother?"

Beth did not answer the first question, but in the dark one hand went involuntarily to her heart as if it were there, with the other she held Jo fast, whispering eagerly, "No, no, don't call her, don't tell her. I shall be better soon. Lie down here and 'poor' my head. I'll be quiet and go to sleep, indeed I will."

Jo obeyed, but as her hand went softly to and fro across Beth's hot forehead and wet eyelids, her heart was very full and she longed to speak. But young as she was, Jo had learned that hearts, like flowers, cannot be rudely handled, but must open naturally, so though she believed she knew the cause of Beth's new pain, she only said, in her tenderest tone, "Does anything trouble you, deary?"

"Yes, Jo," after a long pause.

"Wouldn't it comfort you to tell me what it is?"

"Not now, not yet."

"Then I won't ask, but remember, Bethy, that Mother and Jo are always glad to hear and help you, if they can."

"I know it. I'll tell you by-and-by."

"Is the pain better now?"

"Oh, yes, much better, you are so comfortable, Jo."

"Go to sleep, dear. I'll stay with you."

So cheek to cheek they fell asleep, and on the morrow Beth seemed quite herself again, for at eighteen neither heads nor hearts ache long, and a loving word can medicine most ills.

But Jo had made up her mind, and after pondering over a project for some days, she confided it to her mother.

"You asked me the other day what my wishes were. I'll tell you one of them, Marmee," she began, as they sat along together. "I want to go away somewhere this winter for a change."

"Why, Jo?" and her mother looked up quickly, as if the words suggested a double meaning.

With her eyes on her work Jo answered soberly, "I want something new. I feel restless and anxious to be seeing, doing, and learning more than I am. I brood too much over my own small affairs, and need stirring up, so as I can be spared this winter, I'd like to hop a little way and try my wings."

"Where will you hop?"

"To New York. I had a bright idea yesterday, and this is it. You know Mrs. Kirke wrote to you for some respectable young person to teach her children and sew. It's rather hard to find just the thing, but I think I should suit if I tried."

"My dear, go out to service in that great boarding house!" and Mrs. March looked surprised, but not displeased.

"It's not exactly going out to service, for Mrs. Kirke is your friend—the kindest soul that ever lived—and would make things pleasant for me, I know. Her family is separate from the rest, and no one knows me there. Don't care if they do. It's honest work, and I'm not ashamed of it."

"Nor I. But your writing?"

"All the better for the change. I shall see and hear new things, get new ideas, and even if I haven't much time there, I shall bring home quantities of material for my rubbish."

"I have no doubt of it, but are these your only reasons for this sudden fancy?"

"No, Mother."

"May I know the others?"

Jo looked up and Jo looked down, then said slowly, with sudden color in her cheeks, "It may be vain and wrong to say it, but—I'm afraid—Laurie is getting too fond of me."

"Then you don't care for him in the way it is evident he begins to care for you?" And Mrs. March looked anxious as she put the question.

"Mercy, no! I love the dear boy, as I always have, and am immensely proud of him, but as for anything more, it's out of the question."

"I'm glad of that, Jo."

"Why, please?"

"Because, dear, I don't think you are suited to one another. As friends you are very happy, and your frequent quarrels soon blow over, but I fear you would both rebel if you were mated for life. You are too much alike and too fond of freedom, not to mention hot tempers and strong wills, to get on happily together, in a relation which needs infinite patience and forbearance, as well as love."

"That's just the feeling I had, though I couldn't express it. I'm glad you think he is only beginning to care for me. It would trouble me sadly to make him unhappy, for I couldn't fall in love with the dear old fellow merely out of gratitude, could I?"

"You are sure of his feeling for you?"

The color deepened in Jo's cheeks as she answered, with the look of mingled pleasure, pride, and pain which young girls wear when speaking of first lovers, "I'm afraid it is so, Mother. He hasn't said anything, but he looks a great deal. I think I had better go away before it comes to anything."

"I agree with you, and if it can be managed you shall go."

Jo looked relieved, and after a pause, said, smiling, "How Mrs. Moffat would wonder at your want of management, if she knew, and how she will rejoice that Annie may still hope."

"Ah, Jo, mothers may differ in their management, but the hope is the same in all—the desire to see their children happy. Meg is so, and I am content with her success. You I leave to enjoy your liberty till you tire of it, for only then will you find that there is something sweeter. Amy is my chief care now, but her good sense will help her. For Beth, I indulge no hopes except that she may be well. By the way, she seems brighter this last day or two. Have you spoken to her?'

"Yes, she owned she had a trouble, and promised to tell me by-and-by. I said no more, for I think I know it," and Jo told her little story.

Mrs. March shook her head, and did not take so romantic a view of the case, but looked grave, and repeated her opinion that for Laurie's sake Jo should go away for a time.

"Let us say nothing about it to him till the plan is settled, then I'll run away before he can collect his wits and be tragic. Beth must think I'm going to please myself, as I am, for I can't talk about Laurie to her. But she can pet and comfort him after I'm gone, and so cure him of this romantic notion. He's been through so many little trials of the sort, he's used to it, and will soon get over his lovelornity."

Jo spoke hopefully, but could not rid herself of the foreboding fear that this "little trial" would be harder than the others, and that Laurie would not get over his "lovelornity" as easily as heretofore.

The plan was talked over in a family council and agreed upon, for Mrs. Kirke gladly accepted Jo, and promised to make a pleasant home for her. The teaching would render her independent, and such leisure as she got might be made profitable by writing, while the new scenes and society would be both useful and agreeable. Jo liked the prospect and was eager to be gone, for the home nest was growing too narrow for her restless nature and adventurous spirit. When all was settled, with fear and trembling she told Laurie, but to her surprise he took it very quietly. He had been graver than usual of late, but very pleasant, and when jokingly accused of turning over a new leaf, he answered soberly, "So I am, and I mean this one shall stay turned."

Jo was very much relieved that one of his virtuous fits should come on just then, and made her preparations with a lightened heart, for Beth seemed more cheerful, and hoped she was doing the best for all.

"One thing I leave in your especial care," she said, the night before she left.

"You mean your papers?" asked Beth.

"No, my boy. Be very good to him, won't you?"

"Of course I will, but I can't fill your place, and he'll miss you sadly."

"It won't hurt him, so remember, I leave him in your charge, to plague, pet, and keep in order."

"I'll do my best, for your sake," promised Beth, wondering why Jo looked at her so queerly.

When Laurie said good-by, he whispered significantly, "It won't do a bit of good, Jo. My eye is on you, so mind what you do, or I'll come and bring you home."

CHAPTER XXXIII

JO'S JOURNAL

New York, November

Dear Marmee and Beth,

I'm going to write you a regular volume, for I've got heaps to tell, though I'm not a fine young lady traveling on the continent. When I lost sight of Father's dear old face, I felt a trifle blue, and might have shed a briny drop or two, if an Irish lady with four small children, all crying more or less, hadn't diverted my mind, for I amused myself by dropping gingerbread nuts over the seat every time they opened their mouths to roar.

Soon the sun came out, and taking it as a good omen, I cleared up likewise and enjoyed my journey with all my heart.

Mrs. Kirke welcomed me so kindly I felt at home at once, even in that big house full of strangers. She gave me a funny little sky parlor—all she had, but there is a stove in it, and a nice table in a sunny window, so I can sit here and write whenever I like. A fine view and a church tower opposite atone for the many stairs, and I took a fancy to my den on the spot. The nursery, where I am to teach and sew, is a pleasant room next Mrs. Kirke's private parlor, and the two little girls are pretty children, rather spoiled, I fancy, but they took to me after telling them *The Seven Bad Pigs*, and I've no doubt I shall make a model governess.

I am to have my meals with the children, if I prefer it to the great table, and for the present I do, for I *am* bashful, though no one will believe it.

"Now, my dear, make yourself at home," said Mrs. K. in her motherly way, "I'm on the drive from morning to night, as you may suppose with such a family, but a great anxiety will be off my mind if I know the children are safe with you. My rooms are always open to you, and your own shall be as comfortable as I can make it. There are some pleasant people in the house if you feel sociable, and your evenings are always free. Come to me if anything goes wrong, and be as happy as you can. There's the tea bell, I must run and change my cap." And off she bustled, leaving me to settle myself in my new nest.

As I went downstairs soon after, I saw something I liked. The flights are very long in this tall house, and as I stood waiting at the head of the third one for a little servant girl to lumber up, I saw a gentleman come along behind her, take the heavy hod of coal out of her hand, carry it all the way up, put it down at a door near by, and walk away, saying, with a kind nod and a foreign accent, "It goes better so. The little back is too young to haf such heaviness."

Wasn't it good of him? I like such things, for as Father says, trifles show character. When I mentioned it to Mrs. K., that evening, she laughed, and said, "That must have been Professor Bhaer, he's always doing things of that sort."

Mrs. K. told me he was from Berlin, very learned and good, but poor as a church mouse, and gives lessons to support himself and two little orphan nephews whom he is educating here, according to the wishes of his sister, who married an American. Not a very romantic story, but it interested me, and I was glad to hear that Mrs. K. lends him her parlor for some of his scholars. There is a glass door between it and the nursery, and I mean to peep at him, and then I'll tell you how he looks. He's almost forty, so it's no harm, Marmee.

After tea and a go-to-bed romp with the little girls, I attacked the big workbasket, and had a quiet evening chatting with my new friend. I shall keep a journal-letter, and send it once a week, so goodnight, and more tomorrow.

TUESDAY EVE

Had a lively time in my seminary this morning, for the children acted like Sancho, and at one time I really thought I should shake them all round. Some good angel inspired me to try gymnastics, and I kept it up till they were glad to sit down and keep still. After luncheon, the girl took them out for a walk, and I went to my needlework like little Mabel "with a willing mind." I was thanking my stars that I'd learned to make nice buttonholes, when the parlor door opened and shut, and someone began to hum,

"Kennst du das Land,"

like a big bumblebee. It was dreadfully improper, I know, but I couldn't resist the temptation, and lifting one end of the curtain before the glass door, I peeped in. Professor Bhaer was there, and while he arranged his books, I took a good look at him. A regular German—rather stout, with brown hair tumbled all over his head, a bushy beard, good nose, the kindest eyes I ever saw, and a splendid big voice that does one's ears good, after our sharp or slipshod American gabble. His clothes were rusty, his hands were large, and he hadn't a really handsome feature in his face, except his beautiful teeth, yet I liked him, for he had a fine head, his linen was very nice, and he looked like a gentleman, though two buttons were off his coat and there was a patch on one shoe. He looked sober in spite of his humming, till he went to the window to turn the hyacinth bulbs toward the sun, and stroke the cat, who received him like an old friend. Then he smiled, and when a tap came at the door, called out in a loud, brisk tone,

"Herein!"

I was just going to run, when I caught sight of a morsel of a child carrying a big book, and stopped, to see what was going on.

"Me wants my Bhaer," said the mite, slamming down her book and running to meet him.

"Thou shalt haf thy Bhaer. Come, then, and take a goot hug from him, my Tina," said the Professor, catching her up with a laugh, and holding her so high over his head that she had to stoop her little face to kiss him.

"Now me mus tuddy my lessin," went on the funny little thing. So he put her up at the table, opened the great dictionary she had brought, and gave her a paper and pencil, and she scribbled away, turning a leaf now and then, and passing her little fat finger down the page, as if finding a word, so soberly that I nearly betrayed myself by a laugh, while Mr. Bhaer stood stroking her pretty hair with a fatherly look that made me think she must be his own, though she looked more French than German.

Another knock and the appearance of two young ladies sent me back to my work, and there I virtuously remained through all the noise and gabbling that went on next door. One of the girls kept laughing affectedly, and saying, "Now Professor," in a coquettish tone, and the other pronounced her German with an accent that must have made it hard for him to keep sober.

Both seemed to try his patience sorely, for more than once I heard him say emphatically, "No, no, it is not so, you haf not attend to what I say," and once there was a loud rap, as if he struck the table with his book, followed by the despairing exclamation, "Prut! It all goes bad this day."

Poor man, I pitied him, and when the girls were gone, took just one more peep to see if he survived it. He seemed to have thrown himself back in his chair, tired out, and sat there with his eyes shut till the clock struck two, when he jumped up, put his books in his pocket, as if ready for another lesson, and taking little Tina who had fallen asleep on the sofa in his arms, he carried her quietly away. I fancy he has a hard life of it. Mrs. Kirke asked me if I wouldn't go down to the five o'clock dinner, and feeling a little bit homesick, I thought I would, just to see what sort of people are under the same roof with me. So I made myself respectable and tried to slip in behind Mrs. Kirke, but as she is short and I'm tall, my efforts at concealment were rather a failure. She gave me a seat by her, and after my face cooled off, I plucked up courage and looked about me. The long table was full, and every one intent on getting their dinner, the gentlemen especially, who seemed to be eating on time, for they bolted in every sense of the word, vanishing as soon as they were done. There was the usual assortment of young men absorbed in themselves, young couples absorbed in each other, married ladies in their babies, and old gentlemen in politics. I don't think I shall care to have much to do with any of them, except one sweetfaced maiden lady, who looks as if she had something in her.

Cast away at the very bottom of the table was the Professor, shouting answers to the questions of a very inquisitive, deaf old gentleman on one side, and talking philosophy with a Frenchman on the other. If Amy had been here, she'd have turned her back on him forever because, sad to relate, he had a great appetite, and shoveled in his dinner in a manner which would have horrified "her ladyship." I didn't mind, for I like "to see folks eat with a relish," as Hannah says, and the poor man must have needed a deal of food after teaching idiots all day.

As I went upstairs after dinner, two of the young men were settling their hats before the hall mirror, and I heard one say low to the other, "Who's the new party?"

"Governess, or something of that sort."

"What the deuce is she at our table for?"

"Friend of the old lady's."

"Handsome head, but no style."

"Not a bit of it. Give us a light and come on."

I felt angry at first, and then I didn't care, for a governess is as good as a clerk, and I've got sense, if I haven't style, which is more than some people have, judging from the remarks of the elegant beings who clattered away, smoking like bad chimneys. I hate ordinary people!

THURSDAY

Yesterday was a quiet day spent in teaching, sewing, and writing in my little room, which is very cozy, with a light and fire. I picked up a few bits of news and was introduced to the Professor. It seems that Tina is the child of the Frenchwoman who does the fine ironing in the laundry here. The little thing has lost her heart to Mr. Bhaer, and follows him about the house like a dog whenever he is at home, which delights him, as he is very fond of children, though a "bacheldore." Kitty and Minnie Kirke likewise regard him with affection, and tell all sorts of stories about the plays he invents, the presents he brings, and the splendid tales he tells. The younger men quiz him, it seems, call him Old Fritz, Lager Beer, Ursa Major, and make all manner of jokes on his name. But he enjoys it like a boy, Mrs. Kirke says, and takes it so good-naturedly that they all like him in spite of his foreign ways.

The maiden lady is a Miss Norton—rich, cultivated, and kind. She spoke to me at dinner today (for I went to table again, it's such fun to watch people), and asked me to come and see her at her room. She has fine books and pictures, knows interesting persons, and seems friendly, so I shall make myself agreeable, for I *do* want to get into good society, only it isn't the same sort that Amy likes.

I was in our parlor last evening when Mr. Bhaer came in with some newspapers for Mrs. Kirke. She wasn't there, but Minnie, who is a little old woman, introduced me very prettily. "This is Mamma's friend, Miss March."

"Yes, and she's jolly and we like her lots," added Kitty, who is an *enfant terrible*.

We both bowed, and then we laughed, for the prim introduction and the blunt addition were rather a comical contrast.

"Ah, yes, I hear these naughty ones go to vex you, Mees Marsch. If so again, call at me and I come," he said, with a threatening frown that delighted the little wretches.

I promised I would, and he departed, but it seems as if I was doomed to see a good deal of him, for today as I passed his door on my way out, by accident I knocked against it with my umbrella. It flew open, and there he stood in his dressing gown, with a big blue sock on one hand and a darning needle in the other. He didn't seem at all ashamed of it, for when I explained and hurried on, he waved his hand, sock and all, saying in his loud, cheerful way—

"You haf a fine day to make your walk. Bon voyage, Mademoiselle."

I laughed all the way downstairs, but it was a little pathetic, also to think of the poor man having to mend his own clothes. The German gentlemen embroider, I know, but darning hose is another thing and not so pretty.

SATURDAY

Nothing has happened to write about, except a call on Miss Norton, who has a room full of pretty things, and who was very charming, for she showed me all her treasures, and asked me if I would sometimes go with her to lectures and concerts, as her escort—if I enjoyed them. She put it as a favor, but I'm sure Mrs. Kirke has told her about us, and she does it out of kindness to me. I'm as proud as Lucifer, but such favors from such people don't burden me, and I accepted gratefully.

When I got back to the nursery there was such an uproar in the parlor that I looked in, and there was Mr. Bhaer down on his hands and knees, with Tina on his back, Kitty leading him with a jump rope, and Minnie feeding two small boys with seedcakes, as they roared and ramped in cages built of chairs.

"We are playing *nargerie*," explained Kitty.

"Dis is mine effalunt!" added Tina, holding on by the Professor's hair.

"Mamma always allows us to do what we like Saturday afternoon, when Franz and Emil come, doesn't she, Mr. Bhaer?" said Minnie.

The "effalunt" sat up, looking as much in earnest as any of them, and said soberly to me, "I gif you my wort it is so, if we make too large a noise you shall say Hush! to us, and we go more softly."

I promised to do so, but left the door open and enjoyed the fun as much as they did, for a more glorious frolic I never witnessed. They played tag and soldiers, danced and sang, and when it began to grow dark they all piled onto the sofa about the Professor, while he told charming fairy stories of the storks on the chimney tops, and the little "koblods," who ride the snowflakes as they fall. I wish Americans were as simple and natural as Germans, don't you?

I'm so fond of writing, I should go spinning on forever if motives of economy didn't stop me, for though I've used thin paper and written fine, I tremble to think of the stamps this long letter will need. Pray forward Amy's as soon as you can spare them. My small news will sound very flat after her splendors, but you will like them, I know. Is Teddy studying so hard that he can't find time to write to his friends? Take good care of him for me, Beth, and tell me all about the babies, and give heaps of love to everyone.

From your faithful Jo.

P.S. On reading over my letter, it strikes me as rather Bhaery, but I am always interested in odd people, and I really had nothing else to write about. Bless you!

December

My Precious Betsey,

As this is to be a scribble-scrabble letter, I direct it to you, for it may amuse you, and give you some idea of my goings on, for though quiet, they are rather amusing, for which, oh, be joyful! After what Amy would call Herculaneum efforts, in the way of mental and moral agriculture, my young ideas begin to shoot and my little twigs to bend as I could wish. They are not so interesting to me as Tina and the boys, but I do my duty by them, and they are fond of me. Franz and Emil are jolly little lads, quite after my own heart, for the mixture of German and American spirit in them produces a constant state of effervescence. Saturday afternoons are riotous times, whether spent in the house or out, for on pleasant days they all go to walk, like a seminary, with the Professor and myself to keep order, and then such fun!

We are very good friends now, and I've begun to take lessons. I really couldn't help it, and it all came about in such a droll way that I must tell you. To begin at the beginning, Mrs. Kirke called to me one day as I passed Mr. Bhaer's room where she was rummaging.

"Did you ever see such a den, my dear? Just come and help me put these books to rights, for I've turned everything upside down, trying to discover what he has done with the six new handkerchiefs I gave him not long ago."

I went in, and while we worked I looked about me, for it was "a den" to be sure. Books and papers everywhere, a broken meerschaum, and an old flute over the mantlepiece as if done with, a ragged bird without any tail chirped on one window seat, and a box of white mice adorned the other. Half-finished boats and bits of string lay among the manuscripts. Dirty little boots stood drying before the fire, and traces of the dearly beloved boys, for whom he makes a slave of himself, were to be seen all over the room. After a grand rummage three of the missing articles were found, one over the bird cage, one covered with ink, and a third burned brown, having been used as a holder.

"Such a man!" laughed good-natured Mrs. K., as she put the relics in the rag bay. "I suppose the others are torn up to rig ships, bandage cut fingers, or make kite tails. It's dreadful, but I can't scold him. He's so absent-minded and goodnatured, he lets those boys ride over him roughshod. I agreed to do his washing and mending, but he forgets to give out his things and I forget to look them over, so he comes to a sad pass sometimes."

"Let me mend them," said I. "I don't mind it, and he needn't know. I'd like to, he's so kind to me about bringing my letters and lending books."

So I have got his things in order, and knit heels into two pairs of the socks, for they were boggled out of shape with his queer darns. Nothing was said, and I hoped he wouldn't find it out, but one day last week he caught me at it. Hearing the lessons he gives to others has interested and amused me so much that I took a fancy to learn, for Tina runs in and out, leaving the door open, and I can hear. I had been sitting near this door, finishing off the last sock, and trying to understand what he said to a new scholar, who is as stupid as I am. The girl had gone, and I thought he had also, it was so still, and I was busily gabbling over a verb, and rocking to and fro in a most absurd way, when a little crow made me look up, and there was Mr. Bhaer looking and laughing quietly, while he made signs to Tina not to betray him.

"So!" he said, as I stopped and stared like a goose, "you peep at me, I peep at you, and this is not bad, but see, I am not pleasanting when I say, haf you a wish for German?"

"Yes, but you are too busy. I am too stupid to learn," I blundered out, as red as a peony.

"Prut! We will make the time, and we fail not to find the sense. At efening I shall gif a little lesson with much gladness, for look you, Mees Marsch, I haf this debt to pay." And he pointed to my work "'Yes,' they say to one another, these so kind ladies, 'he is a stupid old fellow, he will see not what we do, he will never observe that his sock heels go not in holes any more, he will think his buttons grow out new when they fall, and believe that strings make theirselves.' Ah! But I haf an eye, and I see much. I haf a heart, and I feel thanks for this. Come, a little lesson then and now, or—no more good fairy works for me and mine."

Of course I couldn't say anything after that, and as it really is a splendid opportunity, I made the bargain, and we began. I took four lessons, and then I stuck fast in a grammatical bog. The Professor was very patient with me, but it must have been torment to him, and now and then he'd look at me with such an expression of mild despair that it was a toss-up with me whether to laugh or cry. I tried both ways, and when it came to a sniff or utter mortification and woe, he just threw the grammar on to the floor and marched out of the room. I felt myself disgraced and deserted forever, but didn't blame him a particle, and was scrambling my papers together, meaning to rush upstairs and shake myself hard, when in he came, as brisk and beaming as if I'd covered myself in glory.

"Now we shall try a new way. You and I will read these pleasant little *Märchen* together, and dig no more in that dry book, that goes in the corner for making us trouble." He spoke so kindly, and opened Hans Anderson's fairy tales so invitingly before me, that I was more ashamed than ever, and went at my lesson in a neck-or-nothing style that seemed to amuse him immensely. I forgot my bashfulness, and pegged away (no other word will express it) with all my might, tumbling over long words, pronouncing according to inspiration of the minute, and doing my very best. When I finished reading my first page, and stopped for breath, he clapped his hands and cried out in his hearty way, "*Das ist gut*! Now we go well! My turn. I do him in German, gif me your ear." And away he went, rumbling out the words with his strong voice and a relish which was good to see as well as hear. Fortunately the story was the *Constant Tin Soldier*, which is droll, you know, so I could laugh, and I did, though I didn't understand half he read, for I couldn't help it, he was so earnest, I so excited, and the whole thing so comical.

After that we got on better, and now I read my lessons pretty well, for this way of studying suits me, and I can see that the grammar gets tucked into the tales and poetry as one gives pills in jelly. I like it very much, and he doesn't seem tired of it yet, which is very good of him, isn't it? I mean to give him something on Christmas, for I dare not offer money. Tell me something nice, Marmee.

I'm glad Laurie seems so happy and busy, that he has given up smoking and lets his hair grow. You see Beth manages him better than I did. I'm not jealous, dear, do your best, only don't make a saint of him. I'm afraid I couldn't like him without a spice of human naughtiness. Read him bits of my letters. I haven't time to write much, and that will do just as well. Thank Heaven Beth continues so comfortable.

JANUARY

A Happy New Year to you all, my dearest family, which of course includes Mr. L. and a young man by the name of Teddy. I can't tell you how much I enjoyed your Christmas bundle, for I didn't get it till night and had given up hoping. Your letter came in the morning, but you said nothing about a parcel, meaning it for a surprise, so I was disappointed, for I'd had a "kind of feeling" that you wouldn't forget me. I felt a little low in my mind as I sat up in my room after tea, and when the big, muddy, battered-looking bundle was brought to me, I just hugged it and pranced. It was so homey and refreshing that I sat down on the floor and read and looked and ate and laughed and cried, in my usual absurd way. The things were just what I wanted, and all the better for being made instead of bought. Beth's new "ink bib" was capital, and Hannah's box of hard gingerbread will be a treasure. I'll be sure and wear the nice flannels you sent, Marmee, and read carefully the books Father has marked. Thank you all, heaps and heaps!

Speaking of books reminds me that I'm getting rich in that line, for on New Year's Day Mr. Bhaer gave me a fine Shakespeare. It is one he values much, and I've often admired it, set up in the place of honor with his German Bible, Plato, Homer, and Milton, so you may imagine how I felt when he brought it down, without its cover, and showed me my own name in it, "from my friend Friedrich Bhaer."

"You say often you wish a library. Here I gif you one, for between these lids (he meant covers) is many books in one. Read him well, and he will help you much, for the study of character in this book will help you to read it in the world and paint it with your pen."

I thanked him as well as I could, and talk now about "my library," as if I had a hundred books. I never knew how much there was in Shakespeare before, but then I never had a Bhaer to explain it to me. Now don't laugh at his horrid name. It isn't pronounced either Bear or Beer, as people will say it, but something between the two, as only Germans can give it. I'm glad you both like what I tell you about him, and hope you will know him some day. Mother would admire his warm heart, Father his wise head. I admire both, and feel rich in my new "friend Friedrich Bhaer."

Not having much money, or knowing what he'd like, I got several little things, and put them about the room, where he would find them unexpectedly. They were useful, pretty, or funny, a new standish on his table, a little vase for his flower, he always has one, or a bit of green in a glass, to keep him fresh, he says, and a holder for his blower, so that he needn't burn up what Amy calls "mouchoirs." I made it like those Beth invented, a big butterfly with a fat body, and black and yellow wings, worsted feelers, and bead eyes. It took his fancy immensely, and he put it on his mantlepiece as an article of virtue, so it was rather a failure after all. Poor as he is, he didn't forget a servant or a child in the house, and not a soul here, from the French laundrywoman to Miss Norton forgot him. I was so glad of that.

They got up a masquerade, and had a gay time New Year's Eve. I didn't mean to go down, having no dress. But at the last minute, Mrs. Kirke remembered some old brocades, and Miss Norton lent me lace and feathers. So I dressed up as Mrs. Malaprop, and sailed in with a mask on. No one knew me, for I disguised my voice, and no one dreamed of the silent, haughty Miss March (for they think I am very stiff and cool, most of them, and so I am to whippersnappers) could dance and dress, and burst out into a "nice derangement of epitaphs, like an allegory on the banks of the Nile." I enjoyed it very much, and when we unmasked it was fun to see them stare at me. I heard one of the young men tell another that he knew I'd been an actress, in fact, he thought he remembered seeing me at one of the minor theaters. Meg will relish that joke. Mr. Bhaer was Nick Bottom, and Tina was Titania, a perfect little fairy in his arms. To see them dance was "quite a landscape," to use a Teddyism.

I had a very happy New Year, after all, and when I thought it over in my room, I felt as if I was getting on a little in spite of my many failures, for I'm cheerful all the time now, work with a will, and take more interest in other people than I used to, which is satisfactory. Bless you all!

Ever your loving
Jo

CHAPTER XXXIV

A FRIEND

Though very happy in the social atmosphere about her, and very busy with the daily work that earned her bread and made it sweeter for the effort, Jo still found time for literary labors. The purpose which now took possession of her was a natural one to a poor and ambitious girl, but the means she took to gain her end were not the best. She saw that money conferred power, money and power, therefore, she resolved to have, not to be used for herself alone, but for those whom she loved more than life.

The dream of filling home with comforts, giving Beth everything she wanted, from strawberries in winter to an organ in her bedroom, going abroad herself, and always having more than enough, so that she might indulge in the luxury of charity, had been for years Jo's most cherished castle in the air.

The prize-story experience had seemed to open a way which might, after long traveling and much uphill work, lead to this delightful *château en Espagne*. But the novel disaster quenched her courage for a time, for public opinion is a giant which has frightened stouter-hearted Jacks on bigger beanstalks than hers. Like that immortal hero, she reposed awhile after the first attempt, which resulted in a tumble and the least lovely of the giant's treasures, if I remember rightly. But the 'up again and take another' spirit was as strong in Jo as in Jack, so she scrambled up on the shady side this time and got more booty, but nearly left behind her what was far more precious than the moneybags.

She took to writing sensation stories, for in those dark ages, even all-perfect America read rubbish. She told no one, but concocted a 'thrilling tale,' and boldly carried it herself to Mr. Dashwood, editor of the *Weekly Volcano*. She had never read *Sartor Resartus*, but she had a womanly instinct that clothes possess an influence more powerful over many than the worth of character or the magic of manners. So she dressed herself in her best, and trying to persuade herself that she was neither excited nor nervous, bravely climbed two pairs of dark and dirty stairs to find herself in a disorderly room, a cloud of cigar smoke, and the presence of three gentlemen, sitting with their heels rather higher than their hats, which articles of dress none of them took the trouble to remove on her appearance. Somewhat daunted by this reception, Jo hesitated on the threshold, murmuring in much embarrassment—

"Excuse me, I was looking for the *Weekly Volcano* office. I wished to see Mr. Dashwood." Down went the highest pair of heels, up rose the smokiest gentleman, and carefully cherishing his cigar between his fingers, he advanced with a nod and a countenance expressive of nothing but sleep. Feeling that she must get through the matter somehow, Jo produced her manuscript and, blushing redder and redder with each sentence, blundered out fragments of the little speech carefully prepared for the occasion.

"A friend of mine desired me to offer—a story—just as an experiment—would like your opinion—be glad to write more if this suits."

While she blushed and blundered, Mr. Dashwood had taken the manuscript, and was turning over the leaves with a pair of rather dirty fingers, and casting critical glances up and down the neat pages.

"Not a first attempt, I take it?" observing that the pages were numbered, covered only on one side, and not tied up with a ribbon—sure sign of a novice.

"No, sir. She has had some experience, and got a prize for a tale in the *Blarneystone Banner*."

"Oh, did she?" and Mr. Dashwood gave Jo a quick look, which seemed to take note of everything she had on, from the bow in her bonnet to the buttons on her boots. "Well, you can leave it, if you like. We've more of this sort of thing on hand than we know what to do with at present, but I'll run my eye over it, and give you an answer next week."

Now, Jo did *not* like to leave it, for Mr. Dashwood didn't suit her at all, but, under the circumstances, there was nothing for her to do but bow and walk away, looking particularly tall and dignified, as she was apt to do when nettled or abashed. Just then she was both, for it was perfectly evident from the knowing glances exchanged among the gentlemen that her little fiction of "my friend" was considered a good joke, and a laugh, produced by some inaudible remark of the editor, as he closed the door, completed her discomfiture. Half resolving never to return, she went home, and worked off her irritation by stitching pinafores vigorously, and in an hour or two was cool enough to laugh over the scene and long for next week.

When she went again, Mr. Dashwood was alone, whereat she rejoiced. Mr. Dashwood was much wider awake than before, which was agreeable, and Mr. Dashwood was not too deeply absorbed in a cigar to remember his manners, so the second interview was much more comfortable than the first.

"We'll take this (editors never say I), if you don't object to a few alterations. It's too long, but omitting the passages I've marked will make it just the right length," he said, in a businesslike tone.

Jo hardly knew her own MS. again, so crumpled and underscored were its pages and paragraphs, but feeling as a tender parent might on being asked to cut off her baby's legs in order that it might fit into a new cradle, she looked at the marked passages and was surprised to find that all the moral reflections—which she had carefully put in as ballast for much romance—had been stricken out.

"But, Sir, I thought every story should have some sort of a moral, so I took care to have a few of my sinners repent."

Mr. Dashwoods's editorial gravity relaxed into a smile, for Jo had forgotten her "friend," and spoken as only an author could.

"People want to be amused, not preached at, you know. Morals don't sell nowadays;" which was not quite a correct statement, by the way.

"You think it would do with these alterations, then?"

"Yes, it's a new plot, and pretty well worked up—language good, and so on," was Mr. Dashwood's affable reply.

"What do you—that is, what compensation—" began Jo, not exactly knowing how to express herself.

"Oh, yes, well, we give from twenty-five to thirty for things of this sort. Pay when it comes out," returned Mr. Dashwood, as if that point had escaped him. Such trifles do escape the editorial mind, it is said.

"Very well, you can have it," said Jo, handing back the story with a satisfied air, for after the dollar-a-column work, even twenty-five seemed good pay.

"Shall I tell my friend you will take another if she has one better than this?" asked Jo, unconscious of her little slip of the tongue, and emboldened by her success.

"Well, we'll look at it. Can't promise to take it. Tell her to make it short and spicy, and never mind the moral. What name would your friend like to put on it?" in a careless tone.

"None at all, if you please, she doesn't wish her name to appear and has no nom de plume," said Jo, blushing in spite of herself.

"Just as she likes, of course. The tale will be out next week. Will you call for the money, or shall I send it?" asked Mr. Dashwood, who felt a natural desire to know who his new contributor might be.

"I'll call. Good morning, Sir."

As she departed, Mr. Dashwood put up his feet, with the graceful remark, "Poor and proud, as usual, but she'll do."

Following Mr. Dashwood's directions, and making Mrs. Northbury her model, Jo rashly took a plunge into the frothy sea of sensational literature, but thanks to the life preserver thrown her by a friend, she came up again not much the worse for her ducking.

Like most young scribblers, she went abroad for her characters and scenery, and banditti, counts, gypsies, nuns, and duchesses appeared upon her stage, and played their parts with as much accuracy and spirit as could be expected. Her readers were not particular about such trifles as grammar, punctuation, and probability, and Mr. Dashwood graciously permitted her to fill his columns at the lowest prices, not thinking it necessary to tell her that the real cause of his hospitality was the fact that one of his hacks, on being offered higher wages, had basely left him in the lurch.

She soon became interested in her work, for her emaciated purse grew stout, and the little hoard she was making to take Beth to the mountains next summer grew slowly but surely as the weeks passed. One thing disturbed her satisfaction, and that was that she did not tell them at home. She had a feeling that Father and Mother would not approve, and preferred to have her own way first, and beg pardon afterward. It was easy to keep her secret, for no name appeared with her stories. Mr. Dashwood had of course found it out very soon, but promised to be dumb, and for a wonder kept his word.

She thought it would do her no harm, for she sincerely meant to write nothing of which she would be ashamed, and quieted all pricks of conscience by anticipations of the happy minute when she should show her earnings and laugh over her well-kept secret.

But Mr. Dashwood rejected any but thrilling tales, and as thrills could not be produced except by harrowing up the souls of the readers, history and romance, land and sea, science and art, police records and lunatic asylums, had to be ransacked for the purpose. Jo soon found that her innocent experience had given her but few glimpses of the tragic world which underlies society, so regarding it in a business light, she set about supplying her deficiencies with characteristic energy. Eager to find material for stories, and bent on making them original in plot, if not masterly in execution, she searched newspapers for accidents, incidents, and crimes. She excited the suspicions of public librarians by asking for works on poisons. She studied faces in the street, and characters, good, bad, and indifferent, all about her. She delved in the dust of ancient times for facts or fictions so old that they were as good as new, and introduced herself to folly, sin, and misery, as well as her limited opportunities allowed. She thought she was prospering finely, but unconsciously she was beginning to desecrate some of the womanliest attributes of a woman's character. She was living in bad society, and imaginary though it was, its influence affected her, for she was feeding heart and fancy on dangerous and unsubstantial food, and was fast brushing the innocent bloom from her nature by a premature acquaintance with the darker side of life, which comes soon enough to all of us.

She was beginning to feel rather than see this, for much describing of other people's passions and feelings set her to studying and speculating about her own, a morbid amusement in which healthy young minds do not voluntarily indulge. Wrongdoing always brings its own punishment, and when Jo most needed hers, she got it.

I don't know whether the study of Shakespeare helped her to read character, or the natural instinct of a woman for what was honest, brave, and strong, but while endowing her imaginary heroes with every perfection under the sun, Jo was discovering a live hero, who interested her in spite of many human imperfections. Mr. Bhaer, in one of their conversations, had advised her to study simple, true, and lovely characters, wherever she found them, as good training for a writer. Jo took him at his word, for she coolly turned round and studied him—a proceeding which would have much surprised him, had he known it, for the worthy Professor was very humble in his own conceit.

Why everybody liked him was what puzzled Jo, at first. He was neither rich nor great, young nor handsome, in no respect what is called fascinating, imposing, or brilliant, and yet he was as attractive as a genial fire, and people seemed to gather about him as naturally as about a warm hearth. He was poor, yet always appeared to be giving something away; a stranger, yet everyone was his friend; no longer young, but as happy-hearted as a boy; plain and peculiar, yet his face looked beautiful to many, and his oddities were freely forgiven for his sake. Jo often watched him, trying to discover the charm, and at last decided that it was benevolence which worked the miracle. If he had any sorrow, 'it sat with its head under its wing,' and he turned only his sunny side to the world. There were lines upon his forehead, but Time seemed to have touched him gently, remembering how kind he was to others. The pleasant curves about his mouth were the memorials of many friendly words and cheery laughs, his eyes were never cold or hard, and his big hand had a warm, strong grasp that was more expressive than words.

His very clothes seemed to partake of the hospitable nature of the wearer. They looked as if they were at ease, and liked to make him comfortable. His capacious waistcoat was suggestive of a large heart underneath. His rusty coat had a social air, and the baggy pockets plainly proved that little hands often went in empty and came out full. His very boots were benevolent, and his collars never stiff and raspy like other people's.

"That's it!" said Jo to herself, when she at length discovered that genuine good will toward one's fellow men could beautify and dignify even a stout German teacher, who shoveled in his dinner, darned his own socks, and was burdened with the name of Bhaer.

Jo valued goodness highly, but she also possessed a most feminine respect for intellect, and a little discovery which she made about the Professor added much to her regard for him. He never spoke of himself, and no one ever knew that in his native city he had been a man much honored and esteemed for learning and integrity, till a countryman came to see him, and in a conversation with Miss Norton divulged the pleasing fact. From her Jo learned it, and liked it all the better because Mr. Bhaer had never told it. She felt proud to know that he was an honored Professor in Berlin, though only a poor language-master in America, and his homely, hard-working life was much beautified by the spice of romance which this discovery gave it.

Another and a better gift than intellect was shown her in a most unexpected manner. Miss Norton had the entree into literary society, which Jo would have had no chance of seeing but for her. The solitary woman felt an interest in the ambitious girl, and kindly conferred many favors of this sort both on Jo and the Professor. She took them with her one night to a select symposium, held in honor of several celebrities.

Jo went prepared to bow down and adore the mighty ones whom she had worshiped with youthful enthusiasm afar off. But her reverence for genius received a severe shock that night, and it took her some time to recover from the discovery that the great creatures were only men and women after all. Imagine her dismay, on stealing a glance of timid admiration at the poet whose lines suggested an ethereal being fed on "spirit, fire, and dew," to behold him devouring his supper with an ardor which flushed his intellectual countenance. Turning as from a fallen idol, she made other discoveries which rapidly dispelled her romantic illusions. The great novelist vibrated between two decanters with the regularity of a pendulum; the famous divine flirted openly with one of the Madame de Staels of the age, who looked daggers at another Corinne, who was amiably satirizing her, after outmaneuvering her in efforts to absorb the profound philosopher, who imbibed tea Johnsonianly and appeared to slumber, the loquacity of the lady rendering speech impossible. The scientific celebrities, forgetting their mollusks and glacial periods, gossiped about art, while devoting themselves to oysters and ices with characteristic energy; the young musician, who was charming the city like a second Orpheus, talked horses; and the specimen of the British nobility present happened to be the most ordinary man of the party.

Before the evening was half over, Jo felt so completely disillusioned, that she sat down in a corner to recover herself. Mr. Bhaer soon joined her, looking rather out of his element, and presently several of the philosophers, each mounted on his hobby, came ambling up to hold an intellectual tournament in the recess. The conversations were miles beyond Jo's comprehension, but she enjoyed it, though Kant and Hegel were unknown gods, the Subjective and Objective unintelligible terms, and the only thing "evolved from her inner consciousness" was a bad headache after it was all over. It dawned upon her gradually that the world was being picked to pieces, and put together on new and, according to the talkers, on infinitely better principles than before, that religion was in a fair way to be reasoned into nothingness, and intellect was to be the only God. Jo knew nothing about philosophy or metaphysics of any sort, but a curious excitement, half pleasurable, half painful, came over her as she listened with a sense of being turned adrift into time and space, like a young balloon out on a holiday.

She looked round to see how the Professor liked it, and found him looking at her with the grimmest expression she had ever seen him wear. He shook his head and beckoned her to come away, but she was fascinated just then by the freedom of Speculative Philosophy, and kept her seat, trying to find out what the wise gentlemen intended to rely upon after they had annihilated all the old beliefs.

Now, Mr. Bhaer was a diffident man and slow to offer his own opinions, not because they were unsettled, but too sincere and earnest to be lightly spoken. As he glanced from Jo to several other young people, attracted by the brilliancy of the philosophic pyrotechnics, he knit his brows and longed to speak, fearing that some inflammable young soul would be led astray by the rockets, to find when the display was over that they had only an empty stick or a scorched hand.

He bore it as long as he could, but when he was appealed to for an opinion, he blazed up with honest indignation and defended religion with all the eloquence of truth—an eloquence which made his broken English musical and his plain face beautiful. He had a hard fight, for the wise men argued well, but he didn't know when he was beaten and stood to his colors like a man. Somehow, as he talked, the world got right again to Jo. The old beliefs, that had lasted so long, seemed better than the new. God was not a blind force, and immortality was not a pretty fable, but a blessed fact. She felt as if she had solid ground under her feet again, and when Mr. Bhaer paused, outtalked but not one whit convinced, Jo wanted to clap her hands and thank him.

She did neither, but she remembered the scene, and gave the Professor her heartiest respect, for she knew it cost him an effort to speak out then and there, because his conscience would not let him be silent. She began to see that character is a better possession than money, rank, intellect, or beauty, and to feel that if greatness is what a wise man has defined it to be, "truth, reverence, and good will," then her friend Friedrich Bhaer was not only good, but great.

This belief strengthened daily. She valued his esteem, she coveted his respect, she wanted to be worthy of his friendship, and just when the wish was sincerest, she came near to losing everything. It all grew out of a cocked hat, for one evening the Professor came in to give Jo her lesson with a paper soldier cap on his head, which Tina had put there and he had forgotten to take off.

"It's evident he doesn't look in his glass before coming down," thought Jo, with a smile, as he said "Goot efening," and sat soberly down, quite unconscious of the ludicrous contrast between his subject and his headgear, for he was going to read her the Death of Wallenstein.

She said nothing at first, for she liked to hear him laugh out his big, hearty laugh when anything funny happened, so she left him to discover it for himself, and presently forgot all about it, for to hear a German read Schiller is rather an absorbing occupation. After the reading came the lesson, which was a lively one, for Jo was in a gay mood that night, and the cocked hat kept her eyes dancing with merriment. The Professor didn't know what to make of her, and stopped at last to ask with an air of mild surprise that was irresistible—

"Mees Marsch, for what do you laugh in your master's face? Haf you no respect for me, that you go on so bad?"

"How can I be respectful, Sir, when you forget to take your hat off?" said Jo.

Lifting his hand to his head, the absent-minded Professor gravely felt and removed the little cocked hat, looked at it a minute, and then threw back his head and laughed like a merry bass viol.

"Ah! I see him now, it is that imp Tina who makes me a fool with my cap. Well, it is nothing, but see you, if this lesson goes not well, you too shall wear him."

But the lesson did not go at all for a few minutes because Mr. Bhaer caught sight of a picture on the hat, and unfolding it, said with great disgust, "I wish these papers did not come in the house. They are not for children to see, nor young people to read. It is not well, and I haf no patience with those who make this harm."

Jo glanced at the sheet and saw a pleasing illustration composed of a lunatic, a corpse, a villain, and a viper. She did not like it, but the impulse that made her turn it over was not one of displeasure but fear, because for a minute she fancied the paper was the *Volcano*. It was not, however, and her panic subsided as she remembered that even if it had been and one of her own tales in it, there would have been no name to betray her. She had betrayed herself, however, by a look and a blush, for though an absent man, the Professor saw a good deal more than people fancied. He knew that Jo wrote, and had met her down among the newspaper offices more than once, but as she never spoke of it, he asked no questions in spite of a strong desire to see her work. Now it occurred to him that she was doing what she was ashamed to own, and it troubled him. He did not say to himself, "It is none of my business. I've no right to say anything," as many people would have done. He only remembered that she was young and poor, a girl far away from mother's love and father's care, and he was moved to help her with an impulse as quick and natural as that which would prompt him to put out his hand to save a baby from a puddle. All this flashed through his mind in a minute, but not a trace of it appeared in his face, and by the time the paper was turned, and Jo's needle threaded, he was ready to say quite naturally, but very gravely—

"Yes, you are right to put it from you. I do not think that good young girls should see such things. They are made pleasant to some, but I would more rather give my boys gunpowder to play with than this bad trash."

"All may not be bad, only silly, you know, and if there is a demand for it, I don't see any harm in supplying it. Many very respectable people make an honest living out of what are called sensation stories," said Jo, scratching gathers so energetically that a row of little slits followed her pin.

"There is a demand for whisky, but I think you and I do not care to sell it. If the respectable people knew what harm they did, they would not feel that the living was honest. They haf no right to put poison in the sugarplum, and let the small ones eat it. No, they should think a little, and sweep mud in the street before they do this thing."

Mr. Bhaer spoke warmly, and walked to the fire, crumpling the paper in his hands. Jo sat still, looking as if the fire had come to her, for her cheeks burned long after the cocked hat had turned to smoke and gone harmlessly up the chimney.

"I should like much to send all the rest after him," muttered the Professor, coming back with a relieved air.

Jo thought what a blaze her pile of papers upstairs would make, and her hard-earned money lay rather heavily on her conscience at that minute. Then she thought consolingly to herself, "Mine are not like that, they are only silly, never bad, so I won't be worried," and taking up her book, she said, with a studious face, "Shall we go on, Sir? I'll be very good and proper now."

"I shall hope so," was all he said, but he meant more than she imagined, and the grave, kind look he gave her made her feel as if the words *Weekly Volcano* were printed in large type on her forehead.

As soon as she went to her room, she got out her papers, and carefully reread every one of her stories. Being a little shortsighted, Mr. Bhaer sometimes used eye glasses, and Jo had tried them once, smiling to see how they magnified the fine print of her book. Now she seemed to have on the Professor's mental or moral spectacles also, for the faults of these poor stories glared at her dreadfully and filled her with dismay.

"They *are* trash, and will soon be worse trash if I go on, for each is more sensational than the last. I've gone blindly on, hurting myself and other people, for the sake of money. I know it's so, for I can't read this stuff in sober earnest without being horribly ashamed of it, and what should I do if they were seen at home or Mr. Bhaer got hold of them?"

Jo turned hot at the bare idea, and stuffed the whole bundle into her stove, nearly setting the chimney afire with the blaze.

"Yes, that's the best place for such inflammable nonsense. I'd better burn the house down, I suppose, than let other people blow themselves up with my gunpowder," she thought as she watched the *Demon of the Jura* whisk away, a little black cinder with fiery eyes.

But when nothing remained of all her three month's work except a heap of ashes and the money in her lap, Jo looked sober, as she sat on the floor, wondering what she ought to do about her wages.

"I think I haven't done much harm yet, and may keep this to pay for my time," she said, after a long meditation, adding impatiently, "I almost wish I hadn't any conscience, it's so inconvenient. If I didn't care about doing right, and didn't feel uncomfortable when doing wrong, I should get on capitally. I can't help wishing sometimes, that Mother and Father hadn't been so particular about such things."

Ah, Jo, instead of wishing that, thank God that "Father and Mother were particular," and pity from your heart those who have no such guardians to hedge them round with principles which may seem like prison walls to impatient youth, but which will prove sure foundations to build character upon in womanhood.

Jo wrote no more sensational stories, deciding that the money did not pay for her share of the sensation, but going to the other extreme, as is the way with people of her stamp, she took a course of Mrs. Sherwood, Miss Edgeworth, and Hannah More, and then produced a tale which might have been more properly called an essay or a sermon, so intensely moral was it. She had her doubts about it from the beginning, for her lively fancy and girlish romance felt as ill at ease in the new style as she would have done masquerading in the stiff and cumbrous costume of the last century. She sent this didactic gem to several markets, but it found no purchaser, and she was inclined to agree with Mr. Dashwood that morals didn't sell.

Then she tried a child's story, which she could easily have disposed of if she had not been mercenary enough to demand filthy lucre for it. The only person who offered enough to make it worth her while to try juvenile literature was a worthy gentleman who felt it his mission to convert all the world to his particular belief. But much as she liked to write for children, Jo could not consent to depict all her naughty boys as being eaten by bears or tossed by mad bulls because they did not go to a particular Sabbath school, nor all the good infants who did go as rewarded by every kind of bliss, from gilded gingerbread to escorts of angels when they departed this life with psalms or sermons on their lisping tongues. So nothing came of these trials, and Jo corked up her inkstand, and said in a fit of very wholesome humility—

"I don't know anything. I'll wait until I do before I try again, and meantime, 'sweep mud in the street' if I can't do better, that's honest, at least." Which decision proved that her second tumble down the beanstalk had done her some good.

While these internal revolutions were going on, her external life had been as busy and uneventful as usual, and if she sometimes looked serious or a little sad no one observed it but Professor Bhaer. He did it so quietly that Jo never knew he was watching to see if she would accept and profit by his reproof, but she stood the test, and he was satisfied, for though no words passed between them, he knew that she had given up writing. Not only did he guess it by the fact that the second finger of her right hand was no longer inky, but she spent her evenings downstairs now, was met no more among newspaper offices, and studied with a dogged patience, which assured him that she was bent on occupying her mind with something useful, if not pleasant.

He helped her in many ways, proving himself a true friend, and Jo was happy, for while her pen lay idle, she was learning other lessons besides German, and laying a foundation for the sensation story of her own life.

It was a pleasant winter and a long one, for she did not leave Mrs. Kirke till June. Everyone seemed sorry when the time came. The children were inconsolable, and Mr. Bhaer's hair stuck straight up all over his head, for he always rumpled it wildly when disturbed in mind.

"Going home? Ah, you are happy that you haf a home to go in," he said, when she told him, and sat silently pulling his beard in the corner, while she held a little levee on that last evening.

She was going early, so she bade them all goodbye overnight, and when his turn came, she said warmly, "Now, Sir, you won't forget to come and see us, if you ever travel our way, will you? I'll never forgive you if you do, for I want them all to know my friend."

"Do you? Shall I come?" he asked, looking down at her with an eager expression which she did not see.

"Yes, come next month. Laurie graduates then, and you'd enjoy commencement as something new."

"That is your best friend, of whom you speak?" he said in an altered tone.

"Yes, my boy Teddy. I'm very proud of him and should like you to see him."

Jo looked up then, quite unconscious of anything but her own pleasure in the prospect of showing them to one another. Something in Mr. Bhaer's face suddenly recalled the fact that she might find Laurie more than a "best friend," and simply because she particularly wished not to look as if anything was the matter, she involuntarily began to blush, and the more she tried not to, the redder she grew. If it had not been for Tina on her knee, she didn't know what would have become of her. Fortunately the child was moved to hug her, so she managed to hide her face an instant, hoping the Professor did not see it. But he did, and his own changed again from that momentary anxiety to its usual expression, as he said cordially—

"I fear I shall not make the time for that, but I wish the friend much success, and you all happiness. Gott bless you!" And with that, he shook hands warmly, shouldered Tina, and went away.

But after the boys were abed, he sat long before his fire with the tired look on his face and the "*heimweh*," or homesickness, lying heavy at his heart. Once, when he remembered Jo as she sat with the little child in her lap and that new softness in her face, he leaned his head on his hands a minute, and then roamed about the room, as if in search of something that he could not find.

"It is not for me, I must not hope it now," he said to himself, with a sigh that was almost a groan. Then, as if reproaching himself for the longing that he could not repress, he went and kissed the two tousled heads upon the pillow, took down his seldom-used meerschaum, and opened his Plato.

He did his best and did it manfully, but I don't think he found that a pair of rampant boys, a pipe, or even the divine Plato, were very satisfactory substitutes for wife and child at home.

Early as it was, he was at the station next morning to see Jo off, and thanks to him, she began her solitary journey with the pleasant memory of a familiar face smiling its farewell, a bunch of violets to keep her company, and best of all, the happy thought, "Well, the winter's gone, and I've written no books, earned no fortune, but I've made a friend worth having and I'll try to keep him all my life."

CHAPTER XXXV

HEARTACHE

Whatever his motive might have been, Laurie studied to some purpose that year, for he graduated with honor, and gave the Latin oration with the grace of a Phillips and the eloquence of a Demosthenes, so his friends said. They were all there, his grandfather—oh, so proud—Mr. and Mrs. March, John and Meg, Jo and Beth, and all exulted over him with the sincere admiration which boys make light of at the time, but fail to win from the world by any after-triumphs.

"I've got to stay for this confounded supper, but I shall be home early tomorrow. You'll come and meet me as usual, girls?" Laurie said, as he put the sisters into the carriage after the joys of the day were over. He said "girls," but he meant Jo, for she was the only one who kept up the old custom. She had not the heart to refuse her splendid, successful boy anything, and answered warmly—

"I'll come, Teddy, rain or shine, and march before you, playing '*Hail the conquering hero comes*' on a jew's-harp."

Laurie thanked her with a look that made her think in a sudden panic, "Oh, deary me! I know he'll say something, and then what shall I do?"

Evening meditation and morning work somewhat allayed her fears, and having decided that she wouldn't be vain enough to think people were going to propose when she had given them every reason to know what her answer would be, she set forth at the appointed time, hoping Teddy wouldn't do anything to make her hurt his poor feelings. A call at Meg's, and a refreshing sniff and sip at the Daisy and Demijohn, still further fortified her for the tête-à-tête, but when she saw a stalwart figure looming in the distance, she had a strong desire to turn about and run away.

"Where's the jew's-harp, Jo?" cried Laurie, as soon as he was within speaking distance.

"I forgot it." And Jo took heart again, for that salutation could not be called lover-like.

She always used to take his arm on these occasions, now she did not, and he made no complaint, which was a bad sign, but talked on rapidly about all sorts of faraway subjects, till they turned from the road into the little path that led homeward through the grove. Then he walked more slowly, suddenly lost his fine flow of language, and now and then a dreadful pause occurred. To rescue the conversation from one of the wells of silence into which it kept falling, Jo said hastily, "Now you must have a good long holiday!"

"I intend to."

Something in his resolute tone made Jo look up quickly to find him looking down at her with an expression that assured her the dreaded moment had come, and made her put out her hand with an imploring, "No, Teddy. Please don't!"

"I will, and you *must* hear me. It's no use, Jo, we've got to have it out, and the sooner the better for both of us," he answered, getting flushed and excited all at once.

"Say what you like then. I'll listen," said Jo, with a desperate sort of patience.

Laurie was a young lover, but he was in earnest, and meant to "have it out," if he died in the attempt, so he plunged into the subject with characteristic impetuousity, saying in a voice that *would* get choky now and then, in spite of manful efforts to keep it steady—

"I've loved you ever since I've known you, Jo, couldn't help it, you've been so good to me. I've tried to show it, but you wouldn't let me. Now I'm going to make you hear, and give me an answer, for I *can't* go on so any longer."

"I wanted to save you this. I thought you'd understand—" began Jo, finding it a great deal harder than she expected.

"I know you did, but the girls are so queer you never know what they mean. They say no when they mean yes, and drive a man out of his wits just for the fun of it," returned Laurie, entrenching himself behind an undeniable fact.

"*I* don't. I never wanted to make you care for me so, and I went away to keep you from it if I could."

"I thought so. It was like you, but it was no use. I only loved you all the more, and I worked hard to please you, and I gave up billiards and everything you didn't like, and waited and never complained, for I hoped you'd love me, though I'm not half good enough—" Here there was a choke that couldn't be controlled, so he decapitated buttercups while he cleared his "confounded throat."

"You, you are, you're a great deal too good for me, and I'm so grateful to you, and so proud and fond of you, I don't know why I can't love you as you want me to. I've tried, but I can't change the feeling, and it would be a lie to say I do when I don't."

"Really, truly, Jo?"

He stopped short, and caught both her hands as he put his question with a look that she did not soon forget.

"Really, truly, dear."

They were in the grove now, close by the stile, and when the last words fell reluctantly from Jo's lips, Laurie dropped her hands and turned as if to go on, but for once in his life the fence was too much for him. So he just laid his head down on the mossy post, and stood so still that Jo was frightened.

"Oh, Teddy, I'm sorry, so desperately sorry, I could kill myself if it would do any good! I wish you wouldn't take it so hard, I can't help it. You know it's impossible for people to make themselves love other people if they don't," cried Jo inelegantly but remorsefully, as she softly patted his shoulder, remembering the time when he had comforted her so long ago.

"They do sometimes," said a muffled voice from the post.

"I don't believe it's the right sort of love, and I'd rather not try it," was the decided answer.

There was a long pause, while a blackbird sung blithely on the willow by the river, and the tall grass rustled in the wind. Presently Jo said very soberly, as she sat down on the step of the stile, "Laurie, I want to tell you something."

He started as if he had been shot, threw up his head, and cried out in a fierce tone, "*Don't* tell me that, Jo, I can't bear it now!"

"Tell what?" she asked, wondering at his violence.

"That you love that old man."

"What old man?" demanded Jo, thinking he must mean his grandfather.

"That devilish Professor you were always writing about. If you say you love him, I know I shall do something desperate;" and he looked as if he would keep his word, as he clenched his hands with a wrathful spark in his eyes.

Jo wanted to laugh, but restrained herself and said warmly, for she too, was getting excited with all this, "Don't swear, Teddy! He isn't old, nor anything bad, but good and kind, and the best friend I've got, next to you. Pray, don't fly into a passion. I want to be kind, but I know I shall get angry if you abuse my Professor. I haven't the least idea of loving him or anybody else."

"But you will after a while, and then what will become of me?"

"You'll love someone else too, like a sensible boy, and forget all this trouble."

"I *can't* love anyone else, and I'll never forget you, Jo, never! Never!" with a stamp to emphasize his passionate words.

"What shall I do with him?" sighed Jo, finding that emotions were more unmanagable than she expected. "You haven't heard what I wanted to tell you. Sit down and listen, for indeed I want to do right and make you happy," she said, hoping to soothe him with a little reason, which proved that she knew nothing about love.

Seeing a ray of hope in that last speech, Laurie threw himself down on the grass at her feet, leaned his arm on the lower step of the stile, and looked up at her with an expectant face. Now that arrangement was not conducive to calm speech or clear thought on Jo's part, for how *could* she say hard things to her boy while he watched her with eyes full of love and longing, and lashes still wet with the bitter drop or two her hardness of heart had wrung from him? She gently turned his head away, saying, as she stroked the wavy hair which had been allowed to grow for her sake—how touching that was, to be sure!

"I agree with Mother that you and I are not suited to each other, because our quick tempers and strong wills would probably make us very miserable, if we were so foolish as to—" Jo paused a little over the last word, but Laurie uttered it with a rapturous expression.

"Marry—no we shouldn't! If you loved me, Jo, I should be a perfect saint, for you could make me anything you like."

"No, I can't. I've tried and failed, and I won't risk our happiness by such a serious experiment. We don't agree and we never shall, so we'll be good friends all our lives, but we won't go and do anything rash."

"Yes, we will if we get the chance," muttered Laurie rebelliously.

"Now do be reasonable, and take a sensible view of the case," implored Jo, almost at her wit's end.

"I won't be reasonable. I don't want to take what you call 'a sensible view.' It won't help me, and it only makes it harder. I don't believe you've got any heart."

"I wish I hadn't."

There was a little quiver in Jo's voice, and thinking it a good omen, Laurie turned round, bringing all his persuasive powers to bear as he said, in the wheedlesome tone that had never been so dangerously wheedlesome before, "Don't disappoint us, dear! Everyone expects it. Grandpa has set his heart upon it, your people like it, and I can't get on without you. Say you will, and let's be happy. Do, do!"

Not until months afterward did Jo understand how she had the strength of mind to hold fast to the resolution she had made when she decided that she did not love her boy, and never could. It was very hard to do, but she did it, knowing that delay was both useless and cruel.

"I can't say 'yes' truly, so I won't say it at all. You'll see that I'm right, by-and-by, and thank me for it—" she began solemnly.

"I'll be hanged if I do!" And Laurie bounced up off the grass, burning with indignation at the very idea.

"Yes, you will!" persisted Jo. "You'll get over this after a while, and find some lovely accomplished girl, who will adore you, and make a fine mistress for your fine house. I shouldn't. I'm homely and awkward and odd and old, and you'd be ashamed of me, and we should quarrel—we can't help it even now, you see—and I shouldn't like elegant society and you would, and you'd hate my scribbling, and I couldn't get on without it, and we should be unhappy, and wish we hadn't done it, and everything would be horrid!"

"Anything more?" asked Laurie, finding it hard to listen patiently to this prophetic burst.

"Nothing more, except that I don't believe I shall ever marry. I'm happy as I am, and love my liberty too well to be in a hurry to give it up for any mortal man."

"I know better!" broke in Laurie. "You think so now, but there'll come a time when you *will* care for somebody, and you'll love him tremendously, and live and die for him. I know you will, it's your way, and I shall have to stand by and see it," and the despairing lover cast his hat upon the ground with a gesture that would have seemed comical, if his face had not been so tragic.

"Yes, I *will* live and die for him, if he ever comes and makes me love him in spite of myself, and you must do the best you can!" cried Jo, losing patience with poor Teddy. "I've done my best, but you *won't* be reasonable, and it's selfish of you to keep teasing for what I can't give. I shall always be fond of you, very fond indeed, as a friend, but I'll never marry you, and the sooner you believe it the better for both of us—so now!"

That speech was like gunpowder. Laurie looked at her a minute as if he did not quite know what to do with himself, then turned sharply away, saying in a desperate sort of tone, "You'll be sorry some day, Jo."

"Oh, where are you going?" she cried, for his face frightened her.

"To the devil!" was the consoling answer.

For a minute Jo's heart stood still, as he swung himself down the bank toward the river, but it takes much folly, sin or misery to send a young man to a violent death, and Laurie was not one of the weak sort who are conquered by a single failure. He had no thought of a melodramatic plunge, but some blind instinct led him to fling hat and coat into his boat, and row away with all his might, making better time up the river than he had done in any race. Jo drew a long breath and unclasped her hands as she watched the poor fellow trying to outstrip the trouble which he carried in his heart.

"That will do him good, and he'll come home in such a tender, penitent state of mind, that I shan't dare to see him," she said, adding, as she went slowly home, feeling as if she had murdered some innocent thing, and buried it under the leaves. "Now I must go and prepare Mr. Laurence to be very kind to my poor boy. I wish he'd love Beth, perhaps he may in time, but I begin to think I was mistaken about her. Oh dear! How can girls like to have lovers and refuse them? I think it's dreadful."

Being sure that no one could do it so well as herself, she went straight to Mr. Laurence, told the hard story bravely through, and then broke down, crying so dismally over her own insensibility that the kind old gentleman, though sorely disappointed, did not utter a reproach. He found it difficult to understand how any girl could help loving Laurie, and hoped she would change her mind, but he knew even better than Jo that love cannot be forced, so he shook his head sadly and resolved to carry his boy out of harm's way, for Young Impetuosity's parting words to Jo disturbed him more than he would confess.

When Laurie came home, dead tired but quite composed, his grandfather met him as if he knew nothing, and kept up the delusion very successfully for an hour or two. But when they sat together in the twilight, the time they used to enjoy so much, it was hard work for the old man to ramble on as usual, and harder still for the young one to listen to praises of the last year's success, which to him now seemed like love's labor lost. He bore it as long as he could, then went to his piano and began to play. The windows were open, and Jo, walking in the garden with Beth, for once understood music better than her sister, for he played the "Sonata Pathétique," and played it as he never did before.

"That's very fine, I dare say, but it's sad enough to make one cry. Give us something gayer, lad," said Mr. Laurence, whose kind old heart was full of sympathy, which he longed to show but knew not how.

Laurie dashed into a livelier strain, played stormily for several minutes, and would have got through bravely, if in a momentary lull Mrs. March's voice had not been heard calling, "Jo, dear, come in. I want you."

Just what Laurie longed to say, with a different meaning! As he listened, he lost his place, the music ended with a broken chord, and the musician sat silent in the dark.

"I can't stand this," muttered the old gentleman. Up he got, groped his way to the piano, laid a kind hand on either of the broad shoulders, and said, as gently as a woman, "I know, my boy, I know."

No answer for an instant, then Laurie asked sharply, "Who told you?"

"Jo herself."

"Then there's an end of it!" And he shook off his grandfather's hands with an impatient motion, for though grateful for the sympathy, his man's pride could not bear a man's pity.

"Not quite. I want to say one thing, and then there shall be an end of it," returned Mr. Laurence with unusual mildness. "You won't care to stay at home now, perhaps?"

"I don't intend to run away from a girl. Jo can't prevent my seeing her, and I shall stay and do it as long as I like," interrupted Laurie in a defiant tone.

"Not if you are the gentleman I think you. I'm disappointed, but the girl can't help it, and the only thing left for you to do is to go away for a time. Where will you go?"

"Anywhere. I don't care what becomes of me," and Laurie got up with a reckless laugh that grated on his grandfather's ear.

"Take it like a man, and don't do anything rash, for God's sake. Why not go abroad, as you planned, and forget it?"

"I can't."

"But you've been wild to go, and I promised you should when you got through college."

"Ah, but I didn't mean to go alone!" and Laurie walked fast through the room with an expression which it was well his grandfather did not see.

"I don't ask you to go alone. There's someone ready and glad to go with you, anywhere in the world."

"Who, Sir?" stopping to listen.

"Myself."

Laurie came back as quickly as he went, and put out his hand, saying huskily, "I'm a selfish brute, but—you know—Grandfather—"

"Lord help me, yes, I do know, for I've been through it all before, once in my own young days, and then with your father. Now, my dear boy, just sit quietly down and hear my plan. It's all settled, and can be carried out at once," said Mr. Laurence, keeping hold of the young man, as if fearful that he would break away as his father had done before him.

"Well, sir, what is it?" and Laurie sat down, without a sign of interest in face or voice.

"There is business in London that needs looking after. I meant you should attend to it, but I can do it better myself, and things here will get on very well with Brooke to manage them. My partners do almost everything, I'm merely holding on until you take my place, and can be off at any time."

"But you hate traveling, Sir. I can't ask it of you at your age," began Laurie, who was grateful for the sacrifice, but much preferred to go alone, if he went at all.

The old gentleman knew that perfectly well, and particularly desired to prevent it, for the mood in which he found his grandson assured him that it would not be wise to leave him to his own devices. So, stifling a natural regret at the thought of the home comforts he would leave behind him, he said stoutly, "Bless your soul, I'm not superannuated yet. I quite enjoy the idea. It will do me good, and my old bones won't suffer, for traveling nowadays is almost as easy as sitting in a chair."

A restless movement from Laurie suggested that *his* chair was not easy, or that he did not like the plan, and made the old man add hastily, "I don't mean to be a marplot or a burden. I go because I think you'd feel happier than if I was left behind. I don't intend to gad about with you, but leave you free to go where you like, while I amuse myself in my own way. I've friends in London and Paris, and should like to visit them. Meantime you can go to Italy, Germany, Switzerland, where you will, and enjoy pictures, music, scenery, and adventures to your heart's content."

Now, Laurie felt just then that his heart was entirely broken and the world a howling wilderness, but at the sound of certain words which the old gentleman artfully introduced into his closing sentence, the broken heart gave an unexpected leap, and a green oasis or two suddenly appeared in the howling wilderness. He sighed, and then said, in a spiritless tone, "Just as you like, sir. It doesn't matter where I go or what I do."

"It does to me, remember that, my lad. I give you entire liberty, but I trust you to make an honest use of it. Promise me that, Laurie."

"Anything you like, sir."

"Good," thought the old gentleman. "You don't care now, but there'll come a time when that promise will keep you out of mischief, or I'm much mistaken."

Being an energetic individual, Mr. Laurence struck while the iron was hot, and before the blighted being recovered spirit enough to rebel, they were off. During the time necessary for preparation, Laurie bore himself as young gentleman usually do in such cases. He was moody, irritable, and pensive by turns, lost his appetite, neglected his dress and devoted much time to playing tempestuously on his piano, avoided Jo, but consoled himself by staring at her from his window, with a tragic face that haunted her dreams by night and oppressed her with a heavy sense of guilt by day. Unlike some sufferers, he never spoke of his unrequited passion, and would allow no one, not even Mrs. March, to attempt consolation or offer sympathy. On some accounts, this was a relief to his friends, but the weeks before his departure were very uncomfortable, and everyone rejoiced that the "poor, dear fellow was going away to forget his trouble, and come home happy." Of course, he smiled darkly at their delusion, but passed it by with the sad superiority of one who knew that his fidelity like his love was unalterable.

When the parting came he affected high spirits, to conceal certain inconvenient emotions which seemed inclined to assert themselves. This gaiety did not impose upon anybody, but they tried to look as if it did for his sake, and he got on very well till Mrs. March kissed him, with a whisper full of motherly solicitude. Then feeling that he was going very fast, he hastily embraced them all round, not forgetting the afflicted Hannah, and ran downstairs as if for his life. Jo followed a minute after to wave her hand to him if he looked round. He did look round, came back, put his arms about her as she stood on the step above him, and looked up at her with a face that made his short appeal eloquent and pathetic.

"Oh, Jo, can't you?"

"Teddy, dear, I wish I could!"

That was all, except a little pause. Then Laurie straightened himself up, said, "It's all right, never mind," and went away without another word. Ah, but it wasn't all right, and Jo *did* mind, for while the curly head lay on her arm a minute after her hard answer, she felt as if she had stabbed her dearest friend, and when he left her without a look behind him, she knew that the boy Laurie never would come again.

CHAPTER XXXVI

BETH'S SECRET

When Jo came home that spring, she had been struck with the change in Beth. No one spoke of it or seemed aware of it, for it had come too gradually to startle those who saw her daily, but to eyes sharpened by absence, it was very plain and a heavy weight fell on Jo's heart as she saw her sister's face. It was no paler and but littler thinner than in the autumn, yet there was a strange, transparent look about it, as if the mortal was being slowly refined away, and the immortal shining through the frail flesh with an indescribably pathetic beauty. Jo saw and felt it, but said nothing at the time, and soon the first impression lost much of its power, for Beth seemed happy, no one appeared to doubt that she was better, and presently in other cares Jo for a time forgot her fear.

But when Laurie was gone, and peace prevailed again, the vague anxiety returned and haunted her. She had confessed her sins and been forgiven, but when she showed her savings and proposed a mountain trip, Beth had thanked her heartily, but begged not to go so far away from home. Another little visit to the seashore would suit her better, and as Grandma could not be prevailed upon to leave the babies, Jo took Beth down to the quiet place, where she could live much in the open air, and let the fresh sea breezes blow a little color into her pale cheeks.

It was not a fashionable place, but even among the pleasant people there, the girls made few friends, preferring to live for one another. Beth was too shy to enjoy society, and Jo too wrapped up in her to care for anyone else. So they were all in all to each other, and came and went, quite unconscious of the interest they excited in those about them, who watched with sympathetic eyes the strong sister and the feeble one, always together, as if they felt instinctively that a long separation was not far away.

They did feel it, yet neither spoke of it, for often between ourselves and those nearest and dearest to us there exists a reserve which it is very hard to overcome. Jo felt as if a veil had fallen between her heart and Beth's, but when she put out her hand to lift it up, there seemed something sacred in the silence, and she waited for Beth to speak. She wondered, and was thankful also, that her parents did not seem to see what she saw, and during the quiet weeks when the shadows grew so plain to her, she said nothing of it to those at home, believing that it would tell itself when Beth came back no better. She wondered still more if her sister really guessed the hard truth, and what thoughts were passing through her mind during the long hours when she lay on the warm rocks with her head in Jo's lap, while the winds blew healthfully over her and the sea made music at her feet.

One day Beth told her. Jo thought she was asleep, she lay so still, and putting down her book, sat looking at her with wistful eyes, trying to see signs of hope in the faint color on Beth's cheeks. But she could not find enough to satisfy her, for the cheeks were very thin, and the hands seemed too feeble to hold even the rosy little shells they had been collecting. It came to her then more bitterly than ever that Beth was slowly drifting away from her, and her arms instinctively tightened their hold upon the dearest treasure she possessed. For a minute her eyes were too dim for seeing, and when they cleared, Beth was looking up at her so tenderly that there was hardly any need for her to say, "Jo, dear, I'm glad you know it. I've tried to tell you, but I couldn't."

There was no answer except her sister's cheek against her own, not even tears, for when most deeply moved, Jo did not cry. She was the weaker then, and Beth tried to comfort and sustain her, with her arms about her and the soothing words she whispered in her ear.

"I've known it for a good while, dear, and now I'm used to it, it isn't hard to think of or to bear. Try to see it so and don't be troubled about me, because it's best, indeed it is."

"Is this what made you so unhappy in the autumn, Beth? You did not feel it then, and keep it to yourself so long, did you?" asked Jo, refusing to see or say that it *was* best, but glad to know that Laurie had no part in Beth's trouble.

"Yes, I gave up hoping then, but I didn't like to own it. I tried to think it was a sick fancy, and would not let it trouble anyone. But when I saw you all so well and strong and full of happy plans, it was hard to feel that I could never be like you, and then I was miserable, Jo."

"Oh, Beth, and you didn't tell me, didn't let me comfort and help you? How could you shut me out, bear it all alone?"

Jo's voice was full of tender reproach, and her heart ached to think of the solitary struggle that must have gone on while Beth learned to say goodbye to health, love, and life, and take up her cross so cheerfully.

"Perhaps it was wrong, but I tried to do right. I wasn't sure, no one said anything, and I hoped I was mistaken. It would have been selfish to frighten you all when Marmee was so anxious about Meg, and Amy away, and you so happy with Laurie—at least I thought so then."

"And I thought you loved him, Beth, and I went away because I couldn't," cried Jo, glad to say all the truth.

Beth looked so amazed at the idea that Jo smiled in spite of her pain, and added softly, "Then you didn't, dearie? I was afraid it was so, and imagined your poor little heart full of lovelornity all that while."

"Why, Jo, how could I, when he was so fond of you?" asked Beth, as innocently as a child. "I do love him dearly. He is so good to me, how can I help It? But he could never be anything to me but my brother. I hope he truly will be, sometime."

"Not through me," said Jo decidedly. "Amy is left for him, and they would suit excellently, but I have no heart for such things, now. I don't care what becomes of anybody but you, Beth. You *must* get well."

"I want to, oh, so much! I try, but every day I lose a little, and feel more sure that I shall never gain it back. It's like the tide, Jo, when it turns, it goes slowly, but it can't be stopped."

"It *shall* be stopped, your tide must not turn so soon, nineteen is too young, Beth. I can't let you go. I'll work and pray and fight against it. I'll keep you in spite of everything. There must be ways, it can't be too late. God won't be so cruel as to take you from me," cried poor Jo rebelliously, for her spirit was far less piously submissive than Beth's.

Simple, sincere people seldom speak much of their piety. It shows itself in acts rather than in words, and has more influence than homilies or protestations. Beth could not reason upon or explain the faith that gave her courage and patience to give up life, and cheerfully wait for death. Like a confiding child, she asked no questions, but left everything to God and nature, Father and Mother of us all, feeling sure that they, and they only, could teach and strengthen heart and spirit for this life and the life to come. She did not rebuke Jo with saintly speeches, only loved her better for her passionate affection, and clung more closely to the dear human love, from which our Father never means us to be weaned, but through which He draws us closer to Himself. She could not say, "I'm glad to go," for life was very sweet for her. She could only sob out, "I try to be willing," while she held fast to Jo, as the first bitter wave of this great sorrow broke over them together.

By and by Beth said, with recovered serenity, "You'll tell them this when we go home?"

"I think they will see it without words," sighed Jo, for now it seemed to her that Beth changed every day.

"Perhaps not. I've heard that the people who love best are often blindest to such things. If they don't see it, you will tell them for me. I don't want any secrets, and it's kinder to prepare them. Meg has John and the babies to comfort her, but you must stand by Father and Mother, won't you Jo?"

"If I can. But, Beth, I don't give up yet. I'm going to believe that it is a sick fancy, and not let you think it's true." said Jo, trying to speak cheerfully.

Beth lay a minute thinking, and then said in her quiet way, "I don't know how to express myself, and shouldn't try to anyone but you, because I can't speak out except to my Jo. I only mean to say that I have a feeling that it never was intended I should live long. I'm not like the rest of you. I never made any plans about what I'd do when I grew up. I never thought of being married, as you all did. I couldn't seem to imagine myself anything but stupid little Beth, trotting about at home, of no use anywhere but there. I never wanted to go away, and the hard part now is the leaving you all. I'm not afraid, but it seems as if I should be homesick for you even in heaven."

Jo could not speak, and for several minutes there was no sound but the sigh of the wind and the lapping of the tide. A white-winged gull flew by, with the flash of sunshine on its silvery breast. Beth watched it till it vanished, and her eyes were full of sadness. A little gray-coated sand bird came tripping over the beach "peeping" softly to itself, as if enjoying the sun and sea. It came quite close to Beth, and looked at her with a friendly eye and sat upon a warm stone, dressing its wet feathers, quite at home. Beth smiled and felt comforted, for the tiny thing seemed to offer its small friendship and remind her that a pleasant world was still to be enjoyed.

"Dear little bird! See, Jo, how tame it is. I like peeps better than the gulls. They are not so wild and handsome, but they seem happy, confiding little things. I used to call them my birds last summer, and

Mother said they reminded her of me—busy, quaker-colored creatures, always near the shore, and always chirping that contented little song of theirs. You are the gull, Jo, strong and wild, fond of the storm and the wind, flying far out to sea, and happy all alone. Meg is the turtledove, and Amy is like the lark she writes about, trying to get up among the clouds, but always dropping down into its nest again. Dear little girl! She's so ambitious, but her heart is good and tender, and no matter how high she flies, she never will forget home. I hope I shall see her again, but she seems so far away."

"She is coming in the spring, and I mean that you shall be all ready to see and enjoy her. I'm going to have you well and rosy by that time," began Jo, feeling that of all the changes in Beth, the talking change was the greatest, for it seemed to cost no effort now, and she thought aloud in a way quite unlike bashful Beth.

"Jo, dear, don't hope any more. It won't do any good. I'm sure of that. We won't be miserable, but enjoy being together while we wait. We'll have happy times, for I don't suffer much, and I think the tide will go out easily, if you help me."

Jo leaned down to kiss the tranquil face, and with that silent kiss, she dedicated herself soul and body to Beth.

She was right: there was no need of any words when they got home, for Father and Mother saw plainly now what they had prayed to be saved from seeing. Tired with her short journey, Beth went at once to bed, saying how glad she was to be home, and when Jo went down, she found that she would be spared the hard task of telling Beth's secret. Her father stood leaning his head on the mantelpiece and did not turn as she came in, but her mother stretched out her arms as if for help, and Jo went to comfort her without a word.

CHAPTER XXXVII

NEW IMPRESSIONS

At three o'clock in the afternoon, all the fashionable world at Nice may be seen on the Promenade des Anglais—a charming place, for the wide walk, bordered with palms, flowers, and tropical shrubs, is bounded on one side by the sea, on the other by the grand drive, lined with hotels and villas, while beyond lie orange orchards and the hills. Many nations are represented, many languages spoken, many costumes worn, and on a sunny day the spectacle is as gay and brilliant as a carnival. Haughty English, lively French, sober Germans, handsome Spaniards, ugly Russians, meek Jews, free-and-easy Americans, all drive, sit, or saunter here, chatting over the news, and criticizing the latest celebrity who has arrived—Ristori or Dickens, Victor Emmanuel or the Queen of the Sandwich Islands. The equipages are as varied as the company and attract as much attention, especially the low basket barouches in which ladies drive themselves, with a pair of dashing ponies, gay nets to keep their voluminous flounces from overflowing the diminutive vehicles, and little grooms on the perch behind.

Along this walk, on Christmas Day, a tall young man walked slowly, with his hands behind him, and a somewhat absent expression of countenance. He looked like an Italian, was dressed like an Englishman, and had the independent air of an American—a combination which caused sundry pairs of feminine eyes to look approvingly after him, and sundry dandies in black velvet suits, with rose-colored neckties, buff gloves, and orange flowers in their buttonholes, to shrug their shoulders, and then envy him his inches. There were plenty of pretty faces to admire, but the young man took little notice of them, except to glance now and then at some blonde girl in blue. Presently he strolled out of the promenade and stood a moment at the crossing, as if undecided whether to go and listen to the band in the Jardin Publique, or to wander along the beach toward Castle Hill. The quick trot of ponies' feet made him look up, as one of the little carriages, containing a single young lady, came rapidly down the street. The lady was young, blonde, and dressed in blue. He stared a minute, then his whole face woke up, and, waving his hat like a boy, he hurried forward to meet her.

"Oh, Laurie, is it really you? I thought you'd never come!" cried Amy, dropping the reins and holding out both hands, to the great scandalization of a French mamma, who hastened her daughter's steps, lest she should be demoralized by beholding the free manners of these "mad English."

"I was detained by the way, but I promised to spend Christmas with you, and here I am."

"How is your grandfather? When did you come? Where are you staying?"

"Very well—last night—at the Chauvain. I called at your hotel, but you were out."

"I have so much to say, I don't know where to begin! Get in and we can talk at our ease. I was going for a drive and longing for company. Flo's saving up for tonight."

"What happens then, a ball?"

"A Christmas party at our hotel. There are many Americans there, and they give it in honor of the day. You'll go with us, of course? Aunt will be charmed."

"Thank you. Where now?" asked Laurie, leaning back and folding his arms, a proceeding which suited Amy, who preferred to drive, for her parasol whip and blue reins over the white ponies' backs afforded her infinite satisfaction.

"I'm going to the bankers first for letters, and then to Castle Hill. The view is so lovely, and I like to feed the peacocks. Have you ever been there?"

"Often, years ago, but I don't mind having a look at it."

"Now tell me all about yourself. The last I heard of you, your grandfather wrote that he expected you from Berlin."

"Yes, I spent a month there and then joined him in Paris, where he has settled for the winter. He has friends there and finds plenty to amuse him, so I go and come, and we get on capitally."

"That's a sociable arrangement," said Amy, missing something in Laurie's manner, though she couldn't tell what.

"Why, you see, he hates to travel, and I hate to keep still, so we each suit ourselves, and there is no trouble. I am often with him, and he enjoys my adventures, while I like to feel that someone is glad to see me when I get back from my wanderings. Dirty old hole, isn't it?" he added, with a look of disgust as they drove along the boulevard to the Place Napoleon in the old city.

"The dirt is picturesque, so I don't mind. The river and the hills are delicious, and these glimpses of the narrow cross streets are my delight. Now we shall have to wait for that procession to pass. It's going to the Church of St. John."

While Laurie listlessly watched the procession of priests under their canopies, white-veiled nuns bearing lighted tapers, and some brotherhood in blue chanting as they walked, Amy watched him, and felt a new sort of shyness steal over her, for he was changed, and she could not find the merry-faced boy she left in the moody-looking man beside her. He was handsomer than ever and greatly improved, she thought, but now that the flush of pleasure at meeting her was over, he looked tired and spiritless—not sick, nor exactly unhappy, but older and graver than a year or two of prosperous life should have made him. She couldn't understand it and did not venture to ask questions, so she shook her head and touched up her ponies, as the procession wound away across the arches of the Paglioni bridge and vanished in the church.

"*Que pensez-vous?*" she said, airing her French, which had improved in quantity, if not in quality, since she came abroad.

"That mademoiselle has made good use of her time, and the result is charming," replied Laurie, bowing with his hand on his heart and an admiring look.

She blushed with pleasure, but somehow the compliment did not satisfy her like the blunt praises he used to give her at home, when he promenaded round her on festival occasions, and told her she was "altogether jolly," with a hearty smile and an approving pat on the head. She didn't like the new tone, for though not blasé, it sounded indifferent in spite of the look.

"If that's the way he's going to grow up, I wish he'd stay a boy," she thought, with a curious sense of disappointment and discomfort, trying meantime to seem quite easy and gay.

At Avigdor's she found the precious home letters and, giving the reins to Laurie, read them luxuriously as they wound up the shady road between green hedges, where tea roses bloomed as freshly as in June.

"Beth is very poorly, Mother says. I often think I ought to go home, but they all say 'stay.' So I do, for I shall never have another chance like this," said Amy, looking sober over one page.

"I think you are right, there. You could do nothing at home, and it is a great comfort to them to know that you are well and happy, and enjoying so much, my dear."

He drew a little nearer, and looked more like his old self as he said that, and the fear that sometimes weighed on Amy's heart was lightened, for the look, the act, the brotherly "my dear," seemed to assure her that if any trouble did come, she would not be alone in a strange land. Presently she laughed and showed him a small sketch of Jo in her scribbling suit, with the bow rampantly erect upon her cap, and issuing from her mouth the words, "Genius burns!"

Laurie smiled, took it, put it in his vest pocket 'to keep it from blowing away,' and listened with interest to the lively letter Amy read him.

"This will be a regularly merry Christmas to me, with presents in the morning, you and letters in the afternoon, and a party at night," said Amy, as they alighted among the ruins of the old fort, and a flock of splendid peacocks came trooping about them, tamely waiting to be fed. While Amy stood laughing on the bank above him as she scattered crumbs to the brilliant birds, Laurie looked at her as she had looked at him, with a natural curiosity to see what changes time and absence had wrought. He found nothing to perplex or disappoint, much to admire and approve, for overlooking a few little affectations of speech and manner, she was as sprightly and graceful as ever, with the addition of that indescribable something in dress and bearing which we call elegance. Always mature for her age, she had gained a certain aplomb in both carriage and conversation, which made her seem more of a woman of the world than she was, but her old petulance now and then showed itself, her strong will still held its own, and her native frankness was unspoiled by foreign polish.

Laurie did not read all this while he watched her feed the peacocks, but he saw enough to satisfy and interest him, and carried away a pretty little picture of a bright-faced girl standing in the sunshine, which brought out the soft hue of her dress, the fresh color of her cheeks, the golden gloss of her hair, and made her a prominent figure in the pleasant scene.

As they came up onto the stone plateau that crowns the hill, Amy waved her hand as if welcoming him to her favorite haunt, and said, pointing here and there, "Do you remember the Cathedral and the Corso, the fishermen dragging their nets in the bay, and the lovely road to Villa Franca, Schubert's Tower, just below, and best of all, that speck far out to sea which they say is Corsica?"

"I remember. It's not much changed," he answered without enthusiasm.

"What Jo would give for a sight of that famous speck!" said Amy, feeling in good spirits and anxious to see him so also.

"Yes," was all he said, but he turned and strained his eyes to see the island which a greater usurper than even Napoleon now made interesting in his sight.

"Take a good look at it for her sake, and then come and tell me what you have been doing with yourself all this while," said Amy, seating herself, ready for a good talk.

But she did not get it, for though he joined her and answered all her questions freely, she could only learn that he had roved about the Continent and been to Greece. So after idling away an hour, they drove home again, and having paid his respects to Mrs. Carrol, Laurie left them, promising to return in the evening.

It must be recorded of Amy that she deliberately prinked that night. Time and absence had done its work on both the young people. She had seen her old friend in a new light, not as "our boy," but as a handsome and agreeable man, and she was conscious of a very natural desire to find favor in his sight. Amy knew her good points, and made the most of them with the taste and skill which is a fortune to a poor and pretty woman.

Tarlatan and tulle were cheap at Nice, so she enveloped herself in them on such occasions, and following the sensible English fashion of simple dress for young girls, got up charming little toilettes with fresh flowers, a few trinkets, and all manner of dainty devices, which were both inexpensive and effective. It must be confessed that the artist sometimes got possession of the woman, and indulged in antique coiffures, statuesque attitudes, and classic draperies. But, dear heart, we all have our little weaknesses, and find it easy to pardon such in the young, who satisfy our eyes with their comeliness, and keep our hearts merry with their artless vanities.

"I do want him to think I look well, and tell them so at home," said

Amy to herself, as she put on Flo's old white silk ball dress, and covered it with a cloud of fresh illusion, out of which her white shoulders and golden head emerged with a most artistic effect. Her hair she had the sense to let alone, after gathering up the thick waves and curls into a Hebe-like knot at the back of her head.

"It's not the fashion, but it's becoming, and I can't afford to make a fright of myself," she used to say, when advised to frizzle, puff, or braid, as the latest style commanded.

Having no ornaments fine enough for this important occasion, Amy looped her fleecy skirts with rosy clusters of azalea, and framed the white shoulders in delicate green vines. Remembering the painted boots, she surveyed her white satin slippers with girlish satisfaction, and chasséd down the room, admiring her aristocratic feet all by herself.

"My new fan just matches my flowers, my gloves fit to a charm, and the real lace on Aunt's *mouchoir* gives an air to my whole dress. If I only had a classical nose and mouth I should be perfectly happy," she said, surveying herself with a critical eye and a candle in each hand.

In spite of this affliction, she looked unusually gay and graceful as she glided away. She seldom ran—it did not suit her style, she thought, for being tall, the stately and Junoesque was more appropriate than the sportive or piquante. She walked up and down the long salon while waiting for Laurie, and once arranged herself under the chandelier, which had a good effect upon her hair, then she thought better of it, and went away to the other end of the room, as if ashamed of the girlish desire to have the first view a propitious one. It so happened that she could not have done a better thing, for Laurie came in so quietly she did not hear him, and as she stood at the distant window, with her head half turned and one hand gathering up her dress, the slender, white figure against the red curtains was as effective as a well-placed statue.

"Good evening, Diana!" said Laurie, with the look of satisfaction she liked to see in his eyes when they rested on her.

"Good evening, Apollo!" she answered, smiling back at him, for he too looked unusually debonair, and the thought of entering the ballroom on the arm of such a personable man caused Amy to pity the four plain Misses Davis from the bottom of her heart.

"Here are your flowers. I arranged them myself, remembering that you didn't like what Hannah calls a 'sot-bookay,'" said Laurie, handing her a delicate nosegay, in a holder that she had long coveted as she daily passed it in Cardiglia's window.

"How kind you are!" she exclaimed gratefully. "If I'd known you were coming I'd have had something ready for you today, though not as pretty as this, I'm afraid."

"Thank you. It isn't what it should be, but you have improved it," he added, as she snapped the silver bracelet on her wrist.

"Please don't."

"I thought you liked that sort of thing."

"Not from you, it doesn't sound natural, and I like your old bluntness better."

"I'm glad of it," he answered, with a look of relief, then buttoned her gloves for her, and asked if his tie was straight, just as he used to do when they went to parties together at home.

The company assembled in the long *salle à manger*, that evening, was such as one sees nowhere but on the Continent. The hospitable Americans had invited every acquaintance they had in Nice, and having no prejudice against titles, secured a few to add luster to their Christmas ball.

A Russian prince condescended to sit in a corner for an hour and talk with a massive lady, dressed like Hamlet's mother in black velvet with a pearl bridle under her chin. A Polish count, aged eighteen, devoted himself to the ladies, who pronounced him, "a fascinating dear," and a German Serene Something, having come to supper alone, roamed vaguely about, seeking what he might devour. Baron Rothschild's private secretary, a large-nosed Jew in tight boots, affably beamed upon the world, as if his master's name crowned him with a golden halo. A stout Frenchman, who knew the Emperor, came to indulge his mania for dancing, and Lady de Jones, a British matron, adorned the scene with her little family of eight. Of course, there were many light-footed, shrill-voiced American girls, handsome, lifeless-looking English ditto, and a few plain but piquante French demoiselles; likewise the usual set of traveling young gentlemen who disported themselves gaily, while mammas of all nations lined the walls and smiled upon them benignly when they danced with their daughters.

Any young girl can imagine Amy's state of mind when she "took the stage" that night, leaning on Laurie's arm. She knew she looked well, she loved to dance, she felt that her foot was on her native heath in a ballroom, and enjoyed the delightful sense of power which comes when young girls first discover the new and lovely kingdom they are born to rule by virtue of beauty, youth, and womanhood. She did pity the Davis girls, who were awkward, plain, and destitute of escort, except a grim papa and three grimmer maiden aunts, and she bowed to them in her friendliest manner as she passed, which was good of her, as it permitted them to see her dress, and burn with curiosity to know who her distinguished-looking friend might be. With the first burst of the band, Amy's color rose, her eyes began to sparkle, and her feet to tap the floor impatiently, for she danced well and wanted Laurie to know it. Therefore the shock she received can better be imagined than described, when he said in a perfectly tranquil tone, "Do you care to dance?"

"One usually does at a ball."

Her amazed look and quick answer caused Laurie to repair his error as fast as possible.

"I meant the first dance. May I have the honor?"

"I can give you one if I put off the Count. He dances devinely, but he will excuse me, as you are an old friend," said Amy, hoping that the name would have a good effect, and show Laurie that she was not to be trifled with.

"Nice little boy, but rather a short Pole to support

> "A daughter of the gods,
> Divinely tall, and most divinely fair,"

was all the satisfaction she got, however.

The set in which they found themselves was composed of English, and Amy was compelled to walk decorously through a cotillion, feeling all the while as if she could dance the tarantella with relish. Laurie resigned her to the "nice little boy," and went to do his duty to Flo, without securing Amy for the joys to come, which reprehensible want of forethought was properly punished, for she immediately engaged herself till supper, meaning to relent if he then gave any signs penitence. She showed him her ball book with demure satisfaction when he strolled instead of rushed up to claim her for the next, a glorious polka redowa. But his polite regrets didn't impose upon her, and when she galloped away with the Count, she saw Laurie sit down by her aunt with an actual expression of relief.

That was unpardonable, and Amy took no more notice of him for a long while, except a word now and then when she came to her chaperon between the dances for a necessary pin or a moment's rest. Her anger had a good effect, however, for she hid it under a smiling face, and seemed unusually blithe and brilliant. Laurie's eyes followed her with pleasure, for she neither romped nor sauntered, but danced with spirit and grace, making the delightsome pastime what it should be. He very naturally fell to studying her from this new point of view, and before the evening was half over, had decided that "little Amy was going to make a very charming woman."

It was a lively scene, for soon the spirit of the social season took possession of everyone, and Christmas merriment made all faces shine, hearts happy, and heels light. The musicians fiddled, tooted, and banged as if they enjoyed it, everybody danced who could, and those who couldn't admired their neighbors with uncommon warmth. The air was dark with Davises, and many Joneses gamboled like a flock of young giraffes. The golden secretary darted through the room like a meteor with a dashing French-woman who carpeted the floor with her pink satin train. The serene Teuton found the supper-table and was happy, eating steadily through the bill of fare, and dismayed the *garçons* by the ravages he committed. But the Emperor's friend covered himself with glory, for he danced everything, whether he knew it or not, and introduced impromptu pirouettes when the figures bewildered him. The boyish abandon of that stout man was charming to behold, for though he "carried weight," he danced like an India-rubber ball. He ran, he flew, he pranced, his face glowed, his bald head shown, his coattails waved wildly, his pumps actually twinkled in the air, and when the music stopped, he wiped the drops from his brow, and beamed upon his fellow men like a French Pickwick without glasses.

Amy and her Pole distinguished themselves by equal enthusiasm but more graceful agility, and Laurie found himself involuntarily keeping time to the rhythmic rise and fall of the white slippers as they flew by as indefatigably as if winged. When little Vladimir finally relinquished her, with assurances that he was "desolated to leave so early," she was ready to rest, and see how her recreant knight had borne his punishment.

It had been successful, for at three-and-twenty, blighted affections find a balm in friendly society, and young nerves will thrill, young blood dance, and healthy young spirits rise, when subjected to the enchantment of beauty, light, music, and motion. Laurie had a waked-up look as he rose to give her his seat, and when he hurried away to bring her some supper, she said to herself, with a satisfied smile, "Ah, I thought that would do him good!"

"You look like Balzac's '*Femme peinte par elle-même*,'" he said, as he fanned her with one hand and held her coffee cup in the other.

"My rouge won't come off." and Amy rubbed her brilliant cheek, and showed him her white glove with a sober simplicity that made him laugh outright.

"What do you call this stuff?" he asked, touching a fold of her dress that had blown over his knee.

"Illusion."

"Good name for it. It's very pretty—new thing, isn't it?"

"It's as old as the hills. You have seen it on dozens of girls, and you never found out that it was pretty till now—*stupide*!"

"I never saw it on you before, which accounts for the mistake, you see."

"None of that, it is forbidden. I'd rather take coffee than compliments just now. No, don't lounge, it makes me nervous."

Laurie sat bold upright, and meekly took her empty plate feeling an odd sort of pleasure in having "little Amy" order him about, for she had lost her shyness now, and felt an irrestible desire to trample on him, as girls have a delightful way of doing when lords of creation show any signs of subjection.

"Where did you learn all this sort of thing?" he asked with a quizzical look.

"As 'this sort of thing' is rather a vague expression, would you kindly explain?" returned Amy, knowing perfectly well what he meant, but wickedly leaving him to describe what is indescribable.

"Well—the general air, the style, the self-possession, the—the—illusion—you know," laughed Laurie, breaking down and helping himself out of his quandary with the new word.

Amy was gratified, but of course didn't show it, and demurely answered, "Foreign life polishes one in spite of one's self. I study as well as play, and as for this"—with a little gesture toward her dress—"why, tulle is cheap, posies to be had for nothing, and I am used to making the most of my poor little things."

Amy rather regretted that last sentence, fearing it wasn't in good taste, but Laurie liked her better for it, and found himself both admiring and respecting the brave patience that made the most of opportunity, and the cheerful spirit that covered poverty with flowers. Amy did not know why he looked at her so kindly, nor why he filled up her book with his own name, and devoted himself to her for the rest of the evening in the most delightful manner; but the impulse that wrought this agreeable change was the result of one of the new impressions which both of them were unconsciously giving and receiving.

CHAPTER XXXVIII

ON THE SHELF

In France the young girls have a dull time of it till they are married, when "*Vive la liberté*!" becomes their motto. In America, as everyone knows, girls early sign the declaration of independence, and enjoy their freedom with republican zest, but the young matrons usually abdicate with the first heir to the throne and go into a seclusion almost as close as a French nunnery, though by no means as quiet. Whether they like it or not, they are virtually put upon the shelf as soon as the wedding excitement is over, and most of them might exclaim, as did a very pretty woman the other day, "I'm as handsome as ever, but no one takes any notice of me because I'm married."

Not being a belle or even a fashionable lady, Meg did not experience this affliction till her babies were a year old, for in her little world primitive customs prevailed, and she found herself more admired and beloved than ever.

As she was a womanly little woman, the maternal instinct was very strong, and she was entirely absorbed in her children, to the utter exclusion of everything and everybody else. Day and night she brooded over them with tireless devotion and anxiety, leaving John to the tender mercies of the help, for an Irish lady now presided over the kitchen department. Being a domestic man, John decidedly missed the wifely attentions he had been accustomed to receive, but as he adored his babies, he cheerfully relinquished his comfort for a time, supposing with masculine ignorance that peace would soon be restored. But three months passed, and there was no return of repose. Meg looked worn and nervous, the babies absorbed every minute of her time, the house was neglected, and Kitty, the cook, who took life "aisy," kept him on short commons. When he went out in the morning he was bewildered by small commissions for the captive mamma, if he came gaily in at night, eager to embrace his family, he was quenched by a "Hush! They are just asleep after worrying all day." If he proposed a little amusement at home, "No, it would disturb the babies." If he hinted at a lecture or a concert, he was answered with a reproachful look, and a decided "Leave my children for pleasure, never!" His sleep was broken by infant wails and visions of a phantom figure pacing noiselessly to and fro in the watches of the night. His meals were interrupted by the frequent flight of the presiding genius, who deserted him, half-helped, if a muffled chirp sounded from the nest above. And when he read his paper of an evening, Demi's colic got into the shipping list and Daisy's fall affected the price of stocks, for Mrs. Brooke was only interested in domestic news.

The poor man was very uncomfortable, for the children had bereft him of his wife, home was merely a nursery and the perpetual "hushing" made him feel like a brutal intruder whenever he entered the sacred precincts of Babyland. He bore it very patiently for six months, and when no signs of amendment appeared, he did what other paternal exiles do—tried to get a little comfort elsewhere. Scott had married and gone to housekeeping not far off, and John fell into the way of running over for an hour or two of an evening, when his own parlor was empty, and his own wife singing lullabies that seemed to have no end. Mrs. Scott was a lively, pretty girl, with nothing to do but be agreeable, and she performed her mission most successfully. The parlor was always bright and attractive, the chessboard ready, the piano in tune, plenty of gay gossip, and a nice little supper set forth in tempting style.

John would have preferred his own fireside if it had not been so lonely, but as it was he gratefully took the next best thing and enjoyed his neighbor's society.

Meg rather approved of the new arrangement at first, and found it a relief to know that John was having a good time instead of dozing in the parlor, or tramping about the house and waking the children. But by-and-by, when the teething worry was over and the idols went to sleep at proper hours, leaving Mamma time to rest, she began to miss John, and find her workbasket dull company, when he was not sitting opposite in his old dressing gown, comfortably scorching his slippers on the fender. She would not ask him to stay at home, but felt injured because he did not know that she wanted him without being told, entirely forgetting the many evenings he had waited for her in vain. She was nervous and worn out with watching and worry, and in that unreasonable frame of mind which the best of mothers occasionally experience when domestic cares oppress them. Want of exercise robs them of cheerfulness, and too much devotion to that idol of American women, the teapot, makes them feel as if they were all nerve and no muscle.

"Yes," she would say, looking in the glass, "I'm getting old and ugly. John doesn't find me interesting any longer, so he leaves his faded wife and goes to see his pretty neighbor, who has no incumbrances. Well, the babies love me, they don't care if I am thin and pale and haven't time to crimp my hair, they are my comfort, and some day John will see what I've gladly sacrificed for them, won't he, my precious?"

To which pathetic appeal Daisy would answer with a coo, or Demi with a crow, and Meg would put by her lamentations for a maternal revel, which soothed her solitude for the time being. But the pain increased as politics absorbed John, who was always running over to discuss interesting points with Scott, quite unconscious that Meg missed him. Not a word did she say, however, till her mother found her in tears one day, and insisted on knowing what the matter was, for Meg's drooping spirits had not escaped her observation.

"I wouldn't tell anyone except you, Mother, but I really do need advice, for if John goes on much longer I might as well be widowed," replied Mrs. Brooke, drying her tears on Daisy's bib with an injured air.

"Goes on how, my dear?" asked her mother anxiously.

"He's away all day, and at night when I want to see him, he is continually going over to the Scotts'. It isn't fair that I should have the hardest work, and never any amusement. Men are very selfish, even the best of them."

"So are women. Don't blame John till you see where you are wrong yourself."

"But it can't be right for him to neglect me."

"Don't you neglect him?"

"Why, Mother, I thought you'd take my part!"

"So I do, as far as sympathizing goes, but I think the fault is yours, Meg."

"I don't see how."

"Let me show you. Did John ever neglect you, as you call it, while you made it a point to give him your society of an evening, his only leisure time?"

"No, but I can't do it now, with two babies to tend."

"I think you could, dear, and I think you ought. May I speak quite freely, and will you remember that it's Mother who blames as well as Mother who sympathizes?"

"Indeed I will! Speak to me as if I were little Meg again. I often feel as if I needed teaching more than ever since these babies look to me for everything."

Meg drew her low chair beside her mother's, and with a little interruption in either lap, the two women rocked and talked lovingly together, feeling that the tie of motherhood made them more one than ever.

"You have only made the mistake that most young wives make—forgotten your duty to your husband in your love for your children. A very natural and forgivable mistake, Meg, but one that had better be remedied before you take to different ways, for children should draw you nearer than ever, not separate you, as if they were all yours, and John had nothing to do but support them. I've seen it for some weeks, but have not spoken, feeling sure it would come right in time."

"I'm afraid it won't. If I ask him to stay, he'll think I'm jealous, and I wouldn't insult him by such an idea. He doesn't see that I want him, and I don't know how to tell him without words."

"Make it so pleasant he won't want to go away. My dear, he's longing for his little home, but it isn't home without you, and you are always in the nursery."

"Oughtn't I to be there?"

"Not all the time, too much confinement makes you nervous, and then you are unfitted for everything. Besides, you owe something to John as well as to the babies. Don't neglect husband for children, don't shut him out of the nursery, but teach him how to help in it. His place is there as well as yours, and the children need him. Let him feel that he has a part to do, and he will do it gladly and faithfully, and it will be better for you all."

"You really think so, Mother?"

"I know it, Meg, for I've tried it, and I seldom give advice unless I've proved its practicability. When you and Jo were little, I went on just as you are, feeling as if I didn't do my duty unless I devoted myself wholly to you. Poor Father took to his books, after I had refused all offers of help, and left me to try my experiment alone. I struggled along as well as I could, but Jo was too much for me. I nearly spoiled her by indulgence. You were poorly, and I worried about you till I fell sick myself. Then Father came to the rescue, quietly managed everything, and made himself so helpful that I saw my mistake, and never have been able to get on without him since. That is the secret of our home happiness. He does not let business wean him from the little cares and duties that affect us all, and I try not to let domestic worries destroy my interest in his pursuits. Each do our part alone in many things, but at home we work together, always."

"It is so, Mother, and my great wish is to be to my husband and children what you have been to yours. Show me how, I'll do anything you say."

"You always were my docile daughter. Well, dear, if I were you, I'd let John have more to do with the management of Demi, for the boy needs training, and it's none too soon to begin. Then I'd do what I have often proposed, let Hannah come and help you. She is a capital nurse, and you may trust the precious babies to her while you do more housework. You need the exercise, Hannah would enjoy the rest, and John would find his wife again. Go out more, keep cheerful as well as busy, for you are the sunshine-maker of the family, and if you get dismal there is no fair weather. Then I'd try to take an interest in whatever John likes—talk with him, let him read to you, exchange ideas, and help each other in that way. Don't shut yourself up in a bandbox because you are a woman, but understand what is going on, and educate yourself to take your part in the world's work, for it all affects you and yours."

"John is so sensible, I'm afraid he will think I'm stupid if I ask questions about politics and things."

"I don't believe he would. Love covers a multitude of sins, and of whom could you ask more freely than of him? Try it, and see if he doesn't find your society far more agreeable than Mrs. Scott's suppers."

"I will. Poor John! I'm afraid I *have* neglected him sadly, but I thought I was right, and he never said anything."

"He tried not to be selfish, but he *has* felt rather forlorn, I fancy. This is just the time, Meg, when young married people are apt to grow apart, and the very time when they ought to be most together, for the first tenderness soon wears off, unless care is taken to preserve it. And no time is so beautiful and precious to parents as the first years of the little lives given to them to train. Don't let John be a stranger to the babies, for they will do more to keep him safe and happy in this world of trial and temptation than anything else, and through them you will learn to know and love one another as you should. Now, dear, good-by. Think over Mother's preachment, act upon it if it seems good, and God bless you all."

Meg did think it over, found it good, and acted upon it, though the first attempt was not made exactly as she planned to have it. Of course the children tyrannized over her, and ruled the house as soon as they found out that kicking and squalling brought them whatever they wanted. Mamma was an abject slave to their caprices, but Papa was not so easily subjugated, and occasionally afflicted his tender spouse by an attempt at paternal discipline with his obstreperous son. For Demi inherited a trifle of his sire's firmness of character, we won't call it obstinacy, and when he made up his little mind to have or to do anything, all the king's horses and all the king's men could not change that pertinacious little mind. Mamma thought the dear too young to be taught to conquer his prejudices, but Papa believed that it never was too soon to learn obedience. So Master Demi early discovered that when he undertook to "wrestle" with "Parpar," he always got the worst of it, yet like the Englishman, baby respected the man who conquered him, and loved the father whose grave "No, no," was more impressive than all Mamma's love pats.

A few days after the talk with her mother, Meg resolved to try a social evening with John, so she ordered a nice supper, set the parlor in order, dressed herself prettily, and put the children to bed early, that nothing should interfere with her experiment. But unfortunately Demi's most unconquerable prejudice was against going to bed, and that night he decided to go on a rampage. So poor Meg sang and rocked, told stories and tried every sleep-prevoking wile she could devise, but all in vain, the big eyes wouldn't shut, and long after Daisy had gone to byelow, like the chubby little bunch of good nature she was, naughty Demi lay staring at the light, with the most discouragingly wide-awake expression of countenance.

"Will Demi lie still like a good boy, while Mamma runs down and gives poor Papa his tea?" asked Meg, as the hall door softly closed, and the well-known step went tip-toeing into the dining room.

"Me has tea!" said Demi, preparing to join in the revel.

"No, but I'll save you some little cakies for breakfast, if you'll go bye-bye like Daisy. Will you, lovey?"

"Iss!" and Demi shut his eyes tight, as if to catch sleep and hurry the desired day.

Taking advantage of the propitious moment, Meg slipped away and ran down to greet her husband with a smiling face and the little blue bow in her hair which was his especial admiration. He saw it at once and said with pleased surprise, "Why, little mother, how gay we are tonight. Do you expect company?"

"Only you, dear."

"Is it a birthday, anniversary, or anything?"

"No, I'm tired of being dowdy, so I dressed up as a change. You always make yourself nice for table, no matter how tired you are, so why shouldn't I when I have the time?"

"I do it out of respect for you, my dear," said old-fashioned John.

"Ditto, ditto, Mr. Brooke," laughed Meg, looking young and pretty again, as she nodded to him over the teapot.

"Well, it's altogether delightful, and like old times. This tastes right. I drink your health, dear." and John sipped his tea with an air of reposeful rapture, which was of very short duration however, for as he put down his cup, the door handle rattled mysteriously, and a little voice was heard, saying impatiently—

"Opy doy. Me's tummin!"

"It's that naughty boy. I told him to go to sleep alone, and here he is, downstairs, getting his death a-cold pattering over that canvas," said Meg, answering the call.

"Mornin' now," announced Demi in joyful tone as he entered, with his long nightgown gracefully festooned over his arm and every curl bobbing gayly as he pranced about the table, eyeing the "cakies" with loving glances.

"No, it isn't morning yet. You must go to bed, and not trouble poor Mamma. Then you can have the little cake with sugar on it."

"Me loves Parpar," said the artful one, preparing to climb the paternal knee and revel in forbidden joys. But John shook his head, and said to Meg—

"If you told him to stay up there, and go to sleep alone, make him do it, or he will never learn to mind you."

"Yes, of course. Come, Demi," and Meg led her son away, feeling a strong desire to spank the little marplot who hopped beside her, laboring under the delusion that the bribe was to be administered as soon as they reached the nursery.

Nor was he disappointed, for that shortsighted woman actually gave him a lump of sugar, tucked him into his bed, and forbade any more promenades till morning.

"Iss!" said Demi the perjured, blissfully sucking his sugar, and regarding his first attempt as eminently successful.

Meg returned to her place, and supper was progressing pleasantly, when the little ghost walked again, and exposed the maternal delinquencies by boldly demanding, "More sudar, Marmar."

"Now this won't do," said John, hardening his heart against the engaging little sinner. "We shall never know any peace till that child learns to go to bed properly. You have made a slave of yourself long enough. Give him one lesson, and then there will be an end of it. Put him in his bed and leave him, Meg."

"He won't stay there, he never does unless I sit by him."

"I'll manage him. Demi, go upstairs, and get into your bed, as Mamma bids you."

"S'ant!" replied the young rebel, helping himself to the coveted "cakie," and beginning to eat the same with calm audacity.

"You must never say that to Papa. I shall carry you if you don't go yourself."

"Go 'way, me don't love Parpar." And Demi retired to his mother's skirts for protection.

But even that refuge proved unavailing, for he was delivered over to the enemy, with a "Be gentle with him, John," which struck the culprit with dismay, for when Mamma deserted him, then the judgment day was at hand. Bereft of his cake, defrauded of his frolic, and borne away by a strong hand to that detested bed, poor Demi could not restrain his wrath, but openly defied Papa, and kicked and screamed lustily all the way upstairs. The minute he was put into bed on one side, he rolled out on the other, and made for the door, only to be ignominiously caught up by the tail of his little toga and put back again, which lively performance was kept up till the young man's strength gave out, when he devoted himself to roaring at the top of his voice. This vocal exercise usually conquered Meg, but John sat as unmoved as the post which is popularly believed to be deaf. No coaxing, no sugar, no lullaby, no story, even the light was put out and only the red glow of the fire enlivened the "big dark" which Demi regarded with curiosity rather than fear. This new order of things disgusted him, and he howled dismally for "Marmar," as his angry passions subsided, and recollections of his tender bondwoman returned to the captive autocrat. The plaintive wail which succeeded the passionate roar went to Meg's heart, and she ran up to say beseechingly—

"Let me stay with him, he'll be good now, John."

"No, my dear. I've told him he must go to sleep, as you bid him, and he must, if I stay here all night."

"But he'll cry himself sick," pleaded Meg, reproaching herself for deserting her boy.

"No, he won't, he's so tired he will soon drop off and then the matter is settled, for he will understand that he has got to mind. Don't interfere, I'll manage him."

"He's my child, and I can't have his spirit broken by harshness."

"He's my child, and I won't have his temper spoiled by indulgence. Go down, my dear, and leave the boy to me."

When John spoke in that masterful tone, Meg always obeyed, and never regretted her docility.

"Please let me kiss him once, John?"

"Certainly. Demi, say good night to Mamma, and let her go and rest, for she is very tired with taking care of you all day."

Meg always insisted upon it that the kiss won the victory, for after it was given, Demi sobbed more quietly, and lay quite still at the bottom of the bed, whither he had wriggled in his anguish of mind.

"Poor little man, he's worn out with sleep and crying. I'll cover him up, and then go and set Meg's heart at rest," thought John, creeping to the bedside, hoping to find his rebellious heir asleep.

But he wasn't, for the moment his father peeped at him, Demi's eyes opened, his little chin began to quiver, and he put up his arms, saying with a penitent hiccough, "Me's dood, now."

Sitting on the stairs outside Meg wondered at the long silence which followed the uproar, and after imagining all sorts of impossible accidents, she slipped into the room to set her fears at rest. Demi lay fast asleep, not in his usual spreadeagle attitude, but in a subdued bunch, cuddled close in the circle of his father's arm and holding his father's finger, as if he felt that justice was tempered with mercy, and had gone to sleep a sadder and wiser baby. So held, John had waited with a womanly patience till the little hand relaxed its hold, and while waiting had fallen asleep, more tired by that tussle with his son than with his whole day's work.

As Meg stood watching the two faces on the pillow, she smiled to herself, and then slipped away again, saying in a satisfied tone, "I never need fear that John will be too harsh with my babies. He *does* know how to manage them, and will be a great help, for Demi *is* getting too much for me."

When John came down at last, expecting to find a pensive or reproachful wife, he was agreeably surprised to find Meg placidly trimming a bonnet, and to be greeted with the request to read something about the election, if he was not too tired. John saw in a minute that a revolution of some kind was going on, but wisely asked no questions, knowing that Meg was such a transparent little person, she couldn't keep a secret to save her life, and therefore the clue would soon appear. He read a long debate with the most amiable readiness and then explained it in his most lucid manner, while Meg tried to look deeply interested, to ask intelligent questions, and keep her thoughts from wandering from the state of the nation to the state of her bonnet. In her secret soul, however, she decided that politics were as bad as mathematics, and that the mission of politicians seemed to be calling each other names, but she kept these feminine ideas to herself, and when John paused, shook her head and said with what she thought diplomatic ambiguity, "Well, I really don't see what we are coming to."

John laughed, and watched her for a minute, as she poised a pretty little preparation of lace and flowers on her hand, and regarded it with the genuine interest which his harangue had failed to waken.

"She is trying to like politics for my sake, so I'll try and like millinery for hers, that's only fair," thought John the Just, adding aloud, "That's very pretty. Is it what you call a breakfast cap?"

"My dear man, it's a bonnet! My very best go-to-concert-and-theater bonnet."

"I beg your pardon, it was so small, I naturally mistook it for one of the flyaway things you sometimes wear. How do you keep it on?"

"These bits of lace are fastened under the chin with a rosebud, so," and Meg illustrated by putting on the bonnet and regarding him with an air of calm satisfaction that was irresistible.

"It's a love of a bonnet, but I prefer the face inside, for it looks young and happy again," and John kissed the smiling face, to the great detriment of the rosebud under the chin.

"I'm glad you like it, for I want you to take me to one of the new concerts some night. I really need some music to put me in tune. Will you, please?"

"Of course I will, with all my heart, or anywhere else you like. You have been shut up so long, it will do you no end of good, and I shall enjoy it, of all things. What put it into your head, little mother?"

"Well, I had a talk with Marmee the other day, and told her how nervous and cross and out of sorts I felt, and she said I needed change and less care, so Hannah is to help me with the children, and I'm to see to things about the house more, and now and then have a little fun, just to keep me from getting to be a fidgety, broken-down old woman before my time. It's only an experiment, John, and I want to try it for your sake as much as for mine, because I've neglected you shamefully lately, and I'm going to make home what it used to be, if I can. You don't object, I hope?"

Never mind what John said, or what a very narrow escape the little bonnet had from utter ruin. All that we have any business to know is that John did *not* appear to object, judging from the changes which gradually took place in the house and its inmates. It was not all Paradise by any means, but everyone was better for the division of labor system. The children throve under the paternal rule, for accurate, steadfast John brought order and obedience into Babydom, while Meg recovered her spirits and composed her nerves by plenty of wholesome exercise, a little pleasure, and much confidential conversation with her sensible husband. Home grew homelike again, and John had no wish to leave it, unless he took Meg with him. The Scotts came to the Brookes' now, and everyone found the little house a cheerful place, full of happiness, content, and family love. Even Sallie Moffat liked to go there. "It is always so quiet and pleasant here, it does me good, Meg," she used to say, looking about her with wistful eyes, as if trying to discover the charm, that she might use it in her great house, full of splendid loneliness, for there were no riotous, sunny-faced babies there, and Ned lived in a world of his own, where there was no place for her.

This household happiness did not come all at once, but John and Meg had found the key to it, and each year of married life taught them how to use it, unlocking the treasuries of real home love and mutual helpfulness, which the poorest may possess, and the richest cannot buy. This is the sort of shelf on which young wives and mothers may consent to be laid, safe from the restless fret and fever of the world, finding loyal lovers in the little sons and daughters who cling to them, undaunted by sorrow, poverty, or age, walking side by side, through fair and stormy weather, with a faithful friend, who is, in the true sense of the good old Saxon word, the "house-band," and learning, as Meg learned, that a woman's happiest kingdom is home, her highest honor the art of ruling it not as a queen, but as a wise wife and mother.

CHAPTER XXXIX

LAZY LAURENCE

Laurie went to Nice intending to stay a week, and remained a month. He was tired of wandering about alone, and Amy's familiar presence seemed to give a homelike charm to the foreign scenes in which she bore a part. He rather missed the "petting" he used to receive, and enjoyed a taste of it again, for no attentions, however flattering, from strangers, were half so pleasant as the sisterly adoration of the girls at home. Amy never would pet him like the others, but she was very glad to see him now, and quite clung to him, feeling that he was the representative of the dear family for whom she longed more than she would confess. They naturally took comfort in each other's society and were much together, riding, walking, dancing, or dawdling, for at Nice no one can be very industrious during the gay season. But, while apparently amusing themselves in the most careless fashion, they were half-consciously making discoveries and forming opinions about each other. Amy rose daily in the estimation of her friend, but he sank in hers, and each felt the truth before a word was spoken. Amy tried to please, and succeeded, for she was grateful for the many pleasures he gave her, and repaid him with the little services to which womanly women know how to lend an indescribable charm. Laurie made no effort of any kind, but just let himself drift along as comfortably as possible, trying to forget, and feeling that all women owed him a kind word because one had been cold to him. It cost him no effort to be generous, and he would have given Amy all the trinkets in Nice if she would have taken them, but at the same time he felt that he could not change the opinion she was forming of him, and he rather dreaded the keen blue eyes that seemed to watch him with such half-sorrowful, half-scornful surprise.

"All the rest have gone to Monaco for the day. I preferred to stay at home and write letters. They are done now, and I am going to Valrosa to sketch, will you come?" said Amy, as she joined Laurie one lovely day when he lounged in as usual, about noon.

"Well, yes, but isn't it rather warm for such a long walk?" he answered slowly, for the shaded *salon* looked inviting after the glare without.

"I'm going to have the little carriage, and Baptiste can drive, so you'll have nothing to do but hold your umbrella, and keep your gloves nice," returned Amy, with a sarcastic glance at the immaculate kids, which were a weak point with Laurie.

"Then I'll go with pleasure." and he put out his hand for her sketchbook. But she tucked it under her arm with a sharp—

"Don't trouble yourself. It's no exertion to me, but *you* don't look equal to it."

Laurie lifted his eyebrows and followed at a leisurely pace as she ran downstairs, but when they got into the carriage he took the reins himself, and left little Baptiste nothing to do but fold his arms and fall asleep on his perch.

The two never quarreled. Amy was too well-bred, and just now Laurie was too lazy, so in a minute he peeped under her hatbrim with an inquiring air. She answered him with a smile, and they went on together in the most amicable manner.

It was a lovely drive, along winding roads rich in the picturesque scenes that delight beauty-loving eyes. Here an ancient monastery, whence the solemn chanting of the monks came down to them. There a bare-legged shepherd, in wooden shoes, pointed hat, and rough jacket over one shoulder, sat piping on a stone while his goats skipped among the rocks or lay at his feet. Meek, mouse-colored donkeys, laden with panniers of freshly cut grass passed by, with a pretty girl in a *capaline* sitting between the green piles, or an old woman spinning with a distaff as she went. Brown, soft-eyed children ran out from the quaint stone hovels to offer nosegays, or bunches of oranges still on the bough. Gnarled olive trees covered the hills with their dusky foliage, fruit hung golden in the orchard, and great scarlet anemones fringed the roadside, while beyond green slopes and craggy heights, the Maritime Alps rose sharp and white against the blue Italian sky.

Valrosa well deserved its name, for in that climate of perpetual summer roses blossomed everywhere. They overhung the archway, thrust themselves between the bars of the great gate with a sweet welcome to passers-by, and lined the avenue, winding through lemon trees and feathery palms up to the villa on the hill. Every shadowy nook, where seats invited one to stop and rest, was a mass of bloom, every cool grotto had its marble nymph smiling from a veil of flowers and every fountain reflected crimson, white, or pale pink roses, leaning down to smile at their own beauty. Roses covered the walls of the house, draped the cornices, climbed the pillars, and ran riot over the balustrade of the wide terrace, whence one looked down on the sunny Mediterranean, and the white-walled city on its shore.

"This is a regular honeymoon paradise, isn't it? Did you ever see such roses?" asked Amy, pausing on the terrace to enjoy the view, and a luxurious whiff of perfume that came wandering by.

"No, nor felt such thorns," returned Laurie, with his thumb in his mouth, after a vain attempt to capture a solitary scarlet flower that grew just beyond his reach.

"Try lower down, and pick those that have no thorns," said Amy, gathering three of the tiny cream-colored ones that starred the wall behind her. She put them in his buttonhole as a peace offering, and he stood a minute looking down at them with a curious expression, for in the Italian part of his nature there was a touch of superstition, and he was just then in that state of half-sweet, half-bitter melancholy, when imaginative young men find significance in trifles and food for romance everywhere. He had thought of Jo in reaching after the thorny red rose, for vivid flowers became her, and she had often worn ones like that from the greenhouse at home. The pale roses Amy gave him were the sort that the Italians lay in dead hands, never in bridal wreaths, and for a moment he wondered if the omen was for Jo or for himself, but the next instant his American common sense got the better of sentimentality, and he laughed a heartier laugh than Amy had heard since he came.

"It's good advice, you'd better take it and save your fingers," she said, thinking her speech amused him.

"Thank you, I will," he answered in jest, and a few months later he did it in earnest.

"Laurie, when are you going to your grandfather?" she asked presently, as she settled herself on a rustic seat.

"Very soon."

"You have said that a dozen times within the last three weeks."

"I dare say, short answers save trouble."

"He expects you, and you really ought to go."

"Hospitable creature! I know it."

"Then why don't you do it?"

"Natural depravity, I suppose."

"Natural indolence, you mean. It's really dreadful!" And Amy looked severe.

"Not so bad as it seems, for I should only plague him if I went, so I might as well stay and plague you a little longer, you can bear it better, in fact I think it agrees with you excellently," and Laurie composed himself for a lounge on the broad ledge of the balustrade.

Amy shook her head and opened her sketchbook with an air of resignation, but she had made up her mind to lecture "that boy" and in a minute she began again.

"What are you doing just now?"

"Watching lizards."

"No, no. I mean what do you intend and wish to do?"

"Smoke a cigarette, if you'll allow me."

"How provoking you are! I don't approve of cigars and I will only allow it on condition that you let me put you into my sketch. I need a figure."

"With all the pleasure in life. How will you have me, full length or three-quarters, on my head or my heels? I should respectfully suggest a recumbent posture, then put yourself in also and call it '*Dolce far niente.*'"

"Stay as you are, and go to sleep if you like. *I* intend to work hard," said Amy in her most energetic tone.

"What delightful enthusiasm!" and he leaned against a tall urn with an air of entire satisfaction.

"What would Jo say if she saw you now?" asked Amy impatiently, hoping to stir him up by the mention of her still more energetic sister's name.

"As usual, 'Go away, Teddy. I'm busy!'" He laughed as he spoke, but the laugh was not natural, and a shade passed over his face, for the utterance of the familiar name touched the wound that was not healed yet. Both tone and shadow struck Amy, for she had seen and heard them before, and now she looked up in time to catch a new expression on Laurie's face—a hard bitter look, full of pain, dissatisfaction, and regret. It was gone before she could study it and the listless expression back again. She watched him for a moment with artistic pleasure, thinking how like an Italian he looked, as he lay basking in the sun with uncovered head and eyes full of southern dreaminess, for he seemed to have forgotten her and fallen into a reverie.

"You look like the effigy of a young knight asleep on his tomb," she said, carefully tracing the well-cut profile defined against the dark stone.

"Wish I was!"

"That's a foolish wish, unless you have spoiled your life. You are so changed, I sometimes think—" There Amy stopped, with a half-timid, half-wistful look, more significant than her unfinished speech.

Laurie saw and understood the affectionate anxiety which she hesitated to express, and looking straight into her eyes, said, just as he used to say it to her mother, "It's all right, ma'am."

That satisfied her and set at rest the doubts that had begun to worry her lately. It also touched her, and she showed that it did, by the cordial tone in which she said—

"I'm glad of that! I didn't think you'd been a very bad boy, but I fancied you might have wasted money at that wicked Baden-Baden, lost your heart to some charming Frenchwoman with a husband, or got into some of the scrapes that young men seem to consider a necessary part of a foreign tour. Don't stay out there in the sun, come and lie on the grass here and 'let us be friendly,' as Jo used to say when we got in the sofa corner and told secrets."

Laurie obediently threw himself down on the turf, and began to amuse himself by sticking daisies into the ribbons of Amy's hat, that lay there.

"I'm all ready for the secrets." And he glanced up with a decided expression of interest in his eyes.

"I've none to tell. You may begin."

"Haven't one to bless myself with. I thought perhaps you'd had some news from home."

"You have heard all that has come lately. Don't you hear often? I fancied Jo would send you volumes."

"She's very busy. I'm roving about so, it's impossible to be regular, you know. When do you begin your great work of art, Raphaella?" he asked, changing the subject abruptly after another pause, in which he had been wondering if Amy knew his secret and wanted to talk about it.

"Never," she answered, with a despondent but decided air. "Rome took all the vanity out of me, for after seeing the wonders there, I felt too insignificant to live and gave up all my foolish hopes in despair."

"Why should you, with so much energy and talent?"

"That's just why, because talent isn't genius, and no amount of energy can make it so. I want to be great, or nothing. I won't be a common-place dauber, so I don't intend to try any more."

"And what are you going to do with yourself now, if I may ask?"

"Polish up my other talents, and be an ornament to society, if I get the chance."

It was a characteristic speech, and sounded daring, but audacity becomes young people, and Amy's ambition had a good foundation. Laurie smiled, but he liked the spirit with which she took up a new purpose when a long-cherished one died, and spent no time lamenting.

"Good! And here is where Fred Vaughn comes in, I fancy."

Amy preserved a discreet silence, but there was a conscious look in her downcast face that made Laurie sit up and say gravely, "Now I'm going to play brother, and ask questions. May I?"

"I don't promise to answer."

"Your face will, if your tongue won't. You aren't woman of the world enough yet to hide your feelings, my dear. I heard rumors about Fred and you last year, and it's my private opinion that if he had not been called home so suddenly and detained so long, something would have come of it—hey?"

"That's not for me to say," was Amy's grim reply, but her lips would smile, and there was a traitorous sparkle of the eye which betrayed that she knew her power and enjoyed the knowledge.

"You are not engaged, I hope?" and Laurie looked very elder-brotherly and grave all of a sudden.

"No."

"But you will be, if he comes back and goes properly down on his knees, won't you?"

"Very likely."

"Then you are fond of old Fred?"

"I could be, if I tried."

"But you don't intend to try till the proper moment? Bless my soul, what unearthly prudence! He's a good fellow, Amy, but not the man I fancied you'd like."

"He is rich, a gentleman, and has delightful manners," began Amy, trying to be quite cool and dignified, but feeling a little ashamed of herself, in spite of the sincerity of her intentions.

"I understand. Queens of society can't get on without money, so you mean to make a good match, and start in that way? Quite right and proper, as the world goes, but it sounds odd from the lips of one of your mother's girls."

"True, nevertheless."

A short speech, but the quiet decision with which it was uttered contrasted curiously with the young speaker. Laurie felt this instinctively and laid himself down again, with a sense of disappointment which he could not explain. His look and silence, as well as a certain inward self-disapproval, ruffled Amy, and made her resolve to deliver her lecture without delay.

"I wish you'd do me the favor to rouse yourself a little," she said sharply.

"Do it for me, there's a dear girl."

"I could, if I tried." And she looked as if she would like doing it in the most summary style.

"Try, then. I give you leave," returned Laurie, who enjoyed having someone to tease, after his long abstinence from his favorite pastime.

"You'd be angry in five minutes."

"I'm never angry with you. It takes two flints to make a fire. You are as cool and soft as snow."

"You don't know what I can do. Snow produces a glow and a tingle, if applied rightly. Your indifference is half affectation, and a good stirring up would prove it."

"Stir away, it won't hurt me and it may amuse you, as the big man said when his little wife beat him. Regard me in the light of a husband or a carpet, and beat till you are tired, if that sort of exercise agrees with you."

Being decidedly nettled herself, and longing to see him shake off the apathy that so altered him, Amy sharpened both tongue and pencil, and began.

"Flo and I have got a new name for you. It's Lazy Laurence. How do you like it?"

She thought it would annoy him, but he only folded his arms under his head, with an imperturbable, "That's not bad. Thank you, ladies."

"Do you want to know what I honestly think of you?"

"Pining to be told."

"Well, I despise you."

If she had even said "I hate you" in a petulant or coquettish tone, he would have laughed and rather liked it, but the grave, almost sad, accent in her voice made him open his eyes, and ask quickly—

"Why, if you please?"

"Because, with every chance for being good, useful, and happy, you are faulty, lazy, and miserable."

"Strong language, mademoiselle."

"If you like it, I'll go on."

"Pray do, it's quite interesting."

"I thought you'd find it so. Selfish people always like to talk about themselves."

"Am *I* selfish?" the question slipped out involuntarily and in a tone of surprise, for the one virtue on which he prided himself was generosity.

"Yes, very selfish," continued Amy, in a calm, cool voice, twice as effective just then as an angry one. "I'll show you how, for I've studied you while we were frolicking, and I'm not at all satisfied with you. Here you have been abroad nearly six months, and done nothing but waste time and money and disappoint your friends."

"Isn't a fellow to have any pleasure after a four-year grind?"

"You don't look as if you'd had much. At any rate, you are none the better for it, as far as I can see. I said when we first met that you had improved. Now I take it all back, for I don't think you half so nice as when I left you at home. You have grown abominably lazy, you like gossip, and waste time on frivolous things, you are contented to be petted and admired by silly people, instead of being loved and respected by wise ones. With money, talent, position, health, and beauty—ah you like that old Vanity! But it's the truth, so I can't help saying it—with all these splendid things to use and enjoy, you can find nothing to do but dawdle, and instead of being the man you ought to be, you are only—" There she stopped, with a look that had both pain and pity in it.

"Saint Laurence on a gridiron," added Laurie, blandly finishing the sentence. But the lecture began to take effect, for there was a wide-awake sparkle in his eyes now and a half-angry, half-injured expression replaced the former indifference.

"I supposed you'd take it so. You men tell us we are angels, and say we can make you what we will, but the instant we honestly try to do you good, you laugh at us and won't listen, which proves how much your flattery is worth." Amy spoke bitterly, and turned her back on the exasperating martyr at her feet.

In a minute a hand came down over the page, so that she could not draw, and Laurie's voice said, with a droll imitation of a penitent child, "I will be good, oh, I will be good!"

But Amy did not laugh, for she was in earnest, and tapping on the outspread hand with her pencil, said soberly, "Aren't you ashamed of a hand like that? It's as soft and white as a woman's, and looks as if it never did anything but wear Jouvin's best gloves and pick flowers for ladies. You are not a dandy, thank Heaven, so I'm glad to see there are no diamonds or big seal rings on it, only the little old one Jo gave you so long ago. Dear soul, I wish she was here to help me!"

"So do I!"

The hand vanished as suddenly as it came, and there was energy enough in the echo of her wish to suit even Amy. She glanced down at him with a new thought in her mind, but he was lying with his hat half over his face, as if for shade, and his mustache hid his mouth. She only saw his chest rise and fall, with a long breath that might have been a sigh, and the hand that wore the ring nestled down into the grass, as if to hide something too precious or too tender to be spoken of. All in a minute various hints and trifles assumed shape and significance in Amy's mind, and told her what her sister never had confided to her. She remembered that Laurie never spoke voluntarily of Jo, she recalled the shadow on his face just now, the change in his character, and the wearing of the little old ring which was no ornament to a handsome hand. Girls are quick to read such signs and feel their eloquence. Amy had fancied that perhaps a love trouble was at the bottom of the alteration, and now she was sure of it. Her keen eyes filled, and when she spoke again, it was in a voice that could be beautifully soft and kind when she chose to make it so.

"I know I have no right to talk so to you, Laurie, and if you weren't the sweetest-tempered fellow in the world, you'd be very angry with me. But we are all so fond and proud of you, I couldn't bear to think they should be disappointed in you at home as I have been, though, perhaps they would understand the change better than I do."

"I think they would," came from under the hat, in a grim tone, quite as touching as a broken one.

"They ought to have told me, and not let me go blundering and scolding, when I should have been more kind and patient than ever. I never did like that Miss Randal and now I hate her!" said artful Amy, wishing to be sure of her facts this time.

"Hang Miss Randal!" and Laurie knocked the hat off his face with a look that left no doubt of his sentiments toward that young lady.

"I beg pardon, I thought—" And there she paused diplomatically.

"No, you didn't, you knew perfectly well I never cared for anyone but Jo," Laurie said that in his old, impetuous tone, and turned his face away as he spoke.

"I did think so, but as they never said anything about it, and you came away, I supposed I was mistaken. And Jo wouldn't be kind to you? Why, I was sure she loved you dearly."

"She *was* kind, but not in the right way, and it's lucky for her she didn't love me, if I'm the good-for-nothing fellow you think me. It's her fault though, and you may tell her so."

The hard, bitter look came back again as he said that, and it troubled Amy, for she did not know what balm to apply.

"I was wrong, I didn't know. I'm very sorry I was so cross, but I can't help wishing you'd bear it better, Teddy, dear."

"Don't, that's her name for me!" and Laurie put up his hand with a quick gesture to stop the words spoken in Jo's half-kind, half-reproachful tone. "Wait till you've tried it yourself," he added in a low voice, as he pulled up the grass by the handful.

"I'd take it manfully, and be respected if I couldn't be loved," said Amy, with the decision of one who knew nothing about it.

Now, Laurie flattered himself that he *had* borne it remarkably well, making no moan, asking no sympathy, and taking his trouble away to live it down alone. Amy's lecture put the matter in a new light, and for the first time it did look weak and selfish to lose heart at the first failure, and shut himself up in moody indifference. He felt as if suddenly shaken out of a pensive dream and found it impossible to go to sleep again. Presently he sat up and asked slowly, "Do you think Jo would despise me as you do?"

"Yes, if she saw you now. She hates lazy people. Why don't you do something splendid, and *make* her love you?"

"I did my best, but it was no use."

"Graduating well, you mean? That was no more than you ought to have done, for your grandfather's sake. It would have been shameful to fail after spending so much time and money, when everyone knew that you *could* do well."

"I did fail, say what you will, for Jo wouldn't love me," began Laurie, leaning his head on his hand in a despondent attitude.

"No, you didn't, and you'll say so in the end, for it did you good, and proved that you could do something if you tried. If you'd only set about another task of some sort, you'd soon be your hearty, happy self again, and forget your trouble."

"That's impossible."

"Try it and see. You needn't shrug your shoulders, and think, 'Much she knows about such things.' I don't pretend to be wise, but I am observing, and I see a great deal more than you'd imagine. I'm interested in other people's experiences and inconsistencies, and though I can't explain, I remember and use them for my own benefit. Love Jo all your days, if you choose, but don't let it spoil you, for it's wicked to throw away so many good gifts because you can't have the one you want. There, I won't lecture any more, for I know you'll wake up and be a man in spite of that hardhearted girl."

Neither spoke for several minutes. Laurie sat turning the little ring on his finger, and Amy put the last touches to the hasty sketch she had been working at while she talked. Presently she put it on his knee, merely saying, "How do you like that?"

He looked and then he smiled, as he could not well help doing, for it was capitally done, the long, lazy figure on the grass, with listless face, half-shut eyes, and one hand holding a cigar, from which came the little wreath of smoke that encircled the dreamer's head.

"How well you draw!" he said, with a genuine surprise and pleasure at her skill, adding, with a half-laugh, "Yes, that's me."

"As you are. This is as you were." And Amy laid another sketch beside the one he held.

It was not nearly so well done, but there was a life and spirit in it which atoned for many faults, and it recalled the past so vividly that a sudden change swept over the young man's face as he looked. Only a rough sketch of Laurie taming a horse. Hat and coat were off, and every line of the active figure, resolute face, and commanding attitude was full of energy and meaning. The handsome brute, just subdued, stood arching his neck under the tightly drawn rein, with one foot impatiently pawing the ground, and ears pricked up as if listening for the voice that had mastered him. In the ruffled mane, the rider's breezy hair and erect attitude, there was a suggestion of suddenly arrested motion, of strength, courage, and youthful buoyancy that contrasted sharply with the supine grace of the "*Dolce far niente*" sketch. Laurie said nothing but as his eye went from one to the other, Amy saw him flush up and fold his lips together as if he read and accepted the little lesson she had given him. That satisfied her, and without waiting for him to speak, she said, in her sprightly way—

"Don't you remember the day you played Rarey with Puck, and we all looked on? Meg and Beth were frightened, but Jo clapped and pranced, and I sat on the fence and drew you. I found that sketch in my portfolio the other day, touched it up, and kept it to show you."

"Much obliged. You've improved immensely since then, and I congratulate you. May I venture to suggest in 'a honeymoon paradise' that five o'clock is the dinner hour at your hotel?"

Laurie rose as he spoke, returned the pictures with a smile and a bow and looked at his watch, as if to remind her that even moral lectures should have an end. He tried to resume his former easy, indifferent air, but it *was* an affectation now, for the rousing had been more effacious than he would confess. Amy felt the shade of coldness in his manner, and said to herself—

"Now, I've offended him. Well, if it does him good, I'm glad, if it makes him hate me, I'm sorry, but it's true, and I can't take back a word of it."

They laughed and chatted all the way home, and little Baptiste, up behind, thought that monsieur and madamoiselle were in charming spirits. But both felt ill at ease. The friendly frankness was disturbed, the sunshine had a shadow over it, and despite their apparent gaiety, there was a secret discontent in the heart of each.

"Shall we see you this evening, *mon frère*?" asked Amy, as they parted at her aunt's door.

"Unfortunately I have an engagement. *Au revoir, madamoiselle*," and Laurie bent as if to kiss her hand, in the foreign fashion, which became him better than many men. Something in his face made Amy say quickly and warmly—

"No, be yourself with me, Laurie, and part in the good old way. I'd rather have a hearty English handshake than all the sentimental salutations in France."

"Goodbye, dear," and with these words, uttered in the tone she liked, Laurie left her, after a handshake almost painful in its heartiness.

Next morning, instead of the usual call, Amy received a note which made her smile at the beginning and sigh at the end:

MY DEAR MENTOR,

Please make my adieux to your aunt, and exult within yourself, for "Lazy Laurence" has gone to his grandpa, like the best of boys. A pleasant winter to you, and may the gods grant you a blissful honeymoon at Valrosa! I think Fred would be benefited by a rouser. Tell him so, with my congratulations.

Yours gratefully,

TELEMACHUS.

"Good boy! I'm glad he's gone," said Amy, with an approving smile. The next minute her face fell as she glanced about the empty room, adding, with an involuntary sigh, "Yes, I *am* glad, but how I shall miss him."

CHAPTER XL

THE VALLEY OF THE SHADOW

When the first bitterness was over, the family accepted the inevitable, and tried to bear it cheerfully, helping one another by the increased affection which comes to bind households tenderly together in times of trouble. They put away their grief, and each did his or her part toward making that last year a happy one.

The pleasantest room in the house was set apart for Beth, and in it was gathered everything that she most loved—flowers, pictures, her piano, the little worktable, and the beloved pussies. Father's best books found their way there, Mother's easy chair, Jo's desk, Amy's finest sketches, and every day Meg brought her babies on a loving pilgrimage, to make sunshine for Aunty Beth. John quietly set apart a little sum, that he might enjoy the pleasure of keeping the invalid supplied with the fruit she loved and longed for. Old Hannah never wearied of concocting dainty dishes to tempt a capricious appetite, dropping tears as she worked, and from across the sea came little gifts and cheerful letters, seeming to bring breaths of warmth and fragrance from lands that know no winter.

Here, cherished like a household saint in its shrine, sat Beth, tranquil and busy as ever, for nothing could change the sweet, unselfish nature, and even while preparing to leave life, she tried to make it happier for those who should remain behind. The feeble fingers were never idle, and one of her pleasures was to make little things for the school children daily passing to and fro—to drop a pair of mittens from her window for a pair of purple hands, a needlebook for some small mother of many dolls, penwipers for young penmen toiling through forests of pothooks, scrapbooks for picture-loving eyes, and all manner of pleasant devices, till the reluctant climbers of the ladder of learning found their way strewn with flowers, as it were, and came to regard the gentle giver as a sort of fairy godmother, who sat above there, and showered down gifts miraculously suited to their tastes and needs. If Beth had wanted any reward, she found it in the bright little faces always turned up to her window, with nods and smiles, and the droll little letters which came to her, full of blots and gratitude.

The first few months were very happy ones, and Beth often used to look round, and say "How beautiful this is!" as they all sat together in her sunny room, the babies kicking and crowing on the floor, mother and sisters working near, and father reading, in his pleasant voice, from the wise old books which seemed rich in good and comfortable words, as applicable now as when written centuries ago, a little chapel, where a paternal priest taught his flock the hard lessons all must learn, trying to show them that hope can comfort love, and faith make resignation possible. Simple sermons, that went straight to the souls of those who listened, for the father's heart was in the minister's religion, and the frequent falter in the voice gave a double eloquence to the words he spoke or read.

It was well for all that this peaceful time was given them as preparation for the sad hours to come, for by-and-by, Beth said the needle was "so heavy," and put it down forever. Talking wearied her, faces troubled her, pain claimed her for its own, and her tranquil spirit was sorrowfully perturbed by the ills that vexed her feeble flesh. Ah me! Such heavy days, such long, long nights, such aching hearts and imploring prayers, when those who loved her best were forced to see the thin hands stretched out to them beseechingly, to hear the bitter cry, "Help me, help me!" and to feel that there was no help. A sad eclipse of the serene soul, a sharp struggle of the young life with death, but both were mercifully brief, and then the natural rebellion over, the old peace returned more beautiful than ever. With the wreck of her frail body, Beth's soul grew strong, and though she said little, those about her felt that she was ready, saw that the first pilgrim called was likewise the fittest, and waited with her on the shore, trying to see the Shining Ones coming to receive her when she crossed the river.

Jo never left her for an hour since Beth had said "I feel stronger when you are here." She slept on a couch in the room, waking often to renew the fire, to feed, lift, or wait upon the patient creature who seldom asked for anything, and "tried not to be a trouble." All day she haunted the room, jealous of any other nurse, and prouder of being chosen then than of any honor her life ever brought her. Precious and helpful hours to Jo, for now her heart received the teaching that it needed. Lessons in patience were so sweetly taught her that she could not fail to learn them, charity for all, the lovely spirit that can forgive and truly forget unkindness, the loyalty to duty that makes the hardest easy, and the sincere faith that fears nothing, but trusts undoubtingly.

Often when she woke Jo found Beth reading in her well-worn little book, heard her singing softly, to beguile the sleepless night, or saw her lean her face upon her hands, while slow tears dropped through the transparent fingers, and Jo would lie watching her with thoughts too deep for tears, feeling that Beth, in her simple, unselfish way, was trying to wean herself from the dear old life, and fit herself for the life to come, by sacred words of comfort, quiet prayers, and the music she loved so well.

Seeing this did more for Jo than the wisest sermons, the saintliest hymns, the most fervent prayers that any voice could utter. For with eyes made clear by many tears, and a heart softened by the tenderest sorrow, she recognized the beauty of her sister's life—uneventful, unambitious, yet full of the genuine virtues which "smell sweet, and blossom in the dust," the self-forgetfulness that makes the humblest on earth remembered soonest in heaven, the true success which is possible to all.

One night when Beth looked among the books upon her table, to find something to make her forget the mortal weariness that was almost as hard to bear as pain, as she turned the leaves of her old favorite, Pilgrims's Progress, she found a little paper, scribbled over in Jo's hand. The name caught her eye and the blurred look of the lines made her sure that tears had fallen on it.

"Poor Jo! She's fast asleep, so I won't wake her to ask leave. She shows me all her things, and I don't think she'll mind if I look at this", thought Beth, with a glance at her sister, who lay on the rug, with the tongs beside her, ready to wake up the minute the log fell apart.

My Beth

Sitting patient in the shadow
Till the blessed light shall come,
A serene and saintly presence
Sanctifies our troubled home.
Earthly joys and hopes and sorrows
Break like ripples on the strand
Of the deep and solemn river
Where her willing feet now stand.

O my sister, passing from me,
Out of human care and strife,
Leave me, as a gift, those virtues
Which have beautified your life.
Dear, bequeath me that great patience
Which has power to sustain
A cheerful, uncomplaining spirit
In its prison-house of pain.

Give me, for I need it sorely,
Of that courage, wise and sweet,
Which has made the path of duty
Green beneath your willing feet.
Give me that unselfish nature,
That with charity devine
Can pardon wrong for love's dear sake—
Meek heart, forgive me mine!

Thus our parting daily loseth
Something of its bitter pain,
And while learning this hard lesson,
My great loss becomes my gain.
For the touch of grief will render
My wild nature more serene,
Give to life new aspirations,
A new trust in the unseen.

Henceforth, safe across the river,
I shall see forever more
A beloved, household spirit
Waiting for me on the shore.
Hope and faith, born of my sorrow,
Guardian angels shall become,
And the sister gone before me
By their hands shall lead me home.

Blurred and blotted, faulty and feeble as the lines were, they brought a look of inexpressible comfort to Beth's face, for her one regret had been that she had done so little, and this seemed to assure her that her life had not been useless, that her death would not bring the despair she feared. As she sat with the paper folded between her hands, the charred log fell asunder. Jo started up, revived the blaze, and crept to the bedside, hoping Beth slept.

"Not asleep, but so happy, dear. See, I found this and read it. I knew you wouldn't care. Have I been all that to you, Jo?" she asked, with wistful, humble earnestness.

"Oh, Beth, so much, so much!" And Jo's head went down upon the pillow beside her sister's.

"Then I don't feel as if I'd wasted my life. I'm not so good as you make me, but I *have* tried to do right. And now, when it's too late to begin even to do better, it's such a comfort to know that someone loves me so much, and feels as if I'd helped them."

"More than any one in the world, Beth. I used to think I couldn't let you go, but I'm learning to feel that I don't lose you, that you'll be more to me than ever, and death can't part us, though it seems to."

"I know it cannot, and I don't fear it any longer, for I'm sure I shall be your Beth still, to love and help you more than ever. You must take my place, Jo, and be everything to Father and Mother when I'm gone. They will turn to you, don't fail them, and if it's hard to work alone, remember that I don't forget you, and that you'll be happier in doing that than writing splendid books or seeing all the world, for love is the only thing that we can carry with us when we go, and it makes the end so easy."

"I'll try, Beth." And then and there Jo renounced her old ambition, pledged herself to a new and better one, acknowledging the poverty of other desires, and feeling the blessed solace of a belief in the immortality of love.

So the spring days came and went, the sky grew clearer, the earth greener, the flowers were up fairly early, and the birds came back in time to say goodbye to Beth, who, like a tired but trustful child, clung to the hands that had led her all her life, as Father and Mother guided her tenderly through the Valley of the Shadow, and gave her up to God.

Seldom except in books do the dying utter memorable words, see visions, or depart with beatified countenances, and those who have sped many parting souls know that to most the end comes as naturally and simply as sleep. As Beth had hoped, the "tide went out easily," and in the dark hour before dawn, on the bosom where she had drawn her first breath, she quietly drew her last, with no farewell but one loving look, one little sigh.

With tears and prayers and tender hands, Mother and sisters made her ready for the long sleep that pain would never mar again, seeing with grateful eyes the beautiful serenity that soon replaced the pathetic patience that had wrung their hearts so long, and feeling with reverent joy that to their darling death was a benignant angel, not a phantom full of dread.

When morning came, for the first time in many months the fire was out, Jo's place was empty, and the room was very still. But a bird sang blithely on a budding bough, close by, the snowdrops blossomed freshly at the window, and the spring sunshine streamed in like a benediction over the placid face upon the pillow, a face so full of painless peace that those who loved it best smiled through their tears, and thanked God that Beth was well at last.

CHAPTER XLI

LEARNING TO FORGET

Amy's lecture did Laurie good, though, of course, he did not own it till long afterward. Men seldom do, for when women are the advisers, the lords of creation don't take the advice till they have persuaded themselves that it is just what they intended to do. Then they act upon it, and, if it succeeds, they give the weaker vessel half the credit of it. If it fails, they generously give her the whole. Laurie went back to his grandfather, and was so dutifully devoted for several weeks that the old gentleman declared the climate of Nice had improved him wonderfully, and he had better try it again. There was nothing the young gentleman would have liked better, but elephants could not have dragged him back after the scolding he had received. Pride forbid, and whenever the longing grew very strong, he fortified his resolution by repeating the words that had made the deepest impression, "I despise you." "Go and do something splendid that will *make* her love you."

Laurie turned the matter over in his mind so often that he soon brought himself to confess that he *had* been selfish and lazy, but then when a man has a great sorrow, he should be indulged in all sorts of vagaries till he has lived it down. He felt that his blighted affections were quite dead now, and though he should never cease to be a faithful mourner, there was no occasion to wear his weeds ostentatiously. Jo *wouldn't* love him, but he might *make* her respect and admire him by doing something which should prove that a girl's "No" had not spoiled his life. He had always meant to do something, and Amy's advice was quite unnecessary. He had only been waiting till the aforesaid blighted affections were decently interred. That being done, he felt that he was ready to "hide his stricken heart, and still toil on."

As Goethe, when he had a joy or a grief, put it into a song, so Laurie resolved to embalm his love sorrow in music, and to compose a Requiem which should harrow up Jo's soul and melt the heart of every hearer. Therefore the next time the old gentleman found him getting restless and moody and ordered him off, he went to Vienna, where he had musical friends, and fell to work with the firm determination to distinguish himself. But whether the sorrow was too vast to be embodied in music, or music too ethereal to uplift a mortal woe, he soon discovered that the Requiem was beyond him just at present. It was evident that his mind was not in working order yet, and his ideas needed clarifying, for often in the middle of a plaintive strain, he would find himself humming a dancing tune that vividly recalled the Christmas ball at Nice, especially the stout Frenchman, and put an effectual stop to tragic composition for the time being.

Then he tried an opera, for nothing seemed impossible in the beginning, but here again unforeseen difficulties beset him. He wanted Jo for his heroine, and called upon his memory to supply him with tender recollections and romantic visions of his love. But memory turned traitor, and as if possessed by the perverse spirit of the girl, would only recall Jo's oddities, faults, and freaks, would only show her in the most unsentimental aspects—beating mats with her head tied up in a bandanna, barricading herself with the sofa pillow, or throwing cold water over his passion a la Gummidge—and an irresistable laugh spoiled the pensive picture he was endeavoring to paint. Jo wouldn't be put into the opera at any price, and he had to give her up with a "Bless that girl, what a torment she is," and a clutch at his hair, as became a distracted composer.

When he looked about him for another and a less intractable damsel to immortalize in melody, memory produced one with the most obliging readiness. This phantom wore many faces, but it always had golden hair, was enveloped in a diaphanous cloud, and floated airily before his mind's eye in a pleasing chaos of roses, peacocks, white ponies, and blue ribbons. He did not give the complacent wraith any name, but he took her for his heroine and grew quite fond of her, as well he might, for he gifted her with every gift and grace under the sun, and escorted her, unscathed, through trials which would have annihilated any mortal woman.

Thanks to this inspiration, he got on swimmingly for a time, but gradually the work lost its charm, and he forgot to compose, while he sat musing, pen in hand, or roamed about the gay city to get some new ideas and refresh his mind, which seemed to be in a somewhat unsettled state that winter. He did not do much, but he thought a great deal and was conscious of a change of some sort going on in spite of himself. "It's genius simmering, perhaps. I'll let it simmer, and see what comes of it," he said, with a secret suspicion all the while that it wasn't genius, but something far more common. Whatever it was, it simmered to some purpose, for he grew more and more discontented with his desultory life, began to long for some real and earnest work to go at, soul and body, and finally came to the wise conclusion that everyone who loved music was not a composer. Returning from one of Mozart's grand operas, splendidly performed at the Royal Theatre, he looked over his own, played a few of the best parts, sat staring at the busts of Mendelssohn, Beethoven, and Bach, who stared benignly back again. Then suddenly he tore up his music sheets, one by one, and as the last fluttered out of his hand, he said soberly to himself—

"She is right! Talent isn't genius, and you can't make it so. That music has taken the vanity out of me as Rome took it out of her, and I won't be a humbug any longer. Now what shall I do?"

That seemed a hard question to answer, and Laurie began to wish he had to work for his daily bread. Now if ever, occurred an eligible opportunity for "going to the devil," as he once forcibly expressed it, for he had plenty of money and nothing to do, and Satan is proverbially fond of providing employment for full and idle hands. The poor fellow had temptations enough from without and from within, but he withstood them pretty well, for much as he valued liberty, he valued good faith and confidence more, so his promise to his grandfather, and his desire to be able to look honestly into the eyes of the women who loved him, and say "All's well," kept him safe and steady.

Very likely some Mrs. Grundy will observe, "I don't believe it, boys will be boys, young men must sow their wild oats, and women must not expect miracles." I dare say *you* don't, Mrs. Grundy, but it's true nevertheless. Women work a good many miracles, and I have a persuasion that they may perform even that of raising the standard of manhood by refusing to echo such sayings. Let the boys be boys, the longer the better, and let the young men sow their wild oats if they must. But mothers, sisters, and friends may help to make the crop a small one, and keep many tares from spoiling the harvest, by believing, and showing that they believe, in the possibility of loyalty to the virtues which make men manliest in good women's eyes. If it is a feminine delusion, leave us to enjoy it while we may, for without it half the beauty and the romance of life is lost, and sorrowful forebodings would embitter all our hopes of the brave, tenderhearted little lads, who still love their mothers better than themselves and are not ashamed to own it.

Laurie thought that the task of forgetting his love for Jo would absorb all his powers for years, but to his great surprise he discovered it grew easier every day. He refused to believe it at first, got angry with himself, and couldn't understand it, but these hearts of ours are curious and contrary things, and time and nature work their will in spite of us. Laurie's heart *wouldn't* ache. The wound persisted in healing with a rapidity that astonished him, and instead of trying to forget, he found himself trying to remember. He had not foreseen this turn of affairs, and was not prepared for it. He was disgusted with himself, surprised at his own fickleness, and full of a queer mixture of disappointment and relief that he could recover from such a tremendous blow so soon. He carefully stirred up the embers of his lost love, but they refused to burst into a blaze. There was only a comfortable glow that warmed and did him good without putting him into a fever, and he was reluctantly obliged to confess that the boyish passion was slowly subsiding into a more tranquil sentiment, very tender, a little sad and resentful still, but that was sure to pass away in time, leaving a brotherly affection which would last unbroken to the end.

As the word "brotherly" passed through his mind in one of his reveries, he smiled, and glanced up at the picture of Mozart that was before him:

"Well, he was a great man, and when he couldn't have one sister he took the other, and was happy."

Laurie did not utter the words, but he thought them, and the next instant kissed the little old ring, saying to himself, "No, I won't! I haven't forgotten, I never can. I'll try again, and if that fails, why then—"

Leaving his sentence unfinished, he seized pen and paper and wrote to Jo, telling her that he could not settle to anything while there was the least hope of her changing her mind. Couldn't she, wouldn't she—and let him come home and be happy? While waiting for an answer he did nothing, but he did it energetically, for he was in a fever of impatience. It came at last, and settled his mind effectually on one point, for Jo decidedly couldn't and wouldn't. She was wrapped up in Beth, and never wished to hear the word love again. Then she begged him to be happy with somebody else, but always keep a little corner of his heart for his loving sister Jo. In a postscript she desired him not to tell Amy that Beth was worse, she was coming home in the spring and there was no need of saddening the remainder of her stay. That would be time enough, please God, but Laurie must write to her often, and not let her feel lonely, homesick or anxious.

"So I will, at once. Poor little girl, it will be a sad going home for her, I'm afraid," and Laurie opened his desk, as if writing to Amy had been the proper conclusion of the sentence left unfinished some weeks before.

But he did not write the letter that day, for as he rummaged out his best paper, he came across something which changed his purpose. Tumbling about in one part of the desk among bills, passports, and business documents of various kinds were several of Jo's letters, and in another compartment were three notes from Amy, carefully tied up with one of her blue ribbons and sweetly suggestive of the little dead roses put away inside. With a half-repentant, half-amused expression, Laurie gathered up all Jo's letters, smoothed, folded, and put them neatly into a small drawer of the desk, stood a minute turning the ring thoughtfully on his finger, then slowly drew it off, laid it with the letters, locked the drawer, and went out to hear High Mass at Saint Stefan's, feeling as if there had been a funeral, and though not overwhelmed with affliction, this seemed a more proper way to spend the rest of the day than in writing letters to charming young ladies.

The letter went very soon, however, and was promptly answered, for Amy was homesick, and confessed it in the most delightfully confiding manner. The correspondence flourished famously, and letters flew to and fro with unfailing regularity all through the early spring. Laurie sold his busts, made allumettes of his opera, and went back to Paris, hoping somebody would arrive before long. He wanted desperately to go to Nice, but would not till he was asked, and Amy would not ask him, for just then she was having little experiences of her own, which made her rather wish to avoid the quizzical eyes of "our boy."

Fred Vaughn had returned, and put the question to which she had once decided to answer, "Yes, thank you," but now she said, "No, thank you," kindly but steadily, for when the time came, her courage failed her, and she found that something more than money and position was needed to satisfy the new longing that filled her heart so full of tender hopes and fears. The words, "Fred is a good fellow, but not at all the man I fancied you would ever like," and Laurie's face when he uttered them, kept returning to her as pertinaciously as her own did when she said in look, if not in words, "I shall marry for money." It troubled her to remember that now, she wished she could take it back, it sounded so unwomanly. She didn't want Laurie to think her a heartless, worldly creature. She didn't care to be a queen of society now half so much as she did to be a lovable woman. She was so glad he didn't hate her for the dreadful things she said, but took them so beautifully and was kinder than ever. His letters were such a comfort, for the home letters were very irregular and not half so satisfactory as his when they did come. It was not only a pleasure, but a duty to answer them, for the poor fellow was forlorn, and needed petting, since Jo persisted in being stonyhearted. She ought to have made an effort and tried to love him. It couldn't be very hard, many people would be proud and glad to have such a dear boy care for them. But Jo never would act like other girls, so there was nothing to do but be very kind and treat him like a brother.

If all brothers were treated as well as Laurie was at this period, they would be a much happier race of beings than they are. Amy never lectured now. She asked his opinion on all subjects, she was interested in everything he did, made charming little presents for him, and sent him two letters a week, full of lively gossip, sisterly confidences, and captivating sketches of the lovely scenes about her. As few brothers are complimented by having their letters carried about in their sister's pockets, read and reread diligently, cried over when short, kissed when long, and treasured carefully, we will not hint that Amy did any of these fond and foolish things. But she certainly did grow a little pale and pensive that spring, lost much of her relish for society, and went out sketching alone a good deal. She never had much to show when she came home, but was studying nature, I dare say, while she sat for hours, with her hands folded, on the terrace at Valrosa, or absently sketched any fancy that occurred to her, a stalwart knight carved on a tomb, a young man asleep in the grass, with his hat over his eyes, or a curly haired girl in gorgeous array, promenading down a ballroom on the arm of a tall gentleman, both faces being left a blur according to the last fashion in art, which was safe but not altogether satisfactory.

Her aunt thought that she regretted her answer to Fred, and finding denials useless and explanations impossible, Amy left her to think what she liked, taking care that Laurie should know that Fred had gone to

Egypt. That was all, but he understood it, and looked relieved, as he said to himself, with a venerable air—

"I was sure she would think better of it. Poor old fellow! I've been through it all, and I can sympathize."

With that he heaved a great sigh, and then, as if he had discharged his duty to the past, put his feet up on the sofa and enjoyed Amy's letter luxuriously.

While these changes were going on abroad, trouble had come at home. But the letter telling that Beth was failing never reached Amy, and when the next found her at Vevay, for the heat had driven them from Nice in May, and they had travelled slowly to Switzerland, by way of Genoa and the Italian lakes. She bore it very well, and quietly submitted to the family decree that she should not shorten her visit, for since it was too late to say goodbye to Beth, she had better stay, and let absence soften her sorrow. But her heart was very heavy, she longed to be at home, and every day looked wistfully across the lake, waiting for Laurie to come and comfort her.

He did come very soon, for the same mail brought letters to them both, but he was in Germany, and it took some days to reach him. The moment he read it, he packed his knapsack, bade adieu to his fellow pedestrians, and was off to keep his promise, with a heart full of joy and sorrow, hope and suspense.

He knew Vevay well, and as soon as the boat touched the little quay, he hurried along the shore to La Tour, where the Carrols were living *en pension*. The *garçon* was in despair that the whole family had gone to take a promenade on the lake, but no, the blonde mademoiselle might be in the château garden. If monsieur would give himself the pain of sitting down, a flash of time should present her. But monsieur could not wait even a "flash of time," and in the middle of the speech departed to find mademoiselle himself.

A pleasant old garden on the borders of the lovely lake, with chestnuts rustling overhead, ivy climbing everywhere, and the black shadow of the tower falling far across the sunny water. At one corner of the wide, low wall was a seat, and here Amy often came to read or work, or console herself with the beauty all about her. She was sitting here that day, leaning her head on her hand, with a homesick heart and heavy eyes, thinking of Beth and wondering why Laurie did not come. She did not hear him cross the courtyard beyond, nor see him pause in the archway that led from the subterranean path into the garden. He stood a minute looking at her with new eyes, seeing what no one had ever seen before, the tender side of Amy's character. Everything about her mutely suggested love and sorrow, the blotted letters in her lap, the black ribbon that tied up her hair, the womanly pain and patience in her face, even the little ebony cross at her throat seemed pathetic to Laurie, for he had given it to her, and she wore it as her only ornament. If he had any doubts about the reception she would give him, they were set at rest the minute she looked up and saw him, for dropping everything, she ran to him, exclaiming in a tone of unmistakable love and longing—

"Oh, Laurie, Laurie, I knew you'd come to me!"

I think everything was said and settled then, for as they stood together quite silent for a moment, with the dark head bent down protectingly over the light one, Amy felt that no one could comfort and sustain her so well as Laurie, and Laurie decided that Amy was the only woman in the world who could fill Jo's place and make him happy. He did not tell her so, but she was not disappointed, for both felt the truth, were satisfied, and gladly left the rest to silence.

In a minute Amy went back to her place, and while she dried her tears, Laurie gathered up the scattered papers, finding in the sight of sundry well-worn letters and suggestive sketches good omens for the future. As he sat down beside her, Amy felt shy again, and turned rosy red at the recollection of her impulsive greeting.

"I couldn't help it, I felt so lonely and sad, and was so very glad to see you. It was such a surprise to look up and find you, just as I was beginning to fear you wouldn't come," she said, trying in vain to speak quite naturally.

"I came the minute I heard. I wish I could say something to comfort you for the loss of dear little Beth, but I can only feel, and—" He could not get any further, for he too turned bashful all of a sudden, and did not quite know what to say. He longed to lay Amy's head down on his shoulder, and tell her to have a good cry, but he did not dare, so took her hand instead, and gave it a sympathetic squeeze that was better than words.

"You needn't say anything, this comforts me," she said softly. "Beth is well and happy, and I mustn't wish her back, but I dread the going home, much as I long to see them all. We won't talk about it now, for it makes me cry, and I want to enjoy you while you stay. You needn't go right back, need you?"

"Not if you want me, dear."

"I do, so much. Aunt and Flo are very kind, but you seem like one of the family, and it would be so comfortable to have you for a little while." Amy spoke and looked so like a homesick child whose heart was full that Laurie forgot his bashfulness all at once, and gave her just what she wanted—the petting she was used to and the cheerful conversation she needed.

"Poor little soul, you look as if you'd grieved yourself half sick! I'm going to take care of you, so don't cry any more, but come and walk about with me, the wind is too chilly for you to sit still," he said, in the half-caressing, half-commanding way that Amy liked, as he tied on her hat, drew her arm through his, and began to pace up and down the sunny walk under the new-leaved chestnuts. He felt more at ease upon his legs, and Amy found it pleasant to have a strong arm to lean upon, a familiar face to smile at her, and a kind voice to talk delightfully for her alone.

The quaint old garden had sheltered many pairs of lovers, and seemed expressly made for them, so sunny and secluded was it, with nothing but the tower to overlook them, and the wide lake to carry away the echo of their words, as it rippled by below. For an hour this new pair walked and talked, or rested on the wall, enjoying the sweet influences which gave such a charm to time and place, and when an unromantic dinner bell warned them away, Amy felt as if she left her burden of loneliness and sorrow behind her in the château garden.

The moment Mrs. Carrol saw the girl's altered face, she was illuminated with a new idea, and exclaimed to herself, "Now I understand it all—the child has been pining for young Laurence. Bless my heart, I never thought of such a thing!"

With praiseworthy discretion, the good lady said nothing, and betrayed no sign of enlightenment, but cordially urged Laurie to stay and begged Amy to enjoy his society, for it would do her more good than so much solitude. Amy was a model of docility, and as her aunt was a good deal occupied with Flo, she was left to entertain her friend, and did it with more than her usual success.

At Nice, Laurie had lounged and Amy had scolded. At Vevay, Laurie was never idle, but always walking, riding, boating, or studying in the most energetic manner, while Amy admired everything he did and followed his example as far and as fast as she could. He said the change was owing to the climate, and she did not contradict him, being glad of a like excuse for her own recovered health and spirits.

The invigorating air did them both good, and much exercise worked wholesome changes in minds as well as bodies. They seemed to get clearer views of life and duty up there among the everlasting hills. The fresh winds blew away desponding doubts, delusive fancies, and moody mists. The warm spring sunshine brought out all sorts of aspiring ideas, tender hopes, and happy thoughts. The lake seemed to wash away the troubles of the past, and the grand old mountains to look benignly down upon them saying, "Little children, love one another."

In spite of the new sorrow, it was a very happy time, so happy that Laurie could not bear to disturb it by a word. It took him a little while to recover from his surprise at the cure of his first, and as he had firmly believed, his last and only love. He consoled himself for the seeming disloyalty by the thought that Jo's sister was almost the same as Jo's self, and the conviction that it would have been impossible to love any other woman but Amy so soon and so well. His first wooing had been of the tempestuous order, and he looked back upon it as if through a long vista of years with a feeling of compassion blended with regret. He was not ashamed of it, but put it away as one of the bitter-sweet experiences of his life, for which he could be grateful when the pain was over. His second wooing, he resolved, should be as calm and simple as possible. There was no need of having a scene, hardly any need of telling Amy that he loved her, she knew it without words and had given him his answer long ago. It all came about so naturally that no one could complain, and he knew that everybody would be pleased, even Jo. But when our first little passion has been crushed, we are apt to be wary and slow in making a second trial, so Laurie let the days pass, enjoying every hour, and leaving to chance the utterance of the word that would put an end to the first and sweetest part of his new romance.

He had rather imagined that the denouement would take place in the château garden by moonlight, and in the most graceful and decorous manner, but it turned out exactly the reverse, for the matter was settled on the lake at noonday in a few blunt words. They had been floating about all the morning, from gloomy St. Gingolf to sunny Montreux, with the Alps of Savoy on one side, Mont St. Bernard and the Dent du Midi on the other, pretty Vevay in the valley, and Lausanne upon the hill beyond, a cloudless blue sky overhead, and the bluer lake below, dotted with the picturesque boats that look like white-winged gulls.

They had been talking of Bonnivard, as they glided past Chillon, and of Rousseau, as they looked up at Clarens, where he wrote his *Héloise*. Neither had read it, but they knew it was a love story, and each privately wondered if it was half as interesting as their own. Amy had been dabbling her hand in the water during the little pause that fell between them, and when she looked up, Laurie was leaning on his oars with an expression in his eyes that made her say hastily, merely for the sake of saying something—

"You must be tired. Rest a little, and let me row. It will do me good, for since you came I have been altogether lazy and luxurious."

"I'm not tired, but you may take an oar, if you like. There's room enough, though I have to sit nearly in the middle, else the boat won't trim," returned Laurie, as if he rather liked the arrangement.

Feeling that she had not mended matters much, Amy took the offered third of a seat, shook her hair over her face, and accepted an oar. She rowed as well as she did many other things, and though she used both hands, and Laurie but one, the oars kept time, and the boat went smoothly through the water.

"How well we pull together, don't we?" said Amy, who objected to silence just then.

"So well that I wish we might always pull in the same boat. Will you, Amy?" very tenderly.

"Yes, Laurie," very low.

Then they both stopped rowing, and unconsciously added a pretty little tableau of human love and happiness to the dissolving views reflected in the lake.

CHAPTER XLII

ALL ALONE

It was easy to promise self-abnegation when self was wrapped up in another, and heart and soul were purified by a sweet example. But when the helpful voice was silent, the daily lesson over, the beloved presence gone, and nothing remained but loneliness and grief, then Jo found her promise very hard to keep. How could she "comfort Father and Mother" when her own heart ached with a ceaseless longing for her sister, how could she "make the house cheerful" when all its light and warmth and beauty seemed to have deserted it when Beth left the old home for the new, and where in all the world could she "find some useful, happy work to do," that would take the place of the loving service which had been its own reward? She tried in a blind, hopeless way to do her duty, secretly rebelling against it all the while, for it seemed unjust that her few joys should be lessened, her burdens made heavier, and life get harder and harder as she toiled along. Some people seemed to get all sunshine, and some all shadow. It was not fair, for she tried more than Amy to be good, but never got any reward, only disappointment, trouble and hard work.

Poor Jo, these were dark days to her, for something like despair came over her when she thought of spending all her life in that quiet house, devoted to humdrum cares, a few small pleasures, and the duty that never seemed to grow any easier. "I can't do it. I wasn't meant for a life like this, and I know I shall break away and do something desperate if somebody doesn't come and help me," she said to herself, when her first efforts failed and she fell into the moody, miserable state of mind which often comes when strong wills have to yield to the inevitable.

But someone did come and help her, though Jo did not recognize her good angels at once because they wore familiar shapes and used the simple spells best fitted to poor humanity. Often she started up at night, thinking Beth called her, and when the sight of the little empty bed made her cry with the bitter cry of unsubmissive sorrow, "Oh, Beth, come back! Come back!" she did not stretch out her yearning arms in vain. For, as quick to hear her sobbing as she had been to hear her sister's faintest whisper, her mother came to comfort her, not with words only, but the patient tenderness that soothes by a touch, tears that were mute reminders of a greater grief than Jo's, and broken whispers, more eloquent than prayers, because hopeful resignation went hand-in-hand with natural sorrow. Sacred moments, when heart talked to heart in the silence of the night, turning affliction to a blessing, which chastened grief and strengthened love. Feeling this, Jo's burden seemed easier to bear, duty grew sweeter, and life looked more endurable, seen from the safe shelter of her mother's arms.

When aching heart was a little comforted, troubled mind likewise found help, for one day she went to the study, and leaning over the good gray head lifted to welcome her with a tranquil smile, she said very humbly, "Father, talk to me as you did to Beth. I need it more than she did, for I'm all wrong."

"My dear, nothing can comfort me like this," he answered, with a falter in his voice, and both arms round her, as if he too, needed help, and did not fear to ask for it.

Then, sitting in Beth's little chair close beside him, Jo told her troubles—the resentful sorrow for her loss, the fruitless efforts that discouraged her, the want of faith that made life look so dark, and all the sad bewilderment which we call despair. She gave him entire confidence, he gave her the help she needed, and both found consolation in the act. For the time had come when they could talk together not only as father and daughter, but as man and woman, able and glad to serve each other with mutual sympathy as well as mutual love. Happy, thoughtful times there in the old study which Jo called "the church of one member," and from which she came with fresh courage, recovered cheerfulness, and a more submissive spirit. For the parents who had taught one child to meet death without fear, were trying now to teach another to accept life without despondency or distrust, and to use its beautiful opportunities with gratitude and power.

Other helps had Jo—humble, wholesome duties and delights that would not be denied their part in serving her, and which she slowly learned to see and value. Brooms and dishcloths never could be as distasteful as they once had been, for Beth had presided over both, and something of her housewifely spirit seemed to linger around the little mop and the old brush, never thrown away. As she used them, Jo found herself humming the songs Beth used to hum, imitating Beth's orderly ways, and giving the little touches here and there that kept everything fresh and cozy, which was the first step toward making home happy, though she didn't know it till Hannah said with an approving squeeze of the hand—

"You thoughtful creter, you're determined we shan't miss that dear lamb ef you can help it. We don't say much, but we see it, and the Lord will bless you for't, see ef He don't."

As they sat sewing together, Jo discovered how much improved her sister Meg was, how well she could talk, how much she knew about good, womanly impulses, thoughts, and feelings, how happy she was in husband and children, and how much they were all doing for each other.

"Marriage is an excellent thing, after all. I wonder if I should blossom out half as well as you have, if I tried it," said Jo, as she constructed a kite for Demi in the topsy-turvy nursery.

"It's just what you need to bring out the tender womanly half of your nature, Jo. You are like a chestnut burr, prickly outside, but silky-soft within, and a sweet kernel, if one can only get at it. Love will make you show your heart one day, and then the rough burr will fall off."

"Frost opens chestnut burrs, ma'am, and it takes a good shake to bring them down. Boys go nutting, and I don't care to be bagged by them," returned Jo, pasting away at the kite which no wind that blows would ever carry up, for Daisy had tied herself on as a bob.

Meg laughed, for she was glad to see a glimmer of Jo's old spirit, but she felt it her duty to enforce her opinion by every argument in her power, and the sisterly chats were not wasted, especially as two of Meg's most effective arguments were the babies, whom Jo loved tenderly. Grief is the best opener of some hearts, and Jo's was nearly ready for the bag. A little more sunshine to ripen the nut, then, not a boy's impatient shake, but a man's hand reached up to pick it gently from the burr, and find the kernal sound and sweet. If she suspected this, she would have shut up tight, and been more prickly than ever, fortunately she wasn't thinking about herself, so when the time came, down she dropped.

Now, if she had been the heroine of a moral storybook, she ought at this period of her life to have become quite saintly, renounced the world, and gone about doing good in a mortified bonnet, with tracts in her pocket. But, you see, Jo wasn't a heroine, she was only a struggling human girl like hundreds of others, and she just acted out her nature, being sad, cross, listless, or energetic, as the mood suggested. It's highly virtuous to say we'll be good, but we can't do it all at once, and it takes a long pull, a strong pull, and a pull all together before some of us even get our feet set in the right way. Jo had got so far, she was learning to do her duty, and to feel unhappy if she did not, but to do it cheerfully—ah, that was another thing! She had often said she wanted to do something splendid, no matter how hard, and now she had her wish, for what could be more beautiful than to devote her life to Father and Mother, trying to make home as happy to them as they had to her? And if difficulties were necessary to increase the splendor of the effort, what could be harder for a restless, ambitious girl than to give up her own hopes, plans, and desires, and cheerfully live for others?

Providence had taken her at her word. Here was the task, not what she had expected, but better because self had no part in it. Now, could she do it? She decided that she would try, and in her first attempt she found the helps I have suggested. Still another was given her, and she took it, not as a reward, but as a comfort, as Christian took the refreshment afforded by the little arbor where he rested, as he climbed the hill called Difficulty.

"Why don't you write? That always used to make you happy," said her mother once, when the desponding fit over-shadowed Jo.

"I've no heart to write, and if I had, nobody cares for my things."

"We do. Write something for us, and never mind the rest of the world. Try it, dear. I'm sure it would do you good, and please us very much."

"Don't believe I can." But Jo got out her desk and began to overhaul her half-finished manuscripts.

An hour afterward her mother peeped in and there she was, scratching away, with her black pinafore on, and an absorbed expression, which caused Mrs. March to smile and slip away, well pleased with the success of her suggestion. Jo never knew how it happened, but something got into that story that went straight to the hearts of those who read it, for when her family had laughed and cried over it, her father sent it, much against her will, to one of the popular magazines, and to her utter surprise, it was not only paid for, but others requested. Letters from several persons, whose praise was honor, followed the appearance of the little story, newspapers copied it, and strangers as well as friends admired it. For a small thing it was a great success, and Jo was more astonished than when her novel was commended and condemned all at once.

"I don't understand it. What *can* there be in a simple little story like that to make people praise it so?" she said, quite bewildered.

"There is truth in it, Jo, that's the secret. Humor and pathos make it alive, and you have found your style at last. You wrote with no thoughts of fame and money, and put your heart into it, my daughter. You have had the bitter, now comes the sweet. Do your best, and grow as happy as we are in your success."

"If there *is* anything good or true in what I write, it isn't mine. I owe it all to you and Mother and Beth," said Jo, more touched by her father's words than by any amount of praise from the world.

So taught by love and sorrow, Jo wrote her little stories, and sent them away to make friends for themselves and her, finding it a very charitable world to such humble wanderers, for they were kindly welcomed, and sent home comfortable tokens to their mother, like dutiful children whom good fortune overtakes.

When Amy and Laurie wrote of their engagement, Mrs. March feared that Jo would find it difficult to rejoice over it, but her fears were soon set at rest, for though Jo looked grave at first, she took it very quietly, and was full of hopes and plans for "the children" before she read the letter twice. It was a sort of written duet, wherein each glorified the other in loverlike fashion, very pleasant to read and satisfactory to think of, for no one had any objection to make.

"You like it, Mother?" said Jo, as they laid down the closely written sheets and looked at one another.

"Yes, I hoped it would be so, ever since Amy wrote that she had refused Fred. I felt sure then that something better than what you call the 'mercenary spirit' had come over her, and a hint here and there in her letters made me suspect that love and Laurie would win the day."

"How sharp you are, Marmee, and how silent! You never said a word to me."

"Mothers have need of sharp eyes and discreet tongues when they have girls to manage. I was half afraid to put the idea into your head, lest you should write and congratulate them before the thing was settled."

"I'm not the scatterbrain I was. You may trust me. I'm sober and sensible enough for anyone's confidante now."

"So you are, my dear, and I should have made you mine, only I fancied it might pain you to learn that your Teddy loved someone else."

"Now, Mother, did you really think I could be so silly and selfish, after I'd refused his love, when it was freshest, if not best?"

"I knew you were sincere then, Jo, but lately I have thought that if he came back, and asked again, you might perhaps, feel like giving another answer. Forgive me, dear, I can't help seeing that you are very lonely, and sometimes there is a hungry look in your eyes that goes to my heart. So I fancied that your boy might fill the empty place if he tried now."

"No, Mother, it is better as it is, and I'm glad Amy has learned to love him. But you are right in one thing. I am lonely, and perhaps if Teddy had tried again, I might have said 'Yes,' not because I love him any more, but because I care more to be loved than when he went away."

"I'm glad of that, Jo, for it shows that you are getting on. There are plenty to love you, so try to be satisfied with Father and Mother, sisters and brothers, friends and babies, till the best lover of all comes to give you your reward."

"Mothers are the *best* lovers in the world, but I don't mind whispering to Marmee that I'd like to try all kinds. It's very curious, but the more I try to satisfy myself with all sorts of natural affections, the more I seem to want. I'd no idea hearts could take in so many. Mine is so elastic, it never seems full now, and I used to be quite contented with my family. I don't understand it."

"I do," and Mrs. March smiled her wise smile, as Jo turned back the leaves to read what Amy said of Laurie.

"It is so beautiful to be loved as Laurie loves me. He isn't sentimental, doesn't say much about it, but I see and feel it in all he says and does, and it makes me so happy and so humble that I don't seem to be the same girl I was. I never knew how good and generous and tender he was till now, for he lets me read his heart, and I find it full of noble impulses and hopes and purposes, and am so proud to know it's mine. He says he feels as if he 'could make a prosperous voyage now with me aboard as mate, and lots of love for ballast.' I pray he may, and try to be all he believes me, for I love my gallant captain with all my heart and soul and might, and never will desert him, while God lets us be together. Oh, Mother, I never knew how much like heaven this world could be, when two people love and live for one another!"

"And that's our cool, reserved, and worldly Amy! Truly, love does work miracles. How very, very happy they must be!" and Jo laid the rustling sheets together with a careful hand, as one might shut the covers of a lovely romance, which holds the reader fast till the end comes, and he finds himself alone in the workaday world again.

By-and-by Jo roamed away upstairs, for it was rainy, and she could not walk. A restless spirit possessed her, and the old feeling came again, not bitter as it once was, but a sorrowfully patient wonder why one sister should have all she asked, the other nothing. It was not true, she knew that and tried to put it away, but the natural craving for affection was strong, and Amy's happiness woke the hungry longing for someone to "love with heart and soul, and cling to while God let them be together."

Up in the garret, where Jo's unquiet wanderings ended stood four little wooden chests in a row, each marked with its owners name, and each filled with relics of the childhood and girlhood ended now for all. Jo glanced into them, and when she came to her own, leaned her chin on the edge, and stared absently at the chaotic collection, till a bundle of old exercise books caught her eye. She drew them out, turned them over, and relived that pleasant winter at kind Mrs. Kirke's. She had smiled at first, then she looked thoughtful, next sad, and when she came to a little message written in the Professor's hand, her lips began to tremble, the books slid out of her lap, and she sat looking at the friendly words, as they took a new meaning, and touched a tender spot in her heart.

"Wait for me, my friend. I may be a little late, but I shall surely come."

"Oh, if he only would! So kind, so good, so patient with me always, my dear old Fritz. I didn't value him half enough when I had him, but now how I should love to see him, for everyone seems going away from me, and I'm all alone."

And holding the little paper fast, as if it were a promise yet to be fulfilled, Jo laid her head down on a comfortable rag bag, and cried, as if in opposition to the rain pattering on the roof.

Was it all self-pity, loneliness, or low spirits? Or was it the waking up of a sentiment which had bided its time as patiently as its inspirer? Who shall say?

CHAPTER XLIII

SURPRISES

Jo was alone in the twilight, lying on the old sofa, looking at the fire, and thinking. It was her favorite way of spending the hour of dusk. No one disturbed her, and she used to lie there on Beth's little red pillow, planning stories, dreaming dreams, or thinking tender thoughts of the sister who never seemed far away. Her face looked tired, grave, and rather sad, for tomorrow was her birthday, and she was thinking how fast the years went by, how old she was getting, and how little she seemed to have accomplished. Almost twenty-five, and nothing to show for it. Jo was mistaken in that. There was a good deal to show, and by-and-by she saw, and was grateful for it.

"An old maid, that's what I'm to be. A literary spinster, with a pen for a spouse, a family of stories for children, and twenty years hence a morsel of fame, perhaps, when, like poor Johnson, I'm old and can't enjoy it, solitary, and can't share it, independent, and don't need it. Well, I needn't be a sour saint nor a selfish sinner, and, I dare say, old maids are very comfortable when they get used to it, but—" and there Jo sighed, as if the prospect was not inviting.

It seldom is, at first, and thirty seems the end of all things to five-and-twenty. But it's not as bad as it looks, and one can get on quite happily if one has something in one's self to fall back upon. At twenty-five, girls begin to talk about being old maids, but secretly resolve that they never will be. At thirty they say nothing about it, but quietly accept the fact, and if sensible, console themselves by remembering that they have twenty more useful, happy years, in which they may be learning to grow old gracefully. Don't laugh at the spinsters, dear girls, for often very tender, tragic romances are hidden away in the hearts that beat so quietly under the sober gowns, and many silent sacrifices of youth, health, ambition, love itself, make the faded faces beautiful in God's sight. Even the sad, sour sisters should be kindly dealt with, because they have missed the sweetest part of life, if for no other reason. And looking at them with compassion, not contempt, girls in their bloom should remember that they too may miss the blossom time. That rosy cheeks don't last forever, that silver threads will come in the bonnie brown hair, and that, by-and-by, kindness and respect will be as sweet as love and admiration now.

Gentlemen, which means boys, be courteous to the old maids, no matter how poor and plain and prim, for the only chivalry worth having is that which is the readiest to pay deference to the old, protect the feeble, and serve womankind, regardless of rank, age, or color. Just recollect the good aunts who have not only lectured and fussed, but nursed and petted, too often without thanks, the scrapes they have helped you out of, the tips they have given you from their small store, the stitches the patient old fingers have set for you, the steps the willing old feet have taken, and gratefully pay the dear old ladies the little attentions that women love to receive as long as they live. The bright-eyed girls are quick to see such traits, and will like you all the better for them, and if death, almost the only power that can part mother and son, should rob you of yours, you will be sure to find a tender welcome and maternal cherishing from some Aunt Priscilla, who has kept the warmest corner of her lonely old heart for "the best nevvy in the world."

Jo must have fallen asleep (as I dare say my reader has during this little homily), for suddenly Laurie's ghost seemed to stand before her, a substantial, lifelike ghost—leaning over her with the very look he used to wear when he felt a good deal and didn't like to show it. But, like Jenny in the ballad—

> "She could not think it he,"

and lay staring up at him in startled silence, till he stooped and kissed her. Then she knew him, and flew up, crying joyfully—

"Oh my Teddy! Oh my Teddy!"

"Dear Jo, you are glad to see me, then?"

"Glad! My blessed boy, words can't express my gladness. Where's Amy?"

"Your mother has got her down at Meg's. We stopped there by the way, and there was no getting my wife out of their clutches."

"Your what?" cried Jo, for Laurie uttered those two words with an unconscious pride and satisfaction which betrayed him.

"Oh, the dickens! Now I've done it," and he looked so guilty that Jo was down on him like a flash.

"You've gone and got married!"

"Yes, please, but I never will again," and he went down upon his knees, with a penitent clasping of hands, and a face full of mischief, mirth, and triumph.

"Actually married?"

"Very much so, thank you."

"Mercy on us. What dreadful thing will you do next?" and Jo fell into her seat with a gasp.

"A characteristic, but not exactly complimentary, congratulation," returned Laurie, still in an abject attitude, but beaming with satisfaction.

"What can you expect, when you take one's breath away, creeping in like a burglar, and letting cats out of bags like that? Get up, you ridiculous boy, and tell me all about it."

"Not a word, unless you let me come in my old place, and promise not to barricade."

Jo laughed at that as she had not done for many a long day, and patted the sofa invitingly, as she said in a cordial tone, "The old pillow is up garret, and we don't need it now. So, come and fess, Teddy."

"How good it sounds to hear you say 'Teddy'! No one ever calls me that but you," and Laurie sat down with an air of great content.

"What does Amy call you?"

"My lord."

"That's like her. Well, you look it." And Jo's eye plainly betrayed that she found her boy comelier than ever.

The pillow was gone, but there was a barricade, nevertheless, a natural one, raised by time, absence, and change of heart. Both felt it, and for a minute looked at one another as if that invisible barrier cast a little shadow over them. It was gone directly however, for Laurie said, with a vain attempt at dignity—

"Don't I look like a married man and the head of a family?"

"Not a bit, and you never will. You've grown bigger and bonnier, but you are the same scapegrace as ever."

"Now really, Jo, you ought to treat me with more respect," began Laurie, who enjoyed it all immensely.

"How can I, when the mere idea of you, married and settled, is so irresistibly funny that I can't keep sober!" answered Jo, smiling all over her face, so infectiously that they had another laugh, and then settled down for a good talk, quite in the pleasant old fashion.

"It's no use your going out in the cold to get Amy, for they are all coming up presently. I couldn't wait. I wanted to be the one to tell you the grand surprise, and have 'first skim' as we used to say when we squabbled about the cream."

"Of course you did, and spoiled your story by beginning at the wrong end. Now, start right, and tell me how it all happened. I'm pining to know."

"Well, I did it to please Amy," began Laurie, with a twinkle that made Jo exclaim—

"Fib number one. Amy did it to please you. Go on, and tell the truth, if you can, sir."

"Now she's beginning to marm it. Isn't it jolly to hear her?" said Laurie to the fire, and the fire glowed and sparkled as if it quite agreed. "It's all the same, you know, she and I being one. We planned to come home with the Carrols, a month or more ago, but they suddenly changed their minds, and decided to pass another winter in Paris. But Grandpa wanted to come home. He went to please me, and I couldn't let him go alone, neither could I leave Amy, and Mrs. Carrol had got English notions about chaperons and such nonsense, and wouldn't let Amy come with us. So I just settled the difficulty by saying, 'Let's be married, and then we can do as we like.'"

"Of course you did. You always have things to suit you."

"Not always." And something in Laurie's voice made Jo say hastily—

"How did you ever get Aunt to agree?"

"It was hard work, but between us, we talked her over, for we had heaps of good reasons on our side. There wasn't time to write and ask leave, but you all liked it, had consented to it by-and-by, and it was only 'taking time by the fetlock,' as my wife says."

"Aren't we proud of those two words, and don't we like to say them?" interrupted Jo, addressing the fire in her turn, and watching with delight the happy light it seemed to kindle in the eyes that had been so tragically gloomy when she saw them last.

"A trifle, perhaps, she's such a captivating little woman I can't help being proud of her. Well, then Uncle and Aunt were there to play propriety. We were so absorbed in one another we were of no mortal use apart, and that charming arrangement would make everything easy all round, so we did it."

"When, where, how?" asked Jo, in a fever of feminine interest and curiosity, for she could not realize it a particle.

"Six weeks ago, at the American consul's, in Paris, a very quiet wedding; of course, for even in our happiness we didn't forget dear little Beth."

Jo put her hand in his as he said that, and Laurie gently smoothed the little red pillow, which he remembered well.

"Why didn't you let us know afterward?" asked Jo, in a quieter tone, when they had sat quite still a minute.

"We wanted to surprise you. We thought we were coming directly home, at first, but the dear old gentleman, as soon as we were married, found he couldn't be ready under a month, at least, and sent us off to spend our honeymoon wherever we liked. Amy had once called Valrosa a regular honeymoon home, so we went there, and were as happy as people are but once in their lives. My faith! Wasn't it love among the roses!"

Laurie seemed to forget Jo for a minute, and Jo was glad of it, for the fact that he told her these things so freely and so naturally assured her that he had quite forgiven and forgotten. She tried to draw away her hand, but as if he guessed the thought that prompted the half-involuntary impulse, Laurie held it fast, and said, with a manly gravity she had never seen in him before—

"Jo, dear, I want to say one thing, and then we'll put it by forever. As I told you in my letter when I wrote that Amy had been so kind to me, I never shall stop loving you, but the love is altered, and I have learned to see that it is better as it is. Amy and you changed places in my heart, that's all. I think it was meant to be so, and would have come about naturally, if I had waited, as you tried to make me, but I never could be patient, and so I got a heartache. I was a boy then, headstrong and violent, and it took a hard lesson to show me my mistake. For it *was* one, Jo, as you said, and I found it out, after making a fool of myself. Upon my word, I was so tumbled up in my mind, at one time, that I didn't know which I loved best, you or Amy, and tried to love you both alike. But I couldn't, and when I saw her in Switzerland, everything seemed to clear up all at once. You both got into your right places, and I felt sure that it was well off with the old love before it was on with the new, that I could honestly share my heart between sister Jo and wife Amy, and love them dearly. Will you believe it, and go back to the happy old times when we first knew one another?"

"I'll believe it, with all my heart, but, Teddy, we never can be boy and girl again. The happy old times can't come back, and we mustn't expect it. We are man and woman now, with sober work to do, for playtime is over, and we must give up frolicking. I'm sure you feel this. I see the change in you, and you'll find it in me. I shall miss my boy, but I shall love the man as much, and admire him more, because he means to be what I hoped he would. We can't be little playmates any longer, but we will be brother and sister, to love and help one another all our lives, won't we, Laurie?"

He did not say a word, but took the hand she offered him, and laid his face down on it for a minute, feeling that out of the grave of a boyish passion, there had risen a beautiful, strong friendship to bless them both. Presently Jo said cheerfully, for she didn't want the coming home to be a sad one, "I can't make it true that you children are really married and going to set up housekeeping. Why, it seems only yesterday that I was buttoning Amy's pinafore, and pulling your hair when you teased. Mercy me, how time does fly!"

"As one of the children is older than yourself, you needn't talk so like a grandma. I flatter myself I'm a 'gentleman growed' as Peggotty said of David, and when you see Amy, you'll find her rather a precocious infant," said Laurie, looking amused at her maternal air.

"You may be a little older in years, but I'm ever so much older in feeling, Teddy. Women always are, and this last year has been such a hard one that I feel forty."

"Poor Jo! We left you to bear it alone, while we went pleasuring. You *are* older. Here's a line, and there's another. Unless you smile, your eyes look sad, and when I touched the cushion, just now, I found a tear on it. You've had a great deal to bear, and had to bear it all alone. What a selfish beast I've been!" and Laurie pulled his own hair, with a remorseful look.

But Jo only turned over the traitorous pillow, and answered, in a tone which she tried to make more cheerful, "No, I had Father and Mother to help me, and the dear babies to comfort me, and the thought that you and Amy were safe and happy, to make the troubles here easier to bear. I am lonely, sometimes, but I dare say it's good for me, and—"

"You never shall be again," broke in Laurie, putting his arm about her, as if to fence out every human ill. "Amy and I can't get on without you, so you must come and teach 'the children' to keep house, and go halves in everything, just as we used to do, and let us pet you, and all be blissfully happy and friendly together."

"If I shouldn't be in the way, it would be very pleasant. I begin to feel quite young already, for somehow all my troubles seemed to fly away when you came. You always were a comfort, Teddy," and Jo leaned her head on his shoulder, just as she did years ago, when Beth lay ill and Laurie told her to hold on to him.

He looked down at her, wondering if she remembered the time, but Jo was smiling to herself, as if in truth her troubles *had* all vanished at his coming.

"You are the same Jo still, dropping tears about one minute, and laughing the next. You look a little wicked now. What is it, Grandma?"

"I was wondering how you and Amy get on together."

"Like angels!"

"Yes, of course, but which rules?"

"I don't mind telling you that she does now, at least I let her think so—it pleases her, you know. By-and-by we shall take turns, for marriage, they say, halves one's rights and doubles one's duties."

"You'll go on as you begin, and Amy will rule you all the days of your life."

"Well, she does it so imperceptibly that I don't think I shall mind much. She is the sort of woman who knows how to rule well. In fact, I rather like it, for she winds one round her finger as softly and prettily as a skein of silk, and makes you feel as if she was doing you a favor all the while."

"That ever I should live to see you a henpecked husband and enjoying it!" cried Jo, with uplifted hands.

It was good to see Laurie square his shoulders, and smile with masculine scorn at that insinuation, as he replied, with his "high and mighty" air, "Amy is too well-bred for that, and I am not the sort of man to submit to it. My wife and I respect ourselves and one another too much ever to tyrannize or quarrel."

Jo liked that, and thought the new dignity very becoming, but the boy seemed changing very fast into the man, and regret mingled with her pleasure.

"I am sure of that. Amy and you never did quarrel as we used to. She is the sun and I the wind, in the fable, and the sun managed the man best, you remember."

"She can blow him up as well as shine on him," laughed Laurie. "Such a lecture as I got at Nice! I give you my word it was a deal worse than any of your scoldings—a regular rouser. I'll tell you all about it sometime—*she* never will, because after telling me that she despised and was ashamed of me, she lost her heart to the despicable party and married the good-for-nothing."

"What baseness! Well, if she abuses you, come to me, and I'll defend you."

"I look as if I needed it, don't I?" said Laurie, getting up and striking an attitude which suddenly changed from the imposing to the rapturous, as Amy's voice was heard calling, "Where is she? Where's my dear old Jo?"

In trooped the whole family, and everyone was hugged and kissed all over again, and after several vain attempts, the three wanderers were set down to be looked at and exulted over. Mr. Laurence, hale and hearty as ever, was quite as much improved as the others by his foreign tour, for the crustiness seemed to be nearly gone, and the old-fashioned courtliness had received a polish which made it kindlier than ever. It was good to see him beam at "my children," as he called the young pair. It was better still to see Amy pay him the daughterly duty and affection which completely won his old heart, and best of all, to watch Laurie revolve about the two, as if never tired of enjoying the pretty picture they made.

The minute she put her eyes upon Amy, Meg became conscious that her own dress hadn't a Parisian air, that young Mrs. Moffat would be entirely eclipsed by young Mrs. Laurence, and that "her ladyship" was altogether a most elegant and graceful woman. Jo thought, as she watched the pair, "How well they look together! I was right, and Laurie has found the beautiful, accomplished girl who will become his home better than clumsy old Jo, and be a pride, not a torment to him." Mrs. March and her husband smiled and nodded at each other with happy faces, for they saw that their youngest had done well, not only in worldly things, but the better wealth of love, confidence, and happiness.

For Amy's face was full of the soft brightness which betokens a peaceful heart, her voice had a new tenderness in it, and the cool, prim carriage was changed to a gentle dignity, both womanly and winning. No little affectations marred it, and the cordial sweetness of her manner was more charming than the new beauty or the old grace, for it stamped her at once with the unmistakable sign of the true gentlewoman she had hoped to become.

"Love has done much for our little girl," said her mother softly.

"She has had a good example before her all her life, my dear," Mr. March whispered back, with a loving look at the worn face and gray head beside him.

Daisy found it impossible to keep her eyes off her "pitty aunty," but attached herself like a lap dog to the wonderful chatelaine full of delightful charms. Demi paused to consider the new relationship before he compromised himself by the rash acceptance of a bribe, which took the tempting form of a family of wooden bears from Berne. A flank movement produced an unconditional surrender, however, for Laurie knew where to have him.

"Young man, when I first had the honor of making your acquaintance you hit me in the face. Now I demand the satisfaction of a gentleman," and with that the tall uncle proceeded to toss and tousle the small nephew in a way that damaged his philosophical dignity as much as it delighted his boyish soul.

"Blest if she ain't in silk from head to foot; ain't it a relishin' sight to see her settin' there as fine as a fiddle, and hear folks calling little Amy 'Mis. Laurence!'" muttered old Hannah, who could not resist frequent "peeks" through the slide as she set the table in a most decidedly promiscuous manner.

Mercy on us, how they did talk! First one, then the other, then all burst out together—trying to tell the history of three years in half an hour. It was fortunate that tea was at hand, to produce a lull and provide refreshment—for they would have been hoarse and faint if they had gone on much longer. Such a happy procession as filed away into the little dining room! Mr. March proudly escorted Mrs. Laurence. Mrs. March as proudly leaned on the arm of "my son." The old gentleman took Jo, with a whispered, "You must be my girl now," and a glance at the empty corner by the fire, that made Jo whisper back, "I'll try to fill her place, sir."

The twins pranced behind, feeling that the millennium was at hand, for everyone was so busy with the newcomers that they were left to revel at their own sweet will, and you may be sure they made the most of the opportunity. Didn't they steal sips of tea, stuff gingerbread ad libitum, get a hot biscuit apiece, and as a crowning trespass, didn't they each whisk a captivating little tart into their tiny pockets, there to stick and crumble treacherously, teaching them that both human nature and a pastry are frail? Burdened with the guilty consciousness of the sequestered tarts, and fearing that Dodo's sharp eyes would pierce the thin disguise of cambric and merino which hid their booty, the little sinners attached themselves to "Dranpa," who hadn't his spectacles on. Amy, who was handed about like refreshments, returned to the parlor on Father Laurence's arm. The others paired off as before, and this arrangement left Jo companionless. She did not mind it at the minute, for she lingered to answer Hannah's eager inquiry.

"Will Miss Amy ride in her coop (coupe), and use all them lovely silver dishes that's stored away over yander?"

"Shouldn't wonder if she drove six white horses, ate off gold plate, and wore diamonds and point lace every day. Teddy thinks nothing too good for her," returned Jo with infinite satisfaction.

"No more there is! Will you have hash or fishballs for breakfast?" asked Hannah, who wisely mingled poetry and prose.

"I don't care," and Jo shut the door, feeling that food was an uncongenial topic just then. She stood a minute looking at the party vanishing above, and as Demi's short plaid legs toiled up the last stair, a sudden sense of loneliness came over her so strongly that she looked about her with dim eyes, as if to find something to lean upon, for even Teddy had deserted her. If she had known what birthday gift was coming every minute nearer and nearer, she would not have said to herself, "I'll weep a little weep when I go to bed. It won't do to be dismal now." Then she drew her hand over her eyes—for one of her boyish habits was never to know where her handkerchief was—and had just managed to call up a smile when there came a knock at the porch door.

She opened with hospitable haste, and started as if another ghost had come to surprise her, for there stood a tall bearded gentleman, beaming on her from the darkness like a midnight sun.

"Oh, Mr. Bhaer, I *am* so glad to see you!" cried Jo, with a clutch, as if she feared the night would swallow him up before she could get him in.

"And I to see Miss Marsch—but no, you haf a party—" And the Professor paused as the sound of voices and the tap of dancing feet came down to them.

"No, we haven't, only the family. My sister and friends have just come home, and we are all very happy. Come in, and make one of us."

Though a very social man, I think Mr. Bhaer would have gone decorously away, and come again another day, but how could he, when Jo shut the door behind him, and bereft him of his hat? Perhaps her face had something to do with it, for she forgot to hide her joy at seeing him, and showed it with a frankness that proved irresistible to the solitary man, whose welcome far exceeded his boldest hopes.

"If I shall not be Monsieur de Trop, I will so gladly see them all. You haf been ill, my friend?"

He put the question abruptly, for, as Jo hung up his coat, the light fell on her face, and he saw a change in it.

"Not ill, but tired and sorrowful. We have had trouble since I saw you last."

"Ah, yes, I know. My heart was sore for you when I heard that," and he shook hands again, with such a sympathetic face that Jo felt as if no comfort could equal the look of the kind eyes, the grasp of the big, warm hand.

"Father, Mother, this is my friend, Professor Bhaer," she said, with a face and tone of such irrepressible pride and pleasure that she might as well have blown a trumpet and opened the door with a flourish.

If the stranger had any doubts about his reception, they were set at rest in a minute by the cordial welcome he received. Everyone greeted him kindly, for Jo's sake at first, but very soon they liked him for his own. They could not help it, for he carried the talisman that opens all hearts, and these simple people warmed to him at once, feeling even the more friendly because he was poor. For poverty enriches those who live above it, and is a sure passport to truly hospitable spirits. Mr. Bhaer sat looking about him with the air of a traveler who knocks at a strange door, and when it opens, finds himself at home. The children went to him like bees to a honeypot, and establishing themselves on each knee, proceeded to captivate him by rifling his pockets, pulling his beard, and investigating his watch, with juvenile audacity. The women telegraphed their approval to one another, and Mr. March, feeling that he had got a kindred spirit, opened his choicest stores for his guest's benefit, while silent John listened and enjoyed the talk, but said not a word, and Mr. Laurence found it impossible to go to sleep.

If Jo had not been otherwise engaged, Laurie's behavior would have amused her, for a faint twinge, not of jealousy, but something like suspicion, caused that gentleman to stand aloof at first, and observe the newcomer with brotherly circumspection. But it did not last long. He got interested in spite of himself, and before he knew it, was drawn into the circle. For Mr. Bhaer talked well in this genial atmosphere, and did himself justice. He seldom spoke to Laurie, but he looked at him often, and a shadow would pass across his face, as if regretting his own lost youth, as he watched the young man in his prime. Then his eyes would turn to Jo so wistfully that she would have surely answered the mute inquiry if she had seen it. But Jo had her own eyes to take care of, and feeling that they could not be trusted, she prudently kept them on the little sock she was knitting, like a model maiden aunt.

A stealthy glance now and then refreshed her like sips of fresh water after a dusty walk, for the sidelong peeps showed her several propitious omens. Mr. Bhaer's face had lost the absent-minded expression, and looked all alive with interest in the present moment, actually young and handsome, she thought, forgetting to compare him with Laurie, as she usually did strange men, to their great detriment. Then he seemed quite inspired, though the burial customs of the ancients, to which the conversation had strayed, might not be considered an exhilarating topic. Jo quite glowed with triumph when Teddy got quenched in an argument, and thought to herself, as she watched her father's absorbed face, "How he would enjoy having such a man as my Professor to talk with every day!" Lastly, Mr. Bhaer was dressed in a new suit of black, which made him look more like a gentleman than ever. His bushy hair had been cut and smoothly brushed, but didn't stay in order long, for in exciting moments, he rumpled it up in the droll way he used to do, and Jo liked it rampantly erect better than flat, because she thought it gave his fine forehead a Jove-like aspect. Poor Jo, how she did glorify that plain man, as she sat knitting away so quietly, yet letting nothing escape her, not even the fact that Mr. Bhaer actually had gold sleeve-buttons in his immaculate wristbands.

"Dear old fellow! He couldn't have got himself up with more care if he'd been going a-wooing," said Jo to herself, and then a sudden thought born of the words made her blush so dreadfully that she had to drop her ball, and go down after it to hide her face.

The maneuver did not succeed as well as she expected, however, for though just in the act of setting fire to a funeral pyre, the Professor dropped his torch, metaphorically speaking, and made a dive after the little blue ball. Of course they bumped their heads smartly together, saw stars, and both came up flushed and laughing, without the ball, to resume their seats, wishing they had not left them.

Nobody knew where the evening went to, for Hannah skillfully abstracted the babies at an early hour, nodding like two rosy poppies, and Mr. Laurence went home to rest. The others sat round the fire, talking away, utterly regardless of the lapse of time, till Meg, whose maternal mind was impressed with a firm conviction that Daisy had tumbled out of bed, and Demi set his nightgown afire studying the structure of matches, made a move to go.

"We must have our sing, in the good old way, for we are all together again once more," said Jo, feeling that a good shout would be a safe and pleasant vent for the jubilant emotions of her soul.

They were not *all* there. But no one found the words thougtless or untrue, for Beth still seemed among them, a peaceful presence, invisible, but dearer than ever, since death could not break the household league that love made disoluble. The little chair stood in its old place. The tidy basket, with the bit of work she left unfinished when the needle grew "so heavy," was still on its accustomed shelf. The beloved instrument, seldom touched now had not been moved, and above it Beth's face, serene and smiling, as in the early days, looked down upon them, seeming to say, "Be happy. I am here."

"Play something, Amy. Let them hear how much you have improved," said Laurie, with pardonable pride in his promising pupil.

But Amy whispered, with full eyes, as she twirled the faded stool, "Not tonight, dear. I can't show off tonight."

But she did show something better than brilliancy or skill, for she sang Beth's songs with a tender music in her voice which the best master could not have taught, and touched the listener's hearts with a sweeter power than any other inspiration could have given her. The room was very still, when the clear voice failed suddenly at the last line of Beth's favorite hymn. It was hard to say—

Earth hath no sorrow that heaven cannot heal;

and Amy leaned against her husband, who stood behind her, feeling that her welcome home was not quite perfect without Beth's kiss.

"Now, we must finish with Mignon's song, for Mr. Bhaer sings that," said Jo, before the pause grew painful. And Mr. Bhaer cleared his throat with a gratified "Hem!" as he stepped into the corner where Jo stood, saying—

"You will sing with me? We go excellently well together."

A pleasing fiction, by the way, for Jo had no more idea of music than a grasshopper. But she would have consented if he had proposed to sing a whole opera, and warbled away, blissfully regardless of time and tune. It didn't much matter, for Mr. Bhaer sang like a true German, heartily and well, and Jo soon subsided into a subdued hum, that she might listen to the mellow voice that seemed to sing for her alone.

> Know'st thou the land where the citron blooms,

used to be the Professor's favorite line, for "das land" meant Germany to him, but now he seemed to dwell, with peculiar warmth and melody, upon the words—

> There, oh there, might I with thee,
> O, my beloved, go

and one listener was so thrilled by the tender invitation that she longed to say she did know the land, and would joyfully depart thither whenever he liked.

The song was considered a great success, and the singer retired covered with laurels. But a few minutes afterward, he forgot his manners entirely, and stared at Amy putting on her bonnet, for she had been introduced simply as "my sister," and no one had called her by her new name since he came. He forgot himself still further when Laurie said, in his most gracious manner, at parting—

"My wife and I are very glad to meet you, sir. Please remember that there is always a welcome waiting for you over the way."

Then the Professor thanked him so heartily, and looked so suddenly illuminated with satisfaction, that Laurie thought him the most delightfully demonstrative old fellow he ever met.

"I too shall go, but I shall gladly come again, if you will gif me leave, dear madame, for a little business in the city will keep me here some days."

He spoke to Mrs. March, but he looked at Jo, and the mother's voice gave as cordial an assent as did the daughter's eyes, for Mrs. March was not so blind to her children's interest as Mrs. Moffat supposed.

"I suspect that is a wise man," remarked Mr. March, with placid satisfaction, from the hearthrug, after the last guest had gone.

"I know he is a good one," added Mrs. March, with decided approval, as she wound up the clock.

"I thought you'd like him," was all Jo said, as she slipped away to her bed.

She wondered what the business was that brought Mr. Bhaer to the city, and finally decided that he had been appointed to some great honor, somewhere, but had been too modest to mention the fact. If she had seen his face when, safe in his own room, he looked at the picture of a severe and rigid young lady, with a good deal of hair, who appeared to be gazing darkly into futurity, it might have thrown some light upon the subject, especially when he turned off the gas, and kissed the picture in the dark.

CHAPTER XLIV

MY LORD AND LADY

"Please, Madam Mother, could you lend me my wife for half an hour? The luggage has come, and I've been making hay of Amy's Paris finery, trying to find some things I want," said Laurie, coming in the next day to find Mrs. Laurence sitting in her mother's lap, as if being made "the baby" again.

"Certainly. Go, dear, I forgot that you have any home but this," and Mrs. March pressed the white hand that wore the wedding ring, as if asking pardon for her maternal covetousness.

"I shouldn't have come over if I could have helped it, but I can't get on without my little woman any more than a—"

"Weathercock can without the wind," suggested Jo, as he paused for a simile. Jo had grown quite her own saucy self again since Teddy came home.

"Exactly, for Amy keeps me pointing due west most of the time, with only an occasional whiffle round to the south, and I haven't had an easterly spell since I was married. Don't know anything about the north, but am altogether salubrious and balmy, hey, my lady?"

"Lovely weather so far. I don't know how long it will last, but I'm not afraid of storms, for I'm learning how to sail my ship. Come home, dear, and I'll find your bootjack. I suppose that's what you are rummaging after among my things. Men are so helpless, Mother," said Amy, with a matronly air, which delighted her husband.

"What are you going to do with yourselves after you get settled?" asked Jo, buttoning Amy's cloak as she used to button her pinafores.

"We have our plans. We don't mean to say much about them yet, because we are such very new brooms, but we don't intend to be idle. I'm going into business with a devotion that shall delight Grandfather, and prove to him that I'm not spoiled. I need something of the sort to keep me steady. I'm tired of dawdling, and mean to work like a man."

"And Amy, what is she going to do?" asked Mrs. March, well pleased at Laurie's decision and the energy with which he spoke.

"After doing the civil all round, and airing our best bonnet, we shall astonish you by the elegant hospitalities of our mansion, the brilliant society we shall draw about us, and the beneficial influence we shall exert over the world at large. That's about it, isn't it, Madame Récamier?" asked Laurie with a quizzical look at Amy.

"Time will show. Come away, Impertinence, and don't shock my family by calling me names before their faces," answered Amy, resolving that there should be a home with a good wife in it before she set up a salon as a queen of society.

"How happy those children seem together!" observed Mr. March, finding it difficult to become absorbed in his Aristotle after the young couple had gone.

"Yes, and I think it will last," added Mrs. March, with the restful expression of a pilot who has brought a ship safely into port.

"I know it will. Happy Amy!" and Jo sighed, then smiled brightly as Professor Bhaer opened the gate with an impatient push.

Later in the evening, when his mind had been set at rest about the bootjack, Laurie said suddenly to his wife, "Mrs. Laurence."

"My Lord!"

"That man intends to marry our Jo!"

"I hope so, don't you, dear?"

"Well, my love, I consider him a trump, in the fullest sense of that expressive word, but I do wish he was a little younger and a good deal richer."

"Now, Laurie, don't be too fastidious and worldly-minded. If they love one another it doesn't matter a particle how old they are nor how poor. Women never should marry for money—" Amy caught herself up short as the words escaped her, and looked at her husband, who replied, with malicious gravity.

"Certainly not, though you do hear charming girls say that they intend to do it sometimes. If my memory serves me, you once thought it your duty to make a rich match. That accounts, perhaps, for your marrying a good-for-nothing like me."

"Oh, my dearest boy, don't, don't say that! I forgot you were rich when I said 'Yes'. I'd have married you if you hadn't a penny, and I sometimes wish you were poor that I might show how much I love you." And Amy, who was very dignified in public and very fond in private, gave convincing proofs of the truth of her words.

"You don't really think I am such a mercenary creature as I tried to be once, do you? It would break my heart if you didn't believe that I'd gladly pull in the same boat with you, even if you had to get your living by rowing on the lake."

"Am I an idiot and a brute? How could I think so, when you refused a richer man for me, and won't let me give you half I want to now, when I have the right? Girls do it every day, poor things, and are taught to think it is their only salvation, but you had better lessons, and though I trembled for you at one time, I was not disappointed, for the daughter was true to the mother's teaching. I told Mamma so yesterday, and she looked as glad and grateful as if I'd given her a check for a million, to be spent in charity. You are not listening to my moral remarks, Mrs. Laurence," and Laurie paused, for Amy's eyes had an absent look, though fixed upon his face.

"Yes, I am, and admiring the mole in your chin at the same time. I don't wish to make you vain, but I must confess that I'm prouder of my handsome husband than of all his money. Don't laugh, but your nose is *such* a comfort to me," and Amy softly caressed the well-cut feature with artistic satisfaction.

Laurie had received many compliments in his life, but never one that suited him better, as he plainly showed though he did laugh at his wife's peculiar taste, while she said slowly, "May I ask you a question, dear?"

"Of course, you may."

"Shall you care if Jo does marry Mr. Bhaer?"

"Oh, that's the trouble is it? I thought there was something in the dimple that didn't quite suit you. Not being a dog in the manger, but the happiest fellow alive, I assure you I can dance at Jo's wedding with a heart as light as my heels. Do you doubt it, my darling?"

Amy looked up at him, and was satisfied. Her little jealous fear vanished forever, and she thanked him, with a face full of love and confidence.

"I wish we could do something for that capital old Professor. Couldn't we invent a rich relation, who shall obligingly die out there in Germany, and leave him a tidy little fortune?" said Laurie, when they began to pace up and down the long drawing room, arm in arm, as they were fond of doing, in memory of the château garden.

"Jo would find us out, and spoil it all. She is very proud of him, just as he is, and said yesterday that she thought poverty was a beautiful thing."

"Bless her dear heart! She won't think so when she has a literary husband, and a dozen little professors and professorins to support. We won't interfere now, but watch our chance, and do them a good turn in spite of themselves. I owe Jo for a part of my education, and she believes in people's paying their honest debts, so I'll get round her in that way."

"How delightful it is to be able to help others, isn't it? That was always one of my dreams, to have the power of giving freely, and thanks to you, the dream has come true."

"Ah, we'll do quantities of good, won't we? There's one sort of poverty that I particularly like to help. Out-and-out beggars get taken care of, but poor gentle folks fare badly, because they won't ask, and people don't dare to offer charity. Yet there are a thousand ways of helping them, if one only knows how to do it so delicately that it does not offend. I must say, I like to serve a decayed gentleman better than a blarneying beggar. I suppose it's wrong, but I do, though it is harder."

"Because it takes a gentleman to do it," added the other member of the domestic admiration society.

"Thank you, I'm afraid I don't deserve that pretty compliment. But I was going to say that while I was dawdling about abroad, I saw a good many talented young fellows making all sorts of sacrifices, and enduring real hardships, that they might realize their dreams. Splendid fellows, some of them, working like heroes, poor and friendless, but so full of courage, patience, and ambition that I was ashamed of myself, and longed to give them a right good lift. Those are people whom it's a satisfaction to help, for if they've got genius, it's an honor to be allowed to serve them, and not let it be lost or delayed for want of fuel to keep the pot boiling. If they haven't, it's a pleasure to comfort the poor souls, and keep them from despair when they find it out."

"Yes, indeed, and there's another class who can't ask, and who suffer in silence. I know something of it, for I belonged to it before you made a princess of me, as the king does the beggarmaid in the old story. Ambitious girls have a hard time, Laurie, and often have to see youth, health, and precious opportunities go by, just for want of a little help at the right minute. People have been very kind to me, and whenever I see girls struggling along, as we used to do, I want to put out my hand and help them, as I was helped."

"And so you shall, like an angel as you are!" cried Laurie, resolving, with a glow of philanthropic zeal, to found and endow an institution for the express benefit of young women with artistic tendencies. "Rich people have no right to sit down and enjoy themselves, or let their money accumulate for others to waste. It's not half so sensible to leave legacies when one dies as it is to use the money wisely while alive, and enjoy making one's fellow creatures happy with it. We'll have a good time ourselves, and add an extra relish to our own pleasure by giving other people a generous taste. Will you be a little Dorcas, going about emptying a big basket of comforts, and filling it up with good deeds?"

"With all my heart, if you will be a brave St. Martin, stopping as you ride gallantly through the world to share your cloak with the beggar."

"It's a bargain, and we shall get the best of it!"

So the young pair shook hands upon it, and then paced happily on again, feeling that their pleasant home was more homelike because they hoped to brighten other homes, believing that their own feet would walk more uprightly along the flowery path before them, if they smoothed rough ways for other feet, and feeling that their hearts were more closely knit together by a love which could tenderly remember those less blest than they.

CHAPTER XLV

DAISY AND DEMI

I cannot feel that I have done my duty as humble historian of the March family, without devoting at least one chapter to the two most precious and important members of it. Daisy and Demi had now arrived at years of discretion, for in this fast age babies of three or four assert their rights, and get them, too, which is more than many of their elders do. If there ever were a pair of twins in danger of being utterly spoiled by adoration, it was these prattling Brookes. Of course they were the most remarkable children ever born, as will be shown when I mention that they walked at eight months, talked fluently at twelve months, and at two years they took their places at table, and behaved with a propriety which charmed all beholders. At three, Daisy demanded a "needler," and actually made a bag with four stitches in it. She likewise set up housekeeping in the sideboard, and managed a microscopic cooking stove with a skill that brought tears of pride to Hannah's eyes, while Demi learned his letters with his grandfather, who invented a new mode of teaching the alphabet by forming letters with his arms and legs, thus uniting gymnastics for head and heels. The boy early developed a mechanical genius which delighted his father and distracted his mother, for he tried to imitate every machine he saw, and kept the nursery in a chaotic condition, with his "sewin-sheen," a mysterious structure of string, chairs, clothespins, and spools, for wheels to go "wound and wound." Also a basket hung over the back of a chair, in which he vainly tried to hoist his too confiding sister, who, with feminine devotion, allowed her little head to be bumped till rescued, when the young inventor indignantly remarked, "Why, Marmar, dat's my lellywaiter, and me's trying to pull her up."

Though utterly unlike in character, the twins got on remarkably well together, and seldom quarreled more than thrice a day. Of course, Demi tyrannized over Daisy, and gallantly defended her from every other aggressor, while Daisy made a galley slave of herself, and adored her brother as the one perfect being in the world. A rosy, chubby, sunshiny little soul was Daisy, who found her way to everybody's heart, and nestled there. One of the captivating children, who seem made to be kissed and cuddled, adorned and adored like little goddesses, and produced for general approval on all festive occasions. Her small virtues were so sweet that she would have been quite angelic if a few small naughtinesses had not kept her delightfully human. It was all fair weather in her world, and every morning she scrambled up to the window in her little nightgown to look out, and say, no matter whether it rained or shone, "Oh, pitty day, oh, pitty day!" Everyone was a friend, and she offered kisses to a stranger so confidingly that the most inveterate bachelor relented, and baby-lovers became faithful worshipers.

"Me loves evvybody," she once said, opening her arms, with her spoon in one hand, and her mug in the other, as if eager to embrace and nourish the whole world.

As she grew, her mother began to feel that the Dovecote would be blessed by the presence of an inmate as serene and loving as that which had helped to make the old house home, and to pray that she might be spared a loss like that which had lately taught them how long they had entertained an angel unawares. Her grandfather often called her "Beth," and her grandmother watched over her with untiring devotion, as if trying to atone for some past mistake, which no eye but her own could see.

Demi, like a true Yankee, was of an inquiring turn, wanting to know everything, and often getting much disturbed because he could not get satisfactory answers to his perpetual "What for?"

He also possessed a philosophic bent, to the great delight of his grandfather, who used to hold Socratic conversations with him, in which the precocious pupil occasionally posed his teacher, to the undisguised satisfaction of the womenfolk.

"What makes my legs go, Dranpa?" asked the young philosopher, surveying those active portions of his frame with a meditative air, while resting after a go-to-bed frolic one night.

"It's your little mind, Demi," replied the sage, stroking the yellow head respectfully.

"What is a little mine?"

"It is something which makes your body move, as the spring made the wheels go in my watch when I showed it to you."

"Open me. I want to see it go wound."

"I can't do that any more than you could open the watch. God winds you up, and you go till He stops you."

"Does I?" and Demi's brown eyes grew big and bright as he took in the new thought. "Is I wounded up like the watch?"

"Yes, but I can't show you how, for it is done when we don't see."

Demi felt his back, as if expecting to find it like that of the watch, and then gravely remarked, "I dess Dod does it when I's asleep."

A careful explanation followed, to which he listened so attentively that his anxious grandmother said, "My dear, do you think it wise to talk about such things to that baby? He's getting great bumps over his eyes, and learning to ask the most unanswerable questions."

"If he is old enough to ask the question he is old enough to receive true answers. I am not putting the thoughts into his head, but helping him unfold those already there. These children are wiser than we are, and I have no doubt the boy understands every word I have said to him. Now, Demi, tell me where you keep your mind."

If the boy had replied like Alcibiades, "By the gods, Socrates, I cannot tell," his grandfather would not have been surprised, but when, after standing a moment on one leg, like a meditative young stork, he answered, in a tone of calm conviction, "In my little belly," the old gentleman could only join in Grandma's laugh, and dismiss the class in metaphysics.

There might have been cause for maternal anxiety, if Demi had not given convincing proofs that he was a true boy, as well as a budding philosopher, for often, after a discussion which caused Hannah to prophesy, with ominous nods, "That child ain't long for this world," he would turn about and set her fears at rest by some of the pranks with which dear, dirty, naughty little rascals distract and delight their parents' souls.

Meg made many moral rules, and tried to keep them, but what mother was ever proof against the winning wiles, the ingenious evasions, or the tranquil audacity of the miniature men and women who so early show themselves accomplished Artful Dodgers?

"No more raisins, Demi. They'll make you sick," says Mamma to the young person who offers his services in the kitchen with unfailing regularity on plum-pudding day.

"Me likes to be sick."

"I don't want to have you, so run away and help Daisy make patty cakes."

He reluctantly departs, but his wrongs weigh upon his spirit, and by-and-by when an opportunity comes to redress them, he outwits Mamma by a shrewd bargain.

"Now you have been good children, and I'll play anything you like," says Meg, as she leads her assistant cooks upstairs, when the pudding is safely bouncing in the pot.

"Truly, Marmar?" asks Demi, with a brilliant idea in his well-powdered head.

"Yes, truly. Anything you say," replies the shortsighted parent, preparing herself to sing, "The Three Little Kittens" half a dozen times over, or to take her family to "Buy a penny bun," regardless of wind or limb. But Demi corners her by the cool reply—

"Then we'll go and eat up all the raisins."

Aunt Dodo was chief playmate and confidante of both children, and the trio turned the little house topsy-turvy. Aunt Amy was as yet only a name to them, Aunt Beth soon faded into a pleasantly vague memory, but Aunt Dodo was a living reality, and they made the most of her, for which compliment she was deeply grateful. But when Mr. Bhaer came, Jo neglected her playfellows, and dismay and desolation fell upon their little souls. Daisy, who was fond of going about peddling kisses, lost her best customer and became bankrupt. Demi, with infantile penetration, soon discovered that Dodo like to play with "the bear-man" better than she did him, but though hurt, he concealed his anguish, for he hadn't the heart to insult a rival who kept a mine of chocolate drops in his waistcoat pocket, and a watch that could be taken out of its case and freely shaken by ardent admirers.

Some persons might have considered these pleasing liberties as bribes, but Demi didn't see it in that light, and continued to patronize the "the bear-man" with pensive affability, while Daisy bestowed her small affections upon him at the third call, and considered his shoulder her throne, his arm her refuge, his gifts treasures surpassing worth.

Gentlemen are sometimes seized with sudden fits of admiration for the young relatives of ladies whom they honor with their regard, but this counterfeit philoprogenitiveness sits uneasily upon them, and does not deceive anybody a particle. Mr. Bhaer's devotion was sincere, however likewise effective—for honesty is the best policy in love as in law. He was one of the men who are at home with children, and looked particularly well when little faces made a pleasant contrast with his manly one. His business, whatever it was, detained him from day to day, but evening seldom failed to bring him out to see—well, he always asked for Mr. March, so I suppose *he* was the attraction. The excellent papa labored under the delusion that he was, and reveled in long discussions with the kindred spirit, till a chance remark of his more observing grandson suddenly enlightened him.

Mr. Bhaer came in one evening to pause on the threshold of the study, astonished by the spectacle that met his eye. Prone upon the floor lay Mr. March, with his respectable legs in the air, and beside him, likewise prone, was Demi, trying to imitate the attitude with his own short, scarlet-stockinged legs, both grovelers so seriously absorbed that they were unconscious of spectators, till Mr. Bhaer laughed his sonorous laugh, and Jo cried out, with a scandalized face—

"Father, Father, here's the Professor!"

Down went the black legs and up came the gray head, as the preceptor said, with undisturbed dignity, "Good evening, Mr. Bhaer. Excuse me for a moment. We are just finishing our lesson. Now, Demi, make the letter and tell its name."

"I knows him!" and, after a few convulsive efforts, the red legs took the shape of a pair of compasses, and the intelligent pupil triumphantly shouted, "It's a We, Dranpa, it's a We!"

"He's a born Weller," laughed Jo, as her parent gathered himself up, and her nephew tried to stand on his head, as the only mode of expressing his satisfaction that school was over.

"What have you been at today, *bübchen*?" asked Mr. Bhaer, picking up the gymnast.

"Me went to see little Mary."

"And what did you there?"

"I kissed her," began Demi, with artless frankness.

"Prut! Thou beginnest early. What did the little Mary say to that?" asked Mr. Bhaer, continuing to confess the young sinner, who stood upon the knee, exploring the waistcoat pocket.

"Oh, she liked it, and she kissed me, and I liked it. Don't little boys like little girls?" asked Demi, with his mouth full, and an air of bland satisfaction.

"You precocious chick! Who put that into your head?" said Jo, enjoying the innocent revelation as much as the Professor.

"'Tisn't in mine head, it's in mine mouf," answered literal Demi, putting out his tongue, with a chocolate drop on it, thinking she alluded to confectionery, not ideas.

"Thou shouldst save some for the little friend. Sweets to the sweet, mannling." And Mr. Bhaer offered Jo some, with a look that made her wonder if chocolate was not the nectar drunk by the gods. Demi also saw the smile, was impressed by it, and artlessy inquired—

"Do great boys like great girls, to, 'Fessor?"

Like young Washington, Mr. Bhaer "couldn't tell a lie," so he gave the somewhat vague reply that he believed they did sometimes, in a tone that made Mr. March put down his clothesbrush, glance at Jo's retiring face, and then sink into his chair, looking as if the "precocious chick" had put an idea into *his* head that was both sweet and sour.

Why Dodo, when she caught him in the china closet half an hour afterward, nearly squeezed the breath out of his little body with a tender embrace, instead of shaking him for being there, and why she followed up this novel performance by the unexpected gift of a big slice of bread and jelly, remained one of the problems over which Demi puzzled his small wits, and was forced to leave unsolved forever.

CHAPTER XLVI

UNDER THE UMBRELLA

While Laurie and Amy were taking conjugal strolls over velvet carpets, as they set their house in order, and planned a blissful future, Mr. Bhaer and Jo were enjoying promenades of a different sort, along muddy roads and sodden fields.

"I always do take a walk toward evening, and I don't know why I should give it up, just because I happen to meet the Professor on his way out," said Jo to herself, after two or three encounters, for though there were two paths to Meg's whichever one she took she was sure to meet him, either going or returning. He was always walking rapidly, and never seemed to see her until quite close, when he would look as if his short-sighted eyes had failed to recognize the approaching lady till that moment. Then, if she was going to Meg's he always had something for the babies. If her face was turned homeward, he had merely strolled down to see the river, and was just returning, unless they were tired of his frequent calls.

Under the circumstances, what could Jo do but greet him civilly, and invite him in? If she *was* tired of his visits, she concealed her weariness with perfect skill, and took care that there should be coffee for supper, "as Friedrich—I mean Mr. Bhaer—doesn't like tea."

By the second week, everyone knew perfectly well what was going on, yet everyone tried to look as if they were stone-blind to the changes in Jo's face. They never asked why she sang about her work, did up her hair three times a day, and got so blooming with her evening exercise. And no one seemed to have the slightest suspicion that Professor Bhaer, while talking philosophy with the father, was giving the daughter lessons in love.

Jo couldn't even lose her heart in a decorous manner, but sternly tried to quench her feelings, and failing to do so, led a somewhat agitated life. She was mortally afraid of being laughed at for surrendering, after her many and vehement declarations of independence. Laurie was her especial dread, but thanks to the new manager, he behaved with praiseworthy propriety, never called Mr. Bhaer "a capital old fellow" in public, never alluded, in the remotest manner, to Jo's improved appearance, or expressed the least surprise at seeing the Professor's hat on the Marches' table nearly every evening. But he exulted in private and longed for the time to come when he could give Jo a piece of plate, with a bear and a ragged staff on it as an appropriate coat of arms.

For a fortnight, the Professor came and went with lover-like regularity. Then he stayed away for three whole days, and made no sign, a proceeding which caused everybody to look sober, and Jo to become pensive, at first, and then—alas for romance—very cross.

"Disgusted, I dare say, and gone home as suddenly as he came. It's nothing to me, of course, but I *should* think he would have come and bid us goodbye like a gentleman," she said to herself, with a despairing look at the gate, as she put on her things for the customary walk one dull afternoon.

"You'd better take the little umbrella, dear. It looks like rain," said her mother, observing that she had on her new bonnet, but not alluding to the fact.

"Yes, Marmee, do you want anything in town? I've got to run in and get some paper," returned Jo, pulling out the bow under her chin before the glass as an excuse for not looking at her mother.

"Yes, I want some twilled silesia, a paper of number nine needles, and two yards of narrow lavender ribbon. Have you got your thick boots on, and something warm under your cloak?"

"I believe so," answered Jo absently.

"If you happen to meet Mr. Bhaer, bring him home to tea. I quite long to see the dear man," added Mrs. March.

Jo heard *that*, but made no answer, except to kiss her mother, and walk rapidly away, thinking with a glow of gratitude, in spite of her heartache, "How good she is to me! What *do* girls do who haven't any mothers to help them through their troubles?"

The dry-goods stores were not down among the counting-houses, banks, and wholesale warerooms, where gentlemen most do congregate, but Jo found herself in that part of the city before she did a single errand, loitering along as if waiting for someone, examining engineering instruments in one window and samples of wool in another, with most unfeminine interest, tumbling over barrels, being half-smothered by descending bales, and hustled unceremoniously by busy men who looked as if they wondered "how the deuce she got there." A drop of rain on her cheek recalled her thoughts from baffled hopes to ruined ribbons. For the drops continued to fall, and being a woman as well as a lover, she felt that, though it was too late to save her heart, she might her bonnet. Now she remembered the little umbrella, which she had forgotten to take in her hurry to be off, but regret was unavailing, and nothing could be done but borrow one or submit to a drenching. She looked up at the lowering sky, down at the crimson bow already flecked with black, forward along the muddy street, then one long, lingering look behind, at a certain grimy warehouse, with "Hoffmann, Swartz, & Co." over the door, and said to herself, with a sternly reproachful air—

"It serves me right! what business had I to put on all my best things and come philandering down here, hoping to see the Professor? Jo, I'm ashamed of you! No, you shall *not* go there to borrow an umbrella, or find out where he is, from his friends. You shall trudge away, and do your errands in the rain, and if you catch your death and ruin your bonnet, it's no more than you deserve. Now then!"

With that she rushed across the street so impetuously that she narrowly escaped annihilation from a passing truck, and precipitated herself into the arms of a stately old gentleman, who said, "I beg pardon, ma'am," and looked mortally offended. Somewhat daunted, Jo righted herself, spread her handkerchief over the devoted ribbons, and putting temptation behind her, hurried on, with increasing dampness about the ankles, and much clashing of umbrellas overhead. The fact that a somewhat dilapidated blue one remained stationary above the unprotected bonnet attracted her attention, and looking up, she saw Mr. Bhaer looking down.

"I feel to know the strong-minded lady who goes so bravely under many horse noses, and so fast through much mud. What do you down here, my friend?"

"I'm shopping."

Mr. Bhaer smiled, as he glanced from the pickle factory on one side to the wholesale hide and leather concern on the other, but he only said politely, "You haf no umbrella. May I go also, and take for you the bundles?"

"Yes, thank you."

Jo's cheeks were as red as her ribbon, and she wondered what he thought of her, but she didn't care, for in a minute she found herself walking away arm in arm with her Professor, feeling as if the sun had suddenly burst out with uncommon brilliancy, that the world was all right again, and that one thoroughly happy woman was paddling through the wet that day.

"We thought you had gone," said Jo hastily, for she knew he was looking at her. Her bonnet wasn't big enough to hide her face, and she feared he might think the joy it betrayed unmaidenly.

"Did you believe that I should go with no farewell to those who haf been so heavenly kind to me?" he asked so reproachfully that she felt as if she had insulted him by the suggestion, and answered heartily—

"No, *I* didn't. I knew you were busy about your own affairs, but we rather missed you—Father and Mother especially."

"And you?"

"I'm always glad to see you, sir."

In her anxiety to keep her voice quite calm, Jo made it rather cool, and the frosty little monosyllable at the end seemed to chill the Professor, for his smile vanished, as he said gravely—

"I thank you, and come one more time before I go."

"You *are* going, then?"

"I haf no longer any business here, it is done."

"Successfully, I hope?" said Jo, for the bitterness of disappointment was in that short reply of his.

"I ought to think so, for I haf a way opened to me by which I can make my bread and gif my Junglings much help."

"Tell me, please! I like to know all about the—the boys," said Jo eagerly.

"That is so kind, I gladly tell you. My friends find for me a place in a college, where I teach as at home, and earn enough to make the way smooth for Franz and Emil. For this I should be grateful, should I not?"

"Indeed you should. How splendid it will be to have you doing what you like, and be able to see you often, and the boys!" cried Jo, clinging to the lads as an excuse for the satisfaction she could not help betraying.

"Ah! But we shall not meet often, I fear, this place is at the West."

"So far away!" and Jo left her skirts to their fate, as if it didn't matter now what became of her clothes or herself.

Mr. Bhaer could read several languages, but he had not learned to read women yet. He flattered himself that he knew Jo pretty well, and was, therefore, much amazed by the contradictions of voice, face, and manner, which she showed him in rapid succession that day, for she was in half a dozen different moods in the course of half an hour. When she met him she looked surprised, though it was impossible to help suspecting that she had come for that express purpose. When he offered her his arm, she took it with a look that filled him with delight, but when he asked if she missed him, she gave such a chilly, formal reply that despair fell upon him. On learning his good fortune she almost clapped her hands. Was the joy all for the boys? Then on hearing his destination, she said, "So far away!" in a tone of despair that lifted him on to a pinnacle of hope, but the next minute she tumbled him down again by observing, like one entirely absorbed in the matter—

"Here's the place for my errands. Will you come in? It won't take long."

Jo rather prided herself upon her shopping capabilities, and particularly wished to impress her escort with the neatness and dispatch with which she would accomplish the business. But owing to the flutter she was in, everything went amiss. She upset the tray of needles, forgot the silesia was to be "twilled" till it was cut off, gave the wrong change, and covered herself with confusion by asking for lavender ribbon at the calico counter. Mr. Bhaer stood by, watching her blush and blunder, and as he watched, his own bewilderment seemed to subside, for he was beginning to see that on some occasions, women, like dreams, go by contraries.

When they came out, he put the parcel under his arm with a more cheerful aspect, and splashed through the puddles as if he rather enjoyed it on the whole.

"Should we now do a little what you call shopping for the babies, and haf a farewell feast tonight if I go for my last call at your so pleasant home?" he asked, stopping before a window full of fruit and flowers.

"What will we buy?" asked Jo, ignoring the latter part of his speech, and sniffing the mingled odors with an affectation of delight as they went in.

"May they haf oranges and figs?" asked Mr. Bhaer, with a paternal air.

"They eat them when they can get them."

"Do you care for nuts?"

"Like a squirrel."

"Hamburg grapes. Yes, we shall drink to the Fatherland in those?"

Jo frowned upon that piece of extravagance, and asked why he didn't buy a frail of dates, a cask of raisins, and a bag of almonds, and be done with it? Whereat Mr. Bhaer confiscated her purse, produced his own, and finished the marketing by buying several pounds of grapes, a pot of rosy daisies, and a pretty jar of honey, to be regarded in the light of a demijohn. Then distorting his pockets with knobby bundles, and giving her the flowers to hold, he put up the old umbrella, and they traveled on again.

"Miss Marsch, I haf a great favor to ask of you," began the Professor, after a moist promenade of half a block.

"Yes, sir?" and Jo's heart began to beat so hard she was afraid he would hear it.

"I am bold to say it in spite of the rain, because so short a time remains to me."

"Yes, sir," and Jo nearly crushed the small flowerpot with the sudden squeeze she gave it.

"I wish to get a little dress for my Tina, and I am too stupid to go alone. Will you kindly gif me a word of taste and help?"

"Yes, sir," and Jo felt as calm and cool all of a sudden as if she had stepped into a refrigerator.

"Perhaps also a shawl for Tina's mother, she is so poor and sick, and the husband is such a care. Yes, yes, a thick, warm shawl would be a friendly thing to take the little mother."

"I'll do it with pleasure, Mr. Bhaer. I'm going very fast, and he's getting dearer every minute," added Jo to herself, then with a mental shake she entered into the business with an energy that was pleasant to behold.

Mr. Bhaer left it all to her, so she chose a pretty gown for Tina, and then ordered out the shawls. The clerk, being a married man, condescended to take an interest in the couple, who appeared to be shopping for their family.

"Your lady may prefer this. It's a superior article, a most desirable color, quite chaste and genteel," he said, shaking out a comfortable gray shawl, and throwing it over Jo's shoulders.

"Does this suit you, Mr. Bhaer?" she asked, turning her back to him, and feeling deeply grateful for the chance of hiding her face.

"Excellently well, we will haf it," answered the Professor, smiling to himself as he paid for it, while Jo continued to rummage the counters like a confirmed bargain-hunter.

"Now shall we go home?" he asked, as if the words were very pleasant to him.

"Yes, it's late, and I'm *so* tired." Jo's voice was more pathetic than she knew. For now the sun seemed to have gone in as suddenly as it came out, and the world grew muddy and miserable again, and for the first time she discovered that her feet were cold, her head ached, and that her heart was colder than the former, fuller of pain than the latter. Mr. Bhaer was going away, he only cared for her as a friend, it was all a mistake, and the sooner it was over the better. With this idea in her head, she hailed an approaching omnibus with such a hasty gesture that the daisies flew out of the pot and were badly damaged.

"This is not our omniboos," said the Professor, waving the loaded vehicle away, and stopping to pick up the poor little flowers.

"I beg your pardon. I didn't see the name distinctly. Never mind, I can walk. I'm used to plodding in the mud," returned Jo, winking hard, because she would have died rather than openly wipe her eyes.

Mr. Bhaer saw the drops on her cheeks, though she turned her head away. The sight seemed to touch him very much, for suddenly stooping down, he asked in a tone that meant a great deal, "Heart's dearest, why do you cry?"

Now, if Jo had not been new to this sort of thing she would have said she wasn't crying, had a cold in her head, or told any other feminine fib proper to the occasion. Instead of which, that undignified creature answered, with an irrepressible sob, "Because you are going away."

"*Ach, mein Gott*, that is *so* good!" cried Mr. Bhaer, managing to clasp his hands in spite of the umbrella and the bundles, "Jo, I haf nothing but much love to gif you. I came to see if you could care for it, and I waited to be sure that I was something more than a friend. Am I? Can you make a little place in your heart for old Fritz?" he added, all in one breath.

"Oh, yes!" said Jo, and he was quite satisfied, for she folded both hands over his arm, and looked up at him with an expression that plainly showed how happy she would be to walk through life beside him, even though she had no better shelter than the old umbrella, if he carried it.

It was certainly proposing under difficulties, for even if he had desired to do so, Mr. Bhaer could not go down upon his knees, on account of the mud. Neither could he offer Jo his hand, except figuratively, for both were full. Much less could he indulge in tender remonstrations in the open street, though he was near it. So the only way in which he could express his rapture was to look at her, with an expression which glorified his face to such a degree that there actually seemed to be little rainbows in the drops that sparkled on his beard. If he had not loved Jo very much, I don't think he could have done it *then*, for she looked far from lovely, with her skirts in a deplorable state, her rubber boots splashed to the ankle, and her bonnet a ruin. Fortunately, Mr. Bhaer considered her the most beautiful woman living, and she found him more "Jove-like" than ever, though his hatbrim was quite limp with the little rills trickling thence upon his shoulders (for he held the umbrella all over Jo), and every finger of his gloves needed mending.

Passers-by probably thought them a pair of harmless lunatics, for they entirely forgot to hail a bus, and strolled leisurely along, oblivious of deepening dusk and fog. Little they cared what anybody thought, for they were enjoying the happy hour that seldom comes but once in any life, the magical moment which bestows youth on the old, beauty on the plain, wealth on the poor, and gives human hearts a foretaste of heaven. The Professor looked as if he had conquered a kingdom, and the world had nothing more to offer him in the way of bliss. While Jo trudged beside him, feeling as if her place had always been there, and wondering how she ever could have chosen any other lot. Of course, she was the first to speak—intelligibly, I mean, for the emotional remarks which followed her impetuous "Oh, yes!" were not of a coherent or reportable character.

"Friedrich, why didn't you—"

"Ah, heaven, she gifs me the name that no one speaks since Minna died!" cried the Professor, pausing in a puddle to regard her with grateful delight.

"I always call you so to myself—I forgot, but I won't unless you like it."

"Like it? It is more sweet to me than I can tell. Say 'thou,' also, and I shall say your language is almost as beautiful as mine."

"Isn't 'thou' a little sentimental?" asked Jo, privately thinking it a lovely monosyllable.

"Sentimental? Yes. Thank Gott, we Germans believe in sentiment, and keep ourselves young mit it. Your English 'you' is so cold, say 'thou,' heart's dearest, it means so much to me," pleaded Mr. Bhaer, more like a romantic student than a grave professor.

"Well, then, why didn't thou tell me all this sooner?" asked Jo bashfully.

"Now I shall haf to show thee all my heart, and I so gladly will, because thou must take care of it hereafter. See, then, my Jo—ah, the dear, funny little name—I had a wish to tell something the day I said goodbye in New York, but I thought the handsome friend was betrothed to thee, and so I spoke not. Wouldst thou have said 'Yes,' then, if I had spoken?"

"I don't know. I'm afraid not, for I didn't have any heart just then."

"Prut! That I do not believe. It was asleep till the fairy prince came through the wood, and waked it up. Ah, well, '*Die erste Liebe ist die beste*,' but that I should not expect."

"Yes, the first love *is* the best, but be so contented, for I never had another. Teddy was only a boy, and soon got over his little fancy," said Jo, anxious to correct the Professor's mistake.

"Good! Then I shall rest happy, and be sure that thou givest me all. I haf waited so long, I am grown selfish, as thou wilt find, Professorin."

"I like that," cried Jo, delighted with her new name. "Now tell me what brought you, at last, just when I wanted you?"

"This," and Mr. Bhaer took a little worn paper out of his waistcoat pocket.

Jo unfolded it, and looked much abashed, for it was one of her own contributions to a paper that paid for poetry, which accounted for her sending it an occasional attempt.

"How could that bring you?" she asked, wondering what he meant.

"I found it by chance. I knew it by the names and the initials, and in it there was one little verse that seemed to call me. Read and find him. I will see that you go not in the wet."

Jo obeyed, and hastily skimmed through the lines which she had christened—

IN THE GARRET

Four little chests all in a row,
Dim with dust, and worn by time,
All fashioned and filled, long ago,
By children now in their prime.
Four little keys hung side by side,

With faded ribbons, brave and gay
When fastened there, with childish pride,
Long ago, on a rainy day.
Four little names, one on each lid,
Carved out by a boyish hand,
And underneath there lieth hid
Histories of the happy band
Once playing here, and pausing oft
To hear the sweet refrain,
That came and went on the roof aloft,
In the falling summer rain.

"Meg" on the first lid, smooth and fair.
I look in with loving eyes,
For folded here, with well-known care,
A goodly gathering lies,
The record of a peaceful life—
Gifts to gentle child and girl,
A bridal gown, lines to a wife,
A tiny shoe, a baby curl.
No toys in this first chest remain,
For all are carried away,
In their old age, to join again
In another small Meg's play.
Ah, happy mother! Well I know
You hear, like a sweet refrain,
Lullabies ever soft and low
In the falling summer rain.

"Jo" on the next lid, scratched and worn,
And within a motley store
Of headless dolls, of schoolbooks torn,
Birds and beasts that speak no more,
Spoils brought home from the fairy ground
Only trod by youthful feet,
Dreams of a future never found,
Memories of a past still sweet,
Half-writ poems, stories wild,
April letters, warm and cold,
Diaries of a wilful child,
Hints of a woman early old,
A woman in a lonely home,

Hearing, like a sad refrain—
"Be worthy, love, and love will come,"
In the falling summer rain.

My Beth! the dust is always swept
From the lid that bears your name,
As if by loving eyes that wept,
By careful hands that often came.
Death canonized for us one saint,
Ever less human than divine,
And still we lay, with tender plaint,
Relics in this household shrine—
The silver bell, so seldom rung,
The little cap which last she wore,
The fair, dead Catherine that hung
By angels borne above her door.
The songs she sang, without lament,
In her prison-house of pain,
Forever are they sweetly blent
With the falling summer rain.

Upon the last lid's polished field—
Legend now both fair and true
A gallant knight bears on his shield,
"Amy" in letters gold and blue.
Within lie snoods that bound her hair,
Slippers that have danced their last,
Faded flowers laid by with care,
Fans whose airy toils are past,
Gay valentines, all ardent flames,
Trifles that have borne their part
In girlish hopes and fears and shames,
The record of a maiden heart
Now learning fairer, truer spells,
Hearing, like a blithe refrain,
The silver sound of bridal bells
In the falling summer rain.

Four little chests all in a row,
Dim with dust, and worn by time,
Four women, taught by weal and woe
To love and labor in their prime.

Four sisters, parted for an hour,
None lost, one only gone before,
Made by love's immortal power,
Nearest and dearest evermore.
Oh, when these hidden stores of ours
Lie open to the Father's sight,
May they be rich in golden hours,
Deeds that show fairer for the light,
Lives whose brave music long shall ring,
Like a spirit-stirring strain,
Souls that shall gladly soar and sing
In the long sunshine after rain.

J.M.

"It's very bad poetry, but I felt it when I wrote it, one day when I was very lonely, and had a good cry on a rag bag. I never thought it would go where it could tell tales," said Jo, tearing up the verses the Professor had treasured so long.

"Let it go, it has done its duty, and I will haf a fresh one when I read all the brown book in which she keeps her little secrets," said Mr. Bhaer with a smile as he watched the fragments fly away on the wind. "Yes," he added earnestly, "I read that, and I think to myself, She has a sorrow, she is lonely, she would find comfort in true love. I haf a heart full, full for her. Shall I not go and say, 'If this is not too poor a thing to gif for what I shall hope to receive, take it in Gott's name?'"

"And so you came to find that it was not too poor, but the one precious thing I needed," whispered Jo.

"I had no courage to think that at first, heavenly kind as was your welcome to me. But soon I began to hope, and then I said, 'I will haf her if I die for it,' and so I will!" cried Mr. Bhaer, with a defiant nod, as if the walls of mist closing round them were barriers which he was to surmount or valiantly knock down.

Jo thought that was splendid, and resolved to be worthy of her knight, though he did not come prancing on a charger in gorgeous array.

"What made you stay away so long?" she asked presently, finding it so pleasant to ask confidential questions and get delightful answers that she could not keep silent.

"It was not easy, but I could not find the heart to take you from that so happy home until I could haf a prospect of one to gif you, after much time, perhaps, and hard work. How could I ask you to gif up so much for a poor old fellow, who has no fortune but a little learning?"

"I'm glad you *are* poor. I couldn't bear a rich husband," said Jo decidedly, adding in a softer tone, "Don't fear poverty. I've known it long enough to lose my dread and be happy working for those I love, and don't call yourself old—forty is the prime of life. I couldn't help loving you if you were seventy!"

The Professor found that so touching that he would have been glad of his handkerchief, if he could have got at it. As he couldn't, Jo wiped his eyes for him, and said, laughing, as she took away a bundle or two—

"I may be strong-minded, but no one can say I'm out of my sphere now, for woman's special mission is supposed to be drying tears and bearing burdens. I'm to carry my share, Friedrich, and help to earn the home. Make up your mind to that, or I'll never go," she added resolutely, as he tried to reclaim his load.

"We shall see. Haf you patience to wait a long time, Jo? I must go away and do my work alone. I must help my boys first, because, even for you, I may not break my word to Minna. Can you forgif that, and be happy while we hope and wait?"

"Yes, I know I can, for we love one another, and that makes all the rest easy to bear. I have my duty, also, and my work. I couldn't enjoy myself if I neglected them even for you, so there's no need of hurry or impatience. You can do your part out West, I can do mine here, and both be happy hoping for the best, and leaving the future to be as God wills."

"Ah! Thou gifest me such hope and courage, and I haf nothing to gif back but a full heart and these empty hands," cried the Professor, quite overcome.

Jo never, never would learn to be proper, for when he said that as they stood upon the steps, she just put both hands into his, whispering tenderly, "Not empty now," and stooping down, kissed her Friedrich under the umbrella. It was dreadful, but she would have done it if the flock of draggle-tailed sparrows on the hedge had been human beings, for she was very far gone indeed, and quite regardless of everything but her own happiness. Though it came in such a very simple guise, that was the crowning moment of both their lives, when, turning from the night and storm and loneliness to the household light and warmth and peace waiting to receive them, with a glad "Welcome home!" Jo led her lover in, and shut the door.

CHAPTER XLVII

HARVEST TIME

For a year Jo and her Professor worked and waited, hoped and loved, met occasionally, and wrote such voluminous letters that the rise in the price of paper was accounted for, Laurie said. The second year began rather soberly, for their prospects did not brighten, and Aunt March died suddenly. But when their first sorrow was over—for they loved the old lady in spite of her sharp tongue—they found they had cause for rejoicing, for she had left Plumfield to Jo, which made all sorts of joyful things possible.

"It's a fine old place, and will bring a handsome sum, for of course you intend to sell it," said Laurie, as they were all talking the matter over some weeks later.

"No, I don't," was Jo's decided answer, as she petted the fat poodle, whom she had adopted, out of respect to his former mistress.

"You don't mean to live there?"

"Yes, I do."

"But, my dear girl, it's an immense house, and will take a power of money to keep it in order. The garden and orchard alone need two or three men, and farming isn't in Bhaer's line, I take it."

"He'll try his hand at it there, if I propose it."

"And you expect to live on the produce of the place? Well, that sounds paradisiacal, but you'll find it desperate hard work."

"The crop we are going to raise is a profitable one," and Jo laughed.

"Of what is this fine crop to consist, ma'am?"

"Boys. I want to open a school for little lads—a good, happy, homelike school, with me to take care of them and Fritz to teach them."

"That's a truly Joian plan for you! Isn't that just like her?" cried Laurie, appealing to the family, who looked as much surprised as he.

"I like it," said Mrs. March decidedly.

"So do I," added her husband, who welcomed the thought of a chance for trying the Socratic method of education on modern youth.

"It will be an immense care for Jo," said Meg, stroking the head of her one all-absorbing son.

"Jo can do it, and be happy in it. It's a splendid idea. Tell us all about it," cried Mr. Laurence, who had been longing to lend the lovers a hand, but knew that they would refuse his help.

"I knew you'd stand by me, sir. Amy does too—I see it in her eyes, though she prudently waits to turn it over in her mind before she speaks. Now, my dear people," continued Jo earnestly, "just understand that this isn't a new idea of mine, but a long cherished plan. Before my Fritz came, I used to think how, when I'd made my fortune, and no one needed me at home, I'd hire a big house, and pick up some poor, forlorn little lads who hadn't any mothers, and take care of them, and make life jolly for them before it was too late. I see so many going to ruin for want of help at the right minute, I love so to do anything for them, I seem to feel their wants, and sympathize with their troubles, and oh, I should so like to be a mother to them!"

Mrs. March held out her hand to Jo, who took it, smiling, with tears in her eyes, and went on in the old enthusiastic way, which they had not seen for a long while.

"I told my plan to Fritz once, and he said it was just what he would like, and agreed to try it when we got rich. Bless his dear heart, he's been doing it all his life—helping poor boys, I mean, not getting rich, that he'll never be. Money doesn't stay in his pocket long enough to lay up any. But now, thanks to my good old aunt, who loved me better than I ever deserved, *I'm* rich, at least I feel so, and we can live at Plumfield perfectly well, if we have a flourishing school. It's just the place for boys, the house is big, and the furniture strong and plain. There's plenty of room for dozens inside, and splendid grounds outside. They could help in the garden and orchard. Such work is healthy, isn't it, sir? Then Fritz could train and teach in his own way, and Father will help him. I can feed and nurse and pet and scold them, and Mother will be my stand-by. I've always longed for lots of boys, and never had enough, now I can fill the house full and revel in the little dears to my heart's content. Think what luxury—Plumfield my own, and a wilderness of boys to enjoy it with me."

As Jo waved her hands and gave a sigh of rapture, the family went off into a gale of merriment, and Mr. Laurence laughed till they thought he'd have an apoplectic fit.

"I don't see anything funny," she said gravely, when she could be heard. "Nothing could be more natural and proper than for my

Professor to open a school, and for me to prefer to reside in my own estate."

"She is putting on airs already," said Laurie, who regarded the idea in the light of a capital joke. "But may I inquire how you intend to support the establishment? If all the pupils are little ragamuffins, I'm afraid your crop won't be profitable in a worldly sense, Mrs. Bhaer."

"Now don't be a wet-blanket, Teddy. Of course I shall have rich pupils, also—perhaps begin with such altogether. Then, when I've got a start, I can take in a ragamuffin or two, just for a relish. Rich people's children often need care and comfort, as well as poor. I've seen unfortunate little creatures left to servants, or backward ones pushed forward, when it's real cruelty. Some are naughty through mismanagment or neglect, and some lose their mothers. Besides, the best have to get through the hobbledehoy age, and that's the very time they need most patience and kindness. People laugh at them, and hustle them about, try to keep them out of sight, and expect them to turn all at once from pretty children into fine young men. They don't complain much—plucky little souls—but they feel it. I've been through something of it, and I know all about it. I've a special interest in such young bears, and like to show them that I see the warm, honest, well-meaning boys' hearts, in spite of the clumsy arms and legs and the topsy-turvy heads. I've had experience, too, for haven't I brought up one boy to be a pride and honor to his family?"

"I'll testify that you tried to do it," said Laurie with a grateful look.

"And I've succeeded beyond my hopes, for here you are, a steady, sensible businessman, doing heaps of good with your money, and laying up the blessings of the poor, instead of dollars. But you are not merely a businessman, you love good and beautiful things, enjoy them yourself, and let others go halves, as you always did in the old times. I am proud of you, Teddy, for you get better every year, and everyone feels it, though you won't let them say so. Yes, and when I have my flock, I'll just point to you, and say 'There's your model, my lads.'"

Poor Laurie didn't know where to look, for, man though he was, something of the old bashfulness came over him as this burst of praise made all faces turn approvingly upon him.

"I say, Jo, that's rather too much," he began, just in his old boyish way. "You have all done more for me than I can ever thank you for, except by doing my best not to disappoint you. You have rather cast me off lately, Jo, but I've had the best of help, nevertheless. So, if I've got on at all, you may thank these two for it," and he laid one hand gently on his grandfather's head, and the other on Amy's golden one, for the three were never far apart.

"I do think that families are the most beautiful things in all the world!" burst out Jo, who was in an unusually up-lifted frame of mind just then. "When I have one of my own, I hope it will be as happy as the three I know and love the best. If John and my Fritz were only here, it would be quite a little heaven on earth," she added more quietly. And that night when she went to her room after a blissful evening of family counsels, hopes, and plans, her heart was so full of happiness that she could only calm it by kneeling beside the empty bed always near her own, and thinking tender thoughts of Beth.

It was a very astonishing year altogether, for things seemed to happen in an unusually rapid and delightful manner. Almost before she knew where she was, Jo found herself married and settled at Plumfield. Then a family of six or seven boys sprung up like mushrooms, and flourished surprisingly, poor boys as well as rich, for Mr. Laurence was continually finding some touching case of destitution, and begging the Bhaers to take pity on the child, and he would gladly pay a trifle for its support. In this way, the sly old gentleman got round proud Jo, and furnished her with the style of boy in which she most delighted.

Of course it was uphill work at first, and Jo made queer mistakes, but the wise Professor steered her safely into calmer waters, and the most rampant ragamuffin was conquered in the end. How Jo did enjoy her "wilderness of boys," and how poor, dear Aunt March would have lamented had she been there to see the sacred precincts of prim, well-ordered Plumfield overrun with Toms, Dicks, and Harrys! There was a sort of poetic justice about it, after all, for the old lady had been the terror of the boys for miles around, and now the exiles feasted freely on forbidden plums, kicked up the gravel with profane boots unreproved, and played cricket in the big field where the irritable "cow with a crumpled horn" used to invite rash youths to come and be tossed. It became a sort of boys' paradise, and Laurie suggested that it should be called the "Bhaer-garten," as a compliment to its master and appropriate to its inhabitants.

It never was a fashionable school, and the Professor did not lay up a fortune, but it *was* just what Jo intended it to be—"a happy, homelike place for boys, who needed teaching, care, and kindness." Every room in the big house was soon full. Every little plot in the garden soon had its owner. A regular menagerie appeared in barn and shed, for pet animals were allowed. And three times a day, Jo smiled at her Fritz from the head of a long table lined on either side with rows of happy young faces, which all turned to her with affectionate eyes, confiding words, and grateful hearts, full of love for "Mother Bhaer." She had boys enough now, and did not tire of them, though they were not angels, by any means, and some of them caused both Professor and Professorin much trouble and anxiety. But her faith in the good spot which exists in the heart of the naughtiest, sauciest, most tantalizing little ragamuffin gave her patience, skill, and in time success, for no mortal boy could hold out long with Father Bhaer shining on him as benevolently as the sun, and Mother Bhaer forgiving him seventy times seven. Very precious to Jo was the friendship of the lads, their penitent sniffs and whispers after wrongdoing, their droll or touching little confidences, their pleasant enthusiasms, hopes, and plans, even their misfortunes, for they only endeared them to her all the more. There were slow boys and bashful boys, feeble boys and riotous boys, boys that lisped and boys that stuttered, one or two lame ones, and a merry little quadroon, who could not be taken in elsewhere, but who was welcome to the "Bhaer-garten," though some people predicted that his admission would ruin the school.

Yes, Jo was a very happy woman there, in spite of hard work, much anxiety, and a perpetual racket. She enjoyed it heartily and found the applause of her boys more satisfying than any praise of the world, for now she told no stories except to her flock of enthusiastic believers and admirers. As the years went on, two little lads of her own came to increase her happiness—Rob, named for Grandpa, and Teddy, a happy-go-lucky baby, who seemed to have inherited his papa's sunshiny temper as well as his mother's lively spirit. How they ever grew up alive in that whirlpool of boys was a mystery to their grandma and aunts, but they flourished like dandelions in spring, and their rough nurses loved and served them well.

There were a great many holidays at Plumfield, and one of the most delightful was the yearly apple-picking. For then the Marches, Laurences, Brookes, and Bhaers turned out in full force and made a day of it. Five years after Jo's wedding, one of these fruitful festivals occurred, a mellow October day, when the air was full of an exhilarating freshness which made the spirits rise and the blood dance healthily in the veins. The old orchard wore its holiday attire. Goldenrod and asters fringed the mossy walls. Grasshoppers skipped briskly in the sere grass, and crickets chirped like fairy pipers at a feast. Squirrels were busy with their small harvesting. Birds twittered their adieux from the alders in the lane, and every tree stood ready to send down its shower of red or yellow apples at the first shake. Everybody was there. Everybody laughed and sang, climbed up and tumbled down. Everybody declared that there never had been such a perfect day or such a jolly set to enjoy it, and everyone gave themselves up to the simple pleasures of the hour as freely as if there were no such things as care or sorrow in the world.

Mr. March strolled placidly about, quoting Tusser, Cowley, and Columella to Mr. Laurence, while enjoying—

> The gentle apple's winey juice.

The Professor charged up and down the green aisles like a stout Teutonic knight, with a pole for a lance, leading on the boys, who made a hook and ladder company of themselves, and performed wonders in the way of ground and lofty tumbling. Laurie devoted himself to the little ones, rode his small daughter in a bushel-basket, took Daisy up among the bird's nests, and kept adventurous Rob from breaking his neck. Mrs. March and Meg sat among the apple piles like a pair of Pomonas, sorting the contributions that kept pouring in, while Amy with a beautiful motherly expression in her face sketched the various groups, and watched over one pale lad, who sat adoring her with his little crutch beside him.

Jo was in her element that day, and rushed about, with her gown pinned up, and her hat anywhere but on her head, and her baby tucked under her arm, ready for any lively adventure which might turn up. Little Teddy bore a charmed life, for nothing ever happened to him, and Jo never felt any anxiety when he was whisked up into a tree by one lad, galloped off on the back of another, or supplied with sour russets by his indulgent papa, who labored under the Germanic delusion that babies could digest anything, from pickled cabbage to buttons, nails, and their own small shoes. She knew that little Ted would turn up again in time, safe and rosy, dirty and serene, and she always received him back with a hearty welcome, for Jo loved her babies tenderly.

At four o'clock a lull took place, and baskets remained empty, while the apple pickers rested and compared rents and bruises. Then Jo and Meg, with a detachment of the bigger boys, set forth the supper on the grass, for an out-of-door tea was always the crowning joy of the day. The land literally flowed with milk and honey on such occasions, for the lads were not required to sit at table, but allowed to partake of refreshment as they liked—freedom being the sauce best beloved by the boyish soul. They availed themselves of the rare privilege to the fullest extent, for some tried the pleasing experiment of drinking milk while standing on their heads, others lent a charm to leapfrog by eating pie in the pauses of the game, cookies were sown broadcast over the field, and apple turnovers roosted in the trees like a new style of bird. The little girls had a private tea party, and Ted roved among the edibles at his own sweet will.

When no one could eat any more, the Professor proposed the first regular toast, which was always drunk at such times—"Aunt March, God bless her!" A toast heartily given by the good man, who never forgot how much he owed her, and quietly drunk by the boys, who had been taught to keep her memory green.

"Now, Grandma's sixtieth birthday! Long life to her, with three times three!"

That was given with a will, as you may well believe, and the cheering once begun, it was hard to stop it. Everybody's health was proposed, from Mr. Laurence, who was considered their special patron, to the astonished guinea pig, who had strayed from its proper sphere in search of its young master. Demi, as the oldest grandchild, then presented the queen of the day with various gifts, so numerous that they were transported to the festive scene in a wheelbarrow. Funny presents, some of them, but what would have been defects to other eyes were ornaments to Grandma's—for the children's gifts were all their own. Every stitch Daisy's patient little fingers had put into the handkerchiefs she hemmed was better than embroidery to Mrs. March. Demi's miracle of mechanical skill, though the cover wouldn't shut, Rob's footstool had a wiggle in its uneven legs that she declared was soothing, and no page of the costly book Amy's child gave her was so fair as that on which appeared in tipsy capitals, the words—"To dear Grandma, from her little Beth."

During the ceremony the boys had mysteriously disappeared, and when Mrs. March had tried to thank her children, and broken down, while Teddy wiped her eyes on his pinafore, the Professor suddenly began to sing. Then, from above him, voice after voice took up the words, and from tree to tree echoed the music of the unseen choir, as the boys sang with all their hearts the little song that Jo had written, Laurie set to music, and the Professor trained his lads to give with the best effect. This was something altogether new, and it proved a grand success, for Mrs. March couldn't get over her surprise, and insisted on shaking hands with every one of the featherless birds, from tall Franz and Emil to the little quadroon, who had the sweetest voice of all.

After this, the boys dispersed for a final lark, leaving Mrs. March and her daughters under the festival tree.

"I don't think I ever ought to call myself 'unlucky Jo' again, when my greatest wish has been so beautifully gratified," said Mrs. Bhaer, taking Teddy's little fist out of the milk pitcher, in which he was rapturously churning.

"And yet your life is very different from the one you pictured so long ago. Do you remember our castles in the air?" asked Amy, smiling as she watched Laurie and John playing cricket with the boys.

"Dear fellows! It does my heart good to see them forget business and frolic for a day," answered Jo, who now spoke in a maternal way of all mankind. "Yes, I remember, but the life I wanted then seems selfish, lonely, and cold to me now. I haven't given up the hope that I may write a good book yet, but I can wait, and I'm sure it will be all the better for such experiences and illustrations as these," and Jo pointed from the lively lads in the distance to her father, leaning on the Professor's arm, as they walked to and fro in the sunshine, deep in one of the conversations which both enjoyed so much, and then to her mother, sitting enthroned among her daughters, with their children in her lap and at her feet, as if all found help and happiness in the face which never could grow old to them.

"My castle was the most nearly realized of all. I asked for splendid things, to be sure, but in my heart I knew I should be satisfied, if I had a little home, and John, and some dear children like these. I've got them all, thank God, and am the happiest woman in the world," and Meg laid her hand on her tall boy's head, with a face full of tender and devout content.

"My castle is very different from what I planned, but I would not alter it, though, like Jo, I don't relinquish all my artistic hopes, or confine myself to helping others fulfill their dreams of beauty. I've begun to model a figure of baby, and Laurie says it is the best thing I've ever done. I think so, myself, and mean to do it in marble, so that, whatever happens, I may at least keep the image of my little angel."

As Amy spoke, a great tear dropped on the golden hair of the sleeping child in her arms, for her one well-beloved daughter was a frail little creature and the dread of losing her was the shadow over Amy's sunshine. This cross was doing much for both father and mother, for one love and sorrow bound them closely together. Amy's nature was growing sweeter, deeper, and more tender. Laurie was growing more serious, strong, and firm, and both were learning that beauty, youth, good fortune, even love itself, cannot keep care and pain, loss and sorrow, from the most blessed for—

> Into each life some rain must fall,
> Some days must be dark and sad and dreary.

"She is growing better, I am sure of it, my dear. Don't despond, but hope and keep happy," said Mrs. March, as tenderhearted Daisy stooped from her knee to lay her rosy cheek against her little cousin's pale one.

"I never ought to, while I have you to cheer me up, Marmee, and Laurie to take more than half of every burden," replied Amy warmly. "He never lets me see his anxiety, but is so sweet and patient with me, so devoted to Beth, and such a stay and comfort to me always that I can't love him enough. So, in spite of my one cross, I can say with Meg, 'Thank God, I'm a happy woman.'"

"There's no need for me to say it, for everyone can see that I'm far happier than I deserve," added Jo, glancing from her good husband to her chubby children, tumbling on the grass beside her. "Fritz is getting gray and stout. I'm growing as thin as a shadow, and am thirty. We never shall be rich, and Plumfield may burn up any night, for that incorrigible Tommy Bangs *will* smoke sweet-fern cigars under the bed-clothes, though he's set himself afire three times already. But in spite of these unromantic facts, I have nothing to complain of, and never was so jolly in my life. Excuse the remark, but living among boys, I can't help using their expressions now and then."

"Yes, Jo, I think your harvest will be a good one," began Mrs.

March, frightening away a big black cricket that was staring Teddy out of countenance.

"Not half so good as yours, Mother. Here it is, and we never can thank you enough for the patient sowing and reaping you have done," cried Jo, with the loving impetuosity which she never would outgrow.

"I hope there will be more wheat and fewer tares every year," said Amy softly.

"A large sheaf, but I know there's room in your heart for it, Marmee dear," added Meg's tender voice.

Touched to the heart, Mrs. March could only stretch out her arms, as if to gather children and grandchildren to herself, and say, with face and voice full of motherly love, gratitude, and humility—

"Oh, my girls, however long you may live, I never can wish you a greater happiness than this!"

Word Cloud Classics

12 Years a Slave

A Christmas Carol and Other Holiday Treasures

Adventures of Huckleberry Finn

The Adventures of Sherlock Holmes

Aesop's Fables

The Age of Innocence

Anna Karenina

Anne of Green Gables

The Art of War

Black Beauty

The Brothers Grimm 101 Fairy Tales

The Brothers Grimm Volume II: 110 Grimmer Fairy Tales

Common Sense and Selected Works of Thomas Paine

The Count of Monte Cristo

Don Quixote

Dracula

Emma

Frankenstein

Great Expectations

Hans Christian Andersen Tales

Inferno

Jane Eyre

The Jungle Book

Lady Chatterley's Lover

Leaves of Grass

Les Misérables

Word Cloud Classics

Little Women

Madame Bovary

Moby-Dick

Narrative of the Life of Frederick Douglass and Other Works

Persuasion

Peter Pan

The Picture of Dorian Gray

The Poetry of Emily Dickinson

Pride and Prejudice

The Prince and Other Writings

The Red Badge of Courage and Other Stories

The Romantic Poets

The Scarlet Letter

The Secret Garden

Sense and Sensibility

Strange Case of Dr. Jekyll and Mr. Hyde & Other Stories

The Three Musketeers

Treasure Island

Twenty Thousand Leagues Under the Sea

Uncle Tom's Cabin, or Life Among the Lowly

The U.S. Constitution and Other Key American Writings

Walden and Civil Disobedience

The Wizard of Oz

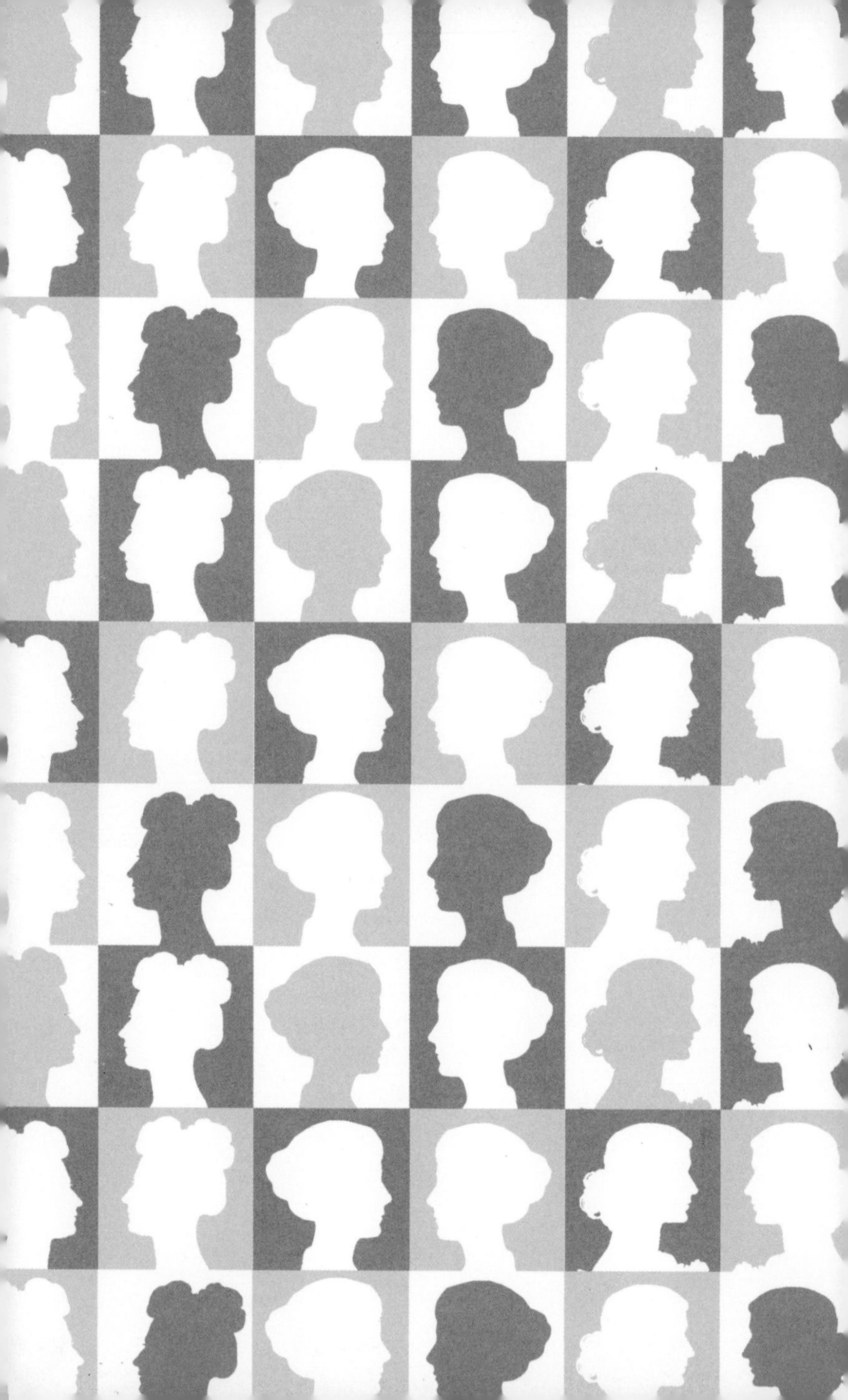

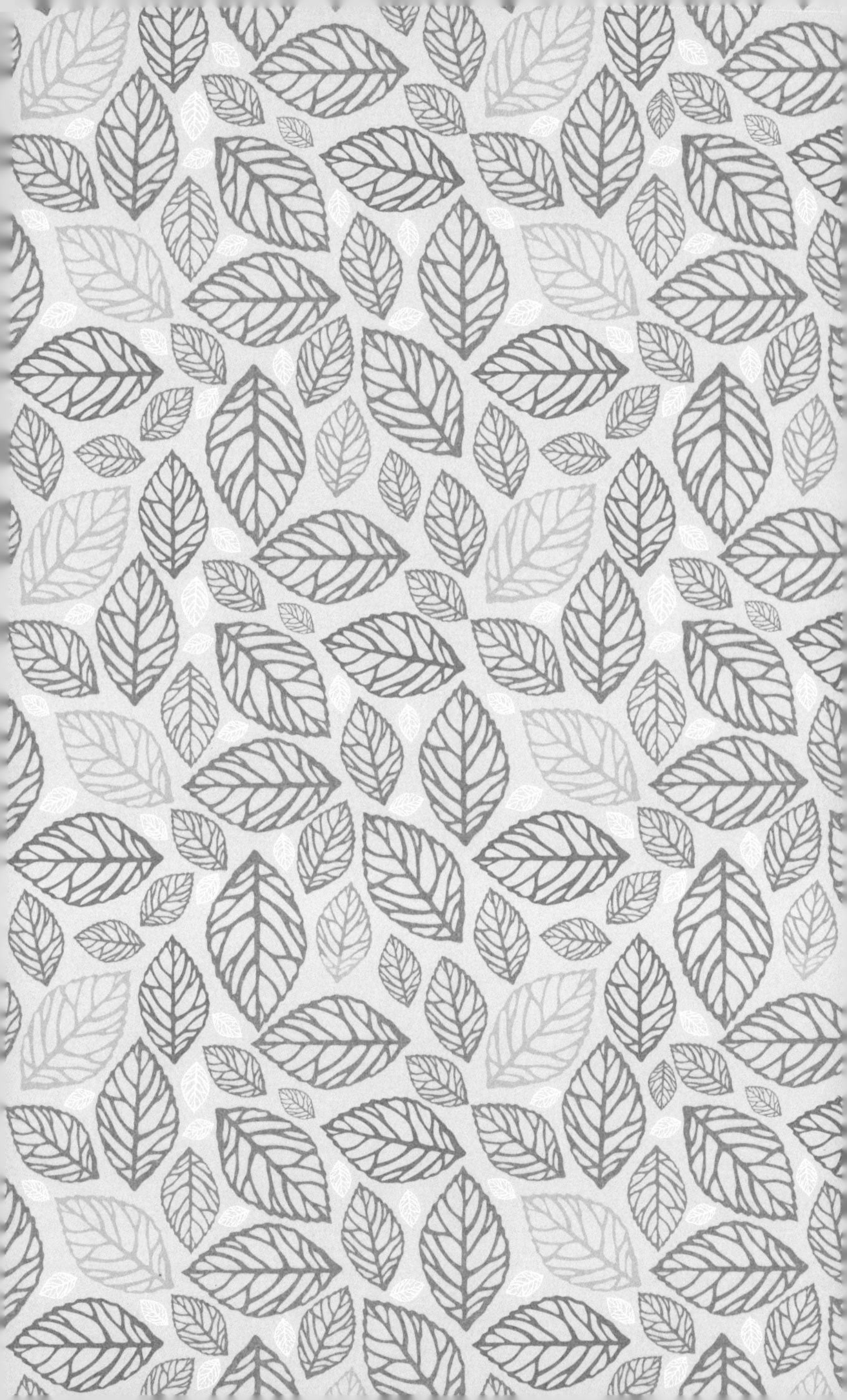

The Secret Garden

Word Cloud Classics

A Christmas Carol and Other Holiday Treasures

Adventures of Huckleberry Finn

The Adventures of Sherlock Holmes

Aesop's Fables

The Age of Innocence

Anna Karenina

Anne of Green Gables

The Art of War

The Brothers Grimm: 101 Fairy Tales

The Brothers Grimm Volume II: 110 Grimmer Fairy Tales

Common Sense and Selected Works of Thomas Paine

The Count of Monte Cristo

Don Quixote

Dracula

Emma

Frankenstein

Great Expectations

Inferno

Jane Eyre

Lady Chatterley's Lover

Les Misérables

Little Women

Madame Bovary

Moby-Dick

Narrative of the Life of Frederick Douglass and Other Works

Persuasion

The Picture of Dorian Gray

Pride and Prejudice

The Prince and Other Writings

The Red Badge of Courage and Other Stories

The Scarlet Letter

Sense and Sensibility

The Three Musketeers

Twenty Thousand Leagues Under the Sea

Uncle Tom's Cabin

Walden and Civil Disobedience

The Wizard of Oz

The Secret Garden

By Frances Hodgson Burnett

CANTERBURY CLASSICS
San Diego

All correspondence concerning the content of
this book should be addressed to:
Canterbury Classics
10350 Barnes Canyon Road, Suite 100
San Diego, CA 92121

Publisher: Peter Norton
Publishing Team: Lori Asbury, Ana Parker
Director Editorial and Production: JoAnn Padgett
Editor: Melinda Allman

Library of Congress Cataloging-in-Publication Data

Burnett, Frances Hodgson, 1849-1924.
The secret garden / Frances Hodgson Burnett.
p. cm.
Summary: Ten-year-old orphan Mary Lennox comes to live in a lonely house on the Yorkshire moors and discovers an invalid cousin and the mysteries of a locked garden.
ISBN 978-1-60710-729-3 (pbk.)
[1. Orphans--Fiction. 2. Gardens--Fiction. 3. Friendship--Fiction. 4. People with disabilities--Fiction. 5. Yorkshire (England)--History--20th century--Fiction. 6. Great Britain--History--Edward VII, 1901-1910--Fiction.] I. Title.

PZ7.B934Se 2013
[Fic]--dc23

2012028130

PRINTED IN CHINA

4 5 6 7 8 19 18 17 16 15

CONTENTS

CHAPTER I

THERE IS NO ONE LEFT

When Mary Lennox was sent to Misselthwaite Manor to live with her uncle everybody said she was the most disagreeable-looking child ever seen. It was true, too. She had a little thin face and a little thin body, thin light hair and a sour expression. Her hair was yellow, and her face was yellow because she had been born in India and had always been ill in one way or another. Her father had held a position under the English Government and had always been busy and ill himself, and her mother had been a great beauty who cared only to go to parties and amuse herself with gay people. She had not wanted a little girl at all, and when Mary was born she handed her over to the care of an Ayah, who was made to understand that if she wished to please the Mem Sahib she must keep the child out of sight as much as possible. So when she was a sickly, fretful, ugly little baby she was kept out of the way, and when she became a sickly, fretful, toddling thing she was kept out of the way also. She never remembered seeing familiarly anything but the dark faces of her Ayah and the other native servants, and as they always obeyed her and gave her her own way in everything, because the Mem Sahib would be angry if she was disturbed by her crying, by the time she was six years old she was as tyrannical and selfish a little pig as ever lived. The young English governess who came to teach her to read and write disliked her so much that she gave up her place in three months, and when other governesses came to try to fill it they always went away in a shorter time than the first one. So if Mary had not chosen to really want to know how to read books she would never have learned her letters at all.

One frightfully hot morning, when she was about nine years old, she awakened feeling very cross, and she became crosser still when she saw that the servant who stood by her bedside was not her Ayah.

"Why did you come?" she said to the strange woman. "I will not let you stay. Send my Ayah to me."

The woman looked frightened, but she only stammered that the Ayah could not come and when Mary threw herself into a passion and beat and kicked her, she looked only more frightened and repeated that it was not possible for the Ayah to come to Missie Sahib.

There was something mysterious in the air that morning. Nothing was done in its regular order and several of the native servants seemed missing, while those whom Mary saw slunk or hurried about with ashy and scared faces. But no one would tell her anything and her Ayah did not come. She was actually left alone as the morning went on, and at last she wandered out into the garden and began to play by herself under a tree near the veranda. She pretended that she was making a flower-bed, and she stuck big scarlet hibiscus blossoms into little heaps of earth, all the time growing more and more angry and muttering to herself the things she would say and the names she would call Saidie when she returned.

"Pig! Pig! Daughter of Pigs!" she said, because to call a native a pig is the worst insult of all.

She was grinding her teeth and saying this over and over again when she heard her mother come out on the veranda with some one. She was with a fair young man and they stood talking together in low strange voices. Mary knew the fair young man who looked like a boy. She had heard that he was a very young officer who had just come from England. The child stared at him, but she stared most at her mother. She always did this when she had a chance to see her, because the Mem Sahib—Mary used to call her that oftener than anything else—was such a tall, slim, pretty person and wore such lovely clothes. Her hair was like curly silk and she had a delicate little nose which seemed to be disdaining things, and she had large laughing eyes. All her clothes were thin and floating, and Mary said they were "full of lace." They looked fuller of lace than ever this morning, but her eyes were not laughing at all. They were large and scared and lifted imploringly to the fair boy officer's face.

"Is it so very bad? Oh, is it?" Mary heard her say.

"Awfully," the young man answered in a trembling voice. "Awfully, Mrs. Lennox. You ought to have gone to the hills two weeks ago."

The Mem Sahib wrung her hands.

"Oh, I know I ought!" she cried. "I only stayed to go to that silly dinner party. What a fool I was!"

At that very moment such a loud sound of wailing broke out from the servants' quarters that she clutched the young man's arm, and Mary stood shivering from head to foot. The wailing grew wilder and wilder. "What is it? What is it?" Mrs. Lennox gasped.

"Some one has died," answered the boy officer. "You did not say it had broken out among your servants."

"I did not know!" the Mem Sahib cried. "Come with me! Come with me!" and she turned and ran into the house.

After that, appalling things happened, and the mysteriousness of the morning was explained to Mary. The cholera had broken out in its most fatal form and people were dying like flies. The Ayah had been taken ill in the night, and it was because she had just died that the servants had wailed in the huts. Before the next day three other servants were dead and others had run away in terror. There was panic on every side, and dying people in all the bungalows.

During the confusion and bewilderment of the second day Mary hid herself in the nursery and was forgotten by everyone. Nobody thought of her, nobody wanted her, and strange things happened of which she knew nothing. Mary alternately cried and slept through the hours. She only knew that people were ill and that she heard mysterious and frightening sounds. Once she crept into the dining-room and found it empty, though a partly finished meal was on the table and chairs and plates looked as if they had been hastily pushed back when the diners rose suddenly for some reason. The child ate some fruit and biscuits, and being thirsty she drank a glass of wine which stood nearly filled. It was sweet, and she did not know how strong it was. Very soon it made her intensely drowsy, and she went back to her nursery and shut herself in again, frightened by cries she heard in the huts and by the hurrying sound of feet. The wine made her so sleepy that she could scarcely keep her eyes open and she lay down on her bed and knew nothing more for a long time.

Many things happened during the hours in which she slept so heavily, but she was not disturbed by the wails and the sound of things being carried in and out of the bungalow.

When she awakened she lay and stared at the wall. The house was perfectly still. She had never known it to be so silent before. She heard neither voices nor footsteps, and wondered if everybody had got well of the cholera and all the trouble was over. She wondered also who would take care of her now her Ayah was dead. There would be a new Ayah, and perhaps she would know some new stories. Mary had been rather tired of the old ones. She did not cry because her nurse had died. She was not an affectionate child and had never cared much for any one. The noise and hurrying about and wailing over the cholera had frightened her, and she had been angry because no one seemed to remember that she was alive. Everyone was too panic-stricken to think of a little girl no one was fond of. When people had the cholera it seemed that they remembered nothing but themselves. But if everyone had got well again, surely some one would remember and come to look for her.

But no one came, and as she lay waiting the house seemed to grow more and more silent. She heard something rustling on the matting and when she looked down she saw a little snake gliding along and watching her with eyes like jewels. She was not frightened, because he was a harmless little thing who would not hurt her and he seemed in a hurry to get out of the room. He slipped under the door as she watched him.

"How queer and quiet it is," she said. "It sounds as if there were no one in the bungalow but me and the snake."

Almost the next minute she heard footsteps in the compound, and then on the veranda. They were men's footsteps, and the men entered the bungalow and talked in low voices. No one went to meet or speak to them and they seemed to open doors and look into rooms. "What desolation!" she heard one voice say. "That pretty, pretty woman! I suppose the child, too. I heard there was a child, though no one ever saw her."

Mary was standing in the middle of the nursery when they opened the door a few minutes later. She looked an ugly, cross little thing and was frowning because she was beginning to be hungry and feel disgracefully neglected. The first man who came in was a large officer she had once seen talking to her father. He looked tired and troubled, but when he saw her he was so startled that he almost jumped back.

"Barney!" he cried out. "There is a child here! A child alone! In a place like this! Mercy on us, who is she!"

"I am Mary Lennox," the little girl said, drawing herself up stiffly. She thought the man was very rude to call her father's bungalow "A place like this!" "I fell asleep when everyone had the cholera and I have only just wakened up. Why does nobody come?"

"It is the child no one ever saw!" exclaimed the man, turning to his companions. "She has actually been forgotten!"

"Why was I forgotten?" Mary said, stamping her foot. "Why does nobody come?"

The young man whose name was Barney looked at her very sadly. Mary even thought she saw him wink his eyes as if to wink tears away.

"Poor little kid!" he said. "There is nobody left to come."

It was in that strange and sudden way that Mary found out that she had neither father nor mother left; that they had died and been carried away in the night, and that the few native servants who had not died also had left the house as quickly as they could get out of it, none of them even remembering that there was a Missie Sahib. That was why the place was so quiet. It was true that there was no one in the bungalow but herself and the little rustling snake.

CHAPTER II

MISTRESS MARY QUITE CONTRARY

Mary had liked to look at her mother from a distance and she had thought her very pretty, but as she knew very little of her she could scarcely have been expected to love her or to miss her very much when she was gone. She did not miss her at all, in fact, and as she was a self-absorbed child she gave her entire thought to herself, as she had always done. If she had been older she would no doubt have been very anxious at being left alone in the world, but she was very young, and as she had always been taken care of, she supposed she always would be. What she thought was that she would like to know if she was going to nice people, who would be polite to her and give her her own way as her Ayah and the other native servants had done.

She knew that she was not going to stay at the English clergyman's house where she was taken at first. She did not want to stay. The English clergyman was poor and he had five children nearly all the same age and they wore shabby clothes and were always quarreling and snatching toys from each other. Mary hated their untidy bungalow and was so disagreeable to them that after the first day or two nobody would play with her. By the second day they had given her a nickname which made her furious.

It was Basil who thought of it first. Basil was a little boy with impudent blue eyes and a turned-up nose, and Mary hated him. She was playing by herself under a tree, just as she had been playing the day the cholera broke out. She was making heaps of earth and paths for a garden and Basil came and stood near to watch her. Presently he got rather interested and suddenly made a suggestion.

"Why don't you put a heap of stones there and pretend it is a rockery?" he said. "There in the middle," and he leaned over her to point.

"Go away!" cried Mary. "I don't want boys. Go away!"

For a moment Basil looked angry, and then he began to tease. He was always teasing his sisters. He danced round and round her and made faces and sang and laughed.

"Mistress Mary, quite contrary,
How does your garden grow?
With silver bells, and cockle shells,
And marigolds all in a row."

He sang it until the other children heard and laughed, too; and the crosser Mary got, the more they sang "Mistress Mary, quite contrary"; and after that as long as she stayed with them they called her "Mistress Mary Quite Contrary" when they spoke of her to each other, and often when they spoke to her.

"You are going to be sent home," Basil said to her, "at the end of the week. And we're glad of it."

"I am glad of it, too," answered Mary. "Where is home?"

"She doesn't know where home is!" said Basil, with seven-year-old scorn. "It's England, of course. Our grandmama lives there and our sister Mabel was sent to her last year. You are not going to your grandmama. You have none. You are going to your uncle. His name is Mr. Archibald Craven."

"I don't know anything about him," snapped Mary.

"I know you don't," Basil answered. "You don't know anything. Girls never do. I heard father and mother talking about him. He lives in a great, big, desolate old house in the country and no one goes near him. He's so cross he won't let them, and they wouldn't come if he would let them. He's a hunchback, and he's horrid."

"I don't believe you," said Mary; and she turned her back and stuck her fingers in her ears, because she would not listen any more.

But she thought over it a great deal afterward; and when Mrs. Crawford told her that night that she was going to sail away to England in a few days and go to her uncle, Mr. Archibald Craven, who lived at Misselthwaite Manor, she looked so stony and stubbornly uninterested that they did not know what to think about her. They tried to be kind to her, but she only turned her face away when Mrs. Crawford attempted to kiss her, and held herself stiffly when Mr. Crawford patted her shoulder.

"She is such a plain child," Mrs. Crawford said pityingly, afterward. "And her mother was such a pretty creature. She had a very pretty manner, too, and Mary has the most unattractive ways I ever saw in a child. The children call her 'Mistress Mary Quite Contrary,' and though it's naughty of them, one can't help understanding it."

"Perhaps if her mother had carried her pretty face and her pretty manners oftener into the nursery Mary might have learned some pretty ways too. It is very sad, now the poor beautiful thing is gone, to remember that many people never even knew that she had a child at all."

"I believe she scarcely ever looked at her," sighed Mrs. Crawford. "When her Ayah was dead there was no one to give a thought to the little thing. Think of the servants running away and leaving her all alone in that deserted bungalow. Colonel McGrew said he nearly jumped out of his skin when he opened the door and found her standing by herself in the middle of the room."

Mary made the long voyage to England under the care of an officer's wife, who was taking her children to leave them in a boarding-school. She was very much absorbed in her own little boy and girl, and was rather glad to hand the child over to the woman Mr. Archibald Craven sent to meet her, in London. The woman was his housekeeper at Misselthwaite Manor, and her name was Mrs. Medlock. She was a stout woman, with very red cheeks and sharp black eyes. She wore a very purple dress, a black silk mantle with jet fringe on it and a black bonnet with purple velvet flowers which stuck up and trembled when she moved her head. Mary did not like her at all, but as she very seldom liked people there was nothing remarkable in that; besides which it was very evident Mrs. Medlock did not think much of her.

"My word! she's a plain little piece of goods!" she said. "And we'd heard that her mother was a beauty. She hasn't handed much of it down, has she, ma'am?"

"Perhaps she will improve as she grows older," the officer's wife said good-naturedly. "If she were not so sallow and had a nicer expression, her features are rather good. Children alter so much."

"She'll have to alter a good deal," answered Mrs. Medlock. "And, there's nothing likely to improve children at Misselthwaite—if you ask me!" They thought Mary was not listening because she was standing a little apart from them at the window of the private hotel they had gone to. She was watching the passing buses and cabs and people, but she heard quite well and was made very curious about her uncle and the place he lived in. What sort of a place was it, and what would he be like? What was a hunchback? She had never seen one. Perhaps there were none in India.

Since she had been living in other people's houses and had had no Ayah, she had begun to feel lonely and to think queer thoughts which were new to her. She had begun to wonder why she had never seemed to belong to anyone even when her father and mother had been alive. Other children seemed to belong to their fathers and mothers, but she had never seemed to really be anyone's little girl. She had had servants, and food and clothes, but no one had taken any notice of her. She did not know that this was because she was a disagreeable child; but then, of course, she did not know she was disagreeable. She often thought that other people were, but she did not know that she was so herself.

She thought Mrs. Medlock the most disagreeable person she had ever seen, with her common, highly colored face and her common fine bonnet. When the next day they set out on their journey to Yorkshire, she walked through the station to the railway carriage with her head up and trying to keep as far away from her as she could, because she did not want to seem to belong to her. It would have made her angry to think people imagined she was her little girl.

But Mrs. Medlock was not in the least disturbed by her and her thoughts. She was the kind of woman who would "stand no nonsense from young ones." At least, that is what she would have said if she had been asked. She had not wanted to go to London just when her sister Maria's daughter was going to be married, but she had a comfortable, well paid place as housekeeper at Misselthwaite Manor and the only way in which she could keep it was to do at once what Mr. Archibald Craven told her to do. She never dared even to ask a question.

"Captain Lennox and his wife died of the cholera," Mr. Craven had said in his short, cold way. "Captain Lennox was my wife's brother and I am their daughter's guardian. The child is to be brought here. You must go to London and bring her yourself."

So she packed her small trunk and made the journey.

Mary sat in her corner of the railway carriage and looked plain and fretful. She had nothing to read or to look at, and she had folded her thin little black-gloved hands in her lap. Her black dress made her look yellower than ever, and her limp light hair straggled from under her black crepe hat.

"A more marred-looking young one I never saw in my life," Mrs. Medlock thought. (Marred is a Yorkshire word and means spoiled and pettish.) She had never seen a child who sat so still without doing anything; and at last she got tired of watching her and began to talk in a brisk, hard voice.

"I suppose I may as well tell you something about where you are going to," she said. "Do you know anything about your uncle?"

"No," said Mary.

"Never heard your father and mother talk about him?"

"No," said Mary frowning. She frowned because she remembered that her father and mother had never talked to her about anything in particular. Certainly they had never told her things.

"Humph," muttered Mrs. Medlock, staring at her queer, unresponsive little face. She did not say any more for a few moments and then she began again.

"I suppose you might as well be told something—to prepare you. You are going to a queer place."

Mary said nothing at all, and Mrs. Medlock looked rather discomfited by her apparent indifference, but, after taking a breath, she went on.

"Not but that it's a grand big place in a gloomy way, and Mr. Craven's proud of it in his way—and that's gloomy enough, too. The house is six hundred years old and it's on the edge of the moor, and there's near a hundred rooms in it, though most of them's shut up and locked. And there's pictures and fine old furniture and things that's been there for ages, and there's a big park round it and gardens and trees with branches trailing to the ground—some of them." She paused and took another breath. "But there's nothing else," she ended suddenly.

Mary had begun to listen in spite of herself. It all sounded so unlike India, and anything new rather attracted her. But she did not intend to look as if she were interested. That was one of her unhappy, disagreeable ways. So she sat still.

"Well," said Mrs. Medlock. "What do you think of it?"

"Nothing," she answered. "I know nothing about such places."

That made Mrs. Medlock laugh a short sort of laugh.

"Eh!" she said, "but you are like an old woman. Don't you care?"

"It doesn't matter" said Mary, "whether I care or not."

"You are right enough there," said Mrs. Medlock. "It doesn't. What you're to be kept at Misselthwaite Manor for I don't know, unless because it's the easiest way. He's not going to trouble himself about you, that's sure and certain. He never troubles himself about no one."

She stopped herself as if she had just remembered something in time.

"He's got a crooked back," she said. "That set him wrong. He was a sour young man and got no good of all his money and big place till he was married."

Mary's eyes turned toward her in spite of her intention not to seem to care. She had never thought of the hunchback's being married and she was a trifle surprised. Mrs. Medlock saw this, and as she was a talkative woman she continued with more interest. This was one way of passing some of the time, at any rate.

"She was a sweet, pretty thing and he'd have walked the world over to get her a blade o' grass she wanted. Nobody thought she'd marry him, but she did, and people said she married him for his money. But she didn't—she didn't," positively. "When she died—"

Mary gave a little involuntary jump.

"Oh! did she die!" she exclaimed, quite without meaning to. She had just remembered a French fairy story she had once read called "Riquet a la Houppe." It had been about a poor hunchback and a beautiful princess and it had made her suddenly sorry for Mr. Archibald Craven.

"Yes, she died," Mrs. Medlock answered. "And it made him queerer than ever. He cares about nobody. He won't see people. Most of the time he goes away, and when he is at Misselthwaite he shuts himself up in the West Wing and won't let any one but Pitcher see him. Pitcher's an old fellow, but he took care of him when he was a child and he knows his ways."

It sounded like something in a book and it did not make Mary feel cheerful. A house with a hundred rooms, nearly all shut up and with their doors locked—a house on the edge of a moor—whatsoever a moor was—sounded dreary. A man with a crooked back who shut himself up also! She stared out of the window with her lips pinched together, and it seemed quite natural that the rain should have begun to pour down in gray slanting lines and splash and stream down the window-panes. If the pretty wife had been alive she might have made things cheerful by being something like her own mother and by running in and out and going to parties as she had done in frocks "full of lace." But she was not there any more.

"You needn't expect to see him, because ten to one you won't," said Mrs. Medlock. "And you mustn't expect that there will be people to talk to you. You'll have to play about and look after yourself. You'll be told what rooms you can go into and what rooms you're to keep out of. There's gardens enough. But when you're in the house don't go wandering and poking about. Mr. Craven won't have it."

"I shall not want to go poking about," said sour little Mary and just as suddenly as she had begun to be rather sorry for Mr. Archibald Craven she began to cease to be sorry and to think he was unpleasant enough to deserve all that had happened to him.

And she turned her face toward the streaming panes of the window of the railway carriage and gazed out at the gray rain-storm which looked as if it would go on forever and ever. She watched it so long and steadily that the grayness grew heavier and heavier before her eyes and she fell asleep.

CHAPTER III

ACROSS THE MOOR

She slept a long time, and when she awakened Mrs. Medlock had bought a lunchbasket at one of the stations and they had some chicken and cold beef and bread and butter and some hot tea. The rain seemed to be streaming down more heavily than ever and everybody in the station wore wet and glistening waterproofs. The guard lighted the lamps in the carriage, and Mrs. Medlock cheered up very much over her tea and chicken and beef. She ate a great deal and afterward fell asleep herself, and Mary sat and stared at her and watched her fine bonnet slip on one side until she herself fell asleep once more in the corner of the carriage, lulled by the splashing of the rain against the windows. It was quite dark when she awakened again. The train had stopped at a station and Mrs. Medlock was shaking her.

"You have had a sleep!" she said. "It's time to open your eyes! We're at Thwaite Station and we've got a long drive before us."

Mary stood up and tried to keep her eyes open while Mrs. Medlock collected her parcels. The little girl did not offer to help her, because in India native servants always picked up or carried things and it seemed quite proper that other people should wait on one.

The station was a small one and nobody but themselves seemed to be getting out of the train. The station-master spoke to Mrs. Medlock in a rough, good-natured way, pronouncing his words in a queer broad fashion which Mary found out afterward was Yorkshire.

"I see tha's got back," he said. "An' tha's browt th' young 'un with thee."

"Aye, that's her," answered Mrs. Medlock, speaking with a Yorkshire accent herself and jerking her head over her shoulder toward Mary. "How's thy Missus?"

"Well enow. Th' carriage is waitin' outside for thee."

A brougham stood on the road before the little outside platform. Mary saw that it was a smart carriage and that it was a smart footman who helped her in. His long waterproof coat and the waterproof covering of his hat were shining and dripping with rain as everything was, the burly station-master included.

When he shut the door, mounted the box with the coachman, and they drove off, the little girl found herself seated in a comfortably cushioned corner, but she was not inclined to go to sleep again. She sat and looked out of the window, curious to see something of the road over which she was being driven to the queer place Mrs. Medlock had spoken of. She was not at all a timid child and she was not exactly frightened, but she felt that there was no knowing what might happen in a house with a hundred rooms nearly all shut up—a house standing on the edge of a moor.

"What is a moor?" she said suddenly to Mrs. Medlock.

"Look out of the window in about ten minutes and you'll see," the woman answered. "We've got to drive five miles across Missel Moor before we get to the Manor. You won't see much because it's a dark night, but you can see something."

Mary asked no more questions but waited in the darkness of her corner, keeping her eyes on the window. The carriage lamps cast rays of light a little distance ahead of them and she caught glimpses of the things they passed. After they had left the station they had driven through a tiny village and she had seen whitewashed cottages and the lights of a public house. Then they had passed a church and a vicarage and a little shop-window or so in a cottage with toys and sweets and odd things set out for sale. Then they were on the highroad and she saw hedges and trees. After that there seemed nothing different for a long time—or at least it seemed a long time to her.

At last the horses began to go more slowly, as if they were climbing up-hill, and presently there seemed to be no more hedges and no more trees. She could see nothing, in fact, but a dense darkness on either side. She leaned forward and pressed her face against the window just as the carriage gave a big jolt.

"Eh! We're on the moor now sure enough," said Mrs. Medlock.

The carriage lamps shed a yellow light on a rough-looking road which seemed to be cut through bushes and low-growing things which ended in the great expanse of dark apparently spread out before and around them. A wind was rising and making a singular, wild, low, rushing sound.

"It's—it's not the sea, is it?" said Mary, looking round at her companion.

"No, not it," answered Mrs. Medlock. "Nor it isn't fields nor mountains, it's just miles and miles and miles of wild land that nothing grows on but heather and gorse and broom, and nothing lives on but wild ponies and sheep."

"I feel as if it might be the sea, if there were water on it," said Mary. "It sounds like the sea just now."

"That's the wind blowing through the bushes," Mrs. Medlock said. "It's a wild, dreary enough place to my mind, though there's plenty that likes it—particularly when the heather's in bloom."

On and on they drove through the darkness, and though the rain stopped, the wind rushed by and whistled and made strange sounds. The road went up and down, and several times the carriage passed over a little bridge beneath which water rushed very fast with a great deal of noise. Mary felt as if the drive would never come to an end and that the wide, bleak moor was a wide expanse of black ocean through which she was passing on a strip of dry land.

"I don't like it," she said to herself. "I don't like it," and she pinched her thin lips more tightly together.

The horses were climbing up a hilly piece of road when she first caught sight of a light. Mrs. Medlock saw it as soon as she did and drew a long sigh of relief.

"Eh, I am glad to see that bit o' light twinkling," she exclaimed. "It's the light in the lodge window. We shall get a good cup of tea after a bit, at all events."

It was "after a bit," as she said, for when the carriage passed through the park gates there was still two miles of avenue to drive through and the trees (which nearly met overhead) made it seem as if they were driving through a long dark vault.

They drove out of the vault into a clear space and stopped before an immensely long but low-built house which seemed to ramble round a stone court. At first Mary thought that there were no lights at all in the windows, but as she got out of the carriage she saw that one room in a corner upstairs showed a dull glow.

The entrance door was a huge one made of massive, curiously shaped panels of oak studded with big iron nails and bound with great iron bars. It opened into an enormous hall, which was so dimly lighted that the faces in the portraits on the walls and the figures in the suits of armor made Mary feel that she did not want to look at them. As she stood on the stone floor she looked a very small, odd little black figure, and she felt as small and lost and odd as she looked.

A neat, thin old man stood near the manservant who opened the door for them.

"You are to take her to her room," he said in a husky voice. "He doesn't want to see her. He's going to London in the morning."

"Very well, Mr. Pitcher," Mrs. Medlock answered. "So long as I know what's expected of me, I can manage."

"What's expected of you, Mrs. Medlock," Mr. Pitcher said, "is that you make sure that he's not disturbed and that he doesn't see what he doesn't want to see."

And then Mary Lennox was led up a broad staircase and down a long corridor and up a short flight of steps and through another corridor and another, until a door opened in a wall and she found herself in a room with a fire in it and a supper on a table.

Mrs. Medlock said unceremoniously:

"Well, here you are! This room and the next are where you'll live—and you must keep to them. Don't you forget that!"

It was in this way Mistress Mary arrived at Misselthwaite Manor and she had perhaps never felt quite so contrary in all her life.

CHAPTER IV

MARTHA

When she opened her eyes in the morning it was because a young housemaid had come into her room to light the fire and was kneeling on the hearth-rug raking out the cinders noisily. Mary lay and watched her for a few moments and then began to look about the room. She had never seen a room at all like it and thought it curious and gloomy. The walls were covered with tapestry with a forest scene embroidered on it. There were fantastically dressed people under the trees and in the distance there was a glimpse of the turrets of a castle. There were hunters and horses and dogs and ladies. Mary felt as if she were in the forest with them. Out of a deep window she could see a great climbing stretch of land which seemed to have no trees on it, and to look rather like an endless, dull, purplish sea.

"What is that?" she said, pointing out of the window.

Martha, the young housemaid, who had just risen to her feet, looked and pointed also. "That there?" she said.

"Yes."

"That's th' moor," with a good-natured grin. "Does tha' like it?"

"No," answered Mary. "I hate it."

"That's because tha'rt not used to it," Martha said, going back to her hearth. "Tha' thinks it's too big an' bare now. But tha' will like it."

"Do you?" inquired Mary.

"Aye, that I do," answered Martha, cheerfully polishing away at the grate. "I just love it. It's none bare. It's covered wi' growin' things as smells sweet. It's fair lovely in spring an' summer when th' gorse an' broom an' heather's in flower. It smells o' honey an' there's such a lot o' fresh air—an' th' sky looks so high an' th' bees an' skylarks makes such a nice noise hummin' an' singin'. Eh! I wouldn't live away from th' moor for anythin'."

Mary listened to her with a grave, puzzled expression. The native servants she had been used to in India were not in the least like this. They were obsequious and servile and did not presume to talk to their masters as if they were their equals. They made salaams and called them "protector of the poor" and names of that sort. Indian servants were commanded to do things, not asked. It was not the custom to say "please" and "thank you" and Mary had always slapped her Ayah in the face when she was angry. She wondered a little what this girl would do if one slapped her in the face. She was a round, rosy, good-natured-looking creature, but she had a sturdy way which made Mistress Mary wonder if she might not even slap back—if the person who slapped her was only a little girl.

"You are a strange servant," she said from her pillows, rather haughtily.

Martha sat up on her heels, with her blacking-brush in her hand, and laughed, without seeming the least out of temper.

"Eh! I know that," she said. "If there was a grand Missus at Misselthwaite I should never have been even one of th' under house-maids. I might have been let to be scullerymaid but I'd never have been let upstairs. I'm too common an' I talk too much Yorkshire. But this is a funny house for all it's so grand. Seems like there's neither Master nor Mistress except Mr. Pitcher an' Mrs. Medlock. Mr. Craven, he won't be troubled about anythin' when he's here, an' he's nearly always away. Mrs. Medlock gave me th' place out o' kindness. She told me she could never have done it if Misselthwaite had been like other big houses."

"Are you going to be my servant?" Mary asked, still in her imperious little Indian way.

Martha began to rub her grate again.

"I'm Mrs. Medlock's servant," she said stoutly. "An' she's Mr. Craven's—but I'm to do the housemaid's work up here an' wait on you a bit. But you won't need much waitin' on."

"Who is going to dress me?" demanded Mary.

Martha sat up on her heels again and stared. She spoke in broad Yorkshire in her amazement.

"Canna' tha' dress thysen!" she said.

"What do you mean? I don't understand your language," said Mary.

"Eh! I forgot," Martha said. "Mrs. Medlock told me I'd have to be careful or you wouldn't know what I was sayin'. I mean can't you put on your own clothes?"

"No," answered Mary, quite indignantly. "I never did in my life. My Ayah dressed me, of course."

"Well," said Martha, evidently not in the least aware that she was impudent, "it's time tha' should learn. Tha' cannot begin younger. It'll do thee good to wait on thysen a bit. My mother always said she couldn't see why grand people's children didn't turn out fair fools—what with nurses an' bein' washed an' dressed an' took out to walk as if they was puppies!"

"It is different in India," said Mistress Mary disdainfully. She could scarcely stand this.

But Martha was not at all crushed.

"Eh! I can see it's different," she answered almost sympathetically. "I dare say it's because there's such a lot o' blacks there instead o' respectable white people. When I heard you was comin' from India I thought you was a black too."

Mary sat up in bed furious.

"What!" she said. "What! You thought I was a native. You—you daughter of a pig!"

Martha stared and looked hot.

"Who are you callin' names?" she said. "You needn't be so vexed. That's not th' way for a young lady to talk. I've nothin' against th' blacks. When you read about 'em in tracts they're always very religious. You always read as a black's a man an' a brother. I've never seen a black an' I was fair pleased to think I was goin' to see one close. When I come in to light your fire this mornin' I crep' up to your bed an' pulled th' cover back careful to look at you. An' there you was," disappointedly, "no more black than me—for all you're so yeller."

Mary did not even try to control her rage and humiliation. "You thought I was a native! You dared! You don't know anything about natives! They are not people—they're servants who must salaam to you. You know nothing about India. You know nothing about anything!"

She was in such a rage and felt so helpless before the girl's simple stare, and somehow she suddenly felt so horribly lonely and far away from everything she understood and which understood her, that she threw herself face downward on the pillows and burst into passionate sobbing. She sobbed so unrestrainedly that good-natured Yorkshire Martha was a little frightened and quite sorry for her. She went to the bed and bent over her.

"Eh! you mustn't cry like that there!" she begged. "You mustn't for sure. I didn't know you'd be vexed. I don't know anythin' about anythin'—just like you said. I beg your pardon, Miss. Do stop cryin'."

There was something comforting and really friendly in her queer Yorkshire speech and sturdy way which had a good effect on Mary. She gradually ceased crying and became quiet. Martha looked relieved.

"It's time for thee to get up now," she said. "Mrs. Medlock said I was to carry tha' breakfast an' tea an' dinner into th' room next to this. It's been made into a nursery for thee. I'll help thee on with thy clothes if tha'll get out o' bed. If th' buttons are at th' back tha' cannot button them up tha'self."

When Mary at last decided to get up, the clothes Martha took from the wardrobe were not the ones she had worn when she arrived the night before with Mrs. Medlock.

"Those are not mine," she said. "Mine are black."

She looked the thick white wool coat and dress over, and added with cool approval:

"Those are nicer than mine."

"These are th' ones tha' must put on," Martha answered. "Mr. Craven ordered Mrs. Medlock to get 'em in London. He said 'I won't have a child dressed in black wanderin' about like a lost soul,' he said. 'It'd make the place sadder than it is. Put color on her.' Mother she said she knew what he meant. Mother always knows what a body means. She doesn't hold with black hersel'."

"I hate black things," said Mary.

The dressing process was one which taught them both something. Martha had "buttoned up" her little sisters and brothers but she had never seen a child who stood still and waited for another person to do things for her as if she had neither hands nor feet of her own.

"Why doesn't tha' put on tha' own shoes?" she said when Mary quietly held out her foot.

"My Ayah did it," answered Mary, staring. "It was the custom."

She said that very often—"It was the custom." The native servants were always saying it. If one told them to do a thing their ancestors had not done for a thousand years they gazed at one mildly and said, "It is not the custom" and one knew that was the end of the matter.

It had not been the custom that Mistress Mary should do anything but stand and allow herself to be dressed like a doll, but before she was ready for breakfast she began to suspect that her life at Misselthwaite Manor would end by teaching her a number of things quite new to her—things such as putting on her own shoes and stockings, and picking up things she let fall. If Martha had been a well-trained fine young lady's maid she would have been more subservient and respectful and would have known that it was her business to brush hair, and button boots, and pick things up and lay them away. She was, however, only an untrained Yorkshire rustic who had been brought up in a moorland cottage with a swarm of little brothers and sisters who had never dreamed of doing anything but waiting on themselves and on the younger ones who were either babies in arms or just learning to totter about and tumble over things.

If Mary Lennox had been a child who was ready to be amused she would perhaps have laughed at Martha's readiness to talk, but Mary only listened to her coldly and wondered at her freedom of manner. At first she was not at all interested, but gradually, as the girl rattled on in her good-tempered, homely way, Mary began to notice what she was saying.

"Eh! you should see 'em all," she said. "There's twelve of us an' my father only gets sixteen shilling a week. I can tell you my mother's put to it to get porridge for 'em all. They tumble about on th' moor an' play there all day an' mother says th' air of th' moor fattens 'em. She says she believes they eat th' grass same as th' wild ponies do. Our Dickon, he's twelve years old and he's got a young pony he calls his own."

"Where did he get it?" asked Mary.

"He found it on th' moor with its mother when it was a little one an' he began to make friends with it an' give it bits o' bread an' pluck young grass for it. And it got to like him so it follows him about an' it lets him get on its back. Dickon's a kind lad an' animals likes him."

Mary had never possessed an animal pet of her own and had always thought she should like one. So she began to feel a slight interest in Dickon, and as she had never before been interested in any one but herself, it was the dawning of a healthy sentiment. When she went into the room which had been made into a nursery for her, she found that it was rather like the one she had slept in. It was not a child's room, but a grown-up person's room, with gloomy old pictures on the walls and heavy old oak chairs. A table in the center was set with a good substantial breakfast. But she had always had a very small appetite, and she looked with something more than indifference at the first plate Martha set before her.

"I don't want it," she said.

"Tha' doesn't want thy porridge!" Martha exclaimed incredulously.

"No."

"Tha' doesn't know how good it is. Put a bit o' treacle on it or a bit o' sugar."

"I don't want it," repeated Mary.

"Eh!" said Martha. "I can't abide to see good victuals go to waste. If our children was at this table they'd clean it bare in five minutes."

"Why?" said Mary coldly.

"Why!" echoed Martha. "Because they scarce ever had their stomachs full in their lives. They're as hungry as young hawks an' foxes."

"I don't know what it is to be hungry," said Mary, with the indifference of ignorance.

Martha looked indignant.

"Well, it would do thee good to try it. I can see that plain enough," she said outspokenly. "I've no patience with folk as sits an' just stares at good bread an' meat. My word! don't I wish Dickon and Phil an' Jane an' th' rest of 'em had what's here under their pinafores."

"Why don't you take it to them?" suggested Mary.

"It's not mine," answered Martha stoutly. "An' this isn't my day out. I get my day out once a month same as th' rest. Then I go home an' clean up for mother an' give her a day's rest."

Mary drank some tea and ate a little toast and some marmalade.

"You wrap up warm an' run out an' play you," said Martha. "It'll do you good and give you some stomach for your meat."

Mary went to the window. There were gardens and paths and big trees, but everything looked dull and wintry.

"Out? Why should I go out on a day like this?"

"Well, if tha' doesn't go out tha'lt have to stay in, an' what has tha' got to do?"

Mary glanced about her. There was nothing to do. When Mrs. Medlock had prepared the nursery she had not thought of amusement. Perhaps it would be better to go and see what the gardens were like.

"Who will go with me?" she inquired.

Martha stared.

"You'll go by yourself," she answered. "You'll have to learn to play like other children does when they haven't got sisters and brothers. Our Dickon goes off on th' moor by himself an' plays for hours. That's how he made friends with th' pony. He's got sheep on th' moor that knows him, an' birds as comes an' eats out of his hand. However little there is to eat, he always saves a bit o' his bread to coax his pets."

It was really this mention of Dickon which made Mary decide to go out, though she was not aware of it. There would be birds outside though there would not be ponies or sheep. They would be different from the birds in India and it might amuse her to look at them.

Martha found her coat and hat for her and a pair of stout little boots and she showed her her way downstairs.

"If tha' goes round that way tha'll come to th' gardens," she said, pointing to a gate in a wall of shrubbery. "There's lots o' flowers in summer-time, but there's nothin' bloomin' now." She seemed to hesitate a second before she added, "One of th' gardens is locked up. No one has been in it for ten years."

"Why?" asked Mary in spite of herself. Here was another locked door added to the hundred in the strange house.

"Mr. Craven had it shut when his wife died so sudden. He won't let no one go inside. It was her garden. He locked th' door an' dug a hole and buried th' key. There's Mrs. Medlock's bell ringing—I must run."

After she was gone Mary turned down the walk which led to the door in the shrubbery. She could not help thinking about the garden which no one had been into for ten years. She wondered what it would look like and whether there were any flowers still alive in it. When she had passed through the shrubbery gate she found herself in great gardens, with wide lawns and winding walks with clipped borders. There were trees, and flower-beds, and evergreens clipped into strange shapes, and a large pool with an old gray fountain in its midst. But the flower-beds were bare and wintry and the fountain was not playing. This was not the garden which was shut up. How could a garden be shut up? You could always walk into a garden.

She was just thinking this when she saw that, at the end of the path she was following, there seemed to be a long wall, with ivy growing over it. She was not familiar enough with England to know that she was coming upon the kitchen-gardens where the vegetables and fruit were growing. She went toward the wall and found that there was a green door in the ivy, and that it stood open. This was not the closed garden, evidently, and she could go into it.

She went through the door and found that it was a garden with walls all round it and that it was only one of several walled gardens which seemed to open into one another. She saw another open green door, revealing bushes and pathways between beds containing winter vegetables. Fruit-trees were trained flat against the wall, and over some of the beds there were glass frames. The place was bare and ugly enough, Mary thought, as she stood and stared about her. It might be nicer in summer when things were green, but there was nothing pretty about it now.

Presently an old man with a spade over his shoulder walked through the door leading from the second garden. He looked startled when he saw Mary, and then touched his cap. He had a surly old face, and did not seem at all pleased to see her—but then she was displeased with his garden and wore her "quite contrary" expression, and certainly did not seem at all pleased to see him.

"What is this place?" she asked.

"One o' th' kitchen-gardens," he answered.

"What is that?" said Mary, pointing through the other green door.

"Another of 'em," shortly. "There's another on t'other side o' th' wall an' there's th' orchard t'other side o' that."

"Can I go in them?" asked Mary.

"If tha' likes. But there's nowt to see."

Mary made no response. She went down the path and through the second green door. There, she found more walls and winter vegetables and glass frames, but in the second wall there was another green door and it was not open. Perhaps it led into the garden which no one had seen for ten years. As she was not at all a timid child and always did what she wanted to do, Mary went to the green door and turned the handle. She hoped the door would not open because she wanted to be sure she had found the mysterious garden—but it did open quite easily and she walked through it and found herself in an orchard. There were walls all round it also and trees trained against them, and there were bare fruit-trees growing in the winter-browned grass—but there was no green door to be seen anywhere. Mary looked for it, and yet when she had entered the upper end of the garden she had noticed that the wall did not seem to end with the orchard but to extend beyond it as if it enclosed a place at the other side. She could see the tops of trees above the wall, and when she stood still she saw a bird with a bright red breast sitting on the topmost branch of one of them, and suddenly he burst into his winter song—almost as if he had caught sight of her and was calling to her.

She stopped and listened to him and somehow his cheerful, friendly little whistle gave her a pleased feeling—even a disagreeable little girl may be lonely, and the big closed house and big bare moor and big bare gardens had made this one feel as if there was no one left in the world but herself. If she had been an affectionate child, who had been used to being loved, she would have broken her heart, but even though she was "Mistress Mary Quite Contrary" she was desolate, and the bright-breasted little bird brought a look into her sour little face which was almost a smile. She listened to him until he flew away. He was not like an Indian bird and she liked him and wondered if she should ever see him again. Perhaps he lived in the mysterious garden and knew all about it.

Perhaps it was because she had nothing whatever to do that she thought so much of the deserted garden. She was curious about it and wanted to see what it was like. Why had Mr. Archibald Craven buried the key? If he had liked his wife so much why did he hate her garden? She wondered if she should ever see him, but she knew that if she did she should not like him, and he would not like her, and that she should only stand and stare at him and say nothing, though she should be wanting dreadfully to ask him why he had done such a queer thing.

"People never like me and I never like people," she thought. "And I never can talk as the Crawford children could. They were always talking and laughing and making noises."

She thought of the robin and of the way he seemed to sing his song at her, and as she remembered the tree-top he perched on she stopped rather suddenly on the path.

"I believe that tree was in the secret garden—I feel sure it was," she said. "There was a wall round the place and there was no door."

She walked back into the first kitchen-garden she had entered and found the old man digging there. She went and stood beside him and watched him a few moments in her cold little way. He took no notice of her and so at last she spoke to him.

"I have been into the other gardens," she said.

"There was nothin' to prevent thee," he answered crustily.

"I went into the orchard."

"There was no dog at th' door to bite thee," he answered.

"There was no door there into the other garden," said Mary.

"What garden?" he said in a rough voice, stopping his digging for a moment.

"The one on the other side of the wall," answered Mistress Mary. "There are trees there—I saw the tops of them. A bird with a red breast was sitting on one of them and he sang."

To her surprise the surly old weather-beaten face actually changed its expression. A slow smile spread over it and the gardener looked quite different. It made her think that it was curious how much nicer a person looked when he smiled. She had not thought of it before.

He turned about to the orchard side of his garden and began to whistle—a low soft whistle. She could not understand how such a surly man could make such a coaxing sound. Almost the next moment a wonderful thing happened. She heard a soft little rushing flight through the air—and it was the bird with the red breast flying to them, and he actually alighted on the big clod of earth quite near to the gardener's foot.

"Here he is," chuckled the old man, and then he spoke to the bird as if he were speaking to a child.

"Where has tha' been, tha' cheeky little beggar?" he said. "I've not seen thee before today. Has tha' begun tha' courtin' this early in th' season? Tha'rt too forrad."

The bird put his tiny head on one side and looked up at him with his soft bright eye which was like a black dewdrop. He seemed quite familiar and not the least afraid. He hopped about and pecked the earth briskly, looking for seeds and insects. It actually gave Mary a queer feeling in her heart, because he was so pretty and cheerful and seemed so like a person. He had a tiny plump body and a delicate beak, and slender delicate legs.

"Will he always come when you call him?" she asked almost in a whisper.

"Aye, that he will. I've knowed him ever since he was a fledgling. He come out of th' nest in th' other garden an' when first he flew over th' wall he was too weak to fly back for a few days an' we got friendly. When he went over th' wall again th' rest of th' brood was gone an' he was lonely an' he come back to me."

"What kind of a bird is he?" Mary asked.

"Doesn't tha' know? He's a robin redbreast an' they're th'

friendliest, curiousest birds alive. They're almost as friendly as dogs—if you know how to get on with 'em. Watch him peckin' about there an' lookin' round at us now an' again. He knows we're talkin' about him."

It was the queerest thing in the world to see the old fellow. He looked at the plump little scarlet-waistcoated bird as if he were both proud and fond of him.

"He's a conceited one," he chuckled. "He likes to hear folk talk about him. An' curious—bless me, there never was his like for curiosity an' meddlin'. He's always comin' to see what I'm plantin'. He knows all th' things Mester Craven never troubles hissel' to find out. He's th' head gardener, he is."

The robin hopped about busily pecking the soil and now and then stopped and looked at them a little. Mary thought his black dewdrop eyes gazed at her with great curiosity. It really seemed as if he were finding out all about her. The queer feeling in her heart increased. "Where did the rest of the brood fly to?" she asked.

"There's no knowin'. The old ones turn 'em out o' their nest an' make 'em fly an' they're scattered before you know it. This one was a knowin' one an' he knew he was lonely."

Mistress Mary went a step nearer to the robin and looked at him very hard.

"I'm lonely," she said.

She had not known before that this was one of the things which made her feel sour and cross. She seemed to find it out when the robin looked at her and she looked at the robin.

The old gardener pushed his cap back on his bald head and stared at her a minute.

"Art tha' th' little wench from India?" he asked.

Mary nodded.

"Then no wonder tha'rt lonely. Tha'lt be lonlier before tha's done," he said.

He began to dig again, driving his spade deep into the rich black garden soil while the robin hopped about very busily employed.

"What is your name?" Mary inquired.

He stood up to answer her.

"Ben Weatherstaff," he answered, and then he added with a surly chuckle, "I'm lonely mysel' except when he's with me," and he jerked his thumb toward the robin. "He's th' only friend I've got."

"I have no friends at all," said Mary. "I never had. My Ayah didn't like me and I never played with any one."

It is a Yorkshire habit to say what you think with blunt frankness, and old Ben Weatherstaff was a Yorkshire moor man.

"Tha' an' me are a good bit alike," he said. "We was wove out of th' same cloth. We're neither of us good lookin' an' we're both of us as sour as we look. We've got the same nasty tempers, both of us, I'll warrant."

This was plain speaking, and Mary Lennox had never heard the truth about herself in her life. Native servants always salaamed and submitted to you, whatever you did. She had never thought much about her looks, but she wondered if she was as unattractive as Ben Weatherstaff and she also wondered if she looked as sour as he had looked before the robin came. She actually began to wonder also if she was "nasty tempered." She felt uncomfortable.

Suddenly a clear rippling little sound broke out near her and she turned round. She was standing a few feet from a young apple-tree and the robin had flown on to one of its branches and had burst out into a scrap of a song. Ben Weatherstaff laughed outright.

"What did he do that for?" asked Mary.

"He's made up his mind to make friends with thee," replied Ben. "Dang me if he hasn't took a fancy to thee."

"To me?" said Mary, and she moved toward the little tree softly and looked up.

"Would you make friends with me?" she said to the robin just as if she was speaking to a person. "Would you?" And she did not say it either in her hard little voice or in her imperious Indian voice, but in a tone so soft and eager and coaxing that Ben Weatherstaff was as surprised as she had been when she heard him whistle.

"Why," he cried out, "tha' said that as nice an' human as if tha' was a real child instead of a sharp old woman. Tha' said it almost like Dickon talks to his wild things on th' moor."

"Do you know Dickon?" Mary asked, turning round rather in a hurry.

"Everybody knows him. Dickon's wanderin' about everywhere. Th' very blackberries an' heather-bells knows him. I warrant th' foxes shows him where their cubs lies an' th' skylarks doesn't hide their nests from him."

Mary would have liked to ask some more questions. She was almost as curious about Dickon as she was about the deserted garden. But just that moment the robin, who had ended his song, gave a little shake of his wings, spread them and flew away. He had made his visit and had other things to do.

"He has flown over the wall!" Mary cried out, watching him. "He has flown into the orchard—he has flown across the other wall—into the garden where there is no door!"

"He lives there," said old Ben. "He came out o' th' egg there. If he's courtin', he's makin' up to some young madam of a robin that lives among th' old rose-trees there."

"Rose-trees," said Mary. "Are there rose-trees?"

Ben Weatherstaff took up his spade again and began to dig.

"There was ten year' ago," he mumbled.

"I should like to see them," said Mary. "Where is the green door? There must be a door somewhere."

Ben drove his spade deep and looked as uncompanionable as he had looked when she first saw him.

"There was ten year' ago, but there isn't now," he said.

"No door!" cried Mary. "There must be."

"None as any one can find, an' none as is any one's business. Don't you be a meddlesome wench an' poke your nose where it's no cause to go. Here, I must go on with my work. Get you gone an' play you. I've no more time."

And he actually stopped digging, threw his spade over his shoulder and walked off, without even glancing at her or saying good-by.

CHAPTER V

THE CRY IN THE CORRIDOR

At first each day which passed by for Mary Lennox was exactly like the others. Every morning she awoke in her tapestried room and found Martha kneeling upon the hearth building her fire; every morning she ate her breakfast in the nursery which had nothing amusing in it; and after each breakfast she gazed out of the window across to the huge moor which seemed to spread out on all sides and climb up to the sky, and after she had stared for a while she realized that if she did not go out she would have to stay in and do nothing—and so she went out. She did not know that this was the best thing she could have done, and she did not know that, when she began to walk quickly or even run along the paths and down the avenue, she was stirring her slow blood and making herself stronger by fighting with the wind which swept down from the moor. She ran only to make herself warm, and she hated the wind which rushed at her face and roared and held her back as if it were some giant she could not see. But the big breaths of rough fresh air blown over the heather filled her lungs with something which was good for her whole thin body and whipped some red color into her cheeks and brightened her dull eyes when she did not know anything about it.

But after a few days spent almost entirely out of doors she wakened one morning knowing what it was to be hungry, and when she sat down to her breakfast she did not glance disdainfully at her porridge and push it away, but took up her spoon and began to eat it and went on eating it until her bowl was empty.

"Tha' got on well enough with that this mornin', didn't tha'?" said Martha.

"It tastes nice today," said Mary, feeling a little surprised herself.

"It's th' air of th' moor that's givin' thee stomach for tha' victuals," answered Martha. "It's lucky for thee that tha's got victuals as well as appetite. There's been twelve in our cottage as had th' stomach an' nothin' to put in it. You go on playin' you out o' doors every day an' you'll get some flesh on your bones an' you won't be so yeller."

"I don't play," said Mary. "I have nothing to play with."

"Nothin' to play with!" exclaimed Martha. "Our children plays with sticks and stones. They just runs about an' shouts an' looks at things."

Mary did not shout, but she looked at things. There was nothing else to do. She walked round and round the gardens and wandered about the paths in the park. Sometimes she looked for Ben Weatherstaff, but though several times she saw him at work he was too busy to look at her or was too surly. Once when she was walking toward him he picked up his spade and turned away as if he did it on purpose.

One place she went to oftener than to any other. It was the long walk outside the gardens with the walls round them. There were bare flower-beds on either side of it and against the walls ivy grew thickly. There was one part of the wall where the creeping dark green leaves were more bushy than elsewhere. It seemed as if for a long time that part had been neglected. The rest of it had been clipped and made to look neat, but at this lower end of the walk it had not been trimmed at all.

A few days after she had talked to Ben Weatherstaff, Mary stopped to notice this and wondered why it was so. She had just paused and was looking up at a long spray of ivy swinging in the wind when she saw a gleam of scarlet and heard a brilliant chirp, and there, on the top of the wall, perched Ben Weatherstaff's robin redbreast, tilting forward to look at her with his small head on one side.

"Oh!" she cried out, "is it you—is it you?" And it did not seem at all queer to her that she spoke to him as if she were sure that he would understand and answer her.

He did answer. He twittered and chirped and hopped along the wall as if he were telling her all sorts of things. It seemed to Mistress Mary as if she understood him, too, though he was not speaking in words. It was as if he said:

"Good morning! Isn't the wind nice? Isn't the sun nice? Isn't everything nice? Let us both chirp and hop and twitter. Come on! Come on!"

Mary began to laugh, and as he hopped and took little flights along the wall she ran after him. Poor little thin, sallow, ugly Mary—she actually looked almost pretty for a moment.

"I like you! I like you!" she cried out, pattering down the walk; and she chirped and tried to whistle, which last she did not know how to do in the least. But the robin seemed to be quite satisfied and chirped and whistled back at her. At last he spread his wings and made a darting flight to the top of a tree, where he perched and sang loudly. That reminded Mary of the first time she had seen him. He had been swinging on a tree-top then and she had been standing in the orchard. Now she was on the other side of the orchard and standing in the path outside a wall—much lower down—and there was the same tree inside.

"It's in the garden no one can go into," she said to herself. "It's the garden without a door. He lives in there. How I wish I could see what it is like!"

She ran up the walk to the green door she had entered the first morning. Then she ran down the path through the other door and then into the orchard, and when she stood and looked up there was the tree on the other side of the wall, and there was the robin just finishing his song and beginning to preen his feathers with his beak.

"It is the garden," she said. "I am sure it is."

She walked round and looked closely at that side of the orchard wall, but she only found what she had found before—that there was no door in it. Then she ran through the kitchen-gardens again and out into the walk outside the long ivy-covered wall, and she walked to the end of it and looked at it, but there was no door; and then she walked to the other end, looking again, but there was no door.

"It's very queer," she said. "Ben Weatherstaff said there was no door and there is no door. But there must have been one ten years ago, because Mr. Craven buried the key."

This gave her so much to think of that she began to be quite interested and feel that she was not sorry that she had come to Misselthwaite Manor. In India she had always felt hot and too languid to care much about anything. The fact was that the fresh wind from the moor had begun to blow the cobwebs out of her young brain and to waken her up a little.

She stayed out of doors nearly all day, and when she sat down to her supper at night she felt hungry and drowsy and comfortable. She did not feel cross when Martha chattered away. She felt as if she rather liked to hear her, and at last she thought she would ask her a question. She asked it after she had finished her supper and had sat down on the hearth-rug before the fire.

"Why did Mr. Craven hate the garden?" she said.

She had made Martha stay with her and Martha had not objected at all. She was very young, and used to a crowded cottage full of brothers and sisters, and she found it dull in the great servants' hall downstairs where the footman and upper-housemaids made fun of her Yorkshire speech and looked upon her as a common little thing, and sat and whispered among themselves. Martha liked to talk, and the strange child who had lived in India, and been waited upon by "blacks," was novelty enough to attract her.

She sat down on the hearth herself without waiting to be asked.

"Art tha' thinkin' about that garden yet?" she said. "I knew tha' would. That was just the way with me when I first heard about it."

"Why did he hate it?" Mary persisted.

Martha tucked her feet under her and made herself quite comfortable.

"Listen to th' wind wutherin' round the house," she said. "You could bare stand up on the moor if you was out on it tonight."

Mary did not know what "wutherin'" meant until she listened, and then she understood. It must mean that hollow shuddering sort of roar which rushed round and round the house as if the giant no one could see were buffeting it and beating at the walls and windows to try to break in. But one knew he could not get in, and somehow it made one feel very safe and warm inside a room with a red coal fire.

"But why did he hate it so?" she asked, after she had listened. She intended to know if Martha did.

Then Martha gave up her store of knowledge.

"Mind," she said, "Mrs. Medlock said it's not to be talked about. There's lots o' things in this place that's not to be talked over. That's Mr. Craven's orders. His troubles are none servants' business, he says. But for th' garden he wouldn't be like he is. It was Mrs. Craven's garden that she had made when first they were married an' she just loved it, an' they used to 'tend the flowers themselves. An' none o' th' gardeners was ever let to go in. Him an' her used to go in an' shut th' door an' stay there hours an' hours, readin' and talkin'. An' she was just a bit of a girl an' there was an old tree with a branch bent like a seat on it. An' she made roses grow over it an' she used to sit there. But one day when she was sittin' there th' branch broke an' she fell on th' ground an' was hurt so bad that next day she died. Th' doctors thought he'd go out o' his mind an' die, too. That's why he hates it. No one's never gone in since, an' he won't let any one talk about it."

Mary did not ask any more questions. She looked at the red fire and listened to the wind "wutherin'." It seemed to be "wutherin'" louder than ever. At that moment a very good thing was happening to her. Four good things had happened to her, in fact, since she came to Misselthwaite Manor. She had felt as if she had understood a robin and that he had understood her; she had run in the wind until her blood had grown warm; she had been healthily hungry for the first time in her life; and she had found out what it was to be sorry for some one.

But as she was listening to the wind she began to listen to something else. She did not know what it was, because at first she could scarcely distinguish it from the wind itself. It was a curious sound—it seemed almost as if a child were crying somewhere. Sometimes the wind sounded rather like a child crying, but presently Mistress Mary felt quite sure this sound was inside the house, not outside it. It was far away, but it was inside. She turned round and looked at Martha.

"Do you hear any one crying?" she said.

Martha suddenly looked confused.

"No," she answered. "It's th' wind. Sometimes it sounds like as if some one was lost on th' moor an' wailin'. It's got all sorts o' sounds."

"But listen," said Mary. "It's in the house—down one of those long corridors."

And at that very moment a door must have been opened somewhere downstairs; for a great rushing draft blew along the passage and the door of the room they sat in was blown open with a crash, and as they both jumped to their feet the light was blown out and the crying sound was swept down the far corridor so that it was to be heard more plainly than ever.

"There!" said Mary. "I told you so! It is some one crying—and it isn't a grown-up person."

Martha ran and shut the door and turned the key, but before she did it they both heard the sound of a door in some far passage shutting with a bang, and then everything was quiet, for even the wind ceased "wutherin'" for a few moments.

"It was th' wind," said Martha stubbornly. "An' if it wasn't, it was little Betty Butterworth, th' scullery-maid. She's had th' toothache all day."

But something troubled and awkward in her manner made Mistress Mary stare very hard at her. She did not believe she was speaking the truth.

CHAPTER VI

"THERE WAS SOME ONE CRYING—THERE WAS!"

The next day the rain poured down in torrents again, and when Mary looked out of her window the moor was almost hidden by gray mist and cloud. There could be no going out today.

"What do you do in your cottage when it rains like this?" she asked Martha.

"Try to keep from under each other's feet mostly," Martha answered. "Eh! there does seem a lot of us then. Mother's a good-tempered woman but she gets fair moithered. The biggest ones goes out in th' cow-shed and plays there. Dickon he doesn't mind th' wet. He goes out just th' same as if th' sun was shinin'. He says he sees things on rainy days as doesn't show when it's fair weather. He once found a little fox cub half drowned in its hole and he brought it home in th' bosom of his shirt to keep it warm. Its mother had been killed nearby an' th' hole was swum out an' th' rest o' th' litter was dead. He's got it at home now. He found a half-drowned young crow another time an' he brought it home, too, an' tamed it. It's named Soot because it's so black, an' it hops an' flies about with him everywhere."

The time had come when Mary had forgotten to resent Martha's familiar talk. She had even begun to find it interesting and to be sorry when she stopped or went away. The stories she had been told by her Ayah when she lived in India had been quite unlike those Martha had to tell about the moorland cottage which held fourteen people who lived in four little rooms and never had quite enough to eat. The children seemed to tumble about and amuse themselves like a litter of rough, good-natured collie puppies. Mary was most attracted by the mother and Dickon. When Martha told stories of what "mother" said or did they always sounded comfortable.

"If I had a raven or a fox cub I could play with it," said Mary. "But I have nothing."

Martha looked perplexed.

"Can tha' knit?" she asked.

"No," answered Mary.

"Can tha' sew?"

"No."

"Can tha' read?"

"Yes."

"Then why doesn't tha' read somethin', or learn a bit o' spellin'? Tha'st old enough to be learnin' thy book a good bit now."

"I haven't any books," said Mary. "Those I had were left in India."

"That's a pity," said Martha. "If Mrs. Medlock'd let thee go into th' library, there's thousands o' books there."

Mary did not ask where the library was, because she was suddenly inspired by a new idea. She made up her mind to go and find it herself. She was not troubled about Mrs. Medlock. Mrs. Medlock seemed always to be in her comfortable housekeeper's sitting-room downstairs. In this queer place one scarcely ever saw any one at all. In fact, there was no one to see but the servants, and when their master was away they lived a luxurious life below stairs, where there was a huge kitchen hung about with shining brass and pewter, and a large servants' hall where there were four or five abundant meals eaten every day, and where a great deal of lively romping went on when Mrs. Medlock was out of the way.

Mary's meals were served regularly, and Martha waited on her, but no one troubled themselves about her in the least. Mrs. Medlock came and looked at her every day or two, but no one inquired what she did or told her what to do. She supposed that perhaps this was the English way of treating children. In India she had always been attended by her Ayah, who had followed her about and waited on her, hand and foot. She had often been tired of her company. Now she was followed by nobody and was learning to dress herself because Martha looked as though she thought she was silly and stupid when she wanted to have things handed to her and put on.

"Hasn't tha' got good sense?" she said once, when Mary had stood waiting for her to put on her gloves for her. "Our Susan Ann is twice as sharp as thee an' she's only four year' old. Sometimes tha' looks fair soft in th' head."

Mary had worn her contrary scowl for an hour after that, but it made her think several entirely new things.

She stood at the window for about ten minutes this morning after Martha had swept up the hearth for the last time and gone downstairs. She was thinking over the new idea which had come to her when she heard of the library. She did not care very much about the library itself, because she had read very few books; but to hear of it brought back to her mind the hundred rooms with closed doors. She wondered if they were all really locked and what she would find if she could get into any of them. Were there a hundred really? Why shouldn't she go and see how many doors she could count? It would be something to do on this morning when she could not go out. She had never been taught to ask permission to do things, and she knew nothing at all about authority, so she would not have thought it necessary to ask Mrs. Medlock if she might walk about the house, even if she had seen her.

She opened the door of the room and went into the corridor, and then she began her wanderings. It was a long corridor and it branched into other corridors and it led her up short flights of steps which mounted to others again. There were doors and doors, and there were pictures on the walls. Sometimes they were pictures of dark, curious landscapes, but oftenest they were portraits of men and women in queer, grand costumes made of satin and velvet. She found herself in one long gallery whose walls were covered with these portraits. She had never thought there could be so many in any house. She walked slowly down this place and stared at the faces which also seemed to stare at her. She felt as if they were wondering what a little girl from India was doing in their house. Some were pictures of children—little girls in thick satin frocks which reached to their feet and stood out about them, and boys with puffed sleeves and lace collars and long hair, or with big ruffs around their necks. She always stopped to look at the children, and wonder what their names were, and where they had gone, and why they wore such odd clothes. There was a stiff, plain little girl rather like herself. She wore a green brocade dress and held a green parrot on her finger. Her eyes had a sharp, curious look.

"Where do you live now?" said Mary aloud to her. "I wish you were here."

Surely no other little girl ever spent such a queer morning. It seemed as if there was no one in all the huge rambling house but her own small self, wandering about upstairs and down, through narrow passages and wide ones, where it seemed to her that no one but herself had ever walked. Since so many rooms had been built, people must have lived in them, but it all seemed so empty that she could not quite believe it true.

It was not until she climbed to the second floor that she thought of turning the handle of a door. All the doors were shut, as Mrs. Medlock had said they were, but at last she put her hand on the handle of one of them and turned it. She was almost frightened for a moment when she felt that it turned without difficulty and that when she pushed upon the door itself it slowly and heavily opened. It was a massive door and opened into a big bedroom. There were embroidered hangings on the wall, and inlaid furniture such as she had seen in India stood about the room. A broad window with leaded panes looked out upon the moor; and over the mantel was another portrait of the stiff, plain little girl who seemed to stare at her more curiously than ever.

"Perhaps she slept here once," said Mary. "She stares at me so that she makes me feel queer."

After that she opened more doors and more. She saw so many rooms that she became quite tired and began to think that there must be a hundred, though she had not counted them. In all of them there were old pictures or old tapestries with strange scenes worked on them. There were curious pieces of furniture and curious ornaments in nearly all of them.

In one room, which looked like a lady's sitting-room, the hangings were all embroidered velvet, and in a cabinet were about a hundred little elephants made of ivory. They were of different sizes, and some had their mahouts or palanquins on their backs. Some were much bigger than the others and some were so tiny that they seemed only babies. Mary had seen carved ivory in India and she knew all about elephants. She opened the door of the cabinet and stood on a footstool and played with these for quite a long time. When she got tired she set the elephants in order and shut the door of the cabinet.

In all her wanderings through the long corridors and the empty rooms, she had seen nothing alive; but in this room she saw something. Just after she had closed the cabinet door she heard a tiny rustling sound. It made her jump and look around at the sofa by the fireplace, from which it seemed to come. In the corner of the sofa there was a cushion, and in the velvet which covered it there was a hole, and out of the hole peeped a tiny head with a pair of frightened eyes in it.

Mary crept softly across the room to look. The bright eyes belonged to a little gray mouse, and the mouse had eaten a hole into the cushion and made a comfortable nest there. Six baby mice were cuddled up asleep near her. If there was no one else alive in the hundred rooms there were seven mice who did not look lonely at all.

"If they wouldn't be so frightened I would take them back with me," said Mary.

She had wandered about long enough to feel too tired to wander any farther, and she turned back. Two or three times she lost her way by turning down the wrong corridor and was obliged to ramble up and down until she found the right one; but at last she reached her own floor again, though she was some distance from her own room and did not know exactly where she was.

"I believe I have taken a wrong turning again," she said, standing still at what seemed the end of a short passage with tapestry on the wall. "I don't know which way to go. How still everything is!"

It was while she was standing here and just after she had said this that the stillness was broken by a sound. It was another cry, but not quite like the one she had heard last night; it was only a short one, a fretful childish whine muffled by passing through walls.

"It's nearer than it was," said Mary, her heart beating rather faster. "And it is crying."

She put her hand accidentally upon the tapestry near her, and then sprang back, feeling quite startled. The tapestry was the covering of a door which fell open and showed her that there was another part of the corridor behind it, and Mrs. Medlock was coming up it with her bunch of keys in her hand and a very cross look on her face.

"What are you doing here?" she said, and she took Mary by the arm and pulled her away. "What did I tell you?"

"I turned round the wrong corner," explained Mary. "I didn't know which way to go and I heard some one crying." She quite hated Mrs. Medlock at the moment, but she hated her more the next.

"You didn't hear anything of the sort," said the housekeeper. "You come along back to your own nursery or I'll box your ears."

And she took her by the arm and half pushed, half pulled her up one passage and down another until she pushed her in at the door of her own room.

"Now," she said, "you stay where you're told to stay or you'll find yourself locked up. The master had better get you a governess, same as he said he would. You're one that needs some one to look sharp after you. I've got enough to do."

She went out of the room and slammed the door after her, and Mary went and sat on the hearth-rug, pale with rage. She did not cry, but ground her teeth.

"There *was* some one crying—there *was*—there *was*!" she said to herself.

She had heard it twice now, and sometime she would find out. She had found out a great deal this morning. She felt as if she had been on a long journey, and at any rate she had had something to amuse her all the time, and she had played with the ivory elephants and had seen the gray mouse and its babies in their nest in the velvet cushion.

CHAPTER VII

THE KEY TO THE GARDEN

Two days after this, when Mary opened her eyes she sat upright in bed immediately, and called to Martha.

"Look at the moor! Look at the moor!"

The rainstorm had ended and the gray mist and clouds had been swept away in the night by the wind. The wind itself had ceased and a brilliant, deep blue sky arched high over the moorland. Never, never had Mary dreamed of a sky so blue. In India skies were hot and blazing; this was of a deep cool blue which almost seemed to sparkle like the waters of some lovely bottomless lake, and here and there, high, high in the arched blueness floated small clouds of snow-white fleece. The far-reaching world of the moor itself looked softly blue instead of gloomy purple-black or awful dreary gray.

"Aye," said Martha with a cheerful grin. "Th' storm's over for a bit. It does like this at this time o' th' year. It goes off in a night like it was pretendin' it had never been here an' never meant to come again. That's because th' springtime's on its way. It's a long way off yet, but it's comin'."

"I thought perhaps it always rained or looked dark in England," Mary said.

"Eh! no!" said Martha, sitting up on her heels among her black lead brushes. "Nowt o' th' soart!"

"What does that mean?" asked Mary seriously. In India the natives spoke different dialects which only a few people understood, so she was not surprised when Martha used words she did not know.

Martha laughed as she had done the first morning.

"There now," she said. "I've talked broad Yorkshire again like Mrs. Medlock said I mustn't. 'Nowt o' th' soart' means 'nothin'-of-the-sort,'" slowly and carefully, "but it takes so long to say it. Yorkshire's th' sunniest place on earth when it is sunny. I told thee tha'd like th' moor after a bit. Just you wait till you see th' gold-colored gorse blossoms an' th' blossoms o' th' broom, an' th' heather flowerin', all purple bells, an' hundreds o' butterflies flutterin' an' bees hummin' an' skylarks soarin' up an' singin'. You'll want to get out on it at sunrise an' live out on it all day like Dickon does."

"Could I ever get there?" asked Mary wistfully, looking through her window at the far-off blue. It was so new and big and wonderful and such a heavenly color.

"I don't know," answered Martha. "Tha's never used tha' legs since tha' was born, it seems to me. Tha' couldn't walk five mile. It's five mile to our cottage."

"I should like to see your cottage."

Martha stared at her a moment curiously before she took up her polishing brush and began to rub the grate again. She was thinking that the small plain face did not look quite as sour at this moment as it had done the first morning she saw it. It looked just a trifle like little Susan Ann's when she wanted something very much.

"I'll ask my mother about it," she said. "She's one o' them that nearly always sees a way to do things. It's my day out today an' I'm goin' home. Eh! I am glad. Mrs. Medlock thinks a lot o' mother. Perhaps she could talk to her."

"I like your mother," said Mary.

"I should think tha' did," agreed Martha, polishing away.

"I've never seen her," said Mary.

"No, tha' hasn't," replied Martha.

She sat up on her heels again and rubbed the end of her nose with the back of her hand as if puzzled for a moment, but she ended quite positively.

"Well, she's that sensible an' hard workin' an' goodnatured an' clean that no one could help likin' her whether they'd seen her or not. When I'm goin' home to her on my day out I just jump for joy when I'm crossin' the moor."

"I like Dickon," added Mary. "And I've never seen him."

"Well," said Martha stoutly, "I've told thee that th' very birds likes him an' th' rabbits an' wild sheep an' ponies, an' th' foxes themselves. I wonder," staring at her reflectively, "what Dickon would think of thee?"

"He wouldn't like me," said Mary in her stiff, cold little way. "No one does."

Martha looked reflective again.

"How does tha' like thysel'?" she inquired, really quite as if she were curious to know.

Mary hesitated a moment and thought it over.

"Not at all—really," she answered. "But I never thought of that before."

Martha grinned a little as if at some homely recollection.

"Mother said that to me once," she said. "She was at her wash-tub an' I was in a bad temper an' talkin' ill of folk, an' she turns round on me an' says: 'Tha' young vixen, tha'! There tha' stands sayin' tha' doesn't like this one an' tha' doesn't like that one. How does tha' like thysel'?' It made me laugh an' it brought me to my senses in a minute."

She went away in high spirits as soon as she had given Mary her breakfast. She was going to walk five miles across the moor to the cottage, and she was going to help her mother with the washing and do the week's baking and enjoy herself thoroughly.

Mary felt lonelier than ever when she knew she was no longer in the house. She went out into the garden as quickly as possible, and the first thing she did was to run round and round the fountain flower garden ten times. She counted the times carefully and when she had finished she felt in better spirits. The sunshine made the whole place look different. The high, deep, blue sky arched over Misselthwaite as well as over the moor, and she kept lifting her face and looking up into it, trying to imagine what it would be like to lie down on one of the little snow-white clouds and float about. She went into the first kitchen-garden and found Ben Weatherstaff working there with two other gardeners. The change in the weather seemed to have done him good. He spoke to her of his own accord. "Springtime's comin,'" he said. "Cannot tha' smell it?"

Mary sniffed and thought she could.

"I smell something nice and fresh and damp," she said.

"That's th' good rich earth," he answered, digging away. "It's in a good humor makin' ready to grow things. It's glad when plantin' time comes. It's dull in th' winter when it's got nowt to do. In th' flower gardens out there things will be stirrin' down below in th' dark. Th' sun's warmin' 'em. You'll see bits o' green spikes stickin' out o' th' black earth after a bit."

"What will they be?" asked Mary.

"Crocuses an' snowdrops an' daffydowndillys. Has tha' never seen them?"

"No. Everything is hot, and wet, and green after the rains in India," said Mary. "And I think things grow up in a night."

"These won't grow up in a night," said Weatherstaff. "Tha'll have to wait for 'em. They'll poke up a bit higher here, an' push out a spike more there, an' uncurl a leaf this day an' another that. You watch 'em."

"I am going to," answered Mary.

Very soon she heard the soft rustling flight of wings again and she knew at once that the robin had come again. He was very pert and lively, and hopped about so close to her feet, and put his head on one side and looked at her so slyly that she asked Ben Weatherstaff a question.

"Do you think he remembers me?" she said.

"Remembers thee!" said Weatherstaff indignantly. "He knows every cabbage stump in th' gardens, let alone th' people. He's never seen a little wench here before, an' he's bent on findin' out all about thee. Tha's no need to try to hide anything from him."

"Are things stirring down below in the dark in that garden where he lives?" Mary inquired.

"What garden?" grunted Weatherstaff, becoming surly again.

"The one where the old rose-trees are." She could not help asking, because she wanted so much to know. "Are all the flowers dead, or do some of them come again in the summer? Are there ever any roses?"

"Ask him," said Ben Weatherstaff, hunching his shoulders toward the robin. "He's the only one as knows. No one else has seen inside it for ten year'."

Ten years was a long time, Mary thought. She had been born ten years ago.

She walked away, slowly thinking. She had begun to like the garden just as she had begun to like the robin and Dickon and Martha's mother. She was beginning to like Martha, too. That seemed a good many people to like—when you were not used to liking. She thought of the robin as one of the people. She went to her walk outside the long, ivy-covered wall over which she could see the tree-tops; and the second time she walked up and down the most interesting and exciting thing happened to her, and it was all through Ben Weatherstaff's robin.

She heard a chirp and a twitter, and when she looked at the bare flower-bed at her left side there he was hopping about and pretending to peck things out of the earth to persuade her that he had not followed her. But she knew he had followed her and the surprise so filled her with delight that she almost trembled a little.

"You do remember me!" she cried out. "You do! You are prettier than anything else in the world!"

She chirped, and talked, and coaxed and he hopped, and flirted his tail and twittered. It was as if he were talking. His red waistcoat was like satin and he puffed his tiny breast out and was so fine and so grand and so pretty that it was really as if he were showing her how important and like a human person a robin could be. Mistress Mary forgot that she had ever been contrary in her life when he allowed her to draw closer and closer to him, and bend down and talk and try to make something like robin sounds.

Oh! to think that he should actually let her come as near to him as that! He knew nothing in the world would make her put out her hand toward him or startle him in the least tiniest way. He knew it because he was a real person—only nicer than any other person in the world. She was so happy that she scarcely dared to breathe.

The flower-bed was not quite bare. It was bare of flowers because the perennial plants had been cut down for their winter rest, but there were tall shrubs and low ones which grew together at the back of the bed, and as the robin hopped about under them she saw him hop over a small pile of freshly turned up earth. He stopped on it to look for a worm. The earth had been turned up because a dog had been trying to dig up a mole and he had scratched quite a deep hole.

Mary looked at it, not really knowing why the hole was there, and as she looked she saw something almost buried in the newly-turned soil. It was something like a ring of rusty iron or brass and when the robin flew up into a tree nearby she put out her hand and picked the ring up. It was more than a ring, however; it was an old key which looked as if it had been buried a long time.

Mistress Mary stood up and looked at it with an almost frightened face as it hung from her finger.

"Perhaps it has been buried for ten years," she said in a whisper. "Perhaps it is the key to the garden!"

CHAPTER VIII

THE ROBIN WHO SHOWED THE WAY

She looked at the key quite a long time. She turned it over and over, and thought about it. As I have said before, she was not a child who had been trained to ask permission or consult her elders about things. All she thought about the key was that if it was the key to the closed garden, and she could find out where the door was, she could perhaps open it and see what was inside the walls, and what had happened to the old rose-trees. It was because it had been shut up so long that she wanted to see it. It seemed as if it must be different from other places and that something strange must have happened to it during ten years. Besides that, if she liked it she could go into it every day and shut the door behind her, and she could make up some play of her own and play it quite alone, because nobody would ever know where she was, but would think the door was still locked and the key buried in the earth. The thought of that pleased her very much.

Living as it were, all by herself in a house with a hundred mysteriously closed rooms and having nothing whatever to do to amuse herself, had set her inactive brain to working and was actually awakening her imagination. There is no doubt that the fresh, strong, pure air from the moor had a great deal to do with it. Just as it had given her an appetite, and fighting with the wind had stirred her blood, so the same things had stirred her mind. In India she had always been too hot and languid and weak to care much about anything, but in this place she was beginning to care and to want to do new things. Already she felt less "contrary," though she did not know why.

She put the key in her pocket and walked up and down her walk. No one but herself ever seemed to come there, so she could walk slowly and look at the wall, or, rather, at the ivy growing on it. The ivy was the baffling thing. Howsoever carefully she looked she could see nothing but thickly growing, glossy, dark green leaves. She was very much disappointed. Something of her contrariness came back to her as she paced the walk and looked over it at the tree-tops inside. It seemed so silly, she said to herself, to be near it and not be able to get in. She took the key in her pocket when she went back to the house, and she made up her mind that she would always carry it with her when she went out, so that if she ever should find the hidden door she would be ready.

Mrs. Medlock had allowed Martha to sleep all night at the cottage, but she was back at her work in the morning with cheeks redder than ever and in the best of spirits.

"I got up at four o'clock," she said. "Eh! it was pretty on th' moor with th' birds gettin' up an' th' rabbits scamperin' about an' th' sun risin'. I didn't walk all th' way. A man gave me a ride in his cart an' I did enjoy myself."

She was full of stories of the delights of her day out. Her mother had been glad to see her and they had got the baking and washing all out of the way. She had even made each of the children a doughcake with a bit of brown sugar in it.

"I had 'em all pipin' hot when they came in from playin' on th' moor. An' th' cottage all smelt o' nice, clean hot bakin' an' there was a good fire, an' they just shouted for joy. Our Dickon he said our cottage was good enough for a king."

In the evening they had all sat round the fire, and Martha and her mother had sewed patches on torn clothes and mended stockings and Martha had told them about the little girl who had come from India and who had been waited on all her life by what Martha called "blacks" until she didn't know how to put on her own stockings.

"Eh! they did like to hear about you," said Martha. "They wanted to know all about th' blacks an' about th' ship you came in. I couldn't tell 'em enough."

Mary reflected a little.

"I'll tell you a great deal more before your next day out," she said, "so that you will have more to talk about. I dare say they would like to hear about riding on elephants and camels, and about the officers going to hunt tigers."

"My word!" cried delighted Martha. "It would set 'em clean off their heads. Would tha' really do that, Miss? It would be same as a wild beast show like we heard they had in York once."

"India is quite different from Yorkshire," Mary said slowly, as she thought the matter over. "I never thought of that. Did Dickon and your mother like to hear you talk about me?"

"Why, our Dickon's eyes nearly started out o' his head, they got that round," answered Martha. "But mother, she was put out about your seemin' to be all by yourself like. She said, 'Hasn't Mr. Craven got no governess for her, nor no nurse?' and I said, 'No, he hasn't, though Mrs. Medlock says he will when he thinks of it, but she says he mayn't think of it for two or three years.'"

"I don't want a governess," said Mary sharply.

"But mother says you ought to be learnin' your book by this time an' you ought to have a woman to look after you, an' she says: 'Now, Martha, you just think how you'd feel yourself, in a big place like that, wanderin' about all alone, an' no mother. You do your best to cheer her up,' she says, an' I said I would."

Mary gave her a long, steady look.

"You do cheer me up," she said. "I like to hear you talk."

Presently Martha went out of the room and came back with something held in her hands under her apron.

"What does tha' think," she said, with a cheerful grin. "I've brought thee a present."

"A present!" exclaimed Mistress Mary. How could a cottage full of fourteen hungry people give any one a present!

"A man was drivin' across the moor peddlin'," Martha explained. "An' he stopped his cart at our door. He had pots an' pans an' odds an' ends, but mother had no money to buy anythin'. Just as he was goin' away our 'Lizabeth Ellen called out, 'Mother, he's got skippin'-ropes with red an' blue handles.' An' mother she calls out quite sudden, 'Here, stop, mister! How much are they?' An' he says 'Tuppence', an' mother she began fumblin' in her pocket an' she says to me, 'Martha, tha's brought me thy wages like a good lass, an' I've got four places to put every penny, but I'm just goin' to take tuppence out of it to buy that child a skippin'-rope,' an' she bought one an' here it is."

She brought it out from under her apron and exhibited it quite proudly. It was a strong, slender rope with a striped red and blue handle at each end, but Mary Lennox had never seen a skipping-rope before. She gazed at it with a mystified expression.

"What is it for?" she asked curiously.

"For!" cried out Martha. "Does tha' mean that they've not got skippin'-ropes in India, for all they've got elephants and tigers and camels! No wonder most of 'em's black. This is what it's for; just watch me."

And she ran into the middle of the room and, taking a handle in each hand, began to skip, and skip, and skip, while Mary turned in her chair to stare at her, and the queer faces in the old portraits seemed to stare at her, too, and wonder what on earth this common little cottager had the impudence to be doing under their very noses. But Martha did not even see them. The interest and curiosity in Mistress Mary's face delighted her, and she went on skipping and counted as she skipped until she had reached a hundred.

"I could skip longer than that," she said when she stopped. "I've skipped as much as five hundred when I was twelve, but I wasn't as fat then as I am now, an' I was in practice."

Mary got up from her chair beginning to feel excited herself.

"It looks nice," she said. "Your mother is a kind woman. Do you think I could ever skip like that?"

"You just try it," urged Martha, handing her the skipping-rope. "You can't skip a hundred at first, but if you practice you'll mount up. That's what mother said. She says, 'Nothin' will do her more good than skippin' rope. It's th' sensiblest toy a child can have. Let her play out in th' fresh air skippin' an' it'll stretch her legs an' arms an' give her some strength in 'em.'"

It was plain that there was not a great deal of strength in Mistress Mary's arms and legs when she first began to skip. She was not very clever at it, but she liked it so much that she did not want to stop.

"Put on tha' things and run an' skip out o' doors," said Martha. "Mother said I must tell you to keep out o' doors as much as you could, even when it rains a bit, so as tha' wrap up warm."

Mary put on her coat and hat and took her skipping-rope over her arm. She opened the door to go out, and then suddenly thought of something and turned back rather slowly.

"Martha," she said, "they were your wages. It was your two-pence really. Thank you." She said it stiffly because she was not used to thanking people or noticing that they did things for her. "Thank you," she said, and held out her hand because she did not know what else to do.

Martha gave her hand a clumsy little shake, as if she was not accustomed to this sort of thing either. Then she laughed.

"Eh! th' art a queer, old-womanish thing," she said. "If tha'd been our 'Lizabeth Ellen tha'd have given me a kiss."

Mary looked stiffer than ever.

"Do you want me to kiss you?"

Martha laughed again.

"Nay, not me," she answered. "If tha' was different, p'raps tha'd want to thysel'. But tha' isn't. Run off outside an' play with thy rope."

Mistress Mary felt a little awkward as she went out of the room. Yorkshire people seemed strange, and Martha was always rather a puzzle to her. At first she had disliked her very much, but now she did not. The skipping-rope was a wonderful thing. She counted and skipped, and skipped and counted, until her cheeks were quite red, and she was more interested than she had ever been since she was born. The sun was shining and a little wind was blowing—not a rough wind, but one which came in delightful little gusts and brought a fresh scent of newly turned earth with it. She skipped round the fountain garden, and up one walk and down another. She skipped at last into the kitchen-garden and saw Ben Weatherstaff digging and talking to his robin, which was hopping about him. She skipped down the walk toward him and he lifted his head and looked at her with a curious expression. She had wondered if he would notice her. She wanted him to see her skip.

"Well!" he exclaimed. "Upon my word. P'raps tha' art a young 'un, after all, an' p'raps tha's got child's blood in thy veins instead of sour buttermilk. Tha's skipped red into thy cheeks as sure as my name's Ben Weatherstaff. I wouldn't have believed tha' could do it."

"I never skipped before," Mary said. "I'm just beginning. I can only go up to twenty."

"Tha' keep on," said Ben. "Tha' shapes well enough at it for a young 'un that's lived with heathen. Just see how he's watchin' thee," jerking his head toward the robin. "He followed after thee yesterday. He'll be at it again today. He'll be bound to find out what th' skippin'-rope is. He's never seen one. Eh!" shaking his head at the bird, "tha' curiosity will be th' death of thee sometime if tha' doesn't look sharp."

Mary skipped round all the gardens and round the orchard, resting every few minutes. At length she went to her own special walk and made up her mind to try if she could skip the whole length of it. It was a good long skip and she began slowly, but before she had gone half-way down the path she was so hot and breathless that she was obliged to stop. She did not mind much, because she had already counted up to thirty. She stopped with a little laugh of pleasure, and there, lo and behold, was the robin swaying on a long branch of ivy. He had followed her and he greeted her with a chirp. As Mary had skipped toward him she felt something heavy in her pocket strike against her at each jump, and when she saw the robin she laughed again.

"You showed me where the key was yesterday," she said. "You ought to show me the door today; but I don't believe you know!"

The robin flew from his swinging spray of ivy on to the top of the wall and he opened his beak and sang a loud, lovely trill, merely to show off. Nothing in the world is quite as adorably lovely as a robin when he shows off—and they are nearly always doing it.

Mary Lennox had heard a great deal about Magic in her Ayah's stories, and she always said that what happened almost at that moment was Magic.

One of the nice little gusts of wind rushed down the walk, and it was a stronger one than the rest. It was strong enough to wave the branches of the trees, and it was more than strong enough to sway the trailing sprays of untrimmed ivy hanging from the wall. Mary had stepped close to the robin, and suddenly the gust of wind swung aside some loose ivy trails, and more suddenly still she jumped toward it and caught it in her hand. This she did because she had seen something under it—a round knob which had been covered by the leaves hanging over it. It was the knob of a door.

She put her hands under the leaves and began to pull and push them aside. Thick as the ivy hung, it nearly all was a loose and swinging curtain, though some had crept over wood and iron. Mary's heart began to thump and her hands to shake a little in her delight and excitement. The robin kept singing and twittering away and tilting his head on one side, as if he were as excited as she was. What was this under her hands which was square and made of iron and which her fingers found a hole in?

It was the lock of the door which had been closed ten years and she put her hand in her pocket, drew out the key and found it fitted the keyhole. She put the key in and turned it. It took two hands to do it, but it did turn.

And then she took a long breath and looked behind her up the long walk to see if any one was coming. No one was coming. No one ever did come, it seemed, and she took another long breath, because she could not help it, and she held back the swinging curtain of ivy and pushed back the door which opened slowly—slowly.

Then she slipped through it, and shut it behind her, and stood with her back against it, looking about her and breathing quite fast with excitement, and wonder, and delight.

She was standing inside the secret garden.

CHAPTER IX

THE STRANGEST HOUSE ANY ONE EVER LIVED IN

It was the sweetest, most mysterious-looking place any one could imagine. The high walls which shut it in were covered with the leafless stems of climbing roses which were so thick that they were matted together. Mary Lennox knew they were roses because she had seen a great many roses in India. All the ground was covered with grass of a wintry brown and out of it grew clumps of bushes which were surely rosebushes if they were alive. There were numbers of standard roses which had so spread their branches that they were like little trees. There were other trees in the garden, and one of the things which made the place look strangest and loveliest was that climbing roses had run all over them and swung down long tendrils which made light swaying curtains, and here and there they had caught at each other or at a far-reaching branch and had crept from one tree to another and made lovely bridges of themselves. There were neither leaves nor roses on them now and Mary did not know whether they were dead or alive, but their thin gray or brown branches and sprays looked like a sort of hazy mantle spreading over everything, walls, and trees, and even brown grass, where they had fallen from their fastenings and run along the ground. It was this hazy tangle from tree to tree which made it all look so mysterious. Mary had thought it must be different from other gardens which had not been left all by themselves so long; and indeed it was different from any other place she had ever seen in her life.

"How still it is!" she whispered. "How still!"

Then she waited a moment and listened at the stillness. The robin, who had flown to his tree-top, was still as all the rest. He did not even flutter his wings; he sat without stirring, and looked at Mary.

"No wonder it is still," she whispered again. "I am the first person who has spoken in here for ten years."

She moved away from the door, stepping as softly as if she were afraid of awakening some one. She was glad that there was grass under her feet and that her steps made no sounds. She walked under one of the fairy-like gray arches between the trees and looked up at the sprays and tendrils which formed them. "I wonder if they are all quite dead," she said. "Is it all a quite dead garden? I wish it wasn't."

If she had been Ben Weatherstaff she could have told whether the wood was alive by looking at it, but she could only see that there were only gray or brown sprays and branches and none showed any signs of even a tiny leaf-bud anywhere.

But she was inside the wonderful garden and she could come through the door under the ivy any time and she felt as if she had found a world all her own.

The sun was shining inside the four walls and the high arch of blue sky over this particular piece of Misselthwaite seemed even more brilliant and soft than it was over the moor. The robin flew down from his tree-top and hopped about or flew after her from one bush to another. He chirped a good deal and had a very busy air, as if he were showing her things. Everything was strange and silent and she seemed to be hundreds of miles away from any one, but somehow she did not feel lonely at all. All that troubled her was her wish that she knew whether all the roses were dead, or if perhaps some of them had lived and might put out leaves and buds as the weather got warmer. She did not want it to be a quite dead garden. If it were a quite alive garden, how wonderful it would be, and what thousands of roses would grow on every side!

Her skipping-rope had hung over her arm when she came in and after she had walked about for a while she thought she would skip round the whole garden, stopping when she wanted to look at things. There seemed to have been grass paths here and there, and in one or two corners there were alcoves of evergreen with stone seats or tall moss-covered flower urns in them.

As she came near the second of these alcoves she stopped skipping. There had once been a flowerbed in it, and she thought she saw something sticking out of the black earth—some sharp little pale green points. She remembered what Ben Weatherstaff had said and she knelt down to look at them.

"Yes, they are tiny growing things and they might be crocuses or snowdrops or daffodils," she whispered.

She bent very close to them and sniffed the fresh scent of the damp earth. She liked it very much.

"Perhaps there are some other ones coming up in other places," she said. "I will go all over the garden and look."

She did not skip, but walked. She went slowly and kept her eyes on the ground. She looked in the old border beds and among the grass, and after she had gone round, trying to miss nothing, she had found ever so many more sharp, pale green points, and she had become quite excited again.

"It isn't a quite dead garden," she cried out softly to herself. "Even if the roses are dead, there are other things alive."

She did not know anything about gardening, but the grass seemed so thick in some of the places where the green points were pushing their way through that she thought they did not seem to have room enough to grow. She searched about until she found a rather sharp piece of wood and knelt down and dug and weeded out the weeds and grass until she made nice little clear places around them.

"Now they look as if they could breathe," she said, after she had finished with the first ones. "I am going to do ever so many more. I'll do all I can see. If I haven't time today I can come tomorrow."

She went from place to place, and dug and weeded, and enjoyed herself so immensely that she was led on from bed to bed and into the grass under the trees. The exercise made her so warm that she first threw her coat off, and then her hat, and without knowing it she was smiling down on to the grass and the pale green points all the time.

The robin was tremendously busy. He was very much pleased to see gardening begun on his own estate. He had often wondered at Ben Weatherstaff. Where gardening is done all sorts of delightful things to eat are turned up with the soil. Now here was this new kind of creature who was not half Ben's size and yet had had the sense to come into his garden and begin at once.

Mistress Mary worked in her garden until it was time to go to her midday dinner. In fact, she was rather late in remembering, and when she put on her coat and hat, and picked up her skipping-rope, she could not believe that she had been working two or three hours. She had been actually happy all the time; and dozens and dozens of the tiny, pale green points were to be seen in cleared places, looking twice as cheerful as they had looked before when the grass and weeds had been smothering them.

"I shall come back this afternoon," she said, looking all round at her new kingdom, and speaking to the trees and the rose-bushes as if they heard her.

Then she ran lightly across the grass, pushed open the slow old door and slipped through it under the ivy. She had such red cheeks and such bright eyes and ate such a dinner that Martha was delighted.

"Two pieces o' meat an' two helps o' rice puddin'!" she said. "Eh! mother will be pleased when I tell her what th' skippin'-rope's done for thee."

In the course of her digging with her pointed stick Mistress Mary had found herself digging up a sort of white root rather like an onion. She had put it back in its place and patted the earth carefully down on it and just now she wondered if Martha could tell her what it was.

"Martha," she said, "what are those white roots that look like onions?"

"They're bulbs," answered Martha. "Lots o' spring flowers grow from 'em. Th' very little ones are snowdrops an' crocuses an' th' big ones are narcissuses an' jonquils and daffydowndillys. Th' biggest of all is lilies an' purple flags. Eh! they are nice. Dickon's got a whole lot of 'em planted in our bit o' garden."

"Does Dickon know all about them?" asked Mary, a new idea taking possession of her.

"Our Dickon can make a flower grow out of a brick walk. Mother says he just whispers things out o' th' ground."

"Do bulbs live a long time? Would they live years and years if no one helped them?" inquired Mary anxiously.

"They're things as helps themselves," said Martha. "That's why poor folk can afford to have 'em. If you don't trouble 'em, most of 'em'll work away underground for a lifetime an' spread out an' have little 'uns. There's a place in th' park woods here where there's snowdrops by thousands. They're the prettiest sight in Yorkshire when th' spring comes. No one knows when they was first planted."

"I wish the spring was here now," said Mary. "I want to see all the things that grow in England."

She had finished her dinner and gone to her favorite seat on the hearth-rug.

"I wish—I wish I had a little spade," she said.

"Whatever does tha' want a spade for?" asked Martha, laughing. "Art tha' goin' to take to diggin'? I must tell mother that, too."

Mary looked at the fire and pondered a little. She must be careful if she meant to keep her secret kingdom. She wasn't doing any harm, but if Mr. Craven found out about the open door he would be fearfully angry and get a new key and lock it up forevermore. She really could not bear that.

"This is such a big lonely place," she said slowly, as if she were turning matters over in her mind. "The house is lonely, and the park is lonely, and the gardens are lonely. So many places seem shut up. I never did many things in India, but there were more people to look at—natives and soldiers marching by—and sometimes bands playing, and my Ayah told me stories. There is no one to talk to here except you and Ben Weatherstaff. And you have to do your work and Ben Weatherstaff won't speak to me often. I thought if I had a little spade I could dig somewhere as he does, and I might make a little garden if he would give me some seeds."

Martha's face quite lighted up.

"There now!" she exclaimed, "if that wasn't one of th' things mother said. She says, 'There's such a lot o' room in that big place, why don't they give her a bit for herself, even if she doesn't plant nothin' but parsley an' radishes? She'd dig an' rake away an' be right down happy over it.' Them was the very words she said."

"Were they?" said Mary. "How many things she knows, doesn't she?"

"Eh!" said Martha. "It's like she says: 'A woman as brings up twelve children learns something besides her A B C. Children's as good as 'rithmetic to set you findin' out things.'"

"How much would a spade cost—a little one?" Mary asked.

"Well," was Martha's reflective answer, "at Thwaite village there's a shop or so an' I saw little garden sets with a spade an' a rake an' a fork all tied together for two shillings. An' they was stout enough to work with, too."

"I've got more than that in my purse," said Mary. "Mrs. Morrison gave me five shillings and Mrs. Medlock gave me some money from Mr. Craven."

"Did he remember thee that much?" exclaimed Martha.

"Mrs. Medlock said I was to have a shilling a week to spend. She gives me one every Saturday. I didn't know what to spend it on."

"My word! that's riches," said Martha. "Tha' can buy anything in th' world tha' wants. Th' rent of our cottage is only one an' threepence an' it's like pullin' eye-teeth to get it. Now I've just thought of somethin'," putting her hands on her hips.

"What?" said Mary eagerly.

"In the shop at Thwaite they sell packages o' flower-seeds for a penny each, and our Dickon he knows which is th' prettiest ones an' how to make 'em grow. He walks over to Thwaite many a day just for th' fun of it. Does tha' know how to print letters?" suddenly.

"I know how to write," Mary answered.

Martha shook her head.

"Our Dickon can only read printin'. If tha' could print we could write a letter to him an' ask him to go an' buy th' garden tools an' th' seeds at th' same time."

"Oh! you're a good girl!" Mary cried. "You are, really! I didn't know you were so nice. I know I can print letters if I try. Let's ask Mrs. Medlock for a pen and ink and some paper."

"I've got some of my own," said Martha. "I bought 'em so I could print a bit of a letter to mother of a Sunday. I'll go and get it." She ran out of the room, and Mary stood by the fire and twisted her thin little hands together with sheer pleasure.

"If I have a spade," she whispered, "I can make the earth nice and soft and dig up weeds. If I have seeds and can make flowers grow the garden won't be dead at all—it will come alive."

She did not go out again that afternoon because when Martha returned with her pen and ink and paper she was obliged to clear the table and carry the plates and dishes downstairs and when she got into the kitchen Mrs. Medlock was there and told her to do something, so Mary waited for what seemed to her a long time before she came back. Then it was a serious piece of work to write to Dickon. Mary had been taught very little because her governesses had disliked her too much to stay with her. She could not spell particularly well but she found that she could print letters when she tried. This was the letter Martha dictated to her:

"My Dear Dickon:

This comes hoping to find you well as it leaves me at present. Miss Mary has plenty of money and will you go to Thwaite and buy her some flower seeds and a set of garden tools to make a flower-bed. Pick the prettiest ones and easy to grow because she has never done it before and lived in India which is different. Give my love to mother and every one of you. Miss Mary is going to tell me a lot more so that on my next day out you can hear about elephants and camels and gentlemen going hunting lions and tigers.

Your loving sister,
Martha Phoebe Sowerby."

"We'll put the money in th' envelope an' I'll get th' butcher boy to take it in his cart. He's a great friend o' Dickon's," said Martha.

"How shall I get the things when Dickon buys them?"

"He'll bring 'em to you himself. He'll like to walk over this way."

"Oh!" exclaimed Mary, "then I shall see him! I never thought I should see Dickon."

"Does tha' want to see him?" asked Martha suddenly, for Mary had looked so pleased.

"Yes, I do. I never saw a boy foxes and crows loved. I want to see him very much."

Martha gave a little start, as if she remembered something. "Now to think," she broke out, "to think o' me forgettin' that there; an' I thought I was goin' to tell you first thing this mornin'. I asked mother—and she said she'd ask Mrs. Medlock her own self."

"Do you mean—" Mary began.

"What I said Tuesday. Ask her if you might be driven over to our cottage some day and have a bit o' mother's hot oat cake, an' butter, an' a glass o' milk."

It seemed as if all the interesting things were happening in one day. To think of going over the moor in the daylight and when the sky was blue! To think of going into the cottage which held twelve children!

"Does she think Mrs. Medlock would let me go?" she asked, quite anxiously.

"Aye, she thinks she would. She knows what a tidy woman mother is and how clean she keeps the cottage."

"If I went I should see your mother as well as Dickon," said Mary, thinking it over and liking the idea very much. "She doesn't seem to be like the mothers in India."

Her work in the garden and the excitement of the afternoon ended by making her feel quiet and thoughtful. Martha stayed with her until tea-time, but they sat in comfortable quiet and talked very little. But just before Martha went downstairs for the tea-tray, Mary asked a question.

"Martha," she said, "has the scullery-maid had the tooth-ache again today?"

Martha certainly started slightly.

"What makes thee ask that?" she said.

"Because when I waited so long for you to come back I opened the door and walked down the corridor to see if you were coming. And I heard that far-off crying again, just as we heard it the other night. There isn't a wind today, so you see it couldn't have been the wind."

"Eh!" said Martha restlessly. "Tha' mustn't go walkin' about in corridors an' listenin'. Mr. Craven would be that there angry there's no knowin' what he'd do."

"I wasn't listening," said Mary. "I was just waiting for you—and I heard it. That's three times."

"My word! There's Mrs. Medlock's bell," said Martha, and she almost ran out of the room.

"It's the strangest house any one ever lived in," said Mary drowsily, as she dropped her head on the cushioned seat of the armchair near her. Fresh air, and digging, and skipping-rope had made her feel so comfortably tired that she fell asleep.

CHAPTER X

DICKON

The sun shone down for nearly a week on the secret garden. The Secret Garden was what Mary called it when she was thinking of it. She liked the name, and she liked still more the feeling that when its beautiful old walls shut her in no one knew where she was. It seemed almost like being shut out of the world in some fairy place. The few books she had read and liked had been fairy-story books, and she had read of secret gardens in some of the stories. Sometimes people went to sleep in them for a hundred years, which she had thought must be rather stupid. She had no intention of going to sleep, and, in fact, she was becoming wider awake every day which passed at Misselthwaite. She was beginning to like to be out of doors; she no longer hated the wind, but enjoyed it. She could run faster, and longer, and she could skip up to a hundred. The bulbs in the secret garden must have been much astonished. Such nice clear places were made round them that they had all the breathing space they wanted, and really, if Mistress Mary had known it, they began to cheer up under the dark earth and work tremendously. The sun could get at them and warm them, and when the rain came down it could reach them at once, so they began to feel very much alive.

Mary was an odd, determined little person, and now she had something interesting to be determined about, she was very much absorbed, indeed. She worked and dug and pulled up weeds steadily, only becoming more pleased with her work every hour instead of tiring of it. It seemed to her like a fascinating sort of play. She found many more of the sprouting pale green points than she had ever hoped to find. They seemed to be starting up everywhere and each day she was sure she found tiny new ones, some so tiny that they barely peeped above the earth. There were so many that she remembered what Martha had said about the "snowdrops by the thousands," and about bulbs spreading and making new ones. These had been left to themselves for ten years and perhaps they had spread, like the snowdrops, into thousands. She wondered how long it would be before they showed that they were flowers. Sometimes she stopped digging to look at the garden and try to imagine what it would be like when it was covered with thousands of lovely things in bloom. During that week of sunshine, she became more intimate with Ben Weatherstaff. She surprised him several times by seeming to start up beside him as if she sprang out of the earth. The truth was that she was afraid that he would pick up his tools and go away if he saw her coming, so she always walked toward him as silently as possible. But, in fact, he did not object to her as strongly as he had at first. Perhaps he was secretly rather flattered by her evident desire for his elderly company. Then, also, she was more civil than she had been. He did not know that when she first saw him she spoke to him as she would have spoken to a native, and had not known that a cross, sturdy old Yorkshire man was not accustomed to salaam to his masters, and be merely commanded by them to do things.

"Tha'rt like th' robin," he said to her one morning when he lifted his head and saw her standing by him. "I never knows when I shall see thee or which side tha'll come from."

"He's friends with me now," said Mary.

"That's like him," snapped Ben Weatherstaff. "Makin' up to th' women folk just for vanity an' flightiness. There's nothin' he wouldn't do for th' sake o' showin' off an' flirtin' his tail-feathers. He's as full o' pride as an egg's full o' meat."

He very seldom talked much and sometimes did not even answer Mary's questions except by a grunt, but this morning he said more than usual. He stood up and rested one hobnailed boot on the top of his spade while he looked her over.

"How long has tha' been here?" he jerked out.

"I think it's about a month," she answered.

"Tha's beginnin' to do Misselthwaite credit," he said. "Tha's a bit fatter than tha' was an' tha's not quite so yeller. Tha' looked like a young plucked crow when tha' first came into this garden. Thinks I to myself I never set eyes on an uglier, sourer faced young 'un."

Mary was not vain and as she had never thought much of her looks she was not greatly disturbed.

"I know I'm fatter," she said. "My stockings are getting tighter. They used to make wrinkles. There's the robin, Ben Weatherstaff."

There, indeed, was the robin, and she thought he looked nicer than ever. His red waistcoat was as glossy as satin and he flirted his wings and tail and tilted his head and hopped about with all sorts of lively graces. He seemed determined to make Ben Weatherstaff admire him. But Ben was sarcastic.

"Aye, there tha' art!" he said. "Tha' can put up with me for a bit sometimes when tha's got no one better. Tha's been reddenin' up thy waistcoat an' polishin' thy feathers this two weeks. I know what tha's up to. Tha's courtin' some bold young madam somewhere tellin' thy lies to her about bein' th' finest cock robin on Missel Moor an' ready to fight all th' rest of 'em."

"Oh! look at him!" exclaimed Mary.

The robin was evidently in a fascinating, bold mood. He hopped closer and closer and looked at Ben Weatherstaff more and more engagingly. He flew on to the nearest currant bush and tilted his head and sang a little song right at him.

"Tha' thinks tha'll get over me by doin' that," said Ben, wrinkling his face up in such a way that Mary felt sure he was trying not to look pleased. "Tha' thinks no one can stand out against thee—that's what tha' thinks."

The robin spread his wings—Mary could scarcely believe her eyes. He flew right up to the handle of Ben Weatherstaff's spade and alighted on the top of it. Then the old man's face wrinkled itself slowly into a new expression. He stood still as if he were afraid to breathe—as if he would not have stirred for the world, lest his robin should start away. He spoke quite in a whisper.

"Well, I'm danged!" he said as softly as if he were saying something quite different. "Tha' does know how to get at a chap—tha' does! Tha's fair unearthly, tha's so knowin'."

And he stood without stirring—almost without drawing his breath—until the robin gave another flirt to his wings and flew away. Then he stood looking at the handle of the spade as if there might be Magic in it, and then he began to dig again and said nothing for several minutes.

But because he kept breaking into a slow grin now and then, Mary was not afraid to talk to him.

"Have you a garden of your own?" she asked.

"No. I'm bachelder an' lodge with Martin at th' gate."

"If you had one," said Mary, "what would you plant?"

"Cabbages an' 'taters an' onions."

"But if you wanted to make a flower garden," persisted Mary, "what would you plant?"

"Bulbs an' sweet-smellin' things—but mostly roses."

Mary's face lighted up.

"Do you like roses?" she said.

Ben Weatherstaff rooted up a weed and threw it aside before he answered.

"Well, yes, I do. I was learned that by a young lady I was gardener to. She had a lot in a place she was fond of, an' she loved 'em like they was children—or robins. I've seen her bend over an' kiss 'em." He dragged out another weed and scowled at it. "That were as much as ten year' ago."

"Where is she now?" asked Mary, much interested.

"Heaven," he answered, and drove his spade deep into the soil, "'cording to what parson says."

"What happened to the roses?" Mary asked again, more interested than ever.

"They was left to themselves."

Mary was becoming quite excited.

"Did they quite die? Do roses quite die when they are left to themselves?" she ventured.

"Well, I'd got to like 'em—an' I liked her—an' she liked 'em," Ben Weatherstaff admitted reluctantly. "Once or twice a year I'd go an' work at 'em a bit—prune 'em an' dig about th' roots. They run wild, but they was in rich soil, so some of 'em lived."

"When they have no leaves and look gray and brown and dry, how can you tell whether they are dead or alive?" inquired Mary.

"Wait till th' spring gets at 'em—wait till th' sun shines on th' rain and th' rain falls on th' sunshine an' then tha'll find out."

"How—how?" cried Mary, forgetting to be careful.

"Look along th' twigs an' branches an' if tha' see a bit of a brown lump swelling here an' there, watch it after th' warm rain an' see what happens." He stopped suddenly and looked curiously at her eager face. "Why does tha' care so much about roses an' such, all of a sudden?" he demanded.

Mistress Mary felt her face grow red. She was almost afraid to answer.

"I—I want to play that—that I have a garden of my own," she

stammered. "I—there is nothing for me to do. I have nothing—and no one."

"Well," said Ben Weatherstaff slowly, as he watched her, "that's true. Tha' hasn't."

He said it in such an odd way that Mary wondered if he was actually a little sorry for her. She had never felt sorry for herself; she had only felt tired and cross, because she disliked people and things so much. But now the world seemed to be changing and getting nicer. If no one found out about the secret garden, she should enjoy herself always.

She stayed with him for ten or fifteen minutes longer and asked him as many questions as she dared. He answered every one of them in his queer grunting way and he did not seem really cross and did not pick up his spade and leave her. He said something about roses just as she was going away and it reminded her of the ones he had said he had been fond of.

"Do you go and see those other roses now?" she asked.

"Not been this year. My rheumatics has made me too stiff in th' joints."

He said it in his grumbling voice, and then quite suddenly he seemed to get angry with her, though she did not see why he should.

"Now look here!" he said sharply. "Don't tha' ask so many questions. Tha'rt th' worst wench for askin' questions I've ever come a cross. Get thee gone an' play thee. I've done talkin' for today."

And he said it so crossly that she knew there was not the least use in staying another minute. She went skipping slowly down the outside walk, thinking him over and saying to herself that, queer as it was, here was another person whom she liked in spite of his crossness. She liked old Ben Weatherstaff. Yes, she did like him. She always wanted to try to make him talk to her. Also she began to believe that he knew everything in the world about flowers.

There was a laurel-hedged walk which curved round the secret garden and ended at a gate which opened into a wood, in the park. She thought she would slip round this walk and look into the wood and see if there were any rabbits hopping about. She enjoyed the skipping very much and when she reached the little gate she opened it and went through because she heard a low, peculiar whistling sound and wanted to find out what it was.

It was a very strange thing indeed. She quite caught her breath as she stopped to look at it. A boy was sitting under a tree, with his back against it, playing on a rough wooden pipe. He was a funny looking boy about twelve. He looked very clean and his nose turned up and his cheeks were as red as poppies and never had Mistress Mary seen such round and such blue eyes in any boy's face. And on the trunk of the tree he leaned against, a brown squirrel was clinging and watching him, and from behind a bush nearby a cock pheasant was delicately stretching his neck to peep out, and quite near him were two rabbits sitting up and sniffing with tremulous noses—and actually it appeared as if they were all drawing near to watch him and listen to the strange low little call his pipe seemed to make.

When he saw Mary he held up his hand and spoke to her in a voice almost as low as and rather like his piping.

"Don't tha' move," he said. "It'd flight 'em." Mary remained motionless. He stopped playing his pipe and began to rise from the ground. He moved so slowly that it scarcely seemed as though he were moving at all, but at last he stood on his feet and then the squirrel scampered back up into the branches of his tree, the pheasant withdrew his head and the rabbits dropped on all fours and began to hop away, though not at all as if they were frightened.

"I'm Dickon," the boy said. "I know tha'rt Miss Mary."

Then Mary realized that somehow she had known at first that he was Dickon. Who else could have been charming rabbits and pheasants as the natives charm snakes in India? He had a wide, red, curving mouth and his smile spread all over his face.

"I got up slow," he explained, "because if tha' makes a quick move it startles 'em. A body 'as to move gentle an' speak low when wild things is about."

He did not speak to her as if they had never seen each other before but as if he knew her quite well. Mary knew nothing about boys and she spoke to him a little stiffly because she felt rather shy.

"Did you get Martha's letter?" she asked.

He nodded his curly, rust-colored head. "That's why I come."

He stooped to pick up something which had been lying on the ground beside him when he piped.

"I've got th' garden tools. There's a little spade an' rake an' a fork an' hoe. Eh! they are good 'uns. There's a trowel, too. An' th' woman in th' shop threw in a packet o' white poppy an' one o' blue larkspur when I bought th' other seeds."

"Will you show the seeds to me?" Mary said.

She wished she could talk as he did. His speech was so quick and easy. It sounded as if he liked her and was not the least afraid she would not like him, though he was only a common moor boy, in patched clothes and with a funny face and a rough, rusty-red head. As she came closer to him she noticed that there was a clean fresh scent of heather and grass and leaves about him, almost as if he were made of them. She liked it very much and when she looked into his funny face with the red cheeks and round blue eyes she forgot that she had felt shy.

"Let us sit down on this log and look at them," she said.

They sat down and he took a clumsy little brown paper package out of his coat pocket. He untied the string and inside there were ever so many neater and smaller packages with a picture of a flower on each one.

"There's a lot o' mignonette an' poppies," he said. "Mignonette's th' sweetest smellin' thing as grows, an' it'll grow wherever you cast it, same as poppies will. Them as'll come up an' bloom if you just whistle to 'em, them's th' nicest of all." He stopped and turned his head quickly, his poppy-cheeked face lighting up.

"Where's that robin as is callin' us?" he said.

The chirp came from a thick holly bush, bright with scarlet berries, and Mary thought she knew whose it was.

"Is it really calling us?" she asked.

"Aye," said Dickon, as if it was the most natural thing in the world, "he's callin' some one he's friends with. That's same as sayin' 'Here I am. Look at me. I wants a bit of a chat.' There he is in the bush. Whose is he?"

"He's Ben Weatherstaff's, but I think he knows me a little," answered Mary.

"Aye, he knows thee," said Dickon in his low voice again. "An' he likes thee. He's took thee on. He'll tell me all about thee in a minute."

He moved quite close to the bush with the slow movement Mary had noticed before, and then he made a sound almost like the robin's own twitter. The robin listened a few seconds, intently, and then answered quite as if he were replying to a question.

"Aye, he's a friend o' yours," chuckled Dickon.

"Do you think he is?" cried Mary eagerly. She did so want to know. "Do you think he really likes me?"

"He wouldn't come near thee if he didn't," answered Dickon. "Birds is rare choosers an' a robin can flout a body worse than a man. See, he's making up to thee now. 'Cannot tha' see a chap?' he's sayin'."

And it really seemed as if it must be true. He so sidled and twittered and tilted as he hopped on his bush.

"Do you understand everything birds say?" said Mary.

Dickon's grin spread until he seemed all wide, red, curving mouth, and he rubbed his rough head.

"I think I do, and they think I do," he said. "I've lived on th' moor with 'em so long. I've watched 'em break shell an' come out an' fledge an' learn to fly an' begin to sing, till I think I'm one of 'em. Sometimes I think p'raps I'm a bird, or a fox, or a rabbit, or a squirrel, or even a beetle, an' I don't know it."

He laughed and came back to the log and began to talk about the flower seeds again. He told her what they looked like when they were flowers; he told her how to plant them, and watch them, and feed and water them.

"See here," he said suddenly, turning round to look at her. "I'll plant them for thee myself. Where is tha' garden?"

Mary's thin hands clutched each other as they lay on her lap. She did not know what to say, so for a whole minute she said nothing. She had never thought of this. She felt miserable. And she felt as if she went red and then pale.

"Tha's got a bit o' garden, hasn't tha'?" Dickon said.

It was true that she had turned red and then pale. Dickon saw her do it, and as she still said nothing, he began to be puzzled.

"Wouldn't they give thee a bit?" he asked. "Hasn't tha' got any yet?"

She held her hands tighter and turned her eyes toward him.

"I don't know anything about boys," she said slowly. "Could you keep a secret, if I told you one? It's a great secret. I don't know what I should do if any one found it out. I believe I should die!" She said the last sentence quite fiercely.

Dickon looked more puzzled than ever and even rubbed his hand over his rough head again, but he answered quite good-humoredly. "I'm keepin' secrets all th' time," he said. "If I couldn't keep secrets from th' other lads, secrets about foxes' cubs, an' birds' nests, an' wild things' holes, there'd be naught safe on th' moor. Aye, I can keep secrets."

Mistress Mary did not mean to put out her hand and clutch his sleeve but she did it.

"I've stolen a garden," she said very fast. "It isn't mine. It isn't anybody's. Nobody wants it, nobody cares for it, nobody ever goes into it. Perhaps everything is dead in it already. I don't know."

She began to feel hot and as contrary as she had ever felt in her life.

"I don't care, I don't care! Nobody has any right to take it from me when I care about it and they don't. They're letting it die, all shut in by itself," she ended passionately, and she threw her arms over her face and burst out crying—poor little Mistress Mary.

Dickon's curious blue eyes grew rounder and rounder. "Eh-h-h!" he said, drawing his exclamation out slowly, and the way he did it meant both wonder and sympathy.

"I've nothing to do," said Mary. "Nothing belongs to me. I found it myself and I got into it myself. I was only just like the robin, and they wouldn't take it from the robin."

"Where is it?" asked Dickon in a dropped voice.

Mistress Mary got up from the log at once. She knew she felt contrary again, and obstinate, and she did not care at all. She was imperious and Indian, and at the same time hot and sorrowful.

"Come with me and I'll show you," she said.

She led him round the laurel path and to the walk where the ivy grew so thickly. Dickon followed her with a queer, almost pitying, look on his face. He felt as if he were being led to look at some strange bird's nest and must move softly. When she stepped to the wall and lifted the hanging ivy he started. There was a door and Mary pushed it slowly open and they passed in together, and then Mary stood and waved her hand round defiantly.

"It's this," she said. "It's a secret garden, and I'm the only one in the world who wants it to be alive."

Dickon looked round and round about it, and round and round again.

"Eh!" he almost whispered, "it is a queer, pretty place! It's like as if a body was in a dream."

CHAPTER XI

THE NEST OF THE MISSEL THRUSH

For two or three minutes he stood looking round him, while Mary watched him, and then he began to walk about softly, even more lightly than Mary had walked the first time she had found herself inside the four walls. His eyes seemed to be taking in everything—the gray trees with the gray creepers climbing over them and hanging from their branches, the tangle on the walls and among the grass, the evergreen alcoves with the stone seats and tall flower urns standing in them.

"I never thought I'd see this place," he said at last, in a whisper.

"Did you know about it?" asked Mary.

She had spoken aloud and he made a sign to her.

"We must talk low," he said, "or some one'll hear us an' wonder what's to do in here."

"Oh! I forgot!" said Mary, feeling frightened and putting her hand quickly against her mouth. "Did you know about the garden?" she asked again when she had recovered herself. Dickon nodded.

"Martha told me there was one as no one ever went inside," he answered. "Us used to wonder what it was like."

He stopped and looked round at the lovely gray tangle about him, and his round eyes looked queerly happy.

"Eh! the nests as'll be here come springtime," he said. "It'd be th' safest nestin' place in England. No one never comin' near an' tangles o' trees an' roses to build in. I wonder all th' birds on th' moor don't build here."

Mistress Mary put her hand on his arm again without knowing it.

"Will there be roses?" she whispered. "Can you tell? I thought perhaps they were all dead."

"Eh! No! Not them—not all of 'em!" he answered. "Look here!"

He stepped over to the nearest tree—an old, old one with gray lichen all over its bark, but upholding a curtain of tangled sprays and branches. He took a thick knife out of his pocket and opened one of its blades.

"There's lots o' dead wood as ought to be cut out," he said. "An' there's a lot o' old wood, but it made some new last year. This here's a new bit," and he touched a shoot which looked brownish green instead of hard, dry gray. Mary touched it herself in an eager, reverent way.

"That one?" she said. "Is that one quite alive—quite?"

Dickon curved his wide smiling mouth.

"It's as wick as you or me," he said; and Mary remembered that Martha had told her that "wick" meant "alive" or "lively."

"I'm glad it's wick!" she cried out in her whisper. "I want them all to be wick. Let us go round the garden and count how many wick ones there are."

She quite panted with eagerness, and Dickon was as eager as she was. They went from tree to tree and from bush to bush. Dickon carried his knife in his hand and showed her things which she thought wonderful.

"They've run wild," he said, "but th' strongest ones has fair thrived on it. The delicatest ones has died out, but th' others has growed an' growed, an' spread an' spread, till they's a wonder. See here!" and he pulled down a thick gray, dry-looking branch. "A body might think this was dead wood, but I don't believe it is—down to th' root. I'll cut it low down an' see."

He knelt and with his knife cut the lifeless-looking branch through, not far above the earth.

"There!" he said exultantly. "I told thee so. There's green in that wood yet. Look at it."

Mary was down on her knees before he spoke, gazing with all her might.

"When it looks a bit greenish an' juicy like that, it's wick," he explained. "When th' inside is dry an' breaks easy, like this here piece I've cut off, it's done for. There's a big root here as all this live wood sprung out of, an' if th' old wood's cut off an' it's dug round, and took care of there'll be—" he stopped and lifted his face to look up at the climbing and hanging sprays above him—"there'll be a fountain o' roses here this summer."

They went from bush to bush and from tree to tree. He was very strong and clever with his knife and knew how to cut the dry and dead wood away, and could tell when an unpromising bough or twig had still green life in it. In the course of half an hour Mary thought she could tell too, and when he cut through a lifeless-looking branch she would cry out joyfully under her breath when she caught sight of the least shade of moist green. The spade, and hoe, and fork were very useful.

He showed her how to use the fork while he dug about roots with the spade and stirred the earth and let the air in.

They were working industriously round one of the biggest standard roses when he caught sight of something which made him utter an exclamation of surprise.

"Why!" he cried, pointing to the grass a few feet away. "Who did that there?"

It was one of Mary's own little clearings round the pale green points.

"I did it," said Mary.

"Why, I thought tha' didn't know nothin' about gardenin'," he exclaimed.

"I don't," she answered, "but they were so little, and the grass was so thick and strong, and they looked as if they had no room to breathe. So I made a place for them. I don't even know what they are."

Dickon went and knelt down by them, smiling his wide smile.

"Tha' was right," he said. "A gardener couldn't have told thee better. They'll grow now like Jack's bean-stalk. They're crocuses an' snowdrops, an' these here is narcissuses," turning to another patch, "an here's daffydowndillys. Eh! they will be a sight."

He ran from one clearing to another.

"Tha' has done a lot o' work for such a little wench," he said, looking her over.

"I'm growing fatter," said Mary, "and I'm growing stronger. I used always to be tired. When I dig I'm not tired at all. I like to smell the earth when it's turned up."

"It's rare good for thee," he said, nodding his head wisely. "There's naught as nice as th' smell o' good clean earth, except th' smell o' fresh growin' things when th' rain falls on 'em. I get out on th' moor many a day when it's rainin' an' I lie under a bush an' listen to th' soft swish o' drops on th' heather an' I just sniff an' sniff. My nose end fair quivers like a rabbit's, mother says."

"Do you never catch cold?" inquired Mary, gazing at him wonderingly. She had never seen such a funny boy, or such a nice one.

"Not me," he said, grinning. "I never ketched cold since I was born. I wasn't brought up nesh enough. I've chased about th' moor in all weathers same as th' rabbits does. Mother says I've sniffed up too much fresh air for twelve year' to ever get to sniffin' with cold. I'm as tough as a white-thorn knobstick."

He was working all the time he was talking and Mary was following him and helping him with her fork or the trowel.

"There's a lot of work to do here!" he said once, looking about quite exultantly.

"Will you come again and help me to do it?" Mary begged. "I'm sure I can help, too. I can dig and pull up weeds, and do whatever you tell me. Oh! do come, Dickon!"

"I'll come every day if tha' wants me, rain or shine," he answered stoutly. "It's the best fun I ever had in my life—shut in here an' wakenin' up a garden."

"If you will come," said Mary, "if you will help me to make it alive I'll—I don't know what I'll do," she ended helplessly. What could you do for a boy like that?

"I'll tell thee what tha'll do," said Dickon, with his happy grin. "Tha'll get fat an' tha'll get as hungry as a young fox an' tha'll learn how to talk to th' robin same as I do. Eh! we'll have a lot o' fun."

He began to walk about, looking up in the trees and at the walls and bushes with a thoughtful expression.

"I wouldn't want to make it look like a gardener's garden, all clipped an' spick an' span, would you?" he said. "It's nicer like this with things runnin' wild, an' swingin' an' catchin' hold of each other."

"Don't let us make it tidy," said Mary anxiously. "It wouldn't seem like a secret garden if it was tidy."

Dickon stood rubbing his rusty-red head with a rather puzzled look. "It's a secret garden sure enough," he said, "but seems like some one besides th' robin must have been in it since it was shut up ten year' ago."

"But the door was locked and the key was buried," said Mary. "No one could get in."

"That's true," he answered. "It's a queer place. Seems to me as if there'd been a bit o' prunin' done here an' there, later than ten year' ago."

"But how could it have been done?" said Mary.

He was examining a branch of a standard rose and he shook his head.

"Aye! how could it!" he murmured. "With th' door locked an' th' key buried."

Mistress Mary always felt that however many years she lived she should never forget that first morning when her garden began to grow.

Of course, it did seem to begin to grow for her that morning. When Dickon began to clear places to plant seeds, she remembered what Basil had sung at her when he wanted to tease her.

"Are there any flowers that look like bells?" she inquired.

"Lilies o' th' valley does," he answered, digging away with the trowel, "an' there's Canterbury bells, an' campanulas."

"Let's plant some," said Mary.

"There's lilies o' th' valley here already; I saw 'em. They'll have growed too close an' we'll have to separate 'em, but there's plenty. Th' other ones takes two years to bloom from seed, but I can bring you some bits o' plants from our cottage garden. Why does tha' want 'em?"

Then Mary told him about Basil and his brothers and sisters in India and of how she had hated them and of their calling her "Mistress Mary Quite Contrary."

"They used to dance round and sing at me. They sang—

'Mistress Mary, quite contrary,
How does your garden grow?
With silver bells, and cockle shells,
And marigolds all in a row.'

I just remembered it and it made me wonder if there were really flowers like silver bells."

She frowned a little and gave her trowel a rather spiteful dig into the earth.

"I wasn't as contrary as they were."

But Dickon laughed.

"Eh!" he said, and as he crumbled the rich black soil she saw he was sniffing up the scent of it. "There doesn't seem to be no need for no one to be contrary when there's flowers an' such like, an' such lots o' friendly wild things runnin' about makin' homes for themselves, or buildin' nests an' singin' an' whistlin', does there?"

Mary, kneeling by him holding the seeds, looked at him and stopped frowning.

"Dickon," she said, "you are as nice as Martha said you were. I like you, and you make the fifth person. I never thought I should like five people."

Dickon sat up on his heels as Martha did when she was polishing the grate. He did look funny and delightful, Mary thought, with his round blue eyes and red cheeks and happy looking turned-up nose.

"Only five folk as tha' likes?" he said. "Who is th' other four?"

"Your mother and Martha," Mary checked them off on her fingers, "and the robin and Ben Weatherstaff."

Dickon laughed so that he was obliged to stifle the sound by putting his arm over his mouth.

"I know tha' thinks I'm a queer lad," he said, "but I think tha' art th' queerest little lass I ever saw."

Then Mary did a strange thing. She leaned forward and asked him a question she had never dreamed of asking any one before. And she tried to ask it in Yorkshire because that was his language, and in India a native was always pleased if you knew his speech.

"Does tha' like me?" she said.

"Eh!" he answered heartily, "that I does. I likes thee wonderful, an' so does th' robin, I do believe!"

"That's two, then," said Mary. "That's two for me."

And then they began to work harder than ever and more joyfully. Mary was startled and sorry when she heard the big clock in the courtyard strike the hour of her midday dinner.

"I shall have to go," she said mournfully. "And you will have to go too, won't you?"

Dickon grinned.

"My dinner's easy to carry about with me," he said. "Mother always lets me put a bit o' somethin' in my pocket."

He picked up his coat from the grass and brought out of a pocket a lumpy little bundle tied up in a quite clean, coarse, blue and white handkerchief. It held two thick pieces of bread with a slice of something laid between them.

"It's oftenest naught but bread," he said, "but I've got a fine slice o' fat bacon with it today."

Mary thought it looked a queer dinner, but he seemed ready to enjoy it.

"Run on an' get thy victuals," he said. "I'll be done with mine first. I'll get some more work done before I start back home."

He sat down with his back against a tree.

"I'll call th' robin up," he said, "and give him th' rind o' th' bacon to peck at. They likes a bit o' fat wonderful."

Mary could scarcely bear to leave him. Suddenly it seemed as if he might be a sort of wood fairy who might be gone when she came into the garden again. He seemed too good to be true. She went slowly half-way to the door in the wall and then she stopped and went back.

"Whatever happens, you—you never would tell?" she said.

His poppy-colored cheeks were distended with his first big bite of bread and bacon, but he managed to smile encouragingly.

"If tha' was a missel thrush an' showed me where thy nest was, does tha' think I'd tell any one? Not me," he said. "Tha' art as safe as a missel thrush."

And she was quite sure she was.

CHAPTER XII

"MIGHT I HAVE A BIT OF EARTH?"

Mary ran so fast that she was rather out of breath when she reached her room. Her hair was ruffled on her forehead and her cheeks were bright pink. Her dinner was waiting on the table, and Martha was waiting near it.

"Tha's a bit late," she said. "Where has tha' been?"

"I've seen Dickon!" said Mary. "I've seen Dickon!"

"I knew he'd come," said Martha exultantly. "How does tha' like him?"

"I think—I think he's beautiful!" said Mary in a determined voice.

Martha looked rather taken aback but she looked pleased, too.

"Well," she said, "he's th' best lad as ever was born, but us never thought he was handsome. His nose turns up too much."

"I like it to turn up," said Mary.

"An' his eyes is so round," said Martha, a trifle doubtful. "Though they're a nice color."

"I like them round," said Mary. "And they are exactly the color of the sky over the moor."

Martha beamed with satisfaction.

"Mother says he made 'em that color with always lookin' up at th' birds an' th' clouds. But he has got a big mouth, hasn't he, now?"

"I love his big mouth," said Mary obstinately. "I wish mine were just like it."

Martha chuckled delightedly.

"It'd look rare an' funny in thy bit of a face," she said. "But I knowed it would be that way when tha' saw him. How did tha' like th' seeds an' th' garden tools?"

"How did you know he brought them?" asked Mary.

"Eh! I never thought of him not bringin' 'em. He'd be sure to bring 'em if they was in Yorkshire. He's such a trusty lad."

Mary was afraid that she might begin to ask difficult questions, but she did not. She was very much interested in the seeds and gardening tools, and there was only one moment when Mary was frightened.

This was when she began to ask where the flowers were to be planted.

"Who did tha' ask about it?" she inquired.

"I haven't asked anybody yet," said Mary, hesitating.

"Well, I wouldn't ask th' head gardener. He's too grand, Mr. Roach is."

"I've never seen him," said Mary. "I've only seen undergardeners and Ben Weatherstaff."

"If I was you, I'd ask Ben Weatherstaff," advised Martha. "He's not half as bad as he looks, for all he's so crabbed. Mr. Craven lets him do what he likes because he was here when Mrs. Craven was alive, an' he used to make her laugh. She liked him. Perhaps he'd find you a corner somewhere out o' the way."

"If it was out of the way and no one wanted it, no one could mind my having it, could they?" Mary said anxiously.

"There wouldn't be no reason," answered Martha. "You wouldn't do no harm."

Mary ate her dinner as quickly as she could and when she rose from the table she was going to run to her room to put on her hat again, but Martha stopped her.

"I've got somethin' to tell you," she said. "I thought I'd let you eat your dinner first. Mr. Craven came back this mornin' and I think he wants to see you."

Mary turned quite pale.

"Oh!" she said. "Why! Why! He didn't want to see me when I came. I heard Pitcher say he didn't."

"Well," explained Martha, "Mrs. Medlock says it's because o' mother. She was walkin' to Thwaite village an' she met him. She'd never spoke to him before, but Mrs. Craven had been to our cottage two or three times. He'd forgot, but mother hadn't an' she made bold to stop him. I don't know what she said to him about you but she said somethin' as put him in th' mind to see you before he goes away again, tomorrow."

"Oh!" cried Mary, "is he going away tomorrow? I am so glad!"

"He's goin' for a long time. He mayn't come back till autumn or winter. He's goin' to travel in foreign places. He's always doin' it."

"Oh! I'm so glad—so glad!" said Mary thankfully.

If he did not come back until winter, or even autumn, there would be time to watch the secret garden come alive. Even if he found out then and took it away from her she would have had that much at least.

"When do you think he will want to see—"

She did not finish the sentence, because the door opened, and Mrs. Medlock walked in. She had on her best black dress and cap, and her collar was fastened with a large brooch with a picture of a man's face on it. It was a colored photograph of Mr. Medlock who had died years ago, and she always wore it when she was dressed up. She looked nervous and excited.

"Your hair's rough," she said quickly. "Go and brush it. Martha, help her to slip on her best dress. Mr. Craven sent me to bring her to him in his study."

All the pink left Mary's cheeks. Her heart began to thump and she felt herself changing into a stiff, plain, silent child again. She did not even answer Mrs. Medlock, but turned and walked into her bedroom, followed by Martha. She said nothing while her dress was changed, and her hair brushed, and after she was quite tidy she followed Mrs. Medlock down the corridors, in silence. What was there for her to say? She was obliged to go and see Mr. Craven and he would not like her, and she would not like him. She knew what he would think of her.

She was taken to a part of the house she had not been into before. At last Mrs. Medlock knocked at a door, and when some one said, "Come in," they entered the room together. A man was sitting in an armchair before the fire, and Mrs. Medlock spoke to him.

"This is Miss Mary, sir," she said.

"You can go and leave her here. I will ring for you when I want you to take her away," said Mr. Craven.

When she went out and closed the door, Mary could only stand waiting, a plain little thing, twisting her thin hands together. She could see that the man in the chair was not so much a hunchback as a man with high, rather crooked shoulders, and he had black hair streaked with white. He turned his head over his high shoulders and spoke to her.

"Come here!" he said.

Mary went to him.

He was not ugly. His face would have been handsome if it had not been so miserable. He looked as if the sight of her worried and fretted him and as if he did not know what in the world to do with her.

"Are you well?" he asked.

"Yes," answered Mary.

"Do they take good care of you?"

"Yes."

He rubbed his forehead fretfully as he looked her over.

"You are very thin," he said.

"I am getting fatter," Mary answered in what she knew was her stiffest way.

What an unhappy face he had! His black eyes seemed as if they scarcely saw her, as if they were seeing something else, and he could hardly keep his thoughts upon her.

"I forgot you," he said. "How could I remember you? I intended to send you a governess or a nurse, or some one of that sort, but I forgot."

"Please," began Mary. "Please—" and then the lump in her throat choked her.

"What do you want to say?" he inquired.

"I am—I am too big for a nurse," said Mary. "And please—please don't make me have a governess yet."

He rubbed his forehead again and stared at her.

"That was what the Sowerby woman said," he muttered absentmindedly.

Then Mary gathered a scrap of courage.

"Is she—is she Martha's mother?" she stammered.

"Yes, I think so," he replied.

"She knows about children," said Mary. "She has twelve. She knows."

He seemed to rouse himself.

"What do you want to do?"

"I want to play out of doors," Mary answered, hoping that her voice did not tremble. "I never liked it in India. It makes me hungry here, and I am getting fatter."

He was watching her.

"Mrs. Sowerby said it would do you good. Perhaps it will," he said. "She thought you had better get stronger before you had a governess."

"It makes me feel strong when I play and the wind comes over the moor," argued Mary.

"Where do you play?" he asked next.

"Everywhere," gasped Mary. "Martha's mother sent me a skipping-rope. I skip and run—and I look about to see if things are beginning to stick up out of the earth. I don't do any harm."

"Don't look so frightened," he said in a worried voice. "You could not do any harm, a child like you! You may do what you like."

Mary put her hand up to her throat because she was afraid he might see the excited lump which she felt jump into it. She came a step nearer to him.

"May I?" she said tremulously.

Her anxious little face seemed to worry him more than ever.

"Don't look so frightened," he exclaimed. "Of course you may. I am your guardian, though I am a poor one for any child. I cannot give you time or attention. I am too ill, and wretched and distracted; but I wish you to be happy and comfortable. I don't know anything about children, but Mrs. Medlock is to see that you have all you need. I sent for you to-day because Mrs. Sowerby said I ought to see you. Her daughter had talked about you. She thought you needed fresh air and freedom and running about."

"She knows all about children," Mary said again in spite of herself.

"She ought to," said Mr. Craven. "I thought her rather bold to stop me on the moor, but she said—Mrs. Craven had been kind to her." It seemed hard for him to speak his dead wife's name. "She is a respectable woman. Now I have seen you I think she said sensible things. Play out of doors as much as you like. It's a big place and you may go where you like and amuse yourself as you like. Is there anything you want?" as if a sudden thought had struck him. "Do you want toys, books, dolls?"

"Might I," quavered Mary, "might I have a bit of earth?"

In her eagerness she did not realize how queer the words would sound and that they were not the ones she had meant to say. Mr. Craven looked quite startled.

"Earth!" he repeated. "What do you mean?"

"To plant seeds in—to make things grow—to see them come alive," Mary faltered.

He gazed at her a moment and then passed his hand quickly over his eyes.

"Do you—care about gardens so much," he said slowly.

"I didn't know about them in India," said Mary. "I was always ill and tired and it was too hot. I sometimes made little beds in the sand and stuck flowers in them. But here it is different."

Mr. Craven got up and began to walk slowly across the room.

"A bit of earth," he said to himself, and Mary thought that somehow she must have reminded him of something. When he stopped and spoke to her his dark eyes looked almost soft and kind.

"You can have as much earth as you want," he said. "You remind me of some one else who loved the earth and things that grow. When you see a bit of earth you want," with something like a smile, "take it, child, and make it come alive."

"May I take it from anywhere—if it's not wanted?"

"Anywhere," he answered. "There! You must go now, I am tired." He touched the bell to call Mrs. Medlock. "Good-by. I shall be away all summer."

Mrs. Medlock came so quickly that Mary thought she must have been waiting in the corridor.

"Mrs. Medlock," Mr. Craven said to her, "now I have seen the child I understand what Mrs. Sowerby meant. She must be less delicate before she begins lessons. Give her simple, healthy food. Let her run wild in the garden. Don't look after her too much. She needs liberty and fresh air and romping about. Mrs. Sowerby is to come and see her now and then and she may sometimes go to the cottage."

Mrs. Medlock looked pleased. She was relieved to hear that she need not "look after" Mary too much. She had felt her a tiresome charge and had indeed seen as little of her as she dared. In addition to this she was fond of Martha's mother.

"Thank you, sir," she said. "Susan Sowerby and me went to school together and she's as sensible and good-hearted a woman as you'd find in a day's walk. I never had any children myself and she's had twelve, and there never was healthier or better ones. Miss Mary can get no harm from them. I'd always take Susan Sowerby's advice about children myself. She's what you might call healthy-minded—if you understand me."

"I understand," Mr. Craven answered. "Take Miss Mary away now and send Pitcher to me."

When Mrs. Medlock left her at the end of her own corridor Mary flew back to her room. She found Martha waiting there. Martha had, in fact, hurried back after she had removed the dinner service.

"I can have my garden!" cried Mary. "I may have it where I like! I am not going to have a governess for a long time! Your mother is coming to see me and I may go to your cottage! He says a little girl like me could not do any harm and I may do what I like—anywhere!"

"Eh!" said Martha delightedly, "that was nice of him wasn't it?"

"Martha," said Mary solemnly, "he is really a nice man, only his face is so miserable and his forehead is all drawn together."

She ran as quickly as she could to the garden. She had been away so much longer than she had thought she should and she knew Dickon would have to set out early on his five-mile walk. When she slipped through the door under the ivy, she saw he was not working where she had left him. The gardening tools were laid together under a tree. She ran to them, looking all round the place, but there was no Dickon to be seen. He had gone away and the secret garden was empty—except for the robin who had just flown across the wall and sat on a standard rose-bush watching her. "He's gone," she said woefully. "Oh! was he—was he—was he only a wood fairy?"

Something white fastened to the standard rose-bush caught her eye. It was a piece of paper, in fact, it was a piece of the letter she had printed for Martha to send to Dickon. It was fastened on the bush with a long thorn, and in a minute she knew Dickon had left it there. There were some roughly printed letters on it and a sort of picture. At first she could not tell what it was. Then she saw it was meant for a nest with a bird sitting on it. Underneath were the printed letters and they said:

"I will cum bak."

CHAPTER XIII

"I AM COLIN"

Mary took the picture back to the house when she went to her supper and she showed it to Martha.

"Eh!" said Martha with great pride. "I never knew our Dickon was as clever as that. That there's a picture of a missel thrush on her nest, as large as life an' twice as natural."

Then Mary knew Dickon had meant the picture to be a message. He had meant that she might be sure he would keep her secret. Her garden was her nest and she was like a missel thrush. Oh, how she did like that queer, common boy!

She hoped he would come back the very next day and she fell asleep looking forward to the morning.

But you never know what the weather will do in Yorkshire, particularly in the springtime. She was awakened in the night by the sound of rain beating with heavy drops against her window. It was pouring down in torrents and the wind was "wuthering" round the corners and in the chimneys of the huge old house. Mary sat up in bed and felt miserable and angry.

"The rain is as contrary as I ever was," she said. "It came because it knew I did not want it."

She threw herself back on her pillow and buried her face. She did not cry, but she lay and hated the sound of the heavily beating rain, she hated the wind and its "wuthering." She could not go to sleep again. The mournful sound kept her awake because she felt mournful herself. If she had felt happy it would probably have lulled her to sleep. How it "wuthered" and how the big raindrops poured down and beat against the pane!

"It sounds just like a person lost on the moor and wandering on and on crying," she said.

She had been lying awake turning from side to side for about an hour, when suddenly something made her sit up in bed and turn her head toward the door listening. She listened and she listened.

"It isn't the wind now," she said in a loud whisper. "That isn't the wind. It is different. It is that crying I heard before."

The door of her room was ajar and the sound came down the corridor, a far-off faint sound of fretful crying. She listened for a few minutes and each minute she became more and more sure. She felt as if she must find out what it was. It seemed even stranger than the secret garden and the buried key. Perhaps the fact that she was in a rebellious mood made her bold. She put her foot out of bed and stood on the floor.

"I am going to find out what it is," she said. "Everybody is in bed and I don't care about Mrs. Medlock—I don't care!"

There was a candle by her bedside and she took it up and went softly out of the room. The corridor looked very long and dark, but she was too excited to mind that. She thought she remembered the corners she must turn to find the short corridor with the door covered with tapestry—the one Mrs. Medlock had come through the day she lost herself. The sound had come up that passage. So she went on with her dim light, almost feeling her way, her heart beating so loud that she fancied she could hear it. The far-off faint crying went on and led her. Sometimes it stopped for a moment or so and then began again. Was this the right corner to turn? She stopped and thought. Yes it was. Down this passage and then to the left, and then up two broad steps, and then to the right again. Yes, there was the tapestry door.

She pushed it open very gently and closed it behind her, and she stood in the corridor and could hear the crying quite plainly, though it was not loud. It was on the other side of the wall at her left and a few yards farther on there was a door. She could see a glimmer of light coming from beneath it. The Someone was crying in that room, and it was quite a young Someone.

So she walked to the door and pushed it open, and there she was standing in the room!

It was a big room with ancient, handsome furniture in it. There was a low fire glowing faintly on the hearth and a night light burning by the side of a carved four-posted bed hung with brocade, and on the bed was lying a boy, crying fretfully.

Mary wondered if she was in a real place or if she had fallen asleep again and was dreaming without knowing it.

The boy had a sharp, delicate face the color of ivory and he seemed to have eyes too big for it. He had also a lot of hair which tumbled over his forehead in heavy locks and made his thin face seem smaller. He looked like a boy who had been ill, but he was crying more as if he were tired and cross than as if he were in pain.

Mary stood near the door with her candle in her hand, holding her breath. Then she crept across the room, and, as she drew nearer, the light attracted the boy's attention and he turned his head on his pillow and stared at her, his gray eyes opening so wide that they seemed immense.

"Who are you?" he said at last in a half-frightened whisper. "Are you a ghost?"

"No, I am not," Mary answered, her own whisper sounding half frightened. "Are you one?"

He stared and stared and stared. Mary could not help noticing what strange eyes he had. They were agate gray and they looked too big for his face because they had black lashes all round them.

"No," he replied after waiting a moment or so. "I am Colin."

"Who is Colin?" she faltered.

"I am Colin Craven. Who are you?"

"I am Mary Lennox. Mr. Craven is my uncle."

"He is my father," said the boy.

"Your father!" gasped Mary. "No one ever told me he had a boy! Why didn't they?"

"Come here," he said, still keeping his strange eyes fixed on her with an anxious expression.

She came close to the bed and he put out his hand and touched her.

"You are real, aren't you?" he said. "I have such real dreams very often. You might be one of them."

Mary had slipped on a woolen wrapper before she left her room and she put a piece of it between his fingers.

"Rub that and see how thick and warm it is," she said. "I will pinch you a little if you like, to show you how real I am. For a minute I thought you might be a dream too."

"Where did you come from?" he asked.

"From my own room. The wind wuthered so I couldn't go to sleep and I heard some one crying and wanted to find out who it was. What were you crying for?"

"Because I couldn't go to sleep either and my head ached. Tell me your name again."

"Mary Lennox. Did no one ever tell you I had come to live here?"

He was still fingering the fold of her wrapper, but he began to look a little more as if he believed in her reality.

"No," he answered. "They daren't."

"Why?" asked Mary.

"Because I should have been afraid you would see me. I won't let people see me and talk me over."

"Why?" Mary asked again, feeling more mystified every moment.

"Because I am like this always, ill and having to lie down. My father won't let people talk me over either. The servants are not allowed to speak about me. If I live I may be a hunchback, but I shan't live. My father hates to think I may be like him."

"Oh, what a queer house this is!" Mary said. "What a queer house! Everything is a kind of secret. Rooms are locked up and gardens are locked up—and you! Have you been locked up?"

"No. I stay in this room because I don't want to be moved out of it. It tires me too much."

"Does your father come and see you?" Mary ventured.

"Sometimes. Generally when I am asleep. He doesn't want to see me."

"Why?" Mary could not help asking again.

A sort of angry shadow passed over the boy's face.

"My mother died when I was born and it makes him wretched to look at me. He thinks I don't know, but I've heard people talking. He almost hates me."

"He hates the garden, because she died," said Mary half speaking to herself.

"What garden?" the boy asked.

"Oh! just—just a garden she used to like," Mary stammered. "Have you been here always?"

"Nearly always. Sometimes I have been taken to places at the seaside, but I won't stay because people stare at me. I used to wear an iron thing to keep my back straight, but a grand doctor came from London to see me and said it was stupid. He told them to take it off and keep me out in the fresh air. I hate fresh air and I don't want to go out."

"I didn't when first I came here," said Mary. "Why do you keep looking at me like that?"

"Because of the dreams that are so real," he answered rather fretfully. "Sometimes when I open my eyes I don't believe I'm awake."

"We're both awake," said Mary. She glanced round the room with its high ceiling and shadowy corners and dim fire-light. "It looks quite like a dream, and it's the middle of the night, and everybody in the house is asleep—everybody but us. We are wide awake."

"I don't want it to be a dream," the boy said restlessly.

Mary thought of something all at once.

"If you don't like people to see you," she began, "do you want me to go away?"

He still held the fold of her wrapper and he gave it a little pull.

"No," he said. "I should be sure you were a dream if you went. If you are real, sit down on that big footstool and talk. I want to hear about you."

Mary put down her candle on the table near the bed and sat down on the cushioned stool. She did not want to go away at all. She wanted to stay in the mysterious hidden-away room and talk to the mysterious boy.

"What do you want me to tell you?" she said.

He wanted to know how long she had been at Misselthwaite; he wanted to know which corridor her room was on; he wanted to know what she had been doing; if she disliked the moor as he disliked it; where she had lived before she came to Yorkshire. She answered all these questions and many more and he lay back on his pillow and listened. He made her tell him a great deal about India and about her voyage across the ocean. She found out that because he had been an invalid he had not learned things as other children had. One of his nurses had taught him to read when he was quite little and he was always reading and looking at pictures in splendid books.

Though his father rarely saw him when he was awake, he was given all sorts of wonderful things to amuse himself with. He never seemed to have been amused, however. He could have anything he asked for and was never made to do anything he did not like to do. "Everyone is obliged to do what pleases me," he said indifferently. "It makes me ill to be angry. No one believes I shall live to grow up."

He said it as if he was so accustomed to the idea that it had ceased to matter to him at all. He seemed to like the sound of Mary's voice. As she went on talking he listened in a drowsy, interested way. Once or twice she wondered if he were not gradually falling into a doze. But at last he asked a question which opened up a new subject.

"How old are you?" he asked.

"I am ten," answered Mary, forgetting herself for the moment, "and so are you."

"How do you know that?" he demanded in a surprised voice.

"Because when you were born the garden door was locked and the key was buried. And it has been locked for ten years."

Colin half sat up, turning toward her, leaning on his elbows.

"What garden door was locked? Who did it? Where was the key buried?" he exclaimed as if he were suddenly very much interested.

"It—it was the garden Mr. Craven hates," said Mary nervously. "He locked the door. No one—no one knew where he buried the key."

"What sort of a garden is it?" Colin persisted eagerly.

"No one has been allowed to go into it for ten years," was Mary's careful answer.

But it was too late to be careful. He was too much like herself. He too had had nothing to think about and the idea of a hidden garden attracted him as it had attracted her. He asked question after question. Where was it? Had she never looked for the door? Had she never asked the gardeners?

"They won't talk about it," said Mary. "I think they have been told not to answer questions."

"I would make them," said Colin.

"Could you?" Mary faltered, beginning to feel frightened. If he could make people answer questions, who knew what might happen!

"Everyone is obliged to please me. I told you that," he said. "If I were to live, this place would sometime belong to me. They all know that. I would make them tell me."

Mary had not known that she herself had been spoiled, but she could see quite plainly that this mysterious boy had been. He thought that the whole world belonged to him. How peculiar he was and how coolly he spoke of not living.

"Do you think you won't live?" she asked, partly because she was curious and partly in hope of making him forget the garden.

"I don't suppose I shall," he answered as indifferently as he had spoken before. "Ever since I remember anything I have heard people say I shan't. At first they thought I was too little to understand and now they think I don't hear. But I do. My doctor is my father's cousin. He is quite poor and if I die he will have all Misselthwaite when my father is dead. I should think he wouldn't want me to live."

"Do you want to live?" inquired Mary.

"No," he answered, in a cross, tired fashion. "But I don't want to die. When I feel ill I lie here and think about it until I cry and cry."

"I have heard you crying three times," Mary said, "but I did not know who it was. Were you crying about that?" She did so want him to forget the garden.

"I dare say," he answered. "Let us talk about something else. Talk about that garden. Don't you want to see it?"

"Yes," answered Mary, in quite a low voice.

"I do," he went on persistently. "I don't think I ever really wanted to see anything before, but I want to see that garden. I want the key dug up. I want the door unlocked. I would let them take me there in my chair. That would be getting fresh air. I am going to make them open the door."

He had become quite excited and his strange eyes began to shine like stars and looked more immense than ever.

"They have to please me," he said. "I will make them take me there and I will let you go, too."

Mary's hands clutched each other. Everything would be spoiled—everything! Dickon would never come back. She would never again feel like a missel thrush with a safe-hidden nest.

"Oh, don't—don't—don't—don't do that!" she cried out.

He stared as if he thought she had gone crazy!

"Why?" he exclaimed. "You said you wanted to see it."

"I do," she answered almost with a sob in her throat, "but if you make them open the door and take you in like that it will never be a secret again."

He leaned still farther forward.

"A secret," he said. "What do you mean? Tell me."

Mary's words almost tumbled over one another.

"You see—you see," she panted, "if no one knows but ourselves—if there was a door, hidden somewhere under the ivy—if there was—and we could find it; and if we could slip through it together and shut it behind us, and no one knew any one was inside and we called it our garden and pretended that—that we were missel thrushes and it was our nest, and if we played there almost every day and dug and planted seeds and made it all come alive—"

"Is it dead?" he interrupted her.

"It soon will be if no one cares for it," she went on. "The bulbs will live but the roses—"

He stopped her again as excited as she was herself.

"What are bulbs?" he put in quickly.

"They are daffodils and lilies and snowdrops. They are working in the earth now—pushing up pale green points because the spring is coming."

"Is the spring coming?" he said. "What is it like? You don't see it in rooms if you are ill."

"It is the sun shining on the rain and the rain falling on the sunshine, and things pushing up and working under the earth," said Mary. "If the garden was a secret and we could get into it we could watch the things grow bigger every day, and see how many roses are alive. Don't you see? Oh, don't you see how much nicer it would be if it was a secret?"

He dropped back on his pillow and lay there with an odd expression on his face.

"I never had a secret," he said, "except that one about not living to grow up. They don't know I know that, so it is a sort of secret. But I like this kind better."

"If you won't make them take you to the garden," pleaded Mary, "perhaps—I feel almost sure I can find out how to get in sometime. And then—if the doctor wants you to go out in your chair, and if you can always do what you want to do, perhaps—perhaps we might find some boy who would push you, and we could go alone and it would always be a secret garden."

"I should—like—that," he said very slowly, his eyes looking dreamy. "I should like that. I should not mind fresh air in a secret garden."

Mary began to recover her breath and feel safer because the idea of keeping the secret seemed to please him. She felt almost sure that if she kept on talking and could make him see the garden in his mind as she had seen it he would like it so much that he could not bear to think that everybody might tramp in to it when they chose.

"I'll tell you what I think it would be like, if we could go into it," she said. "It has been shut up so long things have grown into a tangle perhaps."

He lay quite still and listened while she went on talking about the roses which might have clambered from tree to tree and hung down—about the many birds which might have built their nests there because it was so safe. And then she told him about the robin and Ben Weatherstaff, and there was so much to tell about the robin and it was so easy and safe to talk about it that she ceased to be afraid. The robin pleased him so much that he smiled until he looked almost beautiful, and at first Mary had thought that he was even plainer than herself, with his big eyes and heavy locks of hair.

"I did not know birds could be like that," he said. "But if you stay in a room you never see things. What a lot of things you know. I feel as if you had been inside that garden."

She did not know what to say, so she did not say anything. He evidently did not expect an answer and the next moment he gave her a surprise.

"I am going to let you look at something," he said. "Do you see that rose-colored silk curtain hanging on the wall over the mantel-piece?"

Mary had not noticed it before, but she looked up and saw it. It was a curtain of soft silk hanging over what seemed to be some picture.

"Yes," she answered.

"There is a cord hanging from it," said Colin. "Go and pull it."

Mary got up, much mystified, and found the cord. When she pulled it the silk curtain ran back on rings and when it ran back it uncovered a picture. It was the picture of a girl with a laughing face. She had bright hair tied up with a blue ribbon and her gay, lovely eyes were exactly like Colin's unhappy ones, agate gray and looking twice as big as they really were because of the black lashes all round them.

"She is my mother," said Colin complainingly. "I don't see why she died. Sometimes I hate her for doing it."

"How queer!" said Mary.

"If she had lived I believe I should not have been ill always," he grumbled. "I dare say I should have lived, too. And my father would not have hated to look at me. I dare say I should have had a strong back. Draw the curtain again."

Mary did as she was told and returned to her footstool.

"She is much prettier than you," she said, "but her eyes are just like yours—at least they are the same shape and color. Why is the curtain drawn over her?"

He moved uncomfortably.

"I made them do it," he said. "Sometimes I don't like to see her looking at me. She smiles too much when I am ill and miserable. Besides, she is mine and I don't want everyone to see her." There were a few moments of silence and then Mary spoke.

"What would Mrs. Medlock do if she found out that I had been here?" she inquired.

"She would do as I told her to do," he answered. "And I should tell her that I wanted you to come here and talk to me every day. I am glad you came."

"So am I," said Mary. "I will come as often as I can, but"—she hesitated—"I shall have to look every day for the garden door."

"Yes, you must," said Colin, "and you can tell me about it afterward."

He lay thinking a few minutes, as he had done before, and then he spoke again.

"I think you shall be a secret, too," he said. "I will not tell them until they find out. I can always send the nurse out of the room and say that I want to be by myself. Do you know Martha?"

"Yes, I know her very well," said Mary. "She waits on me."

He nodded his head toward the outer corridor.

"She is the one who is asleep in the other room. The nurse went away yesterday to stay all night with her sister and she always makes Martha attend to me when she wants to go out. Martha shall tell you when to come here."

Then Mary understood Martha's troubled look when she had asked questions about the crying.

"Martha knew about you all the time?" she said.

"Yes; she often attends to me. The nurse likes to get away from me and then Martha comes."

"I have been here a long time," said Mary. "Shall I go away now? Your eyes look sleepy."

"I wish I could go to sleep before you leave me," he said rather shyly.

"Shut your eyes," said Mary, drawing her footstool closer, "and I will do what my Ayah used to do in India. I will pat your hand and stroke it and sing something quite low."

"I should like that perhaps," he said drowsily.

Somehow she was sorry for him and did not want him to lie awake, so she leaned against the bed and began to stroke and pat his hand and sing a very low little chanting song in Hindustani.

"That is nice," he said more drowsily still, and she went on chanting and stroking, but when she looked at him again his black lashes were lying close against his cheeks, for his eyes were shut and he was fast asleep. So she got up softly, took her candle and crept away without making a sound.

CHAPTER XIV

A YOUNG RAJAH

The moor was hidden in mist when the morning came, and the rain had not stopped pouring down. There could be no going out of doors. Martha was so busy that Mary had no opportunity of talking to her, but in the afternoon she asked her to come and sit with her in the nursery. She came bringing the stocking she was always knitting when she was doing nothing else.

"What's the matter with thee?" she asked as soon as they sat down. "Tha' looks as if tha'd somethin' to say."

"I have. I have found out what the crying was," said Mary.

Martha let her knitting drop on her knee and gazed at her with startled eyes.

"Tha' hasn't!" she exclaimed. "Never!"

"I heard it in the night," Mary went on. "And I got up and went to see where it came from. It was Colin. I found him."

Martha's face became red with fright.

"Eh! Miss Mary!" she said half crying. "Tha' shouldn't have done it—tha' shouldn't! Tha'll get me in trouble. I never told thee nothin' about him—but tha'll get me in trouble. I shall lose my place and what'll mother do!"

"You won't lose your place," said Mary. "He was glad I came. We talked and talked and he said he was glad I came."

"Was he?" cried Martha. "Art tha' sure? Tha' doesn't know what he's like when anything vexes him. He's a big lad to cry like a baby, but when he's in a passion he'll fair scream just to frighten us. He knows us daren't call our souls our own."

"He wasn't vexed," said Mary. "I asked him if I should go away and he made me stay. He asked me questions and I sat on a big footstool and talked to him about India and about the robin and gardens. He wouldn't let me go. He let me see his mother's picture. Before I left him I sang him to sleep."

Martha fairly gasped with amazement.

"I can scarcely believe thee!" she protested. "It's as if tha'd walked straight into a lion's den. If he'd been like he is most times he'd have throwed himself into one of his tantrums and roused th' house. He won't let strangers look at him."

"He let me look at him. I looked at him all the time and he looked at me. We stared!" said Mary.

"I don't know what to do!" cried agitated Martha. "If Mrs. Medlock finds out, she'll think I broke orders and told thee and I shall be packed back to mother."

"He is not going to tell Mrs. Medlock anything about it yet. It's to be a sort of secret just at first," said Mary firmly. "And he says everybody is obliged to do as he pleases."

"Aye, that's true enough—th' bad lad!" sighed Martha, wiping her forehead with her apron.

"He says Mrs. Medlock must. And he wants me to come and talk to him every day. And you are to tell me when he wants me."

"Me!" said Martha; "I shall lose my place—I shall for sure!"

"You can't if you are doing what he wants you to do and everybody is ordered to obey him," Mary argued.

"Does tha' mean to say," cried Martha with wide open eyes, "that he was nice to thee!"

"I think he almost liked me," Mary answered.

"Then tha' must have bewitched him!" decided Martha, drawing a long breath.

"Do you mean Magic?" inquired Mary. "I've heard about Magic in India, but I can't make it. I just went into his room and I was so surprised to see him I stood and stared. And then he turned round and stared at me. And he thought I was a ghost or a dream and I thought perhaps he was. And it was so queer being there alone together in the middle of the night and not knowing about each other. And we began to ask each other questions. And when I asked him if I must go away he said I must not."

"Th' world's comin' to a end!" gasped Martha.

"What is the matter with him?" asked Mary.

"Nobody knows for sure and certain," said Martha. "Mr. Craven went off his head like when he was born. Th' doctors thought he'd have to be put in a 'sylum. It was because Mrs. Craven died like I told you. He wouldn't set eyes on th' baby. He just raved and said it'd be another hunchback like him and it'd better die."

"Is Colin a hunchback?" Mary asked. "He didn't look like one."

"He isn't yet," said Martha. "But he began all wrong. Mother said that there was enough trouble and raging in th' house to set any child wrong. They was afraid his back was weak an' they've always been takin' care of it—keepin' him lyin' down and not lettin' him walk. Once they made him wear a brace but he fretted so he was downright ill. Then a big doctor came to see him an' made them take it off. He talked to th' other doctor quite rough—in a polite way. He said there'd been too much medicine and too much lettin' him have his own way."

"I think he's a very spoiled boy," said Mary.

"He's th' worst young nowt as ever was!" said Martha. "I won't say as he hasn't been ill a good bit. He's had coughs an' colds that's nearly killed him two or three times. Once he had rheumatic fever an' once he had typhoid. Eh! Mrs. Medlock did get a fright then. He'd been out of his head an' she was talkin' to th' nurse, thinkin' he didn't know nothin', an' she said, 'He'll die this time sure enough, an' best thing for him an' for everybody.' An' she looked at him an' there he was with his big eyes open, starin' at her as sensible as she was herself. She didn't know wha'd happen but he just stared at her an' says, 'You give me some water an' stop talkin'.'"

"Do you think he will die?" asked Mary.

"Mother says there's no reason why any child should live that gets no fresh air an' doesn't do nothin' but lie on his back an' read picture-books an' take medicine. He's weak and hates th' trouble o' bein' taken out o' doors, an' he gets cold so easy he says it makes him ill."

Mary sat and looked at the fire. "I wonder," she said slowly, "if it would not do him good to go out into a garden and watch things growing. It did me good."

"One of th' worst fits he ever had," said Martha, "was one time they took him out where the roses is by the fountain. He'd been readin' in a paper about people gettin' somethin' he called 'rose cold' an' he began to sneeze an' said he'd got it an' then a new gardener as didn't know th' rules passed by an' looked at him curious. He threw himself into a passion an' he said he'd looked at him because he was going to be a hunchback. He cried himself into a fever an' was ill all night."

"If he ever gets angry at me, I'll never go and see him again," said Mary.

"He'll have thee if he wants thee," said Martha. "Tha' may as well know that at th' start."

Very soon afterward a bell rang and she rolled up her knitting.

"I dare say th' nurse wants me to stay with him a bit," she said. "I hope he's in a good temper."

She was out of the room about ten minutes and then she came back with a puzzled expression.

"Well, tha' has bewitched him," she said. "He's up on his sofa with his picture-books. He's told the nurse to stay away until six o'clock. I'm to wait in the next room. Th' minute she was gone he called me to him an' says, 'I want Mary Lennox to come and talk to me, and remember you're not to tell any one.' You'd better go as quick as you can."

Mary was quite willing to go quickly. She did not want to see Colin as much as she wanted to see Dickon; but she wanted to see him very much.

There was a bright fire on the hearth when she entered his room, and in the daylight she saw it was a very beautiful room indeed. There were rich colors in the rugs and hangings and pictures and books on the walls which made it look glowing and comfortable even in spite of the gray sky and falling rain. Colin looked rather like a picture himself. He was wrapped in a velvet dressing-gown and sat against a big brocaded cushion. He had a red spot on each cheek.

"Come in," he said. "I've been thinking about you all morning."

"I've been thinking about you, too," answered Mary. "You don't know how frightened Martha is. She says Mrs. Medlock will think she told me about you and then she will be sent away."

He frowned.

"Go and tell her to come here," he said. "She is in the next room."

Mary went and brought her back. Poor Martha was shaking in her shoes. Colin was still frowning.

"Have you to do what I please or have you not?" he demanded.

"I have to do what you please, sir," Martha faltered, turning quite red.

"Has Medlock to do what I please?"

"Everybody has, sir," said Martha.

"Well, then, if I order you to bring Miss Mary to me, how can Medlock send you away if she finds it out?"

"Please don't let her, sir," pleaded Martha.

"I'll send her away if she dares to say a word about such a thing," said Master Craven grandly. "She wouldn't like that, I can tell you."

"Thank you, sir," bobbing a curtsy, "I want to do my duty, sir."

"What I want is your duty" said Colin more grandly still. "I'll take care of you. Now go away."

When the door closed behind Martha, Colin found Mistress Mary gazing at him as if he had set her wondering.

"Why do you look at me like that?" he asked her. "What are you thinking about?"

"I am thinking about two things."

"What are they? Sit down and tell me."

"This is the first one," said Mary, seating herself on the big stool. "Once in India I saw a boy who was a Rajah. He had rubies and emeralds and diamonds stuck all over him. He spoke to his people just as you spoke to Martha. Everybody had to do everything he told them—in a minute. I think they would have been killed if they hadn't."

"I shall make you tell me about Rajahs presently," he said, "but first tell me what the second thing was."

"I was thinking," said Mary, "how different you are from Dickon."

"Who is Dickon?" he said. "What a queer name!"

She might as well tell him, she thought she could talk about Dickon without mentioning the secret garden. She had liked to hear Martha talk about him. Besides, she longed to talk about him. It would seem to bring him nearer.

"He is Martha's brother. He is twelve years old," she explained. "He is not like any one else in the world. He can charm foxes and squirrels and birds just as the natives in India charm snakes. He plays a very soft tune on a pipe and they come and listen."

There were some big books on a table at his side and he dragged one suddenly toward him. "There is a picture of a snake-charmer in this," he exclaimed. "Come and look at it."

The book was a beautiful one with superb colored illustrations and he turned to one of them.

"Can he do that?" he asked eagerly.

"He played on his pipe and they listened," Mary explained. "But he doesn't call it Magic. He says it's because he lives on the moor so much and he knows their ways. He says he feels sometimes as if he was a bird or a rabbit himself, he likes them so. I think he asked the robin questions. It seemed as if they talked to each other in soft chirps."

Colin lay back on his cushion and his eyes grew larger and larger and the spots on his cheeks burned.

"Tell me some more about him," he said.

"He knows all about eggs and nests," Mary went on. "And he knows where foxes and badgers and otters live. He keeps them secret so that other boys won't find their holes and frighten them. He knows about everything that grows or lives on the moor."

"Does he like the moor?" said Colin. "How can he when it's such a great, bare, dreary place?"

"It's the most beautiful place," protested Mary. "Thousands of lovely things grow on it and there are thousands of little creatures all busy building nests and making holes and burrows and chippering or singing or squeaking to each other. They are so busy and having such fun under the earth or in the trees or heather. It's their world."

"How do you know all that?" said Colin, turning on his elbow to look at her.

"I have never been there once, really," said Mary suddenly remembering. "I only drove over it in the dark. I thought it was hideous. Martha told me about it first and then Dickon. When Dickon talks about it you feel as if you saw things and heard them and as if you were standing in the heather with the sun shining and the gorse smelling like honey—and all full of bees and butterflies."

"You never see anything if you are ill," said Colin restlessly. He looked like a person listening to a new sound in the distance and wondering what it was.

"You can't if you stay in a room," said Mary.

"I couldn't go on the moor," he said in a resentful tone.

Mary was silent for a minute and then she said something bold.

"You might—sometime."

He moved as if he were startled.

"Go on the moor! How could I? I am going to die."

"How do you know?" said Mary unsympathetically. She didn't like the way he had of talking about dying. She did not feel very sympathetic. She felt rather as if he almost boasted about it.

"Oh, I've heard it ever since I remember," he answered crossly. "They are always whispering about it and thinking I don't notice. They wish I would, too."

Mistress Mary felt quite contrary. She pinched her lips together.

"If they wished I would," she said, "I wouldn't. Who wishes you would?"

"The servants—and of course Dr. Craven because he would get Misselthwaite and be rich instead of poor. He daren't say so, but he always looks cheerful when I am worse. When I had typhoid fever his face got quite fat. I think my father wishes it, too."

"I don't believe he does," said Mary quite obstinately.

That made Colin turn and look at her again.

"Don't you?" he said.

And then he lay back on his cushion and was still, as if he were thinking. And there was quite a long silence. Perhaps they were both of them thinking strange things children do not usually think. "I like the grand doctor from London, because he made them take the iron thing off," said Mary at last. "Did he say you were going to die?"

"No."

"What did he say?"

"He didn't whisper," Colin answered. "Perhaps he knew I hated whispering. I heard him say one thing quite aloud. He said, 'The lad might live if he would make up his mind to it. Put him in the humor.' It sounded as if he was in a temper."

"I'll tell you who would put you in the humor, perhaps," said Mary reflecting. She felt as if she would like this thing to be settled one way or the other. "I believe Dickon would. He's always talking about live things. He never talks about dead things or things that are ill. He's always looking up in the sky to watch birds flying—or looking down at the earth to see something growing. He has such round blue eyes and they are so wide open with looking about. And he laughs such a big laugh with his wide mouth—and his cheeks are as red—as red as cherries." She pulled her stool nearer to the sofa and her expression quite changed at the remembrance of the wide curving mouth and wide open eyes.

"See here," she said. "Don't let us talk about dying; I don't like it. Let us talk about living. Let us talk and talk about Dickon. And then we will look at your pictures."

It was the best thing she could have said. To talk about Dickon meant to talk about the moor and about the cottage and the fourteen people who lived in it on sixteen shillings a week—and the children who got fat on the moor grass like the wild ponies. And about Dickon's mother—and the skipping-rope—and the moor with the sun on it—and about pale green points sticking up out of the black sod. And it was all so alive that Mary talked more than she had ever talked before—and Colin both talked and listened as he had never done either before. And they both began to laugh over nothings as children will when they are happy together. And they laughed so that in the end they were making as much noise as if they had been two ordinary healthy natural ten-year-old creatures—instead of a hard, little, unloving girl and a sickly boy who believed that he was going to die.

They enjoyed themselves so much that they forgot the pictures and they forgot about the time. They had been laughing quite loudly over Ben Weatherstaff and his robin, and Colin was actually sitting up as if he had forgotten about his weak back, when he suddenly remembered something. "Do you know there is one thing we have never once thought of," he said. "We are cousins."

It seemed so queer that they had talked so much and never remembered this simple thing that they laughed more than ever, because they had got into the humor to laugh at anything. And in the midst of the fun the door opened and in walked Dr. Craven and Mrs. Medlock.

Dr. Craven started in actual alarm and Mrs. Medlock almost fell back because he had accidentally bumped against her.

"Good Lord!" exclaimed poor Mrs. Medlock with her eyes almost starting out of her head. "Good Lord!"

"What is this?" said Dr. Craven, coming forward. "What does it mean?"

Then Mary was reminded of the boy Rajah again. Colin answered as if neither the doctor's alarm nor Mrs. Medlock's terror were of the slightest consequence. He was as little disturbed or frightened as if an elderly cat and dog had walked into the room.

"This is my cousin, Mary Lennox," he said. "I asked her to come and talk to me. I like her. She must come and talk to me whenever I send for her."

Dr. Craven turned reproachfully to Mrs. Medlock. "Oh, sir," she panted. "I don't know how it's happened. There's not a servant on the place tha'd dare to talk—they all have their orders."

"Nobody told her anything," said Colin. "She heard me crying and found me herself. I am glad she came. Don't be silly, Medlock."

Mary saw that Dr. Craven did not look pleased, but it was quite plain that he dare not oppose his patient. He sat down by Colin and felt his pulse.

"I am afraid there has been too much excitement. Excitement is not good for you, my boy," he said.

"I should be excited if she kept away," answered Colin, his eyes beginning to look dangerously sparkling. "I am better. She makes me better. The nurse must bring up her tea with mine. We will have tea together."

Mrs. Medlock and Dr. Craven looked at each other in a troubled way, but there was evidently nothing to be done.

"He does look rather better, sir," ventured Mrs. Medlock. "But"—thinking the matter over—"he looked better this morning before she came into the room."

"She came into the room last night. She stayed with me a long time. She sang a Hindustani song to me and it made me go to sleep," said Colin. "I was better when I wakened up. I wanted my breakfast. I want my tea now. Tell nurse, Medlock."

Dr. Craven did not stay very long. He talked to the nurse for a few minutes when she came into the room and said a few words of warning to Colin. He must not talk too much; he must not forget that he was ill; he must not forget that he was very easily tired. Mary thought that there seemed to be a number of uncomfortable things he was not to forget.

Colin looked fretful and kept his strange black-lashed eyes fixed on Dr. Craven's face.

"I want to forget it," he said at last. "She makes me forget it. That is why I want her."

Dr. Craven did not look happy when he left the room. He gave a puzzled glance at the little girl sitting on the large stool. She had become a stiff, silent child again as soon as he entered and he could not see what the attraction was. The boy actually did look brighter, however—and he sighed rather heavily as he went down the corridor.

"They are always wanting me to eat things when I don't want to," said Colin, as the nurse brought in the tea and put it on the table by the sofa. "Now, if you'll eat I will. Those muffins look so nice and hot. Tell me about Rajahs."

CHAPTER XV

NEST BUILDING

After another week of rain the high arch of blue sky appeared again and the sun which poured down was quite hot. Though there had been no chance to see either the secret garden or Dickon, Mistress Mary had enjoyed herself very much. The week had not seemed long. She had spent hours of every day with Colin in his room, talking about Rajahs or gardens or Dickon and the cottage on the moor. They had looked at the splendid books and pictures and sometimes Mary had read things to Colin, and sometimes he had read a little to her. When he was amused and interested she thought he scarcely looked like an invalid at all, except that his face was so colorless and he was always on the sofa.

"You are a sly young one to listen and get out of your bed to go following things up like you did that night," Mrs. Medlock said once. "But there's no saying it's not been a sort of blessing to the lot of us. He's not had a tantrum or a whining fit since you made friends. The nurse was just going to give up the case because she was so sick of him, but she says she doesn't mind staying now you've gone on duty with her," laughing a little.

In her talks with Colin, Mary had tried to be very cautious about the secret garden. There were certain things she wanted to find out from him, but she felt that she must find them out without asking him direct questions. In the first place, as she began to like to be with him, she wanted to discover whether he was the kind of boy you could tell a secret to. He was not in the least like Dickon, but he was evidently so pleased with the idea of a garden no one knew anything about that she thought perhaps he could be trusted. But she had not known him long enough to be sure. The second thing she wanted to find out was this: If he could be trusted—if he really could—wouldn't it be possible to take him to the garden without having any one find it out? The grand doctor had said that he must have fresh air and Colin had said that he would not mind fresh air in a secret garden. Perhaps if he had a great deal of fresh air and knew Dickon and the robin and saw things growing he might not think so much about dying. Mary had seen herself in the glass sometimes lately when she had realized that she looked quite a different creature from the child she had seen when she arrived from India. This child looked nicer. Even Martha had seen a change in her.

"Th' air from th' moor has done thee good already," she had said. "Tha'rt not nigh so yeller and tha'rt not nigh so scrawny. Even tha' hair doesn't slamp down on tha' head so flat. It's got some life in it so as it sticks out a bit."

"It's like me," said Mary. "It's growing stronger and fatter. I'm sure there's more of it."

"It looks it, for sure," said Martha, ruffling it up a little round her face. "Tha'rt not half so ugly when it's that way an' there's a bit o' red in tha' cheeks."

If gardens and fresh air had been good for her perhaps they would be good for Colin. But then, if he hated people to look at him, perhaps he would not like to see Dickon.

"Why does it make you angry when you are looked at?" she inquired one day.

"I always hated it," he answered, "even when I was very little. Then when they took me to the seaside and I used to lie in my carriage everybody used to stare and ladies would stop and talk to my nurse and then they would begin to whisper and I knew then they were saying I shouldn't live to grow up. Then sometimes the ladies would pat my cheeks and say 'Poor child!' Once when a lady did that I screamed out loud and bit her hand. She was so frightened she ran away."

"She thought you had gone mad like a dog," said Mary, not at all admiringly.

"I don't care what she thought," said Colin, frowning.

"I wonder why you didn't scream and bite me when I came into your room?" said Mary. Then she began to smile slowly.

"I thought you were a ghost or a dream," he said. "You can't bite a ghost or a dream, and if you scream they don't care."

"Would you hate it if—if a boy looked at you?" Mary asked uncertainly.

He lay back on his cushion and paused thoughtfully.

"There's one boy," he said quite slowly, as if he were thinking over every word, "there's one boy I believe I shouldn't mind. It's that boy who knows where the foxes live—Dickon."

"I'm sure you wouldn't mind him," said Mary.

"The birds don't and other animals," he said, still thinking it over, "perhaps that's why I shouldn't. He's a sort of animal charmer and I am a boy animal."

Then he laughed and she laughed too; in fact it ended in their both laughing a great deal and finding the idea of a boy animal hiding in his hole very funny indeed.

What Mary felt afterward was that she need not fear about Dickon. On that first morning when the sky was blue again Mary wakened very early. The sun was pouring in slanting rays through the blinds and there was something so joyous in the sight of it that she jumped out of bed and ran to the window. She drew up the blinds and opened the window itself and a great waft of fresh, scented air blew in upon her. The moor was blue and the whole world looked as if something Magic had happened to it. There were tender little fluting sounds here and there and everywhere, as if scores of birds were beginning to tune up for a concert. Mary put her hand out of the window and held it in the sun.

"It's warm—warm!" she said. "It will make the green points push up and up and up, and it will make the bulbs and roots work and struggle with all their might under the earth."

She kneeled down and leaned out of the window as far as she could, breathing big breaths and sniffing the air until she laughed because she remembered what Dickon's mother had said about the end of his nose quivering like a rabbit's. "It must be very early," she said. "The little clouds are all pink and I've never seen the sky look like this. No one is up. I don't even hear the stable boys."

A sudden thought made her scramble to her feet.

"I can't wait! I am going to see the garden!"

She had learned to dress herself by this time and she put on her clothes in five minutes. She knew a small side door which she could unbolt herself and she flew downstairs in her stocking feet and put on her shoes in the hall. She unchained and unbolted and unlocked and when the door was open she sprang across the step with one bound, and there she was standing on the grass, which seemed to have turned green, and with the sun pouring down on her and warm sweet wafts about her and the fluting and twittering and singing coming from every bush and tree. She clasped her hands for pure joy and looked up in the sky and it was so blue and pink and pearly and white and flooded with springtime light that she felt as if she must flute and sing aloud herself and knew that thrushes and robins and skylarks could not possibly help it. She ran around the shrubs and paths towards the secret garden.

"It is all different already," she said. "The grass is greener and things are sticking up everywhere and things are uncurling and green buds of leaves are showing. This afternoon I am sure Dickon will come."

The long warm rain had done strange things to the herbaceous beds which bordered the walk by the lower wall. There were things sprouting and pushing out from the roots of clumps of plants and there were actually here and there glimpses of royal purple and yellow unfurling among the stems of crocuses. Six months before Mistress Mary would not have seen how the world was waking up, but now she missed nothing.

When she had reached the place where the door hid itself under the ivy, she was startled by a curious loud sound. It was the caw—caw of a crow and it came from the top of the wall, and when she looked up, there sat a big glossy-plumaged blue-black bird, looking down at her very wisely indeed. She had never seen a crow so close before and he made her a little nervous, but the next moment he spread his wings and flapped away across the garden. She hoped he was not going to stay inside and she pushed the door open wondering if he would. When she got fairly into the garden she saw that he probably did intend to stay because he had alighted on a dwarf apple-tree and under the apple-tree was lying a little reddish animal with a bushy tail, and both of them were watching the stooping body and rust-red head of Dickon, who was kneeling on the grass working hard.

Mary flew across the grass to him.

"Oh, Dickon! Dickon!" she cried out. "How could you get here so early! How could you! The sun has only just got up!"

He got up himself, laughing and glowing, and tousled; his eyes like a bit of the sky.

"Eh!" he said. "I was up long before him. How could I have stayed abed! Th' world's all fair begun again this mornin', it has. An' it's workin' an' hummin' an' scratchin' an' pipin' an' nest-buildin' an' breathin' out scents, till you've got to be out on it 'stead o' lyin' on your back. When th' sun did jump up, th' moor went mad for joy, an' I was in the midst of th' heather, an' I run like mad myself, shoutin' an' singin'. An' I come straight here. I couldn't have stayed away. Why, th' garden was lyin' here waitin'!"

Mary put her hands on her chest, panting, as if she had been running herself.

"Oh, Dickon! Dickon!" she said. "I'm so happy I can scarcely breathe!"

Seeing him talking to a stranger, the little bushy-tailed animal rose from its place under the tree and came to him, and the rook, cawing once, flew down from its branch and settled quietly on his shoulder.

"This is th' little fox cub," he said, rubbing the little reddish animal's head. "It's named Captain. An' this here's Soot. Soot he flew across th' moor with me an' Captain he run same as if th' hounds had been after him. They both felt same as I did."

Neither of the creatures looked as if he were the least afraid of Mary. When Dickon began to walk about, Soot stayed on his shoulder and Captain trotted quietly close to his side.

"See here!" said Dickon. "See how these has pushed up, an' these an' these! An' Eh! Look at these here!"

He threw himself upon his knees and Mary went down beside him. They had come upon a whole clump of crocuses burst into purple and orange and gold. Mary bent her face down and kissed and kissed them.

"You never kiss a person in that way," she said when she lifted her head. "Flowers are so different."

He looked puzzled but smiled.

"Eh!" he said, "I've kissed mother many a time that way when I come in from th' moor after a day's roamin' an' she stood there at th' door in th' sun, lookin' so glad an' comfortable." They ran from one part of the garden to another and found so many wonders that they were obliged to remind themselves that they must whisper or speak low. He showed her swelling leafbuds on rose branches which had seemed dead. He showed her ten thousand new green points pushing through the mould. They put their eager young noses close to the earth and sniffed its warmed springtime breathing; they dug and pulled and laughed low with rapture until Mistress Mary's hair was as tumbled as Dickon's and her cheeks were almost as poppy red as his.

There was every joy on earth in the secret garden that morning, and in the midst of them came a delight more delightful than all, because it was more wonderful. Swiftly something flew across the wall and darted through the trees to a close grown corner, a little flare of red-breasted bird with something hanging from its beak. Dickon stood quite still and put his hand on Mary almost as if they had suddenly found themselves laughing in a church.

"We munnot stir," he whispered in broad Yorkshire. "We munnot scarce breathe. I knowed he was mate-huntin' when I seed him last. It's Ben Weatherstaff's robin. He's buildin' his nest. He'll stay here if us don't fight him." They settled down softly upon the grass and sat there without moving.

"Us mustn't seem as if us was watchin' him too close," said Dickon. "He'd be out with us for good if he got th' notion us was interferin' now. He'll be a good bit different till all this is over. He's settin' up housekeepin'. He'll be shyer an' readier to take things ill. He's got no time for visitin' an' gossipin'. Us must keep still a bit an' try to look as if us was grass an' trees an' bushes. Then when he's got used to seein' us I'll chirp a bit an' he'll know us'll not be in his way."

Mistress Mary was not at all sure that she knew, as Dickon seemed to, how to try to look like grass and trees and bushes. But he had said the queer thing as if it were the simplest and most natural thing in the world, and she felt it must be quite easy to him, and indeed she watched him for a few minutes carefully, wondering if it was possible for him to quietly turn green and put out branches and leaves. But he only sat wonderfully still, and when he spoke dropped his voice to such a softness that it was curious that she could hear him, but she could.

"It's part o' th' springtime, this nest-buildin' is," he said. "I warrant it's been goin' on in th' same way every year since th' world was begun. They've got their way o' thinkin' and doin' things an' a body had better not meddle. You can lose a friend in springtime easier than any other season if you're too curious."

"If we talk about him I can't help looking at him," Mary said as softly as possible. "We must talk of something else. There is something I want to tell you."

"He'll like it better if us talks o' somethin' else," said Dickon. "What is it tha's got to tell me?"

"Well—do you know about Colin?" she whispered.

He turned his head to look at her.

"What does tha' know about him?" he asked.

"I've seen him. I have been to talk to him every day this week. He wants me to come. He says I'm making him forget about being ill and dying," answered Mary.

Dickon looked actually relieved as soon as the surprise died away from his round face.

"I am glad o' that," he exclaimed. "I'm right down glad. It makes me easier. I knowed I must say nothin' about him an' I don't like havin' to hide things."

"Don't you like hiding the garden?" said Mary.

"I'll never tell about it," he answered. "But I says to mother, 'Mother,' I says, 'I got a secret to keep. It's not a bad 'un, tha' knows that. It's no worse than hidin' where a bird's nest is. Tha' doesn't mind it, does tha'?"

Mary always wanted to hear about mother.

"What did she say?" she asked, not at all afraid to hear.

Dickon grinned sweet-temperedly.

"It was just like her, what she said," he answered. "She give my head a bit of a rub an' laughed an' she says, 'Eh, lad, tha' can have all th' secrets tha' likes. I've knowed thee twelve year'."

"How did you know about Colin?" asked Mary.

"Everybody as knowed about Mester Craven knowed there was a little lad as was like to be a cripple, an' they knowed Mester Craven didn't like him to be talked about. Folks is sorry for Mester Craven because Mrs. Craven was such a pretty young lady an' they was so fond of each other. Mrs. Medlock stops in our cottage whenever she goes to Thwaite an' she doesn't mind talkin' to mother before us children, because she knows us has been brought up to be trusty. How did tha' find out about him? Martha was in fine trouble th' last time she came home. She said tha'd heard him frettin' an' tha' was askin' questions an' she didn't know what to say."

Mary told him her story about the midnight wuthering of the wind which had wakened her and about the faint far-off sounds of the complaining voice which had led her down the dark corridors with her candle and had ended with her opening of the door of the dimly lighted room with the carven four-posted bed in the corner. When she described the small ivory-white face and the strange black-rimmed eyes Dickon shook his head.

"Them's just like his mother's eyes, only hers was always laughin', they say," he said. "They say as Mr. Craven can't bear to see him when he's awake an' it's because his eyes is so like his mother's an' yet looks so different in his miserable bit of a face."

"Do you think he wants to die?" whispered Mary.

"No, but he wishes he'd never been born. Mother she says that's th' worst thing on earth for a child. Them as is not wanted scarce ever thrives. Mester Craven he'd buy anythin' as money could buy for th' poor lad but he'd like to forget as he's on earth. For one thing, he's afraid he'll look at him some day and find he's growed hunchback."

"Colin's so afraid of it himself that he won't sit up," said Mary. "He says he's always thinking that if he should feel a lump coming he should go crazy and scream himself to death."

"Eh! he oughtn't to lie there thinkin' things like that," said Dickon. "No lad could get well as thought them sort o' things."

The fox was lying on the grass close by him, looking up to ask for a pat now and then, and Dickon bent down and rubbed his neck softly and thought a few minutes in silence. Presently he lifted his head and looked round the garden.

"When first we got in here," he said, "it seemed like everything was gray. Look round now and tell me if tha' doesn't see a difference."

Mary looked and caught her breath a little.

"Why!" she cried, "the gray wall is changing. It is as if a green mist were creeping over it. It's almost like a green gauze veil."

"Aye," said Dickon. "An' it'll be greener and greener till th' gray's all gone. Can tha' guess what I was thinkin'?"

"I know it was something nice," said Mary eagerly. "I believe it was something about Colin."

"I was thinkin' that if he was out here he wouldn't be watchin' for lumps to grow on his back; he'd be watchin' for buds to break on th' rose-bushes, an' he'd likely be healthier," explained Dickon. "I was wonderin' if us could ever get him in th' humor to come out here an' lie under th' trees in his carriage."

"I've been wondering that myself. I've thought of it almost every time I've talked to him," said Mary. "I've wondered if he could keep a secret and I've wondered if we could bring him here without any one seeing us. I thought perhaps you could push his carriage. The doctor said he must have fresh air and if he wants us to take him out no one dare disobey him. He won't go out for other people and perhaps they will be glad if he will go out with us. He could order the gardeners to keep away so they wouldn't find out."

Dickon was thinking very hard as he scratched Captain's back.

"It'd be good for him, I'll warrant," he said. "Us'd not be thinkin' he'd better never been born. Us'd be just two children watchin' a garden grow, an' he'd be another. Two lads an' a little lass just lookin' on at th' springtime. I warrant it'd be better than doctor's stuff."

"He's been lying in his room so long and he's always been so afraid of his back that it has made him queer," said Mary. "He knows a good many things out of books but he doesn't know anything else. He says he has been too ill to notice things and he hates going out of doors and hates gardens and gardeners. But he likes to hear about this garden because it is a secret. I daren't tell him much but he said he wanted to see it."

"Us'll have him out here sometime for sure," said Dickon. "I could push his carriage well enough. Has tha' noticed how th' robin an' his mate has been workin' while we've been sittin' here? Look at him perched on that branch wonderin' where it'd be best to put that twig he's got in his beak."

He made one of his low whistling calls and the robin turned his head and looked at him inquiringly, still holding his twig. Dickon spoke to him as Ben Weatherstaff did, but Dickon's tone was one of friendly advice.

"Wheres'ever tha' puts it," he said, "it'll be all right. Tha' knew how to build tha' nest before tha' came out o' th' egg. Get on with thee, lad. Tha'st got no time to lose."

"Oh, I do like to hear you talk to him!" Mary said, laughing delightedly. "Ben Weatherstaff scolds him and makes fun of him, and he hops about and looks as if he understood every word, and I know he likes it. Ben Weatherstaff says he is so conceited he would rather have stones thrown at him than not be noticed."

Dickon laughed too and went on talking.

"Tha' knows us won't trouble thee," he said to the robin. "Us is near bein' wild things ourselves. Us is nest-buildin' too, bless thee. Look out tha' doesn't tell on us."

And though the robin did not answer, because his beak was occupied, Mary knew that when he flew away with his twig to his own corner of the garden the darkness of his dew-bright eye meant that he would not tell their secret for the world.

CHAPTER XVI

"I WON'T!" SAID MARY

They found a great deal to do that morning and Mary was late in returning to the house and was also in such a hurry to get back to her work that she quite forgot Colin until the last moment.

"Tell Colin that I can't come and see him yet," she said to Martha. "I'm very busy in the garden."

Martha looked rather frightened.

"Eh! Miss Mary," she said, "it may put him all out of humor when I tell him that."

But Mary was not as afraid of him as other people were and she was not a self-sacrificing person.

"I can't stay," she answered. "Dickon's waiting for me;" and she ran away.

The afternoon was even lovelier and busier than the morning had been. Already nearly all the weeds were cleared out of the garden and most of the roses and trees had been pruned or dug about. Dickon had brought a spade of his own and he had taught Mary to use all her tools, so that by this time it was plain that though the lovely wild place was not likely to become a "gardener's garden" it would be a wilderness of growing things before the springtime was over.

"There'll be apple blossoms an' cherry blossoms overhead," Dickon said, working away with all his might. "An' there'll be peach an' plum trees in bloom against th' walls, an' th' grass'll be a carpet o' flowers."

The little fox and the rook were as happy and busy as they were, and the robin and his mate flew backward and forward like tiny streaks of lightning. Sometimes the rook flapped his black wings and soared away over the tree-tops in the park. Each time he came back and perched near Dickon and cawed several times as if he were relating his adventures, and Dickon talked to him just as he had talked to the robin. Once when Dickon was so busy that he did not answer him at first, Soot flew on to his shoulders and gently tweaked his ear with his large beak. When Mary wanted to rest a little Dickon sat down with her under a tree and once he took his pipe out of his pocket and played the soft strange little notes and two squirrels appeared on the wall and looked and listened.

"Tha's a good bit stronger than tha' was," Dickon said, looking at her as she was digging. "Tha's beginning to look different, for sure."

Mary was glowing with exercise and good spirits.

"I'm getting fatter and fatter every day," she said quite exultantly. "Mrs. Medlock will have to get me some bigger dresses. Martha says my hair is growing thicker. It isn't so flat and stringy."

The sun was beginning to set and sending deep gold-colored rays slanting under the trees when they parted.

"It'll be fine tomorrow," said Dickon. "I'll be at work by sunrise."

"So will I," said Mary.

She ran back to the house as quickly as her feet would carry her. She wanted to tell Colin about Dickon's fox cub and the rook and about what the springtime had been doing. She felt sure he would like to hear. So it was not very pleasant when she opened the door of her room, to see Martha standing waiting for her with a doleful face.

"What is the matter?" she asked. "What did Colin say when you told him I couldn't come?"

"Eh!" said Martha, "I wish tha'd gone. He was nigh goin' into one o' his tantrums. There's been a nice to do all afternoon to keep him quiet. He would watch the clock all th' time."

Mary's lips pinched themselves together. She was no more used to considering other people than Colin was and she saw no reason why an ill-tempered boy should interfere with the thing she liked best. She knew nothing about the pitifulness of people who had been ill and nervous and who did not know that they could control their tempers and need not make other people ill and nervous, too. When she had had a headache in India she had done her best to see that everybody else also had a headache or something quite as bad. And she felt she was quite right; but of course now she felt that Colin was quite wrong.

He was not on his sofa when she went into his room. He was lying flat on his back in bed and he did not turn his head toward her as she came in. This was a bad beginning and Mary marched up to him with her stiff manner.

"Why didn't you get up?" she said.

"I did get up this morning when I thought you were coming," he answered, without looking at her. "I made them put me back in bed this afternoon. My back ached and my head ached and I was tired. Why didn't you come?"

"I was working in the garden with Dickon," said Mary.

Colin frowned and condescended to look at her.

"I won't let that boy come here if you go and stay with him instead of coming to talk to me," he said.

Mary flew into a fine passion. She could fly into a passion without making a noise. She just grew sour and obstinate and did not care what happened.

"If you send Dickon away, I'll never come into this room again!" she retorted.

"You'll have to if I want you," said Colin.

"I won't!" said Mary.

"I'll make you," said Colin. "They shall drag you in."

"Shall they, Mr. Rajah!" said Mary fiercely. "They may drag me in but they can't make me talk when they get me here. I'll sit and clench my teeth and never tell you one thing. I won't even look at you. I'll stare at the floor!"

They were a nice agreeable pair as they glared at each other. If they had been two little street boys they would have sprung at each other and had a rough-and-tumble fight. As it was, they did the next thing to it.

"You are a selfish thing!" cried Colin.

"What are you?" said Mary. "Selfish people always say that. Any one is selfish who doesn't do what they want. You're more selfish than I am. You're the most selfish boy I ever saw."

"I'm not!" snapped Colin. "I'm not as selfish as your fine Dickon is! He keeps you playing in the dirt when he knows I am all by myself. He's selfish, if you like!"

Mary's eyes flashed fire.

"He's nicer than any other boy that ever lived!" she said. "He's—he's like an angel!" It might sound rather silly to say that but she did not care.

"A nice angel!" Colin sneered ferociously. "He's a common cottage boy off the moor!"

"He's better than a common Rajah!" retorted Mary. "He's a thousand times better!"

Because she was the stronger of the two she was beginning to get the better of him. The truth was that he had never had a fight with any one like himself in his life and, upon the whole, it was rather good for him, though neither he nor Mary knew anything about that. He turned his head on his pillow and shut his eyes and a big tear was squeezed out and ran down his cheek. He was beginning to feel pathetic and sorry for himself—not for any one else.

"I'm not as selfish as you, because I'm always ill, and I'm sure there is a lump coming on my back," he said. "And I am going to die besides."

"You're not!" contradicted Mary unsympathetically.

He opened his eyes quite wide with indignation. He had never heard such a thing said before. He was at once furious and slightly pleased, if a person could be both at one time.

"I'm not?" he cried. "I am! You know I am! Everybody says so."

"I don't believe it!" said Mary sourly. "You just say that to make people sorry. I believe you're proud of it. I don't believe it! If you were a nice boy it might be true—but you're too nasty!"

In spite of his invalid back Colin sat up in bed in quite a healthy rage.

"Get out of the room!" he shouted and he caught hold of his pillow and threw it at her. He was not strong enough to throw it far and it only fell at her feet, but Mary's face looked as pinched as a nutcracker.

"I'm going," she said. "And I won't come back!" She walked to the door and when she reached it she turned round and spoke again.

"I was going to tell you all sorts of nice things," she said. "Dickon brought his fox and his rook and I was going to tell you all about them. Now I won't tell you a single thing!"

She marched out of the door and closed it behind her, and there to her great astonishment she found the trained nurse standing as if she had been listening and, more amazing still—she was laughing. She was a big handsome young woman who ought not to have been a trained nurse at all, as she could not bear invalids and she was always making excuses to leave Colin to Martha or any one else who would take her place. Mary had never liked her, and she simply stood and gazed up at her as she stood giggling into her handkerchief.

"What are you laughing at?" she asked her.

"At you two young ones," said the nurse. "It's the best thing that could happen to the sickly pampered thing to have some one to stand up to him that's as spoiled as himself;" and she laughed into her handkerchief again. "If he'd had a young vixen of a sister to fight with it would have been the saving of him."

"Is he going to die?"

"I don't know and I don't care," said the nurse. "Hysterics and temper are half what ails him."

"What are hysterics?" asked Mary.

"You'll find out if you work him into a tantrum after this—but at any rate you've given him something to have hysterics about, and I'm glad of it."

Mary went back to her room not feeling at all as she had felt when she had come in from the garden. She was cross and disappointed but not at all sorry for Colin. She had looked forward to telling him a great many things and she had meant to try to make up her mind whether it would be safe to trust him with the great secret. She had been beginning to think it would be, but now she had changed her mind entirely. She would never tell him and he could stay in his room and never get any fresh air and die if he liked! It would serve him right! She felt so sour and unrelenting that for a few minutes she almost forgot about Dickon and the green veil creeping over the world and the soft wind blowing down from the moor.

Martha was waiting for her and the trouble in her face had been temporarily replaced by interest and curiosity. There was a wooden box on the table and its cover had been removed and revealed that it was full of neat packages.

"Mr. Craven sent it to you," said Martha. "It looks as if it had picture-books in it."

Mary remembered what he had asked her the day she had gone to his room. "Do you want anything—dolls—toys—books?" She opened the package wondering if he had sent a doll, and also wondering what she should do with it if he had. But he had not sent one. There were several beautiful books such as Colin had, and two of them were about gardens and were full of pictures. There were two or three games and there was a beautiful little writing-case with a gold monogram on it and a gold pen and inkstand.

Everything was so nice that her pleasure began to crowd her anger out of her mind. She had not expected him to remember her at all and her hard little heart grew quite warm.

"I can write better than I can print," she said, "and the first thing I shall write with that pen will be a letter to tell him I am much obliged."

If she had been friends with Colin she would have run to show him her presents at once, and they would have looked at the pictures and read some of the gardening books and perhaps tried playing the games, and he would have enjoyed himself so much he would never once have thought he was going to die or have put his hand on his spine to see if there was a lump coming. He had a way of doing that which she could not bear. It gave her an uncomfortable frightened feeling because he always looked so frightened himself. He said that if he felt even quite a little lump some day he should know his hunch had begun to grow. Something he had heard Mrs. Medlock whispering to the nurse had given him the idea and he had thought over it in secret until it was quite firmly fixed in his mind. Mrs. Medlock had said his father's back had begun to show its crookedness in that way when he was a child. He had never told any one but Mary that most of his "tantrums" as they called them grew out of his hysterical hidden fear. Mary had been sorry for him when he had told her.

"He always began to think about it when he was cross or tired," she said to herself. "And he has been cross today. Perhaps—perhaps he has been thinking about it all afternoon."

She stood still, looking down at the carpet and thinking.

"I said I would never go back again—" she hesitated, knitting her brows—"but perhaps, just perhaps, I will go and see—if he wants me—in the morning. Perhaps he'll try to throw his pillow at me again, but—I think—I'll go."

CHAPTER XVII

A TANTRUM

She had got up very early in the morning and had worked hard in the garden and she was tired and sleepy, so as soon as Martha had brought her supper and she had eaten it, she was glad to go to bed. As she laid her head on the pillow she murmured to herself:

"I'll go out before breakfast and work with Dickon and then afterward—I believe—I'll go to see him."

She thought it was the middle of the night when she was awakened by such dreadful sounds that she jumped out of bed in an instant. What was it—what was it? The next minute she felt quite sure she knew. Doors were opened and shut and there were hurrying feet in the corridors and some one was crying and screaming at the same time, screaming and crying in a horrible way.

"It's Colin," she said. "He's having one of those tantrums the nurse called hysterics. How awful it sounds."

As she listened to the sobbing screams she did not wonder that people were so frightened that they gave him his own way in everything rather than hear them. She put her hands over her ears and felt sick and shivering.

"I don't know what to do. I don't know what to do," she kept saying. "I can't bear it."

Once she wondered if he would stop if she dared go to him and then she remembered how he had driven her out of the room and thought that perhaps the sight of her might make him worse. Even when she pressed her hands more tightly over her ears she could not keep the awful sounds out. She hated them so and was so terrified by them that suddenly they began to make her angry and she felt as if she should like to fly into a tantrum herself and frighten him as he was frightening her. She was not used to any one's tempers but her own. She took her hands from her ears and sprang up and stamped her foot.

"He ought to be stopped! Somebody ought to make him stop! Somebody ought to beat him!" she cried out.

Just then she heard feet almost running down the corridor and her door opened and the nurse came in. She was not laughing now by any means. She even looked rather pale.

"He's worked himself into hysterics," she said in a great hurry. "He'll do himself harm. No one can do anything with him. You come and try, like a good child. He likes you."

"He turned me out of the room this morning," said Mary, stamping her foot with excitement.

The stamp rather pleased the nurse. The truth was that she had been afraid she might find Mary crying and hiding her head under the bedclothes.

"That's right," she said. "You're in the right humor. You go and scold him. Give him something new to think of. Do go, child, as quick as ever you can."

It was not until afterward that Mary realized that the thing had been funny as well as dreadful—that it was funny that all the grown-up people were so frightened that they came to a little girl just because they guessed she was almost as bad as Colin himself.

She flew along the corridor and the nearer she got to the screams the higher her temper mounted. She felt quite wicked by the time she reached the door. She slapped it open with her hand and ran across the room to the four-posted bed.

"You stop!" she almost shouted. "You stop! I hate you! Everybody hates you! I wish everybody would run out of the house and let you scream yourself to death! You will scream yourself to death in a minute, and I wish you would!" A nice sympathetic child could neither have thought nor said such things, but it just happened that the shock of hearing them was the best possible thing for this hysterical boy whom no one had ever dared to restrain or contradict.

He had been lying on his face beating his pillow with his hands and he actually almost jumped around, he turned so quickly at the sound of the furious little voice. His face looked dreadful, white and red and swollen, and he was gasping and choking; but savage little Mary did not care an atom.

"If you scream another scream," she said, "I'll scream too—and I can scream louder than you can and I'll frighten you, I'll frighten you!"

He actually had stopped screaming because she had startled him so. The scream which had been coming almost choked him. The tears were streaming down his face and he shook all over.

"I can't stop!" he gasped and sobbed. "I can't—I can't!"

"You can!" shouted Mary. "Half that ails you is hysterics and temper—just hysterics—hysterics—hysterics!" and she stamped each time she said it.

"I felt the lump—I felt it," choked out Colin. "I knew I should. I shall have a hunch on my back and then I shall die," and he began to writhe again and turned on his face and sobbed and wailed but he didn't scream.

"You didn't feel a lump!" contradicted Mary fiercely. "If you did it was only a hysterical lump. Hysterics makes lumps. There's nothing the matter with your horrid back—nothing but hysterics! Turn over and let me look at it!"

She liked the word "hysterics" and felt somehow as if it had an effect on him. He was probably like herself and had never heard it before.

"Nurse," she commanded, "come here and show me his back this minute!"

The nurse, Mrs. Medlock and Martha had been standing huddled together near the door staring at her, their mouths half open. All three had gasped with fright more than once. The nurse came forward as if she were half afraid. Colin was heaving with great breathless sobs.

"Perhaps he—he won't let me," she hesitated in a low voice.

Colin heard her, however, and he gasped out between two sobs:

"Sh-show her! She-she'll see then!"

It was a poor thin back to look at when it was bared. Every rib could be counted and every joint of the spine, though Mistress Mary did not count them as she bent over and examined them with a solemn savage little face. She looked so sour and old-fashioned that the nurse turned her head aside to hide the twitching of her mouth. There was just a minute's silence, for even Colin tried to hold his breath while Mary looked up and down his spine, and down and up, as intently as if she had been the great doctor from London.

"There's not a single lump there!" she said at last. "There's not a lump as big as a pin—except backbone lumps, and you can only feel them because you're thin. I've got backbone lumps myself, and they used to stick out as much as yours do, until I began to get fatter, and I am not fat enough yet to hide them. There's not a lump as big as a pin! If you ever say there is again, I shall laugh!"

No one but Colin himself knew what effect those crossly spoken childish words had on him. If he had ever had any one to talk to about his secret terrors—if he had ever dared to let himself ask questions—if he had had childish companions and had not lain on his back in the huge closed house, breathing an atmosphere heavy with the fears of people who were most of them ignorant and tired of him, he would have found out that most of his fright and illness was created by himself. But he had lain and thought of himself and his aches and weariness for hours and days and months and years. And now that an angry unsympathetic little girl insisted obstinately that he was not as ill as he thought he was he actually felt as if she might be speaking the truth.

"I didn't know," ventured the nurse, "that he thought he had a lump on his spine. His back is weak because he won't try to sit up. I could have told him there was no lump there." Colin gulped and turned his face a little to look at her.

"C-could you?" he said pathetically.

"Yes, sir."

"There!" said Mary, and she gulped too.

Colin turned on his face again and but for his long-drawn broken breaths, which were the dying down of his storm of sobbing, he lay still for a minute, though great tears streamed down his face and wet the pillow. Actually the tears meant that a curious great relief had come to him. Presently he turned and looked at the nurse again and strangely enough he was not like a Rajah at all as he spoke to her.

"Do you think—I could—live to grow up?" he said.

The nurse was neither clever nor soft-hearted but she could repeat some of the London doctor's words.

"You probably will if you will do what you are told to do and not give way to your temper, and stay out a great deal in the fresh air."

Colin's tantrum had passed and he was weak and worn out with crying and this perhaps made him feel gentle. He put out his hand a little toward Mary, and I am glad to say that, her own tantrum having passed, she was softened too and met him half-way with her hand, so that it was a sort of making up.

"I'll—I'll go out with you, Mary," he said. "I shan't hate fresh air if we can find—" He remembered just in time to stop himself from saying "if we can find the secret garden" and he ended, "I shall like to go out with you if Dickon will come and push my chair. I do so want to see Dickon and the fox and the crow."

The nurse remade the tumbled bed and shook and straightened the pillows. Then she made Colin a cup of beef tea and gave a cup to Mary, who really was very glad to get it after her excitement. Mrs. Medlock and Martha gladly slipped away, and after everything was neat and calm and in order the nurse looked as if she would very gladly slip away also. She was a healthy young woman who resented being robbed of her sleep and she yawned quite openly as she looked at Mary, who had pushed her big footstool close to the four-posted bed and was holding Colin's hand.

"You must go back and get your sleep out," she said. "He'll drop off after a while—if he's not too upset. Then I'll lie down myself in the next room."

"Would you like me to sing you that song I learned from my Ayah?" Mary whispered to Colin.

His hand pulled hers gently and he turned his tired eyes on her appealingly.

"Oh, yes!" he answered. "It's such a soft song. I shall go to sleep in a minute."

"I will put him to sleep," Mary said to the yawning nurse. "You can go if you like."

"Well," said the nurse, with an attempt at reluctance. "If he doesn't go to sleep in half an hour you must call me."

"Very well," answered Mary.

The nurse was out of the room in a minute and as soon as she was gone Colin pulled Mary's hand again.

"I almost told," he said; "but I stopped myself in time. I won't talk and I'll go to sleep, but you said you had a whole lot of nice things to tell me. Have you—do you think you have found out anything at all about the way into the secret garden?"

Mary looked at his poor little tired face and swollen eyes and her heart relented.

"Ye-es," she answered, "I think I have. And if you will go to sleep I will tell you tomorrow." His hand quite trembled.

"Oh, Mary!" he said. "Oh, Mary! If I could get into it I think I should live to grow up! Do you suppose that instead of singing the Ayah song—you could just tell me softly as you did that first day what you imagine it looks like inside? I am sure it will make me go to sleep."

"Yes," answered Mary. "Shut your eyes."

He closed his eyes and lay quite still and she held his hand and began to speak very slowly and in a very low voice.

"I think it has been left alone so long—that it has grown all into a lovely tangle. I think the roses have climbed and climbed and climbed until they hang from the branches and walls and creep over the ground—almost like a strange gray mist. Some of them have died but many—are alive and when the summer comes there will be curtains and fountains of roses. I think the ground is full of daffodils and snowdrops and lilies and iris working their way out of the dark. Now the spring has begun—perhaps—perhaps—"

The soft drone of her voice was making him stiller and stiller and she saw it and went on.

"Perhaps they are coming up through the grass—perhaps there are clusters of purple crocuses and gold ones—even now. Perhaps the leaves are beginning to break out and uncurl—and perhaps—the gray is changing and a green gauze veil is creeping—and creeping over—everything. And the birds are coming to look at it—because it is—so safe and still. And perhaps—perhaps—perhaps—" very softly and slowly indeed, "the robin has found a mate—and is building a nest."

And Colin was asleep.

CHAPTER XVIII

"THA' MUNNOT WASTE NO TIME"

Of course Mary did not waken early the next morning. She slept late because she was tired, and when Martha brought her breakfast she told her that though Colin was quite quiet he was ill and feverish as he always was after he had worn himself out with a fit of crying. Mary ate her breakfast slowly as she listened.

"He says he wishes tha' would please go and see him as soon as tha' can," Martha said. "It's queer what a fancy he's took to thee. Tha' did give it him last night for sure—didn't tha? Nobody else would have dared to do it. Eh! poor lad! He's been spoiled till salt won't save him. Mother says as th' two worst things as can happen to a child is never to have his own way—or always to have it. She doesn't know which is th' worst. Tha' was in a fine temper tha'self, too. But he says to me when I went into his room, 'Please ask Miss Mary if she'll please come an' talk to me?' Think o' him saying please! Will you go, Miss?"

"I'll run and see Dickon first," said Mary. "No, I'll go and see Colin first and tell him—I know what I'll tell him," with a sudden inspiration.

She had her hat on when she appeared in Colin's room and for a second he looked disappointed. He was in bed. His face was pitifully white and there were dark circles round his eyes.

"I'm glad you came," he said. "My head aches and I ache all over because I'm so tired. Are you going somewhere?"

Mary went and leaned against his bed.

"I won't be long," she said. "I'm going to Dickon, but I'll come back. Colin, it's—it's something about the garden."

His whole face brightened and a little color came into it.

"Oh! is it?" he cried out. "I dreamed about it all night. I heard you say something about gray changing into green, and I dreamed I was standing in a place all filled with trembling little green leaves—and there were birds on nests everywhere and they looked so soft and still. I'll lie and think about it until you come back."

In five minutes Mary was with Dickon in their garden. The fox and the crow were with him again and this time he had brought two tame squirrels. "I came over on the pony this mornin'," he said. "Eh! he is a good little chap—Jump is! I brought these two in my pockets. This here one he's called Nut an' this here other one's called Shell."

When he said "Nut" one squirrel leaped on to his right shoulder and when he said "Shell" the other one leaped on to his left shoulder.

When they sat down on the grass with Captain curled at their feet, Soot solemnly listening on a tree and Nut and Shell nosing about close to them, it seemed to Mary that it would be scarcely bearable to leave such delightfulness, but when she began to tell her story somehow the look in Dickon's funny face gradually changed her mind. She could see he felt sorrier for Colin than she did. He looked up at the sky and all about him.

"Just listen to them birds—th' world seems full of 'em—all whistlin' an' pipin'," he said. "Look at 'em dartin' about, an' hearken at 'em callin' to each other. Come springtime seems like as if all th' world's callin'. The leaves is uncurlin' so you can see 'em—an', my word, th' nice smells there is about!" sniffing with his happy turned-up nose. "An' that poor lad lyin' shut up an' seein' so little that he gets to thinkin' o' things as sets him screamin'. Eh! my! we mun get him out here—we mun get him watchin' an listenin' an' sniffin' up th' air an' get him just soaked through wi' sunshine. An' we munnot lose no time about it."

When he was very much interested he often spoke quite broad Yorkshire though at other times he tried to modify his dialect so that Mary could better understand. But she loved his broad Yorkshire and had in fact been trying to learn to speak it herself. So she spoke a little now.

"Aye, that we mun," she said (which meant "Yes, indeed, we must"). "I'll tell thee what us'll do first," she proceeded, and Dickon grinned, because when the little wench tried to twist her tongue into speaking Yorkshire it amused him very much. "He's took a graidely fancy to thee. He wants to see thee and he wants to see Soot an' Captain. When I go back to the house to talk to him I'll ax him if tha' canna' come an' see him tomorrow mornin'—an' bring tha' creatures wi' thee—an' then—in a bit, when there's more leaves out, an' happen a bud or two, we'll get him to come out an' tha' shall push him in his chair an' we'll bring him here an' show him everything."

When she stopped she was quite proud of herself. She had never made a long speech in Yorkshire before and she had remembered very well.

"Tha' mun talk a bit o' Yorkshire like that to Mester Colin," Dickon chuckled. "Tha'll make him laugh an' there's nowt as good for ill folk as laughin' is. Mother says she believes as half a hour's good laugh every mornin' 'ud cure a chap as was makin' ready for typhus fever."

"I'm going to talk Yorkshire to him this very day," said Mary, chuckling herself.

The garden had reached the time when every day and every night it seemed as if Magicians were passing through it drawing loveliness out of the earth and the boughs with wands. It was hard to go away and leave it all, particularly as Nut had actually crept on to her dress and Shell had scrambled down the trunk of the apple-tree they sat under and stayed there looking at her with inquiring eyes. But she went back to the house and when she sat down close to Colin's bed he began to sniff as Dickon did though not in such an experienced way.

"You smell like flowers and—and fresh things," he cried out quite joyously. "What is it you smell of? It's cool and warm and sweet all at the same time."

"It's th' wind from th' moor," said Mary. "It comes o' sittin' on th' grass under a tree wi' Dickon an' wi' Captain an' Soot an' Nut an' Shell. It's th' springtime an' out o' doors an' sunshine as smells so graidely."

She said it as broadly as she could, and you do not know how broadly Yorkshire sounds until you have heard some one speak it. Colin began to laugh.

"What are you doing?" he said. "I never heard you talk like that before. How funny it sounds."

"I'm givin' thee a bit o' Yorkshire," answered Mary triumphantly. "I canna' talk as graidely as Dickon an' Martha can but tha' sees I can shape a bit. Doesn't tha' understand a bit o' Yorkshire when tha' hears it? An' tha' a Yorkshire lad thysel' bred an' born! Eh! I wonder tha'rt not ashamed o' thy face."

And then she began to laugh too and they both laughed until they could not stop themselves and they laughed until the room echoed and Mrs. Medlock opening the door to come in drew back into the corridor and stood listening amazed.

"Well, upon my word!" she said, speaking rather broad Yorkshire herself because there was no one to hear her and she was so astonished. "Whoever heard th' like! Whoever on earth would ha' thought it!"

There was so much to talk about. It seemed as if Colin could never hear enough of Dickon and Captain and Soot and Nut and Shell and the pony whose name was Jump. Mary had run round into the wood with Dickon to see Jump. He was a tiny little shaggy moor pony with thick locks hanging over his eyes and with a pretty face and a nuzzling velvet nose. He was rather thin with living on moor grass but he was as tough and wiry as if the muscle in his little legs had been made of steel springs. He had lifted his head and whinnied softly the moment he saw Dickon and he had trotted up to him and put his head across his shoulder and then Dickon had talked into his ear and Jump had talked back in odd little whinnies and puffs and snorts. Dickon had made him give Mary his small front hoof and kiss her on her cheek with his velvet muzzle.

"Does he really understand everything Dickon says?" Colin asked.

"It seems as if he does," answered Mary. "Dickon says anything will understand if you're friends with it for sure, but you have to be friends for sure."

Colin lay quiet a little while and his strange gray eyes seemed to be staring at the wall, but Mary saw he was thinking.

"I wish I was friends with things," he said at last, "but I'm not. I never had anything to be friends with, and I can't bear people."

"Can't you bear me?" asked Mary.

"Yes, I can," he answered. "It's funny but I even like you."

"Ben Weatherstaff said I was like him," said Mary. "He said he'd warrant we'd both got the same nasty tempers. I think you are like him too. We are all three alike—you and I and Ben Weatherstaff. He said we were neither of us much to look at and we were as sour as we looked. But I don't feel as sour as I used to before I knew the robin and Dickon."

"Did you feel as if you hated people?"

"Yes," answered Mary without any affectation. "I should have detested you if I had seen you before I saw the robin and Dickon."

Colin put out his thin hand and touched her.

"Mary," he said, "I wish I hadn't said what I did about sending Dickon away. I hated you when you said he was like an angel and I laughed at you but—but perhaps he is."

"Well, it was rather funny to say it," she admitted frankly, "because his nose does turn up and he has a big mouth and his clothes have patches all over them and he talks broad Yorkshire, but—but if an angel did come to Yorkshire and live on the moor—if there was a Yorkshire angel—I believe he'd understand the green things and know how to make them grow and he would know how to talk to the wild creatures as Dickon does and they'd know he was friends for sure."

"I shouldn't mind Dickon looking at me," said Colin; "I want to see him."

"I'm glad you said that," answered Mary, "because—because—"

Quite suddenly it came into her mind that this was the minute to tell him. Colin knew something new was coming.

"Because what?" he cried eagerly.

Mary was so anxious that she got up from her stool and came to him and caught hold of both his hands.

"Can I trust you? I trusted Dickon because birds trusted him. Can I trust you—for sure—*for sure*?" she implored.

Her face was so solemn that he almost whispered his answer.

"Yes—yes!"

"Well, Dickon will come to see you tomorrow morning, and he'll bring his creatures with him."

"Oh! Oh!" Colin cried out in delight.

"But that's not all," Mary went on, almost pale with solemn excitement. "The rest is better. There is a door into the garden. I found it. It is under the ivy on the wall."

If he had been a strong healthy boy Colin would probably have shouted "Hooray! Hooray! Hooray!" but he was weak and rather hysterical; his eyes grew bigger and bigger and he gasped for breath.

"Oh! Mary!" he cried out with a half sob. "Shall I see it? Shall I get into it? Shall I live to get into it?" and he clutched her hands and dragged her toward him.

"Of course you'll see it!" snapped Mary indignantly. "Of course you'll live to get into it! Don't be silly!"

And she was so un-hysterical and natural and childish that she brought him to his senses and he began to laugh at himself and a few minutes afterward she was sitting on her stool again telling him not what she imagined the secret garden to be like but what it really was, and Colin's aches and tiredness were forgotten and he was listening enraptured.

"It is just what you thought it would be," he said at last. "It sounds just as if you had really seen it. You know I said that when you told me first."

Mary hesitated about two minutes and then boldly spoke the truth.

"I had seen it—and I had been in," she said. "I found the key and got in weeks ago. But I daren't tell you—I daren't because I was so afraid I couldn't trust you—*for sure*!"

CHAPTER XIX

"IT HAS COME!"

Of course Dr. Craven had been sent for the morning after Colin had had his tantrum. He was always sent for at once when such a thing occurred and he always found, when he arrived, a white shaken boy lying on his bed, sulky and still so hysterical that he was ready to break into fresh sobbing at the least word. In fact, Dr. Craven dreaded and detested the difficulties of these visits. On this occasion he was away from Misselthwaite Manor until afternoon.

"How is he?" he asked Mrs. Medlock rather irritably when he arrived. "He will break a blood-vessel in one of those fits some day. The boy is half insane with hysteria and self-indulgence."

"Well, sir," answered Mrs. Medlock, "you'll scarcely believe your eyes when you see him. That plain sour-faced child that's almost as bad as himself has just bewitched him. How she's done it there's no telling. The Lord knows she's nothing to look at and you scarcely ever hear her speak, but she did what none of us dare do. She just flew at him like a little cat last night, and stamped her feet and ordered him to stop screaming, and somehow she startled him so that he actually did stop, and this afternoon—well just come up and see, sir. It's past crediting."

The scene which Dr. Craven beheld when he entered his patient's room was indeed rather astonishing to him. As Mrs. Medlock opened the door he heard laughing and chattering. Colin was on his sofa in his dressing-gown and he was sitting up quite straight looking at a picture in one of the garden books and talking to the plain child who at that moment could scarcely be called plain at all because her face was so glowing with enjoyment.

"Those long spires of blue ones—we'll have a lot of those," Colin was announcing. "They're called Del-phin-iums."

"Dickon says they're larkspurs made big and grand," cried Mistress Mary. "There are clumps there already."

Then they saw Dr. Craven and stopped. Mary became quite still and Colin looked fretful.

"I am sorry to hear you were ill last night, my boy," Dr. Craven said a trifle nervously. He was rather a nervous man.

"I'm better now—much better," Colin answered, rather like a Rajah. "I'm going out in my chair in a day or two if it is fine. I want some fresh air."

Dr. Craven sat down by him and felt his pulse and looked at him curiously.

"It must be a very fine day," he said, "and you must be very careful not to tire yourself."

"Fresh air won't tire me," said the young Rajah.

As there had been occasions when this same young gentleman had shrieked aloud with rage and had insisted that fresh air would give him cold and kill him, it is not to be wondered at that his doctor felt somewhat startled.

"I thought you did not like fresh air," he said.

"I don't when I am by myself," replied the Rajah; "but my cousin is going out with me."

"And the nurse, of course?" suggested Dr. Craven.

"No, I will not have the nurse," so magnificently that Mary could not help remembering how the young native Prince had looked with his diamonds and emeralds and pearls stuck all over him and the great rubies on the small dark hand he had waved to command his servants to approach with salaams and receive his orders.

"My cousin knows how to take care of me. I am always better when she is with me. She made me better last night. A very strong boy I know will push my carriage."

Dr. Craven felt rather alarmed. If this tiresome hysterical boy should chance to get well he himself would lose all chance of inheriting Misselthwaite; but he was not an unscrupulous man, though he was a weak one, and he did not intend to let him run into actual danger.

"He must be a strong boy and a steady boy," he said. "And I must know something about him. Who is he? What is his name?"

"It's Dickon," Mary spoke up suddenly. She felt somehow that everybody who knew the moor must know Dickon. And she was right, too. She saw that in a moment Dr. Craven's serious face relaxed into a relieved smile.

"Oh, Dickon," he said. "If it is Dickon you will be safe enough. He's as strong as a moor pony, is Dickon."

"And he's trusty," said Mary. "He's th' trustiest lad i' Yorkshire." She had been talking Yorkshire to Colin and she forgot herself.

"Did Dickon teach you that?" asked Dr. Craven, laughing outright.

"I'm learning it as if it was French," said Mary rather coldly. "It's like a native dialect in India. Very clever people try to learn them. I like it and so does Colin."

"Well, well," he said. "If it amuses you perhaps it won't do you any harm. Did you take your bromide last night, Colin?"

"No," Colin answered. "I wouldn't take it at first and after Mary made me quiet she talked me to sleep—in a low voice—about the spring creeping into a garden."

"That sounds soothing," said Dr. Craven, more perplexed than ever and glancing sideways at Mistress Mary sitting on her stool and looking down silently at the carpet. "You are evidently better, but you must remember—"

"I don't want to remember," interrupted the Rajah, appearing again. "When I lie by myself and remember I begin to have pains everywhere and I think of things that make me begin to scream because I hate them so. If there was a doctor anywhere who could make you forget you were ill instead of remembering it I would have him brought here." And he waved a thin hand which ought really to have been covered with royal signet rings made of rubies. "It is because my cousin makes me forget that she makes me better."

Dr. Craven had never made such a short stay after a "tantrum"; usually he was obliged to remain a very long time and do a great many things. This afternoon he did not give any medicine or leave any new orders and he was spared any disagreeable scenes. When he went downstairs he looked very thoughtful and when he talked to Mrs. Medlock in the library she felt that he was a much puzzled man.

"Well, sir," she ventured, "could you have believed it?"

"It is certainly a new state of affairs," said the doctor. "And there's no denying it is better than the old one."

"I believe Susan Sowerby's right—I do that," said Mrs. Medlock. "I stopped in her cottage on my way to Thwaite yesterday and had a bit of talk with her. And she says to me, 'Well, Sarah Ann, she mayn't be a good child, an' she mayn't be a pretty one, but she's a child, an' children needs children.' We went to school together, Susan Sowerby and me."

"She's the best sick nurse I know," said Dr. Craven. "When I find her in a cottage I know the chances are that I shall save my patient."

Mrs. Medlock smiled. She was fond of Susan Sowerby.

"She's got a way with her, has Susan," she went on quite volubly. "I've been thinking all morning of one thing she said yesterday. She says, 'Once when I was givin' th' children a bit of a preach after they'd been fightin' I ses to 'em all, "When I was at school my jography told as th' world was shaped like a orange an' I found out before I was ten that th' whole orange doesn't belong to nobody. No one owns more than his bit of a quarter an' there's times it seems like there's not enow quarters to go round. But don't you—none o' you—think as you own th' whole orange or you'll find out you're mistaken, an' you won't find it out without hard knocks." 'What children learns from children,' she says, 'is that there's no sense in grabbin' at th' whole orange—peel an' all. If you do you'll likely not get even th' pips, an' them's too bitter to eat."

"She's a shrewd woman," said Dr. Craven, putting on his coat.

"Well, she's got a way of saying things," ended Mrs. Medlock, much pleased. "Sometimes I've said to her, 'Eh! Susan, if you was a different woman an' didn't talk such broad Yorkshire I've seen the times when I should have said you was clever."

That night Colin slept without once awakening and when he opened his eyes in the morning he lay still and smiled without knowing it—smiled because he felt so curiously comfortable. It was actually nice to be awake, and he turned over and stretched his limbs luxuriously. He felt as if tight strings which had held him had loosened themselves and let him go. He did not know that Dr. Craven would have said that his nerves had relaxed and rested themselves. Instead of lying and staring at the wall and wishing he had not awakened, his mind was full of the plans he and Mary had made yesterday, of pictures of the garden and of Dickon and his wild creatures. It was so nice to have things to think about. And he had not been awake more than ten minutes when he heard feet running along the corridor and Mary was at the door. The next minute she was in the room and had run across to his bed, bringing with her a waft of fresh air full of the scent of the morning.

"You've been out! You've been out! There's that nice smell of leaves!" he cried.

She had been running and her hair was loose and blown and she was bright with the air and pink-cheeked, though he could not see it.

"It's so beautiful!" she said, a little breathless with her speed. "You never saw anything so beautiful! It has come! I thought it had come that other morning, but it was only coming. It is here now! It has come, the Spring! Dickon says so!"

"Has it?" cried Colin, and though he really knew nothing about it he felt his heart beat. He actually sat up in bed.

"Open the window!" he added, laughing half with joyful excitement and half at his own fancy. "Perhaps we may hear golden trumpets!"

And though he laughed, Mary was at the window in a moment and in a moment more it was opened wide and freshness and softness and scents and birds' songs were pouring through.

"That's fresh air," she said. "Lie on your back and draw in long breaths of it. That's what Dickon does when he's lying on the moor. He says he feels it in his veins and it makes him strong and he feels as if he could live forever and ever. Breathe it and breathe it."

She was only repeating what Dickon had told her, but she caught Colin's fancy.

"'Forever and ever'! Does it make him feel like that?" he said, and he did as she told him, drawing in long deep breaths over and over again until he felt that something quite new and delightful was happening to him.

Mary was at his bedside again.

"Things are crowding up out of the earth," she ran on in a hurry. "And there are flowers uncurling and buds on everything and the green veil has covered nearly all the gray and the birds are in such a hurry about their nests for fear they may be too late that some of them are even fighting for places in the secret garden. And the rose-bushes look as wick as wick can be, and there are primroses in the lanes and woods, and the seeds we planted are up, and Dickon has brought the fox and the crow and the squirrels and a new-born lamb."

And then she paused for breath. The new-born lamb Dickon had found three days before lying by its dead mother among the gorse bushes on the moor. It was not the first motherless lamb he had found and he knew what to do with it. He had taken it to the cottage wrapped in his jacket and he had let it lie near the fire and had fed it with warm milk. It was a soft thing with a darling silly baby face and legs rather long for its body. Dickon had carried it over the moor in his arms and its feeding bottle was in his pocket with a squirrel, and when Mary had sat under a tree with its limp warmness huddled on her lap she had felt as if she were too full of strange joy to speak. A lamb—a lamb! A living lamb who lay on your lap like a baby!

She was describing it with great joy and Colin was listening and drawing in long breaths of air when the nurse entered. She started a little at the sight of the open window. She had sat stifling in the room many a warm day because her patient was sure that open windows gave people cold.

"Are you sure you are not chilly, Master Colin?" she inquired.

"No," was the answer. "I am breathing long breaths of fresh air. It makes you strong. I am going to get up to the sofa for breakfast. My cousin will have breakfast with me."

The nurse went away, concealing a smile, to give the order for two breakfasts. She found the servants' hall a more amusing place than the invalid's chamber and just now everybody wanted to hear the news from upstairs. There was a great deal of joking about the unpopular young recluse who, as the cook said, "had found his master, and good for him." The servants' hall had been very tired of the tantrums, and the butler, who was a man with a family, had more than once expressed his opinion that the invalid would be all the better "for a good hiding."

When Colin was on his sofa and the breakfast for two was put upon the table he made an announcement to the nurse in his most Rajah-like manner.

"A boy, and a fox, and a crow, and two squirrels, and a new-born lamb, are coming to see me this morning. I want them brought upstairs as soon as they come," he said. "You are not to begin playing with the animals in the servants' hall and keep them there. I want them here."

The nurse gave a slight gasp and tried to conceal it with a cough.

"Yes, sir," she answered.

"I'll tell you what you can do," added Colin, waving his hand. "You can tell Martha to bring them here. The boy is Martha's brother. His name is Dickon and he is an animal charmer."

"I hope the animals won't bite, Master Colin," said the nurse.

"I told you he was a charmer," said Colin austerely. "Charmers' animals never bite."

"There are snake-charmers in India," said Mary. "And they can put their snakes' heads in their mouths."

"Goodness!" shuddered the nurse.

They ate their breakfast with the morning air pouring in upon them. Colin's breakfast was a very good one and Mary watched him with serious interest.

"You will begin to get fatter just as I did," she said. "I never wanted my breakfast when I was in India and now I always want it."

"I wanted mine this morning," said Colin. "Perhaps it was the fresh air. When do you think Dickon will come?"

He was not long in coming. In about ten minutes Mary held up her hand.

"Listen!" she said. "Did you hear a caw?"

Colin listened and heard it, the oddest sound in the world to hear inside a house, a hoarse "caw-caw."

"Yes," he answered.

"That's Soot," said Mary. "Listen again. Do you hear a bleat—a tiny one?"

"Oh, yes!" cried Colin, quite flushing.

"That's the new-born lamb," said Mary. "He's coming."

Dickon's moorland boots were thick and clumsy and though he tried to walk quietly they made a clumping sound as he walked through the long corridors. Mary and Colin heard him marching—marching, until he passed through the tapestry door on to the soft carpet of Colin's own passage.

"If you please, sir," announced Martha, opening the door, "if you please, sir, here's Dickon an' his creatures."

Dickon came in smiling his nicest wide smile. The new-born lamb was in his arms and the little red fox trotted by his side. Nut sat on his left shoulder and Soot on his right and Shell's head and paws peeped out of his coat pocket.

Colin slowly sat up and stared and stared—as he had stared when he first saw Mary; but this was a stare of wonder and delight. The truth was that in spite of all he had heard he had not in the least understood what this boy would be like and that his fox and his crow and his squirrels and his lamb were so near to him and his friendliness that they seemed almost to be part of himself. Colin had never talked to a boy in his life and he was so overwhelmed by his own pleasure and curiosity that he did not even think of speaking.

But Dickon did not feel the least shy or awkward. He had not felt embarrassed because the crow had not known his language and had only stared and had not spoken to him the first time they met. Creatures were always like that until they found out about you. He walked over to Colin's sofa and put the new-born lamb quietly on his lap, and immediately the little creature turned to the warm velvet dressing-gown and began to nuzzle and nuzzle into its folds and butt its tight-curled head with soft impatience against his side. Of course no boy could have helped speaking then.

"What is it doing?" cried Colin. "What does it want?"

"It wants its mother," said Dickon, smiling more and more. "I brought it to thee a bit hungry because I knowed tha'd like to see it feed."

He knelt down by the sofa and took a feeding-bottle from his pocket.

"Come on, little 'un," he said, turning the small woolly white head with a gentle brown hand. "This is what tha's after. Tha'll get more out o' this than tha' will out o' silk velvet coats. There now," and he pushed the rubber tip of the bottle into the nuzzling mouth and the lamb began to suck it with ravenous ecstasy.

After that there was no wondering what to say. By the time the lamb fell asleep questions poured forth and Dickon answered them all. He told them how he had found the lamb just as the sun was rising three mornings ago. He had been standing on the moor listening to a skylark and watching him swing higher and higher into the sky until he was only a speck in the heights of blue.

"I'd almost lost him but for his song an' I was wonderin' how a chap could hear it when it seemed as if he'd get out o' th' world in a minute—an' just then I heard somethin' else far off among th' gorse bushes. It was a weak bleatin' an' I knowed it was a new lamb as was hungry an' I knowed it wouldn't be hungry if it hadn't lost its mother somehow, so I set off searchin'. Eh! I did have a look for it. I went in an' out among th' gorse bushes an' round an' round an' I always seemed to take th' wrong turnin'. But at last I seed a bit o' white by a rock on top o' th' moor an' I climbed up an' found th' little 'un half dead wi' cold an' clemmin'." While he talked, Soot flew solemnly in and out of the open window and cawed remarks about the scenery while Nut and Shell made excursions into the big trees outside and ran up and down trunks and explored branches. Captain curled up near Dickon, who sat on the hearth-rug from preference.

They looked at the pictures in the gardening books and Dickon knew all the flowers by their country names and knew exactly which ones were already growing in the secret garden.

"I couldna' say that there name," he said, pointing to one under which was written "Aquilegia," "but us calls that a columbine, an' that there one it's a snapdragon and they both grow wild in hedges, but these is garden ones an' they're bigger an' grander. There's some big clumps o' columbine in th' garden. They'll look like a bed o' blue an' white butterflies flutterin' when they're out."

"I'm going to see them," cried Colin. "I am going to see them!"

"Aye, that tha' mun," said Mary quite seriously. "An' tha' munnot lose no time about it."

CHAPTER XX

"I SHALL LIVE FOREVER—AND EVER—AND EVER!"

But they were obliged to wait more than a week because first there came some very windy days and then Colin was threatened with a cold, which two things happening one after the other would no doubt have thrown him into a rage but that there was so much careful and mysterious planning to do and almost every day Dickon came in, if only for a few minutes, to talk about what was happening on the moor and in the lanes and hedges and on the borders of streams. The things he had to tell about otters' and badgers' and water-rats' houses, not to mention birds' nests and field-mice and their burrows, were enough to make you almost tremble with excitement when you heard all the intimate details from an animal charmer and realized with what thrilling eagerness and anxiety the whole busy underworld was working.

"They're same as us," said Dickon, "only they have to build their homes every year. An' it keeps 'em so busy they fair scuffle to get 'em done."

The most absorbing thing, however, was the preparations to be made before Colin could be transported with sufficient secrecy to the garden. No one must see the chair-carriage and Dickon and Mary after they turned a certain corner of the shrubbery and entered upon the walk outside the ivied walls. As each day passed, Colin had become more and more fixed in his feeling that the mystery surrounding the garden was one of its greatest charms. Nothing must spoil that. No one must ever suspect that they had a secret. People must think that he was simply going out with Mary and Dickon because he liked them and did not object to their looking at him. They had long and quite delightful talks about their route. They would go up this path and down that one and cross the other and go round among the fountain flower-beds as if they were looking at the "bedding-out plants" the head gardener, Mr. Roach, had been having arranged. That would seem such a rational thing to do that no one would think it at all mysterious. They would turn into the shrubbery walks and lose themselves until they came to the long walls. It was almost as serious and elaborately thought out as the plans of march made by great generals in time of war.

Rumors of the new and curious things which were occurring in the invalid's apartments had of course filtered through the servants' hall into the stable yards and out among the gardeners, but notwithstanding this, Mr. Roach was startled one day when he received orders from Master Colin's room to the effect that he must report himself in the apartment no outsider had ever seen, as the invalid himself desired to speak to him.

"Well, well," he said to himself as he hurriedly changed his coat, "what's to do now? His Royal Highness that wasn't to be looked at calling up a man he's never set eyes on."

Mr. Roach was not without curiosity. He had never caught even a glimpse of the boy and had heard a dozen exaggerated stories about his uncanny looks and ways and his insane tempers. The thing he had heard oftenest was that he might die at any moment and there had been numerous fanciful descriptions of a humped back and helpless limbs, given by people who had never seen him.

"Things are changing in this house, Mr. Roach," said Mrs. Medlock, as she led him up the back staircase to the corridor on to which opened the hitherto mysterious chamber.

"Let's hope they're changing for the better, Mrs. Medlock," he answered.

"They couldn't well change for the worse," she continued; "and queer as it all is there's them as finds their duties made a lot easier to stand up under. Don't you be surprised, Mr. Roach, if you find yourself in the middle of a menagerie and Martha Sowerby's Dickon more at home than you or me could ever be."

There really was a sort of Magic about Dickon, as Mary always privately believed. When Mr. Roach heard his name he smiled quite leniently.

"He'd be at home in Buckingham Palace or at the bottom of a coal mine," he said. "And yet it's not impudence, either. He's just fine, is that lad."

It was perhaps well he had been prepared or he might have been startled. When the bedroom door was opened a large crow, which seemed quite at home perched on the high back of a carven chair, announced the entrance of a visitor by saying "Caw—Caw" quite loudly. In spite of Mrs. Medlock's warning, Mr. Roach only just escaped being sufficiently undignified to jump backward.

The young Rajah was neither in bed nor on his sofa. He was sitting in an armchair and a young lamb was standing by him shaking its tail in feeding-lamb fashion as Dickon knelt giving it milk from its bottle. A squirrel was perched on Dickon's bent back attentively nibbling a nut. The little girl from India was sitting on a big footstool looking on.

"Here is Mr. Roach, Master Colin," said Mrs. Medlock.

The young Rajah turned and looked his servitor over—at least that was what the head gardener felt happened.

"Oh, you are Roach, are you?" he said. "I sent for you to give you some very important orders."

"Very good, sir," answered Roach, wondering if he was to receive instructions to fell all the oaks in the park or to transform the orchards into water-gardens.

"I am going out in my chair this afternoon," said Colin. "If the fresh air agrees with me I may go out every day. When I go, none of the gardeners are to be anywhere near the Long Walk by the garden walls. No one is to be there. I shall go out about two o'clock and everyone must keep away until I send word that they may go back to their work."

"Very good, sir," replied Mr. Roach, much relieved to hear that the oaks might remain and that the orchards were safe. "Mary," said Colin, turning to her, "what is that thing you say in India when you have finished talking and want people to go?"

"You say, 'You have my permission to go,'" answered Mary.

The Rajah waved his hand.

"You have my permission to go, Roach," he said. "But, remember, this is very important."

"Caw—Caw!" remarked the crow hoarsely but not impolitely.

"Very good, sir. Thank you, sir," said Mr. Roach, and Mrs. Medlock took him out of the room.

Outside in the corridor, being a rather good-natured man, he smiled until he almost laughed.

"My word!" he said, "he's got a fine lordly way with him, hasn't he? You'd think he was a whole Royal Family rolled into one—Prince Consort and all."

"Eh!" protested Mrs. Medlock, "we've had to let him trample all over every one of us ever since he had feet and he thinks that's what folks was born for."

"Perhaps he'll grow out of it, if he lives," suggested Mr. Roach.

"Well, there's one thing pretty sure," said Mrs. Medlock. "If he does live and that Indian child stays here I'll warrant she teaches him that the whole orange does not belong to him, as Susan Sowerby says. And he'll be likely to find out the size of his own quarter."

Inside the room Colin was leaning back on his cushions.

"It's all safe now," he said. "And this afternoon I shall see it—this afternoon I shall be in it!"

Dickon went back to the garden with his creatures and Mary stayed with Colin. She did not think he looked tired but he was very quiet before their lunch came and he was quiet while they were eating it. She wondered why and asked him about it.

"What big eyes you've got, Colin," she said. "When you are thinking they get as big as saucers. What are you thinking about now?"

"I can't help thinking about what it will look like," he answered.

"The garden?" asked Mary.

"The springtime," he said. "I was thinking that I've really never seen it before. I scarcely ever went out and when I did go I never looked at it. I didn't even think about it."

"I never saw it in India because there wasn't any," said Mary.

Shut in and morbid as his life had been, Colin had more imagination than she had and at least he had spent a good deal of time looking at wonderful books and pictures.

"That morning when you ran in and said 'It's come! It's come!', you made me feel quite queer. It sounded as if things were coming with a great procession and big bursts and wafts of music. I've a picture like it in one of my books—crowds of lovely people and children with garlands and branches with blossoms on them, everyone laughing and dancing and crowding and playing on pipes. That was why I said, 'Perhaps we shall hear golden trumpets' and told you to throw open the window."

"How funny!" said Mary. "That's really just what it feels like. And if all the flowers and leaves and green things and birds and wild creatures danced past at once, what a crowd it would be! I'm sure they'd dance and sing and flute and that would be the wafts of music."

They both laughed but it was not because the idea was laughable but because they both so liked it.

A little later the nurse made Colin ready. She noticed that instead of lying like a log while his clothes were put on he sat up and made some efforts to help himself, and he talked and laughed with Mary all the time.

"This is one of his good days, sir," she said to Dr. Craven, who dropped in to inspect him. "He's in such good spirits that it makes him stronger."

"I'll call in again later in the afternoon, after he has come in," said Dr. Craven. "I must see how the going out agrees with him. I wish," in a very low voice, "that he would let you go with him."

"I'd rather give up the case this moment, sir, than even stay here while it's suggested," answered the nurse with sudden firmness.

"I hadn't really decided to suggest it," said the doctor, with his slight nervousness. "We'll try the experiment. Dickon's a lad I'd trust with a new-born child."

The strongest footman in the house carried Colin downstairs and put him in his wheeled chair near which Dickon waited outside. After the manservant had arranged his rugs and cushions the Rajah waved his hand to him and to the nurse.

"You have my permission to go," he said, and they both disappeared quickly and it must be confessed giggled when they were safely inside the house.

Dickon began to push the wheeled chair slowly and steadily. Mistress Mary walked beside it and Colin leaned back and lifted his face to the sky. The arch of it looked very high and the small snowy clouds seemed like white birds floating on outspread wings below its crystal blueness. The wind swept in soft big breaths down from the moor and was strange with a wild clear scented sweetness. Colin kept lifting his thin chest to draw it in, and his big eyes looked as if it were they which were listening—listening, instead of his ears.

"There are so many sounds of singing and humming and calling out," he said. "What is that scent the puffs of wind bring?"

"It's gorse on th' moor that's openin' out," answered Dickon. "Eh! th' bees are at it wonderful today."

Not a human creature was to be caught sight of in the paths they took. In fact every gardener or gardener's lad had been witched away.

But they wound in and out among the shrubbery and out and round the fountain beds, following their carefully planned route for the mere mysterious pleasure of it. But when at last they turned into the Long Walk by the ivied walls the excited sense of an approaching thrill made them, for some curious reason they could not have explained, begin to speak in whispers.

"This is it," breathed Mary. "This is where I used to walk up and down and wonder and wonder."

"Is it?" cried Colin, and his eyes began to search the ivy with eager curiousness. "But I can see nothing," he whispered. "There is no door."

"That's what I thought," said Mary.

Then there was a lovely breathless silence and the chair wheeled on.

"That is the garden where Ben Weatherstaff works," said Mary.

"Is it?" said Colin.

A few yards more and Mary whispered again.

"This is where the robin flew over the wall," she said.

"Is it?" cried Colin. "Oh! I wish he'd come again!"

"And that," said Mary with solemn delight, pointing under a big lilac bush, "is where he perched on the little heap of earth and showed me the key."

Then Colin sat up.

"Where? Where? There?" he cried, and his eyes were as big as the wolf's in Red Riding-Hood, when Red Riding-Hood felt called upon to remark on them. Dickon stood still and the wheeled chair stopped.

"And this," said Mary, stepping on to the bed close to the ivy, "is where I went to talk to him when he chirped at me from the top of the wall. And this is the ivy the wind blew back," and she took hold of the hanging green curtain.

"Oh! is it—is it!" gasped Colin.

"And here is the handle, and here is the door. Dickon push him in—push him in quickly!"

And Dickon did it with one strong, steady, splendid push.

But Colin had actually dropped back against his cushions, even though he gasped with delight, and he had covered his eyes with his hands and held them there shutting out everything until they were inside and the chair stopped as if by magic and the door was closed. Not till then did he take them away and look round and round and round as Dickon and Mary had done. And over walls and earth and trees and swinging sprays and tendrils the fair green veil of tender little leaves had crept, and in the grass under the trees and the gray urns in the alcoves and here and there everywhere were touches or splashes of gold and purple and white and the trees were showing pink and snow above his head and there were fluttering of wings and faint sweet pipes and humming and scents and scents. And the sun fell warm upon his face like a hand with a lovely touch. And in wonder Mary and Dickon stood and stared at him. He looked so strange and different because a pink glow of color had actually crept all over him—ivory face and neck and hands and all.

"I shall get well! I shall get well!" he cried out. "Mary! Dickon! I shall get well! And I shall live forever and ever and ever!"

CHAPTER XXI

BEN WEATHERSTAFF

One of the strange things about living in the world is that it is only now and then one is quite sure one is going to live forever and ever and ever. One knows it sometimes when one gets up at the tender solemn dawn-time and goes out and stands alone and throws one's head far back and looks up and up and watches the pale sky slowly changing and flushing and marvelous unknown things happening until the East almost makes one cry out and one's heart stands still at the strange unchanging majesty of the rising of the sun—which has been happening every morning for thousands and thousands and thousands of years. One knows it then for a moment or so. And one knows it sometimes when one stands by oneself in a wood at sunset and the mysterious deep gold stillness slanting through and under the branches seems to be saying slowly again and again something one cannot quite hear, however much one tries. Then sometimes the immense quiet of the dark blue at night with millions of stars waiting and watching makes one sure; and sometimes a sound of far-off music makes it true; and sometimes a look in some one's eyes.

And it was like that with Colin when he first saw and heard and felt the Springtime inside the four high walls of a hidden garden. That afternoon the whole world seemed to devote itself to being perfect and radiantly beautiful and kind to one boy. Perhaps out of pure heavenly goodness the spring came and crowned everything it possibly could into that one place. More than once Dickon paused in what he was doing and stood still with a sort of growing wonder in his eyes, shaking his head softly.

"Eh! it is graidely," he said. "I'm twelve goin' on thirteen an' there's a lot o' afternoons in thirteen years, but seems to me like I never seed one as graidely as this 'ere."

"Aye, it is a graidely one," said Mary, and she sighed for mere joy. "I'll warrant it's the graidelest one as ever was in this world."

"Does tha' think," said Colin with dreamy carefulness, "as happen it was made loike this 'ere all o' purpose for me?"

"My word!" cried Mary admiringly, "that there is a bit o' good Yorkshire. Tha'rt shapin' first-rate—that tha' art."

And delight reigned. They drew the chair under the plum-tree, which was snow-white with blossoms and musical with bees. It was like a king's canopy, a fairy king's. There were flowering cherry-trees near and apple-trees whose buds were pink and white, and here and there one had burst open wide. Between the blossoming branches of the canopy bits of blue sky looked down like wonderful eyes.

Mary and Dickon worked a little here and there and Colin watched them. They brought him things to look at—buds which were opening, buds which were tight closed, bits of twig whose leaves were just showing green, the feather of a woodpecker which had dropped on the grass, the empty shell of some bird early hatched. Dickon pushed the chair slowly round and round the garden, stopping every other moment to let him look at wonders springing out of the earth or trailing down from trees. It was like being taken in state round the country of a magic king and queen and shown all the mysterious riches it contained.

"I wonder if we shall see the robin?" said Colin.

"Tha'll see him often enow after a bit," answered Dickon. "When th' eggs hatches out th' little chap he'll be kep' so busy it'll make his head swim. Tha'll see him flyin' backward an' for'ard carryin' worms nigh as big as himsel' an' that much noise goin' on in th' nest when he gets there as fair flusters him so as he scarce knows which big mouth to drop th' first piece in. An' gapin' beaks an' squawks on every side. Mother says as when she sees th' work a robin has to keep them gapin' beaks filled, she feels like she was a lady with nothin' to do. She says she's seen th' little chaps when it seemed like th' sweat must be droppin' off 'em, though folk can't see it."

This made them giggle so delightedly that they were obliged to cover their mouths with their hands, remembering that they must not be heard. Colin had been instructed as to the law of whispers and low voices several days before. He liked the mysteriousness of it and did his best, but in the midst of excited enjoyment it is rather difficult never to laugh above a whisper.

Every moment of the afternoon was full of new things and every hour the sunshine grew more golden. The wheeled chair had been drawn back under the canopy and Dickon had sat down on the grass and had just drawn out his pipe when Colin saw something he had not had time to notice before.

"That's a very old tree over there, isn't it?" he said. Dickon looked across the grass at the tree and Mary looked and there was a brief moment of stillness.

"Yes," answered Dickon, after it, and his low voice had a very gentle sound.

Mary gazed at the tree and thought.

"The branches are quite gray and there's not a single leaf anywhere," Colin went on. "It's quite dead, isn't it?"

"Aye," admitted Dickon. "But them roses as has climbed all over it will near hide every bit o' th' dead wood when they're full o' leaves an' flowers. It won't look dead then. It'll be th' prettiest of all."

Mary still gazed at the tree and thought.

"It looks as if a big branch had been broken off," said Colin. "I wonder how it was done."

"It's been done many a year," answered Dickon. "Eh!" with a sudden relieved start and laying his hand on Colin. "Look at that robin! There he is! He's been foragin' for his mate."

Colin was almost too late but he just caught sight of him, the flash of red-breasted bird with something in his beak. He darted through the greenness and into the close-grown corner and was out of sight. Colin leaned back on his cushion again, laughing a little. "He's taking her tea to her. Perhaps it's five o'clock. I think I'd like some tea myself."

And so they were safe.

"It was Magic which sent the robin," said Mary secretly to Dickon afterward. "I know it was Magic." For both she and Dickon had been afraid Colin might ask something about the tree whose branch had broken off ten years ago and they had talked it over together and Dickon had stood and rubbed his head in a troubled way.

"We mun look as if it wasn't no different from th' other trees," he had said. "We couldn't never tell him how it broke, poor lad. If he says anything about it we mun—we mun try to look cheerful."

"Aye, that we mun," had answered Mary.

But she had not felt as if she looked cheerful when she gazed at the tree. She wondered and wondered in those few moments if there was any reality in that other thing Dickon had said. He had gone on rubbing his rust-red hair in a puzzled way, but a nice comforted look had begun to grow in his blue eyes.

"Mrs. Craven was a very lovely young lady," he had gone on rather hesitatingly. "An' mother she thinks maybe she's about Misselthwaite many a time lookin' after Mester Colin, same as all mothers do when they're took out o' th' world. They have to come back, tha' sees. Happen she's been in the garden an' happen it was her set us to work, an' told us to bring him here."

Mary had thought he meant something about Magic. She was a great believer in Magic. Secretly she quite believed that Dickon worked Magic, of course good Magic, on everything near him and that was why people liked him so much and wild creatures knew he was their friend. She wondered, indeed, if it were not possible that his gift had brought the robin just at the right moment when Colin asked that dangerous question. She felt that his Magic was working all the afternoon and making Colin look like an entirely different boy. It did not seem possible that he could be the crazy creature who had screamed and beaten and bitten his pillow. Even his ivory whiteness seemed to change. The faint glow of color which had shown on his face and neck and hands when he first got inside the garden really never quite died away. He looked as if he were made of flesh instead of ivory or wax.

They saw the robin carry food to his mate two or three times, and it was so suggestive of afternoon tea that Colin felt they must have some.

"Go and make one of the men servants bring some in a basket to the rhododendron walk," he said. "And then you and Dickon can bring it here."

It was an agreeable idea, easily carried out, and when the white cloth was spread upon the grass, with hot tea and buttered toast and crumpets, a delightfully hungry meal was eaten, and several birds on domestic errands paused to inquire what was going on and were led into investigating crumbs with great activity. Nut and Shell whisked up trees with pieces of cake and Soot took the entire half of a buttered crumpet into a corner and pecked at and examined and turned it over and made hoarse remarks about it until he decided to swallow it all joyfully in one gulp.

The afternoon was dragging towards its mellow hour. The sun was deepening the gold of its lances, the bees were going home and the birds were flying past less often. Dickon and Mary were sitting on the grass, the tea-basket was repacked ready to be taken back to the house, and Colin was lying against his cushions with his heavy locks pushed back from his forehead and his face looking quite a natural color.

"I don't want this afternoon to go," he said; "but I shall come back tomorrow, and the day after, and the day after, and the day after."

"You'll get plenty of fresh air, won't you?" said Mary.

"I'm going to get nothing else," he answered. "I've seen the spring now and I'm going to see the summer. I'm going to see everything grow here. I'm going to grow here myself."

"That tha' will," said Dickon. "Us'll have thee walkin' about here an' diggin' same as other folk afore long."

Colin flushed tremendously.

"Walk!" he said. "Dig! Shall I?"

Dickon's glance at him was delicately cautious. Neither he nor Mary had ever asked if anything was the matter with his legs.

"For sure tha' will," he said stoutly. "Tha—tha's got legs o' thine own, same as other folks!"

Mary was rather frightened until she heard Colin's answer.

"Nothing really ails them," he said, "but they are so thin and weak. They shake so that I'm afraid to try to stand on them."

Both Mary and Dickon drew a relieved breath.

"When tha' stops bein' afraid tha'lt stand on 'em," Dickon said with renewed cheer. "An' tha'lt stop bein' afraid in a bit."

"I shall?" said Colin, and he lay still as if he were wondering about things.

They were really very quiet for a little while. The sun was dropping lower. It was that hour when everything stills itself, and they really had had a busy and exciting afternoon. Colin looked as if he were resting luxuriously. Even the creatures had ceased moving about and had drawn together and were resting near them. Soot had perched on a low branch and drawn up one leg and dropped the gray film drowsily over his eyes. Mary privately thought he looked as if he might snore in a minute.

In the midst of this stillness it was rather startling when Colin half lifted his head and exclaimed in a loud suddenly alarmed whisper:

"Who is that man?"

Dickon and Mary scrambled to their feet.

"Man!" they both cried in low quick voices.

Colin pointed to the high wall. "Look!" he whispered excitedly. "Just look!"

Mary and Dickon wheeled about and looked. There was Ben

Weatherstaff's indignant face glaring at them over the wall from the top of a ladder! He actually shook his fist at Mary.

"If I wasn't a bachelder, an' tha' was a wench o' mine," he cried, "I'd give thee a hidin'!"

He mounted another step threateningly as if it were his energetic intention to jump down and deal with her; but as she came toward him he evidently thought better of it and stood on the top step of his ladder shaking his fist down at her.

"I never thowt much o' thee!" he harangued. "I couldna' abide thee th' first time I set eyes on thee. A scrawny buttermilk-faced young besom, allus askin' questions an' pokin' tha' nose where it wasna' wanted. I never knowed how tha' got so thick wi' me. If it hadna' been for th' robin— Drat him—"

"Ben Weatherstaff," called out Mary, finding her breath. She stood below him and called up to him with a sort of gasp. "Ben Weatherstaff, it was the robin who showed me the way!"

Then it did seem as if Ben really would scramble down on her side of the wall, he was so outraged.

"Tha' young bad 'un!" he called down at her. "Layin' tha' badness on a robin—not but what he's impidint enow for anythin'. Him showin' thee th' way! Him! Eh! tha' young nowt"—she could see his next words burst out because he was overpowered by curiosity—"however i' this world did tha' get in?"

"It was the robin who showed me the way," she protested obstinately. "He didn't know he was doing it but he did. And I can't tell you from here while you're shaking your fist at me."

He stopped shaking his fist very suddenly at that very moment and his jaw actually dropped as he stared over her head at something he saw coming over the grass toward him.

At the first sound of his torrent of words Colin had been so surprised that he had only sat up and listened as if he were spellbound. But in the midst of it he had recovered himself and beckoned imperiously to Dickon.

"Wheel me over there!" he commanded. "Wheel me quite close and stop right in front of him!"

And this, if you please, this is what Ben Weatherstaff beheld and which made his jaw drop. A wheeled chair with luxurious cushions and robes which came toward him looking rather like some sort of State

Coach because a young Rajah leaned back in it with royal command in his great black-rimmed eyes and a thin white hand extended haughtily toward him. And it stopped right under Ben Weatherstaff's nose. It was really no wonder his mouth dropped open.

"Do you know who I am?" demanded the Rajah.

How Ben Weatherstaff stared! His red old eyes fixed themselves on what was before him as if he were seeing a ghost. He gazed and gazed and gulped a lump down his throat and did not say a word. "Do you know who I am?" demanded Colin still more imperiously. "Answer!"

Ben Weatherstaff put his gnarled hand up and passed it over his eyes and over his forehead and then he did answer in a queer shaky voice.

"Who tha' art?" he said. "Aye, that I do—wi' tha' mother's eyes starin' at me out o' tha' face. Lord knows how tha' come here. But tha'rt th' poor cripple."

Colin forgot that he had ever had a back. His face flushed scarlet and he sat bolt upright.

"I'm not a cripple!" he cried out furiously. "I'm not!"

"He's not!" cried Mary, almost shouting up the wall in her fierce indignation. "He's not got a lump as big as a pin! I looked and there was none there—not one!"

Ben Weatherstaff passed his hand over his forehead again and gazed as if he could never gaze enough. His hand shook and his mouth shook and his voice shook. He was an ignorant old man and a tactless old man and he could only remember the things he had heard.

"Tha'—tha' hasn't got a crooked back?" he said hoarsely.

"No!" shouted Colin.

"Tha'—tha' hasn't got crooked legs?" quavered Ben more hoarsely yet. It was too much. The strength which Colin usually threw into his tantrums rushed through him now in a new way. Never yet had he been accused of crooked legs—even in whispers—and the perfectly simple belief in their existence which was revealed by Ben Weatherstaff's voice was more than Rajah flesh and blood could endure. His anger and insulted pride made him forget everything but this one moment and filled him with a power he had never known before, an almost unnatural strength.

"Come here!" he shouted to Dickon, and he actually began to tear the coverings off his lower limbs and disentangle himself. "Come here! Come here! This minute!"

Dickon was by his side in a second. Mary caught her breath in a short gasp and felt herself turn pale.

"He can do it! He can do it! He can do it! He can!" she gabbled over to herself under her breath as fast as ever she could.

There was a brief fierce scramble, the rugs were tossed on the ground, Dickon held Colin's arm, the thin legs were out, the thin feet were on the grass. Colin was standing upright—upright—as straight as an arrow and looking strangely tall—his head thrown back and his strange eyes flashing lightning. "Look at me!" he flung up at Ben Weatherstaff. "Just look at me—you! Just look at me!"

"He's as straight as I am!" cried Dickon. "He's as straight as any lad i' Yorkshire!"

What Ben Weatherstaff did Mary thought queer beyond measure. He choked and gulped and suddenly tears ran down his weather-wrinkled cheeks as he struck his old hands together.

"Eh!" he burst forth, "th' lies folk tells! Tha'rt as thin as a lath an' as white as a wraith, but there's not a knob on thee. Tha'lt make a mon yet. God bless thee!"

Dickon held Colin's arm strongly but the boy had not begun to falter. He stood straighter and straighter and looked Ben Weatherstaff in the face.

"I'm your master," he said, "when my father is away. And you are to obey me. This is my garden. Don't dare to say a word about it! You get down from that ladder and go out to the Long Walk and Miss Mary will meet you and bring you here. I want to talk to you. We did not want you, but now you will have to be in the secret. Be quick!"

Ben Weatherstaff's crabbed old face was still wet with that one queer rush of tears. It seemed as if he could not take his eyes from thin straight Colin standing on his feet with his head thrown back.

"Eh! lad," he almost whispered. "Eh! my lad!" And then remembering himself he suddenly touched his hat gardener fashion and said, "Yes, sir! Yes, sir!" and obediently disappeared as he descended the ladder.

CHAPTER XXII

WHEN THE SUN WENT DOWN

When his head was out of sight Colin turned to Mary.

"Go and meet him," he said; and Mary flew across the grass to the door under the ivy.

Dickon was watching him with sharp eyes. There were scarlet spots on his cheeks and he looked amazing, but he showed no signs of falling.

"I can stand," he said, and his head was still held up and he said it quite grandly.

"I told thee tha' could as soon as tha' stopped bein' afraid," answered Dickon. "An' tha's stopped."

"Yes, I've stopped," said Colin.

Then suddenly he remembered something Mary had said.

"Are you making Magic?" he asked sharply.

Dickon's curly mouth spread in a cheerful grin.

"Tha's doin' Magic thysel'," he said. "It's same Magic as made these 'ere work out o' th' earth," and he touched with his thick boot a clump of crocuses in the grass. Colin looked down at them.

"Aye," he said slowly, "there couldna' be bigger Magic than that there—there couldna' be."

He drew himself up straighter than ever.

"I'm going to walk to that tree," he said, pointing to one a few feet away from him. "I'm going to be standing when Weatherstaff comes here. I can rest against the tree if I like. When I want to sit down I will sit down, but not before. Bring a rug from the chair."

He walked to the tree and though Dickon held his arm he was wonderfully steady. When he stood against the tree trunk it was not too plain that he supported himself against it, and he still held himself so straight that he looked tall.

When Ben Weatherstaff came through the door in the wall he saw him standing there and he heard Mary muttering something under her breath.

"What art sayin'?" he asked rather testily because he did not want his attention distracted from the long thin straight boy figure and proud face.

But she did not tell him. What she was saying was this:

"You can do it! You can do it! I told you you could! You can do it! You can do it! You can!" She was saying it to Colin because she wanted to make Magic and keep him on his feet looking like that. She could not bear that he should give in before Ben Weatherstaff. He did not give in. She was uplifted by a sudden feeling that he looked quite beautiful in spite of his thinness. He fixed his eyes on Ben Weatherstaff in his funny imperious way.

"Look at me!" he commanded. "Look at me all over! Am I a hunchback? Have I got crooked legs?"

Ben Weatherstaff had not quite got over his emotion, but he had recovered a little and answered almost in his usual way.

"Not tha'," he said. "Nowt o' th' sort. What's tha' been doin' with thysel'—hidin' out o' sight an' lettin' folk think tha' was cripple an' half-witted?"

"Half-witted!" said Colin angrily. "Who thought that?"

"Lots o' fools," said Ben. "Th' world's full o' jackasses brayin' an' they never bray nowt but lies. What did tha' shut thysel' up for?"

"Everyone thought I was going to die," said Colin shortly. "I'm not!"

And he said it with such decision Ben Weatherstaff looked him over, up and down, down and up.

"Tha' die!" he said with dry exultation. "Nowt o' th' sort! Tha's got too much pluck in thee. When I seed thee put tha' legs on th' ground in such a hurry I knowed tha' was all right. Sit thee down on th' rug a bit young Mester an' give me thy orders."

There was a queer mixture of crabbed tenderness and shrewd understanding in his manner. Mary had poured out speech as rapidly as she could as they had come down the Long Walk. The chief thing to be remembered, she had told him, was that Colin was getting well—getting well. The garden was doing it. No one must let him remember about having humps and dying.

The Rajah condescended to seat himself on a rug under the tree.

"What work do you do in the gardens, Weatherstaff?" he inquired.

"Anythin' I'm told to do," answered old Ben. "I'm kep' on by favor—because she liked me."

"She?" said Colin.

"Tha' mother," answered Ben Weatherstaff.

"My mother?" said Colin, and he looked about him quietly. "This was her garden, wasn't it?"

"Aye, it was that!" and Ben Weatherstaff looked about him too. "She were main fond of it."

"It is my garden now. I am fond of it. I shall come here every day," announced Colin. "But it is to be a secret. My orders are that no one is to know that we come here. Dickon and my cousin have worked and made it come alive. I shall send for you sometimes to help—but you must come when no one can see you."

Ben Weatherstaff's face twisted itself in a dry old smile.

"I've come here before when no one saw me," he said.

"What!" exclaimed Colin. "When?"

"Th' last time I was here," rubbing his chin and looking round, "was about two year' ago."

"But no one has been in it for ten years!" cried Colin. "There was no door!"

"I'm no one," said old Ben dryly. "An' I didn't come through th' door. I come over th' wall. Th' rheumatics held me back th' last two year'."

"Tha' come an' did a bit o' prunin'!" cried Dickon. "I couldn't make out how it had been done."

"She was so fond of it—she was!" said Ben Weatherstaff slowly. "An' she was such a pretty young thing. She says to me once, 'Ben,' says she laughin', 'if ever I'm ill or if I go away you must take care of my roses.' When she did go away th' orders was no one was ever to come nigh. But I come," with grumpy obstinacy. "Over th' wall I come—until th' rheumatics stopped me—an' I did a bit o' work once a year. She'd gave her order first."

"It wouldn't have been as wick as it is if tha' hadn't done it," said Dickon. "I did wonder."

"I'm glad you did it, Weatherstaff," said Colin. "You'll know how to keep the secret."

"Aye, I'll know, sir," answered Ben. "An' it'll be easier for a man wi' rheumatics to come in at th' door."

On the grass near the tree Mary had dropped her trowel. Colin stretched out his hand and took it up. An odd expression came into his face and he began to scratch at the earth. His thin hand was weak enough but presently as they watched him—Mary with quite breathless interest—he drove the end of the trowel into the soil and turned some over.

"You can do it! You can do it!" said Mary to herself. "I tell you, you can!"

Dickon's round eyes were full of eager curiousness but he said not a word. Ben Weatherstaff looked on with interested face.

Colin persevered. After he had turned a few trowelfuls of soil he spoke exultantly to Dickon in his best Yorkshire.

"Tha' said as tha'd have me walkin' about here same as other folk—an' tha' said tha'd have me diggin'. I thowt tha' was just leein' to please me. This is only th' first day an' I've walked—an' here I am diggin'."

Ben Weatherstaff's mouth fell open again when he heard him, but he ended by chuckling.

"Eh!" he said, "that sounds as if tha'd got wits enow. Tha'rt a Yorkshire lad for sure. An' tha'rt diggin', too. How'd tha' like to plant a bit o' somethin'? I can get thee a rose in a pot."

"Go and get it!" said Colin, digging excitedly. "Quick! Quick!"

It was done quickly enough indeed. Ben Weatherstaff went his way forgetting rheumatics. Dickon took his spade and dug the hole deeper and wider than a new digger with thin white hands could make it. Mary slipped out to run and bring back a watering-can. When Dickon had deepened the hole Colin went on turning the soft earth over and over. He looked up at the sky, flushed and glowing with the strangely new exercise, slight as it was.

"I want to do it before the sun goes quite—quite down," he said.

Mary thought that perhaps the sun held back a few minutes just on purpose. Ben Weatherstaff brought the rose in its pot from the greenhouse. He hobbled over the grass as fast as he could. He had begun to be excited, too. He knelt down by the hole and broke the pot from the mould.

"Here, lad," he said, handing the plant to Colin. "Set it in the earth thysel' same as th' king does when he goes to a new place."

The thin white hands shook a little and Colin's flush grew deeper as he set the rose in the mould and held it while old Ben made firm the earth. It was filled in and pressed down and made steady. Mary was leaning forward on her hands and knees. Soot had flown down and marched forward to see what was being done. Nut and Shell chattered about it from a cherry-tree.

"It's planted!" said Colin at last. "And the sun is only slipping over the edge. Help me up, Dickon. I want to be standing when it goes. That's part of the Magic."

And Dickon helped him, and the Magic—or whatever it was—so gave him strength that when the sun did slip over the edge and end the strange lovely afternoon for them there he actually stood on his two feet—laughing.

CHAPTER XXIII

MAGIC

Dr. Craven had been waiting some time at the house when they returned to it. He had indeed begun to wonder if it might not be wise to send some one out to explore the garden paths. When Colin was brought back to his room the poor man looked him over seriously.

"You should not have stayed so long," he said. "You must not overexert yourself."

"I am not tired at all," said Colin. "It has made me well. Tomorrow I am going out in the morning as well as in the afternoon."

"I am not sure that I can allow it," answered Dr. Craven. "I am afraid it would not be wise."

"It would not be wise to try to stop me," said Colin quite seriously. "I am going."

Even Mary had found out that one of Colin's chief peculiarities was that he did not know in the least what a rude little brute he was with his way of ordering people about. He had lived on a sort of desert island all his life and as he had been the king of it he had made his own manners and had had no one to compare himself with. Mary had indeed been rather like him herself and since she had been at Misselthwaite had gradually discovered that her own manners had not been of the kind which is usual or popular. Having made this discovery she naturally thought it of enough interest to communicate to Colin. So she sat and looked at him curiously for a few minutes after Dr. Craven had gone. She wanted to make him ask her why she was doing it and of course she did.

"What are you looking at me for?" he said.

"I'm thinking that I am rather sorry for Dr. Craven."

"So am I," said Colin calmly, but not without an air of some satisfaction. "He won't get Misselthwaite at all now I'm not going to die."

"I'm sorry for him because of that, of course," said Mary, "but I was thinking just then that it must have been very horrid to have had to be polite for ten years to a boy who was always rude. I would never have done it."

"Am I rude?" Colin inquired undisturbedly.

"If you had been his own boy and he had been a slapping sort of man," said Mary, "he would have slapped you."

"But he daren't," said Colin.

"No, he daren't," answered Mistress Mary, thinking the thing out quite without prejudice. "Nobody ever dared to do anything you didn't like—because you were going to die and things like that. You were such a poor thing."

"But," announced Colin stubbornly, "I am not going to be a poor thing. I won't let people think I'm one. I stood on my feet this afternoon."

"It is always having your own way that has made you so queer," Mary went on, thinking aloud.

Colin turned his head, frowning.

"Am I queer?" he demanded.

"Yes," answered Mary, "very. But you needn't be cross," she added impartially, "because so am I queer—and so is Ben Weatherstaff. But I am not as queer as I was before I began to like people and before I found the garden."

"I don't want to be queer," said Colin. "I am not going to be," and he frowned again with determination.

He was a very proud boy. He lay thinking for a while and then Mary saw his beautiful smile begin and gradually change his whole face.

"I shall stop being queer," he said, "if I go every day to the garden. There is Magic in there—good Magic, you know, Mary. I am sure there is."

"So am I," said Mary.

"Even if it isn't real Magic," Colin said, "we can pretend it is. Something is there—something!"

"It's Magic," said Mary, "but not black. It's as white as snow."

They always called it Magic and indeed it seemed like it in the months that followed—the wonderful months—the radiant months—the amazing ones. Oh! the things which happened in that garden! If you have never had a garden you cannot understand, and if you have had a garden you will know that it would take a whole book to describe all that came to pass there. At first it seemed that green things would never cease pushing their way through the earth, in the grass, in the beds, even in the crevices of the walls. Then the green things began to show buds and the buds began to unfurl and show color, every shade of blue, every shade of purple, every tint and hue of crimson. In its happy days flowers had been tucked away into every inch and hole and corner. Ben Weatherstaff had seen it done and had himself scraped out mortar from between the bricks of the wall and made pockets of earth for lovely clinging things to grow on. Iris and white lilies rose out of the grass in sheaves, and the green alcoves filled themselves with amazing armies of the blue and white flower lances of tall delphiniums or columbines or campanulas.

"She was main fond o' them—she was," Ben Weatherstaff said. "She liked them things as was allus pointin' up to th' blue sky, she used to tell. Not as she was one o' them as looked down on th' earth—not her. She just loved it but she said as th' blue sky allus looked so joyful."

The seeds Dickon and Mary had planted grew as if fairies had tended them. Satiny poppies of all tints danced in the breeze by the score, gaily defying flowers which had lived in the garden for years and which it might be confessed seemed rather to wonder how such new people had got there. And the roses—the roses! Rising out of the grass, tangled round the sun-dial, wreathing the tree trunks and hanging from their branches, climbing up the walls and spreading over them with long garlands falling in cascades—they came alive day by day, hour by hour. Fair fresh leaves, and buds—and buds—tiny at first but swelling and working Magic until they burst and uncurled into cups of scent delicately spilling themselves over their brims and filling the garden air.

Colin saw it all, watching each change as it took place. Every morning he was brought out and every hour of each day when it didn't rain he spent in the garden. Even gray days pleased him. He would lie on the grass "watching things growing," he said. If you watched long enough, he declared, you could see buds unsheath themselves. Also you could make the acquaintance of strange busy insect things running about on various unknown but evidently serious errands, sometimes carrying tiny scraps of straw or feather or food, or climbing blades of grass as if they were trees from whose tops one could look out to explore the country. A mole throwing up its mound at the end of its burrow and making its way out at last with the long-nailed paws which looked so like elfish hands, had absorbed him one whole morning. Ants' ways, beetles' ways, bees' ways, frogs' ways, birds' ways, plants' ways, gave him a new world to explore and when Dickon revealed them all and added foxes' ways, otters' ways, ferrets' ways, squirrels' ways, and trouts' and water-rats' and badgers' ways, there was no end to the things to talk about and think over.

And this was not the half of the Magic. The fact that he had really once stood on his feet had set Colin thinking tremendously and when Mary told him of the spell she had worked he was excited and approved of it greatly. He talked of it constantly.

"Of course there must be lots of Magic in the world," he said wisely one day, "but people don't know what it is like or how to make it. Perhaps the beginning is just to say nice things are going to happen until you make them happen. I am going to try and experiment."

The next morning when they went to the secret garden he sent at once for Ben Weatherstaff. Ben came as quickly as he could and found the Rajah standing on his feet under a tree and looking very grand but also very beautifully smiling.

"Good morning, Ben Weatherstaff," he said. "I want you and Dickon and Miss Mary to stand in a row and listen to me because I am going to tell you something very important."

"Aye, aye, sir!" answered Ben Weatherstaff, touching his forehead. (One of the long concealed charms of Ben Weatherstaff was that in his boyhood he had once run away to sea and had made voyages. So he could reply like a sailor.)

"I am going to try a scientific experiment," explained the Rajah. "When I grow up I am going to make great scientific discoveries and I am going to begin now with this experiment."

"Aye, aye, sir!" said Ben Weatherstaff promptly, though this was the first time he had heard of great scientific discoveries.

It was the first time Mary had heard of them, either, but even at this stage she had begun to realize that, queer as he was, Colin had read about a great many singular things and was somehow a very convincing sort of boy. When he held up his head and fixed his strange eyes on you it seemed as if you believed him almost in spite of yourself though he was only ten years old—going on eleven. At this moment he was especially convincing because he suddenly felt the fascination of actually making a sort of speech like a grown-up person.

"The great scientific discoveries I am going to make," he went on, "will be about Magic. Magic is a great thing and scarcely any one knows anything about it except a few people in old books—and Mary a little, because she was born in India where there are fakirs. I believe Dickon knows some Magic, but perhaps he doesn't know he knows it. He charms animals and people. I would never have let him come to see me if he had not been an animal charmer—which is a boy charmer, too, because a boy is an animal. I am sure there is Magic in everything, only we have not sense enough to get hold of it and make it do things for us—like electricity and horses and steam."

This sounded so imposing that Ben Weatherstaff became quite excited and really could not keep still. "Aye, aye, sir," he said and he began to stand up quite straight.

"When Mary found this garden it looked quite dead," the orator proceeded. "Then something began pushing things up out of the soil and making things out of nothing. One day things weren't there and another they were. I had never watched things before and it made me feel very curious. Scientific people are always curious and I am going to be scientific. I keep saying to myself, 'What is it? What is it?' It's something. It can't be nothing! I don't know its name so I call it Magic. I have never seen the sun rise but Mary and Dickon have and from what they tell me I am sure that is Magic too. Something pushes it up and draws it. Sometimes since I've been in the garden I've looked up through the trees at the sky and I have had a strange feeling of being happy as if something were pushing and drawing in my chest and making me breathe fast. Magic is always pushing and drawing and making things out of nothing. Everything is made out of Magic, leaves and trees, flowers and birds, badgers and foxes and squirrels and people. So it must be all around us. In this garden—in all the places. The Magic in this garden has made me stand up and know I am going to live to be a man. I am going to make the scientific experiment of trying to get some and put it in myself and make it push and draw me and make me strong. I don't know how to do it but I think that if you keep thinking about it and calling it perhaps it will come. Perhaps that is the first baby way to get it. When I was going to try to stand that first time Mary kept saying to herself as fast as she could, 'You can do it! You can do it!' and I did. I had to try myself at the same time, of course, but her Magic helped me—and so did Dickon's. Every morning and evening and as often in the daytime as I can remember I am going to say, 'Magic is in me! Magic is making me well! I am going to be as strong as Dickon, as strong as Dickon!' And you must all do it, too. That is my experiment. Will you help, Ben Weatherstaff?"

"Aye, aye, sir!" said Ben Weatherstaff. "Aye, aye!"

"If you keep doing it every day as regularly as soldiers go through drill we shall see what will happen and find out if the experiment succeeds. You learn things by saying them over and over and thinking about them until they stay in your mind forever and I think it will be the same with Magic. If you keep calling it to come to you and help you it will get to be part of you and it will stay and do things."

"I once heard an officer in India tell my mother that there were fakirs who said words over and over thousands of times," said Mary.

"I've heard Jem Fettleworth's wife say th' same thing over thousands o' times—callin' Jem a drunken brute," said Ben Weatherstaff dryly. "Summat allus come o' that, sure enough. He gave her a good hidin' an' went to th' Blue Lion an' got as drunk as a lord."

Colin drew his brows together and thought a few minutes. Then he cheered up.

"Well," he said, "you see something did come of it. She used the wrong Magic until she made him beat her. If she'd used the right Magic and had said something nice perhaps he wouldn't have got as drunk as a lord and perhaps—perhaps he might have bought her a new bonnet."

Ben Weatherstaff chuckled and there was shrewd admiration in his little old eyes.

"Tha'rt a clever lad as well as a straight-legged one, Mester Colin," he said. "Next time I see Bess Fettleworth I'll give her a bit of a hint o' what Magic will do for her. She'd be rare an' pleased if th' sinetifik 'speriment worked—an' so 'ud Jem."

Dickon had stood listening to the lecture, his round eyes shining with curious delight. Nut and Shell were on his shoulders and he held a long-eared white rabbit in his arm and stroked and stroked it softly while it laid its ears along its back and enjoyed itself.

"Do you think the experiment will work?" Colin asked him, wondering what he was thinking. He so often wondered what Dickon was thinking when he saw him looking at him or at one of his "creatures" with his happy wide smile.

He smiled now and his smile was wider than usual.

"Aye," he answered, "that I do. It'll work same as th' seeds do when th' sun shines on 'em. It'll work for sure. Shall us begin it now?"

Colin was delighted and so was Mary. Fired by recollections of fakirs and devotees in illustrations Colin suggested that they should all sit cross-legged under the tree which made a canopy.

"It will be like sitting in a sort of temple," said Colin. "I'm rather tired and I want to sit down."

"Eh!" said Dickon, "tha' mustn't begin by sayin' tha'rt tired. Tha' might spoil th' Magic."

Colin turned and looked at him—into his innocent round eyes.

"That's true," he said slowly. "I must only think of the Magic." It all seemed most majestic and mysterious when they sat down in their circle. Ben Weatherstaff felt as if he had somehow been led into appearing at a prayer-meeting. Ordinarily he was very fixed in being what he called "agen' prayer-meetin's" but this being the Rajah's affair he did not resent it and was indeed inclined to be gratified at being called upon to assist. Mistress Mary felt solemnly enraptured. Dickon held his rabbit in his arm, and perhaps he made some charmer's signal no one heard, for when he sat down, cross-legged like the rest, the crow, the fox, the squirrels and the lamb slowly drew near and made part of the circle, settling each into a place of rest as if of their own desire.

"The 'creatures' have come," said Colin gravely. "They want to help us."

Colin really looked quite beautiful, Mary thought. He held his head high as if he felt like a sort of priest and his strange eyes had a wonderful look in them. The light shone on him through the tree canopy.

"Now we will begin," he said. "Shall we sway backward and forward, Mary, as if we were dervishes?"

"I canna' do no swayin' back'ard and for'ard," said Ben Weatherstaff. "I've got th' rheumatics."

"The Magic will take them away," said Colin in a High Priest tone, "but we won't sway until it has done it. We will only chant."

"I canna' do no chantin'," said Ben Weatherstaff a trifle testily. "They turned me out o' th' church choir th' only time I ever tried it."

No one smiled. They were all too much in earnest. Colin's face was not even crossed by a shadow. He was thinking only of the Magic.

"Then I will chant," he said. And he began, looking like a strange boy spirit. "The sun is shining—the sun is shining. That is the Magic. The flowers are growing—the roots are stirring. That is the Magic. Being alive is the Magic—being strong is the Magic. The Magic is in me—the Magic is in me. It is in me—it is in me. It's in every one of us. It's in Ben Weatherstaff's back. Magic! Magic! Come and help!"

He said it a great many times—not a thousand times but quite a goodly number. Mary listened entranced. She felt as if it were at once queer and beautiful and she wanted him to go on and on. Ben Weatherstaff began to feel soothed into a sort of dream which was quite agreeable. The humming of the bees in the blossoms mingled with the chanting voice and drowsily melted into a doze. Dickon sat cross-legged with his rabbit asleep on his arm and a hand resting on the lamb's back. Soot had pushed away a squirrel and huddled close to him on his shoulder, the gray film dropped over his eyes. At last Colin stopped.

"Now I am going to walk round the garden," he announced.

Ben Weatherstaff's head had just dropped forward and he lifted it with a jerk.

"You have been asleep," said Colin.

"Nowt o' th' sort," mumbled Ben. "Th' sermon was good enow—but I'm bound to get out afore th' collection."

He was not quite awake yet.

"You're not in church," said Colin.

"Not me," said Ben, straightening himself. "Who said I were? I heard every bit of it. You said th' Magic was in my back. Th' doctor calls it rheumatics."

The Rajah waved his hand.

"That was the wrong Magic," he said. "You will get better. You have my permission to go to your work. But come back tomorrow."

"I'd like to see thee walk round the garden," grunted Ben.

It was not an unfriendly grunt, but it was a grunt. In fact, being a stubborn old party and not having entire faith in Magic he had made up his mind that if he were sent away he would climb his ladder and look over the wall so that he might be ready to hobble back if there were any stumbling.

The Rajah did not object to his staying and so the procession was formed. It really did look like a procession. Colin was at its head with Dickon on one side and Mary on the other. Ben Weatherstaff walked behind, and the "creatures" trailed after them, the lamb and the fox cub keeping close to Dickon, the white rabbit hopping along or stopping to nibble and Soot following with the solemnity of a person who felt himself in charge.

It was a procession which moved slowly but with dignity. Every few yards it stopped to rest. Colin leaned on Dickon's arm and privately Ben Weatherstaff kept a sharp lookout, but now and then Colin took his hand from its support and walked a few steps alone. His head was held up all the time and he looked very grand.

"The Magic is in me!" he kept saying. "The Magic is making me strong! I can feel it! I can feel it!"

It seemed very certain that something was upholding and uplifting him. He sat on the seats in the alcoves, and once or twice he sat down on the grass and several times he paused in the path and leaned on Dickon, but he would not give up until he had gone all round the garden. When he returned to the canopy tree his cheeks were flushed and he looked triumphant.

"I did it! The Magic worked!" he cried. "That is my first scientific discovery."

"What will Dr. Craven say?" broke out Mary.

"He won't say anything," Colin answered, "because he will not be told. This is to be the biggest secret of all. No one is to know anything about it until I have grown so strong that I can walk and run like any other boy. I shall come here every day in my chair and I shall be taken back in it. I won't have people whispering and asking questions and I won't let my father hear about it until the experiment has quite succeeded. Then sometime when he comes back to Misselthwaite I shall just walk into his study and say 'Here I am; I am like any other boy. I am quite well and I shall live to be a man. It has been done by a scientific experiment.'"

"He will think he is in a dream," cried Mary. "He won't believe his eyes."

Colin flushed triumphantly. He had made himself believe that he was going to get well, which was really more than half the battle, if he had been aware of it. And the thought which stimulated him more than any other was this imagining what his father would look like when he saw that he had a son who was as straight and strong as other fathers' sons. One of his darkest miseries in the unhealthy morbid past days had been his hatred of being a sickly weak-backed boy whose father was afraid to look at him.

"He'll be obliged to believe them," he said.

"One of the things I am going to do, after the Magic works and before I begin to make scientific discoveries, is to be an athlete."

"We shall have thee takin' to boxin' in a week or so," said Ben Weatherstaff. "Tha'lt end wi' winnin' th' Belt an' bein' champion prize-fighter of all England."

Colin fixed his eyes on him sternly.

"Weatherstaff," he said, "that is disrespectful. You must not take liberties because you are in the secret. However much the Magic works I shall not be a prize-fighter. I shall be a Scientific Discoverer."

"Ax pardon—ax pardon, sir," answered Ben, touching his forehead in salute. "I ought to have seed it wasn't a jokin' matter," but his eyes twinkled and secretly he was immensely pleased. He really did not mind being snubbed since the snubbing meant that the lad was gaining strength and spirit.

CHAPTER XXIV

"LET THEM LAUGH"

The secret garden was not the only one Dickon worked in. Round the cottage on the moor there was a piece of ground enclosed by a low wall of rough stones. Early in the morning and late in the fading twilight and on all the days Colin and Mary did not see him, Dickon worked there planting or tending potatoes and cabbages, turnips and carrots and herbs for his mother. In the company of his "creatures" he did wonders there and was never tired of doing them, it seemed. While he dug or weeded he whistled or sang bits of Yorkshire moor songs or talked to Soot or Captain or the brothers and sisters he had taught to help him.

"We'd never get on as comfortable as we do," Mrs. Sowerby said, "if it wasn't for Dickon's garden. Anything'll grow for him. His 'taters and cabbages is twice th' size of any one else's an' they've got a flavor with 'em as nobody's has."

When she found a moment to spare she liked to go out and talk to him. After supper there was still a long clear twilight to work in and that was her quiet time. She could sit upon the low rough wall and look on and hear stories of the day. She loved this time. There were not only vegetables in this garden. Dickon had bought penny packages of flower seeds now and then and sown bright sweet-scented things among gooseberry bushes and even cabbages and he grew borders of mignonette and pinks and pansies and things whose seeds he could save year after year or whose roots would bloom each spring and spread in time into fine clumps. The low wall was one of the prettiest things in Yorkshire because he had tucked moorland foxglove and ferns and rock-cress and hedgerow flowers into every crevice until only here and there glimpses of the stones were to be seen.

"All a chap's got to do to make 'em thrive, mother," he would say, "is to be friends with 'em for sure. They're just like th' 'creatures.' If they're thirsty give 'em drink and if they're hungry give 'em a bit o' food. They want to live same as we do. If they died I should feel as if I'd been a bad lad and somehow treated them heartless."

It was in these twilight hours that Mrs. Sowerby heard of all that happened at Misselthwaite Manor. At first she was only told that "Mester Colin" had taken a fancy to going out into the grounds with Miss Mary and that it was doing him good. But it was not long before it was agreed between the two children that Dickon's mother might "come into the secret." Somehow it was not doubted that she was "safe for sure."

So one beautiful still evening Dickon told the whole story, with all the thrilling details of the buried key and the robin and the gray haze which had seemed like deadness and the secret Mistress Mary had planned never to reveal. The coming of Dickon and how it had been told to him, the doubt of Mester Colin and the final drama of his introduction to the hidden domain, combined with the incident of Ben Weatherstaff's angry face peering over the wall and Mester Colin's sudden indignant strength, made Mrs. Sowerby's nice-looking face quite change color several times.

"My word!" she said. "It was a good thing that little lass came to th' Manor. It's been th' makin' o' her an' th' savin', o' him. Standin' on his feet! An' us all thinkin' he was a poor half-witted lad with not a straight bone in him."

She asked a great many questions and her blue eyes were full of deep thinking.

"What do they make of it at th' Manor—him being so well an' cheerful an' never complainin'?" she inquired.

"They don't know what to make of it," answered Dickon. "Every day as comes round his face looks different. It's fillin' out and doesn't look so sharp an' th' waxy color is goin'. But he has to do his bit o' complainin'," with a highly entertained grin.

"What for, i' Mercy's name?" asked Mrs. Sowerby.

Dickon chuckled.

"He does it to keep them from guessin' what's happened. If the doctor knew he'd found out he could stand on his feet he'd likely write and tell Mester Craven. Mester Colin's savin' th' secret to tell himself. He's goin' to practise his Magic on his legs every day till his father comes back an' then he's goin' to march into his room an' show him he's as straight as other lads. But him an' Miss Mary thinks it's best plan to do a bit o' groanin' an' frettin' now an' then to throw folk off th' scent."

Mrs. Sowerby was laughing a low comfortable laugh long before he had finished his last sentence.

"Eh!" she said, "that pair's enjoyin' theirselves I'll warrant. They'll get a good bit o' actin' out of it an' there's nothin' children likes as much as play actin'. Let's hear what they do, Dickon lad." Dickon stopped weeding and sat up on his heels to tell her. His eyes were twinkling with fun.

"Mester Colin is carried down to his chair every time he goes out," he explained. "An' he flies out at John, th' footman, for not carryin' him careful enough. He makes himself as helpless lookin' as he can an' never lifts his head until we're out o' sight o' th' house. An' he grunts an' frets a good bit when he's bein' settled into his chair. Him an' Miss Mary's both got to enjoyin' it an' when he groans an' complains she'll say, 'Poor Colin! Does it hurt you so much? Are you so weak as that, poor Colin?'—but th' trouble is that sometimes they can scarce keep from burstin' out laughin'. When we get safe into the garden they laugh till they've no breath left to laugh with. An' they have to stuff their faces into Mester Colin's cushions to keep the gardeners from hearin', if any of 'em's about."

"Th' more they laugh th' better for 'em!" said Mrs. Sowerby, still laughing herself. "Good healthy child laughin's better than pills any day o' th' year. That pair'll plump up for sure."

"They are plumpin' up," said Dickon. "They're that hungry they don't know how to get enough to eat without makin' talk. Mester Colin says if he keeps sendin' for more food they won't believe he's an invalid at all. Miss Mary says she'll let him eat her share, but he says that if she goes hungry she'll get thin an' they mun both get fat at once."

Mrs. Sowerby laughed so heartily at the revelation of this difficulty that she quite rocked backward and forward in her blue cloak, and Dickon laughed with her.

"I'll tell thee what, lad," Mrs. Sowerby said when she could speak. "I've thought of a way to help 'em. When tha' goes to 'em in th' mornin's tha' shall take a pail o' good new milk an' I'll bake 'em a crusty cottage loaf or some buns wi' currants in 'em, same as you children like. Nothin's so good as fresh milk an' bread. Then they could take off th' edge o' their hunger while they were in their garden an' th' fine food they get indoors 'ud polish off th' corners."

"Eh! mother!" said Dickon admiringly, "what a wonder tha' art! Tha' always sees a way out o' things. They was quite in a pother yesterday. They didn't see how they was to manage without orderin' up more food—they felt that empty inside."

"They're two young 'uns growin' fast, an' health's comin' back to both of 'em. Children like that feels like young wolves an' food's flesh an' blood to 'em," said Mrs. Sowerby. Then she smiled Dickon's own curving smile. "Eh! but they're enjoyin' theirselves for sure," she said.

She was quite right, the comfortable wonderful mother creature—and she had never been more so than when she said their "play actin'" would be their joy. Colin and Mary found it one of their most thrilling sources of entertainment. The idea of protecting themselves from suspicion had been unconsciously suggested to them first by the puzzled nurse and then by Dr. Craven himself.

"Your appetite is improving very much, Master Colin," the nurse had said one day. "You used to eat nothing, and so many things disagreed with you."

"Nothing disagrees with me now," replied Colin, and then seeing the nurse looking at him curiously he suddenly remembered that perhaps he ought not to appear too well just yet. "At least things don't so often disagree with me. It's the fresh air."

"Perhaps it is," said the nurse, still looking at him with a mystified expression. "But I must talk to Dr. Craven about it."

"How she stared at you!" said Mary when she went away. "As if she thought there must be something to find out."

"I won't have her finding out things," said Colin. "No one must begin to find out yet." When Dr. Craven came that morning he seemed puzzled, also. He asked a number of questions, to Colin's great annoyance.

"You stay out in the garden a great deal," he suggested. "Where do you go?"

Colin put on his favorite air of dignified indifference to opinion.

"I will not let any one know where I go," he answered. "I go to a place I like. Every one has orders to keep out of the way. I won't be watched and stared at. You know that!"

"You seem to be out all day but I do not think it has done you harm—I do not think so. The nurse says that you eat much more than you have ever done before."

"Perhaps," said Colin, prompted by a sudden inspiration, "perhaps it is an unnatural appetite."

"I do not think so, as your food seems to agree with you," said Dr. Craven. "You are gaining flesh rapidly and your color is better."

"Perhaps—perhaps I am bloated and feverish," said Colin, assuming a discouraging air of gloom. "People who are not going to live are often—different."

Dr. Craven shook his head. He was holding Colin's wrist and he pushed up his sleeve and felt his arm.

"You are not feverish," he said thoughtfully, "and such flesh as you have gained is healthy. If you can keep this up, my boy, we need not talk of dying. Your father will be happy to hear of this remarkable improvement."

"I won't have him told!" Colin broke forth fiercely. "It will only disappoint him if I get worse again—and I may get worse this very night. I might have a raging fever. I feel as if I might be beginning to have one now. I won't have letters written to my father—I won't—I won't! You are making me angry and you know that is bad for me. I feel hot already. I hate being written about and being talked over as much as I hate being stared at!"

"Hush-h! my boy," Dr. Craven soothed him. "Nothing shall be written without your permission. You are too sensitive about things. You must not undo the good which has been done."

He said no more about writing to Mr. Craven and when he saw the nurse he privately warned her that such a possibility must not be mentioned to the patient.

"The boy is extraordinarily better," he said. "His advance seems almost abnormal. But of course he is doing now of his own free will what we could not make him do before. Still, he excites himself very easily and nothing must be said to irritate him."

Mary and Colin were much alarmed and talked together anxiously. From this time dated their plan of "play actin'."

"I may be obliged to have a tantrum," said Colin regretfully. "I don't want to have one and I'm not miserable enough now to work myself into a big one. Perhaps I couldn't have one at all. That lump doesn't come in my throat now and I keep thinking of nice things instead of horrible ones. But if they talk about writing to my father I shall have to do something."

He made up his mind to eat less, but unfortunately it was not possible to carry out this brilliant idea when he wakened each morning with an amazing appetite and the table near his sofa was set with a breakfast of home-made bread and fresh butter, snow-white eggs, raspberry jam and clotted cream. Mary always breakfasted with him and when they found themselves at the table—particularly if there were delicate slices of sizzling ham sending forth tempting odors from under a hot silver cover—they would look into each other's eyes in desperation.

"I think we shall have to eat it all this morning, Mary," Colin always ended by saying. "We can send away some of the lunch and a great deal of the dinner."

But they never found they could send away anything and the highly polished condition of the empty plates returned to the pantry awakened much comment.

"I do wish," Colin would say also, "I do wish the slices of ham were thicker, and one muffin each is not enough for any one."

"It's enough for a person who is going to die," answered Mary when first she heard this, "but it's not enough for a person who is going to live. I sometimes feel as if I could eat three when those nice fresh heather and gorse smells from the moor come pouring in at the open window."

The morning that Dickon—after they had been enjoying themselves in the garden for about two hours—went behind a big rosebush and brought forth two tin pails and revealed that one was full of rich new milk with cream on the top of it, and that the other held cottage-made currant buns folded in a clean blue and white napkin, buns so carefully tucked in that they were still hot, there was a riot of surprised joyfulness. What a wonderful thing for Mrs. Sowerby to think of! What a kind, clever woman she must be! How good the buns were! And what delicious fresh milk!

"Magic is in her just as it is in Dickon," said Colin. "It makes her think of ways to do things—nice things. She is a Magic person. Tell her we are grateful, Dickon—extremely grateful." He was given to using rather grown-up phrases at times. He enjoyed them. He liked this so much that he improved upon it.

"Tell her she has been most bounteous and our gratitude is extreme."

And then forgetting his grandeur he fell to and stuffed himself with buns and drank milk out of the pail in copious draughts in the manner of any hungry little boy who had been taking unusual exercise and breathing in moorland air and whose breakfast was more than two hours behind him.

This was the beginning of many agreeable incidents of the same kind. They actually awoke to the fact that as Mrs. Sowerby had fourteen people to provide food for she might not have enough to satisfy two extra appetites every day. So they asked her to let them send some of their shillings to buy things.

Dickon made the stimulating discovery that in the wood in the park outside the garden where Mary had first found him piping to the wild creatures there was a deep little hollow where you could build a sort of tiny oven with stones and roast potatoes and eggs in it. Roasted eggs were a previously unknown luxury and very hot potatoes with salt and fresh butter in them were fit for a woodland king—besides being deliciously satisfying. You could buy both potatoes and eggs and eat as many as you liked without feeling as if you were taking food out of the mouths of fourteen people.

Every beautiful morning the Magic was worked by the mystic circle under the plum-tree which provided a canopy of thickening green leaves after its brief blossom-time was ended. After the ceremony Colin always took his walking exercise and throughout the day he exercised his newly found power at intervals. Each day he grew stronger and could walk more steadily and cover more ground. And each day his belief in the Magic grew stronger—as well it might. He tried one experiment after another as he felt himself gaining strength and it was Dickon who showed him the best things of all.

"Yesterday," he said one morning after an absence, "I went to Thwaite for mother an' near th' Blue Cow Inn I seed Bob Haworth. He's the strongest chap on th' moor. He's the champion wrestler an' he can jump higher than any other chap an' throw th' hammer farther. He's gone all th' way to Scotland for th' sports some years. He's knowed me ever since I was a little 'un an' he's a friendly sort an' I axed him some questions. Th' gentry calls him a athlete and I thought o' thee, Mester Colin, and I says, 'How did tha' make tha' muscles stick out that way, Bob? Did tha' do anythin' extra to make thysel' so strong?' An' he says, 'Well, yes, lad, I did. A strong man in a show that came to Thwaite once showed me how to exercise my arms an' legs an' every muscle in my body. An' I says, 'Could a delicate chap make himself stronger with 'em, Bob?' an' he laughed an' says, 'Art tha' th' delicate chap?' an' I says, 'No, but I knows a young gentleman that's gettin' well of a long illness an' I wish I knowed some o' them tricks to tell him about.' I didn't say no names an' he didn't ask none. He's friendly same as I said an' he stood up an' showed me good-natured like, an' I imitated what he did till I knowed it by heart."

Colin had been listening excitedly.

"Can you show me?" he cried. "Will you?"

"Aye, to be sure," Dickon answered, getting up. "But he says tha' mun do 'em gentle at first an' be careful not to tire thysel'. Rest in between times an' take deep breaths an' don't overdo."

"I'll be careful," said Colin. "Show me! Show me! Dickon, you are the most Magic boy in the world!"

Dickon stood up on the grass and slowly went through a carefully practical but simple series of muscle exercises. Colin watched them with widening eyes. He could do a few while he was sitting down. Presently he did a few gently while he stood upon his already steadied feet. Mary began to do them also. Soot, who was watching the performance, became much disturbed and left his branch and hopped about restlessly because he could not do them too.

From that time the exercises were part of the day's duties as much as the Magic was. It became possible for both Colin and Mary to do more of them each time they tried, and such appetites were the results that but for the basket Dickon put down behind the bush each morning when he arrived they would have been lost. But the little oven in the hollow and Mrs. Sowerby's bounties were so satisfying that Mrs. Medlock and the nurse and Dr. Craven became mystified again. You can trifle with your breakfast and seem to disdain your dinner if you are full to the brim with roasted eggs and potatoes and richly frothed new milk and oatcakes and buns and heather honey and clotted cream.

"They are eating next to nothing," said the nurse. "They'll die of starvation if they can't be persuaded to take some nourishment. And yet see how they look."

"Look!" exclaimed Mrs. Medlock indignantly. "Eh! I'm moithered to death with them. They're a pair of young Satans. Bursting their jackets one day and the next turning up their noses at the best meals Cook can tempt them with. Not a mouthful of that lovely young fowl and bread sauce did they set a fork into yesterday—and the poor woman fair invented a pudding for them—and back it's sent. She almost cried. She's afraid she'll be blamed if they starve themselves into their graves."

Dr. Craven came and looked at Colin long and carefully. He wore an extremely worried expression when the nurse talked with him and showed him the almost untouched tray of breakfast she had saved for him to look at—but it was even more worried when he sat down by Colin's sofa and examined him. He had been called to London on business and had not seen the boy for nearly two weeks. When young things begin to gain health they gain it rapidly. The waxen tinge had left Colin's skin and a warm rose showed through it; his beautiful eyes were clear and the hollows under them and in his cheeks and temples had filled out. His once dark, heavy locks had begun to look as if they sprang healthily from his forehead and were soft and warm with life. His lips were fuller and of a normal color. In fact as an imitation of a boy who was a confirmed invalid he was a disgraceful sight. Dr. Craven held his chin in his hand and thought him over.

"I am sorry to hear that you do not eat anything," he said. "That will not do. You will lose all you have gained—and you have gained amazingly. You ate so well a short time ago."

"I told you it was an unnatural appetite," answered Colin.

Mary was sitting on her stool nearby and she suddenly made a very queer sound which she tried so violently to repress that she ended by almost choking.

"What is the matter?" said Dr. Craven, turning to look at her.

Mary became quite severe in her manner.

"It was something between a sneeze and a cough," she replied with reproachful dignity, "and it got into my throat."

"But," she said afterward to Colin, "I couldn't stop myself. It just burst out because all at once I couldn't help remembering that last big potato you ate and the way your mouth stretched when you bit through that thick lovely crust with jam and clotted cream on it."

"Is there any way in which those children can get food secretly?" Dr. Craven inquired of Mrs. Medlock.

"There's no way unless they dig it out of the earth or pick it off the trees," Mrs. Medlock answered. "They stay out in the grounds all day and see no one but each other. And if they want anything different to eat from what's sent up to them they need only ask for it."

"Well," said Dr. Craven, "so long as going without food agrees with them we need not disturb ourselves. The boy is a new creature."

"So is the girl," said Mrs. Medlock. "She's begun to be downright pretty since she's filled out and lost her ugly little sour look. Her hair's grown thick and healthy looking and she's got a bright color. The glummest, ill-natured little thing she used to be and now her and Master Colin laugh together like a pair of crazy young ones. Perhaps they're growing fat on that."

"Perhaps they are," said Dr. Craven. "Let them laugh."

CHAPTER XXV

THE CURTAIN

And the secret garden bloomed and bloomed and every morning revealed new miracles. In the robin's nest there were Eggs and the robin's mate sat upon them keeping them warm with her feathery little breast and careful wings. At first she was very nervous and the robin himself was indignantly watchful. Even Dickon did not go near the close-grown corner in those days, but waited until by the quiet working of some mysterious spell he seemed to have conveyed to the soul of the little pair that in the garden there was nothing which was not quite like themselves—nothing which did not understand the wonderfulness of what was happening to them—the immense, tender, terrible, heart-breaking beauty and solemnity of Eggs. If there had been one person in that garden who had not known through all his or her innermost being that if an Egg were taken away or hurt the whole world would whirl round and crash through space and come to an end—if there had been even one who did not feel it and act accordingly there could have been no happiness even in that golden springtime air. But they all knew it and felt it and the robin and his mate knew they knew it.

At first the robin watched Mary and Colin with sharp anxiety. For some mysterious reason he knew he need not watch Dickon. The first moment he set his dew-bright black eye on Dickon he knew he was not a stranger but a sort of robin without beak or feathers. He could speak robin (which is a quite distinct language not to be mistaken for any other). To speak robin to a robin is like speaking French to a Frenchman. Dickon always spoke it to the robin himself, so the queer gibberish he used when he spoke to humans did not matter in the least. The robin thought he spoke this gibberish to them because they were not intelligent enough to understand feathered speech. His movements also were robin. They never startled one by being sudden enough to seem dangerous or threatening. Any robin could understand Dickon, so his presence was not even disturbing.

But at the outset it seemed necessary to be on guard against the other two. In the first place the boy creature did not come into the garden on his legs. He was pushed in on a thing with wheels and the skins of wild animals were thrown over him. That in itself was doubtful. Then when he began to stand up and move about he did it in a queer unaccustomed way and the others seemed to have to help him. The robin used to secrete himself in a bush and watch this anxiously, his head tilted first on one side and then on the other. He thought that the slow movements might mean that he was preparing to pounce, as cats do. When cats are preparing to pounce they creep over the ground very slowly. The robin talked this over with his mate a great deal for a few days but after that he decided not to speak of the subject because her terror was so great that he was afraid it might be injurious to the Eggs.

When the boy began to walk by himself and even to move more quickly it was an immense relief. But for a long time—or it seemed a long time to the robin—he was a source of some anxiety. He did not act as the other humans did. He seemed very fond of walking but he had a way of sitting or lying down for a while and then getting up in a disconcerting manner to begin again.

One day the robin remembered that when he himself had been made to learn to fly by his parents he had done much the same sort of thing. He had taken short flights of a few yards and then had been obliged to rest. So it occurred to him that this boy was learning to fly—or rather to walk. He mentioned this to his mate and when he told her that the Eggs would probably conduct themselves in the same way after they were fledged she was quite comforted and even became eagerly interested and derived great pleasure from watching the boy over the edge of her nest—though she always thought that the Eggs would be much cleverer and learn more quickly. But then she said indulgently that humans were always more clumsy and slow than Eggs and most of them never seemed really to learn to fly at all. You never met them in the air or on tree-tops.

After a while the boy began to move about as the others did, but all three of the children at times did unusual things. They would stand under the trees and move their arms and legs and heads about in a way which was neither walking nor running nor sitting down. They went through these movements at intervals every day and the robin was never able to explain to his mate what they were doing or tying to do. He could only say that he was sure that the Eggs would never flap about in such a manner; but as the boy who could speak robin so fluently was doing the thing with them, birds could be quite sure that the actions were not of a dangerous nature. Of course neither the robin nor his mate had ever heard of the champion wrestler, Bob Haworth, and his exercises for making the muscles stand out like lumps. Robins are not like human beings; their muscles are always exercised from the first and so they develop themselves in a natural manner. If you have to fly about to find every meal you eat, your muscles do not become atrophied (atrophied means wasted away through want of use).

When the boy was walking and running about and digging and weeding like the others, the nest in the corner was brooded over by a great peace and content. Fears for the Eggs became things of the past. Knowing that your Eggs were as safe as if they were locked in a bank vault and the fact that you could watch so many curious things going on made setting a most entertaining occupation. On wet days the Eggs' mother sometimes felt even a little dull because the children did not come into the garden.

But even on wet days it could not be said that Mary and Colin were dull. One morning when the rain streamed down unceasingly and Colin was beginning to feel a little restive, as he was obliged to remain on his sofa because it was not safe to get up and walk about, Mary had an inspiration.

"Now that I am a real boy," Colin had said, "my legs and arms and all my body are so full of Magic that I can't keep them still. They want to be doing things all the time. Do you know that when I waken in the morning, Mary, when it's quite early and the birds are just shouting outside and everything seems just shouting for joy—even the trees and things we can't really hear—I feel as if I must jump out of bed and shout myself. If I did it, just think what would happen!"

Mary giggled inordinately.

"The nurse would come running and Mrs. Medlock would come running and they would be sure you had gone crazy and they'd send for the doctor," she said.

Colin giggled himself. He could see how they would all look—how horrified by his outbreak and how amazed to see him standing upright.

"I wish my father would come home," he said. "I want to tell him myself. I'm always thinking about it—but we couldn't go on like this much longer. I can't stand lying still and pretending, and besides I look too different. I wish it wasn't raining today."

It was then Mistress Mary had her inspiration.

"Colin," she began mysteriously, "do you know how many rooms there are in this house?"

"About a thousand, I suppose," he answered.

"There's about a hundred no one ever goes into," said Mary. "And one rainy day I went and looked into ever so many of them. No one ever knew, though Mrs. Medlock nearly found me out. I lost my way when I was coming back and I stopped at the end of your corridor. That was the second time I heard you crying."

Colin started up on his sofa.

"A hundred rooms no one goes into," he said. "It sounds almost like a secret garden. Suppose we go and look at them. Wheel me in my chair and nobody would know we went."

"That's what I was thinking," said Mary. "No one would dare to follow us. There are galleries where you could run. We could do our exercises. There is a little Indian room where there is a cabinet full of ivory elephants. There are all sorts of rooms."

"Ring the bell," said Colin.

When the nurse came in he gave his orders.

"I want my chair," he said. "Miss Mary and I are going to look at the part of the house which is not used. John can push me as far as the picture-gallery because there are some stairs. Then he must go away and leave us alone until I send for him again."

Rainy days lost their terrors that morning. When the footman had wheeled the chair into the picture-gallery and left the two together in obedience to orders, Colin and Mary looked at each other delighted. As soon as Mary had made sure that John was really on his way back to his own quarters below stairs, Colin got out of his chair.

"I am going to run from one end of the gallery to the other," he said, "and then I am going to jump and then we will do Bob Haworth's exercises."

And they did all these things and many others. They looked at the portraits and found the plain little girl dressed in green brocade and holding the parrot on her finger.

"All these," said Colin, "must be my relations. They lived a long time ago. That parrot one, I believe, is one of my great, great, great, great aunts. She looks rather like you, Mary—not as you look now but as you looked when you came here. Now you are a great deal fatter and better looking."

"So are you," said Mary, and they both laughed.

They went to the Indian room and amused themselves with the ivory elephants. They found the rose-colored brocade boudoir and the hole in the cushion the mouse had left, but the mice had grown up and run away and the hole was empty. They saw more rooms and made more discoveries than Mary had made on her first pilgrimage. They found new corridors and corners and flights of steps and new old pictures they liked and weird old things they did not know the use of. It was a curiously entertaining morning and the feeling of wandering about in the same house with other people but at the same time feeling as if one were miles away from them was a fascinating thing.

"I'm glad we came," Colin said. "I never knew I lived in such a big queer old place. I like it. We will ramble about every rainy day. We shall always be finding new queer corners and things."

That morning they had found among other things such good appetites that when they returned to Colin's room it was not possible to send the luncheon away untouched.

When the nurse carried the tray downstairs she slapped it down on the kitchen dresser so that Mrs. Loomis, the cook, could see the highly polished dishes and plates.

"Look at that!" she said. "This is a house of mystery, and those two children are the greatest mysteries in it."

"If they keep that up every day," said the strong young footman John, "there'd be small wonder that he weighs twice as much today as he did a month ago. I should have to give up my place in time, for fear of doing my muscles an injury."

That afternoon Mary noticed that something new had happened in Colin's room. She had noticed it the day before but had said nothing because she thought the change might have been made by chance. She said nothing today but she sat and looked fixedly at the picture over the mantel. She could look at it because the curtain had been drawn aside. That was the change she noticed.

"I know what you want me to tell you," said Colin, after she had stared a few minutes. "I always know when you want me to tell you something. You are wondering why the curtain is drawn back. I am going to keep it like that."

"Why?" asked Mary.

"Because it doesn't make me angry any more to see her laughing.

I wakened when it was bright moonlight two nights ago and felt as if the Magic was filling the room and making everything so splendid that I couldn't lie still. I got up and looked out of the window. The room was quite light and there was a patch of moonlight on the curtain and somehow that made me go and pull the cord. She looked right down at me as if she were laughing because she was glad I was standing there. It made me like to look at her. I want to see her laughing like that all the time. I think she must have been a sort of Magic person perhaps."

"You are so like her now," said Mary, "that sometimes I think perhaps you are her ghost made into a boy."

That idea seemed to impress Colin. He thought it over and then answered her slowly.

"If I were her ghost—my father would be fond of me."

"Do you want him to be fond of you?" inquired Mary.

"I used to hate it because he was not fond of me. If he grew fond of me I think I should tell him about the Magic. It might make him more cheerful."

CHAPTER XXVI

"IT'S MOTHER!"

Their belief in the Magic was an abiding thing. After the morning's incantations Colin sometimes gave them Magic lectures.

"I like to do it," he explained, "because when I grow up and make great scientific discoveries I shall be obliged to lecture about them and so this is practise. I can only give short lectures now because I am very young, and besides Ben Weatherstaff would feel as if he were in church and he would go to sleep."

"Th' best thing about lecturin'," said Ben, "is that a chap can get up an' say aught he pleases an' no other chap can answer him back. I wouldn't be agen' lecturin' a bit mysel' sometimes."

But when Colin held forth under his tree old Ben fixed devouring eyes on him and kept them there. He looked him over with critical affection. It was not so much the lecture which interested him as the legs which looked straighter and stronger each day, the boyish head which held itself up so well, the once sharp chin and hollow cheeks which had filled and rounded out and the eyes which had begun to hold the light he remembered in another pair. Sometimes when Colin felt Ben's earnest gaze meant that he was much impressed he wondered what he was reflecting on and once when he had seemed quite entranced he questioned him.

"What are you thinking about, Ben Weatherstaff?" he asked.

"I was thinkin'" answered Ben, "as I'd warrant tha's gone up three or four pound this week. I was lookin' at tha' calves an' tha' shoulders. I'd like to get thee on a pair o' scales."

"It's the Magic and—and Mrs. Sowerby's buns and milk and things," said Colin. "You see the scientific experiment has succeeded."

That morning Dickon was too late to hear the lecture. When he came he was ruddy with running and his funny face looked more twinkling than usual. As they had a good deal of weeding to do after the rains they fell to work. They always had plenty to do after a warm deep sinking rain. The moisture which was good for the flowers was also good for the weeds which thrust up tiny blades of grass and points of leaves which must be pulled up before their roots took too firm hold. Colin was as good at weeding as any one in these days and he could lecture while he was doing it. "The Magic works best when you work, yourself," he said this morning. "You can feel it in your bones and muscles. I am going to read books about bones and muscles, but I am going to write a book about Magic. I am making it up now. I keep finding out things."

It was not very long after he had said this that he laid down his trowel and stood up on his feet. He had been silent for several minutes and they had seen that he was thinking out lectures, as he often did. When he dropped his trowel and stood upright it seemed to Mary and Dickon as if a sudden strong thought had made him do it. He stretched himself out to his tallest height and he threw out his arms exultantly. Color glowed in his face and his strange eyes widened with joyfulness. All at once he had realized something to the full.

"Mary! Dickon!" he cried. "Just look at me!"

They stopped their weeding and looked at him.

"Do you remember that first morning you brought me in here?" he demanded.

Dickon was looking at him very hard. Being an animal charmer he could see more things than most people could and many of them were things he never talked about. He saw some of them now in this boy. "Aye, that we do," he answered.

Mary looked hard too, but she said nothing.

"Just this minute," said Colin, "all at once I remembered it myself—when I looked at my hand digging with the trowel—and I had to stand up on my feet to see if it was real. And it is real! I'm well—I'm well!"

"Aye, that th' art!" said Dickon.

"I'm well! I'm well!" said Colin again, and his face went quite red all over.

He had known it before in a way, he had hoped it and felt it and thought about it, but just at that minute something had rushed all through him—a sort of rapturous belief and realization and it had been so strong that he could not help calling out.

"I shall live forever and ever and ever!" he cried grandly. "I shall find out thousands and thousands of things. I shall find out about people and creatures and everything that grows—like Dickon—and I shall never stop making Magic. I'm well! I'm well! I feel—I feel as if I want to shout out something—something thankful, joyful!"

Ben Weatherstaff, who had been working near a rose-bush, glanced round at him.

"Tha' might sing th' Doxology," he suggested in his dryest grunt. He had no opinion of the Doxology and he did not make the suggestion with any particular reverence.

But Colin was of an exploring mind and he knew nothing about the Doxology.

"What is that?" he inquired.

"Dickon can sing it for thee, I'll warrant," replied Ben Weatherstaff.

Dickon answered with his all-perceiving animal charmer's smile.

"They sing it i' church," he said. "Mother says she believes th' skylarks sings it when they gets up i' th' mornin'."

"If she says that, it must be a nice song," Colin answered. "I've never been in a church myself. I was always too ill. Sing it, Dickon. I want to hear it."

Dickon was quite simple and unaffected about it. He understood what Colin felt better than Colin did himself. He understood by a sort of instinct so natural that he did not know it was understanding. He pulled off his cap and looked round still smiling.

"Tha' must take off tha' cap," he said to Colin, "an' so mun tha', Ben—an' tha' mun stand up, tha' knows."

Colin took off his cap and the sun shone on and warmed his thick hair as he watched Dickon intently. Ben Weatherstaff scrambled up from his knees and bared his head too with a sort of puzzled half-resentful look on his old face as if he didn't know exactly why he was doing this remarkable thing.

Dickon stood out among the trees and rose-bushes and began to sing in quite a simple matter-of-fact way and in a nice strong boy voice:

"Praise God from whom all blessings flow,
Praise Him all creatures here below,
Praise Him above ye Heavenly Host,
Praise Father, Son, and Holy Ghost.
Amen."

When he had finished, Ben Weatherstaff was standing quite still with his jaws set obstinately but with a disturbed look in his eyes fixed on Colin. Colin's face was thoughtful and appreciative.

"It is a very nice song," he said. "I like it. Perhaps it means just what

I mean when I want to shout out that I am thankful to the Magic." He stopped and thought in a puzzled way. "Perhaps they are both the same thing. How can we know the exact names of everything? Sing it again, Dickon. Let us try, Mary. I want to sing it, too. It's my song. How does it begin? 'Praise God from whom all blessings flow'?"

And they sang it again, and Mary and Colin lifted their voices as musically as they could and Dickon's swelled quite loud and beautiful—and at the second line Ben Weatherstaff raspingly cleared his throat and at the third line he joined in with such vigor that it seemed almost savage and when the "Amen" came to an end Mary observed that the very same thing had happened to him which had happened when he found out that Colin was not a cripple—his chin was twitching and he was staring and winking and his leathery old cheeks were wet.

"I never seed no sense in th' Doxology afore," he said hoarsely, "but I may change my mind i' time. I should say tha'd gone up five pound this week Mester Colin—five on 'em!"

Colin was looking across the garden at something attracting his attention and his expression had become a startled one.

"Who is coming in here?" he said quickly. "Who is it?"

The door in the ivied wall had been pushed gently open and a woman had entered. She had come in with the last line of their song and she had stood still listening and looking at them. With the ivy behind her, the sunlight drifting through the trees and dappling her long blue cloak, and her nice fresh face smiling across the greenery she was rather like a softly colored illustration in one of Colin's books. She had wonderful affectionate eyes which seemed to take everything in—all of them, even Ben Weatherstaff and the "creatures" and every flower that was in bloom. Unexpectedly as she had appeared, not one of them felt that she was an intruder at all. Dickon's eyes lighted like lamps.

"It's mother—that's who it is!" he cried and went across the grass at a run.

Colin began to move toward her, too, and Mary went with him. They both felt their pulses beat faster.

"It's mother!" Dickon said again when they met halfway. "I knowed tha' wanted to see her an' I told her where th' door was hid."

Colin held out his hand with a sort of flushed royal shyness but his eyes quite devoured her face.

"Even when I was ill I wanted to see you," he said, "you and Dickon and the secret garden. I'd never wanted to see any one or anything before."

The sight of his uplifted face brought about a sudden change in her own. She flushed and the corners of her mouth shook and a mist seemed to sweep over her eyes.

"Eh! dear lad!" she broke out tremulously. "Eh! dear lad!" as if she had not known she were going to say it. She did not say, "Mester Colin," but just "dear lad" quite suddenly. She might have said it to Dickon in the same way if she had seen something in his face which touched her. Colin liked it.

"Are you surprised because I am so well?" he asked. She put her hand on his shoulder and smiled the mist out of her eyes. "Aye, that I am!" she said; "but tha'rt so like thy mother tha' made my heart jump."

"Do you think," said Colin a little awkwardly, "that will make my father like me?"

"Aye, for sure, dear lad," she answered and she gave his shoulder a soft quick pat. "He mun come home—he mun come home."

"Susan Sowerby," said Ben Weatherstaff, getting close to her. "Look at th' lad's legs, wilt tha'? They was like drumsticks i' stockin' two month' ago—an' I heard folk tell as they was bandy an' knock-kneed both at th' same time. Look at 'em now!"

Susan Sowerby laughed a comfortable laugh.

"They're goin' to be fine strong lad's legs in a bit," she said. "Let him go on playin' an' workin' in the garden an' eatin' hearty an' drinkin' plenty o' good sweet milk an' there'll not be a finer pair i' Yorkshire, thank God for it."

She put both hands on Mistress Mary's shoulders and looked her little face over in a motherly fashion.

"An' thee, too!" she said. "Tha'rt grown near as hearty as our 'Lisabeth Ellen. I'll warrant tha'rt like thy mother too. Our Martha told me as Mrs. Medlock heard she was a pretty woman. Tha'lt be like a blush rose when tha' grows up, my little lass, bless thee."

She did not mention that when Martha came home on her "day out" and described the plain sallow child she had said that she had no confidence whatever in what Mrs. Medlock had heard. "It doesn't stand to reason that a pretty woman could be th' mother o' such a fou' little lass," she had added obstinately.

Mary had not had time to pay much attention to her changing face.

She had only known that she looked "different" and seemed to have a great deal more hair and that it was growing very fast. But remembering her pleasure in looking at the Mem Sahib in the past she was glad to hear that she might some day look like her.

Susan Sowerby went round their garden with them and was told the whole story of it and shown every bush and tree which had come alive. Colin walked on one side of her and Mary on the other. Each of them kept looking up at her comfortable rosy face, secretly curious about the delightful feeling she gave them—a sort of warm, supported feeling. It seemed as if she understood them as Dickon understood his "creatures." She stooped over the flowers and talked about them as if they were children. Soot followed her and once or twice cawed at her and flew upon her shoulder as if it were Dickon's. When they told her about the robin and the first flight of the young ones she laughed a motherly little mellow laugh in her throat.

"I suppose learnin' 'em to fly is like learnin' children to walk, but I'm feared I should be all in a worrit if mine had wings instead o' legs," she said.

It was because she seemed such a wonderful woman in her nice moorland cottage way that at last she was told about the Magic.

"Do you believe in Magic?" asked Colin after he had explained about Indian fakirs. "I do hope you do."

"That I do, lad," she answered. "I never knowed it by that name but what does th' name matter? I warrant they call it a different name i' France an' a different one i' Germany. Th' same thing as set th' seeds swellin' an' th' sun shinin' made thee a well lad an' it's th' Good Thing. It isn't like us poor fools as think it matters if us is called out of our names. Th' Big Good Thing doesn't stop to worrit, bless thee. It goes on makin' worlds by th' million—worlds like us. Never thee stop believin' in th' Big Good Thing an' knowin' th' world's full of it—an' call it what tha' likes. Tha' wert singin' to it when I come into th' garden."

"I felt so joyful," said Colin, opening his beautiful strange eyes at her. "Suddenly I felt how different I was—how strong my arms and legs were, you know—and how I could dig and stand—and I jumped up and wanted to shout out something to anything that would listen."

"Th' Magic listened when tha' sung th' Doxology. It would ha' listened to anything tha'd sung. It was th' joy that mattered. Eh! lad,

lad—what's names to th' Joy Maker," and she gave his shoulders a quick soft pat again.

She had packed a basket which held a regular feast this morning, and when the hungry hour came and Dickon brought it out from its hiding place, she sat down with them under their tree and watched them devour their food, laughing and quite gloating over their appetites. She was full of fun and made them laugh at all sorts of odd things. She told them stories in broad Yorkshire and taught them new words. She laughed as if she could not help it when they told her of the increasing difficulty there was in pretending that Colin was still a fretful invalid.

"You see we can't help laughing nearly all the time when we are together," explained Colin. "And it doesn't sound ill at all. We try to choke it back but it will burst out and that sounds worse than ever."

"There's one thing that comes into my mind so often," said Mary, "and I can scarcely ever hold in when I think of it suddenly. I keep thinking suppose Colin's face should get to look like a full moon. It isn't like one yet but he gets a tiny bit fatter every day—and suppose some morning it should look like one—what should we do!"

"Bless us all, I can see tha' has a good bit o' play actin' to do," said Susan Sowerby. "But tha' won't have to keep it up much longer. Mester Craven'll come home."

"Do you think he will?" asked Colin. "Why?"

Susan Sowerby chuckled softly.

"I suppose it 'ud nigh break thy heart if he found out before tha' told him in tha' own way," she said. "Tha's laid awake nights plannin' it."

"I couldn't bear any one else to tell him," said Colin. "I think about different ways every day, I think now I just want to run into his room."

"That'd be a fine start for him," said Susan Sowerby. "I'd like to see his face, lad. I would that! He mun come back—that he mun."

One of the things they talked of was the visit they were to make to her cottage. They planned it all. They were to drive over the moor and lunch out of doors among the heather. They would see all the twelve children and Dickon's garden and would not come back until they were tired.

Susan Sowerby got up at last to return to the house and Mrs. Medlock. It was time for Colin to be wheeled back also. But before he got into his chair he stood quite close to Susan and fixed his eyes on her with a kind of bewildered adoration and he suddenly caught hold of the fold of her blue cloak and held it fast.

"You are just what I—what I wanted," he said. "I wish you were my mother—as well as Dickon's!"

All at once Susan Sowerby bent down and drew him with her warm arms close against the bosom under the blue cloak—as if he had been Dickon's brother. The quick mist swept over her eyes.

"Eh! dear lad!" she said. "Thy own mother's in this 'ere very garden, I do believe. She couldna' keep out of it. Thy father mun come back to thee—he mun!"

CHAPTER XXVII

IN THE GARDEN

In each century since the beginning of the world wonderful things have been discovered. In the last century more amazing things were found out than in any century before. In this new century hundreds of things still more astounding will be brought to light. At first people refuse to believe that a strange new thing can be done, then they begin to hope it can be done, then they see it can be done—then it is done and all the world wonders why it was not done centuries ago. One of the new things people began to find out in the last century was that thoughts—just mere thoughts—are as powerful as electric batteries—as good for one as sunlight is, or as bad for one as poison. To let a sad thought or a bad one get into your mind is as dangerous as letting a scarlet fever germ get into your body. If you let it stay there after it has got in you may never get over it as long as you live.

So long as Mistress Mary's mind was full of disagreeable thoughts about her dislikes and sour opinions of people and her determination not to be pleased by or interested in anything, she was a yellow-faced, sickly, bored and wretched child. Circumstances, however, were very kind to her, though she was not at all aware of it. They began to push her about for her own good. When her mind gradually filled itself with robins, and moorland cottages crowded with children, with queer crabbed old gardeners and common little Yorkshire housemaids, with springtime and with secret gardens coming alive day by day, and also with a moor boy and his "creatures," there was no room left for the disagreeable thoughts which affected her liver and her digestion and made her yellow and tired.

So long as Colin shut himself up in his room and thought only of his fears and weakness and his detestation of people who looked at him and reflected hourly on humps and early death, he was a hysterical half-crazy little hypochondriac who knew nothing of the sunshine and the spring and also did not know that he could get well and could stand upon his feet if he tried to do it. When new beautiful thoughts began to push out the old hideous ones, life began to come back to him, his blood ran healthily through his veins and strength poured into him like a flood. His scientific experiment was quite practical and simple and there was nothing weird about it at all. Much more surprising things can happen to any one who, when a disagreeable or discouraged thought comes into his mind, just has the sense to remember in time and push it out by putting in an agreeable determinedly courageous one. Two things cannot be in one place.

> *"Where, you tend a rose, my lad,*
> *A thistle cannot grow."*

While the secret garden was coming alive and two children were coming alive with it, there was a man wandering about certain far-away beautiful places in the Norwegian fiords and the valleys and mountains of Switzerland and he was a man who for ten years had kept his mind filled with dark and heart-broken thinking. He had not been courageous; he had never tried to put any other thoughts in the place of the dark ones. He had wandered by blue lakes and thought them; he had lain on mountain-sides with sheets of deep blue gentians blooming all about him and flower breaths filling all the air and he had thought them. A terrible sorrow had fallen upon him when he had been happy and he had let his soul fill itself with blackness and had refused obstinately to allow any rift of light to pierce through. He had forgotten and deserted his home and his duties. When he traveled about, darkness so brooded over him that the sight of him was a wrong done to other people because it was as if he poisoned the air about him with gloom. Most strangers thought he must be either half mad or a man with some hidden crime on his soul. He was a tall man with a drawn face and crooked shoulders and the name he always entered on hotel registers was, "Archibald Craven, Misselthwaite Manor, Yorkshire, England."

He had traveled far and wide since the day he saw Mistress Mary in his study and told her she might have her "bit of earth." He had been in the most beautiful places in Europe, though he had remained nowhere more than a few days. He had chosen the quietest and remotest spots. He had been on the tops of mountains whose heads were in the clouds and had looked down on other mountains when the sun rose and touched them with such light as made it seem as if the world were just being born.

But the light had never seemed to touch himself until one day when he realized that for the first time in ten years a strange thing had happened. He was in a wonderful valley in the Austrian Tyrol and he had been walking alone through such beauty as might have lifted any man's soul out of shadow. He had walked a long way and it had not lifted his. But at last he had felt tired and had thrown himself down to rest on a carpet of moss by a stream. It was a clear little stream which ran quite merrily along on its narrow way through the luscious damp greenness. Sometimes it made a sound rather like very low laughter as it bubbled over and round stones. He saw birds come and dip their heads to drink in it and then flick their wings and fly away. It seemed like a thing alive and yet its tiny voice made the stillness seem deeper. The valley was very, very still.

As he sat gazing into the clear running of the water, Archibald Craven gradually felt his mind and body both grow quiet, as quiet as the valley itself. He wondered if he were going to sleep, but he was not. He sat and gazed at the sunlit water and his eyes began to see things growing at its edge. There was one lovely mass of blue forget-me-nots growing so close to the stream that its leaves were wet and at these he found himself looking as he remembered he had looked at such things years ago. He was actually thinking tenderly how lovely it was and what wonders of blue its hundreds of little blossoms were. He did not know that just that simple thought was slowly filling his mind—filling and filling it until other things were softly pushed aside. It was as if a sweet clear spring had begun to rise in a stagnant pool and had risen and risen until at last it swept the dark water away. But of course he did not think of this himself. He only knew that the valley seemed to grow quieter and quieter as he sat and stared at the bright delicate blueness. He did not know how long he sat there or what was happening to him, but at last he moved as if he were awakening and he got up slowly and stood on the moss carpet, drawing a long, deep, soft breath and wondering at himself. Something seemed to have been unbound and released in him, very quietly.

"What is it?" he said, almost in a whisper, and he passed his hand over his forehead. "I almost feel as if—I were alive!"

I do not know enough about the wonderfulness of undiscovered things to be able to explain how this had happened to him. Neither does any one else yet. He did not understand at all himself—but he remembered this strange hour months afterward when he was at Misselthwaite again and he found out quite by accident that on this very day Colin had cried out as he went into the secret garden:

"I am going to live forever and ever and ever!"

The singular calmness remained with him the rest of the evening and he slept a new reposeful sleep; but it was not with him very long. He did not know that it could be kept. By the next night he had opened the doors wide to his dark thoughts and they had come trooping and rushing back. He left the valley and went on his wandering way again. But, strange as it seemed to him, there were minutes—sometimes half-hours—when, without his knowing why, the black burden seemed to lift itself again and he knew he was a living man and not a dead one. Slowly—slowly—for no reason that he knew of—he was "coming alive" with the garden.

As the golden summer changed into the deep golden autumn he went to the Lake of Como. There he found the loveliness of a dream. He spent his days upon the crystal blueness of the lake or he walked back into the soft thick verdure of the hills and tramped until he was tired so that he might sleep. But by this time he had begun to sleep better, he knew, and his dreams had ceased to be a terror to him.

"Perhaps," he thought, "my body is growing stronger."

It was growing stronger but—because of the rare peaceful hours when his thoughts were changed—his soul was slowly growing stronger, too. He began to think of Misselthwaite and wonder if he should not go home. Now and then he wondered vaguely about his boy and asked himself what he should feel when he went and stood by the carved four-posted bed again and looked down at the sharply chiseled ivory-white face while it slept and the black lashes rimmed so startlingly the close-shut eyes. He shrank from it.

One marvel of a day he had walked so far that when he returned the moon was high and full and all the world was purple shadow and silver. The stillness of lake and shore and wood was so wonderful that he did not go into the villa he lived in. He walked down to a little bowered terrace at the water's edge and sat upon a seat and breathed in all the heavenly scents of the night. He felt the strange calmness stealing over him and it grew deeper and deeper until he fell asleep.

He did not know when he fell asleep and when he began to dream; his dream was so real that he did not feel as if he were dreaming. He remembered afterward how intensely wide awake and alert he had thought he was. He thought that as he sat and breathed in the scent of the late roses and listened to the lapping of the water at his feet he heard a voice calling. It was sweet and clear and happy and far away. It seemed very far, but he heard it as distinctly as if it had been at his very side.

"Archie! Archie! Archie!" it said, and then again, sweeter and clearer than before, "Archie! Archie!"

He thought he sprang to his feet not even startled. It was such a real voice and it seemed so natural that he should hear it.

"Lilias! Lilias!" he answered. "Lilias! where are you?"

"In the garden," it came back like a sound from a golden flute. "In the garden!"

And then the dream ended. But he did not awaken. He slept soundly and sweetly all through the lovely night. When he did awake at last it was brilliant morning and a servant was standing staring at him. He was an Italian servant and was accustomed, as all the servants of the villa were, to accepting without question any strange thing his foreign master might do. No one ever knew when he would go out or come in or where he would choose to sleep or if he would roam about the garden or lie in the boat on the lake all night. The man held a salver with some letters on it and he waited quietly until Mr. Craven took them. When he had gone away Mr. Craven sat a few moments holding them in his hand and looking at the lake. His strange calm was still upon him and something more—a lightness as if the cruel thing which had been done had not happened as he thought—as if something had changed. He was remembering the dream—the real—real dream.

"In the garden!" he said, wondering at himself. "In the garden! But the door is locked and the key is buried deep."

When he glanced at the letters a few minutes later he saw that the one lying at the top of the rest was an English letter and came from Yorkshire. It was directed in a plain woman's hand but it was not a hand he knew. He opened it, scarcely thinking of the writer, but the first words attracted his attention at once.

"Dear Sir:

I am Susan Sowerby that made bold to speak to you once on the moor. It was about Miss Mary I spoke. I will make bold to speak again. Please, sir, I would come home if I was you. I

think you would be glad to come and—if you will excuse me, sir—I think your lady would ask you to come if she was here.
Your obedient servant,
Susan Sowerby."

Mr. Craven read the letter twice before he put it back in its envelope. He kept thinking about the dream.

"I will go back to Misselthwaite," he said. "Yes, I'll go at once."

And he went through the garden to the villa and ordered Pitcher to prepare for his return to England.

In a few days he was in Yorkshire again, and on his long railroad journey he found himself thinking of his boy as he had never thought in all the ten years past. During those years he had only wished to forget him. Now, though he did not intend to think about him, memories of him constantly drifted into his mind. He remembered the black days when he had raved like a madman because the child was alive and the mother was dead. He had refused to see it, and when he had gone to look at it at last it had been such a weak wretched thing that everyone had been sure it would die in a few days. But to the surprise of those who took care of it the days passed and it lived and then everyone believed it would be a deformed and crippled creature.

He had not meant to be a bad father, but he had not felt like a father at all. He had supplied doctors and nurses and luxuries, but he had shrunk from the mere thought of the boy and had buried himself in his own misery. The first time after a year's absence he returned to Misselthwaite and the small miserable looking thing languidly and indifferently lifted to his face the great gray eyes with black lashes round them, so like and yet so horribly unlike the happy eyes he had adored, he could not bear the sight of them and turned away pale as death. After that he scarcely ever saw him except when he was asleep, and all he knew of him was that he was a confirmed invalid, with a vicious, hysterical, half-insane temper. He could only be kept from furies dangerous to himself by being given his own way in every detail.

All this was not an uplifting thing to recall, but as the train whirled him through mountain passes and golden plains the man who was "coming alive" began to think in a new way and he thought long and steadily and deeply.

"Perhaps I have been all wrong for ten years," he said to himself. "Ten years is a long time. It may be too late to do anything—quite too late. What have I been thinking of!"

Of course this was the wrong Magic—to begin by saying "too late." Even Colin could have told him that. But he knew nothing of Magic—either black or white. This he had yet to learn. He wondered if Susan Sowerby had taken courage and written to him only because the motherly creature had realized that the boy was much worse—was fatally ill. If he had not been under the spell of the curious calmness which had taken possession of him he would have been more wretched than ever. But the calm had brought a sort of courage and hope with it. Instead of giving way to thoughts of the worst he actually found he was trying to believe in better things.

"Could it be possible that she sees that I may be able to do him good and control him?" he thought. "I will go and see her on my way to Misselthwaite."

But when on his way across the moor he stopped the carriage at the cottage, seven or eight children who were playing about gathered in a group and bobbing seven or eight friendly and polite curtsies told him that their mother had gone to the other side of the moor early in the morning to help a woman who had a new baby. "Our Dickon," they volunteered, was over at the Manor working in one of the gardens where he went several days each week.

Mr. Craven looked over the collection of sturdy little bodies and round red-cheeked faces, each one grinning in its own particular way, and he awoke to the fact that they were a healthy likable lot. He smiled at their friendly grins and took a golden sovereign from his pocket and gave it to "our 'Lizabeth Ellen" who was the oldest.

"If you divide that into eight parts there will be half a crown for each of you," he said.

Then amid grins and chuckles and bobbing of curtsies he drove away, leaving ecstasy and nudging elbows and little jumps of joy behind.

The drive across the wonderfulness of the moor was a soothing thing. Why did it seem to give him a sense of homecoming which he had been sure he could never feel again—that sense of the beauty of land and sky and purple bloom of distance and a warming of the heart at drawing nearer to the great old house which had held those of his blood for six hundred years? How he had driven away from it the last time, shuddering to think of its closed rooms and the boy lying in the four-posted bed with the brocaded hangings. Was it possible that perhaps he might find him changed a little for the better and that he might overcome his shrinking from him? How real that dream had been—how wonderful and clear the voice which called back to him, "In the garden—In the garden!"

"I will try to find the key," he said. "I will try to open the door. I must—though I don't know why."

When he arrived at the Manor the servants who received him with the usual ceremony noticed that he looked better and that he did not go to the remote rooms where he usually lived attended by Pitcher. He went into the library and sent for Mrs. Medlock. She came to him somewhat excited and curious and flustered.

"How is Master Colin, Medlock?" he inquired.

"Well, sir," Mrs. Medlock answered, "he's—he's different, in a manner of speaking."

"Worse?" he suggested.

Mrs. Medlock really was flushed.

"Well, you see, sir," she tried to explain, "neither Dr. Craven, nor the nurse, nor me can exactly make him out."

"Why is that?"

"To tell the truth, sir, Master Colin might be better and he might be changing for the worse. His appetite, sir, is past understanding—and his ways—"

"Has he become more—more peculiar?" her master asked, knitting his brows anxiously.

"That's it, sir. He's growing very peculiar—when you compare him with what he used to be. He used to eat nothing and then suddenly he began to eat something enormous—and then he stopped again all at once and the meals were sent back just as they used to be. You never knew, sir, perhaps, that out of doors he never would let himself be taken. The things we've gone through to get him to go out in his chair would leave a body trembling like a leaf. He'd throw himself into such a state that Dr. Craven said he couldn't be responsible for forcing him. Well, sir, just without warning—not long after one of his worst tantrums he suddenly insisted on being taken out every day by Miss Mary and Susan Sowerby's boy Dickon that could push his chair. He took a fancy to both Miss Mary and Dickon, and Dickon brought his tame animals, and, if you'll credit it, sir, out of doors he will stay from morning until night."

"How does he look?" was the next question.

"If he took his food natural, sir, you'd think he was putting on flesh—but we're afraid it may be a sort of bloat. He laughs sometimes in a queer way when he's alone with Miss Mary. He never used to laugh at all. Dr. Craven is coming to see you at once, if you'll allow him. He never was as puzzled in his life."

"Where is Master Colin now?" Mr. Craven asked.

"In the garden, sir. He's always in the garden—though not a human creature is allowed to go near for fear they'll look at him."

Mr. Craven scarcely heard her last words.

"In the garden," he said, and after he had sent Mrs. Medlock away he stood and repeated it again and again. "In the garden!"

He had to make an effort to bring himself back to the place he was standing in and when he felt he was on earth again he turned and went out of the room. He took his way, as Mary had done, through the door in the shrubbery and among the laurels and the fountain beds. The fountain was playing now and was encircled by beds of brilliant autumn flowers. He crossed the lawn and turned into the Long Walk by the ivied walls. He did not walk quickly, but slowly, and his eyes were on the path. He felt as if he were being drawn back to the place he had so long forsaken, and he did not know why. As he drew near to it his step became still more slow. He knew where the door was even though the ivy hung thick over it—but he did not know exactly where it lay—that buried key.

So he stopped and stood still, looking about him, and almost the moment after he had paused he started and listened—asking himself if he were walking in a dream.

The ivy hung thick over the door, the key was buried under the shrubs, no human being had passed that portal for ten lonely years—and yet inside the garden there were sounds. They were the sounds of running scuffling feet seeming to chase round and round under the trees, they were strange sounds of lowered suppressed voices—exclamations and smothered joyous cries. It seemed actually like the laughter of young things, the uncontrollable laughter of children who were trying not to be heard but who in a moment or so—as their excitement mounted—would burst forth. What in heaven's name was he dreaming of—what in heaven's name did he hear? Was he losing his reason and thinking he heard things which were not for human ears? Was it that the far clear voice had meant?

And then the moment came, the uncontrollable moment when the sounds forgot to hush themselves. The feet ran faster and faster—they were nearing the garden door—there was quick strong young breathing and a wild outbreak of laughing shows which could not be contained—and the door in the wall was flung wide open, the sheet of ivy swinging back, and a boy burst through it at full speed and, without seeing the outsider, dashed almost into his arms.

Mr. Craven had extended them just in time to save him from falling as a result of his unseeing dash against him, and when he held him away to look at him in amazement at his being there he truly gasped for breath.

He was a tall boy and a handsome one. He was glowing with life and his running had sent splendid color leaping to his face. He threw the thick hair back from his forehead and lifted a pair of strange gray eyes—eyes full of boyish laughter and rimmed with black lashes like a fringe. It was the eyes which made Mr. Craven gasp for breath. "Who—What? Who!" he stammered.

This was not what Colin had expected—this was not what he had planned. He had never thought of such a meeting. And yet to come dashing out—winning a race—perhaps it was even better. He drew himself up to his very tallest. Mary, who had been running with him and had dashed through the door too, believed that he managed to make himself look taller than he had ever looked before—inches taller.

"Father," he said, "I'm Colin. You can't believe it. I scarcely can myself. I'm Colin."

Like Mrs. Medlock, he did not understand what his father meant when he said hurriedly:

"In the garden! In the garden!"

"Yes," hurried on Colin. "It was the garden that did it—and Mary and Dickon and the creatures—and the Magic. No one knows. We kept it to tell you when you came. I'm well, I can beat Mary in a race. I'm going to be an athlete."

He said it all so like a healthy boy—his face flushed, his words tumbling over each other in his eagerness—that Mr. Craven's soul shook with unbelieving joy.

Colin put out his hand and laid it on his father's arm.

"Aren't you glad, Father?" he ended. "Aren't you glad? I'm going to live forever and ever and ever!"

Mr. Craven put his hands on both the boy's shoulders and held him still. He knew he dared not even try to speak for a moment.

"Take me into the garden, my boy," he said at last. "And tell me all about it."

And so they led him in.

The place was a wilderness of autumn gold and purple and violet blue and flaming scarlet and on every side were sheaves of late lilies standing together—lilies which were white or white and ruby. He remembered well when the first of them had been planted that just at this season of the year their late glories should reveal themselves. Late roses climbed and hung and clustered and the sunshine deepening the hue of the yellowing trees made one feel that one stood in an embowered temple of gold. The newcomer stood silent just as the children had done when they came into its grayness. He looked round and round.

"I thought it would be dead," he said.

"Mary thought so at first," said Colin. "But it came alive."

Then they sat down under their tree—all but Colin, who wanted to stand while he told the story.

It was the strangest thing he had ever heard, Archibald Craven thought, as it was poured forth in headlong boy fashion. Mystery and Magic and wild creatures, the weird midnight meeting—the coming of the spring—the passion of insulted pride which had dragged the young Rajah to his feet to defy old Ben Weatherstaff to his face. The odd companionship, the play acting, the great secret so carefully kept. The listener laughed until tears came into his eyes and sometimes tears came into his eyes when he was not laughing. The Athlete, the Lecturer, the Scientific Discoverer was a laughable, lovable, healthy young human thing.

"Now," he said at the end of the story, "it need not be a secret any more. I dare say it will frighten them nearly into fits when they see me—but I am never going to get into the chair again. I shall walk back with you, Father—to the house."

Ben Weatherstaff's duties rarely took him away from the gardens, but on this occasion he made an excuse to carry some vegetables to the kitchen and being invited into the servants' hall by Mrs. Medlock to drink a glass of beer he was on the spot—as he had hoped to be—when the most dramatic event Misselthwaite Manor had seen during the present generation actually took place. One of the windows looking upon the courtyard gave also a glimpse of the lawn. Mrs. Medlock, knowing Ben had come from the gardens, hoped that he might have caught sight of his master and even by chance of his meeting with Master Colin.

"Did you see either of them, Weatherstaff?" she asked.

Ben took his beer-mug from his mouth and wiped his lips with the back of his hand.

"Aye, that I did," he answered with a shrewdly significant air.

"Both of them?" suggested Mrs. Medlock.

"Both of 'em," returned Ben Weatherstaff. "Thank ye kindly, ma'am, I could sup up another mug of it."

"Together?" said Mrs. Medlock, hastily overfilling his beer-mug in her excitement.

"Together, ma'am," and Ben gulped down half of his new mug at one gulp.

"Where was Master Colin? How did he look? What did they say to each other?"

"I didna' hear that," said Ben, "along o' only bein' on th' stepladder lookin' over th' wall. But I'll tell thee this. There's been things goin' on outside as you house people knows nowt about. An' what tha'll find out tha'll find out soon."

And it was not two minutes before he swallowed the last of his beer and waved his mug solemnly toward the window which took in through the shrubbery a piece of the lawn.

"Look there," he said, "if tha's curious. Look what's comin' across th' grass."

When Mrs. Medlock looked she threw up her hands and gave a little shriek and every man and woman servant within hearing bolted across the servants' hall and stood looking through the window with their eyes almost starting out of their heads.

Across the lawn came the Master of Misselthwaite and he looked as many of them had never seen him. And by his side with his head up in the air and his eyes full of laughter walked as strongly and steadily as any boy in Yorkshire—Master Colin!

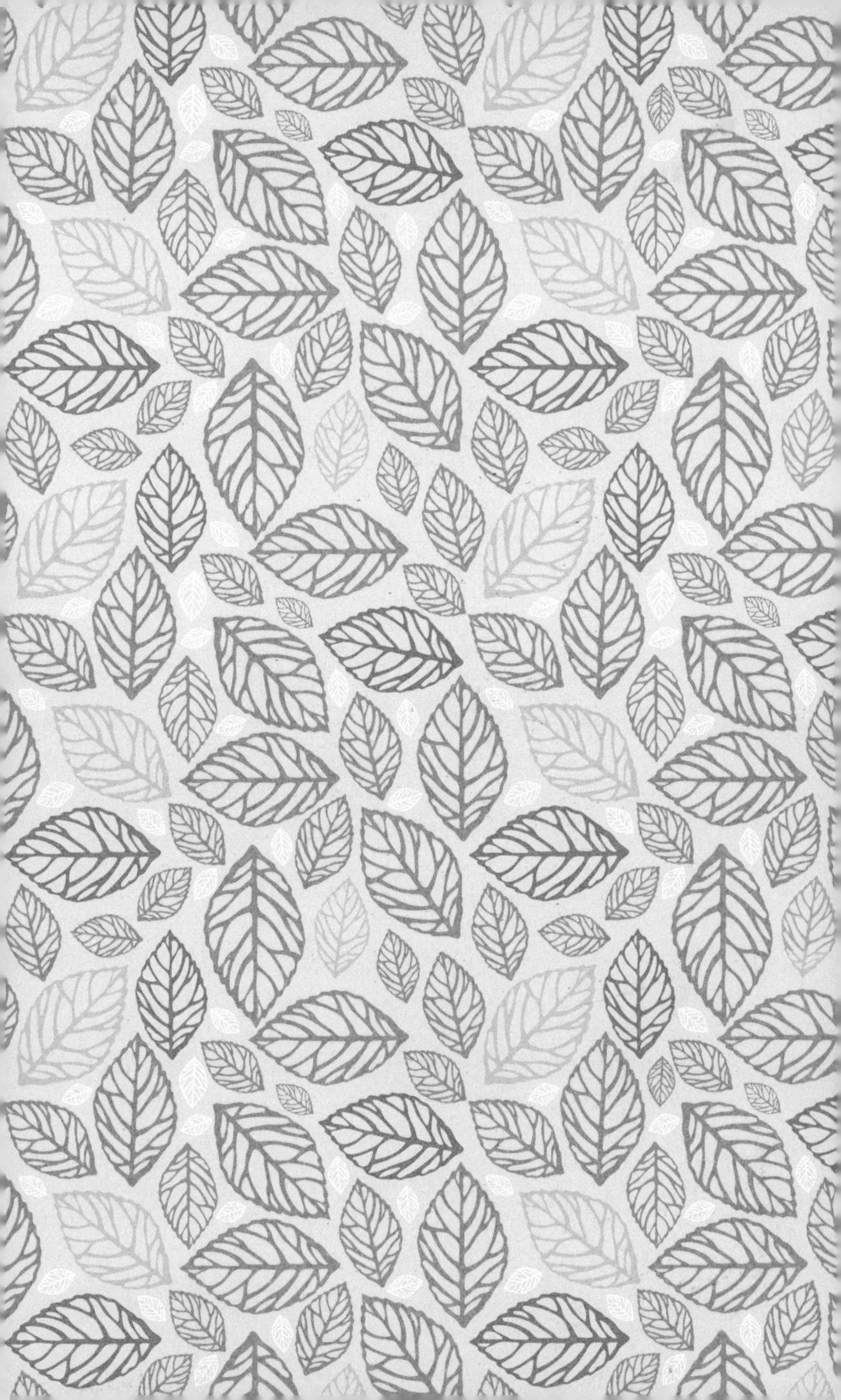